Mark Twain: 10 Books in 1

The Adventures of Tom Sawyer,
Huckleberry Finn,
Tom Sawyer Abroad,
Tom Sawyer, Detective,
Life On The Mississippi,
The Prince and The Pauper,
The Tragedy Of Pudd'nhead Wilson,
A Connecticut Yankee In King Arthur's Court,
Roughing It,
and Following The Equator

Published by Shoes and Ships and Sealing Wax

Visit our website, ShoesAndShipsAndSealingWax.com, for more great books!

This omnibus edition first published in the UK in 2006

Published by Shoes and Ships and Sealing Wax Ltd

Registered in the UK, company number 5180917

ISBN 0-9548401-8-6

"The time has come," the Walrus said,
"To talk of many things:
Of shoes — and ships — and sealing-wax —
Of cabbages — and kings —
And why the sea is boiling hot —
And whether pigs have wings."

Lewis Carroll, The Walrus and The Carpenter, 1872

Contents

The Adventures of Tom Sawyer
By Mark Twain

PREFACE

MOST of the adventures recorded in this book really occurred; one or two were experiences of my own, the rest those of boys who were schoolmates of mine. Huck Finn is drawn from life; Tom Sawyer also, but not from an individual—he is a combination of the characteristics of three boys whom I knew, and therefore belongs to the composite order of architecture.

The odd superstitions touched upon were all prevalent among children and slaves in the West at the period of this story—that is to say, thirty or forty years ago.

Although my book is intended mainly for the entertainment of boys and girls, I hope it will not be shunned by men and women on that account, for part of my plan has been to try to pleasantly remind adults of what they once were themselves, and of how they felt and thought and talked, and what queer enterprises they sometimes engaged in.

The Author, Hartford, 1876.

CHAPTER I

"TOM!"

No answer.

"TOM!"

No answer.

"What's gone with that boy, I wonder? You, TOM!"

No answer.

The old lady pulled her spectacles down and looked over them about the room; then she put them up and looked out under them. She seldom or never looked THROUGH them for so small a thing as a boy; they were her state pair, the pride of her heart, and were built for "style," not service—she could have seen through a pair of stove-lids just as well. She looked perplexed for a moment, and then said, not fiercely, but still loud enough for the furniture to hear:

"Well, I lay if I get hold of you I'll—"

She did not finish, for by this time she was bending down and punching under the bed with the broom, and so she needed breath to punctuate the punches with. She resurrected nothing but the cat.

"I never did see the beat of that boy!"

She went to the open door and stood in it and looked out among the tomato vines and "jimpson" weeds that constituted the garden. No Tom. So she lifted up her voice at an angle calculated for distance and shouted:

"Y-o-u-u TOM!"

There was a slight noise behind her and she turned just in time to seize a small boy by the slack of his roundabout and arrest his flight.

"There! I might 'a' thought of that closet. What you been doing in there?"

"Nothing."

"Nothing! Look at your hands. And look at your mouth. What IS that truck?"

"I don't know, aunt."

"Well, I know. It's jam—that's what it is. Forty times I've said if you didn't let that jam alone I'd skin you. Hand me that switch."

The switch hovered in the air—the peril was desperate—

"My! Look behind you, aunt!"

The old lady whirled round, and snatched her skirts out of danger. The lad fled on the instant, scrambled up the high board-fence, and disappeared over it.

His aunt Polly stood surprised a moment, and then broke into a gentle laugh.

"Hang the boy, can't I never learn anything? Ain't he played me tricks enough like that for me to be looking out for him by this time? But old fools is the biggest fools there is. Can't learn an old dog new tricks, as the saying is. But my goodness, he never plays them alike, two days, and how is a body to know what's coming? He 'pears to know just how long he can torment me before I get my dander up, and he knows if he can make out to put me off for a minute or make me laugh, it's all down again and I can't hit him a lick. I ain't doing my duty by that boy, and that's the Lord's truth, goodness knows. Spare the rod and spile the child, as the Good Book says. I'm a laying up sin and suffering for us both, I know. He's full of the Old Scratch, but laws-a-me! he's my own dead sister's boy, poor thing, and I ain't got the heart to lash him, somehow. Every time I let him off, my conscience does hurt me so, and every time I hit him my old heart most breaks. Well-a-well, man that is born of woman is of few days and full of trouble, as the Scripture says, and I reckon it's so. He'll play hookey this evening*, and I'll just be obleeged to make him work, to-morrow, to punish him. It's mighty hard to make him work Saturdays, when all the boys is having holiday, but he hates work more than he hates anything else, and I've GOT to do some of my duty by him, or I'll be the ruination of the child."

Tom did play hookey, and he had a very good time. He got back home barely in season to help Jim, the small colored boy, saw next-day's wood and split the kindlings before supper—at least he was there in time to tell his adventures to Jim while Jim did three-fourths of the work. Tom's younger brother (or rather half-brother) Sid was already through with his part of the work (picking up chips), for he was a quiet boy, and had no adventurous, troublesome ways.

While Tom was eating his supper, and stealing sugar as opportunity offered, Aunt Polly asked him questions that were full of guile, and very deep—for she wanted to trap him into damaging revealments. Like many other simple-hearted souls, it was her pet vanity to believe she was endowed with a talent for dark and mysterious diplomacy, and she loved to contemplate her most transparent devices as marvels of low

* Southwestern for "afternoon"

cunning. Said she:

"Tom, it was middling warm in school, warn't it?"

"Yes'm."

"Powerful warm, warn't it?"

"Yes'm."

"Didn't you want to go in a-swimming, Tom?"

A bit of a scare shot through Tom—a touch of uncomfortable suspicion. He searched Aunt Polly's face, but it told him nothing. So he said:

"No'm—well, not very much."

The old lady reached out her hand and felt Tom's shirt, and said:

"But you ain't too warm now, though." And it flattered her to reflect that she had discovered that the shirt was dry without anybody knowing that that was what she had in her mind. But in spite of her, Tom knew where the wind lay, now. So he forestalled what might be the next move:

"Some of us pumped on our heads—mine's damp yet. See?"

Aunt Polly was vexed to think she had overlooked that bit of circumstantial evidence, and missed a trick. Then she had a new inspiration:

"Tom, you didn't have to undo your shirt collar where I sewed it, to pump on your head, did you? Unbutton your jacket!"

The trouble vanished out of Tom's face. He opened his jacket. His shirt collar was securely sewed.

"Bother! Well, go 'long with you. I'd made sure you'd played hookey and been a-swimming. But I forgive ye, Tom. I reckon you're a kind of a singed cat, as the saying is—better'n you look. THIS time."

She was half sorry her sagacity had miscarried, and half glad that Tom had stumbled into obedient conduct for once.

But Sidney said:

"Well, now, if I didn't think you sewed his collar with white thread, but it's black."

"Why, I did sew it with white! Tom!"

But Tom did not wait for the rest. As he went out at the door he said:

"Siddy, I'll lick you for that."

In a safe place Tom examined two large needles which were thrust into the lapels of his jacket, and had thread bound about them—one needle carried white thread and the other black. He said:

"She'd never noticed if it hadn't been for Sid. Confound it! sometimes she sews it with white, and sometimes she sews it with black. I wish to geeminy she'd stick to one or t'other—I can't keep the run of 'em. But I bet you I'll lam Sid for that. I'll

learn him!"

He was not the Model Boy of the village. He knew the model boy very well though—and loathed him.

Within two minutes, or even less, he had forgotten all his troubles. Not because his troubles were one whit less heavy and bitter to him than a man's are to a man, but because a new and powerful interest bore them down and drove them out of his mind for the time—just as men's misfortunes are forgotten in the excitement of new enterprises. This new interest was a valued novelty in whistling, which he had just acquired from a negro, and he was suffering to practise it undisturbed. It consisted in a peculiar bird-like turn, a sort of liquid warble, produced by touching the tongue to the roof of the mouth at short intervals in the midst of the music—the reader probably remembers how to do it, if he has ever been a boy. Diligence and attention soon gave him the knack of it, and he strode down the street with his mouth full of harmony and his soul full of gratitude. He felt much as an astronomer feels who has discovered a new planet—no doubt, as far as strong, deep, unalloyed pleasure is concerned, the advantage was with the boy, not the astronomer.

The summer evenings were long. It was not dark, yet. Presently Tom checked his whistle. A stranger was before him—a boy a shade larger than himself. A new-comer of any age or either sex was an impressive curiosity in the poor little shabby village of St. Petersburg. This boy was well dressed, too—well dressed on a week-day. This was simply astounding. His cap was a dainty thing, his close-buttoned blue cloth roundabout was new and natty, and so were his pantaloons. He had shoes on—and it was only Friday. He even wore a necktie, a bright bit of ribbon. He had a citified air about him that ate into Tom's vitals. The more Tom stared at the splendid marvel, the higher he turned up his nose at his finery and the shabbier and shabbier seemed to him his own outfit to grow. Neither boy spoke. If one moved, the other moved—but only sidewise, in a circle; they kept face to face and eye to eye all the time. Finally Tom said:

"I can lick you!"

"I'd like to see you try it."

"Well, I can do it."

"No you can't, either."

"Yes I can."

"No you can't."

"I can."

"You can't."

"Can!"

"Can't!"

An uncomfortable pause. Then Tom said:

"What's your name?"

"'Tisn't any of your business, maybe."

"Well I 'low I'll MAKE it my business."

"Well why don't you?"

"If you say much, I will."

"Much—much—MUCH. There now."

"Oh, you think you're mighty smart, DON'T you? I could lick you with one hand tied behind me, if I wanted to."

"Well why don't you DO it? You SAY you can do it."

"Well I WILL, if you fool with me."

"Oh yes—I've seen whole families in the same fix."

"Smarty! You think you're SOME, now, DON'T you? Oh, what a hat!"

"You can lump that hat if you don't like it. I dare you to knock it off—and anybody that'll take a dare will suck eggs."

"You're a liar!"

"You're another."

"You're a fighting liar and dasn't take it up."

"Aw—take a walk!"

"Say—if you give me much more of your sass I'll take and bounce a rock off'n your head."

"Oh, of COURSE you will."

"Well I WILL."

"Well why don't you DO it then? What do you keep SAYING you will for? Why don't you DO it? It's because you're afraid."

"I AIN'T afraid."

"You are."

"I ain't."

"You are."

Another pause, and more eying and sidling around each other. Presently they were shoulder to shoulder. Tom said:

"Get away from here!"

"Go away yourself!"

"I won't."

"I won't either."

So they stood, each with a foot placed at an angle as a brace, and both shoving with might and main, and glowering at each other with hate. But neither could get an advantage. After struggling till both were hot and flushed, each relaxed his strain with watchful caution, and Tom said:

"You're a coward and a pup. I'll tell my big brother on you, and he can thrash you with his little finger, and I'll make him do it, too."

"What do I care for your big brother? I've got a brother that's bigger than he is—and what's more, he can throw him over that fence, too." [Both brothers were imaginary.]

"That's a lie."

"YOUR saying so don't make it so."

Tom drew a line in the dust with his big toe, and said:

"I dare you to step over that, and I'll lick you till you can't stand up. Anybody that'll take a dare will steal sheep."

The new boy stepped over promptly, and said:

"Now you said you'd do it, now let's see you do it."

"Don't you crowd me now; you better look out."

"Well, you SAID you'd do it—why don't you do it?"

"By jingo! for two cents I WILL do it."

The new boy took two broad coppers out of his pocket and held them out with derision. Tom struck them to the ground. In an instant both boys were rolling and tumbling in the dirt, gripped together like cats; and for the space of a minute they tugged and tore at each other's hair and clothes, punched and scratched each other's nose, and covered themselves with dust and glory. Presently the confusion took form, and through the fog of battle Tom appeared, seated astride the new boy, and pounding him with his fists. "Holler 'nuff!" said he.

The boy only struggled to free himself. He was crying—mainly from rage.

"Holler 'nuff!"—and the pounding went on.

At last the stranger got out a smothered "'Nuff!" and Tom let him up and said:

"Now that'll learn you. Better look out who you're fooling with next time."

The new boy went off brushing the dust from his clothes, sobbing, snuffling, and occasionally looking back and shaking his head and threatening what he would do to Tom the "next time he caught him out." To which Tom responded with jeers, and started off in high feather, and as soon as his back was turned the new boy snatched up a stone, threw it and hit him between the shoulders and then turned tail and ran like an antelope. Tom chased the traitor home, and thus found out where he lived. He then held a position at the gate for some time, daring the enemy to come outside, but the enemy only made faces at him through the window and declined. At last the enemy's mother appeared, and called Tom a bad, vicious, vulgar child, and ordered him away. So he went away; but he said he "'lowed" to "lay" for that boy.

He got home pretty late that night, and when he climbed cautiously in at the window, he uncovered an ambuscade, in the person of his aunt; and when she saw the state his clothes were in her resolution to turn his Saturday holiday into captivity at hard labor became adamantine in its firmness.

CHAPTER II

SATURDAY morning was come, and all the summer world was bright and fresh, and brimming with life. There was a song in every heart; and if the heart was young the music issued at the lips. There was cheer in every face and a spring in every step. The locust-trees were in bloom and the fragrance of the blossoms filled the air. Cardiff Hill, beyond the village and above it, was green with vegetation and it lay just far enough away to seem a Delectable Land, dreamy, reposeful, and inviting.

Tom appeared on the sidewalk with a bucket of whitewash and a long-handled brush. He surveyed the fence, and all gladness left him and a deep melancholy settled down upon his spirit. Thirty yards of board fence nine feet high. Life to him seemed hollow, and existence but a burden. Sighing, he dipped his brush and passed it along the topmost plank; repeated the operation; did it again; compared the insignificant whitewashed streak with the far-reaching continent of unwhitewashed fence, and sat down on a tree-box discouraged. Jim came skipping out at the gate with a tin pail, and singing Buffalo Gals. Bringing water from the town pump had always been hateful work in Tom's eyes, before, but now it did not strike him so. He remembered that there was company at the pump. White, mulatto, and negro boys and girls were always there waiting their turns, resting, trading playthings, quarrelling, fighting, skylarking. And he remembered that although the pump was only a hundred and fifty yards off, Jim never got back with a bucket of water under an hour—and even then somebody generally had to go after him. Tom said:

"Say, Jim, I'll fetch the water if you'll whitewash some."

Jim shook his head and said:

"Can't, Mars Tom. Ole missis, she tole me I got to go an' git dis water an' not stop foolin' roun' wid anybody. She say she spec' Mars Tom gwine to ax me to whitewash, an' so she tole me go 'long an' 'tend to my own business—she 'lowed SHE'D 'tend to de whitewashin'."

"Oh, never you mind what she said, Jim. That's the way she always talks. Gimme the bucket—I won't be gone only a a minute. SHE won't ever know."

"Oh, I dasn't, Mars Tom. Ole missis she'd take an' tar de head off'n me. 'Deed she would."

"SHE! She never licks anybody—whacks 'em over the head with her thimble—and who cares for that, I'd like to know. She talks awful, but talk don't hurt—anyways it don't if she don't cry. Jim, I'll give you a marvel. I'll give you a white alley!"

Jim began to waver.

"White alley, Jim! And it's a bully taw."

"My! Dat's a mighty gay marvel, I tell you! But Mars Tom I's powerful 'fraid ole missis—"

"And besides, if you will I'll show you my sore toe."

Jim was only human—this attraction was too much for him. He put down his pail, took the white alley, and bent over the toe with absorbing interest while the bandage was being unwound. In another moment he was flying down the street with his pail and a tingling rear, Tom was whitewashing with vigor, and Aunt Polly was retiring from the field with a slipper in her hand and triumph in her eye.

But Tom's energy did not last. He began to think of the fun he had planned for this day, and his sorrows multiplied. Soon the free boys would come tripping along on all sorts of delicious expeditions, and they would make a world of fun of him for having to work—the very thought of it burnt him like fire. He got out his worldly wealth and examined it—bits of toys, marbles, and trash; enough to buy an exchange of WORK, maybe, but not half enough to buy so much as half an hour of pure freedom. So he returned his straitened means to his pocket, and gave up the idea of trying to buy the boys. At this dark and hopeless moment an inspiration burst upon him! Nothing less than a great, magnificent inspiration.

He took up his brush and went tranquilly to work. Ben Rogers hove in sight presently—the very boy, of all boys, whose ridicule he had been dreading. Ben's gait was the hop-skip-and-jump—proof enough that his heart was light and his anticipations high. He was eating an apple, and giving a long, melodious whoop, at intervals, followed by a deep-toned ding-dong-dong, ding-dong-dong, for he was personating a steamboat. As he drew near, he slackened speed, took the middle of the street, leaned far over to starboard and rounded to ponderously and with laborious pomp and circumstance—for he was personating the Big Missouri, and considered himself to be drawing nine feet of water. He was boat and captain and engine-bells combined, so he had to imagine himself standing on his own hurricane-deck giving the orders and executing them:

"Stop her, sir! Ting-a-ling-ling!" The headway ran almost out, and he drew up slowly toward the sidewalk.

"Ship up to back! Ting-a-ling-ling!" His arms straightened and stiffened down his sides.

"Set her back on the stabboard! Ting-a-ling-ling! Chow! ch-chow-wow! Chow!" His right hand, meantime, describing stately circles—for it was representing a forty-foot wheel.

"Let her go back on the labboard! Ting-a-lingling! Chow-ch-chow-chow!" The left hand began to describe circles.

"Stop the stabboard! Ting-a-ling-ling! Stop the labboard! Come ahead on the stabboard! Stop her! Let your outside turn over slow! Ting-a-ling-ling! Chow-ow-ow! Get out that head-line! LIVELY now! Come—out with your spring-line—what're you about there! Take a turn round that stump with the bight of it! Stand by that stage, now—let her go! Done with the engines, sir! Ting-a-ling-ling! SH'T! S'H'T! SH'T!" (trying the gauge-cocks).

Tom went on whitewashing—paid no attention to the steamboat. Ben stared a moment and then said: "Hi-YI! YOU'RE up a stump, ain't you!"

No answer. Tom surveyed his last touch with the eye of an artist, then he gave his brush another gentle sweep and surveyed the result, as before. Ben ranged up alongside of him. Tom's mouth watered for the apple, but he stuck to his work. Ben said:

"Hello, old chap, you got to work, hey?"

Tom wheeled suddenly and said:

"Why, it's you, Ben! I warn't noticing."

"Say—I'm going in a-swimming, I am. Don't you wish you could? But of course you'd druther WORK—wouldn't you? Course you would!"

Tom contemplated the boy a bit, and said:

"What do you call work?"

"Why, ain't THAT work?"

Tom resumed his whitewashing, and answered carelessly:

"Well, maybe it is, and maybe it ain't. All I know, is, it suits Tom Sawyer."

"Oh come, now, you don't mean to let on that you LIKE it?"

The brush continued to move.

"Like it? Well, I don't see why I oughtn't to like it. Does a boy get a chance to whitewash a fence every day?"

That put the thing in a new light. Ben stopped nibbling his apple. Tom swept his brush daintily back and forth—stepped back to note the effect—added a touch here and there—criticised the effect again—Ben watching every move and getting more and more interested, more and more absorbed. Presently he said:

"Say, Tom, let ME whitewash a little."

Tom considered, was about to consent; but he altered his mind:

"No—no—I reckon it wouldn't hardly do, Ben. You see, Aunt Polly's awful particular about this fence—right here on the street, you know —but if it was the back fence I wouldn't mind and SHE wouldn't. Yes, she's awful particular about this fence; it's got to be done very careful; I reckon there ain't one boy in a thousand, maybe two thousand, that can do it the way it's got to be done."

"No—is that so? Oh come, now—lemme just try. Only just a little—I'd let YOU, if you was me, Tom."

"Ben, I'd like to, honest injun; but Aunt Polly—well, Jim wanted to do it, but she wouldn't let him; Sid wanted to do it, and she wouldn't let Sid. Now don't you see how I'm fixed? If you was to tackle this fence and anything was to happen to it—"

"Oh, shucks, I'll be just as careful. Now lemme try. Say—I'll give you the core of my apple."

"Well, here—No, Ben, now don't. I'm afeard—"

"I'll give you ALL of it!"

Tom gave up the brush with reluctance in his face, but alacrity in his heart. And while the late steamer Big Missouri worked and sweated in the sun, the retired artist sat on a barrel in the shade close by, dangled his legs, munched his apple, and planned the slaughter of more innocents. There was no lack of material; boys happened along every little while; they came to jeer, but remained to whitewash. By the time Ben was fagged out, Tom had traded the next chance to Billy Fisher for a kite, in good repair; and when he played out, Johnny Miller bought in for a dead rat and a string to swing it with—and so on, and

so on, hour after hour. And when the middle of the afternoon came, from being a poor poverty-stricken boy in the morning, Tom was literally rolling in wealth. He had besides the things before mentioned, twelve marbles, part of a jews-harp, a piece of blue bottle-glass to look through, a spool cannon, a key that wouldn't unlock anything, a fragment of chalk, a glass stopper of a decanter, a tin soldier, a couple of tadpoles, six fire-crackers, a kitten with only one eye, a brass doorknob, a dog-collar—but no dog—the handle of a knife, four pieces of orange-peel, and a dilapidated old window sash.

He had had a nice, good, idle time all the while—plenty of company —and the fence had three coats of whitewash on it! If he hadn't run out of whitewash he would have bankrupted every boy in the village.

Tom said to himself that it was not such a hollow world, after all. He had discovered a great law of human action, without knowing it—namely, that in order to make a man or a boy covet a thing, it is only necessary to make the thing difficult to attain. If he had been a great and wise philosopher, like the writer of this book, he would now have comprehended that Work consists of whatever a body is OBLIGED to do, and that Play consists of whatever a body is not obliged to do. And this would help him to understand why constructing artificial flowers or performing on a tread-mill is work, while rolling ten-pins or climbing Mont Blanc is only amusement. There are wealthy gentlemen in England who drive four-horse passenger-coaches twenty or thirty miles on a daily line, in the summer, because the privilege costs them considerable money; but if they were offered wages for the service, that would turn it into work and then they would resign.

The boy mused awhile over the substantial change which had taken place in his worldly circumstances, and then wended toward headquarters to report.

CHAPTER III

TOM presented himself before Aunt Polly, who was sitting by an open window in a pleasant rearward apartment, which was bedroom, breakfast-room, dining-room, and library, combined. The balmy summer air, the restful quiet, the odor of the flowers, and the drowsing murmur of the bees had had their effect, and she was nodding over her knitting —for she had no company but the cat, and it was asleep in her lap. Her spectacles were propped up on her gray head for safety. She had thought that of course Tom had deserted long ago, and she wondered at seeing him place himself in her power again in this intrepid way. He said: "Mayn't I go and play now, aunt?"

"What, a'ready? How much have you done?"

"It's all done, aunt."

"Tom, don't lie to me—I can't bear it."

"I ain't, aunt; it IS all done."

Aunt Polly placed small trust in such evidence. She went out to see for herself; and she would have been content to find twenty per cent. of Tom's statement true. When she found the entire fence whitewashed, and not only whitewashed but elaborately coated and recoated, and even a streak added to the ground, her astonishment was almost unspeakable. She said:

"Well, I never! There's no getting round it, you can work when you're a mind to, Tom." And then she diluted the compliment by adding, "But it's powerful seldom you're a mind to, I'm bound to say. Well, go 'long and play; but mind you get back some time in a week, or I'll tan you."

She was so overcome by the splendor of his achievement that she took him into the closet and selected a choice apple and delivered it to him, along with an improving lecture upon the added value and flavor a treat took to itself when it came without sin through virtuous effort. And while she closed with a happy Scriptural flourish, he "hooked" a doughnut.

Then he skipped out, and saw Sid just starting up the outside stairway that led to the back rooms on the second floor. Clods were handy and the air was full of them in a twinkling. They raged around Sid like a hail-storm; and before Aunt Polly could collect her surprised faculties and sally to the rescue, six or seven clods had taken personal effect, and Tom was over the fence and gone. There was a gate, but as a general thing he was too crowded for time to make use of it. His soul was at peace, now that he had settled with Sid for calling attention to his black thread and getting him into trouble.

Tom skirted the block, and came round into a muddy alley that led by the back of his aunt's cow-stable. He presently got safely beyond the reach of capture and punishment, and hastened toward the public square of the village, where two "military" companies of boys had met for conflict, according to previous appointment. Tom was General of one of these armies, Joe Harper (a bosom friend) General of the other. These two great commanders did not condescend to fight in person—that being better suited to the still smaller fry—but sat together on an eminence and conducted the field operations by orders delivered through aides-de-camp. Tom's army won a great victory, after a long and hard-fought battle. Then the dead were counted, prisoners exchanged, the terms of the next disagreement agreed upon, and the day for the necessary battle appointed; after which the armies fell into line and marched away, and Tom turned homeward alone.

As he was passing by the house where Jeff Thatcher lived, he saw a new girl in the garden—a lovely little blue-eyed creature with yellow hair plaited into two long-tails, white summer frock and embroidered pantalettes. The fresh-crowned hero fell without firing a shot. A certain Amy Lawrence vanished out of his heart and left not even a memory of herself behind. He had thought he loved her to distraction; he had regarded his passion as adoration; and behold it was only a poor little evanescent partiality. He had been months winning her; she had confessed hardly a week ago; he had been the happiest and the proudest boy in the world only seven short days, and here in one instant of time she had gone out of his heart like a casual stranger whose visit is done.

He worshipped this new angel with furtive eye, till he saw that she had discovered him; then he pretended he did not know she was present, and began to "show off" in all sorts of absurd boyish ways, in order to win her admiration. He kept up this grotesque foolishness for some time; but by-and-by, while he was in the midst of some dangerous gymnastic performances, he glanced aside and saw that the little girl was wending her way toward the house. Tom came up to the fence and leaned on it, grieving, and hoping she would tarry yet awhile longer. She halted a moment on the steps and then moved toward the door. Tom heaved a great sigh as she put her foot on the threshold. But his face lit up, right away, for she tossed a pansy over the fence a moment before she disappeared.

The boy ran around and stopped within a foot or two of the flower, and then shaded his eyes with his hand and began to look down street as if he had discovered something of interest going on in that direction. Presently he picked up a straw and began trying to balance it on his nose, with his head tilted far back; and as he moved from side to side, in his efforts, he edged nearer and nearer toward the pansy; finally his bare foot rested upon it, his pliant toes closed upon it, and he hopped away with the treasure and disappeared round the corner. But only for a minute—only while he could button the flower inside his jacket, next his heart—or next his stomach, possibly, for he was not much posted in anatomy, and not hypercritical, anyway.

He returned, now, and hung about the fence till nightfall, "showing off," as before; but the girl never exhibited herself again, though Tom comforted himself a little with the hope that she had been near some window, meantime, and been aware of his attentions. Finally he strode home reluctantly, with his poor head full of visions.

All through supper his spirits were so high that his aunt wondered "what had got into the child." He took a good scolding about clodding Sid, and did not seem to mind it in the least. He tried to steal sugar under his aunt's very nose, and got his knuckles rapped for it. He said:

"Aunt, you don't whack Sid when he takes it."

"Well, Sid don't torment a body the way you do. You'd be always into that sugar if I warn't watching you."

Presently she stepped into the kitchen, and Sid, happy in his immunity, reached for the sugar-bowl—a sort of glorying over Tom which was wellnigh unbearable. But Sid's fingers slipped and the bowl dropped and broke. Tom was in ecstasies. In such ecstasies that he even controlled his tongue and was silent. He said to himself that he would not speak a word, even when his aunt came in, but would sit perfectly still till she asked who did the mischief; and then he would tell, and there would be nothing so good in the world as to see that pet model "catch it." He was so brimful of exultation that he could hardly hold himself when the old lady came back and stood above the wreck discharging lightnings of wrath from over her spectacles. He said to himself, "Now it's coming!" And the next instant he was sprawling on the floor! The potent palm was uplifted to strike again when Tom cried out:

"Hold on, now, what 'er you belting ME for?—Sid broke it!"

Aunt Polly paused, perplexed, and Tom looked for healing pity. But when she got her tongue again, she only said:

"Umf! Well, you didn't get a lick amiss, I reckon. You been into some other audacious mischief when I wasn't around, like enough."

Then her conscience reproached her, and she yearned to say something kind and loving; but she judged that this would be construed into a confession that she had been in the wrong, and discipline forbade that. So she kept silence, and went about her affairs with a troubled heart. Tom sulked in a corner and exalted his woes. He knew that in her heart his aunt was on her knees to him, and he was morosely gratified by the consciousness of it. He would hang out no signals, he would take notice of none. He knew that a yearning glance fell upon him, now and then, through a film of tears, but he refused recognition of it. He pictured himself lying sick unto death and his aunt bending over him beseeching one little forgiving word, but he would turn his face to the wall, and die with that word unsaid. Ah, how would she feel then? And he pictured himself brought home from the river, dead, with his curls all wet, and his sore heart at rest. How she would throw herself upon him, and how her tears would fall like rain, and her lips pray God to give her back her boy and she would never, never abuse him any more! But he would lie there cold and white and make no sign—a poor little sufferer, whose griefs were at an end. He so worked upon his feelings with the pathos of these dreams, that he had to keep swallowing, he was so like to choke; and his eyes swam in a blur of water, which overflowed when he winked, and ran down and trickled from the end of his nose. And such a luxury to him was this petting of his sorrows, that he could not bear to have any worldly cheeriness or any grating delight intrude upon it; it was too sacred for such contact; and so, presently, when his cousin Mary danced in, all alive with the joy of seeing home again after an age-long visit of one week to the country, he got up and moved in clouds and darkness out at one door as she brought song and sunshine in at the other.

He wandered far from the accustomed haunts of boys, and sought desolate places that were in harmony with his spirit. A log raft in the river invited him, and he seated himself on its outer edge and contemplated the dreary vastness of the stream, wishing, the while, that he could only be drowned, all at once and unconsciously, without undergoing the uncomfortable routine devised by nature. Then he thought of his flower. He got it out, rumpled and wilted, and it mightily increased his dismal felicity. He wondered if she would pity him if she knew? Would she cry, and wish that she had a right to put her arms around his neck and comfort him? Or would she turn coldly away like all the hollow world? This picture brought such an agony of pleasurable suffering that he worked it over and over again in his mind and set it up in new and varied lights, till he wore it threadbare. At last he rose up sighing and departed in the darkness.

About half-past nine or ten o'clock he came along the deserted street to where the Adored Unknown lived; he paused a moment; no sound fell upon his listening ear; a candle was casting a dull glow upon the curtain of a second-story window. Was the sacred presence there? He climbed the fence, threaded his stealthy way through the plants, till he stood under that window; he looked up at it long, and with emotion; then he laid him down on the ground under it, disposing himself upon his back, with his hands clasped upon his breast and holding his poor wilted flower. And thus he would die—out in the cold world, with no shelter over his homeless head, no friendly hand to wipe the death-damps from his brow, no loving face to bend pityingly over him when the great agony came. And thus SHE would see him when she looked out upon the glad morning, and oh! would she drop one little tear upon his poor, lifeless form, would she heave one little sigh to see a bright young life so rudely blighted, so untimely cut down?

The window went up, a maid-servant's discordant voice profaned the holy calm, and a deluge of water drenched the prone martyr's remains!

The strangling hero sprang up with a relieving snort. There was a whiz as of a missile in the air, mingled with the murmur of a curse, a sound as of shivering glass followed, and a small, vague form went over the fence and shot away in the gloom.

Not long after, as Tom, all undressed for bed, was surveying

his drenched garments by the light of a tallow dip, Sid woke up; but if he had any dim idea of making any "references to allusions," he thought better of it and held his peace, for there was danger in Tom's eye.

Tom turned in without the added vexation of prayers, and Sid made mental note of the omission.

CHAPTER IV

THE sun rose upon a tranquil world, and beamed down upon the peaceful village like a benediction. Breakfast over, Aunt Polly had family worship: it began with a prayer built from the ground up of solid courses of Scriptural quotations, welded together with a thin mortar of originality; and from the summit of this she delivered a grim chapter of the Mosaic Law, as from Sinai.

Then Tom girded up his loins, so to speak, and went to work to "get his verses." Sid had learned his lesson days before. Tom bent all his energies to the memorizing of five verses, and he chose part of the Sermon on the Mount, because he could find no verses that were shorter. At the end of half an hour Tom had a vague general idea of his lesson, but no more, for his mind was traversing the whole field of human thought, and his hands were busy with distracting recreations. Mary took his book to hear him recite, and he tried to find his way through the fog:

"Blessed are the—a—a—"

"Poor"—

"Yes—poor; blessed are the poor—a—a—"

"In spirit—"

"In spirit; blessed are the poor in spirit, for they—they—"

"THEIRS—"

"For THEIRS. Blessed are the poor in spirit, for theirs is the kingdom of heaven. Blessed are they that mourn, for they—they—"

"Sh—"

"For they—a—"

"S, H, A—"

"For they S, H—Oh, I don't know what it is!"

"SHALL!"

"Oh, SHALL! for they shall—for they shall—a—a—shall mourn—a—a— blessed are they that shall—they that—a—they that shall mourn, for they shall—a—shall WHAT? Why don't you tell me, Mary?—what do you want to be so mean for?"

"Oh, Tom, you poor thick-headed thing, I'm not teasing you. I wouldn't do that. You must go and learn it again. Don't you be discouraged, Tom, you'll manage it—and if you do, I'll give you something ever so nice. There, now, that's a good boy."

"All right! What is it, Mary, tell me what it is."

"Never you mind, Tom. You know if I say it's nice, it is nice."

"You bet you that's so, Mary. All right, I'll tackle it again."

And he did "tackle it again"—and under the double pressure of curiosity and prospective gain he did it with such spirit that he accomplished a shining success. Mary gave him a brand-new "Barlow" knife worth twelve and a half cents; and the convulsion of delight that swept his system shook him to his foundations. True, the knife would not cut anything, but it was a "sure-enough" Barlow, and there was inconceivable grandeur in that—though where the Western boys ever got the idea that such a weapon could possibly be counterfeited to its injury is an imposing mystery and will always remain so, perhaps. Tom contrived to scarify the cupboard with it, and was arranging to begin on the bureau, when he was called off to dress for Sunday-school.

Mary gave him a tin basin of water and a piece of soap, and he went outside the door and set the basin on a little bench there; then he dipped the soap in the water and laid it down; turned up his sleeves; poured out the water on the ground, gently, and then entered the kitchen and began to wipe his face diligently on the towel behind the door. But Mary removed the towel and said:

"Now ain't you ashamed, Tom. You mustn't be so bad. Water won't hurt you."

Tom was a trifle disconcerted. The basin was refilled, and this time he stood over it a little while, gathering resolution; took in a big breath and began. When he entered the kitchen presently, with both eyes shut and groping for the towel with his hands, an honorable testimony of suds and water was dripping from his face. But when he emerged from the towel, he was not yet satisfactory, for the clean territory stopped short at his chin and his jaws, like a mask; below and beyond this line there was a dark expanse of unirrigated soil that spread downward in front and backward around his neck. Mary took him in hand, and when she was done with him he was a man and a brother, without distinction of color, and his saturated hair was neatly brushed, and its short curls wrought into a dainty and symmetrical general effect. [He privately smoothed out the curls, with labor and difficulty, and plastered his hair close down to his head; for he held curls to be effeminate, and his own filled his life with bitterness.] Then Mary got out a suit of his clothing that had been used only on Sundays during two years—they were simply called his "other clothes"—and so by that we know the size of his wardrobe. The girl "put him to rights" after he had dressed himself; she buttoned his neat roundabout up to his chin, turned his vast shirt collar down over his shoulders, brushed him off and crowned him with his speckled straw hat. He now looked exceedingly improved and uncomfortable. He was fully as uncomfortable as he looked; for there was a restraint about whole clothes and cleanliness that galled him. He hoped that Mary would forget his shoes, but the hope was blighted; she coated them thoroughly with tallow, as was the custom, and brought them out. He lost his temper and said he was always being made to do everything he didn't want to do. But Mary said, persuasively:

"Please, Tom—that's a good boy."

So he got into the shoes snarling. Mary was soon ready, and the three children set out for Sunday-school—a place that Tom hated with his whole heart; but Sid and Mary were fond of it.

Sabbath-school hours were from nine to half-past ten; and

then church service. Two of the children always remained for the sermon voluntarily, and the other always remained too—for stronger reasons. The church's high-backed, uncushioned pews would seat about three hundred persons; the edifice was but a small, plain affair, with a sort of pine board tree-box on top of it for a steeple. At the door Tom dropped back a step and accosted a Sunday-dressed comrade:

"Say, Billy, got a yaller ticket?"

"Yes."

"What'll you take for her?"

"What'll you give?"

"Piece of lickrish and a fish-hook."

"Less see 'em."

Tom exhibited. They were satisfactory, and the property changed hands. Then Tom traded a couple of white alleys for three red tickets, and some small trifle or other for a couple of blue ones. He waylaid other boys as they came, and went on buying tickets of various colors ten or fifteen minutes longer. He entered the church, now, with a swarm of clean and noisy boys and girls, proceeded to his seat and started a quarrel with the first boy that came handy. The teacher, a grave, elderly man, interfered; then turned his back a moment and Tom pulled a boy's hair in the next bench, and was absorbed in his book when the boy turned around; stuck a pin in another boy, presently, in order to hear him say "Ouch!" and got a new reprimand from his teacher. Tom's whole class were of a pattern—restless, noisy, and troublesome. When they came to recite their lessons, not one of them knew his verses perfectly, but had to be prompted all along. However, they worried through, and each got his reward—in small blue tickets, each with a passage of Scripture on it; each blue ticket was pay for two verses of the recitation. Ten blue tickets equalled a red one, and could be exchanged for it; ten red tickets equalled a yellow one; for ten yellow tickets the superintendent gave a very plainly bound Bible (worth forty cents in those easy times) to the pupil. How many of my readers would have the industry and application to memorize two thousand verses, even for a Dore Bible? And yet Mary had acquired two Bibles in this way—it was the patient work of two years—and a boy of German parentage had won four or five. He once recited three thousand verses without stopping; but the strain upon his mental faculties was too great, and he was little better than an idiot from that day forth—a grievous misfortune for the school, for on great occasions, before company, the superintendent (as Tom expressed it) had always made this boy come out and "spread himself." Only the older pupils managed to keep their tickets and stick to their tedious work long enough to get a Bible, and so the delivery of one of these prizes was a rare and noteworthy circumstance; the successful pupil was so great and conspicuous for that day that on the spot every scholar's heart was fired with a fresh ambition that often lasted a couple of weeks. It is possible that Tom's mental stomach had never really hungered for one of those prizes, but unquestionably his entire being had for many a day longed for the glory and the eclat that came with it.

In due course the superintendent stood up in front of the pulpit, with a closed hymn-book in his hand and his forefinger inserted between its leaves, and commanded attention. When a Sunday-school superintendent makes his customary little speech, a hymn-book in the hand is as necessary as is the inevitable sheet of music in the hand of a singer who stands forward on the platform and sings a solo at a concert —though why, is a mystery: for neither the hymn-book nor the sheet of music is ever referred to by the sufferer. This superintendent was a slim creature of thirty-five, with a sandy goatee and short sandy hair; he wore a stiff standing-collar whose upper edge almost reached his ears and whose sharp points curved forward abreast the corners of his mouth—a fence that compelled a straight lookout ahead, and a turning of the whole body when a side view was required; his chin was propped on a spreading cravat which was as broad and as long as a bank-note, and had fringed ends; his boot toes were turned sharply up, in the fashion of the day, like sleigh-runners—an effect patiently and laboriously produced by the young men by sitting with their toes pressed against a wall for hours together. Mr. Walters was very earnest of mien, and very sincere and honest at heart; and he held sacred things and places in such reverence, and so separated them from worldly matters, that unconsciously to himself his Sunday-school voice had acquired a peculiar intonation which was wholly absent on week-days. He began after this fashion:

"Now, children, I want you all to sit up just as straight and pretty as you can and give me all your attention for a minute or two. There —that is it. That is the way good little boys and girls should do. I see one little girl who is looking out of the window—I am afraid she thinks I am out there somewhere— perhaps up in one of the trees making a speech to the little birds. [Applausive titter.] I want to tell you how good it makes me feel to see so many bright, clean little faces assembled in a place like this, learning to do right and be good." And so forth and so on. It is not necessary to set down the rest of the oration. It was of a pattern which does not vary, and so it is familiar to us all.

The latter third of the speech was marred by the resumption of fights and other recreations among certain of the bad boys, and by fidgetings and whisperings that extended far and wide, washing even to the bases of isolated and incorruptible rocks like Sid and Mary. But now every sound ceased suddenly, with the subsidence of Mr. Walters' voice, and the conclusion of the speech was received with a burst of silent gratitude.

A good part of the whispering had been occasioned by an event which was more or less rare—the entrance of visitors: lawyer Thatcher, accompanied by a very feeble and aged man; a fine, portly, middle-aged gentleman with iron-gray hair; and a dignified lady who was doubtless the latter's wife. The lady was leading a child. Tom had been restless and full of chafings and repinings; conscience-smitten, too—he could not meet Amy Lawrence's eye, he could not brook her loving gaze. But when he saw this small new-comer his soul was all ablaze with bliss in a moment. The next moment he was "showing off" with all his might —cuffing boys, pulling hair, making faces— in a word, using every art that seemed likely to fascinate a girl and win her applause. His exaltation had but one alloy—the memory of his humiliation in this angel's garden—and that record in sand was fast washing out, under the waves of happiness that were sweeping over it now.

The visitors were given the highest seat of honor, and as soon as Mr. Walters' speech was finished, he introduced them to the school. The middle-aged man turned out to be a prodigious personage—no less a one than the county judge—altogether the most august creation these children had ever looked upon—and they wondered what kind of material he was made of—and they half wanted to hear him roar, and were half afraid he might, too. He was from Constantinople, twelve

miles away—so he had travelled, and seen the world—these very eyes had looked upon the county court-house—which was said to have a tin roof. The awe which these reflections inspired was attested by the impressive silence and the ranks of staring eyes. This was the great Judge Thatcher, brother of their own lawyer. Jeff Thatcher immediately went forward, to be familiar with the great man and be envied by the school. It would have been music to his soul to hear the whisperings:

"Look at him, Jim! He's a going up there. Say—look! he's a going to shake hands with him—he IS shaking hands with him! By jings, don't you wish you was Jeff?"

Mr. Walters fell to "showing off," with all sorts of official bustlings and activities, giving orders, delivering judgments, discharging directions here, there, everywhere that he could find a target. The librarian "showed off"—running hither and thither with his arms full of books and making a deal of the splutter and fuss that insect authority delights in. The young lady teachers "showed off" —bending sweetly over pupils that were lately being boxed, lifting pretty warning fingers at bad little boys and patting good ones lovingly. The young gentlemen teachers "showed off" with small scoldings and other little displays of authority and fine attention to discipline—and most of the teachers, of both sexes, found business up at the library, by the pulpit; and it was business that frequently had to be done over again two or three times (with much seeming vexation). The little girls "showed off" in various ways, and the little boys "showed off" with such diligence that the air was thick with paper wads and the murmur of scufflings. And above it all the great man sat and beamed a majestic judicial smile upon all the house, and warmed himself in the sun of his own grandeur—for he was "showing off," too.

There was only one thing wanting to make Mr. Walters' ecstasy complete, and that was a chance to deliver a Bible-prize and exhibit a prodigy. Several pupils had a few yellow tickets, but none had enough —he had been around among the star pupils inquiring. He would have given worlds, now, to have that German lad back again with a sound mind.

And now at this moment, when hope was dead, Tom Sawyer came forward with nine yellow tickets, nine red tickets, and ten blue ones, and demanded a Bible. This was a thunderbolt out of a clear sky. Walters was not expecting an application from this source for the next ten years. But there was no getting around it—here were the certified checks, and they were good for their face. Tom was therefore elevated to a place with the Judge and the other elect, and the great news was announced from headquarters. It was the most stunning surprise of the decade, and so profound was the sensation that it lifted the new hero up to the judicial one's altitude, and the school had two marvels to gaze upon in place of one. The boys were all eaten up with envy—but those that suffered the bitterest pangs were those who perceived too late that they themselves had contributed to this hated splendor by trading tickets to Tom for the wealth he had amassed in selling whitewashing privileges. These despised themselves, as being the dupes of a wily fraud, a guileful snake in the grass.

The prize was delivered to Tom with as much effusion as the superintendent could pump up under the circumstances; but it lacked somewhat of the true gush, for the poor fellow's instinct taught him that there was a mystery here that could not well bear the light, perhaps; it was simply preposterous that this boy had warehoused two thousand sheaves of Scriptural wisdom on his premises—a dozen would strain his capacity, without a doubt.

Amy Lawrence was proud and glad, and she tried to make Tom see it in her face—but he wouldn't look. She wondered; then she was just a grain troubled; next a dim suspicion came and went—came again; she watched; a furtive glance told her worlds—and then her heart broke, and she was jealous, and angry, and the tears came and she hated everybody. Tom most of all (she thought).

Tom was introduced to the Judge; but his tongue was tied, his breath would hardly come, his heart quaked—partly because of the awful greatness of the man, but mainly because he was her parent. He would have liked to fall down and worship him, if it were in the dark. The Judge put his hand on Tom's head and called him a fine little man, and asked him what his name was. The boy stammered, gasped, and got it out:

"Tom."

"Oh, no, not Tom—it is—"

"Thomas."

"Ah, that's it. I thought there was more to it, maybe. That's very well. But you've another one I daresay, and you'll tell it to me, won't you?"

"Tell the gentleman your other name, Thomas," said Walters, "and say sir. You mustn't forget your manners."

"Thomas Sawyer—sir."

"That's it! That's a good boy. Fine boy. Fine, manly little fellow. Two thousand verses is a great many—very, very great many. And you never can be sorry for the trouble you took to learn them; for knowledge is worth more than anything there is in the world; it's what makes great men and good men; you'll be a great man and a good man yourself, some day, Thomas, and then you'll look back and say, It's all owing to the precious Sunday-school privileges of my boyhood—it's all owing to my dear teachers that taught me to learn—it's all owing to the good superintendent, who encouraged me, and watched over me, and gave me a beautiful Bible—a splendid elegant Bible—to keep and have it all for my own, always—it's all owing to right bringing up! That is what you will say, Thomas—and you wouldn't take any money for those two thousand verses—no indeed you wouldn't. And now you wouldn't mind telling me and this lady some of the things you've learned—no, I know you wouldn't—for we are proud of little boys that learn. Now, no doubt you know the names of all the twelve disciples. Won't you tell us the names of the first two that were appointed?"

Tom was tugging at a button-hole and looking sheepish. He blushed, now, and his eyes fell. Mr. Walters' heart sank within him. He said to himself, it is not possible that the boy can answer the simplest question—why DID the Judge ask him? Yet he felt obliged to speak up and say:

"Answer the gentleman, Thomas—don't be afraid."

Tom still hung fire.

"Now I know you'll tell me," said the lady. "The names of the first two disciples were—"

"DAVID AND GOLIAH!"

Let us draw the curtain of charity over the rest of the scene.

CHAPTER V

ABOUT half-past ten the cracked bell of the small church began to ring, and presently the people began to gather for the morning sermon. The Sunday-school children distributed themselves about the house and occupied pews with their parents, so as to be under supervision. Aunt Polly came, and Tom and Sid and Mary sat with her—Tom being placed next the aisle, in order that he might be as far away from the open window and the seductive outside summer scenes as possible. The crowd filed up the aisles: the aged and needy postmaster, who had seen better days; the mayor and his wife—for they had a mayor there, among other unnecessaries; the justice of the peace; the widow Douglass, fair, smart, and forty, a generous, good-hearted soul and well-to-do, her hill mansion the only palace in the town, and the most hospitable and much the most lavish in the matter of festivities that St. Petersburg could boast; the bent and venerable Major and Mrs. Ward; lawyer Riverson, the new notable from a distance; next the belle of the village, followed by a troop of lawn-clad and ribbon-decked young heart-breakers; then all the young clerks in town in a body—for they had stood in the vestibule sucking their cane-heads, a circling wall of oiled and simpering admirers, till the last girl had run their gantlet; and last of all came the Model Boy, Willie Mufferson, taking as heedful care of his mother as if she were cut glass. He always brought his mother to church, and was the pride of all the matrons. The boys all hated him, he was so good. And besides, he had been "thrown up to them" so much. His white handkerchief was hanging out of his pocket behind, as usual on Sundays—accidentally. Tom had no handkerchief, and he looked upon boys who had as snobs.

The congregation being fully assembled, now, the bell rang once more, to warn laggards and stragglers, and then a solemn hush fell upon the church which was only broken by the tittering and whispering of the choir in the gallery. The choir always tittered and whispered all through service. There was once a church choir that was not ill-bred, but I have forgotten where it was, now. It was a great many years ago, and I can scarcely remember anything about it, but I think it was in some foreign country.

The minister gave out the hymn, and read it through with a relish, in a peculiar style which was much admired in that part of the country. His voice began on a medium key and climbed steadily up till it reached a certain point, where it bore with strong emphasis upon the topmost word and then plunged down as if from a spring-board:

Shall I be car-ri-ed toe the skies, on flow'ry BEDS of ease,

Whilst others fight to win the prize, and sail thro' BLOODY seas?

He was regarded as a wonderful reader. At church "sociables" he was always called upon to read poetry; and when he was through, the ladies would lift up their hands and let them fall helplessly in their laps, and "wall" their eyes, and shake their heads, as much as to say, "Words cannot express it; it is too beautiful, TOO beautiful for this mortal earth."

After the hymn had been sung, the Rev. Mr. Sprague turned himself into a bulletin-board, and read off "notices" of meetings and societies and things till it seemed that the list would stretch out to the crack of doom—a queer custom which is still kept up in America, even in cities, away here in this age of abundant newspapers. Often, the less there is to justify a traditional custom, the harder it is to get rid of it.

And now the minister prayed. A good, generous prayer it was, and went into details: it pleaded for the church, and the little children of the church; for the other churches of the village; for the village itself; for the county; for the State; for the State officers; for the United States; for the churches of the United States; for Congress; for the President; for the officers of the Government; for poor sailors, tossed by stormy seas; for the oppressed millions groaning under the heel of European monarchies and Oriental despotisms; for such as have the light and the good tidings, and yet have not eyes to see nor ears to hear withal; for the heathen in the far islands of the sea; and closed with a supplication that the words he was about to speak might find grace and favor, and be as seed sown in fertile ground, yielding in time a grateful harvest of good. Amen.

There was a rustling of dresses, and the standing congregation sat down. The boy whose history this book relates did not enjoy the prayer, he only endured it—if he even did that much. He was restive all through it; he kept tally of the details of the prayer, unconsciously —for he was not listening, but he knew the ground of old, and the clergyman's regular route over it— and when a little trifle of new matter was interlarded, his ear detected it and his whole nature resented it; he considered additions unfair, and scoundrelly. In the midst of the prayer a fly had lit on the back of the pew in front of him and tortured his spirit by calmly rubbing its hands together, embracing its head with its arms, and polishing it so vigorously that it seemed to almost part company with the body, and the slender thread of a neck was exposed to view; scraping its wings with its hind legs and smoothing them to its body as if they had been coat-tails; going through its whole toilet as tranquilly as if it knew it was perfectly safe. As indeed it was; for as sorely as Tom's hands itched to grab for it they did not dare—he believed his soul would be instantly destroyed if he did such a thing while the prayer was going on. But with the closing sentence his hand began to curve and steal forward; and the instant the "Amen" was out the fly was a prisoner of war. His aunt detected the act and made him let it go.

The minister gave out his text and droned along monotonously through an argument that was so prosy that many a head by and by began to nod —and yet it was an argument that dealt in limitless fire and brimstone and thinned the predestined elect down to a company so small as to be hardly worth the saving. Tom counted the pages of the sermon; after church he always knew how many pages there had been, but he seldom knew anything else about the discourse. However, this time he was really interested for a little while. The minister made a grand and moving picture of the assembling together of the world's hosts at the millennium when the lion and the lamb should lie down together and a little child should lead them. But the pathos, the lesson, the moral of the great spectacle were lost upon the boy; he only thought of the conspicuousness of the principal character before the on-looking nations; his face lit with the thought, and he said to himself that he wished he could be that child, if it was a tame lion.

Now he lapsed into suffering again, as the dry argument was resumed. Presently he bethought him of a treasure he had and got it out. It was a large black beetle with formidable jaws—a "pinchbug," he called it. It was in a percussion-cap box. The first thing the beetle did was to take him by the finger. A

natural fillip followed, the beetle went floundering into the aisle and lit on its back, and the hurt finger went into the boy's mouth. The beetle lay there working its helpless legs, unable to turn over. Tom eyed it, and longed for it; but it was safe out of his reach. Other people uninterested in the sermon found relief in the beetle, and they eyed it too. Presently a vagrant poodle dog came idling along, sad at heart, lazy with the summer softness and the quiet, weary of captivity, sighing for change. He spied the beetle; the drooping tail lifted and wagged. He surveyed the prize; walked around it; smelt at it from a safe distance; walked around it again; grew bolder, and took a closer smell; then lifted his lip and made a gingerly snatch at it, just missing it; made another, and another; began to enjoy the diversion; subsided to his stomach with the beetle between his paws, and continued his experiments; grew weary at last, and then indifferent and absent-minded. His head nodded, and little by little his chin descended and touched the enemy, who seized it. There was a sharp yelp, a flirt of the poodle's head, and the beetle fell a couple of yards away, and lit on its back once more. The neighboring spectators shook with a gentle inward joy, several faces went behind fans and handkerchiefs, and Tom was entirely happy. The dog looked foolish, and probably felt so; but there was resentment in his heart, too, and a craving for revenge. So he went to the beetle and began a wary attack on it again; jumping at it from every point of a circle, lighting with his fore-paws within an inch of the creature, making even closer snatches at it with his teeth, and jerking his head till his ears flapped again. But he grew tired once more, after a while; tried to amuse himself with a fly but found no relief; followed an ant around, with his nose close to the floor, and quickly wearied of that; yawned, sighed, forgot the beetle entirely, and sat down on it. Then there was a wild yelp of agony and the poodle went sailing up the aisle; the yelps continued, and so did the dog; he crossed the house in front of the altar; he flew down the other aisle; he crossed before the doors; he clamored up the home-stretch; his anguish grew with his progress, till presently he was but a woolly comet moving in its orbit with the gleam and the speed of light. At last the frantic sufferer sheered from its course, and sprang into its master's lap; he flung it out of the window, and the voice of distress quickly thinned away and died in the distance.

By this time the whole church was red-faced and suffocating with suppressed laughter, and the sermon had come to a dead standstill. The discourse was resumed presently, but it went lame and halting, all possibility of impressiveness being at an end; for even the gravest sentiments were constantly being received with a smothered burst of unholy mirth, under cover of some remote pew-back, as if the poor parson had said a rarely facetious thing. It was a genuine relief to the whole congregation when the ordeal was over and the benediction pronounced.

Tom Sawyer went home quite cheerful, thinking to himself that there was some satisfaction about divine service when there was a bit of variety in it. He had but one marring thought; he was willing that the dog should play with his pinchbug, but he did not think it was upright in him to carry it off.

CHAPTER VI

MONDAY morning found Tom Sawyer miserable. Monday morning always found him so—because it began another week's slow suffering in school. He generally began that day with wishing he had had no intervening holiday, it made the going into captivity and fetters again so much more odious.

Tom lay thinking. Presently it occurred to him that he wished he was sick; then he could stay home from school. Here was a vague possibility. He canvassed his system. No ailment was found, and he investigated again. This time he thought he could detect colicky symptoms, and he began to encourage them with considerable hope. But they soon grew feeble, and presently died wholly away. He reflected further. Suddenly he discovered something. One of his upper front teeth was loose. This was lucky; he was about to begin to groan, as a "starter," as he called it, when it occurred to him that if he came into court with that argument, his aunt would pull it out, and that would hurt. So he thought he would hold the tooth in reserve for the present, and seek further. Nothing offered for some little time, and then he remembered hearing the doctor tell about a certain thing that laid up a patient for two or three weeks and threatened to make him lose a finger. So the boy eagerly drew his sore toe from under the sheet and held it up for inspection. But now he did not know the necessary symptoms. However, it seemed well worth while to chance it, so he fell to groaning with considerable spirit.

But Sid slept on unconscious.

Tom groaned louder, and fancied that he began to feel pain in the toe.

No result from Sid.

Tom was panting with his exertions by this time. He took a rest and then swelled himself up and fetched a succession of admirable groans.

Sid snored on.

Tom was aggravated. He said, "Sid, Sid!" and shook him. This course worked well, and Tom began to groan again. Sid yawned, stretched, then brought himself up on his elbow with a snort, and began to stare at Tom. Tom went on groaning. Sid said:

"Tom! Say, Tom!" [No response.] "Here, Tom! TOM! What is the matter, Tom?" And he shook him and looked in his face anxiously.

Tom moaned out:

"Oh, don't, Sid. Don't joggle me."

"Why, what's the matter, Tom? I must call auntie."

"No—never mind. It'll be over by and by, maybe. Don't call anybody."

"But I must! DON'T groan so, Tom, it's awful. How long you been this way?"

"Hours. Ouch! Oh, don't stir so, Sid, you'll kill me."

"Tom, why didn't you wake me sooner? Oh, Tom, DON'T! It makes my flesh crawl to hear you. Tom, what is the matter?"

"I forgive you everything, Sid. [Groan.] Everything you've ever done to me. When I'm gone—"

"Oh, Tom, you ain't dying, are you? Don't, Tom—oh, don't. Maybe—"

"I forgive everybody, Sid. [Groan.] Tell 'em so, Sid. And Sid, you give my window-sash and my cat with one eye to that new girl that's come to town, and tell her—"

But Sid had snatched his clothes and gone. Tom was suffering in reality, now, so handsomely was his imagination working, and so his groans had gathered quite a genuine tone.

Sid flew down-stairs and said:

"Oh, Aunt Polly, come! Tom's dying!"

"Dying!"

"Yes'm. Don't wait—come quick!"

"Rubbage! I don't believe it!"

But she fled up-stairs, nevertheless, with Sid and Mary at her heels. And her face grew white, too, and her lip trembled. When she reached the bedside she gasped out:

"You, Tom! Tom, what's the matter with you?"

"Oh, auntie, I'm—"

"What's the matter with you—what is the matter with you, child?"

"Oh, auntie, my sore toe's mortified!"

The old lady sank down into a chair and laughed a little, then cried a little, then did both together. This restored her and she said:

"Tom, what a turn you did give me. Now you shut up that nonsense and climb out of this."

The groans ceased and the pain vanished from the toe. The boy felt a little foolish, and he said:

"Aunt Polly, it SEEMED mortified, and it hurt so I never minded my tooth at all."

"Your tooth, indeed! What's the matter with your tooth?"

"One of them's loose, and it aches perfectly awful."

"There, there, now, don't begin that groaning again. Open your mouth. Well—your tooth IS loose, but you're not going to die about that. Mary, get me a silk thread, and a chunk of fire out of the kitchen."

Tom said:

"Oh, please, auntie, don't pull it out. It don't hurt any more. I wish I may never stir if it does. Please don't, auntie. I don't want to stay home from school."

"Oh, you don't, don't you? So all this row was because you thought you'd get to stay home from school and go a-fishing? Tom, Tom, I love you so, and you seem to try every way you can to break my old heart with your outrageousness." By this time the dental instruments were ready. The old lady made one end of the silk thread fast to Tom's tooth with a loop and tied the other to the bedpost. Then she seized the chunk of fire and suddenly thrust it almost into the boy's face. The tooth hung dangling by the bedpost, now.

But all trials bring their compensations. As Tom wended to school after breakfast, he was the envy of every boy he met because the gap in his upper row of teeth enabled him to expectorate in a new and admirable way. He gathered quite a following of lads interested in the exhibition; and one that had cut his finger and had been a centre of fascination and homage up to this time, now found himself suddenly without an adherent, and shorn of his glory. His heart was heavy, and he said with a disdain which he did not feel that it wasn't anything to spit like Tom Sawyer; but another boy said, "Sour grapes!" and he wandered away a dismantled hero.

Shortly Tom came upon the juvenile pariah of the village, Huckleberry Finn, son of the town drunkard. Huckleberry was cordially hated and dreaded by all the mothers of the town, because he was idle and lawless and vulgar and bad—and because all their children admired him so, and delighted in his forbidden society, and wished they dared to be like him. Tom was like the rest of the respectable boys, in that he envied Huckleberry his gaudy outcast condition, and was under strict orders not to play with him. So he played with him every time he got a chance. Huckleberry was always dressed in the cast-off clothes of full-grown men, and they were in perennial bloom and fluttering with rags. His hat was a vast ruin with a wide crescent lopped out of its brim; his coat, when he wore one, hung nearly to his heels and had the rearward buttons far down the back; but one suspender supported his trousers; the seat of the trousers bagged low and contained nothing, the fringed legs dragged in the dirt when not rolled up.

Huckleberry came and went, at his own free will. He slept on doorsteps in fine weather and in empty hogsheads in wet; he did not have to go to school or to church, or call any being master or obey anybody; he could go fishing or swimming when and where he chose, and stay as long as it suited him; nobody forbade him to fight; he could sit up as late as he pleased; he was always the first boy that went barefoot in the spring and the last to resume leather in the fall; he never had to wash, nor put on clean clothes; he could swear wonderfully. In a word, everything that goes to make life precious that boy had. So thought every harassed, hampered, respectable boy in St. Petersburg.

Tom hailed the romantic outcast:

"Hello, Huckleberry!"

"Hello yourself, and see how you like it."

"What's that you got?"

"Dead cat."

"Lemme see him, Huck. My, he's pretty stiff. Where'd you get him ?"

"Bought him off'n a boy."

"What did you give?"

"I give a blue ticket and a bladder that I got at the slaughter-house."

"Where'd you get the blue ticket?"

"Bought it off'n Ben Rogers two weeks ago for a hoop-stick."

"Say—what is dead cats good for, Huck?"

"Good for? Cure warts with."

"No! Is that so? I know something that's better."

"I bet you don't. What is it?"

"Why, spunk-water."

"Spunk-water! I wouldn't give a dern for spunk-water."

"You wouldn't, wouldn't you? D'you ever try it?"

"No, I hain't. But Bob Tanner did."

"Who told you so!"

"Why, he told Jeff Thatcher, and Jeff told Johnny Baker, and Johnny told Jim Hollis, and Jim told Ben Rogers, and Ben told a nigger, and the nigger told me. There now!"

"Well, what of it? They'll all lie. Leastways all but the nigger. I don't know HIM. But I never see a nigger that WOULDN'T lie. Shucks! Now you tell me how Bob Tanner done it, Huck."

"Why, he took and dipped his hand in a rotten stump where the rain-water was."

"In the daytime?"

"Certainly."

"With his face to the stump?"

"Yes. Least I reckon so."

"Did he say anything?"

"I don't reckon he did. I don't know."

"Aha! Talk about trying to cure warts with spunk-water such a blame fool way as that! Why, that ain't a-going to do any good. You got to go all by yourself, to the middle of the woods, where you know there's a spunk-water stump, and just as it's midnight you back up against the stump and jam your hand in and say:

'Barley-corn, barley-corn, injun-meal shorts, Spunk-water, spunk-water, swaller these warts,'

and then walk away quick, eleven steps, with your eyes shut, and then turn around three times and walk home without speaking to anybody. Because if you speak the charm's busted."

"Well, that sounds like a good way; but that ain't the way Bob Tanner done."

"No, sir, you can bet he didn't, becuz he's the wartiest boy in this town; and he wouldn't have a wart on him if he'd knowed how to work spunk-water. I've took off thousands of warts off of my hands that way, Huck. I play with frogs so much that I've always got considerable many warts. Sometimes I take 'em off with a bean."

"Yes, bean's good. I've done that."

"Have you? What's your way?"

"You take and split the bean, and cut the wart so as to get some blood, and then you put the blood on one piece of the bean and take and dig a hole and bury it 'bout midnight at the crossroads in the dark of the moon, and then you burn up the rest of the bean. You see that piece that's got the blood on it will keep drawing and drawing, trying to fetch the other piece to it, and so that helps the blood to draw the wart, and pretty soon off she comes."

"Yes, that's it, Huck—that's it; though when you're burying it if you say 'Down bean; off wart; come no more to bother me!' it's better. That's the way Joe Harper does, and he's been nearly to Coonville and most everywheres. But say—how do you cure 'em with dead cats?"

"Why, you take your cat and go and get in the graveyard 'long about midnight when somebody that was wicked has been buried; and when it's midnight a devil will come, or maybe two or three, but you can't see 'em, you can only hear something like the wind, or maybe hear 'em talk; and when they're taking that feller away, you heave your cat after 'em and say, 'Devil follow corpse, cat follow devil, warts follow cat, I'm done with ye!' That'll fetch ANY wart."

"Sounds right. D'you ever try it, Huck?"

"No, but old Mother Hopkins told me."

"Well, I reckon it's so, then. Becuz they say she's a witch."

"Say! Why, Tom, I KNOW she is. She witched pap. Pap says so his own self. He come along one day, and he see she was a-witching him, so he took up a rock, and if she hadn't dodged, he'd a got her. Well, that very night he rolled off'n a shed wher' he was a layin drunk, and broke his arm."

"Why, that's awful. How did he know she was a-witching him?"

"Lord, pap can tell, easy. Pap says when they keep looking at you right stiddy, they're a-witching you. Specially if they mumble. Becuz when they mumble they're saying the Lord's Prayer backards."

"Say, Hucky, when you going to try the cat?"

"To-night. I reckon they'll come after old Hoss Williams to-night."

"But they buried him Saturday. Didn't they get him Saturday night?"

"Why, how you talk! How could their charms work till midnight?—and THEN it's Sunday. Devils don't slosh around much of a Sunday, I don't reckon."

"I never thought of that. That's so. Lemme go with you?"

"Of course—if you ain't afeard."

"Afeard! 'Tain't likely. Will you meow?"

"Yes—and you meow back, if you get a chance. Last time, you kep' me a-meowing around till old Hays went to throwing rocks at me and says 'Dern that cat!' and so I hove a brick through his window—but don't you tell."

"I won't. I couldn't meow that night, becuz auntie was watching me, but I'll meow this time. Say—what's that?"

"Nothing but a tick."

"Where'd you get him?"

"Out in the woods."

"What'll you take for him?"

"I don't know. I don't want to sell him."

"All right. It's a mighty small tick, anyway."

"Oh, anybody can run a tick down that don't belong to them. I'm satisfied with it. It's a good enough tick for me."

"Sho, there's ticks a plenty. I could have a thousand of 'em if I wanted to."

"Well, why don't you? Becuz you know mighty well you can't. This is a pretty early tick, I reckon. It's the first one I've seen this year."

"Say, Huck—I'll give you my tooth for him."

"Less see it."

Tom got out a bit of paper and carefully unrolled it. Huckleberry viewed it wistfully. The temptation was very strong. At last he said:

"Is it genuwyne?"

Tom lifted his lip and showed the vacancy.

"Well, all right," said Huckleberry, "it's a trade."

Tom enclosed the tick in the percussion-cap box that had lately been the pinchbug's prison, and the boys separated, each feeling wealthier than before.

When Tom reached the little isolated frame schoolhouse, he strode in briskly, with the manner of one who had come with all honest speed. He hung his hat on a peg and flung himself into his seat with business-like alacrity. The master, throned on high in his great splint-bottom arm-chair, was dozing, lulled by the drowsy hum of study. The interruption roused him.

"Thomas Sawyer!"

Tom knew that when his name was pronounced in full, it meant trouble.

"Sir!"

"Come up here. Now, sir, why are you late again, as usual?"

Tom was about to take refuge in a lie, when he saw two long tails of yellow hair hanging down a back that he recognized by the electric sympathy of love; and by that form was THE ONLY VACANT PLACE on the girls' side of the schoolhouse. He instantly said:

"I STOPPED TO TALK WITH HUCKLEBERRY FINN!"

The master's pulse stood still, and he stared helplessly. The buzz of study ceased. The pupils wondered if this foolhardy boy had lost his mind. The master said:

"You—you did what?"

"Stopped to talk with Huckleberry Finn."

There was no mistaking the words.

"Thomas Sawyer, this is the most astounding confession I have ever listened to. No mere ferule will answer for this offence. Take off your jacket."

The master's arm performed until it was tired and the stock of switches notably diminished. Then the order followed:

"Now, sir, go and sit with the girls! And let this be a warning to you."

The titter that rippled around the room appeared to abash the boy, but in reality that result was caused rather more by his worshipful awe of his unknown idol and the dread pleasure that lay in his high good fortune. He sat down upon the end of the pine bench and the girl hitched herself away from him with a toss of her head. Nudges and winks and whispers traversed the room, but Tom sat still, with his arms upon the long, low desk before him, and seemed to study his book.

By and by attention ceased from him, and the accustomed school murmur rose upon the dull air once more. Presently the boy began to steal furtive glances at the girl. She observed it, "made a mouth" at him and gave him the back of her head for the space of a minute. When she cautiously faced around again, a peach lay before her. She thrust it away. Tom gently put it back. She thrust it away again, but with less animosity. Tom patiently returned it to its place. Then she let it remain. Tom scrawled on his slate, "Please take it—I got more." The girl glanced at the words, but made no sign. Now the boy began to draw something on the slate, hiding his work with his left hand. For a time the girl refused to notice; but her human curiosity presently began to manifest itself by hardly perceptible signs. The boy worked on, apparently unconscious. The girl made a sort of noncommittal attempt to see, but the boy did not betray that he was aware of it. At last she gave in and hesitatingly whispered:

"Let me see it."

Tom partly uncovered a dismal caricature of a house with two gable ends to it and a corkscrew of smoke issuing from the chimney. Then the girl's interest began to fasten itself upon the work and she forgot everything else. When it was finished, she gazed a moment, then whispered:

"It's nice—make a man."

The artist erected a man in the front yard, that resembled a derrick. He could have stepped over the house; but the girl was not hypercritical; she was satisfied with the monster, and whispered:

"It's a beautiful man—now make me coming along."

Tom drew an hour-glass with a full moon and straw limbs to it and armed the spreading fingers with a portentous fan. The girl said:

"It's ever so nice—I wish I could draw."

"It's easy," whispered Tom, "I'll learn you."

"Oh, will you? When?"

"At noon. Do you go home to dinner?"

"I'll stay if you will."

"Good—that's a whack. What's your name?"

"Becky Thatcher. What's yours? Oh, I know. It's Thomas Sawyer."

"That's the name they lick me by. I'm Tom when I'm good. You call me Tom, will you?"

"Yes."

Now Tom began to scrawl something on the slate, hiding the words from the girl. But she was not backward this time. She begged to see. Tom said:

"Oh, it ain't anything."

"Yes it is."

"No it ain't. You don't want to see."

"Yes I do, indeed I do. Please let me."

"You'll tell."

"No I won't—deed and deed and double deed won't."

"You won't tell anybody at all? Ever, as long as you live?"

"No, I won't ever tell ANYbody. Now let me."

"Oh, YOU don't want to see!"

"Now that you treat me so, I WILL see." And she put her small hand upon his and a little scuffle ensued, Tom pretending to resist in earnest but letting his hand slip by degrees till these words were revealed: "I LOVE YOU."

"Oh, you bad thing!" And she hit his hand a smart rap, but reddened and looked pleased, nevertheless.

Just at this juncture the boy felt a slow, fateful grip closing on his ear, and a steady lifting impulse. In that vise he was borne across the house and deposited in his own seat, under a peppering fire of giggles from the whole school. Then the master stood over him during a few awful moments, and finally moved away to his throne without saying a word. But although Tom's ear tingled, his heart was jubilant.

As the school quieted down Tom made an honest effort to study, but the turmoil within him was too great. In turn he took his place in the reading class and made a botch of it; then in the geography class and turned lakes into mountains, mountains into rivers, and rivers into continents, till chaos was come again; then in the spelling class, and got "turned down," by a succession of mere baby words, till he brought up at the foot and yielded up the pewter medal which he had worn with ostentation for months.

CHAPTER VII

THE harder Tom tried to fasten his mind on his book, the more his ideas wandered. So at last, with a sigh and a yawn, he gave it up. It seemed to him that the noon recess would never come. The air was utterly dead. There was not a breath stirring. It was the sleepiest of sleepy days. The drowsing murmur of the five and twenty studying scholars soothed the soul like the spell that is in the murmur of bees. Away off in the flaming sunshine, Cardiff Hill lifted its soft green sides through a shimmering veil of heat, tinted with the purple of distance; a few birds floated on lazy wing high in the air; no other living thing was visible but some cows, and they were asleep. Tom's heart ached to be free, or else to have something of interest to do to pass the dreary time. His hand wandered into his pocket and his face lit up with a glow of gratitude that was prayer, though he did not know it. Then furtively the percussion-cap box came out. He released the tick and put him on the long flat desk. The creature probably glowed with a gratitude that amounted to prayer, too, at this moment, but it was premature: for when he started thankfully to travel off, Tom turned him aside with a pin and made him take a new direction.

Tom's bosom friend sat next him, suffering just as Tom had been, and now he was deeply and gratefully interested in this entertainment in an instant. This bosom friend was Joe Harper. The two boys were sworn friends all the week, and embattled enemies on Saturdays. Joe took a pin out of his lapel and began to assist in exercising the prisoner. The sport grew in interest momently. Soon Tom said that they were interfering with each other, and neither getting the fullest benefit of the tick. So he put Joe's slate on the desk and drew a line down the middle of it from top to bottom.

"Now," said he, "as long as he is on your side you can stir him up and I'll let him alone; but if you let him get away and get on my side, you're to leave him alone as long as I can keep him from crossing over."

"All right, go ahead; start him up."

The tick escaped from Tom, presently, and crossed the equator. Joe harassed him awhile, and then he got away and crossed back again. This change of base occurred often. While one boy was worrying the tick with absorbing interest, the other would look on with interest as strong, the two heads bowed together over the slate, and the two souls dead to all things else. At last luck seemed to settle and abide with Joe. The tick tried this, that, and the other course, and got as excited and as anxious as the boys themselves, but time and again just as he would have victory in his very grasp, so to speak, and Tom's fingers would be twitching to begin, Joe's pin would deftly head him off, and keep possession. At last Tom could stand it no longer. The temptation was too strong. So he reached out and lent a hand with his pin. Joe was angry in a moment. Said he:

"Tom, you let him alone."

"I only just want to stir him up a little, Joe."

"No, sir, it ain't fair; you just let him alone."

"Blame it, I ain't going to stir him much."

"Let him alone, I tell you."

"I won't!"

"You shall—he's on my side of the line."

"Look here, Joe Harper, whose is that tick?"

"I don't care whose tick he is—he's on my side of the line, and you sha'n't touch him."

"Well, I'll just bet I will, though. He's my tick and I'll do what I blame please with him, or die!"

A tremendous whack came down on Tom's shoulders, and its duplicate on Joe's; and for the space of two minutes the dust continued to fly from the two jackets and the whole school to enjoy it. The boys had been too absorbed to notice the hush that had stolen upon the school awhile before when the master came tiptoeing down the room and stood over them. He had contemplated a good part of the performance before he contributed his bit of variety to it.

When school broke up at noon, Tom flew to Becky Thatcher, and whispered in her ear:

"Put on your bonnet and let on you're going home; and when you get to the corner, give the rest of 'em the slip, and turn down through the lane and come back. I'll go the other way and come it over 'em the same way."

So the one went off with one group of scholars, and the other with another. In a little while the two met at the bottom of the lane, and when they reached the school they had it all to themselves. Then they sat together, with a slate before them, and Tom gave Becky the pencil and held her hand in his, guiding it, and so created another surprising house. When the interest in art began to wane, the two fell to talking. Tom was swimming in bliss. He said:

"Do you love rats?"

"No! I hate them!"

"Well, I do, too—LIVE ones. But I mean dead ones, to swing round your head with a string."

"No, I don't care for rats much, anyway. What I like is chewing-gum."

"Oh, I should say so! I wish I had some now."

"Do you? I've got some. I'll let you chew it awhile, but you must give it back to me."

That was agreeable, so they chewed it turn about, and dangled their legs against the bench in excess of contentment.

"Was you ever at a circus?" said Tom.

"Yes, and my pa's going to take me again some time, if I'm good."

"I been to the circus three or four times—lots of times. Church ain't shucks to a circus. There's things going on at a circus all the time. I'm going to be a clown in a circus when I grow up."

"Oh, are you! That will be nice. They're so lovely, all spotted up."

"Yes, that's so. And they get slathers of money—most a dollar a day, Ben Rogers says. Say, Becky, was you ever engaged?"

"What's that?"

"Why, engaged to be married."

"No."

"Would you like to?"

"I reckon so. I don't know. What is it like?"

"Like? Why it ain't like anything. You only just tell a boy you won't ever have anybody but him, ever ever ever, and then you kiss and that's all. Anybody can do it."

"Kiss? What do you kiss for?"

"Why, that, you know, is to—well, they always do that."

"Everybody?"

"Why, yes, everybody that's in love with each other. Do you remember what I wrote on the slate?"

"Ye—yes."

"What was it?"

"I sha'n't tell you."

"Shall I tell YOU?"

"Ye—yes—but some other time."

"No, now."

"No, not now—to-morrow."

"Oh, no, NOW. Please, Becky—I'll whisper it, I'll whisper it ever so easy."

Becky hesitating, Tom took silence for consent, and passed his arm about her waist and whispered the tale ever so softly, with his mouth close to her ear. And then he added:

"Now you whisper it to me—just the same."

She resisted, for a while, and then said:

"You turn your face away so you can't see, and then I will. But you mustn't ever tell anybody—WILL you, Tom? Now you won't, WILL you?"

"No, indeed, indeed I won't. Now, Becky."

He turned his face away. She bent timidly around till her breath stirred his curls and whispered, "I—love—you!"

Then she sprang away and ran around and around the desks and benches, with Tom after her, and took refuge in a corner at last, with her little white apron to her face. Tom clasped her about her neck and pleaded:

"Now, Becky, it's all done—all over but the kiss. Don't you be afraid of that—it ain't anything at all. Please, Becky." And he

tugged at her apron and the hands.

By and by she gave up, and let her hands drop; her face, all glowing with the struggle, came up and submitted. Tom kissed the red lips and said:

"Now it's all done, Becky. And always after this, you know, you ain't ever to love anybody but me, and you ain't ever to marry anybody but me, ever never and forever. Will you?"

"No, I'll never love anybody but you, Tom, and I'll never marry anybody but you—and you ain't to ever marry anybody but me, either."

"Certainly. Of course. That's PART of it. And always coming to school or when we're going home, you're to walk with me, when there ain't anybody looking—and you choose me and I choose you at parties, because that's the way you do when you're engaged."

"It's so nice. I never heard of it before."

"Oh, it's ever so gay! Why, me and Amy Lawrence—"

The big eyes told Tom his blunder and he stopped, confused.

"Oh, Tom! Then I ain't the first you've ever been engaged to!"

The child began to cry. Tom said:

"Oh, don't cry, Becky, I don't care for her any more."

"Yes, you do, Tom—you know you do."

Tom tried to put his arm about her neck, but she pushed him away and turned her face to the wall, and went on crying. Tom tried again, with soothing words in his mouth, and was repulsed again. Then his pride was up, and he strode away and went outside. He stood about, restless and uneasy, for a while, glancing at the door, every now and then, hoping she would repent and come to find him. But she did not. Then he began to feel badly and fear that he was in the wrong. It was a hard struggle with him to make new advances, now, but he nerved himself to it and entered. She was still standing back there in the corner, sobbing, with her face to the wall. Tom's heart smote him. He went to her and stood a moment, not knowing exactly how to proceed. Then he said hesitatingly:

"Becky, I—I don't care for anybody but you."

No reply—but sobs.

"Becky"—pleadingly. "Becky, won't you say something?"

More sobs.

Tom got out his chiefest jewel, a brass knob from the top of an andiron, and passed it around her so that she could see it, and said:

"Please, Becky, won't you take it?"

She struck it to the floor. Then Tom marched out of the house and over the hills and far away, to return to school no more that day. Presently Becky began to suspect. She ran to the door; he was not in sight; she flew around to the play-yard; he was not there. Then she called:

"Tom! Come back, Tom!"

She listened intently, but there was no answer. She had no companions but silence and loneliness. So she sat down to cry again and upbraid herself; and by this time the scholars began to gather again, and she had to hide her griefs and still her broken heart and take up the cross of a long, dreary, aching afternoon, with none among the strangers about her to exchange sorrows with.

CHAPTER VIII

TOM dodged hither and thither through lanes until he was well out of the track of returning scholars, and then fell into a moody jog. He crossed a small "branch" two or three times, because of a prevailing juvenile superstition that to cross water baffled pursuit. Half an hour later he was disappearing behind the Douglas mansion on the summit of Cardiff Hill, and the schoolhouse was hardly distinguishable away off in the valley behind him. He entered a dense wood, picked his pathless way to the centre of it, and sat down on a mossy spot under a spreading oak. There was not even a zephyr stirring; the dead noonday heat had even stilled the songs of the birds; nature lay in a trance that was broken by no sound but the occasional far-off hammering of a woodpecker, and this seemed to render the pervading silence and sense of loneliness the more profound. The boy's soul was steeped in melancholy; his feelings were in happy accord with his surroundings. He sat long with his elbows on his knees and his chin in his hands, meditating. It seemed to him that life was but a trouble, at best, and he more than half envied Jimmy Hodges, so lately released; it must be very peaceful, he thought, to lie and slumber and dream forever and ever, with the wind whispering through the trees and caressing the grass and the flowers over the grave, and nothing to bother and grieve about, ever any more. If he only had a clean Sunday-school record he could be willing to go, and be done with it all. Now as to this girl. What had he done? Nothing. He had meant the best in the world, and been treated like a dog—like a very dog. She would be sorry some day—maybe when it was too late. Ah, if he could only die TEMPORARILY!

But the elastic heart of youth cannot be compressed into one constrained shape long at a time. Tom presently began to drift insensibly back into the concerns of this life again. What if he turned his back, now, and disappeared mysteriously? What if he went away—ever so far away, into unknown countries beyond the seas—and never came back any more! How would she feel then! The idea of being a clown recurred to him now, only to fill him with disgust. For frivolity and jokes and spotted tights were an offense, when they intruded themselves upon a spirit that was exalted into the vague august realm of the romantic. No, he would be a soldier, and return after long years, all war-worn and illustrious. No—better still, he would join the Indians, and hunt buffaloes and go on the warpath in the mountain ranges and the trackless great plains of the Far West, and away in the future come back a great chief, bristling with feathers, hideous with paint, and prance into Sunday-school, some drowsy summer morning, with a bloodcurdling war-whoop, and sear the eyeballs of all his companions with unappeasable envy. But no, there was something gaudier even than this. He would be a pirate! That was it! NOW his future lay plain before him, and glowing with unimaginable splendor. How his name would fill the world, and make people shudder! How gloriously he would go plowing the dancing seas, in his long, low, black-hulled racer, the Spirit of the Storm, with his grisly flag flying at the fore! And at the zenith of his fame, how he would suddenly appear at the old village and stalk into church, brown and weather-beaten, in his black velvet doublet and trunks, his great jack-boots, his crimson sash, his belt bristling with horse-pistols, his crime-rusted cutlass at his side, his slouch hat with waving plumes, his black flag unfurled, with the skull and crossbones on it, and hear with swelling ecstasy the whisperings, "It's Tom Sawyer the Pirate!—the Black Avenger of the Spanish Main!"

Yes, it was settled; his career was determined. He would run away from home and enter upon it. He would start the very next morning. Therefore he must now begin to get ready. He would collect his resources together. He went to a rotten log near at hand and began to dig under one end of it with his Barlow knife. He soon struck wood that sounded hollow. He put his hand there and uttered this incantation impressively:

"What hasn't come here, come! What's here, stay here!"

Then he scraped away the dirt, and exposed a pine shingle. He took it up and disclosed a shapely little treasure-house whose bottom and sides were of shingles. In it lay a marble. Tom's astonishment was boundless! He scratched his head with a perplexed air, and said:

"Well, that beats anything!"

Then he tossed the marble away pettishly, and stood cogitating. The truth was, that a superstition of his had failed, here, which he and all his comrades had always looked upon as infallible. If you buried a marble with certain necessary incantations, and left it alone a fortnight, and then opened the place with the incantation he had just used, you would find that all the marbles you had ever lost had gathered themselves together there, meantime, no matter how widely they had been separated. But now, this thing had actually and unquestionably failed. Tom's whole structure of faith was shaken to its foundations. He had many a time heard of this thing succeeding but never of its failing before. It did not occur to him that he had tried it several times before, himself, but could never find the hiding-places afterward. He puzzled over the matter some time, and finally decided that some witch had interfered and broken the charm. He thought he would satisfy himself on that point; so he searched around till he found a small sandy spot with a little funnel-shaped depression in it. He laid himself down and put his mouth close to this depression and called—

"Doodle-bug, doodle-bug, tell me what I want to know! Doodle-bug, doodle-bug, tell me what I want to know!"

The sand began to work, and presently a small black bug appeared for a second and then darted under again in a fright.

"He dasn't tell! So it WAS a witch that done it. I just knowed it."

He well knew the futility of trying to contend against witches, so he gave up discouraged. But it occurred to him that he might as well have the marble he had just thrown away, and therefore he went and made a patient search for it. But he could not find it. Now he went back to his treasure-house and carefully placed himself just as he had been standing when he tossed the marble away; then he took another marble from his pocket and tossed it in the same way, saying:

"Brother, go find your brother!"

He watched where it stopped, and went there and looked. But

it must have fallen short or gone too far; so he tried twice more. The last repetition was successful. The two marbles lay within a foot of each other.

Just here the blast of a toy tin trumpet came faintly down the green aisles of the forest. Tom flung off his jacket and trousers, turned a suspender into a belt, raked away some brush behind the rotten log, disclosing a rude bow and arrow, a lath sword and a tin trumpet, and in a moment had seized these things and bounded away, barelegged, with fluttering shirt. He presently halted under a great elm, blew an answering blast, and then began to tiptoe and look warily out, this way and that. He said cautiously—to an imaginary company:

"Hold, my merry men! Keep hid till I blow."

Now appeared Joe Harper, as airily clad and elaborately armed as Tom. Tom called:

"Hold! Who comes here into Sherwood Forest without my pass?"

"Guy of Guisborne wants no man's pass. Who art thou that—that—"

"Dares to hold such language," said Tom, prompting—for they talked "by the book," from memory.

"Who art thou that dares to hold such language?"

"I, indeed! I am Robin Hood, as thy caitiff carcase soon shall know."

"Then art thou indeed that famous outlaw? Right gladly will I dispute with thee the passes of the merry wood. Have at thee!"

They took their lath swords, dumped their other traps on the ground, struck a fencing attitude, foot to foot, and began a grave, careful combat, "two up and two down." Presently Tom said:

"Now, if you've got the hang, go it lively!"

So they "went it lively," panting and perspiring with the work. By and by Tom shouted:

"Fall! fall! Why don't you fall?"

"I sha'n't! Why don't you fall yourself? You're getting the worst of it."

"Why, that ain't anything. I can't fall; that ain't the way it is in the book. The book says, 'Then with one back-handed stroke he slew poor Guy of Guisborne.' You're to turn around and let me hit you in the back."

There was no getting around the authorities, so Joe turned, received the whack and fell.

"Now," said Joe, getting up, "you got to let me kill YOU. That's fair."

"Why, I can't do that, it ain't in the book."

"Well, it's blamed mean—that's all."

"Well, say, Joe, you can be Friar Tuck or Much the miller's son, and lam me with a quarter-staff; or I'll be the Sheriff of

Nottingham and you be Robin Hood a little while and kill me."

This was satisfactory, and so these adventures were carried out. Then Tom became Robin Hood again, and was allowed by the treacherous nun to bleed his strength away through his neglected wound. And at last Joe, representing a whole tribe of weeping outlaws, dragged him sadly forth, gave his bow into his feeble hands, and Tom said, "Where this arrow falls, there bury poor Robin Hood under the greenwood tree." Then he shot the arrow and fell back and would have died, but he lit on a nettle and sprang up too gaily for a corpse.

The boys dressed themselves, hid their accoutrements, and went off grieving that there were no outlaws any more, and wondering what modern civilization could claim to have done to compensate for their loss. They said they would rather be outlaws a year in Sherwood Forest than President of the United States forever.

CHAPTER IX

AT half-past nine, that night, Tom and Sid were sent to bed, as usual. They said their prayers, and Sid was soon asleep. Tom lay awake and waited, in restless impatience. When it seemed to him that it must be nearly daylight, he heard the clock strike ten! This was despair. He would have tossed and fidgeted, as his nerves demanded, but he was afraid he might wake Sid. So he lay still, and stared up into the dark. Everything was dismally still. By and by, out of the stillness, little, scarcely perceptible noises began to emphasize themselves. The ticking of the clock began to bring itself into notice. Old beams began to crack mysteriously. The stairs creaked faintly. Evidently spirits were abroad. A measured, muffled snore issued from Aunt Polly's chamber. And now the tiresome chirping of a cricket that no human ingenuity could locate, began. Next the ghastly ticking of a deathwatch in the wall at the bed's head made Tom shudder—it meant that somebody's days were numbered. Then the howl of a far-off dog rose on the night air, and was answered by a fainter howl from a remoter distance. Tom was in an agony. At last he was satisfied that time had ceased and eternity begun; he began to doze, in spite of himself; the clock chimed eleven, but he did not hear it. And then there came, mingling with his half-formed dreams, a most melancholy caterwauling. The raising of a neighboring window disturbed him. A cry of "Scat! you devil!" and the crash of an empty bottle against the back of his aunt's woodshed brought him wide awake, and a single minute later he was dressed and out of the window and creeping along the roof of the "ell" on all fours. He "meow'd" with caution once or twice, as he went; then jumped to the roof of the woodshed and thence to the ground. Huckleberry Finn was there, with his dead cat. The boys moved off and disappeared in the gloom. At the end of half an hour they were wading through the tall grass of the graveyard.

It was a graveyard of the old-fashioned Western kind. It was on a hill, about a mile and a half from the village. It had a crazy board fence around it, which leaned inward in places, and outward the rest of the time, but stood upright nowhere. Grass and weeds grew rank over the whole cemetery. All the old graves were sunken in, there was not a tombstone on the place; round-topped, worm-eaten boards staggered over the graves, leaning for support and finding none. "Sacred to the memory of" So-and-So had been painted on them once, but it could no longer have been read, on the most of them, now, even if there had been light.

A faint wind moaned through the trees, and Tom feared it

might be the spirits of the dead, complaining at being disturbed. The boys talked little, and only under their breath, for the time and the place and the pervading solemnity and silence oppressed their spirits. They found the sharp new heap they were seeking, and ensconced themselves within the protection of three great elms that grew in a bunch within a few feet of the grave.

Then they waited in silence for what seemed a long time. The hooting of a distant owl was all the sound that troubled the dead stillness. Tom's reflections grew oppressive. He must force some talk. So he said in a whisper:

"Hucky, do you believe the dead people like it for us to be here?"

Huckleberry whispered:

"I wisht I knowed. It's awful solemn like, AIN'T it?"

"I bet it is."

There was a considerable pause, while the boys canvassed this matter inwardly. Then Tom whispered:

"Say, Hucky—do you reckon Hoss Williams hears us talking?"

"O' course he does. Least his sperrit does."

Tom, after a pause:

"I wish I'd said Mister Williams. But I never meant any harm. Everybody calls him Hoss."

"A body can't be too partic'lar how they talk 'bout these-yer dead people, Tom."

This was a damper, and conversation died again.

Presently Tom seized his comrade's arm and said:

"Sh!"

"What is it, Tom?" And the two clung together with beating hearts.

"Sh! There 'tis again! Didn't you hear it?"

"I—"

"There! Now you hear it."

"Lord, Tom, they're coming! They're coming, sure. What'll we do?"

"I dono. Think they'll see us?"

"Oh, Tom, they can see in the dark, same as cats. I wisht I hadn't come."

"Oh, don't be afeard. I don't believe they'll bother us. We ain't doing any harm. If we keep perfectly still, maybe they won't notice us at all."

"I'll try to, Tom, but, Lord, I'm all of a shiver."

"Listen!"

The boys bent their heads together and scarcely breathed. A muffled sound of voices floated up from the far end of the graveyard.

"Look! See there!" whispered Tom. "What is it?"

"It's devil-fire. Oh, Tom, this is awful."

Some vague figures approached through the gloom, swinging an old-fashioned tin lantern that freckled the ground with innumerable little spangles of light. Presently Huckleberry whispered with a shudder:

"It's the devils sure enough. Three of 'em! Lordy, Tom, we're goners! Can you pray?"

"I'll try, but don't you be afeard. They ain't going to hurt us. 'Now I lay me down to sleep, I—'"

"Sh!"

"What is it, Huck?"

"They're HUMANS! One of 'em is, anyway. One of 'em's old Muff Potter's voice."

"No—'tain't so, is it?"

"I bet I know it. Don't you stir nor budge. He ain't sharp enough to notice us. Drunk, the same as usual, likely—blamed old rip!"

"All right, I'll keep still. Now they're stuck. Can't find it. Here they come again. Now they're hot. Cold again. Hot again. Red hot! They're p'inted right, this time. Say, Huck, I know another o' them voices; it's Injun Joe."

"That's so—that murderin' half-breed! I'd druther they was devils a dern sight. What kin they be up to?"

The whisper died wholly out, now, for the three men had reached the grave and stood within a few feet of the boys' hiding-place.

"Here it is," said the third voice; and the owner of it held the lantern up and revealed the face of young Doctor Robinson.

Potter and Injun Joe were carrying a handbarrow with a rope and a couple of shovels on it. They cast down their load and began to open the grave. The doctor put the lantern at the head of the grave and came and sat down with his back against one of the elm trees. He was so close the boys could have touched him.

"Hurry, men!" he said, in a low voice; "the moon might come out at any moment."

They growled a response and went on digging. For some time there was no noise but the grating sound of the spades discharging their freight of mould and gravel. It was very monotonous. Finally a spade struck upon the coffin with a dull woody accent, and within another minute or two the men had hoisted it out on the ground. They pried off the lid with their shovels, got out the body and dumped it rudely on the ground. The moon drifted from behind the clouds and exposed the pallid face. The barrow was got ready and the corpse placed on it, covered with a blanket, and bound to its place with the rope. Potter took out a large spring-knife and cut off the dangling end of the rope and then said:

"Now the cussed thing's ready, Sawbones, and you'll just out with another five, or here she stays."

"That's the talk!" said Injun Joe.

"Look here, what does this mean?" said the doctor. "You required your pay in advance, and I've paid you."

"Yes, and you done more than that," said Injun Joe, approaching the doctor, who was now standing. "Five years ago you drove me away from your father's kitchen one night, when I come to ask for something to eat, and you said I warn't there for any good; and when I swore I'd get even with you if it took a hundred years, your father had me jailed for a vagrant. Did you think I'd forget? The Injun blood ain't in me for nothing. And now I've GOT you, and you got to SETTLE, you know!"

He was threatening the doctor, with his fist in his face, by this time. The doctor struck out suddenly and stretched the ruffian on the ground. Potter dropped his knife, and exclaimed:

"Here, now, don't you hit my pard!" and the next moment he had grappled with the doctor and the two were struggling with might and main, trampling the grass and tearing the ground with their heels. Injun Joe sprang to his feet, his eyes flaming with passion, snatched up Potter's knife, and went creeping, catlike and stooping, round and round about the combatants, seeking an opportunity. All at once the doctor flung himself free, seized the heavy headboard of Williams' grave and felled Potter to the earth with it—and in the same instant the half-breed saw his chance and drove the knife to the hilt in the young man's breast. He reeled and fell partly upon Potter, flooding him with his blood, and in the same moment the clouds blotted out the dreadful spectacle and the two frightened boys went speeding away in the dark.

Presently, when the moon emerged again, Injun Joe was standing over the two forms, contemplating them. The doctor murmured inarticulately, gave a long gasp or two and was still. The half-breed muttered:

"THAT score is settled—damn you."

Then he robbed the body. After which he put the fatal knife in Potter's open right hand, and sat down on the dismantled coffin. Three —four—five minutes passed, and then Potter began to stir and moan. His hand closed upon the knife; he raised it, glanced at it, and let it fall, with a shudder. Then he sat up, pushing the body from him, and gazed at it, and then around him, confusedly. His eyes met Joe's.

"Lord, how is this, Joe?" he said.

"It's a dirty business," said Joe, without moving.

"What did you do it for?"

"I! I never done it!"

"Look here! That kind of talk won't wash."

Potter trembled and grew white.

"I thought I'd got sober. I'd no business to drink to-night. But it's in my head yet—worse'n when we started here. I'm all in a

muddle; can't recollect anything of it, hardly. Tell me, Joe—HONEST, now, old feller—did I do it? Joe, I never meant to—'pon my soul and honor, I never meant to, Joe. Tell me how it was, Joe. Oh, it's awful—and him so young and promising."

"Why, you two was scuffling, and he fetched you one with the headboard and you fell flat; and then up you come, all reeling and staggering like, and snatched the knife and jammed it into him, just as he fetched you another awful clip—and here you've laid, as dead as a wedge til now."

"Oh, I didn't know what I was a-doing. I wish I may die this minute if I did. It was all on account of the whiskey and the excitement, I reckon. I never used a weepon in my life before, Joe. I've fought, but never with weepons. They'll all say that. Joe, don't tell! Say you won't tell, Joe—that's a good feller. I always liked you, Joe, and stood up for you, too. Don't you remember? You WON'T tell, WILL you, Joe?" And the poor creature dropped on his knees before the stolid murderer, and clasped his appealing hands.

"No, you've always been fair and square with me, Muff Potter, and I won't go back on you. There, now, that's as fair as a man can say."

"Oh, Joe, you're an angel. I'll bless you for this the longest day I live." And Potter began to cry.

"Come, now, that's enough of that. This ain't any time for blubbering. You be off yonder way and I'll go this. Move, now, and don't leave any tracks behind you."

Potter started on a trot that quickly increased to a run. The half-breed stood looking after him. He muttered:

"If he's as much stunned with the lick and fuddled with the rum as he had the look of being, he won't think of the knife till he's gone so far he'll be afraid to come back after it to such a place by himself —chicken-heart!"

Two or three minutes later the murdered man, the blanketed corpse, the lidless coffin, and the open grave were under no inspection but the moon's. The stillness was complete again, too.

CHAPTER X

THE two boys flew on and on, toward the village, speechless with horror. They glanced backward over their shoulders from time to time, apprehensively, as if they feared they might be followed. Every stump that started up in their path seemed a man and an enemy, and made them catch their breath; and as they sped by some outlying cottages that lay near the village, the barking of the aroused watch-dogs seemed to give wings to their feet.

"If we can only get to the old tannery before we break down!" whispered Tom, in short catches between breaths. "I can't stand it much longer."

Huckleberry's hard pantings were his only reply, and the boys fixed their eyes on the goal of their hopes and bent to their work to win it. They gained steadily on it, and at last, breast to breast, they burst through the open door and fell grateful and exhausted in the sheltering shadows beyond. By and by their pulses slowed down, and Tom whispered:

"Huckleberry, what do you reckon'll come of this?"

"If Doctor Robinson dies, I reckon hanging'll come of it."

"Do you though?"

"Why, I KNOW it, Tom."

Tom thought a while, then he said:

"Who'll tell? We?"

"What are you talking about? S'pose something happened and Injun Joe DIDN'T hang? Why, he'd kill us some time or other, just as dead sure as we're a laying here."

"That's just what I was thinking to myself, Huck."

"If anybody tells, let Muff Potter do it, if he's fool enough. He's generally drunk enough."

Tom said nothing—went on thinking. Presently he whispered:

"Huck, Muff Potter don't know it. How can he tell?"

"What's the reason he don't know it?"

"Because he'd just got that whack when Injun Joe done it. D'you reckon he could see anything? D'you reckon he knowed anything?"

"By hokey, that's so, Tom!"

"And besides, look-a-here—maybe that whack done for HIM!"

"No, 'taint likely, Tom. He had liquor in him; I could see that; and besides, he always has. Well, when pap's full, you might take and belt him over the head with a church and you couldn't phase him. He says so, his own self. So it's the same with Muff Potter, of course. But if a man was dead sober, I reckon maybe that whack might fetch him; I dono."

After another reflective silence, Tom said:

"Hucky, you sure you can keep mum?"

"Tom, we GOT to keep mum. You know that. That Injun devil wouldn't make any more of drownding us than a couple of cats, if we was to squeak 'bout this and they didn't hang him. Now, look-a-here, Tom, less take and swear to one another—that's what we got to do—swear to keep mum."

"I'm agreed. It's the best thing. Would you just hold hands and swear that we—"

"Oh no, that wouldn't do for this. That's good enough for little rubbishy common things—specially with gals, cuz THEY go back on you anyway, and blab if they get in a huff—but there orter be writing 'bout a big thing like this. And blood."

Tom's whole being applauded this idea. It was deep, and dark, and awful; the hour, the circumstances, the surroundings, were in keeping with it. He picked up a clean pine shingle that lay in the moonlight, took a little fragment of "red keel" out of his pocket, got the moon on his work, and painfully scrawled these lines, emphasizing each slow down-stroke by clamping his tongue between his teeth, and letting up the pressure on the up-strokes.

"Huck Finn and Tom Sawyer swears they will keep mum about This and They wish They may Drop down dead in Their Tracks if They ever Tell and Rot."

Huckleberry was filled with admiration of Tom's facility in writing, and the sublimity of his language. He at once took a pin from his lapel and was going to prick his flesh, but Tom said:

"Hold on! Don't do that. A pin's brass. It might have verdigrease on it."

"What's verdigrease?"

"It's p'ison. That's what it is. You just swaller some of it once — you'll see."

So Tom unwound the thread from one of his needles, and each boy pricked the ball of his thumb and squeezed out a drop of blood. In time, after many squeezes, Tom managed to sign his initials, using the ball of his little finger for a pen. Then he showed Huckleberry how to make an H and an F, and the oath was complete. They buried the shingle close to the wall, with some dismal ceremonies and incantations, and the fetters that bound their tongues were considered to be locked and the key thrown away.

A figure crept stealthily through a break in the other end of the ruined building, now, but they did not notice it.

"Tom," whispered Huckleberry, "does this keep us from EVER telling —ALWAYS?"

"Of course it does. It don't make any difference WHAT happens, we got to keep mum. We'd drop down dead—don't YOU know that?"

"Yes, I reckon that's so."

They continued to whisper for some little time. Presently a dog set up a long, lugubrious howl just outside—within ten feet of them. The boys clasped each other suddenly, in an agony of fright.

"Which of us does he mean?" gasped Huckleberry.

"I dono—peep through the crack. Quick!"

"No, YOU, Tom!"

"I can't—I can't DO it, Huck!"

"Please, Tom. There 'tis again!"

"Oh, lordy, I'm thankful!" whispered Tom. "I know his voice. It's Bull Harbison."*

"Oh, that's good—I tell you, Tom, I was most scared to death; I'd a bet anything it was a STRAY dog."

The dog howled again. The boys' hearts sank once more.

"Oh, my! that ain't no Bull Harbison!" whispered Huckleberry. "DO, Tom!"

---

* If Mr. Harbison owned a slave named Bull, Tom would have spoken of him as "Harbison's Bull," but a son or a dog of that name was "Bull Harbison."

Tom, quaking with fear, yielded, and put his eye to the crack. His whisper was hardly audible when he said:

"Oh, Huck, IT S A STRAY DOG!"

"Quick, Tom, quick! Who does he mean?"

"Huck, he must mean us both—we're right together."

"Oh, Tom, I reckon we're goners. I reckon there ain't no mistake 'bout where I'LL go to. I been so wicked."

"Dad fetch it! This comes of playing hookey and doing everything a feller's told NOT to do. I might a been good, like Sid, if I'd a tried —but no, I wouldn't, of course. But if ever I get off this time, I lay I'll just WALLER in Sunday-schools!" And Tom began to snuffle a little.

"YOU bad!" and Huckleberry began to snuffle too. "Consound it, Tom Sawyer, you're just old pie, 'longside o' what I am. Oh, LORDY, lordy, lordy, I wisht I only had half your chance."

Tom choked off and whispered:

"Look, Hucky, look! He's got his BACK to us!"

Hucky looked, with joy in his heart.

"Well, he has, by jingoes! Did he before?"

"Yes, he did. But I, like a fool, never thought. Oh, this is bully, you know. NOW who can he mean?"

The howling stopped. Tom pricked up his ears.

"Sh! What's that?" he whispered.

"Sounds like—like hogs grunting. No—it's somebody snoring, Tom."

"That IS it! Where 'bouts is it, Huck?"

"I bleeve it's down at 'tother end. Sounds so, anyway. Pap used to sleep there, sometimes, 'long with the hogs, but laws bless you, he just lifts things when HE snores. Besides, I reckon he ain't ever coming back to this town any more."

The spirit of adventure rose in the boys' souls once more.

"Hucky, do you das't to go if I lead?"

"I don't like to, much. Tom, s'pose it's Injun Joe!"

Tom quailed. But presently the temptation rose up strong again and the boys agreed to try, with the understanding that they would take to their heels if the snoring stopped. So they went tiptoeing stealthily down, the one behind the other. When they had got to within five steps of the snorer, Tom stepped on a stick, and it broke with a sharp snap. The man moaned, writhed a little, and his face came into the moonlight. It was Muff Potter. The boys' hearts had stood still, and their hopes too, when the man moved, but their fears passed away now. They tiptoed out, through the broken weather-boarding, and stopped at a little distance to exchange a parting word. That long, lugubrious howl rose on the night air again! They turned and saw the strange dog standing within a few feet of where Potter was lying, and FACING Potter, with his nose

pointing heavenward.

"Oh, geeminy, it's HIM!" exclaimed both boys, in a breath.

"Say, Tom—they say a stray dog come howling around Johnny Miller's house, 'bout midnight, as much as two weeks ago; and a whippoorwill come in and lit on the banisters and sung, the very same evening; and there ain't anybody dead there yet."

"Well, I know that. And suppose there ain't. Didn't Gracie Miller fall in the kitchen fire and burn herself terrible the very next Saturday?"

"Yes, but she ain't DEAD. And what's more, she's getting better, too."

"All right, you wait and see. She's a goner, just as dead sure as Muff Potter's a goner. That's what the niggers say, and they know all about these kind of things, Huck."

Then they separated, cogitating. When Tom crept in at his bedroom window the night was almost spent. He undressed with excessive caution, and fell asleep congratulating himself that nobody knew of his escapade. He was not aware that the gently-snoring Sid was awake, and had been so for an hour.

When Tom awoke, Sid was dressed and gone. There was a late look in the light, a late sense in the atmosphere. He was startled. Why had he not been called—persecuted till he was up, as usual? The thought filled him with bodings. Within five minutes he was dressed and down-stairs, feeling sore and drowsy. The family were still at table, but they had finished breakfast. There was no voice of rebuke; but there were averted eyes; there was a silence and an air of solemnity that struck a chill to the culprit's heart. He sat down and tried to seem gay, but it was up-hill work; it roused no smile, no response, and he lapsed into silence and let his heart sink down to the depths.

After breakfast his aunt took him aside, and Tom almost brightened in the hope that he was going to be flogged; but it was not so. His aunt wept over him and asked him how he could go and break her old heart so; and finally told him to go on, and ruin himself and bring her gray hairs with sorrow to the grave, for it was no use for her to try any more. This was worse than a thousand whippings, and Tom's heart was sorer now than his body. He cried, he pleaded for forgiveness, promised to reform over and over again, and then received his dismissal, feeling that he had won but an imperfect forgiveness and established but a feeble confidence.

He left the presence too miserable to even feel revengeful toward Sid; and so the latter's prompt retreat through the back gate was unnecessary. He moped to school gloomy and sad, and took his flogging, along with Joe Harper, for playing hookey the day before, with the air of one whose heart was busy with heavier woes and wholly dead to trifles. Then he betook himself to his seat, rested his elbows on his desk and his jaws in his hands, and stared at the wall with the stony stare of suffering that has reached the limit and can no further go. His elbow was pressing against some hard substance. After a long time he slowly and sadly changed his position, and took up this object with a sigh. It was in a paper. He unrolled it. A long, lingering, colossal sigh followed, and his heart broke. It was his brass andiron knob!

This final feather broke the camel's back.

CHAPTER XI

CLOSE upon the hour of noon the whole village was suddenly electrified with the ghastly news. No need of the as yet undreamed-of telegraph; the tale flew from man to man, from group to group, from house to house, with little less than telegraphic speed. Of course the schoolmaster gave holiday for that afternoon; the town would have thought strangely of him if he had not.

A gory knife had been found close to the murdered man, and it had been recognized by somebody as belonging to Muff Potter—so the story ran. And it was said that a belated citizen had come upon Potter washing himself in the "branch" about one or two o'clock in the morning, and that Potter had at once sneaked off—suspicious circumstances, especially the washing which was not a habit with Potter. It was also said that the town had been ransacked for this "murderer" (the public are not slow in the matter of sifting evidence and arriving at a verdict), but that he could not be found. Horsemen had departed down all the roads in every direction, and the Sheriff "was confident" that he would be captured before night.

All the town was drifting toward the graveyard. Tom's heartbreak vanished and he joined the procession, not because he would not a thousand times rather go anywhere else, but because an awful, unaccountable fascination drew him on. Arrived at the dreadful place, he wormed his small body through the crowd and saw the dismal spectacle. It seemed to him an age since he was there before. Somebody pinched his arm. He turned, and his eyes met Huckleberry's. Then both looked elsewhere at once, and wondered if anybody had noticed anything in their mutual glance. But everybody was talking, and intent upon the grisly spectacle before them.

"Poor fellow!" "Poor young fellow!" "This ought to be a lesson to grave robbers!" "Muff Potter'll hang for this if they catch him!" This was the drift of remark; and the minister said, "It was a judgment; His hand is here."

Now Tom shivered from head to heel; for his eye fell upon the stolid face of Injun Joe. At this moment the crowd began to sway and struggle, and voices shouted, "It's him! it's him! he's coming himself!"

"Who? Who?" from twenty voices.

"Muff Potter!"

"Hallo, he's stopped!—Look out, he's turning! Don't let him get away!"

People in the branches of the trees over Tom's head said he wasn't trying to get away—he only looked doubtful and perplexed.

"Infernal impudence!" said a bystander; "wanted to come and take a quiet look at his work, I reckon—didn't expect any company."

The crowd fell apart, now, and the Sheriff came through, ostentatiously leading Potter by the arm. The poor fellow's face was haggard, and his eyes showed the fear that was upon him. When he stood before the murdered man, he shook as with a palsy, and he put his face in his hands and burst into tears.

"I didn't do it, friends," he sobbed; "'pon my word and honor I never done it."

"Who's accused you?" shouted a voice.

This shot seemed to carry home. Potter lifted his face and looked around him with a pathetic hopelessness in his eyes. He saw Injun Joe, and exclaimed:

"Oh, Injun Joe, you promised me you'd never—"

"Is that your knife?" and it was thrust before him by the Sheriff.

Potter would have fallen if they had not caught him and eased him to the ground. Then he said:

"Something told me 't if I didn't come back and get—" He shuddered; then waved his nerveless hand with a vanquished gesture and said, "Tell 'em, Joe, tell 'em—it ain't any use any more."

Then Huckleberry and Tom stood dumb and staring, and heard the stony-hearted liar reel off his serene statement, they expecting every moment that the clear sky would deliver God's lightnings upon his head, and wondering to see how long the stroke was delayed. And when he had finished and still stood alive and whole, their wavering impulse to break their oath and save the poor betrayed prisoner's life faded and vanished away, for plainly this miscreant had sold himself to Satan and it would be fatal to meddle with the property of such a power as that.

"Why didn't you leave? What did you want to come here for?" somebody said.

"I couldn't help it—I couldn't help it," Potter moaned. "I wanted to run away, but I couldn't seem to come anywhere but here." And he fell to sobbing again.

Injun Joe repeated his statement, just as calmly, a few minutes afterward on the inquest, under oath; and the boys, seeing that the lightnings were still withheld, were confirmed in their belief that Joe had sold himself to the devil. He was now become, to them, the most balefully interesting object they had ever looked upon, and they could not take their fascinated eyes from his face.

They inwardly resolved to watch him nights, when opportunity should offer, in the hope of getting a glimpse of his dread master.

Injun Joe helped to raise the body of the murdered man and put it in a wagon for removal; and it was whispered through the shuddering crowd that the wound bled a little! The boys thought that this happy circumstance would turn suspicion in the right direction; but they were disappointed, for more than one villager remarked:

"It was within three feet of Muff Potter when it done it."

Tom's fearful secret and gnawing conscience disturbed his sleep for as much as a week after this; and at breakfast one morning Sid said:

"Tom, you pitch around and talk in your sleep so much that you keep me awake half the time."

Tom blanched and dropped his eyes.

"It's a bad sign," said Aunt Polly, gravely. "What you got on your mind, Tom?"

"Nothing. Nothing 't I know of." But the boy's hand shook so that he spilled his coffee.

"And you do talk such stuff," Sid said. "Last night you said, 'It's blood, it's blood, that's what it is!' You said that over and over. And you said, 'Don't torment me so—I'll tell!' Tell WHAT? What is it you'll tell?"

Everything was swimming before Tom. There is no telling what might have happened, now, but luckily the concern passed out of Aunt Polly's face and she came to Tom's relief without knowing it. She said:

"Sho! It's that dreadful murder. I dream about it most every night myself. Sometimes I dream it's me that done it."

Mary said she had been affected much the same way. Sid seemed satisfied. Tom got out of the presence as quick as he plausibly could, and after that he complained of toothache for a week, and tied up his jaws every night. He never knew that Sid lay nightly watching, and frequently slipped the bandage free and then leaned on his elbow listening a good while at a time, and afterward slipped the bandage back to its place again. Tom's distress of mind wore off gradually and the toothache grew irksome and was discarded. If Sid really managed to make anything out of Tom's disjointed mutterings, he kept it to himself.

It seemed to Tom that his schoolmates never would get done holding inquests on dead cats, and thus keeping his trouble present to his mind. Sid noticed that Tom never was coroner at one of these inquiries, though it had been his habit to take the lead in all new enterprises; he noticed, too, that Tom never acted as a witness—and that was strange; and Sid did not overlook the fact that Tom even showed a marked aversion to these inquests, and always avoided them when he could. Sid marvelled, but said nothing. However, even inquests went out of vogue at last, and ceased to torture Tom's conscience.

Every day or two, during this time of sorrow, Tom watched his opportunity and went to the little grated jail-window and smuggled such small comforts through to the "murderer" as he could get hold of. The jail was a trifling little brick den that stood in a marsh at the edge of the village, and no guards were afforded for it; indeed, it was seldom occupied. These offerings greatly helped to ease Tom's conscience.

The villagers had a strong desire to tar-and-feather Injun Joe and ride him on a rail, for body-snatching, but so formidable was his character that nobody could be found who was willing to take the lead in the matter, so it was dropped. He had been careful to begin both of his inquest-statements with the fight, without confessing the grave-robbery that preceded it; therefore it was deemed wisest not to try the case in the courts at present.

CHAPTER XII

ONE of the reasons why Tom's mind had drifted away from its secret troubles was, that it had found a new and weighty matter to interest itself about. Becky Thatcher had stopped coming to school. Tom had struggled with his pride a few days, and tried to "whistle her down the wind," but failed. He began to find himself hanging around her father's house, nights, and feeling very miserable. She was ill. What if she should die!

There was distraction in the thought. He no longer took an interest in war, nor even in piracy. The charm of life was gone; there was nothing but dreariness left. He put his hoop away, and his bat; there was no joy in them any more. His aunt was concerned. She began to try all manner of remedies on him. She was one of those people who are infatuated with patent medicines and all new-fangled methods of producing health or mending it. She was an inveterate experimenter in these things. When something fresh in this line came out she was in a fever, right away, to try it; not on herself, for she was never ailing, but on anybody else that came handy. She was a subscriber for all the "Health" periodicals and phrenological frauds; and the solemn ignorance they were inflated with was breath to her nostrils. All the "rot" they contained about ventilation, and how to go to bed, and how to get up, and what to eat, and what to drink, and how much exercise to take, and what frame of mind to keep one's self in, and what sort of clothing to wear, was all gospel to her, and she never observed that her health-journals of the current month customarily upset everything they had recommended the month before. She was as simple-hearted and honest as the day was long, and so she was an easy victim. She gathered together her quack periodicals and her quack medicines, and thus armed with death, went about on her pale horse, metaphorically speaking, with "hell following after." But she never suspected that she was not an angel of healing and the balm of Gilead in disguise, to the suffering neighbors.

The water treatment was new, now, and Tom's low condition was a windfall to her. She had him out at daylight every morning, stood him up in the woodshed and drowned him with a deluge of cold water; then she scrubbed him down with a towel like a file, and so brought him to; then she rolled him up in a wet sheet and put him away under blankets till she sweated his soul clean and "the yellow stains of it came through his pores"—as Tom said.

Yet notwithstanding all this, the boy grew more and more melancholy and pale and dejected. She added hot baths, sitz baths, shower baths, and plunges. The boy remained as dismal as a hearse. She began to assist the water with a slim oatmeal diet and blister-plasters. She calculated his capacity as she would a jug's, and filled him up every day with quack cure-alls.

Tom had become indifferent to persecution by this time. This phase filled the old lady's heart with consternation. This indifference must be broken up at any cost. Now she heard of Pain-killer for the first time. She ordered a lot at once. She tasted it and was filled with gratitude. It was simply fire in a liquid form. She dropped the water treatment and everything else, and pinned her faith to Pain-killer. She gave Tom a teaspoonful and watched with the deepest anxiety for the result. Her troubles were instantly at rest, her soul at peace again; for the "indifference" was broken up. The boy could not have shown a wilder, heartier interest, if she had built a fire under him.

Tom felt that it was time to wake up; this sort of life might be romantic enough, in his blighted condition, but it was getting to have too little sentiment and too much distracting variety about it. So he thought over various plans for relief, and finally hit upon that of professing to be fond of Pain-killer. He asked for it so often that he became a nuisance, and his aunt ended by telling him to help himself and quit bothering her. If it had been Sid, she would have had no misgivings to alloy her delight; but since it was Tom, she watched the bottle clandestinely. She found that the medicine did really diminish, but it did not occur to her that the boy was mending the health of a crack in the sitting-room floor with it.

One day Tom was in the act of dosing the crack when his aunt's yellow cat came along, purring, eying the teaspoon avariciously, and begging for a taste. Tom said:

"Don't ask for it unless you want it, Peter."

But Peter signified that he did want it.

"You better make sure."

Peter was sure.

"Now you've asked for it, and I'll give it to you, because there ain't anything mean about me; but if you find you don't like it, you mustn't blame anybody but your own self."

Peter was agreeable. So Tom pried his mouth open and poured down the Pain-killer. Peter sprang a couple of yards in the air, and then delivered a war-whoop and set off round and round the room, banging against furniture, upsetting flower-pots, and making general havoc. Next he rose on his hind feet and pranced around, in a frenzy of enjoyment, with his head over his shoulder and his voice proclaiming his unappeasable happiness. Then he went tearing around the house again spreading chaos and destruction in his path. Aunt Polly entered in time to see him throw a few double summersets, deliver a final mighty hurrah, and sail through the open window, carrying the rest of the flower-pots with him. The old lady stood petrified with astonishment, peering over her glasses; Tom lay on the floor expiring with laughter.

"Tom, what on earth ails that cat?"

"I don't know, aunt," gasped the boy.

"Why, I never see anything like it. What did make him act so?"

"Deed I don't know, Aunt Polly; cats always act so when they're having a good time."

"They do, do they?" There was something in the tone that made Tom apprehensive.

"Yes'm. That is, I believe they do."

"You DO?"

"Yes'm."

The old lady was bending down, Tom watching, with interest emphasized by anxiety. Too late he divined her "drift." The handle of the telltale teaspoon was visible under the bed-valance. Aunt Polly took it, held it up. Tom winced, and dropped his eyes. Aunt Polly raised him by the usual handle—his ear—and cracked his head soundly with her thimble.

"Now, sir, what did you want to treat that poor dumb beast so, for?"

"I done it out of pity for him—because he hadn't any aunt."

"Hadn't any aunt!—you numskull. What has that got to do with it?"

"Heaps. Because if he'd had one she'd a burnt him out herself! She'd a roasted his bowels out of him 'thout any more feeling than if he was a human!"

Aunt Polly felt a sudden pang of remorse. This was putting the thing in a new light; what was cruelty to a cat MIGHT be cruelty to a boy, too. She began to soften; she felt sorry. Her eyes watered a little, and she put her hand on Tom's head and said gently:

"I was meaning for the best, Tom. And, Tom, it DID do you good."

Tom looked up in her face with just a perceptible twinkle peeping through his gravity.

"I know you was meaning for the best, aunty, and so was I with Peter. It done HIM good, too. I never see him get around so since—"

"Oh, go 'long with you, Tom, before you aggravate me again. And you try and see if you can't be a good boy, for once, and you needn't take any more medicine."

Tom reached school ahead of time. It was noticed that this strange thing had been occurring every day latterly. And now, as usual of late, he hung about the gate of the schoolyard instead of playing with his comrades. He was sick, he said, and he looked it. He tried to seem to be looking everywhere but whither he really was looking—down the road. Presently Jeff Thatcher hove in sight, and Tom's face lighted; he gazed a moment, and then turned sorrowfully away. When Jeff arrived, Tom accosted him; and "led up" warily to opportunities for remark about Becky, but the giddy lad never could see the bait. Tom watched and watched, hoping whenever a frisking frock came in sight, and hating the owner of it as soon as he saw she was not the right one. At last frocks ceased to appear, and he dropped hopelessly into the dumps; he entered the empty schoolhouse and sat down to suffer. Then one more frock passed in at the gate, and Tom's heart gave a great bound. The next instant he was out, and "going on" like an Indian; yelling, laughing, chasing boys, jumping over the fence at risk of life and limb, throwing handsprings, standing on his head—doing all the heroic things he could conceive of, and keeping a furtive eye out, all the while, to see if Becky Thatcher was noticing. But she seemed to be unconscious of it all; she never looked. Could it be possible that she was not aware that he was there? He carried his exploits to her immediate vicinity; came war-whooping around, snatched a boy's cap, hurled it to the roof of the schoolhouse, broke through a group of boys, tumbling them in every direction, and fell sprawling, himself, under Becky's nose, almost upsetting her—and she turned, with her nose in the air, and he heard her say: "Mf! some people think they're mighty smart—always showing off!"

Tom's cheeks burned. He gathered himself up and sneaked off, crushed and crestfallen.

CHAPTER XIII

TOM'S mind was made up now. He was gloomy and desperate. He was a forsaken, friendless boy, he said; nobody loved him; when they found out what they had driven him to, perhaps they would be sorry; he had tried to do right and get along, but they would not let him; since nothing would do them but to be rid of him, let it be so; and let them blame HIM for the consequences—why shouldn't they? What right had the friendless to complain? Yes, they had forced him to it at last: he would lead a life of crime. There was no choice.

By this time he was far down Meadow Lane, and the bell for school to "take up" tinkled faintly upon his ear. He sobbed, now, to think he should never, never hear that old familiar sound any more—it was very hard, but it was forced on him; since he was driven out into the cold world, he must submit—but he forgave them. Then the sobs came thick and fast.

Just at this point he met his soul's sworn comrade, Joe Harper —hard-eyed, and with evidently a great and dismal purpose in his heart. Plainly here were "two souls with but a single thought." Tom, wiping his eyes with his sleeve, began to blubber out something about a resolution to escape from hard usage and lack of sympathy at home by roaming abroad into the great world never to return; and ended by hoping that Joe would not forget him.

But it transpired that this was a request which Joe had just been going to make of Tom, and had come to hunt him up for that purpose. His mother had whipped him for drinking some cream which he had never tasted and knew nothing about; it was plain that she was tired of him and wished him to go; if she felt that way, there was nothing for him to do but succumb; he hoped she would be happy, and never regret having driven her poor boy out into the unfeeling world to suffer and die.

As the two boys walked sorrowing along, they made a new compact to stand by each other and be brothers and never separate till death relieved them of their troubles. Then they began to lay their plans. Joe was for being a hermit, and living on crusts in a remote cave, and dying, some time, of cold and want and grief; but after listening to Tom, he conceded that there were some conspicuous advantages about a life of crime, and so he consented to be a pirate.

Three miles below St. Petersburg, at a point where the Mississippi River was a trifle over a mile wide, there was a long, narrow, wooded island, with a shallow bar at the head of it, and this offered well as a rendezvous. It was not inhabited; it lay far over toward the further shore, abreast a dense and almost wholly unpeopled forest. So Jackson's Island was chosen. Who were to be the subjects of their piracies was a matter that did not occur to them. Then they hunted up Huckleberry Finn, and he joined them promptly, for all careers were one to him; he was indifferent. They presently separated to meet at a lonely spot on the river-bank two miles above the village at the favorite hour—which was midnight. There was a small log raft there which they meant to capture. Each would bring hooks and lines, and such provision as he could steal in the most dark and mysterious way—as became outlaws. And before the afternoon was done, they had all managed to enjoy the sweet glory of spreading the fact that pretty soon the town would "hear something." All who got this vague hint were cautioned to "be mum and wait."

About midnight Tom arrived with a boiled ham and a few trifles, and stopped in a dense undergrowth on a small bluff overlooking the meeting-place. It was starlight, and very still. The mighty river lay like an ocean at rest. Tom listened a moment, but no sound disturbed the quiet. Then he gave a low, distinct whistle. It was answered from under the bluff. Tom whistled twice more; these signals were answered in the same way. Then a guarded voice said:

"Who goes there?"

"Tom Sawyer, the Black Avenger of the Spanish Main. Name

your names."

"Huck Finn the Red-Handed, and Joe Harper the Terror of the Seas." Tom had furnished these titles, from his favorite literature.

"'Tis well. Give the countersign."

Two hoarse whispers delivered the same awful word simultaneously to the brooding night:

"BLOOD!"

Then Tom tumbled his ham over the bluff and let himself down after it, tearing both skin and clothes to some extent in the effort. There was an easy, comfortable path along the shore under the bluff, but it lacked the advantages of difficulty and danger so valued by a pirate.

The Terror of the Seas had brought a side of bacon, and had about worn himself out with getting it there. Finn the Red-Handed had stolen a skillet and a quantity of half-cured leaf tobacco, and had also brought a few corn-cobs to make pipes with. But none of the pirates smoked or "chewed" but himself. The Black Avenger of the Spanish Main said it would never do to start without some fire. That was a wise thought; matches were hardly known there in that day. They saw a fire smouldering upon a great raft a hundred yards above, and they went stealthily thither and helped themselves to a chunk. They made an imposing adventure of it, saying, "Hist!" every now and then, and suddenly halting with finger on lip; moving with hands on imaginary dagger-hilts; and giving orders in dismal whispers that if "the foe" stirred, to "let him have it to the hilt," because "dead men tell no tales." They knew well enough that the raftsmen were all down at the village laying in stores or having a spree, but still that was no excuse for their conducting this thing in an unpiratical way.

They shoved off, presently, Tom in command, Huck at the after oar and Joe at the forward. Tom stood amidships, gloomy-browed, and with folded arms, and gave his orders in a low, stern whisper:

"Luff, and bring her to the wind!"

"Aye-aye, sir!"

"Steady, steady-y-y-y!"

"Steady it is, sir!"

"Let her go off a point!"

"Point it is, sir!"

As the boys steadily and monotonously drove the raft toward mid-stream it was no doubt understood that these orders were given only for "style," and were not intended to mean anything in particular.

"What sail's she carrying?"

"Courses, tops'ls, and flying-jib, sir."

"Send the r'yals up! Lay out aloft, there, half a dozen of ye — foretopmaststuns'l! Lively, now!"

"Aye-aye, sir!"

"Shake out that maintogalans'l! Sheets and braces! NOW my hearties!"

"Aye-aye, sir!"

"Hellum-a-lee—hard a port! Stand by to meet her when she comes! Port, port! NOW, men! With a will! Stead-y-y-y!"

"Steady it is, sir!"

The raft drew beyond the middle of the river; the boys pointed her head right, and then lay on their oars. The river was not high, so there was not more than a two or three mile current. Hardly a word was said during the next three-quarters of an hour. Now the raft was passing before the distant town. Two or three glimmering lights showed where it lay, peacefully sleeping, beyond the vague vast sweep of star-gemmed water, unconscious of the tremendous event that was happening. The Black Avenger stood still with folded arms, "looking his last" upon the scene of his former joys and his later sufferings, and wishing "she" could see him now, abroad on the wild sea, facing peril and death with dauntless heart, going to his doom with a grim smile on his lips. It was but a small strain on his imagination to remove Jackson's Island beyond eyeshot of the village, and so he "looked his last" with a broken and satisfied heart. The other pirates were looking their last, too; and they all looked so long that they came near letting the current drift them out of the range of the island. But they discovered the danger in time, and made shift to avert it. About two o'clock in the morning the raft grounded on the bar two hundred yards above the head of the island, and they waded back and forth until they had landed their freight. Part of the little raft's belongings consisted of an old sail, and this they spread over a nook in the bushes for a tent to shelter their provisions; but they themselves would sleep in the open air in good weather, as became outlaws.

They built a fire against the side of a great log twenty or thirty steps within the sombre depths of the forest, and then cooked some bacon in the frying-pan for supper, and used up half of the corn "pone" stock they had brought. It seemed glorious sport to be feasting in that wild, free way in the virgin forest of an unexplored and uninhabited island, far from the haunts of men, and they said they never would return to civilization. The climbing fire lit up their faces and threw its ruddy glare upon the pillared tree-trunks of their forest temple, and upon the varnished foliage and festooning vines.

When the last crisp slice of bacon was gone, and the last allowance of corn pone devoured, the boys stretched themselves out on the grass, filled with contentment. They could have found a cooler place, but they would not deny themselves such a romantic feature as the roasting camp-fire.

"AIN'T it gay?" said Joe.

"It's NUTS!" said Tom. "What would the boys say if they could see us?"

"Say? Well, they'd just die to be here—hey, Hucky!"

"I reckon so," said Huckleberry; "anyways, I'm suited. I don't want nothing better'n this. I don't ever get enough to eat, gen'ally—and here they can't come and pick at a feller and bullyrag him so."

"It's just the life for me," said Tom. "You don't have to get up,

mornings, and you don't have to go to school, and wash, and all that blame foolishness. You see a pirate don't have to do ANYTHING, Joe, when he's ashore, but a hermit HE has to do praying considerable, and then he don't have any fun, anyway, all by himself that way."

"Oh yes, that's so," said Joe, "but I hadn't thought much about it, you know. I'd a good deal rather be a pirate, now that I've tried it."

"You see," said Tom, "people don't go much on hermits, nowadays, like they used to in old times, but a pirate's always respected. And a hermit's got to sleep on the hardest place he can find, and put sackcloth and ashes on his head, and stand out in the rain, and—"

"What does he put sackcloth and ashes on his head for?" inquired Huck.

"I dono. But they've GOT to do it. Hermits always do. You'd have to do that if you was a hermit."

"Dern'd if I would," said Huck.

"Well, what would you do?"

"I dono. But I wouldn't do that."

"Why, Huck, you'd HAVE to. How'd you get around it?"

"Why, I just wouldn't stand it. I'd run away."

"Run away! Well, you WOULD be a nice old slouch of a hermit. You'd be a disgrace."

The Red-Handed made no response, being better employed. He had finished gouging out a cob, and now he fitted a weed stem to it, loaded it with tobacco, and was pressing a coal to the charge and blowing a cloud of fragrant smoke—he was in the full bloom of luxurious contentment. The other pirates envied him this majestic vice, and secretly resolved to acquire it shortly. Presently Huck said:

"What does pirates have to do?"

Tom said:

"Oh, they have just a bully time—take ships and burn them, and get the money and bury it in awful places in their island where there's ghosts and things to watch it, and kill everybody in the ships—make 'em walk a plank."

"And they carry the women to the island," said Joe; "they don't kill the women."

"No," assented Tom, "they don't kill the women—they're too noble. And the women's always beautiful, too.

"And don't they wear the bulliest clothes! Oh no! All gold and silver and di'monds," said Joe, with enthusiasm.

"Who?" said Huck.

"Why, the pirates."

Huck scanned his own clothing forlornly.

"I reckon I ain't dressed fitten for a pirate," said he, with a regretful pathos in his voice; "but I ain't got none but these."

But the other boys told him the fine clothes would come fast enough, after they should have begun their adventures. They made him understand that his poor rags would do to begin with, though it was customary for wealthy pirates to start with a proper wardrobe.

Gradually their talk died out and drowsiness began to steal upon the eyelids of the little waifs. The pipe dropped from the fingers of the Red-Handed, and he slept the sleep of the conscience-free and the weary. The Terror of the Seas and the Black Avenger of the Spanish Main had more difficulty in getting to sleep. They said their prayers inwardly, and lying down, since there was nobody there with authority to make them kneel and recite aloud; in truth, they had a mind not to say them at all, but they were afraid to proceed to such lengths as that, lest they might call down a sudden and special thunderbolt from heaven. Then at once they reached and hovered upon the imminent verge of sleep—but an intruder came, now, that would not "down." It was conscience. They began to feel a vague fear that they had been doing wrong to run away; and next they thought of the stolen meat, and then the real torture came. They tried to argue it away by reminding conscience that they had purloined sweetmeats and apples scores of times; but conscience was not to be appeased by such thin plausibilities; it seemed to them, in the end, that there was no getting around the stubborn fact that taking sweetmeats was only "hooking," while taking bacon and hams and such valuables was plain simple stealing—and there was a command against that in the Bible. So they inwardly resolved that so long as they remained in the business, their piracies should not again be sullied with the crime of stealing. Then conscience granted a truce, and these curiously inconsistent pirates fell peacefully to sleep.

CHAPTER XIV

WHEN Tom awoke in the morning, he wondered where he was. He sat up and rubbed his eyes and looked around. Then he comprehended. It was the cool gray dawn, and there was a delicious sense of repose and peace in the deep pervading calm and silence of the woods. Not a leaf stirred; not a sound obtruded upon great Nature's meditation. Beaded dewdrops stood upon the leaves and grasses. A white layer of ashes covered the fire, and a thin blue breath of smoke rose straight into the air. Joe and Huck still slept.

Now, far away in the woods a bird called; another answered; presently the hammering of a woodpecker was heard. Gradually the cool dim gray of the morning whitened, and as gradually sounds multiplied and life manifested itself. The marvel of Nature shaking off sleep and going to work unfolded itself to the musing boy. A little green worm came crawling over a dewy leaf, lifting two-thirds of his body into the air from time to time and "sniffing around," then proceeding again—for he was measuring, Tom said; and when the worm approached him, of its own accord, he sat as still as a stone, with his hopes rising and falling, by turns, as the creature still came toward him or seemed inclined to go elsewhere; and when at last it considered a painful moment with its curved body in the air and then came decisively down upon Tom's leg and began a journey over him, his whole heart was glad—for that meant that he was going to have a new suit of clothes—without the shadow of a doubt a gaudy piratical uniform. Now a procession of ants appeared, from nowhere in particular, and went about their labors; one struggled manfully by with a dead spider five times as big as itself in its arms, and lugged it

straight up a tree-trunk. A brown spotted lady-bug climbed the dizzy height of a grass blade, and Tom bent down close to it and said, "Lady-bug, lady-bug, fly away home, your house is on fire, your children's alone," and she took wing and went off to see about it —which did not surprise the boy, for he knew of old that this insect was credulous about conflagrations, and he had practised upon its simplicity more than once. A tumblebug came next, heaving sturdily at its ball, and Tom touched the creature, to see it shut its legs against its body and pretend to be dead. The birds were fairly rioting by this time. A catbird, the Northern mocker, lit in a tree over Tom's head, and trilled out her imitations of her neighbors in a rapture of enjoyment; then a shrill jay swept down, a flash of blue flame, and stopped on a twig almost within the boy's reach, cocked his head to one side and eyed the strangers with a consuming curiosity; a gray squirrel and a big fellow of the "fox" kind came skurrying along, sitting up at intervals to inspect and chatter at the boys, for the wild things had probably never seen a human being before and scarcely knew whether to be afraid or not. All Nature was wide awake and stirring, now; long lances of sunlight pierced down through the dense foliage far and near, and a few butterflies came fluttering upon the scene.

Tom stirred up the other pirates and they all clattered away with a shout, and in a minute or two were stripped and chasing after and tumbling over each other in the shallow limpid water of the white sandbar. They felt no longing for the little village sleeping in the distance beyond the majestic waste of water. A vagrant current or a slight rise in the river had carried off their raft, but this only gratified them, since its going was something like burning the bridge between them and civilization.

They came back to camp wonderfully refreshed, glad-hearted, and ravenous; and they soon had the camp-fire blazing up again. Huck found a spring of clear cold water close by, and the boys made cups of broad oak or hickory leaves, and felt that water, sweetened with such a wildwood charm as that, would be a good enough substitute for coffee. While Joe was slicing bacon for breakfast, Tom and Huck asked him to hold on a minute; they stepped to a promising nook in the river-bank and threw in their lines; almost immediately they had reward. Joe had not had time to get impatient before they were back again with some handsome bass, a couple of sun-perch and a small catfish—provisions enough for quite a family. They fried the fish with the bacon, and were astonished; for no fish had ever seemed so delicious before. They did not know that the quicker a fresh-water fish is on the fire after he is caught the better he is; and they reflected little upon what a sauce open-air sleeping, open-air exercise, bathing, and a large ingredient of hunger make, too.

They lay around in the shade, after breakfast, while Huck had a smoke, and then went off through the woods on an exploring expedition. They tramped gayly along, over decaying logs, through tangled underbrush, among solemn monarchs of the forest, hung from their crowns to the ground with a drooping regalia of grape-vines. Now and then they came upon snug nooks carpeted with grass and jeweled with flowers.

They found plenty of things to be delighted with, but nothing to be astonished at. They discovered that the island was about three miles long and a quarter of a mile wide, and that the shore it lay closest to was only separated from it by a narrow channel hardly two hundred yards wide. They took a swim about every hour, so it was close upon the middle of the afternoon when they got back to camp. They were too hungry to stop to fish, but they fared sumptuously upon cold ham, and then threw themselves down in the shade to talk. But the talk soon began to drag, and then died. The stillness, the solemnity that brooded in the woods, and the sense of loneliness, began to tell upon the spirits of the boys. They fell to thinking. A sort of undefined longing crept upon them. This took dim shape, presently—it was budding homesickness. Even Finn the Red-Handed was dreaming of his doorsteps and empty hogsheads. But they were all ashamed of their weakness, and none was brave enough to speak his thought.

For some time, now, the boys had been dully conscious of a peculiar sound in the distance, just as one sometimes is of the ticking of a clock which he takes no distinct note of. But now this mysterious sound became more pronounced, and forced a recognition. The boys started, glanced at each other, and then each assumed a listening attitude. There was a long silence, profound and unbroken; then a deep, sullen boom came floating down out of the distance.

"What is it!" exclaimed Joe, under his breath.

"I wonder," said Tom in a whisper.

"'Tain't thunder," said Huckleberry, in an awed tone, "becuz thunder—"

"Hark!" said Tom. "Listen—don't talk."

They waited a time that seemed an age, and then the same muffled boom troubled the solemn hush.

"Let's go and see."

They sprang to their feet and hurried to the shore toward the town. They parted the bushes on the bank and peered out over the water. The little steam ferryboat was about a mile below the village, drifting with the current. Her broad deck seemed crowded with people. There were a great many skiffs rowing about or floating with the stream in the neighborhood of the ferryboat, but the boys could not determine what the men in them were doing. Presently a great jet of white smoke burst from the ferryboat's side, and as it expanded and rose in a lazy cloud, that same dull throb of sound was borne to the listeners again.

"I know now!" exclaimed Tom; "somebody's drownded!"

"That's it!" said Huck; "they done that last summer, when Bill Turner got drownded; they shoot a cannon over the water, and that makes him come up to the top. Yes, and they take loaves of bread and put quicksilver in 'em and set 'em afloat, and wherever there's anybody that's drownded, they'll float right there and stop."

"Yes, I've heard about that," said Joe. "I wonder what makes the bread do that."

"Oh, it ain't the bread, so much," said Tom; "I reckon it's mostly what they SAY over it before they start it out."

"But they don't say anything over it," said Huck. "I've seen 'em and they don't."

"Well, that's funny," said Tom. "But maybe they say it to themselves. Of COURSE they do. Anybody might know that."

The other boys agreed that there was reason in what Tom said, because an ignorant lump of bread, uninstructed by an incantation, could not be expected to act very intelligently when set upon an errand of such gravity.

"By jings, I wish I was over there, now," said Joe.

"I do too" said Huck "I'd give heaps to know who it is."

The boys still listened and watched. Presently a revealing thought flashed through Tom's mind, and he exclaimed:

"Boys, I know who's drownded—it's us!"

They felt like heroes in an instant. Here was a gorgeous triumph; they were missed; they were mourned; hearts were breaking on their account; tears were being shed; accusing memories of unkindness to these poor lost lads were rising up, and unavailing regrets and remorse were being indulged; and best of all, the departed were the talk of the whole town, and the envy of all the boys, as far as this dazzling notoriety was concerned. This was fine. It was worth while to be a pirate, after all.

As twilight drew on, the ferryboat went back to her accustomed business and the skiffs disappeared. The pirates returned to camp. They were jubilant with vanity over their new grandeur and the illustrious trouble they were making. They caught fish, cooked supper and ate it, and then fell to guessing at what the village was thinking and saying about them; and the pictures they drew of the public distress on their account were gratifying to look upon—from their point of view. But when the shadows of night closed them in, they gradually ceased to talk, and sat gazing into the fire, with their minds evidently wandering elsewhere. The excitement was gone, now, and Tom and Joe could not keep back thoughts of certain persons at home who were not enjoying this fine frolic as much as they were. Misgivings came; they grew troubled and unhappy; a sigh or two escaped, unawares. By and by Joe timidly ventured upon a roundabout "feeler" as to how the others might look upon a return to civilization—not right now, but—

Tom withered him with derision! Huck, being uncommitted as yet, joined in with Tom, and the waverer quickly "explained," and was glad to get out of the scrape with as little taint of chicken-hearted homesickness clinging to his garments as he could. Mutiny was effectually laid to rest for the moment.

As the night deepened, Huck began to nod, and presently to snore. Joe followed next. Tom lay upon his elbow motionless, for some time, watching the two intently. At last he got up cautiously, on his knees, and went searching among the grass and the flickering reflections flung by the camp-fire. He picked up and inspected several large semi-cylinders of the thin white bark of a sycamore, and finally chose two which seemed to suit him. Then he knelt by the fire and painfully wrote something upon each of these with his "red keel"; one he rolled up and put in his jacket pocket, and the other he put in Joe's hat and removed it to a little distance from the owner. And he also put into the hat certain schoolboy treasures of almost inestimable value—among them a lump of chalk, an India-rubber ball, three fishhooks, and one of that kind of marbles known as a "sure 'nough crystal." Then he tiptoed his way cautiously among the trees till he felt that he was out of hearing, and straightway broke into a keen run in the direction of the sandbar.

CHAPTER XV

A FEW minutes later Tom was in the shoal water of the bar, wading toward the Illinois shore. Before the depth reached his middle he was half-way over; the current would permit no more wading, now, so he struck out confidently to swim the remaining hundred yards. He swam quartering upstream, but still was swept downward rather faster than he had expected. However, he reached the shore finally, and drifted along till he found a low place and drew himself out. He put his hand on his jacket pocket, found his piece of bark safe, and then struck through the woods, following the shore, with streaming garments. Shortly before ten o'clock he came out into an open place opposite the village, and saw the ferryboat lying in the shadow of the trees and the high bank. Everything was quiet under the blinking stars. He crept down the bank, watching with all his eyes, slipped into the water, swam three or four strokes and climbed into the skiff that did "yawl" duty at the boat's stern. He laid himself down under the thwarts and waited, panting.

Presently the cracked bell tapped and a voice gave the order to "cast off." A minute or two later the skiff's head was standing high up, against the boat's swell, and the voyage was begun. Tom felt happy in his success, for he knew it was the boat's last trip for the night. At the end of a long twelve or fifteen minutes the wheels stopped, and Tom slipped overboard and swam ashore in the dusk, landing fifty yards downstream, out of danger of possible stragglers.

He flew along unfrequented alleys, and shortly found himself at his aunt's back fence. He climbed over, approached the "ell," and looked in at the sitting-room window, for a light was burning there. There sat Aunt Polly, Sid, Mary, and Joe Harper's mother, grouped together, talking. They were by the bed, and the bed was between them and the door. Tom went to the door and began to softly lift the latch; then he pressed gently and the door yielded a crack; he continued pushing cautiously, and quaking every time it creaked, till he judged he might squeeze through on his knees; so he put his head through and began, warily.

"What makes the candle blow so?" said Aunt Polly. Tom hurried up. "Why, that door's open, I believe. Why, of course it is. No end of strange things now. Go 'long and shut it, Sid."

Tom disappeared under the bed just in time. He lay and "breathed" himself for a time, and then crept to where he could almost touch his aunt's foot.

"But as I was saying," said Aunt Polly, "he warn't BAD, so to say —only mischEEvous. Only just giddy, and harum-scarum, you know. He warn't any more responsible than a colt. HE never meant any harm, and he was the best-hearted boy that ever was"—and she began to cry.

"It was just so with my Joe—always full of his devilment, and up to every kind of mischief, but he was just as unselfish and kind as he could be—and laws bless me, to think I went and whipped him for taking that cream, never once recollecting that I throwed it out myself because it was sour, and I never to see him again in this world, never, never, never, poor abused boy!" And Mrs. Harper sobbed as if her heart would break.

"I hope Tom's better off where he is," said Sid, "but if he'd been better in some ways—"

"SID!" Tom felt the glare of the old lady's eye, though he could not see it. "Not a word against my Tom, now that he's gone! God'll take care of HIM—never you trouble YOURself, sir! Oh,

Mrs. Harper, I don't know how to give him up! I don't know how to give him up! He was such a comfort to me, although he tormented my old heart out of me, 'most."

"The Lord giveth and the Lord hath taken away—Blessed be the name of the Lord! But it's so hard—Oh, it's so hard! Only last Saturday my Joe busted a firecracker right under my nose and I knocked him sprawling. Little did I know then, how soon—Oh, if it was to do over again I'd hug him and bless him for it."

"Yes, yes, yes, I know just how you feel, Mrs. Harper, I know just exactly how you feel. No longer ago than yesterday noon, my Tom took and filled the cat full of Pain-killer, and I did think the cretur would tear the house down. And God forgive me, I cracked Tom's head with my thimble, poor boy, poor dead boy. But he's out of all his troubles now. And the last words I ever heard him say was to reproach—"

But this memory was too much for the old lady, and she broke entirely down. Tom was snuffling, now, himself—and more in pity of himself than anybody else. He could hear Mary crying, and putting in a kindly word for him from time to time. He began to have a nobler opinion of himself than ever before. Still, he was sufficiently touched by his aunt's grief to long to rush out from under the bed and overwhelm her with joy—and the theatrical gorgeousness of the thing appealed strongly to his nature, too, but he resisted and lay still.

He went on listening, and gathered by odds and ends that it was conjectured at first that the boys had got drowned while taking a swim; then the small raft had been missed; next, certain boys said the missing lads had promised that the village should "hear something" soon; the wise-heads had "put this and that together" and decided that the lads had gone off on that raft and would turn up at the next town below, presently; but toward noon the raft had been found, lodged against the Missouri shore some five or six miles below the village —and then hope perished; they must be drowned, else hunger would have driven them home by nightfall if not sooner. It was believed that the search for the bodies had been a fruitless effort merely because the drowning must have occurred in mid-channel, since the boys, being good swimmers, would otherwise have escaped to shore. This was Wednesday night. If the bodies continued missing until Sunday, all hope would be given over, and the funerals would be preached on that morning. Tom shuddered.

Mrs. Harper gave a sobbing good-night and turned to go. Then with a mutual impulse the two bereaved women flung themselves into each other's arms and had a good, consoling cry, and then parted. Aunt Polly was tender far beyond her wont, in her good-night to Sid and Mary. Sid snuffled a bit and Mary went off crying with all her heart.

Aunt Polly knelt down and prayed for Tom so touchingly, so appealingly, and with such measureless love in her words and her old trembling voice, that he was weltering in tears again, long before she was through.

He had to keep still long after she went to bed, for she kept making broken-hearted ejaculations from time to time, tossing unrestfully, and turning over. But at last she was still, only moaning a little in her sleep. Now the boy stole out, rose gradually by the bedside, shaded the candle-light with his hand, and stood regarding her. His heart was full of pity for her. He took out his sycamore scroll and placed it by the candle. But something occurred to him, and he lingered considering. His face lighted with a happy solution of his thought; he put the bark hastily in his pocket. Then he bent over and kissed the faded lips, and straightway made his stealthy exit, latching the door behind him.

He threaded his way back to the ferry landing, found nobody at large there, and walked boldly on board the boat, for he knew she was tenantless except that there was a watchman, who always turned in and slept like a graven image. He untied the skiff at the stern, slipped into it, and was soon rowing cautiously upstream. When he had pulled a mile above the village, he started quartering across and bent himself stoutly to his work. He hit the landing on the other side neatly, for this was a familiar bit of work to him. He was moved to capture the skiff, arguing that it might be considered a ship and therefore legitimate prey for a pirate, but he knew a thorough search would be made for it and that might end in revelations. So he stepped ashore and entered the woods.

He sat down and took a long rest, torturing himself meanwhile to keep awake, and then started warily down the home-stretch. The night was far spent. It was broad daylight before he found himself fairly abreast the island bar. He rested again until the sun was well up and gilding the great river with its splendor, and then he plunged into the stream. A little later he paused, dripping, upon the threshold of the camp, and heard Joe say:

"No, Tom's true-blue, Huck, and he'll come back. He won't desert. He knows that would be a disgrace to a pirate, and Tom's too proud for that sort of thing. He's up to something or other. Now I wonder what?"

"Well, the things is ours, anyway, ain't they?"

Pretty near, but not yet, Huck. The writing says they are if he ain't back here to breakfast."

"Which he is!" exclaimed Tom, with fine dramatic effect, stepping grandly into camp.

A sumptuous breakfast of bacon and fish was shortly provided, and as the boys set to work upon it, Tom recounted (and adorned) his adventures. They were a vain and boastful company of heroes when the tale was done. Then Tom hid himself away in a shady nook to sleep till noon, and the other pirates got ready to fish and explore.

CHAPTER XVI

AFTER dinner all the gang turned out to hunt for turtle eggs on the bar. They went about poking sticks into the sand, and when they found a soft place they went down on their knees and dug with their hands. Sometimes they would take fifty or sixty eggs out of one hole. They were perfectly round white things a trifle smaller than an English walnut. They had a famous fried-egg feast that night, and another on Friday morning.

After breakfast they went whooping and prancing out on the bar, and chased each other round and round, shedding clothes as they went, until they were naked, and then continued the frolic far away up the shoal water of the bar, against the stiff current, which latter tripped their legs from under them from time to time and greatly increased the fun. And now and then they stooped in a group and splashed water in each other's faces with their palms, gradually approaching each other, with averted faces to avoid the strangling sprays, and finally gripping and struggling till the best man ducked his neighbor,

and then they all went under in a tangle of white legs and arms and came up blowing, sputtering, laughing, and gasping for breath at one and the same time.

When they were well exhausted, they would run out and sprawl on the dry, hot sand, and lie there and cover themselves up with it, and by and by break for the water again and go through the original performance once more. Finally it occurred to them that their naked skin represented flesh-colored "tights" very fairly; so they drew a ring in the sand and had a circus—with three clowns in it, for none would yield this proudest post to his neighbor.

Next they got their marbles and played "knucks" and "ring-taw" and "keeps" till that amusement grew stale. Then Joe and Huck had another swim, but Tom would not venture, because he found that in kicking off his trousers he had kicked his string of rattlesnake rattles off his ankle, and he wondered how he had escaped cramp so long without the protection of this mysterious charm. He did not venture again until he had found it, and by that time the other boys were tired and ready to rest. They gradually wandered apart, dropped into the "dumps," and fell to gazing longingly across the wide river to where the village lay drowsing in the sun. Tom found himself writing "BECKY" in the sand with his big toe; he scratched it out, and was angry with himself for his weakness. But he wrote it again, nevertheless; he could not help it. He erased it once more and then took himself out of temptation by driving the other boys together and joining them.

But Joe's spirits had gone down almost beyond resurrection. He was so homesick that he could hardly endure the misery of it. The tears lay very near the surface. Huck was melancholy, too. Tom was downhearted, but tried hard not to show it. He had a secret which he was not ready to tell, yet, but if this mutinous depression was not broken up soon, he would have to bring it out. He said, with a great show of cheerfulness:

"I bet there's been pirates on this island before, boys. We'll explore it again. They've hid treasures here somewhere. How'd you feel to light on a rotten chest full of gold and silver—hey?"

But it roused only faint enthusiasm, which faded out, with no reply. Tom tried one or two other seductions; but they failed, too. It was discouraging work. Joe sat poking up the sand with a stick and looking very gloomy. Finally he said:

"Oh, boys, let's give it up. I want to go home. It's so lonesome."

"Oh no, Joe, you'll feel better by and by," said Tom. "Just think of the fishing that's here."

"I don't care for fishing. I want to go home."

"But, Joe, there ain't such another swimming-place anywhere."

"Swimming's no good. I don't seem to care for it, somehow, when there ain't anybody to say I sha'n't go in. I mean to go home."

"Oh, shucks! Baby! You want to see your mother, I reckon."

"Yes, I DO want to see my mother—and you would, too, if you had one. I ain't any more baby than you are." And Joe snuffled a little.

"Well, we'll let the cry-baby go home to his mother, won't we,

Huck? Poor thing—does it want to see its mother? And so it shall. You like it here, don't you, Huck? We'll stay, won't we?"

Huck said, "Y-e-s"—without any heart in it.

"I'll never speak to you again as long as I live," said Joe, rising. "There now!" And he moved moodily away and began to dress himself.

"Who cares!" said Tom. "Nobody wants you to. Go 'long home and get laughed at. Oh, you're a nice pirate. Huck and me ain't cry-babies. We'll stay, won't we, Huck? Let him go if he wants to. I reckon we can get along without him, per'aps."

But Tom was uneasy, nevertheless, and was alarmed to see Joe go sullenly on with his dressing. And then it was discomforting to see Huck eying Joe's preparations so wistfully, and keeping up such an ominous silence. Presently, without a parting word, Joe began to wade off toward the Illinois shore. Tom's heart began to sink. He glanced at Huck. Huck could not bear the look, and dropped his eyes. Then he said:

"I want to go, too, Tom. It was getting so lonesome anyway, and now it'll be worse. Let's us go, too, Tom."

"I won't! You can all go, if you want to. I mean to stay."

"Tom, I better go."

"Well, go 'long—who's hendering you."

Huck began to pick up his scattered clothes. He said:

"Tom, I wisht you'd come, too. Now you think it over. We'll wait for you when we get to shore."

"Well, you'll wait a blame long time, that's all."

Huck started sorrowfully away, and Tom stood looking after him, with a strong desire tugging at his heart to yield his pride and go along too. He hoped the boys would stop, but they still waded slowly on. It suddenly dawned on Tom that it was become very lonely and still. He made one final struggle with his pride, and then darted after his comrades, yelling:

"Wait! Wait! I want to tell you something!"

They presently stopped and turned around. When he got to where they were, he began unfolding his secret, and they listened moodily till at last they saw the "point" he was driving at, and then they set up a war-whoop of applause and said it was "splendid!" and said if he had told them at first, they wouldn't have started away. He made a plausible excuse; but his real reason had been the fear that not even the secret would keep them with him any very great length of time, and so he had meant to hold it in reserve as a last seduction.

The lads came gayly back and went at their sports again with a will, chattering all the time about Tom's stupendous plan and admiring the genius of it. After a dainty egg and fish dinner, Tom said he wanted to learn to smoke, now. Joe caught at the idea and said he would like to try, too. So Huck made pipes and filled them. These novices had never smoked anything before but cigars made of grape-vine, and they "bit" the tongue, and were not considered manly anyway.

Now they stretched themselves out on their elbows and began to puff, charily, and with slender confidence. The smoke had

an unpleasant taste, and they gagged a little, but Tom said:

"Why, it's just as easy! If I'd a knowed this was all, I'd a learnt long ago."

"So would I," said Joe. "It's just nothing."

"Why, many a time I've looked at people smoking, and thought well I wish I could do that; but I never thought I could," said Tom.

"That's just the way with me, hain't it, Huck? You've heard me talk just that way—haven't you, Huck? I'll leave it to Huck if I haven't."

"Yes—heaps of times," said Huck.

"Well, I have too," said Tom; "oh, hundreds of times. Once down by the slaughter-house. Don't you remember, Huck? Bob Tanner was there, and Johnny Miller, and Jeff Thatcher, when I said it. Don't you remember, Huck, 'bout me saying that?"

"Yes, that's so," said Huck. "That was the day after I lost a white alley. No, 'twas the day before."

"There—I told you so," said Tom. "Huck recollects it."

"I bleeve I could smoke this pipe all day," said Joe. "I don't feel sick."

"Neither do I," said Tom. "I could smoke it all day. But I bet you Jeff Thatcher couldn't."

"Jeff Thatcher! Why, he'd keel over just with two draws. Just let him try it once. HE'D see!"

"I bet he would. And Johnny Miller—I wish could see Johnny Miller tackle it once."

"Oh, don't I!" said Joe. "Why, I bet you Johnny Miller couldn't any more do this than nothing. Just one little snifter would fetch HIM."

"'Deed it would, Joe. Say—I wish the boys could see us now."

"So do I."

"Say—boys, don't say anything about it, and some time when they're around, I'll come up to you and say, 'Joe, got a pipe? I want a smoke.' And you'll say, kind of careless like, as if it warn't anything, you'll say, 'Yes, I got my OLD pipe, and another one, but my tobacker ain't very good.' And I'll say, 'Oh, that's all right, if it's STRONG enough.' And then you'll out with the pipes, and we'll light up just as ca'm, and then just see 'em look!"

"By jings, that'll be gay, Tom! I wish it was NOW!"

"So do I! And when we tell 'em we learned when we was off pirating, won't they wish they'd been along?"

"Oh, I reckon not! I'll just BET they will!"

So the talk ran on. But presently it began to flag a trifle, and grow disjointed. The silences widened; the expectoration marvellously increased. Every pore inside the boys' cheeks became a spouting fountain; they could scarcely bail out the cellars under their tongues fast enough to prevent an inundation; little overflowings down their throats occurred in spite of all they could do, and sudden retchings followed every time. Both boys were looking very pale and miserable, now. Joe's pipe dropped from his nerveless fingers. Tom's followed. Both fountains were going furiously and both pumps bailing with might and main. Joe said feebly:

"I've lost my knife. I reckon I better go and find it."

Tom said, with quivering lips and halting utterance:

"I'll help you. You go over that way and I'll hunt around by the spring. No, you needn't come, Huck—we can find it."

So Huck sat down again, and waited an hour. Then he found it lonesome, and went to find his comrades. They were wide apart in the woods, both very pale, both fast asleep. But something informed him that if they had had any trouble they had got rid of it.

They were not talkative at supper that night. They had a humble look, and when Huck prepared his pipe after the meal and was going to prepare theirs, they said no, they were not feeling very well—something they ate at dinner had disagreed with them.

About midnight Joe awoke, and called the boys. There was a brooding oppressiveness in the air that seemed to bode something. The boys huddled themselves together and sought the friendly companionship of the fire, though the dull dead heat of the breathless atmosphere was stifling. They sat still, intent and waiting. The solemn hush continued. Beyond the light of the fire everything was swallowed up in the blackness of darkness. Presently there came a quivering glow that vaguely revealed the foliage for a moment and then vanished. By and by another came, a little stronger. Then another. Then a faint moan came sighing through the branches of the forest and the boys felt a fleeting breath upon their cheeks, and shuddered with the fancy that the Spirit of the Night had gone by. There was a pause. Now a weird flash turned night into day and showed every little grass-blade, separate and distinct, that grew about their feet. And it showed three white, startled faces, too. A deep peal of thunder went rolling and tumbling down the heavens and lost itself in sullen rumblings in the distance. A sweep of chilly air passed by, rustling all the leaves and snowing the flaky ashes broadcast about the fire. Another fierce glare lit up the forest and an instant crash followed that seemed to rend the tree-tops right over the boys' heads. They clung together in terror, in the thick gloom that followed. A few big rain-drops fell pattering upon the leaves.

"Quick! boys, go for the tent!" exclaimed Tom.

They sprang away, stumbling over roots and among vines in the dark, no two plunging in the same direction. A furious blast roared through the trees, making everything sing as it went. One blinding flash after another came, and peal on peal of deafening thunder. And now a drenching rain poured down and the rising hurricane drove it in sheets along the ground. The boys cried out to each other, but the roaring wind and the booming thunder-blasts drowned their voices utterly. However, one by one they straggled in at last and took shelter under the tent, cold, scared, and streaming with water; but to have company in misery seemed something to be grateful for. They could not talk, the old sail flapped so furiously, even if the other noises would have allowed them. The tempest rose higher and higher, and presently the sail tore loose from its fastenings and went winging away on the blast. The boys seized each others' hands and fled, with many tumblings and bruises, to the shelter of a great oak that stood upon the river-bank. Now the battle was at its highest. Under the ceaseless conflagration of lightning that flamed in the skies, everything below stood out in clean-cut and shadowless distinctness: the bending trees, the billowy river, white with foam, the driving spray of spume-flakes, the dim outlines of the high bluffs on the other side, glimpsed through the drifting cloud-rack and the slanting veil of rain. Every little while some giant tree yielded the fight and fell crashing through the younger growth; and the unflagging thunder-peals came now in ear-splitting explosive bursts, keen and sharp, and unspeakably appalling. The storm culminated in one matchless effort that seemed likely to tear the island to pieces, burn it up, drown it to the tree-tops, blow it away, and deafen every creature in it, all at one and the same moment. It was a wild night for homeless young heads to be out in.

But at last the battle was done, and the forces retired with weaker and weaker threatenings and grumblings, and peace resumed her sway. The boys went back to camp, a good deal awed; but they found there was still something to be thankful for, because the great sycamore, the shelter of their beds, was a ruin, now, blasted by the lightnings, and they were not under it when the catastrophe happened.

Everything in camp was drenched, the camp-fire as well; for they were but heedless lads, like their generation, and had made no provision against rain. Here was matter for dismay, for they were soaked through and chilled. They were eloquent in their distress; but they presently discovered that the fire had eaten so far up under the great log it had been built against (where it curved upward and separated itself from the ground), that a handbreadth or so of it had escaped wetting; so they patiently wrought until, with shreds and bark gathered from the under sides of sheltered logs, they coaxed the fire to burn again. Then they piled on great dead boughs till they had a roaring furnace, and were glad-hearted once more. They dried their boiled ham and had a feast, and after that they sat by the fire and expanded and glorified their midnight adventure until morning, for there was not a dry spot to sleep on, anywhere around.

As the sun began to steal in upon the boys, drowsiness came over them, and they went out on the sandbar and lay down to sleep. They got scorched out by and by, and drearily set about getting breakfast. After the meal they felt rusty, and stiff-jointed, and a little homesick once more. Tom saw the signs, and fell to cheering up the pirates as well as he could. But they cared nothing for marbles, or circus, or swimming, or anything. He reminded them of the imposing secret, and raised a ray of cheer. While it lasted, he got them interested in a new device. This was to knock off being pirates, for a while, and be Indians for a change. They were attracted by this idea; so it was not long before they were stripped, and striped from head to heel with black mud, like so many zebras—all of them chiefs, of course—and then they went tearing through the woods to attack an English settlement.

By and by they separated into three hostile tribes, and darted upon each other from ambush with dreadful war-whoops, and killed and scalped each other by thousands. It was a gory day. Consequently it was an extremely satisfactory one.

They assembled in camp toward supper-time, hungry and happy; but now a difficulty arose—hostile Indians could not break the bread of hospitality together without first making peace, and this was a simple impossibility without smoking a pipe of peace. There was no other process that ever they had heard of. Two of the savages almost wished they had remained pirates. However, there was no other way; so with such show of cheerfulness as they could muster they called for the pipe and took their whiff as it passed, in due form.

And behold, they were glad they had gone into savagery, for they had gained something; they found that they could now smoke a little without having to go and hunt for a lost knife; they did not get sick enough to be seriously uncomfortable. They were not likely to fool away this high promise for lack of effort. No, they practised cautiously, after supper, with right fair success, and so they spent a jubilant evening. They were prouder and happier in their new acquirement than they would have been in the scalping and skinning of the Six Nations. We will leave them to smoke and chatter and brag, since we have no further use for them at present.

CHAPTER XVII

BUT there was no hilarity in the little town that same tranquil Saturday afternoon. The Harpers, and Aunt Polly's family, were being put into mourning, with great grief and many tears. An unusual quiet possessed the village, although it was ordinarily quiet enough, in all conscience. The villagers conducted their concerns with an absent air, and talked little; but they sighed often. The Saturday holiday seemed a burden to the children. They had no heart in their sports, and gradually gave them up.

In the afternoon Becky Thatcher found herself moping about the deserted schoolhouse yard, and feeling very melancholy. But she found nothing there to comfort her. She soliloquized:

"Oh, if I only had a brass andiron-knob again! But I haven't got anything now to remember him by." And she choked back a little sob.

Presently she stopped, and said to herself:

"It was right here. Oh, if it was to do over again, I wouldn't say that—I wouldn't say it for the whole world. But he's gone now; I'll never, never, never see him any more."

This thought broke her down, and she wandered away, with tears rolling down her cheeks. Then quite a group of boys and girls—playmates of Tom's and Joe's—came by, and stood looking over the paling fence and talking in reverent tones of how Tom did so-and-so the last time they saw him, and how Joe said this and that small trifle (pregnant with awful prophecy, as they could easily see now!)—and each speaker pointed out the exact spot where the lost lads stood at the time, and then added something like "and I was a-standing just so—just as I am now, and as if you was him—I was as close as that—and he smiled, just this way—and then something seemed to go all over me, like—awful, you know—and I never thought what it meant, of course, but I can see now!"

Then there was a dispute about who saw the dead boys last in life, and many claimed that dismal distinction, and offered evidences, more or less tampered with by the witness; and when it was ultimately decided who DID see the departed last, and exchanged the last words with them, the lucky parties took upon themselves a sort of sacred importance, and were gaped at and envied by all the rest. One poor chap, who had no other grandeur to offer, said with tolerably manifest pride in the remembrance:

"Well, Tom Sawyer he licked me once."

But that bid for glory was a failure. Most of the boys could say that, and so that cheapened the distinction too much. The group loitered away, still recalling memories of the lost heroes, in awed voices.

When the Sunday-school hour was finished, the next morning, the bell began to toll, instead of ringing in the usual way. It was a very still Sabbath, and the mournful sound seemed in keeping with the musing hush that lay upon nature. The villagers began to gather, loitering a moment in the vestibule to converse in whispers about the sad event. But there was no whispering in the house; only the funereal rustling of dresses as the women gathered to their seats disturbed the silence there. None could remember when the little church had been so full before. There was finally a waiting pause, an expectant dumbness, and then Aunt Polly entered, followed by Sid and Mary, and they by the Harper family, all in deep black, and the whole congregation, the old minister as well, rose reverently and stood until the mourners were seated in the front pew. There was another communing silence, broken at intervals by muffled sobs, and then the minister spread his hands abroad and prayed. A moving hymn was sung, and the text followed: "I am the Resurrection and the Life."

As the service proceeded, the clergyman drew such pictures of the graces, the winning ways, and the rare promise of the lost lads that every soul there, thinking he recognized these pictures, felt a pang in remembering that he had persistently blinded himself to them always before, and had as persistently seen only faults and flaws in the poor boys. The minister related many a touching incident in the lives of the departed, too, which illustrated their sweet, generous natures, and the people could easily see, now, how noble and beautiful those episodes were, and remembered with grief that at the time they occurred they had seemed rank rascalities, well deserving of the cowhide. The congregation became more and more moved, as the pathetic tale went on, till at last the whole company broke down and joined the weeping mourners in a chorus of anguished sobs, the preacher himself giving way to his feelings, and crying in the pulpit.

There was a rustle in the gallery, which nobody noticed; a moment later the church door creaked; the minister raised his streaming eyes above his handkerchief, and stood transfixed! First one and then another pair of eyes followed the minister's, and then almost with one impulse the congregation rose and stared while the three dead boys came marching up the aisle, Tom in the lead, Joe next, and Huck, a ruin of drooping rags, sneaking sheepishly in the rear! They had been hid in the unused gallery listening to their own funeral sermon!

Aunt Polly, Mary, and the Harpers threw themselves upon their restored ones, smothered them with kisses and poured out thanksgivings, while poor Huck stood abashed and uncomfortable, not knowing exactly what to do or where to hide from so many unwelcoming eyes. He wavered, and started to slink away, but Tom seized him and said:

"Aunt Polly, it ain't fair. Somebody's got to be glad to see Huck."

"And so they shall. I'm glad to see him, poor motherless thing!" And the loving attentions Aunt Polly lavished upon him were the one thing capable of making him more uncomfortable than he was before.

Suddenly the minister shouted at the top of his voice: "Praise God from whom all blessings flow—SING!—and put your hearts in it!"

And they did. Old Hundred swelled up with a triumphant burst, and while it shook the rafters Tom Sawyer the Pirate looked around upon the envying juveniles about him and confessed in his heart that this was the proudest moment of his life.

As the "sold" congregation trooped out they said they would almost be willing to be made ridiculous again to hear Old Hundred sung like that once more.

Tom got more cuffs and kisses that day—according to Aunt Polly's varying moods—than he had earned before in a year; and he hardly knew which expressed the most gratefulness to God and affection for himself.

CHAPTER XVIII

THAT was Tom's great secret—the scheme to return home with his brother pirates and attend their own funerals. They had paddled over to the Missouri shore on a log, at dusk on Saturday, landing five or six miles below the village; they had slept in the woods at the edge of the town till nearly daylight, and had then crept through back lanes and alleys and finished their sleep in the gallery of the church among a chaos of invalided benches.

At breakfast, Monday morning, Aunt Polly and Mary were very loving to Tom, and very attentive to his wants. There was an unusual amount of talk. In the course of it Aunt Polly said:

"Well, I don't say it wasn't a fine joke, Tom, to keep everybody suffering 'most a week so you boys had a good time, but it is a pity you could be so hard-hearted as to let me suffer so. If you could come over on a log to go to your funeral, you could have come over and give me a hint some way that you warn't dead, but only run off."

"Yes, you could have done that, Tom," said Mary; "and I believe you would if you had thought of it."

"Would you, Tom?" said Aunt Polly, her face lighting wistfully. "Say, now, would you, if you'd thought of it?"

"I—well, I don't know. 'Twould 'a' spoiled everything."

"Tom, I hoped you loved me that much," said Aunt Polly, with a grieved tone that discomforted the boy. "It would have been something if you'd cared enough to THINK of it, even if you didn't DO it."

"Now, auntie, that ain't any harm," pleaded Mary; "it's only Tom's giddy way—he is always in such a rush that he never thinks of anything."

"More's the pity. Sid would have thought. And Sid would have come and DONE it, too. Tom, you'll look back, some day, when it's too late, and wish you'd cared a little more for me when it would have cost you so little."

"Now, auntie, you know I do care for you," said Tom.

"I'd know it better if you acted more like it."

"I wish now I'd thought," said Tom, with a repentant tone; "but I dreamt about you, anyway. That's something, ain't it?"

"It ain't much—a cat does that much—but it's better than nothing. What did you dream?"

"Why, Wednesday night I dreamt that you was sitting over there by the bed, and Sid was sitting by the woodbox, and Mary next to him."

"Well, so we did. So we always do. I'm glad your dreams could take even that much trouble about us."

"And I dreamt that Joe Harper's mother was here."

"Why, she was here! Did you dream any more?"

"Oh, lots. But it's so dim, now."

"Well, try to recollect—can't you?"

"Somehow it seems to me that the wind—the wind blowed the—the—"

"Try harder, Tom! The wind did blow something. Come!"

Tom pressed his fingers on his forehead an anxious minute, and then said:

"I've got it now! I've got it now! It blowed the candle!"

"Mercy on us! Go on, Tom—go on!"

"And it seems to me that you said, 'Why, I believe that that door—'"

"Go ON, Tom!"

"Just let me study a moment—just a moment. Oh, yes—you said you believed the door was open."

"As I'm sitting here, I did! Didn't I, Mary! Go on!"

"And then—and then—well I won't be certain, but it seems like as if you made Sid go and—and—"

"Well? Well? What did I make him do, Tom? What did I make him do?"

"You made him—you—Oh, you made him shut it."

"Well, for the land's sake! I never heard the beat of that in all my days! Don't tell ME there ain't anything in dreams, any more. Sereny Harper shall know of this before I'm an hour older. I'd like to see her get around THIS with her rubbage 'bout superstition. Go on, Tom!"

"Oh, it's all getting just as bright as day, now. Next you said I warn't BAD, only mischeevous and harum-scarum, and not any more responsible than—than—I think it was a colt, or something."

"And so it was! Well, goodness gracious! Go on, Tom!"

"And then you began to cry."

"So I did. So I did. Not the first time, neither. And then—"

"Then Mrs. Harper she began to cry, and said Joe was just the same, and she wished she hadn't whipped him for taking cream when she'd throwed it out her own self—"

"Tom! The sperrit was upon you! You was a prophesying—that's what you was doing! Land alive, go on, Tom!"

"Then Sid he said—he said—"

"I don't think I said anything," said Sid.

"Yes you did, Sid," said Mary.

"Shut your heads and let Tom go on! What did he say, Tom?"

"He said—I THINK he said he hoped I was better off where I was gone to, but if I'd been better sometimes—"

"THERE, d'you hear that! It was his very words!"

"And you shut him up sharp."

"I lay I did! There must 'a' been an angel there. There WAS an angel there, somewheres!"

"And Mrs. Harper told about Joe scaring her with a firecracker, and you told about Peter and the Painkiller—"

"Just as true as I live!"

"And then there was a whole lot of talk 'bout dragging the river for us, and 'bout having the funeral Sunday, and then you and old Miss Harper hugged and cried, and she went."

"It happened just so! It happened just so, as sure as I'm a-sitting in these very tracks. Tom, you couldn't told it more like if you'd 'a' seen it! And then what? Go on, Tom!"

"Then I thought you prayed for me—and I could see you and hear every word you said. And you went to bed, and I was so sorry that I took and wrote on a piece of sycamore bark, 'We ain't dead—we are only off being pirates,' and put it on the table by the candle; and then you looked so good, laying there asleep, that I thought I went and leaned over and kissed you on the lips."

"Did you, Tom, DID you! I just forgive you everything for that!" And she seized the boy in a crushing embrace that made him feel like the guiltiest of villains.

"It was very kind, even though it was only a—dream," Sid soliloquized just audibly.

"Shut up, Sid! A body does just the same in a dream as he'd do if he was awake. Here's a big Milum apple I've been saving for you, Tom, if you was ever found again—now go 'long to school. I'm thankful to the good God and Father of us all I've got you back, that's long-suffering and merciful to them that believe on Him and keep His word, though goodness knows I'm unworthy of it, but if only the worthy ones got His blessings and had His hand to help them over the rough places, there's few enough would smile here or ever enter into His rest when the long night comes. Go 'long Sid, Mary, Tom—take yourselves off—you've hendered me long enough."

The children left for school, and the old lady to call on Mrs. Harper and vanquish her realism with Tom's marvellous dream. Sid had better judgment than to utter the thought that

was in his mind as he left the house. It was this: "Pretty thin—as long a dream as that, without any mistakes in it!"

What a hero Tom was become, now! He did not go skipping and prancing, but moved with a dignified swagger as became a pirate who felt that the public eye was on him. And indeed it was; he tried not to seem to see the looks or hear the remarks as he passed along, but they were food and drink to him. Smaller boys than himself flocked at his heels, as proud to be seen with him, and tolerated by him, as if he had been the drummer at the head of a procession or the elephant leading a menagerie into town. Boys of his own size pretended not to know he had been away at all; but they were consuming with envy, nevertheless. They would have given anything to have that swarthy suntanned skin of his, and his glittering notoriety; and Tom would not have parted with either for a circus.

At school the children made so much of him and of Joe, and delivered such eloquent admiration from their eyes, that the two heroes were not long in becoming insufferably "stuck-up." They began to tell their adventures to hungry listeners—but they only began; it was not a thing likely to have an end, with imaginations like theirs to furnish material. And finally, when they got out their pipes and went serenely puffing around, the very summit of glory was reached.

Tom decided that he could be independent of Becky Thatcher now. Glory was sufficient. He would live for glory. Now that he was distinguished, maybe she would be wanting to "make up." Well, let her—she should see that he could be as indifferent as some other people. Presently she arrived. Tom pretended not to see her. He moved away and joined a group of boys and girls and began to talk. Soon he observed that she was tripping gayly back and forth with flushed face and dancing eyes, pretending to be busy chasing schoolmates, and screaming with laughter when she made a capture; but he noticed that she always made her captures in his vicinity, and that she seemed to cast a conscious eye in his direction at such times, too. It gratified all the vicious vanity that was in him; and so, instead of winning him, it only "set him up" the more and made him the more diligent to avoid betraying that he knew she was about. Presently she gave over skylarking, and moved irresolutely about, sighing once or twice and glancing furtively and wistfully toward Tom. Then she observed that now Tom was talking more particularly to Amy Lawrence than to any one else. She felt a sharp pang and grew disturbed and uneasy at once. She tried to go away, but her feet were treacherous, and carried her to the group instead. She said to a girl almost at Tom's elbow—with sham vivacity:

"Why, Mary Austin! you bad girl, why didn't you come to Sunday-school?"

"I did come—didn't you see me?"

"Why, no! Did you? Where did you sit?"

"I was in Miss Peters' class, where I always go. I saw YOU."

"Did you? Why, it's funny I didn't see you. I wanted to tell you about the picnic."

"Oh, that's jolly. Who's going to give it?"

"My ma's going to let me have one."

"Oh, goody; I hope she'll let ME come."

"Well, she will. The picnic's for me. She'll let anybody come that I want, and I want you."

"That's ever so nice. When is it going to be?"

"By and by. Maybe about vacation."

"Oh, won't it be fun! You going to have all the girls and boys?"

"Yes, every one that's friends to me—or wants to be"; and she glanced ever so furtively at Tom, but he talked right along to Amy Lawrence about the terrible storm on the island, and how the lightning tore the great sycamore tree "all to flinders" while he was "standing within three feet of it."

"Oh, may I come?" said Grace Miller.

"Yes."

"And me?" said Sally Rogers.

"Yes."

"And me, too?" said Susy Harper. "And Joe?"

"Yes."

And so on, with clapping of joyful hands till all the group had begged for invitations but Tom and Amy. Then Tom turned coolly away, still talking, and took Amy with him. Becky's lips trembled and the tears came to her eyes; she hid these signs with a forced gayety and went on chattering, but the life had gone out of the picnic, now, and out of everything else; she got away as soon as she could and hid herself and had what her sex call "a good cry." Then she sat moody, with wounded pride, till the bell rang. She roused up, now, with a vindictive cast in her eye, and gave her plaited tails a shake and said she knew what SHE'D do.

At recess Tom continued his flirtation with Amy with jubilant self-satisfaction. And he kept drifting about to find Becky and lacerate her with the performance. At last he spied her, but there was a sudden falling of his mercury. She was sitting cosily on a little bench behind the schoolhouse looking at a picture-book with Alfred Temple—and so absorbed were they, and their heads so close together over the book, that they did not seem to be conscious of anything in the world besides. Jealousy ran red-hot through Tom's veins. He began to hate himself for throwing away the chance Becky had offered for a reconciliation. He called himself a fool, and all the hard names he could think of. He wanted to cry with vexation. Amy chatted happily along, as they walked, for her heart was singing, but Tom's tongue had lost its function. He did not hear what Amy was saying, and whenever she paused expectantly he could only stammer an awkward assent, which was as often misplaced as otherwise. He kept drifting to the rear of the schoolhouse, again and again, to sear his eyeballs with the hateful spectacle there. He could not help it. And it maddened him to see, as he thought he saw, that Becky Thatcher never once suspected that he was even in the land of the living. But she did see, nevertheless; and she knew she was winning her fight, too, and was glad to see him suffer as she had suffered.

Amy's happy prattle became intolerable. Tom hinted at things he had to attend to; things that must be done; and time was fleeting. But in vain—the girl chirped on. Tom thought, "Oh,

hang her, ain't I ever going to get rid of her?" At last he must be attending to those things—and she said artlessly that she would be "around" when school let out. And he hastened away, hating her for it.

"Any other boy!" Tom thought, grating his teeth. "Any boy in the whole town but that Saint Louis smarty that thinks he dresses so fine and is aristocracy! Oh, all right, I licked you the first day you ever saw this town, mister, and I'll lick you again! You just wait till I catch you out! I'll just take and—"

And he went through the motions of thrashing an imaginary boy —pummelling the air, and kicking and gouging. "Oh, you do, do you? You holler 'nough, do you? Now, then, let that learn you!" And so the imaginary flogging was finished to his satisfaction.

Tom fled home at noon. His conscience could not endure any more of Amy's grateful happiness, and his jealousy could bear no more of the other distress. Becky resumed her picture inspections with Alfred, but as the minutes dragged along and no Tom came to suffer, her triumph began to cloud and she lost interest; gravity and absent-mindedness followed, and then melancholy; two or three times she pricked up her ear at a footstep, but it was a false hope; no Tom came. At last she grew entirely miserable and wished she hadn't carried it so far. When poor Alfred, seeing that he was losing her, he did not know how, kept exclaiming: "Oh, here's a jolly one! look at this!" she lost patience at last, and said, "Oh, don't bother me! I don't care for them!" and burst into tears, and got up and walked away.

Alfred dropped alongside and was going to try to comfort her, but she said:

"Go away and leave me alone, can't you! I hate you!"

So the boy halted, wondering what he could have done—for she had said she would look at pictures all through the nooning—and she walked on, crying. Then Alfred went musing into the deserted schoolhouse. He was humiliated and angry. He easily guessed his way to the truth—the girl had simply made a convenience of him to vent her spite upon Tom Sawyer. He was far from hating Tom the less when this thought occurred to him. He wished there was some way to get that boy into trouble without much risk to himself. Tom's spelling-book fell under his eye. Here was his opportunity. He gratefully opened to the lesson for the afternoon and poured ink upon the page.

Becky, glancing in at a window behind him at the moment, saw the act, and moved on, without discovering herself. She started homeward, now, intending to find Tom and tell him; Tom would be thankful and their troubles would be healed. Before she was half way home, however, she had changed her mind. The thought of Tom's treatment of her when she was talking about her picnic came scorching back and filled her with shame. She resolved to let him get whipped on the damaged spelling-book's account, and to hate him forever, into the bargain.

CHAPTER XIX

TOM arrived at home in a dreary mood, and the first thing his aunt said to him showed him that he had brought his sorrows to an unpromising market:

"Tom, I've a notion to skin you alive!"

"Auntie, what have I done?"

"Well, you've done enough. Here I go over to Sereny Harper, like an old softy, expecting I'm going to make her believe all that rubbage about that dream, when lo and behold you she'd found out from Joe that you was over here and heard all the talk we had that night. Tom, I don't know what is to become of a boy that will act like that. It makes me feel so bad to think you could let me go to Sereny Harper and make such a fool of myself and never say a word."

This was a new aspect of the thing. His smartness of the morning had seemed to Tom a good joke before, and very ingenious. It merely looked mean and shabby now. He hung his head and could not think of anything to say for a moment. Then he said:

"Auntie, I wish I hadn't done it—but I didn't think."

"Oh, child, you never think. You never think of anything but your own selfishness. You could think to come all the way over here from Jackson's Island in the night to laugh at our troubles, and you could think to fool me with a lie about a dream; but you couldn't ever think to pity us and save us from sorrow."

"Auntie, I know now it was mean, but I didn't mean to be mean. I didn't, honest. And besides, I didn't come over here to laugh at you that night."

"What did you come for, then?"

"It was to tell you not to be uneasy about us, because we hadn't got drownded."

"Tom, Tom, I would be the thankfullest soul in this world if I could believe you ever had as good a thought as that, but you know you never did—and I know it, Tom."

"Indeed and 'deed I did, auntie—I wish I may never stir if I didn't."

"Oh, Tom, don't lie—don't do it. It only makes things a hundred times worse."

"It ain't a lie, auntie; it's the truth. I wanted to keep you from grieving—that was all that made me come."

"I'd give the whole world to believe that—it would cover up a power of sins, Tom. I'd 'most be glad you'd run off and acted so bad. But it ain't reasonable; because, why didn't you tell me, child?"

"Why, you see, when you got to talking about the funeral, I just got all full of the idea of our coming and hiding in the church, and I couldn't somehow bear to spoil it. So I just put the bark back in my pocket and kept mum."

"What bark?"

"The bark I had wrote on to tell you we'd gone pirating. I wish, now, you'd waked up when I kissed you—I do, honest."

The hard lines in his aunt's face relaxed and a sudden tenderness dawned in her eyes.

"DID you kiss me, Tom?"

"Why, yes, I did."

"Are you sure you did, Tom?"

"Why, yes, I did, auntie—certain sure."

"What did you kiss me for, Tom?"

"Because I loved you so, and you laid there moaning and I was so sorry."

The words sounded like truth. The old lady could not hide a tremor in her voice when she said:

"Kiss me again, Tom!—and be off with you to school, now, and don't bother me any more."

The moment he was gone, she ran to a closet and got out the ruin of a jacket which Tom had gone pirating in. Then she stopped, with it in her hand, and said to herself:

"No, I don't dare. Poor boy, I reckon he's lied about it—but it's a blessed, blessed lie, there's such a comfort come from it. I hope the Lord—I KNOW the Lord will forgive him, because it was such goodheartedness in him to tell it. But I don't want to find out it's a lie. I won't look."

She put the jacket away, and stood by musing a minute. Twice she put out her hand to take the garment again, and twice she refrained. Once more she ventured, and this time she fortified herself with the thought: "It's a good lie—it's a good lie—I won't let it grieve me." So she sought the jacket pocket. A moment later she was reading Tom's piece of bark through flowing tears and saying: "I could forgive the boy, now, if he'd committed a million sins!"

CHAPTER XX

THERE was something about Aunt Polly's manner, when she kissed Tom, that swept away his low spirits and made him lighthearted and happy again. He started to school and had the luck of coming upon Becky Thatcher at the head of Meadow Lane. His mood always determined his manner. Without a moment's hesitation he ran to her and said:

"I acted mighty mean to-day, Becky, and I'm so sorry. I won't ever, ever do that way again, as long as ever I live—please make up, won't you?"

The girl stopped and looked him scornfully in the face:

"I'll thank you to keep yourself TO yourself, Mr. Thomas Sawyer. I'll never speak to you again."

She tossed her head and passed on. Tom was so stunned that he had not even presence of mind enough to say "Who cares, Miss Smarty?" until the right time to say it had gone by. So he said nothing. But he was in a fine rage, nevertheless. He moped into the schoolyard wishing she were a boy, and imagining how he would trounce her if she were. He presently encountered her and delivered a stinging remark as he passed. She hurled one in return, and the angry breach was complete. It seemed to Becky, in her hot resentment, that she could hardly wait for school to "take in," she was so impatient to see Tom flogged for the injured spelling-book. If she had had any lingering notion of exposing Alfred Temple, Tom's offensive fling had driven it entirely away.

Poor girl, she did not know how fast she was nearing trouble herself. The master, Mr. Dobbins, had reached middle age with an unsatisfied ambition. The darling of his desires was, to be a doctor, but poverty had decreed that he should be nothing higher than a village schoolmaster. Every day he took a mysterious book out of his desk and absorbed himself in it at times when no classes were reciting. He kept that book under lock and key. There was not an urchin in school but was perishing to have a glimpse of it, but the chance never came. Every boy and girl had a theory about the nature of that book; but no two theories were alike, and there was no way of getting at the facts in the case. Now, as Becky was passing by the desk, which stood near the door, she noticed that the key was in the lock! It was a precious moment. She glanced around; found herself alone, and the next instant she had the book in her hands. The title-page—Professor Somebody's ANATOMY—carried no information to her mind; so she began to turn the leaves. She came at once upon a handsomely engraved and colored frontispiece—a human figure, stark naked. At that moment a shadow fell on the page and Tom Sawyer stepped in at the door and caught a glimpse of the picture. Becky snatched at the book to close it, and had the hard luck to tear the pictured page half down the middle. She thrust the volume into the desk, turned the key, and burst out crying with shame and vexation.

"Tom Sawyer, you are just as mean as you can be, to sneak up on a person and look at what they're looking at."

"How could I know you was looking at anything?"

"You ought to be ashamed of yourself, Tom Sawyer; you know you're going to tell on me, and oh, what shall I do, what shall I do! I'll be whipped, and I never was whipped in school."

Then she stamped her little foot and said:

"BE so mean if you want to! I know something that's going to happen. You just wait and you'll see! Hateful, hateful, hateful!"—and she flung out of the house with a new explosion of crying.

Tom stood still, rather flustered by this onslaught. Presently he said to himself:

"What a curious kind of a fool a girl is! Never been licked in school! Shucks! What's a licking! That's just like a girl—they're so thin-skinned and chicken-hearted. Well, of course I ain't going to tell old Dobbins on this little fool, because there's other ways of getting even on her, that ain't so mean; but what of it? Old Dobbins will ask who it was tore his book. Nobody'll answer. Then he'll do just the way he always does—ask first one and then t'other, and when he comes to the right girl he'll know it, without any telling. Girls' faces always tell on them. They ain't got any backbone. She'll get licked. Well, it's a kind of a tight place for Becky Thatcher, because there ain't any way out of it." Tom conned the thing a moment longer, and then added: "All right, though; she'd like to see me in just such a fix—let her sweat it out!"

Tom joined the mob of skylarking scholars outside. In a few moments the master arrived and school "took in." Tom did not feel a strong interest in his studies. Every time he stole a glance at the girls' side of the room Becky's face troubled him. Considering all things, he did not want to pity her, and yet it was all he could do to help it. He could get up no exultation that was really worthy the name. Presently the spelling-book discovery was made, and Tom's mind was entirely full of his own matters for a while after that. Becky roused up from her lethargy of distress and showed good interest in the proceedings. She did not expect that Tom could get out of his trouble by denying that he spilt the ink on the book himself; and she was right. The denial only seemed to make the thing worse for Tom. Becky supposed she would be glad of that, and she tried to believe she was glad of it, but she found she was not certain. When the worst came to the worst, she had an impulse to get up and tell on Alfred Temple, but she made an effort and forced herself to keep still—because, said she to herself, "he'll tell about me tearing the picture sure. I wouldn't say a word, not to save his life!"

Tom took his whipping and went back to his seat not at all broken-hearted, for he thought it was possible that he had unknowingly upset the ink on the spelling-book himself, in some skylarking bout—he had denied it for form's sake and because it was custom, and had stuck to the denial from principle.

A whole hour drifted by, the master sat nodding in his throne, the air was drowsy with the hum of study. By and by, Mr. Dobbins straightened himself up, yawned, then unlocked his desk, and reached for his book, but seemed undecided whether to take it out or leave it. Most of the pupils glanced up languidly, but there were two among them that watched his movements with intent eyes. Mr. Dobbins fingered his book absently for a while, then took it out and settled himself in his chair to read! Tom shot a glance at Becky. He had seen a hunted and helpless rabbit look as she did, with a gun levelled at its head. Instantly he forgot his quarrel with her. Quick—something must be done! done in a flash, too! But the very imminence of the emergency paralyzed his invention. Good!—he had an inspiration! He would run and snatch the book, spring through the door and fly. But his resolution shook for one little instant, and the chance was lost—the master opened the volume. If Tom only had the wasted opportunity back again! Too late. There was no help for Becky now, he said. The next moment the master faced the school. Every eye sank under his gaze. There was that in it which smote even the innocent with fear. There was silence while one might count ten —the master was gathering his wrath. Then he spoke: "Who tore this book?"

There was not a sound. One could have heard a pin drop. The stillness continued; the master searched face after face for signs of guilt.

"Benjamin Rogers, did you tear this book?"

A denial. Another pause.

"Joseph Harper, did you?"

Another denial. Tom's uneasiness grew more and more intense under the slow torture of these proceedings. The master scanned the ranks of boys—considered a while, then turned to the girls:

"Amy Lawrence?"

A shake of the head.

"Gracie Miller?"

The same sign.

"Susan Harper, did you do this?"

Another negative. The next girl was Becky Thatcher. Tom was trembling from head to foot with excitement and a sense of the hopelessness of the situation.

"Rebecca Thatcher" [Tom glanced at her face—it was white with terror] —"did you tear—no, look me in the face" [her hands rose in appeal] —"did you tear this book?"

A thought shot like lightning through Tom's brain. He sprang to his feet and shouted—"I done it!"

The school stared in perplexity at this incredible folly. Tom stood a moment, to gather his dismembered faculties; and when he stepped forward to go to his punishment the surprise, the gratitude, the adoration that shone upon him out of poor Becky's eyes seemed pay enough for a hundred floggings. Inspired by the splendor of his own act, he took without an outcry the most merciless flaying that even Mr. Dobbins had ever administered; and also received with indifference the added cruelty of a command to remain two hours after school should be dismissed—for he knew who would wait for him outside till his captivity was done, and not count the tedious time as loss, either.

Tom went to bed that night planning vengeance against Alfred Temple; for with shame and repentance Becky had told him all, not forgetting her own treachery; but even the longing for vengeance had to give way, soon, to pleasanter musings, and he fell asleep at last with Becky's latest words lingering dreamily in his ear—

"Tom, how COULD you be so noble!"

CHAPTER XXI

VACATION was approaching. The schoolmaster, always severe, grew severer and more exacting than ever, for he wanted the school to make a good showing on "Examination" day. His rod and his ferule were seldom idle now—at least among the smaller pupils. Only the biggest boys, and young ladies of eighteen and twenty, escaped lashing. Mr. Dobbins' lashings were very vigorous ones, too; for although he carried, under his wig, a perfectly bald and shiny head, he had only reached middle age, and there was no sign of feebleness in his muscle. As the great day approached, all the tyranny that was in him came to the surface; he seemed to take a vindictive pleasure in punishing the least shortcomings. The consequence was, that the smaller boys spent their days in terror and suffering and their nights in plotting revenge. They threw away no opportunity to do the master a mischief. But he kept ahead all the time. The retribution that followed every vengeful success was so sweeping and majestic that the boys always retired from the field badly worsted. At last they conspired together and hit upon a plan that promised a dazzling victory. They swore in the sign-painter's boy, told him the scheme, and asked his help. He had his own reasons for being delighted, for the master boarded in his father's family and had given the boy ample cause to hate him. The master's wife would go on a visit to the country in a few days, and there would be nothing to interfere with the plan; the master always prepared himself for great occasions by getting pretty well fuddled, and the sign-painter's boy said that when the dominie had reached the proper condition on Examination Evening he would "manage the thing" while he napped in his chair; then he would have him awakened at the right time and hurried away to school.

In the fulness of time the interesting occasion arrived. At eight in the evening the schoolhouse was brilliantly lighted, and adorned with wreaths and festoons of foliage and flowers. The master sat throned in his great chair upon a raised platform, with his blackboard behind him. He was looking tolerably mellow. Three rows of benches on each side and six rows in front of him were occupied by the dignitaries of the town and by the parents of the pupils. To his left, back of the rows of citizens, was a spacious temporary platform upon which were seated the scholars who were to take part in the exercises of the evening; rows of small boys, washed and dressed to an intolerable state of discomfort; rows of gawky big boys; snowbanks of girls and young ladies clad in lawn and muslin and conspicuously conscious of their bare arms, their grandmothers' ancient trinkets, their bits of pink and blue ribbon and the flowers in their hair. All the rest of the house was filled with non-participating scholars.

The exercises began. A very little boy stood up and sheepishly recited, "You'd scarce expect one of my age to speak in public on the stage," etc.—accompanying himself with the painfully exact and spasmodic gestures which a machine might have used—supposing the machine to be a trifle out of order. But he got through safely, though cruelly scared, and got a fine round of applause when he made his manufactured bow and retired.

A little shamefaced girl lisped, "Mary had a little lamb," etc., performed a compassion-inspiring curtsy, got her meed of applause, and sat down flushed and happy.

Tom Sawyer stepped forward with conceited confidence and soared into the unquenchable and indestructible "Give me liberty or give me death" speech, with fine fury and frantic gesticulation, and broke down in the middle of it. A ghastly stage-fright seized him, his legs quaked under him and he was like to choke. True, he had the manifest sympathy of the house but he had the house's silence, too, which was even worse than its sympathy. The master frowned, and this completed the disaster. Tom struggled awhile and then retired, utterly defeated. There was a weak attempt at applause, but it died early.

"The Boy Stood on the Burning Deck" followed; also "The Assyrian Came Down," and other declamatory gems. Then there were reading exercises, and a spelling fight. The meagre Latin class recited with honor. The prime feature of the evening was in order, now—original "compositions" by the young ladies. Each in her turn stepped forward to the edge of the platform, cleared her throat, held up her manuscript (tied with dainty ribbon), and proceeded to read, with labored attention to "expression" and punctuation. The themes were the same that had been illuminated upon similar occasions by their mothers before them, their grandmothers, and doubtless all their ancestors in the female line clear back to the Crusades. "Friendship" was one; "Memories of Other Days"; "Religion in History"; "Dream Land"; "The Advantages of Culture"; "Forms of Political Government Compared and Contrasted"; "Melancholy"; "Filial Love"; "Heart Longings," etc., etc.

A prevalent feature in these compositions was a nursed and petted melancholy; another was a wasteful and opulent gush of "fine language"; another was a tendency to lug in by the ears particularly prized words and phrases until they were worn entirely out; and a peculiarity that conspicuously marked and marred them was the inveterate and intolerable sermon that wagged its crippled tail at the end of each and every one of them. No matter what the subject might be, a brain-racking effort was made to squirm it into some aspect or other that the moral and religious mind could contemplate with edification. The glaring insincerity of these sermons was not sufficient to compass the banishment of the fashion from the schools, and it is not sufficient to-day; it never will be sufficient while the world stands, perhaps. There is no school in all our land where the young ladies do not feel obliged to close their compositions with a sermon; and you will find that the sermon of the most frivolous and the least religious girl in the school is always the longest and the most relentlessly pious. But enough of this. Homely truth is unpalatable.

Let us return to the "Examination." The first composition that was read was one entitled "Is this, then, Life?" Perhaps the reader can endure an extract from it:

"In the common walks of life, with what delightful emotions does the youthful mind look forward to some anticipated scene of festivity! Imagination is busy sketching rose-tinted pictures of joy. In fancy, the voluptuous votary of fashion sees herself amid the festive throng, 'the observed of all observers.' Her graceful form, arrayed in snowy robes, is whirling through the mazes of the joyous dance; her eye is brightest, her step is lightest in the gay assembly.

"In such delicious fancies time quickly glides by, and the welcome hour arrives for her entrance into the Elysian world, of which she has had such bright dreams. How fairy-like does everything appear to her enchanted vision! Each new scene is more charming than the last. But after a while she finds that beneath this goodly exterior, all is vanity, the flattery which once charmed her soul, now grates harshly upon her ear; the ball-room has lost its charms; and with wasted health and imbittered heart, she turns away with the conviction that earthly pleasures cannot satisfy the longings of the soul!"

And so forth and so on. There was a buzz of gratification from time to time during the reading, accompanied by whispered ejaculations of "How sweet!" "How eloquent!" "So true!" etc., and after the thing had closed with a peculiarly afflicting sermon the applause was enthusiastic.

Then arose a slim, melancholy girl, whose face had the "interesting" paleness that comes of pills and indigestion, and read a "poem." Two stanzas of it will do:

"A MISSOURI MAIDEN'S FAREWELL TO ALABAMA

"Alabama, good-bye! I love thee well! But yet for a while do I leave thee now! Sad, yes, sad thoughts of thee my heart doth swell, And burning recollections throng my brow! For I have wandered through thy flowery woods; Have roamed and read near Tallapoosa's stream; Have listened to Tallassee's warring floods, And wooed on Coosa's side Aurora's beam.

"Yet shame I not to bear an o'er-full heart, Nor blush to turn behind my tearful eyes; 'Tis from no stranger land I now must part, 'Tis to no strangers left I yield these sighs. Welcome and home were mine within this State, Whose vales I leave—whose spires fade fast from me And cold must be mine eyes, and heart, and tete, When, dear Alabama! they turn cold on thee!"

There were very few there who knew what "tete" meant, but the poem was very satisfactory, nevertheless.

Next appeared a dark-complexioned, black-eyed, black-haired young lady, who paused an impressive moment, assumed a tragic expression, and began to read in a measured, solemn tone:

"A VISION

"Dark and tempestuous was night. Around the throne on high not a single star quivered; but the deep intonations of the heavy thunder constantly vibrated upon the ear; whilst the terrific lightning revelled in angry mood through the cloudy chambers of heaven, seeming to scorn the power exerted over its terror by the illustrious Franklin! Even the boisterous winds unanimously came forth from their mystic homes, and blustered about as if to enhance by their aid the wildness of the scene.

"At such a time, so dark, so dreary, for human sympathy my very spirit sighed; but instead thereof,

"'My dearest friend, my counsellor, my comforter and guide— My joy in grief, my second bliss in joy,' came to my side. She moved like one of those bright beings pictured in the sunny walks of fancy's Eden by the romantic and young, a queen of beauty unadorned save by her own transcendent loveliness. So soft was her step, it failed to make even a sound, and but for the magical thrill imparted by her genial touch, as other unobtrusive beauties, she would have glided away unperceived—unsought. A strange sadness rested upon her features, like icy tears upon the robe of December, as she pointed to the contending elements without, and bade me contemplate the two beings presented."

This nightmare occupied some ten pages of manuscript and wound up with a sermon so destructive of all hope to non-Presbyterians that it took the first prize. This composition was considered to be the very finest effort of the evening. The mayor of the village, in delivering the prize to the author of it, made a warm speech in which he said that it was by far the most "eloquent" thing he had ever listened to, and that Daniel Webster himself might well be proud of it.

It may be remarked, in passing, that the number of compositions in which the word "beauteous" was over-fondled, and human experience referred to as "life's page," was up to the usual average.

Now the master, mellow almost to the verge of geniality, put his chair aside, turned his back to the audience, and began to draw a map of America on the blackboard, to exercise the geography class upon. But he made a sad business of it with his unsteady hand, and a smothered titter rippled over the house. He knew what the matter was, and set himself to right it. He sponged out lines and remade them; but he only distorted them more than ever, and the tittering was more pronounced. He threw his entire attention upon his work, now, as if determined not to be put down by the mirth. He felt that all eyes were fastened upon him; he imagined he was succeeding, and yet the tittering continued; it even manifestly increased. And well it might. There was a garret above, pierced with a scuttle over his head; and down through this scuttle came a cat, suspended around the haunches by a string; she had a rag tied about her head and jaws to keep her from mewing; as she slowly descended she curved upward and clawed at the string, she swung downward and clawed at the intangible air. The tittering rose higher and higher—the cat was within six inches of the absorbed teacher's head—down, down, a little lower, and she grabbed his wig with her desperate claws, ·clung to it, and was snatched up into the garret in an instant with her trophy still in her possession! And how the light did blaze abroad from the master's bald pate—for the sign-painter's boy had GILDED it!

That broke up the meeting. The boys were avenged. Vacation had come.

NOTE:—The pretended "compositions" quoted in this chapter are taken without alteration from a volume entitled "Prose and Poetry, by a Western Lady"—but they are exactly and precisely after the schoolgirl pattern, and hence are much happier than any mere imitations could be.

CHAPTER XXII

TOM joined the new order of Cadets of Temperance, being attracted by the showy character of their "regalia." He promised to abstain from smoking, chewing, and profanity as long as he remained a member. Now he found out a new thing—namely, that to promise not to do a thing is the surest way in the world to make a body want to go and do that very thing. Tom soon found himself tormented with a desire to drink and swear; the desire grew to be so intense that nothing but the hope of a chance to display himself in his red sash kept him from withdrawing from the order. Fourth of July was coming; but he soon gave that up —gave it up before he had worn his shackles over forty-eight hours—and fixed his hopes upon old Judge Frazer, justice of the peace, who was apparently on his deathbed and would have a big public funeral, since he was so high an official. During three days Tom was deeply concerned about the Judge's condition and hungry for news of it. Sometimes his hopes ran high—so high that he would venture to get out his regalia and practise before the looking-glass. But the Judge had a most discouraging way of fluctuating. At last he was pronounced upon the mend—and then convalescent. Tom was disgusted; and felt a sense of injury, too. He handed in his resignation at once—and that night the Judge suffered a relapse and died. Tom resolved that he would never trust a man like that again.

The funeral was a fine thing. The Cadets paraded in a style calculated to kill the late member with envy. Tom was a free boy again, however —there was something in that. He could drink and swear, now—but found to his surprise that he did not want to. The simple fact that he could, took the desire away, and the charm of it.

Tom presently wondered to find that his coveted vacation was beginning to hang a little heavily on his hands.

He attempted a diary—but nothing happened during three days, and so he abandoned it.

The first of all the negro minstrel shows came to town, and made a sensation. Tom and Joe Harper got up a band of performers and were happy for two days.

Even the Glorious Fourth was in some sense a failure, for it rained hard, there was no procession in consequence, and the greatest man in the world (as Tom supposed), Mr. Benton, an actual United States Senator, proved an overwhelming disappointment—for he was not twenty-five feet high, nor even anywhere in the neighborhood of it.

A circus came. The boys played circus for three days afterward in tents made of rag carpeting—admission, three pins for boys, two for girls—and then circusing was abandoned.

A phrenologist and a mesmerizer came—and went again and

left the village duller and drearier than ever.

There were some boys-and-girls' parties, but they were so few and so delightful that they only made the aching voids between ache the harder.

Becky Thatcher was gone to her Constantinople home to stay with her parents during vacation—so there was no bright side to life anywhere.

The dreadful secret of the murder was a chronic misery. It was a very cancer for permanency and pain.

Then came the measles.

During two long weeks Tom lay a prisoner, dead to the world and its happenings. He was very ill, he was interested in nothing. When he got upon his feet at last and moved feebly down-town, a melancholy change had come over everything and every creature. There had been a "revival," and everybody had "got religion," not only the adults, but even the boys and girls. Tom went about, hoping against hope for the sight of one blessed sinful face, but disappointment crossed him everywhere. He found Joe Harper studying a Testament, and turned sadly away from the depressing spectacle. He sought Ben Rogers, and found him visiting the poor with a basket of tracts. He hunted up Jim Hollis, who called his attention to the precious blessing of his late measles as a warning. Every boy he encountered added another ton to his depression; and when, in desperation, he flew for refuge at last to the bosom of Huckleberry Finn and was received with a Scriptural quotation, his heart broke and he crept home and to bed realizing that he alone of all the town was lost, forever and forever.

And that night there came on a terrific storm, with driving rain, awful claps of thunder and blinding sheets of lightning. He covered his head with the bedclothes and waited in a horror of suspense for his doom; for he had not the shadow of a doubt that all this hubbub was about him. He believed he had taxed the forbearance of the powers above to the extremity of endurance and that this was the result. It might have seemed to him a waste of pomp and ammunition to kill a bug with a battery of artillery, but there seemed nothing incongruous about the getting up such an expensive thunderstorm as this to knock the turf from under an insect like himself.

By and by the tempest spent itself and died without accomplishing its object. The boy's first impulse was to be grateful, and reform. His second was to wait—for there might not be any more storms.

The next day the doctors were back; Tom had relapsed. The three weeks he spent on his back this time seemed an entire age. When he got abroad at last he was hardly grateful that he had been spared, remembering how lonely was his estate, how companionless and forlorn he was. He drifted listlessly down the street and found Jim Hollis acting as judge in a juvenile court that was trying a cat for murder, in the presence of her victim, a bird. He found Joe Harper and Huck Finn up an alley eating a stolen melon. Poor lads! they—like Tom—had suffered a relapse.

CHAPTER XXIII

AT last the sleepy atmosphere was stirred—and vigorously: the murder trial came on in the court. It became the absorbing topic of village talk immediately. Tom could not get away from it. Every reference to the murder sent a shudder to his heart, for his troubled conscience and fears almost persuaded him that these remarks were put forth in his hearing as "feelers"; he did not see how he could be suspected of knowing anything about the murder, but still he could not be comfortable in the midst of this gossip. It kept him in a cold shiver all the time. He took Huck to a lonely place to have a talk with him. It would be some relief to unseal his tongue for a little while; to divide his burden of distress with another sufferer. Moreover, he wanted to assure himself that Huck had remained discreet.

"Huck, have you ever told anybody about—that?"

"'Bout what?"

"You know what."

"Oh—'course I haven't."

"Never a word?"

"Never a solitary word, so help me. What makes you ask?"

"Well, I was afeard."

"Why, Tom Sawyer, we wouldn't be alive two days if that got found out. YOU know that."

Tom felt more comfortable. After a pause:

"Huck, they couldn't anybody get you to tell, could they?"

"Get me to tell? Why, if I wanted that half-breed devil to drownd me they could get me to tell. They ain't no different way."

"Well, that's all right, then. I reckon we're safe as long as we keep mum. But let's swear again, anyway. It's more surer."

"I'm agreed."

So they swore again with dread solemnities.

"What is the talk around, Huck? I've heard a power of it."

"Talk? Well, it's just Muff Potter, Muff Potter, Muff Potter all the time. It keeps me in a sweat, constant, so's I want to hide som'ers."

"That's just the same way they go on round me. I reckon he's a goner. Don't you feel sorry for him, sometimes?"

"Most always—most always. He ain't no account; but then he hain't ever done anything to hurt anybody. Just fishes a little, to get money to get drunk on—and loafs around considerable; but lord, we all do that—leastways most of us—preachers and such like. But he's kind of good—he give me half a fish, once, when there warn't enough for two; and lots of times he's kind of stood by me when I was out of luck."

"Well, he's mended kites for me, Huck, and knitted hooks on to my line. I wish we could get him out of there."

"My! we couldn't get him out, Tom. And besides, 'twouldn't do any good; they'd ketch him again."

"Yes—so they would. But I hate to hear 'em abuse him so like the dickens when he never done—that."

"I do too, Tom. Lord, I hear 'em say he's the bloodiest looking villain in this country, and they wonder he wasn't ever hung before."

"Yes, they talk like that, all the time. I've heard 'em say that if he was to get free they'd lynch him."

"And they'd do it, too."

The boys had a long talk, but it brought them little comfort. As the twilight drew on, they found themselves hanging about the neighborhood of the little isolated jail, perhaps with an undefined hope that something would happen that might clear away their difficulties. But nothing happened; there seemed to be no angels or fairies interested in this luckless captive.

The boys did as they had often done before—went to the cell grating and gave Potter some tobacco and matches. He was on the ground floor and there were no guards.

His gratitude for their gifts had always smote their consciences before—it cut deeper than ever, this time. They felt cowardly and treacherous to the last degree when Potter said:

"You've been mighty good to me, boys—better'n anybody else in this town. And I don't forget it, I don't. Often I says to myself, says I, 'I used to mend all the boys' kites and things, and show 'em where the good fishin' places was, and befriend 'em what I could, and now they've all forgot old Muff when he's in trouble; but Tom don't, and Huck don't—THEY don't forget him, says I, 'and I don't forget them.' Well, boys, I done an awful thing—drunk and crazy at the time—that's the only way I account for it—and now I got to swing for it, and it's right. Right, and BEST, too, I reckon—hope so, anyway. Well, we won't talk about that. I don't want to make YOU feel bad; you've befriended me. But what I want to say, is, don't YOU ever get drunk—then you won't ever get here. Stand a litter furder west—so—that's it; it's a prime comfort to see faces that's friendly when a body's in such a muck of trouble, and there don't none come here but yourn. Good friendly faces—good friendly faces. Git up on one another's backs and let me touch 'em. That's it. Shake hands—yourn'll come through the bars, but mine's too big. Little hands, and weak—but they've helped Muff Potter a power, and they'd help him more if they could."

Tom went home miserable, and his dreams that night were full of horrors. The next day and the day after, he hung about the court-room, drawn by an almost irresistible impulse to go in, but forcing himself to stay out. Huck was having the same experience. They studiously avoided each other. Each wandered away, from time to time, but the same dismal fascination always brought them back presently. Tom kept his ears open when idlers sauntered out of the court-room, but invariably heard distressing news—the toils were closing more and more relentlessly around poor Potter. At the end of the second day the village talk was to the effect that Injun Joe's evidence stood firm and unshaken, and that there was not the slightest question as to what the jury's verdict would be.

Tom was out late, that night, and came to bed through the window. He was in a tremendous state of excitement. It was hours before he got to sleep. All the village flocked to the court-house the next morning, for this was to be the great day. Both sexes were about equally represented in the packed audience. After a long wait the jury filed in and took their places; shortly afterward, Potter, pale and haggard, timid and hopeless, was brought in, with chains upon him, and seated where all the curious eyes could stare at him; no less conspicuous was Injun Joe, stolid as ever. There was another pause, and then the judge arrived and the sheriff proclaimed the opening of the court. The usual whisperings among the lawyers and gathering together of papers followed. These details and accompanying delays worked up an atmosphere of preparation that was as impressive as it was fascinating.

Now a witness was called who testified that he found Muff Potter washing in the brook, at an early hour of the morning that the murder was discovered, and that he immediately sneaked away. After some further questioning, counsel for the prosecution said:

"Take the witness."

The prisoner raised his eyes for a moment, but dropped them again when his own counsel said:

"I have no questions to ask him."

The next witness proved the finding of the knife near the corpse. Counsel for the prosecution said:

"Take the witness."

"I have no questions to ask him," Potter's lawyer replied.

A third witness swore he had often seen the knife in Potter's possession.

"Take the witness."

Counsel for Potter declined to question him. The faces of the audience began to betray annoyance. Did this attorney mean to throw away his client's life without an effort?

Several witnesses deposed concerning Potter's guilty behavior when brought to the scene of the murder. They were allowed to leave the stand without being cross-questioned.

Every detail of the damaging circumstances that occurred in the graveyard upon that morning which all present remembered so well was brought out by credible witnesses, but none of them were cross-examined by Potter's lawyer. The perplexity and dissatisfaction of the house expressed itself in murmurs and provoked a reproof from the bench. Counsel for the prosecution now said:

"By the oaths of citizens whose simple word is above suspicion, we have fastened this awful crime, beyond all possibility of question, upon the unhappy prisoner at the bar. We rest our case here."

A groan escaped from poor Potter, and he put his face in his hands and rocked his body softly to and fro, while a painful silence reigned in the court-room. Many men were moved, and many women's compassion testified itself in tears. Counsel for the defence rose and said:

"Your honor, in our remarks at the opening of this trial, we foreshadowed our purpose to prove that our client did this fearful deed while under the influence of a blind and irresponsible delirium produced by drink. We have changed our mind. We shall not offer that plea." [Then to the clerk:] "Call Thomas Sawyer!"

A puzzled amazement awoke in every face in the house, not even excepting Potter's. Every eye fastened itself with wondering interest upon Tom as he rose and took his place upon the stand. The boy looked wild enough, for he was badly scared. The oath was administered.

"Thomas Sawyer, where were you on the seventeenth of June, about the hour of midnight?"

Tom glanced at Injun Joe's iron face and his tongue failed him. The audience listened breathless, but the words refused to come. After a few moments, however, the boy got a little of his strength back, and managed to put enough of it into his voice to make part of the house hear:

"In the graveyard!"

"A little bit louder, please. Don't be afraid. You were—"

"In the graveyard."

A contemptuous smile flitted across Injun Joe's face.

"Were you anywhere near Horse Williams' grave?"

"Yes, sir."

"Speak up—just a trifle louder. How near were you?"

"Near as I am to you."

"Were you hidden, or not?"

"I was hid."

"Where?"

"Behind the elms that's on the edge of the grave."

Injun Joe gave a barely perceptible start.

"Any one with you?"

"Yes, sir. I went there with—"

"Wait—wait a moment. Never mind mentioning your companion's name. We will produce him at the proper time. Did you carry anything there with you."

Tom hesitated and looked confused.

"Speak out, my boy—don't be diffident. The truth is always respectable. What did you take there?"

"Only a—a—dead cat."

There was a ripple of mirth, which the court checked.

"We will produce the skeleton of that cat. Now, my boy, tell us everything that occurred—tell it in your own way—don't skip anything, and don't be afraid."

Tom began—hesitatingly at first, but as he warmed to his subject his words flowed more and more easily; in a little while every sound ceased but his own voice; every eye fixed itself upon him; with parted lips and bated breath the audience hung upon his words, taking no note of time, rapt in the ghastly fascinations of the tale. The strain upon pent emotion reached its climax when the boy said:

"—and as the doctor fetched the board around and Muff Potter fell, Injun Joe jumped with the knife and—"

Crash! Quick as lightning the half-breed sprang for a window, tore his way through all opposers, and was gone!

CHAPTER XXIV

TOM was a glittering hero once more—the pet of the old, the envy of the young. His name even went into immortal print, for the village paper magnified him. There were some that believed he would be President, yet, if he escaped hanging.

As usual, the fickle, unreasoning world took Muff Potter to its bosom and fondled him as lavishly as it had abused him before. But that sort of conduct is to the world's credit; therefore it is not well to find fault with it.

Tom's days were days of splendor and exultation to him, but his nights were seasons of horror. Injun Joe infested all his dreams, and always with doom in his eye. Hardly any temptation could persuade the boy to stir abroad after nightfall. Poor Huck was in the same state of wretchedness and terror, for Tom had told the whole story to the lawyer the night before the great day of the trial, and Huck was sore afraid that his share in the business might leak out, yet, notwithstanding Injun Joe's flight had saved him the suffering of testifying in court. The poor fellow had got the attorney to promise secrecy, but what of that? Since Tom's harassed conscience had managed to drive him to the lawyer's house by night and wring a dread tale from lips that had been sealed with the dismalest and most formidable of oaths, Huck's confidence in the human race was well-nigh obliterated.

Daily Muff Potter's gratitude made Tom glad he had spoken; but nightly he wished he had sealed up his tongue.

Half the time Tom was afraid Injun Joe would never be captured; the other half he was afraid he would be. He felt sure he never could draw a safe breath again until that man was dead and he had seen the corpse.

Rewards had been offered, the country had been scoured, but no Injun Joe was found. One of those omniscient and awe-inspiring marvels, a detective, came up from St. Louis, moused around, shook his head, looked wise, and made that sort of astounding success which members of that craft usually achieve. That is to say, he "found a clew." But you can't hang a "clew" for murder, and so after that detective had got through and gone home, Tom felt just as insecure as he was before.

The slow days drifted on, and each left behind it a slightly lightened weight of apprehension.

CHAPTER XXV

THERE comes a time in every rightly-constructed boy's life when he has a raging desire to go somewhere and dig for hidden treasure. This desire suddenly came upon Tom one day. He sallied out to find Joe Harper, but failed of success. Next he sought Ben Rogers; he had gone fishing. Presently he stumbled upon Huck Finn the Red-Handed. Huck would answer. Tom took him to a private place and opened the matter to him confidentially. Huck was willing. Huck was always willing to take a hand in any enterprise that offered

entertainment and required no capital, for he had a troublesome superabundance of that sort of time which is not money. "Where'll we dig?" said Huck.

"Oh, most anywhere."

"Why, is it hid all around?"

"No, indeed it ain't. It's hid in mighty particular places, Huck—sometimes on islands, sometimes in rotten chests under the end of a limb of an old dead tree, just where the shadow falls at midnight; but mostly under the floor in ha'nted houses."

"Who hides it?"

"Why, robbers, of course—who'd you reckon? Sunday-school sup'rintendents?"

"I don't know. If 'twas mine I wouldn't hide it; I'd spend it and have a good time."

"So would I. But robbers don't do that way. They always hide it and leave it there."

"Don't they come after it any more?"

"No, they think they will, but they generally forget the marks, or else they die. Anyway, it lays there a long time and gets rusty; and by and by somebody finds an old yellow paper that tells how to find the marks—a paper that's got to be ciphered over about a week because it's mostly signs and hy'roglyphics."

"HyroQwhich?"

"Hy'roglyphics—pictures and things, you know, that don't seem to mean anything."

"Have you got one of them papers, Tom?"

"No."

"Well then, how you going to find the marks?"

"I don't want any marks. They always bury it under a ha'nted house or on an island, or under a dead tree that's got one limb sticking out. Well, we've tried Jackson's Island a little, and we can try it again some time; and there's the old ha'nted house up the Still-House branch, and there's lots of dead-limb trees—dead loads of 'em."

"Is it under all of them?"

"How you talk! No!"

"Then how you going to know which one to go for?"

"Go for all of 'em!"

"Why, Tom, it'll take all summer."

"Well, what of that? Suppose you find a brass pot with a hundred dollars in it, all rusty and gray, or rotten chest full of di'monds. How's that?"

Huck's eyes glowed.

"That's bully. Plenty bully enough for me. Just you gimme the hundred dollars and I don't want no di'monds."

"All right. But I bet you I ain't going to throw off on di'monds. Some of 'em's worth twenty dollars apiece—there ain't any, hardly, but's worth six bits or a dollar."

"No! Is that so?"

"Cert'nly—anybody'll tell you so. Hain't you ever seen one, Huck?"

"Not as I remember."

"Oh, kings have slathers of them."

"Well, I don' know no kings, Tom."

"I reckon you don't. But if you was to go to Europe you'd see a raft of 'em hopping around."

"Do they hop?"

"Hop?—your granny! No!"

"Well, what did you say they did, for?"

"Shucks, I only meant you'd SEE 'em—not hopping, of course—what do they want to hop for?—but I mean you'd just see 'em—scattered around, you know, in a kind of a general way. Like that old humpbacked Richard."

"Richard? What's his other name?"

"He didn't have any other name. Kings don't have any but a given name."

"No?"

"But they don't."

"Well, if they like it, Tom, all right; but I don't want to be a king and have only just a given name, like a nigger. But say—where you going to dig first?"

"Well, I don't know. S'pose we tackle that old dead-limb tree on the hill t'other side of Still-House branch?"

"I'm agreed."

So they got a crippled pick and a shovel, and set out on their three-mile tramp. They arrived hot and panting, and threw themselves down in the shade of a neighboring elm to rest and have a smoke.

"I like this," said Tom.

"So do I."

"Say, Huck, if we find a treasure here, what you going to do with your share?"

"Well, I'll have pie and a glass of soda every day, and I'll go to every circus that comes along. I bet I'll have a gay time."

"Well, ain't you going to save any of it?"

"Save it? What for?"

"Why, so as to have something to live on, by and by."

"Oh, that ain't any use. Pap would come back to thish-yer town some day and get his claws on it if I didn't hurry up, and I tell you he'd clean it out pretty quick. What you going to do with yourn, Tom?"

"I'm going to buy a new drum, and a sure-'nough sword, and a red necktie and a bull pup, and get married."

"Married!"

"That's it."

"Tom, you—why, you ain't in your right mind."

"Wait—you'll see."

"Well, that's the foolishest thing you could do. Look at pap and my mother. Fight! Why, they used to fight all the time. I remember, mighty well."

"That ain't anything. The girl I'm going to marry won't fight."

"Tom, I reckon they're all alike. They'll all comb a body. Now you better think 'bout this awhile. I tell you you better. What's the name of the gal?"

"It ain't a gal at all—it's a girl."

"It's all the same, I reckon; some says gal, some says girl—both's right, like enough. Anyway, what's her name, Tom?"

"I'll tell you some time—not now."

"All right—that'll do. Only if you get married I'll be more lonesomer than ever."

"No you won't. You'll come and live with me. Now stir out of this and we'll go to digging."

They worked and sweated for half an hour. No result. They toiled another half-hour. Still no result. Huck said:

"Do they always bury it as deep as this?"

"Sometimes—not always. Not generally. I reckon we haven't got the right place."

So they chose a new spot and began again. The labor dragged a little, but still they made progress. They pegged away in silence for some time. Finally Huck leaned on his shovel, swabbed the beaded drops from his brow with his sleeve, and said:

"Where you going to dig next, after we get this one?"

"I reckon maybe we'll tackle the old tree that's over yonder on Cardiff Hill back of the widow's."

"I reckon that'll be a good one. But won't the widow take it away from us, Tom? It's on her land."

"SHE take it away! Maybe she'd like to try it once. Whoever finds one of these hid treasures, it belongs to him. It don't make any difference whose land it's on."

That was satisfactory. The work went on. By and by Huck said:

"Blame it, we must be in the wrong place again. What do you think?"

"It is mighty curious, Huck. I don't understand it. Sometimes witches interfere. I reckon maybe that's what's the trouble now."

"Shucks! Witches ain't got no power in the daytime."

"Well, that's so. I didn't think of that. Oh, I know what the matter is! What a blamed lot of fools we are! You got to find out where the shadow of the limb falls at midnight, and that's where you dig!"

"Then consound it, we've fooled away all this work for nothing. Now hang it all, we got to come back in the night. It's an awful long way. Can you get out?"

"I bet I will. We've got to do it to-night, too, because if somebody sees these holes they'll know in a minute what's here and they'll go for it."

"Well, I'll come around and maow to-night."

"All right. Let's hide the tools in the bushes."

The boys were there that night, about the appointed time. They sat in the shadow waiting. It was a lonely place, and an hour made solemn by old traditions. Spirits whispered in the rustling leaves, ghosts lurked in the murky nooks, the deep baying of a hound floated up out of the distance, an owl answered with his sepulchral note. The boys were subdued by these solemnities, and talked little. By and by they judged that twelve had come; they marked where the shadow fell, and began to dig. Their hopes commenced to rise. Their interest grew stronger, and their industry kept pace with it. The hole deepened and still deepened, but every time their hearts jumped to hear the pick strike upon something, they only suffered a new disappointment. It was only a stone or a chunk. At last Tom said:

"It ain't any use, Huck, we're wrong again."

"Well, but we CAN'T be wrong. We spotted the shadder to a dot."

"I know it, but then there's another thing."

"What's that?".

"Why, we only guessed at the time. Like enough it was too late or too early."

Huck dropped his shovel.

"That's it," said he. "That's the very trouble. We got to give this one up. We can't ever tell the right time, and besides this kind of thing's too awful, here this time of night with witches and ghosts a-fluttering around so. I feel as if something's behind me all the time; and I'm afeard to turn around, becuz maybe there's others in front a-waiting for a chance. I been creeping all over, ever since I got here."

"Well, I've been pretty much so, too, Huck. They most always put in a dead man when they bury a treasure under a tree, to look out for it."

"Lordy!"

"Yes, they do. I've always heard that."

"Tom, I don't like to fool around much where there's dead people. A body's bound to get into trouble with 'em, sure."

"I don't like to stir 'em up, either. S'pose this one here was to stick his skull out and say something!"

"Don't Tom! It's awful."

"Well, it just is. Huck, I don't feel comfortable a bit."

"Say, Tom, let's give this place up, and try somewheres else."

"All right, I reckon we better."

"What'll it be?"

Tom considered awhile; and then said:

"The ha'nted house. That's it!"

"Blame it, I don't like ha'nted houses, Tom. Why, they're a dern sight worse'n dead people. Dead people might talk, maybe, but they don't come sliding around in a shroud, when you ain't noticing, and peep over your shoulder all of a sudden and grit their teeth, the way a ghost does. I couldn't stand such a thing as that, Tom—nobody could."

"Yes, but, Huck, ghosts don't travel around only at night. They won't hender us from digging there in the daytime."

"Well, that's so. But you know mighty well people don't go about that ha'nted house in the day nor the night."

"Well, that's mostly because they don't like to go where a man's been murdered, anyway—but nothing's ever been seen around that house except in the night—just some blue lights slipping by the windows—no regular ghosts."

"Well, where you see one of them blue lights flickering around, Tom, you can bet there's a ghost mighty close behind it. It stands to reason. Becuz you know that they don't anybody but ghosts use 'em."

"Yes, that's so. But anyway they don't come around in the daytime, so what's the use of our being afeard?"

"Well, all right. We'll tackle the ha'nted house if you say so— but I reckon it's taking chances."

They had started down the hill by this time. There in the middle of the moonlit valley below them stood the "ha'nted" house, utterly isolated, its fences gone long ago, rank weeds smothering the very doorsteps, the chimney crumbled to ruin, the window-sashes vacant, a corner of the roof caved in. The boys gazed awhile, half expecting to see a blue light flit past a window; then talking in a low tone, as befitted the time and the circumstances, they struck far off to the right, to give the haunted house a wide berth, and took their way homeward through the woods that adorned the rearward side of Cardiff Hill.

CHAPTER XXVI

ABOUT noon the next day the boys arrived at the dead tree; they had come for their tools. Tom was impatient to go to the haunted house; Huck was measurably so, also—but suddenly said:

"Lookyhere, Tom, do you know what day it is?"

Tom mentally ran over the days of the week, and then quickly lifted his eyes with a startled look in them—

"My! I never once thought of it, Huck!"

"Well, I didn't neither, but all at once it popped onto me that it was Friday."

"Blame it, a body can't be too careful, Huck. We might 'a' got into an awful scrape, tackling such a thing on a Friday."

"MIGHT! Better say we WOULD! There's some lucky days, maybe, but Friday ain't."

"Any fool knows that. I don't reckon YOU was the first that found it out, Huck."

"Well, I never said I was, did I? And Friday ain't all, neither. I had a rotten bad dream last night—dreampt about rats."

"No! Sure sign of trouble. Did they fight?"

"No."

"Well, that's good, Huck. When they don't fight it's only a sign that there's trouble around, you know. All we got to do is to look mighty sharp and keep out of it. We'll drop this thing for to-day, and play. Do you know Robin Hood, Huck?"

"No. Who's Robin Hood?"

"Why, he was one of the greatest men that was ever in England—and the best. He was a robber."

"Cracky, I wisht I was. Who did he rob?"

"Only sheriffs and bishops and rich people and kings, and such like. But he never bothered the poor. He loved 'em. He always divided up with 'em perfectly square."

"Well, he must 'a' been a brick."

"I bet you he was, Huck. Oh, he was the noblest man that ever was. They ain't any such men now, I can tell you. He could lick any man in England, with one hand tied behind him; and he could take his yew bow and plug a ten-cent piece every time, a mile and a half."

"What's a YEW bow?"

"I don't know. It's some kind of a bow, of course. And if he hit that dime only on the edge he would set down and cry—and curse. But we'll play Robin Hood—it's nobby fun. I'll learn you."

"I'm agreed."

So they played Robin Hood all the afternoon, now and then casting a yearning eye down upon the haunted house and passing a remark about the morrow's prospects and possibilities there. As the sun began to sink into the west they took their way homeward athwart the long shadows of the trees and soon were buried from sight in the forests of Cardiff

Hill.

On Saturday, shortly after noon, the boys were at the dead tree again. They had a smoke and a chat in the shade, and then dug a little in their last hole, not with great hope, but merely because Tom said there were so many cases where people had given up a treasure after getting down within six inches of it, and then somebody else had come along and turned it up with a single thrust of a shovel. The thing failed this time, however, so the boys shouldered their tools and went away feeling that they had not trifled with fortune, but had fulfilled all the requirements that belong to the business of treasure-hunting.

When they reached the haunted house there was something so weird and grisly about the dead silence that reigned there under the baking sun, and something so depressing about the loneliness and desolation of the place, that they were afraid, for a moment, to venture in. Then they crept to the door and took a trembling peep. They saw a weed-grown, floorless room, unplastered, an ancient fireplace, vacant windows, a ruinous staircase; and here, there, and everywhere hung ragged and abandoned cobwebs. They presently entered, softly, with quickened pulses, talking in whispers, ears alert to catch the slightest sound, and muscles tense and ready for instant retreat.

In a little while familiarity modified their fears and they gave the place a critical and interested examination, rather admiring their own boldness, and wondering at it, too. Next they wanted to look up-stairs. This was something like cutting off retreat, but they got to daring each other, and of course there could be but one result—they threw their tools into a corner and made the ascent. Up there were the same signs of decay. In one corner they found a closet that promised mystery, but the promise was a fraud—there was nothing in it. Their courage was up now and well in hand. They were about to go down and begin work when—

"Sh!" said Tom.

"What is it?" whispered Huck, blanching with fright.

"Sh! ... There! ... Hear it?"

"Yes! ... Oh, my! Let's run!"

"Keep still! Don't you budge! They're coming right toward the door."

The boys stretched themselves upon the floor with their eyes to knot-holes in the planking, and lay waiting, in a misery of fear.

"They've stopped.... No—coming.... Here they are. Don't whisper another word, Huck. My goodness, I wish I was out of this!"

Two men entered. Each boy said to himself: "There's the old deaf and dumb Spaniard that's been about town once or twice lately—never saw t'other man before."

"T'other" was a ragged, unkempt creature, with nothing very pleasant in his face. The Spaniard was wrapped in a serape; he had bushy white whiskers; long white hair flowed from under his sombrero, and he wore green goggles. When they came in, "t'other" was talking in a low voice; they sat down on the ground, facing the door, with their backs to the wall, and the speaker continued his remarks. His manner became less guarded and his words more distinct as he proceeded:

"No," said he, "I've thought it all over, and I don't like it. It's dangerous."

"Dangerous!" grunted the "deaf and dumb" Spaniard—to the vast surprise of the boys. "Milksop!"

This voice made the boys gasp and quake. It was Injun Joe's! There was silence for some time. Then Joe said:

"What's any more dangerous than that job up yonder—but nothing's come of it."

"That's different. Away up the river so, and not another house about. 'Twon't ever be known that we tried, anyway, long as we didn't succeed."

"Well, what's more dangerous than coming here in the daytime!—anybody would suspicion us that saw us."

"I know that. But there warn't any other place as handy after that fool of a job. I want to quit this shanty. I wanted to yesterday, only it warn't any use trying to stir out of here, with those infernal boys playing over there on the hill right in full view."

"Those infernal boys" quaked again under the inspiration of this remark, and thought how lucky it was that they had remembered it was Friday and concluded to wait a day. They wished in their hearts they had waited a year.

The two men got out some food and made a luncheon. After a long and thoughtful silence, Injun Joe said:

"Look here, lad—you go back up the river where you belong. Wait there till you hear from me. I'll take the chances on dropping into this town just once more, for a look. We'll do that 'dangerous' job after I've spied around a little and think things look well for it. Then for Texas! We'll leg it together!"

This was satisfactory. Both men presently fell to yawning, and Injun Joe said:

"I'm dead for sleep! It's your turn to watch."

He curled down in the weeds and soon began to snore. His comrade stirred him once or twice and he became quiet. Presently the watcher began to nod; his head drooped lower and lower, both men began to snore now.

The boys drew a long, grateful breath. Tom whispered:

"Now's our chance—come!"

Huck said:

"I can't—I'd die if they was to wake."

Tom urged—Huck held back. At last Tom rose slowly and softly, and started alone. But the first step he made wrung such a hideous creak from the crazy floor that he sank down almost dead with fright. He never made a second attempt. The boys lay there counting the dragging moments till it seemed to them that time must be done and eternity growing gray; and then they were grateful to note that at last the sun was setting.

Now one snore ceased. Injun Joe sat up, stared around—

smiled grimly upon his comrade, whose head was drooping upon his knees—stirred him up with his foot and said:

"Here! YOU'RE a watchman, ain't you! All right, though—nothing's happened."

"My! have I been asleep?"

"Oh, partly, partly. Nearly time for us to be moving, pard. What'll we do with what little swag we've got left?"

"I don't know—leave it here as we've always done, I reckon. No use to take it away till we start south. Six hundred and fifty in silver's something to carry."

"Well—all right—it won't matter to come here once more."

"No—but I'd say come in the night as we used to do—it's better."

"Yes: but look here; it may be a good while before I get the right chance at that job; accidents might happen; 'tain't in such a very good place; we'll just regularly bury it—and bury it deep."

"Good idea," said the comrade, who walked across the room, knelt down, raised one of the rearward hearth-stones and took out a bag that jingled pleasantly. He subtracted from it twenty or thirty dollars for himself and as much for Injun Joe, and passed the bag to the latter, who was on his knees in the corner, now, digging with his bowie-knife.

The boys forgot all their fears, all their miseries in an instant. With gloating eyes they watched every movement. Luck!—the splendor of it was beyond all imagination! Six hundred dollars was money enough to make half a dozen boys rich! Here was treasure-hunting under the happiest auspices—there would not be any bothersome uncertainty as to where to dig. They nudged each other every moment—eloquent nudges and easily understood, for they simply meant—"Oh, but ain't you glad NOW we're here!"

Joe's knife struck upon something.

"Hello!" said he.

"What is it?" said his comrade.

"Half-rotten plank—no, it's a box, I believe. Here—bear a hand and we'll see what it's here for. Never mind, I've broke a hole."

He reached his hand in and drew it out—

"Man, it's money!"

The two men examined the handful of coins. They were gold. The boys above were as excited as themselves, and as delighted.

Joe's comrade said:

"We'll make quick work of this. There's an old rusty pick over amongst the weeds in the corner the other side of the fireplace—I saw it a minute ago."

He ran and brought the boys' pick and shovel. Injun Joe took the pick, looked it over critically, shook his head, muttered something to himself, and then began to use it. The box was soon unearthed. It was not very large; it was iron bound and had been very strong before the slow years had injured it. The men contemplated the treasure awhile in blissful silence.

"Pard, there's thousands of dollars here," said Injun Joe.

"'Twas always said that Murrel's gang used to be around here one summer," the stranger observed.

"I know it," said Injun Joe; "and this looks like it, I should say."

"Now you won't need to do that job."

The half-breed frowned. Said he:

"You don't know me. Least you don't know all about that thing. 'Tain't robbery altogether—it's REVENGE!" and a wicked light flamed in his eyes. "I'll need your help in it. When it's finished—then Texas. Go home to your Nance and your kids, and stand by till you hear from me."

"Well—if you say so; what'll we do with this—bury it again?"

"Yes. [Ravishing delight overhead.] NO! by the great Sachem, no! [Profound distress overhead.] I'd nearly forgot. That pick had fresh earth on it! [The boys were sick with terror in a moment.] What business has a pick and a shovel here? What business with fresh earth on them? Who brought them here— and where are they gone? Have you heard anybody?—seen anybody? What! bury it again and leave them to come and see the ground disturbed? Not exactly—not exactly. We'll take it to my den."

"Why, of course! Might have thought of that before. You mean Number One?"

"No—Number Two—under the cross. The other place is bad— too common."

"All right. It's nearly dark enough to start."

Injun Joe got up and went about from window to window cautiously peeping out. Presently he said:

"Who could have brought those tools here? Do you reckon they can be up-stairs?"

The boys' breath forsook them. Injun Joe put his hand on his knife, halted a moment, undecided, and then turned toward the stairway. The boys thought of the closet, but their strength was gone. The steps came creaking up the stairs—the intolerable distress of the situation woke the stricken resolution of the lads—they were about to spring for the closet, when there was a crash of rotten timbers and Injun Joe landed on the ground amid the debris of the ruined stairway. He gathered himself up cursing, and his comrade said:

"Now what's the use of all that? If it's anybody, and they're up there, let them STAY there—who cares? If they want to jump down, now, and get into trouble, who objects? It will be dark in fifteen minutes —and then let them follow us if they want to. I'm willing. In my opinion, whoever hove those things in here caught a sight of us and took us for ghosts or devils or something. I'll bet they're running yet."

Joe grumbled awhile; then he agreed with his friend that what daylight was left ought to be economized in getting things

ready for leaving. Shortly afterward they slipped out of the house in the deepening twilight, and moved toward the river with their precious box.

Tom and Huck rose up, weak but vastly relieved, and stared after them through the chinks between the logs of the house. Follow? Not they. They were content to reach ground again without broken necks, and take the townward track over the hill. They did not talk much. They were too much absorbed in hating themselves—hating the ill luck that made them take the spade and the pick there. But for that, Injun Joe never would have suspected. He would have hidden the silver with the gold to wait there till his "revenge" was satisfied, and then he would have had the misfortune to find that money turn up missing. Bitter, bitter luck that the tools were ever brought there!

They resolved to keep a lookout for that Spaniard when he should come to town spying out for chances to do his revengeful job, and follow him to "Number Two," wherever that might be. Then a ghastly thought occurred to Tom.

"Revenge? What if he means US, Huck!"

"Oh, don't!" said Huck, nearly fainting.

They talked it all over, and as they entered town they agreed to believe that he might possibly mean somebody else—at least that he might at least mean nobody but Tom, since only Tom had testified.

Very, very small comfort it was to Tom to be alone in danger! Company would be a palpable improvement, he thought.

CHAPTER XXVII

THE adventure of the day mightily tormented Tom's dreams that night. Four times he had his hands on that rich treasure and four times it wasted to nothingness in his fingers as sleep forsook him and wakefulness brought back the hard reality of his misfortune. As he lay in the early morning recalling the incidents of his great adventure, he noticed that they seemed curiously subdued and far away—somewhat as if they had happened in another world, or in a time long gone by. Then it occurred to him that the great adventure itself must be a dream! There was one very strong argument in favor of this idea—namely, that the quantity of coin he had seen was too vast to be real. He had never seen as much as fifty dollars in one mass before, and he was like all boys of his age and station in life, in that he imagined that all references to "hundreds" and "thousands" were mere fanciful forms of speech, and that no such sums really existed in the world. He never had supposed for a moment that so large a sum as a hundred dollars was to be found in actual money in any one's possession. If his notions of hidden treasure had been analyzed, they would have been found to consist of a handful of real dimes and a bushel of vague, splendid, ungraspable dollars.

But the incidents of his adventure grew sensibly sharper and clearer under the attrition of thinking them over, and so he presently found himself leaning to the impression that the thing might not have been a dream, after all. This uncertainty must be swept away. He would snatch a hurried breakfast and go and find Huck. Huck was sitting on the gunwale of a flatboat, listlessly dangling his feet in the water and looking very melancholy. Tom concluded to let Huck lead up to the subject. If he did not do it, then the adventure would be proved to have been only a dream.

"Hello, Huck!"

"Hello, yourself."

Silence, for a minute.

"Tom, if we'd 'a' left the blame tools at the dead tree, we'd 'a' got the money. Oh, ain't it awful!"

"'Tain't a dream, then, 'tain't a dream! Somehow I most wish it was. Dog'd if I don't, Huck."

"What ain't a dream?"

"Oh, that thing yesterday. I been half thinking it was."

"Dream! If them stairs hadn't broke down you'd 'a' seen how much dream it was! I've had dreams enough all night—with that patch-eyed Spanish devil going for me all through 'em—rot him!"

"No, not rot him. FIND him! Track the money!"

"Tom, we'll never find him. A feller don't have only one chance for such a pile—and that one's lost. I'd feel mighty shaky if I was to see him, anyway."

"Well, so'd I; but I'd like to see him, anyway—and track him out—to his Number Two."

"Number Two—yes, that's it. I been thinking 'bout that. But I can't make nothing out of it. What do you reckon it is?"

"I dono. It's too deep. Say, Huck—maybe it's the number of a house!"

"Goody! ... No, Tom, that ain't it. If it is, it ain't in this one-horse town. They ain't no numbers here."

"Well, that's so. Lemme think a minute. Here—it's the number of a room—in a tavern, you know!"

"Oh, that's the trick! They ain't only two taverns. We can find out quick."

"You stay here, Huck, till I come."

Tom was off at once. He did not care to have Huck's company in public places. He was gone half an hour. He found that in the best tavern, No. 2 had long been occupied by a young lawyer, and was still so occupied. In the less ostentatious house, No. 2 was a mystery. The tavern-keeper's young son said it was kept locked all the time, and he never saw anybody go into it or come out of it except at night; he did not know any particular reason for this state of things; had had some little curiosity, but it was rather feeble; had made the most of the mystery by entertaining himself with the idea that that room was "ha'nted"; had noticed that there was a light in there the night before.

"That's what I've found out, Huck. I reckon that's the very No. 2 we're after."

"I reckon it is, Tom. Now what you going to do?"

"Lemme think."

Tom thought a long time. Then he said:

"I'll tell you. The back door of that No. 2 is the door that comes out into that little close alley between the tavern and the old rattle trap of a brick store. Now you get hold of all the door-keys you can find, and I'll nip all of auntie's, and the first dark night we'll go there and try 'em. And mind you, keep a lookout for Injun Joe, because he said he was going to drop into town and spy around once more for a chance to get his revenge. If you see him, you just follow him; and if he don't go to that No. 2, that ain't the place."

"Lordy, I don't want to foller him by myself!"

"Why, it'll be night, sure. He mightn't ever see you—and if he did, maybe he'd never think anything."

"Well, if it's pretty dark I reckon I'll track him. I dono—I dono. I'll try."

"You bet I'll follow him, if it's dark, Huck. Why, he might 'a' found out he couldn't get his revenge, and be going right after that money."

"It's so, Tom, it's so. I'll foller him; I will, by jingoes!"

"Now you're TALKING! Don't you ever weaken, Huck, and I won't."

CHAPTER XXVIII

THAT night Tom and Huck were ready for their adventure. They hung about the neighborhood of the tavern until after nine, one watching the alley at a distance and the other the tavern door. Nobody entered the alley or left it; nobody resembling the Spaniard entered or left the tavern door. The night promised to be a fair one; so Tom went home with the understanding that if a considerable degree of darkness came on, Huck was to come and "maow," whereupon he would slip out and try the keys. But the night remained clear, and Huck closed his watch and retired to bed in an empty sugar hogshead about twelve.

Tuesday the boys had the same ill luck. Also Wednesday. But Thursday night promised better. Tom slipped out in good season with his aunt's old tin lantern, and a large towel to blindfold it with. He hid the lantern in Huck's sugar hogshead and the watch began. An hour before midnight the tavern closed up and its lights (the only ones thereabouts) were put out. No Spaniard had been seen. Nobody had entered or left the alley. Everything was auspicious. The blackness of darkness reigned, the perfect stillness was interrupted only by occasional mutterings of distant thunder.

Tom got his lantern, lit it in the hogshead, wrapped it closely in the towel, and the two adventurers crept in the gloom toward the tavern. Huck stood sentry and Tom felt his way into the alley. Then there was a season of waiting anxiety that weighed upon Huck's spirits like a mountain. He began to wish he could see a flash from the lantern—it would frighten him, but it would at least tell him that Tom was alive yet. It seemed hours since Tom had disappeared. Surely he must have fainted; maybe he was dead; maybe his heart had burst under terror and excitement. In his uneasiness Huck found himself drawing closer and closer to the alley; fearing all sorts of dreadful things, and momentarily expecting some catastrophe to happen that would take away his breath. There was not much to take away, for he seemed only able to inhale it by thimblefuls, and his heart would soon wear itself out, the way it was beating. Suddenly there was a flash of light and Tom came tearing by him: "Run!" said he; "run, for your life!"

He needn't have repeated it; once was enough; Huck was making thirty or forty miles an hour before the repetition was uttered. The boys never stopped till they reached the shed of a deserted slaughter-house at the lower end of the village. Just as they got within its shelter the storm burst and the rain poured down. As soon as Tom got his breath he said:

"Huck, it was awful! I tried two of the keys, just as soft as I could; but they seemed to make such a power of racket that I couldn't hardly get my breath I was so scared. They wouldn't turn in the lock, either. Well, without noticing what I was doing, I took hold of the knob, and open comes the door! It warn't locked! I hopped in, and shook off the towel, and, GREAT CAESAR'S GHOST!"

"What!—what'd you see, Tom?"

"Huck, I most stepped onto Injun Joe's hand!"

"No!"

"Yes! He was lying there, sound asleep on the floor, with his old patch on his eye and his arms spread out."

"Lordy, what did you do? Did he wake up?"

"No, never budged. Drunk, I reckon. I just grabbed that towel and started!"

"I'd never 'a' thought of the towel, I bet!"

"Well, I would. My aunt would make me mighty sick if I lost it."

"Say, Tom, did you see that box?"

"Huck, I didn't wait to look around. I didn't see the box, I didn't see the cross. I didn't see anything but a bottle and a tin cup on the floor by Injun Joe; yes, I saw two barrels and lots more bottles in the room. Don't you see, now, what's the matter with that ha'nted room?"

"How?"

"Why, it's ha'nted with whiskey! Maybe ALL the Temperance Taverns have got a ha'nted room, hey, Huck?"

"Well, I reckon maybe that's so. Who'd 'a' thought such a thing? But say, Tom, now's a mighty good time to get that box, if Injun Joe's drunk."

"It is, that! You try it!"

Huck shuddered.

"Well, no—I reckon not."

"And I reckon not, Huck. Only one bottle alongside of Injun Joe ain't enough. If there'd been three, he'd be drunk enough and I'd do it."

There was a long pause for reflection, and then Tom said:

"Lookyhere, Huck, less not try that thing any more till we

know Injun Joe's not in there. It's too scary. Now, if we watch every night, we'll be dead sure to see him go out, some time or other, and then we'll snatch that box quicker'n lightning."

"Well, I'm agreed. I'll watch the whole night long, and I'll do it every night, too, if you'll do the other part of the job."

"All right, I will. All you got to do is to trot up Hooper Street a block and maow—and if I'm asleep, you throw some gravel at the window and that'll fetch me."

"Agreed, and good as wheat!"

"Now, Huck, the storm's over, and I'll go home. It'll begin to be daylight in a couple of hours. You go back and watch that long, will you?"

"I said I would, Tom, and I will. I'll ha'nt that tavern every night for a year! I'll sleep all day and I'll stand watch all night."

"That's all right. Now, where you going to sleep?"

"In Ben Rogers' hayloft. He lets me, and so does his pap's nigger man, Uncle Jake. I tote water for Uncle Jake whenever he wants me to, and any time I ask him he gives me a little something to eat if he can spare it. That's a mighty good nigger, Tom. He likes me, becuz I don't ever act as if I was above him. Sometime I've set right down and eat WITH him. But you needn't tell that. A body's got to do things when he's awful hungry he wouldn't want to do as a steady thing."

"Well, if I don't want you in the daytime, I'll let you sleep. I won't come bothering around. Any time you see something's up, in the night, just skip right around and maow."

CHAPTER XXIX

THE first thing Tom heard on Friday morning was a glad piece of news —Judge Thatcher's family had come back to town the night before. Both Injun Joe and the treasure sunk into secondary importance for a moment, and Becky took the chief place in the boy's interest. He saw her and they had an exhausting good time playing "hi-spy" and "gully-keeper" with a crowd of their school-mates. The day was completed and crowned in a peculiarly satisfactory way: Becky teased her mother to appoint the next day for the long-promised and long-delayed picnic, and she consented. The child's delight was boundless; and Tom's not more moderate. The invitations were sent out before sunset, and straightway the young folks of the village were thrown into a fever of preparation and pleasurable anticipation. Tom's excitement enabled him to keep awake until a pretty late hour, and he had good hopes of hearing Huck's "maow," and of having his treasure to astonish Becky and the picnickers with, next day; but he was disappointed. No signal came that night.

Morning came, eventually, and by ten or eleven o'clock a giddy and rollicking company were gathered at Judge Thatcher's, and everything was ready for a start. It was not the custom for elderly people to mar the picnics with their presence. The children were considered safe enough under the wings of a few young ladies of eighteen and a few young gentlemen of twenty-three or thereabouts. The old steam ferryboat was chartered for the occasion; presently the gay throng filed up the main street laden with provision-baskets. Sid was sick and had to miss the fun; Mary remained at home to entertain him. The last thing Mrs. Thatcher said to Becky, was:

"You'll not get back till late. Perhaps you'd better stay all night with some of the girls that live near the ferry-landing, child."

"Then I'll stay with Susy Harper, mamma."

"Very well. And mind and behave yourself and don't be any trouble."

Presently, as they tripped along, Tom said to Becky:

"Say—I'll tell you what we'll do. 'Stead of going to Joe Harper's we'll climb right up the hill and stop at the Widow Douglas'. She'll have ice-cream! She has it most every day—dead loads of it. And she'll be awful glad to have us."

"Oh, that will be fun!"

Then Becky reflected a moment and said:

"But what will mamma say?"

"How'll she ever know?"

The girl turned the idea over in her mind, and said reluctantly:

"I reckon it's wrong—but—"

"But shucks! Your mother won't know, and so what's the harm? All she wants is that you'll be safe; and I bet you she'd 'a' said go there if she'd 'a' thought of it. I know she would!"

The Widow Douglas' splendid hospitality was a tempting bait. It and Tom's persuasions presently carried the day. So it was decided to say nothing anybody about the night's programme. Presently it occurred to Tom that maybe Huck might come this very night and give the signal. The thought took a deal of the spirit out of his anticipations. Still he could not bear to give up the fun at Widow Douglas'. And why should he give it up, he reasoned—the signal did not come the night before, so why should it be any more likely to come to-night? The sure fun of the evening outweighed the uncertain treasure; and, boy-like, he determined to yield to the stronger inclination and not allow himself to think of the box of money another time that day.

Three miles below town the ferryboat stopped at the mouth of a woody hollow and tied up. The crowd swarmed ashore and soon the forest distances and craggy heights echoed far and near with shoutings and laughter. All the different ways of getting hot and tired were gone through with, and by-and-by the rovers straggled back to camp fortified with responsible appetites, and then the destruction of the good things began. After the feast there was a refreshing season of rest and chat in the shade of spreading oaks. By-and-by somebody shouted:

"Who's ready for the cave?"

Everybody was. Bundles of candles were procured, and straightway there was a general scamper up the hill. The mouth of the cave was up the hillside—an opening shaped like a letter A. Its massive oaken door stood unbarred. Within was a small chamber, chilly as an ice-house, and walled by Nature with solid limestone that was dewy with a cold sweat. It was romantic and mysterious to stand here in the deep gloom and look out upon the green valley shining in the sun. But the impressiveness of the situation quickly wore off, and the romping began again. The moment a candle was lighted there was a general rush upon the owner of it; a struggle and a

gallant defence followed, but the candle was soon knocked down or blown out, and then there was a glad clamor of laughter and a new chase. But all things have an end. By-and-by the procession went filing down the steep descent of the main avenue, the flickering rank of lights dimly revealing the lofty walls of rock almost to their point of junction sixty feet overhead. This main avenue was not more than eight or ten feet wide. Every few steps other lofty and still narrower crevices branched from it on either hand—for McDougal's cave was but a vast labyrinth of crooked aisles that ran into each other and out again and led nowhere. It was said that one might wander days and nights together through its intricate tangle of rifts and chasms, and never find the end of the cave; and that he might go down, and down, and still down, into the earth, and it was just the same—labyrinth under labyrinth, and no end to any of them. No man "knew" the cave. That was an impossible thing. Most of the young men knew a portion of it, and it was not customary to venture much beyond this known portion. Tom Sawyer knew as much of the cave as any one.

The procession moved along the main avenue some three-quarters of a mile, and then groups and couples began to slip aside into branch avenues, fly along the dismal corridors, and take each other by surprise at points where the corridors joined again. Parties were able to elude each other for the space of half an hour without going beyond the "known" ground.

By-and-by, one group after another came straggling back to the mouth of the cave, panting, hilarious, smeared from head to foot with tallow drippings, daubed with clay, and entirely delighted with the success of the day. Then they were astonished to find that they had been taking no note of time and that night was about at hand. The clanging bell had been calling for half an hour. However, this sort of close to the day's adventures was romantic and therefore satisfactory. When the ferryboat with her wild freight pushed into the stream, nobody cared sixpence for the wasted time but the captain of the craft.

Huck was already upon his watch when the ferryboat's lights went glinting past the wharf. He heard no noise on board, for the young people were as subdued and still as people usually are who are nearly tired to death. He wondered what boat it was, and why she did not stop at the wharf—and then he dropped her out of his mind and put his attention upon his business. The night was growing cloudy and dark. Ten o'clock came, and the noise of vehicles ceased, scattered lights began to wink out, all straggling foot-passengers disappeared, the village betook itself to its slumbers and left the small watcher alone with the silence and the ghosts. Eleven o'clock came, and the tavern lights were put out; darkness everywhere, now. Huck waited what seemed a weary long time, but nothing happened. His faith was weakening. Was there any use? Was there really any use? Why not give it up and turn in?

A noise fell upon his ear. He was all attention in an instant. The alley door closed softly. He sprang to the corner of the brick store. The next moment two men brushed by him, and one seemed to have something under his arm. It must be that box! So they were going to remove the treasure. Why call Tom now? It would be absurd—the men would get away with the box and never be found again. No, he would stick to their wake and follow them; he would trust to the darkness for security from discovery. So communing with himself, Huck stepped out and glided along behind the men, cat-like, with bare feet, allowing them to keep just far enough ahead not to be invisible.

They moved up the river street three blocks, then turned to the left up a cross-street. They went straight ahead, then, until they came to the path that led up Cardiff Hill; this they took. They passed by the old Welshman's house, half-way up the hill, without hesitating, and still climbed upward. Good, thought Huck, they will bury it in the old quarry. But they never stopped at the quarry. They passed on, up the summit. They plunged into the narrow path between the tall sumach bushes, and were at once hidden in the gloom. Huck closed up and shortened his distance, now, for they would never be able to see him. He trotted along awhile; then slackened his pace, fearing he was gaining too fast; moved on a piece, then stopped altogether; listened; no sound; none, save that he seemed to hear the beating of his own heart. The hooting of an owl came over the hill—ominous sound! But no footsteps. Heavens, was everything lost! He was about to spring with winged feet, when a man cleared his throat not four feet from him! Huck's heart shot into his throat, but he swallowed it again; and then he stood there shaking as if a dozen agues had taken charge of him at once, and so weak that he thought he must surely fall to the ground. He knew where he was. He knew he was within five steps of the stile leading into Widow Douglas' grounds. Very well, he thought, let them bury it there; it won't be hard to find.

Now there was a voice—a very low voice—Injun Joe's:

"Damn her, maybe she's got company—there's lights, late as it is."

"I can't see any."

This was that stranger's voice—the stranger of the haunted house. A deadly chill went to Huck's heart—this, then, was the "revenge" job! His thought was, to fly. Then he remembered that the Widow Douglas had been kind to him more than once, and maybe these men were going to murder her. He wished he dared venture to warn her; but he knew he didn't dare—they might come and catch him. He thought all this and more in the moment that elapsed between the stranger's remark and Injun Joe's next—which was—

"Because the bush is in your way. Now—this way—now you see, don't you?"

"Yes. Well, there IS company there, I reckon. Better give it up."

"Give it up, and I just leaving this country forever! Give it up and maybe never have another chance. I tell you again, as I've told you before, I don't care for her swag—you may have it. But her husband was rough on me—many times he was rough on me—and mainly he was the justice of the peace that jugged me for a vagrant. And that ain't all. It ain't a millionth part of it! He had me HORSEWHIPPED!—horsewhipped in front of the jail, like a nigger!—with all the town looking on! HORSEWHIPPED!—do you understand? He took advantage of me and died. But I'll take it out of HER."

"Oh, don't kill her! Don't do that!"

"Kill? Who said anything about killing? I would kill HIM if he was here; but not her. When you want to get revenge on a woman you don't kill her—bosh! you go for her looks. You slit her nostrils—you notch her ears like a sow!"

"By God, that's—"

"Keep your opinion to yourself! It will be safest for you. I'll tie

her to the bed. If she bleeds to death, is that my fault? I'll not cry, if she does. My friend, you'll help me in this thing—for MY sake —that's why you're here—I mightn't be able alone. If you flinch, I'll kill you. Do you understand that? And if I have to kill you, I'll kill her—and then I reckon nobody'll ever know much about who done this business."

"Well, if it's got to be done, let's get at it. The quicker the better—I'm all in a shiver."

"Do it NOW? And company there? Look here—I'll get suspicious of you, first thing you know. No—we'll wait till the lights are out—there's no hurry."

Huck felt that a silence was going to ensue—a thing still more awful than any amount of murderous talk; so he held his breath and stepped gingerly back; planted his foot carefully and firmly, after balancing, one-legged, in a precarious way and almost toppling over, first on one side and then on the other. He took another step back, with the same elaboration and the same risks; then another and another, and—a twig snapped under his foot! His breath stopped and he listened. There was no sound—the stillness was perfect. His gratitude was measureless. Now he turned in his tracks, between the walls of sumach bushes—turned himself as carefully as if he were a ship—and then stepped quickly but cautiously along. When he emerged at the quarry he felt secure, and so he picked up his nimble heels and flew. Down, down he sped, till he reached the Welshman's. He banged at the door, and presently the heads of the old man and his two stalwart sons were thrust from windows.

"What's the row there? Who's banging? What do you want?"

"Let me in—quick! I'll tell everything."

"Why, who are you?"

"Huckleberry Finn—quick, let me in!"

"Huckleberry Finn, indeed! It ain't a name to open many doors, I judge! But let him in, lads, and let's see what's the trouble."

"Please don't ever tell I told you," were Huck's first words when he got in. "Please don't—I'd be killed, sure—but the widow's been good friends to me sometimes, and I want to tell—I WILL tell if you'll promise you won't ever say it was me."

"By George, he HAS got something to tell, or he wouldn't act so!" exclaimed the old man; "out with it and nobody here'll ever tell, lad."

Three minutes later the old man and his sons, well armed, were up the hill, and just entering the sumach path on tiptoe, their weapons in their hands. Huck accompanied them no further. He hid behind a great bowlder and fell to listening. There was a lagging, anxious silence, and then all of a sudden there was an explosion of firearms and a cry.

Huck waited for no particulars. He sprang away and sped down the hill as fast as his legs could carry him.

CHAPTER XXX

AS the earliest suspicion of dawn appeared on Sunday morning, Huck came groping up the hill and rapped gently at the old Welshman's door. The inmates were asleep, but it was a sleep that was set on a hair-trigger, on account of the exciting episode of the night. A call came from a window:

"Who's there!"

Huck's scared voice answered in a low tone:

"Please let me in! It's only Huck Finn!"

"It's a name that can open this door night or day, lad!—and welcome!"

These were strange words to the vagabond boy's ears, and the pleasantest he had ever heard. He could not recollect that the closing word had ever been applied in his case before. The door was quickly unlocked, and he entered. Huck was given a seat and the old man and his brace of tall sons speedily dressed themselves.

"Now, my boy, I hope you're good and hungry, because breakfast will be ready as soon as the sun's up, and we'll have a piping hot one, too —make yourself easy about that! I and the boys hoped you'd turn up and stop here last night."

"I was awful scared," said Huck, "and I run. I took out when the pistols went off, and I didn't stop for three mile. I've come now becuz I wanted to know about it, you know; and I come before daylight becuz I didn't want to run across them devils, even if they was dead."

"Well, poor chap, you do look as if you'd had a hard night of it—but there's a bed here for you when you've had your breakfast. No, they ain't dead, lad—we are sorry enough for that. You see we knew right where to put our hands on them, by your description; so we crept along on tiptoe till we got within fifteen feet of them—dark as a cellar that sumach path was—and just then I found I was going to sneeze. It was the meanest kind of luck! I tried to keep it back, but no use —'twas bound to come, and it did come! I was in the lead with my pistol raised, and when the sneeze started those scoundrels a-rustling to get out of the path, I sung out, 'Fire boys!' and blazed away at the place where the rustling was. So did the boys. But they were off in a jiffy, those villains, and we after them, down through the woods. I judge we never touched them. They fired a shot apiece as they started, but their bullets whizzed by and didn't do us any harm. As soon as we lost the sound of their feet we quit chasing, and went down and stirred up the constables. They got a posse together, and went off to guard the river bank, and as soon as it is light the sheriff and a gang are going to beat up the woods. My boys will be with them presently. I wish we had some sort of description of those rascals—'twould help a good deal. But you couldn't see what they were like, in the dark, lad, I suppose?"

"Oh yes; I saw them down-town and follered them."

"Splendid! Describe them—describe them, my boy!"

"One's the old deaf and dumb Spaniard that's ben around here once or twice, and t'other's a mean-looking, ragged—"

"That's enough, lad, we know the men! Happened on them in the woods back of the widow's one day, and they slunk away. Off with you, boys, and tell the sheriff—get your breakfast to-morrow morning!"

The Welshman's sons departed at once. As they were leaving the room Huck sprang up and exclaimed:

"Oh, please don't tell ANYbody it was me that blowed on them! Oh, please!"

"All right if you say it, Huck, but you ought to have the credit of what you did."

"Oh no, no! Please don't tell!"

When the young men were gone, the old Welshman said:

"They won't tell—and I won't. But why don't you want it known?"

Huck would not explain, further than to say that he already knew too much about one of those men and would not have the man know that he knew anything against him for the whole world—he would be killed for knowing it, sure.

The old man promised secrecy once more, and said:

"How did you come to follow these fellows, lad? Were they looking suspicious?"

Huck was silent while he framed a duly cautious reply. Then he said:

"Well, you see, I'm a kind of a hard lot,—least everybody says so, and I don't see nothing agin it—and sometimes I can't sleep much, on account of thinking about it and sort of trying to strike out a new way of doing. That was the way of it last night. I couldn't sleep, and so I come along up-street 'bout midnight, a-turning it all over, and when I got to that old shackly brick store by the Temperance Tavern, I backed up agin the wall to have another think. Well, just then along comes these two chaps slipping along close by me, with something under their arm, and I reckoned they'd stole it. One was a-smoking, and t'other one wanted a light; so they stopped right before me and the cigars lit up their faces and I see that the big one was the deaf and dumb Spaniard, by his white whiskers and the patch on his eye, and t'other one was a rusty, ragged-looking devil."

"Could you see the rags by the light of the cigars?"

This staggered Huck for a moment. Then he said:

"Well, I don't know—but somehow it seems as if I did."

"Then they went on, and you—"

"Follered 'em—yes. That was it. I wanted to see what was up—they sneaked along so. I dogged 'em to the widder's stile, and stood in the dark and heard the ragged one beg for the widder, and the Spaniard swear he'd spile her looks just as I told you and your two—"

"What! The DEAF AND DUMB man said all that!"

Huck had made another terrible mistake! He was trying his best to keep the old man from getting the faintest hint of who the Spaniard might be, and yet his tongue seemed determined to get him into trouble in spite of all he could do. He made several efforts to creep out of his scrape, but the old man's eye was upon him and he made blunder after blunder. Presently the Welshman said:

"My boy, don't be afraid of me. I wouldn't hurt a hair of your head for all the world. No—I'd protect you—I'd protect you. This Spaniard is not deaf and dumb; you've let that slip without intending it; you can't cover that up now. You know something about that Spaniard that you want to keep dark. Now trust me—tell me what it is, and trust me —I won't betray you."

Huck looked into the old man's honest eyes a moment, then bent over and whispered in his ear:

"'Tain't a Spaniard—it's Injun Joe!"

The Welshman almost jumped out of his chair. In a moment he said:

"It's all plain enough, now. When you talked about notching ears and slitting noses I judged that that was your own embellishment, because white men don't take that sort of revenge. But an Injun! That's a different matter altogether."

During breakfast the talk went on, and in the course of it the old man said that the last thing which he and his sons had done, before going to bed, was to get a lantern and examine the stile and its vicinity for marks of blood. They found none, but captured a bulky bundle of—

"Of WHAT?"

If the words had been lightning they could not have leaped with a more stunning suddenness from Huck's blanched lips. His eyes were staring wide, now, and his breath suspended—waiting for the answer. The Welshman started—stared in return—three seconds—five seconds—ten —then replied:

"Of burglar's tools. Why, what's the MATTER with you?"

Huck sank back, panting gently, but deeply, unutterably grateful. The Welshman eyed him gravely, curiously—and presently said:

"Yes, burglar's tools. That appears to relieve you a good deal. But what did give you that turn? What were YOU expecting we'd found?"

Huck was in a close place—the inquiring eye was upon him—he would have given anything for material for a plausible answer—nothing suggested itself—the inquiring eye was boring deeper and deeper—a senseless reply offered—there was no time to weigh it, so at a venture he uttered it—feebly:

"Sunday-school books, maybe."

Poor Huck was too distressed to smile, but the old man laughed loud and joyously, shook up the details of his anatomy from head to foot, and ended by saying that such a laugh was money in a-man's pocket, because it cut down the doctor's bill like everything. Then he added:

"Poor old chap, you're white and jaded—you ain't well a bit—no wonder you're a little flighty and off your balance. But you'll come out of it. Rest and sleep will fetch you out all right, I hope."

Huck was irritated to think he had been such a goose and betrayed such a suspicious excitement, for he had dropped the idea that the parcel brought from the tavern was the treasure, as soon as he had heard the talk at the widow's stile. He had only thought it was not the treasure, however—he had not

known that it wasn't—and so the suggestion of a captured bundle was too much for his self-possession. But on the whole he felt glad the little episode had happened, for now he knew beyond all question that that bundle was not THE bundle, and so his mind was at rest and exceedingly comfortable. In fact, everything seemed to be drifting just in the right direction, now; the treasure must be still in No. 2, the men would be captured and jailed that day, and he and Tom could seize the gold that night without any trouble or any fear of interruption.

Just as breakfast was completed there was a knock at the door. Huck jumped for a hiding-place, for he had no mind to be connected even remotely with the late event. The Welshman admitted several ladies and gentlemen, among them the Widow Douglas, and noticed that groups of citizens were climbing up the hill—to stare at the stile. So the news had spread. The Welshman had to tell the story of the night to the visitors. The widow's gratitude for her preservation was outspoken.

"Don't say a word about it, madam. There's another that you're more beholden to than you are to me and my boys, maybe, but he don't allow me to tell his name. We wouldn't have been there but for him."

Of course this excited a curiosity so vast that it almost belittled the main matter—but the Welshman allowed it to eat into the vitals of his visitors, and through them be transmitted to the whole town, for he refused to part with his secret. When all else had been learned, the widow said:

"I went to sleep reading in bed and slept straight through all that noise. Why didn't you come and wake me?"

"We judged it warn't worth while. Those fellows warn't likely to come again—they hadn't any tools left to work with, and what was the use of waking you up and scaring you to death? My three negro men stood guard at your house all the rest of the night. They've just come back."

More visitors came, and the story had to be told and retold for a couple of hours more.

There was no Sabbath-school during day-school vacation, but everybody was early at church. The stirring event was well canvassed. News came that not a sign of the two villains had been yet discovered. When the sermon was finished, Judge Thatcher's wife dropped alongside of Mrs. Harper as she moved down the aisle with the crowd and said:

"Is my Becky going to sleep all day? I just expected she would be tired to death."

"Your Becky?"

"Yes," with a startled look—"didn't she stay with you last night?"

"Why, no."

Mrs. Thatcher turned pale, and sank into a pew, just as Aunt Polly, talking briskly with a friend, passed by. Aunt Polly said:

"Good-morning, Mrs. Thatcher. Good-morning, Mrs. Harper. I've got a boy that's turned up missing. I reckon my Tom stayed at your house last night—one of you. And now he's afraid to come to church. I've got to settle with him."

Mrs. Thatcher shook her head feebly and turned paler than ever.

"He didn't stay with us," said Mrs. Harper, beginning to look uneasy. A marked anxiety came into Aunt Polly's face.

"Joe Harper, have you seen my Tom this morning?"

"No'm."

"When did you see him last?"

Joe tried to remember, but was not sure he could say. The people had stopped moving out of church. Whispers passed along, and a boding uneasiness took possession of every countenance. Children were anxiously questioned, and young teachers. They all said they had not noticed whether Tom and Becky were on board the ferryboat on the homeward trip; it was dark; no one thought of inquiring if any one was missing. One young man finally blurted out his fear that they were still in the cave! Mrs. Thatcher swooned away. Aunt Polly fell to crying and wringing her hands.

The alarm swept from lip to lip, from group to group, from street to street, and within five minutes the bells were wildly clanging and the whole town was up! The Cardiff Hill episode sank into instant insignificance, the burglars were forgotten, horses were saddled, skiffs were manned, the ferryboat ordered out, and before the horror was half an hour old, two hundred men were pouring down highroad and river toward the cave.

All the long afternoon the village seemed empty and dead. Many women visited Aunt Polly and Mrs. Thatcher and tried to comfort them. They cried with them, too, and that was still better than words. All the tedious night the town waited for news; but when the morning dawned at last, all the word that came was, "Send more candles—and send food." Mrs. Thatcher was almost crazed; and Aunt Polly, also. Judge Thatcher sent messages of hope and encouragement from the cave, but they conveyed no real cheer.

The old Welshman came home toward daylight, spattered with candle-grease, smeared with clay, and almost worn out. He found Huck still in the bed that had been provided for him, and delirious with fever. The physicians were all at the cave, so the Widow Douglas came and took charge of the patient. She said she would do her best by him, because, whether he was good, bad, or indifferent, he was the Lord's, and nothing that was the Lord's was a thing to be neglected. The Welshman said Huck had good spots in him, and the widow said:

"You can depend on it. That's the Lord's mark. He don't leave it off. He never does. Puts it somewhere on every creature that comes from his hands."

Early in the forenoon parties of jaded men began to straggle into the village, but the strongest of the citizens continued searching. All the news that could be gained was that remotenesses of the cavern were being ransacked that had never been visited before; that every corner and crevice was going to be thoroughly searched; that wherever one wandered through the maze of passages, lights were to be seen flitting hither and thither in the distance, and shoutings and pistol-shots sent their hollow reverberations to the ear down the sombre aisles. In one place, far from the section usually traversed by tourists, the names "BECKY & TOM" had been found traced upon the rocky wall with candle-smoke, and near at hand a grease-soiled bit of ribbon. Mrs. Thatcher recognized the ribbon and cried over it. She said it was the last relic she should ever have of her child; and that no other memorial of her could ever be so precious, because this one parted latest from the living body before the awful death came. Some said that now and then, in the cave, a far-away speck of light would glimmer, and then a glorious shout would burst forth and a score of men go trooping down the echoing aisle—and then a sickening disappointment always followed; the children were not there; it was only a searcher's light.

Three dreadful days and nights dragged their tedious hours along, and the village sank into a hopeless stupor. No one had heart for anything. The accidental discovery, just made, that the proprietor of the Temperance Tavern kept liquor on his premises, scarcely fluttered the public pulse, tremendous as the fact was. In a lucid interval, Huck feebly led up to the subject of taverns, and finally asked—dimly dreading the worst—if anything had been discovered at the Temperance Tavern since he had been ill.

"Yes," said the widow.

Huck started up in bed, wild-eyed:

"What? What was it?"

"Liquor!—and the place has been shut up. Lie down, child—what a turn you did give me!"

"Only tell me just one thing—only just one—please! Was it Tom Sawyer that found it?"

The widow burst into tears. "Hush, hush, child, hush! I've told you before, you must NOT talk. You are very, very sick!"

Then nothing but liquor had been found; there would have been a great powwow if it had been the gold. So the treasure was gone forever—gone forever! But what could she be crying about? Curious that she should cry.

These thoughts worked their dim way through Huck's mind, and under the weariness they gave him he fell asleep. The widow said to herself:

"There—he's asleep, poor wreck. Tom Sawyer find it! Pity but somebody could find Tom Sawyer! Ah, there ain't many left, now, that's got hope enough, or strength enough, either, to go on searching."

CHAPTER XXXI

NOW to return to Tom and Becky's share in the picnic. They tripped along the murky aisles with the rest of the company, visiting the familiar wonders of the cave—wonders dubbed with rather over-descriptive names, such as "The Drawing-Room," "The Cathedral," "Aladdin's Palace," and so on. Presently the hide-and-seek frolicking began, and Tom and Becky engaged in it with zeal until the exertion began to grow a trifle wearisome; then they wandered down a sinuous avenue holding their candles aloft and reading the tangled web-work of names, dates, post-office addresses, and mottoes with which the rocky walls had been frescoed (in candle-smoke). Still drifting along and talking, they scarcely noticed that they were now in a part of the cave whose walls were not frescoed. They smoked their own names under an overhanging shelf and moved on. Presently they came to a place where a little stream of water, trickling over a ledge and carrying a limestone sediment with it, had, in the slow-dragging ages, formed a laced and ruffled Niagara in gleaming and imperishable stone. Tom squeezed his small body behind it in order to illuminate it for Becky's gratification. He found that it curtained a sort of steep natural stairway which was enclosed between narrow walls, and at once the ambition to be a discoverer seized him. Becky responded to his call, and they made a smoke-mark for future guidance, and started upon their quest. They wound this way and that, far down into the secret depths of the cave, made another mark, and branched off in search of novelties to tell the upper world about. In one place they found a spacious cavern, from whose ceiling depended a multitude of shining stalactites of the length and circumference of a man's leg; they walked all about it, wondering and admiring, and presently left it by one of the numerous passages that opened into it. This shortly brought them to a bewitching spring, whose basin was incrusted with a frostwork of glittering crystals; it was in the midst of a cavern whose walls were supported by many fantastic pillars which had been formed by the joining of great stalactites and stalagmites together, the result of the ceaseless water-drip of centuries. Under the roof vast knots of bats had packed themselves together, thousands in a bunch; the lights disturbed the creatures and they came flocking down by hundreds, squeaking and darting furiously at the candles. Tom knew their ways and the danger of this sort of conduct. He seized Becky's hand and hurried her into the first corridor that offered; and none too soon, for a bat struck Becky's light out with its wing while she was passing out of the cavern. The bats chased the children a good distance; but the fugitives plunged into every new passage that offered, and at last got rid of the perilous things. Tom found a subterranean lake, shortly, which stretched its dim length away until its shape was lost in the shadows. He wanted to explore its borders, but concluded that it would be best to sit down and rest awhile, first. Now, for the first time, the deep stillness of the place laid a clammy hand upon the spirits of the children. Becky said:

"Why, I didn't notice, but it seems ever so long since I heard any of the others."

"Come to think, Becky, we are away down below them—and I don't know how far away north, or south, or east, or whichever it is. We couldn't hear them here."

Becky grew apprehensive.

"I wonder how long we've been down here, Tom? We better start back."

"Yes, I reckon we better. P'raps we better."

"Can you find the way, Tom? It's all a mixed-up crookedness to me."

"I reckon I could find it—but then the bats. If they put our candles out it will be an awful fix. Let's try some other way, so as not to go through there."

"Well. But I hope we won't get lost. It would be so awful!" and the girl shuddered at the thought of the dreadful possibilities.

They started through a corridor, and traversed it in silence a long way, glancing at each new opening, to see if there was anything familiar about the look of it; but they were all strange. Every time Tom made an examination, Becky would watch his face for an encouraging sign, and he would say cheerily:

"Oh, it's all right. This ain't the one, but we'll come to it right away!"

But he felt less and less hopeful with each failure, and presently began to turn off into diverging avenues at sheer random, in desperate hope of finding the one that was wanted. He still said it was "all right," but there was such a leaden dread at his heart that the words had lost their ring and sounded just as if he had said, "All is lost!" Becky clung to his side in an anguish of fear, and tried hard to keep back the tears, but they would come. At last she said:

"Oh, Tom, never mind the bats, let's go back that way! We seem to get worse and worse off all the time."

"Listen!" said he.

Profound silence; silence so deep that even their breathings were conspicuous in the hush. Tom shouted. The call went echoing down the empty aisles and died out in the distance in a faint sound that resembled a ripple of mocking laughter.

"Oh, don't do it again, Tom, it is too horrid," said Becky.

"It is horrid, but I better, Becky; they might hear us, you know," and he shouted again.

The "might" was even a chillier horror than the ghostly laughter, it so confessed a perishing hope. The children stood still and listened; but there was no result. Tom turned upon the back track at once, and hurried his steps. It was but a little while before a certain indecision in his manner revealed another fearful fact to Becky—he could not find his way back!

"Oh, Tom, you didn't make any marks!"

"Becky, I was such a fool! Such a fool! I never thought we might want to come back! No—I can't find the way. It's all mixed up."

"Tom, Tom, we're lost! we're lost! We never can get out of this awful place! Oh, why DID we ever leave the others!"

She sank to the ground and burst into such a frenzy of crying that Tom was appalled with the idea that she might die, or lose her reason. He sat down by her and put his arms around her; she buried her face in his bosom, she clung to him, she poured out her terrors, her unavailing regrets, and the far echoes turned them all to jeering laughter. Tom begged her to pluck up hope again, and she said she could not. He fell to blaming and abusing himself for getting her into this miserable situation; this had a better effect. She said she would try to hope again, she would get up and follow wherever he might lead if only he would not talk like that any more. For he was no more to blame than she, she said.

So they moved on again—aimlessly—simply at random—all they could do was to move, keep moving. For a little while, hope made a show of reviving—not with any reason to back it, but only because it is its nature to revive when the spring has not been taken out of it by age and familiarity with failure.

By-and-by Tom took Becky's candle and blew it out. This economy meant so much! Words were not needed. Becky understood, and her hope died again. She knew that Tom had a whole candle and three or four pieces in his pockets—yet he must economize.

By-and-by, fatigue began to assert its claims; the children tried to pay attention, for it was dreadful to think of sitting down when time was grown to be so precious, moving, in some direction, in any direction, was at least progress and might bear fruit; but to sit down was to invite death and shorten its pursuit.

At last Becky's frail limbs refused to carry her farther. She sat down. Tom rested with her, and they talked of home, and the friends there, and the comfortable beds and, above all, the light! Becky cried, and Tom tried to think of some way of comforting her, but all his encouragements were grown threadbare with use, and sounded like sarcasms. Fatigue bore so heavily upon Becky that she drowsed off to sleep. Tom was grateful. He sat looking into her drawn face and saw it grow smooth and natural under the influence of pleasant dreams; and by-and-by a smile dawned and rested there. The peaceful face reflected somewhat of peace and healing into his own spirit, and his thoughts wandered away to bygone times and dreamy memories. While he was deep in his musings, Becky woke up with a breezy little laugh—but it was stricken dead upon her lips, and a groan followed it.

"Oh, how COULD I sleep! I wish I never, never had waked! No! No, I don't, Tom! Don't look so! I won't say it again."

"I'm glad you've slept, Becky; you'll feel rested, now, and we'll find the way out."

"We can try, Tom; but I've seen such a beautiful country in my dream. I reckon we are going there."

"Maybe not, maybe not. Cheer up, Becky, and let's go on trying."

They rose up and wandered along, hand in hand and hopeless. They tried to estimate how long they had been in the cave, but all they knew was that it seemed days and weeks, and yet it was plain that this could not be, for their candles were not gone yet. A long time after this—they could not tell how long—Tom said they must go softly and listen for dripping water—they must find a spring. They found one presently, and Tom said it was time to rest again. Both were cruelly tired, yet Becky said she thought she could go a little farther. She was surprised to hear Tom dissent. She could not understand it. They sat down, and Tom fastened his candle to the wall in front of them with some clay. Thought was soon busy; nothing was said for some time. Then Becky broke the silence:

"Tom, I am so hungry!"

Tom took something out of his pocket.

"Do you remember this?" said he.

Becky almost smiled.

"It's our wedding-cake, Tom."

"Yes—I wish it was as big as a barrel, for it's all we've got."

"I saved it from the picnic for us to dream on, Tom, the way grown-up people do with wedding-cake—but it'll be our—"

She dropped the sentence where it was. Tom divided the cake and Becky ate with good appetite, while Tom nibbled at his moiety. There was abundance of cold water to finish the feast with. By-and-by Becky suggested that they move on again.

Tom was silent a moment. Then he said:

"Becky, can you bear it if I tell you something?"

Becky's face paled, but she thought she could.

"Well, then, Becky, we must stay here, where there's water to drink. That little piece is our last candle!"

Becky gave loose to tears and wailings. Tom did what he could to comfort her, but with little effect. At length Becky said:

"Tom!"

"Well, Becky?"

"They'll miss us and hunt for us!"

"Yes, they will! Certainly they will!"

"Maybe they're hunting for us now, Tom."

"Why, I reckon maybe they are. I hope they are."

"When would they miss us, Tom?"

"When they get back to the boat, I reckon."

"Tom, it might be dark then—would they notice we hadn't come?"

"I don't know. But anyway, your mother would miss you as soon as they got home."

A frightened look in Becky's face brought Tom to his senses and he saw that he had made a blunder. Becky was not to have gone home that night! The children became silent and thoughtful. In a moment a new burst of grief from Becky showed Tom that the thing in his mind had struck hers also—that the Sabbath morning might be half spent before Mrs. Thatcher discovered that Becky was not at Mrs. Harper's.

The children fastened their eyes upon their bit of candle and watched it melt slowly and pitilessly away; saw the half inch of wick stand alone at last; saw the feeble flame rise and fall, climb the thin column of smoke, linger at its top a moment, and then—the horror of utter darkness reigned!

How long afterward it was that Becky came to a slow consciousness that she was crying in Tom's arms, neither could tell. All that they knew was, that after what seemed a mighty stretch of time, both awoke out of a dead stupor of sleep and resumed their miseries once more. Tom said it might be Sunday, now—maybe Monday. He tried to get Becky to talk, but her sorrows were too oppressive, all her hopes were gone. Tom said that they must have been missed long ago, and no doubt the search was going on. He would shout and maybe some one would come. He tried it; but in the darkness the distant echoes sounded so hideously that he tried it no more.

The hours wasted away, and hunger came to torment the captives again. A portion of Tom's half of the cake was left; they divided and ate it. But they seemed hungrier than before. The poor morsel of food only whetted desire.

By-and-by Tom said:

"SH! Did you hear that?"

Both held their breath and listened. There was a sound like the faintest, far-off shout. Instantly Tom answered it, and leading Becky by the hand, started groping down the corridor in its direction. Presently he listened again; again the sound was heard, and apparently a little nearer.

"It's them!" said Tom; "they're coming! Come along, Becky—we're all right now!"

The joy of the prisoners was almost overwhelming. Their speed was slow, however, because pitfalls were somewhat common, and had to be guarded against. They shortly came to one and had to stop. It might be three feet deep, it might be a hundred—there was no passing it at any rate. Tom got down on his breast and reached as far down as he could. No bottom. They must stay there and wait until the searchers came. They listened; evidently the distant shoutings were growing more distant! a moment or two more and they had gone altogether. The heart-sinking misery of it! Tom whooped until he was hoarse, but it was of no use. He talked hopefully to Becky; but an age of anxious waiting passed and no sounds came again.

The children groped their way back to the spring. The weary time dragged on; they slept again, and awoke famished and woe-stricken. Tom believed it must be Tuesday by this time.

Now an idea struck him. There were some side passages near at hand. It would be better to explore some of these than bear the weight of the heavy time in idleness. He took a kite-line from his pocket, tied it to a projection, and he and Becky started, Tom in the lead, unwinding the line as he groped along. At the end of twenty steps the corridor ended in a "jumping-off place." Tom got down on his knees and felt below, and then as far around the corner as he could reach with his hands conveniently; he made an effort to stretch yet a little farther to the right, and at that moment, not twenty yards away, a human hand, holding a candle, appeared from behind a rock! Tom lifted up a glorious shout, and instantly that hand was followed by the body it belonged to—Injun Joe's! Tom was paralyzed; he could not move. He was vastly gratified the next moment, to see the "Spaniard" take to his heels and get himself out of sight. Tom wondered that Joe had not recognized his voice and come over and killed him for testifying in court. But the echoes must have disguised the voice. Without doubt, that was it, he reasoned. Tom's fright weakened every muscle in his body. He said to himself that if he had strength enough to get back to the spring he would stay there, and nothing should tempt him to run the risk of meeting Injun Joe again. He was careful to keep from Becky what it was he had seen. He told her he had only shouted "for luck."

But hunger and wretchedness rise superior to fears in the long run. Another tedious wait at the spring and another long sleep brought changes. The children awoke tortured with a raging hunger. Tom believed that it must be Wednesday or Thursday or even Friday or Saturday, now, and that the search had been given over. He proposed to explore another passage. He felt willing to risk Injun Joe and all other terrors. But Becky was very weak. She had sunk into a dreary apathy and would not be roused. She said she would wait, now, where she was, and die—it would not be long. She told Tom to go with the kite-line and explore if he chose; but she implored him to come back every little while and speak to her; and she made him promise that when the awful time came, he would stay by her and hold her hand until all was over.

Tom kissed her, with a choking sensation in his throat, and made a show of being confident of finding the searchers or an escape from the cave; then he took the kite-line in his hand and went groping down one of the passages on his hands and knees, distressed with hunger and sick with bodings of coming doom.

CHAPTER XXXII

TUESDAY afternoon came, and waned to the twilight. The village of St. Petersburg still mourned. The lost children had not been found. Public prayers had been offered up for them, and many and many a private prayer that had the petitioner's whole heart in it; but still no good news came from the cave. The majority of the searchers had given up the quest and gone back to their daily avocations, saying that it was plain the children could never be found. Mrs. Thatcher was very ill, and a great part of the time delirious. People said it was heartbreaking to hear her call her child, and raise her head and listen a whole minute at a time, then lay it wearily down again with a moan. Aunt Polly had drooped into a settled melancholy, and her gray hair had grown almost white. The village went to its rest on Tuesday night, sad and forlorn.

Away in the middle of the night a wild peal burst from the village bells, and in a moment the streets were swarming with frantic half-clad people, who shouted, "Turn out! turn out! they're found! they're found!" Tin pans and horns were added to the din, the population massed itself and moved toward the river, met the children coming in an open carriage drawn by shouting citizens, thronged around it, joined its homeward march, and swept magnificently up the main street roaring huzzah after huzzah!

The village was illuminated; nobody went to bed again; it was the greatest night the little town had ever seen. During the first half-hour a procession of villagers filed through Judge Thatcher's house, seized the saved ones and kissed them, squeezed Mrs. Thatcher's hand, tried to speak but couldn't—and drifted out raining tears all over the place.

Aunt Polly's happiness was complete, and Mrs. Thatcher's nearly so. It would be complete, however, as soon as the messenger dispatched with the great news to the cave should get the word to her husband. Tom lay upon a sofa with an eager auditory about him and told the history of the wonderful adventure, putting in many striking additions to adorn it withal; and closed with a description of how he left Becky and went on an exploring expedition; how he followed two avenues as far as his kite-line would reach; how he followed a third to the fullest stretch of the kite-line, and was about to turn back when he glimpsed a far-off speck that looked like daylight; dropped the line and groped toward it, pushed his head and shoulders through a small hole, and saw the broad Mississippi rolling by! And if it had only happened to be night he would not have seen that speck of daylight and would not have explored that passage any more! He told how he went back for Becky and broke the good news and she told him not to fret her with such stuff, for she was tired, and knew she was going to die, and wanted to. He described how he labored with her and convinced her; and how she almost died for joy when she had groped to where she actually saw the blue speck of daylight; how he pushed his way out at the hole and then helped her out; how they sat there and cried for gladness; how some men came along in a skiff and Tom hailed them and told them their situation and their famished condition; how the men didn't believe the wild tale at first, "because," said they, "you are five miles down the river below the valley the cave is in" —then took them aboard, rowed to a house, gave them supper, made them rest till two or three hours after dark and then brought them home.

Before day-dawn, Judge Thatcher and the handful of searchers with him were tracked out, in the cave, by the twine clews they had strung behind them, and informed of the great news.

Three days and nights of toil and hunger in the cave were not to be shaken off at once, as Tom and Becky soon discovered. They were bedridden all of Wednesday and Thursday, and seemed to grow more and more tired and worn, all the time. Tom got about, a little, on Thursday, was down-town Friday, and nearly as whole as ever Saturday; but Becky did not leave her room until Sunday, and then she looked as if she had passed through a wasting illness.

Tom learned of Huck's sickness and went to see him on Friday, but could not be admitted to the bedroom; neither could he on Saturday or Sunday. He was admitted daily after that, but was warned to keep still about his adventure and introduce no exciting topic. The Widow Douglas stayed by to see that he obeyed. At home Tom learned of the Cardiff Hill event; also that the "ragged man's" body had eventually been found in the river near the ferry-landing; he had been drowned while trying to escape, perhaps.

About a fortnight after Tom's rescue from the cave, he started off to visit Huck, who had grown plenty strong enough, now, to hear exciting talk, and Tom had some that would interest him, he thought. Judge Thatcher's house was on Tom's way, and he stopped to see Becky. The Judge and some friends set Tom to talking, and some one asked him ironically if he wouldn't like to go to the cave again. Tom said he thought he wouldn't mind it. The Judge said:

"Well, there are others just like you, Tom, I've not the least doubt. But we have taken care of that. Nobody will get lost in that cave any more."

"Why?"

"Because I had its big door sheathed with boiler iron two weeks ago, and triple-locked—and I've got the keys."

Tom turned as white as a sheet.

"What's the matter, boy! Here, run, somebody! Fetch a glass of water!"

The water was brought and thrown into Tom's face.

"Ah, now you're all right. What was the matter with you, Tom?"

"Oh, Judge, Injun Joe's in the cave!"

CHAPTER XXXIII

WITHIN a few minutes the news had spread, and a dozen skiff-loads of men were on their way to McDougal's cave, and the ferryboat, well filled with passengers, soon followed. Tom Sawyer was in the skiff that bore Judge Thatcher.

When the cave door was unlocked, a sorrowful sight presented itself in the dim twilight of the place. Injun Joe lay stretched upon the ground, dead, with his face close to the crack of the door, as if his longing eyes had been fixed, to the latest moment, upon the light and the cheer of the free world outside. Tom was touched, for he knew by his own experience how this wretch had suffered. His pity was moved, but nevertheless he felt an abounding sense of relief and security, now, which revealed to him in a degree which he had not fully appreciated before how vast a weight of dread had been lying upon him since the day he lifted his voice against this bloody-minded outcast.

Injun Joe's bowie-knife lay close by, its blade broken in two. The great foundation-beam of the door had been chipped and hacked through, with tedious labor; useless labor, too, it was, for the native rock formed a sill outside it, and upon that stubborn material the knife had wrought no effect; the only damage done was to the knife itself. But if there had been no stony obstruction there the labor would have been useless still, for if the beam had been wholly cut away Injun Joe could not have squeezed his body under the door, and he knew it. So he had only hacked that place in order to be doing something—in order to pass the weary time—in order to employ his tortured faculties. Ordinarily one could find half a dozen bits of candle stuck around in the crevices of this vestibule, left there by tourists; but there were none now. The prisoner had searched them out and eaten them. He had also contrived to catch a few bats, and these, also, he had eaten, leaving only their claws. The poor unfortunate had starved to death. In one place, near at hand, a stalagmite had been slowly growing up from the ground for ages, builded by the water-drip from a stalactite overhead. The captive had broken off the stalagmite, and upon the stump had placed a stone, wherein he had scooped a shallow hollow to catch the precious drop that fell once in every three minutes with the dreary regularity of a clock-tick— a dessertspoonful once in four and twenty hours. That drop was falling when the Pyramids were new; when Troy fell; when the foundations of Rome were laid when Christ was crucified; when the Conqueror created the British empire; when Columbus sailed; when the massacre at Lexington was "news." It is falling now; it will still be falling when all these things shall have sunk down the afternoon of history, and the twilight of tradition, and been swallowed up in the thick night of oblivion. Has everything a purpose and a mission? Did this drop fall patiently during five thousand years to be ready for this flitting human insect's need? and has it another important object to accomplish ten thousand years to come? No matter. It is many and many a year since the hapless half-breed scooped out the stone to catch the priceless drops, but to this day the tourist stares longest at that pathetic stone and that slow-dropping water when he comes to see the wonders of McDougal's cave. Injun Joe's cup stands first in the list of the cavern's marvels; even "Aladdin's Palace" cannot rival it.

Injun Joe was buried near the mouth of the cave; and people flocked there in boats and wagons from the towns and from all the farms and hamlets for seven miles around; they brought their children, and all sorts of provisions, and confessed that they had had almost as satisfactory a time at the funeral as they could have had at the hanging.

This funeral stopped the further growth of one thing—the petition to the governor for Injun Joe's pardon. The petition had been largely signed; many tearful and eloquent meetings had been held, and a committee of sappy women been appointed to go in deep mourning and wail around the governor, and implore him to be a merciful ass and trample his duty under foot. Injun Joe was believed to have killed five citizens of the village, but what of that? If he had been Satan himself there would have been plenty of weaklings ready to scribble their names to a pardon-petition, and drip a tear on it from their permanently impaired and leaky water-works.

The morning after the funeral Tom took Huck to a private place to have an important talk. Huck had learned all about Tom's adventure from the Welshman and the Widow Douglas, by this time, but Tom said he reckoned there was one thing they had not told him; that thing was what he wanted to talk about now. Huck's face saddened. He said:

"I know what it is. You got into No. 2 and never found anything but whiskey. Nobody told me it was you; but I just knowed it must 'a' ben you, soon as I heard 'bout that whiskey business; and I knowed you hadn't got the money becuz you'd 'a' got at me some way or other and told me even if you was mum to everybody else. Tom, something's always told me we'd never get holt of that swag."

"Why, Huck, I never told on that tavern-keeper. YOU know his tavern was all right the Saturday I went to the picnic. Don't you remember you was to watch there that night?"

"Oh yes! Why, it seems 'bout a year ago. It was that very night that I follered Injun Joe to the widder's."

"YOU followed him?"

"Yes—but you keep mum. I reckon Injun Joe's left friends behind him, and I don't want 'em souring on me and doing me mean tricks. If it hadn't ben for me he'd be down in Texas now, all right."

Then Huck told his entire adventure in confidence to Tom, who had only heard of the Welshman's part of it before.

"Well," said Huck, presently, coming back to the main question, "whoever nipped the whiskey in No. 2, nipped the money, too, I reckon —anyways it's a goner for us, Tom."

"Huck, that money wasn't ever in No. 2!"

"What!" Huck searched his comrade's face keenly. "Tom, have you got on the track of that money again?"

"Huck, it's in the cave!"

Huck's eyes blazed.

"Say it again, Tom."

"The money's in the cave!"

"Tom—honest injun, now—is it fun, or earnest?"

"Earnest, Huck—just as earnest as ever I was in my life. Will you go in there with me and help get it out?"

"I bet I will! I will if it's where we can blaze our way to it and not get lost."

"Huck, we can do that without the least little bit of trouble in the world."

"Good as wheat! What makes you think the money's—"

"Huck, you just wait till we get in there. If we don't find it I'll agree to give you my drum and every thing I've got in the world. I will, by jings."

"All right—it's a whiz. When do you say?"

"Right now, if you say it. Are you strong enough?"

"Is it far in the cave? I ben on my pins a little, three or four days, now, but I can't walk more'n a mile, Tom—least I don't think I could."

"It's about five mile into there the way anybody but me would go, Huck, but there's a mighty short cut that they don't anybody but me know about. Huck, I'll take you right to it in a skiff. I'll float the skiff down there, and I'll pull it back again all by myself. You needn't ever turn your hand over."

"Less start right off, Tom."

"All right. We want some bread and meat, and our pipes, and a little bag or two, and two or three kite-strings, and some of these new-fangled things they call lucifer matches. I tell you, many's the time I wished I had some when I was in there before."

A trifle after noon the boys borrowed a small skiff from a citizen who was absent, and got under way at once. When they were several miles below "Cave Hollow," Tom said:

"Now you see this bluff here looks all alike all the way down from the cave hollow—no houses, no wood-yards, bushes all alike. But do you see that white place up yonder where there's been a landslide? Well, that's one of my marks. We'll get ashore, now."

They landed.

"Now, Huck, where we're a-standing you could touch that hole I got out of with a fishing-pole. See if you can find it."

Huck searched all the place about, and found nothing. Tom proudly marched into a thick clump of sumach bushes and said:

"Here you are! Look at it, Huck; it's the snuggest hole in this country. You just keep mum about it. All along I've been wanting to be a robber, but I knew I'd got to have a thing like this, and where to run across it was the bother. We've got it now, and we'll keep it quiet, only we'll let Joe Harper and Ben Rogers in—because of course there's got to be a Gang, or else there wouldn't be any style about it. Tom Sawyer's Gang—it sounds splendid, don't it, Huck?"

"Well, it just does, Tom. And who'll we rob?"

"Oh, most anybody. Waylay people—that's mostly the way."

"And kill them?"

"No, not always. Hive them in the cave till they raise a ransom."

"What's a ransom?"

"Money. You make them raise all they can, off'n their friends; and after you've kept them a year, if it ain't raised then you kill them. That's the general way. Only you don't kill the women. You shut up the women, but you don't kill them. They're always beautiful and rich, and awfully scared. You take their watches and things, but you always take your hat off and talk polite. They ain't anybody as polite as robbers —you'll see that in any book. Well, the women get to loving you, and after they've been in the cave a week or two weeks they stop crying and after that you couldn't get them to leave. If you drove them out they'd turn right around and come back. It's so in all the books."

"Why, it's real bully, Tom. I believe it's better'n to be a pirate."

"Yes, it's better in some ways, because it's close to home and circuses and all that."

By this time everything was ready and the boys entered the hole, Tom in the lead. They toiled their way to the farther end of the tunnel, then made their spliced kite-strings fast and moved on. A few steps brought them to the spring, and Tom felt a shudder quiver all through him. He showed Huck the fragment of candle-wick perched on a lump of clay against the wall, and described how he and Becky had watched the flame struggle and expire.

The boys began to quiet down to whispers, now, for the stillness and gloom of the place oppressed their spirits. They went on, and presently entered and followed Tom's other corridor until they reached the "jumping-off place." The candles revealed the fact that it was not really a precipice, but only a steep clay hill twenty or thirty feet high. Tom whispered:

"Now I'll show you something, Huck."

He held his candle aloft and said:

"Look as far around the corner as you can. Do you see that? There—on the big rock over yonder—done with candle-smoke."

"Tom, it's a CROSS!"

"NOW where's your Number Two? 'UNDER THE CROSS,' hey? Right yonder's where I saw Injun Joe poke up his candle, Huck!"

Huck stared at the mystic sign awhile, and then said with a shaky voice:

"Tom, less git out of here!"

"What! and leave the treasure?"

"Yes—leave it. Injun Joe's ghost is round about there, certain."

"No it ain't, Huck, no it ain't. It would ha'nt the place where he died—away out at the mouth of the cave—five mile from here."

"No, Tom, it wouldn't. It would hang round the money. I know the ways of ghosts, and so do you."

Tom began to fear that Huck was right. Misgivings gathered in his mind. But presently an idea occurred to him—

"Lookyhere, Huck, what fools we're making of ourselves! Injun Joe's ghost ain't a going to come around where there's a cross!"

The point was well taken. It had its effect.

"Tom, I didn't think of that. But that's so. It's luck for us, that

cross is. I reckon we'll climb down there and have a hunt for that box."

Tom went first, cutting rude steps in the clay hill as he descended. Huck followed. Four avenues opened out of the small cavern which the great rock stood in. The boys examined three of them with no result. They found a small recess in the one nearest the base of the rock, with a pallet of blankets spread down in it; also an old suspender, some bacon rind, and the well-gnawed bones of two or three fowls. But there was no money-box. The lads searched and researched this place, but in vain. Tom said:

"He said UNDER the cross. Well, this comes nearest to being under the cross. It can't be under the rock itself, because that sets solid on the ground."

They searched everywhere once more, and then sat down discouraged. Huck could suggest nothing. By-and-by Tom said:

"Lookyhere, Huck, there's footprints and some candle-grease on the clay about one side of this rock, but not on the other sides. Now, what's that for? I bet you the money IS under the rock. I'm going to dig in the clay."

"That ain't no bad notion, Tom!" said Huck with animation.

Tom's "real Barlow" was out at once, and he had not dug four inches before he struck wood.

"Hey, Huck!—you hear that?"

Huck began to dig and scratch now. Some boards were soon uncovered and removed. They had concealed a natural chasm which led under the rock. Tom got into this and held his candle as far under the rock as he could, but said he could not see to the end of the rift. He proposed to explore. He stooped and passed under; the narrow way descended gradually. He followed its winding course, first to the right, then to the left, Huck at his heels. Tom turned a short curve, by-and-by, and exclaimed:

"My goodness, Huck, lookyhere!"

It was the treasure-box, sure enough, occupying a snug little cavern, along with an empty powder-keg, a couple of guns in leather cases, two or three pairs of old moccasins, a leather belt, and some other rubbish well soaked with the water-drip.

"Got it at last!" said Huck, ploughing among the tarnished coins with his hand. "My, but we're rich, Tom!"

"Huck, I always reckoned we'd get it. It's just too good to believe, but we HAVE got it, sure! Say—let's not fool around here. Let's snake it out. Lemme see if I can lift the box."

It weighed about fifty pounds. Tom could lift it, after an awkward fashion, but could not carry it conveniently.

"I thought so," he said; "THEY carried it like it was heavy, that day at the ha'nted house. I noticed that. I reckon I was right to think of fetching the little bags along."

The money was soon in the bags and the boys took it up to the cross rock.

"Now less fetch the guns and things," said Huck.

"No, Huck—leave them there. They're just the tricks to have when we go to robbing. We'll keep them there all the time, and we'll hold our orgies there, too. It's an awful snug place for orgies."

"What orgies?"

"I dono. But robbers always have orgies, and of course we've got to have them, too. Come along, Huck, we've been in here a long time. It's getting late, I reckon. I'm hungry, too. We'll eat and smoke when we get to the skiff."

They presently emerged into the clump of sumach bushes, looked warily out, found the coast clear, and were soon lunching and smoking in the skiff. As the sun dipped toward the horizon they pushed out and got under way. Tom skimmed up the shore through the long twilight, chatting cheerily with Huck, and landed shortly after dark.

"Now, Huck," said Tom, "we'll hide the money in the loft of the widow's woodshed, and I'll come up in the morning and we'll count it and divide, and then we'll hunt up a place out in the woods for it where it will be safe. Just you lay quiet here and watch the stuff till I run and hook Benny Taylor's little wagon; I won't be gone a minute."

He disappeared, and presently returned with the wagon, put the two small sacks into it, threw some old rags on top of them, and started off, dragging his cargo behind him. When the boys reached the Welshman's house, they stopped to rest. Just as they were about to move on, the Welshman stepped out and said:

"Hallo, who's that?"

"Huck and Tom Sawyer."

"Good! Come along with me, boys, you are keeping everybody waiting. Here—hurry up, trot ahead—I'll haul the wagon for you. Why, it's not as light as it might be. Got bricks in it?—or old metal?"

"Old metal," said Tom.

"I judged so; the boys in this town will take more trouble and fool away more time hunting up six bits' worth of old iron to sell to the foundry than they would to make twice the money at regular work. But that's human nature—hurry along, hurry along!"

The boys wanted to know what the hurry was about.

"Never mind; you'll see, when we get to the Widow Douglas'."

Huck said with some apprehension—for he was long used to being falsely accused:

"Mr. Jones, we haven't been doing nothing."

The Welshman laughed.

"Well, I don't know, Huck, my boy. I don't know about that. Ain't you and the widow good friends?"

"Yes. Well, she's ben good friends to me, anyway."

"All right, then. What do you want to be afraid for?"

This question was not entirely answered in Huck's slow mind before he found himself pushed, along with Tom, into Mrs. Douglas' drawing-room. Mr. Jones left the wagon near the door and followed.

The place was grandly lighted, and everybody that was of any consequence in the village was there. The Thatchers were there, the Harpers, the Rogerses, Aunt Polly, Sid, Mary, the minister, the editor, and a great many more, and all dressed in their best. The widow received the boys as heartily as any one could well receive two such looking beings. They were covered with clay and candle-grease. Aunt Polly blushed crimson with humiliation, and frowned and shook her head at Tom. Nobody suffered half as much as the two boys did, however. Mr. Jones said:

"Tom wasn't at home, yet, so I gave him up; but I stumbled on him and Huck right at my door, and so I just brought them along in a hurry."

"And you did just right," said the widow. "Come with me, boys."

She took them to a bedchamber and said:

"Now wash and dress yourselves. Here are two new suits of clothes —shirts, socks, everything complete. They're Huck's— no, no thanks, Huck—Mr. Jones bought one and I the other. But they'll fit both of you. Get into them. We'll wait—come down when you are slicked up enough."

Then she left.

CHAPTER XXXIV

HUCK said: "Tom, we can slope, if we can find a rope. The window ain't high from the ground."

"Shucks! what do you want to slope for?"

"Well, I ain't used to that kind of a crowd. I can't stand it. I ain't going down there, Tom."

"Oh, bother! It ain't anything. I don't mind it a bit. I'll take care of you."

Sid appeared.

"Tom," said he, "auntie has been waiting for you all the afternoon. Mary got your Sunday clothes ready, and everybody's been fretting about you. Say—ain't this grease and clay, on your clothes?"

"Now, Mr. Siddy, you jist 'tend to your own business. What's all this blow-out about, anyway?"

"It's one of the widow's parties that she's always having. This time it's for the Welshman and his sons, on account of that scrape they helped her out of the other night. And say—I can tell you something, if you want to know."

"Well, what?"

"Why, old Mr. Jones is going to try to spring something on the people here to-night, but I overheard him tell auntie to-day about it, as a secret, but I reckon it's not much of a secret now. Everybody knows —the widow, too, for all she tries to let on she don't. Mr. Jones was bound Huck should be here—couldn't get along with his grand secret without Huck, you know!"

"Secret about what, Sid?"

"About Huck tracking the robbers to the widow's. I reckon Mr. Jones was going to make a grand time over his surprise, but I bet you it will drop pretty flat."

Sid chuckled in a very contented and satisfied way.

"Sid, was it you that told?"

"Oh, never mind who it was. SOMEBODY told—that's enough."

"Sid, there's only one person in this town mean enough to do that, and that's you. If you had been in Huck's place you'd 'a' sneaked down the hill and never told anybody on the robbers. You can't do any but mean things, and you can't bear to see anybody praised for doing good ones. There—no thanks, as the widow says"—and Tom cuffed Sid's ears and helped him to the door with several kicks. "Now go and tell auntie if you dare—and to-morrow you'll catch it!"

Some minutes later the widow's guests were at the supper-table, and a dozen children were propped up at little side-tables in the same room, after the fashion of that country and that day. At the proper time Mr. Jones made his little speech, in which he thanked the widow for the honor she was doing himself and his sons, but said that there was another person whose modesty—

And so forth and so on. He sprung his secret about Huck's share in the adventure in the finest dramatic manner he was master of, but the surprise it occasioned was largely counterfeit and not as clamorous and effusive as it might have been under happier circumstances. However, the widow made a pretty fair show of astonishment, and heaped so many compliments and so much gratitude upon Huck that he almost forgot the nearly intolerable discomfort of his new clothes in the entirely intolerable discomfort of being set up as a target for everybody's gaze and everybody's laudations.

The widow said she meant to give Huck a home under her roof and have him educated; and that when she could spare the money she would start him in business in a modest way. Tom's chance was come. He said:

"Huck don't need it. Huck's rich."

Nothing but a heavy strain upon the good manners of the company kept back the due and proper complimentary laugh at this pleasant joke. But the silence was a little awkward. Tom broke it:

"Huck's got money. Maybe you don't believe it, but he's got lots of it. Oh, you needn't smile—I reckon I can show you. You just wait a minute."

Tom ran out of doors. The company looked at each other with a perplexed interest—and inquiringly at Huck, who was tongue-tied.

"Sid, what ails Tom?" said Aunt Polly. "He—well, there ain't ever any making of that boy out. I never—"

Tom entered, struggling with the weight of his sacks, and Aunt Polly did not finish her sentence. Tom poured the mass of yellow coin upon the table and said:

"There—what did I tell you? Half of it's Huck's and half of it's mine!"

The spectacle took the general breath away. All gazed, nobody spoke for a moment. Then there was a unanimous call for an explanation. Tom said he could furnish it, and he did. The tale was long, but brimful of interest. There was scarcely an interruption from any one to break the charm of its flow. When he had finished, Mr. Jones said:

"I thought I had fixed up a little surprise for this occasion, but it don't amount to anything now. This one makes it sing mighty small, I'm willing to allow."

The money was counted. The sum amounted to a little over twelve thousand dollars. It was more than any one present had ever seen at one time before, though several persons were there who were worth considerably more than that in property.

CHAPTER XXXV

THE reader may rest satisfied that Tom's and Huck's windfall made a mighty stir in the poor little village of St. Petersburg. So vast a sum, all in actual cash, seemed next to incredible. It was talked about, gloated over, glorified, until the reason of many of the citizens tottered under the strain of the unhealthy excitement. Every "haunted" house in St. Petersburg and the neighboring villages was dissected, plank by plank, and its foundations dug up and ransacked for hidden treasure—and not by boys, but men—pretty grave, unromantic men, too, some of them. Wherever Tom and Huck appeared they were courted, admired, stared at. The boys were not able to remember that their remarks had possessed weight before; but now their sayings were treasured and repeated; everything they did seemed somehow to be regarded as remarkable; they had evidently lost the power of doing and saying commonplace things; moreover, their past history was raked up and discovered to bear marks of conspicuous originality. The village paper published biographical sketches of the boys.

The Widow Douglas put Huck's money out at six per cent., and Judge Thatcher did the same with Tom's at Aunt Polly's request. Each lad had an income, now, that was simply prodigious—a dollar for every week-day in the year and half of the Sundays. It was just what the minister got —no, it was what he was promised—he generally couldn't collect it. A dollar and a quarter a week would board, lodge, and school a boy in those old simple days—and clothe him and wash him, too, for that matter.

Judge Thatcher had conceived a great opinion of Tom. He said that no commonplace boy would ever have got his daughter out of the cave. When Becky told her father, in strict confidence, how Tom had taken her whipping at school, the Judge was visibly moved; and when she pleaded grace for the mighty lie which Tom had told in order to shift that whipping from her shoulders to his own, the Judge said with a fine outburst that it was a noble, a generous, a magnanimous lie—a lie that was worthy to hold up its head and march down through history breast to breast with George Washington's lauded Truth about the hatchet! Becky thought her father had never looked so tall and so superb as when he walked the floor and stamped his foot and said that. She went straight off and told Tom about it.

Judge Thatcher hoped to see Tom a great lawyer or a great soldier some day. He said he meant to look to it that Tom should be admitted to the National Military Academy and afterward trained in the best law school in the country, in order that he might be ready for either career or both.

Huck Finn's wealth and the fact that he was now under the Widow Douglas' protection introduced him into society—no, dragged him into it, hurled him into it—and his sufferings were almost more than he could bear. The widow's servants kept him clean and neat, combed and brushed, and they bedded him nightly in unsympathetic sheets that had not one little spot or stain which he could press to his heart and know for a friend. He had to eat with a knife and fork; he had to use napkin, cup, and plate; he had to learn his book, he had to go to church; he had to talk so properly that speech was become insipid in his mouth; whithersoever he turned, the bars and shackles of civilization shut him in and bound him hand and foot.

He bravely bore his miseries three weeks, and then one day turned up missing. For forty-eight hours the widow hunted for him everywhere in great distress. The public were profoundly concerned; they searched high and low, they dragged the river for his body. Early the third morning Tom Sawyer wisely went poking among some old empty hogsheads down behind the abandoned slaughter-house, and in one of them he found the refugee. Huck had slept there; he had just breakfasted upon some stolen odds and ends of food, and was lying off, now, in comfort, with his pipe. He was unkempt, uncombed, and clad in the same old ruin of rags that had made him picturesque in the days when he was free and happy. Tom routed him out, told him the trouble he had been causing, and urged him to go home. Huck's face lost its tranquil content, and took a melancholy cast. He said:

"Don't talk about it, Tom. I've tried it, and it don't work; it don't work, Tom. It ain't for me; I ain't used to it. The widder's good to me, and friendly; but I can't stand them ways. She makes me get up just at the same time every morning; she makes me wash, they comb me all to thunder; she won't let me sleep in the woodshed; I got to wear them blamed clothes that just smothers me, Tom; they don't seem to any air git through 'em, somehow; and they're so rotten nice that I can't set down, nor lay down, nor roll around anywher's; I hain't slid on a cellar-door for—well, it 'pears to be years; I got to go to church and sweat and sweat—I hate them ornery sermons! I can't ketch a fly in there, I can't chaw. I got to wear shoes all Sunday. The widder eats by a bell; she goes to bed by a bell; she gits up by a bell—everything's so awful reg'lar a body can't stand it."

"Well, everybody does that way, Huck."

"Tom, it don't make no difference. I ain't everybody, and I can't STAND it. It's awful to be tied up so. And grub comes too easy—I don't take no interest in vittles, that way. I got to ask to go a-fishing; I got to ask to go in a-swimming—dern'd if I hain't got to ask to do everything. Well, I'd got to talk so nice it wasn't no comfort—I'd got to go up in the attic and rip out awhile, every day, to git a taste in my mouth, or I'd a died, Tom. The widder wouldn't let me smoke; she wouldn't let me yell, she wouldn't let me gape, nor stretch, nor scratch, before folks—" [Then with a spasm of special irritation and injury]— "And dad fetch it, she prayed all the time! I never see such a woman! I HAD to shove, Tom—I just had to. And besides, that school's going to open, and I'd a had to go to it—well, I

wouldn't stand THAT, Tom. Looky here, Tom, being rich ain't what it's cracked up to be. It's just worry and worry, and sweat and sweat, and a-wishing you was dead all the time. Now these clothes suits me, and this bar'l suits me, and I ain't ever going to shake 'em any more. Tom, I wouldn't ever got into all this trouble if it hadn't 'a' ben for that money; now you just take my sheer of it along with your'n, and gimme a ten-center sometimes—not many times, becuz I don't give a dern for a thing 'thout it's tollable hard to git—and you go and beg off for me with the widder."

"Oh, Huck, you know I can't do that. 'Tain't fair; and besides if you'll try this thing just a while longer you'll come to like it."

"Like it! Yes—the way I'd like a hot stove if I was to set on it long enough. No, Tom, I won't be rich, and I won't live in them cussed smothery houses. I like the woods, and the river, and hogsheads, and I'll stick to 'em, too. Blame it all! just as we'd got guns, and a cave, and all just fixed to rob, here this dern foolishness has got to come up and spile it all!"

Tom saw his opportunity—

"Lookyhere, Huck, being rich ain't going to keep me back from turning robber."

"No! Oh, good-licks; are you in real dead-wood earnest, Tom?"

"Just as dead earnest as I'm sitting here. But Huck, we can't let you into the gang if you ain't respectable, you know."

Huck's joy was quenched.

"Can't let me in, Tom? Didn't you let me go for a pirate?"

"Yes, but that's different. A robber is more high-toned than what a pirate is—as a general thing. In most countries they're awful high up in the nobility—dukes and such."

"Now, Tom, hain't you always ben friendly to me? You wouldn't shet me out, would you, Tom? You wouldn't do that, now, WOULD you, Tom?"

"Huck, I wouldn't want to, and I DON'T want to—but what would people say? Why, they'd say, 'Mph! Tom Sawyer's Gang! pretty low characters in it!' They'd mean you, Huck. You wouldn't like that, and I wouldn't."

Huck was silent for some time, engaged in a mental struggle. Finally he said:

"Well, I'll go back to the widder for a month and tackle it and see if I can come to stand it, if you'll let me b'long to the gang, Tom."

"All right, Huck, it's a whiz! Come along, old chap, and I'll ask the widow to let up on you a little, Huck."

"Will you, Tom—now will you? That's good. If she'll let up on some of the roughest things, I'll smoke private and cuss private, and crowd through or bust. When you going to start the gang and turn robbers?"

"Oh, right off. We'll get the boys together and have the initiation to-night, maybe."

"Have the which?"

"Have the initiation."

"What's that?"

"It's to swear to stand by one another, and never tell the gang's secrets, even if you're chopped all to flinders, and kill anybody and all his family that hurts one of the gang."

"That's gay—that's mighty gay, Tom, I tell you."

"Well, I bet it is. And all that swearing's got to be done at midnight, in the lonesomest, awfulest place you can find—a ha'nted house is the best, but they're all ripped up now."

"Well, midnight's good, anyway, Tom."

"Yes, so it is. And you've got to swear on a coffin, and sign it with blood."

"Now, that's something LIKE! Why, it's a million times bullier than pirating. I'll stick to the widder till I rot, Tom; and if I git to be a reg'lar ripper of a robber, and everybody talking 'bout it, I reckon she'll be proud she snaked me in out of the wet."

CONCLUSION

SO endeth this chronicle. It being strictly a history of a BOY, it must stop here; the story could not go much further without becoming the history of a MAN. When one writes a novel about grown people, he knows exactly where to stop—that is, with a marriage; but when he writes of juveniles, he must stop where he best can.

Most of the characters that perform in this book still live, and are prosperous and happy. Some day it may seem worth while to take up the story of the younger ones again and see what sort of men and women they turned out to be; therefore it will be wisest not to reveal any of that part of their lives at present.

Huckleberry Finn
By Mark Twain

NOTICE

PERSONS attempting to find a motive in this narrative will be prosecuted; persons attempting to find a moral in it will be banished; persons attempting to find a plot in it will be shot.

BY ORDER OF THE AUTHOR, Per G.G., Chief of Ordnance.

EXPLANATORY

IN this book a number of dialects are used, to wit: the Missouri negro dialect; the extremest form of the backwoods Southwestern dialect; the ordinary "Pike County" dialect; and four modified varieties of this last. The shadings have not been done in a haphazard fashion, or by guesswork; but painstakingly, and with the trustworthy guidance and support of personal familiarity with these several forms of speech.

I make this explanation for the reason that without it many readers would suppose that all these characters were trying to talk alike and not succeeding.

THE AUTHOR.

HUCKLEBERRY FINN

Scene: The Mississippi Valley Time: Forty to fifty years ago

CHAPTER I.

YOU don't know about me without you have read a book by the name of The Adventures of Tom Sawyer; but that ain't no matter. That book was made by Mr. Mark Twain, and he told the truth, mainly. There was things which he stretched, but mainly he told the truth. That is nothing. I never seen anybody but lied one time or another, without it was Aunt Polly, or the widow, or maybe Mary. Aunt Polly—Tom's Aunt Polly, she is—and Mary, and the Widow Douglas is all told about in that book, which is mostly a true book, with some stretchers, as I said before.

Now the way that the book winds up is this: Tom and me found the money that the robbers hid in the cave, and it made us rich. We got six thousand dollars apiece—all gold. It was an awful sight of money when it was piled up. Well, Judge Thatcher he took it and put it out at interest, and it fetched us a dollar a day apiece all the year round —more than a body could tell what to do with. The Widow Douglas she took me for her son, and allowed she would sivilize me; but it was rough living in the house all the time, considering how dismal regular and decent the widow was in all her ways; and so when I couldn't stand it no longer I lit out. I got into my old rags and my sugar-hogshead again, and was free and satisfied. But Tom Sawyer he hunted me up and said he was going to start a band of robbers, and I might join if I would go back to the widow and be respectable. So I went back.

The widow she cried over me, and called me a poor lost lamb, and she called me a lot of other names, too, but she never meant no harm by it. She put me in them new clothes again, and I couldn't do nothing but sweat and sweat, and feel all cramped up. Well, then, the old thing commenced again. The widow rung a bell for supper, and you had to come to time. When you got to the table you couldn't go right to eating, but you had to wait for the widow to tuck down her head and grumble a little over the victuals, though there warn't really anything the matter with them,—that is, nothing only everything was cooked by itself. In a barrel of odds and ends it is different; things get mixed up, and the juice kind of swaps around, and the things go better.

After supper she got out her book and learned me about Moses and the Bulrushers, and I was in a sweat to find out all about him; but by and by she let it out that Moses had been dead a considerable long time; so then I didn't care no more about him, because I don't take no stock in dead people.

Pretty soon I wanted to smoke, and asked the widow to let me. But she wouldn't. She said it was a mean practice and wasn't clean, and I must try to not do it any more. That is just the way with some people. They get down on a thing when they don't know nothing about it. Here she was a-bothering about Moses, which was no kin to her, and no use to anybody, being gone, you see, yet finding a power of fault with me for doing a thing that had some good in it. And she took snuff, too; of course that was all right, because she done it herself.

Her sister, Miss Watson, a tolerable slim old maid, with goggles on, had just come to live with her, and took a set at me now with a spelling-book. She worked me middling hard for about an hour, and then the widow made her ease up. I couldn't stood it much longer. Then for an hour it was deadly dull, and I was fidgety. Miss Watson would say, "Don't put your feet up there, Huckleberry;" and "Don't scrunch up like that, Huckleberry—set up straight;" and pretty soon she would say, "Don't gap and stretch like that, Huckleberry—why don't you try to behave?" Then she told me all about the bad place, and I said I wished I was there. She got mad then, but I didn't mean no harm. All I wanted was to go somewheres; all I wanted was a change, I warn't particular. She said it was wicked to say what I said; said she wouldn't say it for the whole world; she was going to live so as to go to the good place. Well, I couldn't see no advantage in going where she was going, so I made up my mind I wouldn't try for it. But I never said so, because it would only make trouble, and wouldn't do no good.

Now she had got a start, and she went on and told me all about the good place. She said all a body would have to do there was to go around all day long with a harp and sing, forever and ever. So I didn't think much of it. But I never said so. I asked her if she reckoned Tom Sawyer would go there, and she said not by a considerable sight. I was glad about that, because I wanted him and me to be together.

Miss Watson she kept pecking at me, and it got tiresome and lonesome. By and by they fetched the niggers in and had prayers, and then everybody was off to bed. I went up to my room with a piece of candle, and put it on the table. Then I set down in a chair by the window and tried to think of something cheerful, but it warn't no use. I felt so lonesome I most wished I was dead. The stars were shining, and the leaves rustled in the woods ever so mournful; and I heard an owl, away off, who-whooing about somebody that was dead, and a whippowill and a dog crying about somebody that was going to die; and the wind was trying to whisper something to me, and I couldn't make out what it was, and so it made the cold shivers run over me. Then away out in the woods I heard that kind of a sound that a ghost makes when it wants to tell about something that's on its mind and can't make itself understood, and so can't rest easy in its grave, and has to go about that way every night grieving. I got so down-hearted and scared I did wish I had some company. Pretty soon a spider went crawling up my shoulder, and I flipped it off and it lit in the candle; and before I could budge it was all shriveled up. I didn't need anybody to tell me that that was an awful bad sign and would fetch me some bad luck, so I was scared and most shook the clothes off of me. I got up and turned around in my tracks three times and crossed my breast every time; and then I tied up a little lock of my hair with a thread to keep witches away. But I hadn't no confidence. You do that when you've lost a horseshoe that you've found, instead of nailing it up over the door, but I hadn't ever heard anybody say it was any way to keep off bad luck when you'd killed a spider.

I set down again, a-shaking all over, and got out my pipe for a smoke; for the house was all as still as death now, and so the widow wouldn't know. Well, after a long time I heard the clock away off in the town go boom—boom—boom—twelve licks; and all still again—stiller than ever. Pretty soon I heard a twig snap down in the dark amongst the trees —something was a stirring. I set still and listened. Directly I could just barely hear a "me-yow! me-yow!" down there. That was good! Says I, "me-yow! me-yow!" as soft as I could, and then I put out the light and scrambled out of the window on to the shed. Then I slipped down to the ground and crawled in among the trees, and, sure enough, there was Tom Sawyer waiting for me.

CHAPTER II.

WE went tiptoeing along a path amongst the trees back towards the end of the widow's garden, stooping down so as the branches wouldn't scrape our heads. When we was passing by the kitchen I fell over a root and made a noise. We scrouched down and laid still. Miss Watson's big nigger, named Jim, was setting in the kitchen door; we could see him pretty clear, because there was a light behind him. He got up and stretched his neck out about a minute, listening. Then he says:

"Who dah?"

He listened some more; then he come tiptoeing down and stood right between us; we could a touched him, nearly. Well, likely it was minutes and minutes that there warn't a sound, and we all there so close together. There was a place on my ankle that got to itching, but I dasn't scratch it; and then my ear begun to itch; and next my back, right between my shoulders. Seemed like I'd die if I couldn't scratch. Well, I've noticed that thing plenty times since. If you are with the quality, or at a funeral, or trying to go to sleep when you ain't sleepy—if you are anywheres where it won't do for you to scratch, why you will itch all over in upwards of a thousand places. Pretty soon Jim says:

"Say, who is you? Whar is you? Dog my cats ef I didn' hear sumf'n. Well, I know what I's gwyne to do: I's gwyne to set down here and listen tell I hears it agin."

So he set down on the ground betwixt me and Tom. He leaned his back up against a tree, and stretched his legs out till one of them most touched one of mine. My nose begun to itch. It itched till the tears come into my eyes. But I dasn't scratch. Then it begun to itch on the inside. Next I got to itching underneath. I didn't know how I was going to set still. This miserableness went on as much as six or seven minutes; but it seemed a sight longer than that. I was itching in eleven different places now. I reckoned I couldn't stand it more'n a minute longer, but I set my teeth hard and got ready to try. Just then Jim begun to breathe heavy; next he begun to snore—and then I was pretty soon comfortable again.

Tom he made a sign to me—kind of a little noise with his mouth—and we went creeping away on our hands and knees. When we was ten foot off Tom whispered to me, and wanted to tie Jim to the tree for fun. But I said no; he might wake and make a disturbance, and then they'd find out I warn't in. Then Tom said he hadn't got candles enough, and he would slip in the kitchen and get some more. I didn't want him to try. I said Jim might wake up and come. But Tom wanted to resk it; so we slid in there and got three candles, and Tom laid five cents on the table for pay. Then we got out, and I was in a sweat to get away; but nothing would do Tom but he must crawl to where Jim was, on his hands and knees, and play something on him. I waited, and it seemed a good while, everything was so still and lonesome.

As soon as Tom was back we cut along the path, around the garden fence, and by and by fetched up on the steep top of the hill the other side of the house. Tom said he slipped Jim's hat off of his head and hung it on a limb right over him, and Jim stirred a little, but he didn't wake. Afterwards Jim said the witches be witched him and put him in a trance, and rode him all over the State, and then set him under the trees again, and hung his hat on a limb to show who done it. And next time Jim told it he said they rode him down to New Orleans; and, after that, every time he told it he spread it more and more, till by and by he said they rode him all over the world, and tired him most to death, and his back was all over saddle-boils. Jim was monstrous proud about it, and he got so he wouldn't hardly notice the other niggers. Niggers would come miles to hear Jim tell about it, and he was more looked up to than any nigger in that country. Strange niggers would stand with their mouths open and look him all over, same as if he was a wonder. Niggers is always talking about witches in the dark by the kitchen fire; but whenever one was talking and letting on to know all about such things, Jim would happen in and say, "Hm! What you know 'bout witches?" and that nigger was corked up and had to take a back seat. Jim always kept that five-center piece round his neck with a string, and said it was a charm the devil give to him with his own hands, and told him he could cure anybody with it and fetch witches whenever he wanted to just by saying something to it; but he never told what it was he said to it. Niggers would come from all around there and give Jim anything they had, just for a sight of that five-center piece; but they wouldn't touch it, because the devil had had his hands on it. Jim was most ruined for a servant, because he got stuck up on account of having seen the devil and been rode by witches.

Well, when Tom and me got to the edge of the hilltop we looked away down into the village and could see three or four lights twinkling, where there was sick folks, maybe; and the stars over us was sparkling ever so fine; and down by the village was the river, a whole mile broad, and awful still and grand. We went down the hill and found Jo Harper and Ben Rogers, and two or three more of the boys, hid in the old tanyard. So we unhitched a skiff and pulled down the river two mile and a half, to the big scar on the hillside, and went ashore.

We went to a clump of bushes, and Tom made everybody swear to keep the secret, and then showed them a hole in the hill, right in the thickest part of the bushes. Then we lit the candles, and crawled in on our hands and knees. We went about two hundred yards, and then the cave opened up. Tom poked about amongst the passages, and pretty soon ducked under a wall where you wouldn't a noticed that there was a hole. We went along a narrow place and got into a kind of room, all damp and sweaty and cold, and there we stopped. Tom says:

"Now, we'll start this band of robbers and call it Tom Sawyer's Gang. Everybody that wants to join has got to take an oath, and write his name in blood."

Everybody was willing. So Tom got out a sheet of paper that he had wrote the oath on, and read it. It swore every boy to stick to the band, and never tell any of the secrets; and if anybody done anything to any boy in the band, whichever boy was ordered to kill that person and his family must do it, and he mustn't eat and he mustn't sleep till he had killed them and hacked a cross in their breasts, which was the sign of the band. And nobody that didn't belong to the band could use that mark, and if he did he must be sued; and if he done it again he must be killed. And if anybody that belonged to the band told the secrets, he must have his throat cut, and then have his carcass burnt up and the ashes scattered all around, and his name blotted off of the list with blood and never mentioned again by the gang, but have a curse put on it and be forgot forever.

Everybody said it was a real beautiful oath, and asked Tom if he got it out of his own head. He said, some of it, but the rest was out of pirate-books and robber-books, and every gang that was high-toned had it.

Some thought it would be good to kill the FAMILIES of boys that told the secrets. Tom said it was a good idea, so he took a pencil and wrote it in. Then Ben Rogers says:

"Here's Huck Finn, he hain't got no family; what you going to do 'bout him?"

"Well, hain't he got a father?" says Tom Sawyer.

"Yes, he's got a father, but you can't never find him these days. He used to lay drunk with the hogs in the tanyard, but he hain't been seen in these parts for a year or more."

They talked it over, and they was going to rule me out, because they said every boy must have a family or somebody to kill, or else it wouldn't be fair and square for the others. Well, nobody could think of anything to do—everybody was stumped, and set still. I was most ready to cry; but all at once I thought of a way, and so I offered them Miss Watson—they could kill her. Everybody said:

"Oh, she'll do. That's all right. Huck can come in."

Then they all stuck a pin in their fingers to get blood to sign with, and I made my mark on the paper.

"Now," says Ben Rogers, "what's the line of business of this Gang?"

"Nothing only robbery and murder," Tom said.

"But who are we going to rob?—houses, or cattle, or—"

"Stuff! stealing cattle and such things ain't robbery; it's burglary," says Tom Sawyer. "We ain't burglars. That ain't no sort of style. We are highwaymen. We stop stages and carriages on the road, with masks on, and kill the people and take their watches and money."

"Must we always kill the people?"

"Oh, certainly. It's best. Some authorities think different, but mostly it's considered best to kill them—except some that you bring to the cave here, and keep them till they're ransomed."

"Ransomed? What's that?"

"I don't know. But that's what they do. I've seen it in books; and so of course that's what we've got to do."

"But how can we do it if we don't know what it is?"

"Why, blame it all, we've GOT to do it. Don't I tell you it's in the books? Do you want to go to doing different from what's in the books, and get things all muddled up?"

"Oh, that's all very fine to SAY, Tom Sawyer, but how in the nation are these fellows going to be ransomed if we don't know how to do it to them? —that's the thing I want to get at. Now, what do you reckon it is?"

"Well, I don't know. But per'aps if we keep them till they're ransomed, it means that we keep them till they're dead."

"Now, that's something LIKE. That'll answer. Why couldn't you said that before? We'll keep them till they're ransomed to death; and a bothersome lot they'll be, too—eating up everything, and always trying to get loose."

"How you talk, Ben Rogers. How can they get loose when there's a guard over them, ready to shoot them down if they move a peg?"

"A guard! Well, that IS good. So somebody's got to set up all night and never get any sleep, just so as to watch them. I think that's foolishness. Why can't a body take a club and ransom them as soon as they get here?"

"Because it ain't in the books so—that's why. Now, Ben Rogers, do you want to do things regular, or don't you?—that's the idea. Don't you reckon that the people that made the books knows what's the correct thing to do? Do you reckon YOU can learn 'em anything? Not by a good deal. No, sir, we'll just go on and ransom them in the regular way."

"All right. I don't mind; but I say it's a fool way, anyhow. Say, do we kill the women, too?"

"Well, Ben Rogers, if I was as ignorant as you I wouldn't let on. Kill the women? No; nobody ever saw anything in the books like that. You fetch them to the cave, and you're always as polite as pie to them; and by and by they fall in love with you, and never want to go home any more."

"Well, if that's the way I'm agreed, but I don't take no stock in it. Mighty soon we'll have the cave so cluttered up with women, and fellows waiting to be ransomed, that there won't be no place for the robbers. But go ahead, I ain't got nothing to say."

Little Tommy Barnes was asleep now, and when they waked him up he was scared, and cried, and said he wanted to go home to his ma, and didn't want to be a robber any more.

So they all made fun of him, and called him cry-baby, and that made him mad, and he said he would go straight and tell all the secrets. But Tom give him five cents to keep quiet, and said we would all go home and meet next week, and rob somebody and kill some people.

Ben Rogers said he couldn't get out much, only Sundays, and so he wanted to begin next Sunday; but all the boys said it would be wicked to do it on Sunday, and that settled the thing. They agreed to get together and fix a day as soon as they could, and then we elected Tom Sawyer first captain and Jo Harper second captain of the Gang, and so started home.

I clumb up the shed and crept into my window just before day was breaking. My new clothes was all greased up and clayey, and I was dog-tired.

CHAPTER III.

WELL, I got a good going-over in the morning from old Miss Watson on account of my clothes; but the widow she didn't scold, but only cleaned off the grease and clay, and looked so sorry that I thought I would behave awhile if I could. Then Miss Watson she took me in the closet and prayed, but nothing come of it. She told me to pray every day, and whatever I asked for I would get it. But it warn't so. I tried it. Once I got a fish-line, but no hooks. It warn't any good to me without hooks. I tried for the hooks three or four times, but somehow I couldn't make it work. By and by, one day, I asked Miss Watson to try for me, but she said I was a fool. She never told me why, and I couldn't make it out no way.

I set down one time back in the woods, and had a long think about it. I says to myself, if a body can get anything they pray for, why don't Deacon Winn get back the money he lost on pork? Why can't the widow get back her silver snuffbox that was stole? Why can't Miss Watson fat up? No, says I to my self, there ain't nothing in it. I went and told the widow about it, and she said the thing a body could get by praying for it was "spiritual gifts." This was too many for me, but she told me what she meant—I must help other people, and do everything I could for other people, and look out for them all the time, and never think about myself. This was including Miss Watson, as I took it. I went out in the woods and turned it over in my mind a long time, but I couldn't see no advantage about it—except for the other people; so at last I reckoned I wouldn't worry about it any more, but just let it go. Sometimes the widow would take me one side and talk about Providence in a way to make a body's mouth water; but maybe next day Miss Watson would take hold and knock it all down again. I judged I could see that there was two Providences, and a poor chap would stand considerable show with the widow's Providence, but if Miss Watson's got him there warn't no help for him any more. I thought it all out, and reckoned I would belong to the widow's if he wanted me, though I couldn't make out how he was a-going to be any better off then than what he was before, seeing I was so ignorant, and so kind of low-down and ornery.

Pap he hadn't been seen for more than a year, and that was comfortable for me; I didn't want to see him no more. He used to always whale me when he was sober and could get his hands on me; though I used to take to the woods most of the time when he was around. Well, about this time he was found in the river drownded, about twelve mile above town, so people said. They judged it was him, anyway; said this drownded man was just his size, and was ragged, and had uncommon long hair, which was all like pap; but they couldn't make nothing out of the face, because it had been in the water so long it warn't much like a face at all. They said he was floating on his back in the water. They took him and buried him on the bank. But I warn't comfortable long, because I happened to think of something. I knowed mighty well that a drownded man don't float on his back, but on his face. So I knowed, then, that this warn't pap, but a woman dressed up in a man's clothes. So I was uncomfortable again. I judged the old man would turn up again by and by, though I wished he wouldn't.

We played robber now and then about a month, and then I resigned. All the boys did. We hadn't robbed nobody, hadn't killed any people, but only just pretended. We used to hop out of the woods and go charging down on hog-drivers and women in carts taking garden stuff to market, but we never hived any of them. Tom Sawyer called the hogs "ingots," and he called the turnips and stuff "julery," and we would go to the cave and powwow over what we had done, and how many people we had killed and marked. But I couldn't see no profit in it. One time Tom sent a boy to run about town with a blazing stick, which he called a slogan (which was the sign for the Gang to get together), and then he said he had got secret news by his spies that next day a whole parcel of Spanish merchants and rich A-rabs was going to camp in Cave Hollow with two hundred elephants, and six hundred camels, and over a thousand "sumter" mules, all loaded down with di'monds, and they didn't have only a guard of four hundred soldiers, and so we would lay in ambuscade, as he called it, and kill the lot and scoop the things. He said we must slick up our swords and guns, and get ready. He never could go after even a turnip-cart but he must have the swords and guns all scoured up for it, though they was only lath and broomsticks, and you might scour at them till you rotted, and then they warn't worth a mouthful of ashes more than what they was before. I didn't believe we could lick such a crowd of Spaniards and A-rabs, but I wanted to see the camels and elephants, so I was on hand next day, Saturday, in the ambuscade; and when we got the word we rushed out of the woods and down the hill. But there warn't no Spaniards and A-rabs, and there warn't no camels nor no elephants. It warn't anything but a Sunday-school picnic, and only a primer-class at that. We busted it up, and chased the children up the hollow; but we never got anything but some doughnuts and jam, though Ben Rogers got a rag doll, and Jo Harper got a hymn-book and a tract; and then the teacher charged in, and made us drop everything and cut. I didn't see no di'monds, and I told Tom Sawyer so. He said there was loads of them there, anyway; and he said there was A-rabs there, too, and elephants and things. I said, why couldn't we see them, then? He said if I warn't so ignorant, but had read a book called Don Quixote, I would know without asking. He said it was all done by enchantment. He said there was hundreds of soldiers there, and elephants and treasure, and so on, but we had enemies which he called magicians; and they had turned the whole thing into an infant Sunday-school, just out of spite. I said, all right; then the thing for us to do was to go for the magicians. Tom Sawyer said I was a numskull.

"Why," said he, "a magician could call up a lot of genies, and they would hash you up like nothing before you could say Jack Robinson. They are as tall as a tree and as big around as a church."

"Well," I says, "s'pose we got some genies to help US—can't we lick the other crowd then?"

"How you going to get them?"

"I don't know. How do THEY get them?"

"Why, they rub an old tin lamp or an iron ring, and then the genies come tearing in, with the thunder and lightning a-ripping around and the smoke a-rolling, and everything they're told to do they up and do it. They don't think nothing of pulling a shot-tower up by the roots, and belting a Sunday-school superintendent over the head with it—or any other man."

"Who makes them tear around so?"

"Why, whoever rubs the lamp or the ring. They belong to whoever rubs the lamp or the ring, and they've got to do whatever he says. If he tells them to build a palace forty miles long out of di'monds, and fill it full of chewing-gum, or whatever you want, and fetch an emperor's daughter from China for you to marry, they've got to do it—and they've got to do it before sun-up next morning, too. And more: they've got to waltz that palace around over the country wherever you want it, you understand."

"Well," says I, "I think they are a pack of flat-heads for not keeping the palace themselves 'stead of fooling them away like that. And what's more—if I was one of them I would see a man in Jericho before I would drop my business and come to him for the rubbing of an old tin lamp."

"How you talk, Huck Finn. Why, you'd HAVE to come when he rubbed it, whether you wanted to or not."

"What! and I as high as a tree and as big as a church? All right, then; I WOULD come; but I lay I'd make that man climb the highest tree there was in the country."

"Shucks, it ain't no use to talk to you, Huck Finn. You don't seem to know anything, somehow—perfect saphead."

I thought all this over for two or three days, and then I reckoned I would see if there was anything in it. I got an old tin lamp and an iron ring, and went out in the woods and rubbed and rubbed till I sweat like an Injun, calculating to build a palace and sell it; but it warn't no use, none of the genies come. So then I judged that all that stuff was only just one of Tom Sawyer's lies. I reckoned he believed in the A-rabs and the elephants, but as for me I think different. It had all the marks of a Sunday-school.

CHAPTER IV.

WELL, three or four months run along, and it was well into the winter now. I had been to school most all the time and could spell and read and write just a little, and could say the multiplication table up to six times seven is thirty-five, and I don't reckon I could ever get any further than that if I was to live forever. I don't take no stock in mathematics, anyway.

At first I hated the school, but by and by I got so I could stand it. Whenever I got uncommon tired I played hookey, and the hiding I got next day done me good and cheered me up. So the longer I went to school the easier it got to be. I was getting sort of used to the widow's ways, too, and they warn't so raspy on me. Living in a house and sleeping in a bed pulled on me pretty tight mostly, but before the cold weather I used to slide out and sleep in the woods sometimes, and so that was a rest to me. I liked the old ways best, but I was getting so I liked the new ones, too, a little bit. The widow said I was coming along slow but sure, and doing very satisfactory. She said she warn't ashamed of me.

One morning I happened to turn over the salt-cellar at breakfast. I reached for some of it as quick as I could to throw over my left shoulder and keep off the bad luck, but Miss

Watson was in ahead of me, and crossed me off. She says, "Take your hands away, Huckleberry; what a mess you are always making!" The widow put in a good word for me, but that warn't going to keep off the bad luck, I knowed that well enough. I started out, after breakfast, feeling worried and shaky, and wondering where it was going to fall on me, and what it was going to be. There is ways to keep off some kinds of bad luck, but this wasn't one of them kind; so I never tried to do anything, but just poked along low-spirited and on the watch-out.

I went down to the front garden and clumb over the stile where you go through the high board fence. There was an inch of new snow on the ground, and I seen somebody's tracks. They had come up from the quarry and stood around the stile a while, and then went on around the garden fence. It was funny they hadn't come in, after standing around so. I couldn't make it out. It was very curious, somehow. I was going to follow around, but I stooped down to look at the tracks first. I didn't notice anything at first, but next I did. There was a cross in the left boot-heel made with big nails, to keep off the devil.

I was up in a second and shinning down the hill. I looked over my shoulder every now and then, but I didn't see nobody. I was at Judge Thatcher's as quick as I could get there. He said:

"Why, my boy, you are all out of breath. Did you come for your interest?"

"No, sir," I says; "is there some for me?"

"Oh, yes, a half-yearly is in last night—over a hundred and fifty dollars. Quite a fortune for you. You had better let me invest it along with your six thousand, because if you take it you'll spend it."

"No, sir," I says, "I don't want to spend it. I don't want it at all—nor the six thousand, nuther. I want you to take it; I want to give it to you—the six thousand and all."

He looked surprised. He couldn't seem to make it out. He says:

"Why, what can you mean, my boy?"

I says, "Don't you ask me no questions about it, please. You'll take it —won't you?"

He says:

"Well, I'm puzzled. Is something the matter?"

"Please take it," says I, "and don't ask me nothing—then I won't have to tell no lies."

He studied a while, and then he says:

"Oho-o! I think I see. You want to SELL all your property to me—not give it. That's the correct idea."

Then he wrote something on a paper and read it over, and says:

"There; you see it says 'for a consideration.' That means I have bought it of you and paid you for it. Here's a dollar for you. Now you sign it."

So I signed it, and left.

Miss Watson's nigger, Jim, had a hair-ball as big as your fist, which had been took out of the fourth stomach of an ox, and he used to do magic with it. He said there was a spirit inside of it, and it knowed everything. So I went to him that night and told him pap was here again, for I found his tracks in the snow. What I wanted to know was, what he was going to do, and was he going to stay? Jim got out his hair-ball and said something over it, and then he held it up and dropped it on the floor. It fell pretty solid, and only rolled about an inch. Jim tried it again, and then another time, and it acted just the same. Jim got down on his knees, and put his ear against it and listened. But it warn't no use; he said it wouldn't talk. He said sometimes it wouldn't talk without money. I told him I had an old slick counterfeit quarter that warn't no good because the brass showed through the silver a little, and it wouldn't pass nohow, even if the brass didn't show, because it was so slick it felt greasy, and so that would tell on it every time. (I reckoned I wouldn't say nothing about the dollar I got from the judge.) I said it was pretty bad money, but maybe the hair-ball would take it, because maybe it wouldn't know the difference. Jim smelt it and bit it and rubbed it, and said he would manage so the hair-ball would think it was good. He said he would split open a raw Irish potato and stick the quarter in between and keep it there all night, and next morning you couldn't see no brass, and it wouldn't feel greasy no more, and so anybody in town would take it in a minute, let alone a hair-ball. Well, I knowed a potato would do that before, but I had forgot it.

Jim put the quarter under the hair-ball, and got down and listened again. This time he said the hair-ball was all right. He said it would tell my whole fortune if I wanted it to. I says, go on. So the hair-ball talked to Jim, and Jim told it to me. He says:

"Yo' ole father doan' know yit what he's a-gwyne to do. Sometimes he spec he'll go 'way, en den agin he spec he'll stay. De bes' way is to res' easy en let de ole man take his own way. Dey's two angels hoverin' roun' 'bout him. One uv 'em is white en shiny, en t'other one is black. De white one gits him to go right a little while, den de black one sail in en bust it all up. A body can't tell yit which one gwyne to fetch him at de las'. But you is all right. You gwyne to have considable trouble in yo' life, en considable joy. Sometimes you gwyne to git hurt, en sometimes you gwyne to git sick; but every time you's gwyne to git well agin. Dey's two gals flyin' 'bout you in yo' life. One uv 'em's light en t'other one is dark. One is rich en t'other is po'. You's gwyne to marry de po' one fust en de rich one by en by. You wants to keep 'way fum de water as much as you kin, en don't run no resk, 'kase it's down in de bills dat you's gwyne to git hung."

When I lit my candle and went up to my room that night there sat pap—his own self!

CHAPTER V.

I HAD shut the door to. Then I turned around and there he was. I used to be scared of him all the time, he tanned me so much. I reckoned I was scared now, too; but in a minute I see I was mistaken—that is, after the first jolt, as you may say, when my breath sort of hitched, he being so unexpected; but right away after I see I warn't scared of him worth bothring about.

He was most fifty, and he looked it. His hair was long and tangled and greasy, and hung down, and you could see his eyes shining through like he was behind vines. It was all black, no gray; so was his long, mixed-up whiskers. There warn't no color in his face, where his face showed; it was white; not like another man's white, but a white to make a body sick, a white to make a body's flesh crawl—a tree-toad white, a fish-belly white. As for his clothes—just rags, that was all. He had one ankle resting on t'other knee; the boot on that foot was busted, and two of his toes stuck through, and he worked them now and then. His hat was laying on the floor—an old black slouch with the top caved in, like a lid.

I stood a-looking at him; he set there a-looking at me, with his chair tilted back a little. I set the candle down. I noticed the window was up; so he had clumb in by the shed. He kept a-looking me all over. By and by he says:

"Starchy clothes—very. You think you're a good deal of a big-bug, DON'T you?"

"Maybe I am, maybe I ain't," I says.

"Don't you give me none o' your lip," says he. "You've put on considerable many frills since I been away. I'll take you down a peg before I get done with you. You're educated, too, they say—can read and write. You think you're better'n your father, now, don't you, because he can't? I'LL take it out of you. Who told you you might meddle with such hifalut'n foolishness, hey?—who told you you could?"

"The widow. She told me."

"The widow, hey?—and who told the widow she could put in her shovel about a thing that ain't none of her business?"

"Nobody never told her."

"Well, I'll learn her how to meddle. And looky here—you drop that school, you hear? I'll learn people to bring up a boy to put on airs over his own father and let on to be better'n what HE is. You lemme catch you fooling around that school again, you hear? Your mother couldn't read, and she couldn't write, nuther, before she died. None of the family couldn't before THEY died. I can't; and here you're a-swelling yourself up like this. I ain't the man to stand it—you hear? Say, lemme hear you read."

I took up a book and begun something about General Washington and the wars. When I'd read about a half a minute, he fetched the book a whack with his hand and knocked it across the house. He says:

"It's so. You can do it. I had my doubts when you told me. Now looky here; you stop that putting on frills. I won't have it. I'll lay for you, my smarty; and if I catch you about that school I'll tan you good. First you know you'll get religion, too. I never see such a son."

He took up a little blue and yaller picture of some cows and a boy, and says:

"What's this?"

"It's something they give me for learning my lessons good."

He tore it up, and says:

"I'll give you something better—I'll give you a cowhide."

He set there a-mumbling and a-growling a minute, and then he says:

"AIN'T you a sweet-scented dandy, though? A bed; and bedclothes; and a look'n'-glass; and a piece of carpet on the floor—and your own father got to sleep with the hogs in the tanyard. I never see such a son. I bet I'll take some o' these frills out o' you before I'm done with you. Why, there ain't no end to your airs—they say you're rich. Hey?—how's that?"

"They lie—that's how."

"Looky here—mind how you talk to me; I'm a-standing about all I can stand now—so don't gimme no sass. I've been in town two days, and I hain't heard nothing but about you bein' rich. I heard about it away down the river, too. That's why I come. You git me that money to-morrow—I want it."

"I hain't got no money."

"It's a lie. Judge Thatcher's got it. You git it. I want it."

"I hain't got no money, I tell you. You ask Judge Thatcher; he'll tell you the same."

"All right. I'll ask him; and I'll make him pungle, too, or I'll know the reason why. Say, how much you got in your pocket? I want it."

"I hain't got only a dollar, and I want that to—"

"It don't make no difference what you want it for—you just shell it out."

He took it and bit it to see if it was good, and then he said he was going down town to get some whisky; said he hadn't had a drink all day. When he had got out on the shed he put his head in again, and cussed me for putting on frills and trying to be better than him; and when I reckoned he was gone he come back and put his head in again, and told me to mind about that school, because he was going to lay for me and lick me if I didn't drop that.

Next day he was drunk, and he went to Judge Thatcher's and bullyragged him, and tried to make him give up the money; but he couldn't, and then he swore he'd make the law force him.

The judge and the widow went to law to get the court to take me away from him and let one of them be my guardian; but it was a new judge that had just come, and he didn't know the old man; so he said courts mustn't interfere and separate families if they could help it; said he'd druther not take a child away from its father. So Judge Thatcher and the widow had to quit on the business.

That pleased the old man till he couldn't rest. He said he'd cowhide me till I was black and blue if I didn't raise some money for him. I borrowed three dollars from Judge Thatcher, and pap took it and got drunk, and went a-blowing around and cussing and whooping and carrying on; and he kept it up all over town, with a tin pan, till most midnight; then they jailed him, and next day they had him before court, and jailed him again for a week. But he said HE was satisfied; said he was boss of his son, and he'd make it warm for HIM.

When he got out the new judge said he was a-going to make a man of him. So he took him to his own house, and dressed him up clean and nice, and had him to breakfast and dinner and supper with the family, and was just old pie to him, so to

speak. And after supper he talked to him about temperance and such things till the old man cried, and said he'd been a fool, and fooled away his life; but now he was a-going to turn over a new leaf and be a man nobody wouldn't be ashamed of, and he hoped the judge would help him and not look down on him. The judge said he could hug him for them words; so he cried, and his wife she cried again; pap said he'd been a man that had always been misunderstood before, and the judge said he believed it. The old man said that what a man wanted that was down was sympathy, and the judge said it was so; so they cried again. And when it was bedtime the old man rose up and held out his hand, and says:

"Look at it, gentlemen and ladies all; take a-hold of it; shake it. There's a hand that was the hand of a hog; but it ain't so no more; it's the hand of a man that's started in on a new life, and'll die before he'll go back. You mark them words—don't forget I said them. It's a clean hand now; shake it—don't be afeard."

So they shook it, one after the other, all around, and cried. The judge's wife she kissed it. Then the old man he signed a pledge—made his mark. The judge said it was the holiest time on record, or something like that. Then they tucked the old man into a beautiful room, which was the spare room, and in the night some time he got powerful thirsty and clumb out on to the porch-roof and slid down a stanchion and traded his new coat for a jug of forty-rod, and clumb back again and had a good old time; and towards daylight he crawled out again, drunk as a fiddler, and rolled off the porch and broke his left arm in two places, and was most froze to death when somebody found him after sun-up. And when they come to look at that spare room they had to take soundings before they could navigate it.

The judge he felt kind of sore. He said he reckoned a body could reform the old man with a shotgun, maybe, but he didn't know no other way.

CHAPTER VI.

WELL, pretty soon the old man was up and around again, and then he went for Judge Thatcher in the courts to make him give up that money, and he went for me, too, for not stopping school. He catched me a couple of times and thrashed me, but I went to school just the same, and dodged him or outrun him most of the time. I didn't want to go to school much before, but I reckoned. I'd go now to spite pap. That law trial was a slow business—appeared like they warn't ever going to get started on it; so every now and then I'd borrow two or three dollars off of the judge for him, to keep from getting a cowhiding. Every time he got money he got drunk; and every time he got drunk he raised Cain around town; and every time he raised Cain he got jailed. He was just suited—this kind of thing was right in his line.

He got to hanging around the widow's too much and so she told him at last that if he didn't quit using around there she would make trouble for him. Well, WASN'T he mad? He said he would show who was Huck Finn's boss. So he watched out for me one day in the spring, and catched me, and took me up the river about three mile in a skiff, and crossed over to the Illinois shore where it was woody and there warn't no houses but an old log hut in a place where the timber was so thick you couldn't find it if you didn't know where it was.

He kept me with him all the time, and I never got a chance to run off. We lived in that old cabin, and he always locked the door and put the key under his head nights. He had a gun which he had stole, I reckon, and we fished and hunted, and that was what we lived on. Every little while he locked me in and went down to the store, three miles, to the ferry, and traded fish and game for whisky, and fetched it home and got drunk and had a good time, and licked me. The widow she found out where I was by and by, and she sent a man over to try to get hold of me; but pap drove him off with the gun, and it warn't long after that till I was used to being where I was, and liked it—all but the cowhide part.

It was kind of lazy and jolly, laying off comfortable all day, smoking and fishing, and no books nor study. Two months or more run along, and my clothes got to be all rags and dirt, and I didn't see how I'd ever got to like it so well at the widow's, where you had to wash, and eat on a plate, and comb up, and go to bed and get up regular, and be forever bothering over a book, and have old Miss Watson pecking at you all the time. I didn't want to go back no more. I had stopped cussing, because the widow didn't like it; but now I took to it again because pap hadn't no objections. It was pretty good times up in the woods there, take it all around.

But by and by pap got too handy with his hick'ry, and I couldn't stand it. I was all over welts. He got to going away so much, too, and locking me in. Once he locked me in and was gone three days. It was dreadful lonesome. I judged he had got drowned, and I wasn't ever going to get out any more. I was scared. I made up my mind I would fix up some way to leave there. I had tried to get out of that cabin many a time, but I couldn't find no way. There warn't a window to it big enough for a dog to get through. I couldn't get up the chimbly; it was too narrow. The door was thick, solid oak slabs. Pap was pretty careful not to leave a knife or anything in the cabin when he was away; I reckon I had hunted the place over as much as a hundred times; well, I was most all the time at it, because it was about the only way to put in the time. But this time I found something at last; I found an old rusty wood-saw without any handle; it was laid in between a rafter and the clapboards of the roof. I greased it up and went to work. There was an old horse-blanket nailed against the logs at the far end of the cabin behind the table, to keep the wind from blowing through the chinks and putting the candle out. I got under the table and raised the blanket, and went to work to saw a section of the big bottom log out—big enough to let me through. Well, it was a good long job, but I was getting towards the end of it when I heard pap's gun in the woods. I got rid of the signs of my work, and dropped the blanket and hid my saw, and pretty soon pap come in.

Pap warn't in a good humor—so he was his natural self. He said he was down town, and everything was going wrong. His lawyer said he reckoned he would win his lawsuit and get the money if they ever got started on the trial; but then there was ways to put it off a long time, and Judge Thatcher knowed how to do it. And he said people allowed there'd be another trial to get me away from him and give me to the widow for my guardian, and they guessed it would win this time. This shook me up considerable, because I didn't want to go back to the widow's any more and be so cramped up and sivilized, as they called it. Then the old man got to cussing, and cussed everything and everybody he could think of, and then cussed them all over again to make sure he hadn't skipped any, and after that he polished off with a kind of a general cuss all round, including a considerable parcel of people which he didn't know the names of, and so called them what's-his-name when he got to them, and went right along with his cussing.

He said he would like to see the widow get me. He said he would watch out, and if they tried to come any such game on him he knowed of a place six or seven mile off to stow me in, where they might hunt till they dropped and they couldn't find me. That made me pretty uneasy again, but only for a minute; I reckoned I wouldn't stay on hand till he got that chance.

The old man made me go to the skiff and fetch the things he had got. There was a fifty-pound sack of corn meal, and a side of bacon, ammunition, and a four-gallon jug of whisky, and an old book and two newspapers for wadding, besides some tow. I toted up a load, and went back and set down on the bow of the skiff to rest. I thought it all over, and I reckoned I would walk off with the gun and some lines, and take to the woods when I run away. I guessed I wouldn't stay in one place, but just tramp right across the country, mostly night times, and hunt and fish to keep alive, and so get so far away that the old man nor the widow couldn't ever find me any more. I judged I would saw out and leave that night if pap got drunk enough, and I reckoned he would. I got so full of it I didn't notice how long I was staying till the old man hollered and asked me whether I was asleep or drownded.

I got the things all up to the cabin, and then it was about dark. While I was cooking supper the old man took a swig or two and got sort of warmed up, and went to ripping again. He had been drunk over in town, and laid in the gutter all night, and he was a sight to look at. A body would a thought he was Adam—he was just all mud. Whenever his liquor begun to work he most always went for the govment, this time he says:

"Call this a govment! why, just look at it and see what it's like. Here's the law a-standing ready to take a man's son away from him—a man's own son, which he has had all the trouble and all the anxiety and all the expense of raising. Yes, just as that man has got that son raised at last, and ready to go to work and begin to do suthin' for HIM and give him a rest, the law up and goes for him. And they call THAT govment! That ain't all, nuther. The law backs that old Judge Thatcher up and helps him to keep me out o' my property. Here's what the law does: The law takes a man worth six thousand dollars and up'ards, and jams him into an old trap of a cabin like this, and lets him go round in clothes that ain't fitten for a hog. They call that govment! A man can't get his rights in a govment like this. Sometimes I've a mighty notion to just leave the country for good and all. Yes, and I TOLD 'em so; I told old Thatcher so to his face. Lots of 'em heard me, and can tell what I said. Says I, for two cents I'd leave the blamed country and never come a-near it agin. Them's the very words. I says look at my hat—if you call it a hat—but the lid raises up and the rest of it goes down till it's below my chin, and then it ain't rightly a hat at all, but more like my head was shoved up through a jint o' stove-pipe. Look at it, says I—such a hat for me to wear—one of the wealthiest men in this town if I could git my rights.

"Oh, yes, this is a wonderful govment, wonderful. Why, looky here. There was a free nigger there from Ohio—a mulatter, most as white as a white man. He had the whitest shirt on you ever see, too, and the shiniest hat; and there ain't a man in that town that's got as fine clothes as what he had; and he had a gold watch and chain, and a silver-headed cane—the awfulest old gray-headed nabob in the State. And what do you think? They said he was a p'fessor in a college, and could talk all kinds of languages, and knowed everything. And that ain't the wust. They said he could VOTE when he was at home. Well, that let me out. Thinks I, what is the country a-coming to? It was 'lection day, and I was just about to go and vote myself if I warn't too drunk to get there; but when they told me there was a State in this country where they'd let that nigger vote, I drawed out. I says I'll never vote agin. Them's the very words I said; they all heard me; and the country may rot for all me —I'll never vote agin as long as I live. And to see the cool way of that nigger—why, he wouldn't give me the road if I hadn't shoved him out o' the way. I says to the people, why ain't this nigger put up at auction and sold?—that's what I want to know. And what do you reckon they said? Why, they said he couldn't be sold till he'd been in the State six months, and he hadn't been there that long yet. There, now—that's a specimen. They call that a govment that can't sell a free nigger till he's been in the State six months. Here's a govment that calls itself a govment, and lets on to be a govment, and thinks it is a govment, and yet's got to set stock-still for six whole months before it can take a hold of a prowling, thieving, infernal, white-shirted free nigger, and—"

Pap was agoing on so he never noticed where his old limber legs was taking him to, so he went head over heels over the tub of salt pork and barked both shins, and the rest of his speech was all the hottest kind of language—mostly hove at the nigger and the govment, though he give the tub some, too, all along, here and there. He hopped around the cabin considerable, first on one leg and then on the other, holding first one shin and then the other one, and at last he let out with his left foot all of a sudden and fetched the tub a rattling kick. But it warn't good judgment, because that was the boot that had a couple of his toes leaking out of the front end of it; so now he raised a howl that fairly made a body's hair raise, and down he went in the dirt, and rolled there, and held his toes; and the cussing he done then laid over anything he had ever done previous. He said so his own self afterwards. He had heard old Sowberry Hagan in his best days, and he said it laid over him, too; but I reckon that was sort of piling it on, maybe.

After supper pap took the jug, and said he had enough whisky there for two drunks and one delirium tremens. That was always his word. I judged he would be blind drunk in about an hour, and then I would steal the key, or saw myself out, one or t'other. He drank and drank, and tumbled down on his blankets by and by; but luck didn't run my way. He didn't go sound asleep, but was uneasy. He groaned and moaned and thrashed around this way and that for a long time. At last I got so sleepy I couldn't keep my eyes open all I could do, and so before I knowed what I was about I was sound asleep, and the candle burning.

I don't know how long I was asleep, but all of a sudden there was an awful scream and I was up. There was pap looking wild, and skipping around every which way and yelling about snakes. He said they was crawling up his legs; and then he would give a jump and scream, and say one had bit him on the cheek—but I couldn't see no snakes. He started and run round and round the cabin, hollering "Take him off! take him off! he's biting me on the neck!" I never see a man look so wild in the eyes. Pretty soon he was all fagged out, and fell down panting; then he rolled over and over wonderful fast, kicking things every which way, and striking and grabbing at the air with his hands, and screaming and saying there was devils a-hold of him. He wore out by and by, and laid still a while, moaning. Then he laid stiller, and didn't make a sound. I could hear the owls and the wolves away off in the woods, and it seemed terrible still. He was laying over by the corner. By and by he raised up part way and listened, with his head to one side. He says, very low:

"Tramp—tramp—tramp; that's the dead; tramp—tramp—tramp; they're coming after me; but I won't go. Oh, they're

here! don't touch me —don't! hands off—they're cold; let go. Oh, let a poor devil alone!"

Then he went down on all fours and crawled off, begging them to let him alone, and he rolled himself up in his blanket and wallowed in under the old pine table, still a-begging; and then he went to crying. I could hear him through the blanket.

By and by he rolled out and jumped up on his feet looking wild, and he see me and went for me. He chased me round and round the place with a clasp-knife, calling me the Angel of Death, and saying he would kill me, and then I couldn't come for him no more. I begged, and told him I was only Huck; but he laughed SUCH a screechy laugh, and roared and cussed, and kept on chasing me up. Once when I turned short and dodged under his arm he made a grab and got me by the jacket between my shoulders, and I thought I was gone; but I slid out of the jacket quick as lightning, and saved myself. Pretty soon he was all tired out, and dropped down with his back against the door, and said he would rest a minute and then kill me. He put his knife under him, and said he would sleep and get strong, and then he would see who was who.

So he dozed off pretty soon. By and by I got the old split-bottom chair and clumb up as easy as I could, not to make any noise, and got down the gun. I slipped the ramrod down it to make sure it was loaded, then I laid it across the turnip barrel, pointing towards pap, and set down behind it to wait for him to stir. And how slow and still the time did drag along.

CHAPTER VII.

"GIT up! What you 'bout?"

I opened my eyes and looked around, trying to make out where I was. It was after sun-up, and I had been sound asleep. Pap was standing over me looking sour and sick, too. He says:

"What you doin' with this gun?"

I judged he didn't know nothing about what he had been doing, so I says:

"Somebody tried to get in, so I was laying for him."

"Why didn't you roust me out?"

"Well, I tried to, but I couldn't; I couldn't budge you."

"Well, all right. Don't stand there palavering all day, but out with you and see if there's a fish on the lines for breakfast. I'll be along in a minute."

He unlocked the door, and I cleared out up the river-bank. I noticed some pieces of limbs and such things floating down, and a sprinkling of bark; so I knowed the river had begun to rise. I reckoned I would have great times now if I was over at the town. The June rise used to be always luck for me; because as soon as that rise begins here comes cordwood floating down, and pieces of log rafts—sometimes a dozen logs together; so all you have to do is to catch them and sell them to the wood-yards and the sawmill.

I went along up the bank with one eye out for pap and t'other one out for what the rise might fetch along. Well, all at once here comes a canoe; just a beauty, too, about thirteen or fourteen foot long, riding high like a duck. I shot head-first off of the bank like a frog, clothes and all on, and struck out for the canoe. I just expected there'd be somebody laying down in it, because people often done that to fool folks, and when a chap had pulled a skiff out most to it they'd raise up and laugh at him. But it warn't so this time. It was a drift-canoe sure enough, and I clumb in and paddled her ashore. Thinks I, the old man will be glad when he sees this—she's worth ten dollars. But when I got to shore pap wasn't in sight yet, and as I was running her into a little creek like a gully, all hung over with vines and willows, I struck another idea: I judged I'd hide her good, and then, 'stead of taking to the woods when I run off, I'd go down the river about fifty mile and camp in one place for good, and not have such a rough time tramping on foot.

It was pretty close to the shanty, and I thought I heard the old man coming all the time; but I got her hid; and then I out and looked around a bunch of willows, and there was the old man down the path a piece just drawing a bead on a bird with his gun. So he hadn't seen anything.

When he got along I was hard at it taking up a "trot" line. He abused me a little for being so slow; but I told him I fell in the river, and that was what made me so long. I knowed he would see I was wet, and then he would be asking questions. We got five catfish off the lines and went home.

While we laid off after breakfast to sleep up, both of us being about wore out, I got to thinking that if I could fix up some way to keep pap and the widow from trying to follow me, it would be a certainer thing than trusting to luck to get far enough off before they missed me; you see, all kinds of things might happen. Well, I didn't see no way for a while, but by and by pap raised up a minute to drink another barrel of water, and he says:

"Another time a man comes a-prowling round here you roust me out, you hear? That man warn't here for no good. I'd a shot him. Next time you roust me out, you hear?"

Then he dropped down and went to sleep again; but what he had been saying give me the very idea I wanted. I says to myself, I can fix it now so nobody won't think of following me.

About twelve o'clock we turned out and went along up the bank. The river was coming up pretty fast, and lots of driftwood going by on the rise. By and by along comes part of a log raft—nine logs fast together. We went out with the skiff and towed it ashore. Then we had dinner. Anybody but pap would a waited and seen the day through, so as to catch more stuff; but that warn't pap's style. Nine logs was enough for one time; he must shove right over to town and sell. So he locked me in and took the skiff, and started off towing the raft about half-past three. I judged he wouldn't come back that night. I waited till I reckoned he had got a good start; then I out with my saw, and went to work on that log again. Before he was t'other side of the river I was out of the hole; him and his raft was just a speck on the water away off yonder.

I took the sack of corn meal and took it to where the canoe was hid, and shoved the vines and branches apart and put it in; then I done the same with the side of bacon; then the whisky-jug. I took all the coffee and sugar there was, and all the ammunition; I took the wadding; I took the bucket and gourd; I took a dipper and a tin cup, and my old saw and two blankets, and the skillet and the coffee-pot. I took fish-lines and matches and other things—everything that was worth a cent. I cleaned out the place. I wanted an axe, but there wasn't any, only the one out at the woodpile, and I knowed why I was

going to leave that. I fetched out the gun, and now I was done.

I had wore the ground a good deal crawling out of the hole and dragging out so many things. So I fixed that as good as I could from the outside by scattering dust on the place, which covered up the smoothness and the sawdust. Then I fixed the piece of log back into its place, and put two rocks under it and one against it to hold it there, for it was bent up at that place and didn't quite touch ground. If you stood four or five foot away and didn't know it was sawed, you wouldn't never notice it; and besides, this was the back of the cabin, and it warn't likely anybody would go fooling around there.

It was all grass clear to the canoe, so I hadn't left a track. I followed around to see. I stood on the bank and looked out over the river. All safe. So I took the gun and went up a piece into the woods, and was hunting around for some birds when I see a wild pig; hogs soon went wild in them bottoms after they had got away from the prairie farms. I shot this fellow and took him into camp.

I took the axe and smashed in the door. I beat it and hacked it considerable a-doing it. I fetched the pig in, and took him back nearly to the table and hacked into his throat with the axe, and laid him down on the ground to bleed; I say ground because it was ground—hard packed, and no boards. Well, next I took an old sack and put a lot of big rocks in it—all I could drag—and I started it from the pig, and dragged it to the door and through the woods down to the river and dumped it in, and down it sunk, out of sight. You could easy see that something had been dragged over the ground. I did wish Tom Sawyer was there; I knowed he would take an interest in this kind of business, and throw in the fancy touches. Nobody could spread himself like Tom Sawyer in such a thing as that.

Well, last I pulled out some of my hair, and blooded the axe good, and stuck it on the back side, and slung the axe in the corner. Then I took up the pig and held him to my breast with my jacket (so he couldn't drip) till I got a good piece below the house and then dumped him into the river. Now I thought of something else. So I went and got the bag of meal and my old saw out of the canoe, and fetched them to the house. I took the bag to where it used to stand, and ripped a hole in the bottom of it with the saw, for there warn't no knives and forks on the place —pap done everything with his clasp-knife about the cooking. Then I carried the sack about a hundred yards across the grass and through the willows east of the house, to a shallow lake that was five mile wide and full of rushes—and ducks too, you might say, in the season. There was a slough or a creek leading out of it on the other side that went miles away, I don't know where, but it didn't go to the river. The meal sifted out and made a little track all the way to the lake. I dropped pap's whetstone there too, so as to look like it had been done by accident. Then I tied up the rip in the meal sack with a string, so it wouldn't leak no more, and took it and my saw to the canoe again.

It was about dark now; so I dropped the canoe down the river under some willows that hung over the bank, and waited for the moon to rise. I made fast to a willow; then I took a bite to eat, and by and by laid down in the canoe to smoke a pipe and lay out a plan. I says to myself, they'll follow the track of that sackful of rocks to the shore and then drag the river for me. And they'll follow that meal track to the lake and go browsing down the creek that leads out of it to find the robbers that killed me and took the things. They won't ever hunt the river for anything but my dead carcass. They'll soon get tired of that, and won't bother no more about me. All right; I can stop anywhere I want to. Jackson's Island is good enough for me; I know that island pretty well, and nobody ever comes there. And then I can paddle over to town nights, and slink around and pick up things I want. Jackson's Island's the place.

I was pretty tired, and the first thing I knowed I was asleep. When I woke up I didn't know where I was for a minute. I set up and looked around, a little scared. Then I remembered. The river looked miles and miles across. The moon was so bright I could a counted the drift logs that went a-slipping along, black and still, hundreds of yards out from shore. Everything was dead quiet, and it looked late, and SMELT late. You know what I mean—I don't know the words to put it in.

I took a good gap and a stretch, and was just going to unhitch and start when I heard a sound away over the water. I listened. Pretty soon I made it out. It was that dull kind of a regular sound that comes from oars working in rowlocks when it's a still night. I peeped out through the willow branches, and there it was—a skiff, away across the water. I couldn't tell how many was in it. It kept a-coming, and when it was abreast of me I see there warn't but one man in it. Think's I, maybe it's pap, though I warn't expecting him. He dropped below me with the current, and by and by he came a-swinging up shore in the easy water, and he went by so close I could a reached out the gun and touched him. Well, it WAS pap, sure enough—and sober, too, by the way he laid his oars.

I didn't lose no time. The next minute I was a-spinning down stream soft but quick in the shade of the bank. I made two mile and a half, and then struck out a quarter of a mile or more towards the middle of the river, because pretty soon I would be passing the ferry landing, and people might see me and hail me. I got out amongst the driftwood, and then laid down in the bottom of the canoe and let her float. I laid there, and had a good rest and a smoke out of my pipe, looking away into the sky; not a cloud in it. The sky looks ever so deep when you lay down on your back in the moonshine; I never knowed it before. And how far a body can hear on the water such nights! I heard people talking at the ferry landing. I heard what they said, too—every word of it. One man said it was getting towards the long days and the short nights now. T'other one said THIS warn't one of the short ones, he reckoned—and then they laughed, and he said it over again, and they laughed again; then they waked up another fellow and told him, and laughed, but he didn't laugh; he ripped out something brisk, and said let him alone. The first fellow said he 'lowed to tell it to his old woman—she would think it was pretty good; but he said that warn't nothing to some things he had said in his time. I heard one man say it was nearly three o'clock, and he hoped daylight wouldn't wait more than about a week longer. After that the talk got further and further away, and I couldn't make out the words any more; but I could hear the mumble, and now and then a laugh, too, but it seemed a long ways off.

I was away below the ferry now. I rose up, and there was Jackson's Island, about two mile and a half down stream, heavy timbered and standing up out of the middle of the river, big and dark and solid, like a steamboat without any lights. There warn't any signs of the bar at the head—it was all under water now.

It didn't take me long to get there. I shot past the head at a ripping rate, the current was so swift, and then I got into the dead water and landed on the side towards the Illinois shore. I run the canoe into a deep dent in the bank that I knowed about; I had to part the willow branches to get in; and when I

made fast nobody could a seen the canoe from the outside.

I went up and set down on a log at the head of the island, and looked out on the big river and the black driftwood and away over to the town, three mile away, where there was three or four lights twinkling. A monstrous big lumber-raft was about a mile up stream, coming along down, with a lantern in the middle of it. I watched it come creeping down, and when it was most abreast of where I stood I heard a man say, "Stern oars, there! heave her head to stabboard!" I heard that just as plain as if the man was by my side.

There was a little gray in the sky now; so I stepped into the woods, and laid down for a nap before breakfast.

CHAPTER VIII.

THE sun was up so high when I waked that I judged it was after eight o'clock. I laid there in the grass and the cool shade thinking about things, and feeling rested and ruther comfortable and satisfied. I could see the sun out at one or two holes, but mostly it was big trees all about, and gloomy in there amongst them. There was freckled places on the ground where the light sifted down through the leaves, and the freckled places swapped about a little, showing there was a little breeze up there. A couple of squirrels set on a limb and jabbered at me very friendly.

I was powerful lazy and comfortable—didn't want to get up and cook breakfast. Well, I was dozing off again when I thinks I hears a deep sound of "boom!" away up the river. I rouses up, and rests on my elbow and listens; pretty soon I hears it again. I hopped up, and went and looked out at a hole in the leaves, and I see a bunch of smoke laying on the water a long ways up—about abreast the ferry. And there was the ferryboat full of people floating along down. I knowed what was the matter now. "Boom!" I see the white smoke squirt out of the ferryboat's side. You see, they was firing cannon over the water, trying to make my carcass come to the top.

I was pretty hungry, but it warn't going to do for me to start a fire, because they might see the smoke. So I set there and watched the cannon-smoke and listened to the boom. The river was a mile wide there, and it always looks pretty on a summer morning—so I was having a good enough time seeing them hunt for my remainders if I only had a bite to eat. Well, then I happened to think how they always put quicksilver in loaves of bread and float them off, because they always go right to the drownded carcass and stop there. So, says I, I'll keep a lookout, and if any of them's floating around after me I'll give them a show. I changed to the Illinois edge of the island to see what luck I could have, and I warn't disappointed. A big double loaf come along, and I most got it with a long stick, but my foot slipped and she floated out further. Of course I was where the current set in the closest to the shore—I knowed enough for that. But by and by along comes another one, and this time I won. I took out the plug and shook out the little dab of quicksilver, and set my teeth in. It was "baker's bread"—what the quality eat; none of your low-down corn-pone.

I got a good place amongst the leaves, and set there on a log, munching the bread and watching the ferry-boat, and very well satisfied. And then something struck me. I says, now I reckon the widow or the parson or somebody prayed that this bread would find me, and here it has gone and done it. So there ain't no doubt but there is something in that thing —that is, there's something in it when a body like the widow or the parson prays, but it don't work for me, and I reckon it don't work for only just the right kind.

I lit a pipe and had a good long smoke, and went on watching. The ferryboat was floating with the current, and I allowed I'd have a chance to see who was aboard when she come along, because she would come in close, where the bread did. When she'd got pretty well along down towards me, I put out my pipe and went to where I fished out the bread, and laid down behind a log on the bank in a little open place. Where the log forked I could peep through.

By and by she come along, and she drifted in so close that they could a run out a plank and walked ashore. Most everybody was on the boat. Pap, and Judge Thatcher, and Bessie Thatcher, and Jo Harper, and Tom Sawyer, and his old Aunt Polly, and Sid and Mary, and plenty more. Everybody was talking about the murder, but the captain broke in and says:

"Look sharp, now; the current sets in the closest here, and maybe he's washed ashore and got tangled amongst the brush at the water's edge. I hope so, anyway."

"I didn't hope so. They all crowded up and leaned over the rails, nearly in my face, and kept still, watching with all their might. I could see them first-rate, but they couldn't see me. Then the captain sung out:

"Stand away!" and the cannon let off such a blast right before me that it made me deef with the noise and pretty near blind with the smoke, and I judged I was gone. If they'd a had some bullets in, I reckon they'd a got the corpse they was after. Well, I see I warn't hurt, thanks to goodness. The boat floated on and went out of sight around the shoulder of the island. I could hear the booming now and then, further and further off, and by and by, after an hour, I didn't hear it no more. The island was three mile long. I judged they had got to the foot, and was giving it up. But they didn't yet a while. They turned around the foot of the island and started up the channel on the Missouri side, under steam, and booming once in a while as they went. I crossed over to that side and watched them. When they got abreast the head of the island they quit shooting and dropped over to the Missouri shore and went home to the town.

I knowed I was all right now. Nobody else would come a-hunting after me. I got my traps out of the canoe and made me a nice camp in the thick woods. I made a kind of a tent out of my blankets to put my things under so the rain couldn't get at them. I catched a catfish and haggled him open with my saw, and towards sundown I started my camp fire and had supper. Then I set out a line to catch some fish for breakfast.

When it was dark I set by my camp fire smoking, and feeling pretty well satisfied; but by and by it got sort of lonesome, and so I went and set on the bank and listened to the current swashing along, and counted the stars and drift logs and rafts that come down, and then went to bed; there ain't no better way to put in time when you are lonesome; you can't stay so, you soon get over it.

And so for three days and nights. No difference—just the same thing. But the next day I went exploring around down through the island. I was boss of it; it all belonged to me, so to say, and I wanted to know all about it; but mainly I wanted to put in the time. I found plenty strawberries, ripe and prime; and green summer grapes, and green razberries; and the green blackberries was just beginning to show. They would all come

handy by and by, I judged.

Well, I went fooling along in the deep woods till I judged I warn't far from the foot of the island. I had my gun along, but I hadn't shot nothing; it was for protection; thought I would kill some game nigh home. About this time I mighty near stepped on a good-sized snake, and it went sliding off through the grass and flowers, and I after it, trying to get a shot at it. I clipped along, and all of a sudden I bounded right on to the ashes of a camp fire that was still smoking.

My heart jumped up amongst my lungs. I never waited for to look further, but uncocked my gun and went sneaking back on my tiptoes as fast as ever I could. Every now and then I stopped a second amongst the thick leaves and listened, but my breath come so hard I couldn't hear nothing else. I slunk along another piece further, then listened again; and so on, and so on. If I see a stump, I took it for a man; if I trod on a stick and broke it, it made me feel like a person had cut one of my breaths in two and I only got half, and the short half, too.

When I got to camp I warn't feeling very brash, there warn't much sand in my craw; but I says, this ain't no time to be fooling around. So I got all my traps into my canoe again so as to have them out of sight, and I put out the fire and scattered the ashes around to look like an old last year's camp, and then clumb a tree.

I reckon I was up in the tree two hours; but I didn't see nothing, I didn't hear nothing—I only THOUGHT I heard and seen as much as a thousand things. Well, I couldn't stay up there forever; so at last I got down, but I kept in the thick woods and on the lookout all the time. All I could get to eat was berries and what was left over from breakfast.

By the time it was night I was pretty hungry. So when it was good and dark I slid out from shore before moonrise and paddled over to the Illinois bank—about a quarter of a mile. I went out in the woods and cooked a supper, and I had about made up my mind I would stay there all night when I hear a PLUNKETY-PLUNK, PLUNKETY-PLUNK, and says to myself, horses coming; and next I hear people's voices. I got everything into the canoe as quick as I could, and then went creeping through the woods to see what I could find out. I hadn't got far when I hear a man say:

"We better camp here if we can find a good place; the horses is about beat out. Let's look around."

I didn't wait, but shoved out and paddled away easy. I tied up in the old place, and reckoned I would sleep in the canoe.

I didn't sleep much. I couldn't, somehow, for thinking. And every time I waked up I thought somebody had me by the neck. So the sleep didn't do me no good. By and by I says to myself, I can't live this way; I'm a-going to find out who it is that's here on the island with me; I'll find it out or bust. Well, I felt better right off.

So I took my paddle and slid out from shore just a step or two, and then let the canoe drop along down amongst the shadows. The moon was shining, and outside of the shadows it made it most as light as day. I poked along well on to an hour, everything still as rocks and sound asleep. Well, by this time I was most down to the foot of the island. A little ripply, cool breeze begun to blow, and that was as good as saying the night was about done. I give her a turn with the paddle and brung her nose to shore; then I got my gun and slipped out and into the edge of the woods. I sat down there on a log, and looked out through the leaves. I see the moon go off watch, and the darkness begin to blanket the river. But in a little while I see a pale streak over the treetops, and knowed the day was coming. So I took my gun and slipped off towards where I had run across that camp fire, stopping every minute or two to listen. But I hadn't no luck somehow; I couldn't seem to find the place. But by and by, sure enough, I catched a glimpse of fire away through the trees. I went for it, cautious and slow. By and by I was close enough to have a look, and there laid a man on the ground. It most give me the fantods. He had a blanket around his head, and his head was nearly in the fire. I set there behind a clump of bushes in about six foot of him, and kept my eyes on him steady. It was getting gray daylight now. Pretty soon he gapped and stretched himself and hove off the blanket, and it was Miss Watson's Jim! I bet I was glad to see him. I says:

"Hello, Jim!" and skipped out.

He bounced up and stared at me wild. Then he drops down on his knees, and puts his hands together and says:

"Doan' hurt me—don't! I hain't ever done no harm to a ghos'. I alwuz liked dead people, en done all I could for 'em. You go en git in de river agin, whah you b'longs, en doan' do nuffn to Ole Jim, 'at 'uz awluz yo' fren'."

Well, I warn't long making him understand I warn't dead. I was ever so glad to see Jim. I warn't lonesome now. I told him I warn't afraid of HIM telling the people where I was. I talked along, but he only set there and looked at me; never said nothing. Then I says:

"It's good daylight. Le's get breakfast. Make up your camp fire good."

"What's de use er makin' up de camp fire to cook strawbries en sich truck? But you got a gun, hain't you? Den we kin git sumfn better den strawbries."

"Strawberries and such truck," I says. "Is that what you live on?"

"I couldn' git nuffn else," he says.

"Why, how long you been on the island, Jim?"

"I come heah de night arter you's killed."

"What, all that time?"

"Yes—indeedy."

"And ain't you had nothing but that kind of rubbage to eat?"

"No, sah—nuffn else."

"Well, you must be most starved, ain't you?"

"I reck'n I could eat a hoss. I think I could. How long you ben on de islan'?"

"Since the night I got killed."

"No! W'y, what has you lived on? But you got a gun. Oh, yes, you got a gun. Dat's good. Now you kill sumfn en I'll make up de fire."

So we went over to where the canoe was, and while he built a fire in a grassy open place amongst the trees, I fetched meal and bacon and coffee, and coffee-pot and frying-pan, and sugar and tin cups, and the nigger was set back considerable, because he reckoned it was all done with witchcraft. I catched a good big catfish, too, and Jim cleaned him with his knife, and fried him.

When breakfast was ready we lolled on the grass and eat it smoking hot. Jim laid it in with all his might, for he was most about starved. Then when we had got pretty well stuffed, we laid off and lazied. By and by Jim says:

"But looky here, Huck, who wuz it dat 'uz killed in dat shanty ef it warn't you?"

Then I told him the whole thing, and he said it was smart. He said Tom Sawyer couldn't get up no better plan than what I had. Then I says:

"How do you come to be here, Jim, and how'd you get here?"

He looked pretty uneasy, and didn't say nothing for a minute. Then he says:

"Maybe I better not tell."

"Why, Jim?"

"Well, dey's reasons. But you wouldn' tell on me ef I uz to tell you, would you, Huck?"

"Blamed if I would, Jim."

"Well, I b'lieve you, Huck. I—I RUN OFF."

"Jim!"

"But mind, you said you wouldn' tell—you know you said you wouldn' tell, Huck."

"Well, I did. I said I wouldn't, and I'll stick to it. Honest INJUN, I will. People would call me a low-down Abolitionist and despise me for keeping mum—but that don't make no difference. I ain't a-going to tell, and I ain't a-going back there, anyways. So, now, le's know all about it."

"Well, you see, it 'uz dis way. Ole missus—dat's Miss Watson— she pecks on me all de time, en treats me pooty rough, but she awluz said she wouldn' sell me down to Orleans. But I noticed dey wuz a nigger trader roun' de place considable lately, en I begin to git oneasy. Well, one night I creeps to de do' pooty late, en de do' warn't quite shet, en I hear old missus tell de widder she gwyne to sell me down to Orleans, but she didn' want to, but she could git eight hund'd dollars for me, en it 'uz sich a big stack o' money she couldn' resis'. De widder she try to git her to say she wouldn' do it, but I never waited to hear de res'. I lit out mighty quick, I tell you.

"I tuck out en shin down de hill, en 'spec to steal a skift 'long de sho' som'ers 'bove de town, but dey wuz people a-stirring yit, so I hid in de ole tumble-down cooper-shop on de bank to wait for everybody to go 'way. Well, I wuz dah all night. Dey wuz somebody roun' all de time. 'Long 'bout six in de mawnin' skifts begin to go by, en 'bout eight er nine every skift dat went 'long wuz talkin' 'bout how yo' pap come over to de town en say you's killed. Dese las' skifts wuz full o' ladies en genlmen a-goin' over for to see de place. Sometimes dey'd pull up at de sho' en take a res' b'fo' dey started acrost, so by de talk I got to know all 'bout de killin'. I 'uz powerful sorry you's killed, Huck, but I ain't no mo' now.

"I laid dah under de shavin's all day. I 'uz hungry, but I warn't afeard; bekase I knowed ole missus en de widder wuz goin' to start to de camp-meet'n' right arter breakfas' en be gone all day, en dey knows I goes off wid de cattle 'bout daylight, so dey wouldn' 'spec to see me roun' de place, en so dey wouldn' miss me tell arter dark in de evenin'. De yuther servants wouldn' miss me, kase dey'd shin out en take holiday soon as de ole folks 'uz out'n de way.

"Well, when it come dark I tuck out up de river road, en went 'bout two mile er more to whah dey warn't no houses. I'd made up my mine 'bout what I's agwyne to do. You see, ef I kep' on tryin' to git away afoot, de dogs 'ud track me; ef I stole a skift to cross over, dey'd miss dat skift, you see, en dey'd know 'bout whah I'd lan' on de yuther side, en whah to pick up my track. So I says, a raff is what I's arter; it doan' MAKE no track.

"I see a light a-comin' roun' de p'int bymeby, so I wade' in en shove' a log ahead o' me en swum more'n half way acrost de river, en got in 'mongst de drift-wood, en kep' my head down low, en kinder swum agin de current tell de raff come along. Den I swum to de stern uv it en tuck a-holt. It clouded up en 'uz pooty dark for a little while. So I clumb up en laid down on de planks. De men 'uz all 'way yonder in de middle, whah de lantern wuz. De river wuz a-risin', en dey wuz a good current; so I reck'n'd 'at by fo' in de mawnin' I'd be twenty-five mile down de river, en den I'd slip in jis b'fo' daylight en swim asho', en take to de woods on de Illinois side.

"But I didn' have no luck. When we 'uz mos' down to de head er de islan' a man begin to come aft wid de lantern, I see it warn't no use fer to wait, so I slid overboard en struck out fer de islan'. Well, I had a notion I could lan' mos' anywhers, but I couldn't—bank too bluff. I 'uz mos' to de foot er de islan' b'fo' I found' a good place. I went into de woods en jedged I wouldn' fool wid raffs no mo', long as dey move de lantern roun' so. I had my pipe en a plug er dog-leg, en some matches in my cap, en dey warn't wet, so I 'uz all right."

"And so you ain't had no meat nor bread to eat all this time? Why didn't you get mud-turkles?"

"How you gwyne to git 'm? You can't slip up on um en grab um; en how's a body gwyne to hit um wid a rock? How could a body do it in de night? En I warn't gwyne to show mysef on de bank in de daytime."

"Well, that's so. You've had to keep in the woods all the time, of course. Did you hear 'em shooting the cannon?"

"Oh, yes. I knowed dey was arter you. I see um go by heah—watched um thoo de bushes."

Some young birds come along, flying a yard or two at a time and lighting. Jim said it was a sign it was going to rain. He said it was a sign when young chickens flew that way, and so he reckoned it was the same way when young birds done it. I was going to catch some of them, but Jim wouldn't let me. He said it was death. He said his father laid mighty sick once, and some of them catched a bird, and his old granny said his father would die, and he did.

And Jim said you mustn't count the things you are going to

cook for dinner, because that would bring bad luck. The same if you shook the table-cloth after sundown. And he said if a man owned a beehive and that man died, the bees must be told about it before sun-up next morning, or else the bees would all weaken down and quit work and die. Jim said bees wouldn't sting idiots; but I didn't believe that, because I had tried them lots of times myself, and they wouldn't sting me.

I had heard about some of these things before, but not all of them. Jim knowed all kinds of signs. He said he knowed most everything. I said it looked to me like all the signs was about bad luck, and so I asked him if there warn't any good-luck signs. He says:

"Mighty few—an' DEY ain't no use to a body. What you want to know when good luck's a-comin' for? Want to keep it off?" And he said: "Ef you's got hairy arms en a hairy breas', it's a sign dat you's agwyne to be rich. Well, dey's some use in a sign like dat, 'kase it's so fur ahead. You see, maybe you's got to be po' a long time fust, en so you might git discourage' en kill yo'sef 'f you didn' know by de sign dat you gwyne to be rich bymeby."

"Have you got hairy arms and a hairy breast, Jim?"

"What's de use to ax dat question? Don't you see I has?"

"Well, are you rich?"

"No, but I ben rich wunst, and gwyne to be rich agin. Wunst I had foteen dollars, but I tuck to specalat'n', en got busted out."

"What did you speculate in, Jim?"

"Well, fust I tackled stock."

"What kind of stock?"

"Why, live stock—cattle, you know. I put ten dollars in a cow. But I ain' gwyne to resk no mo' money in stock. De cow up 'n' died on my han's."

"So you lost the ten dollars."

"No, I didn't lose it all. I on'y los' 'bout nine of it. I sole de hide en taller for a dollar en ten cents."

"You had five dollars and ten cents left. Did you speculate any more?"

"Yes. You know that one-laigged nigger dat b'longs to old Misto Bradish? Well, he sot up a bank, en say anybody dat put in a dollar would git fo' dollars mo' at de en' er de year. Well, all de niggers went in, but dey didn't have much. I wuz de on'y one dat had much. So I stuck out for mo' dan fo' dollars, en I said 'f I didn' git it I'd start a bank mysef. Well, o' course dat nigger want' to keep me out er de business, bekase he says dey warn't business 'nough for two banks, so he say I could put in my five dollars en he pay me thirty-five at de en' er de year.

"So I done it. Den I reck'n'd I'd inves' de thirty-five dollars right off en keep things a-movin'. Dey wuz a nigger name' Bob, dat had ketched a wood-flat, en his marster didn' know it; en I bought it off'n him en told him to take de thirty-five dollars when de en' er de year come; but somebody stole de wood-flat dat night, en nex' day de one-laigged nigger say de bank's busted. So dey didn' none uv us git no money."

"What did you do with the ten cents, Jim?"

"Well, I 'uz gwyne to spen' it, but I had a dream, en de dream tole me to give it to a nigger name' Balum—Balum's Ass dey call him for short; he's one er dem chuckleheads, you know. But he's lucky, dey say, en I see I warn't lucky. De dream say let Balum inves' de ten cents en he'd make a raise for me. Well, Balum he tuck de money, en when he wuz in church he hear de preacher say dat whoever give to de po' len' to de Lord, en boun' to git his money back a hund'd times. So Balum he tuck en give de ten cents to de po', en laid low to see what wuz gwyne to come of it."

"Well, what did come of it, Jim?"

"Nuffn never come of it. I couldn' manage to k'leck dat money no way; en Balum he couldn'. I ain' gwyne to len' no mo' money 'dout I see de security. Boun' to git yo' money back a hund'd times, de preacher says! Ef I could git de ten CENTS back, I'd call it squah, en be glad er de chanst."

"Well, it's all right anyway, Jim, long as you're going to be rich again some time or other."

"Yes; en I's rich now, come to look at it. I owns mysef, en I's wuth eight hund'd dollars. I wisht I had de money, I wouldn' want no mo'."

CHAPTER IX.

I WANTED to go and look at a place right about the middle of the island that I'd found when I was exploring; so we started and soon got to it, because the island was only three miles long and a quarter of a mile wide.

This place was a tolerable long, steep hill or ridge about forty foot high. We had a rough time getting to the top, the sides was so steep and the bushes so thick. We tramped and clumb around all over it, and by and by found a good big cavern in the rock, most up to the top on the side towards Illinois. The cavern was as big as two or three rooms bunched together, and Jim could stand up straight in it. It was cool in there. Jim was for putting our traps in there right away, but I said we didn't want to be climbing up and down there all the time.

Jim said if we had the canoe hid in a good place, and had all the traps in the cavern, we could rush there if anybody was to come to the island, and they would never find us without dogs. And, besides, he said them little birds had said it was going to rain, and did I want the things to get wet?

So we went back and got the canoe, and paddled up abreast the cavern, and lugged all the traps up there. Then we hunted up a place close by to hide the canoe in, amongst the thick willows. We took some fish off of the lines and set them again, and begun to get ready for dinner.

The door of the cavern was big enough to roll a hogshead in, and on one side of the door the floor stuck out a little bit, and was flat and a good place to build a fire on. So we built it there and cooked dinner.

We spread the blankets inside for a carpet, and eat our dinner in there. We put all the other things handy at the back of the cavern. Pretty soon it darkened up, and begun to thunder and lighten; so the birds was right about it. Directly it begun to rain, and it rained like all fury, too, and I never see the wind blow so. It was one of these regular summer storms. It would get so dark that it looked all blue-black outside, and lovely;

and the rain would thrash along by so thick that the trees off a little ways looked dim and spider-webby; and here would come a blast of wind that would bend the trees down and turn up the pale underside of the leaves; and then a perfect ripper of a gust would follow along and set the branches to tossing their arms as if they was just wild; and next, when it was just about the bluest and blackest—FST! it was as bright as glory, and you'd have a little glimpse of tree-tops a-plunging about away off yonder in the storm, hundreds of yards further than you could see before; dark as sin again in a second, and now you'd hear the thunder let go with an awful crash, and then go rumbling, grumbling, tumbling, down the sky towards the under side of the world, like rolling empty barrels down stairs—where it's long stairs and they bounce a good deal, you know.

"Jim, this is nice," I says. "I wouldn't want to be nowhere else but here. Pass me along another hunk of fish and some hot corn-bread."

"Well, you wouldn't a ben here 'f it hadn't a ben for Jim. You'd a ben down dah in de woods widout any dinner, en gittn' mos' drownded, too; dat you would, honey. Chickens knows when it's gwyne to rain, en so do de birds, chile."

The river went on raising and raising for ten or twelve days, till at last it was over the banks. The water was three or four foot deep on the island in the low places and on the Illinois bottom. On that side it was a good many miles wide, but on the Missouri side it was the same old distance across—a half a mile—because the Missouri shore was just a wall of high bluffs.

Daytimes we paddled all over the island in the canoe, It was mighty cool and shady in the deep woods, even if the sun was blazing outside. We went winding in and out amongst the trees, and sometimes the vines hung so thick we had to back away and go some other way. Well, on every old broken-down tree you could see rabbits and snakes and such things; and when the island had been overflowed a day or two they got so tame, on account of being hungry, that you could paddle right up and put your hand on them if you wanted to; but not the snakes and turtles—they would slide off in the water. The ridge our cavern was in was full of them. We could a had pets enough if we'd wanted them.

One night we catched a little section of a lumber raft—nice pine planks. It was twelve foot wide and about fifteen or sixteen foot long, and the top stood above water six or seven inches—a solid, level floor. We could see saw-logs go by in the daylight sometimes, but we let them go; we didn't show ourselves in daylight.

Another night when we was up at the head of the island, just before daylight, here comes a frame-house down, on the west side. She was a two-story, and tilted over considerable. We paddled out and got aboard —clumb in at an upstairs window. But it was too dark to see yet, so we made the canoe fast and set in her to wait for daylight.

The light begun to come before we got to the foot of the island. Then we looked in at the window. We could make out a bed, and a table, and two old chairs, and lots of things around about on the floor, and there was clothes hanging against the wall. There was something laying on the floor in the far corner that looked like a man. So Jim says:

"Hello, you!"

But it didn't budge. So I hollered again, and then Jim says:

"De man ain't asleep—he's dead. You hold still—I'll go en see."

He went, and bent down and looked, and says:

"It's a dead man. Yes, indeedy; naked, too. He's ben shot in de back. I reck'n he's ben dead two er three days. Come in, Huck, but doan' look at his face—it's too gashly."

I didn't look at him at all. Jim throwed some old rags over him, but he needn't done it; I didn't want to see him. There was heaps of old greasy cards scattered around over the floor, and old whisky bottles, and a couple of masks made out of black cloth; and all over the walls was the ignorantest kind of words and pictures made with charcoal. There was two old dirty calico dresses, and a sun-bonnet, and some women's underclothes hanging against the wall, and some men's clothing, too. We put the lot into the canoe—it might come good. There was a boy's old speckled straw hat on the floor; I took that, too. And there was a bottle that had had milk in it, and it had a rag stopper for a baby to suck. We would a took the bottle, but it was broke. There was a seedy old chest, and an old hair trunk with the hinges broke. They stood open, but there warn't nothing left in them that was any account. The way things was scattered about we reckoned the people left in a hurry, and warn't fixed so as to carry off most of their stuff.

We got an old tin lantern, and a butcher-knife without any handle, and a bran-new Barlow knife worth two bits in any store, and a lot of tallow candles, and a tin candlestick, and a gourd, and a tin cup, and a ratty old bedquilt off the bed, and a reticule with needles and pins and beeswax and buttons and thread and all such truck in it, and a hatchet and some nails, and a fishline as thick as my little finger with some monstrous hooks on it, and a roll of buckskin, and a leather dog-collar, and a horseshoe, and some vials of medicine that didn't have no label on them; and just as we was leaving I found a tolerable good curry-comb, and Jim he found a ratty old fiddle-bow, and a wooden leg. The straps was broke off of it, but, barring that, it was a good enough leg, though it was too long for me and not long enough for Jim, and we couldn't find the other one, though we hunted all around.

And so, take it all around, we made a good haul. When we was ready to shove off we was a quarter of a mile below the island, and it was pretty broad day; so I made Jim lay down in the canoe and cover up with the quilt, because if he set up people could tell he was a nigger a good ways off. I paddled over to the Illinois shore, and drifted down most a half a mile doing it. I crept up the dead water under the bank, and hadn't no accidents and didn't see nobody. We got home all safe.

CHAPTER X.

AFTER breakfast I wanted to talk about the dead man and guess out how he come to be killed, but Jim didn't want to. He said it would fetch bad luck; and besides, he said, he might come and ha'nt us; he said a man that warn't buried was more likely to go a-ha'nting around than one that was planted and comfortable. That sounded pretty reasonable, so I didn't say no more; but I couldn't keep from studying over it and wishing I knowed who shot the man, and what they done it for.

We rummaged the clothes we'd got, and found eight dollars in silver sewed up in the lining of an old blanket overcoat. Jim said he reckoned the people in that house stole the coat, because if they'd a knowed the money was there they wouldn't a left it. I said I reckoned they killed him, too; but Jim didn't want to talk about that. I says:

"Now you think it's bad luck; but what did you say when I fetched in the snake-skin that I found on the top of the ridge day before yesterday? You said it was the worst bad luck in the world to touch a snake-skin with my hands. Well, here's your bad luck! We've raked in all this truck and eight dollars besides. I wish we could have some bad luck like this every day, Jim."

"Never you mind, honey, never you mind. Don't you git too peart. It's a-comin'. Mind I tell you, it's a-comin'."

It did come, too. It was a Tuesday that we had that talk. Well, after dinner Friday we was laying around in the grass at the upper end of the ridge, and got out of tobacco. I went to the cavern to get some, and found a rattlesnake in there. I killed him, and curled him up on the foot of Jim's blanket, ever so natural, thinking there'd be some fun when Jim found him there. Well, by night I forgot all about the snake, and when Jim flung himself down on the blanket while I struck a light the snake's mate was there, and bit him.

He jumped up yelling, and the first thing the light showed was the varmint curled up and ready for another spring. I laid him out in a second with a stick, and Jim grabbed pap's whisky-jug and begun to pour it down.

He was barefooted, and the snake bit him right on the heel. That all comes of my being such a fool as to not remember that wherever you leave a dead snake its mate always comes there and curls around it. Jim told me to chop off the snake's head and throw it away, and then skin the body and roast a piece of it. I done it, and he eat it and said it would help cure him. He made me take off the rattles and tie them around his wrist, too. He said that that would help. Then I slid out quiet and throwed the snakes clear away amongst the bushes; for I warn't going to let Jim find out it was all my fault, not if I could help it.

Jim sucked and sucked at the jug, and now and then he got out of his head and pitched around and yelled; but every time he come to himself he went to sucking at the jug again. His foot swelled up pretty big, and so did his leg; but by and by the drunk begun to come, and so I judged he was all right; but I'd druther been bit with a snake than pap's whisky.

Jim was laid up for four days and nights. Then the swelling was all gone and he was around again. I made up my mind I wouldn't ever take a-holt of a snake-skin again with my hands, now that I see what had come of it. Jim said he reckoned I would believe him next time. And he said that handling a snake-skin was such awful bad luck that maybe we hadn't got to the end of it yet. He said he druther see the new moon over his left shoulder as much as a thousand times than take up a snake-skin in his hand. Well, I was getting to feel that way myself, though I've always reckoned that looking at the new moon over your left shoulder is one of the carelessest and foolishest things a body can do. Old Hank Bunker done it once, and bragged about it; and in less than two years he got drunk and fell off of the shot-tower, and spread himself out so that he was just a kind of a layer, as you may say; and they slid him edgeways between two barn doors for a coffin, and buried him so, so they say, but I didn't see it. Pap told me. But anyway it all come of looking at the moon that way, like a fool.

Well, the days went along, and the river went down between its banks again; and about the first thing we done was to bait one of the big hooks with a skinned rabbit and set it and catch a catfish that was as big as a man, being six foot two inches long, and weighed over two hundred pounds. We couldn't handle him, of course; he would a flung us into Illinois. We just set there and watched him rip and tear around till he drownded. We found a brass button in his stomach and a round ball, and lots of rubbage. We split the ball open with the hatchet, and there was a spool in it. Jim said he'd had it there a long time, to coat it over so and make a ball of it. It was as big a fish as was ever catched in the Mississippi, I reckon. Jim said he hadn't ever seen a bigger one. He would a been worth a good deal over at the village. They peddle out such a fish as that by the pound in the market-house there; everybody buys some of him; his meat's as white as snow and makes a good fry.

Next morning I said it was getting slow and dull, and I wanted to get a stirring up some way. I said I reckoned I would slip over the river and find out what was going on. Jim liked that notion; but he said I must go in the dark and look sharp. Then he studied it over and said, couldn't I put on some of them old things and dress up like a girl? That was a good notion, too. So we shortened up one of the calico gowns, and I turned up my trouser-legs to my knees and got into it. Jim hitched it behind with the hooks, and it was a fair fit. I put on the sun-bonnet and tied it under my chin, and then for a body to look in and see my face was like looking down a joint of stove-pipe. Jim said nobody would know me, even in the daytime, hardly. I practiced around all day to get the hang of the things, and by and by I could do pretty well in them, only Jim said I didn't walk like a girl; and he said I must quit pulling up my gown to get at my britches-pocket. I took notice, and done better.

I started up the Illinois shore in the canoe just after dark.

I started across to the town from a little below the ferry-landing, and the drift of the current fetched me in at the bottom of the town. I tied up and started along the bank. There was a light burning in a little shanty that hadn't been lived in for a long time, and I wondered who had took up quarters there. I slipped up and peeped in at the window. There was a woman about forty year old in there knitting by a candle that was on a pine table. I didn't know her face; she was a stranger, for you couldn't start a face in that town that I didn't know. Now this was lucky, because I was weakening; I was getting afraid I had come; people might know my voice and find me out. But if this woman had been in such a little town two days she could tell me all I wanted to know; so I knocked at the door, and made up my mind I wouldn't forget I was a girl.

CHAPTER XI.

"COME in," says the woman, and I did. She says: "Take a cheer."

I done it. She looked me all over with her little shiny eyes, and says:

"What might your name be?"

"Sarah Williams."

"Where 'bouts do you live? In this neighborhood?'

"No'm. In Hookerville, seven mile below. I've walked all the

way and I'm all tired out."

"Hungry, too, I reckon. I'll find you something."

"No'm, I ain't hungry. I was so hungry I had to stop two miles below here at a farm; so I ain't hungry no more. It's what makes me so late. My mother's down sick, and out of money and everything, and I come to tell my uncle Abner Moore. He lives at the upper end of the town, she says. I hain't ever been here before. Do you know him?"

"No; but I don't know everybody yet. I haven't lived here quite two weeks. It's a considerable ways to the upper end of the town. You better stay here all night. Take off your bonnet."

"No," I says; "I'll rest a while, I reckon, and go on. I ain't afeared of the dark."

She said she wouldn't let me go by myself, but her husband would be in by and by, maybe in a hour and a half, and she'd send him along with me. Then she got to talking about her husband, and about her relations up the river, and her relations down the river, and about how much better off they used to was, and how they didn't know but they'd made a mistake coming to our town, instead of letting well alone—and so on and so on, till I was afeard I had made a mistake coming to her to find out what was going on in the town; but by and by she dropped on to pap and the murder, and then I was pretty willing to let her clatter right along. She told about me and Tom Sawyer finding the six thousand dollars (only she got it ten) and all about pap and what a hard lot he was, and what a hard lot I was, and at last she got down to where I was murdered. I says:

"Who done it? We've heard considerable about these goings on down in Hookerville, but we don't know who 'twas that killed Huck Finn."

"Well, I reckon there's a right smart chance of people HERE that'd like to know who killed him. Some think old Finn done it himself."

"No—is that so?"

"Most everybody thought it at first. He'll never know how nigh he come to getting lynched. But before night they changed around and judged it was done by a runaway nigger named Jim."

"Why HE—"

I stopped. I reckoned I better keep still. She run on, and never noticed I had put in at all:

"The nigger run off the very night Huck Finn was killed. So there's a reward out for him—three hundred dollars. And there's a reward out for old Finn, too—two hundred dollars. You see, he come to town the morning after the murder, and told about it, and was out with 'em on the ferryboat hunt, and right away after he up and left. Before night they wanted to lynch him, but he was gone, you see. Well, next day they found out the nigger was gone; they found out he hadn't ben seen sence ten o'clock the night the murder was done. So then they put it on him, you see; and while they was full of it, next day, back comes old Finn, and went boo-hooing to Judge Thatcher to get money to hunt for the nigger all over Illinois with. The judge gave him some, and that evening he got drunk, and was around till after midnight with a couple of mighty hard-looking strangers, and then went off with them. Well, he hain't come back sence, and they ain't looking for him back till this thing blows over a little, for people thinks now that he killed his boy and fixed things so folks would think robbers done it, and then he'd get Huck's money without having to bother a long time with a lawsuit. People do say he warn't any too good to do it. Oh, he's sly, I reckon. If he don't come back for a year he'll be all right. You can't prove anything on him, you know; everything will be quieted down then, and he'll walk in Huck's money as easy as nothing."

"Yes, I reckon so, 'm. I don't see nothing in the way of it. Has everybody quit thinking the nigger done it?"

"Oh, no, not everybody. A good many thinks he done it. But they'll get the nigger pretty soon now, and maybe they can scare it out of him."

"Why, are they after him yet?"

"Well, you're innocent, ain't you! Does three hundred dollars lay around every day for people to pick up? Some folks think the nigger ain't far from here. I'm one of them—but I hain't talked it around. A few days ago I was talking with an old couple that lives next door in the log shanty, and they happened to say hardly anybody ever goes to that island over yonder that they call Jackson's Island. Don't anybody live there? says I. No, nobody, says they. I didn't say any more, but I done some thinking. I was pretty near certain I'd seen smoke over there, about the head of the island, a day or two before that, so I says to myself, like as not that nigger's hiding over there; anyway, says I, it's worth the trouble to give the place a hunt. I hain't seen any smoke sence, so I reckon maybe he's gone, if it was him; but husband's going over to see —him and another man. He was gone up the river; but he got back to-day, and I told him as soon as he got here two hours ago."

I had got so uneasy I couldn't set still. I had to do something with my hands; so I took up a needle off of the table and went to threading it. My hands shook, and I was making a bad job of it. When the woman stopped talking I looked up, and she was looking at me pretty curious and smiling a little. I put down the needle and thread, and let on to be interested —and I was, too—and says:

"Three hundred dollars is a power of money. I wish my mother could get it. Is your husband going over there to-night?"

"Oh, yes. He went up-town with the man I was telling you of, to get a boat and see if they could borrow another gun. They'll go over after midnight."

"Couldn't they see better if they was to wait till daytime?"

"Yes. And couldn't the nigger see better, too? After midnight he'll likely be asleep, and they can slip around through the woods and hunt up his camp fire all the better for the dark, if he's got one."

"I didn't think of that."

The woman kept looking at me pretty curious, and I didn't feel a bit comfortable. Pretty soon she says"

"What did you say your name was, honey?"

"M—Mary Williams."

Somehow it didn't seem to me that I said it was Mary before, so I didn't look up—seemed to me I said it was Sarah; so I felt sort of cornered, and was afeared maybe I was looking it, too. I wished the woman would say something more; the longer she set still the uneasier I was. But now she says:

"Honey, I thought you said it was Sarah when you first come in?"

"Oh, yes'm, I did. Sarah Mary Williams. Sarah's my first name. Some calls me Sarah, some calls me Mary."

"Oh, that's the way of it?"

"Yes'm."

I was feeling better then, but I wished I was out of there, anyway. I couldn't look up yet.

Well, the woman fell to talking about how hard times was, and how poor they had to live, and how the rats was as free as if they owned the place, and so forth and so on, and then I got easy again. She was right about the rats. You'd see one stick his nose out of a hole in the corner every little while. She said she had to have things handy to throw at them when she was alone, or they wouldn't give her no peace. She showed me a bar of lead twisted up into a knot, and said she was a good shot with it generly, but she'd wrenched her arm a day or two ago, and didn't know whether she could throw true now. But she watched for a chance, and directly banged away at a rat; but she missed him wide, and said "Ouch!" it hurt her arm so. Then she told me to try for the next one. I wanted to be getting away before the old man got back, but of course I didn't let on. I got the thing, and the first rat that showed his nose I let drive, and if he'd a stayed where he was he'd a been a tolerable sick rat. She said that was first-rate, and she reckoned I would hive the next one. She went and got the lump of lead and fetched it back, and brought along a hank of yarn which she wanted me to help her with. I held up my two hands and she put the hank over them, and went on talking about her and her husband's matters. But she broke off to say:

"Keep your eye on the rats. You better have the lead in your lap, handy."

So she dropped the lump into my lap just at that moment, and I clapped my legs together on it and she went on talking. But only about a minute. Then she took off the hank and looked me straight in the face, and very pleasant, and says:

"Come, now, what's your real name?"

"Wh—what, mum?"

"What's your real name? Is it Bill, or Tom, or Bob?—or what is it?"

I reckon I shook like a leaf, and I didn't know hardly what to do. But I says:

"Please to don't poke fun at a poor girl like me, mum. If I'm in the way here, I'll—"

"No, you won't. Set down and stay where you are. I ain't going to hurt you, and I ain't going to tell on you, nuther. You just tell me your secret, and trust me. I'll keep it; and, what's more, I'll help you. So'll my old man if you want him to. You see, you're a runaway 'prentice, that's all. It ain't anything. There ain't no harm in it. You've been treated bad, and you made up your mind to cut. Bless you, child, I wouldn't tell on you. Tell me all about it now, that's a good boy."

So I said it wouldn't be no use to try to play it any longer, and I would just make a clean breast and tell her everything, but she musn't go back on her promise. Then I told her my father and mother was dead, and the law had bound me out to a mean old farmer in the country thirty mile back from the river, and he treated me so bad I couldn't stand it no longer; he went away to be gone a couple of days, and so I took my chance and stole some of his daughter's old clothes and cleared out, and I had been three nights coming the thirty miles. I traveled nights, and hid daytimes and slept, and the bag of bread and meat I carried from home lasted me all the way, and I had a-plenty. I said I believed my uncle Abner Moore would take care of me, and so that was why I struck out for this town of Goshen.

"Goshen, child? This ain't Goshen. This is St. Petersburg. Goshen's ten mile further up the river. Who told you this was Goshen?"

"Why, a man I met at daybreak this morning, just as I was going to turn into the woods for my regular sleep. He told me when the roads forked I must take the right hand, and five mile would fetch me to Goshen."

"He was drunk, I reckon. He told you just exactly wrong."

"Well, he did act like he was drunk, but it ain't no matter now. I got to be moving along. I'll fetch Goshen before daylight."

"Hold on a minute. I'll put you up a snack to eat. You might want it."

So she put me up a snack, and says:

"Say, when a cow's laying down, which end of her gets up first? Answer up prompt now—don't stop to study over it. Which end gets up first?"

"The hind end, mum."

"Well, then, a horse?"

"The for'rard end, mum."

"Which side of a tree does the moss grow on?"

"North side."

"If fifteen cows is browsing on a hillside, how many of them eats with their heads pointed the same direction?"

"The whole fifteen, mum."

"Well, I reckon you HAVE lived in the country. I thought maybe you was trying to hocus me again. What's your real name, now?"

"George Peters, mum."

"Well, try to remember it, George. Don't forget and tell me it's Elexander before you go, and then get out by saying it's George Elexander when I catch you. And don't go about women in that old calico. You do a girl tolerable poor, but you might fool men, maybe. Bless you, child, when you set out to thread a needle don't hold the thread still and fetch the needle up to it;

hold the needle still and poke the thread at it; that's the way a woman most always does, but a man always does t'other way. And when you throw at a rat or anything, hitch yourself up a tiptoe and fetch your hand up over your head as awkward as you can, and miss your rat about six or seven foot. Throw stiff-armed from the shoulder, like there was a pivot there for it to turn on, like a girl; not from the wrist and elbow, with your arm out to one side, like a boy. And, mind you, when a girl tries to catch anything in her lap she throws her knees apart; she don't clap them together, the way you did when you catched the lump of lead. Why, I spotted you for a boy when you was threading the needle; and I contrived the other things just to make certain. Now trot along to your uncle, Sarah Mary Williams George Elexander Peters, and if you get into trouble you send word to Mrs. Judith Loftus, which is me, and I'll do what I can to get you out of it. Keep the river road all the way, and next time you tramp take shoes and socks with you. The river road's a rocky one, and your feet'll be in a condition when you get to Goshen, I reckon."

I went up the bank about fifty yards, and then I doubled on my tracks and slipped back to where my canoe was, a good piece below the house. I jumped in, and was off in a hurry. I went up-stream far enough to make the head of the island, and then started across. I took off the sun-bonnet, for I didn't want no blinders on then. When I was about the middle I heard the clock begin to strike, so I stops and listens; the sound come faint over the water but clear—eleven. When I struck the head of the island I never waited to blow, though I was most winded, but I shoved right into the timber where my old camp used to be, and started a good fire there on a high and dry spot.

Then I jumped in the canoe and dug out for our place, a mile and a half below, as hard as I could go. I landed, and slopped through the timber and up the ridge and into the cavern. There Jim laid, sound asleep on the ground. I roused him out and says:

"Git up and hump yourself, Jim! There ain't a minute to lose. They're after us!"

Jim never asked no questions, he never said a word; but the way he worked for the next half an hour showed about how he was scared. By that time everything we had in the world was on our raft, and she was ready to be shoved out from the willow cove where she was hid. We put out the camp fire at the cavern the first thing, and didn't show a candle outside after that.

I took the canoe out from the shore a little piece, and took a look; but if there was a boat around I couldn't see it, for stars and shadows ain't good to see by. Then we got out the raft and slipped along down in the shade, past the foot of the island dead still—never saying a word.

CHAPTER XII.

IT must a been close on to one o'clock when we got below the island at last, and the raft did seem to go mighty slow. If a boat was to come along we was going to take to the canoe and break for the Illinois shore; and it was well a boat didn't come, for we hadn't ever thought to put the gun in the canoe, or a fishing-line, or anything to eat. We was in ruther too much of a sweat to think of so many things. It warn't good judgment to put EVERYTHING on the raft.

If the men went to the island I just expect they found the camp fire I built, and watched it all night for Jim to come. Anyways, they stayed away from us, and if my building the fire never fooled them it warn't no fault of mine. I played it as low down on them as I could.

When the first streak of day began to show we tied up to a towhead in a big bend on the Illinois side, and hacked off cottonwood branches with the hatchet, and covered up the raft with them so she looked like there had been a cave-in in the bank there. A tow-head is a sandbar that has cottonwoods on it as thick as harrow-teeth.

We had mountains on the Missouri shore and heavy timber on the Illinois side, and the channel was down the Missouri shore at that place, so we warn't afraid of anybody running across us. We laid there all day, and watched the rafts and steamboats spin down the Missouri shore, and up-bound steamboats fight the big river in the middle. I told Jim all about the time I had jabbering with that woman; and Jim said she was a smart one, and if she was to start after us herself she wouldn't set down and watch a camp fire—no, sir, she'd fetch a dog. Well, then, I said, why couldn't she tell her husband to fetch a dog? Jim said he bet she did think of it by the time the men was ready to start, and he believed they must a gone up-town to get a dog and so they lost all that time, or else we wouldn't be here on a towhead sixteen or seventeen mile below the village—no, indeedy, we would be in that same old town again. So I said I didn't care what was the reason they didn't get us as long as they didn't.

When it was beginning to come on dark we poked our heads out of the cottonwood thicket, and looked up and down and across; nothing in sight; so Jim took up some of the top planks of the raft and built a snug wigwam to get under in blazing weather and rainy, and to keep the things dry. Jim made a floor for the wigwam, and raised it a foot or more above the level of the raft, so now the blankets and all the traps was out of reach of steamboat waves. Right in the middle of the wigwam we made a layer of dirt about five or six inches deep with a frame around it for to hold it to its place; this was to build a fire on in sloppy weather or chilly; the wigwam would keep it from being seen. We made an extra steering-oar, too, because one of the others might get broke on a snag or something. We fixed up a short forked stick to hang the old lantern on, because we must always light the lantern whenever we see a steamboat coming down-stream, to keep from getting run over; but we wouldn't have to light it for up-stream boats unless we see we was in what they call a "crossing"; for the river was pretty high yet, very low banks being still a little under water; so up-bound boats didn't always run the channel, but hunted easy water.

This second night we run between seven and eight hours, with a current that was making over four mile an hour. We catched fish and talked, and we took a swim now and then to keep off sleepiness. It was kind of solemn, drifting down the big, still river, laying on our backs looking up at the stars, and we didn't ever feel like talking loud, and it warn't often that we laughed—only a little kind of a low chuckle. We had mighty good weather as a general thing, and nothing ever happened to us at all—that night, nor the next, nor the next.

Every night we passed towns, some of them away up on black hillsides, nothing but just a shiny bed of lights; not a house could you see. The fifth night we passed St. Louis, and it was like the whole world lit up. In St. Petersburg they used to say there was twenty or thirty thousand people in St. Louis, but I never believed it till I see that wonderful spread of lights at two o'clock that still night. There warn't a sound there; everybody was asleep.

Every night now I used to slip ashore towards ten o'clock at some little village, and buy ten or fifteen cents' worth of meal or bacon or other stuff to eat; and sometimes I lifted a chicken that warn't roosting comfortable, and took him along. Pap always said, take a chicken when you get a chance, because if you don't want him yourself you can easy find somebody that does, and a good deed ain't ever forgot. I never see pap when he didn't want the chicken himself, but that is what he used to say, anyway.

Mornings before daylight I slipped into cornfields and borrowed a watermelon, or a mushmelon, or a punkin, or some new corn, or things of that kind. Pap always said it warn't no harm to borrow things if you was meaning to pay them back some time; but the widow said it warn't anything but a soft name for stealing, and no decent body would do it. Jim said he reckoned the widow was partly right and pap was partly right; so the best way would be for us to pick out two or three things from the list and say we wouldn't borrow them any more—then he reckoned it wouldn't be no harm to borrow the others. So we talked it over all one night, drifting along down the river, trying to make up our minds whether to drop the watermelons, or the cantelopes, or the mushmelons, or what. But towards daylight we got it all settled satisfactory, and concluded to drop crabapples and p'simmons. We warn't feeling just right before that, but it was all comfortable now. I was glad the way it come out, too, because crabapples ain't ever good, and the p'simmons wouldn't be ripe for two or three months yet.

We shot a water-fowl now and then that got up too early in the morning or didn't go to bed early enough in the evening. Take it all round, we lived pretty high.

The fifth night below St. Louis we had a big storm after midnight, with a power of thunder and lightning, and the rain poured down in a solid sheet. We stayed in the wigwam and let the raft take care of itself. When the lightning glared out we could see a big straight river ahead, and high, rocky bluffs on both sides. By and by says I, "Hel-LO, Jim, looky yonder!" It was a steamboat that had killed herself on a rock. We was drifting straight down for her. The lightning showed her very distinct. She was leaning over, with part of her upper deck above water, and you could see every little chimbly-guy clean and clear, and a chair by the big bell, with an old slouch hat hanging on the back of it, when the flashes come.

Well, it being away in the night and stormy, and all so mysterious-like, I felt just the way any other boy would a felt when I see that wreck laying there so mournful and lonesome in the middle of the river. I wanted to get aboard of her and slink around a little, and see what there was there. So I says:

"Le's land on her, Jim."

But Jim was dead against it at first. He says:

"I doan' want to go fool'n 'long er no wrack. We's doin' blame' well, en we better let blame' well alone, as de good book says. Like as not dey's a watchman on dat wrack."

"Watchman your grandmother," I says; "there ain't nothing to watch but the texas and the pilot-house; and do you reckon anybody's going to resk his life for a texas and a pilot-house such a night as this, when it's likely to break up and wash off down the river any minute?" Jim couldn't say nothing to that, so he didn't try. "And besides," I says, "we might borrow something worth having out of the captain's stateroom. Seegars, I bet you—and cost five cents apiece, solid cash. Steamboat captains is always rich, and get sixty dollars a month, and THEY don't care a cent what a thing costs, you know, long as they want it. Stick a candle in your pocket; I can't rest, Jim, till we give her a rummaging. Do you reckon Tom Sawyer would ever go by this thing? Not for pie, he wouldn't. He'd call it an adventure—that's what he'd call it; and he'd land on that wreck if it was his last act. And wouldn't he throw style into it? —wouldn't he spread himself, nor nothing? Why, you'd think it was Christopher C'lumbus discovering Kingdom-Come. I wish Tom Sawyer WAS here."

Jim he grumbled a little, but give in. He said we mustn't talk any more than we could help, and then talk mighty low. The lightning showed us the wreck again just in time, and we fetched the stabboard derrick, and made fast there.

The deck was high out here. We went sneaking down the slope of it to labboard, in the dark, towards the texas, feeling our way slow with our feet, and spreading our hands out to fend off the guys, for it was so dark we couldn't see no sign of them. Pretty soon we struck the forward end of the skylight, and clumb on to it; and the next step fetched us in front of the captain's door, which was open, and by Jimminy, away down through the texas-hall we see a light! and all in the same second we seem to hear low voices in yonder!

Jim whispered and said he was feeling powerful sick, and told me to come along. I says, all right, and was going to start for the raft; but just then I heard a voice wail out and say:

"Oh, please don't, boys; I swear I won't ever tell!"

Another voice said, pretty loud:

"It's a lie, Jim Turner. You've acted this way before. You always want more'n your share of the truck, and you've always got it, too, because you've swore 't if you didn't you'd tell. But this time you've said it jest one time too many. You're the meanest, treacherousest hound in this country."

By this time Jim was gone for the raft. I was just a-biling with curiosity; and I says to myself, Tom Sawyer wouldn't back out now, and so I won't either; I'm a-going to see what's going on here. So I dropped on my hands and knees in the little passage, and crept aft in the dark till there warn't but one stateroom betwixt me and the cross-hall of the texas. Then in there I see a man stretched on the floor and tied hand and foot, and two men standing over him, and one of them had a dim lantern in his hand, and the other one had a pistol. This one kept pointing the pistol at the man's head on the floor, and saying:

"I'd LIKE to! And I orter, too—a mean skunk!"

The man on the floor would shrivel up and say, "Oh, please don't, Bill; I hain't ever goin' to tell."

And every time he said that the man with the lantern would laugh and say:

"'Deed you AIN'T! You never said no truer thing 'n that, you bet you." And once he said: "Hear him beg! and yit if we hadn't got the best of him and tied him he'd a killed us both. And what FOR? Jist for noth'n. Jist because we stood on our

RIGHTS—that's what for. But I lay you ain't a-goin' to threaten nobody any more, Jim Turner. Put UP that pistol, Bill."

Bill says:

"I don't want to, Jake Packard. I'm for killin' him—and didn't he kill old Hatfield jist the same way—and don't he deserve it?"

"But I don't WANT him killed, and I've got my reasons for it."

"Bless yo' heart for them words, Jake Packard! I'll never forgit you long's I live!" says the man on the floor, sort of blubbering.

Packard didn't take no notice of that, but hung up his lantern on a nail and started towards where I was there in the dark, and motioned Bill to come. I crawfished as fast as I could about two yards, but the boat slanted so that I couldn't make very good time; so to keep from getting run over and catched I crawled into a stateroom on the upper side. The man came a-pawing along in the dark, and when Packard got to my stateroom, he says:

"Here—come in here."

And in he come, and Bill after him. But before they got in I was up in the upper berth, cornered, and sorry I come. Then they stood there, with their hands on the ledge of the berth, and talked. I couldn't see them, but I could tell where they was by the whisky they'd been having. I was glad I didn't drink whisky; but it wouldn't made much difference anyway, because most of the time they couldn't a treed me because I didn't breathe. I was too scared. And, besides, a body COULDN'T breathe and hear such talk. They talked low and earnest. Bill wanted to kill Turner. He says:

"He's said he'll tell, and he will. If we was to give both our shares to him NOW it wouldn't make no difference after the row and the way we've served him. Shore's you're born, he'll turn State's evidence; now you hear ME. I'm for putting him out of his troubles."

"So'm I," says Packard, very quiet.

"Blame it, I'd sorter begun to think you wasn't. Well, then, that's all right. Le's go and do it."

"Hold on a minute; I hain't had my say yit. You listen to me. Shooting's good, but there's quieter ways if the thing's GOT to be done. But what I say is this: it ain't good sense to go court'n around after a halter if you can git at what you're up to in some way that's jist as good and at the same time don't bring you into no resks. Ain't that so?"

"You bet it is. But how you goin' to manage it this time?"

"Well, my idea is this: we'll rustle around and gather up whatever pickins we've overlooked in the staterooms, and shove for shore and hide the truck. Then we'll wait. Now I say it ain't a-goin' to be more'n two hours befo' this wrack breaks up and washes off down the river. See? He'll be drownded, and won't have nobody to blame for it but his own self. I reckon that's a considerble sight better 'n killin' of him. I'm unfavorable to killin' a man as long as you can git aroun' it; it ain't good sense, it ain't good morals. Ain't I right?"

"Yes, I reck'n you are. But s'pose she DON'T break up and wash off?"

"Well, we can wait the two hours anyway and see, can't we?"

"All right, then; come along."

So they started, and I lit out, all in a cold sweat, and scrambled forward. It was dark as pitch there; but I said, in a kind of a coarse whisper, "Jim !" and he answered up, right at my elbow, with a sort of a moan, and I says:

"Quick, Jim, it ain't no time for fooling around and moaning; there's a gang of murderers in yonder, and if we don't hunt up their boat and set her drifting down the river so these fellows can't get away from the wreck there's one of 'em going to be in a bad fix. But if we find their boat we can put ALL of 'em in a bad fix—for the sheriff 'll get 'em. Quick—hurry! I'll hunt the labboard side, you hunt the stabboard. You start at the raft, and—"

"Oh, my lordy, lordy! RAF'? Dey ain' no raf' no mo'; she done broke loose en gone I—en here we is!"

CHAPTER XIII.

WELL, I catched my breath and most fainted. Shut up on a wreck with such a gang as that! But it warn't no time to be sentimentering. We'd GOT to find that boat now—had to have it for ourselves. So we went a-quaking and shaking down the stabboard side, and slow work it was, too—seemed a week before we got to the stern. No sign of a boat. Jim said he didn't believe he could go any further—so scared he hadn't hardly any strength left, he said. But I said, come on, if we get left on this wreck we are in a fix, sure. So on we prowled again. We struck for the stern of the texas, and found it, and then scrabbled along forwards on the skylight, hanging on from shutter to shutter, for the edge of the skylight was in the water. When we got pretty close to the cross-hall door there was the skiff, sure enough! I could just barely see her. I felt ever so thankful. In another second I would a been aboard of her, but just then the door opened. One of the men stuck his head out only about a couple of foot from me, and I thought I was gone; but he jerked it in again, and says:

"Heave that blame lantern out o' sight, Bill!"

He flung a bag of something into the boat, and then got in himself and set down. It was Packard. Then Bill HE come out and got in. Packard says, in a low voice:

"All ready—shove off!"

I couldn't hardly hang on to the shutters, I was so weak. But Bill says:

"Hold on—'d you go through him?"

"No. Didn't you?"

"No. So he's got his share o' the cash yet."

"Well, then, come along; no use to take truck and leave money."

"Say, won't he suspicion what we're up to?"

"Maybe he won't. But we got to have it anyway. Come along."

So they got out and went in.

The door slammed to because it was on the careened side; and in a half second I was in the boat, and Jim come tumbling after me. I out with my knife and cut the rope, and away we went!

We didn't touch an oar, and we didn't speak nor whisper, nor hardly even breathe. We went gliding swift along, dead silent, past the tip of the paddle-box, and past the stern; then in a second or two more we was a hundred yards below the wreck, and the darkness soaked her up, every last sign of her, and we was safe, and knowed it.

When we was three or four hundred yards down-stream we see the lantern show like a little spark at the texas door for a second, and we knowed by that that the rascals had missed their boat, and was beginning to understand that they was in just as much trouble now as Jim Turner was.

Then Jim manned the oars, and we took out after our raft. Now was the first time that I begun to worry about the men—I reckon I hadn't had time to before. I begun to think how dreadful it was, even for murderers, to be in such a fix. I says to myself, there ain't no telling but I might come to be a murderer myself yet, and then how would I like it? So says I to Jim:

"The first light we see we'll land a hundred yards below it or above it, in a place where it's a good hiding-place for you and the skiff, and then I'll go and fix up some kind of a yarn, and get somebody to go for that gang and get them out of their scrape, so they can be hung when their time comes."

But that idea was a failure; for pretty soon it begun to storm again, and this time worse than ever. The rain poured down, and never a light showed; everybody in bed, I reckon. We boomed along down the river, watching for lights and watching for our raft. After a long time the rain let up, but the clouds stayed, and the lightning kept whimpering, and by and by a flash showed us a black thing ahead, floating, and we made for it.

It was the raft, and mighty glad was we to get aboard of it again. We seen a light now away down to the right, on shore. So I said I would go for it. The skiff was half full of plunder which that gang had stole there on the wreck. We hustled it on to the raft in a pile, and I told Jim to float along down, and show a light when he judged he had gone about two mile, and keep it burning till I come; then I manned my oars and shoved for the light. As I got down towards it three or four more showed—up on a hillside. It was a village. I closed in above the shore light, and laid on my oars and floated. As I went by I see it was a lantern hanging on the jackstaff of a double-hull ferryboat. I skimmed around for the watchman, a-wondering whereabouts he slept; and by and by I found him roosting on the bitts forward, with his head down between his knees. I gave his shoulder two or three little shoves, and begun to cry.

He stirred up in a kind of a startlish way; but when he see it was only me he took a good gap and stretch, and then he says:

"Hello, what's up? Don't cry, bub. What's the trouble?"

I says:

"Pap, and mam, and sis, and—"

Then I broke down. He says:

"Oh, dang it now, DON'T take on so; we all has to have our troubles, and this 'n 'll come out all right. What's the matter with 'em?"

"They're—they're—are you the watchman of the boat?"

"Yes," he says, kind of pretty-well-satisfied like. "I'm the captain and the owner and the mate and the pilot and watchman and head deck-hand; and sometimes I'm the freight and passengers. I ain't as rich as old Jim Hornback, and I can't be so blame' generous and good to Tom, Dick, and Harry as what he is, and slam around money the way he does; but I've told him a many a time 't I wouldn't trade places with him; for, says I, a sailor's life's the life for me, and I'm derned if I'D live two mile out o' town, where there ain't nothing ever goin' on, not for all his spondulicks and as much more on top of it. Says I—"

I broke in and says:

"They're in an awful peck of trouble, and—"

"WHO is?"

"Why, pap and mam and sis and Miss Hooker; and if you'd take your ferryboat and go up there—"

"Up where? Where are they?"

"On the wreck."

"What wreck?"

"Why, there ain't but one."

"What, you don't mean the Walter Scott?"

"Yes."

"Good land! what are they doin' THERE, for gracious sakes?"

"Well, they didn't go there a-purpose."

"I bet they didn't! Why, great goodness, there ain't no chance for 'em if they don't git off mighty quick! Why, how in the nation did they ever git into such a scrape?"

"Easy enough. Miss Hooker was a-visiting up there to the town—"

"Yes, Booth's Landing—go on."

"She was a-visiting there at Booth's Landing, and just in the edge of the evening she started over with her nigger woman in the horse-ferry to stay all night at her friend's house, Miss What-you-may-call-her I disremember her name—and they lost their steering-oar, and swung around and went a-floating down, stern first, about two mile, and saddle-baggsed on the wreck, and the ferryman and the nigger woman and the horses was all lost, but Miss Hooker she made a grab and got aboard the wreck. Well, about an hour after dark we come along down in our trading-scow, and it was so dark we didn't notice the wreck till we was right on it; and so WE saddle-baggsed; but all of us was saved but Bill Whipple—and oh, he WAS the best cretur !—I most wish 't it had been me, I do."

"My George! It's the beatenest thing I ever struck. And THEN

94 *Huckleberry Finn*

what did you all do?"

"Well, we hollered and took on, but it's so wide there we couldn't make nobody hear. So pap said somebody got to get ashore and get help somehow. I was the only one that could swim, so I made a dash for it, and Miss Hooker she said if I didn't strike help sooner, come here and hunt up her uncle, and he'd fix the thing. I made the land about a mile below, and been fooling along ever since, trying to get people to do something, but they said, 'What, in such a night and such a current? There ain't no sense in it; go for the steam ferry.' Now if you'll go and—"

"By Jackson, I'd LIKE to, and, blame it, I don't know but I will; but who in the dingnation's a-going' to PAY for it? Do you reckon your pap—"

"Why THAT'S all right. Miss Hooker she tole me, PARTICULAR, that her uncle Hornback—"

"Great guns! is HE her uncle? Looky here, you break for that light over yonder-way, and turn out west when you git there, and about a quarter of a mile out you'll come to the tavern; tell 'em to dart you out to Jim Hornback's, and he'll foot the bill. And don't you fool around any, because he'll want to know the news. Tell him I'll have his niece all safe before he can get to town. Hump yourself, now; I'm a-going up around the corner here to roust out my engineer."

I struck for the light, but as soon as he turned the corner I went back and got into my skiff and bailed her out, and then pulled up shore in the easy water about six hundred yards, and tucked myself in among some woodboats; for I couldn't rest easy till I could see the ferryboat start. But take it all around, I was feeling ruther comfortable on accounts of taking all this trouble for that gang, for not many would a done it. I wished the widow knowed about it. I judged she would be proud of me for helping these rapscallions, because rapscallions and dead beats is the kind the widow and good people takes the most interest in.

Well, before long here comes the wreck, dim and dusky, sliding along down! A kind of cold shiver went through me, and then I struck out for her. She was very deep, and I see in a minute there warn't much chance for anybody being alive in her. I pulled all around and hollered a little, but there wasn't any answer; all dead still. I felt a little bit heavy-hearted about the gang, but not much, for I reckoned if they could stand it I could.

Then here comes the ferryboat; so I shoved for the middle of the river on a long down-stream slant; and when I judged I was out of eye-reach I laid on my oars, and looked back and see her go and smell around the wreck for Miss Hooker's remainders, because the captain would know her uncle Hornback would want them; and then pretty soon the ferryboat give it up and went for the shore, and I laid into my work and went a-booming down the river.

It did seem a powerful long time before Jim's light showed up; and when it did show it looked like it was a thousand mile off. By the time I got there the sky was beginning to get a little gray in the east; so we struck for an island, and hid the raft, and sunk the skiff, and turned in and slept like dead people.

CHAPTER XIV.

BY and by, when we got up, we turned over the truck the gang had stole off of the wreck, and found boots, and blankets, and clothes, and all sorts of other things, and a lot of books, and a spyglass, and three boxes of seegars. We hadn't ever been this rich before in neither of our lives. The seegars was prime. We laid off all the afternoon in the woods talking, and me reading the books, and having a general good time. I told Jim all about what happened inside the wreck and at the ferryboat, and I said these kinds of things was adventures; but he said he didn't want no more adventures. He said that when I went in the texas and he crawled back to get on the raft and found her gone he nearly died, because he judged it was all up with HIM anyway it could be fixed; for if he didn't get saved he would get drownded; and if he did get saved, whoever saved him would send him back home so as to get the reward, and then Miss Watson would sell him South, sure. Well, he was right; he was most always right; he had an uncommon level head for a nigger.

I read considerable to Jim about kings and dukes and earls and such, and how gaudy they dressed, and how much style they put on, and called each other your majesty, and your grace, and your lordship, and so on, 'stead of mister; and Jim's eyes bugged out, and he was interested. He says:

"I didn' know dey was so many un um. I hain't hearn 'bout none un um, skasely, but ole King Sollermun, onless you counts dem kings dat's in a pack er k'yards. How much do a king git?"

"Get?" I says; "why, they get a thousand dollars a month if they want it; they can have just as much as they want; everything belongs to them."

"AIN' dat gay? En what dey got to do, Huck?"

"THEY don't do nothing! Why, how you talk! They just set around."

"No; is dat so?"

"Of course it is. They just set around—except, maybe, when there's a war; then they go to the war. But other times they just lazy around; or go hawking—just hawking and sp—Sh!—d' you hear a noise?"

We skipped out and looked; but it warn't nothing but the flutter of a steamboat's wheel away down, coming around the point; so we come back.

"Yes," says I, "and other times, when things is dull, they fuss with the parlyment; and if everybody don't go just so he whacks their heads off. But mostly they hang round the harem."

"Roun' de which?"

"Harem."

"What's de harem?"

"The place where he keeps his wives. Don't you know about the harem? Solomon had one; he had about a million wives."

"Why, yes, dat's so; I—I'd done forgot it. A harem's a bo'd'n-house, I reck'n. Mos' likely dey has rackety times in de nussery. En I reck'n de wives quarrels considable; en dat 'crease de racket. Yit dey say Sollermun de wises' man dat ever live'. I doan' take no stock in dat. Bekase why: would a wise man want to live in de mids' er sich a blim-blammin' all de time? No—'deed he wouldn't. A wise man 'ud take en buil' a biler-factry; en den he could shet DOWN de biler-factry when he want to res'."

"Well, but he WAS the wisest man, anyway; because the widow she told me so, her own self."

"I doan k'yer what de widder say, he WARN'T no wise man nuther. He had some er de dad-fetchedes' ways I ever see. Does you know 'bout dat chile dat he 'uz gwyne to chop in two?"

"Yes, the widow told me all about it."

"WELL, den! Warn' dat de beatenes' notion in de worl'? You jes' take en look at it a minute. Dah's de stump, dah—dat's one er de women; heah's you—dat's de yuther one; I's Sollermun; en dish yer dollar bill's de chile. Bofe un you claims it. What does I do? Does I shin aroun' mongs' de neighbors en fine out which un you de bill DO b'long to, en han' it over to de right one, all safe en soun', de way dat anybody dat had any gumption would? No; I take en whack de bill in TWO, en give half un it to you, en de yuther half to de yuther woman. Dat's de way Sollermun was gwyne to do wid de chile. Now I want to ast you: what's de use er dat half a bill?—can't buy noth'n wid it. En what use is a half a chile? I wouldn' give a dern for a million un um."

"But hang it, Jim, you've clean missed the point—blame it, you've missed it a thousand mile."

"Who? Me? Go 'long. Doan' talk to me 'bout yo' pints. I reck'n I knows sense when I sees it; en dey ain' no sense in sich doin's as dat. De 'spute warn't 'bout a half a chile, de 'spute was 'bout a whole chile; en de man dat think he kin settle a 'spute 'bout a whole chile wid a half a chile doan' know enough to come in out'n de rain. Doan' talk to me 'bout Sollermun, Huck, I knows him by de back."

"But I tell you you don't get the point."

"Blame de point! I reck'n I knows what I knows. En mine you, de REAL pint is down furder—it's down deeper. It lays in de way Sollermun was raised. You take a man dat's got on'y one or two chillen; is dat man gwyne to be waseful o' chillen? No, he ain't; he can't 'ford it. HE know how to value 'em. But you take a man dat's got 'bout five million chillen runnin' roun' de house, en it's diffunt. HE as soon chop a chile in two as a cat. Dey's plenty mo'. A chile er two, mo' er less, warn't no consekens to Sollermun, dad fatch him!"

I never see such a nigger. If he got a notion in his head once, there warn't no getting it out again. He was the most down on Solomon of any nigger I ever see. So I went to talking about other kings, and let Solomon slide. I told about Louis Sixteenth that got his head cut off in France long time ago; and about his little boy the dolphin, that would a been a king, but they took and shut him up in jail, and some say he died there.

"Po' little chap."

"But some says he got out and got away, and come to America."

"Dat's good! But he'll be pooty lonesome—dey ain' no kings here, is dey, Huck?"

"No."

"Den he cain't git no situation. What he gwyne to do?"

"Well, I don't know. Some of them gets on the police, and some of them learns people how to talk French."

"Why, Huck, doan' de French people talk de same way we does?"

"NO, Jim; you couldn't understand a word they said—not a single word."

"Well, now, I be ding-busted! How do dat come?"

"I don't know; but it's so. I got some of their jabber out of a book. S'pose a man was to come to you and say Polly-voo-franzy—what would you think?"

"I wouldn' think nuff'n; I'd take en bust him over de head—dat is, if he warn't white. I wouldn't 'low no nigger to call me dat."

"Shucks, it ain't calling you anything. It's only saying, do you know how to talk French?"

"Well, den, why couldn't he SAY it?"

"Why, he IS a-saying it. That's a Frenchman's WAY of saying it."

"Well, it's a blame ridicklous way, en I doan' want to hear no mo' 'bout it. Dey ain' no sense in it."

"Looky here, Jim; does a cat talk like we do?"

"No, a cat don't."

"Well, does a cow?"

"No, a cow don't, nuther."

"Does a cat talk like a cow, or a cow talk like a cat?"

"No, dey don't."

"It's natural and right for 'em to talk different from each other, ain't it?"

"Course."

"And ain't it natural and right for a cat and a cow to talk different from US?"

"Why, mos' sholy it is."

"Well, then, why ain't it natural and right for a FRENCHMAN to talk different from us? You answer me that."

"Is a cat a man, Huck?"

"No."

"Well, den, dey ain't no sense in a cat talkin' like a man. Is a cow a man?—er is a cow a cat?"

"No, she ain't either of them."

"Well, den, she ain't got no business to talk like either one er

the yuther of 'em. Is a Frenchman a man?"

"Yes."

"WELL, den! Dad blame it, why doan' he TALK like a man? You answer me DAT!"

I see it warn't no use wasting words—you can't learn a nigger to argue. So I quit.

CHAPTER XV.

WE judged that three nights more would fetch us to Cairo, at the bottom of Illinois, where the Ohio River comes in, and that was what we was after. We would sell the raft and get on a steamboat and go way up the Ohio amongst the free States, and then be out of trouble.

Well, the second night a fog begun to come on, and we made for a towhead to tie to, for it wouldn't do to try to run in a fog; but when I paddled ahead in the canoe, with the line to make fast, there warn't anything but little saplings to tie to. I passed the line around one of them right on the edge of the cut bank, but there was a stiff current, and the raft come booming down so lively she tore it out by the roots and away she went. I see the fog closing down, and it made me so sick and scared I couldn't budge for most a half a minute it seemed to me—and then there warn't no raft in sight; you couldn't see twenty yards. I jumped into the canoe and run back to the stern, and grabbed the paddle and set her back a stroke. But she didn't come. I was in such a hurry I hadn't untied her. I got up and tried to untie her, but I was so excited my hands shook so I couldn't hardly do anything with them.

As soon as I got started I took out after the raft, hot and heavy, right down the towhead. That was all right as far as it went, but the towhead warn't sixty yards long, and the minute I flew by the foot of it I shot out into the solid white fog, and hadn't no more idea which way I was going than a dead man.

Thinks I, it won't do to paddle; first I know I'll run into the bank or a towhead or something; I got to set still and float, and yet it's mighty fidgety business to have to hold your hands still at such a time. I whooped and listened. Away down there somewheres I hears a small whoop, and up comes my spirits. I went tearing after it, listening sharp to hear it again. The next time it come I see I warn't heading for it, but heading away to the right of it. And the next time I was heading away to the left of it—and not gaining on it much either, for I was flying around, this way and that and t'other, but it was going straight ahead all the time.

I did wish the fool would think to beat a tin pan, and beat it all the time, but he never did, and it was the still places between the whoops that was making the trouble for me. Well, I fought along, and directly I hears the whoop BEHIND me. I was tangled good now. That was somebody else's whoop, or else I was turned around.

I throwed the paddle down. I heard the whoop again; it was behind me yet, but in a different place; it kept coming, and kept changing its place, and I kept answering, till by and by was in front of me again, and I knowed the current had swung the canoe's head down-stream, and I was all right if that was Jim and not some other raftsman hollering. I couldn't tell nothing about voices in a fog, for nothing don't look natural nor sound natural in a fog.

The whooping went on, and in about a minute I come a-booming down on a cut bank with smoky ghosts of big trees on it, and the current throwed me off to the left and shot by, amongst a lot of snags that fairly roared, the currrent was tearing by them so swift.

In another second or two it was solid white and still again. I set perfectly still then, listening to my heart thump, and I reckon I didn't draw a breath while it thumped a hundred.

I just give up then. I knowed what the matter was. That cut bank was an island, and Jim had gone down t'other side of it. It warn't no towhead that you could float by in ten minutes. It had the big timber of a regular island; it might be five or six miles long and more than half a mile wide.

I kept quiet, with my ears cocked, about fifteen minutes, I reckon. I was floating along, of course, four or five miles an hour; but you don't ever think of that. No, you FEEL like you are laying dead still on the water; and if a little glimpse of a snag slips by you don't think to yourself how fast YOU'RE going, but you catch your breath and think, my! how that snag's tearing along. If you think it ain't dismal and lonesome out in a fog that way by yourself in the night, you try it once—you'll see.

Next, for about a half an hour, I whoops now and then; at last I hears the answer a long ways off, and tries to follow it, but I couldn't do it, and directly I judged I'd got into a nest of towheads, for I had little dim glimpses of them on both sides of me—sometimes just a narrow channel between, and some that I couldn't see I knowed was there because I'd hear the wash of the current against the old dead brush and trash that hung over the banks. Well, I warn't long loosing the whoops down amongst the towheads; and I only tried to chase them a little while, anyway, because it was worse than chasing a Jack-o'-lantern. You never knowed a sound dodge around so, and swap places so quick and so much.

I had to claw away from the bank pretty lively four or five times, to keep from knocking the islands out of the river; and so I judged the raft must be butting into the bank every now and then, or else it would get further ahead and clear out of hearing—it was floating a little faster than what I was.

Well, I seemed to be in the open river again by and by, but I couldn't hear no sign of a whoop nowheres. I reckoned Jim had fetched up on a snag, maybe, and it was all up with him. I was good and tired, so I laid down in the canoe and said I wouldn't bother no more. I didn't want to go to sleep, of course; but I was so sleepy I couldn't help it; so I thought I would take jest one little cat-nap.

But I reckon it was more than a cat-nap, for when I waked up the stars was shining bright, the fog was all gone, and I was spinning down a big bend stern first. First I didn't know where I was; I thought I was dreaming; and when things began to come back to me they seemed to come up dim out of last week.

It was a monstrous big river here, with the tallest and the thickest kind of timber on both banks; just a solid wall, as well as I could see by the stars. I looked away down-stream, and seen a black speck on the water. I took after it; but when I got to it it warn't nothing but a couple of sawlogs made fast together. Then I see another speck, and chased that; then another, and this time I was right. It was the raft.

When I got to it Jim was setting there with his head down between his knees, asleep, with his right arm hanging over the steering-oar. The other oar was smashed off, and the raft was littered up with leaves and branches and dirt. So she'd had a rough time.

I made fast and laid down under Jim's nose on the raft, and began to gap, and stretch my fists out against Jim, and says:

"Hello, Jim, have I been asleep? Why didn't you stir me up?"

"Goodness gracious, is dat you, Huck? En you ain' dead—you ain' drownded—you's back agin? It's too good for true, honey, it's too good for true. Lemme look at you chile, lemme feel o' you. No, you ain' dead! you's back agin, 'live en soun', jis de same ole Huck—de same ole Huck, thanks to goodness!"

"What's the matter with you, Jim? You been a-drinking?"

"Drinkin'? Has I ben a-drinkin'? Has I had a chance to be a-drinkin'?"

"Well, then, what makes you talk so wild?"

"How does I talk wild?"

"HOW? Why, hain't you been talking about my coming back, and all that stuff, as if I'd been gone away?"

"Huck—Huck Finn, you look me in de eye; look me in de eye. HAIN'T you ben gone away?"

"Gone away? Why, what in the nation do you mean? I hain't been gone anywheres. Where would I go to?"

"Well, looky here, boss, dey's sumf'n wrong, dey is. Is I ME, or who IS I? Is I heah, or whah IS I? Now dat's what I wants to know."

"Well, I think you're here, plain enough, but I think you're a tangle-headed old fool, Jim."

"I is, is I? Well, you answer me dis: Didn't you tote out de line in de canoe fer to make fas' to de tow-head?"

"No, I didn't. What tow-head? I hain't see no tow-head."

"You hain't seen no towhead? Looky here, didn't de line pull loose en de raf' go a-hummin' down de river, en leave you en de canoe behine in de fog?"

"What fog?"

"Why, de fog!—de fog dat's been aroun' all night. En didn't you whoop, en didn't I whoop, tell we got mix' up in de islands en one un us got los' en t'other one was jis' as good as los', 'kase he didn' know whah he wuz? En didn't I bust up agin a lot er dem islands en have a turrible time en mos' git drownded? Now ain' dat so, boss—ain't it so? You answer me dat."

"Well, this is too many for me, Jim. I hain't seen no fog, nor no islands, nor no troubles, nor nothing. I been setting here talking with you all night till you went to sleep about ten minutes ago, and I reckon I done the same. You couldn't a got drunk in that time, so of course you've been dreaming."

"Dad fetch it, how is I gwyne to dream all dat in ten minutes?"

"Well, hang it all, you did dream it, because there didn't any of it happen."

"But, Huck, it's all jis' as plain to me as—"

"It don't make no difference how plain it is; there ain't nothing in it. I know, because I've been here all the time."

Jim didn't say nothing for about five minutes, but set there studying over it. Then he says:

"Well, den, I reck'n I did dream it, Huck; but dog my cats ef it ain't de powerfullest dream I ever see. En I hain't ever had no dream b'fo' dat's tired me like dis one."

"Oh, well, that's all right, because a dream does tire a body like everything sometimes. But this one was a staving dream; tell me all about it, Jim."

So Jim went to work and told me the whole thing right through, just as it happened, only he painted it up considerable. Then he said he must start in and "'terpret" it, because it was sent for a warning. He said the first towhead stood for a man that would try to do us some good, but the current was another man that would get us away from him. The whoops was warnings that would come to us every now and then, and if we didn't try hard to make out to understand them they'd just take us into bad luck, 'stead of keeping us out of it. The lot of towheads was troubles we was going to get into with quarrelsome people and all kinds of mean folks, but if we minded our business and didn't talk back and aggravate them, we would pull through and get out of the fog and into the big clear river, which was the free States, and wouldn't have no more trouble.

It had clouded up pretty dark just after I got on to the raft, but it was clearing up again now.

"Oh, well, that's all interpreted well enough as far as it goes, Jim," I says; "but what does THESE things stand for?"

It was the leaves and rubbish on the raft and the smashed oar. You could see them first-rate now.

Jim looked at the trash, and then looked at me, and back at the trash again. He had got the dream fixed so strong in his head that he couldn't seem to shake it loose and get the facts back into its place again right away. But when he did get the thing straightened around he looked at me steady without ever smiling, and says:

"What do dey stan' for? I'se gwyne to tell you. When I got all wore out wid work, en wid de callin' for you, en went to sleep, my heart wuz mos' broke bekase you wuz los', en I didn' k'yer no' mo' what become er me en de raf'. En when I wake up en fine you back agin, all safe en soun', de tears come, en I could a got down on my knees en kiss yo' foot, I's so thankful. En all you wuz thinkin' 'bout wuz how you could make a fool uv ole Jim wid a lie. Dat truck dah is TRASH; en trash is what people is dat puts dirt on de head er dey fren's en makes 'em ashamed."

Then he got up slow and walked to the wigwam, and went in there without saying anything but that. But that was enough. It made me feel so mean I could almost kissed HIS foot to get him to take it back.

It was fifteen minutes before I could work myself up to go and humble myself to a nigger; but I done it, and I warn't ever

sorry for it afterwards, neither. I didn't do him no more mean tricks, and I wouldn't done that one if I'd a knowed it would make him feel that way.

CHAPTER XVI.

WE slept most all day, and started out at night, a little ways behind a monstrous long raft that was as long going by as a procession. She had four long sweeps at each end, so we judged she carried as many as thirty men, likely. She had five big wigwams aboard, wide apart, and an open camp fire in the middle, and a tall flag-pole at each end. There was a power of style about her. It AMOUNTED to something being a raftsman on such a craft as that.

We went drifting down into a big bend, and the night clouded up and got hot. The river was very wide, and was walled with solid timber on both sides; you couldn't see a break in it hardly ever, or a light. We talked about Cairo, and wondered whether we would know it when we got to it. I said likely we wouldn't, because I had heard say there warn't but about a dozen houses there, and if they didn't happen to have them lit up, how was we going to know we was passing a town? Jim said if the two big rivers joined together there, that would show. But I said maybe we might think we was passing the foot of an island and coming into the same old river again. That disturbed Jim—and me too. So the question was, what to do? I said, paddle ashore the first time a light showed, and tell them pap was behind, coming along with a trading-scow, and was a green hand at the business, and wanted to know how far it was to Cairo. Jim thought it was a good idea, so we took a smoke on it and waited.

There warn't nothing to do now but to look out sharp for the town, and not pass it without seeing it. He said he'd be mighty sure to see it, because he'd be a free man the minute he seen it, but if he missed it he'd be in a slave country again and no more show for freedom. Every little while he jumps up and says:

"Dah she is?"

But it warn't. It was Jack-o'-lanterns, or lightning bugs; so he set down again, and went to watching, same as before. Jim said it made him all over trembly and feverish to be so close to freedom. Well, I can tell you it made me all over trembly and feverish, too, to hear him, because I begun to get it through my head that he WAS most free—and who was to blame for it? Why, ME. I couldn't get that out of my conscience, no how nor no way. It got to troubling me so I couldn't rest; I couldn't stay still in one place. It hadn't ever come home to me before, what this thing was that I was doing. But now it did; and it stayed with me, and scorched me more and more. I tried to make out to myself that I warn't to blame, because I didn't run Jim off from his rightful owner; but it warn't no use, conscience up and says, every time, "But you knowed he was running for his freedom, and you could a paddled ashore and told somebody." That was so—I couldn't get around that noway. That was where it pinched. Conscience says to me, "What had poor Miss Watson done to you that you could see her nigger go off right under your eyes and never say one single word? What did that poor old woman do to you that you could treat her so mean? Why, she tried to learn you your book, she tried to learn you your manners, she tried to be good to you every way she knowed how. THAT'S what she done."

I got to feeling so mean and so miserable I most wished I was dead. I fidgeted up and down the raft, abusing myself to myself, and Jim was fidgeting up and down past me. We neither of us could keep still. Every time he danced around and says, "Dah's Cairo!" it went through me like a shot, and I thought if it WAS Cairo I reckoned I would die of miserableness.

Jim talked out loud all the time while I was talking to myself. He was saying how the first thing he would do when he got to a free State he would go to saving up money and never spend a single cent, and when he got enough he would buy his wife, which was owned on a farm close to where Miss Watson lived; and then they would both work to buy the two children, and if their master wouldn't sell them, they'd get an Ab'litionist to go and steal them.

It most froze me to hear such talk. He wouldn't ever dared to talk such talk in his life before. Just see what a difference it made in him the minute he judged he was about free. It was according to the old saying, "Give a nigger an inch and he'll take an ell." Thinks I, this is what comes of my not thinking. Here was this nigger, which I had as good as helped to run away, coming right out flat-footed and saying he would steal his children—children that belonged to a man I didn't even know; a man that hadn't ever done me no harm.

I was sorry to hear Jim say that, it was such a lowering of him. My conscience got to stirring me up hotter than ever, until at last I says to it, "Let up on me—it ain't too late yet—I'll paddle ashore at the first light and tell." I felt easy and happy and light as a feather right off. All my troubles was gone. I went to looking out sharp for a light, and sort of singing to myself. By and by one showed. Jim sings out:

"We's safe, Huck, we's safe! Jump up and crack yo' heels! Dat's de good ole Cairo at las', I jis knows it!"

I says:

"I'll take the canoe and go and see, Jim. It mightn't be, you know."

He jumped and got the canoe ready, and put his old coat in the bottom for me to set on, and give me the paddle; and as I shoved off, he says:

"Pooty soon I'll be a-shout'n' for joy, en I'll say, it's all on accounts o' Huck; I's a free man, en I couldn't ever ben free ef it hadn' ben for Huck; Huck done it. Jim won't ever forgit you, Huck; you's de bes' fren' Jim's ever had; en you's de ONLY fren' ole Jim's got now."

I was paddling off, all in a sweat to tell on him; but when he says this, it seemed to kind of take the tuck all out of me. I went along slow then, and I warn't right down certain whether I was glad I started or whether I warn't. When I was fifty yards off, Jim says:

"Dah you goes, de ole true Huck; de on'y white genlman dat ever kep' his promise to ole Jim."

Well, I just felt sick. But I says, I GOT to do it—I can't get OUT of it. Right then along comes a skiff with two men in it with guns, and they stopped and I stopped. One of them says:

"What's that yonder?"

"A piece of a raft," I says.

"Do you belong on it?"

"Yes, sir."

"Any men on it?"

"Only one, sir."

"Well, there's five niggers run off to-night up yonder, above the head of the bend. Is your man white or black?"

I didn't answer up prompt. I tried to, but the words wouldn't come. I tried for a second or two to brace up and out with it, but I warn't man enough—hadn't the spunk of a rabbit. I see I was weakening; so I just give up trying, and up and says:

"He's white."

"I reckon we'll go and see for ourselves."

"I wish you would," says I, "because it's pap that's there, and maybe you'd help me tow the raft ashore where the light is. He's sick—and so is mam and Mary Ann."

"Oh, the devil! we're in a hurry, boy. But I s'pose we've got to. Come, buckle to your paddle, and let's get along."

I buckled to my paddle and they laid to their oars. When we had made a stroke or two, I says:

"Pap'll be mighty much obleeged to you, I can tell you. Everybody goes away when I want them to help me tow the raft ashore, and I can't do it by myself."

"Well, that's infernal mean. Odd, too. Say, boy, what's the matter with your father?"

"It's the—a—the—well, it ain't anything much."

They stopped pulling. It warn't but a mighty little ways to the raft now. One says:

"Boy, that's a lie. What IS the matter with your pap? Answer up square now, and it'll be the better for you."

"I will, sir, I will, honest—but don't leave us, please. It's the—the —Gentlemen, if you'll only pull ahead, and let me heave you the headline, you won't have to come a-near the raft— please do."

"Set her back, John, set her back!" says one. They backed water. "Keep away, boy—keep to looard. Confound it, I just expect the wind has blowed it to us. Your pap's got the small-pox, and you know it precious well. Why didn't you come out and say so? Do you want to spread it all over?"

"Well," says I, a-blubbering, "I've told everybody before, and they just went away and left us."

"Poor devil, there's something in that. We are right down sorry for you, but we—well, hang it, we don't want the small-pox, you see. Look here, I'll tell you what to do. Don't you try to land by yourself, or you'll smash everything to pieces. You float along down about twenty miles, and you'll come to a town on the left-hand side of the river. It will be long after sun-up then, and when you ask for help you tell them your folks are all down with chills and fever. Don't be a fool again, and let people guess what is the matter. Now we're trying to do you a kindness; so you just put twenty miles between us, that's a good boy. It wouldn't do any good to land yonder where the light is—it's only a wood-yard. Say, I reckon your father's poor, and I'm bound to say he's in pretty hard luck. Here, I'll put a twenty-dollar gold piece on this board, and you get it when it floats by. I feel mighty mean to leave you; but my kingdom! it won't do to fool with small-pox, don't you see?"

"Hold on, Parker," says the other man, "here's a twenty to put on the board for me. Good-bye, boy; you do as Mr. Parker told you, and you'll be all right."

"That's so, my boy—good-bye, good-bye. If you see any runaway niggers you get help and nab them, and you can make some money by it."

"Good-bye, sir," says I; "I won't let no runaway niggers get by me if I can help it."

They went off and I got aboard the raft, feeling bad and low, because I knowed very well I had done wrong, and I see it warn't no use for me to try to learn to do right; a body that don't get STARTED right when he's little ain't got no show—when the pinch comes there ain't nothing to back him up and keep him to his work, and so he gets beat. Then I thought a minute, and says to myself, hold on; s'pose you'd a done right and give Jim up, would you felt better than what you do now? No, says I, I'd feel bad—I'd feel just the same way I do now. Well, then, says I, what's the use you learning to do right when it's troublesome to do right and ain't no trouble to do wrong, and the wages is just the same? I was stuck. I couldn't answer that. So I reckoned I wouldn't bother no more about it, but after this always do whichever come handiest at the time.

I went into the wigwam; Jim warn't there. I looked all around; he warn't anywhere. I says:

"Jim!"

"Here I is, Huck. Is dey out o' sight yit? Don't talk loud."

He was in the river under the stern oar, with just his nose out. I told him they were out of sight, so he come aboard. He says:

"I was a-listenin' to all de talk, en I slips into de river en was gwyne to shove for sho' if dey come aboard. Den I was gwyne to swim to de raf' agin when dey was gone. But lawsy, how you did fool 'em, Huck! Dat WUZ de smartes' dodge! I tell you, chile, I 'spec it save' ole Jim—ole Jim ain't going to forget you for dat, honey."

Then we talked about the money. It was a pretty good raise—twenty dollars apiece. Jim said we could take deck passage on a steamboat now, and the money would last us as far as we wanted to go in the free States. He said twenty mile more warn't far for the raft to go, but he wished we was already there.

Towards daybreak we tied up, and Jim was mighty particular about hiding the raft good. Then he worked all day fixing things in bundles, and getting all ready to quit rafting.

That night about ten we hove in sight of the lights of a town away down in a left-hand bend.

I went off in the canoe to ask about it. Pretty soon I found a man out in the river with a skiff, setting a trot-line. I ranged up and says:

"Mister, is that town Cairo?"

"Cairo? no. You must be a blame' fool."

"What town is it, mister?"

"If you want to know, go and find out. If you stay here botherin' around me for about a half a minute longer you'll get something you won't want."

I paddled to the raft. Jim was awful disappointed, but I said never mind, Cairo would be the next place, I reckoned.

We passed another town before daylight, and I was going out again; but it was high ground, so I didn't go. No high ground about Cairo, Jim said. I had forgot it. We laid up for the day on a towhead tolerable close to the left-hand bank. I begun to suspicion something. So did Jim. I says:

"Maybe we went by Cairo in the fog that night."

He says:

"Doan' le's talk about it, Huck. Po' niggers can't have no luck. I awluz 'spected dat rattlesnake-skin warn't done wid its work."

"I wish I'd never seen that snake-skin, Jim—I do wish I'd never laid eyes on it."

"It ain't yo' fault, Huck; you didn' know. Don't you blame yo'self 'bout it."

When it was daylight, here was the clear Ohio water inshore, sure enough, and outside was the old regular Muddy! So it was all up with Cairo.

We talked it all over. It wouldn't do to take to the shore; we couldn't take the raft up the stream, of course. There warn't no way but to wait for dark, and start back in the canoe and take the chances. So we slept all day amongst the cottonwood thicket, so as to be fresh for the work, and when we went back to the raft about dark the canoe was gone!

We didn't say a word for a good while. There warn't anything to say. We both knowed well enough it was some more work of the rattlesnake-skin; so what was the use to talk about it? It would only look like we was finding fault, and that would be bound to fetch more bad luck—and keep on fetching it, too, till we knowed enough to keep still.

By and by we talked about what we better do, and found there warn't no way but just to go along down with the raft till we got a chance to buy a canoe to go back in. We warn't going to borrow it when there warn't anybody around, the way pap would do, for that might set people after us.

So we shoved out after dark on the raft.

Anybody that don't believe yet that it's foolishness to handle a snake-skin, after all that that snake-skin done for us, will believe it now if they read on and see what more it done for us.

The place to buy canoes is off of rafts laying up at shore. But we didn't see no rafts laying up; so we went along during three hours and more. Well, the night got gray and ruther thick, which is the next meanest thing to fog. You can't tell the shape of the river, and you can't see no distance. It got to be very late and still, and then along comes a steamboat up the river. We lit the lantern, and judged she would see it. Up-stream boats didn't generly come close to us; they go out and follow the bars and hunt for easy water under the reefs; but nights like this they bull right up the channel against the whole river.

We could hear her pounding along, but we didn't see her good till she was close. She aimed right for us. Often they do that and try to see how close they can come without touching; sometimes the wheel bites off a sweep, and then the pilot sticks his head out and laughs, and thinks he's mighty smart. Well, here she comes, and we said she was going to try and shave us; but she didn't seem to be sheering off a bit. She was a big one, and she was coming in a hurry, too, looking like a black cloud with rows of glow-worms around it; but all of a sudden she bulged out, big and scary, with a long row of wide-open furnace doors shining like red-hot teeth, and her monstrous bows and guards hanging right over us. There was a yell at us, and a jingling of bells to stop the engines, a powwow of cussing, and whistling of steam—and as Jim went overboard on one side and I on the other, she come smashing straight through the raft.

I dived—and I aimed to find the bottom, too, for a thirty-foot wheel had got to go over me, and I wanted it to have plenty of room. I could always stay under water a minute; this time I reckon I stayed under a minute and a half. Then I bounced for the top in a hurry, for I was nearly busting. I popped out to my armpits and blowed the water out of my nose, and puffed a bit. Of course there was a booming current; and of course that boat started her engines again ten seconds after she stopped them, for they never cared much for raftsmen; so now she was churning along up the river, out of sight in the thick weather, though I could hear her.

I sung out for Jim about a dozen times, but I didn't get any answer; so I grabbed a plank that touched me while I was "treading water," and struck out for shore, shoving it ahead of me. But I made out to see that the drift of the current was towards the left-hand shore, which meant that I was in a crossing; so I changed off and went that way.

It was one of these long, slanting, two-mile crossings; so I was a good long time in getting over. I made a safe landing, and clumb up the bank. I couldn't see but a little ways, but I went poking along over rough ground for a quarter of a mile or more, and then I run across a big old-fashioned double log-house before I noticed it. I was going to rush by and get away, but a lot of dogs jumped out and went to howling and barking at me, and I knowed better than to move another peg.

CHAPTER XVII.

IN about a minute somebody spoke out of a window without putting his head out, and says:

"Be done, boys! Who's there?"

I says:

"It's me."

"Who's me?"

"George Jackson, sir."

"What do you want?"

"I don't want nothing, sir. I only want to go along by, but the dogs won't let me."

"What are you prowling around here this time of night for—hey?"

"I warn't prowling around, sir, I fell overboard off of the steamboat."

"Oh, you did, did you? Strike a light there, somebody. What did you say your name was?"

"George Jackson, sir. I'm only a boy."

"Look here, if you're telling the truth you needn't be afraid—nobody'll hurt you. But don't try to budge; stand right where you are. Rouse out Bob and Tom, some of you, and fetch the guns. George Jackson, is there anybody with you?"

"No, sir, nobody."

I heard the people stirring around in the house now, and see a light. The man sung out:

"Snatch that light away, Betsy, you old fool—ain't you got any sense? Put it on the floor behind the front door. Bob, if you and Tom are ready, take your places."

"All ready."

"Now, George Jackson, do you know the Shepherdsons?"

"No, sir; I never heard of them."

"Well, that may be so, and it mayn't. Now, all ready. Step forward, George Jackson. And mind, don't you hurry—come mighty slow. If there's anybody with you, let him keep back—if he shows himself he'll be shot. Come along now. Come slow; push the door open yourself—just enough to squeeze in, d' you hear?"

I didn't hurry; I couldn't if I'd a wanted to. I took one slow step at a time and there warn't a sound, only I thought I could hear my heart. The dogs were as still as the humans, but they followed a little behind me. When I got to the three log doorsteps I heard them unlocking and unbarring and unbolting. I put my hand on the door and pushed it a little and a little more till somebody said, "There, that's enough—put your head in." I done it, but I judged they would take it off.

The candle was on the floor, and there they all was, looking at me, and me at them, for about a quarter of a minute: Three big men with guns pointed at me, which made me wince, I tell you; the oldest, gray and about sixty, the other two thirty or more—all of them fine and handsome —and the sweetest old gray-headed lady, and back of her two young women which I couldn't see right well. The old gentleman says:

"There; I reckon it's all right. Come in."

As soon as I was in the old gentleman he locked the door and barred it and bolted it, and told the young men to come in with their guns, and they all went in a big parlor that had a new rag carpet on the floor, and got together in a corner that was out of the range of the front windows —there warn't none on the side. They held the candle, and took a good look at me, and all said, "Why, HE ain't a Shepherdson—no, there ain't any Shepherdson about him." Then the old man said he hoped I wouldn't mind being searched for arms, because he didn't mean no harm by it—it was only to make sure. So he didn't pry into my pockets, but only felt outside with his hands, and said it was all right. He told me to make myself easy and at home, and tell all about myself; but the old lady says:

"Why, bless you, Saul, the poor thing's as wet as he can be; and don't you reckon it may be he's hungry?"

"True for you, Rachel—I forgot."

So the old lady says:

"Betsy" (this was a nigger woman), "you fly around and get him something to eat as quick as you can, poor thing; and one of you girls go and wake up Buck and tell him—oh, here he is himself. Buck, take this little stranger and get the wet clothes off from him and dress him up in some of yours that's dry."

Buck looked about as old as me—thirteen or fourteen or along there, though he was a little bigger than me. He hadn't on anything but a shirt, and he was very frowzy-headed. He came in gaping and digging one fist into his eyes, and he was dragging a gun along with the other one. He says:

"Ain't they no Shepherdsons around?"

They said, no, 'twas a false alarm.

"Well," he says, "if they'd a ben some, I reckon I'd a got one."

They all laughed, and Bob says:

"Why, Buck, they might have scalped us all, you've been so slow in coming."

"Well, nobody come after me, and it ain't right I'm always kept down; I don't get no show."

"Never mind, Buck, my boy," says the old man, "you'll have show enough, all in good time, don't you fret about that. Go 'long with you now, and do as your mother told you."

When we got up-stairs to his room he got me a coarse shirt and a roundabout and pants of his, and I put them on. While I was at it he asked me what my name was, but before I could tell him he started to tell me about a bluejay and a young rabbit he had catched in the woods day before yesterday, and he asked me where Moses was when the candle went out. I said I didn't know; I hadn't heard about it before, no way.

"Well, guess," he says.

"How'm I going to guess," says I, "when I never heard tell of it before?"

"But you can guess, can't you? It's just as easy."

"WHICH candle?" I says.

"Why, any candle," he says.

"I don't know where he was," says I; "where was he?"

"Why, he was in the DARK! That's where he was!"

"Well, if you knowed where he was, what did you ask me for?"

"Why, blame it, it's a riddle, don't you see? Say, how long are

you going to stay here? You got to stay always. We can just have booming times—they don't have no school now. Do you own a dog? I've got a dog—and he'll go in the river and bring out chips that you throw in. Do you like to comb up Sundays, and all that kind of foolishness? You bet I don't, but ma she makes me. Confound these ole britches! I reckon I'd better put 'em on, but I'd rather not, it's so warm. Are you all ready? All right. Come along, old hoss."

Cold corn-pone, cold corn-beef, butter and buttermilk—that is what they had for me down there, and there ain't nothing better that ever I've come across yet. Buck and his ma and all of them smoked cob pipes, except the nigger woman, which was gone, and the two young women. They all smoked and talked, and I eat and talked. The young women had quilts around them, and their hair down their backs. They all asked me questions, and I told them how pap and me and all the family was living on a little farm down at the bottom of Arkansaw, and my sister Mary Ann run off and got married and never was heard of no more, and Bill went to hunt them and he warn't heard of no more, and Tom and Mort died, and then there warn't nobody but just me and pap left, and he was just trimmed down to nothing, on account of his troubles; so when he died I took what there was left, because the farm didn't belong to us, and started up the river, deck passage, and fell overboard; and that was how I come to be here. So they said I could have a home there as long as I wanted it. Then it was most daylight and everybody went to bed, and I went to bed with Buck, and when I waked up in the morning, drat it all, I had forgot what my name was. So I laid there about an hour trying to think, and when Buck waked up I says:

"Can you spell, Buck?"

"Yes," he says.

"I bet you can't spell my name," says I.

"I bet you what you dare I can," says he.

"All right," says I, "go ahead."

"G-e-o-r-g-e J-a-x-o-n—there now," he says.

"Well," says I, "you done it, but I didn't think you could. It ain't no slouch of a name to spell—right off without studying."

I set it down, private, because somebody might want ME to spell it next, and so I wanted to be handy with it and rattle it off like I was used to it.

It was a mighty nice family, and a mighty nice house, too. I hadn't seen no house out in the country before that was so nice and had so much style. It didn't have an iron latch on the front door, nor a wooden one with a buckskin string, but a brass knob to turn, the same as houses in town. There warn't no bed in the parlor, nor a sign of a bed; but heaps of parlors in towns has beds in them. There was a big fireplace that was bricked on the bottom, and the bricks was kept clean and red by pouring water on them and scrubbing them with another brick; sometimes they wash them over with red water-paint that they call Spanish-brown, same as they do in town. They had big brass dog-irons that could hold up a saw-log. There was a clock on the middle of the mantelpiece, with a picture of a town painted on the bottom half of the glass front, and a round place in the middle of it for the sun, and you could see the pendulum swinging behind it. It was beautiful to hear that clock tick; and sometimes when one of these peddlers had been along and scoured her up and got her in good shape, she would start in and strike a hundred and fifty before she got tuckered out. They wouldn't took any money for her.

Well, there was a big outlandish parrot on each side of the clock, made out of something like chalk, and painted up gaudy. By one of the parrots was a cat made of crockery, and a crockery dog by the other; and when you pressed down on them they squeaked, but didn't open their mouths nor look different nor interested. They squeaked through underneath. There was a couple of big wild-turkey-wing fans spread out behind those things. On the table in the middle of the room was a kind of a lovely crockery basket that had apples and oranges and peaches and grapes piled up in it, which was much redder and yellower and prettier than real ones is, but they warn't real because you could see where pieces had got chipped off and showed the white chalk, or whatever it was, underneath.

This table had a cover made out of beautiful oilcloth, with a red and blue spread-eagle painted on it, and a painted border all around. It come all the way from Philadelphia, they said. There was some books, too, piled up perfectly exact, on each corner of the table. One was a big family Bible full of pictures. One was Pilgrim's Progress, about a man that left his family, it didn't say why. I read considerable in it now and then. The statements was interesting, but tough. Another was Friendship's Offering, full of beautiful stuff and poetry; but I didn't read the poetry. Another was Henry Clay's Speeches, and another was Dr. Gunn's Family Medicine, which told you all about what to do if a body was sick or dead. There was a hymn book, and a lot of other books. And there was nice split-bottom chairs, and perfectly sound, too—not bagged down in the middle and busted, like an old basket.

They had pictures hung on the walls—mainly Washingtons and Lafayettes, and battles, and Highland Marys, and one called "Signing the Declaration." There was some that they called crayons, which one of the daughters which was dead made her own self when she was only fifteen years old. They was different from any pictures I ever see before —blacker, mostly, than is common. One was a woman in a slim black dress, belted small under the armpits, with bulges like a cabbage in the middle of the sleeves, and a large black scoop-shovel bonnet with a black veil, and white slim ankles crossed about with black tape, and very wee black slippers, like a chisel, and she was leaning pensive on a tombstone on her right elbow, under a weeping willow, and her other hand hanging down her side holding a white handkerchief and a reticule, and underneath the picture it said "Shall I Never See Thee More Alas." Another one was a young lady with her hair all combed up straight to the top of her head, and knotted there in front of a comb like a chair-back, and she was crying into a handkerchief and had a dead bird laying on its back in her other hand with its heels up, and underneath the picture it said "I Shall Never Hear Thy Sweet Chirrup More Alas." There was one where a young lady was at a window looking up at the moon, and tears running down her cheeks; and she had an open letter in one hand with black sealing wax showing on one edge of it, and she was mashing a locket with a chain to it against her mouth, and underneath the picture it said "And Art Thou Gone Yes Thou Art Gone Alas." These was all nice pictures, I reckon, but I didn't somehow seem to take to them, because if ever I was down a little they always give me the fan-tods. Everybody was sorry she died, because she had laid out a lot more of these pictures to do, and a body could see by what she had done what they had lost. But I reckoned that with her disposition she was having a better time in the graveyard. She

was at work on what they said was her greatest picture when she took sick, and every day and every night it was her prayer to be allowed to live till she got it done, but she never got the chance. It was a picture of a young woman in a long white gown, standing on the rail of a bridge all ready to jump off, with her hair all down her back, and looking up to the moon, with the tears running down her face, and she had two arms folded across her breast, and two arms stretched out in front, and two more reaching up towards the moon—and the idea was to see which pair would look best, and then scratch out all the other arms; but, as I was saying, she died before she got her mind made up, and now they kept this picture over the head of the bed in her room, and every time her birthday come they hung flowers on it. Other times it was hid with a little curtain. The young woman in the picture had a kind of a nice sweet face, but there was so many arms it made her look too spidery, seemed to me.

This young girl kept a scrap-book when she was alive, and used to paste obituaries and accidents and cases of patient suffering in it out of the Presbyterian Observer, and write poetry after them out of her own head. It was very good poetry. This is what she wrote about a boy by the name of Stephen Dowling Bots that fell down a well and was drownded:

ODE TO STEPHEN DOWLING BOTS, DEC'D

And did young Stephen sicken, And did young Stephen die? And did the sad hearts thicken, And did the mourners cry?

No; such was not the fate of Young Stephen Dowling Bots; Though sad hearts round him thickened, 'Twas not from sickness' shots.

No whooping-cough did rack his frame, Nor measles drear with spots; Not these impaired the sacred name Of Stephen Dowling Bots.

Despised love struck not with woe That head of curly knots, Nor stomach troubles laid him low, Young Stephen Dowling Bots.

O no. Then list with tearful eye, Whilst I his fate do tell. His soul did from this cold world fly By falling down a well.

They got him out and emptied him; Alas it was too late; His spirit was gone for to sport aloft In the realms of the good and great.

If Emmeline Grangerford could make poetry like that before she was fourteen, there ain't no telling what she could a done by and by. Buck said she could rattle off poetry like nothing. She didn't ever have to stop to think. He said she would slap down a line, and if she couldn't find anything to rhyme with it would just scratch it out and slap down another one, and go ahead. She warn't particular; she could write about anything you choose to give her to write about just so it was sadful. Every time a man died, or a woman died, or a child died, she would be on hand with her "tribute" before he was cold. She called them tributes. The neighbors said it was the doctor first, then Emmeline, then the undertaker—the undertaker never got in ahead of Emmeline but once, and then she hung fire on a rhyme for the dead person's name, which was Whistler. She warn't ever the same after that; she never complained, but she kinder pined away and did not live long. Poor thing, many's the time I made myself go up to the little room that used to be hers and get out her poor old scrap-book and read in it when her pictures had been aggravating me and I had soured on her a little. I liked all that family, dead ones and all, and warn't going to let anything come between us. Poor Emmeline made poetry about all the dead people when she was alive, and it didn't seem right that there warn't nobody to make some about her now she was gone; so I tried to sweat out a verse or two myself, but I couldn't seem to make it go somehow. They kept Emmeline's room trim and nice, and all the things fixed in it just the way she liked to have them when she was alive, and nobody ever slept there. The old lady took care of the room herself, though there was plenty of niggers, and she sewed there a good deal and read her Bible there mostly.

Well, as I was saying about the parlor, there was beautiful curtains on the windows: white, with pictures painted on them of castles with vines all down the walls, and cattle coming down to drink. There was a little old piano, too, that had tin pans in it, I reckon, and nothing was ever so lovely as to hear the young ladies sing "The Last Link is Broken" and play "The Battle of Prague" on it. The walls of all the rooms was plastered, and most had carpets on the floors, and the whole house was whitewashed on the outside.

It was a double house, and the big open place betwixt them was roofed and floored, and sometimes the table was set there in the middle of the day, and it was a cool, comfortable place. Nothing couldn't be better. And warn't the cooking good, and just bushels of it too!

CHAPTER XVIII.

COL. GRANGERFORD was a gentleman, you see. He was a gentleman all over; and so was his family. He was well born, as the saying is, and that's worth as much in a man as it is in a horse, so the Widow Douglas said, and nobody ever denied that she was of the first aristocracy in our town; and pap he always said it, too, though he warn't no more quality than a mudcat himself. Col. Grangerford was very tall and very slim, and had a darkish-paly complexion, not a sign of red in it anywheres; he was clean shaved every morning all over his thin face, and he had the thinnest kind of lips, and the thinnest kind of nostrils, and a high nose, and heavy eyebrows, and the blackest kind of eyes, sunk so deep back that they seemed like they was looking out of caverns at you, as you may say. His forehead was high, and his hair was black and straight and hung to his shoulders. His hands was long and thin, and every day of his life he put on a clean shirt and a full suit from head to foot made out of linen so white it hurt your eyes to look at it; and on Sundays he wore a blue tail-coat with brass buttons on it. He carried a mahogany cane with a silver head to it. There warn't no frivolishness about him, not a bit, and he warn't ever loud. He was as kind as he could be—you could feel that, you know, and so you had confidence. Sometimes he smiled, and it was good to see; but when he straightened himself up like a liberty-pole, and the lightning begun to flicker out from under his eyebrows, you wanted to climb a tree first, and find out what the matter was afterwards. He didn't ever have to tell anybody to mind their manners — everybody was always good-mannered where he was. Everybody loved to have him around, too; he was sunshine most always—I mean he made it seem like good weather. When he turned into a cloudbank it was awful dark for half a minute, and that was enough; there wouldn't nothing go wrong again for a week.

When him and the old lady come down in the morning all the family got up out of their chairs and give them good-day, and didn't set down again till they had set down. Then Tom and

Bob went to the sideboard where the decanter was, and mixed a glass of bitters and handed it to him, and he held it in his hand and waited till Tom's and Bob's was mixed, and then they bowed and said, "Our duty to you, sir, and madam;" and THEY bowed the least bit in the world and said thank you, and so they drank, all three, and Bob and Tom poured a spoonful of water on the sugar and the mite of whisky or apple brandy in the bottom of their tumblers, and give it to me and Buck, and we drank to the old people too.

Bob was the oldest and Tom next—tall, beautiful men with very broad shoulders and brown faces, and long black hair and black eyes. They dressed in white linen from head to foot, like the old gentleman, and wore broad Panama hats.

Then there was Miss Charlotte; she was twenty-five, and tall and proud and grand, but as good as she could be when she warn't stirred up; but when she was she had a look that would make you wilt in your tracks, like her father. She was beautiful.

So was her sister, Miss Sophia, but it was a different kind. She was gentle and sweet like a dove, and she was only twenty.

Each person had their own nigger to wait on them—Buck too. My nigger had a monstrous easy time, because I warn't used to having anybody do anything for me, but Buck's was on the jump most of the time.

This was all there was of the family now, but there used to be more —three sons; they got killed; and Emmeline that died.

The old gentleman owned a lot of farms and over a hundred niggers. Sometimes a stack of people would come there, horseback, from ten or fifteen mile around, and stay five or six days, and have such junketings round about and on the river, and dances and picnics in the woods daytimes, and balls at the house nights. These people was mostly kinfolks of the family. The men brought their guns with them. It was a handsome lot of quality, I tell you.

There was another clan of aristocracy around there—five or six families —mostly of the name of Shepherdson. They was as high-toned and well born and rich and grand as the tribe of Grangerfords. The Shepherdsons and Grangerfords used the same steamboat landing, which was about two mile above our house; so sometimes when I went up there with a lot of our folks I used to see a lot of the Shepherdsons there on their fine horses.

One day Buck and me was away out in the woods hunting, and heard a horse coming. We was crossing the road. Buck says:

"Quick! Jump for the woods!"

We done it, and then peeped down the woods through the leaves. Pretty soon a splendid young man come galloping down the road, setting his horse easy and looking like a soldier. He had his gun across his pommel. I had seen him before. It was young Harney Shepherdson. I heard Buck's gun go off at my ear, and Harney's hat tumbled off from his head. He grabbed his gun and rode straight to the place where we was hid. But we didn't wait. We started through the woods on a run. The woods warn't thick, so I looked over my shoulder to dodge the bullet, and twice I seen Harney cover Buck with his gun; and then he rode away the way he come—to get his hat, I reckon, but I couldn't see. We never stopped running till we got home. The old gentleman's eyes blazed a minute—'twas pleasure, mainly, I judged—then his face sort of smoothed down, and he says, kind of gentle:

"I don't like that shooting from behind a bush. Why didn't you step into the road, my boy?"

"The Shepherdsons don't, father. They always take advantage."

Miss Charlotte she held her head up like a queen while Buck was telling his tale, and her nostrils spread and her eyes snapped. The two young men looked dark, but never said nothing. Miss Sophia she turned pale, but the color come back when she found the man warn't hurt.

Soon as I could get Buck down by the corn-cribs under the trees by ourselves, I says:

"Did you want to kill him, Buck?"

"Well, I bet I did."

"What did he do to you?"

"Him? He never done nothing to me."

"Well, then, what did you want to kill him for?"

"Why, nothing—only it's on account of the feud."

"What's a feud?"

"Why, where was you raised? Don't you know what a feud is?"

"Never heard of it before—tell me about it."

"Well," says Buck, "a feud is this way: A man has a quarrel with another man, and kills him; then that other man's brother kills HIM; then the other brothers, on both sides, goes for one another; then the COUSINS chip in—and by and by everybody's killed off, and there ain't no more feud. But it's kind of slow, and takes a long time."

"Has this one been going on long, Buck?"

"Well, I should RECKON! It started thirty year ago, or som'ers along there. There was trouble 'bout something, and then a lawsuit to settle it; and the suit went agin one of the men, and so he up and shot the man that won the suit—which he would naturally do, of course. Anybody would."

"What was the trouble about, Buck?—land?"

"I reckon maybe—I don't know."

"Well, who done the shooting? Was it a Grangerford or a Shepherdson?"

"Laws, how do I know? It was so long ago."

"Don't anybody know?"

"Oh, yes, pa knows, I reckon, and some of the other old people; but they don't know now what the row was about in the first place."

"Has there been many killed, Buck?"

"Yes; right smart chance of funerals. But they don't always kill. Pa's got a few buckshot in him; but he don't mind it 'cuz he

don't weigh much, anyway. Bob's been carved up some with a bowie, and Tom's been hurt once or twice."

"Has anybody been killed this year, Buck?"

"Yes; we got one and they got one. 'Bout three months ago my cousin Bud, fourteen year old, was riding through the woods on t'other side of the river, and didn't have no weapon with him, which was blame' foolishness, and in a lonesome place he hears a horse a-coming behind him, and sees old Baldy Shepherdson a-linkin' after him with his gun in his hand and his white hair a-flying in the wind; and 'stead of jumping off and taking to the brush, Bud 'lowed he could out-run him; so they had it, nip and tuck, for five mile or more, the old man a-gaining all the time; so at last Bud seen it warn't any use, so he stopped and faced around so as to have the bullet holes in front, you know, and the old man he rode up and shot him down. But he didn't git much chance to enjoy his luck, for inside of a week our folks laid HIM out."

"I reckon that old man was a coward, Buck."

"I reckon he WARN'T a coward. Not by a blame' sight. There ain't a coward amongst them Shepherdsons—not a one. And there ain't no cowards amongst the Grangerfords either. Why, that old man kep' up his end in a fight one day for half an hour against three Grangerfords, and come out winner. They was all a-horseback; he lit off of his horse and got behind a little woodpile, and kep' his horse before him to stop the bullets; but the Grangerfords stayed on their horses and capered around the old man, and peppered away at him, and he peppered away at them. Him and his horse both went home pretty leaky and crippled, but the Grangerfords had to be FETCHED home—and one of 'em was dead, and another died the next day. No, sir; if a body's out hunting for cowards he don't want to fool away any time amongst them Shepherdsons, becuz they don't breed any of that KIND."

Next Sunday we all went to church, about three mile, everybody a-horseback. The men took their guns along, so did Buck, and kept them between their knees or stood them handy against the wall. The Shepherdsons done the same. It was pretty ornery preaching—all about brotherly love, and such-like tiresomeness; but everybody said it was a good sermon, and they all talked it over going home, and had such a powerful lot to say about faith and good works and free grace and preforeordestination, and I don't know what all, that it did seem to me to be one of the roughest Sundays I had run across yet.

About an hour after dinner everybody was dozing around, some in their chairs and some in their rooms, and it got to be pretty dull. Buck and a dog was stretched out on the grass in the sun sound asleep. I went up to our room, and judged I would take a nap myself. I found that sweet Miss Sophia standing in her door, which was next to ours, and she took me in her room and shut the door very soft, and asked me if I liked her, and I said I did; and she asked me if I would do something for her and not tell anybody, and I said I would. Then she said she'd forgot her Testament, and left it in the seat at church between two other books, and would I slip out quiet and go there and fetch it to her, and not say nothing to nobody. I said I would. So I slid out and slipped off up the road, and there warn't anybody at the church, except maybe a hog or two, for there warn't any lock on the door, and hogs likes a puncheon floor in summer-time because it's cool. If you notice, most folks don't go to church only when they've got to; but a hog is different.

Says I to myself, something's up; it ain't natural for a girl to be in such a sweat about a Testament. So I give it a shake, and out drops a little piece of paper with "HALF-PAST TWO" wrote on it with a pencil. I ransacked it, but couldn't find anything else. I couldn't make anything out of that, so I put the paper in the book again, and when I got home and upstairs there was Miss Sophia in her door waiting for me. She pulled me in and shut the door; then she looked in the Testament till she found the paper, and as soon as she read it she looked glad; and before a body could think she grabbed me and give me a squeeze, and said I was the best boy in the world, and not to tell anybody. She was mighty red in the face for a minute, and her eyes lighted up, and it made her powerful pretty. I was a good deal astonished, but when I got my breath I asked her what the paper was about, and she asked me if I had read it, and I said no, and she asked me if I could read writing, and I told her "no, only coarse-hand," and then she said the paper warn't anything but a book-mark to keep her place, and I might go and play now.

I went off down to the river, studying over this thing, and pretty soon I noticed that my nigger was following along behind. When we was out of sight of the house he looked back and around a second, and then comes a-running, and says:

"Mars Jawge, if you'll come down into de swamp I'll show you a whole stack o' water-moccasins."

Thinks I, that's mighty curious; he said that yesterday. He oughter know a body don't love water-moccasins enough to go around hunting for them. What is he up to, anyway? So I says:

"All right; trot ahead."

I followed a half a mile; then he struck out over the swamp, and waded ankle deep as much as another half-mile. We come to a little flat piece of land which was dry and very thick with trees and bushes and vines, and he says:

"You shove right in dah jist a few steps, Mars Jawge; dah's whah dey is. I's seed 'm befo'; I don't k'yer to see 'em no mo'."

Then he slopped right along and went away, and pretty soon the trees hid him. I poked into the place a-ways and come to a little open patch as big as a bedroom all hung around with vines, and found a man laying there asleep—and, by jings, it was my old Jim!

I waked him up, and I reckoned it was going to be a grand surprise to him to see me again, but it warn't. He nearly cried he was so glad, but he warn't surprised. Said he swum along behind me that night, and heard me yell every time, but dasn't answer, because he didn't want nobody to pick HIM up and take him into slavery again. Says he:

"I got hurt a little, en couldn't swim fas', so I wuz a considable ways behine you towards de las'; when you landed I reck'ned I could ketch up wid you on de lan' 'dout havin' to shout at you, but when I see dat house I begin to go slow. I 'uz off too fur to hear what dey say to you—I wuz 'fraid o' de dogs; but when it 'uz all quiet agin I knowed you's in de house, so I struck out for de woods to wait for day. Early in de mawnin' some er de niggers come along, gwyne to de fields, en dey tuk me en showed me dis place, whah de dogs can't track me on accounts o' de water, en dey brings me truck to eat every night, en tells me how you's a-gitt'n along."

"Why didn't you tell my Jack to fetch me here sooner, Jim?"

"Well, 'twarn't no use to 'sturb you, Huck, tell we could do sumfn—but we's all right now. I ben a-buyin' pots en pans en vittles, as I got a chanst, en a-patchin' up de raf' nights when—"

"WHAT raft, Jim?"

"Our ole raf'."

"You mean to say our old raft warn't smashed all to flinders?"

"No, she warn't. She was tore up a good deal—one en' of her was; but dey warn't no great harm done, on'y our traps was mos' all los'. Ef we hadn' dive' so deep en swum so fur under water, en de night hadn' ben so dark, en we warn't so sk'yerd, en ben sich punkin-heads, as de sayin' is, we'd a seed de raf'. But it's jis' as well we didn't, 'kase now she's all fixed up agin mos' as good as new, en we's got a new lot o' stuff, in de place o' what 'uz los'."

"Why, how did you get hold of the raft again, Jim—did you catch her?"

"How I gwyne to ketch her en I out in de woods? No; some er de niggers foun' her ketched on a snag along heah in de ben', en dey hid her in a crick 'mongst de willows, en dey wuz so much jawin' 'bout which un 'um she b'long to de mos' dat I come to heah 'bout it pooty soon, so I ups en settles de trouble by tellin' 'um she don't b'long to none uv um, but to you en me; en I ast 'm if dey gwyne to grab a young white genlman's propaty, en git a hid'n for it? Den I gin 'm ten cents apiece, en dey 'uz mighty well satisfied, en wisht some mo' raf's 'ud come along en make 'm rich agin. Dey's mighty good to me, dese niggers is, en whatever I wants 'm to do fur me I doan' have to ast 'm twice, honey. Dat Jack's a good nigger, en pooty smart."

"Yes, he is. He ain't ever told me you was here; told me to come, and he'd show me a lot of water-moccasins. If anything happens HE ain't mixed up in it. He can say he never seen us together, and it 'll be the truth."

I don't want to talk much about the next day. I reckon I'll cut it pretty short. I waked up about dawn, and was a-going to turn over and go to sleep again when I noticed how still it was—didn't seem to be anybody stirring. That warn't usual. Next I noticed that Buck was up and gone. Well, I gets up, a-wondering, and goes down stairs—nobody around; everything as still as a mouse. Just the same outside. Thinks I, what does it mean? Down by the wood-pile I comes across my Jack, and says:

"What's it all about?"

Says he:

"Don't you know, Mars Jawge?"

"No," says I, "I don't."

"Well, den, Miss Sophia's run off! 'deed she has. She run off in de night some time—nobody don't know jis' when; run off to get married to dat young Harney Shepherdson, you know—leastways, so dey 'spec. De fambly foun' it out 'bout half an hour ago—maybe a little mo'—en' I TELL you dey warn't no time los'. Sich another hurryin' up guns en hosses YOU never see! De women folks has gone for to stir up de relations, en ole

Mars Saul en de boys tuck dey guns en rode up de river road for to try to ketch dat young man en kill him 'fo' he kin git acrost de river wid Miss Sophia. I reck'n dey's gwyne to be mighty rough times."

"Buck went off 'thout waking me up."

"Well, I reck'n he DID! Dey warn't gwyne to mix you up in it. Mars Buck he loaded up his gun en 'lowed he's gwyne to fetch home a Shepherdson or bust. Well, dey'll be plenty un 'm dah, I reck'n, en you bet you he'll fetch one ef he gits a chanst."

I took up the river road as hard as I could put. By and by I begin to hear guns a good ways off. When I came in sight of the log store and the woodpile where the steamboats lands I worked along under the trees and brush till I got to a good place, and then I clumb up into the forks of a cottonwood that was out of reach, and watched. There was a wood-rank four foot high a little ways in front of the tree, and first I was going to hide behind that; but maybe it was luckier I didn't.

There was four or five men cavorting around on their horses in the open place before the log store, cussing and yelling, and trying to get at a couple of young chaps that was behind the wood-rank alongside of the steamboat landing; but they couldn't come it. Every time one of them showed himself on the river side of the woodpile he got shot at. The two boys was squatting back to back behind the pile, so they could watch both ways.

By and by the men stopped cavorting around and yelling. They started riding towards the store; then up gets one of the boys, draws a steady bead over the wood-rank, and drops one of them out of his saddle. All the men jumped off of their horses and grabbed the hurt one and started to carry him to the store; and that minute the two boys started on the run. They got half way to the tree I was in before the men noticed. Then the men see them, and jumped on their horses and took out after them. They gained on the boys, but it didn't do no good, the boys had too good a start; they got to the woodpile that was in front of my tree, and slipped in behind it, and so they had the bulge on the men again. One of the boys was Buck, and the other was a slim young chap about nineteen years old.

The men ripped around awhile, and then rode away. As soon as they was out of sight I sung out to Buck and told him. He didn't know what to make of my voice coming out of the tree at first. He was awful surprised. He told me to watch out sharp and let him know when the men come in sight again; said they was up to some devilment or other —wouldn't be gone long. I wished I was out of that tree, but I dasn't come down. Buck begun to cry and rip, and 'lowed that him and his cousin Joe (that was the other young chap) would make up for this day yet. He said his father and his two brothers was killed, and two or three of the enemy. Said the Shepherdsons laid for them in ambush. Buck said his father and brothers ought to waited for their relations—the Shepherdsons was too strong for them. I asked him what was become of young Harney and Miss Sophia. He said they'd got across the river and was safe. I was glad of that; but the way Buck did take on because he didn't manage to kill Harney that day he shot at him—I hain't ever heard anything like it.

All of a sudden, bang! bang! bang! goes three or four guns—the men had slipped around through the woods and come in from behind without their horses! The boys jumped for the river— both of them hurt—and as they swum down the current the men run along the bank shooting at them and singing out,

"Kill them, kill them!" It made me so sick I most fell out of the tree. I ain't a-going to tell ALL that happened—it would make me sick again if I was to do that. I wished I hadn't ever come ashore that night to see such things. I ain't ever going to get shut of them—lots of times I dream about them.

I stayed in the tree till it begun to get dark, afraid to come down. Sometimes I heard guns away off in the woods; and twice I seen little gangs of men gallop past the log store with guns; so I reckoned the trouble was still a-going on. I was mighty downhearted; so I made up my mind I wouldn't ever go anear that house again, because I reckoned I was to blame, somehow. I judged that that piece of paper meant that Miss Sophia was to meet Harney somewheres at half-past two and run off; and I judged I ought to told her father about that paper and the curious way she acted, and then maybe he would a locked her up, and this awful mess wouldn't ever happened.

When I got down out of the tree I crept along down the river bank a piece, and found the two bodies laying in the edge of the water, and tugged at them till I got them ashore; then I covered up their faces, and got away as quick as I could. I cried a little when I was covering up Buck's face, for he was mighty good to me.

It was just dark now. I never went near the house, but struck through the woods and made for the swamp. Jim warn't on his island, so I tramped off in a hurry for the crick, and crowded through the willows, red-hot to jump aboard and get out of that awful country. The raft was gone! My souls, but I was scared! I couldn't get my breath for most a minute. Then I raised a yell. A voice not twenty-five foot from me says:

"Good lan'! is dat you, honey? Doan' make no noise."

It was Jim's voice—nothing ever sounded so good before. I run along the bank a piece and got aboard, and Jim he grabbed me and hugged me, he was so glad to see me. He says:

"Laws bless you, chile, I 'uz right down sho' you's dead agin. Jack's been heah; he say he reck'n you's ben shot, kase you didn' come home no mo'; so I's jes' dis minute a startin' de raf' down towards de mouf er de crick, so's to be all ready for to shove out en leave soon as Jack comes agin en tells me for certain you IS dead. Lawsy, I's mighty glad to git you back again, honey."

I says:

"All right—that's mighty good; they won't find me, and they'll think I've been killed, and floated down the river—there's something up there that 'll help them think so—so don't you lose no time, Jim, but just shove off for the big water as fast as ever you can."

I never felt easy till the raft was two mile below there and out in the middle of the Mississippi. Then we hung up our signal lantern, and judged that we was free and safe once more. I hadn't had a bite to eat since yesterday, so Jim he got out some corn-dodgers and buttermilk, and pork and cabbage and greens—there ain't nothing in the world so good when it's cooked right—and whilst I eat my supper we talked and had a good time. I was powerful glad to get away from the feuds, and so was Jim to get away from the swamp. We said there warn't no home like a raft, after all. Other places do seem so cramped up and smothery, but a raft don't. You feel mighty free and easy and comfortable on a raft.

CHAPTER XIX.

TWO or three days and nights went by; I reckon I might say they swum by, they slid along so quiet and smooth and lovely. Here is the way we put in the time. It was a monstrous big river down there—sometimes a mile and a half wide; we run nights, and laid up and hid daytimes; soon as night was most gone we stopped navigating and tied up—nearly always in the dead water under a towhead; and then cut young cottonwoods and willows, and hid the raft with them. Then we set out the lines. Next we slid into the river and had a swim, so as to freshen up and cool off; then we set down on the sandy bottom where the water was about knee deep, and watched the daylight come. Not a sound anywheres—perfectly still —just like the whole world was asleep, only sometimes the bullfrogs a-cluttering, maybe. The first thing to see, looking away over the water, was a kind of dull line—that was the woods on t'other side; you couldn't make nothing else out; then a pale place in the sky; then more paleness spreading around; then the river softened up away off, and warn't black any more, but gray; you could see little dark spots drifting along ever so far away—trading scows, and such things; and long black streaks —rafts; sometimes you could hear a sweep screaking; or jumbled up voices, it was so still, and sounds come so far; and by and by you could see a streak on the water which you know by the look of the streak that there's a snag there in a swift current which breaks on it and makes that streak look that way; and you see the mist curl up off of the water, and the east reddens up, and the river, and you make out a log-cabin in the edge of the woods, away on the bank on t'other side of the river, being a woodyard, likely, and piled by them cheats so you can throw a dog through it anywheres; then the nice breeze springs up, and comes fanning you from over there, so cool and fresh and sweet to smell on account of the woods and the flowers; but sometimes not that way, because they've left dead fish laying around, gars and such, and they do get pretty rank; and next you've got the full day, and everything smiling in the sun, and the song-birds just going it!

A little smoke couldn't be noticed now, so we would take some fish off of the lines and cook up a hot breakfast. And afterwards we would watch the lonesomeness of the river, and kind of lazy along, and by and by lazy off to sleep. Wake up by and by, and look to see what done it, and maybe see a steamboat coughing along up-stream, so far off towards the other side you couldn't tell nothing about her only whether she was a stern-wheel or side-wheel; then for about an hour there wouldn't be nothing to hear nor nothing to see—just solid lonesomeness. Next you'd see a raft sliding by, away off yonder, and maybe a galoot on it chopping, because they're most always doing it on a raft; you'd see the axe flash and come down —you don't hear nothing; you see that axe go up again, and by the time it's above the man's head then you hear the K'CHUNK!—it had took all that time to come over the water. So we would put in the day, lazying around, listening to the stillness. Once there was a thick fog, and the rafts and things that went by was beating tin pans so the steamboats wouldn't run over them. A scow or a raft went by so close we could hear them talking and cussing and laughing—heard them plain; but we couldn't see no sign of them; it made you feel crawly; it was like spirits carrying on that way in the air. Jim said he believed it was spirits; but I says:

"No; spirits wouldn't say, 'Dern the dern fog.'"

Soon as it was night out we shoved; when we got her out to about the middle we let her alone, and let her float wherever the current wanted her to; then we lit the pipes, and dangled our legs in the water, and talked about all kinds of things—we was always naked, day and night, whenever the mosquitoes would let us—the new clothes Buck's folks made for me was too good to be comfortable, and besides I didn't go much on clothes, nohow.

Sometimes we'd have that whole river all to ourselves for the longest time. Yonder was the banks and the islands, across the water; and maybe a spark—which was a candle in a cabin window; and sometimes on the water you could see a spark or two—on a raft or a scow, you know; and maybe you could hear a fiddle or a song coming over from one of them crafts. It's lovely to live on a raft. We had the sky up there, all speckled with stars, and we used to lay on our backs and look up at them, and discuss about whether they was made or only just happened. Jim he allowed they was made, but I allowed they happened; I judged it would have took too long to MAKE so many. Jim said the moon could a LAID them; well, that looked kind of reasonable, so I didn't say nothing against it, because I've seen a frog lay most as many, so of course it could be done. We used to watch the stars that fell, too, and see them streak down. Jim allowed they'd got spoiled and was hove out of the nest.

Once or twice of a night we would see a steamboat slipping along in the dark, and now and then she would belch a whole world of sparks up out of her chimbleys, and they would rain down in the river and look awful pretty; then she would turn a corner and her lights would wink out and her powwow shut off and leave the river still again; and by and by her waves would get to us, a long time after she was gone, and joggle the raft a bit, and after that you wouldn't hear nothing for you couldn't tell how long, except maybe frogs or something.

After midnight the people on shore went to bed, and then for two or three hours the shores was black—no more sparks in the cabin windows. These sparks was our clock—the first one that showed again meant morning was coming, so we hunted a place to hide and tie up right away.

One morning about daybreak I found a canoe and crossed over a chute to the main shore—it was only two hundred yards— and paddled about a mile up a crick amongst the cypress woods, to see if I couldn't get some berries. Just as I was passing a place where a kind of a cowpath crossed the crick, here comes a couple of men tearing up the path as tight as they could foot it. I thought I was a goner, for whenever anybody was after anybody I judged it was ME—or maybe Jim. I was about to dig out from there in a hurry, but they was pretty close to me then, and sung out and begged me to save their lives—said they hadn't been doing nothing, and was being chased for it—said there was men and dogs a-coming. They wanted to jump right in, but I says:

"Don't you do it. I don't hear the dogs and horses yet; you've got time to crowd through the brush and get up the crick a little ways; then you take to the water and wade down to me and get in—that'll throw the dogs off the scent."

They done it, and soon as they was aboard I lit out for our towhead, and in about five or ten minutes we heard the dogs and the men away off, shouting. We heard them come along towards the crick, but couldn't see them; they seemed to stop and fool around a while; then, as we got further and further away all the time, we couldn't hardly hear them at all; by the time we had left a mile of woods behind us and struck the river, everything was quiet, and we paddled over to the towhead and hid in the cottonwoods and was safe.

One of these fellows was about seventy or upwards, and had a bald head and very gray whiskers. He had an old battered-up slouch hat on, and a greasy blue woollen shirt, and ragged old blue jeans britches stuffed into his boot-tops, and home-knit galluses—no, he only had one. He had an old long-tailed blue jeans coat with slick brass buttons flung over his arm, and both of them had big, fat, ratty-looking carpet-bags.

The other fellow was about thirty, and dressed about as ornery. After breakfast we all laid off and talked, and the first thing that come out was that these chaps didn't know one another.

"What got you into trouble?" says the baldhead to t'other chap.

"Well, I'd been selling an article to take the tartar off the teeth—and it does take it off, too, and generly the enamel along with it—but I stayed about one night longer than I ought to, and was just in the act of sliding out when I ran across you on the trail this side of town, and you told me they were coming, and begged me to help you to get off. So I told you I was expecting trouble myself, and would scatter out WITH you. That's the whole yarn—what's yourn?

"Well, I'd ben a-running' a little temperance revival thar 'bout a week, and was the pet of the women folks, big and little, for I was makin' it mighty warm for the rummies, I TELL you, and takin' as much as five or six dollars a night—ten cents a head, children and niggers free—and business a-growin' all the time, when somehow or another a little report got around last night that I had a way of puttin' in my time with a private jug on the sly. A nigger rousted me out this mornin', and told me the people was getherin' on the quiet with their dogs and horses, and they'd be along pretty soon and give me 'bout half an hour's start, and then run me down if they could; and if they got me they'd tar and feather me and ride me on a rail, sure. I didn't wait for no breakfast—I warn't hungry."

"Old man," said the young one, "I reckon we might double-team it together; what do you think?"

"I ain't undisposed. What's your line—mainly?"

"Jour printer by trade; do a little in patent medicines; theater-actor —tragedy, you know; take a turn to mesmerism and phrenology when there's a chance; teach singing-geography school for a change; sling a lecture sometimes—oh, I do lots of things—most anything that comes handy, so it ain't work. What's your lay?"

"I've done considerble in the doctoring way in my time. Layin' on o' hands is my best holt—for cancer and paralysis, and sich things; and I k'n tell a fortune pretty good when I've got somebody along to find out the facts for me. Preachin's my line, too, and workin' camp-meetin's, and missionaryin' around."

Nobody never said anything for a while; then the young man hove a sigh and says:

"Alas!"

"What 're you alassin' about?" says the bald-head.

"To think I should have lived to be leading such a life, and be degraded down into such company." And he begun to wipe the corner of his eye with a rag.

"Dern your skin, ain't the company good enough for you?" says the baldhead, pretty pert and uppish.

"Yes, it IS good enough for me; it's as good as I deserve; for who fetched me so low when I was so high? I did myself. I don't blame YOU, gentlemen—far from it; I don't blame anybody. I deserve it all. Let the cold world do its worst; one thing I know—there's a grave somewhere for me. The world may go on just as it's always done, and take everything from me—loved ones, property, everything; but it can't take that. Some day I'll lie down in it and forget it all, and my poor broken heart will be at rest." He went on a-wiping.

"Drot your pore broken heart," says the baldhead; "what are you heaving your pore broken heart at US f'r? WE hain't done nothing."

"No, I know you haven't. I ain't blaming you, gentlemen. I brought myself down—yes, I did it myself. It's right I should suffer—perfectly right—I don't make any moan."

"Brought you down from whar? Whar was you brought down from?"

"Ah, you would not believe me; the world never believes—let it pass —'tis no matter. The secret of my birth—"

"The secret of your birth! Do you mean to say—"

"Gentlemen," says the young man, very solemn, "I will reveal it to you, for I feel I may have confidence in you. By rights I am a duke!"

Jim's eyes bugged out when he heard that; and I reckon mine did, too. Then the baldhead says: "No! you can't mean it?"

"Yes. My great-grandfather, eldest son of the Duke of Bridgewater, fled to this country about the end of the last century, to breathe the pure air of freedom; married here, and died, leaving a son, his own father dying about the same time. The second son of the late duke seized the titles and estates— the infant real duke was ignored. I am the lineal descendant of that infant—I am the rightful Duke of Bridgewater; and here am I, forlorn, torn from my high estate, hunted of men, despised by the cold world, ragged, worn, heart-broken, and degraded to the companionship of felons on a raft!"

Jim pitied him ever so much, and so did I. We tried to comfort him, but he said it warn't much use, he couldn't be much comforted; said if we was a mind to acknowledge him, that would do him more good than most anything else; so we said we would, if he would tell us how. He said we ought to bow when we spoke to him, and say "Your Grace," or "My Lord," or "Your Lordship"—and he wouldn't mind it if we called him plain "Bridgewater," which, he said, was a title anyway, and not a name; and one of us ought to wait on him at dinner, and do any little thing for him he wanted done.

Well, that was all easy, so we done it. All through dinner Jim stood around and waited on him, and says, "Will yo' Grace have some o' dis or some o' dat?" and so on, and a body could see it was mighty pleasing to him.

But the old man got pretty silent by and by—didn't have much to say, and didn't look pretty comfortable over all that petting that was going on around that duke. He seemed to have something on his mind. So, along in the afternoon, he says:

"Looky here, Bilgewater," he says, "I'm nation sorry for you, but you ain't the only person that's had troubles like that."

"No?"

"No you ain't. You ain't the only person that's ben snaked down wrongfully out'n a high place."

"Alas!"

"No, you ain't the only person that's had a secret of his birth." And, by jings, HE begins to cry.

"Hold! What do you mean?"

"Bilgewater, kin I trust you?" says the old man, still sort of sobbing.

"To the bitter death!" He took the old man by the hand and squeezed it, and says, "That secret of your being: speak!"

"Bilgewater, I am the late Dauphin!"

You bet you, Jim and me stared this time. Then the duke says:

"You are what?"

"Yes, my friend, it is too true—your eyes is lookin' at this very moment on the pore disappeared Dauphin, Looy the Seventeen, son of Looy the Sixteen and Marry Antonette."

"You! At your age! No! You mean you're the late Charlemagne; you must be six or seven hundred years old, at the very least."

"Trouble has done it, Bilgewater, trouble has done it; trouble has brung these gray hairs and this premature balditude. Yes, gentlemen, you see before you, in blue jeans and misery, the wanderin', exiled, trampled-on, and sufferin' rightful King of France."

Well, he cried and took on so that me and Jim didn't know hardly what to do, we was so sorry—and so glad and proud we'd got him with us, too. So we set in, like we done before with the duke, and tried to comfort HIM. But he said it warn't no use, nothing but to be dead and done with it all could do him any good; though he said it often made him feel easier and better for a while if people treated him according to his rights, and got down on one knee to speak to him, and always called him "Your Majesty," and waited on him first at meals, and didn't set down in his presence till he asked them. So Jim and me set to majestying him, and doing this and that and t'other for him, and standing up till he told us we might set down. This done him heaps of good, and so he got cheerful and comfortable. But the duke kind of soured on him, and didn't look a bit satisfied with the way things was going; still, the king acted real friendly towards him, and said the duke's great-grandfather and all the other Dukes of Bilgewater was a good deal thought of by HIS father, and was allowed to come to the palace considerable; but the duke stayed huffy a good while, till by and by the king says:

"Like as not we got to be together a blamed long time on this h-yer raft, Bilgewater, and so what's the use o' your bein' sour? It 'll only make things oncomfortable. It ain't my fault I warn't born a duke, it ain't your fault you warn't born a king—so what's the use to worry? Make the best o' things the way you

find 'em, says I—that's my motto. This ain't no bad thing that we've struck here—plenty grub and an easy life—come, give us your hand, duke, and le's all be friends."

The duke done it, and Jim and me was pretty glad to see it. It took away all the uncomfortableness and we felt mighty good over it, because it would a been a miserable business to have any unfriendliness on the raft; for what you want, above all things, on a raft, is for everybody to be satisfied, and feel right and kind towards the others.

It didn't take me long to make up my mind that these liars warn't no kings nor dukes at all, but just low-down humbugs and frauds. But I never said nothing, never let on; kept it to myself; it's the best way; then you don't have no quarrels, and don't get into no trouble. If they wanted us to call them kings and dukes, I hadn't no objections, 'long as it would keep peace in the family; and it warn't no use to tell Jim, so I didn't tell him. If I never learnt nothing else out of pap, I learnt that the best way to get along with his kind of people is to let them have their own way.

CHAPTER XX.

THEY asked us considerable many questions; wanted to know what we covered up the raft that way for, and laid by in the daytime instead of running —was Jim a runaway nigger? Says I:

"Goodness sakes! would a runaway nigger run SOUTH?"

No, they allowed he wouldn't. I had to account for things some way, so I says:

"My folks was living in Pike County, in Missouri, where I was born, and they all died off but me and pa and my brother Ike. Pa, he 'lowed he'd break up and go down and live with Uncle Ben, who's got a little one-horse place on the river, forty-four mile below Orleans. Pa was pretty poor, and had some debts; so when he'd squared up there warn't nothing left but sixteen dollars and our nigger, Jim. That warn't enough to take us fourteen hundred mile, deck passage nor no other way. Well, when the river rose pa had a streak of luck one day; he ketched this piece of a raft; so we reckoned we'd go down to Orleans on it. Pa's luck didn't hold out; a steamboat run over the forrard corner of the raft one night, and we all went overboard and dove under the wheel; Jim and me come up all right, but pa was drunk, and Ike was only four years old, so they never come up no more. Well, for the next day or two we had considerable trouble, because people was always coming out in skiffs and trying to take Jim away from me, saying they believed he was a runaway nigger. We don't run daytimes no more now; nights they don't bother us."

The duke says:

"Leave me alone to cipher out a way so we can run in the daytime if we want to. I'll think the thing over—I'll invent a plan that'll fix it. We'll let it alone for to-day, because of course we don't want to go by that town yonder in daylight—it mightn't be healthy."

Towards night it begun to darken up and look like rain; the heat lightning was squirting around low down in the sky, and the leaves was beginning to shiver—it was going to be pretty ugly, it was easy to see that. So the duke and the king went to overhauling our wigwam, to see what the beds was like. My bed was a straw tick better than Jim's, which was a corn-shuck tick; there's always cobs around about in a shuck tick, and they poke into you and hurt; and when you roll over the dry shucks sound like you was rolling over in a pile of dead leaves; it makes such a rustling that you wake up. Well, the duke allowed he would take my bed; but the king allowed he wouldn't. He says:

"I should a reckoned the difference in rank would a sejested to you that a corn-shuck bed warn't just fitten for me to sleep on. Your Grace 'll take the shuck bed yourself."

Jim and me was in a sweat again for a minute, being afraid there was going to be some more trouble amongst them; so we was pretty glad when the duke says:

"'Tis my fate to be always ground into the mire under the iron heel of oppression. Misfortune has broken my once haughty spirit; I yield, I submit; 'tis my fate. I am alone in the world—let me suffer; can bear it."

We got away as soon as it was good and dark. The king told us to stand well out towards the middle of the river, and not show a light till we got a long ways below the town. We come in sight of the little bunch of lights by and by—that was the town, you know—and slid by, about a half a mile out, all right. When we was three-quarters of a mile below we hoisted up our signal lantern; and about ten o'clock it come on to rain and blow and thunder and lighten like everything; so the king told us to both stay on watch till the weather got better; then him and the duke crawled into the wigwam and turned in for the night. It was my watch below till twelve, but I wouldn't a turned in anyway if I'd had a bed, because a body don't see such a storm as that every day in the week, not by a long sight. My souls, how the wind did scream along! And every second or two there'd come a glare that lit up the white-caps for a half a mile around, and you'd see the islands looking dusty through the rain, and the trees thrashing around in the wind; then comes a H-WHACK!—bum! bum! bumble-umble-um-bum-bum-bum-bum—and the thunder would go rumbling and grumbling away, and quit—and then RIP comes another flash and another sockdolager. The waves most washed me off the raft sometimes, but I hadn't any clothes on, and didn't mind. We didn't have no trouble about snags; the lightning was glaring and flittering around so constant that we could see them plenty soon enough to throw her head this way or that and miss them.

I had the middle watch, you know, but I was pretty sleepy by that time, so Jim he said he would stand the first half of it for me; he was always mighty good that way, Jim was. I crawled into the wigwam, but the king and the duke had their legs sprawled around so there warn't no show for me; so I laid outside—I didn't mind the rain, because it was warm, and the waves warn't running so high now. About two they come up again, though, and Jim was going to call me; but he changed his mind, because he reckoned they warn't high enough yet to do any harm; but he was mistaken about that, for pretty soon all of a sudden along comes a regular ripper and washed me overboard. It most killed Jim a-laughing. He was the easiest nigger to laugh that ever was, anyway.

I took the watch, and Jim he laid down and snored away; and by and by the storm let up for good and all; and the first cabin-light that showed I rousted him out, and we slid the raft into hiding quarters for the day.

The king got out an old ratty deck of cards after breakfast, and him and the duke played seven-up a while, five cents a game.

Then they got tired of it, and allowed they would "lay out a campaign," as they called it. The duke went down into his carpet-bag, and fetched up a lot of little printed bills and read them out loud. One bill said, "The celebrated Dr. Armand de Montalban, of Paris," would "lecture on the Science of Phrenology" at such and such a place, on the blank day of blank, at ten cents admission, and "furnish charts of character at twenty-five cents apiece." The duke said that was HIM. In another bill he was the "world-renowned Shakespearian tragedian, Garrick the Younger, of Drury Lane, London." In other bills he had a lot of other names and done other wonderful things, like finding water and gold with a "divining-rod," "dissipating witch spells," and so on. By and by he says:

"But the histrionic muse is the darling. Have you ever trod the boards, Royalty?"

"No," says the king.

"You shall, then, before you're three days older, Fallen Grandeur," says the duke. "The first good town we come to we'll hire a hall and do the sword fight in Richard III. and the balcony scene in Romeo and Juliet. How does that strike you?"

"I'm in, up to the hub, for anything that will pay, Bilgewater; but, you see, I don't know nothing about play-actin', and hain't ever seen much of it. I was too small when pap used to have 'em at the palace. Do you reckon you can learn me?"

"Easy!"

"All right. I'm jist a-freezn' for something fresh, anyway. Le's commence right away."

So the duke he told him all about who Romeo was and who Juliet was, and said he was used to being Romeo, so the king could be Juliet.

"But if Juliet's such a young gal, duke, my peeled head and my white whiskers is goin' to look oncommon odd on her, maybe."

"No, don't you worry; these country jakes won't ever think of that. Besides, you know, you'll be in costume, and that makes all the difference in the world; Juliet's in a balcony, enjoying the moonlight before she goes to bed, and she's got on her night-gown and her ruffled nightcap. Here are the costumes for the parts."

He got out two or three curtain-calico suits, which he said was meedyevil armor for Richard III. and t'other chap, and a long white cotton nightshirt and a ruffled nightcap to match. The king was satisfied; so the duke got out his book and read the parts over in the most splendid spread-eagle way, prancing around and acting at the same time, to show how it had got to be done; then he give the book to the king and told him to get his part by heart.

There was a little one-horse town about three mile down the bend, and after dinner the duke said he had ciphered out his idea about how to run in daylight without it being dangersome for Jim; so he allowed he would go down to the town and fix that thing. The king allowed he would go, too, and see if he couldn't strike something. We was out of coffee, so Jim said I better go along with them in the canoe and get some.

When we got there there warn't nobody stirring; streets empty, and perfectly dead and still, like Sunday. We found a sick nigger sunning himself in a back yard, and he said everybody that warn't too young or too sick or too old was gone to camp-meeting, about two mile back in the woods. The king got the directions, and allowed he'd go and work that camp-meeting for all it was worth, and I might go, too.

The duke said what he was after was a printing-office. We found it; a little bit of a concern, up over a carpenter shop—carpenters and printers all gone to the meeting, and no doors locked. It was a dirty, littered-up place, and had ink marks, and handbills with pictures of horses and runaway niggers on them, all over the walls. The duke shed his coat and said he was all right now. So me and the king lit out for the camp-meeting.

We got there in about a half an hour fairly dripping, for it was a most awful hot day. There was as much as a thousand people there from twenty mile around. The woods was full of teams and wagons, hitched everywheres, feeding out of the wagon-troughs and stomping to keep off the flies. There was sheds made out of poles and roofed over with branches, where they had lemonade and gingerbread to sell, and piles of watermelons and green corn and such-like truck.

The preaching was going on under the same kinds of sheds, only they was bigger and held crowds of people. The benches was made out of outside slabs of logs, with holes bored in the round side to drive sticks into for legs. They didn't have no backs. The preachers had high platforms to stand on at one end of the sheds. The women had on sun-bonnets; and some had linsey-woolsey frocks, some gingham ones, and a few of the young ones had on calico. Some of the young men was barefooted, and some of the children didn't have on any clothes but just a tow-linen shirt. Some of the old women was knitting, and some of the young folks was courting on the sly.

The first shed we come to the preacher was lining out a hymn. He lined out two lines, everybody sung it, and it was kind of grand to hear it, there was so many of them and they done it in such a rousing way; then he lined out two more for them to sing—and so on. The people woke up more and more, and sung louder and louder; and towards the end some begun to groan, and some begun to shout. Then the preacher begun to preach, and begun in earnest, too; and went weaving first to one side of the platform and then the other, and then a-leaning down over the front of it, with his arms and his body going all the time, and shouting his words out with all his might; and every now and then he would hold up his Bible and spread it open, and kind of pass it around this way and that, shouting, "It's the brazen serpent in the wilderness! Look upon it and live!" And people would shout out, "Glory!—A-a-MEN!" And so he went on, and the people groaning and crying and saying amen:

"Oh, come to the mourners' bench! come, black with sin! (AMEN!) come, sick and sore! (AMEN!) come, lame and halt and blind! (AMEN!) come, pore and needy, sunk in shame! (A-A-MEN!) come, all that's worn and soiled and suffering!—come with a broken spirit! come with a contrite heart! come in your rags and sin and dirt! the waters that cleanse is free, the door of heaven stands open—oh, enter in and be at rest!" (A-A-MEN! GLORY, GLORY HALLELUJAH!)

And so on. You couldn't make out what the preacher said any more, on account of the shouting and crying. Folks got up everywheres in the crowd, and worked their way just by main strength to the mourners' bench, with the tears running down their faces; and when all the mourners had got up there to the front benches in a crowd, they sung and shouted and flung

themselves down on the straw, just crazy and wild.

Well, the first I knowed the king got a-going, and you could hear him over everybody; and next he went a-charging up on to the platform, and the preacher he begged him to speak to the people, and he done it. He told them he was a pirate—been a pirate for thirty years out in the Indian Ocean—and his crew was thinned out considerable last spring in a fight, and he was home now to take out some fresh men, and thanks to goodness he'd been robbed last night and put ashore off of a steamboat without a cent, and he was glad of it; it was the blessedest thing that ever happened to him, because he was a changed man now, and happy for the first time in his life; and, poor as he was, he was going to start right off and work his way back to the Indian Ocean, and put in the rest of his life trying to turn the pirates into the true path; for he could do it better than anybody else, being acquainted with all pirate crews in that ocean; and though it would take him a long time to get there without money, he would get there anyway, and every time he convinced a pirate he would say to him, "Don't you thank me, don't you give me no credit; it all belongs to them dear people in Pokeville camp-meeting, natural brothers and benefactors of the race, and that dear preacher there, the truest friend a pirate ever had!"

And then he busted into tears, and so did everybody. Then somebody sings out, "Take up a collection for him, take up a collection!" Well, a half a dozen made a jump to do it, but somebody sings out, "Let HIM pass the hat around!" Then everybody said it, the preacher too.

So the king went all through the crowd with his hat swabbing his eyes, and blessing the people and praising them and thanking them for being so good to the poor pirates away off there; and every little while the prettiest kind of girls, with the tears running down their cheeks, would up and ask him would he let them kiss him for to remember him by; and he always done it; and some of them he hugged and kissed as many as five or six times—and he was invited to stay a week; and everybody wanted him to live in their houses, and said they'd think it was an honor; but he said as this was the last day of the camp-meeting he couldn't do no good, and besides he was in a sweat to get to the Indian Ocean right off and go to work on the pirates.

When we got back to the raft and he come to count up he found he had collected eighty-seven dollars and seventy-five cents. And then he had fetched away a three-gallon jug of whisky, too, that he found under a wagon when he was starting home through the woods. The king said, take it all around, it laid over any day he'd ever put in in the missionarying line. He said it warn't no use talking, heathens don't amount to shucks alongside of pirates to work a camp-meeting with.

The duke was thinking HE'D been doing pretty well till the king come to show up, but after that he didn't think so so much. He had set up and printed off two little jobs for farmers in that printing-office—horse bills—and took the money, four dollars. And he had got in ten dollars' worth of advertisements for the paper, which he said he would put in for four dollars if they would pay in advance—so they done it. The price of the paper was two dollars a year, but he took in three subscriptions for half a dollar apiece on condition of them paying him in advance; they were going to pay in cordwood and onions as usual, but he said he had just bought the concern and knocked down the price as low as he could afford it, and was going to run it for cash. He set up a little piece of poetry, which he made, himself, out of his own head—three verses—kind of sweet and saddish—the name of it was, "Yes, crush, cold world, this breaking heart"—and he left that all set up and ready to print in the paper, and didn't charge nothing for it. Well, he took in nine dollars and a half, and said he'd done a pretty square day's work for it.

Then he showed us another little job he'd printed and hadn't charged for, because it was for us. It had a picture of a runaway nigger with a bundle on a stick over his shoulder, and "$200 reward" under it. The reading was all about Jim, and just described him to a dot. It said he run away from St. Jacques' plantation, forty mile below New Orleans, last winter, and likely went north, and whoever would catch him and send him back he could have the reward and expenses.

"Now," says the duke, "after to-night we can run in the daytime if we want to. Whenever we see anybody coming we can tie Jim hand and foot with a rope, and lay him in the wigwam and show this handbill and say we captured him up the river, and were too poor to travel on a steamboat, so we got this little raft on credit from our friends and are going down to get the reward. Handcuffs and chains would look still better on Jim, but it wouldn't go well with the story of us being so poor. Too much like jewelry. Ropes are the correct thing—we must preserve the unities, as we say on the boards."

We all said the duke was pretty smart, and there couldn't be no trouble about running daytimes. We judged we could make miles enough that night to get out of the reach of the powwow we reckoned the duke's work in the printing office was going to make in that little town; then we could boom right along if we wanted to.

We laid low and kept still, and never shoved out till nearly ten o'clock; then we slid by, pretty wide away from the town, and didn't hoist our lantern till we was clear out of sight of it.

When Jim called me to take the watch at four in the morning, he says:

"Huck, does you reck'n we gwyne to run acrost any mo' kings on dis trip?"

"No," I says, "I reckon not."

"Well," says he, "dat's all right, den. I doan' mine one er two kings, but dat's enough. Dis one's powerful drunk, en de duke ain' much better."

I found Jim had been trying to get him to talk French, so he could hear what it was like; but he said he had been in this country so long, and had so much trouble, he'd forgot it.

CHAPTER XXI.

IT was after sun-up now, but we went right on and didn't tie up. The king and the duke turned out by and by looking pretty rusty; but after they'd jumped overboard and took a swim it chippered them up a good deal. After breakfast the king he took a seat on the corner of the raft, and pulled off his boots and rolled up his britches, and let his legs dangle in the water, so as to be comfortable, and lit his pipe, and went to getting his Romeo and Juliet by heart. When he had got it pretty good him and the duke begun to practice it together. The duke had to learn him over and over again how to say every speech; and he made him sigh, and put his hand on his heart, and after a while he said he done it pretty well; "only," he says, "you mustn't bellow out ROMEO! that way, like a bull—you must say it soft and sick and languishy, so—R-o-o-meo! that is the idea; for Juliet's a dear sweet mere child of a girl, you know, and she doesn't bray like a jackass."

Well, next they got out a couple of long swords that the duke made out of oak laths, and begun to practice the sword fight—the duke called himself Richard III.; and the way they laid on and pranced around the raft was grand to see. But by and by the king tripped and fell overboard, and after that they took a rest, and had a talk about all kinds of adventures they'd had in other times along the river.

After dinner the duke says:

"Well, Capet, we'll want to make this a first-class show, you know, so I guess we'll add a little more to it. We want a little something to answer encores with, anyway."

"What's onkores, Bilgewater?"

The duke told him, and then says:

"I'll answer by doing the Highland fling or the sailor's hornpipe; and you—well, let me see—oh, I've got it—you can do Hamlet's soliloquy."

"Hamlet's which?"

"Hamlet's soliloquy, you know; the most celebrated thing in Shakespeare. Ah, it's sublime, sublime! Always fetches the house. I haven't got it in the book—I've only got one volume—but I reckon I can piece it out from memory. I'll just walk up and down a minute, and see if I can call it back from recollection's vaults."

So he went to marching up and down, thinking, and frowning horrible every now and then; then he would hoist up his eyebrows; next he would squeeze his hand on his forehead and stagger back and kind of moan; next he would sigh, and next he'd let on to drop a tear. It was beautiful to see him. By and by he got it. He told us to give attention. Then he strikes a most noble attitude, with one leg shoved forwards, and his arms stretched away up, and his head tilted back, looking up at the sky; and then he begins to rip and rave and grit his teeth; and after that, all through his speech, he howled, and spread around, and swelled up his chest, and just knocked the spots out of any acting ever I see before. This is the speech—I learned it, easy enough, while he was learning it to the king:

To be, or not to be; that is the bare bodkin That makes calamity of so long life; For who would fardels bear, till Birnam Wood do come to Dunsinane, But that the fear of something after death Murders the innocent sleep, Great nature's second course, And makes us rather sling the arrows of outrageous fortune Than fly to others that we know not of. There's the respect must give us pause: Wake Duncan with thy knocking! I would thou couldst; For who would bear the whips and scorns of time, The oppressor's wrong, the proud man's contumely, The law's delay, and the quietus which his pangs might take, In the dead waste and middle of the night, when churchyards yawn In customary suits of solemn black, But that the undiscovered country from whose bourne no traveler returns, Breathes forth contagion on the world, And thus the native hue of resolution, like the poor cat i' the adage, Is sicklied o'er with care, And all the clouds that lowered o'er our housetops, With this regard their currents turn awry, And lose the name of action. 'Tis a consummation devoutly to be wished. But soft you, the fair Ophelia: Ope not thy ponderous and marble jaws, But get thee to a nunnery—go!

Well, the old man he liked that speech, and he mighty soon got it so he could do it first-rate. It seemed like he was just born for it; and when he had his hand in and was excited, it was perfectly lovely the way he would rip and tear and rair up behind when he was getting it off.

The first chance we got the duke he had some showbills printed; and after that, for two or three days as we floated along, the raft was a most uncommon lively place, for there warn't nothing but sword fighting and rehearsing—as the duke called it—going on all the time. One morning, when we was pretty well down the State of Arkansaw, we come in sight of a little one-horse town in a big bend; so we tied up about three-quarters of a mile above it, in the mouth of a crick which was shut in like a tunnel by the cypress trees, and all of us but Jim took the canoe and went down there to see if there was any chance in that place for our show.

We struck it mighty lucky; there was going to be a circus there that afternoon, and the country people was already beginning to come in, in all kinds of old shackly wagons, and on horses. The circus would leave before night, so our show would have a pretty good chance. The duke he hired the courthouse, and we went around and stuck up our bills. They read like this:

Shaksperean Revival ! ! ! Wonderful Attraction! For One Night Only!

The world renowned tragedians, David Garrick the Younger, of Drury Lane Theatre London, and Edmund Kean the elder, of the Royal Haymarket Theatre, Whitechapel, Pudding Lane, Piccadilly, London, and the Royal Continental Theatres, in their sublime Shaksperean Spectacle entitled

TheBalcony Scene in Romeo and Juliet ! ! !

      Romeo   Mr. Garrick
      Juliet   Mr. Kean

Assisted by the whole strength of the company! New costumes, new scenes, new appointments! Also: The thrilling, masterly, and blood-curdling Broad-sword conflict In Richard III. ! ! !

      Richard III   Mr. Garrick
      Richmond   Mr. Kean

Also: (by special request) Hamlet's Immortal Soliloquy ! ! By The Illustrious Kean! Done by him 300 consecutive nights in Paris! For One Night Only, On account of imperative European engagements! Admission 25 cents; children and servants, 10 cents.

Then we went loafing around town. The stores and houses was most all old, shackly, dried up frame concerns that hadn't ever been painted; they was set up three or four foot above ground on stilts, so as to be out of reach of the water when the river was over-flowed. The houses had little gardens around them, but they didn't seem to raise hardly anything in them but jimpson-weeds, and sunflowers, and ash piles, and old curled-up boots and shoes, and pieces of bottles, and rags, and played-out tinware. The fences was made of different kinds of boards, nailed on at different times; and they leaned every which way, and had gates that didn't generly have but one hinge—a leather one. Some of the fences had been white-washed some time or another, but the duke said it was in

Clumbus' time, like enough. There was generly hogs in the garden, and people driving them out.

All the stores was along one street. They had white domestic awnings in front, and the country people hitched their horses to the awning-posts. There was empty drygoods boxes under the awnings, and loafers roosting on them all day long, whittling them with their Barlow knives; and chawing tobacco, and gaping and yawning and stretching—a mighty ornery lot. They generly had on yellow straw hats most as wide as an umbrella, but didn't wear no coats nor waistcoats, they called one another Bill, and Buck, and Hank, and Joe, and Andy, and talked lazy and drawly, and used considerable many cuss words. There was as many as one loafer leaning up against every awning-post, and he most always had his hands in his britches-pockets, except when he fetched them out to lend a chaw of tobacco or scratch. What a body was hearing amongst them all the time was:

"Gimme a chaw 'v tobacker, Hank."

"Cain't; I hain't got but one chaw left. Ask Bill."

Maybe Bill he gives him a chaw; maybe he lies and says he ain't got none. Some of them kinds of loafers never has a cent in the world, nor a chaw of tobacco of their own. They get all their chawing by borrowing; they say to a fellow, "I wisht you'd len' me a chaw, Jack, I jist this minute give Ben Thompson the last chaw I had"—which is a lie pretty much everytime; it don't fool nobody but a stranger; but Jack ain't no stranger, so he says:

"YOU give him a chaw, did you? So did your sister's cat's grandmother. You pay me back the chaws you've awready borry'd off'n me, Lafe Buckner, then I'll loan you one or two ton of it, and won't charge you no back intrust, nuther."

"Well, I DID pay you back some of it wunst."

"Yes, you did—'bout six chaws. You borry'd store tobacker and paid back nigger-head."

Store tobacco is flat black plug, but these fellows mostly chaws the natural leaf twisted. When they borrow a chaw they don't generly cut it off with a knife, but set the plug in between their teeth, and gnaw with their teeth and tug at the plug with their hands till they get it in two; then sometimes the one that owns the tobacco looks mournful at it when it's handed back, and says, sarcastic:

"Here, gimme the CHAW, and you take the PLUG."

All the streets and lanes was just mud; they warn't nothing else BUT mud —mud as black as tar and nigh about a foot deep in some places, and two or three inches deep in ALL the places. The hogs loafed and grunted around everywheres. You'd see a muddy sow and a litter of pigs come lazying along the street and whollop herself right down in the way, where folks had to walk around her, and she'd stretch out and shut her eyes and wave her ears whilst the pigs was milking her, and look as happy as if she was on salary. And pretty soon you'd hear a loafer sing out, "Hi! SO boy! sick him, Tige!" and away the sow would go, squealing most horrible, with a dog or two swinging to each ear, and three or four dozen more a-coming; and then you would see all the loafers get up and watch the thing out of sight, and laugh at the fun and look grateful for the noise. Then they'd settle back again till there was a dog fight. There couldn't anything wake them up all over, and make them happy all over, like a dog fight—unless it might be putting turpentine on a stray dog and setting fire to him, or tying a tin pan to his tail and see him run himself to death.

On the river front some of the houses was sticking out over the bank, and they was bowed and bent, and about ready to tumble in, The people had moved out of them. The bank was caved away under one corner of some others, and that corner was hanging over. People lived in them yet, but it was dangersome, because sometimes a strip of land as wide as a house caves in at a time. Sometimes a belt of land a quarter of a mile deep will start in and cave along and cave along till it all caves into the river in one summer. Such a town as that has to be always moving back, and back, and back, because the river's always gnawing at it.

The nearer it got to noon that day the thicker and thicker was the wagons and horses in the streets, and more coming all the time. Families fetched their dinners with them from the country, and eat them in the wagons. There was considerable whisky drinking going on, and I seen three fights. By and by somebody sings out:

"Here comes old Boggs!—in from the country for his little old monthly drunk; here he comes, boys!"

All the loafers looked glad; I reckoned they was used to having fun out of Boggs. One of them says:

"Wonder who he's a-gwyne to chaw up this time. If he'd a-chawed up all the men he's ben a-gwyne to chaw up in the last twenty year he'd have considerable ruputation now."

Another one says, "I wisht old Boggs 'd threaten me, 'cuz then I'd know I warn't gwyne to die for a thousan' year."

Boggs comes a-tearing along on his horse, whooping and yelling like an Injun, and singing out:

"Cler the track, thar. I'm on the waw-path, and the price uv coffins is a-gwyne to raise."

He was drunk, and weaving about in his saddle; he was over fifty year old, and had a very red face. Everybody yelled at him and laughed at him and sassed him, and he sassed back, and said he'd attend to them and lay them out in their regular turns, but he couldn't wait now because he'd come to town to kill old Colonel Sherburn, and his motto was, "Meat first, and spoon vittles to top off on."

He see me, and rode up and says:

"Whar'd you come f'm, boy? You prepared to die?"

Then he rode on. I was scared, but a man says:

"He don't mean nothing; he's always a-carryin' on like that when he's drunk. He's the best naturedest old fool in Arkansaw—never hurt nobody, drunk nor sober."

Boggs rode up before the biggest store in town, and bent his head down so he could see under the curtain of the awning and yells:

"Come out here, Sherburn! Come out and meet the man you've swindled. You're the houn' I'm after, and I'm a-gwyne to have you, too!"

And so he went on, calling Sherburn everything he could lay his tongue to, and the whole street packed with people listening and laughing and going on. By and by a proud-looking man about fifty-five—and he was a heap the best dressed man in that town, too—steps out of the store, and the crowd drops back on each side to let him come. He says to Boggs, mighty ca'm and slow—he says:

"I'm tired of this, but I'll endure it till one o'clock. Till one o'clock, mind—no longer. If you open your mouth against me only once after that time you can't travel so far but I will find you."

Then he turns and goes in. The crowd looked mighty sober; nobody stirred, and there warn't no more laughing. Boggs rode off blackguarding Sherburn as loud as he could yell, all down the street; and pretty soon back he comes and stops before the store, still keeping it up. Some men crowded around him and tried to get him to shut up, but he wouldn't; they told him it would be one o'clock in about fifteen minutes, and so he MUST go home—he must go right away. But it didn't do no good. He cussed away with all his might, and throwed his hat down in the mud and rode over it, and pretty soon away he went a-raging down the street again, with his gray hair a-flying. Everybody that could get a chance at him tried their best to coax him off of his horse so they could lock him up and get him sober; but it warn't no use—up the street he would tear again, and give Sherburn another cussing. By and by somebody says:

"Go for his daughter!—quick, go for his daughter; sometimes he'll listen to her. If anybody can persuade him, she can."

So somebody started on a run. I walked down street a ways and stopped. In about five or ten minutes here comes Boggs again, but not on his horse. He was a-reeling across the street towards me, bare-headed, with a friend on both sides of him a-holt of his arms and hurrying him along. He was quiet, and looked uneasy; and he warn't hanging back any, but was doing some of the hurrying himself. Somebody sings out:

"Boggs!"

I looked over there to see who said it, and it was that Colonel Sherburn. He was standing perfectly still in the street, and had a pistol raised in his right hand—not aiming it, but holding it out with the barrel tilted up towards the sky. The same second I see a young girl coming on the run, and two men with her. Boggs and the men turned round to see who called him, and when they see the pistol the men jumped to one side, and the pistol-barrel come down slow and steady to a level—both barrels cocked. Boggs throws up both of his hands and says, "O Lord, don't shoot!" Bang! goes the first shot, and he staggers back, clawing at the air—bang! goes the second one, and he tumbles backwards on to the ground, heavy and solid, with his arms spread out. That young girl screamed out and comes rushing, and down she throws herself on her father, crying, and saying, "Oh, he's killed him, he's killed him!" The crowd closed up around them, and shouldered and jammed one another, with their necks stretched, trying to see, and people on the inside trying to shove them back and shouting, "Back, back! give him air, give him air!"

Colonel Sherburn he tossed his pistol on to the ground, and turned around on his heels and walked off.

They took Boggs to a little drug store, the crowd pressing

around just the same, and the whole town following, and I rushed and got a good place at the window, where I was close to him and could see in. They laid him on the floor and put one large Bible under his head, and opened another one and spread it on his breast; but they tore open his shirt first, and I seen where one of the bullets went in. He made about a dozen long gasps, his breast lifting the Bible up when he drawed in his breath, and letting it down again when he breathed it out—and after that he laid still; he was dead. Then they pulled his daughter away from him, screaming and crying, and took her off. She was about sixteen, and very sweet and gentle looking, but awful pale and scared.

Well, pretty soon the whole town was there, squirming and scrouging and pushing and shoving to get at the window and have a look, but people that had the places wouldn't give them up, and folks behind them was saying all the time, "Say, now, you've looked enough, you fellows; 'tain't right and 'tain't fair for you to stay thar all the time, and never give nobody a chance; other folks has their rights as well as you."

There was considerable jawing back, so I slid out, thinking maybe there was going to be trouble. The streets was full, and everybody was excited. Everybody that seen the shooting was telling how it happened, and there was a big crowd packed around each one of these fellows, stretching their necks and listening. One long, lanky man, with long hair and a big white fur stovepipe hat on the back of his head, and a crooked-handled cane, marked out the places on the ground where Boggs stood and where Sherburn stood, and the people following him around from one place to t'other and watching everything he done, and bobbing their heads to show they understood, and stooping a little and resting their hands on their thighs to watch him mark the places on the ground with his cane; and then he stood up straight and stiff where Sherburn had stood, frowning and having his hat-brim down over his eyes, and sung out, "Boggs!" and then fetched his cane down slow to a level, and says "Bang!" staggered backwards, says "Bang!" again, and fell down flat on his back. The people that had seen the thing said he done it perfect; said it was just exactly the way it all happened. Then as much as a dozen people got out their bottles and treated him.

Well, by and by somebody said Sherburn ought to be lynched. In about a minute everybody was saying it; so away they went, mad and yelling, and snatching down every clothes-line they come to to do the hanging with.

CHAPTER XXII.

THEY swarmed up towards Sherburn's house, a-whooping and raging like Injuns, and everything had to clear the way or get run over and tromped to mush, and it was awful to see. Children was heeling it ahead of the mob, screaming and trying to get out of the way; and every window along the road was full of women's heads, and there was nigger boys in every tree, and bucks and wenches looking over every fence; and as soon as the mob would get nearly to them they would break and skaddle back out of reach. Lots of the women and girls was crying and taking on, scared most to death.

They swarmed up in front of Sherburn's palings as thick as they could jam together, and you couldn't hear yourself think for the noise. It was a little twenty-foot yard. Some sung out "Tear down the fence! tear down the fence!" Then there was a racket of ripping and tearing and smashing, and down she goes, and the front wall of the crowd begins to roll in like a wave.

Just then Sherburn steps out on to the roof of his little front porch, with a double-barrel gun in his hand, and takes his stand, perfectly ca'm and deliberate, not saying a word. The racket stopped, and the wave sucked back.

Sherburn never said a word—just stood there, looking down. The stillness was awful creepy and uncomfortable. Sherburn run his eye slow along the crowd; and wherever it struck the people tried a little to out-gaze him, but they couldn't; they dropped their eyes and looked sneaky. Then pretty soon Sherburn sort of laughed; not the pleasant kind, but the kind that makes you feel like when you are eating bread that's got sand in it.

Then he says, slow and scornful:

"The idea of YOU lynching anybody! It's amusing. The idea of you thinking you had pluck enough to lynch a MAN! Because you're brave enough to tar and feather poor friendless cast-out women that come along here, did that make you think you had grit enough to lay your hands on a MAN? Why, a MAN'S safe in the hands of ten thousand of your kind—as long as it's daytime and you're not behind him.

"Do I know you? I know you clear through was born and raised in the South, and I've lived in the North; so I know the average all around. The average man's a coward. In the North he lets anybody walk over him that wants to, and goes home and prays for a humble spirit to bear it. In the South one man all by himself, has stopped a stage full of men in the daytime, and robbed the lot. Your newspapers call you a brave people so much that you think you are braver than any other people—whereas you're just AS brave, and no braver. Why don't your juries hang murderers? Because they're afraid the man's friends will shoot them in the back, in the dark—and it's just what they WOULD do.

"So they always acquit; and then a MAN goes in the night, with a hundred masked cowards at his back and lynches the rascal. Your mistake is, that you didn't bring a man with you; that's one mistake, and the other is that you didn't come in the dark and fetch your masks. You brought PART of a man—Buck Harkness, there—and if you hadn't had him to start you, you'd a taken it out in blowing.

"You didn't want to come. The average man don't like trouble and danger. YOU don't like trouble and danger. But if only HALF a man—like Buck Harkness, there—shouts 'Lynch him! lynch him!' you're afraid to back down—afraid you'll be found out to be what you are—COWARDS—and so you raise a yell, and hang yourselves on to that half-a-man's coat-tail, and come raging up here, swearing what big things you're going to do. The pitifulest thing out is a mob; that's what an army is—a mob; they don't fight with courage that's born in them, but with courage that's borrowed from their mass, and from their officers. But a mob without any MAN at the head of it is BENEATH pitifulness. Now the thing for YOU to do is to droop your tails and go home and crawl in a hole. If any real lynching's going to be done it will be done in the dark, Southern fashion; and when they come they'll bring their masks, and fetch a MAN along. Now LEAVE—and take your half-a-man with you"—tossing his gun up across his left arm and cocking it when he says this.

The crowd washed back sudden, and then broke all apart, and went tearing off every which way, and Buck Harkness he heeled it after them, looking tolerable cheap. I could a stayed if

I wanted to, but I didn't want to.

I went to the circus and loafed around the back side till the watchman went by, and then dived in under the tent. I had my twenty-dollar gold piece and some other money, but I reckoned I better save it, because there ain't no telling how soon you are going to need it, away from home and amongst strangers that way. You can't be too careful. I ain't opposed to spending money on circuses when there ain't no other way, but there ain't no use in WASTING it on them.

It was a real bully circus. It was the splendidest sight that ever was when they all come riding in, two and two, a gentleman and lady, side by side, the men just in their drawers and undershirts, and no shoes nor stirrups, and resting their hands on their thighs easy and comfortable —there must a been twenty of them—and every lady with a lovely complexion, and perfectly beautiful, and looking just like a gang of real sure-enough queens, and dressed in clothes that cost millions of dollars, and just littered with diamonds. It was a powerful fine sight; I never see anything so lovely. And then one by one they got up and stood, and went a-weaving around the ring so gentle and wavy and graceful, the men looking ever so tall and airy and straight, with their heads bobbing and skimming along, away up there under the tent-roof, and every lady's rose-leafy dress flapping soft and silky around her hips, and she looking like the most loveliest parasol.

And then faster and faster they went, all of them dancing, first one foot out in the air and then the other, the horses leaning more and more, and the ringmaster going round and round the center-pole, cracking his whip and shouting "Hi!—hi!" and the clown cracking jokes behind him; and by and by all hands dropped the reins, and every lady put her knuckles on her hips and every gentleman folded his arms, and then how the horses did lean over and hump themselves! And so one after the other they all skipped off into the ring, and made the sweetest bow I ever see, and then scampered out, and everybody clapped their hands and went just about wild.

Well, all through the circus they done the most astonishing things; and all the time that clown carried on so it most killed the people. The ringmaster couldn't ever say a word to him but he was back at him quick as a wink with the funniest things a body ever said; and how he ever COULD think of so many of them, and so sudden and so pat, was what I couldn't noway understand. Why, I couldn't a thought of them in a year. And by and by a drunk man tried to get into the ring—said he wanted to ride; said he could ride as well as anybody that ever was. They argued and tried to keep him out, but he wouldn't listen, and the whole show come to a standstill. Then the people begun to holler at him and make fun of him, and that made him mad, and he begun to rip and tear; so that stirred up the people, and a lot of men begun to pile down off of the benches and swarm towards the ring, saying, "Knock him down! throw him out!" and one or two women begun to scream. So, then, the ringmaster he made a little speech, and said he hoped there wouldn't be no disturbance, and if the man would promise he wouldn't make no more trouble he would let him ride if he thought he could stay on the horse. So everybody laughed and said all right, and the man got on. The minute he was on, the horse begun to rip and tear and jump and cavort around, with two circus men hanging on to his bridle trying to hold him, and the drunk man hanging on to his neck, and his heels flying in the air every jump, and the whole crowd of people standing up shouting and laughing till tears rolled down. And at last, sure enough, all the circus men could do, the horse broke loose, and away he went like the very

nation, round and round the ring, with that sot laying down on him and hanging to his neck, with first one leg hanging most to the ground on one side, and then t'other one on t'other side, and the people just crazy. It warn't funny to me, though; I was all of a tremble to see his danger. But pretty soon he struggled up astraddle and grabbed the bridle, a-reeling this way and that; and the next minute he sprung up and dropped the bridle and stood! and the horse a-going like a house afire too. He just stood up there, a-sailing around as easy and comfortable as if he warn't ever drunk in his life—and then he begun to pull off his clothes and sling them. He shed them so thick they kind of clogged up the air, and altogether he shed seventeen suits. And, then, there he was, slim and handsome, and dressed the gaudiest and prettiest you ever saw, and he lit into that horse with his whip and made him fairly hum—and finally skipped off, and made his bow and danced off to the dressing-room, and everybody just a-howling with pleasure and astonishment.

Then the ringmaster he see how he had been fooled, and he WAS the sickest ringmaster you ever see, I reckon. Why, it was one of his own men! He had got up that joke all out of his own head, and never let on to nobody. Well, I felt sheepish enough to be took in so, but I wouldn't a been in that ringmaster's place, not for a thousand dollars. I don't know; there may be bullier circuses than what that one was, but I never struck them yet. Anyways, it was plenty good enough for ME; and wherever I run across it, it can have all of MY custom every time.

Well, that night we had OUR show; but there warn't only about twelve people there—just enough to pay expenses. And they laughed all the time, and that made the duke mad; and everybody left, anyway, before the show was over, but one boy which was asleep. So the duke said these Arkansaw lunkheads couldn't come up to Shakespeare; what they wanted was low comedy—and maybe something ruther worse than low comedy, he reckoned. He said he could size their style. So next morning he got some big sheets of wrapping paper and some black paint, and drawed off some handbills, and stuck them up all over the village. The bills said:

AT THE COURT HOUSE! FOR 3 NIGHTS ONLY! The World-Renowned Tragedians DAVID GARRICK THE YOUNGER! AND EDMUND KEAN THE ELDER! Of the London and Continental Theatres, In their Thrilling Tragedy of THE KING'S CAMELEOPARD, OR THE ROYAL NONESUCH ! ! ! Admission 50 cents.

Then at the bottom was the biggest line of all, which said:

LADIES AND CHILDREN NOT ADMITTED.

"There," says he, "if that line don't fetch them, I don't know Arkansaw!"

CHAPTER XXIII.

WELL, all day him and the king was hard at it, rigging up a stage and a curtain and a row of candles for footlights; and that night the house was jam full of men in no time. When the place couldn't hold no more, the duke he quit tending door and went around the back way and come on to the stage and stood up before the curtain and made a little speech, and praised up this tragedy, and said it was the most thrillingest one that ever was; and so he went on a-bragging about the tragedy, and about Edmund Kean the Elder, which was to play the main principal part in it; and at last when he'd got everybody's expectations up high enough, he rolled up the curtain, and the next minute the king come a-prancing out on all fours, naked; and he was painted all over, ring-streaked-and- striped, all sorts of colors, as splendid as a rainbow. And—but never mind the rest of his outfit; it was just wild, but it was awful funny. The people most killed themselves laughing; and when the king got done capering and capered off behind the scenes, they roared and clapped and stormed and haw-hawed till he come back and done it over again, and after that they made him do it another time. Well, it would make a cow laugh to see the shines that old idiot cut.

Then the duke he lets the curtain down, and bows to the people, and says the great tragedy will be performed only two nights more, on accounts of pressing London engagements, where the seats is all sold already for it in Drury Lane; and then he makes them another bow, and says if he has succeeded in pleasing them and instructing them, he will be deeply obleeged if they will mention it to their friends and get them to come and see it.

Twenty people sings out:

"What, is it over? Is that ALL?"

The duke says yes. Then there was a fine time. Everybody sings out, "Sold!" and rose up mad, and was a-going for that stage and them tragedians. But a big, fine looking man jumps up on a bench and shouts:

"Hold on! Just a word, gentlemen." They stopped to listen. "We are sold—mighty badly sold. But we don't want to be the laughing stock of this whole town, I reckon, and never hear the last of this thing as long as we live. NO. What we want is to go out of here quiet, and talk this show up, and sell the REST of the town! Then we'll all be in the same boat. Ain't that sensible?" ("You bet it is!—the jedge is right!" everybody sings out.) "All right, then—not a word about any sell. Go along home, and advise everybody to come and see the tragedy."

Next day you couldn't hear nothing around that town but how splendid that show was. House was jammed again that night, and we sold this crowd the same way. When me and the king and the duke got home to the raft we all had a supper; and by and by, about midnight, they made Jim and me back her out and float her down the middle of the river, and fetch her in and hide her about two mile below town.

The third night the house was crammed again—and they warn't new-comers this time, but people that was at the show the other two nights. I stood by the duke at the door, and I see that every man that went in had his pockets bulging, or something muffled up under his coat—and I see it warn't no perfumery, neither, not by a long sight. I smelt sickly eggs by the barrel, and rotten cabbages, and such things; and if I know the signs of a dead cat being around, and I bet I do, there was sixty-four of them went in. I shoved in there for a minute, but it was too various for me; I couldn't stand it. Well, when the place couldn't hold no more people the duke he give a fellow a quarter and told him to tend door for him a minute, and then he started around for the stage door, I after him; but the minute we turned the corner and was in the dark he says:

"Walk fast now till you get away from the houses, and then shin for the raft like the dickens was after you!"

I done it, and he done the same. We struck the raft at the same time, and in less than two seconds we was gliding down stream, all dark and still, and edging towards the middle of the

river, nobody saying a word. I reckoned the poor king was in for a gaudy time of it with the audience, but nothing of the sort; pretty soon he crawls out from under the wigwam, and says:

"Well, how'd the old thing pan out this time, duke?" He hadn't been up-town at all.

We never showed a light till we was about ten mile below the village. Then we lit up and had a supper, and the king and the duke fairly laughed their bones loose over the way they'd served them people. The duke says:

"Greenhorns, flatheads! I knew the first house would keep mum and let the rest of the town get roped in; and I knew they'd lay for us the third night, and consider it was THEIR turn now. Well, it IS their turn, and I'd give something to know how much they'd take for it. I WOULD just like to know how they're putting in their opportunity. They can turn it into a picnic if they want to—they brought plenty provisions."

Them rapscallions took in four hundred and sixty-five dollars in that three nights. I never see money hauled in by the wagon-load like that before. By and by, when they was asleep and snoring, Jim says:

"Don't it s'prise you de way dem kings carries on, Huck?"

"No," I says, "it don't."

"Why don't it, Huck?"

"Well, it don't, because it's in the breed. I reckon they're all alike,"

"But, Huck, dese kings o' ourn is reglar rapscallions; dat's jist what dey is; dey's reglar rapscallions."

"Well, that's what I'm a-saying; all kings is mostly rapscallions, as fur as I can make out."

"Is dat so?"

"You read about them once—you'll see. Look at Henry the Eight; this 'n 's a Sunday-school Superintendent to HIM. And look at Charles Second, and Louis Fourteen, and Louis Fifteen, and James Second, and Edward Second, and Richard Third, and forty more; besides all them Saxon heptarchies that used to rip around so in old times and raise Cain. My, you ought to seen old Henry the Eight when he was in bloom. He WAS a blossom. He used to marry a new wife every day, and chop off her head next morning. And he would do it just as indifferent as if he was ordering up eggs. 'Fetch up Nell Gwynn,' he says. They fetch her up. Next morning, 'Chop off her head!' And they chop it off. 'Fetch up Jane Shore,' he says; and up she comes, Next morning, 'Chop off her head'—and they chop it off. 'Ring up Fair Rosamun.' Fair Rosamun answers the bell. Next morning, 'Chop off her head.' And he made every one of them tell him a tale every night; and he kept that up till he had hogged a thousand and one tales that way, and then he put them all in a book, and called it Domesday Book—which was a good name and stated the case. You don't know kings, Jim, but I know them; and this old rip of ourn is one of the cleanest I've struck in history. Well, Henry he takes a notion he wants to get up some trouble with this country. How does he go at it —give notice?—give the country a show? No. All of a sudden he heaves all the tea in Boston Harbor overboard, and whacks out a declaration of independence, and dares them to come on.

That was HIS style—he never give anybody a chance. He had suspicions of his father, the Duke of Wellington. Well, what did he do? Ask him to show up? No—drownded him in a butt of mamsey, like a cat. S'pose people left money laying around where he was—what did he do? He collared it. S'pose he contracted to do a thing, and you paid him, and didn't set down there and see that he done it—what did he do? He always done the other thing. S'pose he opened his mouth—what then? If he didn't shut it up powerful quick he'd lose a lie every time. That's the kind of a bug Henry was; and if we'd a had him along 'stead of our kings he'd a fooled that town a heap worse than ourn done. I don't say that ourn is lambs, because they ain't, when you come right down to the cold facts; but they ain't nothing to THAT old ram, anyway. All I say is, kings is kings, and you got to make allowances. Take them all around, they're a mighty ornery lot. It's the way they're raised."

"But dis one do SMELL so like de nation, Huck."

"Well, they all do, Jim. We can't help the way a king smells; history don't tell no way."

"Now de duke, he's a tolerble likely man in some ways."

"Yes, a duke's different. But not very different. This one's a middling hard lot for a duke. When he's drunk there ain't no near-sighted man could tell him from a king."

"Well, anyways, I doan' hanker for no mo' un um, Huck. Dese is all I kin stan'."

"It's the way I feel, too, Jim. But we've got them on our hands, and we got to remember what they are, and make allowances. Sometimes I wish we could hear of a country that's out of kings."

What was the use to tell Jim these warn't real kings and dukes? It wouldn't a done no good; and, besides, it was just as I said: you couldn't tell them from the real kind.

I went to sleep, and Jim didn't call me when it was my turn. He often done that. When I waked up just at daybreak he was sitting there with his head down betwixt his knees, moaning and mourning to himself. I didn't take notice nor let on. I knowed what it was about. He was thinking about his wife and his children, away up yonder, and he was low and homesick; because he hadn't ever been away from home before in his life; and I do believe he cared just as much for his people as white folks does for their'n. It don't seem natural, but I reckon it's so. He was often moaning and mourning that way nights, when he judged I was asleep, and saying, "Po' little 'Lizabeth! po' little Johnny! it's mighty hard; I spec' I ain't ever gwyne to see you no mo', no mo'!" He was a mighty good nigger, Jim was.

But this time I somehow got to talking to him about his wife and young ones; and by and by he says:

"What makes me feel so bad dis time 'uz bekase I hear sumpn over yonder on de bank like a whack, er a slam, while ago, en it mine me er de time I treat my little 'Lizabeth so ornery. She warn't on'y 'bout fo' year ole, en she tuck de sk'yarlet fever, en had a powful rough spell; but she got well, en one day she was a-stannin' aroun', en I says to her, I says:

"'Shet de do'.'

"She never done it; jis' stood dah, kiner smilin' up at me. It make me mad; en I says agin, mighty loud, I says:

"'Doan' you hear me? Shet de do'!'

"She jis stood de same way, kiner smilin' up. I was a-bilin'! I says:

"'I lay I MAKE you mine!'

"En wid dat I fetch' her a slap side de head dat sont her a-sprawlin'. Den I went into de yuther room, en 'uz gone 'bout ten minutes; en when I come back dah was dat do' a-stannin' open YIT, en dat chile stannin' mos' right in it, a-lookin' down and mournin', en de tears runnin' down. My, but I WUZ mad! I was a-gwyne for de chile, but jis' den—it was a do' dat open innerds—jis' den, 'long come de wind en slam it to, behine de chile, ker-BLAM!—en my lan', de chile never move'! My breff mos' hop outer me; en I feel so—so—I doan' know HOW I feel. I crope out, all a-tremblin', en crope aroun' en open de do' easy en slow, en poke my head in behine de chile, sof' en still, en all uv a sudden I says POW! jis' as loud as I could yell. SHE NEVER BUDGE! Oh, Huck, I bust out a-cryin' en grab her up in my arms, en say, 'Oh, de po' little thing! De Lord God Amighty fogive po' ole Jim, kaze he never gwyne to fogive hisself as long's he live!' Oh, she was plumb deef en dumb, Huck, plumb deef en dumb—en I'd ben a-treat'n her so!"

CHAPTER XXIV.

NEXT day, towards night, we laid up under a little willow towhead out in the middle, where there was a village on each side of the river, and the duke and the king begun to lay out a plan for working them towns. Jim he spoke to the duke, and said he hoped it wouldn't take but a few hours, because it got mighty heavy and tiresome to him when he had to lay all day in the wigwam tied with the rope. You see, when we left him all alone we had to tie him, because if anybody happened on to him all by himself and not tied it wouldn't look much like he was a runaway nigger, you know. So the duke said it WAS kind of hard to have to lay roped all day, and he'd cipher out some way to get around it.

He was uncommon bright, the duke was, and he soon struck it. He dressed Jim up in King Lear's outfit—it was a long curtain-calico gown, and a white horse-hair wig and whiskers; and then he took his theater paint and painted Jim's face and hands and ears and neck all over a dead, dull, solid blue, like a man that's been drownded nine days. Blamed if he warn't the horriblest looking outrage I ever see. Then the duke took and wrote out a sign on a shingle so:

Sick Arab—but harmless when not out of his head.

And he nailed that shingle to a lath, and stood the lath up four or five foot in front of the wigwam. Jim was satisfied. He said it was a sight better than lying tied a couple of years every day, and trembling all over every time there was a sound. The duke told him to make himself free and easy, and if anybody ever come meddling around, he must hop out of the wigwam, and carry on a little, and fetch a howl or two like a wild beast, and he reckoned they would light out and leave him alone. Which was sound enough judgment; but you take the average man, and he wouldn't wait for him to howl. Why, he didn't only look like he was dead, he looked considerable more than that.

These rapscallions wanted to try the Nonesuch again, because there was so much money in it, but they judged it wouldn't be safe, because maybe the news might a worked along down by this time. They couldn't hit no project that suited exactly; so at last the duke said he reckoned he'd lay off and work his brains an hour or two and see if he couldn't put up something on the Arkansaw village; and the king he allowed he would drop over to t'other village without any plan, but just trust in Providence to lead him the profitable way—meaning the devil, I reckon. We had all bought store clothes where we stopped last; and now the king put his'n on, and he told me to put mine on. I done it, of course. The king's duds was all black, and he did look real swell and starchy. I never knowed how clothes could change a body before. Why, before, he looked like the orneriest old rip that ever was; but now, when he'd take off his new white beaver and make a bow and do a smile, he looked that grand and good and pious that you'd say he had walked right out of the ark, and maybe was old Leviticus himself. Jim cleaned up the canoe, and I got my paddle ready. There was a big steamboat laying at the shore away up under the point, about three mile above the town—been there a couple of hours, taking on freight. Says the king:

"Seein' how I'm dressed, I reckon maybe I better arrive down from St. Louis or Cincinnati, or some other big place. Go for the steamboat, Huckleberry; we'll come down to the village on her."

I didn't have to be ordered twice to go and take a steamboat ride. I fetched the shore a half a mile above the village, and then went scooting along the bluff bank in the easy water. Pretty soon we come to a nice innocent-looking young country jake setting on a log swabbing the sweat off of his face, for it was powerful warm weather; and he had a couple of big carpet-bags by him.

"Run her nose in shore," says the king. I done it. "Wher' you bound for, young man?"

"For the steamboat; going to Orleans."

"Git aboard," says the king. "Hold on a minute, my servant 'll he'p you with them bags. Jump out and he'p the gentleman, Adolphus"—meaning me, I see.

I done so, and then we all three started on again. The young chap was mighty thankful; said it was tough work toting his baggage such weather. He asked the king where he was going, and the king told him he'd come down the river and landed at the other village this morning, and now he was going up a few mile to see an old friend on a farm up there. The young fellow says:

"When I first see you I says to myself, 'It's Mr. Wilks, sure, and he come mighty near getting here in time.' But then I says again, 'No, I reckon it ain't him, or else he wouldn't be paddling up the river.' You AIN'T him, are you?"

"No, my name's Blodgett—Elexander Blodgett—REVEREND Elexander Blodgett, I s'pose I must say, as I'm one o' the Lord's poor servants. But still I'm jist as able to be sorry for Mr. Wilks for not arriving in time, all the same, if he's missed anything by it—which I hope he hasn't."

"Well, he don't miss any property by it, because he'll get that all right; but he's missed seeing his brother Peter die—which he mayn't mind, nobody can tell as to that—but his brother would a give anything in this world to see HIM before he died; never talked about nothing else all these three weeks; hadn't seen him since they was boys together—and hadn't ever seen his brother William at all—that's the deef and dumb one—

William ain't more than thirty or thirty-five. Peter and George were the only ones that come out here; George was the married brother; him and his wife both died last year. Harvey and William's the only ones that's left now; and, as I was saying, they haven't got here in time."

"Did anybody send 'em word?"

"Oh, yes; a month or two ago, when Peter was first took; because Peter said then that he sorter felt like he warn't going to get well this time. You see, he was pretty old, and George's g'yirls was too young to be much company for him, except Mary Jane, the red-headed one; and so he was kinder lonesome after George and his wife died, and didn't seem to care much to live. He most desperately wanted to see Harvey—and William, too, for that matter—because he was one of them kind that can't bear to make a will. He left a letter behind for Harvey, and said he'd told in it where his money was hid, and how he wanted the rest of the property divided up so George's g'yirls would be all right—for George didn't leave nothing. And that letter was all they could get him to put a pen to."

"Why do you reckon Harvey don't come? Wher' does he live?"

"Oh, he lives in England—Sheffield—preaches there—hasn't ever been in this country. He hasn't had any too much time—and besides he mightn't a got the letter at all, you know."

"Too bad, too bad he couldn't a lived to see his brothers, poor soul. You going to Orleans, you say?"

"Yes, but that ain't only a part of it. I'm going in a ship, next Wednesday, for Ryo Janeero, where my uncle lives."

"It's a pretty long journey. But it'll be lovely; wisht I was a-going. Is Mary Jane the oldest? How old is the others?"

"Mary Jane's nineteen, Susan's fifteen, and Joanna's about fourteen —that's the one that gives herself to good works and has a hare-lip."

"Poor things! to be left alone in the cold world so."

"Well, they could be worse off. Old Peter had friends, and they ain't going to let them come to no harm. There's Hobson, the Babtis' preacher; and Deacon Lot Hovey, and Ben Rucker, and Abner Shackleford, and Levi Bell, the lawyer; and Dr. Robinson, and their wives, and the widow Bartley, and—well, there's a lot of them; but these are the ones that Peter was thickest with, and used to write about sometimes, when he wrote home; so Harvey 'll know where to look for friends when he gets here."

Well, the old man went on asking questions till he just fairly emptied that young fellow. Blamed if he didn't inquire about everybody and everything in that blessed town, and all about the Wilkses; and about Peter's business—which was a tanner; and about George's—which was a carpenter; and about Harvey's—which was a dissentering minister; and so on, and so on. Then he says:

"What did you want to walk all the way up to the steamboat for?"

"Because she's a big Orleans boat, and I was afeard she mightn't stop there. When they're deep they won't stop for a hail. A Cincinnati boat will, but this is a St. Louis one."

"Was Peter Wilks well off?"

"Oh, yes, pretty well off. He had houses and land, and it's reckoned he left three or four thousand in cash hid up som'ers."

"When did you say he died?"

"I didn't say, but it was last night."

"Funeral to-morrow, likely?"

"Yes, 'bout the middle of the day."

"Well, it's all terrible sad; but we've all got to go, one time or another. So what we want to do is to be prepared; then we're all right."

"Yes, sir, it's the best way. Ma used to always say that."

When we struck the boat she was about done loading, and pretty soon she got off. The king never said nothing about going aboard, so I lost my ride, after all. When the boat was gone the king made me paddle up another mile to a lonesome place, and then he got ashore and says:

"Now hustle back, right off, and fetch the duke up here, and the new carpet-bags. And if he's gone over to t'other side, go over there and git him. And tell him to git himself up regardless. Shove along, now."

I see what HE was up to; but I never said nothing, of course. When I got back with the duke we hid the canoe, and then they set down on a log, and the king told him everything, just like the young fellow had said it —every last word of it. And all the time he was a-doing it he tried to talk like an Englishman; and he done it pretty well, too, for a slouch. I can't imitate him, and so I ain't a-going to try to; but he really done it pretty good. Then he says:

"How are you on the deef and dumb, Bilgewater?"

The duke said, leave him alone for that; said he had played a deef and dumb person on the histronic boards. So then they waited for a steamboat.

About the middle of the afternoon a couple of little boats come along, but they didn't come from high enough up the river; but at last there was a big one, and they hailed her. She sent out her yawl, and we went aboard, and she was from Cincinnati; and when they found we only wanted to go four or five mile they was booming mad, and gave us a cussing, and said they wouldn't land us. But the king was ca'm. He says:

"If gentlemen kin afford to pay a dollar a mile apiece to be took on and put off in a yawl, a steamboat kin afford to carry 'em, can't it?"

So they softened down and said it was all right; and when we got to the village they yawled us ashore. About two dozen men flocked down when they see the yawl a-coming, and when the king says:

"Kin any of you gentlemen tell me wher' Mr. Peter Wilks lives?" they give a glance at one another, and nodded their heads, as much as to say, "What d' I tell you?" Then one of them says, kind of soft and gentle:

"I'm sorry sir, but the best we can do is to tell you where he DID live yesterday evening."

Sudden as winking the ornery old cretur went an to smash, and fell up against the man, and put his chin on his shoulder, and cried down his back, and says:

"Alas, alas, our poor brother—gone, and we never got to see him; oh, it's too, too hard!"

Then he turns around, blubbering, and makes a lot of idiotic signs to the duke on his hands, and blamed if he didn't drop a carpet-bag and bust out a-crying. If they warn't the beatenest lot, them two frauds, that ever I struck.

Well, the men gathered around and sympathized with them, and said all sorts of kind things to them, and carried their carpet-bags up the hill for them, and let them lean on them and cry, and told the king all about his brother's last moments, and the king he told it all over again on his hands to the duke, and both of them took on about that dead tanner like they'd lost the twelve disciples. Well, if ever I struck anything like it, I'm a nigger. It was enough to make a body ashamed of the human race.

CHAPTER XXV.

THE news was all over town in two minutes, and you could see the people tearing down on the run from every which way, some of them putting on their coats as they come. Pretty soon we was in the middle of a crowd, and the noise of the tramping was like a soldier march. The windows and dooryards was full; and every minute somebody would say, over a fence:

"Is it THEM?"

And somebody trotting along with the gang would answer back and say:

"You bet it is."

When we got to the house the street in front of it was packed, and the three girls was standing in the door. Mary Jane WAS red-headed, but that don't make no difference, she was most awful beautiful, and her face and her eyes was all lit up like glory, she was so glad her uncles was come. The king he spread his arms, and Mary Jane she jumped for them, and the hare-lip jumped for the duke, and there they HAD it! Everybody most, leastways women, cried for joy to see them meet again at last and have such good times.

Then the king he hunched the duke private—I see him do it— and then he looked around and see the coffin, over in the corner on two chairs; so then him and the duke, with a hand across each other's shoulder, and t'other hand to their eyes, walked slow and solemn over there, everybody dropping back to give them room, and all the talk and noise stopping, people saying "Sh!" and all the men taking their hats off and drooping their heads, so you could a heard a pin fall. And when they got there they bent over and looked in the coffin, and took one sight, and then they bust out a-crying so you could a heard them to Orleans, most; and then they put their arms around each other's necks, and hung their chins over each other's shoulders; and then for three minutes, or maybe four, I never see two men leak the way they done. And, mind you, everybody was doing the same; and the place was that damp I never see anything like it. Then one of them got on one side of the coffin, and t'other on t'other side, and they kneeled down and rested their foreheads on the coffin, and let on to pray all to themselves. Well, when it come to that it worked the crowd like you never see anything like it, and everybody broke down and went to sobbing right out loud—the poor girls, too; and every woman, nearly, went up to the girls, without saying a word, and kissed them, solemn, on the forehead, and then put their hand on their head, and looked up towards the sky, with the tears running down, and then busted out and went off sobbing and swabbing, and give the next woman a show. I never see anything so disgusting.

Well, by and by the king he gets up and comes forward a little, and works himself up and slobbers out a speech, all full of tears and flapdoodle about its being a sore trial for him and his poor brother to lose the diseased, and to miss seeing diseased alive after the long journey of four thousand mile, but it's a trial that's sweetened and sanctified to us by this dear sympathy and these holy tears, and so he thanks them out of his heart and out of his brother's heart, because out of their mouths they can't, words being too weak and cold, and all that kind of rot and slush, till it was just sickening; and then he blubbers out a pious goody-goody Amen, and turns himself loose and goes to crying fit to bust.

And the minute the words were out of his mouth somebody over in the crowd struck up the doxolojer, and everybody joined in with all their might, and it just warmed you up and made you feel as good as church letting out. Music is a good thing; and after all that soul-butter and hogwash I never see it freshen up things so, and sound so honest and bully.

Then the king begins to work his jaw again, and says how him and his nieces would be glad if a few of the main principal friends of the family would take supper here with them this evening, and help set up with the ashes of the diseased; and says if his poor brother laying yonder could speak he knows who he would name, for they was names that was very dear to him, and mentioned often in his letters; and so he will name the same, to wit, as follows, vizz.:—Rev. Mr. Hobson, and Deacon Lot Hovey, and Mr. Ben Rucker, and Abner Shackleford, and Levi Bell, and Dr. Robinson, and their wives, and the widow Bartley.

Rev. Hobson and Dr. Robinson was down to the end of the town a-hunting together—that is, I mean the doctor was shipping a sick man to t'other world, and the preacher was pinting him right. Lawyer Bell was away up to Louisville on business. But the rest was on hand, and so they all come and shook hands with the king and thanked him and talked to him; and then they shook hands with the duke and didn't say nothing, but just kept a-smiling and bobbing their heads like a passel of sapheads whilst he made all sorts of signs with his hands and said "Goo-goo—goo-goo-goo" all the time, like a baby that can't talk.

So the king he blattered along, and managed to inquire about pretty much everybody and dog in town, by his name, and mentioned all sorts of little things that happened one time or another in the town, or to George's family, or to Peter. And he always let on that Peter wrote him the things; but that was a lie: he got every blessed one of them out of that young flathead that we canoed up to the steamboat.

Then Mary Jane she fetched the letter her father left behind, and the king he read it out loud and cried over it. It give the dwelling-house and three thousand dollars, gold, to the girls; and it give the tanyard (which was doing a good business), along with some other houses and land (worth about seven

thousand), and three thousand dollars in gold to Harvey and William, and told where the six thousand cash was hid down cellar. So these two frauds said they'd go and fetch it up, and have everything square and above-board; and told me to come with a candle. We shut the cellar door behind us, and when they found the bag they spilt it out on the floor, and it was a lovely sight, all them yaller-boys. My, the way the king's eyes did shine! He slaps the duke on the shoulder and says:

"Oh, THIS ain't bully nor noth'n! Oh, no, I reckon not! Why, Billy, it beats the Nonesuch, DON'T it?"

The duke allowed it did. They pawed the yaller-boys, and sifted them through their fingers and let them jingle down on the floor; and the king says:

"It ain't no use talkin'; bein' brothers to a rich dead man and representatives of furrin heirs that's got left is the line for you and me, Bilge. Thish yer comes of trust'n to Providence. It's the best way, in the long run. I've tried 'em all, and ther' ain't no better way."

Most everybody would a been satisfied with the pile, and took it on trust; but no, they must count it. So they counts it, and it comes out four hundred and fifteen dollars short. Says the king:

"Dern him, I wonder what he done with that four hundred and fifteen dollars?"

They worried over that awhile, and ransacked all around for it. Then the duke says:

"Well, he was a pretty sick man, and likely he made a mistake—I reckon that's the way of it. The best way's to let it go, and keep still about it. We can spare it."

"Oh, shucks, yes, we can SPARE it. I don't k'yer noth'n 'bout that—it's the COUNT I'm thinkin' about. We want to be awful square and open and above-board here, you know. We want to lug this h-yer money up stairs and count it before everybody—then ther' ain't noth'n suspicious. But when the dead man says ther's six thous'n dollars, you know, we don't want to—"

"Hold on," says the duke. "Le's make up the deffisit," and he begun to haul out yaller-boys out of his pocket.

"It's a most amaz'n' good idea, duke—you HAVE got a rattlin' clever head on you," says the king. "Blest if the old Nonesuch ain't a heppin' us out agin," and HE begun to haul out yaller-jackets and stack them up.

It most busted them, but they made up the six thousand clean and clear.

"Say," says the duke, "I got another idea. Le's go up stairs and count this money, and then take and GIVE IT TO THE GIRLS."

"Good land, duke, lemme hug you! It's the most dazzling idea 'at ever a man struck. You have cert'nly got the most astonishin' head I ever see. Oh, this is the boss dodge, ther' ain't no mistake 'bout it. Let 'em fetch along their suspicions now if they want to—this 'll lay 'em out."

When we got up-stairs everybody gethered around the table, and the king he counted it and stacked it up, three hundred dollars in a pile—twenty elegant little piles. Everybody looked hungry at it, and licked their chops. Then they raked it into the bag again, and I see the king begin to swell himself up for another speech. He says:

"Friends all, my poor brother that lays yonder has done generous by them that's left behind in the vale of sorrers. He has done generous by these yer poor little lambs that he loved and sheltered, and that's left fatherless and motherless. Yes, and we that knowed him knows that he would a done MORE generous by 'em if he hadn't ben afeard o' woundin' his dear William and me. Now, WOULDN'T he? Ther' ain't no question 'bout it in MY mind. Well, then, what kind o' brothers would it be that 'd stand in his way at sech a time? And what kind o' uncles would it be that 'd rob—yes, ROB—sech poor sweet lambs as these 'at he loved so at sech a time? If I know William—and I THINK I do—he—well, I'll jest ask him." He turns around and begins to make a lot of signs to the duke with his hands, and the duke he looks at him stupid and leather-headed a while; then all of a sudden he seems to catch his meaning, and jumps for the king, goo-gooing with all his might for joy, and hugs him about fifteen times before he lets up. Then the king says, "I knowed it; I reckon THAT 'll convince anybody the way HE feels about it. Here, Mary Jane, Susan, Joanner, take the money—take it ALL. It's the gift of him that lays yonder, cold but joyful."

Mary Jane she went for him, Susan and the hare-lip went for the duke, and then such another hugging and kissing I never see yet. And everybody crowded up with the tears in their eyes, and most shook the hands off of them frauds, saying all the time:

"You DEAR good souls!—how LOVELY!—how COULD you!"

Well, then, pretty soon all hands got to talking about the diseased again, and how good he was, and what a loss he was, and all that; and before long a big iron-jawed man worked himself in there from outside, and stood a-listening and looking, and not saying anything; and nobody saying anything to him either, because the king was talking and they was all busy listening. The king was saying—in the middle of something he'd started in on—

"—they bein' partickler friends o' the diseased. That's why they're invited here this evenin'; but tomorrow we want ALL to come—everybody; for he respected everybody, he liked everybody, and so it's fitten that his funeral orgies sh'd be public."

And so he went a-mooning on and on, liking to hear himself talk, and every little while he fetched in his funeral orgies again, till the duke he couldn't stand it no more; so he writes on a little scrap of paper, "OBSEQUIES, you old fool," and folds it up, and goes to goo-gooing and reaching it over people's heads to him. The king he reads it and puts it in his pocket, and says:

"Poor William, afflicted as he is, his HEART'S aluz right. Asks me to invite everybody to come to the funeral—wants me to make 'em all welcome. But he needn't a worried—it was jest what I was at."

Then he weaves along again, perfectly ca'm, and goes to dropping in his funeral orgies again every now and then, just like he done before. And when he done it the third time he says:

"I say orgies, not because it's the common term, because it ain't —obsequies bein' the common term—but because orgies is the right term. Obsequies ain't used in England no more now—it's gone out. We say orgies now in England. Orgies is better, because it means the thing you're after more exact. It's a word that's made up out'n the Greek ORGO, outside, open, abroad; and the Hebrew JEESUM, to plant, cover up; hence inTER. So, you see, funeral orgies is an open er public funeral."

He was the WORST I ever struck. Well, the iron-jawed man he laughed right in his face. Everybody was shocked. Everybody says, "Why, DOCTOR!" and Abner Shackleford says:

"Why, Robinson, hain't you heard the news? This is Harvey Wilks."

The king he smiled eager, and shoved out his flapper, and says:

"Is it my poor brother's dear good friend and physician? I—"

"Keep your hands off of me!" says the doctor. "YOU talk like an Englishman, DON'T you? It's the worst imitation I ever heard. YOU Peter Wilks's brother! You're a fraud, that's what you are!"

Well, how they all took on! They crowded around the doctor and tried to quiet him down, and tried to explain to him and tell him how Harvey 'd showed in forty ways that he WAS Harvey, and knowed everybody by name, and the names of the very dogs, and begged and BEGGED him not to hurt Harvey's feelings and the poor girl's feelings, and all that. But it warn't no use; he stormed right along, and said any man that pretended to be an Englishman and couldn't imitate the lingo no better than what he did was a fraud and a liar. The poor girls was hanging to the king and crying; and all of a sudden the doctor ups and turns on THEM. He says:

"I was your father's friend, and I'm your friend; and I warn you as a friend, and an honest one that wants to protect you and keep you out of harm and trouble, to turn your backs on that scoundrel and have nothing to do with him, the ignorant tramp, with his idiotic Greek and Hebrew, as he calls it. He is the thinnest kind of an impostor—has come here with a lot of empty names and facts which he picked up somewheres, and you take them for PROOFS, and are helped to fool yourselves by these foolish friends here, who ought to know better. Mary Jane Wilks, you know me for your friend, and for your unselfish friend, too. Now listen to me; turn this pitiful rascal out—I BEG you to do it. Will you?"

Mary Jane straightened herself up, and my, but she was handsome! She says:

"HERE is my answer." She hove up the bag of money and put it in the king's hands, and says, "Take this six thousand dollars, and invest for me and my sisters any way you want to, and don't give us no receipt for it."

Then she put her arm around the king on one side, and Susan and the hare-lip done the same on the other. Everybody clapped their hands and stomped on the floor like a perfect storm, whilst the king held up his head and smiled proud. The doctor says:

"All right; I wash MY hands of the matter. But I warn you all that a time 's coming when you're going to feel sick whenever you think of this day." And away he went.

"All right, doctor," says the king, kinder mocking him; "we'll try and get 'em to send for you;" which made them all laugh, and they said it was a prime good hit.

CHAPTER XXVI.

WELL, when they was all gone the king he asks Mary Jane how they was off for spare rooms, and she said she had one spare room, which would do for Uncle William, and she'd give her own room to Uncle Harvey, which was a little bigger, and she would turn into the room with her sisters and sleep on a cot; and up garret was a little cubby, with a pallet in it. The king said the cubby would do for his valley—meaning me.

So Mary Jane took us up, and she showed them their rooms, which was plain but nice. She said she'd have her frocks and a lot of other traps took out of her room if they was in Uncle Harvey's way, but he said they warn't. The frocks was hung along the wall, and before them was a curtain made out of calico that hung down to the floor. There was an old hair trunk in one corner, and a guitar-box in another, and all sorts of little knickknacks and jimcracks around, like girls brisken up a room with. The king said it was all the more homely and more pleasanter for these fixings, and so don't disturb them. The duke's room was pretty small, but plenty good enough, and so was my cubby.

That night they had a big supper, and all them men and women was there, and I stood behind the king and the duke's chairs and waited on them, and the niggers waited on the rest. Mary Jane she set at the head of the table, with Susan alongside of her, and said how bad the biscuits was, and how mean the preserves was, and how ornery and tough the fried chickens was—and all that kind of rot, the way women always do for to force out compliments; and the people all knowed everything was tiptop, and said so—said "How DO you get biscuits to brown so nice?" and "Where, for the land's sake, DID you get these amaz'n pickles?" and all that kind of humbug talky-talk, just the way people always does at a supper, you know.

And when it was all done me and the hare-lip had supper in the kitchen off of the leavings, whilst the others was helping the niggers clean up the things. The hare-lip she got to pumping me about England, and blest if I didn't think the ice was getting mighty thin sometimes. She says:

"Did you ever see the king?"

"Who? William Fourth? Well, I bet I have—he goes to our church." I knowed he was dead years ago, but I never let on. So when I says he goes to our church, she says:

"What—regular?"

"Yes—regular. His pew's right over opposite ourn—on t'other side the pulpit."

"I thought he lived in London?"

"Well, he does. Where WOULD he live?"

"But I thought YOU lived in Sheffield?"

I see I was up a stump. I had to let on to get choked with a chicken bone, so as to get time to think how to get down again. Then I says:

"I mean he goes to our church regular when he's in Sheffield. That's only in the summer time, when he comes there to take the sea baths."

"Why, how you talk—Sheffield ain't on the sea."

"Well, who said it was?"

"Why, you did."

"I DIDN'T nuther."

"You did!"

"I didn't."

"You did."

"I never said nothing of the kind."

"Well, what DID you say, then?"

"Said he come to take the sea BATHS—that's what I said."

"Well, then, how's he going to take the sea baths if it ain't on the sea?"

"Looky here," I says; "did you ever see any Congress-water?"

"Yes."

"Well, did you have to go to Congress to get it?"

"Why, no."

"Well, neither does William Fourth have to go to the sea to get a sea bath."

"How does he get it, then?"

"Gets it the way people down here gets Congress-water—in barrels. There in the palace at Sheffield they've got furnaces, and he wants his water hot. They can't bile that amount of water away off there at the sea. They haven't got no conveniences for it."

"Oh, I see, now. You might a said that in the first place and saved time."

When she said that I see I was out of the woods again, and so I was comfortable and glad. Next, she says:

"Do you go to church, too?"

"Yes—regular."

"Where do you set?"

"Why, in our pew."

"WHOSE pew?"

"Why, OURN—your Uncle Harvey's."

"His'n? What does HE want with a pew?"

"Wants it to set in. What did you RECKON he wanted with it?"

"Why, I thought he'd be in the pulpit."

Rot him, I forgot he was a preacher. I see I was up a stump again, so I played another chicken bone and got another think. Then I says:

"Blame it, do you suppose there ain't but one preacher to a church?"

"Why, what do they want with more?"

"What!—to preach before a king? I never did see such a girl as you. They don't have no less than seventeen."

"Seventeen! My land! Why, I wouldn't set out such a string as that, not if I NEVER got to glory. It must take 'em a week."

"Shucks, they don't ALL of 'em preach the same day—only ONE of 'em."

"Well, then, what does the rest of 'em do?"

"Oh, nothing much. Loll around, pass the plate—and one thing or another. But mainly they don't do nothing."

"Well, then, what are they FOR?"

"Why, they're for STYLE. Don't you know nothing?"

"Well, I don't WANT to know no such foolishness as that. How is servants treated in England? Do they treat 'em better 'n we treat our niggers?"

"NO! A servant ain't nobody there. They treat them worse than dogs."

"Don't they give 'em holidays, the way we do, Christmas and New Year's week, and Fourth of July?"

"Oh, just listen! A body could tell YOU hain't ever been to England by that. Why, Hare-l—why, Joanna, they never see a holiday from year's end to year's end; never go to the circus, nor theater, nor nigger shows, nor nowheres."

"Nor church?"

"Nor church."

"But YOU always went to church."

Well, I was gone up again. I forgot I was the old man's servant. But next minute I whirled in on a kind of an explanation how a valley was different from a common servant and HAD to go to church whether he wanted to or not, and set with the family, on account of its being the law. But I didn't do it pretty good, and when I got done I see she warn't satisfied. She says:

"Honest injun, now, hain't you been telling me a lot of lies?"

"Honest injun," says I.

"None of it at all?"

"None of it at all. Not a lie in it," says I.

"Lay your hand on this book and say it."

I see it warn't nothing but a dictionary, so I laid my hand on it and said it. So then she looked a little better satisfied, and says:

"Well, then, I'll believe some of it; but I hope to gracious if I'll believe the rest."

"What is it you won't believe, Joe?" says Mary Jane, stepping in with Susan behind her. "It ain't right nor kind for you to talk so to him, and him a stranger and so far from his people. How would you like to be treated so?"

"That's always your way, Maim—always sailing in to help somebody before they're hurt. I hain't done nothing to him. He's told some stretchers, I reckon, and I said I wouldn't swallow it all; and that's every bit and grain I DID say. I reckon he can stand a little thing like that, can't he?"

"I don't care whether 'twas little or whether 'twas big; he's here in our house and a stranger, and it wasn't good of you to say it. If you was in his place it would make you feel ashamed; and so you oughtn't to say a thing to another person that will make THEM feel ashamed."

"Why, Maim, he said—"

"It don't make no difference what he SAID—that ain't the thing. The thing is for you to treat him KIND, and not be saying things to make him remember he ain't in his own country and amongst his own folks."

I says to myself, THIS is a girl that I'm letting that old reptile rob her of her money!

Then Susan SHE waltzed in; and if you'll believe me, she did give Hare-lip hark from the tomb!

Says I to myself, and this is ANOTHER one that I'm letting him rob her of her money!

Then Mary Jane she took another inning, and went in sweet and lovely again—which was her way; but when she got done there warn't hardly anything left o' poor Hare-lip. So she hollered.

"All right, then," says the other girls; "you just ask his pardon."

She done it, too; and she done it beautiful. She done it so beautiful it was good to hear; and I wished I could tell her a thousand lies, so she could do it again.

I says to myself, this is ANOTHER one that I'm letting him rob her of her money. And when she got through they all jest laid theirselves out to make me feel at home and know I was amongst friends. I felt so ornery and low down and mean that I says to myself, my mind's made up; I'll hive that money for them or bust.

So then I lit out—for bed, I said, meaning some time or another. When I got by myself I went to thinking the thing over. I says to myself, shall I go to that doctor, private, and blow on these frauds? No—that won't do. He might tell who told him; then the king and the duke would make it warm for me. Shall I go, private, and tell Mary Jane? No—I dasn't do it. Her face would give them a hint, sure; they've got the money, and they'd slide right out and get away with it. If she was to fetch in help I'd get mixed up in the business before it was done with, I judge. No; there ain't no good way but one. I got to steal that money, somehow; and I got to steal it some way that they won't suspicion that I done it. They've got a good thing here, and they ain't a-going to leave till they've played this family and this town for all they're worth, so I'll find a chance time enough. I'll steal it and hide it; and by and by, when I'm away down the river, I'll write a letter and tell Mary Jane where it's hid. But I better hive it tonight if I can, because the doctor maybe hasn't let up as much as he lets on he has; he might scare them out of here yet.

So, thinks I, I'll go and search them rooms. Upstairs the hall was dark, but I found the duke's room, and started to paw around it with my hands; but I recollected it wouldn't be much like the king to let anybody else take care of that money but his own self; so then I went to his room and begun to paw around there. But I see I couldn't do nothing without a candle, and I dasn't light one, of course. So I judged I'd got to do the other thing—lay for them and eavesdrop. About that time I hears their footsteps coming, and was going to skip under the bed; I reached for it, but it wasn't where I thought it would be; but I touched the curtain that hid Mary Jane's frocks, so I jumped in behind that and snuggled in amongst the gowns, and stood there perfectly still.

They come in and shut the door; and the first thing the duke done was to get down and look under the bed. Then I was glad I hadn't found the bed when I wanted it. And yet, you know, it's kind of natural to hide under the bed when you are up to anything private. They sets down then, and the king says:

"Well, what is it? And cut it middlin' short, because it's better for us to be down there a-whoopin' up the mournin' than up here givin' 'em a chance to talk us over."

"Well, this is it, Capet. I ain't easy; I ain't comfortable. That doctor lays on my mind. I wanted to know your plans. I've got a notion, and I think it's a sound one."

"What is it, duke?"

"That we better glide out of this before three in the morning, and clip it down the river with what we've got. Specially, seeing we got it so easy—GIVEN back to us, flung at our heads, as you may say, when of course we allowed to have to steal it back. I'm for knocking off and lighting out."

That made me feel pretty bad. About an hour or two ago it would a been a little different, but now it made me feel bad and disappointed, The king rips out and says:

"What! And not sell out the rest o' the property? March off like a passel of fools and leave eight or nine thous'n' dollars' worth o' property layin' around jest sufferin' to be scooped in?—and all good, salable stuff, too."

The duke he grumbled; said the bag of gold was enough, and he didn't want to go no deeper—didn't want to rob a lot of orphans of EVERYTHING they had.

"Why, how you talk!" says the king. "We sha'n't rob 'em of nothing at all but jest this money. The people that BUYS the property is the suff'rers; because as soon 's it's found out 'at we didn't own it—which won't be long after we've slid—the sale won't be valid, and it 'll all go back to the estate. These yer orphans 'll git their house back agin, and that's enough for THEM; they're young and spry, and k'n easy earn a livin'. THEY ain't a-goin to suffer. Why, jest think—there's thous'n's and thous'n's that ain't nigh so well off. Bless you, THEY ain't

got noth'n' to complain of."

Well, the king he talked him blind; so at last he give in, and said all right, but said he believed it was blamed foolishness to stay, and that doctor hanging over them. But the king says:

"Cuss the doctor! What do we k'yer for HIM? Hain't we got all the fools in town on our side? And ain't that a big enough majority in any town?"

So they got ready to go down stairs again. The duke says:

"I don't think we put that money in a good place."

That cheered me up. I'd begun to think I warn't going to get a hint of no kind to help me. The king says:

"Why?"

"Because Mary Jane 'll be in mourning from this out; and first you know the nigger that does up the rooms will get an order to box these duds up and put 'em away; and do you reckon a nigger can run across money and not borrow some of it?"

"Your head's level agin, duke," says the king; and he comes a-fumbling under the curtain two or three foot from where I was. I stuck tight to the wall and kept mighty still, though quivery; and I wondered what them fellows would say to me if they catched me; and I tried to think what I'd better do if they did catch me. But the king he got the bag before I could think more than about a half a thought, and he never suspicioned I was around. They took and shoved the bag through a rip in the straw tick that was under the feather-bed, and crammed it in a foot or two amongst the straw and said it was all right now, because a nigger only makes up the feather-bed, and don't turn over the straw tick only about twice a year, and so it warn't in no danger of getting stole now.

But I knowed better. I had it out of there before they was half-way down stairs. I groped along up to my cubby, and hid it there till I could get a chance to do better. I judged I better hide it outside of the house somewheres, because if they missed it they would give the house a good ransacking: I knowed that very well. Then I turned in, with my clothes all on; but I couldn't a gone to sleep if I'd a wanted to, I was in such a sweat to get through with the business. By and by I heard the king and the duke come up; so I rolled off my pallet and laid with my chin at the top of my ladder, and waited to see if anything was going to happen. But nothing did.

So I held on till all the late sounds had quit and the early ones hadn't begun yet; and then I slipped down the ladder.

CHAPTER XXVII.

I CREPT to their doors and listened; they was snoring. So I tiptoed along, and got down stairs all right. There warn't a sound anywheres. I peeped through a crack of the dining-room door, and see the men that was watching the corpse all sound asleep on their chairs. The door was open into the parlor, where the corpse was laying, and there was a candle in both rooms. I passed along, and the parlor door was open; but I see there warn't nobody in there but the remainders of Peter; so I shoved on by; but the front door was locked, and the key wasn't there. Just then I heard somebody coming down the stairs, back behind me. I run in the parlor and took a swift look around, and the only place I see to hide the bag was in the coffin. The lid was shoved along about a foot, showing the dead man's face down in there, with a wet cloth over it, and his shroud on. I tucked the money-bag in under the lid, just down beyond where his hands was crossed, which made me creep, they was so cold, and then I run back across the room and in behind the door.

The person coming was Mary Jane. She went to the coffin, very soft, and kneeled down and looked in; then she put up her handkerchief, and I see she begun to cry, though I couldn't hear her, and her back was to me. I slid out, and as I passed the dining-room I thought I'd make sure them watchers hadn't seen me; so I looked through the crack, and everything was all right. They hadn't stirred.

I slipped up to bed, feeling ruther blue, on accounts of the thing playing out that way after I had took so much trouble and run so much resk about it. Says I, if it could stay where it is, all right; because when we get down the river a hundred mile or two I could write back to Mary Jane, and she could dig him up again and get it; but that ain't the thing that's going to happen; the thing that's going to happen is, the money 'll be found when they come to screw on the lid. Then the king 'll get it again, and it 'll be a long day before he gives anybody another chance to smouch it from him. Of course I WANTED to slide down and get it out of there, but I dasn't try it. Every minute it was getting earlier now, and pretty soon some of them watchers would begin to stir, and I might get catched—catched with six thousand dollars in my hands that nobody hadn't hired me to take care of. I don't wish to be mixed up in no such business as that, I says to myself.

When I got down stairs in the morning the parlor was shut up, and the watchers was gone. There warn't nobody around but the family and the widow Bartley and our tribe. I watched their faces to see if anything had been happening, but I couldn't tell.

Towards the middle of the day the undertaker come with his man, and they set the coffin in the middle of the room on a couple of chairs, and then set all our chairs in rows, and borrowed more from the neighbors till the hall and the parlor and the dining-room was full. I see the coffin lid was the way it was before, but I dasn't go to look in under it, with folks around.

Then the people begun to flock in, and the beats and the girls took seats in the front row at the head of the coffin, and for a half an hour the people filed around slow, in single rank, and looked down at the dead man's face a minute, and some dropped in a tear, and it was all very still and solemn, only the girls and the beats holding handkerchiefs to their eyes and keeping their heads bent, and sobbing a little. There warn't no other sound but the scraping of the feet on the floor and blowing noses—because people always blows them more at a funeral than they do at other places except church.

When the place was packed full the undertaker he slid around in his black gloves with his softy soothering ways, putting on the last touches, and getting people and things all ship-shape and comfortable, and making no more sound than a cat. He never spoke; he moved people around, he squeezed in late ones, he opened up passageways, and done it with nods, and signs with his hands. Then he took his place over against the wall. He was the softest, glidingest, stealthiest man I ever see; and there warn't no more smile to him than there is to a ham.

They had borrowed a melodeum—a sick one; and when everything was ready a young woman set down and worked it,

and it was pretty skreeky and colicky, and everybody joined in and sung, and Peter was the only one that had a good thing, according to my notion. Then the Reverend Hobson opened up, slow and solemn, and begun to talk; and straight off the most outrageous row busted out in the cellar a body ever heard; it was only one dog, but he made a most powerful racket, and he kept it up right along; the parson he had to stand there, over the coffin, and wait—you couldn't hear yourself think. It was right down awkward, and nobody didn't seem to know what to do. But pretty soon they see that long-legged undertaker make a sign to the preacher as much as to say, "Don't you worry—just depend on me." Then he stooped down and begun to glide along the wall, just his shoulders showing over the people's heads. So he glided along, and the powwow and racket getting more and more outrageous all the time; and at last, when he had gone around two sides of the room, he disappears down cellar. Then in about two seconds we heard a whack, and the dog he finished up with a most amazing howl or two, and then everything was dead still, and the parson begun his solemn talk where he left off. In a minute or two here comes this undertaker's back and shoulders gliding along the wall again; and so he glided and glided around three sides of the room, and then rose up, and shaded his mouth with his hands, and stretched his neck out towards the preacher, over the people's heads, and says, in a kind of a coarse whisper, "HE HAD A RAT!" Then he drooped down and glided along the wall again to his place. You could see it was a great satisfaction to the people, because naturally they wanted to know. A little thing like that don't cost nothing, and it's just the little things that makes a man to be looked up to and liked. There warn't no more popular man in town than what that undertaker was.

Well, the funeral sermon was very good, but pison long and tiresome; and then the king he shoved in and got off some of his usual rubbage, and at last the job was through, and the undertaker begun to sneak up on the coffin with his screw-driver. I was in a sweat then, and watched him pretty keen. But he never meddled at all; just slid the lid along as soft as mush, and screwed it down tight and fast. So there I was! I didn't know whether the money was in there or not. So, says I, s'pose somebody has hogged that bag on the sly?—now how do I know whether to write to Mary Jane or not? S'pose she dug him up and didn't find nothing, what would she think of me? Blame it, I says, I might get hunted up and jailed; I'd better lay low and keep dark, and not write at all; the thing's awful mixed now; trying to better it, I've worsened it a hundred times, and I wish to goodness I'd just let it alone, dad fetch the whole business!

They buried him, and we come back home, and I went to watching faces again—I couldn't help it, and I couldn't rest easy. But nothing come of it; the faces didn't tell me nothing.

The king he visited around in the evening, and sweetened everybody up, and made himself ever so friendly; and he give out the idea that his congregation over in England would be in a sweat about him, so he must hurry and settle up the estate right away and leave for home. He was very sorry he was so pushed, and so was everybody; they wished he could stay longer, but they said they could see it couldn't be done. And he said of course him and William would take the girls home with them; and that pleased everybody too, because then the girls would be well fixed and amongst their own relations; and it pleased the girls, too—tickled them so they clean forgot they ever had a trouble in the world; and told him to sell out as quick as he wanted to, they would be ready. Them poor things was that glad and happy it made my heart ache to see them getting fooled and lied to so, but I didn't see no safe way for me to chip in and change the general tune.

Well, blamed if the king didn't bill the house and the niggers and all the property for auction straight off—sale two days after the funeral; but anybody could buy private beforehand if they wanted to.

So the next day after the funeral, along about noon-time, the girls' joy got the first jolt. A couple of nigger traders come along, and the king sold them the niggers reasonable, for three-day drafts as they called it, and away they went, the two sons up the river to Memphis, and their mother down the river to Orleans. I thought them poor girls and them niggers would break their hearts for grief; they cried around each other, and took on so it most made me down sick to see it. The girls said they hadn't ever dreamed of seeing the family separated or sold away from the town. I can't ever get it out of my memory, the sight of them poor miserable girls and niggers hanging around each other's necks and crying; and I reckon I couldn't a stood it all, but would a had to bust out and tell on our gang if I hadn't knowed the sale warn't no account and the niggers would be back home in a week or two.

The thing made a big stir in the town, too, and a good many come out flatfooted and said it was scandalous to separate the mother and the children that way. It injured the frauds some; but the old fool he bulled right along, spite of all the duke could say or do, and I tell you the duke was powerful uneasy.

Next day was auction day. About broad day in the morning the king and the duke come up in the garret and woke me up, and I see by their look that there was trouble. The king says:

"Was you in my room night before last?"

"No, your majesty"—which was the way I always called him when nobody but our gang warn't around.

"Was you in there yisterday er last night?"

"No, your majesty."

"Honor bright, now—no lies."

"Honor bright, your majesty, I'm telling you the truth. I hain't been a-near your room since Miss Mary Jane took you and the duke and showed it to you."

The duke says:

"Have you seen anybody else go in there?"

"No, your grace, not as I remember, I believe."

"Stop and think."

I studied awhile and see my chance; then I says:

"Well, I see the niggers go in there several times."

Both of them gave a little jump, and looked like they hadn't ever expected it, and then like they HAD. Then the duke says:

"What, all of them?"

"No—leastways, not all at once—that is, I don't think I ever see them all come OUT at once but just one time."

"Hello! When was that?"

"It was the day we had the funeral. In the morning. It warn't early, because I overslept. I was just starting down the ladder, and I see them."

"Well, go on, GO on! What did they do? How'd they act?"

"They didn't do nothing. And they didn't act anyway much, as fur as I see. They tiptoed away; so I seen, easy enough, that they'd shoved in there to do up your majesty's room, or something, s'posing you was up; and found you WARN'T up, and so they was hoping to slide out of the way of trouble without waking you up, if they hadn't already waked you up."

"Great guns, THIS is a go!" says the king; and both of them looked pretty sick and tolerable silly. They stood there a-thinking and scratching their heads a minute, and the duke he bust into a kind of a little raspy chuckle, and says:

"It does beat all how neat the niggers played their hand. They let on to be SORRY they was going out of this region! And I believed they WAS sorry, and so did you, and so did everybody. Don't ever tell ME any more that a nigger ain't got any histrionic talent. Why, the way they played that thing it would fool ANYBODY. In my opinion, there's a fortune in 'em. If I had capital and a theater, I wouldn't want a better lay-out than that—and here we've gone and sold 'em for a song. Yes, and ain't privileged to sing the song yet. Say, where IS that song—that draft?"

"In the bank for to be collected. Where WOULD it be?"

"Well, THAT'S all right then, thank goodness."

Says I, kind of timid-like:

"Is something gone wrong?"

The king whirls on me and rips out:

"None o' your business! You keep your head shet, and mind y'r own affairs—if you got any. Long as you're in this town don't you forgit THAT—you hear?" Then he says to the duke, "We got to jest swaller it and say noth'n': mum's the word for US."

As they was starting down the ladder the duke he chuckles again, and says:

"Quick sales AND small profits! It's a good business—yes."

The king snarls around on him and says:

"I was trying to do for the best in sellin' 'em out so quick. If the profits has turned out to be none, lackin' considable, and none to carry, is it my fault any more'n it's yourn?"

"Well, THEY'D be in this house yet and we WOULDN'T if I could a got my advice listened to."

The king sassed back as much as was safe for him, and then swapped around and lit into ME again. He give me down the banks for not coming and TELLING him I see the niggers come out of his room acting that way—said any fool would a KNOWED something was up. And then waltzed in and cussed HIMSELF awhile, and said it all come of him not laying late and taking his natural rest that morning, and he'd be blamed if he'd ever do it again. So they went off a-jawing; and I felt dreadful glad I'd worked it all off on to the niggers, and yet hadn't done the niggers no harm by it.

CHAPTER XXVIII.

BY and by it was getting-up time. So I come down the ladder and started for down-stairs; but as I come to the girls' room the door was open, and I see Mary Jane setting by her old hair trunk, which was open and she'd been packing things in it—getting ready to go to England. But she had stopped now with a folded gown in her lap, and had her face in her hands, crying. I felt awful bad to see it; of course anybody would. I went in there and says:

"Miss Mary Jane, you can't a-bear to see people in trouble, and I can't —most always. Tell me about it."

So she done it. And it was the niggers—I just expected it. She said the beautiful trip to England was most about spoiled for her; she didn't know HOW she was ever going to be happy there, knowing the mother and the children warn't ever going to see each other no more—and then busted out bitterer than ever, and flung up her hands, and says:

"Oh, dear, dear, to think they ain't EVER going to see each other any more!"

"But they WILL—and inside of two weeks—and I KNOW it!" says I.

Laws, it was out before I could think! And before I could budge she throws her arms around my neck and told me to say it AGAIN, say it AGAIN, say it AGAIN!

I see I had spoke too sudden and said too much, and was in a close place. I asked her to let me think a minute; and she set there, very impatient and excited and handsome, but looking kind of happy and eased-up, like a person that's had a tooth pulled out. So I went to studying it out. I says to myself, I reckon a body that ups and tells the truth when he is in a tight place is taking considerable many resks, though I ain't had no experience, and can't say for certain; but it looks so to me, anyway; and yet here's a case where I'm blest if it don't look to me like the truth is better and actuly SAFER than a lie. I must lay it by in my mind, and think it over some time or other, it's so kind of strange and unregular. I never see nothing like it. Well, I says to myself at last, I'm a-going to chance it; I'll up and tell the truth this time, though it does seem most like setting down on a kag of powder and touching it off just to see where you'll go to. Then I says:

"Miss Mary Jane, is there any place out of town a little ways where you could go and stay three or four days?"

"Yes; Mr. Lothrop's. Why?"

"Never mind why yet. If I'll tell you how I know the niggers will see each other again inside of two weeks—here in this house—and PROVE how I know it—will you go to Mr. Lothrop's and stay four days?"

"Four days!" she says; "I'll stay a year!"

"All right," I says, "I don't want nothing more out of YOU than just your word—I druther have it than another man's kiss-the-Bible." She smiled and reddened up very sweet, and I says, "If you don't mind it, I'll shut the door—and bolt it."

Then I come back and set down again, and says:

"Don't you holler. Just set still and take it like a man. I got to tell the truth, and you want to brace up, Miss Mary, because it's a bad kind, and going to be hard to take, but there ain't no help for it. These uncles of yourn ain't no uncles at all; they're a couple of frauds —regular dead-beats. There, now we're over the worst of it, you can stand the rest middling easy."

It jolted her up like everything, of course; but I was over the shoal water now, so I went right along, her eyes a-blazing higher and higher all the time, and told her every blame thing, from where we first struck that young fool going up to the steamboat, clear through to where she flung herself on to the king's breast at the front door and he kissed her sixteen or seventeen times—and then up she jumps, with her face afire like sunset, and says:

"The brute! Come, don't waste a minute—not a SECOND—we'll have them tarred and feathered, and flung in the river!"

Says I:

"Cert'nly. But do you mean BEFORE you go to Mr. Lothrop's, or—"

"Oh," she says, "what am I THINKING about!" she says, and set right down again. "Don't mind what I said—please don't—you WON'T, now, WILL you?" Laying her silky hand on mine in that kind of a way that I said I would die first. "I never thought, I was so stirred up," she says; "now go on, and I won't do so any more. You tell me what to do, and whatever you say I'll do it."

"Well," I says, "it's a rough gang, them two frauds, and I'm fixed so I got to travel with them a while longer, whether I want to or not—I druther not tell you why; and if you was to blow on them this town would get me out of their claws, and I'd be all right; but there'd be another person that you don't know about who'd be in big trouble. Well, we got to save HIM, hain't we? Of course. Well, then, we won't blow on them."

Saying them words put a good idea in my head. I see how maybe I could get me and Jim rid of the frauds; get them jailed here, and then leave. But I didn't want to run the raft in the daytime without anybody aboard to answer questions but me; so I didn't want the plan to begin working till pretty late to-night. I says:

"Miss Mary Jane, I'll tell you what we'll do, and you won't have to stay at Mr. Lothrop's so long, nuther. How fur is it?"

"A little short of four miles—right out in the country, back here."

"Well, that 'll answer. Now you go along out there, and lay low till nine or half-past to-night, and then get them to fetch you home again —tell them you've thought of something. If you get here before eleven put a candle in this window, and if I don't turn up wait TILL eleven, and THEN if I don't turn up it means I'm gone, and out of the way, and safe. Then you come out and spread the news around, and get these beats jailed."

"Good," she says, "I'll do it."

"And if it just happens so that I don't get away, but get took up along with them, you must up and say I told you the whole thing beforehand, and you must stand by me all you can."

"Stand by you! indeed I will. They sha'n't touch a hair of your head!" she says, and I see her nostrils spread and her eyes snap when she said it, too.

"If I get away I sha'n't be here," I says, "to prove these rapscallions ain't your uncles, and I couldn't do it if I WAS here. I could swear they was beats and bummers, that's all, though that's worth something. Well, there's others can do that better than what I can, and they're people that ain't going to be doubted as quick as I'd be. I'll tell you how to find them. Gimme a pencil and a piece of paper. There—'Royal Nonesuch, Bricksville.' Put it away, and don't lose it. When the court wants to find out something about these two, let them send up to Bricksville and say they've got the men that played the Royal Nonesuch, and ask for some witnesses—why, you'll have that entire town down here before you can hardly wink, Miss Mary. And they'll come a-biling, too."

I judged we had got everything fixed about right now. So I says:

"Just let the auction go right along, and don't worry. Nobody don't have to pay for the things they buy till a whole day after the auction on accounts of the short notice, and they ain't going out of this till they get that money; and the way we've fixed it the sale ain't going to count, and they ain't going to get no money. It's just like the way it was with the niggers—it warn't no sale, and the niggers will be back before long. Why, they can't collect the money for the NIGGERS yet—they're in the worst kind of a fix, Miss Mary."

"Well," she says, "I'll run down to breakfast now, and then I'll start straight for Mr. Lothrop's."

"'Deed, THAT ain't the ticket, Miss Mary Jane," I says, "by no manner of means; go BEFORE breakfast."

"Why?"

"What did you reckon I wanted you to go at all for, Miss Mary?"

"Well, I never thought—and come to think, I don't know. What was it?"

"Why, it's because you ain't one of these leather-face people. I don't want no better book than what your face is. A body can set down and read it off like coarse print. Do you reckon you can go and face your uncles when they come to kiss you good-morning, and never—"

"There, there, don't! Yes, I'll go before breakfast—I'll be glad to. And leave my sisters with them?"

"Yes; never mind about them. They've got to stand it yet a while. They might suspicion something if all of you was to go. I don't want you to see them, nor your sisters, nor nobody in this town; if a neighbor was to ask how is your uncles this morning your face would tell something. No, you go right along, Miss Mary Jane, and I'll fix it with all of them. I'll tell Miss Susan to give your love to your uncles and say you've went away for a few hours for to get a little rest and change, or to see a friend, and you'll be back to-night or early in the morning."

"Gone to see a friend is all right, but I won't have my love

given to them."

"Well, then, it sha'n't be." It was well enough to tell HER so—no harm in it. It was only a little thing to do, and no trouble; and it's the little things that smooths people's roads the most, down here below; it would make Mary Jane comfortable, and it wouldn't cost nothing. Then I says: "There's one more thing—that bag of money."

"Well, they've got that; and it makes me feel pretty silly to think HOW they got it."

"No, you're out, there. They hain't got it."

"Why, who's got it?"

"I wish I knowed, but I don't. I HAD it, because I stole it from them; and I stole it to give to you; and I know where I hid it, but I'm afraid it ain't there no more. I'm awful sorry, Miss Mary Jane, I'm just as sorry as I can be; but I done the best I could; I did honest. I come nigh getting caught, and I had to shove it into the first place I come to, and run—and it warn't a good place."

"Oh, stop blaming yourself—it's too bad to do it, and I won't allow it —you couldn't help it; it wasn't your fault. Where did you hide it?"

I didn't want to set her to thinking about her troubles again; and I couldn't seem to get my mouth to tell her what would make her see that corpse laying in the coffin with that bag of money on his stomach. So for a minute I didn't say nothing; then I says:

"I'd rather not TELL you where I put it, Miss Mary Jane, if you don't mind letting me off; but I'll write it for you on a piece of paper, and you can read it along the road to Mr. Lothrop's, if you want to. Do you reckon that 'll do?"

"Oh, yes."

So I wrote: "I put it in the coffin. It was in there when you was crying there, away in the night. I was behind the door, and I was mighty sorry for you, Miss Mary Jane."

It made my eyes water a little to remember her crying there all by herself in the night, and them devils laying there right under her own roof, shaming her and robbing her; and when I folded it up and give it to her I see the water come into her eyes, too; and she shook me by the hand, hard, and says:

"GOOD-bye. I'm going to do everything just as you've told me; and if I don't ever see you again, I sha'n't ever forget you and I'll think of you a many and a many a time, and I'll PRAY for you, too!"—and she was gone.

Pray for me! I reckoned if she knowed me she'd take a job that was more nearer her size. But I bet she done it, just the same—she was just that kind. She had the grit to pray for Judus if she took the notion—there warn't no back-down to her, I judge. You may say what you want to, but in my opinion she had more sand in her than any girl I ever see; in my opinion she was just full of sand. It sounds like flattery, but it ain't no flattery. And when it comes to beauty—and goodness, too—she lays over them all. I hain't ever seen her since that time that I see her go out of that door; no, I hain't ever seen her since, but I reckon I've thought of her a many and a many a million times, and of her saying she would pray for me; and if ever I'd a thought it would do any good for me to pray for HER, blamed if I wouldn't a done it or bust.

Well, Mary Jane she lit out the back way, I reckon; because nobody see her go. When I struck Susan and the hare-lip, I says:

"What's the name of them people over on t'other side of the river that you all goes to see sometimes?"

They says:

"There's several; but it's the Proctors, mainly."

"That's the name," I says; "I most forgot it. Well, Miss Mary Jane she told me to tell you she's gone over there in a dreadful hurry—one of them's sick."

"Which one?"

"I don't know; leastways, I kinder forget; but I thinks it's—"

"Sakes alive, I hope it ain't HANNER?"

"I'm sorry to say it," I says, "but Hanner's the very one."

"My goodness, and she so well only last week! Is she took bad?"

"It ain't no name for it. They set up with her all night, Miss Mary Jane said, and they don't think she'll last many hours."

"Only think of that, now! What's the matter with her?"

I couldn't think of anything reasonable, right off that way, so I says:

"Mumps."

"Mumps your granny! They don't set up with people that's got the mumps."

"They don't, don't they? You better bet they do with THESE mumps. These mumps is different. It's a new kind, Miss Mary Jane said."

"How's it a new kind?"

"Because it's mixed up with other things."

"What other things?"

"Well, measles, and whooping-cough, and erysiplas, and consumption, and yaller janders, and brain-fever, and I don't know what all."

"My land! And they call it the MUMPS?"

"That's what Miss Mary Jane said."

"Well, what in the nation do they call it the MUMPS for?"

"Why, because it IS the mumps. That's what it starts with."

"Well, ther' ain't no sense in it. A body might stump his toe, and take pison, and fall down the well, and break his neck, and bust his brains out, and somebody come along and ask what killed him, and some numskull up and say, 'Why, he stumped

his TOE.' Would ther' be any sense in that? NO. And ther' ain't no sense in THIS, nuther. Is it ketching?"

"Is it KETCHING? Why, how you talk. Is a HARROW catching—in the dark? If you don't hitch on to one tooth, you're bound to on another, ain't you? And you can't get away with that tooth without fetching the whole harrow along, can you? Well, these kind of mumps is a kind of a harrow, as you may say—and it ain't no slouch of a harrow, nuther, you come to get it hitched on good."

"Well, it's awful, I think," says the hare-lip. "I'll go to Uncle Harvey and—"

"Oh, yes," I says, "I WOULD. Of COURSE I would. I wouldn't lose no time."

"Well, why wouldn't you?"

"Just look at it a minute, and maybe you can see. Hain't your uncles obleegd to get along home to England as fast as they can? And do you reckon they'd be mean enough to go off and leave you to go all that journey by yourselves? YOU know they'll wait for you. So fur, so good. Your uncle Harvey's a preacher, ain't he? Very well, then; is a PREACHER going to deceive a steamboat clerk? is he going to deceive a SHIP CLERK? —so as to get them to let Miss Mary Jane go aboard? Now YOU know he ain't. What WILL he do, then? Why, he'll say, 'It's a great pity, but my church matters has got to get along the best way they can; for my niece has been exposed to the dreadful pluribus-unum mumps, and so it's my bounden duty to set down here and wait the three months it takes to show on her if she's got it.' But never mind, if you think it's best to tell your uncle Harvey—"

"Shucks, and stay fooling around here when we could all be having good times in England whilst we was waiting to find out whether Mary Jane's got it or not? Why, you talk like a muggins."

"Well, anyway, maybe you'd better tell some of the neighbors."

"Listen at that, now. You do beat all for natural stupidness. Can't you SEE that THEY'D go and tell? Ther' ain't no way but just to not tell anybody at ALL."

"Well, maybe you're right—yes, I judge you ARE right."

"But I reckon we ought to tell Uncle Harvey she's gone out a while, anyway, so he won't be uneasy about her?"

"Yes, Miss Mary Jane she wanted you to do that. She says, 'Tell them to give Uncle Harvey and William my love and a kiss, and say I've run over the river to see Mr.'—Mr.—what IS the name of that rich family your uncle Peter used to think so much of?—I mean the one that—"

"Why, you must mean the Apthorps, ain't it?"

"Of course; bother them kind of names, a body can't ever seem to remember them, half the time, somehow. Yes, she said, say she has run over for to ask the Apthorps to be sure and come to the auction and buy this house, because she allowed her uncle Peter would ruther they had it than anybody else; and she's going to stick to them till they say they'll come, and then, if she ain't too tired, she's coming home; and if she is, she'll be home in the morning anyway. She said, don't say nothing about the Proctors, but only about the Apthorps—which 'll be perfectly true, because she is going there to speak about their buying the house; I know it, because she told me so herself."

"All right," they said, and cleared out to lay for their uncles, and give them the love and the kisses, and tell them the message.

Everything was all right now. The girls wouldn't say nothing because they wanted to go to England; and the king and the duke would ruther Mary Jane was off working for the auction than around in reach of Doctor Robinson. I felt very good; I judged I had done it pretty neat—I reckoned Tom Sawyer couldn't a done it no neater himself. Of course he would a throwed more style into it, but I can't do that very handy, not being brung up to it.

Well, they held the auction in the public square, along towards the end of the afternoon, and it strung along, and strung along, and the old man he was on hand and looking his level pisonest, up there longside of the auctioneer, and chipping in a little Scripture now and then, or a little goody-goody saying of some kind, and the duke he was around goo-gooing for sympathy all he knowed how, and just spreading himself generly.

But by and by the thing dragged through, and everything was sold —everything but a little old trifling lot in the graveyard. So they'd got to work that off—I never see such a girafft as the king was for wanting to swallow EVERYTHING. Well, whilst they was at it a steamboat landed, and in about two minutes up comes a crowd a-whooping and yelling and laughing and carrying on, and singing out:

"HERE'S your opposition line! here's your two sets o' heirs to old Peter Wilks—and you pays your money and you takes your choice!"

CHAPTER XXIX.

THEY was fetching a very nice-looking old gentleman along, and a nice-looking younger one, with his right arm in a sling. And, my souls, how the people yelled and laughed, and kept it up. But I didn't see no joke about it, and I judged it would strain the duke and the king some to see any. I reckoned they'd turn pale. But no, nary a pale did THEY turn. The duke he never let on he suspicioned what was up, but just went a goo-gooing around, happy and satisfied, like a jug that's googling out buttermilk; and as for the king, he just gazed and gazed down sorrowful on them new-comers like it give him the stomach-ache in his very heart to think there could be such frauds and rascals in the world. Oh, he done it admirable. Lots of the principal people gethered around the king, to let him see they was on his side. That old gentleman that had just come looked all puzzled to death. Pretty soon he begun to speak, and I see straight off he pronounced LIKE an Englishman—not the king's way, though the king's WAS pretty good for an imitation. I can't give the old gent's words, nor I can't imitate him; but he turned around to the crowd, and says, about like this:

"This is a surprise to me which I wasn't looking for; and I'll acknowledge, candid and frank, I ain't very well fixed to meet it and answer it; for my brother and me has had misfortunes; he's broke his arm, and our baggage got put off at a town above here last night in the night by a mistake. I am Peter Wilks' brother Harvey, and this is his brother William, which can't hear nor speak—and can't even make signs to amount to much, now't he's only got one hand to work them with. We are

who we say we are; and in a day or two, when I get the baggage, I can prove it. But up till then I won't say nothing more, but go to the hotel and wait."

So him and the new dummy started off; and the king he laughs, and blethers out:

"Broke his arm—VERY likely, AIN'T it?—and very convenient, too, for a fraud that's got to make signs, and ain't learnt how. Lost their baggage! That's MIGHTY good!—and mighty ingenious—under the CIRCUMSTANCES!"

So he laughed again; and so did everybody else, except three or four, or maybe half a dozen. One of these was that doctor; another one was a sharp-looking gentleman, with a carpet-bag of the old-fashioned kind made out of carpet-stuff, that had just come off of the steamboat and was talking to him in a low voice, and glancing towards the king now and then and nodding their heads—it was Levi Bell, the lawyer that was gone up to Louisville; and another one was a big rough husky that come along and listened to all the old gentleman said, and was listening to the king now. And when the king got done this husky up and says:

"Say, looky here; if you are Harvey Wilks, when'd you come to this town?"

"The day before the funeral, friend," says the king.

"But what time o' day?"

"In the evenin'—'bout an hour er two before sundown."

"HOW'D you come?"

"I come down on the Susan Powell from Cincinnati."

"Well, then, how'd you come to be up at the Pint in the MORNIN'—in a canoe?"

"I warn't up at the Pint in the mornin'."

"It's a lie."

Several of them jumped for him and begged him not to talk that way to an old man and a preacher.

"Preacher be hanged, he's a fraud and a liar. He was up at the Pint that mornin'. I live up there, don't I? Well, I was up there, and he was up there. I see him there. He come in a canoe, along with Tim Collins and a boy."

The doctor he up and says:

"Would you know the boy again if you was to see him, Hines?"

"I reckon I would, but I don't know. Why, yonder he is, now. I know him perfectly easy."

It was me he pointed at. The doctor says:

"Neighbors, I don't know whether the new couple is frauds or not; but if THESE two ain't frauds, I am an idiot, that's all. I think it's our duty to see that they don't get away from here till we've looked into this thing. Come along, Hines; come along, the rest of you. We'll take these fellows to the tavern and affront them with t'other couple, and I reckon we'll find out SOMETHING before we get through."

It was nuts for the crowd, though maybe not for the king's friends; so we all started. It was about sundown. The doctor he led me along by the hand, and was plenty kind enough, but he never let go my hand.

We all got in a big room in the hotel, and lit up some candles, and fetched in the new couple. First, the doctor says:

"I don't wish to be too hard on these two men, but I think they're frauds, and they may have complices that we don't know nothing about. If they have, won't the complices get away with that bag of gold Peter Wilks left? It ain't unlikely. If these men ain't frauds, they won't object to sending for that money and letting us keep it till they prove they're all right—ain't that so?"

Everybody agreed to that. So I judged they had our gang in a pretty tight place right at the outstart. But the king he only looked sorrowful, and says:

"Gentlemen, I wish the money was there, for I ain't got no disposition to throw anything in the way of a fair, open, out-and-out investigation o' this misable business; but, alas, the money ain't there; you k'n send and see, if you want to."

"Where is it, then?"

"Well, when my niece give it to me to keep for her I took and hid it inside o' the straw tick o' my bed, not wishin' to bank it for the few days we'd be here, and considerin' the bed a safe place, and not bein' used to niggers, and suppos'n' 'em honest, like servants in England. The niggers stole it the very next mornin' after I had went down stairs; and when I sold 'em I hadn't missed the money yit, so they got clean away with it. My servant here k'n tell you 'bout it, gentlemen."

The doctor and several said "Shucks!" and I see nobody didn't altogether believe him. One man asked me if I see the niggers steal it. I said no, but I see them sneaking out of the room and hustling away, and I never thought nothing, only I reckoned they was afraid they had waked up my master and was trying to get away before he made trouble with them. That was all they asked me. Then the doctor whirls on me and says:

"Are YOU English, too?"

I says yes; and him and some others laughed, and said, "Stuff!"

Well, then they sailed in on the general investigation, and there we had it, up and down, hour in, hour out, and nobody never said a word about supper, nor ever seemed to think about it—and so they kept it up, and kept it up; and it WAS the worst mixed-up thing you ever see. They made the king tell his yarn, and they made the old gentleman tell his'n; and anybody but a lot of prejudiced chuckleheads would a SEEN that the old gentleman was spinning truth and t'other one lies. And by and by they had me up to tell what I knowed. The king he give me a left-handed look out of the corner of his eye, and so I knowed enough to talk on the right side. I begun to tell about Sheffield, and how we lived there, and all about the English Wilkses, and so on; but I didn't get pretty fur till the doctor begun to laugh; and Levi Bell, the lawyer, says:

"Set down, my boy; I wouldn't strain myself if I was you. I reckon you ain't used to lying, it don't seem to come handy; what you want is practice. You do it pretty awkward."

I didn't care nothing for the compliment, but I was glad to be let off, anyway.

The doctor he started to say something, and turns and says:

"If you'd been in town at first, Levi Bell—" The king broke in and reached out his hand, and says:

"Why, is this my poor dead brother's old friend that he's wrote so often about?"

The lawyer and him shook hands, and the lawyer smiled and looked pleased, and they talked right along awhile, and then got to one side and talked low; and at last the lawyer speaks up and says:

"That 'll fix it. I'll take the order and send it, along with your brother's, and then they'll know it's all right."

So they got some paper and a pen, and the king he set down and twisted his head to one side, and chawed his tongue, and scrawled off something; and then they give the pen to the duke—and then for the first time the duke looked sick. But he took the pen and wrote. So then the lawyer turns to the new old gentleman and says:

"You and your brother please write a line or two and sign your names."

The old gentleman wrote, but nobody couldn't read it. The lawyer looked powerful astonished, and says:

"Well, it beats ME"—and snaked a lot of old letters out of his pocket, and examined them, and then examined the old man's writing, and then THEM again; and then says: "These old letters is from Harvey Wilks; and here's THESE two handwritings, and anybody can see they didn't write them" (the king and the duke looked sold and foolish, I tell you, to see how the lawyer had took them in), "and here's THIS old gentleman's hand writing, and anybody can tell, easy enough, HE didn't write them—fact is, the scratches he makes ain't properly WRITING at all. Now, here's some letters from—"

The new old gentleman says:

"If you please, let me explain. Nobody can read my hand but my brother there—so he copies for me. It's HIS hand you've got there, not mine."

"WELL!" says the lawyer, "this IS a state of things. I've got some of William's letters, too; so if you'll get him to write a line or so we can com—"

"He CAN'T write with his left hand," says the old gentleman. "If he could use his right hand, you would see that he wrote his own letters and mine too. Look at both, please—they're by the same hand."

The lawyer done it, and says:

"I believe it's so—and if it ain't so, there's a heap stronger resemblance than I'd noticed before, anyway. Well, well, well! I thought we was right on the track of a solution, but it's gone to grass, partly. But anyway, one thing is proved—THESE two ain't either of 'em Wilkses"—and he wagged his head towards the king and the duke.

Well, what do you think? That muleheaded old fool wouldn't

give in THEN! Indeed he wouldn't. Said it warn't no fair test. Said his brother William was the cussedest joker in the world, and hadn't tried to write —HE see William was going to play one of his jokes the minute he put the pen to paper. And so he warmed up and went warbling right along till he was actuly beginning to believe what he was saying HIMSELF; but pretty soon the new gentleman broke in, and says:

"I've thought of something. Is there anybody here that helped to lay out my br—helped to lay out the late Peter Wilks for burying?"

"Yes," says somebody, "me and Ab Turner done it. We're both here."

Then the old man turns towards the king, and says:

"Perhaps this gentleman can tell me what was tattooed on his breast?"

Blamed if the king didn't have to brace up mighty quick, or he'd a squshed down like a bluff bank that the river has cut under, it took him so sudden; and, mind you, it was a thing that was calculated to make most ANYBODY sqush to get fetched such a solid one as that without any notice, because how was HE going to know what was tattooed on the man? He whitened a little; he couldn't help it; and it was mighty still in there, and everybody bending a little forwards and gazing at him. Says I to myself, NOW he'll throw up the sponge—there ain't no more use. Well, did he? A body can't hardly believe it, but he didn't. I reckon he thought he'd keep the thing up till he tired them people out, so they'd thin out, and him and the duke could break loose and get away. Anyway, he set there, and pretty soon he begun to smile, and says:

"Mf! It's a VERY tough question, AIN'T it! YES, sir, I k'n tell you what's tattooed on his breast. It's jest a small, thin, blue arrow —that's what it is; and if you don't look clost, you can't see it. NOW what do you say—hey?"

Well, I never see anything like that old blister for clean out-and-out cheek.

The new old gentleman turns brisk towards Ab Turner and his pard, and his eye lights up like he judged he'd got the king THIS time, and says:

"There—you've heard what he said! Was there any such mark on Peter Wilks' breast?"

Both of them spoke up and says:

"We didn't see no such mark."

"Good!" says the old gentleman. "Now, what you DID see on his breast was a small dim P, and a B (which is an initial he dropped when he was young), and a W, with dashes between them, so: P—B—W"—and he marked them that way on a piece of paper. "Come, ain't that what you saw?"

Both of them spoke up again, and says:

"No, we DIDN'T. We never seen any marks at all."

Well, everybody WAS in a state of mind now, and they sings out:

"The whole BILIN' of 'm 's frauds! Le's duck 'em! le's drown

'em! le's ride 'em on a rail!" and everybody was whooping at once, and there was a rattling powwow. But the lawyer he jumps on the table and yells, and says:

"Gentlemen—gentleMEN! Hear me just a word—just a SINGLE word—if you PLEASE! There's one way yet—let's go and dig up the corpse and look."

That took them.

"Hooray!" they all shouted, and was starting right off; but the lawyer and the doctor sung out:

"Hold on, hold on! Collar all these four men and the boy, and fetch THEM along, too!"

"We'll do it!" they all shouted; "and if we don't find them marks we'll lynch the whole gang!"

I WAS scared, now, I tell you. But there warn't no getting away, you know. They gripped us all, and marched us right along, straight for the graveyard, which was a mile and a half down the river, and the whole town at our heels, for we made noise enough, and it was only nine in the evening.

As we went by our house I wished I hadn't sent Mary Jane out of town; because now if I could tip her the wink she'd light out and save me, and blow on our dead-beats.

Well, we swarmed along down the river road, just carrying on like wildcats; and to make it more scary the sky was darking up, and the lightning beginning to wink and flitter, and the wind to shiver amongst the leaves. This was the most awful trouble and most dangersome I ever was in; and I was kinder stunned; everything was going so different from what I had allowed for; stead of being fixed so I could take my own time if I wanted to, and see all the fun, and have Mary Jane at my back to save me and set me free when the close-fit come, here was nothing in the world betwixt me and sudden death but just them tattoo-marks. If they didn't find them—

I couldn't bear to think about it; and yet, somehow, I couldn't think about nothing else. It got darker and darker, and it was a beautiful time to give the crowd the slip; but that big husky had me by the wrist —Hines—and a body might as well try to give Goliar the slip. He dragged me right along, he was so excited, and I had to run to keep up.

When they got there they swarmed into the graveyard and washed over it like an overflow. And when they got to the grave they found they had about a hundred times as many shovels as they wanted, but nobody hadn't thought to fetch a lantern. But they sailed into digging anyway by the flicker of the lightning, and sent a man to the nearest house, a half a mile off, to borrow one.

So they dug and dug like everything; and it got awful dark, and the rain started, and the wind swished and swushed along, and the lightning come brisker and brisker, and the thunder boomed; but them people never took no notice of it, they was so full of this business; and one minute you could see everything and every face in that big crowd, and the shovelfuls of dirt sailing up out of the grave, and the next second the dark wiped it all out, and you couldn't see nothing at all.

At last they got out the coffin and begun to unscrew the lid, and then such another crowding and shouldering and shoving as there was, to scrouge in and get a sight, you never see; and in the dark, that way, it was awful. Hines he hurt my wrist dreadful pulling and tugging so, and I reckon he clean forgot I was in the world, he was so excited and panting.

All of a sudden the lightning let go a perfect sluice of white glare, and somebody sings out:

"By the living jingo, here's the bag of gold on his breast!"

Hines let out a whoop, like everybody else, and dropped my wrist and give a big surge to bust his way in and get a look, and the way I lit out and shinned for the road in the dark there ain't nobody can tell.

I had the road all to myself, and I fairly flew—leastways, I had it all to myself except the solid dark, and the now-and-then glares, and the buzzing of the rain, and the thrashing of the wind, and the splitting of the thunder; and sure as you are born I did clip it along!

When I struck the town I see there warn't nobody out in the storm, so I never hunted for no back streets, but humped it straight through the main one; and when I begun to get towards our house I aimed my eye and set it. No light there; the house all dark—which made me feel sorry and disappointed, I didn't know why. But at last, just as I was sailing by, FLASH comes the light in Mary Jane's window! and my heart swelled up sudden, like to bust; and the same second the house and all was behind me in the dark,.and wasn't ever going to be before me no more in this world. She WAS the best girl I ever see, and had the most sand.

The minute I was far enough above the town to see I could make the towhead, I begun to look sharp for a boat to borrow, and the first time the lightning showed me one that wasn't chained I snatched it and shoved. It was a canoe, and warn't fastened with nothing but a rope. The towhead was a rattling big distance off, away out there in the middle of the river, but I didn't lose no time; and when I struck the raft at last I was so fagged I would a just laid down to blow and gasp if I could afforded it. But I didn't. As I sprung aboard I sung out:

"Out with you, Jim, and set her loose! Glory be to goodness, we're shut of them!"

Jim lit out, and was a-coming for me with both arms spread, he was so full of joy; but when I glimpsed him in the lightning my heart shot up in my mouth and I went overboard backwards; for I forgot he was old King Lear and a drownded A-rab all in one, and it most scared the livers and lights out of me. But Jim fished me out, and was going to hug me and bless me, and so on, he was so glad I was back and we was shut of the king and the duke, but I says:

"Not now; have it for breakfast, have it for breakfast! Cut loose and let her slide!"

So in two seconds away we went a-sliding down the river, and it DID seem so good to be free again and all by ourselves on the big river, and nobody to bother us. I had to skip around a bit, and jump up and crack my heels a few times—I couldn't help it; but about the third crack I noticed a sound that I knowed mighty well, and held my breath and listened and waited; and sure enough, when the next flash busted out over the water, here they come!—and just a-laying to their oars and making their skiff hum! It was the king and the duke.

So I wilted right down on to the planks then, and give up; and it was all I could do to keep from crying.

CHAPTER XXX.

WHEN they got aboard the king went for me, and shook me by the collar, and says:

"Tryin' to give us the slip, was ye, you pup! Tired of our company, hey?"

I says:

"No, your majesty, we warn't—PLEASE don't, your majesty!"

"Quick, then, and tell us what WAS your idea, or I'll shake the insides out o' you!"

"Honest, I'll tell you everything just as it happened, your majesty. The man that had a-holt of me was very good to me, and kept saying he had a boy about as big as me that died last year, and he was sorry to see a boy in such a dangerous fix; and when they was all took by surprise by finding the gold, and made a rush for the coffin, he lets go of me and whispers, 'Heel it now, or they'll hang ye, sure!' and I lit out. It didn't seem no good for ME to stay—I couldn't do nothing, and I didn't want to be hung if I could get away. So I never stopped running till I found the canoe; and when I got here I told Jim to hurry, or they'd catch me and hang me yet, and said I was afeard you and the duke wasn't alive now, and I was awful sorry, and so was Jim, and was awful glad when we see you coming; you may ask Jim if I didn't."

Jim said it was so; and the king told him to shut up, and said, "Oh, yes, it's MIGHTY likely!" and shook me up again, and said he reckoned he'd drownd me. But the duke says:

"Leggo the boy, you old idiot! Would YOU a done any different? Did you inquire around for HIM when you got loose? I don't remember it."

So the king let go of me, and begun to cuss that town and everybody in it. But the duke says:

"You better a blame' sight give YOURSELF a good cussing, for you're the one that's entitled to it most. You hain't done a thing from the start that had any sense in it, except coming out so cool and cheeky with that imaginary blue-arrow mark. That WAS bright—it was right down bully; and it was the thing that saved us. For if it hadn't been for that they'd a jailed us till them Englishmen's baggage come—and then—the penitentiary, you bet! But that trick took 'em to the graveyard, and the gold done us a still bigger kindness; for if the excited fools hadn't let go all holts and made that rush to get a look we'd a slept in our cravats to-night—cravats warranted to WEAR, too—longer than WE'D need 'em."

They was still a minute—thinking; then the king says, kind of absent-minded like:

"Mf! And we reckoned the NIGGERS stole it!"

That made me squirm!

"Yes," says the duke, kinder slow and deliberate and sarcastic, "WE did."

After about a half a minute the king drawls out:

"Leastways, I did."

The duke says, the same way:

"On the contrary, I did."

The king kind of ruffles up, and says:

"Looky here, Bilgewater, what'r you referrin' to?"

The duke says, pretty brisk:

"When it comes to that, maybe you'll let me ask, what was YOU referring to?"

"Shucks!" says the king, very sarcastic; "but I don't know—maybe you was asleep, and didn't know what you was about."

The duke bristles up now, and says:

"Oh, let UP on this cussed nonsense; do you take me for a blame' fool? Don't you reckon I know who hid that money in that coffin?"

"YES, sir! I know you DO know, because you done it yourself!"

"It's a lie!"—and the duke went for him. The king sings out:

"Take y'r hands off!—leggo my throat!—I take it all back!"

The duke says:

"Well, you just own up, first, that you DID hide that money there, intending to give me the slip one of these days, and come back and dig it up, and have it all to yourself."

"Wait jest a minute, duke—answer me this one question, honest and fair; if you didn't put the money there, say it, and I'll b'lieve you, and take back everything I said."

"You old scoundrel, I didn't, and you know I didn't. There, now!"

"Well, then, I b'lieve you. But answer me only jest this one more—now DON'T git mad; didn't you have it in your mind to hook the money and hide it?"

The duke never said nothing for a little bit; then he says:

"Well, I don't care if I DID, I didn't DO it, anyway. But you not only had it in mind to do it, but you DONE it."

"I wisht I never die if I done it, duke, and that's honest. I won't say I warn't goin' to do it, because I WAS; but you—I mean somebody—got in ahead o' me."

"It's a lie! You done it, and you got to SAY you done it, or—"

The king began to gurgle, and then he gasps out:

"'Nough!—I OWN UP!"

I was very glad to hear him say that; it made me feel much more easier than what I was feeling before. So the duke took his hands off and says:

"If you ever deny it again I'll drown you. It's WELL for you to set there and blubber like a baby—it's fitten for you, after the

way you've acted. I never see such an old ostrich for wanting to gobble everything —and I a-trusting you all the time, like you was my own father. You ought to been ashamed of yourself to stand by and hear it saddled on to a lot of poor niggers, and you never say a word for 'em. It makes me feel ridiculous to think I was soft enough to BELIEVE that rubbage. Cuss you, I can see now why you was so anxious to make up the deffisit—you wanted to get what money I'd got out of the Nonesuch and one thing or another, and scoop it ALL!"

The king says, timid, and still a-snuffling:

"Why, duke, it was you that said make up the deffisit; it warn't me."

"Dry up! I don't want to hear no more out of you!" says the duke. "And NOW you see what you GOT by it. They've got all their own money back, and all of OURN but a shekel or two BESIDES. G'long to bed, and don't you deffersit ME no more deffersits, long 's YOU live!"

So the king sneaked into the wigwam and took to his bottle for comfort, and before long the duke tackled HIS bottle; and so in about a half an hour they was as thick as thieves again, and the tighter they got the lovinger they got, and went off a-snoring in each other's arms. They both got powerful mellow, but I noticed the king didn't get mellow enough to forget to remember to not deny about hiding the money-bag again. That made me feel easy and satisfied. Of course when they got to snoring we had a long gabble, and I told Jim everything.

CHAPTER XXXI.

WE dasn't stop again at any town for days and days; kept right along down the river. We was down south in the warm weather now, and a mighty long ways from home. We begun to come to trees with Spanish moss on them, hanging down from the limbs like long, gray beards. It was the first I ever see it growing, and it made the woods look solemn and dismal. So now the frauds reckoned they was out of danger, and they begun to work the villages again.

First they done a lecture on temperance; but they didn't make enough for them both to get drunk on. Then in another village they started a dancing-school; but they didn't know no more how to dance than a kangaroo does; so the first prance they made the general public jumped in and pranced them out of town. Another time they tried to go at yellocution; but they didn't yellocute long till the audience got up and give them a solid good cussing, and made them skip out. They tackled missionarying, and mesmerizing, and doctoring, and telling fortunes, and a little of everything; but they couldn't seem to have no luck. So at last they got just about dead broke, and laid around the raft as she floated along, thinking and thinking, and never saying nothing, by the half a day at a time, and dreadful blue and desperate.

And at last they took a change and begun to lay their heads together in the wigwam and talk low and confidential two or three hours at a time. Jim and me got uneasy. We didn't like the look of it. We judged they was studying up some kind of worse deviltry than ever. We turned it over and over, and at last we made up our minds they was going to break into somebody's house or store, or was going into the counterfeit-money business, or something. So then we was pretty scared, and made up an agreement that we wouldn't have nothing in the world to do with such actions, and if we ever got the least show we would give them the cold shake and clear out and leave them behind. Well, early one morning we hid the raft in a good, safe place about two mile below a little bit of a shabby village named Pikesville, and the king he went ashore and told us all to stay hid whilst he went up to town and smelt around to see if anybody had got any wind of the Royal Nonesuch there yet. ("House to rob, you MEAN," says I to myself; "and when you get through robbing it you'll come back here and wonder what has become of me and Jim and the raft—and you'll have to take it out in wondering.") And he said if he warn't back by midday the duke and me would know it was all right, and we was to come along.

So we stayed where we was. The duke he fretted and sweated around, and was in a mighty sour way. He scolded us for everything, and we couldn't seem to do nothing right; he found fault with every little thing. Something was a-brewing, sure. I was good and glad when midday come and no king; we could have a change, anyway—and maybe a chance for THE chance on top of it. So me and the duke went up to the village, and hunted around there for the king, and by and by we found him in the back room of a little low doggery, very tight, and a lot of loafers bullyragging him for sport, and he a-cussing and a-threatening with all his might, and so tight he couldn't walk, and couldn't do nothing to them. The duke he begun to abuse him for an old fool, and the king begun to sass back, and the minute they was fairly at it I lit out and shook the reefs out of my hind legs, and spun down the river road like a deer, for I see our chance; and I made up my mind that it would be a long day before they ever see me and Jim again. I got down there all out of breath but loaded up with joy, and sung out:

"Set her loose, Jim! we're all right now!"

But there warn't no answer, and nobody come out of the wigwam. Jim was gone! I set up a shout—and then another—and then another one; and run this way and that in the woods, whooping and screeching; but it warn't no use—old Jim was gone. Then I set down and cried; I couldn't help it. But I couldn't set still long. Pretty soon I went out on the road, trying to think what I better do, and I run across a boy walking, and asked him if he'd seen a strange nigger dressed so and so, and he says:

"Yes."

"Whereabouts?" says I.

"Down to Silas Phelps' place, two mile below here. He's a runaway nigger, and they've got him. Was you looking for him?"

"You bet I ain't! I run across him in the woods about an hour or two ago, and he said if I hollered he'd cut my livers out—and told me to lay down and stay where I was; and I done it. Been there ever since; afeard to come out."

"Well," he says, "you needn't be afeard no more, becuz they've got him. He run off f'm down South, som'ers."

"It's a good job they got him."

"Well, I RECKON! There's two hunderd dollars reward on him. It's like picking up money out'n the road."

"Yes, it is—and I could a had it if I'd been big enough; I see him FIRST. Who nailed him?"

"It was an old fellow—a stranger—and he sold out his chance in him for forty dollars, becuz he's got to go up the river and can't wait. Think o' that, now! You bet I'D wait, if it was seven year."

"That's me, every time," says I. "But maybe his chance ain't worth no more than that, if he'll sell it so cheap. Maybe there's something ain't straight about it."

"But it IS, though—straight as a string. I see the handbill myself. It tells all about him, to a dot—paints him like a picture, and tells the plantation he's frum, below NewrLEANS. No-sirree-BOB, they ain't no trouble 'bout THAT speculation, you bet you. Say, gimme a chaw tobacker, won't ye?"

I didn't have none, so he left. I went to the raft, and set down in the wigwam to think. But I couldn't come to nothing. I thought till I wore my head sore, but I couldn't see no way out of the trouble. After all this long journey, and after all we'd done for them scoundrels, here it was all come to nothing, everything all busted up and ruined, because they could have the heart to serve Jim such a trick as that, and make him a slave again all his life, and amongst strangers, too, for forty dirty dollars.

Once I said to myself it would be a thousand times better for Jim to be a slave at home where his family was, as long as he'd GOT to be a slave, and so I'd better write a letter to Tom Sawyer and tell him to tell Miss Watson where he was. But I soon give up that notion for two things: she'd be mad and disgusted at his rascality and ungratefulness for leaving her, and so she'd sell him straight down the river again; and if she didn't, everybody naturally despises an ungrateful nigger, and they'd make Jim feel it all the time, and so he'd feel ornery and disgraced. And then think of ME! It would get all around that Huck Finn helped a nigger to get his freedom; and if I was ever to see anybody from that town again I'd be ready to get down and lick his boots for shame. That's just the way: a person does a low-down thing, and then he don't want to take no consequences of it. Thinks as long as he can hide, it ain't no disgrace. That was my fix exactly. The more I studied about this the more my conscience went to grinding me, and the more wicked and low-down and ornery I got to feeling. And at last, when it hit me all of a sudden that here was the plain hand of Providence slapping me in the face and letting me know my wickedness was being watched all the time from up there in heaven, whilst I was stealing a poor old woman's nigger that hadn't ever done me no harm, and now was showing me there's One that's always on the lookout, and ain't a-going to allow no such miserable doings to go only just so fur and no further, I most dropped in my tracks I was so scared. Well, I tried the best I could to kinder soften it up somehow for myself by saying I was brung up wicked, and so I warn't so much to blame; but something inside of me kept saying, "There was the Sunday-school, you could a gone to it; and if you'd a done it they'd a learnt you there that people that acts as I'd been acting about that nigger goes to everlasting fire."

It made me shiver. And I about made up my mind to pray, and see if I couldn't try to quit being the kind of a boy I was and be better. So I kneeled down. But the words wouldn't come. Why wouldn't they? It warn't no use to try and hide it from Him. Nor from ME, neither. I knowed very well why they wouldn't come. It was because my heart warn't right; it was because I warn't square; it was because I was playing double. I was letting ON to give up sin, but away inside of me I was holding on to the biggest one of all. I was trying to make my mouth SAY I would do the right thing and the clean thing, and go and write to that nigger's owner and tell where he was; but deep down in me I knowed it was a lie, and He knowed it. You can't pray a lie—I found that out.

So I was full of trouble, full as I could be; and didn't know what to do. At last I had an idea; and I says, I'll go and write the letter—and then see if I can pray. Why, it was astonishing, the way I felt as light as a feather right straight off, and my troubles all gone. So I got a piece of paper and a pencil, all glad and excited, and set down and wrote:

Miss Watson, your runaway nigger Jim is down here two mile below Pikesville, and Mr. Phelps has got him and he will give him up for the reward if you send.

HUCK FINN.

I felt good and all washed clean of sin for the first time I had ever felt so in my life, and I knowed I could pray now. But I didn't do it straight off, but laid the paper down and set there thinking—thinking how good it was all this happened so, and how near I come to being lost and going to hell. And went on thinking. And got to thinking over our trip down the river; and I see Jim before me all the time: in the day and in the night-time, sometimes moonlight, sometimes storms, and we a-floating along, talking and singing and laughing. But somehow I couldn't seem to strike no places to harden me against him, but only the other kind. I'd see him standing my watch on top of his'n, 'stead of calling me, so I could go on sleeping; and see him how glad he was when I come back out of the fog; and when I come to him again in the swamp, up there where the feud was; and such-like times; and would always call me honey, and pet me and do everything he could think of for me, and how good he always was; and at last I struck the time I saved him by telling the men we had small-pox aboard, and he was so grateful, and said I was the best friend old Jim ever had in the world, and the ONLY one he's got now; and then I happened to look around and see that paper.

It was a close place. I took it up, and held it in my hand. I was a-trembling, because I'd got to decide, forever, betwixt two things, and I knowed it. I studied a minute, sort of holding my breath, and then says to myself:

"All right, then, I'll GO to hell"—and tore it up.

It was awful thoughts and awful words, but they was said. And I let them stay said; and never thought no more about reforming. I shoved the whole thing out of my head, and said I would take up wickedness again, which was in my line, being brung up to it, and the other warn't. And for a starter I would go to work and steal Jim out of slavery again; and if I could think up anything worse, I would do that, too; because as long as I was in, and in for good, I might as well go the whole hog.

Then I set to thinking over how to get at it, and turned over some considerable many ways in my mind; and at last fixed up a plan that suited me. So then I took the bearings of a woody island that was down the river a piece, and as soon as it was fairly dark I crept out with my raft and went for it, and hid it there, and then turned in. I slept the night through, and got up before it was light, and had my breakfast, and put on my store clothes, and tied up some others and one thing or another in a bundle, and took the canoe and cleared for shore. I landed below where I judged was Phelps's place, and hid my bundle in the woods, and then filled up the canoe with water, and loaded rocks into her and sunk her where I could find her again when I wanted her, about a quarter of a mile below a little steam sawmill that was on the bank.

Then I struck up the road, and when I passed the mill I see a sign on it, "Phelps's Sawmill," and when I come to the farmhouses, two or three hundred yards further along, I kept my eyes peeled, but didn't see nobody around, though it was good daylight now. But I didn't mind, because I didn't want to see nobody just yet—I only wanted to get the lay of the land. According to my plan, I was going to turn up there from the village, not from below. So I just took a look, and shoved along, straight for town. Well, the very first man I see when I got there was the duke. He was sticking up a bill for the Royal Nonesuch—three-night performance—like that other time. They had the cheek, them frauds! I was right on him before I could shirk. He looked astonished, and says:

"Hel-LO! Where'd YOU come from?" Then he says, kind of glad and eager, "Where's the raft?—got her in a good place?"

I says:

"Why, that's just what I was going to ask your grace."

Then he didn't look so joyful, and says:

"What was your idea for asking ME?" he says.

"Well," I says, "when I see the king in that doggery yesterday I says to myself, we can't get him home for hours, till he's soberer; so I went a-loafing around town to put in the time and wait. A man up and offered me ten cents to help him pull a skiff over the river and back to fetch a sheep, and so I went along; but when we was dragging him to the boat, and the man left me a-holt of the rope and went behind him to shove him along, he was too strong for me and jerked loose and run, and we after him. We didn't have no dog, and so we had to chase him all over the country till we tired him out. We never got him till dark; then we fetched him over, and I started down for the raft. When I got there and see it was gone, I says to myself, 'They've got into trouble and had to leave; and they've took my nigger, which is the only nigger I've got in the world, and now I'm in a strange country, and ain't got no property no more, nor nothing, and no way to make my living;' so I set down and cried. I slept in the woods all night. But what DID become of the raft, then?—and Jim—poor Jim!"

"Blamed if I know—that is, what's become of the raft. That old fool had made a trade and got forty dollars, and when we found him in the doggery the loafers had matched half-dollars with him and got every cent but what he'd spent for whisky; and when I got him home late last night and found the raft gone, we said, 'That little rascal has stole our raft and shook us, and run off down the river.'"

"I wouldn't shake my NIGGER, would I?—the only nigger I had in the world, and the only property."

"We never thought of that. Fact is, I reckon we'd come to consider him OUR nigger; yes, we did consider him so—goodness knows we had trouble enough for him. So when we see the raft was gone and we flat broke, there warn't anything for it but to try the Royal Nonesuch another shake. And I've pegged along ever since, dry as a powder-horn. Where's that ten cents? Give it here."

I had considerable money, so I give him ten cents, but begged him to spend it for something to eat, and give me some, because it was all the money I had, and I hadn't had nothing to eat since yesterday. He never said nothing. The next minute he whirls on me and says:

"Do you reckon that nigger would blow on us? We'd skin him if he done that!"

"How can he blow? Hain't he run off?"

"No! That old fool sold him, and never divided with me, and the money's gone."

"SOLD him?" I says, and begun to cry; "why, he was MY nigger, and that was my money. Where is he?—I want my nigger."

"Well, you can't GET your nigger, that's all—so dry up your blubbering. Looky here—do you think YOU'D venture to blow on us? Blamed if I think I'd trust you. Why, if you WAS to blow on us—"

He stopped, but I never see the duke look so ugly out of his eyes before. I went on a-whimpering, and says:

"I don't want to blow on nobody; and I ain't got no time to blow, nohow. I got to turn out and find my nigger."

He looked kinder bothered, and stood there with his bills fluttering on his arm, thinking, and wrinkling up his forehead. At last he says:

"I'll tell you something. We got to be here three days. If you'll promise you won't blow, and won't let the nigger blow, I'll tell you where to find him."

So I promised, and he says:

"A farmer by the name of Silas Ph—" and then he stopped. You see, he started to tell me the truth; but when he stopped that way, and begun to study and think again, I reckoned he was changing his mind. And so he was. He wouldn't trust me; he wanted to make sure of having me out of the way the whole three days. So pretty soon he says:

"The man that bought him is named Abram Foster—Abram G. Foster—and he lives forty mile back here in the country, on the road to Lafayette."

"All right," I says, "I can walk it in three days. And I'll start this very afternoon."

"No you wont, you'll start NOW; and don't you lose any time about it, neither, nor do any gabbling by the way. Just keep a tight tongue in your head and move right along, and then you won't get into trouble with US, d'ye hear?"

That was the order I wanted, and that was the one I played for. I wanted to be left free to work my plans.

"So clear out," he says; "and you can tell Mr. Foster whatever you want to. Maybe you can get him to believe that Jim IS your nigger—some idiots don't require documents—leastways I've heard there's such down South here. And when you tell him the handbill and the reward's bogus, maybe he'll believe you when you explain to him what the idea was for getting 'em out. Go 'long now, and tell him anything you want to; but mind you don't work your jaw any BETWEEN here and there."

So I left, and struck for the back country. I didn't look around, but I kinder felt like he was watching me. But I knowed I could tire him out at that. I went straight out in the country as much as a mile before I stopped; then I doubled back through the woods towards Phelps'. I reckoned I better start in on my plan straight off without fooling around, because I wanted to stop Jim's mouth till these fellows could get away. I didn't want no trouble with their kind. I'd seen all I wanted to of them, and wanted to get entirely shut of them.

CHAPTER XXXII.

WHEN I got there it was all still and Sunday-like, and hot and sunshiny; the hands was gone to the fields; and there was them kind of faint dronings of bugs and flies in the air that makes it seem so lonesome and like everybody's dead and gone; and if a breeze fans along and quivers the leaves it makes you feel mournful, because you feel like it's spirits whispering—spirits that's been dead ever so many years—and you always think they're talking about YOU. As a general thing it makes a body wish HE was dead, too, and done with it all.

Phelps' was one of these little one-horse cotton plantations, and they all look alike. A rail fence round a two-acre yard; a stile made out of logs sawed off and up-ended in steps, like barrels of a different length, to climb over the fence with, and for the women to stand on when they are going to jump on to a horse; some sickly grass-patches in the big yard, but mostly it was bare and smooth, like an old hat with the nap rubbed off; big double log-house for the white folks—hewed logs, with the chinks stopped up with mud or mortar, and these mud-stripes been whitewashed some time or another; round-log kitchen, with a big broad, open but roofed passage joining it to the house; log smoke-house back of the kitchen; three little log nigger-cabins in a row t'other side the smoke-house; one little hut all by itself away down against the back fence, and some outbuildings down a piece the other side; ash-hopper and big kettle to bile soap in by the little hut; bench by the kitchen door, with bucket of water and a gourd; hound asleep there in the sun; more hounds asleep round about; about three shade trees away off in a corner; some currant bushes and gooseberry bushes in one place by the fence; outside of the fence a garden and a watermelon patch; then the cotton fields begins, and after the fields the woods.

I went around and clumb over the back stile by the ash-hopper, and started for the kitchen. When I got a little ways I heard the dim hum of a spinning-wheel wailing along up and sinking along down again; and then I knowed for certain I wished I was dead—for that IS the lonesomest sound in the whole world.

I went right along, not fixing up any particular plan, but just trusting to Providence to put the right words in my mouth when the time come; for I'd noticed that Providence always did put the right words in my mouth if I left it alone.

When I got half-way, first one hound and then another got up and went for me, and of course I stopped and faced them, and kept still. And such another powwow as they made! In a quarter of a minute I was a kind of a hub of a wheel, as you may say—spokes made out of dogs—circle of fifteen of them packed together around me, with their necks and noses stretched up towards me, a-barking and howling; and more a-coming; you could see them sailing over fences and around corners from everywheres.

A nigger woman come tearing out of the kitchen with a rolling-pin in her hand, singing out, "Begone YOU Tige! you Spot! begone sah!" and she fetched first one and then another of them a clip and sent them howling, and then the rest followed; and the next second half of them come back, wagging their tails around me, and making friends with me. There ain't no harm in a hound, nohow.

And behind the woman comes a little nigger girl and two little nigger boys without anything on but tow-linen shirts, and they hung on to their mother's gown, and peeped out from behind her at me, bashful, the way they always do. And here comes the white woman running from the house, about forty-five or fifty year old, bareheaded, and her spinning-stick in her hand; and behind her comes her little white children, acting the same way the little niggers was going. She was smiling all over so she could hardly stand—and says:

"It's YOU, at last!—AIN'T it?"

I out with a "Yes'm" before I thought.

She grabbed me and hugged me tight; and then gripped me by both hands and shook and shook; and the tears come in her eyes, and run down over; and she couldn't seem to hug and shake enough, and kept saying, "You don't look as much like your mother as I reckoned you would; but law sakes, I don't care for that, I'm so glad to see you! Dear, dear, it does seem like I could eat you up! Children, it's your cousin Tom!—tell him howdy."

But they ducked their heads, and put their fingers in their mouths, and hid behind her. So she run on:

"Lize, hurry up and get him a hot breakfast right away—or did you get your breakfast on the boat?"

I said I had got it on the boat. So then she started for the house, leading me by the hand, and the children tagging after. When we got there she set me down in a split-bottomed chair, and set herself down on a little low stool in front of me, holding both of my hands, and says:

"Now I can have a GOOD look at you; and, laws-a-me, I've been hungry for it a many and a many a time, all these long years, and it's come at last! We been expecting you a couple of days and more. What kep' you?—boat get aground?"

"Yes'm—she—"

"Don't say yes'm—say Aunt Sally. Where'd she get aground?"

I didn't rightly know what to say, because I didn't know whether the boat would be coming up the river or down. But I go a good deal on instinct; and my instinct said she would be coming up—from down towards Orleans. That didn't help me much, though; for I didn't know the names of bars down that way. I see I'd got to invent a bar, or forget the name of the one we got aground on—or—Now I struck an idea, and fetched it out:

"It warn't the grounding—that didn't keep us back but a little. We blowed out a cylinder-head."

"Good gracious! anybody hurt?"

"No'm. Killed a nigger."

"Well, it's lucky; because sometimes people do get hurt. Two years ago last Christmas your uncle Silas was coming up from Newrleans on the old Lally Rook, and she blowed out a

cylinder-head and crippled a man. And I think he died afterwards. He was a Baptist. Your uncle Silas knowed a family in Baton Rouge that knowed his people very well. Yes, I remember now, he DID die. Mortification set in, and they had to amputate him. But it didn't save him. Yes, it was mortification—that was it. He turned blue all over, and died in the hope of a glorious resurrection. They say he was a sight to look at. Your uncle's been up to the town every day to fetch you. And he's gone again, not more'n an hour ago; he'll be back any minute now. You must a met him on the road, didn't you?—oldish man, with a—"

"No, I didn't see nobody, Aunt Sally. The boat landed just at daylight, and I left my baggage on the wharf-boat and went looking around the town and out a piece in the country, to put in the time and not get here too soon; and so I come down the back way."

"Who'd you give the baggage to?"

"Nobody."

"Why, child, it 'll be stole!"

"Not where I hid it I reckon it won't," I says.

"How'd you get your breakfast so early on the boat?"

It was kinder thin ice, but I says:

"The captain see me standing around, and told me I better have something to eat before I went ashore; so he took me in the texas to the officers' lunch, and give me all I wanted."

I was getting so uneasy I couldn't listen good. I had my mind on the children all the time; I wanted to get them out to one side and pump them a little, and find out who I was. But I couldn't get no show, Mrs. Phelps kept it up and run on so. Pretty soon she made the cold chills streak all down my back, because she says:

"But here we're a-running on this way, and you hain't told me a word about Sis, nor any of them. Now I'll rest my works a little, and you start up yourn; just tell me EVERYTHING—tell me all about 'm all every one of 'm; and how they are, and what they're doing, and what they told you to tell me; and every last thing you can think of."

Well, I see I was up a stump—and up it good. Providence had stood by me this fur all right, but I was hard and tight aground now. I see it warn't a bit of use to try to go ahead—I'd got to throw up my hand. So I says to myself, here's another place where I got to resk the truth. I opened my mouth to begin; but she grabbed me and hustled me in behind the bed, and says:

"Here he comes! Stick your head down lower—there, that'll do; you can't be seen now. Don't you let on you're here. I'll play a joke on him. Children, don't you say a word."

I see I was in a fix now. But it warn't no use to worry; there warn't nothing to do but just hold still, and try and be ready to stand from under when the lightning struck.

I had just one little glimpse of the old gentleman when he come in; then the bed hid him. Mrs. Phelps she jumps for him, and says:

"Has he come?"

"No," says her husband.

"Good-NESS gracious!" she says, "what in the warld can have become of him?"

"I can't imagine," says the old gentleman; "and I must say it makes me dreadful uneasy."

"Uneasy!" she says; "I'm ready to go distracted! He MUST a come; and you've missed him along the road. I KNOW it's so—something tells me so."

"Why, Sally, I COULDN'T miss him along the road—YOU know that."

"But oh, dear, dear, what WILL Sis say! He must a come! You must a missed him. He—"

"Oh, don't distress me any more'n I'm already distressed. I don't know what in the world to make of it. I'm at my wit's end, and I don't mind acknowledging 't I'm right down scared. But there's no hope that he's come; for he COULDN'T come and me miss him. Sally, it's terrible—just terrible—something's happened to the boat, sure!"

"Why, Silas! Look yonder!—up the road!—ain't that somebody coming?"

He sprung to the window at the head of the bed, and that give Mrs. Phelps the chance she wanted. She stooped down quick at the foot of the bed and give me a pull, and out I come; and when he turned back from the window there she stood, a-beaming and a-smiling like a house afire, and I standing pretty meek and sweaty alongside. The old gentleman stared, and says:

"Why, who's that?"

"Who do you reckon 't is?"

"I hain't no idea. Who IS it?"

"It's TOM SAWYER!"

By jings, I most slumped through the floor! But there warn't no time to swap knives; the old man grabbed me by the hand and shook, and kept on shaking; and all the time how the woman did dance around and laugh and cry; and then how they both did fire off questions about Sid, and Mary, and the rest of the tribe.

But if they was joyful, it warn't nothing to what I was; for it was like being born again, I was so glad to find out who I was. Well, they froze to me for two hours; and at last, when my chin was so tired it couldn't hardly go any more, I had told them more about my family—I mean the Sawyer family—than ever happened to any six Sawyer families. And I explained all about how we blowed out a cylinder-head at the mouth of White River, and it took us three days to fix it. Which was all right, and worked first-rate; because THEY didn't know but what it would take three days to fix it. If I'd a called it a bolthead it would a done just as well.

Now I was feeling pretty comfortable all down one side, and pretty uncomfortable all up the other. Being Tom Sawyer was easy and comfortable, and it stayed easy and comfortable till by and by I hear a steamboat coughing along down the river.

Then I says to myself, s'pose Tom Sawyer comes down on that boat? And s'pose he steps in here any minute, and sings out my name before I can throw him a wink to keep quiet?

Well, I couldn't HAVE it that way; it wouldn't do at all. I must go up the road and waylay him. So I told the folks I reckoned I would go up to the town and fetch down my baggage. The old gentleman was for going along with me, but I said no, I could drive the horse myself, and I druther he wouldn't take no trouble about me.

CHAPTER XXXIII.

SO I started for town in the wagon, and when I was half-way I see a wagon coming, and sure enough it was Tom Sawyer, and I stopped and waited till he come along. I says "Hold on!" and it stopped alongside, and his mouth opened up like a trunk, and stayed so; and he swallowed two or three times like a person that's got a dry throat, and then says:

"I hain't ever done you no harm. You know that. So, then, what you want to come back and ha'nt ME for?"

I says:

"I hain't come back—I hain't been GONE."

When he heard my voice it righted him up some, but he warn't quite satisfied yet. He says:

"Don't you play nothing on me, because I wouldn't on you. Honest injun, you ain't a ghost?"

"Honest injun, I ain't," I says.

"Well—I—I—well, that ought to settle it, of course; but I can't somehow seem to understand it no way. Looky here, warn't you ever murdered AT ALL?"

"No. I warn't ever murdered at all—I played it on them. You come in here and feel of me if you don't believe me."

So he done it; and it satisfied him; and he was that glad to see me again he didn't know what to do. And he wanted to know all about it right off, because it was a grand adventure, and mysterious, and so it hit him where he lived. But I said, leave it alone till by and by; and told his driver to wait, and we drove off a little piece, and I told him the kind of a fix I was in, and what did he reckon we better do? He said, let him alone a minute, and don't disturb him. So he thought and thought, and pretty soon he says:

"It's all right; I've got it. Take my trunk in your wagon, and let on it's your'n; and you turn back and fool along slow, so as to get to the house about the time you ought to; and I'll go towards town a piece, and take a fresh start, and get there a quarter or a half an hour after you; and you needn't let on to know me at first."

I says:

"All right; but wait a minute. There's one more thing—a thing that NOBODY don't know but me. And that is, there's a nigger here that I'm a-trying to steal out of slavery, and his name is JIM—old Miss Watson's Jim."

He says:

"What! Why, Jim is—"

He stopped and went to studying. I says:

"I know what you'll say. You'll say it's dirty, low-down business; but what if it is? I'm low down; and I'm a-going to steal him, and I want you keep mum and not let on. Will you?"

His eye lit up, and he says:

"I'll HELP you steal him!"

Well, I let go all holts then, like I was shot. It was the most astonishing speech I ever heard—and I'm bound to say Tom Sawyer fell considerable in my estimation. Only I couldn't believe it. Tom Sawyer a NIGGER-STEALER!

"Oh, shucks!" I says; "you're joking."

"I ain't joking, either."

"Well, then," I says, "joking or no joking, if you hear anything said about a runaway nigger, don't forget to remember that YOU don't know nothing about him, and I don't know nothing about him."

Then we took the trunk and put it in my wagon, and he drove off his way and I drove mine. But of course I forgot all about driving slow on accounts of being glad and full of thinking; so I got home a heap too quick for that length of a trip. The old gentleman was at the door, and he says:

"Why, this is wonderful! Whoever would a thought it was in that mare to do it? I wish we'd a timed her. And she hain't sweated a hair—not a hair. It's wonderful. Why, I wouldn't take a hundred dollars for that horse now—I wouldn't, honest; and yet I'd a sold her for fifteen before, and thought 'twas all she was worth."

That's all he said. He was the innocentest, best old soul I ever see. But it warn't surprising; because he warn't only just a farmer, he was a preacher, too, and had a little one-horse log church down back of the plantation, which he built it himself at his own expense, for a church and schoolhouse, and never charged nothing for his preaching, and it was worth it, too. There was plenty other farmer-preachers like that, and done the same way, down South.

In about half an hour Tom's wagon drove up to the front stile, and Aunt Sally she see it through the window, because it was only about fifty yards, and says:

"Why, there's somebody come! I wonder who 'tis? Why, I do believe it's a stranger. Jimmy" (that's one of the children) "run and tell Lize to put on another plate for dinner."

Everybody made a rush for the front door, because, of course, a stranger don't come EVERY year, and so he lays over the yaller-fever, for interest, when he does come. Tom was over the stile and starting for the house; the wagon was spinning up the road for the village, and we was all bunched in the front door. Tom had his store clothes on, and an audience—and that was always nuts for Tom Sawyer. In them circumstances it warn't no trouble to him to throw in an amount of style that was suitable. He warn't a boy to meeky along up that yard like a sheep; no, he come ca'm and important, like the ram. When he got a-front of us he lifts his hat ever so gracious and dainty, like it was the lid of a box that had butterflies asleep in it and

he didn't want to disturb them, and says:

"Mr. Archibald Nichols, I presume?"

"No, my boy," says the old gentleman, "I'm sorry to say 't your driver has deceived you; Nichols's place is down a matter of three mile more. Come in, come in."

Tom he took a look back over his shoulder, and says, "Too late—he's out of sight."

"Yes, he's gone, my son, and you must come in and eat your dinner with us; and then we'll hitch up and take you down to Nichols's."

"Oh, I CAN'T make you so much trouble; I couldn't think of it. I'll walk —I don't mind the distance."

"But we won't LET you walk—it wouldn't be Southern hospitality to do it. Come right in."

"Oh, DO," says Aunt Sally; "it ain't a bit of trouble to us, not a bit in the world. You must stay. It's a long, dusty three mile, and we can't let you walk. And, besides, I've already told 'em to put on another plate when I see you coming; so you mustn't disappoint us. Come right in and make yourself at home."

So Tom he thanked them very hearty and handsome, and let himself be persuaded, and come in; and when he was in he said he was a stranger from Hicksville, Ohio, and his name was William Thompson—and he made another bow.

Well, he run on, and on, and on, making up stuff about Hicksville and everybody in it he could invent, and I getting a little nervous, and wondering how this was going to help me out of my scrape; and at last, still talking along, he reached over and kissed Aunt Sally right on the mouth, and then settled back again in his chair comfortable, and was going on talking; but she jumped up and wiped it off with the back of her hand, and says:

"You owdacious puppy!"

He looked kind of hurt, and says:

"I'm surprised at you, m'am."

"You're s'rp—Why, what do you reckon I am? I've a good notion to take and—Say, what do you mean by kissing me?"

He looked kind of humble, and says:

"I didn't mean nothing, m'am. I didn't mean no harm. I—I—thought you'd like it."

"Why, you born fool!" She took up the spinning stick, and it looked like it was all she could do to keep from giving him a crack with it. "What made you think I'd like it?"

"Well, I don't know. Only, they—they—told me you would."

"THEY told you I would. Whoever told you's ANOTHER lunatic. I never heard the beat of it. Who's THEY?"

"Why, everybody. They all said so, m'am."

It was all she could do to hold in; and her eyes snapped, and her fingers worked like she wanted to scratch him; and she says:

"Who's 'everybody'? Out with their names, or ther'll be an idiot short."

He got up and looked distressed, and fumbled his hat, and says:

"I'm sorry, and I warn't expecting it. They told me to. They all told me to. They all said, kiss her; and said she'd like it. They all said it—every one of them. But I'm sorry, m'am, and I won't do it no more —I won't, honest."

"You won't, won't you? Well, I sh'd RECKON you won't!"

"No'm, I'm honest about it; I won't ever do it again—till you ask me."

"Till I ASK you! Well, I never see the beat of it in my born days! I lay you'll be the Methusalem-numskull of creation before ever I ask you —or the likes of you."

"Well," he says, "it does surprise me so. I can't make it out, somehow. They said you would, and I thought you would. But—" He stopped and looked around slow, like he wished he could run across a friendly eye somewheres, and fetched up on the old gentleman's, and says, "Didn't YOU think she'd like me to kiss her, sir?"

"Why, no; I—I—well, no, I b'lieve I didn't."

Then he looks on around the same way to me, and says:

"Tom, didn't YOU think Aunt Sally 'd open out her arms and say, 'Sid Sawyer—'"

"My land!" she says, breaking in and jumping for him, "you impudent young rascal, to fool a body so—" and was going to hug him, but he fended her off, and says:

"No, not till you've asked me first."

So she didn't lose no time, but asked him; and hugged him and kissed him over and over again, and then turned him over to the old man, and he took what was left. And after they got a little quiet again she says:

"Why, dear me, I never see such a surprise. We warn't looking for YOU at all, but only Tom. Sis never wrote to me about anybody coming but him."

"It's because it warn't INTENDED for any of us to come but Tom," he says; "but I begged and begged, and at the last minute she let me come, too; so, coming down the river, me and Tom thought it would be a first-rate surprise for him to come here to the house first, and for me to by and by tag along and drop in, and let on to be a stranger. But it was a mistake, Aunt Sally. This ain't no healthy place for a stranger to come."

"No—not impudent whelps, Sid. You ought to had your jaws boxed; I hain't been so put out since I don't know when. But I don't care, I don't mind the terms—I'd be willing to stand a thousand such jokes to have you here. Well, to think of that performance! I don't deny it, I was most putrified with astonishment when you give me that smack."

We had dinner out in that broad open passage betwixt the house and the kitchen; and there was things enough on that table for seven families —and all hot, too; none of your flabby, tough meat that's laid in a cupboard in a damp cellar all night and tastes like a hunk of old cold cannibal in the morning. Uncle Silas he asked a pretty long blessing over it, but it was worth it; and it didn't cool it a bit, neither, the way I've seen them kind of interruptions do lots of times. There was a considerable good deal of talk all the afternoon, and me and Tom was on the lookout all the time; but it warn't no use, they didn't happen to say nothing about any runaway nigger, and we was afraid to try to work up to it. But at supper, at night, one of the little boys says:

"Pa, mayn't Tom and Sid and me go to the show?"

"No," says the old man, "I reckon there ain't going to be any; and you couldn't go if there was; because the runaway nigger told Burton and me all about that scandalous show, and Burton said he would tell the people; so I reckon they've drove the owdacious loafers out of town before this time."

So there it was!—but I couldn't help it. Tom and me was to sleep in the same room and bed; so, being tired, we bid good-night and went up to bed right after supper, and clumb out of the window and down the lightning-rod, and shoved for the town; for I didn't believe anybody was going to give the king and the duke a hint, and so if I didn't hurry up and give them one they'd get into trouble sure.

On the road Tom he told me all about how it was reckoned I was murdered, and how pap disappeared pretty soon, and didn't come back no more, and what a stir there was when Jim run away; and I told Tom all about our Royal Nonesuch rapscallions, and as much of the raft voyage as I had time to; and as we struck into the town and up through the—here comes a raging rush of people with torches, and an awful whooping and yelling, and banging tin pans and blowing horns; and we jumped to one side to let them go by; and as they went by I see they had the king and the duke astraddle of a rail—that is, I knowed it WAS the king and the duke, though they was all over tar and feathers, and didn't look like nothing in the world that was human—just looked like a couple of monstrous big soldier-plumes. Well, it made me sick to see it; and I was sorry for them poor pitiful rascals, it seemed like I couldn't ever feel any hardness against them any more in the world. It was a dreadful thing to see. Human beings CAN be awful cruel to one another.

We see we was too late—couldn't do no good. We asked some stragglers about it, and they said everybody went to the show looking very innocent; and laid low and kept dark till the poor old king was in the middle of his cavortings on the stage; then somebody give a signal, and the house rose up and went for them.

So we poked along back home, and I warn't feeling so brash as I was before, but kind of ornery, and humble, and to blame, somehow—though I hadn't done nothing. But that's always the way; it don't make no difference whether you do right or wrong, a person's conscience ain't got no sense, and just goes for him anyway. If I had a yaller dog that didn't know no more than a person's conscience does I would pison him. It takes up more room than all the rest of a person's insides, and yet ain't no good, nohow. Tom Sawyer he says the same.

CHAPTER XXXIV.

WE stopped talking, and got to thinking. By and by Tom says:

"Looky here, Huck, what fools we are to not think of it before! I bet I know where Jim is."

"No! Where?"

"In that hut down by the ash-hopper. Why, looky here. When we was at dinner, didn't you see a nigger man go in there with some vittles?"

"Yes."

"What did you think the vittles was for?"

"For a dog."

"So 'd I. Well, it wasn't for a dog."

"Why?"

"Because part of it was watermelon."

"So it was—I noticed it. Well, it does beat all that I never thought about a dog not eating watermelon. It shows how a body can see and don't see at the same time."

"Well, the nigger unlocked the padlock when he went in, and he locked it again when he came out. He fetched uncle a key about the time we got up from table—same key, I bet. Watermelon shows man, lock shows prisoner; and it ain't likely there's two prisoners on such a little plantation, and where the people's all so kind and good. Jim's the prisoner. All right—I'm glad we found it out detective fashion; I wouldn't give shucks for any other way. Now you work your mind, and study out a plan to steal Jim, and I will study out one, too; and we'll take the one we like the best."

What a head for just a boy to have! If I had Tom Sawyer's head I wouldn't trade it off to be a duke, nor mate of a steamboat, nor clown in a circus, nor nothing I can think of. I went to thinking out a plan, but only just to be doing something; I knowed very well where the right plan was going to come from. Pretty soon Tom says:

"Ready?"

"Yes," I says.

"All right—bring it out."

"My plan is this," I says. "We can easy find out if it's Jim in there. Then get up my canoe to-morrow night, and fetch my raft over from the island. Then the first dark night that comes steal the key out of the old man's britches after he goes to bed, and shove off down the river on the raft with Jim, hiding daytimes and running nights, the way me and Jim used to do before. Wouldn't that plan work?"

"WORK? Why, cert'nly it would work, like rats a-fighting. But it's too blame' simple; there ain't nothing TO it. What's the good of a plan that ain't no more trouble than that? It's as mild as goose-milk. Why, Huck, it wouldn't make no more talk than breaking into a soap factory."

I never said nothing, because I warn't expecting nothing different; but I knowed mighty well that whenever he got HIS plan ready it wouldn't have none of them objections to it.

And it didn't. He told me what it was, and I see in a minute it

was worth fifteen of mine for style, and would make Jim just as free a man as mine would, and maybe get us all killed besides. So I was satisfied, and said we would waltz in on it. I needn't tell what it was here, because I knowed it wouldn't stay the way, it was. I knowed he would be changing it around every which way as we went along, and heaving in new bullinesses wherever he got a chance. And that is what he done.

Well, one thing was dead sure, and that was that Tom Sawyer was in earnest, and was actuly going to help steal that nigger out of slavery. That was the thing that was too many for me. Here was a boy that was respectable and well brung up; and had a character to lose; and folks at home that had characters; and he was bright and not leather-headed; and knowing and not ignorant; and not mean, but kind; and yet here he was, without any more pride, or rightness, or feeling, than to stoop to this business, and make himself a shame, and his family a shame, before everybody. I COULDN'T understand it no way at all. It was outrageous, and I knowed I ought to just up and tell him so; and so be his true friend, and let him quit the thing right where he was and save himself. And I DID start to tell him; but he shut me up, and says:

"Don't you reckon I know what I'm about? Don't I generly know what I'm about?"

"Yes."

"Didn't I SAY I was going to help steal the nigger?"

"Yes."

"WELL, then."

That's all he said, and that's all I said. It warn't no use to say any more; because when he said he'd do a thing, he always done it. But I couldn't make out how he was willing to go into this thing; so I just let it go, and never bothered no more about it. If he was bound to have it so, I couldn't help it.

When we got home the house was all dark and still; so we went on down to the hut by the ash-hopper for to examine it. We went through the yard so as to see what the hounds would do. They knowed us, and didn't make no more noise than country dogs is always doing when anything comes by in the night. When we got to the cabin we took a look at the front and the two sides; and on the side I warn't acquainted with—which was the north side—we found a square window-hole, up tolerable high, with just one stout board nailed across it. I says:

"Here's the ticket. This hole's big enough for Jim to get through if we wrench off the board."

Tom says:

"It's as simple as tit-tat-toe, three-in-a-row, and as easy as playing hooky. I should HOPE we can find a way that's a little more complicated than THAT, Huck Finn."

"Well, then," I says, "how 'll it do to saw him out, the way I done before I was murdered that time?"

"That's more LIKE," he says. "It's real mysterious, and troublesome, and good," he says; "but I bet we can find a way that's twice as long. There ain't no hurry; le's keep on looking around."

Betwixt the hut and the fence, on the back side, was a lean-to that joined the hut at the eaves, and was made out of plank. It was as long as the hut, but narrow—only about six foot wide. The door to it was at the south end, and was padlocked. Tom he went to the soap-kettle and searched around, and fetched back the iron thing they lift the lid with; so he took it and prized out one of the staples. The chain fell down, and we opened the door and went in, and shut it, and struck a match, and see the shed was only built against a cabin and hadn't no connection with it; and there warn't no floor to the shed, nor nothing in it but some old rusty played-out hoes and spades and picks and a crippled plow. The match went out, and so did we, and shoved in the staple again, and the door was locked as good as ever. Tom was joyful. He says;

"Now we're all right. We'll DIG him out. It 'll take about a week!"

Then we started for the house, and I went in the back door— you only have to pull a buckskin latch-string, they don't fasten the doors—but that warn't romantical enough for Tom Sawyer; no way would do him but he must climb up the lightning-rod. But after he got up half way about three times, and missed fire and fell every time, and the last time most busted his brains out, he thought he'd got to give it up; but after he was rested he allowed he would give her one more turn for luck, and this time he made the trip.

In the morning we was up at break of day, and down to the nigger cabins to pet the dogs and make friends with the nigger that fed Jim—if it WAS Jim that was being fed. The niggers was just getting through breakfast and starting for the fields; and Jim's nigger was piling up a tin pan with bread and meat and things; and whilst the others was leaving, the key come from the house.

This nigger had a good-natured, chuckle-headed face, and his wool was all tied up in little bunches with thread. That was to keep witches off. He said the witches was pestering him awful these nights, and making him see all kinds of strange things, and hear all kinds of strange words and noises, and he didn't believe he was ever witched so long before in his life. He got so worked up, and got to running on so about his troubles, he forgot all about what he'd been a-going to do. So Tom says:

"What's the vittles for? Going to feed the dogs?"

The nigger kind of smiled around gradually over his face, like when you heave a brickbat in a mud-puddle, and he says:

"Yes, Mars Sid, A dog. Cur'us dog, too. Does you want to go en look at 'im?"

"Yes."

I hunched Tom, and whispers:

"You going, right here in the daybreak? THAT warn't the plan."

"No, it warn't; but it's the plan NOW."

So, drat him, we went along, but I didn't like it much. When we got in we couldn't hardly see anything, it was so dark; but Jim was there, sure enough, and could see us; and he sings out:

"Why, HUCK! En good LAN'! ain' dat Misto Tom?"

I just knowed how it would be; I just expected it. I didn't know nothing to do; and if I had I couldn't a done it, because that nigger busted in and says:

"Why, de gracious sakes! do he know you genlmen?"

We could see pretty well now. Tom he looked at the nigger, steady and kind of wondering, and says:

"Does WHO know us?"

"Why, dis-yer runaway nigger."

"I don't reckon he does; but what put that into your head?"

"What PUT it dar? Didn' he jis' dis minute sing out like he knowed you?"

Tom says, in a puzzled-up kind of way:

"Well, that's mighty curious. WHO sung out? WHEN did he sing out? WHAT did he sing out?" And turns to me, perfectly ca'm, and says, "Did YOU hear anybody sing out?"

Of course there warn't nothing to be said but the one thing; so I says:

"No; I ain't heard nobody say nothing."

Then he turns to Jim, and looks him over like he never see him before, and says:

"Did you sing out?"

"No, sah," says Jim; "I hain't said nothing, sah."

"Not a word?"

"No, sah, I hain't said a word."

"Did you ever see us before?"

"No, sah; not as I knows on."

So Tom turns to the nigger, which was looking wild and distressed, and says, kind of severe:

"What do you reckon's the matter with you, anyway? What made you think somebody sung out?"

"Oh, it's de dad-blame' witches, sah, en I wisht I was dead, I do. Dey's awluz at it, sah, en dey do mos' kill me, dey sk'yers me so. Please to don't tell nobody 'bout it sah, er ole Mars Silas he'll scole me; 'kase he say dey AIN'T no witches. I jis' wish to goodness he was heah now —DEN what would he say! I jis' bet he couldn' fine no way to git aroun' it DIS time. But it's awluz jis' so; people dat's SOT, stays sot; dey won't look into noth'n'en fine it out f'r deyselves, en when YOU fine it out en tell um 'bout it, dey doan' b'lieve you."

Tom give him a dime, and said we wouldn't tell nobody; and told him to buy some more thread to tie up his wool with; and then looks at Jim, and says:

"I wonder if Uncle Silas is going to hang this nigger. If I was to catch a nigger that was ungrateful enough to run away, I wouldn't give him up, I'd hang him." And whilst the nigger stepped to the door to look at the dime and bite it to see if it was good, he whispers to Jim and says:

"Don't ever let on to know us. And if you hear any digging going on nights, it's us; we're going to set you free."

Jim only had time to grab us by the hand and squeeze it; then the nigger come back, and we said we'd come again some time if the nigger wanted us to; and he said he would, more particular if it was dark, because the witches went for him mostly in the dark, and it was good to have folks around then.

CHAPTER XXXV.

IT would be most an hour yet till breakfast, so we left and struck down into the woods; because Tom said we got to have SOME light to see how to dig by, and a lantern makes too much, and might get us into trouble; what we must have was a lot of them rotten chunks that's called fox-fire, and just makes a soft kind of a glow when you lay them in a dark place. We fetched an armful and hid it in the weeds, and set down to rest, and Tom says, kind of dissatisfied:

"Blame it, this whole thing is just as easy and awkward as it can be. And so it makes it so rotten difficult to get up a difficult plan. There ain't no watchman to be drugged—now there OUGHT to be a watchman. There ain't even a dog to give a sleeping-mixture to. And there's Jim chained by one leg, with a ten-foot chain, to the leg of his bed: why, all you got to do is to lift up the bedstead and slip off the chain. And Uncle Silas he trusts everybody; sends the key to the punkin-headed nigger, and don't send nobody to watch the nigger. Jim could a got out of that window-hole before this, only there wouldn't be no use trying to travel with a ten-foot chain on his leg. Why, drat it, Huck, it's the stupidest arrangement I ever see. You got to invent ALL the difficulties. Well, we can't help it; we got to do the best we can with the materials we've got. Anyhow, there's one thing—there's more honor in getting him out through a lot of difficulties and dangers, where there warn't one of them furnished to you by the people who it was their duty to furnish them, and you had to contrive them all out of your own head. Now look at just that one thing of the lantern. When you come down to the cold facts, we simply got to LET ON that a lantern's resky. Why, we could work with a torchlight procession if we wanted to, I believe. Now, whilst I think of it, we got to hunt up something to make a saw out of the first chance we get."

"What do we want of a saw?"

"What do we WANT of a saw? Hain't we got to saw the leg of Jim's bed off, so as to get the chain loose?"

"Why, you just said a body could lift up the bedstead and slip the chain off."

"Well, if that ain't just like you, Huck Finn. You CAN get up the infant-schooliest ways of going at a thing. Why, hain't you ever read any books at all?—Baron Trenck, nor Casanova, nor Benvenuto Chelleeny, nor Henri IV., nor none of them heroes? Who ever heard of getting a prisoner loose in such an old-maidy way as that? No; the way all the best authorities does is to saw the bed-leg in two, and leave it just so, and swallow the sawdust, so it can't be found, and put some dirt and grease around the sawed place so the very keenest seneskal can't see no sign of it's being sawed, and thinks the bed-leg is perfectly sound. Then, the night you're ready, fetch the leg a kick, down

she goes; slip off your chain, and there you are. Nothing to do but hitch your rope ladder to the battlements, shin down it, break your leg in the moat —because a rope ladder is nineteen foot too short, you know—and there's your horses and your trusty vassles, and they scoop you up and fling you across a saddle, and away you go to your native Langudoc, or Navarre, or wherever it is. It's gaudy, Huck. I wish there was a moat to this cabin. If we get time, the night of the escape, we'll dig one."

I says:

"What do we want of a moat when we're going to snake him out from under the cabin?"

But he never heard me. He had forgot me and everything else. He had his chin in his hand, thinking. Pretty soon he sighs and shakes his head; then sighs again, and says:

"No, it wouldn't do—there ain't necessity enough for it."

"For what?" I says.

"Why, to saw Jim's leg off," he says.

"Good land!" I says; "why, there ain't NO necessity for it. And what would you want to saw his leg off for, anyway?"

"Well, some of the best authorities has done it. They couldn't get the chain off, so they just cut their hand off and shoved. And a leg would be better still. But we got to let that go. There ain't necessity enough in this case; and, besides, Jim's a nigger, and wouldn't understand the reasons for it, and how it's the custom in Europe; so we'll let it go. But there's one thing—he can have a rope ladder; we can tear up our sheets and make him a rope ladder easy enough. And we can send it to him in a pie; it's mostly done that way. And I've et worse pies."

"Why, Tom Sawyer, how you talk," I says; "Jim ain't got no use for a rope ladder."

"He HAS got use for it. How YOU talk, you better say; you don't know nothing about it. He's GOT to have a rope ladder; they all do."

"What in the nation can he DO with it?"

"DO with it? He can hide it in his bed, can't he?" That's what they all do; and HE'S got to, too. Huck, you don't ever seem to want to do anything that's regular; you want to be starting something fresh all the time. S'pose he DON'T do nothing with it? ain't it there in his bed, for a clew, after he's gone? and don't you reckon they'll want clews? Of course they will. And you wouldn't leave them any? That would be a PRETTY howdy-do, WOULDN'T it! I never heard of such a thing."

"Well," I says, "if it's in the regulations, and he's got to have it, all right, let him have it; because I don't wish to go back on no regulations; but there's one thing, Tom Sawyer—if we go to tearing up our sheets to make Jim a rope ladder, we're going to get into trouble with Aunt Sally, just as sure as you're born. Now, the way I look at it, a hickry-bark ladder don't cost nothing, and don't waste nothing, and is just as good to load up a pie with, and hide in a straw tick, as any rag ladder you can start; and as for Jim, he ain't had no experience, and so he don't care what kind of a—"

"Oh, shucks, Huck Finn, if I was as ignorant as you I'd keep still —that's what I'D do. Who ever heard of a state prisoner escaping by a hickry-bark ladder? Why, it's perfectly ridiculous."

"Well, all right, Tom, fix it your own way; but if you'll take my advice, you'll let me borrow a sheet off of the clothesline."

He said that would do. And that gave him another idea, and he says:

"Borrow a shirt, too."

"What do we want of a shirt, Tom?"

"Want it for Jim to keep a journal on."

"Journal your granny—JIM can't write."

"S'pose he CAN'T write—he can make marks on the shirt, can't he, if we make him a pen out of an old pewter spoon or a piece of an old iron barrel-hoop?"

"Why, Tom, we can pull a feather out of a goose and make him a better one; and quicker, too."

"PRISONERS don't have geese running around the donjon-keep to pull pens out of, you muggins. They ALWAYS make their pens out of the hardest, toughest, troublesomest piece of old brass candlestick or something like that that they can get their hands on; and it takes them weeks and weeks and months and months to file it out, too, because they've got to do it by rubbing it on the wall. THEY wouldn't use a goose-quill if they had it. It ain't regular."

"Well, then, what'll we make him the ink out of?"

"Many makes it out of iron-rust and tears; but that's the common sort and women; the best authorities uses their own blood. Jim can do that; and when he wants to send any little common ordinary mysterious message to let the world know where he's captivated, he can write it on the bottom of a tin plate with a fork and throw it out of the window. The Iron Mask always done that, and it's a blame' good way, too."

"Jim ain't got no tin plates. They feed him in a pan."

"That ain't nothing; we can get him some."

"Can't nobody READ his plates."

"That ain't got anything to DO with it, Huck Finn. All HE'S got to do is to write on the plate and throw it out. You don't HAVE to be able to read it. Why, half the time you can't read anything a prisoner writes on a tin plate, or anywhere else."

"Well, then, what's the sense in wasting the plates?"

"Why, blame it all, it ain't the PRISONER'S plates."

"But it's SOMEBODY'S plates, ain't it?"

"Well, spos'n it is? What does the PRISONER care whose—"

He broke off there, because we heard the breakfast-horn blowing. So we cleared out for the house.

Along during the morning I borrowed a sheet and a white shirt off of the clothes-line; and I found an old sack and put them in it, and we went down and got the fox-fire, and put that in too. I called it borrowing, because that was what pap always called it; but Tom said it warn't borrowing, it was stealing. He said we was representing prisoners; and prisoners don't care how they get a thing so they get it, and nobody don't blame them for it, either. It ain't no crime in a prisoner to steal the thing he needs to get away with, Tom said; it's his right; and so, as long as we was representing a prisoner, we had a perfect right to steal anything on this place we had the least use for to get ourselves out of prison with. He said if we warn't prisoners it would be a very different thing, and nobody but a mean, ornery person would steal when he warn't a prisoner. So we allowed we would steal everything there was that come handy. And yet he made a mighty fuss, one day, after that, when I stole a watermelon out of the nigger-patch and eat it; and he made me go and give the niggers a dime without telling them what it was for. Tom said that what he meant was, we could steal anything we NEEDED. Well, I says, I needed the watermelon. But he said I didn't need it to get out of prison with; there's where the difference was. He said if I'd a wanted it to hide a knife in, and smuggle it to Jim to kill the seneskal with, it would a been all right. So I let it go at that, though I couldn't see no advantage in my representing a prisoner if I got to set down and chaw over a lot of gold-leaf distinctions like that every time I see a chance to hog a watermelon.

Well, as I was saying, we waited that morning till everybody was settled down to business, and nobody in sight around the yard; then Tom he carried the sack into the lean-to whilst I stood off a piece to keep watch. By and by he come out, and we went and set down on the woodpile to talk. He says:

"Everything's all right now except tools; and that's easy fixed."

"Tools?" I says.

"Yes."

"Tools for what?"

"Why, to dig with. We ain't a-going to GNAW him out, are we?"

"Ain't them old crippled picks and things in there good enough to dig a nigger out with?" I says.

He turns on me, looking pitying enough to make a body cry, and says:

"Huck Finn, did you EVER hear of a prisoner having picks and shovels, and all the modern conveniences in his wardrobe to dig himself out with? Now I want to ask you—if you got any reasonableness in you at all—what kind of a show would THAT give him to be a hero? Why, they might as well lend him the key and done with it. Picks and shovels—why, they wouldn't furnish 'em to a king."

"Well, then," I says, "if we don't want the picks and shovels, what do we want?"

"A couple of case-knives."

"To dig the foundations out from under that cabin with?"

"Yes."

"Confound it, it's foolish, Tom."

"It don't make no difference how foolish it is, it's the RIGHT way—and it's the regular way. And there ain't no OTHER way, that ever I heard of, and I've read all the books that gives any information about these things. They always dig out with a case-knife—and not through dirt, mind you; generly it's through solid rock. And it takes them weeks and weeks and weeks, and for ever and ever. Why, look at one of them prisoners in the bottom dungeon of the Castle Deef, in the harbor of Marseilles, that dug himself out that way; how long was HE at it, you reckon?"

"I don't know."

"Well, guess."

"I don't know. A month and a half."

"THIRTY-SEVEN YEAR—and he come out in China. THAT'S the kind. I wish the bottom of THIS fortress was solid rock."

"JIM don't know nobody in China."

"What's THAT got to do with it? Neither did that other fellow. But you're always a-wandering off on a side issue. Why can't you stick to the main point?"

"All right—I don't care where he comes out, so he COMES out; and Jim don't, either, I reckon. But there's one thing, anyway—Jim's too old to be dug out with a case-knife. He won't last."

"Yes he will LAST, too. You don't reckon it's going to take thirty-seven years to dig out through a DIRT foundation, do you?"

"How long will it take, Tom?"

"Well, we can't resk being as long as we ought to, because it mayn't take very long for Uncle Silas to hear from down there by New Orleans. He'll hear Jim ain't from there. Then his next move will be to advertise Jim, or something like that. So we can't resk being as long digging him out as we ought to. By rights I reckon we ought to be a couple of years; but we can't. Things being so uncertain, what I recommend is this: that we really dig right in, as quick as we can; and after that, we can LET ON, to ourselves, that we was at it thirty-seven years. Then we can snatch him out and rush him away the first time there's an alarm. Yes, I reckon that 'll be the best way."

"Now, there's SENSE in that," I says. "Letting on don't cost nothing; letting on ain't no trouble; and if it's any object, I don't mind letting on we was at it a hundred and fifty year. It wouldn't strain me none, after I got my hand in. So I'll mosey along now, and smouch a couple of case-knives."

"Smouch three," he says; "we want one to make a saw out of."

"Tom, if it ain't unregular and irreligious to sejest it," I says, "there's an old rusty saw-blade around yonder sticking under the weather-boarding behind the smoke-house."

He looked kind of weary and discouraged-like, and says:

"It ain't no use to try to learn you nothing, Huck. Run along and smouch the knives—three of them." So I done it.

AS soon as we reckoned everybody was asleep that night we went down the lightning-rod, and shut ourselves up in the lean-to, and got out our pile of fox-fire, and went to work. We cleared everything out of the way, about four or five foot along the middle of the bottom log. Tom said we was right behind Jim's bed now, and we'd dig in under it, and when we got through there couldn't nobody in the cabin ever know there was any hole there, because Jim's counter-pin hung down most to the ground, and you'd have to raise it up and look under to see the hole. So we dug and dug with the case-knives till most midnight; and then we was dog-tired, and our hands was blistered, and yet you couldn't see we'd done anything hardly. At last I says:

"This ain't no thirty-seven year job; this is a thirty-eight year job, Tom Sawyer."

He never said nothing. But he sighed, and pretty soon he stopped digging, and then for a good little while I knowed that he was thinking. Then he says:

"It ain't no use, Huck, it ain't a-going to work. If we was prisoners it would, because then we'd have as many years as we wanted, and no hurry; and we wouldn't get but a few minutes to dig, every day, while they was changing watches, and so our hands wouldn't get blistered, and we could keep it up right along, year in and year out, and do it right, and the way it ought to be done. But WE can't fool along; we got to rush; we ain't got no time to spare. If we was to put in another night this way we'd have to knock off for a week to let our hands get well—couldn't touch a case-knife with them sooner."

"Well, then, what we going to do, Tom?"

"I'll tell you. It ain't right, and it ain't moral, and I wouldn't like it to get out; but there ain't only just the one way: we got to dig him out with the picks, and LET ON it's case-knives."

"NOW you're TALKING!" I says; "your head gets leveler and leveler all the time, Tom Sawyer," I says. "Picks is the thing, moral or no moral; and as for me, I don't care shucks for the morality of it, nohow. When I start in to steal a nigger, or a watermelon, or a Sunday-school book, I ain't no ways particular how it's done so it's done. What I want is my nigger; or what I want is my watermelon; or what I want is my Sunday-school book; and if a pick's the handiest thing, that's the thing I'm a-going to dig that nigger or that watermelon or that Sunday-school book out with; and I don't give a dead rat what the authorities thinks about it nuther."

"Well," he says, "there's excuse for picks and letting-on in a case like this; if it warn't so, I wouldn't approve of it, nor I wouldn't stand by and see the rules broke—because right is right, and wrong is wrong, and a body ain't got no business doing wrong when he ain't ignorant and knows better. It might answer for YOU to dig Jim out with a pick, WITHOUT any letting on, because you don't know no better; but it wouldn't for me, because I do know better. Gimme a case-knife."

He had his own by him, but I handed him mine. He flung it down, and says:

"Gimme a CASE-KNIFE."

I didn't know just what to do—but then I thought. I scratched around amongst the old tools, and got a pickaxe and give it to him, and he took it and went to work, and never said a word.

He was always just that particular. Full of principle.

So then I got a shovel, and then we picked and shoveled, turn about, and made the fur fly. We stuck to it about a half an hour, which was as long as we could stand up; but we had a good deal of a hole to show for it. When I got up stairs I looked out at the window and see Tom doing his level best with the lightning-rod, but he couldn't come it, his hands was so sore. At last he says:

"It ain't no use, it can't be done. What you reckon I better do? Can't you think of no way?"

"Yes," I says, "but I reckon it ain't regular. Come up the stairs, and let on it's a lightning-rod."

So he done it.

Next day Tom stole a pewter spoon and a brass candlestick in the house, for to make some pens for Jim out of, and six tallow candles; and I hung around the nigger cabins and laid for a chance, and stole three tin plates. Tom says it wasn't enough; but I said nobody wouldn't ever see the plates that Jim throwed out, because they'd fall in the dog-fennel and jimpson weeds under the window-hole—then we could tote them back and he could use them over again. So Tom was satisfied. Then he says:

"Now, the thing to study out is, how to get the things to Jim."

"Take them in through the hole," I says, "when we get it done."

He only just looked scornful, and said something about nobody ever heard of such an idiotic idea, and then he went to studying. By and by he said he had ciphered out two or three ways, but there warn't no need to decide on any of them yet. Said we'd got to post Jim first.

That night we went down the lightning-rod a little after ten, and took one of the candles along, and listened under the window-hole, and heard Jim snoring; so we pitched it in, and it didn't wake him. Then we whirled in with the pick and shovel, and in about two hours and a half the job was done. We crept in under Jim's bed and into the cabin, and pawed around and found the candle and lit it, and stood over Jim awhile, and found him looking hearty and healthy, and then we woke him up gentle and gradual. He was so glad to see us he most cried; and called us honey, and all the pet names he could think of; and was for having us hunt up a cold-chisel to cut the chain off of his leg with right away, and clearing out without losing any time. But Tom he showed him how unregular it would be, and set down and told him all about our plans, and how we could alter them in a minute any time there was an alarm; and not to be the least afraid, because we would see he got away, SURE. So Jim he said it was all right, and we set there and talked over old times awhile, and then Tom asked a lot of questions, and when Jim told him Uncle Silas come in every day or two to pray with him, and Aunt Sally come in to see if he was comfortable and had plenty to eat, and both of them was kind as they could be, Tom says:

"NOW I know how to fix it. We'll send you some things by them."

I said, "Don't do nothing of the kind; it's one of the most jackass ideas I ever struck;" but he never paid no attention to me; went right on. It was his way when he'd got his plans set.

So he told Jim how we'd have to smuggle in the rope-ladder pie and other large things by Nat, the nigger that fed him, and he must be on the lookout, and not be surprised, and not let Nat see him open them; and we would put small things in uncle's coat-pockets and he must steal them out; and we would tie things to aunt's apron-strings or put them in her apron-pocket, if we got a chance; and told him what they would be and what they was for. And told him how to keep a journal on the shirt with his blood, and all that. He told him everything. Jim he couldn't see no sense in the most of it, but he allowed we was white folks and knowed better than him; so he was satisfied, and said he would do it all just as Tom said.

Jim had plenty corn-cob pipes and tobacco; so we had a right down good sociable time; then we crawled out through the hole, and so home to bed, with hands that looked like they'd been chawed. Tom was in high spirits. He said it was the best fun he ever had in his life, and the most intellectural; and said if he only could see his way to it we would keep it up all the rest of our lives and leave Jim to our children to get out; for he believed Jim would come to like it better and better the more he got used to it. He said that in that way it could be strung out to as much as eighty year, and would be the best time on record. And he said it would make us all celebrated that had a hand in it.

In the morning we went out to the woodpile and chopped up the brass candlestick into handy sizes, and Tom put them and the pewter spoon in his pocket. Then we went to the nigger cabins, and while I got Nat's notice off, Tom shoved a piece of candlestick into the middle of a corn-pone that was in Jim's pan, and we went along with Nat to see how it would work, and it just worked noble; when Jim bit into it it most mashed all his teeth out; and there warn't ever anything could a worked better. Tom said so himself. Jim he never let on but what it was only just a piece of rock or something like that that's always getting into bread, you know; but after that he never bit into nothing but what he jabbed his fork into it in three or four places first.

And whilst we was a-standing there in the dimmish light, here comes a couple of the hounds bulging in from under Jim's bed; and they kept on piling in till there was eleven of them, and there warn't hardly room in there to get your breath. By jings, we forgot to fasten that lean-to door! The nigger Nat he only just hollered "Witches" once, and keeled over on to the floor amongst the dogs, and begun to groan like he was dying. Tom jerked the door open and flung out a slab of Jim's meat, and the dogs went for it, and in two seconds he was out himself and back again and shut the door, and I knowed he'd fixed the other door too. Then he went to work on the nigger, coaxing him and petting him, and asking him if he'd been imagining he saw something again. He raised up, and blinked his eyes around, and says:

"Mars Sid, you'll say I's a fool, but if I didn't b'lieve I see most a million dogs, er devils, er some'n, I wisht I may die right heah in dese tracks. I did, mos' sholy. Mars Sid, I FELT um—I FELT um, sah; dey was all over me. Dad fetch it, I jis' wisht I could git my han's on one er dem witches jis' wunst—on'y jis' wunst—it's all I'd ast. But mos'ly I wisht dey'd lemme 'lone, I does."

Tom says:

"Well, I tell you what I think. What makes them come here just at this runaway nigger's breakfast-time? It's because they're hungry; that's the reason. You make them a witch pie; that's the thing for YOU to do."

"But my lan', Mars Sid, how's I gwyne to make 'm a witch pie? I doan' know how to make it. I hain't ever hearn er sich a thing b'fo'."

"Well, then, I'll have to make it myself."

"Will you do it, honey?—will you? I'll wusshup de groun' und' yo' foot, I will!"

"All right, I'll do it, seeing it's you, and you've been good to us and showed us the runaway nigger. But you got to be mighty careful. When we come around, you turn your back; and then whatever we've put in the pan, don't you let on you see it at all. And don't you look when Jim unloads the pan—something might happen, I don't know what. And above all, don't you HANDLE the witch-things."

"HANNEL 'm, Mars Sid? What IS you a-talkin' 'bout? I wouldn' lay de weight er my finger on um, not f'r ten hund'd thous'n billion dollars, I wouldn't."

CHAPTER XXXVII.

THAT was all fixed. So then we went away and went to the rubbage-pile in the back yard, where they keep the old boots, and rags, and pieces of bottles, and wore-out tin things, and all such truck, and scratched around and found an old tin washpan, and stopped up the holes as well as we could, to bake the pie in, and took it down cellar and stole it full of flour and started for breakfast, and found a couple of shingle-nails that Tom said would be handy for a prisoner to scrabble his name and sorrows on the dungeon walls with, and dropped one of them in Aunt Sally's apron-pocket which was hanging on a chair, and t'other we stuck in the band of Uncle Silas's hat, which was on the bureau, because we heard the children say their pa and ma was going to the runaway nigger's house this morning, and then went to breakfast, and Tom dropped the pewter spoon in Uncle Silas's coat-pocket, and Aunt Sally wasn't come yet, so we had to wait a little while.

And when she come she was hot and red and cross, and couldn't hardly wait for the blessing; and then she went to sluicing out coffee with one hand and cracking the handiest child's head with her thimble with the other, and says:

"I've hunted high and I've hunted low, and it does beat all what HAS become of your other shirt."

My heart fell down amongst my lungs and livers and things, and a hard piece of corn-crust started down my throat after it and got met on the road with a cough, and was shot across the table, and took one of the children in the eye and curled him up like a fishing-worm, and let a cry out of him the size of a warwhoop, and Tom he turned kinder blue around the gills, and it all amounted to a considerable state of things for about a quarter of a minute or as much as that, and I would a sold out for half price if there was a bidder. But after that we was all right again—it was the sudden surprise of it that knocked us so kind of cold. Uncle Silas he says:

"It's most uncommon curious, I can't understand it. I know perfectly well I took it OFF, because—"

"Because you hain't got but one ON. Just LISTEN at the man! I know you took it off, and know it by a better way than your

wool-gathering memory, too, because it was on the clo's-line yesterday—I see it there myself. But it's gone, that's the long and the short of it, and you'll just have to change to a red flann'l one till I can get time to make a new one. And it 'll be the third I've made in two years. It just keeps a body on the jump to keep you in shirts; and whatever you do manage to DO with 'm all is more'n I can make out. A body 'd think you WOULD learn to take some sort of care of 'em at your time of life."

"I know it, Sally, and I do try all I can. But it oughtn't to be altogether my fault, because, you know, I don't see them nor have nothing to do with them except when they're on me; and I don't believe I've ever lost one of them OFF of me."

"Well, it ain't YOUR fault if you haven't, Silas; you'd a done it if you could, I reckon. And the shirt ain't all that's gone, nuther. Ther's a spoon gone; and THAT ain't all. There was ten, and now ther's only nine. The calf got the shirt, I reckon, but the calf never took the spoon, THAT'S certain."

"Why, what else is gone, Sally?"

"Ther's six CANDLES gone—that's what. The rats could a got the candles, and I reckon they did; I wonder they don't walk off with the whole place, the way you're always going to stop their holes and don't do it; and if they warn't fools they'd sleep in your hair, Silas—YOU'D never find it out; but you can't lay the SPOON on the rats, and that I know."

"Well, Sally, I'm in fault, and I acknowledge it; I've been remiss; but I won't let to-morrow go by without stopping up them holes."

"Oh, I wouldn't hurry; next year 'll do. Matilda Angelina Araminta PHELPS!"

Whack comes the thimble, and the child snatches her claws out of the sugar-bowl without fooling around any. Just then the nigger woman steps on to the passage, and says:

"Missus, dey's a sheet gone."

"A SHEET gone! Well, for the land's sake!"

"I'll stop up them holes to-day," says Uncle Silas, looking sorrowful.

"Oh, DO shet up!—s'pose the rats took the SHEET? WHERE'S it gone, Lize?"

"Clah to goodness I hain't no notion, Miss' Sally. She wuz on de clo'sline yistiddy, but she done gone: she ain' dah no mo' now."

"I reckon the world IS coming to an end. I NEVER see the beat of it in all my born days. A shirt, and a sheet, and a spoon, and six can—"

"Missus," comes a young yaller wench, "dey's a brass cannelstick miss'n."

"Cler out from here, you hussy, er I'll take a skillet to ye!"

Well, she was just a-biling. I begun to lay for a chance; I reckoned I would sneak out and go for the woods till the weather moderated. She kept a-raging right along, running her insurrection all by herself, and everybody else mighty meek and quiet; and at last Uncle Silas, looking kind of foolish, fishes up that spoon out of his pocket. She stopped, with her mouth open and her hands up; and as for me, I wished I was in Jeruslem or somewheres. But not long, because she says:

"It's JUST as I expected. So you had it in your pocket all the time; and like as not you've got the other things there, too. How'd it get there?"

"I reely don't know, Sally," he says, kind of apologizing, "or you know I would tell. I was a-studying over my text in Acts Seventeen before breakfast, and I reckon I put it in there, not noticing, meaning to put my Testament in, and it must be so, because my Testament ain't in; but I'll go and see; and if the Testament is where I had it, I'll know I didn't put it in, and that will show that I laid the Testament down and took up the spoon, and—"

"Oh, for the land's sake! Give a body a rest! Go 'long now, the whole kit and biling of ye; and don't come nigh me again till I've got back my peace of mind."

I'd a heard her if she'd a said it to herself, let alone speaking it out; and I'd a got up and obeyed her if I'd a been dead. As we was passing through the setting-room the old man he took up his hat, and the shingle-nail fell out on the floor, and he just merely picked it up and laid it on the mantel-shelf, and never said nothing, and went out. Tom see him do it, and remembered about the spoon, and says:

"Well, it ain't no use to send things by HIM no more, he ain't reliable." Then he says: "But he done us a good turn with the spoon, anyway, without knowing it, and so we'll go and do him one without HIM knowing it—stop up his rat-holes."

There was a noble good lot of them down cellar, and it took us a whole hour, but we done the job tight and good and shipshape. Then we heard steps on the stairs, and blowed out our light and hid; and here comes the old man, with a candle in one hand and a bundle of stuff in t'other, looking as absent-minded as year before last. He went a mooning around, first to one rat-hole and then another, till he'd been to them all. Then he stood about five minutes, picking tallow-drip off of his candle and thinking. Then he turns off slow and dreamy towards the stairs, saying:

"Well, for the life of me I can't remember when I done it. I could show her now that I warn't to blame on account of the rats. But never mind —let it go. I reckon it wouldn't do no good."

And so he went on a-mumbling up stairs, and then we left. He was a mighty nice old man. And always is.

Tom was a good deal bothered about what to do for a spoon, but he said we'd got to have it; so he took a think. When he had ciphered it out he told me how we was to do; then we went and waited around the spoon-basket till we see Aunt Sally coming, and then Tom went to counting the spoons and laying them out to one side, and I slid one of them up my sleeve, and Tom says:

"Why, Aunt Sally, there ain't but nine spoons YET."

She says:

"Go 'long to your play, and don't bother me. I know better, I counted 'm myself."

"Well, I've counted them twice, Aunty, and I can't make but nine."

She looked out of all patience, but of course she come to count—anybody would.

"I declare to gracious ther' AIN'T but nine!" she says. "Why, what in the world—plague TAKE the things, I'll count 'm again."

So I slipped back the one I had, and when she got done counting, she says:

"Hang the troublesome rubbage, ther's TEN now!" and she looked huffy and bothered both. But Tom says:

"Why, Aunty, I don't think there's ten."

"You numskull, didn't you see me COUNT 'm?"

"I know, but—"

"Well, I'll count 'm AGAIN."

So I smouched one, and they come out nine, same as the other time. Well, she WAS in a tearing way—just a-trembling all over, she was so mad. But she counted and counted till she got that addled she'd start to count in the basket for a spoon sometimes; and so, three times they come out right, and three times they come out wrong. Then she grabbed up the basket and slammed it across the house and knocked the cat galley-west; and she said cle'r out and let her have some peace, and if we come bothering around her again betwixt that and dinner she'd skin us. So we had the odd spoon, and dropped it in her apron-pocket whilst she was a-giving us our sailing orders, and Jim got it all right, along with her shingle nail, before noon. We was very well satisfied with this business, and Tom allowed it was worth twice the trouble it took, because he said NOW she couldn't ever count them spoons twice alike again to save her life; and wouldn't believe she'd counted them right if she DID; and said that after she'd about counted her head off for the next three days he judged she'd give it up and offer to kill anybody that wanted her to ever count them any more.

So we put the sheet back on the line that night, and stole one out of her closet; and kept on putting it back and stealing it again for a couple of days till she didn't know how many sheets she had any more, and she didn't CARE, and warn't a-going to bullyrag the rest of her soul out about it, and wouldn't count them again not to save her life; she druther die first.

So we was all right now, as to the shirt and the sheet and the spoon and the candles, by the help of the calf and the rats and the mixed-up counting; and as to the candlestick, it warn't no consequence, it would blow over by and by.

But that pie was a job; we had no end of trouble with that pie. We fixed it up away down in the woods, and cooked it there; and we got it done at last, and very satisfactory, too; but not all in one day; and we had to use up three wash-pans full of flour before we got through, and we got burnt pretty much all over, in places, and eyes put out with the smoke; because, you see, we didn't want nothing but a crust, and we couldn't prop it up right, and she would always cave in. But of course we thought of the right way at last—which was to cook the ladder, too, in the pie. So then we laid in with Jim the second night, and tore up the sheet all in little strings and twisted them together, and long before daylight we had a lovely rope that you could a hung a person with. We let on it took nine months to make it.

And in the forenoon we took it down to the woods, but it wouldn't go into the pie. Being made of a whole sheet, that way, there was rope enough for forty pies if we'd a wanted them, and plenty left over for soup, or sausage, or anything you choose. We could a had a whole dinner.

But we didn't need it. All we needed was just enough for the pie, and so we throwed the rest away. We didn't cook none of the pies in the wash-pan—afraid the solder would melt; but Uncle Silas he had a noble brass warming-pan which he thought considerable of, because it belonged to one of his ancesters with a long wooden handle that come over from England with William the Conqueror in the Mayflower or one of them early ships and was hid away up garret with a lot of other old pots and things that was valuable, not on account of being any account, because they warn't, but on account of them being relicts, you know, and we snaked her out, private, and took her down there, but she failed on the first pies, because we didn't know how, but she come up smiling on the last one. We took and lined her with dough, and set her in the coals, and loaded her up with rag rope, and put on a dough roof, and shut down the lid, and put hot embers on top, and stood off five foot, with the long handle, cool and comfortable, and in fifteen minutes she turned out a pie that was a satisfaction to look at. But the person that et it would want to fetch a couple of kags of toothpicks along, for if that rope ladder wouldn't cramp him down to business I don't know nothing what I'm talking about, and lay him in enough stomach-ache to last him till next time, too.

Nat didn't look when we put the witch pie in Jim's pan; and we put the three tin plates in the bottom of the pan under the vittles; and so Jim got everything all right, and as soon as he was by himself he busted into the pie and hid the rope ladder inside of his straw tick, and scratched some marks on a tin plate and throwed it out of the window-hole.

CHAPTER XXXVIII.

MAKING them pens was a distressid tough job, and so was the saw; and Jim allowed the inscription was going to be the toughest of all. That's the one which the prisoner has to scrabble on the wall. But he had to have it; Tom said he'd GOT to; there warn't no case of a state prisoner not scrabbling his inscription to leave behind, and his coat of arms.

"Look at Lady Jane Grey," he says; "look at Gilford Dudley; look at old Northumberland! Why, Huck, s'pose it IS considerble trouble?—what you going to do?—how you going to get around it? Jim's GOT to do his inscription and coat of arms. They all do."

Jim says:

"Why, Mars Tom, I hain't got no coat o' arm; I hain't got nuffn but dish yer ole shirt, en you knows I got to keep de journal on dat."

"Oh, you don't understand, Jim; a coat of arms is very different."

"Well," I says, "Jim's right, anyway, when he says he ain't got no coat of arms, because he hain't."

"I reckon I knowed that," Tom says, "but you bet he'll have one

before he goes out of this—because he's going out RIGHT, and there ain't going to be no flaws in his record."

So whilst me and Jim filed away at the pens on a brickbat apiece, Jim a-making his'n out of the brass and I making mine out of the spoon, Tom set to work to think out the coat of arms. By and by he said he'd struck so many good ones he didn't hardly know which to take, but there was one which he reckoned he'd decide on. He says:

"On the scutcheon we'll have a bend OR in the dexter base, a saltire MURREY in the fess, with a dog, couchant, for common charge, and under his foot a chain embattled, for slavery, with a chevron VERT in a chief engrailed, and three invected lines on a field AZURE, with the nombril points rampant on a dancette indented; crest, a runaway nigger, SABLE, with his bundle over his shoulder on a bar sinister; and a couple of gules for supporters, which is you and me; motto, MAGGIORE FRETTA, MINORE OTTO. Got it out of a book—means the more haste the less speed."

"Geewhillikins," I says, "but what does the rest of it mean?"

"We ain't got no time to bother over that," he says; "we got to dig in like all git-out."

"Well, anyway," I says, "what's SOME of it? What's a fess?"

"A fess—a fess is—YOU don't need to know what a fess is. I'll show him how to make it when he gets to it."

"Shucks, Tom," I says, "I think you might tell a person. What's a bar sinister?"

"Oh, I don't know. But he's got to have it. All the nobility does."

That was just his way. If it didn't suit him to explain a thing to you, he wouldn't do it. You might pump at him a week, it wouldn't make no difference.

He'd got all that coat of arms business fixed, so now he started in to finish up the rest of that part of the work, which was to plan out a mournful inscription—said Jim got to have one, like they all done. He made up a lot, and wrote them out on a paper, and read them off, so:

1. Here a captive heart busted. 2. Here a poor prisoner, forsook by the world and friends, fretted his sorrowful life. 3. Here a lonely heart broke, and a worn spirit went to its rest, after thirty-seven years of solitary captivity. 4. Here, homeless and friendless, after thirty-seven years of bitter captivity, perished a noble stranger, natural son of Louis XIV.

Tom's voice trembled whilst he was reading them, and he most broke down. When he got done he couldn't no way make up his mind which one for Jim to scrabble on to the wall, they was all so good; but at last he allowed he would let him scrabble them all on. Jim said it would take him a year to scrabble such a lot of truck on to the logs with a nail, and he didn't know how to make letters, besides; but Tom said he would block them out for him, and then he wouldn't have nothing to do but just follow the lines. Then pretty soon he says:

"Come to think, the logs ain't a-going to do; they don't have log walls in a dungeon: we got to dig the inscriptions into a rock. We'll fetch a rock."

Jim said the rock was worse than the logs; he said it would take him such a pison long time to dig them into a rock he wouldn't ever get out. But Tom said he would let me help him do it. Then he took a look to see how me and Jim was getting along with the pens. It was most pesky tedious hard work and slow, and didn't give my hands no show to get well of the sores, and we didn't seem to make no headway, hardly; so Tom says:

"I know how to fix it. We got to have a rock for the coat of arms and mournful inscriptions, and we can kill two birds with that same rock. There's a gaudy big grindstone down at the mill, and we'll smouch it, and carve the things on it, and file out the pens and the saw on it, too."

It warn't no slouch of an idea; and it warn't no slouch of a grindstone nuther; but we allowed we'd tackle it. It warn't quite midnight yet, so we cleared out for the mill, leaving Jim at work. We smouched the grindstone, and set out to roll her home, but it was a most nation tough job. Sometimes, do what we could, we couldn't keep her from falling over, and she come mighty near mashing us every time. Tom said she was going to get one of us, sure, before we got through. We got her half way; and then we was plumb played out, and most drownded with sweat. We see it warn't no use; we got to go and fetch Jim So he raised up his bed and slid the chain off of the bed-leg, and wrapt it round and round his neck, and we crawled out through our hole and down there, and Jim and me laid into that grindstone and walked her along like nothing; and Tom superintended. He could out-superintend any boy I ever see. He knowed how to do everything.

Our hole was pretty big, but it warn't big enough to get the grindstone through; but Jim he took the pick and soon made it big enough. Then Tom marked out them things on it with the nail, and set Jim to work on them, with the nail for a chisel and an iron bolt from the rubbage in the lean-to for a hammer, and told him to work till the rest of his candle quit on him, and then he could go to bed, and hide the grindstone under his straw tick and sleep on it. Then we helped him fix his chain back on the bed-leg, and was ready for bed ourselves. But Tom thought of something, and says:

"You got any spiders in here, Jim?"

"No, sah, thanks to goodness I hain't, Mars Tom."

"All right, we'll get you some."

"But bless you, honey, I doan' WANT none. I's afeard un um. I jis' 's soon have rattlesnakes aroun'."

Tom thought a minute or two, and says:

"It's a good idea. And I reckon it's been done. It MUST a been done; it stands to reason. Yes, it's a prime good idea. Where could you keep it?"

"Keep what, Mars Tom?"

"Why, a rattlesnake."

"De goodness gracious alive, Mars Tom! Why, if dey was a rattlesnake to come in heah I'd take en bust right out thoo dat log wall, I would, wid my head."

Why, Jim, you wouldn't be afraid of it after a little. You could tame it."

"TAME it!"

"Yes—easy enough. Every animal is grateful for kindness and petting, and they wouldn't THINK of hurting a person that pets them. Any book will tell you that. You try—that's all I ask; just try for two or three days. Why, you can get him so in a little while that he'll love you; and sleep with you; and won't stay away from you a minute; and will let you wrap him round your neck and put his head in your mouth."

"PLEASE, Mars Tom—DOAN' talk so! I can't STAN' it! He'd LET me shove his head in my mouf—fer a favor, hain't it? I lay he'd wait a pow'ful long time 'fo' I AST him. En mo' en dat, I doan' WANT him to sleep wid me."

"Jim, don't act so foolish. A prisoner's GOT to have some kind of a dumb pet, and if a rattlesnake hain't ever been tried, why, there's more glory to be gained in your being the first to ever try it than any other way you could ever think of to save your life."

"Why, Mars Tom, I doan' WANT no sich glory. Snake take 'n bite Jim's chin off, den WHAH is de glory? No, sah, I doan' want no sich doin's."

"Blame it, can't you TRY? I only WANT you to try—you needn't keep it up if it don't work."

"But de trouble all DONE ef de snake bite me while I's a tryin' him. Mars Tom, I's willin' to tackle mos' anything 'at ain't onreasonable, but ef you en Huck fetches a rattlesnake in heah for me to tame, I's gwyne to LEAVE, dat's SHORE."

"Well, then, let it go, let it go, if you're so bull-headed about it. We can get you some garter-snakes, and you can tie some buttons on their tails, and let on they're rattlesnakes, and I reckon that 'll have to do."

"I k'n stan' DEM, Mars Tom, but blame' 'f I couldn' get along widout um, I tell you dat. I never knowed b'fo' 't was so much bother and trouble to be a prisoner."

"Well, it ALWAYS is when it's done right. You got any rats around here?"

"No, sah, I hain't seed none."

"Well, we'll get you some rats."

"Why, Mars Tom, I doan' WANT no rats. Dey's de dadblamedest creturs to 'sturb a body, en rustle roun' over 'im, en bite his feet, when he's tryin' to sleep, I ever see. No, sah, gimme g'yarter-snakes, 'f I's got to have 'm, but doan' gimme no rats; I hain' got no use fr um, skasely."

"But, Jim, you GOT to have 'em—they all do. So don't make no more fuss about it. Prisoners ain't ever without rats. There ain't no instance of it. And they train them, and pet them, and learn them tricks, and they get to be as sociable as flies. But you got to play music to them. You got anything to play music on?"

"I ain' got nuffn but a coase comb en a piece o' paper, en a juice-harp; but I reck'n dey wouldn' take no stock in a juice-harp."

"Yes they would. THEY don't care what kind of music 'tis. A

jews-harp's plenty good enough for a rat. All animals like music—in a prison they dote on it. Specially, painful music; and you can't get no other kind out of a jews-harp. It always interests them; they come out to see what's the matter with you. Yes, you're all right; you're fixed very well. You want to set on your bed nights before you go to sleep, and early in the mornings, and play your jews-harp; play 'The Last Link is Broken'—that's the thing that 'll scoop a rat quicker 'n anything else; and when you've played about two minutes you'll see all the rats, and the snakes, and spiders, and things begin to feel worried about you, and come. And they'll just fairly swarm over you, and have a noble good time."

"Yes, DEY will, I reck'n, Mars Tom, but what kine er time is JIM havin'? Blest if I kin see de pint. But I'll do it ef I got to. I reck'n I better keep de animals satisfied, en not have no trouble in de house."

Tom waited to think it over, and see if there wasn't nothing else; and pretty soon he says:

"Oh, there's one thing I forgot. Could you raise a flower here, do you reckon?"

"I doan know but maybe I could, Mars Tom; but it's tolable dark in heah, en I ain' got no use f'r no flower, nohow, en she'd be a pow'ful sight o' trouble."

"Well, you try it, anyway. Some other prisoners has done it."

"One er dem big cat-tail-lookin' mullen-stalks would grow in heah, Mars Tom, I reck'n, but she wouldn't be wuth half de trouble she'd coss."

"Don't you believe it. We'll fetch you a little one and you plant it in the corner over there, and raise it. And don't call it mullen, call it Pitchiola—that's its right name when it's in a prison. And you want to water it with your tears."

"Why, I got plenty spring water, Mars Tom."

"You don't WANT spring water; you want to water it with your tears. It's the way they always do."

"Why, Mars Tom, I lay I kin raise one er dem mullen-stalks twyste wid spring water whiles another man's a START'N one wid tears."

"That ain't the idea. You GOT to do it with tears."

"She'll die on my han's, Mars Tom, she sholy will; kase I doan' skasely ever cry."

So Tom was stumped. But he studied it over, and then said Jim would have to worry along the best he could with an onion. He promised he would go to the nigger cabins and drop one, private, in Jim's coffee-pot, in the morning. Jim said he would "jis' 's soon have tobacker in his coffee;" and found so much fault with it, and with the work and bother of raising the mullen, and jews-harping the rats, and petting and flattering up the snakes and spiders and things, on top of all the other work he had to do on pens, and inscriptions, and journals, and things, which made it more trouble and worry and responsibility to be a prisoner than anything he ever undertook, that Tom most lost all patience with him; and said he was just loadened down with more gaudier chances than a prisoner ever had in the world to make a name for himself, and yet he didn't know enough to appreciate them, and they

was just about wasted on him. So Jim he was sorry, and said he wouldn't behave so no more, and then me and Tom shoved for bed.

CHAPTER XXXIX.

IN the morning we went up to the village and bought a wire rat-trap and fetched it down, and unstopped the best rat-hole, and in about an hour we had fifteen of the bulliest kind of ones; and then we took it and put it in a safe place under Aunt Sally's bed. But while we was gone for spiders little Thomas Franklin Benjamin Jefferson Elexander Phelps found it there, and opened the door of it to see if the rats would come out, and they did; and Aunt Sally she come in, and when we got back she was a-standing on top of the bed raising Cain, and the rats was doing what they could to keep off the dull times for her. So she took and dusted us both with the hickry, and we was as much as two hours catching another fifteen or sixteen, drat that meddlesome cub, and they warn't the likeliest, nuther, because the first haul was the pick of the flock. I never see a likelier lot of rats than what that first haul was.

We got a splendid stock of sorted spiders, and bugs, and frogs, and caterpillars, and one thing or another; and we like to got a hornet's nest, but we didn't. The family was at home. We didn't give it right up, but stayed with them as long as we could; because we allowed we'd tire them out or they'd got to tire us out, and they done it. Then we got allycumpain and rubbed on the places, and was pretty near all right again, but couldn't set down convenient. And so we went for the snakes, and grabbed a couple of dozen garters and house-snakes, and put them in a bag, and put it in our room, and by that time it was supper-time, and a rattling good honest day's work: and hungry?—oh, no, I reckon not! And there warn't a blessed snake up there when we went back—we didn't half tie the sack, and they worked out somehow, and left. But it didn't matter much, because they was still on the premises somewheres. So we judged we could get some of them again. No, there warn't no real scarcity of snakes about the house for a considerable spell. You'd see them dripping from the rafters and places every now and then; and they generly landed in your plate, or down the back of your neck, and most of the time where you didn't want them. Well, they was handsome and striped, and there warn't no harm in a million of them; but that never made no difference to Aunt Sally; she despised snakes, be the breed what they might, and she couldn't stand them no way you could fix it; and every time one of them flopped down on her, it didn't make no difference what she was doing, she would just lay that work down and light out. I never see such a woman. And you could hear her whoop to Jericho. You couldn't get her to take a-holt of one of them with the tongs. And if she turned over and found one in bed she would scramble out and lift a howl that you would think the house was afire. She disturbed the old man so that he said he could most wish there hadn't ever been no snakes created. Why, after every last snake had been gone clear out of the house for as much as a week Aunt Sally warn't over it yet; she warn't near over it; when she was setting thinking about something you could touch her on the back of her neck with a feather and she would jump right out of her stockings. It was very curious. But Tom said all women was just so. He said they was made that way for some reason or other.

We got a licking every time one of our snakes come in her way, and she allowed these lickings warn't nothing to what she would do if we ever loaded up the place again with them. I didn't mind the lickings, because they didn't amount to nothing; but I minded the trouble we had to lay in another lot.

But we got them laid in, and all the other things; and you never see a cabin as blithesome as Jim's was when they'd all swarm out for music and go for him. Jim didn't like the spiders, and the spiders didn't like Jim; and so they'd lay for him, and make it mighty warm for him. And he said that between the rats and the snakes and the grindstone there warn't no room in bed for him, skasely; and when there was, a body couldn't sleep, it was so lively, and it was always lively, he said, because THEY never all slept at one time, but took turn about, so when the snakes was asleep the rats was on deck, and when the rats turned in the snakes come on watch, so he always had one gang under him, in his way, and t'other gang having a circus over him, and if he got up to hunt a new place the spiders would take a chance at him as he crossed over. He said if he ever got out this time he wouldn't ever be a prisoner again, not for a salary.

Well, by the end of three weeks everything was in pretty good shape. The shirt was sent in early, in a pie, and every time a rat bit Jim he would get up and write a little in his journal whilst the ink was fresh; the pens was made, the inscriptions and so on was all carved on the grindstone; the bed-leg was sawed in two, and we had et up the sawdust, and it give us a most amazing stomach-ache. We reckoned we was all going to die, but didn't. It was the most undigestible sawdust I ever see; and Tom said the same. But as I was saying, we'd got all the work done now, at last; and we was all pretty much fagged out, too, but mainly Jim. The old man had wrote a couple of times to the plantation below Orleans to come and get their runaway nigger, but hadn't got no answer, because there warn't no such plantation; so he allowed he would advertise Jim in the St. Louis and New Orleans papers; and when he mentioned the St. Louis ones it give me the cold shivers, and I see we hadn't no time to lose. So Tom said, now for the nonnamous letters.

"What's them?" I says.

"Warnings to the people that something is up. Sometimes it's done one way, sometimes another. But there's always somebody spying around that gives notice to the governor of the castle. When Louis XVI. was going to light out of the Tooleries a servant-girl done it. It's a very good way, and so is the nonnamous letters. We'll use them both. And it's usual for the prisoner's mother to change clothes with him, and she stays in, and he slides out in her clothes. We'll do that, too."

"But looky here, Tom, what do we want to WARN anybody for that something's up? Let them find it out for themselves—it's their lookout."

"Yes, I know; but you can't depend on them. It's the way they've acted from the very start—left us to do EVERYTHING. They're so confiding and mullet-headed they don't take notice of nothing at all. So if we don't GIVE them notice there won't be nobody nor nothing to interfere with us, and so after all our hard work and trouble this escape 'll go off perfectly flat; won't amount to nothing—won't be nothing TO it."

"Well, as for me, Tom, that's the way I'd like."

"Shucks!" he says, and looked disgusted. So I says:

"But I ain't going to make no complaint. Any way that suits you suits me. What you going to do about the servant-girl?"

"You'll be her. You slide in, in the middle of the night, and hook that yaller girl's frock."

"Why, Tom, that 'll make trouble next morning; because, of course, she prob'bly hain't got any but that one."

"I know; but you don't want it but fifteen minutes, to carry the nonnamous letter and shove it under the front door."

"All right, then, I'll do it; but I could carry it just as handy in my own togs."

"You wouldn't look like a servant-girl THEN, would you?"

"No, but there won't be nobody to see what I look like, ANYWAY."

"That ain't got nothing to do with it. The thing for us to do is just to do our DUTY, and not worry about whether anybody SEES us do it or not. Hain't you got no principle at all?"

"All right, I ain't saying nothing; I'm the servant-girl. Who's Jim's mother?"

"I'm his mother. I'll hook a gown from Aunt Sally."

"Well, then, you'll have to stay in the cabin when me and Jim leaves."

"Not much. I'll stuff Jim's clothes full of straw and lay it on his bed to represent his mother in disguise, and Jim 'll take the nigger woman's gown off of me and wear it, and we'll all evade together. When a prisoner of style escapes it's called an evasion. It's always called so when a king escapes, f'rinstance. And the same with a king's son; it don't make no difference whether he's a natural one or an unnatural one."

So Tom he wrote the nonnamous letter, and I smouched the yaller wench's frock that night, and put it on, and shoved it under the front door, the way Tom told me to. It said:

Beware. Trouble is brewing. Keep a sharp lookout. UNKNOWN FRIEND.

Next night we stuck a picture, which Tom drawed in blood, of a skull and crossbones on the front door; and next night another one of a coffin on the back door. I never see a family in such a sweat. They couldn't a been worse scared if the place had a been full of ghosts laying for them behind everything and under the beds and shivering through the air. If a door banged, Aunt Sally she jumped and said "ouch!" if anything fell, she jumped and said "ouch!" if you happened to touch her, when she warn't noticing, she done the same; she couldn't face noway and be satisfied, because she allowed there was something behind her every time—so she was always a-whirling around sudden, and saying "ouch," and before she'd got two-thirds around she'd whirl back again, and say it again; and she was afraid to go to bed, but she dasn't set up. So the thing was working very well, Tom said; he said he never see a thing work more satisfactory. He said it showed it was done right.

So he said, now for the grand bulge! So the very next morning at the streak of dawn we got another letter ready, and was wondering what we better do with it, because we heard them say at supper they was going to have a nigger on watch at both doors all night. Tom he went down the lightning-rod to spy around; and the nigger at the back door was asleep, and he stuck it in the back of his neck and come back. This letter said:

Don't betray me, I wish to be your friend. There is a desprate gang of cut-throats from over in the Indian Territory going to steal your runaway nigger to-night, and they have been trying to scare you so as you will stay in the house and not bother them. I am one of the gang, but have got relligion and wish to quit it and lead an honest life again, and will betray the helish design. They will sneak down from northards, along the fence, at midnight exact, with a false key, and go in the nigger's cabin to get him. I am to be off a piece and blow a tin horn if I see any danger; but stead of that I will BA like a sheep soon as they get in and not blow at all; then whilst they are getting his chains loose, you slip there and lock them in, and can kill them at your leasure. Don't do anything but just the way I am telling you; if you do they will suspicion something and raise whoop-jamboreehoo. I do not wish any reward but to know I have done the right thing. UNKNOWN FRIEND.

CHAPTER XL.

WE was feeling pretty good after breakfast, and took my canoe and went over the river a-fishing, with a lunch, and had a good time, and took a look at the raft and found her all right, and got home late to supper, and found them in such a sweat and worry they didn't know which end they was standing on, and made us go right off to bed the minute we was done supper, and wouldn't tell us what the trouble was, and never let on a word about the new letter, but didn't need to, because we knowed as much about it as anybody did, and as soon as we was half up stairs and her back was turned we slid for the cellar cupboard and loaded up a good lunch and took it up to our room and went to bed, and got up about half-past eleven, and Tom put on Aunt Sally's dress that he stole and was going to start with the lunch, but says:

"Where's the butter?"

"I laid out a hunk of it," I says, "on a piece of a corn-pone."

"Well, you LEFT it laid out, then—it ain't here."

"We can get along without it," I says.

"We can get along WITH it, too," he says; "just you slide down cellar and fetch it. And then mosey right down the lightning-rod and come along. I'll go and stuff the straw into Jim's clothes to represent his mother in disguise, and be ready to BA like a sheep and shove soon as you get there."

So out he went, and down cellar went I. The hunk of butter, big as a person's fist, was where I had left it, so I took up the slab of corn-pone with it on, and blowed out my light, and started up stairs very stealthy, and got up to the main floor all right, but here comes Aunt Sally with a candle, and I clapped the truck in my hat, and clapped my hat on my head, and the next second she see me; and she says:

"You been down cellar?"

"Yes'm."

"What you been doing down there?"

"Noth'n."

"NOTH'N!"

"No'm."

"Well, then, what possessed you to go down there this time of

night?"

"I don't know 'm."

"You don't KNOW? Don't answer me that way. Tom, I want to know what you been DOING down there."

"I hain't been doing a single thing, Aunt Sally, I hope to gracious if I have."

I reckoned she'd let me go now, and as a generl thing she would; but I s'pose there was so many strange things going on she was just in a sweat about every little thing that warn't yard-stick straight; so she says, very decided:

"You just march into that setting-room and stay there till I come. You been up to something you no business to, and I lay I'll find out what it is before I'M done with you."

So she went away as I opened the door and walked into the setting-room. My, but there was a crowd there! Fifteen farmers, and every one of them had a gun. I was most powerful sick, and slunk to a chair and set down. They was setting around, some of them talking a little, in a low voice, and all of them fidgety and uneasy, but trying to look like they warn't; but I knowed they was, because they was always taking off their hats, and putting them on, and scratching their heads, and changing their seats, and fumbling with their buttons. I warn't easy myself, but I didn't take my hat off, all the same.

I did wish Aunt Sally would come, and get done with me, and lick me, if she wanted to, and let me get away and tell Tom how we'd overdone this thing, and what a thundering hornet's-nest we'd got ourselves into, so we could stop fooling around straight off, and clear out with Jim before these rips got out of patience and come for us.

At last she come and begun to ask me questions, but I COULDN'T answer them straight, I didn't know which end of me was up; because these men was in such a fidget now that some was wanting to start right NOW and lay for them desperadoes, and saying it warn't but a few minutes to midnight; and others was trying to get them to hold on and wait for the sheep-signal; and here was Aunty pegging away at the questions, and me a-shaking all over and ready to sink down in my tracks I was that scared; and the place getting hotter and hotter, and the butter beginning to melt and run down my neck and behind my ears; and pretty soon, when one of them says, "I'M for going and getting in the cabin FIRST and right NOW, and catching them when they come," I most dropped; and a streak of butter come a-trickling down my forehead, and Aunt Sally she see it, and turns white as a sheet, and says:

"For the land's sake, what IS the matter with the child? He's got the brain-fever as shore as you're born, and they're oozing out!"

And everybody runs to see, and she snatches off my hat, and out comes the bread and what was left of the butter, and she grabbed me, and hugged me, and says:

"Oh, what a turn you did give me! and how glad and grateful I am it ain't no worse; for luck's against us, and it never rains but it pours, and when I see that truck I thought we'd lost you, for I knowed by the color and all it was just like your brains would be if—Dear, dear, whyd'nt you TELL me that was what you'd been down there for, I wouldn't a cared. Now cler out to bed, and don't lemme see no more of you till morning!"

I was up stairs in a second, and down the lightning-rod in another one, and shinning through the dark for the lean-to. I couldn't hardly get my words out, I was so anxious; but I told Tom as quick as I could we must jump for it now, and not a minute to lose—the house full of men, yonder, with guns!

His eyes just blazed; and he says:

"No!—is that so? AIN'T it bully! Why, Huck, if it was to do over again, I bet I could fetch two hundred! If we could put it off till—"

"Hurry! HURRY!" I says. "Where's Jim?"

"Right at your elbow; if you reach out your arm you can touch him. He's dressed, and everything's ready. Now we'll slide out and give the sheep-signal."

But then we heard the tramp of men coming to the door, and heard them begin to fumble with the pad-lock, and heard a man say:

"I TOLD you we'd be too soon; they haven't come—the door is locked. Here, I'll lock some of you into the cabin, and you lay for 'em in the dark and kill 'em when they come; and the rest scatter around a piece, and listen if you can hear 'em coming."

So in they come, but couldn't see us in the dark, and most trod on us whilst we was hustling to get under the bed. But we got under all right, and out through the hole, swift but soft—Jim first, me next, and Tom last, which was according to Tom's orders. Now we was in the lean-to, and heard trampings close by outside. So we crept to the door, and Tom stopped us there and put his eye to the crack, but couldn't make out nothing, it was so dark; and whispered and said he would listen for the steps to get further, and when he nudged us Jim must glide out first, and him last. So he set his ear to the crack and listened, and listened, and listened, and the steps a-scraping around out there all the time; and at last he nudged us, and we slid out, and stooped down, not breathing, and not making the least noise, and slipped stealthy towards the fence in Injun file, and got to it all right, and me and Jim over it; but Tom's britches catched fast on a splinter on the top rail, and then he hear the steps coming, so he had to pull loose, which snapped the splinter and made a noise; and as he dropped in our tracks and started somebody sings out:

"Who's that? Answer, or I'll shoot!"

But we didn't answer; we just unfurled our heels and shoved. Then there was a rush, and a BANG, BANG, BANG! and the bullets fairly whizzed around us! We heard them sing out:

"Here they are! They've broke for the river! After 'em, boys, and turn loose the dogs!"

So here they come, full tilt. We could hear them because they wore boots and yelled, but we didn't wear no boots and didn't yell. We was in the path to the mill; and when they got pretty close on to us we dodged into the bush and let them go by, and then dropped in behind them. They'd had all the dogs shut up, so they wouldn't scare off the robbers; but by this time somebody had let them loose, and here they come, making powwow enough for a million; but they was our dogs; so we stopped in our tracks till they catched up; and when they see it warn't nobody but us, and no excitement to offer them, they only just said howdy, and tore right ahead towards the shouting and clattering; and then we up-steam again, and whizzed along after them till we was nearly to the mill, and then struck up through the bush to where my canoe was tied, and hopped in and pulled for dear life towards the middle of the river, but didn't make no more noise than we was obleeged to. Then we struck out, easy and comfortable, for the island where my raft was; and we could hear them yelling and barking at each other all up and down the bank, till we was so far away the sounds got dim and died out. And when we stepped on to the raft I says:

"NOW, old Jim, you're a free man again, and I bet you won't ever be a slave no more."

"En a mighty good job it wuz, too, Huck. It 'uz planned beautiful, en it 'uz done beautiful; en dey ain't NOBODY kin git up a plan dat's mo' mixed-up en splendid den what dat one wuz."

We was all glad as we could be, but Tom was the gladdest of all because he had a bullet in the calf of his leg.

When me and Jim heard that we didn't feel so brash as what we did before. It was hurting him considerable, and bleeding; so we laid him in the wigwam and tore up one of the duke's shirts for to bandage him, but he says:

"Gimme the rags; I can do it myself. Don't stop now; don't fool around here, and the evasion booming along so handsome; man the sweeps, and set her loose! Boys, we done it elegant!—'deed we did. I wish WE'D a had the handling of Louis XVI., there wouldn't a been no 'Son of Saint Louis, ascend to heaven!' wrote down in HIS biography; no, sir, we'd a whooped him over the BORDER—that's what we'd a done with HIM—and done it just as slick as nothing at all, too. Man the sweeps—man the sweeps!"

But me and Jim was consulting—and thinking. And after we'd thought a minute, I says:

"Say it, Jim."

So he says:

"Well, den, dis is de way it look to me, Huck. Ef it wuz HIM dat 'uz bein' sot free, en one er de boys wuz to git shot, would he say, 'Go on en save me, nemmine 'bout a doctor f'r to save dis one?' Is dat like Mars Tom Sawyer? Would he say dat? You BET he wouldn't! WELL, den, is JIM gywne to say it? No, sah—I doan' budge a step out'n dis place 'dout a DOCTOR, not if it's forty year!"

I knowed he was white inside, and I reckoned he'd say what he did say—so it was all right now, and I told Tom I was a-going for a doctor. He raised considerable row about it, but me and Jim stuck to it and wouldn't budge; so he was for crawling out and setting the raft loose himself; but we wouldn't let him. Then he give us a piece of his mind, but it didn't do no good.

So when he sees me getting the canoe ready, he says:

"Well, then, if you re bound to go, I'll tell you the way to do when you get to the village. Shut the door and blindfold the doctor tight and fast, and make him swear to be silent as the grave, and put a purse full of gold in his hand, and then take and lead him all around the back alleys and everywheres in the dark, and then fetch him here in the canoe, in a roundabout way amongst the islands, and search him and take his chalk away from him, and don't give it back to him till you get him back to the village, or else he will chalk this raft so he can find it again. It's the way they all do."

So I said I would, and left, and Jim was to hide in the woods when he see the doctor coming till he was gone again.

CHAPTER XLI.

THE doctor was an old man; a very nice, kind-looking old man when I got him up. I told him me and my brother was over on Spanish Island hunting yesterday afternoon, and camped on a piece of a raft we found, and about midnight he must a kicked his gun in his dreams, for it went off and shot him in the leg, and we wanted him to go over there and fix it and not say nothing about it, nor let anybody know, because we wanted to come home this evening and surprise the folks.

"Who is your folks?" he says.

"The Phelpses, down yonder."

"Oh," he says. And after a minute, he says:

"How'd you say he got shot?"

"He had a dream," I says, "and it shot him."

"Singular dream," he says.

So he lit up his lantern, and got his saddle-bags, and we started. But when he sees the canoe he didn't like the look of her—said she was big enough for one, but didn't look pretty safe for two. I says:

"Oh, you needn't be afeard, sir, she carried the three of us easy enough."

"What three?"

"Why, me and Sid, and—and—and THE GUNS; that's what I mean."

"Oh," he says.

But he put his foot on the gunnel and rocked her, and shook his head, and said he reckoned he'd look around for a bigger one. But they was all locked and chained; so he took my canoe, and said for me to wait till he come back, or I could hunt around further, or maybe I better go down home and get them ready for the surprise if I wanted to. But I said I didn't; so I told him just how to find the raft, and then he started.

I struck an idea pretty soon. I says to myself, spos'n he can't fix that leg just in three shakes of a sheep's tail, as the saying is? spos'n it takes him three or four days? What are we going to do?—lay around there till he lets the cat out of the bag? No, sir; I know what I'LL do. I'll wait, and when he comes back if he says he's got to go any more I'll get down there, too, if I swim; and we'll take and tie him, and keep him, and shove out down the river; and when Tom's done with him we'll give him what it's worth, or all we got, and then let him get ashore.

So then I crept into a lumber-pile to get some sleep; and next time I waked up the sun was away up over my head! I shot out and went for the doctor's house, but they told me he'd gone away in the night some time or other, and warn't back yet.

Well, thinks I, that looks powerful bad for Tom, and I'll dig out for the island right off. So away I shoved, and turned the corner, and nearly rammed my head into Uncle Silas's stomach! He says:

"Why, TOM! Where you been all this time, you rascal?"

"I hain't been nowheres," I says, "only just hunting for the runaway nigger—me and Sid."

"Why, where ever did you go?" he says. "Your aunt's been mighty uneasy."

"She needn't," I says, "because we was all right. We followed the men and the dogs, but they outrun us, and we lost them; but we thought we heard them on the water, so we got a canoe and took out after them and crossed over, but couldn't find nothing of them; so we cruised along up-shore till we got kind of tired and beat out; and tied up the canoe and went to sleep, and never waked up till about an hour ago; then we paddled over here to hear the news, and Sid's at the post-office to see what he can hear, and I'm a-branching out to get something to eat for us, and then we're going home."

So then we went to the post-office to get "Sid"; but just as I suspicioned, he warn't there; so the old man he got a letter out of the office, and we waited awhile longer, but Sid didn't come; so the old man said, come along, let Sid foot it home, or canoe it, when he got done fooling around—but we would ride. I couldn't get him to let me stay and wait for Sid; and he said there warn't no use in it, and I must come along, and let Aunt Sally see we was all right.

When we got home Aunt Sally was that glad to see me she laughed and cried both, and hugged me, and give me one of them lickings of hern that don't amount to shucks, and said she'd serve Sid the same when he come.

And the place was plum full of farmers and farmers' wives, to dinner; and such another clack a body never heard. Old Mrs. Hotchkiss was the worst; her tongue was a-going all the time. She says:

"Well, Sister Phelps, I've ransacked that-air cabin over, an' I b'lieve the nigger was crazy. I says to Sister Damrell—didn't I, Sister Damrell?—s'I, he's crazy, s'I—them's the very words I said. You all hearn me: he's crazy, s'I; everything shows it, s'I. Look at that-air grindstone, s'I; want to tell ME't any cretur 't's in his right mind 's a goin' to scrabble all them crazy things onto a grindstone, s'I? Here sich 'n' sich a person busted his heart; 'n' here so 'n' so pegged along for thirty-seven year, 'n' all that—natcherl son o' Louis somebody, 'n' sich everlast'n rubbage. He's plumb crazy, s'I; it's what I says in the fust place, it's what I says in the middle, 'n' it's what I says last 'n' all the time—the nigger's crazy—crazy 's Nebokoodneezer, s'I."

"An' look at that-air ladder made out'n rags, Sister Hotchkiss," says old Mrs. Damrell; "what in the name o' goodness COULD he ever want of—"

"The very words I was a-sayin' no longer ago th'n this minute to Sister Utterback, 'n' she'll tell you so herself. Sh-she, look at that-air rag ladder, sh-she; 'n' s'I, yes, LOOK at it, s'I—what COULD he a-wanted of it, s'I. Sh-she, Sister Hotchkiss, sh-she—"

"But how in the nation'd they ever GIT that grindstone IN there, ANYWAY? 'n' who dug that-air HOLE? 'n' who—"

"My very WORDS, Brer Penrod! I was a-sayin'—pass that-air sasser o' m'lasses, won't ye?—I was a-sayin' to Sister Dunlap, jist this minute, how DID they git that grindstone in there, s'I. Without HELP, mind you —'thout HELP! THAT'S wher 'tis. Don't tell ME, s'I; there WUZ help, s'I; 'n' ther' wuz a PLENTY help, too, s'I; ther's ben a DOZEN a-helpin' that nigger, 'n' I lay I'd skin every last nigger on this place but I'D find out who done it, s'I; 'n' moreover, s'I—"

"A DOZEN says you!—FORTY couldn't a done every thing that's been done. Look at them case-knife saws and things, how tedious they've been made; look at that bed-leg sawed off with 'm, a week's work for six men; look at that nigger made out'n straw on the bed; and look at—"

"You may WELL say it, Brer Hightower! It's jist as I was a-sayin' to Brer Phelps, his own self. S'e, what do YOU think of it, Sister Hotchkiss, s'e? Think o' what, Brer Phelps, s'I? Think o' that bed-leg sawed off that a way, s'e? THINK of it, s'I? I lay it never sawed ITSELF off, s'I—somebody SAWED it, s'I; that's my opinion, take it or leave it, it mayn't be no 'count, s'I, but sich as 't is, it's my opinion, s'I, 'n' if any body k'n start a better one, s'I, let him DO it, s'I, that's all. I says to Sister Dunlap, s'I—"

"Why, dog my cats, they must a ben a house-full o' niggers in there every night for four weeks to a done all that work, Sister Phelps. Look at that shirt—every last inch of it kivered over with secret African writ'n done with blood! Must a ben a raft uv 'm at it right along, all the time, amost. Why, I'd give two dollars to have it read to me; 'n' as for the niggers that wrote it, I 'low I'd take 'n' lash 'm t'll—"

"People to HELP him, Brother Marples! Well, I reckon you'd THINK so if you'd a been in this house for a while back. Why, they've stole everything they could lay their hands on—and we a-watching all the time, mind you. They stole that shirt right off o' the line! and as for that sheet they made the rag ladder out of, ther' ain't no telling how many times they DIDN'T steal that; and flour, and candles, and candlesticks, and spoons, and the old warming-pan, and most a thousand things that I disremember now, and my new calico dress; and me and Silas and my Sid and Tom on the constant watch day AND night, as I was a-telling you, and not a one of us could catch hide nor hair nor sight nor sound of them; and here at the last minute, lo and behold you, they slides right in under our noses and fools us, and not only fools US but the Injun Territory robbers too, and actuly gets AWAY with that nigger safe and sound, and that with sixteen men and twenty-two dogs right on their very heels at that very time! I tell you, it just bangs anything I ever HEARD of. Why, SPERITS couldn't a done better and been no smarter. And I reckon they must a BEEN sperits—because, YOU know our dogs, and ther' ain't no better; well, them dogs never even got on the TRACK of 'm once! You explain THAT to me if you can!—ANY of you!"

"Well, it does beat—"

"Laws alive, I never—"

"So help me, I wouldn't a be—"

"HOUSE-thieves as well as—"

"Goodnessgracioussakes, I'd a ben afeard to live in sich a—"

"'Fraid to LIVE!—why, I was that scared I dasn't hardly go to bed, or get up, or lay down, or SET down, Sister Ridgeway. Why, they'd steal the very—why, goodness sakes, you can guess what kind of a fluster I was in by the time midnight come last night. I hope to gracious if I warn't afraid they'd steal some o' the family! I was just to that pass I didn't have no reasoning faculties no more. It looks foolish enough NOW, in the daytime; but I says to myself, there's my two poor boys asleep, 'way up stairs in that lonesome room, and I declare to goodness I was that uneasy 't I crep' up there and locked 'em in! I DID. And anybody would. Because, you know, when you get scared that way, and it keeps running on, and getting worse and worse all the time, and your wits gets to addling, and you get to doing all sorts o' wild things, and by and by you think to yourself, spos'n I was a boy, and was away up there, and the door ain't locked, and you—" She stopped, looking kind of wondering, and then she turned her head around slow, and when her eye lit on me—I got up and took a walk.

Says I to myself, I can explain better how we come to not be in that room this morning if I go out to one side and study over it a little. So I done it. But I dasn't go fur, or she'd a sent for me. And when it was late in the day the people all went, and then I come in and told her the noise and shooting waked up me and "Sid," and the door was locked, and we wanted to see the fun, so we went down the lightning-rod, and both of us got hurt a little, and we didn't never want to try THAT no more. And then I went on and told her all what I told Uncle Silas before; and then she said she'd forgive us, and maybe it was all right enough anyway, and about what a body might expect of boys, for all boys was a pretty harum-scarum lot as fur as she could see; and so, as long as no harm hadn't come of it, she judged she better put in her time being grateful we was alive and well and she had us still, stead of fretting over what was past and done. So then she kissed me, and patted me on the head, and dropped into a kind of a brown study; and pretty soon jumps up, and says:

"Why, lawsamercy, it's most night, and Sid not come yet! What HAS become of that boy?"

I see my chance; so I skips up and says:

"I'll run right up to town and get him," I says.

"No you won't," she says. "You'll stay right wher' you are; ONE'S enough to be lost at a time. If he ain't here to supper, your uncle 'll go."

Well, he warn't there to supper; so right after supper uncle went.

He come back about ten a little bit uneasy; hadn't run across Tom's track. Aunt Sally was a good DEAL uneasy; but Uncle Silas he said there warn't no occasion to be—boys will be boys, he said, and you'll see this one turn up in the morning all sound and right. So she had to be satisfied. But she said she'd set up for him a while anyway, and keep a light burning so he could see it.

And then when I went up to bed she come up with me and fetched her candle, and tucked me in, and mothered me so good I felt mean, and like I couldn't look her in the face; and she set down on the bed and talked with me a long time, and said what a splendid boy Sid was, and didn't seem to want to ever stop talking about him; and kept asking me every now and then if I reckoned he could a got lost, or hurt, or maybe drownded, and might be laying at this minute somewheres suffering or dead, and she not by him to help him, and so the tears would drip down silent, and I would tell her that Sid was all right, and would be home in the morning, sure; and she would squeeze my hand, or maybe kiss me, and tell me to say it again, and keep on saying it, because it done her good, and she was in so much trouble. And when she was going away she looked down in my eyes so steady and gentle, and says:

"The door ain't going to be locked, Tom, and there's the window and the rod; but you'll be good, WON'T you? And you won't go? For MY sake."

Laws knows I WANTED to go bad enough to see about Tom, and was all intending to go; but after that I wouldn't a went, not for kingdoms.

But she was on my mind and Tom was on my mind, so I slept very restless. And twice I went down the rod away in the night, and slipped around front, and see her setting there by her candle in the window with her eyes towards the road and the tears in them; and I wished I could do something for her, but I couldn't, only to swear that I wouldn't never do nothing to grieve her any more. And the third time I waked up at dawn, and slid down, and she was there yet, and her candle was most out, and her old gray head was resting on her hand, and she was asleep.

CHAPTER XLII.

THE old man was uptown again before breakfast, but couldn't get no track of Tom; and both of them set at the table thinking, and not saying nothing, and looking mournful, and their coffee getting cold, and not eating anything. And by and by the old man says:

"Did I give you the letter?"

"What letter?"

"The one I got yesterday out of the post-office."

"No, you didn't give me no letter."

"Well, I must a forgot it."

So he rummaged his pockets, and then went off somewheres where he had laid it down, and fetched it, and give it to her. She says:

"Why, it's from St. Petersburg—it's from Sis."

I allowed another walk would do me good; but I couldn't stir. But before she could break it open she dropped it and run—for she see something. And so did I. It was Tom Sawyer on a mattress; and that old doctor; and Jim, in HER calico dress, with his hands tied behind him; and a lot of people. I hid the letter behind the first thing that come handy, and rushed. She flung herself at Tom, crying, and says:

"Oh, he's dead, he's dead, I know he's dead!"

And Tom he turned his head a little, and muttered something or other, which showed he warn't in his right mind; then she flung up her hands, and says:

"He's alive, thank God! And that's enough!" and she snatched a kiss of him, and flew for the house to get the bed ready, and scattering orders right and left at the niggers and everybody else, as fast as her tongue could go, every jump of the way.

I followed the men to see what they was going to do with Jim; and the old doctor and Uncle Silas followed after Tom into the house. The men was very huffy, and some of them wanted to hang Jim for an example to all the other niggers around there, so they wouldn't be trying to run away like Jim done, and making such a raft of trouble, and keeping a whole family scared most to death for days and nights. But the others said, don't do it, it wouldn't answer at all; he ain't our nigger, and his owner would turn up and make us pay for him, sure. So that cooled them down a little, because the people that's always the most anxious for to hang a nigger that hain't done just right is always the very ones that ain't the most anxious to pay for him when they've got their satisfaction out of him.

They cussed Jim considerble, though, and give him a cuff or two side the head once in a while, but Jim never said nothing, and he never let on to know me, and they took him to the same cabin, and put his own clothes on him, and chained him again, and not to no bed-leg this time, but to a big staple drove into the bottom log, and chained his hands, too, and both legs, and said he warn't to have nothing but bread and water to eat after this till his owner come, or he was sold at auction because he didn't come in a certain length of time, and filled up our hole, and said a couple of farmers with guns must stand watch around about the cabin every night, and a bulldog tied to the door in the daytime; and about this time they was through with the job and was tapering off with a kind of generl good-bye cussing, and then the old doctor comes and takes a look, and says:

"Don't be no rougher on him than you're obleeged to, because he ain't a bad nigger. When I got to where I found the boy I see I couldn't cut the bullet out without some help, and he warn't in no condition for me to leave to go and get help; and he got a little worse and a little worse, and after a long time he went out of his head, and wouldn't let me come a-nigh him any more, and said if I chalked his raft he'd kill me, and no end of wild foolishness like that, and I see I couldn't do anything at all with him; so I says, I got to have HELP somehow; and the minute I says it out crawls this nigger from somewheres and says he'll help, and he done it, too, and done it very well. Of course I judged he must be a runaway nigger, and there I WAS! and there I had to stick right straight along all the rest of the day and all night. It was a fix, I tell you! I had a couple of patients with the chills, and of course I'd of liked to run up to town and see them, but I dasn't, because the nigger might get away, and then I'd be to blame; and yet never a skiff come close enough for me to hail. So there I had to stick plumb until daylight this morning; and I never see a nigger that was a better nuss or faithfuller, and yet he was risking his freedom to do it, and was all tired out, too, and I see plain enough he'd been worked main hard lately. I liked the nigger for that; I tell you, gentlemen, a nigger like that is worth a thousand dollars—and kind treatment, too. I had everything I needed, and the boy was doing as well there as he would a done at home—better, maybe, because it was so quiet; but there I WAS, with both of 'm on my hands, and there I had to stick till about dawn this morning; then some men in a skiff come by, and as good luck would have it the nigger was setting by the pallet with his head propped on his knees sound asleep; so I motioned them in quiet, and they slipped up on him and grabbed him and tied him before he knowed what he was about, and we never had no trouble. And the boy being in a kind of a flighty sleep, too, we muffled the oars and hitched the raft on, and towed her over very nice and quiet, and the nigger never made the least row nor said a word from the start. He ain't no bad nigger, gentlemen; that's what I think about him."

Somebody says:

"Well, it sounds very good, doctor, I'm obleeged to say."

Then the others softened up a little, too, and I was mighty thankful to that old doctor for doing Jim that good turn; and I was glad it was according to my judgment of him, too; because I thought he had a good heart in him and was a good man the first time I see him. Then they all agreed that Jim had acted very well, and was deserving to have some notice took of it, and reward. So every one of them promised, right out and hearty, that they wouldn't cuss him no more.

Then they come out and locked him up. I hoped they was going to say he could have one or two of the chains took off, because they was rotten heavy, or could have meat and greens with his bread and water; but they didn't think of it, and I reckoned it warn't best for me to mix in, but I judged I'd get the doctor's yarn to Aunt Sally somehow or other as soon as I'd got through the breakers that was laying just ahead of me — explanations, I mean, of how I forgot to mention about Sid being shot when I was telling how him and me put in that dratted night paddling around hunting the runaway nigger.

But I had plenty time. Aunt Sally she stuck to the sick-room all day and all night, and every time I see Uncle Silas mooning around I dodged him.

Next morning I heard Tom was a good deal better, and they said Aunt Sally was gone to get a nap. So I slips to the sick-room, and if I found him awake I reckoned we could put up a yarn for the family that would wash. But he was sleeping, and sleeping very peaceful, too; and pale, not fire-faced the way he was when he come. So I set down and laid for him to wake. In about half an hour Aunt Sally comes gliding in, and there I was, up a stump again! She motioned me to be still, and set down by me, and begun to whisper, and said we could all be joyful now, because all the symptoms was first-rate, and he'd been sleeping like that for ever so long, and looking better and peacefuller all the time, and ten to one he'd wake up in his right mind.

So we set there watching, and by and by he stirs a bit, and opened his eyes very natural, and takes a look, and says:

"Hello!—why, I'm at HOME! How's that? Where's the raft?"

"It's all right," I says.

"And JIM?"

"The same," I says, but couldn't say it pretty brash. But he never noticed, but says:

"Good! Splendid! NOW we're all right and safe! Did you tell Aunty?"

I was going to say yes; but she chipped in and says: "About what, Sid?"

"Why, about the way the whole thing was done."

"What whole thing?"

"Why, THE whole thing. There ain't but one; how we set the runaway nigger free—me and Tom."

"Good land! Set the run—What IS the child talking about! Dear, dear, out of his head again!"

"NO, I ain't out of my HEAD; I know all what I'm talking about. We DID set him free—me and Tom. We laid out to do it, and we DONE it. And we done it elegant, too." He'd got a start, and she never checked him up, just set and stared and stared, and let him clip along, and I see it warn't no use for ME to put in. "Why, Aunty, it cost us a power of work —weeks of it— hours and hours, every night, whilst you was all asleep. And we had to steal candles, and the sheet, and the shirt, and your dress, and spoons, and tin plates, and case-knives, and the warming-pan, and the grindstone, and flour, and just no end of things, and you can't think what work it was to make the saws, and pens, and inscriptions, and one thing or another, and you can't think HALF the fun it was. And we had to make up the pictures of coffins and things, and nonnamous letters from the robbers, and get up and down the lightning-rod, and dig the hole into the cabin, and made the rope ladder and send it in cooked up in a pie, and send in spoons and things to work with in your apron pocket—"

"Mercy sakes!"

"—and load up the cabin with rats and snakes and so on, for company for Jim; and then you kept Tom here so long with the butter in his hat that you come near spiling the whole business, because the men come before we was out of the cabin, and we had to rush, and they heard us and let drive at us, and I got my share, and we dodged out of the path and let them go by, and when the dogs come they warn't interested in us, but went for the most noise, and we got our canoe, and made for the raft, and was all safe, and Jim was a free man, and we done it all by ourselves, and WASN'T it bully, Aunty!"

"Well, I never heard the likes of it in all my born days! So it was YOU, you little rapscallions, that's been making all this trouble, and turned everybody's wits clean inside out and scared us all most to death. I've as good a notion as ever I had in my life to take it out o' you this very minute. To think I've been, night after night, a—YOU just get well once, you young scamp, and I lay I'll tan the Old Harry out o' both o' ye!"

But Tom, he WAS so proud and joyful, he just COULDN'T hold in, and his tongue just WENT it—she a-chipping in, and spitting fire all along, and both of them going it at once, like a cat convention; and she says:

"WELL, you get all the enjoyment you can out of it NOW, for mind I tell you if I catch you meddling with him again—"

"Meddling with WHO?" Tom says, dropping his smile and looking surprised.

"With WHO? Why, the runaway nigger, of course. Who'd you reckon?"

Tom looks at me very grave, and says:

"Tom, didn't you just tell me he was all right? Hasn't he got away?"

"HIM?" says Aunt Sally; "the runaway nigger? 'Deed he hasn't. They've got him back, safe and sound, and he's in that cabin again, on bread and water, and loaded down with chains, till he's claimed or sold!"

Tom rose square up in bed, with his eye hot, and his nostrils opening and shutting like gills, and sings out to me:

"They hain't no RIGHT to shut him up! SHOVE!—and don't you lose a minute. Turn him loose! he ain't no slave; he's as free as any cretur that walks this earth!"

"What DOES the child mean?"

"I mean every word I SAY, Aunt Sally, and if somebody don't go, I'LL go. I've knowed him all his life, and so has Tom, there. Old Miss Watson died two months ago, and she was ashamed she ever was going to sell him down the river, and SAID so; and she set him free in her will."

"Then what on earth did YOU want to set him free for, seeing he was already free?"

"Well, that IS a question, I must say; and just like women! Why, I wanted the ADVENTURE of it; and I'd a waded neck-deep in blood to —goodness alive, AUNT POLLY!"

If she warn't standing right there, just inside the door, looking as sweet and contented as an angel half full of pie, I wish I may never!

Aunt Sally jumped for her, and most hugged the head off of her, and cried over her, and I found a good enough place for me under the bed, for it was getting pretty sultry for us, seemed to me. And I peeped out, and in a little while Tom's Aunt Polly shook herself loose and stood there looking across at Tom over her spectacles—kind of grinding him into the earth, you know. And then she says:

"Yes, you BETTER turn y'r head away—I would if I was you, Tom."

"Oh, deary me!" says Aunt Sally; "IS he changed so? Why, that ain't TOM, it's Sid; Tom's—Tom's—why, where is Tom? He was here a minute ago."

"You mean where's Huck FINN—that's what you mean! I reckon I hain't raised such a scamp as my Tom all these years not to know him when I SEE him. That WOULD be a pretty howdy-do. Come out from under that bed, Huck Finn."

So I done it. But not feeling brash.

Aunt Sally she was one of the mixed-upest-looking persons I ever see —except one, and that was Uncle Silas, when he come in and they told it all to him. It kind of made him drunk, as you may say, and he didn't know nothing at all the rest of the day, and preached a prayer-meeting sermon that night that gave him a rattling ruputation, because the oldest man in the world couldn't a understood it. So Tom's Aunt Polly, she told all about who I was, and what; and I had to up and tell how I was in such a tight place that when Mrs. Phelps took me for Tom Sawyer—she chipped in and says, "Oh, go on and call me Aunt Sally, I'm used to it now, and 'tain't no need to change"— that when Aunt Sally took me for Tom Sawyer I had to stand it—there warn't no other way, and I knowed he wouldn't mind, because it would be nuts for him, being a mystery, and he'd make an adventure out of it, and be perfectly satisfied. And so it turned out, and he let on to be Sid, and made things as soft as he could for me.

And his Aunt Polly she said Tom was right about old Miss Watson setting Jim free in her will; and so, sure enough, Tom Sawyer had gone and took all that trouble and bother to set a

free nigger free! and I couldn't ever understand before, until that minute and that talk, how he COULD help a body set a nigger free with his bringing-up.

Well, Aunt Polly she said that when Aunt Sally wrote to her that Tom and SID had come all right and safe, she says to herself:

"Look at that, now! I might have expected it, letting him go off that way without anybody to watch him. So now I got to go and trapse all the way down the river, eleven hundred mile, and find out what that creetur's up to THIS time, as long as I couldn't seem to get any answer out of you about it."

"Why, I never heard nothing from you," says Aunt Sally.

"Well, I wonder! Why, I wrote you twice to ask you what you could mean by Sid being here."

"Well, I never got 'em, Sis."

Aunt Polly she turns around slow and severe, and says:

"You, Tom!"

"Well—WHAT?" he says, kind of pettish.

"Don't you what ME, you impudent thing—hand out them letters."

"What letters?"

"THEM letters. I be bound, if I have to take a-holt of you I'll—"

"They're in the trunk. There, now. And they're just the same as they was when I got them out of the office. I hain't looked into them, I hain't touched them. But I knowed they'd make trouble, and I thought if you warn't in no hurry, I'd—"

"Well, you DO need skinning, there ain't no mistake about it. And I wrote another one to tell you I was coming; and I s'pose he—"

"No, it come yesterday; I hain't read it yet, but IT'S all right, I've got that one."

I wanted to offer to bet two dollars she hadn't, but I reckoned maybe it was just as safe to not to. So I never said nothing.

CHAPTER THE LAST

THE first time I catched Tom private I asked him what was his idea, time of the evasion?—what it was he'd planned to do if the evasion worked all right and he managed to set a nigger free that was already free before? And he said, what he had planned in his head from the start, if we got Jim out all safe, was for us to run him down the river on the raft, and have adventures plumb to the mouth of the river, and then tell him about his being free, and take him back up home on a steamboat, in style, and pay him for his lost time, and write word ahead and get out all the niggers around, and have them waltz him into town with a torchlight procession and a brass-band, and then he would be a hero, and so would we. But I reckoned it was about as well the way it was.

We had Jim out of the chains in no time, and when Aunt Polly and Uncle Silas and Aunt Sally found out how good he helped the doctor nurse Tom, they made a heap of fuss over him, and fixed him up prime, and give him all he wanted to eat, and a good time, and nothing to do. And we had him up to the sick-room, and had a high talk; and Tom give Jim forty dollars for being prisoner for us so patient, and doing it up so good, and Jim was pleased most to death, and busted out, and says:

"DAH, now, Huck, what I tell you?—what I tell you up dah on Jackson islan'? I TOLE you I got a hairy breas', en what's de sign un it; en I TOLE you I ben rich wunst, en gwineter to be rich AGIN; en it's come true; en heah she is! DAH, now! doan' talk to ME—signs is SIGNS, mine I tell you; en I knowed jis' 's well 'at I 'uz gwineter be rich agin as I's a-stannin' heah dis minute!"

And then Tom he talked along and talked along, and says, le's all three slide out of here one of these nights and get an outfit, and go for howling adventures amongst the Injuns, over in the Territory, for a couple of weeks or two; and I says, all right, that suits me, but I ain't got no money for to buy the outfit, and I reckon I couldn't get none from home, because it's likely pap's been back before now, and got it all away from Judge Thatcher and drunk it up.

"No, he hain't," Tom says; "it's all there yet—six thousand dollars and more; and your pap hain't ever been back since. Hadn't when I come away, anyhow."

Jim says, kind of solemn:

"He ain't a-comin' back no mo', Huck."

I says:

"Why, Jim?"

"Nemmine why, Huck—but he ain't comin' back no mo."

But I kept at him; so at last he says:

"Doan' you 'member de house dat was float'n down de river, en dey wuz a man in dah, kivered up, en I went in en unkivered him and didn' let you come in? Well, den, you kin git yo' money when you wants it, kase dat wuz him."

Tom's most well now, and got his bullet around his neck on a watch-guard for a watch, and is always seeing what time it is, and so there ain't nothing more to write about, and I am rotten glad of it, because if I'd a knowed what a trouble it was to make a book I wouldn't a tackled it, and ain't a-going to no more. But I reckon I got to light out for the Territory ahead of the rest, because Aunt Sally she's going to adopt me and sivilize me, and I can't stand it. I been there before.

Tom Sawyer Abroad
By Mark Twain

CHAPTER I. TOM SEEKS NEW ADVENTURES

DO you reckon Tom Sawyer was satisfied after all them adventures? I mean the adventures we had down the river, and the time we set the darky Jim free and Tom got shot in the leg. No, he wasn't. It only just p'isoned him for more. That was all the effect it had. You see, when we three came back up the river in glory, as you may say, from that long travel, and then the village received us with a torchlight procession and speeches, and everybody hurrah'd and shouted, it made us heroes, and that was what Tom Sawyer had always been hankering to be.

For a while he WAS satisfied. Everybody made much of him, and he tilted up his nose and stepped around the town as though he owned it. Some called him Tom Sawyer the Traveler, and that just swelled him up fit to bust. You see he laid over me and Jim considerable, because we only went down the river on a raft and came back by the steamboat, but Tom went by the steamboat both ways. The boys envied me and Jim a good deal, but land! they just knuckled to the dirt before TOM.

Well, I don't know; maybe he might have been satisfied if it hadn't been for old Nat Parsons, which was postmaster, and powerful long and slim, and kind o' good-hearted and silly, and bald-headed, on account of his age, and about the talkiest old cretur I ever see. For as much as thirty years he'd been the only man in the village that had a reputation—I mean a reputation for being a traveler, and of course he was mortal proud of it, and it was reckoned that in the course of that thirty years he had told about that journey over a million times and enjoyed it every time. And now comes along a boy not quite fifteen, and sets everybody admiring and gawking over HIS travels, and it just give the poor old man the high strikes. It made him sick to listen to Tom, and to hear the people say "My land!" "Did you ever!" "My goodness sakes alive!" and all such things; but he couldn't pull away from it, any more than a fly that's got its hind leg fast in the molasses. And always when Tom come to a rest, the poor old cretur would chip in on HIS same old travels and work them for all they were worth; but they were pretty faded, and didn't go for much, and it was pitiful to see. And then Tom would take another innings, and then the old man again—and so on, and so on, for an hour and more, each trying to beat out the other.

You see, Parsons' travels happened like this: When he first got to be postmaster and was green in the business, there come a letter for somebody he didn't know, and there wasn't any such person in the village. Well, he didn't know what to do, nor how to act, and there the letter stayed and stayed, week in and week out, till the bare sight of it gave him a conniption. The postage wasn't paid on it, and that was another thing to worry about. There wasn't any way to collect that ten cents, and he reckon'd the gov'ment would hold him responsible for it and maybe turn him out besides, when they found he hadn't collected it. Well, at last he couldn't stand it any longer. He couldn't sleep nights, he couldn't eat, he was thinned down to a shadder, yet he da'sn't ask anybody's advice, for the very person he asked for advice might go back on him and let the gov'ment know about the letter. He had the letter buried under the floor, but that did no good; if he happened to see a person standing over the place it'd give him the cold shivers, and loaded him up with suspicions, and he would sit up that night till the town was still and dark, and then he would sneak there

and get it out and bury it in another place. Of course, people got to avoiding him and shaking their heads and whispering, because, the way he was looking and acting, they judged he had killed somebody or done something terrible, they didn't know what, and if he had been a stranger they would've lynched him.

Well, as I was saying, it got so he couldn't stand it any longer; so he made up his mind to pull out for Washington, and just go to the President of the United States and make a clean breast of the whole thing, not keeping back an atom, and then fetch the letter out and lay it before the whole gov'ment, and say, "Now, there she is—do with me what you're a mind to; though as heaven is my judge I am an innocent man and not deserving of the full penalties of the law and leaving behind me a family that must starve and yet hadn't had a thing to do with it, which is the whole truth and I can swear to it."

So he did it. He had a little wee bit of steamboating, and some stage-coaching, but all the rest of the way was horseback, and it took him three weeks to get to Washington. He saw lots of land and lots of villages and four cities. He was gone 'most eight weeks, and there never was such a proud man in the village as he when he got back. His travels made him the greatest man in all that region, and the most talked about; and people come from as much as thirty miles back in the country, and from over in the Illinois bottoms, too, just to look at him—and there they'd stand and gawk, and he'd gabble. You never see anything like it.

Well, there wasn't any way now to settle which was the greatest traveler; some said it was Nat, some said it was Tom. Everybody allowed that Nat had seen the most longitude, but they had to give in that whatever Tom was short in longitude he had made up in latitude and climate. It was about a stand-off; so both of them had to whoop up their dangerous adventures, and try to get ahead THAT way. That bullet-wound in Tom's leg was a tough thing for Nat Parsons to buck against, but he bucked the best he could; and at a disadvantage, too, for Tom didn't set still as he'd orter done, to be fair, but always got up and sauntered around and worked his limp while Nat was painting up the adventure that HE had in Washington; for Tom never let go that limp when his leg got well, but practiced it nights at home, and kept it good as new right along.

Nat's adventure was like this; I don't know how true it is; maybe he got it out of a paper, or somewhere, but I will say this for him, that he DID know how to tell it. He could make anybody's flesh crawl, and he'd turn pale and hold his breath when he told it, and sometimes women and girls got so faint they couldn't stick it out. Well, it was this way, as near as I can remember:

He come a-loping into Washington, and put up his horse and shoved out to the President's house with his letter, and they told him the President was up to the Capitol, and just going to start for Philadelphia—not a minute to lose if he wanted to catch him. Nat 'most dropped, it made him so sick. His horse was put up, and he didn't know what to do. But just then along comes a darky driving an old ramshackly hack, and he see his chance. He rushes out and shouts: "A half a dollar if you git me to the Capitol in half an hour, and a quarter extra if you do it in twenty minutes!"

"Done!" says the darky.

Nat he jumped in and slammed the door, and away they went

a-ripping and a-tearing over the roughest road a body ever see, and the racket of it was something awful. Nat passed his arms through the loops and hung on for life and death, but pretty soon the hack hit a rock and flew up in the air, and the bottom fell out, and when it come down Nat's feet was on the ground, and he see he was in the most desperate danger if he couldn't keep up with the hack. He was horrible scared, but he laid into his work for all he was worth, and hung tight to the arm-loops and made his legs fairly fly. He yelled and shouted to the driver to stop, and so did the crowds along the street, for they could see his legs spinning along under the coach, and his head and shoulders bobbing inside through the windows, and he was in awful danger; but the more they all shouted the more the nigger whooped and yelled and lashed the horses and shouted, "Don't you fret, I'se gwine to git you dah in time, boss; I's gwine to do it, sho'!" for you see he thought they were all hurrying him up, and, of course, he couldn't hear anything for the racket he was making. And so they went ripping along, and everybody just petrified to see it; and when they got to the Capitol at last it was the quickest trip that ever was made, and everybody said so. The horses laid down, and Nat dropped, all tuckered out, and he was all dust and rags and barefooted; but he was in time and just in time, and caught the President and give him the letter, and everything was all right, and the President give him a free pardon on the spot, and Nat give the nigger two extra quarters instead of one, because he could see that if he hadn't had the hack he wouldn't'a' got there in time, nor anywhere near it.

It WAS a powerful good adventure, and Tom Sawyer had to work his bullet-wound mighty lively to hold his own against it.

Well, by and by Tom's glory got to paling down gradu'ly, on account of other things turning up for the people to talk about—first a horse-race, and on top of that a house afire, and on top of that the circus, and on top of that the eclipse; and that started a revival, same as it always does, and by that time there wasn't any more talk about Tom, so to speak, and you never see a person so sick and disgusted.

Pretty soon he got to worrying and fretting right along day in and day out, and when I asked him what WAS he in such a state about, he said it 'most broke his heart to think how time was slipping away, and him getting older and older, and no wars breaking out and no way of making a name for himself that he could see. Now that is the way boys is always thinking, but he was the first one I ever heard come out and say it.

So then he set to work to get up a plan to make him celebrated; and pretty soon he struck it, and offered to take me and Jim in. Tom Sawyer was always free and generous that way. There's a-plenty of boys that's mighty good and friendly when YOU'VE got a good thing, but when a good thing happens to come their way they don't say a word to you, and try to hog it all. That warn't ever Tom Sawyer's way, I can say that for him. There's plenty of boys that will come hankering and groveling around you when you've got an apple and beg the core off of you; but when they've got one, and you beg for the core and remind them how you give them a core one time, they say thank you 'most to death, but there ain't a-going to be no core. But I notice they always git come up with; all you got to do is to wait.

Well, we went out in the woods on the hill, and Tom told us what it was. It was a crusade.

"What's a crusade?" I says.

He looked scornful, the way he's always done when he was ashamed of a person, and says:

"Huck Finn, do you mean to tell me you don't know what a crusade is?"

"No," says I, "I don't. And I don't care to, nuther. I've lived till now and done without it, and had my health, too. But as soon as you tell me, I'll know, and that's soon enough. I don't see any use in finding out things and clogging up my head with them when I mayn't ever have any occasion to use 'em. There was Lance Williams, he learned how to talk Choctaw here till one come and dug his grave for him. Now, then, what's a crusade? But I can tell you one thing before you begin; if it's a patent-right, there's no money in it. Bill Thompson he—"

"Patent-right!" says he. "I never see such an idiot. Why, a crusade is a kind of war."

I thought he must be losing his mind. But no, he was in real earnest, and went right on, perfectly ca'm.

"A crusade is a war to recover the Holy Land from the paynim."

"Which Holy Land?"

"Why, the Holy Land—there ain't but one."

"What do we want of it?"

"Why, can't you understand? It's in the hands of the paynim, and it's our duty to take it away from them."

"How did we come to let them git hold of it?"

"We didn't come to let them git hold of it. They always had it."

"Why, Tom, then it must belong to them, don't it?"

"Why of course it does. Who said it didn't?"

I studied over it, but couldn't seem to git at the right of it, no way. I says:

"It's too many for me, Tom Sawyer. If I had a farm and it was mine, and another person wanted it, would it be right for him to—"

"Oh, shucks! you don't know enough to come in when it rains, Huck Finn. It ain't a farm, it's entirely different. You see, it's like this. They own the land, just the mere land, and that's all they DO own; but it was our folks, our Jews and Christians, that made it holy, and so they haven't any business to be there defiling it. It's a shame, and we ought not to stand it a minute. We ought to march against them and take it away from them."

"Why, it does seem to me it's the most mixed-up thing I ever see! Now, if I had a farm and another person—"

"Don't I tell you it hasn't got anything to do with farming? Farming is business, just common low-down business: that's all it is, it's all you can say for it; but this is higher, this is religious, and totally different."

"Religious to go and take the land away from people that owns it?"

"Certainly; it's always been considered so."

Jim he shook his head, and says:

"Mars Tom, I reckon dey's a mistake about it somers—dey mos' sholy is. I's religious myself, en I knows plenty religious people, but I hain't run across none dat acts like dat."

It made Tom hot, and he says:

"Well, it's enough to make a body sick, such mullet-headed ignorance! If either of you'd read anything about history, you'd know that Richard Cur de Loon, and the Pope, and Godfrey de Bulleyn, and lots more of the most noble-hearted and pious people in the world, hacked and hammered at the paynims for more than two hundred years trying to take their land away from them, and swum neck-deep in blood the whole time—and yet here's a couple of sap-headed country yahoos out in the backwoods of Missouri setting themselves up to know more about the rights and wrongs of it than they did! Talk about cheek!"

Well, of course, that put a more different light on it, and me and Jim felt pretty cheap and ignorant, and wished we hadn't been quite so chipper. I couldn't say nothing, and Jim he couldn't for a while; then he says:

"Well, den, I reckon it's all right; beca'se ef dey didn't know, dey ain't no use for po' ignorant folks like us to be trying to know; en so, ef it's our duty, we got to go en tackle it en do de bes' we can. Same time, I feel as sorry for dem paynims as Mars Tom. De hard part gwine to be to kill folks dat a body hain't been 'quainted wid and dat hain't done him no harm. Dat's it, you see. Ef we wuz to go 'mongst 'em, jist we three, en say we's hungry, en ast 'em for a bite to eat, why, maybe dey's jist like yuther people. Don't you reckon dey is? Why, DEY'D give it, I know dey would, en den—"

"Then what?"

"Well, Mars Tom, my idea is like dis. It ain't no use, we CAN'T kill dem po' strangers dat ain't doin' us no harm, till we've had practice—I knows it perfectly well, Mars Tom—'deed I knows it perfectly well. But ef we takes a' axe or two, jist you en me en Huck, en slips acrost de river to-night arter de moon's gone down, en kills dat sick fam'ly dat's over on de Sny, en burns dey house down, en—"

"Oh, you make me tired!" says Tom. "I don't want to argue any more with people like you and Huck Finn, that's always wandering from the subject, and ain't got any more sense than to try to reason out a thing that's pure theology by the laws that protect real estate!"

Now that's just where Tom Sawyer warn't fair. Jim didn't mean no harm, and I didn't mean no harm. We knowed well enough that he was right and we was wrong, and all we was after was to get at the HOW of it, and that was all; and the only reason he couldn't explain it so we could understand it was because we was ignorant—yes, and pretty dull, too, I ain't denying that; but, land! that ain't no crime, I should think.

But he wouldn't hear no more about it—just said if we had tackled the thing in the proper spirit, he would 'a' raised a couple of thousand knights and put them in steel armor from head to heel, and made me a lieutenant and Jim a sutler, and took the command himself and brushed the whole paynim outfit into the sea like flies and come back across the world in

a glory like sunset. But he said we didn't know enough to take the chance when we had it, and he wouldn't ever offer it again. And he didn't. When he once got set, you couldn't budge him.

But I didn't care much. I am peaceable, and don't get up rows with people that ain't doing nothing to me. I allowed if the paynim was satisfied I was, and we would let it stand at that.

Now Tom he got all that notion out of Walter Scott's book, which he was always reading. And it WAS a wild notion, because in my opinion he never could've raised the men, and if he did, as like as not he would've got licked. I took the book and read all about it, and as near as I could make it out, most of the folks that shook farming to go crusading had a mighty rocky time of it.

CHAPTER II. THE BALLOON ASCENSION

WELL, Tom got up one thing after another, but they all had tender spots about 'em somewhere, and he had to shove 'em aside. So at last he was about in despair. Then the St. Louis papers begun to talk a good deal about the balloon that was going to sail to Europe, and Tom sort of thought he wanted to go down and see what it looked like, but couldn't make up his mind. But the papers went on talking, and so he allowed that maybe if he didn't go he mightn't ever have another chance to see a balloon; and next, he found out that Nat Parsons was going down to see it, and that decided him, of course. He wasn't going to have Nat Parsons coming back bragging about seeing the balloon, and him having to listen to it and keep quiet. So he wanted me and Jim to go too, and we went.

It was a noble big balloon, and had wings and fans and all sorts of things, and wasn't like any balloon you see in pictures. It was away out toward the edge of town, in a vacant lot, corner of Twelfth street; and there was a big crowd around it, making fun of it, and making fun of the man,—a lean pale feller with that soft kind of moonlight in his eyes, you know,—and they kept saying it wouldn't go. It made him hot to hear them, and he would turn on them and shake his fist and say they was animals and blind, but some day they would find they had stood face to face with one of the men that lifts up nations and makes civilizations, and was too dull to know it; and right here on this spot their own children and grandchildren would build a monument to him that would outlast a thousand years, but his name would outlast the monument. And then the crowd would burst out in a laugh again, and yell at him, and ask him what was his name before he was married, and what he would take to not do it, and what was his sister's cat's grandmother's name, and all the things that a crowd says when they've got hold of a feller that they see they can plague. Well, some things they said WAS funny,—yes, and mighty witty too, I ain't denying that,—but all the same it warn't fair nor brave, all them people pitching on one, and they so glib and sharp, and him without any gift of talk to answer back with. But, good land! what did he want to sass back for? You see, it couldn't do him no good, and it was just nuts for them. They HAD him, you know. But that was his way. I reckon he couldn't help it; he was made so, I judge. He was a good enough sort of cretur, and hadn't no harm in him, and was just a genius, as the papers said, which wasn't his fault. We can't all be sound: we've got to be the way we're made. As near as I can make out, geniuses think they know it all, and so they won't take people's advice, but always go their own way, which makes everybody forsake them and despise them, and that is perfectly natural. If they was humbler, and listened and tried to learn, it would be better for them.

The part the professor was in was like a boat, and was big and roomy, and had water-tight lockers around the inside to keep all sorts of things in, and a body could sit on them, and make beds on them, too. We went aboard, and there was twenty people there, snooping around and examining, and old Nat Parsons was there, too. The professor kept fussing around getting ready, and the people went ashore, drifting out one at a time, and old Nat he was the last. Of course it wouldn't do to let him go out behind US. We mustn't budge till he was gone, so we could be last ourselves.

But he was gone now, so it was time for us to follow. I heard a big shout, and turned around—the city was dropping from under us like a shot! It made me sick all through, I was so scared. Jim turned gray and couldn't say a word, and Tom didn't say nothing, but looked excited. The city went on dropping down, and down, and down; but we didn't seem to be doing nothing but just hang in the air and stand still. The houses got smaller and smaller, and the city pulled itself together, closer and closer, and the men and wagons got to looking like ants and bugs crawling around, and the streets like threads and cracks; and then it all kind of melted together, and there wasn't any city any more it was only a big scar on the earth, and it seemed to me a body could see up the river and down the river about a thousand miles, though of course it wasn't so much. By and by the earth was a ball—just a round ball, of a dull color, with shiny stripes wriggling and winding around over it, which was rivers. The Widder Douglas always told me the earth was round like a ball, but I never took any stock in a lot of them superstitions o' hers, and of course I paid no attention to that one, because I could see myself that the world was the shape of a plate, and flat. I used to go up on the hill, and take a look around and prove it for myself, because I reckon the best way to get a sure thing on a fact is to go and examine for yourself, and not take anybody's say-so. But I had to give in now that the widder was right. That is, she was right as to the rest of the world, but she warn't right about the part our village is in; that part is the shape of a plate, and flat, I take my oath!

The professor had been quiet all this time, as if he was asleep; but he broke loose now, and he was mighty bitter. He says something like this:

"Idiots! They said it wouldn't go; and they wanted to examine it, and spy around and get the secret of it out of me. But I beat them. Nobody knows the secret but me. Nobody knows what makes it move but me; and it's a new power—a new power, and a thousand times the strongest in the earth! Steam's foolishness to it! They said I couldn't go to Europe. To Europe! Why, there's power aboard to last five years, and feed for three months. They are fools! What do they know about it? Yes, and they said my air-ship was flimsy. Why, she's good for fifty years! I can sail the skies all my life if I want to, and steer where I please, though they laughed at that, and said I couldn't. Couldn't steer! Come here, boy; we'll see. You press these buttons as I tell you."

He made Tom steer the ship all about and every which way, and learnt him the whole thing in nearly no time; and Tom said it was perfectly easy. He made him fetch the ship down 'most to the earth, and had him spin her along so close to the Illinois prairies that a body could talk to the farmers, and hear everything they said perfectly plain; and he flung out printed bills to them that told about the balloon, and said it was going to Europe. Tom got so he could steer straight for a tree till he got nearly to it, and then dart up and skin right along over the top of it. Yes, and he showed Tom how to land her; and he

done it first-rate, too, and set her down in the prairies as soft as wool. But the minute we started to skip out the professor says, "No, you don't!" and shot her up in the air again. It was awful. I begun to beg, and so did Jim; but it only give his temper a rise, and he begun to rage around and look wild out of his eyes, and I was scared of him.

Well, then he got on to his troubles again, and mourned and grumbled about the way he was treated, and couldn't seem to git over it, and especially people's saying his ship was flimsy. He scoffed at that, and at their saying she warn't simple and would be always getting out of order. Get out of order! That graveled him; he said that she couldn't any more get out of order than the solar sister.

He got worse and worse, and I never see a person take on so. It give me the cold shivers to see him, and so it did Jim. By and by he got to yelling and screaming, and then he swore the world shouldn't ever have his secret at all now, it had treated him so mean. He said he would sail his balloon around the globe just to show what he could do, and then he would sink it in the sea, and sink us all along with it, too. Well, it was the awfulest fix to be in, and here was night coming on!

He give us something to eat, and made us go to the other end of the boat, and he laid down on a locker, where he could boss all the works, and put his old pepper-box revolver under his head, and said if anybody come fooling around there trying to land her, he would kill him.

We set scrunched up together, and thought considerable, but didn't say much—only just a word once in a while when a body had to say something or bust, we was so scared and worried. The night dragged along slow and lonesome. We was pretty low down, and the moonshine made everything soft and pretty, and the farmhouses looked snug and homeful, and we could hear the farm sounds, and wished we could be down there; but, laws! we just slipped along over them like a ghost, and never left a track.

Away in the night, when all the sounds was late sounds, and the air had a late feel, and a late smell, too—about a two-o'clock feel, as near as I could make out—Tom said the professor was so quiet this time he must be asleep, and we'd better—

"Better what?" I says in a whisper, and feeling sick all over, because I knowed what he was thinking about.

"Better slip back there and tie him, and land the ship," he says.

I says: "No, sir! Don' you budge, Tom Sawyer."

And Jim—well, Jim was kind o' gasping, he was so scared. He says:

"Oh, Mars Tom, DON'T! Ef you teches him, we's gone—we's gone sho'! I ain't gwine anear him, not for nothin' in dis worl'. Mars Tom, he's plumb crazy."

Tom whispers and says—"That's WHY we've got to do something. If he wasn't crazy I wouldn't give shucks to be anywhere but here; you couldn't hire me to get out—now that I've got used to this balloon and over the scare of being cut loose from the solid ground—if he was in his right mind. But it's no good politics, sailing around like this with a person that's out of his head, and says he's going round the world and then drown us all. We've GOT to do something, I tell you, and do it before he wakes up, too, or we mayn't ever get another chance. Come!"

But it made us turn cold and creepy just to think of it, and we said we wouldn't budge. So Tom was for slipping back there by himself to see if he couldn't get at the steering-gear and land the ship. We begged and begged him not to, but it warn't no use; so he got down on his hands and knees, and begun to crawl an inch at a time, we a-holding our breath and watching. After he got to the middle of the boat he crept slower than ever, and it did seem like years to me. But at last we see him get to the professor's head, and sort of raise up soft and look a good spell in his face and listen. Then we see him begin to inch along again toward the professor's feet where the steering-buttons was. Well, he got there all safe, and was reaching slow and steady toward the buttons, but he knocked down something that made a noise, and we see him slump down flat an' soft in the bottom, and lay still. The professor stirred, and says, "What's that?" But everybody kept dead still and quiet, and he begun to mutter and mumble and nestle, like a person that's going to wake up, and I thought I was going to die, I was so worried and scared.

Then a cloud slid over the moon, and I 'most cried, I was so glad. She buried herself deeper and deeper into the cloud, and it got so dark we couldn't see Tom. Then it began to sprinkle rain, and we could hear the professor fussing at his ropes and things and abusing the weather. We was afraid every minute he would touch Tom, and then we would be goners, and no help; but Tom was already on his way back, and when we felt his hands on our knees my breath stopped sudden, and my heart fell down 'mongst my other works, because I couldn't tell in the dark but it might be the professor! which I thought it WAS.

Dear! I was so glad to have him back that I was just as near happy as a person could be that was up in the air that way with a deranged man. You can't land a balloon in the dark, and so I hoped it would keep on raining, for I didn't want Tom to go meddling any more and make us so awful uncomfortable. Well, I got my wish. It drizzled and drizzled along the rest of the night, which wasn't long, though it did seem so; and at daybreak it cleared, and the world looked mighty soft and gray and pretty, and the forests and fields so good to see again, and the horses and cattle standing sober and thinking. Next, the sun come a-blazing up gay and splendid, and then we began to feel rusty and stretchy, and first we knowed we was all asleep.

CHAPTER III. TOM EXPLAINS

WE went to sleep about four o'clock, and woke up about eight. The professor was setting back there at his end, looking glum. He pitched us some breakfast, but he told us not to come abaft the midship compass. That was about the middle of the boat. Well, when you are sharp-set, and you eat and satisfy yourself, everything looks pretty different from what it done before. It makes a body feel pretty near comfortable, even when he is up in a balloon with a genius. We got to talking together.

There was one thing that kept bothering me, and by and by I says:

"Tom, didn't we start east?"

"Yes."

"How fast have we been going?"

"Well, you heard what the professor said when he was raging round. Sometimes, he said, we was making fifty miles an hour, sometimes ninety, sometimes a hundred; said that with a gale to help he could make three hundred any time, and said if he wanted the gale, and wanted it blowing the right direction, he only had to go up higher or down lower to find it."

"Well, then, it's just as I reckoned. The professor lied."

"Why?"

"Because if we was going so fast we ought to be past Illinois, oughtn't we?"

"Certainly."

"Well, we ain't."

"What's the reason we ain't?"

"I know by the color. We're right over Illinois yet. And you can see for yourself that Indiana ain't in sight."

"I wonder what's the matter with you, Huck. You know by the COLOR?"

"Yes, of course I do."

"What's the color got to do with it?"

"It's got everything to do with it. Illinois is green, Indiana is pink. You show me any pink down here, if you can. No, sir; it's green."

"Indiana PINK? Why, what a lie!"

"It ain't no lie; I've seen it on the map, and it's pink."

You never see a person so aggravated and disgusted. He says:

"Well, if I was such a numbskull as you, Huck Finn, I would jump over. Seen it on the map! Huck Finn, did you reckon the States was the same color out-of-doors as they are on the map?"

"Tom Sawyer, what's a map for? Ain't it to learn you facts?"

"Of course."

"Well, then, how's it going to do that if it tells lies? That's what I want to know."

"Shucks, you muggins! It don't tell lies."

"It don't, don't it?"

"No, it don't."

"All right, then; if it don't, there ain't no two States the same color. You git around THAT if you can, Tom Sawyer."

He see I had him, and Jim see it too; and I tell you, I felt pretty good, for Tom Sawyer was always a hard person to git ahead of. Jim slapped his leg and says:

"I tell YOU! dat's smart, dat's right down smart. Ain't no use, Mars Tom; he got you DIS time, sho'!" He slapped his leg again, and says, "My LAN', but it was smart one!"

I never felt so good in my life; and yet I didn't know I was saying anything much till it was out. I was just mooning along, perfectly careless, and not expecting anything was going to happen, and never THINKING of such a thing at all, when, all of a sudden, out it came. Why, it was just as much a surprise to me as it was to any of them. It was just the same way it is when a person is munching along on a hunk of corn-pone, and not thinking about anything, and all of a sudden bites into a di'mond. Now all that HE knows first off is that it's some kind of gravel he's bit into; but he don't find out it's a di'mond till he gits it out and brushes off the sand and crumbs and one thing or another, and has a look at it, and then he's surprised and glad—yes, and proud too; though when you come to look the thing straight in the eye, he ain't entitled to as much credit as he would 'a' been if he'd been HUNTING di'monds. You can see the difference easy if you think it over. You see, an accident, that way, ain't fairly as big a thing as a thing that's done a-purpose. Anybody could find that di'mond in that corn-pone; but mind you, it's got to be somebody that's got THAT KIND OF A CORN-PONE. That's where that feller's credit comes in, you see; and that's where mine comes in. I don't claim no great things—I don't reckon I could 'a' done it again—but I done it that time; that's all I claim. And I hadn't no more idea I could do such a thing, and warn't any more thinking about it or trying to, than you be this minute. Why, I was just as ca'm, a body couldn't be any ca'mer, and yet, all of a sudden, out it come. I've often thought of that time, and I can remember just the way everything looked, same as if it was only last week. I can see it all: beautiful rolling country with woods and fields and lakes for hundreds and hundreds of miles all around, here and there and yonder; and the professor mooning over a chart on his little table, and Tom's cap flopping in the rigging where it was hung up to dry. And one thing in particular was a bird right alongside, not ten foot off, going our way and trying to keep up, but losing ground all the time; and a railroad train doing the same thing down there, sliding among the trees and farms, and pouring out a long cloud of black smoke and now and then a little puff of white; and when the white was gone so long you had almost forgot it, you would hear a little faint toot, and that was the whistle. And we left the bird and the train both behind, 'WAY behind, and done it easy, too.

But Tom he was huffy, and said me and Jim was a couple of ignorant blatherskites, and then he says:

"Suppose there's a brown calf and a big brown dog, and an artist is making a picture of them. What is the MAIN thing that that artist has got to do? He has got to paint them so you can tell them apart the minute you look at them, hain't he? Of course. Well, then, do you want him to go and paint BOTH of them brown? Certainly you don't. He paints one of them blue, and then you can't make no mistake. It's just the same with the maps. That's why they make every State a different color; it ain't to deceive you, it's to keep you from deceiving yourself."

But I couldn't see no argument about that, and neither could Jim. Jim shook his head, and says:

"Why, Mars Tom, if you knowed what chuckle-heads dem painters is, you'd wait a long time before you'd fetch one er DEM in to back up a fac'. I's gwine to tell you, den you kin see for you'self. I see one of 'em a-paintin' away, one day, down in ole Hank Wilson's back lot, en I went down to see, en he was paintin' dat old brindle cow wid de near horn gone—you knows de one I means. En I ast him what he's paintin' her for,

en he say when he git her painted, de picture's wuth a hundred dollars. Mars Tom, he could a got de cow fer fifteen, en I tole him so. Well, sah, if you'll b'lieve me, he jes' shuck his head, dat painter did, en went on a-dobbin'. Bless you, Mars Tom, DEY don't know nothin'."

Tom lost his temper. I notice a person 'most always does that's got laid out in an argument. He told us to shut up, and maybe we'd feel better. Then he see a town clock away off down yonder, and he took up the glass and looked at it, and then looked at his silver turnip, and then at the clock, and then at the turnip again, and says:

"That's funny! That clock's near about an hour fast."

So he put up his turnip. Then he see another clock, and took a look, and it was an hour fast too. That puzzled him.

"That's a mighty curious thing," he says. "I don't understand it."

Then he took the glass and hunted up another clock, and sure enough it was an hour fast too. Then his eyes began to spread and his breath to come out kinder gaspy like, and he says:

"Ger-reat Scott, it's the LONGITUDE!"

I says, considerably scared:

"Well, what's been and gone and happened now?"

"Why, the thing that's happened is that this old bladder has slid over Illinois and Indiana and Ohio like nothing, and this is the east end of Pennsylvania or New York, or somewheres around there."

"Tom Sawyer, you don't mean it!"

"Yes, I do, and it's dead sure. We've covered about fifteen degrees of longitude since we left St. Louis yesterday afternoon, and them clocks are right. We've come close on to eight hundred miles."

I didn't believe it, but it made the cold streaks trickle down my back just the same. In my experience I knowed it wouldn't take much short of two weeks to do it down the Mississippi on a raft. Jim was working his mind and studying. Pretty soon he says:

"Mars Tom, did you say dem clocks uz right?"

"Yes, they're right."

"Ain't yo' watch right, too?"

"She's right for St. Louis, but she's an hour wrong for here."

"Mars Tom, is you tryin' to let on dat de time ain't de SAME everywheres?"

"No, it ain't the same everywheres, by a long shot."

Jim looked distressed, and says:

"It grieves me to hear you talk like dat, Mars Tom; I's right down ashamed to hear you talk like dat, arter de way you's been raised. Yassir, it'd break yo' Aunt Polly's heart to hear you."

Tom was astonished. He looked Jim over wondering, and didn't say nothing, and Jim went on:

"Mars Tom, who put de people out yonder in St. Louis? De Lord done it. Who put de people here whar we is? De Lord done it. Ain' dey bofe his children? 'Cose dey is. WELL, den! is he gwine to SCRIMINATE 'twixt 'em?"

"Scriminate! I never heard such ignorance. There ain't no discriminating about it. When he makes you and some more of his children black, and makes the rest of us white, what do you call that?"

Jim see the p'int. He was stuck. He couldn't answer. Tom says:

"He does discriminate, you see, when he wants to; but this case HERE ain't no discrimination of his, it's man's. The Lord made the day, and he made the night; but he didn't invent the hours, and he didn't distribute them around. Man did that."

"Mars Tom, is dat so? Man done it?"

"Certainly."

"Who tole him he could?"

"Nobody. He never asked."

Jim studied a minute, and says:

"Well, dat do beat me. I wouldn't 'a' tuck no sich resk. But some people ain't scared o' nothin'. Dey bangs right ahead; DEY don't care what happens. So den dey's allays an hour's diff'unce everywhah, Mars Tom?"

"An hour? No! It's four minutes difference for every degree of longitude, you know. Fifteen of 'em's an hour, thirty of 'em's two hours, and so on. When it's one clock Tuesday morning in England, it's eight o'clock the night before in New York."

Jim moved a little way along the locker, and you could see he was insulted. He kept shaking his head and muttering, and so I slid along to him and patted him on the leg, and petted him up, and got him over the worst of his feelings, and then he says:

"Mars Tom talkin' sich talk as dat! Choosday in one place en Monday in t'other, bofe in the same day! Huck, dis ain't no place to joke—up here whah we is. Two days in one day! How you gwine to get two days inter one day? Can't git two hours inter one hour, kin you? Can't git two niggers inter one nigger skin, kin you? Can't git two gallons of whisky inter a one-gallon jug, kin you? No, sir, 'twould strain de jug. Yes, en even den you couldn't, I don't believe. Why, looky here, Huck, s'posen de Choosday was New Year's—now den! is you gwine to tell me it's dis year in one place en las' year in t'other, bofe in de identical same minute? It's de beatenest rubbage! I can't stan' it—I can't stan' to hear tell 'bout it." Then he begun to shiver and turn gray, and Tom says:

"NOW what's the matter? What's the trouble?"

Jim could hardly speak, but he says:

"Mars Tom, you ain't jokin', en it's SO?"

"No, I'm not, and it is so."

Jim shivered again, and says:

"Den dat Monday could be de las' day, en dey wouldn't be no las' day in England, en de dead wouldn't be called. We mustn't go over dah, Mars Tom. Please git him to turn back; I wants to be whah—"

All of a sudden we see something, and all jumped up, and forgot everything and begun to gaze. Tom says:

"Ain't that the—" He catched his breath, then says: "It IS, sure as you live! It's the ocean!"

That made me and Jim catch our breath, too. Then we all stood petrified but happy, for none of us had ever seen an ocean, or ever expected to. Tom kept muttering:

"Atlantic Ocean—Atlantic. Land, don't it sound great! And that's IT—and WE are looking at it—we! Why, it's just too splendid to believe!"

Then we see a big bank of black smoke; and when we got nearer, it was a city—and a monster she was, too, with a thick fringe of ships around one edge; and we wondered if it was New York, and begun to jaw and dispute about it, and, first we knowed, it slid from under us and went flying behind, and here we was, out over the very ocean itself, and going like a cyclone. Then we woke up, I tell you!

We made a break aft and raised a wail, and begun to beg the professor to turn back and land us, but he jerked out his pistol and motioned us back, and we went, but nobody will ever know how bad we felt.

The land was gone, all but a little streak, like a snake, away off on the edge of the water, and down under us was just ocean, ocean, ocean—millions of miles of it, heaving and pitching and squirming, and white sprays blowing from the wave-tops, and only a few ships in sight, wallowing around and laying over, first on one side and then on t'other, and sticking their bows under and then their sterns; and before long there warn't no ships at all, and we had the sky and the whole ocean all to ourselves, and the roomiest place I ever see and the lonesomest.

CHAPTER IV. STORM

AND it got lonesomer and lonesomer. There was the big sky up there, empty and awful deep; and the ocean down there without a thing on it but just the waves. All around us was a ring, where the sky and the water come together; yes, a monstrous big ring it was, and we right in the dead center of it—plumb in the center. We was racing along like a prairie fire, but it never made any difference, we couldn't seem to git past that center no way. I couldn't see that we ever gained an inch on that ring. It made a body feel creepy, it was so curious and unaccountable.

Well, everything was so awful still that we got to talking in a very low voice, and kept on getting creepier and lonesomer and less and less talky, till at last the talk ran dry altogether, and we just set there and "thunk," as Jim calls it, and never said a word the longest time.

The professor never stirred till the sun was overhead, then he stood up and put a kind of triangle to his eye, and Tom said it was a sextant and he was taking the sun to see whereabouts the balloon was. Then he ciphered a little and looked in a book, and then he begun to carry on again. He said lots of wild things, and, among others, he said he would keep up this hundred-mile gait till the middle of to-morrow afternoon, and then he'd land in London.

We said we would be humbly thankful.

He was turning away, but he whirled around when we said that, and give us a long look of his blackest kind—one of the maliciousest and suspiciousest looks I ever see. Then he says:

"You want to leave me. Don't try to deny it."

We didn't know what to say, so we held in and didn't say nothing at all.

He went aft and set down, but he couldn't seem to git that thing out of his mind. Every now and then he would rip out something about it, and try to make us answer him, but we dasn't.

It got lonesomer and lonesomer right along, and it did seem to me I couldn't stand it. It was still worse when night begun to come on. By and by Tom pinched me and whispers:

"Look!"

I took a glance aft, and see the professor taking a whet out of a bottle. I didn't like the looks of that. By and by he took another drink, and pretty soon he begun to sing. It was dark now, and getting black and stormy. He went on singing, wilder and wilder, and the thunder begun to mutter, and the wind to wheeze and moan among the ropes, and altogether it was awful. It got so black we couldn't see him any more, and wished we couldn't hear him, but we could. Then he got still; but he warn't still ten minutes till we got suspicious, and wished he would start up his noise again, so we could tell where he was. By and by there was a flash of lightning, and we see him start to get up, but he staggered and fell down. We heard him scream out in the dark:

"They don't want to go to England. All right, I'll change the course. They want to leave me. I know they do. Well, they shall—and NOW!"

I 'most died when he said that. Then he was still again—still so long I couldn't bear it, and it did seem to me the lightning wouldn't EVER come again. But at last there was a blessed flash, and there he was, on his hands and knees crawling, and not four feet from us. My, but his eyes was terrible! He made a lunge for Tom, and says, "Overboard YOU go!" but it was already pitch-dark again, and I couldn't see whether he got him or not, and Tom didn't make a sound.

There was another long, horrible wait; then there was a flash, and I see Tom's head sink down outside the boat and disappear. He was on the rope-ladder that dangled down in the air from the gunnel. The professor let off a shout and jumped for him, and straight off it was pitch-dark again, and Jim groaned out, "Po' Mars Tom, he's a goner!" and made a jump for the professor, but the professor warn't there.

Then we heard a couple of terrible screams, and then another not so loud, and then another that was 'way below, and you could only JUST hear it; and I heard Jim say, "Po' Mars Tom!"

Then it was awful still, and I reckon a person could 'a' counted four thousand before the next flash come. When it come I see Jim on his knees, with his arms on the locker and his face buried in them, and he was crying. Before I could look over the edge it was all dark again, and I was glad, because I didn't want to see. But when the next flash come, I was watching, and down there I see somebody a-swinging in the wind on the ladder, and it was Tom!

"Come up!" I shouts; "come up, Tom!"

His voice was so weak, and the wind roared so, I couldn't make out what he said, but I thought he asked was the professor up there. I shouts:

"No, he's down in the ocean! Come up! Can we help you?"

Of course, all this in the dark.

"Huck, who is you hollerin' at?"

"I'm hollerin' at Tom."

"Oh, Huck, how kin you act so, when you know po' Mars Tom—" Then he let off an awful scream, and flung his head and his arms back and let off another one, because there was a white glare just then, and he had raised up his face just in time to see Tom's, as white as snow, rise above the gunnel and look him right in the eye. He thought it was Tom's ghost, you see.

Tom clumb aboard, and when Jim found it WAS him, and not his ghost, he hugged him, and called him all sorts of loving names, and carried on like he was gone crazy, he was so glad. Says I:

"What did you wait for, Tom? Why didn't you come up at first?"

"I dasn't, Huck. I knowed somebody plunged down past me, but I didn't know who it was in the dark. It could 'a' been you, it could 'a' been Jim."

That was the way with Tom Sawyer—always sound. He warn't coming up till he knowed where the professor was.

The storm let go about this time with all its might; and it was dreadful the way the thunder boomed and tore, and the lightning glared out, and the wind sung and screamed in the rigging, and the rain come down. One second you couldn't see your hand before you, and the next you could count the threads in your coat-sleeve, and see a whole wide desert of waves pitching and tossing through a kind of veil of rain. A storm like that is the loveliest thing there is, but it ain't at its best when you are up in the sky and lost, and it's wet and lonesome, and there's just been a death in the family.

We set there huddled up in the bow, and talked low about the poor professor; and everybody was sorry for him, and sorry the world had made fun of him and treated him so harsh, when he was doing the best he could, and hadn't a friend nor nobody to encourage him and keep him from brooding his mind away and going deranged. There was plenty of clothes and blankets and everything at the other end, but we thought we'd ruther take the rain than go meddling back there.

CHAPTER V. LAND

WE tried to make some plans, but we couldn't come to no agreement. Me and Jim was for turning around and going back home, but Tom allowed that by the time daylight come, so we could see our way, we would be so far toward England that we might as well go there, and come back in a ship, and have the glory of saying we done it.

About midnight the storm quit and the moon come out and lit up the ocean, and we begun to feel comfortable and drowsy; so we stretched out on the lockers and went to sleep, and never woke up again till sun-up. The sea was sparkling like di'monds, and it was nice weather, and pretty soon our things was all dry again.

We went aft to find some breakfast, and the first thing we noticed was that there was a dim light burning in a compass back there under a hood. Then Tom was disturbed. He says:

"You know what that means, easy enough. It means that somebody has got to stay on watch and steer this thing the same as he would a ship, or she'll wander around and go wherever the wind wants her to."

"Well," I says, "what's she been doing since—er—since we had the accident?"

"Wandering," he says, kinder troubled—"wandering, without any doubt. She's in a wind now that's blowing her south of east. We don't know how long that's been going on, either."

So then he p'inted her east, and said he would hold her there till we rousted out the breakfast. The professor had laid in everything a body could want; he couldn't 'a' been better fixed. There wasn't no milk for the coffee, but there was water, and everything else you could want, and a charcoal stove and the fixings for it, and pipes and cigars and matches; and wine and liquor, which warn't in our line; and books, and maps, and charts, and an accordion; and furs, and blankets, and no end of rubbish, like brass beads and brass jewelry, which Tom said was a sure sign that he had an idea of visiting among savages. There was money, too. Yes, the professor was well enough fixed.

After breakfast Tom learned me and Jim how to steer, and divided us all up into four-hour watches, turn and turn about; and when his watch was out I took his place, and he got out the professor's papers and pens and wrote a letter home to his aunt Polly, telling her everything that had happened to us, and dated it "IN THE WELKIN, APPROACHING ENGLAND," and folded it together and stuck it fast with a red wafer, and directed it, and wrote above the direction, in big writing, "FROM TOM SAWYER, THE ERRONORT," and said it would stump old Nat Parsons, the postmaster, when it come along in the mail. I says:

"Tom Sawyer, this ain't no welkin, it's a balloon."

"Well, now, who SAID it was a welkin, smarty?"

"You've wrote it on the letter, anyway."

"What of it? That don't mean that the balloon's the welkin."

"Oh, I thought it did. Well, then, what is a welkin?"

I see in a minute he was stuck. He raked and scraped around in his mind, but he couldn't find nothing, so he had to say:

"I don't know, and nobody don't know. It's just a word, and it's a mighty good word, too. There ain't many that lays over it. I

don't believe there's ANY that does."

"Shucks!" I says. "But what does it MEAN?—that's the p'int."

"I don't know what it means, I tell you. It's a word that people uses for—for—well, it's ornamental. They don't put ruffles on a shirt to keep a person warm, do they?"

"Course they don't."

"But they put them ON, don't they?"

"Yes."

"All right, then; that letter I wrote is a shirt, and the welkin's the ruffle on it."

I judged that that would gravel Jim, and it did.

"Now, Mars Tom, it ain't no use to talk like dat; en, moreover, it's sinful. You knows a letter ain't no shirt, en dey ain't no ruffles on it, nuther. Dey ain't no place to put 'em on; you can't put em on, and dey wouldn't stay ef you did."

"Oh DO shut up, and wait till something's started that you know something about."

"Why, Mars Tom, sholy you can't mean to say I don't know about shirts, when, goodness knows, I's toted home de washin' ever sence—"

"I tell you, this hasn't got anything to do with shirts. I only—"

"Why, Mars Tom, you said yo'self dat a letter—"

"Do you want to drive me crazy? Keep still. I only used it as a metaphor."

That word kinder bricked us up for a minute. Then Jim says—rather timid, because he see Tom was getting pretty tetchy:

"Mars Tom, what is a metaphor?"

"A metaphor's a—well, it's a—a—a metaphor's an illustration." He see THAT didn't git home, so he tried again. "When I say birds of a feather flocks together, it's a metaphorical way of saying—"

"But dey DON'T, Mars Tom. No, sir, 'deed dey don't. Dey ain't no feathers dat's more alike den a bluebird en a jaybird, but ef you waits till you catches dem birds together, you'll—"

"Oh, give us a rest! You can't get the simplest little thing through your thick skull. Now don't bother me any more."

Jim was satisfied to stop. He was dreadful pleased with himself for catching Tom out. The minute Tom begun to talk about birds I judged he was a goner, because Jim knowed more about birds than both of us put together. You see, he had killed hundreds and hundreds of them, and that's the way to find out about birds. That's the way people does that writes books about birds, and loves them so that they'll go hungry and tired and take any amount of trouble to find a new bird and kill it. Their name is ornithologers, and I could have been an ornithologer myself, because I always loved birds and creatures; and I started out to learn how to be one, and I see a bird setting on a limb of a high tree, singing with its head tilted back and its mouth open, and before I thought I fired, and his song stopped and he fell straight down from the limb, all limp like a rag, and I run and picked him up and he was dead, and his body was warm in my hand, and his head rolled about this way and that, like his neck was broke, and there was a little white skin over his eyes, and one little drop of blood on the side of his head; and, laws! I couldn't see nothing more for the tears; and I hain't never murdered no creature since that warn't doing me no harm, and I ain't going to.

But I was aggravated about that welkin. I wanted to know. I got the subject up again, and then Tom explained, the best he could. He said when a person made a big speech the newspapers said the shouts of the people made the welkin ring. He said they always said that, but none of them ever told what it was, so he allowed it just meant outdoors and up high. Well, that seemed sensible enough, so I was satisfied, and said so. That pleased Tom and put him in a good humor again, and he says:

"Well, it's all right, then; and we'll let bygones be bygones. I don't know for certain what a welkin is, but when we land in London we'll make it ring, anyway, and don't you forget it."

He said an erronort was a person who sailed around in balloons; and said it was a mighty sight finer to be Tom Sawyer the Erronort than to be Tom Sawyer the Traveler, and we would be heard of all round the world, if we pulled through all right, and so he wouldn't give shucks to be a traveler now.

Toward the middle of the afternoon we got everything ready to land, and we felt pretty good, too, and proud; and we kept watching with the glasses, like Columbus discovering America. But we couldn't see nothing but ocean. The afternoon wasted out and the sun shut down, and still there warn't no land anywheres. We wondered what was the matter, but reckoned it would come out all right, so we went on steering east, but went up on a higher level so we wouldn't hit any steeples or mountains in the dark.

It was my watch till midnight, and then it was Jim's; but Tom stayed up, because he said ship captains done that when they was making the land, and didn't stand no regular watch.

Well, when daylight come, Jim give a shout, and we jumped up and looked over, and there was the land sure enough—land all around, as far as you could see, and perfectly level and yaller. We didn't know how long we'd been over it. There warn't no trees, nor hills, nor rocks, nor towns, and Tom and Jim had took it for the sea. They took it for the sea in a dead ca'm; but we was so high up, anyway, that if it had been the sea and rough, it would 'a' looked smooth, all the same, in the night, that way.

We was all in a powerful excitement now, and grabbed the glasses and hunted everywheres for London, but couldn't find hair nor hide of it, nor any other settlement—nor any sign of a lake or a river, either. Tom was clean beat. He said it warn't his notion of England; he thought England looked like America, and always had that idea. So he said we better have breakfast, and then drop down and inquire the quickest way to London. We cut the breakfast pretty short, we was so impatient. As we slanted along down, the weather began to moderate, and pretty soon we shed our furs. But it kept ON moderating, and in a precious little while it was 'most too moderate. We was close down now, and just blistering!

We settled down to within thirty foot of the land—that is, it was land if sand is land; for this wasn't anything but pure

sand. Tom and me clumb down the ladder and took a run to stretch our legs, and it felt amazing good—that is, the stretching did, but the sand scorched our feet like hot embers. Next, we see somebody coming, and started to meet him; but we heard Jim shout, and looked around and he was fairly dancing, and making signs, and yelling. We couldn't make out what he said, but we was scared anyway, and begun to heel it back to the balloon. When we got close enough, we understood the words, and they made me sick:

"Run! Run fo' yo' life! Hit's a lion; I kin see him thoo de glass! Run, boys; do please heel it de bes' you kin. He's bu'sted outen de menagerie, en dey ain't nobody to stop him!"

It made Tom fly, but it took the stiffening all out of my legs. I could only just gasp along the way you do in a dream when there's a ghost gaining on you.

Tom got to the ladder and shinned up it a piece and waited for me; and as soon as I got a foothold on it he shouted to Jim to soar away. But Jim had clean lost his head, and said he had forgot how. So Tom shinned along up and told me to follow; but the lion was arriving, fetching a most ghastly roar with every lope, and my legs shook so I dasn't try to take one of them out of the rounds for fear the other one would give way under me.

But Tom was aboard by this time, and he started the balloon up a little, and stopped it again as soon as the end of the ladder was ten or twelve feet above ground. And there was the lion, a-ripping around under me, and roaring and springing up in the air at the ladder, and only missing it about a quarter of an inch, it seemed to me. It was delicious to be out of his reach, perfectly delicious, and made me feel good and thankful all up one side; but I was hanging there helpless and couldn't climb, and that made me feel perfectly wretched and miserable all down the other. It is most seldom that a person feels so mixed like that; and it is not to be recommended, either.

Tom asked me what he'd better do, but I didn't know. He asked me if I could hold on whilst he sailed away to a safe place and left the lion behind. I said I could if he didn't go no higher than he was now; but if he went higher I would lose my head and fall, sure. So he said, "Take a good grip," and he started.

"Don't go so fast," I shouted. "It makes my head swim."

He had started like a lightning express. He slowed down, and we glided over the sand slower, but still in a kind of sickening way; for it IS uncomfortable to see things sliding and gliding under you like that, and not a sound.

But pretty soon there was plenty of sound, for the lion was catching up. His noise fetched others. You could see them coming on the lope from every direction, and pretty soon there was a couple of dozen of them under me, jumping up at the ladder and snarling and snapping at each other; and so we went skimming along over the sand, and these fellers doing what they could to help us to not forgit the occasion; and then some other beasts come, without an invite, and they started a regular riot down there.

We see this plan was a mistake. We couldn't ever git away from them at this gait, and I couldn't hold on forever. So Tom took a think, and struck another idea. That was, to kill a lion with the pepper-box revolver, and then sail away while the others stopped to fight over the carcass. So he stopped the

Tom Sawyer Abroad 173

balloon still, and done it, and then we sailed off while the fuss was going on, and come down a quarter of a mile off, and they helped me aboard; but by the time we was out of reach again, that gang was on hand once more. And when they see we was really gone and they couldn't get us, they sat down on their hams and looked up at us so kind of disappointed that it was as much as a person could do not to see THEIR side of the matter.

CHAPTER VI. IT'S A CARAVAN

I WAS so weak that the only thing I wanted was a chance to lay down, so I made straight for my locker-bunk, and stretched myself out there. But a body couldn't get back his strength in no such oven as that, so Tom give the command to soar, and Jim started her aloft.

We had to go up a mile before we struck comfortable weather where it was breezy and pleasant and just right, and pretty soon I was all straight again. Tom had been setting quiet and thinking; but now he jumps up and says:

"I bet you a thousand to one I know where we are. We're in the Great Sahara, as sure as guns!"

He was so excited he couldn't hold still; but I wasn't. I says:

"Well, then, where's the Great Sahara? In England or in Scotland?"

"'Tain't in either; it's in Africa."

Jim's eyes bugged out, and he begun to stare down with no end of interest, because that was where his originals come from; but I didn't more than half believe it. I couldn't, you know; it seemed too awful far away for us to have traveled.

But Tom was full of his discovery, as he called it, and said the lions and the sand meant the Great Desert, sure. He said he could 'a' found out, before we sighted land, that we was crowding the land somewheres, if he had thought of one thing; and when we asked him what, he said:

"These clocks. They're chronometers. You always read about them in sea voyages. One of them is keeping Grinnage time, and the other is keeping St. Louis time, like my watch. When we left St. Louis it was four in the afternoon by my watch and this clock, and it was ten at night by this Grinnage clock. Well, at this time of the year the sun sets at about seven o'clock. Now I noticed the time yesterday evening when the sun went down, and it was half-past five o'clock by the Grinnage clock, and half past 11 A.M. by my watch and the other clock. You see, the sun rose and set by my watch in St. Louis, and the Grinnage clock was six hours fast; but we've come so far east that it comes within less than half an hour of setting by the Grinnage clock now, and I'm away out—more than four hours and a half out. You see, that meant that we was closing up on the longitude of Ireland, and would strike it before long if we was p'inted right—which we wasn't. No, sir, we've been a-wandering—wandering 'way down south of east, and it's my opinion we are in Africa. Look at this map. You see how the shoulder of Africa sticks out to the west. Think how fast we've traveled; if we had gone straight east we would be long past England by this time. You watch for noon, all of you, and we'll stand up, and when we can't cast a shadow we'll find that this Grinnage clock is coming mighty close to marking twelve. Yes, sir, I think we're in Africa; and it's just bully."

Jim was gazing down with the glass. He shook his head and says:

"Mars Tom, I reckon dey's a mistake som'er's, hain't seen no niggers yit."

"That's nothing; they don't live in the desert. What is that, 'way off yonder? Gimme a glass."

He took a long look, and said it was like a black string stretched across the sand, but he couldn't guess what it was.

"Well," I says, "I reckon maybe you've got a chance now to find out whereabouts this balloon is, because as like as not that is one of these lines here, that's on the map, that you call meridians of longitude, and we can drop down and look at its number, and—"

"Oh, shucks, Huck Finn, I never see such a lunkhead as you. Did you s'pose there's meridians of longitude on the EARTH?"

"Tom Sawyer, they're set down on the map, and you know it perfectly well, and here they are, and you can see for yourself."

"Of course they're on the map, but that's nothing; there ain't any on the GROUND."

"Tom, do you know that to be so?"

"Certainly I do."

"Well, then, that map's a liar again. I never see such a liar as that map."

He fired up at that, and I was ready for him, and Jim was warming his opinion, too, and next minute we'd 'a' broke loose on another argument, if Tom hadn't dropped the glass and begun to clap his hands like a maniac and sing out:

"Camels!—Camels!"

So I grabbed a glass and Jim, too, and took a look, but I was disappointed, and says:

"Camels your granny; they're spiders."

"Spiders in a desert, you shad? Spiders walking in a procession? You don't ever reflect, Huck Finn, and I reckon you really haven't got anything to reflect WITH. Don't you know we're as much as a mile up in the air, and that that string of crawlers is two or three miles away? Spiders, good land! Spiders as big as a cow? Perhaps you'd like to go down and milk one of 'em. But they're camels, just the same. It's a caravan, that's what it is, and it's a mile long."

"Well, then, let's go down and look at it. I don't believe in it, and ain't going to till I see it and know it."

"All right," he says, and give the command:

"Lower away."

As we come slanting down into the hot weather, we could see that it was camels, sure enough, plodding along, an everlasting string of them, with bales strapped to them, and several hundred men in long white robes, and a thing like a shawl bound over their heads and hanging down with tassels and fringes; and some of the men had long guns and some hadn't, and some was riding and some was walking. And the weather—well, it was just roasting. And how slow they did creep along! We swooped down now, all of a sudden, and stopped about a hundred yards over their heads.

The men all set up a yell, and some of them fell flat on their stomachs, some begun to fire their guns at us, and the rest broke and scampered every which way, and so did the camels.

We see that we was making trouble, so we went up again about a mile, to the cool weather, and watched them from there. It took them an hour to get together and form the procession again; then they started along, but we could see by the glasses that they wasn't paying much attention to anything but us. We poked along, looking down at them with the glasses, and by and by we see a big sand mound, and something like people the other side of it, and there was something like a man laying on top of the mound that raised his head up every now and then, and seemed to be watching the caravan or us, we didn't know which. As the caravan got nearer, he sneaked down on the other side and rushed to the other men and horses—for that is what they was—and we see them mount in a hurry; and next, here they come, like a house afire, some with lances and some with long guns, and all of them yelling the best they could.

They come a-tearing down on to the caravan, and the next minute both sides crashed together and was all mixed up, and there was such another popping of guns as you never heard, and the air got so full of smoke you could only catch glimpses of them struggling together. There must 'a' been six hundred men in that battle, and it was terrible to see. Then they broke up into gangs and groups, fighting tooth and nail, and scurrying and scampering around, and laying into each other like everything; and whenever the smoke cleared a little you could see dead and wounded people and camels scattered far and wide and all about, and camels racing off in every direction.

At last the robbers see they couldn't win, so their chief sounded a signal, and all that was left of them broke away and went scampering across the plain. The last man to go snatched up a child and carried it off in front of him on his horse, and a woman run screaming and begging after him, and followed him away off across the plain till she was separated a long ways from her people; but it warn't no use, and she had to give it up, and we see her sink down on the sand and cover her face with her hands. Then Tom took the hellum, and started for that yahoo, and we come a-whizzing down and made a swoop, and knocked him out of the saddle, child and all; and he was jarred considerable, but the child wasn't hurt, but laid there working its hands and legs in the air like a tumble-bug that's on its back and can't turn over. The man went staggering off to overtake his horse, and didn't know what had hit him, for we was three or four hundred yards up in the air by this time.

We judged the woman would go and get the child now; but she didn't. We could see her, through the glass, still setting there, with her head bowed down on her knees; so of course she hadn't seen the performance, and thought her child was clean gone with the man. She was nearly a half a mile from her people, so we thought we might go down to the child, which was about a quarter of a mile beyond her, and snake it to her before the caravan people could git to us to do us any harm; and besides, we reckoned they had enough business on their hands for one while, anyway, with the wounded. We thought we'd chance it, and we did. We swooped down and stopped, and Jim shinned down the ladder and fetched up the kid,

which was a nice fat little thing, and in a noble good humor, too, considering it was just out of a battle and been tumbled off of a horse; and then we started for the mother, and stopped back of her and tolerable near by, and Jim slipped down and crept up easy, and when he was close back of her the child goo-goo'd, the way a child does, and she heard it, and whirled and fetched a shriek of joy, and made a jump for the kid and snatched it and hugged it, and dropped it and hugged Jim, and then snatched off a gold chain and hung it around Jim's neck, and hugged him again, and jerked up the child again, a-sobbing and glorifying all the time; and Jim he shoved for the ladder and up it, and in a minute we was back up in the sky and the woman was staring up, with the back of her head between her shoulders and the child with its arms locked around her neck. And there she stood, as long as we was in sight a-sailing away in the sky.

CHAPTER VII. TOM RESPECTS THE FLEA

"NOON!" says Tom, and so it was. His shadder was just a blot around his feet. We looked, and the Grinnage clock was so close to twelve the difference didn't amount to nothing. So Tom said London was right north of us or right south of us, one or t'other, and he reckoned by the weather and the sand and the camels it was north; and a good many miles north, too; as many as from New York to the city of Mexico, he guessed.

Jim said he reckoned a balloon was a good deal the fastest thing in the world, unless it might be some kinds of birds—a wild pigeon, maybe, or a railroad.

But Tom said he had read about railroads in England going nearly a hundred miles an hour for a little ways, and there never was a bird in the world that could do that—except one, and that was a flea.

"A flea? Why, Mars Tom, in de fust place he ain't a bird, strickly speakin'—"

"He ain't a bird, eh? Well, then, what is he?"

"I don't rightly know, Mars Tom, but I speck he's only jist a' animal. No, I reckon dat won't do, nuther, he ain't big enough for a' animal. He mus' be a bug. Yassir, dat's what he is, he's a bug."

"I bet he ain't, but let it go. What's your second place?"

"Well, in de second place, birds is creturs dat goes a long ways, but a flea don't."

"He don't, don't he? Come, now, what IS a long distance, if you know?"

"Why, it's miles, and lots of 'em—anybody knows dat."

"Can't a man walk miles?"

"Yassir, he kin."

"As many as a railroad?"

"Yassir, if you give him time."

"Can't a flea?"

"Well—I s'pose so—ef you gives him heaps of time."

"Now you begin to see, don't you, that DISTANCE ain't the thing to judge by, at all; it's the time it takes to go the distance IN that COUNTS, ain't it?"

"Well, hit do look sorter so, but I wouldn't 'a' b'lieved it, Mars Tom."

"It's a matter of PROPORTION, that's what it is; and when you come to gauge a thing's speed by its size, where's your bird and your man and your railroad, alongside of a flea? The fastest man can't run more than about ten miles in an hour—not much over ten thousand times his own length. But all the books says any common ordinary third-class flea can jump a hundred and fifty times his own length; yes, and he can make five jumps a second too—seven hundred and fifty times his own length, in one little second—for he don't fool away any time stopping and starting—he does them both at the same time; you'll see, if you try to put your finger on him. Now that's a common, ordinary, third-class flea's gait; but you take an Eyetalian FIRST-class, that's been the pet of the nobility all his life, and hasn't ever knowed what want or sickness or exposure was, and he can jump more than three hundred times his own length, and keep it up all day, five such jumps every second, which is fifteen hundred times his own length. Well, suppose a man could go fifteen hundred times his own length in a second—say, a mile and a half. It's ninety miles a minute; it's considerable more than five thousand miles an hour. Where's your man NOW?—yes, and your bird, and your railroad, and your balloon? Laws, they don't amount to shucks 'longside of a flea. A flea is just a comet b'iled down small."

Jim was a good deal astonished, and so was I. Jim said:

"Is dem figgers jist edjackly true, en no jokin' en no lies, Mars Tom?"

"Yes, they are; they're perfectly true."

"Well, den, honey, a body's got to respec' a flea. I ain't had no respec' for um befo', sca'sely, but dey ain't no gittin' roun' it, dey do deserve it, dat's certain."

"Well, I bet they do. They've got ever so much more sense, and brains, and brightness, in proportion to their size, than any other cretur in the world. A person can learn them 'most anything; and they learn it quicker than any other cretur, too. They've been learnt to haul little carriages in harness, and go this way and that way and t'other way according to their orders; yes, and to march and drill like soldiers, doing it as exact, according to orders, as soldiers does it. They've been learnt to do all sorts of hard and troublesome things. S'pose you could cultivate a flea up to the size of a man, and keep his natural smartness a-growing and a-growing right along up, bigger and bigger, and keener and keener, in the same proportion—where'd the human race be, do you reckon? That flea would be President of the United States, and you couldn't any more prevent it than you can prevent lightning."

"My lan', Mars Tom, I never knowed dey was so much TO de beas'. No, sir, I never had no idea of it, and dat's de fac'."

"There's more to him, by a long sight, than there is to any other cretur, man or beast, in proportion to size. He's the interestingest of them all. People have so much to say about an ant's strength, and an elephant's, and a locomotive's. Shucks, they don't begin with a flea. He can lift two or three hundred times his own weight. And none of them can come anywhere

near it. And, moreover, he has got notions of his own, and is very particular, and you can't fool him; his instinct, or his judgment, or whatever it is, is perfectly sound and clear, and don't ever make a mistake. People think all humans are alike to a flea. It ain't so. There's folks that he won't go near, hungry or not hungry, and I'm one of them. I've never had one of them on me in my life."

"Mars Tom!"

"It's so; I ain't joking."

"Well, sah, I hain't ever heard de likes o' dat befo'." Jim couldn't believe it, and I couldn't; so we had to drop down to the sand and git a supply and see. Tom was right. They went for me and Jim by the thousand, but not a one of them lit on Tom. There warn't no explaining it, but there it was and there warn't no getting around it. He said it had always been just so, and he'd just as soon be where there was a million of them as not; they'd never touch him nor bother him.

We went up to the cold weather to freeze 'em out, and stayed a little spell, and then come back to the comfortable weather and went lazying along twenty or twenty-five miles an hour, the way we'd been doing for the last few hours. The reason was, that the longer we was in that solemn, peaceful desert, the more the hurry and fuss got kind of soothed down in us, and the more happier and contented and satisfied we got to feeling, and the more we got to liking the desert, and then loving it. So we had cramped the speed down, as I was saying, and was having a most noble good lazy time, sometimes watching through the glasses, sometimes stretched out on the lockers reading, sometimes taking a nap.

It didn't seem like we was the same lot that was in such a state to find land and git ashore, but it was. But we had got over that—clean over it. We was used to the balloon now and not afraid any more, and didn't want to be anywheres else. Why, it seemed just like home; it 'most seemed as if I had been born and raised in it, and Jim and Tom said the same. And always I had had hateful people around me, a-nagging at me, and pestering of me, and scolding, and finding fault, and fussing and bothering, and sticking to me, and keeping after me, and making me do this, and making me do that and t'other, and always selecting out the things I didn't want to do, and then giving me Sam Hill because I shirked and done something else, and just aggravating the life out of a body all the time; but up here in the sky it was so still and sunshiny and lovely, and plenty to eat, and plenty of sleep, and strange things to see, and no nagging and no pestering, and no good people, and just holiday all the time. Land, I warn't in no hurry to git out and buck at civilization again. Now, one of the worst things about civilization is, that anybody that gits a letter with trouble in it comes and tells you all about it and makes you feel bad, and the newspapers fetches you the troubles of everybody all over the world, and keeps you downhearted and dismal 'most all the time, and it's such a heavy load for a person. I hate them newspapers; and I hate letters; and if I had my way I wouldn't allow nobody to load his troubles on to other folks he ain't acquainted with, on t'other side of the world, that way. Well, up in a balloon there ain't any of that, and it's the darlingest place there is.

We had supper, and that night was one of the prettiest nights I ever see. The moon made it just like daylight, only a heap softer; and once we see a lion standing all alone by himself, just all alone on the earth, it seemed like, and his shadder laid on the sand by him like a puddle of ink. That's the kind of moonlight to have.

Mainly we laid on our backs and talked; we didn't want to go to sleep. Tom said we was right in the midst of the Arabian Nights now. He said it was right along here that one of the cutest things in that book happened; so we looked down and watched while he told about it, because there ain't anything that is so interesting to look at as a place that a book has talked about. It was a tale about a camel-driver that had lost his camel, and he come along in the desert and met a man, and says:

"Have you run across a stray camel to-day?"

And the man says:

"Was he blind in his left eye?"

"Yes."

"Had he lost an upper front tooth?"

"Yes."

"Was his off hind leg lame?"

"Yes."

"Was he loaded with millet-seed on one side and honey on the other?"

"Yes, but you needn't go into no more details—that's the one, and I'm in a hurry. Where did you see him?"

"I hain't seen him at all," the man says.

"Hain't seen him at all? How can you describe him so close, then?"

"Because when a person knows how to use his eyes, everything has got a meaning to it; but most people's eyes ain't any good to them. I knowed a camel had been along, because I seen his track. I knowed he was lame in his off hind leg because he had favored that foot and trod light on it, and his track showed it. I knowed he was blind on his left side because he only nibbled the grass on the right side of the trail. I knowed he had lost an upper front tooth because where he bit into the sod his teeth-print showed it. The millet-seed sifted out on one side—the ants told me that; the honey leaked out on the other—the flies told me that. I know all about your camel, but I hain't seen him."

Jim says:

"Go on, Mars Tom, hit's a mighty good tale, and powerful interestin'."

"That's all," Tom says.

"ALL?" says Jim, astonished. "What 'come o' de camel?"

"I don't know."

"Mars Tom, don't de tale say?"

"No."

Jim puzzled a minute, then he says:

"Well! Ef dat ain't de beatenes' tale ever I struck. Jist gits to de place whah de intrust is gittin' red-hot, en down she breaks. Why, Mars Tom, dey ain't no SENSE in a tale dat acts like dat. Hain't you got no IDEA whether de man got de camel back er not?"

"No, I haven't."

I see myself there warn't no sense in the tale, to chop square off that way before it come to anything, but I warn't going to say so, because I could see Tom was souring up pretty fast over the way it flatted out and the way Jim had popped on to the weak place in it, and I don't think it's fair for everybody to pile on to a feller when he's down. But Tom he whirls on me and says:

"What do YOU think of the tale?"

Of course, then, I had to come out and make a clean breast and say it did seem to me, too, same as it did to Jim, that as long as the tale stopped square in the middle and never got to no place, it really warn't worth the trouble of telling.

Tom's chin dropped on his breast, and 'stead of being mad, as I reckoned he'd be, to hear me scoff at his tale that way, he seemed to be only sad; and he says:

"Some people can see, and some can't—just as that man said. Let alone a camel, if a cyclone had gone by, YOU duffers wouldn't 'a' noticed the track."

I don't know what he meant by that, and he didn't say; it was just one of his irrulevances, I reckon—he was full of them, sometimes, when he was in a close place and couldn't see no other way out—but I didn't mind. We'd spotted the soft place in that tale sharp enough, he couldn't git away from that little fact. It graveled him like the nation, too, I reckon, much as he tried not to let on.

CHAPTER VIII. THE DISAPPEARING LAKE

WE had an early breakfast in the morning, and set looking down on the desert, and the weather was ever so bammy and lovely, although we warn't high up. You have to come down lower and lower after sundown in the desert, because it cools off so fast; and so, by the time it is getting toward dawn, you are skimming along only a little ways above the sand.

We was watching the shadder of the balloon slide along the ground, and now and then gazing off across the desert to see if anything was stirring, and then down on the shadder again, when all of a sudden almost right under us we see a lot of men and camels laying scattered about, perfectly quiet, like they was asleep.

We shut off the power, and backed up and stood over them, and then we see that they was all dead. It give us the cold shivers. And it made us hush down, too, and talk low, like people at a funeral. We dropped down slow and stopped, and me and Tom clumb down and went among them. There was men, and women, and children. They was dried by the sun and dark and shriveled and leathery, like the pictures of mummies you see in books. And yet they looked just as human, you wouldn't 'a' believed it; just like they was asleep.

Some of the people and animals was partly covered with sand, but most of them not, for the sand was thin there, and the bed was gravel and hard. Most of the clothes had rotted away; and when you took hold of a rag, it tore with a touch, like spiderweb. Tom reckoned they had been laying there for years.

Some of the men had rusty guns by them, some had swords on and had shawl belts with long, silver-mounted pistols stuck in them. All the camels had their loads on yet, but the packs had busted or rotted and spilt the freight out on the ground. We didn't reckon the swords was any good to the dead people any more, so we took one apiece, and some pistols. We took a small box, too, because it was so handsome and inlaid so fine; and then we wanted to bury the people; but there warn't no way to do it that we could think of, and nothing to do it with but sand, and that would blow away again, of course.

Then we mounted high and sailed away, and pretty soon that black spot on the sand was out of sight, and we wouldn't ever see them poor people again in this world. We wondered, and reasoned, and tried to guess how they come to be there, and how it all happened to them, but we couldn't make it out. First we thought maybe they got lost, and wandered around and about till their food and water give out and they starved to death; but Tom said no wild animals nor vultures hadn't meddled with them, and so that guess wouldn't do. So at last we give it up, and judged we wouldn't think about it no more, because it made us low-spirited.

Then we opened the box, and it had gems and jewels in it, quite a pile, and some little veils of the kind the dead women had on, with fringes made out of curious gold money that we warn't acquainted with. We wondered if we better go and try to find them again and give it back; but Tom thought it over and said no, it was a country that was full of robbers, and they would come and steal it; and then the sin would be on us for putting the temptation in their way. So we went on; but I wished we had took all they had, so there wouldn't 'a' been no temptation at all left.

We had had two hours of that blazing weather down there, and was dreadful thirsty when we got aboard again. We went straight for the water, but it was spoiled and bitter, besides being pretty near hot enough to scald your mouth. We couldn't drink it. It was Mississippi river water, the best in the world, and we stirred up the mud in it to see if that would help, but no, the mud wasn't any better than the water. Well, we hadn't been so very, very thirsty before, while we was interested in the lost people, but we was now, and as soon as we found we couldn't have a drink, we was more than thirty-five times as thirsty as we was a quarter of a minute before. Why, in a little while we wanted to hold our mouths open and pant like a dog.

Tom said to keep a sharp lookout, all around, everywheres, because we'd got to find an oasis or there warn't no telling what would happen. So we done it. We kept the glasses gliding around all the time, till our arms got so tired we couldn't hold them any more. Two hours—three hours—just gazing and gazing, and nothing but sand, sand, SAND, and you could see the quivering heat-shimmer playing over it. Dear, dear, a body don't know what real misery is till he is thirsty all the way through and is certain he ain't ever going to come to any water any more. At last I couldn't stand it to look around on them baking plains; I laid down on the locker, and give it up.

But by and by Tom raised a whoop, and there she was! A lake, wide and shiny, with pa'm-trees leaning over it asleep, and their shadders in the water just as soft and delicate as ever you see. I never see anything look so good. It was a long ways off, but that warn't anything to us; we just slapped on a hundred-

mile gait, and calculated to be there in seven minutes; but she stayed the same old distance away, all the time; we couldn't seem to gain on her; yes, sir, just as far, and shiny, and like a dream; but we couldn't get no nearer; and at last, all of a sudden, she was gone!

Tom's eyes took a spread, and he says:

"Boys, it was a MYridge!" Said it like he was glad. I didn't see nothing to be glad about. I says:

"Maybe. I don't care nothing about its name, the thing I want to know is, what's become of it?"

Jim was trembling all over, and so scared he couldn't speak, but he wanted to ask that question himself if he could 'a' done it. Tom says:

"What's BECOME of it? Why, you see yourself it's gone."

"Yes, I know; but where's it gone TO?"

He looked me over and says:

"Well, now, Huck Finn, where WOULD it go to! Don't you know what a myridge is?"

"No, I don't. What is it?"

"It ain't anything but imagination. There ain't anything TO it."

It warmed me up a little to hear him talk like that, and I says:

"What's the use you talking that kind of stuff, Tom Sawyer? Didn't I see the lake?"

"Yes—you think you did."

"I don't think nothing about it, I DID see it."

"I tell you you DIDN'T see it either—because it warn't there to see."

It astonished Jim to hear him talk so, and he broke in and says, kind of pleading and distressed:

"Mars Tom, PLEASE don't say sich things in sich an awful time as dis. You ain't only reskin' yo' own self, but you's reskin' us—same way like Anna Nias en Siffra. De lake WUZ dah—I seen it jis' as plain as I sees you en Huck dis minute."

I says:

"Why, he seen it himself! He was the very one that seen it first. NOW, then!"

"Yes, Mars Tom, hit's so—you can't deny it. We all seen it, en dat PROVE it was dah."

"Proves it! How does it prove it?"

"Same way it does in de courts en everywheres, Mars Tom. One pusson might be drunk, or dreamy or suthin', en he could be mistaken; en two might, maybe; but I tell you, sah, when three sees a thing, drunk er sober, it's SO. Dey ain't no gittin' aroun' dat, en you knows it, Mars Tom."

"I don't know nothing of the kind. There used to be forty

thousand million people that seen the sun move from one side of the sky to the other every day. Did that prove that the sun DONE it?"

"Course it did. En besides, dey warn't no 'casion to prove it. A body 'at's got any sense ain't gwine to doubt it. Dah she is now—a sailin' thoo de sky, like she allays done."

Tom turned on me, then, and says:

"What do YOU say—is the sun standing still?"

"Tom Sawyer, what's the use to ask such a jackass question? Anybody that ain't blind can see it don't stand still."

"Well," he says, "I'm lost in the sky with no company but a passel of low-down animals that don't know no more than the head boss of a university did three or four hundred years ago."

It warn't fair play, and I let him know it. I says:

"Throwin' mud ain't arguin', Tom Sawyer."

"Oh, my goodness, oh, my goodness gracious, dah's de lake agi'n!" yelled Jim, just then. "NOW, Mars Tom, what you gwine to say?"

Yes, sir, there was the lake again, away yonder across the desert, perfectly plain, trees and all, just the same as it was before. I says:

"I reckon you're satisfied now, Tom Sawyer."

But he says, perfectly ca'm:

"Yes, satisfied there ain't no lake there."

Jim says:

"DON'T talk so, Mars Tom—it sk'yers me to hear you. It's so hot, en you's so thirsty, dat you ain't in yo' right mine, Mars Tom. Oh, but don't she look good! 'clah I doan' know how I's gwine to wait tell we gits dah, I's SO thirsty."

"Well, you'll have to wait; and it won't do you no good, either, because there ain't no lake there, I tell you."

I says:

"Jim, don't you take your eye off of it, and I won't, either."

"'Deed I won't; en bless you, honey, I couldn't ef I wanted to."

We went a-tearing along toward it, piling the miles behind us like nothing, but never gaining an inch on it—and all of a sudden it was gone again! Jim staggered, and 'most fell down. When he got his breath he says, gasping like a fish:

"Mars Tom, hit's a GHOS', dat's what it is, en I hopes to goodness we ain't gwine to see it no mo'. Dey's BEEN a lake, en suthin's happened, en de lake's dead, en we's seen its ghos'; we's seen it twiste, en dat's proof. De desert's ha'nted, it's ha'nted, sho; oh, Mars Tom, le''s git outen it; I'd ruther die den have de night ketch us in it ag'in en de ghos' er dat lake come a-mournin' aroun' us en we asleep en doan' know de danger we's in."

"Ghost, you gander! It ain't anything but air and heat and thirstiness pasted together by a person's imagination. If I— gimme the glass!"

He grabbed it and begun to gaze off to the right.

"It's a flock of birds," he says. "It's getting toward sundown, and they're making a bee-line across our track for somewheres. They mean business—maybe they're going for food or water, or both. Let her go to starboard!—Port your hellum! Hard down! There—ease up—steady, as you go."

We shut down some of the power, so as not to outspeed them, and took out after them. We went skimming along a quarter of a mile behind them, and when we had followed them an hour and a half and was getting pretty discouraged, and was thirsty clean to unendurableness, Tom says:

"Take the glass, one of you, and see what that is, away ahead of the birds."

Jim got the first glimpse, and slumped down on the locker sick. He was most crying, and says:

"She's dah ag'in, Mars Tom, she's dah ag'in, en I knows I's gwine to die, 'case when a body sees a ghos' de third time, dat's what it means. I wisht I'd never come in dis balloon, dat I does."

He wouldn't look no more, and what he said made me afraid, too, because I knowed it was true, for that has always been the way with ghosts; so then I wouldn't look any more, either. Both of us begged Tom to turn off and go some other way, but he wouldn't, and said we was ignorant superstitious blatherskites. Yes, and he'll git come up with, one of these days, I says to myself, insulting ghosts that way. They'll stand it for a while, maybe, but they won't stand it always, for anybody that knows about ghosts knows how easy they are hurt, and how revengeful they are.

So we was all quiet and still, Jim and me being scared, and Tom busy. By and by Tom fetched the balloon to a standstill, and says:

"NOW get up and look, you sapheads."

We done it, and there was the sure-enough water right under us!—clear, and blue, and cool, and deep, and wavy with the breeze, the loveliest sight that ever was. And all about it was grassy banks, and flowers, and shady groves of big trees, looped together with vines, and all looking so peaceful and comfortable—enough to make a body cry, it was so beautiful.

Jim DID cry, and rip and dance and carry on, he was so thankful and out of his mind for joy. It was my watch, so I had to stay by the works, but Tom and Jim clumb down and drunk a barrel apiece, and fetched me up a lot, and I've tasted a many a good thing in my life, but nothing that ever begun with that water.

Then we went down and had a swim, and then Tom came up and spelled me, and me and Jim had a swim, and then Jim spelled Tom, and me and Tom had a foot-race and a boxing-mill, and I don't reckon I ever had such a good time in my life. It warn't so very hot, because it was close on to evening, and we hadn't any clothes on, anyway. Clothes is well enough in school, and in towns, and at balls, too, but there ain't no sense in them when there ain't no civilization nor other kinds of bothers and fussiness around.

"Lions a-comin'!—lions! Quick, Mars Tom! Jump for yo' life, Huck!"

Oh, and didn't we! We never stopped for clothes, but waltzed up the ladder just so. Jim lost his head straight off—he always done it whenever he got excited and scared; and so now, 'stead of just easing the ladder up from the ground a little, so the animals couldn't reach it, he turned on a raft of power, and we went whizzing up and was dangling in the sky before he got his wits together and seen what a foolish thing he was doing. Then he stopped her, but he had clean forgot what to do next; so there we was, so high that the lions looked like pups, and we was drifting off on the wind.

But Tom he shinned up and went for the works and begun to slant her down, and back toward the lake, where the animals was gathering like a camp-meeting, and I judged he had lost HIS head, too; for he knowed I was too scared to climb, and did he want to dump me among the tigers and things?

But no, his head was level, he knowed what he was about. He swooped down to within thirty or forty feet of the lake, and stopped right over the center, and sung out:

"Leggo, and drop!"

I done it, and shot down, feet first, and seemed to go about a mile toward the bottom; and when I come up, he says:

"Now lay on your back and float till you're rested and got your pluck back, then I'll dip the ladder in the water and you can climb aboard."

I done it. Now that was ever so smart in Tom, because if he had started off somewheres else to drop down on the sand, the menagerie would 'a' come along, too, and might 'a' kept us hunting a safe place till I got tuckered out and fell.

And all this time the lions and tigers was sorting out the clothes, and trying to divide them up so there would be some for all, but there was a misunderstanding about it somewheres, on account of some of them trying to hog more than their share; so there was another insurrection, and you never see anything like it in the world. There must 'a' been fifty of them, all mixed up together, snorting and roaring and snapping and biting and tearing, legs and tails in the air, and you couldn't tell which was which, and the sand and fur a-flying. And when they got done, some was dead and some was limping off crippled, and the rest was setting around on the battlefield, some of them licking their sore places and the others looking up at us and seemed to be kind of inviting us to come down and have some fun, but which we didn't want any.

As for the clothes, they warn't any, any more. Every last rag of them was inside of the animals; and not agreeing with them very well, I don't reckon, for there was considerable many brass buttons on them, and there was knives in the pockets, too, and smoking tobacco, and nails and chalk and marbles and fishhooks and things. But I wasn't caring. All that was bothering me was, that all we had now was the professor's clothes, a big enough assortment, but not suitable to go into company with, if we came across any, because the britches was as long as tunnels, and the coats and things according. Still, there was everything a tailor needed, and Jim was a kind of jack legged tailor, and he allowed he could soon trim a suit or two down for us that would answer.

CHAPTER IX. TOM DISCOURSES ON THE DESERT

STILL, we thought we would drop down there a minute, but on another errand. Most of the professor's cargo of food was put up in cans, in the new way that somebody had just invented; the rest was fresh. When you fetch Missouri beefsteak to the Great Sahara, you want to be particular and stay up in the coolish weather. So we reckoned we would drop down into the lion market and see how we could make out there.

We hauled in the ladder and dropped down till we was just above the reach of the animals, then we let down a rope with a slip-knot in it and hauled up a dead lion, a small tender one, then yanked up a cub tiger. We had to keep the congregation off with the revolver, or they would 'a' took a hand in the proceedings and helped.

We carved off a supply from both, and saved the skins, and hove the rest overboard. Then we baited some of the professor's hooks with the fresh meat and went a-fishing. We stood over the lake just a convenient distance above the water, and catched a lot of the nicest fish you ever see. It was a most amazing good supper we had; lion steak, tiger steak, fried fish, and hot corn-pone. I don't want nothing better than that.

We had some fruit to finish off with. We got it out of the top of a monstrous tall tree. It was a very slim tree that hadn't a branch on it from the bottom plumb to the top, and there it bursted out like a feather-duster. It was a pa'm-tree, of course; anybody knows a pa'm-tree the minute he see it, by the pictures. We went for cocoanuts in this one, but there warn't none. There was only big loose bunches of things like oversized grapes, and Tom allowed they was dates, because he said they answered the description in the Arabian Nights and the other books. Of course they mightn't be, and they might be poison; so we had to wait a spell, and watch and see if the birds et them. They done it; so we done it, too, and they was most amazing good.

By this time monstrous big birds begun to come and settle on the dead animals. They was plucky creturs; they would tackle one end of a lion that was being gnawed at the other end by another lion. If the lion drove the bird away, it didn't do no good; he was back again the minute the lion was busy.

The big birds come out of every part of the sky—you could make them out with the glass while they was still so far away you couldn't see them with your naked eye. Tom said the birds didn't find out the meat was there by the smell; they had to find it out by seeing it. Oh, but ain't that an eye for you! Tom said at the distance of five mile a patch of dead lions couldn't look any bigger than a person's finger-nail, and he couldn't imagine how the birds could notice such a little thing so far off.

It was strange and unnatural to see lion eat lion, and we thought maybe they warn't kin. But Jim said that didn't make no difference. He said a hog was fond of her own children, and so was a spider, and he reckoned maybe a lion was pretty near as unprincipled though maybe not quite. He thought likely a lion wouldn't eat his own father, if he knowed which was him, but reckoned he would eat his brother-in-law if he was uncommon hungry, and eat his mother-in-law any time. But RECKONING don't settle nothing. You can reckon till the cows come home, but that don't fetch you to no decision. So we give it up and let it drop.

Generly it was very still in the Desert nights, but this time there was music. A lot of other animals come to dinner; sneaking yelpers that Tom allowed was jackals, and roached-backed ones that he said was hyenas; and all the whole biling of them kept up a racket all the time. They made a picture in the moonlight that was more different than any picture I ever see. We had a line out and made fast to the top of a tree, and didn't stand no watch, but all turned in and slept; but I was up two or three times to look down at the animals and hear the music. It was like having a front seat at a menagerie for nothing, which I hadn't ever had before, and so it seemed foolish to sleep and not make the most of it; I mightn't ever have such a chance again.

We went a-fishing again in the early dawn, and then lazied around all day in the deep shade on an island, taking turn about to watch and see that none of the animals come a-snooping around there after erronorts for dinner. We was going to leave the next day, but couldn't, it was too lovely.

The day after, when we rose up toward the sky and sailed off eastward, we looked back and watched that place till it warn't nothing but just a speck in the Desert, and I tell you it was like saying good-bye to a friend that you ain't ever going to see any more.

Jim was thinking to himself, and at last he says:

"Mars Tom, we's mos' to de end er de Desert now, I speck."

"Why?"

"Well, hit stan' to reason we is. You knows how long we's been a-skimmin' over it. Mus' be mos' out o' san'. Hit's a wonder to me dat it's hilt out as long as it has."

"Shucks, there's plenty sand, you needn't worry."

"Oh, I ain't a-worryin', Mars Tom, only wonderin', dat's all. De Lord's got plenty san', I ain't doubtin' dat; but nemmine, He ain't gwyne to WAS'E it jist on dat account; en I allows dat dis Desert's plenty big enough now, jist de way she is, en you can't spread her out no mo' 'dout was'in' san'."

"Oh, go 'long! we ain't much more than fairly STARTED across this Desert yet. The United States is a pretty big country, ain't it? Ain't it, Huck?"

"Yes," I says, "there ain't no bigger one, I don't reckon."

"Well," he says, "this Desert is about the shape of the United States, and if you was to lay it down on top of the United States, it would cover the land of the free out of sight like a blanket. There'd be a little corner sticking out, up at Maine and away up northwest, and Florida sticking out like a turtle's tail, and that's all. We've took California away from the Mexicans two or three years ago, so that part of the Pacific coast is ours now, and if you laid the Great Sahara down with her edge on the Pacific, she would cover the United States and stick out past New York six hundred miles into the Atlantic ocean."

I say:

"Good land! have you got the documents for that, Tom Sawyer?"

"Yes, and they're right here, and I've been studying them. You can look for yourself. From New York to the Pacific is 2,600 miles. From one end of the Great Desert to the other is 3,200. The United States contains 3,600,000 square miles, the Desert contains 4,162,000. With the Desert's bulk you could cover up every last inch of the United States, and in under where the edges projected out, you could tuck England, Scotland, Ireland, France, Denmark, and all Germany. Yes, sir, you could hide the home of the brave and all of them countries clean out of sight under the Great Sahara, and you would still have 2,000 square miles of sand left."

"Well," I says, "it clean beats me. Why, Tom, it shows that the Lord took as much pains makin' this Desert as makin' the United States and all them other countries."

Jim says: "Huck, dat don' stan' to reason. I reckon dis Desert wa'n't made at all. Now you take en look at it like dis—you look at it, and see ef I's right. What's a desert good for? 'Taint good for nuthin'. Dey ain't no way to make it pay. Hain't dat so, Huck?"

"Yes, I reckon."

"Hain't it so, Mars Tom?"

"I guess so. Go on."

"Ef a thing ain't no good, it's made in vain, ain't it?"

"Yes."

"NOW, den! Do de Lord make anything in vain? You answer me dat."

"Well—no, He don't."

"Den how come He make a desert?"

"Well, go on. How DID He come to make it?"

"Mars Tom, I b'lieve it uz jes like when you's buildin' a house; dey's allays a lot o' truck en rubbish lef' over. What does you do wid it? Doan' you take en k'yart it off en dump it into a ole vacant back lot? 'Course. Now, den, it's my opinion hit was jes like dat—dat de Great Sahara warn't made at all, she jes HAPPEN'."

I said it was a real good argument, and I believed it was the best one Jim ever made. Tom he said the same, but said the trouble about arguments is, they ain't nothing but THEORIES, after all, and theories don't prove nothing, they only give you a place to rest on, a spell, when you are tuckered out butting around and around trying to find out something there ain't no way TO find out. And he says:

"There's another trouble about theories: there's always a hole in them somewheres, sure, if you look close enough. It's just so with this one of Jim's. Look what billions and billions of stars there is. How does it come that there was just exactly enough star-stuff, and none left over? How does it come there ain't no sand-pile up there?"

But Jim was fixed for him and says:

"What's de Milky Way?—dat's what I want to know. What's de Milky Way? Answer me dat!"

In my opinion it was just a sockdologer. It's only an opinion, it's only MY opinion and others may think different; but I said it then and I stand to it now—it was a sockdologer. And moreover, besides, it landed Tom Sawyer. He couldn't say a word. He had that stunned look of a person that's been shot in the back with a kag of nails. All he said was, as for people like me and Jim, he'd just as soon have intellectual intercourse with a catfish. But anybody can say that—and I notice they always do, when somebody has fetched them a lifter. Tom Sawyer was tired of that end of the subject.

So we got back to talking about the size of the Desert again, and the more we compared it with this and that and t'other thing, the more nobler and bigger and grander it got to look right along. And so, hunting among the figgers, Tom found, by and by, that it was just the same size as the Empire of China. Then he showed us the spread the Empire of China made on the map, and the room she took up in the world. Well, it was wonderful to think of, and I says:

"Why, I've heard talk about this Desert plenty of times, but I never knowed before how important she was."

Then Tom says:

"Important! Sahara important! That's just the way with some people. If a thing's big, it's important. That's all the sense they've got. All they can see is SIZE. Why, look at England. It's the most important country in the world; and yet you could put it in China's vest-pocket; and not only that, but you'd have the dickens's own time to find it again the next time you wanted it. And look at Russia. It spreads all around and everywhere, and yet ain't no more important in this world than Rhode Island is, and hasn't got half as much in it that's worth saving."

Away off now we see a little hill, a-standing up just on the edge of the world. Tom broke off his talk, and reached for a glass very much excited, and took a look, and says:

"That's it—it's the one I've been looking for, sure. If I'm right, it's the one the dervish took the man into and showed him all the treasures."

So we begun to gaze, and he begun to tell about it out of the Arabian Nights.

CHAPTER X. THE TREASURE-HILL

TOM said it happened like this.

A dervish was stumping it along through the Desert, on foot, one blazing hot day, and he had come a thousand miles and was pretty poor, and hungry, and ornery and tired, and along about where we are now he run across a camel-driver with a hundred camels, and asked him for some alms. But the cameldriver he asked to be excused. The dervish said:

"Don't you own these camels?"

"Yes, they're mine."

"Are you in debt?"

"Who—me? No."

"Well, a man that owns a hundred camels and ain't in debt is rich—and not only rich, but very rich. Ain't it so?"

The camel-driver owned up that it was so. Then the dervish says:

"God has made you rich, and He has made me poor. He has His reasons, and they are wise, blessed be His name. But He has willed that His rich shall help His poor, and you have turned away from me, your brother, in my need, and He will remember this, and you will lose by it."

That made the camel-driver feel shaky, but all the same he was born hoggish after money and didn't like to let go a cent; so he begun to whine and explain, and said times was hard, and although he had took a full freight down to Balsora and got a fat rate for it, he couldn't git no return freight, and so he warn't making no great things out of his trip. So the dervish starts along again, and says:

"All right, if you want to take the risk; but I reckon you've made a mistake this time, and missed a chance."

Of course the camel-driver wanted to know what kind of a chance he had missed, because maybe there was money in it; so he run after the dervish, and begged him so hard and earnest to take pity on him that at last the dervish gave in, and says:

"Do you see that hill yonder? Well, in that hill is all the treasures of the earth, and I was looking around for a man with a particular good kind heart and a noble, generous disposition, because if I could find just that man, I've got a kind of a salve I could put on his eyes and he could see the treasures and get them out."

So then the camel-driver was in a sweat; and he cried, and begged, and took on, and went down on his knees, and said he was just that kind of a man, and said he could fetch a thousand people that would say he wasn't ever described so exact before.

"Well, then," says the dervish, "all right. If we load the hundred camels, can I have half of them?"

The driver was so glad he couldn't hardly hold in, and says:

"Now you're shouting."

So they shook hands on the bargain, and the dervish got out his box and rubbed the salve on the driver's right eye, and the hill opened and he went in, and there, sure enough, was piles and piles of gold and jewels sparkling like all the stars in heaven had fell down.

So him and the dervish laid into it, and they loaded every camel till he couldn't carry no more; then they said good-bye, and each of them started off with his fifty. But pretty soon the camel-driver come a-running and overtook the dervish and says:

"You ain't in society, you know, and you don't really need all you've got. Won't you be good, and let me have ten of your camels?"

"Well," the dervish says, "I don't know but what you say is reasonable enough."

So he done it, and they separated and the dervish started off again with his forty. But pretty soon here comes the camel-driver bawling after him again, and whines and slobbers around and begs another ten off of him, saying thirty camel loads of treasures was enough to see a dervish through, because they live very simple, you know, and don't keep house, but board around and give their note.

But that warn't the end yet. That ornery hound kept coming and coming till he had begged back all the camels and had the whole hundred. Then he was satisfied, and ever so grateful, and said he wouldn't ever forgit the dervish as long as he lived, and nobody hadn't been so good to him before, and liberal. So they shook hands good-bye, and separated and started off again.

But do you know, it warn't ten minutes till the camel-driver was unsatisfied again—he was the lowdownest reptyle in seven counties—and he come a-running again. And this time the thing he wanted was to get the dervish to rub some of the salve on his other eye.

"Why?" said the dervish.

"Oh, you know," says the driver.

"Know what?"

"Well, you can't fool me," says the driver. "You're trying to keep back something from me, you know it mighty well. You know, I reckon, that if I had the salve on the other eye I could see a lot more things that's valuable. Come—please put it on."

The dervish says:

"I wasn't keeping anything back from you. I don't mind telling you what would happen if I put it on. You'd never see again. You'd be stone-blind the rest of your days."

But do you know that beat wouldn't believe him. No, he begged and begged, and whined and cried, till at last the dervish opened his box and told him to put it on, if he wanted to. So the man done it, and sure enough he was as blind as a bat in a minute.

Then the dervish laughed at him and mocked at him and made fun of him; and says:

"Good-bye—a man that's blind hain't got no use for jewelry."

And he cleared out with the hundred camels, and left that man to wander around poor and miserable and friendless the rest of his days in the Desert.

Jim said he'd bet it was a lesson to him.

"Yes," Tom says, "and like a considerable many lessons a body gets. They ain't no account, because the thing don't ever happen the same way again—and can't. The time Hen Scovil fell down the chimbly and crippled his back for life, everybody said it would be a lesson to him. What kind of a lesson? How was he going to use it? He couldn't climb chimblies no more, and he hadn't no more backs to break."

"All de same, Mars Tom, dey IS sich a thing as learnin' by expe'ence. De Good Book say de burnt chile shun de fire."

"Well, I ain't denying that a thing's a lesson if it's a thing that can happen twice just the same way. There's lots of such things, and THEY educate a person, that's what Uncle Abner always said; but there's forty MILLION lots of the other kind—the kind that don't happen the same way twice—and they ain't

no real use, they ain't no more instructive than the small-pox. When you've got it, it ain't no good to find out you ought to been vaccinated, and it ain't no good to git vaccinated afterward, because the small-pox don't come but once. But, on the other hand, Uncle Abner said that the person that had took a bull by the tail once had learnt sixty or seventy times as much as a person that hadn't, and said a person that started in to carry a cat home by the tail was gitting knowledge that was always going to be useful to him, and warn't ever going to grow dim or doubtful. But I can tell you, Jim, Uncle Abner was down on them people that's all the time trying to dig a lesson out of everything that happens, no matter whether—"

But Jim was asleep. Tom looked kind of ashamed, because you know a person always feels bad when he is talking uncommon fine and thinks the other person is admiring, and that other person goes to sleep that way. Of course he oughtn't to go to sleep, because it's shabby; but the finer a person talks the certainer it is to make you sleep, and so when you come to look at it it ain't nobody's fault in particular; both of them's to blame.

Jim begun to snore—soft and blubbery at first, then a long rasp, then a stronger one, then a half a dozen horrible ones like the last water sucking down the plug-hole of a bath-tub, then the same with more power to it, and some big coughs and snorts flung in, the way a cow does that is choking to death; and when the person has got to that point he is at his level best, and can wake up a man that is in the next block with a dipperful of loddanum in him, but can't wake himself up although all that awful noise of his'n ain't but three inches from his own ears. And that is the curiosest thing in the world, seems to me. But you rake a match to light the candle, and that little bit of a noise will fetch him. I wish I knowed what was the reason of that, but there don't seem to be no way to find out. Now there was Jim alarming the whole Desert, and yanking the animals out, for miles and miles around, to see what in the nation was going on up there; there warn't nobody nor nothing that was as close to the noise as HE was, and yet he was the only cretur that wasn't disturbed by it. We yelled at him and whooped at him, it never done no good; but the first time there come a little wee noise that wasn't of a usual kind it woke him up. No, sir, I've thought it all over, and so has Tom, and there ain't no way to find out why a snorer can't hear himself snore.

Jim said he hadn't been asleep; he just shut his eyes so he could listen better.

Tom said nobody warn't accusing him.

That made him look like he wished he hadn't said anything. And he wanted to git away from the subject, I reckon, because he begun to abuse the camel-driver, just the way a person does when he has got catched in something and wants to take it out of somebody else. He let into the camel-driver the hardest he knowed how, and I had to agree with him; and he praised up the dervish the highest he could, and I had to agree with him there, too. But Tom says:

"I ain't so sure. You call that dervish so dreadful liberal and good and unselfish, but I don't quite see it. He didn't hunt up another poor dervish, did he? No, he didn't. If he was so unselfish, why didn't he go in there himself and take a pocketful of jewels and go along and be satisfied? No, sir, the person he was hunting for was a man with a hundred camels. He wanted to get away with all the treasure he could."

"Why, Mars Tom, he was willin' to divide, fair and square; he only struck for fifty camels."

"Because he knowed how he was going to get all of them by and by."

"Mars Tom, he TOLE de man de truck would make him bline."

"Yes, because he knowed the man's character. It was just the kind of a man he was hunting for—a man that never believes in anybody's word or anybody's honorableness, because he ain't got none of his own. I reckon there's lots of people like that dervish. They swindle, right and left, but they always make the other person SEEM to swindle himself. They keep inside of the letter of the law all the time, and there ain't no way to git hold of them. THEY don't put the salve on—oh, no, that would be sin; but they know how to fool YOU into putting it on, then it's you that blinds yourself. I reckon the dervish and the camel-driver was just a pair—a fine, smart, brainy rascal, and a dull, coarse, ignorant one, but both of them rascals, just the same."

"Mars Tom, does you reckon dey's any o' dat kind o' salve in de worl' now?"

"Yes, Uncle Abner says there is. He says they've got it in New York, and they put it on country people's eyes and show them all the railroads in the world, and they go in and git them, and then when they rub the salve on the other eye the other man bids them goodbye and goes off with their railroads. Here's the treasure-hill now. Lower away!"

We landed, but it warn't as interesting as I thought it was going to be, because we couldn't find the place where they went in to git the treasure. Still, it was plenty interesting enough, just to see the mere hill itself where such a wonderful thing happened. Jim said he wou'dn't 'a' missed it for three dollars, and I felt the same way.

And to me and Jim, as wonderful a thing as any was the way Tom could come into a strange big country like this and go straight and find a little hump like that and tell it in a minute from a million other humps that was almost just like it, and nothing to help him but only his own learning and his own natural smartness. We talked and talked it over together, but couldn't make out how he done it. He had the best head on him I ever see; and all he lacked was age, to make a name for himself equal to Captain Kidd or George Washington. I bet you it would 'a' crowded either of THEM to find that hill, with all their gifts, but it warn't nothing to Tom Sawyer; he went across Sahara and put his finger on it as easy as you could pick a nigger out of a bunch of angels.

We found a pond of salt water close by and scraped up a raft of salt around the edges, and loaded up the lion's skin and the tiger's so as they would keep till Jim could tan them.

CHAPTER XI. THE SAND-STORM

WE went a-fooling along for a day or two, and then just as the full moon was touching the ground on the other side of the desert, we see a string of little black figgers moving across its big silver face. You could see them as plain as if they was painted on the moon with ink. It was another caravan. We cooled down our speed and tagged along after it, just to have company, though it warn't going our way. It was a rattler, that caravan, and a most bully sight to look at next morning when the sun come a-streaming across the desert and flung the long shadders of the camels on the gold sand like a thousand

grand-daddy-long-legses marching in procession. We never went very near it, because we knowed better now than to act like that and scare people's camels and break up their caravans. It was the gayest outfit you ever see, for rich clothes and nobby style. Some of the chiefs rode on dromedaries, the first we ever see, and very tall, and they go plunging along like they was on stilts, and they rock the man that is on them pretty violent and churn up his dinner considerable, I bet you, but they make noble good time, and a camel ain't nowheres with them for speed.

The caravan camped, during the middle part of the day, and then started again about the middle of the afternoon. Before long the sun begun to look very curious. First it kind of turned to brass, and then to copper, and after that it begun to look like a blood-red ball, and the air got hot and close, and pretty soon all the sky in the west darkened up and looked thick and foggy, but fiery and dreadful—like it looks through a piece of red glass, you know. We looked down and see a big confusion going on in the caravan, and a rushing every which way like they was scared; and then they all flopped down flat in the sand and laid there perfectly still.

Pretty soon we see something coming that stood up like an amazing wide wall, and reached from the Desert up into the sky and hid the sun, and it was coming like the nation, too. Then a little faint breeze struck us, and then it come harder, and grains of sand begun to sift against our faces and sting like fire, and Tom sung out:

"It's a sand-storm—turn your backs to it!"

We done it; and in another minute it was blowing a gale, and the sand beat against us by the shovelful, and the air was so thick with it we couldn't see a thing. In five minutes the boat was level full, and we was setting on the lockers buried up to the chin in sand, and only our heads out and could hardly breathe.

Then the storm thinned, and we see that monstrous wall go a-sailing off across the desert, awful to look at, I tell you. We dug ourselves out and looked down, and where the caravan was before there wasn't anything but just the sand ocean now, and all still and quiet. All them people and camels was smothered and dead and buried—buried under ten foot of sand, we reckoned, and Tom allowed it might be years before the wind uncovered them, and all that time their friends wouldn't ever know what become of that caravan. Tom said:

"NOW we know what it was that happened to the people we got the swords and pistols from."

Yes, sir, that was just it. It was as plain as day now. They got buried in a sand-storm, and the wild animals couldn't get at them, and the wind never uncovered them again until they was dried to leather and warn't fit to eat. It seemed to me we had felt as sorry for them poor people as a person could for anybody, and as mournful, too, but we was mistaken; this last caravan's death went harder with us, a good deal harder. You see, the others was total strangers, and we never got to feeling acquainted with them at all, except, maybe, a little with the man that was watching the girl, but it was different with this last caravan. We was huvvering around them a whole night and 'most a whole day, and had got to feeling real friendly with them, and acquainted. I have found out that there ain't no surer way to find out whether you like people or hate them than to travel with them. Just so with these. We kind of liked them from the start, and traveling with them put on the finisher. The longer we traveled with them, and the more we got used to their ways, the better and better we liked them, and the gladder and gladder we was that we run across them. We had come to know some of them so well that we called them by name when we was talking about them, and soon got so familiar and sociable that we even dropped the Miss and Mister and just used their plain names without any handle, and it did not seem unpolite, but just the right thing. Of course, it wasn't their own names, but names we give them. There was Mr. Elexander Robinson and Miss Adaline Robinson, and Colonel Jacob McDougal and Miss Harryet McDougal, and Judge Jeremiah Butler and young Bushrod Butler, and these was big chiefs mostly that wore splendid great turbans and simmeters, and dressed like the Grand Mogul, and their families. But as soon as we come to know them good, and like them very much, it warn't Mister, nor Judge, nor nothing, any more, but only Elleck, and Addy, and Jake, and Hattie, and Jerry, and Buck, and so on.

And you know the more you join in with people in their joys and their sorrows, the more nearer and dearer they come to be to you. Now we warn't cold and indifferent, the way most travelers is, we was right down friendly and sociable, and took a chance in everything that was going, and the caravan could depend on us to be on hand every time, it didn't make no difference what it was.

When they camped, we camped right over them, ten or twelve hundred feet up in the air. When they et a meal, we et ourn, and it made it ever so much home-liker to have their company. When they had a wedding that night, and Buck and Addy got married, we got ourselves up in the very starchiest of the professor's duds for the blow-out, and when they danced we jined in and shook a foot up there.

But it is sorrow and trouble that brings you the nearest, and it was a funeral that done it with us. It was next morning, just in the still dawn. We didn't know the diseased, and he warn't in our set, but that never made no difference; he belonged to the caravan, and that was enough, and there warn't no more sincerer tears shed over him than the ones we dripped on him from up there eleven hundred foot on high.

Yes, parting with this caravan was much more bitterer than it was to part with them others, which was comparative strangers, and been dead so long, anyway. We had knowed these in their lives, and was fond of them, too, and now to have death snatch them from right before our faces while we was looking, and leave us so lonesome and friendless in the middle of that big desert, it did hurt so, and we wished we mightn't ever make any more friends on that voyage if we was going to lose them again like that.

We couldn't keep from talking about them, and they was all the time coming up in our memory, and looking just the way they looked when we was all alive and happy together. We could see the line marching, and the shiny spearheads a-winking in the sun; we could see the dromedaries lumbering along; we could see the wedding and the funeral; and more oftener than anything else we could see them praying, because they don't allow nothing to prevent that; whenever the call come, several times a day, they would stop right there, and stand up and face to the east, and lift back their heads, and spread out their arms and begin, and four or five times they would go down on their knees, and then fall forward and touch their forehead to the ground.

Well, it warn't good to go on talking about them, lovely as they was in their life, and dear to us in their life and death both, because it didn't do no good, and made us too down-hearted. Jim allowed he was going to live as good a life as he could, so he could see them again in a better world; and Tom kept still and didn't tell him they was only Mohammedans; it warn't no use to disappoint him, he was feeling bad enough just as it was.

When we woke up next morning we was feeling a little cheerfuller, and had had a most powerful good sleep, because sand is the comfortablest bed there is, and I don't see why people that can afford it don't have it more. And it's terrible good ballast, too; I never see the balloon so steady before.

Tom allowed we had twenty tons of it, and wondered what we better do with it; it was good sand, and it didn't seem good sense to throw it away. Jim says:

"Mars Tom, can't we tote it back home en sell it? How long'll it take?"

"Depends on the way we go."

"Well, sah, she's wuth a quarter of a dollar a load at home, en I reckon we's got as much as twenty loads, hain't we? How much would dat be?"

"Five dollars."

"By jings, Mars Tom, le's shove for home right on de spot! Hit's more'n a dollar en a half apiece, hain't it?"

"Yes."

"Well, ef dat ain't makin' money de easiest ever I struck! She jes' rained in—never cos' us a lick o' work. Le's mosey right along, Mars Tom."

But Tom was thinking and ciphering away so busy and excited he never heard him. Pretty soon he says:

"Five dollars—sho! Look here, this sand's worth—worth—why, it's worth no end of money."

"How is dat, Mars Tom? Go on, honey, go on!"

"Well, the minute people knows it's genuwyne sand from the genuwyne Desert of Sahara, they'll just be in a perfect state of mind to git hold of some of it to keep on the what-not in a vial with a label on it for a curiosity. All we got to do is to put it up in vials and float around all over the United States and peddle them out at ten cents apiece. We've got all of ten thousand dollars' worth of sand in this boat."

Me and Jim went all to pieces with joy, and begun to shout whoopjamboreehoo, and Tom says:

"And we can keep on coming back and fetching sand, and coming back and fetching more sand, and just keep it a-going till we've carted this whole Desert over there and sold it out; and there ain't ever going to be any opposition, either, because we'll take out a patent."

"My goodness," I says, "we'll be as rich as Creosote, won't we, Tom?"

"Yes—Creesus, you mean. Why, that dervish was hunting in that little hill for the treasures of the earth, and didn't know he was walking over the real ones for a thousand miles. He was blinder than he made the driver."

"Mars Tom, how much is we gwyne to be worth?"

"Well, I don't know yet. It's got to be ciphered, and it ain't the easiest job to do, either, because it's over four million square miles of sand at ten cents a vial."

Jim was awful excited, but this faded it out considerable, and he shook his head and says:

"Mars Tom, we can't 'ford all dem vials—a king couldn't. We better not try to take de whole Desert, Mars Tom, de vials gwyne to bust us, sho'."

Tom's excitement died out, too, now, and I reckoned it was on account of the vials, but it wasn't. He set there thinking, and got bluer and bluer, and at last he says:

"Boys, it won't work; we got to give it up."

"Why, Tom?"

"On account of the duties."

I couldn't make nothing out of that, neither could Jim. I says:

"What IS our duty, Tom? Because if we can't git around it, why can't we just DO it? People often has to."

But he says:

"Oh, it ain't that kind of duty. The kind I mean is a tax. Whenever you strike a frontier—that's the border of a country, you know—you find a custom-house there, and the gov'ment officers comes and rummages among your things and charges a big tax, which they call a duty because it's their duty to bust you if they can, and if you don't pay the duty they'll hog your sand. They call it confiscating, but that don't deceive nobody, it's just hogging, and that's all it is. Now if we try to carry this sand home the way we're pointed now, we got to climb fences till we git tired—just frontier after frontier—Egypt, Arabia, Hindostan, and so on, and they'll all whack on a duty, and so you see, easy enough, we CAN'T go THAT road."

"Why, Tom," I says, "we can sail right over their old frontiers; how are THEY going to stop us?"

He looked sorrowful at me, and says, very grave:

"Huck Finn, do you think that would be honest?"

I hate them kind of interruptions. I never said nothing, and he went on:

"Well, we're shut off the other way, too. If we go back the way we've come, there's the New York custom-house, and that is worse than all of them others put together, on account of the kind of cargo we've got."

"Why?"

"Well, they can't raise Sahara sand in America, of course, and when they can't raise a thing there, the duty is fourteen hundred thousand per cent. on it if you try to fetch it in from where they do raise it."

"There ain't no sense in that, Tom Sawyer."

"Who said there WAS? What do you talk to me like that for, Huck Finn? You wait till I say a thing's got sense in it before you go to accusing me of saying it."

"All right, consider me crying about it, and sorry. Go on."

Jim says:

"Mars Tom, do dey jam dat duty onto everything we can't raise in America, en don't make no 'stinction 'twix' anything?"

"Yes, that's what they do."

"Mars Tom, ain't de blessin' o' de Lord de mos' valuable thing dey is?"

"Yes, it is."

"Don't de preacher stan' up in de pulpit en call it down on de people?"

"Yes."

"Whah do it come from?"

"From heaven."

"Yassir! you's jes' right, 'deed you is, honey—it come from heaven, en dat's a foreign country. NOW, den! do dey put a tax on dat blessin'?"

"No, they don't."

"Course dey don't; en so it stan' to reason dat you's mistaken, Mars Tom. Dey wouldn't put de tax on po' truck like san', dat everybody ain't 'bleeged to have, en leave it off'n de bes' thing dey is, which nobody can't git along widout."

Tom Sawyer was stumped; he see Jim had got him where he couldn't budge. He tried to wiggle out by saying they had FORGOT to put on that tax, but they'd be sure to remember about it, next session of Congress, and then they'd put it on, but that was a poor lame come-off, and he knowed it. He said there warn't nothing foreign that warn't taxed but just that one, and so they couldn't be consistent without taxing it, and to be consistent was the first law of politics. So he stuck to it that they'd left it out unintentional and would be certain to do their best to fix it before they got caught and laughed at.

But I didn't feel no more interest in such things, as long as we couldn't git our sand through, and it made me low-spirited, and Jim the same. Tom he tried to cheer us up by saying he would think up another speculation for us that would be just as good as this one and better, but it didn't do no good, we didn't believe there was any as big as this. It was mighty hard; such a little while ago we was so rich, and could 'a' bought a country and started a kingdom and been celebrated and happy, and now we was so poor and ornery again, and had our sand left on our hands. The sand was looking so lovely before, just like gold and di'monds, and the feel of it was so soft and so silky and nice, but now I couldn't bear the sight of it, it made me sick to look at it, and I knowed I wouldn't ever feel comfortable again till we got shut of it, and I didn't have it there no more to remind us of what we had been and what we had got degraded down to. The others was feeling the same way about it that I was. I knowed it, because they cheered up so, the minute I says le's throw this truck overboard.

Well, it was going to be work, you know, and pretty solid work, too; so Tom he divided it up according to fairness and strength. He said me and him would clear out a fifth apiece of the sand, and Jim three-fifths. Jim he didn't quite like that arrangement. He says:

"Course I's de stronges', en I's willin' to do a share accordin', but by jings you's kinder pilin' it onto ole Jim, Mars Tom, hain't you?"

"Well, I didn't think so, Jim, but you try your hand at fixing it, and let's see."

So Jim reckoned it wouldn't be no more than fair if me and Tom done a TENTH apiece. Tom he turned his back to git room and be private, and then he smole a smile that spread around and covered the whole Sahara to the westward, back to the Atlantic edge of it where we come from. Then he turned around again and said it was a good enough arrangement, and we was satisfied if Jim was. Jim said he was.

So then Tom measured off our two-tenths in the bow and left the rest for Jim, and it surprised Jim a good deal to see how much difference there was and what a raging lot of sand his share come to, and said he was powerful glad now that he had spoke up in time and got the first arrangement altered, for he said that even the way it was now, there was more sand than enjoyment in his end of the contract, he believed.

Then we laid into it. It was mighty hot work, and tough; so hot we had to move up into cooler weather or we couldn't 'a' stood it. Me and Tom took turn about, and one worked while t'other rested, but there warn't nobody to spell poor old Jim, and he made all that part of Africa damp, he sweated so. We couldn't work good, we was so full of laugh, and Jim he kept fretting and wanting to know what tickled us so, and we had to keep making up things to account for it, and they was pretty poor inventions, but they done well enough, Jim didn't see through them. At last when we got done we was 'most dead, but not with work but with laughing. By and by Jim was 'most dead, too, but: it was with work; then we took turns and spelled him, and he was as thankfull as he could be, and would set on the gunnel and swab the sweat, and heave and pant, and say how good we was to a poor old nigger, and he wouldn't ever forgit us. He was always the gratefulest nigger I ever see, for any little thing you done for him. He was only nigger outside; inside he was as white as you be.

CHAPTER XII. JIM STANDING SIEGE

THE next few meals was pretty sandy, but that don't make no difference when you are hungry; and when you ain't it ain't no satisfaction to eat, anyway, and so a little grit in the meat ain't no particular drawback, as far as I can see.

Then we struck the east end of the Desert at last, sailing on a northeast course. Away off on the edge of the sand, in a soft pinky light, we see three little sharp roofs like tents, and Tom says:

"It's the pyramids of Egypt."

It made my heart fairly jump. You see, I had seen a many and a many a picture of them, and heard tell about them a hundred times, and yet to come on them all of a sudden, that way, and find they was REAL, 'stead of imaginations, 'most knocked the breath out of me with surprise. It's a curious thing, that the more you hear about a grand and big and bully thing or person, the more it kind of dreamies out, as you may say, and gets to be a big dim wavery figger made out of moonshine and nothing solid to it. It's just so with George Washington, and the same with them pyramids.

And moreover, besides, the thing they always said about them seemed to me to be stretchers. There was a feller come to the Sunday-school once, and had a picture of them, and made a speech, and said the biggest pyramid covered thirteen acres, and was most five hundred foot high, just a steep mountain, all built out of hunks of stone as big as a bureau, and laid up in perfectly regular layers, like stair-steps. Thirteen acres, you see, for just one building; it's a farm. If it hadn't been in Sunday-school, I would 'a' judged it was a lie; and outside I was certain of it. And he said there was a hole in the pyramid, and you could go in there with candles, and go ever so far up a long slanting tunnel, and come to a large room in the stomach of that stone mountain, and there you would find a big stone chest with a king in it, four thousand years old. I said to myself, then, if that ain't a lie I will eat that king if they will fetch him, for even Methusalem warn't that old, and nobody claims it.

As we come a little nearer we see the yaller sand come to an end in a long straight edge like a blanket, and on to it was joined, edge to edge, a wide country of bright green, with a snaky stripe crooking through it, and Tom said it was the Nile. It made my heart jump again, for the Nile was another thing that wasn't real to me. Now I can tell you one thing which is dead certain: if you will fool along over three thousand miles of yaller sand, all glimmering with heat so that it makes your eyes water to look at it, and you've been a considerable part of a week doing it, the green country will look so like home and heaven to you that it will make your eyes water AGAIN.

It was just so with me, and the same with Jim.

And when Jim got so he could believe it WAS the land of Egypt he was looking at, he wouldn't enter it standing up, but got down on his knees and took off his hat, because he said it wasn't fitten' for a humble poor nigger to come any other way where such men had been as Moses and Joseph and Pharaoh and the other prophets. He was a Presbyterian, and had a most deep respect for Moses which was a Presbyterian, too, he said. He was all stirred up, and says:

"Hit's de lan' of Egypt, de lan' of Egypt, en I's 'lowed to look at it wid my own eyes! En dah's de river dat was turn' to blood, en I's looking at de very same groun' whah de plagues was, en de lice, en de frogs, en de locus', en de hail, en whah dey marked de door-pos', en de angel o' de Lord come by in de darkness o' de night en slew de fust-born in all de lan' o' Egypt. Ole Jim ain't worthy to see dis day!"

And then he just broke down and cried, he was so thankful. So between him and Tom there was talk enough, Jim being excited because the land was so full of history—Joseph and his brethren, Moses in the bulrushers, Jacob coming down into Egypt to buy corn, the silver cup in the sack, and all them interesting things; and Tom just as excited too, because the land was so full of history that was in HIS line, about Noureddin, and Bedreddin, and such like monstrous giants, that made Jim's wool rise, and a raft of other Arabian Nights folks, which the half of them never done the things they let on they done, I don't believe.

Then we struck a disappointment, for one of them early morning fogs started up, and it warn't no use to sail over the top of it, because we would go by Egypt, sure, so we judged it was best to set her by compass straight for the place where the pyramids was gitting blurred and blotted out, and then drop low and skin along pretty close to the ground and keep a sharp lookout. Tom took the hellum, I stood by to let go the anchor, and Jim he straddled the bow to dig through the fog with his eyes and watch out for danger ahead. We went along a steady gait, but not very fast, and the fog got solider and solider, so solid that Jim looked dim and ragged and smoky through it. It was awful still, and we talked low and was anxious. Now and then Jim would say:

"Highst her a p'int, Mars Tom, highst her!" and up she would skip, a foot or two, and we would slide right over a flat-roofed mud cabin, with people that had been asleep on it just beginning to turn out and gap and stretch; and once when a feller was clear up on his hind legs so he could gap and stretch better, we took him a blip in the back and knocked him off. By and by, after about an hour, and everything dead still and we a-straining our ears for sounds and holding our breath, the fog thinned a little, very sudden, and Jim sung out in an awful scare:

"Oh, for de lan's sake, set her back, Mars Tom, here's de biggest giant outen de 'Rabian Nights a-comin' for us!" and he went over backwards in the boat.

Tom slammed on the back-action, and as we slowed to a standstill a man's face as big as our house at home looked in over the gunnel, same as a house looks out of its windows, and I laid down and died. I must 'a' been clear dead and gone for as much as a minute or more; then I come to, and Tom had hitched a boat-hook on to the lower lip of the giant and was holding the balloon steady with it whilst he canted his head back and got a good long look up at that awful face.

Jim was on his knees with his hands clasped, gazing up at the thing in a begging way, and working his lips, but not getting anything out. I took only just a glimpse, and was fading out again, but Tom says:

"He ain't alive, you fools; it's the Sphinx!"

I never see Tom look so little and like a fly; but that was because the giant's head was so big and awful. Awful, yes, so it was, but not dreadful any more, because you could see it was a noble face, and kind of sad, and not thinking about you, but about other things and larger. It was stone, reddish stone, and its nose and ears battered, and that give it an abused look, and you felt sorrier for it for that.

We stood off a piece, and sailed around it and over it, and it was just grand. It was a man's head, or maybe a woman's, on a tiger's body a hundred and twenty-five foot long, and there was a dear little temple between its front paws. All but the head used to be under the sand, for hundreds of years, maybe thousands, but they had just lately dug the sand away and found that little temple. It took a power of sand to bury that cretur; most as much as it would to bury a steamboat, I reckon.

We landed Jim on top of the head, with an American flag to protect him, it being a foreign land; then we sailed off to this and that and t'other distance, to git what Tom called effects and perspectives and proportions, and Jim he done the best he could, striking all the different kinds of attitudes and positions

he could study up, but standing on his head and working his legs the way a frog does was the best. The further we got away, the littler Jim got, and the grander the Sphinx got, till at last it was only a clothespin on a dome, as you might say. That's the way perspective brings out the correct proportions, Tom said; he said Julus Cesar's niggers didn't know how big he was, they was too close to him.

Then we sailed off further and further, till we couldn't see Jim at all any more, and then that great figger was at its noblest, a-gazing out over the Nile Valley so still and solemn and lonesome, and all the little shabby huts and things that was scattered about it clean disappeared and gone, and nothing around it now but a soft wide spread of yaller velvet, which was the sand.

That was the right place to stop, and we done it. We set there a-looking and a-thinking for a half an hour, nobody a-saying anything, for it made us feel quiet and kind of solemn to remember it had been looking over that valley just that same way, and thinking its awful thoughts all to itself for thousands of years, and nobody can't find out what they are to this day.

At last I took up the glass and see some little black things a-capering around on that velvet carpet, and some more a-climbing up the cretur's back, and then I see two or three wee puffs of white smoke, and told Tom to look. He done it, and says:

"They're bugs. No—hold on; they—why, I believe they're men. Yes, it's men—men and horses both. They're hauling a long ladder up onto the Sphinx's back—now ain't that odd? And now they're trying to lean it up a—there's some more puffs of smoke—it's guns! Huck, they're after Jim."

We clapped on the power, and went for them a-biling. We was there in no time, and come a-whizzing down amongst them, and they broke and scattered every which way, and some that was climbing the ladder after Jim let go all holts and fell. We soared up and found him laying on top of the head panting and most tuckered out, partly from howling for help and partly from scare. He had been standing a siege a long time—a week, HE said, but it warn't so, it only just seemed so to him because they was crowding him so. They had shot at him, and rained the bullets all around him, but he warn't hit, and when they found he wouldn't stand up and the bullets couldn't git at him when he was laying down, they went for the ladder, and then he knowed it was all up with him if we didn't come pretty quick. Tom was very indignant, and asked him why he didn't show the flag and command them to GIT, in the name of the United States. Jim said he done it, but they never paid no attention. Tom said he would have this thing looked into at Washington, and says:

"You'll see that they'll have to apologize for insulting the flag, and pay an indemnity, too, on top of it even if they git off THAT easy."

Jim says:

"What's an indemnity, Mars Tom?"

"It's cash, that's what it is."

"Who gits it, Mars Tom?"

"Why, WE do."

"En who gits de apology?"

"The United States. Or, we can take whichever we please. We can take the apology, if we want to, and let the gov'ment take the money."

"How much money will it be, Mars Tom?"

"Well, in an aggravated case like this one, it will be at least three dollars apiece, and I don't know but more."

"Well, den, we'll take de money, Mars Tom, blame de 'pology. Hain't dat yo' notion, too? En hain't it yourn, Huck?"

We talked it over a little and allowed that that was as good a way as any, so we agreed to take the money. It was a new business to me, and I asked Tom if countries always apologized when they had done wrong, and he says:

"Yes; the little ones does."

We was sailing around examining the pyramids, you know, and now we soared up and roosted on the flat top of the biggest one, and found it was just like what the man said in the Sunday-school. It was like four pairs of stairs that starts broad at the bottom and slants up and comes together in a point at the top, only these stair-steps couldn't be clumb the way you climb other stairs; no, for each step was as high as your chin, and you have to be boosted up from behind. The two other pyramids warn't far away, and the people moving about on the sand between looked like bugs crawling, we was so high above them.

Tom he couldn't hold himself he was so worked up with gladness and astonishment to be in such a celebrated place, and he just dripped history from every pore, seemed to me. He said he couldn't scarcely believe he was standing on the very identical spot the prince flew from on the Bronze Horse. It was in the Arabian Night times, he said. Somebody give the prince a bronze horse with a peg in its shoulder, and he could git on him and fly through the air like a bird, and go all over the world, and steer it by turning the peg, and fly high or low and land wherever he wanted to.

When he got done telling it there was one of them uncomfortable silences that comes, you know, when a person has been telling a whopper and you feel sorry for him and wish you could think of some way to change the subject and let him down easy, but git stuck and don't see no way, and before you can pull your mind together and DO something, that silence has got in and spread itself and done the business. I was embarrassed, Jim he was embarrassed, and neither of us couldn't say a word. Well, Tom he glowered at me a minute, and says:

"Come, out with it. What do you think?"

I says:

"Tom Sawyer, YOU don't believe that, yourself."

"What's the reason I don't? What's to hender me?"

"There's one thing to hender you: it couldn't happen, that's all."

"What's the reason it couldn't happen?"

"You tell me the reason it COULD happen."

"This balloon is a good enough reason it could happen, I should reckon."

"WHY is it?"

"WHY is it? I never saw such an idiot. Ain't this balloon and the bronze horse the same thing under different names?"

"No, they're not. One is a balloon and the other's a horse. It's very different. Next you'll be saying a house and a cow is the same thing."

"By Jackson, Huck's got him ag'in! Dey ain't no wigglin' outer dat!"

"Shut your head, Jim; you don't know what you're talking about. And Huck don't. Look here, Huck, I'll make it plain to you, so you can understand. You see, it ain't the mere FORM that's got anything to do with their being similar or unsimilar, it's the PRINCIPLE involved; and the principle is the same in both. Don't you see, now?"

I turned it over in my mind, and says:

"Tom, it ain't no use. Principles is all very well, but they don't git around that one big fact, that the thing that a balloon can do ain't no sort of proof of what a horse can do."

"Shucks, Huck, you don't get the idea at all. Now look here a minute—it's perfectly plain. Don't we fly through the air?"

"Yes."

"Very well. Don't we fly high or fly low, just as we please?"

"Yes."

"Don't we steer whichever way we want to?"

"Yes."

"And don't we land when and where we please?"

"Yes."

"How do we move the balloon and steer it?"

"By touching the buttons."

"NOW I reckon the thing is clear to you at last. In the other case the moving and steering was done by turning a peg. We touch a button, the prince turned a peg. There ain't an atom of difference, you see. I knowed I could git it through your head if I stuck to it long enough."

He felt so happy he begun to whistle. But me and Jim was silent, so he broke off surprised, and says:

"Looky here, Huck Finn, don't you see it YET?"

I says:

"Tom Sawyer, I want to ask you some questions."

"Go ahead," he says, and I see Jim chirk up to listen.

"As I understand it, the whole thing is in the buttons and the peg—the rest ain't of no consequence. A button is one shape, a peg is another shape, but that ain't any matter?"

"No, that ain't any matter, as long as they've both got the same power."

"All right, then. What is the power that's in a candle and in a match?"

"It's the fire."

"It's the same in both, then?"

"Yes, just the same in both."

"All right. Suppose I set fire to a carpenter shop with a match, what will happen to that carpenter shop?"

"She'll burn up."

"And suppose I set fire to this pyramid with a candle—will she burn up?"

"Of course she won't."

"All right. Now the fire's the same, both times. WHY does the shop burn, and the pyramid don't?"

"Because the pyramid CAN'T burn."

"Aha! and A HORSE CAN'T FLY!"

"My lan', ef Huck ain't got him ag'in! Huck's landed him high en dry dis time, I tell you! Hit's de smartes' trap I ever see a body walk inter—en ef I—"

But Jim was so full of laugh he got to strangling and couldn't go on, and Tom was that mad to see how neat I had floored him, and turned his own argument ag'in him and knocked him all to rags and flinders with it, that all he could manage to say was that whenever he heard me and Jim try to argue it made him ashamed of the human race. I never said nothing; I was feeling pretty well satisfied. When I have got the best of a person that way, it ain't my way to go around crowing about it the way some people does, for I consider that if I was in his place I wouldn't wish him to crow over me. It's better to be generous, that's what I think.

CHAPTER XIII. GOING FOR TOM'S PIPE:

BY AND BY we left Jim to float around up there in the neighborhood of the pyramids, and we clumb down to the hole where you go into the tunnel, and went in with some Arabs and candles, and away in there in the middle of the pyramid we found a room and a big stone box in it where they used to keep that king, just as the man in the Sunday-school said; but he was gone, now; somebody had got him. But I didn't take no interest in the place, because there could be ghosts there, of course; not fresh ones, but I don't like no kind.

So then we come out and got some little donkeys and rode a piece, and then went in a boat another piece, and then more donkeys, and got to Cairo; and all the way the road was as smooth and beautiful a road as ever I see, and had tall date-pa'ms on both sides, and naked children everywhere, and the men was as red as copper, and fine and strong and handsome. And the city was a curiosity. Such narrow streets—why, they

were just lanes, and crowded with people with turbans, and women with veils, and everybody rigged out in blazing bright clothes and all sorts of colors, and you wondered how the camels and the people got by each other in such narrow little cracks, but they done it—a perfect jam, you see, and everybody noisy. The stores warn't big enough to turn around in, but you didn't have to go in; the storekeeper sat tailor fashion on his counter, smoking his snaky long pipe, and had his things where he could reach them to sell, and he was just as good as in the street, for the camel-loads brushed him as they went by.

Now and then a grand person flew by in a carriage with fancy dressed men running and yelling in front of it and whacking anybody with a long rod that didn't get out of the way. And by and by along comes the Sultan riding horseback at the head of a procession, and fairly took your breath away his clothes was so splendid; and everybody fell flat and laid on his stomach while he went by. I forgot, but a feller helped me to remember. He was one that had a rod and run in front.

There was churches, but they don't know enough to keep Sunday; they keep Friday and break the Sabbath. You have to take off your shoes when you go in. There was crowds of men and boys in the church, setting in groups on the stone floor and making no end of noise—getting their lessons by heart, Tom said, out of the Koran, which they think is a Bible, and people that knows better knows enough to not let on. I never see such a big church in my life before, and most awful high, it was; it made you dizzy to look up; our village church at home ain't a circumstance to it; if you was to put it in there, people would think it was a drygoods box.

What I wanted to see was a dervish, because I was interested in dervishes on accounts of the one that played the trick on the camel-driver. So we found a lot in a kind of a church, and they called themselves Whirling Dervishes; and they did whirl, too. I never see anything like it. They had tall sugar-loaf hats on, and linen petticoats; and they spun and spun and spun, round and round like tops, and the petticoats stood out on a slant, and it was the prettiest thing I ever see, and made me drunk to look at it. They was all Moslems, Tom said, and when I asked him what a Moslem was, he said it was a person that wasn't a Presbyterian. So there is plenty of them in Missouri, though I didn't know it before.

We didn't see half there was to see in Cairo, because Tom was in such a sweat to hunt out places that was celebrated in history. We had a most tiresome time to find the granary where Joseph stored up the grain before the famine, and when we found it it warn't worth much to look at, being such an old tumble-down wreck; but Tom was satisfied, and made more fuss over it than I would make if I stuck a nail in my foot. How he ever found that place was too many for me. We passed as much as forty just like it before we come to it, and any of them would 'a' done for me, but none but just the right one would suit him; I never see anybody so particular as Tom Sawyer. The minute he struck the right one he reconnized it as easy as I would reconnize my other shirt if I had one, but how he done it he couldn't any more tell than he could fly; he said so himself.

Then we hunted a long time for the house where the boy lived that learned the cadi how to try the case of the old olives and the new ones, and said it was out of the Arabian Nights, and he would tell me and Jim about it when he got time. Well, we hunted and hunted till I was ready to drop, and I wanted Tom to give it up and come next day and git somebody that knowed the town and could talk Missourian and could go straight to the place; but no, he wanted to find it himself, and nothing else would answer. So on we went. Then at last the remarkablest thing happened I ever see. The house was gone—gone hundreds of years ago—every last rag of it gone but just one mud brick. Now a person wouldn't ever believe that a backwoods Missouri boy that hadn't ever been in that town before could go and hunt that place over and find that brick, but Tom Sawyer done it. I know he done it, because I see him do it. I was right by his very side at the time, and see him see the brick and see him reconnize it. Well, I says to myself, how DOES he do it? Is it knowledge, or is it instink?

Now there's the facts, just as they happened: let everybody explain it their own way. I've ciphered over it a good deal, and it's my opinion that some of it is knowledge but the main bulk of it is instink. The reason is this: Tom put the brick in his pocket to give to a museum with his name on it and the facts when he went home, and I slipped it out and put another brick considerable like it in its place, and he didn't know the difference—but there was a difference, you see. I think that settles it—it's mostly instink, not knowledge. Instink tells him where the exact PLACE is for the brick to be in, and so he reconnizes it by the place it's in, not by the look of the brick. If it was knowledge, not instink, he would know the brick again by the look of it the next time he seen it—which he didn't. So it shows that for all the brag you hear about knowledge being such a wonderful thing, instink is worth forty of it for real unerringness. Jim says the same.

When we got back Jim dropped down and took us in, and there was a young man there with a red skullcap and tassel on and a beautiful silk jacket and baggy trousers with a shawl around his waist and pistols in it that could talk English and wanted to hire to us as guide and take us to Mecca and Medina and Central Africa and everywheres for a half a dollar a day and his keep, and we hired him and left, and piled on the power, and by the time we was through dinner we was over the place where the Israelites crossed the Red Sea when Pharaoh tried to overtake them and was caught by the waters. We stopped, then, and had a good look at the place, and it done Jim good to see it. He said he could see it all, now, just the way it happened; he could see the Israelites walking along between the walls of water, and the Egyptians coming, from away off yonder, hurrying all they could, and see them start in as the Israelites went out, and then when they was all in, see the walls tumble together and drown the last man of them. Then we piled on the power again and rushed away and huvvered over Mount Sinai, and saw the place where Moses broke the tables of stone, and where the children of Israel camped in the plain and worshiped the golden calf, and it was all just as interesting as could be, and the guide knowed every place as well as I knowed the village at home.

But we had an accident, now, and it fetched all the plans to a standstill. Tom's old ornery corn-cob pipe had got so old and swelled and warped that she couldn't hold together any longer, notwithstanding the strings and bandages, but caved in and went to pieces. Tom he didn't know WHAT to do. The professor's pipe wouldn't answer; it warn't anything but a mershum, and a person that's got used to a cob pipe knows it lays a long ways over all the other pipes in this world, and you can't git him to smoke any other. He wouldn't take mine, I couldn't persuade him. So there he was.

He thought it over, and said we must scour around and see if we could roust out one in Egypt or Arabia or around in some of these countries, but the guide said no, it warn't no use, they didn't have them. So Tom was pretty glum for a little while,

then he chirked up and said he'd got the idea and knowed what to do. He says:

"I've got another corn-cob pipe, and it's a prime one, too, and nearly new. It's laying on the rafter that's right over the kitchen stove at home in the village. Jim, you and the guide will go and get it, and me and Huck will camp here on Mount Sinai till you come back."

"But, Mars Tom, we couldn't ever find de village. I could find de pipe, 'case I knows de kitchen, but my lan', we can't ever find de village, nur Sent Louis, nur none o' dem places. We don't know de way, Mars Tom."

That was a fact, and it stumped Tom for a minute. Then he said:

"Looky here, it can be done, sure; and I'll tell you how. You set your compass and sail west as straight as a dart, till you find the United States. It ain't any trouble, because it's the first land you'll strike the other side of the Atlantic. If it's daytime when you strike it, bulge right on, straight west from the upper part of the Florida coast, and in an hour and three quarters you'll hit the mouth of the Mississippi—at the speed that I'm going to send you. You'll be so high up in the air that the earth will be curved considerable—sorter like a washbowl turned upside down—and you'll see a raft of rivers crawling around every which way, long before you get there, and you can pick out the Mississippi without any trouble. Then you can follow the river north nearly, an hour and three quarters, till you see the Ohio come in; then you want to look sharp, because you're getting near. Away up to your left you'll see another thread coming in—that's the Missouri and is a little above St. Louis. You'll come down low then, so as you can examine the villages as you spin along. You'll pass about twenty-five in the next fifteen minutes, and you'll recognize ours when you see it—and if you don't, you can yell down and ask."

"Ef it's dat easy, Mars Tom, I reckon we kin do it—yassir, I knows we kin."

The guide was sure of it, too, and thought that he could learn to stand his watch in a little while.

"Jim can learn you the whole thing in a half an hour," Tom said. "This balloon's as easy to manage as a canoe."

Tom got out the chart and marked out the course and measured it, and says:

"To go back west is the shortest way, you see. It's only about seven thousand miles. If you went east, and so on around, it's over twice as far." Then he says to the guide, "I want you both to watch the tell-tale all through the watches, and whenever it don't mark three hundred miles an hour, you go higher or drop lower till you find a storm-current that's going your way. There's a hundred miles an hour in this old thing without any wind to help. There's two-hundred-mile gales to be found, any time you want to hunt for them."

"We'll hunt for them, sir."

"See that you do. Sometimes you may have to go up a couple of miles, and it'll be p'ison cold, but most of the time you'll find your storm a good deal lower. If you can only strike a cyclone—that's the ticket for you! You'll see by the professor's books that they travel west in these latitudes; and they travel low, too."

Then he ciphered on the time, and says—

"Seven thousand miles, three hundred miles an hour—you can make the trip in a day—twenty-four hours. This is Thursday; you'll be back here Saturday afternoon. Come, now, hustle out some blankets and food and books and things for me and Huck, and you can start right along. There ain't no occasion to fool around—I want a smoke, and the quicker you fetch that pipe the better."

All hands jumped for the things, and in eight minutes our things was out and the balloon was ready for America. So we shook hands good-bye, and Tom gave his last orders:

"It's 10 minutes to 2 P.M. now, Mount Sinai time. In 24 hours you'll be home, and it'll be 6 to-morrow morning, village time. When you strike the village, land a little back of the top of the hill, in the woods, out of sight; then you rush down, Jim, and shove these letters in the post-office, and if you see anybody stirring, pull your slouch down over your face so they won't know you. Then you go and slip in the back way to the kitchen and git the pipe, and lay this piece of paper on the kitchen table, and put something on it to hold it, and then slide out and git away, and don't let Aunt Polly catch a sight of you, nor nobody else. Then you jump for the balloon and shove for Mount Sinai three hundred miles an hour. You won't have lost more than an hour. You'll start back at 7 or 8 A.M., village time, and be here in 24 hours, arriving at 2 or 3 P.M., Mount Sinai time."

Tom he read the piece of paper to us. He had wrote on it:

"THURSDAY AFTERNOON. Tom Sawyer the Erro-nort sends his love to Aunt Polly from Mount Sinai where the Ark was, and so does Huck Finn, and she will get it to-morrow morning half-past six."*

"That'll make her eyes bulge out and the tears come," he says. Then he says:

"Stand by! One—two—three—away you go!"

And away she DID go! Why, she seemed to whiz out of sight in a second.

Then we found a most comfortable cave that looked out over the whole big plain, and there we camped to wait for the pipe.

The balloon come hack all right, and brung the pipe; but Aunt Polly had catched Jim when he was getting it, and anybody can guess what happened: she sent for Tom. So Jim he says:

"Mars Tom, she's out on de porch wid her eye sot on de sky a-layin' for you, en she say she ain't gwyne to budge from dah tell she gits hold of you. Dey's gwyne to be trouble, Mars Tom, 'deed dey is."

So then we shoved for home, and not feeling very gay, neither.

----

* This misplacing of the Ark is probably Huck's error, not Tom's.— M.T.

Tom Sawyer, Detective
By Mark Twain

CHAPTER I. AN INVITATION FOR TOM AND HUCK

WELL, it was the next spring after me and Tom Sawyer set our old nigger Jim free, the time he was chained up for a runaway slave down there on Tom's uncle Silas's farm in Arkansaw. The frost was working out of the ground, and out of the air, too, and it was getting closer and closer onto barefoot time every day; and next it would be marble time, and next mumbletypeg, and next tops and hoops, and next kites, and then right away it would be summer and going in a-swimming. It just makes a boy homesick to look ahead like that and see how far off summer is. Yes, and it sets him to sighing and saddening around, and there's something the matter with him, he don't know what. But anyway, he gets out by himself and mopes and thinks; and mostly he hunts for a lonesome place high up on the hill in the edge of the woods, and sets there and looks away off on the big Mississippi down there a-reaching miles and miles around the points where the timber looks smoky and dim it's so far off and still, and everything's so solemn it seems like everybody you've loved is dead and gone, and you 'most wish you was dead and gone too, and done with it all.

Don't you know what that is? It's spring fever. That is what the name of it is. And when you've got it, you want—oh, you don't quite know what it is you DO want, but it just fairly makes your heart ache, you want it so! It seems to you that mainly what you want is to get away; get away from the same old tedious things you're so used to seeing and so tired of, and set something new. That is the idea; you want to go and be a wanderer; you want to go wandering far away to strange countries where everything is mysterious and wonderful and romantic. And if you can't do that, you'll put up with considerable less; you'll go anywhere you CAN go, just so as to get away, and be thankful of the chance, too.

Well, me and Tom Sawyer had the spring fever, and had it bad, too; but it warn't any use to think about Tom trying to get away, because, as he said, his Aunt Polly wouldn't let him quit school and go traipsing off somers wasting time; so we was pretty blue. We was setting on the front steps one day about sundown talking this way, when out comes his aunt Polly with a letter in her hand and says:

"Tom, I reckon you've got to pack up and go down to Arkansaw—your aunt Sally wants you."

I 'most jumped out of my skin for joy. I reckoned Tom would fly at his aunt and hug her head off; but if you believe me he set there like a rock, and never said a word. It made me fit to cry to see him act so foolish, with such a noble chance as this opening up. Why, we might lose it if he didn't speak up and show he was thankful and grateful. But he set there and studied and studied till I was that distressed I didn't know what to do; then he says, very ca'm, and I could a shot him for it:

"Well," he says, "I'm right down sorry, Aunt Polly, but I reckon I got to be excused—for the present."

Strange as the incidents of this story are, they are not inventions, but facts—even to the public confession of the accused. I take them from an old-time Swedish criminal trial, change the actors, and transfer the scenes to America. I have added some details, but only a couple of them are important ones. — M. T.

His aunt Polly was knocked so stupid and so mad at the cold impudence of it that she couldn't say a word for as much as a half a minute, and this gave me a chance to nudge Tom and whisper:

"Ain't you got any sense? Sp'iling such a noble chance as this and throwing it away?"

But he warn't disturbed. He mumbled back:

"Huck Finn, do you want me to let her SEE how bad I want to go? Why, she'd begin to doubt, right away, and imagine a lot of sicknesses and dangers and objections, and first you know she'd take it all back. You lemme alone; I reckon I know how to work her."

Now I never would 'a' thought of that. But he was right. Tom Sawyer was always right—the levelest head I ever see, and always AT himself and ready for anything you might spring on him. By this time his aunt Polly was all straight again, and she let fly. She says:

"You'll be excused! YOU will! Well, I never heard the like of it in all my days! The idea of you talking like that to ME! Now take yourself off and pack your traps; and if I hear another word out of you about what you'll be excused from and what you won't, I lay I'LL excuse you—with a hickory!"

She hit his head a thump with her thimble as we dodged by, and he let on to be whimpering as we struck for the stairs. Up in his room he hugged me, he was so out of his head for gladness because he was going traveling. And he says:

"Before we get away she'll wish she hadn't let me go, but she won't know any way to get around it now. After what she's said, her pride won't let her take it back."

Tom was packed in ten minutes, all except what his aunt and Mary would finish up for him; then we waited ten more for her to get cooled down and sweet and gentle again; for Tom said it took her ten minutes to unruffle in times when half of her feathers was up, but twenty when they was all up, and this was one of the times when they was all up. Then we went down, being in a sweat to know what the letter said.

She was setting there in a brown study, with it laying in her lap. We set down, and she says:

"They're in considerable trouble down there, and they think you and Huck'll be a kind of diversion for them—'comfort,' they say. Much of that they'll get out of you and Huck Finn, I reckon. There's a neighbor named Brace Dunlap that's been wanting to marry their Benny for three months, and at last they told him point blank and once for all, he COULDN'T; so he has soured on them, and they're worried about it. I reckon he's somebody they think they better be on the good side of, for they've tried to please him by hiring his no-account brother to help on the farm when they can't hardly afford it, and don't want him around anyhow. Who are the Dunlaps?"

"They live about a mile from Uncle Silas's place, Aunt Polly—all the farmers live about a mile apart down there—and Brace Dunlap is a long sight richer than any of the others, and owns a whole grist of niggers. He's a widower, thirty-six years old, without any children, and is proud of his money and overbearing, and everybody is a little afraid of him. I judge he thought he could have any girl he wanted, just for the asking, and it must have set him back a good deal when he found he couldn't get Benny. Why, Benny's only half as old as he is, and just as sweet and lovely as—well, you've seen her. Poor old Uncle Silas—why, it's pitiful, him trying to curry favor that way—so hard pushed and poor, and yet hiring that useless Jubiter Dunlap to please his ornery brother."

"What a name—Jubiter! Where'd he get it?"

"It's only just a nickname. I reckon they've forgot his real name long before this. He's twenty-seven, now, and has had it ever since the first time he ever went in swimming. The school teacher seen a round brown mole the size of a dime on his left leg above his knee, and four little bits of moles around it, when he was naked, and he said it minded him of Jubiter and his moons; and the children thought it was funny, and so they got to calling him Jubiter, and he's Jubiter yet. He's tall, and lazy, and sly, and sneaky, and ruther cowardly, too, but kind of good-natured, and wears long brown hair and no beard, and hasn't got a cent, and Brace boards him for nothing, and gives him his old clothes to wear, and despises him. Jubiter is a twin."

"What's t'other twin like?"

"Just exactly like Jubiter—so they say; used to was, anyway, but he hain't been seen for seven years. He got to robbing when he was nineteen or twenty, and they jailed him; but he broke jail and got away—up North here, somers. They used to hear about him robbing and burglaring now and then, but that was years ago. He's dead, now. At least that's what they say. They don't hear about him any more."

"What was his name?"

"Jake."

There wasn't anything more said for a considerable while; the old lady was thinking. At last she says:

"The thing that is mostly worrying your aunt Sally is the tempers that that man Jubiter gets your uncle into."

Tom was astonished, and so was I. Tom says:

"Tempers? Uncle Silas? Land, you must be joking! I didn't know he HAD any temper."

"Works him up into perfect rages, your aunt Sally says; says he acts as if he would really hit the man, sometimes."

"Aunt Polly, it beats anything I ever heard of. Why, he's just as gentle as mush."

"Well, she's worried, anyway. Says your uncle Silas is like a changed man, on account of all this quarreling. And the neighbors talk about it, and lay all the blame on your uncle, of course, because he's a preacher and hain't got any business to quarrel. Your aunt Sally says he hates to go into the pulpit he's so ashamed; and the people have begun to cool toward him, and he ain't as popular now as he used to was."

"Well, ain't it strange? Why, Aunt Polly, he was always so good and kind and moony and absent-minded and chuckle-headed and lovable—why, he was just an angel! What CAN be the matter of him, do you reckon?"

CHAPTER II. JAKE DUNLAP

WE had powerful good luck; because we got a chance in a stern-wheeler from away North which was bound for one of them bayous or one-horse rivers away down Louisiana way, and so we could go all the way down the Upper Mississippi and all the way down the Lower Mississippi to that farm in Arkansaw without having to change steamboats at St. Louis; not so very much short of a thousand miles at one pull.

A pretty lonesome boat; there warn't but few passengers, and all old folks, that set around, wide apart, dozing, and was very quiet. We was four days getting out of the "upper river," because we got aground so much. But it warn't dull—couldn't be for boys that was traveling, of course.

From the very start me and Tom allowed that there was somebody sick in the stateroom next to ourn, because the meals was always toted in there by the waiters. By and by we asked about it—Tom did and the waiter said it was a man, but he didn't look sick.

"Well, but AIN'T he sick?"

"I don't know; maybe he is, but 'pears to me he's just letting on."

"What makes you think that?"

"Because if he was sick he would pull his clothes off SOME time or other—don't you reckon he would? Well, this one don't. At least he don't ever pull off his boots, anyway."

"The mischief he don't! Not even when he goes to bed?"

"No."

It was always nuts for Tom Sawyer—a mystery was. If you'd lay out a mystery and a pie before me and him, you wouldn't have to say take your choice; it was a thing that would regulate itself. Because in my nature I have always run to pie, whilst in his nature he has always run to mystery. People are made different. And it is the best way. Tom says to the waiter:

"What's the man's name?"

"Phillips."

"Where'd he come aboard?"

"I think he got aboard at Elexandria, up on the Iowa line."

"What do you reckon he's a-playing?"

"I hain't any notion—I never thought of it."

I says to myself, here's another one that runs to pie.

"Anything peculiar about him?—the way he acts or talks?"

"No—nothing, except he seems so scary, and keeps his doors locked night and day both, and when you knock he won't let you in till he opens the door a crack and sees who it is."

"By jimminy, it's int'resting! I'd like to get a look at him. Say—the next time you're going in there, don't you reckon you could spread the door and—"

"No, indeedy! He's always behind it. He would block that game."

Tom studied over it, and then he says:

"Looky here. You lend me your apern and let me take him his breakfast in the morning. I'll give you a quarter."

The boy was plenty willing enough, if the head steward wouldn't mind. Tom says that's all right, he reckoned he could fix it with the head steward; and he done it. He fixed it so as we could both go in with aperns on and toting vittles.

He didn't sleep much, he was in such a sweat to get in there and find out the mystery about Phillips; and moreover he done a lot of guessing about it all night, which warn't no use, for if you are going to find out the facts of a thing, what's the sense in guessing out what ain't the facts and wasting ammunition? I didn't lose no sleep. I wouldn't give a dern to know what's the matter of Phillips, I says to myself.

Well, in the morning we put on the aperns and got a couple of trays of truck, and Tom he knocked on the door. The man opened it a crack, and then he let us in and shut it quick. By Jackson, when we got a sight of him, we 'most dropped the trays! and Tom says:

"Why, Jubiter Dunlap, where'd YOU come from?"

Well, the man was astonished, of course; and first off he looked like he didn't know whether to be scared, or glad, or both, or which, but finally he settled down to being glad; and then his color come back, though at first his face had turned pretty white. So we got to talking together while he et his breakfast. And he says:

"But I aint Jubiter Dunlap. I'd just as soon tell you who I am, though, if you'll swear to keep mum, for I ain't no Phillips, either."

Tom says:

"We'll keep mum, but there ain't any need to tell who you are if you ain't Jubiter Dunlap."

"Why?"

"Because if you ain't him you're t'other twin, Jake. You're the spit'n image of Jubiter."

"Well, I'm Jake. But looky here, how do you come to know us Dunlaps?"

Tom told about the adventures we'd had down there at his uncle Silas's last summer, and when he see that there warn't anything about his folks—or him either, for that matter—that we didn't know, he opened out and talked perfectly free and candid. He never made any bones about his own case; said he'd been a hard lot, was a hard lot yet, and reckoned he'd be a hard lot plumb to the end. He said of course it was a dangerous life, and—He give a kind of gasp, and set his head like a person that's listening. We didn't say anything, and so it was very still for a second or so, and there warn't no sounds but the screaking of the woodwork and the chug-chugging of the machinery down below.

Then we got him comfortable again, telling him about his people, and how Brace's wife had been dead three years, and Brace wanted to marry Benny and she shook him, and Jubiter was working for Uncle Silas, and him and Uncle Silas quarreling all the time—and then he let go and laughed.

"Land!" he says, "it's like old times to hear all this tittle-tattle, and does me good. It's been seven years and more since I heard any. How do they talk about me these days?"

"Who?"

"The farmers—and the family."

"Why, they don't talk about you at all—at least only just a mention, once in a long time."

"The nation!" he says, surprised; "why is that?"

"Because they think you are dead long ago."

"No! Are you speaking true?—honor bright, now." He jumped up, excited.

"Honor bright. There ain't anybody thinks you are alive."

"Then I'm saved, I'm saved, sure! I'll go home. They'll hide me and save my life. You keep mum. Swear you'll keep mum— swear you'll never, never tell on me. Oh, boys, be good to a poor devil that's being hunted day and night, and dasn't show his face! I've never done you any harm; I'll never do you any, as God is in the heavens; swear you'll be good to me and help me save my life."

We'd a swore it if he'd been a dog; and so we done it. Well, he couldn't love us enough for it or be grateful enough, poor cuss; it was all he could do to keep from hugging us.

We talked along, and he got out a little hand-bag and begun to open it, and told us to turn our backs. We done it, and when he told us to turn again he was perfectly different to what he was before. He had on blue goggles and the naturalest-looking long brown whiskers and mustashes you ever see. His own mother wouldn't 'a' knowed him. He asked us if he looked like his brother Jubiter, now.

"No," Tom said; "there ain't anything left that's like him except the long hair."

"All right, I'll get that cropped close to my head before I get there; then him and Brace will keep my secret, and I'll live with them as being a stranger, and the neighbors won't ever guess me out. What do you think?"

Tom he studied awhile, then he says:

"Well, of course me and Huck are going to keep mum there, but if you don't keep mum yourself there's going to be a little bit of a risk—it ain't much, maybe, but it's a little. I mean, if you talk, won't people notice that your voice is just like Jubiter's; and mightn't it make them think of the twin they reckoned was dead, but maybe after all was hid all this time under another name?"

"By George," he says, "you're a sharp one! You're perfectly right. I've got to play deef and dumb when there's a neighbor around. If I'd a struck for home and forgot that little detail— However, I wasn't striking for home. I was breaking for any place where I could get away from these fellows that are after me; then I was going to put on this disguise and get some different clothes, and—"

He jumped for the outside door and laid his ear against it and listened, pale and kind of panting. Presently he whispers:

"Sounded like cocking a gun! Lord, what a life to lead!"

Then he sunk down in a chair all limp and sick like, and wiped the sweat off of his face.

CHAPTER III. A DIAMOND ROBBERY

FROM that time out, we was with him 'most all the time, and one or t'other of us slept in his upper berth. He said he had been so lonesome, and it was such a comfort to him to have company, and somebody to talk to in his troubles. We was in a sweat to find out what his secret was, but Tom said the best way was not to seem anxious, then likely he would drop into it himself in one of his talks, but if we got to asking questions he would get suspicious and shet up his shell. It turned out just so. It warn't no trouble to see that he WANTED to talk about it, but always along at first he would scare away from it when he got on the very edge of it, and go to talking about something else. The way it come about was this: He got to asking us, kind of indifferent like, about the passengers down on deck. We told him about them. But he warn't satisfied; we warn't particular enough. He told us to describe them better. Tom done it. At last, when Tom was describing one of the roughest and raggedest ones, he gave a shiver and a gasp and says:

"Oh, lordy, that's one of them! They're aboard sure—I just knowed it. I sort of hoped I had got away, but I never believed it. Go on."

Presently when Tom was describing another mangy, rough deck passenger, he give that shiver again and says:

"That's him!—that's the other one. If it would only come a good black stormy night and I could get ashore. You see, they've got spies on me. They've got a right to come up and buy drinks at the bar yonder forrard, and they take that chance to bribe somebody to keep watch on me—porter or boots or somebody. If I was to slip ashore without anybody seeing me, they would know it inside of an hour."

So then he got to wandering along, and pretty soon, sure enough, he was telling! He was poking along through his ups and downs, and when he come to that place he went right along. He says:

"It was a confidence game. We played it on a julery-shop in St. Louis. What we was after was a couple of noble big di'monds as big as hazel-nuts, which everybody was running to see. We was dressed up fine, and we played it on them in broad daylight. We ordered the di'monds sent to the hotel for us to see if we wanted to buy, and when we was examining them we had paste counterfeits all ready, and THEM was the things that went back to the shop when we said the water wasn't quite fine enough for twelve thousand dollars."

"Twelve-thousand-dollars!" Tom says. "Was they really worth all that money, do you reckon?"

"Every cent of it."

"And you fellows got away with them?"

"As easy as nothing. I don't reckon the julery people know they've been robbed yet. But it wouldn't be good sense to stay around St. Louis, of course, so we considered where we'd go.

One was for going one way, one another, so we throwed up, heads or tails, and the Upper Mississippi won. We done up the di'monds in a paper and put our names on it and put it in the keep of the hotel clerk, and told him not to ever let either of us have it again without the others was on hand to see it done; then we went down town, each by his own self—because I reckon maybe we all had the same notion. I don't know for certain, but I reckon maybe we had."

"What notion?" Tom says.

"To rob the others."

"What—one take everything, after all of you had helped to get it?"

"Cert'nly."

It disgusted Tom Sawyer, and he said it was the orneriest, low-downest thing he ever heard of. But Jake Dunlap said it warn't unusual in the profession. Said when a person was in that line of business he'd got to look out for his own intrust, there warn't nobody else going to do it for him. And then he went on. He says:

"You see, the trouble was, you couldn't divide up two di'monds amongst three. If there'd been three—But never mind about that, there warn't three. I loafed along the back streets studying and studying. And I says to myself, I'll hog them di'monds the first chance I get, and I'll have a disguise all ready, and I'll give the boys the slip, and when I'm safe away I'll put it on, and then let them find me if they can. So I got the false whiskers and the goggles and this countrified suit of clothes, and fetched them along back in a hand-bag; and when I was passing a shop where they sell all sorts of things, I got a glimpse of one of my pals through the window. It was Bud Dixon. I was glad, you bet. I says to myself, I'll see what he buys. So I kept shady, and watched. Now what do you reckon it was he bought?"

"Whiskers?" said I.

"No."

"Goggles?"

"No."

"Oh, keep still, Huck Finn, can't you, you're only just hendering all you can. What WAS it he bought, Jake?"

"You'd never guess in the world. It was only just a screwdriver—just a wee little bit of a screwdriver."

"Well, I declare! What did he want with that?"

"That's what I thought. It was curious. It clean stumped me. I says to myself, what can he want with that thing? Well, when he come out I stood back out of sight, and then tracked him to a second-hand slop-shop and see him buy a red flannel shirt and some old ragged clothes—just the ones he's got on now, as you've described. Then I went down to the wharf and hid my things aboard the up-river boat that we had picked out, and then started back and had another streak of luck. I seen our other pal lay in HIS stock of old rusty second-handers. We got the di'monds and went aboard the boat.

"But now we was up a stump, for we couldn't go to bed. We

had to set up and watch one another. Pity, that was; pity to put that kind of a strain on us, because there was bad blood between us from a couple of weeks back, and we was only friends in the way of business. Bad anyway, seeing there was only two di'monds betwixt three men. First we had supper, and then tramped up and down the deck together smoking till most midnight; then we went and set down in my stateroom and locked the doors and looked in the piece of paper to see if the di'monds was all right, then laid it on the lower berth right in full sight; and there we set, and set, and by-and-by it got to be dreadful hard to keep awake. At last Bud Dixon he dropped off. As soon as he was snoring a good regular gait that was likely to last, and had his chin on his breast and looked permanent, Hal Clayton nodded towards the di'monds and then towards the outside door, and I understood. I reached and got the paper, and then we stood up and waited perfectly still; Bud never stirred; I turned the key of the outside door very soft and slow, then turned the knob the same way, and we went tiptoeing out onto the guard, and shut the door very soft and gentle.

"There warn't nobody stirring anywhere, and the boat was slipping along, swift and steady, through the big water in the smoky moonlight. We never said a word, but went straight up onto the hurricane-deck and plumb back aft, and set down on the end of the sky-light. Both of us knowed what that meant, without having to explain to one another. Bud Dixon would wake up and miss the swag, and would come straight for us, for he ain't afeard of anything or anybody, that man ain't. He would come, and we would heave him overboard, or get killed trying. It made me shiver, because I ain't as brave as some people, but if I showed the white feather—well, I knowed better than do that. I kind of hoped the boat would land somers, and we could skip ashore and not have to run the risk of this row, I was so scared of Bud Dixon, but she was an upper-river tub and there warn't no real chance of that.

"Well, the time strung along and along, and that fellow never come! Why, it strung along till dawn begun to break, and still he never come. 'Thunder,' I says, 'what do you make out of this?—ain't it suspicious?' 'Land!' Hal says, 'do you reckon he's playing us?—open the paper!' I done it, and by gracious there warn't anything in it but a couple of little pieces of loaf-sugar! THAT'S the reason he could set there and snooze all night so comfortable. Smart? Well, I reckon! He had had them two papers all fixed and ready, and he had put one of them in place of t'other right under our noses.

"We felt pretty cheap. But the thing to do, straight off, was to make a plan; and we done it. We would do up the paper again, just as it was, and slip in, very elaborate and soft, and lay it on the bunk again, and let on WE didn't know about any trick, and hadn't any idea he was a-laughing at us behind them bogus snores of his'n; and we would stick by him, and the first night we was ashore we would get him drunk and search him, and get the di'monds; and DO for him, too, if it warn't too risky. If we got the swag, we'd GOT to do for him, or he would hunt us down and do for us, sure. But I didn't have no real hope. I knowed we could get him drunk—he was always ready for that—but what's the good of it? You might search him a year and never find—Well, right there I catched my breath and broke off my thought! For an idea went ripping through my head that tore my brains to rags—and land, but I felt gay and good! You see, I had had my boots off, to unswell my feet, and just then I took up one of them to put it on, and I catched a glimpse of the heel-bottom, and it just took my breath away. You remember about that puzzlesome little screwdriver?"

"You bet I do," says Tom, all excited.

"Well, when I catched that glimpse of that boot heel, the idea that went smashing through my head was, I know where he's hid the di'monds! You look at this boot heel, now. See, it's bottomed with a steel plate, and the plate is fastened on with little screws. Now there wasn't a screw about that feller anywhere but in his boot heels; so, if he needed a screwdriver, I reckoned I knowed why."

"Huck, ain't it bully!" says Tom.

"Well, I got my boots on, and we went down and slipped in and laid the paper of sugar on the berth, and sat down soft and sheepish and went to listening to Bud Dixon snore. Hal Clayton dropped off pretty soon, but I didn't; I wasn't ever so wide awake in my life. I was spying out from under the shade of my hat brim, searching the floor for leather. It took me a long time, and I begun to think maybe my guess was wrong, but at last I struck it. It laid over by the bulkhead, and was nearly the color of the carpet. It was a little round plug about as thick as the end of your little finger, and I says to myself there's a di'mond in the nest you've come from. Before long I spied out the plug's mate.

"Think of the smartness and coolness of that blatherskite! He put up that scheme on us and reasoned out what we would do, and we went ahead and done it perfectly exact, like a couple of pudd'nheads. He set there and took his own time to unscrew his heelplates and cut out his plugs and stick in the di'monds and screw on his plates again. He allowed we would steal the bogus swag and wait all night for him to come up and get drownded, and by George it's just what we done! I think it was powerful smart."

"You bet your life it was!" says Tom, just full of admiration.

CHAPTER IV. THE THREE SLEEPERS

WELL, all day we went through the humbug of watching one another, and it was pretty sickly business for two of us and hard to act out, I can tell you. About night we landed at one of them little Missouri towns high up toward Iowa, and had supper at the tavern, and got a room upstairs with a cot and a double bed in it, but I dumped my bag under a deal table in the dark hall while we was moving along it to bed, single file, me last, and the landlord in the lead with a tallow candle. We had up a lot of whisky, and went to playing high-low-jack for dimes, and as soon as the whisky begun to take hold of Bud we stopped drinking, but we didn't let him stop. We loaded him till he fell out of his chair and laid there snoring.

"We was ready for business now. I said we better pull our boots off, and his'n too, and not make any noise, then we could pull him and haul him around and ransack him without any trouble. So we done it. I set my boots and Bud's side by side, where they'd be handy. Then we stripped him and searched his seams and his pockets and his socks and the inside of his boots, and everything, and searched his bundle. Never found any di'monds. We found the screwdriver, and Hal says, 'What do you reckon he wanted with that?' I said I didn't know; but when he wasn't looking I hooked it. At last Hal he looked beat and discouraged, and said we'd got to give it up. That was what I was waiting for. I says:

"'There's one place we hain't searched.'

"'What place is that?' he says.

"'His stomach.'

"'By gracious, I never thought of that! NOW we're on the homestretch, to a dead moral certainty. How'll we manage?'

"'Well,' I says, 'just stay by him till I turn out and hunt up a drug store, and I reckon I'll fetch something that'll make them di'monds tired of the company they're keeping.'

"He said that's the ticket, and with him looking straight at me I slid myself into Bud's boots instead of my own, and he never noticed. They was just a shade large for me, but that was considerable better than being too small. I got my bag as I went a-groping through the hall, and in about a minute I was out the back way and stretching up the river road at a five-mile gait.

"And not feeling so very bad, neither—walking on di'monds don't have no such effect. When I had gone fifteen minutes I says to myself, there's more'n a mile behind me, and everything quiet. Another five minutes and I says there's considerable more land behind me now, and there's a man back there that's begun to wonder what's the trouble. Another five and I says to myself he's getting real uneasy—he's walking the floor now. Another five, and I says to myself, there's two mile and a half behind me, and he's AWFUL uneasy—beginning to cuss, I reckon. Pretty soon I says to myself, forty minutes gone—he KNOWS there's something up! Fifty minutes—the truth's a-busting on him now! he is reckoning I found the di'monds whilst he was searching, and shoved them in my pocket and never let on—yes, and he's starting out to hunt for me. He'll hunt for new tracks in the dust, and they'll as likely send him down the river as up.

"Just then I see a man coming down on a mule, and before I thought I jumped into the bush. It was stupid! When he got abreast he stopped and waited a little for me to come out; then he rode on again. But I didn't feel gay any more. I says to myself I've botched my chances by that; I surely have, if he meets up with Hal Clayton.

"Well, about three in the morning I fetched Elexandria and see this stern-wheeler laying there, and was very glad, because I felt perfectly safe, now, you know. It was just daybreak. I went aboard and got this stateroom and put on these clothes and went up in the pilot-house—to watch, though I didn't reckon there was any need of it. I set there and played with my di'monds and waited and waited for the boat to start, but she didn't. You see, they was mending her machinery, but I didn't know anything about it, not being very much used to steamboats.

"Well, to cut the tale short, we never left there till plumb noon; and long before that I was hid in this stateroom; for before breakfast I see a man coming, away off, that had a gait like Hal Clayton's, and it made me just sick. I says to myself, if he finds out I'm aboard this boat, he's got me like a rat in a trap. All he's got to do is to have me watched, and wait—wait till I slip ashore, thinking he is a thousand miles away, then slip after me and dog me to a good place and make me give up the di'monds, and then he'll—oh, I know what he'll do! Ain't it awful—awful! And now to think the OTHER one's aboard, too! Oh, ain't it hard luck, boys—ain't it hard! But you'll help save me, WON'T you?—oh, boys, be good to a poor devil that's being hunted to death, and save me—I'll worship the very ground you walk on!"

We turned in and soothed him down and told him we would plan for him and help him, and he needn't be so afeard; and so by and by he got to feeling kind of comfortable again, and unscrewed his heelplates and held up his di'monds this way and that, admiring them and loving them; and when the light struck into them they WAS beautiful, sure; why, they seemed to kind of bust, and snap fire out all around. But all the same I judged he was a fool. If I had been him I would a handed the di'monds to them pals and got them to go ashore and leave me alone. But he was made different. He said it was a whole fortune and he couldn't bear the idea.

Twice we stopped to fix the machinery and laid a good while, once in the night; but it wasn't dark enough, and he was afeard to skip. But the third time we had to fix it there was a better chance. We laid up at a country woodyard about forty mile above Uncle Silas's place a little after one at night, and it was thickening up and going to storm. So Jake he laid for a chance to slide. We begun to take in wood. Pretty soon the rain come a-drenching down, and the wind blowed hard. Of course every boat-hand fixed a gunny sack and put it on like a bonnet, the way they do when they are toting wood, and we got one for Jake, and he slipped down aft with his hand-bag and come tramping forrard just like the rest, and walked ashore with them, and when we see him pass out of the light of the torch-basket and get swallowed up in the dark, we got our breath again and just felt grateful and splendid. But it wasn't for long. Somebody told, I reckon; for in about eight or ten minutes them two pals come tearing forrard as tight as they could jump and darted ashore and was gone. We waited plumb till dawn for them to come back, and kept hoping they would, but they never did. We was awful sorry and low-spirited. All the hope we had was that Jake had got such a start that they couldn't get on his track, and he would get to his brother's and hide there and be safe.

He was going to take the river road, and told us to find out if Brace and Jubiter was to home and no strangers there, and then slip out about sundown and tell him. Said he would wait for us in a little bunch of sycamores right back of Tom's uncle Silas's tobacker field on the river road, a lonesome place.

We set and talked a long time about his chances, and Tom said he was all right if the pals struck up the river instead of down, but it wasn't likely, because maybe they knowed where he was from; more likely they would go right, and dog him all day, him not suspecting, and kill him when it come dark, and take the boots. So we was pretty sorrowful.

CHAPTER V. A TRAGEDY IN THE WOODS

WE didn't get done tinkering the machinery till away late in the afternoon, and so it was so close to sundown when we got home that we never stopped on our road, but made a break for the sycamores as tight as we could go, to tell Jake what the delay was, and have him wait till we could go to Brace's and find out how things was there. It was getting pretty dim by the time we turned the corner of the woods, sweating and panting with that long run, and see the sycamores thirty yards ahead of us; and just then we see a couple of men run into the bunch and heard two or three terrible screams for help. "Poor Jake is killed, sure," we says. We was scared through and through, and broke for the tobacker field and hid there, trembling so our clothes would hardly stay on; and just as we skipped in there, a couple of men went tearing by, and into the bunch they went, and in a second out jumps four men and took out up the road as tight as they could go, two chasing two.

We laid down, kind of weak and sick, and listened for more sounds, but didn't hear none for a good while but just our hearts. We was thinking of that awful thing laying yonder in the sycamores, and it seemed like being that close to a ghost, and it give me the cold shudders. The moon come a-swelling up out of the ground, now, powerful big and round and bright, behind a comb of trees, like a face looking through prison bars, and the black shadders and white places begun to creep around, and it was miserable quiet and still and night-breezy and graveyardy and scary. All of a sudden Tom whispers:

"Look!—what's that?"

"Don't!" I says. "Don't take a person by surprise that way. I'm 'most ready to die, anyway, without you doing that."

"Look, I tell you. It's something coming out of the sycamores."

"Don't, Tom!"

"It's terrible tall!"

"Oh, lordy-lordy! let's—"

"Keep still—it's a-coming this way."

He was so excited he could hardly get breath enough to whisper. I had to look. I couldn't help it. So now we was both on our knees with our chins on a fence rail and gazing—yes, and gasping too. It was coming down the road—coming in the shadder of the trees, and you couldn't see it good; not till it was pretty close to us; then it stepped into a bright splotch of moonlight and we sunk right down in our tracks—it was Jake Dunlap's ghost! That was what we said to ourselves.

We couldn't stir for a minute or two; then it was gone We talked about it in low voices. Tom says:

"They're mostly dim and smoky, or like they're made out of fog, but this one wasn't."

"No," I says; "I seen the goggles and the whiskers perfectly plain."

"Yes, and the very colors in them loud countrified Sunday clothes—plaid breeches, green and black—"

"Cotton velvet westcot, fire-red and yaller squares—"

"Leather straps to the bottoms of the breeches legs and one of them hanging unbottoned—"

"Yes, and that hat—"

"What a hat for a ghost to wear!"

You see it was the first season anybody wore that kind—a black stiff-brim stove-pipe, very high, and not smooth, with a round top—just like a sugar-loaf.

"Did you notice if its hair was the same, Huck?"

"No—seems to me I did, then again it seems to me I didn't."

"I didn't either; but it had its bag along, I noticed that."

"So did I. How can there be a ghost-bag, Tom?"

"Sho! I wouldn't be as ignorant as that if I was you, Huck Finn. Whatever a ghost has, turns to ghost-stuff. They've got to have their things, like anybody else. You see, yourself, that its clothes was turned to ghost-stuff. Well, then, what's to hender its bag from turning, too? Of course it done it."

That was reasonable. I couldn't find no fault with it. Bill Withers and his brother Jack come along by, talking, and Jack says:

"What do you reckon he was toting?"

"I dunno; but it was pretty heavy."

"Yes, all he could lug. Nigger stealing corn from old Parson Silas, I judged."

"So did I. And so I allowed I wouldn't let on to see him."

"That's me, too."

Then they both laughed, and went on out of hearing. It showed how unpopular old Uncle Silas had got to be now. They wouldn't 'a' let a nigger steal anybody else's corn and never done anything to him.

We heard some more voices mumbling along towards us and getting louder, and sometimes a cackle of a laugh. It was Lem Beebe and Jim Lane. Jim Lane says:

"Who?—Jubiter Dunlap?"

"Yes."

"Oh, I don't know. I reckon so. I seen him spading up some ground along about an hour ago, just before sundown—him and the parson. Said he guessed he wouldn't go to-night, but we could have his dog if we wanted him."

"Too tired, I reckon."

"Yes—works so hard!"

"Oh, you bet!"

They cackled at that, and went on by. Tom said we better jump out and tag along after them, because they was going our way and it wouldn't be comfortable to run across the ghost all by ourselves. So we done it, and got home all right.

That night was the second of September—a Saturday. I sha'n't ever forget it. You'll see why, pretty soon.

CHAPTER VI. PLANS TO SECURE THE DIAMONDS

WE tramped along behind Jim and Lem till we come to the back stile where old Jim's cabin was that he was captivated in, the time we set him free, and here come the dogs piling around us to say howdy, and there was the lights of the house, too; so we warn't afeard any more, and was going to climb over, but Tom says:

"Hold on; set down here a minute. By George!"

"What's the matter?" says I.

"Matter enough!" he says. "Wasn't you expecting we would be the first to tell the family who it is that's been killed yonder in the sycamores, and all about them rapscallions that done it, and about the di'monds they've smouched off of the corpse, and paint it up fine, and have the glory of being the ones that knows a lot more about it than anybody else?"

"Why, of course. It wouldn't be you, Tom Sawyer, if you was to let such a chance go by. I reckon it ain't going to suffer none for lack of paint," I says, "when you start in to scollop the facts."

"Well, now," he says, perfectly ca'm, "what would you say if I was to tell you I ain't going to start in at all?"

I was astonished to hear him talk so. I says:

"I'd say it's a lie. You ain't in earnest, Tom Sawyer?"

"You'll soon see. Was the ghost barefooted?"

"No, it wasn't. What of it?"

"You wait—I'll show you what. Did it have its boots on?"

"Yes. I seen them plain."

"Swear it?"

"Yes, I swear it."

"So do I. Now do you know what that means?"

"No. What does it mean?"

"Means that them thieves DIDN'T GET THE DI'MONDS."

"Jimminy! What makes you think that?"

"I don't only think it, I know it. Didn't the breeches and goggles and whiskers and hand-bag and every blessed thing turn to ghost-stuff? Everything it had on turned, didn't it? It shows that the reason its boots turned too was because it still had them on after it started to go ha'nting around, and if that ain't proof that them blatherskites didn't get the boots, I'd like to know what you'd CALL proof."

Think of that now. I never see such a head as that boy had. Why, I had eyes and I could see things, but they never meant nothing to me. But Tom Sawyer was different. When Tom Sawyer seen a thing it just got up on its hind legs and TALKED to him—told him everything it knowed. I never see such a head.

"Tom Sawyer," I says, "I'll say it again as I've said it a many a time before: I ain't fitten to black your boots. But that's all right—that's neither here nor there. God Almighty made us all, and some He gives eyes that's blind, and some He gives eyes that can see, and I reckon it ain't none of our lookout what He done it for; it's all right, or He'd 'a' fixed it some other way. Go on—I see plenty plain enough, now, that them thieves didn't get way with the di'monds. Why didn't they, do you reckon?"

"Because they got chased away by them other two men before they could pull the boots off of the corpse."

"That's so! I see it now. But looky here, Tom, why ain't we to go and tell about it?"

"Oh, shucks, Huck Finn, can't you see? Look at it. What's a-

going to happen? There's going to be an inquest in the morning. Them two men will tell how they heard the yells and rushed there just in time to not save the stranger. Then the jury'll twaddle and twaddle and twaddle, and finally they'll fetch in a verdict that he got shot or stuck or busted over the head with something, and come to his death by the inspiration of God. And after they've buried him they'll auction off his things for to pay the expenses, and then's OUR chance." "How, Tom?"

"Buy the boots for two dollars!"

Well, it 'most took my breath.

"My land! Why, Tom, WE'LL get the di'monds!"

"You bet. Some day there'll be a big reward offered for them—a thousand dollars, sure. That's our money! Now we'll trot in and see the folks. And mind you we don't know anything about any murder, or any di'monds, or any thieves—don't you forget that."

I had to sigh a little over the way he had got it fixed. I'd 'a' SOLD them di'monds—yes, sir—for twelve thousand dollars; but I didn't say anything. It wouldn't done any good. I says:

"But what are we going to tell your aunt Sally has made us so long getting down here from the village, Tom?"

"Oh, I'll leave that to you," he says. "I reckon you can explain it somehow."

He was always just that strict and delicate. He never would tell a lie himself.

We struck across the big yard, noticing this, that, and t'other thing that was so familiar, and we so glad to see it again, and when we got to the roofed big passageway betwixt the double log house and the kitchen part, there was everything hanging on the wall just as it used to was, even to Uncle Silas's old faded green baize working-gown with the hood to it, and raggedy white patch between the shoulders that always looked like somebody had hit him with a snowball; and then we lifted the latch and walked in. Aunt Sally she was just a-ripping and a-tearing around, and the children was huddled in one corner, and the old man he was huddled in the other and praying for help in time of need. She jumped for us with joy and tears running down her face and give us a whacking box on the ear, and then hugged us and kissed us and boxed us again, and just couldn't seem to get enough of it, she was so glad to see us; and she says:

"Where HAVE you been a-loafing to, you good-for-nothing trash! I've been that worried about you I didn't know what to do. Your traps has been here ever so long, and I've had supper cooked fresh about four times so as to have it hot and good when you come, till at last my patience is just plumb wore out, and I declare I—I—why I could skin you alive! You must be starving, poor things!—set down, set down, everybody; don't lose no more time."

It was good to be there again behind all that noble corn-pone and spareribs, and everything that you could ever want in this world. Old Uncle Silas he peeled off one of his bulliest old-time blessings, with as many layers to it as an onion, and whilst the angels was hauling in the slack of it I was trying to study up what to say about what kept us so long. When our plates was all loadened and we'd got a-going, she asked me, and I says:

"Well, you see,—er—Mizzes—"

"Huck Finn! Since when am I Mizzes to you? Have I ever been stingy of cuffs or kisses for you since the day you stood in this room and I took you for Tom Sawyer and blessed God for sending you to me, though you told me four thousand lies and I believed every one of them like a simpleton? Call me Aunt Sally—like you always done."

So I done it. And I says:

"Well, me and Tom allowed we would come along afoot and take a smell of the woods, and we run across Lem Beebe and Jim Lane, and they asked us to go with them blackberrying to-night, and said they could borrow Jubiter Dunlap's dog, because he had told them just that minute—"

"Where did they see him?" says the old man; and when I looked up to see how HE come to take an intrust in a little thing like that, his eyes was just burning into me, he was that eager. It surprised me so it kind of throwed me off, but I pulled myself together again and says:

"It was when he was spading up some ground along with you, towards sundown or along there."

He only said, "Um," in a kind of a disappointed way, and didn't take no more intrust. So I went on. I says:

"Well, then, as I was a-saying—"

"That'll do, you needn't go no furder." It was Aunt Sally. She was boring right into me with her eyes, and very indignant. "Huck Finn," she says, "how'd them men come to talk about going a-black-berrying in September—in THIS region?"

I see I had slipped up, and I couldn't say a word. She waited, still a-gazing at me, then she says:

"And how'd they come to strike that idiot idea of going a-blackberrying in the night?"

"Well, m'm, they,—er—they told us they had a lantern, and—"

"Oh, SHET up—do! Looky here; what was they going to do with a dog?—hunt blackberries with it?"

"I think, m'm, they—"

"Now, Tom Sawyer, what kind of a lie are you fixing YOUR mouth to contribit to this mess of rubbage? Speak out—and I warn you before you begin, that I don't believe a word of it. You and Huck's been up to something you no business to—I know it perfectly well; I know you, BOTH of you. Now you explain that dog, and them blackberries, and the lantern, and the rest of that rot—and mind you talk as straight as a string—do you hear?"

Tom he looked considerable hurt, and says, very dignified:

"It is a pity if Huck is to be talked to that way, just for making a little bit of a mistake that anybody could make."

"What mistake has he made?"

"Why, only the mistake of saying blackberries when of course he meant strawberries."

"Tom Sawyer, I lay if you aggravate me a little more, I'll—"

"Aunt Sally, without knowing it—and of course without intending it—you are in the wrong. If you'd 'a' studied natural history the way you ought, you would know that all over the world except just here in Arkansaw they ALWAYS hunt strawberries with a dog—and a lantern—"

But she busted in on him there and just piled into him and snowed him under. She was so mad she couldn't get the words out fast enough, and she gushed them out in one everlasting freshet. That was what Tom Sawyer was after. He allowed to work her up and get her started and then leave her alone and let her burn herself out. Then she would be so aggravated with that subject that she wouldn't say another word about it, nor let anybody else. Well, it happened just so. When she was tuckered out and had to hold up, he says, quite ca'm:

"And yet, all the same, Aunt Sally—"

"Shet up!" she says, "I don't want to hear another word out of you."

So we was perfectly safe, then, and didn't have no more trouble about that delay. Tom done it elegant.

CHAPTER VII. A NIGHT'S VIGIL

BENNY she was looking pretty sober, and she sighed some, now and then; but pretty soon she got to asking about Mary, and Sid, and Tom's aunt Polly, and then Aunt Sally's clouds cleared off and she got in a good humor and joined in on the questions and was her lovingest best self, and so the rest of the supper went along gay and pleasant. But the old man he didn't take any hand hardly, and was absent-minded and restless, and done a considerable amount of sighing; and it was kind of heart-breaking to see him so sad and troubled and worried.

By and by, a spell after supper, come a nigger and knocked on the door and put his head in with his old straw hat in his hand bowing and scraping, and said his Marse Brace was out at the stile and wanted his brother, and was getting tired waiting supper for him, and would Marse Silas please tell him where he was? I never see Uncle Silas speak up so sharp and fractious before. He says:

"Am I his brother's keeper?" And then he kind of wilted together, and looked like he wished he hadn't spoken so, and then he says, very gentle: "But you needn't say that, Billy; I was took sudden and irritable, and I ain't very well these days, and not hardly responsible. Tell him he ain't here."

And when the nigger was gone he got up and walked the floor, backwards and forwards, mumbling and muttering to himself and plowing his hands through his hair. It was real pitiful to see him. Aunt Sally she whispered to us and told us not to take notice of him, it embarrassed him. She said he was always thinking and thinking, since these troubles come on, and she allowed he didn't more'n about half know what he was about when the thinking spells was on him; and she said he walked in his sleep considerable more now than he used to, and sometimes wandered around over the house and even outdoors in his sleep, and if we catched him at it we must let him alone and not disturb him. She said she reckoned it didn't do him no harm, and may be it done him good. She said Benny was the only one that was much help to him these days. Said Benny appeared to know just when to try to soothe him and when to leave him alone.

So he kept on tramping up and down the floor and muttering, till by and by he begun to look pretty tired; then Benny she went and snuggled up to his side and put one hand in his and one arm around his waist and walked with him; and he smiled down on her, and reached down and kissed her; and so, little by little the trouble went out of his face and she persuaded him off to his room. They had very petting ways together, and it was uncommon pretty to see.

Aunt Sally she was busy getting the children ready for bed; so by and by it got dull and tedious, and me and Tom took a turn in the moonlight, and fetched up in the watermelon-patch and et one, and had a good deal of talk. And Tom said he'd bet the quarreling was all Jubiter's fault, and he was going to be on hand the first time he got a chance, and see; and if it was so, he was going to do his level best to get Uncle Silas to turn him off.

And so we talked and smoked and stuffed watermelons much as two hours, and then it was pretty late, and when we got back the house was quiet and dark, and everybody gone to bed.

Tom he always seen everything, and now he see that the old green baize work-gown was gone, and said it wasn't gone when he went out; so he allowed it was curious, and then we went up to bed.

We could hear Benny stirring around in her room, which was next to ourn, and judged she was worried a good deal about her father and couldn't sleep. We found we couldn't, neither. So we set up a long time, and smoked and talked in a low voice, and felt pretty dull and down-hearted. We talked the murder and the ghost over and over again, and got so creepy and crawly we couldn't get sleepy nohow and noway.

By and by, when it was away late in the night and all the sounds was late sounds and solemn, Tom nudged me and whispers to me to look, and I done it, and there we see a man poking around in the yard like he didn't know just what he wanted to do, but it was pretty dim and we couldn't see him good. Then he started for the stile, and as he went over it the moon came out strong, and he had a long-handled shovel over his shoulder, and we see the white patch on the old work-gown. So Tom says:

"He's a-walking in his sleep. I wish we was allowed to follow him and see where he's going to. There, he's turned down by the tobacker-field. Out of sight now. It's a dreadful pity he can't rest no better."

We waited a long time, but he didn't come back any more, or if he did he come around the other way; so at last we was tuckered out and went to sleep and had nightmares, a million of them. But before dawn we was awake again, because meantime a storm had come up and been raging, and the thunder and lightning was awful, and the wind was a-thrashing the trees around, and the rain was driving down in slanting sheets, and the gullies was running rivers. Tom says:

"Looky here, Huck, I'll tell you one thing that's mighty curious. Up to the time we went out last night the family hadn't heard about Jake Dunlap being murdered. Now the men that chased Hal Clayton and Bud Dixon away would spread the thing around in a half an hour, and every neighbor that heard it would shin out and fly around from one farm to t'other and try to be the first to tell the news. Land, they don't have such a big

thing as that to tell twice in thirty year! Huck, it's mighty strange; I don't understand it."

So then he was in a fidget for the rain to let up, so we could turn out and run across some of the people and see if they would say anything about it to us. And he said if they did we must be horribly surprised and shocked.

We was out and gone the minute the rain stopped. It was just broad day then. We loafed along up the road, and now and then met a person and stopped and said howdy, and told them when we come, and how we left the folks at home, and how long we was going to stay, and all that, but none of them said a word about that thing; which was just astonishing, and no mistake. Tom said he believed if we went to the sycamores we would find that body laying there solitary and alone, and not a soul around. Said he believed the men chased the thieves so far into the woods that the thieves prob'ly seen a good chance and turned on them at last, and maybe they all killed each other, and so there wasn't anybody left to tell.

First we knowed, gabbling along that away, we was right at the sycamores. The cold chills trickled down my back and I wouldn't budge another step, for all Tom's persuading. But he couldn't hold in; he'd GOT to see if the boots was safe on that body yet. So he crope in—and the next minute out he come again with his eyes bulging he was so excited, and says:

"Huck, it's gone!"

I WAS astonished! I says:

"Tom, you don't mean it."

"It's gone, sure. There ain't a sign of it. The ground is trampled some, but if there was any blood it's all washed away by the storm, for it's all puddles and slush in there."

At last I give in, and went and took a look myself; and it was just as Tom said—there wasn't a sign of a corpse.

"Dern it," I says, "the di'monds is gone. Don't you reckon the thieves slunk back and lugged him off, Tom?"

"Looks like it. It just does. Now where'd they hide him, do you reckon?"

"I don't know," I says, disgusted, "and what's more I don't care. They've got the boots, and that's all I cared about. He'll lay around these woods a long time before I hunt him up."

Tom didn't feel no more intrust in him neither, only curiosity to know what come of him; but he said we'd lay low and keep dark and it wouldn't be long till the dogs or somebody rousted him out.

We went back home to breakfast ever so bothered and put out and disappointed and swindled. I warn't ever so down on a corpse before.

CHAPTER VIII. TALKING WITH THE GHOST

IT warn't very cheerful at breakfast. Aunt Sally she looked old and tired and let the children snarl and fuss at one another and didn't seem to notice it was going on, which wasn't her usual style; me and Tom had a plenty to think about without talking; Benny she looked like she hadn't had much sleep, and whenever she'd lift her head a little and steal a look towards her father you could see there was tears in her eyes; and as for the old man, his things stayed on his plate and got cold without him knowing they was there, I reckon, for he was thinking and thinking all the time, and never said a word and never et a bite.

By and by when it was stillest, that nigger's head was poked in at the door again, and he said his Marse Brace was getting powerful uneasy about Marse Jubiter, which hadn't come home yet, and would Marse Silas please —He was looking at Uncle Silas, and he stopped there, like the rest of his words was froze; for Uncle Silas he rose up shaky and steadied himself leaning his fingers on the table, and he was panting, and his eyes was set on the nigger, and he kept swallowing, and put his other hand up to his throat a couple of times, and at last he got his words started, and says:

"Does he—does he—think—WHAT does he think! Tell him—tell him—" Then he sunk down in his chair limp and weak, and says, so as you could hardly hear him: "Go away—go away!"

The nigger looked scared and cleared out, and we all felt—well, I don't know how we felt, but it was awful, with the old man panting there, and his eyes set and looking like a person that was dying. None of us could budge; but Benny she slid around soft, with her tears running down, and stood by his side, and nestled his old gray head up against her and begun to stroke it and pet it with her hands, and nodded to us to go away, and we done it, going out very quiet, like the dead was there.

Me and Tom struck out for the woods mighty solemn, and saying how different it was now to what it was last summer when we was here and everything was so peaceful and happy and everybody thought so much of Uncle Silas, and he was so cheerful and simple-hearted and pudd'n-headed and good—and now look at him. If he hadn't lost his mind he wasn't muck short of it. That was what we allowed.

It was a most lovely day now, and bright and sunshiny; and the further and further we went over the hills towards the prairie the lovelier and lovelier the trees and flowers got to be and the more it seemed strange and somehow wrong that there had to be trouble in such a world as this. And then all of a sudden I catched my breath and grabbed Tom's arm, and all my livers and lungs and things fell down into my legs.

"There it is!" I says. We jumped back behind a bush shivering, and Tom says:

"'Sh!—don't make a noise."

It was setting on a log right in the edge of a little prairie, thinking. I tried to get Tom to come away, but he wouldn't, and I dasn't budge by myself. He said we mightn't ever get another chance to see one, and he was going to look his fill at this one if he died for it. So I looked too, though it give me the fan-tods to do it. Tom he HAD to talk, but he talked low. He says:

"Poor Jakey, it's got all its things on, just as he said he would. NOW you see what we wasn't certain about—its hair. It's not long now the way it was: it's got it cropped close to its head, the way he said he would. Huck, I never see anything look any more naturaler than what It does."

"Nor I neither," I says; "I'd recognize it anywheres."

"So would I. It looks perfectly solid and genuwyne, just the

way it done before it died."

So we kept a-gazing. Pretty soon Tom says:

"Huck, there's something mighty curious about this one, don't you know? IT oughtn't to be going around in the daytime."

"That's so, Tom—I never heard the like of it before."

"No, sir, they don't ever come out only at night—and then not till after twelve. There's something wrong about this one, now you mark my words. I don't believe it's got any right to be around in the daytime. But don't it look natural! Jake was going to play deef and dumb here, so the neighbors wouldn't know his voice. Do you reckon it would do that if we was to holler at it?"

"Lordy, Tom, don't talk so! If you was to holler at it I'd die in my tracks."

"Don't you worry, I ain't going to holler at it. Look, Huck, it's a-scratching its head—don't you see?"

"Well, what of it?"

"Why, this. What's the sense of it scratching its head? There ain't anything there to itch; its head is made out of fog or something like that, and can't itch. A fog can't itch; any fool knows that."

"Well, then, if it don't itch and can't itch, what in the nation is it scratching it for? Ain't it just habit, don't you reckon?"

"No, sir, I don't. I ain't a bit satisfied about the way this one acts. I've a blame good notion it's a bogus one—I have, as sure as I'm a-sitting here. Because, if it—Huck!"

"Well, what's the matter now?"

"YOU CAN'T SEE THE BUSHES THROUGH IT!"

"Why, Tom, it's so, sure! It's as solid as a cow. I sort of begin to think—"

"Huck, it's biting off a chaw of tobacker! By George, THEY don't chaw—they hain't got anything to chaw WITH. Huck!"

"I'm a-listening."

"It ain't a ghost at all. It's Jake Dunlap his own self!"

"Oh your granny!" I says.

"Huck Finn, did we find any corpse in the sycamores?"

"No."

"Or any sign of one?"

"No."

"Mighty good reason. Hadn't ever been any corpse there."

"Why, Tom, you know we heard—"

"Yes, we did—heard a howl or two. Does that prove anybody was killed? Course it don't. And we seen four men run, then this one come walking out and we took it for a ghost. No more ghost than you are. It was Jake Dunlap his own self, and it's Jake Dunlap now. He's been and got his hair cropped, the way he said he would, and he's playing himself for a stranger, just the same as he said he would. Ghost? Hum!—he's as sound as a nut."

Then I see it all, and how we had took too much for granted. I was powerful glad he didn't get killed, and so was Tom, and we wondered which he would like the best—for us to never let on to know him, or how? Tom reckoned the best way would be to go and ask him. So he started; but I kept a little behind, because I didn't know but it might be a ghost, after all. When Tom got to where he was, he says:

"Me and Huck's mighty glad to see you again, and you needn't be afeared we'll tell. And if you think it'll be safer for you if we don't let on to know you when we run across you, say the word and you'll see you can depend on us, and would ruther cut our hands off than get you into the least little bit of danger."

First off he looked surprised to see us, and not very glad, either; but as Tom went on he looked pleasanter, and when he was done he smiled, and nodded his head several times, and made signs with his hands, and says:

"Goo-goo—goo-goo," the way deef and dummies does.

Just then we see some of Steve Nickerson's people coming that lived t'other side of the prairie, so Tom says:

"You do it elegant; I never see anybody do it better. You're right; play it on us, too; play it on us same as the others; it'll keep you in practice and prevent you making blunders. We'll keep away from you and let on we don't know you, but any time we can be any help, you just let us know."

Then we loafed along past the Nickersons, and of course they asked if that was the new stranger yonder, and where'd he come from, and what was his name, and which communion was he, Babtis' or Methodis', and which politics, Whig or Democrat, and how long is he staying, and all them other questions that humans always asks when a stranger comes, and animals does, too. But Tom said he warn't able to make anything out of deef and dumb signs, and the same with goo-gooing. Then we watched them go and bullyrag Jake; because we was pretty uneasy for him. Tom said it would take him days to get so he wouldn't forget he was a deef and dummy sometimes, and speak out before he thought. When we had watched long enough to see that Jake was getting along all right and working his signs very good, we loafed along again, allowing to strike the schoolhouse about recess time, which was a three-mile tramp.

I was so disappointed not to hear Jake tell about the row in the sycamores, and how near he come to getting killed, that I couldn't seem to get over it, and Tom he felt the same, but said if we was in Jake's fix we would want to go careful and keep still and not take any chances.

The boys and girls was all glad to see us again, and we had a real good time all through recess. Coming to school the Henderson boys had come across the new deef and dummy and told the rest; so all the scholars was chuck full of him and couldn't talk about anything else, and was in a sweat to get a sight of him because they hadn't ever seen a deef and dummy in their lives, and it made a powerful excitement.

Tom said it was tough to have to keep mum now; said we

would be heroes if we could come out and tell all we knowed; but after all, it was still more heroic to keep mum, there warn't two boys in a million could do it. That was Tom Sawyer's idea about it, and reckoned there warn't anybody could better it.

CHAPTER IX. FINDING OF JUBITER DUNLAP

IN the next two or three days Dummy he got to be powerful popular. He went associating around with the neighbors, and they made much of him, and was proud to have such a rattling curiosity among them. They had him to breakfast, they had him to dinner, they had him to supper; they kept him loaded up with hog and hominy, and warn't ever tired staring at him and wondering over him, and wishing they knowed more about him, he was so uncommon and romantic. His signs warn't no good; people couldn't understand them and he prob'ly couldn't himself, but he done a sight of goo-gooing, and so everybody was satisfied, and admired to hear him go it. He toted a piece of slate around, and a pencil; and people wrote questions on it and he wrote answers; but there warn't anybody could read his writing but Brace Dunlap. Brace said he couldn't read it very good, but he could manage to dig out the meaning most of the time. He said Dummy said he belonged away off somers and used to be well off, but got busted by swindlers which he had trusted, and was poor now, and hadn't any way to make a living.

Everybody praised Brace Dunlap for being so good to that stranger. He let him have a little log-cabin all to himself, and had his niggers take care of it, and fetch him all the vittles he wanted.

Dummy was at our house some, because old Uncle Silas was so afflicted himself, these days, that anybody else that was afflicted was a comfort to him. Me and Tom didn't let on that we had knowed him before, and he didn't let on that he had knowed us before. The family talked their troubles out before him the same as if he wasn't there, but we reckoned it wasn't any harm for him to hear what they said. Generly he didn't seem to notice, but sometimes he did.

Well, two or three days went along, and everybody got to getting uneasy about Jubiter Dunlap. Everybody was asking everybody if they had any idea what had become of him. No, they hadn't, they said: and they shook their heads and said there was something powerful strange about it. Another and another day went by; then there was a report got around that praps he was murdered. You bet it made a big stir! Everybody's tongue was clacking away after that. Saturday two or three gangs turned out and hunted the woods to see if they could run across his remainders. Me and Tom helped, and it was noble good times and exciting. Tom he was so brimful of it he couldn't eat nor rest. He said if we could find that corpse we would be celebrated, and more talked about than if we got drownded.

The others got tired and give it up; but not Tom Sawyer—that warn't his style. Saturday night he didn't sleep any, hardly, trying to think up a plan; and towards daylight in the morning he struck it. He snaked me out of bed and was all excited, and says:

"Quick, Huck, snatch on your clothes—I've got it! Bloodhound!"

In two minutes we was tearing up the river road in the dark towards the village. Old Jeff Hooker had a bloodhound, and Tom was going to borrow him. I says:

"The trail's too old, Tom—and besides, it's rained, you know."

"It don't make any difference, Huck. If the body's hid in the woods anywhere around the hound will find it. If he's been murdered and buried, they wouldn't bury him deep, it ain't likely, and if the dog goes over the spot he'll scent him, sure. Huck, we're going to be celebrated, sure as you're born!"

He was just a-blazing; and whenever he got afire he was most likely to get afire all over. That was the way this time. In two minutes he had got it all ciphered out, and wasn't only just going to find the corpse—no, he was going to get on the track of that murderer and hunt HIM down, too; and not only that, but he was going to stick to him till —"Well," I says, "you better find the corpse first; I reckon that's a-plenty for to-day. For all we know, there AIN'T any corpse and nobody hain't been murdered at all. That cuss could 'a' gone off somers and not been killed at all."

That graveled him, and he says:

"Huck Finn, I never see such a person as you to want to spoil everything. As long as YOU can't see anything hopeful in a thing, you won't let anybody else. What good can it do you to throw cold water on that corpse and get up that selfish theory that there ain't been any murder? None in the world. I don't see how you can act so. I wouldn't treat you like that, and you know it. Here we've got a noble good opportunity to make a ruputation, and—"

"Oh, go ahead," I says. "I'm sorry, and I take it all back. I didn't mean nothing. Fix it any way you want it. HE ain't any consequence to me. If he's killed, I'm as glad of it as you are; and if he—"

"I never said anything about being glad; I only—"

"Well, then, I'm as SORRY as you are. Any way you druther have it, that is the way I druther have it. He—"

"There ain't any druthers ABOUT it, Huck Finn; nobody said anything about druthers. And as for—"

He forgot he was talking, and went tramping along, studying. He begun to get excited again, and pretty soon he says:

"Huck, it'll be the bulliest thing that ever happened if we find the body after everybody else has quit looking, and then go ahead and hunt up the murderer. It won't only be an honor to us, but it'll be an honor to Uncle Silas because it was us that done it. It'll set him up again, you see if it don't."

But Old Jeff Hooker he throwed cold water on the whole business when we got to his blacksmith shop and told him what we come for.

"You can take the dog," he says, "but you ain't a-going to find any corpse, because there ain't any corpse to find. Everybody's quit looking, and they're right. Soon as they come to think, they knowed there warn't no corpse. And I'll tell you for why. What does a person kill another person for, Tom Sawyer?—answer me that."

"Why, he—er—"

"Answer up! You ain't no fool. What does he kill him FOR?"

"Well, sometimes it's for revenge, and—"

"Wait. One thing at a time. Revenge, says you; and right you are. Now who ever had anything agin that poor trifling no-account? Who do you reckon would want to kill HIM?—that rabbit!"

Tom was stuck. I reckon he hadn't thought of a person having to have a REASON for killing a person before, and now he sees it warn't likely anybody would have that much of a grudge against a lamb like Jubiter Dunlap. The blacksmith says, by and by:

"The revenge idea won't work, you see. Well, then, what's next? Robbery? B'gosh, that must 'a' been it, Tom! Yes, sirree, I reckon we've struck it this time. Some feller wanted his gallus-buckles, and so he—"

But it was so funny he busted out laughing, and just went on laughing and laughing and laughing till he was 'most dead, and Tom looked so put out and cheap that I knowed he was ashamed he had come, and he wished he hadn't. But old Hooker never let up on him. He raked up everything a person ever could want to kill another person about, and any fool could see they didn't any of them fit this case, and he just made no end of fun of the whole business and of the people that had been hunting the body; and he said:

"If they'd had any sense they'd 'a' knowed the lazy cuss slid out because he wanted a loafing spell after all this work. He'll come pottering back in a couple of weeks, and then how'll you fellers feel? But, laws bless you, take the dog, and go and hunt his remainders. Do, Tom."

Then he busted out, and had another of them forty-rod laughs of hisn. Tom couldn't back down after all this, so he said, "All right, unchain him;" and the blacksmith done it, and we started home and left that old man laughing yet.

It was a lovely dog. There ain't any dog that's got a lovelier disposition than a bloodhound, and this one knowed us and liked us. He capered and raced around ever so friendly, and powerful glad to be free and have a holiday; but Tom was so cut up he couldn't take any intrust in him, and said he wished he'd stopped and thought a minute before he ever started on such a fool errand. He said old Jeff Hooker would tell everybody, and we'd never hear the last of it.

So we loafed along home down the back lanes, feeling pretty glum and not talking. When we was passing the far corner of our tobacker field we heard the dog set up a long howl in there, and we went to the place and he was scratching the ground with all his might, and every now and then canting up his head sideways and fetching another howl.

It was a long square, the shape of a grave; the rain had made it sink down and show the shape. The minute we come and stood there we looked at one another and never said a word. When the dog had dug down only a few inches he grabbed something and pulled it up, and it was an arm and a sleeve. Tom kind of gasped out, and says:

"Come away, Huck—it's found."

I just felt awful. We struck for the road and fetched the first men that come along. They got a spade at the crib and dug out the body, and you never see such an excitement. You couldn't make anything out of the face, but you didn't need to.

Everybody said:

"Poor Jubiter; it's his clothes, to the last rag!"

Some rushed off to spread the news and tell the justice of the peace and have an inquest, and me and Tom lit out for the house. Tom was all afire and 'most out of breath when we come tearing in where Uncle Silas and Aunt Sally and Benny was. Tom sung out:

"Me and Huck's found Jubiter Dunlap's corpse all by ourselves with a bloodhound, after everybody else had quit hunting and given it up; and if it hadn't a been for us it never WOULD 'a' been found; and he WAS murdered too—they done it with a club or something like that; and I'm going to start in and find the murderer, next, and I bet I'll do it!"

Aunt Sally and Benny sprung up pale and astonished, but Uncle Silas fell right forward out of his chair on to the floor and groans out:

"Oh, my God, you've found him NOW!"

CHAPTER X. THE ARREST OF UNCLE SILAS

THEM awful words froze us solid. We couldn't move hand or foot for as much as half a minute. Then we kind of come to, and lifted the old man up and got him into his chair, and Benny petted him and kissed him and tried to comfort him, and poor old Aunt Sally she done the same; but, poor things, they was so broke up and scared and knocked out of their right minds that they didn't hardly know what they was about. With Tom it was awful; it 'most petrified him to think maybe he had got his uncle into a thousand times more trouble than ever, and maybe it wouldn't ever happened if he hadn't been so ambitious to get celebrated, and let the corpse alone the way the others done. But pretty soon he sort of come to himself again and says:

"Uncle Silas, don't you say another word like that. It's dangerous, and there ain't a shadder of truth in it."

Aunt Sally and Benny was thankful to hear him say that, and they said the same; but the old man he wagged his head sorrowful and hopeless, and the tears run down his face, and he says;

"No—I done it; poor Jubiter, I done it!"

It was dreadful to hear him say it. Then he went on and told about it, and said it happened the day me and Tom come—along about sundown. He said Jubiter pestered him and aggravated him till he was so mad he just sort of lost his mind and grabbed up a stick and hit him over the head with all his might, and Jubiter dropped in his tracks. Then he was scared and sorry, and got down on his knees and lifted his head up, and begged him to speak and say he wasn't dead; and before long he come to, and when he see who it was holding his head, he jumped like he was 'most scared to death, and cleared the fence and tore into the woods, and was gone. So he hoped he wasn't hurt bad.

"But laws," he says, "it was only just fear that gave him that last little spurt of strength, and of course it soon played out and he laid down in the bush, and there wasn't anybody to help him, and he died."

Then the old man cried and grieved, and said he was a

murderer and the mark of Cain was on him, and he had disgraced his family and was going to be found out and hung. But Tom said:

"No, you ain't going to be found out. You DIDN'T kill him. ONE lick wouldn't kill him. Somebody else done it."

"Oh, yes," he says, "I done it—nobody else. Who else had anything against him? Who else COULD have anything against him?"

He looked up kind of like he hoped some of us could mention somebody that could have a grudge against that harmless no-account, but of course it warn't no use—he HAD us; we couldn't say a word. He noticed that, and he saddened down again, and I never see a face so miserable and so pitiful to see. Tom had a sudden idea, and says:

"But hold on!—somebody BURIED him. Now who—"

He shut off sudden. I knowed the reason. It give me the cold shudders when he said them words, because right away I remembered about us seeing Uncle Silas prowling around with a long-handled shovel away in the night that night. And I knowed Benny seen him, too, because she was talking about it one day. The minute Tom shut off he changed the subject and went to begging Uncle Silas to keep mum, and the rest of us done the same, and said he MUST, and said it wasn't his business to tell on himself, and if he kept mum nobody would ever know; but if it was found out and any harm come to him it would break the family's hearts and kill them, and yet never do anybody any good. So at last he promised. We was all of us more comfortable, then, and went to work to cheer up the old man. We told him all he'd got to do was to keep still, and it wouldn't be long till the whole thing would blow over and be forgot. We all said there wouldn't anybody ever suspect Uncle Silas, nor ever dream of such a thing, he being so good and kind, and having such a good character; and Tom says, cordial and hearty, he says:

"Why, just look at it a minute; just consider. Here is Uncle Silas, all these years a preacher—at his own expense; all these years doing good with all his might and every way he can think of—at his own expense, all the time; always been loved by everybody, and respected; always been peaceable and minding his own business, the very last man in this whole deestrict to touch a person, and everybody knows it. Suspect HIM? Why, it ain't any more possible than—"

"By authority of the State of Arkansaw, I arrest you for the murder of Jubiter Dunlap!" shouts the sheriff at the door.

It was awful. Aunt Sally and Benny flung themselves at Uncle Silas, screaming and crying, and hugged him and hung to him, and Aunt Sally said go away, she wouldn't ever give him up, they shouldn't have him, and the niggers they come crowding and crying to the door and—well, I couldn't stand it; it was enough to break a person's heart; so I got out.

They took him up to the little one-horse jail in the village, and we all went along to tell him good-bye; and Tom was feeling elegant, and says to me, "We'll have a most noble good time and heaps of danger some dark night getting him out of there, Huck, and it'll be talked about everywheres and we will be celebrated;" but the old man busted that scheme up the minute he whispered to him about it. He said no, it was his duty to stand whatever the law done to him, and he would stick to the jail plumb through to the end, even if there warn't no door to it. It disappointed Tom and graveled him a good deal, but he had to put up with it.

But he felt responsible and bound to get his uncle Silas free; and he told Aunt Sally, the last thing, not to worry, because he was going to turn in and work night and day and beat this game and fetch Uncle Silas out innocent; and she was very loving to him and thanked him and said she knowed he would do his very best. And she told us to help Benny take care of the house and the children, and then we had a good-bye cry all around and went back to the farm, and left her there to live with the jailer's wife a month till the trial in October.

CHAPTER XI. TOM SAWYER DISCOVERS THE MURDERERS

WELL, that was a hard month on us all. Poor Benny, she kept up the best she could, and me and Tom tried to keep things cheerful there at the house, but it kind of went for nothing, as you may say. It was the same up at the jail. We went up every day to see the old people, but it was awful dreary, because the old man warn't sleeping much, and was walking in his sleep considerable and so he got to looking fagged and miserable, and his mind got shaky, and we all got afraid his troubles would break him down and kill him. And whenever we tried to persuade him to feel cheerfuler, he only shook his head and said if we only knowed what it was to carry around a murderer's load in your heart we wouldn't talk that way. Tom and all of us kept telling him it WASN'T murder, but just accidental killing! but it never made any difference—it was murder, and he wouldn't have it any other way. He actu'ly begun to come out plain and square towards trial time and acknowledge that he TRIED to kill the man. Why, that was awful, you know. It made things seem fifty times as dreadful, and there warn't no more comfort for Aunt Sally and Benny. But he promised he wouldn't say a word about his murder when others was around, and we was glad of that.

Tom Sawyer racked the head off of himself all that month trying to plan some way out for Uncle Silas, and many's the night he kept me up 'most all night with this kind of tiresome work, but he couldn't seem to get on the right track no way. As for me, I reckoned a body might as well give it up, it all looked so blue and I was so downhearted; but he wouldn't. He stuck to the business right along, and went on planning and thinking and ransacking his head.

So at last the trial come on, towards the middle of October, and we was all in the court. The place was jammed, of course. Poor old Uncle Silas, he looked more like a dead person than a live one, his eyes was so hollow and he looked so thin and so mournful. Benny she set on one side of him and Aunt Sally on the other, and they had veils on, and was full of trouble. But Tom he set by our lawyer, and had his finger in everywheres, of course. The lawyer let him, and the judge let him. He 'most took the business out of the lawyer's hands sometimes; which was well enough, because that was only a mud-turtle of a back-settlement lawyer and didn't know enough to come in when it rains, as the saying is.

They swore in the jury, and then the lawyer for the prostitution got up and begun. He made a terrible speech against the old man, that made him moan and groan, and made Benny and Aunt Sally cry. The way HE told about the murder kind of knocked us all stupid it was so different from the old man's tale. He said he was going to prove that Uncle Silas was SEEN to kill Jubiter Dunlap by two good witnesses, and done it deliberate, and SAID he was going to kill him the

very minute he hit him with the club; and they seen him hide Jubiter in the bushes, and they seen that Jubiter was stone-dead. And said Uncle Silas come later and lugged Jubiter down into the tobacker field, and two men seen him do it. And said Uncle Silas turned out, away in the night, and buried Jubiter, and a man seen him at it.

I says to myself, poor old Uncle Silas has been lying about it because he reckoned nobody seen him and he couldn't bear to break Aunt Sally's heart and Benny's; and right he was: as for me, I would 'a' lied the same way, and so would anybody that had any feeling, to save them such misery and sorrow which THEY warn't no ways responsible for. Well, it made our lawyer look pretty sick; and it knocked Tom silly, too, for a little spell, but then he braced up and let on that he warn't worried—but I knowed he WAS, all the same. And the people—my, but it made a stir amongst them!

And when that lawyer was done telling the jury what he was going to prove, he set down and begun to work his witnesses.

First, he called a lot of them to show that there was bad blood betwixt Uncle Silas and the diseased; and they told how they had heard Uncle Silas threaten the diseased, at one time and another, and how it got worse and worse and everybody was talking about it, and how diseased got afraid of his life, and told two or three of them he was certain Uncle Silas would up and kill him some time or another.

Tom and our lawyer asked them some questions; but it warn't no use, they stuck to what they said.

Next, they called up Lem Beebe, and he took the stand. It come into my mind, then, how Lem and Jim Lane had come along talking, that time, about borrowing a dog or something from Jubiter Dunlap; and that brought up the blackberries and the lantern; and that brought up Bill and Jack Withers, and how they passed by, talking about a nigger stealing Uncle Silas's corn; and that fetched up our old ghost that come along about the same time and scared us so—and here HE was too, and a privileged character, on accounts of his being deef and dumb and a stranger, and they had fixed him a chair inside the railing, where he could cross his legs and be comfortable, whilst the other people was all in a jam so they couldn't hardly breathe. So it all come back to me just the way it was that day; and it made me mournful to think how pleasant it was up to then, and how miserable ever since.

LEM BEEBE, sworn, said—"I was a-coming along, that day, second of September, and Jim Lane was with me, and it was towards sundown, and we heard loud talk, like quarrelling, and we was very close, only the hazel bushes between (that's along the fence); and we heard a voice say, 'I've told you more'n once I'd kill you,' and knowed it was this prisoner's voice; and then we see a club come up above the bushes and down out of sight again, and heard a smashing thump and then a groan or two: and then we crope soft to where we could see, and there laid Jupiter Dunlap dead, and this prisoner standing over him with the club; and the next he hauled the dead man into a clump of bushes and hid him, and then we stooped low, to be cut of sight, and got away."

Well, it was awful. It kind of froze everybody's blood to hear it, and the house was 'most as still whilst he was telling it as if there warn't nobody in it. And when he was done, you could hear them gasp and sigh, all over the house, and look at one another the same as to say, "Ain't it perfectly terrible—ain't it awful!"

Now happened a thing that astonished me. All the time the first witnesses was proving the bad blood and the threats and all that, Tom Sawyer was alive and laying for them; and the minute they was through, he went for them, and done his level best to catch them in lies and spile their testimony. But now, how different. When Lem first begun to talk, and never said anything about speaking to Jubiter or trying to borrow a dog off of him, he was all alive and laying for Lem, and you could see he was getting ready to cross-question him to death pretty soon, and then I judged him and me would go on the stand by and by and tell what we heard him and Jim Lane say. But the next time I looked at Tom I got the cold shivers. Why, he was in the brownest study you ever see—miles and miles away. He warn't hearing a word Lem Beebe was saying; and when he got through he was still in that brown-study, just the same. Our lawyer joggled him, and then he looked up startled, and says, "Take the witness if you want him. Lemme alone—I want to think."

Well, that beat me. I couldn't understand it. And Benny and her mother—oh, they looked sick, they was so troubled. They shoved their veils to one side and tried to get his eye, but it warn't any use, and I couldn't get his eye either. So the mud-turtle he tackled the witness, but it didn't amount to nothing; and he made a mess of it.

Then they called up Jim Lane, and he told the very same story over again, exact. Tom never listened to this one at all, but set there thinking and thinking, miles and miles away. So the mud-turtle went in alone again and come out just as flat as he done before. The lawyer for the prostitution looked very comfortable, but the judge looked disgusted. You see, Tom was just the same as a regular lawyer, nearly, because it was Arkansaw law for a prisoner to choose anybody he wanted to help his lawyer, and Tom had had Uncle Silas shove him into the case, and now he was botching it and you could see the judge didn't like it much. All that the mud-turtle got out of Lem and Jim was this: he asked them:

"Why didn't you go and tell what you saw?"

"We was afraid we would get mixed up in it ourselves. And we was just starting down the river a-hunting for all the week besides; but as soon as we come back we found out they'd been searching for the body, so then we went and told Brace Dunlap all about it."

"When was that?"

"Saturday night, September 9th."

The judge he spoke up and says:

"Mr. Sheriff, arrest these two witnesses on suspicions of being accessionary after the fact to the murder."

The lawyer for the prostitution jumps up all excited, and says:

"Your honor! I protest against this extraordi—"

"Set down!" says the judge, pulling his bowie and laying it on his pulpit. "I beg you to respect the Court."

So he done it. Then he called Bill Withers.

BILL WITHERS, sworn, said: "I was coming along about sundown, Saturday, September 2d, by the prisoner's field, and

my brother Jack was with me and we seen a man toting off something heavy on his back and allowed it was a nigger stealing corn; we couldn't see distinct; next we made out that it was one man carrying another; and the way it hung, so kind of limp, we judged it was somebody that was drunk; and by the man's walk we said it was Parson Silas, and we judged he had found Sam Cooper drunk in the road, which he was always trying to reform him, and was toting him out of danger."

It made the people shiver to think of poor old Uncle Silas toting off the diseased down to the place in his tobacker field where the dog dug up the body, but there warn't much sympathy around amongst the faces, and I heard one cuss say "'Tis the coldest blooded work I ever struck, lugging a murdered man around like that, and going to bury him like a animal, and him a preacher at that."

Tom he went on thinking, and never took no notice; so our lawyer took the witness and done the best he could, and it was plenty poor enough.

Then Jack Withers he come on the stand and told the same tale, just like Bill done.

And after him comes Brace Dunlap, and he was looking very mournful, and most crying; and there was a rustle and a stir all around, and everybody got ready to listen, and lost of the women folks said, "Poor cretur, poor cretur," and you could see a many of them wiping their eyes.

BRACE DUNLAP, sworn, said: "I was in considerable trouble a long time about my poor brother, but I reckoned things warn't near so bad as he made out, and I couldn't make myself believe anybody would have the heart to hurt a poor harmless cretur like that"—[by jings, I was sure I seen Tom give a kind of a faint little start, and then look disappointed again]—"and you know I COULDN'T think a preacher would hurt him—it warn't natural to think such an onlikely thing—so I never paid much attention, and now I sha'n't ever, ever forgive myself; for if I had a done different, my poor brother would be with me this day, and not laying yonder murdered, and him so harmless." He kind of broke down there and choked up, and waited to get his voice; and people all around said the most pitiful things, and women cried; and it was very still in there, and solemn, and old Uncle Silas, poor thing, he give a groan right out so everybody heard him. Then Brace he went on, "Saturday, September 2d, he didn't come home to supper. By-and-by I got a little uneasy, and one of my niggers went over to this prisoner's place, but come back and said he warn't there. So I got uneasier and uneasier, and couldn't rest. I went to bed, but I couldn't sleep; and turned out, away late in the night, and went wandering over to this prisoner's place and all around about there a good while, hoping I would run across my poor brother, and never knowing he was out of his troubles and gone to a better shore—" So he broke down and choked up again, and most all the women was crying now. Pretty soon he got another start and says: "But it warn't no use; so at last I went home and tried to get some sleep, but couldn't. Well, in a day or two everybody was uneasy, and they got to talking about this prisoner's threats, and took to the idea, which I didn't take no stock in, that my brother was murdered so they hunted around and tried to find his body, but couldn't and give it up. And so I reckoned he was gone off somers to have a little peace, and would come back to us when his troubles was kind of healed. But late Saturday night, the 9th, Lem Beebe and Jim Lane come to my house and told me all—told me the whole awful 'sassination, and my heart was broke. And THEN I remembered something that hadn't took no hold of me at the time, because reports said this prisoner had took to walking in his sleep and doing all kind of things of no consequence, not knowing what he was about. I will tell you what that thing was that come back into my memory. Away late that awful Saturday night when I was wandering around about this prisoner's place, grieving and troubled, I was down by the corner of the tobacker-field and I heard a sound like digging in a gritty soil; and I crope nearer and peeped through the vines that hung on the rail fence and seen this prisoner SHOVELING—shoveling with a long-handled shovel—heaving earth into a big hole that was most filled up; his back was to me, but it was bright moonlight and I knowed him by his old green baize work-gown with a splattery white patch in the middle of the back like somebody had hit him with a snowball. HE WAS BURYING THE MAN HE'D MURDERED!"

And he slumped down in his chair crying and sobbing, and 'most everybody in the house busted out wailing, and crying, and saying, "Oh, it's awful—awful—horrible! and there was a most tremendous excitement, and you couldn't hear yourself think; and right in the midst of it up jumps old Uncle Silas, white as a sheet, and sings out:

"IT'S TRUE, EVERY WORD—I MURDERED HIM IN COLD BLOOD!"

By Jackson, it petrified them! People rose up wild all over the house, straining and staring for a better look at him, and the judge was hammering with his mallet and the sheriff yelling "Order—order in the court—order!"

And all the while the old man stood there a-quaking and his eyes a-burning, and not looking at his wife and daughter, which was clinging to him and begging him to keep still, but pawing them off with his hands and saying he WOULD clear his black soul from crime, he WOULD heave off this load that was more than he could bear, and he WOULDN'T bear it another hour! And then he raged right along with his awful tale, everybody a-staring and gasping, judge, jury, lawyers, and everybody, and Benny and Aunt Sally crying their hearts out. And by George, Tom Sawyer never looked at him once! Never once—just set there gazing with all his eyes at something else, I couldn't tell what. And so the old man raged right along, pouring his words out like a stream of fire:

"I killed him! I am guilty! But I never had the notion in my life to hurt him or harm him, spite of all them lies about my threatening him, till the very minute I raised the club—then my heart went cold!—then the pity all went out of it, and I struck to kill! In that one moment all my wrongs come into my mind; all the insults that that man and the scoundrel his brother, there, had put upon me, and how they laid in together to ruin me with the people, and take away my good name, and DRIVE me to some deed that would destroy me and my family that hadn't ever done THEM no harm, so help me God! And they done it in a mean revenge—for why? Because my innocent pure girl here at my side wouldn't marry that rich, insolent, ignorant coward, Brace Dunlap, who's been sniveling here over a brother he never cared a brass farthing for—"[I see Tom give a jump and look glad THIS time, to a dead certainty]"—and in that moment I've told you about, I forgot my God and remembered only my heart's bitterness, God forgive me, and I struck to kill. In one second I was miserably sorry—oh, filled with remorse; but I thought of my poor family, and I MUST hide what I'd done for their sakes; and I did hide that corpse in the bushes; and presently I carried it to the tobacker field; and in the deep night I went with my shovel and buried it where—"

Up jumps Tom and shouts:

"NOW, I've got it!" and waves his hand, oh, ever so fine and starchy, towards the old man, and says:

"Set down! A murder WAS done, but you never had no hand in it!"

Well, sir, you could a heard a pin drop. And the old man he sunk down kind of bewildered in his seat and Aunt Sally and Benny didn't know it, because they was so astonished and staring at Tom with their mouths open and not knowing what they was about. And the whole house the same. I never seen people look so helpless and tangled up, and I hain't ever seen eyes bug out and gaze without a blink the way theirn did. Tom says, perfectly ca'm:

"Your honor, may I speak?"

"For God's sake, yes—go on!" says the judge, so astonished and mixed up he didn't know what he was about hardly.

Then Tom he stood there and waited a second or two—that was for to work up an "effect," as he calls it—then he started in just as ca'm as ever, and says:

"For about two weeks now there's been a little bill sticking on the front of this courthouse offering two thousand dollars reward for a couple of big di'monds—stole at St. Louis. Them di'monds is worth twelve thousand dollars. But never mind about that till I get to it. Now about this murder. I will tell you all about it—how it happened—who done it—every DEtail."

You could see everybody nestle now, and begin to listen for all they was worth.

"This man here, Brace Dunlap, that's been sniveling so about his dead brother that YOU know he never cared a straw for, wanted to marry that young girl there, and she wouldn't have him. So he told Uncle Silas he would make him sorry. Uncle Silas knowed how powerful he was, and how little chance he had against such a man, and he was scared and worried, and done everything he could think of to smooth him over and get him to be good to him: he even took his no-account brother Jubiter on the farm and give him wages and stinted his own family to pay them; and Jubiter done everything his brother could contrive to insult Uncle Silas, and fret and worry him, and try to drive Uncle Silas into doing him a hurt, so as to injure Uncle Silas with the people. And it done it. Everybody turned against him and said the meanest kind of things about him, and it gradly broke his heart—yes, and he was so worried and distressed that often he warn't hardly in his right mind.

"Well, on that Saturday that we've had so much trouble about, two of these witnesses here, Lem Beebe and Jim Lane, come along by where Uncle Silas and Jubiter Dunlap was at work—and that much of what they've said is true, the rest is lies. They didn't hear Uncle Silas say he would kill Jubiter; they didn't hear no blow struck; they didn't see no dead man, and they didn't see Uncle Silas hide anything in the bushes. Look at them now—how they set there, wishing they hadn't been so handy with their tongues; anyway, they'll wish it before I get done.

"That same Saturday evening Bill and Jack Withers DID see one man lugging off another one. That much of what they said is true, and the rest is lies. First off they thought it was a nigger stealing Uncle Silas's corn—you notice it makes them look silly, now, to find out somebody overheard them say that. That's because they found out by and by who it was that was doing the lugging, and THEY know best why they swore here that they took it for Uncle Silas by the gait—which it WASN'T, and they knowed it when they swore to that lie.

"A man out in the moonlight DID see a murdered person put under ground in the tobacker field—but it wasn't Uncle Silas that done the burying. He was in his bed at that very time.

"Now, then, before I go on, I want to ask you if you've ever noticed this: that people, when they're thinking deep, or when they're worried, are most always doing something with their hands, and they don't know it, and don't notice what it is their hands are doing; some stroke their chins; some stroke their noses; some stroke up UNDER their chin with their hand; some twirl a chain, some fumble a button, then there's some that draws a figure or a letter with their finger on their cheek, or under their chin or on their under lip. That's MY way. When I'm restless, or worried, or thinking hard, I draw capital V's on my cheek or on my under lip or under my chin, and never anything BUT capital V's—and half the time I don't notice it and don't know I'm doing it."

That was odd. That is just what I do; only I make an O. And I could see people nodding to one another, same as they do when they mean "THAT's so."

"Now, then, I'll go on. That same Saturday—no, it was the night before—there was a steamboat laying at Flagler's Landing, forty miles above here, and it was raining and storming like the nation. And there was a thief aboard, and he had them two big di'monds that's advertised out here on this courthouse door; and he slipped ashore with his hand-bag and struck out into the dark and the storm, and he was a-hoping he could get to this town all right and be safe. But he had two pals aboard the boat, hiding, and he knowed they was going to kill him the first chance they got and take the di'monds; because all three stole them, and then this fellow he got hold of them and skipped.

"Well, he hadn't been gone more'n ten minutes before his pals found it out, and they jumped ashore and lit out after him. Prob'ly they burnt matches and found his tracks. Anyway, they dogged along after him all day Saturday and kept out of his sight; and towards sundown he come to the bunch of sycamores down by Uncle Silas's field, and he went in there to get a disguise out of his hand-bag and put it on before he showed himself here in the town—and mind you he done that just a little after the time that Uncle Silas was hitting Jubiter Dunlap over the head with a club—for he DID hit him.

"But the minute the pals see that thief slide into the bunch of sycamores, they jumped out of the bushes and slid in after him.

"They fell on him and clubbed him to death.

"Yes, for all he screamed and howled so, they never had no mercy on him, but clubbed him to death. And two men that was running along the road heard him yelling that way, and they made a rush into the syca-i more bunch—which was where they was bound for, anyway—and when the pals saw them they lit out and the two new men after them a-chasing them as tight as they could go. But only a minute or two—then these two new men slipped back very quiet into the sycamores.

"THEN what did they do? I will tell you what they done. They found where the thief had got his disguise out of his carpet-sack to put on; so one of them strips and puts on that disguise."

Tom waited a little here, for some more "effect"—then he says, very deliberate:

"The man that put on that dead man's disguise was—JUBITER DUNLAP!"

"Great Scott!" everybody shouted, all over the house, and old Uncle Silas he looked perfectly astonished.

"Yes, it was Jubiter Dunlap. Not dead, you see. Then they pulled off the dead man's boots and put Jubiter Dunlap's old ragged shoes on the corpse and put the corpse's boots on Jubiter Dunlap. Then Jubiter Dunlap stayed where he was, and the other man lugged the dead body off in the twilight; and after midnight he went to Uncle Silas's house, and took his old green work-robe off of the peg where it always hangs in the passage betwixt the house and the kitchen and put it on, and stole the long-handled shovel and went off down into the tobacker field and buried the murdered man."

He stopped, and stood half a minute. Then—"And who do you reckon the murdered man WAS? It was—JAKE Dunlap, the long-lost burglar!"

"Great Scott!"

"And the man that buried him was—BRACE Dunlap, his brother!"

"Great Scott!"

"And who do you reckon is this mowing idiot here that's letting on all these weeks to be a deef and dumb stranger? It's—JUBITER Dunlap!"

My land, they all busted out in a howl, and you never see the like of that excitement since the day you was born. And Tom he made a jump for Jubiter and snaked off his goggles and his false whiskers, and there was the murdered man, sure enough, just as alive as anybody! And Aunt Sally and Benny they went to hugging and crying and kissing and smothering old Uncle Silas to that degree he was more muddled and confused and mushed up in his mind than he ever was before, and that is saying considerable. And next, people begun to yell:

"Tom Sawyer! Tom Sawyer! Shut up everybody, and let him go on! Go on, Tom Sawyer!"

Which made him feel uncommon bully, for it was nuts for Tom Sawyer to be a public character that-away, and a hero, as he calls it. So when it was all quiet, he says:

"There ain't much left, only this. When that man there, Bruce Dunlap, had most worried the life and sense out of Uncle Silas till at last he plumb lost his mind and hit this other blatherskite, his brother, with a club, I reckon he seen his chance. Jubiter broke for the woods to hide, and I reckon the game was for him to slide out, in the night, and leave the country. Then Brace would make everybody believe Uncle Silas killed him and hid his body somers; and that would ruin Uncle Silas and drive HIM out of the country—hang him, maybe; I dunno. But when they found their dead brother in the sycamores without knowing him, because he was so battered up, they see they had a better thing; disguise BOTH and bury Jake and dig him up presently all dressed up in Jubiter's clothes, and hire Jim Lane and Bill Withers and the others to swear to some handy lies—which they done. And there they set, now, and I told them they would be looking sick before I got done, and that is the way they're looking now.

"Well, me and Huck Finn here, we come down on the boat with the thieves, and the dead one told us all about the di'monds, and said the others would murder him if they got the chance; and we was going to help him all we could. We was bound for the sycamores when we heard them killing him in there; but we was in there in the early morning after the storm and allowed nobody hadn't been killed, after all. And when we see Jubiter Dunlap here spreading around in the very same disguise Jake told us HE was going to wear, we thought it was Jake his own self—and he was goo-gooing deef and dumb, and THAT was according to agreement.

"Well, me and Huck went on hunting for the corpse after the others quit, and we found it. And was proud, too; but Uncle Silas he knocked us crazy by telling us HE killed the man. So we was mighty sorry we found the body, and was bound to save Uncle Silas's neck if we could; and it was going to be tough work, too, because he wouldn't let us break him out of prison the way we done with our old nigger Jim.

"I done everything I could the whole month to think up some way to save Uncle Silas, but I couldn't strike a thing. So when we come into court to-day I come empty, and couldn't see no chance anywheres. But by and by I had a glimpse of something that set me thinking—just a little wee glimpse—only that, and not enough to make sure; but it set me thinking hard—and WATCHING, when I was only letting on to think; and by and by, sure enough, when Uncle Silas was piling out that stuff about HIM killing Jubiter Dunlap, I catched that glimpse again, and this time I jumped up and shut down the proceedings, because I KNOWED Jubiter Dunlap was a-setting here before me. I knowed him by a thing which I seen him do—and I remembered it. I'd seen him do it when I was here a year ago."

He stopped then, and studied a minute—laying for an "effect"—I knowed it perfectly well. Then he turned off like he was going to leave the platform, and says, kind of lazy and indifferent:

"Well, I believe that is all."

Why, you never heard such a howl!—and it come from the whole house:

"What WAS it you seen him do? Stay where you are, you little devil! You think you are going to work a body up till his mouth's a-watering and stop there? What WAS it he done?"

That was it, you see—he just done it to get an "effect"; you couldn't 'a' pulled him off of that platform with a yoke of oxen.

"Oh, it wasn't anything much," he says. "I seen him looking a little excited when he found Uncle Silas was actly fixing to hang himself for a murder that warn't ever done; and he got more and more nervous and worried, I a-watching him sharp but not seeming to look at him—and all of a sudden his hands begun to work and fidget, and pretty soon his left crept up and HIS FINGER DRAWED A CROSS ON HIS CHEEK, and then I HAD him!"

Well, then they ripped and howled and stomped and clapped their hands till Tom Sawyer was that proud and happy he didn't know what to do with himself.

And then the judge he looked down over his pulpit and says:

"My boy, did you SEE all the various details of this strange conspiracy and tragedy that you've been describing?"

"No, your honor, I didn't see any of them."

"Didn't see any of them! Why, you've told the whole history straight through, just the same as if you'd seen it with your eyes. How did you manage that?"

Tom says, kind of easy and comfortable:

"Oh, just noticing the evidence and piecing this and that together, your honor; just an ordinary little bit of detective work; anybody could 'a' done it."

"Nothing of the kind! Not two in a million could 'a' done it. You are a very remarkable boy."

Then they let go and give Tom another smashing round, and he—well, he wouldn't 'a' sold out for a silver mine. Then the judge says:

"But are you certain you've got this curious history straight?"

"Perfectly, your honor. Here is Brace Dunlap—let him deny his share of it if he wants to take the chance; I'll engage to make him wish he hadn't said anything...... Well, you see HE'S pretty quiet. And his brother's pretty quiet, and them four witnesses that lied so and got paid for it, they're pretty quiet. And as for Uncle Silas, it ain't any use for him to put in his oar, I wouldn't believe him under oath!"

Well, sir, that fairly made them shout; and even the judge he let go and laughed. Tom he was just feeling like a rainbow. When they was done laughing he looks up at the judge and says:

"Your honor, there's a thief in this house."

"A thief?"

"Yes, sir. And he's got them twelve-thousand-dollar di'monds on him."

By gracious, but it made a stir! Everybody went shouting:

"Which is him? which is him? p'int him out!"

And the judge says:

"Point him out, my lad. Sheriff, you will arrest him. Which one is it?"

Tom says:

"This late dead man here—Jubiter Dunlap."

Then there was another thundering let-go of astonishment and excitement; but Jubiter, which was astonished enough before, was just fairly putrified with astonishment this time. And he spoke up, about half crying, and says:

"Now THAT'S a lie. Your honor, it ain't fair; I'm plenty bad enough without that. I done the other things—Brace he put me up to it, and persuaded me, and promised he'd make me rich, some day, and I done it, and I'm sorry I done it, and I wisht I hadn't; but I hain't stole no di'monds, and I hain't GOT no di'monds; I wisht I may never stir if it ain't so. The sheriff can search me and see."

Tom says:

"Your honor, it wasn't right to call him a thief, and I'll let up on that a little. He did steal the di'monds, but he didn't know it. He stole them from his brother Jake when he was laying dead, after Jake had stole them from the other thieves; but Jubiter didn't know he was stealing them; and he's been swelling around here with them a month; yes, sir, twelve thousand dollars' worth of di'monds on him—all that riches, and going around here every day just like a poor man. Yes, your honor, he's got them on him now."

The judge spoke up and says:

"Search him, sheriff."

Well, sir, the sheriff he ransacked him high and low, and everywhere: searched his hat, socks, seams, boots, everything—and Tom he stood there quiet, laying for another of them effects of hisn. Finally the sheriff he give it up, and everybody looked disappointed, and Jubiter says:

"There, now! what'd I tell you?"

And the judge says:

"It appears you were mistaken this time, my boy."

Then Tom took an attitude and let on to be studying with all his might, and scratching his head. Then all of a sudden he glanced up chipper, and says:

"Oh, now I've got it! I'd forgot."

Which was a lie, and I knowed it. Then he says:

"Will somebody be good enough to lend me a little small screwdriver? There was one in your brother's hand-bag that you smouched, Jubiter. but I reckon you didn't fetch it with you."

"No, I didn't. I didn't want it, and I give it away."

"That's because you didn't know what it was for."

Jubiter had his boots on again, by now, and when the thing Tom wanted was passed over the people's heads till it got to him, he says to Jubiter:

"Put up your foot on this chair." And he kneeled down and begun to unscrew the heel-plate, everybody watching; and when he got that big di'mond out of that boot-heel and held it up and let it flash and blaze and squirt sunlight everwhichaway, it just took everybody's breath; and Jubiter he looked so sick and sorry you never see the like of it. And when Tom held up the other di'mond he looked sorrier than ever. Land! he was thinking how he would 'a' skipped out and been rich and independent in a foreign land if he'd only had the luck to guess what the screwdriver was in the carpet-bag for.

Well, it was a most exciting time, take it all around, and Tom got cords of glory. The judge took the di'monds, and stood up in his pulpit, and cleared his throat, and shoved his spectacles back on his head, and says:

"I'll keep them and notify the owners; and when they send for them it will be a real pleasure to me to hand you the two thousand dollars, for you've earned the money—yes, and you've earned the deepest and most sincerest thanks of this community besides, for lifting a wronged and innocent family out of ruin and shame, and saving a good and honorable man from a felon's death, and for exposing to infamy and the punishment of the law a cruel and odious scoundrel and his miserable creatures!"

Well, sir, if there'd been a brass band to bust out some music, then, it would 'a' been just the perfectest thing I ever see, and Tom Sawyer he said the same.

Then the sheriff he nabbed Brace Dunlap and his crowd, and by and by next month the judge had them up for trial and jailed the whole lot. And everybody crowded back to Uncle Silas's little old church, and was ever so loving and kind to him and the family and couldn't do enough for them; and Uncle Silas he preached them the blamedest jumbledest idiotic sermons you ever struck, and would tangle you up so you couldn't find your way home in daylight; but the people never let on but what they thought it was the clearest and brightest and elegantest sermons that ever was; and they would set there and cry, for love and pity; but, by George, they give me the jim-jams and the fan-tods and caked up what brains I had, and turned them solid; but by and by they loved the old man's intellects back into him again, and he was as sound in his skull as ever he was, which ain't no flattery, I reckon. And so the whole family was as happy as birds, and nobody could be gratefuler and lovinger than what they was to Tom Sawyer; and the same to me, though I hadn't done nothing. And when the two thousand dollars come, Tom give half of it to me, and never told anybody so, which didn't surprise me, because I knowed him.

Life On The Mississippi
By Mark Twain

THE 'BODY OF THE NATION'

BUT the basin of the Mississippi is the BODY OF THE NATION. All the other parts are but members, important in themselves, yet more important in their relations to this. Exclusive of the Lake basin and of 300,000 square miles in Texas and New Mexico, which in many aspects form a part of it, this basin contains about 1,250,000 square miles. In extent it is the second great valley of the world, being exceeded only by that of the Amazon. The valley of the frozen Obi approaches it in extent; that of La Plata comes next in space, and probably in habitable capacity, having about eight-ninths of its area; then comes that of the Yenisei, with about seven-ninths; the Lena, Amoor, Hoang-ho, Yang-tse-kiang, and Nile, five-ninths; the Ganges, less than one-half; the Indus, less than one-third; the Euphrates, one-fifth; the Rhine, one-fifteenth. It exceeds in extent the whole of Europe, exclusive of Russia, Norway, and Sweden. IT WOULD CONTAIN AUSTRIA FOUR TIMES, GERMANY OR SPAIN FIVE TIMES, FRANCE SIX TIMES, THE BRITISH ISLANDS OR ITALY TEN TIMES. Conceptions formed from the river-basins of Western Europe are rudely shocked when we consider the extent of the valley of the Mississippi; nor are those formed from the sterile basins of the great rivers of Siberia, the lofty plateaus of Central Asia, or the mighty sweep of the swampy Amazon more adequate. Latitude, elevation, and rainfall all combine to render every part of the Mississippi Valley capable of supporting a dense population. AS A DWELLING-PLACE FOR CIVILIZED MAN IT IS BY FAR THE FIRST UPON OUR GLOBE.

EDITOR'S TABLE, HARPER'S MAGAZINE, FEBRUARY 1863

Chapter 1 The River and Its History

THE Mississippi is well worth reading about. It is not a commonplace river, but on the contrary is in all ways remarkable. Considering the Missouri its main branch, it is the longest river in the world—four thousand three hundred miles. It seems safe to say that it is also the crookedest river in the world, since in one part of its journey it uses up one thousand three hundred miles to cover the same ground that the crow would fly over in six hundred and seventy-five. It discharges three times as much water as the St. Lawrence, twenty-five times as much as the Rhine, and three hundred and thirty-eight times as much as the Thames. No other river has so vast a drainage-basin: it draws its water supply from twenty-eight States and Territories; from Delaware, on the Atlantic seaboard, and from all the country between that and Idaho on the Pacific slope—a spread of forty-five degrees of longitude. The Mississippi receives and carries to the Gulf water from fifty-four subordinate rivers that are navigable by steamboats, and from some hundreds that are navigable by flats and keels. The area of its drainage-basin is as great as the combined areas of England, Wales, Scotland, Ireland, France, Spain, Portugal, Germany, Austria, Italy, and Turkey; and almost all this wide region is fertile; the Mississippi valley, proper, is exceptionally so.

It is a remarkable river in this: that instead of widening toward its mouth, it grows narrower; grows narrower and deeper. From the junction of the Ohio to a point half way down to the sea, the width averages a mile in high water: thence to the sea the width steadily diminishes, until, at the 'Passes,' above the mouth, it is but little over half a mile. At the junction of the Ohio the Mississippi's depth is eighty-seven feet; the depth increases gradually, reaching one hundred and twenty-nine just above the mouth.

The difference in rise and fall is also remarkable—not in the upper, but in the lower river. The rise is tolerably uniform down to Natchez (three hundred and sixty miles above the mouth)—about fifty feet. But at Bayou La Fourche the river rises only twenty-four feet; at New Orleans only fifteen, and just above the mouth only two and one half.

An article in the New Orleans 'Times-Democrat,' based upon reports of able engineers, states that the river annually empties four hundred and six million tons of mud into the Gulf of Mexico—which brings to mind Captain Marryat's rude name for the Mississippi—'the Great Sewer.' This mud, solidified, would make a mass a mile square and two hundred and forty-one feet high.

The mud deposit gradually extends the land—but only gradually; it has extended it not quite a third of a mile in the two hundred years which have elapsed since the river took its place in history. The belief of the scientific people is, that the mouth used to be at Baton Rouge, where the hills cease, and that the two hundred miles of land between there and the Gulf was built by the river. This gives us the age of that piece of country, without any trouble at all—one hundred and twenty thousand years. Yet it is much the youthfullest batch of country that lies around there anywhere.

The Mississippi is remarkable in still another way—its disposition to make prodigious jumps by cutting through narrow necks of land, and thus straightening and shortening itself. More than once it has shortened itself thirty miles at a single jump! These cut-offs have had curious effects: they have thrown several river towns out into the rural districts, and built up sand bars and forests in front of them. The town of Delta used to be three miles below Vicksburg: a recent cutoff has radically changed the position, and Delta is now TWO MILES ABOVE Vicksburg.

Both of these river towns have been retired to the country by that cut-off. A cut-off plays havoc with boundary lines and jurisdictions: for instance, a man is living in the State of Mississippi to-day, a cut-off occurs to-night, and to-morrow the man finds himself and his land over on the other side of the river, within the boundaries and subject to the laws of the State of Louisiana! Such a thing, happening in the upper river in the old times, could have transferred a slave from Missouri to Illinois and made a free man of him.

The Mississippi does not alter its locality by cut-offs alone: it is always changing its habitat BODILY—is always moving bodily SIDEWISE. At Hard Times, La., the river is two miles west of the region it used to occupy. As a result, the original SITE of that settlement is not now in Louisiana at all, but on the other side of the river, in the State of Mississippi. NEARLY THE WHOLE OF THAT ONE THOUSAND THREE HUNDRED MILES OF OLD MISSISSIPPI RIVER WHICH LA SALLE FLOATED DOWN IN HIS CANOES, TWO HUNDRED YEARS AGO, IS GOOD SOLID DRY GROUND NOW. The river lies to the right of it, in places, and to the left of it in other places.

Although the Mississippi's mud builds land but slowly, down at the mouth, where the Gulfs billows interfere with its work, it builds fast enough in better protected regions higher up: for instance, Prophet's Island contained one thousand five hundred acres of land thirty years ago; since then the river has added seven hundred acres to it.

But enough of these examples of the mighty stream's eccentricities for the present—I will give a few more of them further along in the book.

Let us drop the Mississippi's physical history, and say a word about its historical history—so to speak. We can glance briefly at its slumbrous first epoch in a couple of short chapters; at its second and wider-awake epoch in a couple more; at its flushest and widest-awake epoch in a good many succeeding chapters; and then talk about its comparatively tranquil present epoch in what shall be left of the book.

The world and the books are so accustomed to use, and over-use, the word 'new' in connection with our country, that we early get and permanently retain the impression that there is nothing old about it. We do of course know that there are several comparatively old dates in American history, but the mere figures convey to our minds no just idea, no distinct realization, of the stretch of time which they represent. To say that De Soto, the first white man who ever saw the Mississippi River, saw it in 1542, is a remark which states a fact without interpreting it: it is something like giving the dimensions of a sunset by astronomical measurements, and cataloguing the colors by their scientific names;—as a result, you get the bald fact of the sunset, but you don't see the sunset. It would have been better to paint a picture of it.

The date 1542, standing by itself, means little or nothing to us; but when one groups a few neighboring historical dates and facts around it, he adds perspective and color, and then realizes that this is one of the American dates which is quite respectable for age.

For instance, when the Mississippi was first seen by a white man, less than a quarter of a century had elapsed since Francis I.'s defeat at Pavia; the death of Raphael, the death of Bayard, SANS PEUR ET SANS REPROCHE; the driving out of the Knights-Hospitallers from Rhodes by the Turks; and the placarding of the Ninety-Five Propositions,—the act which began the Reformation. When De Soto took his glimpse of the river, Ignatius Loyola was an obscure name; the order of the Jesuits was not yet a year old; Michael Angelo's paint was not yet dry on the Last Judgment in the Sistine Chapel; Mary Queen of Scots was not yet born, but would be before the year closed. Catherine de Medici was a child; Elizabeth of England was not yet in her teens; Calvin, Benvenuto Cellini, and the Emperor Charles V. were at the top of their fame, and each was manufacturing history after his own peculiar fashion; Margaret of Navarre was writing the 'Heptameron' and some religious books,—the first survives, the others are forgotten, wit and indelicacy being sometimes better literature preservers than holiness; lax court morals and the absurd chivalry business were in full feather, and the joust and the tournament were the frequent pastime of titled fine gentlemen who could fight better than they could spell, while religion was the passion of their ladies, and classifying their offspring into children of full rank and children by brevet their pastime. In fact, all around, religion was in a peculiarly blooming condition: the Council of Trent was being called; the Spanish Inquisition was roasting, and racking, and burning, with a free hand; elsewhere on the continent the nations were being persuaded to holy living by the sword and fire; in England, Henry VIII. had suppressed the monasteries, burnt Fisher and another bishop or two, and was getting his English reformation and his harem effectively started. When De Soto stood on the banks of the Mississippi, it was still two years

before Luther's death; eleven years before the burning of Servetus; thirty years before the St. Bartholomew slaughter; Rabelais was not yet published; 'Don Quixote' was not yet written; Shakespeare was not yet born; a hundred long years must still elapse before Englishmen would hear the name of Oliver Cromwell.

Unquestionably the discovery of the Mississippi is a datable fact which considerably mellows and modifies the shiny newness of our country, and gives her a most respectable outside-aspect of rustiness and antiquity.

De Soto merely glimpsed the river, then died and was buried in it by his priests and soldiers. One would expect the priests and the soldiers to multiply the river's dimensions by ten—the Spanish custom of the day— and thus move other adventurers to go at once and explore it. On the contrary, their narratives when they reached home, did not excite that amount of curiosity. The Mississippi was left unvisited by whites during a term of years which seems incredible in our energetic days. One may 'sense' the interval to his mind, after a fashion, by dividing it up in this way: After De Soto glimpsed the river, a fraction short of a quarter of a century elapsed, and then Shakespeare was born; lived a trifle more than half a century, then died; and when he had been in his grave considerably more than half a century, the SECOND white man saw the Mississippi. In our day we don't allow a hundred and thirty years to elapse between glimpses of a marvel. If somebody should discover a creek in the county next to the one that the North Pole is in, Europe and America would start fifteen costly expeditions thither: one to explore the creek, and the other fourteen to hunt for each other.

For more than a hundred and fifty years there had been white settlements on our Atlantic coasts. These people were in intimate communication with the Indians: in the south the Spaniards were robbing, slaughtering, enslaving and converting them; higher up, the English were trading beads and blankets to them for a consideration, and throwing in civilization and whiskey, 'for lagniappe;' and in Canada the French were schooling them in a rudimentary way, missionarying among them, and drawing whole populations of them at a time to Quebec, and later to Montreal, to buy furs of them. Necessarily, then, these various clusters of whites must have heard of the great river of the far west; and indeed, they did hear of it vaguely,—so vaguely and indefinitely, that its course, proportions, and locality were hardly even guessable. The mere mysteriousness of the matter ought to have fired curiosity and compelled exploration; but this did not occur. Apparently nobody happened to want such a river, nobody needed it, nobody was curious about it; so, for a century and a half the Mississippi remained out of the market and undisturbed. When De Soto found it, he was not hunting for a river, and had no present occasion for one; consequently he did not value it or even take any particular notice of it.

But at last La Salle the Frenchman conceived the idea of seeking out that river and exploring it. It always happens that when a man seizes upon a neglected and important idea, people inflamed with the same notion crop up all around. It happened so in this instance.

Naturally the question suggests itself, Why did these people want the river now when nobody had wanted it in the five preceding generations? Apparently it was because at this late day they thought they had discovered a way to make it useful; for it had come to be believed that the Mississippi emptied into the Gulf of California, and therefore afforded a short cut from Canada to China. Previously the supposition had been that it emptied into the Atlantic, or Sea of Virginia.

Chapter 2 The River and Its Explorers

LA SALLE himself sued for certain high privileges, and they were graciously accorded him by Louis XIV of inflated memory. Chief among them was the privilege to explore, far and wide, and build forts, and stake out continents, and hand the same over to the king, and pay the expenses himself; receiving, in return, some little advantages of one sort or another; among them the monopoly of buffalo hides. He spent several years and about all of his money, in making perilous and painful trips between Montreal and a fort which he had built on the Illinois, before he at last succeeded in getting his expedition in such a shape that he could strike for the Mississippi.

And meantime other parties had had better fortune. In 1673 Joliet the merchant, and Marquette the priest, crossed the country and reached the banks of the Mississippi. They went by way of the Great Lakes; and from Green Bay, in canoes, by way of Fox River and the Wisconsin. Marquette had solemnly contracted, on the feast of the Immaculate Conception, that if the Virgin would permit him to discover the great river, he would name it Conception, in her honor. He kept his word. In that day, all explorers traveled with an outfit of priests. De Soto had twenty-four with him. La Salle had several, also. The expeditions were often out of meat, and scant of clothes, but they always had the furniture and other requisites for the mass; they were always prepared, as one of the quaint chroniclers of the time phrased it, to 'explain hell to the savages.'

On the 17th of June, 1673, the canoes of Joliet and Marquette and their five subordinates reached the junction of the Wisconsin with the Mississippi. Mr. Parkman says: 'Before them a wide and rapid current coursed athwart their way, by the foot of lofty heights wrapped thick in forests.' He continues: 'Turning southward, they paddled down the stream, through a solitude unrelieved by the faintest trace of man.'

A big cat-fish collided with Marquette's canoe, and startled him; and reasonably enough, for he had been warned by the Indians that he was on a foolhardy journey, and even a fatal one, for the river contained a demon 'whose roar could be heard at a great distance, and who would engulf them in the abyss where he dwelt.' I have seen a Mississippi cat-fish that was more than six feet long, and weighed two hundred and fifty pounds; and if Marquette's fish was the fellow to that one, he had a fair right to think the river's roaring demon was come.

'At length the buffalo began to appear, grazing in herds on the great prairies which then bordered the river; and Marquette describes the fierce and stupid look of the old bulls as they stared at the intruders through the tangled mane which nearly blinded them.'

The voyagers moved cautiously: 'Landed at night and made a fire to cook their evening meal; then extinguished it, embarked again, paddled some way farther, and anchored in the stream, keeping a man on the watch till morning.'

They did this day after day and night after night; and at the end of two weeks they had not seen a human being. The river was an awful solitude, then. And it is now, over most of its stretch.

But at the close of the fortnight they one day came upon the footprints of men in the mud of the western bank—a Robinson Crusoe experience which carries an electric shiver with it yet, when one stumbles on it in print. They had been warned that the river Indians were as ferocious and pitiless as the river demon, and destroyed all comers without waiting for provocation; but no matter, Joliet and Marquette struck into the country to hunt up the proprietors of the tracks. They found them, by and by, and were hospitably received and well treated—if to be received by an Indian chief who has taken off his last rag in order to appear at his level best is to be received hospitably; and if to be treated abundantly to fish, porridge, and other game, including dog, and have these things forked into one's mouth by the ungloved fingers of Indians is to be well treated. In the morning the chief and six hundred of his tribesmen escorted the Frenchmen to the river and bade them a friendly farewell.

On the rocks above the present city of Alton they found some rude and fantastic Indian paintings, which they describe. A short distance below 'a torrent of yellow mud rushed furiously athwart the calm blue current of the Mississippi, boiling and surging and sweeping in its course logs, branches, and uprooted trees.' This was the mouth of the Missouri, 'that savage river,' which 'descending from its mad career through a vast unknown of barbarism, poured its turbid floods into the bosom of its gentle sister.'

By and by they passed the mouth of the Ohio; they passed cane-brakes; they fought mosquitoes; they floated along, day after day, through the deep silence and loneliness of the river, drowsing in the scant shade of makeshift awnings, and broiling with the heat; they encountered and exchanged civilities with another party of Indians; and at last they reached the mouth of the Arkansas (about a month out from their starting-point), where a tribe of war-whooping savages swarmed out to meet and murder them; but they appealed to the Virgin for help; so in place of a fight there was a feast, and plenty of pleasant palaver and fol-de-rol.

They had proved to their satisfaction, that the Mississippi did not empty into the Gulf of California, or into the Atlantic. They believed it emptied into the Gulf of Mexico. They turned back, now, and carried their great news to Canada.

But belief is not proof. It was reserved for La Salle to furnish the proof. He was provokingly delayed, by one misfortune after another, but at last got his expedition under way at the end of the year 1681. In the dead of winter he and Henri de Tonty, son of Lorenzo Tonty, who invented the tontine, his lieutenant, started down the Illinois, with a following of eighteen Indians brought from New England, and twenty-three Frenchmen. They moved in procession down the surface of the frozen river, on foot, and dragging their canoes after them on sledges.

At Peoria Lake they struck open water, and paddled thence to the Mississippi and turned their prows southward. They plowed through the fields of floating ice, past the mouth of the Missouri; past the mouth of the Ohio, by-and-by; 'and, gliding by the wastes of bordering swamp, landed on the 24th of February near the Third Chickasaw Bluffs,' where they halted and built Fort Prudhomme.

'Again,' says Mr. Parkman, 'they embarked; and with every stage of their adventurous progress, the mystery of this vast new world was more and more unveiled. More and more they entered the realms of spring. The hazy sunlight, the warm and drowsy air, the tender foliage, the opening flowers, betokened the reviving life of nature.'

Day by day they floated down the great bends, in the shadow of the dense forests, and in time arrived at the mouth of the Arkansas. First, they were greeted by the natives of this locality as Marquette had before been greeted by them—with the booming of the war drum and the flourish of arms. The Virgin composed the difficulty in Marquette's case; the pipe of peace did the same office for La Salle. The white man and the red man struck hands and entertained each other during three days. Then, to the admiration of the savages, La Salle set up a cross with the arms of France on it, and took possession of the whole country for the king—the cool fashion of the time—while the priest piously consecrated the robbery with a hymn. The priest explained the mysteries of the faith 'by signs,' for the saving of the savages; thus compensating them with possible possessions in Heaven for the certain ones on earth which they had just been robbed of. And also, by signs, La Salle drew from these simple children of the forest acknowledgments of fealty to Louis the Putrid, over the water. Nobody smiled at these colossal ironies.

These performances took place on the site of the future town of Napoleon, Arkansas, and there the first confiscation-cross was raised on the banks of the great river. Marquette's and Joliet's voyage of discovery ended at the same spot—the site of the future town of Napoleon. When De Soto took his fleeting glimpse of the river, away back in the dim early days, he took it from that same spot—the site of the future town of Napoleon, Arkansas. Therefore, three out of the four memorable events connected with the discovery and exploration of the mighty river, occurred, by accident, in one and the same place. It is a most curious distinction, when one comes to look at it and think about it. France stole that vast country on that spot, the future Napoleon; and by and by Napoleon himself was to give the country back again!—make restitution, not to the owners, but to their white American heirs.

The voyagers journeyed on, touching here and there; 'passed the sites, since become historic, of Vicksburg and Grand Gulf,' and visited an imposing Indian monarch in the Teche country, whose capital city was a substantial one of sun-baked bricks mixed with straw—better houses than many that exist there now. The chiefs house contained an audience room forty feet square; and there he received Tonty in State, surrounded by sixty old men clothed in white cloaks. There was a temple in the town, with a mud wall about it ornamented with skulls of enemies sacrificed to the sun.

The voyagers visited the Natchez Indians, near the site of the present city of that name, where they found a 'religious and political despotism, a privileged class descended from the sun, a temple and a sacred fire.' It must have been like getting home again; it was home with an advantage, in fact, for it lacked Louis XIV.

A few more days swept swiftly by, and La Salle stood in the shadow of his confiscating cross, at the meeting of the waters from Delaware, and from Itaska, and from the mountain ranges close upon the Pacific, with the waters of the Gulf of Mexico, his task finished, his prodigy achieved. Mr. Parkman, in closing his fascinating narrative, thus sums up:

'On that day, the realm of France received on parchment a stupendous accession. The fertile plains of Texas; the vast

basin of the Mississippi, from its frozen northern springs to the sultry borders of the Gulf; from the woody ridges of the Alleghanies to the bare peaks of the Rocky Mountains—a region of savannas and forests, sun-cracked deserts and grassy prairies, watered by a thousand rivers, ranged by a thousand warlike tribes, passed beneath the scepter of the Sultan of Versailles; and all by virtue of a feeble human voice, inaudible at half a mile.'

Chapter 3 Frescoes from the Past

APPARENTLY the river was ready for business, now. But no, the distribution of a population along its banks was as calm and deliberate and time-devouring a process as the discovery and exploration had been.

Seventy years elapsed, after the exploration, before the river's borders had a white population worth considering; and nearly fifty more before the river had a commerce. Between La Salle's opening of the river and the time when it may be said to have become the vehicle of anything like a regular and active commerce, seven sovereigns had occupied the throne of England, America had become an independent nation, Louis XIV. and Louis XV. had rotted and died, the French monarchy had gone down in the red tempest of the revolution, and Napoleon was a name that was beginning to be talked about. Truly, there were snails in those days.

The river's earliest commerce was in great barges—keelboats, broadhorns. They floated and sailed from the upper rivers to New Orleans, changed cargoes there, and were tediously warped and poled back by hand. A voyage down and back sometimes occupied nine months. In time this commerce increased until it gave employment to hordes of rough and hardy men; rude, uneducated, brave, suffering terrific hardships with sailor-like stoicism; heavy drinkers, coarse frolickers in moral sties like the Natchez-under-the-hill of that day, heavy fighters, reckless fellows, every one, elephantinely jolly, foul-witted, profane; prodigal of their money, bankrupt at the end of the trip, fond of barbaric finery, prodigious braggarts; yet, in the main, honest, trustworthy, faithful to promises and duty, and often picturesquely magnanimous.

By and by the steamboat intruded. Then for fifteen or twenty years, these men continued to run their keelboats down-stream, and the steamers did all of the upstream business, the keelboatmen selling their boats in New Orleans, and returning home as deck passengers in the steamers.

But after a while the steamboats so increased in number and in speed that they were able to absorb the entire commerce; and then keelboating died a permanent death. The keelboatman became a deck hand, or a mate, or a pilot on the steamer; and when steamer-berths were not open to him, he took a berth on a Pittsburgh coal-flat, or on a pine-raft constructed in the forests up toward the sources of the Mississippi.

In the heyday of the steamboating prosperity, the river from end to end was flaked with coal-fleets and timber rafts, all managed by hand, and employing hosts of the rough characters whom I have been trying to describe. I remember the annual processions of mighty rafts that used to glide by Hannibal when I was a boy,—an acre or so of white, sweet-smelling boards in each raft, a crew of two dozen men or more, three or four wigwams scattered about the raft's vast level space for storm- quarters,—and I remember the rude ways and the tremendous talk of their big crews, the ex-keelboatmen and their admiringly patterning successors; for we used to swim out a quarter or third of a mile and get on these rafts and have a ride.

By way of illustrating keelboat talk and manners, and that now-departed and hardly-remembered raft-life, I will throw in, in this place, a chapter from a book which I have been working at, by fits and starts, during the past five or six years, and may possibly finish in the course of five or six more. The book is a story which details some passages in the life of an ignorant village boy, Huck Finn, son of the town drunkard of my time out west, there. He has run away from his persecuting father, and from a persecuting good widow who wishes to make a nice, truth-telling, respectable boy of him; and with him a slave of the widow's has also escaped. They have found a fragment of a lumber raft (it is high water and dead summer time), and are floating down the river by night, and hiding in the willows by day,—bound for Cairo,—whence the negro will seek freedom in the heart of the free States. But in a fog, they pass Cairo without knowing it. By and by they begin to suspect the truth, and Huck Finn is persuaded to end the dismal suspense by swimming down to a huge raft which they have seen in the distance ahead of them, creeping aboard under cover of the darkness, and gathering the needed information by eavesdropping:—

But you know a young person can't wait very well when he is impatient to find a thing out. We talked it over, and by and by Jim said it was such a black night, now, that it wouldn't be no risk to swim down to the big raft and crawl aboard and listen—they would talk about Cairo, because they would be calculating to go ashore there for a spree, maybe, or anyway they would send boats ashore to buy whiskey or fresh meat or something. Jim had a wonderful level head, for a nigger: he could most always start a good plan when you wanted one.

I stood up and shook my rags off and jumped into the river, and struck out for the raft's light. By and by, when I got down nearly to her, I eased up and went slow and cautious. But everything was all right— nobody at the sweeps. So I swum down along the raft till I was most abreast the camp fire in the middle, then I crawled aboard and inched along and got in amongst some bundles of shingles on the weather side of the fire. There was thirteen men there—they was the watch on deck of course. And a mighty rough-looking lot, too. They had a jug, and tin cups, and they kept the jug moving. One man was singing—roaring, you may say; and it wasn't a nice song—for a parlor anyway. He roared through his nose, and strung out the last word of every line very long. When he was done they all fetched a kind of Injun war-whoop, and then another was sung. It begun:—

'There was a woman in our towdn, In our towdn did dwed'l (dwell,) She loved her husband dear-i-lee, But another man twyste as wed'l.

Singing too, riloo, riloo, riloo, Ri-too, riloo, rilay - - - e, She loved her husband dear-i-lee, But another man twyste as wed'l.

And so on—fourteen verses. It was kind of poor, and when he was going to start on the next verse one of them said it was the tune the old cow died on; and another one said, 'Oh, give us a rest.' And another one told him to take a walk. They made fun of him till he got mad and jumped up and begun to cuss the crowd, and said he could lame any thief in the lot.

They was all about to make a break for him, but the biggest man there jumped up and says—

'Set whar you are, gentlemen. Leave him to me; he's my meat.'

Then he jumped up in the air three times and cracked his heels together every time. He flung off a buckskin coat that was all hung with fringes, and says, 'You lay thar tell the chawin-up's done;' and flung his hat down, which was all over ribbons, and says, 'You lay thar tell his sufferin's is over.'

Then he jumped up in the air and cracked his heels together again and shouted out—

'Whoo-oop! I'm the old original iron-jawed, brass-mounted, copper- bellied corpse-maker from the wilds of Arkansaw!—Look at me! I'm the man they call Sudden Death and General Desolation! Sired by a hurricane, dam'd by an earthquake, half-brother to the cholera, nearly related to the small-pox on the mother's side! Look at me! I take nineteen alligators and a bar'l of whiskey for breakfast when I'm in robust health, and a bushel of rattlesnakes and a dead body when I'm ailing! I split the everlasting rocks with my glance, and I squench the thunder when I speak! Whoo-oop! Stand back and give me room according to my strength! Blood's my natural drink, and the wails of the dying is music to my ear! Cast your eye on me, gentlemen!—and lay low and hold your breath, for I'm bout to turn myself loose!'

All the time he was getting this off, he was shaking his head and looking fierce, and kind of swelling around in a little circle, tucking up his wrist-bands, and now and then straightening up and beating his breast with his fist, saying, 'Look at me, gentlemen!' When he got through, he jumped up and cracked his heels together three times, and let off a roaring 'Whoo-oop! I'm the bloodiest son of a wildcat that lives!'

Then the man that had started the row tilted his old slouch hat down over his right eye; then he bent stooping forward, with his back sagged and his south end sticking out far, and his fists a-shoving out and drawing in in front of him, and so went around in a little circle about three times, swelling himself up and breathing hard. Then he straightened, and jumped up and cracked his heels together three times, before he lit again (that made them cheer), and he begun to shout like this—

'Whoo-oop! bow your neck and spread, for the kingdom of sorrow's a- coming! Hold me down to the earth, for I feel my powers a-working! whoo- oop! I'm a child of sin, don't let me get a start! Smoked glass, here, for all! Don't attempt to look at me with the naked eye, gentlemen! When I'm playful I use the meridians of longitude and parallels of latitude for a seine, and drag the Atlantic Ocean for whales! I scratch my head with the lightning, and purr myself to sleep with the thunder! When I'm cold, I bile the Gulf of Mexico and bathe in it; when I'm hot I fan myself with an equinoctial storm; when I'm thirsty I reach up and suck a cloud dry like a sponge; when I range the earth hungry, famine follows in my tracks! Whoo-oop! Bow your neck and spread! I put my hand on the sun's face and make it night in the earth; I bite a piece out of the moon and hurry the seasons; I shake myself and crumble the mountains! Contemplate me through leather—don't use the naked eye! I'm the man with a petrified heart and biler-iron bowels! The massacre of isolated communities is the pastime of my idle moments, the destruction of nationalities the serious business of my life! The boundless vastness of the great American desert is my enclosed property, and I bury my dead on my own premises!' He jumped up and cracked his heels together three times before he lit (they cheered him again), and as he come down he shouted out: 'Whoo-oop! bow your neck and spread, for the pet child of calamity's a-coming! '

Then the other one went to swelling around and blowing again—the first one—the one they called Bob; next, the Child of Calamity chipped in again, bigger than ever; then they both got at it at the same time, swelling round and round each other and punching their fists most into each other's faces, and whooping and jawing like Injuns; then Bob called the Child names, and the Child called him names back again: next, Bob called him a heap rougher names and the Child come back at him with the very worst kind of language; next, Bob knocked the Child's hat off, and the Child picked it up and kicked Bob's ribbony hat about six foot; Bob went and got it and said never mind, this warn't going to be the last of this thing, because he was a man that never forgot and never forgive, and so the Child better look out, for there was a time a-coming, just as sure as he was a living man, that he would have to answer to him with the best blood in his body. The Child said no man was willinger than he was for that time to come, and he would give Bob fair warning, now, never to cross his path again, for he could never rest till he had waded in his blood, for such was his nature, though he was sparing him now on account of his family, if he had one.

Both of them was edging away in different directions, growling and shaking their heads and going on about what they was going to do; but a little black-whiskered chap skipped up and says—

'Come back here, you couple of chicken-livered cowards, and I'll thrash the two of ye!'

And he done it, too. He snatched them, he jerked them this way and that, he booted them around, he knocked them sprawling faster than they could get up. Why, it warn't two minutes till they begged like dogs— and how the other lot did yell and laugh and clap their hands all the way through, and shout 'Sail in, Corpse-Maker!' 'Hi! at him again, Child of Calamity!' 'Bully for you, little Davy!' Well, it was a perfect pow- wow for a while. Bob and the Child had red noses and black eyes when they got through. Little Davy made them own up that they were sneaks and cowards and not fit to eat with a dog or drink with a nigger; then Bob and the Child shook hands with each other, very solemn, and said they had always respected each other and was willing to let bygones be bygones. So then they washed their faces in the river; and just then there was a loud order to stand by for a crossing, and some of them went forward to man the sweeps there, and the rest went aft to handle the after-sweeps.

I laid still and waited for fifteen minutes, and had a smoke out of a pipe that one of them left in reach; then the crossing was finished, and they stumped back and had a drink around and went to talking and singing again. Next they got out an old fiddle, and one played and another patted juba, and the rest turned themselves loose on a regular old- fashioned keel-boat break-down. They couldn't keep that up very long without getting winded, so by and by they settled around the jug again.

They sung 'jolly, jolly raftman's the life for me,' with a musing chorus, and then they got to talking about differences betwixt hogs, and their different kind of habits; and next about women and their different ways: and next about the best ways to put out houses that was afire; and next about what ought to be done with the Injuns; and next about what a king had to do, and how much he got; and next about how to make cats fight;

and next about what to do when a man has fits; and next about differences betwixt clear-water rivers and muddy-water ones. The man they called Ed said the muddy Mississippi water was wholesomer to drink than the clear water of the Ohio; he said if you let a pint of this yaller Mississippi water settle, you would have about a half to three-quarters of an inch of mud in the bottom, according to the stage of the river, and then it warn't no better than Ohio water—what you wanted to do was to keep it stirred up—and when the river was low, keep mud on hand to put in and thicken the water up the way it ought to be.

The Child of Calamity said that was so; he said there was nutritiousness in the mud, and a man that drunk Mississippi water could grow corn in his stomach if he wanted to. He says—

'You look at the graveyards; that tells the tale. Trees won't grow worth chucks in a Cincinnati graveyard, but in a Sent Louis graveyard they grow upwards of eight hundred foot high. It's all on account of the water the people drunk before they laid up. A Cincinnati corpse don't richen a soil any.'

And they talked about how Ohio water didn't like to mix with Mississippi water. Ed said if you take the Mississippi on a rise when the Ohio is low, you'll find a wide band of clear water all the way down the east side of the Mississippi for a hundred mile or more, and the minute you get out a quarter of a mile from shore and pass the line, it is all thick and yaller the rest of the way across. Then they talked about how to keep tobacco from getting moldy, and from that they went into ghosts and told about a lot that other folks had seen; but Ed says—

'Why don't you tell something that you've seen yourselves? Now let me have a say. Five years ago I was on a raft as big as this, and right along here it was a bright moonshiny night, and I was on watch and boss of the stabboard oar forrard, and one of my pards was a man named Dick Allbright, and he come along to where I was sitting, forrard—gaping and stretching, he was—and stooped down on the edge of the raft and washed his face in the river, and come and set down by me and got out his pipe, and had just got it filled, when he looks up and says—

'"Why looky-here," he says, "ain't that Buck Miller's place, over yander in the bend."

'"Yes," says I, "it is—why." He laid his pipe down and leant his head on his hand, and says—

'"I thought we'd be furder down." I says—

'"I thought it too, when I went off watch"—we was standing six hours on and six off—"but the boys told me," I says, "that the raft didn't seem to hardly move, for the last hour," says I, "though she's a slipping along all right, now," says I. He give a kind of a groan, and says—

'"I've seed a raft act so before, along here," he says, "'pears to me the current has most quit above the head of this bend durin' the last two years," he says.

'Well, he raised up two or three times, and looked away off and around on the water. That started me at it, too. A body is always doing what he sees somebody else doing, though there mayn't be no sense in it. Pretty soon I see a black something floating on the water away off to stabboard and quartering behind us. I see he was looking at it, too. I says—

'"What's that?" He says, sort of pettish,—

'"Tain't nothing but an old empty bar'l."

'"An empty bar'l!" says I, "why," says I, "a spy-glass is a fool to your eyes. How can you tell it's an empty bar'l?" He says—

'"I don't know; I reckon it ain't a bar'l, but I thought it might be," says he.

'"Yes," I says, "so it might be, and it might be anything else, too; a body can't tell nothing about it, such a distance as that," I says.

'We hadn't nothing else to do, so we kept on watching it. By and by I says—

'"Why looky-here, Dick Allbright, that thing's a-gaining on us, I believe."

'He never said nothing. The thing gained and gained, and I judged it must be a dog that was about tired out. Well, we swung down into the crossing, and the thing floated across the bright streak of the moonshine, and, by George, it was bar'l. Says I—

'"Dick Allbright, what made you think that thing was a bar'l, when it was a half a mile off," says I. Says he—

'"I don't know." Says I—

'"You tell me, Dick Allbright." He says—

'"Well, I knowed it was a bar'l; I've seen it before; lots has seen it; they says it's a haunted bar'l."

'I called the rest of the watch, and they come and stood there, and I told them what Dick said. It floated right along abreast, now, and didn't gain any more. It was about twenty foot off. Some was for having it aboard, but the rest didn't want to. Dick Allbright said rafts that had fooled with it had got bad luck by it. The captain of the watch said he didn't believe in it. He said he reckoned the bar'l gained on us because it was in a little better current than what we was. He said it would leave by and by.

'So then we went to talking about other things, and we had a song, and then a breakdown; and after that the captain of the watch called for another song; but it was clouding up, now, and the bar'l stuck right thar in the same place, and the song didn't seem to have much warm-up to it, somehow, and so they didn't finish it, and there warn't any cheers, but it sort of dropped flat, and nobody said anything for a minute. Then everybody tried to talk at once, and one chap got off a joke, but it warn't no use, they didn't laugh, and even the chap that made the joke didn't laugh at it, which ain't usual. We all just settled down glum, and watched the bar'l, and was oneasy and oncomfortable. Well, sir, it shut down black and still, and then the wind begin to moan around, and next the lightning begin to play and the thunder to grumble. And pretty soon it was a regular storm, and in the middle of it a man that was running aft stumbled and fell and sprained his ankle so that he had to lay up. This made the boys shake their heads. And every time the lightning come, there was that bar'l with the blue lights winking around it. We was always on the look-out for it. But by and by, towards dawn, she was gone. When the day come we couldn't see her anywhere, and we warn't sorry, neither.

'But next night about half-past nine, when there was songs and high jinks going on, here she comes again, and took her old roost on the stabboard side. There warn't no more high jinks. Everybody got solemn; nobody talked; you couldn't get anybody to do anything but set around moody and look at the bar'l. It begun to cloud up again. When the watch changed, the off watch stayed up, 'stead of turning in. The storm ripped and roared around all night, and in the middle of it another man tripped and sprained his ankle, and had to knock off. The bar'l left towards day, and nobody see it go.

'Everybody was sober and down in the mouth all day. I don't mean the kind of sober that comes of leaving liquor alone—not that. They was quiet, but they all drunk more than usual—not together—but each man sidled off and took it private, by himself.

'After dark the off watch didn't turn in; nobody sung, nobody talked; the boys didn't scatter around, neither; they sort of huddled together, forrard; and for two hours they set there, perfectly still, looking steady in the one direction, and heaving a sigh once in a while. And then, here comes the bar'l again. She took up her old place. She staid there all night; nobody turned in. The storm come on again, after midnight. It got awful dark; the rain poured down; hail, too; the thunder boomed and roared and bellowed; the wind blowed a hurricane; and the lightning spread over everything in big sheets of glare, and showed the whole raft as plain as day; and the river lashed up white as milk as far as you could see for miles, and there was that bar'l jiggering along, same as ever. The captain ordered the watch to man the after sweeps for a crossing, and nobody would go—no more sprained ankles for them, they said. They wouldn't even walk aft. Well then, just then the sky split wide open, with a crash, and the lightning killed two men of the after watch, and crippled two more. Crippled them how, says you? Why, sprained their ankles!

'The bar'l left in the dark betwixt lightnings, towards dawn. Well, not a body eat a bite at breakfast that morning. After that the men loafed around, in twos and threes, and talked low together. But none of them herded with Dick Allbright. They all give him the cold shake. If he come around where any of the men was, they split up and sidled away. They wouldn't man the sweeps with him. The captain had all the skiffs hauled up on the raft, alongside of his wigwam, and wouldn't let the dead men be took ashore to be planted; he didn't believe a man that got ashore would come back; and he was right.

'After night come, you could see pretty plain that there was going to be trouble if that bar'l come again; there was such a muttering going on. A good many wanted to kill Dick Allbright, because he'd seen the bar'l on other trips, and that had an ugly look. Some wanted to put him ashore. Some said, let's all go ashore in a pile, if the bar'l comes again.

'This kind of whispers was still going on, the men being bunched together forrard watching for the bar'l, when, lo and behold you, here she comes again. Down she comes, slow and steady, and settles into her old tracks. You could a heard a pin drop. Then up comes the captain, and says:—

'"Boys, don't be a pack of children and fools; I don't want this bar'l to be dogging us all the way to Orleans, and YOU don't; well, then, how's the best way to stop it? Burn it up,—that's the way. I'm going to fetch it aboard," he says. And before anybody could say a word, in he went.

'He swum to it, and as he come pushing it to the raft, the men spread to one side. But the old man got it aboard and busted in the head, and there was a baby in it! Yes, sir, a stark naked baby. It was Dick Allbright's baby; he owned up and said so.

'"Yes," he says, a-leaning over it, "yes, it is my own lamented darling, my poor lost Charles William Allbright deceased," says he,—for he could curl his tongue around the bulliest words in the language when he was a mind to, and lay them before you without a jint started, anywheres. Yes, he said he used to live up at the head of this bend, and one night he choked his child, which was crying, not intending to kill it,—which was prob'ly a lie,—and then he was scared, and buried it in a bar'l, before his wife got home, and off he went, and struck the northern trail and went to rafting; and this was the third year that the bar'l had chased him. He said the bad luck always begun light, and lasted till four men was killed, and then the bar'l didn't come any more after that. He said if the men would stand it one more night,—and was a-going on like that,—but the men had got enough. They started to get out a boat to take him ashore and lynch him, but he grabbed the little child all of a sudden and jumped overboard with it hugged up to his breast and shedding tears, and we never see him again in this life, poor old suffering soul, nor Charles William neither.'

'WHO was shedding tears?' says Bob; 'was it Allbright or the baby?'

'Why, Allbright, of course; didn't I tell you the baby was dead. Been dead three years—how could it cry?'

'Well, never mind how it could cry—how could it KEEP all that time?' says Davy. 'You answer me that.'

'I don't know how it done it,' says Ed. 'It done it though—that's all I know about it.'

'Say—what did they do with the bar'l?' says the Child of Calamity.

'Why, they hove it overboard, and it sunk like a chunk of lead.'

'Edward, did the child look like it was choked?' says one.

'Did it have its hair parted?' says another.

'What was the brand on that bar'l, Eddy?' says a fellow they called Bill.

'Have you got the papers for them statistics, Edmund?' says Jimmy.

'Say, Edwin, was you one of the men that was killed by the lightning.' says Davy.

'Him? O, no, he was both of 'em,' says Bob. Then they all haw-hawed.

'Say, Edward, don't you reckon you'd better take a pill? You look bad— don't you feel pale?' says the Child of Calamity.

'O, come, now, Eddy,' says Jimmy, 'show up; you must a kept part of that bar'l to prove the thing by. Show us the bunghole— do—and we'll all believe you.'

'Say, boys,' says Bill, 'less divide it up. Thar's thirteen of us. I can swaller a thirteenth of the yarn, if you can worry down the rest.'

Ed got up mad and said they could all go to some place which he ripped out pretty savage, and then walked off aft cussing to himself, and they yelling and jeering at him, and roaring and laughing so you could hear them a mile.

'Boys, we'll split a watermelon on that,' says the Child of Calamity; and he come rummaging around in the dark amongst the shingle bundles where I was, and put his hand on me. I was warm and soft and naked; so he says 'Ouch!' and jumped back.

'Fetch a lantern or a chunk of fire here, boys—there's a snake here as big as a cow!'

So they run there with a lantern and crowded up and looked in on me.

'Come out of that, you beggar!' says one.

'Who are you?' says another.

'What are you after here? Speak up prompt, or overboard you go.

'Snake him out, boys. Snatch him out by the heels.'

I began to beg, and crept out amongst them trembling. They looked me over, wondering, and the Child of Calamity says—

'A cussed thief! Lend a hand and less heave him overboard!'

'No,' says Big Bob, 'less get out the paint-pot and paint him a sky blue all over from head to heel, and then heave him over!'

'Good, that 's it. Go for the paint, Jimmy.'

When the paint come, and Bob took the brush and was just going to begin, the others laughing and rubbing their hands, I begun to cry, and that sort of worked on Davy, and he says—

'"Vast there! He 's nothing but a cub. 'I'll paint the man that tetches him!'

So I looked around on them, and some of them grumbled and growled, and Bob put down the paint, and the others didn't take it up.

'Come here to the fire, and less see what you're up to here,' says Davy. 'Now set down there and give an account of yourself. How long have you been aboard here?'

'Not over a quarter of a minute, sir,' says I.

'How did you get dry so quick?'

'I don't know, sir. I'm always that way, mostly.'

'Oh, you are, are you. What's your name?'

I warn't going to tell my name. I didn't know what to say, so I just says—

'Charles William Allbright, sir.'

Then they roared—the whole crowd; and I was mighty glad I said that, because maybe laughing would get them in a better humor.

When they got done laughing, Davy says—

'It won't hardly do, Charles William. You couldn't have growed this much in five year, and you was a baby when you come out of the bar'l, you know, and dead at that. Come, now, tell a straight story, and nobody'll hurt you, if you ain't up to anything wrong. What IS your name?'

'Aleck Hopkins, sir. Aleck James Hopkins.'

'Well, Aleck, where did you come from, here?'

'From a trading scow. She lays up the bend yonder. I was born on her. Pap has traded up and down here all his life; and he told me to swim off here, because when you went by he said he would like to get some of you to speak to a Mr. Jonas Turner, in Cairo, and tell him—'

'Oh, come!'

'Yes, sir; it's as true as the world; Pap he says—'

'Oh, your grandmother!'

They all laughed, and I tried again to talk, but they broke in on me and stopped me.

'Now, looky-here,' says Davy; 'you're scared, and so you talk wild. Honest, now, do you live in a scow, or is it a lie?'

'Yes, sir, in a trading scow. She lays up at the head of the bend. But I warn't born in her. It's our first trip.'

'Now you're talking! What did you come aboard here, for? To steal?'

'No, sir, I didn't.—It was only to get a ride on the raft. All boys does that.'

'Well, I know that. But what did you hide for?'

'Sometimes they drive the boys off.'

'So they do. They might steal. Looky-here; if we let you off this time, will you keep out of these kind of scrapes hereafter?'

"Deed I will, boss. You try me.'

'All right, then. You ain't but little ways from shore. Overboard with you, and don't you make a fool of yourself another time this way.—Blast it, boy, some raftsmen would rawhide you till you were black and blue!'

I didn't wait to kiss good-bye, but went overboard and broke for shore. When Jim come along by and by, the big raft was away out of sight around the point. I swum out and got aboard, and was mighty glad to see home again.

The boy did not get the information he was after, but his adventure has furnished the glimpse of the departed raftsman and keelboatman which I desire to offer in this place.

I now come to a phase of the Mississippi River life of the flush times of steamboating, which seems to me to warrant full examination—the marvelous science of piloting, as displayed there. I believe there has been nothing like it elsewhere in the world.

Chapter 4 The Boys' Ambition

WHEN I was a boy, there was but one permanent ambition among my comrades in our village* on the west bank of the Mississippi River. That was, to be a steamboatman. We had transient ambitions of other sorts, but they were only transient. When a circus came and went, it left us all burning to become clowns; the first negro minstrel show that came to our section left us all suffering to try that kind of life; now and then we had a hope that if we lived and were good, God would permit us to be pirates. These ambitions faded out, each in its turn; but the ambition to be a steamboatman always remained.

Once a day a cheap, gaudy packet arrived upward from St. Louis, and another downward from Keokuk. Before these events, the day was glorious with expectancy; after them, the day was a dead and empty thing. Not only the boys, but the whole village, felt this. After all these years I can picture that old time to myself now, just as it was then: the white town drowsing in the sunshine of a summer's morning; the streets empty, or pretty nearly so; one or two clerks sitting in front of the Water Street stores, with their splint-bottomed chairs tilted back against the wall, chins on breasts, hats slouched over their faces, asleep—with shingle-shavings enough around to show what broke them down; a sow and a litter of pigs loafing along the sidewalk, doing a good business in watermelon rinds and seeds; two or three lonely little freight piles scattered about the 'levee;' a pile of 'skids' on the slope of the stone-paved wharf, and the fragrant town drunkard asleep in the shadow of them; two or three wood flats at the head of the wharf, but nobody to listen to the peaceful lapping of the wavelets against them; the great Mississippi, the majestic, the magnificent Mississippi, rolling its mile-wide tide along, shining in the sun; the dense forest away on the other side; the 'point' above the town, and the 'point' below, bounding the river-glimpse and turning it into a sort of sea, and withal a very still and brilliant and lonely one. Presently a film of dark smoke appears above one of those remote 'points;' instantly a negro drayman, famous for his quick eye and prodigious voice, lifts up the cry, 'S-t-e- a-m-boat a-comin'!' and the scene changes! The town drunkard stirs, the clerks wake up, a furious clatter of drays follows, every house and store pours out a human contribution, and all in a twinkling the dead town is alive and moving. Drays, carts, men, boys, all go hurrying from many quarters to a common center, the wharf. Assembled there, the people fasten their eyes upon the coming boat as upon a wonder they are seeing for the first time. And the boat IS rather a handsome sight, too. She is long and sharp and trim and pretty; she has two tall, fancy-topped chimneys, with a gilded device of some kind swung between them; a fanciful pilot-house, a glass and 'gingerbread', perched on top of the 'texas' deck behind them; the paddle-boxes are gorgeous with a picture or with gilded rays above the boat's name; the boiler deck, the hurricane deck, and the texas deck are fenced and ornamented with clean white railings; there is a flag gallantly flying from the jack-staff; the furnace doors are open and the fires glaring bravely; the upper decks are black with passengers; the captain stands by the big bell, calm, imposing, the envy of all; great volumes of the blackest smoke are rolling and tumbling out of the chimneys—a husbanded grandeur created with a bit of pitch pine just before arriving at a town; the crew are grouped on the forecastle; the broad stage is run far out over the port bow, and an envied deckhand stands picturesquely on the end of it with a coil of rope in his hand;

* Hannibal, Missouri

the pent steam is screaming through the gauge- cocks, the captain lifts his hand, a bell rings, the wheels stop; then they turn back, churning the water to foam, and the steamer is at rest. Then such a scramble as there is to get aboard, and to get ashore, and to take in freight and to discharge freight, all at one and the same time; and such a yelling and cursing as the mates facilitate it all with! Ten minutes later the steamer is under way again, with no flag on the jack-staff and no black smoke issuing from the chimneys. After ten more minutes the town is dead again, and the town drunkard asleep by the skids once more.

My father was a justice of the peace, and I supposed he possessed the power of life and death over all men and could hang anybody that offended him. This was distinction enough for me as a general thing; but the desire to be a steamboatman kept intruding, nevertheless. I first wanted to be a cabin-boy, so that I could come out with a white apron on and shake a tablecloth over the side, where all my old comrades could see me; later I thought I would rather be the deckhand who stood on the end of the stage-plank with the coil of rope in his hand, because he was particularly conspicuous. But these were only day-dreams,—they were too heavenly to be contemplated as real possibilities. By and by one of our boys went away. He was not heard of for a long time. At last he turned up as apprentice engineer or 'striker' on a steamboat. This thing shook the bottom out of all my Sunday-school teachings. That boy had been notoriously worldly, and I just the reverse; yet he was exalted to this eminence, and I left in obscurity and misery. There was nothing generous about this fellow in his greatness. He would always manage to have a rusty bolt to scrub while his boat tarried at our town, and he would sit on the inside guard and scrub it, where we could all see him and envy him and loathe him. And whenever his boat was laid up he would come home and swell around the town in his blackest and greasiest clothes, so that nobody could help remembering that he was a steamboatman; and he used all sorts of steamboat technicalities in his talk, as if he were so used to them that he forgot common people could not understand them. He would speak of the 'labboard' side of a horse in an easy, natural way that would make one wish he was dead. And he was always talking about 'St. Looy' like an old citizen; he would refer casually to occasions when he 'was coming down Fourth Street,' or when he was 'passing by the Planter's House,' or when there was a fire and he took a turn on the brakes of 'the old Big Missouri;' and then he would go on and lie about how many towns the size of ours were burned down there that day. Two or three of the boys had long been persons of consideration among us because they had been to St. Louis once and had a vague general knowledge of its wonders, but the day of their glory was over now. They lapsed into a humble silence, and learned to disappear when the ruthless 'cub'-engineer approached. This fellow had money, too, and hair oil. Also an ignorant silver watch and a showy brass watch chain. He wore a leather belt and used no suspenders. If ever a youth was cordially admired and hated by his comrades, this one was. No girl could withstand his charms. He 'cut out' every boy in the village. When his boat blew up at last, it diffused a tranquil contentment among us such as we had not known for months. But when he came home the next week, alive, renowned, and appeared in church all battered up and bandaged, a shining hero, stared at and wondered over by everybody, it seemed to us that the partiality of Providence for an undeserving reptile had reached a point where it was open to criticism.

This creature's career could produce but one result, and it speedily followed. Boy after boy managed to get on the river.

The minister's son became an engineer. The doctor's and the post-master's sons became 'mud clerks;' the wholesale liquor dealer's son became a barkeeper on a boat; four sons of the chief merchant, and two sons of the county judge, became pilots. Pilot was the grandest position of all. The pilot, even in those days of trivial wages, had a princely salary—from a hundred and fifty to two hundred and fifty dollars a month, and no board to pay. Two months of his wages would pay a preacher's salary for a year. Now some of us were left disconsolate. We could not get on the river—at least our parents would not let us.

So by and by I ran away. I said I never would come home again till I was a pilot and could come in glory. But somehow I could not manage it. I went meekly aboard a few of the boats that lay packed together like sardines at the long St. Louis wharf, and very humbly inquired for the pilots, but got only a cold shoulder and short words from mates and clerks. I had to make the best of this sort of treatment for the time being, but I had comforting daydreams of a future when I should be a great and honored pilot, with plenty of money, and could kill some of these mates and clerks and pay for them.

Chapter 5 I Want to be a Cub-pilot

MONTHS afterward the hope within me struggled to a reluctant death, and I found myself without an ambition. But I was ashamed to go home. I was in Cincinnati, and I set to work to map out a new career. I had been reading about the recent exploration of the river Amazon by an expedition sent out by our government. It was said that the expedition, owing to difficulties, had not thoroughly explored a part of the country lying about the head-waters, some four thousand miles from the mouth of the river. It was only about fifteen hundred miles from Cincinnati to New Orleans, where I could doubtless get a ship. I had thirty dollars left; I would go and complete the exploration of the Amazon. This was all the thought I gave to the subject. I never was great in matters of detail. I packed my valise, and took passage on an ancient tub called the 'Paul Jones,' for New Orleans. For the sum of sixteen dollars I had the scarred and tarnished splendors of 'her' main saloon principally to myself, for she was not a creature to attract the eye of wiser travelers.

When we presently got under way and went poking down the broad Ohio, I became a new being, and the subject of my own admiration. I was a traveler! A word never had tasted so good in my mouth before. I had an exultant sense of being bound for mysterious lands and distant climes which I never have felt in so uplifting a degree since. I was in such a glorified condition that all ignoble feelings departed out of me, and I was able to look down and pity the untraveled with a compassion that had hardly a trace of contempt in it. Still, when we stopped at villages and wood-yards, I could not help lolling carelessly upon the railings of the boiler deck to enjoy the envy of the country boys on the bank. If they did not seem to discover me, I presently sneezed to attract their attention, or moved to a position where they could not help seeing me. And as soon as I knew they saw me I gaped and stretched, and gave other signs of being mightily bored with traveling.

I kept my hat off all the time, and stayed where the wind and the sun could strike me, because I wanted to get the bronzed and weather-beaten look of an old traveler. Before the second day was half gone I experienced a joy which filled me with the purest gratitude; for I saw that the skin had begun to blister and peel off my face and neck. I wished that the boys and girls at home could see me now.

We reached Louisville in time—at least the neighborhood of it. We stuck hard and fast on the rocks in the middle of the river, and lay there four days. I was now beginning to feel a strong sense of being a part of the boat's family, a sort of infant son to the captain and younger brother to the officers. There is no estimating the pride I took in this grandeur, or the affection that began to swell and grow in me for those people. I could not know how the lordly steamboatman scorns that sort of presumption in a mere landsman. I particularly longed to acquire the least trifle of notice from the big stormy mate, and I was on the alert for an opportunity to do him a service to that end. It came at last. The riotous powwow of setting a spar was going on down on the forecastle, and I went down there and stood around in the way—or mostly skipping out of it—till the mate suddenly roared a general order for somebody to bring him a capstan bar. I sprang to his side and said: 'Tell me where it is—I'll fetch it!'

If a rag-picker had offered to do a diplomatic service for the Emperor of Russia, the monarch could not have been more astounded than the mate was. He even stopped swearing. He stood and stared down at me. It took him ten seconds to scrape his disjointed remains together again. Then he said impressively: 'Well, if this don't beat hell!' and turned to his work with the air of a man who had been confronted with a problem too abstruse for solution.

I crept away, and courted solitude for the rest of the day. I did not go to dinner; I stayed away from supper until everybody else had finished. I did not feel so much like a member of the boat's family now as before. However, my spirits returned, in installments, as we pursued our way down the river. I was sorry I hated the mate so, because it was not in (young) human nature not to admire him. He was huge and muscular, his face was bearded and whiskered all over; he had a red woman and a blue woman tattooed on his right arm,—one on each side of a blue anchor with a red rope to it; and in the matter of profanity he was sublime. When he was getting out cargo at a landing, I was always where I could see and hear. He felt all the majesty of his great position, and made the world feel it, too. When he gave even the simplest order, he discharged it like a blast of lightning, and sent a long, reverberating peal of profanity thundering after it. I could not help contrasting the way in which the average landsman would give an order, with the mate's way of doing it. If the landsman should wish the gang-plank moved a foot farther forward, he would probably say: 'James, or William, one of you push that plank forward, please;' but put the mate in his place and he would roar out: 'Here, now, start that gang-plank for'ard! Lively, now! WHAT're you about! Snatch it! SNATCH it! There! there! Aft again! aft again! don't you hear me. Dash it to dash! are you going to SLEEP over it! 'VAST heaving. 'Vast heaving, I tell you! Going to heave it clear astern? WHERE're you going with that barrel! FOR'ARD with it 'fore I make you swallow it, you dash-dash-dash-DASHED split between a tired mud-turtle and a crippled hearse-horse!'

I wished I could talk like that.

When the soreness of my adventure with the mate had somewhat worn off, I began timidly to make up to the humblest official connected with the boat—the night watchman. He snubbed my advances at first, but I presently ventured to offer him a new chalk pipe; and that softened him. So he allowed me to sit with him by the big bell on the hurricane deck, and in time he melted into conversation. He could not well have helped it, I hung with such homage on his

words and so plainly showed that I felt honored by his notice. He told me the names of dim capes and shadowy islands as we glided by them in the solemnity of the night, under the winking stars, and by and by got to talking about himself. He seemed over-sentimental for a man whose salary was six dollars a week— or rather he might have seemed so to an older person than I. But I drank in his words hungrily, and with a faith that might have moved mountains if it had been applied judiciously. What was it to me that he was soiled and seedy and fragrant with gin? What was it to me that his grammar was bad, his construction worse, and his profanity so void of art that it was an element of weakness rather than strength in his conversation? He was a wronged man, a man who had seen trouble, and that was enough for me. As he mellowed into his plaintive history his tears dripped upon the lantern in his lap, and I cried, too, from sympathy. He said he was the son of an English nobleman—either an earl or an alderman, he could not remember which, but believed was both; his father, the nobleman, loved him, but his mother hated him from the cradle; and so while he was still a little boy he was sent to 'one of them old, ancient colleges'—he couldn't remember which; and by and by his father died and his mother seized the property and 'shook' him as he phrased it. After his mother shook him, members of the nobility with whom he was acquainted used their influence to get him the position of 'loblolly-boy in a ship;' and from that point my watchman threw off all trammels of date and locality and branched out into a narrative that bristled all along with incredible adventures; a narrative that was so reeking with bloodshed and so crammed with hair-breadth escapes and the most engaging and unconscious personal villainies, that I sat speechless, enjoying, shuddering, wondering, worshipping.

It was a sore blight to find out afterwards that he was a low, vulgar, ignorant, sentimental, half-witted humbug, an untraveled native of the wilds of Illinois, who had absorbed wildcat literature and appropriated its marvels, until in time he had woven odds and ends of the mess into this yarn, and then gone on telling it to fledglings like me, until he had come to believe it himself.

Chapter 6 A Cub-pilot's Experience

WHAT with lying on the rocks four days at Louisville, and some other delays, the poor old 'Paul Jones' fooled away about two weeks in making the voyage from Cincinnati to New Orleans. This gave me a chance to get acquainted with one of the pilots, and he taught me how to steer the boat, and thus made the fascination of river life more potent than ever for me.

It also gave me a chance to get acquainted with a youth who had taken deck passage—more's the pity; for he easily borrowed six dollars of me on a promise to return to the boat and pay it back to me the day after we should arrive. But he probably died or forgot, for he never came. It was doubtless the former, since he had said his parents were wealthy, and he only traveled deck passage because it was cooler.*

I soon discovered two things. One was that a vessel would not be likely to sail for the mouth of the Amazon under ten or twelve years; and the other was that the nine or ten dollars still left in my pocket would not suffice for so imposing an exploration as I had planned, even if I could afford to wait for a ship. Therefore it followed that I must contrive a new career. The 'Paul Jones' was now bound for St. Louis. I planned a

---

* 'Deck' Passage, i.e. steerage passage.

siege against my pilot, and at the end of three hard days he surrendered. He agreed to teach me the Mississippi River from New Orleans to St. Louis for five hundred dollars, payable out of the first wages I should receive after graduating. I entered upon the small enterprise of 'learning' twelve or thirteen hundred miles of the great Mississippi River with the easy confidence of my time of life. If I had really known what I was about to require of my faculties, I should not have had the courage to begin. I supposed that all a pilot had to do was to keep his boat in the river, and I did not consider that that could be much of a trick, since it was so wide.

The boat backed out from New Orleans at four in the afternoon, and it was 'our watch' until eight. Mr. Bixby, my chief, 'straightened her up,' plowed her along past the sterns of the other boats that lay at the Levee, and then said, 'Here, take her; shave those steamships as close as you'd peel an apple.' I took the wheel, and my heart-beat fluttered up into the hundreds; for it seemed to me that we were about to scrape the side off every ship in the line, we were so close. I held my breath and began to claw the boat away from the danger; and I had my own opinion of the pilot who had known no better than to get us into such peril, but I was too wise to express it. In half a minute I had a wide margin of safety intervening between the 'Paul Jones' and the ships; and within ten seconds more I was set aside in disgrace, and Mr. Bixby was going into danger again and flaying me alive with abuse of my cowardice. I was stung, but I was obliged to admire the easy confidence with which my chief loafed from side to side of his wheel, and trimmed the ships so closely that disaster seemed ceaselessly imminent. When he had cooled a little he told me that the easy water was close ashore and the current outside, and therefore we must hug the bank, up-stream, to get the benefit of the former, and stay well out, down-stream, to take advantage of the latter. In my own mind I resolved to be a down-stream pilot and leave the up-streaming to people dead to prudence.

Now and then Mr. Bixby called my attention to certain things. Said he, 'This is Six-Mile Point.' I assented. It was pleasant enough information, but I could not see the bearing of it. I was not conscious that it was a matter of any interest to me. Another time he said, 'This is Nine-Mile Point.' Later he said, 'This is Twelve-Mile Point.' They were all about level with the water's edge; they all looked about alike to me; they were monotonously unpicturesque. I hoped Mr. Bixby would change the subject. But no; he would crowd up around a point, hugging the shore with affection, and then say: 'The slack water ends here, abreast this bunch of China-trees; now we cross over.' So he crossed over. He gave me the wheel once or twice, but I had no luck. I either came near chipping off the edge of a sugar plantation, or I yawed too far from shore, and so dropped back into disgrace again and got abused.

The watch was ended at last, and we took supper and went to bed. At midnight the glare of a lantern shone in my eyes, and the night watchman said—

'Come! turn out!'

And then he left. I could not understand this extraordinary procedure; so I presently gave up trying to, and dozed off to sleep. Pretty soon the watchman was back again, and this time he was gruff. I was annoyed. I said:—

'What do you want to come bothering around here in the middle of the night for. Now as like as not I'll not get to sleep again to-night.'

The watchman said—

'Well, if this an't good, I'm blest.'

The 'off-watch' was just turning in, and I heard some brutal laughter from them, and such remarks as 'Hello, watchman! an't the new cub turned out yet? He's delicate, likely. Give him some sugar in a rag and send for the chambermaid to sing rock-a-by-baby to him.'

About this time Mr. Bixby appeared on the scene. Something like a minute later I was climbing the pilot-house steps with some of my clothes on and the rest in my arms. Mr. Bixby was close behind, commenting. Here was something fresh—this thing of getting up in the middle of the night to go to work. It was a detail in piloting that had never occurred to me at all. I knew that boats ran all night, but somehow I had never happened to reflect that somebody had to get up out of a warm bed to run them. I began to fear that piloting was not quite so romantic as I had imagined it was; there was something very real and work-like about this new phase of it.

It was a rather dingy night, although a fair number of stars were out. The big mate was at the wheel, and he had the old tub pointed at a star and was holding her straight up the middle of the river. The shores on either hand were not much more than half a mile apart, but they seemed wonderfully far away and ever so vague and indistinct. The mate said:—

'We've got to land at Jones's plantation, sir.'

The vengeful spirit in me exulted. I said to myself, I wish you joy of your job, Mr. Bixby; you'll have a good time finding Mr. Jones's plantation such a night as this; and I hope you never WILL find it as long as you live.

Mr. Bixby said to the mate:—

'Upper end of the plantation, or the lower?'

'Upper.'

'I can't do it. The stumps there are out of water at this stage: It's no great distance to the lower, and you'll have to get along with that.'

'All right, sir. If Jones don't like it he'll have to lump it, I reckon.'

And then the mate left. My exultation began to cool and my wonder to come up. Here was a man who not only proposed to find this plantation on such a night, but to find either end of it you preferred. I dreadfully wanted to ask a question, but I was carrying about as many short answers as my cargo-room would admit of, so I held my peace. All I desired to ask Mr. Bixby was the simple question whether he was ass enough to really imagine he was going to find that plantation on a night when all plantations were exactly alike and all the same color. But I held in. I used to have fine inspirations of prudence in those days.

Mr. Bixby made for the shore and soon was scraping it, just the same as if it had been daylight. And not only that, but singing—

'Father in heaven, the day is declining,' etc.

It seemed to me that I had put my life in the keeping of a

peculiarly reckless outcast. Presently he turned on me and said:—

'What's the name of the first point above New Orleans?'

I was gratified to be able to answer promptly, and I did. I said I didn't know.

'Don't KNOW?'

This manner jolted me. I was down at the foot again, in a moment. But I had to say just what I had said before.

'Well, you're a smart one,' said Mr. Bixby. 'What's the name of the NEXT point?'

Once more I didn't know.

'Well, this beats anything. Tell me the name of ANY point or place I told you.'

I studied a while and decided that I couldn't.

'Look here! What do you start out from, above Twelve-Mile Point, to cross over?'

'I—I—don't know.'

'You—you—don't know?' mimicking my drawling manner of speech. 'What DO you know?'

'I—I—nothing, for certain.'

'By the great Caesar's ghost, I believe you! You're the stupidest dunderhead I ever saw or ever heard of, so help me Moses! The idea of you being a pilot—you! Why, you don't know enough to pilot a cow down a lane.'

Oh, but his wrath was up! He was a nervous man, and he shuffled from one side of his wheel to the other as if the floor was hot. He would boil a while to himself, and then overflow and scald me again.

'Look here! What do you suppose I told you the names of those points for?'

I tremblingly considered a moment, and then the devil of temptation provoked me to say:—

'Well—to—to—be entertaining, I thought.'

This was a red rag to the bull. He raged and stormed so (he was crossing the river at the time) that I judge it made him blind, because he ran over the steering-oar of a trading-scow. Of course the traders sent up a volley of red-hot profanity. Never was a man so grateful as Mr. Bixby was: because he was brim full, and here were subjects who would TALK BACK. He threw open a window, thrust his head out, and such an irruption followed as I never had heard before. The fainter and farther away the scowmen's curses drifted, the higher Mr. Bixby lifted his voice and the weightier his adjectives grew. When he closed the window he was empty. You could have drawn a seine through his system and not caught curses enough to disturb your mother with. Presently he said to me in the gentlest way—

'My boy, you must get a little memorandum book, and every time I tell you a thing, put it down right away. There's only one way to be a pilot, and that is to get this entire river by heart. You have to know it just like A B C.'

That was a dismal revelation to me; for my memory was never loaded with anything but blank cartridges. However, I did not feel discouraged long. I judged that it was best to make some allowances, for doubtless Mr. Bixby was 'stretching.' Presently he pulled a rope and struck a few strokes on the big bell. The stars were all gone now, and the night was as black as ink. I could hear the wheels churn along the bank, but I was not entirely certain that I could see the shore. The voice of the invisible watchman called up from the hurricane deck—

'What's this, sir?'

'Jones's plantation.'

I said to myself, I wish I might venture to offer a small bet that it isn't. But I did not chirp. I only waited to see. Mr. Bixby handled the engine bells, and in due time the boat's nose came to the land, a torch glowed from the forecastle, a man skipped ashore, a darky's voice on the bank said, 'Gimme de k'yarpet-bag, Mars' Jones,' and the next moment we were standing up the river again, all serene. I reflected deeply awhile, and then said—but not aloud—'Well, the finding of that plantation was the luckiest accident that ever happened; but it couldn't happen again in a hundred years.' And I fully believed it was an accident, too.

By the time we had gone seven or eight hundred miles up the river, I had learned to be a tolerably plucky up-stream steersman, in daylight, and before we reached St. Louis I had made a trifle of progress in night- work, but only a trifle. I had a note-book that fairly bristled with the names of towns, 'points,' bars, islands, bends, reaches, etc.; but the information was to be found only in the notebook—none of it was in my head. It made my heart ache to think I had only got half of the river set down; for as our watch was four hours off and four hours on, day and night, there was a long four-hour gap in my book for every time I had slept since the voyage began.

My chief was presently hired to go on a big New Orleans boat, and I packed my satchel and went with him. She was a grand affair. When I stood in her pilot-house I was so far above the water that I seemed perched on a mountain; and her decks stretched so far away, fore and aft, below me, that I wondered how I could ever have considered the little 'Paul Jones' a large craft. There were other differences, too. The 'Paul Jones's' pilot-house was a cheap, dingy, battered rattle-trap, cramped for room: but here was a sumptuous glass temple; room enough to have a dance in; showy red and gold window-curtains; an imposing sofa; leather cushions and a back to the high bench where visiting pilots sit, to spin yarns and 'look at the river;' bright, fanciful 'cuspadores' instead of a broad wooden box filled with sawdust; nice new oil-cloth on the floor; a hospitable big stove for winter; a wheel as high as my head, costly with inlaid work; a wire tiller-rope; bright brass knobs for the bells; and a tidy, white-aproned, black 'texas-tender,' to bring up tarts and ices and coffee during mid-watch, day and night. Now this was 'something like,' and so I began to take heart once more to believe that piloting was a romantic sort of occupation after all. The moment we were under way I began to prowl about the great steamer and fill myself with joy. She was as clean and as dainty as a drawing-room; when I looked down her long, gilded saloon, it was like gazing through a splendid tunnel; she had an oil-picture, by some gifted sign-painter, on every stateroom door; she glittered with no end of prism-fringed chandeliers; the clerk's office was elegant, the bar was marvelous, and the bar-keeper had been barbered and upholstered at incredible cost. The boiler deck (i.e. the second story of the boat, so to speak) was as spacious as a church, it seemed to me; so with the forecastle; and there was no pitiful handful of deckhands, firemen, and roustabouts down there, but a whole battalion of men. The fires were fiercely glaring from a long row of furnaces, and over them were eight huge boilers! This was unutterable pomp. The mighty engines—but enough of this. I had never felt so fine before. And when I found that the regiment of natty servants respectfully 'sir'd' me, my satisfaction was complete.

Chapter 7 A Daring Deed

WHEN I returned to the pilot-house St. Louis was gone and I was lost. Here was a piece of river which was all down in my book, but I could make neither head nor tail of it: you understand, it was turned around. I had seen it when coming up-stream, but I had never faced about to see how it looked when it was behind me. My heart broke again, for it was plain that I had got to learn this troublesome river BOTH WAYS.

The pilot-house was full of pilots, going down to 'look at the river.' What is called the 'upper river' (the two hundred miles between St. Louis and Cairo, where the Ohio comes in) was low; and the Mississippi changes its channel so constantly that the pilots used to always find it necessary to run down to Cairo to take a fresh look, when their boats were to lie in port a week; that is, when the water was at a low stage. A deal of this 'looking at the river' was done by poor fellows who seldom had a berth, and whose only hope of getting one lay in their being always freshly posted and therefore ready to drop into the shoes of some reputable pilot, for a single trip, on account of such pilot's sudden illness, or some other necessity. And a good many of them constantly ran up and down inspecting the river, not because they ever really hoped to get a berth, but because (they being guests of the boat) it was cheaper to 'look at the river' than stay ashore and pay board. In time these fellows grew dainty in their tastes, and only infested boats that had an established reputation for setting good tables. All visiting pilots were useful, for they were always ready and willing, winter or summer, night or day, to go out in the yawl and help buoy the channel or assist the boat's pilots in any way they could. They were likewise welcome because all pilots are tireless talkers, when gathered together, and as they talk only about the river they are always understood and are always interesting. Your true pilot cares nothing about anything on earth but the river, and his pride in his occupation surpasses the pride of kings.

We had a fine company of these river-inspectors along, this trip. There were eight or ten; and there was abundance of room for them in our great pilot-house. Two or three of them wore polished silk hats, elaborate shirt-fronts, diamond breast-pins, kid gloves, and patent-leather boots. They were choice in their English, and bore themselves with a dignity proper to men of solid means and prodigious reputation as pilots. The others were more or less loosely clad, and wore upon their heads tall felt cones that were suggestive of the days of the Commonwealth.

I was a cipher in this august company, and felt subdued, not to say torpid. I was not even of sufficient consequence to assist at the wheel when it was necessary to put the tiller hard down in a hurry; the guest that stood nearest did that when occasion required—and this was pretty much all the time, because of the crookedness of the channel and the scant water. I stood in

a corner; and the talk I listened to took the hope all out of me. One visitor said to another—

'Jim, how did you run Plum Point, coming up?'

'It was in the night, there, and I ran it the way one of the boys on the "Diana" told me; started out about fifty yards above the wood pile on the false point, and held on the cabin under Plum Point till I raised the reef—quarter less twain—then straightened up for the middle bar till I got well abreast the old one-limbed cotton-wood in the bend, then got my stern on the cotton-wood and head on the low place above the point, and came through a-booming—nine and a half.'

'Pretty square crossing, an't it?'

'Yes, but the upper bar 's working down fast.'

Another pilot spoke up and said—

'I had better water than that, and ran it lower down; started out from the false point—mark twain—raised the second reef abreast the big snag in the bend, and had quarter less twain.'

One of the gorgeous ones remarked—

'I don't want to find fault with your leadsmen, but that's a good deal of water for Plum Point, it seems to me.'

There was an approving nod all around as this quiet snub dropped on the boaster and 'settled' him. And so they went on talk-talk-talking. Meantime, the thing that was running in my mind was, 'Now if my ears hear aright, I have not only to get the names of all the towns and islands and bends, and so on, by heart, but I must even get up a warm personal acquaintanceship with every old snag and one-limbed cotton-wood and obscure wood pile that ornaments the banks of this river for twelve hundred miles; and more than that, I must actually know where these things are in the dark, unless these guests are gifted with eyes that can pierce through two miles of solid blackness; I wish the piloting business was in Jericho and I had never thought of it.'

At dusk Mr. Bixby tapped the big bell three times (the signal to land), and the captain emerged from his drawing-room in the forward end of the texas, and looked up inquiringly. Mr. Bixby said—

'We will lay up here all night, captain.'

'Very well, sir.'

That was all. The boat came to shore and was tied up for the night. It seemed to me a fine thing that the pilot could do as he pleased, without asking so grand a captain's permission. I took my supper and went immediately to bed, discouraged by my day's observations and experiences. My late voyage's note-booking was but a confusion of meaningless names. It had tangled me all up in a knot every time I had looked at it in the daytime. I now hoped for respite in sleep; but no, it reveled all through my head till sunrise again, a frantic and tireless nightmare.

Next morning I felt pretty rusty and low-spirited. We went booming along, taking a good many chances, for we were anxious to 'get out of the river' (as getting out to Cairo was called) before night should overtake us. But Mr. Bixby's partner, the other pilot, presently grounded the boat, and we lost so much time in getting her off that it was plain that darkness would overtake us a good long way above the mouth. This was a great misfortune, especially to certain of our visiting pilots, whose boats would have to wait for their return, no matter how long that might be. It sobered the pilot-house talk a good deal. Coming up-stream, pilots did not mind low water or any kind of darkness; nothing stopped them but fog. But down-stream work was different; a boat was too nearly helpless, with a stiff current pushing behind her; so it was not customary to run down-stream at night in low water.

There seemed to be one small hope, however: if we could get through the intricate and dangerous Hat Island crossing before night, we could venture the rest, for we would have plainer sailing and better water. But it would be insanity to attempt Hat Island at night. So there was a deal of looking at watches all the rest of the day, and a constant ciphering upon the speed we were making; Hat Island was the eternal subject; sometimes hope was high and sometimes we were delayed in a bad crossing, and down it went again. For hours all hands lay under the burden of this suppressed excitement; it was even communicated to me, and I got to feeling so solicitous about Hat Island, and under such an awful pressure of responsibility, that I wished I might have five minutes on shore to draw a good, full, relieving breath, and start over again. We were standing no regular watches. Each of our pilots ran such portions of the river as he had run when coming up-stream, because of his greater familiarity with it; but both remained in the pilot house constantly.

An hour before sunset, Mr. Bixby took the wheel and Mr. W— stepped aside. For the next thirty minutes every man held his watch in his hand and was restless, silent, and uneasy. At last somebody said, with a doomful sigh—

'Well, yonder's Hat Island—and we can't make it.' All the watches closed with a snap, everybody sighed and muttered something about its being 'too bad, too bad—ah, if we could only have got here half an hour sooner!' and the place was thick with the atmosphere of disappointment. Some started to go out, but loitered, hearing no bell-tap to land. The sun dipped behind the horizon, the boat went on. Inquiring looks passed from one guest to another; and one who had his hand on the door-knob and had turned it, waited, then presently took away his hand and let the knob turn back again. We bore steadily down the bend. More looks were exchanged, and nods of surprised admiration—but no words. Insensibly the men drew together behind Mr. Bixby, as the sky darkened and one or two dim stars came out. The dead silence and sense of waiting became oppressive. Mr. Bixby pulled the cord, and two deep, mellow notes from the big bell floated off on the night. Then a pause, and one more note was struck. The watchman's voice followed, from the hurricane deck—

'Labboard lead, there! Stabboard lead!'

The cries of the leadsmen began to rise out of the distance, and were gruffly repeated by the word-passers on the hurricane deck.

'M-a-r-k three!.... M-a-r-k three!.... Quarter-less three! .... Half twain! .... Quarter twain! .... M-a-r-k twain! .... Quarter-less—'

Mr. Bixby pulled two bell-ropes, and was answered by faint jinglings far below in the engine room, and our speed slackened. The steam began to whistle through the gauge-cocks. The cries of the leadsmen went on—and it is a weird sound, always, in the night. Every pilot in the lot was watching

now, with fixed eyes, and talking under his breath. Nobody was calm and easy but Mr. Bixby. He would put his wheel down and stand on a spoke, and as the steamer swung into her (to me) utterly invisible marks—for we seemed to be in the midst of a wide and gloomy sea—he would meet and fasten her there. Out of the murmur of half-audible talk, one caught a coherent sentence now and then—such as—

'There; she's over the first reef all right!'

After a pause, another subdued voice—

'Her stern's coming down just exactly right, by George!'

'Now she's in the marks; over she goes!'

Somebody else muttered—

'Oh, it was done beautiful—BEAUTIFUL!'

Now the engines were stopped altogether, and we drifted with the current. Not that I could see the boat drift, for I could not, the stars being all gone by this time. This drifting was the dismalest work; it held one's heart still. Presently I discovered a blacker gloom than that which surrounded us. It was the head of the island. We were closing right down upon it. We entered its deeper shadow, and so imminent seemed the peril that I was likely to suffocate; and I had the strongest impulse to do SOMETHING, anything, to save the vessel. But still Mr. Bixby stood by his wheel, silent, intent as a cat, and all the pilots stood shoulder to shoulder at his back.

'She'll not make it!' somebody whispered.

The water grew shoaler and shoaler, by the leadsman's cries, till it was down to—

'Eight-and-a-half!.... E-i-g-h-t feet!.... E-i-g-h-t feet!.... Seven-and—'

Mr. Bixby said warningly through his speaking tube to the engineer—

'Stand by, now!'

'Aye-aye, sir!'

'Seven-and-a-half! Seven feet! Six-and—'

We touched bottom! Instantly Mr. Bixby set a lot of bells ringing, shouted through the tube, 'NOW, let her have it—every ounce you've got!' then to his partner, 'Put her hard down! snatch her! snatch her!' The boat rasped and ground her way through the sand, hung upon the apex of disaster a single tremendous instant, and then over she went! And such a shout as went up at Mr. Bixby's back never loosened the roof of a pilot-house before!

There was no more trouble after that. Mr. Bixby was a hero that night; and it was some little time, too, before his exploit ceased to be talked about by river men.

Fully to realize the marvelous precision required in laying the great steamer in her marks in that murky waste of water, one should know that not only must she pick her intricate way through snags and blind reefs, and then shave the head of the island so closely as to brush the overhanging foliage with her stern, but at one place she must pass almost within arm's reach of a sunken and invisible wreck that would snatch the hull timbers from under her if she should strike it, and destroy a quarter of a million dollars' worth of steam-boat and cargo in five minutes, and maybe a hundred and fifty human lives into the bargain.

The last remark I heard that night was a compliment to Mr. Bixby, uttered in soliloquy and with unction by one of our guests. He said—

'By the Shadow of Death, but he's a lightning pilot!'

Chapter 8 Perplexing Lessons

At the end of what seemed a tedious while, I had managed to pack my head full of islands, towns, bars, 'points,' and bends; and a curiously inanimate mass of lumber it was, too. However, inasmuch as I could shut my eyes and reel off a good long string of these names without leaving out more than ten miles of river in every fifty, I began to feel that I could take a boat down to New Orleans if I could make her skip those little gaps. But of course my complacency could hardly get start enough to lift my nose a trifle into the air, before Mr. Bixby would think of something to fetch it down again. One day he turned on me suddenly with this settler—

'What is the shape of Walnut Bend?'

He might as well have asked me my grandmother's opinion of protoplasm. I reflected respectfully, and then said I didn't know it had any particular shape. My gunpowdery chief went off with a bang, of course, and then went on loading and firing until he was out of adjectives.

I had learned long ago that he only carried just so many rounds of ammunition, and was sure to subside into a very placable and even remorseful old smooth-bore as soon as they were all gone. That word 'old' is merely affectionate; he was not more than thirty-four. I waited. By and by he said—

'My boy, you've got to know the SHAPE of the river perfectly. It is all there is left to steer by on a very dark night. Everything else is blotted out and gone. But mind you, it hasn't the same shape in the night that it has in the day-time.'

'How on earth am I ever going to learn it, then?'

'How do you follow a hall at home in the dark. Because you know the shape of it. You can't see it.'

'Do you mean to say that I've got to know all the million trifling variations of shape in the banks of this interminable river as well as I know the shape of the front hall at home?'

'On my honor, you've got to know them BETTER than any man ever did know the shapes of the halls in his own house.'

'I wish I was dead!'

'Now I don't want to discourage you, but—'

'Well, pile it on me; I might as well have it now as another time.'

'You see, this has got to be learned; there isn't any getting around it. A clear starlight night throws such heavy shadows that if you didn't know the shape of a shore perfectly you would claw away from every bunch of timber, because you

would take the black shadow of it for a solid cape; and you see you would be getting scared to death every fifteen minutes by the watch. You would be fifty yards from shore all the time when you ought to be within fifty feet of it. You can't see a snag in one of those shadows, but you know exactly where it is, and the shape of the river tells you when you are coming to it. Then there's your pitch- dark night; the river is a very different shape on a pitch-dark night from what it is on a starlight night. All shores seem to be straight lines, then, and mighty dim ones, too; and you'd RUN them for straight lines only you know better. You boldly drive your boat right into what seems to be a solid, straight wall (you knowing very well that in reality there is a curve there), and that wall falls back and makes way for you. Then there's your gray mist. You take a night when there's one of these grisly, drizzly, gray mists, and then there isn't any particular shape to a shore. A gray mist would tangle the head of the oldest man that ever lived. Well, then, different kinds of MOONLIGHT change the shape of the river in different ways. You see—'

'Oh, don't say any more, please! Have I got to learn the shape of the river according to all these five hundred thousand different ways? If I tried to carry all that cargo in my head it would make me stoop- shouldered.'

'NO! you only learn THE shape of the river, and you learn it with such absolute certainty that you can always steer by the shape that's IN YOUR HEAD, and never mind the one that's before your eyes.'

'Very well, I'll try it; but after I have learned it can I depend on it. Will it keep the same form and not go fooling around?'

Before Mr. Bixby could answer, Mr. W— came in to take the watch, and he said—

'Bixby, you'll have to look out for President's Island and all that country clear away up above the Old Hen and Chickens. The banks are caving and the shape of the shores changing like everything. Why, you wouldn't know the point above 40. You can go up inside the old sycamore- snag, now.*

So that question was answered. Here were leagues of shore changing shape. My spirits were down in the mud again. Two things seemed pretty apparent to me. One was, that in order to be a pilot a man had got to learn more than any one man ought to be allowed to know; and the other was, that he must learn it all over again in a different way every twenty-four hours.

That night we had the watch until twelve. Now it was an ancient river custom for the two pilots to chat a bit when the watch changed. While the relieving pilot put on his gloves and lit his cigar, his partner, the retiring pilot, would say something like this—

'I judge the upper bar is making down a little at Hale's Point; had quarter twain with the lower lead and mark twain** with the other.'

'Yes, I thought it was making down a little, last trip. Meet any boats?'

_____

* It may not be necessary, but still it can do no harm to explain that 'inside' means between the snag and the shore.— M.T.
** Two fathoms. 'Quarter twain' is two-and-a-quarter fathoms, thirteen-and-a-half feet. 'Mark three' is three fathoms.

'Met one abreast the head of 21, but she was away over hugging the bar, and I couldn't make her out entirely. I took her for the "Sunny South"--hadn't any skylights forward of the chimneys.'

And so on. And as the relieving pilot took the wheel his partner*** would mention that we were in such-and-such a bend, and say we were abreast of such-and-such a man's wood-yard or plantation. This was courtesy; I supposed it was necessity. But Mr. W— came on watch full twelve minutes late on this particular night,—a tremendous breach of etiquette; in fact, it is the unpardonable sin among pilots. So Mr. Bixby gave him no greeting whatever, but simply surrendered the wheel and marched out of the pilot-house without a word. I was appalled; it was a villainous night for blackness, we were in a particularly wide and blind part of the river, where there was no shape or substance to anything, and it seemed incredible that Mr. Bixby should have left that poor fellow to kill the boat trying to find out where he was. But I resolved that I would stand by him any way. He should find that he was not wholly friendless. So I stood around, and waited to be asked where we were. But Mr. W— plunged on serenely through the solid firmament of black cats that stood for an atmosphere, and never opened his mouth. Here is a proud devil, thought I; here is a limb of Satan that would rather send us all to destruction than put himself under obligations to me, because I am not yet one of the salt of the earth and privileged to snub captains and lord it over everything dead and alive in a steamboat. I presently climbed up on the bench; I did not think it was safe to go to sleep while this lunatic was on watch.

However, I must have gone to sleep in the course of time, because the next thing I was aware of was the fact that day was breaking, Mr. W— gone, and Mr. Bixby at the wheel again. So it was four o'clock and all well—but me; I felt like a skinful of dry bones and all of them trying to ache at once.

Mr. Bixby asked me what I had stayed up there for. I confessed that it was to do Mr. W— a benevolence,—tell him where he was. It took five minutes for the entire preposterousness of the thing to filter into Mr. Bixby's system, and then I judge it filled him nearly up to the chin; because he paid me a compliment— and not much of a one either. He said,

'Well, taking you by-and-large, you do seem to be more different kinds of an ass than any creature I ever saw before. What did you suppose he wanted to know for?'

I said I thought it might be a convenience to him.

'Convenience D-nation! Didn't I tell you that a man's got to know the river in the night the same as he'd know his own front hall?'

'Well, I can follow the front hall in the dark if I know it IS the front hall; but suppose you set me down in the middle of it in the dark and not tell me which hall it is; how am I to know?'

'Well you've GOT to, on the river!'

'All right. Then I'm glad I never said anything to Mr. W— '

'I should say so. Why, he'd have slammed you through the window and utterly ruined a hundred dollars' worth of window-sash and stuff.'

*** 'Partner' is a technical term for 'the other pilot'.

I was glad this damage had been saved, for it would have made me unpopular with the owners. They always hated anybody who had the name of being careless, and injuring things.

I went to work now to learn the shape of the river; and of all the eluding and ungraspable objects that ever I tried to get mind or hands on, that was the chief. I would fasten my eyes upon a sharp, wooded point that projected far into the river some miles ahead of me, and go to laboriously photographing its shape upon my brain; and just as I was beginning to succeed to my satisfaction, we would draw up toward it and the exasperating thing would begin to melt away and fold back into the bank! If there had been a conspicuous dead tree standing upon the very point of the cape, I would find that tree inconspicuously merged into the general forest, and occupying the middle of a straight shore, when I got abreast of it! No prominent hill would stick to its shape long enough for me to make up my mind what its form really was, but it was as dissolving and changeful as if it had been a mountain of butter in the hottest corner of the tropics. Nothing ever had the same shape when I was coming downstream that it had borne when I went up. I mentioned these little difficulties to Mr. Bixby. He said—

'That's the very main virtue of the thing. If the shapes didn't change every three seconds they wouldn't be of any use. Take this place where we are now, for instance. As long as that hill over yonder is only one hill, I can boom right along the way I'm going; but the moment it splits at the top and forms a V, I know I've got to scratch to starboard in a hurry, or I'll bang this boat's brains out against a rock; and then the moment one of the prongs of the V swings behind the other, I've got to waltz to larboard again, or I'll have a misunderstanding with a snag that would snatch the keelson out of this steamboat as neatly as if it were a sliver in your hand. If that hill didn't change its shape on bad nights there would be an awful steamboat grave-yard around here inside of a year.'

It was plain that I had got to learn the shape of the river in all the different ways that could be thought of,—upside down, wrong end first, inside out, fore-and-aft, and 'thortships,'—and then know what to do on gray nights when it hadn't any shape at all. So I set about it. In the course of time I began to get the best of this knotty lesson, and my self-complacency moved to the front once more. Mr. Bixby was all fixed, and ready to start it to the rear again. He opened on me after this fashion—

'How much water did we have in the middle crossing at Hole-in-the-Wall, trip before last?'

I considered this an outrage. I said—

'Every trip, down and up, the leadsmen are singing through that tangled place for three-quarters of an hour on a stretch. How do you reckon I can remember such a mess as that?'

'My boy, you've got to remember it. You've got to remember the exact spot and the exact marks the boat lay in when we had the shoalest water, in everyone of the five hundred shoal places between St. Louis and New Orleans; and you mustn't get the shoal soundings and marks of one trip mixed up with the shoal soundings and marks of another, either, for they're not often twice alike. You must keep them separate.'

When I came to myself again, I said—

'When I get so that I can do that, I'll be able to raise the dead, and then I won't have to pilot a steamboat to make a living. I want to retire from this business. I want a slush-bucket and a brush; I'm only fit for a roustabout. I haven't got brains enough to be a pilot; and if I had I wouldn't have strength enough to carry them around, unless I went on crutches.'

'Now drop that! When I say I'll learn* a man the river, I mean it. And you can depend on it, I'll learn him or kill him.'

Chapter 9 Continued Perplexities

THERE was no use in arguing with a person like this. I promptly put such a strain on my memory that by and by even the shoal water and the countless crossing-marks began to stay with me. But the result was just the same. I never could more than get one knotty thing learned before another presented itself. Now I had often seen pilots gazing at the water and pretending to read it as if it were a book; but it was a book that told me nothing. A time came at last, however, when Mr. Bixby seemed to think me far enough advanced to bear a lesson on water- reading. So he began—

'Do you see that long slanting line on the face of the water? Now, that's a reef. Moreover, it's a bluff reef. There is a solid sand-bar under it that is nearly as straight up and down as the side of a house. There is plenty of water close up to it, but mighty little on top of it. If you were to hit it you would knock the boat's brains out. Do you see where the line fringes out at the upper end and begins to fade away?'

'Yes, sir.'

'Well, that is a low place; that is the head of the reef. You can climb over there, and not hurt anything. Cross over, now, and follow along close under the reef—easy water there—not much current.'

I followed the reef along till I approached the fringed end. Then Mr. Bixby said—

'Now get ready. Wait till I give the word. She won't want to mount the reef; a boat hates shoal water. Stand by—wait— WAIT—keep her well in hand. NOW cramp her down! Snatch her! snatch her!'

He seized the other side of the wheel and helped to spin it around until it was hard down, and then we held it so. The boat resisted, and refused to answer for a while, and next she came surging to starboard, mounted the reef, and sent a long, angry ridge of water foaming away from her bows.

'Now watch her; watch her like a cat, or she'll get away from you. When she fights strong and the tiller slips a little, in a jerky, greasy sort of way, let up on her a trifle; it is the way she tells you at night that the water is too shoal; but keep edging her up, little by little, toward the point. You are well up on the bar, now; there is a bar under every point, because the water that comes down around it forms an eddy and allows the sediment to sink. Do you see those fine lines on the face of the water that branch out like the ribs of a fan. Well, those are little reefs; you want to just miss the ends of them, but run them pretty close. Now look out—look out! Don't you crowd that slick, greasy-looking place; there ain't nine feet there; she won't stand it. She begins to smell it; look sharp, I tell you! Oh blazes, there you go! Stop the starboard wheel! Quick! Ship up to back! Set her back!

---

* 'Teach' is not in the river vocabulary.

The engine bells jingled and the engines answered promptly, shooting white columns of steam far aloft out of the 'scape pipes, but it was too late. The boat had 'smelt' the bar in good earnest; the foamy ridges that radiated from her bows suddenly disappeared, a great dead swell came rolling forward and swept ahead of her, she careened far over to larboard, and went tearing away toward the other shore as if she were about scared to death. We were a good mile from where we ought to have been, when we finally got the upper hand of her again.

During the afternoon watch the next day, Mr. Bixby asked me if I knew how to run the next few miles. I said—

'Go inside the first snag above the point, outside the next one, start out from the lower end of Higgins's wood-yard, make a square crossing and—'

'That's all right. I'll be back before you close up on the next point.'

But he wasn't. He was still below when I rounded it and entered upon a piece of river which I had some misgivings about. I did not know that he was hiding behind a chimney to see how I would perform. I went gaily along, getting prouder and prouder, for he had never left the boat in my sole charge such a length of time before. I even got to 'setting' her and letting the wheel go, entirely, while I vaingloriously turned my back and inspected the stem marks and hummed a tune, a sort of easy indifference which I had prodigiously admired in Bixby and other great pilots. Once I inspected rather long, and when I faced to the front again my heart flew into my mouth so suddenly that if I hadn't clapped my teeth together I should have lost it. One of those frightful bluff reefs was stretching its deadly length right across our bows! My head was gone in a moment; I did not know which end I stood on; I gasped and could not get my breath; I spun the wheel down with such rapidity that it wove itself together like a spider's web; the boat answered and turned square away from the reef, but the reef followed her! I fled, and still it followed, still it kept—right across my bows! I never looked to see where I was going, I only fled. The awful crash was imminent—why didn't that villain come! If I committed the crime of ringing a bell, I might get thrown overboard. But better that than kill the boat. So in blind desperation I started such a rattling 'shivaree' down below as never had astounded an engineer in this world before, I fancy. Amidst the frenzy of the bells the engines began to back and fill in a furious way, and my reason forsook its throne—we were about to crash into the woods on the other side of the river. Just then Mr. Bixby stepped calmly into view on the hurricane deck. My soul went out to him in gratitude. My distress vanished; I would have felt safe on the brink of Niagara, with Mr. Bixby on the hurricane deck. He blandly and sweetly took his tooth-pick out of his mouth between his fingers, as if it were a cigar— we were just in the act of climbing an overhanging big tree, and the passengers were scudding astern like rats—and lifted up these commands to me ever so gently—

'Stop the starboard. Stop the larboard. Set her back on both.'

The boat hesitated, halted, pressed her nose among the boughs a critical instant, then reluctantly began to back away.

'Stop the larboard. Come ahead on it. Stop the starboard. Come ahead on it. Point her for the bar.'

I sailed away as serenely as a summer's morning Mr. Bixby came in and said, with mock simplicity—

'When you have a hail, my boy, you ought to tap the big bell three times before you land, so that the engineers can get ready.'

I blushed under the sarcasm, and said I hadn't had any hail.

'Ah! Then it was for wood, I suppose. The officer of the watch will tell you when he wants to wood up.'·

I went on consuming and said I wasn't after wood.

'Indeed? Why, what could you want over here in the bend, then? Did you ever know of a boat following a bend up-stream at this stage of the river?'

'No sir,—and I wasn't trying to follow it. I was getting away from a bluff reef.'

'No, it wasn't a bluff reef; there isn't one within three miles of where you were.'

'But I saw it. It was as bluff as that one yonder.'

'Just about. Run over it!'

'Do you give it as an order?'

'Yes. Run over it.'

'If I don't, I wish I may die.'

'All right; I am taking the responsibility.' I was just as anxious to kill the boat, now, as I had been to save her before. I impressed my orders upon my memory, to be used at the inquest, and made a straight break for the reef. As it disappeared under our bows I held my breath; but we slid over it like oil.

'Now don't you see the difference? It wasn't anything but a WIND reef. The wind does that.'

'So I see. But it is exactly like a bluff reef. How am I ever going to tell them apart?'

'I can't tell you. It is an instinct. By and by you will just naturally KNOW one from the other, but you never will be able to explain why or how you know them apart'

It turned out to be true. The face of the water, in time, became a wonderful book—a book that was a dead language to the uneducated passenger, but which told its mind to me without reserve, delivering its most cherished secrets as clearly as if it uttered them with a voice. And it was not a book to be read once and thrown aside, for it had a new story to tell every day. Throughout the long twelve hundred miles there was never a page that was void of interest, never one that you could leave unread without loss, never one that you would want to skip, thinking you could find higher enjoyment in some other thing. There never was so wonderful a book written by man; never one whose interest was so absorbing, so unflagging, so sparkingly renewed with every reperusal. The passenger who could not read it was charmed with a peculiar sort of faint dimple on its surface (on the rare occasions when he did not overlook it altogether); but to the pilot that was an ITALICIZED passage; indeed, it was more than that, it was a legend of the largest capitals, with a string of shouting exclamation points at the end of it; for it meant that a wreck or a rock was buried there that could tear the life out of the strongest vessel that ever floated. It is the faintest and simplest expression the water ever makes, and the most hideous to a pilot's eye. In truth, the passenger who could not read this book saw nothing but all manner of pretty pictures in it painted by the sun and shaded by the clouds, whereas to the trained eye these were not pictures at all, but the grimmest and most dead-earnest of reading-matter.

Now when I had mastered the language of this water and had come to know every trifling feature that bordered the great river as familiarly as I knew the letters of the alphabet, I had made a valuable acquisition. But I had lost something, too. I had lost something which could never be restored to me while I lived. All the grace, the beauty, the poetry had gone out of the majestic river! I still keep in mind a certain wonderful sunset which I witnessed when steamboating was new to me. A broad expanse of the river was turned to blood; in the middle distance the red hue brightened into gold, through which a solitary log came floating, black and conspicuous; in one place a long, slanting mark lay sparkling upon the water; in another the surface was broken by boiling, tumbling rings, that were as many-tinted as an opal; where the ruddy flush was faintest, was a smooth spot that was covered with graceful circles and radiating lines, ever so delicately traced; the shore on our left was densely wooded, and the somber shadow that fell from this forest was broken in one place by a long, ruffled trail that shone like silver; and high above the forest wall a clean-stemmed dead tree waved a single leafy bough that glowed like a flame in the unobstructed splendor that was flowing from the sun. There were graceful curves, reflected images, woody heights, soft distances; and over the whole scene, far and near, the dissolving lights drifted steadily, enriching it, every passing moment, with new marvels of coloring.

I stood like one bewitched. I drank it in, in a speechless rapture. The world was new to me, and I had never seen anything like this at home. But as I have said, a day came when I began to cease from noting the glories and the charms which the moon and the sun and the twilight wrought upon the river's face; another day came when I ceased altogether to note them. Then, if that sunset scene had been repeated, I should have looked upon it without rapture, and should have commented upon it, inwardly, after this fashion: This sun means that we are going to have wind to-morrow; that floating log means that the river is rising, small thanks to it; that slanting mark on the water refers to a bluff reef which is going to kill somebody's steamboat one of these nights, if it keeps on stretching out like that; those tumbling 'boils' show a dissolving bar and a changing channel there; the lines and circles in the slick water over yonder are a warning that that troublesome place is shoaling up dangerously; that silver streak in the shadow of the forest is the 'break' from a new snag, and he has located himself in the very best place he could have found to fish for steamboats; that tall dead tree, with a single living branch, is not going to last long, and then how is a body ever going to get through this blind place at night without the friendly old landmark.

No, the romance and the beauty were all gone from the river. All the value any feature of it had for me now was the amount of usefulness it could furnish toward compassing the safe piloting of a steamboat. Since those days, I have pitied doctors from my heart. What does the lovely flush in a beauty's cheek mean to a doctor but a 'break' that ripples above some deadly disease. Are not all her visible charms sown thick with what are to him the signs and symbols of hidden decay? Does he ever see her beauty at all, or doesn't he simply view her professionally, and comment upon her unwholesome condition all to himself? And doesn't he sometimes wonder whether he has gained most or lost most by learning his trade?

Chapter 10 Completing My Education

WHOSOEVER has done me the courtesy to read my chapters which have preceded this may possibly wonder that I deal so minutely with piloting as a science. It was the prime purpose of those chapters; and I am not quite done yet. I wish to show, in the most patient and painstaking way, what a wonderful science it is. Ship channels are buoyed and lighted, and therefore it is a comparatively easy undertaking to learn to run them; clear-water rivers, with gravel bottoms, change their channels very gradually, and therefore one needs to learn them but once; but piloting becomes another matter when you apply it to vast streams like the Mississippi and the Missouri, whose alluvial banks cave and change constantly, whose snags are always hunting up new quarters, whose sandbars are never at rest, whose channels are for ever dodging and shirking, and whose obstructions must be confronted in all nights and all weathers without the aid of a single light-house or a single buoy; for there is neither light nor buoy to be found anywhere in all this three or four thousand miles of villainous river.* I feel justified in enlarging upon this great science for the reason that I feel sure no one has ever yet written a paragraph about it who had piloted a steamboat himself, and so had a practical knowledge of the subject. If the theme were hackneyed, I should be obliged to deal gently with the reader; but since it is wholly new, I have felt at liberty to take up a considerable degree of room with it.

When I had learned the name and position of every visible feature of the river; when I had so mastered its shape that I could shut my eyes and trace it from St. Louis to New Orleans; when I had learned to read the face of the water as one would cull the news from the morning paper; and finally, when I had trained my dull memory to treasure up an endless array of soundings and crossing-marks, and keep fast hold of them, I judged that my education was complete: so I got to tilting my cap to the side of my head, and wearing a tooth-pick in my mouth at the wheel. Mr. Bixby had his eye on these airs. One day he said—

'What is the height of that bank yonder, at Burgess's?'

'How can I tell, sir. It is three-quarters of a mile away.'

'Very poor eye—very poor. Take the glass.'

I took the glass, and presently said—'I can't tell. I suppose that that bank is about a foot and a half high.'

'Foot and a half! That's a six-foot bank. How high was the bank along here last trip?'

'I don't know; I never noticed.'

'You didn't? Well, you must always do it hereafter.'

'Why?'

'Because you'll have to know a good many things that it tells you. For one thing, it tells you the stage of the river—tells you whether there's more water or less in the river along here than there was last trip.'

'The leads tell me that.' I rather thought I had the advantage of him there.

'Yes, but suppose the leads lie? The bank would tell you so, and then you'd stir those leadsmen up a bit. There was a ten-foot bank here last trip, and there is only a six-foot bank now. What does that signify?'

'That the river is four feet higher than it was last trip.'

'Very good. Is the river rising or falling?'

'Rising.'

'No it ain't.'

'I guess I am right, sir. Yonder is some drift-wood floating down the stream.'

'A rise starts the drift-wood, but then it keeps on floating a while after the river is done rising. Now the bank will tell you about this. Wait till you come to a place where it shelves a little. Now here; do you see this narrow belt of fine sediment That was deposited while the water was higher. You see the driftwood begins to strand, too. The bank helps in other ways. Do you see that stump on the false point?'

'Ay, ay, sir.'

'Well, the water is just up to the roots of it. You must make a note of that.'

'Why?'

'Because that means that there's seven feet in the chute of 103.'

'But 103 is a long way up the river yet.'

'That's where the benefit of the bank comes in. There is water enough in 103 NOW, yet there may not be by the time we get there; but the bank will keep us posted all along. You don't run close chutes on a falling river, up-stream, and there are precious few of them that you are allowed to run at all down-stream. There's a law of the United States against it. The river may be rising by the time we get to 103, and in that case we'll run it. We are drawing—how much?'

'Six feet aft,—six and a half forward.'

'Well, you do seem to know something.'

'But what I particularly want to know is, if I have got to keep up an everlasting measuring of the banks of this river, twelve hundred miles, month in and month out?'

'Of course!'

My emotions were too deep for words for a while. Presently I said—'

And how about these chutes. Are there many of them?'

'I should say so. I fancy we shan't run any of the river this trip as you've ever seen it run before—so to speak. If the river begins to rise again, we'll go up behind bars that you've always seen standing out of the river, high and dry like the roof of a house; we'll cut across low places that you've never noticed at

---

* True at the time referred to; not true now (1882).

all, right through the middle of bars that cover three hundred acres of river; we'll creep through cracks where you've always thought was solid land; we'll dart through the woods and leave twenty-five miles of river off to one side; we'll see the hind-side of every island between New Orleans and Cairo.'

'Then I've got to go to work and learn just as much more river as I already know.'

'Just about twice as much more, as near as you can come at it.'

'Well, one lives to find out. I think I was a fool when I went into this business.'

'Yes, that is true. And you are yet. But you'll not be when you've learned it.'

'Ah, I never can learn it.'

'I will see that you DO.'

By and by I ventured again—

'Have I got to learn all this thing just as I know the rest of the river—shapes and all—and so I can run it at night?'

'Yes. And you've got to have good fair marks from one end of the river to the other, that will help the bank tell you when there is water enough in each of these countless places—like that stump, you know. When the river first begins to rise, you can run half a dozen of the deepest of them; when it rises a foot more you can run another dozen; the next foot will add a couple of dozen, and so on: so you see you have to know your banks and marks to a dead moral certainty, and never get them mixed; for when you start through one of those cracks, there's no backing out again, as there is in the big river; you've got to go through, or stay there six months if you get caught on a falling river. There are about fifty of these cracks which you can't run at all except when the river is brim full and over the banks.'

'This new lesson is a cheerful prospect.'

'Cheerful enough. And mind what I've just told you; when you start into one of those places you've got to go through. They are too narrow to turn around in, too crooked to back out of, and the shoal water is always up at the head; never elsewhere. And the head of them is always likely to be filling up, little by little, so that the marks you reckon their depth by, this season, may not answer for next.'

'Learn a new set, then, every year?'

'Exactly. Cramp her up to the bar! What are you standing up through the middle of the river for?'

The next few months showed me strange things. On the same day that we held the conversation above narrated, we met a great rise coming down the river. The whole vast face of the stream was black with drifting dead logs, broken boughs, and great trees that had caved in and been washed away. It required the nicest steering to pick one's way through this rushing raft, even in the day-time, when crossing from point to point; and at night the difficulty was mightily increased; every now and then a huge log, lying deep in the water, would suddenly appear right under our bows, coming head-on; no use to try to avoid it then; we could only stop the engines, and one wheel would walk over that log from one end to the other,

keeping up a thundering racket and careening the boat in a way that was very uncomfortable to passengers. Now and then we would hit one of these sunken logs a rattling bang, dead in the center, with a full head of steam, and it would stun the boat as if she had hit a continent. Sometimes this log would lodge, and stay right across our nose, and back the Mississippi up before it; we would have to do a little craw-fishing, then, to get away from the obstruction. We often hit WHITE logs, in the dark, for we could not see them till we were right on them; but a black log is a pretty distinct object at night. A white snag is an ugly customer when the daylight is gone.

Of course, on the great rise, down came a swarm of prodigious timber- rafts from the head waters of the Mississippi, coal barges from Pittsburgh, little trading scows from everywhere, and broad-horns from 'Posey County,' Indiana, freighted with 'fruit and furniture'—the usual term for describing it, though in plain English the freight thus aggrandized was hoop-poles and pumpkins. Pilots bore a mortal hatred to these craft; and it was returned with usury. The law required all such helpless traders to keep a light burning, but it was a law that was often broken. All of a sudden, on a murky night, a light would hop up, right under our bows, almost, and an agonized voice, with the backwoods 'whang' to it, would wail out—

'Whar'n the — you goin' to! Cain't you see nothin', you dash-dashed aig-suckin', sheep-stealin', one-eyed son of a stuffed monkey!'

Then for an instant, as we whistled by, the red glare from our furnaces would reveal the scow and the form of the gesticulating orator as if under a lightning-flash, and in that instant our firemen and deck-hands would send and receive a tempest of missiles and profanity, one of our wheels would walk off with the crashing fragments of a steering-oar, and down the dead blackness would shut again. And that flatboatman would be sure to go into New Orleans and sue our boat, swearing stoutly that he had a light burning all the time, when in truth his gang had the lantern down below to sing and lie and drink and gamble by, and no watch on deck. Once, at night, in one of those forest-bordered crevices (behind an island) which steamboatmen intensely describe with the phrase 'as dark as the inside of a cow,' we should have eaten up a Posey County family, fruit, furniture, and all, but that they happened to be fiddling down below, and we just caught the sound of the music in time to sheer off, doing no serious damage, unfortunately, but coming so near it that we had good hopes for a moment. These people brought up their lantern, then, of course; and as we backed and filled to get away, the precious family stood in the light of it—both sexes and various ages—and cursed us till everything turned blue. Once a coalboatman sent a bullet through our pilot-house, when we borrowed a steering oar of him in a very narrow place.

Chapter 11 The River Rises

DURING this big rise these small-fry craft were an intolerable nuisance. We were running chute after chute,—a new world to me,—and if there was a particularly cramped place in a chute, we would be pretty sure to meet a broad-horn there; and if he failed to be there, we would find him in a still worse locality, namely, the head of the chute, on the shoal water. And then there would be no end of profane cordialities exchanged.

Sometimes, in the big river, when we would be feeling our way cautiously along through a fog, the deep hush would suddenly be broken by yells and a clamor of tin pans, and all in instant a log raft would appear vaguely through the webby veil, close

Life On The Mississippi 233

upon us; and then we did not wait to swap knives, but snatched our engine bells out by the roots and piled on all the steam we had, to scramble out of the way! One doesn't hit a rock or a solid log craft with a steamboat when he can get excused.

You will hardly believe it, but many steamboat clerks always carried a large assortment of religious tracts with them in those old departed steamboating days. Indeed they did. Twenty times a day we would be cramping up around a bar, while a string of these small-fry rascals were drifting down into the head of the bend away above and beyond us a couple of miles. Now a skiff would dart away from one of them, and come fighting its laborious way across the desert of water. It would 'ease all,' in the shadow of our forecastle, and the panting oarsmen would shout, 'Gimme a pa-a-per!' as the skiff drifted swiftly astern. The clerk would throw over a file of New Orleans journals. If these were picked up without comment, you might notice that now a dozen other skiffs had been drifting down upon us without saying anything. You understand, they had been waiting to see how No. 1 was going to fare. No. 1 making no comment, all the rest would bend to their oars and come on, now; and as fast as they came the clerk would heave over neat bundles of religious tracts, tied to shingles. The amount of hard swearing which twelve packages of religious literature will command when impartially divided up among twelve raftsmen's crews, who have pulled a heavy skiff two miles on a hot day to get them, is simply incredible.

As I have said, the big rise brought a new world under my vision. By the time the river was over its banks we had forsaken our old paths and were hourly climbing over bars that had stood ten feet out of water before; we were shaving stumpy shores, like that at the foot of Madrid Bend, which I had always seen avoided before; we were clattering through chutes like that of 82, where the opening at the foot was an unbroken wall of timber till our nose was almost at the very spot. Some of these chutes were utter solitudes. The dense, untouched forest overhung both banks of the crooked little crack, and one could believe that human creatures had never intruded there before. The swinging grape-vines, the grassy nooks and vistas glimpsed as we swept by, the flowering creepers waving their red blossoms from the tops of dead trunks, and all the spendthrift richness of the forest foliage, were wasted and thrown away there. The chutes were lovely places to steer in; they were deep, except at the head; the current was gentle; under the 'points' the water was absolutely dead, and the invisible banks so bluff that where the tender willow thickets projected you could bury your boat's broadside in them as you tore along, and then you seemed fairly to fly.

Behind other islands we found wretched little farms, and wretcheder little log-cabins; there were crazy rail fences sticking a foot or two above the water, with one or two jeans-clad, chills-racked, yellow-faced male miserables roosting on the top-rail, elbows on knees, jaws in hands, grinding tobacco and discharging the result at floating chips through crevices left by lost teeth; while the rest of the family and the few farm-animals were huddled together in an empty wood-flat riding at her moorings close at hand. In this flat-boat the family would have to cook and eat and sleep for a lesser or greater number of days (or possibly weeks), until the river should fall two or three feet and let them get back to their log-cabin and their chills again—chills being a merciful provision of an all-wise Providence to enable them to take exercise without exertion. And this sort of watery camping out was a thing which these people were rather liable to be treated to a couple of times a year: by the December rise out of the Ohio, and the June rise

out of the Mississippi. And yet these were kindly dispensations, for they at least enabled the poor things to rise from the dead now and then, and look upon life when a steamboat went by. They appreciated the blessing, too, for they spread their mouths and eyes wide open and made the most of these occasions. Now what COULD these banished creatures find to do to keep from dying of the blues during the low-water season!

Once, in one of these lovely island chutes, we found our course completely bridged by a great fallen tree. This will serve to show how narrow some of the chutes were. The passengers had an hour's recreation in a virgin wilderness, while the boat-hands chopped the bridge away; for there was no such thing as turning back, you comprehend.

From Cairo to Baton Rouge, when the river is over its banks, you have no particular trouble in the night, for the thousand-mile wall of dense forest that guards the two banks all the way is only gapped with a farm or wood-yard opening at intervals, and so you can't 'get out of the river' much easier than you could get out of a fenced lane; but from Baton Rouge to New Orleans it is a different matter. The river is more than a mile wide, and very deep—as much as two hundred feet, in places. Both banks, for a good deal over a hundred miles, are shorn of their timber and bordered by continuous sugar plantations, with only here and there a scattering sapling or row of ornamental China-trees. The timber is shorn off clear to the rear of the plantations, from two to four miles. When the first frost threatens to come, the planters snatch off their crops in a hurry. When they have finished grinding the cane, they form the refuse of the stalks (which they call BAGASSE) into great piles and set fire to them, though in other sugar countries the bagasse is used for fuel in the furnaces of the sugar mills. Now the piles of damp bagasse burn slowly, and smoke like Satan's own kitchen.

An embankment ten or fifteen feet high guards both banks of the Mississippi all the way down that lower end of the river, and this embankment is set back from the edge of the shore from ten to perhaps a hundred feet, according to circumstances; say thirty or forty feet, as a general thing. Fill that whole region with an impenetrable gloom of smoke from a hundred miles of burning bagasse piles, when the river is over the banks, and turn a steamboat loose along there at midnight and see how she will feel. And see how you will feel, too! You find yourself away out in the midst of a vague dim sea that is shoreless, that fades out and loses itself in the murky distances; for you cannot discern the thin rib of embankment, and you are always imagining you see a straggling tree when you don't. The plantations themselves are transformed by the smoke, and look like a part of the sea. All through your watch you are tortured with the exquisite misery of uncertainty. You hope you are keeping in the river, but you do not know. All that you are sure about is that you are likely to be within six feet of the bank and destruction, when you think you are a good half-mile from shore. And you are sure, also, that if you chance suddenly to fetch up against the embankment and topple your chimneys overboard, you will have the small comfort of knowing that it is about what you were expecting to do. One of the great Vicksburg packets darted out into a sugar plantation one night, at such a time, and had to stay there a week. But there was no novelty about it; it had often been done before.

I thought I had finished this chapter, but I wish to add a curious thing, while it is in my mind. It is only relevant in that it is connected with piloting. There used to be an excellent pilot on the river, a Mr. X., who was a somnambulist. It was said that if his mind was troubled about a bad piece of river, he was pretty sure to get up and walk in his sleep and do strange things. He was once fellow-pilot for a trip or two with George Ealer, on a great New Orleans passenger packet. During a considerable part of the first trip George was uneasy, but got over it by and by, as X. seemed content to stay in his bed when asleep. Late one night the boat was approaching Helena, Arkansas; the water was low, and the crossing above the town in a very blind and tangled condition. X. had seen the crossing since Ealer had, and as the night was particularly drizzly, sullen, and dark, Ealer was considering whether he had not better have X. called to assist in running the place, when the door opened and X. walked in. Now on very dark nights, light is a deadly enemy to piloting; you are aware that if you stand in a lighted room, on such a night, you cannot see things in the street to any purpose; but if you put out the lights and stand in the gloom you can make out objects in the street pretty well. So, on very dark nights, pilots do not smoke; they allow no fire in the pilot-house stove if there is a crack which can allow the least ray to escape; they order the furnaces to be curtained with huge tarpaulins and the sky-lights to be closely blinded. Then no light whatever issues from the boat. The undefinable shape that now entered the pilot-house had Mr. X.'s voice. This said—

'Let me take her, George; I've seen this place since you have, and it is so crooked that I reckon I can run it myself easier than I could tell you how to do it.'

'It is kind of you, and I swear *I* am willing. I haven't got another drop of perspiration left in me. I have been spinning around and around the wheel like a squirrel. It is so dark I can't tell which way she is swinging till she is coming around like a whirligig.'

So Ealer took a seat on the bench, panting and breathless. The black phantom assumed the wheel without saying anything, steadied the waltzing steamer with a turn or two, and then stood at ease, coaxing her a little to this side and then to that, as gently and as sweetly as if the time had been noonday. When Ealer observed this marvel of steering, he wished he had not confessed! He stared, and wondered, and finally said—

'Well, I thought I knew how to steer a steamboat, but that was another mistake of mine.'

X. said nothing, but went serenely on with his work. He rang for the leads; he rang to slow down the steam; he worked the boat carefully and neatly into invisible marks, then stood at the center of the wheel and peered blandly out into the blackness, fore and aft, to verify his position; as the leads shoaled more and more, he stopped the engines entirely, and the dead silence and suspense of 'drifting' followed when the shoalest water was struck, he cracked on the steam, carried her handsomely over, and then began to work her warily into the next system of shoal marks; the same patient, heedful use of leads and engines followed, the boat slipped through without touching bottom, and entered upon the third and last intricacy of the crossing; imperceptibly she moved through the gloom, crept by inches into her marks, drifted tediously till the shoalest water was cried, and then, under a tremendous head of steam, went swinging over the reef and away into deep water and safety!

Ealer let his long-pent breath pour out in a great, relieving sigh, and said—

'That's the sweetest piece of piloting that was ever done on the Mississippi River! I wouldn't believed it could be done, if I hadn't seen it.'

There was no reply, and he added—

'Just hold her five minutes longer, partner, and let me run down and get a cup of coffee.'

A minute later Ealer was biting into a pie, down in the 'texas,' and comforting himself with coffee. Just then the night watchman happened in, and was about to happen out again, when he noticed Ealer and exclaimed—

'Who is at the wheel, sir?'

'X.'

'Dart for the pilot-house, quicker than lightning!'

The next moment both men were flying up the pilot-house companion way, three steps at a jump! Nobody there! The great steamer was whistling down the middle of the river at her own sweet will! The watchman shot out of the place again; Ealer seized the wheel, set an engine back with power, and held his breath while the boat reluctantly swung away from a 'towhead' which she was about to knock into the middle of the Gulf of Mexico!

By and by the watchman came back and said—

'Didn't that lunatic tell you he was asleep, when he first came up here?'

'NO.'

'Well, he was. I found him walking along on top of the railings just as unconcerned as another man would walk a pavement; and I put him to bed; now just this minute there he was again, away astern, going through that sort of tight-rope deviltry the same as before.'

'Well, I think I'll stay by, next time he has one of those fits. But I hope he'll have them often. You just ought to have seen him take this boat through Helena crossing. I never saw anything so gaudy before. And if he can do such gold-leaf, kid-glove, diamond-breastpin piloting when he is sound asleep, what COULDN'T he do if he was dead!'

Chapter 12 Sounding

WHEN the river is very low, and one's steamboat is 'drawing all the water' there is in the channel,—or a few inches more, as was often the case in the old times,—one must be painfully circumspect in his piloting. We used to have to 'sound' a number of particularly bad places almost every trip when the river was at a very low stage.

Sounding is done in this way. The boat ties up at the shore, just above the shoal crossing; the pilot not on watch takes his 'cub' or steersman and a picked crew of men (sometimes an officer also), and goes out in the yawl—provided the boat has not that rare and sumptuous luxury, a regularly-devised 'sounding-boat'—and proceeds to hunt for the best water, the pilot on duty watching his movements through a spy-glass, meantime, and in some instances assisting by signals of the boat's whistle, signifying 'try higher up' or 'try lower down;' for the surface of the water, like an oil-painting, is more expressive and intelligible when inspected from a little distance than very close at hand. The whistle signals are seldom necessary, however; never, perhaps, except when the wind confuses the significant ripples upon the water's surface. When the yawl has reached the shoal place, the speed is slackened, the pilot begins to sound the depth with a pole ten or twelve feet long, and the steersman at the tiller obeys the order to 'hold her up to starboard;' or, 'let her fall off to larboard*'; or 'steady—steady as you go.'

When the measurements indicate that the yawl is approaching the shoalest part of the reef, the command is given to 'ease all!' Then the men stop rowing and the yawl drifts with the current. The next order is, 'Stand by with the buoy!' The moment the shallowest point is reached, the pilot delivers the order, 'Let go the buoy!' and over she goes. If the pilot is not satisfied, he sounds the place again; if he finds better water higher up or lower down, he removes the buoy to that place. Being finally satisfied, he gives the order, and all the men stand their oars straight up in the air, in line; a blast from the boat's whistle indicates that the signal has been seen; then the men 'give way' on their oars and lay the yawl alongside the buoy; the steamer comes creeping carefully down, is pointed straight at the buoy, husbands her power for the coming struggle, and presently, at the critical moment, turns on all her steam and goes grinding and wallowing over the buoy and the sand, and gains the deep water beyond. Or maybe she doesn't; maybe she 'strikes and swings.' Then she has to while away several hours (or days) sparring herself off.

Sometimes a buoy is not laid at all, but the yawl goes ahead, hunting the best water, and the steamer follows along in its wake. Often there is a deal of fun and excitement about sounding, especially if it is a glorious summer day, or a blustering night. But in winter the cold and the peril take most of the fun out of it.

A buoy is nothing but a board four or five feet long, with one end turned up; it is a reversed school-house bench, with one of the supports left and the other removed. It is anchored on the shoalest part of the reef by a rope with a heavy stone made fast to the end of it. But for the resistance of the turned-up end of the reversed bench, the current would pull the buoy under water. At night, a paper lantern with a candle in it is fastened on top of the buoy, and this can be seen a mile or more, a little glimmering spark in the waste of blackness.

Nothing delights a cub so much as an opportunity to go out sounding. There is such an air of adventure about it; often there is danger; it is so gaudy and man-of-war-like to sit up in the stern-sheets and steer a swift yawl; there is something fine about the exultant spring of the boat when an experienced old sailor crew throw their souls into the oars; it is lovely to see the white foam stream away from the bows; there is music in the rush of the water; it is deliciously exhilarating, in summer, to go speeding over the breezy expanses of the river when the world of wavelets is dancing in the sun. It is such grandeur, too, to the cub, to get a chance to give an order; for often the pilot will simply say, 'Let her go about!' and leave the rest to the cub, who instantly cries, in his sternest tone of command, 'Ease starboard! Strong on the larboard! Starboard give way! With a will, men!' The cub enjoys sounding for the further reason that the eyes of the passengers are watching all the yawl's movements with absorbing interest if the time be daylight; and if it be night he knows that those same

---

* The term 'larboard' is never used at sea now, to signify the left hand; but was always used on the river in my time

wondering eyes are fastened upon the yawl's lantern as it glides out into the gloom and dims away in the remote distance.

One trip a pretty girl of sixteen spent her time in our pilot-house with her uncle and aunt, every day and all day long. I fell in love with her. So did Mr. Thornburg's cub, Tom G—. Tom and I had been bosom friends until this time; but now a coolness began to arise. I told the girl a good many of my river adventures, and made myself out a good deal of a hero; Tom tried to make himself appear to be a hero, too, and succeeded to some extent, but then he always had a way of embroidering. However, virtue is its own reward, so I was a barely perceptible trifle ahead in the contest. About this time something happened which promised handsomely for me: the pilots decided to sound the crossing at the head of 21. This would occur about nine or ten o'clock at night, when the passengers would be still up; it would be Mr. Thornburg's watch, therefore my chief would have to do the sounding. We had a perfect love of a sounding-boat—long, trim, graceful, and as fleet as a greyhound; her thwarts were cushioned; she carried twelve oarsmen; one of the mates was always sent in her to transmit orders to her crew, for ours was a steamer where no end of 'style' was put on.

We tied up at the shore above 21, and got ready. It was a foul night, and the river was so wide, there, that a landsman's uneducated eyes could discern no opposite shore through such a gloom. The passengers were alert and interested; everything was satisfactory. As I hurried through the engine-room, picturesquely gotten up in storm toggery, I met Tom, and could not forbear delivering myself of a mean speech—

'Ain't you glad YOU don't have to go out sounding?'

Tom was passing on, but he quickly turned, and said—

'Now just for that, you can go and get the sounding-pole yourself. I was going after it, but I'd see you in Halifax, now, before I'd do it.'

'Who wants you to get it? I don't. It's in the sounding-boat.'

'It ain't, either. It's been new-painted; and it's been up on the ladies' cabin guards two days, drying.'

I flew back, and shortly arrived among the crowd of watching and wondering ladies just in time to hear the command:

'Give way, men!'

I looked over, and there was the gallant sounding-boat booming away, the unprincipled Tom presiding at the tiller, and my chief sitting by him with the sounding-pole which I had been sent on a fool's errand to fetch. Then that young girl said to me—

'Oh, how awful to have to go out in that little boat on such a night! Do you think there is any danger?'

I would rather have been stabbed. I went off, full of venom, to help in the pilot-house. By and by the boat's lantern disappeared, and after an interval a wee spark glimmered upon the face of the water a mile away. Mr. Thornburg blew the whistle, in acknowledgment, backed the steamer out, and made for it. We flew along for a while, then slackened steam and went cautiously gliding toward the spark. Presently Mr. Thornburg exclaimed—

'Hello, the buoy-lantern's out!'

He stopped the engines. A moment or two later he said—

'Why, there it is again!'

So he came ahead on the engines once more, and rang for the leads. Gradually the water shoaled up, and then began to deepen again! Mr. Thornburg muttered—

'Well, I don't understand this. I believe that buoy has drifted off the reef. Seems to be a little too far to the left. No matter, it is safest to run over it anyhow.'

So, in that solid world of darkness we went creeping down on the light. Just as our bows were in the act of plowing over it, Mr. Thornburg seized the bell-ropes, rang a startling peal, and exclaimed—

'My soul, it's the sounding-boat!'

A sudden chorus of wild alarms burst out far below—a pause—and then the sound of grinding and crashing followed. Mr. Thornburg exclaimed—

'There! the paddle-wheel has ground the sounding-boat to lucifer matches! Run! See who is killed!'

I was on the main deck in the twinkling of an eye. My chief and the third mate and nearly all the men were safe. They had discovered their danger when it was too late to pull out of the way; then, when the great guards overshadowed them a moment later, they were prepared and knew what to do; at my chiefs order they sprang at the right instant, seized the guard, and were hauled aboard. The next moment the sounding-yawl swept aft to the wheel and was struck and splintered to atoms. Two of the men and the cub Tom, were missing—a fact which spread like wildfire over the boat. The passengers came flocking to the forward gangway, ladies and all, anxious-eyed, white-faced, and talked in awed voices of the dreadful thing. And often and again I heard them say, 'Poor fellows! poor boy, poor boy!'

By this time the boat's yawl was manned and away, to search for the missing. Now a faint call was heard, off to the left. The yawl had disappeared in the other direction. Half the people rushed to one side to encourage the swimmer with their shouts; the other half rushed the other way to shriek to the yawl to turn about. By the callings, the swimmer was approaching, but some said the sound showed failing strength. The crowd massed themselves against the boiler-deck railings, leaning over and staring into the gloom; and every faint and fainter cry wrung from them such words as, 'Ah, poor fellow, poor fellow! is there no way to save him?'

But still the cries held out, and drew nearer, and presently the voice said pluckily—

'I can make it! Stand by with a rope!'

What a rousing cheer they gave him! The chief mate took his stand in the glare of a torch-basket, a coil of rope in his hand, and his men grouped about him. The next moment the swimmer's face appeared in the circle of light, and in another one the owner of it was hauled aboard, limp and drenched, while cheer on cheer went up. It was that devil Tom.

The yawl crew searched everywhere, but found no sign of the two men. They probably failed to catch the guard, tumbled back, and were struck by the wheel and killed. Tom had never jumped for the guard at all, but had plunged head-first into the river and dived under the wheel. It was nothing; I could have done it easy enough, and I said so; but everybody went on just the same, making a wonderful to do over that ass, as if he had done something great. That girl couldn't seem to have enough of that pitiful 'hero' the rest of the trip; but little I cared; I loathed her, any way.

The way we came to mistake the sounding-boat's lantern for the buoy- light was this. My chief said that after laying the buoy he fell away and watched it till it seemed to be secure; then he took up a position a hundred yards below it and a little to one side of the steamer's course, headed the sounding-boat up-stream, and waited. Having to wait some time, he and the officer got to talking; he looked up when he judged that the steamer was about on the reef; saw that the buoy was gone, but supposed that the steamer had already run over it; he went on with his talk; he noticed that the steamer was getting very close on him, but that was the correct thing; it was her business to shave him closely, for convenience in taking him aboard; he was expecting her to sheer off, until the last moment; then it flashed upon him that she was trying to run him down, mistaking his lantern for the buoy-light; so he sang out, 'Stand by to spring for the guard, men!' and the next instant the jump was made.

Chapter 13 A Pilot's Needs

BUT I am wandering from what I was intending to do, that is, make plainer than perhaps appears in the previous chapters, some of the peculiar requirements of the science of piloting. First of all, there is one faculty which a pilot must incessantly cultivate until he has brought it to absolute perfection. Nothing short of perfection will do. That faculty is memory. He cannot stop with merely thinking a thing is so and so; he must know it; for this is eminently one of the 'exact' sciences. With what scorn a pilot was looked upon, in the old times, if he ever ventured to deal in that feeble phrase 'I think,' instead of the vigorous one 'I know!' One cannot easily realize what a tremendous thing it is to know every trivial detail of twelve hundred miles of river and know it with absolute exactness. If you will take the longest street in New York, and travel up and down it, conning its features patiently until you know every house and window and door and lamp-post and big and little sign by heart, and know them so accurately that you can instantly name the one you are abreast of when you are set down at random in that street in the middle of an inky black night, you will then have a tolerable notion of the amount and the exactness of a pilot's knowledge who carries the Mississippi River in his head. And then if you will go on until you know every street crossing, the character, size, and position of the crossing-stones, and the varying depth of mud in each of those numberless places, you will have some idea of what the pilot must know in order to keep a Mississippi steamer out of trouble. Next, if you will take half of the signs in that long street, and CHANGE THEIR PLACES once a month, and still manage to know their new positions accurately on dark nights, and keep up with these repeated changes without making any mistakes, you will understand what is required of a pilot's peerless memory by the fickle Mississippi.

I think a pilot's memory is about the most wonderful thing in the world. To know the Old and New Testaments by heart, and be able to recite them glibly, forward or backward, or begin at random anywhere in the book and recite both ways and never trip or make a mistake, is no extravagant mass of knowledge, and no marvelous facility, compared to a pilot's massed knowledge of the Mississippi and his marvelous facility in the handling of it. I make this comparison deliberately, and believe I am not expanding the truth when I do it. Many will think my figure too strong, but pilots will not.

And how easily and comfortably the pilot's memory does its work; how placidly effortless is its way; how UNCONSCIOUSLY it lays up its vast stores, hour by hour, day by day, and never loses or mislays a single valuable package of them all! Take an instance. Let a leadsman cry, 'Half twain! half twain! half twain! half twain! half twain!' until it become as monotonous as the ticking of a clock; let conversation be going on all the time, and the pilot be doing his share of the talking, and no longer consciously listening to the leadsman; and in the midst of this endless string of half twains let a single 'quarter twain!' be interjected, without emphasis, and then the half twain cry go on again, just as before: two or three weeks later that pilot can describe with precision the boat's position in the river when that quarter twain was uttered, and give you such a lot of head-marks, stern-marks, and side- marks to guide you, that you ought to be able to take the boat there and put her in that same spot again yourself! The cry of 'quarter twain' did not really take his mind from his talk, but his trained faculties instantly photographed the bearings, noted the change of depth, and laid up the important details for future reference without requiring any assistance from him in the matter. If you were walking and talking with a friend, and another friend at your side kept up a monotonous repetition of the vowel sound A, for a couple of blocks, and then in the midst interjected an R, thus, A, A, A, A, A, R, A, A, A, etc., and gave the R no emphasis, you would not be able to state, two or three weeks afterward, that the R had been put in, nor be able to tell what objects you were passing at the moment it was done. But you could if your memory had been patiently and laboriously trained to do that sort of thing mechanically.

Give a man a tolerably fair memory to start with, and piloting will develop it into a very colossus of capability. But ONLY IN THE MATTERS IT IS DAILY DRILLED IN. A time would come when the man's faculties could not help noticing landmarks and soundings, and his memory could not help holding on to them with the grip of a vise; but if you asked that same man at noon what he had had for breakfast, it would be ten chances to one that he could not tell you. Astonishing things can be done with the human memory if you will devote it faithfully to one particular line of business.

At the time that wages soared so high on the Missouri River, my chief, Mr. Bixby, went up there and learned more than a thousand miles of that stream with an ease and rapidity that were astonishing. When he had seen each division once in the daytime and once at night, his education was so nearly complete that he took out a 'daylight' license; a few trips later he took out a full license, and went to piloting day and night—and he ranked A 1, too.

Mr. Bixby placed me as steersman for a while under a pilot whose feats of memory were a constant marvel to me. However, his memory was born in him, I think, not built. For instance, somebody would mention a name. Instantly Mr. Brown would break in—

'Oh, I knew HIM. Sallow-faced, red-headed fellow, with a little scar on the side of his throat, like a splinter under the flesh. He was only in the Southern trade six months. That was thirteen years ago. I made a trip with him. There was five feet in the

upper river then; the "Henry Blake" grounded at the foot of Tower Island drawing four and a half; the "George Elliott" unshipped her rudder on the wreck of the "Sunflower"—'

'Why, the "Sunflower" didn't sink until—'

'I know when she sunk; it was three years before that, on the 2nd of December; Asa Hardy was captain of her, and his brother John was first clerk; and it was his first trip in her, too; Tom Jones told me these things a week afterward in New Orleans; he was first mate of the "Sunflower." Captain Hardy stuck a nail in his foot the 6th of July of the next year, and died of the lockjaw on the 15th. His brother died two years after 3rd of March,—erysipelas. I never saw either of the Hardys,—they were Alleghany River men,—but people who knew them told me all these things. And they said Captain Hardy wore yarn socks winter and summer just the same, and his first wife's name was Jane Shook—she was from New England—and his second one died in a lunatic asylum. It was in the blood. She was from Lexington, Kentucky. Name was Horton before she was married.'

And so on, by the hour, the man's tongue would go. He could NOT forget any thing. It was simply impossible. The most trivial details remained as distinct and luminous in his head, after they had lain there for years, as the most memorable events. His was not simply a pilot's memory; its grasp was universal. If he were talking about a trifling letter he had received seven years before, he was pretty sure to deliver you the entire screed from memory. And then without observing that he was departing from the true line of his talk, he was more than likely to hurl in a long-drawn parenthetical biography of the writer of that letter; and you were lucky indeed if he did not take up that writer's relatives, one by one, and give you their biographies, too.

Such a memory as that is a great misfortune. To it, all occurrences are of the same size. Its possessor cannot distinguish an interesting circumstance from an uninteresting one. As a talker, he is bound to clog his narrative with tiresome details and make himself an insufferable bore. Moreover, he cannot stick to his subject. He picks up every little grain of memory he discerns in his way, and so is led aside. Mr. Brown would start out with the honest intention of telling you a vastly funny anecdote about a dog. He would be 'so full of laugh' that he could hardly begin; then his memory would start with the dog's breed and personal appearance; drift into a history of his owner; of his owner's family, with descriptions of weddings and burials that had occurred in it, together with recitals of congratulatory verses and obituary poetry provoked by the same: then this memory would recollect that one of these events occurred during the celebrated 'hard winter' of such and such a year, and a minute description of that winter would follow, along with the names of people who were frozen to death, and statistics showing the high figures which pork and hay went up to. Pork and hay would suggest corn and fodder; corn and fodder would suggest cows and horses; cows and horses would suggest the circus and certain celebrated bareback riders; the transition from the circus to the menagerie was easy and natural; from the elephant to equatorial Africa was but a step; then of course the heathen savages would suggest religion; and at the end of three or four hours' tedious jaw, the watch would change, and Brown would go out of the pilot-house muttering extracts from sermons he had heard years before about the efficacy of prayer as a means of grace. And the original first mention would be all you had learned about that dog, after all this waiting and hungering.

A pilot must have a memory; but there are two higher qualities which he must also have. He must have good and quick judgment and decision, and a cool, calm courage that no peril can shake. Give a man the merest trifle of pluck to start with, and by the time he has become a pilot he cannot be unmanned by any danger a steamboat can get into; but one cannot quite say the same for judgment. Judgment is a matter of brains, and a man must START with a good stock of that article or he will never succeed as a pilot.

The growth of courage in the pilot-house is steady all the time, but it does not reach a high and satisfactory condition until some time after the young pilot has been 'standing his own watch,' alone and under the staggering weight of all the responsibilities connected with the position. When an apprentice has become pretty thoroughly acquainted with the river, he goes clattering along so fearlessly with his steamboat, night or day, that he presently begins to imagine that it is HIS courage that animates him; but the first time the pilot steps out and leaves him to his own devices he finds out it was the other man's. He discovers that the article has been left out of his own cargo altogether. The whole river is bristling with exigencies in a moment; he is not prepared for them; he does not know how to meet them; all his knowledge forsakes him; and within fifteen minutes he is as white as a sheet and scared almost to death. Therefore pilots wisely train these cubs by various strategic tricks to look danger in the face a little more calmly. A favorite way of theirs is to play a friendly swindle upon the candidate.

Mr. Bixby served me in this fashion once, and for years afterward I used to blush even in my sleep when I thought of it. I had become a good steersman; so good, indeed, that I had all the work to do on our watch, night and day; Mr. Bixby seldom made a suggestion to me; all he ever did was to take the wheel on particularly bad nights or in particularly bad crossings, land the boat when she needed to be landed, play gentleman of leisure nine-tenths of the watch, and collect the wages. The lower river was about bank-full, and if anybody had questioned my ability to run any crossing between Cairo and New Orleans without help or instruction, I should have felt irreparably hurt. The idea of being afraid of any crossing in the lot, in the DAY-TIME, was a thing too preposterous for contemplation. Well, one matchless summer's day I was bowling down the bend above island 66, brimful of self-conceit and carrying my nose as high as a giraffe's, when Mr. Bixby said—

'I am going below a while. I suppose you know the next crossing?'

This was almost an affront. It was about the plainest and simplest crossing in the whole river. One couldn't come to any harm, whether he ran it right or not; and as for depth, there never had been any bottom there. I knew all this, perfectly well.

'Know how to RUN it? Why, I can run it with my eyes shut.'

'How much water is there in it?'

'Well, that is an odd question. I couldn't get bottom there with a church steeple.'

'You think so, do you?'

The very tone of the question shook my confidence. That was what Mr. Bixby was expecting. He left, without saying

anything more. I began to imagine all sorts of things. Mr. Bixby, unknown to me, of course, sent somebody down to the forecastle with some mysterious instructions to the leadsmen, another messenger was sent to whisper among the officers, and then Mr. Bixby went into hiding behind a smoke-stack where he could observe results. Presently the captain stepped out on the hurricane deck; next the chief mate appeared; then a clerk. Every moment or two a straggler was added to my audience; and before I got to the head of the island I had fifteen or twenty people assembled down there under my nose. I began to wonder what the trouble was. As I started across, the captain glanced aloft at me and said, with a sham uneasiness in his voice—

'Where is Mr. Bixby?'

'Gone below, sir.'

But that did the business for me. My imagination began to construct dangers out of nothing, and they multiplied faster than I could keep the run of them. All at once I imagined I saw shoal water ahead! The wave of coward agony that surged through me then came near dislocating every joint in me. All my confidence in that crossing vanished. I seized the bell-rope; dropped it, ashamed; seized it again; dropped it once more; clutched it tremblingly one again, and pulled it so feebly that I could hardly hear the stroke myself. Captain and mate sang out instantly, and both together—

'Starboard lead there! and quick about it!'

This was another shock. I began to climb the wheel like a squirrel; but I would hardly get the boat started to port before I would see new dangers on that side, and away I would spin to the other; only to find perils accumulating to starboard, and be crazy to get to port again. Then came the leadsman's sepulchral cry—

'D-e-e-p four!'

Deep four in a bottomless crossing! The terror of it took my breath away.

'M-a-r-k three!... M-a-r-k three... Quarter less three!... Half twain!'

This was frightful! I seized the bell-ropes and stopped the engines.

'Quarter twain! Quarter twain! MARK twain!'

I was helpless. I did not know what in the world to do. I was quaking from head to foot, and I could have hung my hat on my eyes, they stuck out so far.

'Quarter LESS twain! Nine and a HALF!'

We were DRAWING nine! My hands were in a nerveless flutter. I could not ring a bell intelligibly with them. I flew to the speaking-tube and shouted to the engineer—

'Oh, Ben, if you love me, BACK her! Quick, Ben! Oh, back the immortal SOUL out of her!'

I heard the door close gently. I looked around, and there stood Mr. Bixby, smiling a bland, sweet smile. Then the audience on the hurricane deck sent up a thundergust of humiliating laughter. I saw it all, now, and I felt meaner than the meanest man in human history. I laid in the lead, set the boat in her marks, came ahead on the engines, and said—

'It was a fine trick to play on an orphan, WASN'T it? I suppose I'll never hear the last of how I was ass enough to heave the lead at the head of 66.'

'Well, no, you won't, maybe. In fact I hope you won't; for I want you to learn something by that experience. Didn't you KNOW there was no bottom in that crossing?'

'Yes, sir, I did.'

'Very well, then. You shouldn't have allowed me or anybody else to shake your confidence in that knowledge. Try to remember that. And another thing: when you get into a dangerous place, don't turn coward. That isn't going to help matters any.'

It was a good enough lesson, but pretty hardly learned. Yet about the hardest part of it was that for months I so often had to hear a phrase which I had conceived a particular distaste for. It was, 'Oh, Ben, if you love me, back her!'

Chapter 14 Rank and Dignity of Piloting

IN my preceding chapters I have tried, by going into the minutiae of the science of piloting, to carry the reader step by step to a comprehension of what the science consists of; and at the same time I have tried to show him that it is a very curious and wonderful science, too, and very worthy of his attention. If I have seemed to love my subject, it is no surprising thing, for I loved the profession far better than any I have followed since, and I took a measureless pride in it. The reason is plain: a pilot, in those days, was the only unfettered and entirely independent human being that lived in the earth. Kings are but the hampered servants of parliament and people; parliaments sit in chains forged by their constituency; the editor of a newspaper cannot be independent, but must work with one hand tied behind him by party and patrons, and be content to utter only half or two-thirds of his mind; no clergyman is a free man and may speak the whole truth, regardless of his parish's opinions; writers of all kinds are manacled servants of the public. We write frankly and fearlessly, but then we 'modify' before we print. In truth, every man and woman and child has a master, and worries and frets in servitude; but in the day I write of, the Mississippi pilot had none. The captain could stand upon the hurricane deck, in the pomp of a very brief authority, and give him five or six orders while the vessel backed into the stream, and then that skipper's reign was over. The moment that the boat was under way in the river, she was under the sole and unquestioned control of the pilot. He could do with her exactly as he pleased, run her when and whither he chose, and tie her up to the bank whenever his judgment said that that course was best. His movements were entirely free; he consulted no one, he received commands from nobody, he promptly resented even the merest suggestions. Indeed, the law of the United States forbade him to listen to commands or suggestions, rightly considering that the pilot necessarily knew better how to handle the boat than anybody could tell him. So here was the novelty of a king without a keeper, an absolute monarch who was absolute in sober truth and not by a fiction of words. I have seen a boy of eighteen taking a great steamer serenely into what seemed almost certain destruction, and the aged captain standing mutely by, filled with apprehension but powerless to interfere. His interference, in that particular instance, might have been an excellent thing, but to permit it

would have been to establish a most pernicious precedent. It will easily be guessed, considering the pilot's boundless authority, that he was a great personage in the old steamboating days. He was treated with marked courtesy by the captain and with marked deference by all the officers and servants; and this deferential spirit was quickly communicated to the passengers, too. I think pilots were about the only people I ever knew who failed to show, in some degree, embarrassment in the presence of traveling foreign princes. But then, people in one's own grade of life are not usually embarrassing objects.

By long habit, pilots came to put all their wishes in the form of commands. It 'gravels' me, to this day, to put my will in the weak shape of a request, instead of launching it in the crisp language of an order. In those old days, to load a steamboat at St. Louis, take her to New Orleans and back, and discharge cargo, consumed about twenty-five days, on an average. Seven or eight of these days the boat spent at the wharves of St. Louis and New Orleans, and every soul on board was hard at work, except the two pilots; they did nothing but play gentleman up town, and receive the same wages for it as if they had been on duty. The moment the boat touched the wharf at either city, they were ashore; and they were not likely to be seen again till the last bell was ringing and everything in readiness for another voyage.

When a captain got hold of a pilot of particularly high reputation, he took pains to keep him. When wages were four hundred dollars a month on the Upper Mississippi, I have known a captain to keep such a pilot in idleness, under full pay, three months at a time, while the river was frozen up. And one must remember that in those cheap times four hundred dollars was a salary of almost inconceivable splendor. Few men on shore got such pay as that, and when they did they were mightily looked up to. When pilots from either end of the river wandered into our small Missouri village, they were sought by the best and the fairest, and treated with exalted respect. Lying in port under wages was a thing which many pilots greatly enjoyed and appreciated; especially if they belonged in the Missouri River in the heyday of that trade (Kansas times), and got nine hundred dollars a trip, which was equivalent to about eighteen hundred dollars a month. Here is a conversation of that day. A chap out of the Illinois River, with a little stern-wheel tub, accosts a couple of ornate and gilded Missouri River pilots—

'Gentlemen, I've got a pretty good trip for the upcountry, and shall want you about a month. How much will it be?'

'Eighteen hundred dollars apiece.'

'Heavens and earth! You take my boat, let me have your wages, and I'll divide!'

I will remark, in passing, that Mississippi steamboatmen were important in landsmen's eyes (and in their own, too, in a degree) according to the dignity of the boat they were on. For instance, it was a proud thing to be of the crew of such stately craft as the 'Aleck Scott' or the 'Grand Turk.' Negro firemen, deck hands, and barbers belonging to those boats were distinguished personages in their grade of life, and they were well aware of that fact too. A stalwart darkey once gave offense at a negro ball in New Orleans by putting on a good many airs. Finally one of the managers bustled up to him and said—

'Who IS you, any way? Who is you? dat's what I wants to know!'

The offender was not disconcerted in the least, but swelled himself up and threw that into his voice which showed that he knew he was not putting on all those airs on a stinted capital.

'Who IS I? Who IS I? I let you know mighty quick who I is! I want you niggers to understan' dat I fires de middle do'* on de "Aleck Scott!"'

That was sufficient.

The barber of the 'Grand Turk' was a spruce young negro, who aired his importance with balmy complacency, and was greatly courted by the circle in which he moved. The young colored population of New Orleans were much given to flirting, at twilight, on the banquettes of the back streets. Somebody saw and heard something like the following, one evening, in one of those localities. A middle-aged negro woman projected her head through a broken pane and shouted (very willing that the neighbors should hear and envy), 'You Mary Ann, come in de house dis minute! Stannin' out dah foolin' 'long wid dat low trash, an' heah's de barber offn de "Gran' Turk" wants to conwerse wid you!'

My reference, a moment ago, to the fact that a pilot's peculiar official position placed him out of the reach of criticism or command, brings Stephen W— naturally to my mind. He was a gifted pilot, a good fellow, a tireless talker, and had both wit and humor in him. He had a most irreverent independence, too, and was deliciously easy-going and comfortable in the presence of age, official dignity, and even the most august wealth. He always had work, he never saved a penny, he was a most persuasive borrower, he was in debt to every pilot on the river, and to the majority of the captains. He could throw a sort of splendor around a bit of harum-scarum, devil-may-care piloting, that made it almost fascinating—but not to everybody. He made a trip with good old Captain Y—once, and was 'relieved' from duty when the boat got to New Orleans. Somebody expressed surprise at the discharge. Captain Y— shuddered at the mere mention of Stephen. Then his poor, thin old voice piped out something like this:—

'Why, bless me! I wouldn't have such a wild creature on my boat for the world—not for the whole world! He swears, he sings, he whistles, he yells—I never saw such an Injun to yell. All times of the night—it never made any difference to him. He would just yell that way, not for anything in particular, but merely on account of a kind of devilish comfort he got out of it. I never could get into a sound sleep but he would fetch me out of bed, all in a cold sweat, with one of those dreadful war-whoops. A queer being—very queer being; no respect for anything or anybody. Sometimes he called me "Johnny." And he kept a fiddle, and a cat. He played execrably. This seemed to distress the cat, and so the cat would howl. Nobody could sleep where that man—and his family—was. And reckless. There never was anything like it. Now you may believe it or not, but as sure as I am sitting here, he brought my boat a-tilting down through those awful snags at Chicot under a rattling head of steam, and the wind a-blowing like the very nation, at that! My officers will tell you so. They saw it. And, sir, while he was a-tearing right down through those snags, and I a-shaking in my shoes and praying, I wish I may never speak again if he didn't pucker up his mouth and go to WHISTLING! Yes, sir; whistling "Buffalo gals, can't you come out tonight, can't you come out to-night, can't you come out to-night;" and doing it as calmly as if we were attending a

---

* Door

funeral and weren't related to the corpse. And when I remonstrated with him about it, he smiled down on me as if I was his child, and told me to run in the house and try to be good, and not be meddling with my superiors!'

Once a pretty mean captain caught Stephen in New Orleans out of work and as usual out of money. He laid steady siege to Stephen, who was in a very 'close place,' and finally persuaded him to hire with him at one hundred and twenty-five dollars per month, just half wages, the captain agreeing not to divulge the secret and so bring down the contempt of all the guild upon the poor fellow. But the boat was not more than a day out of New Orleans before Stephen discovered that the captain was boasting of his exploit, and that all the officers had been told. Stephen winced, but said nothing. About the middle of the afternoon the captain stepped out on the hurricane deck, cast his eye around, and looked a good deal surprised. He glanced inquiringly aloft at Stephen, but Stephen was whistling placidly, and attending to business. The captain stood around a while in evident discomfort, and once or twice seemed about to make a suggestion; but the etiquette of the river taught him to avoid that sort of rashness, and so he managed to hold his peace. He chafed and puzzled a few minutes longer, then retired to his apartments. But soon he was out again, and apparently more perplexed than ever. Presently he ventured to remark, with deference—

'Pretty good stage of the river now, ain't it, sir?'

'Well, I should say so! Bank-full IS a pretty liberal stage.'

'Seems to be a good deal of current here.'

'Good deal don't describe it! It's worse than a mill-race.'

'Isn't it easier in toward shore than it is out here in the middle?'

'Yes, I reckon it is; but a body can't be too careful with a steamboat. It's pretty safe out here; can't strike any bottom here, you can depend on that.'

The captain departed, looking rueful enough. At this rate, he would probably die of old age before his boat got to St. Louis. Next day he appeared on deck and again found Stephen faithfully standing up the middle of the river, fighting the whole vast force of the Mississippi, and whistling the same placid tune. This thing was becoming serious. In by the shore was a slower boat clipping along in the easy water and gaining steadily; she began to make for an island chute; Stephen stuck to the middle of the river. Speech was WRUNG from the captain. He said—

'Mr. W—, don't that chute cut off a good deal of distance?'

'I think it does, but I don't know.'

'Don't know! Well, isn't there water enough in it now to go through?'

'I expect there is, but I am not certain.'

'Upon my word this is odd! Why, those pilots on that boat yonder are going to try it. Do you mean to say that you don't know as much as they do?'

'THEY! Why, THEY are two-hundred-and-fifty-dollar pilots! But don't you be uneasy; I know as much as any man can afford to know for a hundred and twenty-five!'

The captain surrendered.

Five minutes later Stephen was bowling through the chute and showing the rival boat a two-hundred-and-fifty-dollar pair of heels.

Chapter 15 The Pilots' Monopoly

ONE day, on board the 'Aleck Scott,' my chief, Mr. Bixby, was crawling carefully through a close place at Cat Island, both leads going, and everybody holding his breath. The captain, a nervous, apprehensive man, kept still as long as he could, but finally broke down and shouted from the hurricane deck—

'For gracious' sake, give her steam, Mr. Bixby! give her steam! She'll never raise the reef on this headway!'

For all the effect that was produced upon Mr. Bixby, one would have supposed that no remark had been made. But five minutes later, when the danger was past and the leads laid in, he burst instantly into a consuming fury, and gave the captain the most admirable cursing I ever listened to. No bloodshed ensued; but that was because the captain's cause was weak; for ordinarily he was not a man to take correction quietly.

Having now set forth in detail the nature of the science of piloting, and likewise described the rank which the pilot held among the fraternity of steamboatmen, this seems a fitting place to say a few words about an organization which the pilots once formed for the protection of their guild. It was curious and noteworthy in this, that it was perhaps the compactest, the completest, and the strongest commercial organization ever formed among men.

For a long time wages had been two hundred and fifty dollars a month; but curiously enough, as steamboats multiplied and business increased, the wages began to fall little by little. It was easy to discover the reason of this. Too many pilots were being 'made.' It was nice to have a 'cub,' a steersman, to do all the hard work for a couple of years, gratis, while his master sat on a high bench and smoked; all pilots and captains had sons or nephews who wanted to be pilots. By and by it came to pass that nearly every pilot on the river had a steersman. When a steersman had made an amount of progress that was satisfactory to any two pilots in the trade, they could get a pilot's license for him by signing an application directed to the United States Inspector. Nothing further was needed; usually no questions were asked, no proofs of capacity required.

Very well, this growing swarm of new pilots presently began to undermine the wages, in order to get berths. Too late—apparently—the knights of the tiller perceived their mistake. Plainly, something had to be done, and quickly; but what was to be the needful thing. A close organization. Nothing else would answer. To compass this seemed an impossibility; so it was talked, and talked, and then dropped. It was too likely to ruin whoever ventured to move in the matter. But at last about a dozen of the boldest—and some of them the best—pilots on the river launched themselves into the enterprise and took all the chances. They got a special charter from the legislature, with large powers, under the name of the Pilots' Benevolent Association; elected their officers, completed their organization, contributed capital, put 'association' wages up to two hundred and fifty dollars at once—and then retired to their homes, for they were promptly discharged from employment. But there were two or three unnoticed trifles in

their by-laws which had the seeds of propagation in them. For instance, all idle members of the association, in good standing, were entitled to a pension of twenty-five dollars per month. This began to bring in one straggler after another from the ranks of the new-fledged pilots, in the dull (summer) season. Better have twenty-five dollars than starve; the initiation fee was only twelve dollars, and no dues required from the unemployed.

Also, the widows of deceased members in good standing could draw twenty-five dollars per month, and a certain sum for each of their children. Also, the said deceased would be buried at the association's expense. These things resurrected all the superannuated and forgotten pilots in the Mississippi Valley. They came from farms, they came from interior villages, they came from everywhere. They came on crutches, on drays, in ambulances,—any way, so they got there. They paid in their twelve dollars, and straightway began to draw out twenty-five dollars a month, and calculate their burial bills.

By and by, all the useless, helpless pilots, and a dozen first-class ones, were in the association, and nine-tenths of the best pilots out of it and laughing at it. It was the laughing-stock of the whole river. Everybody joked about the by-law requiring members to pay ten per cent. of their wages, every month, into the treasury for the support of the association, whereas all the members were outcast and tabooed, and no one would employ them. Everybody was derisively grateful to the association for taking all the worthless pilots out of the way and leaving the whole field to the excellent and the deserving; and everybody was not only jocularly grateful for that, but for a result which naturally followed, namely, the gradual advance of wages as the busy season approached. Wages had gone up from the low figure of one hundred dollars a month to one hundred and twenty-five, and in some cases to one hundred and fifty; and it was great fun to enlarge upon the fact that this charming thing had been accomplished by a body of men not one of whom received a particle of benefit from it. Some of the jokers used to call at the association rooms and have a good time chaffing the members and offering them the charity of taking them as steersmen for a trip, so that they could see what the forgotten river looked like. However, the association was content; or at least it gave no sign to the contrary. Now and then it captured a pilot who was 'out of luck,' and added him to its list; and these later additions were very valuable, for they were good pilots; the incompetent ones had all been absorbed before. As business freshened, wages climbed gradually up to two hundred and fifty dollars—the association figure—and became firmly fixed there; and still without benefiting a member of that body, for no member was hired. The hilarity at the association's expense burst all bounds, now. There was no end to the fun which that poor martyr had to put up with.

However, it is a long lane that has no turning. Winter approached, business doubled and trebled, and an avalanche of Missouri, Illinois and Upper Mississippi River boats came pouring down to take a chance in the New Orleans trade. All of a sudden pilots were in great demand, and were correspondingly scarce. The time for revenge was come. It was a bitter pill to have to accept association pilots at last, yet captains and owners agreed that there was no other way. But none of these outcasts offered! So there was a still bitterer pill to be swallowed: they must be sought out and asked for their services. Captain — was the first man who found it necessary to take the dose, and he had been the loudest derider of the organization. He hunted up one of the best of the association pilots and said—

'Well, you boys have rather got the best of us for a little while, so I'll give in with as good a grace as I can. I've come to hire you; get your trunk aboard right away. I want to leave at twelve o'clock.'

'I don't know about that. Who is your other pilot?'

'I've got I. S—. Why?'

'I can't go with him. He don't belong to the association.'

'What!'

'It's so.'

'Do you mean to tell me that you won't turn a wheel with one of the very best and oldest pilots on the river because he don't belong to your association?'

'Yes, I do.'

'Well, if this isn't putting on airs! I supposed I was doing you a benevolence; but I begin to think that I am the party that wants a favor done. Are you acting under a law of the concern?'

'Yes.'

'Show it to me.'

So they stepped into the association rooms, and the secretary soon satisfied the captain, who said—

'Well, what am I to do? I have hired Mr. S— for the entire season.'

'I will provide for you,' said the secretary. 'I will detail a pilot to go with you, and he shall be on board at twelve o'clock.'

'But if I discharge S—, he will come on me for the whole season's wages.'

'Of course that is a matter between you and Mr. S—, captain. We cannot meddle in your private affairs.'

The captain stormed, but to no purpose. In the end he had to discharge S—, pay him about a thousand dollars, and take an association pilot in his place. The laugh was beginning to turn the other way now. Every day, thenceforward, a new victim fell; every day some outraged captain discharged a non-association pet, with tears and profanity, and installed a hated association man in his berth. In a very little while, idle non-associationists began to be pretty plenty, brisk as business was, and much as their services were desired. The laugh was shifting to the other side of their mouths most palpably. These victims, together with the captains and owners, presently ceased to laugh altogether, and began to rage about the revenge they would take when the passing business 'spurt' was over.

Soon all the laughers that were left were the owners and crews of boats that had two non-association pilots. But their triumph was not very long-lived. For this reason: It was a rigid rule of the association that its members should never, under any circumstances whatever, give information about the channel to any 'outsider.' By this time about half the boats had none but association pilots, and the other half had none but outsiders. At the first glance one would suppose that when it came to forbidding information about the river these two parties could play equally at that game; but this was not so. At every good-sized town from one end of the river to the other, there was a 'wharf-boat' to land at, instead of a wharf or a pier. Freight was stored in it for transportation; waiting passengers slept in its cabins. Upon each of these wharf-boats the association's officers placed a strong box fastened with a peculiar lock which was used in no other service but one—the United States mail service. It was the letter-bag lock, a sacred governmental thing. By dint of much beseeching the government had been persuaded to allow the association to use this lock. Every association man carried a key which would open these boxes. That key, or rather a peculiar way of holding it in the hand when its owner was asked for river information by a stranger—for the success of the St. Louis and New Orleans association had now bred tolerably thriving branches in a dozen neighboring steamboat trades—was the association man's sign and diploma of membership; and if the stranger did not respond by producing a similar key and holding it in a certain manner duly prescribed, his question was politely ignored. From the association's secretary each member received a package of more or less gorgeous blanks, printed like a billhead, on handsome paper, properly ruled in columns; a bill-head worded something like this—

STEAMER GREAT REPUBLIC.

JOHN SMITH MASTER

PILOTS, JOHN JONES AND THOMAS BROWN.

CROSSINGS.	SOUNDINGS.	MARKS.	REMARKS.

These blanks were filled up, day by day, as the voyage progressed, and deposited in the several wharf-boat boxes. For instance, as soon as the first crossing, out from St. Louis, was completed, the items would be entered upon the blank, under the appropriate headings, thus—

'St. Louis. Nine and a half (feet). Stern on court-house, head on dead cottonwood above wood-yard, until you raise the first reef, then pull up square.' Then under head of Remarks: 'Go just outside the wrecks; this is important. New snag just where you straighten down; go above it.'

The pilot who deposited that blank in the Cairo box (after adding to it the details of every crossing all the way down from St. Louis) took out and read half a dozen fresh reports (from upward-bound steamers) concerning the river between Cairo and Memphis, posted himself thoroughly, returned them to the box, and went back aboard his boat again so armed against accident that he could not possibly get his boat into trouble without bringing the most ingenious carelessness to his aid.

Imagine the benefits of so admirable a system in a piece of river twelve or thirteen hundred miles long, whose channel was shifting every day! The pilot who had formerly been obliged to put up with seeing a shoal place once or possibly twice a month, had a hundred sharp eyes to watch it for him, now, and bushels of intelligent brains to tell him how to run it. His information about it was seldom twenty-four hours old. If the reports in the last box chanced to leave any misgivings on his mind concerning a treacherous crossing, he had his remedy; he blew his steam- whistle in a peculiar way as soon as he saw a boat approaching; the signal was answered in a peculiar way if that boat's pilots were association men; and then the two steamers ranged alongside and all uncertainties were swept away by fresh information furnished to the inquirer by word of mouth and in minute detail.

The first thing a pilot did when he reached New Orleans or St. Louis was to take his final and elaborate report to the association parlors and hang it up there,—after which he was free to visit his family. In these parlors a crowd was always gathered together, discussing changes in the channel, and the moment there was a fresh arrival, everybody stopped talking till this witness had told the newest news and settled the latest uncertainty. Other craftsmen can 'sink the shop,' sometimes, and interest themselves in other matters. Not so with a pilot; he must devote himself wholly to his profession and talk of nothing else; for it would be small gain to be perfect one day and imperfect the next. He has no time or words to waste if he would keep 'posted.'

But the outsiders had a hard time of it. No particular place to meet and exchange information, no wharf-boat reports, none but chance and unsatisfactory ways of getting news. The consequence was that a man sometimes had to run five hundred miles of river on information that was a week or ten days old. At a fair stage of the river that might have answered; but when the dead low water came it was destructive.

Now came another perfectly logical result. The outsiders began to ground steamboats, sink them, and get into all sorts of trouble, whereas accidents seemed to keep entirely away from the association men. Wherefore even the owners and captains of boats furnished exclusively with outsiders, and previously considered to be wholly independent of the association and free to comfort themselves with brag and laughter, began to feel pretty uncomfortable. Still, they made a show of keeping up the brag, until one black day when every captain of the lot was formally ordered to immediately discharge his outsiders and take association pilots in their stead. And who was it that had the dashing presumption to do that? Alas, it came from a power behind the throne that was greater than the throne itself. It was the underwriters!

It was no time to 'swap knives.' Every outsider had to take his trunk ashore at once. Of course it was supposed that there was collusion between the association and the underwriters, but this was not so. The latter had come to comprehend the excellence of the 'report' system of the association and the safety it secured, and so they had made their decision among themselves and upon plain business principles.

There was weeping and wailing and gnashing of teeth in the camp of the outsiders now. But no matter, there was but one course for them to pursue, and they pursued it. They came forward in couples and groups, and proffered their twelve dollars and asked for membership. They were surprised to learn that several new by-laws had been long ago added. For instance, the initiation fee had been raised to fifty dollars; that sum must be tendered, and also ten per cent. of the wages which the applicant had received each and every month since the founding of the association. In many cases this amounted to three or four hundred dollars. Still, the association would not entertain the application until the money was present. Even then a single adverse vote killed the application. Every member had to vote 'Yes' or 'No' in person and before witnesses; so it took weeks to decide a candidacy, because many pilots were so long absent on voyages. However, the repentant sinners scraped their savings together, and one by one, by our tedious voting process, they were added to the fold. A time came, at last, when only about ten remained

outside. They said they would starve before they would apply. They remained idle a long while, because of course nobody could venture to employ them.

By and by the association published the fact that upon a certain date the wages would be raised to five hundred dollars per month. All the branch associations had grown strong, now, and the Red River one had advanced wages to seven hundred dollars a month. Reluctantly the ten outsiders yielded, in view of these things, and made application. There was another new by-law, by this time, which required them to pay dues not only on all the wages they had received since the association was born, but also on what they would have received if they had continued at work up to the time of their application, instead of going off to pout in idleness. It turned out to be a difficult matter to elect them, but it was accomplished at last. The most virulent sinner of this batch had stayed out and allowed 'dues' to accumulate against him so long that he had to send in six hundred and twenty-five dollars with his application.

The association had a good bank account now, and was very strong. There was no longer an outsider. A by-law was added forbidding the reception of any more cubs or apprentices for five years; after which time a limited number would be taken, not by individuals, but by the association, upon these terms: the applicant must not be less than eighteen years old, and of respectable family and good character; he must pass an examination as to education, pay a thousand dollars in advance for the privilege of becoming an apprentice, and must remain under the commands of the association until a great part of the membership (more than half, I think) should be willing to sign his application for a pilot's license.

All previously-articled apprentices were now taken away from their masters and adopted by the association. The president and secretary detailed them for service on one boat or another, as they chose, and changed them from boat to boat according to certain rules. If a pilot could show that he was in infirm health and needed assistance, one of the cubs would be ordered to go with him.

The widow and orphan list grew, but so did the association's financial resources. The association attended its own funerals in state, and paid for them. When occasion demanded, it sent members down the river upon searches for the bodies of brethren lost by steamboat accidents; a search of this kind sometimes cost a thousand dollars.

The association procured a charter and went into the insurance business, also. It not only insured the lives of its members, but took risks on steamboats.

The organization seemed indestructible. It was the tightest monopoly in the world. By the United States law, no man could become a pilot unless two duly licensed pilots signed his application; and now there was nobody outside of the association competent to sign. Consequently the making of pilots was at an end. Every year some would die and others become incapacitated by age and infirmity; there would be no new ones to take their places. In time, the association could put wages up to any figure it chose; and as long as it should be wise enough not to carry the thing too far and provoke the national government into amending the licensing system, steamboat owners would have to submit, since there would be no help for it.

The owners and captains were the only obstruction that lay between the association and absolute power; and at last this one was removed. Incredible as it may seem, the owners and captains deliberately did it themselves. When the pilots' association announced, months beforehand, that on the first day of September, 1861, wages would be advanced to five hundred dollars per month, the owners and captains instantly put freights up a few cents, and explained to the farmers along the river the necessity of it, by calling their attention to the burdensome rate of wages about to be established. It was a rather slender argument, but the farmers did not seem to detect it. It looked reasonable to them that to add five cents freight on a bushel of corn was justifiable under the circumstances, overlooking the fact that this advance on a cargo of forty thousand sacks was a good deal more than necessary to cover the new wages.

So, straightway the captains and owners got up an association of their own, and proposed to put captains' wages up to five hundred dollars, too, and move for another advance in freights. It was a novel idea, but of course an effect which had been produced once could be produced again. The new association decreed (for this was before all the outsiders had been taken into the pilots' association) that if any captain employed a non-association pilot, he should be forced to discharge him, and also pay a fine of five hundred dollars. Several of these heavy fines were paid before the captains' organization grew strong enough to exercise full authority over its membership; but that all ceased, presently. The captains tried to get the pilots to decree that no member of their corporation should serve under a non-association captain; but this proposition was declined. The pilots saw that they would be backed up by the captains and the underwriters anyhow, and so they wisely refrained from entering into entangling alliances.

As I have remarked, the pilots' association was now the compactest monopoly in the world, perhaps, and seemed simply indestructible. And yet the days of its glory were numbered. First, the new railroad stretching up through Mississippi, Tennessee, and Kentucky, to Northern railway centers, began to divert the passenger travel from the steamers; next the war came and almost entirely annihilated the steamboating industry during several years, leaving most of the pilots idle, and the cost of living advancing all the time; then the treasurer of the St. Louis association put his hand into the till and walked off with every dollar of the ample fund; and finally, the railroads intruding everywhere, there was little for steamers to do, when the war was over, but carry freights; so straightway some genius from the Atlantic coast introduced the plan of towing a dozen steamer cargoes down to New Orleans at the tail of a vulgar little tug-boat; and behold, in the twinkling of an eye, as it were, the association and the noble science of piloting were things of the dead and pathetic past!

Chapter 16 Racing Days

IT was always the custom for the boats to leave New Orleans between four and five o'clock in the afternoon. From three o'clock onward they would be burning rosin and pitch pine (the sign of preparation), and so one had the picturesque spectacle of a rank, some two or three miles long, of tall, ascending columns of coal-black smoke; a colonnade which supported a sable roof of the same smoke blended together and spreading abroad over the city. Every outward-bound boat had its flag flying at the jack-staff, and sometimes a duplicate on the verge staff astern. Two or three miles of mates were commanding and swearing with more than usual emphasis; countless processions of freight barrels and boxes were spinning athwart the levee and flying aboard the stage-planks,

belated passengers were dodging and skipping among these frantic things, hoping to reach the forecastle companion way alive, but having their doubts about it; women with reticules and bandboxes were trying to keep up with husbands freighted with carpet-sacks and crying babies, and making a failure of it by losing their heads in the whirl and roar and general distraction; drays and baggage-vans were clattering hither and thither in a wild hurry, every now and then getting blocked and jammed together, and then during ten seconds one could not see them for the profanity, except vaguely and dimly; every windlass connected with every forehatch, from one end of that long array of steamboats to the other, was keeping up a deafening whiz and whir, lowering freight into the hold, and the half-naked crews of perspiring negroes that worked them were roaring such songs as 'De Las' Sack! De Las' Sack!'—inspired to unimaginable exaltation by the chaos of turmoil and racket that was driving everybody else mad. By this time the hurricane and boiler decks of the steamers would be packed and black with passengers. The 'last bells' would begin to clang, all down the line, and then the powwow seemed to double; in a moment or two the final warning came,—a simultaneous din of Chinese gongs, with the cry, 'All dat ain't goin', please to git asho'!'—and behold, the powwow quadrupled! People came swarming ashore, overturning excited stragglers that were trying to swarm aboard. One more moment later a long array of stage-planks was being hauled in, each with its customary latest passenger clinging to the end of it with teeth, nails, and everything else, and the customary latest procrastinator making a wild spring shoreward over his head.

Now a number of the boats slide backward into the stream, leaving wide gaps in the serried rank of steamers. Citizens crowd the decks of boats that are not to go, in order to see the sight. Steamer after steamer straightens herself up, gathers all her strength, and presently comes swinging by, under a tremendous head of steam, with flag flying, black smoke rolling, and her entire crew of firemen and deck-hands (usually swarthy negroes) massed together on the forecastle, the best 'voice' in the lot towering from the midst (being mounted on the capstan), waving his hat or a flag, and all roaring a mighty chorus, while the parting cannons boom and the multitudinous spectators swing their hats and huzza! Steamer after steamer falls into line, and the stately procession goes winging its flight up the river.

In the old times, whenever two fast boats started out on a race, with a big crowd of people looking on, it was inspiring to hear the crews sing, especially if the time were night-fall, and the forecastle lit up with the red glare of the torch-baskets. Racing was royal fun. The public always had an idea that racing was dangerous; whereas the opposite was the case—that is, after the laws were passed which restricted each boat to just so many pounds of steam to the square inch. No engineer was ever sleepy or careless when his heart was in a race. He was constantly on the alert, trying gauge-cocks and watching things. The dangerous place was on slow, plodding boats, where the engineers drowsed around and allowed chips to get into the 'doctor' and shut off the water supply from the boilers.

In the 'flush times' of steamboating, a race between two notoriously fleet steamers was an event of vast importance. The date was set for it several weeks in advance, and from that time forward, the whole Mississippi Valley was in a state of consuming excitement. Politics and the weather were dropped, and people talked only of the coming race. As the time approached, the two steamers 'stripped' and got ready. Every encumbrance that added weight, or exposed a resisting surface to wind or water, was removed, if the boat could possibly do without it. The 'spars,' and sometimes even their supporting derricks, were sent ashore, and no means left to set the boat afloat in case she got aground. When the 'Eclipse' and the 'A. L. Shotwell' ran their great race many years ago, it was said that pains were taken to scrape the gilding off the fanciful device which hung between the 'Eclipse's' chimneys, and that for that one trip the captain left off his kid gloves and had his head shaved. But I always doubted these things.

If the boat was known to make her best speed when drawing five and a half feet forward and five feet aft, she was carefully loaded to that exact figure—she wouldn't enter a dose of homoeopathic pills on her manifest after that. Hardly any passengers were taken, because they not only add weight but they never will 'trim boat.' They always run to the side when there is anything to see, whereas a conscientious and experienced steamboatman would stick to the center of the boat and part his hair in the middle with a spirit level.

No way-freights and no way-passengers were allowed, for the racers would stop only at the largest towns, and then it would be only 'touch and go.' Coal flats and wood flats were contracted for beforehand, and these were kept ready to hitch on to the flying steamers at a moment's warning. Double crews were carried, so that all work could be quickly done.

The chosen date being come, and all things in readiness, the two great steamers back into the stream, and lie there jockeying a moment, and apparently watching each other's slightest movement, like sentient creatures; flags drooping, the pent steam shrieking through safety- valves, the black smoke rolling and tumbling from the chimneys and darkening all the air. People, people everywhere; the shores, the house-tops, the steamboats, the ships, are packed with them, and you know that the borders of the broad Mississippi are going to be fringed with humanity thence northward twelve hundred miles, to welcome these racers.

Presently tall columns of steam burst from the 'scape-pipes of both steamers, two guns boom a good-bye, two red-shirted heroes mounted on capstans wave their small flags above the massed crews on the forecastles, two plaintive solos linger on the air a few waiting seconds, two mighty choruses burst forth—and here they come! Brass bands bray Hail Columbia, huzza after huzza thunders from the shores, and the stately creatures go whistling by like the wind.

Those boats will never halt a moment between New Orleans and St. Louis, except for a second or two at large towns, or to hitch thirty-cord wood-boats alongside. You should be on board when they take a couple of those wood-boats in tow and turn a swarm of men into each; by the time you have wiped your glasses and put them on, you will be wondering what has become of that wood.

Two nicely matched steamers will stay in sight of each other day after day. They might even stay side by side, but for the fact that pilots are not all alike, and the smartest pilots will win the race. If one of the boats has a 'lightning' pilot, whose 'partner' is a trifle his inferior, you can tell which one is on watch by noting whether that boat has gained ground or lost some during each four-hour stretch. The shrewdest pilot can delay a boat if he has not a fine genius for steering. Steering is a very high art. One must not keep a rudder dragging across a boat's stem if he wants to get up the river fast.

There is a great difference in boats, of course. For a long time I

was on a boat that was so slow we used to forget what year it was we left port in. But of course this was at rare intervals. Ferryboats used to lose valuable trips because their passengers grew old and died, waiting for us to get by. This was at still rarer intervals. I had the documents for these occurrences, but through carelessness they have been mislaid. This boat, the 'John J. Roe,' was so slow that when she finally sunk in Madrid Bend, it was five years before the owners heard of it. That was always a confusing fact to me, but it is according to the record, any way. She was dismally slow; still, we often had pretty exciting times racing with islands, and rafts, and such things. One trip, however, we did rather well. We went to St. Louis in sixteen days. But even at this rattling gait I think we changed watches three times in Fort Adams reach, which is five miles long. A 'reach' is a piece of straight river, and of course the current drives through such a place in a pretty lively way.

That trip we went to Grand Gulf, from New Orleans, in four days (three hundred and forty miles); the 'Eclipse' and 'Shotwell' did it in one. We were nine days out, in the chute of 63 (seven hundred miles); the 'Eclipse' and 'Shotwell' went there in two days. Something over a generation ago, a boat called the 'J. M. White' went from New Orleans to Cairo in three days, six hours, and forty-four minutes. In 1853 the 'Eclipse' made the same trip in three days, three hours, and twenty minutes*. In 1870 the 'R. E. Lee' did it in three days and ONE hour. This last is called the fastest trip on record. I will try to show that it was not. For this reason: the distance between New Orleans and Cairo, when the 'J. M. White' ran it, was about eleven hundred and six miles; consequently her average speed was a trifle over fourteen miles per hour. In the 'Eclipse's' day the distance between the two ports had become reduced to one thousand and eighty miles; consequently her average speed was a shade under fourteen and three-eighths miles per hour. In the 'R. E. Lee's' time the distance had diminished to about one thousand and thirty miles; consequently her average was about fourteen and one-eighth miles per hour. Therefore the 'Eclipse's' was conspicuously the fastest time that has ever been made.

THE RECORD OF SOME FAMOUS TRIPS

(From Commodore Rollingpin's Almanack.)

FAST TIME ON THE WESTERN WATERS

FROM NEW ORLEANS TO NATCHEZ—268 MILES

	D.	H.	M.
1814 Orleans made the run in	6	6	40
1814 Comet	5	10	
1815 Enterprise	4	11	20
1817 Washington	4		
1817 Shelby	3	20	
1818 Paragon	3	8	
1828 Tecumseh	3	1	20
1834 Tuscarora	1	21	
1838 Natchez	1	17	
1840 Ed. Shippen	1	8	
1842 Belle of the West	1	18	
1844 Sultana		19	45
1851 Magnolia		19	50
1853 A. L. Shotwell		19	49
1853 Southern Belle		20	3

* Time disputed. Some authorities add 1 hour and 16 minutes to this.

1853 Princess (No. 4)	20	26
1853 Eclipse	19	47
1855 Princess (New)	18	53
1855 Natchez (New)	17	30
1856 Princess (New)	17	30
1870 Natchez	17	17
1870 R. E. Lee	17	11

FROM NEW ORLEANS TO CAIRO—1,024 MILES

	D.	H.	M.
1844 J. M. White made the run in	3	6	44
1852 Reindeer	3	12	45
1853 Eclipse	3	4	4
1853 A. L. Shotwell	3	3	40
1869 Dexter	3	6	20
1870 Natchez	3	4	34
1870 R. E. Lee	3	1	

FROM NEW ORLEANS TO LOUISVILLE—1,440 MILES

	D.	H.	M.
1815 Enterprise made the run in	25	2	40
1817 Washington	25		
1817 Shelby	20	4	20
1818 Paragon	18	10	
1828 Tecumseh	8	4	
1834 Tuscarora	7	16	
1837 Gen. Brown	6	22	
1837 Randolph	6	22	
1837 Empress	6	17	
1837 Sultana	6	15	
1840 Ed. Shippen	5	14	
1842 Belle of the West	6	14	
1843 Duke of Orleans	5	23	
1844 Sultana	5	12	
1849 Bostona	5	8	
1851 Belle Key	3	4	23
1852 Reindeer	4	20	45
1852 Eclipse	4	19	
1853 A. L. Shotwell	4	10	20
1853 Eclipse	4	9	30

FROM NEW ORLEANS TO DONALDSONVILLE—78 MILES

	H.	M.
1852 A. L. Shotwell made the run in	5	42
1852 Eclipse	5	42
1854 Sultana	4	51
1860 Atlantic	5	11
1860 Gen. Quitman	5	6
1865 Ruth	4	43
1870 R. E. Lee	4	59

FROM NEW ORLEANS TO ST. LOUIS—1,218 MILES

	D.	H.	M.
1844 J. M. White made the run in	3	23	9
1849 Missouri	4	19	
1869 Dexter	4	9	
1870 Natchez	3	21	58
1870 R. E. Lee	3	18	14

FROM LOUISVILLE TO CINCINNATI—141 MILES

	D.	H.	M.
1819 Gen. Pike made the run in	1	16	
1819 Paragon	1	14	20

1822 Wheeling Packet	1	10	
1837 Moselle	1	12	
1843 Duke of Orleans	1	12	
1843 Congress	1	12	20
1846 Ben Franklin (No. 6)	1	11	45
1852 Alleghaney	1	10	38
1852 Pittsburgh	1	10	23
1853 Telegraph No. 3	1	9	52

FROM LOUISVILLE TO ST. LOUIS—750 MILES

	D.	H.	M.
1843 Congress made the run in	2	1	
1854 Pike	1	23	
1854 Northerner	1	22	30
1855 Southerner	1	19	

FROM CINCINNATI TO PITTSBURGH—490 MILES

	D.	H.
1850 Telegraph No. 2 made the run in	1	17
1851 Buckeye State	1	16
1852 Pittsburgh	1	15

FROM ST. LOUIS TO ALTON—30 MILES

	H.	M.
1853 Altona made the run in	1	35
1876 Golden Eagle	1	37
1876 War Eagle	1	37

MISCELLANEOUS RUNS

In June, 1859, the St. Louis and Keokuk Packet, City of Louisiana, made the run from St. Louis to Keokuk (214 miles) in 16 hours and 20 minutes, the best time on record.

In 1868 the steamer Hawkeye State, of the Northern Packet Company, made the run from St. Louis to St. Paul (800 miles) in 2 days and 20 hours. Never was beaten.

In 1853 the steamer Polar Star made the run from St. Louis to St. Joseph, on the Missouri River, in 64 hours. In July, 1856, the steamer Jas. H. Lucas, Andy Wineland, Master, made the same run in 60 hours and 57 minutes. The distance between the ports is 600 miles, and when the difficulties of navigating the turbulent Missouri are taken into consideration, the performance of the Lucas deserves especial mention.

THE RUN OF THE ROBERT E. LEE

The time made by the R. E. Lee from New Orleans to St. Louis in 1870, in her famous race with the Natchez, is the best on record, and, inasmuch as the race created a national interest, we give below her time table from port to port.

Left New Orleans, Thursday, June 30th, 1870, at 4 o'clock and 55 minutes, p.m.; reached

	D.	H.	M.
Carrollton			27½
Harry Hills		1	00½
Red Church		1	39
Bonnet Carre		2	38
College Point		3	50½
Donaldsonville		4	59
Plaquemine		7	05½
Baton Rouge		8	25

Bayou Sara		10	26
Red River		12	56
Stamps		13	56
Bryaro		15	51½
Hinderson's		16	29
Natchez		17	11
Cole's Creek		19	21
Waterproof		18	53
Rodney		20	45
St. Joseph		21	02
Grand Gulf		22	06
Hard Times		22	18
Half Mile below Warrenton	1		
Vicksburg	1		38
Milliken's Bend	1	2	37
Bailey's	1	3	48
Lake Providence	1	5	47
Greenville	1	10	55
Napoleon	1	16	22
White River	1	16	56
Australia	1	19	
Helena	1	23	25
Half Mile Below St. Francis	2		
Memphis	2	6	9
Foot of Island 37	2	9	
Foot of Island 26	2	13	30
Tow-head, Island 14	2	17	23
New Madrid	2	19	50
Dry Bar No. 10	2	20	37
Foot of Island 8	2	21	25
Upper Tow-head—Lucas Bend	3		
Cairo	3	1	
St. Louis	3	18	14

The Lee landed at St. Louis at 11.25 A.M., on July 4th, 1870—6 hours and 36 minutes ahead of the Natchez. The officers of the Natchez claimed 7 hours and 1 minute stoppage on account of fog and repairing machinery. The R. E. Lee was commanded by Captain John W. Cannon, and the Natchez was in charge of that veteran Southern boatman, Captain Thomas P. Leathers.

Chapter 17 Cut-offs and Stephen

THESE dry details are of importance in one particular. They give me an opportunity of introducing one of the Mississippi's oddest peculiarities,—that of shortening its length from time to time. If you will throw a long, pliant apple-paring over your shoulder, it will pretty fairly shape itself into an average section of the Mississippi River; that is, the nine or ten hundred miles stretching from Cairo, Illinois, southward to New Orleans, the same being wonderfully crooked, with a brief straight bit here and there at wide intervals. The two hundred-mile stretch from Cairo northward to St. Louis is by no means so crooked, that being a rocky country which the river cannot cut much.

The water cuts the alluvial banks of the 'lower' river into deep horseshoe curves; so deep, indeed, that in some places if you were to get ashore at one extremity of the horseshoe and walk across the neck, half or three quarters of a mile, you could sit down and rest a couple of hours while your steamer was coming around the long elbow, at a speed of ten miles an hour, to take you aboard again. When the river is rising fast, some scoundrel whose plantation is back in the country, and therefore of inferior value, has only to watch his chance, cut a little gutter across the narrow neck of land some dark night, and turn the water into it, and in a wonderfully short time a miracle has happened: to wit, the whole Mississippi has taken

possession of that little ditch, and placed the countryman's plantation on its bank (quadrupling its value), and that other party's formerly valuable plantation finds itself away out yonder on a big island; the old watercourse around it will soon shoal up, boats cannot approach within ten miles of it, and down goes its value to a fourth of its former worth. Watches are kept on those narrow necks, at needful times, and if a man happens to be caught cutting a ditch across them, the chances are all against his ever having another opportunity to cut a ditch.

Pray observe some of the effects of this ditching business. Once there was a neck opposite Port Hudson, Louisiana, which was only half a mile across, in its narrowest place. You could walk across there in fifteen minutes; but if you made the journey around the cape on a raft, you traveled thirty-five miles to accomplish the same thing. In 1722 the river darted through that neck, deserted its old bed, and thus shortened itself thirty-five miles. In the same way it shortened itself twenty- five miles at Black Hawk Point in 1699. Below Red River Landing, Raccourci cut-off was made (forty or fifty years ago, I think). This shortened the river twenty-eight miles. In our day, if you travel by river from the southernmost of these three cut-offs to the northernmost, you go only seventy miles. To do the same thing a hundred and seventy- six years ago, one had to go a hundred and fifty-eight miles!— shortening of eighty-eight miles in that trifling distance. At some forgotten time in the past, cut-offs were made above Vidalia, Louisiana; at island 92; at island 84; and at Hale's Point. These shortened the river, in the aggregate, seventy-seven miles.

Since my own day on the Mississippi, cut-offs have been made at Hurricane Island; at island 100; at Napoleon, Arkansas; at Walnut Bend; and at Council Bend. These shortened the river, in the aggregate, sixty-seven miles. In my own time a cut-off was made at American Bend, which shortened the river ten miles or more.

Therefore, the Mississippi between Cairo and New Orleans was twelve hundred and fifteen miles long one hundred and seventy-six years ago. It was eleven hundred and eighty after the cut-off of 1722. It was one thousand and forty after the American Bend cut-off. It has lost sixty- seven miles since. Consequently its length is only nine hundred and seventy-three miles at present.

Now, if I wanted to be one of those ponderous scientific people, and 'let on' to prove what had occurred in the remote past by what had occurred in a given time in the recent past, or what will occur in the far future by what has occurred in late years, what an opportunity is here! Geology never had such a chance, nor such exact data to argue from! Nor 'development of species,' either! Glacial epochs are great things, but they are vague—vague. Please observe:—

In the space of one hundred and seventy-six years the Lower Mississippi has shortened itself two hundred and forty-two miles. That is an average of a trifle over one mile and a third per year. Therefore, any calm person, who is not blind or idiotic, can see that in the Old Oolitic Silurian Period, just a million years ago next November, the Lower Mississippi River was upwards of one million three hundred thousand miles long, and stuck out over the Gulf of Mexico like a fishing-rod. And by the same token any person can see that seven hundred and forty- two years from now the Lower Mississippi will be only a mile and three- quarters long, and Cairo and New Orleans will have joined their streets together, and be plodding comfortably along under a single mayor and a mutual board of aldermen. There is something fascinating about science. One gets such wholesale returns of conjecture out of such a trifling investment of fact.

When the water begins to flow through one of those ditches I have been speaking of, it is time for the people thereabouts to move. The water cleaves the banks away like a knife. By the time the ditch has become twelve or fifteen feet wide, the calamity is as good as accomplished, for no power on earth can stop it now. When the width has reached a hundred yards, the banks begin to peel off in slices half an acre wide. The current flowing around the bend traveled formerly only five miles an hour; now it is tremendously increased by the shortening of the distance. I was on board the first boat that tried to go through the cut-off at American Bend, but we did not get through. It was toward midnight, and a wild night it was— thunder, lightning, and torrents of rain. It was estimated that the current in the cut-off was making about fifteen or twenty miles an hour; twelve or thirteen was the best our boat could do, even in tolerably slack water, therefore perhaps we were foolish to try the cut-off. However, Mr. Brown was ambitious, and he kept on trying. The eddy running up the bank, under the 'point,' was about as swift as the current out in the middle; so we would go flying up the shore like a lightning express train, get on a big head of steam, and 'stand by for a surge' when we struck the current that was whirling by the point. But all our preparations were useless. The instant the current hit us it spun us around like a top, the water deluged the forecastle, and the boat careened so far over that one could hardly keep his feet. The next instant we were away down the river, clawing with might and main to keep out of the woods. We tried the experiment four times. I stood on the forecastle companion way to see. It was astonishing to observe how suddenly the boat would spin around and turn tail the moment she emerged from the eddy and the current struck her nose. The sounding concussion and the quivering would have been about the same if she had come full speed against a sand-bank. Under the lightning flashes one could see the plantation cabins and the goodly acres tumble into the river; and the crash they made was not a bad effort at thunder. Once, when we spun around, we only missed a house about twenty feet, that had a light burning in the window; and in the same instant that house went overboard. Nobody could stay on our forecastle; the water swept across it in a torrent every time we plunged athwart the current. At the end of our fourth effort we brought up in the woods two miles below the cut-off; all the country there was overflowed, of course. A day or two later the cut-off was three-quarters of a mile wide, and boats passed up through it without much difficulty, and so saved ten miles.

The old Raccourci cut-off reduced the river's length twenty-eight miles. There used to be a tradition connected with it. It was said that a boat came along there in the night and went around the enormous elbow the usual way, the pilots not knowing that the cut-off had been made. It was a grisly, hideous night, and all shapes were vague and distorted. The old bend had already begun to fill up, and the boat got to running away from mysterious reefs, and occasionally hitting one. The perplexed pilots fell to swearing, and finally uttered the entirely unnecessary wish that they might never get out of that place. As always happens in such cases, that particular prayer was answered, and the others neglected. So to this day that phantom steamer is still butting around in that deserted river, trying to find her way out. More than one grave watchman has sworn to me that on drizzly, dismal nights, he has glanced fearfully down that forgotten river as he passed the head of the island, and seen the faint glow of the specter steamer's lights drifting through the distant gloom, and heard the muffled cough of her 'scape-pipes and the plaintive cry of her leadsmen.

In the absence of further statistics, I beg to close this chapter with one more reminiscence of 'Stephen.'

Most of the captains and pilots held Stephen's note for borrowed sums, ranging from two hundred and fifty dollars upward. Stephen never paid one of these notes, but he was very prompt and very zealous about renewing them every twelve months.

Of course there came a time, at last, when Stephen could no longer borrow of his ancient creditors; so he was obliged to lie in wait for new men who did not know him. Such a victim was good-hearted, simple natured young Yates (I use a fictitious name, but the real name began, as this one does, with a Y). Young Yates graduated as a pilot, got a berth, and when the month was ended and he stepped up to the clerk's office and received his two hundred and fifty dollars in crisp new bills, Stephen was there! His silvery tongue began to wag, and in a very little while Yates's two hundred and fifty dollars had changed hands. The fact was soon known at pilot headquarters, and the amusement and satisfaction of the old creditors were large and generous. But innocent Yates never suspected that Stephen's promise to pay promptly at the end of the week was a worthless one. Yates called for his money at the stipulated time; Stephen sweetened him up and put him off a week. He called then, according to agreement, and came away sugar-coated again, but suffering under another postponement. So the thing went on. Yates haunted Stephen week after week, to no purpose, and at last gave it up. And then straightway Stephen began to haunt Yates! Wherever Yates appeared, there was the inevitable Stephen. And not only there, but beaming with affection and gushing with apologies for not being able to pay. By and by, whenever poor Yates saw him coming, he would turn and fly, and drag his company with him, if he had company; but it was of no use; his debtor would run him down and corner him. Panting and red- faced, Stephen would come, with outstretched hands and eager eyes, invade the conversation, shake both of Yates's arms loose in their sockets, and begin—

'My, what a race I've had! I saw you didn't see me, and so I clapped on all steam for fear I'd miss you entirely. And here you are! there, just stand so, and let me look at you! just the same old noble countenance.' [To Yates's friend:] 'Just look at him! LOOK at him! Ain't it just GOOD to look at him! AIN'T it now? Ain't he just a picture! SOME call him a picture; I call him a panorama! That's what he is—an entire panorama. And now I'm reminded! How I do wish I could have seen you an hour earlier! For twenty-four hours I've been saving up that two hundred and fifty dollars for you; been looking for you everywhere. I waited at the Planter's from six yesterday evening till two o'clock this morning, without rest or food; my wife says, "Where have you been all night?" I said, "This debt lies heavy on my mind." She says, "In all my days I never saw a man take a debt to heart the way you do." I said, "It's my nature; how can I change it?" She says, "Well, do go to bed and get some rest." I said, "Not till that poor, noble young man has got his money." So I set up all night, and this morning out I shot, and the first man I struck told me you had shipped on the "Grand Turk" and gone to New Orleans. Well, sir, I had to lean up against a building and cry. So help me goodness, I couldn't help it. The man that owned the place come out cleaning up with a rag, and said he didn't like to have people cry against his building, and then it seemed to me that the whole world had turned against me, and it wasn't any use to live any more; and coming along an hour ago, suffering no man knows what agony, I met Jim Wilson and paid him the two hundred and fifty dollars on account; and to think that here you are, now, and I haven't got a cent! But as sure as I am standing here on this ground on this particular brick,—there, I've scratched a mark on the brick to remember it by,—I'll borrow that money and pay it over to you at twelve o'clock sharp, tomorrow! Now, stand so; let me look at you just once more.'

And so on. Yates's life became a burden to him. He could not escape his debtor and his debtor's awful sufferings on account of not being able to pay. He dreaded to show himself in the street, lest he should find Stephen lying in wait for him at the corner.

Bogart's billiard saloon was a great resort for pilots in those days. They met there about as much to exchange river news as to play. One morning Yates was there; Stephen was there, too, but kept out of sight. But by and by, when about all the pilots had arrived who were in town, Stephen suddenly appeared in the midst, and rushed for Yates as for a long-lost brother.

'OH, I am so glad to see you! Oh my soul, the sight of you is such a comfort to my eyes! Gentlemen, I owe all of you money; among you I owe probably forty thousand dollars. I want to pay it; I intend to pay it every last cent of it. You all know, without my telling you, what sorrow it has cost me to remain so long under such deep obligations to such patient and generous friends; but the sharpest pang I suffer—by far the sharpest—is from the debt I owe to this noble young man here; and I have come to this place this morning especially to make the announcement that I have at last found a method whereby I can pay off all my debts! And most especially I wanted HIM to be here when I announced it. Yes, my faithful friend,—my benefactor, I've found the method! I've found the method to pay off all my debts, and you'll get your money!' Hope dawned in Yates's eye; then Stephen, beaming benignantly, and placing his hand upon Yates's head, added, 'I am going to pay them off in alphabetical order!'

Then he turned and disappeared. The full significance of Stephen's 'method' did not dawn upon the perplexed and musing crowd for some two minutes; and then Yates murmured with a sigh—

'Well, the Y's stand a gaudy chance. He won't get any further than the C's in THIS world, and I reckon that after a good deal of eternity has wasted away in the next one, I'll still be referred to up there as "that poor, ragged pilot that came here from St. Louis in the early days!"

Chapter 18 I Take a Few Extra Lessons

DURING the two or two and a half years of my apprenticeship, I served under many pilots, and had experience of many kinds of steamboatmen and many varieties of steamboats; for it was not always convenient for Mr. Bixby to have me with him, and in such cases he sent me with somebody else. I am to this day profiting somewhat by that experience; for in that brief, sharp schooling, I got personally and familiarly acquainted with about all the different types of human nature that are to be found in fiction, biography, or history. The fact is daily borne in upon me, that the average shore-employment requires as much as forty years to equip a man with this sort of an education. When I say I am still profiting by this thing, I do not mean that it has constituted me a judge of men—no, it has not done that; for judges of men are born, not made. My profit

is various in kind and degree; but the feature of it which I value most is the zest which that early experience has given to my later reading. When I find a well-drawn character in fiction or biography, I generally take a warm personal interest in him, for the reason that I have known him before—met him on the river.

The figure that comes before me oftenest, out of the shadows of that vanished time, is that of Brown, of the steamer 'Pennsylvania'—the man referred to in a former chapter, whose memory was so good and tiresome. He was a middle-aged, long, slim, bony, smooth-shaven, horse-faced, ignorant, stingy, malicious, snarling, fault hunting, mote-magnifying tyrant. I early got the habit of coming on watch with dread at my heart. No matter how good a time I might have been having with the off-watch below, and no matter how high my spirits might be when I started aloft, my soul became lead in my body the moment I approached the pilot-house.

I still remember the first time I ever entered the presence of that man. The boat had backed out from St. Louis and was 'straightening down;' I ascended to the pilot-house in high feather, and very proud to be semi- officially a member of the executive family of so fast and famous a boat. Brown was at the wheel. I paused in the middle of the room, all fixed to make my bow, but Brown did not look around. I thought he took a furtive glance at me out of the corner of his eye, but as not even this notice was repeated, I judged I had been mistaken. By this time he was picking his way among some dangerous 'breaks' abreast the woodyards; therefore it would not be proper to interrupt him; so I stepped softly to the high bench and took a seat.

There was silence for ten minutes; then my new boss turned and inspected me deliberately and painstakingly from head to heel for about—as it seemed to me—a quarter of an hour. After which he removed his countenance and I saw it no more for some seconds; then it came around once more, and this question greeted me—

'Are you Horace Bigsby's cub?'

'Yes, sir.'

After this there was a pause and another inspection. Then—

'What's your name?'

I told him. He repeated it after me. It was probably the only thing he ever forgot; for although I was with him many months he never addressed himself to me in any other way than 'Here!' and then his command followed.

'Where was you born?'

'In Florida, Missouri.'

A pause. Then—

'Dern sight better staid there!'

By means of a dozen or so of pretty direct questions, he pumped my family history out of me.

The leads were going now, in the first crossing. This interrupted the inquest. When the leads had been laid in, he resumed—

'How long you been on the river?'

I told him. After a pause—

'Where'd you get them shoes?'

I gave him the information.

'Hold up your foot!'

I did so. He stepped back, examined the shoe minutely and contemptuously, scratching his head thoughtfully, tilting his high sugar-loaf hat well forward to facilitate the operation, then ejaculated, 'Well, I'll be dod derned!' and returned to his wheel.

What occasion there was to be dod derned about it is a thing which is still as much of a mystery to me now as it was then. It must have been all of fifteen minutes—fifteen minutes of dull, homesick silence— before that long horse-face swung round upon me again—and then, what a change! It was as red as fire, and every muscle in it was working. Now came this shriek—

'Here!—You going to set there all day?'

I lit in the middle of the floor, shot there by the electric suddenness of the surprise. As soon as I could get my voice I said, apologetically:—'I have had no orders, sir.'

'You've had no ORDERS! My, what a fine bird we are! We must have ORDERS! Our father was a GENTLEMAN—owned slaves—and we've been to SCHOOL. Yes, WE are a gentleman, TOO, and got to have ORDERS! ORDERS, is it? ORDERS is what you want! Dod dern my skin, I'LL learn you to swell yourself up and blow around here about your dod-derned ORDERS! G'way from the wheel!' (I had approached it without knowing it.)

I moved back a step or two, and stood as in a dream, all my senses stupefied by this frantic assault.

'What you standing there for? Take that ice-pitcher down to the texas-tender-come, move along, and don't you be all day about it!'

The moment I got back to the pilot-house, Brown said—

'Here! What was you doing down there all this time?'

'I couldn't find the texas-tender; I had to go all the way to the pantry.'

'Derned likely story! Fill up the stove.'

I proceeded to do so. He watched me like a cat. Presently he shouted—

'Put down that shovel! Deadest numskull I ever saw—ain't even got sense enough to load up a stove.'

All through the watch this sort of thing went on. Yes, and the subsequent watches were much like it, during a stretch of months. As I have said, I soon got the habit of coming on duty with dread. The moment I was in the presence, even in the darkest night, I could feel those yellow eyes upon me, and knew their owner was watching for a pretext to spit out some venom on me. Preliminarily he would say—

'Here! Take the wheel.'

Two minutes later—

'WHERE in the nation you going to? Pull her down! pull her down!'

After another moment—

'Say! You going to hold her all day? Let her go—meet her! meet her!'

Then he would jump from the bench, snatch the wheel from me, and meet her himself, pouring out wrath upon me all the time.

George Ritchie was the other pilot's cub. He was having good times now; for his boss, George Ealer, was as kindhearted as Brown wasn't. Ritchie had steeled for Brown the season before; consequently he knew exactly how to entertain himself and plague me, all by the one operation. Whenever I took the wheel for a moment on Ealer's watch, Ritchie would sit back on the bench and play Brown, with continual ejaculations of 'Snatch her! snatch her! Derndest mud-cat I ever saw!' 'Here! Where you going NOW? Going to run over that snag?' 'Pull her DOWN! Don't you hear me? Pull her DOWN!' 'There she goes! JUST as I expected! I TOLD you not to cramp that reef. G'way from the wheel!'

So I always had a rough time of it, no matter whose watch it was; and sometimes it seemed to me that Ritchie's good-natured badgering was pretty nearly as aggravating as Brown's dead-earnest nagging.

I often wanted to kill Brown, but this would not answer. A cub had to take everything his boss gave, in the way of vigorous comment and criticism; and we all believed that there was a United States law making it a penitentiary offense to strike or threaten a pilot who was on duty. However, I could IMAGINE myself killing Brown; there was no law against that; and that was the thing I used always to do the moment I was abed. Instead of going over my river in my mind as was my duty, I threw business aside for pleasure, and killed Brown. I killed Brown every night for months; not in old, stale, commonplace ways, but in new and picturesque ones;—ways that were sometimes surprising for freshness of design and ghastliness of situation and environment.

Brown was ALWAYS watching for a pretext to find fault; and if he could find no plausible pretext, he would invent one. He would scold you for shaving a shore, and for not shaving it; for hugging a bar, and for not hugging it; for 'pulling down' when not invited, and for not pulling down when not invited; for firing up without orders, and for waiting FOR orders. In a word, it was his invariable rule to find fault with EVERYTHING you did; and another invariable rule of his was to throw all his remarks (to you) into the form of an insult.

One day we were approaching New Madrid, bound down and heavily laden. Brown was at one side of the wheel, steering; I was at the other, standing by to 'pull down' or 'shove up.' He cast a furtive glance at me every now and then. I had long ago learned what that meant; viz., he was trying to invent a trap for me. I wondered what shape it was going to take. By and by he stepped back from the wheel and said in his usual snarly way—

'Here!—See if you've got gumption enough to round her to.'

This was simply BOUND to be a success; nothing could prevent it; for he had never allowed me to round the boat to before; consequently, no matter how I might do the thing, he could find free fault with it. He stood back there with his greedy eye on me, and the result was what might have been foreseen: I lost my head in a quarter of a minute, and didn't know what I was about; I started too early to bring the boat around, but detected a green gleam of joy in Brown's eye, and corrected my mistake; I started around once more while too high up, but corrected myself again in time; I made other false moves, and still managed to save myself; but at last I grew so confused and anxious that I tumbled into the very worst blunder of all—I got too far down before beginning to fetch the boat around. Brown's chance was come.

His face turned red with passion; he made one bound, hurled me across the house with a sweep of his arm, spun the wheel down, and began to pour out a stream of vituperation upon me which lasted till he was out of breath. In the course of this speech he called me all the different kinds of hard names he could think of, and once or twice I thought he was even going to swear—but he didn't this time. 'Dod dern' was the nearest he ventured to the luxury of swearing, for he had been brought up with a wholesome respect for future fire and brimstone.

That was an uncomfortable hour; for there was a big audience on the hurricane deck. When I went to bed that night, I killed Brown in seventeen different ways—all of them new.

Chapter 19 Brown and I Exchange Compliments

Two trips later, I got into serious trouble. Brown was steering; I was 'pulling down.' My younger brother appeared on the hurricane deck, and shouted to Brown to stop at some landing or other a mile or so below. Brown gave no intimation that he had heard anything. But that was his way: he never condescended to take notice of an under clerk. The wind was blowing; Brown was deaf (although he always pretended he wasn't), and I very much doubted if he had heard the order. If I had two heads, I would have spoken; but as I had only one, it seemed judicious to take care of it; so I kept still.

Presently, sure enough, we went sailing by that plantation. Captain Klinefelter appeared on the deck, and said—

'Let her come around, sir, let her come around. Didn't Henry tell you to land here?'

'NO, sir!'

'I sent him up to do, it.'

'He did come up; and that's all the good it done, the dod-derned fool. He never said anything.'

'Didn't YOU hear him?' asked the captain of me.

Of course I didn't want to be mixed up in this business, but there was no way to avoid it; so I said—

'Yes, sir.'

I knew what Brown's next remark would be, before he uttered it; it was—

'Shut your mouth! you never heard anything of the kind.'

I closed my mouth according to instructions. An hour later, Henry entered the pilot-house, unaware of what had been going on. He was a thoroughly inoffensive boy, and I was sorry to see him come, for I knew Brown would have no pity on him. Brown began, straightway—

'Here! why didn't you tell me we'd got to land at that plantation?'

'I did tell you, Mr. Brown.'

'It's a lie!'

I said—

'You lie, yourself. He did tell you.'

Brown glared at me in unaffected surprise; and for as much as a moment he was entirely speechless; then he shouted to me—

'I'll attend to your case in half a minute!' then to Henry, 'And you leave the pilot-house; out with you!'

It was pilot law, and must be obeyed. The boy started out, and even had his foot on the upper step outside the door, when Brown, with a sudden access of fury, picked up a ten-pound lump of coal and sprang after him; but I was between, with a heavy stool, and I hit Brown a good honest blow which stretched-him out.

I had committed the crime of crimes—I had lifted my hand against a pilot on duty! I supposed I was booked for the penitentiary sure, and couldn't be booked any surer if I went on and squared my long account with this person while I had the chance; consequently I stuck to him and pounded him with my fists a considerable time—I do not know how long, the pleasure of it probably made it seem longer than it really was;—but in the end he struggled free and jumped up and sprang to the wheel: a very natural solicitude, for, all this time, here was this steamboat tearing down the river at the rate of fifteen miles an hour and nobody at the helm! However, Eagle Bend was two miles wide at this bank-full stage, and correspondingly long and deep; and the boat was steering herself straight down the middle and taking no chances. Still, that was only luck—a body MIGHT have found her charging into the woods.

Perceiving, at a glance, that the 'Pennsylvania' was in no danger, Brown gathered up the big spy-glass, war-club fashion, and ordered me out of the pilot-house with more than Comanche bluster. But I was not afraid of him now; so, instead of going, I tarried, and criticized his grammar; I reformed his ferocious speeches for him, and put them into good English, calling his attention to the advantage of pure English over the bastard dialect of the Pennsylvanian collieries whence he was extracted. He could have done his part to admiration in a cross-fire of mere vituperation, of course; but he was not equipped for this species of controversy; so he presently laid aside his glass and took the wheel, muttering and shaking his head; and I retired to the bench. The racket had brought everybody to the hurricane deck, and I trembled when I saw the old captain looking up from the midst of the crowd. I said to myself, 'Now I AM done for!'—For although, as a rule, he was so fatherly and indulgent toward the boat's family, and so patient of minor shortcomings, he could be stern enough when the fault was worth it.

I tried to imagine what he WOULD do to a cub pilot who had

been guilty of such a crime as mine, committed on a boat guard-deep with costly freight and alive with passengers. Our watch was nearly ended. I thought I would go and hide somewhere till I got a chance to slide ashore. So I slipped out of the pilot-house, and down the steps, and around to the texas door—and was in the act of gliding within, when the captain confronted me! I dropped my head, and he stood over me in silence a moment or two, then said impressively—

'Follow me.'

I dropped into his wake; he led the way to his parlor in the forward end of the texas. We were alone, now. He closed the after door; then moved slowly to the forward one and closed that. He sat down; I stood before him. He looked at me some little time, then said—

'So you have been fighting Mr. Brown?'

I answered meekly—

'Yes, sir.'

'Do you know that that is a very serious matter?'

'Yes, sir.'

'Are you aware that this boat was plowing down the river fully five minutes with no one at the wheel?'

'Yes, sir.'

'Did you strike him first?'

'Yes, sir.'

'What with?'

'A stool, sir.'

'Hard?'

'Middling, sir.'

'Did it knock him down?'

'He—he fell, sir.'

'Did you follow it up? Did you do anything further?'

'Yes, sir.'

'What did you do?'

'Pounded him, sir.'

'Pounded him?'

'Yes, sir.'

'Did you pound him much?—that is, severely?'

'One might call it that, sir, maybe.'

'I'm deuced glad of it! Hark ye, never mention that I said that. You have been guilty of a great crime; and don't you ever be guilty of it again, on this boat. BUT—lay for him ashore! Give him a good sound thrashing, do you hear? I'll pay the expenses. Now go—and mind you, not a word of this to anybody. Clear out with you!—you've been guilty of a great crime, you whelp!'

I slid out, happy with the sense of a close shave and a mighty deliverance; and I heard him laughing to himself and slapping his fat thighs after I had closed his door.

When Brown came off watch he went straight to the captain, who was talking with some passengers on the boiler deck, and demanded that I be put ashore in New Orleans—and added—

'I'll never turn a wheel on this boat again while that cub stays.'

The captain said—

'But he needn't come round when you are on watch, Mr. Brown.

'I won't even stay on the same boat with him. One of us has got to go ashore.'

'Very well,' said the captain, 'let it be yourself;' and resumed his talk with the passengers.

During the brief remainder of the trip, I knew how an emancipated slave feels; for I was an emancipated slave myself. While we lay at landings, I listened to George Ealer's flute; or to his readings from his two bibles, that is to say, Goldsmith and Shakespeare; or I played chess with him—and would have beaten him sometimes, only he always took back his last move and ran the game out differently.

Chapter 20 A Catastrophe

WE lay three days in New Orleans, but the captain did not succeed in finding another pilot; so he proposed that I should stand a daylight watch, and leave the night watches to George Ealer. But I was afraid; I had never stood a watch of any sort by myself, and I believed I should be sure to get into trouble in the head of some chute, or ground the boat in a near cut through some bar or other. Brown remained in his place; but he would not travel with me. So the captain gave me an order on the captain of the 'A. T. Lacey,' for a passage to St. Louis, and said he would find a new pilot there and my steersman's berth could then be resumed. The 'Lacey' was to leave a couple of days after the 'Pennsylvania.'

The night before the 'Pennsylvania' left, Henry and I sat chatting on a freight pile on the levee till midnight. The subject of the chat, mainly, was one which I think we had not exploited before—steamboat disasters. One was then on its way to us, little as we suspected it; the water which was to make the steam which should cause it, was washing past some point fifteen hundred miles up the river while we talked;—but it would arrive at the right time and the right place. We doubted if persons not clothed with authority were of much use in cases of disaster and attendant panic; still, they might be of SOME use; so we decided that if a disaster ever fell within our experience we would at least stick to the boat, and give such minor service as chance might throw in the way. Henry remembered this, afterward, when the disaster came, and acted accordingly.

The 'Lacey' started up the river two days behind the 'Pennsylvania.' We touched at Greenville, Mississippi, a couple of days out, and somebody shouted—

'The "Pennsylvania" is blown up at Ship Island, and a hundred and fifty lives lost!'

At Napoleon, Arkansas, the same evening, we got an extra, issued by a Memphis paper, which gave some particulars. It mentioned my brother, and said he was not hurt.

Further up the river we got a later extra. My brother was again mentioned; but this time as being hurt beyond help. We did not get full details of the catastrophe until we reached Memphis. This is the sorrowful story—

It was six o'clock on a hot summer morning. The 'Pennsylvania' was creeping along, north of Ship Island, about sixty miles below Memphis on a half-head of steam, towing a wood-flat which was fast being emptied. George Ealer was in the pilot-house-alone, I think; the second engineer and a striker had the watch in the engine room; the second mate had the watch on deck; George Black, Mr. Wood, and my brother, clerks, were asleep, as were also Brown and the head engineer, the carpenter, the chief mate, and one striker; Captain Klinefelter was in the barber's chair, and the barber was preparing to shave him. There were a good many cabin passengers aboard, and three or four hundred deck passengers —so it was said at the time—and not very many of them were astir. The wood being nearly all out of the flat now, Ealer rang to 'come ahead' full steam, and the next moment four of the eight boilers exploded with a thunderous crash, and the whole forward third of the boat was hoisted toward the sky! The main part of the mass, with the chimneys, dropped upon the boat again, a mountain of riddled and chaotic rubbish—and then, after a little, fire broke out.

Many people were flung to considerable distances, and fell in the river; among these were Mr. Wood and my brother, and the carpenter. The carpenter was still stretched upon his mattress when he struck the water seventy-five feet from the boat. Brown, the pilot, and George Black, chief clerk, were never seen or heard of after the explosion. The barber's chair, with Captain Klinefelter in it and unhurt, was left with its back overhanging vacancy—everything forward of it, floor and all, had disappeared; and the stupefied barber, who was also unhurt, stood with one toe projecting over space, still stirring his lather unconsciously, and saying, not a word.

When George Ealer saw the chimneys plunging aloft in front of him, he knew what the matter was; so he muffled his face in the lapels of his coat, and pressed both hands there tightly to keep this protection in its place so that no steam could get to his nose or mouth. He had ample time to attend to these details while he was going up and returning. He presently landed on top of the unexploded boilers, forty feet below the former pilot-house, accompanied by his wheel and a rain of other stuff, and enveloped in a cloud of scalding steam. All of the many who breathed that steam, died; none escaped. But Ealer breathed none of it. He made his way to the free air as quickly as he could; and when the steam cleared away he returned and climbed up on the boilers again, and patiently hunted out each and every one of his chessmen and the several joints of his flute.

By this time the fire was beginning to threaten. Shrieks and groans filled the air. A great many persons had been scalded, a great many crippled; the explosion had driven an iron crowbar through one man's body—I think they said he was a priest. He did not die at once, and his sufferings were very dreadful. A young French naval cadet, of fifteen, son of a French admiral, was fearfully scalded, but bore his tortures manfully. Both

mates were badly scalded, but they stood to their posts, nevertheless. They drew the wood-boat aft, and they and the captain fought back the frantic herd of frightened immigrants till the wounded could be brought there and placed in safety first.

When Mr. Wood and Henry fell in the water, they struck out for shore, which was only a few hundred yards away; but Henry presently said he believed he was not hurt (what an unaccountable error!), and therefore would swim back to the boat and help save the wounded. So they parted, and Henry returned.

By this time the fire was making fierce headway, and several persons who were imprisoned under the ruins were begging piteously for help. All efforts to conquer the fire proved fruitless; so the buckets were presently thrown aside and the officers fell-to with axes and tried to cut the prisoners out. A striker was one of the captives; he said he was not injured, but could not free himself; and when he saw that the fire was likely to drive away the workers, he begged that some one would shoot him, and thus save him from the more dreadful death. The fire did drive the axmen away, and they had to listen, helpless, to this poor fellow's supplications till the flames ended his miseries.

The fire drove all into the wood-flat that could be accommodated there; it was cut adrift, then, and it and the burning steamer floated down the river toward Ship Island. They moored the flat at the head of the island, and there, unsheltered from the blazing sun, the half-naked occupants had to remain, without food or stimulants, or help for their hurts, during the rest of the day. A steamer came along, finally, and carried the unfortunates to Memphis, and there the most lavish assistance was at once forthcoming. By this time Henry was insensible. The physicians examined his injuries and saw that they were fatal, and naturally turned their main attention to patients who could be saved.

Forty of the wounded were placed upon pallets on the floor of a great public hall, and among these was Henry. There the ladies of Memphis came every day, with flowers, fruits, and dainties and delicacies of all kinds, and there they remained and nursed the wounded. All the physicians stood watches there, and all the medical students; and the rest of the town furnished money, or whatever else was wanted. And Memphis knew how to do all these things well; for many a disaster like the 'Pennsylvania's' had happened near her doors, and she was experienced, above all other cities on the river, in the gracious office of the Good Samaritan'

The sight I saw when I entered that large hall was new and strange to me. Two long rows of prostrate forms—more than forty, in all—and every face and head a shapeless wad of loose raw cotton. It was a gruesome spectacle. I watched there six days and nights, and a very melancholy experience it was. There was one daily incident which was peculiarly depressing: this was the removal of the doomed to a chamber apart. It was done in order that the MORALE of the other patients might not be injuriously affected by seeing one of their number in the death-agony. The fated one was always carried out with as little stir as possible, and the stretcher was always hidden from sight by a wall of assistants; but no matter: everybody knew what that cluster of bent forms, with its muffled step and its slow movement meant; and all eyes watched it wistfully, and a shudder went abreast of it like a wave.

I saw many poor fellows removed to the 'death-room,' and saw them no more afterward. But I saw our chief mate carried thither more than once. His hurts were frightful, especially his scalds. He was clothed in linseed oil and raw cotton to his waist, and resembled nothing human. He was often out of his mind; and then his pains would make him rave and shout and sometimes shriek. Then, after a period of dumb exhaustion, his disordered imagination would suddenly transform the great apartment into a forecastle, and the hurrying throng of nurses into the crew; and he would come to a sitting posture and shout, 'Hump yourselves, HUMP yourselves, you petrifactions, snail-bellies, pall-bearers! going to be all DAY getting that hatful of freight out?' and supplement this explosion with a firmament-obliterating irruption or profanity which nothing could stay or stop till his crater was empty. And now and then while these frenzies possessed him, he would tear off handfuls of the cotton and expose his cooked flesh to view. It was horrible. It was bad for the others, of course—this noise and these exhibitions; so the doctors tried to give him morphine to quiet him. But, in his mind or out of it, he would not take it. He said his wife had been killed by that treacherous drug, and he would die before he would take it. He suspected that the doctors were concealing it in his ordinary medicines and in his water—so he ceased from putting either to his lips. Once, when he had been without water during two sweltering days, he took the dipper in his hand, and the sight of the limpid fluid, and the misery of his thirst, tempted him almost beyond his strength; but he mastered himself and threw it away, and after that he allowed no more to be brought near him. Three times I saw him carried to the death-room, insensible and supposed to be dying; but each time he revived, cursed his attendants, and demanded to be taken back. He lived to be mate of a steamboat again.

But he was the only one who went to the death-room and returned alive. Dr. Peyton, a principal physician, and rich in all the attributes that go to constitute high and flawless character, did all that educated judgment and trained skill could do for Henry; but, as the newspapers had said in the beginning, his hurts were past help. On the evening of the sixth day his wandering mind busied itself with matters far away, and his nerveless fingers 'picked at his coverlet.' His hour had struck; we bore him to the death-room, poor boy.

Chapter 21 A Section in My Biography

IN due course I got my license. I was a pilot now, full fledged. I dropped into casual employments; no misfortunes resulting, intermittent work gave place to steady and protracted engagements. Time drifted smoothly and prosperously on, and I supposed—and hoped—that I was going to follow the river the rest of my days, and die at the wheel when my mission was ended. But by and by the war came, commerce was suspended, my occupation was gone.

I had to seek another livelihood. So I became a silver miner in Nevada; next, a newspaper reporter; next, a gold miner, in California; next, a reporter in San Francisco; next, a special correspondent in the Sandwich Islands; next, a roving correspondent in Europe and the East; next, an instructional torch-bearer on the lecture platform; and, finally, I became a scribbler of books, and an immovable fixture among the other rocks of New England.

In so few words have I disposed of the twenty-one slow-drifting years that have come and gone since I last looked from the windows of a pilot- house.

Let us resume, now.

Chapter 22 I Return to My Muttons

AFTER twenty-one years' absence, I felt a very strong desire to see the river again, and the steamboats, and such of the boys as might be left; so I resolved to go out there. I enlisted a poet for company, and a stenographer to 'take him down,' and started westward about the middle of April.

As I proposed to make notes, with a view to printing, I took some thought as to methods of procedure. I reflected that if I were recognized, on the river, I should not be as free to go and come, talk, inquire, and spy around, as I should be if unknown; I remembered that it was the custom of steamboatmen in the old times to load up the confiding stranger with the most picturesque and admirable lies, and put the sophisticated friend off with dull and ineffectual facts: so I concluded, that, from a business point of view, it would be an advantage to disguise our party with fictitious names. The idea was certainly good, but it bred infinite bother; for although Smith, Jones, and Johnson are easy names to remember when there is no occasion to remember them, it is next to impossible to recollect them when they are wanted. How do criminals manage to keep a brand-new ALIAS in mind? This is a great mystery. I was innocent; and yet was seldom able to lay my hand on my new name when it was needed; and it seemed to me that if I had had a crime on my conscience to further confuse me, I could never have kept the name by me at all.

We left per Pennsylvania Railroad, at 8 A.M. April 18.

'EVENING. Speaking of dress. Grace and picturesqueness drop gradually out of it as one travels away from New York.'

I find that among my notes. It makes no difference which direction you take, the fact remains the same. Whether you move north, south, east, or west, no matter: you can get up in the morning and guess how far you have come, by noting what degree of grace and picturesqueness is by that time lacking in the costumes of the new passengers,—I do not mean of the women alone, but of both sexes. It may be that CARRIAGE is at the bottom of this thing; and I think it is; for there are plenty of ladies and gentlemen in the provincial cities whose garments are all made by the best tailors and dressmakers of New York; yet this has no perceptible effect upon the grand fact: the educated eye never mistakes those people for New-Yorkers. No, there is a godless grace, and snap, and style about a born and bred New-Yorker which mere clothing cannot effect.

'APRIL 19. This morning, struck into the region of full goatees— sometimes accompanied by a mustache, but only occasionally.'

It was odd to come upon this thick crop of an obsolete and uncomely fashion; it was like running suddenly across a forgotten acquaintance whom you had supposed dead for a generation. The goatee extends over a wide extent of country; and is accompanied by an iron-clad belief in Adam and the biblical history of creation, which has not suffered from the assaults of the scientists.

'AFTERNOON. At the railway stations the loafers carry BOTH hands in their breeches pockets; it was observable, heretofore, that one hand was sometimes out of doors,—here, never. This is an important fact in geography.'

If the loafers determined the character of a country, it would be still more important, of course.

'Heretofore, all along, the station-loafer has been often observed to scratch one shin with the other foot; here, these remains of activity are wanting. This has an ominous look.'

By and by, we entered the tobacco-chewing region. Fifty years ago, the tobacco-chewing region covered the Union. It is greatly restricted now.

Next, boots began to appear. Not in strong force, however. Later—away down the Mississippi—they became the rule. They disappeared from other sections of the Union with the mud; no doubt they will disappear from the river villages, also, when proper pavements come in.

We reached St. Louis at ten o'clock at night. At the counter of the hotel I tendered a hurriedly-invented fictitious name, with a miserable attempt at careless ease. The clerk paused, and inspected me in the compassionate way in which one inspects a respectable person who is found in doubtful circumstances; then he said—

'It's all right; I know what sort of a room you want. Used to clerk at the St. James, in New York.'

An unpromising beginning for a fraudulent career. We started to the supper room, and met two other men whom I had known elsewhere. How odd and unfair it is: wicked impostors go around lecturing under my NOM DE GUERRE and nobody suspects them; but when an honest man attempts an imposture, he is exposed at once.

One thing seemed plain: we must start down the river the next day, if people who could not be deceived were going to crop up at this rate: an unpalatable disappointment, for we had hoped to have a week in St. Louis. The Southern was a good hotel, and we could have had a comfortable time there. It is large, and well conducted, and its decorations do not make one cry, as do those of the vast Palmer House, in Chicago. True, the billiard-tables were of the Old Silurian Period, and the cues and balls of the Post-Pliocene; but there was refreshment in this, not discomfort; for there is rest and healing in the contemplation of antiquities.

The most notable absence observable in the billiard-room, was the absence of the river man. If he was there he had taken in his sign, he was in disguise. I saw there none of the swell airs and graces, and ostentatious displays of money, and pompous squanderings of it, which used to distinguish the steamboat crowd from the dry-land crowd in the bygone days, in the thronged billiard-rooms of St. Louis. In those times, the principal saloons were always populous with river men; given fifty players present, thirty or thirty-five were likely to be from the river. But I suspected that the ranks were thin now, and the steamboatmen no longer an aristocracy. Why, in my time they used to call the 'barkeep' Bill, or Joe, or Tom, and slap him on the shoulder; I watched for that. But none of these people did it. Manifestly a glory that once was had dissolved and vanished away in these twenty-one years.

When I went up to my room, I found there the young man called Rogers, crying. Rogers was not his name; neither was Jones, Brown, Dexter, Ferguson, Bascom, nor Thompson; but he answered to either of these that a body found handy in an emergency; or to any other name, in fact, if he perceived that you meant him. He said—

'What is a person to do here when he wants a drink of water?—drink this slush?'

'Can't you drink it?'

'I could if I had some other water to wash it with.'

Here was a thing which had not changed; a score of years had not affected this water's mulatto complexion in the least; a score of centuries would succeed no better, perhaps. It comes out of the turbulent, bank-caving Missouri, and every tumblerful of it holds nearly an acre of land in solution. I got this fact from the bishop of the diocese. If you will let your glass stand half an hour, you can separate the land from the water as easy as Genesis; and then you will find them both good: the one good to eat, the other good to drink. The land is very nourishing, the water is thoroughly wholesome. The one appeases hunger; the other, thirst. But the natives do not take them separately, but together, as nature mixed them. When they find an inch of mud in the bottom of a glass, they stir it up, and then take the draught as they would gruel. It is difficult for a stranger to get used to this batter, but once used to it he will prefer it to water. This is really the case. It is good for steamboating, and good to drink; but it is worthless for all other purposes, except baptizing.

Next morning, we drove around town in the rain. The city seemed but little changed. It WAS greatly changed, but it did not seem so; because in St. Louis, as in London and Pittsburgh, you can't persuade a new thing to look new; the coal smoke turns it into an antiquity the moment you take your hand off it. The place had just about doubled its size, since I was a resident of it, and was now become a city of 400,000 inhabitants; still, in the solid business parts, it looked about as it had looked formerly. Yet I am sure there is not as much smoke in St. Louis now as there used to be. The smoke used to bank itself in a dense billowy black canopy over the town, and hide the sky from view. This shelter is very much thinner now; still, there is a sufficiency of smoke there, I think. I heard no complaint.

However, on the outskirts changes were apparent enough; notably in dwelling-house architecture. The fine new homes are noble and beautiful and modern. They stand by themselves, too, with green lawns around them; whereas the dwellings of a former day are packed together in blocks, and are all of one pattern, with windows all alike, set in an arched frame-work of twisted stone; a sort of house which was handsome enough when it was rarer.

There was another change—the Forest Park. This was new to me. It is beautiful and very extensive, and has the excellent merit of having been made mainly by nature. There are other parks, and fine ones, notably Tower Grove and the Botanical Gardens; for St. Louis interested herself in such improvements at an earlier day than did the most of our cities.

The first time I ever saw St. Louis, I could have bought it for six million dollars, and it was the mistake of my life that I did not do it. It was bitter now to look abroad over this domed and steepled metropolis, this solid expanse of bricks and mortar stretching away on every hand into dim, measure-defying distances, and remember that I had allowed that opportunity to go by. Why I should have allowed it to go by seems, of course, foolish and inexplicable to-day, at a first glance; yet there were reasons at the time to justify this course.

A Scotchman, Hon. Charles Augustus Murray, writing some

forty-five or fifty years ago, said—'The streets are narrow, ill paved and ill lighted.' Those streets are narrow still, of course; many of them are ill paved yet; but the reproach of ill lighting cannot be repeated, now. The 'Catholic New Church' was the only notable building then, and Mr. Murray was confidently called upon to admire it, with its 'species of Grecian portico, surmounted by a kind of steeple, much too diminutive in its proportions, and surmounted by sundry ornaments' which the unimaginative Scotchman found himself 'quite unable to describe;' and therefore was grateful when a German tourist helped him out with the exclamation—'By —, they look exactly like bed-posts!' St. Louis is well equipped with stately and noble public buildings now, and the little church, which the people used to be so proud of, lost its importance a long time ago. Still, this would not surprise Mr. Murray, if he could come back; for he prophesied the coming greatness of St. Louis with strong confidence.

The further we drove in our inspection-tour, the more sensibly I realized how the city had grown since I had seen it last; changes in detail became steadily more apparent and frequent than at first, too: changes uniformly evidencing progress, energy, prosperity.

But the change of changes was on the 'levee.' This time, a departure from the rule. Half a dozen sound-asleep steamboats where I used to see a solid mile of wide-awake ones! This was melancholy, this was woeful. The absence of the pervading and jocund steamboatman from the billiard-saloon was explained. He was absent because he is no more. His occupation is gone, his power has passed away, he is absorbed into the common herd, he grinds at the mill, a shorn Samson and inconspicuous. Half a dozen lifeless steamboats, a mile of empty wharves, a negro fatigued with whiskey stretched asleep, in a wide and soundless vacancy, where the serried hosts of commerce used to contend!* Here was desolation, indeed.

'The old, old sea, as one in tears, Comes murmuring, with foamy lips, And knocking at the vacant piers, Calls for his long-lost multitude of ships.'

The towboat and the railroad had done their work, and done it well and completely. The mighty bridge, stretching along over our heads, had done its share in the slaughter and spoliation. Remains of former steamboatmen told me, with wan satisfaction, that the bridge doesn't pay. Still, it can be no sufficient compensation to a corpse, to know that the dynamite that laid him out was not of as good quality as it had been supposed to be.

The pavements along the river front were bad: the sidewalks were rather out of repair; there was a rich abundance of mud. All this was familiar and satisfying; but the ancient armies of drays, and struggling throngs of men, and mountains of freight, were gone; and Sabbath reigned in their stead. The immemorial mile of cheap foul doggeries remained, but business was dull with them; the multitudes of poison-swilling Irishmen had departed, and in their places were a few scattering handfuls of ragged negroes, some drinking, some drunk, some nodding, others asleep. St. Louis is a great and prosperous and advancing city; but the river- edge of it seems dead past resurrection.

---

* Capt. Marryat, writing forty-five years ago says: 'St. Louis has 20,000 inhabitants. THE RIVER ABREAST OF THE TOWN IS CROWDED WITH STEAMBOATS, LYING IN TWO OR THREE TIERS.'

Mississippi steamboating was born about 1812; at the end of thirty years, it had grown to mighty proportions; and in less than thirty more, it was dead! A strangely short life for so majestic a creature. Of course it is not absolutely dead, neither is a crippled octogenarian who could once jump twenty-two feet on level ground; but as contrasted with what it was in its prime vigor, Mississippi steamboating may be called dead.

It killed the old-fashioned keel-boating, by reducing the freight-trip to New Orleans to less than a week. The railroads have killed the steamboat passenger traffic by doing in two or three days what the steamboats consumed a week in doing; and the towing-fleets have killed the through-freight traffic by dragging six or seven steamer-loads of stuff down the river at a time, at an expense so trivial that steamboat competition was out of the question.

Freight and passenger way-traffic remains to the steamers. This is in the hands—along the two thousand miles of river between St. Paul and New Orleans—of two or three close corporations well fortified with capital; and by able and thoroughly business-like management and system, these make a sufficiency of money out of what is left of the once prodigious steamboating industry. I suppose that St. Louis and New Orleans have not suffered materially by the change, but alas for the wood-yard man!

He used to fringe the river all the way; his close-ranked merchandise stretched from the one city to the other, along the banks, and he sold uncountable cords of it every year for cash on the nail; but all the scattering boats that are left burn coal now, and the seldomest spectacle on the Mississippi to-day is a wood-pile. Where now is the once wood-yard man?

Chapter 23 Traveling Incognito

MY idea was, to tarry a while in every town between St. Louis and New Orleans. To do this, it would be necessary to go from place to place by the short packet lines. It was an easy plan to make, and would have been an easy one to follow, twenty years ago—but not now. There are wide intervals between boats, these days.

I wanted to begin with the interesting old French settlements of St. Genevieve and Kaskaskia, sixty miles below St. Louis. There was only one boat advertised for that section—a Grand Tower packet. Still, one boat was enough; so we went down to look at her. She was a venerable rack- heap, and a fraud to boot; for she was playing herself for personal property, whereas the good honest dirt was so thickly caked all over her that she was righteously taxable as real estate. There are places in New England where her hurricane deck would be worth a hundred and fifty dollars an acre. The soil on her forecastle was quite good—the new crop of wheat was already springing from the cracks in protected places. The companionway was of a dry sandy character, and would have been well suited for grapes, with a southern exposure and a little subsoiling. The soil of the boiler deck was thin and rocky, but good enough for grazing purposes. A colored boy was on watch here—nobody else visible. We gathered from him that this calm craft would go, as advertised, 'if she got her trip;' if she didn't get it, she would wait for it.

'Has she got any of her trip?'

'Bless you, no, boss. She ain't unloadened, yit. She only come in dis mawnin'.'

He was uncertain as to when she might get her trip, but thought it might be to-morrow or maybe next day. This would not answer at all; so we had to give up the novelty of sailing down the river on a farm. We had one more arrow in our quiver: a Vicksburg packet, the 'Gold Dust,' was to leave at 5 P.M. We took passage in her for Memphis, and gave up the idea of stopping off here and there, as being impracticable. She was neat, clean, and comfortable. We camped on the boiler deck, and bought some cheap literature to kill time with. The vender was a venerable Irishman with a benevolent face and a tongue that worked easily in the socket, and from him we learned that he had lived in St. Louis thirty-four years and had never been across the river during that period. Then he wandered into a very flowing lecture, filled with classic names and allusions, which was quite wonderful for fluency until the fact became rather apparent that this was not the first time, nor perhaps the fiftieth, that the speech had been delivered. He was a good deal of a character, and much better company than the sappy literature he was selling. A random remark, connecting Irishmen and beer, brought this nugget of information out of him—

They don't drink it, sir. They can't drink it, sir. Give an Irishman lager for a month, and he's a dead man. An Irishman is lined with copper, and the beer corrodes it. But whiskey polishes the copper and is the saving of him, sir.'

At eight o'clock, promptly, we backed out and crossed the river. As we crept toward the shore, in the thick darkness, a blinding glory of white electric light burst suddenly from our forecastle, and lit up the water and the warehouses as with a noon-day glare. Another big change, this— no more flickering, smoky, pitch-dripping, ineffectual torch-baskets, now: their day is past. Next, instead of calling out a score of hands to man the stage, a couple of men and a hatful of steam lowered it from the derrick where it was suspended, launched it, deposited it in just the right spot, and the whole thing was over and done with before in the olden time a mate could have got his profanity-mill adjusted to begin the preparatory services. Why this new and simple method of handling the stages was not thought of when the first steamboat was built, is a mystery which helps one to realize what a dull-witted slug the average human being is.

We finally got away at two in the morning, and when I turned out at six, we were rounding to at a rocky point where there was an old stone warehouse—at any rate, the ruins of it; two or three decayed dwelling- houses were near by, in the shelter of the leafy hills; but there were no evidences of human or other animal life to be seen. I wondered if I had forgotten the river; for I had no recollection whatever of this place; the shape of the river, too, was unfamiliar; there was nothing in sight, anywhere, that I could remember ever having seen before. I was surprised, disappointed, and annoyed.

We put ashore a well-dressed lady and gentleman, and two well-dressed, lady-like young girls, together with sundry Russia-leather bags. A strange place for such folk! No carriage was waiting. The party moved off as if they had not expected any, and struck down a winding country road afoot.

But the mystery was explained when we got under way again; for these people were evidently bound for a large town which lay shut in behind a tow-head (i.e., new island) a couple of miles below this landing. I couldn't remember that town; I couldn't place it, couldn't call its name. So I lost part of my temper. I suspected that it might be St. Genevieve—and so it

proved to be. Observe what this eccentric river had been about: it had built up this huge useless tow-head directly in front of this town, cut off its river communications, fenced it away completely, and made a 'country' town of it. It is a fine old place, too, and deserved a better fate. It was settled by the French, and is a relic of a time when one could travel from the mouths of the Mississippi to Quebec and be on French territory and under French rule all the way.

Presently I ascended to the hurricane deck and cast a longing glance toward the pilot-house.

Chapter 24 My Incognito is Exploded

AFTER a close study of the face of the pilot on watch, I was satisfied that I had never seen him before; so I went up there. The pilot inspected me; I re-inspected the pilot. These customary preliminaries over, I sat down on the high bench, and he faced about and went on with his work. Every detail of the pilot-house was familiar to me, with one exception,—a large-mouthed tube under the breast-board. I puzzled over that thing a considerable time; then gave up and asked what it was for.

'To hear the engine-bells through.'

It was another good contrivance which ought to have been invented half a century sooner. So I was thinking, when the pilot asked—

'Do you know what this rope is for?'

I managed to get around this question, without committing myself.

'Is this the first time you were ever in a pilot-house?'

I crept under that one.

'Where are you from?'

'New England.'

'First time you have ever been West?'

I climbed over this one.

'If you take an interest in such things, I can tell you what all these things are for.'

I said I should like it.

'This,' putting his hand on a backing-bell rope, 'is to sound the fire- alarm; this,' putting his hand on a go-ahead bell, 'is to call the texas-tender; this one,' indicating the whistle-lever, 'is to call the captain'—and so he went on, touching one object after another, and reeling off his tranquil spool of lies.

I had never felt so like a passenger before. I thanked him, with emotion, for each new fact, and wrote it down in my note-book. The pilot warmed to his opportunity, and proceeded to load me up in the good old- fashioned way. At times I was afraid he was going to rupture his invention; but it always stood the strain, and he pulled through all right. He drifted, by easy stages, into revealments of the river's marvelous eccentricities of one sort and another, and backed them up with some pretty gigantic illustrations. For instance—

'Do you see that little boulder sticking out of the water yonder? well, when I first came on the river, that was a solid ridge of rock, over sixty feet high and two miles long. All washed away but that.' [This with a sigh.]

I had a mighty impulse to destroy him, but it seemed to me that killing, in any ordinary way, would be too good for him.

Once, when an odd-looking craft, with a vast coal-scuttle slanting aloft on the end of a beam, was steaming by in the distance, he indifferently drew attention to it, as one might to an object grown wearisome through familiarity, and observed that it was an 'alligator boat.'

'An alligator boat? What's it for?'

'To dredge out alligators with.'

'Are they so thick as to be troublesome?'

'Well, not now, because the Government keeps them down. But they used to be. Not everywhere; but in favorite places, here and there, where the river is wide and shoal-like Plum Point, and Stack Island, and so on— places they call alligator beds.'

'Did they actually impede navigation?'

'Years ago, yes, in very low water; there was hardly a trip, then, that we didn't get aground on alligators.'

It seemed to me that I should certainly have to get out my tomahawk. However, I restrained myself and said—

'It must have been dreadful.'

'Yes, it was one of the main difficulties about piloting. It was so hard to tell anything about the water; the damned things shift around so— never lie still five minutes at a time. You can tell a wind-reef, straight off, by the look of it; you can tell a break; you can tell a sand-reef—that's all easy; but an alligator reef doesn't show up, worth anything. Nine times in ten you can't tell where the water is; and when you do see where it is, like as not it ain't there when YOU get there, the devils have swapped around so, meantime. Of course there were some few pilots that could judge of alligator water nearly as well as they could of any other kind, but they had to have natural talent for it; it wasn't a thing a body could learn, you had to be born with it. Let me see: there was Ben Thornburg, and Beck Jolly, and Squire Bell, and Horace Bixby, and Major Downing, and John Stevenson, and Billy Gordon, and Jim Brady, and George Ealer, and Billy Youngblood—all A 1 alligator pilots. THEY could tell alligator water as far as another Christian could tell whiskey. Read it?—Ah, COULDN'T they, though! I only wish I had as many dollars as they could read alligator water a mile and a half off. Yes, and it paid them to do it, too. A good alligator pilot could always get fifteen hundred dollars a month. Nights, other people had to lay up for alligators, but those fellows never laid up for alligators; they never laid up for anything but fog. They could SMELL the best alligator water it was said; I don't know whether it was so or not, and I think a body's got his hands full enough if he sticks to just what he knows himself, without going around backing up other people's say-so's, though there's a plenty that ain't backward about doing it, as long as they can roust out something wonderful to tell. Which is not the style of Robert Styles, by as much as three fathom—maybe quarter-LESS.'

[My! Was this Rob Styles?—This mustached and stately figure?-A slim enough cub, in my time. How he has improved in comeliness in five-and- twenty year and in the noble art of inflating his facts.] After these musings, I said aloud—

'I should think that dredging out the alligators wouldn't have done much good, because they could come back again right away.'

'If you had had as much experience of alligators as I have, you wouldn't talk like that. You dredge an alligator once and he's CONVINCED. It's the last you hear of HIM. He wouldn't come back for pie. If there's one thing that an alligator is more down on than another, it's being dredged. Besides, they were not simply shoved out of the way; the most of the scoopful were scooped aboard; they emptied them into the hold; and when they had got a trip, they took them to Orleans to the Government works.'

'What for?'

'Why, to make soldier-shoes out of their hides. All the Government shoes are made of alligator hide. It makes the best shoes in the world. They last five years, and they won't absorb water. The alligator fishery is a Government monopoly. All the alligators are Government property—just like the live-oaks. You cut down a live-oak, and Government fines you fifty dollars; you kill an alligator, and up you go for misprision of treason—lucky duck if they don't hang you, too. And they will, if you're a Democrat. The buzzard is the sacred bird of the South, and you can't touch him; the alligator is the sacred bird of the Government, and you've got to let him alone.'

'Do you ever get aground on the alligators now?'

'Oh, no! it hasn't happened for years.'

'Well, then, why do they still keep the alligator boats in service?'

'Just for police duty—nothing more. They merely go up and down now and then. The present generation of alligators know them as easy as a burglar knows a roundsman; when they see one coming, they break camp and go for the woods.'

After rounding-out and finishing-up and polishing-off the alligator business, he dropped easily and comfortably into the historical vein, and told of some tremendous feats of half-a-dozen old-time steamboats of his acquaintance, dwelling at special length upon a certain extraordinary performance of his chief favorite among this distinguished fleet—and then adding—

'That boat was the "Cyclone,"—last trip she ever made—she sunk, that very trip—captain was Tom Ballou, the most immortal liar that ever I struck. He couldn't ever seem to tell the truth, in any kind of weather. Why, he would make you fairly shudder. He WAS the most scandalous liar! I left him, finally; I couldn't stand it. The proverb says, "like master, like man;" and if you stay with that kind of a man, you'll come under suspicion by and by, just as sure as you live. He paid first-class wages; but said I, What's wages when your reputation's in danger? So I let the wages go, and froze to my reputation. And I've never regretted it. Reputation's worth everything, ain't it? That's the way I look at it. He had more selfish organs than any seven men in the world—all packed in the stern-sheets of his skull, of course, where they belonged. They weighed down the back of his head so that it made his nose tilt up in the air. People thought it was vanity, but it wasn't, it was malice. If you only saw his foot, you'd take him to be nineteen feet high, but he wasn't; it was because his foot was out of drawing. He was intended to be nineteen feet high, no doubt, if his foot was made first, but he didn't get there; he was only five feet ten. That's what he was, and that's what he is. You take the lies out of him, and he'll shrink to the size of your hat; you take the malice out of him, and he'll disappear. That "Cyclone" was a rattler to go, and the sweetest thing to steer that ever walked the waters. Set her amidships, in a big river, and just let her go; it was all you had to do. She would hold herself on a star all night, if you let her alone. You couldn't ever feel her rudder. It wasn't any more labor to steer her than it is to count the Republican vote in a South Carolina election. One morning, just at daybreak, the last trip she ever made, they took her rudder aboard to mend it; I didn't know anything about it; I backed her out from the wood-yard and went a-weaving down the river all serene. When I had gone about twenty-three miles, and made four horribly crooked crossings—'

'Without any rudder?'

'Yes—old Capt. Tom appeared on the roof and began to find fault with me for running such a dark night—'

'Such a DARK NIGHT ?—Why, you said—'

'Never mind what I said,—'twas as dark as Egypt now, though pretty soon the moon began to rise, and—'

'You mean the SUN—because you started out just at break of—look here! Was this BEFORE you quitted the captain on account of his lying, or—'

'It was before—oh, a long time before. And as I was saying, he—'

'But was this the trip she sunk, or was—'

'Oh, no!—months afterward. And so the old man, he—'

'Then she made TWO last trips, because you said—'

He stepped back from the wheel, swabbing away his perspiration, and said—

'Here!' (calling me by name), 'YOU take her and lie a while—you're handier at it than I am. Trying to play yourself for a stranger and an innocent!—why, I knew you before you had spoken seven words; and I made up my mind to find out what was your little game. It was to DRAW ME OUT. Well, I let you, didn't I? Now take the wheel and finish the watch; and next time play fair, and you won't have to work your passage.'

Thus ended the fictitious-name business. And not six hours out from St. Louis! but I had gained a privilege, any way, for I had been itching to get my hands on the wheel, from the beginning. I seemed to have forgotten the river, but I hadn't forgotten how to steer a steamboat, nor how to enjoy it, either.

Chapter 25 From Cairo to Hickman

THE scenery, from St. Louis to Cairo—two hundred miles—is varied and beautiful. The hills were clothed in the fresh foliage of spring now, and were a gracious and worthy setting for the broad river flowing between. Our trip began auspiciously, with a perfect day, as to breeze and sunshine, and our boat threw

the miles out behind her with satisfactory despatch.

We found a railway intruding at Chester, Illinois; Chester has also a penitentiary now, and is otherwise marching on. At Grand Tower, too, there was a railway; and another at Cape Girardeau. The former town gets its name from a huge, squat pillar of rock, which stands up out of the water on the Missouri side of the river—a piece of nature's fanciful handiwork—and is one of the most picturesque features of the scenery of that region. For nearer or remoter neighbors, the Tower has the Devil's Bake Oven—so called, perhaps, because it does not powerfully resemble anybody else's bake oven; and the Devil's Tea Table—this latter a great smooth-surfaced mass of rock, with diminishing wine-glass stem, perched some fifty or sixty feet above the river, beside a beflowered and garlanded precipice, and sufficiently like a tea-table to answer for anybody, Devil or Christian. Away down the river we have the Devil's Elbow and the Devil's Race-course, and lots of other property of his which I cannot now call to mind.

The Town of Grand Tower was evidently a busier place than it had been in old times, but it seemed to need some repairs here and there, and a new coat of whitewash all over. Still, it was pleasant to me to see the old coat once more. 'Uncle' Mumford, our second officer, said the place had been suffering from high water, and consequently was not looking its best now. But he said it was not strange that it didn't waste white-wash on itself, for more lime was made there, and of a better quality, than anywhere in the West; and added—'On a dairy farm you never can get any milk for your coffee, nor any sugar for it on a sugar plantation; and it is against sense to go to a lime town to hunt for white-wash.' In my own experience I knew the first two items to be true; and also that people who sell candy don't care for candy; therefore there was plausibility in Uncle Mumford's final observation that 'people who make lime run more to religion than whitewash.' Uncle Mumford said, further, that Grand Tower was a great coaling center and a prospering place.

Cape Girardeau is situated on a hillside, and makes a handsome appearance. There is a great Jesuit school for boys at the foot of the town by the river. Uncle Mumford said it had as high a reputation for thoroughness as any similar institution in Missouri! There was another college higher up on an airy summit—a bright new edifice, picturesquely and peculiarly towered and pinnacled—a sort of gigantic casters, with the cruets all complete. Uncle Mumford said that Cape Girardeau was the Athens of Missouri, and contained several colleges besides those already mentioned; and all of them on a religious basis of one kind or another. He directed my attention to what he called the 'strong and pervasive religious look of the town,' but I could not see that it looked more religious than the other hill towns with the same slope and built of the same kind of bricks. Partialities often make people see more than really exists.

Uncle Mumford has been thirty years a mate on the river. He is a man of practical sense and a level head; has observed; has had much experience of one sort and another; has opinions; has, also, just a perceptible dash of poetry in his composition, an easy gift of speech, a thick growl in his voice, and an oath or two where he can get at them when the exigencies of his office require a spiritual lift. He is a mate of the blessed old-time kind; and goes gravely damning around, when there is work to the fore, in a way to mellow the ex-steamboatman's heart with sweet soft longings for the vanished days that shall come no more. 'GIT up there you! Going to be all day? Why d'n't you SAY you was petrified in your hind legs, before you shipped!'

He is a steady man with his crew; kind and just, but firm; so they like him, and stay with him. He is still in the slouchy garb of the old generation of mates; but next trip the Anchor Line will have him in uniform—a natty blue naval uniform, with brass buttons, along with all the officers of the line—and then he will be a totally different style of scenery from what he is now.

Uniforms on the Mississippi! It beats all the other changes put together, for surprise. Still, there is another surprise—that it was not made fifty years ago. It is so manifestly sensible, that it might have been thought of earlier, one would suppose. During fifty years, out there, the innocent passenger in need of help and information, has been mistaking the mate for the cook, and the captain for the barber—and being roughly entertained for it, too. But his troubles are ended now. And the greatly improved aspect of the boat's staff is another advantage achieved by the dress-reform period.

Steered down the bend below Cape Girardeau. They used to call it 'Steersman's Bend;' plain sailing and plenty of water in it, always; about the only place in the Upper River that a new cub was allowed to take a boat through, in low water.

Thebes, at the head of the Grand Chain, and Commerce at the foot of it, were towns easily rememberable, as they had not undergone conspicuous alteration. Nor the Chain, either—in the nature of things; for it is a chain of sunken rocks admirably arranged to capture and kill steamboats on bad nights. A good many steamboat corpses lie buried there, out of sight; among the rest my first friend the 'Paul Jones;' she knocked her bottom out, and went down like a pot, so the historian told me—Uncle Mumford. He said she had a gray mare aboard, and a preacher. To me, this sufficiently accounted for the disaster; as it did, of course, to Mumford, who added—

'But there are many ignorant people who would scoff at such a matter, and call it superstition. But you will always notice that they are people who have never traveled with a gray mare and a preacher. I went down the river once in such company. We grounded at Bloody Island; we grounded at Hanging Dog; we grounded just below this same Commerce; we jolted Beaver Dam Rock; we hit one of the worst breaks in the 'Graveyard' behind Goose Island; we had a roustabout killed in a fight; we burnt a boiler; broke a shaft; collapsed a flue; and went into Cairo with nine feet of water in the hold—may have been more, may have been less. I remember it as if it were yesterday. The men lost their heads with terror. They painted the mare blue, in sight of town, and threw the preacher overboard, or we should not have arrived at all. The preacher was fished out and saved. He acknowledged, himself, that he had been to blame. I remember it all, as if it were yesterday.'

That this combination—of preacher and gray mare—should breed calamity, seems strange, and at first glance unbelievable; but the fact is fortified by so much unassailable proof that to doubt is to dishonor reason. I myself remember a case where a captain was warned by numerous friends against taking a gray mare and a preacher with him, but persisted in his purpose in spite of all that could be said; and the same day—it may have been the next, and some say it was, though I think it was the same day—he got drunk and fell down the hatchway, and was borne to his home a corpse. This is literally true.

No vestige of Hat Island is left now; every shred of it is washed away. I do not even remember what part of the river it used to be in, except that it was between St. Louis and Cairo somewhere. It was a bad region— all around and about Hat Island, in early days. A farmer who lived on the Illinois shore there, said that twenty-nine steamboats had left their bones strung along within sight from his house. Between St. Louis and Cairo the steamboat wrecks average one to the mile;—two hundred wrecks, altogether.

I could recognize big changes from Commerce down. Beaver Dam Rock was out in the middle of the river now, and throwing a prodigious 'break;' it used to be close to the shore, and boats went down outside of it. A big island that used to be away out in mid-river, has retired to the Missouri shore, and boats do not go near it any more. The island called Jacket Pattern is whittled down to a wedge now, and is booked for early destruction. Goose Island is all gone but a little dab the size of a steamboat. The perilous 'Graveyard,' among whose numberless wrecks we used to pick our way so slowly and gingerly, is far away from the channel now, and a terror to nobody. One of the islands formerly called the Two Sisters is gone entirely; the other, which used to lie close to the Illinois shore, is now on the Missouri side, a mile away; it is joined solidly to the shore, and it takes a sharp eye to see where the seam is—but it is Illinois ground yet, and the people who live on it have to ferry themselves over and work the Illinois roads and pay Illinois taxes: singular state of things!

Near the mouth of the river several islands were missing— washed away. Cairo was still there—easily visible across the long, flat point upon whose further verge it stands; but we had to steam a long way around to get to it. Night fell as we were going out of the 'Upper River' and meeting the floods of the Ohio. We dashed along without anxiety; for the hidden rock which used to lie right in the way has moved up stream a long distance out of the channel; or rather, about one county has gone into the river from the Missouri point, and the Cairo point has 'made down' and added to its long tongue of territory correspondingly. The Mississippi is a just and equitable river; it never tumbles one man's farm overboard without building a new farm just like it for that man's neighbor. This keeps down hard feelings.

Going into Cairo, we came near killing a steamboat which paid no attention to our whistle and then tried to cross our bows. By doing some strong backing, we saved him; which was a great loss, for he would have made good literature.

Cairo is a brisk town now; and is substantially built, and has a city look about it which is in noticeable contrast to its former estate, as per Mr. Dickens's portrait of it. However, it was already building with bricks when I had seen it last—which was when Colonel (now General) Grant was drilling his first command there. Uncle Mumford says the libraries and Sunday-schools have done a good work in Cairo, as well as the brick masons. Cairo has a heavy railroad and river trade, and her situation at the junction of the two great rivers is so advantageous that she cannot well help prospering.

When I turned out, in the morning, we had passed Columbus, Kentucky, and were approaching Hickman, a pretty town, perched on a handsome hill. Hickman is in a rich tobacco region, and formerly enjoyed a great and lucrative trade in that staple, collecting it there in her warehouses from a large area of country and shipping it by boat; but Uncle Mumford says she built a railway to facilitate this commerce a little more, and he thinks it facilitated it the wrong way—took the bulk of the trade out of her hands by 'collaring it along the line without gathering it at her doors.'

Chapter 26 Under Fire

TALK began to run upon the war now, for we were getting down into the upper edge of the former battle-stretch by this time. Columbus was just behind us, so there was a good deal said about the famous battle of Belmont. Several of the boat's officers had seen active service in the Mississippi war-fleet. I gathered that they found themselves sadly out of their element in that kind of business at first, but afterward got accustomed to it, reconciled to it, and more or less at home in it. One of our pilots had his first war experience in the Belmont fight, as a pilot on a boat in the Confederate service. I had often had a curiosity to know how a green hand might feel, in his maiden battle, perched all solitary and alone on high in a pilot house, a target for Tom, Dick and Harry, and nobody at his elbow to shame him from showing the white feather when matters grew hot and perilous around him; so, to me his story was valuable—it filled a gap for me which all histories had left till that time empty.

THE PILOT'S FIRST BATTLE

He said—

It was the 7th of November. The fight began at seven in the morning. I was on the 'R. H. W. Hill.' Took over a load of troops from Columbus. Came back, and took over a battery of artillery. My partner said he was going to see the fight; wanted me to go along. I said, no, I wasn't anxious, I would look at it from the pilot-house. He said I was a coward, and left.

That fight was an awful sight. General Cheatham made his men strip their coats off and throw them in a pile, and said, 'Now follow me to hell or victory!' I heard him say that from the pilot-house; and then he galloped in, at the head of his troops. Old General Pillow, with his white hair, mounted on a white horse, sailed in, too, leading his troops as lively as a boy. By and by the Federals chased the rebels back, and here they came! tearing along, everybody for himself and Devil take the hindmost! and down under the bank they scrambled, and took shelter. I was sitting with my legs hanging out of the pilot-house window. All at once I noticed a whizzing sound passing my ear. Judged it was a bullet. I didn't stop to think about anything, I just tilted over backwards and landed on the floor, and staid there. The balls came booming around. Three cannon-balls went through the chimney; one ball took off the corner of the pilot-house; shells were screaming and bursting all around. Mighty warm times—I wished I hadn't come. I lay there on the pilot-house floor, while the shots came faster and faster. I crept in behind the big stove, in the middle of the pilot-house. Presently a minie-ball came through the stove, and just grazed my head, and cut my hat. I judged it was time to go away from there. The captain was on the roof with a red-headed major from Memphis—a fine-looking man. I heard him say he wanted to leave here, but 'that pilot is killed.' I crept over to the starboard side to pull the bell to set her back; raised up and took a look, and I saw about fifteen shot holes through the window panes; had come so lively I hadn't noticed them. I glanced out on the water, and the spattering shot were like a hailstorm. I thought best to get out of that place. I went down the pilot-house guy, head first—not feet first but head first—slid down—before I struck the deck, the captain said we must leave there. So I climbed up the guy and got on the floor again. About that time, they collared my partner and were bringing him up to the pilot-house between two soldiers. Somebody had said I was killed. He put his head in and saw me on the floor reaching for the backing bells. He said, 'Oh,

262 *Life On The Mississippi*

hell, he ain't shot,' and jerked away from the men who had him by the collar, and ran below. We were there until three o'clock in the afternoon, and then got away all right.

The next time I saw my partner, I said, 'Now, come out, be honest, and tell me the truth. Where did you go when you went to see that battle?' He says, 'I went down in the hold.'

All through that fight I was scared nearly to death. I hardly knew anything, I was so frightened; but you see, nobody knew that but me. Next day General Polk sent for me, and praised me for my bravery and gallant conduct. I never said anything, I let it go at that. I judged it wasn't so, but it was not for me to contradict a general officer.

Pretty soon after that I was sick, and used up, and had to go off to the Hot Springs. When there, I got a good many letters from commanders saying they wanted me to come back. I declined, because I wasn't well enough or strong enough; but I kept still, and kept the reputation I had made.

A plain story, straightforwardly told; but Mumford told me that that pilot had 'gilded that scare of his, in spots;' that his subsequent career in the war was proof of it.

We struck down through the chute of Island No. 8, and I went below and fell into conversation with a passenger, a handsome man, with easy carriage and an intelligent face. We were approaching Island No. 10, a place so celebrated during the war. This gentleman's home was on the main shore in its neighborhood. I had some talk with him about the war times; but presently the discourse fell upon 'feuds,' for in no part of the South has the vendetta flourished more briskly, or held out longer between warring families, than in this particular region. This gentleman said—

'There's been more than one feud around here, in old times, but I reckon the worst one was between the Darnells and the Watsons. Nobody don't know now what the first quarrel was about, it's so long ago; the Darnells and the Watsons don't know, if there's any of them living, which I don't think there is. Some says it was about a horse or a cow— anyway, it was a little matter; the money in it wasn't of no consequence—none in the world—both families was rich. The thing could have been fixed up, easy enough; but no, that wouldn't do. Rough words had been passed; and so, nothing but blood could fix it up after that. That horse or cow, whichever it was, cost sixty years of killing and crippling! Every year or so somebody was shot, on one side or the other; and as fast as one generation was laid out, their sons took up the feud and kept it a-going. And it's just as I say; they went on shooting each other, year in and year out—making a kind of a religion of it, you see —till they'd done forgot, long ago, what it was all about. Wherever a Darnell caught a Watson, or a Watson caught a Darnell, one of 'em was going to get hurt—only question was, which of them got the drop on the other. They'd shoot one another down, right in the presence of the family. They didn't hunt for each other, but when they happened to meet, they puffed and begun. Men would shoot boys, boys would shoot men. A man shot a boy twelve years old—happened on him in the woods, and didn't give him no chance. If he HAD 'a' given him a chance, the boy'd 'a' shot him. Both families belonged to the same church (everybody around here is religious); through all this fifty or sixty years' fuss, both tribes was there every Sunday, to worship. They lived each side of the line, and the church was at a landing called Compromise. Half the church and half the aisle was in Kentucky, the other half in Tennessee. Sundays you'd see the families drive up, all in their Sunday clothes, men, women, and children, and file up the aisle, and set down, quiet and orderly, one lot on the Tennessee side of the church and the other on the Kentucky side; and the men and boys would lean their guns up against the wall, handy, and then all hands would join in with the prayer and praise; though they say the man next the aisle didn't kneel down, along with the rest of the family; kind of stood guard. I don't know; never was at that church in my life; but I remember that that's what used to be said.

'Twenty or twenty-five years ago, one of the feud families caught a young man of nineteen out and killed him. Don't remember whether it was the Darnells and Watsons, or one of the other feuds; but anyway, this young man rode up— steamboat laying there at the time—and the first thing he saw was a whole gang of the enemy. He jumped down behind a wood-pile, but they rode around and begun on him, he firing back, and they galloping and cavorting and yelling and banging away with all their might. Think he wounded a couple of them; but they closed in on him and chased him into the river; and as he swum along down stream, they followed along the bank and kept on shooting at him; and when he struck shore he was dead. Windy Marshall told me about it. He saw it. He was captain of the boat.

'Years ago, the Darnells was so thinned out that the old man and his two sons concluded they'd leave the country. They started to take steamboat just above No. 10; but the Watsons got wind of it; and they arrived just as the two young Darnells was walking up the companion-way with their wives on their arms. The fight begun then, and they never got no further— both of them killed. After that, old Darnell got into trouble with the man that run the ferry, and the ferry-man got the worst of it— and died. But his friends shot old Darnell through and through—filled him full of bullets, and ended him.'

The country gentleman who told me these things had been reared in ease and comfort, was a man of good parts, and was college bred. His loose grammar was the fruit of careless habit, not ignorance. This habit among educated men in the West is not universal, but it is prevalent— prevalent in the towns, certainly, if not in the cities; and to a degree which one cannot help noticing, and marveling at. I heard a Westerner who would be accounted a highly educated man in any country, say 'never mind, it DON'T MAKE NO DIFFERENCE, anyway.' A life-long resident who was present heard it, but it made no impression upon her. She was able to recall the fact afterward, when reminded of it; but she confessed that the words had not grated upon her ear at the time—a confession which suggests that if educated people can hear such blasphemous grammar, from such a source, and be unconscious of the deed, the crime must be tolerably common—so common that the general ear has become dulled by familiarity with it, and is no longer alert, no longer sensitive to such affronts.

No one in the world speaks blemishless grammar; no one has ever written it—NO one, either in the world or out of it (taking the Scriptures for evidence on the latter point); therefore it would not be fair to exact grammatical perfection from the peoples of the Valley; but they and all other peoples may justly be required to refrain from KNOWINGLY and PURPOSELY debauching their grammar.

I found the river greatly changed at Island No. 10. The island which I remembered was some three miles long and a quarter of a mile wide, heavily timbered, and lay near the Kentucky shore—within two hundred yards of it, I should say. Now, however, one had to hunt for it with a spy-glass. Nothing was

left of it but an insignificant little tuft, and this was no longer near the Kentucky shore; it was clear over against the opposite shore, a mile away. In war times the island had been an important place, for it commanded the situation; and, being heavily fortified, there was no getting by it. It lay between the upper and lower divisions of the Union forces, and kept them separate, until a junction was finally effected across the Missouri neck of land; but the island being itself joined to that neck now, the wide river is without obstruction.

In this region the river passes from Kentucky into Tennessee, back into Missouri, then back into Kentucky, and thence into Tennessee again. So a mile or two of Missouri sticks over into Tennessee.

The town of New Madrid was looking very unwell; but otherwise unchanged from its former condition and aspect. Its blocks of frame-houses were still grouped in the same old flat plain, and environed by the same old forests. It was as tranquil as formerly, and apparently had neither grown nor diminished in size. It was said that the recent high water had invaded it and damaged its looks. This was surprising news; for in low water the river bank is very high there (fifty feet), and in my day an overflow had always been considered an impossibility. This present flood of 1882 will doubtless be celebrated in the river's history for several generations before a deluge of like magnitude shall be seen. It put all the unprotected low lands under water, from Cairo to the mouth; it broke down the levees in a great many places, on both sides of the river; and in some regions south, when the flood was at its highest, the Mississippi was SEVENTY MILES wide! a number of lives were lost, and the destruction of property was fearful. The crops were destroyed, houses washed away, and shelterless men and cattle forced to take refuge on scattering elevations here and there in field and forest, and wait in peril and suffering until the boats put in commission by the national and local governments and by newspaper enterprise could come and rescue them. The properties of multitudes of people were under water for months, and the poorer ones must have starved by the hundred if succor had not been promptly afforded*. The water had been falling during a considerable time now, yet as a rule we found the banks still under water.

Chapter 27 Some Imported Articles

WE met two steamboats at New Madrid. Two steamboats in sight at once! an infrequent spectacle now in the lonesome Mississippi. The loneliness of this solemn, stupendous flood is impressive—and depressing. League after league, and still league after league, it pours its chocolate tide along, between its solid forest walls, its almost untenanted shores, with seldom a sail or a moving object of any kind to disturb the surface and break the monotony of the blank, watery solitude; and so the day goes, the night comes, and again the day—and still the same, night after night and day after day—majestic, unchanging sameness of serenity, repose, tranquillity, lethargy, vacancy—symbol of eternity, realization of the heaven pictured by priest and prophet, and longed for by the good and thoughtless!

Immediately after the war of 1812, tourists began to come to America, from England; scattering ones at first, then a sort of procession of them—a procession which kept up its plodding, patient march through the land during many, many years.

---

* For a detailed and interesting description of the great flood, written on board of the New Orleans TIMES-DEMOCRAT'S relief-boat, see Appendix A

Each tourist took notes, and went home and published a book—a book which was usually calm, truthful, reasonable, kind; but which seemed just the reverse to our tender-footed progenitors. A glance at these tourist-books shows us that in certain of its aspects the Mississippi has undergone no change since those strangers visited it, but remains to-day about as it was then. The emotions produced in those foreign breasts by these aspects were not all formed on one pattern, of course; they HAD to be various, along at first, because the earlier tourists were obliged to originate their emotions, whereas in older countries one can always borrow emotions from one's predecessors. And, mind you, emotions are among the toughest things in the world to manufacture out of whole cloth; it is easier to manufacture seven facts than one emotion. Captain Basil Hall. R.N., writing fifty-five years ago, says—

'Here I caught the first glimpse of the object I had so long wished to behold, and felt myself amply repaid at that moment for all the trouble I had experienced in coming so far; and stood looking at the river flowing past till it was too dark to distinguish anything. But it was not till I had visited the same spot a dozen times, that I came to a right comprehension of the grandeur of the scene.'

Following are Mrs. Trollope's emotions. She is writing a few months later in the same year, 1827, and is coming in at the mouth of the Mississippi—

'The first indication of our approach to land was the appearance of this mighty river pouring forth its muddy mass of waters, and mingling with the deep blue of the Mexican Gulf. I never beheld a scene so utterly desolate as this entrance of the Mississippi. Had Dante seen it, he might have drawn images of another Borgia from its horrors. One only object rears itself above the eddying waters; this is the mast of a vessel long since wrecked in attempting to cross the bar, and it still stands, a dismal witness of the destruction that has been, and a boding prophet of that which is to come.'

Emotions of Hon. Charles Augustus Murray (near St. Louis), seven years later—

'It is only when you ascend the mighty current for fifty or a hundred miles, and use the eye of imagination as well as that of nature, that you begin to understand all his might and majesty. You see him fertilizing a boundless valley, bearing along in his course the trophies of his thousand victories over the shattered forest—here carrying away large masses of soil with all their growth, and there forming islands, destined at some future period to be the residence of man; and while indulging in this prospect, it is then time for reflection to suggest that the current before you has flowed through two or three thousand miles, and has yet to travel one thousand three hundred more before reaching its ocean destination.'

Receive, now, the emotions of Captain Marryat, R.N. author of the sea tales, writing in 1837, three years after Mr. Murray—

'Never, perhaps, in the records of nations, was there an instance of a century of such unvarying and unmitigated crime as is to be collected from the history of the turbulent and blood-stained Mississippi. The stream itself appears as if appropriate for the deeds which have been committed. It is not like most rivers, beautiful to the sight, bestowing fertility in its course; not one that the eye loves to dwell upon as it sweeps along, nor can you wander upon its banks, or trust yourself without danger to its stream. It is a furious, rapid, desolating torrent, loaded with alluvial soil; and few of those who are

received into its waters ever rise again*, or can support themselves long upon its surface without assistance from some friendly log. It contains the coarsest and most uneatable of fish, such as the cat-fish and such genus, and as you descend, its banks are occupied with the fetid alligator, while the panther basks at its edge in the cane-brakes, almost impervious to man. Pouring its impetuous waters through wild tracks covered with trees of little value except for firewood, it sweeps down whole forests in its course, which disappear in tumultuous confusion, whirled away by the stream now loaded with the masses of soil which nourished their roots, often blocking up and changing for a time the channel of the river, which, as if in anger at its being opposed, inundates and devastates the whole country round; and as soon as it forces its way through its former channel, plants in every direction the uprooted monarchs of the forest (upon whose branches the bird will never again perch, or the raccoon, the opossum, or the squirrel climb) as traps to the adventurous navigators of its waters by steam, who, borne down upon these concealed dangers which pierce through the planks, very often have not time to steer for and gain the shore before they sink to the bottom. There are no pleasing associations connected with the great common sewer of the Western America, which pours out its mud into the Mexican Gulf, polluting the clear blue sea for many miles beyond its mouth. It is a river of desolation; and instead of reminding you, like other beautiful rivers, of an angel which has descended for the benefit of man, you imagine it a devil, whose energies have been only overcome by the wonderful power of steam.'

It is pretty crude literature for a man accustomed to handling a pen; still, as a panorama of the emotions sent weltering through this noted visitor's breast by the aspect and traditions of the 'great common sewer,' it has a value. A value, though marred in the matter of statistics by inaccuracies; for the catfish is a plenty good enough fish for anybody, and there are no panthers that are 'impervious to man.'

Later still comes Alexander Mackay, of the Middle Temple, Barrister at Law, with a better digestion, and no catfish dinner aboard, and feels as follows—

'The Mississippi! It was with indescribable emotions that I first felt myself afloat upon its waters. How often in my schoolboy dreams, and in my waking visions afterwards, had my imagination pictured to itself the lordly stream, rolling with tumultuous current through the boundless region to which it has given its name, and gathering into itself, in its course to the ocean, the tributary waters of almost every latitude in the temperate zone! Here it was then in its reality, and I, at length, steaming against its tide. I looked upon it with that reverence with which everyone must regard a great feature of external nature.'

So much for the emotions. The tourists, one and all, remark upon the deep, brooding loneliness and desolation of the vast river. Captain Basil Hall, who saw it at flood-stage, says—

'Sometimes we passed along distances of twenty or thirty miles without seeing a single habitation. An artist, in search of hints for a painting of the deluge, would here have found them in abundance.'

The first shall be last, etc. just two hundred years ago, the old

---

* There was a foolish superstition of some little prevalence in that day, that the Mississippi would neither buoy up a swimmer, nor permit a drowned person's body to rise to the surface.

original first and gallantest of all the foreign tourists, pioneer, head of the procession, ended his weary and tedious discovery-voyage down the solemn stretches of the great river—La Salle, whose name will last as long as the river itself shall last. We quote from Mr. Parkman—

'And now they neared their journey's end. On the sixth of April, the river divided itself into three broad channels. La Salle followed that of the west, and D'Autray that of the east; while Tonty took the middle passage. As he drifted down the turbid current, between the low and marshy shores, the brackish water changed to brine, and the breeze grew fresh with the salt breath of the sea. Then the broad bosom of the great Gulf opened on his sight, tossing its restless billows, limitless, voiceless, lonely as when born of chaos, without a sail, without a sign of life.'

Then, on a spot of solid ground, La Salle reared a column 'bearing the arms of France; the Frenchmen were mustered under arms; and while the New England Indians and their squaws looked on in wondering silence, they chanted the TE DEUM, THE EXAUDIAT, and the DOMINE SALVUM FAC REGEM.'

Then, whilst the musketry volleyed and rejoicing shouts burst forth, the victorious discoverer planted the column, and made proclamation in a loud voice, taking formal possession of the river and the vast countries watered by it, in the name of the King. The column bore this inscription—

LOUIS LE GRAND, ROY DE FRANCE ET DE NAVARRE, REGNE; LE NEUVIEME AVRIL, 1682.

New Orleans intended to fittingly celebrate, this present year, the bicentennial anniversary of this illustrious event; but when the time came, all her energies and surplus money were required in other directions, for the flood was upon the land then, making havoc and devastation everywhere.

Chapter 28 Uncle Mumford Unloads

ALL day we swung along down the river, and had the stream almost wholly to ourselves. Formerly, at such a stage of the water, we should have passed acres of lumber rafts, and dozens of big coal barges; also occasional little trading-scows, peddling along from farm to farm, with the peddler's family on board; possibly, a random scow, bearing a humble Hamlet and Co. on an itinerant dramatic trip. But these were all absent. Far along in the day, we saw one steamboat; just one, and no more. She was lying at rest in the shade, within the wooded mouth of the Obion River. The spy-glass revealed the fact that she was named for me —or HE was named for me, whichever you prefer. As this was the first time I had ever encountered this species of honor, it seems excusable to mention it, and at the same time call the attention of the authorities to the tardiness of my recognition of it.

Noted a big change in the river, at Island 21. It was a very large island, and used to be out toward mid-stream; but it is joined fast to the main shore now, and has retired from business as an island.

As we approached famous and formidable Plum Point, darkness fell, but that was nothing to shudder about—in these modern times. For now the national government has turned the Mississippi into a sort of two- thousand-mile torchlight procession. In the head of every crossing, and in the foot of every crossing, the government has set up a clear-burning lamp. You are never entirely in the dark, now; there is always a beacon in sight, either before you, or behind you, or abreast. One might almost say that lamps have been squandered there. Dozens of crossings are lighted which were not shoal when they were created, and have never been shoal since; crossings so plain, too, and also so straight, that a steamboat can take herself through them without any help, after she has been through once. Lamps in such places are of course not wasted; it is much more convenient and comfortable for a pilot to hold on them than on a spread of formless blackness that won't stay still; and money is saved to the boat, at the same time, for she can of course make more miles with her rudder amidships than she can with it squared across her stern and holding her back.

But this thing has knocked the romance out of piloting, to a large extent. It, and some other things together, have knocked all the romance out of it. For instance, the peril from snags is not now what it once was. The government's snag-boats go patrolling up and down, in these matter-of-fact days, pulling the river's teeth; they have rooted out all the old clusters which made many localities so formidable; and they allow no new ones to collect. Formerly, if your boat got away from you, on a black night, and broke for the woods, it was an anxious time with you; so was it also, when you were groping your way through solidified darkness in a narrow chute; but all that is changed now—you flash out your electric light, transform night into day in the twinkling of an eye, and your perils and anxieties are at an end. Horace Bixby and George Ritchie have charted the crossings and laid out the courses by compass; they have invented a lamp to go with the chart, and have patented the whole. With these helps, one may run in the fog now, with considerable security, and with a confidence unknown in the old days.

With these abundant beacons, the banishment of snags, plenty of daylight in a box and ready to be turned on whenever needed, and a chart and compass to fight the fog with, piloting, at a good stage of water, is now nearly as safe and simple as driving stage, and is hardly more than three times as romantic.

And now in these new days, these days of infinite change, the Anchor Line have raised the captain above the pilot by giving him the bigger wages of the two. This was going far, but they have not stopped there. They have decreed that the pilot shall remain at his post, and stand his watch clear through, whether the boat be under way or tied up to the shore. We, that were once the aristocrats of the river, can't go to bed now, as we used to do, and sleep while a hundred tons of freight are lugged aboard; no, we must sit in the pilot-house; and keep awake, too. Verily we are being treated like a parcel of mates and engineers. The Government has taken away the romance of our calling; the Company has taken away its state and dignity.

Plum Point looked as it had always looked by night, with the exception that now there were beacons to mark the crossings, and also a lot of other lights on the Point and along its shore; these latter glinting from the fleet of the United States River Commission, and from a village which the officials have built on the land for offices and for the employees of the service. The military engineers of the Commission have taken upon their shoulders the job of making the Mississippi over again — a job transcended in size by only the original job of creating it. They are building wing-dams here and there, to deflect the current; and dikes to confine it in narrower bounds; and other dikes to make it stay there; and for unnumbered miles along the Mississippi, they are felling the timber-front for fifty yards back, with the purpose of shaving the bank down to low-water mark with the slant of a house roof, and ballasting it with stones; and in many places they have protected the wasting shores with rows of piles. One who knows the Mississippi will promptly aver— not aloud, but to himself—that ten thousand River Commissions, with the mines of the world at their back, cannot tame that lawless stream, cannot curb it or confine it, cannot say to it, Go here, or Go there, and make it obey; cannot save a shore which it has sentenced; cannot bar its path with an obstruction which it will not tear down, dance over, and laugh at. But a discreet man will not put these things into spoken words; for the West Point engineers have not their superiors anywhere; they know all that can be known of their abstruse science; and so, since they conceive that they can fetter and handcuff that river and boss him, it is but wisdom for the unscientific man to keep still, lie low, and wait till they do it. Captain Eads, with his jetties, has done a work at the mouth of the Mississippi which seemed clearly impossible; so we do not feel full confidence now to prophesy against like impossibilities. Otherwise one would pipe out and say the Commission might as well bully the comets in their courses and undertake to make them behave, as try to bully the Mississippi into right and reasonable conduct.

I consulted Uncle Mumford concerning this and cognate matters; and I give here the result, stenographically reported, and therefore to be relied on as being full and correct; except that I have here and there left out remarks which were addressed to the men, such as 'where in blazes are you going with that barrel now?' and which seemed to me to break the flow of the written statement, without compensating by adding to its information or its clearness. Not that I have ventured to strike out all such interjections; I have removed only those which were obviously irrelevant; wherever one occurred which I felt any question about, I have judged it safest to let it remain.

UNCLE MUMFORD'S IMPRESSIONS

Uncle Mumford said—

'As long as I have been mate of a steamboat—thirty years—I have watched this river and studied it. Maybe I could have learnt more about it at West Point, but if I believe it I wish I may be WHAT ARE YOU SUCKING YOUR FINGERS THERE FOR ?—COLLAR THAT KAG OF NAILS! Four years at West Point, and plenty of books and schooling, will learn a man a good deal, I reckon, but it won't learn him the river. You turn one of those little European rivers over to this Commission, with its hard bottom and clear water, and it would just be a holiday job for them to wall it, and pile it, and dike it, and tame it down, and boss it around, and make it go wherever they wanted it to, and stay where they put it, and do just as they said, every time. But this ain't that kind of a river. They have started in here with big confidence, and the best intentions in the world; but they are going to get left. What does Ecclesiastes vii. 13 say? Says enough to knock THEIR little game galley-west, don't it? Now you look at their methods once. There at Devil's Island, in the Upper River, they wanted the water to go one way, the water wanted to go another. So they put up a stone wall. But what does the river care for a stone wall? When it got ready, it just bulged through it. Maybe they can build another that will stay; that is, up there—but not down here they can't. Down here in the Lower River, they drive some pegs to turn the water away from the shore and stop it from slicing off the bank; very well, don't it go straight over and cut somebody else's bank? Certainly. Are

266 *Life On The Mississippi*

they going to peg all the banks? Why, they could buy ground and build a new Mississippi cheaper. They are pegging Bulletin Tow-head now. It won't do any good. If the river has got a mortgage on that island, it will foreclose, sure, pegs or no pegs. Away down yonder, they have driven two rows of piles straight through the middle of a dry bar half a mile long, which is forty foot out of the water when the river is low. What do you reckon that is for? If I know, I wish I may land in-HUMP YOURSELF, YOU SON OF AN UNDERTAKER!—OUT WITH THAT COAL-OIL, NOW, LIVELY, LIVELY! And just look at what they are trying to do down there at Milliken's Bend. There's been a cut-off in that section, and Vicksburg is left out in the cold. It's a country town now. The river strikes in below it; and a boat can't go up to the town except in high water. Well, they are going to build wing-dams in the bend opposite the foot of 103, and throw the water over and cut off the foot of the island and plow down into an old ditch where the river used to be in ancient times; and they think they can persuade the water around that way, and get it to strike in above Vicksburg, as it used to do, and fetch the town back into the world again. That is, they are going to take this whole Mississippi, and twist it around and make it run several miles UP STREAM. Well you've got to admire men that deal in ideas of that size and can tote them around without crutches; but you haven't got to believe they can DO such miracles, have you! And yet you ain't absolutely obliged to believe they can't. I reckon the safe way, where a man can afford it, is to copper the operation, and at the same time buy enough property in Vicksburg to square you up in case they win. Government is doing a deal for the Mississippi, now—spending loads of money on her. When there used to be four thousand steamboats and ten thousand acres of coal-barges, and rafts and trading scows, there wasn't a lantern from St. Paul to New Orleans, and the snags were thicker than bristles on a hog's back; and now when there's three dozen steamboats and nary barge or raft, Government has snatched out all the snags, and lit up the shores like Broadway, and a boat's as safe on the river as she'd be in heaven. And I reckon that by the time there ain't any boats left at all, the Commission will have the old thing all reorganized, and dredged out, and fenced in, and tidied up, to a degree that will make navigation just simply perfect, and absolutely safe and profitable; and all the days will be Sundays, and all the mates will be Sunday-school su-WHAT-IN-THE-NATION-YOU-FOOLING-AROUND-THERE-FOR, YOU SONS OF UNRIGHTEOUSNESS, HEIRS OF PERDITION! GOING TO BE A YEAR GETTING THAT HOGSHEAD ASHORE?'

During our trip to New Orleans and back, we had many conversations with river men, planters, journalists, and officers of the River Commission— with conflicting and confusing results. To wit:—

1. Some believed in the Commission's scheme to arbitrarily and permanently confine (and thus deepen) the channel, preserve threatened shores, etc.

2. Some believed that the Commission's money ought to be spent only on building and repairing the great system of levees.

3. Some believed that the higher you build your levee, the higher the river's bottom will rise; and that consequently the levee system is a mistake.

4. Some believed in the scheme to relieve the river, in flood-time, by turning its surplus waters off into Lake Borgne, etc.

5. Some believed in the scheme of northern lake-reservoirs to replenish the Mississippi in low-water seasons.

Wherever you find a man down there who believes in one of these theories you may turn to the next man and frame your talk upon the hypothesis that he does not believe in that theory; and after you have had experience, you do not take this course doubtfully, or hesitatingly, but with the confidence of a dying murderer—converted one, I mean. For you will have come to know, with a deep and restful certainty, that you are not going to meet two people sick of the same theory, one right after the other. No, there will always be one or two with the other diseases along between. And as you proceed, you will find out one or two other things. You will find out that there is no distemper of the lot but is contagious; and you cannot go where it is without catching it. You may vaccinate yourself with deterrent facts as much as you please—it will do no good; it will seem to 'take,' but it doesn't; the moment you rub against any one of those theorists, make up your mind that it is time to hang out your yellow flag.

Yes, you are his sure victim: yet his work is not all to your hurt— only part of it; for he is like your family physician, who comes and cures the mumps, and leaves the scarlet-fever behind. If your man is a Lake-Borgne-relief theorist, for instance, he will exhale a cloud of deadly facts and statistics which will lay you out with that disease, sure; but at the same time he will cure you of any other of the five theories that may have previously got into your system.

I have had all the five; and had them 'bad;' but ask me not, in mournful numbers, which one racked me hardest, or which one numbered the biggest sick list, for I do not know. In truth, no one can answer the latter question. Mississippi Improvement is a mighty topic, down yonder. Every man on the river banks, south of Cairo, talks about it every day, during such moments as he is able to spare from talking about the war; and each of the several chief theories has its host of zealous partisans; but, as I have said, it is not possible to determine which cause numbers the most recruits.

All were agreed upon one point, however: if Congress would make a sufficient appropriation, a colossal benefit would result. Very well; since then the appropriation has been made—possibly a sufficient one, certainly not too large a one. Let us hope that the prophecy will be amply fulfilled.

One thing will be easily granted by the reader; that an opinion from Mr. Edward Atkinson, upon any vast national commercial matter, comes as near ranking as authority, as can the opinion of any individual in the Union. What he has to say about Mississippi River Improvement will be found in the Appendix*.

Sometimes, half a dozen figures will reveal, as with a lightning-flash, the importance of a subject which ten thousand labored words, with the same purpose in view, had left at last but dim and uncertain. Here is a case of the sort—paragraph from the 'Cincinnati Commercial'—

'The towboat "Jos. B. Williams" is on her way to New Orleans with a tow of thirty-two barges, containing six hundred thousand bushels (seventy- six pounds to the bushel) of coal exclusive of her own fuel, being the largest tow ever taken to New Orleans or anywhere else in the world. Her freight bill, at 3 cents a bushel, amounts to $18,000. It would take eighteen

* See Appendix B.

hundred cars, of three hundred and thirty-three bushels to the car, to transport this amount of coal. At $10 per ton, or $100 per car, which would be a fair price for the distance by rail, the freight bill would amount to $180,000, or $162,000 more by rail than by river. The tow will be taken from Pittsburg to New Orleans in fourteen or fifteen days. It would take one hundred trains of eighteen cars to the train to transport this one tow of six hundred thousand bushels of coal, and even if it made the usual speed of fast freight lines, it would take one whole summer to put it through by rail.'

When a river in good condition can enable one to save $162,000 and a whole summer's time, on a single cargo, the wisdom of taking measures to keep the river in good condition is made plain to even the uncommercial mind.

Chapter 29 A Few Specimen Bricks

WE passed through the Plum Point region, turned Craighead's Point, and glided unchallenged by what was once the formidable Fort Pillow, memorable because of the massacre perpetrated there during the war. Massacres are sprinkled with some frequency through the histories of several Christian nations, but this is almost the only one that can be found in American history; perhaps it is the only one which rises to a size correspondent to that huge and somber title. We have the 'Boston Massacre,' where two or three people were killed; but we must bunch Anglo-Saxon history together to find the fellow to the Fort Pillow tragedy; and doubtless even then we must travel back to the days and the performances of Coeur de Lion, that fine 'hero,' before we accomplish it.

More of the river's freaks. In times past, the channel used to strike above Island 37, by Brandywine Bar, and down towards Island 39. Afterward, changed its course and went from Brandywine down through Vogelman's chute in the Devil's Elbow, to Island 39—part of this course reversing the old order; the river running UP four or five miles, instead of down, and cutting off, throughout, some fifteen miles of distance. This in 1876. All that region is now called Centennial Island.

There is a tradition that Island 37 was one of the principal abiding places of the once celebrated 'Murel's Gang.' This was a colossal combination of robbers, horse-thieves, negro-stealers, and counterfeiters, engaged in business along the river some fifty or sixty years ago. While our journey across the country towards St. Louis was in progress we had had no end of Jesse James and his stirring history; for he had just been assassinated by an agent of the Governor of Missouri, and was in consequence occupying a good deal of space in the newspapers. Cheap histories of him were for sale by train boys. According to these, he was the most marvelous creature of his kind that had ever existed. It was a mistake. Murel was his equal in boldness; in pluck; in rapacity; in cruelty, brutality, heartlessness, treachery, and in general and comprehensive vileness and shamelessness; and very much his superior in some larger aspects. James was a retail rascal; Murel, wholesale. James's modest genius dreamed of no loftier flight than the planning of raids upon cars, coaches, and country banks; Murel projected negro insurrections and the capture of New Orleans; and furthermore, on occasion, this Murel could go into a pulpit and edify the congregation. What are James and his half-dozen vulgar rascals compared with this stately old-time criminal, with his sermons, his meditated insurrections and city-captures, and his majestic following of ten hundred men, sworn to do his evil will!

Here is a paragraph or two concerning this big operator, from a now forgotten book which was published half a century ago—

He appears to have been a most dexterous as well as consummate villain. When he traveled, his usual disguise was that of an itinerant preacher; and it is said that his discourses were very 'soul-moving'—interesting the hearers so much that they forgot to look after their horses, which were carried away by his confederates while he was preaching. But the stealing of horses in one State, and selling them in another, was but a small portion of their business; the most lucrative was the enticing slaves to run away from their masters, that they might sell them in another quarter. This was arranged as follows; they would tell a negro that if he would run away from his master, and allow them to sell him, he should receive a portion of the money paid for him, and that upon his return to them a second time they would send him to a free State, where he would be safe. The poor wretches complied with this request, hoping to obtain money and freedom; they would be sold to another master, and run away again, to their employers; sometimes they would be sold in this manner three or four times, until they had realized three or four thousand dollars by them; but as, after this, there was fear of detection, the usual custom was to get rid of the only witness that could be produced against them, which was the negro himself, by murdering him, and throwing his body into the Mississippi. Even if it was established that they had stolen a negro, before he was murdered, they were always prepared to evade punishment; for they concealed the negro who had run away, until he was advertised, and a reward offered to any man who would catch him. An advertisement of this kind warrants the person to take the property, if found. And then the negro becomes a property in trust, when, therefore, they sold the negro, it only became a breach of trust, not stealing; and for a breach of trust, the owner of the property can only have redress by a civil action, which was useless, as the damages were never paid. It may be inquired, how it was that Murel escaped Lynch law under such circumstances This will be easily understood when it is stated that he had MORE THAN A THOUSAND SWORN CONFEDERATES, all ready at a moment's notice to support any of the gang who might be in trouble. The names of all the principal confederates of Murel were obtained from himself, in a manner which I shall presently explain. The gang was composed of two classes: the Heads or Council, as they were called, who planned and concerted, but seldom acted; they amounted to about four hundred. The other class were the active agents, and were termed strikers, and amounted to about six hundred and fifty. These were the tools in the hands of the others; they ran all the risk, and received but a small portion of the money; they were in the power of the leaders of the gang, who would sacrifice them at any time by handing them over to justice, or sinking their bodies in the Mississippi. The general rendezvous of this gang of miscreants was on the Arkansas side of the river, where they concealed their negroes in the morasses and cane-brakes.

The depredations of this extensive combination were severely felt; but so well were their plans arranged, that although Murel, who was always active, was everywhere suspected, there was no proof to be obtained. It so happened, however, that a young man of the name of Stewart, who was looking after two slaves which Murel had decoyed away, fell in with him and obtained his confidence, took the oath, and was admitted into the gang as one of the General Council. By this means all was discovered; for Stewart turned traitor, although he had taken the oath, and having obtained every information, exposed the whole concern, the names of all the parties, and finally succeeded in bringing home sufficient evidence against

Murel, to procure his conviction and sentence to the Penitentiary (Murel was sentenced to fourteen years' imprisonment); so many people who were supposed to be honest, and bore a respectable name in the different States, were found to be among the list of the Grand Council as published by Stewart, that every attempt was made to throw discredit upon his assertions—his character was vilified, and more than one attempt was made to assassinate him. He was obliged to quit the Southern States in consequence. It is, however, now well ascertained to have been all true; and although some blame Mr. Stewart for having violated his oath, they no longer attempt to deny that his revelations were correct. I will quote one or two portions of Murel's confessions to Mr. Stewart, made to him when they were journeying together. I ought to have observed, that the ultimate intentions of Murel and his associates were, by his own account, on a very extended scale; having no less an object in view than RAISING THE BLACKS AGAINST THE WHITES, TAKING POSSESSION OF, AND PLUNDERING NEW ORLEANS, AND MAKING THEMSELVES POSSESSORS OF THE TERRITORY. The following are a few extracts:—

'I collected all my friends about New Orleans at one of our friends' houses in that place, and we sat in council three days before we got all our plans to our notion; we then determined to undertake the rebellion at every hazard, and make as many friends as we could for that purpose. Every man's business being assigned him, I started to Natchez on foot, having sold my horse in New Orleans,—with the intention of stealing another after I started. I walked four days, and no opportunity offered for me to get a horse. The fifth day, about twelve, I had become tired, and stopped at a creek to get some water and rest a little. While I was sitting on a log, looking down the road the way that I had come, a man came in sight riding on a good-looking horse. The very moment I saw him, I was determined to have his horse, if he was in the garb of a traveler. He rode up, and I saw from his equipage that he was a traveler. I arose and drew an elegant rifle pistol on him and ordered him to dismount. He did so, and I took his horse by the bridle and pointed down the creek, and ordered him to walk before me. He went a few hundred yards and stopped. I hitched his horse, and then made him undress himself, all to his shirt and drawers, and ordered him to turn his back to me. He said, 'If you are determined to kill me, let me have time to pray before I die,' I told him I had no time to hear him pray. He turned around and dropped on his knees, and I shot him through the back of the head. I ripped open his belly and took out his entrails, and sunk him in the creek. I then searched his pockets, and found four hundred dollars and thirty-seven cents, and a number of papers that I did not take time to examine. I sunk the pocket-book and papers and his hat, in the creek. His boots were brand-new, and fitted me genteelly; and I put them on and sunk my old shoes in the creek, to atone for them. I rolled up his clothes and put them into his portmanteau, as they were brand-new cloth of the best quality. I mounted as fine a horse as ever I straddled, and directed my course for Natchez in much better style than I had been for the last five days.

'Myself and a fellow by the name of Crenshaw gathered four good horses and started for Georgia. We got in company with a young South Carolinian just before we got to Cumberland Mountain, and Crenshaw soon knew all about his business. He had been to Tennessee to buy a drove of hogs, but when he got there pork was dearer than he calculated, and he declined purchasing. We concluded he was a prize. Crenshaw winked at me; I understood his idea. Crenshaw had traveled the road before, but I never had; we had traveled several miles on the mountain, when he passed near a great precipice; just before we passed it Crenshaw asked me for my whip, which had a pound of lead in the butt; I handed it to him, and he rode up by the side of the South Carolinian, and gave him a blow on the side of the head and tumbled him from his horse; we lit from our horses and fingered his pockets; we got twelve hundred and sixty-two dollars. Crenshaw said he knew a place to hide him, and he gathered him under his arms, and I by his feet, and conveyed him to a deep crevice in the brow of the precipice, and tumbled him into it, and he went out of sight; we then tumbled in his saddle, and took his horse with us, which was worth two hundred dollars.

'We were detained a few days, and during that time our friend went to a little village in the neighborhood and saw the negro advertised (a negro in our possession), and a description of the two men of whom he had been purchased, and giving his suspicions of the men. It was rather squally times, but any port in a storm: we took the negro that night on the bank of a creek which runs by the farm of our friend, and Crenshaw shot him through the head. We took out his entrails and sunk him in the creek.

'He had sold the other negro the third time on Arkansaw River for upwards of five hundred dollars; and then stole him and delivered him into the hand of his friend, who conducted him to a swamp, and veiled the tragic scene, and got the last gleanings and sacred pledge of secrecy; as a game of that kind will not do unless it ends in a mystery to all but the fraternity. He sold the negro, first and last, for nearly two thousand dollars, and then put him for ever out of the reach of all pursuers; and they can never graze him unless they can find the negro; and that they cannot do, for his carcass has fed many a tortoise and catfish before this time, and the frogs have sung this many a long day to the silent repose of his skeleton.'

We were approaching Memphis, in front of which city, and witnessed by its people, was fought the most famous of the river battles of the Civil War. Two men whom I had served under, in my river days, took part in that fight: Mr. Bixby, head pilot of the Union fleet, and Montgomery, Commodore of the Confederate fleet. Both saw a great deal of active service during the war, and achieved high reputations for pluck and capacity.

As we neared Memphis, we began to cast about for an excuse to stay with the 'Gold Dust' to the end of her course—Vicksburg. We were so pleasantly situated, that we did not wish to make a change. I had an errand of considerable importance to do at Napoleon, Arkansas, but perhaps I could manage it without quitting the 'Gold Dust.' I said as much; so we decided to stick to present quarters.

The boat was to tarry at Memphis till ten the next morning. It is a beautiful city, nobly situated on a commanding bluff overlooking the river. The streets are straight and spacious, though not paved in a way to incite distempered admiration. No, the admiration must be reserved for the town's sewerage system, which is called perfect; a recent reform, however, for it was just the other way, up to a few years ago—a reform resulting from the lesson taught by a desolating visitation of the yellow-fever. In those awful days the people were swept off by hundreds, by thousands; and so great was the reduction caused by flight and by death together, that the population was diminished three-fourths, and so remained for a time. Business stood nearly still, and the streets bore an empty Sunday aspect.

Here is a picture of Memphis, at that disastrous time, drawn by a German tourist who seems to have been an eye-witness of the scenes which he describes. It is from Chapter VII, of his book, just published, in Leipzig, 'Mississippi-Fahrten, von Ernst von Hesse-Warteg.'—

'In August the yellow-fever had reached its extremest height. Daily, hundreds fell a sacrifice to the terrible epidemic. The city was become a mighty graveyard, two-thirds of the population had deserted the place, and only the poor, the aged and the sick, remained behind, a sure prey for the insidious enemy. The houses were closed: little lamps burned in front of many—a sign that here death had entered. Often, several lay dead in a single house; from the windows hung black crape. The stores were shut up, for their owners were gone away or dead.

'Fearful evil! In the briefest space it struck down and swept away even the most vigorous victim. A slight indisposition, then an hour of fever, then the hideous delirium, then—the Yellow Death! On the street corners, and in the squares, lay sick men, suddenly overtaken by the disease; and even corpses, distorted and rigid. Food failed. Meat spoiled in a few hours in the fetid and pestiferous air, and turned black.

'Fearful clamors issue from many houses; then after a season they cease, and all is still: noble, self-sacrificing men come with the coffin, nail it up, and carry it away, to the graveyard. In the night stillness reigns. Only the physicians and the hearses hurry through the streets; and out of the distance, at intervals, comes the muffled thunder of the railway train, which with the speed of the wind, and as if hunted by furies, flies by the pest-ridden city without halting.'

But there is life enough there now. The population exceeds forty thousand and is augmenting, and trade is in a flourishing condition. We drove about the city; visited the park and the sociable horde of squirrels there; saw the fine residences, rose-clad and in other ways enticing to the eye; and got a good breakfast at the hotel.

A thriving place is the Good Samaritan City of the Mississippi: has a great wholesale jobbing trade; foundries, machine shops; and manufactories of wagons, carriages, and cotton-seed oil; and is shortly to have cotton mills and elevators.

Her cotton receipts reached five hundred thousand bales last year—an increase of sixty thousand over the year before. Out from her healthy commercial heart issue five trunk lines of railway; and a sixth is being added.

This is a very different Memphis from the one which the vanished and unremembered procession of foreign tourists used to put into their books long time ago. In the days of the now forgotten but once renowned and vigorously hated Mrs. Trollope, Memphis seems to have consisted mainly of one long street of log-houses, with some outlying cabins sprinkled around rearward toward the woods; and now and then a pig, and no end of mud. That was fifty-five years ago. She stopped at the hotel. Plainly it was not the one which gave us our breakfast. She says—

'The table was laid for fifty persons, and was nearly full. They ate in perfect silence, and with such astonishing rapidity that their dinner was over literally before ours was begun; the only sounds heard were those produced by the knives and forks, with the unceasing chorus of coughing, ETC.'

'Coughing, etc.' The 'etc.' stands for an unpleasant word there, a word which she does not always charitably cover up, but sometimes prints. You will find it in the following description of a steamboat dinner which she ate in company with a lot of aristocratic planters; wealthy, well-born, ignorant swells they were, tinselled with the usual harmless military and judicial titles of that old day of cheap shams and windy pretense—

'The total want of all the usual courtesies of the table; the voracious rapidity with which the viands were seized and devoured; the strange uncouth phrases and pronunciation; the loathsome spitting, from the contamination of which it was absolutely impossible to protect our dresses; the frightful manner of feeding with their knives, till the whole blade seemed to enter into the mouth; and the still more frightful manner of cleaning the teeth afterward with a pocket knife, soon forced us to feel that we were not surrounded by the generals, colonels, and majors of the old world; and that the dinner hour was to be anything rather than an hour of enjoyment.'

Chapter 30 Sketches by the Way

IT was a big river, below Memphis; banks brimming full, everywhere, and very frequently more than full, the waters pouring out over the land, flooding the woods and fields for miles into the interior; and in places, to a depth of fifteen feet; signs, all about, of men's hard work gone to ruin, and all to be done over again, with straitened means and a weakened courage. A melancholy picture, and a continuous one;—hundreds of miles of it. Sometimes the beacon lights stood in water three feet deep, in the edge of dense forests which extended for miles without farm, wood-yard, clearing, or break of any kind; which meant that the keeper of the light must come in a skiff a great distance to discharge his trust,—and often in desperate weather. Yet I was told that the work is faithfully performed, in all weathers; and not always by men, sometimes by women, if the man is sick or absent. The Government furnishes oil, and pays ten or fifteen dollars a month for the lighting and tending. A Government boat distributes oil and pays wages once a month.

The Ship Island region was as woodsy and tenantless as ever. The island has ceased to be an island; has joined itself compactly to the main shore, and wagons travel, now, where the steamboats used to navigate. No signs left of the wreck of the 'Pennsylvania.' Some farmer will turn up her bones with his plow one day, no doubt, and be surprised.

We were getting down now into the migrating negro region. These poor people could never travel when they were slaves; so they make up for the privation now. They stay on a plantation till the desire to travel seizes them; then they pack up, hail a steamboat, and clear out. Not for any particular place; no, nearly any place will answer; they only want to be moving. The amount of money on hand will answer the rest of the conundrum for them. If it will take them fifty miles, very well; let it be fifty. If not, a shorter flight will do.

During a couple of days, we frequently answered these hails. Sometimes there was a group of high-water-stained, tumble-down cabins, populous with colored folk, and no whites visible; with grassless patches of dry ground here and there; a few felled trees, with skeleton cattle, mules, and horses, eating the leaves and gnawing the bark—no other food for them in the flood-wasted land. Sometimes there was a single lonely landing-cabin; near it the colored family that had hailed us;

little and big, old and young, roosting on the scant pile of household goods; these consisting of a rusty gun, some bed-ticks, chests, tinware, stools, a crippled looking-glass, a venerable arm-chair, and six or eight base- born and spiritless yellow curs, attached to the family by strings. They must have their dogs; can't go without their dogs. Yet the dogs are never willing; they always object; so, one after another, in ridiculous procession, they are dragged aboard; all four feet braced and sliding along the stage, head likely to be pulled off; but the tugger marching determinedly forward, bending to his work, with the rope over his shoulder for better purchase. Sometimes a child is forgotten and left on the bank; but never a dog.

The usual river-gossip going on in the pilot-house. Island No. 63—an island with a lovely 'chute,' or passage, behind it in the former times. They said Jesse Jamieson, in the 'Skylark,' had a visiting pilot with him one trip—a poor old broken-down, superannuated fellow—left him at the wheel, at the foot of 63, to run off the watch. The ancient mariner went up through the chute, and down the river outside; and up the chute and down the river again; and yet again and again; and handed the boat over to the relieving pilot, at the end of three hours of honest endeavor, at the same old foot of the island where he had originally taken the wheel! A darkey on shore who had observed the boat go by, about thirteen times, said, 'clar to gracious, I wouldn't be s'prised if dey's a whole line o' dem Sk'ylarks!'

Anecdote illustrative of influence of reputation in the changing of opinion. The 'Eclipse' was renowned for her swiftness. One day she passed along; an old darkey on shore, absorbed in his own matters, did not notice what steamer it was. Presently someone asked—

'Any boat gone up?'

'Yes, sah.'

'Was she going fast?'

'Oh, so-so—loafin' along.'

'Now, do you know what boat that was?'

'No, sah.'

'Why, uncle, that was the "Eclipse."'

'No! Is dat so? Well, I bet it was—cause she jes' went by here a-SPARKLIN'!'

Piece of history illustrative of the violent style of some of the people down along here, During the early weeks of high water, A's fence rails washed down on B's ground, and B's rails washed up in the eddy and landed on A's ground. A said, 'Let the thing remain so; I will use your rails, and you use mine.' But B objected—wouldn't have it so. One day, A came down on B's ground to get his rails. B said, 'I'll kill you!' and proceeded for him with his revolver. A said, 'I'm not armed.' So B, who wished to do only what was right, threw down his revolver; then pulled a knife, and cut A's throat all around, but gave his principal attention to the front, and so failed to sever the jugular. Struggling around, A managed to get his hands on the discarded revolver, and shot B dead with it—and recovered from his own injuries.

Further gossip;—after which, everybody went below to get

afternoon coffee, and left me at the wheel, alone, Something presently reminded me of our last hour in St. Louis, part of which I spent on this boat's hurricane deck, aft. I was joined there by a stranger, who dropped into conversation with me— a brisk young fellow, who said he was born in a town in the interior of Wisconsin, and had never seen a steamboat until a week before. Also said that on the way down from La Crosse he had inspected and examined his boat so diligently and with such passionate interest that he had mastered the whole thing from stem to rudder-blade. Asked me where I was from. I answered, New England. 'Oh, a Yank!' said he; and went chatting straight along, without waiting for assent or denial. He immediately proposed to take me all over the boat and tell me the names of her different parts, and teach me their uses. Before I could enter protest or excuse, he was already rattling glibly away at his benevolent work; and when I perceived that he was misnaming the things, and inhospitably amusing himself at the expense of an innocent stranger from a far country, I held my peace, and let him have his way. He gave me a world of misinformation; and the further he went, the wider his imagination expanded, and the more he enjoyed his cruel work of deceit. Sometimes, after palming off a particularly fantastic and outrageous lie upon me, he was so 'full of laugh' that he had to step aside for a minute, upon one pretext or another, to keep me from suspecting. I staid faithfully by him until his comedy was finished. Then he remarked that he had undertaken to 'learn' me all about a steamboat, and had done it; but that if he had overlooked anything, just ask him and he would supply the lack. 'Anything about this boat that you don't know the name of or the purpose of, you come to me and I'll tell you.' I said I would, and took my departure; disappeared, and approached him from another quarter, whence he could not see me. There he sat, all alone, doubling himself up and writhing this way and that, in the throes of unappeasable laughter. He must have made himself sick; for he was not publicly visible afterward for several days. Meantime, the episode dropped out of my mind.

The thing that reminded me of it now, when I was alone at the wheel, was the spectacle of this young fellow standing in the pilot-house door, with the knob in his hand, silently and severely inspecting me. I don't know when I have seen anybody look so injured as he did. He did not say anything— simply stood there and looked; reproachfully looked and pondered. Finally he shut the door, and started away; halted on the texas a minute; came slowly back and stood in the door again, with that grieved look in his face; gazed upon me awhile in meek rebuke, then said—

'You let me learn you all about a steamboat, didn't you?'

'Yes,' I confessed.

'Yes, you did—DIDN'T you?'

'Yes.'

'You are the feller that—that—'

Language failed. Pause—impotent struggle for further words— then he gave it up, choked out a deep, strong oath, and departed for good. Afterward I saw him several times below during the trip; but he was cold—would not look at me. Idiot, if he had not been in such a sweat to play his witless practical joke upon me, in the beginning, I would have persuaded his thoughts into some other direction, and saved him from committing that wanton and silly impoliteness.

I had myself called with the four o'clock watch, mornings, for one cannot see too many summer sunrises on the Mississippi. They are enchanting. First, there is the eloquence of silence; for a deep hush broods everywhere. Next, there is the haunting sense of loneliness, isolation, remoteness from the worry and bustle of the world. The dawn creeps in stealthily; the solid walls of black forest soften to gray, and vast stretches of the river open up and reveal themselves; the water is glass-smooth, gives off spectral little wreaths of white mist, there is not the faintest breath of wind, nor stir of leaf; the tranquillity is profound and infinitely satisfying. Then a bird pipes up, another follows, and soon the pipings develop into a jubilant riot of music. You see none of the birds; you simply move through an atmosphere of song which seems to sing itself. When the light has become a little stronger, you have one of the fairest and softest pictures imaginable. You have the intense green of the massed and crowded foliage near by; you see it paling shade by shade in front of you; upon the next projecting cape, a mile off or more, the tint has lightened to the tender young green of spring; the cape beyond that one has almost lost color, and the furthest one, miles away under the horizon, sleeps upon the water a mere dim vapor, and hardly separable from the sky above it and about it. And all this stretch of river is a mirror, and you have the shadowy reflections of the leafage and the curving shores and the receding capes pictured in it. Well, that is all beautiful; soft and rich and beautiful; and when the sun gets well up, and distributes a pink flush here and a powder of gold yonder and a purple haze where it will yield the best effect, you grant that you have seen something that is worth remembering.

We had the Kentucky Bend country in the early morning— scene of a strange and tragic accident in the old times, Captain Poe had a small stern-wheel boat, for years the home of himself and his wife. One night the boat struck a snag in the head of Kentucky Bend, and sank with astonishing suddenness; water already well above the cabin floor when the captain got aft. So he cut into his wife's state-room from above with an ax; she was asleep in the upper berth, the roof a flimsier one than was supposed; the first blow crashed down through the rotten boards and clove her skull.

This bend is all filled up now—result of a cut-off; and the same agent has taken the great and once much-frequented Walnut Bend, and set it away back in a solitude far from the accustomed track of passing steamers.

Helena we visited, and also a town I had not heard of before, it being of recent birth—Arkansas City. It was born of a railway; the Little Rock, Mississippi River and Texas Railroad touches the river there. We asked a passenger who belonged there what sort of a place it was. 'Well,' said he, after considering, and with the air of one who wishes to take time and be accurate, 'It's a hell of a place.' A description which was photographic for exactness. There were several rows and clusters of shabby frame-houses, and a supply of mud sufficient to insure the town against a famine in that article for a hundred years; for the overflow had but lately subsided. There were stagnant ponds in the streets, here and there, and a dozen rude scows were scattered about, lying aground wherever they happened to have been when the waters drained off and people could do their visiting and shopping on foot once more. Still, it is a thriving place, with a rich country behind it, an elevator in front of it, and also a fine big mill for the manufacture of cotton-seed oil. I had never seen this kind of a mill before.

Cotton-seed was comparatively valueless in my time; but it is worth $12 or $13 a ton now, and none of it is thrown away. The oil made from it is colorless, tasteless, and almost if not entirely odorless. It is claimed that it can, by proper manipulation, be made to resemble and perform the office of any and all oils, and be produced at a cheaper rate than the cheapest of the originals. Sagacious people shipped it to Italy, doctored it, labeled it, and brought it back as olive oil. This trade grew to be so formidable that Italy was obliged to put a prohibitory impost upon it to keep it from working serious injury to her oil industry.

Helena occupies one of the prettiest situations on the Mississippi. Her perch is the last, the southernmost group of hills which one sees on that side of the river. In its normal condition it is a pretty town; but the flood (or possibly the seepage) had lately been ravaging it; whole streets of houses had been invaded by the muddy water, and the outsides of the buildings were still belted with a broad stain extending upwards from the foundations. Stranded and discarded scows lay all about; plank sidewalks on stilts four feet high were still standing; the board sidewalks on the ground level were loose and ruinous,—a couple of men trotting along them could make a blind man think a cavalry charge was coming; everywhere the mud was black and deep, and in many places malarious pools of stagnant water were standing. A Mississippi inundation is the next most wasting and desolating infliction to a fire.

We had an enjoyable time here, on this sunny Sunday: two full hours' liberty ashore while the boat discharged freight. In the back streets but few white people were visible, but there were plenty of colored folk—mainly women and girls; and almost without exception upholstered in bright new clothes of swell and elaborate style and cut—a glaring and hilarious contrast to the mournful mud and the pensive puddles.

Helena is the second town in Arkansas, in point of population—which is placed at five thousand. The country about it is exceptionally productive. Helena has a good cotton trade; handles from forty to sixty thousand bales annually; she has a large lumber and grain commerce; has a foundry, oil mills, machine shops and wagon factories—in brief has $1,000,000 invested in manufacturing industries. She has two railways, and is the commercial center of a broad and prosperous region. Her gross receipts of money, annually, from all sources, are placed by the New Orleans 'Times-Democrat' at $4,000,000.

Chapter 31 A Thumb-print and What Came of It

WE were approaching Napoleon, Arkansas. So I began to think about my errand there. Time, noonday; and bright and sunny. This was bad—not best, anyway; for mine was not (preferably) a noonday kind of errand. The more I thought, the more that fact pushed itself upon me—now in one form, now in another. Finally, it took the form of a distinct question: is it good common sense to do the errand in daytime, when, by a little sacrifice of comfort and inclination, you can have night for it, and no inquisitive eyes around. This settled it. Plain question and plain answer make the shortest road out of most perplexities.

I got my friends into my stateroom, and said I was sorry to create annoyance and disappointment, but that upon reflection it really seemed best that we put our luggage ashore and stop over at Napoleon. Their disapproval was prompt and loud; their language mutinous. Their main argument was one which has always been the first to come to the surface, in such

cases, since the beginning of time: 'But you decided and AGREED to stick to this boat, etc.; as if, having determined to do an unwise thing, one is thereby bound to go ahead and make TWO unwise things of it, by carrying out that determination.

I tried various mollifying tactics upon them, with reasonably good success: under which encouragement, I increased my efforts; and, to show them that I had not created this annoying errand, and was in no way to blame for it, I presently drifted into its history—substantially as follows:

Toward the end of last year, I spent a few months in Munich, Bavaria. In November I was living in Fraulein Dahlweiner's PENSION, 1a, Karlstrasse; but my working quarters were a mile from there, in the house of a widow who supported herself by taking lodgers. She and her two young children used to drop in every morning and talk German to me—by request. One day, during a ramble about the city, I visited one of the two establishments where the Government keeps and watches corpses until the doctors decide that they are permanently dead, and not in a trance state. It was a grisly place, that spacious room. There were thirty-six corpses of adults in sight, stretched on their backs on slightly slanted boards, in three long rows—all of them with wax-white, rigid faces, and all of them wrapped in white shrouds. Along the sides of the room were deep alcoves, like bay windows; and in each of these lay several marble- visaged babes, utterly hidden and buried under banks of fresh flowers, all but their faces and crossed hands. Around a finger of each of these fifty still forms, both great and small, was a ring; and from the ring a wire led to the ceiling, and thence to a bell in a watch-room yonder, where, day and night, a watchman sits always alert and ready to spring to the aid of any of that pallid company who, waking out of death, shall make a movement—for any, even the slightest, movement will twitch the wire and ring that fearful bell. I imagined myself a death-sentinel drowsing there alone, far in the dragging watches of some wailing, gusty night, and having in a twinkling all my body stricken to quivering jelly by the sudden clamor of that awful summons! So I inquired about this thing; asked what resulted usually? if the watchman died, and the restored corpse came and did what it could to make his last moments easy. But I was rebuked for trying to feed an idle and frivolous curiosity in so solemn and so mournful a place; and went my way with a humbled crest.

Next morning I was telling the widow my adventure, when she exclaimed—

'Come with me! I have a lodger who shall tell you all you want to know. He has been a night-watchman there.'

He was a living man, but he did not look it. He was abed, and had his head propped high on pillows; his face was wasted and colorless, his deep-sunken eyes were shut; his hand, lying on his breast, was talon- like, it was so bony and long-fingered. The widow began her introduction of me. The man's eyes opened slowly, and glittered wickedly out from the twilight of their caverns; he frowned a black frown; he lifted his lean hand and waved us peremptorily away. But the widow kept straight on, till she had got out the fact that I was a stranger and an American. The man's face changed at once; brightened, became even eager—and the next moment he and I were alone together.

I opened up in cast-iron German; he responded in quite flexible English; thereafter we gave the German language a permanent rest.

This consumptive and I became good friends. I visited him every day, and we talked about everything. At least, about everything but wives and children. Let anybody's wife or anybody's child be mentioned, and three things always followed: the most gracious and loving and tender light glimmered in the man's eyes for a moment; faded out the next, and in its place came that deadly look which had flamed there the first time I ever saw his lids unclose; thirdly, he ceased from speech, there and then for that day; lay silent, abstracted, and absorbed; apparently heard nothing that I said; took no notice of my good-byes, and plainly did not know, by either sight or hearing, when I left the room.

When I had been this Karl Ritter's daily and sole intimate during two months, he one day said, abruptly—

'I will tell you my story.'

A DYING MAN S CONFESSION

Then he went on as follows:—

I have never given up, until now. But now I have given up. I am going to die. I made up my mind last night that it must be, and very soon, too. You say you are going to revisit your river, by-and-bye, when you find opportunity. Very well; that, together with a certain strange experience which fell to my lot last night, determines me to tell you my history—for you will see Napoleon, Arkansas; and for my sake you will stop there, and do a certain thing for me—a thing which you will willingly undertake after you shall have heard my narrative.

Let us shorten the story wherever we can, for it will need it, being long. You already know how I came to go to America, and how I came to settle in that lonely region in the South. But you do not know that I had a wife. My wife was young, beautiful, loving, and oh, so divinely good and blameless and gentle! And our little girl was her mother in miniature. It was the happiest of happy households.

One night—it was toward the close of the war—I woke up out of a sodden lethargy, and found myself bound and gagged, and the air tainted with chloroform! I saw two men in the room, and one was saying to the other, in a hoarse whisper, 'I told her I would, if she made a noise, and as for the child—'

The other man interrupted in a low, half-crying voice—

'You said we'd only gag them and rob them, not hurt them; or I wouldn't have come.'

'Shut up your whining; had to change the plan when they waked up; you done all you could to protect them, now let that satisfy you; come, help rummage.'

Both men were masked, and wore coarse, ragged 'nigger' clothes; they had a bull's-eye lantern, and by its light I noticed that the gentler robber had no thumb on his right hand. They rummaged around my poor cabin for a moment; the head bandit then said, in his stage whisper—

'It's a waste of time—he shall tell where it's hid. Undo his gag, and revive him up.'

The other said—

'All right—provided no clubbing.'

'No clubbing it is, then—provided he keeps still.'

They approached me; just then there was a sound outside; a sound of voices and trampling hoofs; the robbers held their breath and listened; the sounds came slowly nearer and nearer; then came a shout—

'HELLO, the house! Show a light, we want water.'

'The captain's voice, by G—!' said the stage-whispering ruffian, and both robbers fled by the way of the back door, shutting off their bull's-eye as they ran.

The strangers shouted several times more, then rode by—there seemed to be a dozen of the horses—and I heard nothing more.

I struggled, but could not free myself from my bonds. I tried to speak, but the gag was effective; I could not make a sound. I listened for my wife's voice and my child's—listened long and intently, but no sound came from the other end of the room where their bed was. This silence became more and more awful, more and more ominous, every moment. Could you have endured an hour of it, do you think? Pity me, then, who had to endure three. Three hours—? it was three ages! Whenever the clock struck, it seemed as if years had gone by since I had heard it last. All this time I was struggling in my bonds; and at last, about dawn, I got myself free, and rose up and stretched my stiff limbs. I was able to distinguish details pretty well. The floor was littered with things thrown there by the robbers during their search for my savings. The first object that caught my particular attention was a document of mine which I had seen the rougher of the two ruffians glance at and then cast away. It had blood on it! I staggered to the other end of the room. Oh, poor unoffending, helpless ones, there they lay, their troubles ended, mine begun!

Did I appeal to the law—I? Does it quench the pauper's thirst if the King drink for him? Oh, no, no, no—I wanted no impertinent interference of the law. Laws and the gallows could not pay the debt that was owing to me! Let the laws leave the matter in my hands, and have no fears: I would find the debtor and collect the debt. How accomplish this, do you say? How accomplish it, and feel so sure about it, when I had neither seen the robbers' faces, nor heard their natural voices, nor had any idea who they might be? Nevertheless, I WAS sure— quite sure, quite confident. I had a clue—a clue which you would not have valued—a clue which would not have greatly helped even a detective, since he would lack the secret of how to apply it. I shall come to that, presently—you shall see. Let us go on, now, taking things in their due order. There was one circumstance which gave me a slant in a definite direction to begin with: Those two robbers were manifestly soldiers in tramp disguise; and not new to military service, but old in it—regulars, perhaps; they did not acquire their soldierly attitude, gestures, carriage, in a day, nor a month, nor yet in a year. So I thought, but said nothing. And one of them had said, 'the captain's voice, by G—!'—the one whose life I would have. Two miles away, several regiments were in camp, and two companies of U.S. cavalry. When I learned that Captain Blakely, of Company C had passed our way, that night, with an escort, I said nothing, but in that company I resolved to seek my man. In conversation I studiously and persistently described the robbers as tramps, camp followers; and among this class the people made useless search, none suspecting the soldiers but me.

Working patiently, by night, in my desolated home, I made a disguise for myself out of various odds and ends of clothing; in the nearest village I bought a pair of blue goggles. By-and-bye, when the military camp broke up, and Company C was ordered a hundred miles north, to Napoleon, I secreted my small hoard of money in my belt, and took my departure in the night. When Company C arrived in Napoleon, I was already there. Yes, I was there, with a new trade—fortune-teller. Not to seem partial, I made friends and told fortunes among all the companies garrisoned there; but I gave Company C the great bulk of my attentions. I made myself limitlessly obliging to these particular men; they could ask me no favor, put upon me no risk, which I would decline. I became the willing butt of their jokes; this perfected my popularity; I became a favorite.

I early found a private who lacked a thumb—what joy it was to me! And when I found that he alone, of all the company, had lost a thumb, my last misgiving vanished; I was SURE I was on the right track. This man's name was Kruger, a German. There were nine Germans in the company. I watched, to see who might be his intimates; but he seemed to have no especial intimates. But I was his intimate; and I took care to make the intimacy grow. Sometimes I so hungered for my revenge that I could hardly restrain myself from going on my knees and begging him to point out the man who had murdered my wife and child; but I managed to bridle my tongue. I bided my time, and went on telling fortunes, as opportunity offered.

My apparatus was simple: a little red paint and a bit of white paper. I painted the ball of the client's thumb, took a print of it on the paper, studied it that night, and revealed his fortune to him next day. What was my idea in this nonsense? It was this: When I was a youth, I knew an old Frenchman who had been a prison-keeper for thirty years, and he told me that there was one thing about a person which never changed, from the cradle to the grave—the lines in the ball of the thumb; and he said that these lines were never exactly alike in the thumbs of any two human beings. In these days, we photograph the new criminal, and hang his picture in the Rogues' Gallery for future reference; but that Frenchman, in his day, used to take a print of the ball of a new prisoner's thumb and put that away for future reference. He always said that pictures were no good—future disguises could make them useless; 'The thumb's the only sure thing,' said he; 'you can't disguise that.' And he used to prove his theory, too, on my friends and acquaintances; it always succeeded.

I went on telling fortunes. Every night I shut myself in, all alone, and studied the day's thumb-prints with a magnifying-glass. Imagine the devouring eagerness with which I pored over those mazy red spirals, with that document by my side which bore the right-hand thumb-and-finger- marks of that unknown murderer, printed with the dearest blood—to me—that was ever shed on this earth! And many and many a time I had to repeat the same old disappointed remark, 'will they NEVER correspond!'

But my reward came at last. It was the print of the thumb of the forty- third man of Company C whom I had experimented on—Private Franz Adler. An hour before, I did not know the murderer's name, or voice, or figure, or face, or nationality; but now I knew all these things! I believed I might feel sure; the Frenchman's repeated demonstrations being so good a warranty. Still, there was a way to MAKE sure. I had an impression of Kruger's left thumb. In the morning I took him aside when he was off duty; and when we were out of sight and hearing of witnesses, I said, impressively—

'A part of your fortune is so grave, that I thought it would be better for you if I did not tell it in public. You and another man, whose fortune I was studying last night,—Private Adler,—have been murdering a woman and a child! You are being dogged: within five days both of you will be assassinated.'

He dropped on his knees, frightened out of his wits; and for five minutes he kept pouring out the same set of words, like a demented person, and in the same half-crying way which was one of my memories of that murderous night in my cabin—

'I didn't do it; upon my soul I didn't do it; and I tried to keep HIM from doing it; I did, as God is my witness. He did it alone.'

This was all I wanted. And I tried to get rid of the fool; but no, he clung to me, imploring me to save him from the assassin. He said—

'I have money—ten thousand dollars—hid away, the fruit of loot and thievery; save me—tell me what to do, and you shall have it, every penny. Two-thirds of it is my cousin Adler's; but you can take it all. We hid it when we first came here. But I hid it in a new place yesterday, and have not told him—shall not tell him. I was going to desert, and get away with it all. It is gold, and too heavy to carry when one is running and dodging; but a woman who has been gone over the river two days to prepare my way for me is going to follow me with it; and if I got no chance to describe the hiding-place to her I was going to slip my silver watch into her hand, or send it to her, and she would understand. There's a piece of paper in the back of the case, which tells it all. Here, take the watch—tell me what to do!'

He was trying to press his watch upon me, and was exposing the paper and explaining it to me, when Adler appeared on the scene, about a dozen yards away. I said to poor Kruger—

'Put up your watch, I don't want it. You shan't come to any harm. Go, now; I must tell Adler his fortune. Presently I will tell you how to escape the assassin; meantime I shall have to examine your thumbmark again. Say nothing to Adler about this thing—say nothing to anybody.'

He went away filled with fright and gratitude, poor devil. I told Adler a long fortune—purposely so long that I could not finish it; promised to come to him on guard, that night, and tell him the really important part of it—the tragical part of it, I said—so must be out of reach of eavesdroppers. They always kept a picket-watch outside the town—mere discipline and ceremony—no occasion for it, no enemy around.

Toward midnight I set out, equipped with the countersign, and picked my way toward the lonely region where Adler was to keep his watch. It was so dark that I stumbled right on a dim figure almost before I could get out a protecting word. The sentinel hailed and I answered, both at the same moment. I added, 'It's only me—the fortune-teller.' Then I slipped to the poor devil's side, and without a word I drove my dirk into his heart! YA WOHL, laughed I, it WAS the tragedy part of his fortune, indeed! As he fell from his horse, he clutched at me, and my blue goggles remained in his hand; and away plunged the beast dragging him, with his foot in the stirrup.

I fled through the woods, and made good my escape, leaving the accusing goggles behind me in that dead man's hand.

This was fifteen or sixteen years ago. Since then I have wandered aimlessly about the earth, sometimes at work, sometimes idle; sometimes with money, sometimes with none; but always tired of life, and wishing it was done, for my mission here was finished, with the act of that night; and the only pleasure, solace, satisfaction I had, in all those tedious years, was in the daily reflection, 'I have killed him!'

Four years ago, my health began to fail. I had wandered into Munich, in my purposeless way. Being out of money, I sought work, and got it; did my duty faithfully about a year, and was then given the berth of night watchman yonder in that dead-house which you visited lately. The place suited my mood. I liked it. I liked being with the dead—liked being alone with them. I used to wander among those rigid corpses, and peer into their austere faces, by the hour. The later the time, the more impressive it was; I preferred the late time. Sometimes I turned the lights low: this gave perspective, you see; and the imagination could play; always, the dim receding ranks of the dead inspired one with weird and fascinating fancies. Two years ago—I had been there a year then—I was sitting all alone in the watch-room, one gusty winter's night, chilled, numb, comfortless; drowsing gradually into unconsciousness; the sobbing of the wind and the slamming of distant shutters falling fainter and fainter upon my dulling ear each moment, when sharp and suddenly that dead-bell rang out a blood-curdling alarum over my head! The shock of it nearly paralyzed me; for it was the first time I had ever heard it.

I gathered myself together and flew to the corpse-room. About midway down the outside rank, a shrouded figure was sitting upright, wagging its head slowly from one side to the other—a grisly spectacle! Its side was toward me. I hurried to it and peered into its face. Heavens, it was Adler!

Can you divine what my first thought was? Put into words, it was this: 'It seems, then, you escaped me once: there will be a different result this time!'

Evidently this creature was suffering unimaginable terrors. Think what it must have been to wake up in the midst of that voiceless hush, and, look out over that grim congregation of the dead! What gratitude shone in his skinny white face when he saw a living form before him! And how the fervency of this mute gratitude was augmented when his eyes fell upon the life-giving cordials which I carried in my hands! Then imagine the horror which came into this pinched face when I put the cordials behind me, and said mockingly—

'Speak up, Franz Adler—call upon these dead. Doubtless they will listen and have pity; but here there is none else that will.'

He tried to speak, but that part of the shroud which bound his jaws, held firm and would not let him. He tried to lift imploring hands, but they were crossed upon his breast and tied. I said—

'Shout, Franz Adler; make the sleepers in the distant streets hear you and bring help. Shout—and lose no time, for there is little to lose. What, you cannot? That is a pity; but it is no matter—it does not always bring help. When you and your cousin murdered a helpless woman and child in a cabin in Arkansas—my wife, it was, and my child!—they shrieked for help, you remember; but it did no good; you remember that it did no good, is it not so? Your teeth chatter—then why cannot you shout? Loosen the bandages with your hands—then you can. Ah, I see— your hands are tied, they cannot aid you. How strangely things repeat themselves, after long years; for MY hands were tied, that night, you remember? Yes, tied much as yours are now—how odd that is. I could not pull free. It did not occur to you to untie me; it does not occur to me to untie you. Sh—! there's a late footstep. It is coming this way. Hark, how near it is! One can count the footfalls—one—two—three. There—it is just outside. Now is the time! Shout, man, shout!—it is the one sole chance between you and eternity! Ah, you see you have delayed too long—it is gone by. There—it is dying out. It is gone! Think of it—reflect upon it—you have heard a human footstep for the last time. How curious it must be, to listen to so common a sound as that, and know that one will never hear the fellow to it again.'

Oh, my friend, the agony in that shrouded face was ecstasy to see! I thought of a new torture, and applied it—assisting myself with a trifle of lying invention—

'That poor Kruger tried to save my wife and child, and I did him a grateful good turn for it when the time came. I persuaded him to rob you; and I and a woman helped him to desert, and got him away in safety.' A look as of surprise and triumph shone out dimly through the anguish in my victim's face. I was disturbed, disquieted. I said—

'What, then—didn't he escape?'

A negative shake of the head.

'No? What happened, then?'

The satisfaction in the shrouded face was still plainer. The man tried to mumble out some words—could not succeed; tried to express something with his obstructed hands—failed; paused a moment, then feebly tilted his head, in a meaning way, toward the corpse that lay nearest him.

'Dead?' I asked. 'Failed to escape?—caught in the act and shot?'

Negative shake of the head.

'How, then?'

Again the man tried to do something with his hands. I watched closely, but could not guess the intent. I bent over and watched still more intently. He had twisted a thumb around and was weakly punching at his breast with it. 'Ah—stabbed, do you mean?'

Affirmative nod, accompanied by a spectral smile of such peculiar devilishness, that it struck an awakening light through my dull brain, and I cried—

'Did I stab him, mistaking him for you?—for that stroke was meant for none but you.'

The affirmative nod of the re-dying rascal was as joyous as his failing strength was able to put into its expression.

'O, miserable, miserable me, to slaughter the pitying soul that, stood a friend to my darlings when they were helpless, and would have saved them if he could! miserable, oh, miserable, miserable me!'

I fancied I heard the muffled gurgle of a, mocking laugh. I took my face out of my hands, and saw my enemy sinking back upon his inclined board.

He was a satisfactory long time dying. He had a wonderful vitality, an astonishing constitution. Yes, he was a pleasant long time at it. I got a chair and a newspaper, and sat down by him and read. Occasionally I took a sip of brandy. This was necessary, on account of the cold. But I did it partly because I saw, that along at first, whenever I reached for the bottle, he thought I was going to give him some. I read aloud: mainly imaginary accounts of people snatched from the grave's threshold and restored to life and vigor by a few spoonsful of liquor and a warm bath. Yes, he had a long, hard death of it—three hours and six minutes, from the time he rang his bell.

It is believed that in all these eighteen years that have elapsed since the institution of the corpse-watch, no shrouded occupant of the Bavarian dead-houses has ever rung its bell. Well, it is a harmless belief. Let it stand at that.

The chill of that death-room had penetrated my bones. It revived and fastened upon me the disease which had been afflicting me, but which, up to that night, had been steadily disappearing. That man murdered my wife and my child; and in three days hence he will have added me to his list. No matter—God! how delicious the memory of it!—I caught him escaping from his grave, and thrust him back into it.

After that night, I was confined to my bed for a week; but as soon as I could get about, I went to the dead-house books and got the number of the house which Adler had died in. A wretched lodging-house, it was. It was my idea that he would naturally have gotten hold of Kruger's effects, being his cousin; and I wanted to get Kruger's watch, if I could. But while I was sick, Adler's things had been sold and scattered, all except a few old letters, and some odds and ends of no value. However, through those letters, I traced out a son of Kruger's, the only relative left. He is a man of thirty now, a shoemaker by trade, and living at No. 14 Konigstrasse, Mannheim—widower, with several small children. Without explaining to him why, I have furnished two-thirds of his support, ever since.

Now, as to that watch—see how strangely things happen! I traced it around and about Germany for more than a year, at considerable cost in money and vexation; and at last I got it. Got it, and was unspeakably glad; opened it, and found nothing in it! Why, I might have known that that bit of paper was not going to stay there all this time. Of course I gave up that ten thousand dollars then; gave it up, and dropped it out of my mind: and most sorrowfully, for I had wanted it for Kruger's son.

Last night, when I consented at last that I must die, I began to make ready. I proceeded to burn all useless papers; and sure enough, from a batch of Adler's, not previously examined with thoroughness, out dropped that long-desired scrap! I recognized it in a moment. Here it is—I will translate it:

'Brick livery stable, stone foundation, middle of town, corner of Orleans and Market. Corner toward Court-house. Third stone, fourth row. Stick notice there, saying how many are to come.'

There—take it, and preserve it. Kruger explained that that stone was removable; and that it was in the north wall of the foundation, fourth row from the top, and third stone from the west. The money is secreted behind it. He said the closing sentence was a blind, to mislead in case the paper should fall into wrong hands. It probably performed that office for Adler.

Now I want to beg that when you make your intended journey

down the river, you will hunt out that hidden money, and send it to Adam Kruger, care of the Mannheim address which I have mentioned. It will make a rich man of him, and I shall sleep the sounder in my grave for knowing that I have done what I could for the son of the man who tried to save my wife and child—albeit my hand ignorantly struck him down, whereas the impulse of my heart would have been to shield and serve him.

Chapter 32 The Disposal of a Bonanza

'SUCH was Ritter's narrative,' said I to my two friends. There was a profound and impressive silence, which lasted a considerable time; then both men broke into a fusillade of exciting and admiring ejaculations over the strange incidents of the tale; and this, along with a rattling fire of questions, was kept up until all hands were about out of breath. Then my friends began to cool down, and draw off, under shelter of occasional volleys, into silence and abysmal reverie. For ten minutes now, there was stillness. Then Rogers said dreamily—

'Ten thousand dollars.'

Adding, after a considerable pause—

'Ten thousand. It is a heap of money.'

Presently the poet inquired—

'Are you going to send it to him right away?'

'Yes,' I said. 'It is a queer question.'

No reply. After a little, Rogers asked, hesitatingly:

'ALL of it?—That is—I mean—'

'Certainly, all of it.'

I was going to say more, but stopped—was stopped by a train of thought which started up in me. Thompson spoke, but my mind was absent, and I did not catch what he said. But I heard Rogers answer—

'Yes, it seems so to me. It ought to be quite sufficient; for I don't see that he has done anything.'

Presently the poet said—

'When you come to look at it, it is more than sufficient. Just look at it—five thousand dollars! Why, he couldn't spend it in a lifetime! And it would injure him, too; perhaps ruin him—you want to look at that. In a little while he would throw his last away, shut up his shop, maybe take to drinking, maltreat his motherless children, drift into other evil courses, go steadily from bad to worse—'

'Yes, that's it,' interrupted Rogers, fervently, 'I've seen it a hundred times—yes, more than a hundred. You put money into the hands of a man like that, if you want to destroy him, that's all; just put money into his hands, it's all you've got to do; and if it don't pull him down, and take all the usefulness out of him, and all the self-respect and everything, then I don't know human nature—ain't that so, Thompson? And even if we were to give him a THIRD of it; why, in less than six months—'

'Less than six WEEKS, you'd better say!' said I, warming up and breaking in. 'Unless he had that three thousand dollars in safe hands where he couldn't touch it, he would no more last you six weeks than—'

'Of COURSE he wouldn't,' said Thompson; 'I've edited books for that kind of people; and the moment they get their hands on the royalty—maybe it's three thousand, maybe it's two thousand—'

'What business has that shoemaker with two thousand dollars, I should like to know?' broke in Rogers, earnestly. 'A man perhaps perfectly contented now, there in Mannheim, surrounded by his own class, eating his bread with the appetite which laborious industry alone can give, enjoying his humble life, honest, upright, pure in heart; and BLEST!— yes, I say blest! blest above all the myriads that go in silk attire and walk the empty artificial round of social folly—but just you put that temptation before him once! just you lay fifteen hundred dollars before a man like that, and say—'

'Fifteen hundred devils!' cried I, 'FIVE hundred would rot his principles, paralyze his industry, drag him to the rumshop, thence to the gutter, thence to the almshouse, thence to —'

'WHY put upon ourselves this crime, gentlemen?' interrupted the poet earnestly and appealingly. 'He is happy where he is, and AS he is. Every sentiment of honor, every sentiment of charity, every sentiment of high and sacred benevolence warns us, beseeches us, commands us to leave him undisturbed. That is real friendship, that is true friendship. We could follow other courses that would be more showy; but none that would be so truly kind and wise, depend upon it.'

After some further talk, it became evident that each of us, down in his heart, felt some misgivings over this settlement of the matter. It was manifest that we all felt that we ought to send the poor shoemaker SOMETHING. There was long and thoughtful discussion of this point; and we finally decided to send him a chromo.

Well, now that everything seemed to be arranged satisfactorily to everybody concerned, a new trouble broke out: it transpired that these two men were expecting to share equally in the money with me. That was not my idea. I said that if they got half of it between them they might consider themselves lucky. Rogers said—

'Who would have had ANY if it hadn't been for me? I flung out the first hint—but for that it would all have gone to the shoemaker.'

Thompson said that he was thinking of the thing himself at the very moment that Rogers had originally spoken.

I retorted that the idea would have occurred to me plenty soon enough, and without anybody's help. I was slow about thinking, maybe, but I was sure.

This matter warmed up into a quarrel; then into a fight; and each man got pretty badly battered. As soon as I had got myself mended up after a fashion, I ascended to the hurricane deck in a pretty sour humor. I found Captain McCord there, and said, as pleasantly as my humor would permit—

'I have come to say good-bye, captain. I wish to go ashore at Napoleon.'

'Go ashore where?'

'Napoleon.'

The captain laughed; but seeing that I was not in a jovial mood, stopped that and said—

'But are you serious?'

'Serious? I certainly am.'

The captain glanced up at the pilot-house and said—

'He wants to get off at Napoleon!'

'Napoleon ?'

'That's what he says.'

'Great Caesar's ghost!'

Uncle Mumford approached along the deck. The captain said—

'Uncle, here's a friend of yours wants to get off at Napoleon!'

'Well, by —?'

I said—

'Come, what is all this about? Can't a man go ashore at Napoleon if he wants to?'

'Why, hang it, don't you know? There ISN'T any Napoleon any more. Hasn't been for years and years. The Arkansas River burst through it, tore it all to rags, and emptied it into the Mississippi!'

'Carried the WHOLE town away?-banks, churches, jails, newspaper-offices, court-house, theater, fire department, livery stable EVERYTHING ?'

'Everything. just a fifteen-minute job.' or such a matter. Didn't leave hide nor hair, shred nor shingle of it, except the fag-end of a shanty and one brick chimney. This boat is paddling along right now, where the dead-center of that town used to be; yonder is the brick chimney-all that's left of Napoleon.. These dense woods on the right used to be a mile back of the town. Take a look behind you—up-stream—now you begin to recognize this country, don't you?'

'Yes, I do recognize it now. It is the most wonderful thing I ever heard of; by a long shot the most wonderful—and unexpected.'

Mr. Thompson and Mr. Rogers had arrived, meantime, with satchels and umbrellas, and had silently listened to the captain's news. Thompson put a half-dollar in my hand and said softly—

'For my share of the chromo.'

Rogers followed suit.

Yes, it was an astonishing thing to see the Mississippi rolling between unpeopled shores and straight over the spot where I used to see a good big self-complacent town twenty years ago. Town that was county-seat of a great and important county; town with a big United States marine hospital; town of innumerable fights—an inquest every day; town where I had used to know the prettiest girl, and the most accomplished in the whole Mississippi Valley; town where we were handed the first printed news of the 'Pennsylvania's' mournful disaster a quarter of a century ago; a town no more—swallowed up, vanished, gone to feed the fishes; nothing left but a fragment of a shanty and a crumbling brick chimney!

Chapter 33 Refreshments and Ethics

IN regard to Island 74, which is situated not far from the former Napoleon, a freak of the river here has sorely perplexed the laws of men and made them a vanity and a jest. When the State of Arkansas was chartered, she controlled 'to the center of the river'—a most unstable line. The State of Mississippi claimed 'to the channel'—another shifty and unstable line. No. 74 belonged to Arkansas. By and by a cut-off threw this big island out of Arkansas, and yet not within Mississippi. 'Middle of the river' on one side of it, 'channel' on the other. That is as I understand the problem. Whether I have got the details right or wrong, this FACT remains: that here is this big and exceedingly valuable island of four thousand acres, thrust out in the cold, and belonging to neither the one State nor the other; paying taxes to neither, owing allegiance to neither. One man owns the whole island, and of right is 'the man without a country.'

Island 92 belongs to Arkansas. The river moved it over and joined it to Mississippi. A chap established a whiskey shop there, without a Mississippi license, and enriched himself upon Mississippi custom under Arkansas protection (where no license was in those days required).

We glided steadily down the river in the usual privacy—steamboat or other moving thing seldom seen. Scenery as always: stretch upon stretch of almost unbroken forest, on both sides of the river; soundless solitude. Here and there a cabin or two, standing in small openings on the gray and grassless banks—cabins which had formerly stood a quarter or half-mile farther to the front, and gradually been pulled farther and farther back as the shores caved in. As at Pilcher's Point, for instance, where the cabins had been moved back three hundred yards in three months, so we were told; but the caving banks had already caught up with them, and they were being conveyed rearward once more.

Napoleon had but small opinion of Greenville, Mississippi, in the old times; but behold, Napoleon is gone to the cat-fishes, and here is Greenville full of life and activity, and making a considerable flourish in the Valley; having three thousand inhabitants, it is said, and doing a gross trade of $2,500,000 annually. A growing town.

There was much talk on the boat about the Calhoun Land Company, an enterprise which is expected to work wholesome results. Colonel Calhoun, a grandson of the statesman, went to Boston and formed a syndicate which purchased a large tract of land on the river, in Chicot County, Arkansas—some ten thousand acres—for cotton-growing. The purpose is to work on a cash basis: buy at first hands, and handle their own product; supply their negro laborers with provisions and necessaries at a trifling profit, say 8 or 10 per cent.; furnish them comfortable quarters, etc., and encourage them to save money and remain on the place. If this proves a financial success, as seems quite certain, they propose to establish a banking-house in Greenville, and lend money at an unburdensome rate of interest—6 per cent. is spoken of.

The trouble heretofore has been—I am quoting remarks of planters and steamboatmen—that the planters, although

owning the land, were without cash capital; had to hypothecate both land and crop to carry on the business. Consequently, the commission dealer who furnishes the money takes some risk and demands big interest—usually 10 per cent., and 2½ per cent. for negotiating the loan. The planter has also to buy his supplies through the same dealer, paying commissions and profits. Then when he ships his crop, the dealer adds his commissions, insurance, etc. So, taking it by and large, and first and last, the dealer's share of that crop is about 25 per cent.*'

A cotton-planter's estimate of the average margin of profit on planting, in his section: One man and mule will raise ten acres of cotton, giving ten bales cotton, worth, say, $500; cost of producing, say $350; net profit, $150, or $15 per acre. There is also a profit now from the cotton-seed, which formerly had little value—none where much transportation was necessary. In sixteen hundred pounds crude cotton four hundred are lint, worth, say, ten cents a pound; and twelve hundred pounds of seed, worth $12 or $13 per ton. Maybe in future even the stems will not be thrown away. Mr. Edward Atkinson says that for each bale of cotton there are fifteen hundred pounds of stems, and that these are very rich in phosphate of lime and potash; that when ground and mixed with ensilage or cotton-seed meal (which is too rich for use as fodder in large quantities), the stem mixture makes a superior food, rich in all the elements needed for the production of milk, meat, and bone. Heretofore the stems have been considered a nuisance.

Complaint is made that the planter remains grouty toward the former slave, since the war; will have nothing but a chill business relation with him, no sentiment permitted to intrude, will not keep a 'store' himself, and supply the negro's wants and thus protect the negro's pocket and make him able and willing to stay on the place and an advantage to him to do it, but lets that privilege to some thrifty Israelite, who encourages the thoughtless negro and wife to buy all sorts of things which they could do without—buy on credit, at big prices, month after month, credit based on the negro's share of the growing crop; and at the end of the season, the negro's share belongs to the Israelite,' the negro is in debt besides, is discouraged, dissatisfied, restless, and both he and the planter are injured; for he will take steamboat and migrate, and the planter must get a stranger in his place who does not know him, does not care for him, will fatten the Israelite a season, and follow his predecessor per steamboat.

It is hoped that the Calhoun Company will show, by its humane and protective treatment of its laborers, that its method is the most profitable for both planter and negro; and it is believed that a general adoption of that method will then follow.

And where so many are saying their say, shall not the barkeeper testify? He is thoughtful, observant, never drinks; endeavors to earn his salary, and WOULD earn it if there were custom enough. He says the people along here in Mississippi and Louisiana will send up the river to buy vegetables rather than raise them, and they will come aboard at the landings and buy fruits of the barkeeper. Thinks they 'don't know anything but cotton;' believes they don't know how to raise vegetables and fruit—'at least the most of them.' Says 'a nigger will go to

* 'But what can the State do where the people are under subjection to rates of interest ranging from 18 to 30 per cent., and are also under the necessity of purchasing their crops in advance even of planting, at these rates, for the privilege of purchasing all their supplies at 100 per cent. profit?'—EDWARD ATKINSON.

H for a watermelon' ('H' is all I find in the stenographer's report—means Halifax probably, though that seems a good way to go for a watermelon). Barkeeper buys watermelons for five cents up the river, brings them down and sells them for fifty. 'Why does he mix such elaborate and picturesque drinks for the nigger hands on the boat?' Because they won't have any other. 'They want a big drink; don't make any difference what you make it of, they want the worth of their money. You give a nigger a plain gill of half-a-dollar brandy for five cents—will he touch it? No. Ain't size enough to it. But you put up a pint of all kinds of worthless rubbish, and heave in some red stuff to make it beautiful—red's the main thing—and he wouldn't put down that glass to go to a circus.' All the bars on this Anchor Line are rented and owned by one firm. They furnish the liquors from their own establishment, and hire the barkeepers 'on salary.' Good liquors? Yes, on some of the boats, where there are the kind of passengers that want it and can pay for it. On the other boats? No. Nobody but the deck hands and firemen to drink it. 'Brandy? Yes, I've got brandy, plenty of it; but you don't want any of it unless you've made your will.' It isn't as it used to be in the old times. Then everybody traveled by steamboat, everybody drank, and everybody treated everybody else. 'Now most everybody goes by railroad, and the rest don't drink.' In the old times the barkeeper owned the bar himself, 'and was gay and smarty and talky and all jeweled up, and was the toniest aristocrat on the boat; used to make $2,000 on a trip. A father who left his son a steamboat bar, left him a fortune. Now he leaves him board and lodging; yes, and washing, if a shirt a trip will do. Yes, indeedy, times are changed. Why, do you know, on the principal line of boats on the Upper Mississippi, they don't have any bar at all! Sounds like poetry, but it's the petrified truth.'

Chapter 34 Tough Yarns

STACK ISLAND. I remembered Stack Island; also Lake Providence, Louisiana—which is the first distinctly Southern-looking town you come to, downward-bound; lies level and low, shade-trees hung with venerable gray beards of Spanish moss; 'restful, pensive, Sunday aspect about the place,' comments Uncle Mumford, with feeling—also with truth.

A Mr. H. furnished some minor details of fact concerning this region which I would have hesitated to believe if I had not known him to be a steamboat mate. He was a passenger of ours, a resident of Arkansas City, and bound to Vicksburg to join his boat, a little Sunflower packet. He was an austere man, and had the reputation of being singularly unworldly, for a river man. Among other things, he said that Arkansas had been injured and kept back by generations of exaggerations concerning the mosquitoes here. One may smile, said he, and turn the matter off as being a small thing; but when you come to look at the effects produced, in the way of discouragement of immigration, and diminished values of property, it was quite the opposite of a small thing, or thing in any wise to be coughed down or sneered at. These mosquitoes had been persistently represented as being formidable and lawless; whereas 'the truth is, they are feeble, insignificant in size, diffident to a fault, sensitive'—and so on, and so on; you would have supposed he was talking about his family. But if he was soft on the Arkansas mosquitoes, he was hard enough on the mosquitoes of Lake Providence to make up for it—'those Lake Providence colossi,' as he finely called them. He said that two of them could whip a dog, and that four of them could hold a man down; and except help come, they would kill him— 'butcher him,' as he expressed it. Referred in a sort of casual way—and yet significant way—to 'the fact that the life policy in its simplest form is unknown in Lake Providence—they take out a mosquito policy besides.' He told many remarkable things about those lawless insects. Among others, said he had seen them try to vote. Noticing that this statement seemed to be a good deal of a strain on us, he modified it a little: said he might have been mistaken, as to that particular, but knew he had seen them around the polls 'canvassing.'

There was another passenger—friend of H.'s—who backed up the harsh evidence against those mosquitoes, and detailed some stirring adventures which he had had with them. The stories were pretty sizable, merely pretty sizable; yet Mr. H. was continually interrupting with a cold, inexorable 'Wait—knock off twenty-five per cent. of that; now go on;' or, 'Wait—you are getting that too strong; cut it down, cut it down— you get a leetle too much costumery on to your statements: always dress a fact in tights, never in an ulster;' or, 'Pardon, once more: if you are going to load anything more on to that statement, you want to get a couple of lighters and tow the rest, because it's drawing all the water there is in the river already; stick to facts—just stick to the cold facts; what these gentlemen want for a book is the frozen truth—ain't that so, gentlemen?' He explained privately that it was necessary to watch this man all the time, and keep him within bounds; it would not do to neglect this precaution, as he, Mr. H., 'knew to his sorrow.' Said he, 'I will not deceive you; he told me such a monstrous lie once, that it swelled my left ear up, and spread it so that I was actually not able to see out around it; it remained so for months, and people came miles to see me fan myself with it.'

Chapter 35 Vicksburg During the Trouble

WE used to plow past the lofty hill-city, Vicksburg, down-stream; but we cannot do that now. A cut-off has made a country town of it, like Osceola, St. Genevieve, and several others. There is currentless water —also a big island—in front of Vicksburg now. You come down the river the other side of the island, then turn and come up to the town; that is, in high water: in low water you can't come up, but must land some distance below it.

Signs and scars still remain, as reminders of Vicksburg's tremendous war experiences; earthworks, trees crippled by the cannon balls, cave- refuges in the clay precipices, etc. The caves did good service during the six weeks' bombardment of the city—May 8 to July 4, 1863. They were used by the non-combatants—mainly by the women and children; not to live in constantly, but to fly to for safety on occasion. They were mere holes, tunnels, driven into the perpendicular clay bank, then branched Y shape, within the hill. Life in Vicksburg, during the six weeks was perhaps—but wait; here are some materials out of which to reproduce it:—

Population, twenty-seven thousand soldiers and three thousand non- combatants; the city utterly cut off from the world—walled solidly in, the frontage by gunboats, the rear by soldiers and batteries; hence, no buying and selling with the outside; no passing to and fro; no God- speeding a parting guest, no welcoming a coming one; no printed acres of world-wide news to be read at breakfast, mornings—a tedious dull absence of such matter, instead; hence, also, no running to see steamboats smoking into view in the distance up or down, and plowing toward the town—for none came, the river lay vacant and undisturbed; no rush and turmoil around the railway station, no struggling over bewildered swarms of passengers by noisy mobs of hackmen—all quiet there; flour two hundred dollars a barrel, sugar thirty, corn ten dollars a bushel, bacon five dollars a pound, rum a hundred dollars a gallon; other things in proportion: consequently, no roar and racket of drays and carriages tearing along the streets; nothing for them to do, among that handful of non-combatants of exhausted means; at three o'clock in the morning, silence; silence so dead that the measured tramp of a sentinel can be heard a seemingly impossible distance; out of hearing of this lonely sound, perhaps the stillness is absolute: all in a moment come ground-shaking thunder-crashes of artillery, the sky is cobwebbed with the crisscrossing red lines streaming from soaring bomb- shells, and a rain of iron fragments descends upon the city; descends upon the empty streets: streets which are not empty a moment later, but mottled with dim figures of frantic women and children scurrying from home and bed toward the cave dungeons—encouraged by the humorous grim soldiery, who shout 'Rats, to your holes!' and laugh.

The cannon-thunder rages, shells scream and crash overhead, the iron rain pours down, one hour, two hours, three, possibly six, then stops; silence follows, but the streets are still empty; the silence continues; by-and-bye a head projects from a cave here and there and yonder, and reconnoitres, cautiously; the silence still continuing, bodies follow heads, and jaded, half smothered creatures group themselves about, stretch their cramped limbs, draw in deep draughts of the grateful fresh air, gossip with the neighbors from the next cave; maybe straggle off home presently, or take a lounge through the town, if the stillness continues; and will scurry to the holes again, by-and-bye, when the war- tempest breaks forth once more.

There being but three thousand of these cave-dwellers—merely the population of a village—would they not come to know each other, after a week or two, and familiarly; insomuch that the fortunate or unfortunate experiences of one would be of interest to all?

Those are the materials furnished by history. From them might not almost anybody reproduce for himself the life of that time in Vicksburg? Could you, who did not experience it, come nearer to reproducing it to the imagination of another non-participant than could a Vicksburger who did experience it? It seems impossible; and yet there are reasons why it might not really be. When one makes his first voyage in a ship, it is an experience which multitudinously bristles with striking novelties; novelties which are in such sharp contrast with all this person's former experiences that they take a seemingly deathless grip upon his imagination and memory. By tongue or pen he can make a landsman live that strange and stirring voyage over with him; make him see it all and feel it all. But if he wait? If he make ten voyages in succession—what then? Why, the thing has lost color, snap, surprise; and has become commonplace. The man would have nothing to tell that would quicken a landsman's pulse.

Years ago, I talked with a couple of the Vicksburg non-combatants—a man and his wife. Left to tell their story in their own way, those people told it without fire, almost without interest.

A week of their wonderful life there would have made their tongues eloquent for ever perhaps; but they had six weeks of it, and that wore the novelty all out; they got used to being bomb-shelled out of home and into the ground; the matter became commonplace. After that, the possibility of their ever being startlingly interesting in their talks about it was gone. What the man said was to this effect:—

'It got to be Sunday all the time. Seven Sundays in the week—to us, anyway. We hadn't anything to do, and time hung heavy.

Seven Sundays, and all of them broken up at one time or another, in the day or in the night, by a few hours of the awful storm of fire and thunder and iron. At first we used to shin for the holes a good deal faster than we did afterwards. The first time, I forgot the children, and Maria fetched them both along. When she was all safe in the cave she fainted. Two or three weeks afterwards, when she was running for the holes, one morning, through a shell-shower, a big shell burst near her, and covered her all over with dirt, and a piece of the iron carried away her game-bag of false hair from the back of her head. Well, she stopped to get that game-bag before she shoved along again! Was getting used to things already, you see. We all got so that we could tell a good deal about shells; and after that we didn't always go under shelter if it was a light shower. Us men would loaf around and talk; and a man would say, 'There she goes!' and name the kind of shell it was from the sound of it, and go on talking—if there wasn't any danger from it. If a shell was bursting close over us, we stopped talking and stood still;— uncomfortable, yes, but it wasn't safe to move. When it let go, we went on talking again, if nobody hurt—maybe saying, 'That was a ripper!' or some such commonplace comment before we resumed; or, maybe, we would see a shell poising itself away high in the air overhead. In that case, every fellow just whipped out a sudden, 'See you again, gents!' and shoved. Often and often I saw gangs of ladies promenading the streets, looking as cheerful as you please, and keeping an eye canted up watching the shells; and I've seen them stop still when they were uncertain about what a shell was going to do, and wait and make certain; and after that they sa'ntered along again, or lit out for shelter, according to the verdict. Streets in some towns have a litter of pieces of paper, and odds and ends of one sort or another lying around. Ours hadn't; they had IRON litter. Sometimes a man would gather up all the iron fragments and unburstedshells in his neighborhood, and pile them into a kind of monument in his front yard—a ton of it, sometimes. No glass left; glass couldn't stand such a bombardment; it was all shivered out. Windows of the houses vacant—looked like eye-holes in a skull. WHOLE panes were as scarce as news.

'We had church Sundays. Not many there, along at first; but by-and-bye pretty good turnouts. I've seen service stop a minute, and everybody sit quiet—no voice heard, pretty funeral-like then—and all the more so on account of the awful boom and crash going on outside and overhead; and pretty soon, when a body could be heard, service would go on again. Organs and church-music mixed up with a bombardment is a powerful queer combination—along at first. Coming out of church, one morning, we had an accident—the only one that happened around me on a Sunday. I was just having a hearty handshake with a friend I hadn't seen for a while, and saying, 'Drop into our cave to-night, after bombardment; we've got hold of a pint of prime wh—.' Whiskey, I was going to say, you know, but a shell interrupted. A chunk of it cut the man's arm off, and left it dangling in my hand. And do you know the thing that is going to stick the longest in my memory, and outlast everything else, little and big, I reckon, is the mean thought I had then? It was 'the whiskey IS SAVED.' And yet, don't you know, it was kind of excusable; because it was as scarce as diamonds, and we had only just that little; never had another taste during the siege.

'Sometimes the caves were desperately crowded, and always hot and close. Sometimes a cave had twenty or twenty-five people packed into it; no turning-room for anybody; air so foul, sometimes, you couldn't have made a candle burn in it. A child was born in one of those caves one night, Think of that; why, it was like having it born in a trunk.

'Twice we had sixteen people in our cave; and a number of times we had a dozen. Pretty suffocating in there. We always had eight; eight belonged there. Hunger and misery and sickness and fright and sorrow, and I don't know what all, got so loaded into them that none of them were ever rightly their old selves after the siege. They all died but three of us within a couple of years. One night a shell burst in front of the hole and caved it in and stopped it up. It was lively times, for a while, digging out. Some of us came near smothering. After that we made two openings—ought to have thought of it at first.

'Mule meat. No, we only got down to that the last day or two. Of course it was good; anything is good when you are starving.

This man had kept a diary during—six weeks? No, only the first six days. The first day, eight close pages; the second, five; the third, one—loosely written; the fourth, three or four lines; a line or two the fifth and sixth days; seventh day, diary abandoned; life in terrific Vicksburg having now become commonplace and matter of course.

The war history of Vicksburg has more about it to interest the general reader than that of any other of the river-towns. It is full of variety, full of incident, full of the picturesque. Vicksburg held out longer than any other important river-town, and saw warfare in all its phases, both land and water—the siege, the mine, the assault, the repulse, the bombardment, sickness, captivity, famine.

The most beautiful of all the national cemeteries is here. Over the great gateway is this inscription:—

"HERE REST IN PEACE 16,600 WHO DIED FOR THEIR COUNTRY IN THE YEARS 1861 TO 1865"

The grounds are nobly situated; being very high and commanding a wide prospect of land and river. They are tastefully laid out in broad terraces, with winding roads and paths; and there is profuse adornment in the way of semi-tropical shrubs and flowers,' and in one part is a piece of native wild-wood, left just as it grew, and, therefore, perfect in its charm. Everything about this cemetery suggests the hand of the national Government. The Government's work is always conspicuous for excellence, solidity, thoroughness, neatness. The Government does its work well in the first place, and then takes care of it.

By winding-roads—which were often cut to so great a depth between perpendicular walls that they were mere roofless tunnels—we drove out a mile or two and visited the monument which stands upon the scene of the surrender of Vicksburg to General Grant by General Pemberton. Its metal will preserve it from the hackings and chippings which so defaced its predecessor, which was of marble; but the brick foundations are crumbling, and it will tumble down by-and-bye. It overlooks a picturesque region of wooded hills and ravines; and is not unpicturesque itself, being well smothered in flowering weeds. The battered remnant of the marble monument has been removed to the National Cemetery.

On the road, a quarter of a mile townward, an aged colored man showed us, with pride, an unexploded bomb-shell which has lain in his yard since the day it fell there during the siege.

'I was a-stannin' heah, an' de dog was a-stannin' heah; de dog he went for de shell, gwine to pick a fuss wid it; but I didn't; I says, "Jes' make you'seff at home heah; lay still whah you is, or bust up de place, jes' as you's a mind to, but I's got business out in de woods, I has!"'

Vicksburg is a town of substantial business streets and pleasant residences; it commands the commerce of the Yazoo and Sunflower Rivers; is pushing railways in several directions, through rich agricultural regions, and has a promising future of prosperity and importance.

Apparently, nearly all the river towns, big and little, have made up their minds that they must look mainly to railroads for wealth and upbuilding, henceforth. They are acting upon this idea. The signs are, that the next twenty years will bring about some noteworthy changes in the Valley, in the direction of increased population and wealth, and in the intellectual advancement and the liberalizing of opinion which go naturally with these. And yet, if one may judge by the past, the river towns will manage to find and use a chance, here and there, to cripple and retard their progress. They kept themselves back in the days of steamboating supremacy, by a system of wharfage-dues so stupidly graded as to prohibit what may be called small RETAIL traffic in freights and passengers. Boats were charged such heavy wharfage that they could not afford to land for one or two passengers or a light lot of freight. Instead of encouraging the bringing of trade to their doors, the towns diligently and effectively discouraged it. They could have had many boats and low rates; but their policy rendered few boats and high rates compulsory. It was a policy which extended—and extends—from New Orleans to St. Paul.

We had a strong desire to make a trip up the Yazoo and the Sunflower—an interesting region at any time, but additionally interesting at this time, because up there the great inundation was still to be seen in force—but we were nearly sure to have to wait a day or more for a New Orleans boat on our return; so we were obliged to give up the project.

Here is a story which I picked up on board the boat that night. I insert it in this place merely because it is a good story, not because it belongs here—for it doesn't. It was told by a passenger—a college professor—and was called to the surface in the course of a general conversation which began with talk about horses, drifted into talk about astronomy, then into talk about the lynching of the gamblers in Vicksburg half a century ago, then into talk about dreams and superstitions; and ended, after midnight, in a dispute over free trade and protection.

Chapter 36 The Professor's Yarn

IT was in the early days. I was not a college professor then. I was a humble-minded young land-surveyor, with the world before me—to survey, in case anybody wanted it done. I had a contract to survey a route for a great mining-ditch in California, and I was on my way thither, by sea —a three or four weeks' voyage. There were a good many passengers, but I had very little to say to them; reading and dreaming were my passions, and I avoided conversation in order to indulge these appetites. There were three professional gamblers on board—rough, repulsive fellows. I never had any talk with them, yet I could not help seeing them with some frequency, for they gambled in an upper-deck stateroom every day and night, and in my promenades I often had glimpses of them through their door, which stood a little ajar to let out the surplus tobacco smoke and profanity. They were an evil and hateful presence, but I had to put up with it, of course,

There was one other passenger who fell under my eye a good deal, for he seemed determined to be friendly with me, and I could not have gotten rid of him without running some chance of hurting his feelings, and I was far from wishing to do that. Besides, there was something engaging in his countrified simplicity and his beaming good-nature. The first time I saw this Mr. John Backus, I guessed, from his clothes and his looks, that he was a grazier or farmer from the backwoods of some western State—doubtless Ohio—and afterward when he dropped into his personal history and I discovered that he WAS a cattle-raiser from interior Ohio, I was so pleased with my own penetration that I warmed toward him for verifying my instinct.

He got to dropping alongside me every day, after breakfast, to help me make my promenade; and so, in the course of time, his easy-working jaw had told me everything about his business, his prospects, his family, his relatives, his politics—in fact everything that concerned a Backus, living or dead. And meantime I think he had managed to get out of me everything I knew about my trade, my tribe, my purposes, my prospects, and myself. He was a gentle and persuasive genius, and this thing showed it; for I was not given to talking about my matters. I said something about triangulation, once; the stately word pleased his ear; he inquired what it meant; I explained; after that he quietly and inoffensively ignored my name, and always called me Triangle.

What an enthusiast he was in cattle! At the bare name of a bull or a cow, his eye would light and his eloquent tongue would turn itself loose. As long as I would walk and listen, he would walk and talk; he knew all breeds, he loved all breeds, he caressed them all with his affectionate tongue. I tramped along in voiceless misery whilst the cattle question was up; when I could endure it no longer, I used to deftly insert a scientific topic into the conversation; then my eye fired and his faded; my tongue fluttered, his stopped; life was a joy to me, and a sadness to him.

One day he said, a little hesitatingly, and with somewhat of diffidence—

'Triangle, would you mind coming down to my stateroom a minute, and have a little talk on a certain matter?'

I went with him at once. Arrived there, he put his head out, glanced up and down the saloon warily, then closed the door and locked it. He sat down on the sofa, and he said—

'I'm a-going to make a little proposition to you, and if it strikes you favorable, it'll be a middling good thing for both of us. You ain't a-going out to Californy for fun, nuther am I—it's business, ain't that so? Well, you can do me a good turn, and so can I you, if we see fit. I've raked and scraped and saved, a considerable many years, and I've got it all here.' He unlocked an old hair trunk, tumbled a chaos of shabby clothes aside, and drew a short stout bag into view for a moment, then buried it again and relocked the trunk. Dropping his voice to a cautious low tone, he continued, 'She's all there—a round ten thousand dollars in yellow-boys; now this is my little idea: What I don't know about raising cattle, ain't worth knowing. There's mints of money in it, in Californy. Well, I know, and you know, that all along a line that's being surveyed, there's little dabs of land that they call "gores," that fall to the surveyor free gratis for nothing. All you've got to do, on your side, is to survey in such a way that the "gores" will fall on good fat land, then you turn 'em over to me, I stock 'em with cattle, in rolls the cash, I plank out your share of the dollars regular, right along, and—'

I was sorry to wither his blooming enthusiasm, but it could not be helped. I interrupted, and said severely—

'I am not that kind of a surveyor. Let us change the subject, Mr. Backus.'

It was pitiful to see his confusion and hear his awkward and shamefaced apologies. I was as much distressed as he was—especially as he seemed so far from having suspected that there was anything improper in his proposition. So I hastened to console him and lead him on to forget his mishap in a conversational orgy about cattle and butchery. We were lying at Acapulco; and, as we went on deck, it happened luckily that the crew were just beginning to hoist some beeves aboard in slings. Backus's melancholy vanished instantly, and with it the memory of his late mistake.

'Now only look at that!' cried he; 'My goodness, Triangle, what WOULD they say to it in OHIO. Wouldn't their eyes bug out, to see 'em handled like that?—wouldn't they, though?'

All the passengers were on deck to look—even the gamblers—and Backus knew them all, and had afflicted them all with his pet topic. As I moved away, I saw one of the gamblers approach and accost him; then another of them; then the third. I halted; waited; watched; the conversation continued between the four men; it grew earnest; Backus drew gradually away; the gamblers followed, and kept at his elbow. I was uncomfortable. However, as they passed me presently, I heard Backus say, with a tone of persecuted annoyance—

'But it ain't any use, gentlemen; I tell you again, as I've told you a half a dozen times before, I warn't raised to it, and I ain't a-going to resk it.'

I felt relieved. 'His level head will be his sufficient protection,' I said to myself.

During the fortnight's run from Acapulco to San Francisco I several times saw the gamblers talking earnestly with Backus, and once I threw out a gentle warning to him. He chuckled comfortably and said—

'Oh, yes! they tag around after me considerable—want me to play a little, just for amusement, they say—but laws-a-me, if my folks have told me once to look out for that sort of live-stock, they've told me a thousand times, I reckon.'

By-and-bye, in due course, we were approaching San Francisco. It was an ugly black night, with a strong wind blowing, but there was not much sea. I was on deck, alone. Toward ten I started below. A figure issued from the gamblers' den, and disappeared in the darkness. I experienced a shock, for I was sure it was Backus. I flew down the companion-way, looked about for him, could not find him, then returned to the deck just in time to catch a glimpse of him as he re-entered that confounded nest of rascality. Had he yielded at last? I feared it. What had he gone below for?—His bag of coin? Possibly. I drew near the door, full of bodings. It was a-crack, and I glanced in and saw a sight that made me bitterly wish I had given my attention to saving my poor cattle-friend, instead of reading and dreaming my foolish time away. He was gambling. Worse still, he was being plied with champagne, and was already showing some effect from it. He praised the 'cider,' as he called it, and said now that he had got a taste of it he almost believed he would drink it if it was spirits, it was so good and so ahead of anything he had ever run across before. Surreptitious smiles, at this, passed from one rascal to another, and they filled all the glasses, and whilst Backus honestly drained his to the bottom they pretended to do the same, but threw the wine over their shoulders.

I could not bear the scene, so I wandered forward and tried to interest myself in the sea and the voices of the wind. But no, my uneasy spirit kept dragging me back at quarter-hour intervals; and always I saw Backus drinking his wine—fairly and squarely, and the others throwing theirs away. It was the painfullest night I ever spent.

The only hope I had was that we might reach our anchorage with speed— that would break up the game. I helped the ship along all I could with my prayers. At last we went booming through the Golden Gate, and my pulses leaped for joy. I hurried back to that door and glanced in. Alas, there was small room for hope—Backus's eyes were heavy and bloodshot, his sweaty face was crimson, his speech maudlin and thick, his body sawed drunkenly about with the weaving motion of the ship. He drained another glass to the dregs, whilst the cards were being dealt.

He took his hand, glanced at it, and his dull eyes lit up for a moment. The gamblers observed it, and showed their gratification by hardly perceptible signs.

'How many cards?'

'None!' said Backus.

One villain—named Hank Wiley—discarded one card, the others three each. The betting began. Heretofore the bets had been trifling—a dollar or two; but Backus started off with an eagle now, Wiley hesitated a moment, then 'saw it' and 'went ten dollars better.' The other two threw up their hands.

Backus went twenty better. Wiley said—

'I see that, and go you a hundred better!' then smiled and reached for the money.

'Let it alone,' said Backus, with drunken gravity.

'What! you mean to say you're going to cover it?'

'Cover it? Well, I reckon I am—and lay another hundred on top of it, too.'

He reached down inside his overcoat and produced the required sum.

'Oh, that's your little game, is it? I see your raise, and raise it five hundred!' said Wiley.

'Five hundred better.' said the foolish bull-driver, and pulled out the amount and showered it on the pile. The three conspirators hardly tried to conceal their exultation.

All diplomacy and pretense were dropped now, and the sharp exclamations came thick and fast, and the yellow pyramid grew higher and higher. At last ten thousand dollars lay in view. Wiley cast a bag of coin on the table, and said with mocking gentleness—

'Five thousand dollars better, my friend from the rural districts—what do you say NOW?'

'I CALL you!' said Backus, heaving his golden shot-bag on the pile. 'What have you got?'

'Four kings, you d—d fool!' and Wiley threw down his cards and surrounded the stakes with his arms.

'Four ACES, you ass!' thundered Backus, covering his man with a cocked revolver. 'I'M A PROFESSIONAL GAMBLER MYSELF, AND I'VE BEEN LAYING FOR YOU DUFFERS ALL THIS VOYAGE!'

Down went the anchor, rumbledy-dum-dum! and the long trip was ended.

Well—well, it is a sad world. One of the three gamblers was Backus's 'pal.' It was he that dealt the fateful hands. According to an understanding with the two victims, he was to have given Backus four queens, but alas, he didn't.

A week later, I stumbled upon Backus—arrayed in the height of fashion— in Montgomery Street. He said, cheerily, as we were parting—

'Ah, by-the-way, you needn't mind about those gores. I don't really know anything about cattle, except what I was able to pick up in a week's apprenticeship over in Jersey just before we sailed. My cattle- culture and cattle-enthusiasm have served their turn—I shan't need them any more.'

Next day we reluctantly parted from the 'Gold Dust' and her officers, hoping to see that boat and all those officers again, some day. A thing which the fates were to render tragically impossible!

Chapter 37 The End of the 'Gold Dust'

FOR, three months later, August 8, while I was writing one of these foregoing chapters, the New York papers brought this telegram—

A TERRIBLE DISASTER.

SEVENTEEN PERSONS KILLED BY AN EXPLOSION ON THE STEAMER 'GOLD DUST.'

'NASHVILLE, Aug. 7.—A despatch from Hickman, Ky., says—

'The steamer "Gold Dust" exploded her boilers at three o'clock to-day, just after leaving Hickman. Forty-seven persons were scalded and seventeen are missing. The boat was landed in the eddy just above the town, and through the exertions of the citizens the cabin passengers, officers, and part of the crew and deck passengers were taken ashore and removed to the hotels and residences. Twenty-four of the injured were lying in Holcomb's dry-goods store at one time, where they received every attention before being removed to more comfortable places.'

A list of the names followed, whereby it appeared that of the seventeen dead, one was the barkeeper; and among the forty-seven wounded, were the captain, chief mate, second mate, and second and third clerks; also Mr. Lem S. Gray, pilot, and several members of the crew.

In answer to a private telegram, we learned that none of these was severely hurt, except Mr. Gray. Letters received afterward confirmed this news, and said that Mr. Gray was improving and would get well. Later letters spoke less hopefully of his case; and finally came one announcing his death. A good man, a most companionable and manly man, and worthy of a kindlier fate.

Chapter 38 The House Beautiful

WE took passage in a Cincinnati boat for New Orleans; or on a Cincinnati boat—either is correct; the former is the eastern form of putting it, the latter the western.

Mr. Dickens declined to agree that the Mississippi steamboats were 'magnificent,' or that they were 'floating palaces,'—terms which had always been applied to them; terms which did not over-express the admiration with which the people viewed them.

Mr. Dickens's position was unassailable, possibly; the people's position was certainly unassailable. If Mr. Dickens was comparing these boats with the crown jewels; or with the Taj, or with the Matterhorn; or with some other priceless or wonderful thing which he had seen, they were not magnificent—he was right. The people compared them with what they had seen; and, thus measured, thus judged, the boats were magnificent—the term was the correct one, it was not at all too strong. The people were as right as was Mr. Dickens. The steamboats were finer than anything on shore. Compared with superior dwelling-houses and first-class hotels in the Valley, they were indubitably magnificent, they were 'palaces.' To a few people living in New Orleans and St. Louis, they were not magnificent, perhaps; not palaces; but to the great majority of those populations, and to the entire populations spread over both banks between Baton Rouge and St. Louis, they were palaces; they tallied with the citizen's dream of what magnificence was, and satisfied it.

Every town and village along that vast stretch of double river-frontage had a best dwelling, finest dwelling, mansion,—the home of its wealthiest and most conspicuous citizen. It is easy to describe it: large grassy yard, with paling fence painted white—in fair repair; brick walk from gate to door; big, square, two-story 'frame' house, painted white and porticoed like a Grecian temple—with this difference, that the imposing fluted columns and Corinthian capitals were a pathetic sham, being made of white pine, and painted; iron knocker; brass door knob—discolored, for lack of polishing.

Within, an uncarpeted hall, of planed boards; opening out of it, a parlor, fifteen feet by fifteen—in some instances five or ten feet larger; ingrain carpet; mahogany center- table; lamp on it, with green-paper shade—standing on a gridiron, so to speak, made of high-colored yarns, by the young ladies of the house, and called a lamp-mat; several books, piled and disposed, with cast-iron exactness, according to an inherited and unchangeable plan; among them, Tupper, much penciled; also, 'Friendship's Offering,' and 'Affection's Wreath,' with their sappy inanities illustrated in die-away mezzotints; also, Ossian; 'Alonzo and Melissa:' maybe 'Ivanhoe:' also 'Album,' full of original 'poetry' of the Thou-hast-wounded-the-spirit-that-loved-thee breed; two or three goody-goody works— 'Shepherd of Salisbury Plain,' etc.; current number of the chaste and innocuous Godey's 'Lady's Book,' with painted fashion-plate of wax-figure women with mouths all alike— lips and eyelids the same size—each five-foot woman with a two-inch wedge sticking out from under her dress and letting-on to be half of her foot.

Polished air-tight stove (new and deadly invention), with pipe passing through a board which closes up the discarded good old fireplace. On each end of the wooden mantel, over the

fireplace, a large basket of peaches and other fruits, natural size, all done in plaster, rudely, or in wax, and painted to resemble the originals—which they don't. Over middle of mantel, engraving—Washington Crossing the Delaware; on the wall by the door, copy of it done in thunder-and- lightning crewels by one of the young ladies—work of art which would have made Washington hesitate about crossing, if he could have foreseen what advantage was going to be taken of it.

Piano—kettle in disguise— with music, bound and unbound, piled on it, and on a stand near by: Battle of Prague; Bird Waltz; Arkansas Traveler; Rosin the Bow; Marseilles Hymn; On a Lone Barren Isle (St. Helena); The Last Link is Broken; She wore a Wreath of Roses the Night when last we met; Go, forget me, Why should Sorrow o'er that Brow a Shadow fling; Hours there were to Memory Dearer; Long, Long Ago; Days of Absence; A Life on the Ocean Wave, a Home on the Rolling Deep; Bird at Sea; and spread open on the rack, where the plaintive singer has left it, RO-holl on, silver MOO-hoon, guide the TRAV-el-lerr his WAY, etc. Tilted pensively against the piano, a guitar—guitar capable of playing the Spanish Fandango by itself, if you give it a start.

Frantic work of art on the wall—pious motto, done on the premises, sometimes in colored yarns, sometimes in faded grasses: progenitor of the 'God Bless Our Home' of modern commerce. Framed in black moldings on the wall, other works of arts, conceived and committed on the premises, by the young ladies; being grim black-and-white crayons; landscapes, mostly: lake, solitary sail-boat, petrified clouds, pre-geological trees on shore, anthracite precipice; name of criminal conspicuous in the corner. Lithograph, Napoleon Crossing the Alps. Lithograph, The Grave at St. Helena. Steel-plates, Trumbull's Battle of Bunker Hill, and the Sally from Gibraltar. Copper-plates, Moses Smiting the Rock, and Return of the Prodigal Son.

In big gilt frame, slander of the family in oil: papa holding a book ('Constitution of the United States'); guitar leaning against mamma, blue ribbons fluttering from its neck; the young ladies, as children, in slippers and scalloped pantelettes, one embracing toy horse, the other beguiling kitten with ball of yarn, and both simpering up at mamma, who simpers back. These persons all fresh, raw, and red—apparently skinned.

Opposite, in gilt frame, grandpa and grandma, at thirty and twenty-two, stiff, old-fashioned, high-collared, puff-sleeved, glaring pallidly out from a background of solid Egyptian night. Under a glass French clock dome, large bouquet of stiff flowers done in corpsy-white wax. Pyramidal what-not in the corner, the shelves occupied chiefly with bric-a-brac of the period, disposed with an eye to best effect: shell, with the Lord's Prayer carved on it; another shell—of the long-oval sort, narrow, straight orifice, three inches long, running from end to end—portrait of Washington carved on it; not well done; the shell had Washington's mouth, originally—artist should have built to that. These two are memorials of the long-ago bridal trip to New Orleans and the French Market. Other bric-a-brac: Californian 'specimens'—quartz, with gold wart adhering; old Guinea-gold locket, with circlet of ancestral hair in it; Indian arrow-heads, of flint; pair of bead moccasins, from uncle who crossed the Plains; three 'alum' baskets of various colors— being skeleton-frame of wire, clothed-on with cubes of crystallized alum in the rock-candy style—works of art which were achieved by the young ladies; their doubles and duplicates to be found upon all what-nots in the land; convention of desiccated bugs and butterflies pinned to a card; painted toy-dog, seated upon bellows-attachment—drops its under jaw and squeaks when pressed upon; sugar-candy rabbit—limbs and features merged together, not strongly defined; pewter presidential-campaign medal; miniature cardboard wood-sawyer, to be attached to the stove-pipe and operated by the heat; small Napoleon, done in wax; spread-open daguerreotypes of dim children, parents, cousins, aunts, and friends, in all attitudes but customary ones; no templed portico at back, and manufactured landscape stretching away in the distance—that came in later, with the photograph; all these vague figures lavishly chained and ringed—metal indicated and secured from doubt by stripes and splashes of vivid gold bronze; all of them too much combed, too much fixed up; and all of them uncomfortable in inflexible Sunday-clothes of a pattern which the spectator cannot realize could ever have been in fashion; husband and wife generally grouped together—husband sitting, wife standing, with hand on his shoulder—and both preserving, all these fading years, some traceable effect of the daguerreotypist's brisk 'Now smile, if you please!' Bracketed over what-not—place of special sacredness—an outrage in water-color, done by the young niece that came on a visit long ago, and died. Pity, too; for she might have repented of this in time.

Horse-hair chairs, horse-hair sofa which keeps sliding from under you. Window shades, of oil stuff, with milk-maids and ruined castles stenciled on them in fierce colors. Lambrequins dependent from gaudy boxings of beaten tin, gilded. Bedrooms with rag carpets; bedsteads of the 'corded' sort, with a sag in the middle, the cords needing tightening; snuffy feather-bed—not aired often enough; cane- seat chairs, splint-bottomed rocker; looking-glass on wall, school-slate size, veneered frame; inherited bureau; wash-bowl and pitcher, possibly —but not certainly; brass candlestick, tallow candle, snuffers.

Nothing else in the room. Not a bathroom in the house; and no visitor likely to come along who has ever seen one.

That was the residence of the principal citizen, all the way from the suburbs of New Orleans to the edge of St. Louis. When he stepped aboard a big fine steamboat, he entered a new and marvelous world: chimney-tops cut to counterfeit a spraying crown of plumes—and maybe painted red; pilot-house, hurricane deck, boiler-deck guards, all garnished with white wooden filigree work of fanciful patterns; gilt acorns topping the derricks; gilt deer-horns over the big bell; gaudy symbolical picture on the paddle-box, possibly; big roomy boiler-deck, painted blue, and furnished with Windsor armchairs; inside, a far-receding snow-white 'cabin;' porcelain knob and oil-picture on every stateroom door; curving patterns of filigree-work touched up with gilding, stretching overhead all down the converging vista; big chandeliers every little way, each an April shower of glittering glass-drops; lovely rainbow-light falling everywhere from the colored glazing of the skylights; the whole a long- drawn, resplendent tunnel, a bewildering and soul-satisfying spectacle! In the ladies' cabin a pink and white Wilton carpet, as soft as mush, and glorified with a ravishing pattern of gigantic flowers. Then the Bridal Chamber—the animal that invented that idea was still alive and unhanged, at that day—Bridal Chamber whose pretentious flummery was necessarily overawing to the now tottering intellect of that hosannahing citizen. Every state-room had its couple of cozy clean bunks, and perhaps a looking-glass and a snug closet; and sometimes there was even a washbowl and pitcher, and part of a towel which could be told from mosquito netting by an expert—though generally these things were absent, and the shirt-sleeved passengers cleansed themselves at a long row of stationary bowls in the barber shop, where were also public towels, public combs, and public soap.

Take the steamboat which I have just described, and you have her in her highest and finest, and most pleasing, and comfortable, and satisfactory estate. Now cake her over with a layer of ancient and obdurate dirt, and you have the Cincinnati steamer awhile ago referred to. Not all over—only inside; for she was ably officered in all departments except the steward's.

But wash that boat and repaint her, and she would be about the counterpart of the most complimented boat of the old flush times: for the steamboat architecture of the West has undergone no change; neither has steamboat furniture and ornamentation undergone any.

Chapter 39 Manufactures and Miscreants

WHERE the river, in the Vicksburg region, used to be corkscrewed, it is now comparatively straight—made so by cut-off; a former distance of seventy miles is reduced to thirty-five. It is a change which threw Vicksburg's neighbor, Delta, Louisiana, out into the country and ended its career as a river town. Its whole river-frontage is now occupied by a vast sand-bar, thickly covered with young trees—a growth which will magnify itself into a dense forest by-and-bye, and completely hide the exiled town.

In due time we passed Grand Gulf and Rodney, of war fame, and reached Natchez, the last of the beautiful hill-cities—for Baton Rouge, yet to come, is not on a hill, but only on high ground. Famous Natchez-under- the-hill has not changed notably in twenty years; in outward aspect— judging by the descriptions of the ancient procession of foreign tourists—it has not changed in sixty; for it is still small, straggling, and shabby. It had a desperate reputation, morally, in the old keel-boating and early steamboating times—plenty of drinking, carousing, fisticuffing, and killing there, among the riff-raff of the river, in those days. But Natchez-on-top-of-the-hill is attractive; has always been attractive. Even Mrs. Trollope (1827) had to confess its charms:

'At one or two points the wearisome level line is relieved by bluffs, as they call the short intervals of high ground. The town of Natchez is beautifully situated on one of those high spots. The contrast that its bright green hill forms with the dismal line of black forest that stretches on every side, the abundant growth of the pawpaw, palmetto and orange, the copious variety of sweet-scented flowers that flourish there, all make it appear like an oasis in the desert. Natchez is the furthest point to the north at which oranges ripen in the open air, or endure the winter without shelter. With the exception of this sweet spot, I thought all the little towns and villages we passed wretched- looking in the extreme.'

Natchez, like her near and far river neighbors, has railways now, and is adding to them—pushing them hither and thither into all rich outlying regions that are naturally tributary to her. And like Vicksburg and New Orleans, she has her ice-factory: she makes thirty tons of ice a day. In Vicksburg and Natchez, in my time, ice was jewelry; none but the rich could wear it. But anybody and everybody can have it now. I visited one of the ice-factories in New Orleans, to see what the polar regions might look like when lugged into the edge of the tropics. But there was nothing striking in the aspect of the place. It was merely a spacious house, with some innocent steam machinery in one end of it and some big porcelain pipes running here and there. No, not porcelain—they merely seemed to be; they were iron, but the ammonia which was being breathed through them had coated them to the thickness of your hand with solid milk-white ice. It ought to have melted; for one did not require winter clothing in that atmosphere: but it did not melt; the inside of the pipe was too cold.

Sunk into the floor were numberless tin boxes, a foot square and two feet long, and open at the top end. These were full of clear water; and around each box, salt and other proper stuff was packed; also, the ammonia gases were applied to the water in some way which will always remain a secret to me, because I was not able to understand the process. While the water in the boxes gradually froze, men gave it a stir or two with a stick occasionally—to liberate the air-bubbles, I think. Other men were continually lifting out boxes whose contents had become hard frozen. They gave the box a single dip into a vat of boiling water, to melt the block of ice free from its tin coffin, then they shot the block out upon a platform car, and it was ready for market. These big blocks were hard, solid, and crystal-clear. In certain of them, big bouquets of fresh and brilliant tropical flowers had been frozen-in; in others, beautiful silken-clad French dolls, and other pretty objects. These blocks were to be set on end in a platter, in the center of dinner- tables, to cool the tropical air; and also to be ornamental, for the flowers and things imprisoned in them could be seen as through plate glass. I was told that this factory could retail its ice, by wagon, throughout New Orleans, in the humblest dwelling-house quantities, at six or seven dollars a ton, and make a sufficient profit. This being the case, there is business for ice-factories in the North; for we get ice on no such terms there, if one take less than three hundred and fifty pounds at a delivery.

The Rosalie Yarn Mill, of Natchez, has a capacity of 6,000 spindles and 160 looms, and employs 100 hands. The Natchez Cotton Mills Company began operations four years ago in a two-story building of 50 x 190 feet, with 4,000 spindles and 128 looms; capital $105,000, all subscribed in the town. Two years later, the same stockholders increased their capital to $225,000; added a third story to the mill, increased its length to 317 feet; added machinery to increase the capacity to 10,300 spindles and 304 looms. The company now employ 250 operatives, many of whom are citizens of Natchez. The mill works 5,000 bales of cotton annually and manufactures the best standard quality of brown shirtings and sheetings and drills, turning out 5,000,000 yards of these goods per year.*' A close corporation—stock held at $5,000 per share, but none in the market.

The changes in the Mississippi River are great and strange, yet were to be expected; but I was not expecting to live to see Natchez and these other river towns become manufacturing strongholds and railway centers.

Speaking of manufactures reminds me of a talk upon that topic which I heard—which I overheard—on board the Cincinnati boat. I awoke out of a fretted sleep, with a dull confusion of voices in my ears. I listened— two men were talking; subject, apparently, the great inundation. I looked out through the open transom. The two men were eating a late breakfast; sitting opposite each other; nobody else around. They closed up the inundation with a few words—having used it, evidently, as a mere ice-breaker and acquaintanceship-breeder—then they dropped into business. It soon transpired that they were drummers—one belonging in Cincinnati, the other in New Orleans. Brisk men, energetic of movement and speech; the dollar their god, how to get it their religion.

* New Orleans Times-Democrat, 26 Aug, 1882.

'Now as to this article,' said Cincinnati, slashing into the ostensible butter and holding forward a slab of it on his knife-blade, 'it's from our house; look at it—smell of it—taste it. Put any test on it you want to. Take your own time—no hurry—make it thorough. There now— what do you say? butter, ain't it. Not by a thundering sight—it's oleomargarine! Yes, sir, that's what it is—oleomargarine. You can't tell it from butter; by George, an EXPERT can't. It's from our house. We supply most of the boats in the West; there's hardly a pound of butter on one of them. We are crawling right along—JUMPING right along is the word. We are going to have that entire trade. Yes, and the hotel trade, too. You are going to see the day, pretty soon, when you can't find an ounce of butter to bless yourself with, in any hotel in the Mississippi and Ohio Valleys, outside of the biggest cities. Why, we are turning out oleomargarine NOW by the thousands of tons. And we can sell it so dirt-cheap that the whole country has GOT to take it—can't get around it you see. Butter don't stand any show—there ain't any chance for competition. Butter's had its DAY—and from this out, butter goes to the wall. There's more money in oleomargarine than—why, you can't imagine the business we do. I've stopped in every town from Cincinnati to Natchez; and I've sent home big orders from every one of them.'

And so-forth and so-on, for ten minutes longer, in the same fervid strain. Then New Orleans piped up and said—

Yes, it's a first-rate imitation, that's a certainty; but it ain't the only one around that's first-rate. For instance, they make olive-oil out of cotton-seed oil, nowadays, so that you can't tell them apart.'

'Yes, that's so,' responded Cincinnati, 'and it was a tip-top business for a while. They sent it over and brought it back from France and Italy, with the United States custom-house mark on it to indorse it for genuine, and there was no end of cash in it; but France and Italy broke up the game—of course they naturally would. Cracked on such a rattling impost that cotton-seed olive-oil couldn't stand the raise; had to hang up and quit.'

'Oh, it DID, did it? You wait here a minute.'

Goes to his state-room, brings back a couple of long bottles, and takes out the corks—says:

'There now, smell them, taste them, examine the bottles, inspect the labels. One of 'm's from Europe, the other's never been out of this country. One's European olive-oil, the other's American cotton-seed olive-oil. Tell 'm apart? 'Course you can't. Nobody can. People that want to, can go to the expense and trouble of shipping their oils to Europe and back—it's their privilege; but our firm knows a trick worth six of that. We turn out the whole thing—clean from the word go—in our factory in New Orleans: labels, bottles, oil, everything. Well, no, not labels: been buying them abroad—get them dirt-cheap there. You see, there's just one little wee speck, essence, or whatever it is, in a gallon of cotton-seed oil, that give it a smell, or a flavor, or something—get that out, and you're all right—perfectly easy then to turn the oil into any kind of oil you want to, and there ain't anybody that can detect the true from the false. Well, we know how to get that one little particle out—and we're the only firm that does. And we turn out an olive-oil that is just simply perfect—undetectable! We are doing a ripping trade, too—as I could easily show you by my order-book for this trip. Maybe you'll butter everybody's bread pretty soon, but we'll cotton-seed his salad for him from the Gulf to

Canada, and that's a dead-certain thing.'

Cincinnati glowed and flashed with admiration. The two scoundrels exchanged business-cards, and rose. As they left the table, Cincinnati said—

'But you have to have custom-house marks, don't you? How do you manage that?'

I did not catch the answer.

We passed Port Hudson, scene of two of the most terrific episodes of the war—the night-battle there between Farragut's fleet and the Confederate land batteries, April 14th, 1863; and the memorable land battle, two months later, which lasted eight hours—eight hours of exceptionally fierce and stubborn fighting—and ended, finally, in the repulse of the Union forces with great slaughter.

Chapter 40 Castles and Culture

BATON ROUGE was clothed in flowers, like a bride—no, much more so; like a greenhouse. For we were in the absolute South now—no modifications, no compromises, no half-way measures. The magnolia-trees in the Capitol grounds were lovely and fragrant, with their dense rich foliage and huge snow-ball blossoms. The scent of the flower is very sweet, but you want distance on it, because it is so powerful. They are not good bedroom blossoms—they might suffocate one in his sleep. We were certainly in the South at last; for here the sugar region begins, and the plantations—vast green levels, with sugar-mill and negro quarters clustered together in the middle distance—were in view. And there was a tropical sun overhead and a tropical swelter in the air.

And at this point, also, begins the pilot's paradise: a wide river hence to New Orleans, abundance of water from shore to shore, and no bars, snags, sawyers, or wrecks in his road.

Sir Walter Scott is probably responsible for the Capitol building; for it is not conceivable that this little sham castle would ever have been built if he had not run the people mad, a couple of generations ago, with his medieval romances. The South has not yet recovered from the debilitating influence of his books. Admiration of his fantastic heroes and their grotesque 'chivalry' doings and romantic juvenilities still survives here, in an atmosphere in which is already perceptible the wholesome and practical nineteenth-century smell of cotton-factories and locomotives; and traces of its inflated language and other windy humbuggeries survive along with it. It is pathetic enough, that a whitewashed castle, with turrets and things—materials all ungenuine within and without, pretending to be what they are not—should ever have been built in this otherwise honorable place; but it is much more pathetic to see this architectural falsehood undergoing restoration and perpetuation in our day, when it would have been so easy to let dynamite finish what a charitable fire began, and then devote this restoration- money to the building of something genuine.

Baton Rouge has no patent on imitation castles, however, and no monopoly of them. Here is a picture from the advertisement of the 'Female Institute' of Columbia, Tennessee. The following remark is from the same advertisement—

'The Institute building has long been famed as a model of striking and beautiful architecture. Visitors are charmed with its resemblance to the old castles of song and story, with its towers, turreted walls, and ivy-mantled porches.'

Keeping school in a castle is a romantic thing; as romantic as keeping hotel in a castle.

By itself the imitation castle is doubtless harmless, and well enough; but as a symbol and breeder and sustainer of maudlin Middle-Age romanticism here in the midst of the plainest and sturdiest and infinitely greatest and worthiest of all the centuries the world has seen, it is necessarily a hurtful thing and a mistake.

Here is an extract from the prospectus of a Kentucky 'Female College.' Female college sounds well enough; but since the phrasing it in that unjustifiable way was done purely in the interest of brevity, it seems to me that she-college would have been still better—because shorter, and means the same thing: that is, if either phrase means anything at all—

'The president is southern by birth, by rearing, by education, and by sentiment; the teachers are all southern in sentiment, and with the exception of those born in Europe were born and raised in the south. Believing the southern to be the highest type of civilization this continent has seen, the young ladies are trained according to the southern ideas of delicacy, refinement, womanhood, religion, and propriety; hence we offer a first-class female college for the south and solicit southern patronage.'*

---

* Illustrations of it thoughtlessly omitted by the advertiser:

KNOXVILLE, Tenn., October 19.—This morning a few minutes after ten o'clock, General Joseph A. Mabry, Thomas O'Connor, and Joseph A. Mabry, Jr., were killed in a shooting affray. The difficulty began yesterday afternoon by General Mabry attacking Major O'Connor and threatening to kill him. This was at the fair grounds, and O'Connor told Mabry that it was not the place to settle their difficulties. Mabry then told O'Connor he should not live. It seems that Mabry was armed and O'Connor was not. The cause of the difficulty was an old feud about the transfer of some property from Mabry to O'Connor. Later in the afternoon Mabry sent word to O'Connor that he would kill him on sight. This morning Major O'Connor was standing in the door of the Mechanics' National Bank, of which he was president. General Mabry and another gentleman walked down Gay Street on the opposite side from the bank. O'Connor stepped into the bank, got a shot gun, took deliberate aim at General Mabry and fired. Mabry fell dead, being shot in the left side. As he fell O'Connor fired again, the shot taking effect in Mabry's thigh. O'Connor then reached into the bank and got another shot gun. About this time Joseph A. Mabry, Jr., son of General Mabry, came rushing down the street, unseen by O'Connor until within forty feet, when the young man fired a pistol, the shot taking effect in O'Connor's right breast, passing through the body near the heart. The instant Mabry shot, O'Connor turned and fired, the load taking effect in young Mabry's right breast and side. Mabry fell pierced with twenty buckshot, and almost instantly O'Connor fell dead without a struggle. Mabry tried to rise, but fell back dead. The whole tragedy occurred within two minutes, and neither of the three spoke after he was shot. General Mabry had about thirty buckshot in his body. A bystander was painfully wounded in the thigh with a buckshot, and another was wounded in the arm. Four other men had their clothing pierced by buckshot. The affair caused great excitement, and Gay Street was thronged with thousands of people. General Mabry and his son Joe were acquitted only a few days ago of the murder of Moses Lusby and Don Lusby, father and son, whom they killed a few weeks ago. Will Mabry was killed by Don Lusby last Christmas. Major Thomas O'Connor was President of the Mechanics' National Bank here, and was the wealthiest man in the

What, warder, ho! the man that can blow so complacent a blast as that, probably blows it from a castle.

From Baton Rouge to New Orleans, the great sugar plantations border both sides of the river all the way, and stretch their league-wide levels back to the dim forest-walls of bearded cypress in the rear. Shores lonely no longer. Plenty of dwellings all the way, on both banks— standing so close together, for long distances, that the broad river lying between the two rows, becomes a sort of spacious street. A most home-like and happy-looking region. And now and then you see a pillared and porticoed great manor-house, embowered in trees. Here is testimony of one or two of the procession of foreign tourists that filed along here half a century ago. Mrs. Trollope says—

'The unbroken flatness of the banks of the Mississippi continued unvaried for many miles above New Orleans; but the graceful and luxuriant palmetto, the dark and noble ilex, and the bright orange, were everywhere to be seen, and it was many days before we were weary of looking at them.'

Captain Basil Hall—

'The district of country which lies adjacent to the Mississippi, in the lower parts of Louisiana, is everywhere thickly peopled by sugar planters, whose showy houses, gay piazzas, trig gardens, and numerous slave-villages, all clean and neat, gave an exceedingly thriving air to the river scenery.

All the procession paint the attractive picture in the same way.

State.—ASSOCIATED PRESS TELEGRAM.

One day last month, Professor Sharpe, of the Somerville, Tenn., Female College, 'a quiet and gentlemanly man,' was told that his brother-in- law, a Captain Burton, had threatened to kill him. Burton, it seems, had already killed one man and driven his knife into another. The Professor armed himself with a double-barreled shot gun, started out in search of his brother-in-law, found him playing billiards in a saloon, and blew his brains out. The 'Memphis Avalanche' reports that the Professor's course met with pretty general approval in the community; knowing that the law was powerless, in the actual condition of public sentiment, to protect him, he protected himself.

About the same time, two young men in North Carolina quarreled about a girl, and 'hostile messages' were exchanged. Friends tried to reconcile them, but had their labor for their pains. On the 24th the young men met in the public highway. One of them had a heavy club in his hand, the other an ax. The man with the club fought desperately for his life, but it was a hopeless fight from the first. A well-directed blow sent his club whirling out of his grasp, and the next moment he was a dead man.

About the same time, two 'highly connected' young Virginians, clerks in a hardware store at Charlottesville, while 'skylarking,' came to blows. Peter Dick threw pepper in Charles Roads's eyes; Roads demanded an apology; Dick refused to give it, and it was agreed that a duel was inevitable; but a difficulty arose; the parties had no pistols, and it was too late at night to procure them. One of them suggested that butcher-knives would answer the purpose, and the other accepted the suggestion; the result was that Roads fell to the floor with a gash in his abdomen that may or may not prove fatal. If Dick has been arrested, the news has not reached us. He 'expressed deep regret,' and we are told by a Staunton correspondent of the PHILADELPHIA PRESS that 'every effort has been made to hush the matter up.'—EXTRACTS FROM THE PUBLIC JOURNALS.

The descriptions of fifty years ago do not need to have a word changed in order to exactly describe the same region as it appears to-day—except as to the 'trigness' of the houses. The whitewash is gone from the negro cabins now; and many, possibly most, of the big mansions, once so shining white, have worn out their paint and have a decayed, neglected look. It is the blight of the war. Twenty-one years ago everything was trim and trig and bright along the 'coast,' just as it had been in 1827, as described by those tourists.

Unfortunate tourists! People humbugged them with stupid and silly lies, and then laughed at them for believing and printing the same. They told Mrs. Trollope that the alligators— or crocodiles, as she calls them— were terrible creatures; and backed up the statement with a blood-curdling account of how one of these slandered reptiles crept into a squatter cabin one night, and ate up a woman and five children. The woman, by herself, would have satisfied any ordinarily-impossible alligator; but no, these liars must make him gorge the five children besides. One would not imagine that jokers of this robust breed would be sensitive—but they were. It is difficult, at this day, to understand, and impossible to justify, the reception which the book of the grave, honest, intelligent, gentle, manly, charitable, well-meaning Capt. Basil Hall got.

Chapter 41 The Metropolis of the South

THE approaches to New Orleans were familiar; general aspects were unchanged. When one goes flying through London along a railway propped in the air on tall arches, he may inspect miles of upper bedrooms through the open windows, but the lower half of the houses is under his level and out of sight. Similarly, in high-river stage, in the New Orleans region, the water is up to the top of the enclosing levee-rim, the flat country behind it lies low—representing the bottom of a dish— and as the boat swims along, high on the flood, one looks down upon the houses and into the upper windows. There is nothing but that frail breastwork of earth between the people and destruction.

The old brick salt-warehouses clustered at the upper end of the city looked as they had always looked; warehouses which had had a kind of Aladdin's lamp experience, however, since I had seen them; for when the war broke out the proprietor went to bed one night leaving them packed with thousands of sacks of vulgar salt, worth a couple of dollars a sack, and got up in the morning and found his mountain of salt turned into a mountain of gold, so to speak, so suddenly and to so dizzy a height had the war news sent up the price of the article.

The vast reach of plank wharves remained unchanged, and there were as many ships as ever: but the long array of steamboats had vanished; not altogether, of course, but not much of it was left.

The city itself had not changed—to the eye. It had greatly increased in spread and population, but the look of the town was not altered. The dust, waste-paper-littered, was still deep in the streets; the deep, trough-like gutters alongside the curbstones were still half full of reposeful water with a dusty surface; the sidewalks were still—in the sugar and bacon region—encumbered by casks and barrels and hogsheads; the great blocks of austerely plain commercial houses were as dusty- looking as ever.

Canal Street was finer, and more attractive and stirring than formerly, with its drifting crowds of people, its several processions of hurrying street-cars, and—toward evening—its broad second-story verandas crowded with gentlemen and ladies clothed according to the latest mode.

Not that there is any 'architecture' in Canal Street: to speak in broad, general terms, there is no architecture in New Orleans, except in the cemeteries. It seems a strange thing to say of a wealthy, far- seeing, and energetic city of a quarter of a million inhabitants, but it is true. There is a huge granite U.S. Custom-house—costly enough, genuine enough, but as a decoration it is inferior to a gasometer. It looks like a state prison. But it was built before the war. Architecture in America may be said to have been born since the war. New Orleans, I believe, has had the good luck—and in a sense the bad luck— to have had no great fire in late years. It must be so. If the opposite had been the case, I think one would be able to tell the 'burnt district' by the radical improvement in its architecture over the old forms. One can do this in Boston and Chicago. The 'burnt district' of Boston was commonplace before the fire; but now there is no commercial district in any city in the world that can surpass it—or perhaps even rival it—in beauty, elegance, and tastefulness.

However, New Orleans has begun—just this moment, as one may say. When completed, the new Cotton Exchange will be a stately and beautiful building; massive, substantial, full of architectural graces; no shams or false pretenses or uglinesses about it anywhere. To the city, it will be worth many times its cost, for it will breed its species. What has been lacking hitherto, was a model to build toward; something to educate eye and taste; a SUGGESTER, so to speak.

The city is well outfitted with progressive men—thinking, sagacious, long-headed men. The contrast between the spirit of the city and the city's architecture is like the contrast between waking and sleep. Apparently there is a 'boom' in everything but that one dead feature. The water in the gutters used to be stagnant and slimy, and a potent disease-breeder; but the gutters are flushed now, two or three times a day, by powerful machinery; in many of the gutters the water never stands still, but has a steady current. Other sanitary improvements have been made; and with such effect that New Orleans claims to be (during the long intervals between the occasional yellow-fever assaults) one of the healthiest cities in the Union. There's plenty of ice now for everybody, manufactured in the town. It is a driving place commercially, and has a great river, ocean, and railway business. At the date of our visit, it was the best lighted city in the Union, electrically speaking. The New Orleans electric lights were more numerous than those of New York, and very much better. One had this modified noonday not only in Canal and some neighboring chief streets, but all along a stretch of five miles of river frontage. There are good clubs in the city now—several of them but recently organized—and inviting modern-style pleasure resorts at West End and Spanish Fort. The telephone is everywhere. One of the most notable advances is in journalism. The newspapers, as I remember them, were not a striking feature. Now they are. Money is spent upon them with a free hand. They get the news, let it cost what it may. The editorial work is not hack- grinding, but literature. As an example of New Orleans journalistic achievement, it may be mentioned that the 'Times-Democrat' of August 26, 1882, contained a report of the year's business of the towns of the Mississippi Valley, from New Orleans all the way to St. Paul—two thousand miles. That issue of the paper consisted of forty pages; seven columns to the page; two hundred and eighty columns in all; fifteen hundred words to the column; an aggregate of four hundred and twenty thousand words. That is to say, not much short of three times as many words as there are in this book. One may with sorrow contrast this with the architecture of New Orleans.

I have been speaking of public architecture only. The domestic article in New Orleans is reproachless, notwithstanding it remains as it always was. All the dwellings are of wood—in the American part of the town, I mean—and all have a comfortable look. Those in the wealthy quarter are spacious; painted snow-white usually, and generally have wide verandas, or double-verandas, supported by ornamental columns. These mansions stand in the center of large grounds, and rise, garlanded with roses, out of the midst of swelling masses .of shining green foliage and many- colored blossoms. No houses could well be in better harmony with their surroundings, or more pleasing to the eye, or more home-like and comfortable-looking.

One even becomes reconciled to the cistern presently; this is a mighty cask, painted green, and sometimes a couple of stories high, which is propped against the house-corner on stilts. There is a mansion-and- brewery suggestion about the combination which seems very incongruous at first. But the people cannot have wells, and so they take rain-water. Neither can they conveniently have cellars, or graves*, the town being built upon 'made' ground; so they do without both, and few of the living complain, and none of the others.

Chapter 42 Hygiene and Sentiment

THEY bury their dead in vaults, above the ground. These vaults have a resemblance to houses—sometimes to temples; are built of marble, generally; are architecturally graceful and shapely; they face the walks and driveways of the cemetery; and when one moves through the midst of a thousand or so of them and sees their white roofs and gables stretching into the distance on every hand, the phrase 'city of the dead' has all at once a meaning to him. Many of the cemeteries are beautiful, and are kept in perfect order. When one goes from the levee or the business streets near it, to a cemetery, he observes to himself that if those people down there would live as neatly while they are alive as they do after they are dead, they would find many advantages in it; and besides, their quarter would be the wonder and admiration of the business world. Fresh flowers, in vases of water, are to be seen at the portals of many of the vaults: placed there by the pious hands of bereaved parents and children, husbands and wives, and renewed daily. A milder form of sorrow finds its inexpensive and lasting remembrancer in the coarse and ugly but indestructible 'immortelle'—which is a wreath or cross or some such emblem, made of rosettes of black linen, with sometimes a yellow rosette at the conjunction of the cross's bars—kind of sorrowful breast-pin, so to say. The immortelle requires no attention: you just hang it up, and there you are; just leave it alone, it will take care of your grief for you, and keep it in mind better than you can; stands weather first-rate, and lasts like boiler-iron.

On sunny days, pretty little chameleons—gracefullest of legged reptiles—creep along the marble fronts of the vaults, and catch flies. Their changes of color—as to variety—are not up to the creature's reputation. They change color when a person comes along and hangs up an immortelle; but that is nothing: any right-feeling reptile would do that.

I will gradually drop this subject of graveyards. I have been

---

* The Israelites are buried in graves—by permission, I take it, not requirement; but none else, except the destitute, who are buried at public expense. The graves are but three or four feet deep.

trying all I could to get down to the sentimental part of it, but I cannot accomplish it. I think there is no genuinely sentimental part to it. It is all grotesque, ghastly, horrible. Graveyards may have been justifiable in the bygone ages, when nobody knew that for every dead body put into the ground, to glut the earth and the plant-roots, and the air with disease-germs, five or fifty, or maybe a hundred persons must die before their proper time; but they are hardly justifiable now, when even the children know that a dead saint enters upon a century-long career of assassination the moment the earth closes over his corpse. It is a grim sort of a thought. The relics of St. Anne, up in Canada, have now, after nineteen hundred years, gone to curing the sick by the dozen. But it is merest matter-of-course that these same relics, within a generation after St. Anne's death and burial, MADE several thousand people sick. Therefore these miracle-performances are simply compensation, nothing more. St. Anne is somewhat slow pay, for a Saint, it is true; but better a debt paid after nineteen hundred years, and outlawed by the statute of limitations, than not paid at all; and most of the knights of the halo do not pay at all. Where you find one that pays--like St. Anne--you find a hundred and fifty that take the benefit of the statute. And none of them pay any more than the principal of what they owe--they pay none of the interest either simple or compound. A Saint can never QUITE return the principal, however; for his dead body KILLS people, whereas his relics HEAL only—they never restore the dead to life. That part of the account is always left unsettled.

'Dr. F. Julius Le Moyne, after fifty years of medical practice, wrote: "The inhumation of human bodies, dead from infectious diseases, results in constantly loading the atmosphere, and polluting the waters, with not only the germs that rise from simply putrefaction, but also with the SPECIFIC germs of the diseases from which death resulted."

'The gases (from buried corpses) will rise to the surface through eight or ten feet of gravel, just as coal-gas will do, and there is practically no limit to their power of escape.

'During the epidemic in New Orleans in 1853, Dr. E. H. Barton reported that in the Fourth District the mortality was four hundred and fifty-two per thousand—more than double that of any other. In this district were three large cemeteries, in which during the previous year more than three thousand bodies had been buried. In other districts the proximity of cemeteries seemed to aggravate the disease.

'In 1828 Professor Bianchi demonstrated how the fearful reappearance of the plague at Modena was caused by excavations in ground where, THREE HUNDRED YEARS PREVIOUSLY, the victims of the pestilence had been buried. Mr. Cooper, in explaining the causes of some epidemics, remarks that the opening of the plague burial-grounds at Eyam resulted in an immediate outbreak of disease.'—NORTH AMERICAN REVIEW, NO. 3, VOL. 135.

In an address before the Chicago Medical Society, in advocacy of cremation, Dr. Charles W. Purdy made some striking comparisons to show what a burden is laid upon society by the burial of the dead:--

'One and one-fourth times more money is expended annually in funerals in the United States than the Government expends for public-school purposes. Funerals cost this country in 1880 enough money to pay the liabilities of all the commercial failures in the United States during the same year, and give each bankrupt a capital of $8,630 with which to resume

business. Funerals cost annually more money than the value of the combined gold and silver yield of the United States in the year 1880! These figures do not include the sums invested in burial-grounds and expended in tombs and monuments, nor the loss from depreciation of property in the vicinity of cemeteries.'

For the rich, cremation would answer as well as burial; for the ceremonies connected with it could be made as costly and ostentatious as a Hindu suttee; while for the poor, cremation would be better than burial, because so cheap*—so cheap until the poor got to imitating the rich, which they would do by-and-bye. The adoption of cremation would relieve us of a muck of threadbare burial-witticisms; but, on the other hand, it would resurrect a lot of mildewed old cremation-jokes that have had a rest for two thousand years.

I have a colored acquaintance who earns his living by odd jobs and heavy manual labor. He never earns above four hundred dollars in a year, and as he has a wife and several young children, the closest scrimping is necessary to get him through to the end of the twelve months debtless. To such a man a funeral is a colossal financial disaster. While I was writing one of the preceding chapters, this man lost a little child. He walked the town over with a friend, trying to find a coffin that was within his means. He bought the very cheapest one he could find, plain wood, stained. It cost him twenty-six dollars. It would have cost less than four, probably, if it had been built to put something useful into. He and his family will feel that outlay a good many months.

Chapter 43 The Art of Inhumation

ABOUT the same time, I encountered a man in the street, whom I had not seen for six or seven years; and something like this talk followed. I said—

'But you used to look sad and oldish; you don't now. Where did you get all this youth and bubbling cheerfulness? Give me the address.'

He chuckled blithely, took off his shining tile, pointed to a notched pink circlet of paper pasted into its crown, with something lettered on it, and went on chuckling while I read, 'J. B—, UNDERTAKER.' Then he clapped his hat on, gave it an irreverent tilt to leeward, and cried out—

'That's what's the matter! It used to be rough times with me when you knew me—insurance-agency business, you know; mighty irregular. Big fire, all right—brisk trade for ten days while people scared; after that, dull policy-business till next fire. Town like this don't have fires often enough—a fellow strikes so many dull weeks in a row that he gets discouraged. But you bet you, this is the business! People don't wait for examples to die. No, sir, they drop off right along—there ain't any dull spots in the undertaker line. I just started in with two or three little old coffins and a hired hearse, and now look at the thing! I've worked up a business here that would satisfy any man, don't care who he is. Five years ago, lodged in an attic; live in a swell house now, with a mansard roof, and all the modern inconveniences.'

'Does a coffin pay so well. Is there much profit on a coffin?'

'Go-way! How you talk!' Then, with a confidential wink, a dropping of the voice, and an impressive laying of his hand on

_____

* Four or five dollars is the minimum cost.

my arm; 'Look here; there's one thing in this world which isn't ever cheap. That's a coffin. There's one thing in this world which a person don't ever try to jew you down on. That's a coffin. There's one thing in this world which a person don't say—"I'll look around a little, and if I find I can't do better I'll come back and take it." That's a coffin. There's one thing in this world which a person won't take in pine if he can go walnut; and won't take in walnut if he can go mahogany; and won't take in mahogany if he can go an iron casket with silver door-plate and bronze handles. That's a coffin. And there's one thing in this world which you don't have to worry around after a person to get him to pay for. And that's a coffin. Undertaking?—why it's the dead-surest business in Christendom, and the nobbiest.

'Why, just look at it. A rich man won't have anything but your very best; and you can just pile it on, too—pile it on and sock it to him— he won't ever holler. And you take in a poor man, and if you work him right he'll bust himself on a single lay-out. Or especially a woman. F'r instance: Mrs. O'Flaherty comes in—widow—wiping her eyes and kind of moaning. Unhandkerchiefs one eye, bats it around tearfully over the stock; says—

'"And fhat might ye ask for that wan?"

'"Thirty-nine dollars, madam," says I.

'"It 's a foine big price, sure, but Pat shall be buried like a gintleman, as he was, if I have to work me fingers off for it. I'll have that wan, sor."

'"Yes, madam," says I, "and it is a very good one, too; not costly, to be sure, but in this life we must cut our garment to our clothes, as the saying is." And as she starts out, I heave in, kind of casually, "This one with the white satin lining is a beauty, but I am afraid—well, sixty-five dollars is a rather—rather—but no matter, I felt obliged to say to Mrs. O'Shaughnessy—"

'"D'ye mane to soy that Bridget O'Shaughnessy bought the mate to that joo-ul box to ship that dhrunken divil to Purgatory in?"

'"Yes, madam."

'"Then Pat shall go to heaven in the twin to it, if it takes the last rap the O'Flaherties can raise; and moind you, stick on some extras, too, and I'll give ye another dollar."

'And as I lay-in with the livery stables, of course I don't forget to mention that Mrs. O'Shaughnessy hired fifty-four dollars' worth of hacks and flung as much style into Dennis's funeral as if he had been a duke or an assassin. And of course she sails in and goes the O'Shaughnessy about four hacks and an omnibus better. That used to be, but that's all played now; that is, in this particular town. The Irish got to piling up hacks so, on their funerals, that a funeral left them ragged and hungry for two years afterward; so the priest pitched in and broke it all up. He don't allow them to have but two hacks now, and sometimes only one.'

'Well,' said I, 'if you are so light-hearted and jolly in ordinary times, what must you be in an epidemic?'

He shook his head.

'No, you're off, there. We don't like to see an epidemic. An epidemic don't pay. Well, of course I don't mean that, exactly; but it don't pay in proportion to the regular thing. Don't it occur to you, why?'

No.

'Think.'

'I can't imagine. What is it?'

'It's just two things.'

'Well, what are they?'

'One's Embamming.'

'And what's the other?'

'Ice.'

'How is that?'

'Well, in ordinary times, a person dies, and we lay him up in ice; one day two days, maybe three, to wait for friends to come. Takes a lot of it—melts fast. We charge jewelry rates for that ice, and war-prices for attendance. Well, don't you know, when there's an epidemic, they rush 'em to the cemetery the minute the breath's out. No market for ice in an epidemic. Same with Embamming. You take a family that's able to embam, and you've got a soft thing. You can mention sixteen different ways to do it—though there AIN'T only one or two ways, when you come down to the bottom facts of it—and they'll take the highest-priced way, every time. It's human nature—human nature in grief. It don't reason, you see. Time being, it don't care a dam. All it wants is physical immortality for deceased, and they're willing to pay for it. All you've got to do is to just be ca'm and stack it up—they'll stand the racket. Why, man, you can take a defunct that you couldn't GIVE away; and get your embamming traps around you and go to work; and in a couple of hours he is worth a cool six hundred—that's what HE'S worth. There ain't anything equal to it but trading rats for di'monds in time of famine. Well, don't you see, when there's an epidemic, people don't wait to embam. No, indeed they don't; and it hurts the business like hell-th, as we say—hurts it like hell-th, HEALTH, see?—Our little joke in the trade. Well, I must be going. Give me a call whenever you need any—I mean, when you're going by, sometime.'

In his joyful high spirits, he did the exaggerating himself, if any has been done. I have not enlarged on him.

With the above brief references to inhumation, let us leave the subject. As for me, I hope to be cremated. I made that remark to my pastor once, who said, with what he seemed to think was an impressive manner—

'I wouldn't worry about that, if I had your chances.' Much he knew about it—the family all so opposed to it.

Chapter 44 City Sights

THE old French part of New Orleans—anciently the Spanish part—bears no resemblance to the American end of the city: the American end which lies beyond the intervening brick business-center. The houses are massed in blocks; are austerely plain and dignified; uniform of pattern, with here and there a departure from it with pleasant effect; all are plastered on the outside, and nearly all have long, iron-railed verandas running along the several stories. Their chief beauty is the deep, warm, varicolored stain with which time and the weather have enriched the plaster. It harmonizes with all the surroundings, and has as natural a look of belonging there as has the flush upon sunset clouds. This charming decoration cannot be successfully imitated; neither is it to be found elsewhere in America.

The iron railings are a specialty, also. The pattern is often exceedingly light and dainty, and airy and graceful—with a large cipher or monogram in the center, a delicate cobweb of baffling, intricate forms, wrought in steel. The ancient railings are hand-made, and are now comparatively rare and proportionately valuable. They are become BRIC-A-BRAC.

The party had the privilege of idling through this ancient quarter of New Orleans with the South's finest literary genius, the author of 'the Grandissimes.' In him the South has found a masterly delineator of its interior life and its history. In truth, I find by experience, that the untrained eye and vacant mind can inspect it, and learn of it, and judge of it, more clearly and profitably in his books than by personal contact with it.

With Mr. Cable along to see for you, and describe and explain and illuminate, a jog through that old quarter is a vivid pleasure. And you have a vivid sense as of unseen or dimly seen things—vivid, and yet fitful and darkling; you glimpse salient features, but lose the fine shades or catch them imperfectly through the vision of the imagination: a case, as it were, of ignorant near-sighted stranger traversing the rim of wide vague horizons of Alps with an inspired and enlightened long-sighted native.

We visited the old St. Louis Hotel, now occupied by municipal offices. There is nothing strikingly remarkable about it; but one can say of it as of the Academy of Music in New York, that if a broom or a shovel has ever been used in it there is no circumstantial evidence to back up the fact. It is curious that cabbages and hay and things do not grow in the Academy of Music; but no doubt it is on account of the interruption of the light by the benches, and the impossibility of hoeing the crop except in the aisles. The fact that the ushers grow their buttonhole- bouquets on the premises shows what might be done if they had the right kind of an agricultural head to the establishment.

We visited also the venerable Cathedral, and the pretty square in front of it; the one dim with religious light, the other brilliant with the worldly sort, and lovely with orange-trees and blossomy shrubs; then we drove in the hot sun through the wilderness of houses and out on to the wide dead level beyond, where the villas are, and the water wheels to drain the town, and the commons populous with cows and children; passing by an old cemetery where we were told lie the ashes of an early pirate; but we took him on trust, and did not visit him. He was a pirate with a tremendous and sanguinary history; and as long as he preserved unspotted, in retirement, the dignity of his name and the grandeur of his ancient calling, homage and reverence were his from high and low; but when at last he descended into politics and became a paltry alderman, the public 'shook' him, and turned aside and wept. When he died, they set up a monument over him; and little by little he has come into respect again; but it is respect for the pirate, not the alderman. To-day the loyal and generous remember only what he was, and charitably forget what he became.

Thence, we drove a few miles across a swamp, along a raised

shell road, with a canal on one hand and a dense wood on the other; and here and there, in the distance, a ragged and angular-limbed and moss-bearded cypress, top standing out, clear cut against the sky, and as quaint of form as the apple-trees in Japanese pictures—such was our course and the surroundings of it. There was an occasional alligator swimming comfortably along in the canal, and an occasional picturesque colored person on the bank, flinging his statue-rigid reflection upon the still water and watching for a bite.

And by-and-bye we reached the West End, a collection of hotels of the usual light summer-resort pattern, with broad verandas all around, and the waves of the wide and blue Lake Pontchartrain lapping the thresholds. We had dinner on a ground-veranda over the water—the chief dish the renowned fish called the pompano, delicious as the less criminal forms of sin.

Thousands of people come by rail and carriage to West End and to Spanish Fort every evening, and dine, listen to the bands, take strolls in the open air under the electric lights, go sailing on the lake, and entertain themselves in various and sundry other ways.

We had opportunities on other days and in other places to test the pompano. Notably, at an editorial dinner at one of the clubs in the city. He was in his last possible perfection there, and justified his fame. In his suite was a tall pyramid of scarlet cray-fish—large ones; as large as one's thumb—delicate, palatable, appetizing. Also deviled whitebait; also shrimps of choice quality; and a platter of small soft- shell crabs of a most superior breed. The other dishes were what one might get at Delmonico's, or Buckingham Palace; those I have spoken of can be had in similar perfection in New Orleans only, I suppose.

In the West and South they have a new institution—the Broom Brigade. It is composed of young ladies who dress in a uniform costume, and go through the infantry drill, with broom in place of musket. It is a very pretty sight, on private view. When they perform on the stage of a theater, in the blaze of colored fires, it must be a fine and fascinating spectacle. I saw them go through their complex manual with grace, spirit, and admirable precision. I saw them do everything which a human being can possibly do with a broom, except sweep. I did not see them sweep. But I know they could learn. What they have already learned proves that. And if they ever should learn, and should go on the war- path down Tchoupitoulas or some of those other streets around there, those thoroughfares would bear a greatly improved aspect in a very few minutes. But the girls themselves wouldn't; so nothing would be really gained, after all.

The drill was in the Washington Artillery building. In this building we saw many interesting relics of the war. Also a fine oil-painting representing Stonewall Jackson's last interview with General Lee. Both men are on horseback. Jackson has just ridden up, and is accosting Lee. The picture is very valuable, on account of the portraits, which are authentic. But, like many another historical picture, it means nothing without its label. And one label will fit it as well as another—

First Interview between Lee and Jackson.
Last Interview between Lee and Jackson.
Jackson Introducing Himself to Lee.
Jackson Accepting Lee's Invitation to Dinner.
Jackson Declining Lee's Invitation to Dinner—with Thanks.
Jackson Apologizing for a Heavy Defeat.

Jackson Reporting a Great Victory.
Jackson Asking Lee for a Match.

It tells ONE story, and a sufficient one; for it says quite plainly and satisfactorily, 'Here are Lee and Jackson together.' The artist would have made it tell that this is Lee and Jackson's last interview if he could have done it. But he couldn't, for there wasn't any way to do it. A good legible label is usually worth, for information, a ton of significant attitude and expression in a historical picture. In Rome, people with fine sympathetic natures stand up and weep in front of the celebrated 'Beatrice Cenci the Day before her Execution.' It shows what a label can do. If they did not know the picture, they would inspect it unmoved, and say, 'Young girl with hay fever; young girl with her head in a bag.'

I found the half-forgotten Southern intonations and elisions as pleasing to my ear as they had formerly been. A Southerner talks music. At least it is music to me, but then I was born in the South. The educated Southerner has no use for an r, except at the beginning of a word. He says 'honah,' and 'dinnah,' and 'Gove'nuh,' and 'befo' the waw,' and so on. The words may lack charm to the eye, in print, but they have it to the ear. When did the r disappear from Southern speech, and how did it come to disappear? The custom of dropping it was not borrowed from the North, nor inherited from England. Many Southerners—most Southerners— put a y into occasional words that begin with the k sound. For instance, they say Mr. K'yahtah (Carter) and speak of playing k'yahds or of riding in the k'yahs. And they have the pleasant custom—long ago fallen into decay in the North—of frequently employing the respectful 'Sir.' Instead of the curt Yes, and the abrupt No, they say 'Yes, Suh', 'No, Suh.'

But there are some infelicities. Such as 'like' for 'as,' and the addition of an 'at' where it isn't needed. I heard an educated gentleman say, 'Like the flag-officer did.' His cook or his butler would have said, 'Like the flag-officer done.' You hear gentlemen say, 'Where have you been at?' And here is the aggravated form—heard a ragged street Arab say it to a comrade: 'I was a-ask'n' Tom whah you was a-sett'n' at.' The very elect carelessly say 'will' when they mean 'shall'; and many of them say, 'I didn't go to do it,' meaning 'I didn't mean to do it.' The Northern word 'guess'—imported from England, where it used to be common, and now regarded by satirical Englishmen as a Yankee original—is but little used among Southerners. They say 'reckon.' They haven't any 'doesn't' in their language; they say 'don't' instead. The unpolished often use 'went' for 'gone.' It is nearly as bad as the Northern 'hadn't ought.' This reminds me that a remark of a very peculiar nature was made here in my neighborhood (in the North) a few days ago: 'He hadn't ought to have went.' How is that? Isn't that a good deal of a triumph? One knows the orders combined in this half- breed's architecture without inquiring: one parent Northern, the other Southern. To-day I heard a schoolmistress ask, 'Where is John gone?' This form is so common—so nearly universal, in fact—that if she had used 'whither' instead of 'where,' I think it would have sounded like an affectation.

We picked up one excellent word—a word worth traveling to New Orleans to get; a nice limber, expressive, handy word— 'lagniappe.' They pronounce it lanny-yap. It is Spanish—so they said. We discovered it at the head of a column of odds and ends in the Picayune, the first day; heard twenty people use it the second; inquired what it meant the third; adopted it and got facility in swinging it the fourth. It has a restricted meaning, but I think the people spread it out a little when they

choose. It is the equivalent of the thirteenth roll in a 'baker's dozen.' It is something thrown in, gratis, for good measure. The custom originated in the Spanish quarter of the city. When a child or a servant buys something in a shop—or even the mayor or the governor, for aught I know—he finishes the operation by saying—

'Give me something for lagniappe.'

The shopman always responds; gives the child a bit of licorice-root, gives the servant a cheap cigar or a spool of thread, gives the governor—I don't know what he gives the governor; support, likely.

When you are invited to drink, and this does occur now and then in New Orleans—and you say, 'What, again?—no, I've had enough;' the other party says, 'But just this one time more—this is for lagniappe.' When the beau perceives that he is stacking his compliments a trifle too high, and sees by the young lady's countenance that the edifice would have been better with the top compliment left off, he puts his 'I beg pardon—no harm intended,' into the briefer form of 'Oh, that's for lagniappe.' If the waiter in the restaurant stumbles and spills a gill of coffee down the back of your neck, he says 'For lagniappe, sah,' and gets you another cup without extra charge.

Chapter 45 Southern Sports

IN the North one hears the war mentioned, in social conversation, once a month; sometimes as often as once a week; but as a distinct subject for talk, it has long ago been relieved of duty. There are sufficient reasons for this. Given a dinner company of six gentlemen to-day, it can easily happen that four of them—and possibly five—were not in the field at all. So the chances are four to two, or five to one, that the war will at no time during the evening become the topic of conversation; and the chances are still greater that if it become the topic it will remain so but a little while. If you add six ladies to the company, you have added six people who saw so little of the dread realities of the war that they ran out of talk concerning them years ago, and now would soon weary of the war topic if you brought it up.

The case is very different in the South. There, every man you meet was in the war; and every lady you meet saw the war. The war is the great chief topic of conversation. The interest in it is vivid and constant; the interest in other topics is fleeting. Mention of the war will wake up a dull company and set their tongues going, when nearly any other topic would fail. In the South, the war is what A.D. is elsewhere: they date from it. All day long you hear things 'placed' as having happened since the waw; or du'in' the waw; or befo' the waw; or right aftah the waw; or 'bout two yeahs or five yeahs or ten yeahs befo' the waw or aftah the waw. It shows how intimately every individual was visited, in his own person, by that tremendous episode. It gives the inexperienced stranger a better idea of what a vast and comprehensive calamity invasion is than he can ever get by reading books at the fireside.

At a club one evening, a gentleman turned to me and said, in an aside—

'You notice, of course, that we are nearly always talking about the war. It isn't because we haven't anything else to talk about, but because nothing else has so strong an interest for us. And there is another reason: In the war, each of us, in his own person, seems to have sampled all the different varieties of human experience; as a consequence, you can't mention an outside matter of any sort but it will certainly remind some listener of something that happened during the war—and out he comes with it. Of course that brings the talk back to the war. You may try all you want to, to keep other subjects before the house, and we may all join in and help, but there can be but one result: the most random topic would load every man up with war reminiscences, and shut him up, too; and talk would be likely to stop presently, because you can't talk pale inconsequentialities when you've got a crimson fact or fancy in your head that you are burning to fetch out.'

The poet was sitting some little distance away; and presently he began to speak—about the moon.

The gentleman who had been talking to me remarked in an 'aside:' 'There, the moon is far enough from the seat of war, but you will see that it will suggest something to somebody about the war; in ten minutes from now the moon, as a topic, will be shelved.'

The poet was saying he had noticed something which was a surprise to him; had had the impression that down here, toward the equator, the moonlight was much stronger and brighter than up North; had had the impression that when he visited New Orleans, many years ago, the moon—

Interruption from the other end of the room—

'Let me explain that. Reminds me of an anecdote. Everything is changed since the war, for better or for worse; but you'll find people down here born grumblers, who see no change except the change for the worse. There was an old negro woman of this sort. A young New-Yorker said in her presence, "What a wonderful moon you have down here!" She sighed and said, "Ah, bless yo' heart, honey, you ought to seen dat moon befo' de waw!"'

The new topic was dead already. But the poet resurrected it, and gave it a new start.

A brief dispute followed, as to whether the difference between Northern and Southern moonlight really existed or was only imagined. Moonlight talk drifted easily into talk about artificial methods of dispelling darkness. Then somebody remembered that when Farragut advanced upon Port Hudson on a dark night—and did not wish to assist the aim of the Confederate gunners—he carried no battle-lanterns, but painted the decks of his ships white, and thus created a dim but valuable light, which enabled his own men to grope their way around with considerable facility. At this point the war got the floor again—the ten minutes not quite up yet.

I was not sorry, for war talk by men who have been in a war is always interesting; whereas moon talk by a poet who has not been in the moon is likely to be dull.

We went to a cockpit in New Orleans on a Saturday afternoon. I had never seen a cock-fight before. There were men and boys there of all ages and all colors, and of many languages and nationalities. But I noticed one quite conspicuous and surprising absence: the traditional brutal faces. There were no brutal faces. With no cock-fighting going on, you could have played the gathering on a stranger for a prayer-meeting; and after it began, for a revival—provided you blindfolded your stranger—for the shouting was something prodigious.

A negro and a white man were in the ring; everybody else

outside. The cocks were brought in in sacks; and when time was called, they were taken out by the two bottle-holders, stroked, caressed, poked toward each other, and finally liberated. The big black cock plunged instantly at the little gray one and struck him on the head with his spur. The gray responded with spirit. Then the Babel of many-tongued shoutings broke out, and ceased not thenceforth. When the cocks had been fighting some little time, I was expecting them momently to drop dead, for both were blind, red with blood, and so exhausted that they frequently fell down. Yet they would not give up, neither would they die. The negro and the white man would pick them up every few seconds, wipe them off, blow cold water on them in a fine spray, and take their heads in their mouths and hold them there a moment—to warm back the perishing life perhaps; I do not know. Then, being set down again, the dying creatures would totter gropingly about, with dragging wings, find each other, strike a guesswork blow or two, and fall exhausted once more.

I did not see the end of the battle. I forced myself to endure it as long as I could, but it was too pitiful a sight; so I made frank confession to that effect, and we retired. We heard afterward that the black cock died in the ring, and fighting to the last.

Evidently there is abundant fascination about this 'sport' for such as have had a degree of familiarity with it. I never saw people enjoy anything more than this gathering enjoyed this fight. The case was the same with old gray-heads and with boys of ten. They lost themselves in frenzies of delight. The 'cocking-main' is an inhuman sort of entertainment, there is no question about that; still, it seems a much more respectable and far less cruel sport than fox-hunting—for the cocks like it; they experience, as well as confer enjoyment; which is not the fox's case.

We assisted—in the French sense—at a mule race, one day. I believe I enjoyed this contest more than any other mule there. I enjoyed it more than I remember having enjoyed any other animal race I ever saw. The grand-stand was well filled with the beauty and the chivalry of New Orleans. That phrase is not original with me. It is the Southern reporter's. He has used it for two generations. He uses it twenty times a day, or twenty thousand times a day; or a million times a day— according to the exigencies. He is obliged to use it a million times a day, if he have occasion to speak of respectable men and women that often; for he has no other phrase for such service except that single one. He never tires of it; it always has a fine sound to him. There is a kind of swell medieval bulliness and tinsel about it that pleases his gaudy barbaric soul. If he had been in Palestine in the early times, we should have had no references to 'much people' out of him. No, he would have said 'the beauty and the chivalry of Galilee' assembled to hear the Sermon on the Mount. It is likely that the men and women of the South are sick enough of that phrase by this time, and would like a change, but there is no immediate prospect of their getting it.

The New Orleans editor has a strong, compact, direct, unflowery style; wastes no words, and does not gush. Not so with his average correspondent. In the Appendix I have quoted a good letter, penned by a trained hand; but the average correspondent hurls a style which differs from that. For instance—

The 'Times-Democrat' sent a relief-steamer up one of the bayous, last April. This steamer landed at a village, up there somewhere, and the Captain invited some of the ladies of the village to make a short trip with him. They accepted and came aboard, and the steamboat shoved out up the creek. That was all there was 'to it.' And that is all that the editor of the 'Times-Democrat' would have got out of it. There was nothing in the thing but statistics, and he would have got nothing else out of it. He would probably have even tabulated them, partly to secure perfect clearness of statement, and partly to save space. But his special correspondent knows other methods of handling statistics. He just throws off all restraint and wallows in them—

'On Saturday, early in the morning, the beauty of the place graced our cabin, and proud of her fair freight the gallant little boat glided up the bayou.'

Twenty-two words to say the ladies came aboard and the boat shoved out up the creek, is a clean waste of ten good words, and is also destructive of compactness of statement.

The trouble with the Southern reporter is—Women. They unsettle him; they throw him off his balance. He is plain, and sensible, and satisfactory, until a woman heaves in sight. Then he goes all to pieces; his mind totters, he becomes flowery and idiotic. From reading the above extract, you would imagine that this student of Sir Walter Scott is an apprentice, and knows next to nothing about handling a pen. On the contrary, he furnishes plenty of proofs, in his long letter, that he knows well enough how to handle it when the women are not around to give him the artificial-flower complaint. For instance—

'At 4 o'clock ominous clouds began to gather in the south-east, and presently from the Gulf there came a blow which increased in severity every moment. It was not safe to leave the landing then, and there was a delay. The oaks shook off long tresses of their mossy beards to the tugging of the wind, and the bayou in its ambition put on miniature waves in mocking of much larger bodies of water. A lull permitted a start, and homewards we steamed, an inky sky overhead and a heavy wind blowing. As darkness crept on, there were few on board who did not wish themselves nearer home.'

There is nothing the matter with that. It is good description, compactly put. Yet there was great temptation, there, to drop into lurid writing.

But let us return to the mule. Since I left him, I have rummaged around and found a full report of the race. In it I find confirmation of the theory which I broached just now—namely, that the trouble with the Southern reporter is Women: Women, supplemented by Walter Scott and his knights and beauty and chivalry, and so on. This is an excellent report, as long as the women stay out of it. But when they intrude, we have this frantic result—

'It will be probably a long time before the ladies' stand presents such a sea of foam-like loveliness as it did yesterday. The New Orleans women are always charming, but never so much so as at this time of the year, when in their dainty spring costumes they bring with them a breath of balmy freshness and an odor of sanctity unspeakable. The stand was so crowded with them that, walking at their feet and seeing no possibility of approach, many a man appreciated as he never did before the Peri's feeling at the Gates of Paradise, and wondered what was the priceless boon that would admit him to their sacred presence. Sparkling on their white-robed breasts or shoulders were the colors of their favorite knights, and were it not for the fact that the doughty heroes appeared on unromantic mules, it would have been easy to imagine one of King Arthur's gala-days.'

There were thirteen mules in the first heat; all sorts of mules, they were; all sorts of complexions, gaits, dispositions, aspects. Some were handsome creatures, some were not; some were sleek, some hadn't had their fur brushed lately; some were innocently gay and frisky; some were full of malice and all unrighteousness; guessing from looks, some of them thought the matter on hand was war, some thought it was a lark, the rest took it for a religious occasion. And each mule acted according to his convictions. The result was an absence of harmony well compensated by a conspicuous presence of variety—variety of a picturesque and entertaining sort.

All the riders were young gentlemen in fashionable society. If the reader has been wondering why it is that the ladies of New Orleans attend so humble an orgy as a mule-race, the thing is explained now. It is a fashion-freak; all connected with it are people of fashion.

It is great fun, and cordially liked. The mule-race is one of the marked occasions of the year. It has brought some pretty fast mules to the front. One of these had to be ruled out, because he was so fast that he turned the thing into a one-mule contest, and robbed it of one of its best features—variety. But every now and then somebody disguises him with a new name and a new complexion, and rings him in again.

The riders dress in full jockey costumes of bright-colored silks, satins, and velvets.

The thirteen mules got away in a body, after a couple of false starts, and scampered off with prodigious spirit. As each mule and each rider had a distinct opinion of his own as to how the race ought to be run, and which side of the track was best in certain circumstances, and how often the track ought to be crossed, and when a collision ought to be accomplished, and when it ought to be avoided, these twenty-six conflicting opinions created a most fantastic and picturesque confusion, and the resulting spectacle was killingly comical.

Mile heat; time 2:22. Eight of the thirteen mules distanced. I had a bet on a mule which would have won if the procession had been reversed. The second heat was good fun; and so was the 'consolation race for beaten mules,' which followed later; but the first heat was the best in that respect.

I think that much the most enjoyable of all races is a steamboat race; but, next to that, I prefer the gay and joyous mule-rush. Two red-hot steamboats raging along, neck-and-neck, straining every nerve—that is to say, every rivet in the boilers—quaking and shaking and groaning from stem to stern, spouting white steam from the pipes, pouring black smoke from the chimneys, raining down sparks, parting the river into long breaks of hissing foam—this is sport that makes a body's very liver curl with enjoyment. A horse-race is pretty tame and colorless in comparison. Still, a horse-race might be well enough, in its way, perhaps, if it were not for the tiresome false starts. But then, nobody is ever killed. At least, nobody was ever killed when I was at a horse-race. They have been crippled, it is true; but this is little to the purpose.

Chapter 46 Enchantments and Enchanters

THE largest annual event in New Orleans is a something which we arrived too late to sample—the Mardi-Gras festivities. I saw the procession of the Mystic Crew of Comus there, twenty-four years ago—with knights and nobles and so on, clothed in silken and golden Paris-made gorgeousnesses, planned and bought for that single night's use; and in their train all manner of giants, dwarfs, monstrosities, and other diverting grotesquerie—a startling and wonderful sort of show, as it filed solemnly and silently down the street in the light of its smoking and flickering torches; but it is said that in these latter days the spectacle is mightily augmented, as to cost, splendor, and variety. There is a chief personage—'Rex;' and if I remember rightly, neither this king nor any of his great following of subordinates is known to any outsider. All these people are gentlemen of position and consequence; and it is a proud thing to belong to the organization; so the mystery in which they hide their personality is merely for romance's sake, and not on account of the police.

Mardi-Gras is of course a relic of the French and Spanish occupation; but I judge that the religious feature has been pretty well knocked out of it now. Sir Walter has got the advantage of the gentlemen of the cowl and rosary, and he will stay. His medieval business, supplemented by the monsters and the oddities, and the pleasant creatures from fairy- land, is finer to look at than the poor fantastic inventions and performances of the reveling rabble of the priest's day, and serves quite as well, perhaps, to emphasize the day and admonish men that the grace-line between the worldly season and the holy one is reached.

This Mardi-Gras pageant was the exclusive possession of New Orleans until recently. But now it has spread to Memphis and St. Louis and Baltimore. It has probably reached its limit. It is a thing which could hardly exist in the practical North; would certainly last but a very brief time; as brief a time as it would last in London. For the soul of it is the romantic, not the funny and the grotesque. Take away the romantic mysteries, the kings and knights and big-sounding titles, and Mardi-Gras would die, down there in the South. The very feature that keeps it alive in the South—girly-girly romance—would kill it in the North or in London. Puck and Punch, and the press universal, would fall upon it and make merciless fun of it, and its first exhibition would be also its last.

Against the crimes of the French Revolution and of Bonaparte may be set two compensating benefactions: the Revolution broke the chains of the ANCIEN REGIME and of the Church, and made of a nation of abject slaves a nation of freemen; and Bonaparte instituted the setting of merit above birth, and also so completely stripped the divinity from royalty, that whereas crowned heads in Europe were gods before, they are only men, since, and can never be gods again, but only figureheads, and answerable for their acts like common clay. Such benefactions as these compensate the temporary harm which Bonaparte and the Revolution did, and leave the world in debt to them for these great and permanent services to liberty, humanity, and progress.

Then comes Sir Walter Scott with his enchantments, and by his single might checks this wave of progress, and even turns it back; sets the world in love with dreams and phantoms; with decayed and swinish forms of religion; with decayed and degraded systems of government; with the sillinesses and emptinesses, sham grandeurs, sham gauds, and sham chivalries of a brainless and worthless long-vanished society. He did measureless harm; more real and lasting harm, perhaps, than any other individual that ever wrote. Most of the world has now outlived good part of these harms, though by no means all of them; but in our South they flourish pretty forcefully still. Not so forcefully as half a generation ago, perhaps, but still forcefully. There, the genuine and wholesome civilization of the nineteenth century is curiously

confused and commingled with the Walter Scott Middle-Age sham civilization; and so you have practical, common-sense, progressive ideas, and progressive works; mixed up with the duel, the inflated speech, and the jejune romanticism of an absurd past that is dead, and out of charity ought to be buried. But for the Sir Walter disease, the character of the Southerner—or Southron, according to Sir Walter's starchier way of phrasing it—would be wholly modern, in place of modern and medieval mixed, and the South would be fully a generation further advanced than it is. It was Sir Walter that made every gentleman in the South a Major or a Colonel, or a General or a Judge, before the war; and it was he, also, that made these gentlemen value these bogus decorations. For it was he that created rank and caste down there, and also reverence for rank and caste, and pride and pleasure in them. Enough is laid on slavery, without fathering upon it these creations and contributions of Sir Walter.

Sir Walter had so large a hand in making Southern character, as it existed before the war, that he is in great measure responsible for the war. It seems a little harsh toward a dead man to say that we never should have had any war but for Sir Walter; and yet something of a plausible argument might, perhaps, be made in support of that wild proposition. The Southerner of the American Revolution owned slaves; so did the Southerner of the Civil War: but the former resembles the latter as an Englishman resembles a Frenchman. The change of character can be traced rather more easily to Sir Walter's influence than to that of any other thing or person.

One may observe, by one or two signs, how deeply that influence penetrated, and how strongly it holds. If one take up a Northern or Southern literary periodical of forty or fifty years ago, he will find it filled with wordy, windy, flowery 'eloquence,' romanticism, sentimentality—all imitated from Sir Walter, and sufficiently badly done, too—innocent travesties of his style and methods, in fact. This sort of literature being the fashion in both sections of the country, there was opportunity for the fairest competition; and as a consequence, the South was able to show as many well-known literary names, proportioned to population, as the North could.

But a change has come, and there is no opportunity now for a fair competition between North and South. For the North has thrown out that old inflated style, whereas the Southern writer still clings to it— clings to it and has a restricted market for his wares, as a consequence. There is as much literary talent in the South, now, as ever there was, of course; but its work can gain but slight currency under present conditions; the authors write for the past, not the present; they use obsolete forms, and a dead language. But when a Southerner of genius writes modern English, his book goes upon crutches no longer, but upon wings; and they carry it swiftly all about America and England, and through the great English reprint publishing houses of Germany—as witness the experience of Mr. Cable and Uncle Remus, two of the very few Southern authors who do not write in the Southern style. Instead of three or four widely-known literary names, the South ought to have a dozen or two—and will have them when Sir Walter's time is out.

A curious exemplification of the power of a single book for good or harm is shown in the effects wrought by 'Don Quixote' and those wrought by 'Ivanhoe.' The first swept the world's admiration for the medieval chivalry-silliness out of existence; and the other restored it. As far as our South is concerned, the good work done by Cervantes is pretty nearly a dead letter, so effectually has Scott's pernicious work undermined it.

Chapter 47 Uncle Remus and Mr. Cable

MR. JOEL CHANDLER HARRIS ('Uncle Remus') was to arrive from Atlanta at seven o'clock Sunday morning; so we got up and received him. We were able to detect him among the crowd of arrivals at the hotel-counter by his correspondence with a description of him which had been furnished us from a trustworthy source. He was said to be undersized, red-haired, and somewhat freckled. He was the only man in the party whose outside tallied with this bill of particulars. He was said to be very shy. He is a shy man. Of this there is no doubt. It may not show on the surface, but the shyness is there. After days of intimacy one wonders to see that it is still in about as strong force as ever. There is a fine and beautiful nature hidden behind it, as all know who have read the Uncle Remus book; and a fine genius, too, as all know by the same sign. I seem to be talking quite freely about this neighbor; but in talking to the public I am but talking to his personal friends, and these things are permissible among friends.

He deeply disappointed a number of children who had flocked eagerly to Mr. Cable's house to get a glimpse of the illustrious sage and oracle of the nation's nurseries. They said—

'Why, he's white!'

They were grieved about it. So, to console them, the book was brought, that they might hear Uncle Remus's Tar-Baby story from the lips of Uncle Remus himself—or what, in their outraged eyes, was left of him. But it turned out that he had never read aloud to people, and was too shy to venture the attempt now. Mr. Cable and I read from books of ours, to show him what an easy trick it was; but his immortal shyness was proof against even this sagacious strategy, so we had to read about Brer Rabbit ourselves.

Mr. Harris ought to be able to read the negro dialect better than anybody else, for in the matter of writing it he is the only master the country has produced. Mr. Cable is the only master in the writing of French dialects that the country has produced; and he reads them in perfection. It was a great treat to hear him read about Jean-ah Poquelin, and about Innerarity and his famous 'pigshoo' representing 'Louisihanna RIF-fusing to Hanter the Union,' along with passages of nicely-shaded German dialect from a novel which was still in manuscript.

It came out in conversation, that in two different instances Mr. Cable got into grotesque trouble by using, in his books, next-to-impossible French names which nevertheless happened to be borne by living and sensitive citizens of New Orleans. His names were either inventions or were borrowed from the ancient and obsolete past, I do not now remember which; but at any rate living bearers of them turned up, and were a good deal hurt at having attention directed to themselves and their affairs in so excessively public a manner.

Mr. Warner and I had an experience of the same sort when we wrote the book called 'The Gilded Age.' There is a character in it called 'Sellers.' I do not remember what his first name was, in the beginning; but anyway, Mr. Warner did not like it, and wanted it improved. He asked me if I was able to imagine a person named 'Eschol Sellers.' Of course I said I could not, without stimulants. He said that away out West, once, he had met, and contemplated, and actually shaken hands with a man bearing that impossible name—'Eschol Sellers.' He added—

'It was twenty years ago; his name has probably carried him off before this; and if it hasn't, he will never see the book anyhow. We will confiscate his name. The name you are using is common, and therefore dangerous; there are probably a thousand Sellerses bearing it, and the whole horde will come after us; but Eschol Sellers is a safe name—it is a rock.'

So we borrowed that name; and when the book had been out about a week, one of the stateliest and handsomest and most aristocratic looking white men that ever lived, called around, with the most formidable libel suit in his pocket that ever—well, in brief, we got his permission to suppress an edition of ten million* copies of the book and change that name to 'Mulberry Sellers' in future editions.

Chapter 48 Sugar and Postage

ONE day, on the street, I encountered the man whom, of all men, I most wished to see—Horace Bixby; formerly pilot under me—or rather, over me—now captain of the great steamer 'City of Baton Rouge,' the latest and swiftest addition to the Anchor Line. The same slender figure, the same tight curls, the same springy step, the same alertness, the same decision of eye and answering decision of hand, the same erect military bearing; not an inch gained or lost in girth, not an ounce gained or lost in weight, not a hair turned. It is a curious thing, to leave a man thirty-five years old, and come back at the end of twenty-one years and find him still only thirty-five. I have not had an experience of this kind before, I believe. There were some crow's-feet, but they counted for next to nothing, since they were inconspicuous.

His boat was just in. I had been waiting several days for her, purposing to return to St. Louis in her. The captain and I joined a party of ladies and gentlemen, guests of Major Wood, and went down the river fifty-four miles, in a swift tug, to ex-Governor Warmouth's sugar plantation. Strung along below the city, were a number of decayed, ram- shackly, superannuated old steamboats, not one of which had I ever seen before. They had all been built, and worn out, and thrown aside, since I was here last. This gives one a realizing sense of the frailness of a Mississippi boat and the briefness of its life.

Six miles below town a fat and battered brick chimney, sticking above the magnolias and live-oaks, was pointed out as the monument erected by an appreciative nation to celebrate the battle of New Orleans—Jackson's victory over the British, January 8, 1815. The war had ended, the two nations were at peace, but the news had not yet reached New Orleans. If we had had the cable telegraph in those days, this blood would not have been spilt, those lives would not have been wasted; and better still, Jackson would probably never have been president. We have gotten over the harms done us by the war of 1812, but not over some of those done us by Jackson's presidency.

The Warmouth plantation covers a vast deal of ground, and the hospitality of the Warmouth mansion is graduated to the same large scale. We saw steam-plows at work, here, for the first time. The traction engine travels about on its own wheels, till it reaches the required spot; then it stands still and by means of a wire rope pulls the huge plow toward itself two or three hundred yards across the field, between the rows of cane. The thing cuts down into the black mold a foot and a half deep. The plow looks like a fore-and-aft brace of a Hudson

---

* Figures taken from memory, and probably incorrect. Think it was more.

river steamer, inverted. When the negro steersman sits on one end of it, that end tilts down near the ground, while the other sticks up high in air. This great see-saw goes rolling and pitching like a ship at sea, and it is not every circus rider that could stay on it.

The plantation contains two thousand six hundred acres; six hundred and fifty are in cane; and there is a fruitful orange grove of five thousand trees. The cane is cultivated after a modern and intricate scientific fashion, too elaborate and complex for me to attempt to describe; but it lost $40,000 last year. I forget the other details. However, this year's crop will reach ten or twelve hundred tons of sugar, consequently last year's loss will not matter. These troublesome and expensive scientific methods achieve a yield of a ton and a half and from that to two tons, to the acre; which is three or four times what the yield of an acre was in my time.

The drainage-ditches were everywhere alive with little crabs—'fiddlers.' One saw them scampering sidewise in every direction whenever they heard a disturbing noise. Expensive pests, these crabs; for they bore into the levees, and ruin them.

The great sugar-house was a wilderness of tubs and tanks and vats and filters, pumps, pipes, and machinery. The process of making sugar is exceedingly interesting. First, you heave your cane into the centrifugals and grind out the juice; then run it through the evaporating pan to extract the fiber; then through the bone-filter to remove the alcohol; then through the clarifying tanks to discharge the molasses; then through the granulating pipe to condense it; then through the vacuum pan to extract the vacuum. It is now ready for market. I have jotted these particulars down from memory. The thing looks simple and easy. Do not deceive yourself. To make sugar is really one of the most difficult things in the world. And to make it right, is next to impossible. If you will examine your own supply every now and then for a term of years, and tabulate the result, you will find that not two men in twenty can make sugar without getting sand into it.

We could have gone down to the mouth of the river and visited Captain Eads' great work, the 'jetties,' where the river has been compressed between walls, and thus deepened to twenty-six feet; but it was voted useless to go, since at this stage of the water everything would be covered up and invisible.

We could have visited that ancient and singular burg, 'Pilot-town,' which stands on stilts in the water—so they say; where nearly all communication is by skiff and canoe, even to the attending of weddings and funerals; and where the littlest boys and girls are as handy with the oar as unamphibious children are with the velocipede.

We could have done a number of other things; but on account of limited time, we went back home. The sail up the breezy and sparkling river was a charming experience, and would have been satisfyingly sentimental and romantic but for the interruptions of the tug's pet parrot, whose tireless comments upon the scenery and the guests were always this- worldly, and often profane. He had also a superabundance of the discordant, ear-splitting, metallic laugh common to his breed—a machine-made laugh, a Frankenstein laugh, with the soul left out of it. He applied it to every sentimental remark, and to every pathetic song. He cackled it out with hideous energy after 'Home again, home again from a foreign shore,' and said he 'wouldn't give a damn for a tug-load of such rot.' Romance and sentiment cannot long survive this sort of discouragement; so the singing and talking presently ceased;

which so delighted the parrot that he cursed himself hoarse for joy.

Then the male members of the party moved to the forecastle, to smoke and gossip. There were several old steamboatmen along, and I learned from them a great deal of what had been happening to my former river friends during my long absence. I learned that a pilot whom I used to steer for is become a spiritualist, and for more than fifteen years has been receiving a letter every week from a deceased relative, through a New York spiritualist medium named Manchester—postage graduated by distance: from the local post-office in Paradise to New York, five dollars; from New York to St. Louis, three cents. I remember Mr. Manchester very well. I called on him once, ten years ago, with a couple of friends, one of whom wished to inquire after a deceased uncle. This uncle had lost his life in a peculiarly violent and unusual way, half a dozen years before: a cyclone blew him some three miles and knocked a tree down with him which was four feet through at the butt and sixty- five feet high. He did not survive this triumph. At the seance just referred to, my friend questioned his late uncle, through Mr. Manchester, and the late uncle wrote down his replies, using Mr. Manchester's hand and pencil for that purpose. The following is a fair example of the questions asked, and also of the sloppy twaddle in the way of answers, furnished by Manchester under the pretense that it came from the specter. If this man is not the paltriest fraud that lives, I owe him an apology—

QUESTION. Where are you?

ANSWER. In the spirit world.

Q. Are you happy?

A. Very happy. Perfectly happy.

Q. How do you amuse yourself?

A. Conversation with friends, and other spirits.

Q. What else?

A. Nothing else. Nothing else is necessary.

Q. What do you talk about?

A. About how happy we are; and about friends left behind in the earth, and how to influence them for their good.

Q. When your friends in the earth all get to the spirit land, what shall you have to talk about then?—nothing but about how happy you all are?

No reply. It is explained that spirits will not answer frivolous questions.

Q. How is it that spirits that are content to spend an eternity in frivolous employments, and accept it as happiness, are so fastidious about frivolous questions upon the subject?

No reply.

Q. Would you like to come back?

A. No.

Q. Would you say that under oath?

A. Yes.

Q. What do you eat there?

A. We do not eat.

Q. What do you drink?

A. We do not drink.

Q. What do you smoke?

A. We do not smoke.

Q. What do you read?

A. We do not read.

Q. Do all the good people go to your place?

A. Yes.

Q. You know my present way of life. Can you suggest any additions to it, in the way of crime, that will reasonably insure my going to some other place.

A. No reply.

Q. When did you die?

A. I did not die, I passed away.

Q. Very well, then, when did you pass away? How long have you been in the spirit land?

A. We have no measurements of time here.

Q. Though you may be indifferent and uncertain as to dates and times in your present condition and environment, this has nothing to do with your former condition. You had dates then. One of these is what I ask for. You departed on a certain day in a certain year. Is not this true?

A. Yes.

Q. Then name the day of the month.

(Much fumbling with pencil, on the part of the medium, accompanied by violent spasmodic jerkings of his head and body, for some little time. Finally, explanation to the effect that spirits often forget dates, such things being without importance to them.)

Q. Then this one has actually forgotten the date of its translation to the spirit land?

This was granted to be the case.

Q. This is very curious. Well, then, what year was it?

(More fumbling, jerking, idiotic spasms, on the part of the medium. Finally, explanation to the effect that the spirit has forgotten the year.)

Q. This is indeed stupendous. Let me put one more question, one last question, to you, before we part to meet no more;—for even if I fail to avoid your asylum, a meeting there will go for

nothing as a meeting, since by that time you will easily have forgotten me and my name: did you die a natural death, or were you cut off by a catastrophe?

A. (After long hesitation and many throes and spasms.) NATURAL DEATH.

This ended the interview. My friend told the medium that when his relative was in this poor world, he was endowed with an extraordinary intellect and an absolutely defectless memory, and it seemed a great pity that he had not been allowed to keep some shred of these for his amusement in the realms of everlasting contentment, and for the amazement and admiration of the rest of the population there.

This man had plenty of clients—has plenty yet. He receives letters from spirits located in every part of the spirit world, and delivers them all over this country through the United States mail. These letters are filled with advice—advice from 'spirits' who don't know as much as a tadpole—and this advice is religiously followed by the receivers. One of these clients was a man whom the spirits (if one may thus plurally describe the ingenious Manchester) were teaching how to contrive an improved railway car-wheel. It is coarse employment for a spirit, but it is higher and wholesomer activity than talking for ever about 'how happy we are.'

Chapter 49 Episodes in Pilot Life

IN the course of the tug-boat gossip, it came out that out of every five of my former friends who had quitted the river, four had chosen farming as an occupation. Of course this was not because they were peculiarly gifted, agriculturally, and thus more likely to succeed as farmers than in other industries: the reason for their choice must be traced to some other source. Doubtless they chose farming because that life is private and secluded from irruptions of undesirable strangers—like the pilot- house hermitage. And doubtless they also chose it because on a thousand nights of black storm and danger they had noted the twinkling lights of solitary farm-houses, as the boat swung by, and pictured to themselves the serenity and security and coziness of such refuges at such times, and so had by-and-bye come to dream of that retired and peaceful life as the one desirable thing to long for, anticipate, earn, and at last enjoy.

But I did not learn that any of these pilot-farmers had astonished anybody with their successes. Their farms do not support them: they support their farms. The pilot-farmer disappears from the river annually, about the breaking of spring, and is seen no more till next frost. Then he appears again, in damaged homespun, combs the hayseed out of his hair, and takes a pilot-house berth for the winter. In this way he pays the debts which his farming has achieved during the agricultural season. So his river bondage is but half broken; he is still the river's slave the hardest half of the year.

One of these men bought a farm, but did not retire to it. He knew a trick worth two of that. He did not propose to pauperize his farm by applying his personal ignorance to working it. No, he put the farm into the hands of an agricultural expert to be worked on shares—out of every three loads of corn the expert to have two and the pilot the third. But at the end of the season the pilot received no corn. The expert explained that his share was not reached. The farm produced only two loads.

Some of the pilots whom I had known had had adventures—

the outcome fortunate, sometimes, but not in all cases. Captain Montgomery, whom I had steered for when he was a pilot, commanded the Confederate fleet in the great battle before Memphis; when his vessel went down, he swam ashore, fought his way through a squad of soldiers, and made a gallant and narrow escape. He was always a cool man; nothing could disturb his serenity. Once when he was captain of the 'Crescent City,' I was bringing the boat into port at New Orleans, and momently expecting orders from the hurricane deck, but received none. I had stopped the wheels, and there my authority and responsibility ceased. It was evening—dim twilight—the captain's hat was perched upon the big bell, and I supposed the intellectual end of the captain was in it, but such was not the case. The captain was very strict; therefore I knew better than to touch a bell without orders. My duty was to hold the boat steadily on her calamitous course, and leave the consequences to take care of themselves—which I did. So we went plowing past the sterns of steamboats and getting closer and closer—the crash was bound to come very soon—and still that hat never budged; for alas, the captain was napping in the texas.... Things were becoming exceedingly nervous and uncomfortable. It seemed to me that the captain was not going to appear in time to see the entertainment. But he did. Just as we were walking into the stern of a steamboat, he stepped out on deck, and said, with heavenly serenity, 'Set her back on both'—which I did; but a trifle late, however, for the next moment we went smashing through that other boat's flimsy outer works with a most prodigious racket. The captain never said a word to me about the matter afterwards, except to remark that I had done right, and that he hoped I would not hesitate to act in the same way again in like circumstances.

One of the pilots whom I had known when I was on the river had died a very honorable death. His boat caught fire, and he remained at the wheel until he got her safe to land. Then he went out over the breast- board with his clothing in flames, and was the last person to get ashore. He died from his injuries in the course of two or three hours, and his was the only life lost.

The history of Mississippi piloting affords six or seven instances of this sort of martyrdom, and half a hundred instances of escapes from a like fate which came within a second or two of being fatally too late; BUT THERE IS NO INSTANCE OF A PILOT DESERTING HIS POST TO SAVE HIS LIFE WHILE BY REMAINING AND SACRIFICING IT HE MIGHT SECURE OTHER LIVES FROM DESTRUCTION. It is well worth while to set down this noble fact, and well worth while to put it in italics, too.

The 'cub' pilot is early admonished to despise all perils connected with a pilot's calling, and to prefer any sort of death to the deep dishonor of deserting his post while there is any possibility of his being useful in it. And so effectively are these admonitions inculcated, that even young and but half-tried pilots can be depended upon to stick to the wheel, and die there when occasion requires. In a Memphis graveyard is buried a young fellow who perished at the wheel a great many years ago, in White River, to save the lives of other men. He said to the captain that if the fire would give him time to reach a sand bar, some distance away, all could be saved, but that to land against the bluff bank of the river would be to insure the loss of many lives. He reached the bar and grounded the boat in shallow water; but by that time the flames had closed around him, and in escaping through them he was fatally burned. He had been urged to fly sooner, but had replied as became a pilot to reply—

'I will not go. If I go, nobody will be saved; if I stay, no one will be lost but me. I will stay.'

There were two hundred persons on board, and no life was lost but the pilot's. There used to be a monument to this young fellow, in that Memphis graveyard. While we tarried in Memphis on our down trip, I started out to look for it, but our time was so brief that I was obliged to turn back before my object was accomplished.

The tug-boat gossip informed me that Dick Kennet was dead—blown up, near Memphis, and killed; that several others whom I had known had fallen in the war—one or two of them shot down at the wheel; that another and very particular friend, whom I had steered many trips for, had stepped out of his house in New Orleans, one night years ago, to collect some money in a remote part of the city, and had never been seen again—was murdered and thrown into the river, it was thought; that Ben Thornburgh was dead long ago; also his wild 'cub' whom I used to quarrel with, all through every daylight watch. A heedless, reckless creature he was, and always in hot water, always in mischief. An Arkansas passenger brought an enormous bear aboard, one day, and chained him to a life-boat on the hurricane deck. Thornburgh's 'cub' could not rest till he had gone there and unchained the bear, to 'see what he would do.' He was promptly gratified. The bear chased him around and around the deck, for miles and miles, with two hundred eager faces grinning through the railings for audience, and finally snatched off the lad's coat-tail and went into the texas to chew it. The off-watch turned out with alacrity, and left the bear in sole possession. He presently grew lonesome, and started out for recreation. He ranged the whole boat—visited every part of it, with an advance guard of fleeing people in front of him and a voiceless vacancy behind him; and when his owner captured him at last, those two were the only visible beings anywhere; everybody else was in hiding, and the boat was a solitude.

I was told that one of my pilot friends fell dead at the wheel, from heart disease, in 1869. The captain was on the roof at the time. He saw the boat breaking for the shore; shouted, and got no answer; ran up, and found the pilot lying dead on the floor.

Mr. Bixby had been blown up, in Madrid bend; was not injured, but the other pilot was lost.

George Ritchie had been blown up near Memphis—blown into the river from the wheel, and disabled. The water was very cold; he clung to a cotton bale—mainly with his teeth—and floated until nearly exhausted, when he was rescued by some deck hands who were on a piece of the wreck. They tore open the bale and packed him in the cotton, and warmed the life back into him, and got him safe to Memphis. He is one of Bixby's pilots on the 'Baton Rouge' now.

Into the life of a steamboat clerk, now dead, had dropped a bit of romance—somewhat grotesque romance, but romance nevertheless. When I knew him he was a shiftless young spendthrift, boisterous, goodhearted, full of careless generosities, and pretty conspicuously promising to fool his possibilities away early, and come to nothing. In a Western city lived a rich and childless old foreigner and his wife; and in their family was a comely young girl—sort of friend, sort of servant. The young clerk of whom I have been speaking—whose name was not George Johnson, but who shall be called George Johnson for the purposes of this narrative—got acquainted with this young girl, and they sinned; and the old foreigner found them out, and rebuked them. Being ashamed, they lied, and said they were married; that they had been privately married. Then the old foreigner's hurt was healed, and he forgave and blessed them. After that, they were able to continue their sin without concealment. By-and-bye the foreigner's wife died; and presently he followed after her. Friends of the family assembled to mourn; and among the mourners sat the two young sinners. The will was opened and solemnly read. It bequeathed every penny of that old man's great wealth to MRS. GEORGE JOHNSON!

And there was no such person. The young sinners fled forth then, and did a very foolish thing: married themselves before an obscure Justice of the Peace, and got him to antedate the thing. That did no sort of good. The distant relatives flocked in and exposed the fraudful date with extreme suddenness and surprising ease, and carried off the fortune, leaving the Johnsons very legitimately, and legally, and irrevocably chained together in honorable marriage, but with not so much as a penny to bless themselves withal. Such are the actual facts; and not all novels have for a base so telling a situation.

Chapter 50 The 'Original Jacobs'

WE had some talk about Captain Isaiah Sellers, now many years dead. He was a fine man, a high-minded man, and greatly respected both ashore and on the river. He was very tall, well built, and handsome; and in his old age—as I remember him—his hair was as black as an Indian's, and his eye and hand were as strong and steady and his nerve and judgment as firm and clear as anybody's, young or old, among the fraternity of pilots. He was the patriarch of the craft; he had been a keelboat pilot before the day of steamboats; and a steamboat pilot before any other steamboat pilot, still surviving at the time I speak of, had ever turned a wheel. Consequently his brethren held him in the sort of awe in which illustrious survivors of a bygone age are always held by their associates. He knew how he was regarded, and perhaps this fact added some trifle of stiffening to his natural dignity, which had been sufficiently stiff in its original state.

He left a diary behind him; but apparently it did not date back to his first steamboat trip, which was said to be 1811, the year the first steamboat disturbed the waters of the Mississippi. At the time of his death a correspondent of the 'St. Louis Republican' culled the following items from the diary—

'In February, 1825, he shipped on board the steamer "Rambler," at Florence, Ala., and made during that year three trips to New Orleans and back—this on the "Gen. Carrol," between Nashville and New Orleans. It was during his stay on this boat that Captain Sellers introduced the tap of the bell as a signal to heave the lead, previous to which time it was the custom for the pilot to speak to the men below when soundings were wanted. The proximity of the forecastle to the pilot-house, no doubt, rendered this an easy matter; but how different on one of our palaces of the present day.

'In 1827 we find him on board the "President," a boat of two hundred and eighty-five tons burden, and plying between Smithland and New Orleans. Thence he joined the "Jubilee" in 1828, and on this boat he did his first piloting in the St. Louis trade; his first watch extending from Herculaneum to St. Genevieve. On May 26, 1836, he completed and left Pittsburgh in charge of the steamer "Prairie," a boat of four hundred tons, and the first steamer with a STATE-ROOM CABIN ever seen at St. Louis. In 1857 he introduced the signal for meeting boats, and which has, with some slight change, been the universal custom of this day; in fact, is rendered obligatory by act of Congress.

'As general items of river history, we quote the following marginal notes from his general log—

'In March, 1825, Gen. Lafayette left New Orleans for St. Louis on the low-pressure steamer "Natchez."

'In January, 1828, twenty-one steamers left the New Orleans wharf to celebrate the occasion of Gen. Jackson's visit to that city.

'In 1830 the "North American" made the run from New Orleans to Memphis in six days—best time on record to that date. It has since been made in two days and ten hours.

'In 1831 the Red River cut-off formed.

'In 1832 steamer "Hudson" made the run from White River to Helena, a distance of seventy-five miles, in twelve hours. This was the source of much talk and speculation among parties directly interested.

'In 1839 Great Horseshoe cut-off formed.

'Up to the present time, a term of thirty-five years, we ascertain, by reference to the diary, he has made four hundred and sixty round trips to New Orleans, which gives a distance of one million one hundred and four thousand miles, or an average of eighty-six miles a day.'

Whenever Captain Sellers approached a body of gossiping pilots, a chill fell there, and talking ceased. For this reason: whenever six pilots were gathered together, there would always be one or two newly fledged ones in the lot, and the elder ones would be always 'showing off' before these poor fellows; making them sorrowfully feel how callow they were, how recent their nobility, and how humble their degree, by talking largely and vaporously of old-time experiences on the river; always making it a point to date everything back as far as they could, so as to make the new men feel their newness to the sharpest degree possible, and envy the old stagers in the like degree. And how these complacent baldheads WOULD swell, and brag, and lie, and date back—ten, fifteen, twenty years,—and how they did enjoy the effect produced upon the marveling and envying youngsters!

And perhaps just at this happy stage of the proceedings, the stately figure of Captain Isaiah Sellers, that real and only genuine Son of Antiquity, would drift solemnly into the midst. Imagine the size of the silence that would result on the instant. And imagine the feelings of those bald-heads, and the exultation of their recent audience when the ancient captain would begin to drop casual and indifferent remarks of a reminiscent nature—about islands that had disappeared, and cutoffs that had been made, a generation before the oldest bald-head in the company had ever set his foot in a pilot-house!

Many and many a time did this ancient mariner appear on the scene in the above fashion, and spread disaster and humiliation around him. If one might believe the pilots, he always dated his islands back to the misty dawn of river history; and he never used the same island twice; and never did he employ an island that still existed, or give one a name which anybody present was old enough to have heard of before. If you might believe the pilots, he was always conscientiously particular about little details; never spoke of 'the State of Mississippi,' for instance —no, he would say, 'When the State of Mississippi was where Arkansas now is,' and would never speak of Louisiana or Missouri in a general way, and leave an incorrect impression on your mind—no, he would say, 'When Louisiana was up the river farther,' or 'When Missouri was on the Illinois side.'

The old gentleman was not of literary turn or capacity, but he used to jot down brief paragraphs of plain practical information about the river, and sign them 'MARK TWAIN,' and give them to the 'New Orleans Picayune.' They related to the stage and condition of the river, and were accurate and valuable; and thus far, they contained no poison. But in speaking of the stage of the river to-day, at a given point, the captain was pretty apt to drop in a little remark about this being the first time he had seen the water so high or so low at that particular point for forty-nine years; and now and then he would mention Island So- and-so, and follow it, in parentheses, with some such observation as 'disappeared in 1807, if I remember rightly.' In these antique interjections lay poison and bitterness for the other old pilots, and they used to chaff the 'Mark Twain' paragraphs with unsparing mockery.

It so chanced that one of these paragraphs*—became the text for my first newspaper article. I burlesqued it broadly, very broadly, stringing my fantastics out to the extent of eight hundred or a thousand words. I was a 'cub' at the time. I showed my performance to some pilots, and they eagerly rushed it into print in the 'New Orleans True Delta.' It was a great pity; for it did nobody any worthy service, and it sent a pang deep into a good man's heart. There was no malice in my rubbish; but it laughed at the captain. It laughed at a man to whom such a thing was new and strange and dreadful. I did not know then, though I do now, that there is no suffering comparable with that which a private person feels when he is for the first time pilloried in print.

Captain Sellers did me the honor to profoundly detest me from that day forth. When I say he did me the honor, I am not using empty words. It was a very real honor to be in the thoughts of so great a man as Captain Sellers, and I had wit enough to appreciate it and be proud of it. It was distinction to be loved by such a man; but it was a much greater distinction to be hated by him, because he loved scores of people; but he didn't sit up nights to hate anybody but me.

He never printed another paragraph while he lived, and he never again signed 'Mark Twain' to anything. At the time that the telegraph brought the news of his death, I was on the Pacific coast. I was a fresh new journalist, and needed a nom de guerre; so I confiscated the ancient mariner's discarded one, and have done my best to make it remain what it was in his hands—a sign and symbol and warrant that whatever is found in its company may be gambled on as being the petrified truth; how I have succeeded, it would not be modest in me to

* The original MS. of it, in the captain's own hand, has been sent to me from New Orleans. It reads as follows—

VICKSBURG May 4, 1859.

'My opinion for the benefit of the citizens of New Orleans: The water is higher this far up than it has been since 8. My opinion is that the water will be feet deep in Canal street before the first of next June. Mrs. Turner's plantation at the head of Big Black Island is all under water, and it has not been since 1815.

I. Sellers.'

say.

The captain had an honorable pride in his profession and an abiding love for it. He ordered his monument before he died, and kept it near him until he did die. It stands over his grave now, in Bellefontaine cemetery, St. Louis. It is his image, in marble, standing on duty at the pilot wheel; and worthy to stand and confront criticism, for it represents a man who in life would have stayed there till he burned to a cinder, if duty required it.

The finest thing we saw on our whole Mississippi trip, we saw as we approached New Orleans in the steam-tug. This was the curving frontage of the crescent city lit up with the white glare of five miles of electric lights. It was a wonderful sight, and very beautiful.

Chapter 51 Reminiscences

WE left for St. Louis in the 'City of Baton Rouge,' on a delightfully hot day, but with the main purpose of my visit but lamely accomplished. I had hoped to hunt up and talk with a hundred steamboatmen, but got so pleasantly involved in the social life of the town that I got nothing more than mere five-minute talks with a couple of dozen of the craft.

I was on the bench of the pilot-house when we backed out and 'straightened up' for the start—the boat pausing for a 'good ready,' in the old-fashioned way, and the black smoke piling out of the chimneys equally in the old-fashioned way. Then we began to gather momentum, and presently were fairly under way and booming along. It was all as natural and familiar— and so were the shoreward sights—as if there had been no break in my river life. There was a 'cub,' and I judged that he would take the wheel now; and he did. Captain Bixby stepped into the pilot- house. Presently the cub closed up on the rank of steamships. He made me nervous, for he allowed too much water to show between our boat and the ships. I knew quite well what was going to happen, because I could date back in my own life and inspect the record. The captain looked on, during a silent half-minute, then took the wheel himself, and crowded the boat in, till she went scraping along within a hand-breadth of the ships. It was exactly the favor which he had done me, about a quarter of a century before, in that same spot, the first time I ever steamed out of the port of New Orleans. It was a very great and sincere pleasure to me to see the thing repeated—with somebody else as victim.

We made Natchez (three hundred miles) in twenty-two hours and a half— much the swiftest passage I have ever made over that piece of water.

The next morning I came on with the four o'clock watch, and saw Ritchie successfully run half a dozen crossings in a fog, using for his guidance the marked chart devised and patented by Bixby and himself. This sufficiently evidenced the great value of the chart.

By and by, when the fog began to clear off, I noticed that the reflection of a tree in the smooth water of an overflowed bank, six hundred yards away, was stronger and blacker than the ghostly tree itself. The faint spectral trees, dimly glimpsed through the shredding fog, were very pretty things to see.

We had a heavy thunder-storm at Natchez, another at Vicksburg, and still another about fifty miles below Memphis. They had an old-fashioned energy which had long been unfamiliar to me. This third storm was accompanied by a raging wind. We tied up to the bank when we saw the tempest coming, and everybody left the pilot-house but me. The wind bent the young trees down, exposing the pale underside of the leaves; and gust after gust followed, in quick succession, thrashing the branches violently up and down, and to this side and that, and creating swift waves of alternating green and white according to the side of the leaf that was exposed, and these waves raced after each other as do their kind over a wind-tossed field of oats. No color that was visible anywhere was quite natural—all tints were charged with a leaden tinge from the solid cloud-bank overhead. The river was leaden; all distances the same; and even the far-reaching ranks of combing white-caps were dully shaded by the dark, rich atmosphere through which their swarming legions marched. The thunder-peals were constant and deafening; explosion followed explosion with but inconsequential intervals between, and the reports grew steadily sharper and higher-keyed, and more trying to the ear; the lightning was as diligent as the thunder, and produced effects which enchanted the eye and sent electric ecstasies of mixed delight and apprehension shivering along every nerve in the body in unintermittent procession. The rain poured down in amazing volume; the ear-splitting thunder-peals broke nearer and nearer; the wind increased in fury and began to wrench off boughs and tree-tops and send them sailing away through space; the pilot-house fell to rocking and straining and cracking and surging, and I went down in the hold to see what time it was.

People boast a good deal about Alpine thunderstorms; but the storms which I have had the luck to see in the Alps were not the equals of some which I have seen in the Mississippi Valley. I may not have seen the Alps do their best, of course, and if they can beat the Mississippi, I don't wish to.

On this up trip I saw a little towhead (infant island) half a mile long, which had been formed during the past nineteen years. Since there was so much time to spare that nineteen years of it could be devoted to the construction of a mere towhead, where was the use, originally, in rushing this whole globe through in six days? It is likely that if more time had been taken, in the first place, the world would have been made right, and this ceaseless improving and repairing would not be necessary now. But if you hurry a world or a house, you are nearly sure to find out by and by that you have left out a towhead, or a broom-closet, or some other little convenience, here and there, which has got to be supplied, no matter how much expense and vexation it may cost.

We had a succession of black nights, going up the river, and it was observable that whenever we landed, and suddenly inundated the trees with the intense sunburst of the electric light, a certain curious effect was always produced: hundreds of birds flocked instantly out from the masses of shining green foliage, and went careering hither and thither through the white rays, and often a song-bird tuned up and fell to singing. We judged that they mistook this superb artificial day for the genuine article. We had a delightful trip in that thoroughly well- ordered steamer, and regretted that it was accomplished so speedily. By means of diligence and activity, we managed to hunt out nearly all the old friends. One was missing, however; he went to his reward, whatever it was, two years ago. But I found out all about him. His case helped me to realize how lasting can be the effect of a very trifling occurrence. When he was an apprentice-blacksmith in our village, and I a schoolboy, a couple of young Englishmen came to the town and sojourned a while; and one day they got themselves up in cheap royal finery and did the Richard III swordfight with maniac energy and prodigious powwow, in the presence of the village boys.

This blacksmith cub was there, and the histrionic poison entered his bones. This vast, lumbering, ignorant, dull-witted lout was stage-struck, and irrecoverably. He disappeared, and presently turned up in St. Louis. I ran across him there, by and by. He was standing musing on a street corner, with his left hand on his hip, the thumb of his right supporting his chin, face bowed and frowning, slouch hat pulled down over his forehead—imagining himself to be Othello or some such character, and imagining that the passing crowd marked his tragic bearing and were awestruck.

I joined him, and tried to get him down out of the clouds, but did not succeed. However, he casually informed me, presently, that he was a member of the Walnut Street theater company—and he tried to say it with indifference, but the indifference was thin, and a mighty exultation showed through it. He said he was cast for a part in Julius Caesar, for that night, and if I should come I would see him. IF I should come! I said I wouldn't miss it if I were dead.

I went away stupefied with astonishment, and saying to myself, 'How strange it is! WE always thought this fellow a fool; yet the moment he comes to a great city, where intelligence and appreciation abound, the talent concealed in this shabby napkin is at once discovered, and promptly welcomed and honored.'

But I came away from the theater that night disappointed and offended; for I had had no glimpse of my hero, and his name was not in the bills. I met him on the street the next morning, and before I could speak, he asked—

'Did you see me?'

'No, you weren't there.'

He looked surprised and disappointed. He said—

'Yes, I was. Indeed I was. I was a Roman soldier.'

'Which one?'

'Why didn't you see them Roman soldiers that stood back there in a rank, and sometimes marched in procession around the stage?'

'Do you mean the Roman army?—those six sandaled roustabouts in nightshirts, with tin shields and helmets, that marched around treading on each other's heels, in charge of a spider-legged consumptive dressed like themselves?'

'That's it! that's it! I was one of them Roman soldiers. I was the next to the last one. A half a year ago I used to always be the last one; but I've been promoted.'

Well, they told me that that poor fellow remained a Roman soldier to the last—a matter of thirty-four years. Sometimes they cast him for a 'speaking part,' but not an elaborate one. He could be trusted to go and say, 'My lord, the carriage waits,' but if they ventured to add a sentence or two to this, his memory felt the strain and he was likely to miss fire. Yet, poor devil, he had been patiently studying the part of Hamlet for more than thirty years, and he lived and died in the belief that some day he would be invited to play it!

And this is what came of that fleeting visit of those young Englishmen to our village such ages and ages ago! What noble horseshoes this man might have made, but for those

Englishmen; and what an inadequate Roman soldier he DID make!

A day or two after we reached St. Louis, I was walking along Fourth Street when a grizzly-headed man gave a sort of start as he passed me, then stopped, came back, inspected me narrowly, with a clouding brow, and finally said with deep asperity—

'Look here, HAVE YOU GOT THAT DRINK YET?'

A maniac, I judged, at first. But all in a flash I recognized him. I made an effort to blush that strained every muscle in me, and answered as sweetly and winningly as ever I knew how—

'Been a little slow, but am just this minute closing in on the place where they keep it. Come in and help.'

He softened, and said make it a bottle of champagne and he was agreeable. He said he had seen my name in the papers, and had put all his affairs aside and turned out, resolved to find me or die; and make me answer that question satisfactorily, or kill me; though the most of his late asperity had been rather counterfeit than otherwise.

This meeting brought back to me the St. Louis riots of about thirty years ago. I spent a week there, at that time, in a boarding-house, and had this young fellow for a neighbor across the hall. We saw some of the fightings and killings; and by and by we went one night to an armory where two hundred young men had met, upon call, to be armed and go forth against the rioters, under command of a military man. We drilled till about ten o'clock at night; then news came that the mob were in great force in the lower end of the town, and were sweeping everything before them. Our column moved at once. It was a very hot night, and my musket was very heavy. We marched and marched; and the nearer we approached the seat of war, the hotter I grew and the thirstier I got. I was behind my friend; so, finally, I asked him to hold my musket while I dropped out and got a drink. Then I branched off and went home. I was not feeling any solicitude about him of course, because I knew he was so well armed, now, that he could take care of himself without any trouble. If I had had any doubts about that, I would have borrowed another musket for him. I left the city pretty early the next morning, and if this grizzled man had not happened to encounter my name in the papers the other day in St. Louis, and felt moved to seek me out, I should have carried to my grave a heart-torturing uncertainty as to whether he ever got out of the riots all right or not. I ought to have inquired, thirty years ago; I know that. And I would have inquired, if I had had the muskets; but, in the circumstances, he seemed better fixed to conduct the investigations than I was.

One Monday, near the time of our visit to St. Louis, the 'Globe-Democrat' came out with a couple of pages of Sunday statistics, whereby it appeared that 119,448 St. Louis people attended the morning and evening church services the day before, and 23,102 children attended Sunday-school. Thus 142,550 persons, out of the city's total of 400,000 population, respected the day religious-wise. I found these statistics, in a condensed form, in a telegram of the Associated Press, and preserved them. They made it apparent that St. Louis was in a higher state of grace than she could have claimed to be in my time. But now that I canvass the figures narrowly, I suspect that the telegraph mutilated them. It cannot be that there are more than 150,000 Catholics in the town; the other 250,000 must be classified as Protestants. Out of these 250,000,

according to this questionable telegram, only 26,362 attended church and Sunday-school, while out of the 150,000 Catholics, 116,188 went to church and Sunday-school.

Chapter 52 A Burning Brand

ALL at once the thought came into my mind, 'I have not sought out Mr. Brown.'

Upon that text I desire to depart from the direct line of my subject, and make a little excursion. I wish to reveal a secret which I have carried with me nine years, and which has become burdensome.

Upon a certain occasion, nine years ago, I had said, with strong feeling, 'If ever I see St. Louis again, I will seek out Mr. Brown, the great grain merchant, and ask of him the privilege of shaking him by the hand.'

The occasion and the circumstances were as follows. A friend of mine, a clergyman, came one evening and said—

'I have a most remarkable letter here, which I want to read to you, if I can do it without breaking down. I must preface it with some explanations, however. The letter is written by an ex-thief and ex-vagabond of the lowest origin and basest rearing, a man all stained with crime and steeped in ignorance; but, thank God, with a mine of pure gold hidden away in him, as you shall see. His letter is written to a burglar named Williams, who is serving a nine-year term in a certain State prison, for burglary. Williams was a particularly daring burglar, and plied that trade during a number of years; but he was caught at last and jailed, to await trial in a town where he had broken into a house at night, pistol in hand, and forced the owner to hand over to him $8,000 in government bonds. Williams was not a common sort of person, by any means; he was a graduate of Harvard College, and came of good New England stock. His father was a clergyman. While lying in jail, his health began to fail, and he was threatened with consumption. This fact, together with the opportunity for reflection afforded by solitary confinement, had its effect—its natural effect. He fell into serious thought; his early training asserted itself with power, and wrought with strong influence upon his mind and heart. He put his old life behind him, and became an earnest Christian. Some ladies in the town heard of this, visited him, and by their encouraging words supported him in his good resolutions and strengthened him to continue in his new life. The trial ended in his conviction and sentence to the State prison for the term of nine years, as I have before said. In the prison he became acquainted with the poor wretch referred to in the beginning of my talk, Jack Hunt, the writer of the letter which I am going to read. You will see that the acquaintanceship bore fruit for Hunt. When Hunt's time was out, he wandered to St. Louis; and from that place he wrote his letter to Williams. The letter got no further than the office of the prison warden, of course; prisoners are not often allowed to receive letters from outside. The prison authorities read this letter, but did not destroy it. They had not the heart to do it. They read it to several persons, and eventually it fell into the hands of those ladies of whom I spoke a while ago. The other day I came across an old friend of mine—a clergyman—who had seen this letter, and was full of it. The mere remembrance of it so moved him that he could not talk of it without his voice breaking. He promised to get a copy of it for me; and here it is —an exact copy, with all the imperfections of the original preserved. It has many slang expressions in it—thieves' argot— but their meaning has been interlined, in parentheses, by the prison authorities'—

St. Louis, June 9th 1872.

Mr. W— friend Charlie if i may call you so: i no you are surprised to get a letter from me, but i hope you won't be mad at my writing to you. i want to tell you my thanks for the way you talked to me when i was in prison—it has led me to try and be a better man; i guess you thought i did not cair for what you said, & at the first go off I didn't, but i noed you was a man who had don big work with good men & want no sucker, nor want gasing & all the boys knod it.

I used to think at nite what you said, & for it i nocked off swearing months before my time was up, for i saw it want no good, nohow—the day my time was up you told me if i would shake the cross (QUIT STEALING) & live on the square for months, it would be the best job i ever done in my life. The state agent give me a ticket to here, & on the car i thought more of what you said to me, but didn't make up my mind. When we got to Chicago on the cars from there to here, I pulled off an old woman's leather; (ROBBED HER OF HER POCKETBOOK) i hadn't no more than got it off when i wished i hadn't done it, for awhile before that i made up my mind to be a square bloke, for months on your word, but forgot it when i saw the leather was a grip (EASY TO GET)—but i kept clos to her & when she got out of the cars at a way place i said, marm have you lost anything. & she tumbled (DISCOVERED) her leather was off (GONE)—is this it says i, giving it to her—well if you aint honest, says she, but i hadn't got cheak enough to stand that sort of talk, so i left her in a hurry. When i got here i had $1 and 25 cents left & i didn't get no work for 3 days as i aint strong enough for roust about on a steam bote (FOR A DECK HAND)—The afternoon of the 3rd day I spent my last 10 cts for moons (LARGE, ROUND SEA-BISCUIT) & cheese & i felt pretty rough & was thinking i would have to go on the dipe (PICKING POCKETS) again, when i thought of what you once said about a fellows calling on the Lord when he was in hard luck, & i thought i would try it once anyhow, but when i tryed it i got stuck on the start, & all i could get off wos, Lord give a poor fellow a chance to square it for 3 months for Christ's sake, amen; & i kept a thinking, of it over and over as i went along—about an hour after that i was in 4th St. & this is what happened & is the cause of my being where i am now & about which i will tell you before i get done writing. As i was walking along herd a big noise & saw a horse running away with a carriage with 2 children in it, & I grabed up a peace of box cover from the side walk & run in the middle of the street, & when the horse came up i smashed him over the head as hard as i could drive—the bord split to peces & the horse checked up a little & I grabbed the reigns & pulled his head down until he stopped—the gentleman what owned him came running up & soon as he saw the children were all rite, he shook hands with me and gave me a $50 green back, & my asking the Lord to help me come into my head, & i was so thunderstruck i couldn't drop the reigns nor say nothing—he saw something was up, & coming back to me said, my boy are you hurt? & the thought come into my head just then to ask him for work; & i asked him to take back the bill and give me a job—says he, jump in here & lets talk about it, but keep the money—he asked me if i could take care of horses & i said yes, for i used to hang round livery stables & often would help clean & drive horses, he told me he wanted a man for that work, & would give me $16 a month & bord me. You bet i took that chance at once. that nite in my little room over the stable i sat a long time thinking over my past life & of what had just happened & i just got down on my nees & thanked the Lord for the job & to help me to square it, & to bless you for putting me up to it, & the next morning i done it again & got me some new

togs (CLOTHES) & a bible for i made up my mind after what the Lord had done for me i would read the bible every nite and morning, & ask him to keep an eye on me. When I had been there about a week Mr. Brown (that's his name) came in my room one nite and saw me reading the bible—he asked me if i was a Christian & i told him no—he asked me how it was i read the bible instead of papers & books—Well Charlie i thought i had better give him a square deal in the start, so i told him all about my being in prison & about you, & how i had almost done give up looking for work & how the Lord got me the job when I asked him; & the only way i had to pay him back was to read the bible & square it, & i asked him to give me a chance for 3 months—he talked to me like a father for a long time, & told me i could stay & then i felt better than ever i had done in my life, for i had given Mr. Brown a fair start with me & now i didn't fear no one giving me a back cap (EXPOSING HIS PAST LIFE) & running me off the job—the next morning he called me into the library & gave me another square talk, & advised me to study some every day, & he would help me one or 2 hours every nite, & he gave me a Arithmetic, a spelling book, a Geography & a writing book, & he hers me every nite—he lets me come into the house to prayers every morning, & got me put in a bible class in the Sunday School which i likes very much for it helps me to understand my bible better.

Now, Charlie the 3 months on the square are up 2 months ago, & as you said, it is the best job i ever did in my life, & i commenced another of the same sort right away, only it is to God helping me to last a lifetime Charlie—i wrote this letter to tell you I do think God has forgiven my sins & herd your prayers, for you told me you should pray for me—i no i love to read his word & tell him all my troubles & he helps me i know for i have plenty of chances to steal but i don't feel to as i once did & now i take more pleasure in going to church than to the theater & that wasnt so once—our minister and others often talk with me & a month ago they wanted me to join the church, but I said no, not now, i may be mistaken in my feelings, i will wait awhile, but now i feel that God has called me & on the first Sunday in July i will join the church—dear friend i wish i could write to you as i feel, but i cant do it yet—you no i learned to read and write while prisons & i aint got well enough along to write as i would talk; i no i aint spelled all the words rite in this & lots of other mistakes but you will excuse it i no, for you no i was brought up in a poor house until i run away, & that i never new who my father and mother was & i dont no my right name, & i hope you wont be mad at me, but i have as much rite to one name as another & i have taken your name, for you wont use it when you get out i no, & you are the man i think most of in the world; so i hope you wont be mad— I am doing well, i put $10 a month in bank with $25 of the $50— if you ever want any or all of it let me know, & it is yours. i wish you would let me send you some now. I send you with this a receipt for a year of Littles Living Age, i didn't know what you would like & i told Mr. Brown & he said he thought you would like it—i wish i was nere you so i could send you chuck (REFRESHMENTS) on holidays; it would spoil this weather from here, but i will send you a box next thanksgiving any way—next week Mr. Brown takes me into his store as lite porter & will advance me as soon as i know a little more—he keeps a big granary store, wholesale—i forgot to tell you of my mission school, sunday school class—the school is in the sunday afternoon, i went out two sunday afternoons, and picked up seven kids (LITTLE BOYS) & got them to come in. two of them new as much as i did & i had them put in a class where they could learn something. i dont no much myself, but as these kids cant read i get on nicely with them. i make sure of them by going after them every Sunday hour before school time, I also got 4 girls to come. tell Mack and Harry about me, if they will come out here when their time is up i will get them jobs at once. i hope you will excuse this long letter & all mistakes, i wish i could see you for i cant write as i would talk—i hope the warm weather is doing your lungs good—i was afraid when you was bleeding you would die—give my respects to all the boys and tell them how i am doing—i am doing well and every one here treats me as kind as they can—Mr. Brown is going to write to you sometime—i hope some day you will write to me, this letter is from your very true friend

C— W—

who you know as Jack Hunt.

I send you Mr. Brown's card. Send my letter to him.

Here was true eloquence; irresistible eloquence; and without a single grace or ornament to help it out. I have seldom been so deeply stirred by any piece of writing. The reader of it halted, all the way through, on a lame and broken voice; yet he had tried to fortify his feelings by several private readings of the letter before venturing into company with it. He was practising upon me to see if there was any hope of his being able to read the document to his prayer-meeting with anything like a decent command over his feelings. The result was not promising. However, he determined to risk it; and did. He got through tolerably well; but his audience broke down early, and stayed in that condition to the end.

The fame of the letter spread through the town. A brother minister came and borrowed the manuscript, put it bodily into a sermon, preached the sermon to twelve hundred people on a Sunday morning, and the letter drowned them in their own tears. Then my friend put it into a sermon and went before his Sunday morning congregation with it. It scored another triumph. The house wept as one individual.

My friend went on summer vacation up into the fishing regions of our northern British neighbors, and carried this sermon with him, since he might possibly chance to need a sermon. He was asked to preach, one day. The little church was full. Among the people present were the late Dr. J. G. Holland, the late Mr. Seymour of the 'New York Times,' Mr. Page, the philanthropist and temperance advocate, and, I think, Senator Frye, of Maine. The marvelous letter did its wonted work; all the people were moved, all the people wept; the tears flowed in a steady stream down Dr. Holland's cheeks, and nearly the same can be said with regard to all who were there. Mr. Page was so full of enthusiasm over the letter that he said he would not rest until he made pilgrimage to that prison, and had speech with the man who had been able to inspire a fellow-unfortunate to write so priceless a tract.

Ah, that unlucky Page!—and another man. If they had only been in Jericho, that letter would have rung through the world and stirred all the hearts of all the nations for a thousand years to come, and nobody might ever have found out that it was the confoundedest, brazenest, ingeniousest piece of fraud and humbuggery that was ever concocted to fool poor confiding mortals with!

The letter was a pure swindle, and that is the truth. And take it by and large, it was without a compeer among swindles. It was perfect, it was rounded, symmetrical, complete, colossal!

The reader learns it at this point; but we didn't learn it till some miles and weeks beyond this stage of the affair. My friend came back from the woods, and he and other clergymen

and lay missionaries began once more to inundate audiences with their tears and the tears of said audiences; I begged hard for permission to print the letter in a magazine and tell the watery story of its triumphs; numbers of people got copies of the letter, with permission to circulate them in writing, but not in print; copies were sent to the Sandwich Islands and other far regions.

Charles Dudley Warner was at church, one day, when the worn letter was read and wept over. At the church door, afterward, he dropped a peculiarly cold iceberg down the clergyman's back with the question—

'Do you know that letter to be genuine?'

It was the first suspicion that had ever been voiced; but it had that sickening effect which first-uttered suspicions against one's idol always have. Some talk followed—

'Why—what should make you suspect that it isn't genuine?'

'Nothing that I know of, except that it is too neat, and compact, and fluent, and nicely put together for an ignorant person, an unpractised hand. I think it was done by an educated man.'

The literary artist had detected the literary machinery. If you will look at the letter now, you will detect it yourself—it is observable in every line.

Straightway the clergyman went off, with this seed of suspicion sprouting in him, and wrote to a minister residing in that town where Williams had been jailed and converted; asked for light; and also asked if a person in the literary line (meaning me) might be allowed to print the letter and tell its history. He presently received this answer—

Rev. — —

MY DEAR FRIEND,—In regard to that 'convict's letter' there can be no doubt as to its genuineness. 'Williams,' to whom it was written, lay in our jail and professed to have been converted, and Rev. Mr. —, the chaplain, had great faith in the genuineness of the change—as much as one can have in any such case.

The letter was sent to one of our ladies, who is a Sunday-school teacher,—sent either by Williams himself, or the chaplain of the State's prison, probably. She has been greatly annoyed in having so much publicity, lest it might seem a breach of confidence, or be an injury to Williams. In regard to its publication, I can give no permission; though if the names and places were omitted, and especially if sent out of the country, I think you might take the responsibility and do it.

It is a wonderful letter, which no Christian genius, much less one unsanctified, could ever have written. As showing the work of grace in a human heart, and in a very degraded and wicked one, it proves its own origin and reproves our weak faith in its power to cope with any form of wickedness.

'Mr. Brown' of St. Louis, some one said, was a Hartford man. Do all whom you send from Hartford serve their Master as well?

P.S.—Williams is still in the State's prison, serving out a long sentence—of nine years, I think. He has been sick and threatened with consumption, but I have not inquired after him lately. This lady that I speak of corresponds with him, I presume, and will be quite sure to look after him.

This letter arrived a few days after it was written—and up went Mr. Williams's stock again. Mr. Warner's low-down suspicion was laid in the cold, cold grave, where it apparently belonged. It was a suspicion based upon mere internal evidence, anyway; and when you come to internal evidence, it's a big field and a game that two can play at: as witness this other internal evidence, discovered by the writer of the note above quoted, that 'it is a wonderful letter—which no Christian genius, much less one unsanctified, could ever have written.'

I had permission now to print—provided I suppressed names and places and sent my narrative out of the country. So I chose an Australian magazine for vehicle, as being far enough out of the country, and set myself to work on my article. And the ministers set the pumps going again, with the letter to work the handles.

But meantime Brother Page had been agitating. He had not visited the penitentiary, but he had sent a copy of the illustrious letter to the chaplain of that institution, and accompanied it with—apparently inquiries. He got an answer, dated four days later than that other Brother's reassuring epistle; and before my article was complete, it wandered into my hands. The original is before me, now, and I here append it. It is pretty well loaded with internal evidence of the most solid description—

STATE'S PRISON, CHAPLAIN'S OFFICE, July 11, 1873.

DEAR BRO. PAGE,—Herewith please find the letter kindly loaned me. I am afraid its genuineness cannot be established. It purports to be addressed to some prisoner here. No such letter ever came to a prisoner here. All letters received are carefully read by officers of the prison before they go into the hands of the convicts, and any such letter could not be forgotten. Again, Charles Williams is not a Christian man, but a dissolute, cunning prodigal, whose father is a minister of the gospel. His name is an assumed one. I am glad to have made your acquaintance. I am preparing a lecture upon life seen through prison bars, and should like to deliver the same in your vicinity.

And so ended that little drama. My poor article went into the fire; for whereas the materials for it were now more abundant and infinitely richer than they had previously been, there were parties all around me, who, although longing for the publication before, were a unit for suppression at this stage and complexion of the game. They said: 'Wait —the wound is too fresh, yet.' All the copies of the famous letter except mine disappeared suddenly; and from that time onward, the aforetime same old drought set in in the churches. As a rule, the town was on a spacious grin for a while, but there were places in it where the grin did not appear, and where it was dangerous to refer to the ex-convict's letter.

A word of explanation. 'Jack Hunt,' the professed writer of the letter, was an imaginary person. The burglar Williams— Harvard graduate, son of a minister—wrote the letter himself, to himself: got it smuggled out of the prison; got it conveyed to persons who had supported and encouraged him in his conversion—where he knew two things would happen: the genuineness of the letter would not be doubted or inquired into; and the nub of it would be noticed, and would have valuable effect—the effect, indeed, of starting a movement to get Mr. Williams pardoned out of prison.

That 'nub' is so ingeniously, so casually, flung in, and immediately left there in the tail of the letter, undwelt upon, that an indifferent reader would never suspect that it was the heart and core of the epistle, if he even took note of it at all, This is the 'nub'—

'i hope the warm weather is doing your lungs good—I WAS AFRAID WHEN YOU WAS BLEEDING YOU WOULD DIE— give my respects,' etc.

That is all there is of it—simply touch and go—no dwelling upon it. Nevertheless it was intended for an eye that would be swift to see it; and it was meant to move a kind heart to try to effect the liberation of a poor reformed and purified fellow lying in the fell grip of consumption.

When I for the first time heard that letter read, nine years ago, I felt that it was the most remarkable one I had ever encountered. And it so warmed me toward Mr. Brown of St. Louis that I said that if ever I visited that city again, I would seek out that excellent man and kiss the hem of his garment if it was a new one. Well, I visited St. Louis, but I did not hunt for Mr. Brown; for, alas! the investigations of long ago had proved that the benevolent Brown, like 'Jack Hunt,' was not a real person, but a sheer invention of that gifted rascal, Williams— burglar, Harvard graduate, son of a clergyman.

Chapter 53 My Boyhood's Home

WE took passage in one of the fast boats of the St. Louis and St. Paul Packet Company, and started up the river.

When I, as a boy, first saw the mouth of the Missouri River, it was twenty-two or twenty-three miles above St. Louis, according to the estimate of pilots; the wear and tear of the banks have moved it down eight miles since then; and the pilots say that within five years the river will cut through and move the mouth down five miles more, which will bring it within ten miles of St. Louis.

About nightfall we passed the large and flourishing town of Alton, Illinois; and before daylight next morning the town of Louisiana, Missouri, a sleepy village in my day, but a brisk railway center now; however, all the towns out there are railway centers now. I could not clearly recognize the place. This seemed odd to me, for when I retired from the rebel army in '61 I retired upon Louisiana in good order; at least in good enough order for a person who had not yet learned how to retreat according to the rules of war, and had to trust to native genius. It seemed to me that for a first attempt at a retreat it was not badly done. I had done no advancing in all that campaign that was at all equal to it.

There was a railway bridge across the river here well sprinkled with glowing lights, and a very beautiful sight it was.

At seven in the morning we reached Hannibal, Missouri, where my boyhood was spent. I had had a glimpse of it fifteen years ago, and another glimpse six years earlier, but both were so brief that they hardly counted. The only notion of the town that remained in my mind was the memory of it as I had known it when I first quitted it twenty-nine years ago. That picture of it was still as clear and vivid to me as a photograph. I stepped ashore with the feeling of one who returns out of a dead-and-gone generation. I had a sort of realizing sense of what the Bastille prisoners must have felt when they used to come out and look upon Paris after years of captivity, and note how curiously the familiar and the strange were mixed together before them. I saw the new houses— saw them plainly enough—but they did not affect the older picture in my mind, for through their solid bricks and mortar I saw the vanished houses, which had formerly stood there, with perfect distinctness.

It was Sunday morning, and everybody was abed yet. So I passed through the vacant streets, still seeing the town as it was, and not as it is, and recognizing and metaphorically shaking hands with a hundred familiar objects which no longer exist; and finally climbed Holiday's Hill to get a comprehensive view. The whole town lay spread out below me then, and I could mark and fix every locality, every detail. Naturally, I was a good deal moved. I said, 'Many of the people I once knew in this tranquil refuge of my childhood are now in heaven; some, I trust, are in the other place.' The things about me and before me made me feel like a boy again—convinced me that I was a boy again, and that I had simply been dreaming an unusually long dream; but my reflections spoiled all that; for they forced me to say, 'I see fifty old houses down yonder, into each of which I could enter and find either a man or a woman who was a baby or unborn when I noticed those houses last, or a grandmother who was a plump young bride at that time.'

From this vantage ground the extensive view up and down the river, and wide over the wooded expanses of Illinois, is very beautiful—one of the most beautiful on the Mississippi, I think; which is a hazardous remark to make, for the eight hundred miles of river between St. Louis and St. Paul afford an unbroken succession of lovely pictures. It may be that my affection for the one in question biases my judgment in its favor; I cannot say as to that. No matter, it was satisfyingly beautiful to me, and it had this advantage over all the other friends whom I was about to greet again: it had suffered no change; it was as young and fresh and comely and gracious as ever it had been; whereas, the faces of the others would be old, and scarred with the campaigns of life, and marked with their griefs and defeats, and would give me no upliftings of spirit.

An old gentleman, out on an early morning walk, came along, and we discussed the weather, and then drifted into other matters. I could not remember his face. He said he had been living here twenty-eight years. So he had come after my time, and I had never seen him before. I asked him various questions; first about a mate of mine in Sunday school—what became of him?

'He graduated with honor in an Eastern college, wandered off into the world somewhere, succeeded at nothing, passed out of knowledge and memory years ago, and is supposed to have gone to the dogs.'

'He was bright, and promised well when he was a boy.'

'Yes, but the thing that happened is what became of it all.'

I asked after another lad, altogether the brightest in our village school when I was a boy.

'He, too, was graduated with honors, from an Eastern college; but life whipped him in every battle, straight along, and he died in one of the Territories, years ago, a defeated man.'

I asked after another of the bright boys.

'He is a success, always has been, always will be, I think.'

308 *Life On The Mississippi*

I inquired after a young fellow who came to the town to study for one of the professions when I was a boy.

'He went at something else before he got through—went from medicine to law, or from law to medicine—then to some other new thing; went away for a year, came back with a young wife; fell to drinking, then to gambling behind the door; finally took his wife and two young children to her father's, and went off to Mexico; went from bad to worse, and finally died there, without a cent to buy a shroud, and without a friend to attend the funeral.'

'Pity, for he was the best-natured, and most cheery and hopeful young fellow that ever was.'

I named another boy.

'Oh, he is all right. Lives here yet; has a wife and children, and is prospering.'

Same verdict concerning other boys.

I named three school-girls.

'The first two live here, are married and have children; the other is long ago dead—never married.'

I named, with emotion, one of my early sweethearts.

'She is all right. Been married three times; buried two husbands, divorced from the third, and I hear she is getting ready to marry an old fellow out in Colorado somewhere. She's got children scattered around here and there, most everywheres.'

The answer to several other inquiries was brief and simple—

'Killed in the war.'

I named another boy.

'Well, now, his case is curious! There wasn't a human being in this town but knew that that boy was a perfect chucklehead; perfect dummy; just a stupid ass, as you may say. Everybody knew it, and everybody said it. Well, if that very boy isn't the first lawyer in the State of Missouri to-day, I'm a Democrat!'

'Is that so?'

'It's actually so. I'm telling you the truth.'

'How do you account for it?'

'Account for it? There ain't any accounting for it, except that if you send a damned fool to St. Louis, and you don't tell them he's a damned fool they'll never find it out. There's one thing sure—if I had a damned fool I should know what to do with him: ship him to St. Louis— it's the noblest market in the world for that kind of property. Well, when you come to look at it all around, and chew at it and think it over, don't it just bang anything you ever heard of?'

'Well, yes, it does seem to. But don't you think maybe it was the Hannibal people who were mistaken about the boy, and not the St. Louis people'

'Oh, nonsense! The people here have known him from the very

cradle— they knew him a hundred times better than the St. Louis idiots could have known him. No, if you have got any damned fools that you want to realize on, take my advice— send them to St. Louis.'

I mentioned a great number of people whom I had formerly known. Some were dead, some were gone away, some had prospered, some had come to naught; but as regarded a dozen or so of the lot, the answer was comforting:

'Prosperous—live here yet—town littered with their children.'

I asked about Miss —.

Died in the insane asylum three or four years ago—never was out of it from the time she went in; and was always suffering, too; never got a shred of her mind back.'

If he spoke the truth, here was a heavy tragedy, indeed. Thirty-six years in a madhouse, that some young fools might have some fun! I was a small boy, at the time; and I saw those giddy young ladies come tiptoeing into the room where Miss — sat reading at midnight by a lamp. The girl at the head of the file wore a shroud and a doughface, she crept behind the victim, touched her on the shoulder, and she looked up and screamed, and then fell into convulsions. She did not recover from the fright, but went mad. In these days it seems incredible that people believed in ghosts so short a time ago. But they did.

After asking after such other folk as I could call to mind, I finally inquired about MYSELF:

'Oh, he succeeded well enough—another case of damned fool. If they'd sent him to St. Louis, he'd have succeeded sooner.'

It was with much satisfaction that I recognized the wisdom of having told this candid gentleman, in the beginning, that my name was Smith.

Chapter 54 Past and Present

Being left to myself, up there, I went on picking out old houses in the distant town, and calling back their former inmates out of the moldy past. Among them I presently recognized the house of the father of Lem Hackett (fictitious name). It carried me back more than a generation in a moment, and landed me in the midst of a time when the happenings of life were not the natural and logical results of great general laws, but of special orders, and were freighted with very precise and distinct purposes—partly punitive in intent, partly admonitory; and usually local in application.

When I was a small boy, Lem Hackett was drowned—on a Sunday. He fell out of an empty flat-boat, where he was playing. Being loaded with sin, he went to the bottom like an anvil. He was the only boy in the village who slept that night. We others all lay awake, repenting. We had not needed the information, delivered from the pulpit that evening, that Lem's was a case of special judgment—we knew that, already. There was a ferocious thunder-storm, that night, and it raged continuously until near dawn. The winds blew, the windows rattled, the rain swept along the roof in pelting sheets, and at the briefest of intervals the inky blackness of the night vanished, the houses over the way glared out white and blinding for a quivering instant, then the solid darkness shut down again and a splitting peal of thunder followed, which seemed to rend everything in the neighborhood to shreds and splinters. I sat up in bed quaking and shuddering, waiting for

the destruction of the world, and expecting it. To me there was nothing strange or incongruous in heaven's making such an uproar about Lem Hackett. Apparently it was the right and proper thing to do. Not a doubt entered my mind that all the angels were grouped together, discussing this boy's case and observing the awful bombardment of our beggarly little village with satisfaction and approval. There was one thing which disturbed me in the most serious way; that was the thought that this centering of the celestial interest on our village could not fail to attract the attention of the observers to people among us who might otherwise have escaped notice for years. I felt that I was not only one of those people, but the very one most likely to be discovered. That discovery could have but one result: I should be in the fire with Lem before the chill of the river had been fairly warmed out of him. I knew that this would be only just and fair. I was increasing the chances against myself all the time, by feeling a secret bitterness against Lem for having attracted this fatal attention to me, but I could not help it—this sinful thought persisted in infesting my breast in spite of me. Every time the lightning glared I caught my breath, and judged I was gone. In my terror and misery, I meanly began to suggest other boys, and mention acts of theirs which were wickeder than mine, and peculiarly needed punishment—and I tried to pretend to myself that I was simply doing this in a casual way, and without intent to divert the heavenly attention to them for the purpose of getting rid of it myself. With deep sagacity I put these mentions into the form of sorrowing recollections and left-handed sham- supplications that the sins of those boys might be allowed to pass unnoticed—'Possibly they may repent.' 'It is true that Jim Smith broke a window and lied about it—but maybe he did not mean any harm. And although Tom Holmes says more bad words than any other boy in the village, he probably intends to repent—though he has never said he would. And whilst it is a fact that John Jones did fish a little on Sunday, once, he didn't really catch anything but only just one small useless mud-cat; and maybe that wouldn't have been so awful if he had thrown it back—as he says he did, but he didn't. Pity but they would repent of these dreadful things— and maybe they will yet.'

But while I was shamefully trying to draw attention to these poor chaps —who were doubtless directing the celestial attention to me at the same moment, though I never once suspected that—I had heedlessly left my candle burning. It was not a time to neglect even trifling precautions. There was no occasion to add anything to the facilities for attracting notice to me—so I put the light out.

It was a long night to me, and perhaps the most distressful one I ever spent. I endured agonies of remorse for sins which I knew I had committed, and for others which I was not certain about, yet was sure that they had been set down against me in a book by an angel who was wiser than I and did not trust such important matters to memory. It struck me, by and by, that I had been making a most foolish and calamitous mistake, in one respect: doubtless I had not only made my own destruction sure by directing attention to those other boys, but had already accomplished theirs!—Doubtless the lightning had stretched them all dead in their beds by this time! The anguish and the fright which this thought gave me made my previous sufferings seem trifling by comparison.

Things had become truly serious. I resolved to turn over a new leaf instantly; I also resolved to connect myself with the church the next day, if I survived to see its sun appear. I resolved to cease from sin in all its forms, and to lead a high and blameless life for ever after. I would be punctual at church

Life On The Mississippi 309

and Sunday-school; visit the sick; carry baskets of victuals to the poor (simply to fulfil the regulation conditions, although I knew we had none among us so poor but they would smash the basket over my head for my pains); I would instruct other boys in right ways, and take the resulting trouncings meekly; I would subsist entirely on tracts; I would invade the rum shop and warn the drunkard— and finally, if I escaped the fate of those who early become too good to live, I would go for a missionary.

The storm subsided toward daybreak, and I dozed gradually to sleep with a sense of obligation to Lem Hackett for going to eternal suffering in that abrupt way, and thus preventing a far more dreadful disaster—my own loss.

But when I rose refreshed, by and by, and found that those other boys were still alive, I had a dim sense that perhaps the whole thing was a false alarm; that the entire turmoil had been on Lem's account and nobody's else. The world looked so bright and safe that there did not seem to be any real occasion to turn over a new leaf. I was a little subdued, during that day, and perhaps the next; after that, my purpose of reforming slowly dropped out of my mind, and I had a peaceful, comfortable time again, until the next storm.

That storm came about three weeks later; and it was the most unaccountable one, to me, that I had ever experienced; for on the afternoon of that day, 'Dutchy' was drowned. Dutchy belonged to our Sunday-school. He was a German lad who did not know enough to come in out of the rain; but he was exasperatingly good, and had a prodigious memory. One Sunday he made himself the envy of all the youth and the talk of all the admiring village, by reciting three thousand verses of Scripture without missing a word; then he went off the very next day and got drowned.

Circumstances gave to his death a peculiar impressiveness. We were all bathing in a muddy creek which had a deep hole in it, and in this hole the coopers had sunk a pile of green hickory hoop poles to soak, some twelve feet under water. We were diving and 'seeing who could stay under longest.' We managed to remain down by holding on to the hoop poles. Dutchy made such a poor success of it that he was hailed with laughter and derision every time his head appeared above water. At last he seemed hurt with the taunts, and begged us to stand still on the bank and be fair with him and give him an honest count— 'be friendly and kind just this once, and not miscount for the sake of having the fun of laughing at him.' Treacherous winks were exchanged, and all said 'All right, Dutchy—go ahead, we'll play fair.'

Dutchy plunged in, but the boys, instead of beginning to count, followed the lead of one of their number and scampered to a range of blackberry bushes close by and hid behind it. They imagined Dutchy's humiliation, when he should rise after a superhuman effort and find the place silent and vacant, nobody there to applaud. They were 'so full of laugh' with the idea, that they were continually exploding into muffled cackles. Time swept on, and presently one who was peeping through the briers, said, with surprise—

'Why, he hasn't come up, yet!'

The laughing stopped.

'Boys, it 's a splendid dive,' said one.

'Never mind that,' said another, 'the joke on him is all the

better for it.'

There was a remark or two more, and then a pause. Talking ceased, and all began to peer through the vines. Before long, the boys' faces began to look uneasy, then anxious, then terrified. Still there was no movement of the placid water. Hearts began to beat fast, and faces to turn pale. We all glided out, silently, and stood on the bank, our horrified eyes wandering back and forth from each other's countenances to the water.

'Somebody must go down and see!'

Yes, that was plain; but nobody wanted that grisly task.

'Draw straws!'

So we did—with hands which shook so, that we hardly knew what we were about. The lot fell to me, and I went down. The water was so muddy I could not see anything, but I felt around among the hoop poles, and presently grasped a limp wrist which gave me no response—and if it had I should not have known it, I let it go with such a frightened suddenness.

The boy had been caught among the hoop poles and entangled there, helplessly. I fled to the surface and told the awful news. Some of us knew that if the boy were dragged out at once he might possibly be resuscitated, but we never thought of that. We did not think of anything; we did not know what to do, so we did nothing—except that the smaller lads cried, piteously, and we all struggled frantically into our clothes, putting on anybody's that came handy, and getting them wrong- side-out and upside-down, as a rule. Then we scurried away and gave the alarm, but none of us went back to see the end of the tragedy. We had a more important thing to attend to: we all flew home, and lost not a moment in getting ready to lead a better life.

The night presently closed down. Then came on that tremendous and utterly unaccountable storm. I was perfectly dazed; I could not understand it. It seemed to me that there must be some mistake. The elements were turned loose, and they rattled and banged and blazed away in the most blind and frantic manner. All heart and hope went out of me, and the dismal thought kept floating through my brain, 'If a boy who knows three thousand verses by heart is not satisfactory, what chance is there for anybody else?'

Of course I never questioned for a moment that the storm was on Dutchy's account, or that he or any other inconsequential animal was worthy of such a majestic demonstration from on high; the lesson of it was the only thing that troubled me; for it convinced me that if Dutchy, with all his perfections, was not a delight, it would be vain for me to turn over a new leaf, for I must infallibly fall hopelessly short of that boy, no matter how hard I might try. Nevertheless I did turn it over—a highly educated fear compelled me to do that—but succeeding days of cheerfulness and sunshine came bothering around, and within a month I had so drifted backward that again I was as lost and comfortable as ever.

Breakfast time approached while I mused these musings and called these ancient happenings back to mind; so I got me back into the present and went down the hill.

On my way through town to the hotel, I saw the house which was my home when I was a boy. At present rates, the people who now occupy it are of no more value than I am; but in my time they would have been worth not less than five hundred dollars apiece. They are colored folk.

After breakfast, I went out alone again, intending to hunt up some of the Sunday-schools and see how this generation of pupils might compare with their progenitors who had sat with me in those places and had probably taken me as a model—though I do not remember as to that now. By the public square there had been in my day a shabby little brick church called the 'Old Ship of Zion,' which I had attended as a Sunday-school scholar; and I found the locality easily enough, but not the old church; it was gone, and a trig and rather hilarious new edifice was in its place. The pupils were better dressed and better looking than were those of my time; consequently they did not resemble their ancestors; and consequently there was nothing familiar to me in their faces. Still, I contemplated them with a deep interest and a yearning wistfulness, and if I had been a girl I would have cried; for they were the offspring, and represented, and occupied the places, of boys and girls some of whom I had loved to love, and some of whom I had loved to hate, but all of whom were dear to me for the one reason or the other, so many years gone by—and, Lord, where be they now!

I was mightily stirred, and would have been grateful to be allowed to remain unmolested and look my fill; but a bald-summited superintendent who had been a tow-headed Sunday-school mate of mine on that spot in the early ages, recognized me, and I talked a flutter of wild nonsense to those children to hide the thoughts which were in me, and which could not have been spoken without a betrayal of feeling that would have been recognized as out of character with me.

Making speeches without preparation is no gift of mine; and I was resolved to shirk any new opportunity, but in the next and larger Sunday-school I found myself in the rear of the assemblage; so I was very willing to go on the platform a moment for the sake of getting a good look at the scholars. On the spur of the moment I could not recall any of the old idiotic talks which visitors used to insult me with when I was a pupil there; and I was sorry for this, since it would have given me time and excuse to dawdle there and take a long and satisfying look at what I feel at liberty to say was an array of fresh young comeliness not matchable in another Sunday-school of the same size. As I talked merely to get a chance to inspect; and as I strung out the random rubbish solely to prolong the inspection, I judged it but decent to confess these low motives, and I did so.

If the Model Boy was in either of these Sunday-schools, I did not see him. The Model Boy of my time—we never had but the one—was perfect: perfect in manners, perfect in dress, perfect in conduct, perfect in filial piety, perfect in exterior godliness; but at bottom he was a prig; and as for the contents of his skull, they could have changed place with the contents of a pie and nobody would have been the worse off for it but the pie. This fellow's reproachlessness was a standing reproach to every lad in the village. He was the admiration of all the mothers, and the detestation of all their sons. I was told what became of him, but as it was a disappointment to me, I will not enter into details. He succeeded in life.

Chapter 55 A Vendetta and Other Things

DURING my three days' stay in the town, I woke up every morning with the impression that I was a boy—for in my dreams the faces were all young again, and looked as they had looked in the old times—but I went to bed a hundred years old, every night—for meantime I had been seeing those faces as they are now.

Of course I suffered some surprises, along at first, before I had become adjusted to the changed state of things. I met young ladies who did not seem to have changed at all; but they turned out to be the daughters of the young ladies I had in mind—sometimes their grand-daughters. When you are told that a stranger of fifty is a grandmother, there is nothing surprising about it; but if, on the contrary, she is a person whom you knew as a little girl, it seems impossible. You say to yourself, 'How can a little girl be a grandmother.' It takes some little time to accept and realize the fact that while you have been growing old, your friends have not been standing still, in that matter.

I noticed that the greatest changes observable were with the women, not the men. I saw men whom thirty years had changed but slightly; but their wives had grown old. These were good women; it is very wearing to be good.

There was a saddler whom I wished to see; but he was gone. Dead, these many years, they said. Once or twice a day, the saddler used to go tearing down the street, putting on his coat as he went; and then everybody knew a steamboat was coming. Everybody knew, also, that John Stavely was not expecting anybody by the boat—or any freight, either; and Stavely must have known that everybody knew this, still it made no difference to him; he liked to seem to himself to be expecting a hundred thousand tons of saddles by this boat, and so he went on all his life, enjoying being faithfully on hand to receive and receipt for those saddles, in case by any miracle they should come. A malicious Quincy paper used always to refer to this town, in derision as 'Stavely's Landing.' Stavely was one of my earliest admirations; I envied him his rush of imaginary business, and the display he was able to make of it, before strangers, as he went flying down the street struggling with his fluttering coat.

But there was a carpenter who was my chiefest hero. He was a mighty liar, but I did not know that; I believed everything he said. He was a romantic, sentimental, melodramatic fraud, and his bearing impressed me with awe. I vividly remember the first time he took me into his confidence. He was planing a board, and every now and then he would pause and heave a deep sigh; and occasionally mutter broken sentences—confused and not intelligible—but out of their midst an ejaculation sometimes escaped which made me shiver and did me good: one was, 'O God, it is his blood!' I sat on the tool-chest and humbly and shudderingly admired him; for I judged he was full of crime. At last he said in a low voice—

'My little friend, can you keep a secret?'

I eagerly said I could.

'A dark and dreadful one?'

I satisfied him on that point.

'Then I will tell you some passages in my history; for oh, I MUST relieve my burdened soul, or I shall die!'

He cautioned me once more to be 'as silent as the grave;' then he told me he was a 'red-handed murderer.' He put down his plane, held his hands out before him, contemplated them sadly, and said—

'Look—with these hands I have taken the lives of thirty human beings!'

The effect which this had upon me was an inspiration to him, and he turned himself loose upon his subject with interest and energy. He left generalizing, and went into details,—began with his first murder; described it, told what measures he had taken to avert suspicion; then passed to his second homicide, his third, his fourth, and so on. He had always done his murders with a bowie-knife, and he made all my hairs rise by suddenly snatching it out and showing it to me.

At the end of this first seance I went home with six of his fearful secrets among my freightage, and found them a great help to my dreams, which had been sluggish for a while back. I sought him again and again, on my Saturday holidays; in fact I spent the summer with him—all of it which was valuable to me. His fascinations never diminished, for he threw something fresh and stirring, in the way of horror, into each successive murder. He always gave names, dates, places—everything. This by and by enabled me to note two things: that he had killed his victims in every quarter of the globe, and that these victims were always named Lynch. The destruction of the Lynches went serenely on, Saturday after Saturday, until the original thirty had multiplied to sixty—and more to be heard from yet; then my curiosity got the better of my timidity, and I asked how it happened that these justly punished persons all bore the same name.

My hero said he had never divulged that dark secret to any living being; but felt that he could trust me, and therefore he would lay bare before me the story of his sad and blighted life. He had loved one 'too fair for earth,' and she had reciprocated 'with all the sweet affection of her pure and noble nature.' But he had a rival, a 'base hireling' named Archibald Lynch, who said the girl should be his, or he would 'dye his hands in her heart's best blood.' The carpenter, 'innocent and happy in love's young dream,' gave no weight to the threat, but led his 'golden- haired darling to the altar,' and there, the two were made one; there also, just as the minister's hands were stretched in blessing over their heads, the fell deed was done—with a knife—and the bride fell a corpse at her husband's feet. And what did the husband do? He plucked forth that knife, and kneeling by the body of his lost one, swore to 'consecrate his life to the extermination of all the human scum that bear the hated name of Lynch.'

That was it. He had been hunting down the Lynches and slaughtering them, from that day to this—twenty years. He had always used that same consecrated knife; with it he had murdered his long array of Lynches, and with it he had left upon the forehead of each victim a peculiar mark—a cross, deeply incised. Said he—

'The cross of the Mysterious Avenger is known in Europe, in America, in China, in Siam, in the Tropics, in the Polar Seas, in the deserts of Asia, in all the earth. Wherever in the uttermost parts of the globe, a Lynch has penetrated, there has the Mysterious Cross been seen, and those who have seen it have shuddered and said, "It is his mark, he has been here." You have heard of the Mysterious Avenger—look upon him, for before you stands no less a person! But beware—breathe not a word to any soul. Be silent, and wait. Some morning this town will flock aghast to view a gory corpse; on its brow will be seen the awful sign, and men will tremble and whisper, "He has been here—it is the Mysterious Avenger's mark!" You will come here, but I shall have vanished; you will see me no more.'

This ass had been reading the 'Jibbenainosay,' no doubt, and had had his poor romantic head turned by it; but as I had not yet seen the book then, I took his inventions for truth, and did not suspect that he was a plagiarist.

However, we had a Lynch living in the town; and the more I reflected upon his impending doom, the more I could not sleep. It seemed my plain duty to save him, and a still plainer and more important duty to get some sleep for myself, so at last I ventured to go to Mr. Lynch and tell him what was about to happen to him—under strict secrecy. I advised him to 'fly,' and certainly expected him to do it. But he laughed at me; and he did not stop there; he led me down to the carpenter's shop, gave the carpenter a jeering and scornful lecture upon his silly pretensions, slapped his face, made him get down on his knees and beg—then went off and left me to contemplate the cheap and pitiful ruin of what, in my eyes, had so lately been a majestic and incomparable hero. The carpenter blustered, flourished his knife, and doomed this Lynch in his usual volcanic style, the size of his fateful words undiminished; but it was all wasted upon me; he was a hero to me no longer, but only a poor, foolish, exposed humbug. I was ashamed of him, and ashamed of myself; I took no further interest in him, and never went to his shop any more. He was a heavy loss to me, for he was the greatest hero I had ever known. The fellow must have had some talent; for some of his imaginary murders were so vividly and dramatically described that I remember all their details yet.

The people of Hannibal are not more changed than is the town. It is no longer a village; it is a city, with a mayor, and a council, and water- works, and probably a debt. It has fifteen thousand people, is a thriving and energetic place, and is paved like the rest of the west and south—where a well-paved street and a good sidewalk are things so seldom seen, that one doubts them when he does see them. The customary half-dozen railways center in Hannibal now, and there is a new depot which cost a hundred thousand dollars. In my time the town had no specialty, and no commercial grandeur; the daily packet usually landed a passenger and bought a catfish, and took away another passenger and a hatful of freight; but now a huge commerce in lumber has grown up and a large miscellaneous commerce is one of the results. A deal of money changes hands there now.

Bear Creek—so called, perhaps, because it was always so particularly bare of bears—is hidden out of sight now, under islands and continents of piled lumber, and nobody but an expert can find it. I used to get drowned in it every summer regularly, and be drained out, and inflated and set going again by some chance enemy; but not enough of it is unoccupied now to drown a person in. It was a famous breeder of chills and fever in its day. I remember one summer when everybody in town had this disease at once. Many chimneys were shaken down, and all the houses were so racked that the town had to be rebuilt. The chasm or gorge between Lover's Leap and the hill west of it is supposed by scientists to have been caused by glacial action. This is a mistake.

There is an interesting cave a mile or two below Hannibal, among the bluffs. I would have liked to revisit it, but had not time. In my time the person who then owned it turned it into a mausoleum for his daughter, aged fourteen. The body of this poor child was put into a copper cylinder filled with alcohol, and this was suspended in one of the dismal avenues of the cave. The top of the cylinder was removable; and it was said to be a common thing for the baser order of tourists to drag the dead face into view and examine it and comment upon it.

Chapter 56 A Question of Law

THE slaughter-house is gone from the mouth of Bear Creek and so is the small jail (or 'calaboose') which once stood in its neighborhood. A citizen asked, 'Do you remember when Jimmy Finn, the town drunkard, was burned to death in the calaboose?'

Observe, now, how history becomes defiled, through lapse of time and the help of the bad memories of men. Jimmy Finn was not burned in the calaboose, but died a natural death in a tan vat, of a combination of delirium tremens and spontaneous combustion. When I say natural death, I mean it was a natural death for Jimmy Finn to die. The calaboose victim was not a citizen; he was a poor stranger, a harmless whiskey-sodden tramp. I know more about his case than anybody else; I knew too much of it, in that bygone day, to relish speaking of it. That tramp was wandering about the streets one chilly evening, with a pipe in his mouth, and begging for a match; he got neither matches nor courtesy; on the contrary, a troop of bad little boys followed him around and amused themselves with nagging and annoying him. I assisted; but at last, some appeal which the wayfarer made for forbearance, accompanying it with a pathetic reference to his forlorn and friendless condition, touched such sense of shame and remnant of right feeling as were left in me, and I went away and got him some matches, and then hied me home and to bed, heavily weighted as to conscience, and unbuoyant in spirit. An hour or two afterward, the man was arrested and locked up in the calaboose by the marshal—large name for a constable, but that was his title. At two in the morning, the church bells rang for fire, and everybody turned out, of course—I with the rest. The tramp had used his matches disastrously: he had set his straw bed on fire, and the oaken sheathing of the room had caught. When I reached the ground, two hundred men, women, and children stood massed together, transfixed with horror, and staring at the grated windows of the jail. Behind the iron bars, and tugging frantically at them, and screaming for help, stood the tramp; he seemed like a black object set against a sun, so white and intense was the light at his back. That marshal could not be found, and he had the only key. A battering-ram was quickly improvised, and the thunder of its blows upon the door had so encouraging a sound that the spectators broke into wild cheering, and believed the merciful battle won. But it was not so. The timbers were too strong; they did not yield. It was said that the man's death-grip still held fast to the bars after he was dead; and that in this position the fires wrapped him about and consumed him. As to this, I do not know. What was seen after I recognized the face that was pleading through the bars was seen by others, not by me.

I saw that face, so situated, every night for a long time afterward; and I believed myself as guilty of the man's death as if I had given him the matches purposely that he might burn himself up with them. I had not a doubt that I should be hanged if my connection with this tragedy were found out. The happenings and the impressions of that time are burnt into my memory, and the study of them entertains me as much now as they themselves distressed me then. If anybody spoke of that grisly matter, I was all ears in a moment, and alert to hear what might be said, for I was always dreading and expecting to find out that I was suspected; and so fine and so delicate was the perception of my guilty conscience, that it often detected suspicion in the most purposeless remarks, and in looks, gestures, glances of the eye which had no significance, but which sent me shivering away in a panic of fright, just the same. And how sick it made me when somebody dropped, howsoever carelessly and barren of intent, the remark that 'murder will out!' For a boy of ten years, I was carrying a pretty weighty cargo.

All this time I was blessedly forgetting one thing—the fact that I was an inveterate talker in my sleep. But one night I awoke and found my bed-mate—my younger brother—sitting up in bed and contemplating me by the light of the moon. I said—

'What is the matter?'

'You talk so much I can't sleep.'

I came to a sitting posture in an instant, with my kidneys in my throat and my hair on end.

'What did I say. Quick—out with it—what did I say?'

'Nothing much.'

'It's a lie—you know everything.'

'Everything about what?'

'You know well enough. About THAT.'

'About WHAT?—I don't know what you are talking about. I think you are sick or crazy or something. But anyway, you're awake, and I'll get to sleep while I've got a chance.'

He fell asleep and I lay there in a cold sweat, turning this new terror over in the whirling chaos which did duty as my mind. The burden of my thought was, How much did I divulge? How much does he know?—what a distress is this uncertainty! But by and by I evolved an idea—I would wake my brother and probe him with a supposititious case. I shook him up, and said—

'Suppose a man should come to you drunk—'

'This is foolish—I never get drunk.'

'I don't mean you, idiot—I mean the man. Suppose a MAN should come to you drunk, and borrow a knife, or a tomahawk, or a pistol, and you forgot to tell him it was loaded, and—'

'How could you load a tomahawk?'

'I don't mean the tomahawk, and I didn't say the tomahawk; I said the pistol. Now don't you keep breaking in that way, because this is serious. There's been a man killed.'

'What! in this town?'

'Yes, in this town.'

'Well, go on—I won't say a single word.'

'Well, then, suppose you forgot to tell him to be careful with it, because it was loaded, and he went off and shot himself with that pistol—fooling with it, you know, and probably doing it by accident, being drunk. Well, would it be murder?'

'No—suicide.'

'No, no. I don't mean HIS act, I mean yours: would you be a murderer for letting him have that pistol?'

After deep thought came this answer—

'Well, I should think I was guilty of something—maybe murder—yes, probably murder, but I don't quite know.'

This made me very uncomfortable. However, it was not a decisive verdict. I should have to set out the real case—there seemed to be no other way. But I would do it cautiously, and keep a watch out for suspicious effects. I said—

'I was supposing a case, but I am coming to the real one now. Do you know how the man came to be burned up in the calaboose?'

'No.'

'Haven't you the least idea?'

'Not the least.'

'Wish you may die in your tracks if you have?'

'Yes, wish I may die in my tracks.'

'Well, the way of it was this. The man wanted some matches to light his pipe. A boy got him some. The man set fire to the calaboose with those very matches, and burnt himself up.'

'Is that so?'

'Yes, it is. Now, is that boy a murderer, do you think?'

'Let me see. The man was drunk?'

'Yes, he was drunk.'

'Very drunk?'

'Yes.'

'And the boy knew it?'

'Yes, he knew it.'

There was a long pause. Then came this heavy verdict—

'If the man was drunk, and the boy knew it, the boy murdered that man. This is certain.'

Faint, sickening sensations crept along all the fibers of my body, and I seemed to know how a person feels who hears his death sentence pronounced from the bench. I waited to hear what my brother would say next. I believed I knew what it would be, and I was right. He said—

'I know the boy.'

I had nothing to say; so I said nothing. I simply shuddered. Then he added—

'Yes, before you got half through telling about the thing, I knew perfectly well who the boy was; it was Ben Coontz!'

I came out of my collapse as one who rises from the dead. I said, with admiration—

'Why, how in the world did you ever guess it?'

'You told it in your sleep.'

I said to myself, 'How splendid that is! This is a habit which must be cultivated.'

My brother rattled innocently on—

'When you were talking in your sleep, you kept mumbling something about "matches," which I couldn't make anything out of; but just now, when you began to tell me about the man and the calaboose and the matches, I remembered that in your sleep you mentioned Ben Coontz two or three times; so I put this and that together, you see, and right away I knew it was Ben that burnt that man up.'

I praised his sagacity effusively. Presently he asked—

'Are you going to give him up to the law?'

'No,' I said; 'I believe that this will be a lesson to him. I shall keep an eye on him, of course, for that is but right; but if he stops where he is and reforms, it shall never be said that I betrayed him.'

'How good you are!'

'Well, I try to be. It is all a person can do in a world like this.'

And now, my burden being shifted to other shoulders, my terrors soon faded away.

The day before we left Hannibal, a curious thing fell under my notice— the surprising spread which longitudinal time undergoes there. I learned it from one of the most unostentatious of men—the colored coachman of a friend of mine, who lives three miles from town. He was to call for me at the Park Hotel at 7.30 P.M., and drive me out. But he missed it considerably—did not arrive till ten. He excused himself by saying—

'De time is mos' an hour en a half slower in de country en what it is in de town; you'll be in plenty time, boss. Sometimes we shoves out early for church, Sunday, en fetches up dah right plum in de middle er de sermon. Diffunce in de time. A body can't make no calculations 'bout it.'

I had lost two hours and a half; but I had learned a fact worth four.

Chapter 57 An Archangel

FROM St. Louis northward there are all the enlivening signs of the presence of active, energetic, intelligent, prosperous, practical nineteenth-century populations. The people don't dream, they work. The happy result is manifest all around in the substantial outside aspect of things, and the suggestions of wholesome life and comfort that everywhere appear.

Quincy is a notable example—a brisk, handsome, well-ordered city; and now, as formerly, interested in art, letters, and other high things.

But Marion City is an exception. Marion City has gone backwards in a most unaccountable way. This metropolis promised so well that the projectors tacked 'city' to its name in the very beginning, with full confidence; but it was bad prophecy. When I first saw Marion City, thirty-five years ago, it contained one street, and nearly or quite six houses. It contains but one house now, and this one, in a state of ruin, is getting ready to follow the former five into the river. Doubtless Marion City was too near to Quincy. It had another disadvantage: it was situated in a flat mud bottom, below high-water mark, whereas Quincy stands high up on the slope of a hill.

In the beginning Quincy had the aspect and ways of a model New England town: and these she has yet: broad, clean streets, trim, neat dwellings and lawns, fine mansions, stately blocks of commercial buildings. And there are ample fair-grounds, a well kept park, and many attractive drives; library, reading-rooms, a couple of colleges, some handsome and costly churches, and a grand court-house, with grounds which occupy a square. The population of the city is thirty thousand. There are some large factories here, and manufacturing, of many sorts, is done on a great scale.

La Grange and Canton are growing towns, but I missed Alexandria; was told it was under water, but would come up to blow in the summer.

Keokuk was easily recognizable. I lived there in 1857—an extraordinary year there in real-estate matters. The 'boom' was something wonderful. Everybody bought, everybody sold—except widows and preachers; they always hold on; and when the tide ebbs, they get left. Anything in the semblance of a town lot, no matter how situated, was salable, and at a figure which would still have been high if the ground had been sodded with greenbacks.

The town has a population of fifteen thousand now, and is progressing with a healthy growth. It was night, and we could not see details, for which we were sorry, for Keokuk has the reputation of being a beautiful city. It was a pleasant one to live in long ago, and doubtless has advanced, not retrograded, in that respect.

A mighty work which was in progress there in my day is finished now. This is the canal over the Rapids. It is eight miles long, three hundred feet wide, and is in no place less than six feet deep. Its masonry is of the majestic kind which the War Department usually deals in, and will endure like a Roman aqueduct. The work cost four or five millions.

After an hour or two spent with former friends, we started up the river again. Keokuk, a long time ago, was an occasional loafing-place of that erratic genius, Henry Clay Dean. I believe I never saw him but once; but he was much talked of when I lived there. This is what was said of him—

He began life poor and without education. But he educated himself—on the curbstones of Keokuk. He would sit down on a curbstone with his book, careless or unconscious of the clatter of commerce and the tramp of the passing crowds, and bury himself in his studies by the hour, never changing his position except to draw in his knees now and then to let a dray pass unobstructed; and when his book was finished, its contents, however abstruse, had been burnt into his memory, and were his permanent possession. In this way he acquired a vast hoard of all sorts of learning, and had it pigeon-holed in his head where he could put his intellectual hand on it whenever it was wanted.

His clothes differed in no respect from a 'wharf-rat's,' except that they were raggeder, more ill-assorted and inharmonious (and therefore more extravagantly picturesque), and several layers dirtier. Nobody could infer the master-mind in the top of that edifice from the edifice itself.

He was an orator—by nature in the first place, and later by the training of experience and practice. When he was out on a canvass, his name was a lodestone which drew the farmers to his stump from fifty miles around. His theme was always politics. He used no notes, for a volcano does not need notes. In 1862, a son of Keokuk's late distinguished citizen, Mr. Claggett, gave me this incident concerning Dean—

The war feeling was running high in Keokuk (in '61), and a great mass meeting was to be held on a certain day in the new Athenaeum. A distinguished stranger was to address the house. After the building had been packed to its utmost capacity with sweltering folk of both sexes, the stage still remained vacant—the distinguished stranger had failed to connect. The crowd grew impatient, and by and by indignant and rebellious. About this time a distressed manager discovered Dean on a curb-stone, explained the dilemma to him, took his book away from him, rushed him into the building the back way, and told him to make for the stage and save his country.

Presently a sudden silence fell upon the grumbling audience, and everybody's eyes sought a single point—the wide, empty, carpetless stage. A figure appeared there whose aspect was familiar to hardly a dozen persons present. It was the scarecrow Dean—in foxy shoes, down at the heels; socks of odd colors, also 'down;' damaged trousers, relics of antiquity, and a world too short, exposing some inches of naked ankle; an unbuttoned vest, also too short, and exposing a zone of soiled and wrinkled linen between it and the waistband; shirt bosom open; long black handkerchief, wound round and round the neck like a bandage; bob-tailed blue coat, reaching down to the small of the back, with sleeves which left four inches of forearm unprotected; small, stiff-brimmed soldier-cap hung on a corner of the bump of—whichever bump it was. This figure moved gravely out upon the stage and, with sedate and measured step, down to the front, where it paused, and dreamily inspected the house, saying no word. The silence of surprise held its own for a moment, then was broken by a just audible ripple of merriment which swept the sea of faces like the wash of a wave. The figure remained as before, thoughtfully inspecting. Another wave started—laughter, this time. It was followed by another, then a third—this last one boisterous.

And now the stranger stepped back one pace, took off his soldier-cap, tossed it into the wing, and began to speak, with deliberation, nobody listening, everybody laughing and whispering. The speaker talked on unembarrassed, and presently delivered a shot which went home, and silence and attention resulted. He followed it quick and fast, with other telling things; warmed to his work and began to pour his words out, instead of dripping them; grew hotter and hotter, and fell to discharging lightnings and thunder—and now the house began to break into applause, to which the speaker gave no heed, but went hammering straight on; unwound his black bandage and cast it away, still thundering; presently discarded the bob tailed coat and flung it aside, firing up higher and higher all the time; finally flung the vest after the coat; and then for an untimed period stood there, like another Vesuvius, spouting smoke and flame, lava and ashes, raining pumice-stone and cinders, shaking the moral earth with intellectual crash upon crash, explosion upon explosion, while the mad multitude stood upon their feet in a solid body, answering back with a ceaseless hurricane of cheers, through a thrashing snowstorm of waving handkerchiefs.

'When Dean came,' said Claggett, 'the people thought he was an escaped lunatic; but when he went, they thought he was an escaped archangel.'

Burlington, home of the sparkling Burdette, is another hill city; and also a beautiful one; unquestionably so; a fine and flourishing city, with a population of twenty-five thousand, and belted with busy factories of nearly every imaginable description. It was a very sober city, too—for the moment—for a most sobering bill was pending; a bill to forbid the manufacture, exportation, importation, purchase, sale, borrowing, lending, stealing, drinking, smelling, or possession, by conquest, inheritance, intent, accident, or otherwise, in the State of Iowa, of each and every deleterious beverage known to the human race, except water. This measure was approved by all the rational people in the State; but not by the bench of Judges.

Burlington has the progressive modern city's full equipment of devices for right and intelligent government; including a paid fire department, a thing which the great city of New Orleans is without, but still employs that relic of antiquity, the independent system.

In Burlington, as in all these Upper-River towns, one breathes a go-ahead atmosphere which tastes good in the nostrils. An opera-house has lately been built there which is in strong contrast with the shabby dens which usually do duty as theaters in cities of Burlington's size.

We had not time to go ashore in Muscatine, but had a daylight view of it from the boat. I lived there awhile, many years ago, but the place, now, had a rather unfamiliar look; so I suppose it has clear outgrown the town which I used to know. In fact, I know it has; for I remember it as a small place—which it isn't now. But I remember it best for a lunatic who caught me out in the fields, one Sunday, and extracted a butcher-knife from his boot and proposed to carve me up with it, unless I acknowledged him to be the only son of the Devil. I tried to compromise on an acknowledgment that he was the only member of the family I had met; but that did not satisfy him; he wouldn't have any half-measures; I must say he was the sole and only son of the Devil—he whetted his knife on his boot. It did not seem worth while to make trouble about a little thing like that; so I swung round to his view of the matter and saved my skin whole. Shortly afterward, he went to visit his father; and as he has not turned up since, I trust he is there yet.

And I remember Muscatine—still more pleasantly—for its summer sunsets. I have never seen any, on either side of the ocean, that equaled them. They used the broad smooth river as a canvas, and painted on it every imaginable dream of color, from the mottled daintinesses and delicacies of the opal, all the way up, through cumulative intensities, to blinding purple and crimson conflagrations which were enchanting to the eye, but sharply tried it at the same time. All the Upper Mississippi region has these extraordinary sunsets as a familiar spectacle. It is the true Sunset Land: I am sure no other country can show so good a right to the name. The sunrises are also said to be exceedingly fine. I do not know.

Chapter 58 On the Upper River

THE big towns drop in, thick and fast, now: and between stretch processions of thrifty farms, not desolate solitude.

Hour by hour, the boat plows deeper and deeper into the great and populous North-west; and with each successive section of it which is revealed, one's surprise and respect gather emphasis and increase. Such a people, and such achievements as theirs, compel homage. This is an independent race who think for themselves, and who are competent to do it, because they are educated and enlightened; they read, they keep abreast of the best and newest thought, they fortify every weak place in their land with a school, a college, a library, and a newspaper; and they live under law. Solicitude for the future of a race like this is not in order.

This region is new; so new that it may be said to be still in its babyhood. By what it has accomplished while still teething, one may forecast what marvels it will do in the strength of its maturity. It is so new that the foreign tourist has not heard of it yet; and has not visited it. For sixty years, the foreign tourist has steamed up and down the river between St. Louis and New Orleans, and then gone home and written his book, believing he had seen all of the river that was worth seeing or that had anything to see. In not six of all these books is there mention of these Upper River towns—for the reason that the five or six tourists who penetrated this region did it before these towns were projected. The latest tourist of them all (1878) made the same old regulation trip—he had not heard that there was anything north of St. Louis.

Yet there was. There was this amazing region, bristling with great towns, projected day before yesterday, so to speak, and built next morning. A score of them number from fifteen hundred to five thousand people. Then we have Muscatine, ten thousand; Winona, ten thousand; Moline, ten thousand; Rock Island, twelve thousand; La Crosse, twelve thousand; Burlington, twenty-five thousand; Dubuque, twenty-five thousand; Davenport, thirty thousand; St. Paul, fifty-eight thousand, Minneapolis, sixty thousand and upward.

The foreign tourist has never heard of these; there is no note of them in his books. They have sprung up in the night, while he slept. So new is this region, that I, who am comparatively young, am yet older than it is. When I was born, St. Paul had a population of three persons, Minneapolis had just a third as many. The then population of Minneapolis died two years ago; and when he died he had seen himself undergo an increase, in forty years, of fifty-nine thousand nine hundred and ninety-nine persons. He had a frog's fertility.

I must explain that the figures set down above, as the population of St. Paul and Minneapolis, are several months old. These towns are far larger now. In fact, I have just seen a newspaper estimate which gives the former seventy-one thousand, and the latter seventy-eight thousand. This book will not reach the public for six or seven months yet; none of the figures will be worth much then.

We had a glimpse of Davenport, which is another beautiful city, crowning a hill—a phrase which applies to all these towns; for they are all comely, all well built, clean, orderly, pleasant to the eye, and cheering to the spirit; and they are all situated upon hills. Therefore we will give that phrase a rest. The Indians have a tradition that Marquette and Joliet camped where Davenport now stands, in 1673. The next white man who camped there, did it about a hundred and seventy years later—in 1834. Davenport has gathered its thirty thousand people within the past thirty years. She sends more children to her schools now, than her whole population numbered twenty-three years ago. She has the usual Upper River quota of factories, newspapers, and institutions of learning; she has telephones, local telegraphs, an electric alarm, and an admirable paid fire department, consisting of six hook and ladder companies, four steam fire engines, and thirty churches. Davenport is the official residence of two bishops—Episcopal and Catholic.

Opposite Davenport is the flourishing town of Rock Island, which lies at the foot of the Upper Rapids. A great railroad bridge connects the two towns—one of the thirteen which fret the Mississippi and the pilots, between St. Louis and St. Paul.

The charming island of Rock Island, three miles long and half a mile wide, belongs to the United States, and the Government has turned it into a wonderful park, enhancing its natural attractions by art, and threading its fine forests with many miles of drives. Near the center of the island one catches glimpses, through the trees, of ten vast stone four-story buildings, each of which covers an acre of ground. These are the Government workshops; for the Rock Island establishment is a national armory and arsenal.

We move up the river—always through enchanting scenery, there being no other kind on the Upper Mississippi—and pass Moline, a center of vast manufacturing industries; and Clinton and Lyons, great lumber centers; and presently reach Dubuque, which is situated in a rich mineral region. The lead mines are very productive, and of wide extent. Dubuque has a great number of manufacturing establishments; among them a plow factory which has for customers all Christendom in general. At least so I was told by an agent of the concern who was on the boat. He said—

'You show me any country under the sun where they really know how to plow, and if I don't show you our mark on the plow they use, I'll eat that plow; and I won't ask for any Woostershyre sauce to flavor it up with, either.'

All this part of the river is rich in Indian history and traditions. Black Hawk's was once a puissant name hereabouts; as was Keokuk's, further down. A few miles below Dubuque is the Tete de Mort—Death's- head rock, or bluff—to the top of which the French drove a band of Indians, in early times, and cooped them up there, with death for a certainty, and only the manner of it matter of choice—to starve, or jump off and kill themselves. Black Hawk adopted the ways of the white people, toward the end of his life; and when he died he was buried, near Des Moines, in Christian fashion, modified by Indian custom; that is to say, clothed in a Christian military uniform, and with a Christian cane in his hand, but deposited in the grave in a sitting posture. Formerly, a horse had always been buried with a chief. The substitution of the cane shows that Black Hawk's haughty nature was really humbled, and he expected to walk when he got over.

We noticed that above Dubuque the water of the Mississippi was olive- green—rich and beautiful and semi-transparent, with the sun on it. Of course the water was nowhere as clear or of as fine a complexion as it is in some other seasons of the year; for now it was at flood stage, and therefore dimmed and blurred by the mud manufactured from caving banks.

The majestic bluffs that overlook the river, along through this region, charm one with the grace and variety of their forms, and the soft beauty of their adornment. The steep verdant slope, whose base is at the water's edge is topped by a lofty rampart of broken, turreted rocks, which are exquisitely rich and mellow in color—mainly dark browns and dull greens, but splashed with other tints. And then you have the shining river, winding here and there and yonder, its sweep interrupted at intervals by clusters of wooded islands threaded by silver channels; and you have glimpses of distant villages, asleep upon capes; and of stealthy rafts slipping along in the shade of the forest walls; and of white steamers vanishing around remote points. And it is all as tranquil and reposeful as dreamland, and has nothing this-worldly about it— nothing to hang a fret or a worry upon.

Until the unholy train comes tearing along—which it presently does, ripping the sacred solitude to rags and tatters with its devil's warwhoop and the roar and thunder of its rushing wheels—and straightway you are back in this world, and with one of its frets ready to hand for your entertainment: for you remember that this is the very road whose stock always goes down after you buy it, and always goes up again as soon as you sell it. It makes me shudder to this day, to remember that I once came near not getting rid of my stock at all. It must be an awful thing to have a railroad left on your hands.

The locomotive is in sight from the deck of the steamboat almost the whole way from St. Louis to St. Paul—eight hundred miles. These railroads have made havoc with the steamboat commerce. The clerk of our boat was a steamboat clerk before these roads were built. In that day the influx of population was so great, and the freight business so heavy, that the boats were not able to keep up with the demands made upon their carrying capacity; consequently the captains were very independent and airy—pretty 'biggity,' as Uncle Remus would say. The clerk nut-shelled the contrast between the former time and the present, thus—

'Boat used to land—captain on hurricane roof—mighty stiff and straight—iron ramrod for a spine—kid gloves, plug tile, hair parted behind—man on shore takes off hat and says—

'"Got twenty-eight tons of wheat, cap'n—be great favor if you can take them."

'Captain says—

'"ll take two of them"—and don't even condescend to look at him.

'But nowadays the captain takes off his old slouch, and smiles all the way around to the back of his ears, and gets off a bow which he hasn't got any ramrod to interfere with, and says—

'"Glad to see you, Smith, glad to see you—you're looking well—haven't seen you looking so well for years—what you got for us?"

'"Nuth'n", says Smith; and keeps his hat on, and just turns his back and goes to talking with somebody else.

'Oh, yes, eight years ago, the captain was on top; but it's Smith's turn now. Eight years ago a boat used to go up the river with every stateroom full, and people piled five and six deep on the cabin floor; and a solid deck-load of immigrants and harvesters down below, into the bargain. To get a first-class stateroom, you'd got to prove sixteen quarterings of nobility and four hundred years of descent, or be personally acquainted with the nigger that blacked the captain's boots. But it's all changed now; plenty staterooms above, no harvesters below—there's a patent self-binder now, and they don't have harvesters any more; they've gone where the woodbine twineth—and they didn't go by steamboat, either; went by the train.'

Up in this region we met massed acres of lumber rafts coming down—but not floating leisurely along, in the old-fashioned way, manned with joyous and reckless crews of fiddling, song-singing, whiskey-drinking, breakdown-dancing rapscallions; no, the whole thing was shoved swiftly along by a powerful stern-wheeler, modern fashion, and the small crews were quiet, orderly men, of a sedate business aspect, with not a suggestion of romance about them anywhere.

Along here, somewhere, on a black night, we ran some exceedingly narrow and intricate island-chutes by aid of the electric light. Behind was solid blackness—a crackless bank of it; ahead, a narrow elbow of water, curving between dense walls of foliage that almost touched our bows on both sides; and here every individual leaf, and every individual ripple stood out in its natural color, and flooded with a glare as of noonday intensified. The effect was strange, and fine, and very striking.

We passed Prairie du Chien, another of Father Marquette's camping- places; and after some hours of progress through varied and beautiful scenery, reached La Crosse. Here is a town of twelve or thirteen thousand population, with electric lighted streets, and with blocks of buildings which are stately enough, and also architecturally fine enough, to command respect in any city. It is a choice town, and we made satisfactory use of the hour allowed us, in roaming it over, though the weather was rainier than necessary.

Chapter 59 Legends and Scenery

WE added several passengers to our list, at La Crosse; among others an old gentleman who had come to this north-western region with the early settlers, and was familiar with every part of it. Pardonably proud of it, too. He said—

'You'll find scenery between here and St. Paul that can give the Hudson points. You'll have the Queen's Bluff—seven hundred feet high, and just as imposing a spectacle as you can find anywheres; and Trempeleau Island, which isn't like any other island in America, I believe, for it is a gigantic mountain, with precipitous sides, and is full of Indian traditions, and used to be full of rattlesnakes; if you catch the sun just right there, you will have a picture that will stay with you. And above Winona you'll have lovely prairies; and then come the Thousand Islands, too beautiful for anything; green? why you never saw foliage so green, nor packed so thick; it's like a thousand plush cushions afloat on a looking-glass—when the water 's still; and then the monstrous bluffs on both sides of the river—ragged, rugged, dark-complected—just the frame that's wanted; you always want a strong frame, you know, to throw up the nice points of a delicate picture and make them stand out.'

The old gentleman also told us a touching Indian legend or two—but not very powerful ones.

After this excursion into history, he came back to the scenery, and described it, detail by detail, from the Thousand Islands to St. Paul; naming its names with such facility, tripping along his theme with such nimble and confident ease, slamming in a three-ton word, here and there, with such a complacent air of 't isn't-anything,-I-can-do-it-any-time-I- want-to, and letting off fine surprises of lurid eloquence at such judicious intervals, that I presently began to suspect—

But no matter what I began to suspect. Hear him—

'Ten miles above Winona we come to Fountain City, nestling sweetly at the feet of cliffs that lift their awful fronts, Jovelike, toward the blue depths of heaven, bathing them in virgin atmospheres that have known no other contact save that of angels' wings.

'And next we glide through silver waters, amid lovely and stupendous aspects of nature that attune our hearts to adoring admiration, about twelve miles, and strike Mount Vernon, six hundred feet high, with romantic ruins of a once first-class hotel perched far among the cloud shadows that mottle its dizzy heights—sole remnant of once-flourishing Mount Vernon, town of early days, now desolate and utterly deserted.

'And so we move on. Past Chimney Rock we fly—noble shaft of six hundred feet; then just before landing at Minnieska our attention is attracted by a most striking promontory rising over five hundred feet— the ideal mountain pyramid. Its conic shape—thickly-wooded surface girding its sides, and its apex like that of a cone, cause the spectator to wonder at nature's workings. From its dizzy heights superb views of the forests, streams, bluffs, hills and dales below and beyond for miles are brought within its focus. What grander river scenery can be conceived, as we gaze upon this enchanting landscape, from the uppermost point of these bluffs upon the valleys below? The primeval wildness and awful loneliness of these sublime creations of nature and nature's God, excite feelings of unbounded admiration, and the recollection of which can never be effaced from the memory, as we view them in any direction.

'Next we have the Lion's Head and the Lioness's Head, carved by nature's hand, to adorn and dominate the beauteous stream; and then anon the river widens, and a most charming and magnificent view of the valley before us suddenly bursts upon our vision; rugged hills, clad with verdant forests from summit to base, level prairie lands, holding in their lap the beautiful Wabasha, City of the Healing Waters, puissant foe of Bright's disease, and that grandest conception of nature's works, incomparable Lake Pepin—these constitute a picture whereon the tourist's eye may gaze uncounted hours, with rapture unappeased and unappeasable.

'And so we glide along; in due time encountering those majestic domes, the mighty Sugar Loaf, and the sublime Maiden's Rock—which latter, romantic superstition has invested with a voice; and oft-times as the birch canoe glides near, at twilight, the dusky paddler fancies he hears the soft sweet music of the long-departed Winona, darling of Indian song and story.

'Then Frontenac looms upon our vision, delightful resort of jaded summer tourists; then progressive Red Wing; and Diamond Bluff, impressive and preponderous in its lone sublimity; then Prescott and the St. Croix; and anon we see bursting upon us the domes and steeples of St. Paul, giant young chief of the North, marching with seven-league stride in the van of progress, banner-bearer of the highest and newest civilization, carving his beneficent way with the tomahawk of commercial enterprise, sounding the warwhoop of Christian culture, tearing off the reeking scalp of sloth and superstition to plant there the steam-plow and the school-house—ever in his front stretch arid lawlessness, ignorance, crime, despair; ever in his wake bloom the jail, the gallows, and the pulpit; and ever—'

'Have you ever traveled with a panorama?'

'I have formerly served in that capacity.'

My suspicion was confirmed.

'Do you still travel with it?'

'No, she is laid up till the fall season opens. I am helping now to work up the materials for a Tourist's Guide which the St. Louis and St. Paul Packet Company are going to issue this summer for the benefit of travelers who go by that line.'

'When you were talking of Maiden's Rock, you spoke of the long-departed Winona, darling of Indian song and story. Is she the maiden of the rock?—and are the two connected by legend?'

'Yes, and a very tragic and painful one. Perhaps the most celebrated, as well as the most pathetic, of all the legends of the Mississippi.'

We asked him to tell it. He dropped out of his conversational vein and back into his lecture-gait without an effort, and rolled on as follows—

'A little distance above Lake City is a famous point known as Maiden's Rock, which is not only a picturesque spot, but is full of romantic interest from the event which gave it its name, Not many years ago this locality was a favorite resort for the Sioux Indians on account of the fine fishing and hunting to be had there, and large numbers of them were always to be found in this locality. Among the families which used to resort here, was one belonging to the tribe of Wabasha. We-no-na (first-born) was the name of a maiden who had plighted her troth to a lover belonging to the same band. But her stern parents had promised her hand to another, a famous warrior, and insisted on her wedding him. The day was fixed by her parents, to her great grief. She appeared to accede to the proposal and accompany them to the rock, for the purpose of gathering flowers for the feast. On reaching the rock, We-no-na ran to its summit and standing on its edge upbraided her parents who were below, for their cruelty, and then singing a death-dirge, threw herself from the precipice and dashed them in pieces on the rock below.'

'Dashed who in pieces—her parents?'

'Yes.'

'Well, it certainly was a tragic business, as you say. And moreover, there is a startling kind of dramatic surprise about it which I was not looking for. It is a distinct improvement upon the threadbare form of Indian legend. There are fifty Lover's Leaps along the Mississippi from whose summit disappointed Indian girls have jumped, but this is the only jump in the lot hat turned out in the right and satisfactory way. What became of Winona?'

'She was a good deal jarred up and jolted: but she got herself together and disappeared before the coroner reached the fatal spot; and 'tis said she sought and married her true love, and wandered with him to some distant clime, where she lived happy ever after, her gentle spirit mellowed and chastened by the romantic incident which had so early deprived her of the sweet guidance of a mother's love and a father's protecting arm, and thrown her, all unfriended, upon the cold charity of a censorious world.'

I was glad to hear the lecturer's description of the scenery, for it assisted my appreciation of what I saw of it, and enabled me to imagine such of it as we lost by the intrusion of night.

As the lecturer remarked, this whole region is blanketed with Indian tales and traditions. But I reminded him that people usually merely mention this fact—doing it in a way to make a body's mouth water—and judiciously stopped there. Why? Because the impression left, was that these tales were full of incident and imagination—a pleasant impression which would be promptly dissipated if the tales were told. I showed him a lot of this sort of literature which I had been collecting, and he confessed that it was poor stuff, exceedingly sorry rubbish; and I ventured to add that the legends which he had himself told us were of this character, with the single exception of the admirable story of Winona. He granted these facts, but said that if I would hunt up Mr. Schoolcraft's book, published near fifty years ago, and now doubtless out of print, I would find some Indian inventions in it that were very far from being barren of incident and imagination; that the tales in Hiawatha were of this sort, and they came from Schoolcraft's book; and that there were others in the same book which Mr. Longfellow could have turned into verse with good effect. For instance, there was the legend of 'The Undying Head.' He could not tell it, for many of the details had grown dim in his memory; but he would recommend me to find it and enlarge my respect for the Indian imagination. He said that this tale, and most of the others in the book, were current among the Indians along this part of the Mississippi when he first came here; and that the contributors to Schoolcraft's book had got them directly from Indian lips, and had written them down with strict exactness, and without embellishments of their own.

I have found the book. The lecturer was right. There are several legends in it which confirm what he said. I will offer two of them— 'The Undying Head,' and 'Peboan and Seegwun, an Allegory of the Seasons.' The latter is used in Hiawatha; but it is worth reading in the original form, if only that one may see how effective a genuine poem can be without the helps and graces of poetic measure and rhythm—

PEBOAN AND SEEGWUN.

An old man was sitting alone in his lodge, by the side of a frozen stream. It was the close of winter, and his fire was almost out, He appeared very old and very desolate. His locks were white with age, and he trembled in every joint. Day after day passed in solitude, and he heard nothing but the sound of the tempest, sweeping before it the new-fallen snow.

One day, as his fire was just dying, a handsome young man approached and entered his dwelling. His cheeks were red with the blood of youth, his eyes sparkled with animation, and a smile played upon his lips. He walked with a light and quick step. His forehead was bound with a wreath of sweet grass, in place of a warrior's frontlet, and he carried a bunch of flowers in his hand.

'Ah, my son,' said the old man, 'I am happy to see you. Come in. Come and tell me of your adventures, and what strange lands you have been to see. Let us pass the night together. I will tell you of my prowess and exploits, and what I can perform. You shall do the same, and we will amuse ourselves.'

He then drew from his sack a curiously wrought antique pipe, and having filled it with tobacco, rendered mild by a mixture of certain leaves, handed it to his guest. When this ceremony was concluded they began to speak.

'I blow my breath,' said the old man, 'and the stream stands still. The water becomes stiff and hard as clear stone.'

'I breathe,' said the young man, 'and flowers spring up over the plain.'

'I shake my locks,' retorted the old man, 'and snow covers the land. The leaves fall from the trees at my command, and my breath blows them away. The birds get up from the water, and fly to a distant land. The animals hide themselves from my breath, and the very ground becomes as hard as flint.'

'I shake my ringlets,' rejoined the young man, 'and warm showers of soft rain fall upon the earth. The plants lift up their heads out of the earth, like the eyes of children glistening with delight. My voice recalls the birds. The warmth of my breath unlocks the streams. Music fills the groves wherever I walk, and all nature rejoices.'

At length the sun began to rise. A gentle warmth came over the place. The tongue of the old man became silent. The robin and bluebird began to sing on the top of the lodge. The stream began to murmur by the door, and the fragrance of growing herbs and flowers came softly on the vernal breeze.

Daylight fully revealed to the young man the character of his entertainer. When he looked upon him, he had the icy visage of Peboan*. Streams began to flow from his eyes. As the sun increased, he grew less and less in stature, and anon had melted completely away. Nothing remained on the place of his lodge-fire but the miskodeed**, a small white flower, with a pink border, which is one of the earliest species of northern plants.

'The Undying Head' is a rather long tale, but it makes up in weird conceits, fairy-tale prodigies, variety of incident, and energy of movement, for what it lacks in brevity.***

Chapter 60 Speculations and Conclusions

WE reached St. Paul, at the head of navigation of the Mississippi, and there our voyage of two thousand miles from New Orleans ended. It is about a ten-day trip by steamer. It can probably be done quicker by rail. I judge so because I know that one may go by rail from St. Louis to Hannibal—a distance of at least a hundred and twenty miles—in seven hours. This is better than walking; unless one is in a hurry.

The season being far advanced when we were in New Orleans, the roses and magnolia blossoms were falling; but here in St. Paul it was the snow, In New Orleans we had caught an occasional withering breath from over a crater, apparently; here in St. Paul we caught a frequent benumbing one from over a glacier, apparently.

But I wander from my theme. St. Paul is a wonderful town. It is put together in solid blocks of honest brick and stone, and has the air of intending to stay. Its post-office was established thirty-six years ago; and by and by, when the postmaster received a letter, he carried it to Washington, horseback, to inquire what was to be done with it. Such is the legend. Two frame houses were built that year, and several persons were added to the population. A recent number of the leading St. Paul paper, the 'Pioneer Press,' gives some statistics which

* Winter.
** The trailing arbutus.
*** See appendix D.

furnish a vivid contrast to that old state of things, to wit: Population, autumn of the present year (1882), 71,000; number of letters handled, first half of the year, 1,209,387; number of houses built during three- quarters of the year, 989; their cost, $3,186,000. The increase of letters over the corresponding six months of last year was fifty per cent. Last year the new buildings added to the city cost above $4,500,000. St. Paul's strength lies in her commerce—I mean his commerce. He is a manufacturing city, of course—all the cities of that region are—but he is peculiarly strong in the matter of commerce. Last year his jobbing trade amounted to upwards of $52,000,000.

He has a custom-house, and is building a costly capitol to replace the one recently burned—for he is the capital of the State. He has churches without end; and not the cheap poor kind, but the kind that the rich Protestant puts up, the kind that the poor Irish 'hired-girl' delights to erect. What a passion for building majestic churches the Irish hired-girl has. It is a fine thing for our architecture but too often we enjoy her stately fanes without giving her a grateful thought. In fact, instead of reflecting that 'every brick and every stone in this beautiful edifice represents an ache or a pain, and a handful of sweat, and hours of heavy fatigue, contributed by the back and forehead and bones of poverty,' it is our habit to forget these things entirely, and merely glorify the mighty temple itself, without vouchsafing one praiseful thought to its humble builder, whose rich heart and withered purse it symbolizes.

This is a land of libraries and schools. St. Paul has three public libraries, and they contain, in the aggregate, some forty thousand books. He has one hundred and sixteen school-houses, and pays out more than seventy thousand dollars a year in teachers' salaries.

There is an unusually fine railway station; so large is it, in fact, that it seemed somewhat overdone, in the matter of size, at first; but at the end of a few months it was perceived that the mistake was distinctly the other way. The error is to be corrected.

The town stands on high ground; it is about seven hundred feet above the sea level. It is so high that a wide view of river and lowland is offered from its streets.

It is a very wonderful town indeed, and is not finished yet. All the streets are obstructed with building material, and this is being compacted into houses as fast as possible, to make room for more—for other people are anxious to build, as soon as they can get the use of the streets to pile up their bricks and stuff in.

How solemn and beautiful is the thought, that the earliest pioneer of civilization, the van-leader of civilization, is never the steamboat, never the railroad, never the newspaper, never the Sabbath-school, never the missionary—but always whiskey! Such is the case. Look history over; you will see. The missionary comes after the whiskey—I mean he arrives after the whiskey has arrived; next comes the poor immigrant, with ax and hoe and rifle; next, the trader; next, the miscellaneous rush; next, the gambler, the desperado, the highwayman, and all their kindred in sin of both sexes; and next, the smart chap who has bought up an old grant that covers all the land; this brings the lawyer tribe; the vigilance committee brings the undertaker. All these interests bring the newspaper; the newspaper starts up politics and a railroad; all hands turn to and build a church and a jail—and behold, civilization is established for ever in the land. But whiskey, you see, was the van- leader in this beneficent work. It always is. It was like a foreigner— and excusable in a foreigner—to be ignorant of this great truth, and wander off into astronomy to borrow a symbol. But if he had been conversant with the facts, he would have said—

Westward the Jug of Empire takes its way.

This great van-leader arrived upon the ground which St. Paul now occupies, in June 1837. Yes, at that date, Pierre Parrant, a Canadian, built the first cabin, uncorked his jug, and began to sell whiskey to the Indians. The result is before us.

All that I have said of the newness, briskness, swift progress, wealth, intelligence, fine and substantial architecture, and general slash and go, and energy of St. Paul, will apply to his near neighbor, Minneapolis—with the addition that the latter is the bigger of the two cities.

These extraordinary towns were ten miles apart, a few months ago, but were growing so fast that they may possibly be joined now, and getting along under a single mayor. At any rate, within five years from now there will be at least such a substantial ligament of buildings stretching between them and uniting them that a stranger will not be able to tell where the one Siamese twin leaves off and the other begins. Combined, they will then number a population of two hundred and fifty thousand, if they continue to grow as they are now growing. Thus, this center of population at the head of Mississippi navigation, will then begin a rivalry as to numbers, with that center of population at the foot of it—New Orleans.

Minneapolis is situated at the falls of St. Anthony, which stretch across the river, fifteen hundred feet, and have a fall of eighty-two feet—a waterpower which, by art, has been made of inestimable value, business-wise, though somewhat to the damage of the Falls as a spectacle, or as a background against which to get your photograph taken.

Thirty flouring-mills turn out two million barrels of the very choicest of flour every year; twenty sawmills produce two hundred million feet of lumber annually; then there are woolen mills, cotton mills, paper and oil mills; and sash, nail, furniture, barrel, and other factories, without number, so to speak. The great flouring-mills here and at St. Paul use the 'new process' and mash the wheat by rolling, instead of grinding it.

Sixteen railroads meet in Minneapolis, and sixty-five passenger trains arrive and depart daily. In this place, as in St. Paul, journalism thrives. Here there are three great dailies, ten weeklies, and three monthlies.

There is a university, with four hundred students—and, better still, its good efforts are not confined to enlightening the one sex. There are sixteen public schools, with buildings which cost $500,000; there are six thousand pupils and one hundred and twenty-eight teachers. There are also seventy churches existing, and a lot more projected. The banks aggregate a capital of $3,000,000, and the wholesale jobbing trade of the town amounts to $50,000,000 a year.

Near St. Paul and Minneapolis are several points of interest— Fort Snelling, a fortress occupying a river-bluff a hundred feet high; the falls of Minnehaha, White-bear Lake, and so forth. The beautiful falls of Minnehaha are sufficiently celebrated— they do not need a lift from me, in that direction. The White-bear Lake is less known. It is a lovely sheet of water, and is

being utilized as a summer resort by the wealth and fashion of the State. It has its club-house, and its hotel, with the modern improvements and conveniences; its fine summer residences; and plenty of fishing, hunting, and pleasant drives. There are a dozen minor summer resorts around about St. Paul and Minneapolis, but the White-bear Lake is the resort. Connected with White-bear Lake is a most idiotic Indian legend. I would resist the temptation to print it here, if I could, but the task is beyond my strength. The guide-book names the preserver of the legend, and compliments his 'facile pen.' Without further comment or delay then, let us turn the said facile pen loose upon the reader—

A LEGEND OF WHITE-BEAR LAKE.

Every spring, for perhaps a century, or as long as there has been a nation of red men, an island in the middle of White-bear Lake has been visited by a band of Indians for the purpose of making maple sugar.

Tradition says that many springs ago, while upon this island, a young warrior loved and wooed the daughter of his chief, and it is said, also, the maiden loved the warrior. He had again and again been refused her hand by her parents, the old chief alleging that he was no brave, and his old consort called him a woman!

The sun had again set upon the 'sugar-bush,' and the bright moon rose high in the bright blue heavens, when the young warrior took down his flute and went out alone, once more to sing the story of his love, the mild breeze gently moved the two gay feathers in his head-dress, and as he mounted on the trunk of a leaning tree, the damp snow fell from his feet heavily. As he raised his flute to his lips, his blanket slipped from his well-formed shoulders, and lay partly on the snow beneath. He began his weird, wild love-song, but soon felt that he was cold, and as he reached back for his blanket, some unseen hand laid it gently on his shoulders; it was the hand of his love, his guardian angel. She took her place beside him, and for the present they were happy; for the Indian has a heart to love, and in this pride he is as noble as in his own freedom, which makes him the child of the forest. As the legend runs, a large white-bear, thinking, perhaps, that polar snows and dismal winter weather extended everywhere, took up his journey southward. He at length approached the northern shore of the lake which now bears his name, walked down the bank and made his way noiselessly through the deep heavy snow toward the island. It was the same spring ensuing that the lovers met. They had left their first retreat, and were now seated among the branches of a large elm which hung far over the lake. (The same tree is still standing, and excites universal curiosity and interest.) For fear of being detected, they talked almost in a whisper, and now, that they might get back to camp in good time and thereby avoid suspicion, they were just rising to return, when the maiden uttered a shriek which was heard at the camp, and bounding toward the young brave, she caught his blanket, but missed the direction of her foot and fell, bearing the blanket with her into the great arms of the ferocious monster. Instantly every man, woman, and child of the band were upon the bank, but all unarmed. Cries and wailings went up from every mouth. What was to be done'? In the meantime this white and savage beast held the breathless maiden in his huge grasp, and fondled with his precious prey as if he were used to scenes like this. One deafening yell from the lover warrior is heard above the cries of hundreds of his tribe, and dashing away to his wigwam he grasps his faithful knife, returns almost at a single bound to the scene of fear and fright, rushes out along the leaning tree to the spot where his treasure fell, and springing with the fury of a mad panther, pounced upon his prey. The animal turned, and with one stroke of his huge paw brought the lovers heart to heart, but the next moment the warrior, with one plunge of the blade of his knife, opened the crimson sluices of death, and the dying bear relaxed his hold.

That night there was no more sleep for the band or the lovers, and as the young and the old danced about the carcass of the dead monster, the gallant warrior was presented with another plume, and ere another moon had set he had a living treasure added to his heart. Their children for many years played upon the skin of the white-bear—from which the lake derives its name—and the maiden and the brave remembered long the fearful scene and rescue that made them one, for Kis-se-me-pa and Ka-go- ka could never forget their fearful encounter with the huge monster that came so near sending them to the happy hunting-ground.

It is a perplexing business. First, she fell down out of the tree— she and the blanket; and the bear caught her and fondled her—her and the blanket; then she fell up into the tree again— leaving the blanket; meantime the lover goes war-whooping home and comes back 'heeled,' climbs the tree, jumps down on the bear, the girl jumps down after him— apparently, for she was up the tree—resumes her place in the bear's arms along with the blanket, the lover rams his knife into the bear, and saves—whom, the blanket? No—nothing of the sort. You get yourself all worked up and excited about that blanket, and then all of a sudden, just when a happy climax seems imminent you are let down flat—nothing saved but the girl. Whereas, one is not interested in the girl; she is not the prominent feature of the legend. Nevertheless, there you are left, and there you must remain; for if you live a thousand years you will never know who got the blanket. A dead man could get up a better legend than this one. I don't mean a fresh dead man either; I mean a man that's been dead weeks and weeks.

We struck the home-trail now, and in a few hours were in that astonishing Chicago—a city where they are always rubbing the lamp, and fetching up the genii, and contriving and achieving new impossibilities. It is hopeless for the occasional visitor to try to keep up with Chicago—she outgrows his prophecies faster than he can make them. She is always a novelty; for she is never the Chicago you saw when you passed through the last time. The Pennsylvania road rushed us to New York without missing schedule time ten minutes anywhere on the route; and there ended one of the most enjoyable five-thousand-mile journeys I have ever had the good fortune to make.

APPENDIX A

(FROM THE NEW ORLEANS TIMES DEMOCRAT OF MARCH 29, 1882.)

VOYAGE OF THE TIMES-DEMOCRAT'S RELIEF BOAT THROUGH THE INUNDATED REGIONS

IT was nine o'clock Thursday morning when the 'Susie' left the Mississippi and entered Old River, or what is now called the mouth of the Red. Ascending on the left, a flood was pouring in through and over the levees on the Chandler plantation, the most northern point in Pointe Coupee parish. The water completely covered the place, although the levees had given way but a short time before. The stock had been gathered in a large flat-boat, where, without food, as we passed, the animals were huddled together, waiting for a boat to tow them off. On

the right-hand side of the river is Turnbull's Island, and on it is a large plantation which formerly was pronounced one of the most fertile in the State. The water has hitherto allowed it to go scot-free in usual floods, but now broad sheets of water told only where fields were. The top of the protecting levee could be seen here and there, but nearly all of it was submerged.

The trees have put on a greener foliage since the water has poured in, and the woods look bright and fresh, but this pleasant aspect to the eye is neutralized by the interminable waste of water. We pass mile after mile, and it is nothing but trees standing up to their branches in water. A water-turkey now and again rises and flies ahead into the long avenue of silence. A pirogue sometimes flits from the bushes and crosses the Red River on its way out to the Mississippi, but the sad-faced paddlers never turn their heads to look at our boat. The puffing of the boat is music in this gloom, which affects one most curiously. It is not the gloom of deep forests or dark caverns, but a peculiar kind of solemn silence and impressive awe that holds one perforce to its recognition. We passed two negro families on a raft tied up in the willows this morning. They were evidently of the well-to-do class, as they had a supply of meal and three or four hogs with them. Their rafts were about twenty feet square, and in front of an improvised shelter earth had been placed, on which they built their fire.

The current running down the Atchafalaya was very swift, the Mississippi showing a predilection in that direction, which needs only to be seen to enforce the opinion of that river's desperate endeavors to find a short way to the Gulf. Small boats, skiffs, pirogues, etc., are in great demand, and many have been stolen by piratical negroes, who take them where they will bring the greatest price. From what was told me by Mr. C. P. Ferguson, a planter near Red River Landing, whose place has just gone under, there is much suffering in the rear of that place. The negroes had given up all thoughts of a crevasse there, as the upper levee had stood so long, and when it did come they were at its mercy. On Thursday a number were taken out of trees and off of cabin roofs and brought in, many yet remaining.

One does not appreciate the sight of earth until he has traveled through a flood. At sea one does not expect or look for it, but here, with fluttering leaves, shadowy forest aisles, house-tops barely visible, it is expected. In fact a grave-yard, if the mounds were above water, would be appreciated. The river here is known only because there is an opening in the trees, and that is all. It is in width, from Fort Adams on the left bank of the Mississippi to the bank of Rapides Parish, a distance of about sixty miles. A large portion of this was under cultivation, particularly along the Mississippi and back of the Red. When Red River proper was entered, a strong current was running directly across it, pursuing the same direction as that of the Mississippi.

After a run of some hours, Black River was reached. Hardly was it entered before signs of suffering became visible. All the willows along the banks were stripped of their leaves. One man, whom your correspondent spoke to, said that he had had one hundred and fifty head of cattle and one hundred head of hogs. At the first appearance of water he had started to drive them to the high lands of Avoyelles, thirty-five miles off, but he lost fifty head of the beef cattle and sixty hogs. Black River is quite picturesque, even if its shores are under water. A dense growth of ash, oak, gum, and hickory make the shores almost impenetrable, and where one can get a view down some avenue in the trees, only the dim outlines of distant trunks can be barely distinguished in the gloom.

A few miles up this river, the depth of water on the banks was fully eight feet, and on all sides could be seen, still holding against the strong current, the tops of cabins. Here and there one overturned was surrounded by drift-wood, forming the nucleus of possibly some future island.

In order to save coal, as it was impossible to get that fuel at any point to be touched during the expedition, a look-out was kept for a wood-pile. On rounding a point a pirogue, skilfully paddled by a youth, shot out, and in its bow was a girl of fifteen, of fair face, beautiful black eyes, and demure manners. The boy asked for a paper, which was thrown to him, and the couple pushed their tiny craft out into the swell of the boat.

Presently a little girl, not certainly over twelve years, paddled out in the smallest little canoe and handled it with all the deftness of an old voyageur. The little one looked more like an Indian than a white child, and laughed when asked if she were afraid. She had been raised in a pirogue and could go anywhere. She was bound out to pick willow leaves for the stock, and she pointed to a house near by with water three inches deep on the floors. At its back door was moored a raft about thirty feet square, with a sort of fence built upon it, and inside of this some sixteen cows and twenty hogs were standing. The family did not complain, except on account of losing their stock, and promptly brought a supply of wood in a flat.

From this point to the Mississippi River, fifteen miles, there is not a spot of earth above water, and to the westward for thirty-five miles there is nothing but the river's flood. Black River had risen during Thursday, the 23rd, 1¾ inches, and was going up at night still. As we progress up the river habitations become more frequent, but are yet still miles apart. Nearly all of them are deserted, and the out-houses floated off. To add to the gloom, almost every living thing seems to have departed, and not a whistle of a bird nor the bark of the squirrel can be heard in this solitude. Sometimes a morose gar will throw his tail aloft and disappear in the river, but beyond this everything is quiet—the quiet of dissolution. Down the river floats now a neatly whitewashed hen-house, then a cluster of neatly split fence- rails, or a door and a bloated carcass, solemnly guarded by a pair of buzzards, the only bird to be seen, which feast on the carcass as it bears them along. A picture-frame in which there was a cheap lithograph of a soldier on horseback, as it floated on told of some hearth invaded by the water and despoiled of this ornament.

At dark, as it was not prudent to run, a place alongside the woods was hunted and to a tall gum-tree the boat was made fast for the night.

A pretty quarter of the moon threw a pleasant light over forest and river, making a picture that would be a delightful piece of landscape study, could an artist only hold it down to his canvas. The motion of the engines had ceased, the puffing of the escaping steam was stilled, and the enveloping silence closed upon us, and such silence it was! Usually in a forest at night one can hear the piping of frogs, the hum of insects, or the dropping of limbs; but here nature was dumb. The dark recesses, those aisles into this cathedral, gave forth no sound, and even the ripplings of the current die away.

At daylight Friday morning all hands were up, and up the Black we started. The morning was a beautiful one, and the river, which is remarkably straight, put on its loveliest garb.

The blossoms of the haw perfumed the air deliciously, and a few birds whistled blithely along the banks. The trees were larger, and the forest seemed of older growth than below. More fields were passed than nearer the mouth, but the same scene presented itself—smoke-houses drifting out in the pastures, negro quarters anchored in confusion against some oak, and the modest residence just showing its eaves above water. The sun came up in a glory of carmine, and the trees were brilliant in their varied shades of green. Not a foot of soil is to be seen anywhere, and the water is apparently growing deeper and deeper, for it reaches up to the branches of the largest trees. All along, the bordering willows have been denuded of leaves, showing how long the people have been at work gathering this fodder for their animals. An old man in a pirogue was asked how the willow leaves agreed with his cattle. He stopped in his work, and with an ominous shake of his head replied: 'Well, sir, it 's enough to keep warmth in their bodies and that's all we expect, but it's hard on the hogs, particularly the small ones. They is dropping off powerful fast. But what can you do? It 's all we've got.'

At thirty miles above the mouth of Black River the water extends from Natchez on the Mississippi across to the pine hills of Louisiana, a distance of seventy-three miles, and there is hardly a spot that is not ten feet under it. The tendency of the current up the Black is toward the west. In fact, so much is this the case, the waters of Red River have been driven down from toward the Calcasieu country, and the waters of the Black enter the Red some fifteen miles above the mouth of the former, a thing never before seen by even the oldest steamboatmen. The water now in sight of us is entirely from the Mississippi.

Up to Trinity, or rather Troy, which is but a short distance below, the people have nearly all moved out, those remaining having enough for their present personal needs. Their cattle, though, are suffering and dying off quite fast, as the confinement on rafts and the food they get breeds disease.

After a short stop we started, and soon came to a section where there were many open fields and cabins thickly scattered about. Here were seen more pictures of distress. On the inside of the houses the inmates had built on boxes a scaffold on which they placed the furniture. The bed- posts were sawed off on top, as the ceiling was not more than four feet from the improvised floor. The buildings looked very insecure, and threatened every moment to float off. Near the houses were cattle standing breast high in the water, perfectly impassive. They did not move in their places, but stood patiently waiting for help to come. The sight was a distressing one, and the poor creatures will be sure to die unless speedily rescued. Cattle differ from horses in this peculiar quality. A horse, after finding no relief comes, will swim off in search of food, whereas a beef will stand in its tracks until with exhaustion it drops in the water and drowns.

At half-past twelve o'clock a hail was given from a flat-boat inside the line of the bank. Rounding to we ran alongside, and General York stepped aboard. He was just then engaged in getting off stock, and welcomed the 'Times-Democrat' boat heartily, as he said there was much need for her. He said that the distress was not exaggerated in the least. People were in a condition it was difficult even for one to imagine. The water was so high there was great danger of their houses being swept away. It had already risen so high that it was approaching the eaves, and when it reaches this point there is always imminent risk of their being swept away. If this occurs, there will be great loss of life. The General spoke of the gallant work of many of the people in their attempts to save their stock, but thought that fully twenty-five per cent. had perished. Already twenty-five hundred people had received rations from Troy, on Black River, and he had towed out a great many cattle, but a very great quantity remained and were in dire need. The water was now eighteen inches higher than in 1874, and there was no land between Vidalia and the hills of Catahoula.

At two o'clock the 'Susie' reached Troy, sixty-five miles above the mouth of Black River. Here on the left comes in Little River; just beyond that the Ouachita, and on the right the Tensas. These three rivers form the Black River. Troy, or a portion of it, is situated on and around three large Indian mounds, circular in shape, which rise above the present water about twelve feet. They are about one hundred and fifty feet in diameter, and are about two hundred yards apart. The houses are all built between these mounds, and hence are all flooded to a depth of eighteen inches on their floors.

These elevations, built by the aborigines, hundreds of years ago, are the only points of refuge for miles. When we arrived we found them crowded with stock, all of which was thin and hardly able to stand up. They were mixed together, sheep, hogs, horses, mules, and cattle. One of these mounds has been used for many years as the grave-yard, and to-day we saw attenuated cows lying against the marble tomb-stones, chewing their cud in contentment, after a meal of corn furnished by General York. Here, as below, the remarkable skill of the women and girls in the management of the smaller pirogues was noticed. Children were paddling about in these most ticklish crafts with all the nonchalance of adepts.

General York has put into operation a perfect system in regard to furnishing relief. He makes a personal inspection of the place where it is asked, sees what is necessary to be done, and then, having two boats chartered, with flats, sends them promptly to the place, when the cattle are loaded and towed to the pine hills and uplands of Catahoula. He has made Troy his headquarters, and to this point boats come for their supply of feed for cattle. On the opposite side of Little River, which branches to the left out of Black, and between it and the Ouachita, is situated the town of Trinity, which is hourly threatened with destruction. It is much lower than Troy, and the water is eight and nine feet deep in the houses. A strong current sweeps through it, and it is remarkable that all of its houses have not gone before. The residents of both Troy and Trinity have been cared for, yet some of their stock have to be furnished with food.

As soon as the 'Susie' reached Troy, she was turned over to General York, and placed at his disposition to carry out the work of relief more rapidly. Nearly all her supplies were landed on one of the mounds to lighten her, and she was headed down stream to relieve those below. At Tom Hooper's place, a few miles from Troy, a large flat, with about fifty head of stock on board, was taken in tow. The animals were fed, and soon regained some strength. To-day we go on Little River, where the suffering is greatest.

DOWN BLACK RIVER

Saturday Evening, March 25.

We started down Black River quite early, under the direction of General York, to bring out what stock could be reached. Going down river a flat in tow was left in a central locality, and from there men poled her back in the rear of plantations, picking up the animals wherever found. In the loft of a gin-house there were seventeen head found, and after a gangway was built they were led down into the flat without difficulty. Taking a skiff with the General, your reporter was pulled up to a little house of two rooms, in which the water was standing two feet on the floors. In one of the large rooms were huddled the horses and cows of the place, while in the other the Widow Taylor and her son were seated on a scaffold raised on the floor. One or two dug-outs were drifting about in the roam ready to be put in service at any time. When the flat was brought up, the side of the house was cut away as the only means of getting the animals out, and the cattle were driven on board the boat. General York, in this as in every case, inquired if the family desired to leave, informing them that Major Burke, of 'The Times-Democrat,' has sent the 'Susie' up for that purpose. Mrs. Taylor said she thanked Major Burke, but she would try and hold out. The remarkable tenacity of the people here to their homes is beyond all comprehension. Just below, at a point sixteen miles from Troy, information was received that the house of Mr. Tom Ellis was in danger, and his family were all in it. We steamed there immediately, and a sad picture was presented. Looking out of the half of the window left above water, was Mrs. Ellis, who is in feeble health, whilst at the door were her seven children, the oldest not fourteen years. One side of the house was given up to the work animals, some twelve head, besides hogs. In the next room the family lived, the water coming within two inches of the bed-rail. The stove was below water, and the cooking was done on a fire on top of it. The house threatened to give way at any moment: one end of it was sinking, and, in fact, the building looked a mere shell. As the boat rounded to, Mr. Ellis came out in a dug-out, and General York told him that he had come to his relief; that 'The Times-Democrat' boat was at his service, and would remove his family at once to the hills, and on Monday a flat would take out his stock, as, until that time, they would be busy. Notwithstanding the deplorable situation himself and family were in, Mr. Ellis did not want to leave. He said he thought he would wait until Monday, and take the risk of his house falling. The children around the door looked perfectly contented, seeming to care little for the danger they were in. These are but two instances of the many. After weeks of privation and suffering, people still cling to their houses and leave only when there is not room between the water and the ceiling to build a scaffold on which to stand. It seemed to be incomprehensible, yet the love for the old place was stronger than that for safety.

After leaving the Ellis place, the next spot touched at was the Oswald place. Here the flat was towed alongside the gin-house where there were fifteen head standing in water; and yet, as they stood on scaffolds, their heads were above the top of the entrance. It was found impossible to get them out without cutting away a portion of the front; and so axes were brought into requisition and a gap made. After much labor the horses and mules were securely placed on the flat.

At each place we stop there are always three, four, or more dug-outs arriving, bringing information of stock in other places in need. Notwithstanding the fact that a great many had driven a part of their stock to the hills some time ago, there yet remains a large quantity, which General York, who is working with indomitable energy, will get landed in the pine hills by Tuesday.

All along Black River the 'Susie' has been visited by scores of planters, whose tales are the repetition of those already heard of suffering and loss. An old planter, who has lived on the river since 1844, said there never was such a rise, and he was satisfied more than one quarter of the stock has been lost.

Luckily the people cared first for their work stock, and when they could find it horses and mules were housed in a place of safety. The rise which still continues, and was two inches last night, compels them to get them out to the hills; hence it is that the work of General York is of such a great value. From daylight to late at night he is going this way and that, cheering by his kindly words and directing with calm judgment what is to be done. One unpleasant story, of a certain merchant in New Orleans, is told all along the river. It appears for some years past the planters have been dealing with this individual, and many of them had balances in his hands. When the overflow came they wrote for coffee, for meal, and, in fact, for such little necessities as were required. No response to these letters came, and others were written, and yet these old customers, with plantations under water, were refused even what was necessary to sustain life. It is needless to say he is not popular now on Back River.

The hills spoken of as the place of refuge for the people and stock on Black River are in Catahoula parish, twenty-four miles from Black River.

After filling the flat with cattle we took on board the family of T. S. Hooper, seven in number, who could not longer remain in their dwelling, and we are now taking them up Little River to the hills.

THE FLOOD STILL RISING

Troy: March 27, 1882, noon.

The flood here is rising about three and a half inches every twenty-four hours, and rains have set in which will increase this. General York feels now that our efforts ought to be directed towards saving life, as the increase of the water has jeopardized many houses. We intend to go up the Tensas in a few minutes, and then we will return and go down Black River to take off families. There is a lack of steam transportation here to meet the emergency. The General has three boats chartered, with flats in tow, but the demand for these to tow out stock is greater than they can meet with promptness. All are working night and day, and the 'Susie' hardly stops for more than an hour anywhere. The rise has placed Trinity in a dangerous plight, and momentarily it is expected that some of the houses will float off. Troy is a little higher, yet all are in the water. Reports have come in that a woman and child have been washed away below here, and two cabins floated off. Their occupants are the same who refused to come off day before yesterday. One would not believe the utter passiveness of the people.

As yet no news has been received of the steamer 'Delia,' which is supposed to be the one sunk in yesterday's storm on Lake Catahoula. She is due here now, but has not arrived. Even the mail here is most uncertain, and this I send by skiff to Natchez to get it to you. It is impossible to get accurate data as to past crops, etc., as those who know much about the matter have gone, and those who remain are not well versed in the production of this section.

General York desires me to say that the amount of rations formerly sent should be duplicated and sent at once. It is impossible to make any estimate, for the people are fleeing to the hills, so rapid is the rise. The residents here are in a state of commotion that can only be appreciated when seen, and complete demoralization has set in,

If rations are drawn for any particular section hereabouts, they would not be certain to be distributed, so everything should be sent to Troy as a center, and the General will have it properly disposed of. He has sent for one hundred tents, and, if all go to the hills who are in motion now, two hundred will be required.

APPENDIX B

THE MISSISSIPPI RIVER COMMISSION

THE condition of this rich valley of the Lower Mississippi, immediately after and since the war, constituted one of the disastrous effects of war most to be deplored. Fictitious property in slaves was not only righteously destroyed, but very much of the work which had depended upon the slave labor was also destroyed or greatly impaired, especially the levee system.

It might have been expected by those who have not investigated the subject, that such important improvements as the construction and maintenance of the levees would have been assumed at once by the several States. But what can the State do where the people are under subjection to rates of interest ranging from 18 to 30 per cent., and are also under the necessity of pledging their crops in advance even of planting, at these rates, for the privilege of purchasing all of their supplies at 100 per cent. profit?

It has needed but little attention to make it perfectly obvious that the control of the Mississippi River, if undertaken at all, must be undertaken by the national government, and cannot be compassed by States. The river must be treated as a unit; its control cannot be compassed under a divided or separate system of administration.

Neither are the States especially interested competent to combine among themselves for the necessary operations. The work must begin far up the river; at least as far as Cairo, if not beyond; and must be conducted upon a consistent general plan throughout the course of the river.

It does not need technical or scientific knowledge to comprehend the elements of the case if one will give a little time and attention to the subject, and when a Mississippi River commission has been constituted, as the existing commission is, of thoroughly able men of different walks in life, may it not be suggested that their verdict in the case should be accepted as conclusive, so far as any a priori theory of construction or control can be considered conclusive?

It should be remembered that upon this board are General Gilmore, General Comstock, and General Suter, of the United States Engineers; Professor Henry Mitchell (the most competent authority on the question of hydrography), of the United States Coast Survey; B. B. Harrod, the State Engineer of Louisiana; Jas. B. Eads, whose success with the jetties at New Orleans is a warrant of his competency, and Judge Taylor, of Indiana.

It would be presumption on the part of any single man, however skilled, to contest the judgment of such a board as this.

The method of improvement proposed by the commission is at once in accord with the results of engineering experience and with observations of nature where meeting our wants. As in nature the growth of trees and their proneness where undermined to fall across the slope and support the bank secures at some points a fair depth of channel and some degree of permanence, so in the project of the engineer the use of timber and brush and the encouragement of forest growth are the main features. It is proposed to reduce the width where excessive by brushwood dykes, at first low, but raised higher and higher as the mud of the river settles under their shelter, and finally slope them back at the angle upon which willows will grow freely. In this work there are many details connected with the forms of these shelter dykes, their arrangements so as to present a series of settling basins, etc., a description of which would only complicate the conception. Through the larger part of the river works of contraction will not be required, but nearly all the banks on the concave side of the beds must be held against the wear of the stream, and much of the opposite banks defended at critical points. The works having in view this conservative object may be generally designated works of revetment; and these also will be largely of brushwood, woven in continuous carpets, or twined into wire-netting. This veneering process has been successfully employed on the Missouri River; and in some cases they have so covered themselves with sediments, and have become so overgrown with willows, that they may be regarded as permanent. In securing these mats rubble-stone is to be used in small quantities, and in some instances the dressed slope between high and low river will have to be more or less paved with stone.

Any one who has been on the Rhine will have observed operations not unlike those to which we have just referred; and, indeed, most of the rivers of Europe flowing among their own alluvia have required similar treatment in the interest of navigation and agriculture.

The levee is the crowning work of bank revetment, although not necessarily in immediate connection. It may be set back a short distance from the revetted bank; but it is, in effect, the requisite parapet. The flood river and the low river cannot be brought into register, and compelled to unite in the excavation of a single permanent channel, without a complete control of all the stages; and even the abnormal rise must be provided against, because this would endanger the levee, and once in force behind the works of revetment would tear them also away.

Under the general principle that the local slope of a river is the result and measure of the resistance of its bed, it is evident that a narrow and deep stream should have less slope, because it has less frictional surface in proportion to capacity; i.e., less perimeter in proportion to area of cross section. The ultimate effect of levees and revetments confining the floods and bringing all the stages of the river into register is to deepen the channel and let down the slope. The first effect of the levees is to raise the surface; but this, by inducing greater velocity of flow, inevitably causes an enlargement of section, and if this enlargement is prevented from being made at the expense of the banks, the bottom must give way and the form of the waterway be so improved as to admit this flow with less rise. The actual experience with levees upon the Mississippi River, with no attempt to hold the banks, has been favorable, and no one can doubt, upon the evidence furnished in the reports of the commission, that if the earliest levees had been accompanied by revetment of banks, and made complete, we should have to-day a river navigable at low water, and an adjacent country safe from inundation.

Of course it would be illogical to conclude that the constrained river can ever lower its flood slope so as to make levees unnecessary, but it is believed that, by this lateral constraint, the river as a conduit may be so improved in form that even

those rare floods which result from the coincident rising of many tributaries will find vent without destroying levees of ordinary height. That the actual capacity of a channel through alluvium depends upon its service during floods has been often shown, but this capacity does not include anomalous, but recurrent, floods.

It is hardly worth while to consider the projects for relieving the Mississippi River floods by creating new outlets, since these sensational propositions have commended themselves only to unthinking minds, and have no support among engineers. Were the river bed cast-iron, a resort to openings for surplus waters might be a necessity; but as the bottom is yielding, and the best form of outlet is a single deep channel, as realizing the least ratio of perimeter to area of cross section, there could not well be a more unphilosophical method of treatment than the multiplication of avenues of escape.

In the foregoing statement the attempt has been made to condense in as limited a space as the importance of the subject would permit, the general elements of the problem, and the general features of the proposed method of improvement which has been adopted by the Mississippi River Commission.

The writer cannot help feeling that it is somewhat presumptuous on his part to attempt to present the facts relating to an enterprise which calls for the highest scientific skill; but it is a matter which interests every citizen of the United States, and is one of the methods of reconstruction which ought to be approved. It is a war claim which implies no private gain, and no compensation except for one of the cases of destruction incident to war, which may well be repaired by the people of the whole country.

EDWARD ATKINSON.

Boston: April 14, 1882.

APPENDIX C

RECEPTION OF CAPTAIN BASIL HALL'S BOOK IN THE UNITED STATES

HAVING now arrived nearly at the end of our travels, I am induced, ere I conclude, again to mention what I consider as one of the most remarkable traits in the national character of the Americans; namely, their exquisite sensitiveness and soreness respecting everything said or written concerning them. Of this, perhaps, the most remarkable example I can give is the effect produced on nearly every class of readers by the appearance of Captain Basil Hall's 'Travels in North America.' In fact, it was a sort of moral earthquake, and the vibration it occasioned through the nerves of the republic, from one corner of the Union to the other, was by no means over when I left the country in July 1831, a couple of years after the shock.

I was in Cincinnati when these volumes came out, but it was not till July 1830, that I procured a copy of them. One bookseller to whom I applied told me that he had had a few copies before he understood the nature of the work, but that, after becoming acquainted with it, nothing should induce him to sell another. Other persons of his profession must, however, have been less scrupulous; for the book was read in city, town, village, and hamlet, steamboat, and stage-coach, and a sort of war-whoop was sent forth perfectly unprecedented in my recollection upon any occasion whatever.

An ardent desire for approbation, and a delicate sensitiveness under censure, have always, I believe, been considered as amiable traits of character; but the condition into which the appearance of Captain Hall's work threw the republic shows plainly that these feelings, if carried to excess, produce a weakness which amounts to imbecility.

It was perfectly astonishing to hear men who, on other subjects, were of some judgment, utter their opinions upon this. I never heard of any instance in which the commonsense generally found in national criticism was so overthrown by passion. I do not speak of the want of justice, and of fair and liberal interpretation: these, perhaps, were hardly to be expected. Other nations have been called thin-skinned, but the citizens of the Union have, apparently, no skins at all; they wince if a breeze blows over them, unless it be tempered with adulation. It was not, therefore, very surprising that the acute and forcible observations of a traveler they knew would be listened to should be received testily. The extraordinary features of the business were, first, the excess of the rage into which they lashed themselves; and, secondly, the puerility of the inventions by which they attempted to account for the severity with which they fancied they had been treated.

Not content with declaring that the volumes contained no word of truth, from beginning to end (which is an assertion I heard made very nearly as often as they were mentioned), the whole country set to work to discover the causes why Captain Hall had visited the United States, and why he had published his book.

I have heard it said with as much precision and gravity as if the statement had been conveyed by an official report, that Captain Hall had been sent out by the British Government expressly for the purpose of checking the growing admiration of England for the Government of the United States,—that it was by a commission from the treasury he had come, and that it was only in obedience to orders that he had found anything to object to.

I do not give this as the gossip of a coterie; I am persuaded that it is the belief of a very considerable portion of the country. So deep is the conviction of this singular people that they cannot be seen without being admired, that they will not admit the possibility that any one should honestly and sincerely find aught to disapprove in them or their country.

The American Reviews are, many of them, I believe, well known in England; I need not, therefore, quote them here, but I sometimes wondered that they, none of them, ever thought of translating Obadiah's curse into classic American; if they had done so, on placing (he, Basil Hall) between brackets, instead of (he, Obadiah) it would have saved them a world of trouble.

I can hardly describe the curiosity with which I sat down at length to peruse these tremendous volumes; still less can I do justice to my surprise at their contents. To say that I found not one exaggerated statement throughout the work is by no means saying enough. It is impossible for any one who knows the country not to see that Captain Hall earnestly sought out things to admire and commend. When he praises, it is with evident pleasure; and when he finds fault, it is with evident reluctance and restraint, excepting where motives purely patriotic urge him to state roundly what it is for the benefit of his country should be known.

In fact, Captain Hall saw the country to the greatest possible advantage. Furnished, of course, with letters of introduction to the most distinguished individuals, and with the still more influential recommendation of his own reputation, he was received in full drawing-room style and state from one end of the Union to the other. He saw the country in full dress, and had little or no opportunity of judging of it unhouselled, unanointed, unannealed, with all its imperfections on its head, as I and my family too often had.

Captain Hall had certainly excellent opportunities of making himself acquainted with the form of the government and the laws; and of receiving, moreover, the best oral commentary upon them, in conversation with the most distinguished citizens. Of these opportunities he made excellent use; nothing important met his eye which did not receive that sort of analytical attention which an experienced and philosophical traveler alone can give. This has made his volumes highly interesting and valuable; but I am deeply persuaded, that were a man of equal penetration to visit the United States with no other means of becoming acquainted with the national character than the ordinary working-day intercourse of life, he would conceive an infinitely lower idea of the moral atmosphere of the country than Captain Hall appears to have done; and the internal conviction on my mind is strong, that if Captain Hall had not placed a firm restraint on himself, he must have given expression to far deeper indignation than any he has uttered against many points in the American character, with which he shows from other circumstances that he was well acquainted. His rule appears to have been to state just so much of the truth as would leave on the mind of his readers a correct impression, at the least cost of pain to the sensitive folks he was writing about. He states his own opinions and feelings, and leaves it to be inferred that he has good grounds for adopting them; but he spares the Americans the bitterness which a detail of the circumstances would have produced.

If any one chooses to say that some wicked antipathy to twelve millions of strangers is the origin of my opinion, I must bear it; and were the question one of mere idle speculation, I certainly would not court the abuse I must meet for stating it. But it is not so.

. . . .

The candor which he expresses, and evidently feels, they mistake for irony, or totally distrust; his unwillingness to give pain to persons from whom he has received kindness, they scornfully reject as affectation, and although they must know right well, in their own secret hearts, how infinitely more they lay at his mercy than he has chosen to betray; they pretend, even to themselves, that he has exaggerated the bad points of their character and institutions; whereas, the truth is, that he has let them off with a degree of tenderness which may be quite suitable for him to exercise, however little merited; while, at the same time, he has most industriously magnified their merits, whenever he could possibly find anything favorable.

APPENDIX D

THE UNDYING HEAD

IN a remote part of the North lived a man and his sister, who had never seen a human being. Seldom, if ever, had the man any cause to go from home; for, as his wants demanded food, he had only to go a little distance from the lodge, and there, in some particular spot, place his arrows, with their barbs in the ground. Telling his sister where they had been placed, every morning she would go in search, and never fail of finding each stuck through the heart of a deer. She had then only to drag them into the lodge and prepare their food. Thus she lived till she attained womanhood, when one day her brother, whose name was Iamo, said to her: 'Sister, the time is at hand when you will be ill. Listen to my advice. If you do not, it will probably be the cause of my death. Take the implements with which we kindle our fires. Go some distance from our lodge and build a separate fire. When you are in want of food, I will tell you where to find it. You must cook for yourself, and I will for myself. When you are ill, do not attempt to come near the lodge, or bring any of the utensils you use. Be sure always to fasten to your belt the implements you need, for you do not know when the time will come. As for myself, I must do the best I can.' His sister promised to obey him in all he had said.

Shortly after, her brother had cause to go from home. She was alone in her lodge, combing her hair. She had just untied the belt to which the implements were fastened, when suddenly the event, to which her brother had alluded, occurred. She ran out of the lodge, but in her haste forgot the belt. Afraid to return, she stood for some time thinking. Finally, she decided to enter the lodge and get it. For, thought she, my brother is not at home, and I will stay but a moment to catch hold of it. She went back. Running in suddenly, she caught hold of it, and was coming out when her brother came in sight. He knew what was the matter. 'Oh,' he said, 'did I not tell you to take care. But now you have killed me.' She was going on her way, but her brother said to her, 'What can you do there now. The accident has happened. Go in, and stay where you have always stayed. And what will become of you? You have killed me.'

He then laid aside his hunting-dress and accoutrements, and soon after both his feet began to turn black, so that he could not move. Still he directed his sister where to place the arrows, that she might always have food. The inflammation continued to increase, and had now reached his first rib; and he said: 'Sister, my end is near. You must do as I tell you. You see my medicine-sack, and my war-club tied to it. It contains all my medicines, and my war-plumes, and my paints of all colors. As soon as the inflammation reaches my breast, you will take my war-club. It has a sharp point, and you will cut off my head. When it is free from my body, take it, place its neck in the sack, which you must open at one end. Then hang it up in its former place. Do not forget my bow and arrows. One of the last you will take to procure food. The remainder, tie in my sack, and then hang it up, so that I can look towards the door. Now and then I will speak to you, but not often.' His sister again promised to obey.

In a little time his breast was affected. 'Now,' said he, 'take the club and strike off my head.' She was afraid, but he told her to muster courage. 'Strike,' said he, and a smile was on his face. Mustering all her courage, she gave the blow and cut off the head. 'Now,' said the head, 'place me where I told you.' And fearfully she obeyed it in all its commands. Retaining its animation, it looked around the lodge as usual, and it would command its sister to go in such places as it thought would procure for her the flesh of different animals she needed. One day the head said: 'The time is not distant when I shall be freed from this situation, and I shall have to undergo many sore evils. So the superior manito decrees, and I must bear all patiently.' In this situation we must leave the head.

In a certain part of the country was a village inhabited by a numerous and warlike band of Indians. In this village was a family of ten young men—brothers. It was in the spring of the year that the youngest of these blackened his face and fasted.

His dreams were propitious. Having ended his fast, he went secretly for his brothers at night, so that none in the village could overhear or find out the direction they intended to go. Though their drum was heard, yet that was a common occurrence. Having ended the usual formalities, he told how favorable his dreams were, and that he had called them together to know if they would accompany him in a war excursion. They all answered they would. The third brother from the eldest, noted for his oddities, coming up with his war-club when his brother had ceased speaking, jumped up. 'Yes,' said he, 'I will go, and this will be the way I will treat those I am going to fight;' and he struck the post in the center of the lodge, and gave a yell. The others spoke to him, saying: 'Slow, slow, Mudjikewis, when you are in other people's lodges.' So he sat down. Then, in turn, they took the drum, and sang their songs, and closed with a feast. The youngest told them not to whisper their intention to their wives, but secretly to prepare for their journey. They all promised obedience, and Mudjikewis was the first to say so.

The time for their departure drew near. Word was given to assemble on a certain night, when they would depart immediately. Mudjikewis was loud in his demands for his moccasins. Several times his wife asked him the reason. 'Besides,' said she, 'you have a good pair on.' 'Quick, quick,' said he, 'since you must know, we are going on a war excursion; so be quick.' He thus revealed the secret. That night they met and started. The snow was on the ground, and they traveled all night, lest others should follow them. When it was daylight, the leader took snow and made a ball of it, then tossing it into the air, he said: 'It was in this way I saw snow fall in a dream, so that I could not be tracked.' And he told them to keep close to each other for fear of losing themselves, as the snow began to fall in very large flakes. Near as they walked, it was with difficulty they could see each other. The snow continued falling all that day and the following night, so it was impossible to track them.

They had now walked for several days, and Mudjikewis was always in the rear. One day, running suddenly forward, he gave the SAW-SAW-QUAN*, and struck a tree with his war-club, and it broke into pieces as if struck with lightning. 'Brothers,' said he, 'this will be the way I will serve those we are going to fight.' The leader answered, 'Slow, slow, Mudjikewis, the one I lead you to is not to be thought of so lightly.' Again he fell back and thought to himself: 'What! what! who can this be he is leading us to?' He felt fearful and was silent. Day after day they traveled on, till they came to an extensive plain, on the borders of which human bones were bleaching in the sun. The leader spoke: 'They are the bones of those who have gone before us. None has ever yet returned to tell the sad tale of their fate.' Again Mudjikewis became restless, and, running forward, gave the accustomed yell. Advancing to a large rock which stood above the ground, he struck it, and it fell to pieces. 'See, brothers,' said he, 'thus will I treat those whom we are going to fight.' 'Still, still,' once more said the leader; 'he to whom I am leading you is not to be compared to the rock.'

Mudjikewis fell back thoughtful, saying to himself: 'I wonder who this can be that he is going to attack;' and he was afraid. Still they continued to see the remains of former warriors, who had been to the place where they were now going, some of whom had retreated as far back as the place where they first saw the bones, beyond which no one had ever escaped. At last they came to a piece of rising ground, from which they plainly

---

* War-whoop.

distinguished, sleeping on a distant mountain, a mammoth bear.

The distance between them was very great, but the size of the animal caused him to be plainly seen. 'There,' said the leader, 'it is he to whom I am leading you; here our troubles will commence, for he is a mishemokwa and a manito. It is he who has that we prize so dearly (i.e. wampum), to obtain which, the warriors whose bones we saw, sacrificed their lives. You must not be fearful: be manly. We shall find him asleep.' Then the leader went forward and touched the belt around the animal's neck. 'This,' said he, 'is what we must get. It contains the wampum.' Then they requested the eldest to try and slip the belt over the bear's head, who appeared to be fast asleep, as he was not in the least disturbed by the attempt to obtain the belt. All their efforts were in vain, till it came to the one next the youngest. He tried, and the belt moved nearly over the monster's head, but he could get it no farther. Then the youngest one, and the leader, made his attempt, and succeeded. Placing it on the back of the oldest, he said, 'Now we must run,' and off they started. When one became fatigued with its weight, another would relieve him. Thus they ran till they had passed the bones of all former warriors, and were some distance beyond, when looking back, they saw the monster slowly rising. He stood some time before he missed his wampum. Soon they heard his tremendous howl, like distant thunder, slowly filling all the sky; and then they heard him speak and say, 'Who can it be that has dared to steal my wampum? earth is not so large but that I can find them;' and he descended from the hill in pursuit. As if convulsed, the earth shook with every jump he made. Very soon he approached the party. They, however, kept the belt, exchanging it from one to another, and encouraging each other; but he gained on them fast. 'Brothers,' said the leader, 'has never any one of you, when fasting, dreamed of some friendly spirit who would aid you as a guardian?' A dead silence followed. 'Well,' said he, 'fasting, I dreamed of being in danger of instant death, when I saw a small lodge, with smoke curling from its top. An old man lived in it, and I dreamed he helped me; and may it be verified soon,' he said, running forward and giving the peculiar yell, and a howl as if the sounds came from the depths of his stomach, and what is called CHECAUDUM. Getting upon a piece of rising ground, behold! a lodge, with smoke curling from its top, appeared. This gave them all new strength, and they ran forward and entered it. The leader spoke to the old man who sat in the lodge, saying, 'Nemesho, help us; we claim your protection, for the great bear will kill us.' 'Sit down and eat, my grandchildren,' said the old man. 'Who is a great manito?' said he. 'There is none but me; but let me look,' and he opened the door of the lodge, when, lo! at a little distance he saw the enraged animal coming on, with slow but powerful leaps. He closed the door. 'Yes,' said he, 'he is indeed a great manito: my grandchildren, you will be the cause of my losing my life; you asked my protection, and I granted it; so now, come what may, I will protect you. When the bear arrives at the door, you must run out of the other door of the lodge.' Then putting his hand to the side of the lodge where he sat, he brought out a bag which he opened. Taking out two small black dogs, he placed them before him. 'These are the ones I use when I fight,' said he; and he commenced patting with both hands the sides of one of them, and he began to swell out, so that he soon filled the lodge by his bulk; and he had great strong teeth. When he attained his full size he growled, and from that moment, as from instinct, he jumped out at the door and met the bear, who in another leap would have reached the lodge. A terrible combat ensued. The skies rang with the howls of the fierce monsters. The remaining dog soon took the field. The

brothers, at the onset, took the advice of the old man, and escaped through the opposite side of the lodge. They had not proceeded far before they heard the dying cry of one of the dogs, and soon after of the other. 'Well,' said the leader, 'the old man will share their fate: so run; he will soon be after us.' They started with fresh vigor, for they had received food from the old man: but very soon the bear came in sight, and again was fast gaining upon them. Again the leader asked the brothers if they could do nothing for their safety. All were silent. The leader, running forward, did as before. 'I dreamed,' he cried, 'that, being in great trouble, an old man helped me who was a manito; we shall soon see his lodge.' Taking courage, they still went on. After going a short distance they saw the lodge of the old manito. They entered immediately and claimed his protection, telling him a manito was after them. The old man, setting meat before them, said: 'Eat! who is a manito? there is no manito but me; there is none whom I fear;' and the earth trembled as the monster advanced. The old man opened the door and saw him coming. He shut it slowly, and said: 'Yes, my grandchildren, you have brought trouble upon me.' Procuring his medicine-sack, he took out his small war-clubs of black stone, and told the young men to run through the other side of the lodge. As he handled the clubs, they became very large, and the old man stepped out just as the bear reached the door. Then striking him with one of the clubs, it broke in pieces; the bear stumbled. Renewing the attempt with the other war-club, that also was broken, but the bear fell senseless. Each blow the old man gave him sounded like a clap of thunder, and the howls of the bear ran along till they filled the heavens.

The young men had now run some distance, when they looked back. They could see that the bear was recovering from the blows. First he moved his paws, and soon they saw him rise on his feet. The old man shared the fate of the first, for they now heard his cries as he was torn in pieces. Again the monster was in pursuit, and fast overtaking them. Not yet discouraged, the young men kept on their way; but the bear was now so close, that the leader once more applied to his brothers, but they could do nothing. 'Well,' said he, 'my dreams will soon be exhausted; after this I have but one more.' He advanced, invoking his guardian spirit to aid him. 'Once,' said he, 'I dreamed that, being sorely pressed, I came to a large lake, on the shore of which was a canoe, partly out of water, having ten paddles all in readiness. Do not fear,' he cried, 'we shall soon get it.' And so it was, even as he had said. Coming to the lake, they saw the canoe with ten paddles, and immediately they embarked. Scarcely had they reached the center of the lake, when they saw the bear arrive at its borders. Lifting himself on his hind legs, he looked all around. Then he waded into the water; then losing his footing he turned back, and commenced making the circuit of the lake. Meantime the party remained stationary in the center to watch his movements. He traveled all around, till at last he came to the place from whence he started. Then he commenced drinking up the water, and they saw the current fast setting in towards his open mouth. The leader encouraged them to paddle hard for the opposite shore. When only a short distance from land, the current had increased so much, that they were drawn back by it, and all their efforts to reach it were in vain.

Then the leader again spoke, telling them to meet their fates manfully. 'Now is the time, Mudjikewis,' said he, 'to show your prowess. Take courage and sit at the bow of the canoe; and when it approaches his mouth, try what effect your club will have on his head.' He obeyed, and stood ready to give the blow; while the leader, who steered, directed the canoe for the open mouth of the monster.

Rapidly advancing, they were just about to enter his mouth, when Mudjikewis struck him a tremendous blow on the head, and gave the SAW- SAW-QUAN. The bear's limbs doubled under him, and he fell, stunned by the blow. But before Mudjikewis could renew it, the monster disgorged all the water he had drank, with a force which sent the canoe with great velocity to the opposite shore. Instantly leaving the canoe, again they fled, and on they went till they were completely exhausted. The earth again shook, and soon they saw the monster hard after them. Their spirits drooped, and they felt discouraged. The leader exerted himself, by actions and words, to cheer them up; and once more he asked them if they thought of nothing, or could do nothing for their rescue; and, as before, all were silent. 'Then,' he said, 'this is the last time I can apply to my guardian spirit. Now, if we do not succeed, our fates are decided.' He ran forward, invoking his spirit with great earnestness, and gave the yell. 'We shall soon arrive,' said he to his brothers, 'at the place where my last guardian spirit dwells. In him I place great confidence. Do not, do not be afraid, or your limbs will be fear-bound. We shall soon reach his lodge. Run, run,' he cried.

Returning now to Iamo, he had passed all the time in the same condition we had left him, the head directing his sister, in order to procure food, where to place the magic arrows, and speaking at long intervals. One day the sister saw the eyes of the head brighten, as if with pleasure. At last it spoke. 'Oh, sister,' it said, 'in what a pitiful situation you have been the cause of placing me! Soon, very soon, a party of young men will arrive and apply to me for aid; but alas! How can I give what I would have done with so much pleasure? Nevertheless, take two arrows, and place them where you have been in the habit of placing the others, and have meat prepared and cooked before they arrive. When you hear them coming and calling on my name, go out and say, "Alas! it is long ago that an accident befell him. I was the cause of it." If they still come near, ask them in, and set meat before them. And now you must follow my directions strictly. When the bear is near, go out and meet him. You will take my medicine-sack, bows and arrows, and my head. You must then untie the sack, and spread out before you my paints of all colors, my war-eagle feathers, my tufts of dried hair, and whatever else it contains. As the bear approaches, you will take all these articles, one by one, and say to him, "This is my deceased brother's paint," and so on with all the other articles, throwing each of them as far as you can. The virtues contained in them will cause him to totter; and, to complete his destruction, you will take my head, and that too you will cast as far off as you can, crying aloud, "See, this is my deceased brother's head." He will then fall senseless. By this time the young men will have eaten, and you will call them to your assistance. You must then cut the carcass into pieces, yes, into small pieces, and scatter them to the four winds; for, unless you do this, he will again revive.' She promised that all should be done as he said. She had only time to prepare the meat, when the voice of the leader was heard calling upon Iamo for aid. The woman went out and said as her brother had directed. But the war party being closely pursued, came up to the lodge. She invited them in, and placed the meat before them. While they were eating, they heard the bear approaching. Untying the medicine-sack and taking the head, she had all in readiness for his approach. When he came up she did as she had been told; and, before she had expended the paints and feathers, the bear began to totter, but, still advancing, came close to the woman. Saying as she was commanded, she then took the head, and cast it as far from her as she could. As it rolled along the ground, the blood, excited by the feelings of the head in this terrible scene,

gushed from the nose and mouth. The bear, tottering, soon fell with a tremendous noise. Then she cried for help, and the young men came rushing out, having partially regained their strength and spirits.

Mudjikewis, stepping up, gave a yell and struck him a blow upon the head. This he repeated, till it seemed like a mass of brains, while the others, as quick as possible, cut him into very small pieces, which they then scattered in every direction. While thus employed, happening to look around where they had thrown the meat, wonderful to behold, they saw starting up and turning off in every direction small black bears, such as are seen at the present day. The country was soon overspread with these black animals. And it was from this monster that the present race of bears derived their origin.

Having thus overcome their pursuer, they returned to the lodge. In the meantime, the woman, gathering the implements she had used, and the head, placed them again in the sack. But the head did not speak again, probably from its great exertion to overcome the monster.

Having spent so much time and traversed so vast a country in their flight, the young men gave up the idea of ever returning to their own country, and game being plenty, they determined to remain where they now were. One day they moved off some distance from the lodge for the purpose of hunting, having left the wampum with the woman. They were very successful, and amused themselves, as all young men do when alone, by talking and jesting with each other. One of them spoke and said, 'We have all this sport to ourselves; let us go and ask our sister if she will not let us bring the head to this place, as it is still alive. It may be pleased to hear us talk, and be in our company. In the meantime take food to our sister.' They went and requested the head. She told them to take it, and they took it to their hunting-grounds, and tried to amuse it, but only at times did they see its eyes beam with pleasure. One day, while busy in their encampment, they were unexpectedly attacked by unknown Indians. The skirmish was long contested and bloody; many of their foes were slain, but still they were thirty to one. The young men fought desperately till they were all killed. The attacking party then retreated to a height of ground, to muster their men, and to count the number of missing and slain. One of their young men had stayed away, and, in endeavoring to overtake them, came to the place where the head was hung up. Seeing that alone retain animation, he eyed it for some time with fear and surprise. However, he took it down and opened the sack, and was much pleased to see the beautiful feathers, one of which he placed on his head.

Starting off, it waved gracefully over him till he reached his party, when he threw down the head and sack, and told them how he had found it, and that the sack was full of paints and feathers. They all looked at the head and made sport of it. Numbers of the young men took the paint and painted themselves, and one of the party took the head by the hair and said—

'Look, you ugly thing, and see your paints on the faces of warriors.'

But the feathers were so beautiful, that numbers of them also placed them on their heads. Then again they used all kinds of indignity to the head, for which they were in turn repaid by the death of those who had used the feathers. Then the chief commanded them to throw away all except the head. 'We will see,' said he, 'when we get home, what we can do with it. We will try to make it shut its eyes.'

When they reached their homes they took it to the council-lodge, and hung it up before the fire, fastening it with raw hide soaked, which would shrink and become tightened by the action of the fire. 'We will then see,' they said, 'if we cannot make it shut its eyes.'

Meantime, for several days, the sister had been waiting for the young men to bring back the head; till, at last, getting impatient, she went in search of it. The young men she found lying within short distances of each other, dead, and covered with wounds. Various other bodies lay scattered in different directions around them. She searched for the head and sack, but they were nowhere to be found. She raised her voice and wept, and blackened her face. Then she walked in different directions, till she came to the place from whence the head had been taken. Then she found the magic bow and arrows, where the young men, ignorant of their qualities, had left them. She thought to herself that she would find her brother's head, and came to a piece of rising ground, and there saw some of his paints and feathers. These she carefully put up, and hung upon the branch of a tree till her return.

At dusk she arrived at the first lodge of a very extensive village. Here she used a charm, common among Indians when they wish to meet with a kind reception. On applying to the old man and woman of the lodge, she was kindly received. She made known her errand. The old man promised to aid her, and told her the head was hung up before the council-fire, and that the chiefs of the village, with their young men, kept watch over it continually. The former are considered as manitoes. She said she only wished to see it, and would be satisfied if she could only get to the door of the lodge. She knew she had not sufficient power to take it by force. 'Come with me,' said the Indian, 'I will take you there.' They went, and they took their seats near the door. The council-lodge was filled with warriors, amusing themselves with games, and constantly keeping up a fire to smoke the head, as they said, to make dry meat. They saw the head move, and not knowing what to make of it, one spoke and said: 'Ha! ha! It is beginning to feel the effects of the smoke.' The sister looked up from the door, and her eyes met those of her brother, and tears rolled down the cheeks of the head. 'Well,' said the chief, 'I thought we would make you do something at last. Look! look at it—shedding tears,' said he to those around him; and they all laughed and passed their jokes upon it. The chief, looking around, and observing the woman, after some time said to the man who came with her: 'Who have you got there? I have never seen that woman before in our village.' 'Yes,' replied the man, 'you have seen her; she is a relation of mine, and seldom goes out. She stays at my lodge, and asked me to allow her to come with me to this place.' In the center of the lodge sat one of those young men who are always forward, and fond of boasting and displaying themselves before others. 'Why,' said he, 'I have seen her often, and it is to this lodge I go almost every night to court her.' All the others laughed and continued their games. The young man did not know he was telling a lie to the woman's advantage, who by that means escaped.

She returned to the man's lodge, and immediately set out for her own country. Coming to the spot where the bodies of her adopted brothers lay, she placed them together, their feet toward the east. Then taking an ax which she had, she cast it up into the air, crying out, 'Brothers, get up from under it, or it will fall on you.' This she repeated three times, and the third time the brothers all arose and stood on their feet.

Mudjikewis commenced rubbing his eyes and stretching

himself. 'Why,' said he, 'I have overslept myself.' 'No, indeed,' said one of the others, 'do you not know we were all killed, and that it is our sister who has brought us to life?' The young men took the bodies of their enemies and burned them. Soon after, the woman went to procure wives for them, in a distant country, they knew not where; but she returned with ten young women, which she gave to the ten young men, beginning with the eldest. Mudjikewis stepped to and fro, uneasy lest he should not get the one he liked. But he was not disappointed, for she fell to his lot. And they were well matched, for she was a female magician. They then all moved into a very large lodge, and their sister told them that the women must now take turns in going to her brother's head every night, trying to untie it. They all said they would do so with pleasure. The eldest made the first attempt, and with a rushing noise she fled through the air.

Toward daylight she returned. She had been unsuccessful, as she succeeded in untying only one of the knots. All took their turns regularly, and each one succeeded in untying only one knot each time. But when the youngest went, she commenced the work as soon as she reached the lodge; although it had always been occupied, still the Indians never could see any one. For ten nights now, the smoke had not ascended, but filled the lodge and drove them out. This last night they were all driven out, and the young woman carried off the head.

The young people and the sister heard the young woman coming high through the air, and they heard her saying: 'Prepare the body of our brother.' And as soon as they heard it, they went to a small lodge where the black body of Iamo lay. His sister commenced cutting the neck part, from which the neck had been severed. She cut so deep as to cause it to bleed; and the others who were present, by rubbing the body and applying medicines, expelled the blackness. In the meantime, the one who brought it, by cutting the neck of the head, caused that also to bleed.

As soon as she arrived, they placed that close to the body, and, by aid of medicines and various other means, succeeded in restoring Iamo to all his former beauty and manliness. All rejoiced in the happy termination of their troubles, and they had spent some time joyfully together, when Iamo said: 'Now I will divide the wampum,' and getting the belt which contained it, he commenced with the eldest, giving it in equal portions. But the youngest got the most splendid and beautiful, as the bottom of the belt held the richest and rarest.

They were told that, since they had all once died, and were restored to life, they were no longer mortal, but spirits, and they were assigned different stations in the invisible world. Only Mudjikewis's place was, however, named. He was to direct the west wind, hence generally called Kebeyun, there to remain for ever. They were commanded, as they had it in their power, to do good to the inhabitants of the earth, and, forgetting their sufferings in procuring the wampum, to give all things with a liberal hand. And they were also commanded that it should also be held by them sacred; those grains or shells of the pale hue to be emblematic of peace, while those of the darker hue would lead to evil and war.

The spirits then, amid songs and shouts, took their flight to their respective abodes on high; while Iamo, with his sister Iamoqua, descended into the depths below.

The Prince and The Pauper
by Mark Twain

Hugh Latimer, Bishop of Worcester, to Lord Cromwell, on the birth of the Prince of Wales (afterward Edward VI.). From the National Manuscripts preserved by the British Government.

Ryght honorable, Salutem in Christo Jesu, and Syr here ys no lesse joynge and rejossynge in thes partees for the byrth of our prynce, hoom we hungurde for so longe, then ther was (I trow), inter vicinos att the byrth of S. J. Baptyste, as thys berer, Master Erance, can telle you. Gode gyffe us alle grace, to yelde dew thankes to our Lorde Gode, Gode of Inglonde, for verely He hathe shoyd Hym selff Gode of Inglonde, or rather an Inglyssh Gode, yf we consydyr and pondyr welle alle Hys procedynges with us from tyme to tyme. He hath over cumme alle our yllnesse with Hys excedynge goodnesse, so that we are now moor then compellyd to serve Hym, seke Hys glory, promott Hys wurde, yf the Devylle of alle Devylles be natt in us. We have now the stooppe of vayne trustes ande the stey of vayne expectations; lett us alle pray for hys preservatione. Ande I for my partt wylle wyssh that hys Grace allways have, and evyn now from the begynynge, Governares, Instructores and offyceres of ryght jugmente, ne optimum ingenium non optima educatione deprevetur.

Butt whatt a grett fowlle am I! So, whatt devotione shoyth many tymys butt lytelle dyscretione! Ande thus the Gode of Inglonde be ever with you in alle your procedynges.

The 19 of October.
Youres, H. L. B. of Wurcestere, now att Hartlebury.

Yf you wolde excytt thys berere to be moore hartye ayen the abuse of ymagry or mor forwarde to promotte the veryte, ytt myght doo goode. Natt that ytt came of me, butt of your selffe, etc.

(Addressed) To the Ryght Honorable Loorde P. Sealle hys synguler gode Lorde.

To those good-mannered and agreeable children Susie and Clara Clemens this book is affectionately inscribed by their father.

I will set down a tale as it was told to me by one who had it of his father, which latter had it of HIS father, this last having in like manner had it of HIS father—and so on, back and still back, three hundred years and more, the fathers transmitting it to the sons and so preserving it. It may be history, it may be only a legend, a tradition. It may have happened, it may not have happened: but it COULD have happened. It may be that the wise and the learned believed it in the old days; it may be that only the unlearned and the simple loved it and credited it.

The quality of mercy . . . is twice bless'd; It blesseth him that gives, and him that takes; 'Tis mightiest in the mightiest: it becomes The thron-ed monarch better than his crown'. Merchant of Venice.

Chapter I. The birth of the Prince and the Pauper.

In the ancient city of London, on a certain autumn day in the second quarter of the sixteenth century, a boy was born to a poor family of the name of Canty, who did not want him. On the same day another English child was born to a rich family of the name of Tudor, who did want him. All England wanted him too. England had so longed for him, and hoped for him, and prayed God for him, that, now that he was really come, the people went nearly mad for joy. Mere acquaintances hugged and kissed each other and cried. Everybody took a holiday, and high and low, rich and poor, feasted and danced and sang, and got very mellow; and they kept this up for days and nights together. By day, London was a sight to see, with gay banners waving from every balcony and housetop, and splendid pageants marching along. By night, it was again a sight to see, with its great bonfires at every corner, and its troops of revellers making merry around them. There was no talk in all England but of the new baby, Edward Tudor, Prince of Wales, who lay lapped in silks and satins, unconscious of all this fuss, and not knowing that great lords and ladies were tending him and watching over him—and not caring, either. But there was no talk about the other baby, Tom Canty, lapped in his poor rags, except among the family of paupers whom he had just come to trouble with his presence.

Chapter II. Tom's early life.

Let us skip a number of years.

London was fifteen hundred years old, and was a great town—for that day. It had a hundred thousand inhabitants—some think double as many. The streets were very narrow, and crooked, and dirty, especially in the part where Tom Canty lived, which was not far from London Bridge. The houses were of wood, with the second story projecting over the first, and the third sticking its elbows out beyond the second. The higher the houses grew, the broader they grew. They were skeletons of strong criss-cross beams, with solid material between, coated with plaster. The beams were painted red or blue or black, according to the owner's taste, and this gave the houses a very picturesque look. The windows were small, glazed with little diamond-shaped panes, and they opened outward, on hinges, like doors.

The house which Tom's father lived in was up a foul little pocket called Offal Court, out of Pudding Lane. It was small, decayed, and rickety, but it was packed full of wretchedly poor families. Canty's tribe occupied a room on the third floor. The mother and father had a sort of bedstead in the corner; but Tom, his grandmother, and his two sisters, Bet and Nan, were not restricted—they had all the floor to themselves, and might sleep where they chose. There were the remains of a blanket or two, and some bundles of ancient and dirty straw, but these could not rightly be called beds, for they were not organised; they were kicked into a general pile, mornings, and selections made from the mass at night, for service.

Bet and Nan were fifteen years old—twins. They were good-hearted girls, unclean, clothed in rags, and profoundly ignorant. Their mother was like them. But the father and the grandmother were a couple of fiends. They got drunk whenever they could; then they fought each other or anybody else who came in the way; they cursed and swore always, drunk or sober; John Canty was a thief, and his mother a beggar. They made beggars of the children, but failed to make thieves of them. Among, but not of, the dreadful rabble that inhabited the house, was a good old priest whom the King had turned out of house and home with a pension of a few farthings, and he used to get the children aside and teach them right ways secretly. Father Andrew also taught Tom a little Latin, and how to read and write; and would have done the same with the girls, but they were afraid of the jeers of their friends, who could not have endured such a queer accomplishment in them.

All Offal Court was just such another hive as Canty's house. Drunkenness, riot and brawling were the order, there, every night and nearly all night long. Broken heads were as common as hunger in that place. Yet little Tom was not unhappy. He had a hard time of it, but did not know it. It was the sort of time that all the Offal Court boys had, therefore he supposed it was the correct and comfortable thing. When he came home empty-handed at night, he knew his father would curse him and thrash him first, and that when he was done the awful grandmother would do it all over again and improve on it; and that away in the night his starving mother would slip to him stealthily with any miserable scrap or crust she had been able to save for him by going hungry herself, notwithstanding she was often caught in that sort of treason and soundly beaten for it by her husband.

No, Tom's life went along well enough, especially in summer. He only begged just enough to save himself, for the laws against mendicancy were stringent, and the penalties heavy; so he put in a good deal of his time listening to good Father Andrew's charming old tales and legends about giants and fairies, dwarfs and genii, and enchanted castles, and gorgeous kings and princes. His head grew to be full of these wonderful things, and many a night as he lay in the dark on his scant and offensive straw, tired, hungry, and smarting from a thrashing, he unleashed his imagination and soon forgot his aches and pains in delicious picturings to himself of the charmed life of a petted prince in a regal palace. One desire came in time to haunt him day and night: it was to see a real prince, with his own eyes. He spoke of it once to some of his Offal Court comrades; but they jeered him and scoffed him so unmercifully that he was glad to keep his dream to himself after that.

He often read the priest's old books and got him to explain and enlarge upon them. His dreamings and readings worked certain changes in him, by-and-by. His dream-people were so fine that he grew to lament his shabby clothing and his dirt, and to wish to be clean and better clad. He went on playing in the mud just the same, and enjoying it, too; but, instead of splashing around in the Thames solely for the fun of it, he began to find an added value in it because of the washings and cleansings it afforded.

Tom could always find something going on around the Maypole in Cheapside, and at the fairs; and now and then he and the rest of London had a chance to see a military parade when some famous unfortunate was carried prisoner to the Tower, by land or boat. One summer's day he saw poor Anne Askew and three men burned at the stake in Smithfield, and heard an ex-Bishop preach a sermon to them which did not interest him. Yes, Tom's life was varied and pleasant enough, on the whole.

By-and-by Tom's reading and dreaming about princely life wrought such a strong effect upon him that he began to ACT the prince, unconsciously. His speech and manners became curiously ceremonious and courtly, to the vast admiration and amusement of his intimates. But Tom's influence among these young people began to grow now, day by day; and in time he came to be looked up to, by them, with a sort of wondering awe, as a superior being. He seemed to know so much! and he could do and say such marvellous things! and withal, he was so deep and wise! Tom's remarks, and Tom's performances, were reported by the boys to their elders; and these, also, presently began to discuss Tom Canty, and to regard him as a most gifted and extraordinary creature. Full-grown people brought their perplexities to Tom for solution, and were often astonished at the wit and wisdom of his decisions. In fact he was become a hero to all who knew him except his own family—these, only, saw nothing in him.

Privately, after a while, Tom organised a royal court! He was the prince; his special comrades were guards, chamberlains, equerries, lords and ladies in waiting, and the royal family. Daily the mock prince was received with elaborate ceremonials borrowed by Tom from his romantic readings; daily the great affairs of the mimic kingdom were discussed in the royal council, and daily his mimic highness issued decrees to his imaginary armies, navies, and viceroyalties.

After which, he would go forth in his rags and beg a few farthings, eat his poor crust, take his customary cuffs and abuse, and then stretch himself upon his handful of foul straw, and resume his empty grandeurs in his dreams.

And still his desire to look just once upon a real prince, in the flesh, grew upon him, day by day, and week by week, until at last it absorbed all other desires, and became the one passion of his life.

One January day, on his usual begging tour, he tramped despondently up and down the region round about Mincing Lane and Little East Cheap, hour after hour, bare-footed and cold, looking in at cook-shop windows and longing for the dreadful pork-pies and other deadly inventions displayed there—for to him these were dainties fit for the angels; that is, judging by the smell, they were—for it had never been his good luck to own and eat one. There was a cold drizzle of rain; the atmosphere was murky; it was a melancholy day. At night Tom reached home so wet and tired and hungry that it was not possible for his father and grandmother to observe his forlorn condition and not be moved—after their fashion; wherefore they gave him a brisk cuffing at once and sent him to bed. For a long time his pain and hunger, and the swearing and fighting going on in the building, kept him awake; but at last his thoughts drifted away to far, romantic lands, and he fell asleep in the company of jewelled and gilded princelings who live in vast palaces, and had servants salaaming before them or flying to execute their orders. And then, as usual, he dreamed that HE was a princeling himself.

All night long the glories of his royal estate shone upon him; he moved among great lords and ladies, in a blaze of light, breathing perfumes, drinking in delicious music, and answering the reverent obeisances of the glittering throng as it parted to make way for him, with here a smile, and there a nod of his princely head.

And when he awoke in the morning and looked upon the wretchedness about him, his dream had had its usual effect—it had intensified the sordidness of his surroundings a thousandfold. Then came bitterness, and heart-break, and tears.

Chapter III. Tom's meeting with the Prince.

Tom got up hungry, and sauntered hungry away, but with his thoughts busy with the shadowy splendours of his night's dreams. He wandered here and there in the city, hardly noticing where he was going, or what was happening around him. People jostled him, and some gave him rough speech; but it was all lost on the musing boy. By-and-by he found himself at Temple Bar, the farthest from home he had ever travelled in that direction. He stopped and considered a moment, then fell into his imaginings again, and passed on outside the walls of London. The Strand had ceased to be a country-road then, and regarded itself as a street, but by a strained construction; for, though there was a tolerably compact row of houses on one side of it, there were only some scattered great buildings on the other, these being palaces of rich nobles, with ample and beautiful grounds stretching to the river—grounds that are now closely packed with grim acres of brick and stone.

Tom discovered Charing Village presently, and rested himself at the beautiful cross built there by a bereaved king of earlier days; then idled down a quiet, lovely road, past the great cardinal's stately palace, toward a far more mighty and majestic palace beyond—Westminster. Tom stared in glad wonder at the vast pile of masonry, the wide-spreading wings, the frowning bastions and turrets, the huge stone gateway, with its gilded bars and its magnificent array of colossal granite lions, and other the signs and symbols of English royalty. Was the desire of his soul to be satisfied at last? Here, indeed, was a king's palace. Might he not hope to see a prince now—a prince of flesh and blood, if Heaven were willing?

At each side of the gilded gate stood a living statue—that is to say, an erect and stately and motionless man-at-arms, clad from head to heel in shining steel armour. At a respectful distance were many country folk, and people from the city, waiting for any chance glimpse of royalty that might offer. Splendid carriages, with splendid people in them and splendid servants outside, were arriving and departing by several other noble gateways that pierced the royal enclosure.

Poor little Tom, in his rags, approached, and was moving slowly and timidly past the sentinels, with a beating heart and a rising hope, when all at once he caught sight through the golden bars of a spectacle that almost made him shout for joy. Within was a comely boy, tanned and brown with sturdy outdoor sports and exercises, whose clothing was all of lovely silks and satins, shining with jewels; at his hip a little jewelled sword and dagger; dainty buskins on his feet, with red heels; and on his head a jaunty crimson cap, with drooping plumes fastened with a great sparkling gem. Several gorgeous gentlemen stood near—his servants, without a doubt. Oh! he was a prince—a prince, a living prince, a real prince—without the shadow of a question; and the prayer of the pauper-boy's heart was answered at last.

Tom's breath came quick and short with excitement, and his eyes grew big with wonder and delight. Everything gave way in his mind instantly to one desire: that was to get close to the prince, and have a good, devouring look at him. Before he knew what he was about, he had his face against the gate-bars. The next instant one of the soldiers snatched him rudely away, and sent him spinning among the gaping crowd of country gawks and London idlers. The soldier said,—

"Mind thy manners, thou young beggar!"

The crowd jeered and laughed; but the young prince sprang to the gate with his face flushed, and his eyes flashing with indignation, and cried out,—

"How dar'st thou use a poor lad like that? How dar'st thou use the King my father's meanest subject so? Open the gates, and let him in!"

You should have seen that fickle crowd snatch off their hats then. You should have heard them cheer, and shout, "Long live the Prince of Wales!"

The soldiers presented arms with their halberds, opened the gates, and presented again as the little Prince of Poverty passed in, in his fluttering rags, to join hands with the Prince of Limitless Plenty.

Edward Tudor said—

"Thou lookest tired and hungry: thou'st been treated ill. Come with me."

Half a dozen attendants sprang forward to—I don't know what; interfere, no doubt. But they were waved aside with a right royal gesture, and they stopped stock still where they were, like so many statues. Edward took Tom to a rich apartment in the palace, which he called his cabinet. By his command a repast was brought such as Tom had never encountered before except in books. The prince, with princely delicacy and breeding, sent away the servants, so that his humble guest might not be embarrassed by their critical presence; then he sat near by, and asked questions while Tom ate.

"What is thy name, lad?"

"Tom Canty, an' it please thee, sir."

"'Tis an odd one. Where dost live?"

"In the city, please thee, sir. Offal Court, out of Pudding Lane."

"Offal Court! Truly 'tis another odd one. Hast parents?"

"Parents have I, sir, and a grand-dam likewise that is but indifferently precious to me, God forgive me if it be offence to say it—also twin sisters, Nan and Bet."

"Then is thy grand-dam not over kind to thee, I take it?"

"Neither to any other is she, so please your worship. She hath a wicked heart, and worketh evil all her days."

"Doth she mistreat thee?"

"There be times that she stayeth her hand, being asleep or overcome with drink; but when she hath her judgment clear again, she maketh it up to me with goodly beatings."

A fierce look came into the little prince's eyes, and he cried out—

"What! Beatings?"

"Oh, indeed, yes, please you, sir."

"BEATINGS!—and thou so frail and little. Hark ye: before the night come, she shall hie her to the Tower. The King my father"—

"In sooth, you forget, sir, her low degree. The Tower is for the great alone."

"True, indeed. I had not thought of that. I will consider of her punishment. Is thy father kind to thee?"

"Not more than Gammer Canty, sir."

"Fathers be alike, mayhap. Mine hath not a doll's temper. He smiteth with a heavy hand, yet spareth me: he spareth me not always with his tongue, though, sooth to say. How doth thy mother use thee?"

"She is good, sir, and giveth me neither sorrow nor pain of any sort. And Nan and Bet are like to her in this."

"How old be these?"

"Fifteen, an' it please you, sir."

"The Lady Elizabeth, my sister, is fourteen, and the Lady Jane Grey, my cousin, is of mine own age, and comely and gracious withal; but my sister the Lady Mary, with her gloomy mien and—Look you: do thy sisters forbid their servants to smile, lest the sin destroy their souls?"

"They? Oh, dost think, sir, that THEY have servants?"

The little prince contemplated the little pauper gravely a moment, then said—

"And prithee, why not? Who helpeth them undress at night? Who attireth them when they rise?"

"None, sir. Would'st have them take off their garment, and sleep without—like the beasts?"

"Their garment! Have they but one?"

"Ah, good your worship, what would they do with more? Truly they have not two bodies each."

"It is a quaint and marvellous thought! Thy pardon, I had not meant to laugh. But thy good Nan and thy Bet shall have raiment and lackeys enow, and that soon, too: my cofferer shall look to it. No, thank me not; 'tis nothing. Thou speakest well; thou hast an easy grace in it. Art learned?"

"I know not if I am or not, sir. The good priest that is called Father Andrew taught me, of his kindness, from his books."

"Know'st thou the Latin?"

"But scantly, sir, I doubt."

"Learn it, lad: 'tis hard only at first. The Greek is harder; but neither these nor any tongues else, I think, are hard to the Lady Elizabeth and my cousin. Thou should'st hear those damsels at it! But tell me of thy Offal Court. Hast thou a pleasant life there?"

"In truth, yes, so please you, sir, save when one is hungry. There be Punch-and-Judy shows, and monkeys—oh such antic creatures! and so bravely dressed!—and there be plays wherein they that play do shout and fight till all are slain, and 'tis so fine to see, and costeth but a farthing—albeit 'tis main hard to get the farthing, please your worship."

"Tell me more."

"We lads of Offal Court do strive against each other with the cudgel, like to the fashion of the 'prentices, sometimes."

The prince's eyes flashed. Said he—

"Marry, that would not I mislike. Tell me more."

"We strive in races, sir, to see who of us shall be fleetest."

"That would I like also. Speak on."

"In summer, sir, we wade and swim in the canals and in the river, and each doth duck his neighbour, and splatter him with water, and dive and shout and tumble and—"

"'Twould be worth my father's kingdom but to enjoy it once! Prithee go on."

"We dance and sing about the Maypole in Cheapside; we play in the sand, each covering his neighbour up; and times we make mud pastry—oh the lovely mud, it hath not its like for delightfulness in all the world!—we do fairly wallow in the mud, sir, saving your worship's presence."

"Oh, prithee, say no more, 'tis glorious! If that I could but clothe me in raiment like to thine, and strip my feet, and revel in the mud once, just once, with none to rebuke me or forbid, meseemeth I could forego the crown!"

"And if that I could clothe me once, sweet sir, as thou art clad—just once—"

"Oho, would'st like it? Then so shall it be. Doff thy rags, and don these splendours, lad! It is a brief happiness, but will be not less keen for that. We will have it while we may, and change again before any come to molest."

A few minutes later the little Prince of Wales was garlanded with Tom's fluttering odds and ends, and the little Prince of Pauperdom was tricked out in the gaudy plumage of royalty. The two went and stood side by side before a great mirror, and lo, a miracle: there did not seem to have been any change made! They stared at each other, then at the glass, then at each other again. At last the puzzled princeling said—

"What dost thou make of this?"

"Ah, good your worship, require me not to answer. It is not meet that one of my degree should utter the thing."

"Then will I utter it. Thou hast the same hair, the same eyes, the same voice and manner, the same form and stature, the same face and countenance that I bear. Fared we forth naked, there is none could say which was you, and which the Prince of Wales. And, now that I am clothed as thou wert clothed, it seemeth I should be able the more nearly to feel as thou didst when the brute soldier—Hark ye, is not this a bruise upon your hand?"

"Yes; but it is a slight thing, and your worship knoweth that the poor man-at-arms—"

"Peace! It was a shameful thing and a cruel!" cried the little prince, stamping his bare foot. "If the King—Stir not a step till I come again! It is a command!"

In a moment he had snatched up and put away an article of national importance that lay upon a table, and was out at the door and flying through the palace grounds in his bannered rags, with a hot face and glowing eyes. As soon as he reached the great gate, he seized the bars, and tried to shake them, shouting—

"Open! Unbar the gates!"

The soldier that had maltreated Tom obeyed promptly; and as the prince burst through the portal, half-smothered with royal wrath, the soldier fetched him a sounding box on the ear that sent him whirling to the roadway, and said—

"Take that, thou beggar's spawn, for what thou got'st me from his Highness!"

The crowd roared with laughter. The prince picked himself out of the mud, and made fiercely at the sentry, shouting—

"I am the Prince of Wales, my person is sacred; and thou shalt hang for laying thy hand upon me!"

The soldier brought his halberd to a present-arms and said mockingly— ʻ

"I salute your gracious Highness." Then angrily—"Be off, thou crazy rubbish!"

Here the jeering crowd closed round the poor little prince, and hustled him far down the road, hooting him, and shouting—

"Way for his Royal Highness! Way for the Prince of Wales!"

Chapter IV. The Prince's troubles begin.

After hours of persistent pursuit and persecution, the little prince was at last deserted by the rabble and left to himself. As long as he had been able to rage against the mob, and threaten it royally, and royally utter commands that were good stuff to laugh at, he was very entertaining; but when weariness finally forced him to be silent, he was no longer of use to his tormentors, and they sought amusement elsewhere. He looked about him, now, but could not recognise the locality. He was within the city of London—that was all he knew. He moved on, aimlessly, and in a little while the houses thinned, and the passers-by were infrequent. He bathed his bleeding feet in the brook which flowed then where Farringdon Street now is; rested a few moments, then passed on, and presently came upon a great space with only a few scattered houses in it, and a prodigious church. He recognised this church. Scaffoldings were about, everywhere, and swarms of workmen; for it was undergoing elaborate repairs. The prince took heart at once—he felt that his troubles were at an end, now. He said to himself, "It is the ancient Grey Friars' Church, which the king my father hath taken from the monks and given for a home for ever for poor and forsaken children, and new-named it Christ's Church. Right gladly will they serve the son of him who hath done so generously by them—and the more that that son is himself as poor and as forlorn as any that be sheltered here this day, or ever shall be."

He was soon in the midst of a crowd of boys who were running, jumping, playing at ball and leap-frog, and otherwise disporting themselves, and right noisily, too. They were all dressed alike, and in the fashion which in that day prevailed among serving-men and 'prentices*—that is to say, each had

---

* Christ's Hospital Costume: It is most reasonable to regard the dress as copied from the costume of the citizens of London of that period, when long blue coats were the common habit of apprentices and serving-men, and yellow stockings were generally worn; the coat fits closely to the body, but has loose sleeves, and beneath is worn a sleeveless yellow under-coat; around the waist is a red leathern girdle; a clerical band around the neck, and a small flat black cap, about the size of a saucer, completes the costume.— Timbs' Curiosities of London.

on the crown of his head a flat black cap about the size of a saucer, which was not useful as a covering, it being of such scanty dimensions, neither was it ornamental; from beneath it the hair fell, unparted, to the middle of the forehead, and was cropped straight around; a clerical band at the neck; a blue gown that fitted closely and hung as low as the knees or lower; full sleeves; a broad red belt; bright yellow stockings, gartered above the knees; low shoes with large metal buckles. It was a sufficiently ugly costume.

The boys stopped their play and flocked about the prince, who said with native dignity—

"Good lads, say to your master that Edward Prince of Wales desireth speech with him."

A great shout went up at this, and one rude fellow said—

"Marry, art thou his grace's messenger, beggar?"

The prince's face flushed with anger, and his ready hand flew to his hip, but there was nothing there. There was a storm of laughter, and one boy said—

"Didst mark that? He fancied he had a sword—belike he is the prince himself."

This sally brought more laughter. Poor Edward drew himself up proudly and said—

"I am the prince; and it ill beseemeth you that feed upon the king my father's bounty to use me so."

This was vastly enjoyed, as the laughter testified. The youth who had first spoken, shouted to his comrades—

"Ho, swine, slaves, pensioners of his grace's princely father, where be your manners? Down on your marrow bones, all of ye, and do reverence to his kingly port and royal rags!"

With boisterous mirth they dropped upon their knees in a body and did mock homage to their prey. The prince spurned the nearest boy with his foot, and said fiercely—

"Take thou that, till the morrow come and I build thee a gibbet!"

Ah, but this was not a joke—this was going beyond fun. The laughter ceased on the instant, and fury took its place. A dozen shouted—

"Hale him forth! To the horse-pond, to the horse-pond! Where be the dogs? Ho, there, Lion! ho, Fangs!"

Then followed such a thing as England had never seen before—the sacred person of the heir to the throne rudely buffeted by plebeian hands, and set upon and torn by dogs.

As night drew to a close that day, the prince found himself far down in the close-built portion of the city. His body was bruised, his hands were bleeding, and his rags were all besmirched with mud. He wandered on and on, and grew more and more bewildered, and so tired and faint he could hardly drag one foot after the other. He had ceased to ask questions of anyone, since they brought him only insult instead of information. He kept muttering to himself, "Offal Court—that is the name; if I can but find it before my strength is wholly spent and I drop, then am I saved—for his people will take me to the palace and prove that I am none of theirs, but the true prince, and I shall have mine own again." And now and then his mind reverted to his treatment by those rude Christ's Hospital boys, and he said, "When I am king, they shall not have bread and shelter only, but also teachings out of books; for a full belly is little worth where the mind is starved, and the heart. I will keep this diligently in my remembrance, that this day's lesson be not lost upon me, and my people suffer thereby; for learning softeneth the heart and breedeth gentleness and charity."*

The lights began to twinkle, it came on to rain, the wind rose, and a raw and gusty night set in. The houseless prince, the homeless heir to the throne of England, still moved on, drifting deeper into the maze of squalid alleys where the swarming hives of poverty and misery were massed together.

Suddenly a great drunken ruffian collared him and said—

"Out to this time of night again, and hast not brought a farthing home, I warrant me! If it be so, an' I do not break all the bones in thy lean body, then am I not John Canty, but some other."

The prince twisted himself loose, unconsciously brushed his profaned shoulder, and eagerly said—

"Oh, art HIS father, truly? Sweet heaven grant it be so—then wilt thou fetch him away and restore me!"

"HIS father? I know not what thou mean'st; I but know I am THY father, as thou shalt soon have cause to—"

"Oh, jest not, palter not, delay not!—I am worn, I am wounded, I can bear no more. Take me to the king my father, and he will make thee rich beyond thy wildest dreams. Believe me, man, believe me!—I speak no lie, but only the truth!—put forth thy hand and save me! I am indeed the Prince of Wales!"

The man stared down, stupefied, upon the lad, then shook his head and muttered—

"Gone stark mad as any Tom o' Bedlam!"—then collared him once more, and said with a coarse laugh and an oath, "But mad or no mad, I and thy Gammer Canty will soon find where the soft places in thy bones lie, or I'm no true man!"

With this he dragged the frantic and struggling prince away, and disappeared up a front court followed by a delighted and noisy swarm of human vermin.

Chapter V. Tom as a patrician.

Tom Canty, left alone in the prince's cabinet, made good use of his opportunity. He turned himself this way and that before the great mirror, admiring his finery; then walked away, imitating the prince's high-bred carriage, and still observing results in the glass. Next he drew the beautiful sword, and bowed, kissing the blade, and laying it across his breast, as he had seen a noble knight do, by way of salute to the lieutenant of the Tower, five or six weeks before, when delivering the great lords of Norfolk and Surrey into his hands for captivity. Tom played with the jewelled dagger that hung upon his thigh; he examined the costly and exquisite ornaments of the room;

* It appears that Christ's Hospital was not originally founded as a SCHOOL; its object was to rescue children from the streets, to shelter, feed, clothe them.—Timbs' Curiosities of London.

he tried each of the sumptuous chairs, and thought how proud he would be if the Offal Court herd could only peep in and see him in his grandeur. He wondered if they would believe the marvellous tale he should tell when he got home, or if they would shake their heads, and say his overtaxed imagination had at last upset his reason.

At the end of half an hour it suddenly occurred to him that the prince was gone a long time; then right away he began to feel lonely; very soon he fell to listening and longing, and ceased to toy with the pretty things about him; he grew uneasy, then restless, then distressed. Suppose some one should come, and catch him in the prince's clothes, and the prince not there to explain. Might they not hang him at once, and inquire into his case afterward? He had heard that the great were prompt about small matters. His fear rose higher and higher; and trembling he softly opened the door to the antechamber, resolved to fly and seek the prince, and, through him, protection and release. Six gorgeous gentlemen-servants and two young pages of high degree, clothed like butterflies, sprang to their feet and bowed low before him. He stepped quickly back and shut the door. He said—

"Oh, they mock at me! They will go and tell. Oh! why came I here to cast away my life?"

He walked up and down the floor, filled with nameless fears, listening, starting at every trifling sound. Presently the door swung open, and a silken page said—

"The Lady Jane Grey."

The door closed and a sweet young girl, richly clad, bounded toward him. But she stopped suddenly, and said in a distressed voice—

"Oh, what aileth thee, my lord?"

Tom's breath was nearly failing him; but he made shift to stammer out—

"Ah, be merciful, thou! In sooth I am no lord, but only poor Tom Canty of Offal Court in the city. Prithee let me see the prince, and he will of his grace restore to me my rags, and let me hence unhurt. Oh, be thou merciful, and save me!"

By this time the boy was on his knees, and supplicating with his eyes and uplifted hands as well as with his tongue. The young girl seemed horror-stricken. She cried out—

"O my lord, on thy knees?—and to ME!"

Then she fled away in fright; and Tom, smitten with despair, sank down, murmuring—

"There is no help, there is no hope. Now will they come and take me."

Whilst he lay there benumbed with terror, dreadful tidings were speeding through the palace. The whisper—for it was whispered always—flew from menial to menial, from lord to lady, down all the long corridors, from story to story, from saloon to saloon, "The prince hath gone mad, the prince hath gone mad!" Soon every saloon, every marble hall, had its groups of glittering lords and ladies, and other groups of dazzling lesser folk, talking earnestly together in whispers, and every face had in it dismay. Presently a splendid official came marching by these groups, making solemn proclamation—

"IN THE NAME OF THE KING!

Let none list to this false and foolish matter, upon pain of death, nor discuss the same, nor carry it abroad. In the name of the King!"

The whisperings ceased as suddenly as if the whisperers had been stricken dumb.

Soon there was a general buzz along the corridors, of "The prince! See, the prince comes!"

Poor Tom came slowly walking past the low-bowing groups, trying to bow in return, and meekly gazing upon his strange surroundings with bewildered and pathetic eyes. Great nobles walked upon each side of him, making him lean upon them, and so steady his steps. Behind him followed the court-physicians and some servants.

Presently Tom found himself in a noble apartment of the palace and heard the door close behind him. Around him stood those who had come with him. Before him, at a little distance, reclined a very large and very fat man, with a wide, pulpy face, and a stern expression. His large head was very grey; and his whiskers, which he wore only around his face, like a frame, were grey also. His clothing was of rich stuff, but old, and slightly frayed in places. One of his swollen legs had a pillow under it, and was wrapped in bandages. There was silence now; and there was no head there but was bent in reverence, except this man's. This stern-countenanced invalid was the dread Henry VIII. He said—and his face grew gentle as he began to speak—

"How now, my lord Edward, my prince? Hast been minded to cozen me, the good King thy father, who loveth thee, and kindly useth thee, with a sorry jest?"

Poor Tom was listening, as well as his dazed faculties would let him, to the beginning of this speech; but when the words 'me, the good King' fell upon his ear, his face blanched, and he dropped as instantly upon his knees as if a shot had brought him there. Lifting up his hands, he exclaimed—

"Thou the KING? Then am I undone indeed!"

This speech seemed to stun the King. His eyes wandered from face to face aimlessly, then rested, bewildered, upon the boy before him. Then he said in a tone of deep disappointment—

"Alack, I had believed the rumour disproportioned to the truth; but I fear me 'tis not so." He breathed a heavy sigh, and said in a gentle voice, "Come to thy father, child: thou art not well."

Tom was assisted to his feet, and approached the Majesty of England, humble and trembling. The King took the frightened face between his hands, and gazed earnestly and lovingly into it awhile, as if seeking some grateful sign of returning reason there, then pressed the curly head against his breast, and patted it tenderly. Presently he said—

"Dost not know thy father, child? Break not mine old heart; say thou know'st me. Thou DOST know me, dost thou not?"

"Yea: thou art my dread lord the King, whom God preserve!"

"True, true—that is well—be comforted, tremble not so; there

is none here would hurt thee; there is none here but loves thee. Thou art better now; thy ill dream passeth—is't not so? Thou wilt not miscall thyself again, as they say thou didst a little while agone?"

"I pray thee of thy grace believe me, I did but speak the truth, most dread lord; for I am the meanest among thy subjects, being a pauper born, and 'tis by a sore mischance and accident I am here, albeit I was therein nothing blameful. I am but young to die, and thou canst save me with one little word. Oh speak it, sir!"

"Die? Talk not so, sweet prince—peace, peace, to thy troubled heart —thou shalt not die!"

Tom dropped upon his knees with a glad cry—

"God requite thy mercy, O my King, and save thee long to bless thy land!" Then springing up, he turned a joyful face toward the two lords in waiting, and exclaimed, "Thou heard'st it! I am not to die: the King hath said it!" There was no movement, save that all bowed with grave respect; but no one spoke. He hesitated, a little confused, then turned timidly toward the King, saying, "I may go now?"

"Go? Surely, if thou desirest. But why not tarry yet a little? Whither would'st go?"

Tom dropped his eyes, and answered humbly—

"Peradventure I mistook; but I did think me free, and so was I moved to seek again the kennel where I was born and bred to misery, yet which harboureth my mother and my sisters, and so is home to me; whereas these pomps and splendours whereunto I am not used—oh, please you, sir, to let me go!"

The King was silent and thoughtful a while, and his face betrayed a growing distress and uneasiness. Presently he said, with something of hope in his voice—

"Perchance he is but mad upon this one strain, and hath his wits unmarred as toucheth other matter. God send it may be so! We will make trial."

Then he asked Tom a question in Latin, and Tom answered him lamely in the same tongue. The lords and doctors manifested their gratification also. The King said—

"'Twas not according to his schooling and ability, but showeth that his mind is but diseased, not stricken fatally. How say you, sir?"

The physician addressed bowed low, and replied—

"It jumpeth with my own conviction, sire, that thou hast divined aright."

The King looked pleased with this encouragement, coming as it did from so excellent authority, and continued with good heart—

"Now mark ye all: we will try him further."

He put a question to Tom in French. Tom stood silent a moment, embarrassed by having so many eyes centred upon him, then said diffidently—

"I have no knowledge of this tongue, so please your majesty."

The King fell back upon his couch. The attendants flew to his assistance; but he put them aside, and said—

"Trouble me not—it is nothing but a scurvy faintness. Raise me! There, 'tis sufficient. Come hither, child; there, rest thy poor troubled head upon thy father's heart, and be at peace. Thou'lt soon be well: 'tis but a passing fantasy. Fear thou not; thou'lt soon be well." Then he turned toward the company: his gentle manner changed, and baleful lightnings began to play from his eyes. He said—

"List ye all! This my son is mad; but it is not permanent. Over-study hath done this, and somewhat too much of confinement. Away with his books and teachers! see ye to it. Pleasure him with sports, beguile him in wholesome ways, so that his health come again." He raised himself higher still, and went on with energy, "He is mad; but he is my son, and England's heir; and, mad or sane, still shall he reign! And hear ye further, and proclaim it: whoso speaketh of this his distemper worketh against the peace and order of these realms, and shall to the gallows! . . . Give me to drink—I burn: this sorrow sappeth my strength. . . . There, take away the cup. . . . Support me. There, that is well. Mad, is he? Were he a thousand times mad, yet is he Prince of Wales, and I the King will confirm it. This very morrow shall he be installed in his princely dignity in due and ancient form. Take instant order for it, my lord Hertford."

One of the nobles knelt at the royal couch, and said—

"The King's majesty knoweth that the Hereditary Great Marshal of England lieth attainted in the Tower. It were not meet that one attainted—"

"Peace! Insult not mine ears with his hated name. Is this man to live for ever? Am I to be baulked of my will? Is the prince to tarry uninstalled, because, forsooth, the realm lacketh an Earl Marshal free of treasonable taint to invest him with his honours? No, by the splendour of God! Warn my Parliament to bring me Norfolk's doom before the sun rise again, else shall they answer for it grievously!"*

Lord Hertford said—

"The King's will is law;" and, rising, returned to his former place.

Gradually the wrath faded out of the old King's face, and he said—

"Kiss me, my prince. There . . . what fearest thou? Am I not thy loving father?"

"Thou art good to me that am unworthy, O mighty and gracious lord: that in truth I know. But—but—it grieveth me to think of him that is to die, and—"

"Ah, 'tis like thee, 'tis like thee! I know thy heart is still the same, even though thy mind hath suffered hurt, for thou wert

---

* The Duke of Norfolk's Condemnation commanded: The King was now approaching fast towards his end; and fearing lest Norfolk should escape him, he sent a message to the Commons, by which he desired them to hasten the Bill, on pretence that Norfolk enjoyed the dignity of Earl Marshal, and it was necessary to appoint another, who might officiate at the ensuing ceremony of installing his son Prince of Wales.—Hume's History of England, vol. iii. p. 307.

ever of a gentle spirit. But this duke standeth between thee and thine honours: I will have another in his stead that shall bring no taint to his great office. Comfort thee, my prince: trouble not thy poor head with this matter."

"But is it not I that speed him hence, my liege? How long might he not live, but for me?"

"Take no thought of him, my prince: he is not worthy. Kiss me once again, and go to thy trifles and amusements; for my malady distresseth me. I am aweary, and would rest. Go with thine uncle Hertford and thy people, and come again when my body is refreshed."

Tom, heavy-hearted, was conducted from the presence, for this last sentence was a death-blow to the hope he had cherished that now he would be set free. Once more he heard the buzz of low voices exclaiming, "The prince, the prince comes!"

His spirits sank lower and lower as he moved between the glittering files of bowing courtiers; for he recognised that he was indeed a captive now, and might remain for ever shut up in this gilded cage, a forlorn and friendless prince, except God in his mercy take pity on him and set him free.

And, turn where he would, he seemed to see floating in the air the severed head and the remembered face of the great Duke of Norfolk, the eyes fixed on him reproachfully.

His old dreams had been so pleasant; but this reality was so dreary!

Chapter VI. Tom receives instructions.

Tom was conducted to the principal apartment of a noble suite, and made to sit down—a thing which he was loth to do, since there were elderly men and men of high degree about him. He begged them to be seated also, but they only bowed their thanks or murmured them, and remained standing. He would have insisted, but his 'uncle' the Earl of Hertford whispered in his ear—

"Prithee, insist not, my lord; it is not meet that they sit in thy presence."

The Lord St. John was announced, and after making obeisance to Tom, he said—

"I come upon the King's errand, concerning a matter which requireth privacy. Will it please your royal highness to dismiss all that attend you here, save my lord the Earl of Hertford?"

Observing that Tom did not seem to know how to proceed, Hertford whispered him to make a sign with his hand, and not trouble himself to speak unless he chose. When the waiting gentlemen had retired, Lord St. John said—

"His majesty commandeth, that for due and weighty reasons of state, the prince's grace shall hide his infirmity in all ways that be within his power, till it be passed and he be as he was before. To wit, that he shall deny to none that he is the true prince, and heir to England's greatness; that he shall uphold his princely dignity, and shall receive, without word or sign of protest, that reverence and observance which unto it do appertain of right and ancient usage; that he shall cease to speak to any of that lowly birth and life his malady hath conjured out of the unwholesome imaginings of o'er-wrought fancy; that he shall strive with diligence to bring unto his memory again those faces which he was wont to know—and where he faileth he shall hold his peace, neither betraying by semblance of surprise or other sign that he hath forgot; that upon occasions of state, whensoever any matter shall perplex him as to the thing he should do or the utterance he should make, he shall show nought of unrest to the curious that look on, but take advice in that matter of the Lord Hertford, or my humble self, which are commanded of the King to be upon this service and close at call, till this commandment be dissolved. Thus saith the King's majesty, who sendeth greeting to your royal highness, and prayeth that God will of His mercy quickly heal you and have you now and ever in His holy keeping."

The Lord St. John made reverence and stood aside. Tom replied resignedly—

"The King hath said it. None may palter with the King's command, or fit it to his ease, where it doth chafe, with deft evasions. The King shall be obeyed."

Lord Hertford said—

"Touching the King's majesty's ordainment concerning books and such like serious matters, it may peradventure please your highness to ease your time with lightsome entertainment, lest you go wearied to the banquet and suffer harm thereby."

Tom's face showed inquiring surprise; and a blush followed when he saw Lord St. John's eyes bent sorrowfully upon him. His lordship said—

"Thy memory still wrongeth thee, and thou hast shown surprise—but suffer it not to trouble thee, for 'tis a matter that will not bide, but depart with thy mending malady. My Lord of Hertford speaketh of the city's banquet which the King's majesty did promise, some two months flown, your highness should attend. Thou recallest it now?"

"It grieves me to confess it had indeed escaped me," said Tom, in a hesitating voice; and blushed again.

At this moment the Lady Elizabeth and the Lady Jane Grey were announced. The two lords exchanged significant glances, and Hertford stepped quickly toward the door. As the young girls passed him, he said in a low voice—

"I pray ye, ladies, seem not to observe his humours, nor show surprise when his memory doth lapse—it will grieve you to note how it doth stick at every trifle."

Meantime Lord St. John was saying in Tom's ear—

"Please you, sir, keep diligently in mind his majesty's desire. Remember all thou canst—SEEM to remember all else. Let them not perceive that thou art much changed from thy wont, for thou knowest how tenderly thy old play-fellows bear thee in their hearts and how 'twould grieve them. Art willing, sir, that I remain?—and thine uncle?"

Tom signified assent with a gesture and a murmured word, for he was already learning, and in his simple heart was resolved to acquit himself as best he might, according to the King's command.

In spite of every precaution, the conversation among the young people became a little embarrassing at times. More than once, in truth, Tom was near to breaking down and confessing

himself unequal to his tremendous part; but the tact of the Princess Elizabeth saved him, or a word from one or the other of the vigilant lords, thrown in apparently by chance, had the same happy effect. Once the little Lady Jane turned to Tom and dismayed him with this question,—

"Hast paid thy duty to the Queen's majesty to-day, my lord?"

Tom hesitated, looked distressed, and was about to stammer out something at hazard, when Lord St. John took the word and answered for him with the easy grace of a courtier accustomed to encounter delicate difficulties and to be ready for them—

"He hath indeed, madam, and she did greatly hearten him, as touching his majesty's condition; is it not so, your highness?"

Tom mumbled something that stood for assent, but felt that he was getting upon dangerous ground. Somewhat later it was mentioned that Tom was to study no more at present, whereupon her little ladyship exclaimed—

"'Tis a pity, 'tis a pity! Thou wert proceeding bravely. But bide thy time in patience: it will not be for long. Thou'lt yet be graced with learning like thy father, and make thy tongue master of as many languages as his, good my prince."

"My father!" cried Tom, off his guard for the moment. "I trow he cannot speak his own so that any but the swine that kennel in the styes may tell his meaning; and as for learning of any sort soever—"

He looked up and encountered a solemn warning in my Lord St. John's eyes.

He stopped, blushed, then continued low and sadly: "Ah, my malady persecuteth me again, and my mind wandereth. I meant the King's grace no irreverence."

"We know it, sir," said the Princess Elizabeth, taking her 'brother's' hand between her two palms, respectfully but caressingly; "trouble not thyself as to that. The fault is none of thine, but thy distemper's."

"Thou'rt a gentle comforter, sweet lady," said Tom, gratefully, "and my heart moveth me to thank thee for't, an' I may be so bold."

Once the giddy little Lady Jane fired a simple Greek phrase at Tom. The Princess Elizabeth's quick eye saw by the serene blankness of the target's front that the shaft was overshot; so she tranquilly delivered a return volley of sounding Greek on Tom's behalf, and then straightway changed the talk to other matters.

Time wore on pleasantly, and likewise smoothly, on the whole. Snags and sandbars grew less and less frequent, and Tom grew more and more at his ease, seeing that all were so lovingly bent upon helping him and overlooking his mistakes. When it came out that the little ladies were to accompany him to the Lord Mayor's banquet in the evening, his heart gave a bound of relief and delight, for he felt that he should not be friendless, now, among that multitude of strangers; whereas, an hour earlier, the idea of their going with him would have been an insupportable terror to him.

Tom's guardian angels, the two lords, had had less comfort in the interview than the other parties to it. They felt much as if they were piloting a great ship through a dangerous channel; they were on the alert constantly, and found their office no child's play. Wherefore, at last, when the ladies' visit was drawing to a close and the Lord Guilford Dudley was announced, they not only felt that their charge had been sufficiently taxed for the present, but also that they themselves were not in the best condition to take their ship back and make their anxious voyage all over again. So they respectfully advised Tom to excuse himself, which he was very glad to do, although a slight shade of disappointment might have been observed upon my Lady Jane's face when she heard the splendid stripling denied admittance.

There was a pause now, a sort of waiting silence which Tom could not understand. He glanced at Lord Hertford, who gave him a sign—but he failed to understand that also. The ready Elizabeth came to the rescue with her usual easy grace. She made reverence and said—

"Have we leave of the prince's grace my brother to go?"

Tom said—

"Indeed your ladyships can have whatsoever of me they will, for the asking; yet would I rather give them any other thing that in my poor power lieth, than leave to take the light and blessing of their presence hence. Give ye good den, and God be with ye!" Then he smiled inwardly at the thought, "'Tis not for nought I have dwelt but among princes in my reading, and taught my tongue some slight trick of their broidered and gracious speech withal!"

When the illustrious maidens were gone, Tom turned wearily to his keepers and said—

"May it please your lordships to grant me leave to go into some corner and rest me?"

Lord Hertford said—

"So please your highness, it is for you to command, it is for us to obey. That thou should'st rest is indeed a needful thing, since thou must journey to the city presently."

He touched a bell, and a page appeared, who was ordered to desire the presence of Sir William Herbert. This gentleman came straightway, and conducted Tom to an inner apartment. Tom's first movement there was to reach for a cup of water; but a silk-and-velvet servitor seized it, dropped upon one knee, and offered it to him on a golden salver.

Next the tired captive sat down and was going to take off his buskins, timidly asking leave with his eye, but another silk-and-velvet discomforter went down upon his knees and took the office from him. He made two or three further efforts to help himself, but being promptly forestalled each time, he finally gave up, with a sigh of resignation and a murmured "Beshrew me, but I marvel they do not require to breathe for me also!" Slippered, and wrapped in a sumptuous robe, he laid himself down at last to rest, but not to sleep, for his head was too full of thoughts and the room too full of people. He could not dismiss the former, so they stayed; he did not know enough to dismiss the latter, so they stayed also, to his vast regret—and theirs.

Tom's departure had left his two noble guardians alone. They mused a while, with much head-shaking and walking the floor, then Lord St. John said—

"Plainly, what dost thou think?"

"Plainly, then, this. The King is near his end; my nephew is mad—mad will mount the throne, and mad remain. God protect England, since she will need it!"

"Verily it promiseth so, indeed. But . . . have you no misgivings as to . . . as to . . ."

The speaker hesitated, and finally stopped. He evidently felt that he was upon delicate ground. Lord Hertford stopped before him, looked into his face with a clear, frank eye, and said—

"Speak on—there is none to hear but me. Misgivings as to what?"

"I am full loth to word the thing that is in my mind, and thou so near to him in blood, my lord. But craving pardon if I do offend, seemeth it not strange that madness could so change his port and manner?—not but that his port and speech are princely still, but that they DIFFER, in one unweighty trifle or another, from what his custom was aforetime. Seemeth it not strange that madness should filch from his memory his father's very lineaments; the customs and observances that are his due from such as be about him; and, leaving him his Latin, strip him of his Greek and French? My lord, be not offended, but ease my mind of its disquiet and receive my grateful thanks. It haunteth me, his saying he was not the prince, and so—"

"Peace, my lord, thou utterest treason! Hast forgot the King's command? Remember I am party to thy crime if I but listen."

St. John paled, and hastened to say—

"I was in fault, I do confess it. Betray me not, grant me this grace out of thy courtesy, and I will neither think nor speak of this thing more. Deal not hardly with me, sir, else am I ruined."

"I am content, my lord. So thou offend not again, here or in the ears of others, it shall be as though thou hadst not spoken. But thou need'st not have misgivings. He is my sister's son; are not his voice, his face, his form, familiar to me from his cradle? Madness can do all the odd conflicting things thou seest in him, and more. Dost not recall how that the old Baron Marley, being mad, forgot the favour of his own countenance that he had known for sixty years, and held it was another's; nay, even claimed he was the son of Mary Magdalene, and that his head was made of Spanish glass; and, sooth to say, he suffered none to touch it, lest by mischance some heedless hand might shiver it? Give thy misgivings easement, good my lord. This is the very prince—I know him well—and soon will be thy king; it may advantage thee to bear this in mind, and more dwell upon it than the other."

After some further talk, in which the Lord St. John covered up his mistake as well as he could by repeated protests that his faith was thoroughly grounded now, and could not be assailed by doubts again, the Lord Hertford relieved his fellow-keeper, and sat down to keep watch and ward alone. He was soon deep in meditation, and evidently the longer he thought, the more he was bothered. By-and-by he began to pace the floor and mutter.

"Tush, he MUST be the prince! Will any he in all the land

maintain there can be two, not of one blood and birth, so marvellously twinned? And even were it so, 'twere yet a stranger miracle that chance should cast the one into the other's place. Nay, 'tis folly, folly, folly!"

Presently he said—

"Now were he impostor and called himself prince, look you THAT would be natural; that would be reasonable. But lived ever an impostor yet, who, being called prince by the king, prince by the court, prince by all, DENIED his dignity and pleaded against his exaltation? NO! By the soul of St. Swithin, no! This is the true prince, gone mad!"

Chapter VII. Tom's first royal dinner.

Somewhat after one in the afternoon, Tom resignedly underwent the ordeal of being dressed for dinner. He found himself as finely clothed as before, but everything different, everything changed, from his ruff to his stockings. He was presently conducted with much state to a spacious and ornate apartment, where a table was already set for one. Its furniture was all of massy gold, and beautified with designs which well-nigh made it priceless, since they were the work of Benvenuto. The room was half-filled with noble servitors. A chaplain said grace, and Tom was about to fall to, for hunger had long been constitutional with him, but was interrupted by my lord the Earl of Berkeley, who fastened a napkin about his neck; for the great post of Diaperers to the Prince of Wales was hereditary in this nobleman's family. Tom's cupbearer was present, and forestalled all his attempts to help himself to wine. The Taster to his highness the Prince of Wales was there also, prepared to taste any suspicious dish upon requirement, and run the risk of being poisoned. He was only an ornamental appendage at this time, and was seldom called upon to exercise his function; but there had been times, not many generations past, when the office of taster had its perils, and was not a grandeur to be desired. Why they did not use a dog or a plumber seems strange; but all the ways of royalty are strange. My Lord d'Arcy, First Groom of the Chamber, was there, to do goodness knows what; but there he was—let that suffice. The Lord Chief Butler was there, and stood behind Tom's chair, overseeing the solemnities, under command of the Lord Great Steward and the Lord Head Cook, who stood near. Tom had three hundred and eighty-four servants beside these; but they were not all in that room, of course, nor the quarter of them; neither was Tom aware yet that they existed.

All those that were present had been well drilled within the hour to remember that the prince was temporarily out of his head, and to be careful to show no surprise at his vagaries. These 'vagaries' were soon on exhibition before them; but they only moved their compassion and their sorrow, not their mirth. It was a heavy affliction to them to see the beloved prince so stricken.

Poor Tom ate with his fingers mainly; but no one smiled at it, or even seemed to observe it. He inspected his napkin curiously, and with deep interest, for it was of a very dainty and beautiful fabric, then said with simplicity—

"Prithee, take it away, lest in mine unheedfulness it be soiled."

The Hereditary Diaperer took it away with reverent manner, and without word or protest of any sort.

Tom examined the turnips and the lettuce with interest, and asked what they were, and if they were to be eaten; for it was only recently that men had begun to raise these things in England in place of importing them as luxuries from Holland.* His question was answered with grave respect, and no surprise manifested. When he had finished his dessert, he filled his pockets with nuts; but nobody appeared to be aware of it, or disturbed by it. But the next moment he was himself disturbed by it, and showed discomposure; for this was the only service he had been permitted to do with his own hands during the meal, and he did not doubt that he had done a most improper and unprincely thing. At that moment the muscles of his nose began to twitch, and the end of that organ to lift and wrinkle. This continued, and Tom began to evince a growing distress. He looked appealingly, first at one and then another of the lords about him, and tears came into his eyes. They sprang forward with dismay in their faces, and begged to know his trouble. Tom said with genuine anguish—

"I crave your indulgence: my nose itcheth cruelly. What is the custom and usage in this emergence? Prithee, speed, for 'tis but a little time that I can bear it."

None smiled; but all were sore perplexed, and looked one to the other in deep tribulation for counsel. But behold, here was a dead wall, and nothing in English history to tell how to get over it. The Master of Ceremonies was not present: there was no one who felt safe to venture upon this uncharted sea, or risk the attempt to solve this solemn problem. Alas! there was no Hereditary Scratcher. Meantime the tears had overflowed their banks, and begun to trickle down Tom's cheeks. His twitching nose was pleading more urgently than ever for relief. At last nature broke down the barriers of etiquette: Tom lifted up an inward prayer for pardon if he was doing wrong, and brought relief to the burdened hearts of his court by scratching his nose himself.

His meal being ended, a lord came and held before him a broad, shallow, golden dish with fragrant rosewater in it, to cleanse his mouth and fingers with; and my lord the Hereditary Diaperer stood by with a napkin for his use. Tom gazed at the dish a puzzled moment or two, then raised it to his lips, and gravely took a draught. Then he returned it to the waiting lord, and said—

"Nay, it likes me not, my lord: it hath a pretty flavour, but it wanteth strength."

This new eccentricity of the prince's ruined mind made all the hearts about him ache; but the sad sight moved none to merriment.

Tom's next unconscious blunder was to get up and leave the table just when the chaplain had taken his stand behind his chair, and with uplifted hands, and closed, uplifted eyes, was in the act of beginning the blessing. Still nobody seemed to perceive that the prince had done a thing unusual.

By his own request our small friend was now conducted to his private cabinet, and left there alone to his own devices. Hanging upon hooks in the oaken wainscoting were the several pieces of a suit of shining steel armour, covered all over with beautiful designs exquisitely inlaid in gold. This

_____
* It was not till the end of this reign (Henry VIII.) that any salads, carrots, turnips, or other edible roots were produced in England. The little of these vegetables that was used was formerly imported from Holland and Flanders. Queen Catherine, when she wanted a salad, was obliged to despatch a messenger thither on purpose.— Hume's History of England, vol. iii. p. 314.

martial panoply belonged to the true prince—a recent present from Madam Parr the Queen. Tom put on the greaves, the gauntlets, the plumed helmet, and such other pieces as he could don without assistance, and for a while was minded to call for help and complete the matter, but bethought him of the nuts he had brought away from dinner, and the joy it would be to eat them with no crowd to eye him, and no Grand Hereditaries to pester him with undesired services; so he restored the pretty things to their several places, and soon was cracking nuts, and feeling almost naturally happy for the first time since God for his sins had made him a prince. When the nuts were all gone, he stumbled upon some inviting books in a closet, among them one about the etiquette of the English court. This was a prize. He lay down upon a sumptuous divan, and proceeded to instruct himself with honest zeal. Let us leave him there for the present.

Chapter VIII. The question of the Seal.

About five o'clock Henry VIII. awoke out of an unrefreshing nap, and muttered to himself, "Troublous dreams, troublous dreams! Mine end is now at hand: so say these warnings, and my failing pulses do confirm it." Presently a wicked light flamed up in his eye, and he muttered, "Yet will not I die till HE go before."

His attendants perceiving that he was awake, one of them asked his pleasure concerning the Lord Chancellor, who was waiting without.

"Admit him, admit him!" exclaimed the King eagerly.

The Lord Chancellor entered, and knelt by the King's couch, saying—

"I have given order, and, according to the King's command, the peers of the realm, in their robes, do now stand at the bar of the House, where, having confirmed the Duke of Norfolk's doom, they humbly wait his majesty's further pleasure in the matter."

The King's face lit up with a fierce joy. Said he—

"Lift me up! In mine own person will I go before my Parliament, and with mine own hand will I seal the warrant that rids me of—"

His voice failed; an ashen pallor swept the flush from his cheeks; and the attendants eased him back upon his pillows, and hurriedly assisted him with restoratives. Presently he said sorrowfully—

"Alack, how have I longed for this sweet hour! and lo, too late it cometh, and I am robbed of this so coveted chance. But speed ye, speed ye! let others do this happy office sith 'tis denied to me. I put my Great Seal in commission: choose thou the lords that shall compose it, and get ye to your work. Speed ye, man! Before the sun shall rise and set again, bring me his head that I may see it."

"According to the King's command, so shall it be. Will't please your majesty to order that the Seal be now restored to me, so that I may forth upon the business?"

"The Seal? Who keepeth the Seal but thou?"

"Please your majesty, you did take it from me two days since, saying it should no more do its office till your own royal hand should use it upon the Duke of Norfolk's warrant."

"Why, so in sooth I did: I do remember . . . What did I with it?. . . I am very feeble . . . So oft these days doth my memory play the traitor with me . . . 'Tis strange, strange—"

The King dropped into inarticulate mumblings, shaking his grey head weakly from time to time, and gropingly trying to recollect what he had done with the Seal. At last my Lord Hertford ventured to kneel and offer information—

"Sire, if that I may be so bold, here be several that do remember with me how that you gave the Great Seal into the hands of his highness the Prince of Wales to keep against the day that—"

"True, most true!" interrupted the King. "Fetch it! Go: time flieth!"

Lord Hertford flew to Tom, but returned to the King before very long, troubled and empty-handed. He delivered himself to this effect—

"It grieveth me; my lord the King, to bear so heavy and unwelcome tidings; but it is the will of God that the prince's affliction abideth still, and he cannot recall to mind that he received the Seal. So came I quickly to report, thinking it were waste of precious time, and little worth withal, that any should attempt to search the long array of chambers and saloons that belong unto his royal high—"

A groan from the King interrupted the lord at this point. After a little while his majesty said, with a deep sadness in his tone—

"Trouble him no more, poor child. The hand of God lieth heavy upon him, and my heart goeth out in loving compassion for him, and sorrow that I may not bear his burden on mine old trouble-weighted shoulders, and so bring him peace."

He closed his eyes, fell to mumbling, and presently was silent. After a time he opened his eyes again, and gazed vacantly around until his glance rested upon the kneeling Lord Chancellor. Instantly his face flushed with wrath—

"What, thou here yet! By the glory of God, an' thou gettest not about that traitor's business, thy mitre shall have holiday the morrow for lack of a head to grace withal!"

The trembling Chancellor answered—

"Good your Majesty, I cry you mercy! I but waited for the Seal."

"Man, hast lost thy wits? The small Seal which aforetime I was wont to take with me abroad lieth in my treasury. And, since the Great Seal hath flown away, shall not it suffice? Hast lost thy wits? Begone! And hark ye—come no more till thou do bring his head."

The poor Chancellor was not long in removing himself from this dangerous vicinity; nor did the commission waste time in giving the royal assent to the work of the slavish Parliament, and appointing the morrow for the beheading of the premier peer of England, the luckless Duke of Norfolk.*

---

* The House of Peers, without examining the prisoner, without trial or evidence, passed a Bill of Attainder against him and sent it down to the Commons . . . The obsequious Commons obeyed his

Chapter IX. The river pageant.

At nine in the evening the whole vast river-front of the palace was blazing with light. The river itself, as far as the eye could reach citywards, was so thickly covered with watermen's boats and with pleasure-barges, all fringed with coloured lanterns, and gently agitated by the waves, that it resembled a glowing and limitless garden of flowers stirred to soft motion by summer winds. The grand terrace of stone steps leading down to the water, spacious enough to mass the army of a German principality upon, was a picture to see, with its ranks of royal halberdiers in polished armour, and its troops of brilliantly costumed servitors flitting up and down, and to and fro, in the hurry of preparation.

Presently a command was given, and immediately all living creatures vanished from the steps. Now the air was heavy with the hush of suspense and expectancy. As far as one's vision could carry, he might see the myriads of people in the boats rise up, and shade their eyes from the glare of lanterns and torches, and gaze toward the palace.

A file of forty or fifty state barges drew up to the steps. They were richly gilt, and their lofty prows and sterns were elaborately carved. Some of them were decorated with banners and streamers; some with cloth-of-gold and arras embroidered with coats-of-arms; others with silken flags that had numberless little silver bells fastened to them, which shook out tiny showers of joyous music whenever the breezes fluttered them; others of yet higher pretensions, since they belonged to nobles in the prince's immediate service, had their sides picturesquely fenced with shields gorgeously emblazoned with armorial bearings. Each state barge was towed by a tender. Besides the rowers, these tenders carried each a number of men-at-arms in glossy helmet and breastplate, and a company of musicians.

The advance-guard of the expected procession now appeared in the great gateway, a troop of halberdiers. They were dressed in striped hose of black and tawny, velvet caps graced at the sides with silver roses, and doublets of murrey and blue cloth, embroidered on the front and back with the three feathers, the prince's blazon, woven in gold. Their halberd staves were covered with crimson velvet, fastened with gilt nails, and ornamented with gold tassels. Filing off on the right and left, they formed two long lines, extending from the gateway of the palace to the water's edge. A thick rayed cloth or carpet was then unfolded, and laid down between them by attendants in the gold-and-crimson liveries of the prince. This done, a flourish of trumpets resounded from within. A lively prelude arose from the musicians on the water; and two ushers with white wands marched with a slow and stately pace from the portal. They were followed by an officer bearing the civic mace, after whom came another carrying the city's sword; then several sergeants of the city guard, in their full accoutrements, and with badges on their sleeves; then the Garter King-at-arms, in his tabard; then several Knights of the Bath, each with a white lace on his sleeve; then their esquires; then the judges, in their robes of scarlet and coifs; then the Lord High Chancellor of England, in a robe of scarlet, open before, and purfled with minever; then a deputation of aldermen, in their scarlet cloaks; and then the heads of the

different civic companies, in their robes of state. Now came twelve French gentlemen, in splendid habiliments, consisting of pourpoints of white damask barred with gold, short mantles of crimson velvet lined with violet taffeta, and carnation coloured hauts-de-chausses, and took their way down the steps. They were of the suite of the French ambassador, and were followed by twelve cavaliers of the suite of the Spanish ambassador, clothed in black velvet, unrelieved by any ornament. Following these came several great English nobles with their attendants.'

There was a flourish of trumpets within; and the Prince's uncle, the future great Duke of Somerset, emerged from the gateway, arrayed in a 'doublet of black cloth-of-gold, and a cloak of crimson satin flowered with gold, and ribanded with nets of silver.' He turned, doffed his plumed cap, bent his body in a low reverence, and began to step backward, bowing at each step. A prolonged trumpet-blast followed, and a proclamation, "Way for the high and mighty the Lord Edward, Prince of Wales!" High aloft on the palace walls a long line of red tongues of flame leapt forth with a thunder-crash; the massed world on the river burst into a mighty roar of welcome; and Tom Canty, the cause and hero of it all, stepped into view and slightly bowed his princely head.

He was 'magnificently habited in a doublet of white satin, with a front-piece of purple cloth-of-tissue, powdered with diamonds, and edged with ermine. Over this he wore a mantle of white cloth-of-gold, pounced with the triple-feathered crest, lined with blue satin, set with pearls and precious stones, and fastened with a clasp of brilliants. About his neck hung the order of the Garter, and several princely foreign orders;' and wherever light fell upon him jewels responded with a blinding flash. O Tom Canty, born in a hovel, bred in the gutters of London, familiar with rags and dirt and misery, what a spectacle is this!

Chapter X. The Prince in the toils.

We left John Canty dragging the rightful prince into Offal Court, with a noisy and delighted mob at his heels. There was but one person in it who offered a pleading word for the captive, and he was not heeded; he was hardly even heard, so great was the turmoil. The Prince continued to struggle for freedom, and to rage against the treatment he was suffering, until John Canty lost what little patience was left in him, and raised his oaken cudgel in a sudden fury over the Prince's head. The single pleader for the lad sprang to stop the man's arm, and the blow descended upon his own wrist. Canty roared out—

"Thou'lt meddle, wilt thou? Then have thy reward."

His cudgel crashed down upon the meddler's head: there was a groan, a dim form sank to the ground among the feet of the crowd, and the next moment it lay there in the dark alone. The mob pressed on, their enjoyment nothing disturbed by this episode.

Presently the Prince found himself in John Canty's abode, with the door closed against the outsiders. By the vague light of a tallow candle which was thrust into a bottle, he made out the main features of the loathsome den, and also the occupants of it. Two frowsy girls and a middle-aged woman cowered against the wall in one corner, with the aspect of animals habituated to harsh usage, and expecting and dreading it now. From another corner stole a withered hag with streaming grey hair and malignant eyes. John Canty said to this one—

(the King's) directions; and the King, having affixed the Royal assent to the Bill by commissioners, issued orders for the execution of Norfolk on the morning of January 29 (the next day).—Hume's History of England, vol iii. p 306.

"Tarry! There's fine mummeries here. Mar them not till thou'st enjoyed them: then let thy hand be heavy as thou wilt. Stand forth, lad. Now say thy foolery again, an thou'st not forgot it. Name thy name. Who art thou?"

The insulted blood mounted to the little prince's cheek once more, and he lifted a steady and indignant gaze to the man's face and said—

"'Tis but ill-breeding in such as thou to command me to speak. I tell thee now, as I told thee before, I am Edward, Prince of Wales, and none other."

The stunning surprise of this reply nailed the hag's feet to the floor where she stood, and almost took her breath. She stared at the Prince in stupid amazement, which so amused her ruffianly son, that he burst into a roar of laughter. But the effect upon Tom Canty's mother and sisters was different. Their dread of bodily injury gave way at once to distress of a different sort. They ran forward with woe and dismay in their faces, exclaiming—

"Oh, poor Tom, poor lad!"

The mother fell on her knees before the Prince, put her hands upon his shoulders, and gazed yearningly into his face through her rising tears. Then she said—

"Oh, my poor boy! Thy foolish reading hath wrought its woeful work at last, and ta'en thy wit away. Ah! why did'st thou cleave to it when I so warned thee 'gainst it? Thou'st broke thy mother's heart."

The Prince looked into her face, and said gently—

"Thy son is well, and hath not lost his wits, good dame. Comfort thee: let me to the palace where he is, and straightway will the King my father restore him to thee."

"The King thy father! Oh, my child! unsay these words that be freighted with death for thee, and ruin for all that be near to thee. Shake of this gruesome dream. Call back thy poor wandering memory. Look upon me. Am not I thy mother that bore thee, and loveth thee?"

The Prince shook his head and reluctantly said—

"God knoweth I am loth to grieve thy heart; but truly have I never looked upon thy face before."

The woman sank back to a sitting posture on the floor, and, covering her eyes with her hands, gave way to heart-broken sobs and wailings.

"Let the show go on!" shouted Canty. "What, Nan!—what, Bet! mannerless wenches! will ye stand in the Prince's presence? Upon your knees, ye pauper scum, and do him reverence!"

He followed this with another horse-laugh. The girls began to plead timidly for their brother; and Nan said—

"An thou wilt but let him to bed, father, rest and sleep will heal his madness: prithee, do."

"Do, father," said Bet; "he is more worn than is his wont. To-morrow will he be himself again, and will beg with diligence, and come not empty home again."

This remark sobered the father's joviality, and brought his mind to business. He turned angrily upon the Prince, and said—

"The morrow must we pay two pennies to him that owns this hole; two pennies, mark ye—all this money for a half-year's rent, else out of this we go. Show what thou'st gathered with thy lazy begging."

The Prince said—

"Offend me not with thy sordid matters. I tell thee again I am the King's son."

A sounding blow upon the Prince's shoulder from Canty's broad palm sent him staggering into goodwife Canty's arms, who clasped him to her breast, and sheltered him from a pelting rain of cuffs and slaps by interposing her own person. The frightened girls retreated to their corner; but the grandmother stepped eagerly forward to assist her son. The Prince sprang away from Mrs. Canty, exclaiming—

"Thou shalt not suffer for me, madam. Let these swine do their will upon me alone."

This speech infuriated the swine to such a degree that they set about their work without waste of time. Between them they belaboured the boy right soundly, and then gave the girls and their mother a beating for showing sympathy for the victim.

"Now," said Canty, "to bed, all of ye. The entertainment has tired me."

The light was put out, and the family retired. As soon as the snorings of the head of the house and his mother showed that they were asleep, the young girls crept to where the Prince lay, and covered him tenderly from the cold with straw and rags; and their mother crept to him also, and stroked his hair, and cried over him, whispering broken words of comfort and compassion in his ear the while. She had saved a morsel for him to eat, also; but the boy's pains had swept away all appetite—at least for black and tasteless crusts. He was touched by her brave and costly defence of him, and by her commiseration; and he thanked her in very noble and princely words, and begged her to go to her sleep and try to forget her sorrows. And he added that the King his father would not let her loyal kindness and devotion go unrewarded. This return to his 'madness' broke her heart anew, and she strained him to her breast again and again, and then went back, drowned in tears, to her bed.

As she lay thinking and mourning, the suggestion began to creep into her mind that there was an undefinable something about this boy that was lacking in Tom Canty, mad or sane. She could not describe it, she could not tell just what it was, and yet her sharp mother-instinct seemed to detect it and perceive it. What if the boy were really not her son, after all? Oh, absurd! She almost smiled at the idea, spite of her griefs and troubles. No matter, she found that it was an idea that would not 'down,' but persisted in haunting her. It pursued her, it harassed her, it clung to her, and refused to be put away or ignored. At last she perceived that there was not going to be any peace for her until she should devise a test that should prove, clearly and without question, whether this lad was her son or not, and so banish these wearing and worrying doubts. Ah, yes, this was plainly the right way out of the difficulty; therefore she set her wits to work at once to contrive that test.

But it was an easier thing to propose than to accomplish. She turned over in her mind one promising test after another, but was obliged to relinquish them all—none of them were absolutely sure, absolutely perfect; and an imperfect one could not satisfy her. Evidently she was racking her head in vain—it seemed manifest that she must give the matter up. While this depressing thought was passing through her mind, her ear caught the regular breathing of the boy, and she knew he had fallen asleep. And while she listened, the measured breathing was broken by a soft, startled cry, such as one utters in a troubled dream. This chance occurrence furnished her instantly with a plan worth all her laboured tests combined. She at once set herself feverishly, but noiselessly, to work to relight her candle, muttering to herself, "Had I but seen him THEN, I should have known! Since that day, when he was little, that the powder burst in his face, he hath never been startled of a sudden out of his dreams or out of his thinkings, but he hath cast his hand before his eyes, even as he did that day; and not as others would do it, with the palm inward, but always with the palm turned outward—I have seen it a hundred times, and it hath never varied nor ever failed. Yes, I shall soon know, now!"

By this time she had crept to the slumbering boy's side, with the candle, shaded, in her hand. She bent heedfully and warily over him, scarcely breathing in her suppressed excitement, and suddenly flashed the light in his face and struck the floor by his ear with her knuckles. The sleeper's eyes sprang wide open, and he cast a startled stare about him —but he made no special movement with his hands.

The poor woman was smitten almost helpless with surprise and grief; but she contrived to hide her emotions, and to soothe the boy to sleep again; then she crept apart and communed miserably with herself upon the disastrous result of her experiment. She tried to believe that her Tom's madness had banished this habitual gesture of his; but she could not do it. "No," she said, "his HANDS are not mad; they could not unlearn so old a habit in so brief a time. Oh, this is a heavy day for me!"

Still, hope was as stubborn now as doubt had been before; she could not bring herself to accept the verdict of the test; she must try the thing again—the failure must have been only an accident; so she startled the boy out of his sleep a second and a third time, at intervals—with the same result which had marked the first test; then she dragged herself to bed, and fell sorrowfully asleep, saying, "But I cannot give him up—oh no, I cannot, I cannot—he MUST be my boy!"

The poor mother's interruptions having ceased, and the Prince's pains having gradually lost their power to disturb him, utter weariness at last sealed his eyes in a profound and restful sleep. Hour after hour slipped away, and still he slept like the dead. Thus four or five hours passed. Then his stupor began to lighten. Presently, while half asleep and half awake, he murmured—

"Sir William!"

After a moment—

"Ho, Sir William Herbert! Hie thee hither, and list to the strangest dream that ever . . . Sir William! dost hear? Man, I did think me changed to a pauper, and . . . Ho there! Guards! Sir William! What! is there no groom of the chamber in waiting? Alack! it shall go hard with—"

"What aileth thee?" asked a whisper near him. "Who art thou calling?"

"Sir William Herbert. Who art thou?"

"I? Who should I be, but thy sister Nan? Oh, Tom, I had forgot! Thou'rt mad yet—poor lad, thou'rt mad yet: would I had never woke to know it again! But prithee master thy tongue, lest we be all beaten till we die!"

The startled Prince sprang partly up, but a sharp reminder from his stiffened bruises brought him to himself, and he sank back among his foul straw with a moan and the ejaculation—

"Alas! it was no dream, then!"

In a moment all the heavy sorrow and misery which sleep had banished were upon him again, and he realised that he was no longer a petted prince in a palace, with the adoring eyes of a nation upon him, but a pauper, an outcast, clothed in rags, prisoner in a den fit only for beasts, and consorting with beggars and thieves.

In the midst of his grief he began to be conscious of hilarious noises and shoutings, apparently but a block or two away. The next moment there were several sharp raps at the door; John Canty ceased from snoring and said—

"Who knocketh? What wilt thou?"

A voice answered—

"Know'st thou who it was thou laid thy cudgel on?"

"No. Neither know I, nor care."

"Belike thou'lt change thy note eftsoons. An thou would save thy neck, nothing but flight may stead thee. The man is this moment delivering up the ghost. 'Tis the priest, Father Andrew!"

"God-a-mercy!" exclaimed Canty. He roused his family, and hoarsely commanded, "Up with ye all and fly—or bide where ye are and perish!"

Scarcely five minutes later the Canty household were in the street and flying for their lives. John Canty held the Prince by the wrist, and hurried him along the dark way, giving him this caution in a low voice—

"Mind thy tongue, thou mad fool, and speak not our name. I will choose me a new name, speedily, to throw the law's dogs off the scent. Mind thy tongue, I tell thee!"

He growled these words to the rest of the family—

"If it so chance that we be separated, let each make for London Bridge; whoso findeth himself as far as the last linen-draper's shop on the bridge, let him tarry there till the others be come, then will we flee into Southwark together."

At this moment the party burst suddenly out of darkness into light; and not only into light, but into the midst of a multitude of singing, dancing, and shouting people, massed together on the river frontage. There was a line of bonfires stretching as far as one could see, up and down the Thames; London Bridge was illuminated; Southwark Bridge likewise; the entire river was aglow with the flash and sheen of coloured lights; and constant explosions of fireworks filled the skies with an intricate commingling of shooting splendours and a thick rain of dazzling sparks that almost turned night into day; everywhere were crowds of revellers; all London seemed to be at large.

John Canty delivered himself of a furious curse and commanded a retreat; but it was too late. He and his tribe were swallowed up in that swarming hive of humanity, and hopelessly separated from each other in an instant. We are not considering that the Prince was one of his tribe; Canty still kept his grip upon him. The Prince's heart was beating high with hopes of escape, now. A burly waterman, considerably exalted with liquor, found himself rudely shoved by Canty in his efforts to plough through the crowd; he laid his great hand on Canty's shoulder and said—

"Nay, whither so fast, friend? Dost canker thy soul with sordid business when all that be leal men and true make holiday?"

"Mine affairs are mine own, they concern thee not," answered Canty, roughly; "take away thy hand and let me pass."

"Sith that is thy humour, thou'lt NOT pass, till thou'st drunk to the Prince of Wales, I tell thee that," said the waterman, barring the way resolutely.

"Give me the cup, then, and make speed, make speed!"

Other revellers were interested by this time. They cried out—

"The loving-cup, the loving-cup! make the sour knave drink the loving-cup, else will we feed him to the fishes."

So a huge loving-cup was brought; the waterman, grasping it by one of its handles, and with the other hand bearing up the end of an imaginary napkin, presented it in due and ancient form to Canty, who had to grasp the opposite handle with one of his hands and take off the lid with the other, according to ancient custom.* This left the Prince hand-free for a second, of course. He wasted no time, but dived among the forest of legs about him and disappeared. In another moment he could not have been harder to find, under that tossing sea of life, if its billows had been the Atlantic's and he a lost sixpence.

He very soon realised this fact, and straightway busied himself about his own affairs without further thought of John Canty. He quickly realised another thing, too. To wit, that a spurious Prince of Wales was being feasted by the city in his stead. He easily concluded that the pauper lad, Tom Canty, had deliberately taken advantage of his stupendous opportunity and become a usurper.

Therefore there was but one course to pursue—find his way to the Guildhall, make himself known, and denounce the impostor. He also made up his mind that Tom should be allowed a reasonable time for spiritual preparation, and then be hanged, drawn and quartered, according to the law and

* The loving-cup, and the peculiar ceremonies observed in drinking from it, are older than English history. It is thought that both are Danish importations. As far back as knowledge goes, the loving-cup has always been drunk at English banquets. Tradition explains the ceremonies in this way. In the rude ancient times it was deemed a wise precaution to have both hands of both drinkers employed, lest while the pledger pledged his love and fidelity to the pledgee, the pledgee take that opportunity to slip a dirk into him!

usage of the day in cases of high treason.

Chapter XI. At Guildhall.

The royal barge, attended by its gorgeous fleet, took its stately way down the Thames through the wilderness of illuminated boats. The air was laden with music; the river banks were beruffled with joy-flames; the distant city lay in a soft luminous glow from its countless invisible bonfires; above it rose many a slender spire into the sky, incrusted with sparkling lights, wherefore in their remoteness they seemed like jewelled lances thrust aloft; as the fleet swept along, it was greeted from the banks with a continuous hoarse roar of cheers and the ceaseless flash and boom of artillery.

To Tom Canty, half buried in his silken cushions, these sounds and this spectacle were a wonder unspeakably sublime and astonishing. To his little friends at his side, the Princess Elizabeth and the Lady Jane Grey, they were nothing.

Arrived at the Dowgate, the fleet was towed up the limpid Walbrook (whose channel has now been for two centuries buried out of sight under acres of buildings) to Bucklersbury, past houses and under bridges populous with merry-makers and brilliantly lighted, and at last came to a halt in a basin where now is Barge Yard, in the centre of the ancient city of London. Tom disembarked, and he and his gallant procession crossed Cheapside and made a short march through the Old Jewry and Basinghall Street to the Guildhall.

Tom and his little ladies were received with due ceremony by the Lord Mayor and the Fathers of the City, in their gold chains and scarlet robes of state, and conducted to a rich canopy of state at the head of the great hall, preceded by heralds making proclamation, and by the Mace and the City Sword. The lords and ladies who were to attend upon Tom and his two small friends took their places behind their chairs.

At a lower table the Court grandees and other guests of noble degree were seated, with the magnates of the city; the commoners took places at a multitude of tables on the main floor of the hall. From their lofty vantage-ground the giants Gog and Magog, the ancient guardians of the city, contemplated the spectacle below them with eyes grown familiar to it in forgotten generations. There was a bugle-blast and a proclamation, and a fat butler appeared in a high perch in the leftward wall, followed by his servitors bearing with impressive solemnity a royal baron of beef, smoking hot and ready for the knife.

After grace, Tom (being instructed) rose—and the whole house with him —and drank from a portly golden loving-cup with the Princess Elizabeth; from her it passed to the Lady Jane, and then traversed the general assemblage. So the banquet began.

By midnight the revelry was at its height. Now came one of those picturesque spectacles so admired in that old day. A description of it is still extant in the quaint wording of a chronicler who witnessed it:

'Space being made, presently entered a baron and an earl appareled after the Turkish fashion in long robes of bawdkin powdered with gold; hats on their heads of crimson velvet, with great rolls of gold, girded with two swords, called scimitars, hanging by great bawdricks of gold. Next came yet another baron and another earl, in two long gowns of yellow satin, traversed with white satin, and in every bend of white was a bend of crimson satin, after the fashion of Russia, with furred hats of gray on their heads; either of them having an hatchet in their hands, and boots with pykes' (points a foot long), 'turned up. And after them came a knight, then the Lord High Admiral, and with him five nobles, in doublets of crimson velvet, voyded low on the back and before to the cannell-bone, laced on the breasts with chains of silver; and over that, short cloaks of crimson satin, and on their heads hats after the dancers' fashion, with pheasants' feathers in them. These were appareled after the fashion of Prussia. The torchbearers, which were about an hundred, were appareled in crimson satin and green, like Moors, their faces black. Next came in a mommarye. Then the minstrels, which were disguised, danced; and the lords and ladies did wildly dance also, that it was a pleasure to behold.'

And while Tom, in his high seat, was gazing upon this 'wild' dancing, lost in admiration of the dazzling commingling of kaleidoscopic colours which the whirling turmoil of gaudy figures below him presented, the ragged but real little Prince of Wales was proclaiming his rights and his wrongs, denouncing the impostor, and clamouring for admission at the gates of Guildhall! The crowd enjoyed this episode prodigiously, and pressed forward and craned their necks to see the small rioter. Presently they began to taunt him and mock at him, purposely to goad him into a higher and still more entertaining fury. Tears of mortification sprang to his eyes, but he stood his ground and defied the mob right royally. Other taunts followed, added mockings stung him, and he exclaimed—

"I tell ye again, you pack of unmannerly curs, I am the Prince of Wales! And all forlorn and friendless as I be, with none to give me word of grace or help me in my need, yet will not I be driven from my ground, but will maintain it!"

"Though thou be prince or no prince, 'tis all one, thou be'st a gallant lad, and not friendless neither! Here stand I by thy side to prove it; and mind I tell thee thou might'st have a worser friend than Miles Hendon and yet not tire thy legs with seeking. Rest thy small jaw, my child; I talk the language of these base kennel-rats like to a very native."

The speaker was a sort of Don Caesar de Bazan in dress, aspect, and bearing. He was tall, trim-built, muscular. His doublet and trunks were of rich material, but faded and threadbare, and their gold-lace adornments were sadly tarnished; his ruff was rumpled and damaged; the plume in his slouched hat was broken and had a bedraggled and disreputable look; at his side he wore a long rapier in a rusty iron sheath; his swaggering carriage marked him at once as a ruffler of the camp. The speech of this fantastic figure was received with an explosion of jeers and laughter. Some cried, "'Tis another prince in disguise!" "'Ware thy tongue, friend: belike he is dangerous!" "Marry, he looketh it—mark his eye!" "Pluck the lad from him—to the horse-pond wi' the cub!"

Instantly a hand was laid upon the Prince, under the impulse of this happy thought; as instantly the stranger's long sword was out and the meddler went to the earth under a sounding thump with the flat of it. The next moment a score of voices shouted, "Kill the dog! Kill him! Kill him!" and the mob closed in on the warrior, who backed himself against a wall and began to lay about him with his long weapon like a madman. His victims sprawled this way and that, but the mob-tide poured over their prostrate forms and dashed itself against the champion with undiminished fury. His moments seemed numbered, his destruction certain, when suddenly a trumpet-blast sounded, a voice shouted, "Way for the King's

messenger!" and a troop of horsemen came charging down upon the mob, who fled out of harm's reach as fast as their legs could carry them. The bold stranger caught up the Prince in his arms, and was soon far away from danger and the multitude.

Return we within the Guildhall. Suddenly, high above the jubilant roar and thunder of the revel, broke the clear peal of a bugle-note. There was instant silence—a deep hush; then a single voice rose—that of the messenger from the palace—and began to pipe forth a proclamation, the whole multitude standing listening.

The closing words, solemnly pronounced, were—

"The King is dead!"

The great assemblage bent their heads upon their breasts with one accord; remained so, in profound silence, a few moments; then all sank upon their knees in a body, stretched out their hands toward Tom, and a mighty shout burst forth that seemed to shake the building—

"Long live the King!"

Poor Tom's dazed eyes wandered abroad over this stupefying spectacle, and finally rested dreamily upon the kneeling princesses beside him, a moment, then upon the Earl of Hertford. A sudden purpose dawned in his face. He said, in a low tone, at Lord Hertford's ear—

"Answer me truly, on thy faith and honour! Uttered I here a command, the which none but a king might hold privilege and prerogative to utter, would such commandment be obeyed, and none rise up to say me nay?"

"None, my liege, in all these realms. In thy person bides the majesty of England. Thou art the king—thy word is law."

Tom responded, in a strong, earnest voice, and with great animation—

"Then shall the king's law be law of mercy, from this day, and never more be law of blood! Up from thy knees and away! To the Tower, and say the King decrees the Duke of Norfolk shall not die!"*

The words were caught up and carried eagerly from lip to lip far and wide over the hall, and as Hertford hurried from the presence, another prodigious shout burst forth—

"The reign of blood is ended! Long live Edward, King of England!"

Chapter XII. The Prince and his deliverer.

As soon as Miles Hendon and the little prince were clear of the mob, they struck down through back lanes and alleys toward the river. Their way was unobstructed until they approached

---

* Had Henry VIII. survived a few hours longer, his order for the duke's execution would have been carried into effect. 'But news being carried to the Tower that the King himself had expired that night, the lieutenant deferred obeying the warrant; and it was not thought advisable by the Council to begin a new reign by the death of the greatest nobleman in the kingdom, who had been condemned by a sentence so unjust and tyrannical.' —Hume's History of England, vol. iii, p. 307.

London Bridge; then they ploughed into the multitude again, Hendon keeping a fast grip upon the Prince's —no, the King's—wrist. The tremendous news was already abroad, and the boy learned it from a thousand voices at once—"The King is dead!" The tidings struck a chill to the heart of the poor little waif, and sent a shudder through his frame. He realised the greatness of his loss, and was filled with a bitter grief; for the grim tyrant who had been such a terror to others had always been gentle with him. The tears sprang to his eyes and blurred all objects. For an instant he felt himself the most forlorn, outcast, and forsaken of God's creatures—then another cry shook the night with its far-reaching thunders: "Long live King Edward the Sixth!" and this made his eyes kindle, and thrilled him with pride to his fingers' ends. "Ah," he thought, "how grand and strange it seems—I AM KING!"

Our friends threaded their way slowly through the throngs upon the bridge. This structure, which had stood for six hundred years, and had been a noisy and populous thoroughfare all that time, was a curious affair, for a closely packed rank of stores and shops, with family quarters overhead, stretched along both sides of it, from one bank of the river to the other. The Bridge was a sort of town to itself; it had its inn, its beer-houses, its bakeries, its haberdasheries, its food markets, its manufacturing industries, and even its church. It looked upon the two neighbours which it linked together—London and Southwark—as being well enough as suburbs, but not otherwise particularly important. It was a close corporation, so to speak; it was a narrow town, of a single street a fifth of a mile long, its population was but a village population and everybody in it knew all his fellow-townsmen intimately, and had known their fathers and mothers before them—and all their little family affairs into the bargain. It had its aristocracy, of course—its fine old families of butchers, and bakers, and what-not, who had occupied the same old premises for five or six hundred years, and knew the great history of the Bridge from beginning to end, and all its strange legends; and who always talked bridgy talk, and thought bridgy thoughts, and lied in a long, level, direct, substantial bridgy way. It was just the sort of population to be narrow and ignorant and self-conceited. Children were born on the Bridge, were reared there, grew to old age, and finally died without ever having set a foot upon any part of the world but London Bridge alone. Such people would naturally imagine that the mighty and interminable procession which moved through its street night and day, with its confused roar of shouts and cries, its neighings and bellowing and bleatings and its muffled thunder-tramp, was the one great thing in this world, and themselves somehow the proprietors of it. And so they were, in effect—at least they could exhibit it from their windows, and did—for a consideration—whenever a returning king or hero gave it a fleeting splendour, for there was no place like it for affording a long, straight, uninterrupted view of marching columns.

Men born and reared upon the Bridge found life unendurably dull and inane elsewhere. History tells of one of these who left the Bridge at the age of seventy-one and retired to the country. But he could only fret and toss in his bed; he could not go to sleep, the deep stillness was so painful, so awful, so oppressive. When he was worn out with it, at last, he fled back to his old home, a lean and haggard spectre, and fell peacefully to rest and pleasant dreams under the lulling music of the lashing waters and the boom and crash and thunder of London Bridge.

In the times of which we are writing, the Bridge furnished 'object lessons' in English history for its children—namely, the livid and decaying heads of renowned men impaled upon iron spikes atop of its gateways. But we digress.

Hendon's lodgings were in the little inn on the Bridge. As he neared the door with his small friend, a rough voice said—

"So, thou'rt come at last! Thou'lt not escape again, I warrant thee; and if pounding thy bones to a pudding can teach thee somewhat, thou'lt not keep us waiting another time, mayhap"—and John Canty put out his hand to seize the boy.

Miles Hendon stepped in the way and said—

"Not too fast, friend. Thou art needlessly rough, methinks. What is the lad to thee?"

"If it be any business of thine to make and meddle in others' affairs, he is my son."

"'Tis a lie!" cried the little King, hotly.

"Boldly said, and I believe thee, whether thy small headpiece be sound or cracked, my boy. But whether this scurvy ruffian be thy father or no, 'tis all one, he shall not have thee to beat thee and abuse, according to his threat, so thou prefer to bide with me."

"I do, I do—I know him not, I loathe him, and will die before I will go with him."

"Then 'tis settled, and there is nought more to say."

"We will see, as to that!" exclaimed John Canty, striding past Hendon to get at the boy; "by force shall he—"

"If thou do but touch him, thou animated offal, I will spit thee like a goose!" said Hendon, barring the way and laying his hand upon his sword hilt. Canty drew back. "Now mark ye," continued Hendon, "I took this lad under my protection when a mob of such as thou would have mishandled him, mayhap killed him; dost imagine I will desert him now to a worser fate?—for whether thou art his father or no—and sooth to say, I think it is a lie—a decent swift death were better for such a lad than life in such brute hands as thine. So go thy ways, and set quick about it, for I like not much bandying of words, being not over-patient in my nature."

John Canty moved off, muttering threats and curses, and was swallowed from sight in the crowd. Hendon ascended three flights of stairs to his room, with his charge, after ordering a meal to be sent thither. It was a poor apartment, with a shabby bed and some odds and ends of old furniture in it, and was vaguely lighted by a couple of sickly candles. The little King dragged himself to the bed and lay down upon it, almost exhausted with hunger and fatigue. He had been on his feet a good part of a day and a night (for it was now two or three o'clock in the morning), and had eaten nothing meantime. He murmured drowsily—

"Prithee call me when the table is spread," and sank into a deep sleep immediately.

A smile twinkled in Hendon's eye, and he said to himself—

"By the mass, the little beggar takes to one's quarters and usurps one's bed with as natural and easy a grace as if he owned them—with never a by-your-leave or so-please-it-you, or anything of the sort. In his diseased ravings he called himself the Prince of Wales, and bravely doth he keep up the character. Poor little friendless rat, doubtless his mind has been disordered with ill-usage. Well, I will be his friend; I have saved him, and it draweth me strongly to him; already I love the bold-tongued little rascal. How soldier-like he faced the smutty rabble and flung back his high defiance! And what a comely, sweet and gentle face he hath, now that sleep hath conjured away its troubles and its griefs. I will teach him; I will cure his malady; yea, I will be his elder brother, and care for him and watch over him; and whoso would shame him or do him hurt may order his shroud, for though I be burnt for it he shall need it!"

He bent over the boy and contemplated him with kind and pitying interest, tapping the young cheek tenderly and smoothing back the tangled curls with his great brown hand. A slight shiver passed over the boy's form. Hendon muttered—

"See, now, how like a man it was to let him lie here uncovered and fill his body with deadly rheums. Now what shall I do? 'twill wake him to take him up and put him within the bed, and he sorely needeth sleep."

He looked about for extra covering, but finding none, doffed his doublet and wrapped the lad in it, saying, "I am used to nipping air and scant apparel, 'tis little I shall mind the cold!"—then walked up and down the room, to keep his blood in motion, soliloquising as before.

"His injured mind persuades him he is Prince of Wales; 'twill be odd to have a Prince of Wales still with us, now that he that WAS the prince is prince no more, but king—for this poor mind is set upon the one fantasy, and will not reason out that now it should cast by the prince and call itself the king. . . If my father liveth still, after these seven years that I have heard nought from home in my foreign dungeon, he will welcome the poor lad and give him generous shelter for my sake; so will my good elder brother, Arthur; my other brother, Hugh—but I will crack his crown an HE interfere, the fox-hearted, ill-conditioned animal! Yes, thither will we fare—and straightway, too."

A servant entered with a smoking meal, disposed it upon a small deal table, placed the chairs, and took his departure, leaving such cheap lodgers as these to wait upon themselves. The door slammed after him, and the noise woke the boy, who sprang to a sitting posture, and shot a glad glance about him; then a grieved look came into his face and he murmured to. himself, with a deep sigh, "Alack, it was but a dream, woe is me!" Next he noticed Miles Hendon's doublet—glanced from that to Hendon, comprehended the sacrifice that had been made for him, and said, gently—

"Thou art good to me, yes, thou art very good to me. Take it and put it on—I shall not need it more."

Then he got up and walked to the washstand in the corner and stood there, waiting. Hendon said in a cheery voice—

"We'll have a right hearty sup and bite, now, for everything is savoury and smoking hot, and that and thy nap together will make thee a little man again, never fear!"

The boy made no answer, but bent a steady look, that was filled with grave surprise, and also somewhat touched with impatience, upon the tall knight of the sword. Hendon was puzzled, and said—

"What's amiss?"

"Good sir, I would wash me."

"Oh, is that all? Ask no permission of Miles Hendon for aught thou cravest. Make thyself perfectly free here, and welcome, with all that are his belongings."

Still the boy stood, and moved not; more, he tapped the floor once or twice with his small impatient foot. Hendon was wholly perplexed. Said he—

"Bless us, what is it?"

"Prithee pour the water, and make not so many words!"

Hendon, suppressing a horse-laugh, and saying to himself, "By all the saints, but this is admirable!" stepped briskly forward and did the small insolent's bidding; then stood by, in a sort of stupefaction, until the command, "Come—the towel!" woke him sharply up. He took up a towel, from under the boy's nose, and handed it to him without comment. He now proceeded to comfort his own face with a wash, and while he was at it his adopted child seated himself at the table and prepared to fall to. Hendon despatched his ablutions with alacrity, then drew back the other chair and was about to place himself at table, when the boy said, indignantly—

"Forbear! Wouldst sit in the presence of the King?"

This blow staggered Hendon to his foundations. He muttered to himself, "Lo, the poor thing's madness is up with the time! It hath changed with the great change that is come to the realm, and now in fancy is he KING! Good lack, I must humour the conceit, too—there is no other way—faith, he would order me to the Tower, else!"

And pleased with this jest, he removed the chair from the table, took his stand behind the King, and proceeded to wait upon him in the courtliest way he was capable of.

While the King ate, the rigour of his royal dignity relaxed a little, and with his growing contentment came a desire to talk. He said—"I think thou callest thyself Miles Hendon, if I heard thee aright?"

"Yes, Sire," Miles replied; then observed to himself, "If I MUST humour the poor lad's madness, I must 'Sire' him, I must 'Majesty' him, I must not go by halves, I must stick at nothing that belongeth to the part I play, else shall I play it ill and work evil to this charitable and kindly cause."

The King warmed his heart with a second glass of wine, and said—"I would know thee—tell me thy story. Thou hast a gallant way with thee, and a noble—art nobly born?"

"We are of the tail of the nobility, good your Majesty. My father is a baronet—one of the smaller lords by knight service*—Sir Richard Hendon of Hendon Hall, by Monk's Holm in Kent."

"The name has escaped my memory. Go on—tell me thy story."

"'Tis not much, your Majesty, yet perchance it may beguile a

---

* He refers to the order of baronets, or baronettes; the barones minores, as distinct from the parliamentary barons—not, it need hardly be said, to the baronets of later creation.

short half-hour for want of a better. My father, Sir Richard, is very rich, and of a most generous nature. My mother died whilst I was yet a boy. I have two brothers: Arthur, my elder, with a soul like to his father's; and Hugh, younger than I, a mean spirit, covetous, treacherous, vicious, underhanded—a reptile. Such was he from the cradle; such was he ten years past, when I last saw him—a ripe rascal at nineteen, I being twenty then, and Arthur twenty-two. There is none other of us but the Lady Edith, my cousin—she was sixteen then—beautiful, gentle, good, the daughter of an earl, the last of her race, heiress of a great fortune and a lapsed title. My father was her guardian. I loved her and she loved me; but she was betrothed to Arthur from the cradle, and Sir Richard would not suffer the contract to be broken. Arthur loved another maid, and bade us be of good cheer and hold fast to the hope that delay and luck together would some day give success to our several causes. Hugh loved the Lady Edith's fortune, though in truth he said it was herself he loved—but then 'twas his way, alway, to say the one thing and mean the other. But he lost his arts upon the girl; he could deceive my father, but none else. My father loved him best of us all, and trusted and believed him; for he was the youngest child, and others hated him—these qualities being in all ages sufficient to win a parent's dearest love; and he had a smooth persuasive tongue, with an admirable gift of lying —and these be qualities which do mightily assist a blind affection to cozen itself. I was wild—in troth I might go yet farther and say VERY wild, though 'twas a wildness of an innocent sort, since it hurt none but me, brought shame to none, nor loss, nor had in it any taint of crime or baseness, or what might not beseem mine honourable degree.

"Yet did my brother Hugh turn these faults to good account—he seeing that our brother Arthur's health was but indifferent, and hoping the worst might work him profit were I swept out of the path—so—but 'twere a long tale, good my liege, and little worth the telling. Briefly, then, this brother did deftly magnify my faults and make them crimes; ending his base work with finding a silken ladder in mine apartments—conveyed thither by his own means—and did convince my father by this, and suborned evidence of servants and other lying knaves, that I was minded to carry off my Edith and marry with her in rank defiance of his will.

"Three years of banishment from home and England might make a soldier and a man of me, my father said, and teach me some degree of wisdom. I fought out my long probation in the continental wars, tasting sumptuously of hard knocks, privation, and adventure; but in my last battle I was taken captive, and during the seven years that have waxed and waned since then, a foreign dungeon hath harboured me. Through wit and courage I won to the free air at last, and fled hither straight; and am but just arrived, right poor in purse and raiment, and poorer still in knowledge of what these dull seven years have wrought at Hendon Hall, its people and belongings. So please you, sir, my meagre tale is told."

"Thou hast been shamefully abused!" said the little King, with a flashing eye. "But I will right thee—by the cross will I! The King hath said it."

Then, fired by the story of Miles's wrongs, he loosed his tongue and poured the history of his own recent misfortunes into the ears of his astonished listener. When he had finished, Miles said to himself—

"Lo, what an imagination he hath! Verily, this is no common mind; else, crazed or sane, it could not weave so straight and

gaudy a tale as this out of the airy nothings wherewith it hath wrought this curious romaunt. Poor ruined little head, it shall not lack friend or shelter whilst I bide with the living. He shall never leave my side; he shall be my pet, my little comrade. And he shall be cured!—ay, made whole and sound —then will he make himself a name—and proud shall I be to say, 'Yes, he is mine—I took him, a homeless little ragamuffin, but I saw what was in him, and I said his name would be heard some day—behold him, observe him—was I right?'"

The King spoke—in a thoughtful, measured voice—

"Thou didst save me injury and shame, perchance my life, and so my crown. Such service demandeth rich reward. Name thy desire, and so it be within the compass of my royal power, it is thine."

This fantastic suggestion startled Hendon out of his reverie. He was about to thank the King and put the matter aside with saying he had only done his duty and desired no reward, but a wiser thought came into his head, and he asked leave to be silent a few moments and consider the gracious offer—an idea which the King gravely approved, remarking that it was best to be not too hasty with a thing of such great import.

Miles reflected during some moments, then said to himself, "Yes, that is the thing to do—by any other means it were impossible to get at it—and certes, this hour's experience has taught me 'twould be most wearing and inconvenient to continue it as it is. Yes, I will propose it; 'twas a happy accident that I did not throw the chance away." Then he dropped upon one knee and said—

"My poor service went not beyond the limit of a subject's simple duty, and therefore hath no merit; but since your Majesty is pleased to hold it worthy some reward, I take heart of grace to make petition to this effect. Near four hundred years ago, as your grace knoweth, there being ill blood betwixt John, King of England, and the King of France, it was decreed that two champions should fight together in the lists, and so settle the dispute by what is called the arbitrament of God. These two kings, and the Spanish king, being assembled to witness and judge the conflict, the French champion appeared; but so redoubtable was he, that our English knights refused to measure weapons with him. So the matter, which was a weighty one, was like to go against the English monarch by default. Now in the Tower lay the Lord de Courcy, the mightiest arm in England, stripped of his honours and possessions, and wasting with long captivity. Appeal was made to him; he gave assent, and came forth arrayed for battle; but no sooner did the Frenchman glimpse his huge frame and hear his famous name but he fled away, and the French king's cause was lost. King John restored De Courcy's titles and possessions, and said, 'Name thy wish and thou shalt have it, though it cost me half my kingdom;' whereat De Courcy, kneeling, as I do now, made answer, 'This, then, I ask, my liege; that I and my successors may have and hold the privilege of remaining covered in the presence of the kings of England, henceforth while the throne shall last.' The boon was granted, as your Majesty knoweth; and there hath been no time, these four hundred years, that that line has failed of an heir; and so, even unto this day, the head of that ancient house still weareth his hat or helm before the King's Majesty, without let or hindrance, and this none other may do.* Invoking this precedent in aid of my prayer, I beseech the King to grant to

* The lords of Kingsale, descendants of De Courcy, still enjoy this curious privilege.

me but this one grace and privilege—to my more than sufficient reward—and none other, to wit: that I and my heirs, for ever, may SIT in the presence of the Majesty of England!"

"Rise, Sir Miles Hendon, Knight," said the King, gravely—giving the accolade with Hendon's sword—"rise, and seat thyself. Thy petition is granted. Whilst England remains, and the crown continues, the privilege shall not lapse."

His Majesty walked apart, musing, and Hendon dropped into a chair at table, observing to himself, "'Twas a brave thought, and hath wrought me a mighty deliverance; my legs are grievously wearied. An I had not thought of that, I must have had to stand for weeks, till my poor lad's wits are cured." After a little, he went on, "And so I am become a knight of the Kingdom of Dreams and Shadows! A most odd and strange position, truly, for one so matter-of-fact as I. I will not laugh—no, God forbid, for this thing which is so substanceless to me is REAL to him. And to me, also, in one way, it is not a falsity, for it reflects with truth the sweet and generous spirit that is in him." After a pause: "Ah, what if he should call me by my fine title before folk!—there'd be a merry contrast betwixt my glory and my raiment! But no matter, let him call me what he will, so it please him; I shall be content."

Chapter XIII. The disappearance of the Prince.

A heavy drowsiness presently fell upon the two comrades. The King said—

"Remove these rags"—meaning his clothing.

Hendon disapparelled the boy without dissent or remark, tucked him up in bed, then glanced about the room, saying to himself, ruefully, "He hath taken my bed again, as before—marry, what shall *I* do?" The little King observed his perplexity, and dissipated it with a word. He said, sleepily—

"Thou wilt sleep athwart the door, and guard it." In a moment more he was out of his troubles, in a deep slumber.

"Dear heart, he should have been born a king!" muttered Hendon, admiringly; "he playeth the part to a marvel."

Then he stretched himself across the door, on the floor, saying contentedly—

"I have lodged worse for seven years; 'twould be but ill gratitude to Him above to find fault with this."

He dropped asleep as the dawn appeared. Toward noon he rose, uncovered his unconscious ward—a section at a time—and took his measure with a string. The King awoke, just as he had completed his work, complained of the cold, and asked what he was doing.

"'Tis done, now, my liege," said Hendon; "I have a bit of business outside, but will presently return; sleep thou again—thou needest it. There—let me cover thy head also—thou'lt be warm the sooner."

The King was back in dreamland before this speech was ended. Miles slipped softly out, and slipped as softly in again, in the course of thirty or forty minutes, with a complete second-hand suit of boy's clothing, of cheap material, and showing signs of wear; but tidy, and suited to the season of the year. He seated himself, and began to overhaul his purchase, mumbling to himself—

"A longer purse would have got a better sort, but when one has not the long purse one must be content with what a short one may do—

"'There was a woman in our town, In our town did dwell—'

"He stirred, methinks—I must sing in a less thunderous key; 'tis not good to mar his sleep, with this journey before him, and he so wearied out, poor chap . . . This garment—'tis well enough—a stitch here and another one there will set it aright. This other is better, albeit a stitch or two will not come amiss in it, likewise . . . THESE be very good and sound, and will keep his small feet warm and dry—an odd new thing to him, belike, since he has doubtless been used to foot it bare, winters and summers the same . . . Would thread were bread, seeing one getteth a year's sufficiency for a farthing, and such a brave big needle without cost, for mere love. Now shall I have the demon's own time to thread it!"

And so he had. He did as men have always done, and probably always will do, to the end of time—held the needle still, and tried to thrust the thread through the eye, which is the opposite of a woman's way. Time and time again the thread missed the mark, going sometimes on one side of the needle, sometimes on the other, sometimes doubling up against the shaft; but he was patient, having been through these experiences before, when he was soldiering. He succeeded at last, and took up the garment that had lain waiting, meantime, across his lap, and began his work.

"The inn is paid—the breakfast that is to come, included—and there is wherewithal left to buy a couple of donkeys and meet our little costs for the two or three days betwixt this and the plenty that awaits us at Hendon Hall—

"'She loved her hus—'

"Body o' me! I have driven the needle under my nail! . . . It matters little—'tis not a novelty—yet 'tis not a convenience, neither . . .We shall be merry there, little one, never doubt it! Thy troubles will vanish there, and likewise thy sad distemper—

"'She loved her husband dearilee, But another man—'

"These be noble large stitches!"—holding the garment up and viewing it admiringly—"they have a grandeur and a majesty that do cause these small stingy ones of the tailor-man to look mightily paltry and plebeian—

"'She loved her husband dearilee, But another man he loved she,—'

"Marry, 'tis done—a goodly piece of work, too, and wrought with expedition. Now will I wake him, apparel him, pour for him, feed him, and then will we hie us to the mart by the Tabard Inn in Southwark and —be pleased to rise, my liege!—he answereth not—what ho, my liege!—of a truth must I profane his sacred person with a touch, sith his slumber is deaf to speech. What!"

He threw back the covers—the boy was gone!

He stared about him in speechless astonishment for a moment; noticed for the first time that his ward's ragged raiment was also missing; then he began to rage and storm and shout for the innkeeper. At that moment a servant entered with the breakfast.

"Explain, thou limb of Satan, or thy time is come!" roared the man of war, and made so savage a spring toward the waiter that this latter could not find his tongue, for the instant, for fright and surprise. "Where is the boy?"

In disjointed and trembling syllables the man gave the information desired.

"You were hardly gone from the place, your worship, when a youth came running and said it was your worship's will that the boy come to you straight, at the bridge-end on the Southwark side. I brought him hither; and when he woke the lad and gave his message, the lad did grumble some little for being disturbed 'so early,' as he called it, but straightway trussed on his rags and went with the youth, only saying it had been better manners that your worship came yourself, not sent a stranger—and so—"

"And so thou'rt a fool!—a fool and easily cozened—hang all thy breed! Yet mayhap no hurt is done. Possibly no harm is meant the boy. I will go fetch him. Make the table ready. Stay! the coverings of the bed were disposed as if one lay beneath them—happened that by accident?"

"I know not, good your worship. I saw the youth meddle with them—he that came for the boy."

"Thousand deaths! 'Twas done to deceive me—'tis plain 'twas done to gain time. Hark ye! Was that youth alone?"

"All alone, your worship."

"Art sure?"

"Sure, your worship."

"Collect thy scattered wits—bethink thee—take time, man."

After a moment's thought, the servant said—

"When he came, none came with him; but now I remember me that as the two stepped into the throng of the Bridge, a ruffian-looking man plunged out from some near place; and just as he was joining them—"

"What THEN?—out with it!" thundered the impatient Hendon, interrupting.

"Just then the crowd lapped them up and closed them in, and I saw no more, being called by my master, who was in a rage because a joint that the scrivener had ordered was forgot, though I take all the saints to witness that to blame ME for that miscarriage were like holding the unborn babe to judgment for sins com—"

"Out of my sight, idiot! Thy prating drives me mad! Hold! Whither art flying? Canst not bide still an instant? Went they toward Southwark?"

"Even so, your worship—for, as I said before, as to that detestable joint, the babe unborn is no whit more blameless than—"

"Art here YET! And prating still! Vanish, lest I throttle thee!" The servitor vanished. Hendon followed after him, passed him, and plunged down the stairs two steps at a stride,

muttering, "'Tis that scurvy villain that claimed he was his son. I have lost thee, my poor little mad master—it is a bitter thought—and I had come to love thee so! No! by book and bell, NOT lost! Not lost, for I will ransack the land till I find thee again. Poor child, yonder is his breakfast—and mine, but I have no hunger now; so, let the rats have it—speed, speed! that is the word!" As he wormed his swift way through the noisy multitudes upon the Bridge he several times said to himself—clinging to the thought as if it were a particularly pleasing one—"He grumbled, but he WENT—he went, yes, because he thought Miles Hendon asked it, sweet lad—he would ne'er have done it for another, I know it well."

Chapter XIV. 'Le Roi est mort—vive le Roi.'

Toward daylight of the same morning, Tom Canty stirred out of a heavy sleep and opened his eyes in the dark. He lay silent a few moments, trying to analyse his confused thoughts and impressions, and get some sort of meaning out of them; then suddenly he burst out in a rapturous but guarded voice—

"I see it all, I see it all! Now God be thanked, I am indeed awake at last! Come, joy! vanish, sorrow! Ho, Nan! Bet! kick off your straw and hie ye hither to my side, till I do pour into your unbelieving ears the wildest madcap dream that ever the spirits of night did conjure up to astonish the soul of man withal! . . . Ho, Nan, I say! Bet!"

A dim form appeared at his side, and a voice said—

"Wilt deign to deliver thy commands?"

"Commands? . . . O, woe is me, I know thy voice! Speak thou—who am I?"

"Thou? In sooth, yesternight wert thou the Prince of Wales; to-day art thou my most gracious liege, Edward, King of England."

Tom buried his head among his pillows, murmuring plaintively—

"Alack, it was no dream! Go to thy rest, sweet sir—leave me to my sorrows."

Tom slept again, and after a time he had this pleasant dream. He thought it was summer, and he was playing, all alone, in the fair meadow called Goodman's Fields, when a dwarf only a foot high, with long red whiskers and a humped back, appeared to him suddenly and said, "Dig by that stump." He did so, and found twelve bright new pennies—wonderful riches! Yet this was not the best of it; for the dwarf said—

"I know thee. Thou art a good lad, and a deserving; thy distresses shall end, for the day of thy reward is come. Dig here every seventh day, and thou shalt find always the same treasure, twelve bright new pennies. Tell none—keep the secret."

Then the dwarf vanished, and Tom flew to Offal Court with his prize, saying to himself, "Every night will I give my father a penny; he will think I begged it, it will glad his heart, and I shall no more be beaten. One penny every week the good priest that teacheth me shall have; mother, Nan, and Bet the other four. We be done with hunger and rags, now, done with fears and frets and savage usage."

In his dream he reached his sordid home all out of breath, but with eyes dancing with grateful enthusiasm; cast four of his pennies into his mother's lap and cried out—

"They are for thee!—all of them, every one!—for thee and Nan and Bet —and honestly come by, not begged nor stolen!"

The happy and astonished mother strained him to her breast and exclaimed—

"It waxeth late—may it please your Majesty to rise?"

Ah! that was not the answer he was expecting. The dream had snapped asunder—he was awake.

He opened his eyes—the richly clad First Lord of the Bedchamber was kneeling by his couch. The gladness of the lying dream faded away—the poor boy recognised that he was still a captive and a king. The room was filled with courtiers clothed in purple mantles—the mourning colour—and with noble servants of the monarch. Tom sat up in bed and gazed out from the heavy silken curtains upon this fine company.

The weighty business of dressing began, and one courtier after another knelt and paid his court and offered to the little King his condolences upon his heavy loss, whilst the dressing proceeded. In the beginning, a shirt was taken up by the Chief Equerry in Waiting, who passed it to the First Lord of the Buckhounds, who passed it to the Second Gentleman of the Bedchamber, who passed it to the Head Ranger of Windsor Forest, who passed it to the Third Groom of the Stole, who passed it to the Chancellor Royal of the Duchy of Lancaster, who passed it to the Master of the Wardrobe, who passed it to Norroy King-at-Arms, who passed it to the Constable of the Tower, who passed it to the Chief Steward of the Household, who passed it to the Hereditary Grand Diaperer, who passed it to the Lord High Admiral of England, who passed it to the Archbishop of Canterbury, who passed it to the First Lord of the Bedchamber, who took what was left of it and put it on Tom. Poor little wondering chap, it reminded him of passing buckets at a fire.

Each garment in its turn had to go through this slow and solemn process; consequently Tom grew very weary of the ceremony; so weary that he felt an almost gushing gratefulness when he at last saw his long silken hose begin the journey down the line and knew that the end of the matter was drawing near. But he exulted too soon. The First Lord of the Bedchamber received the hose and was about to encase Tom's legs in them, when a sudden flush invaded his face and he hurriedly hustled the things back into the hands of the Archbishop of Canterbury with an astounded look and a whispered, "See, my lord!" pointing to a something connected with the hose. The Archbishop paled, then flushed, and passed the hose to the Lord High Admiral, whispering, "See, my lord!" The Admiral passed the hose to the Hereditary Grand Diaperer, and had hardly breath enough in his body to ejaculate, "See, my lord!" The hose drifted backward along the line, to the Chief Steward of the Household, the Constable of the Tower, Norroy King-at-Arms, the Master of the Wardrobe, the Chancellor Royal of the Duchy of Lancaster, the Third Groom of the Stole, the Head Ranger of Windsor Forest, the Second Gentleman of the Bedchamber, the First Lord of the Buckhounds,—accompanied always with that amazed and frightened "See! see!"—till they finally reached the hands of the Chief Equerry in Waiting, who gazed a moment, with a pallid face, upon what had caused all this dismay, then hoarsely whispered, "Body of my life, a tag gone from a truss-point!—to the Tower with the Head Keeper of the King's

Hose!"—after which he leaned upon the shoulder of the First Lord of the Buckhounds to regather his vanished strength whilst fresh hose, without any damaged strings to them, were brought.

But all things must have an end, and so in time Tom Canty was in a condition to get out of bed. The proper official poured water, the proper official engineered the washing, the proper official stood by with a towel, and by-and-by Tom got safely through the purifying stage and was ready for the services of the Hairdresser-royal. When he at length emerged from this master's hands, he was a gracious figure and as pretty as a girl, in his mantle and trunks of purple satin, and purple-plumed cap. He now moved in state toward his breakfast-room, through the midst of the courtly assemblage; and as he passed, these fell back, leaving his way free, and dropped upon their knees.

After breakfast he was conducted, with regal ceremony, attended by his great officers and his guard of fifty Gentlemen Pensioners bearing gilt battle-axes, to the throne-room, where he proceeded to transact business of state. His 'uncle,' Lord Hertford, took his stand by the throne, to assist the royal mind with wise counsel.

The body of illustrious men named by the late King as his executors appeared, to ask Tom's approval of certain acts of theirs—rather a form, and yet not wholly a form, since there was no Protector as yet. The Archbishop of Canterbury made report of the decree of the Council of Executors concerning the obsequies of his late most illustrious Majesty, and finished by reading the signatures of the Executors, to wit: the Archbishop of Canterbury; the Lord Chancellor of England; William Lord St. John; John Lord Russell; Edward Earl of Hertford; John Viscount Lisle; Cuthbert Bishop of Durham—

Tom was not listening—an earlier clause of the document was puzzling him. At this point he turned and whispered to Lord Hertford—

"What day did he say the burial hath been appointed for?"

"The sixteenth of the coming month, my liege."

"'Tis a strange folly. Will he keep?"

Poor chap, he was still new to the customs of royalty; he was used to seeing the forlorn dead of Offal Court hustled out of the way with a very different sort of expedition. However, the Lord Hertford set his mind at rest with a word or two.

A secretary of state presented an order of the Council appointing the morrow at eleven for the reception of the foreign ambassadors, and desired the King's assent.

Tom turned an inquiring look toward Hertford, who whispered—

"Your Majesty will signify consent. They come to testify their royal masters' sense of the heavy calamity which hath visited your Grace and the realm of England."

Tom did as he was bidden. Another secretary began to read a preamble concerning the expenses of the late King's household, which had amounted to 28,000 pounds during the preceding six months—a sum so vast that it made Tom Canty gasp; he gasped again when the fact appeared that 20,000 pounds of this money was still owing and unpaid*; and once more when it appeared that the King's coffers were about empty, and his twelve hundred servants much embarrassed for lack of the wages due them, Tom spoke out, with lively apprehension—

"We be going to the dogs, 'tis plain. 'Tis meet and necessary that we take a smaller house and set the servants at large, sith they be of no value but to make delay, and trouble one with offices that harass the spirit and shame the soul, they misbecoming any but a doll, that hath nor brains nor hands to help itself withal. I remember me of a small house that standeth over against the fish-market, by Billingsgate—"

A sharp pressure upon Tom's arm stopped his foolish tongue and sent a blush to his face; but no countenance there betrayed any sign that this strange speech had been remarked or given concern.

A secretary made report that forasmuch as the late King had provided in his will for conferring the ducal degree upon the Earl of Hertford and raising his brother, Sir Thomas Seymour, to the peerage, and likewise Hertford's son to an earldom, together with similar aggrandisements to other great servants of the Crown, the Council had resolved to hold a sitting on the 16th of February for the delivering and confirming of these honours, and that meantime, the late King not having granted, in writing, estates suitable to the support of these dignities, the Council, knowing his private wishes in that regard, had thought proper to grant to Seymour '500 pound lands,' and to Hertford's son '800 pound lands, and 300 pound of the next bishop's lands which should fall vacant,'—his present Majesty being willing.*

Tom was about to blurt out something about the propriety of paying the late King's debts first, before squandering all this money, but a timely touch upon his arm, from the thoughtful Hertford, saved him this indiscretion; wherefore he gave the royal assent, without spoken comment, but with much inward discomfort. While he sat reflecting a moment over the ease with which he was doing strange and glittering miracles, a happy thought shot into his mind: why not make his mother Duchess of Offal Court, and give her an estate? But a sorrowful thought swept it instantly away: he was only a king in name, these grave veterans and great nobles were his masters; to them his mother was only the creature of a diseased mind; they would simply listen to his project with unbelieving ears, then send for the doctor.

The dull work went tediously on. Petitions were read, and proclamations, patents, and all manner of wordy, repetitious, and wearisome papers relating to the public business; and at last Tom sighed pathetically and murmured to himself, "In what have I offended, that the good God should take me away from the fields and the free air and the sunshine, to shut me up here and make me a king and afflict me so?" Then his poor muddled head nodded a while and presently drooped to his shoulder; and the business of the empire came to a standstill for want of that august factor, the ratifying power. Silence ensued around the slumbering child, and the sages of the realm ceased from their deliberations.

During the forenoon, Tom had an enjoyable hour, by permission of his keepers, Hertford and St. John, with the Lady Elizabeth and the little Lady Jane Grey; though the

* Hume.
* Ib.

spirits of the princesses were rather subdued by the mighty stroke that had fallen upon the royal house; and at the end of the visit his 'elder sister'—afterwards the 'Bloody Mary' of history —chilled him with a solemn interview which had but one merit in his eyes, its brevity. He had a few moments to himself, and then a slim lad of about twelve years of age was admitted to his presence, whose clothing, except his snowy ruff and the laces about his wrists, was of black, —doublet, hose, and all. He bore no badge of mourning but a knot of purple ribbon on his shoulder. He advanced hesitatingly, with head bowed and bare, and dropped upon one knee in front of Tom. Tom sat still and contemplated him soberly a moment. Then he said—

"Rise, lad. Who art thou. What wouldst have?"

The boy rose, and stood at graceful ease, but with an aspect of concern in his face. He said—

"Of a surety thou must remember me, my lord. I am thy whipping-boy."

"My WHIPPING-boy?"

"The same, your Grace. I am Humphrey—Humphrey Marlow."

Tom perceived that here was someone whom his keepers ought to have posted him about. The situation was delicate. What should he do?—pretend he knew this lad, and then betray by his every utterance that he had never heard of him before? No, that would not do. An idea came to his relief: accidents like this might be likely to happen with some frequency, now that business urgencies would often call Hertford and St. John from his side, they being members of the Council of Executors; therefore perhaps it would be well to strike out a plan himself to meet the requirements of such emergencies. Yes, that would be a wise course—he would practise on this boy, and see what sort of success he might achieve. So he stroked his brow perplexedly a moment or two, and presently said—

"Now I seem to remember thee somewhat—but my wit is clogged and dim with suffering—"

"Alack, my poor master!" ejaculated the whipping-boy, with feeling; adding, to himself, "In truth 'tis as they said—his mind is gone—alas, poor soul! But misfortune catch me, how am I forgetting! They said one must not seem to observe that aught is wrong with him."

"'Tis strange how my memory doth wanton with me these days," said Tom. "But mind it not—I mend apace—a little clue doth often serve to bring me back again the things and names which had escaped me. (And not they, only, forsooth, but e'en such as I ne'er heard before—as this lad shall see.) Give thy business speech."

"'Tis matter of small weight, my liege, yet will I touch upon it, an' it please your Grace. Two days gone by, when your Majesty faulted thrice in your Greek—in the morning lessons,—dost remember it?"

"Y-e-s—methinks I do. (It is not much of a lie—an' I had meddled with the Greek at all, I had not faulted simply thrice, but forty times.) Yes, I do recall it, now—go on."

"The master, being wroth with what he termed such slovenly and doltish work, did promise that he would soundly whip me

The Prince and The Pauper 355

for it—and—"

"Whip THEE!" said Tom, astonished out of his presence of mind. "Why should he whip THEE for faults of mine?"

"Ah, your Grace forgetteth again. He always scourgeth me when thou dost fail in thy lessons."

"True, true—I had forgot. Thou teachest me in private—then if I fail, he argueth that thy office was lamely done, and—"

"Oh, my liege, what words are these? I, the humblest of thy servants, presume to teach THEE?"

"Then where is thy blame? What riddle is this? Am I in truth gone mad, or is it thou? Explain—speak out."

"But, good your Majesty, there's nought that needeth simplifying.—None may visit the sacred person of the Prince of Wales with blows; wherefore, when he faulteth, 'tis I that take them; and meet it is and right, for that it is mine office and my livelihood."*

Tom stared at the tranquil boy, observing to himself, "Lo, it is a wonderful thing,—a most strange and curious trade; I marvel they have not hired a boy to take my combings and my dressings for me—would heaven they would!—an' they will do this thing, I will take my lashings in mine own person, giving God thanks for the change." Then he said aloud—

"And hast thou been beaten, poor friend, according to the promise?"

"No, good your Majesty, my punishment was appointed for this day, and peradventure it may be annulled, as unbefitting the season of mourning that is come upon us; I know not, and so have made bold to come hither and remind your Grace about your gracious promise to intercede in my behalf—"

"With the master? To save thee thy whipping?"

"Ah, thou dost remember!"

"My memory mendeth, thou seest. Set thy mind at ease—thy back shall go unscathed—I will see to it."

"Oh, thanks, my good lord!" cried the boy, dropping upon his knee again. "Mayhap I have ventured far enow; and yet—"

Seeing Master Humphrey hesitate, Tom encouraged him to go on, saying he was "in the granting mood."

"Then will I speak it out, for it lieth near my heart. Sith thou art no more Prince of Wales but King, thou canst order matters as thou wilt, with none to say thee nay; wherefore it is not in reason that thou wilt longer vex thyself with dreary studies, but wilt burn thy books and turn thy mind to things less irksome. Then am I ruined, and mine orphan sisters with me!"

"Ruined? Prithee how?"

"My back is my bread, O my gracious liege! if it go idle, I

---

* The Whipping-boy: James I. and Charles II. had whipping-boys, when they were little fellows, to take their punishment for them when they fell short in their lessons; so I have ventured to furnish my small prince with one, for my own purposes.

starve. An' thou cease from study mine office is gone thou'lt need no whipping-boy. Do not turn me away!"

Tom was touched with this pathetic distress. He said, with a right royal burst of generosity—

"Discomfort thyself no further, lad. Thine office shall be permanent in thee and thy line for ever." Then he struck the boy a light blow on the shoulder with the flat of his sword, exclaiming, "Rise, Humphrey Marlow, Hereditary Grand Whipping-Boy to the Royal House of England! Banish sorrow—I will betake me to my books again, and study so ill that they must in justice treble thy wage, so mightily shall the business of thine office be augmented."

The grateful Humphrey responded fervidly—

"Thanks, O most noble master, this princely lavishness doth far surpass my most distempered dreams of fortune. Now shall I be happy all my days, and all the house of Marlow after me."

Tom had wit enough to perceive that here was a lad who could be useful to him. He encouraged Humphrey to talk, and he was nothing loath. He was delighted to believe that he was helping in Tom's 'cure'; for always, as soon as he had finished calling back to Tom's diseased mind the various particulars of his experiences and adventures in the royal school-room and elsewhere about the palace, he noticed that Tom was then able to 'recall' the circumstances quite clearly. At the end of an hour Tom found himself well freighted with very valuable information concerning personages and matters pertaining to the Court; so he resolved to draw instruction from this source daily; and to this end he would give order to admit Humphrey to the royal closet whenever he might come, provided the Majesty of England was not engaged with other people. Humphrey had hardly been dismissed when my Lord Hertford arrived with more trouble for Tom.

He said that the Lords of the Council, fearing that some overwrought report of the King's damaged health might have leaked out and got abroad, they deemed it wise and best that his Majesty should begin to dine in public after a day or two— his wholesome complexion and vigorous step, assisted by a carefully guarded repose of manner and ease and grace of demeanour, would more surely quiet the general pulse—in case any evil rumours HAD gone about—than any other scheme that could be devised.

Then the Earl proceeded, very delicately, to instruct Tom as to the observances proper to the stately occasion, under the rather thin disguise of 'reminding' him concerning things already known to him; but to his vast gratification it turned out that Tom needed very little help in this line—he had been making use of Humphrey in that direction, for Humphrey had mentioned that within a few days he was to begin to dine in public; having gathered it from the swift-winged gossip of the Court. Tom kept these facts to himself, however.

Seeing the royal memory so improved, the Earl ventured to apply a few tests to it, in an apparently casual way, to find out how far its amendment had progressed. The results were happy, here and there, in spots—spots where Humphrey's tracks remained—and on the whole my lord was greatly pleased and encouraged. So encouraged was he, indeed, that he spoke up and said in a quite hopeful voice—

"Now am I persuaded that if your Majesty will but tax your memory yet a little further, it will resolve the puzzle of the

Great Seal—a loss which was of moment yesterday, although of none to-day, since its term of service ended with our late lord's life. May it please your Grace to make the trial?"

Tom was at sea—a Great Seal was something which he was totally unacquainted with. After a moment's hesitation he looked up innocently and asked—

"What was it like, my lord?"

The Earl started, almost imperceptibly, muttering to himself, "Alack, his wits are flown again!—it was ill wisdom to lead him on to strain them" —then he deftly turned the talk to other matters, with the purpose of sweeping the unlucky seal out of Tom's thoughts—a purpose which easily succeeded.

Chapter XV. Tom as King.

The next day the foreign ambassadors came, with their gorgeous trains; and Tom, throned in awful state, received them. The splendours of the scene delighted his eye and fired his imagination at first, but the audience was long and dreary, and so were most of the addresses —wherefore, what began as a pleasure grew into weariness and home-sickness by-and-by. Tom said the words which Hertford* put into his mouth from time to time, and tried hard to acquit himself satisfactorily, but he was too new to such things, and too ill at ease to accomplish more than a tolerable success. He looked sufficiently like a king, but he was ill able to feel like one. He was cordially glad when the ceremony was ended.

The larger part of his day was 'wasted'—as he termed it, in his own mind—in labours pertaining to his royal office. Even the two hours devoted to certain princely pastimes and recreations were rather a burden to him than otherwise, they were so fettered by restrictions and ceremonious observances. However, he had a private hour with his whipping-boy which he counted clear gain, since he got both entertainment and needful information out of it.

The third day of Tom Canty's kingship came and went much as the others had done, but there was a lifting of his cloud in one way—he felt less uncomfortable than at first; he was getting a little used to his circumstances and surroundings; his chains still galled, but not all the time; he found that the presence and homage of the great afflicted and embarrassed him less and less sharply with every hour that drifted over his head.

---

* Character of Hertford: The young King discovered an extreme attachment to his uncle, who was, in the main, a man of moderation and probity.—Hume's History of England, vol. iii, p324.

But if he (the Protector) gave offence by assuming too much state, he deserves great praise on account of the laws passed this session, by which the rigour of former statutes was much mitigated, and some security given to the freedom of the constitution. All laws were repealed which extended the crime of treason beyond the statute of the twenty-fifth of Edward III.; all laws enacted during the late reign extending the crime of felony; all the former laws against Lollardy or heresy, together with the statute of the Six Articles. None were to be accused for words, but within a month after they were spoken. By these repeals several of the most rigorous laws that ever had passed in England were annulled; and some dawn, both of civil and religious liberty, began to appear to the people. A repeal also passed of that law, the destruction of all laws, by which the King's proclamation was made of equal force with a statute. —Ibid. vol. iii. p. 339.

But for one single dread, he could have seen the fourth day approach without serious distress—the dining in public; it was to begin that day. There were greater matters in the programme—for on that day he would have to preside at a council which would take his views and commands concerning the policy to be pursued toward various foreign nations scattered far and near over the great globe; on that day, too, Hertford would be formally chosen to the grand office of Lord Protector; other things of note were appointed for that fourth day, also; but to Tom they were all insignificant compared with the ordeal of dining all by himself with a multitude of curious eyes fastened upon him and a multitude of mouths whispering comments upon his performance,—and upon his mistakes, if he should be so unlucky as to make any.

Still, nothing could stop that fourth day, and so it came. It found poor Tom low-spirited and absent-minded, and this mood continued; he could not shake it off. The ordinary duties of the morning dragged upon his hands, and wearied him. Once more he felt the sense of captivity heavy upon him.

Late in the forenoon he was in a large audience-chamber, conversing with the Earl of Hertford and dully awaiting the striking of the hour appointed for a visit of ceremony from a considerable number of great officials and courtiers.

After a little while, Tom, who had wandered to a window and become interested in the life and movement of the great highway beyond the palace gates—and not idly interested, but longing with all his heart to take part in person in its stir and freedom—saw the van of a hooting and shouting mob of disorderly men, women, and children of the lowest and poorest degree approaching from up the road.

"I would I knew what 'tis about!" he exclaimed, with all a boy's curiosity in such happenings.

"Thou art the King!" solemnly responded the Earl, with a reverence. "Have I your Grace's leave to act?"

"O blithely, yes! O gladly, yes!" exclaimed Tom excitedly, adding to himself with a lively sense of satisfaction, "In truth, being a king is not all dreariness—it hath its compensations and conveniences."

The Earl called a page, and sent him to the captain of the guard with the order—

"Let the mob be halted, and inquiry made concerning the occasion of its movement. By the King's command!"

A few seconds later a long rank of the royal guards, cased in flashing steel, filed out at the gates and formed across the highway in front of the multitude. A messenger returned, to report that the crowd were following a man, a woman, and a young girl to execution for crimes committed against the peace and dignity of the realm.

Death—and a violent death—for these poor unfortunates! The thought wrung Tom's heart-strings. The spirit of compassion took control of him, to the exclusion of all other considerations; he never thought of the offended laws, or of the grief or loss which these three criminals had inflicted upon their victims; he could think of nothing but the scaffold and the grisly fate hanging over the heads of the condemned. His concern made him even forget, for the moment, that he was but the false shadow of a king, not the substance; and before he knew it he had blurted out the command—

"Bring them here!"

Then he blushed scarlet, and a sort of apology sprung to his lips; but observing that his order had wrought no sort of surprise in the Earl or the waiting page, he suppressed the words he was about to utter. The page, in the most matter-of-course way, made a profound obeisance and retired backwards out of the room to deliver the command. Tom experienced a glow of pride and a renewed sense of the compensating advantages of the kingly office. He said to himself, "Truly it is like what I was used to feel when I read the old priest's tales, and did imagine mine own self a prince, giving law and command to all, saying 'Do this; do that,' whilst none durst offer let or hindrance to my will."

Now the doors swung open; one high-sounding title after another was announced, the personages owning them followed, and the place was quickly half-filled with noble folk and finery. But Tom was hardly conscious of the presence of these people, so wrought up was he and so intensely absorbed in that other and more interesting matter. He seated himself absently in his chair of state, and turned his eyes upon the door with manifestations of impatient expectancy; seeing which, the company forbore to trouble him, and fell to chatting a mixture of public business and court gossip one with another.

In a little while the measured tread of military men was heard approaching, and the culprits entered the presence in charge of an under-sheriff and escorted by a detail of the king's guard. The civil officer knelt before Tom, then stood aside; the three doomed persons knelt, also, and remained so; the guard took position behind Tom's chair. Tom scanned the prisoners curiously. Something about the dress or appearance of the man had stirred a vague memory in him. "Methinks I have seen this man ere now . . . but the when or the where fail me"—such was Tom's thought. Just then the man glanced quickly up and quickly dropped his face again, not being able to endure the awful port of sovereignty; but the one full glimpse of the face which Tom got was sufficient. He said to himself: "Now is the matter clear; this is the stranger that plucked Giles Witt out of the Thames, and saved his life, that windy, bitter, first day of the New Year—a brave good deed—pity he hath been doing baser ones and got himself in this sad case . . . I have not forgot the day, neither the hour; by reason that an hour after, upon the stroke of eleven, I did get a hiding by the hand of Gammer Canty which was of so goodly and admired severity that all that went before or followed after it were but fondlings and caresses by comparison."

Tom now ordered that the woman and the girl be removed from the presence for a little time; then addressed himself to the under-sheriff, saying—

"Good sir, what is this man's offence?"

The officer knelt, and answered—

"So please your Majesty, he hath taken the life of a subject by poison."

Tom's compassion for the prisoner, and admiration of him as the daring rescuer of a drowning boy, experienced a most damaging shock.

"The thing was proven upon him?" he asked.

"Most clearly, sire."

Tom sighed, and said—

"Take him away—he hath earned his death. 'Tis a pity, for he was a brave heart—na—na, I mean he hath the LOOK of it!"

The prisoner clasped his hands together with sudden energy, and wrung them despairingly, at the same time appealing imploringly to the 'King' in broken and terrified phrases—

"O my lord the King, an' thou canst pity the lost, have pity upon me! I am innocent—neither hath that wherewith I am charged been more than but lamely proved—yet I speak not of that; the judgment is gone forth against me and may not suffer alteration; yet in mine extremity I beg a boon, for my doom is more than I can bear. A grace, a grace, my lord the King! in thy royal compassion grant my prayer—give commandment that I be hanged!"

Tom was amazed. This was not the outcome he had looked for.

"Odds my life, a strange BOON! Was it not the fate intended thee?"

"O good my liege, not so! It is ordered that I be BOILED ALIVE!*"

The hideous surprise of these words almost made Tom spring from his chair. As soon as he could recover his wits he cried out—

"Have thy wish, poor soul! an' thou had poisoned a hundred men thou shouldst not suffer so miserable a death."

The prisoner bowed his face to the ground and burst into passionate expressions of gratitude—ending with—

"If ever thou shouldst know misfortune—which God forefend!—may thy goodness to me this day be remembered and requited!"

Tom turned to the Earl of Hertford, and said—

"My lord, is it believable that there was warrant for this man's ferocious doom?"

"It is the law, your Grace—for poisoners. In Germany coiners be boiled to death in OIL—not cast in of a sudden, but by a rope let down into the oil by degrees, and slowly; first the feet, then the legs, then—"

"O prithee no more, my lord, I cannot bear it!" cried Tom,

---

* Boiling to Death: In the reign of Henry VIII. poisoners were, by Act of Parliament, condemned to be BOILED TO DEATH. This Act was repealed in the following reign.

In Germany, even in the seventeenth century, this horrible punishment was inflicted on coiners and counterfeiters. Taylor, the Water Poet, describes an execution he witnessed in Hamburg in 1616. The judgment pronounced against a coiner of false money was that he should 'BE BOILED TO DEATH IN OIL; not thrown into the vessel at once, but with a pulley or rope to be hanged under the armpits, and then let down into the oil BY DEGREES; first the feet, and next the legs, and so to boil his flesh from his bones alive.'—Dr. J. Hammond Trumbull's Blue Laws, True and False, p. 13.

covering his eyes with his hands to shut out the picture. "I beseech your good lordship that order be taken to change this law—oh, let no more poor creatures be visited with its tortures."

The Earl's face showed profound gratification, for he was a man of merciful and generous impulses—a thing not very common with his class in that fierce age. He said—

"These your Grace's noble words have sealed its doom. History will remember it to the honour of your royal house."

The under-sheriff was about to remove his prisoner; Tom gave him a sign to wait; then he said—

"Good sir, I would look into this matter further. The man has said his deed was but lamely proved. Tell me what thou knowest."

"If the King's grace please, it did appear upon the trial that this man entered into a house in the hamlet of Islington where one lay sick—three witnesses say it was at ten of the clock in the morning, and two say it was some minutes later—the sick man being alone at the time, and sleeping—and presently the man came forth again and went his way. The sick man died within the hour, being torn with spasms and retchings."

"Did any see the poison given? Was poison found?"

"Marry, no, my liege."

"Then how doth one know there was poison given at all?"

"Please your Majesty, the doctors testified that none die with such symptoms but by poison."

Weighty evidence, this, in that simple age. Tom recognised its formidable nature, and said—

"The doctor knoweth his trade—belike they were right. The matter hath an ill-look for this poor man."

"Yet was not this all, your Majesty; there is more and worse. Many testified that a witch, since gone from the village, none know whither, did foretell, and speak it privately in their ears, that the sick man WOULD DIE BY POISON—and more, that a stranger would give it—a stranger with brown hair and clothed in a worn and common garb; and surely this prisoner doth answer woundily to the bill. Please your Majesty to give the circumstance that solemn weight which is its due, seeing it was FORETOLD."

This was an argument of tremendous force in that superstitious day. Tom felt that the thing was settled; if evidence was worth anything, this poor fellow's guilt was proved. Still he offered the prisoner a chance, saying—

"If thou canst say aught in thy behalf, speak."

"Nought that will avail, my King. I am innocent, yet cannot I make it appear. I have no friends, else might I show that I was not in Islington that day; so also might I show that at that hour they name I was above a league away, seeing I was at Wapping Old Stairs; yea more, my King, for I could show, that whilst they say I was TAKING life, I was SAVING it. A drowning boy—"

"Peace! Sheriff, name the day the deed was done!"

"At ten in the morning, or some minutes later, the first day of the New Year, most illustrious—"

"Let the prisoner go free—it is the King's will!"

Another blush followed this unregal outburst, and he covered his indecorum as well as he could by adding—

"It enrageth me that a man should be hanged upon such idle, hare-brained evidence!"

A low buzz of admiration swept through the assemblage. It was not admiration of the decree that had been delivered by Tom, for the propriety or expediency of pardoning a convicted poisoner was a thing which few there would have felt justified in either admitting or admiring—no, the admiration was for the intelligence and spirit which Tom had displayed. Some of the low-voiced remarks were to this effect—

"This is no mad king—he hath his wits sound."

"How sanely he put his questions—how like his former natural self was this abrupt imperious disposal of the matter!"

"God be thanked, his infirmity is spent! This is no weakling, but a king. He hath borne himself like to his own father."

The air being filled with applause, Tom's ear necessarily caught a little of it. The effect which this had upon him was to put him greatly at his ease, and also to charge his system with very gratifying sensations.

However, his juvenile curiosity soon rose superior to these pleasant thoughts and feelings; he was eager to know what sort of deadly mischief the woman and the little girl could have been about; so, by his command, the two terrified and sobbing creatures were brought before him.

"What is it that these have done?" he inquired of the sheriff.

"Please your Majesty, a black crime is charged upon them, and clearly proven; wherefore the judges have decreed, according to the law, that they be hanged. They sold themselves to the devil—such is their crime."

Tom shuddered. He had been taught to abhor people who did this wicked thing. Still, he was not going to deny himself the pleasure of feeding his curiosity for all that; so he asked—

"Where was this done?—and when?"

"On a midnight in December, in a ruined church, your Majesty."

Tom shuddered again.

"Who was there present?"

"Only these two, your grace—and THAT OTHER."

"Have these confessed?"

"Nay, not so, sire—they do deny it."

"Then prithee, how was it known?"

"Certain witness did see them wending thither, good your

Majesty; this bred the suspicion, and dire effects have since confirmed and justified it. In particular, it is in evidence that through the wicked power so obtained, they did invoke and bring about a storm that wasted all the region round about. Above forty witnesses have proved the storm; and sooth one might have had a thousand, for all had reason to remember it, sith all had suffered by it."

"Certes this is a serious matter." Tom turned this dark piece of scoundrelism over in his mind a while, then asked—

"Suffered the woman also by the storm?"

Several old heads among the assemblage nodded their recognition of the wisdom of this question. The sheriff, however, saw nothing consequential in the inquiry; he answered, with simple directness—

"Indeed did she, your Majesty, and most righteously, as all aver. Her habitation was swept away, and herself and child left shelterless."

"Methinks the power to do herself so ill a turn was dearly bought. She had been cheated, had she paid but a farthing for it; that she paid her soul, and her child's, argueth that she is mad; if she is mad she knoweth not what she doth, therefore sinneth not."

The elderly heads nodded recognition of Tom's wisdom once more, and one individual murmured, "An' the King be mad himself, according to report, then is it a madness of a sort that would improve the sanity of some I wot of, if by the gentle providence of God they could but catch it."

"What age hath the child?" asked Tom.

"Nine years, please your Majesty."

"By the law of England may a child enter into covenant and sell itself, my lord?" asked Tom, turning to a learned judge.

"The law doth not permit a child to make or meddle in any weighty matter, good my liege, holding that its callow wit unfitteth it to cope with the riper wit and evil schemings of them that are its elders. The DEVIL may buy a child, if he so choose, and the child agree thereto, but not an Englishman—in this latter case the contract would be null and void."

"It seemeth a rude unchristian thing, and ill contrived, that English law denieth privileges to Englishmen to waste them on the devil!" cried Tom, with honest heat.

This novel view of the matter excited many smiles, and was stored away in many heads to be repeated about the Court as evidence of Tom's originality as well as progress toward mental health.

The elder culprit had ceased from sobbing, and was hanging upon Tom's words with an excited interest and a growing hope. Tom noticed this, and it strongly inclined his sympathies toward her in her perilous and unfriended situation. Presently he asked—

"How wrought they to bring the storm?"

"BY PULLING OFF THEIR STOCKINGS, sire."

This astonished Tom, and also fired his curiosity to fever heat.

He said, eagerly—

"It is wonderful! Hath it always this dread effect?"

"Always, my liege—at least if the woman desire it, and utter the needful words, either in her mind or with her tongue."

Tom turned to the woman, and said with impetuous zeal—

"Exert thy power—I would see a storm!"

There was a sudden paling of cheeks in the superstitious assemblage, and a general, though unexpressed, desire to get out of the place—all of which was lost upon Tom, who was dead to everything but the proposed cataclysm. Seeing a puzzled and astonished look in the woman's face, he added, excitedly—

"Never fear—thou shalt be blameless. More—thou shalt go free—none shall touch thee. Exert thy power."

"Oh, my lord the King, I have it not—I have been falsely accused."

"Thy fears stay thee. Be of good heart, thou shalt suffer no harm. Make a storm—it mattereth not how small a one—I require nought great or harmful, but indeed prefer the opposite—do this and thy life is spared —thou shalt go out free, with thy child, bearing the King's pardon, and safe from hurt or malice from any in the realm."

The woman prostrated herself, and protested, with tears, that she had no power to do the miracle, else she would gladly win her child's life alone, and be content to lose her own, if by obedience to the King's command so precious a grace might be acquired.

Tom urged—the woman still adhered to her declarations. Finally he said—

"I think the woman hath said true. An' MY mother were in her place and gifted with the devil's functions, she had not stayed a moment to call her storms and lay the whole land in ruins, if the saving of my forfeit life were the price she got! It is argument that other mothers are made in like mould. Thou art free, goodwife—thou and thy child—for I do think thee innocent. NOW thou'st nought to fear, being pardoned—pull off thy stockings!—an' thou canst make me a storm, thou shalt be rich!"

The redeemed creature was loud in her gratitude, and proceeded to obey, whilst Tom looked on with eager expectancy, a little marred by apprehension; the courtiers at the same time manifesting decided discomfort and uneasiness. The woman stripped her own feet and her little girl's also, and plainly did her best to reward the King's generosity with an earthquake, but it was all a failure and a disappointment. Tom sighed, and said—

"There, good soul, trouble thyself no further, thy power is departed out of thee. Go thy way in peace; and if it return to thee at any time, forget me not, but fetch me a storm."*

---

* The Famous Stocking Case: A woman and her daughter, NINE YEARS OLD, were hanged in Huntingdon for selling their souls to the devil, and raising a storm by pulling off their stockings!—Dr. J. Hammond Trumbull's Blue Laws, True and False, p. 20.

Chapter XVI. The State Dinner.

The dinner hour drew near—yet strangely enough, the thought brought but slight discomfort to Tom, and hardly any terror. The morning's experiences had wonderfully built up his confidence; the poor little ash-cat was already more wonted to his strange garret, after four days' habit, than a mature person could have become in a full month. A child's facility in accommodating itself to circumstances was never more strikingly illustrated.

Let us privileged ones hurry to the great banqueting-room and have a glance at matters there whilst Tom is being made ready for the imposing occasion. It is a spacious apartment, with gilded pillars and pilasters, and pictured walls and ceilings. At the door stand tall guards, as rigid as statues, dressed in rich and picturesque costumes, and bearing halberds. In a high gallery which runs all around the place is a band of musicians and a packed company of citizens of both sexes, in brilliant attire. In the centre of the room, upon a raised platform, is Tom's table. Now let the ancient chronicler speak:

"A gentleman enters the room bearing a rod, and along with him another bearing a tablecloth, which, after they have both kneeled three times with the utmost veneration, he spreads upon the table, and after kneeling again they both retire; then come two others, one with the rod again, the other with a salt-cellar, a plate, and bread; when they have kneeled as the others had done, and placed what was brought upon the table, they too retire with the same ceremonies performed by the first; at last come two nobles, richly clothed, one bearing a tasting-knife, who, after prostrating themselves three times in the most graceful manner, approach and rub the table with bread and salt, with as much awe as if the King had been present."*

So end the solemn preliminaries. Now, far down the echoing corridors we hear a bugle-blast, and the indistinct cry, "Place for the King! Way for the King's most excellent majesty!" These sounds are momently repeated —they grow nearer and nearer—and presently, almost in our faces, the martial note peals and the cry rings out, "Way for the King!" At this instant the shining pageant appears, and files in at the door, with a measured march. Let the chronicler speak again:—

"First come Gentlemen, Barons, Earls, Knights of the Garter, all richly dressed and bareheaded; next comes the Chancellor, between two, one of which carries the royal sceptre, the other the Sword of State in a red scabbard, studded with golden fleurs-de-lis, the point upwards; next comes the King himself—whom, upon his appearing, twelve trumpets and many drums salute with a great burst of welcome, whilst all in the galleries rise in their places, crying 'God save the King!' After him come nobles attached to his person, and on his right and left march his guard of honour, his fifty Gentlemen Pensioners, with gilt battle-axes."

This was all fine and pleasant. Tom's pulse beat high, and a glad light was in his eye. He bore himself right gracefully, and all the more so because he was not thinking of how he was doing it, his mind being charmed and occupied with the blithe sights and sounds about him—and besides, nobody can be very ungraceful in nicely-fitting beautiful clothes after he has grown a little used to them—especially if he is for the moment unconscious of them. Tom remembered his instructions, and acknowledged his greeting with a slight inclination of his

---

* Leigh Hunt's 'The Town,' p.408, quotation from an early tourist.

plumed head, and a courteous "I thank ye, my good people."

He seated himself at table, without removing his cap; and did it without the least embarrassment; for to eat with one's cap on was the one solitary royal custom upon which the kings and the Cantys met upon common ground, neither party having any advantage over the other in the matter of old familiarity with it. The pageant broke up and grouped itself picturesquely, and remained bareheaded.

Now to the sound of gay music the Yeomen of the Guard entered,—"the tallest and mightiest men in England, they being carefully selected in this regard"—but we will let the chronicler tell about it:—

"The Yeomen of the Guard entered, bareheaded, clothed in scarlet, with golden roses upon their backs; and these went and came, bringing in each turn a course of dishes, served in plate. These dishes were received by a gentleman in the same order they were brought, and placed upon the table, while the taster gave to each guard a mouthful to eat of the particular dish he had brought, for fear of any poison."

Tom made a good dinner, notwithstanding he was conscious that hundreds of eyes followed each morsel to his mouth and watched him eat it with an interest which could not have been more intense if it had been a deadly explosive and was expected to blow him up and scatter him all about the place. He was careful not to hurry, and equally careful not to do anything whatever for himself, but wait till the proper official knelt down and did it for him. He got through without a mistake—flawless and precious triumph.

When the meal was over at last and he marched away in the midst of his bright pageant, with the happy noises in his ears of blaring bugles, rolling drums, and thundering acclamations, he felt that if he had seen the worst of dining in public it was an ordeal which he would be glad to endure several times a day if by that means he could but buy himself free from some of the more formidable requirements of his royal office.

Chapter XVII. Foo-foo the First.

Miles Hendon hurried along toward the Southwark end of the bridge, keeping a sharp look-out for the persons he sought, and hoping and expecting to overtake them presently. He was disappointed in this, however. By asking questions, he was enabled to track them part of the way through Southwark; then all traces ceased, and he was perplexed as to how to proceed. Still, he continued his efforts as best he could during the rest of the day. Nightfall found him leg-weary, half-famished, and his desire as far from accomplishment as ever; so he supped at the Tabard Inn and went to bed, resolved to make an early start in the morning, and give the town an exhaustive search. As he lay thinking and planning, he presently began to reason thus: The boy would escape from the ruffian, his reputed father, if possible; would he go back to London and seek his former haunts? No, he would not do that, he would avoid recapture. What, then, would he do? Never having had a friend in the world, or a protector, until he met Miles Hendon, he would naturally try to find that friend again, provided the effort did not require him to go toward London and danger. He would strike for Hendon Hall, that is what he would do, for he knew Hendon was homeward bound and there he might expect to find him. Yes, the case was plain to Hendon—he must lose no more time in Southwark, but move at once through Kent, toward Monk's Holm, searching the wood and inquiring as he went. Let us return to the vanished little King now.

The ruffian whom the waiter at the inn on the bridge saw 'about to join' the youth and the King did not exactly join them, but fell in close behind them and followed their steps. He said nothing. His left arm was in a sling, and he wore a large green patch over his left eye; he limped slightly, and used an oaken staff as a support. The youth led the King a crooked course through Southwark, and by-and-by struck into the high road beyond. The King was irritated, now, and said he would stop here—it was Hendon's place to come to him, not his to go to Hendon. He would not endure such insolence; he would stop where he was. The youth said—

"Thou'lt tarry here, and thy friend lying wounded in the wood yonder? So be it, then."

The King's manner changed at once. He cried out—

"Wounded? And who hath dared to do it? But that is apart; lead on, lead on! Faster, sirrah! Art shod with lead? Wounded, is he? Now though the doer of it be a duke's son he shall rue it!"

It was some distance to the wood, but the space was speedily traversed. The youth looked about him, discovered a bough sticking in the ground, with a small bit of rag tied to it, then led the way into the forest, watching for similar boughs and finding them at intervals; they were evidently guides to the point he was aiming at. By-and-by an open place was reached, where were the charred remains of a farm-house, and near them a barn which was falling to ruin and decay. There was no sign of life anywhere, and utter silence prevailed. The youth entered the barn, the King following eagerly upon his heels. No one there! The King shot a surprised and suspicious glance at the youth, and asked—

"Where is he?"

A mocking laugh was his answer. The King was in a rage in a moment; he seized a billet of wood and was in the act of charging upon the youth when another mocking laugh fell upon his ear. It was from the lame ruffian who had been following at a distance. The King turned and said angrily—

"Who art thou? What is thy business here?"

"Leave thy foolery," said the man, "and quiet thyself. My disguise is none so good that thou canst pretend thou knowest not thy father through it."

"Thou art not my father. I know thee not. I am the King. If thou hast hid my servant, find him for me, or thou shalt sup sorrow for what thou hast done."

John Canty replied, in a stern and measured voice—

"It is plain thou art mad, and I am loath to punish thee; but if thou provoke me, I must. Thy prating doth no harm here, where there are no ears that need to mind thy follies; yet it is well to practise thy tongue to wary speech, that it may do no hurt when our quarters change. I have done a murder, and may not tarry at home—neither shalt thou, seeing I need thy service. My name is changed, for wise reasons; it is Hobbs — John Hobbs; thine is Jack—charge thy memory accordingly. Now, then, speak. Where is thy mother? Where are thy sisters? They came not to the place appointed—knowest thou whither they went?"

The King answered sullenly—

"Trouble me not with these riddles. My mother is dead; my sisters are in the palace."

The youth near by burst into a derisive laugh, and the King would have assaulted him, but Canty—or Hobbs, as he now called himself—prevented him, and said—

"Peace, Hugo, vex him not; his mind is astray, and thy ways fret him. Sit thee down, Jack, and quiet thyself; thou shalt have a morsel to eat, anon."

Hobbs and Hugo fell to talking together, in low voices, and the King removed himself as far as he could from their disagreeable company. He withdrew into the twilight of the farther end of the barn, where he found the earthen floor bedded a foot deep with straw. He lay down here, drew straw over himself in lieu of blankets, and was soon absorbed in thinking. He had many griefs, but the minor ones were swept almost into forgetfulness by the supreme one, the loss of his father. To the rest of the world the name of Henry VIII. brought a shiver, and suggested an ogre whose nostrils breathed destruction and whose hand dealt scourgings and death; but to this boy the name brought only sensations of pleasure; the figure it invoked wore a countenance that was all gentleness and affection. He called to mind a long succession of loving passages between his father and himself, and dwelt fondly upon them, his unstinted tears attesting how deep and real was the grief that possessed his heart. As the afternoon wasted away, the lad, wearied with his troubles, sank gradually into a tranquil and healing slumber.

After a considerable time—he could not tell how long—his senses struggled to a half-consciousness, and as he lay with closed eyes vaguely wondering where he was and what had been happening, he noted a murmurous sound, the sullen beating of rain upon the roof. A snug sense of comfort stole over him, which was rudely broken, the next moment, by a chorus of piping cackles and coarse laughter. It startled him disagreeably, and he unmuffled his head to see whence this interruption proceeded. A grim and unsightly picture met his eye. A bright fire was burning in the middle of the floor, at the other end of the barn; and around it, and lit weirdly up by the red glare, lolled and sprawled the motliest company of tattered gutter-scum and ruffians, of both sexes, he had ever read or dreamed of. There were huge stalwart men, brown with exposure, long-haired, and clothed in fantastic rags; there were middle-sized youths, of truculent countenance, and similarly clad; there were blind mendicants, with patched or bandaged eyes; crippled ones, with wooden legs and crutches; diseased ones, with running sores peeping from ineffectual wrappings; there was a villain-looking pedlar with his pack; a knife-grinder, a tinker, and a barber-surgeon, with the implements of their trades; some of the females were hardly-grown girls, some were at prime, some were old and wrinkled hags, and all were loud, brazen, foul-mouthed; and all soiled and slatternly; there were three sore-faced babies; there were a couple of starveling curs, with strings about their necks, whose office was to lead the blind.

The night was come, the gang had just finished feasting, an orgy was beginning; the can of liquor was passing from mouth to mouth. A general cry broke forth—

"A song! a song from the Bat and Dick and Dot-and-go-One!"

One of the blind men got up, and made ready by casting aside the patches that sheltered his excellent eyes, and the pathetic placard which recited the cause of his calamity. Dot-and-go-One disencumbered himself of his timber leg and took his place, upon sound and healthy limbs, beside his fellow-rascal; then they roared out a rollicking ditty, and were reinforced by the whole crew, at the end of each stanza, in a rousing chorus. By the time the last stanza was reached, the half-drunken enthusiasm had risen to such a pitch, that everybody joined in and sang it clear through from the beginning, producing a volume of villainous sound that made the rafters quake. These were the inspiring words:—

'Bien Darkman's then, Bouse Mort and Ken, The bien Coves bings awast, On Chates to trine by Rome Coves dine For his long lib at last. Bing'd out bien Morts and toure, and toure, Bing out of the Rome vile bine, And toure the Cove that cloy'd your duds, Upon the Chates to trine.' (From 'The English Rogue.' London, 1665.)

Conversation followed; not in the thieves' dialect of the song, for that was only used in talk when unfriendly ears might be listening. In the course of it, it appeared that 'John Hobbs' was not altogether a new recruit, but had trained in the gang at some former time. His later history was called for, and when he said he had 'accidentally' killed a man, considerable satisfaction was expressed; when he added that the man was a priest, he was roundly applauded, and had to take a drink with everybody. Old acquaintances welcomed him joyously, and new ones were proud to shake him by the hand. He was asked why he had 'tarried away so many months.' He answered—

"London is better than the country, and safer, these late years, the laws be so bitter and so diligently enforced. An' I had not had that accident, I had stayed there. I had resolved to stay, and never more venture country-wards—but the accident has ended that."

He inquired how many persons the gang numbered now. The 'ruffler,' or chief, answered—

"Five and twenty sturdy budges, bulks, files, clapperdogeons and maunders, counting the dells and doxies and other morts*. Most are here, the rest are wandering eastward, along the winter lay. We follow at dawn."

"I do not see the Wen among the honest folk about me. Where may he be?"

"Poor lad, his diet is brimstone, now, and over hot for a delicate taste. He was killed in a brawl, somewhere about midsummer."

"I sorrow to hear that; the Wen was a capable man, and brave."

"That was he, truly. Black Bess, his dell, is of us yet, but absent on the eastward tramp; a fine lass, of nice ways and orderly conduct, none ever seeing her drunk above four days in the seven."

"She was ever strict—I remember it well—a goodly wench and worthy all commendation. Her mother was more free and less particular; a troublesome and ugly-tempered beldame, but furnished with a wit above the common."

---

* Canting terms for various kinds of thieves, beggars and vagabonds, and their female companions.

"We lost her through it. Her gift of palmistry and other sorts of fortune-telling begot for her at last a witch's name and fame. The law roasted her to death at a slow fire. It did touch me to a sort of tenderness to see the gallant way she met her lot—cursing and reviling all the crowd that gaped and gazed around her, whilst the flames licked upward toward her face and catched her thin locks and crackled about her old gray head—cursing them! why an' thou should'st live a thousand years thoud'st never hear so masterful a cursing. Alack, her art died with her. There be base and weakling imitations left, but no true blasphemy."

The Ruffler sighed; the listeners sighed in sympathy; a general depression fell upon the company for a moment, for even hardened outcasts like these are not wholly dead to sentiment, but are able to feel a fleeting sense of loss and affliction at wide intervals and under peculiarly favouring circumstances—as in cases like to this, for instance, when genius and culture depart and leave no heir. However, a deep drink all round soon restored the spirits of the mourners.

"Have any others of our friends fared hardly?" asked Hobbs.

"Some—yes. Particularly new comers—such as small husbandmen turned shiftless and hungry upon the world because their farms were taken from them to be changed to sheep ranges. They begged, and were whipped at the cart's tail, naked from the girdle up, till the blood ran; then set in the stocks to be pelted; they begged again, were whipped again, and deprived of an ear; they begged a third time—poor devils, what else could they do?—and were branded on the cheek with a red-hot iron, then sold for slaves; they ran away, were hunted down, and hanged. 'Tis a brief tale, and quickly told. Others of us have fared less hardly. Stand forth, Yokel, Burns, and Hodge—show your adornments!"

These stood up and stripped away some of their rags, exposing their backs, criss-crossed with ropy old welts left by the lash; one turned up his hair and showed the place where a left ear had once been; another showed a brand upon his shoulder—the letter V—and a mutilated ear; the third said—

"I am Yokel, once a farmer and prosperous, with loving wife and kids—now am I somewhat different in estate and calling; and the wife and kids are gone; mayhap they are in heaven, mayhap in—in the other place—but the kindly God be thanked, they bide no more in ENGLAND! My good old blameless mother strove to earn bread by nursing the sick; one of these died, the doctors knew not how, so my mother was burnt for a witch, whilst my babes looked on and wailed. English law!—up, all, with your cups!—now all together and with a cheer!—drink to the merciful English law that delivered HER from the English hell! Thank you, mates, one and all. I begged, from house to house—I and the wife—bearing with us the hungry kids—but it was crime to be hungry in England—so they stripped us and lashed us through three towns. Drink ye all again to the merciful English law!—for its lash drank deep of my Mary's blood and its blessed deliverance came quick. She lies there, in the potter's field, safe from all harms. And the kids—well, whilst the law lashed me from town to town, they starved. Drink, lads—only a drop—a drop to the poor kids, that never did any creature harm. I begged again—begged, for a crust, and got the stocks and lost an ear—see, here bides the stump; I begged again, and here is the stump of the other to keep me minded of it. And still I begged again, and was sold for a slave—here on my cheek under this stain, if I washed it off, ye might see the red S the branding-iron left there! A

SLAVE! Do you understand that word? An English SLAVE! — that is he that stands before ye. I have run from my master, and when I am found—the heavy curse of heaven fall on the law of the land that hath commanded it!—I shall hang!"*

A ringing voice came through the murky air—

"Thou shalt NOT!—and this day the end of that law is come!"

All turned, and saw the fantastic figure of the little King approaching hurriedly; as it emerged into the light and was clearly revealed, a general explosion of inquiries broke out—

"Who is it? WHAT is it? Who art thou, manikin?"

The boy stood unconfused in the midst of all those surprised and questioning eyes, and answered with princely dignity—

"I am Edward, King of England."

A wild burst of laughter followed, partly of derision and partly of delight in the excellence of the joke. The King was stung. He said sharply—

"Ye mannerless vagrants, is this your recognition of the royal boon I have promised?"

He said more, with angry voice and excited gesture, but it was lost in a whirlwind of laughter and mocking exclamations. 'John Hobbs' made several attempts to make himself heard above the din, and at last succeeded—saying—

"Mates, he is my son, a dreamer, a fool, and stark mad—mind him not—he thinketh he IS the King."

"I AM the King," said Edward, turning toward him, "as thou shalt know to thy cost, in good time. Thou hast confessed a murder—thou shalt swing for it."

"THOU'LT betray me?—THOU? An' I get my hands upon thee—"

"Tut-tut!" said the burly Ruffler, interposing in time to save the King, and emphasising this service by knocking Hobbs down with his fist, "hast respect for neither Kings NOR Rufflers? An' thou insult my presence so again, I'll hang thee up myself." Then he said to his Majesty, "Thou must make no threats against thy mates, lad; and thou must guard thy tongue from saying evil of them elsewhere. BE King, if it please thy mad humour, but be not harmful in it. Sink the title thou hast uttered—'tis treason; we be bad men in some few trifling ways, but none among us is so base as to be traitor to his King; we be loving and loyal hearts, in that regard. Note if I speak truth. Now—all together: 'Long live Edward, King of England!'"

"LONG LIVE EDWARD, KING OF ENGLAND!"

The response came with such a thundergust from the motley crew that the crazy building vibrated to the sound. The little King's face lighted with pleasure for an instant, and he slightly

---

* So young a King and so ignorant a peasant were likely to make mistakes; and this is an instance in point. This peasant was suffering from this law BY ANTICIPATION; the King was venting his indignation against a law which was not yet in existence; for this hideous statute was to have birth in this little King's OWN REIGN. However, we know, from the humanity of his character, that it could never have been suggested by him.

inclined his head, and said with grave simplicity—

"I thank you, my good people."

This unexpected result threw the company into convulsions of merriment. When something like quiet was presently come again, the Ruffler said, firmly, but with an accent of good nature—

"Drop it, boy, 'tis not wise, nor well. Humour thy fancy, if thou must, but choose some other title."

A tinker shrieked out a suggestion—

"Foo-foo the First, King of the Mooncalves!"

The title 'took,' at once, every throat responded, and a roaring shout went up, of—

"Long live Foo-foo the First, King of the Mooncalves!" followed by hootings, cat-calls, and peals of laughter.

"Hale him forth, and crown him!"

"Robe him!"

"Sceptre him!"

"Throne him!"

These and twenty other cries broke out at once! and almost before the poor little victim could draw a breath he was crowned with a tin basin, robed in a tattered blanket, throned upon a barrel, and sceptred with the tinker's soldering-iron. Then all flung themselves upon their knees about him and sent up a chorus of ironical wailings, and mocking supplications, whilst they swabbed their eyes with their soiled and ragged sleeves and aprons—

"Be gracious to us, O sweet King!"

"Trample not upon thy beseeching worms, O noble Majesty!"

"Pity thy slaves, and comfort them with a royal kick!"

"Cheer us and warm us with thy gracious rays, O flaming sun of sovereignty!"

"Sanctify the ground with the touch of thy foot, that we may eat the dirt and be ennobled!"

"Deign to spit upon us, O Sire, that our children's children may tell of thy princely condescension, and be proud and happy for ever!"

But the humorous tinker made the 'hit' of the evening and carried off the honours. Kneeling, he pretended to kiss the King's foot, and was indignantly spurned; whereupon he went about begging for a rag to paste over the place upon his face which had been touched by the foot, saying it must be preserved from contact with the vulgar air, and that he should make his fortune by going on the highway and exposing it to view at the rate of a hundred shillings a sight. He made himself so killingly funny that he was the envy and admiration of the whole mangy rabble.

Tears of shame and indignation stood in the little monarch's eyes; and the thought in his heart was, "Had I offered them a deep wrong they could not be more cruel—yet have I proffered nought but to do them a kindness —and it is thus they use me for it!"

Chapter XVIII. The Prince with the tramps.

The troop of vagabonds turned out at early dawn, and set forward on their march. There was a lowering sky overhead, sloppy ground under foot, and a winter chill in the air. All gaiety was gone from the company; some were sullen and silent, some were irritable and petulant, none were gentle-humoured, all were thirsty.

The Ruffler put 'Jack' in Hugo's charge, with some brief instructions, and commanded John Canty to keep away from him and let him alone; he also warned Hugo not to be too rough with the lad.

After a while the weather grew milder, and the clouds lifted somewhat. The troop ceased to shiver, and their spirits began to improve. They grew more and more cheerful, and finally began to chaff each other and insult passengers along the highway. This showed that they were awaking to an appreciation of life and its joys once more. The dread in which their sort was held was apparent in the fact that everybody gave them the road, and took their ribald insolences meekly, without venturing to talk back. They snatched linen from the hedges, occasionally in full view of the owners, who made no protest, but only seemed grateful that they did not take the hedges, too.

By-and-by they invaded a small farmhouse and made themselves at home while the trembling farmer and his people swept the larder clean to furnish a breakfast for them. They chucked the housewife and her daughters under the chin whilst receiving the food from their hands, and made coarse jests about them, accompanied with insulting epithets and bursts of horse-laughter. They threw bones and vegetables at the farmer and his sons, kept them dodging all the time, and applauded uproariously when a good hit was made. They ended by buttering the head of one of the daughters who resented some of their familiarities. When they took their leave they threatened to come back and burn the house over the heads of the family if any report of their doings got to the ears of the authorities.

About noon, after a long and weary tramp, the gang came to a halt behind a hedge on the outskirts of a considerable village. An hour was allowed for rest, then the crew scattered themselves abroad to enter the village at different points to ply their various trades—'Jack' was sent with Hugo. They wandered hither and thither for some time, Hugo watching for opportunities to do a stroke of business, but finding none—so he finally said—

"I see nought to steal; it is a paltry place. Wherefore we will beg."

"WE, forsooth! Follow thy trade—it befits thee. But *I* will not beg."

"Thou'lt not beg!" exclaimed Hugo, eyeing the King with surprise. "Prithee, since when hast thou reformed?"

"What dost thou mean?"

"Mean? Hast thou not begged the streets of London all thy life?"

"I? Thou idiot!"

"Spare thy compliments—thy stock will last the longer. Thy father says thou hast begged all thy days. Mayhap he lied. Peradventure you will even make so bold as to SAY he lied," scoffed Hugo.

"Him YOU call my father? Yes, he lied."

"Come, play not thy merry game of madman so far, mate; use it for thy amusement, not thy hurt. An' I tell him this, he will scorch thee finely for it."

"Save thyself the trouble. I will tell him."

"I like thy spirit, I do in truth; but I do not admire thy judgment. Bone-rackings and bastings be plenty enow in this life, without going out of one's way to invite them. But a truce to these matters; *I* believe your father. I doubt not he can lie; I doubt not he DOTH lie, upon occasion, for the best of us do that; but there is no occasion here. A wise man does not waste so good a commodity as lying for nought. But come; sith it is thy humour to give over begging, wherewithal shall we busy ourselves? With robbing kitchens?"

The King said, impatiently—

"Have done with this folly—you weary me!"

Hugo replied, with temper—

"Now harkee, mate; you will not beg, you will not rob; so be it. But I will tell you what you WILL do. You will play decoy whilst *I* beg. Refuse, an' you think you may venture!"

The King was about to reply contemptuously, when Hugo said, interrupting—

"Peace! Here comes one with a kindly face. Now will I fall down in a fit. When the stranger runs to me, set you up a wail, and fall upon your knees, seeming to weep; then cry out as all the devils of misery were in your belly, and say, 'Oh, sir, it is my poor afflicted brother, and we be friendless; o' God's name cast through your merciful eyes one pitiful look upon a sick, forsaken, and most miserable wretch; bestow one little penny out of thy riches upon one smitten of God and ready to perish!' —and mind you, keep you ON wailing, and abate not till we bilk him of his penny, else shall you rue it."

Then immediately Hugo began to moan, and groan, and roll his eyes, and reel and totter about; and when the stranger was close at hand, down he sprawled before him, with a shriek, and began to writhe and wallow in the dirt, in seeming agony.

"O, dear, O dear!" cried the benevolent stranger, "O poor soul, poor soul, how he doth suffer! There—let me help thee up."

"O noble sir, forbear, and God love you for a princely gentleman—but it giveth me cruel pain to touch me when I am taken so. My brother there will tell your worship how I am racked with anguish when these fits be upon me. A penny, dear sir, a penny, to buy a little food; then leave me to my sorrows."

"A penny! thou shalt have three, thou hapless creature"—and he fumbled in his pocket with nervous haste and got them out. "There, poor lad, take them and most welcome. Now come hither, my boy, and help me carry thy stricken brother to yon house, where—"

"I am not his brother," said the King, interrupting.

"What! not his brother?"

"Oh, hear him!" groaned Hugo, then privately ground his teeth. "He denies his own brother—and he with one foot in the grave!"

"Boy, thou art indeed hard of heart, if this is thy brother. For shame! —and he scarce able to move hand or foot. If he is not thy brother, who is he, then?"

"A beggar and a thief! He has got your money and has picked your pocket likewise. An' thou would'st do a healing miracle, lay thy staff over his shoulders and trust Providence for the rest."

But Hugo did not tarry for the miracle. In a moment he was up and off like the wind, the gentleman following after and raising the hue and cry lustily as he went. The King, breathing deep gratitude to Heaven for his own release, fled in the opposite direction, and did not slacken his pace until he was out of harm's reach. He took the first road that offered, and soon put the village behind him. He hurried along, as briskly as he could, during several hours, keeping a nervous watch over his shoulder for pursuit; but his fears left him at last, and a grateful sense of security took their place. He recognised, now, that he was hungry, and also very tired. So he halted at a farmhouse; but when he was about to speak, he was cut short and driven rudely away. His clothes were against him.

He wandered on, wounded and indignant, and was resolved to put himself in the way of like treatment no more. But hunger is pride's master; so, as the evening drew near, he made an attempt at another farmhouse; but here he fared worse than before; for he was called hard names and was promised arrest as a vagrant except he moved on promptly.

The night came on, chilly and overcast; and still the footsore monarch laboured slowly on. He was obliged to keep moving, for every time he sat down to rest he was soon penetrated to the bone with the cold. All his sensations and experiences, as he moved through the solemn gloom and the empty vastness of the night, were new and strange to him. At intervals he heard voices approach, pass by, and fade into silence; and as he saw nothing more of the bodies they belonged to than a sort of formless drifting blur, there was something spectral and uncanny about it all that made him shudder. Occasionally he caught the twinkle of a light—always far away, apparently—almost in another world; if he heard the tinkle of a sheep's bell, it was vague, distant, indistinct; the muffled lowing of the herds floated to him on the night wind in vanishing cadences, a mournful sound; now and then came the complaining howl of a dog over viewless expanses of field and forest; all sounds were remote; they made the little King feel that all life and activity were far removed from him, and that he stood solitary, companionless, in the centre of a measureless solitude.

He stumbled along, through the gruesome fascinations of this new experience, startled occasionally by the soft rustling of the dry leaves overhead, so like human whispers they seemed to sound; and by-and-by he came suddenly upon the freckled light of a tin lantern near at hand. He stepped back into the shadows and waited. The lantern stood by the open door of a barn. The King waited some time—there was no sound, and

nobody stirring. He got so cold, standing still, and the hospitable barn looked so enticing, that at last he resolved to risk everything and enter. He started swiftly and stealthily, and just as he was crossing the threshold he heard voices behind him. He darted behind a cask, within the barn, and stooped down. Two farm-labourers came in, bringing the lantern with them, and fell to work, talking meanwhile. Whilst they moved about with the light, the King made good use of his eyes and took the bearings of what seemed to be a good-sized stall at the further end of the place, purposing to grope his way to it when he should be left to himself. He also noted the position of a pile of horse blankets, midway of the route, with the intent to levy upon them for the service of the crown of England for one night.

By-and-by the men finished and went away, fastening the door behind them and taking the lantern with them. The shivering King made for the blankets, with as good speed as the darkness would allow; gathered them up, and then groped his way safely to the stall. Of two of the blankets he made a bed, then covered himself with the remaining two. He was a glad monarch, now, though the blankets were old and thin, and not quite warm enough; and besides gave out a pungent horsey odour that was almost suffocatingly powerful.

Although the King was hungry and chilly, he was also so tired and so drowsy that these latter influences soon began to get the advantage of the former, and he presently dozed off into a state of semi-consciousness. Then, just as he was on the point of losing himself wholly, he distinctly felt something touch him! He was broad awake in a moment, and gasping for breath. The cold horror of that mysterious touch in the dark almost made his heart stand still. He lay motionless, and listened, scarcely breathing. But nothing stirred, and there was no sound. He continued to listen, and wait, during what seemed a long time, but still nothing stirred, and there was no sound. So he began to drop into a drowse once more, at last; and all at once he felt that mysterious touch again! It was a grisly thing, this light touch from this noiseless and invisible presence; it made the boy sick with ghostly fears. What should he do? That was the question; but he did not know how to answer it. Should he leave these reasonably comfortable quarters and fly from this inscrutable horror? But fly whither? He could not get out of the barn; and the idea of scurrying blindly hither and thither in the dark, within the captivity of the four walls, with this phantom gliding after him, and visiting him with that soft hideous touch upon cheek or shoulder at every turn, was intolerable. But to stay where he was, and endure this living death all night—was that better? No. What, then, was there left to do? Ah, there was but one course; he knew it well—he must put out his hand and find that thing!

It was easy to think this; but it was hard to brace himself up to try it. Three times he stretched his hand a little way out into the dark, gingerly; and snatched it suddenly back, with a gasp—not because it had encountered anything, but because he had felt so sure it was just GOING to. But the fourth time, he groped a little further, and his hand lightly swept against something soft and warm. This petrified him, nearly, with fright; his mind was in such a state that he could imagine the thing to be nothing else than a corpse, newly dead and still warm. He thought he would rather die than touch it again. But he thought this false thought because he did not know the immortal strength of human curiosity. In no long time his hand was tremblingly groping again —against his judgment, and without his consent—but groping persistently on, just the same. It encountered a bunch of long hair; he shuddered, but followed up the hair and found what seemed to be a warm rope; followed up the rope and found an innocent calf!—for the rope was not a rope at all, but the calf's tail.

The King was cordially ashamed of himself for having gotten all that fright and misery out of so paltry a matter as a slumbering calf; but he need not have felt so about it, for it was not the calf that frightened him, but a dreadful non-existent something which the calf stood for; and any other boy, in those old superstitious times, would have acted and suffered just as he had done.

The King was not only delighted to find that the creature was only a calf, but delighted to have the calf's company; for he had been feeling so lonesome and friendless that the company and comradeship of even this humble animal were welcome. And he had been so buffeted, so rudely entreated by his own kind, that it was a real comfort to him to feel that he was at last in the society of a fellow-creature that had at least a soft heart and a gentle spirit, whatever loftier attributes might be lacking. So he resolved to waive rank and make friends with the calf.

While stroking its sleek warm back—for it lay near him and within easy reach—it occurred to him that this calf might be utilised in more ways than one. Whereupon he re-arranged his bed, spreading it down close to the calf; then he cuddled himself up to the calf's back, drew the covers up over himself and his friend, and in a minute or two was as warm and comfortable as he had ever been in the downy couches of the regal palace of Westminster.

Pleasant thoughts came at once; life took on a cheerfuller seeming. He was free of the bonds of servitude and crime, free of the companionship of base and brutal outlaws; he was warm; he was sheltered; in a word, he was happy. The night wind was rising; it swept by in fitful gusts that made the old barn quake and rattle, then its forces died down at intervals, and went moaning and wailing around corners and projections —but it was all music to the King, now that he was snug and comfortable: let it blow and rage, let it batter and bang, let it moan and wail, he minded it not, he only enjoyed it. He merely snuggled the closer to his friend, in a luxury of warm contentment, and drifted blissfully out of consciousness into a deep and dreamless sleep that was full of serenity and peace. The distant dogs howled, the melancholy kine complained, and the winds went on raging, whilst furious sheets of rain drove along the roof; but the Majesty of England slept on, undisturbed, and the calf did the same, it being a simple creature, and not easily troubled by storms or embarrassed by sleeping with a king.

Chapter XIX. The Prince with the peasants.

When the King awoke in the early morning, he found that a wet but thoughtful rat had crept into the place during the night and made a cosy bed for itself in his bosom. Being disturbed now, it scampered away. The boy smiled, and said, "Poor fool, why so fearful? I am as forlorn as thou. 'Twould be a sham in me to hurt the helpless, who am myself so helpless. Moreover, I owe you thanks for a good omen; for when a king has fallen so low that the very rats do make a bed of him, it surely meaneth that his fortunes be upon the turn, since it is plain he can no lower go."

He got up and stepped out of the stall, and just then he heard the sound of children's voices. The barn door opened and a couple of little girls came in. As soon as they saw him their talking and laughing ceased, and they stopped and stood still, gazing at him with strong curiosity; they presently began to whisper together, then they approached nearer, and stopped again to gaze and whisper. By-and-by they gathered courage and began to discuss him aloud. One said—

"He hath a comely face."

The other added—

"And pretty hair."

"But is ill clothed enow."

"And how starved he looketh."

They came still nearer, sidling shyly around and about him, examining him minutely from all points, as if he were some strange new kind of animal, but warily and watchfully the while, as if they half feared he might be a sort of animal that would bite, upon occasion. Finally they halted before him, holding each other's hands for protection, and took a good satisfying stare with their innocent eyes; then one of them plucked up all her courage and inquired with honest directness—

"Who art thou, boy?"

"I am the King," was the grave answer.

The children gave a little start, and their eyes spread themselves wide open and remained so during a speechless half minute. Then curiosity broke the silence—

"The KING? What King?"

"The King of England."

The children looked at each other—then at him—then at each other again —wonderingly, perplexedly; then one said—

"Didst hear him, Margery?—he said he is the King. Can that be true?"

"How can it be else but true, Prissy? Would he say a lie? For look you, Prissy, an' it were not true, it WOULD be a lie. It surely would be. Now think on't. For all things that be not true, be lies—thou canst make nought else out of it."

It was a good tight argument, without a leak in it anywhere; and it left Prissy's half-doubts not a leg to stand on. She considered a moment, then put the King upon his honour with the simple remark—

"If thou art truly the King, then I believe thee."

"I am truly the King."

This settled the matter. His Majesty's royalty was accepted without further question or discussion, and the two little girls began at once to inquire into how he came to be where he was, and how he came to be so unroyally clad, and whither he was bound, and all about his affairs. It was a mighty relief to him to pour out his troubles where they would not be scoffed at or doubted; so he told his tale with feeling, forgetting even his hunger for the time; and it was received with the deepest and tenderest sympathy by the gentle little maids. But when he got down to his latest experiences and they learned how long he had been without food, they cut him short and hurried him away to the farmhouse to find a breakfast for him.

The King was cheerful and happy now, and said to himself, "When I am come to mine own again, I will always honour little children, remembering how that these trusted me and believed in me in my time of trouble; whilst they that were older, and thought themselves wiser, mocked at me and held me for a liar."

The children's mother received the King kindly, and was full of pity; for his forlorn condition and apparently crazed intellect touched her womanly heart. She was a widow, and rather poor; consequently she had seen trouble enough to enable her to feel for the unfortunate. She imagined that the demented boy had wandered away from his friends or keepers; so she tried to find out whence he had come, in order that she might take measures to return him; but all her references to neighbouring towns and villages, and all her inquiries in the same line went for nothing—the boy's face, and his answers, too, showed that the things she was talking of were not familiar to him. He spoke earnestly and simply about court matters, and broke down, more than once, when speaking of the late King 'his father'; but whenever the conversation changed to baser topics, he lost interest and became silent.

The woman was mightily puzzled; but she did not give up. As she proceeded with her cooking, she set herself to contriving devices to surprise the boy into betraying his real secret. She talked about cattle—he showed no concern; then about sheep—the same result: so her guess that he had been a shepherd boy was an error; she talked about mills; and about weavers, tinkers, smiths, trades and tradesmen of all sorts; and about Bedlam, and jails, and charitable retreats: but no matter, she was baffled at all points. Not altogether, either; for she argued that she had narrowed the thing down to domestic service. Yes, she was sure she was on the right track, now; he must have been a house servant. So she led up to that. But the result was discouraging. The subject of sweeping appeared to weary him; fire-building failed to stir him; scrubbing and scouring awoke no enthusiasm. The goodwife touched, with a perishing hope, and rather as a matter of form, upon the subject of cooking. To her surprise, and her vast delight, the King's face lighted at once! Ah, she had hunted him down at last, she thought; and she was right proud, too, of the devious shrewdness and tact which had accomplished it.

Her tired tongue got a chance to rest, now; for the King's, inspired by gnawing hunger and the fragrant smells that came from the sputtering pots and pans, turned itself loose and delivered itself up to such an eloquent dissertation upon certain toothsome dishes, that within three minutes the woman said to herself, "Of a truth I was right—he hath holpen in a kitchen!" Then he broadened his bill of fare, and discussed it with such appreciation and animation, that the goodwife said to herself, "Good lack! how can he know so many dishes, and so fine ones withal? For these belong only upon the tables of the rich and great. Ah, now I see! ragged outcast as he is, he must have served in the palace before his reason went astray; yes, he must have helped in the very kitchen of the King himself! I will test him."

Full of eagerness to prove her sagacity, she told the King to mind the cooking a moment—hinting that he might manufacture and add a dish or two, if he chose; then she went out of the room and gave her children a sign to follow after. The King muttered—

"Another English king had a commission like to this, in a bygone time—it is nothing against my dignity to undertake an office which the great Alfred stooped to assume. But I will try to better serve my trust than he; for he let the cakes burn."

The intent was good, but the performance was not answerable to it, for this King, like the other one, soon fell into deep thinkings concerning his vast affairs, and the same calamity resulted—the cookery got burned. The woman returned in time to save the breakfast from entire destruction; and she promptly brought the King out of his dreams with a brisk and cordial tongue-lashing. Then, seeing how troubled he was over his violated trust, she softened at once, and was all goodness and gentleness toward him.

The boy made a hearty and satisfying meal, and was greatly refreshed and gladdened by it. It was a meal which was distinguished by this curious feature, that rank was waived on both sides; yet neither recipient of the favour was aware that it had been extended. The goodwife had intended to feed this young tramp with broken victuals in a corner, like any other tramp or like a dog; but she was so remorseful for the scolding she had given him, that she did what she could to atone for it by allowing him to sit at the family table and eat with his betters, on ostensible terms of equality with them; and the King, on his side, was so remorseful for having broken his trust, after the family had been so kind to him, that he forced himself to atone for it by humbling himself to the family level, instead of requiring the woman and her children to stand and wait upon him, while he occupied their table in the solitary state due to his birth and dignity. It does us all good to unbend sometimes. This good woman was made happy all the day long by the applauses which she got out of herself for her magnanimous condescension to a tramp; and the King was just as self-complacent over his gracious humility toward a humble peasant woman.

When breakfast was over, the housewife told the King to wash up the dishes. This command was a staggerer, for a moment, and the King came near rebelling; but then he said to himself, "Alfred the Great watched the cakes; doubtless he would have washed the dishes too—therefore will I essay it."

He made a sufficiently poor job of it; and to his surprise too, for the cleaning of wooden spoons and trenchers had seemed an easy thing to do. It was a tedious and troublesome piece of work, but he finished it at last. He was becoming impatient to get away on his journey now; however, he was not to lose this thrifty dame's society so easily. She furnished him some little odds and ends of employment, which he got through with after a fair fashion and with some credit. Then she set him and the little girls to paring some winter apples; but he was so awkward at this service that she retired him from it and gave him a butcher knife to grind. Afterwards she kept him carding wool until he began to think he had laid the good King Alfred about far enough in the shade for the present in the matter of showy menial heroisms that would read picturesquely in story-books and histories, and so he was half-minded to resign. And when, just after the noonday dinner, the goodwife gave him a basket of kittens to drown, he did resign. At least he was just going to resign—for he felt that he must draw the line somewhere, and it seemed to him that to draw it at kitten-drowning was about the right thing—when there was an interruption. The interruption was John Canty—with a peddler's pack on his back—and Hugo.

The King discovered these rascals approaching the front gate before they had had a chance to see him; so he said nothing about drawing the line, but took up his basket of kittens and stepped quietly out the back way, without a word. He left the creatures in an out-house, and hurried on, into a narrow lane at the rear.

Chapter XX. The Prince and the hermit.

The high hedge hid him from the house, now; and so, under the impulse of a deadly fright, he let out all his forces and sped toward a wood in the distance. He never looked back until he had almost gained the shelter of the forest; then he turned and descried two figures in the distance. That was sufficient; he did not wait to scan them critically, but hurried on, and never abated his pace till he was far within the twilight depths of the wood. Then he stopped; being persuaded that he was now tolerably safe. He listened intently, but the stillness was profound and solemn —awful, even, and depressing to the spirits. At wide intervals his straining ear did detect sounds, but they were so remote, and hollow, and mysterious, that they seemed not to be real sounds, but only the moaning and complaining ghosts of departed ones. So the sounds were yet more dreary than the silence which they interrupted.

It was his purpose, in the beginning, to stay where he was the rest of the day; but a chill soon invaded his perspiring body, and he was at last obliged to resume movement in order to get warm. He struck straight through the forest, hoping to pierce to a road presently, but he was disappointed in this. He travelled on and on; but the farther he went, the denser the wood became, apparently. The gloom began to thicken, by-and-by, and the King realised that the night was coming on. It made him shudder to think of spending it in such an uncanny place; so he tried to hurry faster, but he only made the less speed, for he could not now see well enough to choose his steps judiciously; consequently he kept tripping over roots and tangling himself in vines and briers.

And how glad he was when at last he caught the glimmer of a light! He approached it warily, stopping often to look about him and listen. It came from an unglazed window-opening in a shabby little hut. He heard a voice, now, and felt a disposition to run and hide; but he changed his mind at once, for this voice was praying, evidently. He glided to the one window of the hut, raised himself on tiptoe, and stole a glance within. The room was small; its floor was the natural earth, beaten hard by use; in a corner was a bed of rushes and a ragged blanket or two; near it was a pail, a cup, a basin, and two or three pots and pans; there was a short bench and a three-legged stool; on the hearth the remains of a faggot fire were smouldering; before a shrine, which was lighted by a single candle, knelt an aged man, and on an old wooden box at his side lay an open book and a human skull. The man was of large, bony frame; his hair and whiskers were very long and snowy white; he was clothed in a robe of sheepskins which reached from his neck to his heels.

"A holy hermit!" said the King to himself; "now am I indeed fortunate."

The hermit rose from his knees; the King knocked. A deep voice responded—

"Enter!—but leave sin behind, for the ground whereon thou shalt stand is holy!"

The King entered, and paused. The hermit turned a pair of gleaming, unrestful eyes upon him, and said—

"Who art thou?"

"I am the King," came the answer, with placid simplicity.

"Welcome, King!" cried the hermit, with enthusiasm. Then, bustling about with feverish activity, and constantly saying, "Welcome, welcome," he arranged his bench, seated the King on it, by the hearth, threw some faggots on the fire, and finally fell to pacing the floor with a nervous stride.

"Welcome! Many have sought sanctuary here, but they were not worthy, and were turned away. But a King who casts his crown away, and despises the vain splendours of his office, and clothes his body in rags, to devote his life to holiness and the mortification of the flesh—he is worthy, he is welcome!—here shall he abide all his days till death come." The King hastened to interrupt and explain, but the hermit paid no attention to him—did not even hear him, apparently, but went right on with his talk, with a raised voice and a growing energy. "And thou shalt be at peace here. None shall find out thy refuge to disquiet thee with supplications to return to that empty and foolish life which God hath moved thee to abandon. Thou shalt pray here; thou shalt study the Book; thou shalt meditate upon the follies and delusions of this world, and upon the sublimities of the world to come; thou shalt feed upon crusts and herbs, and scourge thy body with whips, daily, to the purifying of thy soul. Thou shalt wear a hair shirt next thy skin; thou shalt drink water only; and thou shalt be at peace; yes, wholly at peace; for whoso comes to seek thee shall go his way again, baffled; he shall not find thee, he shall not molest thee."

The old man, still pacing back and forth, ceased to speak aloud, and began to mutter. The King seized this opportunity to state his case; and he did it with an eloquence inspired by uneasiness and apprehension. But the hermit went on muttering, and gave no heed. And still muttering, he approached the King and said impressively—

"'Sh! I will tell you a secret!" He bent down to impart it, but checked himself, and assumed a listening attitude. After a moment or two he went on tiptoe to the window-opening, put his head out, and peered around in the gloaming, then came tiptoeing back again, put his face close down to the King's, and whispered—

"I am an archangel!"

The King started violently, and said to himself, "Would God I were with the outlaws again; for lo, now am I the prisoner of a madman!" His apprehensions were heightened, and they showed plainly in his face. In a low excited voice the hermit continued—

"I see you feel my atmosphere! There's awe in your face! None may be in this atmosphere and not be thus affected; for it is the very atmosphere of heaven. I go thither and return, in the twinkling of an eye. I was made an archangel on this very spot, it is five years ago, by angels sent from heaven to confer that awful dignity. Their presence filled this place with an intolerable brightness. And they knelt to me, King! yes, they knelt to me! for I was greater than they. I have walked in the courts of heaven, and held speech with the patriarchs. Touch my hand—be not afraid—touch it. There—now thou hast touched a hand which has been clasped by Abraham and Isaac and Jacob! For I have walked in the golden courts; I have seen the Deity face to face!" He paused, to give this speech effect; then his face suddenly changed, and he started to his feet again saying, with angry energy, "Yes, I am an archangel; A MERE ARCHANGEL!—I that might have been pope! It is verily true. I was told it from heaven in a dream, twenty years ago; ah, yes, I was to be pope! —and I SHOULD have been pope, for Heaven had said it—but the King dissolved my religious house, and I, poor obscure unfriended monk, was cast homeless upon the world, robbed of my mighty destiny!" Here he began to mumble again, and beat his forehead in futile rage, with his fist; now and then articulating a venomous curse, and now and then a pathetic "Wherefore I am nought but an archangel—I that should have been pope!"

So he went on, for an hour, whilst the poor little King sat and suffered. Then all at once the old man's frenzy departed, and he became all gentleness. His voice softened, he came down out of his clouds, and fell to prattling along so simply and so humanly, that he soon won the King's heart completely. The old devotee moved the boy nearer to the fire and made him comfortable; doctored his small bruises and abrasions with a deft and tender hand; and then set about preparing and cooking a supper —chatting pleasantly all the time, and occasionally stroking the lad's cheek or patting his head, in such a gently caressing way that in a little while all the fear and repulsion inspired by the archangel were changed to reverence and affection for the man.

This happy state of things continued while the two ate the supper; then, after a prayer before the shrine, the hermit put the boy to bed, in a small adjoining room, tucking him in as snugly and lovingly as a mother might; and so, with a parting caress, left him and sat down by the fire, and began to poke the brands about in an absent and aimless way. Presently he paused; then tapped his forehead several times with his fingers, as if trying to recall some thought which had escaped from his mind. Apparently he was unsuccessful. Now he started quickly up, and entered his guest's room, and said—

"Thou art King?"

"Yes," was the response, drowsily uttered.

"What King?"

"Of England."

"Of England? Then Henry is gone!"

"Alack, it is so. I am his son."

A black frown settled down upon the hermit's face, and he clenched his bony hands with a vindictive energy. He stood a few moments, breathing fast and swallowing repeatedly, then said in a husky voice—

"Dost know it was he that turned us out into the world houseless and homeless?"

There was no response. The old man bent down and scanned the boy's reposeful face and listened to his placid breathing. "He sleeps—sleeps soundly;" and the frown vanished away and gave place to an expression of evil satisfaction. A smile flitted across the dreaming boy's features. The hermit muttered, "So—his heart is happy;" and he turned away. He went stealthily about the place, seeking here and there for something; now and then halting to listen, now and then jerking his head around and casting a quick glance toward the bed; and always muttering, always mumbling to himself. At last he found what he seemed to want—a rusty old butcher

knife and a whetstone. Then he crept to his place by the fire, sat himself down, and began to whet the knife softly on the stone, still muttering, mumbling, ejaculating. The winds sighed around the lonely place, the mysterious voices of the night floated by out of the distances. The shining eyes of venturesome mice and rats peered out at the old man from cracks and coverts, but he went on with his work, rapt, absorbed, and noted none of these things.

At long intervals he drew his thumb along the edge of his knife, and nodded his head with satisfaction. "It grows sharper," he said; "yes, it grows sharper."

He took no note of the flight of time, but worked tranquilly on, entertaining himself with his thoughts, which broke out occasionally in articulate speech—

"His father wrought us evil, he destroyed us—and is gone down into the eternal fires! Yes, down into the eternal fires! He escaped us—but it was God's will, yes it was God's will, we must not repine. But he hath not escaped the fires! No, he hath not escaped the fires, the consuming, unpitying, remorseless fires—and THEY are everlasting!"

And so he wrought, and still wrought—mumbling, chuckling a low rasping chuckle at times—and at times breaking again into words—

"It was his father that did it all. I am but an archangel; but for him I should be pope!"

The King stirred. The hermit sprang noiselessly to the bedside, and went down upon his knees, bending over the prostrate form with his knife uplifted. The boy stirred again; his eyes came open for an instant, but there was no speculation in them, they saw nothing; the next moment his tranquil breathing showed that his sleep was sound once more.

The hermit watched and listened, for a time, keeping his position and scarcely breathing; then he slowly lowered his arms, and presently crept away, saying,—

"It is long past midnight; it is not best that he should cry out, lest by accident someone be passing."

He glided about his hovel, gathering a rag here, a thong there, and another one yonder; then he returned, and by careful and gentle handling he managed to tie the King's ankles together without waking him. Next he essayed to tie the wrists; he made several attempts to cross them, but the boy always drew one hand or the other away, just as the cord was ready to be applied; but at last, when the archangel was almost ready to despair, the boy crossed his hands himself, and the next moment they were bound. Now a bandage was passed under the sleeper's chin and brought up over his head and tied fast— and so softly, so gradually, and so deftly were the knots drawn together and compacted, that the boy slept peacefully through it all without stirring.

Chapter XXI. Hendon to the rescue.

The old man glided away, stooping, stealthy, cat-like, and brought the low bench. He seated himself upon it, half his body in the dim and flickering light, and the other half in shadow; and so, with his craving eyes bent upon the slumbering boy, he kept his patient vigil there, heedless of the drift of time, and softly whetted his knife, and mumbled and chuckled; and in aspect and attitude he resembled nothing so much as a grizzly, monstrous spider, gloating over some hapless insect that lay bound and helpless in his web.

After a long while, the old man, who was still gazing,—yet not seeing, his mind having settled into a dreamy abstraction,—observed, on a sudden, that the boy's eyes were open! wide open and staring!—staring up in frozen horror at the knife. The smile of a gratified devil crept over the old man's face, and he said, without changing his attitude or his occupation—

"Son of Henry the Eighth, hast thou prayed?"

The boy struggled helplessly in his bonds, and at the same time forced a smothered sound through his closed jaws, which the hermit chose to interpret as an affirmative answer to his question.

"Then pray again. Pray the prayer for the dying!"

A shudder shook the boy's frame, and his face blenched. Then he struggled again to free himself—turning and twisting himself this way and that; tugging frantically, fiercely, desperately—but uselessly—to burst his fetters; and all the while the old ogre smiled down upon him, and nodded his head, and placidly whetted his knife; mumbling, from time to time, "The moments are precious, they are few and precious—pray the prayer for the dying!"

The boy uttered a despairing groan, and ceased from his struggles, panting. The tears came, then, and trickled, one after the other, down his face; but this piteous sight wrought no softening effect upon the savage old man.

The dawn was coming now; the hermit observed it, and spoke up sharply, with a touch of nervous apprehension in his voice—

"I may not indulge this ecstasy longer! The night is already gone. It seems but a moment—only a moment; would it had endured a year! Seed of the Church's spoiler, close thy perishing eyes, an' thou fearest to look upon—"

The rest was lost in inarticulate mutterings. The old man sank upon his knees, his knife in his hand, and bent himself over the moaning boy.

Hark! There was a sound of voices near the cabin—the knife dropped from the hermit's hand; he cast a sheepskin over the boy and started up, trembling. The sounds increased, and presently the voices became rough and angry; then came blows, and cries for help; then a clatter of swift footsteps, retreating. Immediately came a succession of thundering knocks upon the cabin door, followed by—

"Hullo-o-o! Open! And despatch, in the name of all the devils!"

Oh, this was the blessedest sound that had ever made music in the King's ears; for it was Miles Hendon's voice!

The hermit, grinding his teeth in impotent rage, moved swiftly out of the bedchamber, closing the door behind him; and straightway the King heard a talk, to this effect, proceeding from the 'chapel':—

"Homage and greeting, reverend sir! Where is the boy—MY boy?"

"What boy, friend?"

"What boy! Lie me no lies, sir priest, play me no deceptions!—I am not in the humour for it. Near to this place I caught the scoundrels who I judged did steal him from me, and I made them confess; they said he was at large again, and they had tracked him to your door. They showed me his very footprints. Now palter no more; for look you, holy sir, an' thou produce him not—Where is the boy?"

"O good sir, peradventure you mean the ragged regal vagrant that tarried here the night. If such as you take an interest in such as he, know, then, that I have sent him of an errand. He will be back anon."

"How soon? How soon? Come, waste not the time—cannot I overtake him? How soon will he be back?"

"Thou need'st not stir; he will return quickly."

"So be it, then. I will try to wait. But stop!—YOU sent him of an errand?—you! Verily this is a lie—he would not go. He would pull thy old beard, an' thou didst offer him such an insolence. Thou hast lied, friend; thou hast surely lied! He would not go for thee, nor for any man."

"For any MAN—no; haply not. But I am not a man."

"WHAT! Now o' God's name what art thou, then?"

"It is a secret—mark thou reveal it not. I am an archangel!"

There was a tremendous ejaculation from Miles Hendon—not altogether unprofane—followed by—

"This doth well and truly account for his complaisance! Right well I knew he would budge nor hand nor foot in the menial service of any mortal; but, lord, even a king must obey when an archangel gives the word o' command! Let me—'sh! What noise was that?"

All this while the little King had been yonder, alternately quaking with terror and trembling with hope; and all the while, too, he had thrown all the strength he could into his anguished moanings, constantly expecting them to reach Hendon's ear, but always realising, with bitterness, that they failed, or at least made no impression. So this last remark of his servant came as comes a reviving breath from fresh fields to the dying; and he exerted himself once more, and with all his energy, just as the hermit was saying—

"Noise? I heard only the wind."

"Mayhap it was. Yes, doubtless that was it. I have been hearing it faintly all the—there it is again! It is not the wind! What an odd sound! Come, we will hunt it out!"

Now the King's joy was nearly insupportable. His tired lungs did their utmost—and hopefully, too—but the sealed jaws and the muffling sheepskin sadly crippled the effort. Then the poor fellow's heart sank, to hear the hermit say—

"Ah, it came from without—I think from the copse yonder. Come, I will lead the way."

The King heard the two pass out, talking; heard their footsteps die quickly away—then he was alone with a boding, brooding, awful silence.

It seemed an age till he heard the steps and voices approaching again —and this time he heard an added sound,— the trampling of hoofs, apparently. Then he heard Hendon say—

"I will not wait longer. I CANNOT wait longer. He has lost his way in this thick wood. Which direction took he? Quick—point it out to me."

"He—but wait; I will go with thee."

"Good—good! Why, truly thou art better than thy looks. Marry I do not think there's not another archangel with so right a heart as thine. Wilt ride? Wilt take the wee donkey that's for my boy, or wilt thou fork thy holy legs over this ill-conditioned slave of a mule that I have provided for myself?—and had been cheated in too, had he cost but the indifferent sum of a month's usury on a brass farthing let to a tinker out of work."

"No—ride thy mule, and lead thine ass; I am surer on mine own feet, and will walk."

"Then prithee mind the little beast for me while I take my life in my hands and make what success I may toward mounting the big one."

Then followed a confusion of kicks, cuffs, tramplings and plungings, accompanied by a thunderous intermingling of volleyed curses, and finally a bitter apostrophe to the mule, which must have broken its spirit, for hostilities seemed to cease from that moment.

With unutterable misery the fettered little King heard the voices and footsteps fade away and die out. All hope forsook him, now, for the moment, and a dull despair settled down upon his heart. "My only friend is deceived and got rid of," he said; "the hermit will return and—" He finished with a gasp; and at once fell to struggling so frantically with his bonds again, that he shook off the smothering sheepskin.

And now he heard the door open! The sound chilled him to the marrow —already he seemed to feel the knife at his throat. Horror made him close his eyes; horror made him open them again—and before him stood John Canty and Hugo!

He would have said "Thank God!" if his jaws had been free.

A moment or two later his limbs were at liberty, and his captors, each gripping him by an arm, were hurrying him with all speed through the forest.

Chapter XXII. A victim of treachery.

Once more 'King Foo-foo the First' was roving with the tramps and outlaws, a butt for their coarse jests and dull-witted railleries, and sometimes the victim of small spitefulness at the hands of Canty and Hugo when the Ruffler's back was turned. None but Canty and Hugo really disliked him. Some of the others liked him, and all admired his pluck and spirit. During two or three days, Hugo, in whose ward and charge the King was, did what he covertly could to make the boy uncomfortable; and at night, during the customary orgies, he amused the company by putting small indignities upon him— always as if by accident. Twice he stepped upon the King's toes—accidentally—and the King, as became his royalty, was contemptuously unconscious of it and indifferent to it; but the third time Hugo entertained himself in that way, the King felled him to the ground with a cudgel, to the prodigious

delight of the tribe. Hugo, consumed with anger and shame, sprang up, seized a cudgel, and came at his small adversary in a fury. Instantly a ring was formed around the gladiators, and the betting and cheering began. But poor Hugo stood no chance whatever. His frantic and lubberly 'prentice-work found but a poor market for itself when pitted against an arm which had been trained by the first masters of Europe in single-stick, quarter-staff, and every art and trick of swordsmanship. The little King stood, alert but at graceful ease, and caught and turned aside the thick rain of blows with a facility and precision which set the motley on-lookers wild with admiration; and every now and then, when his practised eye detected an opening, and a lightning-swift rap upon Hugo's head followed as a result, the storm of cheers and laughter that swept the place was something wonderful to hear. At the end of fifteen minutes, Hugo, all battered, bruised, and the target for a pitiless bombardment of ridicule, slunk from the field; and the unscathed hero of the fight was seized and borne aloft upon the shoulders of the joyous rabble to the place of honour beside the Ruffler, where with vast ceremony he was crowned King of the Game-Cocks; his meaner title being at the same time solemnly cancelled and annulled, and a decree of banishment from the gang pronounced against any who should thenceforth utter it.

All attempts to make the King serviceable to the troop had failed. He had stubbornly refused to act; moreover, he was always trying to escape. He had been thrust into an unwatched kitchen, the first day of his return; he not only came forth empty-handed, but tried to rouse the housemates. He was sent out with a tinker to help him at his work; he would not work; moreover, he threatened the tinker with his own soldering-iron; and finally both Hugo and the tinker found their hands full with the mere matter of keeping his from getting away. He delivered the thunders of his royalty upon the heads of all who hampered his liberties or tried to force him to service. He was sent out, in Hugo's charge, in company with a slatternly woman and a diseased baby, to beg; but the result was not encouraging—he declined to plead for the mendicants, or be a party to their cause in any way.

Thus several days went by; and the miseries of this tramping life, and the weariness and sordidness and meanness and vulgarity of it, became gradually and steadily so intolerable to the captive that he began at last to feel that his release from the hermit's knife must prove only a temporary respite from death, at best.

But at night, in his dreams, these things were forgotten, and he was on his throne, and master again. This, of course, intensified the sufferings of the awakening—so the mortifications of each succeeding morning of the few that passed between his return to bondage and the combat with Hugo, grew bitterer and bitterer, and harder and harder to bear.

The morning after that combat, Hugo got up with a heart filled with vengeful purposes against the King. He had two plans, in particular. One was to inflict upon the lad what would be, to his proud spirit and 'imagined' royalty, a peculiar humiliation; and if he failed to accomplish this, his other plan was to put a crime of some kind upon the King, and then betray him into the implacable clutches of the law.

In pursuance of the first plan, he purposed to put a 'clime' upon the King's leg; rightly judging that that would mortify him to the last and perfect degree; and as soon as the clime should operate, he meant to get Canty's help, and FORCE the

King to expose his leg in the highway and beg for alms. 'Clime' was the cant term for a sore, artificially created. To make a clime, the operator made a paste or poultice of unslaked lime, soap, and the rust of old iron, and spread it upon a piece of leather, which was then bound tightly upon the leg. This would presently fret off the skin, and make the flesh raw and angry-looking; blood was then rubbed upon the limb, which, being fully dried, took on a dark and repulsive colour. Then a bandage of soiled rags was put on in a cleverly careless way which would allow the hideous ulcer to be seen, and move the compassion of the passer-by.*

Hugo got the help of the tinker whom the King had cowed with the soldering-iron; they took the boy out on a tinkering tramp, and as soon as they were out of sight of the camp they threw him down and the tinker held him while Hugo bound the poultice tight and fast upon his leg.

The King raged and stormed, and promised to hang the two the moment the sceptre was in his hand again; but they kept a firm grip upon him and enjoyed his impotent struggling and jeered at his threats. This continued until the poultice began to bite; and in no long time its work would have been perfected, if there had been no interruption. But there was; for about this time the 'slave' who had made the speech denouncing England's laws, appeared on the scene, and put an end to the enterprise, and stripped off the poultice and bandage.

The King wanted to borrow his deliverer's cudgel and warm the jackets of the two rascals on the spot; but the man said no, it would bring trouble —leave the matter till night; the whole tribe being together, then, the outside world would not venture to interfere or interrupt. He marched the party back to camp and reported the affair to the Ruffler, who listened, pondered, and then decided that the King should not be again detailed to beg, since it was plain he was worthy of something higher and better—wherefore, on the spot he promoted him from the mendicant rank and appointed him to steal!

Hugo was overjoyed. He had already tried to make the King steal, and failed; but there would be no more trouble of that sort, now, for of course the King would not dream of defying a distinct command delivered directly from head-quarters. So he planned a raid for that very afternoon, purposing to get the King in the law's grip in the course of it; and to do it, too, with such ingenious strategy, that it should seem to be accidental and unintentional; for the King of the Game-Cocks was popular now, and the gang might not deal over-gently with an unpopular member who played so serious a treachery upon him as the delivering him over to the common enemy, the law.

Very well. All in good time Hugo strolled off to a neighbouring village with his prey; and the two drifted slowly up and down one street after another, the one watching sharply for a sure chance to achieve his evil purpose, and the other watching as sharply for a chance to dart away and get free of his infamous captivity for ever.

Both threw away some tolerably fair-looking opportunities; for both, in their secret hearts, were resolved to make absolutely sure work this time, and neither meant to allow his fevered desires to seduce him into any venture that had much uncertainty about it.

Hugo's chance came first. For at last a woman approached who carried a fat package of some sort in a basket. Hugo's eyes

* From 'The English Rogue.' London, 1665.

sparkled with sinful pleasure as he said to himself, "Breath o' my life, an' I can but put THAT upon him, 'tis good-den and God keep thee, King of the Game-Cocks!" He waited and watched—outwardly patient, but inwardly consuming with excitement—till the woman had passed by, and the time was ripe; then said, in a low voice—

"Tarry here till I come again," and darted stealthily after the prey.

The King's heart was filled with joy—he could make his escape, now, if Hugo's quest only carried him far enough away.

But he was to have no such luck. Hugo crept behind the woman, snatched the package, and came running back, wrapping it in an old piece of blanket which he carried on his arm. The hue and cry was raised in a moment, by the woman, who knew her loss by the lightening of her burden, although she had not seen the pilfering done. Hugo thrust the bundle into the King's hands without halting, saying—

"Now speed ye after me with the rest, and cry 'Stop thief!' but mind ye lead them astray!"

The next moment Hugo turned a corner and darted down a crooked alley—and in another moment or two he lounged into view again, looking innocent and indifferent, and took up a position behind a post to watch results.

The insulted King threw the bundle on the ground; and the blanket fell away from it just as the woman arrived, with an augmenting crowd at her heels; she seized the King's wrist with one hand, snatched up her bundle with the other, and began to pour out a tirade of abuse upon the boy while he struggled, without success, to free himself from her grip.

Hugo had seen enough—his enemy was captured and the law would get him, now—so he slipped away, jubilant and chuckling, and wended campwards, framing a judicious version of the matter to give to the Ruffler's crew as he strode along.

The King continued to struggle in the woman's strong grasp, and now and then cried out in vexation—

"Unhand me, thou foolish creature; it was not I that bereaved thee of thy paltry goods."

The crowd closed around, threatening the King and calling him names; a brawny blacksmith in leather apron, and sleeves rolled to his elbows, made a reach for him, saying he would trounce him well, for a lesson; but just then a long sword flashed in the air and fell with convincing force upon the man's arm, flat side down, the fantastic owner of it remarking pleasantly, at the same time—

"Marry, good souls, let us proceed gently, not with ill blood and uncharitable words. This is matter for the law's consideration, not private and unofficial handling. Loose thy hold from the boy, goodwife."

The blacksmith averaged the stalwart soldier with a glance, then went muttering away, rubbing his arm; the woman released the boy's wrist reluctantly; the crowd eyed the stranger unlovingly, but prudently closed their mouths. The King sprang to his deliverer's side, with flushed cheeks and sparkling eyes, exclaiming—

"Thou hast lagged sorely, but thou comest in good season, now, Sir Miles; carve me this rabble to rags!"

Chapter XXIII. The Prince a prisoner.

Hendon forced back a smile, and bent down and whispered in the King's ear—

"Softly, softly, my prince, wag thy tongue warily—nay, suffer it not to wag at all. Trust in me—all shall go well in the end." Then he added to himself: "SIR Miles! Bless me, I had totally forgot I was a knight! Lord, how marvellous a thing it is, the grip his memory doth take upon his quaint and crazy fancies! . . . An empty and foolish title is mine, and yet it is something to have deserved it; for I think it is more honour to be held worthy to be a spectre-knight in his Kingdom of Dreams and Shadows, than to be held base enough to be an earl in some of the REAL kingdoms of this world."

The crowd fell apart to admit a constable, who approached and was about to lay his hand upon the King's shoulder, when Hendon said—

"Gently, good friend, withhold your hand—he shall go peaceably; I am responsible for that. Lead on, we will follow."

The officer led, with the woman and her bundle; Miles and the King followed after, with the crowd at their heels. The King was inclined to rebel; but Hendon said to him in a low voice—

"Reflect, Sire—your laws are the wholesome breath of your own royalty; shall their source resist them, yet require the branches to respect them? Apparently one of these laws has been broken; when the King is on his throne again, can it ever grieve him to remember that when he was seemingly a private person he loyally sank the king in the citizen and submitted to its authority?"

"Thou art right; say no more; thou shalt see that whatsoever the King of England requires a subject to suffer, under the law, he will himself suffer while he holdeth the station of a subject."

When the woman was called upon to testify before the justice of the peace, she swore that the small prisoner at the bar was the person who had committed the theft; there was none able to show the contrary, so the King stood convicted. The bundle was now unrolled, and when the contents proved to be a plump little dressed pig, the judge looked troubled, whilst Hendon turned pale, and his body was thrilled with an electric shiver of dismay; but the King remained unmoved, protected by his ignorance. The judge meditated, during an ominous pause, then turned to the woman, with the question—

"What dost thou hold this property to be worth?"

The woman courtesied and replied—

"Three shillings and eightpence, your worship—I could not abate a penny and set forth the value honestly."

The justice glanced around uncomfortably upon the crowd, then nodded to the constable, and said—

"Clear the court and close the doors."

It was done. None remained but the two officials, the accused, the accuser, and Miles Hendon. This latter was rigid and colourless, and on his forehead big drops of cold sweat

gathered, broke and blended together, and trickled down his face. The judge turned to the woman again, and said, in a compassionate voice—

"'Tis a poor ignorant lad, and mayhap was driven hard by hunger, for these be grievous times for the unfortunate; mark you, he hath not an evil face—but when hunger driveth—Good woman! dost know that when one steals a thing above the value of thirteenpence ha'penny the law saith he shall HANG for it?"

The little King started, wide-eyed with consternation, but controlled himself and held his peace; but not so the woman. She sprang to her feet, shaking with fright, and cried out—

"Oh, good lack, what have I done! God-a-mercy, I would not hang the poor thing for the whole world! Ah, save me from this, your worship—what shall I do, what CAN I do?"

The justice maintained his judicial composure, and simply said—

"Doubtless it is allowable to revise the value, since it is not yet writ upon the record."

"Then in God's name call the pig eightpence, and heaven bless the day that freed my conscience of this awesome thing!"

Miles Hendon forgot all decorum in his delight; and surprised the King and wounded his dignity, by throwing his arms around him and hugging him. The woman made her grateful adieux and started away with her pig; and when the constable opened the door for her, he followed her out into the narrow hall. The justice proceeded to write in his record book. Hendon, always alert, thought he would like to know why the officer followed the woman out; so he slipped softly into the dusky hall and listened. He heard a conversation to this effect—

"It is a fat pig, and promises good eating; I will buy it of thee; here is the eightpence."

"Eightpence, indeed! Thou'lt do no such thing. It cost me three shillings and eightpence, good honest coin of the last reign, that old Harry that's just dead ne'er touched or tampered with. A fig for thy eightpence!"

"Stands the wind in that quarter? Thou wast under oath, and so swore falsely when thou saidst the value was but eightpence. Come straightway back with me before his worship, and answer for the crime!—and then the lad will hang."

"There, there, dear heart, say no more, I am content. Give me the eightpence, and hold thy peace about the matter."

The woman went off crying: Hendon slipped back into the court room, and the constable presently followed, after hiding his prize in some convenient place. The justice wrote a while longer, then read the King a wise and kindly lecture, and sentenced him to a short imprisonment in the common jail, to be followed by a public flogging. The astounded King opened his mouth, and was probably going to order the good judge to be beheaded on the spot; but he caught a warning sign from Hendon, and succeeded in closing his mouth again before he lost anything out of it. Hendon took him by the hand, now, made reverence to the justice, and the two departed in the wake of the constable toward the jail. The moment the street was reached, the inflamed monarch halted, snatched away his hand, and exclaimed—

"Idiot, dost imagine I will enter a common jail ALIVE?"

Hendon bent down and said, somewhat sharply—

"WILL you trust in me? Peace! and forbear to worsen our chances with dangerous speech. What God wills, will happen; thou canst not hurry it, thou canst not alter it; therefore wait, and be patient—'twill be time enow to rail or rejoice when what is to happen has happened."*

Chapter XXIV. The escape.

The short winter day was nearly ended. The streets were deserted, save for a few random stragglers, and these hurried straight along, with the intent look of people who were only anxious to accomplish their errands as quickly as possible, and then snugly house themselves from the rising wind and the gathering twilight. They looked neither to the right nor to the left; they paid no attention to our party, they did not even seem to see them. Edward the Sixth wondered if the spectacle of a king on his way to jail had ever encountered such marvellous indifference before. By-and-by the constable arrived at a deserted market-square, and proceeded to cross it. When he had reached the middle of it, Hendon laid his hand upon his arm, and said in a low voice—

"Bide a moment, good sir, there is none in hearing, and I would say a word to thee."

"My duty forbids it, sir; prithee hinder me not, the night comes on."

"Stay, nevertheless, for the matter concerns thee nearly. Turn thy back a moment and seem not to see: LET THIS POOR LAD ESCAPE."

"This to me, sir! I arrest thee in—"

"Nay, be not too hasty. See thou be careful and commit no foolish error"—then he shut his voice down to a whisper, and said in the man's ear—"the pig thou hast purchased for eightpence may cost thee thy neck, man!"

The poor constable, taken by surprise, was speechless, at first, then found his tongue and fell to blustering and threatening; but Hendon was tranquil, and waited with patience till his breath was spent; then said—

"I have a liking to thee, friend, and would not willingly see thee come to harm. Observe, I heard it all—every word. I will prove it to thee." Then he repeated the conversation which the officer and the woman had had together in the hall, word for word, and ended with—

"There—have I set it forth correctly? Should not I be able to set

---

* Death for Trifling Larcenies: When Connecticut and New Haven were framing their first codes, larceny above the value of twelve pence was a capital crime in England—as it had been since the time of Henry I.—Dr. J. Hammond Trumbull's Blue Laws, True and False, p. 17.

The curious old book called The English Rogue makes the limit thirteen pence ha'penny: death being the portion of any who steal a thing 'above the value of thirteen pence ha'penny.'

it forth correctly before the judge, if occasion required?"

The man was dumb with fear and distress, for a moment; then he rallied, and said with forced lightness—

"'Tis making a mighty matter, indeed, out of a jest; I but plagued the woman for mine amusement."

"Kept you the woman's pig for amusement?"

The man answered sharply—

"Nought else, good sir—I tell thee 'twas but a jest."

"I do begin to believe thee," said Hendon, with a perplexing mixture of mockery and half-conviction in his tone; "but tarry thou here a moment whilst I run and ask his worship—for nathless, he being a man experienced in law, in jests, in—"

He was moving away, still talking; the constable hesitated, fidgeted, spat out an oath or two, then cried out—

"Hold, hold, good sir—prithee wait a little—the judge! Why, man, he hath no more sympathy with a jest than hath a dead corpse!—come, and we will speak further. Ods body! I seem to be in evil case—and all for an innocent and thoughtless pleasantry. I am a man of family; and my wife and little ones—List to reason, good your worship: what wouldst thou of me?"

"Only that thou be blind and dumb and paralytic whilst one may count a hundred thousand—counting slowly," said Hendon, with the expression of a man who asks but a reasonable favour, and that a very little one.

"It is my destruction!" said the constable despairingly. "Ah, be reasonable, good sir; only look at this matter, on all its sides, and see how mere a jest it is—how manifestly and how plainly it is so. And even if one granted it were not a jest, it is a fault so small that e'en the grimmest penalty it could call forth would be but a rebuke and warning from the judge's lips."

Hendon replied with a solemnity which chilled the air about him—

"This jest of thine hath a name, in law,—wot you what it is?"

"I knew it not! Peradventure I have been unwise. I never dreamed it had a name—ah, sweet heaven, I thought it was original."

"Yes, it hath a name. In the law this crime is called Non compos mentis lex talionis sic transit gloria mundi."

"Ah, my God!"

"And the penalty is death!"

"God be merciful to me a sinner!"

"By advantage taken of one in fault, in dire peril, and at thy mercy, thou hast seized goods worth above thirteenpence ha'penny, paying but a trifle for the same; and this, in the eye of the law, is constructive barratry, misprision of treason, malfeasance in office, ad hominem expurgatis in statu quo—and the penalty is death by the halter, without ransom, commutation, or benefit of clergy."

"Bear me up, bear me up, sweet sir, my legs do fail me! Be

thou merciful—spare me this doom, and I will turn my back and see nought that shall happen."

"Good! now thou'rt wise and reasonable. And thou'lt restore the pig?"

"I will, I will indeed—nor ever touch another, though heaven send it and an archangel fetch it. Go—I am blind for thy sake—I see nothing. I will say thou didst break in and wrest the prisoner from my hands by force. It is but a crazy, ancient door—I will batter it down myself betwixt midnight and the morning."

"Do it, good soul, no harm will come of it; the judge hath a loving charity for this poor lad, and will shed no tears and break no jailer's bones for his escape."

Chapter XXV. Hendon Hall.

As soon as Hendon and the King were out of sight of the constable, his Majesty was instructed to hurry to a certain place outside the town, and wait there, whilst Hendon should go to the inn and settle his account. Half an hour later the two friends were blithely jogging eastward on Hendon's sorry steeds. The King was warm and comfortable, now, for he had cast his rags and clothed himself in the second-hand suit which Hendon had bought on London Bridge.

Hendon wished to guard against over-fatiguing the boy; he judged that hard journeys, irregular meals, and illiberal measures of sleep would be bad for his crazed mind; whilst rest, regularity, and moderate exercise would be pretty sure to hasten its cure; he longed to see the stricken intellect made well again and its diseased visions driven out of the tormented little head; therefore he resolved to move by easy stages toward the home whence he had so long been banished, instead of obeying the impulse of his impatience and hurrying along night and day.

When he and the King had journeyed about ten miles, they reached a considerable village, and halted there for the night, at a good inn. The former relations were resumed; Hendon stood behind the King's chair, while he dined, and waited upon him; undressed him when he was ready for bed; then took the floor for his own quarters, and slept athwart the door, rolled up in a blanket.

The next day, and the day after, they jogged lazily along talking over the adventures they had met since their separation, and mightily enjoying each other's narratives. Hendon detailed all his wide wanderings in search of the King, and described how the archangel had led him a fool's journey all over the forest, and taken him back to the hut, finally, when he found he could not get rid of him. Then—he said—the old man went into the bedchamber and came staggering back looking broken-hearted, and saying he had expected to find that the boy had returned and laid down in there to rest, but it was not so. Hendon had waited at the hut all day; hope of the King's return died out, then, and he departed upon the quest again.

"And old Sanctum Sanctorum WAS truly sorry your highness came not back," said Hendon; "I saw it in his face."

"Marry I will never doubt THAT!" said the King—and then told his own story; after which, Hendon was sorry he had not destroyed the archangel.

During the last day of the trip, Hendon's spirits were soaring. His tongue ran constantly. He talked about his old father, and his brother Arthur, and told of many things which illustrated their high and generous characters; he went into loving frenzies over his Edith, and was so glad-hearted that he was even able to say some gentle and brotherly things about Hugh. He dwelt a deal on the coming meeting at Hendon Hall; what a surprise it would be to everybody, and what an outburst of thanksgiving and delight there would be.

It was a fair region, dotted with cottages and orchards, and the road led through broad pasture lands whose receding expanses, marked with gentle elevations and depressions, suggested the swelling and subsiding undulations of the sea. In the afternoon the returning prodigal made constant deflections from his course to see if by ascending some hillock he might not pierce the distance and catch a glimpse of his home. At last he was successful, and cried out excitedly—

"There is the village, my Prince, and there is the Hall close by! You may see the towers from here; and that wood there—that is my father's park. Ah, NOW thou'lt know what state and grandeur be! A house with seventy rooms—think of that!—and seven and twenty servants! A brave lodging for such as we, is it not so? Come, let us speed—my impatience will not brook further delay."

All possible hurry was made; still, it was after three o'clock before the village was reached. The travellers scampered through it, Hendon's tongue going all the time. "Here is the church—covered with the same ivy—none gone, none added." "Yonder is the inn, the old Red Lion,—and yonder is the market-place." "Here is the Maypole, and here the pump — nothing is altered; nothing but the people, at any rate; ten years make a change in people; some of these I seem to know, but none know me." So his chat ran on. The end of the village was soon reached; then the travellers struck into a crooked, narrow road, walled in with tall hedges, and hurried briskly along it for half a mile, then passed into a vast flower garden through an imposing gateway, whose huge stone pillars bore sculptured armorial devices. A noble mansion was before them.

"Welcome to Hendon Hall, my King!" exclaimed Miles. "Ah, 'tis a great day! My father and my brother, and the Lady Edith will be so mad with joy that they will have eyes and tongue for none but me in the first transports of the meeting, and so thou'lt seem but coldly welcomed—but mind it not; 'twill soon seem otherwise; for when I say thou art my ward, and tell them how costly is my love for thee, thou'lt see them take thee to their breasts for Miles Hendon's sake, and make their house and hearts thy home for ever after!"

The next moment Hendon sprang to the ground before the great door, helped the King down, then took him by the hand and rushed within. A few steps brought him to a spacious apartment; he entered, seated the King with more hurry than ceremony, then ran toward a young man who sat at a writing-table in front of a generous fire of logs.

"Embrace me, Hugh," he cried, "and say thou'rt glad I am come again! and call our father, for home is not home till I shall touch his hand, and see his face, and hear his voice once more!"

But Hugh only drew back, after betraying a momentary surprise, and bent a grave stare upon the intruder—a stare which indicated somewhat of offended dignity, at first, then changed, in response to some inward thought or purpose, to an expression of marvelling curiosity, mixed with a real or assumed compassion. Presently he said, in a mild voice—

"Thy wits seem touched, poor stranger; doubtless thou hast suffered privations and rude buffetings at the world's hands; thy looks and dress betoken it. Whom dost thou take me to be?"

"Take thee? Prithee for whom else than whom thou art? I take thee to be Hugh Hendon," said Miles, sharply.

The other continued, in the same soft tone—

"And whom dost thou imagine thyself to be?"

"Imagination hath nought to do with it! Dost thou pretend thou knowest me not for thy brother Miles Hendon?"

An expression of pleased surprise flitted across Hugh's face, and he exclaimed—

"What! thou art not jesting? can the dead come to life? God be praised if it be so! Our poor lost boy restored to our arms after all these cruel years! Ah, it seems too good to be true, it IS too good to be true—I charge thee, have pity, do not trifle with me! Quick—come to the light—let me scan thee well!"

He seized Miles by the arm, dragged him to the window, and began to devour him from head to foot with his eyes, turning him this way and that, and stepping briskly around him and about him to prove him from all points of view; whilst the returned prodigal, all aglow with gladness, smiled, laughed, and kept nodding his head and saying—

"Go on, brother, go on, and fear not; thou'lt find nor limb nor feature that cannot bide the test. Scour and scan me to thy content, my good old Hugh—I am indeed thy old Miles, thy same old Miles, thy lost brother, is't not so? Ah, 'tis a great day—I SAID 'twas a great day! Give me thy hand, give me thy cheek—lord, I am like to die of very joy!"

He was about to throw himself upon his brother; but Hugh put up his hand in dissent, then dropped his chin mournfully upon his breast, saying with emotion—

"Ah, God of his mercy give me strength to bear this grievous disappointment!"

Miles, amazed, could not speak for a moment; then he found his tongue, and cried out—

"WHAT disappointment? Am I not thy brother?"

Hugh shook his head sadly, and said—

"I pray heaven it may prove so, and that other eyes may find the resemblances that are hid from mine. Alack, I fear me the letter spoke but too truly."

"What letter?"

"One that came from over sea, some six or seven years ago. It said my brother died in battle."

"It was a lie! Call thy father—he will know me."

"One may not call the dead."

"Dead?" Miles's voice was subdued, and his lips trembled. "My father dead!—oh, this is heavy news. Half my new joy is withered now. Prithee let me see my brother Arthur—he will know me; he will know me and console me."

"He, also, is dead."

"God be merciful to me, a stricken man! Gone,—both gone—the worthy taken and the worthless spared, in me! Ah! I crave your mercy!—do not say the Lady Edith—"

"Is dead? No, she lives."

"Then, God be praised, my joy is whole again! Speed thee, brother—let her come to me! An' SHE say I am not myself—but she will not; no, no, SHE will know me, I were a fool to doubt it. Bring her—bring the old servants; they, too, will know me."

"All are gone but five—Peter, Halsey, David, Bernard, and Margaret."

So saying, Hugh left the room. Miles stood musing a while, then began to walk the floor, muttering—

"The five arch-villains have survived the two-and-twenty leal and honest —'tis an odd thing."

He continued walking back and forth, muttering to himself; he had forgotten the King entirely. By-and-by his Majesty said gravely, and with a touch of genuine compassion, though the words themselves were capable of being interpreted ironically—

"Mind not thy mischance, good man; there be others in the world whose identity is denied, and whose claims are derided. Thou hast company."

"Ah, my King," cried Hendon, colouring slightly, "do not thou condemn me —wait, and thou shalt see. I am no impostor—she will say it; you shall hear it from the sweetest lips in England. I an impostor? Why, I know this old hall, these pictures of my ancestors, and all these things that are about us, as a child knoweth its own nursery. Here was I born and bred, my lord; I speak the truth; I would not deceive thee; and should none else believe, I pray thee do not THOU doubt me—I could not bear it."

"I do not doubt thee," said the King, with a childlike simplicity and faith.

"I thank thee out of my heart!" exclaimed Hendon with a fervency which showed that he was touched. The King added, with the same gentle simplicity—

"Dost thou doubt ME?"

A guilty confusion seized upon Hendon, and he was grateful that the door opened to admit Hugh, at that moment, and saved him the necessity of replying.

A beautiful lady, richly clothed, followed Hugh, and after her came several liveried servants. The lady walked slowly, with her head bowed and her eyes fixed upon the floor. The face was unspeakably sad. Miles Hendon sprang forward, crying out—

"Oh, my Edith, my darling—"

But Hugh waved him back, gravely, and said to the lady—

"Look upon him. Do you know him?"

At the sound of Miles's voice the woman had started slightly, and her cheeks had flushed; she was trembling now. She stood still, during an impressive pause of several moments; then slowly lifted up her head and looked into Hendon's eyes with a stony and frightened gaze; the blood sank out of her face, drop by drop, till nothing remained but the grey pallor of death; then she said, in a voice as dead as the face, "I know him not!" and turned, with a moan and a stifled sob, and tottered out of the room.

Miles Hendon sank into a chair and covered his face with his hands. After a pause, his brother said to the servants—

"You have observed him. Do you know him?"

They shook their heads; then the master said—

"The servants know you not, sir. I fear there is some mistake. You have seen that my wife knew you not."

"Thy WIFE!" In an instant Hugh was pinned to the wall, with an iron grip about his throat. "Oh, thou fox-hearted slave, I see it all! Thou'st writ the lying letter thyself, and my stolen bride and goods are its fruit. There—now get thee gone, lest I shame mine honourable soldiership with the slaying of so pitiful a mannikin!"

Hugh, red-faced, and almost suffocated, reeled to the nearest chair, and commanded the servants to seize and bind the murderous stranger. They hesitated, and one of them said—

"He is armed, Sir Hugh, and we are weaponless."

"Armed! What of it, and ye so many? Upon him, I say!"

But Miles warned them to be careful what they did, and added—

"Ye know me of old—I have not changed; come on, an' it like you."

This reminder did not hearten the servants much; they still held back.

"Then go, ye paltry cowards, and arm yourselves and guard the doors, whilst I send one to fetch the watch!" said Hugh. He turned at the threshold, and said to Miles, "You'll find it to your advantage to offend not with useless endeavours at escape."

"Escape? Spare thyself discomfort, an' that is all that troubles thee. For Miles Hendon is master of Hendon Hall and all its belongings. He will remain—doubt it not."

Chapter XXVI. Disowned.

The King sat musing a few moments, then looked up and said—

"'Tis strange—most strange. I cannot account for it."

"No, it is not strange, my liege. I know him, and this conduct is

but natural. He was a rascal from his birth."

"Oh, I spake not of HIM, Sir Miles."

"Not of him? Then of what? What is it that is strange?"

"That the King is not missed."

"How? Which? I doubt I do not understand."

"Indeed? Doth it not strike you as being passing strange that the land is not filled with couriers and proclamations describing my person and making search for me? Is it no matter for commotion and distress that the Head of the State is gone; that I am vanished away and lost?"

"Most true, my King, I had forgot." Then Hendon sighed, and muttered to himself, "Poor ruined mind—still busy with its pathetic dream."

"But I have a plan that shall right us both—I will write a paper, in three tongues—Latin, Greek and English—and thou shalt haste away with it to London in the morning. Give it to none but my uncle, the Lord Hertford; when he shall see it, he will know and say I wrote it. Then he will send for me."

"Might it not be best, my Prince, that we wait here until I prove myself and make my rights secure to my domains? I should be so much the better able then to—"

The King interrupted him imperiously—

"Peace! What are thy paltry domains, thy trivial interests, contrasted with matters which concern the weal of a nation and the integrity of a throne?" Then, he added, in a gentle voice, as if he were sorry for his severity, "Obey, and have no fear; I will right thee, I will make thee whole—yes, more than whole. I shall remember, and requite."

So saying, he took the pen, and set himself to work. Hendon contemplated him lovingly a while, then said to himself—

"An' it were dark, I should think it WAS a king that spoke; there's no denying it, when the humour's upon on him he doth thunder and lighten like your true King; now where got he that trick? See him scribble and scratch away contentedly at his meaningless pot-hooks, fancying them to be Latin and Greek—and except my wit shall serve me with a lucky device for diverting him from his purpose, I shall be forced to pretend to post away to-morrow on this wild errand he hath invented for me."

The next moment Sir Miles's thoughts had gone back to the recent episode. So absorbed was he in his musings, that when the King presently handed him the paper which he had been writing, he received it and pocketed it without being conscious of the act. "How marvellous strange she acted," he muttered. "I think she knew me—and I think she did NOT know me. These opinions do conflict, I perceive it plainly; I cannot reconcile them, neither can I, by argument, dismiss either of the two, or even persuade one to outweigh the other. The matter standeth simply thus: she MUST have known my face, my figure, my voice, for how could it be otherwise? Yet she SAID she knew me not, and that is proof perfect, for she cannot lie. But stop—I think I begin to see. Peradventure he hath influenced her, commanded her, compelled her to lie. That is the solution. The riddle is unriddled. She seemed dead with fear—yes, she was under his compulsion. I will seek her; I will find her; now that he is away, she will speak her true mind. She will remember the old times when we were little playfellows together, and this will soften her heart, and she will no more betray me, but will confess me. There is no treacherous blood in her—no, she was always honest and true. She has loved me, in those old days—this is my security; for whom one has loved, one cannot betray."

He stepped eagerly toward the door; at that moment it opened, and the Lady Edith entered. She was very pale, but she walked with a firm step, and her carriage was full of grace and gentle dignity. Her face was as sad as before.

Miles sprang forward, with a happy confidence, to meet her, but she checked him with a hardly perceptible gesture, and he stopped where he was. She seated herself, and asked him to do likewise. Thus simply did she take the sense of old comradeship out of him, and transform him into a stranger and a guest. The surprise of it, the bewildering unexpectedness of it, made him begin to question, for a moment, if he WAS the person he was pretending to be, after all. The Lady Edith said—

"Sir, I have come to warn you. The mad cannot be persuaded out of their delusions, perchance; but doubtless they may be persuaded to avoid perils. I think this dream of yours hath the seeming of honest truth to you, and therefore is not criminal—but do not tarry here with it; for here it is dangerous." She looked steadily into Miles's face a moment, then added, impressively, "It is the more dangerous for that you ARE much like what our lost lad must have grown to be if he had lived."

"Heavens, madam, but I AM he!"

"I truly think you think it, sir. I question not your honesty in that; I but warn you, that is all. My husband is master in this region; his power hath hardly any limit; the people prosper or starve, as he wills. If you resembled not the man whom you profess to be, my husband might bid you pleasure yourself with your dream in peace; but trust me, I know him well; I know what he will do; he will say to all that you are but a mad impostor, and straightway all will echo him." She bent upon Miles that same steady look once more, and added: "If you WERE Miles Hendon, and he knew it and all the region knew it—consider what I am saying, weigh it well—you would stand in the same peril, your punishment would be no less sure; he would deny you and denounce you, and none would be bold enough to give you countenance."

"Most truly I believe it," said Miles, bitterly. "The power that can command one life-long friend to betray and disown another, and be obeyed, may well look to be obeyed in quarters where bread and life are on the stake and no cobweb ties of loyalty and honour are concerned."

A faint tinge appeared for a moment in the lady's cheek, and she dropped her eyes to the floor; but her voice betrayed no emotion when she proceeded—

"I have warned you—I must still warn you—to go hence. This man will destroy you, else. He is a tyrant who knows no pity. I, who am his fettered slave, know this. Poor Miles, and Arthur, and my dear guardian, Sir Richard, are free of him, and at rest: better that you were with them than that you bide here in the clutches of this miscreant. Your pretensions are a menace to his title and possessions; you have assaulted him in his own house: you are ruined if you stay. Go—do not hesitate. If you lack money, take this purse, I beg of you, and bribe the servants to let you pass. Oh, be warned, poor soul, and escape while you may."

Miles declined the purse with a gesture, and rose up and stood before her.

"Grant me one thing," he said. "Let your eyes rest upon mine, so that I may see if they be steady. There—now answer me. Am I Miles Hendon?"

"No. I know you not."

"Swear it!"

The answer was low, but distinct—

"I swear."

"Oh, this passes belief!"

"Fly! Why will you waste the precious time? Fly, and save yourself."

At that moment the officers burst into the room, and a violent struggle began; but Hendon was soon overpowered and dragged away. The King was taken also, and both were bound and led to prison.

Chapter XXVII. In prison.

The cells were all crowded; so the two friends were chained in a large room where persons charged with trifling offences were commonly kept. They had company, for there were some twenty manacled and fettered prisoners here, of both sexes and of varying ages,—an obscene and noisy gang. The King chafed bitterly over the stupendous indignity thus put upon his royalty, but Hendon was moody and taciturn. He was pretty thoroughly bewildered; he had come home, a jubilant prodigal, expecting to find everybody wild with joy over his return; and instead had got the cold shoulder and a jail. The promise and the fulfilment differed so widely that the effect was stunning; he could not decide whether it was most tragic or most grotesque. He felt much as a man might who had danced blithely out to enjoy a rainbow, and got struck by lightning.

But gradually his confused and tormenting thoughts settled down into some sort of order, and then his mind centred itself upon Edith. He turned her conduct over, and examined it in all lights, but he could not make anything satisfactory out of it. Did she know him—or didn't she know him? It was a perplexing puzzle, and occupied him a long time; but he ended, finally, with the conviction that she did know him, and had repudiated him for interested reasons. He wanted to load her name with curses now; but this name had so long been sacred to him that he found he could not bring his tongue to profane it.

Wrapped in prison blankets of a soiled and tattered condition, Hendon and the King passed a troubled night. For a bribe the jailer had furnished liquor to some of the prisoners; singing of ribald songs, fighting, shouting, and carousing was the natural consequence. At last, a while after midnight, a man attacked a woman and nearly killed her by beating her over the head with his manacles before the jailer could come to the rescue. The jailer restored peace by giving the man a sound clubbing about the head and shoulders—then the carousing ceased; and after that, all had an opportunity to sleep who did not mind the annoyance of the moanings and groanings of the two wounded people.

During the ensuing week, the days and nights were of a monotonous sameness as to events; men whose faces Hendon remembered more or less distinctly, came, by day, to gaze at the 'impostor' and repudiate and insult him; and by night the carousing and brawling went on with symmetrical regularity. However, there was a change of incident at last. The jailer brought in an old man, and said to him—

"The villain is in this room—cast thy old eyes about and see if thou canst say which is he."

Hendon glanced up, and experienced a pleasant sensation for the first time since he had been in the jail. He said to himself, "This is Blake Andrews, a servant all his life in my father's family—a good honest soul, with a right heart in his breast. That is, formerly. But none are true now; all are liars. This man will know me—and will deny me, too, like the rest."

The old man gazed around the room, glanced at each face in turn, and finally said—

"I see none here but paltry knaves, scum o' the streets. Which is he?"

The jailer laughed.

"Here," he said; "scan this big animal, and grant me an opinion."

The old man approached, and looked Hendon over, long and earnestly, then shook his head and said—

"Marry, THIS is no Hendon—nor ever was!"

"Right! Thy old eyes are sound yet. An' I were Sir Hugh, I would take the shabby carle and—"

The jailer finished by lifting himself a-tip-toe with an imaginary halter, at the same time making a gurgling noise in his throat suggestive of suffocation. The old man said, vindictively—

"Let him bless God an' he fare no worse. An' I had the handling o' the villain he should roast, or I am no true man!"

The jailer laughed a pleasant hyena laugh, and said—

"Give him a piece of thy mind, old man—they all do it. Thou'lt find it good diversion."

Then he sauntered toward his ante-room and disappeared. The old man dropped upon his knees and whispered—

"God be thanked, thou'rt come again, my master! I believed thou wert dead these seven years, and lo, here thou art alive! I knew thee the moment I saw thee; and main hard work it was to keep a stony countenance and seem to see none here but tuppenny knaves and rubbish o' the streets. I am old and poor, Sir Miles; but say the word and I will go forth and proclaim the truth though I be strangled for it."

"No," said Hendon; "thou shalt not. It would ruin thee, and yet help but little in my cause. But I thank thee, for thou hast given me back somewhat of my lost faith in my kind."

The old servant became very valuable to Hendon and the King; for he dropped in several times a day to 'abuse' the former, and always smuggled in a few delicacies to help out the prison bill of fare; he also furnished the current news. Hendon reserved the dainties for the King; without them his Majesty might not have survived, for he was not able to eat the coarse and wretched food provided by the jailer. Andrews was obliged to confine himself to brief visits, in order to avoid suspicion; but he managed to impart a fair degree of information each time —information delivered in a low voice, for Hendon's benefit, and interlarded with insulting epithets delivered in a louder voice for the benefit of other hearers.

So, little by little, the story of the family came out. Arthur had been dead six years. This loss, with the absence of news from Hendon, impaired the father's health; he believed he was going to die, and he wished to see Hugh and Edith settled in life before he passed away; but Edith begged hard for delay, hoping for Miles's return; then the letter came which brought the news of Miles's death; the shock prostrated Sir Richard; he believed his end was very near, and he and Hugh insisted upon the marriage; Edith begged for and obtained a month's respite, then another, and finally a third; the marriage then took place by the death-bed of Sir Richard. It had not proved a happy one. It was whispered about the country that shortly after the nuptials the bride found among her husband's papers several rough and incomplete drafts of the fatal letter, and had accused him of precipitating the marriage—and Sir Richard's death, too—by a wicked forgery. Tales of cruelty to the Lady Edith and the servants were to be heard on all hands; and since the father's death Sir Hugh had thrown off all soft disguises and become a pitiless master toward all who in any way depended upon him and his domains for bread.

There was a bit of Andrew's gossip which the King listened to with a lively interest—

"There is rumour that the King is mad. But in charity forbear to say *I* mentioned it, for 'tis death to speak of it, they say."

His Majesty glared at the old man and said—

"The King is NOT mad, good man—and thou'lt find it to thy advantage to busy thyself with matters that nearer concern thee than this seditious prattle."

"What doth the lad mean?" said Andrews, surprised at this brisk assault from such an unexpected quarter. Hendon gave him a sign, and he did not pursue his question, but went on with his budget—

"The late King is to be buried at Windsor in a day or two—the 16th of the month—and the new King will be crowned at Westminster the 20th."

"Methinks they must needs find him first," muttered his Majesty; then added, confidently, "but they will look to that—and so also shall I."

"In the name of—"

But the old man got no further—a warning sign from Hendon checked his remark. He resumed the thread of his gossip—

"Sir Hugh goeth to the coronation—and with grand hopes. He confidently looketh to come back a peer, for he is high in favour with the Lord Protector."

"What Lord Protector?" asked his Majesty.

"His Grace the Duke of Somerset."

"What Duke of Somerset?"

"Marry, there is but one—Seymour, Earl of Hertford."

The King asked sharply—

"Since when is HE a duke, and Lord Protector?"

"Since the last day of January."

"And prithee who made him so?"

"Himself and the Great Council—with help of the King."

His Majesty started violently. "The KING!" he cried. "WHAT king, good sir?"

"What king, indeed! (God-a-mercy, what aileth the boy?) Sith we have but one, 'tis not difficult to answer—his most sacred Majesty King Edward the Sixth—whom God preserve! Yea, and a dear and gracious little urchin is he, too; and whether he be mad or no—and they say he mendeth daily —his praises are on all men's lips; and all bless him, likewise, and offer prayers that he may be spared to reign long in England; for he began humanely with saving the old Duke of Norfolk's life, and now is he bent on destroying the cruellest of the laws that harry and oppress the people."

This news struck his Majesty dumb with amazement, and plunged him into so deep and dismal a reverie that he heard no more of the old man's gossip. He wondered if the 'little urchin' was the beggar-boy whom he left dressed in his own garments in the palace. It did not seem possible that this could be, for surely his manners and speech would betray him if he pretended to be the Prince of Wales—then he would be driven out, and search made for the true prince. Could it be that the Court had set up some sprig of the nobility in his place? No, for his uncle would not allow that—he was all-powerful and could and would crush such a movement, of course. The boy's musings profited him nothing; the more he tried to unriddle the mystery the more perplexed he became, the more his head ached, and the worse he slept. His impatience to get to London grew hourly, and his captivity became almost unendurable.

Hendon's arts all failed with the King—he could not be comforted; but a couple of women who were chained near him succeeded better. Under their gentle ministrations he found peace and learned a degree of patience. He was very grateful, and came to love them dearly and to delight in the sweet and soothing influence of their presence. He asked them why they were in prison, and when they said they were Baptists, he smiled, and inquired—

"Is that a crime to be shut up for in a prison? Now I grieve, for I shall lose ye—they will not keep ye long for such a little thing."

They did not answer; and something in their faces made him uneasy. He said, eagerly—

"You do not speak; be good to me, and tell me—there will be no other punishment? Prithee tell me there is no fear of that."

They tried to change the topic, but his fears were aroused, and he pursued it—

"Will they scourge thee? No, no, they would not be so cruel! Say they would not. Come, they WILL not, will they?"

The women betrayed confusion and distress, but there was no avoiding an answer, so one of them said, in a voice choked with emotion—

"Oh, thou'lt break our hearts, thou gentle spirit!—God will help us to bear our—"

"It is a confession!" the King broke in. "Then they WILL scourge thee, the stony-hearted wretches! But oh, thou must not weep, I cannot bear it. Keep up thy courage—I shall come to my own in time to save thee from this bitter thing, and I will do it!"

When the King awoke in the morning, the women were gone.

"They are saved!" he said, joyfully; then added, despondently, "but woe is me!—for they were my comforters."

Each of them had left a shred of ribbon pinned to his clothing, in token of remembrance. He said he would keep these things always; and that soon he would seek out these dear good friends of his and take them under his protection.

Just then the jailer came in with some subordinates, and commanded that the prisoners be conducted to the jail-yard. The King was overjoyed—it would be a blessed thing to see the blue sky and breathe the fresh air once more. He fretted and chafed at the slowness of the officers, but his turn came at last, and he was released from his staple and ordered to follow the other prisoners with Hendon.

The court or quadrangle was stone-paved, and open to the sky. The prisoners entered it through a massive archway of masonry, and were placed in file, standing, with their backs against the wall. A rope was stretched in front of them, and they were also guarded by their officers. It was a chill and lowering morning, and a light snow which had fallen during the night whitened the great empty space and added to the general dismalness of its aspect. Now and then a wintry wind shivered through the place and sent the snow eddying hither and thither.

In the centre of the court stood two women, chained to posts. A glance showed the King that these were his good friends. He shuddered, and said to himself, "Alack, they are not gone free, as I had thought. To think that such as these should know the lash!—in England! Ay, there's the shame of it—not in Heathennesse, Christian England! They will be scourged; and I, whom they have comforted and kindly entreated, must look on and see the great wrong done; it is strange, so strange, that I, the very source of power in this broad realm, am helpless to protect them. But let these miscreants look well to themselves, for there is a day coming when I will require of them a heavy reckoning for this work. For every blow they strike now, they shall feel a hundred then."

A great gate swung open, and a crowd of citizens poured in. They flocked around the two women, and hid them from the King's view. A clergyman entered and passed through the crowd, and he also was hidden. The King now heard talking, back and forth, as if questions were being asked and answered, but he could not make out what was said. Next there was a deal of bustle and preparation, and much passing and repassing of officials through that part of the crowd that stood on the further side of the women; and whilst this proceeded a deep hush gradually fell upon the people.

Now, by command, the masses parted and fell aside, and the King saw a spectacle that froze the marrow in his bones. Faggots had been piled about the two women, and a kneeling man was lighting them!

The women bowed their heads, and covered their faces with their hands; the yellow flames began to climb upward among the snapping and crackling faggots, and wreaths of blue smoke to stream away on the wind; the clergyman lifted his hands and began a prayer—just then two young girls came flying through the great gate, uttering piercing screams, and threw themselves upon the women at the stake. Instantly they were torn away by the officers, and one of them was kept in a tight grip, but the other broke loose, saying she would die with her mother; and before she could be stopped she had flung her arms about her mother's neck again. She was torn away once more, and with her gown on fire. Two or three men held her, and the burning portion of her gown was snatched off and thrown flaming aside, she struggling all the while to free herself, and saying she would be alone in the world, now; and begging to be allowed to die with her mother. Both the girls screamed continually, and fought for freedom; but suddenly this tumult was drowned under a volley of heart-piercing shrieks of mortal agony—the King glanced from the frantic girls to the stake, then turned away and leaned his ashen face against the wall, and looked no more. He said, "That which I have seen, in that one little moment, will never go out from my memory, but will abide there; and I shall see it all the days, and dream of it all the nights, till I die. Would God I had been blind!"

Hendon was watching the King. He said to himself, with satisfaction, "His disorder mendeth; he hath changed, and groweth gentler. If he had followed his wont, he would have stormed at these varlets, and said he was King, and commanded that the women be turned loose unscathed. Soon his delusion will pass away and be forgotten, and his poor mind will be whole again. God speed the day!"

That same day several prisoners were brought in to remain over night, who were being conveyed, under guard, to various places in the kingdom, to undergo punishment for crimes committed. The King conversed with these —he had made it a point, from the beginning, to instruct himself for the kingly office by questioning prisoners whenever the opportunity offered —and the tale of their woes wrung his heart. One of them was a poor half-witted woman who had stolen a yard or two of cloth from a weaver —she was to be hanged for it. Another was a man who had been accused of stealing a horse; he said the proof had failed, and he imagined that he was safe from the halter; but no—he was hardly free before he was arraigned for killing a deer in the King's park; this was proved against him, and now he was on his way to the gallows. There was a tradesman's apprentice whose case particularly distressed the King; this youth said he found a hawk, one evening, that had escaped from its owner, and he took it home with him, imagining himself entitled to it; but the court convicted him of stealing it, and sentenced him to death.

The King was furious over these inhumanities, and wanted Hendon to break jail and fly with him to Westminster, so that he could mount his throne and hold out his sceptre in mercy over these unfortunate people and save their lives. "Poor child," sighed Hendon, "these woeful tales have brought his

malady upon him again; alack, but for this evil hap, he would have been well in a little time."

Among these prisoners was an old lawyer—a man with a strong face and a dauntless mien. Three years past, he had written a pamphlet against the Lord Chancellor, accusing him of injustice, and had been punished for it by the loss of his ears in the pillory, and degradation from the bar, and in addition had been fined 3,000 pounds and sentenced to imprisonment for life. Lately he had repeated his offence; and in consequence was now under sentence to lose WHAT REMAINED OF HIS EARS, pay a fine of 5,000 pounds, be branded on both cheeks, and remain in prison for life.

"These be honourable scars," he said, and turned back his grey hair and showed the mutilated stubs of what had once been his ears.

The King's eye burned with passion. He said—

"None believe in me—neither wilt thou. But no matter—within the compass of a month thou shalt be free; and more, the laws that have dishonoured thee, and shamed the English name, shall be swept from the statute books. The world is made wrong; kings should go to school to their own laws, at times, and so learn mercy."*

Chapter XXVIII. The sacrifice.

Meantime Miles was growing sufficiently tired of confinement and inaction. But now his trial came on, to his great gratification, and he thought he could welcome any sentence provided a further imprisonment should not be a part of it. But he was mistaken about that. He was in a fine fury when he found himself described as a 'sturdy vagabond' and sentenced to sit two hours in the stocks for bearing that character and for assaulting the master of Hendon Hall. His pretensions as to brothership with his prosecutor, and rightful heirship to the Hendon honours and estates, were left contemptuously unnoticed, as being not even worth examination.

He raged and threatened on his way to punishment, but it did no good; he was snatched roughly along by the officers, and got an occasional cuff, besides, for his irreverent conduct.

The King could not pierce through the rabble that swarmed behind; so he was obliged to follow in the rear, remote from his good friend and servant. The King had been nearly condemned to the stocks himself for being in such bad company, but had been let off with a lecture and a warning, in consideration of his youth. When the crowd at last halted, he flitted feverishly from point to point around its outer rim,

---

* From many descriptions of larceny the law expressly took away the benefit of clergy: to steal a horse, or a HAWK, or woollen cloth from the weaver, was a hanging matter. So it was to kill a deer from the King's forest, or to export sheep from the kingdom.—Dr. J. Hammond Trumbull's Blue Laws, True and False, p.13.

William Prynne, a learned barrister, was sentenced (long after Edward VI.'s time) to lose both his ears in the pillory, to degradation from the bar, a fine of 3,000 pounds, and imprisonment for life. Three years afterwards he gave new offence to Laud by publishing a pamphlet against the hierarchy. He was again prosecuted, and was sentenced to lose WHAT REMAINED OF HIS EARS, to pay a fine of 5,000 pounds, to be BRANDED ON BOTH HIS CHEEKS with the letters S. L. (for Seditious Libeller), and to remain in prison for life. The severity of this sentence was equalled by the savage rigour of its execution.—Ibid. p. 12.

hunting a place to get through; and at last, after a deal of difficulty and delay, succeeded. There sat his poor henchman in the degrading stocks, the sport and butt of a dirty mob—he, the body servant of the King of England! Edward had heard the sentence pronounced, but he had not realised the half that it meant. His anger began to rise as the sense of this new indignity which had been put upon him sank home; it jumped to summer heat, the next moment, when he saw an egg sail through the air and crush itself against Hendon's cheek, and heard the crowd roar its enjoyment of the episode. He sprang across the open circle and confronted the officer in charge, crying—

"For shame! This is my servant—set him free! I am the—"

"Oh, peace!" exclaimed Hendon, in a panic, "thou'lt destroy thyself. Mind him not, officer, he is mad."

"Give thyself no trouble as to the matter of minding him, good man, I have small mind to mind him; but as to teaching him somewhat, to that I am well inclined." He turned to a subordinate and said, "Give the little fool a taste or two of the lash, to mend his manners."

"Half a dozen will better serve his turn," suggested Sir Hugh, who had ridden up, a moment before, to take a passing glance at the proceedings.

The King was seized. He did not even struggle, so paralysed was he with the mere thought of the monstrous outrage that was proposed to be inflicted upon his sacred person. History was already defiled with the record of the scourging of an English king with whips—it was an intolerable reflection that he must furnish a duplicate of that shameful page. He was in the toils, there was no help for him; he must either take this punishment or beg for its remission. Hard conditions; he would take the stripes—a king might do that, but a king could not beg.

But meantime, Miles Hendon was resolving the difficulty. "Let the child go," said he; "ye heartless dogs, do ye not see how young and frail he is? Let him go—I will take his lashes."

"Marry, a good thought—and thanks for it," said Sir Hugh, his face lighting with a sardonic satisfaction. "Let the little beggar go, and give this fellow a dozen in his place—an honest dozen, well laid on." The King was in the act of entering a fierce protest, but Sir Hugh silenced him with the potent remark, "Yes, speak up, do, and free thy mind—only, mark ye, that for each word you utter he shall get six strokes the more."

Hendon was removed from the stocks, and his back laid bare; and whilst the lash was applied the poor little King turned away his face and allowed unroyal tears to channel his cheeks unchecked. "Ah, brave good heart," he said to himself, "this loyal deed shall never perish out of my memory. I will not forget it—and neither shall THEY!" he added, with passion. Whilst he mused, his appreciation of Hendon's magnanimous conduct grew to greater and still greater dimensions in his mind, and so also did his gratefulness for it. Presently he said to himself, "Who saves his prince from wounds and possible death—and this he did for me —performs high service; but it is little—it is nothing—oh, less than nothing!—when 'tis weighed against the act of him who saves his prince from SHAME!"

Hendon made no outcry under the scourge, but bore the heavy blows with soldierly fortitude. This, together with his redeeming the boy by taking his stripes for him, compelled the respect of even that forlorn and degraded mob that was gathered there; and its gibes and hootings died away, and no sound remained but the sound of the falling blows. The stillness that pervaded the place, when Hendon found himself once more in the stocks, was in strong contrast with the insulting clamour which had prevailed there so little a while before. The King came softly to Hendon's side, and whispered in his ear—

"Kings cannot ennoble thee, thou good, great soul, for One who is higher than kings hath done that for thee; but a king can confirm thy nobility to men." He picked up the scourge from the ground, touched Hendon's bleeding shoulders lightly with it, and whispered, "Edward of England dubs thee Earl!"

Hendon was touched. The water welled to his eyes, yet at the same time the grisly humour of the situation and circumstances so undermined his gravity that it was all he could do to keep some sign of his inward mirth from showing outside. To be suddenly hoisted, naked and gory, from the common stocks to the Alpine altitude and splendour of an Earldom, seemed to him the last possibility in the line of the grotesque. He said to himself, "Now am I finely tinselled, indeed! The spectre-knight of the Kingdom of Dreams and Shadows is become a spectre-earl—a dizzy flight for a callow wing! An' this go on, I shall presently be hung like a very maypole with fantastic gauds and make-believe honours. But I shall value them, all valueless as they are, for the love that doth bestow them. Better these poor mock dignities of mine, that come unasked, from a clean hand and a right spirit, than real ones bought by servility from grudging and interested power."

The dreaded Sir Hugh wheeled his horse about, and as he spurred away, the living wall divided silently to let him pass, and as silently closed together again. And so remained; nobody went so far as to venture a remark in favour of the prisoner, or in compliment to him; but no matter —the absence of abuse was a sufficient homage in itself. A late comer who was not posted as to the present circumstances, and who delivered a sneer at the 'impostor,' and was in the act of following it with a dead cat, was promptly knocked down and kicked out, without any words, and then the deep quiet resumed sway once more.

Chapter XXIX. To London.

When Hendon's term of service in the stocks was finished, he was released and ordered to quit the region and come back no more. His sword was restored to him, and also his mule and his donkey. He mounted and rode off, followed by the King, the crowd opening with quiet respectfulness to let them pass, and then dispersing when they were gone.

Hendon was soon absorbed in thought. There were questions of high import to be answered. What should he do? Whither should he go? Powerful help must be found somewhere, or he must relinquish his inheritance and remain under the imputation of being an impostor besides. Where could he hope to find this powerful help? Where, indeed! It was a knotty question. By-and-by a thought occurred to him which pointed to a possibility—the slenderest of slender possibilities, certainly, but still worth considering, for lack of any other that promised anything at all. He remembered what old Andrews had said about the young King's goodness and his generous championship of the wronged and unfortunate. Why not go and try to get speech of him and beg for justice? Ah, yes, but could so fantastic a pauper get admission to the august presence of a monarch? Never mind—let that matter take care of itself; it was a bridge that would not need to be crossed till he should come to it. He was an old campaigner, and used to inventing shifts and expedients: no doubt he would be able to find a way. Yes, he would strike for the capital. Maybe his father's old friend Sir Humphrey Marlow would help him— 'good old Sir Humphrey, Head Lieutenant of the late King's kitchen, or stables, or something'—Miles could not remember just what or which. Now that he had something to turn his energies to, a distinctly defined object to accomplish, the fog of humiliation and depression which had settled down upon his spirits lifted and blew away, and he raised his head and looked about him. He was surprised to see how far he had come; the village was away behind him. The King was jogging along in his wake, with his head bowed; for he, too, was deep in plans and thinkings. A sorrowful misgiving clouded Hendon's new-born cheerfulness: would the boy be willing to go again to a city where, during all his brief life, he had never known anything but ill-usage and pinching want? But the question must be asked; it could not be avoided; so Hendon reined up, and called out—

"I had forgotten to inquire whither we are bound. Thy commands, my liege!"

"To London!"

Hendon moved on again, mightily contented with the answer—but astounded at it too.

The whole journey was made without an adventure of importance. But it ended with one. About ten o'clock on the night of the 19th of February they stepped upon London Bridge, in the midst of a writhing, struggling jam of howling and hurrahing people, whose beer-jolly faces stood out strongly in the glare from manifold torches—and at that instant the decaying head of some former duke or other grandee tumbled down between them, striking Hendon on the elbow and then bounding off among the hurrying confusion of feet. So evanescent and unstable are men's works in this world!—the late good King is but three weeks dead and three days in his grave, and already the adornments which he took such pains to select from prominent people for his noble bridge are falling. A citizen stumbled over that head, and drove his own head into the back of somebody in front of him, who turned and knocked down the first person that came handy, and was promptly laid out himself by that person's friend. It was the right ripe time for a free fight, for the festivities of the morrow —Coronation Day—were already beginning; everybody was full of strong drink and patriotism; within five minutes the free fight was occupying a good deal of ground; within ten or twelve it covered an acre of so, and was become a riot. By this time Hendon and the King were hopelessly separated from each other and lost in the rush and turmoil of the roaring masses of humanity. And so we leave them.

Chapter XXX. Tom's progress.

Whilst the true King wandered about the land poorly clad, poorly fed, cuffed and derided by tramps one while, herding with thieves and murderers in a jail another, and called idiot and impostor by all impartially, the mock King Tom Canty enjoyed quite a different experience.

When we saw him last, royalty was just beginning to have a bright side for him. This bright side went on brightening more and more every day: in a very little while it was become almost

all sunshine and delightfulness. He lost his fears; his misgivings faded out and died; his embarrassments departed, and gave place to an easy and confident bearing. He worked the whipping-boy mine to ever-increasing profit.

He ordered my Lady Elizabeth and my Lady Jane Grey into his presence when he wanted to play or talk, and dismissed them when he was done with them, with the air of one familiarly accustomed to such performances. It no longer confused him to have these lofty personages kiss his hand at parting.

He came to enjoy being conducted to bed in state at night, and dressed with intricate and solemn ceremony in the morning. It came to be a proud pleasure to march to dinner attended by a glittering procession of officers of state and gentlemen-at-arms; insomuch, indeed, that he doubled his guard of gentlemen-at-arms, and made them a hundred. He liked to hear the bugles sounding down the long corridors, and the distant voices responding, "Way for the King!"

He even learned to enjoy sitting in throned state in council, and seeming to be something more than the Lord Protector's mouthpiece. He liked to receive great ambassadors and their gorgeous trains, and listen to the affectionate messages they brought from illustrious monarchs who called him brother. O happy Tom Canty, late of Offal Court!

He enjoyed his splendid clothes, and ordered more: he found his four hundred servants too few for his proper grandeur, and trebled them. The adulation of salaaming courtiers came to be sweet music to his ears. He remained kind and gentle, and a sturdy and determined champion of all that were oppressed, and he made tireless war upon unjust laws: yet upon occasion, being offended, he could turn upon an earl, or even a duke, and give him a look that would make him tremble. Once, when his royal 'sister,' the grimly holy Lady Mary, set herself to reason with him against the wisdom of his course in pardoning so many people who would otherwise be jailed, or hanged, or burned, and reminded him that their august late father's prisons had sometimes contained as high as sixty thousand convicts at one time, and that during his admirable reign he had delivered seventy-two thousand thieves and robbers over to death by the executioner*, the boy was filled with generous indignation, and commanded her to go to her closet, and beseech God to take away the stone that was in her breast, and give her a human heart.

Did Tom Canty never feel troubled about the poor little rightful prince who had treated him so kindly, and flown out with such hot zeal to avenge him upon the insolent sentinel at the palace-gate? Yes; his first royal days and nights were pretty well sprinkled with painful thoughts about the lost prince, and with sincere longings for his return, and happy restoration to his native rights and splendours. But as time wore on, and the prince did not come, Tom's mind became more and more occupied with his new and enchanting experiences, and by little and little the vanished monarch faded almost out of his thoughts; and finally, when he did intrude upon them at intervals, he was become an unwelcome spectre, for he made Tom feel guilty and ashamed.

Tom's poor mother and sisters travelled the same road out of his mind. At first he pined for them, sorrowed for them, longed to see them, but later, the thought of their coming some day in their rags and dirt, and betraying him with their kisses, and pulling him down from his lofty place, and

---

* Hume's England.

dragging him back to penury and degradation and the slums, made him shudder. At last they ceased to trouble his thoughts almost wholly. And he was content, even glad: for, whenever their mournful and accusing faces did rise before him now, they made him feel more despicable than the worms that crawl.

At midnight of the 19th of February, Tom Canty was sinking to sleep in his rich bed in the palace, guarded by his loyal vassals, and surrounded by the pomps of royalty, a happy boy; for tomorrow was the day appointed for his solemn crowning as King of England. At that same hour, Edward, the true king, hungry and thirsty, soiled and draggled, worn with travel, and clothed in rags and shreds—his share of the results of the riot—was wedged in among a crowd of people who were watching with deep interest certain hurrying gangs of workmen who streamed in and out of Westminster Abbey, busy as ants: they were making the last preparation for the royal coronation.

Chapter XXXI. The Recognition procession.

When Tom Canty awoke the next morning, the air was heavy with a thunderous murmur: all the distances were charged with it. It was music to him; for it meant that the English world was out in its strength to give loyal welcome to the great day.

Presently Tom found himself once more the chief figure in a wonderful floating pageant on the Thames; for by ancient custom the 'recognition procession' through London must start from the Tower, and he was bound thither.

When he arrived there, the sides of the venerable fortress seemed suddenly rent in a thousand places, and from every rent leaped a red tongue of flame and a white gush of smoke; a deafening explosion followed, which drowned the shoutings of the multitude, and made the ground tremble; the flame-jets, the smoke, and the explosions, were repeated over and over again with marvellous celerity, so that in a few moments the old Tower disappeared in the vast fog of its own smoke, all but the very top of the tall pile called the White Tower; this, with its banners, stood out above the dense bank of vapour as a mountain-peak projects above a cloud-rack.

Tom Canty, splendidly arrayed, mounted a prancing war-steed, whose rich trappings almost reached to the ground; his 'uncle,' the Lord Protector Somerset, similarly mounted, took place in his rear; the King's Guard formed in single ranks on either side, clad in burnished armour; after the Protector followed a seemingly interminable procession of resplendent nobles attended by their vassals; after these came the lord mayor and the aldermanic body, in crimson velvet robes, and with their gold chains across their breasts; and after these the officers and members of all the guilds of London, in rich raiment, and bearing the showy banners of the several corporations. Also in the procession, as a special guard of honour through the city, was the Ancient and Honourable Artillery Company—an organisation already three hundred years old at that time, and the only military body in England possessing the privilege (which it still possesses in our day) of holding itself independent of the commands of Parliament. It was a brilliant spectacle, and was hailed with acclamations all along the line, as it took its stately way through the packed multitudes of citizens. The chronicler says, 'The King, as he entered the city, was received by the people with prayers, welcomings, cries, and tender words, and all signs which argue an earnest love of subjects toward their sovereign; and the

King, by holding up his glad countenance to such as stood afar off, and most tender language to those that stood nigh his Grace, showed himself no less thankful to receive the people's goodwill than they to offer it. To all that wished him well, he gave thanks. To such as bade "God save his Grace," he said in return, "God save you all!" and added that "he thanked them with all his heart." Wonderfully transported were the people with the loving answers and gestures of their King.'

In Fenchurch Street a 'fair child, in costly apparel,' stood on a stage to welcome his Majesty to the city. The last verse of his greeting was in these words—

'Welcome, O King! as much as hearts can think; Welcome, again, as much as tongue can tell,—Welcome to joyous tongues, and hearts that will not shrink: God thee preserve, we pray, and wish thee ever well.'

The people burst forth in a glad shout, repeating with one voice what the child had said. Tom Canty gazed abroad over the surging sea of eager faces, and his heart swelled with exultation; and he felt that the one thing worth living for in this world was to be a king, and a nation's idol. Presently he caught sight, at a distance, of a couple of his ragged Offal Court comrades—one of them the lord high admiral in his late mimic court, the other the first lord of the bedchamber in the same pretentious fiction; and his pride swelled higher than ever. Oh, if they could only recognise him now! What unspeakable glory it would be, if they could recognise him, and realise that the derided mock king of the slums and back alleys was become a real King, with illustrious dukes and princes for his humble menials, and the English world at his feet! But he had to deny himself, and choke down his desire, for such a recognition might cost more than it would come to: so he turned away his head, and left the two soiled lads to go on with their shoutings and glad adulations, unsuspicious of whom it was they were lavishing them upon.

Every now and then rose the cry, "A largess! a largess!" and Tom responded by scattering a handful of bright new coins abroad for the multitude to scramble for.

The chronicler says, 'At the upper end of Gracechurch Street, before the sign of the Eagle, the city had erected a gorgeous arch, beneath which was a stage, which stretched from one side of the street to the other. This was an historical pageant, representing the King's immediate progenitors. There sat Elizabeth of York in the midst of an immense white rose, whose petals formed elaborate furbelows around her; by her side was Henry VII., issuing out of a vast red rose, disposed in the same manner: the hands of the royal pair were locked together, and the wedding-ring ostentatiously displayed. From the red and white roses proceeded a stem, which reached up to a second stage, occupied by Henry VIII., issuing from a red and white rose, with the effigy of the new King's mother, Jane Seymour, represented by his side. One branch sprang from this pair, which mounted to a third stage, where sat the effigy of Edward VI. himself, enthroned in royal majesty; and the whole pageant was framed with wreaths of roses, red and white.'

This quaint and gaudy spectacle so wrought upon the rejoicing people, that their acclamations utterly smothered the small voice of the child whose business it was to explain the thing in eulogistic rhymes. But Tom Canty was not sorry; for this loyal uproar was sweeter music to him than any poetry, no matter what its quality might be. Whithersoever Tom turned his happy young face, the people recognised the exactness of his effigy's likeness to himself, the flesh and blood counterpart; and new whirlwinds of applause burst forth.

The great pageant moved on, and still on, under one triumphal arch after another, and past a bewildering succession of spectacular and symbolical tableaux, each of which typified and exalted some virtue, or talent, or merit, of the little King's. Throughout the whole of Cheapside, from every penthouse and window, hung banners and streamers; and the richest carpets, stuffs, and cloth-of-gold tapestried the streets—specimens of the great wealth of the stores within; and the splendour of this thoroughfare was equalled in the other streets, and in some even surpassed.'

"And all these wonders and these marvels are to welcome me—me!" murmured Tom Canty.

The mock King's cheeks were flushed with excitement, his eyes were flashing, his senses swam in a delirium of pleasure. At this point, just as he was raising his hand to fling another rich largess, he caught sight of a pale, astounded face, which was strained forward out of the second rank of the crowd, its intense eyes riveted upon him. A sickening consternation struck through him; he recognised his mother! and up flew his hand, palm outward, before his eyes—that old involuntary gesture, born of a forgotten episode, and perpetuated by habit. In an instant more she had torn her way out of the press, and past the guards, and was at his side. She embraced his leg, she covered it with kisses, she cried, "O my child, my darling!" lifting toward him a face that was transfigured with joy and love. The same instant an officer of the King's Guard snatched her away with a curse, and sent her reeling back whence she came with a vigorous impulse from his strong arm. The words "I do not know you, woman!" were falling from Tom Canty's lips when this piteous thing occurred; but it smote him to the heart to see her treated so; and as she turned for a last glimpse of him, whilst the crowd was swallowing her from his sight, she seemed so wounded, so broken-hearted, that a shame fell upon him which consumed his pride to ashes, and withered his stolen royalty. His grandeurs were stricken valueless: they seemed to fall away from him like rotten rags.

The procession moved on, and still on, through ever augmenting splendours and ever augmenting tempests of welcome; but to Tom Canty they were as if they had not been. He neither saw nor heard. Royalty had lost its grace and sweetness; its pomps were become a reproach. Remorse was eating his heart out. He said, "Would God I were free of my captivity!"

He had unconsciously dropped back into the phraseology of the first days of his compulsory greatness.

The shining pageant still went winding like a radiant and interminable serpent down the crooked lanes of the quaint old city, and through the huzzaing hosts; but still the King rode with bowed head and vacant eyes, seeing only his mother's face and that wounded look in it.

"Largess, largess!" The cry fell upon an unheeding ear.

"Long live Edward of England!" It seemed as if the earth shook with the explosion; but there was no response from the King. He heard it only as one hears the thunder of the surf when it is blown to the ear out of a great distance, for it was smothered under another sound which was still nearer, in his own breast, in his accusing conscience—a voice which kept repeating those shameful words, "I do not know you, woman!"

The words smote upon the King's soul as the strokes of a funeral bell smite upon the soul of a surviving friend when they remind him of secret treacheries suffered at his hands by him that is gone.

New glories were unfolded at every turning; new wonders, new marvels, sprang into view; the pent clamours of waiting batteries were released; new raptures poured from the throats of the waiting multitudes: but the King gave no sign, and the accusing voice that went moaning through his comfortless breast was all the sound he heard.

By-and-by the gladness in the faces of the populace changed a little, and became touched with a something like solicitude or anxiety: an abatement in the volume of the applause was observable too. The Lord Protector was quick to notice these things: he was as quick to detect the cause. He spurred to the King's side, bent low in his saddle, uncovered, and said—

"My liege, it is an ill time for dreaming. The people observe thy downcast head, thy clouded mien, and they take it for an omen. Be advised: unveil the sun of royalty, and let it shine upon these boding vapours, and disperse them. Lift up thy face, and smile upon the people."

So saying, the Duke scattered a handful of coins to right and left, then retired to his place. The mock King did mechanically as he had been bidden. His smile had no heart in it, but few eyes were near enough or sharp enough to detect that. The noddings of his plumed head as he saluted his subjects were full of grace and graciousness; the largess which he delivered from his hand was royally liberal: so the people's anxiety vanished, and the acclamations burst forth again in as mighty a volume as before.

Still once more, a little before the progress was ended, the Duke was obliged to ride forward, and make remonstrance. He whispered—

"O dread sovereign! shake off these fatal humours; the eyes of the world are upon thee." Then he added with sharp annoyance, "Perdition catch that crazy pauper! 'twas she that hath disturbed your Highness."

The gorgeous figure turned a lustreless eye upon the Duke, and said in a dead voice—

"She was my mother!"

"My God!" groaned the Protector as he reined his horse backward to his post, "the omen was pregnant with prophecy. He is gone mad again!"

Chapter XXXII. Coronation Day.

Let us go backward a few hours, and place ourselves in Westminster Abbey, at four o'clock in the morning of this memorable Coronation Day. We are not without company; for although it is still night, we find the torch-lighted galleries already filling up with people who are well content to sit still and wait seven or eight hours till the time shall come for them to see what they may not hope to see twice in their lives —the coronation of a King. Yes, London and Westminster have been astir ever since the warning guns boomed at three o'clock, and already crowds of untitled rich folk who have bought the privilege of trying to find sitting-room in the galleries are flocking in at the entrances reserved for their sort.

The hours drag along tediously enough. All stir has ceased for some time, for every gallery has long ago been packed. We may sit, now, and look and think at our leisure. We have glimpses, here and there and yonder, through the dim cathedral twilight, of portions of many galleries and balconies, wedged full with other people, the other portions of these galleries and balconies being cut off from sight by intervening pillars and architectural projections. We have in view the whole of the great north transept—empty, and waiting for England's privileged ones. We see also the ample area or platform, carpeted with rich stuffs, whereon the throne stands. The throne occupies the centre of the platform, and is raised above it upon an elevation of four steps. Within the seat of the throne is enclosed a rough flat rock—the stone of Scone—which many generations of Scottish kings sat on to be crowned, and so it in time became holy enough to answer a like purpose for English monarchs. Both the throne and its footstool are covered with cloth of gold.

Stillness reigns, the torches blink dully, the time drags heavily. But at last the lagging daylight asserts itself, the torches are extinguished, and a mellow radiance suffuses the great spaces. All features of the noble building are distinct now, but soft and dreamy, for the sun is lightly veiled with clouds.

At seven o'clock the first break in the drowsy monotony occurs; for on the stroke of this hour the first peeress enters the transept, clothed like Solomon for splendour, and is conducted to her appointed place by an official clad in satins and velvets, whilst a duplicate of him gathers up the lady's long train, follows after, and, when the lady is seated, arranges the train across her lap for her. He then places her footstool according to her desire, after which he puts her coronet where it will be convenient to her hand when the time for the simultaneous coroneting of the nobles shall arrive.

By this time the peeresses are flowing in in a glittering stream, and the satin-clad officials are flitting and glinting everywhere, seating them and making them comfortable. The scene is animated enough now. There is stir and life, and shifting colour everywhere. After a time, quiet reigns again; for the peeresses are all come and are all in their places, a solid acre or such a matter, of human flowers, resplendent in variegated colours, and frosted like a Milky Way with diamonds. There are all ages here: brown, wrinkled, white-haired dowagers who are able to go back, and still back, down the stream of time, and recall the crowning of Richard III. and the troublous days of that old forgotten age; and there are handsome middle-aged dames; and lovely and gracious young matrons; and gentle and beautiful young girls, with beaming eyes and fresh complexions, who may possibly put on their jewelled coronets awkwardly when the great time comes; for the matter will be new to them, and their excitement will be a sore hindrance. Still, this may not happen, for the hair of all these ladies has been arranged with a special view to the swift and successful lodging of the crown in its place when the signal comes.

We have seen that this massed array of peeresses is sown thick with diamonds, and we also see that it is a marvellous spectacle—but now we are about to be astonished in earnest. About nine, the clouds suddenly break away and a shaft of sunshine cleaves the mellow atmosphere, and drifts slowly along the ranks of ladies; and every rank it touches flames into a dazzling splendour of many-coloured fires, and we tingle to our finger-tips with the electric thrill that is shot through us by the surprise and the beauty of the spectacle! Presently a special envoy from some distant corner of the Orient,

marching with the general body of foreign ambassadors, crosses this bar of sunshine, and we catch our breath, the glory that streams and flashes and palpitates about him is so overpowering; for he is crusted from head to heel with gems, and his slightest movement showers a dancing radiance all around him.

Let us change the tense for convenience. The time drifted along—one hour—two hours—two hours and a half; then the deep booming of artillery told that the King and his grand procession had arrived at last; so the waiting multitude rejoiced. All knew that a further delay must follow, for the King must be prepared and robed for the solemn ceremony; but this delay would be pleasantly occupied by the assembling of the peers of the realm in their stately robes. These were conducted ceremoniously to their seats, and their coronets placed conveniently at hand; and meanwhile the multitude in the galleries were alive with interest, for most of them were beholding for the first time, dukes, earls, and barons, whose names had been historical for five hundred years. When all were finally seated, the spectacle from the galleries and all coigns of vantage was complete; a gorgeous one to look upon and to remember.

Now the robed and mitred great heads of the church, and their attendants, filed in upon the platform and took their appointed places; these were followed by the Lord Protector and other great officials, and these again by a steel-clad detachment of the Guard.

There was a waiting pause; then, at a signal, a triumphant peal of music burst forth, and Tom Canty, clothed in a long robe of cloth of gold, appeared at a door, and stepped upon the platform. The entire multitude rose, and the ceremony of the Recognition ensued.

Then a noble anthem swept the Abbey with its rich waves of sound; and thus heralded and welcomed, Tom Canty was conducted to the throne. The ancient ceremonies went on, with impressive solemnity, whilst the audience gazed; and as they drew nearer and nearer to completion, Tom Canty grew pale, and still paler, and a deep and steadily deepening woe and despondency settled down upon his spirits and upon his remorseful heart.

At last the final act was at hand. The Archbishop of Canterbury lifted up the crown of England from its cushion and held it out over the trembling mock-King's head. In the same instant a rainbow-radiance flashed along the spacious transept; for with one impulse every individual in the great concourse of nobles lifted a coronet and poised it over his or her head—and paused in that attitude.

A deep hush pervaded the Abbey. At this impressive moment, a startling apparition intruded upon the scene—an apparition observed by none in the absorbed multitude, until it suddenly appeared, moving up the great central aisle. It was a boy, bareheaded, ill shod, and clothed in coarse plebeian garments that were falling to rags. He raised his hand with a solemnity which ill comported with his soiled and sorry aspect, and delivered this note of warning—

"I forbid you to set the crown of England upon that forfeited head. I am the King!"

In an instant several indignant hands were laid upon the boy; but in the same instant Tom Canty, in his regal vestments, made a swift step forward, and cried out in a ringing voice—

"Loose him and forbear! He IS the King!"

A sort of panic of astonishment swept the assemblage, and they partly rose in their places and stared in a bewildered way at one another and at the chief figures in this scene, like persons who wondered whether they were awake and in their senses, or asleep and dreaming. The Lord Protector was as amazed as the rest, but quickly recovered himself, and exclaimed in a voice of authority—

"Mind not his Majesty, his malady is upon him again—seize the vagabond!"

He would have been obeyed, but the mock-King stamped his foot and cried out—

"On your peril! Touch him not, he is the King!"

The hands were withheld; a paralysis fell upon the house; no one moved, no one spoke; indeed, no one knew how to act or what to say, in so strange and surprising an emergency. While all minds were struggling to right themselves, the boy still moved steadily forward, with high port and confident mien; he had never halted from the beginning; and while the tangled minds still floundered helplessly, he stepped upon the platform, and the mock-King ran with a glad face to meet him; and fell on his knees before him and said—

"Oh, my lord the King, let poor Tom Canty be first to swear fealty to thee, and say, 'Put on thy crown and enter into thine own again!'"

The Lord Protector's eye fell sternly upon the new-comer's face; but straightway the sternness vanished away, and gave place to an expression of wondering surprise. This thing happened also to the other great officers. They glanced at each other, and retreated a step by a common and unconscious impulse. The thought in each mind was the same: "What a strange resemblance!"

The Lord Protector reflected a moment or two in perplexity, then he said, with grave respectfulness—

"By your favour, sir, I desire to ask certain questions which—"

"I will answer them, my lord."

The Duke asked him many questions about the Court, the late King, the prince, the princesses—the boy answered them correctly and without hesitating. He described the rooms of state in the palace, the late King's apartments, and those of the Prince of Wales.

It was strange; it was wonderful; yes, it was unaccountable—so all said that heard it. The tide was beginning to turn, and Tom Canty's hopes to run high, when the Lord Protector shook his head and said—

"It is true it is most wonderful—but it is no more than our lord the King likewise can do." This remark, and this reference to himself as still the King, saddened Tom Canty, and he felt his hopes crumbling from under him. "These are not PROOFS," added the Protector.

The tide was turning very fast now, very fast indeed—but in the wrong direction; it was leaving poor Tom Canty stranded on the throne, and sweeping the other out to sea. The Lord

Protector communed with himself —shook his head—the thought forced itself upon him, "It is perilous to the State and to us all, to entertain so fateful a riddle as this; it could divide the nation and undermine the throne." He turned and said—

"Sir Thomas, arrest this—No, hold!" His face lighted, and he confronted the ragged candidate with this question—

"Where lieth the Great Seal? Answer me this truly, and the riddle is unriddled; for only he that was Prince of Wales CAN so answer! On so trivial a thing hang a throne and a dynasty!"

It was a lucky thought, a happy thought. That it was so considered by the great officials was manifested by the silent applause that shot from eye to eye around their circle in the form of bright approving glances. Yes, none but the true prince could dissolve the stubborn mystery of the vanished Great Seal—this forlorn little impostor had been taught his lesson well, but here his teachings must fail, for his teacher himself could not answer THAT question—ah, very good, very good indeed; now we shall be rid of this troublesome and perilous business in short order! And so they nodded invisibly and smiled inwardly with satisfaction, and looked to see this foolish lad stricken with a palsy of guilty confusion. How surprised they were, then, to see nothing of the sort happen— how they marvelled to hear him answer up promptly, in a confident and untroubled voice, and say—

"There is nought in this riddle that is difficult." Then, without so much as a by-your-leave to anybody, he turned and gave this command, with the easy manner of one accustomed to doing such things: "My Lord St. John, go you to my private cabinet in the palace—for none knoweth the place better than you—and, close down to the floor, in the left corner remotest from the door that opens from the ante-chamber, you shall find in the wall a brazen nail-head; press upon it and a little jewel-closet will fly open which not even you do know of—no, nor any soul else in all the world but me and the trusty artisan that did contrive it for me. The first thing that falleth under your eye will be the Great Seal—fetch it hither."

All the company wondered at this speech, and wondered still more to see the little mendicant pick out this peer without hesitancy or apparent fear of mistake, and call him by name with such a placidly convincing air of having known him all his life. The peer was almost surprised into obeying. He even made a movement as if to go, but quickly recovered his tranquil attitude and confessed his blunder with a blush. Tom Canty turned upon him and said, sharply—

"Why dost thou hesitate? Hast not heard the King's command? Go!"

The Lord St. John made a deep obeisance—and it was observed that it was a significantly cautious and non-committal one, it not being delivered at either of the kings, but at the neutral ground about half-way between the two—and took his leave.

Now began a movement of the gorgeous particles of that official group which was slow, scarcely perceptible, and yet steady and persistent—a movement such as is observed in a kaleidoscope that is turned slowly, whereby the components of one splendid cluster fall away and join themselves to another—a movement which, little by little, in the present case, dissolved the glittering crowd that stood about Tom Canty and clustered it together again in the neighbourhood of the new-comer. Tom Canty stood almost alone. Now ensued a brief season of deep suspense and waiting—during which even the few faint hearts still remaining near Tom Canty gradually scraped together courage enough to glide, one by one, over to the majority. So at last Tom Canty, in his royal robes and jewels, stood wholly alone and isolated from the world, a conspicuous figure, occupying an eloquent vacancy.

Now the Lord St. John was seen returning. As he advanced up the mid-aisle the interest was so intense that the low murmur of conversation in the great assemblage died out and was succeeded by a profound hush, a breathless stillness, through which his footfalls pulsed with a dull and distant sound. Every eye was fastened upon him as he moved along. He reached the platform, paused a moment, then moved toward Tom Canty with a deep obeisance, and said—

"Sire, the Seal is not there!"

A mob does not melt away from the presence of a plague-patient with more haste than the band of pallid and terrified courtiers melted away from the presence of the shabby little claimant of the Crown. In a moment he stood all alone, without friend or supporter, a target upon which was concentrated a bitter fire of scornful and angry looks. The Lord Protector called out fiercely—

"Cast the beggar into the street, and scourge him through the town—the paltry knave is worth no more consideration!"

Officers of the guard sprang forward to obey, but Tom Canty waved them off and said—

"Back! Whoso touches him perils his life!"

The Lord Protector was perplexed in the last degree. He said to the Lord St. John—

"Searched you well?—but it boots not to ask that. It doth seem passing strange. Little things, trifles, slip out of one's ken, and one does not think it matter for surprise; but how so bulky a thing as the Seal of England can vanish away and no man be able to get track of it again—a massy golden disk—"

Tom Canty, with beaming eyes, sprang forward and shouted—

"Hold, that is enough! Was it round?—and thick?—and had it letters and devices graved upon it?—yes? Oh, NOW I know what this Great Seal is that there's been such worry and pother about. An' ye had described it to me, ye could have had it three weeks ago. Right well I know where it lies; but it was not I that put it there—first."

"Who, then, my liege?" asked the Lord Protector.

"He that stands there—the rightful King of England. And he shall tell you himself where it lies—then you will believe he knew it of his own knowledge. Bethink thee, my King—spur thy memory—it was the last, the very LAST thing thou didst that day before thou didst rush forth from the palace, clothed in my rags, to punish the soldier that insulted me."

A silence ensued, undisturbed by a movement or a whisper, and all eyes were fixed upon the new-comer, who stood, with bent head and corrugated brow, groping in his memory among a thronging multitude of valueless recollections for one single little elusive fact, which, found, would seat him upon a throne—unfound, would leave him as he was, for good and all—a pauper and an outcast. Moment after moment passed—

the moments built themselves into minutes—still the boy struggled silently on, and gave no sign. But at last he heaved a sigh, shook his head slowly, and said, with a trembling lip and in a despondent voice—

"I call the scene back—all of it—but the Seal hath no place in it." He paused, then looked up, and said with gentle dignity, "My lords and gentlemen, if ye will rob your rightful sovereign of his own for lack of this evidence which he is not able to furnish, I may not stay ye, being powerless. But—"

"Oh, folly, oh, madness, my King!" cried Tom Canty, in a panic, "wait! —think! Do not give up!—the cause is not lost! Nor SHALL be, neither! List to what I say—follow every word—I am going to bring that morning back again, every hap just as it happened. We talked—I told you of my sisters, Nan and Bet—ah, yes, you remember that; and about mine old grandam—and the rough games of the lads of Offal Court—yes, you remember these things also; very well, follow me still, you shall recall everything. You gave me food and drink, and did with princely courtesy send away the servants, so that my low breeding might not shame me before them—ah, yes, this also you remember."

As Tom checked off his details, and the other boy nodded his head in recognition of them, the great audience and the officials stared in puzzled wonderment; the tale sounded like true history, yet how could this impossible conjunction between a prince and a beggar-boy have come about? Never was a company of people so perplexed, so interested, and so stupefied, before.

"For a jest, my prince, we did exchange garments. Then we stood before a mirror; and so alike were we that both said it seemed as if there had been no change made—yes, you remember that. Then you noticed that the soldier had hurt my hand—look! here it is, I cannot yet even write with it, the fingers are so stiff. At this your Highness sprang up, vowing vengeance upon that soldier, and ran towards the door—you passed a table—that thing you call the Seal lay on that table—you snatched it up and looked eagerly about, as if for a place to hide it—your eye caught sight of—"

"There, 'tis sufficient!—and the good God be thanked!" exclaimed the ragged claimant, in a mighty excitement. "Go, my good St. John—in an arm-piece of the Milanese armour that hangs on the wall, thou'lt find the Seal!"

"Right, my King! right!" cried Tom Canty; "NOW the sceptre of England is thine own; and it were better for him that would dispute it that he had been born dumb! Go, my Lord St. John, give thy feet wings!"

The whole assemblage was on its feet now, and well-nigh out of its mind with uneasiness, apprehension, and consuming excitement. On the floor and on the platform a deafening buzz of frantic conversation burst forth, and for some time nobody knew anything or heard anything or was interested in anything but what his neighbour was shouting into his ear, or he was shouting into his neighbour's ear. Time—nobody knew how much of it—swept by unheeded and unnoted. At last a sudden hush fell upon the house, and in the same moment St. John appeared upon the platform, and held the Great Seal aloft in his hand. Then such a shout went up—

"Long live the true King!"

For five minutes the air quaked with shouts and the crash of musical instruments, and was white with a storm of waving handkerchiefs; and through it all a ragged lad, the most conspicuous figure in England, stood, flushed and happy and proud, in the centre of the spacious platform, with the great vassals of the kingdom kneeling around him.

Then all rose, and Tom Canty cried out—

"Now, O my King, take these regal garments back, and give poor Tom, thy servant, his shreds and remnants again."

The Lord Protector spoke up—

"Let the small varlet be stripped and flung into the Tower."

But the new King, the true King, said—

"I will not have it so. But for him I had not got my crown again—none shall lay a hand upon him to harm him. And as for thee, my good uncle, my Lord Protector, this conduct of thine is not grateful toward this poor lad, for I hear he hath made thee a duke"—the Protector blushed—"yet he was not a king; wherefore what is thy fine title worth now? To-morrow you shall sue to me, THROUGH HIM, for its confirmation, else no duke, but a simple earl, shalt thou remain."

Under this rebuke, his Grace the Duke of Somerset retired a little from the front for the moment. The King turned to Tom, and said kindly—"My poor boy, how was it that you could remember where I hid the Seal when I could not remember it myself?"

"Ah, my King, that was easy, since I used it divers days."

"Used it—yet could not explain where it was?"

"I did not know it was THAT they wanted. They did not describe it, your Majesty."

"Then how used you it?"

The red blood began to steal up into Tom's cheeks, and he dropped his eyes and was silent.

"Speak up, good lad, and fear nothing," said the King. "How used you the Great Seal of England?"

Tom stammered a moment, in a pathetic confusion, then got it out—

"To crack nuts with!"

Poor child, the avalanche of laughter that greeted this nearly swept him off his feet. But if a doubt remained in any mind that Tom Canty was not the King of England and familiar with the august appurtenances of royalty, this reply disposed of it utterly.

Meantime the sumptuous robe of state had been removed from Tom's shoulders to the King's, whose rags were effectually hidden from sight under it. Then the coronation ceremonies were resumed; the true King was anointed and the crown set upon his head, whilst cannon thundered the news to the city, and all London seemed to rock with applause.

Chapter XXXIII. Edward as King.

Miles Hendon was picturesque enough before he got into the

riot on London Bridge—he was more so when he got out of it. He had but little money when he got in, none at all when he got out. The pickpockets had stripped him of his last farthing.

But no matter, so he found his boy. Being a soldier, he did not go at his task in a random way, but set to work, first of all, to arrange his campaign.

What would the boy naturally do? Where would he naturally go? Well —argued Miles—he would naturally go to his former haunts, for that is the instinct of unsound minds, when homeless and forsaken, as well as of sound ones. Whereabouts were his former haunts? His rags, taken together with the low villain who seemed to know him and who even claimed to be his father, indicated that his home was in one or another of the poorest and meanest districts of London. Would the search for him be difficult, or long? No, it was likely to be easy and brief. He would not hunt for the boy, he would hunt for a crowd; in the centre of a big crowd or a little one, sooner or later, he should find his poor little friend, sure; and the mangy mob would be entertaining itself with pestering and aggravating the boy, who would be proclaiming himself King, as usual. Then Miles Hendon would cripple some of those people, and carry off his little ward, and comfort and cheer him with loving words, and the two would never be separated any more.

So Miles started on his quest. Hour after hour he tramped through back alleys and squalid streets, seeking groups and crowds, and finding no end of them, but never any sign of the boy. This greatly surprised him, but did not discourage him. To his notion, there was nothing the matter with his plan of campaign; the only miscalculation about it was that the campaign was becoming a lengthy one, whereas he had expected it to be short.

When daylight arrived, at last, he had made many a mile, and canvassed many a crowd, but the only result was that he was tolerably tired, rather hungry and very sleepy. He wanted some breakfast, but there was no way to get it. To beg for it did not occur to him; as to pawning his sword, he would as soon have thought of parting with his honour; he could spare some of his clothes—yes, but one could as easily find a customer for a disease as for such clothes.

At noon he was still tramping—among the rabble which followed after the royal procession, now; for he argued that this regal display would attract his little lunatic powerfully. He followed the pageant through all its devious windings about London, and all the way to Westminster and the Abbey. He drifted here and there amongst the multitudes that were massed in the vicinity for a weary long time, baffled and perplexed, and finally wandered off, thinking, and trying to contrive some way to better his plan of campaign. By-and-by, when he came to himself out of his musings, he discovered that the town was far behind him and that the day was growing old. He was near the river, and in the country; it was a region of fine rural seats—not the sort of district to welcome clothes like his.

It was not at all cold; so he stretched himself on the ground in the lee of a hedge to rest and think. Drowsiness presently began to settle upon his senses; the faint and far-off boom of cannon was wafted to his ear, and he said to himself, "The new King is crowned," and straightway fell asleep. He had not slept or rested, before, for more than thirty hours. He did not wake again until near the middle of the next morning.

He got up, lame, stiff, and half famished, washed himself in the river, stayed his stomach with a pint or two of water, and trudged off toward Westminster, grumbling at himself for having wasted so much time. Hunger helped him to a new plan, now; he would try to get speech with old Sir Humphrey Marlow and borrow a few marks, and—but that was enough of a plan for the present; it would be time enough to enlarge it when this first stage should be accomplished.

Toward eleven o'clock he approached the palace; and although a host of showy people were about him, moving in the same direction, he was not inconspicuous—his costume took care of that. He watched these people's faces narrowly, hoping to find a charitable one whose possessor might be willing to carry his name to the old lieutenant—as to trying to get into the palace himself, that was simply out of the question.

Presently our whipping-boy passed him, then wheeled about and scanned his figure well, saying to himself, "An' that is not the very vagabond his Majesty is in such a worry about, then am I an ass—though belike I was that before. He answereth the description to a rag—that God should make two such would be to cheapen miracles by wasteful repetition. I would I could contrive an excuse to speak with him."

Miles Hendon saved him the trouble; for he turned about, then, as a man generally will when somebody mesmerises him by gazing hard at him from behind; and observing a strong interest in the boy's eyes, he stepped toward him and said—

"You have just come out from the palace; do you belong there?"

"Yes, your worship."

"Know you Sir Humphrey Marlow?"

The boy started, and said to himself, "Lord! mine old departed father!" Then he answered aloud, "Right well, your worship."

"Good—is he within?"

"Yes," said the boy; and added, to himself, "within his grave."

"Might I crave your favour to carry my name to him, and say I beg to say a word in his ear?"

"I will despatch the business right willingly, fair sir."

"Then say Miles Hendon, son of Sir Richard, is here without—I shall be greatly bounden to you, my good lad."

The boy looked disappointed. "The King did not name him so," he said to himself; "but it mattereth not, this is his twin brother, and can give his Majesty news of t'other Sir-Odds-and-Ends, I warrant." So he said to Miles, "Step in there a moment, good sir, and wait till I bring you word."

Hendon retired to the place indicated—it was a recess sunk in the palace wall, with a stone bench in it—a shelter for sentinels in bad weather. He had hardly seated himself when some halberdiers, in charge of an officer, passed by. The officer saw him, halted his men, and commanded Hendon to come forth. He obeyed, and was promptly arrested as a suspicious character prowling within the precincts of the palace. Things began to look ugly. Poor Miles was going to explain, but the officer roughly silenced him, and ordered his men to disarm him and search him.

"God of his mercy grant that they find somewhat," said poor Miles; "I have searched enow, and failed, yet is my need greater than theirs."

Nothing was found but a document. The officer tore it open, and Hendon smiled when he recognised the 'pot-hooks' made by his lost little friend that black day at Hendon Hall. The officer's face grew dark as he read the English paragraph, and Miles blenched to the opposite colour as he listened.

"Another new claimant of the Crown!" cried the officer. "Verily they breed like rabbits, to-day. Seize the rascal, men, and see ye keep him fast whilst I convey this precious paper within and send it to the King."

He hurried away, leaving the prisoner in the grip of the halberdiers.

"Now is my evil luck ended at last," muttered Hendon, "for I shall dangle at a rope's end for a certainty, by reason of that bit of writing. And what will become of my poor lad!—ah, only the good God knoweth."

By-and-by he saw the officer coming again, in a great hurry; so he plucked his courage together, purposing to meet his trouble as became a man. The officer ordered the men to loose the prisoner and return his sword to him; then bowed respectfully, and said—

"Please you, sir, to follow me."

Hendon followed, saying to himself, "An' I were not travelling to death and judgment, and so must needs economise in sin, I would throttle this knave for his mock courtesy."

The two traversed a populous court, and arrived at the grand entrance of the palace, where the officer, with another bow, delivered Hendon into the hands of a gorgeous official, who received him with profound respect and led him forward through a great hall, lined on both sides with rows of splendid flunkeys (who made reverential obeisance as the two passed along, but fell into death-throes of silent laughter at our stately scarecrow the moment his back was turned), and up a broad staircase, among flocks of fine folk, and finally conducted him into a vast room, clove a passage for him through the assembled nobility of England, then made a bow, reminded him to take his hat off, and left him standing in the middle of the room, a mark for all eyes, for plenty of indignant frowns, and for a sufficiency of amused and derisive smiles.

Miles Hendon was entirely bewildered. There sat the young King, under a canopy of state, five steps away, with his head bent down and aside, speaking with a sort of human bird of paradise—a duke, maybe. Hendon observed to himself that it was hard enough to be sentenced to death in the full vigour of life, without having this peculiarly public humiliation added. He wished the King would hurry about it—some of the gaudy people near by were becoming pretty offensive. At this moment the King raised his head slightly, and Hendon caught a good view of his face. The sight nearly took his breath away!—He stood gazing at the fair young face like one transfixed; then presently ejaculated—

"Lo, the Lord of the Kingdom of Dreams and Shadows on his throne!"

He muttered some broken sentences, still gazing and marvelling; then turned his eyes around and about, scanning the gorgeous throng and the splendid saloon, murmuring, "But these are REAL—verily these are REAL —surely it is not a dream."

He stared at the King again—and thought, "IS it a dream . . . or IS he the veritable Sovereign of England, and not the friendless poor Tom o' Bedlam I took him for—who shall solve me this riddle?"

A sudden idea flashed in his eye, and he strode to the wall, gathered up a chair, brought it back, planted it on the floor, and sat down in it!

A buzz of indignation broke out, a rough hand was laid upon him and a voice exclaimed—

"Up, thou mannerless clown! would'st sit in the presence of the King?"

The disturbance attracted his Majesty's attention, who stretched forth his hand and cried out—

"Touch him not, it is his right!"

The throng fell back, stupefied. The King went on—

"Learn ye all, ladies, lords, and gentlemen, that this is my trusty and well-beloved servant, Miles Hendon, who interposed his good sword and saved his prince from bodily harm and possible death—and for this he is a knight, by the King's voice. Also learn, that for a higher service, in that he saved his sovereign stripes and shame, taking these upon himself, he is a peer of England, Earl of Kent, and shall have gold and lands meet for the dignity. More—the privilege which he hath just exercised is his by royal grant; for we have ordained that the chiefs of his line shall have and hold the right to sit in the presence of the Majesty of England henceforth, age after age, so long as the crown shall endure. Molest him not."

Two persons, who, through delay, had only arrived from the country during this morning, and had now been in this room only five minutes, stood listening to these words and looking at the King, then at the scarecrow, then at the King again, in a sort of torpid bewilderment. These were Sir Hugh and the Lady Edith. But the new Earl did not see them. He was still staring at the monarch, in a dazed way, and muttering—

"Oh, body o' me! THIS my pauper! This my lunatic! This is he whom *I* would show what grandeur was, in my house of seventy rooms and seven-and-twenty servants! This is he who had never known aught but rags for raiment, kicks for comfort, and offal for diet! This is he whom *I* adopted and would make respectable! Would God I had a bag to hide my head in!"

Then his manners suddenly came back to him, and he dropped upon his knees, with his hands between the King's, and swore allegiance and did homage for his lands and titles. Then he rose and stood respectfully aside, a mark still for all eyes—and much envy, too.

Now the King discovered Sir Hugh, and spoke out with wrathful voice and kindling eye—

"Strip this robber of his false show and stolen estates, and put him under lock and key till I have need of him."

The late Sir Hugh was led away.

There was a stir at the other end of the room, now; the assemblage fell apart, and Tom Canty, quaintly but richly clothed, marched down, between these living walls, preceded by an usher. He knelt before the King, who said—

"I have learned the story of these past few weeks, and am well pleased with thee. Thou hast governed the realm with right royal gentleness and mercy. Thou hast found thy mother and thy sisters again? Good; they shall be cared for—and thy father shall hang, if thou desire it and the law consent. Know, all ye that hear my voice, that from this day, they that abide in the shelter of Christ's Hospital and share the King's bounty shall have their minds and hearts fed, as well as their baser parts; and this boy shall dwell there, and hold the chief place in its honourable body of governors, during life. And for that he hath been a king, it is meet that other than common observance shall be his due; wherefore note this his dress of state, for by it he shall be known, and none shall copy it; and wheresoever he shall come, it shall remind the people that he hath been royal, in his time, and none shall deny him his due of reverence or fail to give him salutation. He hath the throne's protection, he hath the crown's support, he shall be known and called by the honourable title of the King's Ward."

The proud and happy Tom Canty rose and kissed the King's hand, and was conducted from the presence. He did not waste any time, but flew to his mother, to tell her and Nan and Bet all about it and get them to help him enjoy the great news.*

---

* Christ's Hospital, or Bluecoat School, 'the noblest institution in the world.'

The ground on which the Priory of the Grey Friars stood was conferred by Henry VIII. on the Corporation of London (who caused the institution there of a home for poor boys and girls). Subsequently, Edward VI. caused the old Priory to be properly repaired, and founded within it that noble establishment called the Bluecoat School, or Christ's Hospital, for the EDUCATION and maintenance of orphans and the children of indigent persons . . . Edward would not let him (Bishop Ridley) depart till the letter was written (to the Lord Mayor), and then charged him to deliver it himself, and signify his special request and commandment that no time might be lost in proposing what was convenient, and apprising him of the proceedings. The work was zealously undertaken, Ridley himself engaging in it; and the result was the founding of Christ's Hospital for the education of poor children. (The King endowed several other charities at the same time.) "Lord God," said he, "I yield Thee most hearty thanks that Thou hast given me life thus long to finish this work to the glory of Thy name!" That innocent and most exemplary life was drawing rapidly to its close, and in a few days he rendered up his spirit to his Creator, praying God to defend the realm from Papistry.—J. Heneage Jesse's London: its Celebrated Characters and Places.

In the Great Hall hangs a large picture of King Edward VI. seated on his throne, in a scarlet and ermined robe, holding the sceptre in his left hand, and presenting with the other the Charter to the kneeling Lord Mayor. By his side stands the Chancellor, holding the seals, and next to him are other officers of state. Bishop Ridley kneels before him with uplifted hands, as if supplicating a blessing on the event; whilst the Aldermen, etc., with the Lord Mayor, kneel on both sides, occupying the middle ground of the picture; and lastly, in front, are a double row of boys on one side and girls on the other, from the master and matron down to the boy and girl who have stepped forward from their respective rows, and kneel with raised hands before the King.—Timbs' Curiosities of London, p. 98.

Conclusion. Justice and retribution.

When the mysteries were all cleared up, it came out, by confession of Hugh Hendon, that his wife had repudiated Miles by his command, that day at Hendon Hall—a command assisted and supported by the perfectly trustworthy promise that if she did not deny that he was Miles Hendon, and stand firmly to it, he would have her life; whereupon she said, "Take it!"—she did not value it—and she would not repudiate Miles; then the husband said he would spare her life but have Miles assassinated! This was a different matter; so she gave her word and kept it.

Hugh was not prosecuted for his threats or for stealing his brother's estates and title, because the wife and brother would not testify against him—and the former would not have been allowed to do it, even if she had wanted to. Hugh deserted his wife and went over to the continent, where he presently died; and by-and-by the Earl of Kent married his relict. There were grand times and rejoicings at Hendon village when the couple paid their first visit to the Hall.

Tom Canty's father was never heard of again.

The King sought out the farmer who had been branded and sold as a slave, and reclaimed him from his evil life with the Ruffler's gang, and put him in the way of a comfortable livelihood.

Christ's Hospital, by ancient custom, possesses the privilege of addressing the Sovereign on the occasion of his or her coming into the City to partake of the hospitality of the Corporation of London.—Ibid.

The Dining Hall, with its lobby and organ-gallery, occupies the entire storey, which is 187 feet long, 51 feet wide, and 47 feet high; it is lit by nine large windows, filled with stained glass on the south side; and is, next to Westminster Hall, the noblest room in the metropolis. Here the boys, now about 800 in number, dine; and here are held the 'Suppings in Public,' to which visitors are admitted by tickets issued by the Treasurer and by the Governors of Christ's Hospital. The tables are laid with cheese in wooden bowls, beer in wooden piggins, poured from leathern jacks, and bread brought in large baskets. The official company enter; the Lord Mayor, or President, takes his seat in a state chair made of oak from St. Catherine's Church, by the Tower; a hymn is sung, accompanied by the organ; a 'Grecian,' or head boy, reads the prayers from the pulpit, silence being enforced by three drops of a wooden hammer. After prayer the supper commences, and the visitors walk between the tables. At its close the 'trade-boys' take up the baskets, bowls, jacks, piggins, and candlesticks, and pass in procession, the bowing to the Governors being curiously formal. This spectacle was witnessed by Queen Victoria and Prince Albert in 1845.

Among the more eminent Bluecoat boys are Joshua Barnes, editor of Anacreon and Euripides; Jeremiah Markland, the eminent critic, particularly in Greek Literature; Camden, the antiquary; Bishop Stillingfleet; Samuel Richardson, the novelist; Thomas Mitchell, the translator of Aristophanes; Thomas Barnes, many years editor of the London Times; Coleridge, Charles Lamb, and Leigh Hunt.

No boy is admitted before he is seven years old, or after he is nine; and no boy can remain in the school after he is fifteen, King's boys and 'Grecians' alone excepted. There are about 500 Governors, at the head of whom are the Sovereign and the Prince of Wales. The qualification for a Governor is payment of 500 pounds.—Ibid.

He also took that old lawyer out of prison and remitted his fine. He provided good homes for the daughters of the two Baptist women whom he saw burned at the stake, and roundly punished the official who laid the undeserved stripes upon Miles Hendon's back.

He saved from the gallows the boy who had captured the stray falcon, and also the woman who had stolen a remnant of cloth from a weaver; but he was too late to save the man who had been convicted of killing a deer in the royal forest.

He showed favour to the justice who had pitied him when he was supposed to have stolen a pig, and he had the gratification of seeing him grow in the public esteem and become a great and honoured man.

As long as the King lived he was fond of telling the story of his adventures, all through, from the hour that the sentinel cuffed him away from the palace gate till the final midnight when he deftly mixed himself into a gang of hurrying workmen and so slipped into the Abbey and climbed up and hid himself in the Confessor's tomb, and then slept so long, next day, that he came within one of missing the Coronation altogether. He said that the frequent rehearsing of the precious lesson kept him strong in his purpose to make its teachings yield benefits to his people; and so, whilst his life was spared he should continue to tell the story, and thus keep its sorrowful spectacles fresh in his memory and the springs of pity replenished in his heart.

Miles Hendon and Tom Canty were favourites of the King, all through his brief reign, and his sincere mourners when he died. The good Earl of Kent had too much sense to abuse his peculiar privilege; but he exercised it twice after the instance we have seen of it before he was called from this world—once at the accession of Queen Mary, and once at the accession of Queen Elizabeth. A descendant of his exercised it at the accession of James I. Before this one's son chose to use the privilege, near a quarter of a century had elapsed, and the 'privilege of the Kents' had faded out of most people's memories; so, when the Kent of that day appeared before Charles I. and his court and sat down in the sovereign's presence to assert and perpetuate the right of his house, there was a fine stir indeed! But the matter was soon explained, and the right confirmed. The last Earl of the line fell in the wars of the Commonwealth fighting for the King, and the odd privilege ended with him.

Tom Canty lived to be a very old man, a handsome, white-haired old fellow, of grave and benignant aspect. As long as he lasted he was honoured; and he was also reverenced, for his striking and peculiar costume kept the people reminded that 'in his time he had been royal;' so, wherever he appeared the crowd fell apart, making way for him, and whispering, one to another, "Doff thy hat, it is the King's Ward!"—and so they saluted, and got his kindly smile in return—and they valued it, too, for his was an honourable history.

Yes, King Edward VI. lived only a few years, poor boy, but he lived them worthily. More than once, when some great dignitary, some gilded vassal of the crown, made argument against his leniency, and urged that some law which he was bent upon amending was gentle enough for its purpose, and wrought no suffering or oppression which any one need mightily mind, the young King turned the mournful eloquence of his great compassionate eyes upon him and answered—

"What dost THOU know of suffering and oppression? I and my people know, but not thou."

The reign of Edward VI. was a singularly merciful one for those harsh times. Now that we are taking leave of him, let us try to keep this in our minds, to his credit.

GENERAL NOTE.

One hears much about the 'hideous Blue Laws of Connecticut,' and is accustomed to shudder piously when they are mentioned. There are people in America—and even in England!—who imagine that they were a very monument of malignity, pitilessness, and inhumanity; whereas in reality they were about the first SWEEPING DEPARTURE FROM JUDICIAL ATROCITY which the 'civilised' world had seen. This humane and kindly Blue Law Code, of two hundred and forty years ago, stands all by itself, with ages of bloody law on the further side of it, and a century and three-quarters of bloody English law on THIS side of it.

There has never been a time—under the Blue Laws or any other— when above FOURTEEN crimes were punishable by death in Connecticut. But in England, within the memory of men who are still hale in body and mind, TWO HUNDRED AND TWENTY-THREE crimes were punishable by death! (See Dr. J. Hammond Trumbull's Blue Laws, True and False, p. 11.) These facts are worth knowing—and worth thinking about, too.

The Tragedy Of Pudd'nhead Wilson
By Mark Twain

A WHISPER TO THE READER

There is no character, howsoever good and fine, but it can be destroyed by ridicule, howsoever poor and witless. Observe the ass, for instance: his character is about perfect, he is the choicest spirit among all the humbler animals, yet see what ridicule has brought him to. Instead of feeling complimented when we are called an ass, we are left in doubt. —Pudd'nhead Wilson's Calendar

A person who is ignorant of legal matters is always liable to make mistakes when he tries to photograph a court scene with his pen; and so I was not willing to let the law chapters in this book go to press without first subjecting them to rigid and exhausting revision and correction by a trained barrister—if that is what they are called. These chapters are right, now, in every detail, for they were rewritten under the immediate eye of William Hicks, who studied law part of a while in southwest Missouri thirty-five years ago and then came over here to Florence for his health and is still helping for exercise and board in Macaroni Vermicelli's horse-feed shed, which is up the back alley as you turn around the corner out of the Piazza del Duomo just beyond the house where that stone that Dante used to sit on six hundred years ago is let into the wall when he let on to be watching them build Giotto's campanile and yet always got tired looking as Beatrice passed along on her way to get a chunk of chestnut cake to defend herself with in case of a Ghibelline outbreak before she got to school, at the same old stand where they sell the same old cake to this day and it is just as light and good as it was then, too, and this is not flattery, far from it. He was a little rusty on his law, but he rubbed up for this book, and those two or three legal chapters are right and straight, now. He told me so himself.

Given under my hand this second day of January, 1893, at the Villa Viviani, village of Settignano, three miles back of Florence, on the hills—the same certainly affording the most charming view to be found on this planet, and with it the most dreamlike and enchanting sunsets to be found in any planet or even in any solar system—and given, too, in the swell room of the house, with the busts of Cerretani senators and other grandees of this line looking approvingly down upon me, as they used to look down upon Dante, and mutely asking me to adopt them into my family, which I do with pleasure, for my remotest ancestors are but spring chickens compared with these robed and stately antiques, and it will be a great and satisfying lift for me, that six hundred years will.

Mark Twain.

CHAPTER 1 — Pudd'nhead Wins His Name

Tell the truth or trump—but get the trick. —Pudd'nhead Wilson's Calendar

The scene of this chronicle is the town of Dawson's Landing, on the Missouri side of the Mississippi, half a day's journey, per steamboat, below St. Louis.

In 1830 it was a snug collection of modest one- and two-story frame dwellings, whose whitewashed exteriors were almost concealed from sight by climbing tangles of rose vines, honeysuckles, and morning glories. Each of these pretty homes had a garden in front fenced with white palings and opulently stocked with hollyhocks, marigolds, touch-me-nots, prince's-feathers, and other old-fashioned flowers; while on the windowsills of the houses stood wooden boxes containing moss rose plants and terra-cotta pots in which grew a breed of geranium whose spread of intensely red blossoms accented the prevailing pink tint of the rose-clad house-front like an explosion of flame. When there was room on the ledge outside of the pots and boxes for a cat, the cat was there—in sunny weather—stretched at full length, asleep and blissful, with her furry belly to the sun and a paw curved over her nose. Then that house was complete, and its contentment and peace were made manifest to the world by this symbol, whose testimony is infallible. A home without a cat—and a well-fed, well-petted, and properly revered cat—may be a perfect home, perhaps, but how can it prove title?

All along the streets, on both sides, at the outer edge of the brick sidewalks, stood locust trees with trunks protected by wooden boxing, and these furnished shade for summer and a sweet fragrancer in spring, when the clusters of buds came forth. The main street, one block back from the river, and running parallel with it, was the sole business street. It was six blocks long, and in each block two or three brick stores, three stories high, towered above interjected bunches of little frame shops. Swinging signs creaked in the wind the street's whole length. The candy-striped pole, which indicates nobility proud and ancient along the palace-bordered canals of Venice, indicated merely the humble barbershop along the main street of Dawson's Landing. On a chief corner stood a lofty unpainted pole wreathed from top to bottom with tin pots and pans and cups, the chief tinmonger's noisy notice to the world (when the wind blew) that his shop was on hand for business at that corner.

The hamlet's front was washed by the clear waters of the great river; its body stretched itself rearward up a gentle incline; its most rearward border fringed itself out and scattered its houses about its base line of the hills; the hills rose high, enclosing the town in a half-moon curve, clothed with forests from foot to summit.

Steamboats passed up and down every hour or so. Those belonging to the little Cairo line and the little Memphis line always stopped; the big Orleans liners stopped for hails only, or to land passengers or freight; and this was the case also with the great flotilla of "transients." These latter came out of a dozen rivers—the Illinois, the Missouri, the Upper Mississippi, the Ohio, the Monongahela, the Tennessee, the Red River, the White River, and so on—and were bound every whither and stocked with every imaginable comfort or necessity, which the Mississippi's communities could want, from the frosty Falls of St. Anthony down through nine climates to torrid New Orleans.

Dawson's Landing was a slaveholding town, with a rich, slave-worked grain and pork country back of it. The town was sleepy and comfortable and contented. It was fifty years old, and was growing slowly—very slowly, in fact, but still it was growing.

The chief citizen was York Leicester Driscoll, about forty years old, judge of the county court. He was very proud of his old Virginian ancestry, and in his hospitalities and his rather formal and stately manners, he kept up its traditions. He was fine and just and generous. To be a gentleman—a gentleman without stain or blemish—was his only religion, and to it he was always faithful. He was respected, esteemed, and beloved by all of the community. He was well off, and was gradually adding to his store. He and his wife were very nearly happy, but not quite, for they had no children. The longing for the treasure of a child had grown stronger and stronger as the years slipped away, but the blessing never came—and was never to come.

With this pair lived the judge's widowed sister, Mrs. Rachel Pratt, and she also was childless—childless, and sorrowful for that reason, and not to be comforted. The women were good and commonplace people, and did their duty, and had their reward in clear consciences and the community's approbation. They were Presbyterians, the judge was a freethinker.

Pembroke Howard, lawyer and bachelor, aged almost forty, was another old Virginian grandee with proved descent from the First Families. He was a fine, majestic creature, a gentleman according to the nicest requirements of the Virginia rule, a devoted Presbyterian, an authority on the "code", and a man always courteously ready to stand up before you in the field if any act or word of his had seemed doubtful or suspicious to you, and explain it with any weapon you might prefer from bradawls to artillery. He was very popular with the people, and was the judge's dearest friend.

Then there was Colonel Cecil Burleigh Essex, another F.F.V. of formidable caliber—however, with him we have no concern.

Percy Northumberland Driscoll, brother to the judge, and younger than he by five years, was a married man, and had had children around his hearthstone; but they were attacked in detail by measles, croup, and scarlet fever, and this had given the doctor a chance with his effective antediluvian methods; so the cradles were empty. He was a prosperous man, with a good head for speculations, and his fortune was growing. On the first of February, 1830, two boy babes were born in his house; one to him, one to one of his slave girls, Roxana by name. Roxana was twenty years old. She was up and around the same day, with her hands full, for she was tending both babes.

Mrs. Percy Driscoll died within the week. Roxy remained in charge of the children. She had her own way, for Mr. Driscoll soon absorbed himself in his speculations and left her to her own devices.

In that same month of February, Dawson's Landing gained a new citizen. This was Mr. David Wilson, a young fellow of Scotch parentage. He had wandered to this remote region from his birthplace in the interior of the State of New York, to seek his fortune. He was twenty-five years old, college bred, and had finished a post-college course in an Eastern law school a couple of years before.

He was a homely, freckled, sandy-haired young fellow, with an intelligent blue eye that had frankness and comradeship in it and a covert twinkle of a pleasant sort. But for an unfortunate remark of his, he would no doubt have entered at once upon a successful career at Dawson's Landing. But he made his fatal remark the first day he spent in the village, and it "gaged" him. He had just made the acquaintance of a group of citizens when an invisible dog began to yelp and snarl and howl and make himself very comprehensively disagreeable, whereupon young Wilson said, much as one who is thinking aloud:

"I wish I owned half of that dog."

"Why?" somebody asked.

"Because I would kill my half."

The group searched his face with curiosity, with anxiety even, but found no light there, no expression that they could read. They fell away from him as from something uncanny, and went into privacy to discuss him. One said:

"'Pears to be a fool."

"'Pears?" said another. "*Is*, I reckon you better say."

"Said he wished he owned *half* of the dog, the idiot," said a third. "What did he reckon would become of the other half if he killed his half? Do you reckon he thought it would live?"

"Why, he must have thought it, unless he IS the downrightest fool in the world; because if he hadn't thought it, he would have wanted to own the whole dog, knowing that if he killed his half and the other half died, he would be responsible for that half just the same as if he had killed that half instead of his own. Don't it look that way to you, gents?"

"Yes, it does. If he owned one half of the general dog, it would be so; if he owned one end of the dog and another person owned the other end, it would be so, just the same; particularly in the first case, because if you kill one half of a general dog, there ain't any man that can tell whose half it was; but if he owned one end of the dog, maybe he could kill his end of it and—"

"No, he couldn't either; he couldn't and not be responsible if the other end died, which it would. In my opinion that man ain't in his right mind."

"In my opinion he hain't *got* any mind."

No. 3 said: "Well, he's a lummox, anyway."

"That's what he is;" said No. 4. "He's a labrick—just a Simon-pure labrick, if there was one."

"Yes, sir, he's a dam fool. That's the way I put him up," said No. 5. "Anybody can think different that wants to, but those are my sentiments."

"I'm with you, gentlemen," said No. 6. "Perfect jackass—yes, and it ain't going too far to say he is a pudd'nhead. If he ain't a pudd'nhead, I ain't no judge, that's all."

Mr. Wilson stood elected. The incident was told all over the town, and gravely discussed by everybody. Within a week he had lost his first name; Pudd'nhead took its place. In time he came to be liked, and well liked too; but by that time the nickname had got well stuck on, and it stayed. That first day's verdict made him a fool, and he was not able to get it set aside, or even modified. The nickname soon ceased to carry any harsh or unfriendly feeling with it, but it held its place, and was to continue to hold its place for twenty long years.

CHAPTER 2 — Driscoll Spares His Slaves

Adam was but human—this explains it all. He did not want the apple for the apple's sake, he wanted it only because it was forbidden. The mistake was in not forbidding the serpent; then he would have eaten the serpent. —Pudd'nhead Wilson's Calendar

Pudd'nhead Wilson had a trifle of money when he arrived, and he bought a small house on the extreme western verge of the town. Between it and Judge Driscoll's house there was only a grassy yard, with a paling fence dividing the properties in the middle. He hired a small office down in the town and hung out a tin sign with these words on it:

DAVID WILSON
ATTORNEY AND COUNSELOR-AT-LAW
SURVEYING, CONVEYANCING, ETC.

But his deadly remark had ruined his chance—at least in the law. No clients came. He took down his sign, after a while, and put it up on his own house with the law features knocked out of it. It offered his services now in the humble capacities of land surveyor and expert accountant. Now and then he got a job of surveying to do, and now and then a merchant got him to straighten out his books. With Scotch patience and pluck he resolved to live down his reputation and work his way into the legal field yet. Poor fellow, he could foresee that it was going to take him such a weary long time to do it.

He had a rich abundance of idle time, but it never hung heavy on his hands, for he interested himself in every new thing that was born into the universe of ideas, and studied it, and experimented upon it at his house. One of his pet fads was palmistry. To another one he gave no name, neither would he explain to anybody what its purpose was, but merely said it was an amusement. In fact, he had found that his fads added to his reputation as a pudd'nhead; there, he was growing chary of being too communicative about them. The fad without a name was one which dealt with people's finger marks. He carried in his coat pocket a shallow box with grooves in it, and in the grooves strips of glass five inches long and three inches wide. Along the lower edge of each strip was pasted a slip of white paper. He asked people to pass their hands through their hair (thus collecting upon them a thin coating of the natural oil) and then making a thumb-mark on a glass strip, following it with the mark of the ball of each finger in succession. Under this row of faint grease prints he would write a record on the strip of white paper—thus:

JOHN SMITH, right hand—

and add the day of the month and the year, then take Smith's left hand on another glass strip, and add name and date and the words "left hand." The strips were now returned to the grooved box, and took their place among what Wilson called his "records."

He often studied his records, examining and poring over them with absorbing interest until far into the night; but what he found there—if he found anything—he revealed to no one. Sometimes he copied on paper the involved and delicate pattern left by the ball of the finger, and then vastly enlarged it with a pantograph so that he could examine its web of curving lines with ease and convenience.

One sweltering afternoon—it was the first day of July, 1830—

he was at work over a set of tangled account books in his workroom, which looked westward over a stretch of vacant lots, when a conversation outside disturbed him. It was carried on in yells, which showed that the people engaged in it were not close together.

"Say, Roxy, how does yo' baby come on?" This from the distant voice.

"Fust-rate. How does *you* come on, Jasper?" This yell was from close by.

"Oh, I's middlin'; hain't got noth'n' to complain of, I's gwine to come a-court'n you bimeby, Roxy."

"*You* is, you black mud cat! Yah—yah—yah! I got somep'n' better to do den 'sociat'n' wid niggers as black as you is. Is ole Miss Cooper's Nancy done give you de mitten?" Roxy followed this sally with another discharge of carefree laughter.

"You's jealous, Roxy, dat's what's de matter wid you, you hussy—yah—yah—yah! Dat's de time I got you!"

"Oh, yes, *you* got me, hain't you. 'Clah to goodness if dat conceit o' yo'n strikes in, Jasper, it gwine to kill you sho'. If you b'longed to me, I'd sell you down de river 'fo' you git too fur gone. Fust time I runs acrost yo' marster, I's gwine to tell him so."

This idle and aimless jabber went on and on, both parties enjoying the friendly duel and each well satisfied with his own share of the wit exchanged—for wit they considered it.

Wilson stepped to the window to observe the combatants; he could not work while their chatter continued. Over in the vacant lots was Jasper, young, coal black, and of magnificent build, sitting on a wheelbarrow in the pelting sun—at work, supposably, whereas he was in fact only preparing for it by taking an hour's rest before beginning. In front of Wilson's porch stood Roxy, with a local handmade baby wagon, in which sat her two charges—one at each end and facing each other. From Roxy's manner of speech, a stranger would have expected her to be black, but she was not. Only one sixteenth of her was black, and that sixteenth did not show. She was of majestic form and stature, her attitudes were imposing and statuesque, and her gestures and movements distinguished by a noble and stately grace. Her complexion was very fair, with the rosy glow of vigorous health in her cheeks, her face was full of character and expression, her eyes were brown and liquid, and she had a heavy suit of fine soft hair which was also brown, but the fact was not apparent because her head was bound about with a checkered handkerchief and the hair was concealed under it. Her face was shapely, intelligent, and comely—even beautiful. She had an easy, independent carriage—when she was among her own caste—and a high and "sassy" way, withal; but of course she was meek and humble enough where white people were.

To all intents and purposes Roxy was as white as anybody, but the one sixteenth of her which was black outvoted the other fifteen parts and made her a Negro. She was a slave, and salable as such. Her child was thirty-one parts white, and he, too, was a slave, and by a fiction of law and custom a Negro. He had blue eyes and flaxen curls like his white comrade, but even the father of the white child was able to tell the children apart—little as he had commerce with them—by their clothes; for the white babe wore ruffled soft muslin and a coral necklace, while the other wore merely a coarse tow-linen shirt which barely reached to its knees, and no jewelry.

The white child's name was Thomas a Becket Driscoll, the other's name was Valet de Chambre: no surname—slaves hadn't the privilege. Roxana had heard that phrase somewhere, the fine sound of it had pleased her ear, and as she had supposed it was a name, she loaded it on to her darling. It soon got shorted to "Chambers," of course.

Wilson knew Roxy by sight, and when the duel of wits begun to play out, he stepped outside to gather in a record or two. Jasper went to work energetically, at once, perceiving that his leisure was observed. Wilson inspected the children and asked:

"How old are they, Roxy?"

"Bofe de same age, sir—five months. Bawn de fust o' Feb'uary."

"They're handsome little chaps. One's just as handsome as the other, too."

A delighted smile exposed the girl's white teeth, and she said:

"Bless yo' soul, Misto Wilson, it's pow'ful nice o' you to say dat, 'ca'se one of 'em ain't on'y a nigger. Mighty prime little nigger, I al'ays says, but dat's 'ca'se it's mine, o' course."

"How do you tell them apart, Roxy, when they haven't any clothes on?"

Roxy laughed a laugh proportioned to her size, and said:

"Oh, I kin tell 'em 'part, Misto Wilson, but I bet Marse Percy couldn't, not to save his life."

Wilson chatted along for awhile, and presently got Roxy's fingerprints for his collection—right hand and left—on a couple of his glass strips; then labeled and dated them, and took the "records" of both children, and labeled and dated them also.

Two months later, on the third of September, he took this trio of finger marks again. He liked to have a "series," two or three "takings" at intervals during the period of childhood, these to be followed at intervals of several years.

The next day—that is to say, on the fourth of September—something occurred which profoundly impressed Roxana. Mr. Driscoll missed another small sum of money—which is a way of saying that this was not a new thing, but had happened before. In truth, it had happened three times before. Driscoll's patience was exhausted. He was a fairly humane man toward slaves and other animals; he was an exceedingly humane man toward the erring of his own race. Theft he could not abide, and plainly there was a thief in his house. Necessarily the thief must be one of his Negros. Sharp measures must be taken. He called his servants before him. There were three of these, besides Roxy: a man, a woman, and a boy twelve years old. They were not related. Mr. Driscoll said:

"You have all been warned before. It has done no good. This time I will teach you a lesson. I will sell the thief. Which of you is the guilty one?"

They all shuddered at the threat, for here they had a good home, and a new one was likely to be a change for the worse. The denial was general. None had stolen anything—not

money, anyway—a little sugar, or cake, or honey, or something like that, that "Marse Percy wouldn't mind or miss" but not money—never a cent of money. They were eloquent in their protestations, but Mr. Driscoll was not moved by them. He answered each in turn with a stern "Name the thief!"

The truth was, all were guilty but Roxana; she suspected that the others were guilty, but she did not know them to be so. She was horrified to think how near she had come to being guilty herself; she had been saved in the nick of time by a revival in the colored Methodist Church, a fortnight before, at which time and place she "got religion." The very next day after that gracious experience, while her change of style was fresh upon her and she was vain of her purified condition, her master left a couple dollars unprotected on his desk, and she happened upon that temptation when she was polishing around with a dustrag. She looked at the money awhile with a steady rising resentment, then she burst out with:

"Dad blame dat revival, I wisht it had 'a' be'n put off till tomorrow!"

Then she covered the tempter with a book, and another member of the kitchen cabinet got it. She made this sacrifice as a matter of religious etiquette; as a thing necessary just now, but by no means to be wrested into a precedent; no, a week or two would limber up her piety, then she would be rational again, and the next two dollars that got left out in the cold would find a comforter—and she could name the comforter.

Was she bad? Was she worse than the general run of her race? No. They had an unfair show in the battle of life, and they held it no sin to take military advantage of the enemy—in a small way; in a small way, but not in a large one. They would smouch provisions from the pantry whenever they got a chance; or a brass thimble, or a cake of wax, or an emery bag, or a paper of needles, or a silver spoon, or a dollar bill, or small articles of clothing, or any other property of light value; and so far were they from considering such reprisals sinful, that they would go to church and shout and pray the loudest and sincerest with their plunder in their pockets. A farm smokehouse had to be kept heavily padlocked, or even the colored deacon himself could not resist a ham when Providence showed him in a dream, or otherwise, where such a thing hung lonesome, and longed for someone to love. But with a hundred hanging before him, the deacon would not take two—that is, on the same night. On frosty nights the humane Negro prowler would warm the end of the plank and put it up under the cold claws of chickens roosting in a tree; a drowsy hen would step on to the comfortable board, softly clucking her gratitude, and the prowler would dump her into his bag, and later into his stomach, perfectly sure that in taking this trifle from the man who daily robbed him of an inestimable treasure—his liberty—he was not committing any sin that God would remember against him in the Last Great Day.

"Name the thief!"

For the fourth time Mr. Driscoll had said it, and always in the same hard tone. And now he added these words of awful import:

"I give you one minute." He took out his watch. "If at the end of that time, you have not confessed, I will not only sell all four of you, BUT—I will sell you DOWN THE RIVER!"

It was equivalent to condemning them to hell! No Missouri

Negro doubted this. Roxy reeled in her tracks, and the color vanished out of her face; the others dropped to their knees as if they had been shot; tears gushed from their eyes, their supplicating hands went up, and three answers came in the one instant.

"I done it!"

"I done it!"

"I done it!—have mercy, marster—Lord have mercy on us po' niggers!"

"Very good," said the master, putting up his watch, "I will sell you *here* though you don't deserve it. You ought to be sold down the river."

The culprits flung themselves prone, in an ecstasy of gratitude, and kissed his feet, declaring that they would never forget his goodness and never cease to pray for him as long as they lived. They were sincere, for like a god he had stretched forth his mighty hand and closed the gates of hell against them. He knew, himself, that he had done a noble and gracious thing, and was privately well pleased with his magnanimity; and that night he set the incident down in his diary, so that his son might read it in after years, and be thereby moved to deeds of gentleness and humanity himself.

CHAPTER 3 — Roxy Plays a Shrewd Trick

Whoever has lived long enough to find out what life is, knows how deep a debt of gratitude we owe to Adam, the first great benefactor of our race. He brought death into the world. — Pudd'nhead Wilson's Calendar

Percy Driscoll slept well the night he saved his house minions from going down the river, but no wink of sleep visited Roxy's eyes. A profound terror had taken possession of her. Her child could grow up and be sold down the river! The thought crazed her with horror. If she dozed and lost herself for a moment, the next moment she was on her feet flying to her child's cradle to see if it was still there. Then she would gather it to her heart and pour out her love upon it in a frenzy of kisses, moaning, crying, and saying, "Dey sha'n't, oh, dey *sha'nt'!'—* yo' po' mammy will kill you fust!"

Once, when she was tucking him back in its cradle again, the other child nestled in its sleep and attracted her attention. She went and stood over it a long time communing with herself.

"What has my po' baby done, dat he couldn't have yo' luck? He hain't done nuth'n. God was good to you; why warn't he good to him? Dey can't sell *you* down de river. I hates yo' pappy; he hain't got no heart—for niggers, he hain't, anyways. I hates him, en I could kill him!" She paused awhile, thinking; then she burst into wild sobbings again, and turned away, saying, "Oh, I got to kill my chile, dey ain't no yuther way—killin' *him* wouldn't save de chile fum goin' down de river. Oh, I got to do it, yo' po' mammy's got to kill you to save you, honey." She gathered her baby to her bosom now, and began to smother it with caresses. "Mammy's got to kill you—how *kin* I do it! But yo' mammy ain't gwine to desert you—no, no, *dah*, don't cry—she gwine *wid* you, she gwine to kill herself too. Come along, honey, come along wid mammy; we gwine to jump in de river, den troubles o' dis worl' is all over—dey don't sell po' niggers down the river over *yonder.*"

She stared toward the door, crooning to the child and hushing

it; midway she stopped, suddenly. She had caught sight of her new Sunday gown—a cheap curtain-calico thing, a conflagration of gaudy colors and fantastic figures. She surveyed it wistfully, longingly.

"Hain't ever wore it yet," she said, "en it's just lovely." Then she nodded her head in response to a pleasant idea, and added, "No, I ain't gwine to be fished out, wid everybody lookin' at me, in dis mis'able ole linsey-woolsey."

She put down the child and made the change. She looked in the glass and was astonished at her beauty. She resolved to make her death toilet perfect. She took off her handkerchief turban and dressed her glossy wealth of hair "like white folks"; she added some odds and ends of rather lurid ribbon and a spray of atrocious artificial flowers; finally she threw over her shoulders a fluffy thing called a "cloud" in that day, which was of a blazing red complexion. Then she was ready for the tomb.

She gathered up her baby once more; but when her eye fell upon its miserably short little gray tow-linen shirt and noted the contrast between its pauper shabbiness and her own volcanic eruption of infernal splendors, her mother-heart was touched, and she was ashamed.

"No, dolling mammy ain't gwine to treat you so. De angels is gwine to 'mire you jist as much as dey does yo' mammy. Ain't gwine to have 'em putt'n dey han's up 'fo' dey eyes en sayin' to David and Goliah en dem yuther prophets, 'Dat chile is dress' to indelicate fo' dis place.'"

By this time she had stripped off the shirt. Now she clothed the naked little creature in one of Thomas `a Becket's snowy, long baby gowns, with its bright blue bows and dainty flummery of ruffles.

"Dah—now you's fixed." She propped the child in a chair and stood off to inspect it. Straightway her eyes begun to widen with astonishment and admiration, and she clapped her hands and cried out, "Why, it do beat all! I *never* knowed you was so lovely. Marse Tommy ain't a bit puttier—not a single bit."

She stepped over and glanced at the other infant; she flung a glance back at her own; then one more at the heir of the house. Now a strange light dawned in her eyes, and in a moment she was lost in thought. She seemed in a trance; when she came out of it, she muttered, "When I 'uz a-washin' 'em in de tub, yistiddy, he own pappy asked me which of 'em was his'n."

She began to move around like one in a dream. She undressed Thomas `a Becket, stripping him of everything, and put the tow-linen shirt on him. She put his coral necklace on her own child's neck. Then she placed the children side by side, and after earnest inspection she muttered:

"Now who would b'lieve clo'es could do de like o' dat? Dog my cats if it ain't all *I* kin do to tell t' other fum which, let alone his pappy."

She put her cub in Tommy's elegant cradle and said:

"You's young Marse *Tom* fum dis out, en I got to practice and git used to 'memberin' to call you dat, honey, or I's gwine to make a mistake sometime en git us bofe into trouble. Dah—now you lay still en don't fret no mo', Marse Tom. Oh, thank de lord in heaven, you's saved, you's saved! Dey ain't no man kin ever sell mammy's po' little honey down de river now!"

She put the heir of the house in her own child's unpainted pine cradle, and said, contemplating its slumbering form uneasily:

"I's sorry for you, honey; I's sorry, God knows I is—but what *kin* I do, what *could* I do? Yo' pappy would sell him to somebody, sometime, en den he'd go down de river, sho', en I couldn't, couldn't, *couldn't* stan' it."

She flung herself on her bed and began to think and toss, toss and think. By and by she sat suddenly upright, for a comforting thought had flown through her worried mind—

"'T ain't no sin—*white* folks has done it! It ain't no sin, glory to goodness it ain't no sin! *Dey's* done it—yes, en dey was de biggest quality in de whole bilin', too—*kings!*"

She began to muse; she was trying to gather out of her memory the dim particulars of some tale she had heard some time or other. At last she said—

"Now I's got it; now I 'member. It was dat ole nigger preacher dat tole it, de time he come over here fum Illinois en preached in de nigger church. He said dey ain't nobody kin save his own self—can't do it by faith, can't do it by works, can't do it no way at all. Free grace is de *on'y* way, en dat don't come fum nobody but jis' de Lord; en *he* kin give it to anybody He please, saint or sinner—*he* don't kyer. He do jis' as He's a mineter. He s'lect out anybody dat suit Him, en put another one in his place, en make de fust one happy forever en leave t' other one to burn wid Satan. De preacher said it was jist like dey done in Englan' one time, long time ago. De queen she lef' her baby layin' aroun' one day, en went out callin'; an one 'o de niggers roun'bout de place dat was 'mos' white, she come in en see de chile layin' aroun', en tuck en put her own chile's clo's on de queen's chile, en put de queen's chile's clo'es on her own chile, en den lef' her own chile layin' aroun', en tuck en toted de queen's chile home to de nigger quarter, en nobody ever foun' it out, en her chile was de king bimeby, en sole de queen's chile down de river one time when dey had to settle up de estate. Dah, now—de preacher said it his own self, en it ain't no sin, 'ca'se white folks done it. DEY done it—yes, DEY done it; en not on'y jis' common white folks nuther, but de biggest quality dey is in de whole bilin'. Oh, I's *so* glad I 'member 'bout dat!"

She got lighthearted and happy, and went to the cradles, and spent what was left of the night "practicing." She would give her own child a light pat and say humbly, "Lay still, Marse Tom," then give the real Tom a pat and say with severity, "Lay *still*, Chambers! Does you want me to take somep'n *to* you?"

As she progressed with her practice, she was surprised to see how steadily and surely the awe which had kept her tongue reverent and her manner humble toward her young master was transferring itself to her speech and manner toward the usurper, and how similarly handy she was becoming in transferring her motherly curtness of speech and peremptoriness of manner to the unlucky heir of the ancient house of Driscoll.

She took occasional rests from practicing, and absorbed herself in calculating her chances.

"Dey'll sell dese niggers today fo' stealin' de money, den dey'll buy some mo' dat don't now de chillen—so *dat's* all right. When I takes de chillen out to git de air, de minute I's roun' de corner I's gwine to gaum dey mouths all roun' wid jam, den dey can't *nobody* notice dey's changed. Yes, I gwine ter do dat till I's safe, if it's a year.

"Dey ain't but one man dat I's afeard of, en dat's dat Pudd'nhead Wilson. Dey calls him a pudd'nhead, en says he's a fool. My lan, dat man ain't no mo' fool den I is! He's de smartes' man in dis town, lessn' it's Jedge Driscoll or maybe Pem Howard. Blame dat man, he worries me wid dem ornery glasses o' his'n; *I* b'lieve he's a witch. But nemmine, I's gwine to happen aroun' dah one o' dese days en let on dat I reckon he wants to print a chillen's fingers ag'in; en if HE don't notice dey's changed, I bound dey ain't nobody gwine to notice it, en den I's safe, sho'. But I reckon I'll tote along a hoss-shoe to keep off de witch work."

The new Negros gave Roxy no trouble, of course. The master gave her none, for one of his speculations was in jeopardy, and his mind was so occupied that he hardly saw the children when he looked at them, and all Roxy had to do was to get them both into a gale of laughter when he came about; then their faces were mainly cavities exposing gums, and he was gone again before the spasm passed and the little creatures resumed a human aspect.

Within a few days the fate of the speculation became so dubious that Mr. Percy went away with his brother, the judge, to see what could be done with it. It was a land speculation as usual, and it had gotten complicated with a lawsuit. The men were gone seven weeks. Before they got back, Roxy had paid her visit to Wilson, and was satisfied. Wilson took the fingerprints, labeled them with the names and with the date — October the first—put them carefully away, and continued his chat with Roxy, who seemed very anxious that he should admire the great advance in flesh and beauty which the babes had made since he took their fingerprints a month before. He complimented their improvement to her contentment; and as they were without any disguise of jam or other stain, she trembled all the while and was miserably frightened lest at any moment he—

But he didn't. He discovered nothing; and she went home jubilant, and dropped all concern about the matter permanently out of her mind.

CHAPTER 4 — The Ways of the Changelings

Adam and Eve had many advantages, but the principal one was, that they escaped teething. —Pudd'nhead Wilson's Calendar

There is this trouble about special providences—namely, there is so often a doubt as to which party was intended to be the beneficiary. In the case of the children, the bears, and the prophet, the bears got more real satisfaction out of the episode than the prophet did, because they got the children. — Pudd'nhead Wilson's Calendar

This history must henceforth accommodate itself to the change which Roxana has consummated, and call the real heir "Chambers" and the usurping little slave, "Thomas `a Becket"—shortening this latter name to "Tom," for daily use, as the people about him did.

"Tom" was a bad baby, from the very beginning of his usurpation. He would cry for nothing; he would burst into storms of devilish temper without notice, and let go scream after scream and squall after squall, then climax the thing with "holding his breath"—that frightful specialty of the teething nursling, in the throes of which the creature exhausts its lungs, then is convulsed with noiseless squirmings and twistings and kickings in the effort to get its breath, while the lips turn blue and the mouth stands wide and rigid, offering for inspection one wee tooth set in the lower rim of a hoop of red gums; and when the appalling stillness has endured until one is sure the lost breath will never return, a nurse comes flying, and dashes water in the child's face, and—presto! the lungs fill, and instantly discharge a shriek, or a yell, or a howl which bursts the listening ear and surprises the owner of it into saying words which would not go well with a halo if he had one. The baby Tom would claw anybody who came within reach of his nails, and pound anybody he could reach with his rattle. He would scream for water until he got it, and then throw cup and all on the floor and scream for more. He was indulged in all his caprices, howsoever troublesome and exasperating they might be; he was allowed to eat anything he wanted, particularly things that would give him the stomach-ache.

When he got to be old enough to begin to toddle about and say broken words and get an idea of what his hands were for, he was a more consummate pest than ever. Roxy got no rest while he was awake. He would call for anything and everything he saw, simply saying, "Awnt it!" (want it), which was a command. When it was brought, he said in a frenzy, and motioning it away with his hands, "Don't awnt it! don't awnt it!" and the moment it was gone he set up frantic yells of "Awnt it! awnt it!" and Roxy had to give wings to her heels to get that thing back to him again before he could get time to carry out his intention of going into convulsions about it.

What he preferred above all other things was the tongs. This was because his "father" had forbidden him to have them lest he break windows and furniture with them. The moment Roxy's back was turned he would toddle to the presence of the tongs and say, "Like it!" and cock his eye to one side or see if Roxy was observed; then, "Awnt it!" and cock his eye again; then, "Hab it!" with another furtive glace; and finally, "Take it!"—and the prize was his. The next moment the heavy implement was raised aloft; the next, there was a crash and a squall, and the cat was off on three legs to meet an engagement; Roxy would arrive just as the lamp or a window went to irremediable smash.

Tom got all the petting, Chambers got none. Tom got all the delicacies, Chambers got mush and milk, and clabber without sugar. In consequence Tom was a sickly child and Chambers wasn't. Tom was "fractious," as Roxy called it, and overbearing; Chambers was meek and docile.

With all her splendid common sense and practical everyday ability, Roxy was a doting fool of a mother. She was this toward her child—and she was also more than this: by the fiction created by herself, he was become her master; the necessity of recognizing this relation outwardly and of perfecting herself in the forms required to express the recognition, had moved her to such diligence and faithfulness in practicing these forms that this exercise soon concreted itself into habit; it became automatic and unconscious; then a natural result followed: deceptions intended solely for others gradually grew practically into self-deceptions as well; the mock reverence became real reverence, the mock homage real homage; the little counterfeit rift of separation between imitation-slave and imitation-master widened and widened, and became an abyss, and a very real one—and on one side of it stood Roxy, the dupe of her own deceptions, and on the other stood her child, no longer a usurper to her, but her accepted and recognized master. He was her darling, her master, and her deity all in one, and in her worship of him she forgot who she was and what he had been.

In babyhood Tom cuffed and banged and scratched Chambers unrebuked, and Chambers early learned that between meekly bearing it and resenting it, the advantage all lay with the former policy. The few times that his persecutions had moved him beyond control and made him fight back had cost him very dear at headquarters; not at the hands of Roxy, for if she ever went beyond scolding him sharply for "forgett'n' who his young marster was," she at least never extended her punishment beyond a box on the ear. No, Percy Driscoll was the person. He told Chambers that under no provocation whatever was he privileged to lift his hand against his little master. Chambers overstepped the line three times, and got three such convincing canings from the man who was his father and didn't know it, that he took Tom's cruelties in all humility after that, and made no more experiments.

Outside the house the two boys were together all through their boyhood. Chambers was strong beyond his years, and a good fighter; strong because he was coarsely fed and hard worked about the house, and a good fighter because Tom furnished him plenty of practice—on white boys whom he hated and was afraid of. Chambers was his constant bodyguard, to and from school; he was present on the playground at recess to protect his charge. He fought himself into such a formidable reputation, by and by, that Tom could have changed clothes with him, and "ridden in peace," like Sir Kay in Launcelot's armor.

He was good at games of skill, too. Tom staked him with marbles to play "keeps" with, and then took all the winnings away from him. In the winter season Chambers was on hand, in Tom's worn-out clothes, with "holy" red mittens, and "holy" shoes, and pants "holy" at the knees and seat, to drag a sled up the hill for Tom, warmly clad, to ride down on; but he never got a ride himself. He built snowmen and snow fortifications under Tom's directions. He was Tom's patient target when Tom wanted to do some snowballing, but the target couldn't fire back. Chambers carried Tom's skates to the river and strapped them on him, then trotted around after him on the ice, so as to be on hand when he wanted; but he wasn't ever asked to try the skates himself.

In summer the pet pastime of the boys of Dawson's Landing was to steal apples, peaches, and melons from the farmer's fruit wagons—mainly on account of the risk they ran of getting their heads laid open with the butt of the farmer's whip. Tom was a distinguished adept at these thefts—by proxy. Chambers did his stealing, and got the peach stones, apple cores, and melon rinds for his share.

Tom always made Chambers go in swimming with him, and stay by him as a protection. When Tom had had enough, he would slip out and tie knots in Chamber's shirt, dip the knots in the water and make them hard to undo, then dress himself and sit by and laugh while the naked shiverer tugged at the stubborn knots with his teeth.

Tom did his humble comrade these various ill turns partly out of native viciousness, and partly because he hated him for his superiorities of physique and pluck, and for his manifold cleverness. Tom couldn't dive, for it gave him splitting headaches. Chambers could dive without inconvenience, and was fond of doing it. He excited so much admiration, one day, among a crowd of white boys, by throwing back somersaults from the stern of a canoe, that it wearied Tom's spirit, and at last he shoved the canoe underneath Chambers while he was in the air—so he came down on his head in the canoe bottom;

and while he lay unconscious, several of Tom's ancient adversaries saw that their long-desired opportunity was come, and they gave the false heir such a drubbing that with Chamber's best help he was hardly able to drag himself home afterward.

When the boys was fifteen and upward, Tom was "showing off" in the river one day, when he was taken with a cramp, and shouted for help. It was a common trick with the boys—particularly if a stranger was present—to pretend a cramp and howl for help; then when the stranger came tearing hand over hand to the rescue, the howler would go on struggling and howling till he was close at hand, then replace the howl with a sarcastic smile and swim blandly away, while the town boys assailed the dupe with a volley of jeers and laughter. Tom had never tried this joke as yet, but was supposed to be trying it now, so the boys held warily back; but Chambers believed his master was in earnest; therefore, he swam out, and arrived in time, unfortunately, and saved his life.

This was the last feather. Tom had managed to endure everything else, but to have to remain publicly and permanently under such an obligation as this to a nigger, and to this nigger of all niggers—this was too much. He heaped insults upon Chambers for "pretending" to think he was in earnest in calling for help, and said that anybody but a blockheaded nigger would have known he was funning and left him alone.

Tom's enemies were in strong force here, so they came out with their opinions quite freely. The laughed at him, and called him coward, liar, sneak, and other sorts of pet names, and told him they meant to call Chambers by a new name after this, and make it common in the town—"Tom Driscoll's nigger pappy,"—to signify that he had had a second birth into this life, and that Chambers was the author of his new being. Tom grew frantic under these taunts, and shouted:

"Knock their heads off, Chambers! Knock their heads off! What do you stand there with your hands in your pockets for?"

Chambers expostulated, and said, "But, Marse Tom, dey's too many of 'em—dey's—"

"Do you hear me?"

"Please, Marse Tom, don't make me! Dey's so many of 'em dat—"

Tom sprang at him and drove his pocketknife into him two or three times before the boys could snatch him away and give the wounded lad a chance to escape. He was considerably hurt, but not seriously. If the blade had been a little longer, his career would have ended there.

Tom had long ago taught Roxy "her place." It had been many a day now since she had ventured a caress or a fondling epithet in his quarter. Such things, from a "nigger," were repulsive to him, and she had been warned to keep her distance and remember who she was. She saw her darling gradually cease from being her son, she saw THAT detail perish utterly; all that was left was master—master, pure and simple, and it was not a gentle mastership, either. She saw herself sink from the sublime height of motherhood to the somber depths of unmodified slavery, the abyss of separation between her and her boy was complete. She was merely his chattel now, his convenience, his dog, his cringing and helpless slave, the humble and unresisting victim of his capricious temper and

vicious nature.

Sometimes she could not go to sleep, even when worn out with fatigue, because her rage boiled so high over the day's experiences with her boy. She would mumble and mutter to herself:

"He struck me en I warn't no way to blame—struck me in de face, right before folks. En he's al'ays callin' me nigger wench, en hussy, en all dem mean names, when I's doin' de very bes' I kin. Oh, Lord, I done so much for him—I lif' him away up to what he is—en dis is what I git for it."

Sometimes when some outrage of peculiar offensiveness stung her to the heart, she would plan schemes of vengeance and revel in the fancied spectacle of his exposure to the world as an imposter and a slave; but in the midst of these joys fear would strike her; she had made him too strong; she could prove nothing, and—heavens, she might get sold down the river for her pains! So her schemes always went for nothing, and she laid them aside in impotent rage against the fates, and against herself for playing the fool on that fatal September day in not providing herself with a witness for use in the day when such a thing might be needed for the appeasing of her vengeance-hungry heart.

And yet the moment Tom happened to be good to her, and kind—and this occurred every now and then—all her sore places were healed, and she was happy; happy and proud, for this was her son, her nigger son, lording it among the whites and securely avenging their crimes against her race.

There were two grand funerals in Dawson's Landing that fall—the fall of 1845. One was that of Colonel Cecil Burleigh Essex, the other that of Percy Driscoll.

On his deathbed Driscoll set Roxy free and delivered his idolized ostensible son solemnly into the keeping of his brother, the judge, and his wife. Those childless people were glad to get him. Childless people are not difficult to please.

Judge Driscoll had gone privately to his brother, a month before, and bought Chambers. He had heard that Tom had been trying to get his father to sell the boy down the river, and he wanted to prevent the scandal—for public sentiment did not approve of that way of treating family servants for light cause or for no cause.

Percy Driscoll had worn himself out in trying to save his great speculative landed estate, and had died without succeeding. He was hardly in his grave before the boom collapsed and left his envied young devil of an heir a pauper. But that was nothing; his uncle told him he should be his heir and have all his fortune when he died; so Tom was comforted.

Roxy had no home now; so she resolved to go around and say good-by to her friends and then clear out and see the world—that is to say, she would go chambermaiding on a steamboat, the darling ambition of her race and sex.

Her last call was on the black giant, Jasper. She found him chopping Pudd'nhead Wilson's winter provision of wood.

Wilson was chatting with him when Roxy arrived. He asked her how she could bear to go off chambermaiding and leave her boys; and chaffingly offered to copy off a series of their fingerprints, reaching up to their twelfth year, for her to remember them by; but she sobered in a moment, wondering if he suspected anything; then she said she believed she didn't want them. Wilson said to himself, "The drop of black blood in her is superstitious; she thinks there's some devilry, some witch business about my glass mystery somewhere; she used to come here with an old horseshoe in her hand; it could have been an accident, but I doubt it."

CHAPTER 5 — The Twins Thrill Dawson's Landing

Training is everything. The peach was once a bitter almond; cauliflower is nothing but cabbage with a college education.
—Pudd'nhead Wilson's Calendar

Remark of Dr. Baldwin's, concerning upstarts: We don't care to eat toadstools that think they are truffles. — Pudd'nhead Wilson's Calendar

Mrs. York Driscoll enjoyed two years of bliss with that prize, Tom—bliss that was troubled a little at times, it is true, but bliss nevertheless; then she died, and her husband and his childless sister, Mrs. Pratt, continued this bliss-business at the old stand. Tom was petted and indulged and spoiled to his entire content—or nearly that. This went on till he was nineteen, then he was sent to Yale. He went handsomely equipped with "conditions," but otherwise he was not an object of distinction there. He remained at Yale two years, and then threw up the struggle. He came home with his manners a good deal improved; he had lost his surliness and brusqueness, and was rather pleasantly soft and smooth, now; he was furtively, and sometimes openly, ironical of speech, and given to gently touching people on the raw, but he did it with a good-natured semiconscious air that carried it off safely, and kept him from getting into trouble. He was as indolent as ever and showed no very strenuous desire to hunt up an occupation. People argued from this that he preferred to be supported by his uncle until his uncle's shoes should become vacant. He brought back one or two new habits with him, one of which he rather openly practiced—tippling—but concealed another, which was gambling. It would not do to gamble where his uncle could hear of it; he knew that quite well.

Tom's Eastern polish was not popular among the young people. They could have endured it, perhaps, if Tom had stopped there; but he wore gloves, and that they couldn't stand, and wouldn't; so he was mainly without society. He brought home with him a suit of clothes of such exquisite style and cut in fashion—Eastern fashion, city fashion—that it filled everybody with anguish and was regarded as a peculiarly wanton affront. He enjoyed the feeling which he was exciting, and paraded the town serene and happy all day; but the young fellows set a tailor to work that night, and when Tom started out on his parade next morning, he found the old deformed Negro bell ringer straddling along in his wake tricked out in a flamboyant curtain-calico exaggeration of his finery, and imitating his fancy Eastern graces as well as he could.

Tom surrendered, and after that clothed himself in the local fashion. But the dull country town was tiresome to him, since his acquaintanceship with livelier regions, and it grew daily more and more so. He began to make little trips to St. Louis for refreshment. There he found companionship to suit him, and pleasures to his taste, along with more freedom, in some particulars, than he could have at home. So, during the next two years, his visits to the city grew in frequency and his tarryings there grew steadily longer in duration.

He was getting into deep waters. He was taking chances, privately, which might get him into trouble some day—in fact, *did.*

Judge Driscoll had retired from the bench and from all business activities in 1850, and had now been comfortably idle three years. He was president of the Freethinkers' Society, and Pudd'nhead Wilson was the other member. The society's weekly discussions were now the old lawyer's main interest in life. Pudd'nhead was still toiling in obscurity at the bottom of the ladder, under the blight of that unlucky remark which he had let fall twenty-three years before about the dog.

Judge Driscoll was his friend, and claimed that he had a mind above the average, but that was regarded as one of the judge's whims, and it failed to modify the public opinion. Or rather, that was one of the reason why it failed, but there was another and better one. If the judge had stopped with bare assertion, it would have had a good deal of effect; but he made the mistake of trying to prove his position. For some years Wilson had been privately at work on a whimsical almanac, for his amusement—a calendar, with a little dab of ostensible philosophy, usually in ironical form, appended to each date; and the judge thought that these quips and fancies of Wilson's were neatly turned and cute; so he carried a handful of them around one day, and read them to some of the chief citizens. But irony was not for those people; their mental vision was not focused for it. They read those playful trifles in the solidest terms, and decided without hesitancy that if there had ever been any doubt that Dave Wilson was a pudd'nhead—which there hadn't—this revelation removed that doubt for good and all. That is just the way in this world; an enemy can partly ruin a man, but it takes a good-natured injudicious friend to complete the thing and make it perfect. After this the judge felt tenderer than ever toward Wilson, and surer than ever that his calendar had merit.

Judge Driscoll could be a freethinker and still hold his place in society because he was the person of most consequence to the community, and therefore could venture to go his own way and follow out his own notions. The other member of his pet organization was allowed the like liberty because he was a cipher in the estimation of the public, and nobody attached any importance to what he thought or did. He was liked, he was welcome enough all around, but he simply didn't count for anything.

The Widow Cooper—affectionately called "Aunt Patsy" by everybody—lived in a snug and comely cottage with her daughter Rowena, who was nineteen, romantic, amiable, and very pretty, but otherwise of no consequence. Rowena had a couple of young brothers—also of no consequence.

The widow had a large spare room, which she let to a lodger, with board, when she could find one, but this room had been empty for a year now, to her sorrow. Her income was only sufficient for the family support, and she needed the lodging money for trifling luxuries. But now, at last, on a flaming June day, she found herself happy; her tedious wait was ended; her year-worn advertisement had been answered; and not by a village applicant, no, no!—this letter was from away off yonder in the dim great world to the North; it was from St. Louis. She sat on her porch gazing out with unseeing eyes upon the shining reaches of the mighty Mississippi, her thoughts steeped in her good fortune. Indeed it was specially good fortune, for she was to have two lodgers instead of one.

She had read the letter to the family, and Rowena had danced away to see to the cleaning and airing of the room by the slave woman, Nancy, and the boys had rushed abroad in the town to spread the great news, for it was a matter of public interest, and the public would wonder and not be pleased if not informed. Presently Rowena returned, all ablush with joyous excitement, and begged for a rereading of the letter. It was framed thus:

HONORED MADAM: My brother and I have seen your advertisement, by chance, and beg leave to take the room you offer. We are twenty-four years of age and twins. We are Italians by birth, but have lived long in the various countries of Europe, and several years in the United States. Our names are Luigi and Angelo Capello. You desire but one guest; but, dear madam, if you will allow us to pay for two, we will not incommode you. We shall be down Thursday.

"Italians! How romantic! Just think, Ma—there's never been one in this town, and everybody will be dying to see them, and they're all OURS! Think of that!"

"Yes, I reckon they'll make a grand stir."

"Oh, indeed they will. The whole town will be on its head! Think—they've been in Europe and everywhere! There's never been a traveler in this town before, Ma, I shouldn't wonder if they've seen kings!"

"Well, a body can't tell, but they'll make stir enough, without that."

"Yes, that's of course. Luigi—Angelo. They're lovely names; and so grand and foreign—not like Jones and Robinson and such. Thursday they are coming, and this is only Tuesday; it's a cruel long time to wait. Here comes Judge Driscoll in at the gate. He's heard about it. I'll go and open the door."

The judge was full of congratulations and curiosity. The letter was read and discussed. Soon Justice Robinson arrived with more congratulations, and there was a new reading and a new discussion. This was the beginning. Neighbor after neighbor, of both sexes, followed, and the procession drifted in and out all day and evening and all Wednesday and Thursday. The letter was read and reread until it was nearly worn out; everybody admired its courtly and gracious tone, and smooth and practiced style, everybody was sympathetic and excited, and the Coopers were steeped in happiness all the while.

The boats were very uncertain in low water in these primitive times. This time the Thursday boat had not arrived at ten at night—so the people had waited at the landing all day for nothing; they were driven to their homes by a heavy storm without having had a view of the illustrious foreigners.

Eleven o'clock came; and the Cooper house was the only one in the town that still had lights burning. The rain and thunder were booming yet, and the anxious family were still waiting, still hoping. At last there was a knock at the door, and the family jumped to open it. Two Negro men entered, each carrying a trunk, and proceeded upstairs toward the guest room. Then entered the twins—the handsomest, the best dressed, the most distinguished-looking pair of young fellows the West had ever seen. One was a little fairer than the other, but otherwise they were exact duplicates.

CHAPTER 6 — Swimming in Glory

Let us endeavor so to live that when we come to die even the undertaker will be sorry. —Pudd'nhead Wilson's Calendar

Habit is habit, and not to be flung out of the window by any man, but coaxed downstairs a step at a time. — Pudd'nhead Wilson's Calendar

At breakfast in the morning, the twins' charm of manner and easy and polished bearing made speedy conquest of the family's good graces. All constraint and formality quickly disappeared, and the friendliest feeling succeeded. Aunt Patsy called them by their Christian names almost from the beginning. She was full of the keenest curiosity about them, and showed it; they responded by talking about themselves, which pleased her greatly. It presently appeared that in their early youth they had known poverty and hardship. As the talk wandered along, the old lady watched for the right place to drop in a question or two concerning that matter, and when she found it, she said to the blond twin, who was now doing the biographies in his turn while the brunette one rested:

"If it ain't asking what I ought not to ask, Mr. Angelo, how did you come to be so friendless and in such trouble when you were little? Do you mind telling? But don't, if you do."

"Oh, we don't mind it at all, madam; in our case it was merely misfortune, and nobody's fault. Our parents were well to do, there in Italy, and we were their only child. We were of the old Florentine nobility"—Rowena's heart gave a great bound, her nostrils expanded, and a fine light played in her eyes—"and when the war broke out, my father was on the losing side and had to fly for his life. His estates were confiscated, his personal property seized, and there we were, in Germany, strangers, friendless, and in fact paupers. My brother and I were ten years old, and well educated for that age, very studious, very fond of our books, and well grounded in the German, French, Spanish, and English languages. Also, we were marvelous musical prodigies—if you will allow me to say it, it being only the truth.

"Our father survived his misfortunes only a month, our mother soon followed him, and we were alone in the world. Our parents could have made themselves comfortable by exhibiting us as a show, and they had many and large offers; but the thought revolted their pride, and they said they would starve and die first. But what they wouldn't consent to do, we had to do without the formality of consent. We were seized for the debts occasioned by their illness and their funerals, and placed among the attractions of a cheap museum in Berlin to earn the liquidation money. It took us two years to get out of that slavery. We traveled all about Germany, receiving no wages, and not even our keep. We had to be exhibited for nothing, and beg our bread.

"Well, madam, the rest is not of much consequence. When we escaped from that slavery at twelve years of age, we were in some respects men. Experience had taught us some valuable things; among others, how to take care of ourselves, how to avoid and defeat sharks and sharpers, and how to conduct our own business for our own profit and without other people's help. We traveled everywhere—years and years—picking up smatterings of strange tongues, familiarizing ourselves with strange sights and strange customs, accumulating an education of a wide and varied and curious sort. It was a pleasant life. We went to Venice—to London, Paris, Russia, India, China, Japan—"

At this point Nancy, the slave woman, thrust her head in at the door and exclaimed:

"Ole Missus, de house is plum' jam full o' people, en dey's jes a-spi'lin' to see de gen'lemen!" She indicated the twins with a nod of her head, and tucked it back out of sight again.

It was a proud occasion for the widow, and she promised herself high satisfaction in showing off her fine foreign birds before her neighbors and friends—simple folk who had hardly ever seen a foreigner of any kind, and never one of any distinction or style. Yet her feeling was moderate indeed when contrasted with Rowena's. Rowena was in the clouds, she walked on air; this was to be the greatest day, the most romantic episode in the colorless history of that dull country town. She was to be familiarly near the source of its glory and feel the full flood of it pour over her and about her; the other girls could only gaze and envy, not partake.

The widow was ready, Rowena was ready, so also were the foreigners.

The party moved along the hall, the twins in advance, and entered the open parlor door, whence issued a low hum of conversation. The twins took a position near the door, the widow stood at Luigi's side, Rowena stood beside Angelo, and the march-past and the introductions began. The widow was all smiles and contentment. She received the procession and passed it on to Rowena.

"Good mornin', Sister Cooper"—handshake.

"Good morning, Brother Higgins—Count Luigi Capello, Mr. Higgins" —handshake, followed by a devouring stare and "I'm glad to see ye," on the part of Higgins, and a courteous inclination of the head and a pleasant "Most happy!" on the part of Count Luigi.

"Good mornin', Roweny"—handshake.

"Good morning, Mr. Higgins—present you to Count Angelo Capello." Handshake, admiring stare, "Glad to see ye"—courteous nod, smily "Most happy!" and Higgins passes on.

None of these visitors was at ease, but, being honest people, they didn't pretend to be. None of them had ever seen a person bearing a title of nobility before, and none had been expecting to see one now, consequently the title came upon them as a kind of pile-driving surprise and caught them unprepared. A few tried to rise to the emergency, and got out an awkward "My lord," or "Your lordship," or something of that sort, but the great majority were overwhelmed by the unaccustomed word and its dim and awful associations with gilded courts and stately ceremony and anointed kingship, so they only fumbled through the handshake and passed on, speechless. Now and then, as happens at all receptions everywhere, a more than ordinary friendly soul blocked the procession and kept it waiting while he inquired how the brothers liked the village, and how long they were going to stay, and if their family was well, and dragged in the weather, and hoped it would get cooler soon, and all that sort of thing, so as to be able to say, when he got home, "I had quite a long talk with them"; but nobody did or said anything of a regrettable kind, and so the great affair went through to the end in a creditable and satisfactory fashion.

General conversation followed, and the twins drifted about from group to group, talking easily and fluently and winning approval, compelling admiration and achieving favor from all. The widow followed their conquering march with a proud eye, and every now and then Rowena said to herself with deep

satisfaction, "And to think they are ours—all ours!"

There were no idle moments for mother or daughter. Eager inquiries concerning the twins were pouring into their enchanted ears all the time; each was the constant center of a group of breathless listeners; each recognized that she knew now for the first time the real meaning of that great word Glory, and perceived the stupendous value of it, and understood why men in all ages had been willing to throw away meaner happiness, treasure, life itself, to get a taste of its sublime and supreme joy. Napoleon and all his kind stood accounted for—and justified.

When Rowena had at last done all her duty by the people in the parlor, she went upstairs to satisfy the longings of an overflow meeting there, for the parlor was not big enough to hold all the comers. Again she was besieged by eager questioners, and again she swam in sunset seas of glory. When the forenoon was nearly gone, she recognized with a pang that this most splendid episode of her life was almost over, that nothing could prolong it, that nothing quite its equal could ever fall to her fortune again. But never mind, it was sufficient unto itself, the grand occasion had moved on an ascending scale from the start, and was a noble and memorable success. If the twins could but do some crowning act now to climax it, something usual, something startling, something to concentrate upon themselves the company's loftiest admiration, something in the nature of an electric surprise—

Here a prodigious slam-banging broke out below, and everybody rushed down to see. It was the twins, knocking out a classic four-handed piece on the piano in great style. Rowena was satisfied—satisfied down to the bottom of her heart.

The young strangers were kept long at the piano. The villagers were astonished and enchanted with the magnificence of their performance, and could not bear to have them stop. All the music that they had ever heard before seemed spiritless prentice-work and barren of grace and charm when compared with these intoxicating floods of melodious sound. They realized that for once in their lives they were hearing masters.

CHAPTER 7 — The Unknown Nymph

One of the most striking differences between a cat and a lie is that a cat has only nine lives. —Pudd'nhead Wilson's Calendar

The company broke up reluctantly, and drifted toward their several homes, chatting with vivacity and all agreeing that it would be many a long day before Dawson's Landing would see the equal of this one again. The twins had accepted several invitations while the reception was in progress, and had also volunteered to play some duets at an amateur entertainment for the benefit of a local charity. Society was eager to receive them to its bosom. Judge Driscoll had the good fortune to secure them for an immediate drive, and to be the first to display them in public. They entered his buggy with him and were paraded down the main street, everybody flocking to the windows and sidewalks to see.

The judge showed the strangers the new graveyard, and the jail, and where the richest man lived, and the Freemasons' hall, and the Methodist church, and the Presbyterian church, and where the Baptist church was going to be when they got some money to build it with, and showed them the town hall and the slaughterhouse, and got out of the independent fire company in uniform and had them put out an imaginary fire; then he let them inspect the muskets of the militia company, and poured out an exhaustless stream of enthusiasm over all these splendors, and seemed very well satisfied with the responses he got, for the twins admired his admiration, and paid him back the best they could, though they could have done better if some fifteen or sixteen hundred thousand previous experiences of this sort in various countries had not already rubbed off a considerable part of the novelty in it.

The judge laid himself out hospitality to make them have a good time, and if there was a defect anywhere, it was not his fault. He told them a good many humorous anecdotes, and always forgot the nub, but they were always able to furnish it, for these yarns were of a pretty early vintage, and they had had many a rejuvenating pull at them before. And he told them all about his several dignities, and how he had held this and that and the other place of honor or profit, and had once been to the legislature, and was now president of the Society of Freethinkers. He said the society had been in existence four years, and already had two members, and was firmly established. He would call for the brothers in the evening, if they would like to attend a meeting of it.

Accordingly he called for them, and on the way he told them all about Pudd'nhead Wilson, in order that they might get a favorable impression of him in advance and be prepared to like him. This scheme succeeded—the favorable impression was achieved. Later it was confirmed and solidified when Wilson proposed that out of courtesy to the strangers the usual topics be put aside and the hour be devoted to conversation upon ordinary subjects and the cultivation of friendly relations and good-fellowship—a proposition which was put to vote and carried.

The hour passed quickly away in lively talk, and when it was ended, the lonesome and neglected Wilson was richer by two friends than he had been when it began. He invited the twins to look in at his lodgings presently, after disposing of an intervening engagement, and they accepted with pleasure.

Toward the middle of the evening, they found themselves on the road to his house. Pudd'nhead was at home waiting for them and putting in his time puzzling over a thing which had come under his notice that morning. The matter was this: He happened to be up very early—at dawn, in fact; and he crossed the hall, which divided his cottage through the center, and entered a room to get something there. The window of the room had no curtains, for that side of the house had long been unoccupied, and through this window he caught sight of something which surprised and interested him. It was a young woman—a young woman where properly no young woman belonged; for she was in Judge Driscoll's house, and in the bedroom over the judge's private study or sitting room. This was young Tom Driscoll's bedroom. He and the judge, the judge's widowed sister Mrs. Pratt, and three Negro servants were the only people who belonged in the house. Who, then, might this young lady be? The two houses were separated by an ordinary yard, with a low fence running back through its middle from the street in front to the lane in the rear. The distance was not great, and Wilson was able to see the girl very well, the window shades of the room she was in being up, and the window also. The girl had on a neat and trim summer dress, patterned in broad stripes of pink and white, and her bonnet was equipped with a pink veil. She was practicing steps, gaits and attitudes, apparently; she was doing the thing gracefully, and was very much absorbed in her work. Who could she be, and how came she to be in young Tom Driscoll's room?

Wilson had quickly chosen a position from which he could watch the girl without running much risk of being seen by her, and he remained there hoping she would raise her veil and betray her face. But she disappointed him. After a matter of twenty minutes she disappeared and although he stayed at his post half an hour longer, she came no more.

Toward noon he dropped in at the judge's and talked with Mrs. Pratt about the great event of the day, the levee of the distinguished foreigners at Aunt Patsy Cooper's. He asked after her nephew Tom, and she said he was on his way home and that she was expecting him to arrive a little before night, and added that she and the judge were gratified to gather from his letters that he was conducting himself very nicely and creditably—at which Wilson winked to himself privately. Wilson did not ask if there was a newcomer in the house, but he asked questions that would have brought light-throwing answers as to that matter if Mrs. Pratt had had any light to throw; so he went away satisfied that he knew of things that were going on in her house of which she herself was not aware.

He was now awaiting for the twins, and still puzzling over the problem of who that girl might be, and how she happened to be in that young fellow's room at daybreak in the morning.

CHAPTER 8 — Marse Tom Tramples His Chance

The holy passion of Friendship is of so sweet and steady and loyal and enduring a nature that it will last through a whole lifetime, if not asked to lend money. —Pudd'nhead Wilson's Calendar

Consider well the proportions of things. It is better to be a young June bug than an old bird of paradise. —Pudd'nhead Wilson's Calendar

It is necessary now to hunt up Roxy.

At the time she was set free and went away chambermaiding, she was thirty-five. She got a berth as second chambermaid on a Cincinnati boat in the New Orleans trade, the *Grand Mogul*. A couple of trips made her wonted and easygoing at the work, and infatuated her with the stir and adventure and independence of steamboat life. Then she was promoted and become head chambermaid. She was a favorite with the officers, and exceedingly proud of their joking and friendly way with her.

During eight years she served three parts of the year on that boat, and the winters on a Vicksburg packet. But now for two months, she had had rheumatism in her arms, and was obliged to let the washtub alone. So she resigned. But she was well fixed—rich, as she would have described it; for she had lived a steady life, and had banked four dollars every month in New Orleans as a provision for her old age. She said in the start that she had "put shoes on one bar'footed nigger to tromple on her with," and that one mistake like that was enough; she would be independent of the human race thenceforth forevermore if hard work and economy could accomplish it. When the boat touched the levee at New Orleans she bade good-by to her comrades on the *Grand Mogul* and moved her kit ashore.

But she was back in an hour. The bank had gone to smash and carried her four hundred dollars with it. She was a pauper and homeless. Also disabled bodily, at least for the present. The officers were full of sympathy for her in her trouble, and made up a little purse for her. She resolved to go to her birthplace;

she had friends there among the Negros, and the unfortunate always help the unfortunate, she was well aware of that; those lowly comrades of her youth would not let her starve.

She took the little local packet at Cairo, and now she was on the homestretch. Time had worn away her bitterness against her son, and she was able to think of him with serenity. She put the vile side of him out of her mind, and dwelt only on recollections of his occasional acts of kindness to her. She gilded and otherwise decorated these, and made them very pleasant to contemplate. She began to long to see him. She would go and fawn upon him slavelike—for this would have to be her attitude, of course—and maybe she would find that time had modified him, and that he would be glad to see his long-forgotten old nurse and treat her gently. That would be lovely; that would make her forget her woes and her poverty.

Her poverty! That thought inspired her to add another castle to her dream: maybe he would give her a trifle now and then— maybe a dollar, once a month, say; any little thing like that would help, oh, ever so much.

By the time she reached Dawson's Landing, she was her old self again; her blues were gone, she was in high feather. She would get along, surely; there were many kitchens where the servants would share their meals with her, and also steal sugar and apples and other dainties for her to carry home—or give her a chance to pilfer them herself, which would answer just as well. And there was the church. She was a more rabid and devoted Methodist than ever, and her piety was no sham, but was strong and sincere. Yes, with plenty of creature comforts and her old place in the amen corner in her possession again, she would be perfectly happy and at peace thenceforward to the end.

She went to Judge Driscoll's kitchen first of all. She was received there in great form and with vast enthusiasm. Her wonderful travels, and the strange countries she had seen, and the adventures she had had, made her a marvel and a heroine of romance. The Negros hung enchanted upon a great story of her experiences, interrupting her all along with eager questions, with laughter, exclamations of delight, and expressions of applause; and she was obliged to confess to herself that if there was anything better in this world than steamboating, it was the glory to be got by telling about it. The audience loaded her stomach with their dinners, and then stole the pantry bare to load up her basket.

Tom was in St. Louis. The servants said he had spent the best part of his time there during the previous two years. Roxy came every day, and had many talks about the family and its affairs. Once she asked why Tom was away so much. The ostensible "Chambers" said:

"De fac' is, ole marster kin git along better when young marster's away den he kin when he's in de town; yes, en he love him better, too; so he gives him fifty dollahs a month—"

"No, is dat so? Chambers, you's a-jokin', ain't you?"

"'Clah to goodness I ain't, Mammy; Marse Tom tole me so his own self. But nemmine, 'tain't enough."

"My lan', what de reason 'tain't enough?"

"Well, I's gwine to tell you, if you gimme a chanst, Mammy. De reason it ain't enough is 'ca'se Marse Tom gambles."

Roxy threw up her hands in astonishment, and Chambers went on:

"Ole marster found it out, 'ca'se he had to pay two hundred dollahs for Marse Tom's gamblin' debts, en dat's true, Mammy, jes as dead certain as you's bawn."

"Two—hund'd dollahs! Why, what is you talkin' 'bout? Two—hund'd—dollahs. Sakes alive, it's 'mos' enough to buy a tol'able good secondhand nigger wid. En you ain't lyin', honey? You wouldn't lie to you' old Mammy?"

"It's God's own truth, jes as I tell you—two hund'd dollahs—I wisht I may never stir outen my tracks if it ain't so. En, oh, my lan', ole Marse was jes a-hoppin'! He was b'ilin' mad, I tell you! He tuck 'n' dissenhurrit him."

"Disen*whiched* him?"

"Dissenhurrit him."

"What's dat? What do you mean?"

"Means he bu'sted de will."

"Bu's—ted de will! He wouldn't *ever* treat him so! Take it back, you mis'able imitation nigger dat I bore in sorrow en tribbilation."

Roxy's pet castle—an occasional dollar from Tom's pocket— was tumbling to ruin before her eyes. She could not abide such a disaster as that; she couldn't endure the thought of it. Her remark amused Chambers.

"Yah-yah-yah! Jes listen to dat! If I's imitation, what is you? Bofe of us is imitation *white*—dat's what we is—en pow'ful good imitation, too. Yah-yah-yah! We don't 'mount to noth'n as imitation *niggers*; en as for—"

"Shet up yo' foolin', 'fo' I knock you side de head, en tell me 'bout de will. Tell me 'tain't bu'sted—do, honey, en I'll never forgit you."

"Well, *'tain't*—'ca'se dey's a new one made, en Marse Tom's all right ag'in. But what is you in sich a sweat 'bout it for, Mammy? 'Tain't none o' your business I don't reckon."

"'Tain't none o' my business? Whose business is it den, I'd like to know? Wuz I his mother tell he was fifteen years old, or wusn't I?—you answer me dat. En you speck I could see him turned out po' and ornery on de worl' en never care noth'n' 'bout it? I reckon if you'd ever be'n a mother yo'self, Valet de Chambers, you wouldn't talk sich foolishness as dat."

"Well, den, ole Marse forgive him en fixed up de will ag'in—do dat satisfy you?"

Yes, she was satisfied now, and quite happy and sentimental over it. She kept coming daily, and at last she was told that Tom had come home. She began to tremble with emotion, and straightway sent to beg him to let his "po' ole nigger Mammy have jes one sight of him en die for joy."

Tom was stretched at his lazy ease on a sofa when Chambers brought the petition. Time had not modified his ancient detestation of the humble drudge and protector of his boyhood; it was still bitter and uncompromising. He sat up and bent a severe gaze upon the face of the young fellow whose name he was unconsciously using and whose family rights he was enjoying. He maintained the gaze until the victim of it had become satisfactorily pallid with terror, then he said:

"What does the old rip want with me?"

The petition was meekly repeated.

"Who gave you permission to come and disturb me with the social attentions of niggers?"

Tom had risen. The other young man was trembling now, visibly. He saw what was coming, and bent his head sideways, and put up his left arm to shield it. Tom rained cuffs upon the head and its shield, saying no word: the victim received each blow with a beseeching, "Please, Marse Tom!—oh, please, Marse Tom!" Seven blows—then Tom said, "Face the door—march!" He followed behind with one, two, three solid kicks. The last one helped the pure-white slave over the door-sill, and he limped away mopping his eyes with his old, ragged sleeve. Tom shouted after him, "Send her in!"

Then he flung himself panting on the sofa again, and rasped out the remark, "He arrived just at the right moment; I was full to the brim with bitter thinkings, and nobody to take it out of. How refreshing it was! I feel better."

Tom's mother entered now, closing the door behind her, and approached her son with all the wheedling and supplication servilities that fear and interest can impart to the words and attitudes of the born slave. She stopped a yard from her boy and made two or three admiring exclamations over his manly stature and general handsomeness, and Tom put an arm under his head and hoisted a leg over the sofa back in order to look properly indifferent.

"My lan', how you is growed, honey! 'Clah to goodness, I wouldn't a-knowed you, Marse Tom! 'Deed I wouldn't! Look at me good; does you 'member old Roxy? Does you know yo' old nigger mammy, honey? Well now, I kin lay down en die in peace, 'ca'se I'se seed—"

"Cut it short, Goddamn it, cut it short! What is it you want?"

"You heah dat? Jes the same old Marse Tom, al'ays so gay and funnin' wid de ole mammy. I'uz jes as shore—"

"Cut it short, I tell you, and get along! What do you want?"

This was a bitter disappointment. Roxy had for so many days nourished and fondled and petted her notion that Tom would be glad to see his old nurse, and would make her proud and happy to the marrow with a cordial word or two, that it took two rebuffs to convince her that he was not funning, and that her beautiful dream was a fond and foolish variety, a shabby and pitiful mistake. She was hurt to the heart, and so ashamed that for a moment she did not quite know what to do or how to act. Then her breast began to heave, the tears came, and in her forlornness she was moved to try that other dream of hers—an appeal to her boy's charity; and so, upon the impulse, and without reflection, she offered her supplication:

"Oh, Marse Tom, de po' ole mammy is in sich hard luck dese days; en she's kinder crippled in de arms en can't work, en if you could gimme a dollah—on'y jes one little dol—"

Tom was on his feet so suddenly that the supplicant was startled into a jump herself.

"A dollar!—give you a dollar! I've a notion to strangle you! Is *that* your errand here? Clear out! And be quick about it!"

Roxy backed slowly toward the door. When she was halfway she stopped, and said mournfully:

"Marse Tom, I nussed you when you was a little baby, en I raised you all by myself tell you was 'most a young man; en now you is young en rich, en I is po' en gitt'n ole, en I come heah b'leavin' dat you would he'p de ole mammy 'long down de little road dat's lef' 'twix' her en de grave, en—"

Tom relished this tune less than any that he preceded it, for it began to wake up a sort of echo in his conscience; so he interrupted and said with decision, though without asperity, that he was not in a situation to help her, and wasn't going to do it.

"Ain't you ever gwine to he'p me, Marse Tom?"

"No! Now go away and don't bother me any more."

Roxy's head was down, in an attitude of humility. But now the fires of her old wrongs flamed up in her breast and began to burn fiercely. She raised her head slowly, till it was well up, and at the same time her great frame unconsciously assumed an erect and masterful attitude, with all the majesty and grace of her vanished youth in it. She raised her finger and punctuated with it.

"You has said de word. You has had yo' chance, en you has trompled it under yo' foot. When you git another one, you'll git down on yo' knees en *beg* for it!"

A cold chill went to Tom's heart, he didn't know why; for he did not reflect that such words, from such an incongruous source, and so solemnly delivered, could not easily fail of that effect. However, he did the natural thing: he replied with bluster and mockery.

"*You'll* give me a chance—*you*! Perhaps I'd better get down on my knees now! But in case I don't—just for argument's sake—what's going to happen, pray?"

"Dis is what is gwine to happen, I's gwine as straight to yo' uncle as I kin walk, en tell him every las' thing I knows 'bout you."

Tom's cheek blenched, and she saw it. Disturbing thoughts began to chase each other through his head. "How can she know? And yet she must have found out—she looks it. I've had the will back only three months, and am already deep in debt again, and moving heaven and earth to save myself from exposure and destruction, with a reasonably fair show of getting the thing covered up if I'm let alone, and now this fiend has gone and found me out somehow or other. I wonder how much she knows? Oh, oh, oh, it's enough to break a body's heart! But I've got to humor her—there's no other way."

Then he worked up a rather sickly sample of a gay laugh and a hollow chipperness of manner, and said:

"Well, well, Roxy dear, old friends like you and me mustn't quarrel. Here's your dollar—now tell me what you know."

He held out the wildcat bill; she stood as she was, and made no movement. It was her turn to scorn persuasive foolery now, and she did not waste it. She said, with a grim implacability in voice and manner which made Tom almost realize that even a former slave can remember for ten minutes insults and injuries returned for compliments and flatteries received, and can also enjoy taking revenge for them when the opportunity offers:

"What does I know? I'll tell you what I knows, I knows enough to bu'st dat will to flinders—en more, mind you, *more!*"

Tom was aghast.

"More?" he said, "What do you call more? Where's there any room for more?"

Roxy laughed a mocking laugh, and said scoffingly, with a toss of her head, and her hands on her hips:

"Yes!—oh, I reckon! *co'se* you'd like to know—wid yo' po' little ole rag dollah. What you reckon I's gwine to tell *you* for?—you ain't got no money. I's gwine to tell yo' uncle—en I'll do it dis minute, too—he'll gimme FIVE dollahs for de news, en mighty glad, too."

She swung herself around disdainfully, and started away. Tom was in a panic. He seized her skirts, and implored her to wait. She turned and said, loftily:

"Look-a-heah, what 'uz it I tole you?"

"You—you—I don't remember anything. What was it you told me?"

"I tole you dat de next time I give you a chance you'd git down on yo' knees en beg for it."

Tom was stupefied for a moment. He was panting with excitement. Then he said:

"Oh, Roxy, you wouldn't require your young master to do such a horrible thing. You can't mean it."

"I'll let you know mighty quick whether I means it or not! You call me names, en as good as spit on me when I comes here, po' en ornery en 'umble, to praise you for bein' growed up so fine and handsome, en tell you how I used to nuss you en tend you en watch you when you 'uz sick en hadn't no mother but me in de whole worl', en beg you to give de po' ole nigger a dollah for to get her som'n' to eat, en you call me names— *names*, dad blame you! Yassir, I gives you jes one chance mo', and dat's *now*, en it las' on'y half a second—you hear?"

Tom slumped to his knees and began to beg, saying:

"You see I'm begging, and it's honest begging, too! Now tell me, Roxy, tell me."

The heir of two centuries of unatoned insult and outrage looked down on him and seemed to drink in deep draughts of satisfaction. Then she said:

"Fine nice young white gen'l'man kneelin' down to a nigger wench! I's wanted to see dat jes once befo' I's called. Now, Gabr'el, blow de hawn, I's ready . . . Git up!"

Tom did it. He said, humbly:

"Now, Roxy, don't punish me any more. I deserved what I've got, but be good and let me off with that. Don't go to uncle. Tell me—I'll give you the five dollars."

"Yes, I bet you will; en you won't stop dah, nuther. But I ain't gwine to tell you heah—"

"Good gracious, no!"

"Is you 'feared o' de ha'nted house?"

"N-no."

"Well, den, you come to de ha'nted house 'bout ten or 'leven tonight, en climb up de ladder, 'ca'se de sta'rsteps is broke down, en you'll find me. I's a-roostin' in de ha'nted house 'ca'se I can't 'ford to roos' nowher's else." She started toward the door, but stopped and said, "Gimme de dollah bill!" He gave it to her. She examined it and said, "H'm—like enough de bank's bu'sted." She started again, but halted again. "Has you got any whisky?"

"Yes, a little."

"Fetch it!"

He ran to his room overhead and brought down a bottle which was two-thirds full. She tilted it up and took a drink. Her eyes sparkled with satisfaction, and she tucked the bottle under her shawl, saying, "It's prime. I'll take it along."

Tom humbly held the door for her, and she marched out as grim and erect as a grenadier.

CHAPTER 9 — Tom Practices Sycophancy

Why is it that we rejoice at a birth and grieve at a funeral? It is because we are not the person involved. — Pudd'nhead Wilson's Calendar

It is easy to find fault, if one has that disposition. There was once a man who, not being able to find any other fault with his coal, complained that there were too many prehistoric toads in it. —Pudd'nhead Wilson's Calendar

Tom flung himself on the sofa, and put his throbbing head in his hands, and rested his elbows on his knees. He rocked himself back and forth and moaned.

"I've knelt to a nigger wench!" he muttered. "I thought I had struck the deepest depths of degradation before, but oh, dear, it was nothing to this. . . . Well, there is one consolation, such as it is—I've struck bottom this time; there's nothing lower."

But that was a hasty conclusion.

At ten that night he climbed the ladder in the haunted house, pale, weak, and wretched. Roxy was standing in the door of one of the rooms, waiting, for she had heard him.

This was a two-story log house which had acquired the reputation a few years ago of being haunted, and that was the end of its usefulness. Nobody would live in it afterward, or go near it by night, and most people even gave it a wide berth in the daytime. As it had no competition, it was called *the* haunted house. It was getting crazy and ruinous now, from long neglect. It stood three hundred yards beyond Pudd'nhead Wilson's house, with nothing between but vacancy. It was the last house in the town at that end.

Tom followed Roxy into the room. She had a pile of clean straw in the corner for a bed, some cheap but well-kept clothing was hanging on the wall, there was a tin lantern freckling the floor with little spots of light, and there were various soap and candle boxes scattered about, which served for chairs. The two sat down. Roxy said:

"Now den, I'll tell you straight off, en I'll begin to k'leck de money later on; I ain't in no hurry. What does you reckon I's gwine to tell you?"

"Well, you—you—oh, Roxy, don't make it too hard for me! Come right out and tell me you've found out somehow what a shape I'm in on account of dissipation and foolishness."

"Disposition en foolishness! NO sir, dat ain't it. Dat jist ain't nothin' at all, 'longside o' what *I* knows."

Tom stared at her, and said:

"Why, Roxy, what do you mean?"

She rose, and gloomed above him like a Fate.

"I means dis—en it's de Lord's truth. You ain't no more kin to ole Marse Driscoll den I is! *dat's* what I means!" and her eyes flamed with triumph.

"What?"

"Yassir, en *dat* ain't all! You's a *nigger!—bawn* a nigger and a *slave!—*en you's a nigger en a slave dis minute; en if I opens my mouf ole Marse Driscoll'll sell you down de river befo' you is two days older den what you is now!"

"It's a thundering lie, you miserable old blatherskite!"

"It ain't no lie, nuther. It's just de truth, en nothin' *but* de truth, so he'p me. Yassir—you's my *son*—"

"You devil!"

"En dat po' boy dat you's be'n a-kickin' en a-cuffin' today is Percy Driscoll's son en yo' *marster*—"

"You beast!"

"En *his* name is Tom Driscoll, en *yo's* name's Valet de Chambers, en you ain't GOT no fambly name, beca'se niggers don't *have* em!"

Tom sprang up and seized a billet of wood and raised it, but his mother only laughed at him, and said:

"Set down, you pup! Does you think you kin skyer me? It ain't in you, nor de likes of you. I reckon you'd shoot me in de back, maybe, if you got a chance, for dat's jist yo' style—*I* knows you, throo en throo—but I don't mind gitt'n killed, beca'se all dis is down in writin' and it's in safe hands, too, en de man dat's got it knows whah to look for de right man when I gits killed. Oh, bless yo' soul, if you puts yo' mother up for as big a fool as *you* is, you's pow'ful mistaken, I kin tell you! Now den, you set still en behave yo'self; en don't you git up ag'in till I tell you!"

Tom fretted and chafed awhile in a whirlwind of disorganizing sensations and emotions, and finally said, with something like settled conviction:

"The whole thing is moonshine; now then, go ahead and do your worst; I'm done with you."

Roxy made no answer. She took the lantern and started for the door. Tom was in a cold panic in a moment.

"Come back, come back!" he wailed. "I didn't mean it, Roxy; I take it all back, and I'll never say it again! Please come back, Roxy!"

The woman stood a moment, then she said gravely:

"Dat's one thing you's got to stop, Valet de Chambers. You can't call me *Roxy*, same as if you was my equal. Chillen don't speak to dey mammies like dat. You'll call me ma or mammy, dat's what you'll call me—leastways when de ain't nobody aroun'. *Say* it!"

It cost Tom a struggle, but he got it out.

"Dat's all right, don't you ever forgit it ag'in, if you knows what's good for you. Now den, you had said you wouldn't ever call it lies en moonshine ag'in. I'll tell you dis, for a warnin': if you ever does say it ag'in, it's de LAS' time you'll ever say it to me; I'll tramp as straight to de judge as I kin walk, en tell him who you is, en *prove* it. Does you b'lieve me when I says dat?"

"Oh," groaned Tom, "I more than believe it; I *know* it."

Roxy knew her conquest was complete. She could have proved nothing to anybody, and her threat of writings was a lie; but she knew the person she was dealing with, and had made both statements without any doubt as to the effect they would produce.

She went and sat down on her candle box, and the pride and pomp of her victorious attitude made it a throne. She said:

"Now den, Chambers, we's gwine to talk business, en dey ain't gwine to be no mo' foolishness. In de fust place, you gits fifty dollahs a month; you's gwine to han' over half of it to yo' ma. Plank it out!"

But Tom had only six dollars in the world. He gave her that, and promised to start fair on next month's pension.

"Chambers, how much is you in debt?"

Tom shuddered, and said:

"Nearly three hundred dollars."

"How is you gwine to pay it?"

Tom groaned out: "Oh, I don't know; don't ask me such awful questions."

But she stuck to her point until she wearied a confession out of him: he had been prowling about in disguise, stealing small valuables from private houses; in fact, he made a good deal of a raid on his fellow villagers a fortnight before, when he was supposed to be in St. Louis; but he doubted if he had sent away enough stuff to realize the required amount, and was afraid to make a further venture in the present excited state of the town. His mother approved of his conduct, and offered to help, but this frightened him. He tremblingly ventured to say that if she would retire from the town he should feel better and safer, and could hold his head higher—and was going on to make an argument, but she interrupted and surprised him pleasantly by saying she was ready; it didn't make any difference to her where she stayed, so that she got her share of the pension regularly. She said she would not go far, and would call at the haunted house once a month for her money. Then she said:

"I don't hate you so much now, but I've hated you a many a year—and anybody would. Didn't I change you off, en give you a good fambly en a good name, en made you a white gen'l'man en rich, wid store clothes on—en what did I git for it? You despised me all de time, en was al'ays sayin' mean hard things to me befo' folks, en wouldn't ever let me forgit I's a nigger—en—en—"

She fell to sobbing, and broke down. Tom said: "But you know I didn't know you were my mother; and besides—"

"Well, nemmine 'bout dat, now; let it go. I's gwine to fo'git it." Then she added fiercely, "En don't ever make me remember it ag'in, or you'll be sorry, *I* tell you."

When they were parting, Tom said, in the most persuasive way he could command:

"Ma, would you mind telling me who was my father?"

He had supposed he was asking an embarrassing question. He was mistaken. Roxy drew herself up with a proud toss of her head, and said:

"Does I mine tellin' you? No, dat I don't! You ain't got no 'casion to be shame' o' yo' father, *I* kin tell you. He wuz de highest quality in dis whole town—ole Virginny stock. Fust famblies, he wuz. Jes as good stock as de Driscolls en de Howards, de bes' day dey ever seed." She put on a little prouder air, if possible, and added impressively: "Does you 'member Cunnel Cecil Burleigh Essex, dat died de same year yo' young Marse Tom Driscoll's pappy died, en all de Masons en Odd Fellers en Churches turned out en give him de bigges' funeral dis town ever seed? Dat's de man."

Under the inspiration of her soaring complacency the departed graces of her earlier days returned to her, and her bearing took to itself a dignity and state that might have passed for queenly if her surroundings had been a little more in keeping with it.

"Dey ain't another nigger in dis town dat's as highbawn as you is. Now den, go 'long! En jes you hold yo' head up as high as you want to—you has de right, en dat I kin swah."

CHAPTER 10 — The Nymph Revealed

All say, "How hard it is that we have to die"—a strange complaint to come from the mouths of people who have had to live. —Pudd'nhead Wilson's Calendar

When angry, count four; when very angry, swear. — Pudd'nhead Wilson's Calendar

Every now and then, after Tom went to bed, he had sudden wakings out of his sleep, and his first thought was, "Oh, joy, it was all a dream!" Then he laid himself heavily down again, with a groan and the muttered words, "A nigger! I am a nigger! Oh, I wish I was dead!"

He woke at dawn with one more repetition of this horror, and then he resolved to meddle no more with that treacherous sleep. He began to think. Sufficiently bitter thinkings they were. They wandered along something after this fashion:

"Why were niggers *and* whites made? What crime did the uncreated first nigger commit that the curse of birth was decreed for him? And why is this awful difference made between white and black? . . . How hard the nigger's fate seems, this morning!—yet until last night such a thought never entered my head."

He sighed and groaned an hour or more away. Then "Chambers" came humbly in to say that breakfast was nearly ready. "Tom" blushed scarlet to see this aristocratic white youth cringe to him, a nigger, and call him "Young Marster." He said roughly:

"Get out of my sight!" and when the youth was gone, he muttered, "He has done me no harm, poor wretch, but he is an eyesore to me now, for he is Driscoll, the young gentleman, and I am a—oh, I wish I was dead!"

A gigantic eruption, like that of Krakatoa a few years ago, with the accompanying earthquakes, tidal waves, and clouds of volcanic dust, changes the face of the surrounding landscape beyond recognition, bringing down the high lands, elevating the low, making fair lakes where deserts had been, and deserts where green prairies had smiled before. The tremendous catastrophe which had befallen Tom had changed his moral landscape in much the same way. Some of his low places he found lifted to ideals, some of his ideas had sunk to the valleys, and lay there with the sackcloth and ashes of pumice stone and sulphur on their ruined heads.

For days he wandered in lonely places, thinking, thinking, thinking —trying to get his bearings. It was new work. If he met a friend, he found that the habit of a lifetime had in some mysterious way vanished —his arm hung limp, instead of involuntarily extending the hand for a shake. It was the "nigger" in him asserting its humility, and he blushed and was abashed. And the "nigger" in him was surprised when the white friend put out his hand for a shake with him. He found the "nigger" in him involuntarily giving the road, on the sidewalk, to a white rowdy and loafer. When Rowena, the dearest thing his heart knew, the idol of his secret worship, invited him in, the "nigger" in him made an embarrassed excuse and was afraid to enter and sit with the dread white folks on equal terms. The "nigger" in him went shrinking and skulking here and there and yonder, and fancying it saw suspicion and maybe detection in all faces, tones, and gestures. So strange and uncharacteristic was Tom's conduct that people noticed it, and turned to look after him when he passed on; and when he glanced back—as he could not help doing, in spite of his best resistance—and caught that puzzled expression in a person's face, it gave him a sick feeling, and he took himself out of view as quickly as he could. He presently came to have a hunted sense and a hunted look, and then he fled away to the hilltops and the solitudes. He said to himself that the curse of Ham was upon him.

He dreaded his meals; the "nigger" in him was ashamed to sit at the white folk's table, and feared discovery all the time; and once when Judge Driscoll said, "What's the matter with you? You look as meek as a nigger," he felt as secret murderers are said to feel when the accuser says, "Thou art the man!" Tom said he was not well, and left the table.

His ostensible "aunt's" solicitudes and endearments were

become a terror to him, and he avoided them.

And all the time, hatred of his ostensible "uncle" was steadily growing in his heart; for he said to himself, "He is white; and I am his chattel, his property, his goods, and he can sell me, just as he could his dog."

For as much as a week after this, Tom imagined that his character had undergone a pretty radical change. But that was because he did not know himself.

In several ways his opinions were totally changed, and would never go back to what they were before, but the main structure of his character was not changed, and could not be changed. One or two very important features of it were altered, and in time effects would result from this, if opportunity offered—effects of a quite serious nature, too. Under the influence of a great mental and moral upheaval, his character and his habits had taken on the appearance of complete change, but after a while with the subsidence of the storm, both began to settle toward their former places. He dropped gradually back into his old frivolous and easygoing ways and conditions of feeling and manner of speech, and no familiar of his could have detected anything in him that differentiated him from the weak and careless Tom of other days.

The theft raid which he had made upon the village turned out better than he had ventured to hope. It produced the sum necessary to pay his gaming debts, and saved him from exposure to his uncle and another smashing of the will. He and his mother learned to like each other fairly well. She couldn't love him, as yet, because there "warn't nothing to him," as she expressed it, but her nature needed something or somebody to rule over, and he was better than nothing. Her strong character and aggressive and commanding ways compelled Tom's admiration in spite of the fact that he got more illustrations of them than he needed for his comfort. However, as a rule her conversation was made up of racy tales about the privacies of the chief families of the town (for she went harvesting among their kitchens every time she came to the village), and Tom enjoyed this. It was just in his line. She always collected her half of his pension punctually, and he was always at the haunted house to have a chat with her on these occasions. Every now and then, she paid him a visit there on between-days also.

Occasions he would run up to St. Louis for a few weeks, and at last temptation caught him again. He won a lot of money, but lost it, and with it a deal more besides, which he promised to raise as soon as possible.

For this purpose he projected a new raid on his town. He never meddled with any other town, for he was afraid to venture into houses whose ins and outs he did not know and the habits of whose households he was not acquainted with. He arrived at the haunted house in disguise on the Wednesday before the advent of the twins—after writing his Aunt Pratt that he would not arrive until two days after—and laying in hiding there with his mother until toward daylight Friday morning, when he went to his uncle's house and entered by the back way with his own key, and slipped up to his room where he could have the use of the mirror and toilet articles. He had a suit of girl's clothes with him in a bundle as a disguise for his raid, and was wearing a suit of his mother's clothing, with black gloves and veil. By dawn he was tricked out for his raid, but he caught a glimpse of Pudd'nhead Wilson through the window over the way, and knew that Pudd'nhead had caught a glimpse of him. So he entertained Wilson with some airs and graces and

attitudes for a while, then stepped out of sight and resumed the other disguise, and by and by went down and out the back way and started downtown to reconnoiter the scene of his intended labors.

But he was ill at ease. He had changed back to Roxy's dress, with the stoop of age added to the disguise, so that Wilson would not bother himself about a humble old women leaving a neighbor's house by the back way in the early morning, in case he was still spying. But supposing Wilson had seen him leave, and had thought it suspicious, and had also followed him? The thought made Tom cold. He gave up the raid for the day, and hurried back to the haunted house by the obscurest route he knew. His mother was gone; but she came back, by and by, with the news of the grand reception at Patsy Cooper's, and soon persuaded him that the opportunity was like a special Providence, it was so inviting and perfect. So he went raiding, after all, and made a nice success of it while everybody was gone to Patsy Cooper's. Success gave him nerve and even actual intrepidity; insomuch, indeed, that after he had conveyed his harvest to his mother in a back alley, he went to the reception himself, and added several of the valuables of that house to his takings.

After this long digression we have now arrived once more at the point where Pudd'nhead Wilson, while waiting for the arrival of the twins on that same Friday evening, sat puzzling over the strange apparition of that morning—a girl in young Tom Driscoll's bedroom; fretting, and guessing, and puzzling over it, and wondering who the shameless creature might be.

CHAPTER 11 — Pudd'nhead's Thrilling Discovery

There are three infallible ways of pleasing an author, and the three form a rising scale of compliment: 1—to tell him you have read one of his books; 2—to tell him you have read all of his books; 3—to ask him to let you read the manuscript of his forthcoming book. No. 1 admits you to his respect; No. 2 admits you to his admiration; No. 3 carries you clear into his heart. —Pudd'nhead Wilson's Calendar

As to the Adjective: when in doubt, strike it out. —Pudd'nhead Wilson's Calendar

The twins arrived presently, and talk began. It flowed along chattily and sociably, and under its influence the new friendship gathered ease and strength. Wilson got out his Calendar, by request, and read a passage or two from it, which the twins praised quite cordially. This pleased the author so much that he complied gladly when they asked him to lend them a batch of the work to read at home. In the course of their wide travels, they had found out that there are three sure ways of pleasing an author; they were now working the best of the three.

There was an interruption now. Young Driscoll appeared, and joined the party. He pretended to be seeing the distinguished strangers for the first time when they rose to shake hands; but this was only a blind, as he had already had a glimpse of them, at the reception, while robbing the house. The twins made mental note that he was smooth-faced and rather handsome, and smooth and undulatory in his movements—graceful, in fact. Angelo thought he had a good eye; Luigi thought there was something veiled and sly about it. Angelo thought he had a pleasant free-and-easy way of talking; Luigi thought it was more so than was agreeable. Angelo thought he was a sufficiently nice young man; Luigi reserved his decision. Tom's first contribution to the conversation was a question which he had put to Wilson a hundred times before. It was always cheerily and good-natured put, and always inflicted a little pang, for it touched a secret sore; but this time the pang was sharp, since strangers were present.

"Well, how does the law come on? Had a case yet?"

Wilson bit his lip, but answered, "No—not yet," with as much indifference as he could assume. Judge Driscoll had generously left the law feature out of Wilson's biography which he had furnished to the twins. Young Tom laughed pleasantly, and said:

"Wilson's a lawyer, gentlemen, but he doesn't practice now."

The sarcasm bit, but Wilson kept himself under control, and said without passion:

"I don't practice, it is true. It is true that I have never had a case, and have had to earn a poor living for twenty years as an expert accountant in a town where I can't get a hold of a set of books to untangle as often as I should like. But it is also true that I did myself well for the practice of the law. By the time I was your age, Tom, I had chosen a profession, and was soon competent to enter upon it." Tom winced. "I never got a chance to try my hand at it, and I may never get a chance; and yet if I ever do get it, I shall be found ready, for I have kept up my law studies all these years."

"That's it; that's good grit! I like to see it. I've a notion to throw all my business your way. My business and your law practice ought to make a pretty gay team, Dave," and the young fellow laughed again.

"If you will throw—" Wilson had thought of the girl in Tom's bedroom, and was going to say, "If you will throw the surreptitious and disreputable part of your business my way, it may amount to something," but thought better of it and said,

"However, this matter doesn't fit well in a general conversation."

"All right, we'll change the subject; I guess you were about to give me another dig, anyway, so I'm willing to change. How's the Awful Mystery flourishing these days? Wilson's got a scheme for driving plain window glass panes out of the market by decorating it with greasy finger marks, and getting rich by selling it at famine prices to the crowned heads over in Europe to outfit their palaces with. Fetch it out, Dave."

Wilson brought three of his glass strips, and said:

"I get the subject to pass the fingers of his right hand through his hair, so as to get a little coating of the natural oil on them, and then press the balls of them on the glass. A fine and delicate print of the lines in the skin results, and is permanent, if it doesn't come in contact with something able to rub it off. You begin, Tom."

"Why, I think you took my finger marks once or twice before."

"Yes, but you were a little boy the last time, only about twelve years old."

"That's so. Of course, I've changed entirely since then, and variety is what the crowned heads want, I guess."

He passed his fingers through his crop of short hair, and

pressed them one at a time on the glass. Angelo made a print of his fingers on another glass, and Luigi followed with a third. Wilson marked the glasses with names and dates, and put them away. Tom gave one of his little laughs, and said:

"I thought I wouldn't say anything, but if variety is what you are after, you have wasted a piece of glass. The hand print of one twin is the same as the hand print of the fellow twin."

"Well, it's done now, and I like to have them both, anyway," said Wilson, returned to his place.

"But look here, Dave," said Tom, "you used to tell people's fortunes, too, when you took their finger marks. Dave's just an all-round genius—a genius of the first water, gentlemen; a great scientist running to seed here in this village, a prophet with the kind of honor that prophets generally get at home—for here they don't give shucks for his scientifics, and they call his skull a notion factory—hey, Dave, ain't it so? But never mind, he'll make his mark someday—finger mark, you know, he-he! But really, you want to let him take a shy at your palms once; it's worth twice the price of admission or your money's returned at the door. Why, he'll read your wrinkles as easy as a book, and not only tell you fifty or sixty things that's going to happen to you, but fifty or sixty thousand that ain't. Come, Dave, show the gentlemen what an inspired jack-at-all-science we've got in this town, and don't know it."

Wilson winced under this nagging and not very courteous chaff, and the twins suffered with him and for him. They rightly judged, now, that the best way to relieve him would be to take the thing in earnest and treat it with respect, ignoring Tom's rather overdone raillery; so Luigi said:

"We have seen something of palmistry in our wanderings, and know very well what astonishing things it can do. If it isn't a science, and one of the greatest of them too, I don't know what its other name ought to be. In the Orient—"

Tom looked surprised and incredulous. He said:

"That juggling a science? But really, you ain't serious, are you?"

"Yes, entirely so. Four years ago we had our hands read out to us as if our plans had been covered with print."

"Well, do you mean to say there was actually anything in it?" asked Tom, his incredulity beginning to weaken a little.

"There was this much in it," said Angelo: "what was told us of our characters was minutely exact—we could have not have bettered it ourselves. Next, two or three memorable things that have happened to us were laid bare—things which no one present but ourselves could have known about."

"Why, it's rank sorcery!" exclaimed Tom, who was now becoming very much interested. "And how did they make out with what was going to happen to you in the future?"

"On the whole, quite fairly," said Luigi. "Two or three of the most striking things foretold have happened since; much the most striking one of all happened within that same year. Some of the minor prophesies have come true; some of the minor and some of the major ones have not been fulfilled yet, and of course may never be: still, I should be more surprised if they failed to arrive than if they didn't."

Tom was entirely sobered, and profoundly impressed. He said, apologetically:

"Dave, I wasn't meaning to belittle that science; I was only chaffing —chattering, I reckon I'd better say. I wish you would look at their palms. Come, won't you?"

"Why certainly, if you want me to; but you know I've had no chance to become an expert, and don't claim to be one. When a past event is somewhat prominently recorded in the palm, I can generally detect that, but minor ones often escape me—not always, of course, but often—but I haven't much confidence in myself when it comes to reading the future. I am talking as if palmistry was a daily study with me, but that is not so. I haven't examined half a dozen hands in the last half dozen years; you see, the people got to joking about it, and I stopped to let the talk die down. I'll tell you what we'll do, Count Luigi: I'll make a try at your past, and if I have any success there—no, on the whole, I'll let the future alone; that's really the affair of an expert."

He took Luigi's hand. Tom said:

"Wait—don't look yet, Dave! Count Luigi, here's paper and pencil. Set down that thing that you said was the most striking one that was foretold to you, and happened less than a year afterward, and give it to me so I can see if Dave finds it in your hand."

Luigi wrote a line privately, and folded up the piece of paper, and handed it to Tom, saying:

"I'll tell you when to look at it, if he finds it."

Wilson began to study Luigi's palm, tracing life lines, heart lines, head lines, and so on, and noting carefully their relations with the cobweb of finer and more delicate marks and lines that enmeshed them on all sides; he felt of the fleshy cushion at the base of the thumb and noted its shape; he felt of the fleshy side of the hand between the wrist and the base of the little finger and noted its shape also; he painstakingly examined the fingers, observing their form, proportions, and natural manner of disposing themselves when in repose. All this process was watched by the three spectators with absorbing interest, their heads bent together over Luigi's palm, and nobody disturbing the stillness with a word. Wilson now entered upon a close survey of the palm again, and his revelations began.

He mapped out Luigi's character and disposition, his tastes, aversions, proclivities, ambitions, and eccentricities in a way which sometimes made Luigi wince and the others laugh, but both twins declared that the chart was artistically drawn and was correct.

Next, Wilson took up Luigi's history. He proceeded cautiously and with hesitation now, moving his finger slowly along the great lines of the palm, and now and then halting it at a "star" or some such landmark, and examining that neighborhood minutely. He proclaimed one or two past events, Luigi confirmed his correctness, and the search went on. Presently Wilson glanced up suddenly with a surprised expression.

"Here is a record of an incident which you would perhaps not wish me to—"

"Bring it out," said Luigi, good-naturedly. "I promise you sha'n't embarrass me."

But Wilson still hesitated, and did not seem quite to know what to do. Then he said:

"I think it is too delicate a matter to—to—I believe I would rather write it or whisper it to you, and let you decide for yourself whether you want it talked out or not."

"That will answer," said Luigi. "Write it."

Wilson wrote something on a slip of paper and handed it to Luigi, who read it to himself and said to Tom:

"Unfold your slip and read it, Mr. Driscoll."

Tom said:

"'It was prophesied that I would kill a man. It came true before the year was out.'"

Tom added, "Great Scott!"

Luigi handed Wilson's paper to Tom, and said:

"Now read this one."

Tom read:

"'You have killed someone, but whether man, woman, or child, I do not make out.'"

"Caesar's ghost!" commented Tom, with astonishment. "It beats anything that was ever heard of! Why, a man's own hand is his deadliest enemy! Just think of that—a man's own hand keeps a record of the deepest and fatalest secrets of his life, and is treacherously ready to expose himself to any black-magic stranger that comes along. But what do you let a person look at your hand for, with that awful thing printed on it?"

"Oh," said Luigi, reposefully, "I don't mind it. I killed the man for good reasons, and I don't regret it."

"What were the reasons?"

"Well, he needed killing."

"I'll tell you why he did it, since he won't say himself," said Angelo, warmly. "He did it to save my life, that's what he did it for. So it was a noble act, and not a thing to be hid in the dark."

"So it was, so it was," said Wilson. "To do such a thing to save a brother's life is a great and fine action."

"Now come," said Luigi, "it is very pleasant to hear you say these things, but for unselfishness, or heroism, or magnanimity, the circumstances won't stand scrutiny. You overlook one detail; suppose I hadn't saved Angelo's life, what would have become of mine? If I had let the man kill him, wouldn't he have killed me, too? I saved my own life, you see."

"Yes, that is your way of talking," said Angelo, "but I know you—I don't believe you thought of yourself at all. I keep that weapon yet that Luigi killed the man with, and I'll show it to you sometime. That incident makes it interesting, and it had a history before it came into Luigi's hands which adds to its interest. It was given to Luigi by a great Indian prince, the Gaikowar of Baroda, and it had been in his family two or three centuries. It killed a good many disagreeable people who troubled the hearthstone at one time or another. It isn't much too look at, except it isn't shaped like other knives, or dirks, or whatever it may be called—here, I'll draw it for you." He took a sheet of paper and made a rapid sketch. "There it is—a broad and murderous blade, with edges like a razor for sharpness. The devices engraved on it are the ciphers or names of its long line of possessors—I had Luigi's name added in Roman letters myself with our coat of arms, as you see. You notice what a curious handle the thing has. It is solid ivory, polished like a mirror, and is four or five inches long—round, and as thick as a large man's wrist, with the end squared off flat, for your thumb to rest on; for you grasp it, with your thumb resting on the blunt end—so—and lift it along and strike downward. The Gaikowar showed us how the thing was done when he gave it to Luigi, and before that night was ended, Luigi had used the knife, and the Gaikowar was a man short by reason of it. The sheath is magnificently ornamented with gems of great value. You will find a sheath more worth looking at than the knife itself, of course."

Tom said to himself:

"It's lucky I came here. I would have sold that knife for a song; I supposed the jewels were glass."

"But go on; don't stop," said Wilson. "Our curiosity is up now, to hear about the homicide. Tell us about that."

"Well, briefly, the knife was to blame for that, all around. A native servant slipped into our room in the palace in the night, to kill us and steal the knife on account of the fortune encrusted on its sheath, without a doubt. Luigi had it under his pillow; we were in bed together. There was a dim night-light burning. I was asleep, but Luigi was awake, and he thought he detected a vague form nearing the bed. He slipped the knife out of the sheath and was ready and unembarrassed by hampering bedclothes, for the weather was hot and we hadn't any. Suddenly that native rose at the bedside, and bent over me with his right hand lifted and a dirk in it aimed at my throat; but Luigi grabbed his wrist, pulled him downward, and drove his own knife into the man's neck. That is the whole story."

Wilson and Tom drew deep breaths, and after some general chat about the tragedy, Pudd'nhead said, taking Tom's hand:

"Now, Tom, I've never had a look at your palms, as it happens; perhaps you've got some little questionable privacies that need—hel-lo!"

Tom had snatched away his hand, and was looking a good deal confused.

"Why, he's blushing!" said Luigi.

Tom darted an ugly look at him, and said sharply:

"Well, if I am, it ain't because I'm a murderer!" Luigi's dark face flushed, but before he could speak or move, Tom added with anxious haste: "Oh, I beg a thousand pardons. I didn't mean that; it was out before I thought, and I'm very, very sorry—you must forgive me!"

Wilson came to the rescue, and smoothed things down as well as he could; and in fact was entirely successful as far as the twins were concerned, for they felt sorrier for the affront put upon him by his guest's outburst of ill manners than for the

insult offered to Luigi. But the success was not so pronounced with the offender. Tom tried to seem at his ease, and he went through the motions fairly well, but at bottom he felt resentful toward all the three witnesses of his exhibition; in fact, he felt so annoyed at them for having witnessed it and noticed it that he almost forgot to feel annoyed at himself for placing it before them. However, something presently happened which made him almost comfortable, and brought him nearly back to a state of charity and friendliness. This was a little spat between the twins; not much of a spat, but still a spat; and before they got far with it, they were in a decided condition of irritation while pretending to be actuated by more respectable motives. By his help the fire got warmed up to the blazing point, and he might have had the happiness of seeing the flames show up in another moment, but for the interruption of a knock on the door—an interruption which fretted him as much as it gratified Wilson. Wilson opened the door.

The visitor was a good-natured, ignorant, energetic middle-aged Irishman named John Buckstone, who was a great politician in a small way, and always took a large share in public matters of every sort. One of the town's chief excitements, just now, was over the matter of rum. There was a strong rum party and a strong anti-rum party. Buckstone was training with the rum party, and he had been sent to hunt up the twins and invite them to attend a mass meeting of that faction. He delivered his errand, and said the clans were already gathering in the big hall over the market house. Luigi accepted the invitation cordially. Angelo less cordially, since he disliked crowds, and did not drink the powerful intoxicants of America. In fact, he was even a teetotaler sometimes —when it was judicious to be one.

The twins left with Buckstone, and Tom Driscoll joined the company with them uninvited.

In the distance, one could see a long wavering line of torches drifting down the main street, and could hear the throbbing of the bass drum, the clash of cymbals, the squeaking of a fife or two, and the faint roar of remote hurrahs. The tail end of this procession was climbing the market house stairs when the twins arrived in its neighborhood; when they reached the hall, it was full of people, torches, smoke, noise, and enthusiasm. They were conducted to the platform by Buckstone—Tom Driscoll still following—and were delivered to the chairman in the midst of a prodigious explosion of welcome. When the noise had moderated a little, the chair proposed that "our illustrious guests be at once elected, by complimentary acclamation, to membership in our ever-glorious organization, the paradise of the free and the perdition of the slave."

This eloquent discharge opened the floodgates of enthusiasm again, and the election was carried with thundering unanimity. Then arose a storm of cries:

"Wet them down! Wet them down! Give them a drink!"

Glasses of whisky were handed to the twins. Luigi waves his aloft, then brought it to his lips; but Angelo set his down. There was another storm of cries.

"What's the matter with the other one?" "What is the blond one going back on us for?" "Explain! Explain!"

The chairman inquired, and then reported:

"We have made an unfortunate mistake, gentlemen. I find that the Count Angelo Capello is opposed to our creed—is a teetotaler, in fact, and was not intending to apply for membership with us. He desires that we reconsider the vote by which he was elected. What is the pleasure of the house?"

There was a general burst of laughter, plentifully accented with whistlings and catcalls, but the energetic use of the gavel presently restored something like order. Then a man spoke from the crowd, and said that while he was very sorry that the mistake had been made, it would not be possible to rectify it at the present meeting. According to the bylaws, it must go over to the next regular meeting for action. He would not offer a motion, as none was required. He desired to apologize to the gentlemen in the name of the house, and begged to assure him that as far as it might lie in the power of the Sons of Liberty, his temporary membership in the order would be made pleasant to him.

This speech was received with great applause, mixed with cries of:

"That's the talk!" "He's a good fellow, anyway, if he *is* a teetotaler!" "Drink his health!" "Give him a rouser, and no heeltaps!"

Glasses were handed around, and everybody on the platform drank Angelo's health, while the house bellowed forth in song:

For he's a jolly good fel-low, For he's a jolly good fel-low, For he's a jolly good fe-el-low, Which nobody can deny.

Tom Driscoll drank. It was his second glass, for he had drunk Angelo's the moment that Angelo had set it down. The two drinks made him very merry—almost idiotically so, and he began to take a most lively and prominent part in the proceedings, particularly in the music and catcalls and side remarks.

The chairman was still standing at the front, the twins at his side. The extraordinarily close resemblance of the brothers to each other suggested a witticism to Tom Driscoll, and just as the chairman began a speech he skipped forward and said, with an air of tipsy confidence, to the audience:

"Boys, I move that he keeps still and lets this human philopena snip you out a speech."

The descriptive aptness of the phrase caught the house, and a mighty burst of laughter followed.

Luigi's southern blood leaped to the boiling point in a moment under the sharp humiliation of this insult delivered in the presence of four hundred strangers. It was not in the young man's nature to let the matter pass, or to delay the squaring of the account. He took a couple of strides and halted behind the unsuspecting joker. Then he drew back and delivered a kick of such titanic vigor that it lifted Tom clear over the footlights and landed him on the heads of the front row of the Sons of Liberty.

Even a sober person does not like to have a human being emptied on him when he is not going any harm; a person who is not sober cannot endure such an attention at all. The nest of Sons of Liberty that Driscoll landed in had not a sober bird in it; in fact there was probably not an entirely sober one in the auditorium. Driscoll was promptly and indignantly flung on the heads of Sons in the next row, and these Sons passed him on toward the rear, and then immediately began to pummel the front row Sons who had passed him to them. This course

was strictly followed by bench after bench as Driscoll traveled in his tumultuous and airy flight toward the door; so he left behind him an ever-lengthening wake of raging and plunging and fighting and swearing humanity. Down went group after group of torches, and presently above the deafening clatter of the gavel, roar of angry voices, and crash of succumbing benches, rose the paralyzing cry of "*fire!*"

The fighting ceased instantly; the cursing ceased; for one distinctly defined moment, there was a dead hush, a motionless calm, where the tempest had been; then with one impulse the multitude awoke to life and energy again, and went surging and struggling and swaying, this way and that, its outer edges melting away through windows and doors and gradually lessening the pressure and relieving the mass.

The fireboys were never on hand so suddenly before; for there was no distance to go this time, their quarters being in the rear end of the market house, There was an engine company and a hook-and-ladder company. Half of each was composed of rummies and the other half of anti-rummies, after the moral and political share-and-share-alike fashion of the frontier town of the period. Enough anti-rummies were loafing in quarters to man the engine and the ladders. In two minutes they had their red shirts and helmets on—they never stirred officially in unofficial costume—and as the mass meeting overhead smashed through the long row of windows and poured out upon the roof of the arcade, the deliverers were ready for them with a powerful stream of water, which washed some of them off the roof and nearly drowned the rest. But water was preferable to fire, and still the stampede from the windows continued, and still the pitiless drenching assailed it until the building was empty; then the fireboys mounted to the hall and flooded it with water enough to annihilate forty times as much fire as there was there; for a village fire company does not often get a chance to show off, and so when it does get a chance, it makes the most of it. Such citizens of that village as were of a thoughtful and judicious temperament did not insure against fire; they insured against the fire company.

CHAPTER 12 — The Shame of Judge Driscoll

Courage is resistance to fear, mastery of fear—not absence of fear. Except a creature be part coward, it is not a compliment to say it is brave; it is merely a loose misapplication of the word. Consider the flea!—incomparably the bravest of all the creatures of God, if ignorance of fear were courage. Whether you are asleep or awake he will attack you, caring nothing for the fact that in bulk and strength you are to him as are the massed armies of the earth to a sucking child; he lives both day and night and all days and nights in the very lap of peril and the immediate presence of death, and yet is no more afraid than is the man who walks the streets of a city that was threatened by an earthquake ten centuries before. When we speak of Clive, Nelson, and Putnam as men who "didn't know what fear was," we ought always to add the flea—and put him at the head of the procession. —Pudd'nhead Wilson's Calendar

Judge Driscoll was in bed and asleep by ten o'clock on Friday night, and he was up and gone a-fishing before daylight in the morning with his friend Pembroke Howard. These two had been boys together in Virginia when that state still ranked as the chief and most imposing member of the Union, and they still coupled the proud and affectionate adjective "old" with her name when they spoke of her. In Missouri a recognized superiority attached to any person who hailed from Old Virginia; and this superiority was exalted to supremacy when a person of such nativity could also prove descent from the First Families of that great commonwealth. The Howards and Driscolls were of this aristocracy. In their eyes, it was a nobility. It had its unwritten laws, and they were as clearly defined and as strict as any that could be found among the printed statues of the land. The F.F.V. was born a gentleman; his highest duty in life was to watch over that great inheritance and keep it unsmirched. He must keep his honor spotless. Those laws were his chart; his course was marked out on it; if he swerved from it by so much as half a point of the compass, it meant shipwreck to his honor; that is to say, degradation from his rank as a gentleman. These laws required certain things of him which his religion might forbid: then his religion must yield—the laws could not be relaxed to accommodate religions or anything else. Honor stood first; and the laws defined what it was and wherein it differed in certain details from honor as defined by church creeds and by the social laws and customs of some of the minor divisions of the globe that had got crowded out when the sacred boundaries of Virginia were staked out.

If Judge Driscoll was the recognized first citizen of Dawson's Landing, Pembroke Howard was easily its recognized second citizen. He was called "the great lawyer"—an earned title. He and Driscoll were of the same age—a year or two past sixty.

Although Driscoll was a freethinker and Howard a strong and determined Presbyterian, their warm intimacy suffered no impairment in consequence. They were men whose opinions were their own property and not subject to revision and amendment, suggestion or criticism, by anybody, even their friends.

The day's fishing finished, they came floating downstream in their skiff, talking national politics and other high matters, and presently met a skiff coming up from town, with a man in it who said:

"I reckon you know one of the new twins gave your nephew a kicking last night, Judge?"

"Did WHAT?"

"Gave him a kicking."

The old judge's lips paled, and his eyes began to flame. He choked with anger for a moment, then he got out what he was trying to say:

"Well—well—go on! Give me the details!"

The man did it. At the finish the judge was silent a minute, turning over in his mind the shameful picture of Tom's flight over the footlights; then he said, as if musing aloud,

"H'm—I don't understand it. I was asleep at home. He didn't wake me. Thought he was competent to manage his affair without my help, I reckon." His face lit up with pride and pleasure at that thought, and he said with a cheery complacency, "I like that—it's the true old blood—hey, Pembroke?"

Howard smiled an iron smile, and nodded his head approvingly. Then the news-bringer spoke again.

"But Tom beat the twin on the trial."

The judge looked at the man wonderingly, and said:

"The trial? What trial?"

"Why, Tom had him up before Judge Robinson for assault and battery."

The old man shrank suddenly together like one who has received a death stroke. Howard sprang for him as he sank forward in a swoon, and took him in his arms, and bedded him on his back in the boat. He sprinkled water in his face, and said to the startled visitor:

"Go, now—don't let him come to and find you here. You see what an effect your heedless speech has had; you ought to have been more considerate than to blurt out such a cruel piece of slander as that."

"I'm right down sorry I did it now, Mr. Howard, and I wouldn't have done it if I had thought; but it ain't slander; it's perfectly true, just as I told him."

He rowed away. Presently the old judge came out of his faint and looked up piteously into the sympathetic face that was bent over him.

"Say it ain't true, Pembroke; tell me it ain't true!" he said in a weak voice.

There was nothing weak in the deep organ tones that responded:

"You know it's a lie as well as I do, old friend. He is of the best blood of the Old Dominion."

"God bless you for saying it!" said the old gentleman, fervently. "Ah, Pembroke, it was such a blow!"

Howard stayed by his friend, and saw him home, and entered the house with him. It was dark, and past supper-time, but the judge was not thinking of supper; he was eager to hear the slander refuted from headquarters, and as eager to have Howard hear it, too. Tom was sent for, and he came immediately. He was bruised and lame, and was not a happy-looking object. His uncle made him sit down, and said:

"We have been hearing about your adventure, Tom, with a handsome lie added for embellishment. Now pulverize that lie to dust! What measures have you taken? How does the thing stand?"

Tom answered guilelessly: "It don't stand at all; it's all over. I had him up in court and beat him. Pudd'nhead Wilson defended him—first case he ever had, and lost it. The judge fined the miserable hound five dollars for the assault."

Howard and the judge sprang to their feet with the opening sentence —why, neither knew; then they stood gazing vacantly at each other. Howard stood a moment, then sat mournfully down without saying anything. The judge's wrath began to kindle, and he burst out:

"You cur! You scum! You vermin! Do you mean to tell me that blood of my race has suffered a blow and crawled to a court of law about it? Answer me!"

Tom's head drooped, and he answered with an eloquent silence. His uncle stared at him with a mixed expression of amazement and shame and incredulity that was sorrowful to see. At last he said:

"Which of the twins was it?"

"Count Luigi."

"You have challenged him?"

"N—no," hesitated Tom, turning pale.

"You will challenge him tonight. Howard will carry it."

Tom began to turn sick, and to show it. He turned his hat round and round in his hand, his uncle glowering blacker and blacker upon him as the heavy seconds drifted by; then at last he began to stammer, and said piteously:

"Oh, please, don't ask me to do it, uncle! He is a murderous devil—I never could—I—I'm afraid of him!"

Old Driscoll's mouth opened and closed three times before he could get it to perform its office; then he stormed out:

"A coward in my family! A Driscoll a coward! Oh, what have I done to deserve this infamy!" He tottered to his secretary in the corner, repeated that lament again and again in heartbreaking tones, and got out of a drawer a paper, which he slowly tore to bits, scattering the bits absently in his track as he walked up and down the room, still grieving and lamenting. At last he said:

"There it is, shreds and fragments once more—my will. Once more you have forced me to disinherit you, you base son of a most noble father! Leave my sight! Go—before I spit on you!"

The young man did not tarry. Then the judge turned to Howard:

"You will be my second, old friend?"

"Of course."

"There is pen and paper. Draft the cartel, and lose no time."

"The Count shall have it in his hands in fifteen minutes," said Howard.

Tom was very heavyhearted. His appetite was gone with his property and his self-respect. He went out the back way and wandered down the obscure lane grieving, and wondering if any course of future conduct, however discreet and carefully perfected and watched over, could win back his uncle's favor and persuade him to reconstruct once more that generous will which had gone to ruin before his eyes. He finally concluded that it could. He said to himself that he had accomplished this sort of triumph once already, and that what had been done once could be done again. He would set about it. He would bend every energy to the task, and he would score that triumph once more, cost what it might to his convenience, limit as it might his frivolous and liberty-loving life.

"To begin," he says to himself, "I'll square up with the proceeds of my raid, and then gambling has got to be stopped—and stopped short off. It's the worst vice I've got—from my standpoint, anyway, because it's the one he can most easily find out, through the impatience of my creditors. He thought it expensive to have to pay two hundred dollars to them for me once. Expensive—*that!* Why, it cost me the whole

of his fortune—but, of course, he never thought of that; some people can't think of any but their own side of a case. If he had known how deep I am in now, the will would have gone to pot without waiting for a duel to help. Three hundred dollars! It's a pile! But he'll never hear of it, I'm thankful to say. The minute I've cleared it off, I'm safe; and I'll never touch a card again. Anyway, I won't while he lives, I make oath to that. I'm entering on my last reform—I know it—yes, and I'll win; but after that, if I ever slip again I'm gone."

CHAPTER 13 — Tom Stares at Ruin

When I reflect upon the number of disagreeable people who I know have gone to a better world, I am moved to lead a different life. —Pudd'nhead Wilson's Calendar

October. This is one of the peculiarly dangerous months to speculate in stocks in. The others are July, January, September, April, November, May, March, June, December, August, and February. —Pudd'nhead Wilson's Calendar

Thus mournfully communing with himself, Tom moped along the lane past Pudd'nhead Wilson's house, and still on and on between fences enclosing vacant country on each hand till he neared the haunted house, then he came moping back again, with many sighs and heavy with trouble. He sorely wanted cheerful company. Rowena! His heart gave a bound at the thought, but the next thought quieted it—the detested twins would be there.

He was on the inhabited side of Wilson's house, and now as he approached it, he noticed that the sitting room was lighted. This would do; others made him feel unwelcome sometimes, but Wilson never failed in courtesy toward him, and a kindly courtesy does at least save one's feelings, even if it is not professing to stand for a welcome. Wilson heard footsteps at his threshold, then the clearing of a throat.

"It's that fickle-tempered, dissipated young goose—poor devil, he find friends pretty scarce today, likely, after the disgrace of carrying a personal assault case into a law-court."

A dejected knock. "Come in!"

Tom entered, and dropped into a chair, without saying anything. Wilson said kindly:

"Why, my boy, you look desolate. Don't take it so hard. Try and forget you have been kicked."

"Oh, dear," said Tom, wretchedly, "it's not that, Pudd'nhead—it's not that. It's a thousand times worse than that—oh, yes, a million times worse."

"Why, Tom, what do you mean? Has Rowena—"

"Flung me? *No*, but the old man has."

Wilson said to himself, "Aha!" and thought of the mysterious girl in the bedroom. "The Driscolls have been making discoveries!" Then he said aloud, gravely:

"Tom, there are some kinds of dissipation which—"

"Oh, shucks, this hasn't got anything to do with dissipation. He wanted me to challenge that derned Italian savage, and I wouldn't do it."

"Yes, of course he would do that," said Wilson in a meditative matter-of-course way, "but the thing that puzzled me was, why he didn't look to that last night, for one thing, and why he let you carry such a matter into a court of law at all, either before the duel or after it. It's no place for it. It was not like him. I couldn't understand it. How did it happen?"

"It happened because he didn't know anything about it. He was asleep when I got home last night."

"And you didn't wake him? Tom, is that possible?"

Tom was not getting much comfort here. He fidgeted a moment, then said:

"I didn't choose to tell him—that's all. He was going a-fishing before dawn, with Pembroke Howard, and if I got the twins into the common calaboose—and I thought sure I could—I never dreamed of their slipping out on a paltry fine for such an outrageous offense—well, once in the calaboose they would be disgraced, and uncle wouldn't want any duels with that sort of characters, and wouldn't allow any.

"Tom, I am ashamed of you! I don't see how you could treat your good old uncle so. I am a better friend of his than you are; for if I had known the circumstances I would have kept that case out of court until I got word to him and let him have the gentleman's chance."

"You would?" exclaimed Tom, with lively surprise. "And it your first case! And you know perfectly well there never would have been any case if he had got that chance, don't you? And you'd have finished your days a pauper nobody, instead of being an actually launched and recognized lawyer today. And you would really have done that, would you?"

"Certainly."

Tom looked at him a moment or two, then shook his head sorrowfully and said:

"I believe you—upon my word I do. I don't know why I do, but I do. Pudd'nhead Wilson, I think you're the biggest fool I ever saw."

"Thank you."

"Don't mention it."

"Well, he has been requiring you to fight the Italian, and you have refused. You degenerate remnant of an honorable line! I'm thoroughly ashamed of you, Tom!"

"Oh, that's nothing! I don't care for anything, now that the will's torn up again."

"Tom, tell me squarely—didn't he find any fault with you for anything but those two things—carrying the case into court and refusing to fight?"

He watched the young fellow's face narrowly, but it was entirely reposeful, and so also was the voice that answered:

"No, he didn't find any other fault with me. If he had had any to find, he would have begun yesterday, for he was just in the humor for it. He drove that jack-pair around town and showed them the sights, and when he came home he couldn't find his father's old silver watch that don't keep time and he thinks so

much of, and couldn't remember what he did with it three or four days ago when he saw it last, and when I suggested that it probably wasn't lost but stolen, it put him in a regular passion, and he said I was a fool—which convinced me, without any trouble, that that was just what he was afraid *had* happened, himself, but did not want to believe it, because lost things stand a better chance of being found again than stolen ones."

"Whe-ew!" whistled Wilson. "Score another one the list."

"Another what?"

"Another theft!"

"Theft?"

"Yes, theft. That watch isn't lost, it's stolen. There's been another raid on the town—and just the same old mysterious sort of thing that has happened once before, as you remember."

"You don't mean it!"

"It's as sure as you are born! Have you missed anything yourself?"

"No. That is, I did miss a silver pencil case that Aunt Mary Pratt gave me last birthday—"

"You'll find it stolen—that's what you'll find."

"No, I sha'n't; for when I suggested theft about the watch and got such a rap, I went and examined my room, and the pencil case was missing, but it was only mislaid, and I found it again."

"You are sure you missed nothing else?"

"Well, nothing of consequence. I missed a small plain gold ring worth two or three dollars, but that will turn up. I'll look again."

"In my opinion you'll not find it. There's been a raid, I tell you. Come *in!*"

Mr. Justice Robinson entered, followed by Buckstone and the town constable, Jim Blake. They sat down, and after some wandering and aimless weather-conversation Wilson said:

"By the way, We've just added another to the list of thefts, maybe two. Judge Driscoll's old silver watch is gone, and Tom here has missed a gold ring."

"Well, it is a bad business," said the justice, "and gets worse the further it goes. The Hankses, the Dobsons, the Pilligrews, the Ortons, the Grangers, the Hales, the Fullers, the Holcombs, in fact everybody that lives around about Patsy Cooper's had been robbed of little things like trinkets and teaspoons and suchlike small valuables that are easily carried off. It's perfectly plain that the thief took advantage of the reception at Patsy Cooper's when all the neighbors were in her house and all their niggers hanging around her fence for a look at the show, to raid the vacant houses undisturbed. Patsy is miserable about it; miserable on account of the neighbors, and particularly miserable on account of her foreigners, of course; so miserable on their account that she hasn't any room to worry about her own little losses."

The Tragedy Of Pudd'nhead Wilson 419

"It's the same old raider," said Wilson. "I suppose there isn't any doubt about that."

"Constable Blake doesn't think so."

"No, you're wrong there," said Blake. "The other times it was a man; there was plenty of signs of that, as we know, in the profession, thought we never got hands on him; but this time it's a woman."

Wilson thought of the mysterious girl straight off. She was always in his mind now. But she failed him again. Blake continued:

"She's a stoop-shouldered old woman with a covered basket on her arm, in a black veil, dressed in mourning. I saw her going aboard the ferryboat yesterday. Lives in Illinois, I reckon; but I don't care where she lives, I'm going to get her—she can make herself sure of that."

"What makes you think she's the thief?"

"Well, there ain't any other, for one thing; and for another, some nigger draymen that happened to be driving along saw her coming out of or going into houses, and told me so—and it just happens that they was *robbed*, every time."

It was granted that this was plenty good enough circumstantial evidence. A pensive silence followed, which lasted some moments, then Wilson said:

"There's one good thing, anyway. She can't either pawn or sell Count Luigi's costly Indian dagger."

"My!" said Tom. "Is *that* gone?"

"Yes."

"Well, that was a haul! But why can't she pawn it or sell it?"

"Because when the twins went home from the Sons of Liberty meeting last night, news of the raid was sifting in from everywhere, and Aunt Patsy was in distress to know if they had lost anything. They found that the dagger was gone, and they notified the police and pawnbrokers everywhere. It was a great haul, yes, but the old woman won't get anything out of it, because she'll get caught."

"Did they offer a reward?" asked Buckstone.

"Yes, five hundred dollars for the knife, and five hundred more for the thief."

"What a leather-headed idea!" exclaimed the constable. "The thief das'n't go near them, nor send anybody. Whoever goes is going to get himself nabbed, for their ain't any pawnbroker that's going to lose the chance to—"

If anybody had noticed Tom's face at that time, the gray-green color of it might have provoked curiosity; but nobody did. He said to himself: "I'm gone! I never can square up; the rest of the plunder won't pawn or sell for half of the bill. Oh, I know it—I'm gone, I'm gone—and this time it's for good. Oh, this is awful—I don't know what to do, nor which way to turn!"

"Softly, softly," said Wilson to Blake. "I planned their scheme for them at midnight last night, and it was all finished up shipshape by two this morning. They'll get their dagger back,

and then I'll explain to you how the thing was done."

There were strong signs of a general curiosity, and Buckstone said:

"Well, you have whetted us up pretty sharp. Wilson, and I'm free to say that if you don't mind telling us in confidence—"

"Oh, I'd as soon tell as not, Buckstone, but as long as the twins and I agreed to say nothing about it, we must let it stand so. But you can take my word for it, you won't be kept waiting three days. Somebody will apply for that reward pretty promptly, and I'll show you the thief and the dagger both very soon afterward."

The constable was disappointed, and also perplexed. He said:

"It may all be—yes, and I hope it will, but I'm blamed if I can see my way through it. It's too many for yours truly."

The subject seemed about talked out. Nobody seemed to have anything further to offer. After a silence the justice of the peace informed Wilson that he and Buckstone and the constable had come as a committee, on the part of the Democratic party, to ask him to run for mayor—for the little town was about to become a city and the first charter election was approaching. It was the first attention which Wilson had ever received at the hands of any party; it was a sufficiently humble one, but it was a recognition of his debut into the town's life and activities at last; it was a step upward, and he was deeply gratified. He accepted, and the committee departed, followed by young Tom.

CHAPTER 14 — Roxana Insists Upon Reform

The true Southern watermelon is a boon apart, and not to be mentioned with commoner things. It is chief of this world's luxuries, king by the grace of God over all the fruits of the earth. When one has tasted it, he knows what the angels eat. It was not a Southern watermelon that Eve took: we know it because she repented. —Pudd'nhead Wilson's Calendar

About the time that Wilson was bowing the committee out, Pembroke Howard was entering the next house to report. He found the old judge sitting grim and straight in his chair, waiting.

"Well, Howard—the news?"

"The best in the world."

"Accepts, does he?" and the light of battle gleamed joyously in the Judge's eye.

"Accepts? Why he jumped at it."

"Did, did he? Now that's fine—that's very fine. I like that. When is it to be?"

"Now! Straight off! Tonight! An admirable fellow—admirable!"

"Admirable? He's a darling! Why, it's an honor as well as a pleasure to stand up before such a man. Come—off with you! Go and arrange everything—and give him my heartiest compliments. A rare fellow, indeed; an admirable fellow, as you have said!"

"I'll have him in the vacant stretch between Wilson's and the haunted house within the hour, and I'll bring my own pistols."

Judge Driscoll began to walk the floor in a state of pleased excitement; but presently he stopped, and began to think—began to think of Tom. Twice he moved toward the secretary, and twice he turned away again; but finally he said:

"This may be my last night in the world—I must not take the chance. He is worthless and unworthy, but it is largely my fault. He was entrusted to me by my brother on his dying bed, and I have indulged him to his hurt, instead of training him up severely, and making a man of him, I have violated my trust, and I must not add the sin of desertion to that. I have forgiven him once already, and would subject him to a long and hard trial before forgiving him again, if I could live; but I must not run that risk. No, I must restore the will. But if I survive the duel, I will hide it away, and he will not know, and I will not tell him until he reforms, and I see that his reformation is going to be permanent."

He redrew the will, and his ostensible nephew was heir to a fortune again. As he was finishing his task, Tom, wearied with another brooding tramp, entered the house and went tiptoeing past the sitting room door. He glanced in, and hurried on, for the sight of his uncle was nothing but terrors for him tonight. But his uncle was writing! That was unusual at this late hour. What could he be writing? A chill of anxiety settled down upon Tom's heart. Did that writing concern him? He was afraid so. He reflected that when ill luck begins, it does not come in sprinkles, but in showers. He said he would get a glimpse of that document or know the reason why. He heard someone coming, and stepped out of sight and hearing. It was Pembroke Howard. What could be hatching?

Howard said, with great satisfaction:

"Everything's right and ready. He's gone to the battleground with his second and the surgeon—also with his brother. I've arranged it all with Wilson—Wilson's his second. We are to have three shots apiece."

"Good! How is the moon?"

"Bright as day, nearly. Perfect, for the distance—fifteen yards. No wind—not a breath; hot and still."

"All good; all first-rate. Here, Pembroke, read this, and witness it."

Pembroke read and witnessed the will, then gave the old man's hand a hearty shake and said:

"Now that's right, York—but I knew you would do it. You couldn't leave that poor chap to fight along without means or profession, with certain defeat before him, and I knew you wouldn't, for his father's sake if not for his own."

"For his dead father's sake, I couldn't, I know; for poor Percy—but you know what Percy was to me. But mind—Tom is not to know of this unless I fall tonight."

"I understand. I'll keep the secret."

The judge put the will away, and the two started for the battleground. In another minute the will was in Tom's hands. His misery vanished, his feelings underwent a tremendous revulsion. He put the will carefully back in its place, and spread his mouth and swung his hat once, twice, three times

around his head, in imitation of three rousing huzzahs, no sound issuing from his lips. He fell to communing with himself excitedly and joyously, but every now and then he let off another volley of dumb hurrahs.

He said to himself: "I've got the fortune again, but I'll not let on that I know about it. And this time I'm gong to hang on to it. I take no more risks. I'll gamble no more, I'll drink no more, because—well, because I'll not go where there is any of that sort of thing going on, again. It's the sure way, and the only sure way; I might have thought of that sooner—well, yes, if I had wanted to. But now—dear me, I've had a scare this time, and I'll take no more chances. Not a single chance more. Land! I persuaded myself this evening that I could fetch him around without any great amount of effort, but I've been getting more and more heavyhearted and doubtful straight along, ever since. If he tells me about this thing, all right; but if he doesn't, I sha'n't let on. I—well, I'd like to tell Pudd'nhead Wilson, but—no, I'll think about that; perhaps I won't." He whirled off another dead huzzah, and said, "I'm reformed, and this time I'll stay so, sure!"

He was about to close with a final grand silent demonstration, when he suddenly recollected that Wilson had put it out of his power to pawn or sell the Indian knife, and that he was once more in awful peril of exposure by his creditors for that reason. His joy collapsed utterly, and he turned away and moped toward the door moaning and lamenting over the bitterness of his luck. He dragged himself upstairs, and brooded in his room a long time, disconsolate and forlorn, with Luigi's Indian knife for a text. At last he sighed and said:

"When I supposed these stones were glass and this ivory bone, the thing hadn't any interest for me because it hadn't any value, and couldn't help me out of my trouble. But now—why, now it is full of interest; yes, and of a sort to break a body's heart. It's a bag of gold that has turned to dirt and ashes in my hands. It could save me, and save me so easily, and yet I've got to go to ruin. It's like drowning with a life preserver in my reach. All the hard luck comes to me, and all the good luck goes to other people—Pudd'nhead Wilson, for instance; even his career has got a sort of a little start at last, and what has he done to deserve it, I should like to know? Yes, he has opened his own road, but he isn't content with that, but must block mine. It's a sordid, selfish world, and I wish I was out of it." He allowed the light of the candle to play upon the jewels of the sheath, but the flashings and sparklings had no charm for his eye; they were only just so many pangs to his heart. "I must not say anything to Roxy about this thing," he said. "She is too daring. She would be for digging these stones out and selling them, and then—why, she would be arrested and the stones traced, and then—" The thought made him quake, and he hid the knife away, trembling all over and glancing furtively about, like a criminal who fancies that the accuser is already at hand.

Should he try to sleep? Oh, no, sleep was not for him; his trouble was too haunting, too afflicting for that. He must have somebody to mourn with. He would carry his despair to Roxy.

He had heard several distant gunshots, but that sort of thing was not uncommon, and they had made no impression upon him. He went out at the back door, and turned westward. He passed Wilson's house and proceeded along the lane, and presently saw several figures approaching Wilson's place through the vacant lots. These were the duelists returning from the fight; he thought he recognized them, but as he had no desire for white people's company, he stooped down behind the fence until they were out of his way.

Roxy was feeling fine. She said:

"Whah was you, child? Warn't you in it?"

"In what?"

"In de duel."

"Duel? Has there been a duel?"

"Co'se dey has. De ole Jedge has be'n havin' a duel wid one o' dem twins."

"Great Scott!" Then he added to himself: "That's what made him remake the will; he thought he might get killed, and it softened him toward me. And that's what he and Howard were so busy about. . . . Oh dear, if the twin had only killed him, I should be out of my—"

"What is you mumblin' 'bout, Chambers? Whah was you? Didn't you know dey was gwine to be a duel?"

"No, I didn't. The old man tried to get me to fight one with Count Luigi, but he didn't succeed, so I reckon he concluded to patch up the family honor himself."

He laughed at the idea, and went rambling on with a detailed account of his talk with the judge, and how shocked and ashamed the judge was to find that he had a coward in his family. He glanced up at last, and got a shock himself. Roxana's bosom was heaving with suppressed passion, and she was glowering down upon him with measureless contempt written in her face.

"En you refuse' to fight a man dat kicked you, 'stid o' jumpin' at de chance! En you ain't got no mo' feelin' den to come en tell me, dat fetched sich a po' lowdown ornery rabbit into de worl'! Pah! it make me sick! It's de nigger in you, dat's what it is. Thirty-one parts o' you is white, en on'y one part nigger, en dat po' little one part is yo' *soul*. 'Tain't wuth savin'; 'tain't wuth totin' out on a shovel en throwin' en de gutter. You has disgraced yo' birth. What would yo' pa think o' you? It's enough to make him turn in his grave."

The last three sentences stung Tom into a fury, and he said to himself that if his father were only alive and in reach of assassination his mother would soon find that he had a very clear notion of the size of his indebtedness to that man, and was willing to pay it up in full, and would do it too, even at risk of his life; but he kept this thought to himself; that was safest in his mother's present state.

"Whatever has come o' yo' Essex blood? Dat's what I can't understan'. En it ain't on'y jist Essex blood dat's in you, not by a long sight—'deed it ain't! My great-great-great-gran'father en yo' great-great-great-great-gran'father was Ole Cap'n John Smith, de highest blood dat Ole Virginny ever turned out, en *his* great-great-gran'mother, or somers along back dah, was Pocahontas de Injun queen, en her husbun' was a nigger king outen Africa—en yit here you is, a slinkin' outen a duel en disgracin' our whole line like a ornery lowdown hound! Yes, it's de nigger in you!"

She sat down on her candle box and fell into a reverie. Tom did not disturb her; he sometimes lacked prudence, but it was not in circumstances of this kind, Roxana's storm went gradually down, but it died hard, and even when it seemed to

be quite gone, it would now and then break out in a distant rumble, so to speak, in the form of muttered ejaculations. One of these was, "Ain't nigger enough in him to show in his fingernails, en dat takes mighty little—yit dey's enough to pain his soul."

Presently she muttered. "Yassir, enough to paint a whole thimbleful of 'em." At last her ramblings ceased altogether, and her countenance began to clear—a welcome sight to Tom, who had learned her moods, and knew she was on the threshold of good humor now. He noticed that from time to time she unconsciously carried her finger to the end of her nose. He looked closer and said:

"Why, Mammy, the end of your nose is skinned. How did that come?"

She sent out the sort of wholehearted peal of laughter which God had vouchsafed in its perfection to none but the happy angels in heaven and the bruised and broken black slave on the earth, and said:

"Dad fetch dat duel, I be'n in it myself."

"Gracious! did a bullet to that?"

"Yassir, you bet it did!"

"Well, I declare! Why, how did that happen?"

"Happened dis-away. I 'uz a-sett'n' here kinder dozin' in de dark, en *che-bang!* goes a gun, right out dah. I skips along out towards t'other end o' de house to see what's gwine on, en stops by de ole winder on de side towards Pudd'nhead Wilson's house dat ain't got no sash in it—but dey ain't none of 'em got any sashes, for as dat's concerned—en I stood dah in de dark en look out, en dar in the moonlight, right down under me 'uz one o' de twins a-cussin'—not much, but jist a-cussin' soft—it 'uz de brown one dat 'uz cussin', 'ca'se he 'uz hit in de shoulder. En Doctor Claypool he 'uz a-workin' at him, en Pudd'nhead Wilson he 'uz a-he'pin', en ole Jedge Driscoll en Pem Howard 'uz a-standin' out yonder a little piece waitin' for 'em to get ready agin. En treckly dey squared off en give de word, en *bang-bang* went de pistols, en de twin he say, 'Ouch!'—hit him on de han' dis time—en I hear dat same bullet go *spat!* ag'in de logs under de winder; en de nex' time dey shoot, de twin say, 'Ouch!' ag'in, en I done it too, 'ca'se de bullet glance' on his cheekbone en skip up here en glance' on de side o' de winder en whiz right acrost my face en tuck de hide off'n my nose—why, if I'd 'a' be'n jist a inch or a inch en a half furder 't would 'a' tuck de whole nose en disfiggered me. Here's de bullet; I hunted her up."

"Did you stand there all the time?"

"Dat's a question to ask, ain't it! What else would I do? Does I git a chance to see a duel every day?"

"Why, you were right in range! Weren't you afraid?"

The woman gave a sniff of scorn.

"'Fraid! De Smith-Pocahontases ain't 'fraid o' nothin', let alone bullets."

"They've got pluck enough, I suppose; what they lack is judgment. *I* wouldn't have stood there."

"Nobody's accusin' you!"

"Did anybody else get hurt?"

"Yes, we all got hit 'cep' de blon' twin en de doctor en de seconds. De Jedge didn't git hurt, but I hear Pudd'nhead say de bullet snip some o' his ha'r off."

"'George!' said Tom to himself, "to come so near being out of my trouble, and miss it by an inch. Oh dear, dear, he will live to find me out and sell me to some nigger trader yet—yes, and he would do it in a minute." Then he said aloud, in a grave tone:

"Mother, we are in an awful fix."

Roxana caught her breath with a spasm, and said:

"Chile! What you hit a body so sudden for, like dat? What's be'n en gone en happen'?"

"Well, there's one thing I didn't tell you. When I wouldn't fight, he tore up the will again, and—"

Roxana's face turned a dead white, and she said:

"Now you's done!—done forever! Dat's de end. Bofe un us is gwine to starve to—"

"Wait and hear me through, can't you! I reckon that when he resolved to fight, himself, he thought he might get killed and not have a chance to forgive me any more in this life, so he made the will again, and I've seen it, and it's all right. But—"

"Oh, thank goodness, den we's safe ag'in!—safe! en so what did you want to come here en talk sich dreadful—"

"Hold ON, I tell you, and let me finish. The swag I gathered won't half square me up, and the first thing we know, my creditors—well, you know what'll happen."

Roxana dropped her chin, and told her son to leave her alone—she must think this matter out. Presently she said impressively:

"You got to go mighty keerful now, I tell you! En here's what you got to do. He didn't git killed, en if you gives him de least reason, he'll bust de will ag'in, en dat's de *las'* time, now you hear me! So—you's got to show him what you kin do in de nex' few days. You got to be pison good, en let him see it; you got to do everything dat'll make him b'lieve in you, en you got to sweeten aroun' ole Aunt Pratt, too—she's pow'ful strong with de Jedge, en de bes' frien' you got. Nex', you'll go 'long away to Sent Louis, en dat'll *keep* him in yo' favor. Den you go en make a bargain wid dem people. You tell 'em he ain't gwine to live long—en dat's de fac', too—en tell 'em you'll pay 'em intrust, en big intrust, too—ten per—what you call it?"

"Ten percent a month?"

"Dat's it. Den you take and sell yo' truck aroun', a little at a time, en pay de intrust. How long will it las'?"

"I think there's enough to pay the interest five or six months." "Den you's all right. If he don't die in six months, dat don't make no diff'rence—Providence'll provide. You's gwine to be safe—if you behaves." She bent an austere eye on him and added, "En you IS gwine to behave—does you know dat?"

He laughed and said he was going to try, anyway. She did not unbend. She said gravely:

"Tryin' ain't de thing. You's gwine to *do* it. You ain't gwine to steal a pin—'ca'se it ain't safe no mo'; en you ain't gwine into no bad comp'ny—not even once, you understand; en you ain't gwine to drink a drop—nary a single drop; en you ain't gwine to gamble one single gamble—not one! Dis ain't what you's gwine to try to do, it's what you's gwine to DO. En I'll tell you how I knows it. Dis is how. I's gwine to foller along to Sent Louis my own self; en you's gwine to come to me every day o' your life, en I'll look you over; en if you fails in one single one o' dem things—jist *one*—I take my oath I'll come straight down to dis town en tell de Jedge you's a nigger en a slave—en *prove* it!" She paused to let her words sink home. Then she added, "Chambers, does you b'lieve me when I says dat?"

Tom was sober enough now. There was no levity in his voice when he answered:

"Yes, Mother, I know, now, that I am reformed—and permanently. Permanently—and beyond the reach of any human temptation."

"Den g'long home en begin!"

CHAPTER 15 — The Robber Robbed

Nothing so needs reforming as other people's habits. — Pudd'nhead Wilson's Calendar

Behold, the fool saith, "Put not all thine eggs in the one basket" —which is but a manner of saying, "Scatter your money and your attention"; but the wise man saith, "Put all your eggs in the one basket and—WATCH THAT BASKET!" — Pudd'nhead Wilson's Calendar

What a time of it Dawson's Landing was having! All its life it had been asleep, but now it hardly got a chance for a nod, so swiftly did big events and crashing surprises come along in one another's wake: Friday morning, first glimpse of Real Nobility, also grand reception at Aunt Patsy Cooper's, also great robber raid; Friday evening, dramatic kicking of the heir of the chief citizen in presence of four hundred people; Saturday morning, emergence as practicing lawyer of the long-submerged Pudd'nhead Wilson; Saturday night, duel between chief citizen and titled stranger.

The people took more pride in the duel than in all the other events put together, perhaps. It was a glory to their town to have such a thing happen there. In their eyes the principals had reached the summit of human honor. Everybody paid homage to their names; their praises were in all mouths. Even the duelists' subordinates came in for a handsome share of the public approbation: wherefore Pudd'nhead Wilson was suddenly become a man of consequence. When asked to run for the mayoralty Saturday night, he was risking defeat, but Sunday morning found him a made man and his success assured.

The twins were prodigiously great now; the town took them to its bosom with enthusiasm. Day after day, and night after night, they went dining and visiting from house to house, making friends, enlarging and solidifying their popularity, and charming and surprising all with their musical prodigies, and now and then heightening the effects with samples of what they could do in other directions, out of their stock of rare and curious accomplishments. They were so pleased that they gave the regulation thirty days' notice, the required preparation for citizenship, and resolved to finish their days in this pleasant place. That was the climax. The delighted community rose as one man and applauded; and when the twins were asked to stand for seats in the forthcoming aldermanic board, and consented, the public contentment was rounded and complete.

Tom Driscoll was not happy over these things; they sunk deep, and hurt all the way down. He hated the one twin for kicking him, and the other one for being the kicker's brother.

Now and then the people wondered why nothing was heard of the raider, or of the stolen knife or the other plunder, but nobody was able to throw any light on that matter. Nearly a week had drifted by, and still the thing remained a vexed mystery.

On Sunday Constable Blake and Pudd'nhead Wilson met on the street, and Tom Driscoll joined them in time to open their conversation for them. He said to Blake: "You are not looking well, Blake; you seem to be annoyed about something. Has anything gone wrong in the detective business? I believe you fairly and justifiably claim to have a pretty good reputation in that line, isn't it so?"—which made Blake feel good, and look it; but Tom added, "for a country detective"—which made Blake feel the other way, and not only look it, but betray it in his voice.

"Yes, sir, I *have* got a reputation; and it's as good as anybody's in the profession, too, country or no country."

"Oh, I beg pardon; I didn't mean any offense. What I started out to ask was only about the old woman that raided the town—the stoop-shouldered old woman, you know, that you said you were going to catch; and I knew you would, too, because you have the reputation of never boasting, and—well, you—you've caught the old woman?"

"Damn the old woman!"

"Why, sho! you don't mean to say you haven't caught her?"

"No, I haven't caught her. If anybody could have caught her, I could; but nobody couldn't, I don't care who he is."

"I am sorry, real sorry—for your sake; because, when it gets around that a detective has expressed himself confidently, and then—"

"Don't you worry, that's all—don't you worry; and as for the town, the town needn't worry either. She's my meat—make yourself easy about that. I'm on her track; I've got clues that—"

"That's good! Now if you could get an old veteran detective down from St. Louis to help you find out what the clues mean, and where they lead to, and then—"

"I'm plenty veteran enough myself, and I don't need anybody's help. I'll have her inside of a we—inside of a month. That I'll swear to!"

Tom said carelessly:

"I suppose that will answer—yes, that will answer. But I reckon she is pretty old, and old people don't often outlive the cautious pace of the professional detective when he has got his clues together and is out on his still-hunt."

Blake's dull face flushed under this gibe, but before he could set his retort in order Tom had turned to Wilson, and was saying, with placid indifference of manner and voice:

"Who got the reward, Pudd'nhead?"

Wilson winced slightly, and saw that his own turn was come.

"What reward?"

"Why, the reward for the thief, and the other one for the knife."

Wilson answered—and rather uncomfortably, to judge by his hesitating fashion of delivering himself:

"Well, the—well, in face, nobody has claimed it yet."

Tom seemed surprised.

"Why, is that so?"

Wilson showed a trifle of irritation when he replied:

"Yes, it's so. And what of it?"

"Oh, nothing. Only I thought you had struck out a new idea, and invented a scheme that was going to revolutionize the timeworn and ineffectual methods of the—" He stopped, and turned to Blake, who was happy now that another had taken his place on the gridiron. "Blake, didn't you understand him to intimate that it wouldn't be necessary for you to hunt the old woman down?"

"'B'George, he said he'd have thief and swag both inside of three days —he did, by hokey! and that's just about a week ago. Why, I said at the time that no thief and no thief's pal was going to try to pawn or sell a thing where he knowed the pawnbroker could get both rewards by taking HIM into camp *with* the swag. It was the blessedest idea that ever I struck!"

"You'd change your mind," said Wilson, with irritated bluntness, "if you knew the entire scheme instead of only part of it."

"Well," said the constable, pensively, "I had the idea that it wouldn't work, and up to now I'm right anyway."

"Very well, then, let it stand at that, and give it a further show. It has worked at least as well as your own methods, you perceive."

The constable hadn't anything handy to hit back with, so he discharged a discontented sniff, and said nothing.

After the night that Wilson had partly revealed his scheme at his house, Tom had tried for several days to guess out the secret of the rest of it, but had failed. Then it occurred to him to give Roxana's smarter head a chance at it. He made up a supposititious case, and laid it before her. She thought it over, and delivered her verdict upon it. Tom said to himself, "She's hit it, sure!" He thought he would test that verdict now, and watch Wilson's face; so he said reflectively:

"Wilson, you're not a fool—a fact of recent discovery. Whatever your scheme was, it had sense in it, Blake's opinion to the contrary notwithstanding. I don't ask you to reveal it, but I will suppose a case—a case which you will answer as a starting point for the real thing I am going to come at, and that's all I want. You offered five hundred dollars for the knife, and five hundred for the thief. We will suppose, for argument's sake, that the first reward is *advertised* and the second offered by *private letter* to pawnbrokers and—"

Blake slapped his thigh, and cried out:

"By Jackson, he's got you, Pudd'nhead! Now why couldn't I or *any* fool have thought of that?"

Wilson said to himself, "Anybody with a reasonably good head would have thought of it. I am not surprised that Blake didn't detect it; I am only surprised that Tom did. There is more to him than I supposed." He said nothing aloud, and Tom went on:

"Very well. The thief would not suspect that there was a trap, and he would bring or send the knife, and say he bought it for a song, or found it in the road, or something like that, and try to collect the reward, and be arrested—wouldn't he?"

"Yes," said Wilson.

"I think so," said Tom. "There can't be any doubt of it. Have you ever seen that knife?"

"No."

"Has any friend of yours?"

"Not that I know of."

"Well, I begin to think I understand why your scheme failed."

"What do you mean, Tom? What are you driving at?" asked Wilson, with a dawning sense of discomfort.

"Why, that there *isn't* any such knife."

"Look here, Wilson," said Blake, "Tom Driscoll's right, for a thousand dollars—if I had it."

Wilson's blood warmed a little, and he wondered if he had been played upon by those strangers; it certainly had something of that look. But what could they gain by it? He threw out that suggestion. Tom replied:

"Gain? Oh, nothing that you would value, maybe. But they are strangers making their way in a new community. Is it nothing to them to appear as pets of an Oriental prince—at no expense? Is it nothing to them to be able to dazzle this poor town with thousand-dollar rewards—at no expense? Wilson, there isn't any such knife, or your scheme would have fetched it to light. Or if there is any such knife, they've got it yet. I believe, myself, that they've seen such a knife, for Angelo pictured it out with his pencil too swiftly and handily for him to have been inventing it, and of course I can't swear that they've never had it; but this I'll go bail for—if they had it when they came to this town, they've got it yet."

Blake said:

"It looks mighty reasonable, the way Tom puts it; it most certainly does."

Tom responded, turning to leave:

"You find the old woman, Blake, and if she can't furnish the knife, go and search the twins!"

Tom sauntered away. Wilson felt a good deal depressed. He hardly knew what to think. He was loath to withdraw his faith from the twins, and was resolved not to do it on the present indecisive evidence; but—well, he would think, and then decide how to act.

"Blake, what do you think of this matter?"

"Well, Pudd'nhead, I'm bound to say I put it up the way Tom does. They hadn't the knife; or if they had it, they've got it yet."

The men parted. Wilson said to himself:

"I believe they had it; if it had been stolen, the scheme would have restored it, that is certain. And so I believe they've got it."

Tom had no purpose in his mind when he encountered those two men. When he began his talk he hoped to be able to gall them a little and get a trifle of malicious entertainment out of it. But when he left, he left in great spirits, for he perceived that just by pure luck and no troublesome labor he had accomplished several delightful things: he had touched both men on a raw spot and seen them squirm; he had modified Wilson's sweetness for the twins with one small bitter taste that he wouldn't be able to get out of his mouth right away; and, best of all, he had taken the hated twins down a peg with the community; for Blake would gossip around freely, after the manner of detectives, and within a week the town would be laughing at them in its sleeve for offering a gaudy reward for a bauble which they either never possessed or hadn't lost. Tom was very well satisfied with himself.

Tom's behavior at home had been perfect during the entire week. His uncle and aunt had seen nothing like it before. They could find no fault with him anywhere.

Saturday evening he said to the Judge:

"I've had something preying on my mind, uncle, and as I am going away, and might never see you again, I can't bear it any longer. I made you believe I was afraid to fight that Italian adventurer. I had to get out of it on some pretext or other, and maybe I chose badly, being taken unawares, but no honorable person could consent to meet him in the field, knowing what I knew about him."

"Indeed? What was that?"

"Count Luigi is a confessed assassin."

"Incredible."

"It's perfectly true. Wilson detected it in his hand, by palmistry, and charged him with it, and cornered him up so close that he had to confess; but both twins begged us on their knees to keep the secret, and swore they would lead straight lives here; and it was all so pitiful that we gave our word of honor never to expose them while they kept the promise. You would have done it yourself, uncle."

"You are right, my boy; I would. A man's secret is still his own property, and sacred, when it has been surprised out of him like that. You did well, and I am proud of you." Then he added mournfully, "But I wish I could have been saved the shame of meeting an assassin on the field on honor."

"It couldn't be helped, uncle. If I had known you were going to challenge him, I should have felt obliged to sacrifice my pledged word in order to stop it, but Wilson couldn't be expected to do otherwise than keep silent."

"Oh, no, Wilson did right, and is in no way to blame. Tom, Tom, you have lifted a heavy load from my heart; I was stung to the very soul when I seemed to have discovered that I had a coward in my family."

"You may imagine what it cost ME to assume such a part, uncle."

"Oh, I know it, poor boy, I know it. And I can understand how much it has cost you to remain under that unjust stigma to this time. But it is all right now, and no harm is done. You have restored my comfort of mind, and with it your own; and both of us had suffered enough."

The old man sat awhile plunged in thought; then he looked up with a satisfied light in his eye, and said: "That this assassin should have put the affront upon me of letting me meet him on the field of honor as if he were a gentleman is a matter which I will presently settle—but not now. I will not shoot him until after election. I see a way to ruin them both before; I will attend to that first. Neither of them shall be elected, that I promise. You are sure that the fact that he is an assassin has not got abroad?"

"Perfectly certain of it, sir."

"It will be a good card. I will fling a hint at it from the stump on the polling day. It will sweep the ground from under both of them."

"There's not a doubt of it. It will finish them."

"That and outside work among the voters will, to a certainty. I want you to come down here by and by and work privately among the rag-tag and bobtail. You shall spend money among them; I will furnish it."

Another point scored against the detested twins! Really it was a great day for Tom. He was encouraged to chance a parting shot, now, at the same target, and did it.

"You know that wonderful Indian knife that the twins have been making such a to-do about? Well, there's no track or trace of it yet; so the town is beginning to sneer and gossip and laugh. Half the people believe they never had any such knife, the other half believe they had it and have got it still. I've heard twenty people talking like that today."

Yes, Tom's blemishless week had restored him to the favor of his aunt and uncle.

His mother was satisfied with him, too. Privately, she believed she was coming to love him, but she did not say so. She told him to go along to St. Louis now, and she would get ready and follow. Then she smashed her whisky bottle and said:

"Dah now! I's a-gwine to make you walk as straight as a string, Chambers, en so I's bown, you ain't gwine to git no bad example out o' yo' mammy. I tole you you couldn't go into no bad comp'ny. Well, you's gwine into my comp'ny, en I's gwine to fill de bill. Now, den, trot along, trot along!"

Tom went aboard one of the big transient boats that night with his heavy satchel of miscellaneous plunder, and slept the sleep of the unjust, which is serener and sounder than the other kind, as we know by the hanging-eve history of a million rascals. But when he got up in the morning, luck was against him again: a brother thief had robbed him while he slept, and gone ashore at some intermediate landing.

CHAPTER 16 — Sold Down the River

If you pick up a starving dog and make him prosperous, he will not bite you. This is the principal difference between a dog and a man. —Pudd'nhead Wilson's Calendar

We all know about the habits of the ant, we know all about the habits of the bee, but we know nothing at all about the habits of the oyster. It seems almost certain that we have been choosing the wrong time for studying the oyster. — Pudd'nhead Wilson's Calendar

When Roxana arrived, she found her son in such despair and misery that her heart was touched and her motherhood rose up strong in her. He was ruined past hope now; his destruction would be immediate and sure, and he would be an outcast and friendless. That was reason enough for a mother to love a child; so she loved him, and told him so. It made him wince, secretly—for she was a "nigger." That he was one himself was far from reconciling him to that despised race.

Roxana poured out endearments upon him, to which he responded uncomfortably, but as well as he could. And she tried to comfort him, but that was not possible. These intimacies quickly became horrible to him, and within the hour he began to try to get up courage enough to tell her so, and require that they be discontinued or very considerably modified. But he was afraid of her; and besides, there came a lull now, for she had begun to think. She was trying to invent a saving plan. Finally she started up, and said she had found a way out. Tom was almost suffocated by the joy of this sudden good news. Roxana said:

"Here is de plan, en she'll win, sure. I's a nigger, en nobody ain't gwine to doubt it dat hears me talk. I's wuth six hund'd dollahs. Take en sell me, en pay off dese gamblers."

Tom was dazed. He was not sure he had heard aright. He was dumb for a moment; then he said:

"Do you mean that you would be sold into slavery to save me?"

"Ain't you my chile? En does you know anything dat a mother won't do for her chile? Day ain't nothin' a white mother won't do for her chile. Who made 'em so? De Lord done it. En who made de niggers? De Lord made 'em. In de inside, mothers is all de same. De good lord he made 'em so. I's gwine to be sole into slavery, en in a year you's gwine to buy yo' ole mammy free ag'in. I'll show you how. Dat's de plan."

Tom's hopes began to rise, and his spirits along with them. He said:

"It's lovely of you, Mammy—it's just—"

"Say it ag'in! En keep on sayin' it! It's all de pay a body kin want in dis worl', en it's mo' den enough. Laws bless you, honey, when I's slav' aroun', en dey 'buses me, if I knows you's a-sayin' dat, 'way off yonder somers, it'll heal up all de sore places, en I kin stan' 'em."

"I DO say it again, Mammy, and I'll keep on saying it, too. But how am I going to sell you? You're free, you know."

"Much diff'rence dat make! White folks ain't partic'lar. De law kin sell me now if dey tell me to leave de state in six months en I don't go. You draw up a paper—bill o' sale—en put it 'way off yonder, down in de middle o' Kaintuck somers, en sign some names to it, en say you'll sell me cheap 'ca'se you's hard up; you'll find you ain't gwine to have no trouble. You take me up de country a piece, en sell me on a farm; dem people ain't gwine to ask no questions if I's a bargain."

Tom forged a bill of sale and sold his mother to an Arkansas cotton planter for a trifle over six hundred dollars. He did not want to commit this treachery, but luck threw the man in his way, and this saved him the necessity of going up-country to hunt up a purchaser, with the added risk of having to answer a lot of questions, whereas this planter was so pleased with Roxy that he asked next to none at all. Besides, the planter insisted that Roxy wouldn't know where she was, at first, and that by the time she found out she would already have been contented.

So Tom argued with himself that it was an immense advantaged for Roxy to have a master who was pleased with her, as this planter manifestly was. In almost no time his flowing reasonings carried him to the point of even half believing he was doing Roxy a splendid surreptitious service in selling her "down the river." And then he kept diligently saying to himself all the time: "It's for only a year. In a year I buy her free again; she'll keep that in mind, and it'll reconcile her." Yes; the little deception could do no harm, and everything would come out right and pleasant in the end, anyway. By agreement, the conversation in Roxy's presence was all about the man's "up-country" farm, and how pleasant a place it was, and how happy the slaves were there; so poor Roxy was entirely deceived; and easily, for she was not dreaming that her own son could be guilty of treason to a mother who, in voluntarily going into slavery—slavery of any kind, mild or severe, or of any duration, brief or long—was making a sacrifice for him compared with which death would have been a poor and commonplace one. She lavished tears and loving caresses upon him privately, and then went away with her owner —went away brokenhearted, and yet proud to do it.

Tom scored his accounts, and resolved to keep to the very letter of his reform, and never to put that will in jeopardy again. He had three hundred dollars left. According to his mother's plan, he was to put that safely away, and add her half of his pension to it monthly. In one year this fund would buy her free again.

For a whole week he was not able to sleep well, so much the villainy which he had played upon his trusting mother preyed upon his rag of conscience; but after that he began to get comfortable again, and was presently able to sleep like any other miscreant.

The boat bore Roxy away from St. Louis at four in the afternoon, and she stood on the lower guard abaft the paddle box and watched Tom through a blur of tears until he melted into the throng of people and disappeared; then she looked no more, but sat there on a coil of cable crying till far into the night. When she went to her foul steerage bunk at last, between the clashing engines, it was not to sleep, but only to wait for the morning, and, waiting, grieve.

It had been imagined that she "would not know," and would think she was traveling upstream. She! Why, she had been steamboating for years. At dawn she got up and went listlessly and sat down on the cable coil again. She passed many a snag whose "break" could have told her a thing to break her heart, for it showed a current moving in the same direction that the boat was going; but her thoughts were elsewhere, and she did not notice. But at last the roar of a bigger and nearer break than usual brought her out of her torpor, and she looked up, and her practiced eye fell upon that telltale rush of water. For one moment her petrified gaze fixed itself there. Then her head dropped upon her breast, and she said:

"Oh, de good Lord God have mercy on po' sinful me—I'S SOLE DOWN DE RIVER!"

CHAPTER 17 — The Judge Utters Dire Prophesy

Even popularity can be overdone. In Rome, along at first, you are full of regrets that Michelangelo died; but by and by, you only regret that you didn't see him do it. — Pudd'nhead Wilson's Calendar

JULY 4. Statistics show that we lose more fools on this day than in all the other days of the year put together. This proves, by the number left in stock, that one Fourth of July per year is now inadequate, the country has grown so. — Pudd'nhead Wilson's Calendar

The summer weeks dragged by, and then the political campaign opened —opened in pretty warm fashion, and waxed hotter and hotter daily. The twins threw themselves into it with their whole heart, for their self-love was engaged. Their popularity, so general at first, had suffered afterward; mainly because they had been TOO popular, and so a natural reaction had followed. Besides, it had been diligently whispered around that it was curious—indeed, VERY curious—that that wonderful knife of theirs did not turn up—IF it was so valuable, or IF it had ever existed. And with the whisperings went chucklings and nudgings and winks, and such things have an effect. The twins considered that success in the election would reinstate them, and that defeat would work them irreparable damage. Therefore they worked hard, but not harder than Judge Driscoll and Tom worked against them in the closing days of the canvass. Tom's conduct had remained so letter-perfect during two whole months now, that his uncle not only trusted him with money with which to persuade voters, but trusted him to go and get it himself out of the safe in the private sitting room.

The closing speech of the campaign was made by Judge Driscoll, and he made it against both of the foreigners. It was disastrously effective. He poured out rivers of ridicule upon them, and forced the big mass meeting to laugh and applaud. He scoffed at them as adventures, mountebanks, sideshow riffraff, dime museum freaks; he assailed their showy titles with measureless derision; he said they were back-alley barbers disguised as nobilities, peanut peddlers masquerading as gentlemen, organ-grinders bereft of their brother monkey. At last he stopped and stood still. He waited until the place had become absolutely silent and expectant, then he delivered his deadliest shot; delivered it with ice-cold seriousness and deliberation, with a significant emphasis upon the closing words: he said he believed that the reward offered for the lost knife was humbug and bunkum, and that its owner would know where to find it whenever he should have occasion TO ASSASSINATE SOMEBODY.

Then he stepped from the stand, leaving a startled and impressive hush behind him instead of the customary explosion of cheers and party cries.

The strange remark flew far and wide over the town and made an extraordinary sensation. Everybody was asking, "What could he mean by that?" And everybody went on asking that question, but in vain; for the judge only said he knew what he was talking about, and stopped there; Tom said he hadn't any idea what his uncle meant, and Wilson, whenever he was asked what he thought it meant, parried the question by asking the questioner what HE thought it meant.

Wilson was elected, the twins were defeated—crushed, in fact, and left forlorn and substantially friendless. Tom went back to St. Louis happy.

Dawson's Landing had a week of repose now, and it needed it. But it was in an expectant state, for the air was full of rumors of a new duel. Judge Driscoll's election labors had prostrated him, but it was said that as soon as he was well enough to entertain a challenge he would get one from Count Luigi.

The brothers withdrew entirely from society, and nursed their humiliation in privacy. They avoided the people, and went out for exercise only late at night, when the streets were deserted.

CHAPTER 18 — Roxana Commands

Gratitude and treachery are merely the two extremities of the same procession. You have seen all of it that is worth staying for when the band and the gaudy officials have gone by. —Pudd'nhead Wilson's Calendar

THANKSGIVING DAY. Let us all give humble, hearty, and sincere thanks now, but the turkeys. In the island of Fiji they do not use turkeys; they use plumbers. It does not become you and me to sneer at Fiji. —Pudd'nhead Wilson's Calendar

The Friday after the election was a rainy one in St. Louis. It rained all day long, and rained hard, apparently trying its best to wash that soot-blackened town white, but of course not succeeding. Toward midnight Tom Driscoll arrived at his lodgings from the theater in the heavy downpour, and closed his umbrella and let himself in; but when he would have shut the door, he found that there was another person entering—doubtless another lodger; this person closed the door and tramped upstairs behind Tom. Tom found his door in the dark, and entered it, and turned up the gas. When he faced about, lightly whistling, he saw the back of a man. The man was closing and locking his door from him. His whistle faded out and he felt uneasy. The man turned around, a wreck of shabby old clothes, sodden with rain and all a-drip, and showed a black face under an old slouch hat. Tom was frightened. He tried to order the man out, but the words refused to come, and the other man got the start. He said, in a low voice:

"Keep still—I's yo' mother!"

Tom sunk in a heap on a chair, and gasped out:

"It was mean of me, and base—I know it; but I meant it for the best, I did indeed—I can swear it."

Roxana stood awhile looking mutely down on him while he writhed in shame and went on incoherently babbling self-

accusations mixed with pitiful attempts at explanation and palliation of his crime; then she seated herself and took off her hat, and her unkept masses of long brown hair tumbled down about her shoulders.

"It warn't no fault o' yo'n dat dat ain't gray," she said sadly, noticing the hair.

"I know it, I know it! I'm a scoundrel. But I swear I meant it for the best. It was a mistake, of course, but I thought it was for the best, I truly did."

Roxana began to cry softly, and presently words began to find their way out between her sobs. They were uttered lamentingly, rather than angrily.

"Sell a pusson down de river—DOWN DE RIVER!—for de bes'! I wouldn't treat a dog so! I is all broke down en wore out now, en so I reckon it ain't in me to storm aroun' no mo', like I used to when I 'uz trompled on en 'bused. I don't know—but maybe it's so. Leastways, I's suffered so much dat mournin' seem to come mo' handy to me now den stormin'."

These words should have touched Tom Driscoll, but if they did, that effect was obliterated by a stronger one—one which removed the heavy weight of fear which lay upon him, and gave his crushed spirit a most grateful rebound, and filled all his small soul with a deep sense of relief. But he kept prudently still, and ventured no comment. There was a voiceless interval of some duration now, in which no sounds were heard but the beating of the rain upon the panes, the sighing and complaining of the winds, and now and then a muffled sob from Roxana. The sobs became more and more infrequent, and at last ceased. Then the refugee began to talk again.

"Shet down dat light a little. More. More yit. A pusson dat is hunted don't like de light. Dah—dat'll do. I kin see whah you is, en dat's enough. I's gwine to tell you de tale, en cut it jes as short as I kin, en den I'll tell you what you's got to do. Dat man dat bought me ain't a bad man; he's good enough, as planters goes; en if he could 'a' had his way I'd 'a' be'n a house servant in his fambly en be'n comfortable: but his wife she was a Yank, en not right down good lookin', en she riz up agin me straight off; so den dey sent me out to de quarter 'mongst de common fiel' han's. Dat woman warn't satisfied even wid dat, but she worked up de overseer ag'in' me, she 'uz dat jealous en hateful; so de overseer he had me out befo' day in de mawnin's en worked me de whole long day as long as dey'uz any light to see by; en many's de lashin's I got 'ca'se I couldn't come up to de work o' de stronges'. Dat overseer wuz a Yank too, outen New Englan', en anybody down South kin tell you what dat mean. DEY knows how to work a nigger to death, en dey knows how to whale 'em too—whale 'em till dey backs is welted like a washboard. 'Long at fust my marster say de good word for me to de overseer, but dat 'uz bad for me; for de mistis she fine it out, en arter dat I jist ketched it at every turn—dey warn't no mercy for me no mo'."

Tom's heart was fired—with fury against the planter's wife; and he said to himself, "But for that meddlesome fool, everything would have gone all right." He added a deep and bitter curse against her.

The expression of this sentiment was fiercely written in his face, and stood thus revealed to Roxana by a white glare of lightning which turned the somber dusk of the room into dazzling day at that moment. She was pleased—pleased and grateful; for did not that expression show that her child was capable of grieving for his mother's wrongs and a feeling resentment toward her persecutors?—a thing which she had been doubting. But her flash of happiness was only a flash, and went out again and left her spirit dark; for she said to herself, "He sole me down de river—he can't feel for a body long; dis'll pass en go." Then she took up her tale again.

"'Bout ten days ago I 'uz sayin' to myself dat I couldn't las' many mo' weeks I 'uz so wore out wid de awful work en de lashin's, en so downhearted en misable. En I didn't care no mo', nuther—life warn't wuth noth'n' to me, if I got to go on like dat. Well, when a body is in a frame o' mine like dat, what do a body care what a body do? Dey was a little sickly nigger wench 'bout ten year ole dat 'uz good to me, en hadn't no mammy, po' thing, en I loved her en she loved me; en she come out whah I 'uz workin' en she had a roasted tater, en tried to slip it to me—robbin' herself, you see, 'ca'se she knowed de overseer didn't give me enough to eat—en he ketched her at it, en giver her a lick acrost de back wid his stick, which 'uz as thick as a broom handle, en she drop' screamin' on de groun', en squirmin' en wallerin' aroun' in de dust like a spider dat's got crippled. I couldn't stan' it. All de hellfire dat 'uz ever in my heart flame' up, en I snatch de stick outen his han' en laid him flat. He laid dah moanin' en cussin', en all out of his head, you know, en de niggers 'uz plumb sk'yred to death. Dey gathered roun' him to he'p him, en I jumped on his hoss en took out for de river as tight as I could go. I knowed what dey would do wid me. Soon as he got well he would start in en work me to death if marster let him; en if dey didn't do dat, they'd sell me furder down de river, en dat's de same thing, so I 'lowed to drown myself en git out o' my troubles. It 'uz gitt'n' towards dark. I 'uz at de river in two minutes. Den I see a canoe, en I says dey ain't no use to drown myself tell I got to; so I ties de hoss in de edge o' de timber en shove out down de river, keepin' in under de shelter o' de bluff bank en prayin' for de dark to shet down quick. I had a pow'ful good start, 'ca'se de big house 'uz three mile back f'om de river en on'y de work mules to ride dah on, en on'y niggers ride 'em, en DEY warn't gwine to hurry—dey'd gimme all de chance dey could. Befo' a body could go to de house en back it would be long pas' dark, en dey couldn't track de hoss en fine out which way I went tell mawnin', en de niggers would tell 'em all de lies dey could 'bout it.

"Well, de dark come, en I went on a-spinnin' down de river. I paddled mo'n two hours, den I warn't worried no mo', so I quit paddlin' en floated down de current, considerin' what I 'uz gwine to do if I didn't have to drown myself. I made up some plans, en floated along, turnin' 'em over in my mine. Well, when it 'uz a little pas' midnight, as I reckoned, en I had come fifteen or twenty mile, I see de lights o' a steamboat layin' at de bank, whah dey warn't no town en no woodyard, en putty soon I ketched de shape o' de chimbly tops ag'in' de stars, en den good gracious me, I 'most jumped out o' my skin for joy! It 'uz de GRAN' MOGUL—I 'uz chambermaid on her for eight seasons in de Cincinnati en Orleans trade. I slid 'long pas'—don't see nobody stirrin' nowhah—hear 'em a-hammerin' away in de engine room, den I knowed what de matter was—some o' de machinery's broke. I got asho' below de boat en turn' de canoe loose, den I goes 'long up, en dey 'uz jes one plank out, en I step' 'board de boat. It 'uz pow'ful hot, deckhan's en roustabouts 'uz sprawled aroun' asleep on de fo'cas'l, de second mate, Jim Bangs, he sot dah on de bitts wid his head down, asleep—'ca'se dat's de way de second mate stan' de cap'n's watch!—en ole watchman, Billy Hatch, he 'uz a-noddin' on de companionway;—en I knowed 'em all; en, lan', but dey did look good! I says to myself, I wished old marster'd

come along NOW en try to take me—bless yo' heart, I's 'mong frien's, I is. So I tromped right along 'mongst 'em, en went up on de b'iler deck en 'way back aft to de ladies' cabin guard, en sot down dah in de same cheer dat I'd sot in 'mos' a hund'd million times, I reckon; en it 'uz jist home ag'in, I tell you!

"In 'bout an hour I heard de ready bell jingle, en den de racket begin. Putty soon I hear de gong strike. 'Set her back on de outside,' I says to myself. 'I reckon I knows dat music!' I hear de gong ag'in. 'Come ahead on de inside,' I says. Gong ag'in. 'Stop outside.' gong ag'in. 'Come ahead on de outside—now we's pinted for Sent Louis, en I's outer de woods en ain't got to drown myself at all.' I knowed de MOGUL 'uz in de Sent Louis trade now, you see. It 'uz jes fair daylight when we passed our plantation, en I seed a gang o' niggers en white folks huntin' up en down de sho', en troublin' deyselves a good deal 'bout me; but I warn't troublin' myself none 'bout dem.

"'Bout dat time Sally Jackson, dat used to be my second chambermaid en 'uz head chambermaid now, she come out on de guard, en 'uz pow'ful glad to see me, en so 'uz all de officers; en I tole 'em I'd got kidnapped en sole down de river, en dey made me up twenty dollahs en give it to me, en Sally she rigged me out wid good clo'es, en when I got here I went straight to whah you used to wuz, en den I come to dis house, en dey say you's away but 'spected back every day; so I didn't dast to go down de river to Dawson's, 'ca'se I might miss you.

"Well, las' Monday I 'uz pass'n by one o' dem places in fourth street whah deh sticks up runaway nigger bills, en he'ps to ketch 'em, en I seed my marster! I 'mos' flopped down on de groun', I felt so gone. He had his back to me, en 'uz talkin' to de man en givin' him some bills—nigger bills, I reckon, en I's de nigger. He's offerin' a reward—dat's it. Ain't I right, don't you reckon?"

Tom had been gradually sinking into a state of ghastly terror, and he said to himself, now: "I'm lost, no matter what turn things take! This man has said to me that he thinks there was something suspicious about that sale; he said he had a letter from a passenger on the GRAND MOGUL saying that Roxy came here on that boat and that everybody on board knew all about the case; so he says that her coming here instead of flying to a free state looks bad for me, and that if I don't find her for him, and that pretty soon, he will make trouble for me. I never believed that story; I couldn't believe she would be so dead to all motherly instincts as to come here, knowing the risk she would run of getting me into irremediable trouble. And after all, here she is! And I stupidly swore I would help find her, thinking it was a perfectly safe thing to promise. If I venture to deliver her up, she—she—but how can I help myself? I've got to do that or pay the money, and where's the money to come from? I—I—well, I should think that if he would swear to treat her kindly hereafter—and she says, herself, that he is a good man—and if he would swear to never allow her to be overworked, or ill fed, or—"

A flash of lightning exposed Tom's pallid face, drawn and rigid with these worrying thoughts. Roxana spoke up sharply now, and there was apprehension in her voice.

"Turn up dat light! I want to see yo' face better. Dah now—lemme look at you. Chambers, you's as white as yo' shirt! Has you see dat man? Has he be'n to see you?"

"Ye-s."

"When?"

"Monday noon."

"Monday noon! Was he on my track?"

"He—well, he thought he was. That is, he hoped he was. This is the bill you saw." He took it out of his pocket.

"Read it to me!"

She was panting with excitement, and there was a dusky glow in her eyes that Tom could not translate with certainty, but there seemed to be something threatening about it. The handbill had the usual rude woodcut of a turbaned Negro woman running, with the customary bundle on a stick over her shoulder, and the heading in bold type, "$100 REWARD." Tom read the bill aloud—at least the part that described Roxana and named the master and his St. Louis address and the address of the Fourth street agency; but he left out the item that applicants for the reward might also apply to Mr. Thomas Driscoll.

"Gimme de bill!"

Tom had folded it and was putting it in his pocket. He felt a chilly streak creeping down his back, but said as carelessly as he could:

"The bill? Why, it isn't any use to you, you can't read it. What do you want with it?"

"Gimme de bill!" Tom gave it to her, but with a reluctance which he could not entirely disguise. "Did you read it ALL to me?"

"Certainly I did."

"Hole up yo' han' en swah to it."

Tom did it. Roxana put the bill carefully away in her pocket, with her eyes fixed upon Tom's face all the while; then she said:

"Yo's lyin'!"

"What would I want to lie about it for?"

"I don't know—but you is. Dat's my opinion, anyways. But nemmine 'bout dat. When I seed dat man I 'uz dat sk'yerd dat I could sca'cely wobble home. Den I give a nigger man a dollar for dese clo'es, en I ain't be'in in a house sence, night ner day, till now. I blacked my face en laid hid in de cellar of a ole house dat's burnt down, daytimes, en robbed de sugar hogsheads en grain sacks on de wharf, nights, to git somethin' to eat, en never dast to try to buy noth'n', en I's 'mos' starved. En I never dast to come near dis place till dis rainy night, when dey ain't no people roun' sca'cely. But tonight I be'n a-stanin' in de dark alley ever sence night come, waitin' for you to go by. En here I is."

She fell to thinking. Presently she said:

"You seed dat man at noon, las' Monday?"

"Yes."

"I seed him de middle o' dat arternoon. He hunted you up, didn't he?"

430 *The Tragedy Of Pudd'nhead Wilson*

"Yes."

"Did he give you de bill dat time?"

"No, he hadn't got it printed yet."

Roxana darted a suspicious glance at him.

"Did you he'p him fix up de bill?"

Tom cursed himself for making that stupid blunder, and tried to rectify it by saying he remember now that it WAS at noon Monday that the man gave him the bill. Roxana said:

"You's lyin' ag'in, sho." Then she straightened up and raised her finger:

"Now den! I's gwine to ask you a question, en I wants to know how you's gwine to git aroun' it. You knowed he 'uz arter me; en if you run off, 'stid o' stayin' here to he'p him, he'd know dey 'uz somethin' wrong 'bout dis business, en den he would inquire 'bout you, en dat would take him to yo' uncle, en yo' uncle would read de bill en see dat you be'n sellin' a free nigger down de river, en you know HIM, I reckon! He'd t'ar up de will en kick you outen de house. Now, den, you answer me dis question: hain't you tole dat man dat I would be sho' to come here, en den you would fix it so he could set a trap en ketch me?"

Tom recognized that neither lies nor arguments could help him any longer—he was in a vise, with the screw turned on, and out of it there was no budging. His face began to take on an ugly look, and presently he said, with a snarl:

"Well, what could I do? You see, yourself, that I was in his grip and couldn't get out."

Roxy scorched him with a scornful gaze awhile, then she said:

"What could you do? You could be Judas to yo' own mother to save yo' wuthless hide! Would anybody b'lieve it? No—a dog couldn't! You is de lowdownest orneriest hound dat was ever pup'd into dis worl'—en I's 'sponsible for it!"—and she spat on him.

He made no effort to resent this. Roxy reflected a moment, then she said:

"Now I'll tell you what you's gwine to do. You's gwine to give dat man de money dat you's got laid up, en make him wait till you kin go to de judge en git de res' en buy me free agin."

"Thunder! What are you thinking of? Go and ask him for three hundred dollars and odd? What would I tell him I want it for, pray?"

Roxy's answer was delivered in a serene and level voice.

"You'll tell him you's sole me to pay yo' gamblin' debts en dat you lied to me en was a villain, en dat I 'quires you to git dat money en buy me back ag'in."

"Why, you've gone stark mad! He would tear the will to shreds in a minute—don't you know that?"

"Yes, I does."

"Then you don't believe I'm idiot enough to go to him, do you?"

"I don't b'lieve nothin' 'bout it—I KNOWS you's a-goin'. I knows it 'ca'se you knows dat if you don't raise dat money I'll go to him myself, en den he'll sell YOU down de river, en you kin see how you like it!"

Tom rose, trembling and excited, and there was an evil light in his eye. He strode to the door and said he must get out of this suffocating place for a moment and clear his brain in the fresh air so that he could determine what to do. The door wouldn't open. Roxy smiled grimly, and said:

"I's got the key, honey—set down. You needn't cle'r up yo' brain none to fine out what you gwine to do—I knows what you's gwine to do." Tom sat down and began to pass his hands through his hair with a helpless and desperate air. Roxy said, "Is dat man in dis house?"

Tom glanced up with a surprised expression, and asked:

"What gave you such an idea?"

"You done it. Gwine out to cle'r yo' brain! In de fust place you ain't got none to cle'r, en in de second place yo' ornery eye tole on you. You's de lowdownest hound dat ever—but I done told you dat befo'. Now den, dis is Friday. You kin fix it up wid dat man, en tell him you's gwine away to git de res' o' de money, en dat you'll be back wid it nex' Tuesday, or maybe Wednesday. You understan'?"

Tom answered sullenly: "Yes."

"En when you gits de new bill o' sale dat sells me to my own self, take en send it in de mail to Mr. Pudd'nhead Wilson, en write on de back dat he's to keep it tell I come. You understan'?"

"Yes."

"Dat's all den. Take yo' umbreller, en put on yo' hat."

"Why?"

"Beca'se you's gwine to see me home to de wharf. You see dis knife? I's toted it aroun' sence de day I seed dat man en bought dese clo'es en it. If he ketch me, I's gwine to kill myself wid it. Now start along, en go sof', en lead de way; en if you gives a sign in dis house, or if anybody comes up to you in de street, I's gwine to jam it right into you. Chambers, does you b'lieve me when I says dat?"

"It's no use to bother me with that question. I know your word's good."

"Yes, it's diff'rent from yo'n! Shet de light out en move along—here's de key."

They were not followed. Tom trembled every time a late straggler brushed by them on the street, and half expected to feel the cold steel in his back. Roxy was right at his heels and always in reach. After tramping a mile they reached a wide vacancy on the deserted wharves, and in this dark and rainy desert they parted.

As Tom trudged home his mind was full of dreary thoughts and wild plans; but at last he said to himself, wearily:

"There is but the one way out. I must follow her plan. But with a variation—I will not ask for the money and ruin myself; I will ROB the old skinflint."

CHAPTER 19 — The Prophesy Realized

Few things are harder to put up with than the annoyance of a good example. —Pudd'nhead Wilson's Calendar

It were not best that we should all think alike; it is difference of opinion that makes horse races. —Pudd'nhead Wilson's Calendar

Dawson's Landing was comfortably finishing its season of dull repose and waiting patiently for the duel. Count Luigi was waiting, too; but not patiently, rumor said. Sunday came, and Luigi insisted on having his challenge conveyed. Wilson carried it. Judge Driscoll declined to fight with an assassin—"that is," he added significantly, "in the field of honor."

Elsewhere, of course, he would be ready. Wilson tried to convince him that if he had been present himself when Angelo told him about the homicide committed by Luigi, he would not have considered the act discreditable to Luigi; but the obstinate old man was not to be moved.

Wilson went back to his principal and reported the failure of his mission. Luigi was incensed, and asked how it could be that the old gentleman, who was by no means dull-witted, held his trifling nephew's evidence in inferences to be of more value than Wilson's. But Wilson laughed, and said:

"That is quite simple; that is easily explicable. I am not his doll—his baby—his infatuation: his nature is. The judge and his late wife never had any children. The judge and his wife were past middle age when this treasure fell into their lap. One must make allowances for a parental instinct that has been starving for twenty-five or thirty years. It is famished, it is crazed with hunger by that time, and will be entirely satisfied with anything that comes handy; its taste is atrophied, it can't tell mud cat from shad. A devil born to a young couple is measurably recognizable by them as a devil before long, but a devil adopted by an old couple is an angel to them, and remains so, through thick and thin. Tom is this old man's angel; he is infatuated with him. Tom can persuade him into things which other people can't—not all things; I don't mean that, but a good many—particularly one class of things: the things that create or abolish personal partialities or prejudices in the old man's mind. The old man liked both of you. Tom conceived a hatred for you. That was enough; it turned the old man around at once. The oldest and strongest friendship must go to the ground when one of these late-adopted darlings throws a brick at it."

"It's a curious philosophy," said Luigi.

"It ain't philosophy at all—it's a fact. And there is something pathetic and beautiful about it, too. I think there is nothing more pathetic than to see one of these poor old childless couples taking a menagerie of yelping little worthless dogs to their hearts; and then adding some cursing and squawking parrots and a jackass-voiced macaw; and next a couple of hundred screeching songbirds, and presently some fetid guinea pigs and rabbits, and a howling colony of cats. It is all a groping and ignorant effort to construct out of base metal and brass filings, so to speak, something to take the place of that golden treasure denied them by Nature, a child. But this is a digression. The unwritten law of this region requires you to kill Judge Driscoll on sight, and he and the community will expect that attention at your hands—though of course your own death by his bullet will answer every purpose. Look out for him! Are you healed—that is, fixed?"

"Yes, he shall have his opportunity. If he attacks me, I will respond."

As Wilson was leaving, he said:

"The judge is still a little used up by his campaign work, and will not get out for a day or so; but when he does get out, you want to be on the alert."

About eleven at night the twins went out for exercise, and started on a long stroll in the veiled moonlight.

Tom Driscoll had landed at Hackett's Store, two miles below Dawson's, just about half an hour earlier, the only passenger for that lonely spot, and had walked up the shore road and entered Judge Driscoll's house without having encountered anyone either on the road or under the roof.

He pulled down his window blinds and lighted his candle. He laid off his coat and hat and began his preparations. He unlocked his trunk and got his suit of girl's clothes out from under the male attire in it, and laid it by. Then he blacked his face with burnt cork and put the cork in his pocket. His plan was to slip down to his uncle's private sitting room below, pass into the bedroom, steal the safe key from the old gentleman's clothes, and then go back and rob the safe. He took up his candle to start. His courage and confidence were high, up to this point, but both began to waver a little now. Suppose he should make a noise, by some accident, and get caught—say, in the act of opening the safe? Perhaps it would be well to go armed. He took the Indian knife from its hiding place, and felt a pleasant return of his wandering courage. He slipped stealthily down the narrow stair, his hair rising and his pulses halting at the slightest creak. When he was halfway down, he was disturbed to perceive that the landing below was touched by a faint glow of light. What could that mean? Was his uncle still up? No, that was not likely; he must have left his night taper there when he went to bed. Tom crept on down, pausing at every step to listen. He found the door standing open, and glanced it. What he saw pleased him beyond measure. His uncle was asleep on the sofa; on a small table at the head of the sofa a lamp was burning low, and by it stood the old man's small cashbox, closed. Near the box was a pile of bank notes and a piece of paper covered with figured in pencil. The safe door was not open. Evidently the sleeper had wearied himself with work upon his finances, and was taking a rest.

Tom set his candle on the stairs, and began to make his way toward the pile of notes, stooping low as he went. When he was passing his uncle, the old man stirred in his sleep, and Tom stopped instantly—stopped, and softly drew the knife from its sheath, with his heart thumping, and his eyes fastened upon his benefactor's face. After a moment or two he ventured forward again—one step—reached for his prize and seized it, dropping the knife sheath. Then he felt the old man's strong grip upon him, and a wild cry of "Help! help!" rang in his ear. Without hesitation he drove the knife home—and was free. Some of the notes escaped from his left hand and fell in the blood on the floor. He dropped the knife and snatched them up and started to fly; transferred them to his left hand, and seized the knife again, in his fright and confusion, but remembered himself and flung it from him, as being a

dangerous witness to carry away with him.

He jumped for the stair-foot, and closed the door behind him; and as he snatched his candle and fled upward, the stillness of the night was broken by the sound of urgent footsteps approaching the house. In another moment he was in his room, and the twins were standing aghast over the body of the murdered man!

Tom put on his coat, buttoned his hat under it, threw on his suit of girl's clothes, dropped the veil, blew out his light, locked the room door by which he had just entered, taking the key, passed through his other door into the black hall, locked that door and kept the key, then worked his way along in the dark and descended the black stairs. He was not expecting to meet anybody, for all interest was centered in the other part of the house now; his calculation proved correct. By the time he was passing through the backyard, Mrs. Pratt, her servants, and a dozen half-dressed neighbors had joined the twins and the dead, and accessions were still arriving at the front door.

As Tom, quaking as with a palsy, passed out at the gate, three women came flying from the house on the opposite side of the lane. They rushed by him and in at the gate, asking him what the trouble was there, but not waiting for an answer. Tom said to himself, "Those old maids waited to dress—they did the same thing the night Stevens's house burned down next door." In a few minutes he was in the haunted house. He lighted a candle and took off his girl-clothes. There was blood on him all down his left side, and his right hand was red with the stains of the blood-soaked notes which he has crushed in it; but otherwise he was free from this sort of evidence. He cleansed his hand on the straw, and cleaned most of the smut from his face. Then he burned the male and female attire to ashes, scattered the ashes, and put on a disguise proper for a tramp. He blew out his light, went below, and was soon loafing down the river road with the intent to borrow and use one of Roxy's devices. He found a canoe and paddled down downstream, setting the canoe adrift as dawn approached, and making his way by land to the next village, where he kept out of sight till a transient steamer came along, and then took deck passage for St. Louis. He was ill at ease Dawson's Landing was behind him; then he said to himself, "All the detectives on earth couldn't trace me now; there's not a vestige of a clue left in the world; that homicide will take its place with the permanent mysteries, and people won't get done trying to guess out the secret of it for fifty years."

In St. Louis, next morning, he read this brief telegram in the papers—dated at Dawson's Landing:

Judge Driscoll, an old and respected citizen, was assassinated here about midnight by a profligate Italian nobleman or a barber on account of a quarrel growing out of the recent election. The assassin will probably be lynched.

"One of the twins!" soliloquized Tom. "How lucky! It is the knife that has done him this grace. We never know when fortune is trying to favor us. I actually cursed Pudd'nhead Wilson in my heart for putting it out of my power to sell that knife. I take it back now."

Tom was now rich and independent. He arranged with the planter, and mailed to Wilson the new bill of sale which sold Roxana to herself; then he telegraphed his Aunt Pratt:

Have seen the awful news in the papers and am almost prostrated with grief. Shall start by packet today. Try to bear up till I come.

When Wilson reached the house of mourning and had gathered such details as Mrs. Pratt and the rest of the crowd could tell him, he took command as mayor, and gave orders that nothing should be touched, but everything left as it was until Justice Robinson should arrive and take the proper measures as coroner. He cleared everybody out of the room but the twins and himself. The sheriff soon arrived and took the twins away to jail. Wilson told them to keep heart, and promised to do it best in their defense when the case should come to trial. Justice Robinson came presently, and with him Constable Blake. They examined the room thoroughly. They found the knife and the sheath. Wilson noticed that there were fingerprints on the knife's handle. That pleased him, for the twins had required the earliest comers to make a scrutiny of their hands and clothes, and neither these people nor Wilson himself had found any bloodstains upon them. Could there be a possibility that the twins had spoken the truth when they had said they found the man dead when they ran into the house in answer to the cry for help? He thought of that mysterious girl at once. But this was not the sort of work for a girl to be engaged in. No matter; Tom Driscoll's room must be examined.

After the coroner's jury had viewed the body and its surroundings, Wilson suggested a search upstairs, and he went along. The jury forced an entrance to Tom's room, but found nothing, of course.

The coroner's jury found that the homicide was committed by Luigi, and that Angelo was accessory to it.

The town was bitter against the misfortunates, and for the first few days after the murder they were in constant danger of being lynched. The grand jury presently indicted Luigi for murder in the first degree, and Angelo as accessory before the fact. The twins were transferred from the city jail to the county prison to await trial.

Wilson examined the finger marks on the knife handle and said to himself, "Neither of the twins made those marks. Then manifestly there was another person concerned, either in his own interest or as hired assassin."

But who could it be? That, he must try to find out. The safe was not opened, the cashbox was closed, and had three thousand dollars in it. Then robbery was not the motive, and revenge was. Where had the murdered man an enemy except Luigi? There was but that one person in the world with a deep grudge against him.

The mysterious girl! The girl was a great trial to Wilson. If the motive had been robbery, the girl might answer; but there wasn't any girl that would want to take this old man's life for revenge. He had no quarrels with girls; he was a gentleman.

Wilson had perfect tracings of the finger marks of the knife handle; and among his glass records he had a great array of fingerprints of women and girls, collected during the last fifteen or eighteen years, but he scanned them in vain, they successfully withstood every test; among them were no duplicates of the prints on the knife.

The presence of the knife on the stage of the murder was a worrying circumstance for Wilson. A week previously he had as good as admitted to himself that he believed Luigi had possessed such a knife, and that he still possessed it notwithstanding his pretense that it had been stolen. And now here was the knife, and with it the twins. Half the town had said the twins were humbugging when they claimed they had lost their knife, and now these people were joyful, and said, "I told you so!"

If their fingerprints had been on the handle—but useless to bother any further about that; the fingerprints on the handle were NOT theirs—that he knew perfectly.

Wilson refused to suspect Tom; for first, Tom couldn't murder anybody—he hadn't character enough; secondly, if he could murder a person he wouldn't select his doting benefactor and nearest relative; thirdly, self-interest was in the way; for while the uncle lived, Tom was sure of a free support and a chance to get the destroyed will revived again, but with the uncle gone, that chance was gone too. It was true the will had really been revived, as was now discovered, but Tom could not have been aware of it, or he would have spoken of it, in his native talky, unsecretive way. Finally, Tom was in St. Louis when the murder was done, and got the news out of the morning journals, as was shown by his telegram to his aunt. These speculations were unemphasized sensations rather than articulated thoughts, for Wilson would have laughed at the idea of seriously connecting Tom with the murder.

Wilson regarded the case of the twins as desperate—in fact, about hopeless. For he argued that if a confederate was not found, an enlightened Missouri jury would hang them; sure; if a confederate was found, that would not improve the matter, but simply furnish one more person for the sheriff to hang. Nothing could save the twins but the discovery of a person who did the murder on his sole personal account—an undertaking which had all the aspect of the impossible. Still, the person who made the fingerprints must be sought. The twins might have no case WITH them, but they certainly would have none without him.

So Wilson mooned around, thinking, thinking, guessing, guessing, day and night, and arriving nowhere. Whenever he ran across a girl or a woman he was not acquainted with, he got her fingerprints, on one pretext or another; and they always cost him a sigh when he got home, for they never tallied with the finger marks on the knife handle.

As to the mysterious girl, Tom swore he knew no such girl, and did not remember ever seeing a girl wearing a dress like the one described by Wilson. He admitted that he did not always lock his room, and that sometimes the servants forgot to lock the house doors; still, in his opinion the girl must have made but few visits or she would have been discovered. When Wilson tried to connect her with the stealing raid, and thought she might have been the old woman's confederate, if not the very thief disguised as an old woman, Tom seemed stuck, and also much interested, and said he would keep a sharp eye out for this person or persons, although he was afraid that she or they would be too smart to venture again into a town where everybody would now be on the watch for a good while to come.

Everybody was pitying Tom, he looked so quiet and sorrowful, and seemed to feel his great loss so deeply. He was playing a part, but it was not all a part. The picture of his alleged uncle, as he had last seen him, was before him in the dark pretty frequently, when he was away, and called again in his dreams, when he was asleep. He wouldn't go into the room where the tragedy had happened. This charmed the doting Mrs. Pratt, who realized now, "as she had never done before," she said, what a sensitive and delicate nature her darling had, and how he adored his poor uncle.

CHAPTER 20 — The Murderer Chuckles

Even the clearest and most perfect circumstantial evidence is likely to be at fault, after all, and therefore ought to be received with great caution. Take the case of any pencil, sharpened by any woman; if you have witnesses, you will find she did it with a knife; but if you take simply the aspect of the pencil, you will say she did it with her teeth. — Pudd'nhead Wilson's Calendar

The weeks dragged along, no friend visiting the jailed twins but their counsel and Aunt Patsy Cooper, and the day of trial came at last—the heaviest day in Wilson's life; for with all his tireless diligence he had discovered no sign or trace of the missing confederate. "Confederate" was the term he had long ago privately accepted for that person—not as being unquestionably the right term, but as being the least possibly the right one, though he was never able to understand why the twins did not vanish and escape, as the confederate had done, instead of remaining by the murdered man and getting caught there.

The courthouse was crowded, of course, and would remain so to the finish, for not only in the town itself, but in the country for miles around, the trial was the one topic of conversation among the people. Mrs. Pratt, in deep mourning, and Tom with a weed on his hat, had seats near Pembroke Howard, the public prosecutor, and back of them sat a great array of friends of the family. The twins had but one friend present to keep their counsel in countenance, their poor old sorrowing landlady. She sat near Wilson, and looked her friendliest. In the "nigger corner" sat Chambers; also Roxy, with good clothes on, and her bill of sale in her pocket. It was her most precious possession, and she never parted with it, day or night. Tom had allowed her thirty-five dollars a month ever since he came into his property, and had said that he and she ought to be grateful to the twins for making them rich; but had roused such a temper in her by this speech that he did not repeat the argument afterward. She said the old judge had treated her child a thousand times better than he deserved, and had never done her an unkindness in his life; so she hated these outlandish devils for killing him, and shouldn't ever sleep satisfied till she saw them hanged for it. She was here to watch the trial now, and was going to lift up just one "hooraw" over it if the county judge put her in jail a year for it. She gave her turbaned head a toss and said, "When dat verdic' comes, I's gwine to lif' dat ROOF, now, I TELL you."

Pembroke Howard briefly sketched the state's case. He said he would show by a chain of circumstantial evidence without break or fault in it anywhere, that the principal prisoner at the bar committed the murder; that the motive was partly revenge, and partly a desire to take his own life out of jeopardy, and that his brother, by his presence, was a consenting accessory to the crime; a crime which was the basest known to the calendar of human misdeeds—assassination; that it was conceived by the blackest of hearts and consummated by the cowardliest of hands; a crime which had broken a loving sister's heart, blighted the happiness of a young nephew who was as dear as a son, brought inconsolable grief to many friends, and sorrow and loss to the whole community. The utmost penalty of the outraged law would be exacted, and upon the accused, now present at the bar, that penalty would unquestionably be executed. He would reserve further remark until his closing speech.

He was strongly moved, and so also was the whole house; Mrs. Pratt and several other women were weeping when he sat down, and many an eye that was full of hate was riveted upon the unhappy prisoners.

Witness after witness was called by the state, and questioned at length; but the cross questioning was brief. Wilson knew they could furnish nothing valuable for his side. People were sorry for Pudd'nhead Wilson; his budding career would get hurt by this trial.

Several witnesses swore they heard Judge Driscoll say in his public speech that the twins would be able to find their lost knife again when they needed it to assassinate somebody with. This was not news, but now it was seen to have been sorrowfully prophetic, and a profound sensation quivered through the hushed courtroom when those dismal words were repeated.

The public prosecutor rose and said that it was within his knowledge, through a conversation held with Judge Driscoll on the last day of his life, that counsel for the defense had brought him a challenge from the person charged at the bar with murder; that he had refused to fight with a confessed assassin—"that is, on the field of honor," but had added significantly, that he would be ready for him elsewhere. Presumably the person here charged with murder was warned that he must kill or be killed the first time he should meet Judge Driscoll. If counsel for the defense chose to let the statement stand so, he would not call him to the witness stand. Mr. Wilson said he would offer no denial. [Murmurs in the house: "It is getting worse and worse for Wilson's case."]

Mrs. Pratt testified that she heard no outcry, and did not know what woke her up, unless it was the sound of rapid footsteps approaching the front door. She jumped up and ran out in the hall just as she was, and heard the footsteps flying up the front steps and then following behind her as she ran to the sitting room. There she found the accused standing over her murdered brother. [Here she broke down and sobbed. Sensation in the court.] Resuming, she said the persons entered behind her were Mr. Rogers and Mr. Buckstone.

Cross-examined by Wilson, she said the twins proclaimed their innocence; declared that they had been taking a walk, and had hurried to the house in response to a cry for help which was so loud and strong that they had heard it at a considerable distance; that they begged her and the gentlemen just mentioned to examine their hands and clothes—which was done, and no blood stains found.

Confirmatory evidence followed from Rogers and Buckstone.

The finding of the knife was verified, the advertisement minutely describing it and offering a reward for it was put in evidence, and its exact correspondence with that description proved. Then followed a few minor details, and the case for the state was closed.

Wilson said that he had three witnesses, the Misses Clarkson, who would testify that they met a veiled young woman leaving Judge Driscoll's premises by the back gate a few minutes after the cries for help were heard, and that their evidence, taken with certain circumstantial evidence which he would call the court's attention to, would in his opinion convince the court that there was still one person concerned in this crime who had not yet been found, and also that a stay of proceedings ought to be granted, in justice to his clients, until that person should be discovered. As it was late, he would ask leave to defer the examination of his three witnesses until the next morning.

The crowd poured out of the place and went flocking away in excited groups and couples, taking the events of the session over with vivacity and consuming interest, and everybody seemed to have had a satisfactory and enjoyable day except the accused, their counsel, and their old lady friend. There was no cheer among these, and no substantial hope.

In parting with the twins Aunt Patsy did attempt a good-night with a gay pretense of hope and cheer in it, but broke down without finishing.

Absolutely secure as Tom considered himself to be, the opening solemnities of the trial had nevertheless oppressed him with a vague uneasiness, his being a nature sensitive to even the smallest alarms; but from the moment that the poverty and weakness of Wilson's case lay exposed to the court, he was comfortable once more, even jubilant. He left the courtroom sarcastically sorry for Wilson. "The Clarksons met an unknown woman in the back lane," he said to himself, "THAT is his case! I'll give him a century to find her in—a couple of them if he likes. A woman who doesn't exist any longer, and the clothes that gave her her sex burnt up and the ashes thrown away—oh, certainly, he'll find HER easy enough!" This reflection set him to admiring, for the hundredth time, the shrewd ingenuities by which he had insured himself against detection—more, against even suspicion.

"Nearly always in cases like this there is some little detail or other overlooked, some wee little track or trace left behind, and detection follows; but here there's not even the faintest suggestion of a trace left. No more than a bird leaves when it flies through the air—yes, through the night, you may say. The man that can track a bird through the air in the dark and find that bird is the man to track me out and find the judge's assassin—no other need apply. And that is the job that has been laid out for poor Pudd'nhead Wilson, of all people in the world! Lord, it will be pathetically funny to see him grubbing and groping after that woman that don't exist, and the right person sitting under his very nose all the time!" The more he thought the situation over, the more the humor of it struck him. Finally he said, "I'll never let him hear the last of that woman. Every time I catch him in company, to his dying day, I'll ask him in the guileless affectionate way that used to gravel him so when I inquired how his unborn law business was coming along, 'Got on her track yet—hey, Pudd'nhead?'" He wanted to laugh, but that would not have answered; there were people about, and he was mourning for his uncle. He made up his mind that it would be good entertainment to look in on Wilson that night and watch him worry over his barren law case and goad him with an exasperating word or two of sympathy and commiseration now and then.

Wilson wanted no supper, he had no appetite. He got out all the fingerprints of girls and women in his collection of records and pored gloomily over them an hour or more, trying to convince himself that that troublesome girl's marks were there somewhere and had been overlooked. But it was not so. He drew back his chair, clasped his hands over his head, and gave himself up to dull and arid musings.

Tom Driscoll dropped in, an hour after dark, and said with a pleasant laugh as he took a seat:

"Hello, we've gone back to the amusements of our days of neglect and obscurity for consolation, have we?" and he took up one of the glass strips and held it against the light to inspect it. "Come, cheer up, old man; there's no use in losing your grip and going back to this child's play merely because this big sunspot is drifting across your shiny new disk. It'll pass, and you'll be all right again"—and he laid the glass down. "Did you think you could win always?"

"Oh, no," said Wilson, with a sigh, "I didn't expect that, but I can't believe Luigi killed your uncle, and I feel very sorry for him. It makes me blue. And you would feel as I do, Tom, if you were not prejudiced against those young fellows."

"I don't know about that," and Tom's countenance darkened, for his memory reverted to his kicking. "I owe them no good will, considering the brunet one's treatment of me that night. Prejudice or no prejudice, Pudd'nhead, I don't like them, and when they get their deserts you're not going to find me sitting on the mourner's bench."

He took up another strip of glass, and exclaimed:

"Why, here's old Roxy's label! Are you going to ornament the royal palaces with nigger paw marks, too? By the date here, I was seven months old when this was done, and she was nursing me and her little nigger cub. There's a line straight across her thumbprint. How comes that?" and Tom held out the piece of glass to Wilson.

"That is common," said the bored man, wearily. "Scar of a cut or a scratch, usually"—and he took the strip of glass indifferently, and raised it toward the lamp.

All the blood sank suddenly out of his face; his hand quaked, and he gazed at the polished surface before him with the glassy stare of a corpse.

"Great heavens, what's the matter with you, Wilson? Are you going to faint?"

Tom sprang for a glass of water and offered it, but Wilson shrank shuddering from him and said:

"No, no!—take it away!" His breast was rising and falling, and he moved his head about in a dull and wandering way, like a person who had been stunned. Presently he said, "I shall feel better when I get to bed; I have been overwrought today; yes, and overworked for many days."

"Then I'll leave you and let you get to your rest. Good night, old man." But as Tom went out he couldn't deny himself a small parting gibe: "Don't take it so hard; a body can't win every time; you'll hang somebody yet."

Wilson muttered to himself, "It is no lie to say I am sorry I have to begin with you, miserable dog though you are!"

He braced himself up with a glass of cold whisky, and went to work again. He did not compare the new finger marks unintentionally left by Tom a few minutes before on Roxy's glass with the tracings of the marks left on the knife handle, there being no need for that (for his trained eye), but busied himself with another matter, muttering from time to time, "Idiot that I was!—Nothing but a GIRL would do me—a man in girl's clothes never occurred to me." First, he hunted out the plate containing the fingerprints made by Tom when he was

The Tragedy Of Pudd'nhead Wilson 435

twelve years old, and laid it by itself; then he brought forth the marks made by Tom's baby fingers when he was a suckling of seven months, and placed these two plates with the one containing this subject's newly (and unconsciously) made record.

"Now the series is complete," he said with satisfaction, and sat down to inspect these things and enjoy them.

But his enjoyment was brief. He stared a considerable time at the three strips, and seemed stupefied with astonishment. At last he put them down and said, "I can't make it out at all—hang it, the baby's don't tally with the others!"

He walked the floor for half an hour puzzling over his enigma, then he hunted out the other glass plates.

He sat down and puzzled over these things a good while, but kept muttering, "It's no use; I can't understand it. They don't tally right, and yet I'll swear the names and dates are right, and so of course they OUGHT to tally. I never labeled one of these thing carelessly in my life. There is a most extraordinary mystery here."

He was tired out now, and his brains were beginning to clog. He said he would sleep himself fresh, and then see what he could do with this riddle. He slept through a troubled and unrestful hour, then unconsciousness began to shred away, and presently he rose drowsily to a sitting posture. "Now what was that dream?" he said, trying to recall it. "What was that dream? It seemed to unravel that puz—"

He landed in the middle of the floor at a bound, without finishing the sentence, and ran and turned up his light and seized his "records." He took a single swift glance at them and cried out:

"It's so! Heavens, what a revelation! And for twenty-three years no man has ever suspected it!"

CHAPTER 21 — Doom

He is useless on top of the ground; he ought to be under it, inspiring the cabbages. —Pudd'nhead Wilson's Calendar

APRIL 1. This is the day upon which we are reminded of what we are on the other three hundred and sixty-four. — Pudd'nhead Wilson's Calendar

Wilson put on enough clothes for business purposes and went to work under a high pressure of steam. He was awake all over. All sense of weariness had been swept away by the invigorating refreshment of the great and hopeful discovery which he had made. He made fine and accurate reproductions of a number of his "records," and then enlarged them on a scale of ten to one with his pantograph. He did these pantograph enlargements on sheets of white cardboard, and made each individual line of the bewildering maze of whorls or curves or loops which consisted of the "pattern" of a "record" stand out bold and black by reinforcing it with ink. To the untrained eye the collection of delicate originals made by the human finger on the glass plates looked about alike; but when enlarged ten times they resembled the markings of a block of wood that has been sawed across the grain, and the dullest eye could detect at a glance, and at a distance of many feet, that no two of the patterns were alike. When Wilson had at last finished his tedious and difficult work, he arranged his results according to a plan in which a progressive order and sequence

was a principal feature; then he added to the batch several pantograph enlargements which he had made from time to time in bygone years.

The night was spent and the day well advanced now. By the time he had snatched a trifle of breakfast, it was nine o'clock, and the court was ready to begin its sitting. He was in his place twelve minutes later with his "records."

Tom Driscoll caught a slight glimpse of the records, and nudged his nearest friend and said, with a wink, "Pudd'nhead's got a rare eye to business—thinks that as long as he can't win his case it's at least a noble good chance to advertise his window palace decorations without any expense." Wilson was informed that his witnesses had been delayed, but would arrive presently; but he rose and said he should probably not have occasion to make use of their testimony. [An amused murmur ran through the room: "It's a clean backdown! he gives up without hitting a lick!"] Wilson continued: "I have other testimony—and better. [This compelled interest, and evoked murmurs of surprise that had a detectable ingredient of disappointment in them.] If I seem to be springing this evidence upon the court, I offer as my justification for this, that I did not discover its existence until late last night, and have been engaged in examining and classifying it ever since, until half an hour ago. I shall offer it presently; but first I wish to say a few preliminary words.

"May it please the court, the claim given the front place, the claim most persistently urged, the claim most strenuously and I may even say aggressively and defiantly insisted upon by the prosecution is this—that the person whose hand left the bloodstained fingerprints upon the handle of the Indian knife is the person who committed the murder." Wilson paused, during several moments, to give impressiveness to what he was about to say, and then added tranquilly, "WE GRANT THAT CLAIM."

It was an electrical surprise. No one was prepared for such an admission. A buzz of astonishment rose on all sides, and people were heard to intimate that the overworked lawyer had lost his mind. Even the veteran judge, accustomed as he was to legal ambushes and masked batteries in criminal procedure, was not sure that his ears were not deceiving him, and asked counsel what it was he had said. Howard's impassive face betrayed no sign, but his attitude and bearing lost something of their careless confidence for a moment. Wilson resumed:

"We not only grant that claim, but we welcome it and strongly endorse it. Leaving that matter for the present, we will now proceed to consider other points in the case which we propose to establish by evidence, and shall include that one in the chain in its proper place."

He had made up his mind to try a few hardy guesses, in mapping out his theory of the origin and motive of the murder—guesses designed to fill up gaps in it—guesses which could help if they hit, and would probably do no harm if they didn't.

"To my mind, certain circumstances of the case before the court seem to suggest a motive for the homicide quite different from the one insisted on by the state. It is my conviction that the motive was not revenge, but robbery. It has been urged that the presence of the accused brothers in that fatal room, just after notification that one of them must take the life of Judge Driscoll or lose his own the moment the parties should meet, clearly signifies that the natural instinct of self-preservation moved my clients to go there secretly and save Count Luigi by destroying his adversary.

"Then why did they stay there, after the deed was done? Mrs. Pratt had time, although she did not hear the cry for help, but woke up some moments later, to run to that room—and there she found these men standing and making no effort to escape. If they were guilty, they ought to have been running out of the house at the same time that she was running to that room. If they had had such a strong instinct toward self-preservation as to move them to kill that unarmed man, what had become of it now, when it should have been more alert than ever. Would any of us have remained there? Let us not slander our intelligence to that degree.

"Much stress has been laid upon the fact that the accused offered a very large reward for the knife with which this murder was done; that no thief came forward to claim that extraordinary reward; that the latter fact was good circumstantial evidence that the claim that the knife had been stolen was a vanity and a fraud; that these details taken in connection with the memorable and apparently prophetic speech of the deceased concerning that knife, and the finally discovery of that very knife in the fatal room where no living person was found present with the slaughtered man but the owner of the knife and his brother, form an indestructible chain of evidence which fixed the crime upon those unfortunate strangers.

"But I shall presently ask to be sworn, and shall testify that there was a large reward offered for the THIEF, also; and it was offered secretly and not advertised; that this fact was indiscreetly mentioned—or at least tacitly admitted—in what was supposed to be safe circumstances, but may NOT have been. The thief may have been present himself. [Tom Driscoll had been looking at the speaker, but dropped his eyes at this point.] In that case he would retain the knife in his possession, not daring to offer it for sale, or for pledge in a pawnshop. [There was a nodding of heads among the audience by way of admission that this was not a bad stroke.] I shall prove to the satisfaction of the jury that there WAS a person in Judge Driscoll's room several minutes before the accused entered it. [This produced a strong sensation; the last drowsy head in the courtroom roused up now, and made preparation to listen.] If it shall seem necessary, I will prove by the Misses Clarkson that they met a veiled person—ostensibly a woman—coming out of the back gate a few minutes after the cry for help was heard. This person was not a woman, but a man dressed in woman's clothes." Another sensation. Wilson had his eye on Tom when he hazarded this guess, to see what effect it would produce. He was satisfied with the result, and said to himself, "It was a success—he's hit!"

The object of that person in that house was robbery, not murder. It is true that the safe was not open, but there was an ordinary cashbox on the table, with three thousand dollars in it. It is easily supposable that the thief was concealed in the house; that he knew of this box, and of its owner's habit of counting its contents and arranging his accounts at night—if he had that habit, which I do not assert, of course—that he tried to take the box while its owner slept, but made a noise and was seized, and had to use the knife to save himself from capture; and that he fled without his booty because he heard help coming.

"I have now done with my theory, and will proceed to the evidences by which I propose to try to prove its soundness." Wilson took up several of his strips of glass. When the audience recognized these familiar mementos of Pudd'nhead's old time childish "puttering" and folly, the tense and funereal interest vanished out of their faces, and the house burst into volleys of relieving and refreshing laughter, and Tom chirked up and joined in the fun himself; but Wilson was apparently not disturbed. He arranged his records on the table before him, and said:

"I beg the indulgence of the court while I make a few remarks in explanation of some evidence which I am about to introduce, and which I shall presently ask to be allowed to verify under oath on the witness stand. Every human being carries with him from his cradle to his grave certain physical marks which do not change their character, and by which he can always be identified—and that without shade of doubt or question. These marks are his signature, his physiological autograph, so to speak, and this autograph can not be counterfeited, nor can he disguise it or hide it away, nor can it become illegible by the wear and mutations of time. This signature is not his face—age can change that beyond recognition; it is not his hair, for that can fall out; it is not his height, for duplicates of that exist; it is not his form, for duplicates of that exist also, whereas this signature is each man's very own—there is no duplicate of it among the swarming populations of the globe! [The audience were interested once more.]

"This autograph consists of the delicate lines or corrugations with which Nature marks the insides of the hands and the soles of the feet. If you will look at the balls of your fingers— you that have very sharp eyesight—you will observe that these dainty curving lines lie close together, like those that indicate the borders of oceans in maps, and that they form various clearly defined patterns, such as arches, circles, long curves, whorls, etc., and that these patterns differ on the different fingers. [Every man in the room had his hand up to the light now, and his head canted to one side, and was minutely scrutinizing the balls of his fingers; there were whispered ejaculations of 'Why, it's so—I never noticed that before!'] The patterns on the right hand are not the same as those on the left. [Ejaculations of 'Why, that's so, too!'] Taken finger for finger, your patterns differ from your neighbor's. [Comparisons were made all over the house—even the judge and jury were absorbed in this curious work.] The patterns of a twin's right hand are not the same as those on his left. One twin's patterns are never the same as his fellow twin's patterns—the jury will find that the patterns upon the finger balls of the twins' hands follow this rule. [An examination of the twins' hands was begun at once.] You have often heard of twins who were so exactly alike that when dressed alike their own parents could not tell them apart. Yet there was never a twin born in to this world that did not carry from birth to death a sure identifier in this mysterious and marvelous natal autograph. That once known to you, his fellow twin could never personate him and deceive you."

Wilson stopped and stood silent. Inattention dies a quick and sure death when a speaker does that. The stillness gives warning that something is coming. All palms and finger balls went down now, all slouching forms straightened, all heads came up, all eyes were fastened upon Wilson's face. He waited yet one, two, three moments, to let his pause complete and perfect its spell upon the house; then, when through the profound hush he could hear the ticking of the clock on the wall, he put out his hand and took the Indian knife by the blade and held it aloft where all could see the sinister spots upon its ivory handle; then he said, in a level and passionless voice:

"Upon this haft stands the assassin's natal autograph, written in the blood of that helpless and unoffending old man who loved you and whom you all loved. There is but one man in the whole earth whose hand can duplicate that crimson sign"—he paused and raised his eyes to the pendulum swinging back and forth—"and please God we will produce that man in this room before the clock strikes noon!"

Stunned, distraught, unconscious of its own movement, the house half rose, as if expecting to see the murderer appear at the door, and a breeze of muttered ejaculations swept the place. "Order in the court!—sit down!" This from the sheriff. He was obeyed, and quiet reigned again. Wilson stole a glance at Tom, and said to himself, "He is flying signals of distress now; even people who despise him are pitying him; they think this is a hard ordeal for a young fellow who has lost his benefactor by so cruel a stroke—and they are right." He resumed his speech:

"For more than twenty years I have amused my compulsory leisure with collecting these curious physical signatures in this town. At my house I have hundreds upon hundreds of them. Each and every one is labeled with name and date; not labeled the next day or even the next hour, but in the very minute that the impression was taken. When I go upon the witness stand I will repeat under oath the things which I am now saying. I have the fingerprints of the court, the sheriff, and every member of the jury. There is hardly a person in this room, white or black, whose natal signature I cannot produce, and not one of them can so disguise himself that I cannot pick him out from a multitude of his fellow creatures and unerringly identify him by his hands. And if he and I should live to be a hundred I could still do it. [The interest of the audience was steadily deepening now.]

"I have studied some of these signatures so much that I know them as well as the bank cashier knows the autograph of his oldest customer. While I turn my back now, I beg that several persons will be so good as to pass their fingers through their hair, and then press them upon one of the panes of the window near the jury, and that among them the accused may set THEIR finger marks. Also, I beg that these experimenters, or others, will set their fingers upon another pane, and add again the marks of the accused, but not placing them in the same order or relation to the other signatures as before—for, by one chance in a million, a person might happen upon the right marks by pure guesswork, ONCE, therefore I wish to be tested twice."

He turned his back, and the two panes were quickly covered with delicately lined oval spots, but visible only to such persons as could get a dark background for them—the foliage of a tree, outside, for instance. Then upon call, Wilson went to the window, made his examination, and said:

"This is Count Luigi's right hand; this one, three signatures below, is his left. Here is Count Angelo's right; down here is his left. Now for the other pane: here and here are Count Luigi's, here and here are his brother's." He faced about. "Am I right?"

A deafening explosion of applause was the answer. The bench said:

"This certainly approaches the miraculous!"

Wilson turned to the window again and remarked, pointing

with his finger:

"This is the signature of Mr. Justice Robinson. [Applause.] This, of Constable Blake. [Applause.] This of John Mason, juryman. [Applause.] This, of the sheriff. [Applause.] I cannot name the others, but I have them all at home, named and dated, and could identify them all by my fingerprint records."

He moved to his place through a storm of applause—which the sheriff stopped, and also made the people sit down, for they were all standing and struggling to see, of course. Court, jury, sheriff, and everybody had been too absorbed in observing Wilson's performance to attend to the audience earlier.

"Now then," said Wilson, "I have here the natal autographs of the two children—thrown up to ten times the natural size by the pantograph, so that anyone who can see at all can tell the markings apart at a glance. We will call the children A and B. Here are A's finger marks, taken at the age of five months. Here they are again taken at seven months. [Tom started.] They are alike, you see. Here are B's at five months, and also at seven months. They, too, exactly copy each other, but the patterns are quite different from A's, you observe. I shall refer to these again presently, but we will turn them face down now.

"Here, thrown up ten sizes, are the natal autographs of the two persons who are here before you accused of murdering Judge Driscoll. I made these pantograph copies last night, and will so swear when I go upon the witness stand. I ask the jury to compare them with the finger marks of the accused upon the windowpanes, and tell the court if they are the same."

He passed a powerful magnifying glass to the foreman.

One juryman after another took the cardboard and the glass and made the comparison. Then the foreman said to the judge:

"Your honor, we are all agreed that they are identical."

Wilson said to the foreman:

"Please turn that cardboard face down, and take this one, and compare it searchingly, by the magnifier, with the fatal signature upon the knife handle, and report your finding to the court."

Again the jury made minute examinations, and again reported:

"We find them to be exactly identical, your honor."

Wilson turned toward the counsel for the prosecution, and there was a clearly recognizable note of warning in his voice when he said:

"May it please the court, the state has claimed, strenuously and persistently, that the bloodstained fingerprints upon that knife handle were left there by the assassin of Judge Driscoll. You have heard us grant that claim, and welcome it." He turned to the jury: "Compare the fingerprints of the accused with the fingerprints left by the assassin—and report."

The comparison began. As it proceeded, all movement and all sound ceased, and the deep silence of an absorbed and waiting suspense settled upon the house; and when at last the words came, "THEY DO NOT EVEN RESEMBLE," a thundercrash of applause followed and the house sprang to its feet, but was quickly repressed by official force and brought to order again.

Tom was altering his position every few minutes now, but none of his changes brought repose nor any small trifle of comfort. When the house's attention was become fixed once more, Wilson said gravely, indicating the twins with a gesture:

"These men are innocent—I have no further concern with them. [Another outbreak of applause began, but was promptly checked.] We will now proceed to find the guilty. [Tom's eyes were starting from their sockets—yes, it was a cruel day for the bereaved youth, everybody thought.] We will return to the infant autographs of A and B. I will ask the jury to take these large pantograph facsimilies of A's marked five months and seven months. Do they tally?"

The foreman responded: "Perfectly."

"Now examine this pantograph, taken at eight months, and also marked A. Does it tally with the other two?"

The surprised response was:

"NO—THEY DIFFER WIDELY!"

"You are quite right. Now take these two pantographs of B's autograph, marked five months and seven months. Do they tally with each other?"

"Yes—perfectly."

"Take this third pantograph marked B, eight months. Does it tally with B's other two?"

"BY NO MEANS!"

"Do you know how to account for those strange discrepancies? I will tell you. For a purpose unknown to us, but probably a selfish one, somebody changed those children in the cradle."

This produced a vast sensation, naturally; Roxana was astonished at this admirable guess, but not disturbed by it. To guess the exchange was one thing, to guess who did it quite another. Pudd'nhead Wilson could do wonderful things, no doubt, but he couldn't do impossible ones. Safe? She was perfectly safe. She smiled privately.

"Between the ages of seven months and eight months those children were changed in the cradle"—he made one of this effect—collecting pauses, and added—"and the person who did it is in this house!"

Roxy's pulses stood still! The house was thrilled as with an electric shock, and the people half rose as if to seek a glimpse of the person who had made that exchange. Tom was growing limp; the life seemed oozing out of him. Wilson resumed:

"A was put into B's cradle in the nursery; B was transferred to the kitchen and became a Negro and a slave [Sensation— confusion of angry ejaculations]—but within a quarter of an hour he will stand before you white and free! [Burst of applause, checked by the officers.] From seven months onward until now, A has still been a usurper, and in my finger record he bears B's name. Here is his pantograph at the age of twelve. Compare it with the assassin's signature upon the knife handle. Do they tally?"

The foreman answered:

"TO THE MINUTEST DETAIL!"

Wilson said, solemnly:

"The murderer of your friend and mine—York Driscoll of the generous hand and the kindly spirit—sits in among you. Valet de Chambre, Negro and slave—falsely called Thomas a Becket Driscoll—make upon the window the fingerprints that will hang you!"

Tom turned his ashen face imploring toward the speaker, made some impotent movements with his white lips, then slid limp and lifeless to the floor.

Wilson broke the awed silence with the words:

"There is no need. He has confessed."

Roxy flung herself upon her knees, covered her face with her hands, and out through her sobs the words struggled:

"De Lord have mercy on me, po' misasble sinner dat I is!"

The clock struck twelve.

The court rose; the new prisoner, handcuffed, was removed.

CONCLUSION

It is often the case that the man who can't tell a lie thinks he is the best judge of one. —Pudd'nhead Wilson's Calendar

OCTOBER 12, THE DISCOVERY. It was wonderful to find America, but it would have been more wonderful to miss it. — Pudd'nhead Wilson's Calendar

The town sat up all night to discuss the amazing events of the day and swap guesses as to when Tom's trial would begin. Troop after troop of citizens came to serenade Wilson, and require a speech, and shout themselves hoarse over every sentence that fell from his lips—for all his sentences were golden, now, all were marvelous. His long fight against hard luck and prejudice was ended; he was a made man for good. And as each of these roaring gangs of enthusiasts marched away, some remorseful member of it was quite sure to raise his voice and say:

"And this is the man the likes of us have called a pudd'nhead for more than twenty years. He has resigned from that position, friends."

"Yes, but it isn't vacant—we're elected."

The twins were heroes of romance, now, and with rehabilitated reputations. But they were weary of Western adventure, and straightway retired to Europe.

Roxy's heart was broken. The young fellow upon whom she had inflicted twenty-three years of slavery continued the false heir's pension of thirty-five dollars a month to her, but her hurts were too deep for money to heal; the spirit in her eye was quenched, her martial bearing departed with it, and the voice of her laughter ceased in the land. In her church and its affairs she found her only solace.

The real heir suddenly found himself rich and free, but in a most embarrassing situation. He could neither read nor write, and his speech was the basest dialect of the Negro quarter. His gait, his attitudes, his gestures, his bearing, his laugh—all were vulgar and uncouth; his manners were the manners of a slave. Money and fine clothes could not mend these defects or cover them up; they only made them more glaring and the more pathetic. The poor fellow could not endure the terrors of the white man's parlor, and felt at home and at peace nowhere but in the kitchen. The family pew was a misery to him, yet he could nevermore enter into the solacing refuge of the "nigger gallery"—that was closed to him for good and all. But we cannot follow his curious fate further—that would be a long story.

The false heir made a full confession and was sentenced to imprisonment for life. But now a complication came up. The Percy Driscoll estate was in such a crippled shape when its owner died that it could pay only sixty percent of its great indebtedness, and was settled at that rate. But the creditors came forward now, and complained that inasmuch as through an error for which THEY were in no way to blame the false heir was not inventoried at the time with the rest of the property, great wrong and loss had thereby been inflicted upon them. They rightly claimed that "Tom" was lawfully their property and had been so for eight years; that they had already lost sufficiently in being deprived of his services during that long period, and ought not to be required to add anything to that loss; that if he had been delivered up to them in the first place, they would have sold him and he could not have murdered Judge Driscoll; therefore it was not that he had really committed the murder, the guilt lay with the erroneous inventory. Everybody saw that there was reason in this. Everybody granted that if "Tom" were white and free it would be unquestionably right to punish him—it would be no loss to anybody; but to shut up a valuable slave for life—that was quite another matter.

As soon as the Governor understood the case, he pardoned Tom at once, and the creditors sold him down the river.

AUTHOR'S NOTE TO "THOSE EXTRAORDINARY TWINS"

A man who is not born with the novel-writing gift has a troublesome time of it when he tries to build a novel. I know this from experience. He has no clear idea of his story; in fact he has no story. He merely has some people in his mind, and an incident or two, also a locality, and he trusts he can plunge those people into those incidents with interesting results. So he goes to work. To write a novel? No—that is a thought which comes later; in the beginning he is only proposing to tell a little tale, a very little tale, a six-page tale. But as it is a tale which he is not acquainted with, and can only find out what it is by listening as it goes along telling itself, it is more than apt to go on and on and on till it spreads itself into a book. I know about this, because it has happened to me so many times.

And I have noticed another thing: that as the short tale grows into the long tale, the original intention (or motif) is apt to get abolished and find itself superseded by a quite different one. It was so in the case of a magazine sketch which I once started to write—a funny and fantastic sketch about a prince and a pauper; it presently assumed a grave cast of its own accord, and in that new shape spread itself out into a book. Much the same thing happened with PUDD'NHEAD WILSON. I had a sufficiently hard time with that tale, because it changed itself from a farce to a tragedy while I was going along with it—a most embarrassing circumstance. But what was a great deal worse, was that it was not one story, but two stories tangled together; and they obstructed and interrupted each other at every turn and created no end of confusion and annoyance. I could not offer the book for publication, for I was afraid it

would unseat the reader's reason, I did not know what was the matter with it, for I had not noticed, as yet, that it was two stories in one. It took me months to make that discovery. I carried the manuscript back and forth across the Atlantic two or three times, and read it and studied over it on shipboard; and at last I saw where the difficulty lay. I had no further trouble. I pulled one of the stories out by the roots, and left the other—a kind of literary Caesarean operation.

Would the reader care to know something about the story which I pulled out? He has been told many a time how the born-and-trained novelist works; won't he let me round and complete his knowledge by telling him how the jackleg does it?

Originally the story was called THOSE EXTRAORDINARY TWINS. I meant to make it very short. I had seen a picture of a youthful Italian "freak"—or "freaks"—which was—or which were—on exhibition in our cities—a combination consisting of two heads and four arms joined to a single body and a single pair of legs—and I thought I would write an extravagantly fantastic little story with this freak of nature for hero—or heroes—a silly young miss for heroine, and two old ladies and two boys for the minor parts. I lavishly elaborated these people and their doings, of course. But the tale kept spreading along and spreading along, and other people got to intruding themselves and taking up more and more room with their talk and their affairs. Among them came a stranger named Pudd'nhead Wilson, and woman named Roxana; and presently the doings of these two pushed up into prominence a young fellow named Tom Driscoll, whose proper place was away in the obscure background. Before the book was half finished those three were taking things almost entirely into their own hands and working the whole tale as a private venture of their own—a tale which they had nothing at all to do with, by rights.

When the book was finished and I came to look around to see what had become of the team I had originally started out with—Aunt Patsy Cooper, Aunt Betsy Hale, and two boys, and Rowena the lightweight heroine—they were nowhere to be seen; they had disappeared from the story some time or other. I hunted about and found them—found them stranded, idle, forgotten, and permanently useless. It was very awkward. It was awkward all around, but more particularly in the case of Rowena, because there was a love match on, between her and one of the twins that constituted the freak, and I had worked it up to a blistering heat and thrown in a quite dramatic love quarrel, wherein Rowena scathingly denounced her betrothed for getting drunk, and scoffed at his explanation of how it had happened, and wouldn't listen to it, and had driven him from her in the usual "forever" way; and now here she sat crying and brokenhearted; for she had found that he had spoken only the truth; that is was not he, but the other of the freak that had drunk the liquor that made him drunk; that her half was a prohibitionist and had never drunk a drop in his life, and altogether tight as a brick three days in the week, was wholly innocent of blame; and indeed, when sober, was constantly doing all he could to reform his brother, the other half, who never got any satisfaction out of drinking, anyway, because liquor never affected him. Yes, here she was, stranded with that deep injustice of hers torturing her poor torn heart.

I didn't know what to do with her. I was as sorry for her as anybody could be, but the campaign was over, the book was finished, she was sidetracked, and there was no possible way of crowding her in, anywhere. I could not leave her there, of course; it would not do. After spreading her out so, and making such a to-do over her affairs, it would be absolutely necessary to account to the reader for her. I thought and thought and studied and studied; but I arrived at nothing. I finally saw plainly that there was really no way but one—I must simply give her the grand bounce. It grieved me to do it, for after associating with her so much I had come to kind of like her after a fashion, notwithstanding she was such an ass and said such stupid, irritating things and was so nauseatingly sentimental. Still it had to be done. So at the top of Chapter XVII I put a "Calendar" remark concerning July the Fourth, and began the chapter with this statistic:

"Rowena went out in the backyard after supper to see the fireworks and fell down the well and got drowned."

It seemed abrupt, but I thought maybe the reader wouldn't notice it, because I changed the subject right away to something else. Anyway it loosened up Rowena from where she was stuck and got her out of the way, and that was the main thing. It seemed a prompt good way of weeding out people that had got stalled, and a plenty good enough way for those others; so I hunted up the two boys and said, "They went out back one night to stone the cat and fell down the well and got drowned." Next I searched around and found old Aunt Patsy and Aunt Betsy Hale where they were around, and said, "They went out back one night to visit the sick and fell down the well and got drowned." I was going to drown some others, but I gave up the idea, partly because I believed that if I kept that up it would arouse attention, and perhaps sympathy with those people, and partly because it was not a large well and would not hold any more anyway.

Still the story was unsatisfactory. Here was a set of new characters who were become inordinately prominent and who persisted in remaining so to the end; and back yonder was an older set who made a large noise and a great to-do for a little while and then suddenly played out utterly and fell down the well. There was a radical defect somewhere, and I must search it out and cure it.

The defect turned out to be the one already spoken of—two stories in one, a farce and a tragedy. So I pulled out the farce and left the tragedy. This left the original team in, but only as mere names, not as characters. Their prominence was wholly gone; they were not even worth drowning; so I removed that detail. Also I took the twins apart and made two separate men of them. They had no occasion to have foreign names now, but it was too much trouble to remove them all through, so I left them christened as they were and made no explanation.

A Connecticut Yankee In King Arthur's Court
By Mark Twain

PREFACE

The ungentle laws and customs touched upon in this tale are historical, and the episodes which are used to illustrate them are also historical. It is not pretended that these laws and customs existed in England in the sixth century; no, it is only pretended that inasmuch as they existed in the English and other civilizations of far later times, it is safe to consider that it is no libel upon the sixth century to suppose them to have been in practice in that day also. One is quite justified in inferring that whatever one of these laws or customs was lacking in that remote time, its place was competently filled by a worse one.

The question as to whether there is such a thing as divine right of kings is not settled in this book. It was found too difficult. That the executive head of a nation should be a person of lofty character and extraordinary ability, was manifest and indisputable; that none but the Deity could select that head unerringly, was also manifest and indisputable; that the Deity ought to make that selection, then, was likewise manifest and indisputable; consequently, that He does make it, as claimed, was an unavoidable deduction. I mean, until the author of this book encountered the Pompadour, and Lady Castlemaine, and some other executive heads of that kind; these were found so difficult to work into the scheme, that it was judged better to take the other tack in this book (which must be issued this fall), and then go into training and settle the question in another book. It is, of course, a thing which ought to be settled, and I am not going to have anything particular to do next winter anyway.

Mark Twain, Hartford, July 21, 1889

A Word Of Explanation

It was in Warwick Castle that I came across the curious stranger whom I am going to talk about. He attracted me by three things: his candid simplicity, his marvelous familiarity with ancient armor, and the restfulness of his company—for he did all the talking. We fell together, as modest people will, in the tail of the herd that was being shown through, and he at once began to say things which interested me. As he talked along, softly, pleasantly, flowingly, he seemed to drift away imperceptibly out of this world and time, and into some remote era and old forgotten country; and so he gradually wove such a spell about me that I seemed to move among the specters and shadows and dust and mold of a gray antiquity, holding speech with a relic of it! Exactly as I would speak of my nearest personal friends or enemies, or my most familiar neighbors, he spoke of Sir Bedivere, Sir Bors de Ganis, Sir Launcelot of the Lake, Sir Galahad, and all the other great names of the Table Round—and how old, old, unspeakably old and faded and dry and musty and ancient he came to look as he went on! Presently he turned to me and said, just as one might speak of the weather, or any other common matter—

"You know about transmigration of souls; do you know about transposition of epochs—and bodies?"

I said I had not heard of it. He was so little interested—just as when people speak of the weather—that he did not notice whether I made him any answer or not. There was half a moment of silence, immediately interrupted by the droning

voice of the salaried cicerone:

"Ancient hauberk, date of the sixth century, time of King Arthur and the Round Table; said to have belonged to the knight Sir Sagramor le Desirous; observe the round hole through the chain-mail in the left breast; can't be accounted for; supposed to have been done with a bullet since invention of firearms—perhaps maliciously by Cromwell's soldiers."

My acquaintance smiled—not a modern smile, but one that must have gone out of general use many, many centuries ago—and muttered apparently to himself:

"Wit ye well, *I saw it done.*" Then, after a pause, added: "I did it myself."

By the time I had recovered from the electric surprise of this remark, he was gone.

All that evening I sat by my fire at the Warwick Arms, steeped in a dream of the olden time, while the rain beat upon the windows, and the wind roared about the eaves and corners. From time to time I dipped into old Sir Thomas Malory's enchanting book, and fed at its rich feast of prodigies and adventures, breathed in the fragrance of its obsolete names, and dreamed again. Midnight being come at length, I read another tale, for a nightcap—this which here follows, to wit:

HOW SIR LAUNCELOT SLEW TWO GIANTS, AND MADE A CASTLE FREE

Anon withal came there upon him two great giants, well armed, all save the heads, with two horrible clubs in their hands. Sir Launcelot put his shield afore him, and put the stroke away of the one giant, and with his sword he clave his head asunder. When his fellow saw that, he ran away as he were wood*, for fear of the horrible strokes, and Sir Launcelot after him with all his might, and smote him on the shoulder, and clave him to the middle. Then Sir Launcelot went into the hall, and there came afore him three score ladies and damsels, and all kneeled unto him, and thanked God and him of their deliverance. For, sir, said they, the most part of us have been here this seven year their prisoners, and we have worked all manner of silk works for our meat, and we are all great gentle-women born, and blessed be the time, knight, that ever thou wert born; for thou hast done the most worship that ever did knight in the world, that will we bear record, and we all pray you to tell us your name, that we may tell our friends who delivered us out of prison. Fair damsels, he said, my name is Sir Launcelot du Lake. And so he departed from them and betaught them unto God. And then he mounted upon his horse, and rode into many strange and wild countries, and through many waters and valleys, and evil was he lodged. And at the last by fortune him happened against a night to come to a fair courtilage, and therein he found an old gentle-woman that lodged him with a good-will, and there he had good cheer for him and his horse. And when time was, his host brought him into a fair garret over the gate to his bed. There Sir Launcelot unarmed him, and set his harness by him, and went to bed, and anon he fell on sleep. So, soon after there came one on horseback, and knocked at the gate in great haste. And when Sir Launcelot heard this he rose up, and looked out at the window, and saw by the moonlight three knights come riding after that one man, and all three lashed on him at once with swords, and that one knight turned on them knightly again and defended him. Truly, said Sir Launcelot, yonder one

---

* demented

knight shall I help, for it were shame for me to see three knights on one, and if he be slain I am partner of his death. And therewith he took his harness and went out at a window by a sheet down to the four knights, and then Sir Launcelot said on high, Turn you knights unto me, and leave your fighting with that knight. And then they all three left Sir Kay, and turned unto Sir Launcelot, and there began great battle, for they alight all three, and strake many strokes at Sir Launcelot, and assailed him on every side. Then Sir Kay dressed him for to have holpen Sir Launcelot. Nay, sir, said he, I will none of your help, therefore as ye will have my help let me alone with them. Sir Kay for the pleasure of the knight suffered him for to do his will, and so stood aside. And then anon within six strokes Sir Launcelot had stricken them to the earth.

And then they all three cried, Sir Knight, we yield us unto you as man of might matchless. As to that, said Sir Launcelot, I will not take your yielding unto me, but so that ye yield you unto Sir Kay the seneschal, on that covenant I will save your lives and else not. Fair knight, said they, that were we loath to do; for as for Sir Kay we chased him hither, and had overcome him had ye not been; therefore, to yield us unto him it were no reason. Well, as to that, said Sir Launcelot, advise you well, for ye may choose whether ye will die or live, for an ye be yielden, it shall be unto Sir Kay. Fair knight, then they said, in saving our lives we will do as thou commandest us. Then shall ye, said Sir Launcelot, on Whitsunday next coming go unto the court of King Arthur, and there shall ye yield you unto Queen Guenever, and put you all three in her grace and mercy, and say that Sir Kay sent you thither to be her prisoners. On the morn Sir Launcelot arose early, and left Sir Kay sleeping; and Sir Launcelot took Sir Kay's armor and his shield and armed him, and so he went to the stable and took his horse, and took his leave of his host, and so he departed. Then soon after arose Sir Kay and missed Sir Launcelot; and then he espied that he had his armor and his horse. Now by my faith I know well that he will grieve some of the court of King Arthur; for on him knights will be bold, and deem that it is I, and that will beguile them; and because of his armor and shield I am sure I shall ride in peace. And then soon after departed Sir Kay, and thanked his host.

As I laid the book down there was a knock at the door, and my stranger came in. I gave him a pipe and a chair, and made him welcome. I also comforted him with a hot Scotch whisky; gave him another one; then still another—hoping always for his story. After a fourth persuader, he drifted into it himself, in a quite simple and natural way:

THE STRANGER'S HISTORY

I am an American. I was born and reared in Hartford, in the State of Connecticut—anyway, just over the river, in the country. So I am a Yankee of the Yankees—and practical; yes, and nearly barren of sentiment, I suppose—or poetry, in other words. My father was a blacksmith, my uncle was a horse doctor, and I was both, along at first. Then I went over to the great arms factory and learned my real trade; learned all there was to it; learned to make everything: guns, revolvers, cannon, boilers, engines, all sorts of labor-saving machinery. Why, I could make anything a body wanted—anything in the world, it didn't make any difference what; and if there wasn't any quick new-fangled way to make a thing, I could invent one—and do it as easy as rolling off a log. I became head superintendent; had a couple of thousand men under me.

Well, a man like that is a man that is full of fight—that goes

without saying. With a couple of thousand rough men under one, one has plenty of that sort of amusement. I had, anyway. At last I met my match, and I got my dose. It was during a misunderstanding conducted with crowbars with a fellow we used to call Hercules. He laid me out with a crusher alongside the head that made everything crack, and seemed to spring every joint in my skull and made it overlap its neighbor. Then the world went out in darkness, and I didn't feel anything more, and didn't know anything at all —at least for a while.

When I came to again, I was sitting under an oak tree, on the grass, with a whole beautiful and broad country landscape all to myself—nearly. Not entirely; for there was a fellow on a horse, looking down at me—a fellow fresh out of a picture-book. He was in old-time iron armor from head to heel, with a helmet on his head the shape of a nail-keg with slits in it; and he had a shield, and a sword, and a prodigious spear; and his horse had armor on, too, and a steel horn projecting from his forehead, and gorgeous red and green silk trappings that hung down all around him like a bedquilt, nearly to the ground.

"Fair sir, will ye just?" said this fellow.

"Will I which?"

"Will ye try a passage of arms for land or lady or for—"

"What are you giving me?" I said. "Get along back to your circus, or I'll report you."

Now what does this man do but fall back a couple of hundred yards and then come rushing at me as hard as he could tear, with his nail-keg bent down nearly to his horse's neck and his long spear pointed straight ahead. I saw he meant business, so I was up the tree when he arrived.

He allowed that I was his property, the captive of his spear. There was argument on his side—and the bulk of the advantage —so I judged it best to humor him. We fixed up an agreement whereby I was to go with him and he was not to hurt me. I came down, and we started away, I walking by the side of his horse. We marched comfortably along; through glades and over brooks which I could not remember to have seen before—which puzzled me and made me wonder—and yet we did not come to any circus or sign of a circus. So I gave up the idea of a circus, and concluded he was from an asylum. But we never came to an asylum—so I was up a stump, as you may say. I asked him how far we were from Hartford. He said he had never heard of the place; which I took to be a lie, but allowed it to go at that. At the end of an hour we saw a far-away town sleeping in a valley by a winding river; and beyond it on a hill, a vast gray fortress, with towers and turrets, the first I had ever seen out of a picture.

"Bridgeport?" said I, pointing.

"Camelot," said he.

My stranger had been showing signs of sleepiness. He caught himself nodding, now, and smiled one of those pathetic, obsolete smiles of his, and said:

"I find I can't go on; but come with me, I've got it all written out, and you can read it if you like."

In his chamber, he said: "First, I kept a journal; then by and by, after years, I took the journal and turned it into a book. How long ago that was!"

He handed me his manuscript, and pointed out the place where I should begin:

"Begin here—I've already told you what goes before." He was steeped in drowsiness by this time. As I went out at his door I heard him murmur sleepily: "Give you good den, fair sir."

I sat down by my fire and examined my treasure. The first part of it—the great bulk of it—was parchment, and yellow with age. I scanned a leaf particularly and saw that it was a palimpsest. Under the old dim writing of the Yankee historian appeared traces of a penmanship which was older and dimmer still—Latin words and sentences: fragments from old monkish legends, evidently. I turned to the place indicated by my stranger and began to read —as follows:

THE TALE OF THE LOST LAND

CHAPTER I

CAMELOT

"Camelot—Camelot," said I to myself. "I don't seem to remember hearing of it before. Name of the asylum, likely."

It was a soft, reposeful summer landscape, as lovely as a dream, and as lonesome as Sunday. The air was full of the smell of flowers, and the buzzing of insects, and the twittering of birds, and there were no people, no wagons, there was no stir of life, nothing going on. The road was mainly a winding path with hoof-prints in it, and now and then a faint trace of wheels on either side in the grass—wheels that apparently had a tire as broad as one's hand.

Presently a fair slip of a girl, about ten years old, with a cataract of golden hair streaming down over her shoulders, came along. Around her head she wore a hoop of flame-red poppies. It was as sweet an outfit as ever I saw, what there was of it. She walked indolently along, with a mind at rest, its peace reflected in her innocent face. The circus man paid no attention to her; didn't even seem to see her. And she—she was no more startled at his fantastic make-up than if she was used to his like every day of her life. She was going by as indifferently as she might have gone by a couple of cows; but when she happened to notice me, *then* there was a change! Up went her hands, and she was turned to stone; her mouth dropped open, her eyes stared wide and timorously, she was the picture of astonished curiosity touched with fear. And there she stood gazing, in a sort of stupefied fascination, till we turned a corner of the wood and were lost to her view. That she should be startled at me instead of at the other man, was too many for me; I couldn't make head or tail of it. And that she should seem to consider me a spectacle, and totally overlook her own merits in that respect, was another puzzling thing, and a display of magnanimity, too, that was surprising in one so young. There was food for thought here. I moved along as one in a dream.

As we approached the town, signs of life began to appear. At intervals we passed a wretched cabin, with a thatched roof, and about it small fields and garden patches in an indifferent state of cultivation. There were people, too; brawny men, with long, coarse, uncombed hair that hung down over their faces and made them look like animals. They and the women, as a rule, wore a coarse tow-linen robe that came well below the knee, and a rude sort of sandal, and many wore an iron collar. The small boys and girls were always naked; but nobody

seemed to know it. All of these people stared at me, talked about me, ran into the huts and fetched out their families to gape at me; but nobody ever noticed that other fellow, except to make him humble salutation and get no response for their pains.

In the town were some substantial windowless houses of stone scattered among a wilderness of thatched cabins; the streets were mere crooked alleys, and unpaved; troops of dogs and nude children played in the sun and made life and noise; hogs roamed and rooted contentedly about, and one of them lay in a reeking wallow in the middle of the main thoroughfare and suckled her family. Presently there was a distant blare of military music; it came nearer, still nearer, and soon a noble cavalcade wound into view, glorious with plumed helmets and flashing mail and flaunting banners and rich doublets and horse-cloths and gilded spearheads; and through the muck and swine, and naked brats, and joyous dogs, and shabby huts, it took its gallant way, and in its wake we followed. Followed through one winding alley and then another,—and climbing, always climbing—till at last we gained the breezy height where the huge castle stood. There was an exchange of bugle blasts; then a parley from the walls, where men-at-arms, in hauberk and morion, marched back and forth with halberd at shoulder under flapping banners with the rude figure of a dragon displayed upon them; and then the great gates were flung open, the drawbridge was lowered, and the head of the cavalcade swept forward under the frowning arches; and we, following, soon found ourselves in a great paved court, with towers and turrets stretching up into the blue air on all the four sides; and all about us the dismount was going on, and much greeting and ceremony, and running to and fro, and a gay display of moving and intermingling colors, and an altogether pleasant stir and noise and confusion.

CHAPTER II

KING ARTHUR'S COURT

The moment I got a chance I slipped aside privately and touched an ancient common looking man on the shoulder and said, in an insinuating, confidential way:

"Friend, do me a kindness. Do you belong to the asylum, or are you just on a visit or something like that?"

He looked me over stupidly, and said:

"Marry, fair sir, me seemeth—"

"That will do," I said; "I reckon you are a patient."

I moved away, cogitating, and at the same time keeping an eye out for any chance passenger in his right mind that might come along and give me some light. I judged I had found one, presently; so I drew him aside and said in his ear:

"If I could see the head keeper a minute—only just a minute—"

"Prithee do not let me."

"Let you *what?*"

"*Hinder* me, then, if the word please thee better. Then he went on to say he was an under-cook and could not stop to gossip, though he would like it another time; for it would comfort his very liver to know where I got my clothes. As he started away he pointed and said yonder was one who was idle enough for my purpose, and was seeking me besides, no doubt. This was an airy slim boy in shrimp-colored tights that made him look like a forked carrot, the rest of his gear was blue silk and dainty laces and ruffles; and he had long yellow curls, and wore a plumed pink satin cap tilted complacently over his ear. By his look, he was good-natured; by his gait, he was satisfied with himself. He was pretty enough to frame. He arrived, looked me over with a smiling and impudent curiosity; said he had come for me, and informed me that he was a page.

"Go 'long," I said; "you ain't more than a paragraph."

It was pretty severe, but I was nettled. However, it never phazed him; he didn't appear to know he was hurt. He began to talk and laugh, in happy, thoughtless, boyish fashion, as we walked along, and made himself old friends with me at once; asked me all sorts of questions about myself and about my clothes, but never waited for an answer—always chattered straight ahead, as if he didn't know he had asked a question and wasn't expecting any reply, until at last he happened to mention that he was born in the beginning of the year 513.

It made the cold chills creep over me! I stopped and said, a little faintly:

"Maybe I didn't hear you just right. Say it again—and say it slow. What year was it?"

"513."

"513! You don't look it! Come, my boy, I am a stranger and friendless; be honest and honorable with me. Are you in your right mind?"

He said he was.

"Are these other people in their right minds?"

He said they were.

"And this isn't an asylum? I mean, it isn't a place where they cure crazy people?"

He said it wasn't.

"Well, then," I said, "either I am a lunatic, or something just as awful has happened. Now tell me, honest and true, where am I?"

"IN KING ARTHUR'S COURT."

I waited a minute, to let that idea shudder its way home, and then said:

"And according to your notions, what year is it now?"

"528—nineteenth of June."

I felt a mournful sinking at the heart, and muttered: "I shall never see my friends again—never, never again. They will not be born for more than thirteen hundred years yet."

I seemed to believe the boy, I didn't know why. *Something* in me seemed to believe him—my consciousness, as you may say; but my reason didn't. My reason straightway began to clamor; that was natural. I didn't know how to go about satisfying it, because I knew that the testimony of men wouldn't serve—my reason would say they were lunatics, and throw out their

evidence. But all of a sudden I stumbled on the very thing, just by luck. I knew that the only total eclipse of the sun in the first half of the sixth century occurred on the 21st of June, A.D. 528, O.S., and began at 3 minutes after 12 noon. I also knew that no total eclipse of the sun was due in what to *me* was the present year—i.e., 1879. So, if I could keep my anxiety and curiosity from eating the heart out of me for forty-eight hours, I should then find out for certain whether this boy was telling me the truth or not.

Wherefore, being a practical Connecticut man, I now shoved this whole problem clear out of my mind till its appointed day and hour should come, in order that I might turn all my attention to the circumstances of the present moment, and be alert and ready to make the most out of them that could be made. One thing at a time, is my motto—and just play that thing for all it is worth, even if it's only two pair and a jack. I made up my mind to two things: if it was still the nineteenth century and I was among lunatics and couldn't get away, I would presently boss that asylum or know the reason why; and if, on the other hand, it was really the sixth century, all right, I didn't want any softer thing: I would boss the whole country inside of three months; for I judged I would have the start of the best-educated man in the kingdom by a matter of thirteen hundred years and upward. I'm not a man to waste time after my mind's made up and there's work on hand; so I said to the page:

"Now, Clarence, my boy—if that might happen to be your name —I'll get you to post me up a little if you don't mind. What is the name of that apparition that brought me here?"

"My master and thine? That is the good knight and great lord Sir Kay the Seneschal, foster brother to our liege the king."

"Very good; go on, tell me everything."

He made a long story of it; but the part that had immediate interest for me was this: He said I was Sir Kay's prisoner, and that in the due course of custom I would be flung into a dungeon and left there on scant commons until my friends ransomed me—unless I chanced to rot, first. I saw that the last chance had the best show, but I didn't waste any bother about that; time was too precious. The page said, further, that dinner was about ended in the great hall by this time, and that as soon as the sociability and the heavy drinking should begin, Sir Kay would have me in and exhibit me before King Arthur and his illustrious knights seated at the Table Round, and would brag about his exploit in capturing me, and would probably exaggerate the facts a little, but it wouldn't be good form for me to correct him, and not over safe, either; and when I was done being exhibited, then ho for the dungeon; but he, Clarence, would find a way to come and see me every now and then, and cheer me up, and help me get word to my friends.

Get word to my friends! I thanked him; I couldn't do less; and about this time a lackey came to say I was wanted; so Clarence led me in and took me off to one side and sat down by me.

Well, it was a curious kind of spectacle, and interesting. It was an immense place, and rather naked—yes, and full of loud contrasts. It was very, very lofty; so lofty that the banners depending from the arched beams and girders away up there floated in a sort of twilight; there was a stone-railed gallery at each end, high up, with musicians in the one, and women, clothed in stunning colors, in the other. The floor was of big stone flags laid in black and white squares, rather battered by age and use, and needing repair. As to ornament, there wasn't any, strictly speaking; though on the walls hung some huge tapestries which were probably taxed as works of art; battle-pieces, they were, with horses shaped like those which children cut out of paper or create in gingerbread; with men on them in scale armor whose scales are represented by round holes—so that the man's coat looks as if it had been done with a biscuit-punch. There was a fireplace big enough to camp in; and its projecting sides and hood, of carved and pillared stonework, had the look of a cathedral door. Along the walls stood men-at-arms, in breastplate and morion, with halberds for their only weapon —rigid as statues; and that is what they looked like.

In the middle of this groined and vaulted public square was an oaken table which they called the Table Round. It was as large as a circus ring; and around it sat a great company of men dressed in such various and splendid colors that it hurt one's eyes to look at them. They wore their plumed hats, right along, except that whenever one addressed himself directly to the king, he lifted his hat a trifle just as he was beginning his remark.

Mainly they were drinking—from entire ox horns; but a few were still munching bread or gnawing beef bones. There was about an average of two dogs to one man; and these sat in expectant attitudes till a spent bone was flung to them, and then they went for it by brigades and divisions, with a rush, and there ensued a fight which filled the prospect with a tumultuous chaos of plunging heads and bodies and flashing tails, and the storm of howlings and barkings deafened all speech for the time; but that was no matter, for the dog-fight was always a bigger interest anyway; the men rose, sometimes, to observe it the better and bet on it, and the ladies and the musicians stretched themselves out over their balusters with the same object; and all broke into delighted ejaculations from time to time. In the end, the winning dog stretched himself out comfortably with his bone between his paws, and proceeded to growl over it, and gnaw it, and grease the floor with it, just as fifty others were already doing; and the rest of the court resumed their previous industries and entertainments.

As a rule, the speech and behavior of these people were gracious and courtly; and I noticed that they were good and serious listeners when anybody was telling anything—I mean in a dog-fightless interval. And plainly, too, they were a childlike and innocent lot; telling lies of the stateliest pattern with a most gentle and winning naivety, and ready and willing to listen to anybody else's lie, and believe it, too. It was hard to associate them with anything cruel or dreadful; and yet they dealt in tales of blood and suffering with a guileless relish that made me almost forget to shudder.

I was not the only prisoner present. There were twenty or more. Poor devils, many of them were maimed, hacked, carved, in a frightful way; and their hair, their faces, their clothing, were caked with black and stiffened drenchings of blood. They were suffering sharp physical pain, of course; and weariness, and hunger and thirst, no doubt; and at least none had given them the comfort of a wash, or even the poor charity of a lotion for their wounds; yet you never heard them utter a moan or a groan, or saw them show any sign of restlessness, or any disposition to complain. The thought was forced upon me: "The rascals—*they* have served other people so in their day; it being their own turn, now, they were not expecting any better treatment than this; so their philosophical bearing is not an outcome of mental training, intellectual fortitude, reasoning; it is mere animal training; they are white Indians."

CHAPTER III

KNIGHTS OF THE TABLE ROUND

Mainly the Round Table talk was monologues—narrative accounts of the adventures in which these prisoners were captured and their friends and backers killed and stripped of their steeds and armor. As a general thing—as far as I could make out—these murderous adventures were not forays undertaken to avenge injuries, nor to settle old disputes or sudden fallings out; no, as a rule they were simply duels between strangers—duels between people who had never even been introduced to each other, and between whom existed no cause of offense whatever. Many a time I had seen a couple of boys, strangers, meet by chance, and say simultaneously, "I can lick you," and go at it on the spot; but I had always imagined until now that that sort of thing belonged to children only, and was a sign and mark of childhood; but here were these big boobies sticking to it and taking pride in it clear up into full age and beyond. Yet there was something very engaging about these great simple-hearted creatures, something attractive and lovable. There did not seem to be brains enough in the entire nursery, so to speak, to bait a fish-hook with; but you didn't seem to mind that, after a little, because you soon saw that brains were not needed in a society like that, and indeed would have marred it, hindered it, spoiled its symmetry—perhaps rendered its existence impossible.

There was a fine manliness observable in almost every face; and in some a certain loftiness and sweetness that rebuked your belittling criticisms and stilled them. A most noble benignity and purity reposed in the countenance of him they called Sir Galahad, and likewise in the king's also; and there was majesty and greatness in the giant frame and high bearing of Sir Launcelot of the Lake.

There was presently an incident which centered the general interest upon this Sir Launcelot. At a sign from a sort of master of ceremonies, six or eight of the prisoners rose and came forward in a body and knelt on the floor and lifted up their hands toward the ladies' gallery and begged the grace of a word with the queen. The most conspicuously situated lady in that massed flower-bed of feminine show and finery inclined her head by way of assent, and then the spokesman of the prisoners delivered himself and his fellows into her hands for free pardon, ransom, captivity, or death, as she in her good pleasure might elect; and this, as he said, he was doing by command of Sir Kay the Seneschal, whose prisoners they were, he having vanquished them by his single might and prowess in sturdy conflict in the field.

Surprise and astonishment flashed from face to face all over the house; the queen's gratified smile faded out at the name of Sir Kay, and she looked disappointed; and the page whispered in my ear with an accent and manner expressive of extravagant derision—

"Sir *Kay*, forsooth! Oh, call me pet names, dearest, call me a marine! In twice a thousand years shall the unholy invention of man labor at odds to beget the fellow to this majestic lie!"

Every eye was fastened with severe inquiry upon Sir Kay. But he was equal to the occasion. He got up and played his hand like a major—and took every trick. He said he would state the case exactly according to the facts; he would tell the simple straightforward tale, without comment of his own; "and then," said he, "if ye find glory and honor due, ye will give it unto him who is the mightiest man of his hands that ever bare shield or strake with sword in the ranks of Christian battle—even him that sitteth there!" and he pointed to Sir Launcelot. Ah, he fetched them; it was a rattling good stroke. Then he went on and told how Sir Launcelot, seeking adventures, some brief time gone by, killed seven giants at one sweep of his sword, and set a hundred and forty-two captive maidens free; and then went further, still seeking adventures, and found him (Sir Kay) fighting a desperate fight against nine foreign knights, and straightway took the battle solely into his own hands, and conquered the nine; and that night Sir Launcelot rose quietly, and dressed him in Sir Kay's armor and took Sir Kay's horse and gat him away into distant lands, and vanquished sixteen knights in one pitched battle and thirty-four in another; and all these and the former nine he made to swear that about Whitsuntide they would ride to Arthur's court and yield them to Queen Guenever's hands as captives of Sir Kay the Seneschal, spoil of his knightly prowess; and now here were these half dozen, and the rest would be along as soon as they might be healed of their desperate wounds.

Well, it was touching to see the queen blush and smile, and look embarrassed and happy, and fling furtive glances at Sir Launcelot that would have got him shot in Arkansas, to a dead certainty.

Everybody praised the valor and magnanimity of Sir Launcelot; and as for me, I was perfectly amazed, that one man, all by himself, should have been able to beat down and capture such battalions of practiced fighters. I said as much to Clarence; but this mocking featherhead only said:

"An Sir Kay had had time to get another skin of sour wine into him, ye had seen the accompt doubled."

I looked at the boy in sorrow; and as I looked I saw the cloud of a deep despondency settle upon his countenance. I followed the direction of his eye, and saw that a very old and white-bearded man, clothed in a flowing black gown, had risen and was standing at the table upon unsteady legs, and feebly swaying his ancient head and surveying the company with his watery and wandering eye. The same suffering look that was in the page's face was observable in all the faces around—the look of dumb creatures who know that they must endure and make no moan.

"Marry, we shall have it again," sighed the boy; "that same old weary tale that he hath told a thousand times in the same words, and that he *will* tell till he dieth, every time he hath gotten his barrel full and feeleth his exaggeration-mill a-working. Would God I had died or I saw this day!"

"Who is it?"

"Merlin, the mighty liar and magician, perdition singe him for the weariness he worketh with his one tale! But that men fear him for that he hath the storms and the lightnings and all the devils that be in hell at his beck and call, they would have dug his entrails out these many years ago to get at that tale and squelch it. He telleth it always in the third person, making believe he is too modest to glorify himself—maledictions light upon him, misfortune be his dole! Good friend, prithee call me for evensong."

The boy nestled himself upon my shoulder and pretended to go to sleep. The old man began his tale; and presently the lad was asleep in reality; so also were the dogs, and the court, the lackeys, and the files of men-at-arms. The droning voice droned on; a soft snoring arose on all sides and supported it like a deep and subdued accompaniment of wind instruments. Some heads were bowed upon folded arms, some lay back with open mouths that issued unconscious music; the flies buzzed and bit, unmolested, the rats swarmed softly out from a hundred holes, and pattered about, and made themselves at home everywhere; and one of them sat up like a squirrel on the king's head and held a bit of cheese in its hands and nibbled it, and dribbled the crumbs in the king's face with naive and impudent irreverence. It was a tranquil scene, and restful to the weary eye and the jaded spirit.

This was the old man's tale. He said:

"Right so the king and Merlin departed, and went until an hermit that was a good man and a great leech. So the hermit searched all his wounds and gave him good salves; so the king was there three days, and then were his wounds well amended that he might ride and go, and so departed. And as they rode, Arthur said, I have no sword. No force*, said Merlin, hereby is a sword that shall be yours and I may. So they rode till they came to a lake, the which was a fair water and broad, and in the midst of the lake Arthur was ware of an arm clothed in white samite, that held a fair sword in that hand. Lo, said Merlin, yonder is that sword that I spake of. With that they saw a damsel going upon the lake. What damsel is that? said Arthur. That is the Lady of the lake, said Merlin; and within that lake is a rock, and therein is as fair a place as any on earth, and richly beseen, and this damsel will come to you anon, and then speak ye fair to her that she will give you that sword. Anon withal came the damsel unto Arthur and saluted him, and he her again. Damsel, said Arthur, what sword is that, that yonder the arm holdeth above the water? I would it were mine, for I have no sword. Sir Arthur King, said the damsel, that sword is mine, and if ye will give me a gift when I ask it you, ye shall have it. By my faith, said Arthur, I will give you what gift ye will ask. Well, said the damsel, go ye into yonder barge and row yourself to the sword, and take it and the scabbard with you, and I will ask my gift when I see my time. So Sir Arthur and Merlin alight, and tied their horses to two trees, and so they went into the ship, and when they came to the sword that the hand held, Sir Arthur took it up by the handles, and took it with him. And the arm and the hand went under the water; and so they came unto the land and rode forth. And then Sir Arthur saw a rich pavilion. What signifieth yonder pavilion? It is the knight's pavilion, said Merlin, that ye fought with last, Sir Pellinore, but he is out, he is not there; he hath ado with a knight of yours, that hight Egglame, and they have fought together, but at the last Egglame fled, and else he had been dead, and he hath chased him even to Carlion, and we shall meet with him anon in the highway. That is well said, said Arthur, now have I a sword, now will I wage battle with him, and be avenged on him. Sir, ye shall not so, said Merlin, for the knight is weary of fighting and chasing, so that ye shall have no worship to have ado with him; also, he will not lightly be matched of one knight living; and therefore it is my counsel, let him pass, for he shall do you good service in short time, and his sons, after his days. Also ye shall see that day in short space ye shall be right glad to give him your sister to wed. When I see him, I will do as ye advise me, said Arthur. Then Sir Arthur looked on the sword, and liked it passing well. Whether liketh you better, said Merlin, the sword or the scabbard? Me liketh better the sword, said Arthur. Ye are more unwise, said Merlin, for the scabbard is worth ten of the sword, for while ye have the scabbard upon you ye shall never

---

* No matter. — M. T.

lose no blood, be ye never so sore wounded; therefore, keep well the scabbard always with you. So they rode into Carlion, and by the way they met with Sir Pellinore; but Merlin had done such a craft that Pellinore saw not Arthur, and he passed by without any words. I marvel, said Arthur, that the knight would not speak. Sir, said Merlin, he saw you not; for and he had seen you ye had not lightly departed. So they came unto Carlion, whereof his knights were passing glad. And when they heard of his adventures they marveled that he would jeopard his person so alone. But all men of worship said it was merry to be under such a chieftain that would put his person in adventure as other poor knights did."

CHAPTER IV

SIR DINADAN THE HUMORIST

It seemed to me that this quaint lie was most simply and beautifully told; but then I had heard it only once, and that makes a difference; it was pleasant to the others when it was fresh, no doubt.

Sir Dinadan the Humorist was the first to awake, and he soon roused the rest with a practical joke of a sufficiently poor quality. He tied some metal mugs to a dog's tail and turned him loose, and he tore around and around the place in a frenzy of fright, with all the other dogs bellowing after him and battering and crashing against everything that came in their way and making altogether a chaos of confusion and a most deafening din and turmoil; at which every man and woman of the multitude laughed till the tears flowed, and some fell out of their chairs and wallowed on the floor in ecstasy. It was just like so many children. Sir Dinadan was so proud of his exploit that he could not keep from telling over and over again, to weariness, how the immortal idea happened to occur to him; and as is the way with humorists of his breed, he was still laughing at it after everybody else had got through. He was so set up that he concluded to make a speech —of course a humorous speech. I think I never heard so many old played-out jokes strung together in my life. He was worse than the minstrels, worse than the clown in the circus. It seemed peculiarly sad to sit here, thirteen hundred years before I was born, and listen again to poor, flat, worm-eaten jokes that had given me the dry gripes when I was a boy thirteen hundred years afterwards. It about convinced me that there isn't any such thing as a new joke possible. Everybody laughed at these antiquities —but then they always do; I had noticed that, centuries later. However, of course the scoffer didn't laugh—I mean the boy. No, he scoffed; there wasn't anything he wouldn't scoff at. He said the most of Sir Dinadan's jokes were rotten and the rest were petrified. I said "petrified" was good; as I believed, myself, that the only right way to classify the majestic ages of some of those jokes was by geologic periods. But that neat idea hit the boy in a blank place, for geology hadn't been invented yet. However, I made a note of the remark, and calculated to educate the commonwealth up to it if I pulled through. It is no use to throw a good thing away merely because the market isn't ripe yet.

Now Sir Kay arose and began to fire up on his history-mill with me for fuel. It was time for me to feel serious, and I did. Sir Kay told how he had encountered me in a far land of barbarians, who all wore the same ridiculous garb that I did—a garb that was a work of enchantment, and intended to make the wearer secure from hurt by human hands. However he had nullified the force of the enchantment by prayer, and had killed my thirteen knights in a three hours' battle, and taken me prisoner, sparing my life in order that so strange a

curiosity as I was might be exhibited to the wonder and admiration of the king and the court. He spoke of me all the time, in the blandest way, as "this prodigious giant," and "this horrible sky-towering monster," and "this tusked and taloned man-devouring ogre", and everybody took in all this bosh in the naivest way, and never smiled or seemed to notice that there was any discrepancy between these watered statistics and me. He said that in trying to escape from him I sprang into the top of a tree two hundred cubits high at a single bound, but he dislodged me with a stone the size of a cow, which "all-to brast" the most of my bones, and then swore me to appear at Arthur's court for sentence. He ended by condemning me to die at noon on the 21st; and was so little concerned about it that he stopped to yawn before he named the date.

I was in a dismal state by this time; indeed, I was hardly enough in my right mind to keep the run of a dispute that sprung up as to how I had better be killed, the possibility of the killing being doubted by some, because of the enchantment in my clothes. And yet it was nothing but an ordinary suit of fifteen-dollar slop-shops. Still, I was sane enough to notice this detail, to wit: many of the terms used in the most matter-of-fact way by this great assemblage of the first ladies and gentlemen in the land would have made a Comanche blush. Indelicacy is too mild a term to convey the idea. However, I had read "Tom Jones," and "Roderick Random," and other books of that kind, and knew that the highest and first ladies and gentlemen in England had remained little or no cleaner in their talk, and in the morals and conduct which such talk implies, clear up to a hundred years ago; in fact clear into our own nineteenth century—in which century, broadly speaking, the earliest samples of the real lady and real gentleman discoverable in English history— or in European history, for that matter—may be said to have made their appearance. Suppose Sir Walter, instead of putting the conversations into the mouths of his characters, had allowed the characters to speak for themselves? We should have had talk from Rebecca and Ivanhoe and the soft lady Rowena which would embarrass a tramp in our day. However, to the unconsciously indelicate all things are delicate. King Arthur's people were not aware that they were indecent and I had presence of mind enough not to mention it.

They were so troubled about my enchanted clothes that they were mightily relieved, at last, when old Merlin swept the difficulty away for them with a common-sense hint. He asked them why they were so dull—why didn't it occur to them to strip me. In half a minute I was as naked as a pair of tongs! And dear, dear, to think of it: I was the only embarrassed person there. Everybody discussed me; and did it as unconcernedly as if I had been a cabbage. Queen Guenever was as naively interested as the rest, and said she had never seen anybody with legs just like mine before. It was the only compliment I got—if it was a compliment.

Finally I was carried off in one direction, and my perilous clothes in another. I was shoved into a dark and narrow cell in a dungeon, with some scant remnants for dinner, some moldy straw for a bed, and no end of rats for company.

CHAPTER V

AN INSPIRATION

I was so tired that even my fears were not able to keep me awake long.

When I next came to myself, I seemed to have been asleep a very long time. My first thought was, "Well, what an astonishing dream I've had! I reckon I've waked only just in time to keep from being hanged or drowned or burned or something.... I'll nap again till the whistle blows, and then I'll go down to the arms factory and have it out with Hercules."

But just then I heard the harsh music of rusty chains and bolts, a light flashed in my eyes, and that butterfly, Clarence, stood before me! I gasped with surprise; my breath almost got away from me.

"What!" I said, "you here yet? Go along with the rest of the dream! scatter!"

But he only laughed, in his light-hearted way, and fell to making fun of my sorry plight.

"All right," I said resignedly, "let the dream go on; I'm in no hurry."

"Prithee what dream?"

"What dream? Why, the dream that I am in Arthur's court—a person who never existed; and that I am talking to you, who are nothing but a work of the imagination."

"Oh, la, indeed! and is it a dream that you're to be burned to-morrow? Ho-ho—answer me that!"

The shock that went through me was distressing. I now began to reason that my situation was in the last degree serious, dream or no dream; for I knew by past experience of the lifelike intensity of dreams, that to be burned to death, even in a dream, would be very far from being a jest, and was a thing to be avoided, by any means, fair or foul, that I could contrive. So I said beseechingly:

"Ah, Clarence, good boy, only friend I've got,—for you *are* my friend, aren't you?—don't fail me; help me to devise some way of escaping from this place!"

"Now do but hear thyself! Escape? Why, man, the corridors are in guard and keep of men-at-arms."

"No doubt, no doubt. But how many, Clarence? Not many, I hope?"

"Full a score. One may not hope to escape." After a pause — hesitatingly: "and there be other reasons—and weightier."

"Other ones? What are they?"

"Well, they say—oh, but I daren't, indeed daren't!"

"Why, poor lad, what is the matter? Why do you blench? Why do you tremble so?"

"Oh, in sooth, there is need! I do want to tell you, but—"

"Come, come, be brave, be a man—speak out, there's a good lad!"

He hesitated, pulled one way by desire, the other way by fear; then he stole to the door and peeped out, listening; and finally crept close to me and put his mouth to my ear and told me his fearful news in a whisper, and with all the cowering apprehension of one who was venturing upon awful ground

and speaking of things whose very mention might be freighted with death.

"Merlin, in his malice, has woven a spell about this dungeon, and there bides not the man in these kingdoms that would be desperate enough to essay to cross its lines with you! Now God pity me, I have told it! Ah, be kind to me, be merciful to a poor boy who means thee well; for an thou betray me I am lost!"

I laughed the only really refreshing laugh I had had for some time; and shouted:

"Merlin has wrought a spell! *Merlin*, forsooth! That cheap old humbug, that maundering old ass? Bosh, pure bosh, the silliest bosh in the world! Why, it does seem to me that of all the childish, idiotic, chuckle-headed, chicken-livered superstitions that ev —oh, damn Merlin!"

But Clarence had slumped to his knees before I had half finished, and he was like to go out of his mind with fright.

"Oh, beware! These are awful words! Any moment these walls may crumble upon us if you say such things. Oh call them back before it is too late!"

Now this strange exhibition gave me a good idea and set me to thinking. If everybody about here was so honestly and sincerely afraid of Merlin's pretended magic as Clarence was, certainly a superior man like me ought to be shrewd enough to contrive some way to take advantage of such a state of things. I went on thinking, and worked out a plan. Then I said:

"Get up. Pull yourself together; look me in the eye. Do you know why I laughed?"

"No—but for our blessed Lady's sake, do it no more."

"Well, I'll tell you why I laughed. Because I'm a magician myself."

"Thou!" The boy recoiled a step, and caught his breath, for the thing hit him rather sudden; but the aspect which he took on was very, very respectful. I took quick note of that; it indicated that a humbug didn't need to have a reputation in this asylum; people stood ready to take him at his word, without that. I resumed.

"I've known Merlin seven hundred years, and he—"

"Seven hun—"

"Don't interrupt me. He has died and come alive again thirteen times, and traveled under a new name every time: Smith, Jones, Robinson, Jackson, Peters, Haskins, Merlin—a new alias every time he turns up. I knew him in Egypt three hundred years ago; I knew him in India five hundred years ago—he is always blethering around in my way, everywhere I go; he makes me tired. He don't amount to shucks, as a magician; knows some of the old common tricks, but has never got beyond the rudiments, and never will. He is well enough for the provinces—one-night stands and that sort of thing, you know—but dear me, *he* oughtn't to set up for an expert—anyway not where there's a real artist. Now look here, Clarence, I am going to stand your friend, right along, and in return you must be mine. I want you to do me a favor. I want you to get word to the king that I am a magician myself—and the Supreme Grand High-yu-Muck-amuck and head of the tribe, at that; and I want him to be made to understand that I am just quietly arranging a little calamity here that will make the fur fly in these realms if Sir Kay's project is carried out and any harm comes to me. Will you get that to the king for me?"

The poor boy was in such a state that he could hardly answer me. It was pitiful to see a creature so terrified, so unnerved, so demoralized. But he promised everything; and on my side he made me promise over and over again that I would remain his friend, and never turn against him or cast any enchantments upon him. Then he worked his way out, staying himself with his hand along the wall, like a sick person.

Presently this thought occurred to me: how heedless I have been! When the boy gets calm, he will wonder why a great magician like me should have begged a boy like him to help me get out of this place; he will put this and that together, and will see that I am a humbug.

I worried over that heedless blunder for an hour, and called myself a great many hard names, meantime. But finally it occurred to me all of a sudden that these animals didn't reason; that *they* never put this and that together; that all their talk showed that they didn't know a discrepancy when they saw it. I was at rest, then.

But as soon as one is at rest, in this world, off he goes on something else to worry about. It occurred to me that I had made another blunder: I had sent the boy off to alarm his betters with a threat—I intending to invent a calamity at my leisure; now the people who are the readiest and eagerest and willingest to swallow miracles are the very ones who are hungriest to see you perform them; suppose I should be called on for a sample? Suppose I should be asked to name my calamity? Yes, I had made a blunder; I ought to have invented my calamity first. "What shall I do? what can I say, to gain a little time?" I was in trouble again; in the deepest kind of trouble...

"There's a footstep!—they're coming. If I had only just a moment to think.... Good, I've got it. I'm all right."

You see, it was the eclipse. It came into my mind in the nick of time, how Columbus, or Cortez, or one of those people, played an eclipse as a saving trump once, on some savages, and I saw my chance. I could play it myself, now, and it wouldn't be any plagiarism, either, because I should get it in nearly a thousand years ahead of those parties.

Clarence came in, subdued, distressed, and said:

"I hasted the message to our liege the king, and straightway he had me to his presence. He was frighted even to the marrow, and was minded to give order for your instant enlargement, and that you be clothed in fine raiment and lodged as befitted one so great; but then came Merlin and spoiled all; for he persuaded the king that you are mad, and know not whereof you speak; and said your threat is but foolishness and idle vaporing. They disputed long, but in the end, Merlin, scoffing, said, 'Wherefore hath he not *named* his brave calamity? Verily it is because he cannot.' This thrust did in a most sudden sort close the king's mouth, and he could offer naught to turn the argument; and so, reluctant, and full loth to do you the discourtesy, he yet prayeth you to consider his perplexed case, as noting how the matter stands, and name the calamity—if so be you have determined the nature of it and the time of its coming. Oh, prithee delay not; to delay at such a time were to double and treble the perils that already compass thee about. Oh, be thou wise—name the calamity!"

I allowed silence to accumulate while I got my impressiveness together, and then said:

"How long have I been shut up in this hole?"

"Ye were shut up when yesterday was well spent. It is 9 of the morning now."

"No! Then I have slept well, sure enough. Nine in the morning now! And yet it is the very complexion of midnight, to a shade. This is the 20th, then?"

"The 20th—yes."

"And I am to be burned alive to-morrow." The boy shuddered.

"At what hour?"

"At high noon."

"Now then, I will tell you what to say." I paused, and stood over that cowering lad a whole minute in awful silence; then, in a voice deep, measured, charged with doom, I began, and rose by dramatically graded stages to my colossal climax, which I delivered in as sublime and noble a way as ever I did such a thing in my life: "Go back and tell the king that at that hour I will smother the whole world in the dead blackness of midnight; I will blot out the sun, and he shall never shine again; the fruits of the earth shall rot for lack of light and warmth, and the peoples of the earth shall famish and die, to the last man!"

I had to carry the boy out myself, he sunk into such a collapse. I handed him over to the soldiers, and went back.

CHAPTER VI

THE ECLIPSE

In the stillness and the darkness, realization soon began to supplement knowledge. The mere knowledge of a fact is pale; but when you come to *realize* your fact, it takes on color. It is all the difference between hearing of a man being stabbed to the heart, and seeing it done. In the stillness and the darkness, the knowledge that I was in deadly danger took to itself deeper and deeper meaning all the time; a something which was realization crept inch by inch through my veins and turned me cold.

But it is a blessed provision of nature that at times like these, as soon as a man's mercury has got down to a certain point there comes a revulsion, and he rallies. Hope springs up, and cheerfulness along with it, and then he is in good shape to do something for himself, if anything can be done. When my rally came, it came with a bound. I said to myself that my eclipse would be sure to save me, and make me the greatest man in the kingdom besides; and straightway my mercury went up to the top of the tube, and my solicitudes all vanished. I was as happy a man as there was in the world. I was even impatient for to-morrow to come, I so wanted to gather in that great triumph and be the center of all the nation's wonder and reverence. Besides, in a business way it would be the making of me; I knew that.

Meantime there was one thing which had got pushed into the background of my mind. That was the half-conviction that when the nature of my proposed calamity should be reported to those superstitious people, it would have such an effect that they would want to compromise. So, by and by when I heard footsteps coming, that thought was recalled to me, and I said to myself, "As sure as anything, it's the compromise. Well, if it is good, all right, I will accept; but if it isn't, I mean to stand my ground and play my hand for all it is worth."

The door opened, and some men-at-arms appeared. The leader said:

"The stake is ready. Come!"

The stake! The strength went out of me, and I almost fell down. It is hard to get one's breath at such a time, such lumps come into one's throat, and such gaspings; but as soon as I could speak, I said:

"But this is a mistake—the execution is to-morrow."

"Order changed; been set forward a day. Haste thee!"

I was lost. There was no help for me. I was dazed, stupefied; I had no command over myself, I only wandered purposely about, like one out of his mind; so the soldiers took hold of me, and pulled me along with them, out of the cell and along the maze of underground corridors, and finally into the fierce glare of daylight and the upper world. As we stepped into the vast enclosed court of the castle I got a shock; for the first thing I saw was the stake, standing in the center, and near it the piled fagots and a monk. On all four sides of the court the seated multitudes rose rank above rank, forming sloping terraces that were rich with color. The king and the queen sat in their thrones, the most conspicuous figures there, of course.

To note all this, occupied but a second. The next second Clarence had slipped from some place of concealment and was pouring news into my ear, his eyes beaming with triumph and gladness. He said:

"'Tis through *me* the change was wrought! And main hard have I worked to do it, too. But when I revealed to them the calamity in store, and saw how mighty was the terror it did engender, then saw I also that this was the time to strike! Wherefore I diligently pretended, unto this and that and the other one, that your power against the sun could not reach its full until the morrow; and so if any would save the sun and the world, you must be slain to-day, while your enchantments are but in the weaving and lack potency. Odsbodikins, it was but a dull lie, a most indifferent invention, but you should have seen them seize it and swallow it, in the frenzy of their fright, as it were salvation sent from heaven; and all the while was I laughing in my sleeve the one moment, to see them so cheaply deceived, and glorifying God the next, that He was content to let the meanest of His creatures be His instrument to the saving of thy life. Ah how happy has the matter sped! You will not need to do the sun a *real* hurt—ah, forget not that, on your soul forget it not! Only make a little darkness—only the littlest little darkness, mind, and cease with that. It will be sufficient. They will see that I spoke falsely,—being ignorant, as they will fancy —and with the falling of the first shadow of that darkness you shall see them go mad with fear; and they will set you free and make you great! Go to thy triumph, now! But remember—ah, good friend, I implore thee remember my supplication, and do the blessed sun no hurt. For *my* sake, thy true friend."

I choked out some words through my grief and misery; as much as to say I would spare the sun; for which the lad's eyes paid me back with such deep and loving gratitude that I had not the heart to tell him his good-hearted foolishness had ruined me and sent me to my death.

As the soldiers assisted me across the court the stillness was so profound that if I had been blindfold I should have supposed I was in a solitude instead of walled in by four thousand people. There was not a movement perceptible in those masses of humanity; they were as rigid as stone images, and as pale; and dread sat upon every countenance. This hush continued while I was being chained to the stake; it still continued while the fagots were carefully and tediously piled about my ankles, my knees, my thighs, my body. Then there was a pause, and a deeper hush, if possible, and a man knelt down at my feet with a blazing torch; the multitude strained forward, gazing, and parting slightly from their seats without knowing it; the monk raised his hands above my head, and his eyes toward the blue sky, and began some words in Latin; in this attitude he droned on and on, a little while, and then stopped. I waited two or three moments; then looked up; he was standing there petrified. With a common impulse the multitude rose slowly up and stared into the sky. I followed their eyes, as sure as guns, there was my eclipse beginning! The life went boiling through my veins; I was a new man! The rim of black spread slowly into the sun's disk, my heart beat higher and higher, and still the assemblage and the priest stared into the sky, motionless. I knew that this gaze would be turned upon me, next. When it was, I was ready. I was in one of the most grand attitudes I ever struck, with my arm stretched up pointing to the sun. It was a noble effect. You could *see* the shudder sweep the mass like a wave. Two shouts rang out, one close upon the heels of the other:

"Apply the torch!"

"I forbid it!"

The one was from Merlin, the other from the king. Merlin started from his place—to apply the torch himself, I judged. I said:

"Stay where you are. If any man moves—even the king—before I give him leave, I will blast him with thunder, I will consume him with lightnings!"

The multitude sank meekly into their seats, and I was just expecting they would. Merlin hesitated a moment or two, and I was on pins and needles during that little while. Then he sat down, and I took a good breath; for I knew I was master of the situation now. The king said:

"Be merciful, fair sir, and essay no further in this perilous matter, lest disaster follow. It was reported to us that your powers could not attain unto their full strength until the morrow; but—"

"Your Majesty thinks the report may have been a lie? It *was* a lie."

That made an immense effect; up went appealing hands everywhere, and the king was assailed with a storm of supplications that I might be bought off at any price, and the calamity stayed. The king was eager to comply. He said:

"Name any terms, reverend sir, even to the halving of my kingdom; but banish this calamity, spare the sun!"

My fortune was made. I would have taken him up in a minute,

but I couldn't stop an eclipse; the thing was out of the question. So I asked time to consider. The king said:

"How long—ah, how long, good sir? Be merciful; look, it groweth darker, moment by moment. Prithee how long?"

"Not long. Half an hour—maybe an hour."

There were a thousand pathetic protests, but I couldn't shorten up any, for I couldn't remember how long a total eclipse lasts. I was in a puzzled condition, anyway, and wanted to think. Something was wrong about that eclipse, and the fact was very unsettling. If this wasn't the one I was after, how was I to tell whether this was the sixth century, or nothing but a dream? Dear me, if I could only prove it was the latter! Here was a glad new hope. If the boy was right about the date, and this was surely the 20th, it *wasn't* the sixth century. I reached for the monk's sleeve, in considerable excitement, and asked him what day of the month it was.

Hang him, he said it was the *twenty-first*! It made me turn cold to hear him. I begged him not to make any mistake about it; but he was sure; he knew it was the 21st. So, that feather-headed boy had botched things again! The time of the day was right for the eclipse; I had seen that for myself, in the beginning, by the dial that was near by. Yes, I was in King Arthur's court, and I might as well make the most out of it I could.

The darkness was steadily growing, the people becoming more and more distressed. I now said:

"I have reflected, Sir King. For a lesson, I will let this darkness proceed, and spread night in the world; but whether I blot out the sun for good, or restore it, shall rest with you. These are the terms, to wit: You shall remain king over all your dominions, and receive all the glories and honors that belong to the kingship; but you shall appoint me your perpetual minister and executive, and give me for my services one per cent of such actual increase of revenue over and above its present amount as I may succeed in creating for the state. If I can't live on that, I sha'n't ask anybody to give me a lift. Is it satisfactory?"

There was a prodigious roar of applause, and out of the midst of it the king's voice rose, saying:

"Away with his bonds, and set him free! and do him homage, high and low, rich and poor, for he is become the king's right hand, is clothed with power and authority, and his seat is upon the highest step of the throne! Now sweep away this creeping night, and bring the light and cheer again, that all the world may bless thee."

But I said:

"That a common man should be shamed before the world, is nothing; but it were dishonor to the *king* if any that saw his minister naked should not also see him delivered from his shame. If I might ask that my clothes be brought again—"

"They are not meet," the king broke in. "Fetch raiment of another sort; clothe him like a prince!"

My idea worked. I wanted to keep things as they were till the eclipse was total, otherwise they would be trying again to get me to dismiss the darkness, and of course I couldn't do it. Sending for the clothes gained some delay, but not enough. So

I had to make another excuse. I said it would be but natural if the king should change his mind and repent to some extent of what he had done under excitement; therefore I would let the darkness grow a while, and if at the end of a reasonable time the king had kept his mind the same, the darkness should be dismissed. Neither the king nor anybody else was satisfied with that arrangement, but I had to stick to my point.

It grew darker and darker and blacker and blacker, while I struggled with those awkward sixth-century clothes. It got to be pitch dark, at last, and the multitude groaned with horror to feel the cold uncanny night breezes fan through the place and see the stars come out and twinkle in the sky. At last the eclipse was total, and I was very glad of it, but everybody else was in misery; which was quite natural. I said:

"The king, by his silence, still stands to the terms." Then I lifted up my hands—stood just so a moment—then I said, with the most awful solemnity: "Let the enchantment dissolve and pass harmless away!"

There was no response, for a moment, in that deep darkness and that graveyard hush. But when the silver rim of the sun pushed itself out, a moment or two later, the assemblage broke loose with a vast shout and came pouring down like a deluge to smother me with blessings and gratitude; and Clarence was not the last of the wash, to be sure.

CHAPTER VII

MERLIN'S TOWER

Inasmuch as I was now the second personage in the Kingdom, as far as political power and authority were concerned, much was made of me. My raiment was of silks and velvets and cloth of gold, and by consequence was very showy, also uncomfortable. But habit would soon reconcile me to my clothes; I was aware of that. I was given the choicest suite of apartments in the castle, after the king's. They were aglow with loud-colored silken hangings, but the stone floors had nothing but rushes on them for a carpet, and they were misfit rushes at that, being not all of one breed. As for conveniences, properly speaking, there weren't any. I mean *little* conveniences; it is the little conveniences that make the real comfort of life. The big oaken chairs, graced with rude carvings, were well enough, but that was the stopping place. There was no soap, no matches, no looking-glass—except a metal one, about as powerful as a pail of water. And not a chromo. I had been used to chromos for years, and I saw now that without my suspecting it a passion for art had got worked into the fabric of my being, and was become a part of me. It made me homesick to look around over this proud and gaudy but heartless barrenness and remember that in our house in East Hartford, all unpretending as it was, you couldn't go into a room but you would find an insurance-chromo, or at least a three-color God-Bless-Our-Home over the door; and in the parlor we had nine. But here, even in my grand room of state, there wasn't anything in the nature of a picture except a thing the size of a bedquilt, which was either woven or knitted (it had darned places in it), and nothing in it was the right color or the right shape; and as for proportions, even Raphael himself couldn't have botched them more formidably, after all his practice on those nightmares they call his "celebrated Hampton Court cartoons." Raphael was a bird. We had several of his chromos; one was his "Miraculous Draught of Fishes," where he puts in a miracle of his own—puts three men into a canoe which wouldn't have held a dog without upsetting. I always admired to study R.'s art, it was so fresh and unconventional.

There wasn't even a bell or a speaking-tube in the castle. I had a great many servants, and those that were on duty lolled in the anteroom; and when I wanted one of them I had to go and call for him. There was no gas, there were no candles; a bronze dish half full of boarding-house butter with a blazing rag floating in it was the thing that produced what was regarded as light. A lot of these hung along the walls and modified the dark, just toned it down enough to make it dismal. If you went out at night, your servants carried torches. There were no books, pens, paper or ink, and no glass in the openings they believed to be windows. It is a little thing—glass is—until it is absent, then it becomes a big thing. But perhaps the worst of all was, that there wasn't any sugar, coffee, tea, or tobacco. I saw that I was just another Robinson Crusoe cast away on an uninhabited island, with no society but some more or less tame animals, and if I wanted to make life bearable I must do as he did—invent, contrive, create, reorganize things; set brain and hand to work, and keep them busy. Well, that was in my line.

One thing troubled me along at first—the immense interest which people took in me. Apparently the whole nation wanted a look at me. It soon transpired that the eclipse had scared the British world almost to death; that while it lasted the whole country, from one end to the other, was in a pitiable state of panic, and the churches, hermitages, and monkeries overflowed with praying and weeping poor creatures who thought the end of the world was come. Then had followed the news that the producer of this awful event was a stranger, a mighty magician at Arthur's court; that he could have blown out the sun like a candle, and was just going to do it when his mercy was purchased, and he then dissolved his enchantments, and was now recognized and honored as the man who had by his unaided might saved the globe from destruction and its peoples from extinction. Now if you consider that everybody believed that, and not only believed it, but never even dreamed of doubting it, you will easily understand that there was not a person in all Britain that would not have walked fifty miles to get a sight of me. Of course I was all the talk—all other subjects were dropped; even the king became suddenly a person of minor interest and notoriety. Within twenty-four hours the delegations began to arrive, and from that time onward for a fortnight they kept coming. The village was crowded, and all the countryside. I had to go out a dozen times a day and show myself to these reverent and awe-stricken multitudes. It came to be a great burden, as to time and trouble, but of course it was at the same time compensatingly agreeable to be so celebrated and such a center of homage. It turned Brer Merlin green with envy and spite, which was a great satisfaction to me. But there was one thing I couldn't understand—nobody had asked for an autograph. I spoke to Clarence about it. By George! I had to explain to him what it was. Then he said nobody in the country could read or write but a few dozen priests. Land! think of that.

There was another thing that troubled me a little. Those multitudes presently began to agitate for another miracle. That was natural. To be able to carry back to their far homes the boast that they had seen the man who could command the sun, riding in the heavens, and be obeyed, would make them great in the eyes of their neighbors, and envied by them all; but to be able to also say they had seen him work a miracle themselves—why, people would come a distance to see *them*. The pressure got to be pretty strong. There was going to be an eclipse of the moon, and I knew the date and hour, but it was

too far away. Two years. I would have given a good deal for license to hurry it up and use it now when there was a big market for it. It seemed a great pity to have it wasted so, and come lagging along at a time when a body wouldn't have any use for it, as like as not. If it had been booked for only a month away, I could have sold it short; but, as matters stood, I couldn't seem to cipher out any way to make it do me any good, so I gave up trying. Next, Clarence found that old Merlin was making himself busy on the sly among those people. He was spreading a report that I was a humbug, and that the reason I didn't accommodate the people with a miracle was because I couldn't. I saw that I must do something. I presently thought out a plan.

By my authority as executive I threw Merlin into prison—the same cell I had occupied myself. Then I gave public notice by herald and trumpet that I should be busy with affairs of state for a fortnight, but about the end of that time I would take a moment's leisure and blow up Merlin's stone tower by fires from heaven; in the meantime, whoso listened to evil reports about me, let him beware. Furthermore, I would perform but this one miracle at this time, and no more; if it failed to satisfy and any murmured, I would turn the murmurers into horses, and make them useful. Quiet ensued.

I took Clarence into my confidence, to a certain degree, and we went to work privately. I told him that this was a sort of miracle that required a trifle of preparation, and that it would be sudden death to ever talk about these preparations to anybody. That made his mouth safe enough. Clandestinely we made a few bushels of first-rate blasting powder, and I superintended my armorers while they constructed a lightning-rod and some wires. This old stone tower was very massive—and rather ruinous, too, for it was Roman, and four hundred years old. Yes, and handsome, after a rude fashion, and clothed with ivy from base to summit, as with a shirt of scale mail. It stood on a lonely eminence, in good view from the castle, and about half a mile away.

Working by night, we stowed the powder in the tower—dug stones out, on the inside, and buried the powder in the walls themselves, which were fifteen feet thick at the base. We put in a peck at a time, in a dozen places. We could have blown up the Tower of London with these charges. When the thirteenth night was come we put up our lightning-rod, bedded it in one of the batches of powder, and ran wires from it to the other batches. Everybody had shunned that locality from the day of my proclamation, but on the morning of the fourteenth I thought best to warn the people, through the heralds, to keep clear away—a quarter of a mile away. Then added, by command, that at some time during the twenty-four hours I would consummate the miracle, but would first give a brief notice; by flags on the castle towers if in the daytime, by torch-baskets in the same places if at night.

Thunder-showers had been tolerably frequent of late, and I was not much afraid of a failure; still, I shouldn't have cared for a delay of a day or two; I should have explained that I was busy with affairs of state yet, and the people must wait.

Of course, we had a blazing sunny day—almost the first one without a cloud for three weeks; things always happen so. I kept secluded, and watched the weather. Clarence dropped in from time to time and said the public excitement was growing and growing all the time, and the whole country filling up with human masses as far as one could see from the battlements. At last the wind sprang up and a cloud appeared—in the right quarter, too, and just at nightfall. For a little while I watched that distant cloud spread and blacken, then I judged it was time for me to appear. I ordered the torch-baskets to be lit, and Merlin liberated and sent to me. A quarter of an hour later I ascended the parapet and there found the king and the court assembled and gazing off in the darkness toward Merlin's Tower. Already the darkness was so heavy that one could not see far; these people and the old turrets, being partly in deep shadow and partly in the red glow from the great torch-baskets overhead, made a good deal of a picture.

Merlin arrived in a gloomy mood. I said:

"You wanted to burn me alive when I had not done you any harm, and latterly you have been trying to injure my professional reputation. Therefore I am going to call down fire and blow up your tower, but it is only fair to give you a chance; now if you think you can break my enchantments and ward off the fires, step to the bat, it's your innings."

"I can, fair sir, and I will. Doubt it not."

He drew an imaginary circle on the stones of the roof, and burnt a pinch of powder in it, which sent up a small cloud of aromatic smoke, whereat everybody fell back and began to cross themselves and get uncomfortable. Then he began to mutter and make passes in the air with his hands. He worked himself up slowly and gradually into a sort of frenzy, and got to thrashing around with his arms like the sails of a windmill. By this time the storm had about reached us; the gusts of wind were flaring the torches and making the shadows swash about, the first heavy drops of rain were falling, the world abroad was black as pitch, the lightning began to wink fitfully. Of course, my rod would be loading itself now. In fact, things were imminent. So I said:

"You have had time enough. I have given you every advantage, and not interfered. It is plain your magic is weak. It is only fair that I begin now."

I made about three passes in the air, and then there was an awful crash and that old tower leaped into the sky in chunks, along with a vast volcanic fountain of fire that turned night to noonday, and showed a thousand acres of human beings groveling on the ground in a general collapse of consternation. Well, it rained mortar and masonry the rest of the week. This was the report; but probably the facts would have modified it.

It was an effective miracle. The great bothersome temporary population vanished. There were a good many thousand tracks in the mud the next morning, but they were all outward bound. If I had advertised another miracle I couldn't have raised an audience with a sheriff.

Merlin's stock was flat. The king wanted to stop his wages; he even wanted to banish him, but I interfered. I said he would be useful to work the weather, and attend to small matters like that, and I would give him a lift now and then when his poor little parlor-magic soured on him. There wasn't a rag of his tower left, but I had the government rebuild it for him, and advised him to take boarders; but he was too high-toned for that. And as for being grateful, he never even said thank you. He was a rather hard lot, take him how you might; but then you couldn't fairly expect a man to be sweet that had been set back so.

CHAPTER VIII

THE BOSS

To be vested with enormous authority is a fine thing; but to have the on-looking world consent to it is a finer. The tower episode solidified my power, and made it impregnable. If any were perchance disposed to be jealous and critical before that, they experienced a change of heart, now. There was not any one in the kingdom who would have considered it good judgment to meddle with my matters.

I was fast getting adjusted to my situation and circumstances. For a time, I used to wake up, mornings, and smile at my "dream," and listen for the Colt's factory whistle; but that sort of thing played itself out, gradually, and at last I was fully able to realize that I was actually living in the sixth century, and in Arthur's court, not a lunatic asylum. After that, I was just as much at home in that century as I could have been in any other; and as for preference, I wouldn't have traded it for the twentieth. Look at the opportunities here for a man of knowledge, brains, pluck, and enterprise to sail in and grow up with the country. The grandest field that ever was; and all my own; not a competitor; not a man who wasn't a baby to me in acquirements and capacities; whereas, what would I amount to in the twentieth century? I should be foreman of a factory, that is about all; and could drag a seine down street any day and catch a hundred better men than myself.

What a jump I had made! I couldn't keep from thinking about it, and contemplating it, just as one does who has struck oil. There was nothing back of me that could approach it, unless it might be Joseph's case; and Joseph's only approached it, it didn't equal it, quite. For it stands to reason that as Joseph's splendid financial ingenuities advantaged nobody but the king, the general public must have regarded him with a good deal of disfavor, whereas I had done my entire public a kindness in sparing the sun, and was popular by reason of it.

I was no shadow of a king; I was the substance; the king himself was the shadow. My power was colossal; and it was not a mere name, as such things have generally been, it was the genuine article. I stood here, at the very spring and source of the second great period of the world's history; and could see the trickling stream of that history gather and deepen and broaden, and roll its mighty tides down the far centuries; and I could note the upspringing of adventurers like myself in the shelter of its long array of thrones: De Montforts, Gavestons, Mortimers, Villierses; the war-making, campaign-directing wantons of France, and Charles the Second's scepter-wielding drabs; but nowhere in the procession was my full-sized fellow visible. I was a Unique; and glad to know that that fact could not be dislodged or challenged for thirteen centuries and a half, for sure. Yes, in power I was equal to the king. At the same time there was another power that was a trifle stronger than both of us put together. That was the Church. I do not wish to disguise that fact. I couldn't, if I wanted to. But never mind about that, now; it will show up, in its proper place, later on. It didn't cause me any trouble in the beginning —at least any of consequence.

Well, it was a curious country, and full of interest. And the people! They were the quaintest and simplest and trustingest race; why, they were nothing but rabbits. It was pitiful for a person born in a wholesome free atmosphere to listen to their humble and hearty outpourings of loyalty toward their king and Church and nobility; as if they had any more occasion to love and honor king and Church and noble than a slave has to love and honor the lash, or a dog has to love and honor the stranger that kicks him! Why, dear me, *any* kind of royalty, howsoever modified, *any* kind of aristocracy, howsoever pruned, is rightly an insult; but if you are born and brought up under that sort of arrangement you probably never find it out for yourself, and don't believe it when somebody else tells you. It is enough to make a body ashamed of his race to think of the sort of froth that has always occupied its thrones without shadow of right or reason, and the seventh-rate people that have always figured as its aristocracies—a company of monarchs and nobles who, as a rule, would have achieved only poverty and obscurity if left, like their betters, to their own exertions.

The most of King Arthur's British nation were slaves, pure and simple, and bore that name, and wore the iron collar on their necks; and the rest were slaves in fact, but without the name; they imagined themselves men and freemen, and called themselves so. The truth was, the nation as a body was in the world for one object, and one only: to grovel before king and Church and noble; to slave for them, sweat blood for them, starve that they might be fed, work that they might play, drink misery to the dregs that they might be happy, go naked that they might wear silks and jewels, pay taxes that they might be spared from paying them, be familiar all their lives with the degrading language and postures of adulation that they might walk in pride and think themselves the gods of this world. And for all this, the thanks they got were cuffs and contempt; and so poor-spirited were they that they took even this sort of attention as an honor.

Inherited ideas are a curious thing, and interesting to observe and examine. I had mine, the king and his people had theirs. In both cases they flowed in ruts worn deep by time and habit, and the man who should have proposed to divert them by reason and argument would have had a long contract on his hands. For instance, those people had inherited the idea that all men without title and a long pedigree, whether they had great natural gifts and acquirements or hadn't, were creatures of no more consideration than so many animals, bugs, insects; whereas I had inherited the idea that human daws who can consent to masquerade in the peacock-shams of inherited dignities and unearned titles, are of no good but to be laughed at. The way I was looked upon was odd, but it was natural. You know how the keeper and the public regard the elephant in the menagerie: well, that is the idea. They are full of admiration of his vast bulk and his prodigious strength; they speak with pride of the fact that he can do a hundred marvels which are far and away beyond their own powers; and they speak with the same pride of the fact that in his wrath he is able to drive a thousand men before him. But does that make him one of *them*? No; the raggedest tramp in the pit would smile at the idea. He couldn't comprehend it; couldn't take it in; couldn't in any remote way conceive of it. Well, to the king, the nobles, and all the nation, down to the very slaves and tramps, I was just that kind of an elephant, and nothing more. I was admired, also feared; but it was as an animal is admired and feared. The animal is not reverenced, neither was I; I was not even respected. I had no pedigree, no inherited title; so in the king's and nobles' eyes I was mere dirt; the people regarded me with wonder and awe, but there was no reverence mixed with it; through the force of inherited ideas they were not able to conceive of anything being entitled to that except pedigree and lordship. There you see the hand of that awful power, the Roman Catholic Church. In two or three little centuries it had converted a nation of men to a nation of worms. Before the day of the Church's supremacy in the world, men were men, and held their heads up, and had a man's pride and spirit and independence; and what of greatness and position a person got, he got mainly by achievement, not by birth. But then the Church came to the front, with an axe to grind; and she was

wise, subtle, and knew more than one way to skin a cat—or a nation; she invented "divine right of kings," and propped it all around, brick by brick, with the Beatitudes —wrenching them from their good purpose to make them fortify an evil one; she preached (to the commoner) humility, obedience to superiors, the beauty of self-sacrifice; she preached (to the commoner) meekness under insult; preached (still to the commoner, always to the commoner) patience, meanness of spirit, non-resistance under oppression; and she introduced heritable ranks and aristocracies, and taught all the Christian populations of the earth to bow down to them and worship them. Even down to my birth-century that poison was still in the blood of Christendom, and the best of English commoners was still content to see his inferiors impudently continuing to hold a number of positions, such as lordships and the throne, to which the grotesque laws of his country did not allow him to aspire; in fact, he was not merely contented with this strange condition of things, he was even able to persuade himself that he was proud of it. It seems to show that there isn't anything you can't stand, if you are only born and bred to it. Of course that taint, that reverence for rank and title, had been in our American blood, too—I know that; but when I left America it had disappeared—at least to all intents and purposes. The remnant of it was restricted to the dudes and dudesses. When a disease has worked its way down to that level, it may fairly be said to be out of the system.

But to return to my anomalous position in King Arthur's kingdom. Here I was, a giant among pigmies, a man among children, a master intelligence among intellectual moles: by all rational measurement the one and only actually great man in that whole British world; and yet there and then, just as in the remote England of my birth-time, the sheep-witted earl who could claim long descent from a king's leman, acquired at second-hand from the slums of London, was a better man than I was. Such a personage was fawned upon in Arthur's realm and reverently looked up to by everybody, even though his dispositions were as mean as his intelligence, and his morals as base as his lineage. There were times when *he* could sit down in the king's presence, but I couldn't. I could have got a title easily enough, and that would have raised me a large step in everybody's eyes; even in the king's, the giver of it. But I didn't ask for it; and I declined it when it was offered. I couldn't have enjoyed such a thing with my notions; and it wouldn't have been fair, anyway, because as far back as I could go, our tribe had always been short of the bar sinister. I couldn't have felt really and satisfactorily fine and proud and set-up over any title except one that should come from the nation itself, the only legitimate source; and such an one I hoped to win; and in the course of years of honest and honorable endeavor, I did win it and did wear it with a high and clean pride. This title fell casually from the lips of a blacksmith, one day, in a village, was caught up as a happy thought and tossed from mouth to mouth with a laugh and an affirmative vote; in ten days it had swept the kingdom, and was become as familiar as the king's name. I was never known by any other designation afterward, whether in the nation's talk or in grave debate upon matters of state at the council-board of the sovereign. This title, translated into modern speech, would be THE BOSS. Elected by the nation. That suited me. And it was a pretty high title. There were very few THE'S, and I was one of them. If you spoke of the duke, or the earl, or the bishop, how could anybody tell which one you meant? But if you spoke of The King or The Queen or The Boss, it was different.

Well, I liked the king, and as king I respected him—respected the office; at least respected it as much as I was capable of respecting any unearned supremacy; but as MEN I looked down upon him and his nobles—privately. And he and they liked me, and respected my office; but as an animal, without birth or sham title, they looked down upon me—and were not particularly private about it, either. I didn't charge for my opinion about them, and they didn't charge for their opinion about me: the account was square, the books balanced, everybody was satisfied.

CHAPTER IX

THE TOURNAMENT

They were always having grand tournaments there at Camelot; and very stirring and picturesque and ridiculous human bull-fights they were, too, but just a little wearisome to the practical mind. However, I was generally on hand—for two reasons: a man must not hold himself aloof from the things which his friends and his community have at heart if he would be liked—especially as a statesman; and both as business man and statesman I wanted to study the tournament and see if I couldn't invent an improvement on it. That reminds me to remark, in passing, that the very first official thing I did, in my administration—and it was on the very first day of it, too—was to start a patent office; for I knew that a country without a patent office and good patent laws was just a crab, and couldn't travel any way but sideways or backways.

Things ran along, a tournament nearly every week; and now and then the boys used to want me to take a hand—I mean Sir Launcelot and the rest—but I said I would by and by; no hurry yet, and too much government machinery to oil up and set to rights and start a-going.

We had one tournament which was continued from day to day during more than a week, and as many as five hundred knights took part in it, from first to last. They were weeks gathering. They came on horseback from everywhere; from the very ends of the country, and even from beyond the sea; and many brought ladies, and all brought squires and troops of servants. It was a most gaudy and gorgeous crowd, as to costumery, and very characteristic of the country and the time, in the way of high animal spirits, innocent indecencies of language, and happy-hearted indifference to morals. It was fight or look on, all day and every day; and sing, gamble, dance, carouse half the night every night. They had a most noble good time. You never saw such people. Those banks of beautiful ladies, shining in their barbaric splendors, would see a knight sprawl from his horse in the lists with a lanceshaft the thickness of your ankle clean through him and the blood spouting, and instead of fainting they would clap their hands and crowd each other for a better view; only sometimes one would dive into her handkerchief, and look ostentatiously broken-hearted, and then you could lay two to one that there was a scandal there somewhere and she was afraid the public hadn't found it out.

The noise at night would have been annoying to me ordinarily, but I didn't mind it in the present circumstances, because it kept me from hearing the quacks detaching legs and arms from the day's cripples. They ruined an uncommon good old cross-cut saw for me, and broke the saw-buck, too, but I let it pass. And as for my axe—well, I made up my mind that the next time I lent an axe to a surgeon I would pick my century.

I not only watched this tournament from day to day, but detailed an intelligent priest from my Department of Public Morals and Agriculture, and ordered him to report it; for it was my purpose by and by, when I should have gotten the people along far enough, to start a newspaper. The first thing you want in a new country, is a patent office; then work up your school system; and after that, out with your paper. A newspaper has its faults, and plenty of them, but no matter, it's hark from the tomb for a dead nation, and don't you forget it. You can't resurrect a dead nation without it; there isn't any way. So I wanted to sample things, and be finding out what sort of reporter-material I might be able to rake together out of the sixth century when I should come to need it.

Well, the priest did very well, considering. He got in all the details, and that is a good thing in a local item: you see, he had kept books for the undertaker-department of his church when he was younger, and there, you know, the money's in the details; the more details, the more swag: bearers, mutes, candles, prayers —everything counts; and if the bereaved don't buy prayers enough you mark up your candles with a forked pencil, and your bill shows up all right. And he had a good knack at getting in the complimentary thing here and there about a knight that was likely to advertise—no, I mean a knight that had influence; and he also had a neat gift of exaggeration, for in his time he had kept door for a pious hermit who lived in a sty and worked miracles.

Of course this novice's report lacked whoop and crash and lurid description, and therefore wanted the true ring; but its antique wording was quaint and sweet and simple, and full of the fragrances and flavors of the time, and these little merits made up in a measure for its more important lacks. Here is an extract from it:

Then Sir Brian de les Isles and Grummore Grummorsum, knights of the castle, encountered with Sir Aglovale and Sir Tor, and Sir Tor smote down Sir Grummore Grummorsum to the earth. Then came Sir Carados of the dolorous tower, and Sir Turquine, knights of the castle, and there encountered with them Sir Percivale de Galis and Sir Lamorak de Galis, that were two brethren, and there encountered Sir Percivale with Sir Carados, and either brake their spears unto their hands, and then Sir Turquine with Sir Lamorak, and either of them smote down other, horse and all, to the earth, and either parties rescued other and horsed them again. And Sir Arnold, and Sir Gauter, knights of the castle, encountered with Sir Brandiles and Sir Kay, and these four knights encountered mightily, and brake their spears to their hands. Then came Sir Pertolope from the castle, and there encountered with him Sir Lionel, and there Sir Pertolope the green knight smote down Sir Lionel, brother to Sir Launcelot. All this was marked by noble heralds, who bare him best, and their names. Then Sir Bleobaris brake his spear upon Sir Gareth, but of that stroke Sir Bleobaris fell to the earth. When Sir Galihodin saw that, he bad Sir Gareth keep him, and Sir Gareth smote him to the earth. Then Sir Galihud gat a spear to avenge his brother, and in the same wise Sir Gareth served him, and Sir Dinadan and his brother La Cote Male Taile, and Sir Sagramore le Disirous, and Sir Dodinas le Savage; all these he bare down with one spear. When King Aswisance of Ireland saw Sir Gareth fare so he marvelled what he might be, that one time seemed green, and another time, at his again coming, he seemed blue. And thus at every course that he rode to and fro he changed his color, so that there might neither king nor knight have ready cognizance of him. Then Sir Agwisance the King of Ireland encountered with Sir Gareth, and there Sir Gareth smote him from his horse, saddle and all. And then came King Carados of Scotland, and Sir Gareth smote him down horse and man. And in the same wise he served King Uriens of the land of Gore. And then there came in Sir Bagdemagus, and Sir Gareth smote him down horse and man to the earth. And Bagdemagus's son

Meliganus brake a spear upon Sir Gareth mightily and knightly. And then Sir Galahault the noble prince cried on high, Knight with the many colors, well hast thou justed; now make thee ready that I may just with thee. Sir Gareth heard him, and he gat a great spear, and so they encountered together, and there the prince brake his spear; but Sir Gareth smote him upon the left side of the helm, that he reeled here and there, and he had fallen down had not his men recovered him. Truly, said King Arthur, that knight with the many colors is a good knight. Wherefore the king called unto him Sir Launcelot, and prayed him to encounter with that knight. Sir, said Launcelot, I may as well find in my heart for to forbear him at this time, for he hath had travail enough this day, and when a good knight doth so well upon some day, it is no good knight's part to let him of his worship, and, namely, when he seeth a knight hath done so great labour; for peradventure, said Sir Launcelot, his quarrel is here this day, and peradventure he is best beloved with this lady of all that be here, for I see well he paineth himself and enforceth him to do great deeds, and therefore, said Sir Launcelot, as for me, this day he shall have the honour; though it lay in my power to put him from it, I would not.

There was an unpleasant little episode that day, which for reasons of state I struck out of my priest's report. You will have noticed that Garry was doing some great fighting in the engagement. When I say Garry I mean Sir Gareth. Garry was my private pet name for him; it suggests that I had a deep affection for him, and that was the case. But it was a private pet name only, and never spoken aloud to any one, much less to him; being a noble, he would not have endured a familiarity like that from me. Well, to proceed: I sat in the private box set apart for me as the king's minister. While Sir Dinadan was waiting for his turn to enter the lists, he came in there and sat down and began to talk; for he was always making up to me, because I was a stranger and he liked to have a fresh market for his jokes, the most of them having reached that stage of wear where the teller has to do the laughing himself while the other person looks sick. I had always responded to his efforts as well as I could, and felt a very deep and real kindness for him, too, for the reason that if by malice of fate he knew the one particular anecdote which I had heard oftenest and had most hated and most loathed all my life, he had at least spared it me. It was one which I had heard attributed to every humorous person who had ever stood on American soil, from Columbus down to Artemus Ward. It was about a humorous lecturer who flooded an ignorant audience with the killingest jokes for an hour and never got a laugh; and then when he was leaving, some gray simpletons wrung him gratefully by the hand and said it had been the funniest thing they had ever heard, and "it was all they could do to keep from laughin' right out in meetin'." That anecdote never saw the day that it was worth the telling; and yet I had sat under the telling of it hundreds and thousands and millions and billions of times, and cried and cursed all the way through. Then who can bear to know what my feelings were, to hear this armor-plated ass start in on it again, in the murky twilight of tradition, before the dawn of history, while even Lactantius might be referred to as "the late Lactantius," and the Crusades wouldn't be born for five hundred years yet? Just as he finished, the call-boy came; so, haw-hawing like a demon, he went rattling and clanking out like a crate of loose castings, and I knew nothing more. It was some minutes before I came to, and then I opened my eyes just in time to see Sir Gareth fetch him an awful welt, and I unconsciously out with the prayer, "I hope to gracious he's killed!" But by ill-luck, before I had got half through with the words, Sir Gareth crashed into Sir Sagramor le Desirous and sent him thundering over his horse's crupper, and Sir Sagramor caught my remark and thought I meant it for *him*.

Well, whenever one of those people got a thing into his head, there was no getting it out again. I knew that, so I saved my breath, and offered no explanations. As soon as Sir Sagramor got well, he notified me that there was a little account to settle between us, and he named a day three or four years in the future; place of settlement, the lists where the offense had been given. I said I would be ready when he got back. You see, he was going for the Holy Grail. The boys all took a flier at the Holy Grail now and then. It was a several years' cruise. They always put in the long absence snooping around, in the most conscientious way, though none of them had any idea where the Holy Grail really was, and I don't think any of them actually expected to find it, or would have known what to do with it if he *had* run across it. You see, it was just the Northwest Passage of that day, as you may say; that was all. Every year expeditions went out holy grailing, and next year relief expeditions went out to hunt for *them*. There was worlds of reputation in it, but no money. Why, they actually wanted *me* to put in! Well, I should smile.

CHAPTER X

BEGINNINGS OF CIVILIZATION

The Round Table soon heard of the challenge, and of course it was a good deal discussed, for such things interested the boys. The king thought I ought now to set forth in quest of adventures, so that I might gain renown and be the more worthy to meet Sir Sagramor when the several years should have rolled away. I excused myself for the present; I said it would take me three or four years yet to get things well fixed up and going smoothly; then I should be ready; all the chances were that at the end of that time Sir Sagramor would still be out grailing, so no valuable time would be lost by the postponement; I should then have been in office six or seven years, and I believed my system and machinery would be so well developed that I could take a holiday without its working any harm.

I was pretty well satisfied with what I had already accomplished. In various quiet nooks and corners I had the beginnings of all sorts of industries under way—nuclei of future vast factories, the iron and steel missionaries of my future civilization. In these were gathered together the brightest young minds I could find, and I kept agents out raking the country for more, all the time. I was training a crowd of ignorant folk into experts—experts in every sort of handiwork and scientific calling. These nurseries of mine went smoothly and privately along undisturbed in their obscure country retreats, for nobody was allowed to come into their precincts without a special permit—for I was afraid of the Church.

I had started a teacher-factory and a lot of Sunday-schools the first thing; as a result, I now had an admirable system of graded schools in full blast in those places, and also a complete variety of Protestant congregations all in a prosperous and growing condition. Everybody could be any kind of a Christian he wanted to; there was perfect freedom in that matter. But I confined public religious teaching to the churches and the Sunday-schools, permitting nothing of it in my other educational buildings. I could have given my own sect the preference and made everybody a Presbyterian without any trouble, but that would have been to affront a law of human nature: spiritual wants and instincts are as various in the human family as are physical appetites, complexions, and features, and a man is only at his best, morally, when he is equipped with the religious garment whose color and shape and size most nicely accommodate themselves to the spiritual complexion, angularities, and stature of the individual who wears it; and, besides, I was afraid of a united Church; it makes a mighty power, the mightiest conceivable, and then when it by and by gets into selfish hands, as it is always bound to do, it means death to human liberty and paralysis to human thought.

All mines were royal property, and there were a good many of them. They had formerly been worked as savages always work mines—holes grubbed in the earth and the mineral brought up in sacks of hide by hand, at the rate of a ton a day; but I had begun to put the mining on a scientific basis as early as I could.

Yes, I had made pretty handsome progress when Sir Sagramor's challenge struck me.

Four years rolled by—and then! Well, you would never imagine it in the world. Unlimited power is the ideal thing when it is in safe hands. The despotism of heaven is the one absolutely perfect government. An earthly despotism would be the absolutely perfect earthly government, if the conditions were the same, namely, the despot the perfectest individual of the human race, and his lease of life perpetual. But as a perishable perfect man must die, and leave his despotism in the hands of an imperfect successor, an earthly despotism is not merely a bad form of government, it is the worst form that is possible.

My works showed what a despot could do with the resources of a kingdom at his command. Unsuspected by this dark land, I had the civilization of the nineteenth century booming under its very nose! It was fenced away from the public view, but there it was, a gigantic and unassailable fact—and to be heard from, yet, if I lived and had luck. There it was, as sure a fact and as substantial a fact as any serene volcano, standing innocent with its smokeless summit in the blue sky and giving no sign of the rising hell in its bowels. My schools and churches were children four years before; they were grown-up now; my shops of that day were vast factories now; where I had a dozen trained men then, I had a thousand now; where I had one brilliant expert then, I had fifty now. I stood with my hand on the cock, so to speak, ready to turn it on and flood the midnight world with light at any moment. But I was not going to do the thing in that sudden way. It was not my policy. The people could not have stood it; and, moreover, I should have had the Established Roman Catholic Church on my back in a minute.

No, I had been going cautiously all the while. I had had confidential agents trickling through the country some time, whose office was to undermine knighthood by imperceptible degrees, and to gnaw a little at this and that and the other superstition, and so prepare the way gradually for a better order of things. I was turning on my light one-candle-power at a time, and meant to continue to do so.

I had scattered some branch schools secretly about the kingdom, and they were doing very well. I meant to work this racket more and more, as time wore on, if nothing occurred to frighten me. One of my deepest secrets was my West Point—my military academy. I kept that most jealously out of sight; and I did the same with my naval academy which I had established at a remote seaport. Both were prospering to my satisfaction.

Clarence was twenty-two now, and was my head executive, my right hand. He was a darling; he was equal to anything; there wasn't anything he couldn't turn his hand to. Of late I had been training him for journalism, for the time seemed about right for a start in the newspaper line; nothing big, but just a small weekly for experimental circulation in my civilization-nurseries. He took to it like a duck; there was an editor concealed in him, sure. Already he had doubled himself in one way; he talked sixth century and wrote nineteenth. His journalistic style was climbing, steadily; it was already up to the back settlement Alabama mark, and couldn't be told from the editorial output of that region either by matter or flavor.

We had another large departure on hand, too. This was a telegraph and a telephone; our first venture in this line. These wires were for private service only, as yet, and must be kept private until a riper day should come. We had a gang of men on the road, working mainly by night. They were stringing ground wires; we were afraid to put up poles, for they would attract too much inquiry. Ground wires were good enough, in both instances, for my wires were protected by an insulation of my own invention which was perfect. My men had orders to strike across country, avoiding roads, and establishing connection with any considerable towns whose lights betrayed their presence, and leaving experts in charge. Nobody could tell you how to find any place in the kingdom, for nobody ever went intentionally to any place, but only struck it by accident in his wanderings, and then generally left it without thinking to inquire what its name was. At one time and another we had sent out topographical expeditions to survey and map the kingdom, but the priests had always interfered and raised trouble. So we had given the thing up, for the present; it would be poor wisdom to antagonize the Church.

As for the general condition of the country, it was as it had been when I arrived in it, to all intents and purposes. I had made changes, but they were necessarily slight, and they were not noticeable. Thus far, I had not even meddled with taxation, outside of the taxes which provided the royal revenues. I had systematized those, and put the service on an effective and righteous basis. As a result, these revenues were already quadrupled, and yet the burden was so much more equably distributed than before, that all the kingdom felt a sense of relief, and the praises of my administration were hearty and general.

Personally, I struck an interruption, now, but I did not mind it, it could not have happened at a better time. Earlier it could have annoyed me, but now everything was in good hands and swimming right along. The king had reminded me several times, of late, that the postponement I had asked for, four years before, had about run out now. It was a hint that I ought to be starting out to seek adventures and get up a reputation of a size to make me worthy of the honor of breaking a lance with Sir Sagramor, who was still out grailing, but was being hunted for by various relief expeditions, and might be found any year, now. So you see I was expecting this interruption; it did not take me by surprise.

CHAPTER XI

THE YANKEE IN SEARCH OF ADVENTURES

There never was such a country for wandering liars; and they were of both sexes. Hardly a month went by without one of these tramps arriving; and generally loaded with a tale about some princess or other wanting help to get her out of some far-away castle where she was held in captivity by a lawless scoundrel, usually a giant. Now you would think that the first thing the king would do after listening to such a novelette from an entire stranger, would be to ask for credentials—yes, and a pointer or two as to locality of castle, best route to it, and so on. But nobody ever thought of so simple and common-sense a thing at that. No, everybody swallowed these people's lies whole, and never asked a question of any sort or about anything. Well, one day when I was not around, one of these people came along—it was a she one, this time—and told a tale of the usual pattern. Her mistress was a captive in a vast and gloomy castle, along with forty-four other young and beautiful girls, pretty much all of them princesses; they had been languishing in that cruel captivity for twenty-six years; the masters of the castle were three stupendous brothers, each with four arms and one eye—the eye in the center of the forehead, and as big as a fruit. Sort of fruit not mentioned; their usual slovenliness in statistics.

Would you believe it? The king and the whole Round Table were in raptures over this preposterous opportunity for adventure. Every knight of the Table jumped for the chance, and begged for it; but to their vexation and chagrin the king conferred it upon me, who had not asked for it at all.

By an effort, I contained my joy when Clarence brought me the news. But he—he could not contain his. His mouth gushed delight and gratitude in a steady discharge—delight in my good fortune, gratitude to the king for this splendid mark of his favor for me. He could keep neither his legs nor his body still, but pirouetted about the place in an airy ecstasy of happiness.

On my side, I could have cursed the kindness that conferred upon me this benefaction, but I kept my vexation under the surface for policy's sake, and did what I could to let on to be glad. Indeed, I *said* I was glad. And in a way it was true; I was as glad as a person is when he is scalped.

Well, one must make the best of things, and not waste time with useless fretting, but get down to business and see what can be done. In all lies there is wheat among the chaff; I must get at the wheat in this case: so I sent for the girl and she came. She was a comely enough creature, and soft and modest, but, if signs went for anything, she didn't know as much as a lady's watch. I said:

"My dear, have you been questioned as to particulars?"

She said she hadn't.

"Well, I didn't expect you had, but I thought I would ask, to make sure; it's the way I've been raised. Now you mustn't take it unkindly if I remind you that as we don't know you, we must go a little slow. You may be all right, of course, and we'll hope that you are; but to take it for granted isn't business. *You* understand that. I'm obliged to ask you a few questions; just answer up fair and square, and don't be afraid. Where do you live, when you are at home?"

"In the land of Moder, fair sir."

"Land of Moder. I don't remember hearing of it before. Parents living?"

"As to that, I know not if they be yet on live, sith it is many years that I have lain shut up in the castle."

"Your name, please?"

"I hight the Demoiselle Alisande la Carteloise, an it please you."

"Do you know anybody here who can identify you?"

"That were not likely, fair lord, I being come hither now for the first time."

"Have you brought any letters—any documents—any proofs that you are trustworthy and truthful?"

"Of a surety, no; and wherefore should I? Have I not a tongue, and cannot I say all that myself?"

"But *your* saying it, you know, and somebody else's saying it, is different."

"Different? How might that be? I fear me I do not understand."

"Don't *understand*? Land of—why, you see—you see—why, great Scott, can't you understand a little thing like that? Can't you understand the difference between your—*why* do you look so innocent and idiotic!"

"I? In truth I know not, but an it were the will of God."

"Yes, yes, I reckon that's about the size of it. Don't mind my seeming excited; I'm not. Let us change the subject. Now as to this castle, with forty-five princesses in it, and three ogres at the head of it, tell me—where is this harem?"

"Harem?"

"The *castle*, you understand; where is the castle?"

"Oh, as to that, it is great, and strong, and well beseen, and lieth in a far country. Yes, it is many leagues."

"*How* many?"

"Ah, fair sir, it were woundily hard to tell, they are so many, and do so lap the one upon the other, and being made all in the same image and tincted with the same color, one may not know the one league from its fellow, nor how to count them except they be taken apart, and ye wit well it were God's work to do that, being not within man's capacity; for ye will note—"

"Hold on, hold on, never mind about the distance; *whereabouts* does the castle lie? What's the direction from here?"

"Ah, please you sir, it hath no direction from here; by reason that the road lieth not straight, but turneth evermore; wherefore the direction of its place abideth not, but is some time under the one sky and anon under another, whereso if ye be minded that it is in the east, and wend thitherward, ye shall observe that the way of the road doth yet again turn upon itself by the space of half a circle, and this marvel happing again and yet again and still again, it will grieve you that you had thought by vanities of the mind to thwart and bring to naught the will of Him that giveth not a castle a direction from a place except it pleaseth Him, and if it please Him not, will the rather that even all castles and all directions thereunto vanish out of the earth, leaving the places wherein they tarried desolate and vacant, so warning His creatures that where He will He will, and where He will not He—"

"Oh, that's all right, that's all right, give us a rest; never mind about the direction, *hang* the direction—I beg pardon, I beg a thousand pardons, I am not well to-day; pay no attention when I soliloquize, it is an old habit, an old, bad habit, and hard to get rid of when one's digestion is all disordered with eating food that was raised forever and ever before he was born; good land! a man can't keep his functions regular on spring chickens thirteen hundred years old. But come—never mind about that; let's—have you got such a thing as a map of that region about you? Now a good map—"

"Is it peradventure that manner of thing which of late the unbelievers have brought from over the great seas, which, being boiled in oil, and an onion and salt added thereto, doth—"

"What, a map? What are you talking about? Don't you know what a map is? There, there, never mind, don't explain, I hate explanations; they fog a thing up so that you can't tell anything about it. Run along, dear; good-day; show her the way, Clarence."

Oh, well, it was reasonably plain, now, why these donkeys didn't prospect these liars for details. It may be that this girl had a fact in her somewhere, but I don't believe you could have sluiced it out with a hydraulic; nor got it with the earlier forms of blasting, even; it was a case for dynamite. Why, she was a perfect ass; and yet the king and his knights had listened to her as if she had been a leaf out of the gospel. It kind of sizes up the whole party. And think of the simple ways of this court: this wandering wench hadn't any more trouble to get access to the king in his palace than she would have had to get into the poorhouse in my day and country. In fact, he was glad to see her, glad to hear her tale; with that adventure of hers to offer, she was as welcome as a corpse is to a coroner.

Just as I was ending-up these reflections, Clarence came back. I remarked upon the barren result of my efforts with the girl; hadn't got hold of a single point that could help me to find the castle. The youth looked a little surprised, or puzzled, or something, and intimated that he had been wondering to himself what I had wanted to ask the girl all those questions for.

"Why, great guns," I said, "don't I want to find the castle? And how else would I go about it?"

"La, sweet your worship, one may lightly answer that, I ween. She will go with thee. They always do. She will ride with thee."

"Ride with me? Nonsense!"

"But of a truth she will. She will ride with thee. Thou shalt see."

"What? She browse around the hills and scour the woods with me —alone—and I as good as engaged to be married? Why, it's scandalous. Think how it would look."

My, the dear face that rose before me! The boy was eager to know all about this tender matter. I swore him to secrecy and then whispered her name—"Puss Flanagan." He looked disappointed, and said he didn't remember the countess. How natural it was for the little courtier to give her a rank. He asked me where she lived.

"In East Har—" I came to myself and stopped, a little confused; then I said, "Never mind, now; I'll tell you some time."

And might he see her? Would I let him see her some day?

It was but a little thing to promise—thirteen hundred years or so—and he so eager; so I said Yes. But I sighed; I couldn't help it. And yet there was no sense in sighing, for she wasn't born yet. But that is the way we are made: we don't reason, where we feel; we just feel.

My expedition was all the talk that day and that night, and the boys were very good to me, and made much of me, and seemed to have forgotten their vexation and disappointment, and come to be as anxious for me to hive those ogres and set those ripe old virgins loose as if it were themselves that had the contract. Well, they *were* good children—but just children, that is all. And they gave me no end of points about how to scout for giants, and how to scoop them in; and they told me all sorts of charms against enchantments, and gave me salves and other rubbish to put on my wounds. But it never occurred to one of them to reflect that if I was such a wonderful necromancer as I was pretending to be, I ought not to need salves or instructions, or charms against enchantments, and, least of all, arms and armor, on a foray of any kind—even against fire-spouting dragons, and devils hot from perdition, let alone such poor adversaries as these I was after, these commonplace ogres of the back settlements.

I was to have an early breakfast, and start at dawn, for that was the usual way; but I had the demon's own time with my armor, and this delayed me a little. It is troublesome to get into, and there is so much detail. First you wrap a layer or two of blanket around your body, for a sort of cushion and to keep off the cold iron; then you put on your sleeves and shirt of chain mail—these are made of small steel links woven together, and they form a fabric so flexible that if you toss your shirt onto the floor, it slumps into a pile like a peck of wet fish-net; it is very heavy and is nearly the uncomfortablest material in the world for a night shirt, yet plenty used it for that—tax collectors, and reformers, and one-horse kings with a defective title, and those sorts of people; then you put on your shoes—flat-boats roofed over with interleaving bands of steel—and screw your clumsy spurs into the heels. Next you buckle your greaves on your legs, and your cuisses on your thighs; then come your backplate and your breastplate, and you begin to feel crowded; then you hitch onto the breastplate the half-petticoat of broad overlapping bands of steel which hangs down in front but is scolloped out behind so you can sit down, and isn't any real improvement on an inverted coal scuttle, either for looks or for wear, or to wipe your hands on; next you belt on your sword; then you put your stove-pipe joints onto your arms, your iron gauntlets onto your hands, your iron rat-trap onto your head, with a rag of steel web hitched onto it to hang over the back of your neck—and there you are, snug as a candle in a candle-mould. This is no time to dance. Well, a man that is packed away like that is a nut that isn't worth the cracking, there is so little of the meat, when you get down to it, by comparison with the shell.

The boys helped me, or I never could have got in. Just as we finished, Sir Bedivere happened in, and I saw that as like as not I hadn't chosen the most convenient outfit for a long trip. How stately he looked; and tall and broad and grand. He had on his head a conical steel casque that only came down to his ears, and for visor had only a narrow steel bar that extended down to his upper lip and protected his nose; and all the rest of him, from neck to heel, was flexible chain mail, trousers and all. But pretty much all of him was hidden under his outside garment, which of course was of chain mail, as I said, and hung straight from his shoulders to his ankles; and from his middle to the bottom, both before and behind, was divided, so that he could ride and let the skirts hang down on each side. He was going grailing, and it was just the outfit for it, too. I would have given a good deal for that ulster, but it was too late now to be fooling around. The sun was just up, the king and the court were all on hand to see me off and wish me luck; so it wouldn't be etiquette for me to tarry. You don't get on your horse yourself; no, if you tried it you would get disappointed. They carry you out, just as they carry a sun-struck man to the drug store, and put you on, and help get you to rights, and fix your feet in the stirrups; and all the while you do feel so strange and stuffy and like somebody else—like somebody that has been married on a sudden, or struck by lightning, or something like that, and hasn't quite fetched around yet, and is sort of numb, and can't just get his bearings. Then they stood up the mast they called a spear, in its socket by my left foot, and I gripped it with my hand; lastly they hung my shield around my neck, and I was all complete and ready to up anchor and get to sea. Everybody was as good to me as they could be, and a maid of honor gave me the stirrup-cup her own self. There was nothing more to do now, but for that damsel to get up behind me on a pillion, which she did, and put an arm or so around me to hold on.

And so we started, and everybody gave us a goodbye and waved their handkerchiefs or helmets. And everybody we met, going down the hill and through the village was respectful to us, except some shabby little boys on the outskirts. They said:

"Oh, what a guy!" And hove clods at us.

In my experience boys are the same in all ages. They don't respect anything, they don't care for anything or anybody. They say "Go up, baldhead" to the prophet going his unoffending way in the gray of antiquity; they sass me in the holy gloom of the Middle Ages; and I had seen them act the same way in Buchanan's administration; I remember, because I was there and helped. The prophet had his bears and settled with his boys; and I wanted to get down and settle with mine, but it wouldn't answer, because I couldn't have got up again. I hate a country without a derrick.

CHAPTER XII

SLOW TORTURE

Straight off, we were in the country. It was most lovely and pleasant in those sylvan solitudes in the early cool morning in the first freshness of autumn. From hilltops we saw fair green valleys lying spread out below, with streams winding through them, and island groves of trees here and there, and huge lonely oaks scattered about and casting black blots of shade; and beyond the valleys we saw the ranges of hills, blue with haze, stretching away in billowy perspective to the horizon, with at wide intervals a dim fleck of white or gray on a wave-summit, which we knew was a castle. We crossed broad natural lawns sparkling with dew, and we moved like spirits, the cushioned turf giving out no sound of footfall; we dreamed along through glades in a mist of green light that got its tint from the sun-drenched roof of leaves overhead, and by our feet the clearest and coldest of runlets went frisking and gossiping over its reefs and making a sort of whispering music, comfortable to hear; and at times we left the world behind and entered into the solemn great deeps and rich gloom of the forest, where furtive wild things whisked and scurried by and were gone before you could even get your eye on the place where the noise was; and where only the earliest birds were turning out and getting to business with a song here and a quarrel yonder and a mysterious far-off hammering and drumming for worms on a tree trunk away somewhere in the impenetrable remotenesses of the woods. And by and by out we would swing again into the glare.

About the third or fourth or fifth time that we swung out into the glare—it was along there somewhere, a couple of hours or so after sun-up—it wasn't as pleasant as it had been. It was beginning to get hot. This was quite noticeable. We had a very long pull, after that, without any shade. Now it is curious how progressively little frets grow and multiply after they once get a start. Things which I didn't mind at all, at first, I began to mind now—and more and more, too, all the time. The first ten or fifteen times I wanted my handkerchief I didn't seem to care; I got along, and said never mind, it isn't any matter, and dropped it out of my mind. But now it was different; I wanted it all the time; it was nag, nag, nag, right along, and no rest; I couldn't get it out of my mind; and so at last I lost my temper and said hang a man that would make a suit of armor without any pockets in it. You see I had my handkerchief in my helmet; and some other things; but it was that kind of a helmet that you can't take off by yourself. That hadn't occurred to me when I put it there; and in fact I didn't know it. I supposed it would be particularly convenient there. And so now, the thought of its being there, so handy and close by, and yet not get-at-able, made it all the worse and the harder to bear. Yes, the thing that you can't get is the thing that you want, mainly; every one has noticed that. Well, it took my mind off from everything else; took it clear off, and centered it in my helmet; and mile after mile, there it stayed, imagining the handkerchief, picturing the handkerchief; and it was bitter and aggravating to have the salt sweat keep trickling down into my eyes, and I couldn't get at it. It seems like a little thing, on paper, but it was not a little thing at all; it was the most real kind of misery. I would not say it if it was not so. I made up my mind that I would carry along a reticule next time, let it look how it might, and people say what they would. Of course these iron dudes of the Round Table would think it was scandalous, and maybe raise Sheol about it, but as for me, give me comfort first, and style afterwards. So we jogged along, and now and then we struck a stretch of dust, and it would tumble up in clouds and get into my nose and make me sneeze and cry; and of course I said things I oughtn't to have said, I don't deny that. I am not better than others.

We couldn't seem to meet anybody in this lonesome Britain, not even an ogre; and, in the mood I was in then, it was well for the ogre; that is, an ogre with a handkerchief. Most knights would have thought of nothing but getting his armor; but so I got his bandanna, he could keep his hardware, for all of me.

Meantime, it was getting hotter and hotter in there. You see, the sun was beating down and warming up the iron more and more all the time. Well, when you are hot, that way, every little thing irritates you. When I trotted, I rattled like a crate of dishes, and that annoyed me; and moreover I couldn't seem to stand that shield slatting and banging, now about my breast, now around my back; and if I dropped into a walk my joints creaked and screeched in that wearisome way that a wheelbarrow does, and as we didn't create any breeze at that gait, I was like to get fried in that stove; and besides, the quieter you went the heavier the iron settled down on you and the more and more tons you seemed to weigh every minute. And you had to be always changing hands, and passing your spear over to the other foot, it got so irksome for one hand to hold it long at a time.

Well, you know, when you perspire that way, in rivers, there comes a time when you—when you—well, when you itch. You are inside, your hands are outside; so there you are; nothing but iron between. It is not a light thing, let it sound as it may. First it is one place; then another; then some more; and it goes on spreading and spreading, and at last the territory is all occupied, and nobody can imagine what you feel like, nor how unpleasant it is. And when it had got to the worst, and it seemed to me that I could not stand anything more, a fly got in through the bars and settled on my nose, and the bars were stuck and wouldn't work, and I couldn't get the visor up; and I could only shake my head, which was baking hot by this time, and the fly—well, you know how a fly acts when he has got a certainty—he only minded the shaking enough to change from nose to lip, and lip to ear, and buzz and buzz all around in there, and keep on lighting and biting, in a way that a person, already so distressed as I was, simply could not stand. So I gave in, and got Alisande to unship the helmet and relieve me of it. Then she emptied the conveniences out of it and fetched it full of water, and I drank and then stood up, and she poured the rest down inside the armor. One cannot think how refreshing it was. She continued to fetch and pour until I was well soaked and thoroughly comfortable.

It was good to have a rest—and peace. But nothing is quite perfect in this life, at any time. I had made a pipe a while back, and also some pretty fair tobacco; not the real thing, but what some of the Indians use: the inside bark of the willow, dried. These comforts had been in the helmet, and now I had them again, but no matches.

Gradually, as the time wore along, one annoying fact was borne in upon my understanding—that we were weather-bound. An armed novice cannot mount his horse without help and plenty of it. Sandy was not enough; not enough for me, anyway. We had to wait until somebody should come along. Waiting, in silence, would have been agreeable enough, for I was full of matter for reflection, and wanted to give it a chance to work. I wanted to try and think out how it was that rational or even half-rational men could ever have learned to wear armor, considering its inconveniences; and how they had managed to keep up such a fashion for generations when it was plain that what I had suffered to-day they had had to suffer all the days of their lives. I wanted to think that out; and moreover I wanted to think out some way to reform this evil and persuade the people to let the foolish fashion die out; but thinking was out of the question in the circumstances. You couldn't think, where Sandy was.

She was a quite biddable creature and good-hearted, but she had a flow of talk that was as steady as a mill, and made your head sore like the drays and wagons in a city. If she had had a cork she would have been a comfort. But you can't cork that kind; they would die. Her clack was going all day, and you would think something would surely happen to her works, by and by; but no, they never got out of order; and she never had to slack up for words. She could grind, and pump, and churn, and buzz by the week, and never stop to oil up or blow out. And yet the result was just nothing but wind. She never had any ideas, any more than a fog has. She was a perfect blatherskite; I mean for jaw, jaw, jaw, talk, talk, talk, jabber, jabber, jabber; but just as good as she could be. I hadn't minded her mill that morning, on account of having that hornets' nest of other troubles; but more than once in the afternoon I had to say:

"Take a rest, child; the way you are using up all the domestic air, the kingdom will have to go to importing it by to-morrow, and it's a low enough treasury without that."

CHAPTER XIII

FREEMEN

Yes, it is strange how little a while at a time a person can be contented. Only a little while back, when I was riding and suffering, what a heaven this peace, this rest, this sweet serenity in this secluded shady nook by this purling stream would have seemed, where I could keep perfectly comfortable all the time by pouring a dipper of water into my armor now and then; yet already I was getting dissatisfied; partly because I could not light my pipe—for, although I had long ago started a match factory, I had forgotten to bring matches with me—and partly because we had nothing to eat. Here was another illustration of the childlike improvidence of this age and people. A man in armor always trusted to chance for his food on a journey, and would have been scandalized at the idea of hanging a basket of sandwiches on his spear. There was probably not a knight of all the Round Table combination who would not rather have died than been caught carrying such a thing as that on his flagstaff. And yet there could not be anything more sensible. It had been my intention to smuggle a couple of sandwiches into my helmet, but I was interrupted in the act, and had to make an excuse and lay them aside, and a dog got them.

Night approached, and with it a storm. The darkness came on fast. We must camp, of course. I found a good shelter for the demoiselle under a rock, and went off and found another for myself. But I was obliged to remain in my armor, because I could not get it off by myself and yet could not allow Alisande to help, because it would have seemed so like undressing before folk. It would not have amounted to that in reality, because I had clothes on underneath; but the prejudices of one's breeding are not gotten rid of just at a jump, and I knew that when it came to stripping off that bob-tailed iron petticoat I should be embarrassed.

With the storm came a change of weather; and the stronger the wind blew, and the wilder the rain lashed around, the colder and colder it got. Pretty soon, various kinds of bugs and ants and worms and things began to flock in out of the wet and crawl down inside my armor to get warm; and while some of them behaved well enough, and snuggled up amongst my clothes and got quiet, the majority were of a restless, uncomfortable sort, and never stayed still, but went on prowling and hunting for they did not know what; especially the ants, which went tickling along in wearisome procession from one end of me to the other by the hour, and are a kind of creatures which I never wish to sleep with again. It would be my advice to persons situated in this way, to not roll or thrash around, because this excites the interest of all the different sorts of animals and makes every last one of them want to turn out and see what is going on, and this makes things worse than they were before, and of course makes you objurgate harder, too, if you can. Still, if one did not roll and thrash around he would die; so perhaps it is as well to do one way as the other; there is no real choice. Even after I was frozen solid I could still distinguish that tickling, just as a corpse does when he is taking electric treatment. I said I would never wear armor after this trip.

All those trying hours whilst I was frozen and yet was in a

living fire, as you may say, on account of that swarm of crawlers, that same unanswerable question kept circling and circling through my tired head: How do people stand this miserable armor? How have they managed to stand it all these generations? How can they sleep at night for dreading the tortures of next day?

When the morning came at last, I was in a bad enough plight: seedy, drowsy, fagged, from want of sleep; weary from thrashing around, famished from long fasting; pining for a bath, and to get rid of the animals; and crippled with rheumatism. And how had it fared with the nobly born, the titled aristocrat, the Demoiselle Alisande la Carteloise? Why, she was as fresh as a squirrel; she had slept like the dead; and as for a bath, probably neither she nor any other noble in the land had ever had one, and so she was not missing it. Measured by modern standards, they were merely modified savages, those people. This noble lady showed no impatience to get to breakfast—and that smacks of the savage, too. On their journeys those Britons were used to long fasts, and knew how to bear them; and also how to freight up against probable fasts before starting, after the style of the Indian and the anaconda. As like as not, Sandy was loaded for a three-day stretch.

We were off before sunrise, Sandy riding and I limping along behind. In half an hour we came upon a group of ragged poor creatures who had assembled to mend the thing which was regarded as a road. They were as humble as animals to me; and when I proposed to breakfast with them, they were so flattered, so overwhelmed by this extraordinary condescension of mine that at first they were not able to believe that I was in earnest. My lady put up her scornful lip and withdrew to one side; she said in their hearing that she would as soon think of eating with the other cattle—a remark which embarrassed these poor devils merely because it referred to them, and not because it insulted or offended them, for it didn't. And yet they were not slaves, not chattels. By a sarcasm of law and phrase they were freemen. Seven-tenths of the free population of the country were of just their class and degree: small "independent" farmers, artisans, etc.; which is to say, they were the nation, the actual Nation; they were about all of it that was useful, or worth saving, or really respect-worthy, and to subtract them would have been to subtract the Nation and leave behind some dregs, some refuse, in the shape of a king, nobility and gentry, idle, unproductive, acquainted mainly with the arts of wasting and destroying, and of no sort of use or value in any rationally constructed world. And yet, by ingenious contrivance, this gilded minority, instead of being in the tail of the procession where it belonged, was marching head up and banners flying, at the other end of it; had elected itself to be the Nation, and these innumerable clams had permitted it so long that they had come at last to accept it as a truth; and not only that, but to believe it right and as it should be. The priests had told their fathers and themselves that this ironical state of things was ordained of God; and so, not reflecting upon how unlike God it would be to amuse himself with sarcasms, and especially such poor transparent ones as this, they had dropped the matter there and become respectfully quiet.

The talk of these meek people had a strange enough sound in a formerly American ear. They were freemen, but they could not leave the estates of their lord or their bishop without his permission; they could not prepare their own bread, but must have their corn ground and their bread baked at his mill and his bakery, and pay roundly for the same; they could not sell a piece of their own property without paying him a handsome percentage of the proceeds, nor buy a piece of somebody else's without remembering him in cash for the privilege; they had to harvest his grain for him gratis, and be ready to come at a moment's notice, leaving their own crop to destruction by the threatened storm; they had to let him plant fruit trees in their fields, and then keep their indignation to themselves when his heedless fruit-gatherers trampled the grain around the trees; they had to smother their anger when his hunting parties galloped through their fields laying waste the result of their patient toil; they were not allowed to keep doves themselves, and when the swarms from my lord's dovecote settled on their crops they must not lose their temper and kill a bird, for awful would the penalty be; when the harvest was at last gathered, then came the procession of robbers to levy their blackmail upon it: first the Church carted off its fat tenth, then the king's commissioner took his twentieth, then my lord's people made a mighty inroad upon the remainder; after which, the skinned freeman had liberty to bestow the remnant in his barn, in case it was worth the trouble; there were taxes, and taxes, and taxes, and more taxes, and taxes again, and yet other taxes—upon this free and independent pauper, but none upon his lord the baron or the bishop, none upon the wasteful nobility or the all-devouring Church; if the baron would sleep unvexed, the freeman must sit up all night after his day's work and whip the ponds to keep the frogs quiet; if the freeman's daughter—but no, that last infamy of monarchical government is unprintable; and finally, if the freeman, grown desperate with his tortures, found his life unendurable under such conditions, and sacrificed it and fled to death for mercy and refuge, the gentle Church condemned him to eternal fire, the gentle law buried him at midnight at the cross-roads with a stake through his back, and his master the baron or the bishop confiscated all his property and turned his widow and his orphans out of doors.

And here were these freemen assembled in the early morning to work on their lord the bishop's road three days each—gratis; every head of a family, and every son of a family, three days each, gratis, and a day or so added for their servants. Why, it was like reading about France and the French, before the ever memorable and blessed Revolution, which swept a thousand years of such villany away in one swift tidal-wave of blood—one: a settlement of that hoary debt in the proportion of half a drop of blood for each hogshead of it that had been pressed by slow tortures out of that people in the weary stretch of ten centuries of wrong and shame and misery the like of which was not to be mated but in hell. There were two "Reigns of Terror," if we would but remember it and consider it; the one wrought murder in hot passion, the other in heartless cold blood; the one lasted mere months, the other had lasted a thousand years; the one inflicted death upon ten thousand persons, the other upon a hundred millions; but our shudders are all for the "horrors" of the minor Terror, the momentary Terror, so to speak; whereas, what is the horror of swift death by the axe, compared with lifelong death from hunger, cold, insult, cruelty, and heart-break? What is swift death by lightning compared with death by slow fire at the stake? A city cemetery could contain the coffins filled by that brief Terror which we have all been so diligently taught to shiver at and mourn over; but all France could hardly contain the coffins filled by that older and real Terror —that unspeakably bitter and awful Terror which none of us has been taught to see in its vastness or pity as it deserves.

These poor ostensible freemen who were sharing their breakfast and their talk with me, were as full of humble reverence for their king and Church and nobility as their worst enemy could desire. There was something pitifully ludicrous about it. I asked them if they supposed a nation of people ever existed, who, with a free vote in every man's hand, would elect that a single family and its descendants should reign over it forever, whether gifted or boobies, to the exclusion of all other families—including the voter's; and would also elect that a certain hundred families should be raised to dizzy summits of rank, and clothed on with offensive transmissible glories and privileges to the exclusion of the rest of the nation's families—*including his own.*

They all looked unhit, and said they didn't know; that they had never thought about it before, and it hadn't ever occurred to them that a nation could be so situated that every man *could* have a say in the government. I said I had seen one—and that it would last until it had an Established Church. Again they were all unhit—at first. But presently one man looked up and asked me to state that proposition again; and state it slowly, so it could soak into his understanding. I did it; and after a little he had the idea, and he brought his fist down and said *he* didn't believe a nation where every man had a vote would voluntarily get down in the mud and dirt in any such way; and that to steal from a nation its will and preference must be a crime and the first of all crimes. I said to myself:

"This one's a man. If I were backed by enough of his sort, I would make a strike for the welfare of this country, and try to prove myself its loyalest citizen by making a wholesome change in its system of government."

You see my kind of loyalty was loyalty to one's country, not to its institutions or its office-holders. The country is the real thing, the substantial thing, the eternal thing; it is the thing to watch over, and care for, and be loyal to; institutions are extraneous, they are its mere clothing, and clothing can wear out, become ragged, cease to be comfortable, cease to protect the body from winter, disease, and death. To be loyal to rags, to shout for rags, to worship rags, to die for rags—that is a loyalty of unreason, it is pure animal; it belongs to monarchy, was invented by monarchy; let monarchy keep it. I was from Connecticut, whose Constitution declares "that all political power is inherent in the people, and all free governments are founded on their authority and instituted for their benefit; and that they have *at all times* an undeniable and indefeasible right to *alter their form of government* in such a manner as they may think expedient."

Under that gospel, the citizen who thinks he sees that the commonwealth's political clothes are worn out, and yet holds his peace and does not agitate for a new suit, is disloyal; he is a traitor. That he may be the only one who thinks he sees this decay, does not excuse him; it is his duty to agitate anyway, and it is the duty of the others to vote him down if they do not see the matter as he does.

And now here I was, in a country where a right to say how the country should be governed was restricted to six persons in each thousand of its population. For the nine hundred and ninety-four to express dissatisfaction with the regnant system and propose to change it, would have made the whole six shudder as one man, it would have been so disloyal, so dishonorable, such putrid black treason. So to speak, I was become a stockholder in a corporation where nine hundred and ninety-four of the members furnished all the money and did all the work, and the other six elected themselves a permanent board of direction and took all the dividends. It seemed to me that what the nine hundred and ninety-four dupes needed was a new deal. The thing that would have best suited the circus side of my nature would have been to resign

the Boss-ship and get up an insurrection and turn it into a revolution; but I knew that the Jack Cade or the Wat Tyler who tries such a thing without first educating his materials up to revolution grade is almost absolutely certain to get left. I had never been accustomed to getting left, even if I do say it myself. Wherefore, the "deal" which had been for some time working into shape in my mind was of a quite different pattern from the Cade-Tyler sort.

So I did not talk blood and insurrection to that man there who sat munching black bread with that abused and mistaught herd of human sheep, but took him aside and talked matter of another sort to him. After I had finished, I got him to lend me a little ink from his veins; and with this and a sliver I wrote on a piece of bark—

Put him in the Man-factory—

and gave it to him, and said:

"Take it to the palace at Camelot and give it into the hands of Amyas le Poulet, whom I call Clarence, and he will understand."

"He is a priest, then," said the man, and some of the enthusiasm went out of his face.

"How—a priest? Didn't I tell you that no chattel of the Church, no bond-slave of pope or bishop can enter my Man-Factory? Didn't I tell you that *you* couldn't enter unless your religion, whatever it might be, was your own free property?"

"Marry, it is so, and for that I was glad; wherefore it liked me not, and bred in me a cold doubt, to hear of this priest being there."

"But he isn't a priest, I tell you."

The man looked far from satisfied. He said:

"He is not a priest, and yet can read?"

"He is not a priest and yet can read—yes, and write, too, for that matter. I taught him myself." The man's face cleared. "And it is the first thing that you yourself will be taught in that Factory—"

"I? I would give blood out of my heart to know that art. Why, I will be your slave, your—"

"No you won't, you won't be anybody's slave. Take your family and go along. Your lord the bishop will confiscate your small property, but no matter. Clarence will fix you all right."

CHAPTER XIV

"DEFEND THEE, LORD"

I paid three pennies for my breakfast, and a most extravagant price it was, too, seeing that one could have breakfasted a dozen persons for that money; but I was feeling good by this time, and I had always been a kind of spendthrift anyway; and then these people had wanted to give me the food for nothing, scant as their provision was, and so it was a grateful pleasure to emphasize my appreciation and sincere thankfulness with a good big financial lift where the money would do so much more good than it would in my helmet, where, these pennies being made of iron and not stinted in weight, my half-dollar's worth was a good deal of a burden to me. I spent money rather too freely in those days, it is true; but one reason for it was that I hadn't got the proportions of things entirely adjusted, even yet, after so long a sojourn in Britain—hadn't got along to where I was able to absolutely realize that a penny in Arthur's land and a couple of dollars in Connecticut were about one and the same thing: just twins, as you may say, in purchasing power. If my start from Camelot could have been delayed a very few days I could have paid these people in beautiful new coins from our own mint, and that would have pleased me; and them, too, not less. I had adopted the American values exclusively. In a week or two now, cents, nickels, dimes, quarters, and half-dollars, and also a trifle of gold, would be trickling in thin but steady streams all through the commercial veins of the kingdom, and I looked to see this new blood freshen up its life.

The farmers were bound to throw in something, to sort of offset my liberality, whether I would or no; so I let them give me a flint and steel; and as soon as they had comfortably bestowed Sandy and me on our horse, I lit my pipe. When the first blast of smoke shot out through the bars of my helmet, all those people broke for the woods, and Sandy went over backwards and struck the ground with a dull thud. They thought I was one of those fire-belching dragons they had heard so much about from knights and other professional liars. I had infinite trouble to persuade those people to venture back within explaining distance. Then I told them that this was only a bit of enchantment which would work harm to none but my enemies. And I promised, with my hand on my heart, that if all who felt no enmity toward me would come forward and pass before me they should see that only those who remained behind would be struck dead. The procession moved with a good deal of promptness. There were no casualties to report, for nobody had curiosity enough to remain behind to see what would happen.

I lost some time, now, for these big children, their fears gone, became so ravished with wonder over my awe-compelling fireworks that I had to stay there and smoke a couple of pipes out before they would let me go. Still the delay was not wholly unproductive, for it took all that time to get Sandy thoroughly wonted to the new thing, she being so close to it, you know. It plugged up her conversation mill, too, for a considerable while, and that was a gain. But above all other benefits accruing, I had learned something. I was ready for any giant or any ogre that might come along, now.

We tarried with a holy hermit, that night, and my opportunity came about the middle of the next afternoon. We were crossing a vast meadow by way of short-cut, and I was musing absently, hearing nothing, seeing nothing, when Sandy suddenly interrupted a remark which she had begun that morning, with the cry:

"Defend thee, lord!—peril of life is toward!"

And she slipped down from the horse and ran a little way and stood. I looked up and saw, far off in the shade of a tree, half a dozen armed knights and their squires; and straightway there was bustle among them and tightening of saddle-girths for the mount. My pipe was ready and would have been lit, if I had not been lost in thinking about how to banish oppression from this land and restore to all its people their stolen rights and manhood without disobliging anybody. I lit up at once, and by the time I had got a good head of reserved steam on, here they came. All together, too; none of those chivalrous magnanimities which one reads so much about —one courtly

rascal at a time, and the rest standing by to see fair play. No, they came in a body, they came with a whirr and a rush, they came like a volley from a battery; came with heads low down, plumes streaming out behind, lances advanced at a level. It was a handsome sight, a beautiful sight—for a man up a tree. I laid my lance in rest and waited, with my heart beating, till the iron wave was just ready to break over me, then spouted a column of white smoke through the bars of my helmet. You should have seen the wave go to pieces and scatter! This was a finer sight than the other one.

But these people stopped, two or three hundred yards away, and this troubled me. My satisfaction collapsed, and fear came; I judged I was a lost man. But Sandy was radiant; and was going to be eloquent—but I stopped her, and told her my magic had miscarried, somehow or other, and she must mount, with all despatch, and we must ride for life. No, she wouldn't. She said that my enchantment had disabled those knights; they were not riding on, because they couldn't; wait, they would drop out of their saddles presently, and we would get their horses and harness. I could not deceive such trusting simplicity, so I said it was a mistake; that when my fireworks killed at all, they killed instantly; no, the men would not die, there was something wrong about my apparatus, I couldn't tell what; but we must hurry and get away, for those people would attack us again, in a minute. Sandy laughed, and said:

"Lack-a-day, sir, they be not of that breed! Sir Launcelot will give battle to dragons, and will abide by them, and will assail them again, and yet again, and still again, until he do conquer and destroy them; and so likewise will Sir Pellinore and Sir Aglovale and Sir Carados, and mayhap others, but there be none else that will venture it, let the idle say what the idle will. And, la, as to yonder base rufflers, think ye they have not their fill, but yet desire more?"

"Well, then, what are they waiting for? Why don't they leave? Nobody's hindering. Good land, I'm willing to let bygones be bygones, I'm sure."

"Leave, is it? Oh, give thyself easement as to that. They dream not of it, no, not they. They wait to yield them."

"Come—really, is that 'sooth'—as you people say? If they want to, why don't they?"

"It would like them much; but an ye wot how dragons are esteemed, ye would not hold them blamable. They fear to come."

"Well, then, suppose I go to them instead, and—"

"Ah, wit ye well they would not abide your coming. I will go."

And she did. She was a handy person to have along on a raid. I would have considered this a doubtful errand, myself. I presently saw the knights riding away, and Sandy coming back. That was a relief. I judged she had somehow failed to get the first innings —I mean in the conversation; otherwise the interview wouldn't have been so short. But it turned out that she had managed the business well; in fact, admirably. She said that when she told those people I was The Boss, it hit them where they lived: "smote them sore with fear and dread" was her word; and then they were ready to put up with anything she might require. So she swore them to appear at Arthur's court within two days and yield them, with horse and harness, and be my knights henceforth, and subject to my command. How much better she managed that thing than I should have done it myself! She was a daisy.

CHAPTER XV

SANDY'S TALE

"And so I'm proprietor of some knights," said I, as we rode off. "Who would ever have supposed that I should live to list up assets of that sort. I shan't know what to do with them; unless I raffle them off. How many of them are there, Sandy?"

"Seven, please you, sir, and their squires."

"It is a good haul. Who are they? Where do they hang out?"

"Where do they hang out?"

"Yes, where do they live?"

"Ah, I understood thee not. That will I tell eftsoons." Then she said musingly, and softly, turning the words daintily over her tongue: "Hang they out—hang they out—where hang—where do they hang out; eh, right so; where do they hang out. Of a truth the phrase hath a fair and winsome grace, and is prettily worded withal. I will repeat it anon and anon in mine idlesse, whereby I may peradventure learn it. Where do they hang out. Even so! already it falleth trippingly from my tongue, and forasmuch as—"

"Don't forget the cowboys, Sandy."

"Cowboys?"

"Yes; the knights, you know: You were going to tell me about them. A while back, you remember. Figuratively speaking, game's called."

"Game—"

"Yes, yes, yes! Go to the bat. I mean, get to work on your statistics, and don't burn so much kindling getting your fire started. Tell me about the knights."

"I will well, and lightly will begin. So they two departed and rode into a great forest. And—"

"Great Scott!"

You see, I recognized my mistake at once. I had set her works a-going; it was my own fault; she would be thirty days getting down to those facts. And she generally began without a preface and finished without a result. If you interrupted her she would either go right along without noticing, or answer with a couple of words, and go back and say the sentence over again. So, interruptions only did harm; and yet I had to interrupt, and interrupt pretty frequently, too, in order to save my life; a person would die if he let her monotony drip on him right along all day.

"Great Scott!" I said in my distress. She went right back and began over again:

"So they two departed and rode into a great forest. And—"

"*Which* two?"

"Sir Gawaine and Sir Uwaine. And so they came to an abbey of monks, and there were well lodged. So on the morn they heard

their masses in the abbey, and so they rode forth till they came to a great forest; then was Sir Gawaine ware in a valley by a turret, of twelve fair damsels, and two knights armed on great horses, and the damsels went to and fro by a tree. And then was Sir Gawaine ware how there hung a white shield on that tree, and ever as the damsels came by it they spit upon it, and some threw mire upon the shield—"

"Now, if I hadn't seen the like myself in this country, Sandy, I wouldn't believe it. But I've seen it, and I can just see those creatures now, parading before that shield and acting like that. The women here do certainly act like all possessed. Yes, and I mean your best, too, society's very choicest brands. The humblest hello-girl along ten thousand miles of wire could teach gentleness, patience, modesty, manners, to the highest duchess in Arthur's land."

"Hello-girl?"

"Yes, but don't you ask me to explain; it's a new kind of a girl; they don't have them here; one often speaks sharply to them when they are not the least in fault, and he can't get over feeling sorry for it and ashamed of himself in thirteen hundred years, it's such shabby mean conduct and so unprovoked; the fact is, no gentleman ever does it—though I—well, I myself, if I've got to confess—"

"Peradventure she—"

"Never mind her; never mind her; I tell you I couldn't ever explain her so you would understand."

"Even so be it, sith ye are so minded. Then Sir Gawaine and Sir Uwaine went and saluted them, and asked them why they did that despite to the shield. Sirs, said the damsels, we shall tell you. There is a knight in this country that owneth this white shield, and he is a passing good man of his hands, but he hateth all ladies and gentlewomen, and therefore we do all this despite to the shield. I will say you, said Sir Gawaine, it beseemeth evil a good knight to despise all ladies and gentlewomen, and peradventure though he hate you he hath some cause, and peradventure he loveth in some other places ladies and gentlewomen, and to be loved again, and he such a man of prowess as ye speak of—"

"Man of prowess—yes, that is the man to please them, Sandy. Man of brains—that is a thing they never think of. Tom Sayers—John Heenan—John L. Sullivan—pity but you could be here. You would have your legs under the Round Table and a 'Sir' in front of your names within the twenty-four hours; and you could bring about a new distribution of the married princesses and duchesses of the Court in another twenty-four. The fact is, it is just a sort of polished-up court of Comanches, and there isn't a squaw in it who doesn't stand ready at the dropping of a hat to desert to the buck with the biggest string of scalps at his belt."

"—and he be such a man of prowess as ye speak of, said Sir Gawaine. Now, what is his name? Sir, said they, his name is Marhaus the king's son of Ireland."

"Son of the king of Ireland, you mean; the other form doesn't mean anything. And look out and hold on tight, now, we must jump this gully.... There, we are all right now. This horse belongs in the circus; he is born before his time."

"I know him well, said Sir Uwaine, he is a passing good knight as any is on live."

"*On live*. If you've got a fault in the world, Sandy, it is that you are a shade too archaic. But it isn't any matter."

"—for I saw him once proved at a justs where many knights were gathered, and that time there might no man withstand him. Ah, said Sir Gawaine, damsels, methinketh ye are to blame, for it is to suppose he that hung that shield there will not be long therefrom, and then may those knights match him on horseback, and that is more your worship than thus; for I will abide no longer to see a knight's shield dishonored. And therewith Sir Uwaine and Sir Gawaine departed a little from them, and then were they ware where Sir Marhaus came riding on a great horse straight toward them. And when the twelve damsels saw Sir Marhaus they fled into the turret as they were wild, so that some of them fell by the way. Then the one of the knights of the tower dressed his shield, and said on high, Sir Marhaus defend thee. And so they ran together that the knight brake his spear on Marhaus, and Sir Marhaus smote him so hard that he brake his neck and the horse's back—"

"Well, that is just the trouble about this state of things, it ruins so many horses."

"That saw the other knight of the turret, and dressed him toward Marhaus, and they went so eagerly together, that the knight of the turret was soon smitten down, horse and man, stark dead—"

"*Another* horse gone; I tell you it is a custom that ought to be broken up. I don't see how people with any feeling can applaud and support it."

. . . .

"So these two knights came together with great random—"

I saw that I had been asleep and missed a chapter, but I didn't say anything. I judged that the Irish knight was in trouble with the visitors by this time, and this turned out to be the case.

"—that Sir Uwaine smote Sir Marhaus that his spear brast in pieces on the shield, and Sir Marhaus smote him so sore that horse and man he bare to the earth, and hurt Sir Uwaine on the left side—"

"The truth is, Alisande, these archaics are a little *too* simple; the vocabulary is too limited, and so, by consequence, descriptions suffer in the matter of variety; they run too much to level Saharas of fact, and not enough to picturesque detail; this throws about them a certain air of the monotonous; in fact the fights are all alike: a couple of people come together with great random —random is a good word, and so is exegesis, for that matter, and so is holocaust, and defalcation, and usufruct and a hundred others, but land! a body ought to discriminate—they come together with great random, and a spear is brast, and one party brake his shield and the other one goes down, horse and man, over his horse-tail and brake his neck, and then the next candidate comes randoming in, and brast *his* spear, and the other man brast his shield, and down *he* goes, horse and man, over his horse-tail, and brake *his* neck, and then there's another elected, and another and another and still another, till the material is all used up; and when you come to figure up results, you can't tell one fight from another, nor who whipped; and as a *picture*, of living, raging, roaring battle, sho! why, it's pale and noiseless—just ghosts scuffling in a fog. Dear me, what would this barren vocabulary get out of the mightiest spectacle?—the burning of

Rome in Nero's time, for instance? Why, it would merely say, 'Town burned down; no insurance; boy brast a window, fireman brake his neck!' Why, *that* ain't a picture!"

It was a good deal of a lecture, I thought, but it didn't disturb Sandy, didn't turn a feather; her steam soared steadily up again, the minute I took off the lid:

"Then Sir Marhaus turned his horse and rode toward Gawaine with his spear. And when Sir Gawaine saw that, he dressed his shield, and they aventred their spears, and they came together with all the might of their horses, that either knight smote other so hard in the midst of their shields, but Sir Gawaine's spear brake—"

"I knew it would."

—"but Sir Marhaus's spear held; and therewith Sir Gawaine and his horse rushed down to the earth—"

"Just so—and brake his back."

—"and lightly Sir Gawaine rose upon his feet and pulled out his sword, and dressed him toward Sir Marhaus on foot, and therewith either came unto other eagerly, and smote together with their swords, that their shields flew in cantels, and they bruised their helms and their hauberks, and wounded either other. But Sir Gawaine, fro it passed nine of the clock, waxed by the space of three hours ever stronger and stronger and thrice his might was increased. All this espied Sir Marhaus, and had great wonder how his might increased, and so they wounded other passing sore; and then when it was come noon—"

The pelting sing-song of it carried me forward to scenes and sounds of my boyhood days:

"N-e-e-ew Haven! ten minutes for refreshments—knductr'll strike the gong-bell two minutes before train leaves—passengers for the Shore line please take seats in the rear k'yar, this k'yar don't go no furder—*ahh*-pls, *aw*-rnjz, b'*nan*ners, s-a-n-d'ches, p—*op*-corn!"

—"and waxed past noon and drew toward evensong. Sir Gawaine's strength feebled and waxed passing faint, that unnethes he might dure any longer, and Sir Marhaus was then bigger and bigger—"

"Which strained his armor, of course; and yet little would one of these people mind a small thing like that."

—"and so, Sir Knight, said Sir Marhaus, I have well felt that ye are a passing good knight, and a marvelous man of might as ever I felt any, while it lasteth, and our quarrels are not great, and therefore it were a pity to do you hurt, for I feel you are passing feeble. Ah, said Sir Gawaine, gentle knight, ye say the word that I should say. And therewith they took off their helms and either kissed other, and there they swore together either to love other as brethren—"

But I lost the thread there, and dozed off to slumber, thinking about what a pity it was that men with such superb strength — strength enabling them to stand up cased in cruelly burdensome iron and drenched with perspiration, and hack and batter and bang each other for six hours on a stretch—should not have been born at a time when they could put it to some useful purpose. Take a jackass, for instance: a jackass has that kind of strength, and puts it to a useful purpose, and is valuable to this world because he is a jackass; but a nobleman is not valuable because he is a jackass. It is a mixture that is always ineffectual, and should never have been attempted in the first place. And yet, once you start a mistake, the trouble is done and you never know what is going to come of it.

When I came to myself again and began to listen, I perceived that I had lost another chapter, and that Alisande had wandered a long way off with her people.

"And so they rode and came into a deep valley full of stones, and thereby they saw a fair stream of water; above thereby was the head of the stream, a fair fountain, and three damsels sitting thereby. In this country, said Sir Marhaus, came never knight since it was christened, but he found strange adventures—"

"This is not good form, Alisande. Sir Marhaus the king's son of Ireland talks like all the rest; you ought to give him a brogue, or at least a characteristic expletive; by this means one would recognize him as soon as he spoke, without his ever being named. It is a common literary device with the great authors. You should make him say, 'In this country, be jabers, came never knight since it was christened, but he found strange adventures, be jabers.' You see how much better that sounds."

—"came never knight but he found strange adventures, be jabers. Of a truth it doth indeed, fair lord, albeit 'tis passing hard to say, though peradventure that will not tarry but better speed with usage. And then they rode to the damsels, and either saluted other, and the eldest had a garland of gold about her head, and she was threescore winter of age or more—"

"The *damsel* was?"

"Even so, dear lord—and her hair was white under the garland—"

"Celluloid teeth, nine dollars a set, as like as not—the loose-fit kind, that go up and down like a portcullis when you eat, and fall out when you laugh."

"The second damsel was of thirty winter of age, with a circlet of gold about her head. The third damsel was but fifteen year of age—"

Billows of thought came rolling over my soul, and the voice faded out of my hearing!

Fifteen! Break—my heart! oh, my lost darling! Just her age who was so gentle, and lovely, and all the world to me, and whom I shall never see again! How the thought of her carries me back over wide seas of memory to a vague dim time, a happy time, so many, many centuries hence, out of sweet dreams of her, and say "Hello, Central!" just to hear her dear voice come melting back to me with a "Hello, Hank!" that was music of the spheres to my enchanted ear. She got three dollars a week, but she was worth it.

I could not follow Alisande's further explanation of who our captured knights were, now—I mean in case she should ever get to explaining who they were. My interest was gone, my thoughts were far away, and sad. By fitful glimpses of the drifting tale, caught here and there and now and then, I merely noted in a vague way that each of these three knights took one of these three damsels up behind him on his horse, and one

rode north, another east, the other south, to seek adventures, and meet again and lie, after year and day. Year and day—and without baggage. It was of a piece with the general simplicity of the country.

The sun was now setting. It was about three in the afternoon when Alisande had begun to tell me who the cowboys were; so she had made pretty good progress with it—for her. She would arrive some time or other, no doubt, but she was not a person who could be hurried.

We were approaching a castle which stood on high ground; a huge, strong, venerable structure, whose gray towers and battlements were charmingly draped with ivy, and whose whole majestic mass was drenched with splendors flung from the sinking sun. It was the largest castle we had seen, and so I thought it might be the one we were after, but Sandy said no. She did not know who owned it; she said she had passed it without calling, when she went down to Camelot.

CHAPTER XVI

MORGAN LE FAY

If knights errant were to be believed, not all castles were desirable places to seek hospitality in. As a matter of fact, knights errant were *not* persons to be believed—that is, measured by modern standards of veracity; yet, measured by the standards of their own time, and scaled accordingly, you got the truth. It was very simple: you discounted a statement ninety-seven per cent; the rest was fact. Now after making this allowance, the truth remained that if I could find out something about a castle before ringing the door-bell—I mean hailing the warders—it was the sensible thing to do. So I was pleased when I saw in the distance a horseman making the bottom turn of the road that wound down from this castle.

As we approached each other, I saw that he wore a plumed helmet, and seemed to be otherwise clothed in steel, but bore a curious addition also—a stiff square garment like a herald's tabard. However, I had to smile at my own forgetfulness when I got nearer and read this sign on his tabard:

"Persimmon's Soap — All the Prime-Donna Use It."

That was a little idea of my own, and had several wholesome purposes in view toward the civilizing and uplifting of this nation. In the first place, it was a furtive, underhand blow at this nonsense of knight errantry, though nobody suspected that but me. I had started a number of these people out—the bravest knights I could get—each sandwiched between bulletin-boards bearing one device or another, and I judged that by and by when they got to be numerous enough they would begin to look ridiculous; and then, even the steel-clad ass that *hadn't* any board would himself begin to look ridiculous because he was out of the fashion.

Secondly, these missionaries would gradually, and without creating suspicion or exciting alarm, introduce a rudimentary cleanliness among the nobility, and from them it would work down to the people, if the priests could be kept quiet. This would undermine the Church. I mean would be a step toward that. Next, education—next, freedom —and then she would begin to crumble. It being my conviction that any Established Church is an established crime, an established slave-pen, I had no scruples, but was willing to assail it in any way or with any weapon that promised to hurt it. Why, in my own former day— in remote centuries not yet stirring in the womb of time—there were old Englishmen who imagined that they had been born in a free country: a "free" country with the Corporation Act and the Test still in force in it—timbers propped against men's liberties and dishonored consciences to shore up an Established Anachronism with.

My missionaries were taught to spell out the gilt signs on their tabards—the showy gilding was a neat idea, I could have got the king to wear a bulletin-board for the sake of that barbaric splendor—they were to spell out these signs and then explain to the lords and ladies what soap was; and if the lords and ladies were afraid of it, get them to try it on a dog. The missionary's next move was to get the family together and try it on himself; he was to stop at no experiment, however desperate, that could convince the nobility that soap was harmless; if any final doubt remained, he must catch a hermit—the woods were full of them; saints they called themselves, and saints they were believed to be. They were unspeakably holy, and worked miracles, and everybody stood in awe of them. If a hermit could survive a wash, and that failed to convince a duke, give him up, let him alone.

Whenever my missionaries overcame a knight errant on the road they washed him, and when he got well they swore him to go and get a bulletin-board and disseminate soap and civilization the rest of his days. As a consequence the workers in the field were increasing by degrees, and the reform was steadily spreading. My soap factory felt the strain early. At first I had only two hands; but before I had left home I was already employing fifteen, and running night and day; and the atmospheric result was getting so pronounced that the king went sort of fainting and gasping around and said he did not believe he could stand it much longer, and Sir Launcelot got so that he did hardly anything but walk up and down the roof and swear, although I told him it was worse up there than anywhere else, but he said he wanted plenty of air; and he was always complaining that a palace was no place for a soap factory anyway, and said if a man was to start one in his house he would be damned if he wouldn't strangle him. There were ladies present, too, but much these people ever cared for that; they would swear before children, if the wind was their way when the factory was going.

This missionary knight's name was La Cote Male Taile, and he said that this castle was the abode of Morgan le Fay, sister of King Arthur, and wife of King Uriens, monarch of a realm about as big as the District of Columbia—you could stand in the middle of it and throw bricks into the next kingdom. "Kings" and "Kingdoms" were as thick in Britain as they had been in little Palestine in Joshua's time, when people had to sleep with their knees pulled up because they couldn't stretch out without a passport.

La Cote was much depressed, for he had scored here the worst failure of his campaign. He had not worked off a cake; yet he had tried all the tricks of the trade, even to the washing of a hermit; but the hermit died. This was, indeed, a bad failure, for this animal would now be dubbed a martyr, and would take his place among the saints of the Roman calendar. Thus made he his moan, this poor Sir La Cote Male Taile, and sorrowed passing sore. And so my heart bled for him, and I was moved to comfort and stay him. Wherefore I said:

"Forbear to grieve, fair knight, for this is not a defeat. We have brains, you and I; and for such as have brains there are no defeats, but only victories. Observe how we will turn this seeming disaster into an advertisement; an advertisement for our soap; and the biggest one, to draw, that was ever thought

of; an advertisement that will transform that Mount Washington defeat into a Matterhorn victory. We will put on your bulletin-board, '*Patronized by the elect.*' How does that strike you?"

"Verily, it is wonderly bethought!"

"Well, a body is bound to admit that for just a modest little one-line ad, it's a corker."

So the poor colporteur's griefs vanished away. He was a brave fellow, and had done mighty feats of arms in his time. His chief celebrity rested upon the events of an excursion like this one of mine, which he had once made with a damsel named Maledisant, who was as handy with her tongue as was Sandy, though in a different way, for her tongue churned forth only railings and insult, whereas Sandy's music was of a kindlier sort. I knew his story well, and so I knew how to interpret the compassion that was in his face when he bade me farewell. He supposed I was having a bitter hard time of it.

Sandy and I discussed his story, as we rode along, and she said that La Cote's bad luck had begun with the very beginning of that trip; for the king's fool had overthrown him on the first day, and in such cases it was customary for the girl to desert to the conqueror, but Maledisant didn't do it; and also persisted afterward in sticking to him, after all his defeats. But, said I, suppose the victor should decline to accept his spoil? She said that that wouldn't answer—he must. He couldn't decline; it wouldn't be regular. I made a note of that. If Sandy's music got to be too burdensome, some time, I would let a knight defeat me, on the chance that she would desert to him.

In due time we were challenged by the warders, from the castle walls, and after a parley admitted. I have nothing pleasant to tell about that visit. But it was not a disappointment, for I knew Mrs. le Fay by reputation, and was not expecting anything pleasant. She was held in awe by the whole realm, for she had made everybody believe she was a great sorceress. All her ways were wicked, all her instincts devilish. She was loaded to the eyelids with cold malice. All her history was black with crime; and among her crimes murder was common. I was most curious to see her; as curious as I could have been to see Satan. To my surprise she was beautiful; black thoughts had failed to make her expression repulsive, age had failed to wrinkle her satin skin or mar its bloomy freshness. She could have passed for old Uriens' granddaughter, she could have been mistaken for sister to her own son.

As soon as we were fairly within the castle gates we were ordered into her presence. King Uriens was there, a kind-faced old man with a subdued look; and also the son, Sir Uwaine le Blanchemains, in whom I was, of course, interested on account of the tradition that he had once done battle with thirty knights, and also on account of his trip with Sir Gawaine and Sir Marhaus, which Sandy had been aging me with. But Morgan was the main attraction, the conspicuous personality here; she was head chief of this household, that was plain. She caused us to be seated, and then she began, with all manner of pretty graces and graciousnesses, to ask me questions. Dear me, it was like a bird or a flute, or something, talking. I felt persuaded that this woman must have been misrepresented, lied about. She trilled along, and trilled along, and presently a handsome young page, clothed like the rainbow, and as easy and undulatory of movement as a wave, came with something on a golden salver, and, kneeling to present it to her, overdid his graces and lost his balance, and so fell lightly against her knee. She slipped a dirk into him in as matter-of-course a way as another person would have harpooned a rat!

Poor child! he slumped to the floor, twisted his silken limbs in one great straining contortion of pain, and was dead. Out of the old king was wrung an involuntary "O-h!" of compassion. The look he got, made him cut it suddenly short and not put any more hyphens in it. Sir Uwaine, at a sign from his mother, went to the anteroom and called some servants, and meanwhile madame went rippling sweetly along with her talk.

I saw that she was a good housekeeper, for while she talked she kept a corner of her eye on the servants to see that they made no balks in handling the body and getting it out; when they came with fresh clean towels, she sent back for the other kind; and when they had finished wiping the floor and were going, she indicated a crimson fleck the size of a tear which their duller eyes had overlooked. It was plain to me that La Cote Male Taile had failed to see the mistress of the house. Often, how louder and clearer than any tongue, does dumb circumstantial evidence speak.

Morgan le Fay rippled along as musically as ever. Marvelous woman. And what a glance she had: when it fell in reproof upon those servants, they shrunk and quailed as timid people do when the lightning flashes out of a cloud. I could have got the habit myself. It was the same with that poor old Brer Uriens; he was always on the ragged edge of apprehension; she could not even turn toward him but he winced.

In the midst of the talk I let drop a complimentary word about King Arthur, forgetting for the moment how this woman hated her brother. That one little compliment was enough. She clouded up like storm; she called for her guards, and said:

"Hale me these varlets to the dungeons."

That struck cold on my ears, for her dungeons had a reputation. Nothing occurred to me to say—or do. But not so with Sandy. As the guard laid a hand upon me, she piped up with the tranquilest confidence, and said:

"God's wounds, dost thou covet destruction, thou maniac? It is The Boss!"

Now what a happy idea that was!—and so simple; yet it would never have occurred to me. I was born modest; not all over, but in spots; and this was one of the spots.

The effect upon madame was electrical. It cleared her countenance and brought back her smiles and all her persuasive graces and blandishments; but nevertheless she was not able to entirely cover up with them the fact that she was in a ghastly fright. She said:

"La, but do list to thine handmaid! as if one gifted with powers like to mine might say the thing which I have said unto one who has vanquished Merlin, and not be jesting. By mine enchantments I foresaw your coming, and by them I knew you when you entered here. I did but play this little jest with hope to surprise you into some display of your art, as not doubting you would blast the guards with occult fires, consuming them to ashes on the spot, a marvel much beyond mine own ability, yet one which I have long been childishly curious to see."

The guards were less curious, and got out as soon as they got permission.

CHAPTER XVII

A ROYAL BANQUET

Madame, seeing me pacific and unresentful, no doubt judged that I was deceived by her excuse; for her fright dissolved away, and she was soon so importunate to have me give an exhibition and kill somebody, that the thing grew to be embarrassing. However, to my relief she was presently interrupted by the call to prayers. I will say this much for the nobility: that, tyrannical, murderous, rapacious, and morally rotten as they were, they were deeply and enthusiastically religious. Nothing could divert them from the regular and faithful performance of the pieties enjoined by the Church. More than once I had seen a noble who had gotten his enemy at a disadvantage, stop to pray before cutting his throat; more than once I had seen a noble, after ambushing and despatching his enemy, retire to the nearest wayside shrine and humbly give thanks, without even waiting to rob the body. There was to be nothing finer or sweeter in the life of even Benvenuto Cellini, that rough-hewn saint, ten centuries later. All the nobles of Britain, with their families, attended divine service morning and night daily, in their private chapels, and even the worst of them had family worship five or six times a day besides. The credit of this belonged entirely to the Church. Although I was no friend to that Catholic Church, I was obliged to admit this. And often, in spite of me, I found myself saying, "What would this country be without the Church?"

After prayers we had dinner in a great banqueting hall which was lighted by hundreds of grease-jets, and everything was as fine and lavish and rudely splendid as might become the royal degree of the hosts. At the head of the hall, on a dais, was the table of the king, queen, and their son, Prince Uwaine. Stretching down the hall from this, was the general table, on the floor. At this, above the salt, sat the visiting nobles and the grown members of their families, of both sexes,—the resident Court, in effect—sixty-one persons; below the salt sat minor officers of the household, with their principal subordinates: altogether a hundred and eighteen persons sitting, and about as many liveried servants standing behind their chairs, or serving in one capacity or another. It was a very fine show. In a gallery a band with cymbals, horns, harps, and other horrors, opened the proceedings with what seemed to be the crude first-draft or original agony of the wail known to later centuries as "In the Sweet Bye and Bye." It was new, and ought to have been rehearsed a little more. For some reason or other the queen had the composer hanged, after dinner.

After this music, the priest who stood behind the royal table said a noble long grace in ostensible Latin. Then the battalion of waiters broke away from their posts, and darted, rushed, flew, fetched and carried, and the mighty feeding began; no words anywhere, but absorbing attention to business. The rows of chops opened and shut in vast unison, and the sound of it was like to the muffled burr of subterranean machinery.

The havoc continued an hour and a half, and unimaginable was the destruction of substantials. Of the chief feature of the feast —the huge wild boar that lay stretched out so portly and imposing at the start—nothing was left but the semblance of a hoop-skirt; and he was but the type and symbol of what had happened to all the other dishes.

With the pastries and so on, the heavy drinking began—and the talk. Gallon after gallon of wine and mead disappeared, and everybody got comfortable, then happy, then sparklingly joyous—both sexes, —and by and by pretty noisy. Men told anecdotes that were terrific to hear, but nobody blushed; and when the nub was sprung, the assemblage let go with a horse-laugh that shook the fortress. Ladies answered back with historiettes that would almost have made Queen Margaret of Navarre or even the great Elizabeth of England hide behind a handkerchief, but nobody hid here, but only laughed — howled, you may say. In pretty much all of these dreadful stories, ecclesiastics were the hardy heroes, but that didn't worry the chaplain any, he had his laugh with the rest; more than that, upon invitation he roared out a song which was of as daring a sort as any that was sung that night.

By midnight everybody was fagged out, and sore with laughing; and, as a rule, drunk: some weepingly, some affectionately, some hilariously, some quarrelsomely, some dead and under the table. Of the ladies, the worst spectacle was a lovely young duchess, whose wedding-eve this was; and indeed she was a spectacle, sure enough. Just as she was she could have sat in advance for the portrait of the young daughter of the Regent d'Orleans, at the famous dinner whence she was carried, foul-mouthed, intoxicated, and helpless, to her bed, in the lost and lamented days of the Ancient Regime.

Suddenly, even while the priest was lifting his hands, and all conscious heads were bowed in reverent expectation of the coming blessing, there appeared under the arch of the far-off door at the bottom of the hall an old and bent and white-haired lady, leaning upon a crutch-stick; and she lifted the stick and pointed it toward the queen and cried out:

"The wrath and curse of God fall upon you, woman without pity, who have slain mine innocent grandchild and made desolate this old heart that had nor chick, nor friend nor stay nor comfort in all this world but him!"

Everybody crossed himself in a grisly fright, for a curse was an awful thing to those people; but the queen rose up majestic, with the death-light in her eye, and flung back this ruthless command:

"Lay hands on her! To the stake with her!"

The guards left their posts to obey. It was a shame; it was a cruel thing to see. What could be done? Sandy gave me a look; I knew she had another inspiration. I said:

"Do what you choose."

She was up and facing toward the queen in a moment. She indicated me, and said:

"Madame, *he* saith this may not be. Recall the commandment, or he will dissolve the castle and it shall vanish away like the instable fabric of a dream!"

Confound it, what a crazy contract to pledge a person to! What if the queen—

But my consternation subsided there, and my panic passed off; for the queen, all in a collapse, made no show of resistance but gave a countermanding sign and sunk into her seat. When she reached it she was sober. So were many of the others. The assemblage rose, whiffed ceremony to the winds, and rushed for the door like a mob; overturning chairs, smashing crockery, tugging, struggling, shouldering, crowding—anything to get out before I should change my mind and puff the castle into the measureless dim vacancies of space. Well,

well, well, they *were* a superstitious lot. It is all a body can do to conceive of it.

The poor queen was so scared and humbled that she was even afraid to hang the composer without first consulting me. I was very sorry for her—indeed, any one would have been, for she was really suffering; so I was willing to do anything that was reasonable, and had no desire to carry things to wanton extremities. I therefore considered the matter thoughtfully, and ended by having the musicians ordered into our presence to play that Sweet Bye and Bye again, which they did. Then I saw that she was right, and gave her permission to hang the whole band. This little relaxation of sternness had a good effect upon the queen. A statesman gains little by the arbitrary exercise of iron-clad authority upon all occasions that offer, for this wounds the just pride of his subordinates, and thus tends to undermine his strength. A little concession, now and then, where it can do no harm, is the wiser policy.

Now that the queen was at ease in her mind once more, and measurably happy, her wine naturally began to assert itself again, and it got a little the start of her. I mean it set her music going—her silver bell of a tongue. Dear me, she was a master talker. It would not become me to suggest that it was pretty late and that I was a tired man and very sleepy. I wished I had gone off to bed when I had the chance. Now I must stick it out; there was no other way. So she tinkled along and along, in the otherwise profound and ghostly hush of the sleeping castle, until by and by there came, as if from deep down under us, a far-away sound, as of a muffled shriek —with an expression of agony about it that made my flesh crawl. The queen stopped, and her eyes lighted with pleasure; she tilted her graceful head as a bird does when it listens. The sound bored its way up through the stillness again.

"What is it?" I said.

"It is truly a stubborn soul, and endureth long. It is many hours now."

"Endureth what?"

"The rack. Come—ye shall see a blithe sight. An he yield not his secret now, ye shall see him torn asunder."

What a silky smooth hellion she was; and so composed and serene, when the cords all down my legs were hurting in sympathy with that man's pain. Conducted by mailed guards bearing flaring torches, we tramped along echoing corridors, and down stone stairways dank and dripping, and smelling of mould and ages of imprisoned night —a chill, uncanny journey and a long one, and not made the shorter or the cheerier by the sorceress's talk, which was about this sufferer and his crime. He had been accused by an anonymous informer, of having killed a stag in the royal preserves. I said:

"Anonymous testimony isn't just the right thing, your Highness. It were fairer to confront the accused with the accuser."

"I had not thought of that, it being but of small consequence. But an I would, I could not, for that the accuser came masked by night, and told the forester, and straightway got him hence again, and so the forester knoweth him not."

"Then is this Unknown the only person who saw the stag killed?"

"Marry, *no* man *saw* the killing, but this Unknown saw this hardy wretch near to the spot where the stag lay, and came with right loyal zeal and betrayed him to the forester."

"So the Unknown was near the dead stag, too? Isn't it just possible that he did the killing himself? His loyal zeal—in a mask—looks just a shade suspicious. But what is your highness's idea for racking the prisoner? Where is the profit?"

"He will not confess, else; and then were his soul lost. For his crime his life is forfeited by the law—and of a surety will I see that he payeth it!—but it were peril to my own soul to let him die unconfessed and unabsolved. Nay, I were a fool to fling me into hell for *his* accommodation."

"But, your Highness, suppose he has nothing to confess?"

"As to that, we shall see, anon. An I rack him to death and he confess not, it will peradventure show that he had indeed naught to confess—ye will grant that that is sooth? Then shall I not be damned for an unconfessed man that had naught to confess —wherefore, I shall be safe."

It was the stubborn unreasoning of the time. It was useless to argue with her. Arguments have no chance against petrified training; they wear it as little as the waves wear a cliff. And her training was everybody's. The brightest intellect in the land would not have been able to see that her position was defective.

As we entered the rack-cell I caught a picture that will not go from me; I wish it would. A native young giant of thirty or thereabouts lay stretched upon the frame on his back, with his wrists and ankles tied to ropes which led over windlasses at either end. There was no color in him; his features were contorted and set, and sweat-drops stood upon his forehead. A priest bent over him on each side; the executioner stood by; guards were on duty; smoking torches stood in sockets along the walls; in a corner crouched a poor young creature, her face drawn with anguish, a half-wild and hunted look in her eyes, and in her lap lay a little child asleep. Just as we stepped across the threshold the executioner gave his machine a slight turn, which wrung a cry from both the prisoner and the woman; but I shouted, and the executioner released the strain without waiting to see who spoke. I could not let this horror go on; it would have killed me to see it. I asked the queen to let me clear the place and speak to the prisoner privately; and when she was going to object I spoke in a low voice and said I did not want to make a scene before her servants, but I must have my way; for I was King Arthur's representative, and was speaking in his name. She saw she had to yield. I asked her to indorse me to these people, and then leave me. It was not pleasant for her, but she took the pill; and even went further than I was meaning to require. I only wanted the backing of her own authority; but she said:

"Ye will do in all things as this lord shall command. It is The Boss."

It was certainly a good word to conjure with: you could see it by the squirming of these rats. The queen's guards fell into line, and she and they marched away, with their torch-bearers, and woke the echoes of the cavernous tunnels with the measured beat of their retreating footfalls. I had the prisoner taken from the rack and placed upon his bed, and medicaments applied to his hurts, and wine given him to drink. The woman crept near and looked on, eagerly, lovingly, but timorously,—like one who fears a repulse; indeed, she

tried furtively to touch the man's forehead, and jumped back, the picture of fright, when I turned unconsciously toward her. It was pitiful to see.

"Lord," I said, "stroke him, lass, if you want to. Do anything you're a mind to; don't mind me."

Why, her eyes were as grateful as an animal's, when you do it a kindness that it understands. The baby was out of her way and she had her cheek against the man's in a minute and her hands fondling his hair, and her happy tears running down. The man revived and caressed his wife with his eyes, which was all he could do. I judged I might clear the den, now, and I did; cleared it of all but the family and myself. Then I said:

"Now, my friend, tell me your side of this matter; I know the other side."

The man moved his head in sign of refusal. But the woman looked pleased—as it seemed to me—pleased with my suggestion. I went on—

"You know of me?"

"Yes. All do, in Arthur's realms."

"If my reputation has come to you right and straight, you should not be afraid to speak."

The woman broke in, eagerly:

"Ah, fair my lord, do thou persuade him! Thou canst an thou wilt. Ah, he suffereth so; and it is for me—for *me*! And how can I bear it? I would I might see him die—a sweet, swift death; oh, my Hugo, I cannot bear this one!"

And she fell to sobbing and grovelling about my feet, and still imploring. Imploring what? The man's death? I could not quite get the bearings of the thing. But Hugo interrupted her and said:

"Peace! Ye wit not what ye ask. Shall I starve whom I love, to win a gentle death? I wend thou knewest me better."

"Well," I said, "I can't quite make this out. It is a puzzle. Now—"

"Ah, dear my lord, an ye will but persuade him! Consider how these his tortures wound me! Oh, and he will not speak!—whereas, the healing, the solace that lie in a blessed swift death—"

"What *are* you maundering about? He's going out from here a free man and whole—he's not going to die."

The man's white face lit up, and the woman flung herself at me in a most surprising explosion of joy, and cried out:

"He is saved!—for it is the king's word by the mouth of the king's servant—Arthur, the king whose word is gold!"

"Well, then you do believe I can be trusted, after all. Why didn't you before?"

"Who doubted? Not I, indeed; and not she."

"Well, why wouldn't you tell me your story, then?"

"Ye had made no promise; else had it been otherwise."

"I see, I see.... And yet I believe I don't quite see, after all. You stood the torture and refused to confess; which shows plain enough to even the dullest understanding that you had nothing to confess—"

"I, my lord? How so? It was I that killed the deer!"

"You *did*? Oh, dear, this is the most mixed-up business that ever—"

"Dear lord, I begged him on my knees to confess, but—"

"You *did*! It gets thicker and thicker. What did you want him to do that for?"

"Sith it would bring him a quick death and save him all this cruel pain."

"Well—yes, there is reason in that. But *he* didn't want the quick death."

"He? Why, of a surety he *did*."

"Well, then, why in the world *didn't* he confess?"

"Ah, sweet sir, and leave my wife and chick without bread and shelter?"

"Oh, heart of gold, now I see it! The bitter law takes the convicted man's estate and beggars his widow and his orphans. They could torture you to death, but without conviction or confession they could not rob your wife and baby. You stood by them like a man; and *you*—true wife and the woman that you are—you would have bought him release from torture at cost to yourself of slow starvation and death—well, it humbles a body to think what your sex can do when it comes to self-sacrifice. I'll book you both for my colony; you'll like it there; it's a Factory where I'm going to turn groping and grubbing automata into *men*."

CHAPTER XVIII

IN THE QUEEN'S DUNGEONS

Well, I arranged all that; and I had the man sent to his home. I had a great desire to rack the executioner; not because he was a good, painstaking and paingiving official,—for surely it was not to his discredit that he performed his functions well—but to pay him back for wantonly cuffing and otherwise distressing that young woman. The priests told me about this, and were generously hot to have him punished. Something of this disagreeable sort was turning up every now and then. I mean, episodes that showed that not all priests were frauds and self-seekers, but that many, even the great majority, of these that were down on the ground among the common people, were sincere and right-hearted, and devoted to the alleviation of human troubles and sufferings. Well, it was a thing which could not be helped, so I seldom fretted about it, and never many minutes at a time; it has never been my way to bother much about things which you can't cure. But I did not like it, for it was just the sort of thing to keep people reconciled to an Established Church. We *must* have a religion —it goes without saying—but my idea is, to have it cut up into forty free sects, so that they will police each other, as had been the case in the United States in my time. Concentration of power in a political machine is bad; and and an Established Church is only a

political machine; it was invented for that; it is nursed, cradled, preserved for that; it is an enemy to human liberty, and does no good which it could not better do in a split-up and scattered condition. That wasn't law; it wasn't gospel: it was only an opinion—my opinion, and I was only a man, one man: so it wasn't worth any more than the pope's—or any less, for that matter.

Well, I couldn't rack the executioner, neither would I overlook the just complaint of the priests. The man must be punished somehow or other, so I degraded him from his office and made him leader of the band—the new one that was to be started. He begged hard, and said he couldn't play—a plausible excuse, but too thin; there wasn't a musician in the country that could.

The queen was a good deal outraged, next morning when she found she was going to have neither Hugo's life nor his property. But I told her she must bear this cross; that while by law and custom she certainly was entitled to both the man's life and his property, there were extenuating circumstances, and so in Arthur the king's name I had pardoned him. The deer was ravaging the man's fields, and he had killed it in sudden passion, and not for gain; and he had carried it into the royal forest in the hope that that might make detection of the misdoer impossible. Confound her, I couldn't make her see that sudden passion is an extenuating circumstance in the killing of venison—or of a person—so I gave it up and let her sulk it out. I *did* think I was going to make her see it by remarking that her own sudden passion in the case of the page modified that crime.

"Crime!" she exclaimed. "How thou talkest! Crime, forsooth! Man, I am going to *pay* for him!"

Oh, it was no use to waste sense on her. Training—training is everything; training is all there is *to* a person. We speak of nature; it is folly; there is no such thing as nature; what we call by that misleading name is merely heredity and training. We have no thoughts of our own, no opinions of our own; they are transmitted to us, trained into us. All that is original in us, and therefore fairly creditable or discreditable to us, can be covered up and hidden by the point of a cambric needle, all the rest being atoms contributed by, and inherited from, a procession of ancestors that stretches back a billion years to the Adam-clam or grasshopper or monkey from whom our race has been so tediously and ostentatiously and unprofitably developed. And as for me, all that I think about in this plodding sad pilgrimage, this pathetic drift between the eternities, is to look out and humbly live a pure and high and blameless life, and save that one microscopic atom in me that is truly *me*: the rest may land in Sheol and welcome for all I care.

No, confound her, her intellect was good, she had brains enough, but her training made her an ass—that is, from a many-centuries-later point of view. To kill the page was no crime—it was her right; and upon her right she stood, serenely and unconscious of offense. She was a result of generations of training in the unexamined and unassailed belief that the law which permitted her to kill a subject when she chose was a perfectly right and righteous one.

Well, we must give even Satan his due. She deserved a compliment for one thing; and I tried to pay it, but the words stuck in my throat. She had a right to kill the boy, but she was in no wise obliged to pay for him. That was law for some other people, but not for her. She knew quite well that she was doing a large and generous thing to pay for that lad, and that I ought in common fairness to come out with something handsome about it, but I couldn't—my mouth refused. I couldn't help seeing, in my fancy, that poor old grandma with the broken heart, and that fair young creature lying butchered, his little silken pomps and vanities laced with his golden blood. How could she *pay* for him! *Whom* could she pay? And so, well knowing that this woman, trained as she had been, deserved praise, even adulation, I was yet not able to utter it, trained as I had been. The best I could do was to fish up a compliment from outside, so to speak—and the pity of it was, that it was true:

"Madame, your people will adore you for this."

Quite true, but I meant to hang her for it some day if I lived. Some of those laws were too bad, altogether too bad. A master might kill his slave for nothing—for mere spite, malice, or to pass the time—just as we have seen that the crowned head could do it with *his* slave, that is to say, anybody. A gentleman could kill a free commoner, and pay for him—cash or garden-truck. A noble could kill a noble without expense, as far as the law was concerned, but reprisals in kind were to be expected. *Anybody* could kill *somebody*, except the commoner and the slave; these had no privileges. If they killed, it was murder, and the law wouldn't stand murder. It made short work of the experimenter—and of his family, too, if he murdered somebody who belonged up among the ornamental ranks. If a commoner gave a noble even so much as a Damiens-scratch which didn't kill or even hurt, he got Damiens' dose for it just the same; they pulled him to rags and tatters with horses, and all the world came to see the show, and crack jokes, and have a good time; and some of the performances of the best people present were as tough, and as properly unprintable, as any that have been printed by the pleasant Casanova in his chapter about the dismemberment of Louis XV's poor awkward enemy.

I had had enough of this grisly place by this time, and wanted to leave, but I couldn't, because I had something on my mind that my conscience kept prodding me about, and wouldn't let me forget. If I had the remaking of man, he wouldn't have any conscience. It is one of the most disagreeable things connected with a person; and although it certainly does a great deal of good, it cannot be said to pay, in the long run; it would be much better to have less good and more comfort. Still, this is only my opinion, and I am only one man; others, with less experience, may think differently. They have a right to their view. I only stand to this: I have noticed my conscience for many years, and I know it is more trouble and bother to me than anything else I started with. I suppose that in the beginning I prized it, because we prize anything that is ours; and yet how foolish it was to think so. If we look at it in another way, we see how absurd it is: if I had an anvil in me would I prize it? Of course not. And yet when you come to think, there is no real difference between a conscience and an anvil—I mean for comfort. I have noticed it a thousand times. And you could dissolve an anvil with acids, when you couldn't stand it any longer; but there isn't any way that you can work off a conscience—at least so it will stay worked off; not that I know of, anyway.

There was something I wanted to do before leaving, but it was a disagreeable matter, and I hated to go at it. Well, it bothered me all the morning. I could have mentioned it to the old king, but what would be the use?—he was but an extinct volcano; he had been active in his time, but his fire was out, this good while, he was only a stately ash-pile now; gentle enough, and kindly enough for my purpose, without doubt, but not usable.

He was nothing, this so-called king: the queen was the only power there. And she was a Vesuvius. As a favor, she might consent to warm a flock of sparrows for you, but then she might take that very opportunity to turn herself loose and bury a city. However, I reflected that as often as any other way, when you are expecting the worst, you get something that is not so bad, after all.

So I braced up and placed my matter before her royal Highness. I said I had been having a general jail-delivery at Camelot and among neighboring castles, and with her permission I would like to examine her collection, her bric-a-brac—that is to say, her prisoners. She resisted; but I was expecting that. But she finally consented. I was expecting that, too, but not so soon. That about ended my discomfort. She called her guards and torches, and we went down into the dungeons. These were down under the castle's foundations, and mainly were small cells hollowed out of the living rock. Some of these cells had no light at all. In one of them was a woman, in foul rags, who sat on the ground, and would not answer a question or speak a word, but only looked up at us once or twice, through a cobweb of tangled hair, as if to see what casual thing it might be that was disturbing with sound and light the meaningless dull dream that was become her life; after that, she sat bowed, with her dirt-caked fingers idly interlocked in her lap, and gave no further sign. This poor rack of bones was a woman of middle age, apparently; but only apparently; she had been there nine years, and was eighteen when she entered. She was a commoner, and had been sent here on her bridal night by Sir Breuse Sance Pite, a neighboring lord whose vassal her father was, and to which said lord she had refused what has since been called le droit du seigneur, and, moreover, had opposed violence to violence and spilt half a gill of his almost sacred blood. The young husband had interfered at that point, believing the bride's life in danger, and had flung the noble out into the midst of the humble and trembling wedding guests, in the parlor, and left him there astonished at this strange treatment, and implacably embittered against both bride and groom. The said lord being cramped for dungeon-room had asked the queen to accommodate his two criminals, and here in her bastile they had been ever since; hither, indeed, they had come before their crime was an hour old, and had never seen each other since. Here they were, kenneled like toads in the same rock; they had passed nine pitch dark years within fifty feet of each other, yet neither knew whether the other was alive or not. All the first years, their only question had been—asked with beseechings and tears that might have moved stones, in time, perhaps, but hearts are not stones: "Is he alive?" "Is she alive?" But they had never got an answer; and at last that question was not asked any more—or any other.

I wanted to see the man, after hearing all this. He was thirty-four years old, and looked sixty. He sat upon a squared block of stone, with his head bent down, his forearms resting on his knees, his long hair hanging like a fringe before his face, and he was muttering to himself. He raised his chin and looked us slowly over, in a listless dull way, blinking with the distress of the torchlight, then dropped his head and fell to muttering again and took no further notice of us. There were some pathetically suggestive dumb witnesses present. On his wrists and ankles were cicatrices, old smooth scars, and fastened to the stone on which he sat was a chain with manacles and fetters attached; but this apparatus lay idle on the ground, and was thick with rust. Chains cease to be needed after the spirit has gone out of a prisoner.

I could not rouse the man; so I said we would take him to her, and see—to the bride who was the fairest thing in the earth to him, once—roses, pearls, and dew made flesh, for him; a wonder-work, the master-work of nature: with eyes like no other eyes, and voice like no other voice, and a freshness, and lithe young grace, and beauty, that belonged properly to the creatures of dreams—as he thought—and to no other. The sight of her would set his stagnant blood leaping; the sight of her—

But it was a disappointment. They sat together on the ground and looked dimly wondering into each other's faces a while, with a sort of weak animal curiosity; then forgot each other's presence, and dropped their eyes, and you saw that they were away again and wandering in some far land of dreams and shadows that we know nothing about.

I had them taken out and sent to their friends. The queen did not like it much. Not that she felt any personal interest in the matter, but she thought it disrespectful to Sir Breuse Sance Pite. However, I assured her that if he found he couldn't stand it I would fix him so that he could.

I set forty-seven prisoners loose out of those awful rat-holes, and left only one in captivity. He was a lord, and had killed another lord, a sort of kinsman of the queen. That other lord had ambushed him to assassinate him, but this fellow had got the best of him and cut his throat. However, it was not for that that I left him jailed, but for maliciously destroying the only public well in one of his wretched villages. The queen was bound to hang him for killing her kinsman, but I would not allow it: it was no crime to kill an assassin. But I said I was willing to let her hang him for destroying the well; so she concluded to put up with that, as it was better than nothing.

Dear me, for what trifling offenses the most of those forty-seven men and women were shut up there! Indeed, some were there for no distinct offense at all, but only to gratify somebody's spite; and not always the queen's by any means, but a friend's. The newest prisoner's crime was a mere remark which he had made. He said he believed that men were about all alike, and one man as good as another, barring clothes. He said he believed that if you were to strip the nation naked and send a stranger through the crowd, he couldn't tell the king from a quack doctor, nor a duke from a hotel clerk. Apparently here was a man whose brains had not been reduced to an ineffectual mush by idiotic training. I set him loose and sent him to the Factory.

Some of the cells carved in the living rock were just behind the face of the precipice, and in each of these an arrow-slit had been pierced outward to the daylight, and so the captive had a thin ray from the blessed sun for his comfort. The case of one of these poor fellows was particularly hard. From his dusky swallow's hole high up in that vast wall of native rock he could peer out through the arrow-slit and see his own home off yonder in the valley; and for twenty-two years he had watched it, with heartache and longing, through that crack. He could see the lights shine there at night, and in the daytime he could see figures go in and come out—his wife and children, some of them, no doubt, though he could not make out at that distance. In the course of years he noted festivities there, and tried to rejoice, and wondered if they were weddings or what they might be. And he noted funerals; and they wrung his heart. He could make out the coffin, but he could not determine its size, and so could not tell whether it was wife or child. He could see the procession form, with priests and mourners, and move solemnly away, bearing the secret with them. He had left behind him five children and a wife; and in

nineteen years he had seen five funerals issue, and none of them humble enough in pomp to denote a servant. So he had lost five of his treasures; there must still be one remaining— one now infinitely, unspeakably precious,—but *which* one? wife, or child? That was the question that tortured him, by night and by day, asleep and awake. Well, to have an interest, of some sort, and half a ray of light, when you are in a dungeon, is a great support to the body and preserver of the intellect. This man was in pretty good condition yet. By the time he had finished telling me his distressful tale, I was in the same state of mind that you would have been in yourself, if you have got average human curiosity; that is to say, I was as burning up as he was to find out which member of the family it was that was left. So I took him over home myself; and an amazing kind of a surprise party it was, too —typhoons and cyclones of frantic joy, and whole Niagaras of happy tears; and by George! we found the aforetime young matron graying toward the imminent verge of her half century, and the babies all men and women, and some of them married and experimenting familywise themselves—for not a soul of the tribe was dead! Conceive of the ingenious devilishness of that queen: she had a special hatred for this prisoner, and she had *invented* all those funerals herself, to scorch his heart with; and the sublimest stroke of genius of the whole thing was leaving the family-invoice a funeral *short*, so as to let him wear his poor old soul out guessing.

But for me, he never would have got out. Morgan le Fay hated him with her whole heart, and she never would have softened toward him. And yet his crime was committed more in thoughtlessness than deliberate depravity. He had said she had red hair. Well, she had; but that was no way to speak of it. When red-headed people are above a certain social grade their hair is auburn.

Consider it: among these forty-seven captives there were five whose names, offenses, and dates of incarceration were no longer known! One woman and four men—all bent, and wrinkled, and mind-extinguished patriarchs. They themselves had long ago forgotten these details; at any rate they had mere vague theories about them, nothing definite and nothing that they repeated twice in the same way. The succession of priests whose office it had been to pray daily with the captives and remind them that God had put them there, for some wise purpose or other, and teach them that patience, humbleness, and submission to oppression was what He loved to see in parties of a subordinate rank, had traditions about these poor old human ruins, but nothing more. These traditions went but little way, for they concerned the length of the incarceration only, and not the names of the offenses. And even by the help of tradition the only thing that could be proven was that none of the five had seen daylight for thirty-five years: how much longer this privation has lasted was not guessable. The king and the queen knew nothing about these poor creatures, except that they were heirlooms, assets inherited, along with the throne, from the former firm. Nothing of their history had been transmitted with their persons, and so the inheriting owners had considered them of no value, and had felt no interest in them. I said to the queen:

"Then why in the world didn't you set them free?"

The question was a puzzler. She didn't know *why* she hadn't, the thing had never come up in her mind. So here she was, forecasting the veritable history of future prisoners of the Castle d'If, without knowing it. It seemed plain to me now, that with her training, those inherited prisoners were merely property—nothing more, nothing less. Well, when we inherit property, it does not occur to us to throw it away, even when we do not value it.

When I brought my procession of human bats up into the open world and the glare of the afternoon sun—previously blindfolding them, in charity for eyes so long untortured by light—they were a spectacle to look at. Skeletons, scarecrows, goblins, pathetic frights, every one; legitimatest possible children of Monarchy by the Grace of God and the Established Church. I muttered absently:

"I *wish* I could photograph them!"

You have seen that kind of people who will never let on that they don't know the meaning of a new big word. The more ignorant they are, the more pitifully certain they are to pretend you haven't shot over their heads. The queen was just one of that sort, and was always making the stupidest blunders by reason of it. She hesitated a moment; then her face brightened up with sudden comprehension, and she said she would do it for me.

I thought to myself: She? why what can she know about photography? But it was a poor time to be thinking. When I looked around, she was moving on the procession with an axe!

Well, she certainly was a curious one, was Morgan le Fay. I have seen a good many kinds of women in my time, but she laid over them all for variety. And how sharply characteristic of her this episode was. She had no more idea than a horse of how to photograph a procession; but being in doubt, it was just like her to try to do it with an axe.

CHAPTER XIX

KNIGHT-ERRANTRY AS A TRADE

Sandy and I were on the road again, next morning, bright and early. It was so good to open up one's lungs and take in whole luscious barrels-ful of the blessed God's untainted, dew-fashioned, woodland-scented air once more, after suffocating body and mind for two days and nights in the moral and physical stenches of that intolerable old buzzard-roost! I mean, for me: of course the place was all right and agreeable enough for Sandy, for she had been used to high life all her days.

Poor girl, her jaws had had a wearisome rest now for a while, and I was expecting to get the consequences. I was right; but she had stood by me most helpfully in the castle, and had mightily supported and reinforced me with gigantic foolishnesses which were worth more for the occasion than wisdoms double their size; so I thought she had earned a right to work her mill for a while, if she wanted to, and I felt not a pang when she started it up:

"Now turn we unto Sir Marhaus that rode with the damsel of thirty winter of age southward—"

"Are you going to see if you can work up another half-stretch on the trail of the cowboys, Sandy?"

"Even so, fair my lord."

"Go ahead, then. I won't interrupt this time, if I can help it. Begin over again; start fair, and shake out all your reefs, and I will load my pipe and give good attention."

"Now turn we unto Sir Marhaus that rode with the damsel of thirty winter of age southward. And so they came into a deep forest, and by fortune they were nighted, and rode along in a deep way, and at the last they came into a courtelage where abode the duke of South Marches, and there they asked harbour. And on the morn the duke sent unto Sir Marhaus, and bad him make him ready. And so Sir Marhaus arose and armed him, and there was a mass sung afore him, and he brake his fast, and so mounted on horseback in the court of the castle, there they should do the battle. So there was the duke already on horseback, clean armed, and his six sons by him, and every each had a spear in his hand, and so they encountered, whereas the duke and his two sons brake their spears upon him, but Sir Marhaus held up his spear and touched none of them. Then came the four sons by couples, and two of them brake their spears, and so did the other two. And all this while Sir Marhaus touched them not. Then Sir Marhaus ran to the duke, and smote him with his spear that horse and man fell to the earth. And so he served his sons. And then Sir Marhaus alight down, and bad the duke yield him or else he would slay him. And then some of his sons recovered, and would have set upon Sir Marhaus. Then Sir Marhaus said to the duke, Cease thy sons, or else I will do the uttermost to you all. When the duke saw he might not escape the death, he cried to his sons, and charged them to yield them to Sir Marhaus. And they kneeled all down and put the pommels of their swords to the knight, and so he received them. And then they holp up their father, and so by their common assent promised unto Sir Marhaus never to be foes unto King Arthur, and thereupon at Whitsuntide after, to come he and his sons, and put them in the king's grace.*

"Even so standeth the history, fair Sir Boss. Now ye shall wit that that very duke and his six sons are they whom but few days past you also did overcome and send to Arthur's court!"

"Why, Sandy, you can't mean it!"

"An I speak not sooth, let it be the worse for me."

"Well, well, well,—now who would ever have thought it? One whole duke and six dukelets; why, Sandy, it was an elegant haul. Knight-errantry is a most chuckle-headed trade, and it is tedious hard work, too, but I begin to see that there *is* money in it, after all, if you have luck. Not that I would ever engage in it as a business, for I wouldn't. No sound and legitimate business can be established on a basis of speculation. A successful whirl in the knight-errantry line—now what is it when you blow away the nonsense and come down to the cold facts? It's just a corner in pork, that's all, and you can't make anything else out of it. You're rich—yes,—suddenly rich—for about a day, maybe a week; then somebody corners the market on *you*, and down goes your bucket-shop; ain't that so, Sandy?"

"Whethersoever it be that my mind miscarrieth, bewraying simple language in such sort that the words do seem to come endlong and overthwart—"

"There's no use in beating about the bush and trying to get around it that way, Sandy, it's *so*, just as I say. I *know* it's so. And, moreover, when you come right down to the bedrock, knight-errantry is *worse* than pork; for whatever happens, the pork's left, and so somebody's benefited anyway; but when the market breaks, in a knight-errantry whirl, and every knight in

---

* The story is borrowed, language and all, from the Morte d'Arthur.—M.T.

the pool passes in his checks, what have you got for assets? Just a rubbish-pile of battered corpses and a barrel or two of busted hardware. Can you call *those* assets? Give me pork, every time. Am I right?"

"Ah, peradventure my head being distraught by the manifold matters whereunto the confusions of these but late adventured haps and fortunings whereby not I alone nor you alone, but every each of us, meseemeth—"

"No, it's not your head, Sandy. Your head's all right, as far as it goes, but you don't know business; that's where the trouble is. It unfits you to argue about business, and you're wrong to be always trying. However, that aside, it was a good haul, anyway, and will breed a handsome crop of reputation in Arthur's court. And speaking of the cowboys, what a curious country this is for women and men that never get old. Now there's Morgan le Fay, as fresh and young as a Vassar pullet, to all appearances, and here is this old duke of the South Marches still slashing away with sword and lance at his time of life, after raising such a family as he has raised. As I understand it, Sir Gawaine killed seven of his sons, and still he had six left for Sir Marhaus and me to take into camp. And then there was that damsel of sixty winter of age still excursioning around in her frosty bloom—How old are you, Sandy?"

It was the first time I ever struck a still place in her. The mill had shut down for repairs, or something.

CHAPTER XX

THE OGRE'S CASTLE

Between six and nine we made ten miles, which was plenty for a horse carrying triple—man, woman, and armor; then we stopped for a long nooning under some trees by a limpid brook.

Right so came by and by a knight riding; and as he drew near he made dolorous moan, and by the words of it I perceived that he was cursing and swearing; yet nevertheless was I glad of his coming, for that I saw he bore a bulletin-board whereon in letters all of shining gold was writ:

"USE PETERSON'S PROPHYLACTIC TOOTH-BRUSH—ALL THE GO."

I was glad of his coming, for even by this token I knew him for knight of mine. It was Sir Madok de la Montaine, a burly great fellow whose chief distinction was that he had come within an ace of sending Sir Launcelot down over his horse-tail once. He was never long in a stranger's presence without finding some pretext or other to let out that great fact. But there was another fact of nearly the same size, which he never pushed upon anybody unasked, and yet never withheld when asked: that was, that the reason he didn't quite succeed was, that he was interrupted and sent down over horse-tail himself. This innocent vast lubber did not see any particular difference between the two facts. I liked him, for he was earnest in his work, and very valuable. And he was so fine to look at, with his broad mailed shoulders, and the grand leonine set of his plumed head, and his big shield with its quaint device of a gauntleted hand clutching a prophylactic tooth-brush, with motto: "Try Noyoudont." This was a tooth-wash that I was introducing.

He was aweary, he said, and indeed he looked it; but he would not alight. He said he was after the stove-polish man; and with

this he broke out cursing and swearing anew. The bulletin-boarder referred to was Sir Ossaise of Surluse, a brave knight, and of considerable celebrity on account of his having tried conclusions in a tournament once, with no less a Mogul than Sir Gaheris himself—although not successfully. He was of a light and laughing disposition, and to him nothing in this world was serious. It was for this reason that I had chosen him to work up a stove-polish sentiment. There were no stoves yet, and so there could be nothing serious about stove-polish. All that the agent needed to do was to deftly and by degrees prepare the public for the great change, and have them established in predilections toward neatness against the time when the stove should appear upon the stage.

Sir Madok was very bitter, and brake out anew with cursings. He said he had cursed his soul to rags; and yet he would not get down from his horse, neither would he take any rest, or listen to any comfort, until he should have found Sir Ossaise and settled this account. It appeared, by what I could piece together of the unprofane fragments of his statement, that he had chanced upon Sir Ossaise at dawn of the morning, and been told that if he would make a short cut across the fields and swamps and broken hills and glades, he could head off a company of travelers who would be rare customers for prophylactics and tooth-wash. With characteristic zeal Sir Madok had plunged away at once upon this quest, and after three hours of awful crosslot riding had overhauled his game. And behold, it was the five patriarchs that had been released from the dungeons the evening before! Poor old creatures, it was all of twenty years since any one of them had known what it was to be equipped with any remaining snag or remnant of a tooth.

"Blank-blank-blank him," said Sir Madok, "an I do not stove-polish him an I may find him, leave it to me; for never no knight that hight Ossaise or aught else may do me this disservice and bide on live, an I may find him, the which I have thereunto sworn a great oath this day."

And with these words and others, he lightly took his spear and gat him thence. In the middle of the afternoon we came upon one of those very patriarchs ourselves, in the edge of a poor village. He was basking in the love of relatives and friends whom he had not seen for fifty years; and about him and caressing him were also descendants of his own body whom he had never seen at all till now; but to him these were all strangers, his memory was gone, his mind was stagnant. It seemed incredible that a man could outlast half a century shut up in a dark hole like a rat, but here were his old wife and some old comrades to testify to it. They could remember him as he was in the freshness and strength of his young manhood, when he kissed his child and delivered it to its mother's hands and went away into that long oblivion. The people at the castle could not tell within half a generation the length of time the man had been shut up there for his unrecorded and forgotten offense; but this old wife knew; and so did her old child, who stood there among her married sons and daughters trying to realize a father who had been to her a name, a thought, a formless image, a tradition, all her life, and now was suddenly concreted into actual flesh and blood and set before her face.

It was a curious situation; yet it is not on that account that I have made room for it here, but on account of a thing which seemed to me still more curious. To wit, that this dreadful matter brought from these downtrodden people no outburst of rage against these oppressors. They had been heritors and subjects of cruelty and outrage so long that nothing could have startled them but a kindness. Yes, here was a curious revelation, indeed, of the depth to which this people had been sunk in slavery. Their entire being was reduced to a monotonous dead level of patience, resignation, dumb uncomplaining acceptance of whatever might befall them in this life. Their very imagination was dead. When you can say that of a man, he has struck bottom, I reckon; there is no lower deep for him.

I rather wished I had gone some other road. This was not the sort of experience for a statesman to encounter who was planning out a peaceful revolution in his mind. For it could not help bringing up the unget-aroundable fact that, all gentle cant and philosophizing to the contrary notwithstanding, no people in the world ever did achieve their freedom by goody-goody talk and moral suasion: it being immutable law that all revolutions that will succeed must *begin* in blood, whatever may answer afterward. If history teaches anything, it teaches that. What this folk needed, then, was a Reign of Terror and a guillotine, and I was the wrong man for them.

Two days later, toward noon, Sandy began to show signs of excitement and feverish expectancy. She said we were approaching the ogre's castle. I was surprised into an uncomfortable shock. The object of our quest had gradually dropped out of my mind; this sudden resurrection of it made it seem quite a real and startling thing for a moment, and roused up in me a smart interest. Sandy's excitement increased every moment; and so did mine, for that sort of thing is catching. My heart got to thumping. You can't reason with your heart; it has its own laws, and thumps about things which the intellect scorns. Presently, when Sandy slid from the horse, motioned me to stop, and went creeping stealthily, with her head bent nearly to her knees, toward a row of bushes that bordered a declivity, the thumpings grew stronger and quicker. And they kept it up while she was gaining her ambush and getting her glimpse over the declivity; and also while I was creeping to her side on my knees. Her eyes were burning now, as she pointed with her finger, and said in a panting whisper:

"The castle! The castle! Lo, where it looms!"

What a welcome disappointment I experienced! I said:

"Castle? It is nothing but a pigsty; a pigsty with a wattled fence around it."

She looked surprised and distressed. The animation faded out of her face; and during many moments she was lost in thought and silent. Then:

"It was not enchanted aforetime," she said in a musing fashion, as if to herself. "And how strange is this marvel, and how awful —that to the one perception it is enchanted and dight in a base and shameful aspect; yet to the perception of the other it is not enchanted, hath suffered no change, but stands firm and stately still, girt with its moat and waving its banners in the blue air from its towers. And God shield us, how it pricks the heart to see again these gracious captives, and the sorrow deepened in their sweet faces! We have tarried along, and are to blame."

I saw my cue. The castle was enchanted to *me*, not to her. It would be wasted time to try to argue her out of her delusion, it couldn't be done; I must just humor it. So I said:

"This is a common case—the enchanting of a thing to one eye and leaving it in its proper form to another. You have heard of it before, Sandy, though you haven't happened to experience

it. But no harm is done. In fact, it is lucky the way it is. If these ladies were hogs to everybody and to themselves, it would be necessary to break the enchantment, and that might be impossible if one failed to find out the particular process of the enchantment. And hazardous, too; for in attempting a disenchantment without the true key, you are liable to err, and turn your hogs into dogs, and the dogs into cats, the cats into rats, and so on, and end by reducing your materials to nothing finally, or to an odorless gas which you can't follow—which, of course, amounts to the same thing. But here, by good luck, no one's eyes but mine are under the enchantment, and so it is of no consequence to dissolve it. These ladies remain ladies to you, and to themselves, and to everybody else; and at the same time they will suffer in no way from my delusion, for when I know that an ostensible hog is a lady, that is enough for me, I know how to treat her."

"Thanks, oh, sweet my lord, thou talkest like an angel. And I know that thou wilt deliver them, for that thou art minded to great deeds and art as strong a knight of your hands and as brave to will and to do, as any that is on live."

"I will not leave a princess in the sty, Sandy. Are those three yonder that to my disordered eyes are starveling swine-herds—"

"The ogres, Are *they* changed also? It is most wonderful. Now am I fearful; for how canst thou strike with sure aim when five of their nine cubits of stature are to thee invisible? Ah, go warily, fair sir; this is a mightier emprise than I wend."

"You be easy, Sandy. All I need to know is, how *much* of an ogre is invisible; then I know how to locate his vitals. Don't you be afraid, I will make short work of these bunco-steerers. Stay where you are."

I left Sandy kneeling there, corpse-faced but plucky and hopeful, and rode down to the pigsty, and struck up a trade with the swine-herds. I won their gratitude by buying out all the hogs at the lump sum of sixteen pennies, which was rather above latest quotations. I was just in time; for the Church, the lord of the manor, and the rest of the tax-gatherers would have been along next day and swept off pretty much all the stock, leaving the swine-herds very short of hogs and Sandy out of princesses. But now the tax people could be paid in cash, and there would be a stake left besides. One of the men had ten children; and he said that last year when a priest came and of his ten pigs took the fattest one for tithes, the wife burst out upon him, and offered him a child and said:

"Thou beast without bowels of mercy, why leave me my child, yet rob me of the wherewithal to feed it?"

How curious. The same thing had happened in the Wales of my day, under this same old Established Church, which was supposed by many to have changed its nature when it changed its disguise.

I sent the three men away, and then opened the sty gate and beckoned Sandy to come—which she did; and not leisurely, but with the rush of a prairie fire. And when I saw her fling herself upon those hogs, with tears of joy running down her cheeks, and strain them to her heart, and kiss them, and caress them, and call them reverently by grand princely names, I was ashamed of her, ashamed of the human race.

We had to drive those hogs home—ten miles; and no ladies were ever more fickle-minded or contrary. They would stay in no road, no path; they broke out through the brush on all sides, and flowed away in all directions, over rocks, and hills, and the roughest places they could find. And they must not be struck, or roughly accosted; Sandy could not bear to see them treated in ways unbecoming their rank. The troublesomest old sow of the lot had to be called my Lady, and your Highness, like the rest. It is annoying and difficult to scour around after hogs, in armor. There was one small countess, with an iron ring in her snout and hardly any hair on her back, that was the devil for perversity. She gave me a race of an hour, over all sorts of country, and then we were right where we had started from, having made not a rod of real progress. I seized her at last by the tail, and brought her along squealing. When I overtook Sandy she was horrified, and said it was in the last degree indelicate to drag a countess by her train.

We got the hogs home just at dark—most of them. The princess Nerovens de Morganore was missing, and two of her ladies in waiting: namely, Miss Angela Bohun, and the Demoiselle Elaine Courtemains, the former of these two being a young black sow with a white star in her forehead, and the latter a brown one with thin legs and a slight limp in the forward shank on the starboard side—a couple of the tryingest blisters to drive that I ever saw. Also among the missing were several mere baronesses—and I wanted them to stay missing; but no, all that sausage-meat had to be found; so servants were sent out with torches to scour the woods and hills to that end.

Of course, the whole drove was housed in the house, and, great guns!—well, I never saw anything like it. Nor ever heard anything like it. And never smelt anything like it. It was like an insurrection in a gasometer.

CHAPTER XXI

THE PILGRIMS

When I did get to bed at last I was unspeakably tired; the stretching out, and the relaxing of the long-tense muscles, how luxurious, how delicious! but that was as far as I could get—sleep was out of the question for the present. The ripping and tearing and squealing of the nobility up and down the halls and corridors was pandemonium come again, and kept me broad awake. Being awake, my thoughts were busy, of course; and mainly they busied themselves with Sandy's curious delusion. Here she was, as sane a person as the kingdom could produce; and yet, from my point of view she was acting like a crazy woman. My land, the power of training! of influence! of education! It can bring a body up to believe anything. I had to put myself in Sandy's place to realize that she was not a lunatic. Yes, and put her in mine, to demonstrate how easy it is to seem a lunatic to a person who has not been taught as you have been taught. If I had told Sandy I had seen a wagon, uninfluenced by enchantment, spin along fifty miles an hour; had seen a man, unequipped with magic powers, get into a basket and soar out of sight among the clouds; and had listened, without any necromancer's help, to the conversation of a person who was several hundred miles away, Sandy would not merely have supposed me to be crazy, she would have thought she knew it. Everybody around her believed in enchantments; nobody had any doubts; to doubt that a castle could be turned into a sty, and its occupants into hogs, would have been the same as my doubting among Connecticut people the actuality of the telephone and its wonders,—and in both cases would be absolute proof of a diseased mind, an unsettled reason. Yes, Sandy was sane; that must be admitted. If I also would be sane—to Sandy —I must keep my superstitions about

unenchanted and unmiraculous locomotives, balloons, and telephones, to myself. Also, I believed that the world was not flat, and hadn't pillars under it to support it, nor a canopy over it to turn off a universe of water that occupied all space above; but as I was the only person in the kingdom afflicted with such impious and criminal opinions, I recognized that it would be good wisdom to keep quiet about this matter, too, if I did not wish to be suddenly shunned and forsaken by everybody as a madman.

The next morning Sandy assembled the swine in the dining-room and gave them their breakfast, waiting upon them personally and manifesting in every way the deep reverence which the natives of her island, ancient and modern, have always felt for rank, let its outward casket and the mental and moral contents be what they may. I could have eaten with the hogs if I had had birth approaching my lofty official rank; but I hadn't, and so accepted the unavoidable slight and made no complaint. Sandy and I had our breakfast at the second table. The family were not at home. I said:

"How many are in the family, Sandy, and where do they keep themselves?"

"Family?"

"Yes."

"Which family, good my lord?"

"Why, this family; your own family."

"Sooth to say, I understand you not. I have no family."

"No family? Why, Sandy, isn't this your home?"

"Now how indeed might that be? I have no home."

"Well, then, whose house is this?"

"Ah, wit you well I would tell you an I knew myself."

"Come—you don't even know these people? Then who invited us here?"

"None invited us. We but came; that is all."

"Why, woman, this is a most extraordinary performance. The effrontery of it is beyond admiration. We blandly march into a man's house, and cram it full of the only really valuable nobility the sun has yet discovered in the earth, and then it turns out that we don't even know the man's name. How did you ever venture to take this extravagant liberty? I supposed, of course, it was your home. What will the man say?"

"What will he say? Forsooth what can he say but give thanks?"

"Thanks for what?"

Her face was filled with a puzzled surprise:

"Verily, thou troublest mine understanding with strange words. Do ye dream that one of his estate is like to have the honor twice in his life to entertain company such as we have brought to grace his house withal?"

"Well, no—when you come to that. No, it's an even bet that this is the first time he has had a treat like this."

A Connecticut Yankee In King Arthur's Court 479

"Then let him be thankful, and manifest the same by grateful speech and due humility; he were a dog, else, and the heir and ancestor of dogs."

To my mind, the situation was uncomfortable. It might become more so. It might be a good idea to muster the hogs and move on. So I said:

"The day is wasting, Sandy. It is time to get the nobility together and be moving."

"Wherefore, fair sir and Boss?"

"We want to take them to their home, don't we?"

"La, but list to him! They be of all the regions of the earth! Each must hie to her own home; wend you we might do all these journeys in one so brief life as He hath appointed that created life, and thereto death likewise with help of Adam, who by sin done through persuasion of his helpmeet, she being wrought upon and bewrayed by the beguilements of the great enemy of man, that serpent hight Satan, aforetime consecrated and set apart unto that evil work by overmastering spite and envy begotten in his heart through fell ambitions that did blight and mildew a nature erst so white and pure whenso it hove with the shining multitudes its brethren-born in glade and shade of that fair heaven wherein all such as native be to that rich estate and—"

"Great Scott!"

"My lord?"

"Well, you know we haven't got time for this sort of thing. Don't you see, we could distribute these people around the earth in less time than it is going to take you to explain that we can't. We mustn't talk now, we must act. You want to be careful; you mustn't let your mill get the start of you that way, at a time like this. To business now—and sharp's the word. Who is to take the aristocracy home?"

"Even their friends. These will come for them from the far parts of the earth."

This was lightning from a clear sky, for unexpectedness; and the relief of it was like pardon to a prisoner. She would remain to deliver the goods, of course.

"Well, then, Sandy, as our enterprise is handsomely and successfully ended, I will go home and report; and if ever another one—"

"I also am ready; I will go with thee."

This was recalling the pardon.

"How? You will go with me? Why should you?"

"Will I be traitor to my knight, dost think? That were dishonor. I may not part from thee until in knightly encounter in the field some overmatching champion shall fairly win and fairly wear me. I were to blame an I thought that that might ever hap."

"Elected for the long term," I sighed to myself. "I may as well make the best of it." So then I spoke up and said:

"All right; let us make a start."

While she was gone to cry her farewells over the pork, I gave that whole peerage away to the servants. And I asked them to take a duster and dust around a little where the nobilities had mainly lodged and promenaded; but they considered that that would be hardly worth while, and would moreover be a rather grave departure from custom, and therefore likely to make talk. A departure from custom—that settled it; it was a nation capable of committing any crime but that. The servants said they would follow the fashion, a fashion grown sacred through immemorial observance; they would scatter fresh rushes in all the rooms and halls, and then the evidence of the aristocratic visitation would be no longer visible. It was a kind of satire on Nature: it was the scientific method, the geologic method; it deposited the history of the family in a stratified record; and the antiquary could dig through it and tell by the remains of each period what changes of diet the family had introduced successively for a hundred years.

The first thing we struck that day was a procession of pilgrims. It was not going our way, but we joined it, nevertheless; for it was hourly being borne in upon me now, that if I would govern this country wisely, I must be posted in the details of its life, and not at second hand, but by personal observation and scrutiny.

This company of pilgrims resembled Chaucer's in this: that it had in it a sample of about all the upper occupations and professions the country could show, and a corresponding variety of costume. There were young men and old men, young women and old women, lively folk and grave folk. They rode upon mules and horses, and there was not a side-saddle in the party; for this specialty was to remain unknown in England for nine hundred years yet.

It was a pleasant, friendly, sociable herd; pious, happy, merry and full of unconscious coarsenesses and innocent indecencies. What they regarded as the merry tale went the continual round and caused no more embarrassment than it would have caused in the best English society twelve centuries later. Practical jokes worthy of the English wits of the first quarter of the far-off nineteenth century were sprung here and there and yonder along the line, and compelled the delightedest applause; and sometimes when a bright remark was made at one end of the procession and started on its travels toward the other, you could note its progress all the way by the sparkling spray of laughter it threw off from its bows as it plowed along; and also by the blushes of the mules in its wake.

Sandy knew the goal and purpose of this pilgrimage, and she posted me. She said:

"They journey to the Valley of Holiness, for to be blessed of the godly hermits and drink of the miraculous waters and be cleansed from sin."

"Where is this watering place?"

"It lieth a two-day journey hence, by the borders of the land that hight the Cuckoo Kingdom."

"Tell me about it. Is it a celebrated place?"

"Oh, of a truth, yes. There be none more so. Of old time there lived there an abbot and his monks. Belike were none in the world more holy than these; for they gave themselves to study of pious books, and spoke not the one to the other, or indeed to any, and ate decayed herbs and naught thereto, and slept hard, and prayed much, and washed never; also they wore the same garment until it fell from their bodies through age and decay. Right so came they to be known of all the world by reason of these holy austerities, and visited by rich and poor, and reverenced."

"Proceed."

"But always there was lack of water there. Whereas, upon a time, the holy abbot prayed, and for answer a great stream of clear water burst forth by miracle in a desert place. Now were the fickle monks tempted of the Fiend, and they wrought with their abbot unceasingly by beggings and beseechings that he would construct a bath; and when he was become aweary and might not resist more, he said have ye your will, then, and granted that they asked. Now mark thou what 'tis to forsake the ways of purity the which He loveth, and wanton with such as be worldly and an offense. These monks did enter into the bath and come thence washed as white as snow; and lo, in that moment His sign appeared, in miraculous rebuke! for His insulted waters ceased to flow, and utterly vanished away."

"They fared mildly, Sandy, considering how that kind of crime is regarded in this country."

"Belike; but it was their first sin; and they had been of perfect life for long, and differing in naught from the angels. Prayers, tears, torturings of the flesh, all was vain to beguile that water to flow again. Even processions; even burnt-offerings; even votive candles to the Virgin, did fail every each of them; and all in the land did marvel."

"How odd to find that even this industry has its financial panics, and at times sees its assignats and greenbacks languish to zero, and everything come to a standstill. Go on, Sandy."

"And so upon a time, after year and day, the good abbot made humble surrender and destroyed the bath. And behold, His anger was in that moment appeased, and the waters gushed richly forth again, and even unto this day they have not ceased to flow in that generous measure."

"Then I take it nobody has washed since."

"He that would essay it could have his halter free; yes, and swiftly would he need it, too."

"The community has prospered since?"

"Even from that very day. The fame of the miracle went abroad into all lands. From every land came monks to join; they came even as the fishes come, in shoals; and the monastery added building to building, and yet others to these, and so spread wide its arms and took them in. And nuns came, also; and more again, and yet more; and built over against the monastery on the yon side of the vale, and added building to building, until mighty was that nunnery. And these were friendly unto those, and they joined their loving labors together, and together they built a fair great foundling asylum midway of the valley between."

"You spoke of some hermits, Sandy."

"These have gathered there from the ends of the earth. A hermit thriveth best where there be multitudes of pilgrims. Ye shall not find no hermit of no sort wanting. If any shall mention a hermit of a kind he thinketh new and not to be found but in some far strange land, let him but scratch among the holes and caves and swamps that line that Valley of Holiness, and whatsoever be his breed, it skills not, he shall find a sample of it there."

I closed up alongside of a burly fellow with a fat good-humored face, purposing to make myself agreeable and pick up some further crumbs of fact; but I had hardly more than scraped acquaintance with him when he began eagerly and awkwardly to lead up, in the immemorial way, to that same old anecdote—the one Sir Dinadan told me, what time I got into trouble with Sir Sagramor and was challenged of him on account of it. I excused myself and dropped to the rear of the procession, sad at heart, willing to go hence from this troubled life, this vale of tears, this brief day of broken rest, of cloud and storm, of weary struggle and monotonous defeat; and yet shrinking from the change, as remembering how long eternity is, and how many have wended thither who know that anecdote.

Early in the afternoon we overtook another procession of pilgrims; but in this one was no merriment, no jokes, no laughter, no playful ways, nor any happy giddiness, whether of youth or age. Yet both were here, both age and youth; gray old men and women, strong men and women of middle age, young husbands, young wives, little boys and girls, and three babies at the breast. Even the children were smileless; there was not a face among all these half a hundred people but was cast down, and bore that set expression of hopelessness which is bred of long and hard trials and old acquaintance with despair. They were slaves. Chains led from their fettered feet and their manacled hands to a sole-leather belt about their waists; and all except the children were also linked together in a file six feet apart, by a single chain which led from collar to collar all down the line. They were on foot, and had tramped three hundred miles in eighteen days, upon the cheapest odds and ends of food, and stingy rations of that. They had slept in these chains every night, bundled together like swine. They had upon their bodies some poor rags, but they could not be said to be clothed. Their irons had chafed the skin from their ankles and made sores which were ulcerated and wormy. Their naked feet were torn, and none walked without a limp. Originally there had been a hundred of these unfortunates, but about half had been sold on the trip. The trader in charge of them rode a horse and carried a whip with a short handle and a long heavy lash divided into several knotted tails at the end. With this whip he cut the shoulders of any that tottered from weariness and pain, and straightened them up. He did not speak; the whip conveyed his desire without that. None of these poor creatures looked up as we rode along by; they showed no consciousness of our presence. And they made no sound but one; that was the dull and awful clank of their chains from end to end of the long file, as forty-three burdened feet rose and fell in unison. The file moved in a cloud of its own making.

All these faces were gray with a coating of dust. One has seen the like of this coating upon furniture in unoccupied houses, and has written his idle thought in it with his finger. I was reminded of this when I noticed the faces of some of those women, young mothers carrying babes that were near to death and freedom, how a something in their hearts was written in the dust upon their faces, plain to see, and lord, how plain to read! for it was the track of tears. One of these young mothers was but a girl, and it hurt me to the heart to read that writing, and reflect that it was come up out of the breast of such a child, a breast that ought not to know trouble yet, but only the

A Connecticut Yankee In King Arthur's Court 481

gladness of the morning of life; and no doubt—

She reeled just then, giddy with fatigue, and down came the lash and flicked a flake of skin from her naked shoulder. It stung me as if I had been hit instead. The master halted the file and jumped from his horse. He stormed and swore at this girl, and said she had made annoyance enough with her laziness, and as this was the last chance he should have, he would settle the account now. She dropped on her knees and put up her hands and began to beg, and cry, and implore, in a passion of terror, but the master gave no attention. He snatched the child from her, and then made the men-slaves who were chained before and behind her throw her on the ground and hold her there and expose her body; and then he laid on with his lash like a madman till her back was flayed, she shrieking and struggling the while piteously. One of the men who was holding her turned away his face, and for this humanity he was reviled and flogged.

All our pilgrims looked on and commented—on the expert way in which the whip was handled. They were too much hardened by lifelong everyday familiarity with slavery to notice that there was anything else in the exhibition that invited comment. This was what slavery could do, in the way of ossifying what one may call the superior lobe of human feeling; for these pilgrims were kind-hearted people, and they would not have allowed that man to treat a horse like that.

I wanted to stop the whole thing and set the slaves free, but that would not do. I must not interfere too much and get myself a name for riding over the country's laws and the citizen's rights roughshod. If I lived and prospered I would be the death of slavery, that I was resolved upon; but I would try to fix it so that when I became its executioner it should be by command of the nation.

Just here was the wayside shop of a smith; and now arrived a landed proprietor who had bought this girl a few miles back, deliverable here where her irons could be taken off. They were removed; then there was a squabble between the gentleman and the dealer as to which should pay the blacksmith. The moment the girl was delivered from her irons, she flung herself, all tears and frantic sobbings, into the arms of the slave who had turned away his face when she was whipped. He strained her to his breast and smothered her face and the child's with kisses, and washed them with the rain of his tears. I suspected. I inquired. Yes, I was right; it was husband and wife. They had to be torn apart by force; the girl had to be dragged away, and she struggled and fought and shrieked like one gone mad till a turn of the road hid her from sight; and even after that, we could still make out the fading plaint of those receding shrieks. And the husband and father, with his wife and child gone, never to be seen by him again in life?— well, the look of him one might not bear at all, and so I turned away; but I knew I should never get his picture out of my mind again, and there it is to this day, to wring my heartstrings whenever I think of it.

We put up at the inn in a village just at nightfall, and when I rose next morning and looked abroad, I was ware where a knight came riding in the golden glory of the new day, and recognized him for knight of mine—Sir Ozana le Cure Hardy. He was in the gentlemen's furnishing line, and his missionarying specialty was plug hats. He was clothed all in steel, in the beautifulest armor of the time—up to where his helmet ought to have been; but he hadn't any helmet, he wore a shiny stove-pipe hat, and was ridiculous a spectacle as one might want to see. It was another of my surreptitious schemes

for extinguishing knighthood by making it grotesque and absurd. Sir Ozana's saddle was hung about with leather hat boxes, and every time he overcame a wandering knight he swore him into my service and fitted him with a plug and made him wear it. I dressed and ran down to welcome Sir Ozana and get his news.

"How is trade?" I asked.

"Ye will note that I have but these four left; yet were they sixteen whenas I got me from Camelot."

"Why, you have certainly done nobly, Sir Ozana. Where have you been foraging of late?"

"I am but now come from the Valley of Holiness, please you sir."

"I am pointed for that place myself. Is there anything stirring in the monkery, more than common?"

"By the mass ye may not question it!.... Give him good feed, boy, and stint it not, an thou valuest thy crown; so get ye lightly to the stable and do even as I bid.... Sir, it is parlous news I bring, and—be these pilgrims? Then ye may not do better, good folk, than gather and hear the tale I have to tell, sith it concerneth you, forasmuch as ye go to find that ye will not find, and seek that ye will seek in vain, my life being hostage for my word, and my word and message being these, namely: That a hap has happened whereof the like has not been seen no more but once this two hundred years, which was the first and last time that that said misfortune strake the holy valley in that form by commandment of the Most High whereto by reasons just and causes thereunto contributing, wherein the matter—"

"The miraculous fount hath ceased to flow!" This shout burst from twenty pilgrim mouths at once.

"Ye say well, good people. I was verging to it, even when ye spake."

"Has somebody been washing again?"

"Nay, it is suspected, but none believe it. It is thought to be some other sin, but none wit what."

"How are they feeling about the calamity?"

"None may describe it in words. The fount is these nine days dry. The prayers that did begin then, and the lamentations in sackcloth and ashes, and the holy processions, none of these have ceased nor night nor day; and so the monks and the nuns and the foundlings be all exhausted, and do hang up prayers writ upon parchment, sith that no strength is left in man to lift up voice. And at last they sent for thee, Sir Boss, to try magic and enchantment; and if you could not come, then was the messenger to fetch Merlin, and he is there these three days now, and saith he will fetch that water though he burst the globe and wreck its kingdoms to accomplish it; and right bravely doth he work his magic and call upon his hellions to hie them hither and help, but not a whiff of moisture hath he started yet, even so much as might qualify as mist upon a copper mirror an ye count not the barrel of sweat he sweateth betwixt sun and sun over the dire labors of his task; and if ye—"

Breakfast was ready. As soon as it was over I showed to Sir

Ozana these words which I had written on the inside of his hat: "Chemical Department, Laboratory extension, Section G. Pxxp. Send two of first size, two of No. 3, and six of No. 4, together with the proper complementary details—and two of my trained assistants." And I said:

"Now get you to Camelot as fast as you can fly, brave knight, and show the writing to Clarence, and tell him to have these required matters in the Valley of Holiness with all possible dispatch."

"I will well, Sir Boss," and he was off.

CHAPTER XXII

THE HOLY FOUNTAIN

The pilgrims were human beings. Otherwise they would have acted differently. They had come a long and difficult journey, and now when the journey was nearly finished, and they learned that the main thing they had come for had ceased to exist, they didn't do as horses or cats or angle-worms would probably have done—turn back and get at something profitable—no, anxious as they had before been to see the miraculous fountain, they were as much as forty times as anxious now to see the place where it had used to be. There is no accounting for human beings.

We made good time; and a couple of hours before sunset we stood upon the high confines of the Valley of Holiness, and our eyes swept it from end to end and noted its features. That is, its large features. These were the three masses of buildings. They were distant and isolated temporalities shrunken to toy constructions in the lonely waste of what seemed a desert—and was. Such a scene is always mournful, it is so impressively still, and looks so steeped in death. But there was a sound here which interrupted the stillness only to add to its mournfulness; this was the faint far sound of tolling bells which floated fitfully to us on the passing breeze, and so faintly, so softly, that we hardly knew whether we heard it with our ears or with our spirits.

We reached the monastery before dark, and there the males were given lodging, but the women were sent over to the nunnery. The bells were close at hand now, and their solemn booming smote upon the ear like a message of doom. A superstitious despair possessed the heart of every monk and published itself in his ghastly face. Everywhere, these black-robed, soft-sandaled, tallow-visaged specters appeared, flitted about and disappeared, noiseless as the creatures of a troubled dream, and as uncanny.

The old abbot's joy to see me was pathetic. Even to tears; but he did the shedding himself. He said:

"Delay not, son, but get to thy saving work. An we bring not the water back again, and soon, we are ruined, and the good work of two hundred years must end. And see thou do it with enchantments that be holy, for the Church will not endure that work in her cause be done by devil's magic."

"When I work, Father, be sure there will be no devil's work connected with it. I shall use no arts that come of the devil, and no elements not created by the hand of God. But is Merlin working strictly on pious lines?"

"Ah, he said he would, my son, he said he would, and took oath to make his promise good."

"Well, in that case, let him proceed."

"But surely you will not sit idle by, but help?"

"It will not answer to mix methods, Father; neither would it be professional courtesy. Two of a trade must not underbid each other. We might as well cut rates and be done with it; it would arrive at that in the end. Merlin has the contract; no other magician can touch it till he throws it up."

"But I will take it from him; it is a terrible emergency and the act is thereby justified. And if it were not so, who will give law to the Church? The Church giveth law to all; and what she wills to do, that she may do, hurt whom it may. I will take it from him; you shall begin upon the moment."

"It may not be, Father. No doubt, as you say, where power is supreme, one can do as one likes and suffer no injury; but we poor magicians are not so situated. Merlin is a very good magician in a small way, and has quite a neat provincial reputation. He is struggling along, doing the best he can, and it would not be etiquette for me to take his job until he himself abandons it."

The abbot's face lighted.

"Ah, that is simple. There are ways to persuade him to abandon it."

"No-no, Father, it skills not, as these people say. If he were persuaded against his will, he would load that well with a malicious enchantment which would balk me until I found out its secret. It might take a month. I could set up a little enchantment of mine which I call the telephone, and he could not find out its secret in a hundred years. Yes, you perceive, he might block me for a month. Would you like to risk a month in a dry time like this?"

"A month! The mere thought of it maketh me to shudder. Have it thy way, my son. But my heart is heavy with this disappointment. Leave me, and let me wear my spirit with weariness and waiting, even as I have done these ten long days, counterfeiting thus the thing that is called rest, the prone body making outward sign of repose where inwardly is none."

Of course, it would have been best, all round, for Merlin to waive etiquette and quit and call it half a day, since he would never be able to start that water, for he was a true magician of the time; which is to say, the big miracles, the ones that gave him his reputation, always had the luck to be performed when nobody but Merlin was present; he couldn't start this well with all this crowd around to see; a crowd was as bad for a magician's miracle in that day as it was for a spiritualist's miracle in mine; there was sure to be some skeptic on hand to turn up the gas at the crucial moment and spoil everything. But I did not want Merlin to retire from the job until I was ready to take hold of it effectively myself; and I could not do that until I got my things from Camelot, and that would take two or three days.

My presence gave the monks hope, and cheered them up a good deal; insomuch that they ate a square meal that night for the first time in ten days. As soon as their stomachs had been properly reinforced with food, their spirits began to rise fast; when the mead began to go round they rose faster. By the time everybody was half-seas over, the holy community was in good shape to make a night of it; so we stayed by the board and put it through on that line. Matters got to be very jolly. Good old questionable stories were told that made the tears run down and cavernous mouths stand wide and the round bellies shake with laughter; and questionable songs were bellowed out in a mighty chorus that drowned the boom of the tolling bells.

At last I ventured a story myself; and vast was the success of it. Not right off, of course, for the native of those islands does not, as a rule, dissolve upon the early applications of a humorous thing; but the fifth time I told it, they began to crack in places; the eight time I told it, they began to crumble; at the twelfth repetition they fell apart in chunks; and at the fifteenth they disintegrated, and I got a broom and swept them up. This language is figurative. Those islanders—well, they are slow pay at first, in the matter of return for your investment of effort, but in the end they make the pay of all other nations poor and small by contrast.

I was at the well next day betimes. Merlin was there, enchanting away like a beaver, but not raising the moisture. He was not in a pleasant humor; and every time I hinted that perhaps this contract was a shade too hefty for a novice he unlimbered his tongue and cursed like a bishop—French bishop of the Regency days, I mean.

Matters were about as I expected to find them. The "fountain" was an ordinary well, it had been dug in the ordinary way, and stoned up in the ordinary way. There was no miracle about it. Even the lie that had created its reputation was not miraculous; I could have told it myself, with one hand tied behind me. The well was in a dark chamber which stood in the center of a cut-stone chapel, whose walls were hung with pious pictures of a workmanship that would have made a chromo feel good; pictures historically commemorative of curative miracles which had been achieved by the waters when nobody was looking. That is, nobody but angels; they are always on deck when there is a miracle to the fore—so as to get put in the picture, perhaps. Angels are as fond of that as a fire company; look at the old masters.

The well-chamber was dimly lighted by lamps; the water was drawn with a windlass and chain by monks, and poured into troughs which delivered it into stone reservoirs outside in the chapel—when there was water to draw, I mean—and none but monks could enter the well-chamber. I entered it, for I had temporary authority to do so, by courtesy of my professional brother and subordinate. But he hadn't entered it himself. He did everything by incantations; he never worked his intellect. If he had stepped in there and used his eyes, instead of his disordered mind, he could have cured the well by natural means, and then turned it into a miracle in the customary way; but no, he was an old numskull, a magician who believed in his own magic; and no magician can thrive who is handicapped with a superstition like that.

I had an idea that the well had sprung a leak; that some of the wall stones near the bottom had fallen and exposed fissures that allowed the water to escape. I measured the chain—98 feet. Then I called in a couple of monks, locked the door, took a candle, and made them lower me in the bucket. When the chain was all paid out, the candle confirmed my suspicion; a considerable section of the wall was gone, exposing a good big fissure.

I almost regretted that my theory about the well's trouble was correct, because I had another one that had a showy point or two about it for a miracle. I remembered that in America, many centuries later, when an oil well ceased to flow, they

used to blast it out with a dynamite torpedo. If I should find this well dry and no explanation of it, I could astonish these people most nobly by having a person of no especial value drop a dynamite bomb into it. It was my idea to appoint Merlin. However, it was plain that there was no occasion for the bomb. One cannot have everything the way he would like it. A man has no business to be depressed by a disappointment, anyway; he ought to make up his mind to get even. That is what I did. I said to myself, I am in no hurry, I can wait; that bomb will come good yet. And it did, too.

When I was above ground again, I turned out the monks, and let down a fish-line; the well was a hundred and fifty feet deep, and there was forty-one feet of water in it. I called in a monk and asked:

"How deep is the well?"

"That, sir, I wit not, having never been told."

"How does the water usually stand in it?"

"Near to the top, these two centuries, as the testimony goeth, brought down to us through our predecessors."

It was true—as to recent times at least—for there was witness to it, and better witness than a monk; only about twenty or thirty feet of the chain showed wear and use, the rest of it was unworn and rusty. What had happened when the well gave out that other time? Without doubt some practical person had come along and mended the leak, and then had come up and told the abbot he had discovered by divination that if the sinful bath were destroyed the well would flow again. The leak had befallen again now, and these children would have prayed, and processioned, and tolled their bells for heavenly succor till they all dried up and blew away, and no innocent of them all would ever have thought to drop a fish-line into the well or go down in it and find out what was really the matter. Old habit of mind is one of the toughest things to get away from in the world. It transmits itself like physical form and feature; and for a man, in those days, to have had an idea that his ancestors hadn't had, would have brought him under suspicion of being illegitimate. I said to the monk:

"It is a difficult miracle to restore water in a dry well, but we will try, if my brother Merlin fails. Brother Merlin is a very passable artist, but only in the parlor-magic line, and he may not succeed; in fact, is not likely to succeed. But that should be nothing to his discredit; the man that can do *this* kind of miracle knows enough to keep hotel."

"Hotel? I mind not to have heard—"

"Of hotel? It's what you call hostel. The man that can do this miracle can keep hostel. I can do this miracle; I shall do this miracle; yet I do not try to conceal from you that it is a miracle to tax the occult powers to the last strain."

"None knoweth that truth better than the brotherhood, indeed; for it is of record that aforetime it was parlous difficult and took a year. Natheless, God send you good success, and to that end will we pray."

As a matter of business it was a good idea to get the notion around that the thing was difficult. Many a small thing has been made large by the right kind of advertising. That monk was filled up with the difficulty of this enterprise; he would fill up the others. In two days the solicitude would be booming.

On my way home at noon, I met Sandy. She had been sampling the hermits. I said:

"I would like to do that myself. This is Wednesday. Is there a matinee?"

"A which, please you, sir?"

"Matinee. Do they keep open afternoons?"

"Who?"

"The hermits, of course."

"Keep open?"

"Yes, keep open. Isn't that plain enough? Do they knock off at noon?"

"Knock off?"

"Knock off?—yes, knock off. What is the matter with knock off? I never saw such a dunderhead; can't you understand anything at all? In plain terms, do they shut up shop, draw the game, bank the fires—"

"Shut up shop, draw—"

"There, never mind, let it go; you make me tired. You can't seem to understand the simplest thing."

"I would I might please thee, sir, and it is to me dole and sorrow that I fail, albeit sith I am but a simple damsel and taught of none, being from the cradle unbaptized in those deep waters of learning that do anoint with a sovereignty him that partaketh of that most noble sacrament, investing him with reverend state to the mental eye of the humble mortal who, by bar and lack of that great consecration seeth in his own unlearned estate but a symbol of that other sort of lack and loss which men do publish to the pitying eye with sackcloth trappings whereon the ashes of grief do lie bepowdered and bestrewn, and so, when such shall in the darkness of his mind encounter these golden phrases of high mystery, these shut-up-shops, and draw-the-game, and bank-the-fires, it is but by the grace of God that he burst not for envy of the mind that can beget, and tongue that can deliver so great and mellow-sounding miracles of speech, and if there do ensue confusion in that humbler mind, and failure to divine the meanings of these wonders, then if so be this miscomprehension is not vain but sooth and true, wit ye well it is the very substance of worshipful dear homage and may not lightly be misprized, nor had been, an ye had noted this complexion of mood and mind and understood that that I would I could not, and that I could not I might not, nor yet nor might *nor* could, nor might-not nor could-not, might be by advantage turned to the desired *would*, and so I pray you mercy of my fault, and that ye will of your kindness and your charity forgive it, good my master and most dear lord."

I couldn't make it all out—that is, the details—but I got the general idea; and enough of it, too, to be ashamed. It was not fair to spring those nineteenth century technicalities upon the untutored infant of the sixth and then rail at her because she couldn't get their drift; and when she was making the honest best drive at it she could, too, and no fault of hers that she couldn't fetch the home plate; and so I apologized. Then we meandered pleasantly away toward the hermit holes in

sociable converse together, and better friends than ever.

I was gradually coming to have a mysterious and shuddery reverence for this girl; nowadays whenever she pulled out from the station and got her train fairly started on one of those horizonless transcontinental sentences of hers, it was borne in upon me that I was standing in the awful presence of the Mother of the German Language. I was so impressed with this, that sometimes when she began to empty one of these sentences on me I unconsciously took the very attitude of reverence, and stood uncovered; and if words had been water, I had been drowned, sure. She had exactly the German way; whatever was in her mind to be delivered, whether a mere remark, or a sermon, or a cyclopedia, or the history of a war, she would get it into a single sentence or die. Whenever the literary German dives into a sentence, that is the last you are going to see of him till he emerges on the other side of his Atlantic with his verb in his mouth.

We drifted from hermit to hermit all the afternoon. It was a most strange menagerie. The chief emulation among them seemed to be, to see which could manage to be the uncleanest and most prosperous with vermin. Their manner and attitudes were the last expression of complacent self-righteousness. It was one anchorite's pride to lie naked in the mud and let the insects bite him and blister him unmolested; it was another's to lean against a rock, all day long, conspicuous to the admiration of the throng of pilgrims and pray; it was another's to go naked and crawl around on all fours; it was another's to drag about with him, year in and year out, eighty pounds of iron; it was another's to never lie down when he slept, but to stand among the thorn-bushes and snore when there were pilgrims around to look; a woman, who had the white hair of age, and no other apparel, was black from crown to heel with forty-seven years of holy abstinence from water. Groups of gazing pilgrims stood around all and every of these strange objects, lost in reverent wonder, and envious of the fleckless sanctity which these pious austerities had won for them from an exacting heaven.

By and by we went to see one of the supremely great ones. He was a mighty celebrity; his fame had penetrated all Christendom; the noble and the renowned journeyed from the remotest lands on the globe to pay him reverence. His stand was in the center of the widest part of the valley; and it took all that space to hold his crowds.

His stand was a pillar sixty feet high, with a broad platform on the top of it. He was now doing what he had been doing every day for twenty years up there—bowing his body ceaselessly and rapidly almost to his feet. It was his way of praying. I timed him with a stop watch, and he made 1,244 revolutions in 24 minutes and 46 seconds. It seemed a pity to have all this power going to waste. It was one of the most useful motions in mechanics, the pedal movement; so I made a note in my memorandum book, purposing some day to apply a system of elastic cords to him and run a sewing machine with it. I afterward carried out that scheme, and got five years' good service out of him; in which time he turned out upward of eighteen thousand first-rate tow-linen shirts, which was ten a day. I worked him Sundays and all; he was going, Sundays, the same as week days, and it was no use to waste the power. These shirts cost me nothing but just the mere trifle for the materials—I furnished those myself, it would not have been right to make him do that—and they sold like smoke to pilgrims at a dollar and a half apiece, which was the price of fifty cows or a blooded race horse in Arthurdom. They were regarded as a perfect protection against sin, and advertised as such by my knights everywhere, with the paint-pot and stencil-plate; insomuch that there was not a cliff or a bowlder or a dead wall in England but you could read on it at a mile distance:

"Buy the only genuine St. Stylite; patronized by the Nobility. Patent applied for."

There was more money in the business than one knew what to do with. As it extended, I brought out a line of goods suitable for kings, and a nobby thing for duchesses and that sort, with ruffles down the forehatch and the running-gear clewed up with a featherstitch to leeward and then hauled aft with a back-stay and triced up with a half-turn in the standing rigging forward of the weather-gaskets. Yes, it was a daisy.

But about that time I noticed that the motive power had taken to standing on one leg, and I found that there was something the matter with the other one; so I stocked the business and unloaded, taking Sir Bors de Ganis into camp financially along with certain of his friends; for the works stopped within a year, and the good saint got him to his rest. But he had earned it. I can say that for him.

When I saw him that first time—however, his personal condition will not quite bear description here. You can read it in the Lives of the Saints.*

CHAPTER XXIII

RESTORATION OF THE FOUNTAIN

Saturday noon I went to the well and looked on a while. Merlin was still burning smoke-powders, and pawing the air, and muttering gibberish as hard as ever, but looking pretty down-hearted, for of course he had not started even a perspiration in that well yet. Finally I said:

"How does the thing promise by this time, partner?"

"Behold, I am even now busied with trial of the powerfulest enchantment known to the princes of the occult arts in the lands of the East; an it fail me, naught can avail. Peace, until I finish."

He raised a smoke this time that darkened all the region, and must have made matters uncomfortable for the hermits, for the wind was their way, and it rolled down over their dens in a dense and billowy fog. He poured out volumes of speech to match, and contorted his body and sawed the air with his hands in a most extraordinary way. At the end of twenty minutes he dropped down panting, and about exhausted. Now arrived the abbot and several hundred monks and nuns, and behind them a multitude of pilgrims and a couple of acres of foundlings, all drawn by the prodigious smoke, and all in a grand state of excitement. The abbot inquired anxiously for results. Merlin said:

"If any labor of mortal might break the spell that binds these waters, this which I have but just essayed had done it. It has failed; whereby I do now know that that which I had feared is a truth established; the sign of this failure is, that the most potent spirit known to the magicians of the East, and whose

_____

* All the details concerning the hermits, in this chapter, are from Lecky—but greatly modified. This book not being a history but only a tale, the majority of the historian's frank details were too strong for reproduction in it.—*Editor*

name none may utter and live, has laid his spell upon this well. The mortal does not breathe, nor ever will, who can penetrate the secret of that spell, and without that secret none can break it. The water will flow no more forever, good Father. I have done what man could. Suffer me to go."

Of course this threw the abbot into a good deal of a consternation. He turned to me with the signs of it in his face, and said:

"Ye have heard him. Is it true?"

"Part of it is."

"Not all, then, not all! What part is true?"

"That that spirit with the Russian name has put his spell upon the well."

"God's wounds, then are we ruined!"

"Possibly."

"But not certainly? Ye mean, not certainly?"

"That is it."

"Wherefore, ye also mean that when he saith none can break the spell—"

"Yes, when he says that, he says what isn't necessarily true. There are conditions under which an effort to break it may have some chance—that is, some small, some trifling chance—of success."

"The conditions—"

"Oh, they are nothing difficult. Only these: I want the well and the surroundings for the space of half a mile, entirely to myself from sunset to-day until I remove the ban—and nobody allowed to cross the ground but by my authority."

"Are these all?"

"Yes."

"And you have no fear to try?"

"Oh, none. One may fail, of course; and one may also succeed. One can try, and I am ready to chance it. I have my conditions?"

"These and all others ye may name. I will issue commandment to that effect."

"Wait," said Merlin, with an evil smile. "Ye wit that he that would break this spell must know that spirit's name?"

"Yes, I know his name."

"And wit you also that to know it skills not of itself, but ye must likewise pronounce it? Ha-ha! Knew ye that?"

"Yes, I knew that, too."

"You had that knowledge! Art a fool? Are ye minded to utter that name and die?"

"Utter it? Why certainly. I would utter it if it was Welsh."

"Ye are even a dead man, then; and I go to tell Arthur."

"That's all right. Take your gripsack and get along. The thing for *you* to do is to go home and work the weather, John W. Merlin."

It was a home shot, and it made him wince; for he was the worst weather-failure in the kingdom. Whenever he ordered up the danger-signals along the coast there was a week's dead calm, sure, and every time he prophesied fair weather it rained brickbats. But I kept him in the weather bureau right along, to undermine his reputation. However, that shot raised his bile, and instead of starting home to report my death, he said he would remain and enjoy it.

My two experts arrived in the evening, and pretty well fagged, for they had traveled double tides. They had pack-mules along, and had brought everything I needed—tools, pump, lead pipe, Greek fire, sheaves of big rockets, roman candles, colored fire sprays, electric apparatus, and a lot of sundries—everything necessary for the stateliest kind of a miracle. They got their supper and a nap, and about midnight we sallied out through a solitude so wholly vacant and complete that it quite overpassed the required conditions. We took possession of the well and its surroundings. My boys were experts in all sorts of things, from the stoning up of a well to the constructing of a mathematical instrument. An hour before sunrise we had that leak mended in ship-shape fashion, and the water began to rise. Then we stowed our fireworks in the chapel, locked up the place, and went home to bed.

Before the noon mass was over, we were at the well again; for there was a deal to do yet, and I was determined to spring the miracle before midnight, for business reasons: for whereas a miracle worked for the Church on a week-day is worth a good deal, it is worth six times as much if you get it in on a Sunday. In nine hours the water had risen to its customary level—that is to say, it was within twenty-three feet of the top. We put in a little iron pump, one of the first turned out by my works near the capital; we bored into a stone reservoir which stood against the outer wall of the well-chamber and inserted a section of lead pipe that was long enough to reach to the door of the chapel and project beyond the threshold, where the gushing water would be visible to the two hundred and fifty acres of people I was intending should be present on the flat plain in front of this little holy hillock at the proper time.

We knocked the head out of an empty hogshead and hoisted this hogshead to the flat roof of the chapel, where we clamped it down fast, poured in gunpowder till it lay loosely an inch deep on the bottom, then we stood up rockets in the hogshead as thick as they could loosely stand, all the different breeds of rockets there are; and they made a portly and imposing sheaf, I can tell you. We grounded the wire of a pocket electrical battery in that powder, we placed a whole magazine of Greek fire on each corner of the roof—blue on one corner, green on another, red on another, and purple on the last—and grounded a wire in each.

About two hundred yards off, in the flat, we built a pen of scantlings, about four feet high, and laid planks on it, and so made a platform. We covered it with swell tapestries borrowed for the occasion, and topped it off with the abbot's own throne. When you are going to do a miracle for an ignorant race, you want to get in every detail that will count; you want to make all the properties impressive to the public eye; you want to make

matters comfortable for your head guest; then you can turn yourself loose and play your effects for all they are worth. I know the value of these things, for I know human nature. You can't throw too much style into a miracle. It costs trouble, and work, and sometimes money; but it pays in the end. Well, we brought the wires to the ground at the chapel, and then brought them under the ground to the platform, and hid the batteries there. We put a rope fence a hundred feet square around the platform to keep off the common multitude, and that finished the work. My idea was, doors open at 10:30, performance to begin at 11:25 sharp. I wished I could charge admission, but of course that wouldn't answer. I instructed my boys to be in the chapel as early as 10, before anybody was around, and be ready to man the pumps at the proper time, and make the fur fly. Then we went home to supper.

The news of the disaster to the well had traveled far by this time; and now for two or three days a steady avalanche of people had been pouring into the valley. The lower end of the valley was become one huge camp; we should have a good house, no question about that. Criers went the rounds early in the evening and announced the coming attempt, which put every pulse up to fever heat. They gave notice that the abbot and his official suite would move in state and occupy the platform at 10:30, up to which time all the region which was under my ban must be clear; the bells would then cease from tolling, and this sign should be permission to the multitudes to close in and take their places.

I was at the platform and all ready to do the honors when the abbot's solemn procession hove in sight—which it did not do till it was nearly to the rope fence, because it was a starless black night and no torches permitted. With it came Merlin, and took a front seat on the platform; he was as good as his word for once. One could not see the multitudes banked together beyond the ban, but they were there, just the same. The moment the bells stopped, those banked masses broke and poured over the line like a vast black wave, and for as much as a half hour it continued to flow, and then it solidified itself, and you could have walked upon a pavement of human heads to—well, miles.

We had a solemn stage-wait, now, for about twenty minutes—a thing I had counted on for effect; it is always good to let your audience have a chance to work up its expectancy. At length, out of the silence a noble Latin chant—men's voices—broke and swelled up and rolled away into the night, a majestic tide of melody. I had put that up, too, and it was one of the best effects I ever invented. When it was finished I stood up on the platform and extended my hands abroad, for two minutes, with my face uplifted—that always produces a dead hush—and then slowly pronounced this ghastly word with a kind of awfulness which caused hundreds to tremble, and many women to faint:

"Constantinopolitanischerdudelsackspfeifenmachersgesellsch afft!"

Just as I was moaning out the closing hunks of that word, I touched off one of my electric connections and all that murky world of people stood revealed in a hideous blue glare! It was immense —that effect! Lots of people shrieked, women curled up and quit in every direction, foundlings collapsed by platoons. The abbot and the monks crossed themselves nimbly and their lips fluttered with agitated prayers. Merlin held his grip, but he was astonished clear down to his corns; he had never seen anything to begin with that, before. Now was the time to pile in the effects. I lifted my hands and groaned out

A Connecticut Yankee In King Arthur's Court 487

this word—as it were in agony:

"Nihilistendynamittheaterkaestchenssprengungsattentaetsver suchungen!"

—and turned on the red fire! You should have heard that Atlantic of people moan and howl when that crimson hell joined the blue! After sixty seconds I shouted:

"Transvaaltruppentropentransporttrampelthiertreibertrauung sthraenen- tragoedie!"

—and lit up the green fire! After waiting only forty seconds this time, I spread my arms abroad and thundered out the devastating syllables of this word of words:

"Mekkamuselmannenmassenmenchenmoerdermohrenmutter marmormonumentenmacher!"

—and whirled on the purple glare! There they were, all going at once, red, blue, green, purple!—four furious volcanoes pouring vast clouds of radiant smoke aloft, and spreading a blinding rainbowed noonday to the furthest confines of that valley. In the distance one could see that fellow on the pillar standing rigid against the background of sky, his seesaw stopped for the first time in twenty years. I knew the boys were at the pump now and ready. So I said to the abbot:

"The time is come, Father. I am about to pronounce the dread name and command the spell to dissolve. You want to brace up, and take hold of something." Then I shouted to the people: "Behold, in another minute the spell will be broken, or no mortal can break it. If it break, all will know it, for you will see the sacred water gush from the chapel door!"

I stood a few moments, to let the hearers have a chance to spread my announcement to those who couldn't hear, and so convey it to the furthest ranks, then I made a grand exhibition of extra posturing and gesturing, and shouted:

"Lo, I command the fell spirit that possesses the holy fountain to now disgorge into the skies all the infernal fires that still remain in him, and straightway dissolve his spell and flee hence to the pit, there to lie bound a thousand years. By his own dread name I command it—BGWJJILLIGKKK!"

Then I touched off the hogshead of rockets, and a vast fountain of dazzling lances of fire vomited itself toward the zenith with a hissing rush, and burst in mid-sky into a storm of flashing jewels! One mighty groan of terror started up from the massed people —then suddenly broke into a wild hosannah of joy—for there, fair and plain in the uncanny glare, they saw the freed water leaping forth! The old abbot could not speak a word, for tears and the chokings in his throat; without utterance of any sort, he folded me in his arms and mashed me. It was more eloquent than speech. And harder to get over, too, in a country where there were really no doctors that were worth a damaged nickel.

You should have seen those acres of people throw themselves down in that water and kiss it; kiss it, and pet it, and fondle it, and talk to it as if it were alive, and welcome it back with the dear names they gave their darlings, just as if it had been a friend who was long gone away and lost, and was come home again. Yes, it was pretty to see, and made me think more of them than I had done before.

I sent Merlin home on a shutter. He had caved in and gone

down like a landslide when I pronounced that fearful name, and had never had that name before,—neither had I—but to him it was the right one. Any jumble would have been the right one. He admitted, afterward, that that spirit's own mother could not have pronounced that name better than I did. He never could understand how I survived it, and I didn't tell him. It is only young magicians that give away a secret like that. Merlin spent three months working enchantments to try to find out the deep trick of how to pronounce that name and outlive it. But he didn't arrive.

When I started to the chapel, the populace uncovered and fell back reverently to make a wide way for me, as if I had been some kind of a superior being—and I was. I was aware of that. I took along a night shift of monks, and taught them the mystery of the pump, and set them to work, for it was plain that a good part of the people out there were going to sit up with the water all night, consequently it was but right that they should have all they wanted of it. To those monks that pump was a good deal of a miracle itself, and they were full of wonder over it; and of admiration, too, of the exceeding effectiveness of its performance.

It was a great night, an immense night. There was reputation in it. I could hardly get to sleep for glorying over it.

CHAPTER XXIV

A RIVAL MAGICIAN

My influence in the Valley of Holiness was something prodigious now. It seemed worth while to try to turn it to some valuable account. The thought came to me the next morning, and was suggested by my seeing one of my knights who was in the soap line come riding in. According to history, the monks of this place two centuries before had been worldly minded enough to want to wash. It might be that there was a leaven of this unrighteousness still remaining. So I sounded a Brother:

"Wouldn't you like a bath?"

He shuddered at the thought—the thought of the peril of it to the well—but he said with feeling:

"One needs not to ask that of a poor body who has not known that blessed refreshment sith that he was a boy. Would God I might wash me! but it may not be, fair sir, tempt me not; it is forbidden."

And then he sighed in such a sorrowful way that I was resolved he should have at least one layer of his real estate removed, if it sized up my whole influence and bankrupted the pile. So I went to the abbot and asked for a permit for this Brother. He blenched at the idea—I don't mean that you could see him blench, for of course you couldn't see it without you scraped him, and I didn't care enough about it to scrape him, but I knew the blench was there, just the same, and within a book-cover's thickness of the surface, too—blenched, and trembled. He said:

"Ah, son, ask aught else thou wilt, and it is thine, and freely granted out of a grateful heart—but this, oh, this! Would you drive away the blessed water again?"

"No, Father, I will not drive it away. I have mysterious knowledge which teaches me that there was an error that other time when it was thought the institution of the bath banished the fountain." A large interest began to show up in the old man's face. "My knowledge informs me that the bath was innocent of that misfortune, which was caused by quite another sort of sin."

"These are brave words—but—but right welcome, if they be true."

"They are true, indeed. Let me build the bath again, Father. Let me build it again, and the fountain shall flow forever."

"You promise this?—you promise it? Say the word—say you promise it!"

"I do promise it."

"Then will I have the first bath myself! Go—get ye to your work. Tarry not, tarry not, but go."

I and my boys were at work, straight off. The ruins of the old bath were there yet in the basement of the monastery, not a stone missing. They had been left just so, all these lifetimes, and avoided with a pious fear, as things accursed. In two days we had it all done and the water in—a spacious pool of clear pure water that a body could swim in. It was running water, too. It came in, and went out, through the ancient pipes. The old abbot kept his word, and was the first to try it. He went down black and shaky, leaving the whole black community above troubled and worried and full of bodings; but he came back white and joyful, and the game was made! another triumph scored.

It was a good campaign that we made in that Valley of Holiness, and I was very well satisfied, and ready to move on now, but I struck a disappointment. I caught a heavy cold, and it started up an old lurking rheumatism of mine. Of course the rheumatism hunted up my weakest place and located itself there. This was the place where the abbot put his arms about me and mashed me, what time he was moved to testify his gratitude to me with an embrace.

When at last I got out, I was a shadow. But everybody was full of attentions and kindnesses, and these brought cheer back into my life, and were the right medicine to help a convalescent swiftly up toward health and strength again; so I gained fast.

Sandy was worn out with nursing; so I made up my mind to turn out and go a cruise alone, leaving her at the nunnery to rest up. My idea was to disguise myself as a freeman of peasant degree and wander through the country a week or two on foot. This would give me a chance to eat and lodge with the lowliest and poorest class of free citizens on equal terms. There was no other way to inform myself perfectly of their everyday life and the operation of the laws upon it. If I went among them as a gentleman, there would be restraints and conventionalities which would shut me out from their private joys and troubles, and I should get no further than the outside shell.

One morning I was out on a long walk to get up muscle for my trip, and had climbed the ridge which bordered the northern extremity of the valley, when I came upon an artificial opening in the face of a low precipice, and recognized it by its location as a hermitage which had often been pointed out to me from a distance as the den of a hermit of high renown for dirt and austerity. I knew he had lately been offered a situation in the Great Sahara, where lions and sandflies made the hermit-life

peculiarly attractive and difficult, and had gone to Africa to take possession, so I thought I would look in and see how the atmosphere of this den agreed with its reputation.

My surprise was great: the place was newly swept and scoured. Then there was another surprise. Back in the gloom of the cavern I heard the clink of a little bell, and then this exclamation:

"Hello Central! Is this you, Camelot?—Behold, thou mayst glad thy heart an thou hast faith to believe the wonderful when that it cometh in unexpected guise and maketh itself manifest in impossible places—here standeth in the flesh his mightiness The Boss, and with thine own ears shall ye hear him speak!"

Now what a radical reversal of things this was; what a jumbling together of extravagant incongruities; what a fantastic conjunction of opposites and irreconcilables—the home of the bogus miracle become the home of a real one, the den of a mediaeval hermit turned into a telephone office!

The telephone clerk stepped into the light, and I recognized one of my young fellows. I said:

"How long has this office been established here, Ulfius?"

"But since midnight, fair Sir Boss, an it please you. We saw many lights in the valley, and so judged it well to make a station, for that where so many lights be needs must they indicate a town of goodly size."

"Quite right. It isn't a town in the customary sense, but it's a good stand, anyway. Do you know where you are?"

"Of that I have had no time to make inquiry; for whenas my comradeship moved hence upon their labors, leaving me in charge, I got me to needed rest, purposing to inquire when I waked, and report the place's name to Camelot for record."

"Well, this is the Valley of Holiness."

It didn't take; I mean, he didn't start at the name, as I had supposed he would. He merely said:

"I will so report it."

"Why, the surrounding regions are filled with the noise of late wonders that have happened here! You didn't hear of them?"

"Ah, ye will remember we move by night, and avoid speech with all. We learn naught but that we get by the telephone from Camelot."

"Why *they* know all about this thing. Haven't they told you anything about the great miracle of the restoration of a holy fountain?"

"Oh, *that*? Indeed yes. But the name of *this* valley doth woundily differ from the name of *that* one; indeed to differ wider were not pos—"

"What was that name, then?"

"The Valley of Hellishness."

"*That* explains it. Confound a telephone, anyway. It is the very demon for conveying similarities of sound that are miracles of divergence from similarity of sense. But no matter, you know the name of the place now. Call up Camelot."

He did it, and had Clarence sent for. It was good to hear my boy's voice again. It was like being home. After some affectionate interchanges, and some account of my late illness, I said:

"What is new?"

"The king and queen and many of the court do start even in this hour, to go to your valley to pay pious homage to the waters ye have restored, and cleanse themselves of sin, and see the place where the infernal spirit spouted true hell-flames to the clouds —an ye listen sharply ye may hear me wink and hear me likewise smile a smile, sith 'twas I that made selection of those flames from out our stock and sent them by your order."

"Does the king know the way to this place?"

"The king?—no, nor to any other in his realms, mayhap; but the lads that holp you with your miracle will be his guide and lead the way, and appoint the places for rests at noons and sleeps at night."

"This will bring them here—when?"

"Mid-afternoon, or later, the third day."

"Anything else in the way of news?"

"The king hath begun the raising of the standing army ye suggested to him; one regiment is complete and officered."

"The mischief! I wanted a main hand in that myself. There is only one body of men in the kingdom that are fitted to officer a regular army."

"Yes—and now ye will marvel to know there's not so much as one West Pointer in that regiment."

"What are you talking about? Are you in earnest?"

"It is truly as I have said."

"Why, this makes me uneasy. Who were chosen, and what was the method? Competitive examination?"

"Indeed, I know naught of the method. I but know this—these officers be all of noble family, and are born—what is it you call it?—chuckleheads."

"There's something wrong, Clarence."

"Comfort yourself, then; for two candidates for a lieutenancy do travel hence with the king—young nobles both—and if you but wait where you are you will hear them questioned."

"That is news to the purpose. I will get one West Pointer in, anyway. Mount a man and send him to that school with a message; let him kill horses, if necessary, but he must be there before sunset to-night and say—"

"There is no need. I have laid a ground wire to the school. Prithee let me connect you with it."

It sounded good! In this atmosphere of telephones and lightning communication with distant regions, I was breathing

the breath of life again after long suffocation. I realized, then, what a creepy, dull, inanimate horror this land had been to me all these years, and how I had been in such a stifled condition of mind as to have grown used to it almost beyond the power to notice it.

I gave my order to the superintendent of the Academy personally. I also asked him to bring me some paper and a fountain pen and a box or so of safety matches. I was getting tired of doing without these conveniences. I could have them now, as I wasn't going to wear armor any more at present, and therefore could get at my pockets.

When I got back to the monastery, I found a thing of interest going on. The abbot and his monks were assembled in the great hall, observing with childish wonder and faith the performances of a new magician, a fresh arrival. His dress was the extreme of the fantastic; as showy and foolish as the sort of thing an Indian medicine-man wears. He was mowing, and mumbling, and gesticulating, and drawing mystical figures in the air and on the floor,—the regular thing, you know. He was a celebrity from Asia—so he said, and that was enough. That sort of evidence was as good as gold, and passed current everywhere.

How easy and cheap it was to be a great magician on this fellow's terms. His specialty was to tell you what any individual on the face of the globe was doing at the moment; and what he had done at any time in the past, and what he would do at any time in the future. He asked if any would like to know what the Emperor of the East was doing now? The sparkling eyes and the delighted rubbing of hands made eloquent answer—this reverend crowd *would* like to know what that monarch was at, just as this moment. The fraud went through some more mummery, and then made grave announcement:

"The high and mighty Emperor of the East doth at this moment put money in the palm of a holy begging friar—one, two, three pieces, and they be all of silver."

A buzz of admiring exclamations broke out, all around:

"It is marvelous!" "Wonderful!" "What study, what labor, to have acquired a so amazing power as this!"

Would they like to know what the Supreme Lord of Inde was doing? Yes. He told them what the Supreme Lord of Inde was doing. Then he told them what the Sultan of Egypt was at; also what the King of the Remote Seas was about. And so on and so on; and with each new marvel the astonishment at his accuracy rose higher and higher. They thought he must surely strike an uncertain place some time; but no, he never had to hesitate, he always knew, and always with unerring precision. I saw that if this thing went on I should lose my supremacy, this fellow would capture my following, I should be left out in the cold. I must put a cog in his wheel, and do it right away, too. I said:

"If I might ask, I should very greatly like to know what a certain person is doing."

"Speak, and freely. I will tell you."

"It will be difficult—perhaps impossible."

"My art knoweth not that word. The more difficult it is, the more certainly will I reveal it to you."

You see, I was working up the interest. It was getting pretty high, too; you could see that by the craning necks all around, and the half-suspended breathing. So now I climaxed it:

"If you make no mistake—if you tell me truly what I want to know—I will give you two hundred silver pennies."

"The fortune is mine! I will tell you what you would know."

"Then tell me what I am doing with my right hand."

"Ah-h!" There was a general gasp of surprise. It had not occurred to anybody in the crowd—that simple trick of inquiring about somebody who wasn't ten thousand miles away. The magician was hit hard; it was an emergency that had never happened in his experience before, and it corked him; he didn't know how to meet it. He looked stunned, confused; he couldn't say a word. "Come," I said, "what are you waiting for? Is it possible you can answer up, right off, and tell what anybody on the other side of the earth is doing, and yet can't tell what a person is doing who isn't three yards from you? Persons behind me know what I am doing with my right hand—they will indorse you if you tell it correctly." He was still dumb. "Very well, I'll tell you why you don't speak up and tell; it is because you don't know. *You* a magician! Good friends, this tramp is a mere fraud and liar."

This distressed the monks and terrified them. They were not used to hearing these awful beings called names, and they did not know what might be the consequence. There was a dead silence now; superstitious bodings were in every mind. The magician began to pull his wits together, and when he presently smiled an easy, nonchalant smile, it spread a mighty relief around; for it indicated that his mood was not destructive. He said:

"It hath struck me speechless, the frivolity of this person's speech. Let all know, if perchance there be any who know it not, that enchanters of my degree deign not to concern themselves with the doings of any but kings, princes, emperors, them that be born in the purple and them only. Had ye asked me what Arthur the great king is doing, it were another matter, and I had told ye; but the doings of a subject interest me not."

"Oh, I misunderstood you. I thought you said 'anybody,' and so I supposed 'anybody' included—well, anybody; that is, everybody."

"It doth—anybody that is of lofty birth; and the better if he be royal."

"That, it meseemeth, might well be," said the abbot, who saw his opportunity to smooth things and avert disaster, "for it were not likely that so wonderful a gift as this would be conferred for the revelation of the concerns of lesser beings than such as be born near to the summits of greatness. Our Arthur the king—"

"Would you know of him?" broke in the enchanter.

"Most gladly, yea, and gratefully."

Everybody was full of awe and interest again right away, the incorrigible idiots. They watched the incantations absorbingly, and looked at me with a "There, now, what can you say to that?" air, when the announcement came:

"The king is weary with the chase, and lieth in his palace these two hours sleeping a dreamless sleep."

"God's benison upon him!" said the abbot, and crossed himself; "may that sleep be to the refreshment of his body and his soul."

"And so it might be, if he were sleeping," I said, "but the king is not sleeping, the king rides."

Here was trouble again—a conflict of authority. Nobody knew which of us to believe; I still had some reputation left. The magician's scorn was stirred, and he said:

"Lo, I have seen many wonderful soothsayers and prophets and magicians in my life days, but none before that could sit idle and see to the heart of things with never an incantation to help."

"You have lived in the woods, and lost much by it. I use incantations myself, as this good brotherhood are aware—but only on occasions of moment."

When it comes to sarcasming, I reckon I know how to keep my end up. That jab made this fellow squirm. The abbot inquired after the queen and the court, and got this information:

"They be all on sleep, being overcome by fatigue, like as to the king."

I said:

"That is merely another lie. Half of them are about their amusements, the queen and the other half are not sleeping, they ride. Now perhaps you can spread yourself a little, and tell us where the king and queen and all that are this moment riding with them are going?"

"They sleep now, as I said; but on the morrow they will ride, for they go a journey toward the sea."

"And where will they be the day after to-morrow at vespers?"

"Far to the north of Camelot, and half their journey will be done."

"That is another lie, by the space of a hundred and fifty miles. Their journey will not be merely half done, it will be all done, and they will be *here*, in this valley."

That was a noble shot! It set the abbot and the monks in a whirl of excitement, and it rocked the enchanter to his base. I followed the thing right up:

"If the king does not arrive, I will have myself ridden on a rail: if he does I will ride you on a rail instead."

Next day I went up to the telephone office and found that the king had passed through two towns that were on the line. I spotted his progress on the succeeding day in the same way. I kept these matters to myself. The third day's reports showed that if he kept up his gait he would arrive by four in the afternoon. There was still no sign anywhere of interest in his coming; there seemed to be no preparations making to receive him in state; a strange thing, truly. Only one thing could explain this: that other magician had been cutting under me, sure. This was true. I asked a friend of mine, a monk, about it, and he said, yes, the magician had tried some further enchantments and found out that the court had concluded to make no journey at all, but stay at home. Think of that! Observe how much a reputation was worth in such a country. These people had seen me do the very showiest bit of magic in history, and the only one within their memory that had a positive value, and yet here they were, ready to take up with an adventurer who could offer no evidence of his powers but his mere unproven word.

However, it was not good politics to let the king come without any fuss and feathers at all, so I went down and drummed up a procession of pilgrims and smoked out a batch of hermits and started them out at two o'clock to meet him. And that was the sort of state he arrived in. The abbot was helpless with rage and humiliation when I brought him out on a balcony and showed him the head of the state marching in and never a monk on hand to offer him welcome, and no stir of life or clang of joy-bell to glad his spirit. He took one look and then flew to rouse out his forces. The next minute the bells were dinning furiously, and the various buildings were vomiting monks and nuns, who went swarming in a rush toward the coming procession; and with them went that magician —and he was on a rail, too, by the abbot's order; and his reputation was in the mud, and mine was in the sky again. Yes, a man can keep his trademark current in such a country, but he can't sit around and do it; he has got to be on deck and attending to business right along.

CHAPTER XXV

A COMPETITIVE EXAMINATION

When the king traveled for change of air, or made a progress, or visited a distant noble whom he wished to bankrupt with the cost of his keep, part of the administration moved with him. It was a fashion of the time. The Commission charged with the examination of candidates for posts in the army came with the king to the Valley, whereas they could have transacted their business just as well at home. And although this expedition was strictly a holiday excursion for the king, he kept some of his business functions going just the same. He touched for the evil, as usual; he held court in the gate at sunrise and tried cases, for he was himself Chief Justice of the King's Bench.

He shone very well in this latter office. He was a wise and humane judge, and he clearly did his honest best and fairest,— according to his lights. That is a large reservation. His lights—I mean his rearing—often colored his decisions. Whenever there was a dispute between a noble or gentleman and a person of lower degree, the king's leanings and sympathies were for the former class always, whether he suspected it or not. It was impossible that this should be otherwise. The blunting effects of slavery upon the slaveholder's moral perceptions are known and conceded, the world over; and a privileged class, an aristocracy, is but a band of slaveholders under another name. This has a harsh sound, and yet should not be offensive to any—even to the noble himself—unless the fact itself be an offense: for the statement simply formulates a fact. The repulsive feature of slavery is the *thing*, not its name. One needs but to hear an aristocrat speak of the classes that are below him to recognize—and in but indifferently modified measure —the very air and tone of the actual slaveholder; and behind these are the slaveholder's spirit, the slaveholder's blunted feeling. They are the result of the same cause in both cases: the possessor's old and inbred custom of regarding himself as a superior being. The king's judgments wrought

frequent injustices, but it was merely the fault of his training, his natural and unalterable sympathies. He was as unfitted for a judgeship as would be the average mother for the position of milk-distributor to starving children in famine-time; her own children would fare a shade better than the rest.

One very curious case came before the king. A young girl, an orphan, who had a considerable estate, married a fine young fellow who had nothing. The girl's property was within a seigniory held by the Church. The bishop of the diocese, an arrogant scion of the great nobility, claimed the girl's estate on the ground that she had married privately, and thus had cheated the Church out of one of its rights as lord of the seigniory—the one heretofore referred to as le droit du seigneur. The penalty of refusal or avoidance was confiscation. The girl's defense was, that the lordship of the seigniory was vested in the bishop, and the particular right here involved was not transferable, but must be exercised by the lord himself or stand vacated; and that an older law, of the Church itself, strictly barred the bishop from exercising it. It was a very odd case, indeed.

It reminded me of something I had read in my youth about the ingenious way in which the aldermen of London raised the money that built the Mansion House. A person who had not taken the Sacrament according to the Anglican rite could not stand as a candidate for sheriff of London. Thus Dissenters were ineligible; they could not run if asked, they could not serve if elected. The aldermen, who without any question were Yankees in disguise, hit upon this neat device: they passed a by-law imposing a fine of £400 upon any one who should refuse to be a candidate for sheriff, and a fine of £600 upon any person who, after being elected sheriff, refused to serve. Then they went to work and elected a lot of Dissenters, one after another, and kept it up until they had collected £15,000 in fines; and there stands the stately Mansion House to this day, to keep the blushing citizen in mind of a long past and lamented day when a band of Yankees slipped into London and played games of the sort that has given their race a unique and shady reputation among all truly good and holy peoples that be in the earth.

The girl's case seemed strong to me; the bishop's case was just as strong. I did not see how the king was going to get out of this hole. But he got out. I append his decision:

"Truly I find small difficulty here, the matter being even a child's affair for simpleness. An the young bride had conveyed notice, as in duty bound, to her feudal lord and proper master and protector the bishop, she had suffered no loss, for the said bishop could have got a dispensation making him, for temporary conveniency, eligible to the exercise of his said right, and thus would she have kept all she had. Whereas, failing in her first duty, she hath by that failure failed in all; for whoso, clinging to a rope, severeth it above his hands, must fall; it being no defense to claim that the rest of the rope is sound, neither any deliverance from his peril, as he shall find. Pardy, the woman's case is rotten at the source. It is the decree of the court that she forfeit to the said lord bishop all her goods, even to the last farthing that she doth possess, and be thereto mulcted in the costs. Next!"

Here was a tragic end to a beautiful honeymoon not yet three months old. Poor young creatures! They had lived these three months lapped to the lips in worldly comforts. These clothes and trinkets they were wearing were as fine and dainty as the shrewdest stretch of the sumptuary laws allowed to people of their degree; and in these pretty clothes, she crying on his shoulder, and he trying to comfort her with hopeful words set to the music of despair, they went from the judgment seat out into the world homeless, bedless, breadless; why, the very beggars by the roadsides were not so poor as they.

Well, the king was out of the hole; and on terms satisfactory to the Church and the rest of the aristocracy, no doubt. Men write many fine and plausible arguments in support of monarchy, but the fact remains that where every man in a State has a vote, brutal laws are impossible. Arthur's people were of course poor material for a republic, because they had been debased so long by monarchy; and yet even they would have been intelligent enough to make short work of that law which the king had just been administering if it had been submitted to their full and free vote. There is a phrase which has grown so common in the world's mouth that it has come to seem to have sense and meaning—the sense and meaning implied when it is used; that is the phrase which refers to this or that or the other nation as possibly being "capable of self-government"; and the implied sense of it is, that there has been a nation somewhere, some time or other which *wasn't* capable of it—wasn't as able to govern itself as some self-appointed specialists were or would be to govern it. The master minds of all nations, in all ages, have sprung in affluent multitude from the mass of the nation, and from the mass of the nation only—not from its privileged classes; and so, no matter what the nation's intellectual grade was; whether high or low, the bulk of its ability was in the long ranks of its nameless and its poor, and so it never saw the day that it had not the material in abundance whereby to govern itself. Which is to assert an always self-proven fact: that even the best governed and most free and most enlightened monarchy is still behind the best condition attainable by its people; and that the same is true of kindred governments of lower grades, all the way down to the lowest.

King Arthur had hurried up the army business altogether beyond my calculations. I had not supposed he would move in the matter while I was away; and so I had not mapped out a scheme for determining the merits of officers; I had only remarked that it would be wise to submit every candidate to a sharp and searching examination; and privately I meant to put together a list of military qualifications that nobody could answer to but my West Pointers. That ought to have been attended to before I left; for the king was so taken with the idea of a standing army that he couldn't wait but must get about it at once, and get up as good a scheme of examination as he could invent out of his own head.

I was impatient to see what this was; and to show, too, how much more admirable was the one which I should display to the Examining Board. I intimated this, gently, to the king, and it fired his curiosity. When the Board was assembled, I followed him in; and behind us came the candidates. One of these candidates was a bright young West Pointer of mine, and with him were a couple of my West Point professors.

When I saw the Board, I did not know whether to cry or to laugh. The head of it was the officer known to later centuries as Norroy King-at-Arms! The two other members were chiefs of bureaus in his department; and all three were priests, of course; all officials who had to know how to read and write were priests.

My candidate was called first, out of courtesy to me, and the head of the Board opened on him with official solemnity:

"Name?"

"Mal-ease."

"Son of?"

"Webster."

"Webster—Webster. H'm—I—my memory faileth to recall the name. Condition?"

"Weaver."

"Weaver!—God keep us!"

The king was staggered, from his summit to his foundations; one clerk fainted, and the others came near it. The chairman pulled himself together, and said indignantly:

"It is sufficient. Get you hence."

But I appealed to the king. I begged that my candidate might be examined. The king was willing, but the Board, who were all well-born folk, implored the king to spare them the indignity of examining the weaver's son. I knew they didn't know enough to examine him anyway, so I joined my prayers to theirs and the king turned the duty over to my professors. I had had a blackboard prepared, and it was put up now, and the circus began. It was beautiful to hear the lad lay out the science of war, and wallow in details of battle and siege, of supply, transportation, mining and countermining, grand tactics, big strategy and little strategy, signal service, infantry, cavalry, artillery, and all about siege guns, field guns, gatling guns, rifled guns, smooth bores, musket practice, revolver practice—and not a solitary word of it all could these catfish make head or tail of, you understand—and it was handsome to see him chalk off mathematical nightmares on the blackboard that would stump the angels themselves, and do it like nothing, too—all about eclipses, and comets, and solstices, and constellations, and mean time, and sidereal time, and dinner time, and bedtime, and every other imaginable thing above the clouds or under them that you could harry or bullyrag an enemy with and make him wish he hadn't come—and when the boy made his military salute and stood aside at last, I was proud enough to hug him, and all those other people were so dazed they looked partly petrified, partly drunk, and wholly caught out and snowed under. I judged that the cake was ours, and by a large majority.

Education is a great thing. This was the same youth who had come to West Point so ignorant that when I asked him, "If a general officer should have a horse shot under him on the field of battle, what ought he to do?" answered up naively and said:

"Get up and brush himself."

One of the young nobles was called up now. I thought I would question him a little myself. I said:

"Can your lordship read?"

His face flushed indignantly, and he fired this at me:

"Takest me for a clerk? I trow I am not of a blood that—"

"Answer the question!"

He crowded his wrath down and made out to answer "No."

"Can you write?"

He wanted to resent this, too, but I said:

"You will confine yourself to the questions, and make no comments. You are not here to air your blood or your graces, and nothing of the sort will be permitted. Can you write?"

"No."

"Do you know the multiplication table?"

"I wit not what ye refer to."

"How much is 9 times 6?"

"It is a mystery that is hidden from me by reason that the emergency requiring the fathoming of it hath not in my life-days occurred, and so, not having no need to know this thing, I abide barren of the knowledge."

"If A trade a barrel of onions to B, worth 2 pence the bushel, in exchange for a sheep worth 4 pence and a dog worth a penny, and C kill the dog before delivery, because bitten by the same, who mistook him for D, what sum is still due to A from B, and which party pays for the dog, C or D, and who gets the money? If A, is the penny sufficient, or may he claim consequential damages in the form of additional money to represent the possible profit which might have inured from the dog, and classifiable as earned increment, that is to say, usufruct?"

"Verily, in the all-wise and unknowable providence of God, who moveth in mysterious ways his wonders to perform, have I never heard the fellow to this question for confusion of the mind and congestion of the ducts of thought. Wherefore I beseech you let the dog and the onions and these people of the strange and godless names work out their several salvations from their piteous and wonderful difficulties without help of mine, for indeed their trouble is sufficient as it is, whereas an I tried to help I should but damage their cause the more and yet mayhap not live myself to see the desolation wrought."

"What do you know of the laws of attraction and gravitation?"

"If there be such, mayhap his grace the king did promulgate them whilst that I lay sick about the beginning of the year and thereby failed to hear his proclamation."

"What do you know of the science of optics?"

"I know of governors of places, and seneschals of castles, and sheriffs of counties, and many like small offices and titles of honor, but him you call the Science of Optics I have not heard of before; peradventure it is a new dignity."

"Yes, in this country."

Try to conceive of this mollusk gravely applying for an official position, of any kind under the sun! Why, he had all the earmarks of a typewriter copyist, if you leave out the disposition to contribute uninvited emendations of your grammar and punctuation. It was unaccountable that he didn't attempt a little help of that sort out of his majestic supply of incapacity for the job. But that didn't prove that he hadn't material in him for the disposition, it only proved that he wasn't a typewriter copyist yet. After nagging him a little more, I let the professors loose on him and they turned him inside out, on the line of scientific war, and found him empty, of

course. He knew somewhat about the warfare of the time—bushwhacking around for ogres, and bull-fights in the tournament ring, and such things—but otherwise he was empty and useless. Then we took the other young noble in hand, and he was the first one's twin, for ignorance and incapacity. I delivered them into the hands of the chairman of the Board with the comfortable consciousness that their cake was dough. They were examined in the previous order of precedence.

"Name, so please you?"

"Pertipole, son of Sir Pertipole, Baron of Barley Mash."

"Grandfather?"

"Also Sir Pertipole, Baron of Barley Mash."

"Great-grandfather?"

"The same name and title."

"Great-great-grandfather?"

"We had none, worshipful sir, the line failing before it had reached so far back."

"It mattereth not. It is a good four generations, and fulfilleth the requirements of the rule."

"Fulfills what rule?" I asked.

"The rule requiring four generations of nobility or else the candidate is not eligible."

"A man not eligible for a lieutenancy in the army unless he can prove four generations of noble descent?"

"Even so; neither lieutenant nor any other officer may be commissioned without that qualification."

"Oh, come, this is an astonishing thing. What good is such a qualification as that?"

"What good? It is a hardy question, fair sir and Boss, since it doth go far to impugn the wisdom of even our holy Mother Church herself."

"As how?"

"For that she hath established the self-same rule regarding saints. By her law none may be canonized until he hath lain dead four generations."

"I see, I see—it is the same thing. It is wonderful. In the one case a man lies dead-alive four generations—mummified in ignorance and sloth—and that qualifies him to command live people, and take their weal and woe into his impotent hands; and in the other case, a man lies bedded with death and worms four generations, and that qualifies him for office in the celestial camp. Does the king's grace approve of this strange law?"

The king said:

"Why, truly I see naught about it that is strange. All places of honor and of profit do belong, by natural right, to them that be of noble blood, and so these dignities in the army are their property and would be so without this or any rule. The rule is but to mark a limit. Its purpose is to keep out too recent blood, which would bring into contempt these offices, and men of lofty lineage would turn their backs and scorn to take them. I were to blame an I permitted this calamity. *You* can permit it an you are minded so to do, for you have the delegated authority, but that the king should do it were a most strange madness and not comprehensible to any."

"I yield. Proceed, sir Chief of the Herald's College."

The chairman resumed as follows:

"By what illustrious achievement for the honor of the Throne and State did the founder of your great line lift himself to the sacred dignity of the British nobility?"

"He built a brewery."

"Sire, the Board finds this candidate perfect in all the requirements and qualifications for military command, and doth hold his case open for decision after due examination of his competitor."

The competitor came forward and proved exactly four generations of nobility himself. So there was a tie in military qualifications that far.

He stood aside a moment, and Sir Pertipole was questioned further:

"Of what condition was the wife of the founder of your line?"

"She came of the highest landed gentry, yet she was not noble; she was gracious and pure and charitable, of a blameless life and character, insomuch that in these regards was she peer of the best lady in the land."

"That will do. Stand down." He called up the competing lordling again, and asked: "What was the rank and condition of the great-grandmother who conferred British nobility upon your great house?"

"She was a king's leman and did climb to that splendid eminence by her own unholpen merit from the sewer where she was born."

"Ah, this, indeed, is true nobility, this is the right and perfect intermixture. The lieutenancy is yours, fair lord. Hold it not in contempt; it is the humble step which will lead to grandeurs more worthy of the splendor of an origin like to thine."

I was down in the bottomless pit of humiliation. I had promised myself an easy and zenith-scouring triumph, and this was the outcome!

I was almost ashamed to look my poor disappointed cadet in the face. I told him to go home and be patient, this wasn't the end.

I had a private audience with the king, and made a proposition. I said it was quite right to officer that regiment with nobilities, and he couldn't have done a wiser thing. It would also be a good idea to add five hundred officers to it; in fact, add as many officers as there were nobles and relatives of nobles in the country, even if there should finally be five times as many officers as privates in it; and thus make it the crack regiment, the envied regiment, the King's Own regiment, and

entitled to fight on its own hook and in its own way, and go whither it would and come when it pleased, in time of war, and be utterly swell and independent. This would make that regiment the heart's desire of all the nobility, and they would all be satisfied and happy. Then we would make up the rest of the standing army out of commonplace materials, and officer it with nobodies, as was proper—nobodies selected on a basis of mere efficiency—and we would make this regiment toe the line, allow it no aristocratic freedom from restraint, and force it to do all the work and persistent hammering, to the end that whenever the King's Own was tired and wanted to go off for a change and rummage around amongst ogres and have a good time, it could go without uneasiness, knowing that matters were in safe hands behind it, and business going to be continued at the old stand, same as usual. The king was charmed with the idea.

When I noticed that, it gave me a valuable notion. I thought I saw my way out of an old and stubborn difficulty at last. You see, the royalties of the Pendragon stock were a long-lived race and very fruitful. Whenever a child was born to any of these — and it was pretty often—there was wild joy in the nation's mouth, and piteous sorrow in the nation's heart. The joy was questionable, but the grief was honest. Because the event meant another call for a Royal Grant. Long was the list of these royalties, and they were a heavy and steadily increasing burden upon the treasury and a menace to the crown. Yet Arthur could not believe this latter fact, and he would not listen to any of my various projects for substituting something in the place of the royal grants. If I could have persuaded him to now and then provide a support for one of these outlying scions from his own pocket, I could have made a grand to-do over it, and it would have had a good effect with the nation; but no, he wouldn't hear of such a thing. He had something like a religious passion for royal grant; he seemed to look upon it as a sort of sacred swag, and one could not irritate him in any way so quickly and so surely as by an attack upon that venerable institution. If I ventured to cautiously hint that there was not another respectable family in England that would humble itself to hold out the hat—however, that is as far as I ever got; he always cut me short there, and peremptorily, too.

But I believed I saw my chance at last. I would form this crack regiment out of officers alone—not a single private. Half of it should consist of nobles, who should fill all the places up to Major-General, and serve gratis and pay their own expenses; and they would be glad to do this when they should learn that the rest of the regiment would consist exclusively of princes of the blood. These princes of the blood should range in rank from Lieutenant-General up to Field Marshal, and be gorgeously salaried and equipped and fed by the state. Moreover—and this was the master stroke—it should be decreed that these princely grandees should be always addressed by a stunningly gaudy and awe-compelling title (which I would presently invent), and they and they only in all England should be so addressed. Finally, all princes of the blood should have free choice; join that regiment, get that great title, and renounce the royal grant, or stay out and receive a grant. Neatest touch of all: unborn but imminent princes of the blood could be *born* into the regiment, and start fair, with good wages and a permanent situation, upon due notice from the parents.

All the boys would join, I was sure of that; so, all existing grants would be relinquished; that the newly born would always join was equally certain. Within sixty days that quaint and bizarre anomaly, the Royal Grant, would cease to be a living fact, and take its place among the curiosities of the past.

CHAPTER XXVI

THE FIRST NEWSPAPER

When I told the king I was going out disguised as a petty freeman to scour the country and familiarize myself with the humbler life of the people, he was all afire with the novelty of the thing in a minute, and was bound to take a chance in the adventure himself—nothing should stop him—he would drop everything and go along—it was the prettiest idea he had run across for many a day. He wanted to glide out the back way and start at once; but I showed him that that wouldn't answer. You see, he was billed for the king's-evil—to touch for it, I mean—and it wouldn't be right to disappoint the house and it wouldn't make a delay worth considering, anyway, it was only a one-night stand. And I thought he ought to tell the queen he was going away. He clouded up at that and looked sad. I was sorry I had spoken, especially when he said mournfully:

"Thou forgettest that Launcelot is here; and where Launcelot is, she noteth not the going forth of the king, nor what day he returneth."

Of course, I changed the Subject. Yes, Guenever was beautiful, it is true, but take her all around she was pretty slack. I never meddled in these matters, they weren't my affair, but I did hate to see the way things were going on, and I don't mind saying that much. Many's the time she had asked me, "Sir Boss, hast seen Sir Launcelot about?" but if ever she went fretting around for the king I didn't happen to be around at the time.

There was a very good lay-out for the king's-evil business—very tidy and creditable. The king sat under a canopy of state; about him were clustered a large body of the clergy in full canonicals. Conspicuous, both for location and personal outfit, stood Marinel, a hermit of the quack-doctor species, to introduce the sick. All abroad over the spacious floor, and clear down to the doors, in a thick jumble, lay or sat the scrofulous, under a strong light. It was as good as a tableau; in fact, it had all the look of being gotten up for that, though it wasn't. There were eight hundred sick people present. The work was slow; it lacked the interest of novelty for me, because I had seen the ceremonies before; the thing soon became tedious, but the proprieties required me to stick it out. The doctor was there for the reason that in all such crowds there were many people who only imagined something was the matter with them, and many who were consciously sound but wanted the immortal honor of fleshly contact with a king, and yet others who pretended to illness in order to get the piece of coin that went with the touch. Up to this time this coin had been a wee little gold piece worth about a third of a dollar. When you consider how much that amount of money would buy, in that age and country, and how usual it was to be scrofulous, when not dead, you would understand that the annual king's-evil appropriation was just the River and Harbor bill of that government for the grip it took on the treasury and the chance it afforded for skinning the surplus. So I had privately concluded to touch the treasury itself for the king's-evil. I covered six-sevenths of the appropriation into the treasury a week before starting from Camelot on my adventures, and ordered that the other seventh be inflated into five-cent nickels and delivered into the hands of the head clerk of the King's Evil Department; a nickel to take the place of each gold coin, you see, and do its work for it. It might strain the nickel some, but I judged it could stand it. As a rule, I do

not approve of watering stock, but I considered it square enough in this case, for it was just a gift, anyway. Of course, you can water a gift as much as you want to; and I generally do. The old gold and silver coins of the country were of ancient and unknown origin, as a rule, but some of them were Roman; they were ill-shapen, and seldom rounder than a moon that is a week past the full; they were hammered, not minted, and they were so worn with use that the devices upon them were as illegible as blisters, and looked like them. I judged that a sharp, bright new nickel, with a first-rate likeness of the king on one side of it and Guenever on the other, and a blooming pious motto, would take the tuck out of scrofula as handy as a nobler coin and please the scrofulous fancy more; and I was right. This batch was the first it was tried on, and it worked to a charm. The saving in expense was a notable economy. You will see that by these figures: We touched a trifle over 700 of the 800 patients; at former rates, this would have cost the government about $240; at the new rate we pulled through for about $35, thus saving upward of $200 at one swoop. To appreciate the full magnitude of this stroke, consider these other figures: the annual expenses of a national government amount to the equivalent of a contribution of three days' average wages of every individual of the population, counting every individual as if he were a man. If you take a nation of 60,000,000, where average wages are $2 per day, three days' wages taken from each individual will provide $360,000,000 and pay the government's expenses. In my day, in my own country, this money was collected from imposts, and the citizen imagined that the foreign importer paid it, and it made him comfortable to think so; whereas, in fact, it was paid by the American people, and was so equally and exactly distributed among them that the annual cost to the 100-millionaire and the annual cost to the sucking child of the day-laborer was precisely the same—each paid $6. Nothing could be equaler than that, I reckon. Well, Scotland and Ireland were tributary to Arthur, and the united populations of the British Islands amounted to something less than 1,000,000. A mechanic's average wage was 3 cents a day, when he paid his own keep. By this rule the national government's expenses were $90,000 a year, or about $250 a day. Thus, by the substitution of nickels for gold on a king's-evil day, I not only injured no one, dissatisfied no one, but pleased all concerned and saved four-fifths of that day's national expense into the bargain—a saving which would have been the equivalent of $800,000 in my day in America. In making this substitution I had drawn upon the wisdom of a very remote source—the wisdom of my boyhood—for the true statesman does not despise any wisdom, howsoever lowly may be its origin: in my boyhood I had always saved my pennies and contributed buttons to the foreign missionary cause. The buttons would answer the ignorant savage as well as the coin, the coin would answer me better than the buttons; all hands were happy and nobody hurt.

Marinel took the patients as they came. He examined the candidate; if he couldn't qualify he was warned off; if he could he was passed along to the king. A priest pronounced the words, "They shall lay their hands on the sick, and they shall recover." Then the king stroked the ulcers, while the reading continued; finally, the patient graduated and got his nickel—the king hanging it around his neck himself—and was dismissed. Would you think that that would cure? It certainly did. Any mummery will cure if the patient's faith is strong in it. Up by Astolat there was a chapel where the Virgin had once appeared to a girl who used to herd geese around there—the girl said so herself—and they built the chapel upon that spot and hung a picture in it representing the occurrence—a picture which you would think it dangerous for a sick person to approach; whereas, on the contrary, thousands of the lame and the sick came and prayed before it every year and went away whole and sound; and even the well could look upon it and live. Of course, when I was told these things I did not believe them; but when I went there and saw them I had to succumb. I saw the cures effected myself; and they were real cures and not questionable. I saw cripples whom I had seen around Camelot for years on crutches, arrive and pray before that picture, and put down their crutches and walk off without a limp. There were piles of crutches there which had been left by such people as a testimony.

In other places people operated on a patient's mind, without saying a word to him, and cured him. In others, experts assembled patients in a room and prayed over them, and appealed to their faith, and those patients went away cured. Wherever you find a king who can't cure the king's-evil you can be sure that the most valuable superstition that supports his throne—the subject's belief in the divine appointment of his sovereign—has passed away. In my youth the monarchs of England had ceased to touch for the evil, but there was no occasion for this diffidence: they could have cured it forty-nine times in fifty.

Well, when the priest had been droning for three hours, and the good king polishing the evidences, and the sick were still pressing forward as plenty as ever, I got to feeling intolerably bored. I was sitting by an open window not far from the canopy of state. For the five hundredth time a patient stood forward to have his repulsivenesses stroked; again those words were being droned out: "they shall lay their hands on the sick"—when outside there rang clear as a clarion a note that enchanted my soul and tumbled thirteen worthless centuries about my ears: "Camelot *Weekly Hosannah and Literary Volcano!*—latest irruption—only two cents —all about the big miracle in the Valley of Holiness!" One greater than kings had arrived—the newsboy. But I was the only person in all that throng who knew the meaning of this mighty birth, and what this imperial magician was come into the world to do.

I dropped a nickel out of the window and got my paper; the Adam-newsboy of the world went around the corner to get my change; is around the corner yet. It was delicious to see a newspaper again, yet I was conscious of a secret shock when my eye fell upon the first batch of display head-lines. I had lived in a clammy atmosphere of reverence, respect, deference, so long that they sent a quivery little cold wave through me:

HIGH TIMES IN THE VALLEY OF HOLINESS!

THE WATER-WORKS CORKED!

BRER MERLIN WORKS HIS ARTS, BUT GETS LEFT?
But the Boss scores on his first Innings!

The Miraculous Well Uncorked amid awful outbursts of
INFERNAL FIRE AND SMOKE ATHUNDER!

THE BUZZARD-ROOST ASTONISHED!

UNPARALLELED REJOICINGS!

—and so on, and so on. Yes, it was too loud. Once I could have enjoyed it and seen nothing out of the way about it, but now its note was discordant. It was good Arkansas journalism, but this was not Arkansas. Moreover, the next to the last line was calculated to give offense to the hermits, and perhaps lose us their advertising. Indeed, there was too lightsome a tone of

flippancy all through the paper. It was plain I had undergone a considerable change without noticing it. I found myself unpleasantly affected by pert little irreverencies which would have seemed but proper and airy graces of speech at an earlier period of my life. There was an abundance of the following breed of items, and they discomforted me:

LOCAL SMOKE AND CINDERS.

Sir Launcelot met up with old King Agrivance of Ireland unexpectedly last weok over on the moor south of Sir Balmoral le Merveilleuse's hog dasture. The widow has been notified.

Expedition No. 3 will start adout the first of mext month on a search f8r Sir Sagramour le Desirous. It is in com- and of the renowned Knight of the Red Lawns, assissted by Sir Persant of Inde, who is compete9t. intelligent, courte- ous, and in every way a brick, and fur- tHer assisted by Sir Palamides the Sara- cen, who is no huckleberry hinself. This is no pic-nic, these boys mean busine&s.

The readers of the Hosannah will re- gret to learn that the hadndsome and popular Sir Charolais of Gaul, who dur- ing his four weeks' stay at the Bull and Halibut, this city, has won every heart by his polished manners and elegant cPnversation, will pUll out to-day for home. Give us another call, Charley!

The bdsiness end of the funeral of the late Sir Dalliance the duke's son of Cornwall, killed in an encounter with the Giant of the Knotted Bludgeon last Tuesday on the borders of the Plain of Enchantment was in the hands of the ever affable and efficient Mumble, prince of un3ertakers, then whom there exists none by whom it were a more satisfying pleasure to have the last sad offices performed. Give him a trial.

The cordial thanks of the Hosannah office are due, from editor down to devil, to the ever courteous and thought- ful Lord High Stew d of the Palace's Third Assistant V t for several sau- ceTs of ice crEam a quality calculated to make the ey of the recipients hu- mid with grt ude; and it done it. When this administration wants to chalk up a desirable name for early promotion, the Hosannah would like a chance to sudgest.

The Demoiselle Irene Dewlap, of South Astolat, is visiting her uncle, the popular host of the Cattlemen's Board- ing Ho&se, Liver Lane, this city.

Young Barker the bellows-mender is hoMe again, and looks much improved by his vacation round-up among the out- lying smithies. See his ad.

Of course it was good enough journalism for a beginning; I knew that quite well, and yet it was somehow disappointing. The "Court Circular" pleased me better; indeed, its simple and dignified respectfulness was a distinct refreshment to me after all those disgraceful familiarities. But even it could have been improved. Do what one may, there is no getting an air of variety into a court circular, I acknowledge that. There is a profound monotonousness about its facts that baffles and defeats one's sincerest efforts to make them sparkle and enthuse. The best way to manage—in fact, the only sensible way—is to disguise repetitiousness of fact under variety of form: skin your fact each time and lay on a new cuticle of words. It deceives the eye; you think it is a new fact; it gives you the idea that the court is carrying on like everything; this excites you, and you drain the whole column, with a good appetite, and perhaps never notice that it's a barrel of soup made out of a single bean. Clarence's way was good, it was simple, it was dignified, it was direct and business-like; all I say is, it was not the best way:

COURT CIRCULAR.

On Monday, the king rode in the park.
" Tuesday,   "   "   "
" Wendesday   "   "   "
" Thursday   "   "   "
" Friday,   "   "   "
" Saturday   "   "   "
" Sunday,   "   "   "

However, take the paper by and large, I was vastly pleased with it. Little crudities of a mechanical sort were observable here and there, but there were not enough of them to amount to anything, and it was good enough Arkansas proof-reading, anyhow, and better than was needed in Arthur's day and realm. As a rule, the grammar was leaky and the construction more or less lame; but I did not much mind these things. They are common defects of my own, and one mustn't criticise other people on grounds where he can't stand perpendicular himself.

I was hungry enough for literature to want to take down the whole paper at this one meal, but I got only a few bites, and then had to postpone, because the monks around me besieged me so with eager questions: What is this curious thing? What is it for? Is it a handkerchief?—saddle blanket?—part of a shirt? What is it made of? How thin it is, and how dainty and frail; and how it rattles. Will it wear, do you think, and won't the rain injure it? Is it writing that appears on it, or is it only ornamentation? They suspected it was writing, because those among them who knew how to read Latin and had a smattering of Greek, recognized some of the letters, but they could make nothing out of the result as a whole. I put my information in the simplest form I could: .

"It is a public journal; I will explain what that is, another time. It is not cloth, it is made of paper; some time I will explain what paper is. The lines on it are reading matter; and not written by hand, but printed; by and by I will explain what printing is. A thousand of these sheets have been made, all exactly like this, in every minute detail—they can't be told apart." Then they all broke out with exclamations of surprise and admiration:

"A thousand! Verily a mighty work—a year's work for many men."

"No—merely a day's work for a man and a boy."

They crossed themselves, and whiffed out a protective prayer or two.

"Ah-h—a miracle, a wonder! Dark work of enchantment."

I let it go at that. Then I read in a low voice, to as many as could crowd their shaven heads within hearing distance, part of the account of the miracle of the restoration of the well, and was accompanied by astonished and reverent ejaculations all through: "Ah-h-h!" "How true!" "Amazing, amazing!" "These be the very haps as they happened, in marvelous exactness!" And might they take this strange thing in their hands, and feel of it and examine it?—they would be very careful. Yes. So they took it, handling it as cautiously and devoutly as if it had been some holy thing come from some supernatural region; and gently felt of its texture, caressed its pleasant smooth surface

with lingering touch, and scanned the mysterious characters with fascinated eyes. These grouped bent heads, these charmed faces, these speaking eyes —how beautiful to me! For was not this my darling, and was not all this mute wonder and interest and homage a most eloquent tribute and unforced compliment to it? I knew, then, how a mother feels when women, whether strangers or friends, take her new baby, and close themselves about it with one eager impulse, and bend their heads over it in a tranced adoration that makes all the rest of the universe vanish out of their consciousness and be as if it were not, for that time. I knew how she feels, and that there is no other satisfied ambition, whether of king, conqueror, or poet, that ever reaches half-way to that serene far summit or yields half so divine a contentment.

During all the rest of the seance my paper traveled from group to group all up and down and about that huge hall, and my happy eye was upon it always, and I sat motionless, steeped in satisfaction, drunk with enjoyment. Yes, this was heaven; I was tasting it once, if I might never taste it more.

CHAPTER XXVII

THE YANKEE AND THE KING TRAVEL INCOGNITO

About bedtime I took the king to my private quarters to cut his hair and help him get the hang of the lowly raiment he was to wear. The high classes wore their hair banged across the forehead but hanging to the shoulders the rest of the way around, whereas the lowest ranks of commoners were banged fore and aft both; the slaves were bangless, and allowed their hair free growth. So I inverted a bowl over his head and cut away all the locks that hung below it. I also trimmed his whiskers and mustache until they were only about a half-inch long; and tried to do it inartistically, and succeeded. It was a villainous disfigurement. When he got his lubberly sandals on, and his long robe of coarse brown linen cloth, which hung straight from his neck to his ankle-bones, he was no longer the comeliest man in his kingdom, but one of the unhandsomest and most commonplace and unattractive. We were dressed and barbered alike, and could pass for small farmers, or farm bailiffs, or shepherds, or carters; yes, or for village artisans, if we chose, our costume being in effect universal among the poor, because of its strength and cheapness. I don't mean that it was really cheap to a very poor person, but I do mean that it was the cheapest material there was for male attire— manufactured material, you understand.

We slipped away an hour before dawn, and by broad sun-up had made eight or ten miles, and were in the midst of a sparsely settled country. I had a pretty heavy knapsack; it was laden with provisions—provisions for the king to taper down on, till he could take to the coarse fare of the country without damage.

I found a comfortable seat for the king by the roadside, and then gave him a morsel or two to stay his stomach with. Then I said I would find some water for him, and strolled away. Part of my project was to get out of sight and sit down and rest a little myself. It had always been my custom to stand when in his presence; even at the council board, except upon those rare occasions when the sitting was a very long one, extending over hours; then I had a trifling little backless thing which was like a reversed culvert and was as comfortable as the toothache. I didn't want to break him in suddenly, but do it by degrees. We should have to sit together now when in company, or people would notice; but it would not be good politics for me to be playing equality with him when there was no necessity for it.

I found the water some three hundred yards away, and had been resting about twenty minutes, when I heard voices. That is all right, I thought—peasants going to work; nobody else likely to be stirring this early. But the next moment these comers jingled into sight around a turn of the road—smartly clad people of quality, with luggage-mules and servants in their train! I was off like a shot, through the bushes, by the shortest cut. For a while it did seem that these people would pass the king before I could get to him; but desperation gives you wings, you know, and I canted my body forward, inflated my breast, and held my breath and flew. I arrived. And in plenty good enough time, too.

"Pardon, my king, but it's no time for ceremony—jump! Jump to your feet—some quality are coming!"

"Is that a marvel? Let them come."

"But my liege! You must not be seen sitting. Rise!—and stand in humble posture while they pass. You are a peasant, you know."

"True—I had forgot it, so lost was I in planning of a huge war with Gaul"—he was up by this time, but a farm could have got up quicker, if there was any kind of a boom in real estate—"and right-so a thought came randoming overthwart this majestic dream the which—"

"A humbler attitude, my lord the king—and quick! Duck your head! —more!—still more!—droop it!"

He did his honest best, but lord, it was no great things. He looked as humble as the leaning tower at Pisa. It is the most you could say of it. Indeed, it was such a thundering poor success that it raised wondering scowls all along the line, and a gorgeous flunkey at the tail end of it raised his whip; but I jumped in time and was under it when it fell; and under cover of the volley of coarse laughter which followed, I spoke up sharply and warned the king to take no notice. He mastered himself for the moment, but it was a sore tax; he wanted to eat up the procession. I said:

"It would end our adventures at the very start; and we, being without weapons, could do nothing with that armed gang. If we are going to succeed in our emprise, we must not only look the peasant but act the peasant."

"It is wisdom; none can gainsay it. Let us go on, Sir Boss. I will take note and learn, and do the best I may."

He kept his word. He did the best he could, but I've seen better. If you have ever seen an active, heedless, enterprising child going diligently out of one mischief and into another all day long, and an anxious mother at its heels all the while, and just saving it by a hair from drowning itself or breaking its neck with each new experiment, you've seen the king and me.

If I could have foreseen what the thing was going to be like, I should have said, No, if anybody wants to make his living exhibiting a king as a peasant, let him take the layout; I can do better with a menagerie, and last longer. And yet, during the first three days I never allowed him to enter a hut or other dwelling. If he could pass muster anywhere during his early novitiate it would be in small inns and on the road; so to these places we confined ourselves. Yes, he certainly did the best he could, but what of that? He didn't improve a bit that I could see.

He was always frightening me, always breaking out with fresh astonishers, in new and unexpected places. Toward evening on the second day, what does he do but blandly fetch out a dirk from inside his robe!

"Great guns, my liege, where did you get that?"

"From a smuggler at the inn, yester eve."

"What in the world possessed you to buy it?"

"We have escaped divers dangers by wit—thy wit—but I have bethought me that it were but prudence if I bore a weapon, too. Thine might fail thee in some pinch."

"But people of our condition are not allowed to carry arms. What would a lord say—yes, or any other person of whatever condition —if he caught an upstart peasant with a dagger on his person?"

It was a lucky thing for us that nobody came along just then. I persuaded him to throw the dirk away; and it was as easy as persuading a child to give up some bright fresh new way of killing itself. We walked along, silent and thinking. Finally the king said:

"When ye know that I meditate a thing inconvenient, or that hath a peril in it, why do you not warn me to cease from that project?"

It was a startling question, and a puzzler. I didn't quite know how to take hold of it, or what to say, and so, of course, I ended by saying the natural thing:

"But, sire, how can I know what your thoughts are?"

The king stopped dead in his tracks, and stared at me.

"I believed thou wert greater than Merlin; and truly in magic thou art. But prophecy is greater than magic. Merlin is a prophet."

I saw I had made a blunder. I must get back my lost ground. After a deep reflection and careful planning, I said:

"Sire, I have been misunderstood. I will explain. There are two kinds of prophecy. One is the gift to foretell things that are but a little way off, the other is the gift to foretell things that are whole ages and centuries away. Which is the mightier gift, do you think?"

"Oh, the last, most surely!"

"True. Does Merlin possess it?"

"Partly, yes. He foretold mysteries about my birth and future kingship that were twenty years away."

"Has he ever gone beyond that?"

"He would not claim more, I think."

"It is probably his limit. All prophets have their limit. The limit of some of the great prophets has been a hundred years."

"These are few, I ween."

"There have been two still greater ones, whose limit was four hundred and six hundred years, and one whose limit compassed even seven hundred and twenty."

"Gramercy, it is marvelous!"

"But what are these in comparison with me? They are nothing."

"What? Canst thou truly look beyond even so vast a stretch of time as—"

"Seven hundred years? My liege, as clear as the vision of an eagle does my prophetic eye penetrate and lay bare the future of this world for nearly thirteen centuries and a half!"

My land, you should have seen the king's eyes spread slowly open, and lift the earth's entire atmosphere as much as an inch! That settled Brer Merlin. One never had any occasion to prove his facts, with these people; all he had to do was to state them. It never occurred to anybody to doubt the statement.

"Now, then," I continued, "I *could* work both kinds of prophecy —the long and the short—if I chose to take the trouble to keep in practice; but I seldom exercise any but the long kind, because the other is beneath my dignity. It is properer to Merlin's sort —stump-tail prophets, as we call them in the profession. Of course, I whet up now and then and flirt out a minor prophecy, but not often—hardly ever, in fact. You will remember that there was great talk, when you reached the Valley of Holiness, about my having prophesied your coming and the very hour of your arrival, two or three days beforehand."

"Indeed, yes, I mind it now."

"Well, I could have done it as much as forty times easier, and piled on a thousand times more detail into the bargain, if it had been five hundred years away instead of two or three days."

"How amazing that it should be so!"

"Yes, a genuine expert can always foretell a thing that is five hundred years away easier than he can a thing that's only five hundred seconds off."

"And yet in reason it should clearly be the other way; it should be five hundred times as easy to foretell the last as the first, for, indeed, it is so close by that one uninspired might almost see it. In truth, the law of prophecy doth contradict the likelihoods, most strangely making the difficult easy, and the easy difficult."

It was a wise head. A peasant's cap was no safe disguise for it; you could know it for a king's under a diving-bell, if you could hear it work its intellect.

I had a new trade now, and plenty of business in it. The king was as hungry to find out everything that was going to happen during the next thirteen centuries as if he were expecting to live in them. From that time out, I prophesied myself bald-headed trying to supply the demand. I have done some indiscreet things in my day, but this thing of playing myself for a prophet was the worst. Still, it had its ameliorations. A prophet doesn't have to have any brains. They are good to have, of course, for the ordinary exigencies of life, but they are no use in professional work. It is the restfulest vocation there

is. When the spirit of prophecy comes upon you, you merely cake your intellect and lay it off in a cool place for a rest, and unship your jaw and leave it alone; it will work itself: the result is prophecy.

Every day a knight-errant or so came along, and the sight of them fired the king's martial spirit every time. He would have forgotten himself, sure, and said something to them in a style a suspicious shade or so above his ostensible degree, and so I always got him well out of the road in time. Then he would stand and look with all his eyes; and a proud light would flash from them, and his nostrils would inflate like a war-horse's, and I knew he was longing for a brush with them. But about noon of the third day I had stopped in the road to take a precaution which had been suggested by the whip-stroke that had fallen to my share two days before; a precaution which I had afterward decided to leave untaken, I was so loath to institute it; but now I had just had a fresh reminder: while striding heedlessly along, with jaw spread and intellect at rest, for I was prophesying, I stubbed my toe and fell sprawling. I was so pale I couldn't think for a moment; then I got softly and carefully up and unstrapped my knapsack. I had that dynamite bomb in it, done up in wool in a box. It was a good thing to have along; the time would come when I could do a valuable miracle with it, maybe, but it was a nervous thing to have about me, and I didn't like to ask the king to carry it. Yet I must either throw it away or think up some safe way to get along with its society. I got it out and slipped it into my scrip, and just then here came a couple of knights. The king stood, stately as a statue, gazing toward them—had forgotten himself again, of course—and before I could get a word of warning out, it was time for him to skip, and well that he did it, too. He supposed they would turn aside. Turn aside to avoid trampling peasant dirt under foot? When had he ever turned aside himself—or ever had the chance to do it, if a peasant saw him or any other noble knight in time to judiciously save him the trouble? The knights paid no attention to the king at all; it was his place to look out himself, and if he hadn't skipped he would have been placidly ridden down, and laughed at besides.

The king was in a flaming fury, and launched out his challenge and epithets with a most royal vigor. The knights were some little distance by now. They halted, greatly surprised, and turned in their saddles and looked back, as if wondering if it might be worth while to bother with such scum as we. Then they wheeled and started for us. Not a moment must be lost. I started for *them*. I passed them at a rattling gait, and as I went by I flung out a hair-lifting soul-scorching thirteen-jointed insult which made the king's effort poor and cheap by comparison. I got it out of the nineteenth century where they know how. They had such headway that they were nearly to the king before they could check up; then, frantic with rage, they stood up their horses on their hind hoofs and whirled them around, and the next moment here they came, breast to breast. I was seventy yards off, then, and scrambling up a great bowlder at the roadside. When they were within thirty yards of me they let their long lances droop to a level, depressed their mailed heads, and so, with their horse-hair plumes streaming straight out behind, most gallant to see, this lightning express came tearing for me! When they were within fifteen yards, I sent that bomb with a sure aim, and it struck the ground just under the horses' noses.

Yes, it was a neat thing, very neat and pretty to see. It resembled a steamboat explosion on the Mississippi; and during the next fifteen minutes we stood under a steady drizzle of microscopic fragments of knights and hardware and horse-flesh. I say we, for the king joined the audience, of course, as soon as he had got his breath again. There was a hole there which would afford steady work for all the people in that region for some years to come —in trying to explain it, I mean; as for filling it up, that service would be comparatively prompt, and would fall to the lot of a select few—peasants of that seignory; and they wouldn't get anything for it, either.

But I explained it to the king myself. I said it was done with a dynamite bomb. This information did him no damage, because it left him as intelligent as he was before. However, it was a noble miracle, in his eyes, and was another settler for Merlin. I thought it well enough to explain that this was a miracle of so rare a sort that it couldn't be done except when the atmospheric conditions were just right. Otherwise he would be encoring it every time we had a good subject, and that would be inconvenient, because I hadn't any more bombs along.

CHAPTER XXVIII

DRILLING THE KING

On the morning of the fourth day, when it was just sunrise, and we had been tramping an hour in the chill dawn, I came to a resolution: the king *must* be drilled; things could not go on so, he must be taken in hand and deliberately and conscientiously drilled, or we couldn't ever venture to enter a dwelling; the very cats would know this masquerader for a humbug and no peasant. So I called a halt and said:

"Sire, as between clothes and countenance, you are all right, there is no discrepancy; but as between your clothes and your bearing, you are all wrong, there is a most noticeable discrepancy. Your soldierly stride, your lordly port—these will not do. You stand too straight, your looks are too high, too confident. The cares of a kingdom do not stoop the shoulders, they do not droop the chin, they do not depress the high level of the eye-glance, they do not put doubt and fear in the heart and hang out the signs of them in slouching body and unsure step. It is the sordid cares of the lowly born that do these things. You must learn the trick; you must imitate the trademarks of poverty, misery, oppression, insult, and the other several and common inhumanities that sap the manliness out of a man and make him a loyal and proper and approved subject and a satisfaction to his masters, or the very infants will know you for better than your disguise, and we shall go to pieces at the first hut we stop at. Pray try to walk like this."

The king took careful note, and then tried an imitation.

"Pretty fair—pretty fair. Chin a little lower, please—there, very good. Eyes too high; pray don't look at the horizon, look at the ground, ten steps in front of you. Ah—that is better, that is very good. Wait, please; you betray too much vigor, too much decision; you want more of a shamble. Look at me, please— this is what I mean.... Now you are getting it; that is the idea— at least, it sort of approaches it.... Yes, that is pretty fair. *But!* There is a great big something wanting, I don't quite know what it is. Please walk thirty yards, so that I can get a perspective on the thing.... Now, then—your head's right, speed's right, shoulders right, eyes right, chin right, gait, carriage, general style right—everything's right! And yet the fact remains, the aggregate's wrong. The account don't balance. Do it again, please.... *Now* I think I begin to see what it is. Yes, I've struck it. You see, the genuine spiritlessness is wanting; that's what's the trouble. It's all *amateur*— mechanical details all right, almost to a hair; everything about

the delusion perfect, except that it don't delude."

"What, then, must one do, to prevail?"

"Let me think... I can't seem to quite get at it. In fact, there isn't anything that can right the matter but practice. This is a good place for it: roots and stony ground to break up your stately gait, a region not liable to interruption, only one field and one hut in sight, and they so far away that nobody could see us from there. It will be well to move a little off the road and put in the whole day drilling you, sire."

After the drill had gone on a little while, I said:

"Now, sire, imagine that we are at the door of the hut yonder, and the family are before us. Proceed, please—accost the head of the house."

The king unconsciously straightened up like a monument, and said, with frozen austerity:

"Varlet, bring a seat; and serve to me what cheer ye have."

"Ah, your grace, that is not well done."

"In what lacketh it?"

"These people do not call *each other* varlets."

"Nay, is that true?"

"Yes; only those above them call them so."

"Then must I try again. I will call him villein."

"No-no; for he may be a freeman."

"Ah—so. Then peradventure I should call him goodman."

"That would answer, your grace, but it would be still better if you said friend, or brother."

"Brother!—to dirt like that?"

"Ah, but *we* are pretending to be dirt like that, too."

"It is even true. I will say it. Brother, bring a seat, and thereto what cheer ye have, withal. Now 'tis right."

"Not quite, not wholly right. You have asked for one, not *us* — for one, not both; food for one, a seat for one."

The king looked puzzled—he wasn't a very heavy weight, intellectually. His head was an hour-glass; it could stow an idea, but it had to do it a grain at a time, not the whole idea at once.

"Would *you* have a seat also—and sit?"

"If I did not sit, the man would perceive that we were only pretending to be equals—and playing the deception pretty poorly, too."

"It is well and truly said! How wonderful is truth, come it in whatsoever unexpected form it may! Yes, he must bring out seats and food for both, and in serving us present not ewer and napkin with more show of respect to the one than to the other."

"And there is even yet a detail that needs correcting. He must bring nothing outside; we will go in—in among the dirt, and possibly other repulsive things,—and take the food with the household, and after the fashion of the house, and all on equal terms, except the man be of the serf class; and finally, there will be no ewer and no napkin, whether he be serf or free. Please walk again, my liege. There—it is better—it is the best yet; but not perfect. The shoulders have known no ignobler burden than iron mail, and they will not stoop."

"Give me, then, the bag. I will learn the spirit that goeth with burdens that have not honor. It is the spirit that stoopeth the shoulders, I ween, and not the weight; for armor is heavy, yet it is a proud burden, and a man standeth straight in it.... Nay, but me no buts, offer me no objections. I will have the thing. Strap it upon my back."

He was complete now with that knapsack on, and looked as little like a king as any man I had ever seen. But it was an obstinate pair of shoulders; they could not seem to learn the trick of stooping with any sort of deceptive naturalness. The drill went on, I prompting and correcting:

"Now, make believe you are in debt, and eaten up by relentless creditors; you are out of work—which is horse-shoeing, let us say—and can get none; and your wife is sick, your children are crying because they are hungry—"

And so on, and so on. I drilled him as representing in turn all sorts of people out of luck and suffering dire privations and misfortunes. But lord, it was only just words, words—they meant nothing in the world to him, I might just as well have whistled. Words realize nothing, vivify nothing to you, unless you have suffered in your own person the thing which the words try to describe. There are wise people who talk ever so knowingly and complacently about "the working classes," and satisfy themselves that a day's hard intellectual work is very much harder than a day's hard manual toil, and is righteously entitled to much bigger pay. Why, they really think that, you know, because they know all about the one, but haven't tried the other. But I know all about both; and so far as I am concerned, there isn't money enough in the universe to hire me to swing a pickaxe thirty days, but I will do the hardest kind of intellectual work for just as near nothing as you can cipher it down—and I will be satisfied, too.

Intellectual "work" is misnamed; it is a pleasure, a dissipation, and is its own highest reward. The poorest paid architect, engineer, general, author, sculptor, painter, lecturer, advocate, legislator, actor, preacher, singer is constructively in heaven when he is at work; and as for the musician with the fiddle-bow in his hand who sits in the midst of a great orchestra with the ebbing and flowing tides of divine sound washing over him—why, certainly, he is at work, if you wish to call it that, but lord, it's a sarcasm just the same. The law of work does seem utterly unfair—but there it is, and nothing can change it: the higher the pay in enjoyment the worker gets out of it, the higher shall be his pay in cash, also. And it's also the very law of those transparent swindles, transmissible nobility and kingship.

CHAPTER XXIX

THE SMALLPOX HUT

When we arrived at that hut at mid-afternoon, we saw no signs of life about it. The field near by had been denuded of its crop

some time before, and had a skinned look, so exhaustively had it been harvested and gleaned. Fences, sheds, everything had a ruined look, and were eloquent of poverty. No animal was around anywhere, no living thing in sight. The stillness was awful, it was like the stillness of death. The cabin was a one-story one, whose thatch was black with age, and ragged from lack of repair.

The door stood a trifle ajar. We approached it stealthily—on tiptoe and at half-breath—for that is the way one's feeling makes him do, at such a time. The king knocked. We waited. No answer. Knocked again. No answer. I pushed the door softly open and looked in. I made out some dim forms, and a woman started up from the ground and stared at me, as one does who is wakened from sleep. Presently she found her voice:

"Have mercy!" she pleaded. "All is taken, nothing is left."

"I have not come to take anything, poor woman."

"You are not a priest?"

"No."

"Nor come not from the lord of the manor?"

"No, I am a stranger."

"Oh, then, for the fear of God, who visits with misery and death such as be harmless, tarry not here, but fly! This place is under his curse—and his Church's."

"Let me come in and help you—you are sick and in trouble."

I was better used to the dim light now. I could see her hollow eyes fixed upon me. I could see how emaciated she was.

"I tell you the place is under the Church's ban. Save yourself — and go, before some straggler see thee here, and report it."

"Give yourself no trouble about me; I don't care anything for the Church's curse. Let me help you."

"Now all good spirits—if there be any such—bless thee for that word. Would God I had a sup of water!—but hold, hold, forget I said it, and fly; for there is that here that even he that feareth not the Church must fear: this disease whereof we die. Leave us, thou brave, good stranger, and take with thee such whole and sincere blessing as them that be accursed can give."

But before this I had picked up a wooden bowl and was rushing past the king on my way to the brook. It was ten yards away. When I got back and entered, the king was within, and was opening the shutter that closed the window-hole, to let in air and light. The place was full of a foul stench. I put the bowl to the woman's lips, and as she gripped it with her eager talons the shutter came open and a strong light flooded her face. Smallpox!

I sprang to the king, and said in his ear:

"Out of the door on the instant, sire! the woman is dying of that disease that wasted the skirts of Camelot two years ago."

He did not budge.

"Of a truth I shall remain—and likewise help."

I whispered again:

"King, it must not be. You must go."

"Ye mean well, and ye speak not unwisely. But it were shame that a king should know fear, and shame that belted knight should withhold his hand where be such as need succor. Peace, I will not go. It is you who must go. The Church's ban is not upon me, but it forbiddeth you to be here, and she will deal with you with a heavy hand an word come to her of your trespass."

It was a desperate place for him to be in, and might cost him his life, but it was no use to argue with him. If he considered his knightly honor at stake here, that was the end of argument; he would stay, and nothing could prevent it; I was aware of that. And so I dropped the subject. The woman spoke:

"Fair sir, of your kindness will ye climb the ladder there, and bring me news of what ye find? Be not afraid to report, for times can come when even a mother's heart is past breaking — being already broke."

"Abide," said the king, "and give the woman to eat. I will go." And he put down the knapsack.

I turned to start, but the king had already started. He halted, and looked down upon a man who lay in a dim light, and had not noticed us thus far, or spoken.

"Is it your husband?" the king asked.

"Yes."

"Is he asleep?"

"God be thanked for that one charity, yes—these three hours. Where shall I pay to the full, my gratitude! for my heart is bursting with it for that sleep he sleepeth now."

I said:

"We will be careful. We will not wake him."

"Ah, no, that ye will not, for he is dead."

"Dead?"

"Yes, what triumph it is to know it! None can harm him, none insult him more. He is in heaven now, and happy; or if not there, he bides in hell and is content; for in that place he will find neither abbot nor yet bishop. We were boy and girl together; we were man and wife these five and twenty years, and never separated till this day. Think how long that is to love and suffer together. This morning was he out of his mind, and in his fancy we were boy and girl again and wandering in the happy fields; and so in that innocent glad converse wandered he far and farther, still lightly gossiping, and entered into those other fields we know not of, and was shut away from mortal sight. And so there was no parting, for in his fancy I went with him; he knew not but I went with him, my hand in his—my young soft hand, not this withered claw. Ah, yes, to go, and know it not; to separate and know it not; how could one go peace—fuller than that? It was his reward for a cruel life patiently borne."

There was a slight noise from the direction of the dim corner

where the ladder was. It was the king descending. I could see that he was bearing something in one arm, and assisting himself with the other. He came forward into the light; upon his breast lay a slender girl of fifteen. She was but half conscious; she was dying of smallpox. Here was heroism at its last and loftiest possibility, its utmost summit; this was challenging death in the open field unarmed, with all the odds against the challenger, no reward set upon the contest, and no admiring world in silks and cloth of gold to gaze and applaud; and yet the king's bearing was as serenely brave as it had always been in those cheaper contests where knight meets knight in equal fight and clothed in protecting steel. He was great now; sublimely great. The rude statues of his ancestors in his palace should have an addition—I would see to that; and it would not be a mailed king killing a giant or a dragon, like the rest, it would be a king in commoner's garb bearing death in his arms that a peasant mother might look her last upon her child and be comforted.

He laid the girl down by her mother, who poured out endearments and caresses from an overflowing heart, and one could detect a flickering faint light of response in the child's eyes, but that was all. The mother hung over her, kissing her, petting her, and imploring her to speak, but the lips only moved and no sound came. I snatched my liquor flask from my knapsack, but the woman forbade me, and said:

"No—she does not suffer; it is better so. It might bring her back to life. None that be so good and kind as ye are would do her that cruel hurt. For look you—what is left to live for? Her brothers are gone, her father is gone, her mother goeth, the Church's curse is upon her, and none may shelter or befriend her even though she lay perishing in the road. She is desolate. I have not asked you, good heart, if her sister be still on live, here overhead; I had no need; ye had gone back, else, and not left the poor thing forsaken—"

"She lieth at peace," interrupted the king, in a subdued voice.

"I would not change it. How rich is this day in happiness! Ah, my Annis, thou shalt join thy sister soon—thou'rt on thy way, and these be merciful friends that will not hinder."

And so she fell to murmuring and cooing over the girl again, and softly stroking her face and hair, and kissing her and calling her by endearing names; but there was scarcely sign of response now in the glazing eyes. I saw tears well from the king's eyes, and trickle down his face. The woman noticed them, too, and said:

"Ah, I know that sign: thou'st a wife at home, poor soul, and you and she have gone hungry to bed, many's the time, that the little ones might have your crust; you know what poverty is, and the daily insults of your betters, and the heavy hand of the Church and the king."

The king winced under this accidental home-shot, but kept still; he was learning his part; and he was playing it well, too, for a pretty dull beginner. I struck up a diversion. I offered the woman food and liquor, but she refused both. She would allow nothing to come between her and the release of death. Then I slipped away and brought the dead child from aloft, and laid it by her. This broke her down again, and there was another scene that was full of heartbreak. By and by I made another diversion, and beguiled her to sketch her story.

"Ye know it well yourselves, having suffered it—for truly none of our condition in Britain escape it. It is the old, weary tale.

We fought and struggled and succeeded; meaning by success, that we lived and did not die; more than that is not to be claimed. No troubles came that we could not outlive, till this year brought them; then came they all at once, as one might say, and overwhelmed us. Years ago the lord of the manor planted certain fruit trees on our farm; in the best part of it, too—a grievous wrong and shame—"

"But it was his right," interrupted the king.

"None denieth that, indeed; an the law mean anything, what is the lord's is his, and what is mine is his also. Our farm was ours by lease, therefore 'twas likewise his, to do with it as he would. Some little time ago, three of those trees were found hewn down. Our three grown sons ran frightened to report the crime. Well, in his lordship's dungeon there they lie, who saith there shall they lie and rot till they confess. They have naught to confess, being innocent, wherefore there will they remain until they die. Ye know that right well, I ween. Think how this left us; a man, a woman and two children, to gather a crop that was planted by so much greater force, yes, and protect it night and day from pigeons and prowling animals that be sacred and must not be hurt by any of our sort. When my lord's crop was nearly ready for the harvest, so also was ours; when his bell rang to call us to his fields to harvest his crop for nothing, he would not allow that I and my two girls should count for our three captive sons, but for only two of them; so, for the lacking one were we daily fined. All this time our own crop was perishing through neglect; and so both the priest and his lordship fined us because their shares of it were suffering through damage. In the end the fines ate up our crop—and they took it all; they took it all and made us harvest it for them, without pay or food, and we starving. Then the worst came when I, being out of my mind with hunger and loss of my boys, and grief to see my husband and my little maids in rags and misery and despair, uttered a deep blasphemy—oh! a thousand of them! —against the Church and the Church's ways. It was ten days ago. I had fallen sick with this disease, and it was to the priest I said the words, for he was come to chide me for lack of due humility under the chastening hand of God. He carried my trespass to his betters; I was stubborn; wherefore, presently upon my head and upon all heads that were dear to me, fell the curse of Rome.

"Since that day we are avoided, shunned with horror. None has come near this hut to know whether we live or not. The rest of us were taken down. Then I roused me and got up, as wife and mother will. It was little they could have eaten in any case; it was less than little they had to eat. But there was water, and I gave them that. How they craved it! and how they blessed it! But the end came yesterday; my strength broke down. Yesterday was the last time I ever saw my husband and this youngest child alive. I have lain here all these hours—these ages, ye may say—listening, listening for any sound up there that—"

She gave a sharp quick glance at her eldest daughter, then cried out, "Oh, my darling!" and feebly gathered the stiffening form to her sheltering arms. She had recognized the death-rattle.

CHAPTER XXX

THE TRAGEDY OF THE MANOR-HOUSE

At midnight all was over, and we sat in the presence of four corpses. We covered them with such rags as we could find, and started away, fastening the door behind us. Their home must

be these people's grave, for they could not have Christian burial, or be admitted to consecrated ground. They were as dogs, wild beasts, lepers, and no soul that valued its hope of eternal life would throw it away by meddling in any sort with these rebuked and smitten outcasts.

We had not moved four steps when I caught a sound as of footsteps upon gravel. My heart flew to my throat. We must not be seen coming from that house. I plucked at the king's robe and we drew back and took shelter behind the corner of the cabin.

"Now we are safe," I said, "but it was a close call—so to speak. If the night had been lighter he might have seen us, no doubt, he seemed to be so near."

"Mayhap it is but a beast and not a man at all."

"True. But man or beast, it will be wise to stay here a minute and let it get by and out of the way."

"Hark! It cometh hither."

True again. The step was coming toward us—straight toward the hut. It must be a beast, then, and we might as well have saved our trepidation. I was going to step out, but the king laid his hand upon my arm. There was a moment of silence, then we heard a soft knock on the cabin door. It made me shiver. Presently the knock was repeated, and then we heard these words in a guarded voice:

"Mother! Father! Open—we have got free, and we bring news to pale your cheeks but glad your hearts; and we may not tarry, but must fly! And—but they answer not. Mother! father!—"

I drew the king toward the other end of the hut and whispered:

"Come—now we can get to the road."

The king hesitated, was going to demur; but just then we heard the door give way, and knew that those desolate men were in the presence of their dead.

"Come, my liege! in a moment they will strike a light, and then will follow that which it would break your heart to hear."

He did not hesitate this time. The moment we were in the road I ran; and after a moment he threw dignity aside and followed. I did not want to think of what was happening in the hut—I couldn't bear it; I wanted to drive it out of my mind; so I struck into the first subject that lay under that one in my mind:

"I have had the disease those people died of, and so have nothing to fear; but if you have not had it also—"

He broke in upon me to say he was in trouble, and it was his conscience that was troubling him:

"These young men have got free, they say—but *how*? It is not likely that their lord hath set them free."

"Oh, no, I make no doubt they escaped."

"That is my trouble; I have a fear that this is so, and your suspicion doth confirm it, you having the same fear."

"I should not call it by that name though. I do suspect that they escaped, but if they did, I am not sorry, certainly."

"I am not sorry, I *think*—but—"

"What is it? What is there for one to be troubled about?"

"*If* they did escape, then are we bound in duty to lay hands upon them and deliver them again to their lord; for it is not seemly that one of his quality should suffer a so insolent and high-handed outrage from persons of their base degree."

There it was again. He could see only one side of it. He was born so, educated so, his veins were full of ancestral blood that was rotten with this sort of unconscious brutality, brought down by inheritance from a long procession of hearts that had each done its share toward poisoning the stream. To imprison these men without proof, and starve their kindred, was no harm, for they were merely peasants and subject to the will and pleasure of their lord, no matter what fearful form it might take; but for these men to break out of unjust captivity was insult and outrage, and a thing not to be countenanced by any conscientious person who knew his duty to his sacred caste.

I worked more than half an hour before I got him to change the subject—and even then an outside matter did it for me. This was a something which caught our eyes as we struck the summit of a small hill—a red glow, a good way off.

"That's a fire," said I.

Fires interested me considerably, because I was getting a good deal of an insurance business started, and was also training some horses and building some steam fire-engines, with an eye to a paid fire department by and by. The priests opposed both my fire and life insurance, on the ground that it was an insolent attempt to hinder the decrees of God; and if you pointed out that they did not hinder the decrees in the least, but only modified the hard consequences of them if you took out policies and had luck, they retorted that that was gambling against the decrees of God, and was just as bad. So they managed to damage those industries more or less, but I got even on my Accident business. As a rule, a knight is a lummox, and some times even a labrick, and hence open to pretty poor arguments when they come glibly from a superstition-monger, but even *he* could see the practical side of a thing once in a while; and so of late you couldn't clean up a tournament and pile the result without finding one of my accident-tickets in every helmet.

We stood there awhile, in the thick darkness and stillness, looking toward the red blur in the distance, and trying to make out the meaning of a far-away murmur that rose and fell fitfully on the night. Sometimes it swelled up and for a moment seemed less remote; but when we were hopefully expecting it to betray its cause and nature, it dulled and sank again, carrying its mystery with it. We started down the hill in its direction, and the winding road plunged us at once into almost solid darkness—darkness that was packed and crammed in between two tall forest walls. We groped along down for half a mile, perhaps, that murmur growing more and more distinct all the time. The coming storm threatening more and more, with now and then a little shiver of wind, a faint show of lightning, and dull grumblings of distant thunder. I was in the lead. I ran against something—a soft heavy something which gave, slightly, to the impulse of my weight; at the same moment the lightning glared out, and within a foot of

my face was the writhing face of a man who was hanging from the limb of a tree! That is, it seemed to be writhing, but it was not. It was a grewsome sight. Straightway there was an ear-splitting explosion of thunder, and the bottom of heaven fell out; the rain poured down in a deluge. No matter, we must try to cut this man down, on the chance that there might be life in him yet, mustn't we? The lightning came quick and sharp now, and the place was alternately noonday and midnight. One moment the man would be hanging before me in an intense light, and the next he was blotted out again in the darkness. I told the king we must cut him down. The king at once objected.

"If he hanged himself, he was willing to lose him property to his lord; so let him be. If others hanged him, belike they had the right—let him hang."

"But—"

"But me no buts, but even leave him as he is. And for yet another reason. When the lightning cometh again—there, look abroad."

Two others hanging, within fifty yards of us!

"It is not weather meet for doing useless courtesies unto dead folk. They are past thanking you. Come—it is unprofitable to tarry here."

There was reason in what he said, so we moved on. Within the next mile we counted six more hanging forms by the blaze of the lightning, and altogether it was a grisly excursion. That murmur was a murmur no longer, it was a roar; a roar of men's voices. A man came flying by now, dimly through the darkness, and other men chasing him. They disappeared. Presently another case of the kind occurred, and then another and another. Then a sudden turn of the road brought us in sight of that fire—it was a large manor-house, and little or nothing was left of it—and everywhere men were flying and other men raging after them in pursuit.

I warned the king that this was not a safe place for strangers. We would better get away from the light, until matters should improve. We stepped back a little, and hid in the edge of the wood. From this hiding-place we saw both men and women hunted by the mob. The fearful work went on until nearly dawn. Then, the fire being out and the storm spent, the voices and flying footsteps presently ceased, and darkness and stillness reigned again.

We ventured out, and hurried cautiously away; and although we were worn out and sleepy, we kept on until we had put this place some miles behind us. Then we asked hospitality at the hut of a charcoal burner, and got what was to be had. A woman was up and about, but the man was still asleep, on a straw shake-down, on the clay floor. The woman seemed uneasy until I explained that we were travelers and had lost our way and been wandering in the woods all night. She became talkative, then, and asked if we had heard of the terrible goings-on at the manor-house of Abblasoure. Yes, we had heard of them, but what we wanted now was rest and sleep. The king broke in:

"Sell us the house and take yourselves away, for we be perilous company, being late come from people that died of the Spotted Death."

It was good of him, but unnecessary. One of the commonest

decorations of the nation was the waffle-iron face. I had early noticed that the woman and her husband were both so decorated. She made us entirely welcome, and had no fears; and plainly she was immensely impressed by the king's proposition; for, of course, it was a good deal of an event in her life to run across a person of the king's humble appearance who was ready to buy a man's house for the sake of a night's lodging. It gave her a large respect for us, and she strained the lean possibilities of her hovel to the utmost to make us comfortable.

We slept till far into the afternoon, and then got up hungry enough to make cotter fare quite palatable to the king, the more particularly as it was scant in quantity. And also in variety; it consisted solely of onions, salt, and the national black bread made out of horse-feed. The woman told us about the affair of the evening before. At ten or eleven at night, when everybody was in bed, the manor-house burst into flames. The country-side swarmed to the rescue, and the family were saved, with one exception, the master. He did not appear. Everybody was frantic over this loss, and two brave yeomen sacrificed their lives in ransacking the burning house seeking that valuable personage. But after a while he was found—what was left of him—which was his corpse. It was in a copse three hundred yards away, bound, gagged, stabbed in a dozen places.

Who had done this? Suspicion fell upon a humble family in the neighborhood who had been lately treated with peculiar harshness by the baron; and from these people the suspicion easily extended itself to their relatives and familiars. A suspicion was enough; my lord's liveried retainers proclaimed an instant crusade against these people, and were promptly joined by the community in general. The woman's husband had been active with the mob, and had not returned home until nearly dawn. He was gone now to find out what the general result had been. While we were still talking he came back from his quest. His report was revolting enough. Eighteen persons hanged or butchered, and two yeomen and thirteen prisoners lost in the fire.

"And how many prisoners were there altogether in the vaults?"

"Thirteen."

"Then every one of them was lost?"

"Yes, all."

"But the people arrived in time to save the family; how is it they could save none of the prisoners?"

The man looked puzzled, and said:

"Would one unlock the vaults at such a time? Marry, some would have escaped."

"Then you mean that nobody *did* unlock them?"

"None went near them, either to lock or unlock. It standeth to reason that the bolts were fast; wherefore it was only needful to establish a watch, so that if any broke the bonds he might not escape, but be taken. None were taken."

"Natheless, three did escape," said the king, "and ye will do well to publish it and set justice upon their track, for these murthered the baron and fired the house."

I was just expecting he would come out with that. For a moment the man and his wife showed an eager interest in this news and an impatience to go out and spread it; then a sudden something else betrayed itself in their faces, and they began to ask questions. I answered the questions myself, and narrowly watched the effects produced. I was soon satisfied that the knowledge of who these three prisoners were had somehow changed the atmosphere; that our hosts' continued eagerness to go and spread the news was now only pretended and not real. The king did not notice the change, and I was glad of that. I worked the conversation around toward other details of the night's proceedings, and noted that these people were relieved to have it take that direction.

The painful thing observable about all this business was the alacrity with which this oppressed community had turned their cruel hands against their own class in the interest of the common oppressor. This man and woman seemed to feel that in a quarrel between a person of their own class and his lord, it was the natural and proper and rightful thing for that poor devil's whole caste to side with the master and fight his battle for him, without ever stopping to inquire into the rights or wrongs of the matter. This man had been out helping to hang his neighbors, and had done his work with zeal, and yet was aware that there was nothing against them but a mere suspicion, with nothing back of it describable as evidence, still neither he nor his wife seemed to see anything horrible about it.

This was depressing—to a man with the dream of a republic in his head. It reminded me of a time thirteen centuries away, when the "poor whites" of our South who were always despised and frequently insulted by the slave-lords around them, and who owed their base condition simply to the presence of slavery in their midst, were yet pusillanimously ready to side with the slave-lords in all political moves for the upholding and perpetuating of slavery, and did also finally shoulder their muskets and pour out their lives in an effort to prevent the destruction of that very institution which degraded them. And there was only one redeeming feature connected with that pitiful piece of history; and that was, that secretly the "poor white" did detest the slave-lord, and did feel his own shame. That feeling was not brought to the surface, but the fact that it was there and could have been brought out, under favoring circumstances, was something—in fact, it was enough; for it showed that a man is at bottom a man, after all, even if it doesn't show on the outside.

Well, as it turned out, this charcoal burner was just the twin of the Southern "poor white" of the far future. The king presently showed impatience, and said:

"An ye prattle here all the day, justice will miscarry. Think ye the criminals will abide in their father's house? They are fleeing, they are not waiting. You should look to it that a party of horse be set upon their track."

The woman paled slightly, but quite perceptibly, and the man looked flustered and irresolute. I said:

"Come, friend, I will walk a little way with you, and explain which direction I think they would try to take. If they were merely resisters of the gabelle or some kindred absurdity I would try to protect them from capture; but when men murder a person of high degree and likewise burn his house, that is another matter."

The last remark was for the king—to quiet him. On the road

the man pulled his resolution together, and began the march with a steady gait, but there was no eagerness in it. By and by I said:

"What relation were these men to you—cousins?"

He turned as white as his layer of charcoal would let him, and stopped, trembling.

"Ah, my God, how know ye that?"

"I didn't know it; it was a chance guess."

"Poor lads, they are lost. And good lads they were, too."

"Were you actually going yonder to tell on them?"

He didn't quite know how to take that; but he said, hesitatingly:

"Ye-s."

"Then I think you are a damned scoundrel!"

It made him as glad as if I had called him an angel.

"Say the good words again, brother! for surely ye mean that ye would not betray me an I failed of my duty."

"Duty? There is no duty in the matter, except the duty to keep still and let those men get away. They've done a righteous deed."

He looked pleased; pleased, and touched with apprehension at the same time. He looked up and down the road to see that no one was coming, and then said in a cautious voice:

"From what land come you, brother, that you speak such perilous words, and seem not to be afraid?"

"They are not perilous words when spoken to one of my own caste, I take it. You would not tell anybody I said them?"

"I? I would be drawn asunder by wild horses first."

"Well, then, let me say my say. I have no fears of your repeating it. I think devil's work has been done last night upon those innocent poor people. That old baron got only what he deserved. If I had my way, all his kind should have the same luck."

Fear and depression vanished from the man's manner, and gratefulness and a brave animation took their place:

"Even though you be a spy, and your words a trap for my undoing, yet are they such refreshment that to hear them again and others like to them, I would go to the gallows happy, as having had one good feast at least in a starved life. And I will say my say now, and ye may report it if ye be so minded. I helped to hang my neighbors for that it were peril to my own life to show lack of zeal in the master's cause; the others helped for none other reason. All rejoice to-day that he is dead, but all do go about seemingly sorrowing, and shedding the hypocrite's tear, for in that lies safety. I have said the words, I have said the words! the only ones that have ever tasted good in my mouth, and the reward of that taste is sufficient. Lead on, an ye will, be it even to the scaffold, for I am ready."

There it was, you see. A man is a man, at bottom. Whole ages of abuse and oppression cannot crush the manhood clear out of him. Whoever thinks it a mistake is himself mistaken. Yes, there is plenty good enough material for a republic in the most degraded people that ever existed—even the Russians; plenty of manhood in them—even in the Germans—if one could but force it out of its timid and suspicious privacy, to overthrow and trample in the mud any throne that ever was set up and any nobility that ever supported it. We should see certain things yet, let us hope and believe. First, a modified monarchy, till Arthur's days were done, then the destruction of the throne, nobility abolished, every member of it bound out to some useful trade, universal suffrage instituted, and the whole government placed in the hands of the men and women of the nation there to remain. Yes, there was no occasion to give up my dream yet a while.

CHAPTER XXXI

MARCO

We strolled along in a sufficiently indolent fashion now, and talked. We must dispose of about the amount of time it ought to take to go to the little hamlet of Abblasoure and put justice on the track of those murderers and get back home again. And meantime I had an auxiliary interest which had never paled yet, never lost its novelty for me since I had been in Arthur's kingdom: the behavior—born of nice and exact subdivisions of caste—of chance passers-by toward each other. Toward the shaven monk who trudged along with his cowl tilted back and the sweat washing down his fat jowls, the coal-burner was deeply reverent; to the gentleman he was abject; with the small farmer and the free mechanic he was cordial and gossipy; and when a slave passed by with a countenance respectfully lowered, this chap's nose was in the air—he couldn't even see him. Well, there are times when one would like to hang the whole human race and finish the farce.

Presently we struck an incident. A small mob of half-naked boys and girls came tearing out of the woods, scared and shrieking. The eldest among them were not more than twelve or fourteen years old. They implored help, but they were so beside themselves that we couldn't make out what the matter was. However, we plunged into the wood, they skurrying in the lead, and the trouble was quickly revealed: they had hanged a little fellow with a bark rope, and he was kicking and struggling, in the process of choking to death. We rescued him, and fetched him around. It was some more human nature; the admiring little folk imitating their elders; they were playing mob, and had achieved a success which promised to be a good deal more serious than they had bargained for.

It was not a dull excursion for me. I managed to put in the time very well. I made various acquaintanceships, and in my quality of stranger was able to ask as many questions as I wanted to. A thing which naturally interested me, as a statesman, was the matter of wages. I picked up what I could under that head during the afternoon. A man who hasn't had much experience, and doesn't think, is apt to measure a nation's prosperity or lack of prosperity by the mere size of the prevailing wages; if the wages be high, the nation is prosperous; if low, it isn't. Which is an error. It isn't what sum you get, it's how much you can buy with it, that's the important thing; and it's that that tells whether your wages are high in fact or only high in name. I could remember how it was in the time of our great civil war in the nineteenth century. In the North a carpenter got three dollars a day, gold valuation;

in the South he got fifty—payable in Confederate shinplasters worth a dollar a bushel. In the North a suit of overalls cost three dollars—a day's wages; in the South it cost seventy-five—which was two days' wages. Other things were in proportion. Consequently, wages were twice as high in the North as they were in the South, because the one wage had that much more purchasing power than the other had.

Yes, I made various acquaintances in the hamlet and a thing that gratified me a good deal was to find our new coins in circulation —lots of milrays, lots of mills, lots of cents, a good many nickels, and some silver; all this among the artisans and commonalty generally; yes, and even some gold—but that was at the bank, that is to say, the goldsmith's. I dropped in there while Marco, the son of Marco, was haggling with a shopkeeper over a quarter of a pound of salt, and asked for change for a twenty-dollar gold piece. They furnished it—that is, after they had chewed the piece, and rung it on the counter, and tried acid on it, and asked me where I got it, and who I was, and where I was from, and where I was going to, and when I expected to get there, and perhaps a couple of hundred more questions; and when they got aground, I went right on and furnished them a lot of information voluntarily; told them I owned a dog, and his name was Watch, and my first wife was a Free Will Baptist, and her grandfather was a Prohibitionist, and I used to know a man who had two thumbs on each hand and a wart on the inside of his upper lip, and died in the hope of a glorious resurrection, and so on, and so on, and so on, till even that hungry village questioner began to look satisfied, and also a shade put out; but he had to respect a man of my financial strength, and so he didn't give me any lip, but I noticed he took it out of his underlings, which was a perfectly natural thing to do. Yes, they changed my twenty, but I judged it strained the bank a little, which was a thing to be expected, for it was the same as walking into a paltry village store in the nineteenth century and requiring the boss of it to change a two thousand-dollar bill for you all of a sudden. He could do it, maybe; but at the same time he would wonder how a small farmer happened to be carrying so much money around in his pocket; which was probably this goldsmith's thought, too; for he followed me to the door and stood there gazing after me with reverent admiration.

Our new money was not only handsomely circulating, but its language was already glibly in use; that is to say, people had dropped the names of the former moneys, and spoke of things as being worth so many dollars or cents or mills or milrays now. It was very gratifying. We were progressing, that was sure.

I got to know several master mechanics, but about the most interesting fellow among them was the blacksmith, Dowley. He was a live man and a brisk talker, and had two journeymen and three apprentices, and was doing a raging business. In fact, he was getting rich, hand over fist, and was vastly respected. Marco was very proud of having such a man for a friend. He had taken me there ostensibly to let me see the big establishment which bought so much of his charcoal, but really to let me see what easy and almost familiar terms he was on with this great man. Dowley and I fraternized at once; I had had just such picked men, splendid fellows, under me in the Colt Arms Factory. I was bound to see more of him, so I invited him to come out to Marco's Sunday, and dine with us. Marco was appalled, and held his breath; and when the grandee accepted, he was so grateful that he almost forgot to be astonished at the condescension.

Marco's joy was exuberant—but only for a moment; then he grew thoughtful, then sad; and when he heard me tell Dowley I should have Dickon, the boss mason, and Smug, the boss wheelwright, out there, too, the coal-dust on his face turned to chalk, and he lost his grip. But I knew what was the matter with him; it was the expense. He saw ruin before him; he judged that his financial days were numbered. However, on our way to invite the others, I said:

"You must allow me to have these friends come; and you must also allow me to pay the costs."

His face cleared, and he said with spirit:

"But not all of it, not all of it. Ye cannot well bear a burden like to this alone."

I stopped him, and said:

"Now let's understand each other on the spot, old friend. I am only a farm bailiff, it is true; but I am not poor, nevertheless. I have been very fortunate this year—you would be astonished to know how I have thriven. I tell you the honest truth when I say I could squander away as many as a dozen feasts like this and never care *that* for the expense!" and I snapped my fingers. I could see myself rise a foot at a time in Marco's estimation, and when I fetched out those last words I was become a very tower for style and altitude. "So you see, you must let me have my way. You can't contribute a cent to this orgy, that's *settled*."

"It's grand and good of you—"

"No, it isn't. You've opened your house to Jones and me in the most generous way; Jones was remarking upon it to-day, just before you came back from the village; for although he wouldn't be likely to say such a thing to you—because Jones isn't a talker, and is diffident in society—he has a good heart and a grateful, and knows how to appreciate it when he is well treated; yes, you and your wife have been very hospitable toward us—"

"Ah, brother, 'tis nothing—*such* hospitality!"

"But it *is* something; the best a man has, freely given, is always something, and is as good as a prince can do, and ranks right along beside it—for even a prince can but do his best. And so we'll shop around and get up this layout now, and don't you worry about the expense. I'm one of the worst spendthrifts that ever was born. Why, do you know, sometimes in a single week I spend —but never mind about that—you'd never believe it anyway."

And so we went gadding along, dropping in here and there, pricing things, and gossiping with the shopkeepers about the riot, and now and then running across pathetic reminders of it, in the persons of shunned and tearful and houseless remnants of families whose homes had been taken from them and their parents butchered or hanged. The raiment of Marco and his wife was of coarse tow-linen and linsey-woolsey respectively, and resembled township maps, it being made up pretty exclusively of patches which had been added, township by township, in the course of five or six years, until hardly a hand's-breadth of the original garments was surviving and present. Now I wanted to fit these people out with new suits, on account of that swell company, and I didn't know just how to get at it —with delicacy, until at last it struck me that as I had already been liberal in inventing wordy gratitude for the king, it would be just the thing to back it up with evidence of a substantial sort; so I said:

"And Marco, there's another thing which you must permit—out of kindness for Jones—because you wouldn't want to offend him. He was very anxious to testify his appreciation in some way, but he is so diffident he couldn't venture it himself, and so he begged me to buy some little things and give them to you and Dame Phyllis and let him pay for them without your ever knowing they came from him—you know how a delicate person feels about that sort of thing —and so I said I would, and we would keep mum. Well, his idea was, a new outfit of clothes for you both—"

"Oh, it is wastefulness! It may not be, brother, it may not be. Consider the vastness of the sum—"

"Hang the vastness of the sum! Try to keep quiet for a moment, and see how it would seem; a body can't get in a word edgeways, you talk so much. You ought to cure that, Marco; it isn't good form, you know, and it will grow on you if you don't check it. Yes, we'll step in here now and price this man's stuff—and don't forget to remember to not let on to Jones that you know he had anything to do with it. You can't think how curiously sensitive and proud he is. He's a farmer—pretty fairly well-to-do farmer —an I'm his bailiff; *but*—the imagination of that man! Why, sometimes when he forgets himself and gets to blowing off, you'd think he was one of the swells of the earth; and you might listen to him a hundred years and never take him for a farmer—especially if he talked agriculture. He *thinks* he's a Sheol of a farmer; thinks he's old Grayback from Wayback; but between you and me privately he don't know as much about farming as he does about running a kingdom—still, whatever he talks about, you want to drop your underjaw and listen, the same as if you had never heard such incredible wisdom in all your life before, and were afraid you might die before you got enough of it. That will please Jones."

It tickled Marco to the marrow to hear about such an odd character; but it also prepared him for accidents; and in my experience when you travel with a king who is letting on to be something else and can't remember it more than about half the time, you can't take too many precautions.

This was the best store we had come across yet; it had everything in it, in small quantities, from anvils and drygoods all the way down to fish and pinchbeck jewelry. I concluded I would bunch my whole invoice right here, and not go pricing around any more. So I got rid of Marco, by sending him off to invite the mason and the wheelwright, which left the field free to me. For I never care to do a thing in a quiet way; it's got to be theatrical or I don't take any interest in it. I showed up money enough, in a careless way, to corral the shopkeeper's respect, and then I wrote down a list of the things I wanted, and handed it to him to see if he could read it. He could, and was proud to show that he could. He said he had been educated by a priest, and could both read and write. He ran it through, and remarked with satisfaction that it was a pretty heavy bill. Well, and so it was, for a little concern like that. I was not only providing a swell dinner, but some odds and ends of extras. I ordered that the things be carted out and delivered at the dwelling of Marco, the son of Marco, by Saturday evening, and send me the bill at dinner-time Sunday. He said I could depend upon his promptness and exactitude, it was the rule of the house. He also observed that he would throw in a couple of miller-guns for the Marcos gratis—that everybody was using them now. He had a mighty opinion of that clever device. I said:

"And please fill them up to the middle mark, too; and add that to the bill."

He would, with pleasure. He filled them, and I took them with me. I couldn't venture to tell him that the miller-gun was a little invention of my own, and that I had officially ordered that every shopkeeper in the kingdom keep them on hand and sell them at government price—which was the merest trifle, and the shopkeeper got that, not the government. We furnished them for nothing.

The king had hardly missed us when we got back at nightfall. He had early dropped again into his dream of a grand invasion of Gaul with the whole strength of his kingdom at his back, and the afternoon had slipped away without his ever coming to himself again.

CHAPTER XXXII

DOWLEY'S HUMILIATION

Well, when that cargo arrived toward sunset, Saturday afternoon, I had my hands full to keep the Marcos from fainting. They were sure Jones and I were ruined past help, and they blamed themselves as accessories to this bankruptcy. You see, in addition to the dinner-materials, which called for a sufficiently round sum, I had bought a lot of extras for the future comfort of the family: for instance, a big lot of wheat, a delicacy as rare to the tables of their class as was ice-cream to a hermit's; also a sizeable deal dinner-table; also two entire pounds of salt, which was another piece of extravagance in those people's eyes; also crockery, stools, the clothes, a small cask of beer, and so on. I instructed the Marcos to keep quiet about this sumptuousness, so as to give me a chance to surprise the guests and show off a little. Concerning the new clothes, the simple couple were like children; they were up and down, all night, to see if it wasn't nearly daylight, so that they could put them on, and they were into them at last as much as an hour before dawn was due. Then their pleasure—not to say delirium—was so fresh and novel and inspiring that the sight of it paid me well for the interruptions which my sleep had suffered. The king had slept just as usual—like the dead. The Marcos could not thank him for their clothes, that being forbidden; but they tried every way they could think of to make him see how grateful they were. Which all went for nothing: he didn't notice any change.

It turned out to be one of those rich and rare fall days which is just a June day toned down to a degree where it is heaven to be out of doors. Toward noon the guests arrived, and we assembled under a great tree and were soon as sociable as old acquaintances. Even the king's reserve melted a little, though it was some little trouble to him to adjust himself to the name of Jones along at first. I had asked him to try to not forget that he was a farmer; but I had also considered it prudent to ask him to let the thing stand at that, and not elaborate it any. Because he was just the kind of person you could depend on to spoil a little thing like that if you didn't warn him, his tongue was so handy, and his spirit so willing, and his information so uncertain.

Dowley was in fine feather, and I early got him started, and then adroitly worked him around onto his own history for a text and himself for a hero, and then it was good to sit there and hear him hum. Self-made man, you know. They know how to talk. They do deserve more credit than any other breed of men, yes, that is true; and they are among the very first to find it out, too. He told how he had begun life an orphan lad without money and without friends able to help him; how he had lived as the slaves of the meanest master lived; how his day's work was from sixteen to eighteen hours long, and yielded him only enough black bread to keep him in a half-fed condition; how his faithful endeavors finally attracted the attention of a good blacksmith, who came near knocking him dead with kindness by suddenly offering, when he was totally unprepared, to take him as his bound apprentice for nine years and give him board and clothes and teach him the trade—or "mystery" as Dowley called it. That was his first great rise, his first gorgeous stroke of fortune; and you saw that he couldn't yet speak of it without a sort of eloquent wonder and delight that such a gilded promotion should have fallen to the lot of a common human being. He got no new clothing during his apprenticeship, but on his graduation day his master tricked him out in spang-new tow-linens and made him feel unspeakably rich and fine.

"I remember me of that day!" the wheelwright sang out, with enthusiasm.

"And I likewise!" cried the mason. "I would not believe they were thine own; in faith I could not."

"Nor other!" shouted Dowley, with sparkling eyes. "I was like to lose my character, the neighbors wending I had mayhap been stealing. It was a great day, a great day; one forgetteth not days like that."

Yes, and his master was a fine man, and prosperous, and always had a great feast of meat twice in the year, and with it white bread, true wheaten bread; in fact, lived like a lord, so to speak. And in time Dowley succeeded to the business and married the daughter.

"And now consider what is come to pass," said he, impressively. "Two times in every month there is fresh meat upon my table." He made a pause here, to let that fact sink home, then added —"and eight times salt meat."

"It is even true," said the wheelwright, with bated breath.

"I know it of mine own knowledge," said the mason, in the same reverent fashion.

"On my table appeareth white bread every Sunday in the year," added the master smith, with solemnity. "I leave it to your own consciences, friends, if this is not also true?"

"By my head, yes," cried the mason.

"I can testify it—and I do," said the wheelwright.

"And as to furniture, ye shall say yourselves what mine equipment is." He waved his hand in fine gesture of granting frank and unhampered freedom of speech, and added: "Speak as ye are moved; speak as ye would speak; an I were not here."

"Ye have five stools, and of the sweetest workmanship at that, albeit your family is but three," said the wheelwright, with deep respect.

"And six wooden goblets, and six platters of wood and two of pewter to eat and drink from withal," said the mason, impressively. "And I say it as knowing God is my judge, and we tarry not here alway, but must answer at the last day for the things said in the body, be they false or be they sooth."

"Now ye know what manner of man I am, brother Jones," said the smith, with a fine and friendly condescension, "and doubtless ye would look to find me a man jealous of his due of respect and but sparing of outgo to strangers till their rating and quality be assured, but trouble yourself not, as concerning that; wit ye well ye shall find me a man that regardeth not these matters but is willing to receive any he as his fellow and equal that carrieth a right heart in his body, be his worldly estate howsoever modest. And in token of it, here is my hand; and I say with my own mouth we are equals—equals"—and he smiled around on the company with the satisfaction of a god who is doing the handsome and gracious thing and is quite well aware of it.

The king took the hand with a poorly disguised reluctance, and let go of it as willingly as a lady lets go of a fish; all of which had a good effect, for it was mistaken for an embarrassment natural to one who was being called upon by greatness.

The dame brought out the table now, and set it under the tree. It caused a visible stir of surprise, it being brand new and a sumptuous article of deal. But the surprise rose higher still when the dame, with a body oozing easy indifference at every pore, but eyes that gave it all away by absolutely flaming with vanity, slowly unfolded an actual simon-pure tablecloth and spread it. That was a notch above even the blacksmith's domestic grandeurs, and it hit him hard; you could see it. But Marco was in Paradise; you could see that, too. Then the dame brought two fine new stools—whew! that was a sensation; it was visible in the eyes of every guest. Then she brought two more—as calmly as she could. Sensation again—with awed murmurs. Again she brought two —walking on air, she was so proud. The guests were petrified, and the mason muttered:

"There is that about earthly pomps which doth ever move to reverence."

As the dame turned away, Marco couldn't help slapping on the climax while the thing was hot; so he said with what was meant for a languid composure but was a poor imitation of it:

"These suffice; leave the rest."

So there were more yet! It was a fine effect. I couldn't have played the hand better myself.

From this out, the madam piled up the surprises with a rush that fired the general astonishment up to a hundred and fifty in the shade, and at the same time paralyzed expression of it down to gasped "Oh's" and "Ah's," and mute upliftings of hands and eyes. She fetched crockery—new, and plenty of it; new wooden goblets and other table furniture; and beer, fish, chicken, a goose, eggs, roast beef, roast mutton, a ham, a small roast pig, and a wealth of genuine white wheaten bread. Take it by and large, that spread laid everything far and away in the shade that ever that crowd had seen before. And while they sat there just simply stupefied with wonder and awe, I sort of waved my hand as if by accident, and the storekeeper's son emerged from space and said he had come to collect.

"That's all right," I said, indifferently. "What is the amount? give us the items."

Then he read off this bill, while those three amazed men listened, and serene waves of satisfaction rolled over my soul and alternate waves of terror and admiration surged over Marco's:

2 pounds salt	200
8 dozen pints beer, in the wood	800
3 bushels wheat	2,700
2 pounds fish	100
3 hens	400
1 goose	400
3 dozen eggs	150
1 roast of beef	450
1 roast of mutton	400
1 ham	800
1 sucking pig	500
2 crockery dinner sets	6,000
2 men's suits and underwear	2,800
1 stuff and 1 linsey-woolsey gown and underwear	
	1,600
8 wooden goblets	800
Various table furniture	10,000
1 deal table	3,000
8 stools	4,000
2 miller guns, loaded	3,000

He ceased. There was a pale and awful silence. Not a limb stirred. Not a nostril betrayed the passage of breath.

"Is that all?" I asked, in a voice of the most perfect calmness.

"All, fair sir, save that certain matters of light moment are placed together under a head hight sundries. If it would like you, I will sepa—"

"It is of no consequence," I said, accompanying the words with a gesture of the most utter indifference; "give me the grand total, please."

The clerk leaned against the tree to stay himself, and said:

"Thirty-nine thousand one hundred and fifty milrays!"

The wheelwright fell off his stool, the others grabbed the table to save themselves, and there was a deep and general ejaculation of:

"God be with us in the day of disaster!"

The clerk hastened to say:

"My father chargeth me to say he cannot honorably require you to pay it all at this time, and therefore only prayeth you—"

I paid no more heed than if it were the idle breeze, but, with an air of indifference amounting almost to weariness, got out my money and tossed four dollars on to the table. Ah, you should have seen them stare!

The clerk was astonished and charmed. He asked me to retain one of the dollars as security, until he could go to town and —I interrupted:

"What, and fetch back nine cents? Nonsense! Take the whole. Keep the change."

There was an amazed murmur to this effect:

"Verily this being is *made* of money! He throweth it away even as if it were dirt."

The blacksmith was a crushed man.

The clerk took his money and reeled away drunk with fortune. I said to Marco and his wife:

"Good folk, here is a little trifle for you"—handing the miller-guns as if it were a matter of no consequence, though each of them contained fifteen cents in solid cash; and while the poor creatures went to pieces with astonishment and gratitude, I turned to the others and said as calmly as one would ask the time of day:

"Well, if we are all ready, I judge the dinner is. Come, fall to."

Ah, well, it was immense; yes, it was a daisy. I don't know that I ever put a situation together better, or got happier spectacular effects out of the materials available. The blacksmith—well, he was simply mashed. Land! I wouldn't have felt what that man was feeling, for anything in the world. Here he had been blowing and bragging about his grand meat-feast twice a year, and his fresh meat twice a month, and his salt meat twice a week, and his white bread every Sunday the year round—all for a family of three; the entire cost for the year not above 69.2.6 (sixty-nine cents, two mills and six milrays), and all of a sudden here comes along a man who slashes out nearly four dollars on a single blow-out; and not only that, but acts as if it made him tired to handle such small sums. Yes, Dowley was a good deal wilted, and shrunk-up and collapsed; he had the aspect of a bladder-balloon that's been stepped on by a cow.

CHAPTER XXXIII

SIXTH CENTURY POLITICAL ECONOMY

However, I made a dead set at him, and before the first third of the dinner was reached, I had him happy again. It was easy to do—in a country of ranks and castes. You see, in a country where they have ranks and castes, a man isn't ever a man, he is only part of a man, he can't ever get his full growth. You prove your superiority over him in station, or rank, or fortune, and that's the end of it—he knuckles down. You can't insult him after that. No, I don't mean quite that; of course you *can* insult him, I only mean it's difficult; and so, unless you've got a lot of useless time on your hands it doesn't pay to try. I had the smith's reverence now, because I was apparently immensely prosperous and rich; I could have had his adoration if I had had some little gimcrack title of nobility. And not only his, but any commoner's in the land, though he were the mightiest production of all the ages, in intellect, worth, and character, and I bankrupt in all three. This was to remain so, as long as England should exist in the earth. With the spirit of prophecy upon me, I could look into the future and see her erect statues and monuments to her unspeakable Georges and other royal and noble clothes-horses, and leave unhonored the creators of this world—after God—Gutenburg, Watt, Arkwright, Whitney, Morse, Stephenson, Bell.

The king got his cargo aboard, and then, the talk not turning upon battle, conquest, or iron-clad duel, he dulled down to drowsiness and went off to take a nap. Mrs. Marco cleared the table, placed the beer keg handy, and went away to eat her dinner of leavings in humble privacy, and the rest of us soon drifted into matters near and dear to the hearts of our sort—business and wages, of course. At a first glance, things appeared to be exceeding prosperous in this little tributary kingdom—whose lord was King Bagdemagus—as compared with the state of things in my own region. They had the "protection" system in full force here, whereas we were working along down toward free-trade, by easy stages, and were now about half way. Before long, Dowley and I were doing all the talking, the others hungrily listening. Dowley warmed to his work, snuffed an advantage in the air, and began to put questions which he considered pretty awkward ones for me, and they did have something of that look:

"In your country, brother, what is the wage of a master bailiff, master hind, carter, shepherd, swineherd?"

"Twenty-five milrays a day; that is to say, a quarter of a cent."

The smith's face beamed with joy. He said:

"With us they are allowed the double of it! And what may a mechanic get—carpenter, dauber, mason, painter, blacksmith, wheelwright, and the like?"

"On the average, fifty milrays; half a cent a day."

"Ho-ho! With us they are allowed a hundred! With us any good mechanic is allowed a cent a day! I count out the tailor, but not the others—they are all allowed a cent a day, and in driving times they get more—yes, up to a hundred and ten and even fifteen milrays a day. I've paid a hundred and fifteen myself, within the week. 'Rah for protection—to Sheol with free-trade!"

And his face shone upon the company like a sunburst. But I didn't scare at all. I rigged up my pile-driver, and allowed myself fifteen minutes to drive him into the earth—drive him *all* in —drive him in till not even the curve of his skull should show above ground. Here is the way I started in on him. I asked:

"What do you pay a pound for salt?"

"A hundred milrays."

"We pay forty. What do you pay for beef and mutton—when you buy it?" That was a neat hit; it made the color come.

"It varieth somewhat, but not much; one may say seventy-five milrays the pound."

"*We* pay thirty-three. What do you pay for eggs?"

"Fifty milrays the dozen."

"We pay twenty. What do you pay for beer?"

"It costeth us eight and one-half milrays the pint."

"We get it for four; twenty-five bottles for a cent. What do you pay for wheat?"

"At the rate of nine hundred milrays the bushel."

"We pay four hundred. What do you pay for a man's tow-linen suit?"

"Thirteen cents."

"We pay six. What do you pay for a stuff gown for the wife of the laborer or the mechanic?"

"We pay eight cents, four mills."

"Well, observe the difference: you pay eight cents and four

mills, we pay only four cents." I prepared now to sock it to him. I said: "Look here, dear friend, *what's become of your high wages you were bragging so about a few minutes ago?*"—and I looked around on the company with placid satisfaction, for I had slipped up on him gradually and tied him hand and foot, you see, without his ever noticing that he was being tied at all. "What's become of those noble high wages of yours?—I seem to have knocked the stuffing all out of them, it appears to me."

But if you will believe me, he merely looked surprised, that is all! he didn't grasp the situation at all, didn't know he had walked into a trap, didn't discover that he was *in* a trap. I could have shot him, from sheer vexation. With cloudy eye and a struggling intellect he fetched this out:

"Marry, I seem not to understand. It is *proved* that our wages be double thine; how then may it be that thou'st knocked therefrom the stuffing?—an miscall not the wonderly word, this being the first time under grace and providence of God it hath been granted me to hear it."

Well, I was stunned; partly with this unlooked-for stupidity on his part, and partly because his fellows so manifestly sided with him and were of his mind—if you might call it mind. My position was simple enough, plain enough; how could it ever be simplified more? However, I must try:

"Why, look here, brother Dowley, don't you see? Your wages are merely higher than ours in *name*, not in *fact*."

"Hear him! They are the *double*—ye have confessed it yourself."

"Yes-yes, I don't deny that at all. But that's got nothing to do with it; the *amount* of the wages in mere coins, with meaningless names attached to them to know them by, has got nothing to do with it. The thing is, how much can you *buy* with your wages? —that's the idea. While it is true that with you a good mechanic is allowed about three dollars and a half a year, and with us only about a dollar and seventy-five—"

"There—ye're confessing it again, ye're confessing it again!"

"Confound it, I've never denied it, I tell you! What I say is this. With us *half* a dollar buys more than a *dollar* buys with you— and THEREFORE it stands to reason and the commonest kind of common-sense, that our wages are *higher* than yours."

He looked dazed, and said, despairingly:

"Verily, I cannot make it out. Ye've just said ours are the higher, and with the same breath ye take it back."

"Oh, great Scott, isn't it possible to get such a simple thing through your head? Now look here—let me illustrate. We pay four cents for a woman's stuff gown, you pay 8.4.0, which is four mills more than *double*. What do you allow a laboring woman who works on a farm?"

"Two mills a day."

"Very good; we allow but half as much; we pay her only a tenth of a cent a day; and—"

"Again ye're conf—"

"Wait! Now, you see, the thing is very simple; this time you'll understand it. For instance, it takes your woman 42 days to earn her gown, at 2 mills a day—7 weeks' work; but ours earns hers in forty days—two days *short* of 7 weeks. Your woman has a gown, and her whole seven weeks wages are gone; ours has a gown, and two days' wages left, to buy something else with. There—*now* you understand it!"

He looked—well, he merely looked dubious, it's the most I can say; so did the others. I waited—to let the thing work. Dowley spoke at last—and betrayed the fact that he actually hadn't gotten away from his rooted and grounded superstitions yet. He said, with a trifle of hesitancy:

"But—but—ye cannot fail to grant that two mills a day is better than one."

Shucks! Well, of course, I hated to give it up. So I chanced another flyer:

"Let us suppose a case. Suppose one of your journeymen goes out and buys the following articles:

"1 pound of salt; 1 dozen eggs; 1 dozen pints of beer; 1 bushel of wheat; 1 tow-linen suit; 5 pounds of beef; 5 pounds of mutton.

"The lot will cost him 32 cents. It takes him 32 working days to earn the money—5 weeks and 2 days. Let him come to us and work 32 days at *half* the wages; he can buy all those things for a shade under 14½ cents; they will cost him a shade under 29 days' work, and he will have about half a week's wages over. Carry it through the year; he would save nearly a week's wages every two months, *your* man nothing; thus saving five or six weeks' wages in a year, your man not a cent. *Now* I reckon you understand that 'high wages' and 'low wages' are phrases that don't mean anything in the world until you find out which of them will *buy* the most!"

It was a crusher.

But, alas! it didn't crush. No, I had to give it up. What those people valued was *high wages*; it didn't seem to be a matter of any consequence to them whether the high wages would buy anything or not. They stood for "protection," and swore by it, which was reasonable enough, because interested parties had gulled them into the notion that it was protection which had created their high wages. I proved to them that in a quarter of a century their wages had advanced but 30 per cent., while the cost of living had gone up 100; and that with us, in a shorter time, wages had advanced 40 per cent. while the cost of living had gone steadily down. But it didn't do any good. Nothing could unseat their strange beliefs.

Well, I was smarting under a sense of defeat. Undeserved defeat, but what of that? That didn't soften the smart any. And to think of the circumstances! the first statesman of the age, the capablest man, the best-informed man in the entire world, the loftiest uncrowned head that had moved through the clouds of any political firmament for centuries, sitting here apparently defeated in argument by an ignorant country blacksmith! And I could see that those others were sorry for me—which made me blush till I could smell my whiskers scorching. Put yourself in my place; feel as mean as I did, as ashamed as I felt—wouldn't *you* have struck below the belt to get even? Yes, you would; it is simply human nature. Well, that is what I did. I am not trying to justify it; I'm only saying that I was mad, and *anybody* would have done it.

Well, when I make up my mind to hit a man, I don't plan out a love-tap; no, that isn't my way; as long as I'm going to hit him at all, I'm going to hit him a lifter. And I don't jump at him all of a sudden, and risk making a blundering half-way business of it; no, I get away off yonder to one side, and work up on him gradually, so that he never suspects that I'm going to hit him at all; and by and by, all in a flash, he's flat on his back, and he can't tell for the life of him how it all happened. That is the way I went for brother Dowley. I started to talking lazy and comfortable, as if I was just talking to pass the time; and the oldest man in the world couldn't have taken the bearings of my starting place and guessed where I was going to fetch up:

"Boys, there's a good many curious things about law, and custom, and usage, and all that sort of thing, when you come to look at it; yes, and about the drift and progress of human opinion and movement, too. There are written laws—they perish; but there are also unwritten laws—*they* are eternal. Take the unwritten law of wages: it says they've got to advance, little by little, straight through the centuries. And notice how it works. We know what wages are now, here and there and yonder; we strike an average, and say that's the wages of to-day. We know what the wages were a hundred years ago, and what they were two hundred years ago; that's as far back as we can get, but it suffices to give us the law of progress, the measure and rate of the periodical augmentation; and so, without a document to help us, we can come pretty close to determining what the wages were three and four and five hundred years ago. Good, so far. Do we stop there? No. We stop looking backward; we face around and apply the law to the future. My friends, I can tell you what people's wages are going to be at any date in the future you want to know, for hundreds and hundreds of years."

"What, goodman, what!"

"Yes. In seven hundred years wages will have risen to six times what they are now, here in your region, and farm hands will be allowed 3 cents a day, and mechanics 6."

"I would't I might die now and live then!" interrupted Smug, the wheelwright, with a fine avaricious glow in his eye.

"And that isn't all; they'll get their board besides—such as it is: it won't bloat them. Two hundred and fifty years later—pay attention now—a mechanic's wages will be—mind you, this is law, not guesswork; a mechanic's wages will then be *twenty* cents a day!"

There was a general gasp of awed astonishment, Dickon the mason murmured, with raised eyes and hands:

"More than three weeks' pay for one day's work!"

"Riches!—of a truth, yes, riches!" muttered Marco, his breath coming quick and short, with excitement.

"Wages will keep on rising, little by little, little by little, as steadily as a tree grows, and at the end of three hundred and forty years more there'll be at least *one* country where the mechanic's average wage will be *two hundred* cents a day!"

It knocked them absolutely dumb! Not a man of them could get his breath for upwards of two minutes. Then the coal-burner said prayerfully:

"Might I but live to see it!"

"It is the income of an earl!" said Smug.

"An earl, say ye?" said Dowley; "ye could say more than that and speak no lie; there's no earl in the realm of Bagdemagus that hath an income like to that. Income of an earl—mf! it's the income of an angel!"

"Now, then, that is what is going to happen as regards wages. In that remote day, that man will earn, with *one* week's work, that bill of goods which it takes you upwards of *fifty* weeks to earn now. Some other pretty surprising things are going to happen, too. Brother Dowley, who is it that determines, every spring, what the particular wage of each kind of mechanic, laborer, and servant shall be for that year?"

"Sometimes the courts, sometimes the town council; but most of all, the magistrate. Ye may say, in general terms, it is the magistrate that fixes the wages."

"Doesn't ask any of those poor devils to *help* him fix their wages for them, does he?"

"Hm! That *were* an idea! The master that's to pay him the money is the one that's rightly concerned in that matter, ye will notice."

"Yes—but I thought the other man might have some little trifle at stake in it, too; and even his wife and children, poor creatures. The masters are these: nobles, rich men, the prosperous generally. These few, who do no work, determine what pay the vast hive shall have who *do* work. You see? They're a 'combine'—a trade union, to coin a new phrase—who band themselves together to force their lowly brother to take what they choose to give. Thirteen hundred years hence—so says the unwritten law—the 'combine' will be the other way, and then how these fine people's posterity will fume and fret and grit their teeth over the insolent tyranny of trade unions! Yes, indeed! the magistrate will tranquilly arrange the wages from now clear away down into the nineteenth century; and then all of a sudden the wage-earner will consider that a couple of thousand years or so is enough of this one-sided sort of thing; and he will rise up and take a hand in fixing his wages himself. Ah, he will have a long and bitter account of wrong and humiliation to settle."

"Do ye believe—"

"That he actually will help to fix his own wages? Yes, indeed. And he will be strong and able, then."

"Brave times, brave times, of a truth!" sneered the prosperous smith.

"Oh,—and there's another detail. In that day, a master may hire a man for only just one day, or one week, or one month at a time, if he wants to."

"What?"

"It's true. Moreover, a magistrate won't be able to force a man to work for a master a whole year on a stretch whether the man wants to or not."

"Will there be *no* law or sense in that day?"

"Both of them, Dowley. In that day a man will be his own property, not the property of magistrate and master. And he can leave town whenever he wants to, if the wages don't suit

him!—and they can't put him in the pillory for it."

"Perdition catch such an age!" shouted Dowley, in strong indignation. "An age of dogs, an age barren of reverence for superiors and respect for authority! The pillory—"

"Oh, wait, brother; say no good word for that institution. I think the pillory ought to be abolished."

"A most strange idea. Why?"

"Well, I'll tell you why. Is a man ever put in the pillory for a capital crime?"

"No."

"Is it right to condemn a man to a slight punishment for a small offense and then kill him?"

There was no answer. I had scored my first point! For the first time, the smith wasn't up and ready. The company noticed it. Good effect.

"You don't answer, brother. You were about to glorify the pillory a while ago, and shed some pity on a future age that isn't going to use it. I think the pillory ought to be abolished. What usually happens when a poor fellow is put in the pillory for some little offense that didn't amount to anything in the world? The mob try to have some fun with him, don't they?"

"Yes."

"They begin by clodding him; and they laugh themselves to pieces to see him try to dodge one clod and get hit with another?"

"Yes."

"Then they throw dead cats at him, don't they?"

"Yes."

"Well, then, suppose he has a few personal enemies in that mob and here and there a man or a woman with a secret grudge against him—and suppose especially that he is unpopular in the community, for his pride, or his prosperity, or one thing or another—stones and bricks take the place of clods and cats presently, don't they?"

"There is no doubt of it."

"As a rule he is crippled for life, isn't he?—jaws broken, teeth smashed out?—or legs mutilated, gangrened, presently cut off? —or an eye knocked out, maybe both eyes?"

"It is true, God knoweth it."

"And if he is unpopular he can depend on *dying*, right there in the stocks, can't he?"

"He surely can! One may not deny it."

"I take it none of *you* are unpopular—by reason of pride or insolence, or conspicuous prosperity, or any of those things that excite envy and malice among the base scum of a village? *You* wouldn't think it much of a risk to take a chance in the stocks?"

Dowley winced, visibly. I judged he was hit. But he didn't betray it by any spoken word. As for the others, they spoke out plainly, and with strong feeling. They said they had seen enough of the stocks to know what a man's chance in them was, and they would never consent to enter them if they could compromise on a quick death by hanging.

"Well, to change the subject—for I think I've established my point that the stocks ought to be abolished. I think some of our laws are pretty unfair. For instance, if I do a thing which ought to deliver me to the stocks, and you know I did it and yet keep still and don't report me, *you* will get the stocks if anybody informs on you."

"Ah, but that would serve you but right," said Dowley, "for you *must* inform. So saith the law."

The others coincided.

"Well, all right, let it go, since you vote me down. But there's one thing which certainly isn't fair. The magistrate fixes a mechanic's wage at one cent a day, for instance. The law says that if any master shall venture, even under utmost press of business, to pay anything *over* that cent a day, even for a single day, he shall be both fined and pilloried for it; and whoever knows he did it and doesn't inform, they also shall be fined and pilloried. Now it seems to me unfair, Dowley, and a deadly peril to all of us, that because you thoughtlessly confessed, a while ago, that within a week you have paid a cent and fifteen mil—"

Oh, I tell *you* it was a smasher! You ought to have seen them to go to pieces, the whole gang. I had just slipped up on poor smiling and complacent Dowley so nice and easy and softly, that he never suspected anything was going to happen till the blow came crashing down and knocked him all to rags.

A fine effect. In fact, as fine as any I ever produced, with so little time to work it up in.

But I saw in a moment that I had overdone the thing a little. I was expecting to scare them, but I wasn't expecting to scare them to death. They were mighty near it, though. You see they had been a whole lifetime learning to appreciate the pillory; and to have that thing staring them in the face, and every one of them distinctly at the mercy of me, a stranger, if I chose to go and report—well, it was awful, and they couldn't seem to recover from the shock, they couldn't seem to pull themselves together. Pale, shaky, dumb, pitiful? Why, they weren't any better than so many dead men. It was very uncomfortable. Of course, I thought they would appeal to me to keep mum, and then we would shake hands, and take a drink all round, and laugh it off, and there an end. But no; you see I was an unknown person, among a cruelly oppressed and suspicious people, a people always accustomed to having advantage taken of their helplessness, and never expecting just or kind treatment from any but their own families and very closest intimates. Appeal to *me* to be gentle, to be fair, to be generous? Of course, they wanted to, but they couldn't dare.

CHAPTER XXXIV

THE YANKEE AND THE KING SOLD AS SLAVES

Well, what had I better do? Nothing in a hurry, sure. I must get up a diversion; anything to employ me while I could think, and while these poor fellows could have a chance to come to life again. There sat Marco, petrified in the act of trying to get

the hang of his miller-gun—turned to stone, just in the attitude he was in when my pile-driver fell, the toy still gripped in his unconscious fingers. So I took it from him and proposed to explain its mystery. Mystery! a simple little thing like that; and yet it was mysterious enough, for that race and that age.

I never saw such an awkward people, with machinery; you see, they were totally unused to it. The miller-gun was a little double-barreled tube of toughened glass, with a neat little trick of a spring to it, which upon pressure would let a shot escape. But the shot wouldn't hurt anybody, it would only drop into your hand. In the gun were two sizes—wee mustard-seed shot, and another sort that were several times larger. They were money. The mustard-seed shot represented milrays, the larger ones mills. So the gun was a purse; and very handy, too; you could pay out money in the dark with it, with accuracy; and you could carry it in your mouth; or in your vest pocket, if you had one. I made them of several sizes —one size so large that it would carry the equivalent of a dollar. Using shot for money was a good thing for the government; the metal cost nothing, and the money couldn't be counterfeited, for I was the only person in the kingdom who knew how to manage a shot tower. "Paying the shot" soon came to be a common phrase. Yes, and I knew it would still be passing men's lips, away down in the nineteenth century, yet none would suspect how and when it originated.

The king joined us, about this time, mightily refreshed by his nap, and feeling good. Anything could make me nervous now, I was so uneasy—for our lives were in danger; and so it worried me to detect a complacent something in the king's eye which seemed to indicate that he had been loading himself up for a performance of some kind or other; confound it, why must he go and choose such a time as this?

I was right. He began, straight off, in the most innocently artful, and transparent, and lubberly way, to lead up to the subject of agriculture. The cold sweat broke out all over me. I wanted to whisper in his ear, "Man, we are in awful danger! every moment is worth a principality till we get back these men's confidence; *don't* waste any of this golden time." But of course I couldn't do it. Whisper to him? It would look as if we were conspiring. So I had to sit there and look calm and pleasant while the king stood over that dynamite mine and mooned along about his damned onions and things. At first the tumult of my own thoughts, summoned by the danger-signal and swarming to the rescue from every quarter of my skull, kept up such a hurrah and confusion and fifing and drumming that I couldn't take in a word; but presently when my mob of gathering plans began to crystallize and fall into position and form line of battle, a sort of order and quiet ensued and I caught the boom of the king's batteries, as if out of remote distance:

"—were not the best way, methinks, albeit it is not to be denied that authorities differ as concerning this point, some contending that the onion is but an unwholesome berry when stricken early from the tree—"

The audience showed signs of life, and sought each other's eyes in a surprised and troubled way.

"—whileas others do yet maintain, with much show of reason, that this is not of necessity the case, instancing that plums and other like cereals do be always dug in the unripe state—"

The audience exhibited distinct distress; yes, and also fear.

"—yet are they clearly wholesome, the more especially when one doth assuage the asperities of their nature by admixture of the tranquilizing juice of the wayward cabbage—"

The wild light of terror began to glow in these men's eyes, and one of them muttered, "These be errors, every one—God hath surely smitten the mind of this farmer." I was in miserable apprehension; I sat upon thorns.

"—and further instancing the known truth that in the case of animals, the young, which may be called the green fruit of the creature, is the better, all confessing that when a goat is ripe, his fur doth heat and sore engame his flesh, the which defect, taken in connection with his several rancid habits, and fulsome appetites, and godless attitudes of mind, and bilious quality of morals—"

They rose and went for him! With a fierce shout, "The one would betray us, the other is mad! Kill them! Kill them!" they flung themselves upon us. What joy flamed up in the king's eye! He might be lame in agriculture, but this kind of thing was just in his line. He had been fasting long, he was hungry for a fight. He hit the blacksmith a crack under the jaw that lifted him clear off his feet and stretched him flat on his back. "St. George for Britain!" and he downed the wheelwright. The mason was big, but I laid him out like nothing. The three gathered themselves up and came again; went down again; came again; and kept on repeating this, with native British pluck, until they were battered to jelly, reeling with exhaustion, and so blind that they couldn't tell us from each other; and yet they kept right on, hammering away with what might be left in them. Hammering each other—for we stepped aside and looked on while they rolled, and struggled, and gouged, and pounded, and bit, with the strict and wordless attention to business of so many bulldogs. We looked on without apprehension, for they were fast getting past ability to go for help against us, and the arena was far enough from the public road to be safe from intrusion.

Well, while they were gradually playing out, it suddenly occurred to me to wonder what had become of Marco. I looked around; he was nowhere to be seen. Oh, but this was ominous! I pulled the king's sleeve, and we glided away and rushed for the hut. No Marco there, no Phyllis there! They had gone to the road for help, sure. I told the king to give his heels wings, and I would explain later. We made good time across the open ground, and as we darted into the shelter of the wood I glanced back and saw a mob of excited peasants swarm into view, with Marco and his wife at their head. They were making a world of noise, but that couldn't hurt anybody; the wood was dense, and as soon as we were well into its depths we would take to a tree and let them whistle. Ah, but then came another sound—dogs! Yes, that was quite another matter. It magnified our contract—we must find running water.

We tore along at a good gait, and soon left the sounds far behind and modified to a murmur. We struck a stream and darted into it. We waded swiftly down it, in the dim forest light, for as much as three hundred yards, and then came across an oak with a great bough sticking out over the water. We climbed up on this bough, and began to work our way along it to the body of the tree; now we began to hear those sounds more plainly; so the mob had struck our trail. For a while the sounds approached pretty fast. And then for another while they didn't. No doubt the dogs had found the place where we had entered the stream, and were now waltzing up and down the shores trying to pick up the trail again.

When we were snugly lodged in the tree and curtained with foliage, the king was satisfied, but I was doubtful. I believed we could crawl along a branch and get into the next tree, and I judged it worth while to try. We tried it, and made a success of it, though the king slipped, at the junction, and came near failing to connect. We got comfortable lodgment and satisfactory concealment among the foliage, and then we had nothing to do but listen to the hunt.

Presently we heard it coming—and coming on the jump, too; yes, and down both sides of the stream. Louder—louder—next minute it swelled swiftly up into a roar of shoutings, barkings, tramplings, and swept by like a cyclone.

"I was afraid that the overhanging branch would suggest something to them," said I, "but I don't mind the disappointment. Come, my liege, it were well that we make good use of our time. We've flanked them. Dark is coming on, presently. If we can cross the stream and get a good start, and borrow a couple of horses from somebody's pasture to use for a few hours, we shall be safe enough."

We started down, and got nearly to the lowest limb, when we seemed to hear the hunt returning. We stopped to listen.

"Yes," said I, "they're baffled, they've given it up, they're on their way home. We will climb back to our roost again, and let them go by."

So we climbed back. The king listened a moment and said:

"They still search—I wit the sign. We did best to abide."

He was right. He knew more about hunting than I did. The noise approached steadily, but not with a rush. The king said:

"They reason that we were advantaged by no parlous start of them, and being on foot are as yet no mighty way from where we took the water."

"Yes, sire, that is about it, I am afraid, though I was hoping better things."

The noise drew nearer and nearer, and soon the van was drifting under us, on both sides of the water. A voice called a halt from the other bank, and said:

"An they were so minded, they could get to yon tree by this branch that overhangs, and yet not touch ground. Ye will do well to send a man up it."

"Marry, that we will do!"

I was obliged to admire my cuteness in foreseeing this very thing and swapping trees to beat it. But, don't you know, there are some things that can beat smartness and foresight? Awkwardness and stupidity can. The best swordsman in the world doesn't need to fear the second best swordsman in the world; no, the person for him to be afraid of is some ignorant antagonist who has never had a sword in his hand before; he doesn't do the thing he ought to do, and so the expert isn't prepared for him; he does the thing he ought not to do; and often it catches the expert out and ends him on the spot. Well, how could I, with all my gifts, make any valuable preparation against a near-sighted, cross-eyed, pudding-headed clown who would aim himself at the wrong tree and hit the right one? And that is what he did. He went for the wrong tree, which was, of course, the right one by mistake, and up he started.

Matters were serious now. We remained still, and awaited developments. The peasant toiled his difficult way up. The king raised himself up and stood; he made a leg ready, and when the comer's head arrived in reach of it there was a dull thud, and down went the man floundering to the ground. There was a wild outbreak of anger below, and the mob swarmed in from all around, and there we were treed, and prisoners. Another man started up; the bridging bough was detected, and a volunteer started up the tree that furnished the bridge. The king ordered me to play Horatius and keep the bridge. For a while the enemy came thick and fast; but no matter, the head man of each procession always got a buffet that dislodged him as soon as he came in reach. The king's spirits rose, his joy was limitless. He said that if nothing occurred to mar the prospect we should have a beautiful night, for on this line of tactics we could hold the tree against the whole country-side.

However, the mob soon came to that conclusion themselves; wherefore they called off the assault and began to debate other plans. They had no weapons, but there were plenty of stones, and stones might answer. We had no objections. A stone might possibly penetrate to us once in a while, but it wasn't very likely; we were well protected by boughs and foliage, and were not visible from any good aiming point. If they would but waste half an hour in stone-throwing, the dark would come to our help. We were feeling very well satisfied. We could smile; almost laugh.

But we didn't; which was just as well, for we should have been interrupted. Before the stones had been raging through the leaves and bouncing from the boughs fifteen minutes, we began to notice a smell. A couple of sniffs of it was enough of an explanation —it was smoke! Our game was up at last. We recognized that. When smoke invites you, you have to come. They raised their pile of dry brush and damp weeds higher and higher, and when they saw the thick cloud begin to roll up and smother the tree, they broke out in a storm of joy-clamors. I got enough breath to say:

"Proceed, my liege; after you is manners."

The king gasped:

"Follow me down, and then back thyself against one side of the trunk, and leave me the other. Then will we fight. Let each pile his dead according to his own fashion and taste."

Then he descended, barking and coughing, and I followed. I struck the ground an instant after him; we sprang to our appointed places, and began to give and take with all our might. The powwow and racket were prodigious; it was a tempest of riot and confusion and thick-falling blows. Suddenly some horsemen tore into the midst of the crowd, and a voice shouted:

"Hold—or ye are dead men!"

How good it sounded! The owner of the voice bore all the marks of a gentleman: picturesque and costly raiment, the aspect of command, a hard countenance, with complexion and features marred by dissipation. The mob fell humbly back, like so many spaniels. The gentleman inspected us critically, then said sharply to the peasants:

"What are ye doing to these people?"

"They be madmen, worshipful sir, that have come wandering we know not whence, and—"

"Ye know not whence? Do ye pretend ye know them not?"

"Most honored sir, we speak but the truth. They are strangers and unknown to any in this region; and they be the most violent and bloodthirsty madmen that ever—"

"Peace! Ye know not what ye say. They are not mad. Who are ye? And whence are ye? Explain."

"We are but peaceful strangers, sir," I said, "and traveling upon our own concerns. We are from a far country, and unacquainted here. We have purposed no harm; and yet but for your brave interference and protection these people would have killed us. As you have divined, sir, we are not mad; neither are we violent or bloodthirsty."

The gentleman turned to his retinue and said calmly: "Lash me these animals to their kennels!"

The mob vanished in an instant; and after them plunged the horsemen, laying about them with their whips and pitilessly riding down such as were witless enough to keep the road instead of taking to the bush. The shrieks and supplications presently died away in the distance, and soon the horsemen began to straggle back. Meantime the gentleman had been questioning us more closely, but had dug no particulars out of us. We were lavish of recognition of the service he was doing us, but we revealed nothing more than that we were friendless strangers from a far country. When the escort were all returned, the gentleman said to one of his servants:

"Bring the led-horses and mount these people."

"Yes, my lord."

We were placed toward the rear, among the servants. We traveled pretty fast, and finally drew rein some time after dark at a roadside inn some ten or twelve miles from the scene of our troubles. My lord went immediately to his room, after ordering his supper, and we saw no more of him. At dawn in the morning we breakfasted and made ready to start.

My lord's chief attendant sauntered forward at that moment with indolent grace, and said:

"Ye have said ye should continue upon this road, which is our direction likewise; wherefore my lord, the earl Grip, hath given commandment that ye retain the horses and ride, and that certain of us ride with ye a twenty mile to a fair town that hight Cambenet, whenso ye shall be out of peril."

We could do nothing less than express our thanks and accept the offer. We jogged along, six in the party, at a moderate and comfortable gait, and in conversation learned that my lord Grip was a very great personage in his own region, which lay a day's journey beyond Cambenet. We loitered to such a degree that it was near the middle of the forenoon when we entered the market square of the town. We dismounted, and left our thanks once more for my lord, and then approached a crowd assembled in the center of the square, to see what might be the object of interest. It was the remnant of that old peregrinating band of slaves! So they had been dragging their chains about, all this weary time. That poor husband was gone, and also many others; and some few purchases had been added to the gang. The king was not interested, and wanted to move along, but I was absorbed, and full of pity. I could not take my eyes away from these worn and wasted wrecks of humanity. There they sat, grounded upon the ground, silent, uncomplaining, with bowed heads, a pathetic sight. And by hideous contrast, a redundant orator was making a speech to another gathering not thirty steps away, in fulsome laudation of "our glorious British liberties!"

I was boiling. I had forgotten I was a plebeian, I was remembering I was a man. Cost what it might, I would mount that rostrum and—

Click! the king and I were handcuffed together! Our companions, those servants, had done it; my lord Grip stood looking on. The king burst out in a fury, and said:

"What meaneth this ill-mannered jest?"

My lord merely said to his head miscreant, coolly:

"Put up the slaves and sell them!"

Slaves! The word had a new sound—and how unspeakably awful! The king lifted his manacles and brought them down with a deadly force; but my lord was out of the way when they arrived. A dozen of the rascal's servants sprang forward, and in a moment we were helpless, with our hands bound behind us. We so loudly and so earnestly proclaimed ourselves freemen, that we got the interested attention of that liberty-mouthing orator and his patriotic crowd, and they gathered about us and assumed a very determined attitude. The orator said:

"If, indeed, ye are freemen, ye have nought to fear—the God-given liberties of Britain are about ye for your shield and shelter! (Applause.) Ye shall soon see. Bring forth your proofs."

"What proofs?"

"Proof that ye are freemen."

Ah—I remembered! I came to myself; I said nothing. But the king stormed out:

"Thou'rt insane, man. It were better, and more in reason, that this thief and scoundrel here prove that we are *not* freemen."

You see, he knew his own laws just as other people so often know the laws; by words, not by effects. They take a *meaning*, and get to be very vivid, when you come to apply them to yourself.

All hands shook their heads and looked disappointed; some turned away, no longer interested. The orator said—and this time in the tones of business, not of sentiment:

"An ye do not know your country's laws, it were time ye learned them. Ye are strangers to us; ye will not deny that. Ye may be freemen, we do not deny that; but also ye may be slaves. The law is clear: it doth not require the claimant to prove ye are slaves, it requireth you to prove ye are not."

I said:

"Dear sir, give us only time to send to Astolat; or give us only time to send to the Valley of Holiness—"

"Peace, good man, these are extraordinary requests, and you may not hope to have them granted. It would cost much time, and would unwarrantably inconvenience your master—"

"*Master*, idiot!" stormed the king. "I have no master, I myself am the m—"

"Silence, for God's sake!"

I got the words out in time to stop the king. We were in trouble enough already; it could not help us any to give these people the notion that we were lunatics.

There is no use in stringing out the details. The earl put us up and sold us at auction. This same infernal law had existed in our own South in my own time, more than thirteen hundred years later, and under it hundreds of freemen who could not prove that they were freemen had been sold into lifelong slavery without the circumstance making any particular impression upon me; but the minute law and the auction block came into my personal experience, a thing which had been merely improper before became suddenly hellish. Well, that's the way we are made.

Yes, we were sold at auction, like swine. In a big town and an active market we should have brought a good price; but this place was utterly stagnant and so we sold at a figure which makes me ashamed, every time I think of it. The King of England brought seven dollars, and his prime minister nine; whereas the king was easily worth twelve dollars and I as easily worth fifteen. But that is the way things always go; if you force a sale on a dull market, I don't care what the property is, you are going to make a poor business of it, and you can make up your mind to it. If the earl had had wit enough to—

However, there is no occasion for my working my sympathies up on his account. Let him go, for the present; I took his number, so to speak.

The slave-dealer bought us both, and hitched us onto that long chain of his, and we constituted the rear of his procession. We took up our line of march and passed out of Cambenet at noon; and it seemed to me unaccountably strange and odd that the King of England and his chief minister, marching manacled and fettered and yoked, in a slave convoy, could move by all manner of idle men and women, and under windows where sat the sweet and the lovely, and yet never attract a curious eye, never provoke a single remark. Dear, dear, it only shows that there is nothing diviner about a king than there is about a tramp, after all. He is just a cheap and hollow artificiality when you don't know he is a king. But reveal his quality, and dear me it takes your very breath away to look at him. I reckon we are all fools. Born so, no doubt.

CHAPTER XXXV

A PITIFUL INCIDENT

It's a world of surprises. The king brooded; this was natural. What would he brood about, should you say? Why, about the prodigious nature of his fall, of course—from the loftiest place in the world to the lowest; from the most illustrious station in the world to the obscurest; from the grandest vocation among men to the basest. No, I take my oath that the thing that graveled him most, to start with, was not this, but the price he had fetched! He couldn't seem to get over that seven dollars. Well, it stunned me so, when I first found it out, that I couldn't believe it; it didn't seem natural. But as soon as my mental sight cleared and I got a right focus on it, I saw I was mistaken; it *was* natural. For this reason: a king is a mere artificiality, and so a king's feelings, like the impulses of an automatic doll, are mere artificialities; but as a man, he is a reality, and his feelings, as a man, are real, not phantoms. It shames the average man to be valued below his own estimate of his worth, and the king certainly wasn't anything more than an average man, if he was up that high.

Confound him, he wearied me with arguments to show that in anything like a fair market he would have fetched twenty-five dollars, sure—a thing which was plainly nonsense, and full or the baldest conceit; I wasn't worth it myself. But it was tender ground for me to argue on. In fact, I had to simply shirk argument and do the diplomatic instead. I had to throw conscience aside, and brazenly concede that he ought to have brought twenty-five dollars; whereas I was quite well aware that in all the ages, the world had never seen a king that was worth half the money, and during the next thirteen centuries wouldn't see one that was worth the fourth of it. Yes, he tired me. If he began to talk about the crops; or about the recent weather; or about the condition of politics; or about dogs, or cats, or morals, or theology—no matter what —I sighed, for I knew what was coming; he was going to get out of it a palliation of that tiresome seven-dollar sale. Wherever we halted where there was a crowd, he would give me a look which said plainly: "if that thing could be tried over again now, with this kind of folk, you would see a different result." Well, when he was first sold, it secretly tickled me to see him go for seven dollars; but before he was done with his sweating and worrying I wished he had fetched a hundred. The thing never got a chance to die, for every day, at one place or another, possible purchasers looked us over, and, as often as any other way, their comment on the king was something like this:

"Here's a two-dollar-and-a-half chump with a thirty-dollar style. Pity but style was marketable."

At last this sort of remark produced an evil result. Our owner was a practical person and he perceived that this defect must be mended if he hoped to find a purchaser for the king. So he went to work to take the style out of his sacred majesty. I could have given the man some valuable advice, but I didn't; you mustn't volunteer advice to a slave-driver unless you want to damage the cause you are arguing for. I had found it a sufficiently difficult job to reduce the king's style to a peasant's style, even when he was a willing and anxious pupil; now then, to undertake to reduce the king's style to a slave's style—and by force—go to! it was a stately contract. Never mind the details—it will save me trouble to let you imagine them. I will only remark that at the end of a week there was plenty of evidence that lash and club and fist had done their work well; the king's body was a sight to see—and to weep over; but his spirit?—why, it wasn't even phased. Even that dull clod of a slave-driver was able to see that there can be such a thing as a slave who will remain a man till he dies; whose bones you can break, but whose manhood you can't. This man found that from his first effort down to his latest, he couldn't ever come within reach of the king, but the king was ready to plunge for him, and did it. So he gave up at last, and left the king in possession of his style unimpaired. The fact is, the king was a good deal more than a king, he was a man; and when a man is a man, you can't knock it out of him.

We had a rough time for a month, tramping to and fro in the earth, and suffering. And what Englishman was the most interested in the slavery question by that time? His grace the king! Yes; from being the most indifferent, he was become the

most interested. He was become the bitterest hater of the institution I had ever heard talk. And so I ventured to ask once more a question which I had asked years before and had gotten such a sharp answer that I had not thought it prudent to meddle in the matter further. Would he abolish slavery?

His answer was as sharp as before, but it was music this time; I shouldn't ever wish to hear pleasanter, though the profanity was not good, being awkwardly put together, and with the crash-word almost in the middle instead of at the end, where, of course, it ought to have been.

I was ready and willing to get free now; I hadn't wanted to get free any sooner. No, I cannot quite say that. I had wanted to, but I had not been willing to take desperate chances, and had always dissuaded the king from them. But now—ah, it was a new atmosphere! Liberty would be worth any cost that might be put upon it now. I set about a plan, and was straightway charmed with it. It would require time, yes, and patience, too, a great deal of both. One could invent quicker ways, and fully as sure ones; but none that would be as picturesque as this; none that could be made so dramatic. And so I was not going to give this one up. It might delay us months, but no matter, I would carry it out or break something.

Now and then we had an adventure. One night we were overtaken by a snow-storm while still a mile from the village we were making for. Almost instantly we were shut up as in a fog, the driving snow was so thick. You couldn't see a thing, and we were soon lost. The slave-driver lashed us desperately, for he saw ruin before him, but his lashings only made matters worse, for they drove us further from the road and from likelihood of succor. So we had to stop at last and slump down in the snow where we were. The storm continued until toward midnight, then ceased. By this time two of our feebler men and three of our women were dead, and others past moving and threatened with death. Our master was nearly beside himself. He stirred up the living, and made us stand, jump, slap ourselves, to restore our circulation, and he helped as well as he could with his whip.

Now came a diversion. We heard shrieks and yells, and soon a woman came running and crying; and seeing our group, she flung herself into our midst and begged for protection. A mob of people came tearing after her, some with torches, and they said she was a witch who had caused several cows to die by a strange disease, and practiced her arts by help of a devil in the form of a black cat. This poor woman had been stoned until she hardly looked human, she was so battered and bloody. The mob wanted to burn her.

Well, now, what do you suppose our master did? When we closed around this poor creature to shelter her, he saw his chance. He said, burn her here, or they shouldn't have her at all. Imagine that! They were willing. They fastened her to a post; they brought wood and piled it about her; they applied the torch while she shrieked and pleaded and strained her two young daughters to her breast; and our brute, with a heart solely for business, lashed us into position about the stake and warmed us into life and commercial value by the same fire which took away the innocent life of that poor harmless mother. That was the sort of master we had. I took *his* number. That snow-storm cost him nine of his flock; and he was more brutal to us than ever, after that, for many days together, he was so enraged over his loss.

We had adventures all along. One day we ran into a procession. And such a procession! All the riffraff of the kingdom seemed to be comprehended in it; and all drunk at that. In the van was a cart with a coffin in it, and on the coffin sat a comely young girl of about eighteen suckling a baby, which she squeezed to her breast in a passion of love every little while, and every little while wiped from its face the tears which her eyes rained down upon it; and always the foolish little thing smiled up at her, happy and content, kneading her breast with its dimpled fat hand, which she patted and fondled right over her breaking heart.

Men and women, boys and girls, trotted along beside or after the cart, hooting, shouting profane and ribald remarks, singing snatches of foul song, skipping, dancing—a very holiday of hellions, a sickening sight. We had struck a suburb of London, outside the walls, and this was a sample of one sort of London society. Our master secured a good place for us near the gallows. A priest was in attendance, and he helped the girl climb up, and said comforting words to her, and made the under-sheriff provide a stool for her. Then he stood there by her on the gallows, and for a moment looked down upon the mass of upturned faces at his feet, then out over the solid pavement of heads that stretched away on every side occupying the vacancies far and near, and then began to tell the story of the case. And there was pity in his voice —how seldom a sound that was in that ignorant and savage land! I remember every detail of what he said, except the words he said it in; and so I change it into my own words:

"Law is intended to mete out justice. Sometimes it fails. This cannot be helped. We can only grieve, and be resigned, and pray for the soul of him who falls unfairly by the arm of the law, and that his fellows may be few. A law sends this poor young thing to death—and it is right. But another law had placed her where she must commit her crime or starve with her child—and before God that law is responsible for both her crime and her ignominious death!

"A little while ago this young thing, this child of eighteen years, was as happy a wife and mother as any in England; and her lips were blithe with song, which is the native speech of glad and innocent hearts. Her young husband was as happy as she; for he was doing his whole duty, he worked early and late at his handicraft, his bread was honest bread well and fairly earned, he was prospering, he was furnishing shelter and sustenance to his family, he was adding his mite to the wealth of the nation. By consent of a treacherous law, instant destruction fell upon this holy home and swept it away! That young husband was waylaid and impressed, and sent to sea. The wife knew nothing of it. She sought him everywhere, she moved the hardest hearts with the supplications of her tears, the broken eloquence of her despair. Weeks dragged by, she watching, waiting, hoping, her mind going slowly to wreck under the burden of her misery. Little by little all her small possessions went for food. When she could no longer pay her rent, they turned her out of doors. She begged, while she had strength; when she was starving at last, and her milk failing, she stole a piece of linen cloth of the value of a fourth part of a cent, thinking to sell it and save her child. But she was seen by the owner of the cloth. She was put in jail and brought to trial. The man testified to the facts. A plea was made for her, and her sorrowful story was told in her behalf. She spoke, too, by permission, and said she did steal the cloth, but that her mind was so disordered of late by trouble that when she was overborne with hunger all acts, criminal or other, swam meaningless through her brain and she knew nothing rightly, except that she was so hungry! For a moment all were touched, and there was disposition to deal mercifully with her, seeing that she was so young and friendless, and her case so piteous,

520 A Connecticut Yankee In King Arthur's Court

and the law that robbed her of her support to blame as being the first and only cause of her transgression; but the prosecuting officer replied that whereas these things were all true, and most pitiful as well, still there was much small theft in these days, and mistimed mercy here would be a danger to property—oh, my God, is there no property in ruined homes, and orphaned babes, and broken hearts that British law holds precious!—and so he must require sentence.

"When the judge put on his black cap, the owner of the stolen linen rose trembling up, his lip quivering, his face as gray as ashes; and when the awful words came, he cried out, 'Oh, poor child, poor child, I did not know it was death!' and fell as a tree falls. When they lifted him up his reason was gone; before the sun was set, he had taken his own life. A kindly man; a man whose heart was right, at bottom; add his murder to this that is to be now done here; and charge them both where they belong —to the rulers and the bitter laws of Britain. The time is come, my child; let me pray over thee—not *for* thee, dear abused poor heart and innocent, but for them that be guilty of thy ruin and death, who need it more."

After his prayer they put the noose around the young girl's neck, and they had great trouble to adjust the knot under her ear, because she was devouring the baby all the time, wildly kissing it, and snatching it to her face and her breast, and drenching it with tears, and half moaning, half shrieking all the while, and the baby crowing, and laughing, and kicking its feet with delight over what it took for romp and play. Even the hangman couldn't stand it, but turned away. When all was ready the priest gently pulled and tugged and forced the child out of the mother's arms, and stepped quickly out of her reach; but she clasped her hands, and made a wild spring toward him, with a shriek; but the rope—and the under-sheriff—held her short. Then she went on her knees and stretched out her hands and cried:

"One more kiss—oh, my God, one more, one more,—it is the dying that begs it!"

She got it; she almost smothered the little thing. And when they got it away again, she cried out:

"Oh, my child, my darling, it will die! It has no home, it has no father, no friend, no mother—"

"It has them all!" said that good priest. "All these will I be to it till I die."

You should have seen her face then! Gratitude? Lord, what do you want with words to express that? Words are only painted fire; a look is the fire itself. She gave that look, and carried it away to the treasury of heaven, where all things that are divine belong.

CHAPTER XXXVI

AN ENCOUNTER IN THE DARK

London—to a slave—was a sufficiently interesting place. It was merely a great big village; and mainly mud and thatch. The streets were muddy, crooked, unpaved. The populace was an ever flocking and drifting swarm of rags, and splendors, of nodding plumes and shining armor. The king had a palace there; he saw the outside of it. It made him sigh; yes, and swear a little, in a poor juvenile sixth century way. We saw knights and grandees whom we knew, but they didn't know us in our rags and dirt and raw welts and bruises, and wouldn't have recognized us if we had hailed them, nor stopped to answer, either, it being unlawful to speak with slaves on a chain. Sandy passed within ten yards of me on a mule—hunting for me, I imagined. But the thing which clean broke my heart was something which happened in front of our old barrack in a square, while we were enduring the spectacle of a man being boiled to death in oil for counterfeiting pennies. It was the sight of a newsboy—and I couldn't get at him! Still, I had one comfort—here was proof that Clarence was still alive and banging away. I meant to be with him before long; the thought was full of cheer.

I had one little glimpse of another thing, one day, which gave me a great uplift. It was a wire stretching from housetop to housetop. Telegraph or telephone, sure. I did very much wish I had a little piece of it. It was just what I needed, in order to carry out my project of escape. My idea was to get loose some night, along with the king, then gag and bind our master, change clothes with him, batter him into the aspect of a stranger, hitch him to the slave-chain, assume possession of the property, march to Camelot, and—

But you get my idea; you see what a stunning dramatic surprise I would wind up with at the palace. It was all feasible, if I could only get hold of a slender piece of iron which I could shape into a lock-pick. I could then undo the lumbering padlocks with which our chains were fastened, whenever I might choose. But I never had any luck; no such thing ever happened to fall in my way. However, my chance came at last. A gentleman who had come twice before to dicker for me, without any result, or indeed any approach to a result, came again. I was far from expecting ever to belong to him, for the price asked for me from the time I was first enslaved was exorbitant, and always provoked either anger or derision, yet my master stuck stubbornly to it—twenty-two dollars. He wouldn't bate a cent. The king was greatly admired, because of his grand physique, but his kingly style was against him, and he wasn't salable; nobody wanted that kind of a slave. I considered myself safe from parting from him because of my extravagant price. No, I was not expecting to ever belong to this gentleman whom I have spoken of, but he had something which I expected would belong to me eventually, if he would but visit us often enough. It was a steel thing with a long pin to it, with which his long cloth outside garment was fastened together in front. There were three of them. He had disappointed me twice, because he did not come quite close enough to me to make my project entirely safe; but this time I succeeded; I captured the lower clasp of the three, and when he missed it he thought he had lost it on the way.

I had a chance to be glad about a minute, then straightway a chance to be sad again. For when the purchase was about to fail, as usual, the master suddenly spoke up and said what would be worded thus —in modern English:

"I'll tell you what I'll do. I'm tired supporting these two for no good. Give me twenty-two dollars for this one, and I'll throw the other one in."

The king couldn't get his breath, he was in such a fury. He began to choke and gag, and meantime the master and the gentleman moved away discussing.

"An ye will keep the offer open—"

"'Tis open till the morrow at this hour."

"Then I will answer you at that time," said the gentleman, and disappeared, the master following him.

I had a time of it to cool the king down, but I managed it. I whispered in his ear, to this effect:

"Your grace *will* go for nothing, but after another fashion. And so shall I. To-night we shall both be free."

"Ah! How is that?"

"With this thing which I have stolen, I will unlock these locks and cast off these chains to-night. When he comes about nine-thirty to inspect us for the night, we will seize him, gag him, batter him, and early in the morning we will march out of this town, proprietors of this caravan of slaves."

That was as far as I went, but the king was charmed and satisfied. That evening we waited patiently for our fellow-slaves to get to sleep and signify it by the usual sign, for you must not take many chances on those poor fellows if you can avoid it. It is best to keep your own secrets. No doubt they fidgeted only about as usual, but it didn't seem so to me. It seemed to me that they were going to be forever getting down to their regular snoring. As the time dragged on I got nervously afraid we shouldn't have enough of it left for our needs; so I made several premature attempts, and merely delayed things by it; for I couldn't seem to touch a padlock, there in the dark, without starting a rattle out of it which interrupted somebody's sleep and made him turn over and wake some more of the gang.

But finally I did get my last iron off, and was a free man once more. I took a good breath of relief, and reached for the king's irons. Too late! in comes the master, with a light in one hand and his heavy walking-staff in the other. I snuggled close among the wallow of snorers, to conceal as nearly as possible that I was naked of irons; and I kept a sharp lookout and prepared to spring for my man the moment he should bend over me.

But he didn't approach. He stopped, gazed absently toward our dusky mass a minute, evidently thinking about something else; then set down his light, moved musingly toward the door, and before a body could imagine what he was going to do, he was out of the door and had closed it behind him.

"Quick!" said the king. "Fetch him back!"

Of course, it was the thing to do, and I was up and out in a moment. But, dear me, there were no lamps in those days, and it was a dark night. But I glimpsed a dim figure a few steps away. I darted for it, threw myself upon it, and then there was a state of things and lively! We fought and scuffled and struggled, and drew a crowd in no time. They took an immense interest in the fight and encouraged us all they could, and, in fact, couldn't have been pleasanter or more cordial if it had been their own fight. Then a tremendous row broke out behind us, and as much as half of our audience left us, with a rush, to invest some sympathy in that. Lanterns began to swing in all directions; it was the watch gathering from far and near. Presently a halberd fell across my back, as a reminder, and I knew what it meant. I was in custody. So was my adversary. We were marched off toward prison, one on each side of the watchman. Here was disaster, here was a fine scheme gone to sudden destruction! I tried to imagine what would happen when the master should discover that it was I who had been fighting him; and what would happen if they jailed us together in the general apartment for brawlers and petty law-breakers, as was the custom; and what might—

Just then my antagonist turned his face around in my direction, the freckled light from the watchman's tin lantern fell on it, and, by George, he was the wrong man!

CHAPTER XXXVII

AN AWFUL PREDICAMENT

Sleep? It was impossible. It would naturally have been impossible in that noisome cavern of a jail, with its mangy crowd of drunken, quarrelsome, and song-singing rapscallions. But the thing that made sleep all the more a thing not to be dreamed of, was my racking impatience to get out of this place and find out the whole size of what might have happened yonder in the slave-quarters in consequence of that intolerable miscarriage of mine.

It was a long night, but the morning got around at last. I made a full and frank explanation to the court. I said I was a slave, the property of the great Earl Grip, who had arrived just after dark at the Tabard inn in the village on the other side of the water, and had stopped there over night, by compulsion, he being taken deadly sick with a strange and sudden disorder. I had been ordered to cross to the city in all haste and bring the best physician; I was doing my best; naturally I was running with all my might; the night was dark, I ran against this common person here, who seized me by the throat and began to pummel me, although I told him my errand, and implored him, for the sake of the great earl my master's mortal peril—

The common person interrupted and said it was a lie; and was going to explain how I rushed upon him and attacked him without a word—

"Silence, sirrah!" from the court. "Take him hence and give him a few stripes whereby to teach him how to treat the servant of a nobleman after a different fashion another time. Go!"

Then the court begged my pardon, and hoped I would not fail to tell his lordship it was in no wise the court's fault that this high-handed thing had happened. I said I would make it all right, and so took my leave. Took it just in time, too; he was starting to ask me why I didn't fetch out these facts the moment I was arrested. I said I would if I had thought of it—which was true —but that I was so battered by that man that all my wit was knocked out of me—and so forth and so on, and got myself away, still mumbling. I didn't wait for breakfast. No grass grew under my feet. I was soon at the slave quarters. Empty—everybody gone! That is, everybody except one body—the slave-master's. It lay there all battered to pulp; and all about were the evidences of a terrific fight. There was a rude board coffin on a cart at the door, and workmen, assisted by the police, were thinning a road through the gaping crowd in order that they might bring it in.

I picked out a man humble enough in life to condescend to talk with one so shabby as I, and got his account of the matter.

"There were sixteen slaves here. They rose against their master in the night, and thou seest how it ended."

"Yes. How did it begin?"

"There was no witness but the slaves. They said the slave that was most valuable got free of his bonds and escaped in some

522 *A Connecticut Yankee In King Arthur's Court*

strange way—by magic arts 'twas thought, by reason that he had no key, and the locks were neither broke nor in any wise injured. When the master discovered his loss, he was mad with despair, and threw himself upon his people with his heavy stick, who resisted and brake his back and in other and divers ways did give him hurts that brought him swiftly to his end."

"This is dreadful. It will go hard with the slaves, no doubt, upon the trial."

"Marry, the trial is over."

"Over!"

"Would they be a week, think you—and the matter so simple? They were not the half of a quarter of an hour at it."

"Why, I don't see how they could determine which were the guilty ones in so short a time."

"*Which* ones? Indeed, they considered not particulars like to that. They condemned them in a body. Wit ye not the law?—which men say the Romans left behind them here when they went—that if one slave killeth his master all the slaves of that man must die for it."

"True. I had forgotten. And when will these die?"

"Belike within a four and twenty hours; albeit some say they will wait a pair of days more, if peradventure they may find the missing one meantime."

The missing one! It made me feel uncomfortable.

"Is it likely they will find him?"

"Before the day is spent—yes. They seek him everywhere. They stand at the gates of the town, with certain of the slaves who will discover him to them if he cometh, and none can pass out but he will be first examined."

"Might one see the place where the rest are confined?"

"The outside of it—yes. The inside of it—but ye will not want to see that."

I took the address of that prison for future reference and then sauntered off. At the first second-hand clothing shop I came to, up a back street, I got a rough rig suitable for a common seaman who might be going on a cold voyage, and bound up my face with a liberal bandage, saying I had a toothache. This concealed my worst bruises. It was a transformation. I no longer resembled my former self. Then I struck out for that wire, found it and followed it to its den. It was a little room over a butcher's shop—which meant that business wasn't very brisk in the telegraphic line. The young chap in charge was drowsing at his table. I locked the door and put the vast key in my bosom. This alarmed the young fellow, and he was going to make a noise; but I said:

"Save your wind; if you open your mouth you are dead, sure. Tackle your instrument. Lively, now! Call Camelot."

"This doth amaze me! How should such as you know aught of such matters as—"

"Call Camelot! I am a desperate man. Call Camelot, or get away from the instrument and I will do it myself."

"What—you?"

"Yes—certainly. Stop gabbling. Call the palace."

He made the call.

"Now, then, call Clarence."

"Clarence *who*?"

"Never mind Clarence who. Say you want Clarence; you'll get an answer."

He did so. We waited five nerve-straining minutes—ten minutes —how long it did seem!—and then came a click that was as familiar to me as a human voice; for Clarence had been my own pupil.

"Now, my lad, vacate! They would have known *my* touch, maybe, and so your call was surest; but I'm all right now."

He vacated the place and cocked his ear to listen—but it didn't win. I used a cipher. I didn't waste any time in sociabilities with Clarence, but squared away for business, straight-off—thus:

"The king is here and in danger. We were captured and brought here as slaves. We should not be able to prove our identity —and the fact is, I am not in a position to try. Send a telegram for the palace here which will carry conviction with it."

His answer came straight back:

"They don't know anything about the telegraph; they haven't had any experience yet, the line to London is so new. Better not venture that. They might hang you. Think up something else."

Might hang us! Little he knew how closely he was crowding the facts. I couldn't think up anything for the moment. Then an idea struck me, and I started it along:

"Send five hundred picked knights with Launcelot in the lead; and send them on the jump. Let them enter by the southwest gate, and look out for the man with a white cloth around his right arm."

The answer was prompt:

"They shall start in half an hour."

"All right, Clarence; now tell this lad here that I'm a friend of yours and a dead-head; and that he must be discreet and say nothing about this visit of mine."

The instrument began to talk to the youth and I hurried away. I fell to ciphering. In half an hour it would be nine o'clock. Knights and horses in heavy armor couldn't travel very fast. These would make the best time they could, and now that the ground was in good condition, and no snow or mud, they would probably make a seven-mile gait; they would have to change horses a couple of times, and they would arrive about six, or a little after; it would still be plenty light enough; they would see the white cloth which I should tie around my right arm, and I would take command. We would surround that prison and have the king out in no time. It would be showy

and picturesque enough, all things considered, though I would have preferred noonday, on account of the more theatrical aspect the thing would have.

Now, then, in order to increase the strings to my bow, I thought I would look up some of those people whom I had formerly recognized, and make myself known. That would help us out of our scrape, without the knights. But I must proceed cautiously, for it was a risky business. I must get into sumptuous raiment, and it wouldn't do to run and jump into it. No, I must work up to it by degrees, buying suit after suit of clothes, in shops wide apart, and getting a little finer article with each change, until I should finally reach silk and velvet, and be ready for my project. So I started.

But the scheme fell through like scat! The first corner I turned, I came plump upon one of our slaves, snooping around with a watchman. I coughed at the moment, and he gave me a sudden look that bit right into my marrow. I judge he thought he had heard that cough before. I turned immediately into a shop and worked along down the counter, pricing things and watching out of the corner of my eye. Those people had stopped, and were talking together and looking in at the door. I made up my mind to get out the back way, if there was a back way, and I asked the shopwoman if I could step out there and look for the escaped slave, who was believed to be in hiding back there somewhere, and said I was an officer in disguise, and my pard was yonder at the door with one of the murderers in charge, and would she be good enough to step there and tell him he needn't wait, but had better go at once to the further end of the back alley and be ready to head him off when I rousted him out.

She was blazing with eagerness to see one of those already celebrated murderers, and she started on the errand at once. I slipped out the back way, locked the door behind me, put the key in my pocket and started off, chuckling to myself and comfortable.

Well, I had gone and spoiled it again, made another mistake. A double one, in fact. There were plenty of ways to get rid of that officer by some simple and plausible device, but no, I must pick out a picturesque one; it is the crying defect of my character. And then, I had ordered my procedure upon what the officer, being human, would *naturally* do; whereas when you are least expecting it, a man will now and then go and do the very thing which it's *not* natural for him to do. The natural thing for the officer to do, in this case, was to follow straight on my heels; he would find a stout oaken door, securely locked, between him and me; before he could break it down, I should be far away and engaged in slipping into a succession of baffling disguises which would soon get me into a sort of raiment which was a surer protection from meddling law-dogs in Britain than any amount of mere innocence and purity of character. But instead of doing the natural thing, the officer took me at my word, and followed my instructions. And so, as I came trotting out of that cul de sac, full of satisfaction with my own cleverness, he turned the corner and I walked right into his handcuffs. If I had known it was a cul de sac—however, there isn't any excusing a blunder like that, let it go. Charge it up to profit and loss.

Of course, I was indignant, and swore I had just come ashore from a long voyage, and all that sort of thing—just to see, you know, if it would deceive that slave. But it didn't. He knew me. Then I reproached him for betraying me. He was more surprised than hurt. He stretched his eyes wide, and said:

"What, wouldst have me let thee, of all men, escape and not hang with us, when thou'rt the very *cause* of our hanging? Go to!"

"Go to" was their way of saying "I should smile!" or "I like that!" Queer talkers, those people.

Well, there was a sort of bastard justice in his view of the case, and so I dropped the matter. When you can't cure a disaster by argument, what is the use to argue? It isn't my way. So I only said:

"You're not going to be hanged. None of us are."

Both men laughed, and the slave said:

"Ye have not ranked as a fool—before. You might better keep your reputation, seeing the strain would not be for long."

"It will stand it, I reckon. Before to-morrow we shall be out of prison, and free to go where we will, besides."

The witty officer lifted at his left ear with his thumb, made a rasping noise in his throat, and said:

"Out of prison—yes—ye say true. And free likewise to go where ye will, so ye wander not out of his grace the Devil's sultry realm."

I kept my temper, and said, indifferently:

"Now I suppose you really think we are going to hang within a day or two."

"I thought it not many minutes ago, for so the thing was decided and proclaimed."

"Ah, then you've changed your mind, is that it?"

"Even that. I only *thought*, then; I *know*, now."

I felt sarcastical, so I said:

"Oh, sapient servant of the law, condescend to tell us, then, what you *know*."

"That ye will all be hanged *to-day*, at mid-afternoon! Oho! that shot hit home! Lean upon me."

The fact is I did need to lean upon somebody. My knights couldn't arrive in time. They would be as much as three hours too late. Nothing in the world could save the King of England; nor me, which was more important. More important, not merely to me, but to the nation—the only nation on earth standing ready to blossom into civilization. I was sick. I said no more, there wasn't anything to say. I knew what the man meant; that if the missing slave was found, the postponement would be revoked, the execution take place to-day. Well, the missing slave was found.

CHAPTER XXXVIII

SIR LAUNCELOT AND KNIGHTS TO THE RESCUE

Nearing four in the afternoon. The scene was just outside the walls of London. A cool, comfortable, superb day, with a brilliant sun; the kind of day to make one want to live, not die. The multitude was prodigious and far-reaching; and yet we

fifteen poor devils hadn't a friend in it. There was something painful in that thought, look at it how you might. There we sat, on our tall scaffold, the butt of the hate and mockery of all those enemies. We were being made a holiday spectacle. They had built a sort of grand stand for the nobility and gentry, and these were there in full force, with their ladies. We recognized a good many of them.

The crowd got a brief and unexpected dash of diversion out of the king. The moment we were freed of our bonds he sprang up, in his fantastic rags, with face bruised out of all recognition, and proclaimed himself Arthur, King of Britain, and denounced the awful penalties of treason upon every soul there present if hair of his sacred head were touched. It startled and surprised him to hear them break into a vast roar of laughter. It wounded his dignity, and he locked himself up in silence. Then, although the crowd begged him to go on, and tried to provoke him to it by catcalls, jeers, and shouts of:

"Let him speak! The king! The king! his humble subjects hunger and thirst for words of wisdom out of the mouth of their master his Serene and Sacred Raggedness!"

But it went for nothing. He put on all his majesty and sat under this rain of contempt and insult unmoved. He certainly was great in his way. Absently, I had taken off my white bandage and wound it about my right arm. When the crowd noticed this, they began upon me. They said:

"Doubtless this sailor-man is his minister—observe his costly badge of office!"

I let them go on until they got tired, and then I said:

"Yes, I am his minister, The Boss; and to-morrow you will hear that from Camelot which—"

I got no further. They drowned me out with joyous derision. But presently there was silence; for the sheriffs of London, in their official robes, with their subordinates, began to make a stir which indicated that business was about to begin. In the hush which followed, our crime was recited, the death warrant read, then everybody uncovered while a priest uttered a prayer.

Then a slave was blindfolded; the hangman unslung his rope. There lay the smooth road below us, we upon one side of it, the banked multitude wailing its other side—a good clear road, and kept free by the police—how good it would be to see my five hundred horsemen come tearing down it! But no, it was out of the possibilities. I followed its receding thread out into the distance—not a horseman on it, or sign of one.

There was a jerk, and the slave hung dangling; dangling and hideously squirming, for his limbs were not tied.

A second rope was unslung, in a moment another slave was dangling.

In a minute a third slave was struggling in the air. It was dreadful. I turned away my head a moment, and when I turned back I missed the king! They were blindfolding him! I was paralyzed; I couldn't move, I was choking, my tongue was petrified. They finished blindfolding him, they led him under the rope. I couldn't shake off that clinging impotence. But when I saw them put the noose around his neck, then everything let go in me and I made a spring to the rescue—and as I made it I shot one more glance abroad—by George! here they came, a-tilting!—five hundred mailed and belted knights on bicycles!

The grandest sight that ever was seen. Lord, how the plumes streamed, how the sun flamed and flashed from the endless procession of webby wheels!

I waved my right arm as Launcelot swept in—he recognized my rag —I tore away noose and bandage, and shouted:

"On your knees, every rascal of you, and salute the king! Who fails shall sup in hell to-night!"

I always use that high style when I'm climaxing an effect. Well, it was noble to see Launcelot and the boys swarm up onto that scaffold and heave sheriffs and such overboard. And it was fine to see that astonished multitude go down on their knees and beg their lives of the king they had just been deriding and insulting. And as he stood apart there, receiving this homage in rags, I thought to myself, well, really there is something peculiarly grand about the gait and bearing of a king, after all.

I was immensely satisfied. Take the whole situation all around, it was one of the gaudiest effects I ever instigated.

And presently up comes Clarence, his own self! and winks, and says, very modernly:

"Good deal of a surprise, wasn't it? I knew you'd like it. I've had the boys practicing this long time, privately; and just hungry for a chance to show off."

CHAPTER XXXIX

THE YANKEE'S FIGHT WITH THE KNIGHTS

Home again, at Camelot. A morning or two later I found the paper, damp from the press, by my plate at the breakfast table. I turned to the advertising columns, knowing I should find something of personal interest to me there. It was this:

DE PAR LE ROI.

Know that the great lord and illus- trious Kni8ht, SIR SAGRAMOR LE DESIROUS having condescended to meet the King's Minister, Hank Mor- gan, the which is surnamed The Boss, for satisfgction of offence anciently given, these wiLL engage in the lists by Camelot about the fourth hour of the morning of the sixteenth day of this next succeeding month. The battle will be a l outrance, sith the said offence was of a deadly sort, admitting of no comPosition.

DE PAR LE ROI

Clarence's editorial reference to this affair was to this effect:

It will be observed, by a gl7nce at our advertising columns, that the commu- nity is to be favored with a treat of un- usual interest in the tournament line. The n ames of the artists are warrant of good enterTemment. The box-office will be open at noon of the 13th; ad- mission 3 cents, reserved seatsh 5; proceeds to go to the hospital fund The royal pair and all the Court will be pres- ent. With these exceptions, and the press and the clergy, the free list is strict- ly susPended. Parties are hereby warn- ed against buying tickets of speculators; they will not be good at the door. Everybody knows and likes The Boss, everybody knows and likes Sir Sag.; come, let us give the lads a good send- off. ReMember, the proceeds go to a great and free charity, and one whose broad begevolence stretches out its help- ing hand, warm with the blood of a lov- ing heart, to all that suffer, regardless of race, creed, condition or color—the only charity yet established in the earth which has no politico-religious stop- cock on its compassion, but says Here flows the stream, let ALL come and drink! Turn out, all hands! fetch along your dou3hnuts and your gum-drops and have a good time. Pie for sale on the grounds, and rocks to crack it with; and ciRcus-lemonade—three drops of lime juice to a barrel of water. N.B. This is the first tournament under the new law, whidh allow each combatant to use any weapon he may prefer. You may want to make a note of that.

Up to the day set, there was no talk in all Britain of anything but this combat. All other topics sank into insignificance and passed out of men's thoughts and interest. It was not because a tournament was a great matter, it was not because Sir Sagramor had found the Holy Grail, for he had not, but had failed; it was not because the second (official) personage in the kingdom was one of the duellists; no, all these features were commonplace. Yet there was abundant reason for the extraordinary interest which this coming fight was creating. It was born of the fact that all the nation knew that this was not to be a duel between mere men, so to speak, but a duel between two mighty magicians; a duel not of muscle but of mind, not of human skill but of superhuman art and craft; a final struggle for supremacy between the two master enchanters of the age. It was realized that the most prodigious achievements of the most renowned knights could not be worthy of comparison with a spectacle like this; they could be but child's play, contrasted with this mysterious and awful battle of the gods. Yes, all the world knew it was going to be in reality a duel between Merlin and me, a measuring of his magic powers against mine. It was known that Merlin had been busy whole days and nights together, imbuing Sir Sagramor's arms and armor with supernal powers of offense and defense, and that he had procured for him from the spirits of the air a fleecy veil which would render the wearer invisible to his antagonist while still visible to other men. Against Sir Sagramor, so weaponed and protected, a thousand knights could accomplish nothing; against him no known enchantments could prevail. These facts were sure; regarding them there was no doubt, no reason for doubt. There was but one question: might there be still other enchantments, *unknown* to Merlin, which could render Sir Sagramor's veil transparent to me, and make his enchanted mail vulnerable to my weapons? This was the one thing to be decided in the lists. Until then the world must remain in suspense.

So the world thought there was a vast matter at stake here, and the world was right, but it was not the one they had in their minds. No, a far vaster one was upon the cast of this die: *the life of knight-errantry.* I was a champion, it was true, but not the champion of the frivolous black arts, I was the champion of hard unsentimental common-sense and reason. I was entering the lists to either destroy knight-errantry or be its victim.

Vast as the show-grounds were, there were no vacant spaces in them outside of the lists, at ten o'clock on the morning of the 16th. The mammoth grand-stand was clothed in flags, streamers, and rich tapestries, and packed with several acres of small-fry tributary kings, their suites, and the British aristocracy; with our own royal gang in the chief place, and each and every individual a flashing prism of gaudy silks and velvets—well, I never saw anything to begin with it but a fight between an Upper Mississippi sunset and the aurora borealis. The huge camp of beflagged and gay-colored tents at one end of the lists, with a stiff-standing sentinel at every door and a shining shield hanging by him for challenge, was another fine sight. You see, every knight was there who had any ambition or any caste feeling; for my feeling toward their order was not much of a secret, and so here was their chance. If I won my fight with Sir Sagramor, others would have the right to call me out as long as I might be willing to respond.

Down at our end there were but two tents; one for me, and another for my servants. At the appointed hour the king made a sign, and the heralds, in their tabards, appeared and made proclamation, naming the combatants and stating the cause of quarrel. There was a pause, then a ringing bugle-blast, which was the signal for us to come forth. All the multitude caught their breath, and an eager curiosity flashed into every face.

Out from his tent rode great Sir Sagramor, an imposing tower of iron, stately and rigid, his huge spear standing upright in its socket and grasped in his strong hand, his grand horse's face and breast cased in steel, his body clothed in rich trappings that almost dragged the ground—oh, a most noble picture. A great shout went up, of welcome and admiration.

And then out I came. But I didn't get any shout. There was a wondering and eloquent silence for a moment, then a great wave of laughter began to sweep along that human sea, but a warning bugle-blast cut its career short. I was in the simplest and comfortablest of gymnast costumes—flesh-colored tights from neck to heel, with blue silk puffings about my loins, and bareheaded. My horse was not above medium size, but he was alert, slender-limbed, muscled with watchsprings, and just a greyhound to go. He was a beauty, glossy as silk, and naked as he was when he was born, except for bridle and ranger-saddle.

The iron tower and the gorgeous bedquilt came cumbrously but gracefully pirouetting down the lists, and we tripped lightly up to meet them. We halted; the tower saluted, I responded; then we wheeled and rode side by side to the grand-stand and faced our king and queen, to whom we made obeisance. The queen exclaimed:

"Alack, Sir Boss, wilt fight naked, and without lance or sword or—"

But the king checked her and made her understand, with a polite phrase or two, that this was none of her business. The bugles rang again; and we separated and rode to the ends of the lists, and took position. Now old Merlin stepped into view and cast a dainty web of gossamer threads over Sir Sagramor which turned him into Hamlet's ghost; the king made a sign, the bugles blew, Sir Sagramor laid his great lance in rest, and the next moment here he came thundering down the course with his veil flying out behind, and I went whistling through the air like an arrow to meet him —cocking my ear the while, as if noting the invisible knight's position and progress by hearing, not sight. A chorus of encouraging shouts burst out for him, and one brave voice flung out a heartening word for me—said:

"Go it, slim Jim!"

It was an even bet that Clarence had procured that favor for me —and furnished the language, too. When that formidable lance-point was within a yard and a half of my breast I twitched my horse aside without an effort, and the big knight swept by, scoring a blank. I got plenty of applause that time. We turned, braced up, and down we came again. Another blank for the knight, a roar of applause for me. This same

thing was repeated once more; and it fetched such a whirlwind of applause that Sir Sagramor lost his temper, and at once changed his tactics and set himself the task of chasing me down. Why, he hadn't any show in the world at that; it was a game of tag, with all the advantage on my side; I whirled out of his path with ease whenever I chose, and once I slapped him on the back as I went to the rear. Finally I took the chase into my own hands; and after that, turn, or twist, or do what he would, he was never able to get behind me again; he found himself always in front at the end of his maneuver. So he gave up that business and retired to his end of the lists. His temper was clear gone now, and he forgot himself and flung an insult at me which disposed of mine. I slipped my lasso from the horn of my saddle, and grasped the coil in my right hand. This time you should have seen him come!—it was a business trip, sure; by his gait there was blood in his eye. I was sitting my horse at ease, and swinging the great loop of my lasso in wide circles about my head; the moment he was under way, I started for him; when the space between us had narrowed to forty feet, I sent the snaky spirals of the rope a-cleaving through the air, then darted aside and faced about and brought my trained animal to a halt with all his feet braced under him for a surge. The next moment the rope sprang taut and yanked Sir Sagramor out of the saddle! Great Scott, but there was a sensation!

Unquestionably, the popular thing in this world is novelty. These people had never seen anything of that cowboy business before, and it carried them clear off their feet with delight. From all around and everywhere, the shout went up:

"Encore! encore!"

I wondered where they got the word, but there was no time to cipher on philological matters, because the whole knight-errantry hive was just humming now, and my prospect for trade couldn't have been better. The moment my lasso was released and Sir Sagramor had been assisted to his tent, I hauled in the slack, took my station and began to swing my loop around my head again. I was sure to have use for it as soon as they could elect a successor for Sir Sagramor, and that couldn't take long where there were so many hungry candidates. Indeed, they elected one straight off —Sir Hervis de Revel.

Bzz! Here he came, like a house afire; I dodged: he passed like a flash, with my horse-hair coils settling around his neck; a second or so later, *fst!* his saddle was empty.

I got another encore; and another, and another, and still another. When I had snaked five men out, things began to look serious to the ironclads, and they stopped and consulted together. As a result, they decided that it was time to waive etiquette and send their greatest and best against me. To the astonishment of that little world, I lassoed Sir Lamorak de Galis, and after him Sir Galahad. So you see there was simply nothing to be done now, but play their right bower—bring out the superbest of the superb, the mightiest of the mighty, the great Sir Launcelot himself!

A proud moment for me? I should think so. Yonder was Arthur, King of Britain; yonder was Guenever; yes, and whole tribes of little provincial kings and kinglets; and in the tented camp yonder, renowned knights from many lands; and likewise the selectest body known to chivalry, the Knights of the Table Round, the most illustrious in Christendom; and biggest fact of all, the very sun of their shining system was yonder couching his lance, the focal point of forty thousand adoring eyes; and all by myself, here was I laying for him. Across my mind flitted the dear image of a certain hello-girl of West Hartford, and I wished she could see me now. In that moment, down came the Invincible, with the rush of a whirlwind—the courtly world rose to its feet and bent forward —the fateful coils went circling through the air, and before you could wink I was towing Sir Launcelot across the field on his back, and kissing my hand to the storm of waving kerchiefs and the thunder-crash of applause that greeted me!

Said I to myself, as I coiled my lariat and hung it on my saddle-horn, and sat there drunk with glory, "The victory is perfect—no other will venture against me—knight-errantry is dead." Now imagine my astonishment—and everybody else's, too—to hear the peculiar bugle-call which announces that another competitor is about to enter the lists! There was a mystery here; I couldn't account for this thing. Next, I noticed Merlin gliding away from me; and then I noticed that my lasso was gone! The old sleight-of-hand expert had stolen it, sure, and slipped it under his robe.

The bugle blew again. I looked, and down came Sagramor riding again, with his dust brushed off and his veil nicely re-arranged. I trotted up to meet him, and pretended to find him by the sound of his horse's hoofs. He said:

"Thou'rt quick of ear, but it will not save thee from this!" and he touched the hilt of his great sword. "An ye are not able to see it, because of the influence of the veil, know that it is no cumbrous lance, but a sword—and I ween ye will not be able to avoid it."

His visor was up; there was death in his smile. I should never be able to dodge his sword, that was plain. Somebody was going to die this time. If he got the drop on me, I could name the corpse. We rode forward together, and saluted the royalties. This time the king was disturbed. He said:

"Where is thy strange weapon?"

"It is stolen, sire."

"Hast another at hand?"

"No, sire, I brought only the one."

Then Merlin mixed in:

"He brought but the one because there was but the one to bring. There exists none other but that one. It belongeth to the king of the Demons of the Sea. This man is a pretender, and ignorant, else he had known that that weapon can be used in but eight bouts only, and then it vanisheth away to its home under the sea."

"Then is he weaponless," said the king. "Sir Sagramore, ye will grant him leave to borrow."

"And I will lend!" said Sir Launcelot, limping up. "He is as brave a knight of his hands as any that be on live, and he shall have mine."

He put his hand on his sword to draw it, but Sir Sagramor said:

"Stay, it may not be. He shall fight with his own weapons; it was his privilege to choose them and bring them. If he has erred, on his head be it."

"Knight!" said the king. "Thou'rt overwrought with passion; it disorders thy mind. Wouldst kill a naked man?"

"An he do it, he shall answer it to me," said Sir Launcelot.

"I will answer it to any he that desireth!" retorted Sir Sagramor hotly.

Merlin broke in, rubbing his hands and smiling his lowdownest smile of malicious gratification:

"'Tis well said, right well said! And 'tis enough of parleying, let my lord the king deliver the battle signal."

The king had to yield. The bugle made proclamation, and we turned apart and rode to our stations. There we stood, a hundred yards apart, facing each other, rigid and motionless, like horsed statues. And so we remained, in a soundless hush, as much as a full minute, everybody gazing, nobody stirring. It seemed as if the king could not take heart to give the signal. But at last he lifted his hand, the clear note of the bugle followed, Sir Sagramor's long blade described a flashing curve in the air, and it was superb to see him come. I sat still. On he came. I did not move. People got so excited that they shouted to me:

"Fly, fly! Save thyself! This is murther!"

I never budged so much as an inch till that thundering apparition had got within fifteen paces of me; then I snatched a dragoon revolver out of my holster, there was a flash and a roar, and the revolver was back in the holster before anybody could tell what had happened.

Here was a riderless horse plunging by, and yonder lay Sir Sagramor, stone dead.

The people that ran to him were stricken dumb to find that the life was actually gone out of the man and no reason for it visible, no hurt upon his body, nothing like a wound. There was a hole through the breast of his chain-mail, but they attached no importance to a little thing like that; and as a bullet wound there produces but little blood, none came in sight because of the clothing and swaddlings under the armor. The body was dragged over to let the king and the swells look down upon it. They were stupefied with astonishment naturally. I was requested to come and explain the miracle. But I remained in my tracks, like a statue, and said:

"If it is a command, I will come, but my lord the king knows that I am where the laws of combat require me to remain while any desire to come against me."

I waited. Nobody challenged. Then I said:

"If there are any who doubt that this field is well and fairly won, I do not wait for them to challenge me, I challenge them."

"It is a gallant offer," said the king, "and well beseems you. Whom will you name first?"

"I name none, I challenge all! Here I stand, and dare the chivalry of England to come against me—not by individuals, but in mass!"

"What!" shouted a score of knights.

"You have heard the challenge. Take it, or I proclaim you recreant knights and vanquished, every one!"

It was a "bluff" you know. At such a time it is sound judgment to put on a bold face and play your hand for a hundred times what it is worth; forty-nine times out of fifty nobody dares to "call," and you rake in the chips. But just this once—well, things looked squally! In just no time, five hundred knights were scrambling into their saddles, and before you could wink a widely scattering drove were under way and clattering down upon me. I snatched both revolvers from the holsters and began to measure distances and calculate chances.

Bang! One saddle empty. Bang! another one. Bang—bang, and I bagged two. Well, it was nip and tuck with us, and I knew it. If I spent the eleventh shot without convincing these people, the twelfth man would kill me, sure. And so I never did feel so happy as I did when my ninth downed its man and I detected the wavering in the crowd which is premonitory of panic. An instant lost now could knock out my last chance. But I didn't lose it. I raised both revolvers and pointed them—the halted host stood their ground just about one good square moment, then broke and fled.

The day was mine. Knight-errantry was a doomed institution. The march of civilization was begun. How did I feel? Ah, you never could imagine it.

And Brer Merlin? His stock was flat again. Somehow, every time the magic of fol-de-rol tried conclusions with the magic of science, the magic of fol-de-rol got left.

CHAPTER XL

THREE YEARS LATER

When I broke the back of knight-errantry that time, I no longer felt obliged to work in secret. So, the very next day I exposed my hidden schools, my mines, and my vast system of clandestine factories and workshops to an astonished world. That is to say, I exposed the nineteenth century to the inspection of the sixth.

Well, it is always a good plan to follow up an advantage promptly. The knights were temporarily down, but if I would keep them so I must just simply paralyze them—nothing short of that would answer. You see, I was "bluffing" that last time in the field; it would be natural for them to work around to that conclusion, if I gave them a chance. So I must not give them time; and I didn't.

I renewed my challenge, engraved it on brass, posted it up where any priest could read it to them, and also kept it standing in the advertising columns of the paper.

I not only renewed it, but added to its proportions. I said, name the day, and I would take fifty assistants and stand up *against the massed chivalry of the whole earth and destroy it.*

I was not bluffing this time. I meant what I said; I could do what I promised. There wasn't any way to misunderstand the language of that challenge. Even the dullest of the chivalry perceived that this was a plain case of "put up, or shut up." They were wise and did the latter. In all the next three years they gave me no trouble worth mentioning.

Consider the three years sped. Now look around on England. A happy and prosperous country, and strangely altered. Schools

everywhere, and several colleges; a number of pretty good newspapers. Even authorship was taking a start; Sir Dinadan the Humorist was first in the field, with a volume of gray-headed jokes which I had been familiar with during thirteen centuries. If he had left out that old rancid one about the lecturer I wouldn't have said anything; but I couldn't stand that one. I suppressed the book and hanged the author.

Slavery was dead and gone; all men were equal before the law; taxation had been equalized. The telegraph, the telephone, the phonograph, the typewriter, the sewing-machine, and all the thousand willing and handy servants of steam and electricity were working their way into favor. We had a steamboat or two on the Thames, we had steam warships, and the beginnings of a steam commercial marine; I was getting ready to send out an expedition to discover America.

We were building several lines of railway, and our line from Camelot to London was already finished and in operation. I was shrewd enough to make all offices connected with the passenger service places of high and distinguished honor. My idea was to attract the chivalry and nobility, and make them useful and keep them out of mischief. The plan worked very well, the competition for the places was hot. The conductor of the 4.33 express was a duke; there wasn't a passenger conductor on the line below the degree of earl. They were good men, every one, but they had two defects which I couldn't cure, and so had to wink at: they wouldn't lay aside their armor, and they would "knock down" fare —I mean rob the company.

There was hardly a knight in all the land who wasn't in some useful employment. They were going from end to end of the country in all manner of useful missionary capacities; their penchant for wandering, and their experience in it, made them altogether the most effective spreaders of civilization we had. They went clothed in steel and equipped with sword and lance and battle-axe, and if they couldn't persuade a person to try a sewing-machine on the installment plan, or a melodeon, or a barbed-wire fence, or a prohibition journal, or any of the other thousand and one things they canvassed for, they removed him and passed on.

I was very happy. Things were working steadily toward a secretly longed-for point. You see, I had two schemes in my head which were the vastest of all my projects. The one was to overthrow the Catholic Church and set up the Protestant faith on its ruins —not as an Established Church, but a go-as-you-please one; and the other project was to get a decree issued by and by, commanding that upon Arthur's death unlimited suffrage should be introduced, and given to men and women alike—at any rate to all men, wise or unwise, and to all mothers who at middle age should be found to know nearly as much as their sons at twenty-one. Arthur was good for thirty years yet, he being about my own age—that is to say, forty— and I believed that in that time I could easily have the active part of the population of that day ready and eager for an event which should be the first of its kind in the history of the world—a rounded and complete governmental revolution without bloodshed. The result to be a republic. Well, I may as well confess, though I do feel ashamed when I think of it: I was beginning to have a base hankering to be its first president myself. Yes, there was more or less human nature in me; I found that out.

Clarence was with me as concerned the revolution, but in a modified way. His idea was a republic, without privileged orders, but with a hereditary royal family at the head of it instead of an elective chief magistrate. He believed that no nation that had ever known the joy of worshiping a royal family could ever be robbed of it and not fade away and die of melancholy. I urged that kings were dangerous. He said, then have cats. He was sure that a royal family of cats would answer every purpose. They would be as useful as any other royal family, they would know as much, they would have the same virtues and the same treacheries, the same disposition to get up shindies with other royal cats, they would be laughably vain and absurd and never know it, they would be wholly inexpensive; finally, they would have as sound a divine right as any other royal house, and "Tom VII, or Tom XI, or Tom XIV by the grace of God King," would sound as well as it would when applied to the ordinary royal tomcat with tights on. "And as a rule," said he, in his neat modern English, "the character of these cats would be considerably above the character of the average king, and this would be an immense moral advantage to the nation, for the reason that a nation always models its morals after its monarch's. The worship of royalty being founded in unreason, these graceful and harmless cats would easily become as sacred as any other royalties, and indeed more so, because it would presently be noticed that they hanged nobody, beheaded nobody, imprisoned nobody, inflicted no cruelties or injustices of any sort, and so must be worthy of a deeper love and reverence than the customary human king, and would certainly get it. The eyes of the whole harried world would soon be fixed upon this humane and gentle system, and royal butchers would presently begin to disappear; their subjects would fill the vacancies with catlings from our own royal house; we should become a factory; we should supply the thrones of the world; within forty years all Europe would be governed by cats, and we should furnish the cats. The reign of universal peace would begin then, to end no more forever.... Me-e-e-yow-ow-ow-ow—fzt!—wow!"

Hang him, I supposed he was in earnest, and was beginning to be persuaded by him, until he exploded that cat-howl and startled me almost out of my clothes. But he never could be in earnest. He didn't know what it was. He had pictured a distinct and perfectly rational and feasible improvement upon constitutional monarchy, but he was too feather-headed to know it, or care anything about it, either. I was going to give him a scolding, but Sandy came flying in at that moment, wild with terror, and so choked with sobs that for a minute she could not get her voice. I ran and took her in my arms, and lavished caresses upon her and said, beseechingly:

"Speak, darling, speak! What is it?"

Her head fell limp upon my bosom, and she gasped, almost inaudibly:

"HELLO-CENTRAL!"

"Quick!" I shouted to Clarence; "telephone the king's homeopath to come!"

In two minutes I was kneeling by the child's crib, and Sandy was dispatching servants here, there, and everywhere, all over the palace. I took in the situation almost at a glance—membranous croup! I bent down and whispered:

"Wake up, sweetheart! Hello-Central."

She opened her soft eyes languidly, and made out to say:

"Papa."

That was a comfort. She was far from dead yet. I sent for preparations of sulphur, I rousted out the croup-kettle myself; for I don't sit down and wait for doctors when Sandy or the child is sick. I knew how to nurse both of them, and had had experience. This little chap had lived in my arms a good part of its small life, and often I could soothe away its troubles and get it to laugh through the tear-dews on its eye-lashes when even its mother couldn't.

Sir Launcelot, in his richest armor, came striding along the great hall now on his way to the stock-board; he was president of the stock-board, and occupied the Siege Perilous, which he had bought of Sir Galahad; for the stock-board consisted of the Knights of the Round Table, and they used the Round Table for business purposes now. Seats at it were worth—well, you would never believe the figure, so it is no use to state it. Sir Launcelot was a bear, and he had put up a corner in one of the new lines, and was just getting ready to squeeze the shorts to-day; but what of that? He was the same old Launcelot, and when he glanced in as he was passing the door and found out that his pet was sick, that was enough for him; bulls and bears might fight it out their own way for all him, he would come right in here and stand by little Hello-Central for all he was worth. And that was what he did. He shied his helmet into the corner, and in half a minute he had a new wick in the alcohol lamp and was firing up on the croup-kettle. By this time Sandy had built a blanket canopy over the crib, and everything was ready.

Sir Launcelot got up steam, he and I loaded up the kettle with unslaked lime and carbolic acid, with a touch of lactic acid added thereto, then filled the thing up with water and inserted the steam-spout under the canopy. Everything was ship-shape now, and we sat down on either side of the crib to stand our watch. Sandy was so grateful and so comforted that she charged a couple of church-wardens with willow-bark and sumach-tobacco for us, and told us to smoke as much as we pleased, it couldn't get under the canopy, and she was used to smoke, being the first lady in the land who had ever seen a cloud blown. Well, there couldn't be a more contented or comfortable sight than Sir Launcelot in his noble armor sitting in gracious serenity at the end of a yard of snowy church-warden. He was a beautiful man, a lovely man, and was just intended to make a wife and children happy. But, of course Guenever—however, it's no use to cry over what's done and can't be helped.

Well, he stood watch-and-watch with me, right straight through, for three days and nights, till the child was out of danger; then he took her up in his great arms and kissed her, with his plumes falling about her golden head, then laid her softly in Sandy's lap again and took his stately way down the vast hall, between the ranks of admiring men-at-arms and menials, and so disappeared. And no instinct warned me that I should never look upon him again in this world! Lord, what a world of heart-break it is.

The doctors said we must take the child away, if we would coax her back to health and strength again. And she must have sea-air. So we took a man-of-war, and a suite of two hundred and sixty persons, and went cruising about, and after a fortnight of this we stepped ashore on the French coast, and the doctors thought it would be a good idea to make something of a stay there. The little king of that region offered us his hospitalities, and we were glad to accept. If he had had as many conveniences as he lacked, we should have been plenty comfortable enough; even as it was, we made out very well, in his queer old castle, by the help of comforts and luxuries from the ship.

At the end of a month I sent the vessel home for fresh supplies, and for news. We expected her back in three or four days. She would bring me, along with other news, the result of a certain experiment which I had been starting. It was a project of mine to replace the tournament with something which might furnish an escape for the extra steam of the chivalry, keep those bucks entertained and out of mischief, and at the same time preserve the best thing in them, which was their hardy spirit of emulation. I had had a choice band of them in private training for some time, and the date was now arriving for their first public effort.

This experiment was baseball. In order to give the thing vogue from the start, and place it out of the reach of criticism, I chose my nines by rank, not capacity. There wasn't a knight in either team who wasn't a sceptered sovereign. As for material of this sort, there was a glut of it always around Arthur. You couldn't throw a brick in any direction and not cripple a king. Of course, I couldn't get these people to leave off their armor; they wouldn't do that when they bathed. They consented to differentiate the armor so that a body could tell one team from the other, but that was the most they would do. So, one of the teams wore chain-mail ulsters, and the other wore plate-armor made of my new Bessemer steel. Their practice in the field was the most fantastic thing I ever saw. Being ball-proof, they never skipped out of the way, but stood still and took the result; when a Bessemer was at the bat and a ball hit him, it would bound a hundred and fifty yards sometimes. And when a man was running, and threw himself on his stomach to slide to his base, it was like an iron-clad coming into port. At first I appointed men of no rank to act as umpires, but I had to discontinue that. These people were no easier to please than other nines. The umpire's first decision was usually his last; they broke him in two with a bat, and his friends toted him home on a shutter. When it was noticed that no umpire ever survived a game, umpiring got to be unpopular. So I was obliged to appoint somebody whose rank and lofty position under the government would protect him.

Here are the names of the nines:

BESSEMERS ULSTERS

KING ARTHUR. EMPEROR LUCIUS. KING LOT OF LOTHIAN. KING LOGRIS. KING OF NORTHGALIS. KING MARHALT OF IRELAND. KING MARSIL. KING MORGANORE. KING OF LITTLE BRITAIN. KING MARK OF CORNWALL. KING LABOR. KING NENTRES OF GARLOT. KING PELLAM OF LISTENGESE. KING MELIODAS OF LIONES. KING BAGDEMAGUS. KING OF THE LAKE. KING TOLLEME LA FEINTES. THE SOWDAN OF SYRIA.

Umpire—CLARENCE.

The first public game would certainly draw fifty thousand people; and for solid fun would be worth going around the world to see. Everything would be favorable; it was balmy and beautiful spring weather now, and Nature was all tailored out in her new clothes.

CHAPTER XLI

THE INTERDICT

However, my attention was suddenly snatched from such matters; our child began to lose ground again, and we had to

go to sitting up with her, her case became so serious. We couldn't bear to allow anybody to help in this service, so we two stood watch-and-watch, day in and day out. Ah, Sandy, what a right heart she had, how simple, and genuine, and good she was! She was a flawless wife and mother; and yet I had married her for no other particular reasons, except that by the customs of chivalry she was my property until some knight should win her from me in the field. She had hunted Britain over for me; had found me at the hanging-bout outside of London, and had straightway resumed her old place at my side in the placidest way and as of right. I was a New Englander, and in my opinion this sort of partnership would compromise her, sooner or later. She couldn't see how, but I cut argument short and we had a wedding.

Now I didn't know I was drawing a prize, yet that was what I did draw. Within the twelvemonth I became her worshiper; and ours was the dearest and perfectest comradeship that ever was. People talk about beautiful friendships between two persons of the same sex. What is the best of that sort, as compared with the friendship of man and wife, where the best impulses and highest ideals of both are the same? There is no place for comparison between the two friendships; the one is earthly, the other divine.

In my dreams, along at first, I still wandered thirteen centuries away, and my unsatisfied spirit went calling and harking all up and down the unreplying vacancies of a vanished world. Many a time Sandy heard that imploring cry come from my lips in my sleep. With a grand magnanimity she saddled that cry of mine upon our child, conceiving it to be the name of some lost darling of mine. It touched me to tears, and it also nearly knocked me off my feet, too, when she smiled up in my face for an earned reward, and played her quaint and pretty surprise upon me:

"The name of one who was dear to thee is here preserved, here made holy, and the music of it will abide alway in our ears. Now thou'lt kiss me, as knowing the name I have given the child."

But I didn't know it, all the same. I hadn't an idea in the world; but it would have been cruel to confess it and spoil her pretty game; so I never let on, but said:

"Yes, I know, sweetheart—how dear and good it is of you, too! But I want to hear these lips of yours, which are also mine, utter it first—then its music will be perfect."

Pleased to the marrow, she murmured:

"HELLO-CENTRAL!"

I didn't laugh—I am always thankful for that—but the strain ruptured every cartilage in me, and for weeks afterward I could hear my bones clack when I walked. She never found out her mistake. The first time she heard that form of salute used at the telephone she was surprised, and not pleased; but I told her I had given order for it: that henceforth and forever the telephone must always be invoked with that reverent formality, in perpetual honor and remembrance of my lost friend and her small namesake. This was not true. But it answered.

Well, during two weeks and a half we watched by the crib, and in our deep solicitude we were unconscious of any world outside of that sick-room. Then our reward came: the center of the universe turned the corner and began to mend. Grateful?

It isn't the term. There *isn't* any term for it. You know that yourself, if you've watched your child through the Valley of the Shadow and seen it come back to life and sweep night out of the earth with one all-illuminating smile that you could cover with your hand.

Why, we were back in this world in one instant! Then we looked the same startled thought into each other's eyes at the same moment; more than two weeks gone, and that ship not back yet!

In another minute I appeared in the presence of my train. They had been steeped in troubled bodings all this time—their faces showed it. I called an escort and we galloped five miles to a hilltop overlooking the sea. Where was my great commerce that so lately had made these glistening expanses populous and beautiful with its white-winged flocks? Vanished, every one! Not a sail, from verge to verge, not a smoke-bank—just a dead and empty solitude, in place of all that brisk and breezy life.

I went swiftly back, saying not a word to anybody. I told Sandy this ghastly news. We could imagine no explanation that would begin to explain. Had there been an invasion? an earthquake? a pestilence? Had the nation been swept out of existence? But guessing was profitless. I must go—at once. I borrowed the king's navy—a "ship" no bigger than a steam launch—and was soon ready.

The parting—ah, yes, that was hard. As I was devouring the child with last kisses, it brisked up and jabbered out its vocabulary! —the first time in more than two weeks, and it made fools of us for joy. The darling mispronunciations of childhood!—dear me, there's no music that can touch it; and how one grieves when it wastes away and dissolves into correctness, knowing it will never visit his bereaved ear again. Well, how good it was to be able to carry that gracious memory away with me!

I approached England the next morning, with the wide highway of salt water all to myself. There were ships in the harbor, at Dover, but they were naked as to sails, and there was no sign of life about them. It was Sunday; yet at Canterbury the streets were empty; strangest of all, there was not even a priest in sight, and no stroke of a bell fell upon my ear. The mournfulness of death was everywhere. I couldn't understand it. At last, in the further edge of that town I saw a small funeral procession —just a family and a few friends following a coffin—no priest; a funeral without bell, book, or candle; there was a church there close at hand, but they passed it by weeping, and did not enter it; I glanced up at the belfry, and there hung the bell, shrouded in black, and its tongue tied back. Now I knew! Now I understood the stupendous calamity that had overtaken England. Invasion? Invasion is a triviality to it. It was the INTERDICT!

I asked no questions; I didn't need to ask any. The Church had struck; the thing for me to do was to get into a disguise, and go warily. One of my servants gave me a suit of clothes, and when we were safe beyond the town I put them on, and from that time I traveled alone; I could not risk the embarrassment of company.

A miserable journey. A desolate silence everywhere. Even in London itself. Traffic had ceased; men did not talk or laugh, or go in groups, or even in couples; they moved aimlessly about, each man by himself, with his head down, and woe and terror at his heart. The Tower showed recent war-scars. Verily, much

had been happening.

Of course, I meant to take the train for Camelot. Train! Why, the station was as vacant as a cavern. I moved on. The journey to Camelot was a repetition of what I had already seen. The Monday and the Tuesday differed in no way from the Sunday. I arrived far in the night. From being the best electric-lighted town in the kingdom and the most like a recumbent sun of anything you ever saw, it was become simply a blot—a blot upon darkness—that is to say, it was darker and solider than the rest of the darkness, and so you could see it a little better; it made me feel as if maybe it was symbolical—a sort of sign that the Church was going to *keep* the upper hand now, and snuff out all my beautiful civilization just like that. I found no life stirring in the somber streets. I groped my way with a heavy heart. The vast castle loomed black upon the hilltop, not a spark visible about it. The drawbridge was down, the great gate stood wide, I entered without challenge, my own heels making the only sound I heard—and it was sepulchral enough, in those huge vacant courts.

CHAPTER XLII

WAR!

I found Clarence alone in his quarters, drowned in melancholy; and in place of the electric light, he had reinstituted the ancient rag-lamp, and sat there in a grisly twilight with all curtains drawn tight. He sprang up and rushed for me eagerly, saying:

"Oh, it's worth a billion milrays to look upon a live person again!"

He knew me as easily as if I hadn't been disguised at all. Which frightened me; one may easily believe that.

"Quick, now, tell me the meaning of this fearful disaster," I said. "How did it come about?"

"Well, if there hadn't been any Queen Guenever, it wouldn't have come so early; but it would have come, anyway. It would have come on your own account by and by; by luck, it happened to come on the queen's."

"*And* Sir Launcelot's?"

"Just so."

"Give me the details."

"I reckon you will grant that during some years there has been only one pair of eyes in these kingdoms that has not been looking steadily askance at the queen and Sir Launcelot—"

"Yes, King Arthur's."

"—and only one heart that was without suspicion—"

"Yes—the king's; a heart that isn't capable of thinking evil of a friend."

"Well, the king might have gone on, still happy and unsuspecting, to the end of his days, but for one of your modern improvements —the stock-board. When you left, three miles of the London, Canterbury and Dover were ready for the rails, and also ready and ripe for manipulation in the stock-market. It was wildcat, and everybody knew it. The stock was

A Connecticut Yankee In King Arthur's Court 531

for sale at a give-away. What does Sir Launcelot do, but—"

"Yes, I know; he quietly picked up nearly all of it for a song; then he bought about twice as much more, deliverable upon call; and he was about to call when I left."

"Very well, he did call. The boys couldn't deliver. Oh, he had them—and he just settled his grip and squeezed them. They were laughing in their sleeves over their smartness in selling stock to him at 15 and 16 and along there that wasn't worth 10. Well, when they had laughed long enough on that side of their mouths, they rested-up that side by shifting the laugh to the other side. That was when they compromised with the Invincible at 283!"

"Good land!"

"He skinned them alive, and they deserved it—anyway, the whole kingdom rejoiced. Well, among the flayed were Sir Agravaine and Sir Mordred, nephews to the king. End of the first act. Act second, scene first, an apartment in Carlisle castle, where the court had gone for a few days' hunting. Persons present, the whole tribe of the king's nephews. Mordred and Agravaine propose to call the guileless Arthur's attention to Guenever and Sir Launcelot. Sir Gawaine, Sir Gareth, and Sir Gaheris will have nothing to do with it. A dispute ensues, with loud talk; in the midst of it enter the king. Mordred and Agravaine spring their devastating tale upon him. *Tableau.* A trap is laid for Launcelot, by the king's command, and Sir Launcelot walks into it. He made it sufficiently uncomfortable for the ambushed witnesses—to wit, Mordred, Agravaine, and twelve knights of lesser rank, for he killed every one of them but Mordred; but of course that couldn't straighten matters between Launcelot and the king, and didn't."

"Oh, dear, only one thing could result—I see that. War, and the knights of the realm divided into a king's party and a Sir Launcelot's party."

"Yes—that was the way of it. The king sent the queen to the stake, proposing to purify her with fire. Launcelot and his knights rescued her, and in doing it slew certain good old friends of yours and mine—in fact, some of the best we ever had; to wit, Sir Belias le Orgulous, Sir Segwarides, Sir Griflet le Fils de Dieu, Sir Brandiles, Sir Aglovale—"

"Oh, you tear out my heartstrings."

"—wait, I'm not done yet—Sir Tor, Sir Gauter, Sir Gillimer—"

"The very best man in my subordinate nine. What a handy right-fielder he was!"

"—Sir Reynold's three brothers, Sir Damus, Sir Priamus, Sir Kay the Stranger—"

"My peerless short-stop! I've seen him catch a daisy-cutter in his teeth. Come, I can't stand this!"

"—Sir Driant, Sir Lambegus, Sir Herminde, Sir Pertilope, Sir Perimones, and—whom do you think?"

"Rush! Go on."

"Sir Gaheris, and Sir Gareth—both!"

"Oh, incredible! Their love for Launcelot was indestructible."

"Well, it was an accident. They were simply onlookers; they were unarmed, and were merely there to witness the queen's punishment. Sir Launcelot smote down whoever came in the way of his blind fury, and he killed these without noticing who they were. Here is an instantaneous photograph one of our boys got of the battle; it's for sale on every news-stand. There—the figures nearest the queen are Sir Launcelot with his sword up, and Sir Gareth gasping his latest breath. You can catch the agony in the queen's face through the curling smoke. It's a rattling battle-picture."

"Indeed, it is. We must take good care of it; its historical value is incalculable. Go on."

"Well, the rest of the tale is just war, pure and simple. Launcelot retreated to his town and castle of Joyous Gard, and gathered there a great following of knights. The king, with a great host, went there, and there was desperate fighting during several days, and, as a result, all the plain around was paved with corpses and cast-iron. Then the Church patched up a peace between Arthur and Launcelot and the queen and everybody—everybody but Sir Gawaine. He was bitter about the slaying of his brothers, Gareth and Gaheris, and would not be appeased. He notified Launcelot to get him thence, and make swift preparation, and look to be soon attacked. So Launcelot sailed to his Duchy of Guienne with his following, and Gawaine soon followed with an army, and he beguiled Arthur to go with him. Arthur left the kingdom in Sir Mordred's hands until you should return—"

"Ah—a king's customary wisdom!"

"Yes. Sir Mordred set himself at once to work to make his kingship permanent. He was going to marry Guenever, as a first move; but she fled and shut herself up in the Tower of London. Mordred attacked; the Bishop of Canterbury dropped down on him with the Interdict. The king returned; Mordred fought him at Dover, at Canterbury, and again at Barham Down. Then there was talk of peace and a composition. Terms, Mordred to have Cornwall and Kent during Arthur's life, and the whole kingdom afterward."

"Well, upon my word! My dream of a republic to *be* a dream, and so remain."

"Yes. The two armies lay near Salisbury. Gawaine—Gawaine's head is at Dover Castle, he fell in the fight there—Gawaine appeared to Arthur in a dream, at least his ghost did, and warned him to refrain from conflict for a month, let the delay cost what it might. But battle was precipitated by an accident. Arthur had given order that if a sword was raised during the consultation over the proposed treaty with Mordred, sound the trumpet and fall on! for he had no confidence in Mordred. Mordred had given a similar order to *his* people. Well, by and by an adder bit a knight's heel; the knight forgot all about the order, and made a slash at the adder with his sword. Inside of half a minute those two prodigious hosts came together with a crash! They butchered away all day. Then the king—however, we have started something fresh since you left—our paper has."

"No? What is that?"

"War correspondence!"

"Why, that's good."

"Yes, the paper was booming right along, for the Interdict made no impression, got no grip, while the war lasted. I had war correspondents with both armies. I will finish that battle by reading you what one of the boys says:

'Then the king looked about him, and then was he ware of all his host and of all his good knights were left no more on live but two knights, that was Sir Lucan de Butlere, and his brother Sir Bedivere: and they were full sore wounded. Jesu mercy, said the king, where are all my noble knights becomen? Alas that ever I should see this doleful day. For now, said Arthur, I am come to mine end. But would to God that I wist where were that traitor Sir Mordred, that hath caused all this mischief. Then was King Arthur ware where Sir Mordred leaned upon his sword among a great heap of dead men. Now give me my spear, said Arthur unto Sir Lucan, for yonder I have espied the traitor that all this woe hath wrought. Sir, let him be, said Sir Lucan, for he is unhappy; and if ye pass this unhappy day, ye shall be right well revenged upon him. Good lord, remember ye of your night's dream, and what the spirit of Sir Gawaine told you this night, yet God of his great goodness hath preserved you hitherto. Therefore, for God's sake, my lord, leave off by this. For blessed be God ye have won the field: for here we be three on live, and with Sir Mordred is none on live. And if ye leave off now, this wicked day of destiny is past. Tide me death, betide me life, saith the king, now I see him yonder alone, he shall never escape mine hands, for at a better avail shall I never have him. God speed you well, said Sir Bedivere. Then the king gat his spear in both his hands, and ran toward Sir Mordred crying, Traitor, now is thy death day come. And when Sir Mordred heard Sir Arthur, he ran until him with his sword drawn in his hand. And then King Arthur smote Sir Mordred under the shield, with a foin of his spear throughout the body more than a fathom. And when Sir Mordred felt that he had his death's wound, he thrust himself, with the might that he had, up to the butt of King Arthur's spear. And right so he smote his father Arthur with his sword holden in both his hands, on the side of the head, that the sword pierced the helmet and the brain-pan, and therewithal Sir Mordred fell stark dead to the earth. And the noble Arthur fell in a swoon to the earth, and there he swooned oft-times—'"

"That is a good piece of war correspondence, Clarence; you are a first-rate newspaper man. Well—is the king all right? Did he get well?"

"Poor soul, no. He is dead."

I was utterly stunned; it had not seemed to me that any wound could be mortal to him.

"And the queen, Clarence?"

"She is a nun, in Almesbury."

"What changes! and in such a short while. It is inconceivable. What next, I wonder?"

"I can tell you what next."

"Well?"

"Stake our lives and stand by them!"

"What do you mean by that?"

"The Church is master now. The Interdict included you with Mordred; it is not to be removed while you remain alive. The clans are gathering. The Church has gathered all the knights that are left alive, and as soon as you are discovered we shall have business on our hands."

"Stuff! With our deadly scientific war-material; with our hosts of trained—"

"Save your breath—we haven't sixty faithful left!"

"What are you saying? Our schools, our colleges, our vast workshops, our—"

"When those knights come, those establishments will empty themselves and go over to the enemy. Did you think you had educated the superstition out of those people?"

"I certainly did think it."

"Well, then, you may unthink it. They stood every strain easily —until the Interdict. Since then, they merely put on a bold outside—at heart they are quaking. Make up your mind to it — when the armies come, the mask will fall."

"It's hard news. We are lost. They will turn our own science against us."

"No they won't."

"Why?"

"Because I and a handful of the faithful have blocked that game. I'll tell you what I've done, and what moved me to it. Smart as you are, the Church was smarter. It was the Church that sent you cruising—through her servants, the doctors."

"Clarence!"

"It is the truth. I know it. Every officer of your ship was the Church's picked servant, and so was every man of the crew."

"Oh, come!"

"It is just as I tell you. I did not find out these things at once, but I found them out finally. Did you send me verbal information, by the commander of the ship, to the effect that upon his return to you, with supplies, you were going to leave Cadiz—"

"Cadiz! I haven't been at Cadiz at all!"

"—going to leave Cadiz and cruise in distant seas indefinitely, for the health of your family? Did you send me that word?"

"Of course not. I would have written, wouldn't I?"

"Naturally. I was troubled and suspicious. When the commander sailed again I managed to ship a spy with him. I have never heard of vessel or spy since. I gave myself two weeks to hear from you in. Then I resolved to send a ship to Cadiz. There was a reason why I didn't."

"What was that?"

"Our navy had suddenly and mysteriously disappeared! Also, as suddenly and as mysteriously, the railway and telegraph and telephone service ceased, the men all deserted, poles were cut down, the Church laid a ban upon the electric light! I had to be up and doing—and straight off. Your life was safe—nobody in these kingdoms but Merlin would venture to touch such a magician as you without ten thousand men at his back—I had nothing to think of but how to put preparations in the best trim against your coming. I felt safe myself—nobody would be anxious to touch a pet of yours. So this is what I did. From our various works I selected all the men—boys I mean—whose faithfulness under whatsoever pressure I could swear to, and I called them together secretly and gave them their instructions. There are fifty-two of them; none younger than fourteen, and none above seventeen years old."

"Why did you select boys?"

"Because all the others were born in an atmosphere of superstition and reared in it. It is in their blood and bones. We imagined we had educated it out of them; they thought so, too; the Interdict woke them up like a thunderclap! It revealed them to themselves, and it revealed them to me, too. With boys it was different. Such as have been under our training from seven to ten years have had no acquaintance with the Church's terrors, and it was among these that I found my fifty-two. As a next move, I paid a private visit to that old cave of Merlin's—not the small one—the big one—"

"Yes, the one where we secretly established our first great electric plant when I was projecting a miracle."

"Just so. And as that miracle hadn't become necessary then, I thought it might be a good idea to utilize the plant now. I've provisioned the cave for a siege—"

"A good idea, a first-rate idea."

"I think so. I placed four of my boys there as a guard—inside, and out of sight. Nobody was to be hurt—while outside; but any attempt to enter—well, we said just let anybody try it! Then I went out into the hills and uncovered and cut the secret wires which connected your bedroom with the wires that go to the dynamite deposits under all our vast factories, mills, workshops, magazines, etc., and about midnight I and my boys turned out and connected that wire with the cave, and nobody but you and I suspects where the other end of it goes to. We laid it under ground, of course, and it was all finished in a couple of hours or so. We sha'n't have to leave our fortress now when we want to blow up our civilization."

"It was the right move—and the natural one; military necessity, in the changed condition of things. Well, what changes *have* come! We expected to be besieged in the palace some time or other, but —however, go on."

"Next, we built a wire fence."

"Wire fence?"

"Yes. You dropped the hint of it yourself, two or three years ago."

"Oh, I remember—the time the Church tried her strength against us the first time, and presently thought it wise to wait for a hopefuler season. Well, how have you arranged the fence?"

"I start twelve immensely strong wires—naked, not insulated —from a big dynamo in the cave—dynamo with no brushes except a positive and a negative one—"

"Yes, that's right."

"The wires go out from the cave and fence in a circle of level ground a hundred yards in diameter; they make twelve independent fences, ten feet apart—that is to say, twelve circles within circles—and their ends come into the cave again."

"Right; go on."

"The fences are fastened to heavy oaken posts only three feet apart, and these posts are sunk five feet in the ground."

"That is good and strong."

"Yes. The wires have no ground-connection outside of the cave. They go out from the positive brush of the dynamo; there is a ground-connection through the negative brush; the other ends of the wire return to the cave, and each is grounded independently."

"No, no, that won't do!"

"Why?"

"It's too expensive—uses up force for nothing. You don't want any ground-connection except the one through the negative brush. The other end of every wire must be brought back into the cave and fastened independently, and *without* any ground-connection. Now, then, observe the economy of it. A cavalry charge hurls itself against the fence; you are using no power, you are spending no money, for there is only one ground-connection till those horses come against the wire; the moment they touch it they form a connection with the negative brush *through the ground*, and drop dead. Don't you see?—you are using no energy until it is needed; your lightning is there, and ready, like the load in a gun; but it isn't costing you a cent till you touch it off. Oh, yes, the single ground-connection—"

"Of course! I don't know how I overlooked that. It's not only cheaper, but it's more effectual than the other way, for if wires break or get tangled, no harm is done."

"No, especially if we have a tell-tale in the cave and disconnect the broken wire. Well, go on. The gatlings?"

"Yes—that's arranged. In the center of the inner circle, on a spacious platform six feet high, I've grouped a battery of thirteen gatling guns, and provided plenty of ammunition."

"That's it. They command every approach, and when the Church's knights arrive, there's going to be music. The brow of the precipice over the cave—"

"I've got a wire fence there, and a gatling. They won't drop any rocks down on us."

"Well, and the glass-cylinder dynamite torpedoes?"

"That's attended to. It's the prettiest garden that was ever planted. It's a belt forty feet wide, and goes around the outer fence—distance between it and the fence one hundred yards—kind of neutral ground that space is. There isn't a single square yard of that whole belt but is equipped with a torpedo. We laid them on the surface of the ground, and sprinkled a layer of sand over them. It's an innocent looking garden, but you let a man start in to hoe it once, and you'll see."

"You tested the torpedoes?"

"Well, I was going to, but—"

"But what? Why, it's an immense oversight not to apply a—"

"Test? Yes, I know; but they're all right; I laid a few in the public road beyond our lines and they've been tested."

"Oh, that alters the case. Who did it?"

"A Church committee."

"How kind!"

"Yes. They came to command us to make submission. You see they didn't really come to test the torpedoes; that was merely an incident."

"Did the committee make a report?"

"Yes, they made one. You could have heard it a mile."

"Unanimous?"

"That was the nature of it. After that I put up some signs, for the protection of future committees, and we have had no intruders since."

"Clarence, you've done a world of work, and done it perfectly."

"We had plenty of time for it; there wasn't any occasion for hurry."

We sat silent awhile, thinking. Then my mind was made up, and I said:

"Yes, everything is ready; everything is shipshape, no detail is wanting. I know what to do now."

"So do I; sit down and wait."

"No, *sir*! rise up and *strike*!"

"Do you mean it?"

"Yes, indeed! The *defensive* isn't in my line, and the *offensive* is. That is, when I hold a fair hand—two-thirds as good a hand as the enemy. Oh, yes, we'll rise up and strike; that's our game."

"A hundred to one you are right. When does the performance begin?"

"*Now!* We'll proclaim the Republic."

"Well, that *will* precipitate things, sure enough!"

"It will make them buzz, I tell you! England will be a hornets' nest before noon to-morrow, if the Church's hand hasn't lost its cunning—and we know it hasn't. Now you write and I'll dictate thus:

"PROCLAMATION

—

"BE IT KNOWN UNTO ALL. Whereas the king having died and left no heir, it becomes my duty to continue the executive authority vested in me, until a government shall have been created and set in motion. The monarchy has lapsed, it no longer exists. By consequence, all political power has reverted to its original source, the people of the nation. With the monarchy, its several adjuncts died also; wherefore there is no longer a nobility, no longer a privileged class, no longer an Established Church; all men are become exactly equal; they are upon one common level, and religion is free. *A Republic is hereby proclaimed*, as being the natural estate of a nation when other authority has ceased. It is the duty of the British people to meet together immediately, and by their votes elect representatives and deliver into their hands the government."

I signed it "The Boss," and dated it from Merlin's Cave. Clarence said—

"Why, that tells where we are, and invites them to call right away."

"That is the idea. We *strike*—by the Proclamation—then it's their innings. Now have the thing set up and printed and posted, right off; that is, give the order; then, if you've got a couple of bicycles handy at the foot of the hill, ho for Merlin's Cave!"

"I shall be ready in ten minutes. What a cyclone there is going to be to-morrow when this piece of paper gets to work!... It's a pleasant old palace, this is; I wonder if we shall ever again — but never mind about that."

CHAPTER XLIII

THE BATTLE OF THE SAND BELT

In Merlin's Cave— Clarence and I and fifty-two fresh, bright, well-educated, clean-minded young British boys. At dawn I sent an order to the factories and to all our great works to stop operations and remove all life to a safe distance, as everything was going to be blown up by secret mines, "*and no telling at what moment—therefore, vacate at once.*" These people knew me, and had confidence in my word. They would clear out without waiting to part their hair, and I could take my own time about dating the explosion. You couldn't hire one of them to go back during the century, if the explosion was still impending.

We had a week of waiting. It was not dull for me, because I was writing all the time. During the first three days, I finished turning my old diary into this narrative form; it only required a chapter or so to bring it down to date. The rest of the week I took up in writing letters to my wife. It was always my habit to write to Sandy every day, whenever we were separate, and now I kept up the habit for love of it, and of her, though I couldn't do anything with the letters, of course, after I had written them. But it put in the time, you see, and was almost like talking; it was almost as if I was saying, "Sandy, if you and Hello-Central were here in the cave, instead of only your photographs, what good times we could have!" And then, you know, I could imagine the baby goo-gooing something out in reply, with its fists in its mouth and itself stretched across its mother's lap on its back, and she a-laughing and admiring and worshipping, and now and then tickling under the baby's chin to set it cackling, and then maybe throwing in a word of answer to me herself—and so on and so on —well, don't you know, I could sit there in the cave with my pen, and keep it up, that way, by the hour with them. Why, it was almost like having us all together again.

I had spies out every night, of course, to get news. Every report made things look more and more impressive. The hosts were gathering, gathering; down all the roads and paths of England the knights were riding, and priests rode with them, to hearten these original Crusaders, this being the Church's war. All the nobilities, big and little, were on their way, and all the gentry. This was all as was expected. We should thin out this sort of folk to such a degree that the people would have nothing to do but just step to the front with their republic and—

Ah, what a donkey I was! Toward the end of the week I began to get this large and disenchanting fact through my head: that the mass of the nation had swung their caps and shouted for the republic for about one day, and there an end! The Church, the nobles, and the gentry then turned one grand, all-disapproving frown upon them and shriveled them into sheep! From that moment the sheep had begun to gather to the fold— that is to say, the camps—and offer their valueless lives and their valuable wool to the "righteous cause." Why, even the very men who had lately been slaves were in the "righteous cause," and glorifying it, praying for it, sentimentally slabbering over it, just like all the other commoners. Imagine such human muck as this; conceive of this folly!

Yes, it was now "Death to the Republic!" everywhere—not a dissenting voice. All England was marching against us! Truly, this was more than I had bargained for.

I watched my fifty-two boys narrowly; watched their faces, their walk, their unconscious attitudes: for all these are a language —a language given us purposely that it may betray us in times of emergency, when we have secrets which we want to keep. I knew that that thought would keep saying itself over and over again in their minds and hearts, *All England is marching against us!* and ever more strenuously imploring attention with each repetition, ever more sharply realizing itself to their imaginations, until even in their sleep they would find no rest from it, but hear the vague and flitting creatures of the dreams say, *All England —ALL ENGLAND!—is marching against you*! I knew all this would happen; I knew that ultimately the pressure would become so great that it would compel utterance; therefore, I must be ready with an answer at that time—an answer well chosen and tranquilizing.

I was right. The time came. They HAD to speak. Poor lads, it was pitiful to see, they were so pale, so worn, so troubled. At first their spokesman could hardly find voice or words; but he presently got both. This is what he said—and he put it in the neat modern English taught him in my schools:

"We have tried to forget what we are—English boys! We have tried to put reason before sentiment, duty before love; our minds approve, but our hearts reproach us. While apparently it was only the nobility, only the gentry, only the twenty-five or thirty thousand knights left alive out of the late wars, we were of one mind, and undisturbed by any troubling doubt; each and every one of these fifty-two lads who stand here before you, said, 'They have chosen—it is their affair.' But think!—the matter is altered—*All England is marching against us*! Oh, sir, consider! —reflect!—these people are our people, they are bone of our bone, flesh of our flesh, we love them—do not ask us to destroy our nation!"

Well, it shows the value of looking ahead, and being ready for a thing when it happens. If I hadn't foreseen this thing and been fixed, that boy would have had me!—I couldn't have said

a word. But I was fixed. I said:

"My boys, your hearts are in the right place, you have thought the worthy thought, you have done the worthy thing. You are English boys, you will remain English boys, and you will keep that name unsmirched. Give yourselves no further concern, let your minds be at peace. Consider this: while all England is marching against us, who is in the van? Who, by the commonest rules of war, will march in the front? Answer me."

"The mounted host of mailed knights."

"True. They are thirty thousand strong. Acres deep they will march. Now, observe: none but *they* will ever strike the sand-belt! Then there will be an episode! Immediately after, the civilian multitude in the rear will retire, to meet business engagements elsewhere. None but nobles and gentry are knights, and *none but these* will remain to dance to our music after that episode. It is absolutely true that we shall have to fight nobody but these thirty thousand knights. Now speak, and it shall be as you decide. Shall we avoid the battle, retire from the field?"

"NO!!!"

The shout was unanimous and hearty.

"Are you—are you—well, afraid of these thirty thousand knights?"

That joke brought out a good laugh, the boys' troubles vanished away, and they went gaily to their posts. Ah, they were a darling fifty-two! As pretty as girls, too.

I was ready for the enemy now. Let the approaching big day come along—it would find us on deck.

The big day arrived on time. At dawn the sentry on watch in the corral came into the cave and reported a moving black mass under the horizon, and a faint sound which he thought to be military music. Breakfast was just ready; we sat down and ate it.

This over, I made the boys a little speech, and then sent out a detail to man the battery, with Clarence in command of it.

The sun rose presently and sent its unobstructed splendors over the land, and we saw a prodigious host moving slowly toward us, with the steady drift and aligned front of a wave of the sea. Nearer and nearer it came, and more and more sublimely imposing became its aspect; yes, all England was there, apparently. Soon we could see the innumerable banners fluttering, and then the sun struck the sea of armor and set it all aflash. Yes, it was a fine sight; I hadn't ever seen anything to beat it.

At last we could make out details. All the front ranks, no telling how many acres deep, were horsemen—plumed knights in armor. Suddenly we heard the blare of trumpets; the slow walk burst into a gallop, and then—well, it was wonderful to see! Down swept that vast horse-shoe wave—it approached the sand-belt—my breath stood still; nearer, nearer—the strip of green turf beyond the yellow belt grew narrow—narrower still—became a mere ribbon in front of the horses—then disappeared under their hoofs. Great Scott! Why, the whole front of that host shot into the sky with a thunder-crash, and became a whirling tempest of rags and fragments; and along the ground lay a thick wall of smoke that hid what was left of the multitude from our sight.

Time for the second step in the plan of campaign! I touched a button, and shook the bones of England loose from her spine!

In that explosion all our noble civilization-factories went up in the air and disappeared from the earth. It was a pity, but it was necessary. We could not afford to let the enemy turn our own weapons against us.

Now ensued one of the dullest quarter-hours I had ever endured. We waited in a silent solitude enclosed by our circles of wire, and by a circle of heavy smoke outside of these. We couldn't see over the wall of smoke, and we couldn't see through it. But at last it began to shred away lazily, and by the end of another quarter-hour the land was clear and our curiosity was enabled to satisfy itself. No living creature was in sight! We now perceived that additions had been made to our defenses. The dynamite had dug a ditch more than a hundred feet wide, all around us, and cast up an embankment some twenty-five feet high on both borders of it. As to destruction of life, it was amazing. Moreover, it was beyond estimate. Of course, we could not *count* the dead, because they did not exist as individuals, but merely as homogeneous protoplasm, with alloys of iron and buttons.

No life was in sight, but necessarily there must have been some wounded in the rear ranks, who were carried off the field under cover of the wall of smoke; there would be sickness among the others—there always is, after an episode like that. But there would be no reinforcements; this was the last stand of the chivalry of England; it was all that was left of the order, after the recent annihilating wars. So I felt quite safe in believing that the utmost force that could for the future be brought against us would be but small; that is, of knights. I therefore issued a congratulatory proclamation to my army in these words:

SOLDIERS, CHAMPIONS OF HUMAN LIBERTY AND EQUALITY: Your General congratulates you! In the pride of his strength and the vanity of his renown, an arrogant enemy came against you. You were ready. The conflict was brief; on your side, glorious. This mighty victory, having been achieved utterly without loss, stands without example in history. So long as the planets shall continue to move in their orbits, the BATTLE OF THE SAND-BELT will not perish out of the memories of men.

THE BOSS.

I read it well, and the applause I got was very gratifying to me. I then wound up with these remarks:

"The war with the English nation, as a nation, is at an end. The nation has retired from the field and the war. Before it can be persuaded to return, war will have ceased. This campaign is the only one that is going to be fought. It will be brief —the briefest in history. Also the most destructive to life, considered from the standpoint of proportion of casualties to numbers engaged. We are done with the nation; henceforth we deal only with the knights. English knights can be killed, but they cannot be conquered. We know what is before us. While one of these men remains alive, our task is not finished, the war is not ended. We will kill them all." [Loud and long continued applause.]

I picketed the great embankments thrown up around our lines by the dynamite explosion—merely a lookout of a couple of boys to announce the enemy when he should appear again.

Next, I sent an engineer and forty men to a point just beyond our lines on the south, to turn a mountain brook that was there, and bring it within our lines and under our command, arranging it in such a way that I could make instant use of it in an emergency. The forty men were divided into two shifts of twenty each, and were to relieve each other every two hours. In ten hours the work was accomplished.

It was nightfall now, and I withdrew my pickets. The one who had had the northern outlook reported a camp in sight, but visible with the glass only. He also reported that a few knights had been feeling their way toward us, and had driven some cattle across our lines, but that the knights themselves had not come very near. That was what I had been expecting. They were feeling us, you see; they wanted to know if we were going to play that red terror on them again. They would grow bolder in the night, perhaps. I believed I knew what project they would attempt, because it was plainly the thing I would attempt myself if I were in their places and as ignorant as they were. I mentioned it to Clarence.

"I think you are right," said he; "it is the obvious thing for them to try."

"Well, then," I said, "if they do it they are doomed."

"Certainly."

"They won't have the slightest show in the world."

"Of course they won't."

"It's dreadful, Clarence. It seems an awful pity."

The thing disturbed me so that I couldn't get any peace of mind for thinking of it and worrying over it. So, at last, to quiet my conscience, I framed this message to the knights:

TO THE HONORABLE THE COMMANDER OF THE INSURGENT CHIVALRY OF ENGLAND: YOU fight in vain. We know your strength—if one may call it by that name. We know that at the utmost you cannot bring against us above five and twenty thousand knights. Therefore, you have no chance— none whatever. Reflect: we are well equipped, well fortified, we number 54. Fifty-four what? Men? No, MINDS—the capablest in the world; a force against which mere animal might may no more hope to prevail than may the idle waves of the sea hope to prevail against the granite barriers of England. Be advised. We offer you your lives; for the sake of your families, do not reject the gift. We offer you this chance, and it is the last: throw down your arms; surrender unconditionally to the Republic, and all will be forgiven.

(Signed) THE BOSS.

I read it to Clarence, and said I proposed to send it by a flag of truce. He laughed the sarcastic laugh he was born with, and said:

"Somehow it seems impossible for you to ever fully realize what these nobilities are. Now let us save a little time and trouble. Consider me the commander of the knights yonder. Now, then, you are the flag of truce; approach and deliver me your message, and I will give you your answer."

I humored the idea. I came forward under an imaginary guard

of the enemy's soldiers, produced my paper, and read it through. For answer, Clarence struck the paper out of my hand, pursed up a scornful lip and said with lofty disdain:

"Dismember me this animal, and return him in a basket to the base-born knave who sent him; other answer have I none!"

How empty is theory in presence of fact! And this was just fact, and nothing else. It was the thing that would have happened, there was no getting around that. I tore up the paper and granted my mistimed sentimentalities a permanent rest.

Then, to business. I tested the electric signals from the gatling platform to the cave, and made sure that they were all right; I tested and retested those which commanded the fences—these were signals whereby I could break and renew the electric current in each fence independently of the others at will. I placed the brook-connection under the guard and authority of three of my best boys, who would alternate in two-hour watches all night and promptly obey my signal, if I should have occasion to give it —three revolver-shots in quick succession. Sentry-duty was discarded for the night, and the corral left empty of life; I ordered that quiet be maintained in the cave, and the electric lights turned down to a glimmer.

As soon as it was good and dark, I shut off the current from all the fences, and then groped my way out to the embankment bordering our side of the great dynamite ditch. I crept to the top of it and lay there on the slant of the muck to watch. But it was too dark to see anything. As for sounds, there were none. The stillness was deathlike. True, there were the usual night-sounds of the country—the whir of night-birds, the buzzing of insects, the barking of distant dogs, the mellow lowing of far-off kine —but these didn't seem to break the stillness, they only intensified it, and added a grewsome melancholy to it into the bargain.

I presently gave up looking, the night shut down so black, but I kept my ears strained to catch the least suspicious sound, for I judged I had only to wait, and I shouldn't be disappointed. However, I had to wait a long time. At last I caught what you may call in distinct glimpses of sound dulled metallic sound. I pricked up my ears, then, and held my breath, for this was the sort of thing I had been waiting for. This sound thickened, and approached—from toward the north. Presently, I heard it at my own level—the ridge-top of the opposite embankment, a hundred feet or more away. Then I seemed to see a row of black dots appear along that ridge—human heads? I couldn't tell; it mightn't be anything at all; you can't depend on your eyes when your imagination is out of focus. However, the question was soon settled. I heard that metallic noise descending into the great ditch. It augmented fast, it spread all along, and it unmistakably furnished me this fact: an armed host was taking up its quarters in the ditch. Yes, these people were arranging a little surprise party for us. We could expect entertainment about dawn, possibly earlier.

I groped my way back to the corral now; I had seen enough. I went to the platform and signaled to turn the current on to the two inner fences. Then I went into the cave, and found everything satisfactory there—nobody awake but the working-watch. I woke Clarence and told him the great ditch was filling up with men, and that I believed all the knights were coming for us in a body. It was my notion that as soon as dawn approached we could expect the ditch's ambuscaded thousands to swarm up over the embankment and make an assault, and be followed immediately by the rest of their army.

Clarence said:

"They will be wanting to send a scout or two in the dark to make preliminary observations. Why not take the lightning off the outer fences, and give them a chance?"

"I've already done it, Clarence. Did you ever know me to be inhospitable?"

"No, you are a good heart. I want to go and—"

"Be a reception committee? I will go, too."

We crossed the corral and lay down together between the two inside fences. Even the dim light of the cave had disordered our eyesight somewhat, but the focus straightway began to regulate itself and soon it was adjusted for present circumstances. We had had to feel our way before, but we could make out to see the fence posts now. We started a whispered conversation, but suddenly Clarence broke off and said:

"What is that?"

"What is what?"

"That thing yonder."

"What thing—where?"

"There beyond you a little piece—dark something—a dull shape of some kind—against the second fence."

I gazed and he gazed. I said:

"Could it be a man, Clarence?"

"No, I think not. If you notice, it looks a lit—why, it *is* a man!—leaning on the fence."

"I certainly believe it is; let us go and see."

We crept along on our hands and knees until we were pretty close, and then looked up. Yes, it was a man—a dim great figure in armor, standing erect, with both hands on the upper wire—and, of course, there was a smell of burning flesh. Poor fellow, dead as a door-nail, and never knew what hurt him. He stood there like a statue—no motion about him, except that his plumes swished about a little in the night wind. We rose up and looked in through the bars of his visor, but couldn't make out whether we knew him or not—features too dim and shadowed.

We heard muffled sounds approaching, and we sank down to the ground where we were. We made out another knight vaguely; he was coming very stealthily, and feeling his way. He was near enough now for us to see him put out a hand, find an upper wire, then bend and step under it and over the lower one. Now he arrived at the first knight—and started slightly when he discovered him. He stood a moment—no doubt wondering why the other one didn't move on; then he said, in a low voice, "Why dreamest thou here, good Sir Mar—" then he laid his hand on the corpse's shoulder—and just uttered a little soft moan and sunk down dead. Killed by a dead man, you see—killed by a dead friend, in fact. There was something awful about it.

These early birds came scattering along after each other, about one every five minutes in our vicinity, during half an hour. They brought no armor of offense but their swords; as a rule, they carried the sword ready in the hand, and put it forward and found the wires with it. We would now and then see a blue spark when the knight that caused it was so far away as to be invisible to us; but we knew what had happened, all the same; poor fellow, he had touched a charged wire with his sword and been elected. We had brief intervals of grim stillness, interrupted with piteous regularity by the clash made by the falling of an iron-clad; and this sort of thing was going on, right along, and was very creepy there in the dark and lonesomeness.

We concluded to make a tour between the inner fences. We elected to walk upright, for convenience's sake; we argued that if discerned, we should be taken for friends rather than enemies, and in any case we should be out of reach of swords, and these gentry did not seem to have any spears along. Well, it was a curious trip. Everywhere dead men were lying outside the second fence—not plainly visible, but still visible; and we counted fifteen of those pathetic statues—dead knights standing with their hands on the upper wire.

One thing seemed to be sufficiently demonstrated: our current was so tremendous that it killed before the victim could cry out. Pretty soon we detected a muffled and heavy sound, and next moment we guessed what it was. It was a surprise in force coming! whispered Clarence to go and wake the army, and notify it to wait in silence in the cave for further orders. He was soon back, and we stood by the inner fence and watched the silent lightning do its awful work upon that swarming host. One could make out but little of detail; but he could note that a black mass was piling itself up beyond the second fence. That swelling bulk was dead men! Our camp was enclosed with a solid wall of the dead—a bulwark, a breastwork, of corpses, you may say. One terrible thing about this thing was the absence of human voices; there were no cheers, no war cries; being intent upon a surprise, these men moved as noiselessly as they could; and always when the front rank was near enough to their goal to make it proper for them to begin to get a shout ready, of course they struck the fatal line and went down without testifying.

I sent a current through the third fence now; and almost immediately through the fourth and fifth, so quickly were the gaps filled up. I believed the time was come now for my climax; I believed that that whole army was in our trap. Anyway, it was high time to find out. So I touched a button and set fifty electric suns aflame on the top of our precipice.

Land, what a sight! We were enclosed in three walls of dead men! All the other fences were pretty nearly filled with the living, who were stealthily working their way forward through the wires. The sudden glare paralyzed this host, petrified them, you may say, with astonishment; there was just one instant for me to utilize their immobility in, and I didn't lose the chance. You see, in another instant they would have recovered their faculties, then they'd have burst into a cheer and made a rush, and my wires would have gone down before it; but that lost instant lost them their opportunity forever; while even that slight fragment of time was still unspent, I shot the current through all the fences and struck the whole host dead in their tracks! *There* was a groan you could *hear*! It voiced the death-pang of eleven thousand men. It swelled out on the night with awful pathos.

A glance showed that the rest of the enemy—perhaps ten thousand strong—were between us and the encircling ditch,

and pressing forward to the assault. Consequently we had them *all!* and had them past help. Time for the last act of the tragedy. I fired the three appointed revolver shots—which meant:

"Turn on the water!"

There was a sudden rush and roar, and in a minute the mountain brook was raging through the big ditch and creating a river a hundred feet wide and twenty-five deep.

"Stand to your guns, men! Open fire!"

The thirteen gatlings began to vomit death into the fated ten thousand. They halted, they stood their ground a moment against that withering deluge of fire, then they broke, faced about and swept toward the ditch like chaff before a gale. A full fourth part of their force never reached the top of the lofty embankment; the three-fourths reached it and plunged over—to death by drowning.

Within ten short minutes after we had opened fire, armed resistance was totally annihilated, the campaign was ended, we fifty-four were masters of England. Twenty-five thousand men lay dead around us.

But how treacherous is fortune! In a little while—say an hour—happened a thing, by my own fault, which—but I have no heart to write that. Let the record end here.

CHAPTER XLIV

A POSTSCRIPT BY CLARENCE

I, Clarence, must write it for him. He proposed that we two go out and see if any help could be accorded the wounded. I was strenuous against the project. I said that if there were many, we could do but little for them; and it would not be wise for us to trust ourselves among them, anyway. But he could seldom be turned from a purpose once formed; so we shut off the electric current from the fences, took an escort along, climbed over the enclosing ramparts of dead knights, and moved out upon the field. The first wounded mall who appealed for help was sitting with his back against a dead comrade. When The Boss bent over him and spoke to him, the man recognized him and stabbed him. That knight was Sir Meliagraunce, as I found out by tearing off his helmet. He will not ask for help any more.

We carried The Boss to the cave and gave his wound, which was not very serious, the best care we could. In this service we had the help of Merlin, though we did not know it. He was disguised as a woman, and appeared to be a simple old peasant goodwife. In this disguise, with brown-stained face and smooth shaven, he had appeared a few days after The Boss was hurt and offered to cook for us, saying her people had gone off to join certain new camps which the enemy were forming, and that she was starving. The Boss had been getting along very well, and had amused himself with finishing up his record.

We were glad to have this woman, for we were short handed. We were in a trap, you see—a trap of our own making. If we stayed where we were, our dead would kill us; if we moved out of our defenses, we should no longer be invincible. We had conquered; in turn we were conquered. The Boss recognized this; we all recognized it. If we could go to one of those new camps and patch up some kind of terms with the enemy—yes, but The Boss could not go, and neither could I, for I was among the first that were made sick by the poisonous air bred by those dead thousands. Others were taken down, and still others. To-morrow—

To-morrow. It is here. And with it the end. About midnight I awoke, and saw that hag making curious passes in the air about The Boss's head and face, and wondered what it meant. Everybody but the dynamo-watch lay steeped in sleep; there was no sound. The woman ceased from her mysterious foolery, and started tip-toeing toward the door. I called out:

"Stop! What have you been doing?"

She halted, and said with an accent of malicious satisfaction:

"Ye were conquerors; ye are conquered! These others are perishing —you also. Ye shall all die in this place—every one—except *him*. He sleepeth now—and shall sleep thirteen centuries. I am Merlin!"

Then such a delirium of silly laughter overtook him that he reeled about like a drunken man, and presently fetched up against one of our wires. His mouth is spread open yet; apparently he is still laughing. I suppose the face will retain that petrified laugh until the corpse turns to dust.

The Boss has never stirred—sleeps like a stone. If he does not wake to-day we shall understand what kind of a sleep it is, and his body will then be borne to a place in one of the remote recesses of the cave where none will ever find it to desecrate it. As for the rest of us—well, it is agreed that if any one of us ever escapes alive from this place, he will write the fact here, and loyally hide this Manuscript with The Boss, our dear good chief, whose property it is, be he alive or dead.

THE END OF THE MANUSCRIPT

FINAL P.S. BY M.T.

The dawn was come when I laid the Manuscript aside. The rain had almost ceased, the world was gray and sad, the exhausted storm was sighing and sobbing itself to rest. I went to the stranger's room, and listened at his door, which was slightly ajar. I could hear his voice, and so I knocked. There was no answer, but I still heard the voice. I peeped in. The man lay on his back in bed, talking brokenly but with spirit, and punctuating with his arms, which he thrashed about, restlessly, as sick people do in delirium. I slipped in softly and bent over him. His mutterings and ejaculations went on. I spoke—merely a word, to call his attention. His glassy eyes and his ashy face were alight in an instant with pleasure, gratitude, gladness, welcome:

"Oh, Sandy, you are come at last—how I have longed for you! Sit by me—do not leave me—never leave me again, Sandy, never again. Where is your hand?—give it me, dear, let me hold it—there —now all is well, all is peace, and I am happy again—*we* are happy again, isn't it so, Sandy? You are so dim, so vague, you are but a mist, a cloud, but you are *here*, and that is blessedness sufficient; and I have your hand; don't take it away—it is for only a little while, I shall not require it long.... Was that the child?... Hello-Central!... she doesn't answer. Asleep, perhaps? Bring her when she wakes, and let me touch her hands, her face, her hair, and tell her good-bye.... Sandy! Yes, you are there. I lost myself a moment, and I thought you were gone.... Have I been sick long? It must be so; it seems months to me. And such dreams! such strange and awful

dreams, Sandy! Dreams that were as real as reality—delirium, of course, but *so* real! Why, I thought the king was dead, I thought you were in Gaul and couldn't get home, I thought there was a revolution; in the fantastic frenzy of these dreams, I thought that Clarence and I and a handful of my cadets fought and exterminated the whole chivalry of England! But even that was not the strangest. I seemed to be a creature out of a remote unborn age, centuries hence, and even *that* was as real as the rest! Yes, I seemed to have flown back out of that age into this of ours, and then forward to it again, and was set down, a stranger and forlorn in that strange England, with an abyss of thirteen centuries yawning between me and you! between me and my home and my friends! between me and all that is dear to me, all that could make life worth the living! It was awful —awfuler than you can ever imagine, Sandy. Ah, watch by me, Sandy —stay by me every moment—*don't* let me go out of my mind again; death is nothing, let it come, but not with those dreams, not with the torture of those hideous dreams—I cannot endure *that* again.... Sandy?..."

He lay muttering incoherently some little time; then for a time he lay silent, and apparently sinking away toward death. Presently his fingers began to pick busily at the coverlet, and by that sign I knew that his end was at hand with the first suggestion of the death-rattle in his throat he started up slightly, and seemed to listen: then he said:

"A bugle?... It is the king! The drawbridge, there! Man the battlements!—turn out the—"

He was getting up his last "effect"; but he never finished it.

Roughing It
By Mark Twain, 1880

To Calvin H. Higbie, of California, an honest man, a genial comrade, and a steadfast friend, this book is inscribed by the author, in memory of the curious time when we two were millionaires for ten days.

PREFATORY.

This book is merely a personal narrative, and not a pretentious history or a philosophical dissertation. It is a record of several years of variegated vagabondizing, and its object is rather to help the resting reader while away an idle hour than afflict him with metaphysics, or goad him with science. Still, there is information in the volume; information concerning an interesting episode in the history of the Far West, about which no books have been written by persons who were on the ground in person, and saw the happenings of the time with their own eyes. I allude to the rise, growth and culmination of the silver-mining fever in Nevada -a curious episode, in some respects; the only one, of its peculiar kind, that has occurred in the land; and the only one, indeed, that is likely to occur in it.

Yes, take it all around, there is quite a good deal of information in the book. I regret this very much; but really it could not be helped: information appears to stew out of me naturally, like the precious ottar of roses out of the otter. Sometimes it has seemed to me that I would give worlds if I could retain my facts; but it cannot be. The more I calk up the sources, and the tighter I get, the more I leak wisdom. Therefore, I can only claim indulgence at the hands of the reader, not justification.

THE AUTHOR.

CHAPTER I.

My brother had just been appointed Secretary of Nevada Territory—an office of such majesty that it concentrated in itself the duties and dignities of Treasurer, Comptroller, Secretary of State, and Acting Governor in the Governor's absence. A salary of eighteen hundred dollars a year and the title of "Mr. Secretary," gave to the great position an air of wild and imposing grandeur. I was young and ignorant, and I envied my brother. I coveted his distinction and his financial splendor, but particularly and especially the long, strange journey he was going to make, and the curious new world he was going to explore. He was going to travel! I never had been away from home, and that word "travel" had a seductive charm for me. Pretty soon he would be hundreds and hundreds of miles away on the great plains and deserts, and among the mountains of the Far West, and would see buffaloes and Indians, and prairie dogs, and antelopes, and have all kinds of adventures, and may be get hanged or scalped, and have ever such a fine time, and write home and tell us all about it, and be a hero. And he would see the gold mines and the silver mines, and maybe go about of an afternoon when his work was done, and pick up two or three pailfuls of shining slugs, and nuggets of gold and silver on the hillside. And by and by he would become very rich, and return home by sea, and be able to talk as calmly about San Francisco and the ocean, and "the isthmus" as if it was nothing of any consequence to have seen those marvels face to face. What I suffered in contemplating his happiness, pen cannot describe. And so, when he offered me, in cold blood, the sublime position of private secretary under him, it appeared to me that

the heavens and the earth passed away, and the firmament was rolled together as a scroll! I had nothing more to desire. My contentment was complete.

At the end of an hour or two I was ready for the journey. Not much packing up was necessary, because we were going in the overland stage from the Missouri frontier to Nevada, and passengers were only allowed a small quantity of baggage apiece. There was no Pacific railroad in those fine times of ten or twelve years ago—not a single rail of it. I only proposed to stay in Nevada three months—I had no thought of staying longer than that. I meant to see all I could that was new and strange, and then hurry home to business. I little thought that I would not see the end of that three-month pleasure excursion for six or seven uncommonly long years!

I dreamed all night about Indians, deserts, and silver bars, and in due time, next day, we took shipping at the St. Louis wharf on board a steamboat bound up the Missouri River.

We were six days going from St. Louis to "St. Jo."—a trip that was so dull, and sleepy, and eventless that it has left no more impression on my memory than if its duration had been six minutes instead of that many days. No record is left in my mind, now, concerning it, but a confused jumble of savage-looking snags, which we deliberately walked over with one wheel or the other; and of reefs which we butted and butted, and then retired from and climbed over in some softer place; and of sand-bars which we roosted on occasionally, and rested, and then got out our crutches and sparred over.

In fact, the boat might almost as well have gone to St. Jo. by land, for she was walking most of the time, anyhow—climbing over reefs and clambering over snags patiently and laboriously all day long. The captain said she was a "bully" boat, and all she wanted was more "shear" and a bigger wheel. I thought she wanted a pair of stilts, but I had the deep sagacity not to say so.

CHAPTER II.

The first thing we did on that glad evening that landed us at St. Joseph was to hunt up the stage-office, and pay a hundred and fifty dollars apiece for tickets per overland coach to Carson City, Nevada.

The next morning, bright and early, we took a hasty breakfast, and hurried to the starting-place. Then an inconvenience presented itself which we had not properly appreciated before, namely, that one cannot make a heavy traveling trunk stand for twenty-five pounds of baggage —because it weighs a good deal more. But that was all we could take —twenty-five pounds each. So we had to snatch our trunks open, and make a selection in a good deal of a hurry. We put our lawful twenty-five pounds apiece all in one valise, and shipped the trunks back to St. Louis again. It was a sad parting, for now we had no swallow-tail coats and white kid gloves to wear at Pawnee receptions in the Rocky Mountains, and no stove-pipe hats nor patent-leather boots, nor anything else necessary to make life calm and peaceful. We were reduced to a war-footing. Each of us put on a rough, heavy suit of clothing, woolen army shirt and "stogy" boots included; and into the valise we crowded a few white shirts, some under-clothing and such things. My brother, the Secretary, took along about four pounds of United States statutes and six pounds of Unabridged Dictionary; for we did not know—poor innocents—that such things could be bought in San Francisco on one day and received in Carson City the next. I was armed to the teeth with a pitiful little

Smith & Wesson's seven-shooter, which carried a ball like a homoeopathic pill, and it took the whole seven to make a dose for an adult. But I thought it was grand. It appeared to me to be a dangerous weapon. It only had one fault—you could not hit anything with it. One of our "conductors" practiced awhile on a cow with it, and as long as she stood still and behaved herself she was safe; but as soon as she went to moving about, and he got to shooting at other things, she came to grief. The Secretary had a small-sized Colt's revolver strapped around him for protection against the Indians, and to guard against accidents he carried it uncapped. Mr. George Bemis was dismally formidable. George Bemis was our fellow-traveler.

We had never seen him before. He wore in his belt an old original "Allen" revolver, such as irreverent people called a "pepper-box." Simply drawing the trigger back, cocked and fired the pistol. As the trigger came back, the hammer would begin to rise and the barrel to turn over, and presently down would drop the hammer, and away would speed the ball. To aim along the turning barrel and hit the thing aimed at was a feat which was probably never done with an "Allen" in the world. But George's was a reliable weapon, nevertheless, because, as one of the stage-drivers afterward said, "If she didn't get what she went after, she would fetch something else." And so she did. She went after a deuce of spades nailed against a tree, once, and fetched a mule standing about thirty yards to the left of it. Bemis did not want the mule; but the owner came out with a double-barreled shotgun and persuaded him to buy it, anyhow. It was a cheerful weapon—the "Allen." Sometimes all its six barrels would go off at once, and then there was no safe place in all the region round about, but behind it.

We took two or three blankets for protection against frosty weather in the mountains. In the matter of luxuries we were modest—we took none along but some pipes and five pounds of smoking tobacco. We had two large canteens to carry water in, between stations on the Plains, and we also took with us a little shot-bag of silver coin for daily expenses in the way of breakfasts and dinners.

By eight o'clock everything was ready, and we were on the other side of the river. We jumped into the stage, the driver cracked his whip, and we bowled away and left "the States" behind us. It was a superb summer morning, and all the landscape was brilliant with sunshine. There was a freshness and breeziness, too, and an exhilarating sense of emancipation from all sorts of cares and responsibilities, that almost made us feel that the years we had spent in the close, hot city, toiling and slaving, had been wasted and thrown away. We were spinning along through Kansas, and in the course of an hour and a half we were fairly abroad on the great Plains. Just here the land was rolling—a grand sweep of regular elevations and depressions as far as the eye could reach—like the stately heave and swell of the ocean's bosom after a storm. And everywhere were cornfields, accenting with squares of deeper green, this limitless expanse of grassy land. But presently this sea upon dry ground was to lose its "rolling" character and stretch away for seven hundred miles as level as a floor!

Our coach was a great swinging and swaying stage, of the most sumptuous description—an imposing cradle on wheels. It was drawn by six handsome horses, and by the side of the driver sat the "conductor," the legitimate captain of the craft; for it was his business to take charge and care of the mails, baggage, express matter, and passengers. We three were the only passengers, this trip. We sat on the back seat, inside. About all the rest of the coach was full of mail bags—for we had three

days' delayed mails with us. Almost touching our knees, a perpendicular wall of mail matter rose up to the roof. There was a great pile of it strapped on top of the stage, and both the fore and hind boots were full. We had twenty-seven hundred pounds of it aboard, the driver said—"a little for Brigham, and Carson, and 'Frisco, but the heft of it for the Injuns, which is powerful troublesome 'thout they get plenty of truck to read." But as he just then got up a fearful convulsion of his countenance which was suggestive of a wink being swallowed by an earthquake, we guessed that his remark was intended to be facetious, and to mean that we would unload the most of our mail matter somewhere on the Plains and leave it to the Indians, or whosoever wanted it.

We changed horses every ten miles, all day long, and fairly flew over the hard, level road. We jumped out and stretched our legs every time the coach stopped, and so the night found us still vivacious and unfatigued.

After supper a woman got in, who lived about fifty miles further on, and we three had to take turns at sitting outside with the driver and conductor. Apparently she was not a talkative woman. She would sit there in the gathering twilight and fasten her steadfast eyes on a mosquito rooting into her arm, and slowly she would raise her other hand till she had got his range, and then she would launch a slap at him that would have jolted a cow; and after that she would sit and contemplate the corpse with tranquil satisfaction—for she never missed her mosquito; she was a dead shot at short range. She never removed a carcase, but left them there for bait. I sat by this grim Sphynx and watched her kill thirty or forty mosquitoes—watched her, and waited for her to say something, but she never did. So I finally opened the conversation myself. I said:

"The mosquitoes are pretty bad, about here, madam."

"You bet!"

"What did I understand you to say, madam?"

"You BET!"

Then she cheered up, and faced around and said:

"Danged if I didn't begin to think you fellers was deaf and dumb. I did, b'gosh. Here I've sot, and sot, and sot, a-bust'n muskeeters and wonderin' what was ailin' ye. Fust I thot you was deaf and dumb, then I thot you was sick or crazy, or suthin', and then by and by I begin to reckon you was a passel of sickly fools that couldn't think of nothing to say. Wher'd ye come from?"

The Sphynx was a Sphynx no more! The fountains of her great deep were broken up, and she rained the nine parts of speech forty days and forty nights, metaphorically speaking, and buried us under a desolating deluge of trivial gossip that left not a crag or pinnacle of rejoinder projecting above the tossing waste of dislocated grammar and decomposed pronunciation!

How we suffered, suffered, suffered! She went on, hour after hour, till I was sorry I ever opened the mosquito question and gave her a start. She never did stop again until she got to her journey's end toward daylight; and then she stirred us up as she was leaving the stage (for we were nodding, by that time), and said:

"Now you git out at Cottonwood, you fellers, and lay over a

couple o' days, and I'll be along some time to-night, and if I can do ye any good by edgin' in a word now and then, I'm right thar. Folks'll tell you't I've always ben kind o' offish and partic'lar for a gal that's raised in the woods, and I am, with the rag-tag and bob-tail, and a gal has to be, if she wants to be anything, but when people comes along which is my equals, I reckon I'm a pretty sociable heifer after all."

We resolved not to "lay by at Cottonwood."

CHAPTER III.

About an hour and a half before daylight we were bowling along smoothly over the road—so smoothly that our cradle only rocked in a gentle, lulling way, that was gradually soothing us to sleep, and dulling our consciousness—when something gave away under us! We were dimly aware of it, but indifferent to it. The coach stopped. We heard the driver and conductor talking together outside, and rummaging for a lantern, and swearing because they could not find it—but we had no interest in whatever had happened, and it only added to our comfort to think of those people out there at work in the murky night, and we snug in our nest with the curtains drawn. But presently, by the sounds, there seemed to be an examination going on, and then the driver's voice said:

"By George, the thoroughbrace is broke!"

This startled me broad awake—as an undefined sense of calamity is always apt to do. I said to myself: "Now, a thoroughbrace is probably part of a horse; and doubtless a vital part, too, from the dismay in the driver's voice. Leg, maybe—and yet how could he break his leg waltzing along such a road as this? No, it can't be his leg. That is impossible, unless he was reaching for the driver. Now, what can be the thoroughbrace of a horse, I wonder? Well, whatever comes, I shall not air my ignorance in this crowd, anyway."

Just then the conductor's face appeared at a lifted curtain, and his lantern glared in on us and our wall of mail matter. He said: "Gents, you'll have to turn out a spell. Thoroughbrace is broke."

We climbed out into a chill drizzle, and felt ever so homeless and dreary. When I found that the thing they called a "thoroughbrace" was the massive combination of belts and springs which the coach rocks itself in, I said to the driver:

"I never saw a thoroughbrace used up like that, before, that I can remember. How did it happen?"

"Why, it happened by trying to make one coach carry three days' mail —that's how it happened," said he. "And right here is the very direction which is wrote on all the newspaper-bags which was to be put out for the Injuns for to keep 'em quiet. It's most uncommon lucky, becuz it's so nation dark I should 'a' gone by unbeknowns if that air thoroughbrace hadn't broke."

I knew that he was in labor with another of those winks of his, though I could not see his face, because he was bent down at work; and wishing him a safe delivery, I turned to and helped the rest get out the mail-sacks. It made a great pyramid by the roadside when it was all out. When they had mended the thoroughbrace we filled the two boots again, but put no mail on top, and only half as much inside as there was before. The conductor bent all the seat-backs down, and then filled the coach just half full of mail-bags from end to end. We objected loudly to this, for it left us no seats. But the conductor was wiser than we, and said a bed was better than seats, and moreover, this plan would protect his thoroughbraces. We never wanted any seats after that. The lazy bed was infinitely preferable. I had many an exciting day, subsequently, lying on it reading the statutes and the dictionary, and wondering how the characters would turn out.

The conductor said he would send back a guard from the next station to take charge of the abandoned mail-bags, and we drove on.

It was now just dawn; and as we stretched our cramped legs full length on the mail sacks, and gazed out through the windows across the wide wastes of greensward clad in cool, powdery mist, to where there was an expectant look in the eastern horizon, our perfect enjoyment took the form of a tranquil and contented ecstasy. The stage whirled along at a spanking gait, the breeze flapping curtains and suspended coats in a most exhilarating way; the cradle swayed and swung luxuriously, the pattering of the horses' hoofs, the cracking of the driver's whip, and his "Hi-yi! g'lang!" were music; the spinning ground and the waltzing trees appeared to give us a mute hurrah as we went by, and then slack up and look after us with interest, or envy, or something; and as we lay and smoked the pipe of peace and compared all this luxury with the years of tiresome city life that had gone before it, we felt that there was only one complete and satisfying happiness in the world, and we had found it.

After breakfast, at some station whose name I have forgotten, we three climbed up on the seat behind the driver, and let the conductor have our bed for a nap. And by and by, when the sun made me drowsy, I lay down on my face on top of the coach, grasping the slender iron railing, and slept for an hour or more. That will give one an appreciable idea of those matchless roads. Instinct will make a sleeping man grip a fast hold of the railing when the stage jolts, but when it only swings and sways, no grip is necessary. Overland drivers and conductors used to sit in their places and sleep thirty or forty minutes at a time, on good roads, while spinning along at the rate of eight or ten miles an hour. I saw them do it, often. There was no danger about it; a sleeping man will seize the irons in time when the coach jolts. These men were hard worked, and it was not possible for them to stay awake all the time.

By and by we passed through Marysville, and over the Big Blue and Little Sandy; thence about a mile, and entered Nebraska. About a mile further on, we came to the Big Sandy—one hundred and eighty miles from St. Joseph.

As the sun was going down, we saw the first specimen of an animal known familiarly over two thousand miles of mountain and desert—from Kansas clear to the Pacific Ocean—as the "jackass rabbit." He is well named. He is just like any other rabbit, except that he is from one third to twice as large, has longer legs in proportion to his size, and has the most preposterous ears that ever were mounted on any creature but a jackass.

When he is sitting quiet, thinking about his sins, or is absent-minded or unapprehensive of danger, his majestic ears project above him conspicuously; but the breaking of a twig will scare him nearly to death, and then he tilts his ears back gently and starts for home. All you can see, then, for the next minute, is his long gray form stretched out straight and "streaking it" through the low sage-brush, head erect, eyes right, and ears just canted a little to the rear, but showing you where the animal is, all the time, the same as if he carried a jib. Now and then he makes a marvelous spring with his long legs, high over the stunted sage-brush, and scores a leap that would make a horse envious. Presently he comes down to a long, graceful "lope," and shortly he mysteriously disappears. He has crouched behind a sage-bush, and will sit there and listen and tremble until you get within six feet of him, when he will get under way again. But one must shoot at this creature once, if he wishes to see him throw his heart into his heels, and do the best he knows how. He is frightened clear through, now, and he lays his long ears down on his back, straightens himself out like a yard-stick every spring he makes, and scatters miles behind him with an easy indifference that is enchanting.

Our party made this specimen "hump himself," as the conductor said. The secretary started him with a shot from the Colt; I commenced spitting at him with my weapon; and all in the same instant the old "Allen's" whole broadside let go with a rattling crash, and it is not putting it too strong to say that the rabbit was frantic! He dropped his ears, set up his tail, and left for San Francisco at a speed which can only be described as a flash and a vanish! Long after he was out of sight we could hear him whiz.

I do not remember where we first came across "sage-brush," but as I have been speaking of it I may as well describe it.

This is easily done, for if the reader can imagine a gnarled and venerable live oak-tree reduced to a little shrub two feet-high, with its rough bark, its foliage, its twisted boughs, all complete, he can picture the "sage-brush" exactly. Often, on lazy afternoons in the mountains, I have lain on the ground with my face under a sage-bush, and entertained myself with fancying that the gnats among its foliage were liliputian birds, and that the ants marching and countermarching about its base were liliputian flocks and herds, and myself some vast loafer from Brobdignag waiting to catch a little citizen and eat him.

It is an imposing monarch of the forest in exquisite miniature, is the "sage-brush." Its foliage is a grayish green, and gives that tint to desert and mountain. It smells like our domestic sage, and "sage-tea" made from it taste like the sage-tea which all boys are so well acquainted with. The sage-brush is a singularly hardy plant, and grows right in the midst of deep sand, and among barren rocks, where nothing else in the vegetable world would try to grow, except "bunch-grass." — ["Bunch-grass" grows on the bleak mountain-sides of Nevada and neighboring territories, and offers excellent feed for stock, even in the dead of winter, wherever the snow is blown aside and exposes it; notwithstanding its unpromising home, bunch-grass is a better and more nutritious diet for cattle and horses than almost any other hay or grass that is known—so stock-men say.]—The sage-bushes grow from three to six or seven feet apart, all over the mountains and deserts of the Far West, clear to the borders of California. There is not a tree of any kind in the deserts, for hundreds of miles—there is no vegetation at all in a regular desert, except the sage-brush and its cousin the "greasewood," which is so much like the sage-brush that the difference amounts to little. Camp-fires and hot suppers in the deserts would be impossible but for the friendly sage-brush. Its trunk is as large as a boy's wrist (and from that up to a man's arm), and its crooked branches are half as large as its trunk—all good, sound, hard wood, very like oak.

When a party camps, the first thing to be done is to cut sage-brush; and in a few minutes there is an opulent pile of it ready

for use. A hole a foot wide, two feet deep, and two feet long, is dug, and sage-brush chopped up and burned in it till it is full to the brim with glowing coals. Then the cooking begins, and there is no smoke, and consequently no swearing. Such a fire will keep all night, with very little replenishing; and it makes a very sociable camp-fire, and one around which the most impossible reminiscences sound plausible, instructive, and profoundly entertaining.

Sage-brush is very fair fuel, but as a vegetable it is a distinguished failure. Nothing can abide the taste of it but the jackass and his illegitimate child the mule. But their testimony to its nutritiousness is worth nothing, for they will eat pine knots, or anthracite coal, or brass filings, or lead pipe, or old bottles, or anything that comes handy, and then go off looking as grateful as if they had had oysters for dinner. Mules and donkeys and camels have appetites that anything will relieve temporarily, but nothing satisfy.

In Syria, once, at the head-waters of the Jordan, a camel took charge of my overcoat while the tents were being pitched, and examined it with a critical eye, all over, with as much interest as if he had an idea of getting one made like it; and then, after he was done figuring on it as an article of apparel, he began to contemplate it as an article of diet. He put his foot on it, and lifted one of the sleeves out with his teeth, and chewed and chewed at it, gradually taking it in, and all the while opening and closing his eyes in a kind of religious ecstasy, as if he had never tasted anything as good as an overcoat before, in his life. Then he smacked his lips once or twice, and reached after the other sleeve. Next he tried the velvet collar, and smiled a smile of such contentment that it was plain to see that he regarded that as the daintiest thing about an overcoat. The tails went next, along with some percussion caps and cough candy, and some fig-paste from Constantinople. And then my newspaper correspondence dropped out, and he took a chance in that — manuscript letters written for the home papers. But he was treading on dangerous ground, now. He began to come across solid wisdom in those documents that was rather weighty on his stomach; and occasionally he would take a joke that would shake him up till it loosened his teeth; it was getting to be perilous times with him, but he held his grip with good courage and hopefully, till at last he began to stumble on statements that not even a camel could swallow with impunity. He began to gag and gasp, and his eyes to stand out, and his forelegs to spread, and in about a quarter of a minute he fell over as stiff as a carpenter's work-bench, and died a death of indescribable agony. I went and pulled the manuscript out of his mouth, and found that the sensitive creature had choked to death on one of the mildest and gentlest statements of fact that I ever laid before a trusting public.

I was about to say, when diverted from my subject, that occasionally one finds sage-bushes five or six feet high, and with a spread of branch and foliage in proportion, but two or two and a half feet is the usual height.

CHAPTER IV.

As the sun went down and the evening chill came on, we made preparation for bed. We stirred up the hard leather letter-sacks, and the knotty canvas bags of printed matter (knotty and uneven because of projecting ends and corners of magazines, boxes and books). We stirred them up and redisposed them in such a way as to make our bed as level as possible. And we did improve it, too, though after all our work it had an upheaved and billowy look about it, like a little piece of a stormy sea. Next we hunted up our boots from odd nooks among the mail-bags where they had settled, and put them on. Then we got down our coats, vests, pantaloons and heavy woolen shirts, from the arm-loops where they had been swinging all day, and clothed ourselves in them—for, there being no ladies either at the stations or in the coach, and the weather being hot, we had looked to our comfort by stripping to our underclothing, at nine o'clock in the morning. All things being now ready, we stowed the uneasy Dictionary where it would lie as quiet as possible, and placed the water-canteens and pistols where we could find them in the dark. Then we smoked a final pipe, and swapped a final yarn; after which, we put the pipes, tobacco and bag of coin in snug holes and caves among the mail-bags, and then fastened down the coach curtains all around, and made the place as "dark as the inside of a cow," as the conductor phrased it in his picturesque way. It was certainly as dark as any place could be—nothing was even dimly visible in it. And finally, we rolled ourselves up like silk-worms, each person in his own blanket, and sank peacefully to sleep.

Whenever the stage stopped to change horses, we would wake up, and try to recollect where we were—and succeed—and in a minute or two the stage would be off again, and we likewise. We began to get into country, now, threaded here and there with little streams. These had high, steep banks on each side, and every time we flew down one bank and scrambled up the other, our party inside got mixed somewhat. First we would all be down in a pile at the forward end of the stage, nearly in a sitting posture, and in a second we would shoot to the other end, and stand on our heads. And we would sprawl and kick, too, and ward off ends and corners of mail-bags that came lumbering over us and about us; and as the dust rose from the tumult, we would all sneeze in chorus, and the majority of us would grumble, and probably say some hasty thing, like: "Take your elbow out of my ribs!—can't you quit crowding?"

Every time we avalanched from one end of the stage to the other, the Unabridged Dictionary would come too; and every time it came it damaged somebody. One trip it "barked" the Secretary's elbow; the next trip it hurt me in the stomach, and the third it tilted Bemis's nose up till he could look down his nostrils—he said. The pistols and coin soon settled to the bottom, but the pipes, pipe-stems, tobacco and canteens clattered and floundered after the Dictionary every time it made an assault on us, and aided and abetted the book by spilling tobacco in our eyes, and water down our backs.

Still, all things considered, it was a very comfortable night. It wore gradually away, and when at last a cold gray light was visible through the puckers and chinks in the curtains, we yawned and stretched with satisfaction, shed our cocoons, and felt that we had slept as much as was necessary. By and by, as the sun rose up and warmed the world, we pulled off our clothes and got ready for breakfast. We were just pleasantly in time, for five minutes afterward the driver sent the weird music of his bugle winding over the grassy solitudes, and presently we detected a low hut or two in the distance. Then the rattling of the coach, the clatter of our six horses' hoofs, and the driver's crisp commands, awoke to a louder and stronger emphasis, and we went sweeping down on the station at our smartest speed. It was fascinating—that old overland stagecoaching.

We jumped out in undress uniform. The driver tossed his gathered reins out on the ground, gaped and stretched complacently, drew off his heavy buckskin gloves with great deliberation and insufferable dignity—taking not the slightest notice of a dozen solicitous inquires after his health, and

humbly facetious and flattering accostings, and obsequious tenders of service, from five or six hairy and half-civilized station-keepers and hostlers who were nimbly unhitching our steeds and bringing the fresh team out of the stables—for in the eyes of the stage-driver of that day, station-keepers and hostlers were a sort of good enough low creatures, useful in their place, and helping to make up a world, but not the kind of beings which a person of distinction could afford to concern himself with; while, on the contrary, in the eyes of the station-keeper and the hostler, the stage-driver was a hero—a great and shining dignitary, the world's favorite son, the envy of the people, the observed of the nations. When they spoke to him they received his insolent silence meekly, and as being the natural and proper conduct of so great a man; when he opened his lips they all hung on his words with admiration (he never honored a particular individual with a remark, but addressed it with a broad generality to the horses, the stables, the surrounding country and the human underlings); when he discharged a facetious insulting personality at a hostler, that hostler was happy for the day; when he uttered his one jest— old as the hills, coarse, profane, witless, and inflicted on the same audience, in the same language, every time his coach drove up there—the varlets roared, and slapped their thighs, and swore it was the best thing they'd ever heard in all their lives. And how they would fly around when he wanted a basin of water, a gourd of the same, or a light for his pipe!—but they would instantly insult a passenger if he so far forgot himself as to crave a favor at their hands. They could do that sort of insolence as well as the driver they copied it from—for, let it be borne in mind, the overland driver had but little less contempt for his passengers than he had for his hostlers.

The hostlers and station-keepers treated the really powerful conductor of the coach merely with the best of what was their idea of civility, but the driver was the only being they bowed down to and worshipped. How admiringly they would gaze up at him in his high seat as he gloved himself with lingering deliberation, while some happy hostler held the bunch of reins aloft, and waited patiently for him to take it! And how they would bombard him with glorifying ejaculations as he cracked his long whip and went careering away.

The station buildings were long, low huts, made of sundried, mud-colored bricks, laid up without mortar (adobes, the Spaniards call these bricks, and Americans shorten it to 'dobies). The roofs, which had no slant to them worth speaking of, were thatched and then sodded or covered with a thick layer of earth, and from this sprung a pretty rank growth of weeds and grass. It was the first time we had ever seen a man's front yard on top of his house. The building consisted of barns, stable-room for twelve or fifteen horses, and a hut for an eating-room for passengers. This latter had bunks in it for the station-keeper and a hostler or two. You could rest your elbow on its eaves, and you had to bend in order to get in at the door. In place of a window there was a square hole about large enough for a man to crawl through, but this had no glass in it. There was no flooring, but the ground was packed hard. There was no stove, but the fire-place served all needful purposes. There were no shelves, no cupboards, no closets. In a corner stood an open sack of flour, and nestling against its base were a couple of black and venerable tin coffee-pots, a tin teapot, a little bag of salt, and a side of bacon.

By the door of the station-keeper's den, outside, was a tin wash-basin, on the ground. Near it was a pail of water and a piece of yellow bar soap, and from the eaves hung a hoary blue woolen shirt, significantly —but this latter was the station-keeper's private towel, and only two persons in all the party might venture to use it—the stage-driver and the conductor. The latter would not, from a sense of decency; the former would not, because did not choose to encourage the advances of a station-keeper. We had towels—in the valise; they might as well have been in Sodom and Gomorrah. We (and the conductor) used our handkerchiefs, and the driver his pantaloons and sleeves. By the door, inside, was fastened a small old-fashioned looking-glass frame, with two little fragments of the original mirror lodged down in one corner of it. This arrangement afforded a pleasant double-barreled portrait of you when you looked into it, with one half of your head set up a couple of inches above the other half. From the glass frame hung the half of a comb by a string—but if I had to describe that patriarch or die, I believe I would order some sample coffins.

It had come down from Esau and Samson, and had been accumulating hair ever since—along with certain impurities. In one corner of the room stood three or four rifles and muskets, together with horns and pouches of ammunition. The station-men wore pantaloons of coarse, country-woven stuff, and into the seat and the inside of the legs were sewed ample additions of buckskin, to do duty in place of leggings, when the man rode horseback—so the pants were half dull blue and half yellow, and unspeakably picturesque. The pants were stuffed into the tops of high boots, the heels whereof were armed with great Spanish spurs, whose little iron clogs and chains jingled with every step. The man wore a huge beard and mustachios, an old slouch hat, a blue woolen shirt, no suspenders, no vest, no coat—in a leathern sheath in his belt, a great long "navy" revolver (slung on right side, hammer to the front), and projecting from his boot a horn-handled bowie-knife. The furniture of the hut was neither gorgeous nor much in the way. The rocking-chairs and sofas were not present, and never had been, but they were represented by two three-legged stools, a pine-board bench four feet long, and two empty candle-boxes. The table was a greasy board on stilts, and the table-cloth and napkins had not come—and they were not looking for them, either. A battered tin platter, a knife and fork, and a tin pint cup, were at each man's place, and the driver had a queens-ware saucer that had seen better days. Of course this duke sat at the head of the table. There was one isolated piece of table furniture that bore about it a touching air of grandeur in misfortune. This was the caster. It was German silver, and crippled and rusty, but it was so preposterously out of place there that it was suggestive of a tattered exiled king among barbarians, and the majesty of its native position compelled respect even in its degradation.

There was only one cruet left, and that was a stopperless, fly-specked, broken-necked thing, with two inches of vinegar in it, and a dozen preserved flies with their heels up and looking sorry they had invested there.

The station-keeper upended a disk of last week's bread, of the shape and size of an old-time cheese, and carved some slabs from it which were as good as Nicholson pavement, and tenderer.

He sliced off a piece of bacon for each man, but only the experienced old hands made out to eat it, for it was condemned army bacon which the United States would not feed to its soldiers in the forts, and the stage company had bought it cheap for the sustenance of their passengers and employees. We may have found this condemned army bacon further out on the plains than the section I am locating it in, but we found it—there is no gainsaying that.

Then he poured for us a beverage which he called "Slum gullion," and it is hard to think he was not inspired when he named it. It really pretended to be tea, but there was too much dish-rag, and sand, and old bacon-rind in it to deceive the intelligent traveler.

He had no sugar and no milk—not even a spoon to stir the ingredients with.

We could not eat the bread or the meat, nor drink the "slumgullion." And when I looked at that melancholy vinegar-cruet, I thought of the anecdote (a very, very old one, even at that day) of the traveler who sat down to a table which had nothing on it but a mackerel and a pot of mustard. He asked the landlord if this was all. The landlord said:

"All! Why, thunder and lightning, I should think there was mackerel enough there for six."

"But I don't like mackerel."

"Oh—then help yourself to the mustard."

In other days I had considered it a good, a very good, anecdote, but there was a dismal plausibility about it, here, that took all the humor out of it.

Our breakfast was before us, but our teeth were idle.

I tasted and smelt, and said I would take coffee, I believed. The station-boss stopped dead still, and glared at me speechless. At last, when he came to, he turned away and said, as one who communes with himself upon a matter too vast to grasp:

"Coffee! Well, if that don't go clean ahead of me, I'm d—d!"

We could not eat, and there was no conversation among the hostlers and herdsmen—we all sat at the same board. At least there was no conversation further than a single hurried request, now and then, from one employee to another. It was always in the same form, and always gruffly friendly. Its western freshness and novelty startled me, at first, and interested me; but it presently grew monotonous, and lost its charm. It was:

"Pass the bread, you son of a skunk!" No, I forget—skunk was not the word; it seems to me it was still stronger than that; I know it was, in fact, but it is gone from my memory, apparently. However, it is no matter—probably it was too strong for print, anyway. It is the landmark in my memory which tells me where I first encountered the vigorous new vernacular of the occidental plains and mountains.

We gave up the breakfast, and paid our dollar apiece and went back to our mail-bag bed in the coach, and found comfort in our pipes. Right here we suffered the first diminution of our princely state. We left our six fine horses and took six mules in their place. But they were wild Mexican fellows, and a man had to stand at the head of each of them and hold him fast while the driver gloved and got himself ready. And when at last he grasped the reins and gave the word, the men sprung suddenly away from the mules' heads and the coach shot from the station as if it had issued from a cannon. How the frantic animals did scamper! It was a fierce and furious gallop—and the gait never altered for a moment till we reeled off ten or twelve miles and swept up to the next collection of little station-huts and stables.

So we flew along all day. At 2 P.M. the belt of timber that fringes the North Platte and marks its windings through the vast level floor of the Plains came in sight. At 4 P.M. we crossed a branch of the river, and at 5 P.M. we crossed the Platte itself, and landed at Fort Kearney, fifty-six hours out from St. Joe—THREE HUNDRED MILES!

Now that was stage-coaching on the great overland, ten or twelve years ago, when perhaps not more than ten men in America, all told, expected to live to see a railroad follow that route to the Pacific. But the railroad is there, now, and it pictures a thousand odd comparisons and contrasts in my mind to read the following sketch, in the New York Times, of a recent trip over almost the very ground I have been describing. I can scarcely comprehend the new state of things:

"ACROSS THE CONTINENT.

"At 4.20 P.M., Sunday, we rolled out of the station at Omaha, and started westward on our long jaunt. A couple of hours out, dinner was announced—an "event" to those of us who had yet to experience what it is to eat in one of Pullman's hotels on wheels; so, stepping into the car next forward of our sleeping palace, we found ourselves in the dining-car. It was a revelation to us, that first dinner on Sunday. And though we continued to dine for four days, and had as many breakfasts and suppers, our whole party never ceased to admire the perfection of the arrangements, and the marvelous results achieved. Upon tables covered with snowy linen, and garnished with services of solid silver, Ethiop waiters, flitting about in spotless white, placed as by magic a repast at which Delmonico himself could have had no occasion to blush; and, indeed, in some respects it would be hard for that distinguished chef to match our menu; for, in addition to all that ordinarily makes up a first-chop dinner, had we not our antelope steak (the gormand who has not experienced this — bah! what does he know of the feast of fat things?) our delicious mountain-brook trout, and choice fruits and berries, and (sauce piquant and unpurchasable!) our sweet-scented, appetite-compelling air of the prairies?

"You may depend upon it, we all did justice to the good things, and as we washed them down with bumpers of sparkling Krug, whilst we sped along at the rate of thirty miles an hour, agreed it was the fastest living we had ever experienced. (We beat that, however, two days afterward when we made twenty-seven miles in twenty-seven minutes, while our Champagne glasses filled to the brim spilled not a drop!) After dinner we repaired to our drawing-room car, and, as it was Sabbath eve, intoned some of the grand old hymns— "Praise God from whom," etc.; "Shining Shore," "Coronation," etc.—the voices of the men singers and of the women singers blending sweetly in the evening air, while our train, with its great, glaring Polyphemus eye, lighting up long vistas of prairie, rushed into the night and the Wild. Then to bed in luxurious couches, where we slept the sleep of the just and only awoke the next morning (Monday) at eight o'clock, to find ourselves at the crossing of the North Platte, three hundred miles from Omaha—fifteen hours and forty minutes out."

CHAPTER V.

Another night of alternate tranquillity and turmoil. But morning came, by and by. It was another glad awakening to fresh breezes, vast expanses of level greensward, bright sunlight, an impressive solitude utterly without visible human beings or human habitations, and an atmosphere of such amazing magnifying properties that trees that seemed close at hand were more than three mile away. We resumed undress uniform, climbed a-top of the flying coach, dangled our legs over the side, shouted occasionally at our frantic mules, merely to see them lay their ears back and scamper faster, tied our hats on to keep our hair from blowing away, and leveled an outlook over the world-wide carpet about us for things new and strange to gaze at. Even at this day it thrills me through and through to think of the life, the gladness and the wild sense of freedom that used to make the blood dance in my veins on those fine overland mornings!

Along about an hour after breakfast we saw the first prairie-dog villages, the first antelope, and the first wolf. If I remember rightly, this latter was the regular cayote (pronounced ky-o-te) of the farther deserts. And if it was, he was not a pretty creature or respectable either, for I got well acquainted with his race afterward, and can speak with confidence. The cayote is a long, slim, sick and sorry-looking skeleton, with a gray wolf-skin stretched over it, a tolerably bushy tail that forever sags down with a despairing expression of forsakenness and misery, a furtive and evil eye, and a long, sharp face, with slightly lifted lip and exposed teeth. He has a general slinking expression all over. The cayote is a living, breathing allegory of Want. He is always hungry.

He is always poor, out of luck and friendless. The meanest creatures despise him, and even the fleas would desert him for a velocipede. He is so spiritless and cowardly that even while his exposed teeth are pretending a threat, the rest of his face is apologizing for it. And he is so homely!—so scrawny, and ribby, and coarse-haired, and pitiful. When he sees you he lifts his lip and lets a flash of his teeth out, and then turns a little out of the course he was pursuing, depresses his head a bit, and strikes a long, soft-footed trot through the sage-brush, glancing over his shoulder at you, from time to time, till he is about out of easy pistol range, and then he stops and takes a deliberate survey of you; he will trot fifty yards and stop again—another fifty and stop again; and finally the gray of his gliding body blends with the gray of the sage-brush, and he disappears. All this is when you make no demonstration against him; but if you do, he develops a livelier interest in his journey, and instantly electrifies his heels and puts such a deal of real estate between himself and your weapon, that by the time you have raised the hammer you see that you need a minie rifle, and by the time you have got him in line you need a rifled cannon, and by the time you have "drawn a bead" on him you see well enough that nothing but an unusually long-winded streak of lightning could reach him where he is now. But if you start a swift-footed dog after him, you will enjoy it ever so much—especially if it is a dog that has a good opinion of himself, and has been brought up to think he knows something about speed.

The cayote will go swinging gently off on that deceitful trot of his, and every little while he will smile a fraudful smile over his shoulder that will fill that dog entirely full of encouragement and worldly ambition, and make him lay his head still lower to the ground, and stretch his neck further to the front, and pant more fiercely, and stick his tail out straighter behind, and move his furious legs with a yet wilder frenzy, and leave a broader and broader, and higher and denser cloud of desert sand smoking behind, and marking his long wake across the level plain! And all this time the dog is only a short twenty feet behind the cayote, and to save the soul of him he cannot understand why it is that he cannot get perceptibly closer; and he begins to get aggravated, and it makes him madder and madder to see how gently the cayote glides along and never pants or sweats or ceases to smile; and he grows still more and

Roughing It 547

more incensed to see how shamefully he has been taken in by an entire stranger, and what an ignoble swindle that long, calm, soft-footed trot is; and next he notices that he is getting fagged, and that the cayote actually has to slacken speed a little to keep from running away from him—and then that town-dog is mad in earnest, and he begins to strain and weep and swear, and paw the sand higher than ever, and reach for the cayote with concentrated and desperate energy. This "spurt" finds him six feet behind the gliding enemy, and two miles from his friends. And then, in the instant that a wild new hope is lighting up his face, the cayote turns and smiles blandly upon him once more, and with a something about it which seems to say: "Well, I shall have to tear myself away from you, bub—business is business, and it will not do for me to be fooling along this way all day"—and forthwith there is a rushing sound, and the sudden splitting of a long crack through the atmosphere, and behold that dog is solitary and alone in the midst of a vast solitude!

It makes his head swim. He stops, and looks all around; climbs the nearest sand-mound, and gazes into the distance; shakes his head reflectively, and then, without a word, he turns and jogs along back to his train, and takes up a humble position under the hindmost wagon, and feels unspeakably mean, and looks ashamed, and hangs his tail at half-mast for a week. And for as much as a year after that, whenever there is a great hue and cry after a cayote, that dog will merely glance in that direction without emotion, and apparently observe to himself, "I believe I do not wish any of the pie."

The cayote lives chiefly in the most desolate and forbidding desert, along with the lizard, the jackass-rabbit and the raven, and gets an uncertain and precarious living, and earns it. He seems to subsist almost wholly on the carcases of oxen, mules and horses that have dropped out of emigrant trains and died, and upon windfalls of carrion, and occasional legacies of offal bequeathed to him by white men who have been opulent enough to have something better to butcher than condemned army bacon.

He will eat anything in the world that his first cousins, the desert-frequenting tribes of Indians will, and they will eat anything they can bite. It is a curious fact that these latter are the only creatures known to history who will eat nitro-glycerine and ask for more if they survive.

The cayote of the deserts beyond the Rocky Mountains has a peculiarly hard time of it, owing to the fact that his relations, the Indians, are just as apt to be the first to detect a seductive scent on the desert breeze, and follow the fragrance to the late ox it emanated from, as he is himself; and when this occurs he has to content himself with sitting off at a little distance watching those people strip off and dig out everything edible, and walk off with it. Then he and the waiting ravens explore the skeleton and polish the bones. It is considered that the cayote, and the obscene bird, and the Indian of the desert, testify their blood kinship with each other in that they live together in the waste places of the earth on terms of perfect confidence and friendship, while hating all other creature and yearning to assist at their funerals. He does not mind going a hundred miles to breakfast, and a hundred and fifty to dinner, because he is sure to have three or four days between meals, and he can just as well be traveling and looking at the scenery as lying around doing nothing and adding to the burdens of his parents.

We soon learned to recognize the sharp, vicious bark of the cayote as it came across the murky plain at night to disturb

our dreams among the mail-sacks; and remembering his forlorn aspect and his hard fortune, made shift to wish him the blessed novelty of a long day's good luck and a limitless larder the morrow.

CHAPTER VI.

Our new conductor (just shipped) had been without sleep for twenty hours. Such a thing was very frequent. From St. Joseph, Missouri, to Sacramento, California, by stage-coach, was nearly nineteen hundred miles, and the trip was often made in fifteen days (the cars do it in four and a half, now), but the time specified in the mail contracts, and required by the schedule, was eighteen or nineteen days, if I remember rightly. This was to make fair allowance for winter storms and snows, and other unavoidable causes of detention. The stage company had everything under strict discipline and good system. Over each two hundred and fifty miles of road they placed an agent or superintendent, and invested him with great authority. His beat or jurisdiction of two hundred and fifty miles was called a "division." He purchased horses, mules harness, and food for men and beasts, and distributed these things among his stage stations, from time to time, according to his judgment of what each station needed. He erected station buildings and dug wells. He attended to the paying of the station-keepers, hostlers, drivers and blacksmiths, and discharged them whenever he chose. He was a very, very great man in his "division"—a kind of Grand Mogul, a Sultan of the Indies, in whose presence common men were modest of speech and manner, and in the glare of whose greatness even the dazzling stage-driver dwindled to a penny dip. There were about eight of these kings, all told, on the overland route.

Next in rank and importance to the division-agent came the "conductor." His beat was the same length as the agent's—two hundred and fifty miles. He sat with the driver, and (when necessary) rode that fearful distance, night and day, without other rest or sleep than what he could get perched thus on top of the flying vehicle. Think of it! He had absolute charge of the mails, express matter, passengers and stage, coach, until he delivered them to the next conductor, and got his receipt for them.

Consequently he had to be a man of intelligence, decision and considerable executive ability. He was usually a quiet, pleasant man, who attended closely to his duties, and was a good deal of a gentleman. It was not absolutely necessary that the division-agent should be a gentleman, and occasionally he wasn't. But he was always a general in administrative ability, and a bull-dog in courage and determination —otherwise the chieftainship over the lawless underlings of the overland service would never in any instance have been to him anything but an equivalent for a month of insolence and distress and a bullet and a coffin at the end of it. There were about sixteen or eighteen conductors on the overland, for there was a daily stage each way, and a conductor on every stage.

Next in real and official rank and importance, after the conductor, came my delight, the driver—next in real but not in apparent importance—for we have seen that in the eyes of the common herd the driver was to the conductor as an admiral is to the captain of the flag-ship. The driver's beat was pretty long, and his sleeping-time at the stations pretty short, sometimes; and so, but for the grandeur of his position his would have been a sorry life, as well as a hard and a wearing one. We took a new driver every day or every night (for they drove backward and forward over the same piece of road all the time), and therefore we never got as well acquainted with them as we did with the conductors; and besides, they would have been above being familiar with such rubbish as passengers, anyhow, as a general thing. Still, we were always eager to get a sight of each and every new driver as soon as the watch changed, for each and every day we were either anxious to get rid of an unpleasant one, or loath to part with a driver we had learned to like and had come to be sociable and friendly with. And so the first question we asked the conductor whenever we got to where we were to exchange drivers, was always, "Which is him?" The grammar was faulty, maybe, but we could not know, then, that it would go into a book some day. As long as everything went smoothly, the overland driver was well enough situated, but if a fellow driver got sick suddenly it made trouble, for the coach must go on, and so the potentate who was about to climb down and take a luxurious rest after his long night's siege in the midst of wind and rain and darkness, had to stay where he was and do the sick man's work. Once, in the Rocky Mountains, when I found a driver sound asleep on the box, and the mules going at the usual break-neck pace, the conductor said never mind him, there was no danger, and he was doing double duty—had driven seventy-five miles on one coach, and was now going back over it on this without rest or sleep. A hundred and fifty miles of holding back of six vindictive mules and keeping them from climbing the trees! It sounds incredible, but I remember the statement well enough.

The station-keepers, hostlers, etc., were low, rough characters, as already described; and from western Nebraska to Nevada a considerable sprinkling of them might be fairly set down as outlaws—fugitives from justice, criminals whose best security was a section of country which was without law and without even the pretence of it. When the "division-agent" issued an order to one of these parties he did it with the full understanding that he might have to enforce it with a navy six-shooter, and so he always went "fixed" to make things go along smoothly.

Now and then a division-agent was really obliged to shoot a hostler through the head to teach him some simple matter that he could have taught him with a club if his circumstances and surroundings had been different. But they were snappy, able men, those division-agents, and when they tried to teach a subordinate anything, that subordinate generally "got it through his head."

A great portion of this vast machinery—these hundreds of men and coaches, and thousands of mules and horses—was in the hands of Mr. Ben Holliday. All the western half of the business was in his hands. This reminds me of an incident of Palestine travel which is pertinent here, so I will transfer it just in the language in which I find it set down in my Holy Land note-book:

No doubt everybody has heard of Ben Holliday—a man of prodigious energy, who used to send mails and passengers flying across the continent in his overland stage-coaches like a very whirlwind—two thousand long miles in fifteen days and a half, by the watch! But this fragment of history is not about Ben Holliday, but about a young New York boy by the name of Jack, who traveled with our small party of pilgrims in the Holy Land (and who had traveled to California in Mr. Holliday's overland coaches three years before, and had by no means forgotten it or lost his gushing admiration of Mr. H.) Aged nineteen. Jack was a good boy—a good-hearted and always well-meaning boy, who had been reared in the city of New York, and although he was bright and knew a great many useful things, his Scriptural education had been a good deal neglected—to such a degree, indeed, that all Holy Land history was fresh and new to him, and all Bible names mysteries that had never disturbed his virgin ear.

Also in our party was an elderly pilgrim who was the reverse of Jack, in that he was learned in the Scriptures and an enthusiast concerning them. He was our encyclopedia, and we were never tired of listening to his speeches, nor he of making them. He never passed a celebrated locality, from Bashan to Bethlehem, without illuminating it with an oration. One day, when camped near the ruins of Jericho, he burst forth with something like this:

"Jack, do you see that range of mountains over yonder that bounds the Jordan valley? The mountains of Moab, Jack! Think of it, my boy—the actual mountains of Moab—renowned in Scripture history! We are actually standing face to face with those illustrious crags and peaks—and for all we know" [dropping his voice impressively], "our eyes may be resting at this very moment upon the spot WHERE LIES THE MYSTERIOUS GRAVE OF MOSES! Think of it, Jack!"

"Moses who?" (falling inflection).

"Moses who! Jack, you ought to be ashamed of yourself—you ought to be ashamed of such criminal ignorance. Why, Moses, the great guide, soldier, poet, lawgiver of ancient Israel! Jack, from this spot where we stand, to Egypt, stretches a fearful desert three hundred miles in extent—and across that desert that wonderful man brought the children of Israel!—guiding them with unfailing sagacity for forty years over the sandy desolation and among the obstructing rocks and hills, and landed them at last, safe and sound, within sight of this very spot; and where we now stand they entered the Promised Land with anthems of rejoicing! It was a wonderful, wonderful thing to do, Jack! Think of it!"

"Forty years? Only three hundred miles? Humph! Ben Holliday would have fetched them through in thirty-six hours!"

The boy meant no harm. He did not know that he had said anything that was wrong or irreverent. And so no one scolded him or felt offended with him—and nobody could but some ungenerous spirit incapable of excusing the heedless blunders of a boy.

At noon on the fifth day out, we arrived at the "Crossing of the South Platte," alias "Julesburg," alias "Overland City," four hundred and seventy miles from St. Joseph—the strangest, quaintest, funniest frontier town that our untraveled eyes had ever stared at and been astonished with.

CHAPTER VII.

It did seem strange enough to see a town again after what appeared to us such a long acquaintance with deep, still, almost lifeless and houseless solitude! We tumbled out into the busy street feeling like meteoric people crumbled off the corner of some other world, and wakened up suddenly in this. For an hour we took as much interest in Overland City as if we had never seen a town before. The reason we had an hour to spare was because we had to change our stage (for a less sumptuous affair, called a "mud-wagon") and transfer our freight of mails.

Presently we got under way again. We came to the shallow, yellow, muddy South Platte, with its low banks and its scattering flat sand-bars and pigmy islands—a melancholy stream straggling through the centre of the enormous flat plain, and only saved from being impossible to find with the naked eye by its sentinel rank of scattering trees standing on either bank. The Platte was "up," they said—which made me wish I could see it when it was down, if it could look any sicker and sorrier. They said it was a dangerous stream to cross, now, because its quicksands were liable to swallow up horses, coach and passengers if an attempt was made to ford it. But the mails had to go, and we made the attempt. Once or twice in midstream the wheels sunk into the yielding sands so threateningly that we half believed we had dreaded and avoided the sea all our lives to be shipwrecked in a "mud-wagon" in the middle of a desert at last. But we dragged through and sped away toward the setting sun.

Next morning, just before dawn, when about five hundred and fifty miles from St. Joseph, our mud-wagon broke down. We were to be delayed five or six hours, and therefore we took horses, by invitation, and joined a party who were just starting on a buffalo hunt. It was noble sport galloping over the plain in the dewy freshness of the morning, but our part of the hunt ended in disaster and disgrace, for a wounded buffalo bull chased the passenger Bemis nearly two miles, and then he forsook his horse and took to a lone tree. He was very sullen about the matter for some twenty-four hours, but at last he began to soften little by little, and finally he said:

"Well, it was not funny, and there was no sense in those gawks making themselves so facetious over it. I tell you I was angry in earnest for awhile. I should have shot that long gangly lubber they called Hank, if I could have done it without crippling six or seven other people—but of course I couldn't, the old 'Allen's' so confounded comprehensive. I wish those loafers had been up in the tree; they wouldn't have wanted to laugh so. If I had had a horse worth a cent—but no, the minute he saw that buffalo bull wheel on him and give a bellow, he raised straight up in the air and stood on his heels. The saddle began to slip, and I took him round the neck and laid close to him, and began to pray. Then he came down and stood up on the other end awhile, and the bull actually stopped pawing sand and bellowing to contemplate the inhuman spectacle.

"Then the bull made a pass at him and uttered a bellow that sounded perfectly frightful, it was so close to me, and that seemed to literally prostrate my horse's reason, and make a raving distracted maniac of him, and I wish I may die if he didn't stand on his head for a quarter of a minute and shed tears. He was absolutely out of his mind—he was, as sure as truth itself, and he really didn't know what he was doing. Then the bull came charging at us, and my horse dropped down on all fours and took a fresh start—and then for the next ten minutes he would actually throw one hand-spring after another so fast that the bull began to get unsettled, too, and didn't know where to start in—and so he stood there sneezing, and shovelling dust over his back, and bellowing every now and then, and thinking he had got a fifteen-hundred dollar circus horse for breakfast, certain. Well, I was first out on his neck—the horse's, not the bull's—and then underneath, and next on his rump, and sometimes head up, and sometimes heels—but I tell you it seemed solemn and awful to be ripping and tearing and carrying on so in the presence of death, as you might say. Pretty soon the bull made a snatch for us and brought away some of my horse's tail (I suppose, but do not know, being pretty busy at the time), but something made him hungry for solitude and suggested to him to get up and hunt for it.

"And then you ought to have seen that spider legged old skeleton go! and you ought to have seen the bull cut out after him, too—head down, tongue out, tail up, bellowing like everything, and actually mowing down the weeds, and tearing up the earth, and boosting up the sand like a whirlwind! By George, it was a hot race! I and the saddle were back on the rump, and I had the bridle in my teeth and holding on to the pommel with both hands. First we left the dogs behind; then we passed a jackass rabbit; then we overtook a cayote, and were gaining on an antelope when the rotten girth let go and threw me about thirty yards off to the left, and as the saddle went down over the horse's rump he gave it a lift with his heels that sent it more than four hundred yards up in the air, I wish I may die in a minute if he didn't. I fell at the foot of the only solitary tree there was in nine counties adjacent (as any creature could see with the naked eye), and the next second I had hold of the bark with four sets of nails and my teeth, and the next second after that I was astraddle of the main limb and blaspheming my luck in a way that made my breath smell of brimstone. I had the bull, now, if he did not think of one thing. But that one thing I dreaded. I dreaded it very seriously. There was a possibility that the bull might not think of it, but there were greater chances that he would. I made up my mind what I would do in case he did. It was a little over forty feet to the ground from where I sat. I cautiously unwound the lariat from the pommel of my saddle—"

"Your saddle? Did you take your saddle up in the tree with you?"

"Take it up in the tree with me? Why, how you talk. Of course I didn't. No man could do that. It fell in the tree when it came down."

"Oh—exactly."

"Certainly. I unwound the lariat, and fastened one end of it to the limb. It was the very best green raw-hide, and capable of sustaining tons. I made a slip-noose in the other end, and then hung it down to see the length. It reached down twenty-two feet—half way to the ground. I then loaded every barrel of the Allen with a double charge. I felt satisfied. I said to myself, if he never thinks of that one thing that I dread, all right—but if he does, all right anyhow—I am fixed for him. But don't you know that the very thing a man dreads is the thing that always happens? Indeed it is so. I watched the bull, now, with anxiety —anxiety which no one can conceive of who has not been in such a situation and felt that at any moment death might come. Presently a thought came into the bull's eye. I knew it! said I—if my nerve fails now, I am lost. Sure enough, it was just as I had dreaded, he started in to climb the tree—"

"What, the bull?"

"Of course—who else?"

"But a bull can't climb a tree."

"He can't, can't he? Since you know so much about it, did you ever see a bull try?"

"No! I never dreamt of such a thing."

"Well, then, what is the use of your talking that way, then? Because you never saw a thing done, is that any reason why it can't be done?"

"Well, all right—go on. What did you do?"

"The bull started up, and got along well for about ten feet, then slipped and slid back. I breathed easier. He tried it again—got up a little higher—slipped again. But he came at it once more, and this time he was careful. He got gradually higher and higher, and my spirits went down more and more. Up he came—an inch at a time—with his eyes hot, and his tongue hanging out. Higher and higher—hitched his foot over the stump of a limb, and looked up, as much as to say, 'You are my meat, friend.' Up again—higher and higher, and getting more excited the closer he got. He was within ten feet of me! I took a long breath,—and then said I, 'It is now or never.' I had the coil of the lariat all ready; I paid it out slowly, till it hung right over his head; all of a sudden I let go of the slack, and the slipnoose fell fairly round his neck! Quicker than lightning I out with the Allen and let him have it in the face. It was an awful roar, and must have scared the bull out of his senses. When the smoke cleared away, there he was, dangling in the air, twenty foot from the ground, and going out of one convulsion into another faster than you could count! I didn't stop to count, anyhow—I shinned down the tree and shot for home."

"Bemis, is all that true, just as you have stated it?"

"I wish I may rot in my tracks and die the death of a dog if it isn't."

"Well, we can't refuse to believe it, and we don't. But if there were some proofs—"

"Proofs! Did I bring back my lariat?"

"No."

"Did I bring back my horse?"

"No."

"Did you ever see the bull again?"

"No."

"Well, then, what more do you want? I never saw anybody as particular as you are about a little thing like that."

I made up my mind that if this man was not a liar he only missed it by the skin of his teeth. This episode reminds me of an incident of my brief sojourn in Siam, years afterward. The European citizens of a town in the neighborhood of Bangkok had a prodigy among them by the name of Eckert, an Englishman—a person famous for the number, ingenuity and imposing magnitude of his lies. They were always repeating his most celebrated falsehoods, and always trying to "draw him out" before strangers; but they seldom succeeded. Twice he was invited to the house where I was visiting, but nothing could seduce him into a specimen lie. One day a planter named Bascom, an influential man, and a proud and sometimes irascible one, invited me to ride over with him and call on Eckert. As we jogged along, said he:

"Now, do you know where the fault lies? It lies in putting Eckert on his guard. The minute the boys go to pumping at Eckert he knows perfectly well what they are after, and of course he shuts up his shell. Anybody might know he would. But when we get there, we must play him finer than that. Let him shape the conversation to suit himself—let him drop it or change it whenever he wants to. Let him see that nobody is trying to draw him out. Just let him have his own way. He will

soon forget himself and begin to grind out lies like a mill. Don't get impatient —just keep quiet, and let me play him. I will make him lie. It does seem to me that the boys must be blind to overlook such an obvious and simple trick as that."

Eckert received us heartily—a pleasant-spoken, gentle-mannered creature. We sat in the veranda an hour, sipping English ale, and talking about the king, and the sacred white elephant, the Sleeping Idol, and all manner of things; and I noticed that my comrade never led the conversation himself or shaped it, but simply followed Eckert's lead, and betrayed no solicitude and no anxiety about anything. The effect was shortly perceptible. Eckert began to grow communicative; he grew more and more at his ease, and more and more talkative and sociable. Another hour passed in the same way, and then all of a sudden Eckert said:

"Oh, by the way! I came near forgetting. I have got a thing here to astonish you. Such a thing as neither you nor any other man ever heard of—I've got a cat that will eat cocoanut! Common green cocoanut—and not only eat the meat, but drink the milk. It is so—I'll swear to it."

A quick glance from Bascom—a glance that I understood—then:

"Why, bless my soul, I never heard of such a thing. Man, it is impossible."

"I knew you would say it. I'll fetch the cat."

He went in the house. Bascom said:

"There—what did I tell you? Now, that is the way to handle Eckert. You see, I have petted him along patiently, and put his suspicions to sleep. I am glad we came. You tell the boys about it when you go back. Cat eat a cocoanut—oh, my! Now, that is just his way, exactly—he will tell the absurdest lie, and trust to luck to get out of it again.

"Cat eat a cocoanut—the innocent fool!"

Eckert approached with his cat, sure enough.

Bascom smiled. Said he:

"I'll hold the cat—you bring a cocoanut."

Eckert split one open, and chopped up some pieces. Bascom smuggled a wink to me, and proffered a slice of the fruit to puss. She snatched it, swallowed it ravenously, and asked for more!

We rode our two miles in silence, and wide apart. At least I was silent, though Bascom cuffed his horse and cursed him a good deal, notwithstanding the horse was behaving well enough. When I branched off homeward, Bascom said:

"Keep the horse till morning. And—you need not speak of this —foolishness to the boys."

CHAPTER VIII.

In a little while all interest was taken up in stretching our necks and watching for the "pony-rider"—the fleet messenger who sped across the continent from St. Joe to Sacramento, carrying letters nineteen hundred miles in eight days! Think of that for perishable horse and human flesh and blood to do!

The pony-rider was usually a little bit of a man, brimful of spirit and endurance. No matter what time of the day or night his watch came on, and no matter whether it was winter or summer, raining, snowing, hailing, or sleeting, or whether his "beat" was a level straight road or a crazy trail over mountain crags and precipices, or whether it led through peaceful regions or regions that swarmed with hostile Indians, he must be always ready to leap into the saddle and be off like the wind! There was no idling-time for a pony-rider on duty. He rode fifty miles without stopping, by daylight, moonlight, starlight, or through the blackness of darkness—just as it happened. He rode a splendid horse that was born for a racer and fed and lodged like a gentleman; kept him at his utmost speed for ten miles, and then, as he came crashing up to the station where stood two men holding fast a fresh, impatient steed, the transfer of rider and mail-bag was made in the twinkling of an eye, and away flew the eager pair and were out of sight before the spectator could get hardly the ghost of a look. Both rider and horse went "flying light." The rider's dress was thin, and fitted close; he wore a "round-about," and a skull-cap, and tucked his pantaloons into his boot-tops like a race-rider. He carried no arms—he carried nothing that was not absolutely necessary, for even the postage on his literary freight was worth five dollars a letter.

He got but little frivolous correspondence to carry—his bag had business letters in it, mostly. His horse was stripped of all unnecessary weight, too. He wore a little wafer of a racing-saddle, and no visible blanket. He wore light shoes, or none at all. The little flat mail-pockets strapped under the rider's thighs would each hold about the bulk of a child's primer. They held many and many an important business chapter and newspaper letter, but these were written on paper as airy and thin as gold-leaf, nearly, and thus bulk and weight were economized. The stage-coach traveled about a hundred to a hundred and twenty-five miles a day (twenty-four hours), the pony-rider about two hundred and fifty. There were about eighty pony-riders in the saddle all the time, night and day, stretching in a long, scattering procession from Missouri to California, forty flying eastward, and forty toward the west, and among them making four hundred gallant horses earn a stirring livelihood and see a deal of scenery every single day in the year.

We had had a consuming desire, from the beginning, to see a pony-rider, but somehow or other all that passed us and all that met us managed to streak by in the night, and so we heard only a whiz and a hail, and the swift phantom of the desert was gone before we could get our heads out of the windows. But now we were expecting one along every moment, and would see him in broad daylight. Presently the driver exclaims:

"HERE HE COMES!"

Every neck is stretched further, and every eye strained wider. Away across the endless dead level of the prairie a black speck appears against the sky, and it is plain that it moves. Well, I should think so!

In a second or two it becomes a horse and rider, rising and falling, rising and falling—sweeping toward us nearer and nearer—growing more and more distinct, more and more sharply defined—nearer and still nearer, and the flutter of the hoofs comes faintly to the ear—another instant a whoop and a hurrah from our upper deck, a wave of the rider's hand, but no reply, and man and horse burst past our excited faces, and go winging away like a belated fragment of a storm!

So sudden is it all, and so like a flash of unreal fancy, that but for the flake of white foam left quivering and perishing on a mail-sack after the vision had flashed by and disappeared, we might have doubted whether we had seen any actual horse and man at all, maybe.

We rattled through Scott's Bluffs Pass, by and by. It was along here somewhere that we first came across genuine and unmistakable alkali water in the road, and we cordially hailed it as a first-class curiosity, and a thing to be mentioned with eclat in letters to the ignorant at home. This water gave the road a soapy appearance, and in many places the ground looked as if it had been whitewashed. I think the strange alkali water excited us as much as any wonder we had come upon yet, and I know we felt very complacent and conceited, and better satisfied with life after we had added it to our list of things which we had seen and some other people had not. In a small way we were the same sort of simpletons as those who climb unnecessarily the perilous peaks of Mont Blanc and the Matterhorn, and derive no pleasure from it except the reflection that it isn't a common experience. But once in a while one of those parties trips and comes darting down the long mountain-crags in a sitting posture, making the crusted snow smoke behind him, flitting from bench to bench, and from terrace to terrace, jarring the earth where he strikes, and still glancing and flitting on again, sticking an iceberg into himself every now and then, and tearing his clothes, snatching at things to save himself, taking hold of trees and fetching them along with him, roots and all, starting little rocks now and then, then big boulders, then acres of ice and snow and patches of forest, gathering and still gathering as he goes, adding and still adding to his massed and sweeping grandeur as he nears a three thousand-foot precipice, till at last he waves his hat magnificently and rides into eternity on the back of a raging and tossing avalanche!

This is all very fine, but let us not be carried away by excitement, but ask calmly, how does this person feel about it in his cooler moments next day, with six or seven thousand feet of snow and stuff on top of him?

We crossed the sand hills near the scene of the Indian mail robbery and massacre of 1856, wherein the driver and conductor perished, and also all the passengers but one, it was supposed; but this must have been a mistake, for at different times afterward on the Pacific coast I was personally acquainted with a hundred and thirty-three or four people who were wounded during that massacre, and barely escaped with their lives. There was no doubt of the truth of it—I had it from their own lips. One of these parties told me that he kept coming across arrow-heads in his system for nearly seven years after the massacre; and another of them told me that he was struck so literally full of arrows that after the Indians were gone and he could raise up and examine himself, he could not restrain his tears, for his clothes were completely ruined.

The most trustworthy tradition avers, however, that only one man, a person named Babbitt, survived the massacre, and he was desperately wounded. He dragged himself on his hands and knee (for one leg was broken) to a station several miles away. He did it during portions of two nights, lying concealed one day and part of another, and for more than forty hours suffering unimaginable anguish from hunger, thirst and bodily pain. The Indians robbed the coach of everything it contained, including quite an amount of treasure.

CHAPTER IX.

We passed Fort Laramie in the night, and on the seventh morning out we found ourselves in the Black Hills, with Laramie Peak at our elbow (apparently) looming vast and solitary—a deep, dark, rich indigo blue in hue, so portentously did the old colossus frown under his beetling brows of storm-cloud. He was thirty or forty miles away, in reality, but he only seemed removed a little beyond the low ridge at our right. We breakfasted at Horse-Shoe Station, six hundred and seventy-six miles out from St. Joseph. We had now reached a hostile Indian country, and during the afternoon we passed Laparelle Station, and enjoyed great discomfort all the time we were in the neighborhood, being aware that many of the trees we dashed by at arm's length concealed a lurking Indian or two. During the preceding night an ambushed savage had sent a bullet through the pony-rider's jacket, but he had ridden on, just the same, because pony-riders were not allowed to stop and inquire into such things except when killed. As long as they had life enough left in them they had to stick to the horse and ride, even if the Indians had been waiting for them a week, and were entirely out of patience. About two hours and a half before we arrived at Laparelle Station, the keeper in charge of it had fired four times at an Indian, but he said with an injured air that the Indian had "skipped around so's to spile everything—and ammunition's blamed skurse, too." The most natural inference conveyed by his manner of speaking was, that in "skipping around," the Indian had taken an unfair advantage.

The coach we were in had a neat hole through its front—a reminiscence of its last trip through this region. The bullet that made it wounded the driver slightly, but he did not mind it much. He said the place to keep a man "huffy" was down on the Southern Overland, among the Apaches, before the company moved the stage line up on the northern route. He said the Apaches used to annoy him all the time down there, and that he came as near as anything to starving to death in the midst of abundance, because they kept him so leaky with bullet holes that he "couldn't hold his vittles."

This person's statement were not generally believed.

We shut the blinds down very tightly that first night in the hostile Indian country, and lay on our arms. We slept on them some, but most of the time we only lay on them. We did not talk much, but kept quiet and listened. It was an inky-black night, and occasionally rainy. We were among woods and rocks, hills and gorges—so shut in, in fact, that when we peeped through a chink in a curtain, we could discern nothing. The driver and conductor on top were still, too, or only spoke at long intervals, in low tones, as is the way of men in the midst of invisible dangers. We listened to rain-drops pattering on the roof; and the grinding of the wheels through the muddy gravel; and the low wailing of the wind; and all the time we had that absurd sense upon us, inseparable from travel at night in a close-curtained vehicle, the sense of remaining perfectly still in one place, notwithstanding the jolting and swaying of the vehicle, the trampling of the horses, and the grinding of the wheels. We listened a long time, with intent faculties and bated breath; every time one of us would relax, and draw a long sigh of relief and start to say something, a comrade would be sure to utter a sudden "Hark!" and instantly the experimenter was rigid and listening again. So the tiresome minutes and decades of minutes dragged away, until at last our tense forms filmed over with a dulled consciousness, and we slept, if one might call such a condition by so strong a name—for it was a sleep set with a hair-trigger. It was a sleep seething and teeming with a weird and distressful confusion of shreds and fag-ends of dreams—a

sleep that was a chaos. Presently, dreams and sleep and the sullen hush of the night were startled by a ringing report, and cloven by such a long, wild, agonizing shriek! Then we heard—ten steps from the stage—

"Help! help! help!" [It was our driver's voice.]

"Kill him! Kill him like a dog!"

"I'm being murdered! Will no man lend me a pistol?"

"Look out! head him off! head him off!"

[Two pistol shots; a confusion of voices and the trampling of many feet, as if a crowd were closing and surging together around some object; several heavy, dull blows, as with a club; a voice that said appealingly, "Don't, gentlemen, please don't—I'm a dead man!" Then a fainter groan, and another blow, and away sped the stage into the darkness, and left the grisly mystery behind us.]

What a startle it was! Eight seconds would amply cover the time it occupied—maybe even five would do it. We only had time to plunge at a curtain and unbuckle and unbutton part of it in an awkward and hindering flurry, when our whip cracked sharply overhead, and we went rumbling and thundering away, down a mountain "grade."

We fed on that mystery the rest of the night—what was left of it, for it was waning fast. It had to remain a present mystery, for all we could get from the conductor in answer to our hails was something that sounded, through the clatter of the wheels, like "Tell you in the morning!"

So we lit our pipes and opened the corner of a curtain for a chimney, and lay there in the dark, listening to each other's story of how he first felt and how many thousand Indians he first thought had hurled themselves upon us, and what his remembrance of the subsequent sounds was, and the order of their occurrence. And we theorized, too, but there was never a theory that would account for our driver's voice being out there, nor yet account for his Indian murderers talking such good English, if they were Indians.

So we chatted and smoked the rest of the night comfortably away, our boding anxiety being somehow marvelously dissipated by the real presence of something to be anxious about.

We never did get much satisfaction about that dark occurrence. All that we could make out of the odds and ends of the information we gathered in the morning, was that the disturbance occurred at a station; that we changed drivers there, and that the driver that got off there had been talking roughly about some of the outlaws that infested the region ("for there wasn't a man around there but had a price on his head and didn't dare show himself in the settlements," the conductor said); he had talked roughly about these characters, and ought to have "drove up there with his pistol cocked and ready on the seat alongside of him, and begun business himself, because any softy would know they would be laying for him."

That was all we could gather, and we could see that neither the conductor nor the new driver were much concerned about the matter. They plainly had little respect for a man who would deliver offensive opinions of people and then be so simple as to come into their presence unprepared to "back his judgment," as they pleasantly phrased the killing of any fellow-being who did not like said opinions. And likewise they plainly had a contempt for the man's poor discretion in venturing to rouse the wrath of such utterly reckless wild beasts as those outlaws—and the conductor added:

"I tell you it's as much as Slade himself want to do!"

This remark created an entire revolution in my curiosity. I cared nothing now about the Indians, and even lost interest in the murdered driver. There was such magic in that name, SLADE! Day or night, now, I stood always ready to drop any subject in hand, to listen to something new about Slade and his ghastly exploits. Even before we got to Overland City, we had begun to hear about Slade and his "division" (for he was a "division-agent") on the Overland; and from the hour we had left Overland City we had heard drivers and conductors talk about only three things —"Californy," the Nevada silver mines, and this desperado Slade. And a deal the most of the talk was about Slade. We had gradually come to have a realizing sense of the fact that Slade was a man whose heart and hands and soul were steeped in the blood of offenders against his dignity; a man who awfully avenged all injuries, affront, insults or slights, of whatever kind—on the spot if he could, years afterward if lack of earlier opportunity compelled it; a man whose hate tortured him day and night till vengeance appeased it—and not an ordinary vengeance either, but his enemy's absolute death—nothing less; a man whose face would light up with a terrible joy when he surprised a foe and had him at a disadvantage. A high and efficient servant of the Overland, an outlaw among outlaws and yet their relentless scourge, Slade was at once the most bloody, the most dangerous and the most valuable citizen that inhabited the savage fastnesses of the mountains.

CHAPTER X.

Really and truly, two thirds of the talk of drivers and conductors had been about this man Slade, ever since the day before we reached Julesburg. In order that the eastern reader may have a clear conception of what a Rocky Mountain desperado is, in his highest state of development, I will reduce all this mass of overland gossip to one straightforward narrative, and present it in the following shape:

Slade was born in Illinois, of good parentage. At about twenty-six years of age he killed a man in a quarrel and fled the country. At St. Joseph, Missouri, he joined one of the early California-bound emigrant trains, and was given the post of train-master. One day on the plains he had an angry dispute with one of his wagon-drivers, and both drew their revolvers. But the driver was the quicker artist, and had his weapon cocked first. So Slade said it was a pity to waste life on so small a matter, and proposed that the pistols be thrown on the ground and the quarrel settled by a fist-fight. The unsuspecting driver agreed, and threw down his pistol—whereupon Slade laughed at his simplicity, and shot him dead!

He made his escape, and lived a wild life for awhile, dividing his time between fighting Indians and avoiding an Illinois sheriff, who had been sent to arrest him for his first murder. It is said that in one Indian battle he killed three savages with his own hand, and afterward cut their ears off and sent them, with his compliments, to the chief of the tribe.

Slade soon gained a name for fearless resolution, and this was sufficient merit to procure for him the important post of overland division-agent at Julesburg, in place of Mr. Jules,

removed. For some time previously, the company's horses had been frequently stolen, and the coaches delayed, by gangs of outlaws, who were wont to laugh at the idea of any man's having the temerity to resent such outrages. Slade resented them promptly.

The outlaws soon found that the new agent was a man who did not fear anything that breathed the breath of life. He made short work of all offenders. The result was that delays ceased, the company's property was let alone, and no matter what happened or who suffered, Slade's coaches went through, every time! True, in order to bring about this wholesome change, Slade had to kill several men—some say three, others say four, and others six—but the world was the richer for their loss. The first prominent difficulty he had was with the ex-agent Jules, who bore the reputation of being a reckless and desperate man himself. Jules hated Slade for supplanting him, and a good fair occasion for a fight was all he was waiting for. By and by Slade dared to employ a man whom Jules had once discharged. Next, Slade seized a team of stage-horses which he accused Jules of having driven off and hidden somewhere for his own use. War was declared, and for a day or two the two men walked warily about the streets, seeking each other, Jules armed with a double-barreled shot gun, and Slade with his history-creating revolver. Finally, as Slade stepped into a store Jules poured the contents of his gun into him from behind the door. Slade was plucky, and Jules got several bad pistol wounds in return.

Then both men fell, and were carried to their respective lodgings, both swearing that better aim should do deadlier work next time. Both were bedridden a long time, but Jules got to his feet first, and gathering his possessions together, packed them on a couple of mules, and fled to the Rocky Mountains to gather strength in safety against the day of reckoning. For many months he was not seen or heard of, and was gradually dropped out of the remembrance of all save Slade himself. But Slade was not the man to forget him. On the contrary, common report said that Slade kept a reward standing for his capture, dead or alive!

After awhile, seeing that Slade's energetic administration had restored peace and order to one of the worst divisions of the road, the overland stage company transferred him to the Rocky Ridge division in the Rocky Mountains, to see if he could perform a like miracle there. It was the very paradise of outlaws and desperadoes. There was absolutely no semblance of law there. Violence was the rule. Force was the only recognized authority. The commonest misunderstandings were settled on the spot with the revolver or the knife. Murders were done in open day, and with sparkling frequency, and nobody thought of inquiring into them. It was considered that the parties who did the killing had their private reasons for it; for other people to meddle would have been looked upon as indelicate. After a murder, all that Rocky Mountain etiquette required of a spectator was, that he should help the gentleman bury his game —otherwise his churlishness would surely be remembered against him the first time he killed a man himself and needed a neighborly turn in interring him.

Slade took up his residence sweetly and peacefully in the midst of this hive of horse-thieves and assassins, and the very first time one of them aired his insolent swaggerings in his presence he shot him dead! He began a raid on the outlaws, and in a singularly short space of time he had completely stopped their depredations on the stage stock, recovered a large number of stolen horses, killed several of the worst desperadoes of the district, and gained such a dread ascendancy over the rest that they respected him, admired him, feared him, obeyed him! He wrought the same marvelous change in the ways of the community that had marked his administration at Overland City. He captured two men who had stolen overland stock, and with his own hands he hanged them. He was supreme judge in his district, and he was jury and executioner likewise—and not only in the case of offences against his employers, but against passing emigrants as well. On one occasion some emigrants had their stock lost or stolen, and told Slade, who chanced to visit their camp. With a single companion he rode to a ranch, the owners of which he suspected, and opening the door, commenced firing, killing three, and wounding the fourth.

From a bloodthirstily interesting little Montana book.—["The Vigilantes of Montana," by Prof. Thos. J. Dimsdale.]—I take this paragraph:

"While on the road, Slade held absolute sway. He would ride down to a station, get into a quarrel, turn the house out of windows, and maltreat the occupants most cruelly. The unfortunates had no means of redress, and were compelled to recuperate as best they could."

On one of these occasions, it is said he killed the father of the fine little half-breed boy Jemmy, whom he adopted, and who lived with his widow after his execution. Stories of Slade's hanging men, and of innumerable assaults, shootings, stabbings and beatings, in which he was a principal actor, form part of the legends of the stage line. As for minor quarrels and shootings, it is absolutely certain that a minute history of Slade's life would be one long record of such practices.

Slade was a matchless marksman with a navy revolver. The legends say that one morning at Rocky Ridge, when he was feeling comfortable, he saw a man approaching who had offended him some days before—observe the fine memory he had for matters like that—and, "Gentlemen," said Slade, drawing, "it is a good twenty-yard shot—I'll clip the third button on his coat!" Which he did. The bystanders all admired it. And they all attended the funeral, too.

On one occasion a man who kept a little whisky-shelf at the station did something which angered Slade—and went and made his will. A day or two afterward Slade came in and called for some brandy. The man reached under the counter (ostensibly to get a bottle—possibly to get something else), but Slade smiled upon him that peculiarly bland and satisfied smile of his which the neighbors had long ago learned to recognize as a death-warrant in disguise, and told him to "none of that!—pass out the high-priced article." So the poor bar-keeper had to turn his back and get the high-priced brandy from the shelf; and when he faced around again he was looking into the muzzle of Slade's pistol. "And the next instant," added my informant, impressively, "he was one of the deadest men that ever lived."

The stage-drivers and conductors told us that sometimes Slade would leave a hated enemy wholly unmolested, unnoticed and unmentioned, for weeks together—had done it once or twice at any rate. And some said they believed he did it in order to lull the victims into unwatchfulness, so that he could get the advantage of them, and others said they believed he saved up an enemy that way, just as a schoolboy saves up a cake, and made the pleasure go as far as it would by gloating over the anticipation. One of these cases was that of a Frenchman who had offended Slade. To the surprise of everybody Slade did not

kill him on the spot, but let him alone for a considerable time. Finally, however, he went to the Frenchman's house very late one night, knocked, and when his enemy opened the door, shot him dead—pushed the corpse inside the door with his foot, set the house on fire and burned up the dead man, his widow and three children! I heard this story from several different people, and they evidently believed what they were saying. It may be true, and it may not. "Give a dog a bad name," etc.

Slade was captured, once, by a party of men who intended to lynch him. They disarmed him, and shut him up in a strong log-house, and placed a guard over him. He prevailed on his captors to send for his wife, so that he might have a last interview with her. She was a brave, loving, spirited woman. She jumped on a horse and rode for life and death. When she arrived they let her in without searching her, and before the door could be closed she whipped out a couple of revolvers, and she and her lord marched forth defying the party. And then, under a brisk fire, they mounted double and galloped away unharmed!

In the fulness of time Slade's myrmidons captured his ancient enemy Jules, whom they found in a well-chosen hiding-place in the remote fastnesses of the mountains, gaining a precarious livelihood with his rifle. They brought him to Rocky Ridge, bound hand and foot, and deposited him in the middle of the cattle-yard with his back against a post. It is said that the pleasure that lit Slade's face when he heard of it was something fearful to contemplate. He examined his enemy to see that he was securely tied, and then went to bed, content to wait till morning before enjoying the luxury of killing him. Jules spent the night in the cattle-yard, and it is a region where warm nights are never known. In the morning Slade practised on him with his revolver, nipping the flesh here and there, and occasionally clipping off a finger, while Jules begged him to kill him outright and put him out of his misery. Finally Slade reloaded, and walking up close to his victim, made some characteristic remarks and then dispatched him. The body lay there half a day, nobody venturing to touch it without orders, and then Slade detailed a party and assisted at the burial himself. But he first cut off the dead man's ears and put them in his vest pocket, where he carried them for some time with great satisfaction. That is the story as I have frequently heard it told and seen it in print in California newspapers. It is doubtless correct in all essential particulars.

In due time we rattled up to a stage-station, and sat down to breakfast with a half-savage, half-civilized company of armed and bearded mountaineers, ranchmen and station employees. The most gentlemanly-appearing, quiet and affable officer we had yet found along the road in the Overland Company's service was the person who sat at the head of the table, at my elbow. Never youth stared and shivered as I did when I heard them call him SLADE!

Here was romance, and I sitting face to face with it!—looking upon it —touching it—hobnobbing with it, as it were! Here, right by my side, was the actual ogre who, in fights and brawls and various ways, had taken the lives of twenty-six human beings, or all men lied about him! I suppose I was the proudest stripling that ever traveled to see strange lands and wonderful people.

He was so friendly and so gentle-spoken that I warmed to him in spite of his awful history. It was hardly possible to realize that this pleasant person was the pitiless scourge of the outlaws, the raw-head-and-bloody-bones the nursing mothers of the mountains terrified their children with. And to this day I can remember nothing remarkable about Slade except that his face was rather broad across the cheek bones, and that the cheek bones were low and the lips peculiarly thin and straight. But that was enough to leave something of an effect upon me, for since then I seldom see a face possessing those characteristics without fancying that the owner of it is a dangerous man.

The coffee ran out. At least it was reduced to one tin-cupful, and Slade was about to take it when he saw that my cup was empty.

He politely offered to fill it, but although I wanted it, I politely declined. I was afraid he had not killed anybody that morning, and might be needing diversion. But still with firm politeness he insisted on filling my cup, and said I had traveled all night and better deserved it than he—and while he talked he placidly poured the fluid, to the last drop. I thanked him and drank it, but it gave me no comfort, for I could not feel sure that he would not be sorry, presently, that he had given it away, and proceed to kill me to distract his thoughts from the loss. But nothing of the kind occurred. We left him with only twenty-six dead people to account for, and I felt a tranquil satisfaction in the thought that in so judiciously taking care of No. 1 at that breakfast-table I had pleasantly escaped being No. 27. Slade came out to the coach and saw us off, first ordering certain rearrangements of the mail-bags for our comfort, and then we took leave of him, satisfied that we should hear of him again, some day, and wondering in what connection.

CHAPTER XI.

And sure enough, two or three years afterward, we did hear him again. News came to the Pacific coast that the Vigilance Committee in Montana (whither Slade had removed from Rocky Ridge) had hanged him. I find an account of the affair in the thrilling little book I quoted a paragraph from in the last chapter—"The Vigilantes of Montana; being a Reliable Account of the Capture, Trial and Execution of Henry Plummer's Notorious Road Agent Band: By Prof. Thos. J. Dimsdale, Virginia City, M.T." Mr. Dimsdale's chapter is well worth reading, as a specimen of how the people of the frontier deal with criminals when the courts of law prove inefficient. Mr. Dimsdale makes two remarks about Slade, both of which are accurately descriptive, and one of which is exceedingly picturesque: "Those who saw him in his natural state only, would pronounce him to be a kind husband, a most hospitable host and a courteous gentleman; on the contrary, those who met him when maddened with liquor and surrounded by a gang of armed roughs, would pronounce him a fiend incarnate." And this: "From Fort Kearney, west, he was feared a great deal more than the almighty." For compactness, simplicity and vigor of expression, I will "back" that sentence against anything in literature. Mr. Dimsdale's narrative is as follows. In all places where italics occur, they are mine:

After the execution of the five men on the 14th of January, the Vigilantes considered that their work was nearly ended. They had freed the country of highwaymen and murderers to a great extent, and they determined that in the absence of the regular civil authority they would establish a People's Court where all offenders should be tried by judge and jury. This was the nearest approach to social order that the circumstances permitted, and, though strict legal authority was wanting, yet the people were firmly determined to maintain its efficiency, and to enforce its decrees. It may here be mentioned that the overt act which was the last round on the fatal ladder leading

to the scaffold on which Slade perished, was the tearing in pieces and stamping upon a writ of this court, followed by his arrest of the Judge Alex. Davis, by authority of a presented Derringer, and with his own hands.

J. A. Slade was himself, we have been informed, a Vigilante; he openly boasted of it, and said he knew all that they knew. He was never accused, or even suspected, of either murder or robbery, committed in this Territory (the latter crime was never laid to his charge, in any place); but that he had killed several men in other localities was notorious, and his bad reputation in this respect was a most powerful argument in determining his fate, when he was finally arrested for the offence above mentioned. On returning from Milk River he became more and more addicted to drinking, until at last it was a common feat for him and his friends to "take the town." He and a couple of his dependents might often be seen on one horse, galloping through the streets, shouting and yelling, firing revolvers, etc. On many occasions he would ride his horse into stores, break up bars, toss the scales out of doors and use most insulting language to parties present. Just previous to the day of his arrest, he had given a fearful beating to one of his followers; but such was his influence over them that the man wept bitterly at the gallows, and begged for his life with all his power. It had become quite common, when Slade was on a spree, for the shop-keepers and citizens to close the stores and put out all the lights; being fearful of some outrage at his hands. For his wanton destruction of goods and furniture, he was always ready to pay, when sober, if he had money; but there were not a few who regarded payment as small satisfaction for the outrage, and these men were his personal enemies.

From time to time Slade received warnings from men that he well knew would not deceive him, of the certain end of his conduct. There was not a moment, for weeks previous to his arrest, in which the public did not expect to hear of some bloody outrage. The dread of his very name, and the presence of the armed band of hangers-on who followed him alone prevented a resistance which must certainly have ended in the instant murder or mutilation of the opposing party.

Slade was frequently arrested by order of the court whose organization we have described, and had treated it with respect by paying one or two fines and promising to pay the rest when he had money; but in the transaction that occurred at this crisis, he forgot even this caution, and goaded by passion and the hatred of restraint, he sprang into the embrace of death.

Slade had been drunk and "cutting up" all night. He and his companions had made the town a perfect hell. In the morning, J. M. Fox, the sheriff, met him, arrested him, took him into court and commenced reading a warrant that he had for his arrest, by way of arraignment. He became uncontrollably furious, and seizing the writ, he tore it up, threw it on the ground and stamped upon it.

The clicking of the locks of his companions' revolvers was instantly heard, and a crisis was expected. The sheriff did not attempt his retention; but being at least as prudent as he was valiant, he succumbed, leaving Slade the master of the situation and the conqueror and ruler of the courts, law and law-makers. This was a declaration of war, and was so accepted. The Vigilance Committee now felt that the question of social order and the preponderance of the law-abiding citizens had then and there to be decided. They knew the character of Slade, and they were well aware that they must submit to his rule without murmur, or else that he must be dealt with in such fashion as would prevent his being able to wreak his vengeance on the committee, who could never have hoped to live in the Territory secure from outrage or death, and who could never leave it without encountering his friend, whom his victory would have emboldened and stimulated to a pitch that would have rendered them reckless of consequences. The day previous he had ridden into Dorris's store, and on being requested to leave, he drew his revolver and threatened to kill the gentleman who spoke to him. Another saloon he had led his horse into, and buying a bottle of wine, he tried to make the animal drink it. This was not considered an uncommon performance, as he had often entered saloons and commenced firing at the lamps, causing a wild stampede.

A leading member of the committee met Slade, and informed him in the quiet, earnest manner of one who feels the importance of what he is saying: "Slade, get your horse at once, and go home, or there will be — to pay." Slade started and took a long look, with his dark and piercing eyes, at the gentleman. "What do you mean?" said he. "You have no right to ask me what I mean," was the quiet reply, "get your horse at once, and remember what I tell you." After a short pause he promised to do so, and actually got into the saddle; but, being still intoxicated, he began calling aloud to one after another of his friends, and at last seemed to have forgotten the warning he had received and became again uproarious, shouting the name of a well-known courtezan in company with those of two men whom he considered heads of the committee, as a sort of challenge; perhaps, however, as a simple act of bravado. It seems probable that the intimation of personal danger he had received had not been forgotten entirely; though fatally for him, he took a foolish way of showing his remembrance of it. He sought out Alexander Davis, the Judge of the Court, and drawing a cocked Derringer, he presented it at his head, and told him that he should hold him as a hostage for his own safety. As the judge stood perfectly quiet, and offered no resistance to his captor, no further outrage followed on this score. Previous to this, on account of the critical state of affairs, the committee had met, and at last resolved to arrest him. His execution had not been agreed upon, and, at that time, would have been negatived, most assuredly. A messenger rode down to Nevada to inform the leading men of what was on hand, as it was desirable to show that there was a feeling of unanimity on the subject, all along the gulch.

The miners turned out almost en masse, leaving their work and forming in solid column about six hundred strong, armed to the teeth, they marched up to Virginia. The leader of the body well knew the temper of his men on the subject. He spurred on ahead of them, and hastily calling a meeting of the executive, he told them plainly that the miners meant "business," and that, if they came up, they would not stand in the street to be shot down by Slade's friends; but that they would take him and hang him. The meeting was small, as the Virginia men were loath to act at all. This momentous announcement of the feeling of the Lower Town was made to a cluster of men, who were deliberation behind a wagon, at the rear of a store on Main street.

The committee were most unwilling to proceed to extremities. All the duty they had ever performed seemed as nothing to the task before them; but they had to decide, and that quickly. It was finally agreed that if the whole body of the miners were of the opinion that he should be hanged, that the committee left it in their hands to deal with him. Off, at hot speed, rode the leader of the Nevada men to join his command.

Slade had found out what was intended, and the news sobered him instantly. He went into P. S. Pfouts' store, where Davis was, and apologized for his conduct, saying that he would take it all back.

The head of the column now wheeled into Wallace street and marched up at quick time. Halting in front of the store, the executive officer of the committee stepped forward and arrested Slade, who was at once informed of his doom, and inquiry was made as to whether he had any business to settle. Several parties spoke to him on the subject; but to all such inquiries he turned a deaf ear, being entirely absorbed in the terrifying reflections on his own awful position. He never ceased his entreaties for life, and to see his dear wife. The unfortunate lady referred to, between whom and Slade there existed a warm affection, was at this time living at their ranch on the Madison. She was possessed of considerable personal attractions; tall, well-formed, of graceful carriage, pleasing manners, and was, withal, an accomplished horsewoman.

A messenger from Slade rode at full speed to inform her of her husband's arrest. In an instant she was in the saddle, and with all the energy that love and despair could lend to an ardent temperament and a strong physique, she urged her fleet charger over the twelve miles of rough and rocky ground that intervened between her and the object of her passionate devotion.

Meanwhile a party of volunteers had made the necessary preparations for the execution, in the valley traversed by the branch. Beneath the site of Pfouts and Russell's stone building there was a corral, the gate-posts of which were strong and high. Across the top was laid a beam, to which the rope was fastened, and a dry-goods box served for the platform. To this place Slade was marched, surrounded by a guard, composing the best armed and most numerous force that has ever appeared in Montana Territory.

The doomed man had so exhausted himself by tears, prayers and lamentations, that he had scarcely strength left to stand under the fatal beam. He repeatedly exclaimed, "My God! my God! must I die? Oh, my dear wife!"

On the return of the fatigue party, they encountered some friends of Slade, staunch and reliable citizens and members of the committee, but who were personally attached to the condemned. On hearing of his sentence, one of them, a stout-hearted man, pulled out his handkerchief and walked away, weeping like a child. Slade still begged to see his wife, most piteously, and it seemed hard to deny his request; but the bloody consequences that were sure to follow the inevitable attempt at a rescue, that her presence and entreaties would have certainly incited, forbade the granting of his request. Several gentlemen were sent for to see him, in his last moments, one of whom (Judge Davis) made a short address to the people; but in such low tones as to be inaudible, save to a few in his immediate vicinity. One of his friends, after exhausting his powers of entreaty, threw off his coat and declared that the prisoner could not be hanged until he himself was killed. A hundred guns were instantly leveled at him; whereupon he turned and fled; but, being brought back, he was compelled to resume his coat, and to give a promise of future peaceable demeanor.

Scarcely a leading man in Virginia could be found, though numbers of the citizens joined the ranks of the guard when the arrest was made. All lamented the stern necessity which dictated the execution.

Everything being ready, the command was given, "Men, do your duty," and the box being instantly slipped from beneath his feet, he died almost instantaneously.

The body was cut down and carried to the Virginia Hotel, where, in a darkened room, it was scarcely laid out, when the unfortunate and bereaved companion of the deceased arrived, at headlong speed, to find that all was over, and that she was a widow. Her grief and heart-piercing cries were terrible evidences of the depth of her attachment for her lost husband, and a considerable period elapsed before she could regain the command of her excited feelings.

There is something about the desperado-nature that is wholly unaccountable—at least it looks unaccountable. It is this. The true desperado is gifted with splendid courage, and yet he will take the most infamous advantage of his enemy; armed and free, he will stand up before a host and fight until he is shot all to pieces, and yet when he is under the gallows and helpless he will cry and plead like a child. Words are cheap, and it is easy to call Slade a coward (all executed men who do not "die game" are promptly called cowards by unreflecting people), and when we read of Slade that he "had so exhausted himself by tears, prayers and lamentations, that he had scarcely strength left to stand under the fatal beam," the disgraceful word suggests itself in a moment—yet in frequently defying and inviting the vengeance of banded Rocky Mountain cut-throats by shooting down their comrades and leaders, and never offering to hide or fly, Slade showed that he was a man of peerless bravery. No coward would dare that. Many a notorious coward, many a chicken-livered poltroon, coarse, brutal, degraded, has made his dying speech without a quaver in his voice and been swung into eternity with what looked liked the calmest fortitude, and so we are justified in believing, from the low intellect of such a creature, that it was not moral courage that enabled him to do it. Then, if moral courage is not the requisite quality, what could it have been that this stout-hearted Slade lacked?—this bloody, desperate, kindly-mannered, urbane gentleman, who never hesitated to warn his most ruffianly enemies that he would kill them whenever or wherever he came across them next! I think it is a conundrum worth investigating.

CHAPTER XII.

Just beyond the breakfast-station we overtook a Mormon emigrant train of thirty-three wagons; and tramping wearily along and driving their herd of loose cows, were dozens of coarse-clad and sad-looking men, women and children, who had walked as they were walking now, day after day for eight lingering weeks, and in that time had compassed the distance our stage had come in eight days and three hours—seven hundred and ninety-eight miles! They were dusty and uncombed, hatless, bonnetless and ragged, and they did look so tired!

After breakfast, we bathed in Horse Creek, a (previously) limpid, sparkling stream—an appreciated luxury, for it was very seldom that our furious coach halted long enough for an indulgence of that kind. We changed horses ten or twelve times in every twenty-four hours—changed mules, rather—six mules—and did it nearly every time in four minutes. It was lively work. As our coach rattled up to each station six harnessed mules stepped gayly from the stable; and in the twinkling of an eye, almost, the old team was out, and the new one in and we off and away again.

During the afternoon we passed Sweetwater Creek, Independence Rock, Devil's Gate and the Devil's Gap. The latter were wild specimens of rugged scenery, and full of interest—we were in the heart of the Rocky Mountains, now. And we also passed by "Alkali" or "Soda Lake," and we woke up to the fact that our journey had stretched a long way across the world when the driver said that the Mormons often came there from Great Salt Lake City to haul away saleratus. He said that a few days gone by they had shoveled up enough pure saleratus from the ground (it was a dry lake) to load two wagons, and that when they got these two wagons-loads of a drug that cost them nothing, to Salt Lake, they could sell it for twenty-five cents a pound.

In the night we sailed by a most notable curiosity, and one we had been hearing a good deal about for a day or two, and were suffering to see. This was what might be called a natural ice-house. It was August, now, and sweltering weather in the daytime, yet at one of the stations the men could scape the soil on the hill-side under the lee of a range of boulders, and at a depth of six inches cut out pure blocks of ice—hard, compactly frozen, and clear as crystal!

Toward dawn we got under way again, and presently as we sat with raised curtains enjoying our early-morning smoke and contemplating the first splendor of the rising sun as it swept down the long array of mountain peaks, flushing and gilding crag after crag and summit after summit, as if the invisible Creator reviewed his gray veterans and they saluted with a smile, we hove in sight of South Pass City. The hotel-keeper, the postmaster, the blacksmith, the mayor, the constable, the city marshal and the principal citizen and property holder, all came out and greeted us cheerily, and we gave him good day. He gave us a little Indian news, and a little Rocky Mountain news, and we gave him some Plains information in return. He then retired to his lonely grandeur and we climbed on up among the bristling peaks and the ragged clouds. South Pass City consisted of four log cabins, one if which was unfinished, and the gentleman with all those offices and titles was the chiefest of the ten citizens of the place. Think of hotel-keeper, postmaster, blacksmith, mayor, constable, city marshal and principal citizen all condensed into one person and crammed into one skin. Bemis said he was "a perfect Allen's revolver of dignities." And he said that if he were to die as postmaster, or as blacksmith, or as postmaster and blacksmith both, the people might stand it; but if he were to die all over, it would be a frightful loss to the community.

Two miles beyond South Pass City we saw for the first time that mysterious marvel which all Western untraveled boys have heard of and fully believe in, but are sure to be astounded at when they see it with their own eyes, nevertheless—banks of snow in dead summer time. We were now far up toward the sky, and knew all the time that we must presently encounter lofty summits clad in the "eternal snow" which was so common place a matter of mention in books, and yet when I did see it glittering in the sun on stately domes in the distance and knew the month was August and that my coat was hanging up because it was too warm to wear it, I was full as much amazed as if I never had heard of snow in August before. Truly, "seeing is believing"—and many a man lives a long life through, thinking he believes certain universally received and well established things, and yet never suspects that if he were confronted by those things once, he would discover that he did not really believe them before, but only thought he believed them.

In a little while quite a number of peaks swung into view with long claws of glittering snow clasping them; and with here and there, in the shade, down the mountain side, a little solitary patch of snow looking no larger than a lady's pocket-handkerchief but being in reality as large as a "public square."

And now, at last, we were fairly in the renowned SOUTH PASS, and whirling gayly along high above the common world. We were perched upon the extreme summit of the great range of the Rocky Mountains, toward which we had been climbing, patiently climbing, ceaselessly climbing, for days and nights together—and about us was gathered a convention of Nature's kings that stood ten, twelve, and even thirteen thousand feet high—grand old fellows who would have to stoop to see Mount Washington, in the twilight. We were in such an airy elevation above the creeping populations of the earth, that now and then when the obstructing crags stood out of the way it seemed that we could look around and abroad and contemplate the whole great globe, with its dissolving views of mountains, seas and continents stretching away through the mystery of the summer haze.

As a general thing the Pass was more suggestive of a valley than a suspension bridge in the clouds—but it strongly suggested the latter at one spot. At that place the upper third of one or two majestic purple domes projected above our level on either hand and gave us a sense of a hidden great deep of mountains and plains and valleys down about their bases which we fancied we might see if we could step to the edge and look over. These Sultans of the fastnesses were turbaned with tumbled volumes of cloud, which shredded away from time to time and drifted off fringed and torn, trailing their continents of shadow after them; and catching presently on an intercepting peak, wrapped it about and brooded there —then shredded away again and left the purple peak, as they had left the purple domes, downy and white with new-laid snow. In passing, these monstrous rags of cloud hung low and swept along right over the spectator's head, swinging their tatters so nearly in his face that his impulse was to shrink when they came closet. In the one place I speak of, one could look below him upon a world of diminishing crags and canyons leading down, down, and away to a vague plain with a thread in it which was a road, and bunches of feathers in it which were trees,—a pretty picture sleeping in the sunlight—but with a darkness stealing over it and glooming its features deeper and deeper under the frown of a coming storm; and then, while no film or shadow marred the noon brightness of his high perch, he could watch the tempest break forth down there and see the lightnings leap from crag to crag and the sheeted rain drive along the canyon-sides, and hear the thunders peal and crash and roar. We had this spectacle; a familiar one to many, but to us a novelty.

We bowled along cheerily, and presently, at the very summit (though it had been all summit to us, and all equally level, for half an hour or more), we came to a spring which spent its water through two outlets and sent it in opposite directions. The conductor said that one of those streams which we were looking at, was just starting on a journey westward to the Gulf of California and the Pacific Ocean, through hundreds and even thousands of miles of desert solitudes. He said that the other was just leaving its home among the snow-peaks on a similar journey eastward —and we knew that long after we should have forgotten the simple rivulet it would still be plodding its patient way down the mountain sides, and canyon-beds, and between the banks of the Yellowstone; and by and by would join the broad Missouri and flow through unknown plains and deserts and unvisited wildernesses; and

add a long and troubled pilgrimage among snags and wrecks and sandbars; and enter the Mississippi, touch the wharves of St. Louis and still drift on, traversing shoals and rocky channels, then endless chains of bottomless and ample bends, walled with unbroken forests, then mysterious byways and secret passages among woody islands, then the chained bends again, bordered with wide levels of shining sugar-cane in place of the sombre forests; then by New Orleans and still other chains of bends—and finally, after two long months of daily and nightly harassment, excitement, enjoyment, adventure, and awful peril of parched throats, pumps and evaporation, pass the Gulf and enter into its rest upon the bosom of the tropic sea, never to look upon its snow-peaks again or regret them.

I freighted a leaf with a mental message for the friends at home, and dropped it in the stream. But I put no stamp on it and it was held for postage somewhere.

On the summit we overtook an emigrant train of many wagons, many tired men and women, and many a disgusted sheep and cow.

In the wofully dusty horseman in charge of the expedition I recognized John —. Of all persons in the world to meet on top of the Rocky Mountains thousands of miles from home, he was the last one I should have looked for. We were school-boys together and warm friends for years. But a boyish prank of mine had disruptured this friendship and it had never been renewed. The act of which I speak was this. I had been accustomed to visit occasionally an editor whose room was in the third story of a building and overlooked the street. One day this editor gave me a watermelon which I made preparations to devour on the spot, but chancing to look out of the window, I saw John standing directly under it and an irresistible desire came upon me to drop the melon on his head, which I immediately did. I was the loser, for it spoiled the melon, and John never forgave me and we dropped all intercourse and parted, but now met again under these circumstances.

We recognized each other simultaneously, and hands were grasped as warmly as if no coldness had ever existed between us, and no allusion was made to any. All animosities were buried and the simple fact of meeting a familiar face in that isolated spot so far from home, was sufficient to make us forget all things but pleasant ones, and we parted again with sincere "good-bye" and "God bless you" from both.

We had been climbing up the long shoulders of the Rocky Mountains for many tedious hours—we started down them, now. And we went spinning away at a round rate too.

We left the snowy Wind River Mountains and Uinta Mountains behind, and sped away, always through splendid scenery but occasionally through long ranks of white skeletons of mules and oxen—monuments of the huge emigration of other days—and here and there were up-ended boards or small piles of stones which the driver said marked the resting-place of more precious remains.

It was the loneliest land for a grave! A land given over to the cayote and the raven—which is but another name for desolation and utter solitude. On damp, murky nights, these scattered skeletons gave forth a soft, hideous glow, like very faint spots of moonlight starring the vague desert. It was because of the phosphorus in the bones. But no scientific explanation could keep a body from shivering when he drifted by one of those ghostly lights and knew that a skull held it.

At midnight it began to rain, and I never saw anything like it—indeed, I did not even see this, for it was too dark. We fastened down the curtains and even caulked them with clothing, but the rain streamed in in twenty places, nothwithstanding. There was no escape. If one moved his feet out of a stream, he brought his body under one; and if he moved his body he caught one somewhere else. If he struggled out of the drenched blankets and sat up, he was bound to get one down the back of his neck. Meantime the stage was wandering about a plain with gaping gullies in it, for the driver could not see an inch before his face nor keep the road, and the storm pelted so pitilessly that there was no keeping the horses still. With the first abatement the conductor turned out with lanterns to look for the road, and the first dash he made was into a chasm about fourteen feet deep, his lantern following like a meteor. As soon as he touched bottom he sang out frantically:

"Don't come here!"

To which the driver, who was looking over the precipice where he had disappeared, replied, with an injured air: "Think I'm a dam fool?"

The conductor was more than an hour finding the road—a matter which showed us how far we had wandered and what chances we had been taking. He traced our wheel-tracks to the imminent verge of danger, in two places. I have always been glad that we were not killed that night. I do not know any particular reason, but I have always been glad. In the morning, the tenth day out, we crossed Green River, a fine, large, limpid stream—stuck in it with the water just up to the top of our mail-bed, and waited till extra teams were put on to haul us up the steep bank. But it was nice cool water, and besides it could not find any fresh place on us to wet.

At the Green River station we had breakfast—hot biscuits, fresh antelope steaks, and coffee—the only decent meal we tasted between the United States and Great Salt Lake City, and the only one we were ever really thankful for.

Think of the monotonous execrableness of the thirty that went before it, to leave this one simple breakfast looming up in my memory like a shot-tower after all these years have gone by!

At five P.M. we reached Fort Bridger, one hundred and seventeen miles from the South Pass, and one thousand and twenty-five miles from St. Joseph. Fifty-two miles further on, near the head of Echo Canyon, we met sixty United States soldiers from Camp Floyd. The day before, they had fired upon three hundred or four hundred Indians, whom they supposed gathered together for no good purpose. In the fight that had ensued, four Indians were captured, and the main body chased four miles, but nobody killed. This looked like business. We had a notion to get out and join the sixty soldiers, but upon reflecting that there were four hundred of the Indians, we concluded to go on and join the Indians.

Echo Canyon is twenty miles long. It was like a long, smooth, narrow street, with a gradual descending grade, and shut in by enormous perpendicular walls of coarse conglomerate, four hundred feet high in many places, and turreted like mediaeval castles. This was the most faultless piece of road in the mountains, and the driver said he would "let his team out." He did, and if the Pacific express trains whiz through there now any faster than we did then in the stage-coach, I envy the passengers the exhilaration of it. We fairly seemed to pick up our wheels and fly—and the mail matter was lifted up free

from everything and held in solution! I am not given to exaggeration, and when I say a thing I mean it.

However, time presses. At four in the afternoon we arrived on the summit of Big Mountain, fifteen miles from Salt Lake City, when all the world was glorified with the setting sun, and the most stupendous panorama of mountain peaks yet encountered burst on our sight. We looked out upon this sublime spectacle from under the arch of a brilliant rainbow! Even the overland stage-driver stopped his horses and gazed!

Half an hour or an hour later, we changed horses, and took supper with a Mormon "Destroying Angel."

"Destroying Angels," as I understand it, are Latter-Day Saints who are set apart by the Church to conduct permanent disappearances of obnoxious citizens. I had heard a deal about these Mormon Destroying Angels and the dark and bloody deeds they had done, and when I entered this one's house I had my shudder all ready. But alas for all our romances, he was nothing but a loud, profane, offensive, old blackguard! He was murderous enough, possibly, to fill the bill of a Destroyer, but would you have any kind of an Angel devoid of dignity? Could you abide an Angel in an unclean shirt and no suspenders? Could you respect an Angel with a horse-laugh and a swagger like a buccaneer?

There were other blackguards present—comrades of this one. And there was one person that looked like a gentleman—Heber C. Kimball's son, tall and well made, and thirty years old, perhaps. A lot of slatternly women flitted hither and thither in a hurry, with coffee-pots, plates of bread, and other appurtenances to supper, and these were said to be the wives of the Angel—or some of them, at least. And of course they were; for if they had been hired "help" they would not have let an angel from above storm and swear at them as he did, let alone one from the place this one hailed from.

This was our first experience of the western "peculiar institution," and it was not very prepossessing. We did not tarry long to observe it, but hurried on to the home of the Latter-Day Saints, the stronghold of the prophets, the capital of the only absolute monarch in America—Great Salt Lake City. As the night closed in we took sanctuary in the Salt Lake House and unpacked our baggage.

CHAPTER XIII.

We had a fine supper, of the freshest meats and fowls and vegetables—a great variety and as great abundance. We walked about the streets some, afterward, and glanced in at shops and stores; and there was fascination in surreptitiously staring at every creature we took to be a Mormon. This was fairy-land to us, to all intents and purposes—a land of enchantment, and goblins, and awful mystery. We felt a curiosity to ask every child how many mothers it had, and if it could tell them apart; and we experienced a thrill every time a dwelling-house door opened and shut as we passed, disclosing a glimpse of human heads and backs and shoulders—for we so longed to have a good satisfying look at a Mormon family in all its comprehensive ampleness, disposed in the customary concentric rings of its home circle.

By and by the Acting Governor of the Territory introduced us to other "Gentiles," and we spent a sociable hour with them. "Gentiles" are people who are not Mormons. Our fellow-passenger, Bemis, took care of himself, during this part of the evening, and did not make an overpowering success of it, either, for he came into our room in the hotel about eleven o'clock, full of cheerfulness, and talking loosely, disjointedly and indiscriminately, and every now and then tugging out a ragged word by the roots that had more hiccups than syllables in it. This, together with his hanging his coat on the floor on one side of a chair, and his vest on the floor on the other side, and piling his pants on the floor just in front of the same chair, and then comtemplating the general result with superstitious awe, and finally pronouncing it "too many for him" and going to bed with his boots on, led us to fear that something he had eaten had not agreed with him.

But we knew afterward that it was something he had been drinking. It was the exclusively Mormon refresher, "valley tan."

Valley tan (or, at least, one form of valley tan) is a kind of whisky, or first cousin to it; is of Mormon invention and manufactured only in Utah. Tradition says it is made of (imported) fire and brimstone. If I remember rightly no public drinking saloons were allowed in the kingdom by Brigham Young, and no private drinking permitted among the faithful, except they confined themselves to "valley tan."

Next day we strolled about everywhere through the broad, straight, level streets, and enjoyed the pleasant strangeness of a city of fifteen thousand inhabitants with no loafers perceptible in it; and no visible drunkards or noisy people; a limpid stream rippling and dancing through every street in place of a filthy gutter; block after block of trim dwellings, built of "frame" and sunburned brick—a great thriving orchard and garden behind every one of them, apparently—branches from the street stream winding and sparkling among the garden beds and fruit trees—and a grand general air of neatness, repair, thrift and comfort, around and about and over the whole. And everywhere were workshops, factories, and all manner of industries; and intent faces and busy hands were to be seen wherever one looked; and in one's ears was the ceaseless clink of hammers, the buzz of trade and the contented hum of drums and fly-wheels.

The armorial crest of my own State consisted of two dissolute bears holding up the head of a dead and gone cask between them and making the pertinent remark, "UNITED, WE STAND—(hic!)—DIVIDED, WE FALL." It was always too figurative for the author of this book. But the Mormon crest was easy. And it was simple, unostentatious, and fitted like a glove. It was a representation of a GOLDEN BEEHIVE, with the bees all at work!

The city lies in the edge of a level plain as broad as the State of Connecticut, and crouches close down to the ground under a curving wall of mighty mountains whose heads are hidden in the clouds, and whose shoulders bear relics of the snows of winter all the summer long.

Seen from one of these dizzy heights, twelve or fifteen miles off, Great Salt Lake City is toned down and diminished till it is suggestive of a child's toy-village reposing under the majestic protection of the Chinese wall.

On some of those mountains, to the southwest, it had been raining every day for two weeks, but not a drop had fallen in the city. And on hot days in late spring and early autumn the citizens could quit fanning and growling and go out and cool off by looking at the luxury of a glorious snow-storm going on in the mountains. They could enjoy it at a distance, at those seasons, every day, though no snow would fall in their streets, or anywhere near them.

Salt Lake City was healthy—an extremely healthy city.

They declared there was only one physician in the place and he was arrested every week regularly and held to answer under the vagrant act for having "no visible means of support." They always give you a good substantial article of truth in Salt Lake, and good measure and good weight, too. [Very often, if you wished to weigh one of their airiest little commonplace statements you would want the hay scales.]

We desired to visit the famous inland sea, the American "Dead Sea," the great Salt Lake—seventeen miles, horseback, from the city—for we had dreamed about it, and thought about it, and talked about it, and yearned to see it, all the first part of our trip; but now when it was only arm's length away it had suddenly lost nearly every bit of its interest. And so we put it off, in a sort of general way, till next day—and that was the last we ever thought of it. We dined with some hospitable Gentiles; and visited the foundation of the prodigious temple; and talked long with that shrewd Connecticut Yankee, Heber C. Kimball (since deceased), a saint of high degree and a mighty man of commerce.

We saw the "Tithing-House," and the "Lion House," and I do not know or remember how many more church and government buildings of various kinds and curious names. We flitted hither and thither and enjoyed every hour, and picked up a great deal of useful information and entertaining nonsense, and went to bed at night satisfied.

The second day, we made the acquaintance of Mr. Street (since deceased) and put on white shirts and went and paid a state visit to the king. He seemed a quiet, kindly, easy-mannered, dignified, self-possessed old gentleman of fifty-five or sixty, and had a gentle craft in his eye that probably belonged there. He was very simply dressed and was just taking off a straw hat as we entered. He talked about Utah, and the Indians, and Nevada, and general American matters and questions, with our secretary and certain government officials who came with us. But he never paid any attention to me, notwithstanding I made several attempts to "draw him out" on federal politics and his high handed attitude toward Congress. I thought some of the things I said were rather fine. But he merely looked around at me, at distant intervals, something as I have seen a benignant old cat look around to see which kitten was meddling with her tail.

By and by I subsided into an indignant silence, and so sat until the end, hot and flushed, and execrating him in my heart for an ignorant savage. But he was calm. His conversation with those gentlemen flowed on as sweetly and peacefully and musically as any summer brook. When the audience was ended and we were retiring from the presence, he put his hand on my head, beamed down on me in an admiring way and said to my brother:

"Ah—your child, I presume? Boy, or girl?"

CHAPTER XIV.

Mr. Street was very busy with his telegraphic matters—and considering that he had eight or nine hundred miles of rugged, snowy, uninhabited mountains, and waterless, treeless, melancholy deserts to traverse with his wire, it was natural and needful that he should be as busy as possible. He could not go comfortably along and cut his poles by the road-side, either, but they had to be hauled by ox teams across those exhausting deserts—and it was two days' journey from water to water, in one or two of them. Mr. Street's contract was a vast work, every way one looked at it; and yet to comprehend what the vague words "eight hundred miles of rugged mountains and dismal deserts" mean, one must go over the ground in person—pen and ink descriptions cannot convey the dreary reality to the reader. And after all, Mr. S.'s mightiest difficulty turned out to be one which he had never taken into the account at all. Unto Mormons he had sub-let the hardest and heaviest half of his great undertaking, and all of a sudden they concluded that they were going to make little or nothing, and so they tranquilly threw their poles overboard in mountain or desert, just as it happened when they took the notion, and drove home and went about their customary business! They were under written contract to Mr. Street, but they did not care anything for that. They said they would "admire" to see a "Gentile" force a Mormon to fulfil a losing contract in Utah! And they made themselves very merry over the matter. Street said—for it was he that told us these things:

"I was in dismay. I was under heavy bonds to complete my contract in a given time, and this disaster looked very much like ruin. It was an astounding thing; it was such a wholly unlooked-for difficulty, that I was entirely nonplussed. I am a business man—have always been a business man—do not know anything but business—and so you can imagine how like being struck by lightning it was to find myself in a country where written contracts were worthless!—that main security, that sheet-anchor, that absolute necessity, of business. My confidence left me. There was no use in making new contracts—that was plain. I talked with first one prominent citizen and then another. They all sympathized with me, first rate, but they did not know how to help me. But at last a Gentile said, 'Go to Brigham Young!—these small fry cannot do you any good.' I did not think much of the idea, for if the law could not help me, what could an individual do who had not even anything to do with either making the laws or executing them? He might be a very good patriarch of a church and preacher in its tabernacle, but something sterner than religion and moral suasion was needed to handle a hundred refractory, half-civilized sub-contractors. But what was a man to do? I thought if Mr. Young could not do anything else, he might probably be able to give me some advice and a valuable hint or two, and so I went straight to him and laid the whole case before him. He said very little, but he showed strong interest all the way through. He examined all the papers in detail, and whenever there seemed anything like a hitch, either in the papers or my statement, he would go back and take up the thread and follow it patiently out to an intelligent and satisfactory result. Then he made a list of the contractors' names. Finally he said:

"'Mr. Street, this is all perfectly plain. These contracts are strictly and legally drawn, and are duly signed and certified. These men manifestly entered into them with their eyes open. I see no fault or flaw anywhere.'

"Then Mr. Young turned to a man waiting at the other end of the room and said: 'Take this list of names to So-and-so, and tell him to have these men here at such-and-such an hour.'

"They were there, to the minute. So was I. Mr. Young asked them a number of questions, and their answers made my statement good. Then he said to them:

"'You signed these contracts and assumed these obligations of your own free will and accord?'

"'Yes.'

"'Then carry them out to the letter, if it makes paupers of you! Go!'

"And they did go, too! They are strung across the deserts now, working like bees. And I never hear a word out of them.

"There is a batch of governors, and judges, and other officials here, shipped from Washington, and they maintain the semblance of a republican form of government—but the petrified truth is that Utah is an absolute monarchy and Brigham Young is king!"

Mr. Street was a fine man, and I believe his story. I knew him well during several years afterward in San Francisco.

Our stay in Salt Lake City amounted to only two days, and therefore we had no time to make the customary inquisition into the workings of polygamy and get up the usual statistics and deductions preparatory to calling the attention of the nation at large once more to the matter.

I had the will to do it. With the gushing self-sufficiency of youth I was feverish to plunge in headlong and achieve a great reform here—until I saw the Mormon women. Then I was touched. My heart was wiser than my head. It warmed toward these poor, ungainly and pathetically "homely" creatures, and as I turned to hide the generous moisture in my eyes, I said, "No—the man that marries one of them has done an act of Christian charity which entitles him to the kindly applause of mankind, not their harsh censure—and the man that marries sixty of them has done a deed of open-handed generosity so sublime that the nations should stand uncovered in his presence and worship in silence."

[For a brief sketch of Mormon history, and the noted Mountain Meadow massacre, see Appendices A and B.]

CHAPTER XV.

It is a luscious country for thrilling evening stories about assassinations of intractable Gentiles. I cannot easily conceive of anything more cosy than the night in Salt Lake which we spent in a Gentile den, smoking pipes and listening to tales of how Burton galloped in among the pleading and defenceless "Morisites" and shot them down, men and women, like so many dogs. And how Bill Hickman, a Destroying Angel, shot Drown and Arnold dead for bringing suit against him for a debt. And how Porter Rockwell did this and that dreadful thing. And how heedless people often come to Utah and make remarks about Brigham, or polygamy, or some other sacred matter, and the very next morning at daylight such parties are sure to be found lying up some back alley, contentedly waiting for the hearse.

And the next most interesting thing is to sit and listen to these Gentiles talk about polygamy; and how some portly old frog of an elder, or a bishop, marries a girl—likes her, marries her sister—likes her, marries another sister—likes her, takes another—likes her, marries her mother—likes her, marries her father, grandfather, great grandfather, and then comes back hungry and asks for more. And how the pert young thing of eleven will chance to be the favorite wife and her own venerable grandmother have to rank away down toward D 4 in their mutual husband's esteem, and have to sleep in the kitchen, as like as not. And how this dreadful sort of thing, this hiving together in one foul nest of mother and daughters, and the making a young daughter superior to her own mother in rank and authority, are things which Mormon women submit to because their religion teaches them that the more wives a man has on earth, and the more children he rears, the higher the place they will all have in the world to come—and the warmer, maybe, though they do not seem to say anything about that.

According to these Gentile friends of ours, Brigham Young's harem contains twenty or thirty wives. They said that some of them had grown old and gone out of active service, but were comfortably housed and cared for in the henery—or the Lion House, as it is strangely named. Along with each wife were her children—fifty altogether. The house was perfectly quiet and orderly, when the children were still. They all took their meals in one room, and a happy and home-like sight it was pronounced to be. None of our party got an opportunity to take dinner with Mr. Young, but a Gentile by the name of Johnson professed to have enjoyed a sociable breakfast in the Lion House. He gave a preposterous account of the "calling of the roll," and other preliminaries, and the carnage that ensued when the buckwheat cakes came in. But he embellished rather too much. He said that Mr. Young told him several smart sayings of certain of his "two-year-olds," observing with some pride that for many years he had been the heaviest contributor in that line to one of the Eastern magazines; and then he wanted to show Mr. Johnson one of the pets that had said the last good thing, but he could not find the child.

He searched the faces of the children in detail, but could not decide which one it was. Finally he gave it up with a sigh and said:

"I thought I would know the little cub again but I don't." Mr. Johnson said further, that Mr. Young observed that life was a sad, sad thing —"because the joy of every new marriage a man contracted was so apt to be blighted by the inopportune funeral of a less recent bride." And Mr. Johnson said that while he and Mr. Young were pleasantly conversing in private, one of the Mrs. Youngs came in and demanded a breast-pin, remarking that she had found out that he had been giving a breast-pin to No. 6, and she, for one, did not propose to let this partiality go on without making a satisfactory amount of trouble about it. Mr. Young reminded her that there was a stranger present. Mrs. Young said that if the state of things inside the house was not agreeable to the stranger, he could find room outside. Mr. Young promised the breast-pin, and she went away. But in a minute or two another Mrs. Young came in and demanded a breast-pin. Mr. Young began a remonstrance, but Mrs. Young cut him short. She said No. 6 had got one, and No. 11 was promised one, and it was "no use for him to try to impose on her—she hoped she knew her rights." He gave his promise, and she went. And presently three Mrs. Youngs entered in a body and opened on their husband a tempest of tears, abuse, and entreaty. They had heard all about No. 6, No. 11, and No. 14. Three more breast-pins were promised. They were hardly gone when nine more Mrs. Youngs filed into the presence, and a new tempest burst forth and raged round about the prophet and his guest. Nine breast-pins were promised, and the weird sisters filed out again. And in came eleven more, weeping and wailing and gnashing their teeth. Eleven promised breast-pins purchased peace once more.

"That is a specimen," said Mr. Young. "You see how it is. You see what a life I lead. A man can't be wise all the time. In a heedless moment I gave my darling No. 6—excuse my calling her thus, as her other name has escaped me for the moment—a breast-pin. It was only worth twenty-five dollars—that is, apparently that was its whole cost—but its ultimate cost was inevitably bound to be a good deal more. You yourself have seen it climb up to six hundred and fifty dollars—and alas, even that is not the end! For I have wives all over this Territory of Utah. I have dozens of wives whose numbers, even, I do not know without looking in the family Bible. They are scattered far and wide among the mountains and valleys of my realm. And mark you, every solitary one of them will hear of this wretched breast pin, and every last one of them will have one or die. No. 6's breast pin will cost me twenty-five hundred dollars before I see the end of it. And these creatures will compare these pins together, and if one is a shade finer than the rest, they will all be thrown on my hands, and I will have to order a new lot to keep peace in the family. Sir, you probably did not know it, but all the time you were present with my children your every movement was watched by vigilant servitors of mine. If you had offered to give a child a dime, or a stick of candy, or any trifle of the kind, you would have been snatched out of the house instantly, provided it could be done before your gift left your hand. Otherwise it would be absolutely necessary for you to make an exactly similar gift to all my children—and knowing by experience the importance of the thing, I would have stood by and seen to it myself that you did it, and did it thoroughly. Once a gentleman gave one of my children a tin whistle—a veritable invention of Satan, sir, and one which I have an unspeakable horror of, and so would you if you had eighty or ninety children in your house. But the deed was done—the man escaped. I knew what the result was going to be, and I thirsted for vengeance. I ordered out a flock of Destroying Angels, and they hunted the man far into the fastnesses of the Nevada mountains. But they never caught him. I am not cruel, sir—I am not vindictive except when sorely outraged—but if I had caught him, sir, so help me Joseph Smith, I would have locked him into the nursery till the brats whistled him to death. By the slaughtered body of St. Parley Pratt (whom God assail!) there was never anything on this earth like it! I knew who gave the whistle to the child, but I could, not make those jealous mothers believe me. They believed I did it, and the result was just what any man of reflection could have foreseen: I had to order a hundred and ten whistles—I think we had a hundred and ten children in the house then, but some of them are off at college now—I had to order a hundred and ten of those shrieking things, and I wish I may never speak another word if we didn't have to talk on our fingers entirely, from that time forth until the children got tired of the whistles. And if ever another man gives a whistle to a child of mine and I get my hands on him, I will hang him higher than Haman! That is the word with the bark on it! Shade of Nephi! You don't know anything about married life. I am rich, and everybody knows it. I am benevolent, and everybody takes advantage of it. I have a strong fatherly instinct and all the foundlings are foisted on me.

"Every time a woman wants to do well by her darling, she puzzles her brain to cipher out some scheme for getting it into my hands. Why, sir, a woman came here once with a child of a curious lifeless sort of complexion (and so had the woman), and swore that the child was mine and she my wife—that I had married her at such-and-such a time in such-and-such a place, but she had forgotten her number, and of course I could not remember her name. Well, sir, she called my attention to the fact that the child looked like me, and really it did seem to resemble me—a common thing in the Territory—and, to cut the story short, I put it in my nursery, and she left. And by the ghost of Orson Hyde, when they came to wash the paint off that child it was an Injun! Bless my soul, you don't know

Roughing It 563

anything about married life. It is a perfect dog's life, sir—a perfect dog's life. You can't economize. It isn't possible. I have tried keeping one set of bridal attire for all occasions. But it is of no use. First you'll marry a combination of calico and consumption that's as thin as a rail, and next you'll get a creature that's nothing more than the dropsy in disguise, and then you've got to eke out that bridal dress with an old balloon. That is the way it goes. And think of the wash-bill—(excuse these tears)—nine hundred and eighty-four pieces a week! No, sir, there is no such thing as economy in a family like mine. Why, just the one item of cradles—think of it! And vermifuge! Soothing syrup! Teething rings! And 'papa's watches' for the babies to play with! And things to scratch the furniture with! And lucifer matches for them to eat, and pieces of glass to cut themselves with! The item of glass alone would support your family, I venture to say, sir. Let me scrimp and squeeze all I can, I still can't get ahead as fast as I feel I ought to, with my opportunities. Bless you, sir, at a time when I had seventy-two wives in this house, I groaned under the pressure of keeping thousands of dollars tied up in seventy-two bedsteads when the money ought to have been out at interest; and I just sold out the whole stock, sir, at a sacrifice, and built a bedstead seven feet long and ninety-six feet wide. But it was a failure, sir. I could not sleep. It appeared to me that the whole seventy-two women snored at once. The roar was deafening. And then the danger of it! That was what I was looking at. They would all draw in their breath at once, and you could actually see the walls of the house suck in—and then they would all exhale their breath at once, and you could see the walls swell out, and strain, and hear the rafters crack, and the shingles grind together. My friend, take an old man's advice, and don't encumber yourself with a large family—mind, I tell you, don't do it. In a small family, and in a small family only, you will find that comfort and that peace of mind which are the best at last of the blessings this world is able to afford us, and for the lack of which no accumulation of wealth, and no acquisition of fame, power, and greatness can ever compensate us. Take my word for it, ten or eleven wives is all you need—never go over it."

Some instinct or other made me set this Johnson down as being unreliable. And yet he was a very entertaining person, and I doubt if some of the information he gave us could have been acquired from any other source. He was a pleasant contrast to those reticent Mormons.

CHAPTER XVI.

All men have heard of the Mormon Bible, but few except the "elect" have seen it, or, at least, taken the trouble to read it. I brought away a copy from Salt Lake. The book is a curiosity to me, it is such a pretentious affair, and yet so "slow," so sleepy; such an insipid mess of inspiration. It is chloroform in print. If Joseph Smith composed this book, the act was a miracle—keeping awake while he did it was, at any rate. If he, according to tradition, merely translated it from certain ancient and mysteriously-engraved plates of copper, which he declares he found under a stone, in an out-of-the-way locality, the work of translating was equally a miracle, for the same reason.

The book seems to be merely a prosy detail of imaginary history, with the Old Testament for a model; followed by a tedious plagiarism of the New Testament. The author labored to give his words and phrases the quaint, old-fashioned sound and structure of our King James's translation of the Scriptures; and the result is a mongrel—half modern glibness, and half ancient simplicity and gravity. The latter is awkward and constrained; the former natural, but grotesque by the

contrast. Whenever he found his speech growing too modern—which was about every sentence or two—he ladled in a few such Scriptural phrases as "exceeding sore," "and it came to pass," etc., and made things satisfactory again. "And it came to pass" was his pet. If he had left that out, his Bible would have been only a pamphlet.

The title-page reads as follows:

The book of Mormon:
An Account Written by the Hand of Mormon, upon Plates
Taken From the Plates of Nephi.

Wherefore it is an abridgment of the record of the people of Nephi, and also of the Lamanites; written to the Lamanites, who are a remnant of the House of Israel; and also to Jew and Gentile; written by way of commandment, and also by the spirit of prophecy and of revelation. Written and sealed up, and hid up unto the Lord, that they might not be destroyed; to come forth by the gift and power of God unto the interpretation thereof; sealed by the hand of Moroni, and hid up unto the Lord, to come forth in due time by the way of Gentile; the interpretation thereof by the gift of God. An abridgment taken from the Book of Ether also; which is a record of the people of Jared; who were scattered at the time the Lord confounded the language of the people when they were building a tower to get to Heaven.

"Hid up" is good. And so is "wherefore"—though why "wherefore"? Any other word would have answered as well—though—in truth it would not have sounded so Scriptural.

Next comes:

THE TESTIMONY OF THREE WITNESSES. Be it known unto all nations, kindreds, tongues, and people unto whom this work shall come, that we, through the grace of God the Father, and our Lord Jesus Christ, have seen the plates which contain this record, which is a record of the people of Nephi, and also of the Lamanites, their brethren, and also of the people of Jared, who came from the tower of which hath been spoken; and we also know that they have been translated by the gift and power of God, for His voice hath declared it unto us; wherefore we know of a surety that the work is true. And we also testify that we have seen the engravings which are upon the plates; and they have been shown unto us by the power of God, and not of man. And we declare with words of soberness, that an angel of God came down from heaven, and he brought and laid before our eyes, that we beheld and saw the plates, and the engravings thereon; and we know that it is by the grace of God the Father, and our Lord Jesus Christ, that we beheld and bear record that these things are true; and it is marvellous in our eyes; nevertheless the voice of the Lord commanded us that we should bear record of it; wherefore, to be obedient unto the commandments of God, we bear testimony of these things. And we know that if we are faithful in Christ, we shall rid our garments of the blood of all men, and be found spotless before the judgment-seat of Christ, and shall dwell with Him eternally in the heavens. And the honor be to the Father, and to the Son, and to the Holy Ghost, which is one God. Amen. Oliver Cowdery, David Whitmer, Martin Harris.

Some people have to have a world of evidence before they can come anywhere in the neighborhood of believing anything; but for me, when a man tells me that he has "seen the engravings which are upon the plates," and not only that, but an angel was there at the time, and saw him see them, and probably took his receipt for it, I am very far on the road to conviction, no matter whether I ever heard of that man before or not, and even if I do not know the name of the angel, or his nationality either.

Next is this:

AND ALSO THE TESTIMONY OF EIGHT WITNESSES. Be it known unto all nations, kindreds, tongues, and people unto whom this work shall come, that Joseph Smith, Jr., the translator of this work, has shown unto us the plates of which hath been spoken, which have the appearance of gold; and as many of the leaves as the said Smith has translated, we did handle with our hands; and we also saw the engravings thereon, all of which has the appearance of ancient work, and of curious workmanship. And this we bear record with words of soberness, that the said Smith has shown unto us, for we have seen and hefted, and know of a surety that the said Smith has got the plates of which we have spoken. And we give our names unto the world, to witness unto the world that which we have seen; and we lie not, God bearing witness of it. Christian Whitmer, Jacob Whitmer, Peter Whitmer, Jr., John Whitmer, Hiram Page, Joseph Smith Sr., Hyrum Smith, Samuel H. Smith.

And when I am far on the road to conviction, and eight men, be they grammatical or otherwise, come forward and tell me that they have seen the plates too; and not only seen those plates but "hefted" them, I am convinced. I could not feel more satisfied and at rest if the entire Whitmer family had testified.

The Mormon Bible consists of fifteen "books"—being the books of Jacob, Enos, Jarom, Omni, Mosiah, Zeniff, Alma, Helaman, Ether, Moroni, two "books" of Mormon, and three of Nephi.

In the first book of Nephi is a plagiarism of the Old Testament, which gives an account of the exodus from Jerusalem of the "children of Lehi"; and it goes on to tell of their wanderings in the wilderness, during eight years, and their supernatural protection by one of their number, a party by the name of Nephi. They finally reached the land of "Bountiful," and camped by the sea. After they had remained there "for the space of many days"—which is more Scriptural than definite—Nephi was commanded from on high to build a ship wherein to "carry the people across the waters." He travestied Noah's ark—but he obeyed orders in the matter of the plan. He finished the ship in a single day, while his brethren stood by and made fun of it—and of him, too—"saying, our brother is a fool, for he thinketh that he can build a ship." They did not wait for the timbers to dry, but the whole tribe or nation sailed the next day. Then a bit of genuine nature cropped out, and is revealed by outspoken Nephi with Scriptural frankness—they all got on a spree! They, "and also their wives, began to make themselves merry, insomuch that they began to dance, and to sing, and to speak with much rudeness; yea, they were lifted up unto exceeding rudeness."

Nephi tried to stop these scandalous proceedings; but they tied him neck and heels, and went on with their lark. But observe how Nephi the prophet circumvented them by the aid of the invisible powers:

And it came to pass that after they had bound me, insomuch that I could not move, the compass, which had been prepared of the Lord, did cease to work; wherefore, they knew not whither they should steer the ship, insomuch that there arose a great storm, yea, a great and terrible tempest, and we were driven back upon the waters for the space of three days; and

they began to be frightened exceedingly, lest they should be drowned in the sea; nevertheless they did not loose me. And on the fourth day, which we had been driven back, the tempest began to be exceeding sore. And it came to pass that we were about to be swallowed up in the depths of the sea.

Then they untied him.

And it came to pass after they had loosed me, behold, I took the compass, and it did work whither I desired it. And it came to pass that I prayed unto the Lord; and after I had prayed, the winds did cease, and the storm did cease, and there was a great calm.

Equipped with their compass, these ancients appear to have had the advantage of Noah.

Their voyage was toward a "promised land"—the only name they give it. They reached it in safety.

Polygamy is a recent feature in the Mormon religion, and was added by Brigham Young after Joseph Smith's death. Before that, it was regarded as an "abomination." This verse from the Mormon Bible occurs in Chapter II. of the book of Jacob:

For behold, thus saith the Lord, this people begin to wax in iniquity; they understand not the Scriptures; for they seek to excuse themselves in committing whoredoms, because of the things which were written concerning David, and Solomon his son. Behold, David and Solomon truly had many wives and concubines, which thing was abominable before me, saith the Lord; wherefore, thus saith the Lord, I have led this people forth out of the land of Jerusalem, by the power of mine arm, that I might raise up unto me a righteous branch from the fruit of the loins of Joseph. Wherefore, I the Lord God, will no suffer that this people shall do like unto them of old.

However, the project failed—or at least the modern Mormon end of it—for Brigham "suffers" it. This verse is from the same chapter:

Behold, the Lamanites your brethren, whom ye hate, because of their filthiness and the cursings which hath come upon their skins, are more righteous than you; for they have not forgotten the commandment of the Lord, which was given unto our fathers, that they should have, save it were one wife; and concubines they should have none.

The following verse (from Chapter IX. of the Book of Nephi) appears to contain information not familiar to everybody:

And now it came to pass that when Jesus had ascended into heaven, the multitude did disperse, and every man did take his wife and his children, and did return to his own home.

And it came to pass that on the morrow, when the multitude was gathered together, behold, Nephi and his brother whom he had raised from the dead, whose name was Timothy, and also his son, whose name was Jonas, and also Mathoni, and Mathonihah, his brother, and Kumen, and Kumenenhi, and Jeremiah, and Shemnon, and Jonas, and Zedekiah, and Isaiah; now these were the names of the disciples whom Jesus had chosen.

In order that the reader may observe how much more grandeur and picturesqueness (as seen by these Mormon twelve) accompanied on of the tenderest episodes in the life of our Saviour than other eyes seem to have been aware of, I quote the following from the same "book"—Nephi:

And it came to pass that Jesus spake unto them, and bade them arise. And they arose from the earth, and He said unto them, Blessed are ye because of your faith. And now behold, My joy is full. And when He had said these words, He wept, and the multitude bear record of it, and He took their little children, one by one, and blessed them, and prayed unto the Father for them. And when He had done this He wept again, and He spake unto the multitude, and saith unto them, Behold your little ones. And as they looked to behold, they cast their eyes toward heaven, and they saw the heavens open, and they saw angels descending out of heaven as it were, in the midst of fire; and they came down and encircled those little ones about, and they were encircled about with fire; and the angels did minister unto them, and the multitude did see and hear and bear record; and they know that their record is true, for they all of them did see and hear, every man for himself; and they were in number about two thousand and five hundred souls; and they did consist of men, women, and children.

And what else would they be likely to consist of?

The Book of Ether is an incomprehensible medley of "history," much of it relating to battles and sieges among peoples whom the reader has possibly never heard of; and who inhabited a country which is not set down in the geography. These was a King with the remarkable name of Coriantumr, and he warred with Shared, and Lib, and Shiz, and others, in the "plains of Heshlon"; and the "valley of Gilgal"; and the "wilderness of Akish"; and the "land of Moran"; and the "plains of Agosh"; and "Ogath," and "Ramah," and the "land of Corihor," and the "hill Comnor," by "the waters of Ripliancum," etc., etc., etc. "And it came to pass," after a deal of fighting, that Coriantumr, upon making calculation of his losses, found that "there had been slain two millions of mighty men, and also their wives and their children"—say 5,000,000 or 6,000,000 in all—"and he began to sorrow in his heart." Unquestionably it was time. So he wrote to Shiz, asking a cessation of hostilities, and offering to give up his kingdom to save his people. Shiz declined, except upon condition that Coriantumr would come and let him cut his head off first—a thing which Coriantumr would not do. Then there was more fighting for a season; then four years were devoted to gathering the forces for a final struggle—after which ensued a battle, which, I take it, is the most remarkable set forth in history,—except, perhaps, that of the Kilkenny cats, which it resembles in some respects. This is the account of the gathering and the battle:

7. And it came to pass that they did gather together all the people, upon all the face of the land, who had not been slain, save it was Ether. And it came to pass that Ether did behold all the doings of the people; and he beheld that the people who were for Coriantumr, were gathered together to the army of Coriantumr; and the people who were for Shiz, were gathered together to the army of Shiz; wherefore they were for the space of four years gathering together the people, that they might get all who were upon the face of the land, and that they might receive all the strength which it was possible that they could receive. And it came to pass that when they were all gathered together, every one to the army which he would, with their wives and their children; both men, women, and children being armed with weapons of war, having shields, and breast-plates, and head-plates, and being clothed after the manner of war, they did march forth one against another, to battle; and they fought all that day, and conquered not. And it came to pass that when it was night they were weary, and retired to

their camps; and after they had retired to their camps, they took up a howling and a lamentation for the loss of the slain of their people; and so great were their cries, their howlings and lamentations, that it did rend the air exceedingly. And it came to pass that on the morrow they did go again to battle, and great and terrible was that day; nevertheless they conquered not, and when the night came again, they did rend the air with their cries, and their howlings, and their mournings, for the loss of the slain of their people.

8. And it came to pass that Coriantumr wrote again an epistle unto Shiz, desiring that he would not come again to battle, but that he would take the kingdom, and spare the lives of the people. But behold, the Spirit of the Lord had ceased striving with them, and Satan had full power over the hearts of the people, for they were given up unto the hardness of their hearts, and the blindness of their minds that they might be destroyed; wherefore they went again to battle. And it came to pass that they fought all that day, and when the night came they slept upon their swords; and on the morrow they fought even until the night came; and when the night came they were drunken with anger, even as a man who is drunken with wine; and they slept again upon their swords; and on the morrow they fought again; and when the night came they had all fallen by the sword save it were fifty and two of the people of Coriantumr, and sixty and nine of the people of Shiz. And it came to pass that they slept upon their swords that night, and on the morrow they fought again, and they contended in their mights with their swords, and with their shields, all that day; and when the night came there were thirty and two of the people of Shiz, and twenty and seven of the people of Coriantumr.

9. And it came to pass that they ate and slept, and prepared for death on the morrow. And they were large and mighty men, as to the strength of men. And it came to pass that they fought for the space of three hours, and they fainted with the loss of blood. And it came to pass that when the men of Coriantumr had received sufficient strength, that they could walk, they were about to flee for their lives, but behold, Shiz arose, and also his men, and he swore in his wrath that he would slay Coriantumr, or he would perish by the sword: wherefore he did pursue them, and on the morrow he did overtake them; and they fought again with the sword. And it came to pass that when they had all fallen by the sword, save it were Coriantumr and Shiz, behold Shiz had fainted with loss of blood. And it came to pass that when Coriantumr had leaned upon his sword, that he rested a little, he smote off the head of Shiz. And it came to pass that after he had smote off the head of Shiz, that Shiz raised upon his hands and fell; and after that he had struggled for breath, he died. And it came to pass that Coriantumr fell to the earth, and became as if he had no life. And the Lord spake unto Ether, and said unto him, go forth. And he went forth, and beheld that the words of the Lord had all been fulfilled; and he finished his record; and the hundredth part I have not written.

It seems a pity he did not finish, for after all his dreary former chapters of commonplace, he stopped just as he was in danger of becoming interesting.

The Mormon Bible is rather stupid and tiresome to read, but there is nothing vicious in its teachings. Its code of morals is unobjectionable —it is "smouched" [Milton] from the New Testament and no credit given.

CHAPTER XVII.

At the end of our two days' sojourn, we left Great Salt Lake City hearty and well fed and happy—physically superb but not so very much wiser, as regards the "Mormon question," than we were when we arrived, perhaps. We had a deal more "information" than we had before, of course, but we did not know what portion of it was reliable and what was not—for it all came from acquaintances of a day—strangers, strictly speaking. We were told, for instance, that the dreadful "Mountain Meadows Massacre" was the work of the Indians entirely, and that the Gentiles had meanly tried to fasten it upon the Mormons; we were told, likewise, that the Indians were to blame, partly, and partly the Mormons; and we were told, likewise, and just as positively, that the Mormons were almost if not wholly and completely responsible for that most treacherous and pitiless butchery. We got the story in all these different shapes, but it was not till several years afterward that Mrs. Waite's book, "The Mormon Prophet," came out with Judge Cradlebaugh's trial of the accused parties in it and revealed the truth that the latter version was the correct one and that the Mormons were the assassins. All our "information" had three sides to it, and so I gave up the idea that I could settle the "Mormon question" in two days. Still I have seen newspaper correspondents do it in one.

I left Great Salt Lake a good deal confused as to what state of things existed there—and sometimes even questioning in my own mind whether a state of things existed there at all or not. But presently I remembered with a lightening sense of relief that we had learned two or three trivial things there which we could be certain of; and so the two days were not wholly lost. For instance, we had learned that we were at last in a pioneer land, in absolute and tangible reality.

The high prices charged for trifles were eloquent of high freights and bewildering distances of freightage. In the east, in those days, the smallest moneyed denomination was a penny and it represented the smallest purchasable quantity of any commodity. West of Cincinnati the smallest coin in use was the silver five-cent piece and no smaller quantity of an article could be bought than "five cents' worth." In Overland City the lowest coin appeared to be the ten-cent piece; but in Salt Lake there did not seem to be any money in circulation smaller than a quarter, or any smaller quantity purchasable of any commodity than twenty-five cents' worth. We had always been used to half dimes and "five cents' worth" as the minimum of financial negotiations; but in Salt Lake if one wanted a cigar, it was a quarter; if he wanted a chalk pipe, it was a quarter; if he wanted a peach, or a candle, or a newspaper, or a shave, or a little Gentile whiskey to rub on his corns to arrest indigestion and keep him from having the toothache, twenty-five cents was the price, every time. When we looked at the shot-bag of silver, now and then, we seemed to be wasting our substance in riotous living, but if we referred to the expense account we could see that we had not been doing anything of the kind.

But people easily get reconciled to big money and big prices, and fond and vain of both—it is a descent to little coins and cheap prices that is hardest to bear and slowest to take hold upon one's toleration. After a month's acquaintance with the twenty-five cent minimum, the average human being is ready to blush every time he thinks of his despicable five-cent days. How sunburnt with blushes I used to get in gaudy Nevada, every time I thought of my first financial experience in Salt Lake. It was on this wise (which is a favorite expression of great authors, and a very neat one, too, but I never hear anybody say on this wise when they are talking). A young half-breed with a complexion like a yellow-jacket asked me if I would have my boots blacked. It was at the Salt Lake House

the morning after we arrived. I said yes, and he blacked them. Then I handed him a silver five-cent piece, with the benevolent air of a person who is conferring wealth and blessedness upon poverty and suffering. The yellow-jacket took it with what I judged to be suppressed emotion, and laid it reverently down in the middle of his broad hand. Then he began to contemplate it, much as a philosopher contemplates a gnat's ear in the ample field of his microscope. Several mountaineers, teamsters, stage-drivers, etc., drew near and dropped into the tableau and fell to surveying the money with that attractive indifference to formality which is noticeable in the hardy pioneer. Presently the yellow-jacket handed the half dime back to me and told me I ought to keep my money in my pocket-book instead of in my soul, and then I wouldn't get it cramped and shriveled up so!

What a roar of vulgar laughter there was! I destroyed the mongrel reptile on the spot, but I smiled and smiled all the time I was detaching his scalp, for the remark he made was good for an "Injun."

Yes, we had learned in Salt Lake to be charged great prices without letting the inward shudder appear on the surface—for even already we had overheard and noted the tenor of conversations among drivers, conductors, and hostlers, and finally among citizens of Salt Lake, until we were well aware that these superior beings despised "emigrants." We permitted no tell-tale shudders and winces in our countenances, for we wanted to seem pioneers, or Mormons, half-breeds, teamsters, stage-drivers, Mountain Meadow assassins—anything in the world that the plains and Utah respected and admired—but we were wretchedly ashamed of being "emigrants," and sorry enough that we had white shirts and could not swear in the presence of ladies without looking the other way.

And many a time in Nevada, afterwards, we had occasion to remember with humiliation that we were "emigrants," and consequently a low and inferior sort of creatures. Perhaps the reader has visited Utah, Nevada, or California, even in these latter days, and while communing with himself upon the sorrowful banishment of these countries from what he considers "the world," has had his wings clipped by finding that he is the one to be pitied, and that there are entire populations around him ready and willing to do it for him—yea, who are complacently doing it for him already, wherever he steps his foot.

Poor thing, they are making fun of his hat; and the cut of his New York coat; and his conscientiousness about his grammar; and his feeble profanity; and his consumingly ludicrous ignorance of ores, shafts, tunnels, and other things which he never saw before, and never felt enough interest in to read about. And all the time that he is thinking what a sad fate it is to be exiled to that far country, that lonely land, the citizens around him are looking down on him with a blighting compassion because he is an "emigrant" instead of that proudest and blessedest creature that exists on all the earth, a "FORTY-NINER."

The accustomed coach life began again, now, and by midnight it almost seemed as if we never had been out of our snuggery among the mail sacks at all. We had made one alteration, however. We had provided enough bread, boiled ham and hard boiled eggs to last double the six hundred miles of staging we had still to do.

And it was comfort in those succeeding days to sit up and contemplate the majestic panorama of mountains and valleys spread out below us and eat ham and hard boiled eggs while our spiritual natures revelled alternately in rainbows, thunderstorms, and peerless sunsets. Nothing helps scenery like ham and eggs. Ham and eggs, and after these a pipe—an old, rank, delicious pipe—ham and eggs and scenery, a "down grade," a flying coach, a fragrant pipe and a contented heart— these make happiness. It is what all the ages have struggled for.

CHAPTER XVIII.

At eight in the morning we reached the remnant and ruin of what had been the important military station of "Camp Floyd," some forty-five or fifty miles from Salt Lake City. At four P.M. we had doubled our distance and were ninety or a hundred miles from Salt Lake. And now we entered upon one of that species of deserts whose concentrated hideousness shames the diffused and diluted horrors of Sahara—an "alkali" desert. For sixty-eight miles there was but one break in it. I do not remember that this was really a break; indeed it seems to me that it was nothing but a watering depot in the midst of the stretch of sixty-eight miles. If my memory serves me, there was no well or spring at this place, but the water was hauled there by mule and ox teams from the further side of the desert. There was a stage station there. It was forty-five miles from the beginning of the desert, and twenty-three from the end of it.

We plowed and dragged and groped along, the whole live-long night, and at the end of this uncomfortable twelve hours we finished the forty-five-mile part of the desert and got to the stage station where the imported water was. The sun was just rising. It was easy enough to cross a desert in the night while we were asleep; and it was pleasant to reflect, in the morning, that we in actual person had encountered an absolute desert and could always speak knowingly of deserts in presence of the ignorant thenceforward. And it was pleasant also to reflect that this was not an obscure, back country desert, but a very celebrated one, the metropolis itself, as you may say. All this was very well and very comfortable and satisfactory—but now we were to cross a desert in daylight. This was fine—novel— romantic—dramatically adventurous —this, indeed, was worth living for, worth traveling for! We would write home all about it.

This enthusiasm, this stern thirst for adventure, wilted under the sultry August sun and did not last above one hour. One poor little hour—and then we were ashamed that we had "gushed" so. The poetry was all in the anticipation—there is none in the reality. Imagine a vast, waveless ocean stricken dead and turned to ashes; imagine this solemn waste tufted with ash-dusted sage-bushes; imagine the lifeless silence and solitude that belong to such a place; imagine a coach, creeping like a bug through the midst of this shoreless level, and sending up tumbled volumes of dust as if it were a bug that went by steam; imagine this aching monotony of toiling and plowing kept up hour after hour, and the shore still as far away as ever, apparently; imagine team, driver, coach and passengers so deeply coated with ashes that they are all one colorless color; imagine ash-drifts roosting above moustaches and eyebrows like snow accumulations on boughs and bushes. This is the reality of it.

The sun beats down with dead, blistering, relentless malignity; the perspiration is welling from every pore in man and beast, but scarcely a sign of it finds its way to the surface—it is absorbed before it gets there; there is not the faintest breath of air stirring; there is not a merciful shred of cloud in all the

brilliant firmament; there is not a living creature visible in any direction whither one searches the blank level that stretches its monotonous miles on every hand; there is not a sound—not a sigh—not a whisper—not a buzz, or a whir of wings, or distant pipe of bird—not even a sob from the lost souls that doubtless people that dead air. And so the occasional sneezing of the resting mules, and the champing of the bits, grate harshly on the grim stillness, not dissipating the spell but accenting it and making one feel more lonesome and forsaken than before.

The mules, under violent swearing, coaxing and whip-cracking, would make at stated intervals a "spurt," and drag the coach a hundred or may be two hundred yards, stirring up a billowy cloud of dust that rolled back, enveloping the vehicle to the wheel-tops or higher, and making it seem afloat in a fog. Then a rest followed, with the usual sneezing and bit-champing. Then another "spurt" of a hundred yards and another rest at the end of it. All day long we kept this up, without water for the mules and without ever changing the team. At least we kept it up ten hours, which, I take it, is a day, and a pretty honest one, in an alkali desert. It was from four in the morning till two in the afternoon. And it was so hot! and so close! and our water canteens went dry in the middle of the day and we got so thirsty! It was so stupid and tiresome and dull! and the tedious hours did lag and drag and limp along with such a cruel deliberation! It was so trying to give one's watch a good long undisturbed spell and then take it out and find that it had been fooling away the time and not trying to get ahead any! The alkali dust cut through our lips, it persecuted our eyes, it ate through the delicate membranes and made our noses bleed and kept them bleeding—and truly and seriously the romance all faded far away and disappeared, and left the desert trip nothing but a harsh reality—a thirsty, sweltering, longing, hateful reality!

Two miles and a quarter an hour for ten hours—that was what we accomplished. It was hard to bring the comprehension away down to such a snail-pace as that, when we had been used to making eight and ten miles an hour. When we reached the station on the farther verge of the desert, we were glad, for the first time, that the dictionary was along, because we never could have found language to tell how glad we were, in any sort of dictionary but an unabridged one with pictures in it. But there could not have been found in a whole library of dictionaries language sufficient to tell how tired those mules were after their twenty-three mile pull. To try to give the reader an idea of how thirsty they were, would be to "gild refined gold or paint the lily."

Somehow, now that it is there, the quotation does not seem to fit—but no matter, let it stay, anyhow. I think it is a graceful and attractive thing, and therefore have tried time and time again to work it in where it would fit, but could not succeed. These efforts have kept my mind distracted and ill at ease, and made my narrative seem broken and disjointed, in places. Under these circumstances it seems to me best to leave it in, as above, since this will afford at least a temporary respite from the wear and tear of trying to "lead up" to this really apt and beautiful quotation.

CHAPTER XIX.

On the morning of the sixteenth day out from St. Joseph we arrived at the entrance of Rocky Canyon, two hundred and fifty miles from Salt Lake. It was along in this wild country somewhere, and far from any habitation of white men, except the stage stations, that we came across the wretchedest type of mankind I have ever seen, up to this writing. I refer to the Goshoot Indians. From what we could see and all we could learn, they are very considerably inferior to even the despised Digger Indians of California; inferior to all races of savages on our continent; inferior to even the Terra del Fuegans; inferior to the Hottentots, and actually inferior in some respects to the Kytches of Africa. Indeed, I have been obliged to look the bulky volumes of Wood's "Uncivilized Races of Men" clear through in order to find a savage tribe degraded enough to take rank with the Goshoots. I find but one people fairly open to that shameful verdict. It is the Bosjesmans (Bushmen) of South Africa. Such of the Goshoots as we saw, along the road and hanging about the stations, were small, lean, "scrawny" creatures; in complexion a dull black like the ordinary American negro; their faces and hands bearing dirt which they had been hoarding and accumulating for months, years, and even generations, according to the age of the proprietor; a silent, sneaking, treacherous looking race; taking note of everything, covertly, like all the other "Noble Red Men" that we (do not) read about, and betraying no sign in their countenances; indolent, everlastingly patient and tireless, like all other Indians; prideless beggars—for if the beggar instinct were left out of an Indian he would not "go," any more than a clock without a pendulum; hungry, always hungry, and yet never refusing anything that a hog would eat, though often eating what a hog would decline; hunters, but having no higher ambition than to kill and eat jack-ass rabbits, crickets and grasshoppers, and embezzle carrion from the buzzards and cayotes; savages who, when asked if they have the common Indian belief in a Great Spirit show a something which almost amounts to emotion, thinking whiskey is referred to; a thin, scattering race of almost naked black children, these Goshoots are, who produce nothing at all, and have no villages, and no gatherings together into strictly defined tribal communities—a people whose only shelter is a rag cast on a bush to keep off a portion of the snow, and yet who inhabit one of the most rocky, wintry, repulsive wastes that our country or any other can exhibit.

The Bushmen and our Goshoots are manifestly descended from the self-same gorilla, or kangaroo, or Norway rat, which-ever animal—Adam the Darwinians trace them to.

One would as soon expect the rabbits to fight as the Goshoots, and yet they used to live off the offal and refuse of the stations a few months and then come some dark night when no mischief was expected, and burn down the buildings and kill the men from ambush as they rushed out. And once, in the night, they attacked the stage-coach when a District Judge, of Nevada Territory, was the only passenger, and with their first volley of arrows (and a bullet or two) they riddled the stage curtains, wounded a horse or two and mortally wounded the driver. The latter was full of pluck, and so was his passenger. At the driver's call Judge Mott swung himself out, clambered to the box and seized the reins of the team, and away they plunged, through the racing mob of skeletons and under a hurtling storm of missiles. The stricken driver had sunk down on the boot as soon as he was wounded, but had held on to the reins and said he would manage to keep hold of them until relieved.

And after they were taken from his relaxing grasp, he lay with his head between Judge Mott's feet, and tranquilly gave directions about the road; he said he believed he could live till the miscreants were outrun and left behind, and that if he managed that, the main difficulty would be at an end, and then if the Judge drove so and so (giving directions about bad places in the road, and general course) he would reach the next station without trouble. The Judge distanced the enemy and at last rattled up to the station and knew that the night's perils were done; but there was no comrade-in-arms for him to rejoice with, for the soldierly driver was dead.

Let us forget that we have been saying harsh things about the Overland drivers, now. The disgust which the Goshoots gave me, a disciple of Cooper and a worshipper of the Red Man—even of the scholarly savages in the "Last of the Mohicans" who are fittingly associated with backwoodsmen who divide each sentence into two equal parts: one part critically grammatical, refined and choice of language, and the other part just such an attempt to talk like a hunter or a mountaineer, as a Broadway clerk might make after eating an edition of Emerson Bennett's works and studying frontier life at the Bowery Theatre a couple of weeks—I say that the nausea which the Goshoots gave me, an Indian worshipper, set me to examining authorities, to see if perchance I had been over-estimating the Red Man while viewing him through the mellow moonshine of romance. The revelations that came were disenchanting. It was curious to see how quickly the paint and tinsel fell away from him and left him treacherous, filthy and repulsive—and how quickly the evidences accumulated that wherever one finds an Indian tribe he has only found Goshoots more or less modified by circumstances and surroundings—but Goshoots, after all. They deserve pity, poor creatures; and they can have mine—at this distance. Nearer by, they never get anybody's.

There is an impression abroad that the Baltimore and Washington Railroad Company and many of its employees are Goshoots; but it is an error. There is only a plausible resemblance, which, while it is apt enough to mislead the ignorant, cannot deceive parties who have contemplated both tribes. But seriously, it was not only poor wit, but very wrong to start the report referred to above; for however innocent the motive may have been, the necessary effect was to injure the reputation of a class who have a hard enough time of it in the pitiless deserts of the Rocky Mountains, Heaven knows! If we cannot find it in our hearts to give those poor naked creatures our Christian sympathy and compassion, in God's name let us at least not throw mud at them.

CHAPTER XX.

On the seventeenth day we passed the highest mountain peaks we had yet seen, and although the day was very warm the night that followed upon its heels was wintry cold and blankets were next to useless.

On the eighteenth day we encountered the eastward-bound telegraph-constructors at Reese River station and sent a message to his Excellency Gov. Nye at Carson City (distant one hundred and fifty-six miles).

On the nineteenth day we crossed the Great American Desert—forty memorable miles of bottomless sand, into which the coach wheels sunk from six inches to a foot. We worked our passage most of the way across. That is to say, we got out and walked. It was a dreary pull and a long and thirsty one, for we had no water. From one extremity of this desert to the other, the road was white with the bones of oxen and horses. It would hardly be an exaggeration to say that we could have walked the forty miles and set our feet on a bone at every step! The desert was one prodigious graveyard. And the log-chains, wagon tyres, and rotting wrecks of vehicles were almost as thick as the bones. I think we saw log-chains enough rusting there in the desert, to reach across any State in the Union. Do not these relics suggest something of an idea of the fearful suffering and privation the early emigrants to California endured?

At the border of the Desert lies Carson Lake, or The "Sink" of the Carson, a shallow, melancholy sheet of water some eighty or a hundred miles in circumference. Carson River empties into it and is lost—sinks mysteriously into the earth and never appears in the light of the sun again—for the lake has no outlet whatever.

There are several rivers in Nevada, and they all have this mysterious fate. They end in various lakes or "sinks," and that is the last of them. Carson Lake, Humboldt Lake, Walker Lake, Mono Lake, are all great sheets of water without any visible outlet. Water is always flowing into them; none is ever seen to flow out of them, and yet they remain always level full, neither receding nor overflowing. What they do with their surplus is only known to the Creator.

On the western verge of the Desert we halted a moment at Ragtown. It consisted of one log house and is not set down on the map.

This reminds me of a circumstance. Just after we left Julesburg, on the Platte, I was sitting with the driver, and he said:

"I can tell you a most laughable thing indeed, if you would like to listen to it. Horace Greeley went over this road once. When he was leaving Carson City he told the driver, Hank Monk, that he had an engagement to lecture at Placerville and was very anxious to go through quick. Hank Monk cracked his whip and started off at an awful pace. The coach bounced up and down in such a terrific way that it jolted the buttons all off of Horace's coat, and finally shot his head clean through the roof of the stage, and then he yelled at Hank Monk and begged him to go easier—said he warn't in as much of a hurry as he was awhile ago. But Hank Monk said, 'Keep your seat, Horace, and I'll get you there on time'—and you bet you he did, too, what was left of him!"

A day or two after that we picked up a Denver man at the cross roads, and he told us a good deal about the country and the Gregory Diggings. He seemed a very entertaining person and a man well posted in the affairs of Colorado. By and by he remarked:

"I can tell you a most laughable thing indeed, if you would like to listen to it. Horace Greeley went over this road once. When he was leaving Carson City he told the driver, Hank Monk, that he had an engagement to lecture at Placerville and was very anxious to go through quick. Hank Monk cracked his whip and started off at an awful pace. The coach bounced up and down in such a terrific way that it jolted the buttons all off of Horace's coat, and finally shot his head clean through the roof of the stage, and then he yelled at Hank Monk and begged him to go easier—said he warn't in as much of a hurry as he was awhile ago. But Hank Monk said, 'Keep your seat, Horace, and I'll get you there on time!'—and you bet you he did, too, what was left of him!"

At Fort Bridger, some days after this, we took on board a cavalry sergeant, a very proper and soldierly person indeed. From no other man during the whole journey, did we gather such a store of concise and well-arranged military information. It was surprising to find in the desolate wilds of our country a man so thoroughly acquainted with everything

useful to know in his line of life, and yet of such inferior rank and unpretentious bearing. For as much as three hours we listened to him with unabated interest. Finally he got upon the subject of trans-continental travel, and presently said:

"I can tell you a very laughable thing indeed, if you would like to listen to it. Horace Greeley went over this road once. When he was leaving Carson City he told the driver, Hank Monk, that he had an engagement to lecture at Placerville and was very anxious to go through quick. Hank Monk cracked his whip and started off at an awful pace. The coach bounced up and down in such a terrific way that it jolted the buttons all off of Horace's coat, and finally shot his head clean through the roof of the stage, and then he yelled at Hank Monk and begged him to go easier—said he warn't in as much of a hurry as he was awhile ago. But Hank Monk said, 'Keep your seat, Horace, and I'll get you there on time!'—and you bet you he did, too, what was left of him!"

When we were eight hours out from Salt Lake City a Mormon preacher got in with us at a way station—a gentle, soft-spoken, kindly man, and one whom any stranger would warm to at first sight. I can never forget the pathos that was in his voice as he told, in simple language, the story of his people's wanderings and unpitied sufferings. No pulpit eloquence was ever so moving and so beautiful as this outcast's picture of the first Mormon pilgrimage across the plains, struggling sorrowfully onward to the land of its banishment and marking its desolate way with graves and watering it with tears. His words so wrought upon us that it was a relief to us all when the conversation drifted into a more cheerful channel and the natural features of the curious country we were in came under treatment. One matter after another was pleasantly discussed, and at length the stranger said:

"I can tell you a most laughable thing indeed, if you would like to listen to it. Horace Greeley went over this road once. When he was leaving Carson City he told the driver, Hank Monk, that he had an engagement to lecture in Placerville, and was very anxious to go through quick. Hank Monk cracked his whip and started off at an awful pace. The coach bounced up and down in such a terrific way that it jolted the buttons all off of Horace's coat, and finally shot his head clean through the roof of the stage, and then he yelled at Hank Monk and begged him to go easier—said he warn't in as much of a hurry as he was awhile ago. But Hank Monk said, 'Keep your seat, Horace, and I'll get you there on time!'—and you bet you bet you he did, too, what was left of him!"

Ten miles out of Ragtown we found a poor wanderer who had lain down to die. He had walked as long as he could, but his limbs had failed him at last. Hunger and fatigue had conquered him. It would have been inhuman to leave him there. We paid his fare to Carson and lifted him into the coach. It was some little time before he showed any very decided signs of life; but by dint of chafing him and pouring brandy between his lips we finally brought him to a languid consciousness. Then we fed him a little, and by and by he seemed to comprehend the situation and a grateful light softened his eye. We made his mail-sack bed as comfortable as possible, and constructed a pillow for him with our coats. He seemed very thankful. Then he looked up in our faces, and said in a feeble voice that had a tremble of honest emotion in it:

"Gentlemen, I know not who you are, but you have saved my life; and although I can never be able to repay you for it, I feel that I can at least make one hour of your long journey lighter. I take it you are strangers to this great thorough fare, but I am entirely familiar with it. In this connection I can tell you a most laughable thing indeed, if you would like to listen to it. Horace Greeley—"

I said, impressively:

"Suffering stranger, proceed at your peril. You see in me the melancholy wreck of a once stalwart and magnificent manhood. What has brought me to this? That thing which you are about to tell. Gradually but surely, that tiresome old anecdote has sapped my strength, undermined my constitution, withered my life. Pity my helplessness. Spare me only just this once, and tell me about young George Washington and his little hatchet for a change."

We were saved. But not so the invalid. In trying to retain the anecdote in his system he strained himself and died in our arms.

I am aware, now, that I ought not to have asked of the sturdiest citizen of all that region, what I asked of that mere shadow of a man; for, after seven years' residence on the Pacific coast, I know that no passenger or driver on the Overland ever corked that anecdote in, when a stranger was by, and survived. Within a period of six years I crossed and recrossed the Sierras between Nevada and California thirteen times by stage and listened to that deathless incident four hundred and eighty-one or eighty-two times. I have the list somewhere. Drivers always told it, conductors told it, landlords told it, chance passengers told it, the very Chinamen and vagrant Indians recounted it. I have had the same driver tell it to me two or three times in the same afternoon. It has come to me in all the multitude of tongues that Babel bequeathed to earth, and flavored with whiskey, brandy, beer, cologne, sozodont, tobacco, garlic, onions, grasshoppers—everything that has a fragrance to it through all the long list of things that are gorged or guzzled by the sons of men. I never have smelt any anecdote as often as I have smelt that one; never have smelt any anecdote that smelt so variegated as that one. And you never could learn to know it by its smell, because every time you thought you had learned the smell of it, it would turn up with a different smell. Bayard Taylor has written about this hoary anecdote, Richardson has published it; so have Jones, Smith, Johnson, Ross Browne, and every other correspondence-inditing being that ever set his foot upon the great overland road anywhere between Julesburg and San Francisco; and I have heard that it is in the Talmud. I have seen it in print in nine different foreign languages; I have been told that it is employed in the inquisition in Rome; and I now learn with regret that it is going to be set to music. I do not think that such things are right.

Stage-coaching on the Overland is no more, and stage drivers are a race defunct. I wonder if they bequeathed that bald-headed anecdote to their successors, the railroad brakemen and conductors, and if these latter still persecute the helpless passenger with it until he concludes, as did many a tourist of other days, that the real grandeurs of the Pacific coast are not Yo Semite and the Big Trees, but Hank Monk and his adventure with Horace Greeley. [And what makes that worn anecdote the more aggravating, is, that the adventure it celebrates never occurred. If it were a good anecdote, that seeming demerit would be its chiefest virtue, for creative power belongs to greatness; but what ought to be done to a man who would wantonly contrive so flat a one as this? If I were to suggest what ought to be done to him, I should be called extravagant—but what does the sixteenth chapter of Daniel say? Aha!]

CHAPTER XXI.

We were approaching the end of our long journey. It was the morning of the twentieth day. At noon we would reach Carson City, the capital of Nevada Territory. We were not glad, but sorry. It had been a fine pleasure trip; we had fed fat on wonders every day; we were now well accustomed to stage life, and very fond of it; so the idea of coming to a stand-still and settling down to a humdrum existence in a village was not agreeable, but on the contrary depressing.

Visibly our new home was a desert, walled in by barren, snow-clad mountains. There was not a tree in sight. There was no vegetation but the endless sage-brush and greasewood. All nature was gray with it. We were plowing through great deeps of powdery alkali dust that rose in thick clouds and floated across the plain like smoke from a burning house.

We were coated with it like millers; so were the coach, the mules, the mail-bags, the driver—we and the sage-brush and the other scenery were all one monotonous color. Long trains of freight wagons in the distance envelope in ascending masses of dust suggested pictures of prairies on fire. These teams and their masters were the only life we saw. Otherwise we moved in the midst of solitude, silence and desolation. Every twenty steps we passed the skeleton of some dead beast of burthen, with its dust-coated skin stretched tightly over its empty ribs. Frequently a solemn raven sat upon the skull or the hips and contemplated the passing coach with meditative serenity.

By and by Carson City was pointed out to us. It nestled in the edge of a great plain and was a sufficient number of miles away to look like an assemblage of mere white spots in the shadow of a grim range of mountains overlooking it, whose summits seemed lifted clear out of companionship and consciousness of earthly things.

We arrived, disembarked, and the stage went on. It was a "wooden" town; its population two thousand souls. The main street consisted of four or five blocks of little white frame stores which were too high to sit down on, but not too high for various other purposes; in fact, hardly high enough. They were packed close together, side by side, as if room were scarce in that mighty plain.

The sidewalk was of boards that were more or less loose and inclined to rattle when walked upon. In the middle of the town, opposite the stores, was the "plaza" which is native to all towns beyond the Rocky Mountains —a large, unfenced, level vacancy, with a liberty pole in it, and very useful as a place for public auctions, horse trades, and mass meetings, and likewise for teamsters to camp in. Two other sides of the plaza were faced by stores, offices and stables.

The rest of Carson City was pretty scattering.

We were introduced to several citizens, at the stage-office and on the way up to the Governor's from the hotel—among others, to a Mr. Harris, who was on horseback; he began to say something, but interrupted himself with the remark:

"I'll have to get you to excuse me a minute; yonder is the witness that swore I helped to rob the California coach—a piece of impertinent intermeddling, sir, for I am not even acquainted with the man."

Then he rode over and began to rebuke the stranger with a six-shooter, and the stranger began to explain with another. When the pistols were emptied, the stranger resumed his work (mending a whip-lash), and Mr. Harris rode by with a polite nod, homeward bound, with a bullet through one of his lungs, and several in his hips; and from them issued little rivulets of blood that coursed down the horse's sides and made the animal look quite picturesque. I never saw Harris shoot a man after that but it recalled to mind that first day in Carson.

This was all we saw that day, for it was two o'clock, now, and according to custom the daily "Washoe Zephyr" set in; a soaring dust-drift about the size of the United States set up edgewise came with it, and the capital of Nevada Territory disappeared from view.

Still, there were sights to be seen which were not wholly uninteresting to new comers; for the vast dust cloud was thickly freckled with things strange to the upper air—things living and dead, that flitted hither and thither, going and coming, appearing and disappearing among the rolling billows of dust—hats, chickens and parasols sailing in the remote heavens; blankets, tin signs, sage-brush and shingles a shade lower; door-mats and buffalo robes lower still; shovels and coal scuttles on the next grade; glass doors, cats and little children on the next; disrupted lumber yards, light buggies and wheelbarrows on the next; and down only thirty or forty feet above ground was a scurrying storm of emigrating roofs and vacant lots.

It was something to see that much. I could have seen more, if I could have kept the dust out of my eyes.

But seriously a Washoe wind is by no means a trifling matter. It blows flimsy houses down, lifts shingle roofs occasionally, rolls up tin ones like sheet music, now and then blows a stage coach over and spills the passengers; and tradition says the reason there are so many bald people there, is, that the wind blows the hair off their heads while they are looking skyward after their hats. Carson streets seldom look inactive on Summer afternoons, because there are so many citizens skipping around their escaping hats, like chambermaids trying to head off a spider.

The "Washoe Zephyr" (Washoe is a pet nickname for Nevada) is a peculiar Scriptural wind, in that no man knoweth "whence it cometh." That is to say, where it originates. It comes right over the mountains from the West, but when one crosses the ridge he does not find any of it on the other side! It probably is manufactured on the mountain-top for the occasion, and starts from there. It is a pretty regular wind, in the summer time. Its office hours are from two in the afternoon till two the next morning; and anybody venturing abroad during those twelve hours needs to allow for the wind or he will bring up a mile or two to leeward of the point he is aiming at. And yet the first complaint a Washoe visitor to San Francisco makes, is that the sea winds blow so, there! There is a good deal of human nature in that.

We found the state palace of the Governor of Nevada Territory to consist of a white frame one-story house with two small rooms in it and a stanchion supported shed in front—for grandeur—it compelled the respect of the citizen and inspired the Indians with awe. The newly arrived Chief and Associate Justices of the Territory, and other machinery of the government, were domiciled with less splendor. They were boarding around privately, and had their offices in their bedrooms.

The Secretary and I took quarters in the "ranch" of a worthy French lady by the name of Bridget O'Flannigan, a camp follower of his Excellency the Governor. She had known him in his prosperity as commander-in-chief of the Metropolitan Police of New York, and she would not desert him in his adversity as Governor of Nevada.

Our room was on the lower floor, facing the plaza, and when we had got our bed, a small table, two chairs, the government fire-proof safe, and the Unabridged Dictionary into it, there was still room enough left for a visitor—may be two, but not without straining the walls. But the walls could stand it—at least the partitions could, for they consisted simply of one thickness of white "cotton domestic" stretched from corner to corner of the room. This was the rule in Carson—any other kind of partition was the rare exception. And if you stood in a dark room and your neighbors in the next had lights, the shadows on your canvas told queer secrets sometimes! Very often these partitions were made of old flour sacks basted together; and then the difference between the common herd and the aristocracy was, that the common herd had unornamented sacks, while the walls of the aristocrat were overpowering with rudimental fresco—i.e., red and blue mill brands on the flour sacks.

Occasionally, also, the better classes embellished their canvas by pasting pictures from Harper's Weekly on them. In many cases, too, the wealthy and the cultured rose to spittoons and other evidences of a sumptuous and luxurious taste. [Washoe people take a joke so hard that I must explain that the above description was only the rule; there were many honorable exceptions in Carson—plastered ceilings and houses that had considerable furniture in them.—M. T.]

We had a carpet and a genuine queen's-ware washbowl. Consequently we were hated without reserve by the other tenants of the O'Flannigan "ranch." When we added a painted oilcloth window curtain, we simply took our lives into our own hands. To prevent bloodshed I removed up stairs and took up quarters with the untitled plebeians in one of the fourteen white pine cot-bedsteads that stood in two long ranks in the one sole room of which the second story consisted.

It was a jolly company, the fourteen. They were principally voluntary camp-followers of the Governor, who had joined his retinue by their own election at New York and San Francisco and came along, feeling that in the scuffle for little territorial crumbs and offices they could not make their condition more precarious than it was, and might reasonably expect to make it better. They were popularly known as the "Irish Brigade," though there were only four or five Irishmen among all the Governor's retainers.

His good-natured Excellency was much annoyed at the gossip his henchmen created—especially when there arose a rumor that they were paid assassins of his, brought along to quietly reduce the democratic vote when desirable!

Mrs. O'Flannigan was boarding and lodging them at ten dollars a week apiece, and they were cheerfully giving their notes for it. They were perfectly satisfied, but Bridget presently found that notes that could not be discounted were but a feeble constitution for a Carson boarding-house. So she began to harry the Governor to find employment for the "Brigade." Her importunities and theirs together drove him to a gentle desperation at last, and he finally summoned the Brigade to the presence. Then, said he:

"Gentlemen, I have planned a lucrative and useful service for you —a service which will provide you with recreation amid noble landscapes, and afford you never ceasing opportunities for enriching your minds by observation and study. I want you to survey a railroad from Carson City westward to a certain point! When the legislature meets I will have the necessary bill passed and the remuneration arranged."

"What, a railroad over the Sierra Nevada Mountains?"

"Well, then, survey it eastward to a certain point!"

He converted them into surveyors, chain-bearers and so on, and turned them loose in the desert. It was "recreation" with a vengeance! Recreation on foot, lugging chains through sand and sage-brush, under a sultry sun and among cattle bones, cayotes and tarantulas.

"Romantic adventure" could go no further. They surveyed very slowly, very deliberately, very carefully. They returned every night during the first week, dusty, footsore, tired, and hungry, but very jolly. They brought in great store of prodigious hairy spiders—tarantulas—and imprisoned them in covered tumblers up stairs in the "ranch." After the first week, they had to camp on the field, for they were getting well eastward. They made a good many inquiries as to the location of that indefinite "certain point," but got no information. At last, to a peculiarly urgent inquiry of "How far eastward?" Governor Nye telegraphed back:

"To the Atlantic Ocean, blast you!—and then bridge it and go on!"

This brought back the dusty toilers, who sent in a report and ceased from their labors. The Governor was always comfortable about it; he said Mrs. O'Flannigan would hold him for the Brigade's board anyhow, and he intended to get what entertainment he could out of the boys; he said, with his old-time pleasant twinkle, that he meant to survey them into Utah and then telegraph Brigham to hang them for trespass!

The surveyors brought back more tarantulas with them, and so we had quite a menagerie arranged along the shelves of the room. Some of these spiders could straddle over a common saucer with their hairy, muscular legs, and when their feelings were hurt, or their dignity offended, they were the wickedest-looking desperadoes the animal world can furnish. If their glass prison-houses were touched ever so lightly they were up and spoiling for a fight in a minute. Starchy?—proud? Indeed, they would take up a straw and pick their teeth like a member of Congress. There was as usual a furious "zephyr" blowing the first night of the brigade's return, and about midnight the roof of an adjoining stable blew off, and a corner of it came crashing through the side of our ranch. There was a simultaneous awakening, and a tumultuous muster of the brigade in the dark, and a general tumbling and sprawling over each other in the narrow aisle between the bedrows. In the midst of the turmoil, Bob H— sprung up out of a sound sleep, and knocked down a shelf with his head. Instantly he shouted:

"Turn out, boys—the tarantulas is loose!"

No warning ever sounded so dreadful. Nobody tried, any longer, to leave the room, lest he might step on a tarantula. Every man groped for a trunk or a bed, and jumped on it. Then followed the strangest silence—a silence of grisly suspense it was, too—waiting, expectancy, fear. It was as dark as pitch,

and one had to imagine the spectacle of those fourteen scant-clad men roosting gingerly on trunks and beds, for not a thing could be seen. Then came occasional little interruptions of the silence, and one could recognize a man and tell his locality by his voice, or locate any other sound a sufferer made by his gropings or changes of position. The occasional voices were not given to much speaking—you simply heard a gentle ejaculation of "Ow!" followed by a solid thump, and you knew the gentleman had felt a hairy blanket or something touch his bare skin and had skipped from a bed to the floor. Another silence. Presently you would hear a gasping voice say:

"Su—su—something's crawling up the back of my neck!"

Every now and then you could hear a little subdued scramble and a sorrowful "O Lord!" and then you knew that somebody was getting away from something he took for a tarantula, and not losing any time about it, either. Directly a voice in the corner rang out wild and clear:

"I've got him! I've got him!" [Pause, and probable change of circumstances.] "No, he's got me! Oh, ain't they never going to fetch a lantern!"

The lantern came at that moment, in the hands of Mrs. O'Flannigan, whose anxiety to know the amount of damage done by the assaulting roof had not prevented her waiting a judicious interval, after getting out of bed and lighting up, to see if the wind was done, now, up stairs, or had a larger contract.

The landscape presented when the lantern flashed into the room was picturesque, and might have been funny to some people, but was not to us. Although we were perched so strangely upon boxes, trunks and beds, and so strangely attired, too, we were too earnestly distressed and too genuinely miserable to see any fun about it, and there was not the semblance of a smile anywhere visible. I know I am not capable of suffering more than I did during those few minutes of suspense in the dark, surrounded by those creeping, bloody-minded tarantulas. I had skipped from bed to bed and from box to box in a cold agony, and every time I touched anything that was furzy I fancied I felt the fangs. I had rather go to war than live that episode over again. Nobody was hurt. The man who thought a tarantula had "got him" was mistaken—only a crack in a box had caught his finger. Not one of those escaped tarantulas was ever seen again. There were ten or twelve of them. We took candles and hunted the place high and low for them, but with no success. Did we go back to bed then? We did nothing of the kind. Money could not have persuaded us to do it. We sat up the rest of the night playing cribbage and keeping a sharp lookout for the enemy.

CHAPTER XXII.

It was the end of August, and the skies were cloudless and the weather superb. In two or three weeks I had grown wonderfully fascinated with the curious new country and concluded to put off my return to "the States" awhile. I had grown well accustomed to wearing a damaged slouch hat, blue woolen shirt, and pants crammed into boot-tops, and gloried in the absence of coat, vest and braces. I felt rowdyish and "bully," (as the historian Josephus phrases it, in his fine chapter upon the destruction of the Temple). It seemed to me that nothing could be so fine and so romantic. I had become an officer of the government, but that was for mere sublimity. The office was an unique sinecure. I had nothing to do and no salary. I was private Secretary to his majesty the Secretary and there was not yet writing enough for two of us. So Johnny K— and I devoted our time to amusement. He was the young son of an Ohio nabob and was out there for recreation. He got it. We had heard a world of talk about the marvellous beauty of Lake Tahoe, and finally curiosity drove us thither to see it. Three or four members of the Brigade had been there and located some timber lands on its shores and stored up a quantity of provisions in their camp. We strapped a couple of blankets on our shoulders and took an axe apiece and started—for we intended to take up a wood ranch or so ourselves and become wealthy. We were on foot. The reader will find it advantageous to go horseback. We were told that the distance was eleven miles. We tramped a long time on level ground, and then toiled laboriously up a mountain about a thousand miles high and looked over. No lake there. We descended on the other side, crossed the valley and toiled up another mountain three or four thousand miles high, apparently, and looked over again. No lake yet. We sat down tired and perspiring, and hired a couple of Chinamen to curse those people who had beguiled us. Thus refreshed, we presently resumed the march with renewed vigor and determination. We plodded on, two or three hours longer, and at last the Lake burst upon us—a noble sheet of blue water lifted six thousand three hundred feet above the level of the sea, and walled in by a rim of snow-clad mountain peaks that towered aloft full three thousand feet higher still! It was a vast oval, and one would have to use up eighty or a hundred good miles in traveling around it. As it lay there with the shadows of the mountains brilliantly photographed upon its still surface I thought it must surely be the fairest picture the whole earth affords.

We found the small skiff belonging to the Brigade boys, and without loss of time set out across a deep bend of the lake toward the landmarks that signified the locality of the camp. I got Johnny to row—not because I mind exertion myself, but because it makes me sick to ride backwards when I am at work. But I steered. A three-mile pull brought us to the camp just as the night fell, and we stepped ashore very tired and wolfishly hungry. In a "cache" among the rocks we found the provisions and the cooking utensils, and then, all fatigued as I was, I sat down on a boulder and superintended while Johnny gathered wood and cooked supper. Many a man who had gone through what I had, would have wanted to rest.

It was a delicious supper—hot bread, fried bacon, and black coffee. It was a delicious solitude we were in, too. Three miles away was a saw-mill and some workmen, but there were not fifteen other human beings throughout the wide circumference of the lake. As the darkness closed down and the stars came out and spangled the great mirror with jewels, we smoked meditatively in the solemn hush and forgot our troubles and our pains. In due time we spread our blankets in the warm sand between two large boulders and soon feel asleep, careless of the procession of ants that passed in through rents in our clothing and explored our persons. Nothing could disturb the sleep that fettered us, for it had been fairly earned, and if our consciences had any sins on them they had to adjourn court for that night, any way. The wind rose just as we were losing consciousness, and we were lulled to sleep by the beating of the surf upon the shore.

It is always very cold on that lake shore in the night, but we had plenty of blankets and were warm enough. We never moved a muscle all night, but waked at early dawn in the original positions, and got up at once, thoroughly refreshed, free from soreness, and brim full of friskiness. There is no end of wholesome medicine in such an experience. That morning

we could have whipped ten such people as we were the day before —sick ones at any rate. But the world is slow, and people will go to "water cures" and "movement cures" and to foreign lands for health. Three months of camp life on Lake Tahoe would restore an Egyptian mummy to his pristine vigor, and give him an appetite like an alligator. I do not mean the oldest and driest mummies, of course, but the fresher ones. The air up there in the clouds is very pure and fine, bracing and delicious. And why shouldn't it be?—it is the same the angels breathe. I think that hardly any amount of fatigue can be gathered together that a man cannot sleep off in one night on the sand by its side. Not under a roof, but under the sky; it seldom or never rains there in the summer time. I know a man who went there to die. But he made a failure of it. He was a skeleton when he came, and could barely stand. He had no appetite, and did nothing but read tracts and reflect on the future. Three months later he was sleeping out of doors regularly, eating all he could hold, three times a day, and chasing game over mountains three thousand feet high for recreation. And he was a skeleton no longer, but weighed part of a ton. This is no fancy sketch, but the truth. His disease was consumption. I confidently commend his experience to other skeletons.

I superintended again, and as soon as we had eaten breakfast we got in the boat and skirted along the lake shore about three miles and disembarked. We liked the appearance of the place, and so we claimed some three hundred acres of it and stuck our "notices" on a tree. It was yellow pine timber land—a dense forest of trees a hundred feet high and from one to five feet through at the butt. It was necessary to fence our property or we could not hold it. That is to say, it was necessary to cut down trees here and there and make them fall in such a way as to form a sort of enclosure (with pretty wide gaps in it). We cut down three trees apiece, and found it such heart-breaking work that we decided to "rest our case" on those; if they held the property, well and good; if they didn't, let the property spill out through the gaps and go; it was no use to work ourselves to death merely to save a few acres of land. Next day we came back to build a house—for a house was also necessary, in order to hold the property. We decided to build a substantial log-house and excite the envy of the Brigade boys; but by the time we had cut and trimmed the first log it seemed unnecessary to be so elaborate, and so we concluded to build it of saplings. However, two saplings, duly cut and trimmed, compelled recognition of the fact that a still modester architecture would satisfy the law, and so we concluded to build a "brush" house. We devoted the next day to this work, but we did so much "sitting around" and discussing, that by the middle of the afternoon we had achieved only a half-way sort of affair which one of us had to watch while the other cut brush, lest if both turned our backs we might not be able to find it again, it had such a strong family resemblance to the surrounding vegetation. But we were satisfied with it.

We were land owners now, duly seized and possessed, and within the protection of the law. Therefore we decided to take up our residence on our own domain and enjoy that large sense of independence which only such an experience can bring. Late the next afternoon, after a good long rest, we sailed away from the Brigade camp with all the provisions and cooking utensils we could carry off—borrow is the more accurate word —and just as the night was falling we beached the boat at our own landing.

CHAPTER XXIII.

If there is any life that is happier than the life we led on our timber ranch for the next two or three weeks, it must be a sort of life which I have not read of in books or experienced in person. We did not see a human being but ourselves during the time, or hear any sounds but those that were made by the wind and the waves, the sighing of the pines, and now and then the far-off thunder of an avalanche. The forest about us was dense and cool, the sky above us was cloudless and brilliant with sunshine, the broad lake before us was glassy and clear, or rippled and breezy, or black and storm-tossed, according to Nature's mood; and its circling border of mountain domes, clothed with forests, scarred with land-slides, cloven by canons and valleys, and helmeted with glittering snow, fitly framed and finished the noble picture. The view was always fascinating, bewitching, entrancing. The eye was never tired of gazing, night or day, in calm or storm; it suffered but one grief, and that was that it could not look always, but must close sometimes in sleep.

We slept in the sand close to the water's edge, between two protecting boulders, which took care of the stormy night-winds for us. We never took any paregoric to make us sleep. At the first break of dawn we were always up and running foot-races to tone down excess of physical vigor and exuberance of spirits. That is, Johnny was—but I held his hat. While smoking the pipe of peace after breakfast we watched the sentinel peaks put on the glory of the sun, and followed the conquering light as it swept down among the shadows, and set the captive crags and forests free. We watched the tinted pictures grow and brighten upon the water till every little detail of forest, precipice and pinnacle was wrought in and finished, and the miracle of the enchanter complete. Then to "business."

That is, drifting around in the boat. We were on the north shore. There, the rocks on the bottom are sometimes gray, sometimes white. This gives the marvelous transparency of the water a fuller advantage than it has elsewhere on the lake. We usually pushed out a hundred yards or so from shore, and then lay down on the thwarts, in the sun, and let the boat drift by the hour whither it would. We seldom talked. It interrupted the Sabbath stillness, and marred the dreams the luxurious rest and indolence brought. The shore all along was indented with deep, curved bays and coves, bordered by narrow sand-beaches; and where the sand ended, the steep mountain-sides rose right up aloft into space—rose up like a vast wall a little out of the perpendicular, and thickly wooded with tall pines.

So singularly clear was the water, that where it was only twenty or thirty feet deep the bottom was so perfectly distinct that the boat seemed floating in the air! Yes, where it was even eighty feet deep. Every little pebble was distinct, every speckled trout, every hand's-breadth of sand. Often, as we lay on our faces, a granite boulder, as large as a village church, would start out of the bottom apparently, and seem climbing up rapidly to the surface, till presently it threatened to touch our faces, and we could not resist the impulse to seize an oar and avert the danger. But the boat would float on, and the boulder descend again, and then we could see that when we had been exactly above it, it must still have been twenty or thirty feet below the surface. Down through the transparency of these great depths, the water was not merely transparent, but dazzlingly, brilliantly so. All objects seen through it had a bright, strong vividness, not only of outline, but of every minute detail, which they would not have had when seen simply through the same depth of atmosphere. So empty and airy did all spaces seem below us, and so strong was the sense of floating high aloft in mid-nothingness, that we called these boat-excursions "balloon-voyages."

We fished a good deal, but we did not average one fish a week. We could see trout by the thousand winging about in the emptiness under us, or sleeping in shoals on the bottom, but they would not bite—they could see the line too plainly, perhaps. We frequently selected the trout we wanted, and rested the bait patiently and persistently on the end of his nose at a depth of eighty feet, but he would only shake it off with an annoyed manner, and shift his position.

We bathed occasionally, but the water was rather chilly, for all it looked so sunny. Sometimes we rowed out to the "blue water," a mile or two from shore. It was as dead blue as indigo there, because of the immense depth. By official measurement the lake in its centre is one thousand five hundred and twenty-five feet deep!

Sometimes, on lazy afternoons, we lolled on the sand in camp, and smoked pipes and read some old well-worn novels. At night, by the camp-fire, we played euchre and seven-up to strengthen the mind—and played them with cards so greasy and defaced that only a whole summer's acquaintance with them could enable the student to tell the ace of clubs from the jack of diamonds.

We never slept in our "house." It never recurred to us, for one thing; and besides, it was built to hold the ground, and that was enough. We did not wish to strain it.

By and by our provisions began to run short, and we went back to the old camp and laid in a new supply. We were gone all day, and reached home again about night-fall, pretty tired and hungry. While Johnny was carrying the main bulk of the provisions up to our "house" for future use, I took the loaf of bread, some slices of bacon, and the coffee-pot, ashore, set them down by a tree, lit a fire, and went back to the boat to get the frying-pan. While I was at this, I heard a shout from Johnny, and looking up I saw that my fire was galloping all over the premises! Johnny was on the other side of it. He had to run through the flames to get to the lake shore, and then we stood helpless and watched the devastation.

The ground was deeply carpeted with dry pine-needles, and the fire touched them off as if they were gunpowder. It was wonderful to see with what fierce speed the tall sheet of flame traveled! My coffee-pot was gone, and everything with it. In a minute and a half the fire seized upon a dense growth of dry manzanita chapparal six or eight feet high, and then the roaring and popping and crackling was something terrific. We were driven to the boat by the intense heat, and there we remained, spell-bound.

Within half an hour all before us was a tossing, blinding tempest of flame! It went surging up adjacent ridges—surmounted them and disappeared in the canons beyond—burst into view upon higher and farther ridges, presently—shed a grander illumination abroad, and dove again —flamed out again, directly, higher and still higher up the mountain-side—threw out skirmishing parties of fire here and there, and sent them trailing their crimson spirals away among remote ramparts and ribs and gorges, till as far as the eye could reach the lofty mountain-fronts were webbed as it were with a tangled network of red lava streams. Away across the water the crags and domes were lit with a ruddy glare, and the firmament above was a reflected hell!

Every feature of the spectacle was repeated in the glowing mirror of the lake! Both pictures were sublime, both were beautiful; but that in the lake had a bewildering richness about it that enchanted the eye and held it with the stronger fascination.

We sat absorbed and motionless through four long hours. We never thought of supper, and never felt fatigue. But at eleven o'clock the conflagration had traveled beyond our range of vision, and then darkness stole down upon the landscape again.

Hunger asserted itself now, but there was nothing to eat. The provisions were all cooked, no doubt, but we did not go to see. We were homeless wanderers again, without any property. Our fence was gone, our house burned down; no insurance. Our pine forest was well scorched, the dead trees all burned up, and our broad acres of manzanita swept away. Our blankets were on our usual sand-bed, however, and so we lay down and went to sleep. The next morning we started back to the old camp, but while out a long way from shore, so great a storm came up that we dared not try to land. So I baled out the seas we shipped, and Johnny pulled heavily through the billows till we had reached a point three or four miles beyond the camp. The storm was increasing, and it became evident that it was better to take the hazard of beaching the boat than go down in a hundred fathoms of water; so we ran in, with tall white-caps following, and I sat down in the stern-sheets and pointed her head-on to the shore. The instant the bow struck, a wave came over the stern that washed crew and cargo ashore, and saved a deal of trouble. We shivered in the lee of a boulder all the rest of the day, and froze all the night through. In the morning the tempest had gone down, and we paddled down to the camp without any unnecessary delay. We were so starved that we ate up the rest of the Brigade's provisions, and then set out to Carson to tell them about it and ask their forgiveness. It was accorded, upon payment of damages.

We made many trips to the lake after that, and had many a hair-breadth escape and blood-curdling adventure which will never be recorded in any history.

CHAPTER XXIV.

I resolved to have a horse to ride. I had never seen such wild, free, magnificent horsemanship outside of a circus as these picturesquely-clad Mexicans, Californians and Mexicanized Americans displayed in Carson streets every day. How they rode! Leaning just gently forward out of the perpendicular, easy and nonchalant, with broad slouch-hat brim blown square up in front, and long riata swinging above the head, they swept through the town like the wind! The next minute they were only a sailing puff of dust on the far desert. If they trotted, they sat up gallantly and gracefully, and seemed part of the horse; did not go jiggering up and down after the silly Miss-Nancy fashion of the riding-schools. I had quickly learned to tell a horse from a cow, and was full of anxiety to learn more. I was resolved to buy a horse.

While the thought was rankling in my mind, the auctioneer came skurrying through the plaza on a black beast that had as many humps and corners on him as a dromedary, and was necessarily uncomely; but he was "going, going, at twenty-two!—horse, saddle and bridle at twenty-two dollars, gentlemen!" and I could hardly resist.

A man whom I did not know (he turned out to be the auctioneer's brother) noticed the wistful look in my eye, and observed that that was a very remarkable horse to be going at such a price; and added that the saddle alone was worth the money. It was a Spanish saddle, with ponderous 'tapidaros',

and furnished with the ungainly sole-leather covering with the unspellable name. I said I had half a notion to bid. Then this keen-eyed person appeared to me to be "taking my measure"; but I dismissed the suspicion when he spoke, for his manner was full of guileless candor and truthfulness. Said he:

"I know that horse—know him well. You are a stranger, I take it, and so you might think he was an American horse, maybe, but I assure you he is not. He is nothing of the kind; but—excuse my speaking in a low voice, other people being near—he is, without the shadow of a doubt, a Genuine Mexican Plug!"

I did not know what a Genuine Mexican Plug was, but there was something about this man's way of saying it, that made me swear inwardly that I would own a Genuine Mexican Plug, or die.

"Has he any other—er—advantages?" I inquired, suppressing what eagerness I could.

He hooked his forefinger in the pocket of my army-shirt, led me to one side, and breathed in my ear impressively these words:

"He can out-buck anything in America!"

"Going, going, going—at twent—ty—four dollars and a half, gen—"

"Twenty-seven!" I shouted, in a frenzy.

"And sold!" said the auctioneer, and passed over the Genuine Mexican Plug to me.

I could scarcely contain my exultation. I paid the money, and put the animal in a neighboring livery-stable to dine and rest himself.

In the afternoon I brought the creature into the plaza, and certain citizens held him by the head, and others by the tail, while I mounted him. As soon as they let go, he placed all his feet in a bunch together, lowered his back, and then suddenly arched it upward, and shot me straight into the air a matter of three or four feet! I came as straight down again, lit in the saddle, went instantly up again, came down almost on the high pommel, shot up again, and came down on the horse's neck—all in the space of three or four seconds. Then he rose and stood almost straight up on his hind feet, and I, clasping his lean neck desperately, slid back into the saddle and held on. He came down, and immediately hoisted his heels into the air, delivering a vicious kick at the sky, and stood on his forefeet. And then down he came once more, and began the original exercise of shooting me straight up again. The third time I went up I heard a stranger say:

"Oh, don't he buck, though!"

While I was up, somebody struck the horse a sounding thwack with a leathern strap, and when I arrived again the Genuine Mexican Plug was not there. A California youth chased him up and caught him, and asked if he might have a ride. I granted him that luxury. He mounted the Genuine, got lifted into the air once, but sent his spurs home as he descended, and the horse darted away like a telegram. He soared over three fences like a bird, and disappeared down the road toward the Washoe Valley.

I sat down on a stone, with a sigh, and by a natural impulse one of my hands sought my forehead, and the other the base of my stomach. I believe I never appreciated, till then, the poverty of the human machinery—for I still needed a hand or two to place elsewhere. Pen cannot describe how I was jolted up. Imagination cannot conceive how disjointed I was—how internally, externally and universally I was unsettled, mixed up and ruptured. There was a sympathetic crowd around me, though.

One elderly-looking comforter said:

"Stranger, you've been taken in. Everybody in this camp knows that horse. Any child, any Injun, could have told you that he'd buck; he is the very worst devil to buck on the continent of America. You hear me. I'm Curry. Old Curry. Old Abe Curry. And moreover, he is a simon-pure, out-and-out, genuine d—d Mexican plug, and an uncommon mean one at that, too. Why, you turnip, if you had laid low and kept dark, there's chances to buy an American horse for mighty little more than you paid for that bloody old foreign relic."

I gave no sign; but I made up my mind that if the auctioneer's brother's funeral took place while I was in the Territory I would postpone all other recreations and attend it.

After a gallop of sixteen miles the Californian youth and the Genuine Mexican Plug came tearing into town again, shedding foam-flakes like the spume-spray that drives before a typhoon, and, with one final skip over a wheelbarrow and a Chinaman, cast anchor in front of the "ranch."

Such panting and blowing! Such spreading and contracting of the red equine nostrils, and glaring of the wild equine eye! But was the imperial beast subjugated? Indeed he was not.

His lordship the Speaker of the House thought he was, and mounted him to go down to the Capitol; but the first dash the creature made was over a pile of telegraph poles half as high as a church; and his time to the Capitol—one mile and three quarters—remains unbeaten to this day. But then he took an advantage—he left out the mile, and only did the three quarters. That is to say, he made a straight cut across lots, preferring fences and ditches to a crooked road; and when the Speaker got to the Capitol he said he had been in the air so much he felt as if he had made the trip on a comet.

In the evening the Speaker came home afoot for exercise, and got the Genuine towed back behind a quartz wagon. The next day I loaned the animal to the Clerk of the House to go down to the Dana silver mine, six miles, and he walked back for exercise, and got the horse towed. Everybody I loaned him to always walked back; they never could get enough exercise any other way.

Still, I continued to loan him to anybody who was willing to borrow him, my idea being to get him crippled, and throw him on the borrower's hands, or killed, and make the borrower pay for him. But somehow nothing ever happened to him. He took chances that no other horse ever took and survived, but he always came out safe. It was his daily habit to try experiments that had always before been considered impossible, but he always got through. Sometimes he miscalculated a little, and did not get his rider through intact, but he always got through himself. Of course I had tried to sell him; but that was a stretch of simplicity which met with little sympathy. The auctioneer stormed up and down the streets on him for four days, dispersing the populace, interrupting business, and destroying children, and never got a bid—at least never any but the eighteen-dollar one he hired a notoriously substanceless bummer to make. The people only smiled pleasantly, and restrained their desire to buy, if they had any. Then the auctioneer brought in his bill, and I withdrew the horse from the market. We tried to trade him off at private vendue next, offering him at a sacrifice for second-hand tombstones, old iron, temperance tracts—any kind of property. But holders were stiff, and we retired from the market again. I never tried to ride the horse any more. Walking was good enough exercise for a man like me, that had nothing the matter with him except ruptures, internal injuries, and such things. Finally I tried to give him away. But it was a failure. Parties said earthquakes were handy enough on the Pacific coast—they did not wish to own one. As a last resort I offered him to the Governor for the use of the "Brigade." His face lit up eagerly at first, but toned down again, and he said the thing would be too palpable.

Just then the livery stable man brought in his bill for six weeks' keeping—stall-room for the horse, fifteen dollars; hay for the horse, two hundred and fifty! The Genuine Mexican Plug had eaten a ton of the article, and the man said he would have eaten a hundred if he had let him.

I will remark here, in all seriousness, that the regular price of hay during that year and a part of the next was really two hundred and fifty dollars a ton. During a part of the previous year it had sold at five hundred a ton, in gold, and during the winter before that there was such scarcity of the article that in several instances small quantities had brought eight hundred dollars a ton in coin! The consequence might be guessed without my telling it: peopled turned their stock loose to starve, and before the spring arrived Carson and Eagle valleys were almost literally carpeted with their carcases! Any old settler there will verify these statements.

I managed to pay the livery bill, and that same day I gave the Genuine Mexican Plug to a passing Arkansas emigrant whom fortune delivered into my hand. If this ever meets his eye, he will doubtless remember the donation.

Now whoever has had the luck to ride a real Mexican plug will recognize the animal depicted in this chapter, and hardly consider him exaggerated —but the uninitiated will feel justified in regarding his portrait as a fancy sketch, perhaps.

CHAPTER XXV.

Originally, Nevada was a part of Utah and was called Carson county; and a pretty large county it was, too. Certain of its valleys produced no end of hay, and this attracted small colonies of Mormon stock-raisers and farmers to them. A few orthodox Americans straggled in from California, but no love was lost between the two classes of colonists. There was little or no friendly intercourse; each party staid to itself. The Mormons were largely in the majority, and had the additional advantage of being peculiarly under the protection of the Mormon government of the Territory. Therefore they could afford to be distant, and even peremptory toward their neighbors. One of the traditions of Carson Valley illustrates the condition of things that prevailed at the time I speak of. The hired girl of one of the American families was Irish, and a Catholic; yet it was noted with surprise that she was the only person outside of the Mormon ring who could get favors from the Mormons. She asked kindnesses of them often, and always got them. It was a mystery to everybody. But one day as she was passing out at the door, a large bowie knife dropped from under her apron, and when her mistress asked for an explanation she observed that she was going out to "borry a wash-tub from the Mormons!"

In 1858 silver lodes were discovered in "Carson County," and then the aspect of things changed. Californians began to flock in, and the American element was soon in the majority. Allegiance to Brigham Young and Utah was renounced, and a temporary territorial government for "Washoe" was instituted by the citizens. Governor Roop was the first and only chief magistrate of it. In due course of time Congress passed a bill to organize "Nevada Territory," and President Lincoln sent out Governor Nye to supplant Roop.

At this time the population of the Territory was about twelve or fifteen thousand, and rapidly increasing. Silver mines were being vigorously developed and silver mills erected. Business of all kinds was active and prosperous and growing more so day by day.

The people were glad to have a legitimately constituted government, but did not particularly enjoy having strangers from distant States put in authority over them—a sentiment that was natural enough. They thought the officials should have been chosen from among themselves from among prominent citizens who had earned a right to such promotion, and who would be in sympathy with the populace and likewise thoroughly acquainted with the needs of the Territory. They were right in viewing the matter thus, without doubt. The new officers were "emigrants," and that was no title to anybody's affection or admiration either.

The new government was received with considerable coolness. It was not only a foreign intruder, but a poor one. It was not even worth plucking —except by the smallest of small fry office-seekers and such. Everybody knew that Congress had appropriated only twenty thousand dollars a year in greenbacks for its support—about money enough to run a quartz mill a month. And everybody knew, also, that the first year's money was still in Washington, and that the getting hold of it would be a tedious and difficult process. Carson City was too wary and too wise to open up a credit account with the imported bantling with anything like indecent haste.

There is something solemnly funny about the struggles of a new-born Territorial government to get a start in this world. Ours had a trying time of it. The Organic Act and the "instructions" from the State Department commanded that a legislature should be elected at such-and-such a time, and its sittings inaugurated at such-and-such a date. It was easy to get legislators, even at three dollars a day, although board was four dollars and fifty cents, for distinction has its charm in Nevada as well as elsewhere, and there were plenty of patriotic souls out of employment; but to get a legislative hall for them to meet in was another matter altogether. Carson blandly declined to give a room rent-free, or let one to the government on credit.

But when Curry heard of the difficulty, he came forward, solitary and alone, and shouldered the Ship of State over the bar and got her afloat again. I refer to "Curry—Old Curry—Old Abe Curry." But for him the legislature would have been obliged to sit in the desert. He offered his large stone building just outside the capital limits, rent-free, and it was gladly accepted. Then he built a horse-railroad from town to the capitol, and carried the legislators gratis.

He also furnished pine benches and chairs for the legislature,

and covered the floors with clean saw-dust by way of carpet and spittoon combined. But for Curry the government would have died in its tender infancy. A canvas partition to separate the Senate from the House of Representatives was put up by the Secretary, at a cost of three dollars and forty cents, but the United States declined to pay for it. Upon being reminded that the "instructions" permitted the payment of a liberal rent for a legislative hall, and that that money was saved to the country by Mr. Curry's generosity, the United States said that did not alter the matter, and the three dollars and forty cents would be subtracted from the Secretary's eighteen hundred dollar salary—and it was!

The matter of printing was from the beginning an interesting feature of the new government's difficulties. The Secretary was sworn to obey his volume of written "instructions," and these commanded him to do two certain things without fail, viz.:

1. Get the House and Senate journals printed; and, 2. For this work, pay one dollar and fifty cents per "thousand" for composition, and one dollar and fifty cents per "token" for press-work, in greenbacks.

It was easy to swear to do these two things, but it was entirely impossible to do more than one of them. When greenbacks had gone down to forty cents on the dollar, the prices regularly charged everybody by printing establishments were one dollar and fifty cents per "thousand" and one dollar and fifty cents per "token," in gold. The "instructions" commanded that the Secretary regard a paper dollar issued by the government as equal to any other dollar issued by the government. Hence the printing of the journals was discontinued. Then the United States sternly rebuked the Secretary for disregarding the "instructions," and warned him to correct his ways. Wherefore he got some printing done, forwarded the bill to Washington with full exhibits of the high prices of things in the Territory, and called attention to a printed market report wherein it would be observed that even hay was two hundred and fifty dollars a ton. The United States responded by subtracting the printing-bill from the Secretary's suffering salary—and moreover remarked with dense gravity that he would find nothing in his "instructions" requiring him to purchase hay!

Nothing in this world is palled in such impenetrable obscurity as a U.S. Treasury Comptroller's understanding. The very fires of the hereafter could get up nothing more than a fitful glimmer in it. In the days I speak of he never could be made to comprehend why it was that twenty thousand dollars would not go as far in Nevada, where all commodities ranged at an enormous figure, as it would in the other Territories, where exceeding cheapness was the rule. He was an officer who looked out for the little expenses all the time. The Secretary of the Territory kept his office in his bedroom, as I before remarked; and he charged the United States no rent, although his "instructions" provided for that item and he could have justly taken advantage of it (a thing which I would have done with more than lightning promptness if I had been Secretary myself). But the United States never applauded this devotion. Indeed, I think my country was ashamed to have so improvident a person in its employ.

Those "instructions" (we used to read a chapter from them every morning, as intellectual gymnastics, and a couple of chapters in Sunday school every Sabbath, for they treated of all subjects under the sun and had much valuable religious matter in them along with the other statistics) those "instructions" commanded that pen-knives, envelopes, pens and writing-paper be furnished the members of the legislature.

So the Secretary made the purchase and the distribution. The knives cost three dollars apiece. There was one too many, and the Secretary gave it to the Clerk of the House of Representatives. The United States said the Clerk of the House was not a "member" of the legislature, and took that three dollars out of the Secretary's salary, as usual.

White men charged three or four dollars a "load" for sawing up stove-wood. The Secretary was sagacious enough to know that the United States would never pay any such price as that; so he got an Indian to saw up a load of office wood at one dollar and a half. He made out the usual voucher, but signed no name to it—simply appended a note explaining that an Indian had done the work, and had done it in a very capable and satisfactory way, but could not sign the voucher owing to lack of ability in the necessary direction. The Secretary had to pay that dollar and a half. He thought the United States would admire both his economy and his honesty in getting the work done at half price and not putting a pretended Indian's signature to the voucher, but the United States did not see it in that light.

The United States was too much accustomed to employing dollar-and-a-half thieves in all manner of official capacities to regard his explanation of the voucher as having any foundation in fact.

But the next time the Indian sawed wood for us I taught him to make a cross at the bottom of the voucher—it looked like a cross that had been drunk a year—and then I "witnessed" it and it went through all right. The United States never said a word. I was sorry I had not made the voucher for a thousand loads of wood instead of one.

The government of my country snubs honest simplicity but fondles artistic villainy, and I think I might have developed into a very capable pickpocket if I had remained in the public service a year or two.

That was a fine collection of sovereigns, that first Nevada legislature. They levied taxes to the amount of thirty or forty thousand dollars and ordered expenditures to the extent of about a million. Yet they had their little periodical explosions of economy like all other bodies of the kind. A member proposed to save three dollars a day to the nation by dispensing with the Chaplain. And yet that short-sighted man needed the Chaplain more than any other member, perhaps, for he generally sat with his feet on his desk, eating raw turnips, during the morning prayer.

The legislature sat sixty days, and passed private tollroad franchises all the time. When they adjourned it was estimated that every citizen owned about three franchises, and it was believed that unless Congress gave the Territory another degree of longitude there would not be room enough to accommodate the toll-roads. The ends of them were hanging over the boundary line everywhere like a fringe.

The fact is, the freighting business had grown to such important proportions that there was nearly as much excitement over suddenly acquired toll-road fortunes as over the wonderful silver mines.

CHAPTER XXVI.

By and by I was smitten with the silver fever. "Prospecting parties" were leaving for the mountains every day, and discovering and taking possession of rich silver-bearing lodes and ledges of quartz. Plainly this was the road to fortune. The great "Gould and Curry" mine was held at three or four hundred dollars a foot when we arrived; but in two months it had sprung up to eight hundred. The "Ophir" had been worth only a mere trifle, a year gone by, and now it was selling at nearly four thousand dollars a foot! Not a mine could be named that had not experienced an astonishing advance in value within a short time. Everybody was talking about these marvels. Go where you would, you heard nothing else, from morning till far into the night. Tom So-and-So had sold out of the "Amanda Smith" for $40,000—hadn't a cent when he "took up" the ledge six months ago. John Jones had sold half his interest in the "Bald Eagle and Mary Ann" for $65,000, gold coin, and gone to the States for his family. The widow Brewster had "struck it rich" in the "Golden Fleece" and sold ten feet for $18,000—hadn't money enough to buy a crape bonnet when Sing-Sing Tommy killed her husband at Baldy Johnson's wake last spring. The "Last Chance" had found a "clay casing" and knew they were "right on the ledge"—consequence, "feet" that went begging yesterday were worth a brick house apiece to-day, and seedy owners who could not get trusted for a drink at any bar in the country yesterday were roaring drunk on champagne to-day and had hosts of warm personal friends in a town where they had forgotten how to bow or shake hands from long-continued want of practice. Johnny Morgan, a common loafer, had gone to sleep in the gutter and waked up worth a hundred thousand dollars, in consequence of the decision in the "Lady Franklin and Rough and Ready" lawsuit. And so on—day in and day out the talk pelted our ears and the excitement waxed hotter and hotter around us.

I would have been more or less than human if I had not gone mad like the rest. Cart-loads of solid silver bricks, as large as pigs of lead, were arriving from the mills every day, and such sights as that gave substance to the wild talk about me. I succumbed and grew as frenzied as the craziest.

Every few days news would come of the discovery of a bran-new mining region; immediately the papers would teem with accounts of its richness, and away the surplus population would scamper to take possession. By the time I was fairly inoculated with the disease, "Esmeralda" had just had a run and "Humboldt" was beginning to shriek for attention. "Humboldt! Humboldt!" was the new cry, and straightway Humboldt, the newest of the new, the richest of the rich, the most marvellous of the marvellous discoveries in silver-land was occupying two columns of the public prints to "Esmeralda's" one. I was just on the point of starting to Esmeralda, but turned with the tide and got ready for Humboldt. That the reader may see what moved me, and what would as surely have moved him had he been there, I insert here one of the newspaper letters of the day. It and several other letters from the same calm hand were the main means of converting me. I shall not garble the extract, but put it in just as it appeared in the Daily Territorial Enterprise:

But what about our mines? I shall be candid with you. I shall express an honest opinion, based upon a thorough examination. Humboldt county is the richest mineral region upon God's footstool. Each mountain range is gorged with the precious ores. Humboldt is the true Golconda.

The other day an assay of mere croppings yielded exceeding four thousand dollars to the ton. A week or two ago an assay of just such surface developments made returns of seven thousand dollars to the ton. Our mountains are full of rambling prospectors. Each day and almost every hour reveals new and more startling evidences of the profuse and intensified wealth of our favored county. The metal is not silver alone. There are distinct ledges of auriferous ore. A late discovery plainly evinces cinnabar. The coarser metals are in gross abundance. Lately evidences of bituminous coal have been detected. My theory has ever been that coal is a ligneous formation. I told Col. Whitman, in times past, that the neighborhood of Dayton (Nevada) betrayed no present or previous manifestations of a ligneous foundation, and that hence I had no confidence in his lauded coal mines. I repeated the same doctrine to the exultant coal discoverers of Humboldt. I talked with my friend Captain Burch on the subject. My pyrhanism vanished upon his statement that in the very region referred to he had seen petrified trees of the length of two hundred feet. Then is the fact established that huge forests once cast their grim shadows over this remote section. I am firm in the coal faith.

Have no fears of the mineral resources of Humboldt county. They are immense—incalculable.

Let me state one or two things which will help the reader to better comprehend certain items in the above. At this time, our near neighbor, Gold Hill, was the most successful silver mining locality in Nevada. It was from there that more than half the daily shipments of silver bricks came. "Very rich" (and scarce) Gold Hill ore yielded from $100 to $400 to the ton; but the usual yield was only $20 to $40 per ton—that is to say, each hundred pounds of ore yielded from one dollar to two dollars. But the reader will perceive by the above extract, that in Humboldt from one fourth to nearly half the mass was silver! That is to say, every one hundred pounds of the ore had from two hundred dollars up to about three hundred and fifty in it. Some days later this same correspondent wrote:

I have spoken of the vast and almost fabulous wealth of this region—it is incredible. The intestines of our mountains are gorged with precious ore to plethora. I have said that nature has so shaped our mountains as to furnish most excellent facilities for the working of our mines. I have also told you that the country about here is pregnant with the finest mill sites in the world. But what is the mining history of Humboldt? The Sheba mine is in the hands of energetic San Francisco capitalists. It would seem that the ore is combined with metals that render it difficult of reduction with our imperfect mountain machinery. The proprietors have combined the capital and labor hinted at in my exordium. They are toiling and probing. Their tunnel has reached the length of one hundred feet. From primal assays alone, coupled with the development of the mine and public confidence in the continuance of effort, the stock had reared itself to eight hundred dollars market value. I do not know that one ton of the ore has been converted into current metal. I do know that there are many lodes in this section that surpass the Sheba in primal assay value. Listen a moment to the calculations of the Sheba operators. They purpose transporting the ore concentrated to Europe. The conveyance from Star City (its locality) to Virginia City will cost seventy dollars per ton; from Virginia to San Francisco, forty dollars per ton; from thence to Liverpool, its destination, ten dollars per ton. Their idea is that its conglomerate metals will reimburse them their cost of original extraction, the price of transportation, and the expense of reduction, and that then a ton of the raw ore will net them twelve hundred dollars. The estimate may be extravagant. Cut it in twain, and the product is enormous, far transcending any previous developments of our racy Territory.

A very common calculation is that many of our mines will

yield five hundred dollars to the ton. Such fecundity throws the Gould & Curry, the Ophir and the Mexican, of your neighborhood, in the darkest shadow. I have given you the estimate of the value of a single developed mine. Its richness is indexed by its market valuation. The people of Humboldt county are feet crazy. As I write, our towns are near deserted. They look as languid as a consumptive girl. What has become of our sinewy and athletic fellow-citizens? They are coursing through ravines and over mountain tops. Their tracks are visible in every direction. Occasionally a horseman will dash among us. His steed betrays hard usage. He alights before his adobe dwelling, hastily exchanges courtesies with his townsmen, hurries to an assay office and from thence to the District Recorder's. In the morning, having renewed his provisional supplies, he is off again on his wild and unbeaten route. Why, the fellow numbers already his feet by the thousands. He is the horse-leech. He has the craving stomach of the shark or anaconda. He would conquer metallic worlds.

This was enough. The instant we had finished reading the above article, four of us decided to go to Humboldt. We commenced getting ready at once. And we also commenced upbraiding ourselves for not deciding sooner—for we were in terror lest all the rich mines would be found and secured before we got there, and we might have to put up with ledges that would not yield more than two or three hundred dollars a ton, maybe. An hour before, I would have felt opulent if I had owned ten feet in a Gold Hill mine whose ore produced twenty-five dollars to the ton; now I was already annoyed at the prospect of having to put up with mines the poorest of which would be a marvel in Gold Hill.

CHAPTER XXVII.

Hurry, was the word! We wasted no time. Our party consisted of four persons—a blacksmith sixty years of age, two young lawyers, and myself. We bought a wagon and two miserable old horses. We put eighteen hundred pounds of provisions and mining tools in the wagon and drove out of Carson on a chilly December afternoon. The horses were so weak and old that we soon found that it would be better if one or two of us got out and walked. It was an improvement. Next, we found that it would be better if a third man got out. That was an improvement also. It was at this time that I volunteered to drive, although I had never driven a harnessed horse before and many a man in such a position would have felt fairly excused from such a responsibility. But in a little while it was found that it would be a fine thing if the drive got out and walked also. It was at this time that I resigned the position of driver, and never resumed it again. Within the hour, we found that it would not only be better, but was absolutely necessary, that we four, taking turns, two at a time, should put our hands against the end of the wagon and push it through the sand, leaving the feeble horses little to do but keep out of the way and hold up the tongue. Perhaps it is well for one to know his fate at first, and get reconciled to it. We had learned ours in one afternoon. It was plain that we had to walk through the sand and shove that wagon and those horses two hundred miles. So we accepted the situation, and from that time forth we never rode. More than that, we stood regular and nearly constant watches pushing up behind.

We made seven miles, and camped in the desert. Young Clagett (now member of Congress from Montana) unharnessed and fed and watered the horses; Oliphant and I cut sagebrush, built the fire and brought water to cook with; and old Mr. Ballou the blacksmith did the cooking. This division of labor, and this appointment, was adhered to throughout the journey. We had no tent, and so we slept under our blankets in the open plain. We were so tired that we slept soundly.

We were fifteen days making the trip—two hundred miles; thirteen, rather, for we lay by a couple of days, in one place, to let the horses rest.

We could really have accomplished the journey in ten days if we had towed the horses behind the wagon, but we did not think of that until it was too late, and so went on shoving the horses and the wagon too when we might have saved half the labor. Parties who met us, occasionally, advised us to put the horses in the wagon, but Mr. Ballou, through whose iron-clad earnestness no sarcasm could pierce, said that that would not do, because the provisions were exposed and would suffer, the horses being "bituminous from long deprivation." The reader will excuse me from translating. What Mr. Ballou customarily meant, when he used a long word, was a secret between himself and his Maker. He was one of the best and kindest hearted men that ever graced a humble sphere of life. He was gentleness and simplicity itself—and unselfishness, too. Although he was more than twice as old as the eldest of us, he never gave himself any airs, privileges, or exemptions on that account. He did a young man's share of the work; and did his share of conversing and entertaining from the general stand-point of any age—not from the arrogant, overawing summit-height of sixty years. His one striking peculiarity was his Partingtonian fashion of loving and using big words for their own sakes, and independent of any bearing they might have upon the thought he was purposing to convey. He always let his ponderous syllables fall with an easy unconsciousness that left them wholly without offensiveness. In truth his air was so natural and so simple that one was always catching himself accepting his stately sentences as meaning something, when they really meant nothing in the world. If a word was long and grand and resonant, that was sufficient to win the old man's love, and he would drop that word into the most out-of-the-way place in a sentence or a subject, and be as pleased with it as if it were perfectly luminous with meaning.

We four always spread our common stock of blankets together on the frozen ground, and slept side by side; and finding that our foolish, long-legged hound pup had a deal of animal heat in him, Oliphant got to admitting him to the bed, between himself and Mr. Ballou, hugging the dog's warm back to his breast and finding great comfort in it. But in the night the pup would get stretchy and brace his feet against the old man's back and shove, grunting complacently the while; and now and then, being warm and snug, grateful and happy, he would paw the old man's back simply in excess of comfort; and at yet other times he would dream of the chase and in his sleep tug at the old man's back hair and bark in his ear. The old gentleman complained mildly about these familiarities, at last, and when he got through with his statement he said that such a dog as that was not a proper animal to admit to bed with tired men, because he was "so meretricious in his movements and so organic in his emotions." We turned the dog out.

It was a hard, wearing, toilsome journey, but it had its bright side; for after each day was done and our wolfish hunger appeased with a hot supper of fried bacon, bread, molasses and black coffee, the pipe-smoking, song-singing and yarn-spinning around the evening camp-fire in the still solitudes of the desert was a happy, care-free sort of recreation that seemed the very summit and culmination of earthly luxury.

It is a kind of life that has a potent charm for all men, whether city or country-bred. We are descended from desert-lounging Arabs, and countless ages of growth toward perfect civilization have failed to root out of us the nomadic instinct. We all confess to a gratified thrill at the thought of "camping out."

Once we made twenty-five miles in a day, and once we made forty miles (through the Great American Desert), and ten miles beyond—fifty in all —in twenty-three hours, without halting to eat, drink or rest. To stretch out and go to sleep, even on stony and frozen ground, after pushing a wagon and two horses fifty miles, is a delight so supreme that for the moment it almost seems cheap at the price.

We camped two days in the neighborhood of the "Sink of the Humboldt." We tried to use the strong alkaline water of the Sink, but it would not answer. It was like drinking lye, and not weak lye, either. It left a taste in the mouth, bitter and every way execrable, and a burning in the stomach that was very uncomfortable. We put molasses in it, but that helped it very little; we added a pickle, yet the alkali was the prominent taste and so it was unfit for drinking.

The coffee we made of this water was the meanest compound man has yet invented. It was really viler to the taste than the unameliorated water itself. Mr. Ballou, being the architect and builder of the beverage felt constrained to endorse and uphold it, and so drank half a cup, by little sips, making shift to praise it faintly the while, but finally threw out the remainder, and said frankly it was "too technical for him."

But presently we found a spring of fresh water, convenient, and then, with nothing to mar our enjoyment, and no stragglers to interrupt it, we entered into our rest.

CHAPTER XXVIII.

After leaving the Sink, we traveled along the Humboldt river a little way. People accustomed to the monster mile-wide Mississippi, grow accustomed to associating the term "river" with a high degree of watery grandeur. Consequently, such people feel rather disappointed when they stand on the shores of the Humboldt or the Carson and find that a "river" in Nevada is a sickly rivulet which is just the counterpart of the Erie canal in all respects save that the canal is twice as long and four times as deep. One of the pleasantest and most invigorating exercises one can contrive is to run and jump across the Humboldt river till he is overheated, and then drink it dry.

On the fifteenth day we completed our march of two hundred miles and entered Unionville, Humboldt county, in the midst of a driving snow-storm. Unionville consisted of eleven cabins and a liberty-pole. Six of the cabins were strung along one side of a deep canyon, and the other five faced them. The rest of the landscape was made up of bleak mountain walls that rose so high into the sky from both sides of the canyon that the village was left, as it were, far down in the bottom of a crevice. It was always daylight on the mountain tops a long time before the darkness lifted and revealed Unionville.

We built a small, rude cabin in the side of the crevice and roofed it with canvas, leaving a corner open to serve as a chimney, through which the cattle used to tumble occasionally, at night, and mash our furniture and interrupt our sleep. It was very cold weather and fuel was scarce. Indians brought brush and bushes several miles on their backs; and when we could catch a laden Indian it was well—and when we could not (which was the rule, not the exception), we shivered and bore it.

I confess, without shame, that I expected to find masses of silver lying all about the ground. I expected to see it glittering in the sun on the mountain summits. I said nothing about this, for some instinct told me that I might possibly have an exaggerated idea about it, and so if I betrayed my thought I might bring derision upon myself. Yet I was as perfectly satisfied in my own mind as I could be of anything, that I was going to gather up, in a day or two, or at furthest a week or two, silver enough to make me satisfactorily wealthy—and so my fancy was already busy with plans for spending this money. The first opportunity that offered, I sauntered carelessly away from the cabin, keeping an eye on the other boys, and stopping and contemplating the sky when they seemed to be observing me; but as soon as the coast was manifestly clear, I fled away as guiltily as a thief might have done and never halted till I was far beyond sight and call. Then I began my search with a feverish excitement that was brimful of expectation—almost of certainty. I crawled about the ground, seizing and examining bits of stone, blowing the dust from them or rubbing them on my clothes, and then peering at them with anxious hope. Presently I found a bright fragment and my heart bounded! I hid behind a boulder and polished it and scrutinized it with a nervous eagerness and a delight that was more pronounced than absolute certainty itself could have afforded. The more I examined the fragment the more I was convinced that I had found the door to fortune. I marked the spot and carried away my specimen. Up and down the rugged mountain side I searched, with always increasing interest and always augmenting gratitude that I had come to Humboldt and come in time. Of all the experiences of my life, this secret search among the hidden treasures of silver-land was the nearest to unmarred ecstasy. It was a delirious revel.

By and by, in the bed of a shallow rivulet, I found a deposit of shining yellow scales, and my breath almost forsook me! A gold mine, and in my simplicity I had been content with vulgar silver! I was so excited that I half believed my overwrought imagination was deceiving me. Then a fear came upon me that people might be observing me and would guess my secret. Moved by this thought, I made a circuit of the place, and ascended a knoll to reconnoiter. Solitude. No creature was near. Then I returned to my mine, fortifying myself against possible disappointment, but my fears were groundless—the shining scales were still there. I set about scooping them out, and for an hour I toiled down the windings of the stream and robbed its bed. But at last the descending sun warned me to give up the quest, and I turned homeward laden with wealth. As I walked along I could not help smiling at the thought of my being so excited over my fragment of silver when a nobler metal was almost under my nose. In this little time the former had so fallen in my estimation that once or twice I was on the point of throwing it away.

The boys were as hungry as usual, but I could eat nothing. Neither could I talk. I was full of dreams and far away. Their conversation interrupted the flow of my fancy somewhat, and annoyed me a little, too. I despised the sordid and commonplace things they talked about. But as they proceeded, it began to amuse me. It grew to be rare fun to hear them planning their poor little economies and sighing over possible privations and distresses when a gold mine, all our own, lay within sight of the cabin and I could point it out at any moment. Smothered hilarity began to oppress me, presently. It was hard to resist the impulse to burst out with exultation and reveal everything; but I did resist. I said within myself that I would filter the great news through my lips calmly and be

serene as a summer morning while I watched its effect in their faces. I said:

"Where have you all been?"

"Prospecting."

"What did you find?"

"Nothing."

"Nothing? What do you think of the country?"

"Can't tell, yet," said Mr. Ballou, who was an old gold miner, and had likewise had considerable experience among the silver mines.

"Well, haven't you formed any sort of opinion?"

"Yes, a sort of a one. It's fair enough here, may be, but overrated. Seven thousand dollar ledges are scarce, though.

"That Sheba may be rich enough, but we don't own it; and besides, the rock is so full of base metals that all the science in the world can't work it. We'll not starve, here, but we'll not get rich, I'm afraid."

"So you think the prospect is pretty poor?"

"No name for it!"

"Well, we'd better go back, hadn't we?"

"Oh, not yet—of course not. We'll try it a riffle, first."

"Suppose, now—this is merely a supposition, you know—suppose you could find a ledge that would yield, say, a hundred and fifty dollars a ton —would that satisfy you?"

"Try us once!" from the whole party.

"Or suppose—merely a supposition, of course—suppose you were to find a ledge that would yield two thousand dollars a ton—would that satisfy you?"

"Here—what do you mean? What are you coming at? Is there some mystery behind all this?"

"Never mind. I am not saying anything. You know perfectly well there are no rich mines here—of course you do. Because you have been around and examined for yourselves. Anybody would know that, that had been around. But just for the sake of argument, suppose—in a kind of general way—suppose some person were to tell you that two-thousand-dollar ledges were simply contemptible—contemptible, understand—and that right yonder in sight of this very cabin there were piles of pure gold and pure silver—oceans of it—enough to make you all rich in twenty-four hours! Come!"

"I should say he was as crazy as a loon!" said old Ballou, but wild with excitement, nevertheless.

"Gentlemen," said I, "I don't say anything—I haven't been around, you know, and of course don't know anything—but all I ask of you is to cast your eye on that, for instance, and tell me what you think of it!" and I tossed my treasure before them.

There was an eager scramble for it, and a closing of heads

together over it under the candle-light. Then old Ballou said:

"Think of it? I think it is nothing but a lot of granite rubbish and nasty glittering mica that isn't worth ten cents an acre!"

So vanished my dream. So melted my wealth away. So toppled my airy castle to the earth and left me stricken and forlorn.

Moralizing, I observed, then, that "all that glitters is not gold."

Mr. Ballou said I could go further than that, and lay it up among my treasures of knowledge, that nothing that glitters is gold. So I learned then, once for all, that gold in its native state is but dull, unornamental stuff, and that only low-born metals excite the admiration of the ignorant with an ostentatious glitter. However, like the rest of the world, I still go on underrating men of gold and glorifying men of mica. Commonplace human nature cannot rise above that.

CHAPTER XXIX.

True knowledge of the nature of silver mining came fast enough. We went out "prospecting" with Mr. Ballou. We climbed the mountain sides, and clambered among sage-brush, rocks and snow till we were ready to drop with exhaustion, but found no silver—nor yet any gold. Day after day we did this. Now and then we came upon holes burrowed a few feet into the declivities and apparently abandoned; and now and then we found one or two listless men still burrowing. But there was no appearance of silver. These holes were the beginnings of tunnels, and the purpose was to drive them hundreds of feet into the mountain, and some day tap the hidden ledge where the silver was. Some day! It seemed far enough away, and very hopeless and dreary. Day after day we toiled, and climbed and searched, and we younger partners grew sicker and still sicker of the promiseless toil. At last we halted under a beetling rampart of rock which projected from the earth high upon the mountain. Mr. Ballou broke off some fragments with a hammer, and examined them long and attentively with a small eye-glass; threw them away and broke off more; said this rock was quartz, and quartz was the sort of rock that contained silver. Contained it! I had thought that at least it would be caked on the outside of it like a kind of veneering. He still broke off pieces and critically examined them, now and then wetting the piece with his tongue and applying the glass. At last he exclaimed:

"We've got it!"

We were full of anxiety in a moment. The rock was clean and white, where it was broken, and across it ran a ragged thread of blue. He said that that little thread had silver in it, mixed with base metal, such as lead and antimony, and other rubbish, and that there was a speck or two of gold visible. After a great deal of effort we managed to discern some little fine yellow specks, and judged that a couple of tons of them massed together might make a gold dollar, possibly. We were not jubilant, but Mr. Ballou said there were worse ledges in the world than that. He saved what he called the "richest" piece of the rock, in order to determine its value by the process called the "fire-assay." Then we named the mine "Monarch of the Mountains" (modesty of nomenclature is not a prominent feature in the mines), and Mr. Ballou wrote out and stuck up the following "notice," preserving a copy to be entered upon the books in the mining recorder's office in the town.

"NOTICE."

"We the undersigned claim three claims, of three hundred feet each (and one for discovery), on this silver-bearing quartz lead or lode, extending north and south from this notice, with all its dips, spurs, and angles, variations and sinuosities, together with fifty feet of ground on either side for working the same."

We put our names to it and tried to feel that our fortunes were made. But when we talked the matter all over with Mr. Ballou, we felt depressed and dubious. He said that this surface quartz was not all there was of our mine; but that the wall or ledge of rock called the "Monarch of the Mountains," extended down hundreds and hundreds of feet into the earth —he illustrated by saying it was like a curb-stone, and maintained a nearly uniform thickness-say twenty feet—away down into the bowels of the earth, and was perfectly distinct from the casing rock on each side of it; and that it kept to itself, and maintained its distinctive character always, no matter how deep it extended into the earth or how far it stretched itself through and across the hills and valleys. He said it might be a mile deep and ten miles long, for all we knew; and that wherever we bored into it above ground or below, we would find gold and silver in it, but no gold or silver in the meaner rock it was cased between. And he said that down in the great depths of the ledge was its richness, and the deeper it went the richer it grew. Therefore, instead of working here on the surface, we must either bore down into the rock with a shaft till we came to where it was rich—say a hundred feet or so —or else we must go down into the valley and bore a long tunnel into the mountain side and tap the ledge far under the earth. To do either was plainly the labor of months; for we could blast and bore only a few feet a day—some five or six. But this was not all. He said that after we got the ore out it must be hauled in wagons to a distant silver-mill, ground up, and the silver extracted by a tedious and costly process. Our fortune seemed a century away!

But we went to work. We decided to sink a shaft. So, for a week we climbed the mountain, laden with picks, drills, gads, crowbars, shovels, cans of blasting powder and coils of fuse and strove with might and main. At first the rock was broken and loose and we dug it up with picks and threw it out with shovels, and the hole progressed very well. But the rock became more compact, presently, and gads and crowbars came into play. But shortly nothing could make an impression but blasting powder.

That was the weariest work! One of us held the iron drill in its place and another would strike with an eight-pound sledge—it was like driving nails on a large scale. In the course of an hour or two the drill would reach a depth of two or three feet, making a hole a couple of inches in diameter. We would put in a charge of powder, insert half a yard of fuse, pour in sand and gravel and ram it down, then light the fuse and run. When the explosion came and the rocks and smoke shot into the air, we would go back and find about a bushel of that hard, rebellious quartz jolted out. Nothing more. One week of this satisfied me. I resigned. Clagget and Oliphant followed. Our shaft was only twelve feet deep. We decided that a tunnel was the thing we wanted.

So we went down the mountain side and worked a week; at the end of which time we had blasted a tunnel about deep enough to hide a hogshead in, and judged that about nine hundred feet more of it would reach the ledge. I resigned again, and the other boys only held out one day longer. We decided that a tunnel was not what we wanted. We wanted a ledge that was already "developed." There were none in the camp.

We dropped the "Monarch" for the time being.

Meantime the camp was filling up with people, and there was a constantly growing excitement about our Humboldt mines. We fell victims to the epidemic and strained every nerve to acquire more "feet." We prospected and took up new claims, put "notices" on them and gave them grandiloquent names. We traded some of our "feet" for "feet" in other people's claims. In a little while we owned largely in the "Gray Eagle," the "Columbiana," the "Branch Mint," the "Maria Jane," the "Universe," the "Root-Hog-or-Die," the "Samson and Delilah," the "Treasure Trove," the "Golconda," the "Sultana," the "Boomerang," the "Great Republic," the "Grand Mogul," and fifty other "mines" that had never been molested by a shovel or scratched with a pick. We had not less than thirty thousand "feet" apiece in the "richest mines on earth" as the frenzied cant phrased it—and were in debt to the butcher. We were stark mad with excitement—drunk with happiness—smothered under mountains of prospective wealth—arrogantly compassionate toward the plodding millions who knew not our marvellous canyon—but our credit was not good at the grocer's.

It was the strangest phase of life one can imagine. It was a beggars' revel. There was nothing doing in the district—no mining—no milling —no productive effort—no income—and not enough money in the entire camp to buy a corner lot in an eastern village, hardly; and yet a stranger would have supposed he was walking among bloated millionaires. Prospecting parties swarmed out of town with the first flush of dawn, and swarmed in again at nightfall laden with spoil—rocks. Nothing but rocks. Every man's pockets were full of them; the floor of his cabin was littered with them; they were disposed in labeled rows on his shelves.

CHAPTER XXX.

I met men at every turn who owned from one thousand to thirty thousand "feet" in undeveloped silver mines, every single foot of which they believed would shortly be worth from fifty to a thousand dollars—and as often as any other way they were men who had not twenty-five dollars in the world. Every man you met had his new mine to boast of, and his "specimens" ready; and if the opportunity offered, he would infallibly back you into a corner and offer as a favor to you, not to him, to part with just a few feet in the "Golden Age," or the "Sarah Jane," or some other unknown stack of croppings, for money enough to get a "square meal" with, as the phrase went. And you were never to reveal that he had made you the offer at such a ruinous price, for it was only out of friendship for you that he was willing to make the sacrifice. Then he would fish a piece of rock out of his pocket, and after looking mysteriously around as if he feared he might be waylaid and robbed if caught with such wealth in his possession, he would dab the rock against his tongue, clap an eyeglass to it, and exclaim:

"Look at that! Right there in that red dirt! See it? See the specks of gold? And the streak of silver? That's from the Uncle Abe. There's a hundred thousand tons like that in sight! Right in sight, mind you! And when we get down on it and the ledge comes in solid, it will be the richest thing in the world! Look at the assay! I don't want you to believe me—look at the assay!"

Then he would get out a greasy sheet of paper which showed that the portion of rock assayed had given evidence of containing silver and gold in the proportion of so many hundreds or thousands of dollars to the ton.

I little knew, then, that the custom was to hunt out the richest

piece of rock and get it assayed! Very often, that piece, the size of a filbert, was the only fragment in a ton that had a particle of metal in it—and yet the assay made it pretend to represent the average value of the ton of rubbish it came from!

On such a system of assaying as that, the Humboldt world had gone crazy. On the authority of such assays its newspaper correspondents were frothing about rock worth four and seven thousand dollars a ton!

And does the reader remember, a few pages back, the calculations, of a quoted correspondent, whereby the ore is to be mined and shipped all the way to England, the metals extracted, and the gold and silver contents received back by the miners as clear profit, the copper, antimony and other things in the ore being sufficient to pay all the expenses incurred? Everybody's head was full of such "calculations" as those —such raving insanity, rather. Few people took work into their calculations—or outlay of money either; except the work and expenditures of other people.

We never touched our tunnel or our shaft again. Why? Because we judged that we had learned the real secret of success in silver mining—which was, not to mine the silver ourselves by the sweat of our brows and the labor of our hands, but to sell the ledges to the dull slaves of toil and let them do the mining!

Before leaving Carson, the Secretary and I had purchased "feet" from various Esmeralda stragglers. We had expected immediate returns of bullion, but were only afflicted with regular and constant "assessments" instead—demands for money wherewith to develop the said mines. These assessments had grown so oppressive that it seemed necessary to look into the matter personally. Therefore I projected a pilgrimage to Carson and thence to Esmeralda. I bought a horse and started, in company with Mr. Ballou and a gentleman named Ollendorff, a Prussian—not the party who has inflicted so much suffering on the world with his wretched foreign grammars, with their interminable repetitions of questions which never have occurred and are never likely to occur in any conversation among human beings. We rode through a snow-storm for two or three days, and arrived at "Honey Lake Smith's," a sort of isolated inn on the Carson river. It was a two-story log house situated on a small knoll in the midst of the vast basin or desert through which the sickly Carson winds its melancholy way. Close to the house were the Overland stage stables, built of sun-dried bricks. There was not another building within several leagues of the place. Towards sunset about twenty hay-wagons arrived and camped around the house and all the teamsters came in to supper—a very, very rough set. There were one or two Overland stage drivers there, also, and half a dozen vagabonds and stragglers; consequently the house was well crowded.

We walked out, after supper, and visited a small Indian camp in the vicinity. The Indians were in a great hurry about something, and were packing up and getting away as fast as they could. In their broken English they said, "By'm-by, heap water!" and by the help of signs made us understand that in their opinion a flood was coming. The weather was perfectly clear, and this was not the rainy season. There was about a foot of water in the insignificant river—or maybe two feet; the stream was not wider than a back alley in a village, and its banks were scarcely higher than a man's head.

So, where was the flood to come from? We canvassed the subject awhile and then concluded it was a ruse, and that the

Indians had some better reason for leaving in a hurry than fears of a flood in such an exceedingly dry time.

At seven in the evening we went to bed in the second story—with our clothes on, as usual, and all three in the same bed, for every available space on the floors, chairs, etc., was in request, and even then there was barely room for the housing of the inn's guests. An hour later we were awakened by a great turmoil, and springing out of bed we picked our way nimbly among the ranks of snoring teamsters on the floor and got to the front windows of the long room. A glance revealed a strange spectacle, under the moonlight. The crooked Carson was full to the brim, and its waters were raging and foaming in the wildest way—sweeping around the sharp bends at a furious speed, and bearing on their surface a chaos of logs, brush and all sorts of rubbish. A depression, where its bed had once been, in other times, was already filling, and in one or two places the water was beginning to wash over the main bank. Men were flying hither and thither, bringing cattle and wagons close up to the house, for the spot of high ground on which it stood extended only some thirty feet in front and about a hundred in the rear. Close to the old river bed just spoken of, stood a little log stable, and in this our horses were lodged.

While we looked, the waters increased so fast in this place that in a few minutes a torrent was roaring by the little stable and its margin encroaching steadily on the logs. We suddenly realized that this flood was not a mere holiday spectacle, but meant damage—and not only to the small log stable but to the Overland buildings close to the main river, for the waves had now come ashore and were creeping about the foundations and invading the great hay-corral adjoining. We ran down and joined the crowd of excited men and frightened animals. We waded knee-deep into the log stable, unfastened the horses and waded out almost waist-deep, so fast the waters increased. Then the crowd rushed in a body to the hay-corral and began to tumble down the huge stacks of baled hay and roll the bales up on the high ground by the house. Meantime it was discovered that Owens, an overland driver, was missing, and a man ran to the large stable, and wading in, boot-top deep, discovered him asleep in his bed, awoke him, and waded out again. But Owens was drowsy and resumed his nap; but only for a minute or two, for presently he turned in his bed, his hand dropped over the side and came in contact with the cold water! It was up level with the mattress! He waded out, breast-deep, almost, and the next moment the sun-burned bricks melted down like sugar and the big building crumbled to a ruin and was washed away in a twinkling.

At eleven o'clock only the roof of the little log stable was out of water, and our inn was on an island in mid-ocean. As far as the eye could reach, in the moonlight, there was no desert visible, but only a level waste of shining water. The Indians were true prophets, but how did they get their information? I am not able to answer the question. We remained cooped up eight days and nights with that curious crew. Swearing, drinking and card playing were the order of the day, and occasionally a fight was thrown in for variety. Dirt and vermin—but let us forget those features; their profusion is simply inconceivable—it is better that they remain so.

There were two men—however, this chapter is long enough.

CHAPTER XXXI.

There were two men in the company who caused me particular discomfort. One was a little Swede, about twenty-five years old, who knew only one song, and he was forever singing it. By day we were all crowded into one small, stifling bar-room, and so there was no escaping this person's music. Through all the profanity, whisky-guzzling, "old sledge" and quarreling, his monotonous song meandered with never a variation in its tiresome sameness, and it seemed to me, at last, that I would be content to die, in order to be rid of the torture. The other man was a stalwart ruffian called "Arkansas," who carried two revolvers in his belt and a bowie knife projecting from his boot, and who was always drunk and always suffering for a fight. But he was so feared, that nobody would accommodate him. He would try all manner of little wary ruses to entrap somebody into an offensive remark, and his face would light up now and then when he fancied he was fairly on the scent of a fight, but invariably his victim would elude his toils and then he would show a disappointment that was almost pathetic. The landlord, Johnson, was a meek, well-meaning fellow, and Arkansas fastened on him early, as a promising subject, and gave him no rest day or night, for awhile. On the fourth morning, Arkansas got drunk and sat himself down to wait for an opportunity. Presently Johnson came in, just comfortably sociable with whisky, and said:

"I reckon the Pennsylvania 'lection—"

Arkansas raised his finger impressively and Johnson stopped. Arkansas rose unsteadily and confronted him. Said he:

"Wha-what do you know a—about Pennsylvania? Answer me that. Wha—what do you know 'bout Pennsylvania?"

"I was only goin' to say—"

"You was only goin' to say. You was! You was only goin' to say—what was you goin' to say? That's it! That's what I want to know. I want to know wha—what you ('ic) what you know about Pennsylvania, since you're makin' yourself so d—d free. Answer me that!"

"Mr. Arkansas, if you'd only let me—"

"Who's a henderin' you? Don't you insinuate nothing agin me!—don't you do it. Don't you come in here bullyin' around, and cussin' and goin' on like a lunatic—don't you do it. 'Coz I won't stand it. If fight's what you want, out with it! I'm your man! Out with it!"

Said Johnson, backing into a corner, Arkansas following, menacingly:

"Why, I never said nothing, Mr. Arkansas. You don't give a man no chance. I was only goin' to say that Pennsylvania was goin' to have an election next week—that was all—that was everything I was goin' to say —I wish I may never stir if it wasn't."

"Well then why d'n't you say it? What did you come swellin' around that way for, and tryin' to raise trouble?"

"Why I didn't come swellin' around, Mr. Arkansas—I just—"

"I'm a liar am I! Ger-reat Caesar's ghost—"

"Oh, please, Mr. Arkansas, I never meant such a thing as that, I wish I may die if I did. All the boys will tell you that I've always spoke well of you, and respected you more'n any man in the house. Ask Smith. Ain't it so, Smith? Didn't I say, no longer ago than last night, that for a man that was a gentleman all the time and every way you took him, give me Arkansas? I'll leave it to any gentleman here if them warn't the very words I used. Come, now, Mr. Arkansas, le's take a drink—le's shake hands and take a drink. Come up—everybody! It's my treat. Come up, Bill, Tom, Bob, Scotty—come up. I want you all to take a drink with me and Arkansas—old Arkansas, I call him—bully old Arkansas. Gimme your hand agin. Look at him, boys—just take a look at him. Thar stands the whitest man in America!—and the man that denies it has got to fight me, that's all. Gimme that old flipper agin!"

They embraced, with drunken affection on the landlord's part and unresponsive toleration on the part of Arkansas, who, bribed by a drink, was disappointed of his prey once more. But the foolish landlord was so happy to have escaped butchery, that he went on talking when he ought to have marched himself out of danger. The consequence was that Arkansas shortly began to glower upon him dangerously, and presently said:

"Lan'lord, will you p-please make that remark over agin if you please?"

"I was a-sayin' to Scotty that my father was up'ards of eighty year old when he died."

"Was that all that you said?"

"Yes, that was all."

"Didn't say nothing but that?"

"No—nothing."

Then an uncomfortable silence.

Arkansas played with his glass a moment, lolling on his elbows on the counter. Then he meditatively scratched his left shin with his right boot, while the awkward silence continued. But presently he loafed away toward the stove, looking dissatisfied; roughly shouldered two or three men out of a comfortable position; occupied it himself, gave a sleeping dog a kick that sent him howling under a bench, then spread his long legs and his blanket-coat tails apart and proceeded to warm his back. In a little while he fell to grumbling to himself, and soon he slouched back to the bar and said:

"Lan'lord, what's your idea for rakin' up old personalities and blowin' about your father? Ain't this company agreeable to you? Ain't it? If this company ain't agreeable to you, p'r'aps we'd better leave. Is that your idea? Is that what you're coming at?"

"Why bless your soul, Arkansas, I warn't thinking of such a thing. My father and my mother—"

"Lan'lord, don't crowd a man! Don't do it. If nothing'll do you but a disturbance, out with it like a man ('ic)—but don't rake up old bygones and fling'em in the teeth of a passel of people that wants to be peaceable if they could git a chance. What's the matter with you this mornin', anyway? I never see a man carry on so."

"Arkansas, I reely didn't mean no harm, and I won't go on with it if it's onpleasant to you. I reckon my licker's got into my head, and what with the flood, and havin' so many to feed and look out for—"

"So that's what's a-ranklin' in your heart, is it? You want us to

leave do you? There's too many on us. You want us to pack up and swim. Is that it? Come!"

"Please be reasonable, Arkansas. Now you know that I ain't the man to—"

"Are you a threatenin' me? Are you? By George, the man don't live that can skeer me! Don't you try to come that game, my chicken—'cuz I can stand a good deal, but I won't stand that. Come out from behind that bar till I clean you! You want to drive us out, do you, you sneakin' underhanded hound! Come out from behind that bar! I'll learn you to bully and badger and browbeat a gentleman that's forever trying to befriend you and keep you out of trouble!"

"Please, Arkansas, please don't shoot! If there's got to be bloodshed—"

"Do you hear that, gentlemen? Do you hear him talk about bloodshed? So it's blood you want, is it, you ravin' desperado! You'd made up your mind to murder somebody this mornin'—I knowed it perfectly well. I'm the man, am I? It's me you're goin' to murder, is it? But you can't do it 'thout I get one chance first, you thievin' black-hearted, white-livered son of a nigger! Draw your weepon!"

With that, Arkansas began to shoot, and the landlord to clamber over benches, men and every sort of obstacle in a frantic desire to escape. In the midst of the wild hubbub the landlord crashed through a glass door, and as Arkansas charged after him the landlord's wife suddenly appeared in the doorway and confronted the desperado with a pair of scissors! Her fury was magnificent. With head erect and flashing eye she stood a moment and then advanced, with her weapon raised. The astonished ruffian hesitated, and then fell back a step. She followed. She backed him step by step into the middle of the bar-room, and then, while the wondering crowd closed up and gazed, she gave him such another tongue-lashing as never a cowed and shamefaced braggart got before, perhaps! As she finished and retired victorious, a roar of applause shook the house, and every man ordered "drinks for the crowd" in one and the same breath.

The lesson was entirely sufficient. The reign of terror was over, and the Arkansas domination broken for good. During the rest of the season of island captivity, there was one man who sat apart in a state of permanent humiliation, never mixing in any quarrel or uttering a boast, and never resenting the insults the once cringing crew now constantly leveled at him, and that man was "Arkansas."

By the fifth or sixth morning the waters had subsided from the land, but the stream in the old river bed was still high and swift and there was no possibility of crossing it. On the eighth it was still too high for an entirely safe passage, but life in the inn had become next to insupportable by reason of the dirt, drunkenness, fighting, etc., and so we made an effort to get away. In the midst of a heavy snow-storm we embarked in a canoe, taking our saddles aboard and towing our horses after us by their halters. The Prussian, Ollendorff, was in the bow, with a paddle, Ballou paddled in the middle, and I sat in the stern holding the halters. When the horses lost their footing and began to swim, Ollendorff got frightened, for there was great danger that the horses would make our aim uncertain, and it was plain that if we failed to land at a certain spot the current would throw us off and almost surely cast us into the main Carson, which was a boiling torrent, now. Such a catastrophe would be death, in all probability, for we would be swept to sea in the "Sink" or overturned and drowned. We warned Ollendorff to keep his wits about him and handle himself carefully, but it was useless; the moment the bow touched the bank, he made a spring and the canoe whirled upside down in ten-foot water.

Ollendorff seized some brush and dragged himself ashore, but Ballou and I had to swim for it, encumbered with our overcoats. But we held on to the canoe, and although we were washed down nearly to the Carson, we managed to push the boat ashore and make a safe landing. We were cold and water-soaked, but safe. The horses made a landing, too, but our saddles were gone, of course. We tied the animals in the sage-brush and there they had to stay for twenty-four hours. We baled out the canoe and ferried over some food and blankets for them, but we slept one more night in the inn before making another venture on our journey.

The next morning it was still snowing furiously when we got away with our new stock of saddles and accoutrements. We mounted and started. The snow lay so deep on the ground that there was no sign of a road perceptible, and the snow-fall was so thick that we could not see more than a hundred yards ahead, else we could have guided our course by the mountain ranges. The case looked dubious, but Ollendorff said his instinct was as sensitive as any compass, and that he could "strike a bee-line" for Carson city and never diverge from it. He said that if he were to straggle a single point out of the true line his instinct would assail him like an outraged conscience. Consequently we dropped into his wake happy and content. For half an hour we poked along warily enough, but at the end of that time we came upon a fresh trail, and Ollendorff shouted proudly:

"I knew I was as dead certain as a compass, boys! Here we are, right in somebody's tracks that will hunt the way for us without any trouble. Let's hurry up and join company with the party."

So we put the horses into as much of a trot as the deep snow would allow, and before long it was evident that we were gaining on our predecessors, for the tracks grew more distinct. We hurried along, and at the end of an hour the tracks looked still newer and fresher—but what surprised us was, that the number of travelers in advance of us seemed to steadily increase. We wondered how so large a party came to be traveling at such a time and in such a solitude. Somebody suggested that it must be a company of soldiers from the fort, and so we accepted that solution and jogged along a little faster still, for they could not be far off now. But the tracks still multiplied, and we began to think the platoon of soldiers was miraculously expanding into a regiment—Ballou said they had already increased to five hundred! Presently he stopped his horse and said:

"Boys, these are our own tracks, and we've actually been circussing round and round in a circle for more than two hours, out here in this blind desert! By George this is perfectly hydraulic!"

Then the old man waxed wroth and abusive. He called Ollendorff all manner of hard names—said he never saw such a lurid fool as he was, and ended with the peculiarly venomous opinion that he "did not know as much as a logarythm!"

We certainly had been following our own tracks. Ollendorff and his "mental compass" were in disgrace from that moment.

After all our hard travel, here we were on the bank of the stream again, with the inn beyond dimly outlined through the driving snow-fall. While we were considering what to do, the young Swede landed from the canoe and took his pedestrian way Carson-wards, singing his same tiresome song about his "sister and his brother" and "the child in the grave with its mother," and in a short minute faded and disappeared in the white oblivion. He was never heard of again. He no doubt got bewildered and lost, and Fatigue delivered him over to Sleep and Sleep betrayed him to Death. Possibly he followed our treacherous tracks till he became exhausted and dropped.

Presently the Overland stage forded the now fast receding stream and started toward Carson on its first trip since the flood came. We hesitated no longer, now, but took up our march in its wake, and trotted merrily along, for we had good confidence in the driver's bump of locality. But our horses were no match for the fresh stage team. We were soon left out of sight; but it was no matter, for we had the deep ruts the wheels made for a guide. By this time it was three in the afternoon, and consequently it was not very long before night came—and not with a lingering twilight, but with a sudden shutting down like a cellar door, as is its habit in that country. The snowfall was still as thick as ever, and of course we could not see fifteen steps before us; but all about us the white glare of the snow-bed enabled us to discern the smooth sugar-loaf mounds made by the covered sage-bushes, and just in front of us the two faint grooves which we knew were the steadily filling and slowly disappearing wheel-tracks.

Now those sage-bushes were all about the same height—three or four feet; they stood just about seven feet apart, all over the vast desert; each of them was a mere snow-mound, now; in any direction that you proceeded (the same as in a well laid out orchard) you would find yourself moving down a distinctly defined avenue, with a row of these snow-mounds an either side of it—an avenue the customary width of a road, nice and level in its breadth, and rising at the sides in the most natural way, by reason of the mounds. But we had not thought of this. Then imagine the chilly thrill that shot through us when it finally occurred to us, far in the night, that since the last faint trace of the wheel-tracks had long ago been buried from sight, we might now be wandering down a mere sage-brush avenue, miles away from the road and diverging further and further away from it all the time. Having a cake of ice slipped down one's back is placid comfort compared to it. There was a sudden leap and stir of blood that had been asleep for an hour, and as sudden a rousing of all the drowsing activities in our minds and bodies. We were alive and awake at once—and shaking and quaking with consternation, too. There was an instant halting and dismounting, a bending low and an anxious scanning of the road-bed. Useless, of course; for if a faint depression could not be discerned from an altitude of four or five feet above it, it certainly could not with one's nose nearly against it.

CHAPTER XXXII.

We seemed to be in a road, but that was no proof. We tested this by walking off in various directions—the regular snow-mounds and the regular avenues between them convinced each man that he had found the true road, and that the others had found only false ones. Plainly the situation was desperate. We were cold and stiff and the horses were tired. We decided to build a sage-brush fire and camp out till morning. This was wise, because if we were wandering from the right road and the snow-storm continued another day our case would be the next thing to hopeless if we kept on.

All agreed that a camp fire was what would come nearest to saving us, now, and so we set about building it. We could find no matches, and so we tried to make shift with the pistols. Not a man in the party had ever tried to do such a thing before, but not a man in the party doubted that it could be done, and without any trouble—because every man in the party had read about it in books many a time and had naturally come to believe it, with trusting simplicity, just as he had long ago accepted and believed that other common book-fraud about Indians and lost hunters making a fire by rubbing two dry sticks together.

We huddled together on our knees in the deep snow, and the horses put their noses together and bowed their patient heads over us; and while the feathery flakes eddied down and turned us into a group of white statuary, we proceeded with the momentous experiment. We broke twigs from a sage bush and piled them on a little cleared place in the shelter of our bodies. In the course of ten or fifteen minutes all was ready, and then, while conversation ceased and our pulses beat low with anxious suspense, Ollendorff applied his revolver, pulled the trigger and blew the pile clear out of the county! It was the flattest failure that ever was.

This was distressing, but it paled before a greater horror—the horses were gone! I had been appointed to hold the bridles, but in my absorbing anxiety over the pistol experiment I had unconsciously dropped them and the released animals had walked off in the storm. It was useless to try to follow them, for their footfalls could make no sound, and one could pass within two yards of the creatures and never see them. We gave them up without an effort at recovering them, and cursed the lying books that said horses would stay by their masters for protection and companionship in a distressful time like ours.

We were miserable enough, before; we felt still more forlorn, now. Patiently, but with blighted hope, we broke more sticks and piled them, and once more the Prussian shot them into annihilation. Plainly, to light a fire with a pistol was an art requiring practice and experience, and the middle of a desert at midnight in a snow-storm was not a good place or time for the acquiring of the accomplishment. We gave it up and tried the other. Each man took a couple of sticks and fell to chafing them together. At the end of half an hour we were thoroughly chilled, and so were the sticks. We bitterly execrated the Indians, the hunters and the books that had betrayed us with the silly device, and wondered dismally what was next to be done. At this critical moment Mr. Ballou fished out four matches from the rubbish of an overlooked pocket. To have found four gold bars would have seemed poor and cheap good luck compared to this.

One cannot think how good a match looks under such circumstances—or how lovable and precious, and sacredly beautiful to the eye. This time we gathered sticks with high hopes; and when Mr. Ballou prepared to light the first match, there was an amount of interest centred upon him that pages of writing could not describe. The match burned hopefully a moment, and then went out. It could not have carried more regret with it if it had been a human life. The next match simply flashed and died. The wind puffed the third one out just as it was on the imminent verge of success. We gathered together closer than ever, and developed a solicitude that was rapt and painful, as Mr. Ballou scratched our last hope on his leg. It lit, burned blue and sickly, and then budded into a robust flame. Shading it with his hands, the old gentleman bent gradually down and every heart went with him—

everybody, too, for that matter—and blood and breath stood still. The flame touched the sticks at last, took gradual hold upon them—hesitated—took a stronger hold —hesitated again—held its breath five heart-breaking seconds, then gave a sort of human gasp and went out.

Nobody said a word for several minutes. It was a solemn sort of silence; even the wind put on a stealthy, sinister quiet, and made no more noise than the falling flakes of snow. Finally a sad-voiced conversation began, and it was soon apparent that in each of our hearts lay the conviction that this was our last night with the living. I had so hoped that I was the only one who felt so. When the others calmly acknowledged their conviction, it sounded like the summons itself. Ollendorff said:

"Brothers, let us die together. And let us go without one hard feeling towards each other. Let us forget and forgive bygones. I know that you have felt hard towards me for turning over the canoe, and for knowing too much and leading you round and round in the snow—but I meant well; forgive me. I acknowledge freely that I have had hard feelings against Mr. Ballou for abusing me and calling me a logarythm, which is a thing I do not know what, but no doubt a thing considered disgraceful and unbecoming in America, and it has scarcely been out of my mind and has hurt me a great deal—but let it go; I forgive Mr. Ballou with all my heart, and—"

Poor Ollendorff broke down and the tears came. He was not alone, for I was crying too, and so was Mr. Ballou. Ollendorff got his voice again and forgave me for things I had done and said. Then he got out his bottle of whisky and said that whether he lived or died he would never touch another drop. He said he had given up all hope of life, and although ill-prepared, was ready to submit humbly to his fate; that he wished he could be spared a little longer, not for any selfish reason, but to make a thorough reform in his character, and by devoting himself to helping the poor, nursing the sick, and pleading with the people to guard themselves against the evils of intemperance, make his life a beneficent example to the young, and lay it down at last with the precious reflection that it had not been lived in vain. He ended by saying that his reform should begin at this moment, even here in the presence of death, since no longer time was to be vouchsafed wherein to prosecute it to men's help and benefit—and with that he threw away the bottle of whisky.

Mr. Ballou made remarks of similar purport, and began the reform he could not live to continue, by throwing away the ancient pack of cards that had solaced our captivity during the flood and made it bearable.

He said he never gambled, but still was satisfied that the meddling with cards in any way was immoral and injurious, and no man could be wholly pure and blemishless without eschewing them. "And therefore," continued he, "in doing this act I already feel more in sympathy with that spiritual saturnalia necessary to entire and obsolete reform." These rolling syllables touched him as no intelligible eloquence could have done, and the old man sobbed with a mournfulness not unmingled with satisfaction.

My own remarks were of the same tenor as those of my comrades, and I know that the feelings that prompted them were heartfelt and sincere. We were all sincere, and all deeply moved and earnest, for we were in the presence of death and without hope. I threw away my pipe, and in doing it felt that at last I was free of a hated vice and one that had ridden me like a tyrant all my days. While I yet talked, the thought of the good I might have done in the world and the still greater good I might now do, with these new incentives and higher and better aims to guide me if I could only be spared a few years longer, overcame me and the tears came again. We put our arms about each other's necks and awaited the warning drowsiness that precedes death by freezing.

It came stealing over us presently, and then we bade each other a last farewell. A delicious dreaminess wrought its web about my yielding senses, while the snow-flakes wove a winding sheet about my conquered body. Oblivion came. The battle of life was done.

CHAPTER XXXIII.

I do not know how long I was in a state of forgetfulness, but it seemed an age. A vague consciousness grew upon me by degrees, and then came a gathering anguish of pain in my limbs and through all my body. I shuddered. The thought flitted through my brain, "this is death—this is the hereafter."

Then came a white upheaval at my side, and a voice said, with bitterness:

"Will some gentleman be so good as to kick me behind?"

It was Ballou—at least it was a towzled snow image in a sitting posture, with Ballou's voice.

I rose up, and there in the gray dawn, not fifteen steps from us, were the frame buildings of a stage station, and under a shed stood our still saddled and bridled horses!

An arched snow-drift broke up, now, and Ollendorff emerged from it, and the three of us sat and stared at the houses without speaking a word. We really had nothing to say. We were like the profane man who could not "do the subject justice," the whole situation was so painfully ridiculous and humiliating that words were tame and we did not know where to commence anyhow.

The joy in our hearts at our deliverance was poisoned; well-nigh dissipated, indeed. We presently began to grow pettish by degrees, and sullen; and then, angry at each other, angry at ourselves, angry at everything in general, we moodily dusted the snow from our clothing and in unsociable single file plowed our way to the horses, unsaddled them, and sought shelter in the station.

I have scarcely exaggerated a detail of this curious and absurd adventure. It occurred almost exactly as I have stated it. We actually went into camp in a snow-drift in a desert, at midnight in a storm, forlorn and hopeless, within fifteen steps of a comfortable inn.

For two hours we sat apart in the station and ruminated in disgust. The mystery was gone, now, and it was plain enough why the horses had deserted us. Without a doubt they were under that shed a quarter of a minute after they had left us, and they must have overheard and enjoyed all our confessions and lamentations.

After breakfast we felt better, and the zest of life soon came back. The world looked bright again, and existence was as dear to us as ever. Presently an uneasiness came over me—grew upon me—assailed me without ceasing. Alas, my regeneration was not complete—I wanted to smoke! I resisted with all my strength, but the flesh was weak. I wandered away alone and

wrestled with myself an hour. I recalled my promises of reform and preached to myself persuasively, upbraidingly, exhaustively. But it was all vain, I shortly found myself sneaking among the snow-drifts hunting for my pipe. I discovered it after a considerable search, and crept away to hide myself and enjoy it. I remained behind the barn a good while, asking myself how I would feel if my braver, stronger, truer comrades should catch me in my degradation. At last I lit the pipe, and no human being can feel meaner and baser than I did then. I was ashamed of being in my own pitiful company. Still dreading discovery, I felt that perhaps the further side of the barn would be somewhat safer, and so I turned the corner. As I turned the one corner, smoking, Ollendorff turned the other with his bottle to his lips, and between us sat unconscious Ballou deep in a game of "solitaire" with the old greasy cards!

Absurdity could go no farther. We shook hands and agreed to say no more about "reform" and "examples to the rising generation."

The station we were at was at the verge of the Twenty-six-Mile Desert. If we had approached it half an hour earlier the night before, we must have heard men shouting there and firing pistols; for they were expecting some sheep drovers and their flocks and knew that they would infallibly get lost and wander out of reach of help unless guided by sounds.

While we remained at the station, three of the drovers arrived, nearly exhausted with their wanderings, but two others of their party were never heard of afterward.

We reached Carson in due time, and took a rest. This rest, together with preparations for the journey to Esmeralda, kept us there a week, and the delay gave us the opportunity to be present at the trial of the great land-slide case of Hyde vs. Morgan—an episode which is famous in Nevada to this day. After a word or two of necessary explanation, I will set down the history of this singular affair just as it transpired.

CHAPTER XXXIV.

The mountains are very high and steep about Carson; Eagle and Washoe Valleys—very high and very steep, and so when the snow gets to melting off fast in the Spring and the warm surface-earth begins to moisten and soften, the disastrous land-slides commence. The reader cannot know what a land-slide is, unless he has lived in that country and seen the whole side of a mountain taken off some fine morning and deposited down in the valley, leaving a vast, treeless, unsightly scar upon the mountain's front to keep the circumstance fresh in his memory all the years that he may go on living within seventy miles of that place.

General Buncombe was shipped out to Nevada in the invoice of Territorial officers, to be United States Attorney. He considered himself a lawyer of parts, and he very much wanted an opportunity to manifest it—partly for the pure gratification of it and partly because his salary was Territorially meagre (which is a strong expression). Now the older citizens of a new territory look down upon the rest of the world with a calm, benevolent compassion, as long as it keeps out of the way—when it gets in the way they snub it. Sometimes this latter takes the shape of a practical joke.

One morning Dick Hyde rode furiously up to General Buncombe's door in Carson city and rushed into his presence without stopping to tie his horse. He seemed much excited. He told the General that he wanted him to conduct a suit for him and would pay him five hundred dollars if he achieved a victory. And then, with violent gestures and a world of profanity, he poured out his grief. He said it was pretty well known that for some years he had been farming (or ranching as the more customary term is) in Washoe District, and making a successful thing of it, and furthermore it was known that his ranch was situated just in the edge of the valley, and that Tom Morgan owned a ranch immediately above it on the mountain side.

And now the trouble was, that one of those hated and dreaded land-slides had come and slid Morgan's ranch, fences, cabins, cattle, barns and everything down on top of his ranch and exactly covered up every single vestige of his property, to a depth of about thirty-eight feet. Morgan was in possession and refused to vacate the premises—said he was occupying his own cabin and not interfering with anybody else's—and said the cabin was standing on the same dirt and same ranch it had always stood on, and he would like to see anybody make him vacate.

"And when I reminded him," said Hyde, weeping, "that it was on top of my ranch and that he was trespassing, he had the infernal meanness to ask me why didn't I stay on my ranch and hold possession when I see him a-coming! Why didn't I stay on it, the blathering lunatic—by George, when I heard that racket and looked up that hill it was just like the whole world was a-ripping and a-tearing down that mountain side — splinters, and cord-wood, thunder and lightning, hail and snow, odds and ends of hay stacks, and awful clouds of dust!— trees going end over end in the air, rocks as big as a house jumping 'bout a thousand feet high and busting into ten million pieces, cattle turned inside out and a-coming head on with their tails hanging out between their teeth!—and in the midst of all that wrack and destruction sot that cussed Morgan on his gate-post, a-wondering why I didn't stay and hold possession! Laws bless me, I just took one glimpse, General, and lit out'n the county in three jumps exactly.

"But what grinds me is that that Morgan hangs on there and won't move off'n that ranch—says it's his'n and he's going to keep it—likes it better'n he did when it was higher up the hill. Mad! Well, I've been so mad for two days I couldn't find my way to town—been wandering around in the brush in a starving condition—got anything here to drink, General? But I'm here now, and I'm a-going to law. You hear me!"

Never in all the world, perhaps, were a man's feelings so outraged as were the General's. He said he had never heard of such high-handed conduct in all his life as this Morgan's. And he said there was no use in going to law—Morgan had no shadow of right to remain where he was —nobody in the wide world would uphold him in it, and no lawyer would take his case and no judge listen to it. Hyde said that right there was where he was mistaken—everybody in town sustained Morgan; Hal Brayton, a very smart lawyer, had taken his case; the courts being in vacation, it was to be tried before a referee, and ex-Governor Roop had already been appointed to that office and would open his court in a large public hall near the hotel at two that afternoon.

The General was amazed. He said he had suspected before that the people of that Territory were fools, and now he knew it. But he said rest easy, rest easy and collect the witnesses, for the victory was just as certain as if the conflict were already over. Hyde wiped away his tears and left.

At two in the afternoon referee Roop's Court opened and Roop appeared throned among his sheriffs, the witnesses, and spectators, and wearing upon his face a solemnity so awe-inspiring that some of his fellow-conspirators had misgivings that maybe he had not comprehended, after all, that this was merely a joke. An unearthly stillness prevailed, for at the slightest noise the judge uttered sternly the command:

"Order in the Court!"

And the sheriffs promptly echoed it. Presently the General elbowed his way through the crowd of spectators, with his arms full of law-books, and on his ears fell an order from the judge which was the first respectful recognition of his high official dignity that had ever saluted them, and it trickled pleasantly through his whole system:

"Way for the United States Attorney!"

The witnesses were called—legislators, high government officers, ranchmen, miners, Indians, Chinamen, negroes. Three fourths of them were called by the defendant Morgan, but no matter, their testimony invariably went in favor of the plaintiff Hyde. Each new witness only added new testimony to the absurdity of a man's claiming to own another man's property because his farm had slid down on top of it. Then the Morgan lawyers made their speeches, and seemed to make singularly weak ones —they did really nothing to help the Morgan cause. And now the General, with exultation in his face, got up and made an impassioned effort; he pounded the table, he banged the law-books, he shouted, and roared, and howled, he quoted from everything and everybody, poetry, sarcasm, statistics, history, pathos, bathos, blasphemy, and wound up with a grand war-whoop for free speech, freedom of the press, free schools, the Glorious Bird of America and the principles of eternal justice! [Applause.]

When the General sat down, he did it with the conviction that if there was anything in good strong testimony, a great speech and believing and admiring countenances all around, Mr. Morgan's case was killed. Ex-Governor Roop leant his head upon his hand for some minutes, thinking, and the still audience waited for his decision. Then he got up and stood erect, with bended head, and thought again. Then he walked the floor with long, deliberate strides, his chin in his hand, and still the audience waited. At last he returned to his throne, seated himself, and began impressively:

"Gentlemen, I feel the great responsibility that rests upon me this day. This is no ordinary case. On the contrary it is plain that it is the most solemn and awful that ever man was called upon to decide. Gentlemen, I have listened attentively to the evidence, and have perceived that the weight of it, the overwhelming weight of it, is in favor of the plaintiff Hyde. I have listened also to the remarks of counsel, with high interest—and especially will I commend the masterly and irrefutable logic of the distinguished gentleman who represents the plaintiff. But gentlemen, let us beware how we allow mere human testimony, human ingenuity in argument and human ideas of equity, to influence us at a moment so solemn as this. Gentlemen, it ill becomes us, worms as we are, to meddle with the decrees of Heaven. It is plain to me that Heaven, in its inscrutable wisdom, has seen fit to move this defendant's ranch for a purpose. We are but creatures, and we must submit. If Heaven has chosen to favor the defendant Morgan in this marked and wonderful manner; and if Heaven, dissatisfied with the position of the Morgan ranch upon the mountain side, has chosen to remove it to a position more eligible and more advantageous for its owner, it ill becomes us, insects as we are, to question the legality of the act or inquire into the reasons that prompted it. No—Heaven created the ranches and it is Heaven's prerogative to rearrange them, to experiment with them around at its pleasure. It is for us to submit, without repining.

"I warn you that this thing which has happened is a thing with which the sacrilegious hands and brains and tongues of men must not meddle. Gentlemen, it is the verdict of this court that the plaintiff, Richard Hyde, has been deprived of his ranch by the visitation of God! And from this decision there is no appeal."

Buncombe seized his cargo of law-books and plunged out of the court-room frantic with indignation. He pronounced Roop to be a miraculous fool, an inspired idiot. In all good faith he returned at night and remonstrated with Roop upon his extravagant decision, and implored him to walk the floor and think for half an hour, and see if he could not figure out some sort of modification of the verdict. Roop yielded at last and got up to walk. He walked two hours and a half, and at last his face lit up happily and he told Buncombe it had occurred to him that the ranch underneath the new Morgan ranch still belonged to Hyde, that his title to the ground was just as good as it had ever been, and therefore he was of opinion that Hyde had a right to dig it out from under there and—

The General never waited to hear the end of it. He was always an impatient and irascible man, that way. At the end of two months the fact that he had been played upon with a joke had managed to bore itself, like another Hoosac Tunnel, through the solid adamant of his understanding.

CHAPTER XXXV.

When we finally left for Esmeralda, horseback, we had an addition to the company in the person of Capt. John Nye, the Governor's brother. He had a good memory, and a tongue hung in the middle. This is a combination which gives immortality to conversation. Capt. John never suffered the talk to flag or falter once during the hundred and twenty miles of the journey. In addition to his conversational powers, he had one or two other endowments of a marked character. One was a singular "handiness" about doing anything and everything, from laying out a railroad or organizing a political party, down to sewing on buttons, shoeing a horse, or setting a broken leg, or a hen. Another was a spirit of accommodation that prompted him to take the needs, difficulties and perplexities of anybody and everybody upon his own shoulders at any and all times, and dispose of them with admirable facility and alacrity—hence he always managed to find vacant beds in crowded inns, and plenty to eat in the emptiest larders. And finally, wherever he met a man, woman or child, in camp, inn or desert, he either knew such parties personally or had been acquainted with a relative of the same. Such another traveling comrade was never seen before. I cannot forbear giving a specimen of the way in which he overcame difficulties. On the second day out, we arrived, very tired and hungry, at a poor little inn in the desert, and were told that the house was full, no provisions on hand, and neither hay nor barley to spare for the horses—must move on. The rest of us wanted to hurry on while it was yet light, but Capt. John insisted on stopping awhile. We dismounted and entered. There was no welcome for us on any face. Capt. John began his blandishments, and within twenty minutes he had accomplished the following things, viz.: found old acquaintances in three teamsters; discovered that he used to

go to school with the landlord's mother; recognized his wife as a lady whose life he had saved once in California, by stopping her runaway horse; mended a child's broken toy and won the favor of its mother, a guest of the inn; helped the hostler bleed a horse, and prescribed for another horse that had the "heaves"; treated the entire party three times at the landlord's bar; produced a later paper than anybody had seen for a week and sat himself down to read the news to a deeply interested audience. The result, summed up, was as follows: The hostler found plenty of feed for our horses; we had a trout supper, an exceedingly sociable time after it, good beds to sleep in, and a surprising breakfast in the morning—and when we left, we left lamented by all! Capt. John had some bad traits, but he had some uncommonly valuable ones to offset them with.

Esmeralda was in many respects another Humboldt, but in a little more forward state. The claims we had been paying assessments on were entirely worthless, and we threw them away. The principal one cropped out of the top of a knoll that was fourteen feet high, and the inspired Board of Directors were running a tunnel under that knoll to strike the ledge. The tunnel would have to be seventy feet long, and would then strike the ledge at the same dept that a shaft twelve feet deep would have reached! The Board were living on the "assessments." [N.B.—This hint comes too late for the enlightenment of New York silver miners; they have already learned all about this neat trick by experience.] The Board had no desire to strike the ledge, knowing that it was as barren of silver as a curbstone. This reminiscence calls to mind Jim Townsend's tunnel. He had paid assessments on a mine called the "Daley" till he was well-nigh penniless. Finally an assessment was levied to run a tunnel two hundred and fifty feet on the Daley, and Townsend went up on the hill to look into matters.

He found the Daley cropping out of the apex of an exceedingly sharp-pointed peak, and a couple of men up there "facing" the proposed tunnel. Townsend made a calculation. Then he said to the men:

"So you have taken a contract to run a tunnel into this hill two hundred and fifty feet to strike this ledge?"

"Yes, sir."

"Well, do you know that you have got one of the most expensive and arduous undertakings before you that was ever conceived by man?"

"Why no—how is that?"

"Because this hill is only twenty-five feet through from side to side; and so you have got to build two hundred and twenty-five feet of your tunnel on trestle-work!"

The ways of silver mining Boards are exceedingly dark and sinuous.

We took up various claims, and commenced shafts and tunnels on them, but never finished any of them. We had to do a certain amount of work on each to "hold" it, else other parties could seize our property after the expiration of ten days. We were always hunting up new claims and doing a little work on them and then waiting for a buyer—who never came. We never found any ore that would yield more than fifty dollars a ton; and as the mills charged fifty dollars a ton for working ore and extracting the silver, our pocket-money melted steadily away and none returned to take its place. We lived in a little cabin and cooked for ourselves; and altogether it was a hard life, though a hopeful one—for we never ceased to expect fortune and a customer to burst upon us some day.

At last, when flour reached a dollar a pound, and money could not be borrowed on the best security at less than eight per cent a month (I being without the security, too), I abandoned mining and went to milling. That is to say, I went to work as a common laborer in a quartz mill, at ten dollars a week and board.

CHAPTER XXXVI.

I had already learned how hard and long and dismal a task it is to burrow down into the bowels of the earth and get out the coveted ore; and now I learned that the burrowing was only half the work; and that to get the silver out of the ore was the dreary and laborious other half of it. We had to turn out at six in the morning and keep at it till dark. This mill was a six-stamp affair, driven by steam. Six tall, upright rods of iron, as large as a man's ankle, and heavily shod with a mass of iron and steel at their lower ends, were framed together like a gate, and these rose and fell, one after the other, in a ponderous dance, in an iron box called a "battery." Each of these rods or stamps weighed six hundred pounds. One of us stood by the battery all day long, breaking up masses of silver-bearing rock with a sledge and shoveling it into the battery. The ceaseless dance of the stamps pulverized the rock to powder, and a stream of water that trickled into the battery turned it to a creamy paste. The minutest particles were driven through a fine wire screen which fitted close around the battery, and were washed into great tubs warmed by super-heated steam—amalgamating pans, they are called. The mass of pulp in the pans was kept constantly stirred up by revolving "mullers." A quantity of quicksilver was kept always in the battery, and this seized some of the liberated gold and silver particles and held on to them; quicksilver was shaken in a fine shower into the pans, also, about every half hour, through a buckskin sack. Quantities of coarse salt and sulphate of copper were added, from time to time to assist the amalgamation by destroying base metals which coated the gold and silver and would not let it unite with the quicksilver.

All these tiresome things we had to attend to constantly. Streams of dirty water flowed always from the pans and were carried off in broad wooden troughs to the ravine. One would not suppose that atoms of gold and silver would float on top of six inches of water, but they did; and in order to catch them, coarse blankets were laid in the troughs, and little obstructing "riffles" charged with quicksilver were placed here and there across the troughs also. These riffles had to be cleaned and the blankets washed out every evening, to get their precious accumulations—and after all this eternity of trouble one third of the silver and gold in a ton of rock would find its way to the end of the troughs in the ravine at last and have to be worked over again some day. There is nothing so aggravating as silver milling. There never was any idle time in that mill. There was always something to do. It is a pity that Adam could not have gone straight out of Eden into a quartz mill, in order to understand the full force of his doom to "earn his bread by the sweat of his brow." Every now and then, during the day, we had to scoop some pulp out of the pans, and tediously "wash" it in a horn spoon—wash it little by little over the edge till at last nothing was left but some little dull globules of quicksilver in the bottom. If they were soft and yielding, the pan needed some salt or some sulphate of copper or some other chemical rubbish to assist digestion; if they were crisp to the touch and would retain a dint, they were freighted with all the silver and

gold they could seize and hold, and consequently the pan needed a fresh charge of quicksilver. When there was nothing else to do, one could always "screen tailings." That is to say, he could shovel up the dried sand that had washed down to the ravine through the troughs and dash it against an upright wire screen to free it from pebbles and prepare it for working over.

The process of amalgamation differed in the various mills, and this included changes in style of pans and other machinery, and a great diversity of opinion existed as to the best in use, but none of the methods employed, involved the principle of milling ore without "screening the tailings." Of all recreations in the world, screening tailings on a hot day, with a long-handled shovel, is the most undesirable.

At the end of the week the machinery was stopped and we "cleaned up." That is to say, we got the pulp out of the pans and batteries, and washed it patiently till nothing was left but the long accumulating mass of quicksilver, with its imprisoned treasures. This we made into heavy, compact snow-balls, and piled them up in a bright, luxurious heap for inspection. Making these snow-balls cost me a fine gold ring—that and ignorance together; for the quicksilver invaded the ring with the same facility with which water saturates a sponge—separated its particles and the ring crumbled to pieces.

We put our pile of quicksilver balls into an iron retort that had a pipe leading from it to a pail of water, and then applied a roasting heat. The quicksilver turned to vapor, escaped through the pipe into the pail, and the water turned it into good wholesome quicksilver again. Quicksilver is very costly, and they never waste it. On opening the retort, there was our week's work—a lump of pure white, frosty looking silver, twice as large as a man's head. Perhaps a fifth of the mass was gold, but the color of it did not show—would not have shown if two thirds of it had been gold. We melted it up and made a solid brick of it by pouring it into an iron brick-mould.

By such a tedious and laborious process were silver bricks obtained. This mill was but one of many others in operation at the time. The first one in Nevada was built at Egan Canyon and was a small insignificant affair and compared most unfavorably with some of the immense establishments afterwards located at Virginia City and elsewhere.

From our bricks a little corner was chipped off for the "fire-assay"—a method used to determine the proportions of gold, silver and base metals in the mass. This is an interesting process. The chip is hammered out as thin as paper and weighed on scales so fine and sensitive that if you weigh a two-inch scrap of paper on them and then write your name on the paper with a course, soft pencil and weigh it again, the scales will take marked notice of the addition.

Then a little lead (also weighed) is rolled up with the flake of silver and the two are melted at a great heat in a small vessel called a cupel, made by compressing bone ashes into a cup-shape in a steel mold. The base metals oxydize and are absorbed with the lead into the pores of the cupel. A button or globule of perfectly pure gold and silver is left behind, and by weighing it and noting the loss, the assayer knows the proportion of base metal the brick contains. He has to separate the gold from the silver now. The button is hammered out flat and thin, put in the furnace and kept some time at a red heat; after cooling it off it is rolled up like a quill and heated in a glass vessel containing nitric acid; the acid dissolves the silver and leaves the gold pure and ready to be weighed on its own merits. Then salt water is poured into the vessel containing the dissolved silver and the silver returns to palpable form again and sinks to the bottom. Nothing now remains but to weigh it; then the proportions of the several metals contained in the brick are known, and the assayer stamps the value of the brick upon its surface.

The sagacious reader will know now, without being told, that the speculative miner, in getting a "fire-assay" made of a piece of rock from his mine (to help him sell the same), was not in the habit of picking out the least valuable fragment of rock on his dump-pile, but quite the contrary. I have seen men hunt over a pile of nearly worthless quartz for an hour, and at last find a little piece as large as a filbert, which was rich in gold and silver—and this was reserved for a fire-assay! Of course the fire-assay would demonstrate that a ton of such rock would yield hundreds of dollars—and on such assays many an utterly worthless mine was sold.

Assaying was a good business, and so some men engaged in it, occasionally, who were not strictly scientific and capable. One assayer got such rich results out of all specimens brought to him that in time he acquired almost a monopoly of the business. But like all men who achieve success, he became an object of envy and suspicion. The other assayers entered into a conspiracy against him, and let some prominent citizens into the secret in order to show that they meant fairly. Then they broke a little fragment off a carpenter's grindstone and got a stranger to take it to the popular scientist and get it assayed. In the course of an hour the result came—whereby it appeared that a ton of that rock would yield $1,184.40 in silver and $366.36 in gold!

Due publication of the whole matter was made in the paper, and the popular assayer left town "between two days."

I will remark, in passing, that I only remained in the milling business one week. I told my employer I could not stay longer without an advance in my wages; that I liked quartz milling, indeed was infatuated with it; that I had never before grown so tenderly attached to an occupation in so short a time; that nothing, it seemed to me, gave such scope to intellectual activity as feeding a battery and screening tailings, and nothing so stimulated the moral attributes as retorting bullion and washing blankets—still, I felt constrained to ask an increase of salary. He said he was paying me ten dollars a week, and thought it a good round sum. How much did I want?

I said about four hundred thousand dollars a month, and board, was about all I could reasonably ask, considering the hard times.

I was ordered off the premises! And yet, when I look back to those days and call to mind the exceeding hardness of the labor I performed in that mill, I only regret that I did not ask him seven hundred thousand.

Shortly after this I began to grow crazy, along with the rest of the population, about the mysterious and wonderful "cement mine," and to make preparations to take advantage of any opportunity that might offer to go and help hunt for it.

CHAPTER XXXVII.

It was somewhere in the neighborhood of Mono Lake that the marvellous Whiteman cement mine was supposed to lie. Every now and then it would be reported that Mr. W. had passed stealthily through Esmeralda at dead of night, in disguise, and then we would have a wild excitement—because he must be steering for his secret mine, and now was the time to follow him. In less than three hours after daylight all the horses and mules and donkeys in the vicinity would be bought, hired or stolen, and half the community would be off for the mountains, following in the wake of Whiteman. But W. would drift about through the mountain gorges for days together, in a purposeless sort of way, until the provisions of the miners ran out, and they would have to go back home. I have known it reported at eleven at night, in a large mining camp, that Whiteman had just passed through, and in two hours the streets, so quiet before, would be swarming with men and animals. Every individual would be trying to be very secret, but yet venturing to whisper to just one neighbor that W. had passed through. And long before daylight—this in the dead of Winter—the stampede would be complete, the camp deserted, and the whole population gone chasing after W.

The tradition was that in the early immigration, more than twenty years ago, three young Germans, brothers, who had survived an Indian massacre on the Plains, wandered on foot through the deserts, avoiding all trails and roads, and simply holding a westerly direction and hoping to find California before they starved, or died of fatigue. And in a gorge in the mountains they sat down to rest one day, when one of them noticed a curious vein of cement running along the ground, shot full of lumps of dull yellow metal. They saw that it was gold, and that here was a fortune to be acquired in a single day. The vein was about as wide as a curbstone, and fully two thirds of it was pure gold. Every pound of the wonderful cement was worth well-nigh $200.

Each of the brothers loaded himself with about twenty-five pounds of it, and then they covered up all traces of the vein, made a rude drawing of the locality and the principal landmarks in the vicinity, and started westward again. But troubles thickened about them. In their wanderings one brother fell and broke his leg, and the others were obliged to go on and leave him to die in the wilderness. Another, worn out and starving, gave up by and by, and laid down to die, but after two or three weeks of incredible hardships, the third reached the settlements of California exhausted, sick, and his mind deranged by his sufferings. He had thrown away all his cement but a few fragments, but these were sufficient to set everybody wild with excitement. However, he had had enough of the cement country, and nothing could induce him to lead a party thither. He was entirely content to work on a farm for wages. But he gave Whiteman his map, and described the cement region as well as he could and thus transferred the curse to that gentleman—for when I had my one accidental glimpse of Mr. W. in Esmeralda he had been hunting for the lost mine, in hunger and thirst, poverty and sickness, for twelve or thirteen years. Some people believed he had found it, but most people believed he had not. I saw a piece of cement as large as my fist which was said to have been given to Whiteman by the young German, and it was of a seductive nature. Lumps of virgin gold were as thick in it as raisins in a slice of fruit cake. The privilege of working such a mine one week would be sufficient for a man of reasonable desires.

A new partner of ours, a Mr. Higbie, knew Whiteman well by sight, and a friend of ours, a Mr. Van Dorn, was well acquainted with him, and not only that, but had Whiteman's promise that he should have a private hint in time to enable him to join the next cement expedition. Van Dorn had promised to extend the hint to us. One evening Higbie came in greatly excited, and said he felt certain he had recognized

Whiteman, up town, disguised and in a pretended state of intoxication. In a little while Van Dorn arrived and confirmed the news; and so we gathered in our cabin and with heads close together arranged our plans in impressive whispers.

We were to leave town quietly, after midnight, in two or three small parties, so as not to attract attention, and meet at dawn on the "divide" overlooking Mono Lake, eight or nine miles distant. We were to make no noise after starting, and not speak above a whisper under any circumstances. It was believed that for once Whiteman's presence was unknown in the town and his expedition unsuspected. Our conclave broke up at nine o'clock, and we set about our preparation diligently and with profound secrecy. At eleven o'clock we saddled our horses, hitched them with their long riatas (or lassos), and then brought out a side of bacon, a sack of beans, a small sack of coffee, some sugar, a hundred pounds of flour in sacks, some tin cups and a coffee pot, frying pan and some few other necessary articles. All these things were "packed" on the back of a led horse—and whoever has not been taught, by a Spanish adept, to pack an animal, let him never hope to do the thing by natural smartness. That is impossible. Higbie had had some experience, but was not perfect. He put on the pack saddle (a thing like a saw-buck), piled the property on it and then wound a rope all over and about it and under it, "every which way," taking a hitch in it every now and then, and occasionally surging back on it till the horse's sides sunk in and he gasped for breath—but every time the lashings grew tight in one place they loosened in another. We never did get the load tight all over, but we got it so that it would do, after a fashion, and then we started, in single file, close order, and without a word. It was a dark night. We kept the middle of the road, and proceeded in a slow walk past the rows of cabins, and whenever a miner came to his door I trembled for fear the light would shine on us an excite curiosity. But nothing happened. We began the long winding ascent of the canyon, toward the "divide," and presently the cabins began to grow infrequent, and the intervals between them wider and wider, and then I began to breathe tolerably freely and feel less like a thief and a murderer. I was in the rear, leading the pack horse. As the ascent grew steeper he grew proportionately less satisfied with his cargo, and began to pull back on his riata occasionally and delay progress. My comrades were passing out of sight in the gloom. I was getting anxious. I coaxed and bullied the pack horse till I presently got him into a trot, and then the tin cups and pans strung about his person frightened him and he ran. His riata was wound around the pummel of my saddle, and so, as he went by he dragged me from my horse and the two animals traveled briskly on without me. But I was not alone—the loosened cargo tumbled overboard from the pack horse and fell close to me. It was abreast of almost the last cabin.

A miner came out and said:

"Hello!"

I was thirty steps from him, and knew he could not see me, it was so very dark in the shadow of the mountain. So I lay still. Another head appeared in the light of the cabin door, and presently the two men walked toward me. They stopped within ten steps of me, and one said:

"Sh! Listen."

I could not have been in a more distressed state if I had been escaping justice with a price on my head. Then the miners appeared to sit down on a boulder, though I could not see

them distinctly enough to be very sure what they did. One said:

"I heard a noise, as plain as I ever heard anything. It seemed to be about there—"

A stone whizzed by my head. I flattened myself out in the dust like a postage stamp, and thought to myself if he mended his aim ever so little he would probably hear another noise. In my heart, now, I execrated secret expeditions. I promised myself that this should be my last, though the Sierras were ribbed with cement veins. Then one of the men said:

"I'll tell you what! Welch knew what he was talking about when he said he saw Whiteman to-day. I heard horses—that was the noise. I am going down to Welch's, right away."

They left and I was glad. I did not care whither they went, so they went. I was willing they should visit Welch, and the sooner the better.

As soon as they closed their cabin door my comrades emerged from the gloom; they had caught the horses and were waiting for a clear coast again. We remounted the cargo on the pack horse and got under way, and as day broke we reached the "divide" and joined Van Dorn. Then we journeyed down into the valley of the Lake, and feeling secure, we halted to cook breakfast, for we were tired and sleepy and hungry. Three hours later the rest of the population filed over the "divide" in a long procession, and drifted off out of sight around the borders of the Lake!

Whether or not my accident had produced this result we never knew, but at least one thing was certain—the secret was out and Whiteman would not enter upon a search for the cement mine this time. We were filled with chagrin.

We held a council and decided to make the best of our misfortune and enjoy a week's holiday on the borders of the curious Lake. Mono, it is sometimes called, and sometimes the "Dead Sea of California." It is one of the strangest freaks of Nature to be found in any land, but it is hardly ever mentioned in print and very seldom visited, because it lies away off the usual routes of travel and besides is so difficult to get at that only men content to endure the roughest life will consent to take upon themselves the discomforts of such a trip. On the morning of our second day, we traveled around to a remote and particularly wild spot on the borders of the Lake, where a stream of fresh, ice-cold water entered it from the mountain side, and then we went regularly into camp. We hired a large boat and two shot-guns from a lonely ranchman who lived some ten miles further on, and made ready for comfort and recreation. We soon got thoroughly acquainted with the Lake and all its peculiarities.

CHAPTER XXXVIII.

Mono Lake lies in a lifeless, treeless, hideous desert, eight thousand feet above the level of the sea, and is guarded by mountains two thousand feet higher, whose summits are always clothed in clouds. This solemn, silent, sail-less sea—this lonely tenant of the loneliest spot on earth —is little graced with the picturesque. It is an unpretending expanse of grayish water, about a hundred miles in circumference, with two islands in its centre, mere upheavals of rent and scorched and blistered lava, snowed over with gray banks and drifts of pumice-stone and ashes, the winding sheet of the dead volcano, whose vast crater the lake has seized upon and occupied.

The lake is two hundred feet deep, and its sluggish waters are so strong with alkali that if you only dip the most hopelessly soiled garment into them once or twice, and wring it out, it will be found as clean as if it had been through the ablest of washerwomen's hands. While we camped there our laundry work was easy. We tied the week's washing astern of our boat, and sailed a quarter of a mile, and the job was complete, all to the wringing out. If we threw the water on our heads and gave them a rub or so, the white lather would pile up three inches high. This water is not good for bruised places and abrasions of the skin. We had a valuable dog. He had raw places on him. He had more raw places on him than sound ones. He was the rawest dog I almost ever saw. He jumped overboard one day to get away from the flies. But it was bad judgment. In his condition, it would have been just as comfortable to jump into the fire.

The alkali water nipped him in all the raw places simultaneously, and he struck out for the shore with considerable interest. He yelped and barked and howled as he went—and by the time he got to the shore there was no bark to him—for he had barked the bark all out of his inside, and the alkali water had cleaned the bark all off his outside, and he probably wished he had never embarked in any such enterprise. He ran round and round in a circle, and pawed the earth and clawed the air, and threw double somersaults, sometimes backward and sometimes forward, in the most extraordinary manner. He was not a demonstrative dog, as a general thing, but rather of a grave and serious turn of mind, and I never saw him take so much interest in anything before. He finally struck out over the mountains, at a gait which we estimated at about two hundred and fifty miles an hour, and he is going yet. This was about nine years ago. We look for what is left of him along here every day.

A white man cannot drink the water of Mono Lake, for it is nearly pure lye. It is said that the Indians in the vicinity drink it sometimes, though. It is not improbable, for they are among the purest liars I ever saw. [There will be no additional charge for this joke, except to parties requiring an explanation of it. This joke has received high commendation from some of the ablest minds of the age.]

There are no fish in Mono Lake—no frogs, no snakes, no polliwigs —nothing, in fact, that goes to make life desirable. Millions of wild ducks and sea-gulls swim about the surface, but no living thing exists under the surface, except a white feathery sort of worm, one half an inch long, which looks like a bit of white thread frayed out at the sides. If you dip up a gallon of water, you will get about fifteen thousand of these. They give to the water a sort of grayish-white appearance. Then there is a fly, which looks something like our house fly. These settle on the beach to eat the worms that wash ashore— and any time, you can see there a belt of flies an inch deep and six feet wide, and this belt extends clear around the lake—a belt of flies one hundred miles long. If you throw a stone among them, they swarm up so thick that they look dense, like a cloud. You can hold them under water as long as you please—they do not mind it—they are only proud of it. When you let them go, they pop up to the surface as dry as a patent office report, and walk off as unconcernedly as if they had been educated especially with a view to affording instructive entertainment to man in that particular way. Providence leaves nothing to go by chance. All things have their uses and their part and proper place in Nature's economy: the ducks eat the flies—the flies eat the worms—the Indians eat all three— the wild cats eat the Indians—the white folks eat the wild cats—and thus all things are lovely.

Mono Lake is a hundred miles in a straight line from the ocean—and between it and the ocean are one or two ranges of mountains—yet thousands of sea-gulls go there every season to lay their eggs and rear their young. One would as soon expect to find sea-gulls in Kansas. And in this connection let us observe another instance of Nature's wisdom. The islands in the lake being merely huge masses of lava, coated over with ashes and pumice-stone, and utterly innocent of vegetation or anything that would burn; and sea-gull's eggs being entirely useless to anybody unless they be cooked, Nature has provided an unfailing spring of boiling water on the largest island, and you can put your eggs in there, and in four minutes you can boil them as hard as any statement I have made during the past fifteen years. Within ten feet of the boiling spring is a spring of pure cold water, sweet and wholesome.

So, in that island you get your board and washing free of charge—and if nature had gone further and furnished a nice American hotel clerk who was crusty and disobliging, and didn't know anything about the time tables, or the railroad routes—or—anything—and was proud of it—I would not wish for a more desirable boarding-house.

Half a dozen little mountain brooks flow into Mono Lake, but not a stream of any kind flows out of it. It neither rises nor falls, apparently, and what it does with its surplus water is a dark and bloody mystery.

There are only two seasons in the region round about Mono Lake—and these are, the breaking up of one Winter and the beginning of the next. More than once (in Esmeralda) I have seen a perfectly blistering morning open up with the thermometer at ninety degrees at eight o'clock, and seen the snow fall fourteen inches deep and that same identical thermometer go down to forty-four degrees under shelter, before nine o'clock at night. Under favorable circumstances it snows at least once in every single month in the year, in the little town of Mono. So uncertain is the climate in Summer that a lady who goes out visiting cannot hope to be prepared for all emergencies unless she takes her fan under one arm and her snow shoes under the other. When they have a Fourth of July procession it generally snows on them, and they do say that as a general thing when a man calls for a brandy toddy there, the bar keeper chops it off with a hatchet and wraps it up in a paper, like maple sugar. And it is further reported that the old soakers haven't any teeth—wore them out eating gin cocktails and brandy punches. I do not endorse that statement—I simply give it for what it is worth—and it is worth—well, I should say, millions, to any man who can believe it without straining himself. But I do endorse the snow on the Fourth of July—because I know that to be true.

CHAPTER XXXIX.

About seven o'clock one blistering hot morning—for it was now dead summer time—Higbie and I took the boat and started on a voyage of discovery to the two islands. We had often longed to do this, but had been deterred by the fear of storms; for they were frequent, and severe enough to capsize an ordinary row-boat like ours without great difficulty—and once capsized, death would ensue in spite of the bravest swimming, for that venomous water would eat a man's eyes out like fire, and burn him out inside, too, if he shipped a sea. It was called twelve miles, straight out to the islands—a long pull and a warm one—but the morning was so quiet and sunny, and the lake so smooth and glassy and dead, that we could not resist the temptation. So we filled two large tin canteens with water (since we were not acquainted with the locality of the spring said to exist on the large island), and started. Higbie's brawny muscles gave the boat good speed, but by the time we reached our destination we judged that we had pulled nearer fifteen miles than twelve.

We landed on the big island and went ashore. We tried the water in the canteens, now, and found that the sun had spoiled it; it was so brackish that we could not drink it; so we poured it out and began a search for the spring—for thirst augments fast as soon as it is apparent that one has no means at hand of quenching it. The island was a long, moderately high hill of ashes—nothing but gray ashes and pumice-stone, in which we sunk to our knees at every step—and all around the top was a forbidding wall of scorched and blasted rocks. When we reached the top and got within the wall, we found simply a shallow, far-reaching basin, carpeted with ashes, and here and there a patch of fine sand. In places, picturesque jets of steam shot up out of crevices, giving evidence that although this ancient crater had gone out of active business, there was still some fire left in its furnaces. Close to one of these jets of steam stood the only tree on the island—a small pine of most graceful shape and most faultless symmetry; its color was a brilliant green, for the steam drifted unceasingly through its branches and kept them always moist. It contrasted strangely enough, did this vigorous and beautiful outcast, with its dead and dismal surroundings. It was like a cheerful spirit in a mourning household.

We hunted for the spring everywhere, traversing the full length of the island (two or three miles), and crossing it twice—climbing ash-hills patiently, and then sliding down the other side in a sitting posture, plowing up smothering volumes of gray dust. But we found nothing but solitude, ashes and a heart-breaking silence. Finally we noticed that the wind had risen, and we forgot our thirst in a solicitude of greater importance; for, the lake being quiet, we had not taken pains about securing the boat. We hurried back to a point overlooking our landing place, and then—but mere words cannot describe our dismay—the boat was gone! The chances were that there was not another boat on the entire lake. The situation was not comfortable—in truth, to speak plainly, it was frightful. We were prisoners on a desolate island, in aggravating proximity to friends who were for the present helpless to aid us; and what was still more uncomfortable was the reflection that we had neither food nor water. But presently we sighted the boat. It was drifting along, leisurely, about fifty yards from shore, tossing in a foamy sea. It drifted, and continued to drift, but at the same safe distance from land, and we walked along abreast it and waited for fortune to favor us. At the end of an hour it approached a jutting cape, and Higbie ran ahead and posted himself on the utmost verge and prepared for the assault. If we failed there, there was no hope for us. It was driving gradually shoreward all the time, now; but whether it was driving fast enough to make the connection or not was the momentous question. When it got within thirty steps of Higbie I was so excited that I fancied I could hear my own heart beat. When, a little later, it dragged slowly along and seemed about to go by, only one little yard out of reach, it seemed as if my heart stood still; and when it was exactly abreast him and began to widen away, and he still standing like a watching statue, I knew my heart did stop. But when he gave a great spring, the next instant, and lit fairly in the stern, I discharged a war-whoop that woke the solitudes!

But it dulled my enthusiasm, presently, when he told me he

had not been caring whether the boat came within jumping distance or not, so that it passed within eight or ten yards of him, for he had made up his mind to shut his eyes and mouth and swim that trifling distance. Imbecile that I was, I had not thought of that. It was only a long swim that could be fatal.

The sea was running high and the storm increasing. It was growing late, too—three or four in the afternoon. Whether to venture toward the mainland or not, was a question of some moment. But we were so distressed by thirst that we decide to try it, and so Higbie fell to work and I took the steering-oar. When we had pulled a mile, laboriously, we were evidently in serious peril, for the storm had greatly augmented; the billows ran very high and were capped with foaming crests, the heavens were hung with black, and the wind blew with great fury. We would have gone back, now, but we did not dare to turn the boat around, because as soon as she got in the trough of the sea she would upset, of course. Our only hope lay in keeping her head-on to the seas. It was hard work to do this, she plunged so, and so beat and belabored the billows with her rising and falling bows. Now and then one of Higbie's oars would trip on the top of a wave, and the other one would snatch the boat half around in spite of my cumbersome steering apparatus. We were drenched by the sprays constantly, and the boat occasionally shipped water. By and by, powerful as my comrade was, his great exertions began to tell on him, and he was anxious that I should change places with him till he could rest a little. But I told him this was impossible; for if the steering oar were dropped a moment while we changed, the boat would slue around into the trough of the sea, capsize, and in less than five minutes we would have a hundred gallons of soap-suds in us and be eaten up so quickly that we could not even be present at our own inquest.

But things cannot last always. Just as the darkness shut down we came booming into port, head on. Higbie dropped his oars to hurrah—I dropped mine to help—the sea gave the boat a twist, and over she went!

The agony that alkali water inflicts on bruises, chafes and blistered hands, is unspeakable, and nothing but greasing all over will modify it —but we ate, drank and slept well, that night, notwithstanding.

In speaking of the peculiarities of Mono Lake, I ought to have mentioned that at intervals all around its shores stand picturesque turret-looking masses and clusters of a whitish, coarse-grained rock that resembles inferior mortar dried hard; and if one breaks off fragments of this rock he will find perfectly shaped and thoroughly petrified gulls' eggs deeply imbedded in the mass. How did they get there? I simply state the fact —for it is a fact—and leave the geological reader to crack the nut at his leisure and solve the problem after his own fashion.

At the end of a week we adjourned to the Sierras on a fishing excursion, and spent several days in camp under snowy Castle Peak, and fished successfully for trout in a bright, miniature lake whose surface was between ten and eleven thousand feet above the level of the sea; cooling ourselves during the hot August noons by sitting on snow banks ten feet deep, under whose sheltering edges fine grass and dainty flowers flourished luxuriously; and at night entertaining ourselves by almost freezing to death. Then we returned to Mono Lake, and finding that the cement excitement was over for the present, packed up and went back to Esmeralda. Mr. Ballou reconnoitred awhile, and not liking the prospect, set out alone for Humboldt.

About this time occurred a little incident which has always had a sort of interest to me, from the fact that it came so near "instigating" my funeral. At a time when an Indian attack had been expected, the citizens hid their gunpowder where it would be safe and yet convenient to hand when wanted. A neighbor of ours hid six cans of rifle powder in the bake-oven of an old discarded cooking stove which stood on the open ground near a frame out-house or shed, and from and after that day never thought of it again. We hired a half-tamed Indian to do some washing for us, and he took up quarters under the shed with his tub. The ancient stove reposed within six feet of him, and before his face. Finally it occurred to him that hot water would be better than cold, and he went out and fired up under that forgotten powder magazine and set on a kettle of water. Then he returned to his tub.

I entered the shed presently and threw down some more clothes, and was about to speak to him when the stove blew up with a prodigious crash, and disappeared, leaving not a splinter behind. Fragments of it fell in the streets full two hundred yards away. Nearly a third of the shed roof over our heads was destroyed, and one of the stove lids, after cutting a small stanchion half in two in front of the Indian, whizzed between us and drove partly through the weather-boarding beyond. I was as white as a sheet and as weak as a kitten and speechless. But the Indian betrayed no trepidation, no distress, not even discomfort. He simply stopped washing, leaned forward and surveyed the clean, blank ground a moment, and then remarked:

"Mph! Dam stove heap gone!"—and resumed his scrubbing as placidly as if it were an entirely customary thing for a stove to do. I will explain, that "heap" is "Injun-English" for "very much." The reader will perceive the exhaustive expressiveness of it in the present instance.

CHAPTER XL. I now come to a curious episode—the most curious, I think, that had yet accented my slothful, valueless, heedless career. Out of a hillside toward the upper end of the town, projected a wall of reddish looking quartz-croppings, the exposed comb of a silver-bearing ledge that extended deep down into the earth, of course. It was owned by a company entitled the "Wide West." There was a shaft sixty or seventy feet deep on the under side of the croppings, and everybody was acquainted with the rock that came from it—and tolerably rich rock it was, too, but nothing extraordinary. I will remark here, that although to the inexperienced stranger all the quartz of a particular "district" looks about alike, an old resident of the camp can take a glance at a mixed pile of rock, separate the fragments and tell you which mine each came from, as easily as a confectioner can separate and classify the various kinds and qualities of candy in a mixed heap of the article.

All at once the town was thrown into a state of extraordinary excitement. In mining parlance the Wide West had "struck it rich!" Everybody went to see the new developments, and for some days there was such a crowd of people about the Wide West shaft that a stranger would have supposed there was a mass meeting in session there. No other topic was discussed but the rich strike, and nobody thought or dreamed about anything else. Every man brought away a specimen, ground it up in a hand mortar, washed it out in his horn spoon, and glared speechless upon the marvelous result. It was not hard rock, but black, decomposed stuff which could be crumbled in the hand like a baked potato, and when spread out on a paper exhibited a thick sprinkling of gold and particles of "native" silver. Higbie brought a handful to the cabin, and when he had

washed it out his amazement was beyond description. Wide West stock soared skywards. It was said that repeated offers had been made for it at a thousand dollars a foot, and promptly refused. We have all had the "blues"—the mere sky-blues—but mine were indigo, now—because I did not own in the Wide West. The world seemed hollow to me, and existence a grief. I lost my appetite, and ceased to take an interest in anything. Still I had to stay, and listen to other people's rejoicings, because I had no money to get out of the camp with.

The Wide West company put a stop to the carrying away of "specimens," and well they might, for every handful of the ore was worth a sun of some consequence. To show the exceeding value of the ore, I will remark that a sixteen-hundred-pounds parcel of it was sold, just as it lay, at the mouth of the shaft, at one dollar a pound; and the man who bought it "packed" it on mules a hundred and fifty or two hundred miles, over the mountains, to San Francisco, satisfied that it would yield at a rate that would richly compensate him for his trouble. The Wide West people also commanded their foreman to refuse any but their own operatives permission to enter the mine at any time or for any purpose. I kept up my "blue" meditations and Higbie kept up a deal of thinking, too, but of a different sort. He puzzled over the "rock," examined it with a glass, inspected it in different lights and from different points of view, and after each experiment delivered himself, in soliloquy, of one and the same unvarying opinion in the same unvarying formula:

"It is not Wide West rock!"

He said once or twice that he meant to have a look into the Wide West shaft if he got shot for it. I was wretched, and did not care whether he got a look into it or not. He failed that day, and tried again at night; failed again; got up at dawn and tried, and failed again. Then he lay in ambush in the sage brush hour after hour, waiting for the two or three hands to adjourn to the shade of a boulder for dinner; made a start once, but was premature—one of the men came back for something; tried it again, but when almost at the mouth of the shaft, another of the men rose up from behind the boulder as if to reconnoitre, and he dropped on the ground and lay quiet; presently he crawled on his hands and knees to the mouth of the shaft, gave a quick glance around, then seized the rope and slid down the shaft.

He disappeared in the gloom of a "side drift" just as a head appeared in the mouth of the shaft and somebody shouted "Hello!"—which he did not answer. He was not disturbed any more. An hour later he entered the cabin, hot, red, and ready to burst with smothered excitement, and exclaimed in a stage whisper:

"I knew it! We are rich! IT'S A BLIND LEAD!"

I thought the very earth reeled under me. Doubt—conviction—doubt again—exultation—hope, amazement, belief, unbelief—every emotion imaginable swept in wild procession through my heart and brain, and I could not speak a word. After a moment or two of this mental fury, I shook myself to rights, and said:

"Say it again!"

"It's blind lead!"

"Cal, let's—let's burn the house—or kill somebody! Let's get out where there's room to hurrah! But what is the use? It is a hundred times too good to be true."

"It's a blind lead, for a million!—hanging wall—foot wall—clay casings—everything complete!" He swung his hat and gave three cheers, and I cast doubt to the winds and chimed in with a will. For I was worth a million dollars, and did not care "whether school kept or not!"

But perhaps I ought to explain. A "blind lead" is a lead or ledge that does not "crop out" above the surface. A miner does not know where to look for such leads, but they are often stumbled upon by accident in the course of driving a tunnel or sinking a shaft. Higbie knew the Wide West rock perfectly well, and the more he had examined the new developments the more he was satisfied that the ore could not have come from the Wide West vein. And so had it occurred to him alone, of all the camp, that there was a blind lead down in the shaft, and that even the Wide West people themselves did not suspect it. He was right. When he went down the shaft, he found that the blind lead held its independent way through the Wide West vein, cutting it diagonally, and that it was enclosed in its own well-defined casing-rocks and clay. Hence it was public property. Both leads being perfectly well defined, it was easy for any miner to see which one belonged to the Wide West and which did not.

We thought it well to have a strong friend, and therefore we brought the foreman of the Wide West to our cabin that night and revealed the great surprise to him. Higbie said:

"We are going to take possession of this blind lead, record it and establish ownership, and then forbid the Wide West company to take out any more of the rock. You cannot help your company in this matter —nobody can help them. I will go into the shaft with you and prove to your entire satisfaction that it is a blind lead. Now we propose to take you in with us, and claim the blind lead in our three names. What do you say?"

What could a man say who had an opportunity to simply stretch forth his hand and take possession of a fortune without risk of any kind and without wronging any one or attaching the least taint of dishonor to his name? He could only say, "Agreed."

The notice was put up that night, and duly spread upon the recorder's books before ten o'clock. We claimed two hundred feet each—six hundred feet in all—the smallest and compactest organization in the district, and the easiest to manage.

No one can be so thoughtless as to suppose that we slept, that night. Higbie and I went to bed at midnight, but it was only to lie broad awake and think, dream, scheme. The floorless, tumble-down cabin was a palace, the ragged gray blankets silk, the furniture rosewood and mahogany. Each new splendor that burst out of my visions of the future whirled me bodily over in bed or jerked me to a sitting posture just as if an electric battery had been applied to me. We shot fragments of conversation back and forth at each other. Once Higbie said:

"When are you going home—to the States?"

"To-morrow!"—with an evolution or two, ending with a sitting position. "Well—no—but next month, at furthest."

"We'll go in the same steamer."

"Agreed."

A pause.

"Steamer of the 10th?"

"Yes. No, the 1st."

"All right."

Another pause.

"Where are you going to live?" said Higbie.

"San Francisco."

"That's me!"

Pause.

"Too high—too much climbing"—from Higbie.

"What is?"

"I was thinking of Russian Hill—building a house up there."

"Too much climbing? Shan't you keep a carriage?"

"Of course. I forgot that."

Pause.

"Cal., what kind of a house are you going to build?"

"I was thinking about that. Three-story and an attic."

"But what kind?"

"Well, I don't hardly know. Brick, I suppose."

"Brick—bosh."

"Why? What is your idea?"

"Brown stone front—French plate glass—billiard-room off the dining-room—statuary and paintings—shrubbery and two-acre grass plat —greenhouse—iron dog on the front stoop—gray horses—landau, and a coachman with a bug on his hat!"

"By George!"

A long pause.

"Cal., when are you going to Europe?"

"Well—I hadn't thought of that. When are you?"

"In the Spring."

"Going to be gone all summer?"

"All summer! I shall remain there three years."

"No—but are you in earnest?"

"Indeed I am."

"I will go along too."

"Why of course you will."

"What part of Europe shall you go to?"

"All parts. France, England, Germany—Spain, Italy, Switzerland, Syria, Greece, Palestine, Arabia, Persia, Egypt—all over—everywhere."

"I'm agreed."

"All right."

"Won't it be a swell trip!"

"We'll spend forty or fifty thousand dollars trying to make it one, anyway."

Another long pause.

"Higbie, we owe the butcher six dollars, and he has been threatening to stop our—"

"Hang the butcher!"

"Amen."

And so it went on. By three o'clock we found it was no use, and so we got up and played cribbage and smoked pipes till sunrise. It was my week to cook. I always hated cooking—now, I abhorred it.

The news was all over town. The former excitement was great—this one was greater still. I walked the streets serene and happy. Higbie said the foreman had been offered two hundred thousand dollars for his third of the mine. I said I would like to see myself selling for any such price. My ideas were lofty. My figure was a million. Still, I honestly believe that if I had been offered it, it would have had no other effect than to make me hold off for more.

I found abundant enjoyment in being rich. A man offered me a three-hundred-dollar horse, and wanted to take my simple, unendorsed note for it. That brought the most realizing sense I had yet had that I was actually rich, beyond shadow of doubt. It was followed by numerous other evidences of a similar nature—among which I may mention the fact of the butcher leaving us a double supply of meat and saying nothing about money.

By the laws of the district, the "locators" or claimants of a ledge were obliged to do a fair and reasonable amount of work on their new property within ten days after the date of the location, or the property was forfeited, and anybody could go and seize it that chose. So we determined to go to work the next day. About the middle of the afternoon, as I was coming out of the post office, I met a Mr. Gardiner, who told me that Capt. John Nye was lying dangerously ill at his place (the "Nine-Mile Ranch"), and that he and his wife were not able to give him nearly as much care and attention as his case demanded. I said if he would wait for me a moment, I would go down and help in the sick room. I ran to the cabin to tell Higbie. He was not there, but I left a note on the table for him, and a few minutes later I left town in Gardiner's wagon.

CHAPTER XLI.

Captain Nye was very ill indeed, with spasmodic rheumatism. But the old gentleman was himself—which is to say, he was kind-hearted and agreeable when comfortable, but a singularly violent wild-cat when things did not go well. He would be smiling along pleasantly enough, when a sudden spasm of his disease would take him and he would go out of his smile into a perfect fury. He would groan and wail and howl with the anguish, and fill up the odd chinks with the most elaborate profanity that strong convictions and a fine fancy could contrive. With fair opportunity he could swear very well and handle his adjectives with considerable judgment; but when the spasm was on him it was painful to listen to him, he was so awkward. However, I had seen him nurse a sick man himself and put up patiently with the inconveniences of the situation, and consequently I was willing that he should have full license now that his own turn had come. He could not disturb me, with all his raving and ranting, for my mind had work on hand, and it labored on diligently, night and day, whether my hands were idle or employed. I was altering and amending the plans for my house, and thinking over the propriety of having the billard-room in the attic, instead of on the same floor with the dining-room; also, I was trying to decide between green and blue for the upholstery of the drawing-room, for, although my preference was blue I feared it was a color that would be too easily damaged by dust and sunlight; likewise while I was content to put the coachman in a modest livery, I was uncertain about a footman—I needed one, and was even resolved to have one, but wished he could properly appear and perform his functions out of livery, for I somewhat dreaded so much show; and yet, inasmuch as my late grandfather had had a coachman and such things, but no liveries, I felt rather drawn to beat him;—or beat his ghost, at any rate; I was also systematizing the European trip, and managed to get it all laid out, as to route and length of time to be devoted to it — everything, with one exception—namely, whether to cross the desert from Cairo to Jerusalem per camel, or go by sea to Beirut, and thence down through the country per caravan. Meantime I was writing to the friends at home every day, instructing them concerning all my plans and intentions, and directing them to look up a handsome homestead for my mother and agree upon a price for it against my coming, and also directing them to sell my share of the Tennessee land and tender the proceeds to the widows' and orphans' fund of the typographical union of which I had long been a member in good standing. [This Tennessee land had been in the possession of the family many years, and promised to confer high fortune upon us some day; it still promises it, but in a less violent way.]

When I had been nursing the Captain nine days he was somewhat better, but very feeble. During the afternoon we lifted him into a chair and gave him an alcoholic vapor bath, and then set about putting him on the bed again. We had to be exceedingly careful, for the least jar produced pain. Gardiner had his shoulders and I his legs; in an unfortunate moment I stumbled and the patient fell heavily on the bed in an agony of torture. I never heard a man swear so in my life. He raved like a maniac, and tried to snatch a revolver from the table—but I got it. He ordered me out of the house, and swore a world of oaths that he would kill me wherever he caught me when he got on his feet again. It was simply a passing fury, and meant nothing. I knew he would forget it in an hour, and maybe be sorry for it, too; but it angered me a little, at the moment. So much so, indeed, that I determined to go back to Esmeralda. I thought he was able to get along alone, now, since he was on the war path. I took supper, and as soon as the moon rose, began my nine-mile journey, on foot.

Even millionaires needed no horses, in those days, for a mere nine-mile jaunt without baggage.

As I "raised the hill" overlooking the town, it lacked fifteen minutes of twelve. I glanced at the hill over beyond the canyon, and in the bright moonlight saw what appeared to be about half the population of the village massed on and around the Wide West croppings. My heart gave an exulting bound, and I said to myself, "They have made a new strike to-night—and struck it richer than ever, no doubt." I started over there, but gave it up. I said the "strick" would keep, and I had climbed hill enough for one night. I went on down through the town, and as I was passing a little German bakery, a woman ran out and begged me to come in and help her. She said her husband had a fit. I went in, and judged she was right—he appeared to have a hundred of them, compressed into one. Two Germans were there, trying to hold him, and not making much of a success of it. I ran up the street half a block or so and routed out a sleeping doctor, brought him down half dressed, and we four wrestled with the maniac, and doctored, drenched and bled him, for more than an hour, and the poor German woman did the crying. He grew quiet, now, and the doctor and I withdrew and left him to his friends.

It was a little after one o'clock. As I entered the cabin door, tired but jolly, the dingy light of a tallow candle revealed Higbie, sitting by the pine table gazing stupidly at my note, which he held in his fingers, and looking pale, old, and haggard. I halted, and looked at him. He looked at me, stolidly. I said:

"Higbie, what—what is it?"

"We're ruined—we didn't do the work—THE BLIND LEAD'S RELOCATED!"

It was enough. I sat down sick, grieved—broken-hearted, indeed. A minute before, I was rich and brimful of vanity; I was a pauper now, and very meek. We sat still an hour, busy with thought, busy with vain and useless self-upbraidings, busy with "Why didn't I do this, and why didn't I do that," but neither spoke a word. Then we dropped into mutual explanations, and the mystery was cleared away. It came out that Higbie had depended on me, as I had on him, and as both of us had on the foreman. The folly of it! It was the first time that ever staid and steadfast Higbie had left an important matter to chance or failed to be true to his full share of a responsibility.

But he had never seen my note till this moment, and this moment was the first time he had been in the cabin since the day he had seen me last. He, also, had left a note for me, on that same fatal afternoon—had ridden up on horseback, and looked through the window, and being in a hurry and not seeing me, had tossed the note into the cabin through a broken pane. Here it was, on the floor, where it had remained undisturbed for nine days:

"Don't fail to do the work before the ten days expire. W. has passed through and given me notice. I am to join him at Mono Lake, and we shall go on from there to-night. He says he will find it this time, sure. CAL."

"W." meant Whiteman, of course. That thrice accursed "cement!"

That was the way of it. An old miner, like Higbie, could no more withstand the fascination of a mysterious mining excitement like this "cement" foolishness, than he could refrain from eating when he was famishing. Higbie had been

dreaming about the marvelous cement for months; and now, against his better judgment, he had gone off and "taken the chances" on my keeping secure a mine worth a million undiscovered cement veins. They had not been followed this time. His riding out of town in broad daylight was such a common-place thing to do that it had not attracted any attention. He said they prosecuted their search in the fastnesses of the mountains during nine days, without success; they could not find the cement. Then a ghastly fear came over him that something might have happened to prevent the doing of the necessary work to hold the blind lead (though indeed he thought such a thing hardly possible), and forthwith he started home with all speed. He would have reached Esmeralda in time, but his horse broke down and he had to walk a great part of the distance. And so it happened that as he came into Esmeralda by one road, I entered it by another. His was the superior energy, however, for he went straight to the Wide West, instead of turning aside as I had done—and he arrived there about five or ten minutes too late! The "notice" was already up, the "relocation" of our mine completed beyond recall, and the crowd rapidly dispersing. He learned some facts before he left the ground. The foreman had not been seen about the streets since the night we had located the mine—a telegram had called him to California on a matter of life and death, it was said. At any rate he had done no work and the watchful eyes of the community were taking note of the fact. At midnight of this woful tenth day, the ledge would be "relocatable," and by eleven o'clock the hill was black with men prepared to do the relocating. That was the crowd I had seen when I fancied a new "strike" had been made—idiot that I was.

[We three had the same right to relocate the lead that other people had, provided we were quick enough.] As midnight was announced, fourteen men, duly armed and ready to back their proceedings, put up their "notice" and proclaimed their ownership of the blind lead, under the new name of the "Johnson." But A. D. Allen our partner (the foreman) put in a sudden appearance about that time, with a cocked revolver in his hand, and said his name must be added to the list, or he would "thin out the Johnson company some." He was a manly, splendid, determined fellow, and known to be as good as his word, and therefore a compromise was effected. They put in his name for a hundred feet, reserving to themselves the customary two hundred feet each. Such was the history of the night's events, as Higbie gathered from a friend on the way home.

Higbie and I cleared out on a new mining excitement the next morning, glad to get away from the scene of our sufferings, and after a month or two of hardship and disappointment, returned to Esmeralda once more. Then we learned that the Wide West and the Johnson companies had consolidated; that the stock, thus united, comprised five thousand feet, or shares; that the foreman, apprehending tiresome litigation, and considering such a huge concern unwieldy, had sold his hundred feet for ninety thousand dollars in gold and gone home to the States to enjoy it. If the stock was worth such a gallant figure, with five thousand shares in the corporation, it makes me dizzy to think what it would have been worth with only our original six hundred in it. It was the difference between six hundred men owning a house and five thousand owning it. We would have been millionaires if we had only worked with pick and spade one little day on our property and so secured our ownership!

It reads like a wild fancy sketch, but the evidence of many witnesses, and likewise that of the official records of

Esmeralda District, is easily obtainable in proof that it is a true history. I can always have it to say that I was absolutely and unquestionably worth a million dollars, once, for ten days.

A year ago my esteemed and in every way estimable old millionaire partner, Higbie, wrote me from an obscure little mining camp in California that after nine or ten years of buffetings and hard striving, he was at last in a position where he could command twenty-five hundred dollars, and said he meant to go into the fruit business in a modest way. How such a thought would have insulted him the night we lay in our cabin planning European trips and brown stone houses on Russian Hill!

CHAPTER XLII.

What to do next?

It was a momentous question. I had gone out into the world to shift for myself, at the age of thirteen (for my father had endorsed for friends; and although he left us a sumptuous legacy of pride in his fine Virginian stock and its national distinction, I presently found that I could not live on that alone without occasional bread to wash it down with). I had gained a livelihood in various vocations, but had not dazzled anybody with my successes; still the list was before me, and the amplest liberty in the matter of choosing, provided I wanted to work—which I did not, after being so wealthy. I had once been a grocery clerk, for one day, but had consumed so much sugar in that time that I was relieved from further duty by the proprietor; said he wanted me outside, so that he could have my custom. I had studied law an entire week, and then given it up because it was so prosy and tiresome. I had engaged briefly in the study of blacksmithing, but wasted so much time trying to fix the bellows so that it would blow itself, that the master turned me adrift in disgrace, and told me I would come to no good. I had been a bookseller's clerk for awhile, but the customers bothered me so much I could not read with any comfort, and so the proprietor gave me a furlough and forgot to put a limit to it. I had clerked in a drug store part of a summer, but my prescriptions were unlucky, and we appeared to sell more stomach pumps than soda water. So I had to go. I had made of myself a tolerable printer, under the impression that I would be another Franklin some day, but somehow had missed the connection thus far. There was no berth open in the Esmeralda Union, and besides I had always been such a slow compositor that I looked with envy upon the achievements of apprentices of two years' standing; and when I took a "take," foremen were in the habit of suggesting that it would be wanted "some time during the year."

I was a good average St. Louis and New Orleans pilot and by no means ashamed of my abilities in that line; wages were two hundred and fifty dollars a month and no board to pay, and I did long to stand behind a wheel again and never roam any more—but I had been making such an ass of myself lately in grandiloquent letters home about my blind lead and my European excursion that I did what many and many a poor disappointed miner had done before; said "It is all over with me now, and I will never go back home to be pitied—and snubbed." I had been a private secretary, a silver miner and a silver mill operative, and amounted to less than nothing in each, and now—

What to do next?

I yielded to Higbie's appeals and consented to try the mining once more. We climbed far up on the mountain side and went to work on a little rubbishy claim of ours that had a shaft on it eight feet deep. Higbie descended into it and worked bravely with his pick till he had loosened up a deal of rock and dirt and then I went down with a long-handled shovel (the most awkward invention yet contrived by man) to throw it out. You must brace the shovel forward with the side of your knee till it is full, and then, with a skilful toss, throw it backward over your left shoulder. I made the toss, and landed the mess just on the edge of the shaft and it all came back on my head and down the back of my neck. I never said a word, but climbed out and walked home. I inwardly resolved that I would starve before I would make a target of myself and shoot rubbish at it with a long-handled shovel.

I sat down, in the cabin, and gave myself up to solid misery—so to speak. Now in pleasanter days I had amused myself with writing letters to the chief paper of the Territory, the Virginia Daily Territorial Enterprise, and had always been surprised when they appeared in print. My good opinion of the editors had steadily declined; for it seemed to me that they might have found something better to fill up with than my literature. I had found a letter in the post office as I came home from the hill side, and finally I opened it. Eureka! [I never did know what Eureka meant, but it seems to be as proper a word to heave in as any when no other that sounds pretty offers.] It was a deliberate offer to me of Twenty-Five Dollars a week to come up to Virginia and be city editor of the Enterprise.

I would have challenged the publisher in the "blind lead" days—I wanted to fall down and worship him, now. Twenty-Five Dollars a week—it looked like bloated luxury—a fortune a sinful and lavish waste of money. But my transports cooled when I thought of my inexperience and consequent unfitness for the position—and straightway, on top of this, my long array of failures rose up before me. Yet if I refused this place I must presently become dependent upon somebody for my bread, a thing necessarily distasteful to a man who had never experienced such a humiliation since he was thirteen years old. Not much to be proud of, since it is so common—but then it was all I had to be proud of. So I was scared into being a city editor. I would have declined, otherwise. Necessity is the mother of "taking chances." I do not doubt that if, at that time, I had been offered a salary to translate the Talmud from the original Hebrew, I would have accepted—albeit with diffidence and some misgivings—and thrown as much variety into it as I could for the money.

I went up to Virginia and entered upon my new vocation. I was a rusty looking city editor, I am free to confess—coatless, slouch hat, blue woolen shirt, pantaloons stuffed into boot-tops, whiskered half down to the waist, and the universal navy revolver slung to my belt. But I secured a more Christian costume and discarded the revolver.

I had never had occasion to kill anybody, nor ever felt a desire to do so, but had worn the thing in deference to popular sentiment, and in order that I might not, by its absence, be offensively conspicuous, and a subject of remark. But the other editors, and all the printers, carried revolvers. I asked the chief editor and proprietor (Mr. Goodman, I will call him, since it describes him as well as any name could do) for some instructions with regard to my duties, and he told me to go all over town and ask all sorts of people all sorts of questions, make notes of the information gained, and write them out for publication. And he added:

"Never say 'We learn' so-and-so, or 'It is reported,' or 'It is rumored,' or 'We understand' so-and-so, but go to headquarters and get the absolute facts, and then speak out and say 'It is so-and-so.' Otherwise, people will not put confidence in your news. Unassailable certainly is the thing that gives a newspaper the firmest and most valuable reputation."

It was the whole thing in a nut-shell; and to this day when I find a reporter commencing his article with "We understand," I gather a suspicion that he has not taken as much pains to inform himself as he ought to have done. I moralize well, but I did not always practise well when I was a city editor; I let fancy get the upper hand of fact too often when there was a dearth of news. I can never forget my first day's experience as a reporter. I wandered about town questioning everybody, boring everybody, and finding out that nobody knew anything. At the end of five hours my notebook was still barren. I spoke to Mr. Goodman. He said:

"Dan used to make a good thing out of the hay wagons in a dry time when there were no fires or inquests. Are there no hay wagons in from the Truckee? If there are, you might speak of the renewed activity and all that sort of thing, in the hay business, you know.

"It isn't sensational or exciting, but it fills up and looks business like."

I canvassed the city again and found one wretched old hay truck dragging in from the country. But I made affluent use of it. I multiplied it by sixteen, brought it into town from sixteen different directions, made sixteen separate items out of it, and got up such another sweat about hay as Virginia City had never seen in the world before.

This was encouraging. Two nonpareil columns had to be filled, and I was getting along. Presently, when things began to look dismal again, a desperado killed a man in a saloon and joy returned once more. I never was so glad over any mere trifle before in my life. I said to the murderer:

"Sir, you are a stranger to me, but you have done me a kindness this day which I can never forget. If whole years of gratitude can be to you any slight compensation, they shall be yours. I was in trouble and you have relieved me nobly and at a time when all seemed dark and drear. Count me your friend from this time forth, for I am not a man to forget a favor."

If I did not really say that to him I at least felt a sort of itching desire to do it. I wrote up the murder with a hungry attention to details, and when it was finished experienced but one regret—namely, that they had not hanged my benefactor on the spot, so that I could work him up too.

Next I discovered some emigrant wagons going into camp on the plaza and found that they had lately come through the hostile Indian country and had fared rather roughly. I made the best of the item that the circumstances permitted, and felt that if I were not confined within rigid limits by the presence of the reporters of the other papers I could add particulars that would make the article much more interesting. However, I found one wagon that was going on to California, and made some judicious inquiries of the proprietor. When I learned, through his short and surly answers to my cross-questioning, that he was certainly going on and would not be in the city next day to make trouble, I got ahead of the other papers, for I took down his list of names and added his party to the killed and wounded. Having more scope here, I put this wagon through an Indian fight that to this day has no parallel in

history.

My two columns were filled. When I read them over in the morning I felt that I had found my legitimate occupation at last. I reasoned within myself that news, and stirring news, too, was what a paper needed, and I felt that I was peculiarly endowed with the ability to furnish it. Mr. Goodman said that I was as good a reporter as Dan. I desired no higher commendation. With encouragement like that, I felt that I could take my pen and murder all the immigrants on the plains if need be and the interests of the paper demanded it.

CHAPTER XLIII.

However, as I grew better acquainted with the business and learned the run of the sources of information I ceased to require the aid of fancy to any large extent, and became able to fill my columns without diverging noticeably from the domain of fact.

I struck up friendships with the reporters of the other journals, and we swapped "regulars" with each other and thus economized work. "Regulars" are permanent sources of news, like courts, bullion returns, "clean-ups" at the quartz mills, and inquests. Inasmuch as everybody went armed, we had an inquest about every day, and so this department was naturally set down among the "regulars." We had lively papers in those days. My great competitor among the reporters was Boggs of the Union. He was an excellent reporter. Once in three or four months he would get a little intoxicated, but as a general thing he was a wary and cautious drinker although always ready to tamper a little with the enemy. He had the advantage of me in one thing; he could get the monthly public school report and I could not, because the principal hated the Enterprise. One snowy night when the report was due, I started out sadly wondering how I was going to get it. Presently, a few steps up the almost deserted street I stumbled on Boggs and asked him where he was going.

"After the school report."

"I'll go along with you."

"No, sir. I'll excuse you."

"Just as you say."

A saloon-keeper's boy passed by with a steaming pitcher of hot punch, and Boggs snuffed the fragrance gratefully. He gazed fondly after the boy and saw him start up the Enterprise stairs. I said:

"I wish you could help me get that school business, but since you can't, I must run up to the Union office and see if I can get them to let me have a proof of it after they have set it up, though I don't begin to suppose they will. Good night."

"Hold on a minute. I don't mind getting the report and sitting around with the boys a little, while you copy it, if you're willing to drop down to the principal's with me."

"Now you talk like a rational being. Come along."

We plowed a couple of blocks through the snow, got the report and returned to our office. It was a short document and soon copied. Meantime Boggs helped himself to the punch. I gave the manuscript back to him and we started out to get an inquest, for we heard pistol shots near by. We got the particulars with little loss of time, for it was only an inferior sort of bar-room murder, and of little interest to the public, and then we separated. Away at three o'clock in the morning, when we had gone to press and were having a relaxing concert as usual —for some of the printers were good singers and others good performers on the guitar and on that atrocity the accordion—the proprietor of the Union strode in and desired to know if anybody had heard anything of Boggs or the school report. We stated the case, and all turned out to help hunt for the delinquent. We found him standing on a table in a saloon, with an old tin lantern in one hand and the school report in the other, haranguing a gang of intoxicated Cornish miners on the iniquity of squandering the public moneys on education "when hundreds and hundreds of honest hard-working men are literally starving for whiskey." [Riotous applause.] He had been assisting in a regal spree with those parties for hours. We dragged him away and put him to bed.

Of course there was no school report in the Union, and Boggs held me accountable, though I was innocent of any intention or desire to compass its absence from that paper and was as sorry as any one that the misfortune had occurred.

But we were perfectly friendly. The day that the school report was next due, the proprietor of the "Genessee" mine furnished us a buggy and asked us to go down and write something about the property—a very common request and one always gladly acceded to when people furnished buggies, for we were as fond of pleasure excursions as other people. In due time we arrived at the "mine"—nothing but a hole in the ground ninety feet deep, and no way of getting down into it but by holding on to a rope and being lowered with a windlass. The workmen had just gone off somewhere to dinner. I was not strong enough to lower Boggs's bulk; so I took an unlighted candle in my teeth, made a loop for my foot in the end of the rope, implored Boggs not to go to sleep or let the windlass get the start of him, and then swung out over the shaft. I reached the bottom muddy and bruised about the elbows, but safe. I lit the candle, made an examination of the rock, selected some specimens and shouted to Boggs to hoist away. No answer. Presently a head appeared in the circle of daylight away aloft, and a voice came down:

"Are you all set?"

"All set—hoist away."

"Are you comfortable?"

"Perfectly."

"Could you wait a little?"

"Oh certainly—no particular hurry."

"Well—good by."

"Why? Where are you going?"

"After the school report!"

And he did. I staid down there an hour, and surprised the workmen when they hauled up and found a man on the rope instead of a bucket of rock. I walked home, too—five miles—up hill. We had no school report next morning; but the Union had.

Six months after my entry into journalism the grand "flush times" of Silverland began, and they continued with unabated splendor for three years. All difficulty about filling up the "local department" ceased, and the only trouble now was how to make the lengthened columns hold the world of incidents and happenings that came to our literary net every day. Virginia had grown to be the "livest" town, for its age and population, that America had ever produced. The sidewalks swarmed with people—to such an extent, indeed, that it was generally no easy matter to stem the human tide. The streets themselves were just as crowded with quartz wagons, freight teams and other vehicles. The procession was endless. So great was the pack, that buggies frequently had to wait half an hour for an opportunity to cross the principal street. Joy sat on every countenance, and there was a glad, almost fierce, intensity in every eye, that told of the money-getting schemes that were seething in every brain and the high hope that held sway in every heart. Money was as plenty as dust; every individual considered himself wealthy, and a melancholy countenance was nowhere to be seen. There were military companies, fire companies, brass bands, banks, hotels, theatres, "hurdy-gurdy houses," wide-open gambling palaces, political pow-wows, civic processions, street fights, murders, inquests, riots, a whiskey mill every fifteen steps, a Board of Aldermen, a Mayor, a City Surveyor, a City Engineer, a Chief of the Fire Department, with First, Second and Third Assistants, a Chief of Police, City Marshal and a large police force, two Boards of Mining Brokers, a dozen breweries and half a dozen jails and station-houses in full operation, and some talk of building a church. The "flush times" were in magnificent flower! Large fire-proof brick buildings were going up in the principal streets, and the wooden suburbs were spreading out in all directions. Town lots soared up to prices that were amazing.

The great "Comstock lode" stretched its opulent length straight through the town from north to south, and every mine on it was in diligent process of development. One of these mines alone employed six hundred and seventy-five men, and in the matter of elections the adage was, "as the 'Gould and Curry' goes, so goes the city." Laboring men's wages were four and six dollars a day, and they worked in three "shifts" or gangs, and the blasting and picking and shoveling went on without ceasing, night and day.

The "city" of Virginia roosted royally midway up the steep side of Mount Davidson, seven thousand two hundred feet above the level of the sea, and in the clear Nevada atmosphere was visible from a distance of fifty miles! It claimed a population of fifteen thousand to eighteen thousand, and all day long half of this little army swarmed the streets like bees and the other half swarmed among the drifts and tunnels of the "Comstock," hundreds of feet down in the earth directly under those same streets. Often we felt our chairs jar, and heard the faint boom of a blast down in the bowels of the earth under the office.

The mountain side was so steep that the entire town had a slant to it like a roof. Each street was a terrace, and from each to the next street below the descent was forty or fifty feet. The fronts of the houses were level with the street they faced, but their rear first floors were propped on lofty stilts; a man could stand at a rear first floor window of a C street house and look down the chimneys of the row of houses below him facing D street. It was a laborious climb, in that thin atmosphere, to ascend from D to A street, and you were panting and out of breath when you got there; but you could turn around and go down again like a house a-fire—so to speak. The atmosphere was so rarified, on account of the great altitude, that one's blood lay near the surface always, and the scratch of a pin was a disaster worth worrying about, for the chances were that a grievous erysipelas would ensue. But to offset this, the thin atmosphere seemed to carry healing to gunshot wounds, and therefore, to simply shoot your adversary through both lungs was a thing not likely to afford you any permanent satisfaction, for he would be nearly certain to be around looking for you within the month, and not with an opera glass, either.

From Virginia's airy situation one could look over a vast, far-reaching panorama of mountain ranges and deserts; and whether the day was bright or overcast, whether the sun was rising or setting, or flaming in the zenith, or whether night and the moon held sway, the spectacle was always impressive and beautiful. Over your head Mount Davidson lifted its gray dome, and before and below you a rugged canyon clove the battlemented hills, making a sombre gateway through which a soft-tinted desert was glimpsed, with the silver thread of a river winding through it, bordered with trees which many miles of distance diminished to a delicate fringe; and still further away the snowy mountains rose up and stretched their long barrier to the filmy horizon—far enough beyond a lake that burned in the desert like a fallen sun, though that, itself, lay fifty miles removed. Look from your window where you would, there was fascination in the picture. At rare intervals—but very rare—there were clouds in our skies, and then the setting sun would gild and flush and glorify this mighty expanse of scenery with a bewildering pomp of color that held the eye like a spell and moved the spirit like music.

CHAPTER XLIV.

My salary was increased to forty dollars a week. But I seldom drew it. I had plenty of other resources, and what were two broad twenty-dollar gold pieces to a man who had his pockets full of such and a cumbersome abundance of bright half dollars besides? [Paper money has never come into use on the Pacific coast.] Reporting was lucrative, and every man in town was lavish with his money and his "feet." The city and all the great mountain side were riddled with mining shafts. There were more mines than miners. True, not ten of these mines were yielding rock worth hauling to a mill, but everybody said, "Wait till the shaft gets down where the ledge comes in solid, and then you will see!" So nobody was discouraged. These were nearly all "wild cat" mines, and wholly worthless, but nobody believed it then. The "Ophir," the "Gould & Curry," the "Mexican," and other great mines on the Comstock lead in Virginia and Gold Hill were turning out huge piles of rich rock every day, and every man believed that his little wild cat claim was as good as any on the "main lead" and would infallibly be worth a thousand dollars a foot when he "got down where it came in solid." Poor fellow, he was blessedly blind to the fact that he never would see that day. So the thousand wild cat shafts burrowed deeper and deeper into the earth day by day, and all men were beside themselves with hope and happiness. How they labored, prophesied, exulted! Surely nothing like it was ever seen before since the world began. Every one of these wild cat mines—not mines, but holes in the ground over imaginary mines—was incorporated and had handsomely engraved "stock" and the stock was salable, too. It was bought and sold with a feverish avidity in the boards every day. You could go up on the mountain side, scratch around and find a ledge (there was no lack of them), put up a "notice" with a grandiloquent name in it, start a shaft, get your stock printed, and with nothing whatever to prove that your mine was worth a straw, you could put your stock on the market and sell out for hundreds and even thousands of dollars. To make money, and make it fast, was as easy as it was

to eat your dinner.

Every man owned "feet" in fifty different wild cat mines and considered his fortune made. Think of a city with not one solitary poor man in it! One would suppose that when month after month went by and still not a wild cat mine (by wild cat I mean, in general terms, any claim not located on the mother vein, i.e., the "Comstock") yielded a ton of rock worth crushing, the people would begin to wonder if they were not putting too much faith in their prospective riches; but there was not a thought of such a thing. They burrowed away, bought and sold, and were happy.

New claims were taken up daily, and it was the friendly custom to run straight to the newspaper offices, give the reporter forty or fifty "feet," and get them to go and examine the mine and publish a notice of it. They did not care a fig what you said about the property so you said something. Consequently we generally said a word or two to the effect that the "indications" were good, or that the ledge was "six feet wide," or that the rock "resembled the Comstock" (and so it did—but as a general thing the resemblance was not startling enough to knock you down). If the rock was moderately promising, we followed the custom of the country, used strong adjectives and frothed at the mouth as if a very marvel in silver discoveries had transpired. If the mine was a "developed" one, and had no pay ore to show (and of course it hadn't), we praised the tunnel; said it was one of the most infatuating tunnels in the land; driveled and driveled about the tunnel till we ran entirely out of ecstasies—but never said a word about the rock. We would squander half a column of adulation on a shaft, or a new wire rope, or a dressed pine windlass, or a fascinating force pump, and close with a burst of admiration of the "gentlemanly and efficient Superintendent" of the mine — but never utter a whisper about the rock. And those people were always pleased, always satisfied. Occasionally we patched up and varnished our reputation for discrimination and stern, undeviating accuracy, by giving some old abandoned claim a blast that ought to have made its dry bones rattle—and then somebody would seize it and sell it on the fleeting notoriety thus conferred upon it.

There was nothing in the shape of a mining claim that was not salable. We received presents of "feet" every day. If we needed a hundred dollars or so, we sold some; if not, we hoarded it away, satisfied that it would ultimately be worth a thousand dollars a foot. I had a trunk about half full of "stock." When a claim made a stir in the market and went up to a high figure, I searched through my pile to see if I had any of its stock —and generally found it.

The prices rose and fell constantly; but still a fall disturbed us little, because a thousand dollars a foot was our figure, and so we were content to let it fluctuate as much as it pleased till it reached it. My pile of stock was not all given to me by people who wished their claims "noticed." At least half of it was given me by persons who had no thought of such a thing, and looked for nothing more than a simple verbal "thank you;" and you were not even obliged by law to furnish that. If you are coming up the street with a couple of baskets of apples in your hands, and you meet a friend, you naturally invite him to take a few. That describes the condition of things in Virginia in the "flush times." Every man had his pockets full of stock, and it was the actual custom of the country to part with small quantities of it to friends without the asking.

Very often it was a good idea to close the transaction instantly, when a man offered a stock present to a friend, for the offer was only good and binding at that moment, and if the price went up to a high figure shortly afterward the procrastination was a thing to be regretted. Mr. Stewart (Senator, now, from Nevada) one day told me he would give me twenty feet of "Justis" stock if I would walk over to his office. It was worth five or ten dollars a foot. I asked him to make the offer good for next day, as I was just going to dinner. He said he would not be in town; so I risked it and took my dinner instead of the stock. Within the week the price went up to seventy dollars and afterward to a hundred and fifty, but nothing could make that man yield. I suppose he sold that stock of mine and placed the guilty proceeds in his own pocket. [My revenge will be found in the accompanying portrait.] I met three friends one afternoon, who said they had been buying "Overman" stock at auction at eight dollars a foot. One said if I would come up to his office he would give me fifteen feet; another said he would add fifteen; the third said he would do the same. But I was going after an inquest and could not stop. A few weeks afterward they sold all their "Overman" at six hundred dollars a foot and generously came around to tell me about it—and also to urge me to accept of the next forty-five feet of it that people tried to force on me.

These are actual facts, and I could make the list a long one and still confine myself strictly to the truth. Many a time friends gave us as much as twenty-five feet of stock that was selling at twenty-five dollars a foot, and they thought no more of it than they would of offering a guest a cigar. These were "flush times" indeed! I thought they were going to last always, but somehow I never was much of a prophet.

To show what a wild spirit possessed the mining brain of the community, I will remark that "claims" were actually "located" in excavations for cellars, where the pick had exposed what seemed to be quartz veins—and not cellars in the suburbs, either, but in the very heart of the city; and forthwith stock would be issued and thrown on the market. It was small matter who the cellar belonged to—the "ledge" belonged to the finder, and unless the United States government interfered (inasmuch as the government holds the primary right to mines of the noble metals in Nevada—or at least did then), it was considered to be his privilege to work it. Imagine a stranger staking out a mining claim among the costly shrubbery in your front yard and calmly proceeding to lay waste the ground with pick and shovel and blasting powder! It has been often done in California. In the middle of one of the principal business streets of Virginia, a man "located" a mining claim and began a shaft on it. He gave me a hundred feet of the stock and I sold it for a fine suit of clothes because I was afraid somebody would fall down the shaft and sue for damages. I owned in another claim that was located in the middle of another street; and to show how absurd people can be, that "East India" stock (as it was called) sold briskly although there was an ancient tunnel running directly under the claim and any man could go into it and see that it did not cut a quartz ledge or anything that remotely resembled one.

One plan of acquiring sudden wealth was to "salt" a wild cat claim and sell out while the excitement was up. The process was simple.

The schemer located a worthless ledge, sunk a shaft on it, bought a wagon load of rich "Comstock" ore, dumped a portion of it into the shaft and piled the rest by its side, above ground. Then he showed the property to a simpleton and sold it to him at a high figure. Of course the wagon load of rich ore was all that the victim ever got out of his purchase. A most remarkable case of "salting" was that of the "North Ophir." It

was claimed that this vein was a "remote extension" of the original "Ophir," a valuable mine on the "Comstock." For a few days everybody was talking about the rich developments in the North Ophir. It was said that it yielded perfectly pure silver in small, solid lumps. I went to the place with the owners, and found a shaft six or eight feet deep, in the bottom of which was a badly shattered vein of dull, yellowish, unpromising rock. One would as soon expect to find silver in a grindstone. We got out a pan of the rubbish and washed it in a puddle, and sure enough, among the sediment we found half a dozen black, bullet-looking pellets of unimpeachable "native" silver. Nobody had ever heard of such a thing before; science could not account for such a queer novelty. The stock rose to sixty-five dollars a foot, and at this figure the world-renowned tragedian, McKean Buchanan, bought a commanding interest and prepared to quit the stage once more—he was always doing that. And then it transpired that the mine had been "salted"—and not in any hackneyed way, either, but in a singularly bold, barefaced and peculiarly original and outrageous fashion. On one of the lumps of "native" silver was discovered the minted legend, "TED STATES OF," and then it was plainly apparent that the mine had been "salted" with melted half-dollars! The lumps thus obtained had been blackened till they resembled native silver, and were then mixed with the shattered rock in the bottom of the shaft. It is literally true. Of course the price of the stock at once fell to nothing, and the tragedian was ruined. But for this calamity we might have lost McKean Buchanan from the stage.

CHAPTER XLV.

The "flush times" held bravely on. Something over two years before, Mr. Goodman and another journeyman printer, had borrowed forty dollars and set out from San Francisco to try their fortunes in the new city of Virginia. They found the Territorial Enterprise, a poverty-stricken weekly journal, gasping for breath and likely to die. They bought it, type, fixtures, good-will and all, for a thousand dollars, on long time. The editorial sanctum, news-room, press-room, publication office, bed-chamber, parlor, and kitchen were all compressed into one apartment and it was a small one, too. The editors and printers slept on the floor, a Chinaman did their cooking, and the "imposing-stone" was the general dinner table. But now things were changed. The paper was a great daily, printed by steam; there were five editors and twenty-three compositors; the subscription price was sixteen dollars a year; the advertising rates were exorbitant, and the columns crowded. The paper was clearing from six to ten thousand dollars a month, and the "Enterprise Building" was finished and ready for occupation—a stately fireproof brick. Every day from five all the way up to eleven columns of "live" advertisements were left out or crowded into spasmodic and irregular "supplements."

The "Gould & Curry" company were erecting a monster hundred-stamp mill at a cost that ultimately fell little short of a million dollars. Gould & Curry stock paid heavy dividends—a rare thing, and an experience confined to the dozen or fifteen claims located on the "main lead," the "Comstock." The Superintendent of the Gould & Curry lived, rent free, in a fine house built and furnished by the company. He drove a fine pair of horses which were a present from the company, and his salary was twelve thousand dollars a year. The superintendent of another of the great mines traveled in grand state, had a salary of twenty-eight thousand dollars a year, and in a law suit in after days claimed that he was to have had one per cent. on the gross yield of the bullion likewise.

Money was wonderfully plenty. The trouble was, not how to get it,—but how to spend it, how to lavish it, get rid of it, squander it. And so it was a happy thing that just at this juncture the news came over the wires that a great United States Sanitary Commission had been formed and money was wanted for the relief of the wounded sailors and soldiers of the Union languishing in the Eastern hospitals. Right on the heels of it came word that San Francisco had responded superbly before the telegram was half a day old. Virginia rose as one man! A Sanitary Committee was hurriedly organized, and its chairman mounted a vacant cart in C street and tried to make the clamorous multitude understand that the rest of the committee were flying hither and thither and working with all their might and main, and that if the town would only wait an hour, an office would be ready, books opened, and the Commission prepared to receive contributions. His voice was drowned and his information lost in a ceaseless roar of cheers, and demands that the money be received now —they swore they would not wait. The chairman pleaded and argued, but, deaf to all entreaty, men plowed their way through the throng and rained checks of gold coin into the cart and skurried away for more. Hands clutching money, were thrust aloft out of the jam by men who hoped this eloquent appeal would cleave a road their strugglings could not open. The very Chinamen and Indians caught the excitement and dashed their half dollars into the cart without knowing or caring what it was all about. Women plunged into the crowd, trimly attired, fought their way to the cart with their coin, and emerged again, by and by, with their apparel in a state of hopeless dilapidation. It was the wildest mob Virginia had ever seen and the most determined and ungovernable; and when at last it abated its fury and dispersed, it had not a penny in its pocket.

To use its own phraseology, it came there "flush" and went away "busted."

After that, the Commission got itself into systematic working order, and for weeks the contributions flowed into its treasury in a generous stream. Individuals and all sorts of organizations levied upon themselves a regular weekly tax for the sanitary fund, graduated according to their means, and there was not another grand universal outburst till the famous "Sanitary Flour Sack" came our way. Its history is peculiar and interesting. A former schoolmate of mine, by the name of Reuel Gridley, was living at the little city of Austin, in the Reese river country, at this time, and was the Democratic candidate for mayor. He and the Republican candidate made an agreement that the defeated man should be publicly presented with a fifty-pound sack of flour by the successful one, and should carry it home on his shoulder. Gridley was defeated. The new mayor gave him the sack of flour, and he shouldered it and carried it a mile or two, from Lower Austin to his home in Upper Austin, attended by a band of music and the whole population. Arrived there, he said he did not need the flour, and asked what the people thought he had better do with it. A voice said:

"Sell it to the highest bidder, for the benefit of the Sanitary fund."

The suggestion was greeted with a round of applause, and Gridley mounted a dry-goods box and assumed the role of auctioneer. The bids went higher and higher, as the sympathies of the pioneers awoke and expanded, till at last the sack was knocked down to a mill man at two hundred and fifty dollars, and his check taken. He was asked where he would have the flour delivered, and he said:

"Nowhere—sell it again."

Now the cheers went up royally, and the multitude were fairly in the spirit of the thing. So Gridley stood there and shouted and perspired till the sun went down; and when the crowd dispersed he had sold the sack to three hundred different people, and had taken in eight thousand dollars in gold. And still the flour sack was in his possession.

The news came to Virginia, and a telegram went back:

"Fetch along your flour sack!"

Thirty-six hours afterward Gridley arrived, and an afternoon mass meeting was held in the Opera House, and the auction began. But the sack had come sooner than it was expected; the people were not thoroughly aroused, and the sale dragged. At nightfall only five thousand dollars had been secured, and there was a crestfallen feeling in the community. However, there was no disposition to let the matter rest here and acknowledge vanquishment at the hands of the village of Austin. Till late in the night the principal citizens were at work arranging the morrow's campaign, and when they went to bed they had no fears for the result. At eleven the next morning a procession of open carriages, attended by clamorous bands of music and adorned with a moving display of flags, filed along C street and was soon in danger of blockade by a huzzaing multitude of citizens. In the first carriage sat Gridley, with the flour sack in prominent view, the latter splendid with bright paint and gilt lettering; also in the same carriage sat the mayor and the recorder. The other carriages contained the Common Council, the editors and reporters, and other people of imposing consequence. The crowd pressed to the corner of C and Taylor streets, expecting the sale to begin there, but they were disappointed, and also unspeakably surprised; for the cavalcade moved on as if Virginia had ceased to be of importance, and took its way over the "divide," toward the small town of Gold Hill. Telegrams had gone ahead to Gold Hill, Silver City and Dayton, and those communities were at fever heat and rife for the conflict. It was a very hot day, and wonderfully dusty. At the end of a short half hour we descended into Gold Hill with drums beating and colors flying, and enveloped in imposing clouds of dust. The whole population—men, women and children, Chinamen and Indians, were massed in the main street, all the flags in town were at the mast head, and the blare of the bands was drowned in cheers. Gridley stood up and asked who would make the first bid for the National Sanitary Flour Sack. Gen. W. said:

"The Yellow Jacket silver mining company offers a thousand dollars, coin!"

A tempest of applause followed. A telegram carried the news to Virginia, and fifteen minutes afterward that city's population was massed in the streets devouring the tidings— for it was part of the programme that the bulletin boards should do a good work that day. Every few minutes a new dispatch was bulletined from Gold Hill, and still the excitement grew. Telegrams began to return to us from Virginia beseeching Gridley to bring back the flour sack; but such was not the plan of the campaign. At the end of an hour Gold Hill's small population had paid a figure for the flour sack that awoke all the enthusiasm of Virginia when the grand total was displayed upon the bulletin boards. Then the Gridley cavalcade moved on, a giant refreshed with new lager beer and plenty of it—for the people brought it to the carriages without waiting to measure it—and within three hours more the expedition had carried Silver City and Dayton by storm and was on its way back covered with glory. Every move had been telegraphed and bulletined, and as the procession entered Virginia and filed down C street at half past eight in the evening the town was abroad in the thoroughfares, torches were glaring, flags flying, bands playing, cheer on cheer cleaving the air, and the city ready to surrender at discretion. The auction began, every bid was greeted with bursts of applause, and at the end of two hours and a half a population of fifteen thousand souls had paid in coin for a fifty-pound sack of flour a sum equal to forty thousand dollars in greenbacks! It was at a rate in the neighborhood of three dollars for each man, woman and child of the population. The grand total would have been twice as large, but the streets were very narrow, and hundreds who wanted to bid could not get within a block of the stand, and could not make themselves heard. These grew tired of waiting and many of them went home long before the auction was over. This was the greatest day Virginia ever saw, perhaps.

Gridley sold the sack in Carson city and several California towns; also in San Francisco. Then he took it east and sold it in one or two Atlantic cities, I think. I am not sure of that, but I know that he finally carried it to St. Louis, where a monster Sanitary Fair was being held, and after selling it there for a large sum and helping on the enthusiasm by displaying the portly silver bricks which Nevada's donation had produced, he had the flour baked up into small cakes and retailed them at high prices.

It was estimated that when the flour sack's mission was ended it had been sold for a grand total of a hundred and fifty thousand dollars in greenbacks! This is probably the only instance on record where common family flour brought three thousand dollars a pound in the public market.

It is due to Mr. Gridley's memory to mention that the expenses of his sanitary flour sack expedition of fifteen thousand miles, going and returning, were paid in large part if not entirely, out of his own pocket. The time he gave to it was not less than three months. Mr. Gridley was a soldier in the Mexican war and a pioneer Californian. He died at Stockton, California, in December, 1870, greatly regretted.

CHAPTER XLVI.

There were nabobs in those days—in the "flush times," I mean. Every rich strike in the mines created one or two. I call to mind several of these. They were careless, easy-going fellows, as a general thing, and the community at large was as much benefited by their riches as they were themselves—possibly more, in some cases.

Two cousins, teamsters, did some hauling for a man and had to take a small segregated portion of a silver mine in lieu of $300 cash. They gave an outsider a third to open the mine, and they went on teaming. But not long. Ten months afterward the mine was out of debt and paying each owner $8,000 to $10,000 a month—say $100,000 a year.

One of the earliest nabobs that Nevada was delivered of wore $6,000 worth of diamonds in his bosom, and swore he was unhappy because he could not spend his money as fast as he made it.

Another Nevada nabob boasted an income that often reached $16,000 a month; and he used to love to tell how he had worked in the very mine that yielded it, for five dollars a day, when he first came to the country.

The silver and sage-brush State has knowledge of another of these pets of fortune—lifted from actual poverty to affluence almost in a single night—who was able to offer $100,000 for a position of high official distinction, shortly afterward, and did offer it—but failed to get it, his politics not being as sound as his bank account.

Then there was John Smith. He was a good, honest, kind-hearted soul, born and reared in the lower ranks of life, and miraculously ignorant. He drove a team, and owned a small ranch—a ranch that paid him a comfortable living, for although it yielded but little hay, what little it did yield was worth from $250 to $300 in gold per ton in the market. Presently Smith traded a few acres of the ranch for a small undeveloped silver mine in Gold Hill. He opened the mine and built a little unpretending ten-stamp mill. Eighteen months afterward he retired from the hay business, for his mining income had reached a most comfortable figure. Some people said it was $30,000 a month, and others said it was $60,000. Smith was very rich at any rate.

And then he went to Europe and traveled. And when he came back he was never tired of telling about the fine hogs he had seen in England, and the gorgeous sheep he had seen in Spain, and the fine cattle he had noticed in the vicinity of Rome. He was full of wonders of the old world, and advised everybody to travel. He said a man never imagined what surprising things there were in the world till he had traveled.

One day, on board ship, the passengers made up a pool of $500, which was to be the property of the man who should come nearest to guessing the run of the vessel for the next twenty-four hours. Next day, toward noon, the figures were all in the purser's hands in sealed envelopes. Smith was serene and happy, for he had been bribing the engineer. But another party won the prize! Smith said:

"Here, that won't do! He guessed two miles wider of the mark than I did."

The purser said, "Mr. Smith, you missed it further than any man on board. We traveled two hundred and eight miles yesterday."

"Well, sir," said Smith, "that's just where I've got you, for I guessed two hundred and nine. If you'll look at my figgers again you'll find a 2 and two o's, which stands for 200, don't it?—and after 'em you'll find a 9 (2009), which stands for two hundred and nine. I reckon I'll take that money, if you please."

The Gould & Curry claim comprised twelve hundred feet, and it all belonged originally to the two men whose names it bears. Mr. Curry owned two thirds of it—and he said that he sold it out for twenty-five hundred dollars in cash, and an old plug horse that ate up his market value in hay and barley in seventeen days by the watch. And he said that Gould sold out for a pair of second-hand government blankets and a bottle of whisky that killed nine men in three hours, and that an unoffending stranger that smelt the cork was disabled for life. Four years afterward the mine thus disposed of was worth in the San Francisco market seven millions six hundred thousand dollars in gold coin.

In the early days a poverty-stricken Mexican who lived in a canyon directly back of Virginia City, had a stream of water as large as a man's wrist trickling from the hill-side on his premises. The Ophir Company segregated a hundred feet of their mine and traded it to him for the stream of water. The hundred feet proved to be the richest part of the entire mine; four years after the swap, its market value (including its mill) was $1,500,000.

An individual who owned twenty feet in the Ophir mine before its great riches were revealed to men, traded it for a horse, and a very sorry looking brute he was, too. A year or so afterward, when Ophir stock went up to $3,000 a foot, this man, who had not a cent, used to say he was the most startling example of magnificence and misery the world had ever seen—because he was able to ride a sixty-thousand-dollar horse—yet could not scrape up cash enough to buy a saddle, and was obliged to borrow one or ride bareback. He said if fortune were to give him another sixty-thousand-dollar horse it would ruin him.

A youth of nineteen, who was a telegraph operator in Virginia on a salary of a hundred dollars a month, and who, when he could not make out German names in the list of San Francisco steamer arrivals, used to ingeniously select and supply substitutes for them out of an old Berlin city directory, made himself rich by watching the mining telegrams that passed through his hands and buying and selling stocks accordingly, through a friend in San Francisco. Once when a private dispatch was sent from Virginia announcing a rich strike in a prominent mine and advising that the matter be kept secret till a large amount of the stock could be secured, he bought forty "feet" of the stock at twenty dollars a foot, and afterward sold half of it at eight hundred dollars a foot and the rest at double that figure. Within three months he was worth $150,000, and had resigned his telegraphic position.

Another telegraph operator who had been discharged by the company for divulging the secrets of the office, agreed with a moneyed man in San Francisco to furnish him the result of a great Virginia mining lawsuit within an hour after its private reception by the parties to it in San Francisco. For this he was to have a large percentage of the profits on purchases and sales made on it by his fellow-conspirator. So he went, disguised as a teamster, to a little wayside telegraph office in the mountains, got acquainted with the operator, and sat in the office day after day, smoking his pipe, complaining that his team was fagged out and unable to travel—and meantime listening to the dispatches as they passed clicking through the machine from Virginia. Finally the private dispatch announcing the result of the lawsuit sped over the wires, and as soon as he heard it he telegraphed his friend in San Francisco:

"Am tired waiting. Shall sell the team and go home."

It was the signal agreed upon. The word "waiting" left out, would have signified that the suit had gone the other way.

The mock teamster's friend picked up a deal of the mining stock, at low figures, before the news became public, and a fortune was the result.

For a long time after one of the great Virginia mines had been incorporated, about fifty feet of the original location were still in the hands of a man who had never signed the incorporation papers. The stock became very valuable, and every effort was made to find this man, but he had disappeared. Once it was heard that he was in New York, and one or two speculators went east but failed to find him. Once the news came that he was in the Bermudas, and straightway a speculator or two hurried east and sailed for Bermuda—but he was not there. Finally he was heard of in Mexico, and a friend of his, a bar-

keeper on a salary, scraped together a little money and sought him out, bought his "feet" for a hundred dollars, returned and sold the property for $75,000.

But why go on? The traditions of Silverland are filled with instances like these, and I would never get through enumerating them were I to attempt do it. I only desired to give, the reader an idea of a peculiarity of the "flush times" which I could not present so strikingly in any other way, and which some mention of was necessary to a realizing comprehension of the time and the country.

I was personally acquainted with the majority of the nabobs I have referred to, and so, for old acquaintance sake, I have shifted their occupations and experiences around in such a way as to keep the Pacific public from recognizing these once notorious men. No longer notorious, for the majority of them have drifted back into poverty and obscurity again.

In Nevada there used to be current the story of an adventure of two of her nabobs, which may or may not have occurred. I give it for what it is worth:

Col. Jim had seen somewhat of the world, and knew more or less of its ways; but Col. Jack was from the back settlements of the States, had led a life of arduous toil, and had never seen a city. These two, blessed with sudden wealth, projected a visit to New York,—Col. Jack to see the sights, and Col. Jim to guard his unsophistication from misfortune. They reached San Francisco in the night, and sailed in the morning. Arrived in New York, Col. Jack said:

"I've heard tell of carriages all my life, and now I mean to have a ride in one; I don't care what it costs. Come along."

They stepped out on the sidewalk, and Col. Jim called a stylish barouche. But Col. Jack said:

"No, sir! None of your cheap-John turn-outs for me. I'm here to have a good time, and money ain't any object. I mean to have the nobbiest rig that's going. Now here comes the very trick. Stop that yaller one with the pictures on it—don't you fret—I'll stand all the expenses myself."

So Col. Jim stopped an empty omnibus, and they got in. Said Col. Jack:

"Ain't it gay, though? Oh, no, I reckon not! Cushions, and windows, and pictures, till you can't rest. What would the boys say if they could see us cutting a swell like this in New York? By George, I wish they could see us."

Then he put his head out of the window, and shouted to the driver:

"Say, Johnny, this suits me!—suits yours truly, you bet, you! I want this shebang all day. I'm on it, old man! Let 'em out! Make 'em go! We'll make it all right with you, sonny!"

The driver passed his hand through the strap-hole, and tapped for his fare—it was before the gongs came into common use. Col. Jack took the hand, and shook it cordially. He said:

"You twig me, old pard! All right between gents. Smell of that, and see how you like it!"

And he put a twenty-dollar gold piece in the driver's hand. After a moment the driver said he could not make change.

"Bother the change! Ride it out. Put it in your pocket."

Then to Col. Jim, with a sounding slap on his thigh:

"Ain't it style, though? Hanged if I don't hire this thing every day for a week."

The omnibus stopped, and a young lady got in. Col. Jack stared a moment, then nudged Col. Jim with his elbow:

"Don't say a word," he whispered. "Let her ride, if she wants to. Gracious, there's room enough."

The young lady got out her porte-monnaie, and handed her fare to Col. Jack.

"What's this for?" said he.

"Give it to the driver, please."

"Take back your money, madam. We can't allow it. You're welcome to ride here as long as you please, but this shebang's chartered, and we can't let you pay a cent."

The girl shrunk into a corner, bewildered. An old lady with a basket climbed in, and proffered her fare.

"Excuse me," said Col. Jack. "You're perfectly welcome here, madam, but we can't allow you to pay. Set right down there, mum, and don't you be the least uneasy. Make yourself just as free as if you was in your own turn-out."

Within two minutes, three gentlemen, two fat women, and a couple of children, entered.

"Come right along, friends," said Col. Jack; "don't mind us. This is a free blow-out." Then he whispered to Col. Jim,

"New York ain't no sociable place, I don't reckon—it ain't no name for it!"

He resisted every effort to pass fares to the driver, and made everybody cordially welcome. The situation dawned on the people, and they pocketed their money, and delivered themselves up to covert enjoyment of the episode. Half a dozen more passengers entered.

"Oh, there's plenty of room," said Col. Jack. "Walk right in, and make yourselves at home. A blow-out ain't worth anything as a blow-out, unless a body has company." Then in a whisper to Col. Jim: "But ain't these New Yorkers friendly? And ain't they cool about it, too? Icebergs ain't anywhere. I reckon they'd tackle a hearse, if it was going their way."

More passengers got in; more yet, and still more. Both seats were filled, and a file of men were standing up, holding on to the cleats overhead. Parties with baskets and bundles were climbing up on the roof. Half-suppressed laughter rippled up from all sides.

"Well, for clean, cool, out-and-out cheek, if this don't bang anything that ever I saw, I'm an Injun!" whispered Col. Jack.

A Chinaman crowded his way in.

"I weaken!" said Col. Jack. "Hold on, driver! Keep your seats, ladies, and gents. Just make yourselves free—everything's paid for. Driver, rustle these folks around as long as they're a mind to go—friends of ours, you know. Take them everywheres—and if you want more money, come to the St. Nicholas, and we'll make it all right. Pleasant journey to you, ladies and gents—go it just as long as you please—it shan't cost you a cent!"

The two comrades got out, and Col. Jack said:

"Jimmy, it's the sociablest place I ever saw. The Chinaman waltzed in as comfortable as anybody. If we'd staid awhile, I reckon we'd had some niggers. B' George, we'll have to barricade our doors to-night, or some of these ducks will be trying to sleep with us."

CHAPTER XLVII.

Somebody has said that in order to know a community, one must observe the style of its funerals and know what manner of men they bury with most ceremony. I cannot say which class we buried with most eclat in our "flush times," the distinguished public benefactor or the distinguished rough—possibly the two chief grades or grand divisions of society honored their illustrious dead about equally; and hence, no doubt the philosopher I have quoted from would have needed to see two representative funerals in Virginia before forming his estimate of the people.

There was a grand time over Buck Fanshaw when he died. He was a representative citizen. He had "killed his man"—not in his own quarrel, it is true, but in defence of a stranger unfairly beset by numbers. He had kept a sumptuous saloon. He had been the proprietor of a dashing helpmeet whom he could have discarded without the formality of a divorce. He had held a high position in the fire department and been a very Warwick in politics. When he died there was great lamentation throughout the town, but especially in the vast bottom-stratum of society.

On the inquest it was shown that Buck Fanshaw, in the delirium of a wasting typhoid fever, had taken arsenic, shot himself through the body, cut his throat, and jumped out of a four-story window and broken his neck—and after due deliberation, the jury, sad and tearful, but with intelligence unblinded by its sorrow, brought in a verdict of death "by the visitation of God." What could the world do without juries?

Prodigious preparations were made for the funeral. All the vehicles in town were hired, all the saloons put in mourning, all the municipal and fire-company flags hung at half-mast, and all the firemen ordered to muster in uniform and bring their machines duly draped in black. Now —let us remark in parenthesis—as all the peoples of the earth had representative adventurers in the Silverland, and as each adventurer had brought the slang of his nation or his locality with him, the combination made the slang of Nevada the richest and the most infinitely varied and copious that had ever existed anywhere in the world, perhaps, except in the mines of California in the "early days." Slang was the language of Nevada. It was hard to preach a sermon without it, and be understood. Such phrases as "You bet!" "Oh, no, I reckon not!" "No Irish need apply," and a hundred others, became so common as to fall from the lips of a speaker unconsciously—and very often when they did not touch the subject under discussion and consequently failed to mean anything.

After Buck Fanshaw's inquest, a meeting of the short-haired brotherhood was held, for nothing can be done on the Pacific coast without a public meeting and an expression of sentiment. Regretful resolutions were passed and various committees appointed; among others, a committee of one was deputed to call on the minister, a fragile, gentle, spiritual new fledgling from an Eastern theological seminary, and as yet unacquainted with the ways of the mines. The committeeman, "Scotty" Briggs, made his visit; and in after days it was worth something to hear the minister tell about it. Scotty was a stalwart rough, whose customary suit, when on weighty official business, like committee work, was a fire helmet, flaming red flannel shirt, patent leather belt with spanner and revolver attached, coat hung over arm, and pants stuffed into boot tops. He formed something of a contrast to the pale theological student. It is fair to say of Scotty, however, in passing, that he had a warm heart, and a strong love for his friends, and never entered into a quarrel when he could reasonably keep out of it. Indeed, it was commonly said that whenever one of Scotty's fights was investigated, it always turned out that it had originally been no affair of his, but that out of native good-heartedness he had dropped in of his own accord to help the man who was getting the worst of it. He and Buck Fanshaw were bosom friends, for years, and had often taken adventurous "pot-luck" together. On one occasion, they had thrown off their coats and taken the weaker side in a fight among strangers, and after gaining a hard-earned victory, turned and found that the men they were helping had deserted early, and not only that, but had stolen their coats and made off with them! But to return to Scotty's visit to the minister. He was on a sorrowful mission, now, and his face was the picture of woe. Being admitted to the presence he sat down before the clergyman, placed his fire-hat on an unfinished manuscript sermon under the minister's nose, took from it a red silk handkerchief, wiped his brow and heaved a sigh of dismal impressiveness, explanatory of his business.

He choked, and even shed tears; but with an effort he mastered his voice and said in lugubrious tones:

"Are you the duck that runs the gospel-mill next door?"

"Am I the—pardon me, I believe I do not understand?"

With another sigh and a half-sob, Scotty rejoined:

"Why you see we are in a bit of trouble, and the boys thought maybe you would give us a lift, if we'd tackle you—that is, if I've got the rights of it and you are the head clerk of the doxology-works next door."

"I am the shepherd in charge of the flock whose fold is next door."

"The which?"

"The spiritual adviser of the little company of believers whose sanctuary adjoins these premises."

Scotty scratched his head, reflected a moment, and then said:

"You ruther hold over me, pard. I reckon I can't call that hand. Ante and pass the buck."

"How? I beg pardon. What did I understand you to say?"

"Well, you've ruther got the bulge on me. Or maybe we've both got the bulge, somehow. You don't smoke me and I don't smoke you. You see, one of the boys has passed in his checks and we want to give him a good send-off, and so the thing I'm on now is to roust out somebody to jerk a little chin-music for

us and waltz him through handsome."

"My friend, I seem to grow more and more bewildered. Your observations are wholly incomprehensible to me. Cannot you simplify them in some way? At first I thought perhaps I understood you, but I grope now. Would it not expedite matters if you restricted yourself to categorical statements of fact unencumbered with obstructing accumulations of metaphor and allegory?"

Another pause, and more reflection. Then, said Scotty:

"I'll have to pass, I judge."

"How?"

"You've raised me out, pard."

"I still fail to catch your meaning."

"Why, that last lead of yourn is too many for me—that's the idea. I can't neither-trump nor follow suit."

The clergyman sank back in his chair perplexed. Scotty leaned his head on his hand and gave himself up to thought.

Presently his face came up, sorrowful but confident.

"I've got it now, so's you can savvy," he said. "What we want is a gospel-sharp. See?"

"A what?"

"Gospel-sharp. Parson."

"Oh! Why did you not say so before? I am a clergyman—a parson."

"Now you talk! You see my blind and straddle it like a man. Put it there!"—extending a brawny paw, which closed over the minister's small hand and gave it a shake indicative of fraternal sympathy and fervent gratification.

"Now we're all right, pard. Let's start fresh. Don't you mind my snuffling a little—becuz we're in a power of trouble. You see, one of the boys has gone up the flume—"

"Gone where?"

"Up the flume—throwed up the sponge, you understand."

"Thrown up the sponge?"

"Yes—kicked the bucket—"

"Ah—has departed to that mysterious country from whose bourne no traveler returns."

"Return! I reckon not. Why pard, he's dead!"

"Yes, I understand."

"Oh, you do? Well I thought maybe you might be getting tangled some more. Yes, you see he's dead again—"

"Again? Why, has he ever been dead before?"

"Dead before? No! Do you reckon a man has got as many lives

as a cat? But you bet you he's awful dead now, poor old boy, and I wish I'd never seen this day. I don't want no better friend than Buck Fanshaw. I knowed him by the back; and when I know a man and like him, I freeze to him—you hear me. Take him all round, pard, there never was a bullier man in the mines. No man ever knowed Buck Fanshaw to go back on a friend. But it's all up, you know, it's all up. It ain't no use. They've scooped him."

"Scooped him?"

"Yes—death has. Well, well, well, we've got to give him up. Yes indeed. It's a kind of a hard world, after all, ain't it? But pard, he was a rustler! You ought to seen him get started once. He was a bully boy with a glass eye! Just spit in his face and give him room according to his strength, and it was just beautiful to see him peel and go in. He was the worst son of a thief that ever drawed breath. Pard, he was on it! He was on it bigger than an Injun!"

"On it? On what?"

"On the shoot. On the shoulder. On the fight, you understand. He didn't give a continental for any body. Beg your pardon, friend, for coming so near saying a cuss-word—but you see I'm on an awful strain, in this palaver, on account of having to cramp down and draw everything so mild. But we've got to give him up. There ain't any getting around that, I don't reckon. Now if we can get you to help plant him—"

"Preach the funeral discourse? Assist at the obsequies?"

"Obs'quies is good. Yes. That's it—that's our little game. We are going to get the thing up regardless, you know. He was always nifty himself, and so you bet you his funeral ain't going to be no slouch —solid silver door-plate on his coffin, six plumes on the hearse, and a nigger on the box in a biled shirt and a plug hat—how's that for high? And we'll take care of you, pard. We'll fix you all right. There'll be a kerridge for you; and whatever you want, you just 'scape out and we'll 'tend to it. We've got a shebang fixed up for you to stand behind, in No. 1's house, and don't you be afraid. Just go in and toot your horn, if you don't sell a clam. Put Buck through as bully as you can, pard, for anybody that knowed him will tell you that he was one of the whitest men that was ever in the mines. You can't draw it too strong. He never could stand it to see things going wrong. He's done more to make this town quiet and peaceable than any man in it. I've seen him lick four Greasers in eleven minutes, myself. If a thing wanted regulating, he warn't a man to go browsing around after somebody to do it, but he would prance in and regulate it himself. He warn't a Catholic. Scasely. He was down on 'em. His word was, 'No Irish need apply!' But it didn't make no difference about that when it came down to what a man's rights was—and so, when some roughs jumped the Catholic bone-yard and started in to stake out town-lots in it he went for 'em! And he cleaned 'em, too! I was there, pard, and I seen it myself."

"That was very well indeed—at least the impulse was—whether the act was strictly defensible or not. Had deceased any religious convictions? That is to say, did he feel a dependence upon, or acknowledge allegiance to a higher power?"

More reflection.

"I reckon you've stumped me again, pard. Could you say it over once more, and say it slow?"

"Well, to simplify it somewhat, was he, or rather had he ever been connected with any organization sequestered from secular concerns and devoted to self-sacrifice in the interests of morality?"

"All down but nine—set 'em up on the other alley, pard."

"What did I understand you to say?"

"Why, you're most too many for me, you know. When you get in with your left I hunt grass every time. Every time you draw, you fill; but I don't seem to have any luck. Lets have a new deal."

"How? Begin again?"

"That's it."

"Very well. Was he a good man, and—"

"There—I see that; don't put up another chip till I look at my hand. A good man, says you? Pard, it ain't no name for it. He was the best man that ever—pard, you would have doted on that man. He could lam any galoot of his inches in America. It was him that put down the riot last election before it got a start; and everybody said he was the only man that could have done it. He waltzed in with a spanner in one hand and a trumpet in the other, and sent fourteen men home on a shutter in less than three minutes. He had that riot all broke up and prevented nice before anybody ever got a chance to strike a blow. He was always for peace, and he would have peace—he could not stand disturbances. Pard, he was a great loss to this town. It would please the boys if you could chip in something like that and do him justice. Here once when the Micks got to throwing stones through the Methodis' Sunday school windows, Buck Fanshaw, all of his own notion, shut up his saloon and took a couple of six-shooters and mounted guard over the Sunday school. Says he, 'No Irish need apply!' And they didn't. He was the bulliest man in the mountains, pard! He could run faster, jump higher, hit harder, and hold more tangle-foot whisky without spilling it than any man in seventeen counties. Put that in, pard—it'll please the boys more than anything you could say. And you can say, pard, that he never shook his mother."

"Never shook his mother?"

"That's it—any of the boys will tell you so."

"Well, but why should he shake her?"

"That's what I say—but some people does."

"Not people of any repute?"

"Well, some that averages pretty so-so."

"In my opinion the man that would offer personal violence to his own mother, ought to—"

"Cheese it, pard; you've banked your ball clean outside the string. What I was a drivin' at, was, that he never throwed off on his mother —don't you see? No indeedy. He give her a house to live in, and town lots, and plenty of money; and he looked after her and took care of her all the time; and when she was down with the small-pox I'm d—d if he didn't set up nights and nuss her himself! Beg your pardon for saying it, but it hopped out too quick for yours truly.

"You've treated me like a gentleman, pard, and I ain't the man to hurt your feelings intentional. I think you're white. I think you're a square man, pard. I like you, and I'll lick any man that don't. I'll lick him till he can't tell himself from a last year's corpse! Put it there!" [Another fraternal hand-shake—and exit.]

The obsequies were all that "the boys" could desire. Such a marvel of funeral pomp had never been seen in Virginia. The plumed hearse, the dirge-breathing brass bands, the closed marts of business, the flags drooping at half mast, the long, plodding procession of uniformed secret societies, military battalions and fire companies, draped engines, carriages of officials, and citizens in vehicles and on foot, attracted multitudes of spectators to the sidewalks, roofs and windows; and for years afterward, the degree of grandeur attained by any civic display in Virginia was determined by comparison with Buck Fanshaw's funeral.

Scotty Briggs, as a pall-bearer and a mourner, occupied a prominent place at the funeral, and when the sermon was finished and the last sentence of the prayer for the dead man's soul ascended, he responded, in a low voice, but with feelings:

"AMEN. No Irish need apply."

As the bulk of the response was without apparent relevancy, it was probably nothing more than a humble tribute to the memory of the friend that was gone; for, as Scotty had once said, it was "his word."

Scotty Briggs, in after days, achieved the distinction of becoming the only convert to religion that was ever gathered from the Virginia roughs; and it transpired that the man who had it in him to espouse the quarrel of the weak out of inborn nobility of spirit was no mean timber whereof to construct a Christian. The making him one did not warp his generosity or diminish his courage; on the contrary it gave intelligent direction to the one and a broader field to the other.

If his Sunday-school class progressed faster than the other classes, was it matter for wonder? I think not. He talked to his pioneer small-fry in a language they understood! It was my large privilege, a month before he died, to hear him tell the beautiful story of Joseph and his brethren to his class "without looking at the book." I leave it to the reader to fancy what it was like, as it fell, riddled with slang, from the lips of that grave, earnest teacher, and was listened to by his little learners with a consuming interest that showed that they were as unconscious as he was that any violence was being done to the sacred proprieties!

CHAPTER XLVIII.

The first twenty-six graves in the Virginia cemetery were occupied by murdered men. So everybody said, so everybody believed, and so they will always say and believe. The reason why there was so much slaughtering done, was, that in a new mining district the rough element predominates, and a person is not respected until he has "killed his man." That was the very expression used.

If an unknown individual arrived, they did not inquire if he was capable, honest, industrious, but—had he killed his man? If he had not, he gravitated to his natural and proper position, that of a man of small consequence; if he had, the cordiality of his reception was graduated according to the number of his

dead. It was tedious work struggling up to a position of influence with bloodless hands; but when a man came with the blood of half a dozen men on his soul, his worth was recognized at once and his acquaintance sought.

In Nevada, for a time, the lawyer, the editor, the banker, the chief desperado, the chief gambler, and the saloon keeper, occupied the same level in society, and it was the highest. The cheapest and easiest way to become an influential man and be looked up to by the community at large, was to stand behind a bar, wear a cluster-diamond pin, and sell whisky. I am not sure but that the saloon-keeper held a shade higher rank than any other member of society. His opinion had weight. It was his privilege to say how the elections should go. No great movement could succeed without the countenance and direction of the saloon-keepers. It was a high favor when the chief saloon-keeper consented to serve in the legislature or the board of aldermen.

Youthful ambition hardly aspired so much to the honors of the law, or the army and navy as to the dignity of proprietorship in a saloon.

To be a saloon-keeper and kill a man was to be illustrious. Hence the reader will not be surprised to learn that more than one man was killed in Nevada under hardly the pretext of provocation, so impatient was the slayer to achieve reputation and throw off the galling sense of being held in indifferent repute by his associates. I knew two youths who tried to "kill their men" for no other reason—and got killed themselves for their pains. "There goes the man that killed Bill Adams" was higher praise and a sweeter sound in the ears of this sort of people than any other speech that admiring lips could utter.

The men who murdered Virginia's original twenty-six cemetery-occupants were never punished. Why? Because Alfred the Great, when he invented trial by jury and knew that he had admirably framed it to secure justice in his age of the world, was not aware that in the nineteenth century the condition of things would be so entirely changed that unless he rose from the grave and altered the jury plan to meet the emergency, it would prove the most ingenious and infallible agency for defeating justice that human wisdom could contrive. For how could he imagine that we simpletons would go on using his jury plan after circumstances had stripped it of its usefulness, any more than he could imagine that we would go on using his candle-clock after we had invented chronometers? In his day news could not travel fast, and hence he could easily find a jury of honest, intelligent men who had not heard of the case they were called to try —but in our day of telegraphs and newspapers his plan compels us to swear in juries composed of fools and rascals, because the system rigidly excludes honest men and men of brains.

I remember one of those sorrowful farces, in Virginia, which we call a jury trial. A noted desperado killed Mr. B., a good citizen, in the most wanton and cold-blooded way. Of course the papers were full of it, and all men capable of reading, read about it. And of course all men not deaf and dumb and idiotic, talked about it. A jury-list was made out, and Mr. B. L., a prominent banker and a valued citizen, was questioned precisely as he would have been questioned in any court in America:

"Have you heard of this homicide?"

"Yes."

"Have you held conversations upon the subject?"

"Yes."

"Have you formed or expressed opinions about it?"

"Yes."

"Have you read the newspaper accounts of it?"

"Yes."

"We do not want you."

A minister, intelligent, esteemed, and greatly respected; a merchant of high character and known probity; a mining superintendent of intelligence and unblemished reputation; a quartz mill owner of excellent standing, were all questioned in the same way, and all set aside. Each said the public talk and the newspaper reports had not so biased his mind but that sworn testimony would overthrow his previously formed opinions and enable him to render a verdict without prejudice and in accordance with the facts. But of course such men could not be trusted with the case. Ignoramuses alone could mete out unsullied justice.

When the peremptory challenges were all exhausted, a jury of twelve men was impaneled—a jury who swore they had neither heard, read, talked about nor expressed an opinion concerning a murder which the very cattle in the corrals, the Indians in the sage-brush and the stones in the streets were cognizant of! It was a jury composed of two desperadoes, two low beer-house politicians, three bar-keepers, two ranchmen who could not read, and three dull, stupid, human donkeys! It actually came out afterward, that one of these latter thought that incest and arson were the same thing.

The verdict rendered by this jury was, Not Guilty. What else could one expect?

The jury system puts a ban upon intelligence and honesty, and a premium upon ignorance, stupidity and perjury. It is a shame that we must continue to use a worthless system because it was good a thousand years ago. In this age, when a gentleman of high social standing, intelligence and probity, swears that testimony given under solemn oath will outweigh, with him, street talk and newspaper reports based upon mere hearsay, he is worth a hundred jurymen who will swear to their own ignorance and stupidity, and justice would be far safer in his hands than in theirs. Why could not the jury law be so altered as to give men of brains and honesty and equal chance with fools and miscreants? Is it right to show the present favoritism to one class of men and inflict a disability on another, in a land whose boast is that all its citizens are free and equal? I am a candidate for the legislature. I desire to tamper with the jury law. I wish to so alter it as to put a premium on intelligence and character, and close the jury box against idiots, blacklegs, and people who do not read newspapers. But no doubt I shall be defeated —every effort I make to save the country "misses fire."

My idea, when I began this chapter, was to say something about desperadoism in the "flush times" of Nevada. To attempt a portrayal of that era and that land, and leave out the blood and carnage, would be like portraying Mormondom and leaving out polygamy. The desperado stalked the streets with a swagger graded according to the number of his homicides, and a nod of recognition from him was sufficient to make a humble admirer happy for the rest of the day. The deference that was paid to a desperado of wide reputation, and who "kept his private graveyard," as the phrase went, was marked, and cheerfully accorded. When he moved along the sidewalk in his excessively long-tailed frock-coat, shiny stump-toed boots, and with dainty little slouch hat tipped over left eye, the small-fry roughs made room for his majesty; when he entered the restaurant, the waiters deserted bankers and merchants to overwhelm him with obsequious service; when he shouldered his way to a bar, the shouldered parties wheeled indignantly, recognized him, and —apologized.

They got a look in return that froze their marrow, and by that time a curled and breast-pinned bar keeper was beaming over the counter, proud of the established acquaintanceship that permitted such a familiar form of speech as:

"How're ye, Billy, old fel? Glad to see you. What'll you take—the old thing?"

The "old thing" meant his customary drink, of course.

The best known names in the Territory of Nevada were those belonging to these long-tailed heroes of the revolver. Orators, Governors, capitalists and leaders of the legislature enjoyed a degree of fame, but it seemed local and meagre when contrasted with the fame of such men as Sam Brown, Jack Williams, Billy Mulligan, Farmer Pease, Sugarfoot Mike, Pock Marked Jake, El Dorado Johnny, Jack McNabb, Joe McGee, Jack Harris, Six-fingered Pete, etc., etc. There was a long list of them. They were brave, reckless men, and traveled with their lives in their hands. To give them their due, they did their killing principally among themselves, and seldom molested peaceable citizens, for they considered it small credit to add to their trophies so cheap a bauble as the death of a man who was "not on the shoot," as they phrased it. They killed each other on slight provocation, and hoped and expected to be killed themselves —for they held it almost shame to die otherwise than "with their boots on," as they expressed it.

I remember an instance of a desperado's contempt for such small game as a private citizen's life. I was taking a late supper in a restaurant one night, with two reporters and a little printer named—Brown, for instance—any name will do. Presently a stranger with a long-tailed coat on came in, and not noticing Brown's hat, which was lying in a chair, sat down on it. Little Brown sprang up and became abusive in a moment. The stranger smiled, smoothed out the hat, and offered it to Brown with profuse apologies couched in caustic sarcasm, and begged Brown not to destroy him. Brown threw off his coat and challenged the man to fight —abused him, threatened him, impeached his courage, and urged and even implored him to fight; and in the meantime the smiling stranger placed himself under our protection in mock distress. But presently he assumed a serious tone, and said:

"Very well, gentlemen, if we must fight, we must, I suppose. But don't rush into danger and then say I gave you no warning. I am more than a match for all of you when I get started. I will give you proofs, and then if my friend here still insists, I will try to accommodate him."

The table we were sitting at was about five feet long, and unusually cumbersome and heavy. He asked us to put our hands on the dishes and hold them in their places a moment— one of them was a large oval dish with a portly roast on it. Then he sat down, tilted up one end of the table, set two of the legs on his knees, took the end of the table between his teeth, took his hands away, and pulled down with his teeth till the table came up to a level position, dishes and all! He said he could lift a keg of nails with his teeth. He picked up a common glass tumbler and bit a semi-circle out of it. Then he opened his bosom and showed us a net-work of knife and bullet scars; showed us more on his arms and face, and said he believed he had bullets enough in his body to make a pig of lead. He was armed to the teeth. He closed with the remark that he was Mr. — of Cariboo—a celebrated name whereat we shook in our shoes. I would publish the name, but for the suspicion that he might come and carve me. He finally inquired if Brown still thirsted for blood. Brown turned the thing over in his mind a moment, and then—asked him to supper.

With the permission of the reader, I will group together, in the next chapter, some samples of life in our small mountain village in the old days of desperadoism. I was there at the time. The reader will observe peculiarities in our official society; and he will observe also, an instance of how, in new countries, murders breed murders.

CHAPTER XLIX.

An extract or two from the newspapers of the day will furnish a photograph that can need no embellishment:

FATAL SHOOTING AFFRAY.—An affray occurred, last evening, in a billiard saloon on C street, between Deputy Marshal Jack Williams and Wm. Brown, which resulted in the immediate death of the latter. There had been some difficulty between the parties for several months.

An inquest was immediately held, and the following testimony adduced:

Officer GEO. BIRDSALL, sworn, says:—I was told Wm. Brown was drunk and was looking for Jack Williams; so soon as I heard that I started for the parties to prevent a collision; went into the billiard saloon; saw Billy Brown running around, saying if anybody had anything against him to show cause; he was talking in a boisterous manner, and officer Perry took him to the other end of the room to talk to him; Brown came back to me; remarked to me that he thought he was as good as anybody, and knew how to take care of himself; he passed by me and went to the bar; don't know whether he drank or not; Williams was at the end of the billiard-table, next to the stairway; Brown, after going to the bar, came back and said he was as good as any man in the world; he had then walked out to the end of the first billiard-table from the bar; I moved closer to them, supposing there would be a fight; as Brown drew his pistol I caught hold of it; he had fired one shot at Williams; don't know the effect of it; caught hold of him with one hand, and took hold of the pistol and turned it up; think he fired once after I caught hold of the pistol; I wrenched the pistol from him; walked to the end of the billiard-table and told a party that I had Brown's pistol, and to stop shooting; I think four shots were fired in all; after walking out, Mr. Foster remarked that Brown was shot dead.

Oh, there was no excitement about it—he merely "remarked" the small circumstance!

Four months later the following item appeared in the same paper (the Enterprise). In this item the name of one of the city officers above referred to (Deputy Marshal Jack Williams) occurs again:

ROBBERY AND DESPERATE AFFRAY.—On Tuesday night, a

German named Charles Hurtzal, engineer in a mill at Silver City, came to this place, and visited the hurdy-gurdy house on B street. The music, dancing and Teutonic maidens awakened memories of Faderland until our German friend was carried away with rapture. He evidently had money, and was spending if freely. Late in the evening Jack Williams and Andy Blessington invited him down stairs to take a cup of coffee. Williams proposed a game of cards and went up stairs to procure a deck, but not finding any returned. On the stairway he met the German, and drawing his pistol knocked him down and rifled his pockets of some seventy dollars. Hurtzal dared give no alarm, as he was told, with a pistol at his head, if he made any noise or exposed them, they would blow his brains out. So effectually was he frightened that he made no complaint, until his friends forced him. Yesterday a warrant was issued, but the culprits had disappeared.

This efficient city officer, Jack Williams, had the common reputation of being a burglar, a highwayman and a desperado. It was said that he had several times drawn his revolver and levied money contributions on citizens at dead of night in the public streets of Virginia.

Five months after the above item appeared, Williams was assassinated while sitting at a card table one night; a gun was thrust through the crack of the door and Williams dropped from his chair riddled with balls. It was said, at the time, that Williams had been for some time aware that a party of his own sort (desperadoes) had sworn away his life; and it was generally believed among the people that Williams's friends and enemies would make the assassination memorable—and useful, too—by a wholesale destruction of each other.

It did not so happen, but still, times were not dull during the next twenty-four hours, for within that time a woman was killed by a pistol shot, a man was brained with a slung shot, and a man named Reeder was also disposed of permanently. Some matters in the Enterprise account of the killing of Reeder are worth nothing—especially the accommodating complaisance of a Virginia justice of the peace. The italics in the following narrative are mine:

MORE CUTTING AND SHOOTING.—The devil seems to have again broken loose in our town. Pistols and guns explode and knives gleam in our streets as in early times. When there has been a long season of quiet, people are slow to wet their hands in blood; but once blood is spilled, cutting and shooting come easy. Night before last Jack Williams was assassinated, and yesterday forenoon we had more bloody work, growing out of the killing of Williams, and on the same street in which he met his death. It appears that Tom Reeder, a friend of Williams, and George Gumbert were talking, at the meat market of the latter, about the killing of Williams the previous night, when Reeder said it was a most cowardly act to shoot a man in such a way, giving him "no show." Gumbert said that Williams had "as good a show as he gave Billy Brown," meaning the man killed by Williams last March. Reeder said it was a d—d lie, that Williams had no show at all. At this, Gumbert drew a knife and stabbed Reeder, cutting him in two places in the back. One stroke of the knife cut into the sleeve of Reeder's coat and passed downward in a slanting direction through his clothing, and entered his body at the small of the back; another blow struck more squarely, and made a much more dangerous wound. Gumbert gave himself up to the officers of justice, and was shortly after discharged by Justice Atwill, on his own recognizance, *to appear for trial at six o'clock in the evening.* In the meantime Reeder had been taken into the office of Dr. Owens, where his wounds were properly dressed.

One of his wounds was considered quite dangerous, and it was thought by many that it would prove fatal. But being considerably under the influence of liquor, Reeder did not feel his wounds as he otherwise would, and he got up and went into the street. He went to the meat market and renewed his quarrel with Gumbert, threatening his life. Friends tried to interfere to put a stop to the quarrel and get the parties away from each other. In the Fashion Saloon Reeder made threats against the life of Gumbert, saying he would kill him, and it is said that he requested the officers not to arrest Gumbert, as he intended to kill him. After these threats Gumbert went off and procured a double-barreled shot gun, loaded with buck-shot or revolver balls, and went after Reeder. Two or three persons were assisting him along the street, trying to get him home, and had him just in front of the store of Klopstock & Harris, when Gumbert came across toward him from the opposite side of the street with his gun. He came up within about ten or fifteen feet of Reeder, and called out to those with him to "look out! get out of the way!" and they had only time to heed the warning, when he fired. Reeder was at the time attempting to screen himself behind a large cask, which stood against the awning post of Klopstock & Harris's store, but some of the balls took effect in the lower part of his breast, and he reeled around forward and fell in front of the cask. Gumbert then raised his gun and fired the second barrel, which missed Reeder and entered the ground. At the time that this occurred, there were a great many persons on the street in the vicinity, and a number of them called out to Gumbert, when they saw him raise his gun, to "hold on," and "don't shoot!" The cutting took place about ten o'clock and the shooting about twelve. After the shooting the street was instantly crowded with the inhabitants of that part of the town, some appearing much excited and laughing—declaring that it looked like the "good old times of '60." Marshal Perry and officer Birdsall were near when the shooting occurred, and Gumbert was immediately arrested and his gun taken from him, when he was marched off to jail. Many persons who were attracted to the spot where this bloody work had just taken place, looked bewildered and seemed to be asking themselves what was to happen next, appearing in doubt as to whether the killing mania had reached its climax, or whether we were to turn in and have a grand killing spell, shooting whoever might have given us offence. It was whispered around that it was not all over yet — five or six more were to be killed before night. Reeder was taken to the Virginia City Hotel, and doctors called in to examine his wounds. They found that two or three balls had entered his right side; one of them appeared to have passed through the substance of the lungs, while another passed into the liver. Two balls were also found to have struck one of his legs. As some of the balls struck the cask, the wounds in Reeder's leg were probably from these, glancing downwards, though they might have been caused by the second shot fired. After being shot, Reeder said when he got on his feet —smiling as he spoke—"It will take better shooting than that to kill me." The doctors consider it almost impossible for him to recover, but as he has an excellent constitution he may survive, notwithstanding the number and dangerous character of the wounds he has received. The town appears to be perfectly quiet at present, as though the late stormy times had cleared our moral atmosphere; but who can tell in what quarter clouds are lowering or plots ripening?

Reeder—or at least what was left of him—survived his wounds two days! Nothing was ever done with Gumbert.

Trial by jury is the palladium of our liberties. I do not know what a palladium is, having never seen a palladium, but it is a good thing no doubt at any rate. Not less than a hundred men have been murdered in Nevada—perhaps I would be within bounds if I said three hundred—and as far as I can learn, only two persons have suffered the death penalty there. However, four or five who had no money and no political influence have been punished by imprisonment—one languished in prison as much as eight months, I think. However, I do not desire to be extravagant—it may have been less.

However, one prophecy was verified, at any rate. It was asserted by the desperadoes that one of their brethren (Joe McGee, a special policeman) was known to be the conspirator chosen by lot to assassinate Williams; and they also asserted that doom had been pronounced against McGee, and that he would be assassinated in exactly the same manner that had been adopted for the destruction of Williams—a prophecy which came true a year later. After twelve months of distress (for McGee saw a fancied assassin in every man that approached him), he made the last of many efforts to get out of the country unwatched. He went to Carson and sat down in a saloon to wait for the stage—it would leave at four in the morning. But as the night waned and the crowd thinned, he grew uneasy, and told the bar-keeper that assassins were on his track. The bar-keeper told him to stay in the middle of the room, then, and not go near the door, or the window by the stove. But a fatal fascination seduced him to the neighborhood of the stove every now and then, and repeatedly the bar-keeper brought him back to the middle of the room and warned him to remain there. But he could not. At three in the morning he again returned to the stove and sat down by a stranger. Before the bar-keeper could get to him with another warning whisper, some one outside fired through the window and riddled McGee's breast with slugs, killing him almost instantly. By the same discharge the stranger at McGee's side also received attentions which proved fatal in the course of two or three days.

CHAPTER L.

These murder and jury statistics remind me of a certain very extraordinary trial and execution of twenty years ago; it is a scrap of history familiar to all old Californians, and worthy to be known by other peoples of the earth that love simple, straightforward justice unencumbered with nonsense. I would apologize for this digression but for the fact that the information I am about to offer is apology enough in itself. And since I digress constantly anyhow, perhaps it is as well to eschew apologies altogether and thus prevent their growing irksome.

Capt. Ned Blakely—that name will answer as well as any other fictitious one (for he was still with the living at last accounts, and may not desire to be famous)—sailed ships out of the harbor of San Francisco for many years. He was a stalwart, warm-hearted, eagle-eyed veteran, who had been a sailor nearly fifty years—a sailor from early boyhood. He was a rough, honest creature, full of pluck, and just as full of hard-headed simplicity, too. He hated trifling conventionalities— "business" was the word, with him. He had all a sailor's vindictiveness against the quips and quirks of the law, and steadfastly believed that the first and last aim and object of the law and lawyers was to defeat justice.

He sailed for the Chincha Islands in command of a guano ship. He had a fine crew, but his negro mate was his pet—on him he had for years lavished his admiration and esteem. It was Capt. Ned's first voyage to the Chinchas, but his fame had gone before him—the fame of being a man who would fight at the dropping of a handkerchief, when imposed upon, and would stand no nonsense. It was a fame well earned. Arrived in the islands, he found that the staple of conversation was the exploits of one Bill Noakes, a bully, the mate of a trading ship. This man had created a small reign of terror there. At nine o'clock at night, Capt. Ned, all alone, was pacing his deck in the starlight. A form ascended the side, and approached him. Capt. Ned said:

"Who goes there?"

"I'm Bill Noakes, the best man in the islands."

"What do you want aboard this ship?"

"I've heard of Capt. Ned Blakely, and one of us is a better man than 'tother—I'll know which, before I go ashore."

"You've come to the right shop—I'm your man. I'll learn you to come aboard this ship without an invite."

He seized Noakes, backed him against the mainmast, pounded his face to a pulp, and then threw him overboard.

Noakes was not convinced. He returned the next night, got the pulp renewed, and went overboard head first, as before.

He was satisfied.

A week after this, while Noakes was carousing with a sailor crowd on shore, at noonday, Capt. Ned's colored mate came along, and Noakes tried to pick a quarrel with him. The negro evaded the trap, and tried to get away. Noakes followed him up; the negro began to run; Noakes fired on him with a revolver and killed him. Half a dozen sea-captains witnessed the whole affair. Noakes retreated to the small after-cabin of his ship, with two other bullies, and gave out that death would be the portion of any man that intruded there. There was no attempt made to follow the villains; there was no disposition to do it, and indeed very little thought of such an enterprise. There were no courts and no officers; there was no government; the islands belonged to Peru, and Peru was far away; she had no official representative on the ground; and neither had any other nation.

However, Capt. Ned was not perplexing his head about such things. They concerned him not. He was boiling with rage and furious for justice. At nine o'clock at night he loaded a double-barreled gun with slugs, fished out a pair of handcuffs, got a ship's lantern, summoned his quartermaster, and went ashore. He said:

"Do you see that ship there at the dock?"

"Ay-ay, sir."

"It's the Venus."

"Ay-ay, sir."

"You—you know me."

"Ay-ay, sir."

"Very well, then. Take the lantern. Carry it just under your chin. I'll walk behind you and rest this gun-barrel on your shoulder, p'inting forward—so. Keep your lantern well up so's I can see things ahead of you good. I'm going to march in on Noakes—and take him—and jug the other chaps. If you

flinch—well, you know me."

"Ay-ay, sir."

In this order they filed aboard softly, arrived at Noakes's den, the quartermaster pushed the door open, and the lantern revealed the three desperadoes sitting on the floor. Capt. Ned said:

"I'm Ned Blakely. I've got you under fire. Don't you move without orders—any of you. You two kneel down in the corner; faces to the wall —now. Bill Noakes, put these handcuffs on; now come up close. Quartermaster, fasten 'em. All right. Don't stir, sir. Quartermaster, put the key in the outside of the door. Now, men, I'm going to lock you two in; and if you try to burst through this door—well, you've heard of me. Bill Noakes, fall in ahead, and march. All set. Quartermaster, lock the door."

Noakes spent the night on board Blakely's ship, a prisoner under strict guard. Early in the morning Capt. Ned called in all the sea-captains in the harbor and invited them, with nautical ceremony, to be present on board his ship at nine o'clock to witness the hanging of Noakes at the yard-arm!

"What! The man has not been tried."

"Of course he hasn't. But didn't he kill the nigger?"

"Certainly he did; but you are not thinking of hanging him without a trial?"

"Trial! What do I want to try him for, if he killed the nigger?"

"Oh, Capt. Ned, this will never do. Think how it will sound."

"Sound be hanged! Didn't he kill the nigger?"

"Certainly, certainly, Capt. Ned,—nobody denies that,—but—"

"Then I'm going to hang him, that's all. Everybody I've talked to talks just the same way you do. Everybody says he killed the nigger, everybody knows he killed the nigger, and yet every lubber of you wants him tried for it. I don't understand such bloody foolishness as that. Tried! Mind you, I don't object to trying him, if it's got to be done to give satisfaction; and I'll be there, and chip in and help, too; but put it off till afternoon—put it off till afternoon, for I'll have my hands middling full till after the burying—"

"Why, what do you mean? Are you going to hang him any how—and try him afterward?"

"Didn't I say I was going to hang him? I never saw such people as you. What's the difference? You ask a favor, and then you ain't satisfied when you get it. Before or after's all one—you know how the trial will go. He killed the nigger. Say—I must be going. If your mate would like to come to the hanging, fetch him along. I like him."

There was a stir in the camp. The captains came in a body and pleaded with Capt. Ned not to do this rash thing. They promised that they would create a court composed of captains of the best character; they would empanel a jury; they would conduct everything in a way becoming the serious nature of the business in hand, and give the case an impartial hearing and the accused a fair trial. And they said it would be murder, and punishable by the American courts if he persisted and hung the accused on his ship. They pleaded hard. Capt. Ned said:

"Gentlemen, I'm not stubborn and I'm not unreasonable. I'm always willing to do just as near right as I can. How long will it take?"

"Probably only a little while."

"And can I take him up the shore and hang him as soon as you are done?"

"If he is proven guilty he shall be hanged without unnecessary delay."

"If he's proven guilty. Great Neptune, ain't he guilty? This beats my time. Why you all know he's guilty."

But at last they satisfied him that they were projecting nothing underhanded. Then he said:

"Well, all right. You go on and try him and I'll go down and overhaul his conscience and prepare him to go—like enough he needs it, and I don't want to send him off without a show for hereafter."

This was another obstacle. They finally convinced him that it was necessary to have the accused in court. Then they said they would send a guard to bring him.

"No, sir, I prefer to fetch him myself—he don't get out of my hands. Besides, I've got to go to the ship to get a rope, anyway."

The court assembled with due ceremony, empaneled a jury, and presently Capt. Ned entered, leading the prisoner with one hand and carrying a Bible and a rope in the other. He seated himself by the side of his captive and told the court to "up anchor and make sail." Then he turned a searching eye on the jury, and detected Noakes's friends, the two bullies.

He strode over and said to them confidentially:

"You're here to interfere, you see. Now you vote right, do you hear?—or else there'll be a double-barreled inquest here when this trial's off, and your remainders will go home in a couple of baskets."

The caution was not without fruit. The jury was a unit—the verdict. "Guilty."

Capt. Ned sprung to his feet and said:

"Come along—you're my meat now, my lad, anyway. Gentlemen you've done yourselves proud. I invite you all to come and see that I do it all straight. Follow me to the canyon, a mile above here."

The court informed him that a sheriff had been appointed to do the hanging, and—

Capt. Ned's patience was at an end. His wrath was boundless. The subject of a sheriff was judiciously dropped.

When the crowd arrived at the canyon, Capt. Ned climbed a tree and arranged the halter, then came down and noosed his man. He opened his Bible, and laid aside his hat. Selecting a chapter at random, he read it through, in a deep bass voice and with sincere solemnity. Then he said:

"Lad, you are about to go aloft and give an account of yourself; and the lighter a man's manifest is, as far as sin's concerned, the better for him. Make a clean breast, man, and carry a log with you that'll bear inspection. You killed the nigger?"

No reply. A long pause.

The captain read another chapter, pausing, from time to time, to impress the effect. Then he talked an earnest, persuasive sermon to him, and ended by repeating the question:

"Did you kill the nigger?"

No reply—other than a malignant scowl. The captain now read the first and second chapters of Genesis, with deep feeling—paused a moment, closed the book reverently, and said with a perceptible savor of satisfaction:

"There. Four chapters. There's few that would have took the pains with you that I have."

Then he swung up the condemned, and made the rope fast; stood by and timed him half an hour with his watch, and then delivered the body to the court. A little after, as he stood contemplating the motionless figure, a doubt came into his face; evidently he felt a twinge of conscience—a misgiving—and he said with a sigh:

"Well, p'raps I ought to burnt him, maybe. But I was trying to do for the best."

When the history of this affair reached California (it was in the "early days") it made a deal of talk, but did not diminish the captain's popularity in any degree. It increased it, indeed. California had a population then that "inflicted" justice after a fashion that was simplicity and primitiveness itself, and could therefore admire appreciatively when the same fashion was followed elsewhere.

CHAPTER LI.

Vice flourished luxuriantly during the hey-day of our "flush times." The saloons were overburdened with custom; so were the police courts, the gambling dens, the brothels and the jails—unfailing signs of high prosperity in a mining region—in any region for that matter. Is it not so? A crowded police court docket is the surest of all signs that trade is brisk and money plenty. Still, there is one other sign; it comes last, but when it does come it establishes beyond cavil that the "flush times" are at the flood. This is the birth of the "literary" paper. The Weekly Occidental, "devoted to literature," made its appearance in Virginia. All the literary people were engaged to write for it. Mr. F. was to edit it. He was a felicitous skirmisher with a pen, and a man who could say happy things in a crisp, neat way. Once, while editor of the Union, he had disposed of a labored, incoherent, two-column attack made upon him by a contemporary, with a single line, which, at first glance, seemed to contain a solemn and tremendous compliment—viz.: "THE LOGIC OF OUR ADVERSARY RESEMBLES THE PEACE OF GOD,"—and left it to the reader's memory and after-thought to invest the remark with another and "more different" meaning by supplying for himself and at his own leisure the rest of the Scripture—"in that it passeth understanding." He once said of a little, half-starved, wayside community that had no subsistence except what they could get by preying upon chance passengers who stopped over with them a day when traveling by the overland stage, that in their Church service they had altered the Lord's Prayer to read: "Give us this day our daily stranger!"

We expected great things of the Occidental. Of course it could not get along without an original novel, and so we made arrangements to hurl into the work the full strength of the company. Mrs. F. was an able romancist of the ineffable school—I know no other name to apply to a school whose heroes are all dainty and all perfect. She wrote the opening chapter, and introduced a lovely blonde simpleton who talked nothing but pearls and poetry and who was virtuous to the verge of eccentricity. She also introduced a young French Duke of aggravated refinement, in love with the blonde. Mr. F. followed next week, with a brilliant lawyer who set about getting the Duke's estates into trouble, and a sparkling young lady of high society who fell to fascinating the Duke and impairing the appetite of the blonde. Mr. D., a dark and bloody editor of one of the dailies, followed Mr. F., the third week, introducing a mysterious Roscicrucian who transmuted metals, held consultations with the devil in a cave at dead of night, and cast the horoscope of the several heroes and heroines in such a way as to provide plenty of trouble for their future careers and breed a solemn and awful public interest in the novel. He also introduced a cloaked and masked melodramatic miscreant, put him on a salary and set him on the midnight track of the Duke with a poisoned dagger. He also created an Irish coachman with a rich brogue and placed him in the service of the society-young-lady with an ulterior mission to carry billet-doux to the Duke.

About this time there arrived in Virginia a dissolute stranger with a literary turn of mind—rather seedy he was, but very quiet and unassuming; almost diffident, indeed. He was so gentle, and his manners were so pleasing and kindly, whether he was sober or intoxicated, that he made friends of all who came in contact with him. He applied for literary work, offered conclusive evidence that he wielded an easy and practiced pen, and so Mr. F. engaged him at once to help write the novel. His chapter was to follow Mr. D.'s, and mine was to come next. Now what does this fellow do but go off and get drunk and then proceed to his quarters and set to work with his imagination in a state of chaos, and that chaos in a condition of extravagant activity. The result may be guessed. He scanned the chapters of his predecessors, found plenty of heroes and heroines already created, and was satisfied with them; he decided to introduce no more; with all the confidence that whisky inspires and all the easy complacency it gives to its servant, he then launched himself lovingly into his work: he married the coachman to the society-young-lady for the sake of the scandal; married the Duke to the blonde's stepmother, for the sake of the sensation; stopped the desperado's salary; created a misunderstanding between the devil and the Roscicrucian; threw the Duke's property into the wicked lawyer's hands; made the lawyer's upbraiding conscience drive him to drink, thence to delirium tremens, thence to suicide; broke the coachman's neck; let his widow succumb to contumely, neglect, poverty and consumption; caused the blonde to drown herself, leaving her clothes on the bank with the customary note pinned to them forgiving the Duke and hoping he would be happy; revealed to the Duke, by means of the usual strawberry mark on left arm, that he had married his own long-lost mother and destroyed his long-lost sister; instituted the proper and necessary suicide of the Duke and the Duchess in order to compass poetical justice; opened the earth and let the Roscicrucian through, accompanied with the accustomed smoke and thunder and smell of brimstone, and finished with the promise that in the next chapter, after holding a general inquest, he would take up the surviving

character of the novel and tell what became of the devil! It read with singular smoothness, and with a "dead" earnestness that was funny enough to suffocate a body. But there was war when it came in. The other novelists were furious. The mild stranger, not yet more than half sober, stood there, under a scathing fire of vituperation, meek and bewildered, looking from one to another of his assailants, and wondering what he could have done to invoke such a storm. When a lull came at last, he said his say gently and appealingly—said he did not rightly remember what he had written, but was sure he had tried to do the best he could, and knew his object had been to make the novel not only pleasant and plausible but instructive and—

The bombardment began again. The novelists assailed his ill-chosen adjectives and demolished them with a storm of denunciation and ridicule. And so the siege went on. Every time the stranger tried to appease the enemy he only made matters worse. Finally he offered to rewrite the chapter. This arrested hostilities. The indignation gradually quieted down, peace reigned again and the sufferer retired in safety and got him to his own citadel.

But on the way thither the evil angel tempted him and he got drunk again. And again his imagination went mad. He led the heroes and heroines a wilder dance than ever; and yet all through it ran that same convincing air of honesty and earnestness that had marked his first work. He got the characters into the most extraordinary situations, put them through the most surprising performances, and made them talk the strangest talk! But the chapter cannot be described. It was symmetrically crazy; it was artistically absurd; and it had explanatory footnotes that were fully as curious as the text. I remember one of the "situations," and will offer it as an example of the whole. He altered the character of the brilliant lawyer, and made him a great-hearted, splendid fellow; gave him fame and riches, and set his age at thirty-three years. Then he made the blonde discover, through the help of the Roscicrucian and the melodramatic miscreant, that while the Duke loved her money ardently and wanted it, he secretly felt a sort of leaning toward the society-young-lady. Stung to the quick, she tore her affections from him and bestowed them with tenfold power upon the lawyer, who responded with consuming zeal. But the parents would none of it. What they wanted in the family was a Duke; and a Duke they were determined to have; though they confessed that next to the Duke the lawyer had their preference. Necessarily the blonde now went into a decline. The parents were alarmed. They pleaded with her to marry the Duke, but she steadfastly refused, and pined on. Then they laid a plan. They told her to wait a year and a day, and if at the end of that time she still felt that she could not marry the Duke, she might marry the lawyer with their full consent. The result was as they had foreseen: gladness came again, and the flush of returning health. Then the parents took the next step in their scheme. They had the family physician recommend a long sea voyage and much land travel for the thorough restoration of the blonde's strength; and they invited the Duke to be of the party. They judged that the Duke's constant presence and the lawyer's protracted absence would do the rest—for they did not invite the lawyer.

So they set sail in a steamer for America—and the third day out, when their sea-sickness called truce and permitted them to take their first meal at the public table, behold there sat the lawyer! The Duke and party made the best of an awkward situation; the voyage progressed, and the vessel neared America.

But, by and by, two hundred miles off New Bedford, the ship took fire; she burned to the water's edge; of all her crew and passengers, only thirty were saved. They floated about the sea half an afternoon and all night long. Among them were our friends. The lawyer, by superhuman exertions, had saved the blonde and her parents, swimming back and forth two hundred yards and bringing one each time—(the girl first). The Duke had saved himself. In the morning two whale ships arrived on the scene and sent their boats. The weather was stormy and the embarkation was attended with much confusion and excitement. The lawyer did his duty like a man; helped his exhausted and insensible blonde, her parents and some others into a boat (the Duke helped himself in); then a child fell overboard at the other end of the raft and the lawyer rushed thither and helped half a dozen people fish it out, under the stimulus of its mother's screams. Then he ran back—a few seconds too late—the blonde's boat was under way. So he had to take the other boat, and go to the other ship. The storm increased and drove the vessels out of sight of each other—drove them whither it would.

When it calmed, at the end of three days, the blonde's ship was seven hundred miles north of Boston and the other about seven hundred south of that port. The blonde's captain was bound on a whaling cruise in the North Atlantic and could not go back such a distance or make a port without orders; such being nautical law. The lawyer's captain was to cruise in the North Pacific, and he could not go back or make a port without orders. All the lawyer's money and baggage were in the blonde's boat and went to the blonde's ship—so his captain made him work his passage as a common sailor. When both ships had been cruising nearly a year, the one was off the coast of Greenland and the other in Behring's Strait. The blonde had long ago been well-nigh persuaded that her lawyer had been washed overboard and lost just before the whale ships reached the raft, and now, under the pleadings of her parents and the Duke she was at last beginning to nerve herself for the doom of the covenant, and prepare for the hated marriage.

But she would not yield a day before the date set. The weeks dragged on, the time narrowed, orders were given to deck the ship for the wedding—a wedding at sea among icebergs and walruses. Five days more and all would be over. So the blonde reflected, with a sigh and a tear. Oh where was her true love—and why, why did he not come and save her? At that moment he was lifting his harpoon to strike a whale in Behring's Strait, five thousand miles away, by the way of the Arctic Ocean, or twenty thousand by the way of the Horn—that was the reason. He struck, but not with perfect aim—his foot slipped and he fell in the whale's mouth and went down his throat. He was insensible five days. Then he came to himself and heard voices; daylight was streaming through a hole cut in the whale's roof. He climbed out and astonished the sailors who were hoisting blubber up a ship's side. He recognized the vessel, flew aboard, surprised the wedding party at the altar and exclaimed:

"Stop the proceedings—I'm here! Come to my arms, my own!"

There were foot-notes to this extravagant piece of literature wherein the author endeavored to show that the whole thing was within the possibilities; he said he got the incident of the whale traveling from Behring's Strait to the coast of Greenland, five thousand miles in five days, through the Arctic Ocean, from Charles Reade's "Love Me Little Love Me Long," and considered that that established the fact that the thing could be done; and he instanced Jonah's adventure as proof that a man could live in a whale's belly, and added that if a

preacher could stand it three days a lawyer could surely stand it five!

There was a fiercer storm than ever in the editorial sanctum now, and the stranger was peremptorily discharged, and his manuscript flung at his head. But he had already delayed things so much that there was not time for some one else to rewrite the chapter, and so the paper came out without any novel in it. It was but a feeble, struggling, stupid journal, and the absence of the novel probably shook public confidence; at any rate, before the first side of the next issue went to press, the Weekly Occidental died as peacefully as an infant.

An effort was made to resurrect it, with the proposed advantage of a telling new title, and Mr. F. said that The Phenix would be just the name for it, because it would give the idea of a resurrection from its dead ashes in a new and undreamed of condition of splendor; but some low-priced smarty on one of the dailies suggested that we call it the Lazarus; and inasmuch as the people were not profound in Scriptural matters but thought the resurrected Lazarus and the dilapidated mendicant that begged in the rich man's gateway were one and the same person, the name became the laughing stock of the town, and killed the paper for good and all.

I was sorry enough, for I was very proud of being connected with a literary paper—prouder than I have ever been of anything since, perhaps. I had written some rhymes for it—poetry I considered it—and it was a great grief to me that the production was on the "first side" of the issue that was not completed, and hence did not see the light. But time brings its revenges—I can put it in here; it will answer in place of a tear dropped to the memory of the lost Occidental. The idea (not the chief idea, but the vehicle that bears it) was probably suggested by the old song called "The Raging Canal," but I cannot remember now. I do remember, though, that at that time I thought my doggerel was one of the ablest poems of the age:

THE AGED PILOT MAN.

On the Erie Canal, it was, All on a summer's day, I sailed forth with my parents Far away to Albany.

From out the clouds at noon that day There came a dreadful storm, That piled the billows high about, And filled us with alarm.

A man came rushing from a house, Saying, "Snub up your boat I pray, [The customary canal technicality for "tie up."] Snub up your boat, snub up, alas, Snub up while yet you may."

Our captain cast one glance astern, Then forward glanced he, And said, "My wife and little ones I never more shall see."

Said Dollinger the pilot man, In noble words, but few, —"Fear not, but lean on Dollinger, And he will fetch you through."

The boat drove on, the frightened mules Tore through the rain and wind, And bravely still, in danger's post, The whip-boy strode behind.

"Come 'board, come 'board," the captain cried, "Nor tempt so wild a storm;" But still the raging mules advanced, And still the boy strode on.

Then said the captain to us all, "Alas, 'tis plain to me, The greater danger is not there, But here upon the sea.

"So let us strive, while life remains, To save all souls on board, And then if die at last we must, Let . . . . I cannot speak the word!"

Said Dollinger the pilot man, Tow'ring above the crew, "Fear not, but trust in Dollinger, And he will fetch you through."

"Low bridge! low bridge!" all heads went down, The laboring bark sped on; A mill we passed, we passed church, Hamlets, and fields of corn; And all the world came out to see, And chased along the shore Crying, "Alas, alas, the sheeted rain, The wind, the tempest's roar! Alas, the gallant ship and crew, Can nothing help them more?"

And from our deck sad eyes looked out Across the stormy scene: The tossing wake of billows aft, The bending forests green, The chickens sheltered under carts In lee of barn the cows, The skurrying swine with straw in mouth, The wild spray from our bows!

"She balances! She wavers! Now let her go about! If she misses stays and broaches to, We're all"—then with a shout, "Huray! huray! Avast! belay! Take in more sail! Lord, what a gale! Ho, boy, haul taut on the hind mule's tail!" "Ho! lighten ship! ho! man the pump! Ho, hostler, heave the lead!"

"A quarter-three!—'tis shoaling fast! Three feet large!—t-h-r-e-e feet! —Three feet scant!" I cried in fright "Oh, is there no retreat?"

Said Dollinger, the pilot man, As on the vessel flew, "Fear not, but trust in Dollinger, And he will fetch you through."

A panic struck the bravest hearts, The boldest cheek turned pale; For plain to all, this shoaling said A leak had burst the ditch's bed! And, straight as bolt from crossbow sped, Our ship swept on, with shoaling lead, Before the fearful gale!

"Sever the tow-line! Cripple the mules!" Too late! There comes a shock! Another length, and the fated craft Would have swum in the saving lock!

Then gathered together the shipwrecked crew And took one last embrace, While sorrowful tears from despairing eyes Ran down each hopeless face; And some did think of their little ones Whom they never more might see, And others of waiting wives at home, And mothers that grieved would be.

But of all the children of misery there On that poor sinking frame, But one spake words of hope and faith, And I worshipped as they came: Said Dollinger the pilot man, —(O brave heart, strong and true!) —"Fear not, but trust in Dollinger, For he will fetch you through."

Lo! scarce the words have passed his lips The dauntless prophet say'th, When every soul about him seeth A wonder crown his faith!

"And count ye all, both great and small, As numbered with the dead: For mariner for forty year, On Erie, boy and man, I never yet saw such a storm, Or one't with it began!"

So overboard a keg of nails And anvils three we threw, Likewise four bales of gunny-sacks, Two hundred pounds of glue, Two sacks of corn, four ditto wheat, A box of books, a cow, A violin, Lord Byron's works, A rip-saw and a sow.

A curve! a curve! the dangers grow! "Labbord!—stabbord!—s-t-e-a-d-y!—so! —Hard-a-port, Dol!—hellum-a-lee! Haw the head mule!—the aft one gee! Luff!—bring her to the wind!"

For straight a farmer brought a plank, —(Mysteriously inspired) —And laying it unto the ship, In silent awe retired.

Then every sufferer stood amazed That pilot man before; A moment stood. Then wondering turned, And speechless walked ashore.

CHAPTER LII.

Since I desire, in this chapter, to say an instructive word or two about the silver mines, the reader may take this fair warning and skip, if he chooses. The year 1863 was perhaps the very top blossom and culmination of the "flush times." Virginia swarmed with men and vehicles to that degree that the place looked like a very hive—that is when one's vision could pierce through the thick fog of alkali dust that was generally blowing in summer. I will say, concerning this dust, that if you drove ten miles through it, you and your horses would be coated with it a sixteenth of an inch thick and present an outside appearance that was a uniform pale yellow color, and your buggy would have three inches of dust in it, thrown there by the wheels. The delicate scales used by the assayers were inclosed in glass cases intended to be air-tight, and yet some of this dust was so impalpable and so invisibly fine that it would get in, somehow, and impair the accuracy of those scales.

Speculation ran riot, and yet there was a world of substantial business going on, too. All freights were brought over the mountains from California (150 miles) by pack-train partly, and partly in huge wagons drawn by such long mule teams that each team amounted to a procession, and it did seem, sometimes, that the grand combined procession of animals stretched unbroken from Virginia to California. Its long route was traceable clear across the deserts of the Territory by the writhing serpent of dust it lifted up. By these wagons, freights over that hundred and fifty miles were $200 a ton for small lots (same price for all express matter brought by stage), and $100 a ton for full loads. One Virginia firm received one hundred tons of freight a month, and paid $10,000 a month freightage. In the winter the freights were much higher. All the bullion was shipped in bars by stage to San Francisco (a bar was usually about twice the size of a pig of lead and contained from $1,500 to $3,000 according to the amount of gold mixed with the silver), and the freight on it (when the shipment was large) was one and a quarter per cent. of its intrinsic value.

So, the freight on these bars probably averaged something more than $25 each. Small shippers paid two per cent. There were three stages a day, each way, and I have seen the outgoing stages carry away a third of a ton of bullion each, and more than once I saw them divide a two-ton lot and take it off. However, these were extraordinary events. [Mr. Valentine, Wells Fargo's agent, has handled all the bullion shipped through the Virginia office for many a month. To his memory—which is excellent—we are indebted for the following exhibit of the company's business in the Virginia office since the first of January, 1862: From January 1st to April 1st, about $270,000 worth of bullion passed through that office, during the next quarter, $570,000; next quarter, $800,000; next quarter, $956,000; next quarter, $1,275,000; and for the quarter ending on the 30th of last June, about $1,600,000. Thus in a year and a half, the Virginia office only shipped

$5,330,000 in bullion. During the year 1862 they shipped $2,615,000, so we perceive the average shipments have more than doubled in the last six months. This gives us room to promise for the Virginia office $500,000 a month for the year 1863 (though perhaps, judging by the steady increase in the business, we are under estimating, somewhat). This gives us $6,000,000 for the year. Gold Hill and Silver City together can beat us—we will give them $10,000,000. To Dayton, Empire City, Ophir and Carson City, we will allow an aggregate of $8,000,000, which is not over the mark, perhaps, and may possibly be a little under it. To Esmeralda we give $4,000,000. To Reese River and Humboldt $2,000,000, which is liberal now, but may not be before the year is out. So we prognosticate that the yield of bullion this year will be about $30,000,000. Placing the number of mills in the Territory at one hundred, this gives to each the labor of producing $300,000 in bullion during the twelve months. Allowing them to run three hundred days in the year (which none of them more than do), this makes their work average $1,000 a day. Say the mills average twenty tons of rock a day and this rock worth $50 as a general thing, and you have the actual work of our one hundred mills figured down "to a spot"—$1,000 a day each, and $30,000,000 a year in the aggregate.—Enterprise. [A considerable over estimate—M. T.]]

Two tons of silver bullion would be in the neighborhood of forty bars, and the freight on it over $1,000. Each coach always carried a deal of ordinary express matter beside, and also from fifteen to twenty passengers at from $25 to $30 a head. With six stages going all the time, Wells, Fargo and Co.'s Virginia City business was important and lucrative.

All along under the centre of Virginia and Gold Hill, for a couple of miles, ran the great Comstock silver lode—a vein of ore from fifty to eighty feet thick between its solid walls of rock—a vein as wide as some of New York's streets. I will remind the reader that in Pennsylvania a coal vein only eight feet wide is considered ample.

Virginia was a busy city of streets and houses above ground. Under it was another busy city, down in the bowels of the earth, where a great population of men thronged in and out among an intricate maze of tunnels and drifts, flitting hither and thither under a winking sparkle of lights, and over their heads towered a vast web of interlocking timbers that held the walls of the gutted Comstock apart. These timbers were as large as a man's body, and the framework stretched upward so far that no eye could pierce to its top through the closing gloom. It was like peering up through the clean-picked ribs and bones of some colossal skeleton. Imagine such a framework two miles long, sixty feet wide, and higher than any church spire in America. Imagine this stately lattice-work stretching down Broadway, from the St. Nicholas to Wall street, and a Fourth of July procession, reduced to pigmies, parading on top of it and flaunting their flags, high above the pinnacle of Trinity steeple. One can imagine that, but he cannot well imagine what that forest of timbers cost, from the time they were felled in the pineries beyond Washoe Lake, hauled up and around Mount Davidson at atrocious rates of freightage, then squared, let down into the deep maw of the mine and built up there. Twenty ample fortunes would not timber one of the greatest of those silver mines. The Spanish proverb says it requires a gold mine to "run" a silver one, and it is true. A beggar with a silver mine is a pitiable pauper indeed if he cannot sell.

I spoke of the underground Virginia as a city. The Gould and Curry is only one single mine under there, among a great many others; yet the Gould and Curry's streets of dismal drifts and tunnels were five miles in extent, altogether, and its population five hundred miners. Taken as a whole, the underground city had some thirty miles of streets and a population of five or six thousand. In this present day some of those populations are at work from twelve to sixteen hundred feet under Virginia and Gold Hill, and the signal-bells that tell them what the superintendent above ground desires them to do are struck by telegraph as we strike a fire alarm. Sometimes men fall down a shaft, there, a thousand feet deep. In such cases, the usual plan is to hold an inquest.

If you wish to visit one of those mines, you may walk through a tunnel about half a mile long if you prefer it, or you may take the quicker plan of shooting like a dart down a shaft, on a small platform. It is like tumbling down through an empty steeple, feet first. When you reach the bottom, you take a candle and tramp through drifts and tunnels where throngs of men are digging and blasting; you watch them send up tubs full of great lumps of stone—silver ore; you select choice specimens from the mass, as souvenirs; you admire the world of skeleton timbering; you reflect frequently that you are buried under a mountain, a thousand feet below daylight; being in the bottom of the mine you climb from "gallery" to "gallery," up endless ladders that stand straight up and down; when your legs fail you at last, you lie down in a small box-car in a cramped "incline" like a half-up-ended sewer and are dragged up to daylight feeling as if you are crawling through a coffin that has no end to it. Arrived at the top, you find a busy crowd of men receiving the ascending cars and tubs and dumping the ore from an elevation into long rows of bins capable of holding half a dozen tons each; under the bins are rows of wagons loading from chutes and trap-doors in the bins, and down the long street is a procession of these wagons wending toward the silver mills with their rich freight. It is all "done," now, and there you are. You need never go down again, for you have seen it all. If you have forgotten the process of reducing the ore in the mill and making the silver bars, you can go back and find it again in my Esmeralda chapters if so disposed.

Of course these mines cave in, in places, occasionally, and then it is worth one's while to take the risk of descending into them and observing the crushing power exerted by the pressing weight of a settling mountain. I published such an experience in the Enterprise, once, and from it I will take an extract:

AN HOUR IN THE CAVED MINES.—We journeyed down into the Ophir mine, yesterday, to see the earthquake. We could not go down the deep incline, because it still has a propensity to cave in places. Therefore we traveled through the long tunnel which enters the hill above the Ophir office, and then by means of a series of long ladders, climbed away down from the first to the fourth gallery. Traversing a drift, we came to the Spanish line, passed five sets of timbers still uninjured, and found the earthquake. Here was as complete a chaos as ever was seen—vast masses of earth and splintered and broken timbers piled confusedly together, with scarcely an aperture left large enough for a cat to creep through. Rubbish was still falling at intervals from above, and one timber which had braced others earlier in the day, was now crushed down out of its former position, showing that the caving and settling of the tremendous mass was still going on. We were in that portion of the Ophir known as the "north mines." Returning to the surface, we entered a tunnel leading into the Central, for the purpose of getting into the main Ophir. Descending a long incline in this tunnel, we traversed a drift or so, and then went down a deep shaft from whence we proceeded into the fifth gallery of the Ophir. From a side-drift we crawled through a small hole and got into the midst of the earthquake again—earth and broken timbers mingled together without regard to grace or symmetry. A large portion of the second, third and fourth galleries had caved in and gone to destruction—the two latter at seven o'clock on the previous evening.

At the turn-table, near the northern extremity of the fifth gallery, two big piles of rubbish had forced their way through from the fifth gallery, and from the looks of the timbers, more was about to come. These beams are solid—eighteen inches square; first, a great beam is laid on the floor, then upright ones, five feet high, stand on it, supporting another horizontal beam, and so on, square above square, like the framework of a window. The superincumbent weight was sufficient to mash the ends of those great upright beams fairly into the solid wood of the horizontal ones three inches, compressing and bending the upright beam till it curved like a bow. Before the Spanish caved in, some of their twelve-inch horizontal timbers were compressed in this way until they were only five inches thick! Imagine the power it must take to squeeze a solid log together in that way. Here, also, was a range of timbers, for a distance of twenty feet, tilted six inches out of the perpendicular by the weight resting upon them from the caved galleries above. You could hear things cracking and giving way, and it was not pleasant to know that the world overhead was slowly and silently sinking down upon you. The men down in the mine do not mind it, however.

Returning along the fifth gallery, we struck the safe part of the Ophir incline, and went down it to the sixth; but we found ten inches of water there, and had to come back. In repairing the damage done to the incline, the pump had to be stopped for two hours, and in the meantime the water gained about a foot. However, the pump was at work again, and the flood-water was decreasing. We climbed up to the fifth gallery again and sought a deep shaft, whereby we might descend to another part of the sixth, out of reach of the water, but suffered disappointment, as the men had gone to dinner, and there was no one to man the windlass. So, having seen the earthquake, we climbed out at the Union incline and tunnel, and adjourned, all dripping with candle grease and perspiration, to lunch at the Ophir office.

During the great flush year of 1863, Nevada [claims to have] produced $25,000,000 in bullion—almost, if not quite, a round million to each thousand inhabitants, which is very well, considering that she was without agriculture and manufactures. Silver mining was her sole productive industry. [Since the above was in type, I learn from an official source that the above figure is too high, and that the yield for 1863 did not exceed $20,000,000.] However, the day for large figures is approaching; the Sutro Tunnel is to plow through the Comstock lode from end to end, at a depth of two thousand feet, and then mining will be easy and comparatively inexpensive; and the momentous matters of drainage, and hoisting and hauling of ore will cease to be burdensome. This vast work will absorb many years, and millions of dollars, in its completion; but it will early yield money, for that desirable epoch will begin as soon as it strikes the first end of the vein. The tunnel will be some eight miles long, and will develop astonishing riches. Cars will carry the ore through the tunnel and dump it in the mills and thus do away with the present costly system of double handling and transportation by mule teams. The water from the tunnel will furnish the motive power for the mills. Mr. Sutro, the originator of this prodigious enterprise, is one of the few men in the world who is gifted with the pluck and perseverance necessary to follow up and

hound such an undertaking to its completion. He has converted several obstinate Congresses to a deserved friendliness toward his important work, and has gone up and down and to and fro in Europe until he has enlisted a great moneyed interest in it there.

CHAPTER LIII.

Every now and then, in these days, the boys used to tell me I ought to get one Jim Blaine to tell me the stirring story of his grandfather's old ram—but they always added that I must not mention the matter unless Jim was drunk at the time—just comfortably and sociably drunk. They kept this up until my curiosity was on the rack to hear the story. I got to haunting Blaine; but it was of no use, the boys always found fault with his condition; he was often moderately but never satisfactorily drunk. I never watched a man's condition with such absorbing interest, such anxious solicitude; I never so pined to see a man uncompromisingly drunk before. At last, one evening I hurried to his cabin, for I learned that this time his situation was such that even the most fastidious could find no fault with it—he was tranquilly, serenely, symmetrically drunk—not a hiccup to mar his voice, not a cloud upon his brain thick enough to obscure his memory. As I entered, he was sitting upon an empty powder-keg, with a clay pipe in one hand and the other raised to command silence. His face was round, red, and very serious; his throat was bare and his hair tumbled; in general appearance and costume he was a stalwart miner of the period. On the pine table stood a candle, and its dim light revealed "the boys" sitting here and there on bunks, candle-boxes, powder-kegs, etc. They said:

"Sh—! Don't speak—he's going to commence."

THE STORY OF THE OLD RAM.

I found a seat at once, and Blaine said:

'I don't reckon them times will ever come again. There never was a more bullier old ram than what he was. Grandfather fetched him from Illinois —got him of a man by the name of Yates—Bill Yates—maybe you might have heard of him; his father was a deacon—Baptist—and he was a rustler, too; a man had to get up ruther early to get the start of old Thankful Yates; it was him that put the Greens up to jining teams with my grandfather when he moved west.

'Seth Green was prob'ly the pick of the flock; he married a Wilkerson —Sarah Wilkerson—good cretur, she was—one of the likeliest heifers that was ever raised in old Stoddard, everybody said that knowed her. She could heft a bar'l of flour as easy as I can flirt a flapjack. And spin? Don't mention it! Independent? Humph! When Sile Hawkins come a browsing around her, she let him know that for all his tin he couldn't trot in harness alongside of her. You see, Sile Hawkins was—no, it warn't Sile Hawkins, after all—it was a galoot by the name of Filkins —I disremember his first name; but he was a stump—come into pra'r meeting drunk, one night, hooraying for Nixon, becuz he thought it was a primary; and old deacon Ferguson up and scooted him through the window and he lit on old Miss Jefferson's head, poor old filly. She was a good soul—had a glass eye and used to lend it to old Miss Wagner, that hadn't any, to receive company in; it warn't big enough, and when Miss Wagner warn't noticing, it would get twisted around in the socket, and look up, maybe, or out to one side, and every which way, while t' other one was looking as straight ahead as a spy-glass.

'Grown people didn't mind it, but it most always made the children cry, it was so sort of scary. She tried packing it in raw cotton, but it wouldn't work, somehow—the cotton would get loose and stick out and look so kind of awful that the children couldn't stand it no way. She was always dropping it out, and turning up her old dead-light on the company empty, and making them oncomfortable, becuz she never could tell when it hopped out, being blind on that side, you see. So somebody would have to hunch her and say, "Your game eye has fetched loose. Miss Wagner dear" —and then all of them would have to sit and wait till she jammed it in again—wrong side before, as a general thing, and green as a bird's egg, being a bashful cretur and easy sot back before company. But being wrong side before warn't much difference, anyway; becuz her own eye was sky-blue and the glass one was yaller on the front side, so whichever way she turned it it didn't match nohow.

'Old Miss Wagner was considerable on the borrow, she was. When she had a quilting, or Dorcas S'iety at her house she gen'ally borrowed Miss Higgins's wooden leg to stump around on; it was considerable shorter than her other pin, but much she minded that. She said she couldn't abide crutches when she had company, becuz they were so slow; said when she had company and things had to be done, she wanted to get up and hump herself. She was as bald as a jug, and so she used to borrow Miss Jacops's wig —Miss Jacops was the coffin-peddler's wife—a ratty old buzzard, he was, that used to go roosting around where people was sick, waiting for 'em; and there that old rip would sit all day, in the shade, on a coffin that he judged would fit the can'idate; and if it was a slow customer and kind of uncertain, he'd fetch his rations and a blanket along and sleep in the coffin nights. He was anchored out that way, in frosty weather, for about three weeks, once, before old Robbins's place, waiting for him; and after that, for as much as two years, Jacops was not on speaking terms with the old man, on account of his disapp'inting him. He got one of his feet froze, and lost money, too, becuz old Robbins took a favorable turn and got well. The next time Robbins got sick, Jacops tried to make up with him, and varnished up the same old coffin and fetched it along; but old Robbins was too many for him; he had him in, and 'peared to be powerful weak; he bought the coffin for ten dollars and Jacops was to pay it back and twenty-five more besides if Robbins didn't like the coffin after he'd tried it. And then Robbins died, and at the funeral he bursted off the lid and riz up in his shroud and told the parson to let up on the performances, becuz he could not stand such a coffin as that. You see he had been in a trance once before, when he was young, and he took the chances on another, cal'lating that if he made the trip it was money in his pocket, and if he missed fire he couldn't lose a cent. And by George he sued Jacops for the rhino and got jedgment; and he set up the coffin in his back parlor and said he 'lowed to take his time, now. It was always an aggravation to Jacops, the way that miserable old thing acted. He moved back to Indiany pretty soon—went to Wellsville —Wellsville was the place the Hogadorns was from. Mighty fine family. Old Maryland stock. Old Squire Hogadorn could carry around more mixed licker, and cuss better than most any man I ever see. His second wife was the widder Billings—she that was Becky Martin; her dam was deacon Dunlap's first wife. Her oldest child, Maria, married a missionary and died in grace—et up by the savages. They et him, too, poor feller —biled him. It warn't the custom, so they say, but they explained to friends of his'n that went down there to bring away his things, that they'd tried missionaries every other way and never could get any good out of 'em—and so it annoyed all his relations to find out that that man's life was fooled away just out of a dern'd experiment, so to speak. But mind you, there ain't anything ever reely lost; everything that people can't understand and don't see the reason of does good if you only hold on and give it a fair shake; Prov'dence don't fire no blank ca'tridges, boys. That there missionary's substance, unbeknowns to himself, actu'ly converted every last one of them heathens that took a chance at the barbacue. Nothing ever fetched them but that. Don't tell me it was an accident that he was biled. There ain't no such a thing as an accident.

'When my uncle Lem was leaning up agin a scaffolding once, sick, or drunk, or suthin, an Irishman with a hod full of bricks fell on him out of the third story and broke the old man's back in two places. People said it was an accident. Much accident there was about that. He didn't know what he was there for, but he was there for a good object. If he hadn't been there the Irishman would have been killed. Nobody can ever make me believe anything different from that. Uncle Lem's dog was there. Why didn't the Irishman fall on the dog? Becuz the dog would seen him a coming and stood from under. That's the reason the dog warn't appinted. A dog can't be depended on to carry out a special providence. Mark my words it was a put-up thing. Accidents don't happen, boys. Uncle Lem's dog—I wish you could a seen that dog. He was a reglar shepherd—or ruther he was part bull and part shepherd—splendid animal; belonged to parson Hagar before Uncle Lem got him. Parson Hagar belonged to the Western Reserve Hagars; prime family; his mother was a Watson; one of his sisters married a Wheeler; they settled in Morgan county, and he got nipped by the machinery in a carpet factory and went through in less than a quarter of a minute; his widder bought the piece of carpet that had his remains wove in, and people come a hundred mile to 'tend the funeral. There was fourteen yards in the piece.

'She wouldn't let them roll him up, but planted him just so—full length. The church was middling small where they preached the funeral, and they had to let one end of the coffin stick out of the window. They didn't bury him—they planted one end, and let him stand up, same as a monument. And they nailed a sign on it and put—put on—put on it—sacred to—the m-e-m-o-r-y—of fourteen y-a-r-d-s—of three-ply—car—pet—containing all that was—m-o-r-t-a-l—of—of—W-i-l-l-i-a-m—W-h-e—'

Jim Blaine had been growing gradually drowsy and drowsier—his head nodded, once, twice, three times—dropped peacefully upon his breast, and he fell tranquilly asleep. The tears were running down the boys' cheeks —they were suffocating with suppressed laughter—and had been from the start, though I had never noticed it. I perceived that I was "sold." I learned then that Jim Blaine's peculiarity was that whenever he reached a certain stage of intoxication, no human power could keep him from setting out, with impressive unction, to tell about a wonderful adventure which he had once had with his grandfather's old ram—and the mention of the ram in the first sentence was as far as any man had ever heard him get, concerning it. He always maundered off, interminably, from one thing to another, till his whisky got the best of him and he fell asleep. What the thing was that happened to him and his grandfather's old ram is a dark mystery to this day, for nobody has ever yet found out.

CHAPTER LIV.

Of course there was a large Chinese population in Virginia—it is the case with every town and city on the Pacific coast. They are a harmless race when white men either let them alone or treat them no worse than dogs; in fact they are almost entirely harmless anyhow, for they seldom think of resenting the vilest insults or the cruelest injuries. They are quiet, peaceable, tractable, free from drunkenness, and they are as industrious as the day is long. A disorderly Chinaman is rare, and a lazy one does not exist. So long as a Chinaman has strength to use his hands he needs no support from anybody; white men often complain of want of work, but a Chinaman offers no such complaint; he always manages to find something to do. He is a great convenience to everybody—even to the worst class of white men, for he bears the most of their sins, suffering fines for their petty thefts, imprisonment for their robberies, and death for their murders. Any white man can swear a Chinaman's life away in the courts, but no Chinaman can testify against a white man. Ours is the "land of the free"—nobody denies that—nobody challenges it. [Maybe it is because we won't let other people testify.] As I write, news comes that in broad daylight in San Francisco, some boys have stoned an inoffensive Chinaman to death, and that although a large crowd witnessed the shameful deed, no one interfered.

There are seventy thousand (and possibly one hundred thousand) Chinamen on the Pacific coast. There were about a thousand in Virginia. They were penned into a "Chinese quarter"—a thing which they do not particularly object to, as they are fond of herding together. Their buildings were of wood; usually only one story high, and set thickly together along streets scarcely wide enough for a wagon to pass through. Their quarter was a little removed from the rest of the town. The chief employment of Chinamen in towns is to wash clothing. They always send a bill, like this below, pinned to the clothes. It is mere ceremony, for it does not enlighten the customer much. Their price for washing was $2.50 per dozen—rather cheaper than white people could afford to wash for at that time. A very common sign on the Chinese houses was: "See Yup, Washer and Ironer"; "Hong Wo, Washer"; "Sam Sing & Ah Hop, Washing." The house servants, cooks, etc., in California and Nevada, were chiefly Chinamen. There were few white servants and no Chinawomen so employed. Chinamen make good house servants, being quick, obedient, patient, quick to learn and tirelessly industrious. They do not need to be taught a thing twice, as a general thing. They are imitative. If a Chinaman were to see his master break up a centre table, in a passion, and kindle a fire with it, that Chinaman would be likely to resort to the furniture for fuel forever afterward.

All Chinamen can read, write and cipher with easy facility—pity but all our petted voters could. In California they rent little patches of ground and do a deal of gardening. They will raise surprising crops of vegetables on a sand pile. They waste nothing. What is rubbish to a Christian, a Chinaman carefully preserves and makes useful in one way or another. He gathers up all the old oyster and sardine cans that white people throw away, and procures marketable tin and solder from them by melting. He gathers up old bones and turns them into manure. In California he gets a living out of old mining claims that white men have abandoned as exhausted and worthless—and then the officers come down on him once a month with an exorbitant swindle to which the legislature has given the broad, general name of "foreign" mining tax, but it is usually inflicted on no foreigners but Chinamen. This swindle has in some cases been repeated once or twice on the same victim in the course of the same month—but the public treasury was no additionally enriched by it, probably.

Chinamen hold their dead in great reverence—they worship their departed ancestors, in fact. Hence, in China, a man's front yard, back yard, or any other part of his premises, is

made his family burying ground, in order that he may visit the graves at any and all times. Therefore that huge empire is one mighty cemetery; it is ridged and wringled from its centre to its circumference with graves—and inasmuch as every foot of ground must be made to do its utmost, in China, lest the swarming population suffer for food, the very graves are cultivated and yield a harvest, custom holding this to be no dishonor to the dead. Since the departed are held in such worshipful reverence, a Chinaman cannot bear that any indignity be offered the places where they sleep. Mr. Burlingame said that herein lay China's bitter opposition to railroads; a road could not be built anywhere in the empire without disturbing the graves of their ancestors or friends.

A Chinaman hardly believes he could enjoy the hereafter except his body lay in his beloved China; also, he desires to receive, himself, after death, that worship with which he has honored his dead that preceded him. Therefore, if he visits a foreign country, he makes arrangements to have his bones returned to China in case he dies; if he hires to go to a foreign country on a labor contract, there is always a stipulation that his body shall be taken back to China if he dies; if the government sells a gang of Coolies to a foreigner for the usual five-year term, it is specified in the contract that their bodies shall be restored to China in case of death. On the Pacific coast the Chinamen all belong to one or another of several great companies or organizations, and these companies keep track of their members, register their names, and ship their bodies home when they die. The See Yup Company is held to be the largest of these. The Ning Yeong Company is next, and numbers eighteen thousand members on the coast. Its headquarters are at San Francisco, where it has a costly temple, several great officers (one of whom keeps regal state in seclusion and cannot be approached by common humanity), and a numerous priesthood. In it I was shown a register of its members, with the dead and the date of their shipment to China duly marked. Every ship that sails from San Francisco carries away a heavy freight of Chinese corpses—or did, at least, until the legislature, with an ingenious refinement of Christian cruelty, forbade the shipments, as a neat underhanded way of deterring Chinese immigration. The bill was offered, whether it passed or not. It is my impression that it passed. There was another bill—it became a law—compelling every incoming Chinaman to be vaccinated on the wharf and pay a duly appointed quack (no decent doctor would defile himself with such legalized robbery) ten dollars for it. As few importers of Chinese would want to go to an expense like that, the law-makers thought this would be another heavy blow to Chinese immigration.

What the Chinese quarter of Virginia was like—or, indeed, what the Chinese quarter of any Pacific coast town was and is like—may be gathered from this item which I printed in the Enterprise while reporting for that paper:

CHINATOWN.—Accompanied by a fellow reporter, we made a trip through our Chinese quarter the other night. The Chinese have built their portion of the city to suit themselves; and as they keep neither carriages nor wagons, their streets are not wide enough, as a general thing, to admit of the passage of vehicles. At ten o'clock at night the Chinaman may be seen in all his glory. In every little cooped-up, dingy cavern of a hut, faint with the odor of burning Josh-lights and with nothing to see the gloom by save the sickly, guttering tallow candle, were two or three yellow, long-tailed vagabonds, coiled up on a sort of short truckle-bed, smoking opium, motionless and with their lustreless eyes turned inward from excess of satisfaction—or rather the recent smoker looks thus, immediately after having passed the pipe to his neighbor—for opium-smoking is a comfortless operation, and requires constant attention. A lamp sits on the bed, the length of the long pipe-stem from the smoker's mouth; he puts a pellet of opium on the end of a wire, sets it on fire, and plasters it into the pipe much as a Christian would fill a hole with putty; then he applies the bowl to the lamp and proceeds to smoke—and the stewing and frying of the drug and the gurgling of the juices in the stem would well-nigh turn the stomach of a statue. John likes it, though; it soothes him, he takes about two dozen whiffs, and then rolls over to dream, Heaven only knows what, for we could not imagine by looking at the soggy creature. Possibly in his visions he travels far away from the gross world and his regular washing, and feast on succulent rats and birds'-nests in Paradise.

Mr. Ah Sing keeps a general grocery and provision store at No. 13 Wang street. He lavished his hospitality upon our party in the friendliest way. He had various kinds of colored and colorless wines and brandies, with unpronounceable names, imported from China in little crockery jugs, and which he offered to us in dainty little miniature wash-basins of porcelain. He offered us a mess of birds'-nests; also, small, neat sausages, of which we could have swallowed several yards if we had chosen to try, but we suspected that each link contained the corpse of a mouse, and therefore refrained. Mr. Sing had in his store a thousand articles of merchandise, curious to behold, impossible to imagine the uses of, and beyond our ability to describe.

His ducks, however, and his eggs, we could understand; the former were split open and flattened out like codfish, and came from China in that shape, and the latter were plastered over with some kind of paste which kept them fresh and palatable through the long voyage.

We found Mr. Hong Wo, No. 37 Chow-chow street, making up a lottery scheme—in fact we found a dozen others occupied in the same way in various parts of the quarter, for about every third Chinaman runs a lottery, and the balance of the tribe "buck" at it. "Tom," who speaks faultless English, and used to be chief and only cook to the Territorial Enterprise, when the establishment kept bachelor's hall two years ago, said that "Sometime Chinaman buy ticket one dollar hap, ketch um two tree hundred, sometime no ketch um anything; lottery like one man fight um seventy—may-be he whip, may-be he get whip heself, welly good."

However, the percentage being sixty-nine against him, the chances are, as a general thing, that "he get whip heself." We could not see that these lotteries differed in any respect from our own, save that the figures being Chinese, no ignorant white man might ever hope to succeed in telling "t'other from which;" the manner of drawing is similar to ours.

Mr. See Yup keeps a fancy store on Live Fox street. He sold us fans of white feathers, gorgeously ornamented; perfumery that smelled like Limburger cheese, Chinese pens, and watch-charms made of a stone unscratchable with steel instruments, yet polished and tinted like the inner coat of a sea-shell. As tokens of his esteem, See Yup presented the party with gaudy plumes made of gold tinsel and trimmed with peacocks' feathers.

We ate chow-chow with chop-sticks in the celestial restaurants; our comrade chided the moon-eyed damsels in front of the houses for their want of feminine reserve; we received protecting Josh-lights from our hosts and "dickered"

for a pagan God or two. Finally, we were impressed with the genius of a Chinese book-keeper; he figured up his accounts on a machine like a gridiron with buttons strung on its bars; the different rows represented units, tens, hundreds and thousands. He fingered them with incredible rapidity—in fact, he pushed them from place to place as fast as a musical professor's fingers travel over the keys of a piano.

They are a kindly disposed, well-meaning race, and are respected and well treated by the upper classes, all over the Pacific coast. No Californian gentleman or lady ever abuses or oppresses a Chinaman, under any circumstances, an explanation that seems to be much needed in the East. Only the scum of the population do it—they and their children; they, and, naturally and consistently, the policemen and politicians, likewise, for these are the dust-licking pimps and slaves of the scum, there as well as elsewhere in America.

CHAPTER LV.

I began to get tired of staying in one place so long.

There was no longer satisfying variety in going down to Carson to report the proceedings of the legislature once a year, and horse-races and pumpkin-shows once in three months; (they had got to raising pumpkins and potatoes in Washoe Valley, and of course one of the first achievements of the legislature was to institute a ten-thousand-dollar Agricultural Fair to show off forty dollars' worth of those pumpkins in—however, the territorial legislature was usually spoken of as the "asylum"). I wanted to see San Francisco. I wanted to go somewhere. I wanted—I did not know what I wanted. I had the "spring fever" and wanted a change, principally, no doubt. Besides, a convention had framed a State Constitution; nine men out of every ten wanted an office; I believed that these gentlemen would "treat" the moneyless and the irresponsible among the population into adopting the constitution and thus well-nigh killing the country (it could not well carry such a load as a State government, since it had nothing to tax that could stand a tax, for undeveloped mines could not, and there were not fifty developed ones in the land, there was but little realty to tax, and it did seem as if nobody was ever going to think of the simple salvation of inflicting a money penalty on murder). I believed that a State government would destroy the "flush times," and I wanted to get away. I believed that the mining stocks I had on hand would soon be worth $100,000, and thought if they reached that before the Constitution was adopted, I would sell out and make myself secure from the crash the change of government was going to bring. I considered $100,000 sufficient to go home with decently, though it was but a small amount compared to what I had been expecting to return with. I felt rather down-hearted about it, but I tried to comfort myself with the reflection that with such a sum I could not fall into want. About this time a schoolmate of mine whom I had not seen since boyhood, came tramping in on foot from Reese River, a very allegory of Poverty. The son of wealthy parents, here he was, in a strange land, hungry, bootless, mantled in an ancient horse-blanket, roofed with a brimless hat, and so generally and so extravagantly dilapidated that he could have "taken the shine out of the Prodigal Son himself," as he pleasantly remarked.

He wanted to borrow forty-six dollars—twenty-six to take him to San Francisco, and twenty for something else; to buy some soap with, maybe, for he needed it. I found I had but little more than the amount wanted, in my pocket; so I stepped in and borrowed forty-six dollars of a banker (on twenty days' time, without the formality of a note), and gave it him, rather than walk half a block to the office, where I had some specie laid up. If anybody had told me that it would take me two years to pay back that forty-six dollars to the banker (for I did not expect it of the Prodigal, and was not disappointed), I would have felt injured. And so would the banker.

I wanted a change. I wanted variety of some kind. It came. Mr. Goodman went away for a week and left me the post of chief editor. It destroyed me. The first day, I wrote my "leader" in the forenoon. The second day, I had no subject and put it off till the afternoon. The third day I put it off till evening, and then copied an elaborate editorial out of the "American Cyclopedia," that steadfast friend of the editor, all over this land. The fourth day I "fooled around" till midnight, and then fell back on the Cyclopedia again. The fifth day I cudgeled my brain till midnight, and then kept the press waiting while I penned some bitter personalities on six different people. The sixth day I labored in anguish till far into the night and brought forth—nothing. The paper went to press without an editorial. The seventh day I resigned. On the eighth, Mr. Goodman returned and found six duels on his hands—my personalities had borne fruit.

Nobody, except he has tried it, knows what it is to be an editor. It is easy to scribble local rubbish, with the facts all before you; it is easy to clip selections from other papers; it is easy to string out a correspondence from any locality; but it is unspeakable hardship to write editorials. Subjects are the trouble—the dreary lack of them, I mean. Every day, it is drag, drag, drag—think, and worry and suffer—all the world is a dull blank, and yet the editorial columns must be filled. Only give the editor a subject, and his work is done—it is no trouble to write it up; but fancy how you would feel if you had to pump your brains dry every day in the week, fifty-two weeks in the year. It makes one low spirited simply to think of it. The matter that each editor of a daily paper in America writes in the course of a year would fill from four to eight bulky volumes like this book! Fancy what a library an editor's work would make, after twenty or thirty years' service. Yet people often marvel that Dickens, Scott, Bulwer, Dumas, etc., have been able to produce so many books. If these authors had wrought as voluminously as newspaper editors do, the result would be something to marvel at, indeed. How editors can continue this tremendous labor, this exhausting consumption of brain fibre (for their work is creative, and not a mere mechanical laying-up of facts, like reporting), day after day and year after year, is incomprehensible. Preachers take two months' holiday in midsummer, for they find that to produce two sermons a week is wearing, in the long run. In truth it must be so, and is so; and therefore, how an editor can take from ten to twenty texts and build upon them from ten to twenty painstaking editorials a week and keep it up all the year round, is farther beyond comprehension than ever. Ever since I survived my week as editor, I have found at least one pleasure in any newspaper that comes to my hand; it is in admiring the long columns of editorial, and wondering to myself how in the mischief he did it!

Mr. Goodman's return relieved me of employment, unless I chose to become a reporter again. I could not do that; I could not serve in the ranks after being General of the army. So I thought I would depart and go abroad into the world somewhere. Just at this juncture, Dan, my associate in the reportorial department, told me, casually, that two citizens had been trying to persuade him to go with them to New York and aid in selling a rich silver mine which they had discovered and secured in a new mining district in our neighborhood. He said they offered to pay his expenses and give him one third of

the proceeds of the sale. He had refused to go. It was the very opportunity I wanted. I abused him for keeping so quiet about it, and not mentioning it sooner. He said it had not occurred to him that I would like to go, and so he had recommended them to apply to Marshall, the reporter of the other paper. I asked Dan if it was a good, honest mine, and no swindle. He said the men had shown him nine tons of the rock, which they had got out to take to New York, and he could cheerfully say that he had seen but little rock in Nevada that was richer; and moreover, he said that they had secured a tract of valuable timber and a mill-site, near the mine. My first idea was to kill Dan. But I changed my mind, notwithstanding I was so angry, for I thought maybe the chance was not yet lost. Dan said it was by no means lost; that the men were absent at the mine again, and would not be in Virginia to leave for the East for some ten days; that they had requested him to do the talking to Marshall, and he had promised that he would either secure Marshall or somebody else for them by the time they got back; he would now say nothing to anybody till they returned, and then fulfil his promise by furnishing me to them.

It was splendid. I went to bed all on fire with excitement; for nobody had yet gone East to sell a Nevada silver mine, and the field was white for the sickle. I felt that such a mine as the one described by Dan would bring a princely sum in New York, and sell without delay or difficulty. I could not sleep, my fancy so rioted through its castles in the air. It was the "blind lead" come again.

Next day I got away, on the coach, with the usual eclat attending departures of old citizens,—for if you have only half a dozen friends out there they will make noise for a hundred rather than let you seem to go away neglected and unregretted—and Dan promised to keep strict watch for the men that had the mine to sell.

The trip was signalized but by one little incident, and that occurred just as we were about to start. A very seedy looking vagabond passenger got out of the stage a moment to wait till the usual ballast of silver bricks was thrown in. He was standing on the pavement, when an awkward express employee, carrying a brick weighing a hundred pounds, stumbled and let it fall on the bummer's foot. He instantly dropped on the ground and began to howl in the most heart-breaking way. A sympathizing crowd gathered around and were going to pull his boot off; but he screamed louder than ever and they desisted; then he fell to gasping, and between the gasps ejaculated "Brandy! for Heaven's sake, brandy!" They poured half a pint down him, and it wonderfully restored and comforted him. Then he begged the people to assist him to the stage, which was done. The express people urged him to have a doctor at their expense, but he declined, and said that if he only had a little brandy to take along with him, to soothe his paroxyms of pain when they came on, he would be grateful and content. He was quickly supplied with two bottles, and we drove off. He was so smiling and happy after that, that I could not refrain from asking him how he could possibly be so comfortable with a crushed foot.

"Well," said he, "I hadn't had a drink for twelve hours, and hadn't a cent to my name. I was most perishing—and so, when that duffer dropped that hundred-pounder on my foot, I see my chance. Got a cork leg, you know!" and he pulled up his pantaloons and proved it.

He was as drunk as a lord all day long, and full of chucklings over his timely ingenuity.

One drunken man necessarily reminds one of another. I once heard a gentleman tell about an incident which he witnessed in a Californian bar-room. He entitled it "Ye Modest Man Taketh a Drink." It was nothing but a bit of acting, but it seemed to me a perfect rendering, and worthy of Toodles himself. The modest man, tolerably far gone with beer and other matters, enters a saloon (twenty-five cents is the price for anything and everything, and specie the only money used) and lays down a half dollar; calls for whiskey and drinks it; the bar-keeper makes change and lays the quarter in a wet place on the counter; the modest man fumbles at it with nerveless fingers, but it slips and the water holds it; he contemplates it, and tries again; same result; observes that people are interested in what he is at, blushes; fumbles at the quarter again—blushes—puts his forefinger carefully, slowly down, to make sure of his aim—pushes the coin toward the bar-keeper, and says with a sigh:

"Gimme a cigar!"

Naturally, another gentleman present told about another drunken man. He said he reeled toward home late at night; made a mistake and entered the wrong gate; thought he saw a dog on the stoop; and it was—an iron one.

He stopped and considered; wondered if it was a dangerous dog; ventured to say "Be (hic) begone!" No effect. Then he approached warily, and adopted conciliation; pursed up his lips and tried to whistle, but failed; still approached, saying, "Poor dog!—doggy, doggy, doggy!—poor doggy-dog!" Got up on the stoop, still petting with fond names; till master of the advantages; then exclaimed, "Leave, you thief!"—planted a vindictive kick in his ribs, and went head-over-heels overboard, of course. A pause; a sigh or two of pain, and then a remark in a reflective voice:

"Awful solid dog. What could he ben eating? ('ic!) Rocks, p'raps. Such animals is dangerous.—' At's what I say—they're dangerous. If a man—('ic!)—if a man wants to feed a dog on rocks, let him feed him on rocks; 'at's all right; but let him keep him at home—not have him layin' round promiscuous, where ('ic!) where people's liable to stumble over him when they ain't noticin'!"

It was not without regret that I took a last look at the tiny flag (it was thirty-five feet long and ten feet wide) fluttering like a lady's handkerchief from the topmost peak of Mount Davidson, two thousand feet above Virginia's roofs, and felt that doubtless I was bidding a permanent farewell to a city which had afforded me the most vigorous enjoyment of life I had ever experienced. And this reminds me of an incident which the dullest memory Virginia could boast at the time it happened must vividly recall, at times, till its possessor dies. Late one summer afternoon we had a rain shower.

That was astonishing enough, in itself, to set the whole town buzzing, for it only rains (during a week or two weeks) in the winter in Nevada, and even then not enough at a time to make it worth while for any merchant to keep umbrellas for sale. But the rain was not the chief wonder. It only lasted five or ten minutes; while the people were still talking about it all the heavens gathered to themselves a dense blackness as of midnight. All the vast eastern front of Mount Davidson, over-looking the city, put on such a funereal gloom that only the nearness and solidity of the mountain made its outlines even faintly distinguishable from the dead blackness of the heavens they rested against. This unaccustomed sight turned all eyes toward the mountain; and as they looked, a little tongue of

rich golden flame was seen waving and quivering in the heart of the midnight, away up on the extreme summit! In a few minutes the streets were packed with people, gazing with hardly an uttered word, at the one brilliant mote in the brooding world of darkness. It flicked like a candle-flame, and looked no larger; but with such a background it was wonderfully bright, small as it was. It was the flag!—though no one suspected it at first, it seemed so like a supernatural visitor of some kind—a mysterious messenger of good tidings, some were fain to believe. It was the nation's emblem transfigured by the departing rays of a sun that was entirely palled from view; and on no other object did the glory fall, in all the broad panorama of mountain ranges and deserts. Not even upon the staff of the flag—for that, a needle in the distance at any time, was now untouched by the light and undistinguishable in the gloom. For a whole hour the weird visitor winked and burned in its lofty solitude, and still the thousands of uplifted eyes watched it with fascinated interest. How the people were wrought up! The superstition grew apace that this was a mystic courier come with great news from the war—the poetry of the idea excusing and commending it—and on it spread, from heart to heart, from lip to lip and from street to street, till there was a general impulse to have out the military and welcome the bright waif with a salvo of artillery!

And all that time one sorely tried man, the telegraph operator sworn to official secrecy, had to lock his lips and chain his tongue with a silence that was like to rend them; for he, and he only, of all the speculating multitude, knew the great things this sinking sun had seen that day in the east—Vicksburg fallen, and the Union arms victorious at Gettysburg!

But for the journalistic monopoly that forbade the slightest revealment of eastern news till a day after its publication in the California papers, the glorified flag on Mount Davidson would have been saluted and re-saluted, that memorable evening, as long as there was a charge of powder to thunder with; the city would have been illuminated, and every man that had any respect for himself would have got drunk,—as was the custom of the country on all occasions of public moment. Even at this distant day I cannot think of this needlessly marred supreme opportunity without regret. What a time we might have had!

CHAPTER LVI.

We rumbled over the plains and valleys, climbed the Sierras to the clouds, and looked down upon summer-clad California. And I will remark here, in passing, that all scenery in California requires distance to give it its highest charm. The mountains are imposing in their sublimity and their majesty of form and altitude, from any point of view—but one must have distance to soften their ruggedness and enrich their tintings; a Californian forest is best at a little distance, for there is a sad poverty of variety in species, the trees being chiefly of one monotonous family—redwood, pine, spruce, fir—and so, at a near view there is a wearisome sameness of attitude in their rigid arms, stretched downward and outward in one continued and reiterated appeal to all men to "Sh! —don't say a word!—you might disturb somebody!" Close at hand, too, there is a reliefless and relentless smell of pitch and turpentine; there is a ceaseless melancholy in their sighing and complaining foliage; one walks over a soundless carpet of beaten yellow bark and dead spines of the foliage till he feels like a wandering spirit bereft of a footfall; he tires of the endless tufts of needles and yearns for substantial, shapely leaves; he looks for moss and grass to loll upon, and finds none, for where there is no bark there is naked clay and dirt, enemies to pensive musing and clean apparel. Often a grassy plain in California, is what it should be, but often, too, it is best contemplated at a distance, because although its grass blades are tall, they stand up vindictively straight and self-sufficient, and are unsociably wide apart, with uncomely spots of barren sand between.

One of the queerest things I know of, is to hear tourists from "the States" go into ecstasies over the loveliness of "ever-blooming California." And they always do go into that sort of ecstasies. But perhaps they would modify them if they knew how old Californians, with the memory full upon them of the dust-covered and questionable summer greens of Californian "verdure," stand astonished, and filled with worshipping admiration, in the presence of the lavish richness, the brilliant green, the infinite freshness, the spend-thrift variety of form and species and foliage that make an Eastern landscape a vision of Paradise itself. The idea of a man falling into raptures over grave and sombre California, when that man has seen New England's meadow-expanses and her maples, oaks and cathedral-windowed elms decked in summer attire, or the opaline splendors of autumn descending upon her forests, comes very near being funny—would be, in fact, but that it is so pathetic. No land with an unvarying climate can be very beautiful. The tropics are not, for all the sentiment that is wasted on them. They seem beautiful at first, but sameness impairs the charm by and by. Change is the handmaiden Nature requires to do her miracles with. The land that has four well-defined seasons, cannot lack beauty, or pall with monotony. Each season brings a world of enjoyment and interest in the watching of its unfolding, its gradual, harmonious development, its culminating graces—and just as one begins to tire of it, it passes away and a radical change comes, with new witcheries and new glories in its train. And I think that to one in sympathy with nature, each season, in its turn, seems the loveliest.

San Francisco, a truly fascinating city to live in, is stately and handsome at a fair distance, but close at hand one notes that the architecture is mostly old-fashioned, many streets are made up of decaying, smoke-grimed, wooden houses, and the barren sand-hills toward the outskirts obtrude themselves too prominently. Even the kindly climate is sometimes pleasanter when read about than personally experienced, for a lovely, cloudless sky wears out its welcome by and by, and then when the longed for rain does come it stays. Even the playful earthquake is better contemplated at a dis—

However there are varying opinions about that.

The climate of San Francisco is mild and singularly equable. The thermometer stands at about seventy degrees the year round. It hardly changes at all. You sleep under one or two light blankets Summer and Winter, and never use a mosquito bar. Nobody ever wears Summer clothing. You wear black broadcloth—if you have it—in August and January, just the same. It is no colder, and no warmer, in the one month than the other. You do not use overcoats and you do not use fans. It is as pleasant a climate as could well be contrived, take it all around, and is doubtless the most unvarying in the whole world. The wind blows there a good deal in the summer months, but then you can go over to Oakland, if you choose—three or four miles away—it does not blow there. It has only snowed twice in San Francisco in nineteen years, and then it only remained on the ground long enough to astonish the children, and set them to wondering what the feathery stuff was.

During eight months of the year, straight along, the skies are bright and cloudless, and never a drop of rain falls. But when the other four months come along, you will need to go and steal an umbrella. Because you will require it. Not just one day, but one hundred and twenty days in hardly varying succession. When you want to go visiting, or attend church, or the theatre, you never look up at the clouds to see whether it is likely to rain or not—you look at the almanac. If it is Winter, it will rain—and if it is Summer, it won't rain, and you cannot help it. You never need a lightning-rod, because it never thunders and it never lightens. And after you have listened for six or eight weeks, every night, to the dismal monotony of those quiet rains, you will wish in your heart the thunder would leap and crash and roar along those drowsy skies once, and make everything alive—you will wish the prisoned lightnings would cleave the dull firmament asunder and light it with a blinding glare for one little instant. You would give anything to hear the old familiar thunder again and see the lightning strike somebody. And along in the Summer, when you have suffered about four months of lustrous, pitiless sunshine, you are ready to go down on your knees and plead for rain—hail—snow—thunder and lightning—anything to break the monotony —you will take an earthquake, if you cannot do any better. And the chances are that you'll get it, too.

San Francisco is built on sand hills, but they are prolific sand hills. They yield a generous vegetation. All the rare flowers which people in "the States" rear with such patient care in parlor flower-pots and green-houses, flourish luxuriantly in the open air there all the year round. Calla lilies, all sorts of geraniums, passion flowers, moss roses—I do not know the names of a tenth part of them. I only know that while New Yorkers are burdened with banks and drifts of snow, Californians are burdened with banks and drifts of flowers, if they only keep their hands off and let them grow. And I have heard that they have also that rarest and most curious of all the flowers, the beautiful Espiritu Santo, as the Spaniards call it—or flower of the Holy Spirit —though I thought it grew only in Central America—down on the Isthmus. In its cup is the daintiest little facsimile of a dove, as pure as snow. The Spaniards have a superstitious reverence for it. The blossom has been conveyed to the States, submerged in ether; and the bulb has been taken thither also, but every attempt to make it bloom after it arrived, has failed.

I have elsewhere spoken of the endless Winter of Mono, California, and but this moment of the eternal Spring of San Francisco. Now if we travel a hundred miles in a straight line, we come to the eternal Summer of Sacramento. One never sees Summer-clothing or mosquitoes in San Francisco—but they can be found in Sacramento. Not always and unvaryingly, but about one hundred and forty-three months out of twelve years, perhaps. Flowers bloom there, always, the reader can easily believe—people suffer and sweat, and swear, morning, noon and night, and wear out their stanchest energies fanning themselves. It gets hot there, but if you go down to Fort Yuma you will find it hotter. Fort Yuma is probably the hottest place on earth. The thermometer stays at one hundred and twenty in the shade there all the time—except when it varies and goes higher. It is a U.S. military post, and its occupants get so used to the terrific heat that they suffer without it. There is a tradition (attributed to John Phenix [It has been purloined by fifty different scribblers who were too poor to invent a fancy but not ashamed to steal one.—M. T.]) that a very, very wicked soldier died there, once, and of course, went straight to the hottest corner of perdition, —and the next day he telegraphed back for his blankets. There is no doubt about the truth of this statement—there can be no doubt about it. I have seen the place where that soldier used to board. In Sacramento it is fiery Summer always, and you can gather roses, and eat strawberries and ice-cream, and wear white linen clothes, and pant and perspire, at eight or nine o'clock in the morning, and then take the cars, and at noon put on your furs and your skates, and go skimming over frozen Donner Lake, seven thousand feet above the valley, among snow banks fifteen feet deep, and in the shadow of grand mountain peaks that lift their frosty crags ten thousand feet above the level of the sea.

There is a transition for you! Where will you find another like it in the Western hemisphere? And some of us have swept around snow-walled curves of the Pacific Railroad in that vicinity, six thousand feet above the sea, and looked down as the birds do, upon the deathless Summer of the Sacramento Valley, with its fruitful fields, its feathery foliage, its silver streams, all slumbering in the mellow haze of its enchanted atmosphere, and all infinitely softened and spiritualized by distance—a dreamy, exquisite glimpse of fairyland, made all the more charming and striking that it was caught through a forbidden gateway of ice and snow, and savage crags and precipices.

CHAPTER LVII.

It was in this Sacramento Valley, just referred to, that a deal of the most lucrative of the early gold mining was done, and you may still see, in places, its grassy slopes and levels torn and guttered and disfigured by the avaricious spoilers of fifteen and twenty years ago. You may see such disfigurements far and wide over California—and in some such places, where only meadows and forests are visible—not a living creature, not a house, no stick or stone or remnant of a ruin, and not a sound, not even a whisper to disturb the Sabbath stillness—you will find it hard to believe that there stood at one time a fiercely-flourishing little city, of two thousand or three thousand souls, with its newspaper, fire company, brass band, volunteer militia, bank, hotels, noisy Fourth of July processions and speeches, gambling hells crammed with tobacco smoke, profanity, and rough-bearded men of all nations and colors, with tables heaped with gold dust sufficient for the revenues of a German principality—streets crowded and rife with business—town lots worth four hundred dollars a front foot—labor, laughter, music, dancing, swearing, fighting, shooting, stabbing—a bloody inquest and a man for breakfast every morning—everything that delights and adorns existence —all the appointments and appurtenances of a thriving and prosperous and promising young city,—and now nothing is left of it all but a lifeless, homeless solitude. The men are gone, the houses have vanished, even the name of the place is forgotten. In no other land, in modern times, have towns so absolutely died and disappeared, as in the old mining regions of California.

It was a driving, vigorous, restless population in those days. It was a curious population. It was the only population of the kind that the world has ever seen gathered together, and it is not likely that the world will ever see its like again. For observe, it was an assemblage of two hundred thousand young men—not simpering, dainty, kid-gloved weaklings, but stalwart, muscular, dauntless young braves, brimful of push and energy, and royally endowed with every attribute that goes to make up a peerless and magnificent manhood—the very pick and choice of the world's glorious ones. No women, no children, no gray and stooping veterans,—none but erect, bright-eyed, quick-moving, strong-handed young giants—the strangest population, the finest population, the most gallant host that ever trooped down the startled solitudes of an unpeopled land. And where are they now? Scattered to the ends of the earth—or prematurely aged and decrepit—or shot or stabbed in street affrays—or dead of disappointed hopes and broken hearts—all gone, or nearly all —victims devoted upon the altar of the golden calf—the noblest holocaust that ever wafted its sacrificial incense heavenward. It is pitiful to think upon.

It was a splendid population—for all the slow, sleepy, sluggish-brained sloths staid at home—you never find that sort of people among pioneers —you cannot build pioneers out of that sort of material. It was that population that gave to California a name for getting up astounding enterprises and rushing them through with a magnificent dash and daring and a recklessness of cost or consequences, which she bears unto this day—and when she projects a new surprise, the grave world smiles as usual, and says "Well, that is California all over."

But they were rough in those times! They fairly reveled in gold, whisky, fights, and fandangoes, and were unspeakably happy. The honest miner raked from a hundred to a thousand dollars out of his claim a day, and what with the gambling dens and the other entertainments, he hadn't a cent the next morning, if he had any sort of luck. They cooked their own bacon and beans, sewed on their own buttons, washed their own shirts — blue woollen ones; and if a man wanted a fight on his hands without any annoying delay, all he had to do was to appear in public in a white shirt or a stove-pipe hat, and he would be accommodated. For those people hated aristocrats. They had a particular and malignant animosity toward what they called a "biled shirt."

It was a wild, free, disorderly, grotesque society! Men—only swarming hosts of stalwart men—nothing juvenile, nothing feminine, visible anywhere!

In those days miners would flock in crowds to catch a glimpse of that rare and blessed spectacle, a woman! Old inhabitants tell how, in a certain camp, the news went abroad early in the morning that a woman was come! They had seen a calico dress hanging out of a wagon down at the camping-ground—sign of emigrants from over the great plains. Everybody went down there, and a shout went up when an actual, bona fide dress was discovered fluttering in the wind! The male emigrant was visible. The miners said:

"Fetch her out!"

He said: "It is my wife, gentlemen—she is sick—we have been robbed of money, provisions, everything, by the Indians—we want to rest."

"Fetch her out! We've got to see her!"

"But, gentlemen, the poor thing, she—"

"FETCH HER OUT!"

He "fetched her out," and they swung their hats and sent up three rousing cheers and a tiger; and they crowded around and gazed at her, and touched her dress, and listened to her voice with the look of men who listened to a memory rather than a present reality—and then they collected twenty-five hundred dollars in gold and gave it to the man, and swung their hats again and gave three more cheers, and went home satisfied.

Once I dined in San Francisco with the family of a pioneer, and talked with his daughter, a young lady whose first experience in San Francisco was an adventure, though she herself did not remember it, as she was only two or three years old at the time. Her father said that, after landing from the ship, they were walking up the street, a servant leading the party with the little girl in her arms. And presently a huge miner, bearded, belted, spurred, and bristling with deadly weapons—just down from a long campaign in the mountains, evidently—barred the way, stopped the servant, and stood gazing, with a face all alive with gratification and astonishment. Then he said, reverently:

"Well, if it ain't a child!" And then he snatched a little leather sack out of his pocket and said to the servant:

"There's a hundred and fifty dollars in dust, there, and I'll give it to you to let me kiss the child!"

That anecdote is true.

But see how things change. Sitting at that dinner-table, listening to that anecdote, if I had offered double the money for the privilege of kissing the same child, I would have been refused. Seventeen added years have far more than doubled the price.

And while upon this subject I will remark that once in Star City, in the Humboldt Mountains, I took my place in a sort of long, post-office single file of miners, to patiently await my chance to peep through a crack in the cabin and get a sight of the splendid new sensation—a genuine, live Woman! And at the end of half of an hour my turn came, and I put my eye to the crack, and there she was, with one arm akimbo, and tossing flap-jacks in a frying-pan with the other.

And she was one hundred and sixty-five [Being in calmer mood, now, I voluntarily knock off a hundred from that.—M.T.] years old, and hadn't a tooth in her head.

CHAPTER LVIII.

For a few months I enjoyed what to me was an entirely new phase of existence—a butterfly idleness; nothing to do, nobody to be responsible to, and untroubled with financial uneasiness. I fell in love with the most cordial and sociable city in the Union. After the sage-brush and alkali deserts of Washoe, San Francisco was Paradise to me. I lived at the best hotel, exhibited my clothes in the most conspicuous places, infested the opera, and learned to seem enraptured with music which oftener afflicted my ignorant ear than enchanted it, if I had had the vulgar honesty to confess it. However, I suppose I was not greatly worse than the most of my countrymen in that. I had longed to be a butterfly, and I was one at last. I attended private parties in sumptuous evening dress, simpered and aired my graces like a born beau, and polkad and schottisched with a step peculiar to myself—and the kangaroo. In a word, I kept the due state of a man worth a hundred thousand dollars (prospectively,) and likely to reach absolute affluence when that silver-mine sale should be ultimately achieved in the East. I spent money with a free hand, and meantime watched the stock sales with an interested eye and looked to see what might happen in Nevada.

Something very important happened. The property holders of Nevada voted against the State Constitution; but the folks who had nothing to lose were in the majority, and carried the measure over their heads. But after all it did not immediately

look like a disaster, though unquestionably it was one I hesitated, calculated the chances, and then concluded not to sell. Stocks went on rising; speculation went mad; bankers, merchants, lawyers, doctors, mechanics, laborers, even the very washerwomen and servant girls, were putting up their earnings on silver stocks, and every sun that rose in the morning went down on paupers enriched and rich men beggared. What a gambling carnival it was! Gould and Curry soared to six thousand three hundred dollars a foot! And then —all of a sudden, out went the bottom and everything and everybody went to ruin and destruction! The wreck was complete.

The bubble scarcely left a microscopic moisture behind it. I was an early beggar and a thorough one. My hoarded stocks were not worth the paper they were printed on. I threw them all away. I, the cheerful idiot that had been squandering money like water, and thought myself beyond the reach of misfortune, had not now as much as fifty dollars when I gathered together my various debts and paid them. I removed from the hotel to a very private boarding house. I took a reporter's berth and went to work. I was not entirely broken in spirit, for I was building confidently on the sale of the silver mine in the east. But I could not hear from Dan. My letters miscarried or were not answered.

One day I did not feel vigorous and remained away from the office. The next day I went down toward noon as usual, and found a note on my desk which had been there twenty-four hours. It was signed "Marshall"—the Virginia reporter—and contained a request that I should call at the hotel and see him and a friend or two that night, as they would sail for the east in the morning. A postscript added that their errand was a big mining speculation! I was hardly ever so sick in my life. I abused myself for leaving Virginia and entrusting to another man a matter I ought to have attended to myself; I abused myself for remaining away from the office on the one day of all the year that I should have been there. And thus berating myself I trotted a mile to the steamer wharf and arrived just in time to be too late. The ship was in the stream and under way.

I comforted myself with the thought that may be the speculation would amount to nothing—poor comfort at best— and then went back to my slavery, resolved to put up with my thirty-five dollars a week and forget all about it.

A month afterward I enjoyed my first earthquake. It was one which was long called the "great" earthquake, and is doubtless so distinguished till this day. It was just after noon, on a bright October day. I was coming down Third street. The only objects in motion anywhere in sight in that thickly built and populous quarter, were a man in a buggy behind me, and a street car wending slowly up the cross street. Otherwise, all was solitude and a Sabbath stillness. As I turned the corner, around a frame house, there was a great rattle and jar, and it occurred to me that here was an item!—no doubt a fight in that house. Before I could turn and seek the door, there came a really terrific shock; the ground seemed to roll under me in waves, interrupted by a violent joggling up and down, and there was a heavy grinding noise as of brick houses rubbing together. I fell up against the frame house and hurt my elbow. I knew what it was, now, and from mere reportorial instinct, nothing else, took out my watch and noted the time of day; at that moment a third and still severer shock came, and as I reeled about on the pavement trying to keep my footing, I saw a sight! The entire front of a tall four-story brick building in Third street sprung outward like a door and fell sprawling across the street, raising a dust like a great volume of smoke! And here came the buggy—overboard went the man, and in less time than I can tell it the vehicle was distributed in small fragments along three hundred yards of street.

One could have fancied that somebody had fired a charge of chair-rounds and rags down the thoroughfare. The street car had stopped, the horses were rearing and plunging, the passengers were pouring out at both ends, and one fat man had crashed half way through a glass window on one side of the car, got wedged fast and was squirming and screaming like an impaled madman. Every door, of every house, as far as the eye could reach, was vomiting a stream of human beings; and almost before one could execute a wink and begin another, there was a massed multitude of people stretching in endless procession down every street my position commanded. Never was solemn solitude turned into teeming life quicker.

Of the wonders wrought by "the great earthquake," these were all that came under my eye; but the tricks it did, elsewhere, and far and wide over the town, made toothsome gossip for nine days.

The destruction of property was trifling—the injury to it was wide-spread and somewhat serious.

The "curiosities" of the earthquake were simply endless. Gentlemen and ladies who were sick, or were taking a siesta, or had dissipated till a late hour and were making up lost sleep, thronged into the public streets in all sorts of queer apparel, and some without any at all. One woman who had been washing a naked child, ran down the street holding it by the ankles as if it were a dressed turkey. Prominent citizens who were supposed to keep the Sabbath strictly, rushed out of saloons in their shirt-sleeves, with billiard cues in their hands. Dozens of men with necks swathed in napkins, rushed from barber-shops, lathered to the eyes or with one cheek clean shaved and the other still bearing a hairy stubble. Horses broke from stables, and a frightened dog rushed up a short attic ladder and out on to a roof, and when his scare was over had not the nerve to go down again the same way he had gone up.

A prominent editor flew down stairs, in the principal hotel, with nothing on but one brief undergarment—met a chambermaid, and exclaimed:

"Oh, what shall I do! Where shall I go!"

She responded with naive serenity:

"If you have no choice, you might try a clothing-store!"

A certain foreign consul's lady was the acknowledged leader of fashion, and every time she appeared in anything new or extraordinary, the ladies in the vicinity made a raid on their husbands' purses and arrayed themselves similarly. One man who had suffered considerably and growled accordingly, was standing at the window when the shocks came, and the next instant the consul's wife, just out of the bath, fled by with no other apology for clothing than—a bath-towel! The sufferer rose superior to the terrors of the earthquake, and said to his wife:

"Now that is something like! Get out your towel my dear!"

The plastering that fell from ceilings in San Francisco that day, would have covered several acres of ground. For some days afterward, groups of eyeing and pointing men stood about many a building, looking at long zig-zag cracks that extended from the eaves to the ground. Four feet of the tops of three chimneys on one house were broken square off and turned around in such a way as to completely stop the draft.

A crack a hundred feet long gaped open six inches wide in the middle of one street and then shut together again with such force, as to ridge up the meeting earth like a slender grave. A lady sitting in her rocking and quaking parlor, saw the wall part at the ceiling, open and shut twice, like a mouth, and then-drop the end of a brick on the floor like a tooth. She was a woman easily disgusted with foolishness, and she arose and went out of there. One lady who was coming down stairs was astonished to see a bronze Hercules lean forward on its pedestal as if to strike her with its club. They both reached the bottom of the flight at the same time,—the woman insensible from the fright. Her child, born some little time afterward, was club-footed. However—on second thought,—if the reader sees any coincidence in this, he must do it at his own risk.

The first shock brought down two or three huge organ-pipes in one of the churches. The minister, with uplifted hands, was just closing the services. He glanced up, hesitated, and said:

"However, we will omit the benediction!"—and the next instant there was a vacancy in the atmosphere where he had stood.

After the first shock, an Oakland minister said:

"Keep your seats! There is no better place to die than this"—

And added, after the third:

"But outside is good enough!" He then skipped out at the back door.

Such another destruction of mantel ornaments and toilet bottles as the earthquake created, San Francisco never saw before. There was hardly a girl or a matron in the city but suffered losses of this kind. Suspended pictures were thrown down, but oftener still, by a curious freak of the earthquake's humor, they were whirled completely around with their faces to the wall! There was great difference of opinion, at first, as to the course or direction the earthquake traveled, but water that splashed out of various tanks and buckets settled that. Thousands of people were made so sea-sick by the rolling and pitching of floors and streets that they were weak and bed-ridden for hours, and some few for even days afterward.—Hardly an individual escaped nausea entirely.

The queer earthquake—episodes that formed the staple of San Francisco gossip for the next week would fill a much larger book than this, and so I will diverge from the subject.

By and by, in the due course of things, I picked up a copy of the Enterprise one day, and fell under this cruel blow:

NEVADA MINES IN NEW YORK.—G. M. Marshall, Sheba Hurs and Amos H. Rose, who left San Francisco last July for New York City, with ores from mines in Pine Wood District, Humboldt County, and on the Reese River range, have disposed of a mine containing six thousand feet and called the Pine Mountains Consolidated, for the sum of $3,000,000. The stamps on the deed, which is now on its way to Humboldt County, from New York, for record, amounted to $3,000, which is said to be the largest amount of stamps ever placed on one document. A working capital of $1,000,000 has been paid into the treasury, and machinery has already been purchased for a large quartz mill, which will be put up as soon as possible. The stock in this company is all full paid and entirely unassessable. The ores of the mines in this district somewhat resemble those of the Sheba mine in Humboldt. Sheba Hurst, the discoverer of the mines, with his friends corralled all the best leads and all the land and timber they desired before making public their whereabouts. Ores from there, assayed in this city, showed them to be exceedingly rich in silver and gold—silver predominating. There is an abundance of wood and water in the District. We are glad to know that New York capital has been enlisted in the development of the mines of this region. Having seen the ores and assays, we are satisfied that the mines of the District are very valuable—anything but wild-cat.

Once more native imbecility had carried the day, and I had lost a million! It was the "blind lead" over again.

Let us not dwell on this miserable matter. If I were inventing these things, I could be wonderfully humorous over them; but they are too true to be talked of with hearty levity, even at this distant day. [True, and yet not exactly as given in the above figures, possibly. I saw Marshall, months afterward, and although he had plenty of money he did not claim to have captured an entire million. In fact I gathered that he had not then received $50,000. Beyond that figure his fortune appeared to consist of uncertain vast expectations rather than prodigious certainties. However, when the above item appeared in print I put full faith in it, and incontinently wilted and went to seed under it.] Suffice it that I so lost heart, and so yielded myself up to repinings and sighings and foolish regrets, that I neglected my duties and became about worthless, as a reporter for a brisk newspaper. And at last one of the proprietors took me aside, with a charity I still remember with considerable respect, and gave me an opportunity to resign my berth and so save myself the disgrace of a dismissal.

CHAPTER LIX.

For a time I wrote literary screeds for the Golden Era. C. H. Webb had established a very excellent literary weekly called the Californian, but high merit was no guaranty of success; it languished, and he sold out to three printers, and Bret Harte became editor at $20 a week, and I was employed to contribute an article a week at $12. But the journal still languished, and the printers sold out to Captain Ogden, a rich man and a pleasant gentleman who chose to amuse himself with such an expensive luxury without much caring about the cost of it. When he grew tired of the novelty, he re-sold to the printers, the paper presently died a peaceful death, and I was out of work again. I would not mention these things but for the fact that they so aptly illustrate the ups and downs that characterize life on the Pacific coast. A man could hardly stumble into such a variety of queer vicissitudes in any other country.

For two months my sole occupation was avoiding acquaintances; for during that time I did not earn a penny, or buy an article of any kind, or pay my board. I became a very adept at "slinking." I slunk from back street to back street, I slunk away from approaching faces that looked familiar, I slunk to my meals, ate them humbly and with a mute apology for every mouthful I robbed my generous landlady of, and at midnight, after wanderings that were but slinkings away from cheerfulness and light, I slunk to my bed. I felt meaner, and lowlier and more despicable than the worms. During all this

time I had but one piece of money—a silver ten cent piece—and I held to it and would not spend it on any account, lest the consciousness coming strong upon me that I was entirely penniless, might suggest suicide. I had pawned every thing but the clothes I had on; so I clung to my dime desperately, till it was smooth with handling.

However, I am forgetting. I did have one other occupation beside that of "slinking." It was the entertaining of a collector (and being entertained by him,) who had in his hands the Virginia banker's bill for forty-six dollars which I had loaned my schoolmate, the "Prodigal." This man used to call regularly once a week and dun me, and sometimes oftener. He did it from sheer force of habit, for he knew he could get nothing. He would get out his bill, calculate the interest for me, at five per cent a month, and show me clearly that there was no attempt at fraud in it and no mistakes; and then plead, and argue and dun with all his might for any sum—any little trifle—even a dollar—even half a dollar, on account. Then his duty was accomplished and his conscience free. He immediately dropped the subject there always; got out a couple of cigars and divided, put his feet in the window, and then we would have a long, luxurious talk about everything and everybody, and he would furnish me a world of curious dunning adventures out of the ample store in his memory. By and by he would clap his hat on his head, shake hands and say briskly:

"Well, business is business—can't stay with you always!"—and was off in a second.

The idea of pining for a dun! And yet I used to long for him to come, and would get as uneasy as any mother if the day went by without his visit, when I was expecting it. But he never collected that bill, at last nor any part of it. I lived to pay it to the banker myself.

Misery loves company. Now and then at night, in out-of-the way, dimly lighted places, I found myself happening on another child of misfortune. He looked so seedy and forlorn, so homeless and friendless and forsaken, that I yearned toward him as a brother. I wanted to claim kinship with him and go about and enjoy our wretchedness together. The drawing toward each other must have been mutual; at any rate we got to falling together oftener, though still seemingly by accident; and although we did not speak or evince any recognition, I think the dull anxiety passed out of both of us when we saw each other, and then for several hours we would idle along contentedly, wide apart, and glancing furtively in at home lights and fireside gatherings, out of the night shadows, and very much enjoying our dumb companionship.

Finally we spoke, and were inseparable after that. For our woes were identical, almost. He had been a reporter too, and lost his berth, and this was his experience, as nearly as I can recollect it. After losing his berth he had gone down, down, down, with never a halt: from a boarding house on Russian Hill to a boarding house in Kearney street; from thence to Dupont; from thence to a low sailor den; and from thence to lodgings in goods boxes and empty hogsheads near the wharves. Then; for a while, he had gained a meagre living by sewing up bursted sacks of grain on the piers; when that failed he had found food here and there as chance threw it in his way. He had ceased to show his face in daylight, now, for a reporter knows everybody, rich and poor, high and low, and cannot well avoid familiar faces in the broad light of day.

This mendicant Blucher—I call him that for convenience—was a splendid creature. He was full of hope, pluck and philosophy; he was well read and a man of cultivated taste; he had a bright wit and was a master of satire; his kindliness and his generous spirit made him royal in my eyes and changed his curb-stone seat to a throne and his damaged hat to a crown.

He had an adventure, once, which sticks fast in my memory as the most pleasantly grotesque that ever touched my sympathies. He had been without a penny for two months. He had shirked about obscure streets, among friendly dim lights, till the thing had become second nature to him. But at last he was driven abroad in daylight. The cause was sufficient; he had not tasted food for forty-eight hours, and he could not endure the misery of his hunger in idle hiding. He came along a back street, glowering at the loaves in bake-shop windows, and feeling that he could trade his life away for a morsel to eat. The sight of the bread doubled his hunger; but it was good to look at it, any how, and imagine what one might do if one only had it.

Presently, in the middle of the street he saw a shining spot— looked again—did not, and could not, believe his eyes—turned away, to try them, then looked again. It was a verity—no vain, hunger-inspired delusion—it was a silver dime!

He snatched it—gloated over it; doubted it—bit it—found it genuine —choked his heart down, and smothered a halleluiah. Then he looked around—saw that nobody was looking at him— threw the dime down where it was before—walked away a few steps, and approached again, pretending he did not know it was there, so that he could re-enjoy the luxury of finding it. He walked around it, viewing it from different points; then sauntered about with his hands in his pockets, looking up at the signs and now and then glancing at it and feeling the old thrill again. Finally he took it up, and went away, fondling it in his pocket. He idled through unfrequented streets, stopping in doorways and corners to take it out and look at it. By and by he went home to his lodgings—an empty queens-ware hogshead,—and employed himself till night trying to make up his mind what to buy with it. But it was hard to do. To get the most for it was the idea. He knew that at the Miner's Restaurant he could get a plate of beans and a piece of bread for ten cents; or a fish-ball and some few trifles, but they gave "no bread with one fish-ball" there. At French Pete's he could get a veal cutlet, plain, and some radishes and bread, for ten cents; or a cup of coffee—a pint at least—and a slice of bread; but the slice was not thick enough by the eighth of an inch, and sometimes they were still more criminal than that in the cutting of it. At seven o'clock his hunger was wolfish; and still his mind was not made up. He turned out and went up Merchant street, still ciphering; and chewing a bit of stick, as is the way of starving men.

He passed before the lights of Martin's restaurant, the most aristocratic in the city, and stopped. It was a place where he had often dined, in better days, and Martin knew him well. Standing aside, just out of the range of the light, he worshiped the quails and steaks in the show window, and imagined that may be the fairy times were not gone yet and some prince in disguise would come along presently and tell him to go in there and take whatever he wanted. He chewed his stick with a hungry interest as he warmed to his subject. Just at this juncture he was conscious of some one at his side, sure enough; and then a finger touched his arm. He looked up, over his shoulder, and saw an apparition—a very allegory of Hunger! It was a man six feet high, gaunt, unshaven, hung with rags; with a haggard face and sunken cheeks, and eyes that pleaded piteously. This phantom said:

"Come with me—please."

He locked his arm in Blucher's and walked up the street to where the passengers were few and the light not strong, and then facing about, put out his hands in a beseeching way, and said:

"Friend—stranger—look at me! Life is easy to you—you go about, placid and content, as I did once, in my day—you have been in there, and eaten your sumptuous supper, and picked your teeth, and hummed your tune, and thought your pleasant thoughts, and said to yourself it is a good world —but you've never suffered! You don't know what trouble is—you don't know what misery is—nor hunger! Look at me! Stranger have pity on a poor friendless, homeless dog! As God is my judge, I have not tasted food for eight and forty hours!—look in my eyes and see if I lie! Give me the least trifle in the world to keep me from starving—anything —twenty-five cents! Do it, stranger—do it, please. It will be nothing to you, but life to me. Do it, and I will go down on my knees and lick the dust before you! I will kiss your footprints—I will worship the very ground you walk on! Only twenty-five cents! I am famishing — perishing—starving by inches! For God's sake don't desert me!"

Blucher was bewildered—and touched, too—stirred to the depths. He reflected. Thought again. Then an idea struck him, and he said:

"Come with me."

He took the outcast's arm, walked him down to Martin's restaurant, seated him at a marble table, placed the bill of fare before him, and said:

"Order what you want, friend. Charge it to me, Mr. Martin."

"All right, Mr. Blucher," said Martin.

Then Blucher stepped back and leaned against the counter and watched the man stow away cargo after cargo of buckwheat cakes at seventy-five cents a plate; cup after cup of coffee, and porter house steaks worth two dollars apiece; and when six dollars and a half's worth of destruction had been accomplished, and the stranger's hunger appeased, Blucher went down to French Pete's, bought a veal cutlet plain, a slice of bread, and three radishes, with his dime, and set to and feasted like a king!

Take the episode all around, it was as odd as any that can be culled from the myriad curiosities of Californian life, perhaps.

CHAPTER LX.

By and by, an old friend of mine, a miner, came down from one of the decayed mining camps of Tuolumne, California, and I went back with him. We lived in a small cabin on a verdant hillside, and there were not five other cabins in view over the wide expanse of hill and forest. Yet a flourishing city of two or three thousand population had occupied this grassy dead solitude during the flush times of twelve or fifteen years before, and where our cabin stood had once been the heart of the teeming hive, the centre of the city. When the mines gave out the town fell into decay, and in a few years wholly disappeared—streets, dwellings, shops, everything—and left no sign. The grassy slopes were as green and smooth and desolate of life as if they had never been disturbed. The mere handful of miners still remaining, had seen the town spring up spread, grow and flourish in its pride; and they had seen it sicken and die, and pass away like a dream. With it their hopes had died, and their zest of life. They had long ago resigned themselves to their exile, and ceased to correspond with their distant friends or turn longing eyes toward their early homes. They had accepted banishment, forgotten the world and been forgotten of the world. They were far from telegraphs and railroads, and they stood, as it were, in a living grave, dead to the events that stirred the globe's great populations, dead to the common interests of men, isolated and outcast from brotherhood with their kind. It was the most singular, and almost the most touching and melancholy exile that fancy can imagine.—One of my associates in this locality, for two or three months, was a man who had had a university education; but now for eighteen years he had decayed there by inches, a bearded, rough-clad, clay-stained miner, and at times, among his sighings and soliloquizings, he unconsciously interjected vaguely remembered Latin and Greek sentences—dead and musty tongues, meet vehicles for the thoughts of one whose dreams were all of the past, whose life was a failure; a tired man, burdened with the present, and indifferent to the future; a man without ties, hopes, interests, waiting for rest and the end.

In that one little corner of California is found a species of mining which is seldom or never mentioned in print. It is called "pocket mining" and I am not aware that any of it is done outside of that little corner. The gold is not evenly distributed through the surface dirt, as in ordinary placer mines, but is collected in little spots, and they are very wide apart and exceedingly hard to find, but when you do find one you reap a rich and sudden harvest. There are not now more than twenty pocket miners in that entire little region. I think I know every one of them personally. I have known one of them to hunt patiently about the hill-sides every day for eight months without finding gold enough to make a snuff-box—his grocery bill running up relentlessly all the time—and then find a pocket and take out of it two thousand dollars in two dips of his shovel. I have known him to take out three thousand dollars in two hours, and go and pay up every cent of his indebtedness, then enter on a dazzling spree that finished the last of his treasure before the night was gone. And the next day he bought his groceries on credit as usual, and shouldered his pan and shovel and went off to the hills hunting pockets again happy and content. This is the most fascinating of all the different kinds of mining, and furnishes a very handsome percentage of victims to the lunatic asylum.

Pocket hunting is an ingenious process. You take a spadeful of earth from the hill-side and put it in a large tin pan and dissolve and wash it gradually away till nothing is left but a teaspoonful of fine sediment. Whatever gold was in that earth has remained, because, being the heaviest, it has sought the bottom. Among the sediment you will find half a dozen yellow particles no larger than pin-heads. You are delighted. You move off to one side and wash another pan. If you find gold again, you move to one side further, and wash a third pan. If you find no gold this time, you are delighted again, because you know you are on the right scent.

You lay an imaginary plan, shaped like a fan, with its handle up the hill—for just where the end of the handle is, you argue that the rich deposit lies hidden, whose vagrant grains of gold have escaped and been washed down the hill, spreading farther and farther apart as they wandered. And so you proceed up the hill, washing the earth and narrowing your lines every time the absence of gold in the pan shows that you are outside the spread of the fan; and at last, twenty yards up

the hill your lines have converged to a point—a single foot from that point you cannot find any gold. Your breath comes short and quick, you are feverish with excitement; the dinner-bell may ring its clapper off, you pay no attention; friends may die, weddings transpire, houses burn down, they are nothing to you; you sweat and dig and delve with a frantic interest—and all at once you strike it! Up comes a spadeful of earth and quartz that is all lovely with soiled lumps and leaves and sprays of gold. Sometimes that one spadeful is all—$500. Sometimes the nest contains $10,000, and it takes you three or four days to get it all out. The pocket-miners tell of one nest that yielded $60,000 and two men exhausted it in two weeks, and then sold the ground for $10,000 to a party who never got $300 out of it afterward.

The hogs are good pocket hunters. All the summer they root around the bushes, and turn up a thousand little piles of dirt, and then the miners long for the rains; for the rains beat upon these little piles and wash them down and expose the gold, possibly right over a pocket. Two pockets were found in this way by the same man in one day. One had $5,000 in it and the other $8,000. That man could appreciate it, for he hadn't had a cent for about a year.

In Tuolumne lived two miners who used to go to the neighboring village in the afternoon and return every night with household supplies. Part of the distance they traversed a trail, and nearly always sat down to rest on a great boulder that lay beside the path. In the course of thirteen years they had worn that boulder tolerably smooth, sitting on it. By and by two vagrant Mexicans came along and occupied the seat. They began to amuse themselves by chipping off flakes from the boulder with a sledge-hammer. They examined one of these flakes and found it rich with gold. That boulder paid them $800 afterward. But the aggravating circumstance was that these "Greasers" knew that there must be more gold where that boulder came from, and so they went panning up the hill and found what was probably the richest pocket that region has yet produced. It took three months to exhaust it, and it yielded $120,000. The two American miners who used to sit on the boulder are poor yet, and they take turn about in getting up early in the morning to curse those Mexicans—and when it comes down to pure ornamental cursing, the native American is gifted above the sons of men.

I have dwelt at some length upon this matter of pocket mining because it is a subject that is seldom referred to in print, and therefore I judged that it would have for the reader that interest which naturally attaches to novelty.

CHAPTER LXI.

One of my comrades there—another of those victims of eighteen years of unrequited toil and blighted hopes—was one of the gentlest spirits that ever bore its patient cross in a weary exile: grave and simple Dick Baker, pocket-miner of Dead-House Gulch.—He was forty-six, gray as a rat, earnest, thoughtful, slenderly educated, slouchily dressed and clay-soiled, but his heart was finer metal than any gold his shovel ever brought to light—than any, indeed, that ever was mined or minted.

Whenever he was out of luck and a little down-hearted, he would fall to mourning over the loss of a wonderful cat he used to own (for where women and children are not, men of kindly impulses take up with pets, for they must love something). And he always spoke of the strange sagacity of that cat with the air of a man who believed in his secret heart that there was something human about it—may be even supernatural.

I heard him talking about this animal once. He said:

"Gentlemen, I used to have a cat here, by the name of Tom Quartz, which you'd a took an interest in I reckon—most any body would. I had him here eight year—and he was the remarkablest cat I ever see. He was a large gray one of the Tom specie, an' he had more hard, natchral sense than any man in this camp—'n' a power of dignity—he wouldn't let the Gov'ner of Californy be familiar with him. He never ketched a rat in his life—'peared to be above it. He never cared for nothing but mining. He knowed more about mining, that cat did, than any man I ever, ever see. You couldn't tell him noth'n 'bout placer diggin's—'n' as for pocket mining, why he was just born for it.

"He would dig out after me an' Jim when we went over the hills prospect'n', and he would trot along behind us for as much as five mile, if we went so fur. An' he had the best judgment about mining ground—why you never see anything like it. When we went to work, he'd scatter a glance around, 'n' if he didn't think much of the indications, he would give a look as much as to say, 'Well, I'll have to get you to excuse me,' 'n' without another word he'd hyste his nose into the air 'n' shove for home. But if the ground suited him, he would lay low 'n' keep dark till the first pan was washed, 'n' then he would sidle up 'n' take a look, an' if there was about six or seven grains of gold he was satisfied—he didn't want no better prospect 'n' that—'n' then he would lay down on our coats and snore like a steamboat till we'd struck the pocket, an' then get up 'n' superintend. He was nearly lightnin' on superintending.

"Well, bye an' bye, up comes this yer quartz excitement. Every body was into it—every body was pick'n' 'n' blast'n' instead of shovelin' dirt on the hill side—every body was put'n' down a shaft instead of scrapin' the surface. Noth'n' would do Jim, but we must tackle the ledges, too, 'n' so we did. We commenced put'n' down a shaft, 'n' Tom Quartz he begin to wonder what in the Dickens it was all about. He hadn't ever seen any mining like that before, 'n' he was all upset, as you may say—he couldn't come to a right understanding of it no way—it was too many for him. He was down on it, too, you bet you—he was down on it powerful —'n' always appeared to consider it the cussedest foolishness out. But that cat, you know, was always agin new fangled arrangements—somehow he never could abide'em. You know how it is with old habits. But by an' by Tom Quartz begin to git sort of reconciled a little, though he never could altogether understand that eternal sinkin' of a shaft an' never pannin' out any thing. At last he got to comin' down in the shaft, hisself, to try to cipher it out. An' when he'd git the blues, 'n' feel kind o'scruffy, 'n' aggravated 'n' disgusted—knowin' as he did, that the bills was runnin' up all the time an' we warn't makin' a cent—he would curl up on a gunny sack in the corner an' go to sleep. Well, one day when the shaft was down about eight foot, the rock got so hard that we had to put in a blast—the first blast'n' we'd ever done since Tom Quartz was born. An' then we lit the fuse 'n' clumb out 'n' got off 'bout fifty yards—'n' forgot 'n' left Tom Quartz sound asleep on the gunny sack.

"In 'bout a minute we seen a puff of smoke bust up out of the hole, 'n' then everything let go with an awful crash, 'n' about four million ton of rocks 'n' dirt 'n' smoke 'n; splinters shot up 'bout a mile an' a half into the air, an' by George, right in the dead centre of it was old Tom Quartz a goin' end over end, an' a snortin' an' a sneez'n', an' a clawin' an' a reachin' for things like all possessed. But it warn't no use, you know, it warn't no

use. An' that was the last we see of him for about two minutes 'n' a half, an' then all of a sudden it begin to rain rocks and rubbage, an' directly he come down ker-whop about ten foot off f'm where we stood Well, I reckon he was p'raps the orneriest lookin' beast you ever see. One ear was sot back on his neck, 'n' his tail was stove up, 'n' his eye-winkers was swinged off, 'n' he was all blacked up with powder an' smoke, an' all sloppy with mud 'n' slush f'm one end to the other.

"Well sir, it warn't no use to try to apologize—we couldn't say a word. He took a sort of a disgusted look at hisself, 'n' then he looked at us —an' it was just exactly the same as if he had said—'Gents, may be you think it's smart to take advantage of a cat that 'ain't had no experience of quartz minin', but I think different'—an' then he turned on his heel 'n' marched off home without ever saying another word.

"That was jest his style. An' may be you won't believe it, but after that you never see a cat so prejudiced agin quartz mining as what he was. An' by an' bye when he did get to goin' down in the shaft agin, you'd 'a been astonished at his sagacity. The minute we'd tetch off a blast 'n' the fuse'd begin to sizzle, he'd give a look as much as to say: 'Well, I'll have to git you to excuse me,' an' it was surpris'n' the way he'd shin out of that hole 'n' go f'r a tree. Sagacity? It ain't no name for it. 'Twas inspiration!"

I said, "Well, Mr. Baker, his prejudice against quartz-mining was remarkable, considering how he came by it. Couldn't you ever cure him of it?"

"Cure him! No! When Tom Quartz was sot once, he was always sot—and you might a blowed him up as much as three million times 'n' you'd never a broken him of his cussed prejudice agin quartz mining."

The affection and the pride that lit up Baker's face when he delivered this tribute to the firmness of his humble friend of other days, will always be a vivid memory with me.

At the end of two months we had never "struck" a pocket. We had panned up and down the hillsides till they looked plowed like a field; we could have put in a crop of grain, then, but there would have been no way to get it to market. We got many good "prospects," but when the gold gave out in the pan and we dug down, hoping and longing, we found only emptiness— the pocket that should have been there was as barren as our own.—At last we shouldered our pans and shovels and struck out over the hills to try new localities. We prospected around Angel's Camp, in Calaveras county, during three weeks, but had no success. Then we wandered on foot among the mountains, sleeping under the trees at night, for the weather was mild, but still we remained as centless as the last rose of summer. That is a poor joke, but it is in pathetic harmony with the circumstances, since we were so poor ourselves. In accordance with the custom of the country, our door had always stood open and our board welcome to tramping miners—they drifted along nearly every day, dumped their paust shovels by the threshold and took "pot luck" with us— and now on our own tramp we never found cold hospitality.

Our wanderings were wide and in many directions; and now I could give the reader a vivid description of the Big Trees and the marvels of the Yo Semite—but what has this reader done to me that I should persecute him? I will deliver him into the hands of less conscientious tourists and take his blessing. Let me be charitable, though I fail in all virtues else.

Note: Some of the phrases in the above are mining technicalities, purely, and may be a little obscure to the general reader. In "placer diggings" the gold is scattered all through the surface dirt; in "pocket" diggings it is concentrated in one little spot; in "quartz" the gold is in a solid, continuous vein of rock, enclosed between distinct walls of some other kind of stone—and this is the most laborious and expensive of all the different kinds of mining. "Prospecting" is hunting for a "placer"; "indications" are signs of its presence; "panning out" refers to the washing process by which the grains of gold are separated from the dirt; a "prospect" is what one finds in the first panful of dirt—and its value determines whether it is a good or a bad prospect, and whether it is worth while to tarry there or seek further.

CHAPTER LXII.

After a three months' absence, I found myself in San Francisco again, without a cent. When my credit was about exhausted, (for I had become too mean and lazy, now, to work on a morning paper, and there were no vacancies on the evening journals,) I was created San Francisco correspondent of the Enterprise, and at the end of five months I was out of debt, but my interest in my work was gone; for my correspondence being a daily one, without rest or respite, I got unspeakably tired of it. I wanted another change. The vagabond instinct was strong upon me. Fortune favored and I got a new berth and a delightful one. It was to go down to the Sandwich Islands and write some letters for the Sacramento Union, an excellent journal and liberal with employees.

We sailed in the propeller Ajax, in the middle of winter. The almanac called it winter, distinctly enough, but the weather was a compromise between spring and summer. Six days out of port, it became summer altogether. We had some thirty passengers; among them a cheerful soul by the name of Williams, and three sea-worn old whaleship captains going down to join their vessels. These latter played euchre in the smoking room day and night, drank astonishing quantities of raw whisky without being in the least affected by it, and were the happiest people I think I ever saw. And then there was "the old Admiral—" a retired whaleman. He was a roaring, terrific combination of wind and lightning and thunder, and earnest, whole-souled profanity. But nevertheless he was tender-hearted as a girl. He was a raving, deafening, devastating typhoon, laying waste the cowering seas but with an unvexed refuge in the centre where all comers were safe and at rest. Nobody could know the "Admiral" without liking him; and in a sudden and dire emergency I think no friend of his would know which to choose—to be cursed by him or prayed for by a less efficient person.

His Title of "Admiral" was more strictly "official" than any ever worn by a naval officer before or since, perhaps—for it was the voluntary offering of a whole nation, and came direct from the people themselves without any intermediate red tape—the people of the Sandwich Islands. It was a title that came to him freighted with affection, and honor, and appreciation of his unpretending merit. And in testimony of the genuineness of the title it was publicly ordained that an exclusive flag should be devised for him and used solely to welcome his coming and wave him God-speed in his going. From that time forth, whenever his ship was signaled in the offing, or he catted his anchor and stood out to sea, that ensign streamed from the royal halliards on the parliament house and the nation lifted their hats to it with spontaneous accord.

Yet he had never fired a gun or fought a battle in his life. When

I knew him on board the Ajax, he was seventy-two years old and had plowed the salt water sixty-one of them. For sixteen years he had gone in and out of the harbor of Honolulu in command of a whaleship, and for sixteen more had been captain of a San Francisco and Sandwich Island passenger packet and had never had an accident or lost a vessel. The simple natives knew him for a friend who never failed them, and regarded him as children regard a father. It was a dangerous thing to oppress them when the roaring Admiral was around.

Two years before I knew the Admiral, he had retired from the sea on a competence, and had sworn a colossal nine-jointed oath that he would "never go within smelling distance of the salt water again as long as he lived." And he had conscientiously kept it. That is to say, he considered he had kept it, and it would have been more than dangerous to suggest to him, even in the gentlest way, that making eleven long sea voyages, as a passenger, during the two years that had transpired since he "retired," was only keeping the general spirit of it and not the strict letter.

The Admiral knew only one narrow line of conduct to pursue in any and all cases where there was a fight, and that was to shoulder his way straight in without an inquiry as to the rights or the merits of it, and take the part of the weaker side.—And this was the reason why he was always sure to be present at the trial of any universally execrated criminal to oppress and intimidate the jury with a vindictive pantomime of what he would do to them if he ever caught them out of the box. And this was why harried cats and outlawed dogs that knew him confidently took sanctuary under his chair in time of trouble. In the beginning he was the most frantic and bloodthirsty Union man that drew breath in the shadow of the Flag; but the instant the Southerners began to go down before the sweep of the Northern armies, he ran up the Confederate colors and from that time till the end was a rampant and inexorable secessionist.

He hated intemperance with a more uncompromising animosity than any individual I have ever met, of either sex; and he was never tired of storming against it and beseeching friends and strangers alike to be wary and drink with moderation. And yet if any creature had been guileless enough to intimate that his absorbing nine gallons of "straight" whiskey during our voyage was any fraction short of rigid or inflexible abstemiousness, in that self-same moment the old man would have spun him to the uttermost parts of the earth in the whirlwind of his wrath. Mind, I am not saying his whisky ever affected his head or his legs, for it did not, in even the slightest degree. He was a capacious container, but he did not hold enough for that. He took a level tumblerful of whisky every morning before he put his clothes on—"to sweeten his bilgewater," he said.—He took another after he got the most of his clothes on, "to settle his mind and give him his bearings." He then shaved, and put on a clean shirt; after which he recited the Lord's Prayer in a fervent, thundering bass that shook the ship to her kelson and suspended all conversation in the main cabin. Then, at this stage, being invariably "by the head," or "by the stern," or "listed to port or starboard," he took one more to "put him on an even keel so that he would mind his hellum and not miss stays and go about, every time he came up in the wind."—And now, his state-room door swung open and the sun of his benignant face beamed redly out upon men and women and children, and he roared his "Shipmets a'hoy!" in a way that was calculated to wake the dead and precipitate the final resurrection; and forth he strode, a picture to look at and a presence to enforce attention.

Stalwart and portly; not a gray hair; broadbrimmed slouch hat; semi-sailor toggery of blue navy flannel—roomy and ample; a stately expanse of shirt-front and a liberal amount of black silk neck-cloth tied with a sailor knot; large chain and imposing seals impending from his fob; awe-inspiring feet, and "a hand like the hand of Providence," as his whaling brethren expressed it; wrist-bands and sleeves pushed back half way to the elbow, out of respect for the warm weather, and exposing hairy arms, gaudy with red and blue anchors, ships, and goddesses of liberty tattooed in India ink. But these details were only secondary matters—his face was the lodestone that chained the eye. It was a sultry disk, glowing determinedly out through a weather beaten mask of mahogany, and studded with warts, seamed with scars, "blazed" all over with unfailing fresh slips of the razor; and with cheery eyes, under shaggy brows, contemplating the world from over the back of a gnarled crag of a nose that loomed vast and lonely out of the undulating immensity that spread away from its foundations. At his heels frisked the darling of his bachelor estate, his terrier "Fan," a creature no larger than a squirrel. The main part of his daily life was occupied in looking after "Fan," in a motherly way, and doctoring her for a hundred ailments which existed only in his imagination.

The Admiral seldom read newspapers; and when he did he never believed anything they said. He read nothing, and believed in nothing, but "The Old Guard," a secession periodical published in New York. He carried a dozen copies of it with him, always, and referred to them for all required information. If it was not there, he supplied it himself, out of a bountiful fancy, inventing history, names, dates, and every thing else necessary to make his point good in an argument. Consequently he was a formidable antagonist in a dispute. Whenever he swung clear of the record and began to create history, the enemy was helpless and had to surrender. Indeed, the enemy could not keep from betraying some little spark of indignation at his manufactured history—and when it came to indignation, that was the Admiral's very "best hold." He was always ready for a political argument, and if nobody started one he would do it himself. With his third retort his temper would begin to rise, and within five minutes he would be blowing a gale, and within fifteen his smoking-room audience would be utterly stormed away and the old man left solitary and alone, banging the table with his fist, kicking the chairs, and roaring a hurricane of profanity. It got so, after a while, that whenever the Admiral approached, with politics in his eye, the passengers would drop out with quiet accord, afraid to meet him; and he would camp on a deserted field.

But he found his match at last, and before a full company. At one time or another, everybody had entered the lists against him and been routed, except the quiet passenger Williams. He had never been able to get an expression of opinion out of him on politics. But now, just as the Admiral drew near the door and the company were about to slip out, Williams said:

"Admiral, are you certain about that circumstance concerning the clergymen you mentioned the other day?"—referring to a piece of the Admiral's manufactured history.

Every one was amazed at the man's rashness. The idea of deliberately inviting annihilation was a thing incomprehensible. The retreat came to a halt; then everybody sat down again wondering, to await the upshot of it. The Admiral himself was as surprised as any one. He paused in the door, with his red handkerchief half raised to his sweating face, and contemplated the daring reptile in the corner.

"Certain of it? Am I certain of it? Do you think I've been lying about it? What do you take me for? Anybody that don't know that circumstance, don't know anything; a child ought to know it. Read up your history! Read it up—, and don't come asking a man if he's certain about a bit of ABC stuff that the very southern niggers know all about."

Here the Admiral's fires began to wax hot, the atmosphere thickened, the coming earthquake rumbled, he began to thunder and lighten. Within three minutes his volcano was in full irruption and he was discharging flames and ashes of indignation, belching black volumes of foul history aloft, and vomiting red-hot torrents of profanity from his crater. Meantime Williams sat silent, and apparently deeply and earnestly interested in what the old man was saying. By and by, when the lull came, he said in the most deferential way, and with the gratified air of a man who has had a mystery cleared up which had been puzzling him uncomfortably:

"Now I understand it. I always thought I knew that piece of history well enough, but was still afraid to trust it, because there was not that convincing particularity about it that one likes to have in history; but when you mentioned every name, the other day, and every date, and every little circumstance, in their just order and sequence, I said to myself, this sounds something like—this is history—this is putting it in a shape that gives a man confidence; and I said to myself afterward, I will just ask the Admiral if he is perfectly certain about the details, and if he is I will come out and thank him for clearing this matter up for me. And that is what I want to do now—for until you set that matter right it was nothing but just a confusion in my mind, without head or tail to it."

Nobody ever saw the Admiral look so mollified before, and so pleased. Nobody had ever received his bogus history as gospel before; its genuineness had always been called in question either by words or looks; but here was a man that not only swallowed it all down, but was grateful for the dose. He was taken a back; he hardly knew what to say; even his profanity failed him. Now, Williams continued, modestly and earnestly:

"But Admiral, in saying that this was the first stone thrown, and that this precipitated the war, you have overlooked a circumstance which you are perfectly familiar with, but which has escaped your memory. Now I grant you that what you have stated is correct in every detail—to wit: that on the 16th of October, 1860, two Massachusetts clergymen, named Waite and Granger, went in disguise to the house of John Moody, in Rockport, at dead of night, and dragged forth two southern women and their two little children, and after tarring and feathering them conveyed them to Boston and burned them alive in the State House square; and I also grant your proposition that this deed is what led to the secession of South Carolina on the 20th of December following. Very well." [Here the company were pleasantly surprised to hear Williams proceed to come back at the Admiral with his own invincible weapon—clean, pure, manufactured history, without a word of truth in it.] "Very well, I say. But Admiral, why overlook the Willis and Morgan case in South Carolina? You are too well informed a man not to know all about that circumstance. Your arguments and your conversations have shown you to be intimately conversant with every detail of this national quarrel. You develop matters of history every day that show plainly that you are no smatterer in it, content to nibble about the surface, but a man who has searched the depths and possessed yourself of everything that has a bearing upon the great question. Therefore, let me just recall to your mind that

Willis and Morgan case—though I see by your face that the whole thing is already passing through your memory at this moment. On the 12th of August, 1860, two months before the Waite and Granger affair, two South Carolina clergymen, named John H. Morgan and Winthrop L. Willis, one a Methodist and the other an Old School Baptist, disguised themselves, and went at midnight to the house of a planter named Thompson—Archibald F. Thompson, Vice President under Thomas Jefferson,—and took thence, at midnight, his widowed aunt, (a Northern woman,) and her adopted child, an orphan—named Mortimer Highie, afflicted with epilepsy and suffering at the time from white swelling on one of his legs, and compelled to walk on crutches in consequence; and the two ministers, in spite of the pleadings of the victims, dragged them to the bush, tarred and feathered them, and afterward burned them at the stake in the city of Charleston. You remember perfectly well what a stir it made; you remember perfectly well that even the Charleston Courier stigmatized the act as being unpleasant, of questionable propriety, and scarcely justifiable, and likewise that it would not be matter of surprise if retaliation ensued. And you remember also, that this thing was the cause of the Massachusetts outrage. Who, indeed, were the two Massachusetts ministers? and who were the two Southern women they burned? I do not need to remind you, Admiral, with your intimate knowledge of history, that Waite was the nephew of the woman burned in Charleston; that Granger was her cousin in the second degree, and that the woman they burned in Boston was the wife of John H. Morgan, and the still loved but divorced wife of Winthrop L. Willis. Now, Admiral, it is only fair that you should acknowledge that the first provocation came from the Southern preachers and that the Northern ones were justified in retaliating. In your arguments you never yet have shown the least disposition to withhold a just verdict or be in anywise unfair, when authoritative history condemned your position, and therefore I have no hesitation in asking you to take the original blame from the Massachusetts ministers, in this matter, and transfer it to the South Carolina clergymen where it justly belongs."

The Admiral was conquered. This sweet spoken creature who swallowed his fraudulent history as if it were the bread of life; basked in his furious blasphemy as if it were generous sunshine; found only calm, even-handed justice in his rampart partisanship; and flooded him with invented history so sugarcoated with flattery and deference that there was no rejecting it, was "too many" for him. He stammered some awkward, profane sentences about the—Willis and Morgan business having escaped his memory, but that he "remembered it now," and then, under pretence of giving Fan some medicine for an imaginary cough, drew out of the battle and went away, a vanquished man. Then cheers and laughter went up, and Williams, the ship's benefactor was a hero. The news went about the vessel, champagne was ordered, and enthusiastic reception instituted in the smoking room, and everybody flocked thither to shake hands with the conqueror. The wheelman said afterward, that the Admiral stood up behind the pilot house and "ripped and cursed all to himself" till he loosened the smokestack guys and becalmed the mainsail.

The Admiral's power was broken. After that, if he began argument, somebody would bring Williams, and the old man would grow weak and begin to quiet down at once. And as soon as he was done, Williams in his dulcet, insinuating way, would invent some history (referring for proof, to the old man's own excellent memory and to copies of "The Old Guard" known not to be in his possession) that would turn the tables

completely and leave the Admiral all abroad and helpless. By and by he came to so dread Williams and his gilded tongue that he would stop talking when he saw him approach, and finally ceased to mention politics altogether, and from that time forward there was entire peace and serenity in the ship.

CHAPTER LXIII.

On a certain bright morning the Islands hove in sight, lying low on the lonely sea, and everybody climbed to the upper deck to look. After two thousand miles of watery solitude the vision was a welcome one. As we approached, the imposing promontory of Diamond Head rose up out of the ocean its rugged front softened by the hazy distance, and presently the details of the land began to make themselves manifest: first the line of beach; then the plumed coacoanut trees of the tropics; then cabins of the natives; then the white town of Honolulu, said to contain between twelve and fifteen thousand inhabitants spread over a dead level; with streets from twenty to thirty feet wide, solid and level as a floor, most of them straight as a line and few as crooked as a corkscrew.

The further I traveled through the town the better I liked it. Every step revealed a new contrast—disclosed something I was unaccustomed to. In place of the grand mud-colored brown fronts of San Francisco, I saw dwellings built of straw, adobies, and cream-colored pebble-and-shell-conglomerated coral, cut into oblong blocks and laid in cement; also a great number of neat white cottages, with green window-shutters; in place of front yards like billiard-tables with iron fences around them, I saw these homes surrounded by ample yards, thickly clad with green grass, and shaded by tall trees, through whose dense foliage the sun could scarcely penetrate; in place of the customary geranium, calla lily, etc., languishing in dust and general debility, I saw luxurious banks and thickets of flowers, fresh as a meadow after a rain, and glowing with the richest dyes; in place of the dingy horrors of San Francisco's pleasure grove, the "Willows," I saw huge-bodied, wide-spreading forest trees, with strange names and stranger appearance —trees that cast a shadow like a thunder-cloud, and were able to stand alone without being tied to green poles; in place of gold fish, wiggling around in glass globes, assuming countless shades and degrees of distortion through the magnifying and diminishing qualities of their transparent prison houses, I saw cats—Tom-cats, Mary Ann cats, long-tailed cats, bob-tailed cats, blind cats, one-eyed cats, wall-eyed cats, cross-eyed cats, gray cats, black cats, white cats, yellow cats, striped cats, spotted cats, tame cats, wild cats, singed cats, individual cats, groups of cats, platoons of cats, companies of cats, regiments of cats, armies of cats, multitudes of cats, millions of cats, and all of them sleek, fat, lazy and sound asleep. I looked on a multitude of people, some white, in white coats, vests, pantaloons, even white cloth shoes, made snowy with chalk duly laid on every morning; but the majority of the people were almost as dark as negroes—women with comely features, fine black eyes, rounded forms, inclining to the voluptuous, clad in a single bright red or white garment that fell free and unconfined from shoulder to heel, long black hair falling loose, gypsy hats, encircled with wreaths of natural flowers of a brilliant carmine tint; plenty of dark men in various costumes, and some with nothing on but a battered stove-pipe hat tilted on the nose, and a very scant breech-clout; —certain smoke-dried children were clothed in nothing but sunshine —a very neat fitting and picturesque apparel indeed.

In place of roughs and rowdies staring and blackguarding on the corners, I saw long-haired, saddle-colored Sandwich Island maidens sitting on the ground in the shade of corner houses, gazing indolently at whatever or whoever happened along; instead of wretched cobble-stone pavements, I walked on a firm foundation of coral, built up from the bottom of the sea by the absurd but persevering insect of that name, with a light layer of lava and cinders overlying the coral, belched up out of fathomless perdition long ago through the seared and blackened crater that stands dead and harmless in the distance now; instead of cramped and crowded street-cars, I met dusky native women sweeping by, free as the wind, on fleet horses and astride, with gaudy riding-sashes, streaming like banners behind them; instead of the combined stenches of Chinadom and Brannan street slaughter-houses, I breathed the balmy fragrance of jessamine, oleander, and the Pride of India; in place of the hurry and bustle and noisy confusion of San Francisco, I moved in the midst of a Summer calm as tranquil as dawn in the Garden of Eden; in place of the Golden City's skirting sand hills and the placid bay, I saw on the one side a frame-work of tall, precipitous mountains close at hand, clad in refreshing green, and cleft by deep, cool, chasm-like valleys—and in front the grand sweep of the ocean; a brilliant, transparent green near the shore, bound and bordered by a long white line of foamy spray dashing against the reef, and further out the dead blue water of the deep sea, flecked with "white caps," and in the far horizon a single, lonely sail —a mere accent-mark to emphasize a slumberous calm and a solitude that were without sound or limit. When the sun sunk down—the one intruder from other realms and persistent in suggestions of them—it was tranced luxury to sit in the perfumed air and forget that there was any world but these enchanted islands.

It was such ecstacy to dream, and dream—till you got a bite.

A scorpion bite. Then the first duty was to get up out of the grass and kill the scorpion; and the next to bathe the bitten place with alcohol or brandy; and the next to resolve to keep out of the grass in future. Then came an adjournment to the bed-chamber and the pastime of writing up the day's journal with one hand and the destruction of mosquitoes with the other—a whole community of them at a slap. Then, observing an enemy approaching,—a hairy tarantula on stilts—why not set the spittoon on him? It is done, and the projecting ends of his paws give a luminous idea of the magnitude of his reach. Then to bed and become a promenade for a centipede with forty-two legs on a side and every foot hot enough to burn a hole through a raw-hide. More soaking with alcohol, and a resolution to examine the bed before entering it, in future. Then wait, and suffer, till all the mosquitoes in the neighborhood have crawled in under the bar, then slip out quickly, shut them in and sleep peacefully on the floor till morning. Meantime it is comforting to curse the tropics in occasional wakeful intervals.

We had an abundance of fruit in Honolulu, of course. Oranges, pine-apples, bananas, strawberries, lemons, limes, mangoes, guavas, melons, and a rare and curious luxury called the chirimoya, which is deliciousness itself. Then there is the tamarind. I thought tamarinds were made to eat, but that was probably not the idea. I ate several, and it seemed to me that they were rather sour that year. They pursed up my lips, till they resembled the stem-end of a tomato, and I had to take my sustenance through a quill for twenty-four hours.

They sharpened my teeth till I could have shaved with them, and gave them a "wire edge" that I was afraid would stay; but a citizen said "no, it will come off when the enamel does"— which was comforting, at any rate. I found, afterward, that only strangers eat tamarinds—but they only eat them once.

CHAPTER LXIV.

In my diary of our third day in Honolulu, I find this:

I am probably the most sensitive man in Hawaii to-night—especially about sitting down in the presence of my betters. I have ridden fifteen or twenty miles on horse-back since 5 P.M. and to tell the honest truth, I have a delicacy about sitting down at all.

An excursion to Diamond Head and the King's Coacoanut Grove was planned to-day—time, 4:30 P.M.—the party to consist of half a dozen gentlemen and three ladies. They all started at the appointed hour except myself. I was at the Government prison, (with Captain Fish and another whaleship-skipper, Captain Phillips,) and got so interested in its examination that I did not notice how quickly the time was passing. Somebody remarked that it was twenty minutes past five o'clock, and that woke me up. It was a fortunate circumstance that Captain Phillips was along with his "turn out," as he calls a top-buggy that Captain Cook brought here in 1778, and a horse that was here when Captain Cook came. Captain Phillips takes a just pride in his driving and in the speed of his horse, and to his passion for displaying them I owe it that we were only sixteen minutes coming from the prison to the American Hotel—a distance which has been estimated to be over half a mile. But it took some fearful driving. The Captain's whip came down fast, and the blows started so much dust out of the horse's hide that during the last half of the journey we rode through an impenetrable fog, and ran by a pocket compass in the hands of Captain Fish, a whaler of twenty-six years experience, who sat there through the perilous voyage as self-possessed as if he had been on the euchre-deck of his own ship, and calmly said, "Port your helm—port," from time to time, and "Hold her a little free — steady—so—so," and "Luff—hard down to starboard!" and never once lost his presence of mind or betrayed the least anxiety by voice or manner. When we came to anchor at last, and Captain Phillips looked at his watch and said, "Sixteen minutes—I told you it was in her! that's over three miles an hour!" I could see he felt entitled to a compliment, and so I said I had never seen lightning go like that horse. And I never had.

The landlord of the American said the party had been gone nearly an hour, but that he could give me my choice of several horses that could overtake them. I said, never mind—I preferred a safe horse to a fast one—I would like to have an excessively gentle horse—a horse with no spirit whatever—a lame one, if he had such a thing. Inside of five minutes I was mounted, and perfectly satisfied with my outfit. I had no time to label him "This is a horse," and so if the public took him for a sheep I cannot help it. I was satisfied, and that was the main thing. I could see that he had as many fine points as any man's horse, and so I hung my hat on one of them, behind the saddle, and swabbed the perspiration from my face and started. I named him after this island, "Oahu" (pronounced O-waw-hee). The first gate he came to he started in; I had neither whip nor spur, and so I simply argued the case with him. He resisted argument, but ultimately yielded to insult and abuse. He backed out of that gate and steered for another one on the other side of the street. I triumphed by my former process. Within the next six hundred yards he crossed the street fourteen times and attempted thirteen gates, and in the meantime the tropical sun was beating down and threatening to cave the top of my head in, and I was literally dripping with perspiration. He abandoned the gate business after that and went along peaceably enough, but absorbed in meditation. I noticed this latter circumstance, and it soon began to fill me with apprehension. I said to my self, this creature is planning some new outrage, some fresh deviltry or other—no horse ever thought over a subject so profoundly as this one is doing just for nothing. The more this thing preyed upon my mind the more uneasy I became, until the suspense became almost unbearable and I dismounted to see if there was anything wild in his eye—for I had heard that the eye of this noblest of our domestic animals is very expressive.

I cannot describe what a load of anxiety was lifted from my mind when I found that he was only asleep. I woke him up and started him into a faster walk, and then the villainy of his nature came out again. He tried to climb over a stone wall, five or six feet high. I saw that I must apply force to this horse, and that I might as well begin first as last. I plucked a stout switch from a tamarind tree, and the moment he saw it, he surrendered. He broke into a convulsive sort of a canter, which had three short steps in it and one long one, and reminded me alternately of the clattering shake of the great earthquake, and the sweeping plunging of the Ajax in a storm.

And now there can be no fitter occasion than the present to pronounce a left-handed blessing upon the man who invented the American saddle. There is no seat to speak of about it—one might as well sit in a shovel —and the stirrups are nothing but an ornamental nuisance. If I were to write down here all the abuse I expended on those stirrups, it would make a large book, even without pictures. Sometimes I got one foot so far through, that the stirrup partook of the nature of an anklet; sometimes both feet were through, and I was handcuffed by the legs; and sometimes my feet got clear out and left the stirrups wildly dangling about my shins. Even when I was in proper position and carefully balanced upon the balls of my feet, there was no comfort in it, on account of my nervous dread that they were going to slip one way or the other in a moment. But the subject is too exasperating to write about.

A mile and a half from town, I came to a grove of tall cocoanut trees, with clean, branchless stems reaching straight up sixty or seventy feet and topped with a spray of green foliage sheltering clusters of cocoa-nuts—not more picturesque than a forest of collossal ragged parasols, with bunches of magnified grapes under them, would be.

I once heard a gouty northern invalid say that a cocoanut tree might be poetical, possibly it was; but it looked like a feather-duster struck by lightning. I think that describes it better than a picture—and yet, without any question, there is something fascinating about a cocoa-nut tree—and graceful, too.

About a dozen cottages, some frame and the others of native grass, nestled sleepily in the shade here and there. The grass cabins are of a grayish color, are shaped much like our own cottages, only with higher and steeper roofs usually, and are made of some kind of weed strongly bound together in bundles. The roofs are very thick, and so are the walls; the latter have square holes in them for windows. At a little distance these cabins have a furry appearance, as if they might be made of bear skins. They are very cool and pleasant inside. The King's flag was flying from the roof of one of the cottages, and His Majesty was probably within. He owns the whole concern thereabouts, and passes his time there frequently, on sultry days "laying off." The spot is called "The King's Grove."

Near by is an interesting ruin—the meagre remains of an ancient heathen temple—a place where human sacrifices were

offered up in those old bygone days when the simple child of nature, yielding momentarily to sin when sorely tempted, acknowledged his error when calm reflection had shown it him, and came forward with noble frankness and offered up his grandmother as an atoning sacrifice—in those old days when the luckless sinner could keep on cleansing his conscience and achieving periodical happiness as long as his relations held out; long, long before the missionaries braved a thousand privations to come and make them permanently miserable by telling them how beautiful and how blissful a place heaven is, and how nearly impossible it is to get there; and showed the poor native how dreary a place perdition is and what unnecessarily liberal facilities there are for going to it; showed him how, in his ignorance he had gone and fooled away all his kinfolks to no purpose; showed him what rapture it is to work all day long for fifty cents to buy food for next day with, as compared with fishing for pastime and lolling in the shade through eternal Summer, and eating of the bounty that nobody labored to provide but Nature. How sad it is to think of the multitudes who have gone to their graves in this beautiful island and never knew there was a hell!

This ancient temple was built of rough blocks of lava, and was simply a roofless inclosure a hundred and thirty feet long and seventy wide —nothing but naked walls, very thick, but not much higher than a man's head. They will last for ages no doubt, if left unmolested. Its three altars and other sacred appurtenances have crumbled and passed away years ago. It is said that in the old times thousands of human beings were slaughtered here, in the presence of naked and howling savages. If these mute stones could speak, what tales they could tell, what pictures they could describe, of fettered victims writhing under the knife; of massed forms straining forward out of the gloom, with ferocious faces lit up by the sacrificial fires; of the background of ghostly trees; of the dark pyramid of Diamond Head standing sentinel over the uncanny scene, and the peaceful moon looking down upon it through rifts in the cloud-rack!

When Kamehameha (pronounced Ka-may-ha-may-ah) the Great—who was a sort of a Napoleon in military genius and uniform success—invaded this island of Oahu three quarters of a century ago, and exterminated the army sent to oppose him, and took full and final possession of the country, he searched out the dead body of the King of Oahu, and those of the principal chiefs, and impaled their heads on the walls of this temple.

Those were savage times when this old slaughter-house was in its prime. The King and the chiefs ruled the common herd with a rod of iron; made them gather all the provisions the masters needed; build all the houses and temples; stand all the expenses, of whatever kind; take kicks and cuffs for thanks; drag out lives well flavored with misery, and then suffer death for trifling offences or yield up their lives on the sacrificial altars to purchase favors from the gods for their hard rulers. The missionaries have clothed them, educated them, broken up the tyrannous authority of their chiefs, and given them freedom and the right to enjoy whatever their hands and brains produce with equal laws for all, and punishment for all alike who transgress them. The contrast is so strong—the benefit conferred upon this people by the missionaries is so prominent, so palpable and so unquestionable, that the frankest compliment I can pay them, and the best, is simply to point to the condition of the Sandwich Islanders of Captain Cook's time, and their condition to-day.

Their work speaks for itself.

CHAPTER LXV.

By and by, after a rugged climb, we halted on the summit of a hill which commanded a far-reaching view. The moon rose and flooded mountain and valley and ocean with a mellow radiance, and out of the shadows of the foliage the distant lights of Honolulu glinted like an encampment of fireflies. The air was heavy with the fragrance of flowers. The halt was brief.—Gayly laughing and talking, the party galloped on, and I clung to the pommel and cantered after. Presently we came to a place where no grass grew—a wide expanse of deep sand. They said it was an old battle ground. All around everywhere, not three feet apart, the bleached bones of men gleamed white in the moonlight. We picked up a lot of them for mementoes. I got quite a number of arm bones and leg bones —of great chiefs, may be, who had fought savagely in that fearful battle in the old days, when blood flowed like wine where we now stood—and wore the choicest of them out on Oahu afterward, trying to make him go. All sorts of bones could be found except skulls; but a citizen said, irreverently, that there had been an unusual number of "skull-hunters" there lately—a species of sportsmen I had never heard of before.

Nothing whatever is known about this place—its story is a secret that will never be revealed. The oldest natives make no pretense of being possessed of its history. They say these bones were here when they were children. They were here when their grandfathers were children—but how they came here, they can only conjecture. Many people believe this spot to be an ancient battle-ground, and it is usual to call it so; and they believe that these skeletons have lain for ages just where their proprietors fell in the great fight. Other people believe that Kamehameha I. fought his first battle here. On this point, I have heard a story, which may have been taken from one of the numerous books which have been written concerning these islands—I do not know where the narrator got it. He said that when Kamehameha (who was at first merely a subordinate chief on the island of Hawaii), landed here, he brought a large army with him, and encamped at Waikiki. The Oahuans marched against him, and so confident were they of success that they readily acceded to a demand of their priests that they should draw a line where these bones now lie, and take an oath that, if forced to retreat at all, they would never retreat beyond this boundary. The priests told them that death and everlasting punishment would overtake any who violated the oath, and the march was resumed. Kamehameha drove them back step by step; the priests fought in the front rank and exhorted them both by voice and inspiriting example to remember their oath—to die, if need be, but never cross the fatal line. The struggle was manfully maintained, but at last the chief priest fell, pierced to the heart with a spear, and the unlucky omen fell like a blight upon the brave souls on his back; with a triumphant shout the invaders pressed forward— the line was crossed—the offended gods deserted the despairing army, and, accepting the doom their perjury had brought upon them, they broke and fled over the plain where Honolulu stands now—up the beautiful Nuuanu Valley — paused a moment, hemmed in by precipitous mountains on either hand and the frightful precipice of the Pari in front, and then were driven over —a sheer plunge of six hundred feet!

The story is pretty enough, but Mr. Jarves' excellent history says the Oahuans were intrenched in Nuuanu Valley; that Kamehameha ousted them, routed them, pursued them up the valley and drove them over the precipice. He makes no mention of our bone-yard at all in his book.

Impressed by the profound silence and repose that rested over the beautiful landscape, and being, as usual, in the rear, I gave voice to my thoughts. I said:

"What a picture is here slumbering in the solemn glory of the moon! How strong the rugged outlines of the dead volcano stand out against the clear sky! What a snowy fringe marks the bursting of the surf over the long, curved reef! How calmly the dim city sleeps yonder in the plain! How soft the shadows lie upon the stately mountains that border the dream-haunted Mauoa Valley! What a grand pyramid of billowy clouds towers above the storied Pari! How the grim warriors of the past seem flocking in ghostly squadrons to their ancient battlefield again—how the wails of the dying well up from the—"

At this point the horse called Oahu sat down in the sand. Sat down to listen, I suppose. Never mind what he heard, I stopped apostrophising and convinced him that I was not a man to allow contempt of Court on the part of a horse. I broke the back-bone of a Chief over his rump and set out to join the cavalcade again.

Very considerably fagged out we arrived in town at 9 o'clock at night, myself in the lead—for when my horse finally came to understand that he was homeward bound and hadn't far to go, he turned his attention strictly to business.

This is a good time to drop in a paragraph of information. There is no regular livery stable in Honolulu, or, indeed, in any part of the Kingdom of Hawaii; therefore unless you are acquainted with wealthy residents (who all have good horses), you must hire animals of the wretchedest description from the Kanakas. (i.e. natives.) Any horse you hire, even though it be from a white man, is not often of much account, because it will be brought in for you from some ranch, and has necessarily been leading a hard life. If the Kanakas who have been caring for him (inveterate riders they are) have not ridden him half to death every day themselves, you can depend upon it they have been doing the same thing by proxy, by clandestinely hiring him out. At least, so I am informed. The result is, that no horse has a chance to eat, drink, rest, recuperate, or look well or feel well, and so strangers go about the Islands mounted as I was to-day.

In hiring a horse from a Kanaka, you must have all your eyes about you, because you can rest satisfied that you are dealing with a shrewd unprincipled rascal. You may leave your door open and your trunk unlocked as long as you please, and he will not meddle with your property; he has no important vices and no inclination to commit robbery on a large scale; but if he can get ahead of you in the horse business, he will take a genuine delight in doing it. This traits is characteristic of horse jockeys, the world over, is it not? He will overcharge you if he can; he will hire you a fine-looking horse at night (anybody's— may be the King's, if the royal steed be in convenient view), and bring you the mate to my Oahu in the morning, and contend that it is the same animal. If you make trouble, he will get out by saying it was not himself who made the bargain with you, but his brother, "who went out in the country this morning." They have always got a "brother" to shift the responsibility upon. A victim said to one of these fellows one day:

"But I know I hired the horse of you, because I noticed that scar on your cheek."

The reply was not bad: "Oh, yes—yes—my brother all same— we twins!"

A friend of mine, J. Smith, hired a horse yesterday, the Kanaka warranting him to be in excellent condition.

Smith had a saddle and blanket of his own, and he ordered the Kanaka to put these on the horse. The Kanaka protested that he was perfectly willing to trust the gentleman with the saddle that was already on the animal, but Smith refused to use it. The change was made; then Smith noticed that the Kanaka had only changed the saddles, and had left the original blanket on the horse; he said he forgot to change the blankets, and so, to cut the bother short, Smith mounted and rode away. The horse went lame a mile from town, and afterward got to cutting up some extraordinary capers. Smith got down and took off the saddle, but the blanket stuck fast to the horse—glued to a procession of raw places. The Kanaka's mysterious conduct stood explained.

Another friend of mine bought a pretty good horse from a native, a day or two ago, after a tolerably thorough examination of the animal. He discovered today that the horse was as blind as a bat, in one eye. He meant to have examined that eye, and came home with a general notion that he had done it; but he remembers now that every time he made the attempt his attention was called to something else by his victimizer.

One more instance, and then I will pass to something else. I am informed that when a certain Mr. L., a visiting stranger, was here, he bought a pair of very respectable-looking match horses from a native. They were in a little stable with a partition through the middle of it—one horse in each apartment. Mr. L. examined one of them critically through a window (the Kanaka's "brother" having gone to the country with the key), and then went around the house and examined the other through a window on the other side. He said it was the neatest match he had ever seen, and paid for the horses on the spot. Whereupon the Kanaka departed to join his brother in the country. The fellow had shamefully swindled L. There was only one "match" horse, and he had examined his starboard side through one window and his port side through another! I decline to believe this story, but I give it because it is worth something as a fanciful illustration of a fixed fact—namely, that the Kanaka horse-jockey is fertile in invention and elastic in conscience.

You can buy a pretty good horse for forty or fifty dollars, and a good enough horse for all practical purposes for two dollars and a half. I estimate "Oahu" to be worth somewhere in the neighborhood of thirty-five cents. A good deal better animal than he is was sold here day before yesterday for a dollar and seventy-five cents, and sold again to-day for two dollars and twenty-five cents; Williams bought a handsome and lively little pony yesterday for ten dollars; and about the best common horse on the island (and he is a really good one) sold yesterday, with Mexican saddle and bridle, for seventy dollars—a horse which is well and widely known, and greatly respected for his speed, good disposition and everlasting bottom.

You give your horse a little grain once a day; it comes from San Francisco, and is worth about two cents a pound; and you give him as much hay as he wants; it is cut and brought to the market by natives, and is not very good it is baled into long, round bundles, about the size of a large man; one of them is stuck by the middle on each end of a six foot pole, and the Kanaka shoulders the pole and walks about the streets between the upright bales in search of customers. These hay

bales, thus carried, have a general resemblance to a colossal capital 'H.'

The hay-bundles cost twenty-five cents apiece, and one will last a horse about a day. You can get a horse for a song, a week's hay for another song, and you can turn your animal loose among the luxuriant grass in your neighbor's broad front yard without a song at all—you do it at midnight, and stable the beast again before morning. You have been at no expense thus far, but when you come to buy a saddle and bridle they will cost you from twenty to thirty-five dollars. You can hire a horse, saddle and bridle at from seven to ten dollars a week, and the owner will take care of them at his own expense.

It is time to close this day's record—bed time. As I prepare for sleep, a rich voice rises out of the still night, and, far as this ocean rock is toward the ends of the earth, I recognize a familiar home air. But the words seem somewhat out of joint:

"Waikiki lantoni oe Kaa hooly hooly wawhoo."

Translated, that means "When we were marching through Georgia."

CHAPTER LXVI.

Passing through the market place we saw that feature of Honolulu under its most favorable auspices—that is, in the full glory of Saturday afternoon, which is a festive day with the natives. The native girls by twos and threes and parties of a dozen, and sometimes in whole platoons and companies, went cantering up and down the neighboring streets astride of fleet but homely horses, and with their gaudy riding habits streaming like banners behind them. Such a troop of free and easy riders, in their natural home, the saddle, makes a gay and graceful spectacle. The riding habit I speak of is simply a long, broad scarf, like a tavern table cloth brilliantly colored, wrapped around the loins once, then apparently passed between the limbs and each end thrown backward over the same, and floating and flapping behind on both sides beyond the horse's tail like a couple of fancy flags; then, slipping the stirrup-irons between her toes, the girl throws her chest forward, sits up like a Major General and goes sweeping by like the wind.

The girls put on all the finery they can on Saturday afternoon—fine black silk robes; flowing red ones that nearly put your eyes out; others as white as snow; still others that discount the rainbow; and they wear their hair in nets, and trim their jaunty hats with fresh flowers, and encircle their dusky throats with home-made necklaces of the brilliant vermillion-tinted blossom of the ohia; and they fill the markets and the adjacent street with their bright presences, and smell like a rag factory on fire with their offensive cocoanut oil.

Occasionally you see a heathen from the sunny isles away down in the South Seas, with his face and neck tatooed till he looks like the customary mendicant from Washoe who has been blown up in a mine. Some are tattooed a dead blue color down to the upper lip—masked, as it were —leaving the natural light yellow skin of Micronesia unstained from thence down; some with broad marks drawn down from hair to neck, on both sides of the face, and a strip of the original yellow skin, two inches wide, down the center—a gridiron with a spoke broken out; and some with the entire face discolored with the popular mortification tint, relieved only by one or two thin, wavy threads of natural yellow running across the face from ear to ear, and eyes twinkling out of this darkness, from under shadowing hat-brims, like stars in the dark of the moon.

Moving among the stirring crowds, you come to the poi merchants, squatting in the shade on their hams, in true native fashion, and surrounded by purchasers. (The Sandwich Islanders always squat on their hams, and who knows but they may be the old original "ham sandwiches?" The thought is pregnant with interest.) The poi looks like common flour paste, and is kept in large bowls formed of a species of gourd, and capable of holding from one to three or four gallons. Poi is the chief article of food among the natives, and is prepared from the taro plant.

The taro root looks like a thick, or, if you please, a corpulent sweet potato, in shape, but is of a light purple color when boiled. When boiled it answers as a passable substitute for bread. The buck Kanakas bake it under ground, then mash it up well with a heavy lava pestle, mix water with it until it becomes a paste, set it aside and let if ferment, and then it is poi—and an unseductive mixture it is, almost tasteless before it ferments and too sour for a luxury afterward. But nothing is more nutritious. When solely used, however, it produces acrid humors, a fact which sufficiently accounts for the humorous character of the Kanakas. I think there must be as much of a knack in handling poi as there is in eating with chopsticks. The forefinger is thrust into the mess and stirred quickly round several times and drawn as quickly out, thickly coated, just as it it were poulticed; the head is thrown back, the finger inserted in the mouth and the delicacy stripped off and swallowed—the eye closing gently, meanwhile, in a languid sort of ecstasy. Many a different finger goes into the same bowl and many a different kind of dirt and shade and quality of flavor is added to the virtues of its contents.

Around a small shanty was collected a crowd of natives buying the awa root. It is said that but for the use of this root the destruction of the people in former times by certain imported diseases would have been far greater than it was, and by others it is said that this is merely a fancy. All agree that poi will rejuvenate a man who is used up and his vitality almost annihilated by hard drinking, and that in some kinds of diseases it will restore health after all medicines have failed; but all are not willing to allow to the awa the virtues claimed for it. The natives manufacture an intoxicating drink from it which is fearful in its effects when persistently indulged in. It covers the body with dry, white scales, inflames the eyes, and causes premature decripitude. Although the man before whose establishment we stopped has to pay a Government license of eight hundred dollars a year for the exclusive right to sell awa root, it is said that he makes a small fortune every twelve-month; while saloon keepers, who pay a thousand dollars a year for the privilege of retailing whiskey, etc., only make a bare living.

We found the fish market crowded; for the native is very fond of fish, and eats the article raw and alive! Let us change the subject.

In old times here Saturday was a grand gala day indeed. All the native population of the town forsook their labors, and those of the surrounding country journeyed to the city. Then the white folks had to stay indoors, for every street was so packed with charging cavaliers and cavalieresses that it was next to impossible to thread one's way through the cavalcades without getting crippled.

At night they feasted and the girls danced the lascivious hula hula—a dance that is said to exhibit the very perfection of educated notion of limb and arm, hand, head and body, and the exactest uniformity of movement and accuracy of "time." It was performed by a circle of girls with no raiment on them to speak of, who went through an infinite variety of motions and figures without prompting, and yet so true was their "time," and in such perfect concert did they move that when they were placed in a straight line, hands, arms, bodies, limbs and heads waved, swayed, gesticulated, bowed, stooped, whirled, squirmed, twisted and undulated as if they were part and parcel of a single individual; and it was difficult to believe they were not moved in a body by some exquisite piece of mechanism.

Of late years, however, Saturday has lost most of its quondam gala features. This weekly stampede of the natives interfered too much with labor and the interests of the white folks, and by sticking in a law here, and preaching a sermon there, and by various other means, they gradually broke it up. The demoralizing hula hula was forbidden to be performed, save at night, with closed doors, in presence of few spectators, and only by permission duly procured from the authorities and the payment of ten dollars for the same. There are few girls now-a-days able to dance this ancient national dance in the highest perfection of the art.

The missionaries have christianized and educated all the natives. They all belong to the Church, and there is not one of them, above the age of eight years, but can read and write with facility in the native tongue. It is the most universally educated race of people outside of China. They have any quantity of books, printed in the Kanaka language, and all the natives are fond of reading. They are inveterate church-goers —nothing can keep them away. All this ameliorating cultivation has at last built up in the native women a profound respect for chastity—in other people. Perhaps that is enough to say on that head. The national sin will die out when the race does, but perhaps not earlier.—But doubtless this purifying is not far off, when we reflect that contact with civilization and the whites has reduced the native population from four hundred thousand (Captain Cook's estimate,) to fifty-five thousand in something over eighty years!

Society is a queer medley in this notable missionary, whaling and governmental centre. If you get into conversation with a stranger and experience that natural desire to know what sort of ground you are treading on by finding out what manner of man your stranger is, strike out boldly and address him as "Captain." Watch him narrowly, and if you see by his countenance that you are on the wrong tack, ask him where he preaches. It is a safe bet that he is either a missionary or captain of a whaler. I am now personally acquainted with seventy-two captains and ninety-six missionaries. The captains and ministers form one-half of the population; the third fourth is composed of common Kanakas and mercantile foreigners and their families, and the final fourth is made up of high officers of the Hawaiian Government. And there are just about cats enough for three apiece all around.

A solemn stranger met me in the suburbs the other day, and said:

"Good morning, your reverence. Preach in the stone church yonder, no doubt?"

"No, I don't. I'm not a preacher."

"Really, I beg your pardon, Captain. I trust you had a good season. How much oil"—

"Oil? What do you take me for? I'm not a whaler."

"Oh, I beg a thousand pardons, your Excellency.

"Major General in the household troops, no doubt? Minister of the Interior, likely? Secretary of war? First Gentleman of the Bed-chamber? Commissioner of the Royal"—

"Stuff! I'm no official. I'm not connected in any way with the Government."

"Bless my life! Then, who the mischief are you? what the mischief are you? and how the mischief did you get here, and where in thunder did you come from?"

"I'm only a private personage—an unassuming stranger—lately arrived from America."

"No? Not a missionary! Not a whaler! not a member of his Majesty's Government! not even Secretary of the Navy! Ah, Heaven! it is too blissful to be true; alas, I do but dream. And yet that noble, honest countenance—those oblique, ingenuous eyes—that massive head, incapable of—of—anything; your hand; give me your hand, bright waif. Excuse these tears. For sixteen weary years I have yearned for a moment like this, and"—

Here his feelings were too much for him, and he swooned away. I pitied this poor creature from the bottom of my heart. I was deeply moved. I shed a few tears on him and kissed him for his mother. I then took what small change he had and "shoved".

CHAPTER LXVII.

I still quote from my journal:

I found the national Legislature to consist of half a dozen white men and some thirty or forty natives. It was a dark assemblage. The nobles and Ministers (about a dozen of them altogether) occupied the extreme left of the hall, with David Kalakaua (the King's Chamberlain) and Prince William at the head. The President of the Assembly, His Royal Highness M. Kekuanaoa, [Kekuanaoa is not of the blood royal. He derives his princely rank from his wife, who was a daughter of Kamehameha the Great. Under other monarchies the male line takes precedence of the female in tracing genealogies, but here the opposite is the case—the female line takes precedence. Their reason for this is exceedingly sensible, and I recommend it to the aristocracy of Europe: They say it is easy to know who a man's mother was, but, etc., etc.] and the Vice President (the latter a white man,) sat in the pulpit, if I may so term it. The President is the King's father. He is an erect, strongly built, massive featured, white-haired, tawny old gentleman of eighty years of age or thereabouts. He was simply but well dressed, in a blue cloth coat and white vest, and white pantaloons, without spot, dust or blemish upon them. He bears himself with a calm, stately dignity, and is a man of noble presence. He was a young man and a distinguished warrior under that terrific fighter, Kamehameha I., more than half a century ago. A knowledge of his career suggested some such thought as this: "This man, naked as the day he was born, and war-club and spear in hand, has charged at the head of a horde of savages against other hordes of savages more than a generation and a half ago, and reveled in slaughter and carnage; has worshipped wooden images on his devout knees; has seen hundreds of his race offered up in

heathen temples as sacrifices to wooden idols, at a time when no missionary's foot had ever pressed this soil, and he had never heard of the white man's God; has believed his enemy could secretly pray him to death; has seen the day, in his childhood, when it was a crime punishable by death for a man to eat with his wife, or for a plebeian to let his shadow fall upon the King—and now look at him; an educated Christian; neatly and handsomely dressed; a high-minded, elegant gentleman; a traveler, in some degree, and one who has been the honored guest of royalty in Europe; a man practiced in holding the reins of an enlightened government, and well versed in the politics of his country and in general, practical information. Look at him, sitting there presiding over the deliberations of a legislative body, among whom are white men—a grave, dignified, statesmanlike personage, and as seemingly natural and fitted to the place as if he had been born in it and had never been out of it in his life time. How the experiences of this old man's eventful life shame the cheap inventions of romance!"

The christianizing of the natives has hardly even weakened some of their barbarian superstitions, much less destroyed them. I have just referred to one of these. It is still a popular belief that if your enemy can get hold of any article belonging to you he can get down on his knees over it and pray you to death. Therefore many a native gives up and dies merely because he imagines that some enemy is putting him through a course of damaging prayer. This praying an individual to death seems absurd enough at a first glance, but then when we call to mind some of the pulpit efforts of certain of our own ministers the thing looks plausible.

In former times, among the Islanders, not only a plurality of wives was customary, but a plurality of husbands likewise. Some native women of noble rank had as many as six husbands. A woman thus supplied did not reside with all her husbands at once, but lived several months with each in turn. An understood sign hung at her door during these months. When the sign was taken down, it meant "NEXT."

In those days woman was rigidly taught to "know her place." Her place was to do all the work, take all the cuffs, provide all the food, and content herself with what was left after her lord had finished his dinner. She was not only forbidden, by ancient law, and under penalty of death, to eat with her husband or enter a canoe, but was debarred, under the same penalty, from eating bananas, pine-apples, oranges and other choice fruits at any time or in any place. She had to confine herself pretty strictly to "poi" and hard work. These poor ignorant heathen seem to have had a sort of groping idea of what came of woman eating fruit in the garden of Eden, and they did not choose to take any more chances. But the missionaries broke up this satisfactory arrangement of things. They liberated woman and made her the equal of man.

The natives had a romantic fashion of burying some of their children alive when the family became larger than necessary. The missionaries interfered in this matter too, and stopped it.

To this day the natives are able to lie down and die whenever they want to, whether there is anything the matter with them or not. If a Kanaka takes a notion to die, that is the end of him; nobody can persuade him to hold on; all the doctors in the world could not save him.

A luxury which they enjoy more than anything else, is a large funeral. If a person wants to get rid of a troublesome native, it is only necessary to promise him a fine funeral and name the hour and he will be on hand to the minute—at least his remains will.

All the natives are Christians, now, but many of them still desert to the Great Shark God for temporary succor in time of trouble. An irruption of the great volcano of Kilauea, or an earthquake, always brings a deal of latent loyalty to the Great Shark God to the surface. It is common report that the King, educated, cultivated and refined Christian gentleman as he undoubtedly is, still turns to the idols of his fathers for help when disaster threatens. A planter caught a shark, and one of his christianized natives testified his emancipation from the thrall of ancient superstition by assisting to dissect the shark after a fashion forbidden by his abandoned creed. But remorse shortly began to torture him. He grew moody and sought solitude; brooded over his sin, refused food, and finally said he must die and ought to die, for he had sinned against the Great Shark God and could never know peace any more. He was proof against persuasion and ridicule, and in the course of a day or two took to his bed and died, although he showed no symptom of disease. His young daughter followed his lead and suffered a like fate within the week. Superstition is ingrained in the native blood and bone and it is only natural that it should crop out in time of distress. Wherever one goes in the Islands, he will find small piles of stones by the wayside, covered with leafy offerings, placed there by the natives to appease evil spirits or honor local deities belonging to the mythology of former days.

In the rural districts of any of the Islands, the traveler hourly comes upon parties of dusky maidens bathing in the streams or in the sea without any clothing on and exhibiting no very intemperate zeal in the matter of hiding their nakedness. When the missionaries first took up their residence in Honolulu, the native women would pay their families frequent friendly visits, day by day, not even clothed with a blush. It was found a hard matter to convince them that this was rather indelicate. Finally the missionaries provided them with long, loose calico robes, and that ended the difficulty—for the women would troop through the town, stark naked, with their robes folded under their arms, march to the missionary houses and then proceed to dress!—The natives soon manifested a strong proclivity for clothing, but it was shortly apparent that they only wanted it for grandeur. The missionaries imported a quantity of hats, bonnets, and other male and female wearing apparel, instituted a general distribution, and begged the people not to come to church naked, next Sunday, as usual. And they did not; but the national spirit of unselfishness led them to divide up with neighbors who were not at the distribution, and next Sabbath the poor preachers could hardly keep countenance before their vast congregations. In the midst of the reading of a hymn a brown, stately dame would sweep up the aisle with a world of airs, with nothing in the world on but a "stovepipe" hat and a pair of cheap gloves; another dame would follow, tricked out in a man's shirt, and nothing else; another one would enter with a flourish, with simply the sleeves of a bright calico dress tied around her waist and the rest of the garment dragging behind like a peacock's tail off duty; a stately "buck" Kanaka would stalk in with a woman's bonnet on, wrong side before—only this, and nothing more; after him would stride his fellow, with the legs of a pair of pantaloons tied around his neck, the rest of his person untrammeled; in his rear would come another gentleman simply gotten up in a fiery neck-tie and a striped vest.

The poor creatures were beaming with complacency and wholly unconscious of any absurdity in their appearance. They gazed at each other with happy admiration, and it was plain to see that the young girls were taking note of what each other had on, as naturally as if they had always lived in a land of Bibles and knew what churches were made for; here was the evidence of a dawning civilization. The spectacle which the congregation presented was so extraordinary and withal so moving, that the missionaries found it difficult to keep to the text and go on with the services; and by and by when the simple children of the sun began a general swapping of garments in open meeting and produced some irresistibly grotesque effects in the course of re-dressing, there was nothing for it but to cut the thing short with the benediction and dismiss the fantastic assemblage.

In our country, children play "keep house;" and in the same high-sounding but miniature way the grown folk here, with the poor little material of slender territory and meagre population, play "empire." There is his royal Majesty the King, with a New York detective's income of thirty or thirty-five thousand dollars a year from the "royal civil list" and the "royal domain." He lives in a two-story frame "palace."

And there is the "royal family"—the customary hive of royal brothers, sisters, cousins and other noble drones and vagrants usual to monarchy, —all with a spoon in the national pap-dish, and all bearing such titles as his or her Royal Highness the Prince or Princess So-and-so. Few of them can carry their royal splendors far enough to ride in carriages, however; they sport the economical Kanaka horse or "hoof it" with the plebeians.

Then there is his Excellency the "royal Chamberlain"—a sinecure, for his majesty dresses himself with his own hands, except when he is ruralizing at Waikiki and then he requires no dressing.

Next we have his Excellency the Commander-in-chief of the Household Troops, whose forces consist of about the number of soldiers usually placed under a corporal in other lands.

Next comes the royal Steward and the Grand Equerry in Waiting—high dignitaries with modest salaries and little to do.

Then we have his Excellency the First Gentleman of the Bedchamber—an office as easy as it is magnificent.

Next we come to his Excellency the Prime Minister, a renegade American from New Hampshire, all jaw, vanity, bombast and ignorance, a lawyer of "shyster" calibre, a fraud by nature, a humble worshipper of the sceptre above him, a reptile never tired of sneering at the land of his birth or glorifying the ten-acre kingdom that has adopted him—salary, $4,000 a year, vast consequence, and no perquisites.

Then we have his Excellency the Imperial Minister of Finance, who handles a million dollars of public money a year, sends in his annual "budget" with great ceremony, talks prodigiously of "finance," suggests imposing schemes for paying off the "national debt" (of $150,000,) and does it all for $4,000 a year and unimaginable glory.

Next we have his Excellency the Minister of War, who holds sway over the royal armies—they consist of two hundred and thirty uniformed Kanakas, mostly Brigadier Generals, and if the country ever gets into trouble with a foreign power we shall probably hear from them. I knew an American whose copper-plate visiting card bore this impressive legend: "Lieutenant-Colonel in the Royal Infantry." To say that he was proud of this distinction is stating it but tamely. The Minister of War has also in his charge some venerable swivels on Punch-Bowl Hill wherewith royal salutes are fired when foreign vessels of war enter the port.

Next comes his Excellency the Minister of the Navy—a nabob who rules the "royal fleet," (a steam-tug and a sixty-ton schooner.)

And next comes his Grace the Lord Bishop of Honolulu, the chief dignitary of the "Established Church"—for when the American Presbyterian missionaries had completed the reduction of the nation to a compact condition of Christianity, native royalty stepped in and erected the grand dignity of an "Established (Episcopal) Church" over it, and imported a cheap ready-made Bishop from England to take charge. The chagrin of the missionaries has never been comprehensively expressed, to this day, profanity not being admissible.

Next comes his Excellency the Minister of Public Instruction.

Next, their Excellencies the Governors of Oahu, Hawaii, etc., and after them a string of High Sheriffs and other small fry too numerous for computation.

Then there are their Excellencies the Envoy Extraordinary and Minister Plenipotentiary of his Imperial Majesty the Emperor of the French; her British Majesty's Minister; the Minister Resident, of the United States; and some six or eight representatives of other foreign nations, all with sounding titles, imposing dignity and prodigious but economical state.

Imagine all this grandeur in a play-house "kingdom" whose population falls absolutely short of sixty thousand souls!

The people are so accustomed to nine-jointed titles and colossal magnates that a foreign prince makes very little more stir in Honolulu than a Western Congressman does in New York.

And let it be borne in mind that there is a strictly defined "court costume" of so "stunning" a nature that it would make the clown in a circus look tame and commonplace by comparison; and each Hawaiian official dignitary has a gorgeous vari-colored, gold-laced uniform peculiar to his office—no two of them are alike, and it is hard to tell which one is the "loudest." The King had a "drawing-room" at stated intervals, like other monarchs, and when these varied uniforms congregate there—weak-eyed people have to contemplate the spectacle through smoked glass. Is there not a gratifying contrast between this latter-day exhibition and the one the ancestors of some of these magnates afforded the missionaries the Sunday after the old-time distribution of clothing? Behold what religion and civilization have wrought!

CHAPTER LXVIII.

While I was in Honolulu I witnessed the ceremonious funeral of the King's sister, her Royal Highness the Princess Victoria. According to the royal custom, the remains had lain in state at the palace thirty days, watched day and night by a guard of honor. And during all that time a great multitude of natives from the several islands had kept the palace grounds well crowded and had made the place a pandemonium every night with their howlings and wailings, beating of tom-toms and dancing of the (at other times) forbidden "hula-hula" by half-clad maidens to the music of songs of questionable decency chanted in honor of the deceased. The printed programme of

the funeral procession interested me at the time; and after what I have just said of Hawaiian grandiloquence in the matter of "playing empire," I am persuaded that a perusal of it may interest the reader:

After reading the long list of dignitaries, etc., and remembering the sparseness of the population, one is almost inclined to wonder where the material for that portion of the procession devoted to "Hawaiian Population Generally" is going to be procured:

Undertaker. Royal School. Kawaiahao School. Roman Catholic School. Maemae School. Honolulu Fire Department. Mechanics' Benefit Union. Attending Physicians. Knonohikis (Superintendents) of the Crown Lands, Konohikis of the Private Lands of His Majesty Konohikis of the Private Lands of Her late Royal Highness. Governor of Oahu and Staff. Hulumanu (Military Company). Household Troops. The Prince of Hawaii's Own (Military Company). The King's household servants. Servants of Her late Royal Highness. Protestant Clergy. The Clergy of the Roman Catholic Church. His Lordship Louis Maigret, The Right Rev. Bishop of Arathea, Vicar-Apostolic of the Hawaiian Islands. The Clergy of the Hawaiian Reformed Catholic Church. His Lordship the Right Rev. Bishop of Honolulu. Her Majesty Queen Emma's Carriage. His Majesty's Staff. Carriage of Her late Royal Highness. Carriage of Her Majesty the Queen Dowager. The King's Chancellor. Cabinet Ministers. His Excellency the Minister Resident of the United States. H. B. M's Commissioner. H. B. M's Acting Commissioner. Judges of Supreme Court. Privy Councillors. Members of Legislative Assembly. Consular Corps. Circuit Judges. Clerks of Government Departments. Members of the Bar. Collector General, Custom-house Officers and Officers of the Customs. Marshal and Sheriffs of the different Islands. King's Yeomanry. Foreign Residents. Ahahui Kaahumanu. Hawaiian Population Generally. Hawaiian Cavalry. Police Force.

I resume my journal at the point where the procession arrived at the royal mausoleum:

As the procession filed through the gate, the military deployed handsomely to the right and left and formed an avenue through which the long column of mourners passed to the tomb. The coffin was borne through the door of the mausoleum, followed by the King and his chiefs, the great officers of the kingdom, foreign Consuls, Embassadors and distinguished guests (Burlingame and General Van Valkenburgh). Several of the kahilis were then fastened to a frame-work in front of the tomb, there to remain until they decay and fall to pieces, or, forestalling this, until another scion of royalty dies. At this point of the proceedings the multitude set up such a heart-broken wailing as I hope never to hear again.

The soldiers fired three volleys of musketry—the wailing being previously silenced to permit of the guns being heard. His Highness Prince William, in a showy military uniform (the "true prince," this —scion of the house over-thrown by the present dynasty—he was formerly betrothed to the Princess but was not allowed to marry her), stood guard and paced back and forth within the door. The privileged few who followed the coffin into the mausoleum remained sometime, but the King soon came out and stood in the door and near one side of it. A stranger could have guessed his rank (although he was so simply and unpretentiously dressed) by the profound deference paid him by all persons in his vicinity; by seeing his high officers receive his quiet orders and suggestions with bowed and uncovered heads; and by observing how careful those persons who came out of the mausoleum were to avoid "crowding" him (although there was room enough in the doorway for a wagon to pass, for that matter); how respectfully they edged out sideways, scraping their backs against the wall and always presenting a front view of their persons to his Majesty, and never putting their hats on until they were well out of the royal presence.

He was dressed entirely in black—dress-coat and silk hat—and looked rather democratic in the midst of the showy uniforms about him. On his breast he wore a large gold star, which was half hidden by the lapel of his coat. He remained at the door a half hour, and occasionally gave an order to the men who were erecting the kahilis [Ranks of long-handled mops made of gaudy feathers—sacred to royalty. They are stuck in the ground around the tomb and left there.] before the tomb. He had the good taste to make one of them substitute black crape for the ordinary hempen rope he was about to tie one of them to the frame-work with. Finally he entered his carriage and drove away, and the populace shortly began to drop into his wake. While he was in view there was but one man who attracted more attention than himself, and that was Harris (the Yankee Prime Minister). This feeble personage had crape enough around his hat to express the grief of an entire nation, and as usual he neglected no opportunity of making himself conspicuous and exciting the admiration of the simple Kanakas. Oh! noble ambition of this modern Richelieu!

It is interesting to contrast the funeral ceremonies of the Princess Victoria with those of her noted ancestor Kamehameha the Conqueror, who died fifty years ago—in 1819, the year before the first missionaries came.

"On the 8th of May, 1819, at the age of sixty-six, he died, as he had lived, in the faith of his country. It was his misfortune not to have come in contact with men who could have rightly influenced his religious aspirations. Judged by his advantages and compared with the most eminent of his countrymen he may be justly styled not only great, but good. To this day his memory warms the heart and elevates the national feelings of Hawaiians. They are proud of their old warrior King; they love his name; his deeds form their historical age; and an enthusiasm everywhere prevails, shared even by foreigners who knew his worth, that constitutes the firmest pillar of the throne of his dynasty.

"In lieu of human victims (the custom of that age), a sacrifice of three hundred dogs attended his obsequies—no mean holocaust when their national value and the estimation in which they were held are considered. The bones of Kamehameha, after being kept for a while, were so carefully concealed that all knowledge of their final resting place is now lost. There was a proverb current among the common people that the bones of a cruel King could not be hid; they made fish-hooks and arrows of them, upon which, in using them, they vented their abhorrence of his memory in bitter execrations."

The account of the circumstances of his death, as written by the native historians, is full of minute detail, but there is scarcely a line of it which does not mention or illustrate some by-gone custom of the country. In this respect it is the most comprehensive document I have yet met with. I will quote it entire:

"When Kamehameha was dangerously sick, and the priests were unable to cure him, they said: 'Be of good courage and build a house for the god' (his own private god or idol), that thou mayest recover.' The chiefs corroborated this advice of the priests, and a place of worship was prepared for Kukailimoku, and consecrated in the evening. They proposed also to the King, with a view to prolong his life, that human victims should be sacrificed to his deity; upon which the greater part of the people absconded through fear of death, and concealed themselves in hiding places till the tabu [Tabu (pronounced tah-boo,) means prohibition (we have borrowed it,) or sacred. The tabu was sometimes permanent, sometimes temporary; and the person or thing placed under tabu was for the time being sacred to the purpose for which it was set apart. In the above case the victims selected under the tabu would be sacred to the sacrifice] in which destruction impended, was past. It is doubtful whether Kamehameha approved of the plan of the chiefs and priests to sacrifice men, as he was known to say, 'The men are sacred for the King;' meaning that they were for the service of his successor. This information was derived from Liholiho, his son.

"After this, his sickness increased to such a degree that he had not strength to turn himself in his bed. When another season, consecrated for worship at the new temple (heiau) arrived, he said to his son, Liholiho, 'Go thou and make supplication to thy god; I am not able to go, and will offer my prayers at home.' When his devotions to his feathered god, Kukailimoku, were concluded, a certain religiously disposed individual, who had a bird god, suggested to the King that through its influence his sickness might be removed. The name of this god was Pua; its body was made of a bird, now eaten by the Hawaiians, and called in their language alae. Kamehameha was willing that a trial should be made, and two houses were constructed to facilitate the experiment; but while dwelling in them he became so very weak as not to receive food. After lying there three days, his wives, children and chiefs, perceiving that he was very low, returned him to his own house. In the evening he was carried to the eating house, where he took a little food in his mouth which he did not swallow; also a cup of water. The chiefs requested him to give them his counsel; but he made no reply, and was carried back to the dwelling house; but when near midnight—ten o'clock, perhaps—he was carried again to the place to eat; but, as before, he merely tasted of what was presented to him. Then Kaikioewa addressed him thus: 'Here we all are, your younger brethren, your son Liholiho and your foreigner; impart to us your dying charge, that Liholiho and Kaahumanu may hear.' Then Kamehameha inquired, 'What do you say?' Kaikioewa repeated, 'Your counsels for us.'

"He then said, 'Move on in my good way and—.' He could proceed no further. The foreigner, Mr. Young, embraced and kissed him. Hoapili also embraced him, whispering something in his ear, after which he was taken back to the house. About twelve he was carried once more to the house for eating, into which his head entered, while his body was in the dwelling house immediately adjoining. It should be remarked that this frequent carrying of a sick chief from one house to another resulted from the tabu system, then in force. There were at that time six houses (huts) connected with an establishment—one was for worship, one for the men to eat in, an eating house for the women, a house to sleep in, a house in which to manufacture kapa (native cloth) and one where, at certain intervals, the women might dwell in seclusion.

"The sick was once more taken to his house, when he expired; this was at two o'clock, a circumstance from which Leleiohoku derived his name. As he breathed his last, Kalaimoku came to the eating house to order those in it to go out. There were two aged persons thus directed to depart; one went, the other remained on account of love to the King, by whom he had formerly been kindly sustained. The children also were sent away. Then Kalaimoku came to the house, and the chiefs had a consultation. One of them spoke thus: 'This is my thought—we will eat him raw. [This sounds suspicious, in view of the fact that all Sandwich Island historians, white and black, protest that cannibalism never existed in the islands. However, since they only proposed to "eat him raw" we "won't count that". But it would certainly have been cannibalism if they had cooked him.—M. T.] Kaahumanu (one of the dead King's widows) replied, 'Perhaps his body is not at our disposal; that is more properly with his successor. Our part in him—his breath—has departed; his remains will be disposed of by Liholiho.'

"After this conversation the body was taken into the consecrated house for the performance of the proper rites by the priest and the new King. The name of this ceremony is uko; and when the sacred hog was baked the priest offered it to the dead body, and it became a god, the King at the same time repeating the customary prayers.

"Then the priest, addressing himself to the King and chiefs, said: 'I will now make known to you the rules to be observed respecting persons to be sacrificed on the burial of this body. If you obtain one man before the corpse is removed, one will be sufficient; but after it leaves this house four will be required. If delayed until we carry the corpse to the grave there must be ten; but after it is deposited in the grave there must be fifteen. To-morrow morning there will be a tabu, and, if the sacrifice be delayed until that time, forty men must die.'

"Then the high priest, Hewahewa, inquired of the chiefs, 'Where shall be the residence of King Liholiho?' They replied, 'Where, indeed? You, of all men, ought to know.' Then the priest observed, 'There are two suitable places; one is Kau, the other is Kohala.' The chiefs preferred the latter, as it was more thickly inhabited. The priest added, 'These are proper places for the King's residence; but he must not remain in Kona, for it is polluted.' This was agreed to. It was now break of day. As he was being carried to the place of burial the people perceived that their King was dead, and they wailed. When the corpse was removed from the house to the tomb, a distance of one chain, the procession was met by a certain man who was ardently attached to the deceased. He leaped upon the chiefs who were carrying the King's body; he desired to die with him on account of his love. The chiefs drove him away. He persisted in making numerous attempts, which were unavailing. Kalaimoka also had it in his heart to die with him, but was prevented by Hookio.

"The morning following Kamehameha's death, Liholiho and his train departed for Kohala, according to the suggestions of the priest, to avoid the defilement occasioned by the dead. At this time if a chief died the land was polluted, and the heirs sought a residence in another part of the country until the corpse was dissected and the bones tied in a bundle, which being done, the season of defilement terminated. If the deceased were not a chief, the house only was defiled which became pure again on the burial of the body. Such were the laws on this subject.

"On the morning on which Liholiho sailed in his canoe for Kohala, the chiefs and people mourned after their manner on occasion of a chief's death, conducting themselves like madmen and like beasts. Their conduct was such as to forbid description; The priests, also, put into action the sorcery apparatus, that the person who had prayed the King to death might die; for it was not believed that Kamehameha's

departure was the effect either of sickness or old age. When the sorcerers set up by their fire-places sticks with a strip of kapa flying at the top, the chief Keeaumoku, Kaahumaun's brother, came in a state of intoxication and broke the flag-staff of the sorcerers, from which it was inferred that Kaahumanu and her friends had been instrumental in the King's death. On this account they were subjected to abuse."

You have the contrast, now, and a strange one it is. This great Queen, Kaahumanu, who was "subjected to abuse" during the frightful orgies that followed the King's death, in accordance with ancient custom, afterward became a devout Christian and a steadfast and powerful friend of the missionaries.

Dogs were, and still are, reared and fattened for food, by the natives —hence the reference to their value in one of the above paragraphs.

Forty years ago it was the custom in the Islands to suspend all law for a certain number of days after the death of a royal personage; and then a saturnalia ensued which one may picture to himself after a fashion, but not in the full horror of the reality. The people shaved their heads, knocked out a tooth or two, plucked out an eye sometimes, cut, bruised, mutilated or burned their flesh, got drunk, burned each other's huts, maimed or murdered one another according to the caprice of the moment, and both sexes gave themselves up to brutal and unbridled licentiousness.

And after it all, came a torpor from which the nation slowly emerged bewildered and dazed, as if from a hideous half-remembered nightmare. They were not the salt of the earth, those "gentle children of the sun."

The natives still keep up an old custom of theirs which cannot be comforting to an invalid. When they think a sick friend is going to die, a couple of dozen neighbors surround his hut and keep up a deafening wailing night and day till he either dies or gets well. No doubt this arrangement has helped many a subject to a shroud before his appointed time.

They surround a hut and wail in the same heart-broken way when its occupant returns from a journey. This is their dismal idea of a welcome. A very little of it would go a great way with most of us.

CHAPTER LXIX.

Bound for Hawaii (a hundred and fifty miles distant,) to visit the great volcano and behold the other notable things which distinguish that island above the remainder of the group, we sailed from Honolulu on a certain Saturday afternoon, in the good schooner Boomerang.

The Boomerang was about as long as two street cars, and about as wide as one. She was so small (though she was larger than the majority of the inter-island coasters) that when I stood on her deck I felt but little smaller than the Colossus of Rhodes must have felt when he had a man-of-war under him. I could reach the water when she lay over under a strong breeze. When the Captain and my comrade (a Mr. Billings,) myself and four other persons were all assembled on the little after portion of the deck which is sacred to the cabin passengers, it was full—there was not room for any more quality folks. Another section of the deck, twice as large as ours, was full of natives of both sexes, with their customary dogs, mats, blankets, pipes, calabashes of poi, fleas, and other luxuries and baggage of minor importance. As soon as we set sail the natives all lay down on the deck as thick as negroes in a slave-pen, and smoked, conversed, and spit on each other, and were truly sociable.

The little low-ceiled cabin below was rather larger than a hearse, and as dark as a vault. It had two coffins on each side—I mean two bunks. A small table, capable of accommodating three persons at dinner, stood against the forward bulkhead, and over it hung the dingiest whale oil lantern that ever peopled the obscurity of a dungeon with ghostly shapes. The floor room unoccupied was not extensive. One might swing a cat in it, perhaps, but not a long cat. The hold forward of the bulkhead had but little freight in it, and from morning till night a portly old rooster, with a voice like Baalam's ass, and the same disposition to use it, strutted up and down in that part of the vessel and crowed. He usually took dinner at six o'clock, and then, after an hour devoted to meditation, he mounted a barrel and crowed a good part of the night. He got hoarser all the time, but he scorned to allow any personal consideration to interfere with his duty, and kept up his labors in defiance of threatened diphtheria.

Sleeping was out of the question when he was on watch. He was a source of genuine aggravation and annoyance. It was worse than useless to shout at him or apply offensive epithets to him—he only took these things for applause, and strained himself to make more noise. Occasionally, during the day, I threw potatoes at him through an aperture in the bulkhead, but he only dodged and went on crowing.

The first night, as I lay in my coffin, idly watching the dim lamp swinging to the rolling of the ship, and snuffing the nauseous odors of bilge water, I felt something gallop over me. I turned out promptly. However, I turned in again when I found it was only a rat. Presently something galloped over me once more. I knew it was not a rat this time, and I thought it might be a centipede, because the Captain had killed one on deck in the afternoon. I turned out. The first glance at the pillow showed me repulsive sentinel perched upon each end of it—cockroaches as large as peach leaves—fellows with long, quivering antennae and fiery, malignant eyes. They were grating their teeth like tobacco worms, and appeared to be dissatisfied about something. I had often heard that these reptiles were in the habit of eating off sleeping sailors' toe nails down to the quick, and I would not get in the bunk any more. I lay down on the floor. But a rat came and bothered me, and shortly afterward a procession of cockroaches arrived and camped in my hair. In a few moments the rooster was crowing with uncommon spirit and a party of fleas were throwing double somersaults about my person in the wildest disorder, and taking a bite every time they struck. I was beginning to feel really annoyed. I got up and put my clothes on and went on deck.

The above is not overdrawn; it is a truthful sketch of inter-island schooner life. There is no such thing as keeping a vessel in elegant condition, when she carries molasses and Kanakas.

It was compensation for my sufferings to come unexpectedly upon so beautiful a scene as met my eye—to step suddenly out of the sepulchral gloom of the cabin and stand under the strong light of the moon—in the centre, as it were, of a glittering sea of liquid silver—to see the broad sails straining in the gale, the ship heeled over on her side, the angry foam hissing past her lee bulwarks, and sparkling sheets of spray dashing high over her bows and raining upon her decks; to brace myself and hang fast to the first object that presented itself, with hat jammed down and coat tails whipping in the breeze, and feel that exhilaration that thrills in one's hair and quivers down his back bone when he knows that every inch of canvas is drawing and the vessel cleaving through the waves at her utmost speed. There was no darkness, no dimness, no obscurity there. All was brightness, every object was vividly defined. Every prostrate Kanaka; every coil of rope; every calabash of poi; every puppy; every seam in the flooring; every bolthead; every object; however minute, showed sharp and distinct in its every outline; and the shadow of the broad mainsail lay black as a pall upon the deck, leaving Billings's white upturned face glorified and his body in a total eclipse. Monday morning we were close to the island of Hawaii. Two of its high mountains were in view—Mauna Loa and Hualaiai.

The latter is an imposing peak, but being only ten thousand feet high is seldom mentioned or heard of. Mauna Loa is said to be sixteen thousand feet high. The rays of glittering snow and ice, that clasped its summit like a claw, looked refreshing when viewed from the blistering climate we were in. One could stand on that mountain (wrapped up in blankets and furs to keep warm), and while he nibbled a snowball or an icicle to quench his thirst he could look down the long sweep of its sides and see spots where plants are growing that grow only where the bitter cold of Winter prevails; lower down he could see sections devoted to production that thrive in the temperate zone alone; and at the bottom of the mountain he could see the home of the tufted cocoa-palms and other species of vegetation that grow only in the sultry atmosphere of eternal Summer. He could see all the climes of the world at a single glance of the eye, and that glance would only pass over a distance of four or five miles as the bird flies!

By and by we took boat and went ashore at Kailua, designing to ride horseback through the pleasant orange and coffee region of Kona, and rejoin the vessel at a point some leagues distant. This journey is well worth taking. The trail passes along on high ground—say a thousand feet above sea level—and usually about a mile distant from the ocean, which is always in sight, save that occasionally you find yourself buried in the forest in the midst of a rank tropical vegetation and a dense growth of trees, whose great bows overarch the road and shut out sun and sea and everything, and leave you in a dim, shady tunnel, haunted with invisible singing birds and fragrant with the odor of flowers. It was pleasant to ride occasionally in the warm sun, and feast the eye upon the ever-changing panorama of the forest (beyond and below us), with its many tints, its softened lights and shadows, its billowy undulations sweeping gently down from the mountain to the sea. It was pleasant also, at intervals, to leave the sultry sun and pass into the cool, green depths of this forest and indulge in sentimental reflections under the inspiration of its brooding twilight and its whispering foliage. We rode through one orange grove that had ten thousand tree in it! They were all laden with fruit.

At one farmhouse we got some large peaches of excellent flavor. This fruit, as a general thing, does not do well in the Sandwich Islands. It takes a sort of almond shape, and is small and bitter. It needs frost, they say, and perhaps it does; if this be so, it will have a good opportunity to go on needing it, as it will not be likely to get it. The trees from which the fine fruit I have spoken of, came, had been planted and replanted sixteen times, and to this treatment the proprietor of the orchard attributed his-success.

We passed several sugar plantations—new ones and not very extensive. The crops were, in most cases, third rattoons. [NOTE.—The first crop is called "plant cane;" subsequent crops which spring from the original roots, without replanting, are called "rattoons."] Almost everywhere on the island of Hawaii sugar-cane matures in twelve months, both rattoons and plant, and although it ought to be taken off as soon as it tassels, no doubt, it is not absolutely necessary to do it until about four months afterward. In Kona, the average yield of an acre of ground is two tons of sugar, they say. This is only a moderate yield for these islands, but would be astounding for Louisiana and most other sugar growing countries. The plantations in Kona being on pretty high ground—up among the light and frequent rains—no irrigation whatever is required.

CHAPTER LXX.

We stopped some time at one of the plantations, to rest ourselves and refresh the horses. We had a chatty conversation with several gentlemen present; but there was one person, a middle aged man, with an absent look in his face, who simply glanced up, gave us good-day and lapsed again into the meditations which our coming had interrupted. The planters whispered us not to mind him—crazy. They said he was in the Islands for his health; was a preacher; his home, Michigan. They said that if he woke up presently and fell to talking about a correspondence which he had some time held with Mr. Greeley about a trifle of some kind, we must humor him and listen with interest; and we must humor his fancy that this correspondence was the talk of the world.

It was easy to see that he was a gentle creature and that his madness had nothing vicious in it. He looked pale, and a little worn, as if with perplexing thought and anxiety of mind. He sat a long time, looking at the floor, and at intervals muttering to himself and nodding his head acquiescingly or shaking it in mild protest. He was lost in his thought, or in his memories. We continued our talk with the planters, branching from subject to subject. But at last the word "circumstance," casually dropped, in the course of conversation, attracted his attention and brought an eager look into his countenance. He faced about in his chair and said:

"Circumstance? What circumstance? Ah, I know—I know too well. So you have heard of it too." [With a sigh.] "Well, no matter—all the world has heard of it. All the world. The whole world. It is a large world, too, for a thing to travel so far in—now isn't it? Yes, yes—the Greeley correspondence with Erickson has created the saddest and bitterest controversy on both sides of the ocean—and still they keep it up! It makes us famous, but at what a sorrowful sacrifice! I was so sorry when I heard that it had caused that bloody and distressful war over there in Italy. It was little comfort to me, after so much bloodshed, to know that the victors sided with me, and the vanquished with Greeley.—It is little comfort to know that Horace Greeley is responsible for the battle of Sadowa, and not me.

"Queen Victoria wrote me that she felt just as I did about it— she said that as much as she was opposed to Greeley and the spirit he showed in the correspondence with me, she would not have had Sadowa happen for hundreds of dollars. I can show you her letter, if you would like to see it. But gentlemen, much as you may think you know about that unhappy correspondence, you cannot know the straight of it till you hear it from my lips. It has always been garbled in the journals, and even in history. Yes, even in history—think of it! Let me—please let me, give you the matter, exactly as it occurred. I truly will not abuse your confidence."

Then he leaned forward, all interest, all earnestness, and told his story—and told it appealingly, too, and yet in the simplest and most unpretentious way; indeed, in such a way as to suggest to one, all the time, that this was a faithful, honorable witness, giving evidence in the sacred interest of justice, and under oath. He said:

"Mrs. Beazeley—Mrs. Jackson Beazeley, widow, of the village of Campbellton, Kansas,—wrote me about a matter which was near her heart —a matter which many might think trivial, but to her it was a thing of deep concern. I was living in Michigan, then—serving in the ministry. She was, and is, an estimable woman—a woman to whom poverty and hardship have proven incentives to industry, in place of discouragements. Her only treasure was her son William, a youth just verging upon manhood; religious, amiable, and sincerely attached to agriculture. He was the widow's comfort and her pride. And so, moved by her love for him, she wrote me about a matter, as I have said before, which lay near her heart —because it lay near her boy's. She desired me to confer with Mr. Greeley about turnips. Turnips were the dream of her child's young ambition. While other youths were frittering away in frivolous amusements the precious years of budding vigor which God had given them for useful preparation, this boy was patiently enriching his mind with information concerning turnips. The sentiment which he felt toward the turnip was akin to adoration. He could not think of the turnip without emotion; he could not speak of it calmly; he could not contemplate it without exaltation. He could not eat it without shedding tears. All the poetry in his sensitive nature was in sympathy with the gracious vegetable. With the earliest pipe of dawn he sought his patch, and when the curtaining night drove him from it he shut himself up with his books and garnered statistics till sleep overcame him. On rainy days he sat and talked hours together with his mother about turnips. When company came, he made it his loving duty to put aside everything else and converse with them all the day long of his great joy in the turnip.

"And yet, was this joy rounded and complete? Was there no secret alloy of unhappiness in it? Alas, there was. There was a canker gnawing at his heart; the noblest inspiration of his soul eluded his endeavor—viz: he could not make of the turnip a climbing vine. Months went by; the bloom forsook his cheek, the fire faded out of his eye; sighings and abstraction usurped the place of smiles and cheerful converse. But a watchful eye noted these things and in time a motherly sympathy unsealed the secret. Hence the letter to me. She pleaded for attention— she said her boy was dying by inches.

"I was a stranger to Mr. Greeley, but what of that? The matter was urgent. I wrote and begged him to solve the difficult problem if possible and save the student's life. My interest grew, until it partook of the anxiety of the mother. I waited in much suspense.—At last the answer came.

"I found that I could not read it readily, the handwriting being unfamiliar and my emotions somewhat wrought up. It seemed to refer in part to the boy's case, but chiefly to other and irrelevant matters—such as paving-stones, electricity, oysters, and something which I took to be 'absolution' or 'agrarianism,' I could not be certain which; still, these appeared to be simply casual mentions, nothing more; friendly in spirit, without doubt, but lacking the connection or coherence necessary to make them useful.—I judged that my understanding was affected by my feelings, and so laid the letter away till morning.

"In the morning I read it again, but with difficulty and

uncertainty still, for I had lost some little rest and my mental vision seemed clouded. The note was more connected, now, but did not meet the emergency it was expected to meet. It was too discursive. It appeared to read as follows, though I was not certain of some of the words:

"Polygamy dissembles majesty; extracts redeem polarity; causes hitherto exist. Ovations pursue wisdom, or warts inherit and condemn. Boston, botany, cakes, folony undertakes, but who shall allay? We fear not. Yrxwly, HEVACE EVEELOJ.'

"But there did not seem to be a word about turnips. There seemed to be no suggestion as to how they might be made to grow like vines. There was not even a reference to the Beazeleys. I slept upon the matter; I ate no supper, neither any breakfast next morning. So I resumed my work with a brain refreshed, and was very hopeful. Now the letter took a different aspect-all save the signature, which latter I judged to be only a harmless affectation of Hebrew. The epistle was necessarily from Mr. Greeley, for it bore the printed heading of The Tribune, and I had written to no one else there. The letter, I say, had taken a different aspect, but still its language was eccentric and avoided the issue. It now appeared to say:

"Bolivia extemporizes mackerel; borax esteems polygamy; sausages wither in the east. Creation perdu, is done; for woes inherent one can damn. Buttons, buttons, corks, geology underrates but we shall allay. My beer's out. Yrxwly, HEVACE EVEELOJ.'

"I was evidently overworked. My comprehension was impaired. Therefore I gave two days to recreation, and then returned to my task greatly refreshed. The letter now took this form:

"Poultices do sometimes choke swine; tulips reduce posterity; causes leather to resist. Our notions empower wisdom, her let's afford while we can. Butter but any cakes, fill any undertaker, we'll wean him from his filly. We feel hot. Yrxwly, HEVACE EVEELOJ.'

"I was still not satisfied. These generalities did not meet the question. They were crisp, and vigorous, and delivered with a confidence that almost compelled conviction; but at such a time as this, with a human life at stake, they seemed inappropriate, worldly, and in bad taste. At any other time I would have been not only glad, but proud, to receive from a man like Mr. Greeley a letter of this kind, and would have studied it earnestly and tried to improve myself all I could; but now, with that poor boy in his far home languishing for relief, I had no heart for learning.

"Three days passed by, and I read the note again. Again its tenor had changed. It now appeared to say:

"Potations do sometimes wake wines; turnips restrain passion; causes necessary to state. Infest the poor widow; her lord's effects will be void. But dirt, bathing, etc., etc., followed unfairly, will worm him from his folly—so swear not. Yrxwly, HEVACE EVEELOJ.'

"This was more like it. But I was unable to proceed. I was too much worn. The word 'turnips' brought temporary joy and encouragement, but my strength was so much impaired, and the delay might be so perilous for the boy, that I relinquished the idea of pursuing the translation further, and resolved to do what I ought to have done at first. I sat down and wrote Mr.

Greeley as follows:

"DEAR SIR: I fear I do not entirely comprehend your kind note. It cannot be possible, Sir, that 'turnips restrain passion'—at least the study or contemplation of turnips cannot—for it is this very employment that has scorched our poor friend's mind and sapped his bodily strength.—But if they do restrain it, will you bear with us a little further and explain how they should be prepared? I observe that you say 'causes necessary to state,' but you have omitted to state them.

"Under a misapprehension, you seem to attribute to me interested motives in this matter—to call it by no harsher term. But I assure you, dear sir, that if I seem to be 'infesting the widow,' it is all seeming, and void of reality. It is from no seeking of mine that I am in this position. She asked me, herself, to write you. I never have infested her—indeed I scarcely know her. I do not infest anybody. I try to go along, in my humble way, doing as near right as I can, never harming anybody, and never throwing out insinuations. As for 'her lord and his effects,' they are of no interest to me. I trust I have effects enough of my own—shall endeavor to get along with them, at any rate, and not go mousing around to get hold of somebody's that are 'void.' But do you not see?—this woman is a widow—she has no 'lord.' He is dead—or pretended to be, when they buried him. Therefore, no amount of 'dirt, bathing,' etc., etc., howsoever 'unfairly followed' will be likely to 'worm him from his folly'—if being dead and a ghost is 'folly.' Your closing remark is as unkind as it was uncalled for; and if report says true you might have applied it to yourself, sir, with more point and less impropriety. Very Truly Yours, SIMON ERICKSON.

"In the course of a few days, Mr. Greely did what would have saved a world of trouble, and much mental and bodily suffering and misunderstanding, if he had done it sooner. To wit, he sent an intelligible rescript or translation of his original note, made in a plain hand by his clerk. Then the mystery cleared, and I saw that his heart had been right, all the time. I will recite the note in its clarified form:

[Translation.] 'Potatoes do sometimes make vines; turnips remain passive: cause unnecessary to state. Inform the poor widow her lad's efforts will be vain. But diet, bathing, etc. etc., followed uniformly, will wean him from his folly—so fear not. Yours, HORACE GREELEY.'

"But alas, it was too late, gentlemen—too late. The criminal delay had done its work—young Beazely was no more. His spirit had taken its flight to a land where all anxieties shall be charmed away, all desires gratified, all ambitions realized. Poor lad, they laid him to his rest with a turnip in each hand."

So ended Erickson, and lapsed again into nodding, mumbling, and abstraction. The company broke up, and left him so.... But they did not say what drove him crazy. In the momentary confusion, I forgot to ask.

CHAPTER LXXI.

At four o'clock in the afternoon we were winding down a mountain of dreary and desolate lava to the sea, and closing our pleasant land journey. This lava is the accumulation of ages; one torrent of fire after another has rolled down here in old times, and built up the island structure higher and higher. Underneath, it is honey-combed with caves; it would be of no use to dig wells in such a place; they would not hold water— you would not find any for them to hold, for that matter.

Consequently, the planters depend upon cisterns.

The last lava flow occurred here so long ago that there are none now living who witnessed it. In one place it enclosed and burned down a grove of cocoa-nut trees, and the holes in the lava where the trunks stood are still visible; their sides retain the impression of the bark; the trees fell upon the burning river, and becoming partly submerged, left in it the perfect counterpart of every knot and branch and leaf, and even nut, for curiosity seekers of a long distant day to gaze upon and wonder at.

There were doubtless plenty of Kanaka sentinels on guard hereabouts at that time, but they did not leave casts of their figures in the lava as the Roman sentinels at Herculaneum and Pompeii did. It is a pity it is so, because such things are so interesting; but so it is. They probably went away. They went away early, perhaps. However, they had their merits; the Romans exhibited the higher pluck, but the Kanakas showed the sounder judgment.

Shortly we came in sight of that spot whose history is so familiar to every school-boy in the wide world—Kealakekua Bay—the place where Captain Cook, the great circumnavigator, was killed by the natives, nearly a hundred years ago. The setting sun was flaming upon it, a Summer shower was falling, and it was spanned by two magnificent rainbows. Two men who were in advance of us rode through one of these and for a moment their garments shone with a more than regal splendor. Why did not Captain Cook have taste enough to call his great discovery the Rainbow Islands? These charming spectacles are present to you at every turn; they are common in all the islands; they are visible every day, and frequently at night also—not the silvery bow we see once in an age in the States, by moonlight, but barred with all bright and beautiful colors, like the children of the sun and rain. I saw one of them a few nights ago. What the sailors call "raindogs"—little patches of rainbow —are often seen drifting about the heavens in these latitudes, like stained cathedral windows.

Kealakekua Bay is a little curve like the last kink of a snail-shell, winding deep into the land, seemingly not more than a mile wide from shore to shore. It is bounded on one side—where the murder was done—by a little flat plain, on which stands a cocoanut grove and some ruined houses; a steep wall of lava, a thousand feet high at the upper end and three or four hundred at the lower, comes down from the mountain and bounds the inner extremity of it. From this wall the place takes its name, Kealakekua, which in the native tongue signifies "The Pathway of the Gods." They say, (and still believe, in spite of their liberal education in Christianity), that the great god Lono, who used to live upon the hillside, always traveled that causeway when urgent business connected with heavenly affairs called him down to the seashore in a hurry.

As the red sun looked across the placid ocean through the tall, clean stems of the cocoanut trees, like a blooming whiskey bloat through the bars of a city prison, I went and stood in the edge of the water on the flat rock pressed by Captain Cook's feet when the blow was dealt which took away his life, and tried to picture in my mind the doomed man struggling in the midst of the multitude of exasperated savages—the men in the ship crowding to the vessel's side and gazing in anxious dismay toward the shore—the—but I discovered that I could not do it.

It was growing dark, the rain began to fall, we could see that the distant Boomerang was helplessly becalmed at sea, and so I adjourned to the cheerless little box of a warehouse and sat down to smoke and think, and wish the ship would make the land—for we had not eaten much for ten hours and were viciously hungry.

Plain unvarnished history takes the romance out of Captain Cook's assassination, and renders a deliberate verdict of justifiable homicide. Wherever he went among the islands, he was cordially received and welcomed by the inhabitants, and his ships lavishly supplied with all manner of food. He returned these kindnesses with insult and ill-treatment.· Perceiving that the people took him for the long vanished and lamented god Lono, he encouraged them in the delusion for the sake of the limitless power it gave him; but during the famous disturbance at this spot, and while he and his comrades were surrounded by fifteen thousand maddened savages, he received a hurt and betrayed his earthly origin with a groan. It was his death-warrant. Instantly a shout went up: "He groans!—he is not a god!" So they closed in upon him and dispatched him.

His flesh was stripped from the bones and burned (except nine pounds of it which were sent on board the ships). The heart was hung up in a native hut, where it was found and eaten by three children, who mistook it for the heart of a dog. One of these children grew to be a very old man, and died in Honolulu a few years ago. Some of Cook's bones were recovered and consigned to the deep by the officers of the ships.

Small blame should attach to the natives for the killing of Cook. They treated him well. In return, he abused them. He and his men inflicted bodily injury upon many of them at different times, and killed at least three of them before they offered any proportionate retaliation.

Near the shore we found "Cook's Monument"—only a cocoanut stump, four feet high and about a foot in diameter at the butt. It had lava boulders piled around its base to hold it up and keep it in its place, and it was entirely sheathed over, from top to bottom, with rough, discolored sheets of copper, such as ships' bottoms are coppered with. Each sheet had a rude inscription scratched upon it—with a nail, apparently—and in every case the execution was wretched. Most of these merely recorded the visits of British naval commanders to the spot, but one of them bore this legend:

"Near this spot fell CAPTAIN JAMES COOK, The Distinguished Circumnavigator, Who Discovered these Islands A. D. 1778."

After Cook's murder, his second in command, on board the ship, opened fire upon the swarms of natives on the beach, and one of his cannon balls cut this cocoanut tree short off and left this monumental stump standing. It looked sad and lonely enough to us, out there in the rainy twilight. But there is no other monument to Captain Cook. True, up on the mountain side we had passed by a large inclosure like an ample hog-pen, built of lava blocks, which marks the spot where Cook's flesh was stripped from his bones and burned; but this is not properly a monument since it was erected by the natives themselves, and less to do honor to the circumnavigator than for the sake of convenience in roasting him. A thing like a guide-board was elevated above this pen on a tall pole, and formerly there was an inscription upon it describing the memorable occurrence that had there taken place; but the sun and the wind have long ago so defaced it as to render it illegible.

Toward midnight a fine breeze sprang up and the schooner soon worked herself into the bay and cast anchor. The boat came ashore for us, and in a little while the clouds and the rain were all gone. The moon was beaming tranquilly down on land and sea, and we two were stretched upon the deck sleeping the refreshing sleep and dreaming the happy dreams that are only vouchsafed to the weary and the innocent.

CHAPTER LXXII.

In the breezy morning we went ashore and visited the ruined temple of the last god Lono. The high chief cook of this temple—the priest who presided over it and roasted the human sacrifices—was uncle to Obookia, and at one time that youth was an apprentice-priest under him. Obookia was a young native of fine mind, who, together with three other native boys, was taken to New England by the captain of a whaleship during the reign of Kamehameha I, and they were the means of attracting the attention of the religious world to their country. This resulted in the sending of missionaries there. And this Obookia was the very same sensitive savage who sat down on the church steps and wept because his people did not have the Bible. That incident has been very elaborately painted in many a charming Sunday School book—aye, and told so plaintively and so tenderly that I have cried over it in Sunday School myself, on general principles, although at a time when I did not know much and could not understand why the people of the Sandwich Islands needed to worry so much about it as long as they did not know there was a Bible at all.

Obookia was converted and educated, and was to have returned to his native land with the first missionaries, had he lived. The other native youths made the voyage, and two of them did good service, but the third, William Kanui, fell from grace afterward, for a time, and when the gold excitement broke out in California he journeyed thither and went to mining, although he was fifty years old. He succeeded pretty well, but the failure of Page, Bacon & Co. relieved him of six thousand dollars, and then, to all intents and purposes, he was a bankrupt in his old age and he resumed service in the pulpit again. He died in Honolulu in 1864.

Quite a broad tract of land near the temple, extending from the sea to the mountain top, was sacred to the god Lono in olden times—so sacred that if a common native set his sacrilegious foot upon it it was judicious for him to make his will, because his time had come. He might go around it by water, but he could not cross it. It was well sprinkled with pagan temples and stocked with awkward, homely idols carved out of logs of wood. There was a temple devoted to prayers for rain—and with fine sagacity it was placed at a point so well up on the mountain side that if you prayed there twenty-four times a day for rain you would be likely to get it every time. You would seldom get to your Amen before you would have to hoist your umbrella.

And there was a large temple near at hand which was built in a single night, in the midst of storm and thunder and rain, by the ghastly hands of dead men! Tradition says that by the weird glare of the lightning a noiseless multitude of phantoms were seen at their strange labor far up the mountain side at dead of night—flitting hither and thither and bearing great lava-blocks clasped in their nerveless fingers—appearing and disappearing as the pallid lustre fell upon their forms and faded away again. Even to this day, it is said, the natives hold this dread structure in awe and reverence, and will not pass by it in the night.

At noon I observed a bevy of nude native young ladies bathing in the sea, and went and sat down on their clothes to keep them from being stolen. I begged them to come out, for the sea was rising and I was satisfied that they were running some risk. But they were not afraid, and presently went on with their sport. They were finished swimmers and divers, and enjoyed themselves to the last degree.

They swam races, splashed and ducked and tumbled each other about, and filled the air with their laughter. It is said that the first thing an Islander learns is how to swim; learning to walk being a matter of smaller consequence, comes afterward. One hears tales of native men and women swimming ashore from vessels many miles at sea—more miles, indeed, than I dare vouch for or even mention. And they tell of a native diver who went down in thirty or forty-foot waters and brought up an anvil! I think he swallowed the anvil afterward, if my memory serves me. However I will not urge this point.

I have spoken, several times, of the god Lono—I may as well furnish two or three sentences concerning him.

The idol the natives worshipped for him was a slender, unornamented staff twelve feet long. Tradition says he was a favorite god on the Island of Hawaii—a great king who had been deified for meritorious services—just our own fashion of rewarding heroes, with the difference that we would have made him a Postmaster instead of a god, no doubt. In an angry moment he slew his wife, a goddess named Kaikilani Aiii. Remorse of conscience drove him mad, and tradition presents us the singular spectacle of a god traveling "on the shoulder;" for in his gnawing grief he wandered about from place to place boxing and wrestling with all whom he met. Of course this pastime soon lost its novelty, inasmuch as it must necessarily have been the case that when so powerful a deity sent a frail human opponent "to grass" he never came back any more. Therefore, he instituted games called makahiki, and ordered that they should be held in his honor, and then sailed for foreign lands on a three-cornered raft, stating that he would return some day—and that was the last of Lono. He was never seen any more; his raft got swamped, perhaps. But the people always expected his return, and thus they were easily led to accept Captain Cook as the restored god.

Some of the old natives believed Cook was Lono to the day of their death; but many did not, for they could not understand how he could die if he was a god.

Only a mile or so from Kealakekua Bay is a spot of historic interest—the place where the last battle was fought for idolatry. Of course we visited it, and came away as wise as most people do who go and gaze upon such mementoes of the past when in an unreflective mood.

While the first missionaries were on their way around the Horn, the idolatrous customs which had obtained in the island, as far back as tradition reached were suddenly broken up. Old Kamehameha I., was dead, and his son, Liholiho, the new King was a free liver, a roystering, dissolute fellow, and hated the restraints of the ancient tabu. His assistant in the Government, Kaahumanu, the Queen dowager, was proud and high-spirited, and hated the tabu because it restricted the privileges of her sex and degraded all women very nearly to the level of brutes. So the case stood. Liholiho had half a mind to put his foot down, Kaahumahu had a whole mind to badger him into doing it, and whiskey did the rest. It was probably the rest. It was probably the first time whiskey ever prominently figured as an aid to civilization. Liholiho came up to Kailua as drunk as a piper, and attended a great feast; the determined Queen spurred his drunken courage up to a reckless pitch, and then, while all the multitude stared in blank dismay, he moved deliberately forward and sat down with the women!

They saw him eat from the same vessel with them, and were appalled! Terrible moments drifted slowly by, and still the King ate, still he lived, still the lightnings of the insulted gods were withheld! Then conviction came like a revelation—the superstitions of a hundred generations passed from before the people like a cloud, and a shout went up, "the tabu is broken! the tabu is broken!"

Thus did King Liholiho and his dreadful whiskey preach the first sermon and prepare the way for the new gospel that was speeding southward over the waves of the Atlantic.

The tabu broken and destruction failing to follow the awful sacrilege, the people, with that childlike precipitancy which has always characterized them, jumped to the conclusion that their gods were a weak and wretched swindle, just as they formerly jumped to the conclusion that Captain Cook was no god, merely because he groaned, and promptly killed him without stopping to inquire whether a god might not groan as well as a man if it suited his convenience to do it; and satisfied that the idols were powerless to protect themselves they went to work at once and pulled them down—hacked them to pieces—applied the torch—annihilated them!

The pagan priests were furious. And well they might be; they had held the fattest offices in the land, and now they were beggared; they had been great—they had stood above the chiefs—and now they were vagabonds. They raised a revolt; they scared a number of people into joining their standard, and Bekuokalani, an ambitious offshoot of royalty, was easily persuaded to become their leader.

In the first skirmish the idolaters triumphed over the royal army sent against them, and full of confidence they resolved to march upon Kailua. The King sent an envoy to try and conciliate them, and came very near being an envoy short by the operation; the savages not only refused to listen to him, but wanted to kill him. So the King sent his men forth under Major General Kalaimoku and the two host met a Kuamoo. The battle was long and fierce—men and women fighting side by side, as was the custom—and when the day was done the rebels were flying in every direction in hopeless panic, and idolatry and the tabu were dead in the land!

The royalists marched gayly home to Kailua glorifying the new dispensation. "There is no power in the gods," said they; "they are a vanity and a lie. The army with idols was weak; the army without idols was strong and victorious!"

The nation was without a religion.

The missionary ship arrived in safety shortly afterward, timed by providential exactness to meet the emergency, and the Gospel was planted as in a virgin soil.

CHAPTER LXXIII.

At noon, we hired a Kanaka to take us down to the ancient ruins at Honaunan in his canoe—price two dollars—reasonable enough, for a sea voyage of eight miles, counting both ways.

The native canoe is an irresponsible looking contrivance. I cannot think of anything to liken it to but a boy's sled runner hollowed out, and that does not quite convey the correct idea. It is about fifteen feet long, high and pointed at both ends, is a foot and a half or two feet deep, and so narrow that if you wedged a fat man into it you might not get him out again. It sits on top of the water like a duck, but it has an outrigger and does not upset easily, if you keep still. This outrigger is formed of two long bent sticks like plow handles, which project from one side, and to their outer ends is bound a curved beam composed of an extremely light wood, which skims along the surface of the water and thus saves you from an upset on that side, while the outrigger's weight is not so easily lifted as to make an upset on the other side a thing to be greatly feared. Still, until one gets used to sitting perched upon this knifeblade, he is apt to reason within himself that it would be more comfortable if there were just an outrigger or so on the other side also. I had the bow seat, and Billings sat amidships and faced the Kanaka, who occupied the stern of the craft and did the paddling. With the first stroke the trim shell of a thing shot out from the shore like an arrow. There was not much to see. While we were on the shallow water of the reef, it was pastime to look down into the limpid depths at the large bunches of branching coral—the unique shrubbery of the sea. We lost that, though, when we got out into the dead blue water of the deep. But we had the picture of the surf, then, dashing angrily against the crag-bound shore and sending a foaming spray high into the air.

There was interest in this beetling border, too, for it was honey-combed with quaint caves and arches and tunnels, and had a rude semblance of the dilapidated architecture of ruined keeps and castles rising out of the restless sea. When this novelty ceased to be a novelty, we turned our eyes shoreward and gazed at the long mountain with its rich green forests stretching up into the curtaining clouds, and at the specks of houses in the rearward distance and the diminished schooner riding sleepily at anchor. And when these grew tiresome we dashed boldly into the midst of a school of huge, beastly porpoises engaged at their eternal game of arching over a wave and disappearing, and then doing it over again and keeping it up—always circling over, in that way, like so many well-submerged wheels. But the porpoises wheeled themselves away, and then we were thrown upon our own resources. It did not take many minutes to discover that the sun was blazing like a bonfire, and that the weather was of a melting temperature. It had a drowsing effect, too. In one place we came upon a large company of naked natives, of both sexes and all ages, amusing themselves with the national pastime of surf-bathing. Each heathen would paddle three or four hundred yards out to sea, (taking a short board with him), then face the shore and wait for a particularly prodigious billow to come along; at the right moment he would fling his board upon its foamy crest and himself upon the board, and here he would come whizzing by like a bombshell! It did not seem that a lightning express train could shoot along at a more hair-lifting speed. I tried surf-bathing once, subsequently, but made a failure of it. I got the board placed right, and at the right moment, too; but missed the connection myself.—The board struck the shore in three quarters of a second, without any cargo, and I struck the bottom about the same time, with a couple of barrels of water in me. None but natives ever master the art of surf-bathing thoroughly.

At the end of an hour, we had made the four miles, and landed on a level point of land, upon which was a wide extent of old ruins, with many a tall cocoanut tree growing among them. Here was the ancient City of Refuge—a vast inclosure, whose stone walls were twenty feet thick at the base, and fifteen feet high; an oblong square, a thousand and forty feet one way and a fraction under seven hundred the other. Within this inclosure, in early times, has been three rude temples; each two hundred and ten feet long by one hundred wide, and thirteen high.

In those days, if a man killed another anywhere on the island the relatives were privileged to take the murderer's life; and then a chase for life and liberty began—the outlawed criminal flying through pathless forests and over mountain and plain, with his hopes fixed upon the protecting walls of the City of Refuge, and the avenger of blood following hotly after him!

Sometimes the race was kept up to the very gates of the temple, and the panting pair sped through long files of excited natives, who watched the contest with flashing eye and dilated nostril, encouraging the hunted refugee with sharp, inspiriting ejaculations, and sending up a ringing shout of exultation when the saving gates closed upon him and the cheated pursuer sank exhausted at the threshold. But sometimes the flying criminal fell under the hand of the avenger at the very door, when one more brave stride, one more brief second of time would have brought his feet upon the sacred ground and barred him against all harm. Where did these isolated pagans get this idea of a City of Refuge—this ancient Oriental custom?

This old sanctuary was sacred to all—even to rebels in arms and invading armies. Once within its walls, and confession made to the priest and absolution obtained, the wretch with a price upon his head could go forth without fear and without danger—he was tabu, and to harm him was death. The routed rebels in the lost battle for idolatry fled to this place to claim sanctuary, and many were thus saved.

Close to the corner of the great inclosure is a round structure of stone, some six or eight feet high, with a level top about ten or twelve in diameter. This was the place of execution. A high palisade of cocoanut piles shut out the cruel scenes from the vulgar multitude. Here criminals were killed, the flesh stripped from the bones and burned, and the bones secreted in holes in the body of the structure. If the man had been guilty of a high crime, the entire corpse was burned.

The walls of the temple are a study. The same food for speculation that is offered the visitor to the Pyramids of Egypt he will find here—the mystery of how they were constructed by a people unacquainted with science and mechanics. The natives have no invention of their own for hoisting heavy weights, they had no beasts of burden, and they have never even shown any knowledge of the properties of the lever. Yet some of the lava blocks quarried out, brought over rough, broken ground, and built into this wall, six or seven feet from the ground, are of prodigious size and would weigh tons. How did they transport and how raise them?

Both the inner and outer surfaces of the walls present a smooth front and are very creditable specimens of masonry. The blocks are of all manner of shapes and sizes, but yet are fitted together with the neatest exactness. The gradual narrowing of the wall from the base upward is accurately preserved.

No cement was used, but the edifice is firm and compact and is capable of resisting storm and decay for centuries. Who built this temple, and how was it built, and when, are mysteries that may never be unraveled. Outside of these ancient walls lies a sort of coffin-shaped stone eleven feet four inches long and

three feet square at the small end (it would weigh a few thousand pounds), which the high chief who held sway over this district many centuries ago brought thither on his shoulder one day to use as a lounge! This circumstance is established by the most reliable traditions. He used to lie down on it, in his indolent way, and keep an eye on his subjects at work for him and see that there was no "soldiering" done. And no doubt there was not any done to speak of, because he was a man of that sort of build that incites to attention to business on the part of an employee.

He was fourteen or fifteen feet high. When he stretched himself at full length on his lounge, his legs hung down over the end, and when he snored he woke the dead. These facts are all attested by irrefragable tradition.

On the other side of the temple is a monstrous seven-ton rock, eleven feet long, seven feet wide and three feet thick. It is raised a foot or a foot and a half above the ground, and rests upon half a dozen little stony pedestals. The same old fourteen-footer brought it down from the mountain, merely for fun (he had his own notions about fun), and propped it up as we find it now and as others may find it a century hence, for it would take a score of horses to budge it from its position. They say that fifty or sixty years ago the proud Queen Kaahumanu used to fly to this rock for safety, whenever she had been making trouble with her fierce husband, and hide under it until his wrath was appeased. But these Kanakas will lie, and this statement is one of their ablest efforts—for Kaahumanu was six feet high—she was bulky—she was built like an ox—and she could no more have squeezed herself under that rock than she could have passed between the cylinders of a sugar mill. What could she gain by it, even if she succeeded? To be chased and abused by a savage husband could not be otherwise than humiliating to her high spirit, yet it could never make her feel so flat as an hour's repose under that rock would.

We walked a mile over a raised macadamized road of uniform width; a road paved with flat stones and exhibiting in its every detail a considerable degree of engineering skill. Some say that that wise old pagan, Kamehameha I planned and built it, but others say it was built so long before his time that the knowledge of who constructed it has passed out of the traditions. In either case, however, as the handiwork of an untaught and degraded race it is a thing of pleasing interest. The stones are worn and smooth, and pushed apart in places, so that the road has the exact appearance of those ancient paved highways leading out of Rome which one sees in pictures.

The object of our tramp was to visit a great natural curiosity at the base of the foothills—a congealed cascade of lava. Some old forgotten volcanic eruption sent its broad river of fire down the mountain side here, and it poured down in a great torrent from an overhanging bluff some fifty feet high to the ground below. The flaming torrent cooled in the winds from the sea, and remains there to-day, all seamed, and frothed and rippled a petrified Niagara. It is very picturesque, and withal so natural that one might almost imagine it still flowed. A smaller stream trickled over the cliff and built up an isolated pyramid about thirty feet high, which has the semblance of a mass of large gnarled and knotted vines and roots and stems intricately twisted and woven together.

We passed in behind the cascade and the pyramid, and found the bluff pierced by several cavernous tunnels, whose crooked courses we followed a long distance.

Two of these winding tunnels stand as proof of Nature's mining abilities. Their floors are level, they are seven feet wide, and their roofs are gently arched. Their height is not uniform, however. We passed through one a hundred feet long, which leads through a spur of the hill and opens out well up in the sheer wall of a precipice whose foot rests in the waves of the sea. It is a commodious tunnel, except that there are occasional places in it where one must stoop to pass under. The roof is lava, of course, and is thickly studded with little lava-pointed icicles an inch long, which hardened as they dripped. They project as closely together as the iron teeth of a corn-sheller, and if one will stand up straight and walk any distance there, he can get his hair combed free of charge.

CHAPTER LXXIV.

We got back to the schooner in good time, and then sailed down to Kau, where we disembarked and took final leave of the vessel. Next day we bought horses and bent our way over the summer-clad mountain-terraces, toward the great volcano of Kilauea (Ke-low-way-ah). We made nearly a two days' journey of it, but that was on account of laziness. Toward sunset on the second day, we reached an elevation of some four thousand feet above sea level, and as we picked our careful way through billowy wastes of lava long generations ago stricken dead and cold in the climax of its tossing fury, we began to come upon signs of the near presence of the volcano—signs in the nature of ragged fissures that discharged jets of sulphurous vapor into the air, hot from the molten ocean down in the bowels of the mountain.

Shortly the crater came into view. I have seen Vesuvius since, but it was a mere toy, a child's volcano, a soup-kettle, compared to this. Mount Vesuvius is a shapely cone thirty-six hundred feet high; its crater an inverted cone only three hundred feet deep, and not more than a thousand feet in diameter, if as much as that; its fires meagre, modest, and docile.—But here was a vast, perpendicular, walled cellar, nine hundred feet deep in some places, thirteen hundred in others, level-floored, and ten miles in circumference! Here was a yawning pit upon whose floor the armies of Russia could camp, and have room to spare.

Perched upon the edge of the crater, at the opposite end from where we stood, was a small look-out house—say three miles away. It assisted us, by comparison, to comprehend and appreciate the great depth of the basin —it looked like a tiny martin-box clinging at the eaves of a cathedral. After some little time spent in resting and looking and ciphering, we hurried on to the hotel.

By the path it is half a mile from the Volcano House to the lookout-house. After a hearty supper we waited until it was thoroughly dark and then started to the crater. The first glance in that direction revealed a scene of wild beauty. There was a heavy fog over the crater and it was splendidly illuminated by the glare from the fires below. The illumination was two miles wide and a mile high, perhaps; and if you ever, on a dark night and at a distance beheld the light from thirty or forty blocks of distant buildings all on fire at once, reflected strongly against over-hanging clouds, you can form a fair idea of what this looked like.

A colossal column of cloud towered to a great height in the air immediately above the crater, and the outer swell of every one of its vast folds was dyed with a rich crimson luster, which was subdued to a pale rose tint in the depressions between. It

glowed like a muffled torch and stretched upward to a dizzy height toward the zenith. I thought it just possible that its like had not been seen since the children of Israel wandered on their long march through the desert so many centuries ago over a path illuminated by the mysterious "pillar of fire." And I was sure that I now had a vivid conception of what the majestic "pillar of fire" was like, which almost amounted to a revelation.

Arrived at the little thatched lookout house, we rested our elbows on the railing in front and looked abroad over the wide crater and down over the sheer precipice at the seething fires beneath us. The view was a startling improvement on my daylight experience. I turned to see the effect on the balance of the company and found the reddest-faced set of men I almost ever saw. In the strong light every countenance glowed like red-hot iron, every shoulder was suffused with crimson and shaded rearward into dingy, shapeless obscurity! The place below looked like the infernal regions and these men like half-cooled devils just come up on a furlough.

I turned my eyes upon the volcano again. The "cellar" was tolerably well lighted up. For a mile and a half in front of us and half a mile on either side, the floor of the abyss was magnificently illuminated; beyond these limits the mists hung down their gauzy curtains and cast a deceptive gloom over all that made the twinkling fires in the remote corners of the crater seem countless leagues removed—made them seem like the camp-fires of a great army far away. Here was room for the imagination to work! You could imagine those lights the width of a continent away—and that hidden under the intervening darkness were hills, and winding rivers, and weary wastes of plain and desert—and even then the tremendous vista stretched on, and on, and on!—to the fires and far beyond! You could not compass it—it was the idea of eternity made tangible—and the longest end of it made visible to the naked eye!

The greater part of the vast floor of the desert under us was as black as ink, and apparently smooth and level; but over a mile square of it was ringed and streaked and striped with a thousand branching streams of liquid and gorgeously brilliant fire! It looked like a colossal railroad map of the State of Massachusetts done in chain lightning on a midnight sky. Imagine it—imagine a coal-black sky shivered into a tangled net-work of angry fire!

Here and there were gleaming holes a hundred feet in diameter, broken in the dark crust, and in them the melted lava—the color a dazzling white just tinged with yellow—was boiling and surging furiously; and from these holes branched numberless bright torrents in many directions, like the spokes of a wheel, and kept a tolerably straight course for a while and then swept round in huge rainbow curves, or made a long succession of sharp worm-fence angles, which looked precisely like the fiercest jagged lightning. These streams met other streams, and they mingled with and crossed and recrossed each other in every conceivable direction, like skate tracks on a popular skating ground. Sometimes streams twenty or thirty feet wide flowed from the holes to some distance without dividing —and through the opera-glasses we could see that they ran down small, steep hills and were genuine cataracts of fire, white at their source, but soon cooling and turning to the richest red, grained with alternate lines of black and gold. Every now and then masses of the dark crust broke away and floated slowly down these streams like rafts down a river. Occasionally the molten lava flowing under the superincumbent crust broke through—split a dazzling streak, from five hundred to a thousand feet long, like a sudden flash of lightning, and then acre after acre of the cold lava parted into fragments, turned up edgewise like cakes of ice when a great river breaks up, plunged downward and were swallowed in the crimson cauldron. Then the wide expanse of the "thaw" maintained a ruddy glow for a while, but shortly cooled and became black and level again. During a "thaw," every dismembered cake was marked by a glittering white border which was superbly shaded inward by aurora borealis rays, which were a flaming yellow where they joined the white border, and from thence toward their points tapered into glowing crimson, then into a rich, pale carmine, and finally into a faint blush that held its own a moment and then dimmed and turned black. Some of the streams preferred to mingle together in a tangle of fantastic circles, and then they looked something like the confusion of ropes one sees on a ship's deck when she has just taken in sail and dropped anchor—provided one can imagine those ropes on fire.

Through the glasses, the little fountains scattered about looked very beautiful. They boiled, and coughed, and spluttered, and discharged sprays of stringy red fire—of about the consistency of mush, for instance—from ten to fifteen feet into the air, along with a shower of brilliant white sparks—a quaint and unnatural mingling of gouts of blood and snow-flakes!

We had circles and serpents and streaks of lightning all twined and wreathed and tied together, without a break throughout an area more than a mile square (that amount of ground was covered, though it was not strictly "square"), and it was with a feeling of placid exultation that we reflected that many years had elapsed since any visitor had seen such a splendid display—since any visitor had seen anything more than the now snubbed and insignificant "North" and "South" lakes in action. We had been reading old files of Hawaiian newspapers and the "Record Book" at the Volcano House, and were posted.

I could see the North Lake lying out on the black floor away off in the outer edge of our panorama, and knitted to it by a web-work of lava streams. In its individual capacity it looked very little more respectable than a schoolhouse on fire. True, it was about nine hundred feet long and two or three hundred wide, but then, under the present circumstances, it necessarily appeared rather insignificant, and besides it was so distant from us.

I forgot to say that the noise made by the bubbling lava is not great, heard as we heard it from our lofty perch. It makes three distinct sounds—a rushing, a hissing, and a coughing or puffing sound; and if you stand on the brink and close your eyes it is no trick at all to imagine that you are sweeping down a river on a large low-pressure steamer, and that you hear the hissing of the steam about her boilers, the puffing from her escape-pipes and the churning rush of the water abaft her wheels. The smell of sulphur is strong, but not unpleasant to a sinner.

We left the lookout house at ten o'clock in a half cooked condition, because of the heat from Pele's furnaces, and wrapping up in blankets, for the night was cold, we returned to our Hotel.

CHAPTER LXXV.

The next night was appointed for a visit to the bottom of the crater, for we desired to traverse its floor and see the "North Lake" (of fire) which lay two miles away, toward the further wall. After dark half a dozen of us set out, with lanterns and native guides, and climbed down a crazy, thousand-foot pathway in a crevice fractured in the crater wall, and reached the bottom in safety.

The irruption of the previous evening had spent its force and the floor looked black and cold; but when we ran out upon it we found it hot yet, to the feet, and it was likewise riven with crevices which revealed the underlying fires gleaming vindictively. A neighboring cauldron was threatening to overflow, and this added to the dubiousness of the situation. So the native guides refused to continue the venture, and then every body deserted except a stranger named Marlette. He said he had been in the crater a dozen times in daylight and believed he could find his way through it at night. He thought that a run of three hundred yards would carry us over the hottest part of the floor and leave us our shoe-soles. His pluck gave me back-bone. We took one lantern and instructed the guides to hang the other to the roof of the look-out house to serve as a beacon for us in case we got lost, and then the party started back up the precipice and Marlette and I made our run. We skipped over the hot floor and over the red crevices with brisk dispatch and reached the cold lava safe but with pretty warm feet. Then we took things leisurely and comfortably, jumping tolerably wide and probably bottomless chasms, and threading our way through picturesque lava upheavals with considerable confidence. When we got fairly away from the cauldrons of boiling fire, we seemed to be in a gloomy desert, and a suffocatingly dark one, surrounded by dim walls that seemed to tower to the sky. The only cheerful objects were the glinting stars high overhead.

By and by Marlette shouted "Stop!" I never stopped quicker in my life. I asked what the matter was. He said we were out of the path. He said we must not try to go on till we found it again, for we were surrounded with beds of rotten lava through which we could easily break and plunge down a thousand feet. I thought eight hundred would answer for me, and was about to say so when Marlette partly proved his statement by accidentally crushing through and disappearing to his arm-pits.

He got out and we hunted for the path with the lantern. He said there was only one path and that it was but vaguely defined. We could not find it. The lava surface was all alike in the lantern light. But he was an ingenious man. He said it was not the lantern that had informed him that we were out of the path, but his feet. He had noticed a crisp grinding of fine lava-needles under his feet, and some instinct reminded him that in the path these were all worn away. So he put the lantern behind him, and began to search with his boots instead of his eyes. It was good sagacity. The first time his foot touched a surface that did not grind under it he announced that the trail was found again; and after that we kept up a sharp listening for the rasping sound and it always warned us in time.

It was a long tramp, but an exciting one. We reached the North Lake between ten and eleven o'clock, and sat down on a huge overhanging lava-shelf, tired but satisfied. The spectacle presented was worth coming double the distance to see. Under us, and stretching away before us, was a heaving sea of molten fire of seemingly limitless extent. The glare from it was so blinding that it was some time before we could bear to look upon it steadily.

It was like gazing at the sun at noon-day, except that the glare was not quite so white. At unequal distances all around the shores of the lake were nearly white-hot chimneys or hollow drums of lava, four or five feet high, and up through them were bursting gorgeous sprays of lava-gouts and gem spangles, some white, some red and some golden—a ceaseless bombardment, and one that fascinated the eye with its unapproachable splendor. The mere distant jets, sparkling up through an intervening gossamer veil of vapor, seemed miles away; and the further the curving ranks of fiery fountains receded, the more fairy-like and beautiful they appeared.

Now and then the surging bosom of the lake under our noses would calm down ominously and seem to be gathering strength for an enterprise; and then all of a sudden a red dome of lava of the bulk of an ordinary dwelling would heave itself aloft like an escaping balloon, then burst asunder, and out of its heart would flit a pale-green film of vapor, and float upward and vanish in the darkness—a released soul soaring homeward from captivity with the damned, no doubt. The crashing plunge of the ruined dome into the lake again would send a world of seething billows lashing against the shores and shaking the foundations of our perch. By and by, a loosened mass of the hanging shelf we sat on tumbled into the lake, jarring the surroundings like an earthquake and delivering a suggestion that may have been intended for a hint, and may not. We did not wait to see.

We got lost again on our way back, and were more than an hour hunting for the path. We were where we could see the beacon lantern at the look-out house at the time, but thought it was a star and paid no attention to it. We reached the hotel at two o'clock in the morning pretty well fagged out.

Kilauea never overflows its vast crater, but bursts a passage for its lava through the mountain side when relief is necessary, and then the destruction is fearful. About 1840 it rent its overburdened stomach and sent a broad river of fire careering down to the sea, which swept away forests, huts, plantations and every thing else that lay in its path. The stream was five miles broad, in places, and two hundred feet deep, and the distance it traveled was forty miles. It tore up and bore away acre-patches of land on its bosom like rafts—rocks, trees and all intact. At night the red glare was visible a hundred miles at sea; and at a distance of forty miles fine print could be read at midnight. The atmosphere was poisoned with sulphurous vapors and choked with falling ashes, pumice stones and cinders; countless columns of smoke rose up and blended together in a tumbled canopy that hid the heavens and glowed with a ruddy flush reflected from the fires below; here and there jets of lava sprung hundreds of feet into the air and burst into rocket-sprays that returned to earth in a crimson rain; and all the while the laboring mountain shook with Nature's great palsy and voiced its distress in moanings and the muffled booming of subterranean thunders.

Fishes were killed for twenty miles along the shore, where the lava entered the sea. The earthquakes caused some loss of human life, and a prodigious tidal wave swept inland, carrying every thing before it and drowning a number of natives. The devastation consummated along the route traversed by the river of lava was complete and incalculable. Only a Pompeii and a Herculaneum were needed at the foot of Kilauea to make the story of the irruption immortal.

CHAPTER LXXVI.

We rode horseback all around the island of Hawaii (the crooked road making the distance two hundred miles), and enjoyed the journey very much. We were more than a week making the trip, because our Kanaka horses would not go by a

house or a hut without stopping—whip and spur could not alter their minds about it, and so we finally found that it economized time to let them have their way. Upon inquiry the mystery was explained: the natives are such thorough-going gossips that they never pass a house without stopping to swap news, and consequently their horses learn to regard that sort of thing as an essential part of the whole duty of man, and his salvation not to be compassed without it. However, at a former crisis of my life I had once taken an aristocratic young lady out driving, behind a horse that had just retired from a long and honorable career as the moving impulse of a milk wagon, and so this present experience awoke a reminiscent sadness in me in place of the exasperation more natural to the occasion. I remembered how helpless I was that day, and how humiliated; how ashamed I was of having intimated to the girl that I had always owned the horse and was accustomed to grandeur; how hard I tried to appear easy, and even vivacious, under suffering that was consuming my vitals; how placidly and maliciously the girl smiled, and kept on smiling, while my hot blushes baked themselves into a permanent blood-pudding in my face; how the horse ambled from one side of the street to the other and waited complacently before every third house two minutes and a quarter while I belabored his back and reviled him in my heart; how I tried to keep him from turning corners and failed; how I moved heaven and earth to get him out of town, and did not succeed; how he traversed the entire settlement and delivered imaginary milk at a hundred and sixty-two different domiciles, and how he finally brought up at a dairy depot and refused to budge further, thus rounding and completing the revealment of what the plebeian service of his life had been; how, in eloquent silence, I walked the girl home, and how, when I took leave of her, her parting remark scorched my soul and appeared to blister me all over: she said that my horse was a fine, capable animal, and I must have taken great comfort in him in my time—but that if I would take along some milk-tickets next time, and appear to deliver them at the various halting places, it might expedite his movements a little. There was a coolness between us after that.

In one place in the island of Hawaii, we saw a laced and ruffled cataract of limpid water leaping from a sheer precipice fifteen hundred feet high; but that sort of scenery finds its stanchest ally in the arithmetic rather than in spectacular effect. If one desires to be so stirred by a poem of Nature wrought in the happily commingled graces of picturesque rocks, glimpsed distances, foliage, color, shifting lights and shadows, and falling water, that the tears almost come into his eyes so potent is the charm exerted, he need not go away from America to enjoy such an experience. The Rainbow Fall, in Watkins Glen (N.Y.), on the Erie railway, is an example. It would recede into pitiable insignificance if the callous tourist drew on arithmetic on it; but left to compete for the honors simply on scenic grace and beauty—the grand, the august and the sublime being barred the contest—it could challenge the old world and the new to produce its peer.

In one locality, on our journey, we saw some horses that had been born and reared on top of the mountains, above the range of running water, and consequently they had never drank that fluid in their lives, but had been always accustomed to quenching their thirst by eating dew-laden or shower-wetted leaves. And now it was destructively funny to see them sniff suspiciously at a pail of water, and then put in their noses and try to take a bite out of the fluid, as if it were a solid. Finding it liquid, they would snatch away their heads and fall to trembling, snorting and showing other evidences of fright. When they became convinced at last that the water was friendly and harmless, they thrust in their noses up to their eyes, brought out a mouthful of water, and proceeded to chew it complacently. We saw a man coax, kick and spur one of them five or ten minutes before he could make it cross a running stream. It spread its nostrils, distended its eyes and trembled all over, just as horses customarily do in the presence of a serpent—and for aught I know it thought the crawling stream was a serpent.

In due course of time our journey came to an end at Kawaehae (usually pronounced To-a-hi—and before we find fault with this elaborate orthographical method of arriving at such an unostentatious result, let us lop off the ugh from our word "though"). I made this horseback trip on a mule. I paid ten dollars for him at Kau (Kah-oo), added four to get him shod, rode him two hundred miles, and then sold him for fifteen dollars. I mark the circumstance with a white stone (in the absence of chalk—for I never saw a white stone that a body could mark anything with, though out of respect for the ancients I have tried it often enough); for up to that day and date it was the first strictly commercial transaction I had ever entered into, and come out winner. We returned to Honolulu, and from thence sailed to the island of Maui, and spent several weeks there very pleasantly. I still remember, with a sense of indolent luxury, a picnicing excursion up a romantic gorge there, called the Iao Valley. The trail lay along the edge of a brawling stream in the bottom of the gorge—a shady route, for it was well roofed with the verdant domes of forest trees. Through openings in the foliage we glimpsed picturesque scenery that revealed ceaseless changes and new charms with every step of our progress. Perpendicular walls from one to three thousand feet high guarded the way, and were sumptuously plumed with varied foliage, in places, and in places swathed in waving ferns. Passing shreds of cloud trailed their shadows across these shining fronts, mottling them with blots; billowy masses of white vapor hid the turreted summits, and far above the vapor swelled a background of gleaming green crags and cones that came and went, through the veiling mists, like islands drifting in a fog; sometimes the cloudy curtain descended till half the canon wall was hidden, then shredded gradually away till only airy glimpses of the ferny front appeared through it—then swept aloft and left it glorified in the sun again. Now and then, as our position changed, rocky bastions swung out from the wall, a mimic ruin of castellated ramparts and crumbling towers clothed with mosses and hung with garlands of swaying vines, and as we moved on they swung back again and hid themselves once more in the foliage. Presently a verdure-clad needle of stone, a thousand feet high, stepped out from behind a corner, and mounted guard over the mysteries of the valley. It seemed to me that if Captain Cook needed a monument, here was one ready made—therefore, why not put up his sign here, and sell out the venerable cocoanut stump?

But the chief pride of Maui is her dead volcano of Haleakala—which means, translated, "the house of the sun." We climbed a thousand feet up the side of this isolated colossus one afternoon; then camped, and next day climbed the remaining nine thousand feet, and anchored on the summit, where we built a fire and froze and roasted by turns, all night. With the first pallor of dawn we got up and saw things that were new to us. Mounted on a commanding pinnacle, we watched Nature work her silent wonders. The sea was spread abroad on every hand, its tumbled surface seeming only wrinkled and dimpled in the distance. A broad valley below appeared like an ample checker-board, its velvety green sugar plantations alternating with dun squares of barrenness and groves of trees diminished to mossy tufts. Beyond the valley were mountains picturesquely grouped together; but bear in mind, we fancied that we were looking up at these things—not down. We seemed to sit in the bottom of a symmetrical bowl ten thousand feet deep, with the valley and the skirting sea lifted away into the sky above us! It was curious; and not only curious, but aggravating; for it was having our trouble all for nothing, to climb ten thousand feet toward heaven and then have to look up at our scenery. However, we had to be content with it and make the best of it; for, all we could do we could not coax our landscape down out of the clouds. Formerly, when I had read an article in which Poe treated of this singular fraud perpetrated upon the eye by isolated great altitudes, I had looked upon the matter as an invention of his own fancy.

I have spoken of the outside view—but we had an inside one, too. That was the yawning dead crater, into which we now and then tumbled rocks, half as large as a barrel, from our perch, and saw them go careering down the almost perpendicular sides, bounding three hundred feet at a jump; kicking up cast-clouds wherever they struck; diminishing to our view as they sped farther into distance; growing invisible, finally, and only betraying their course by faint little puffs of dust; and coming to a halt at last in the bottom of the abyss, two thousand five hundred feet down from where they started! It was magnificent sport. We wore ourselves out at it.

The crater of Vesuvius, as I have before remarked, is a modest pit about a thousand feet deep and three thousand in circumference; that of Kilauea is somewhat deeper, and ten miles in circumference. But what are either of them compared to the vacant stomach of Haleakala? I will not offer any figures of my own, but give official ones—those of Commander Wilkes, U.S.N., who surveyed it and testifies that it is twenty-seven miles in circumference! If it had a level bottom it would make a fine site for a city like London. It must have afforded a spectacle worth contemplating in the old days when its furnaces gave full rein to their anger.

Presently vagrant white clouds came drifting along, high over the sea and the valley; then they came in couples and groups; then in imposing squadrons; gradually joining their forces, they banked themselves solidly together, a thousand feet under us, and totally shut out land and ocean —not a vestige of anything was left in view but just a little of the rim of the crater, circling away from the pinnacle whereon we sat (for a ghostly procession of wanderers from the filmy hosts without had drifted through a chasm in the crater wall and filed round and round, and gathered and sunk and blended together till the abyss was stored to the brim with a fleecy fog). Thus banked, motion ceased, and silence reigned. Clear to the horizon, league on league, the snowy floor stretched without a break—not level, but in rounded folds, with shallow creases between, and with here and there stately piles of vapory architecture lifting themselves aloft out of the common plain—some near at hand, some in the middle distances, and others relieving the monotony of the remote solitudes. There was little conversation, for the impressive scene overawed speech. I felt like the Last Man, neglected of the judgment, and left pinnacled in mid-heaven, a forgotten relic of a vanished world.

While the hush yet brooded, the messengers of the coming resurrection appeared in the East. A growing warmth suffused the horizon, and soon the sun emerged and looked out over the cloud-waste, flinging bars of ruddy light across it, staining its folds and billow-caps with blushes, purpling the shaded troughs between, and glorifying the massy vapor-palaces and cathedrals with a wasteful splendor of all blendings and combinations of rich coloring.

It was the sublimest spectacle I ever witnessed, and I think the memory of it will remain with me always.

CHAPTER LXXVII.

I stumbled upon one curious character in the Island of Mani. He became a sore annoyance to me in the course of time. My first glimpse of him was in a sort of public room in the town of Lahaina. He occupied a chair at the opposite side of the apartment, and sat eyeing our party with interest for some minutes, and listening as critically to what we were saying as if he fancied we were talking to him and expecting him to reply. I thought it very sociable in a stranger. Presently, in the course of conversation, I made a statement bearing upon the subject under discussion—and I made it with due modesty, for there was nothing extraordinary about it, and it was only put forth in illustration of a point at issue. I had barely finished when this person spoke out with rapid utterance and feverish anxiety:

"Oh, that was certainly remarkable, after a fashion, but you ought to have seen my chimney—you ought to have seen my chimney, sir! Smoke! I wish I may hang if—Mr. Jones, you remember that chimney—you must remember that chimney! No, no—I recollect, now, you warn't living on this side of the island then. But I am telling you nothing but the truth, and I wish I may never draw another breath if that chimney didn't smoke so that the smoke actually got caked in it and I had to dig it out with a pickaxe! You may smile, gentlemen, but the High Sheriff's got a hunk of it which I dug out before his eyes, and so it's perfectly easy for you to go and examine for yourselves."

The interruption broke up the conversation, which had already begun to lag, and we presently hired some natives and an outrigger canoe or two, and went out to overlook a grand surf-bathing contest.

Two weeks after this, while talking in a company, I looked up and detected this same man boring through and through me with his intense eye, and noted again his twitching muscles and his feverish anxiety to speak. The moment I paused, he said:

"Beg your pardon, sir, beg your pardon, but it can only be considered remarkable when brought into strong outline by isolation. Sir, contrasted with a circumstance which occurred in my own experience, it instantly becomes commonplace. No, not that—for I will not speak so discourteously of any experience in the career of a stranger and a gentleman—but I am obliged to say that you could not, and you would not ever again refer to this tree as a large one, if you could behold, as I have, the great Yakmatack tree, in the island of Ounaska, sea of Kamtchatka—a tree, sir, not one inch less than four hundred and fifteen feet in solid diameter!—and I wish I may die in a minute if it isn't so! Oh, you needn't look so questioning, gentlemen; here's old Cap Saltmarsh can say whether I know what I'm talking about or not. I showed him the tree."

Captain Saltmarsh—"Come, now, cat your anchor, lad—you're heaving too taut. You promised to show me that stunner, and I walked more than eleven mile with you through the cussedest jungle I ever see, a hunting for it; but the tree you showed me finally warn't as big around as a beer cask, and you know that your own self, Markiss."

"Hear the man talk! Of course the tree was reduced that way, but didn't I explain it? Answer me, didn't I? Didn't I say I

wished you could have seen it when I first saw it? When you got up on your ear and called me names, and said I had brought you eleven miles to look at a sapling, didn't I explain to you that all the whale-ships in the North Seas had been wooding off of it for more than twenty-seven years? And did you s'pose the tree could last for-ever, con-found it? I don't see why you want to keep back things that way, and try to injure a person that's never done you any harm."

Somehow this man's presence made me uncomfortable, and I was glad when a native arrived at that moment to say that Muckawow, the most companionable and luxurious among the rude war-chiefs of the Islands, desired us to come over and help him enjoy a missionary whom he had found trespassing on his grounds.

I think it was about ten days afterward that, as I finished a statement I was making for the instruction of a group of friends and acquaintances, and which made no pretence of being extraordinary, a familiar voice chimed instantly in on the heels of my last word, and said:

"But, my dear sir, there was nothing remarkable about that horse, or the circumstance either—nothing in the world! I mean no sort of offence when I say it, sir, but you really do not know anything whatever about speed. Bless your heart, if you could only have seen my mare Margaretta; there was a beast!—there was lightning for you! Trot! Trot is no name for it—she flew! How she could whirl a buggy along! I started her out once, sir—Colonel Bilgewater, you recollect that animal perfectly well —I started her out about thirty or thirty-five yards ahead of the awfullest storm I ever saw in my life, and it chased us upwards of eighteen miles! It did, by the everlasting hills! And I'm telling you nothing but the unvarnished truth when I say that not one single drop of rain fell on me—not a single drop, sir! And I swear to it! But my dog was a-swimming behind the wagon all the way!"

For a week or two I stayed mostly within doors, for I seemed to meet this person everywhere, and he had become utterly hateful to me. But one evening I dropped in on Captain Perkins and his friends, and we had a sociable time. About ten o'clock I chanced to be talking about a merchant friend of mine, and without really intending it, the remark slipped out that he was a little mean and parsimonious about paying his workmen. Instantly, through the steam of a hot whiskey punch on the opposite side of the room, a remembered voice shot—and for a moment I trembled on the imminent verge of profanity:

"Oh, my dear sir, really you expose yourself when you parade that as a surprising circumstance. Bless your heart and hide, you are ignorant of the very A B C of meanness! ignorant as the unborn babe! ignorant as unborn twins! You don't know anything about it! It is pitiable to see you, sir, a well-spoken and prepossessing stranger, making such an enormous pow-wow here about a subject concerning which your ignorance is perfectly humiliating! Look me in the eye, if you please; look me in the eye. John James Godfrey was the son of poor. but honest parents in the State of Mississippi—boyhood friend of mine—bosom comrade in later years. Heaven rest his noble spirit, he is gone from us now. John James Godfrey was hired by the Hayblossom Mining Company in California to do some blasting for them—the "Incorporated Company of Mean Men," the boys used to call it.

"Well, one day he drilled a hole about four feet deep and put in an awful blast of powder, and was standing over it ramming it down with an iron crowbar about nine foot long, when the cussed thing struck a spark and fired the powder, and scat! away John Godfrey whizzed like a skyrocket, him and his crowbar! Well, sir, he kept on going up in the air higher and higher, till he didn't look any bigger than a boy—and he kept going on up higher and higher, till he didn't look any bigger than a doll—and he kept on going up higher and higher, till he didn't look any bigger than a little small bee—and then he went out of sight! Presently he came in sight again, looking like a little small bee—and he came along down further and further, till he looked as big as a doll again—and down further and further, till he was as big as a boy again—and further and further, till he was a full-sized man once more; and then him and his crowbar came a wh-izzing down and lit right exactly in the same old tracks and went to r-ramming down, and r-ramming down, and r-ramming down again, just the same as if nothing had happened! Now do you know, that poor cuss warn't gone only sixteen minutes, and yet that Incorporated Company of Mean Men DOCKED HIM FOR THE LOST TIME!"

I said I had the headache, and so excused myself and went home. And on my diary I entered "another night spoiled" by this offensive loafer. And a fervent curse was set down with it to keep the item company. And the very next day I packed up, out of all patience, and left the Island.

Almost from the very beginning, I regarded that man as a liar.

The line of points represents an interval of years. At the end of which time the opinion hazarded in that last sentence came to be gratifyingly and remarkably endorsed, and by wholly disinterested persons. The man Markiss was found one morning hanging to a beam of his own bedroom (the doors and windows securely fastened on the inside), dead; and on his breast was pinned a paper in his own handwriting begging his friends to suspect no innocent person of having any thing to do with his death, for that it was the work of his own hands entirely. Yet the jury brought in the astounding verdict that deceased came to his death "by the hands of some person or persons unknown!" They explained that the perfectly undeviating consistency of Markiss's character for thirty years towered aloft as colossal and indestructible testimony, that whatever statement he chose to make was entitled to instant and unquestioning acceptance as a lie. And they furthermore stated their belief that he was not dead, and instanced the strong circumstantial evidence of his own word that he was dead—and beseeched the coroner to delay the funeral as long as possible, which was done. And so in the tropical climate of Lahaina the coffin stood open for seven days, and then even the loyal jury gave him up. But they sat on him again, and changed their verdict to "suicide induced by mental aberration"—because, said they, with penetration, "he said he was dead, and he was dead; and would he have told the truth if he had been in his right mind? No, sir."

CHAPTER LXXVIII.

After half a year's luxurious vagrancy in the islands, I took shipping in a sailing vessel, and regretfully returned to San Francisco—a voyage in every way delightful, but without an incident: unless lying two long weeks in a dead calm, eighteen hundred miles from the nearest land, may rank as an incident. Schools of whales grew so tame that day after day they played about the ship among the porpoises and the sharks without the least apparent fear of us, and we pelted them with empty bottles for lack of better sport. Twenty-four hours afterward these bottles would be still lying on the glassy water under our

noses, showing that the ship had not moved out of her place in all that time. The calm was absolutely breathless, and the surface of the sea absolutely without a wrinkle. For a whole day and part of a night we lay so close to another ship that had drifted to our vicinity, that we carried on conversations with her passengers, introduced each other by name, and became pretty intimately acquainted with people we had never heard of before, and have never heard of since. This was the only vessel we saw during the whole lonely voyage. We had fifteen passengers, and to show how hard pressed they were at last for occupation and amusement, I will mention that the gentlemen gave a good part of their time every day, during the calm, to trying to sit on an empty champagne bottle (lying on its side), and thread a needle without touching their heels to the deck, or falling over; and the ladies sat in the shade of the mainsail, and watched the enterprise with absorbing interest. We were at sea five Sundays; and yet, but for the almanac, we never would have known but that all the other days were Sundays too.

I was home again, in San Francisco, without means and without employment. I tortured my brain for a saving scheme of some kind, and at last a public lecture occurred to me! I sat down and wrote one, in a fever of hopeful anticipation. I showed it to several friends, but they all shook their heads. They said nobody would come to hear me, and I would make a humiliating failure of it.

They said that as I had never spoken in public, I would break down in the delivery, anyhow. I was disconsolate now. But at last an editor slapped me on the back and told me to "go ahead." He said, "Take the largest house in town, and charge a dollar a ticket." The audacity of the proposition was charming; it seemed fraught with practical worldly wisdom, however. The proprietor of the several theatres endorsed the advice, and said I might have his handsome new opera-house at half price —fifty dollars. In sheer desperation I took it—on credit, for sufficient reasons. In three days I did a hundred and fifty dollars' worth of printing and advertising, and was the most distressed and frightened creature on the Pacific coast. I could not sleep—who could, under such circumstances? For other people there was facetiousness in the last line of my posters, but to me it was plaintive with a pang when I wrote it:

"Doors open at 7½. The trouble will begin at 8."

That line has done good service since. Showmen have borrowed it frequently. I have even seen it appended to a newspaper advertisement reminding school pupils in vacation what time next term would begin. As those three days of suspense dragged by, I grew more and more unhappy. I had sold two hundred tickets among my personal friends, but I feared they might not come. My lecture, which had seemed "humorous" to me, at first, grew steadily more and more dreary, till not a vestige of fun seemed left, and I grieved that I could not bring a coffin on the stage and turn the thing into a funeral. I was so panic-stricken, at last, that I went to three old friends, giants in stature, cordial by nature, and stormy-voiced, and said:

"This thing is going to be a failure; the jokes in it are so dim that nobody will ever see them; I would like to have you sit in the parquette, and help me through."

They said they would. Then I went to the wife of a popular citizen, and said that if she was willing to do me a very great kindness, I would be glad if she and her husband would sit prominently in the left-hand stage-box, where the whole house could see them. I explained that I should need help, and would turn toward her and smile, as a signal, when I had been delivered of an obscure joke—"and then," I added, "don't wait to investigate, but respond!"

She promised. Down the street I met a man I never had seen before. He had been drinking, and was beaming with smiles and good nature. He said:

"My name's Sawyer. You don't know me, but that don't matter. I haven't got a cent, but if you knew how bad I wanted to laugh, you'd give me a ticket. Come, now, what do you say?"

"Is your laugh hung on a hair-trigger?—that is, is it critical, or can you get it off easy?"

My drawling infirmity of speech so affected him that he laughed a specimen or two that struck me as being about the article I wanted, and I gave him a ticket, and appointed him to sit in the second circle, in the centre, and be responsible for that division of the house. I gave him minute instructions about how to detect indistinct jokes, and then went away, and left him chuckling placidly over the novelty of the idea.

I ate nothing on the last of the three eventful days—I only suffered. I had advertised that on this third day the box-office would be opened for the sale of reserved seats. I crept down to the theater at four in the afternoon to see if any sales had been made. The ticket seller was gone, the box-office was locked up. I had to swallow suddenly, or my heart would have got out. "No sales," I said to myself; "I might have known it." I thought of suicide, pretended illness, flight. I thought of these things in earnest, for I was very miserable and scared. But of course I had to drive them away, and prepare to meet my fate. I could not wait for half-past seven—I wanted to face the horror, and end it —the feeling of many a man doomed to hang, no doubt. I went down back streets at six o'clock, and entered the theatre by the back door. I stumbled my way in the dark among the ranks of canvas scenery, and stood on the stage. The house was gloomy and silent, and its emptiness depressing. I went into the dark among the scenes again, and for an hour and a half gave myself up to the horrors, wholly unconscious of everything else. Then I heard a murmur; it rose higher and higher, and ended in a crash, mingled with cheers. It made my hair raise, it was so close to me, and so loud.

There was a pause, and then another; presently came a third, and before I well knew what I was about, I was in the middle of the stage, staring at a sea of faces, bewildered by the fierce glare of the lights, and quaking in every limb with a terror that seemed like to take my life away. The house was full, aisles and all!

The tumult in my heart and brain and legs continued a full minute before I could gain any command over myself. Then I recognized the charity and the friendliness in the faces before me, and little by little my fright melted away, and I began to talk Within three or four minutes I was comfortable, and even content. My three chief allies, with three auxiliaries, were on hand, in the parquette, all sitting together, all armed with bludgeons, and all ready to make an onslaught upon the feeblest joke that might show its head. And whenever a joke did fall, their bludgeons came down and their faces seemed to split from ear to ear.

Sawyer, whose hearty countenance was seen looming redly in the centre of the second circle, took it up, and the house was carried handsomely. Inferior jokes never fared so royally

before. Presently I delivered a bit of serious matter with impressive unction (it was my pet), and the audience listened with an absorbed hush that gratified me more than any applause; and as I dropped the last word of the clause, I happened to turn and catch Mrs.—'s intent and waiting eye; my conversation with her flashed upon me, and in spite of all I could do I smiled. She took it for the signal, and promptly delivered a mellow laugh that touched off the whole audience; and the explosion that followed was the triumph of the evening. I thought that that honest man Sawyer would choke himself; and as for the bludgeons, they performed like pile-drivers. But my poor little morsel of pathos was ruined. It was taken in good faith as an intentional joke, and the prize one of the entertainment, and I wisely let it go at that.

All the papers were kind in the morning; my appetite returned; I had a abundance of money. All's well that ends well.

CHAPTER LXXIX.

I launched out as a lecturer, now, with great boldness. I had the field all to myself, for public lectures were almost an unknown commodity in the Pacific market. They are not so rare, now, I suppose. I took an old personal friend along to play agent for me, and for two or three weeks we roamed through Nevada and California and had a very cheerful time of it. Two days before I lectured in Virginia City, two stagecoaches were robbed within two miles of the town. The daring act was committed just at dawn, by six masked men, who sprang up alongside the coaches, presented revolvers at the heads of the drivers and passengers, and commanded a general dismount. Everybody climbed down, and the robbers took their watches and every cent they had. Then they took gunpowder and blew up the express specie boxes and got their contents. The leader of the robbers was a small, quick-spoken man, and the fame of his vigorous manner and his intrepidity was in everybody's mouth when we arrived.

The night after instructing Virginia, I walked over the desolate "divide" and down to Gold Hill, and lectured there. The lecture done, I stopped to talk with a friend, and did not start back till eleven. The "divide" was high, unoccupied ground, between the towns, the scene of twenty midnight murders and a hundred robberies. As we climbed up and stepped out on this eminence, the Gold Hill lights dropped out of sight at our backs, and the night closed down gloomy and dismal. A sharp wind swept the place, too, and chilled our perspiring bodies through.

"I tell you I don't like this place at night," said Mike the agent.

"Well, don't speak so loud," I said. "You needn't remind anybody that we are here."

Just then a dim figure approached me from the direction of Virginia—a man, evidently. He came straight at me, and I stepped aside to let him pass; he stepped in the way and confronted me again. Then I saw that he had a mask on and was holding something in my face—I heard a click-click and recognized a revolver in dim outline. I pushed the barrel aside with my hand and said:

"Don't!"

He ejaculated sharply:

"Your watch! Your money!"

I said:

"You can have them with pleasure—but take the pistol away from my face, please. It makes me shiver."

"No remarks! Hand out your money!"

"Certainly—I—"

"Put up your hands! Don't you go for a weapon! Put 'em up! Higher!"

I held them above my head.

A pause. Then:

"Are you going to hand out your money or not?"

I dropped my hands to my pockets and said:

Certainly! I—"

"Put up your hands! Do you want your head blown off? Higher!"

I put them above my head again.

Another pause.

Are you going to hand out your money or not? Ah-ah—again? Put up your hands! By George, you want the head shot off you awful bad!"

"Well, friend, I'm trying my best to please you. You tell me to give up my money, and when I reach for it you tell me to put up my hands. If you would only—. Oh, now—don't! All six of you at me! That other man will get away while.—Now please take some of those revolvers out of my face—do, if you please! Every time one of them clicks, my liver comes up into my throat! If you have a mother—any of you—or if any of you have ever had a mother—or a—grandmother—or a—"

"Cheese it! Will you give up your money, or have we got to—. There —there—none of that! Put up your hands!"

"Gentlemen—I know you are gentlemen by your—"

"Silence! If you want to be facetious, young man, there are times and places more fitting. This is a serious business."

"You prick the marrow of my opinion. The funerals I have attended in my time were comedies compared to it. Now I think—"

"Curse your palaver! Your money!—your money!—your money! Hold!—put up your hands!"

"Gentlemen, listen to reason. You see how I am situated—now don't put those pistols so close—I smell the powder.

"You see how I am situated. If I had four hands—so that I could hold up two and—"

"Throttle him! Gag him! Kill him!"

"Gentlemen, don't! Nobody's watching the other fellow. Why don't some of you—. Ouch! Take it away, please!

"Gentlemen, you see that I've got to hold up my hands; and so I can't take out my money—but if you'll be so kind as to take it out for me, I will do as much for you some—"

"Search him Beauregard—and stop his jaw with a bullet, quick, if he wags it again. Help Beauregard, Stonewall."

Then three of them, with the small, spry leader, adjourned to Mike and fell to searching him. I was so excited that my lawless fancy tortured me to ask my two men all manner of facetious questions about their rebel brother-generals of the South, but, considering the order they had received, it was but common prudence to keep still. When everything had been taken from me,—watch, money, and a multitude of trifles of small value,—I supposed I was free, and forthwith put my cold hands into my empty pockets and began an inoffensive jig to warm my feet and stir up some latent courage—but instantly all pistols were at my head, and the order came again:

They stood Mike up alongside of me, with strict orders to keep his hands above his head, too, and then the chief highwayman said:

"Beauregard, hide behind that boulder; Phil Sheridan, you hide behind that other one; Stonewall Jackson, put yourself behind that sage-bush there. Keep your pistols bearing on these fellows, and if they take down their hands within ten minutes, or move a single peg, let them have it!"

Then three disappeared in the gloom toward the several ambushes, and the other three disappeared down the road toward Virginia.

It was depressingly still, and miserably cold. Now this whole thing was a practical joke, and the robbers were personal friends of ours in disguise, and twenty more lay hidden within ten feet of us during the whole operation, listening. Mike knew all this, and was in the joke, but I suspected nothing of it. To me it was most uncomfortably genuine. When we had stood there in the middle of the road five minutes, like a couple of idiots, with our hands aloft, freezing to death by inches, Mike's interest in the joke began to wane. He said:

"The time's up, now, aint it?"

"No, you keep still. Do you want to take any chances with these bloody savages?"

Presently Mike said:

"Now the time's up, anyway. I'm freezing."

"Well freeze. Better freeze than carry your brains home in a basket. Maybe the time is up, but how do we know?—got no watch to tell by. I mean to give them good measure. I calculate to stand here fifteen minutes or die. Don't you move."

So, without knowing it, I was making one joker very sick of his contract. When we took our arms down at last, they were aching with cold and fatigue, and when we went sneaking off, the dread I was in that the time might not yet be up and that we would feel bullets in a moment, was not sufficient to draw all my attention from the misery that racked my stiffened body.

The joke of these highwayman friends of ours was mainly a joke upon themselves; for they had waited for me on the cold hill-top two full hours before I came, and there was very little fun in that; they were so chilled that it took them a couple of weeks to get warm again. Moreover, I never had a thought that they would kill me to get money which it was so perfectly easy to get without any such folly, and so they did not really frighten me bad enough to make their enjoyment worth the trouble they had taken. I was only afraid that their weapons would go off accidentally. Their very numbers inspired me with confidence that no blood would be intentionally spilled. They were not smart; they ought to have sent only one highwayman, with a double-barrelled shot gun, if they desired to see the author of this volume climb a tree.

However, I suppose that in the long run I got the largest share of the joke at last; and in a shape not foreseen by the highwaymen; for the chilly exposure on the "divide" while I was in a perspiration gave me a cold which developed itself into a troublesome disease and kept my hands idle some three months, besides costing me quite a sum in doctor's bills. Since then I play no practical jokes on people and generally lose my temper when one is played upon me.

When I returned to San Francisco I projected a pleasure journey to Japan and thence westward around the world; but a desire to see home again changed my mind, and I took a berth in the steamship, bade good-bye to the friendliest land and livest, heartiest community on our continent, and came by the way of the Isthmus to New York—a trip that was not much of a pic-nic excursion, for the cholera broke out among us on the passage and we buried two or three bodies at sea every day. I found home a dreary place after my long absence; for half the children I had known were now wearing whiskers or waterfalls, and few of the grown people I had been acquainted with remained at their hearthstones prosperous and happy— some of them had wandered to other scenes, some were in jail, and the rest had been hanged. These changes touched me deeply, and I went away and joined the famous Quaker City European Excursion and carried my tears to foreign lands.

Thus, after seven years of vicissitudes, ended a "pleasure trip" to the silver mines of Nevada which had originally been intended to occupy only three months. However, I usually miss my calculations further than that.

MORAL.

If the reader thinks he is done, now, and that this book has no moral to it, he is in error. The moral of it is this: If you are of any account, stay at home and make your way by faithful diligence; but if you are "no account," go away from home, and then you will have to work, whether you want to or not. Thus you become a blessing to your friends by ceasing to be a nuisance to them—if the people you go among suffer by the operation.

APPENDIX. A.

BRIEF SKETCH OF MORMON HISTORY.

Mormonism is only about forty years old, but its career has been full of stir and adventure from the beginning, and is likely to remain so to the end. Its adherents have been hunted and hounded from one end of the country to the other, and the result is that for years they have hated all "Gentiles" indiscriminately and with all their might. Joseph Smith, the finder of the Book of Mormon and founder of the religion, was driven from State to State with his mysterious copperplates and the miraculous stones he read their inscriptions with.

Finally he instituted his "church" in Ohio and Brigham Young joined it. The neighbors began to persecute, and apostasy commenced. Brigham held to the faith and worked hard. He arrested desertion. He did more—he added converts in the midst of the trouble. He rose in favor and importance with the brethren. He was made one of the Twelve Apostles of the Church. He shortly fought his way to a higher post and a more powerful—President of the Twelve. The neighbors rose up and drove the Mormons out of Ohio, and they settled in Missouri. Brigham went with them. The Missourians drove them out and they retreated to Nauvoo, Illinois. They prospered there, and built a temple which made some pretensions to architectural grace and achieved some celebrity in a section of country where a brick court-house with a tin dome and a cupola on it was contemplated with reverential awe. But the Mormons were badgered and harried again by their neighbors. All the proclamations Joseph Smith could issue denouncing polygamy and repudiating it as utterly anti-Mormon were of no avail; the people of the neighborhood, on both sides of the Mississippi, claimed that polygamy was practised by the Mormons, and not only polygamy but a little of everything that was bad. Brigham returned from a mission to England, where he had established a Mormon newspaper, and he brought back with him several hundred converts to his preaching. His influence among the brethren augmented with every move he made. Finally Nauvoo was invaded by the Missouri and Illinois Gentiles, and Joseph Smith killed. A Mormon named Rigdon assumed the Presidency of the Mormon church and government, in Smith's place, and even tried his hand at a prophecy or two. But a greater than he was at hand. Brigham seized the advantage of the hour and without other authority than superior brain and nerve and will, hurled Rigdon from his high place and occupied it himself. He did more. He launched an elaborate curse at Rigdon and his disciples; and he pronounced Rigdon's "prophecies" emanations from the devil, and ended by "handing the false prophet over to the buffetings of Satan for a thousand years"—probably the longest term ever inflicted in Illinois. The people recognized their master. They straightway elected Brigham Young President, by a prodigious majority, and have never faltered in their devotion to him from that day to this. Brigham had forecast—a quality which no other prominent Mormon has probably ever possessed. He recognized that it was better to move to the wilderness than be moved. By his command the people gathered together their meagre effects, turned their backs upon their homes, and their faces toward the wilderness, and on a bitter night in February filed in sorrowful procession across the frozen Mississippi, lighted on their way by the glare from their burning temple, whose sacred furniture their own hands had fired! They camped, several days afterward, on the western verge of Iowa, and poverty, want, hunger, cold, sickness, grief and persecution did their work, and many succumbed and died—martyrs, fair and true, whatever else they might have been. Two years the remnant remained there, while Brigham and a small party crossed the country and founded Great Salt Lake City, purposely choosing a land which was outside the ownership and jurisdiction of the hated American nation. Note that. This was in 1847. Brigham moved his people there and got them settled just in time to see disaster fall again. For the war closed and Mexico ceded Brigham's refuge to the enemy—the United States! In 1849 the Mormons organized a "free and independent" government and erected the "State of Deseret," with Brigham Young as its head. But the very next year Congress deliberately snubbed it and created the "Territory of Utah" out of the same accumulation of mountains, sage-brush, alkali and general desolation,—but made Brigham Governor of it. Then for years the enormous migration across the plains to California poured through the land of the Mormons and yet the church remained staunch and true to its lord and master. Neither hunger, thirst, poverty, grief, hatred, contempt, nor persecution could drive the Mormons from their faith or their allegiance; and even the thirst for gold, which gleaned the flower of the youth and strength of many nations was not able to entice them! That was the final test. An experiment that could survive that was an experiment with some substance to it somewhere.

Great Salt Lake City throve finely, and so did Utah. One of the last things which Brigham Young had done before leaving Iowa, was to appear in the pulpit dressed to personate the worshipped and lamented prophet Smith, and confer the prophetic succession, with all its dignities, emoluments and authorities, upon "President Brigham Young!" The people accepted the pious fraud with the maddest enthusiasm, and Brigham's power was sealed and secured for all time. Within five years afterward he openly added polygamy to the tenets of the church by authority of a "revelation" which he pretended had been received nine years before by Joseph Smith, albeit Joseph is amply on record as denouncing polygamy to the day of his death.

Now was Brigham become a second Andrew Johnson in the small beginning and steady progress of his official grandeur. He had served successively as a disciple in the ranks; home missionary; foreign missionary; editor and publisher; Apostle; President of the Board of Apostles; President of all Mormondom, civil and ecclesiastical; successor to the great Joseph by the will of heaven; "prophet," "seer," "revelator." There was but one dignity higher which he could aspire to, and he reached out modestly and took that—he proclaimed himself a God!

He claims that he is to have a heaven of his own hereafter, and that he will be its God, and his wives and children its goddesses, princes and princesses. Into it all faithful Mormons will be admitted, with their families, and will take rank and consequence according to the number of their wives and children. If a disciple dies before he has had time to accumulate enough wives and children to enable him to be respectable in the next world any friend can marry a few wives and raise a few children for him after he is dead, and they are duly credited to his account and his heavenly status advanced accordingly.

Let it be borne in mind that the majority of the Mormons have always been ignorant, simple, of an inferior order of intellect, unacquainted with the world and its ways; and let it be borne in mind that the wives of these Mormons are necessarily after the same pattern and their children likely to be fit representatives of such a conjunction; and then let it be remembered that for forty years these creatures have been driven, driven, driven, relentlessly! and mobbed, beaten, and shot down; cursed, despised, expatriated; banished to a remote desert, whither they journeyed gaunt with famine and disease, disturbing the ancient solitudes with their lamentations and marking the long way with graves of their dead—and all because they were simply trying to live and worship God in the way which they believed with all their hearts and souls to be the true one. Let all these things be borne in mind, and then it will not be hard to account for the deathless hatred which the Mormons bear our people and our government.

That hatred has "fed fat its ancient grudge" ever since Mormon Utah developed into a self-supporting realm and the church waxed rich and strong. Brigham as Territorial Governor made it plain that Mormondom was for the Mormons. The United States tried to rectify all that by appointing territorial officers from New England and other anti-Mormon localities, but Brigham prepared to make their entrance into his dominions difficult. Three thousand United States troops had to go across the plains and put these gentlemen in office. And after they were in office they were as helpless as so many stone images. They made laws which nobody minded and which could not be executed. The federal judges opened court in a land filled with crime and violence and sat as holiday spectacles for insolent crowds to gape at—for there was nothing to try, nothing to do nothing on the dockets! And if a Gentile brought a suit, the Mormon jury would do just as it pleased about bringing in a verdict, and when the judgment of the court was rendered no Mormon cared for it and no officer could execute it. Our Presidents shipped one cargo of officials after another to Utah, but the result was always the same—they sat in a blight for awhile they fairly feasted on scowls and insults day by day, they saw every attempt to do their official duties find its reward in darker and darker looks, and in secret threats and warnings of a more and more dismal nature—and at last they either succumbed and became despised tools and toys of the Mormons, or got scared and discomforted beyond all endurance and left the Territory. If a brave officer kept on courageously till his pluck was proven, some pliant Buchanan or Pierce would remove him and appoint a stick in his place. In 1857 General Harney came very near being appointed Governor of Utah. And so it came very near being Harney governor and Cradlebaugh judge! —two men who never had any idea of fear further than the sort of murky comprehension of it which they were enabled to gather from the dictionary. Simply (if for nothing else) for the variety they would have made in a rather monotonous history of Federal servility and helplessness, it is a pity they were not fated to hold office together in Utah.

Up to the date of our visit to Utah, such had been the Territorial record. The Territorial government established there had been a hopeless failure, and Brigham Young was the only real power in the land. He was an absolute monarch—a monarch who defied our President—a monarch who laughed at our armies when they camped about his capital—a monarch who received without emotion the news that the august Congress of the United States had enacted a solemn law against polygamy, and then went forth calmly and married twenty-five or thirty more wives.

B. THE MOUNTAIN MEADOWS MASSACRE.

The persecutions which the Mormons suffered so long—and which they consider they still suffer in not being allowed to govern themselves —they have endeavored and are still endeavoring to repay. The now almost forgotten "Mountain Meadows massacre" was their work. It was very famous in its day. The whole United States rang with its horrors. A few items will refresh the reader's memory. A great emigrant train from Missouri and Arkansas passed through Salt Lake City and a few disaffected Mormons joined it for the sake of the strong protection it afforded for their escape. In that matter lay sufficient cause for hot retaliation by the Mormon chiefs. Besides, these one hundred and forty-five or one hundred and fifty unsuspecting emigrants being in part from Arkansas, where a noted Mormon missionary had lately been killed, and in part from Missouri, a State remembered with execrations as a bitter persecutor of the saints when they were few and poor and friendless, here were substantial additional grounds for lack of love for these wayfarers. And finally, this train was rich, very rich in cattle, horses, mules and other property—and how could the Mormons consistently keep up their coveted resemblance to the Israelitish tribes and not seize the "spoil" of an enemy when the Lord had so manifestly "delivered it into their hand?"

Wherefore, according to Mrs. C. V. Waite's entertaining book, "The Mormon Prophet," it transpired that—

"A 'revelation' from Brigham Young, as Great Grand Archee or God, was dispatched to President J. C. Haight, Bishop Higbee and J. D. Lee (adopted son of Brigham), commanding them to raise all the forces they could muster and trust, follow those cursed Gentiles (so read the revelation), attack them disguised as Indians, and with the arrows of the Almighty make a clean sweep of them, and leave none to tell the tale; and if they needed any assistance they were commanded to hire the Indians as their allies, promising them a share of the booty. They were to be neither slothful nor negligent in their duty, and to be punctual in sending the teams back to him before winter set in, for this was the mandate of Almighty God."

The command of the "revelation" was faithfully obeyed. A large party of Mormons, painted and tricked out as Indians, overtook the train of emigrant wagons some three hundred miles south of Salt Lake City, and made an attack. But the emigrants threw up earthworks, made fortresses of their wagons and defended themselves gallantly and successfully for five days! Your Missouri or Arkansas gentleman is not much afraid of the sort of scurvy apologies for "Indians" which the southern part of Utah affords. He would stand up and fight five hundred of them.

At the end of the five days the Mormons tried military strategy. They retired to the upper end of the "Meadows," resumed civilized apparel, washed off their paint, and then, heavily armed, drove down in wagons to the beleaguered emigrants, bearing a flag of truce! When the emigrants saw white men coming they threw down their guns and welcomed them with cheer after cheer! And, all unconscious of the poetry of it, no doubt, they lifted a little child aloft, dressed in white, in answer to the flag of truce!

The leaders of the timely white "deliverers" were President Haight and Bishop John D. Lee, of the Mormon Church. Mr. Cradlebaugh, who served a term as a Federal Judge in Utah and afterward was sent to Congress from Nevada, tells in a speech delivered in Congress how these leaders next proceeded:

"They professed to be on good terms with the Indians, and represented them as being very mad. They also proposed to intercede and settle the matter with the Indians. After several hours parley they, having (apparently) visited the Indians, gave the ultimatum of the savages; which was, that the emigrants should march out of their camp, leaving everything behind them, even their guns. It was promised by the Mormon bishops that they would bring a force and guard the emigrants back to the settlements. The terms were agreed to, the emigrants being desirous of saving the lives of their families. The Mormons retired, and subsequently appeared with thirty or forty armed men. The emigrants were marched out, the women and children in front and the men behind, the Mormon guard being in the rear. When they had marched in this way about a mile, at a given signal the slaughter commenced. The men were almost all shot down at the first fire from the guard. Two only escaped, who fled to the desert, and were followed one hundred and fifty miles before they were overtaken and slaughtered. The women and children ran

on, two or three hundred yards further, when they were overtaken and with the aid of the Indians they were slaughtered. Seventeen individuals only, of all the emigrant party, were spared, and they were little children, the eldest of them being only seven years old. Thus, on the 10th day of September, 1857, was consummated one of the most cruel, cowardly and bloody murders known in our history."

The number of persons butchered by the Mormons on this occasion was one hundred and twenty.

With unheard-of temerity Judge Cradlebaugh opened his court and proceeded to make Mormondom answer for the massacre. And what a spectacle it must have been to see this grim veteran, solitary and alone in his pride and his pluck, glowering down on his Mormon jury and Mormon auditory, deriding them by turns, and by turns "breathing threatenings and slaughter!"

An editorial in the Territorial Enterprise of that day says of him and of the occasion:

"He spoke and acted with the fearlessness and resolution of a Jackson; but the jury failed to indict, or even report on the charges, while threats of violence were heard in every quarter, and an attack on the U.S. troops intimated, if he persisted in his course.

"Finding that nothing could be done with the juries, they were discharged with a scathing rebuke from the judge. And then, sitting as a committing magistrate, he commenced his task alone. He examined witnesses, made arrests in every quarter, and created a consternation in the camps of the saints greater than any they had ever witnessed before, since Mormondom was born. At last accounts terrified elders and bishops were decamping to save their necks; and developments of the most starling character were being made, implicating the highest Church dignitaries in the many murders and robberies committed upon the Gentiles during the past eight years."

Had Harney been Governor, Cradlebaugh would have been supported in his work, and the absolute proofs adduced by him of Mormon guilt in this massacre and in a number of previous murders, would have conferred gratuitous coffins upon certain citizens, together with occasion to use them. But Cumming was the Federal Governor, and he, under a curious pretense of impartiality, sought to screen the Mormons from the demands of justice. On one occasion he even went so far as to publish his protest against the use of the U.S. troops in aid of Cradlebaugh's proceedings.

Mrs. C. V. Waite closes her interesting detail of the great massacre with the following remark and accompanying summary of the testimony—and the summary is concise, accurate and reliable:

"For the benefit of those who may still be disposed to doubt the guilt of Young and his Mormons in this transaction, the testimony is here collated and circumstances given which go not merely to implicate but to fasten conviction upon them by 'confirmations strong as proofs of Holy Writ:'

"1. The evidence of Mormons themselves, engaged in the affair, as shown by the statements of Judge Cradlebaugh and Deputy U.S. Marshall Rodgers.

"2. The failure of Brigham Young to embody any account of it in his Report as Superintendent of Indian Affairs. Also his failure to make any allusion to it whatever from the pulpit, until several years after the occurrence

"3. The flight to the mountains of men high in authority in the Mormon Church and State, when this affair was brought to the ordeal of a judicial investigation.

"4. The failure of the Deseret News, the Church organ, and the only paper then published in the Territory, to notice the massacre until several months afterward, and then only to deny that Mormons were engaged in it.

"5. The testimony of the children saved from the massacre.

"6. The children and the property of the emigrants found in possession of the Mormons, and that possession traced back to the very day after the massacre.

"7. The statements of Indians in the neighborhood of the scene of the massacre: these statements are shown, not only by Cradlebaugh and Rodgers, but by a number of military officers, and by J. Forney, who was, in 1859, Superintendent of Indian Affairs for the Territory. To all these were such statements freely and frequently made by the Indians.

"8. The testimony of R. P. Campbell, Capt. 2d Dragoons, who was sent in the Spring of 1859 to Santa Clara, to protect travelers on the road to California and to inquire into Indian depredations."

C. CONCERNING A FRIGHTFUL ASSASSINATION THAT WAS NEVER CONSUMMATED

If ever there was a harmless man, it is Conrad Wiegand, of Gold Hill, Nevada. If ever there was a gentle spirit that thought itself unfired gunpowder and latent ruin, it is Conrad Wiegand. If ever there was an oyster that fancied itself a whale; or a jack-o'lantern, confined to a swamp, that fancied itself a planet with a billion-mile orbit; or a summer zephyr that deemed itself a hurricane, it is Conrad Wiegand. Therefore, what wonder is it that when he says a thing, he thinks the world listens; that when he does a thing the world stands still to look; and that when he suffers, there is a convulsion of nature? When I met Conrad, he was "Superintendent of the Gold Hill Assay Office"—and he was not only its Superintendent, but its entire force. And he was a street preacher, too, with a mongrel religion of his own invention, whereby he expected to regenerate the universe. This was years ago. Here latterly he has entered journalism; and his journalism is what it might be expected to be: colossal to ear, but pigmy to the eye. It is extravagant grandiloquence confined to a newspaper about the size of a double letter sheet. He doubtless edits, sets the type, and prints his paper, all alone; but he delights to speak of the concern as if it occupies a block and employs a thousand men.

[Something less than two years ago, Conrad assailed several people mercilessly in his little "People's Tribune," and got himself into trouble. Straightway he airs the affair in the "Territorial Enterprise," in a communication over his own signature, and I propose to reproduce it here, in all its native simplicity and more than human candor. Long as it is, it is well worth reading, for it is the richest specimen of journalistic literature the history of America can furnish, perhaps:]

From the Territorial Enterprise, Jan. 20, 1870.

SEEMING PLOT FOR ASSASSINATION MISCARRIED.

TO THE EDITOR OF THE ENTERPRISE: Months ago, when Mr. Sutro incidentally exposed mining management on the Comstock, and among others roused me to protest against its continuance, in great kindness you warned me that any attempt by publications, by public meetings and by legislative action, aimed at the correction of chronic mining evils in Storey County, must entail upon me (a) business ruin, (b) the burden of all its costs, (c) personal violence, and if my purpose were persisted in, then (d) assassination, and after all nothing would be effected.

YOUR PROPHECY FULFILLING. In large part at least your prophecies have been fulfilled, for (a) assaying, which was well attended to in the Gold Hill Assay Office (of which I am superintendent), in consequence of my publications, has been taken elsewhere, so the President of one of the companies assures me. With no reason assigned, other work has been taken away. With but one or two important exceptions, our assay business now consists simply of the gleanings of the vicinity. (b) Though my own personal donations to the People's Tribune Association have already exceeded $1,500, outside of our own numbers we have received (in money) less than $300 as contributions and subscriptions for the journal. (c) On Thursday last, on the main street in Gold Hill, near noon, with neither warning nor cause assigned, by a powerful blow I was felled to the ground, and while down I was kicked by a man who it would seem had been led to believe that I had spoken derogatorily of him. By whom he was so induced to believe I am as yet unable to say. On Saturday last I was again assailed and beaten by a man who first informed me why he did so, and who persisted in making his assault even after the erroneous impression under which he also was at first laboring had been clearly and repeatedly pointed out. This same man, after failing through intimidation to elicit from me the names of our editorial contributors, against giving which he knew me to be pledged, beat himself weary upon me with a raw hide, I not resisting, and then pantingly threatened me with permanent disfiguring mayhem, if ever again I should introduce his name into print, and who but a few minutes before his attack upon me assured me that the only reason I was "permitted" to reach home alive on Wednesday evening last (at which time the PEOPLE'S TRIBUNE was issued) was, that he deems me only half-witted, and be it remembered the very next morning I was knocked down and kicked by a man who seemed to be prepared for flight.

[He sees doom impending:]

WHEN WILL THE CIRCLE JOIN? How long before the whole of your prophecy will be fulfilled I cannot say, but under the shadow of so much fulfillment in so short a time, and with such threats from a man who is one of the most prominent exponents of the San Francisco mining-ring staring me and this whole community defiantly in the face and pointing to a completion of your augury, do you blame me for feeling that this communication is the last I shall ever write for the Press, especially when a sense alike of personal self-respect, of duty to this money-oppressed and fear-ridden community, and of American fealty to the spirit of true Liberty all command me, and each more loudly than love of life itself, to declare the name of that prominent man to be JOHN B. WINTERS, President of the Yellow Jacket Company, a political aspirant and a military General? The name of his partially duped accomplice and abettor in this last marvelous assault, is no other than PHILIP LYNCH, Editor and Proprietor of the Gold Hill News.

Despite the insult and wrong heaped upon me by John B. Winters, on Saturday afternoon, only a glimpse of which I shall be able to afford your readers, so much do I deplore clinching (by publicity) a serious mistake of any one, man or woman, committed under natural and not self-wrought passion, in view of his great apparent excitement at the time and in view of the almost perfect privacy of the assault, I am far from sure that I should not have given him space for repentance before exposing him, were it not that he himself has so far exposed the matter as to make it the common talk of the town that he has horsewhipped me. That fact having been made public, all the facts in connection need to be also, or silence on my part would seem more than singular, and with many would be proof either that I was conscious of some unworthy aim in publishing the article, or else that my "non-combatant" principles are but a convenient cloak alike of physical and moral cowardice. I therefore shall try to present a graphic but truthful picture of this whole affair, but shall forbear all comments, presuming that the editors of our own journal, if others do not, will speak freely and fittingly upon this subject in our next number, whether I shall then be dead or living, for my death will not stop, though it may suspend, the publication of the PEOPLE'S TRIBUNE. [The "non-combatant" sticks to principle, but takes along a friend or two of a conveniently different stripe:]

THE TRAP SET. On Saturday morning John B. Winters sent verbal word to the Gold Hill Assay Office that he desired to see me at the Yellow Jacket office. Though such a request struck me as decidedly cool in view of his own recent discourtesies to me there alike as a publisher and as a stockholder in the Yellow Jacket mine, and though it seemed to me more like a summons than the courteous request by one gentleman to another for a favor, hoping that some conference with Sharon looking to the betterment of mining matters in Nevada might arise from it, I felt strongly inclined to overlook what possibly was simply an oversight in courtesy. But as then it had only been two days since I had been bruised and beaten under a hasty and false apprehension of facts, my caution was somewhat aroused. Moreover I remembered sensitively his contemptuousness of manner to me at my last interview in his office. I therefore felt it needful, if I went at all, to go accompanied by a friend whom he would not dare to treat with incivility, and whose presence with me might secure exemption from insult. Accordingly I asked a neighbor to accompany me.

THE TRAP ALMOST DETECTED. Although I was not then aware of this fact, it would seem that previous to my request this same neighbor had heard Dr. Zabriskie state publicly in a saloon, that Mr. Winters had told him he had decided either to kill or to horsewhip me, but had not finally decided on which. My neighbor, therefore, felt unwilling to go down with me until he had first called on Mr. Winters alone. He therefore paid him a visit. From that interview he assured me that he gathered the impression that he did not believe I would have any difficulty with Mr. Winters, and that he (Winters) would call on me at four o'clock in my own office.

MY OWN PRECAUTIONS. As Sheriff Cummings was in Gold Hill that afternoon, and as I desired to converse with him about the previous assault, I invited him to my office, and he came. Although a half hour had passed beyond four o'clock, Mr. Winters had not called, and we both of us began preparing to go home. Just then, Philip Lynch, Publisher of the Gold Hill News, came in and said, blandly and cheerily, as if bringing good news:

"Hello, John B. Winters wants to see you."

I replied, "Indeed! Why he sent me word that he would call on me here this afternoon at four o'clock!"

"O, well, it don't do to be too ceremonious just now, he's in my office, and that will do as well—come on in, Winters wants to consult with you alone. He's got something to say to you."

Though slightly uneasy at this change of programme, yet believing that in an editor's house I ought to be safe, and anyhow that I would be within hail of the street, I hurriedly, and but partially whispered my dim apprehensions to Mr. Cummings, and asked him if he would not keep near enough to hear my voice in case I should call. He consented to do so while waiting for some other parties, and to come in if he heard my voice or thought I had need of protection.

On reaching the editorial part of the News office, which viewed from the street is dark, I did not see Mr. Winters, and again my misgivings arose. Had I paused long enough to consider the case, I should have invited Sheriff Cummings in, but as Lynch went down stairs, he said: "This way, Wiegand—it's best to be private," or some such remark.

[I do not desire to strain the reader's fancy, hurtfully, and yet it would be a favor to me if he would try to fancy this lamb in battle, or the duelling ground or at the head of a vigilance committee—M. T.:]

I followed, and without Mr. Cummings, and without arms, which I never do or will carry, unless as a soldier in war, or unless I should yet come to feel I must fight a duel, or to join and aid in the ranks of a necessary Vigilance Committee. But by following I made a fatal mistake. Following was entering a trap, and whatever animal suffers itself to be caught should expect the common fate of a caged rat, as I fear events to come will prove.

Traps commonly are not set for benevolence. [His body-guard is shut out:]

THE TRAP INSIDE. I followed Lynch down stairs. At their foot a door to the left opened into a small room. From that room another door opened into yet another room, and once entered I found myself inveigled into what many will ever henceforth regard as a private subterranean Gold Hill den, admirably adapted in proper hands to the purposes of murder, raw or disguised, for from it, with both or even one door closed, when too late, I saw that I could not be heard by Sheriff Cummings, and from it, BY VIOLENCE AND BY FORCE, I was prevented from making a peaceable exit, when I thought I saw the studious object of this "consultation" was no other than to compass my killing, in the presence of Philip Lynch as a witness, as soon as by insult a proverbially excitable man should be exasperated to the point of assailing Mr. Winters, so that Mr. Lynch, by his conscience and by his well known tenderness of heart toward the rich and potent would be compelled to testify that he saw Gen. John B. Winters kill Conrad Wiegand in "self-defence." But I am going too fast.

OUR HOST. Mr. Lynch was present during the most of the time (say a little short of an hour), but three times he left the room. His testimony, therefore, would be available only as to the bulk of what transpired. On entering this carpeted den I was invited to a seat near one corner of the room. Mr. Lynch took a seat near the window. J. B. Winters sat (at first) near the door, and began his remarks essentially as follows:

"I have come here to exact of you a retraction, in black and white, of those damnably false charges which you have preferred against me in that—infamous lying sheet of yours, and you must declare yourself their author, that you published them knowing them to be false, and that your motives were malicious."

"Hold, Mr. Winters. Your language is insulting and your demand an enormity. I trust I was not invited here either to be insulted or coerced. I supposed myself here by invitation of Mr. Lynch, at your request."

"Nor did I come here to insult you. I have already told you that I am here for a very different purpose."

"Yet your language has been offensive, and even now shows strong excitement. If insult is repeated I shall either leave the room or call in Sheriff Cummings, whom I just left standing and waiting for me outside the door."

"No, you won't, sir. You may just as well understand it at once as not. Here you are my man, and I'll tell you why! Months ago you put your property out of your hands, boasting that you did so to escape losing it on prosecution for libel."

"It is true that I did convert all my immovable property into personal property, such as I could trust safely to others, and chiefly to escape ruin through possible libel suits."

"Very good, sir. Having placed yourself beyond the pale of the law, may God help your soul if you DON'T make precisely such a retraction as I have demanded. I've got you now, and by— before you can get out of this room you've got to both write and sign precisely the retraction I have demanded, and before you go, anyhow—you—low-lived—lying—, I'll teach you what personal responsibility is outside of the law; and, by—, Sheriff Cummings and all the friends you've got in the world besides, can't save you, you—, etc.! No, sir. I'm alone now, and I'm prepared to be shot right here and now rather than be villified by you as I have been, and suffer you to escape me after publishing those charges, not only here where I am known and universally respected, but where I am not personally known and may be injured."

I confess this speech, with its terrible and but too plainly implied threat of killing me if I did not sign the paper he demanded, terrified me, especially as I saw he was working himself up to the highest possible pitch of passion, and instinct told me that any reply other than one of seeming concession to his demands would only be fuel to a raging fire, so I replied:

"Well, if I've got to sign—," and then I paused some time. Resuming, I said, "But, Mr. Winters, you are greatly excited. Besides, I see you are laboring under a total misapprehension. It is your duty not to inflame but to calm yourself. I am prepared to show you, if you will only point out the article that you allude to, that you regard as 'charges' what no calm and logical mind has any right to regard as such. Show me the charges, and I will try, at all events; and if it becomes plain that no charges have been preferred, then plainly there can be nothing to retract, and no one could rightly urge you to demand a retraction. You should beware of making so serious a mistake, for however honest a man may be, every one is liable to misapprehend. Besides you assume that I am the author of some certain article which you have not pointed out. It is hasty to do so."

He then pointed to some numbered paragraphs in a TRIBUNE article, headed "What's the Matter with Yellow Jacket?" saying "That's what I refer to."

To gain time for general reflection and resolution, I took up the paper and looked it over for awhile, he remaining silent, and as I hoped, cooling. I then resumed saying, "As I supposed. I do not admit having written that article, nor have you any right to assume so important a point, and then base important action upon your assumption. You might deeply regret it afterwards. In my published Address to the People, I notified the world that no information as to the authorship of any article would be given without the consent of the writer. I therefore cannot honorably tell you who wrote that article, nor can you exact it."

"If you are not the author, then I do demand to know who is?"

"I must decline to say."

"Then, by—, I brand you as its author, and shall treat you accordingly."

"Passing that point, the most important misapprehension which I notice is, that you regard them as 'charges' at all, when their context, both at their beginning and end, show they are not. These words introduce them: 'Such an investigation [just before indicated], we think MIGHT result in showing some of the following points.' Then follow eleven specifications, and the succeeding paragraph shows that the suggested investigation 'might EXONERATE those who are generally believed guilty.' You see, therefore, the context proves they are not preferred as charges, and this you seem to have overlooked."

While making those comments, Mr. Winters frequently interrupted me in such a way as to convince me that he was resolved not to consider candidly the thoughts contained in my words. He insisted upon it that they were charges, and "By—," he would make me take them back as charges, and he referred the question to Philip Lynch, to whom I then appealed as a literary man, as a logician, and as an editor, calling his attention especially to the introductory paragraph just before quoted. He replied, "if they are not charges, they certainly are insinuations," whereupon Mr. Winters renewed his demands for retraction precisely such as he had before named, except that he would allow me to state who did write the article if I did not myself, and this time shaking his fist in my face with more cursings and epithets.

When he threatened me with his clenched fist, instinctively I tried to rise from my chair, but Winters then forcibly thrust me down, as he did every other time (at least seven or eight), when under similar imminent danger of bruising by his fist (or for aught I could know worse than that after the first stunning blow), which he could easily and safely to himself have dealt me so long as he kept me down and stood over me.

This fact it was, which more than anything else, convinced me that by plan and plot I was purposely made powerless in Mr. Winters' hands, and that he did not mean to allow me that advantage of being afoot, which he possessed. Moreover, I then became convinced, that Philip Lynch (and for what reason I wondered) would do absolutely nothing to protect me in his own house. I realized then the situation thoroughly. I had found it equally vain to protest or argue, and I would make no unmanly appeal for pity, still less apologize. Yet my life had been by the plainest possible implication threatened. I was a weak man. I was unarmed. I was helplessly down, and Winters was afoot and probably armed. Lynch was the only "witness." The statements demanded, if given and not explained, would utterly sink me in my own self-respect, in my family's eyes, and in the eyes of the community. On the other hand, should I give the author's name how could I ever expect that confidence of the People which I should no longer deserve, and how much dearer to me and to my family was my life than the life of the real author to his friends. Yet life seemed dear and each minute that remained seemed precious if not solemn. I sincerely trust that neither you nor any of your readers, and especially none with families, may ever be placed in such seeming direct proximity to death while obliged to decide the one question I was compelled to, viz.: What should I do—I, a man of family, and not as Mr. Winters is, "alone." [The reader is requested not to skip the following.—M. T.:]

STRATEGY AND MESMERISM. To gain time for further reflection, and hoping that by a seeming acquiescence I might regain my personal liberty, at least till I could give an alarm, or take advantage of some momentary inadvertence of Winters, and then without a cowardly flight escape, I resolved to write a certain kind of retraction, but previously had inwardly decided:

First.—That I would studiously avoid every action which might be construed into the drawing of a weapon, even by a self-infuriated man, no matter what amount of insult might be heaped upon me, for it seemed to me that this great excess of compound profanity, foulness and epithet must be more than a mere indulgence, and therefore must have some object. "Surely in vain the net is spread in the sight of any bird." Therefore, as before without thought, I thereafter by intent kept my hands away from my pockets, and generally in sight and spread upon my knees.

Second.—I resolved to make no motion with my arms or hands which could possibly be construed into aggression.

Third.—I resolved completely to govern my outward manner and suppress indignation. To do this, I must govern my spirit. To do that, by force of imagination I was obliged like actors on the boards to resolve myself into an unnatural mental state and see all things through the eyes of an assumed character.

Fourth.—I resolved to try on Winters, silently, and unconsciously to himself a mesmeric power which I possess over certain kinds of people, and which at times I have found to work even in the dark over the lower animals.

Does any one smile at these last counts? God save you from ever being obliged to beat in a game of chess, whose stake is your life, you having but four poor pawns and pieces and your adversary with his full force unshorn. But if you are, provided you have any strength with breadth of will, do not despair. Though mesmeric power may not save you, it may help you; try it at all events. In this instance I was conscious of power coming into me, and by a law of nature, I know Winters was correspondingly weakened. If I could have gained more time I am sure he would not even have struck me.

It takes time both to form such resolutions and to recite them. That time, however, I gained while thinking of my retraction, which I first wrote in pencil, altering it from time to time till I got it to suit me, my aim being to make it look like a concession to demands, while in fact it should tersely speak the truth into Mr. Winters' mind. When it was finished, I

copied it in ink, and if correctly copied from my first draft it should read as follows. In copying I do not think I made any material change.

COPY. To Philip Lynch, Editor of the Gold Hill News: I learn that Gen. John B. Winters believes the following (pasted on) clipping from the PEOPLE'S TRIBUNE of January to contain distinct charges of mine against him personally, and that as such he desires me to retract them unqualifiedly.

In compliance with his request, permit me to say that, although Mr. Winters and I see this matter differently, in view of his strong feelings in the premises, I hereby declare that I do not know those "charges" (if such they are) to be true, and I hope that a critical examination would altogether disprove them. CONRAD WIEGAND. Gold Hill, January 15, 1870.

I then read what I had written and handed it to Mr. Lynch, whereupon Mr. Winters said:

"That's not satisfactory, and it won't do;" and then addressing himself to Mr. Lynch, he further said: "How does it strike you?"

"Well, I confess I don't see that it retracts anything."

"Nor do I," said Winters; "in fact, I regard it as adding insult to injury. Mr. Wiegand you've got to do better than that. You are not the man who can pull wool over my eyes."

"That, sir, is the only retraction I can write."

"No it isn't, sir, and if you so much as say so again you do it at your peril, for I'll thrash you to within an inch of your life, and, by—, sir, I don't pledge myself to spare you even that inch either. I want you to understand I have asked you for a very different paper, and that paper you've got to sign."

"Mr. Winters, I assure you that I do not wish to irritate you, but, at the same time, it is utterly impossible for me to write any other paper than that which I have written. If you are resolved to compel me to sign something, Philip Lynch's hand must write at your dictation, and if, when written, I can sign it I will do so, but such a document as you say you must have from me, I never can sign. I mean what I say."

"Well, sir, what's to be done must be done quickly, for I've been here long enough already. I'll put the thing in another shape (and then pointing to the paper); don't you know those charges to be false?"

"I do not."

"Do you know them to be true?"

"Of my own personal knowledge I do not."

"Why then did you print them?"

"Because rightly considered in their connection they are not charges, but pertinent and useful suggestions in answer to the queries of a correspondent who stated facts which are inexplicable."

"Don't you know that I know they are false?"

"If you do, the proper course is simply to deny them and court an investigation."

"And do YOU claim the right to make ME come out and deny anything you may choose to write and print?"

To that question I think I made no reply, and he then further said:

"Come, now, we've talked about the matter long enough. I want your final answer—did you write that article or not?"

"I cannot in honor tell you who wrote it."

"Did you not see it before it was printed?"

"Most certainly, sir."

"And did you deem it a fit thing to publish?"

"Most assuredly, sir, or I would never have consented to its appearance. Of its authorship I can say nothing whatever, but for its publication I assume full, sole and personal responsibility."

"And do you then retract it or not?"

"Mr. Winters, if my refusal to sign such a paper as you have demanded must entail upon me all that your language in this room fairly implies, then I ask a few minutes for prayer."

"Prayer!—you, this is not your hour for prayer—your time to pray was when you were writing those—lying charges. Will you sign or not?"

"You already have my answer."

"What! do you still refuse?"

"I do, sir."

"Take that, then," and to my amazement and inexpressible relief he drew only a rawhide instead of what I expected—a bludgeon or pistol. With it, as he spoke, he struck at my left ear downwards, as if to tear it off, and afterwards on the side of the head. As he moved away to get a better chance for a more effective shot, for the first time I gained a chance under peril to rise, and I did so pitying him from the very bottom of my soul, to think that one so naturally capable of true dignity, power and nobility could, by the temptations of this State, and by unfortunate associations and aspirations, be so deeply debased as to find in such brutality anything which he could call satisfaction—but the great hope for us all is in progress and growth, and John B. Winters, I trust, will yet be able to comprehend my feelings.

He continued to beat me with all his great force, until absolutely weary, exhausted and panting for breath. I still adhered to my purpose of non-aggressive defence, and made no other use of my arms than to defend my head and face from further disfigurement. The mere pain arising from the blows he inflicted upon my person was of course transient, and my clothing to some extent deadened its severity, as it now hides all remaining traces.

When I supposed he was through, taking the butt end of his weapon and shaking it in my face, he warned me, if I correctly understood him, of more yet to come, and furthermore said, if ever I again dared introduce his name to print, in either my own or any other public journal, he would cut off my left ear (and I do not think he was jesting) and send me home to my family a visibly mutilated man, to be a standing warning to all low-lived puppies who seek to blackmail gentlemen and to injure their good names. And when he did so operate, he informed me that his implement would not be a whip but a knife.

When he had said this, unaccompanied by Mr. Lynch, as I remember it, he left the room, for I sat down by Mr. Lynch, exclaiming: "The man is mad —he is utterly mad—this step is his ruin—it is a mistake—it would be ungenerous in me, despite of all the ill usage I have here received, to expose him, at least until he has had an opportunity to reflect upon the matter. I shall be in no haste."

"Winters is very mad just now," replied Mr. Lynch, "but when he is himself he is one of the finest men I ever met. In fact, he told me the reason he did not meet you upstairs was to spare you the humiliation of a beating in the sight of others."

I submit that that unguarded remark of Philip Lynch convicts him of having been privy in advance to Mr. Winters' intentions whatever they may have been, or at least to his meaning to make an assault upon me, but I leave to others to determine how much censure an editor deserves for inveigling a weak, non-combatant man, also a publisher, to a pen of his own to be horsewhipped, if no worse, for the simple printing of what is verbally in the mouth of nine out of ten men, and women too, upon the street.

While writing this account two theories have occurred to me as possibly true respecting this most remarkable assault: First— The aim may have been simply to extort from me such admissions as in the hands of money and influence would have sent me to the Penitentiary for libel. This, however, seems unlikely, because any statements elicited by fear or force could not be evidence in law or could be so explained as to have no force. The statements wanted so badly must have been desired for some other purpose. Second—The other theory has so dark and wilfully murderous a look that I shrink from writing it, yet as in all probability my death at the earliest practicable moment has already been decreed, I feel I should do all I can before my hour arrives, at least to show others how to break up that aristocratic rule and combination which has robbed all Nevada of true freedom, if not of manhood itself. Although I do not prefer this hypothesis as a "charge," I feel that as an American citizen I still have a right both to think and to speak my thoughts even in the land of Sharon and Winters, and as much so respecting the theory of a brutal assault (especially when I have been its subject) as respecting any other apparent enormity. I give the matter simply as a suggestion which may explain to the proper authorities and to the people whom they should represent, a well ascertained but notwithstanding a darkly mysterious fact. The scheme of the assault may have been:

First—To terrify me by making me conscious of my own helplessness after making actual though not legal threats against my life.

Second—To imply that I could save my life only by writing or signing certain specific statements which if not subsequently explained would eternally have branded me as infamous and would have consigned my family to shame and want, and to the dreadful compassion and patronage of the rich.

Third—To blow my brains out the moment I had signed, thereby preventing me from making any subsequent explanation such as could remove the infamy.

Fourth—Philip Lynch to be compelled to testify that I was killed by John B. Winters in self-defence, for the conviction of Winters would bring him in as an accomplice. If that was the programme in John B. Winters' mind nothing saved my life but my persistent refusal to sign, when that refusal seemed clearly to me to be the choice of death.

The remarkable assertion made to me by Mr. Winters, that pity only spared my life on Wednesday evening last, almost compels me to believe that at first he could not have intended me to leave that room alive; and why I was allowed to, unless through mesmeric or some other invisible influence, I cannot divine. The more I reflect upon this matter, the more probable as true does this horrible interpretation become.

The narration of these things I might have spared both to Mr. Winters and to the public had he himself observed silence, but as he has both verbally spoken and suffered a thoroughly garbled statement of facts to appear in the Gold Hill News I feel it due to myself no less than to this community, and to the entire independent press of America and Great Britain, to give a true account of what even the Gold Hill News has pronounced a disgraceful affair, and which it deeply regrets because of some alleged telegraphic mistake in the account of it. [Who received the erroneous telegrams?]

Though he may not deem it prudent to take my life just now, the publication of this article I feel sure must compel Gen. Winters (with his peculiar views about his right to exemption from criticism by me) to resolve on my violent death, though it may take years to compass it. Notwithstanding I bear him no ill will; and if W. C. Ralston and William Sharon, and other members of the San Francisco mining and milling Ring feel that he above all other men in this State and California is the most fitting man to supervise and control Yellow Jacket matters, until I am able to vote more than half their stock I presume he will be retained to grace his present post.

Meantime, I cordially invite all who know of any sort of important villainy which only can be cured by exposure (and who would expose it if they felt sure they would not be betrayed under bullying threats), to communicate with the PEOPLE'S TRIBUNE; for until I am murdered, so long as I can raise the means to publish, I propose to continue my efforts at least to revive the liberties of the State, to curb oppression, and to benefit man's world and God's earth.

CONRAD WIEGAND.

[It does seem a pity that the Sheriff was shut out, since the good sense of a general of militia and of a prominent editor failed to teach them that the merited castigation of this weak, half-witted child was a thing that ought to have been done in the street, where the poor thing could have a chance to run. When a journalist maligns a citizen, or attacks his good name on hearsay evidence, he deserves to be thrashed for it, even if he is a "non-combatant" weakling; but a generous adversary would at least allow such a lamb the use of his legs at such a time.—M. T.]

Following The Equator
A Journey Around The World
By Mark Twain
Hartford, Connecticut

This book is affectionately inscribed to my young friend Harry Rogers with recognition of what he is, and apprehension of what he may become unless he form himself a little more closely upon the model of the author.

The Pudd'nhead Maxims: These wisdoms are for the luring of youth toward high moral altitudes. The author did not gather them from practice, but from observation. To be good is noble; but to show others how to be good is nobler and no trouble.

CHAPTER I.

A man may have no bad habits and have worse. — Pudd'nhead Wilson's New Calendar.

The starting point of this lecturing-trip around the world was Paris, where we had been living a year or two.

We sailed for America, and there made certain preparations. This took but little time. Two members of my family elected to go with me. Also a carbuncle. The dictionary says a carbuncle is a kind of jewel. Humor is out of place in a dictionary.

We started westward from New York in midsummer, with Major Pond to manage the platform-business as far as the Pacific. It was warm work, all the way, and the last fortnight of it was suffocatingly smoky, for in Oregon and Columbia the forest fires were raging. We had an added week of smoke at the seaboard, where we were obliged awhile for our ship. She had been getting herself ashore in the smoke, and she had to be docked and repaired.

We sailed at last; and so ended a snail-paced march across the continent, which had lasted forty days.

We moved westward about mid-afternoon over a rippled and summer sea; an enticing sea, a clean and cool sea, and apparently a welcome sea to all on board; it certainly was to the distressful dustings and smokings and swelterings of the past weeks. The voyage would furnish a three-weeks holiday, with hardly a break in it. We had the whole Pacific Ocean in front of us, with nothing to do but do nothing and be comfortable. The city of Victoria was twinkling dim in the deep heart of her smoke-cloud, and getting ready to vanish and now we closed the field-glasses and sat down on our steamer chairs contented and at peace. But they went to wreck and ruin under us and brought us to shame before all the passengers. They had been furnished by the largest furniture-dealing house in Victoria, and were worth a couple of farthings a dozen, though they had cost us the price of honest chairs. In the Pacific and Indian Oceans one must still bring his own deck-chair on board or go without, just as in the old forgotten Atlantic times—those Dark Ages of sea travel.

Ours was a reasonably comfortable ship, with the customary sea-going fare —plenty of good food furnished by the Deity and cooked by the devil. The discipline observable on board was perhaps as good as it is anywhere in the Pacific and Indian Oceans. The ship was not very well arranged for tropical service; but that is nothing, for this is the rule for ships which ply in the tropics. She had an over-supply of cockroaches, but this is also the rule with ships doing business in the summer

seas—at least such as have been long in service. Our young captain was a very handsome man, tall and perfectly formed, the very figure to show up a smart uniform's best effects. He was a man of the best intentions and was polite and courteous even to courtliness. There was a soft and finish about his manners which made whatever place he happened to be in seem for the moment a drawing room. He avoided the smoking room. He had no vices. He did not smoke or chew tobacco or take snuff; he did not swear, or use slang or rude, or coarse, or indelicate language, or make puns, or tell anecdotes, or laugh intemperately, or raise his voice above the moderate pitch enjoined by the canons of good form. When he gave an order, his manner modified it into a request. After dinner he and his officers joined the ladies and gentlemen in the ladies' saloon, and shared in the singing and piano playing, and helped turn the music. He had a sweet and sympathetic tenor voice, and used it with taste and effect the music he played whist there, always with the same partner and opponents, until the ladies' bedtime. The electric lights burned there as late as the ladies and their friends might desire; but they were not allowed to burn in the smoking-room after eleven. There were many laws on the ship's statute book of course; but so far as I could see, this and one other were the only ones that were rigidly enforced. The captain explained that he enforced this one because his own cabin adjoined the smoking-room, and the smell of tobacco smoke made him sick. I did not see how our smoke could reach him, for the smoking-room and his cabin were on the upper deck, targets for all the winds that blew; and besides there was no crack of communication between them, no opening of any sort in the solid intervening bulkhead. Still, to a delicate stomach even imaginary smoke can convey damage.

The captain, with his gentle nature, his polish, his sweetness, his moral and verbal purity, seemed pathetically out of place in his rude and autocratic vocation. It seemed another instance of the irony of fate.

He was going home under a cloud. The passengers knew about his trouble, and were sorry for him. Approaching Vancouver through a narrow and difficult passage densely befogged with smoke from the forest fires, he had had the ill-luck to lose his bearings and get his ship on the rocks. A matter like this would rank merely as an error with you and me; it ranks as a crime with the directors of steamship companies. The captain had been tried by the Admiralty Court at Vancouver, and its verdict had acquitted him of blame. But that was insufficient comfort. A sterner court would examine the case in Sydney— the Court of Directors, the lords of a company in whose ships the captain had served as mate a number of years. This was his first voyage as captain.

The officers of our ship were hearty and companionable young men, and they entered into the general amusements and helped the passengers pass the time. Voyages in the Pacific and Indian Oceans are but pleasure excursions for all hands. Our purser was a young Scotchman who was equipped with a grit that was remarkable. He was an invalid, and looked it, as far as his body was concerned, but illness could not subdue his spirit. He was full of life, and had a gay and capable tongue. To all appearances he was a sick man without being aware of it, for he did not talk about his ailments, and his bearing and conduct were those of a person in robust health; yet he was the prey, at intervals, of ghastly sieges of pain in his heart. These lasted many hours, and while the attack continued he could neither sit nor lie. In one instance he stood on his feet twenty-four hours fighting for his life with these sharp agonies, and yet was as full of life and cheer and activity the next day as if nothing had happened.

The brightest passenger in the ship, and the most interesting and felicitous talker, was a young Canadian who was not able to let the whisky bottle alone. He was of a rich and powerful family, and could have had a distinguished career and abundance of effective help toward it if he could have conquered his appetite for drink; but he could not do it, so his great equipment of talent was of no use to him. He had often taken the pledge to drink no more, and was a good sample of what that sort of unwisdom can do for a man—for a man with anything short of an iron will. The system is wrong in two ways: it does not strike at the root of the trouble, for one thing, and to make a pledge of any kind is to declare war against nature; for a pledge is a chain that is always clanking and reminding the wearer of it that he is not a free man.

I have said that the system does not strike at the root of the trouble, and I venture to repeat that. The root is not the drinking, but the desire to drink. These are very different things. The one merely requires will—and a great deal of it, both as to bulk and staying capacity—the other merely requires watchfulness—and for no long time. The desire of course precedes the act, and should have one's first attention; it can do but little good to refuse the act over and over again, always leaving the desire unmolested, unconquered; the desire will continue to assert itself, and will be almost sure to win in the long run. When the desire intrudes, it should be at once banished out of the mind. One should be on the watch for it all the time—otherwise it will get in. It must be taken in time and not allowed to get a lodgment. A desire constantly repulsed for a fortnight should die, then. That should cure the drinking habit. The system of refusing the mere act of drinking, and leaving the desire in full force, is unintelligent war tactics, it seems to me. I used to take pledges—and soon violate them. My will was not strong, and I could not help it. And then, to be tied in any way naturally irks an otherwise free person and makes him chafe in his bonds and want to get his liberty. But when I finally ceased from taking definite pledges, and merely resolved that I would kill an injurious desire, but leave myself free to resume the desire and the habit whenever I should choose to do so, I had no more trouble. In five days I drove out the desire to smoke and was not obliged to keep watch after that; and I never experienced any strong desire to smoke again. At the end of a year and a quarter of idleness I began to write a book, and presently found that the pen was strangely reluctant to go. I tried a smoke to see if that would help me out of the difficulty. It did. I smoked eight or ten cigars and as many pipes a day for five months; finished the book, and did not smoke again until a year had gone by and another book had to be begun.

I can quit any of my nineteen injurious habits at any time, and without discomfort or inconvenience. I think that the Dr. Tanners and those others who go forty days without eating do it by resolutely keeping out the desire to eat, in the beginning, and that after a few hours the desire is discouraged and comes no more.

Once I tried my scheme in a large medical way. I had been confined to my bed several days with lumbago. My case refused to improve. Finally the doctor said,—

"My remedies have no fair chance. Consider what they have to fight, besides the lumbago. You smoke extravagantly, don't you?"

"Yes."

"You take coffee immoderately?"

"Yes."

"And some tea?"

"Yes."

"You eat all kinds of things that are dissatisfied with each other's company?"

"Yes."

"You drink two hot Scotches every night?"

"Yes."

"Very well, there you see what I have to contend against. We can't make progress the way the matter stands. You must make a reduction in these things; you must cut down your consumption of them considerably for some days."

"I can't, doctor."

"Why can't you."

"I lack the will-power. I can cut them off entirely, but I can't merely moderate them."

He said that that would answer, and said he would come around in twenty-four hours and begin work again. He was taken ill himself and could not come; but I did not need him. I cut off all those things for two days and nights; in fact, I cut off all kinds of food, too, and all drinks except water, and at the end of the forty-eight hours the lumbago was discouraged and left me. I was a well man; so I gave thanks and took to those delicacies again.

It seemed a valuable medical course, and I recommended it to a lady. She had run down and down and down, and had at last reached a point where medicines no longer had any helpful effect upon her. I said I knew I could put her upon her feet in a week. It brightened her up, it filled her with hope, and she said she would do everything I told her to do. So I said she must stop swearing and drinking, and smoking and eating for four days, and then she would be all right again. And it would have happened just so, I know it; but she said she could not stop swearing, and smoking, and drinking, because she had never done those things. So there it was. She had neglected her habits, and hadn't any. Now that they would have come good, there were none in stock. She had nothing to fall back on. She was a sinking vessel, with no freight in her to throw over or lighten ship withal. Why, even one or two little bad habits could have saved her, but she was just a moral pauper. When she could have acquired them she was dissuaded by her parents, who were ignorant people though reared in the best society, and it was too late to begin now. It seemed such a pity; but there was no help for it. These things ought to be attended to while a person is young; otherwise, when age and disease come, there is nothing effectual to fight them with.

When I was a youth I used to take all kinds of pledges, and do my best to keep them, but I never could, because I didn't strike at the root of the habit—the desire; I generally broke down within the month. Once I tried limiting a habit. That worked tolerably well for a while. I pledged myself to smoke but one cigar a day. I kept the cigar waiting until bedtime, then I had a luxurious time with it. But desire persecuted me every day and all day long; so, within the week I found myself hunting for larger cigars than I had been used to smoke; then larger ones still, and still larger ones. Within the fortnight I was getting cigars made for me—on a yet larger pattern. They still grew and grew in size. Within the month my cigar had grown to such proportions that I could have used it as a crutch. It now seemed to me that a one-cigar limit was no real protection to a person, so I knocked my pledge on the head and resumed my liberty.

To go back to that young Canadian. He was a "remittance man," the first one I had ever seen or heard of. Passengers explained the term to me. They said that dissipated ne'er-do-wells belonging to important families in England and Canada were not cast off by their people while there was any hope of reforming them, but when that last hope perished at last, the ne'er-do-well was sent abroad to get him out of the way. He was shipped off with just enough money in his pocket—no, in the purser's pocket—for the needs of the voyage—and when he reached his destined port he would find a remittance awaiting him there. Not a large one, but just enough to keep him a month. A similar remittance would come monthly thereafter. It was the remittance-man's custom to pay his month's board and lodging straightway—a duty which his landlord did not allow him to forget—then spree away the rest of his money in a single night, then brood and mope and grieve in idleness till the next remittance came. It is a pathetic life.

We had other remittance-men on board, it was said. At least they said they were R. M.'s. There were two. But they did not resemble the Canadian; they lacked his tidiness, and his brains, and his gentlemanly ways, and his resolute spirit, and his humanities and generosities. One of them was a lad of nineteen or twenty, and he was a good deal of a ruin, as to clothes, and morals, and general aspect. He said he was a scion of a ducal house in England, and had been shipped to Canada for the house's relief, that he had fallen into trouble there, and was now being shipped to Australia. He said he had no title. Beyond this remark he was economical of the truth. The first thing he did in Australia was to get into the lockup, and the next thing he did was to proclaim himself an earl in the police court in the morning and fail to prove it.

CHAPTER II.

When in doubt, tell the truth. —Pudd'nhead Wilson's New Calendar.

About four days out from Victoria we plunged into hot weather, and all the male passengers put on white linen clothes. One or two days later we crossed the 25th parallel of north latitude, and then, by order, the officers of the ship laid away their blue uniforms and came out in white linen ones. All the ladies were in white by this time. This prevalence of snowy costumes gave the promenade deck an invitingly cool, and cheerful and picnicky aspect.

From my diary:

There are several sorts of ills in the world from which a person can never escape altogether, let him journey as far as he will. One escapes from one breed of an ill only to encounter another breed of it. We have come far from the snake liar and the fish liar, and there was rest and peace in the thought; but now we have reached the realm of the boomerang liar, and sorrow is with us once more. The first officer has seen a man try to escape from his enemy by getting behind a tree; but the enemy

sent his boomerang sailing into the sky far above and beyond the tree; then it turned, descended, and killed the man. The Australian passenger has seen this thing done to two men, behind two trees—and by the one arrow. This being received with a large silence that suggested doubt, he buttressed it with the statement that his brother once saw the boomerang kill a bird away off a hundred yards and bring it to the thrower. But these are ills which must be borne. There is no other way.

The talk passed from the boomerang to dreams—usually a fruitful subject, afloat or ashore—but this time the output was poor. Then it passed to instances of extraordinary memory—with better results. Blind Tom, the negro pianist, was spoken of, and it was said that he could accurately play any piece of music, howsoever long and difficult, after hearing it once; and that six months later he could accurately play it again, without having touched it in the interval. One of the most striking of the stories told was furnished by a gentleman who had served on the staff of the Viceroy of India. He read the details from his note-book, and explained that he had written them down, right after the consummation of the incident which they described, because he thought that if he did not put them down in black and white he might presently come to think he had dreamed them or invented them.

The Viceroy was making a progress, and among the shows offered by the Maharajah of Mysore for his entertainment was a memory-exhibition. The Viceroy and thirty gentlemen of his suite sat in a row, and the memory-expert, a high-caste Brahmin, was brought in and seated on the floor in front of them. He said he knew but two languages, the English and his own, but would not exclude any foreign tongue from the tests to be applied to his memory. Then he laid before the assemblage his program —a sufficiently extraordinary one. He proposed that one gentleman should give him one word of a foreign sentence, and tell him its place in the sentence. He was furnished with the French word 'est', and was told it was second in a sentence of three words. The next, gentleman gave him the German word 'verloren' and said it was the third in a sentence of four words. He asked the next gentleman for one detail in a sum in addition; another for one detail in a sum of subtraction; others for single details in mathematical problems of various kinds; he got them. Intermediates gave him single words from sentences in Greek, Latin, Spanish, Portuguese, Italian, and other languages, and told him their places in the sentences. When at last everybody had furnished him a single rag from a foreign sentence or a figure from a problem, he went over the ground again, and got a second word and a second figure and was told their places in the sentences and the sums; and so on and so on. He went over the ground again and again until he had collected all the parts of the sums and all the parts of the sentences—and all in disorder, of course, not in their proper rotation. This had occupied two hours.

The Brahmin now sat silent and thinking, a while, then began and repeated all the sentences, placing the words in their proper order, and untangled the disordered arithmetical problems and gave accurate answers to them all.

In the beginning he had asked the company to throw almonds at him during the two hours, he to remember how many each gentleman had thrown; but none were thrown, for the Viceroy said that the test would be a sufficiently severe strain without adding that burden to it.

General Grant had a fine memory for all kinds of things, including even names and faces, and I could have furnished an instance of it if I had thought of it. The first time I ever saw him was early in his first term as President. I had just arrived in Washington from the Pacific coast, a stranger and wholly unknown to the public, and was passing the White House one morning when I met a friend, a Senator from Nevada. He asked me if I would like to see the President. I said I should be very glad; so we entered. I supposed that the President would be in the midst of a crowd, and that I could look at him in peace and security from a distance, as another stray cat might look at another king. But it was in the morning, and the Senator was using a privilege of his office which I had not heard of—the privilege of intruding upon the Chief Magistrate's working hours. Before I knew it, the Senator and I were in the presence, and there was none there but we three. General Grant got slowly up from his table, put his pen down, and stood before me with the iron expression of a man who had not smiled for seven years, and was not intending to smile for another seven. He looked me steadily in the eyes—mine lost confidence and fell. I had never confronted a great man before, and was in a miserable state of funk and inefficiency. The Senator said:—

"Mr. President, may I have the privilege of introducing Mr. Clemens?"

The President gave my hand an unsympathetic wag and dropped it. He did not say a word but just stood. In my trouble I could not think of anything to say, I merely wanted to resign. There was an awkward pause, a dreary pause, a horrible pause. Then I thought of something, and looked up into that unyielding face, and said timidly:—

"Mr. President, I—I am embarrassed. Are you?"

His face broke—just a little—a wee glimmer, the momentary flicker of a summer-lightning smile, seven years ahead of time—and I was out and gone as soon as it was.

Ten years passed away before I saw him the second time. Meantime I was become better known; and was one of the people appointed to respond to toasts at the banquet given to General Grant in Chicago—by the Army of the Tennessee when he came back from his tour around the world. I arrived late at night and got up late in the morning. All the corridors of the hotel were crowded with people waiting to get a glimpse of General Grant when he should pass to the place whence he was to review the great procession. I worked my way by the suite of packed drawing-rooms, and at the corner of the house I found a window open where there was a roomy platform decorated with flags, and carpeted. I stepped out on it, and saw below me millions of people blocking all the streets, and other millions caked together in all the windows and on all the house-tops around. These masses took me for General Grant, and broke into volcanic explosions and cheers; but it was a good place to see the procession, and I stayed. Presently I heard the distant blare of military music, and far up the street I saw the procession come in sight, cleaving its way through the huzzaing multitudes, with Sheridan, the most martial figure of the War, riding at its head in the dress uniform of a Lieutenant-General.

And now General Grant, arm-in-arm with Major Carter Harrison, stepped out on the platform, followed two and two by the badged and uniformed reception committee. General Grant was looking exactly as he had looked upon that trying occasion of ten years before—all iron and bronze self-possession. Mr. Harrison came over and led me to the General and formally introduced me. Before I could put together the

proper remark, General Grant said—

"Mr. Clemens, I am not embarrassed. Are you?"—and that little seven-year smile twinkled across his face again.

Seventeen years have gone by since then, and to-day, in New York, the streets are a crush of people who are there to honor the remains of the great soldier as they pass to their final resting-place under the monument; and the air is heavy with dirges and the boom of artillery, and all the millions of America are thinking of the man who restored the Union and the flag, and gave to democratic government a new lease of life, and, as we may hope and do believe, a permanent place among the beneficent institutions of men.

We had one game in the ship which was a good time-passer—at least it was at night in the smoking-room when the men were getting freshened up from the day's monotonies and dullnesses. It was the completing of non-complete stories. That is to say, a man would tell all of a story except the finish, then the others would try to supply the ending out of their own invention. When every one who wanted a chance had had it, the man who had introduced the story would give it its original ending—then you could take your choice. Sometimes the new endings turned out to be better than the old one. But the story which called out the most persistent and determined and ambitious effort was one which had no ending, and so there was nothing to compare the new-made endings with. The man who told it said he could furnish the particulars up to a certain point only, because that was as much of the tale as he knew. He had read it in a volume of `sketches twenty-five years ago, and was interrupted before the end was reached. He would give any one fifty dollars who would finish the story to the satisfaction of a jury to be appointed by ourselves. We appointed a jury and wrestled with the tale. We invented plenty of endings, but the jury voted them all down. The jury was right. It was a tale which the author of it may possibly have completed satisfactorily, and if he really had that good fortune I would like to know what the ending was. Any ordinary man will find that the story's strength is in its middle, and that there is apparently no way to transfer it to the close, where of course it ought to be. In substance the storiette was as follows:

John Brown, aged thirty-one, good, gentle, bashful, timid, lived in a quiet village in Missouri. He was superintendent of the Presbyterian Sunday-school. It was but a humble distinction; still, it was his only official one, and he was modestly proud of it and was devoted to its work and its interests. The extreme kindliness of his nature was recognized by all; in fact, people said that he was made entirely out of good impulses and bashfulness; that he could always be counted upon for help when it was needed, and for bashfulness both when it was needed and when it wasn't.

Mary Taylor, twenty-three, modest, sweet, winning, and in character and person beautiful, was all in all to him. And he was very nearly all in all to her. She was wavering, his hopes were high. Her mother had been in opposition from the first. But she was wavering, too; he could see it. She was being touched by his warm interest in her two charity-proteges and by his contributions toward their support. These were two forlorn and aged sisters who lived in a log hut in a lonely place up a cross road four miles from Mrs. Taylor's farm. One of the sisters was crazy, and sometimes a little violent, but not often.

At last the time seemed ripe for a final advance, and Brown gathered his courage together and resolved to make it. He would take along a contribution of double the usual size, and win the mother over; with her opposition annulled, the rest of the conquest would be sure and prompt.

He took to the road in the middle of a placid Sunday afternoon in the soft Missourian summer, and he was equipped properly for his mission. He was clothed all in white linen, with a blue ribbon for a necktie, and he had on dressy tight boots. His horse and buggy were the finest that the livery stable could furnish. The lap robe was of white linen, it was new, and it had a hand-worked border that could not be rivaled in that region for beauty and elaboration.

When he was four miles out on the lonely road and was walking his horse over a wooden bridge, his straw hat blew off and fell in the creek, and floated down and lodged against a bar. He did not quite know what to do. He must have the hat, that was manifest; but how was he to get it?

Then he had an idea. The roads were empty, nobody was stirring. Yes, he would risk it. He led the horse to the roadside and set it to cropping the grass; then he undressed and put his clothes in the buggy, petted the horse a moment to secure its compassion and its loyalty, then hurried to the stream. He swam out and soon had the hat. When he got to the top of the bank the horse was gone!

His legs almost gave way under him. The horse was walking leisurely along the road. Brown trotted after it, saying, "Whoa, whoa, there's a good fellow;" but whenever he got near enough to chance a jump for the buggy, the horse quickened its pace a little and defeated him. And so this went on, the naked man perishing with anxiety, and expecting every moment to see people come in sight. He tagged on and on, imploring the horse, beseeching the horse, till he had left a mile behind him, and was closing up on the Taylor premises; then at last he was successful, and got into the buggy. He flung on his shirt, his necktie, and his coat; then reached for—but he was too late; he sat suddenly down and pulled up the lap-robe, for he saw some one coming out of the gate—a woman; he thought. He wheeled the horse to the left, and struck briskly up the cross-road. It was perfectly straight, and exposed on both sides; but there were woods and a sharp turn three miles ahead, and he was very grateful when he got there. As he passed around the turn he slowed down to a walk, and reached for his tr— too late again.

He had come upon Mrs. Enderby, Mrs. Glossop, Mrs. Taylor, and Mary. They were on foot, and seemed tired and excited. They came at once to the buggy and shook hands, and all spoke at once, and said eagerly and earnestly, how glad they were that he was come, and how fortunate it was. And Mrs. Enderby said, impressively:

"It looks like an accident, his coming at such a time; but let no one profane it with such a name; he was sent—sent from on high."

They were all moved, and Mrs. Glossop said in an awed voice:

"Sarah Enderby, you never said a truer word in your life. This is no accident, it is a special Providence. He was sent. He is an angel—an angel as truly as ever angel was—an angel of deliverance. I say angel, Sarah Enderby, and will have no other word. Don't let any one ever say to me again, that there's no such thing as special Providences; for if this isn't one, let them account for it that can."

"I know it's so," said Mrs. Taylor, fervently. "John Brown, I could worship you; I could go down on my knees to you. Didn't something tell you?—didn't you feel that you were sent? I could kiss the hem of your laprobe."

He was not able to speak; he was helpless with shame and fright. Mrs. Taylor went on:

"Why, just look at it all around, Julia Glossop. Any person can see the hand of Providence in it. Here at noon what do we see? We see the smoke rising. I speak up and say, 'That's the Old People's cabin afire.' Didn't I, Julia Glossop?"

"The very words you said, Nancy Taylor. I was as close to you as I am now, and I heard them. You may have said hut instead of cabin, but in substance it's the same. And you were looking pale, too."

"Pale? I was that pale that if—why, you just compare it with this laprobe. Then the next thing I said was, 'Mary Taylor, tell the hired man to rig up the team-we'll go to the rescue.' And she said, 'Mother, don't you know you told him he could drive to see his people, and stay over Sunday?' And it was just so. I declare for it, I had forgotten it. 'Then,' said I, 'we'll go afoot.' And go we did. And found Sarah Enderby on the road."

"And we all went together," said Mrs. Enderby. "And found the cabin set fire to and burnt down by the crazy one, and the poor old things so old and feeble that they couldn't go afoot. And we got them to a shady place and made them as comfortable as we could, and began to wonder which way to turn to find some way to get them conveyed to Nancy Taylor's house. And I spoke up and said—now what did I say? Didn't I say, 'Providence will provide'?"

"Why sure as you live, so you did! I had forgotten it."

"So had I," said Mrs. Glossop and Mrs. Taylor; "but you certainly said it. Now wasn't that remarkable?"

"Yes, I said it. And then we went to Mr. Moseley's, two miles, and all of them were gone to the camp meeting over on Stony Fork; and then we came all the way back, two miles, and then here, another mile—and Providence has provided. You see it yourselves"

They gazed at each other awe-struck, and lifted their hands and said in unison:

"It's per-fectly wonderful."

"And then," said Mrs. Glossop, "what do you think we had better do let Mr. Brown drive the Old People to Nancy Taylor's one at a time, or put both of them in the buggy, and him lead the horse?"

Brown gasped.

"Now, then, that's a question," said Mrs. Enderby. "You see, we are all tired out, and any way we fix it it's going to be difficult. For if Mr. Brown takes both of them, at least one of us must, go back to help him, for he can't load them into the buggy by himself, and they so helpless."

"That is so," said Mrs. Taylor. "It doesn't look-oh, how would this do? —one of us drive there with Mr. Brown, and the rest of you go along to my house and get things ready. I'll go with him. He and I together can lift one of the Old People into the buggy; then drive her to my house and—

"But who will take care of the other one?" said Mrs. Enderby. "We musn't leave her there in the woods alone, you know—especially the crazy one. There and back is eight miles, you see."

They had all been sitting on the grass beside the buggy for a while, now, trying to rest their weary bodies. They fell silent a moment or two, and struggled in thought over the baffling situation; then Mrs. Enderby brightened and said:

"I think I've got the idea, now. You see, we can't walk any more. Think what we've done: four miles there, two to Moseley's, is six, then back to here—nine miles since noon, and not a bite to eat; I declare I don't see how we've done it; and as for me, I am just famishing. Now, somebody's got to go back, to help Mr. Brown—there's no getting mound that; but whoever goes has got to ride, not walk. So my idea is this: one of us to ride back with Mr. Brown, then ride to Nancy Taylor's house with one of the Old People, leaving Mr. Brown to keep the other old one company, you all to go now to Nancy's and rest and wait; then one of you drive back and get the other one and drive her to Nancy's, and Mr. Brown walk."

"Splendid!" they all cried. "Oh, that will do—that will answer perfectly." And they all said that Mrs. Enderby had the best head for planning, in the company; and they said that they wondered that they hadn't thought of this simple plan themselves. They hadn't meant to take back the compliment, good simple souls, and didn't know they had done it. After a consultation it was decided that Mrs. Enderby should drive back with Brown, she being entitled to the distinction because she had invented the plan. Everything now being satisfactorily arranged and settled, the ladies rose, relieved and happy, and brushed down their gowns, and three of them started homeward; Mrs. Enderby set her foot on the buggy-step and was about to climb in, when Brown found a remnant of his voice and gasped out—

"Please Mrs. Enderby, call them back—I am very weak; I can't walk, I can't, indeed."

"Why, dear Mr. Brown! You do look pale; I am ashamed of myself that I didn't notice it sooner. Come back—all of you! Mr. Brown is not well. Is there anything I can do for you, Mr. Brown?—I'm real sorry. Are you in pain?"

"No, madam, only weak; I am not sick, but only just weak—lately; not long, but just lately."

The others came back, and poured out their sympathies and commiserations, and were full of self-reproaches for not having noticed how pale he was.

And they at once struck out a new plan, and soon agreed that it was by far the best of all. They would all go to Nancy Taylor's house and see to Brown's needs first. He could lie on the sofa in the parlor, and while Mrs. Taylor and Mary took care of him the other two ladies would take the buggy and go and get one of the Old People, and leave one of themselves with the other one, and—

By this time, without any solicitation, they were at the horse's head and were beginning to turn him around. The danger was imminent, but Brown found his voice again and saved himself. He said—

"But ladies, you are overlooking something which makes the plan impracticable. You see, if you bring one of them home, and one remains behind with the other, there will be three persons there when one of you comes back for that other, for some one must drive the buggy back, and three can't come home in it."

They all exclaimed, "Why, sure-ly, that is so!" and they were, all perplexed again.

"Dear, dear, what can we do?" said Mrs. Glossop; "it is the most mixed-up thing that ever was. The fox and the goose and the corn and things— Oh, dear, they are nothing to it."

They sat wearily down once more, to further torture their tormented heads for a plan that would work. Presently Mary offered a plan; it was her first effort. She said:

"I am young and strong, and am refreshed, now. Take Mr. Brown to our house, and give him help—you see how plainly he needs it. I will go back and take care of the Old People; I can be there in twenty minutes. You can go on and do what you first started to do—wait on the main road at our house until somebody comes along with a wagon; then send and bring away the three of us. You won't have to wait long; the farmers will soon be coming back from town, now. I will keep old Polly patient and cheered up—the crazy one doesn't need it."

This plan was discussed and accepted; it seemed the best that could be done, in the circumstances, and the Old People must be getting discouraged by this time.

Brown felt relieved, and was deeply thankful. Let him once get to the main road and he would find a way to escape.

Then Mrs. Taylor said:

"The evening chill will be coming on, pretty soon, and those poor old burnt-out things will need some kind of covering. Take the lap-robe with you, dear."

"Very well, Mother, I will."

She stepped to the buggy and put out her hand to take it—

That was the end of the tale. The passenger who told it said that when he read the story twenty-five years ago in a train he was interrupted at that point—the train jumped off a bridge.

At first we thought we could finish the story quite easily, and we set to work with confidence; but it soon began to appear that it was not a simple thing, but difficult and baffling. This was on account of Brown's character—great generosity and kindliness, but complicated with unusual shyness and diffidence, particularly in the presence of ladies. There was his love for Mary, in a hopeful state but not yet secure—just in a condition, indeed, where its affair must be handled with great tact, and no mistakes made, no offense given. And there was the mother wavering, half willing—by adroit and flawless diplomacy to be won over, now, or perhaps never at all. Also, there was the helpless Old People yonder in the woods waiting—their fate and Brown's happiness to be determined by what Brown should do within the next two seconds. Mary was reaching for the lap-robe; Brown must decide—there was no time to be lost.

Of course none but a happy ending of the story would be

accepted by the jury; the finish must find Brown in high credit with the ladies, his behavior without blemish, his modesty unwounded, his character for self sacrifice maintained, the Old People rescued through him, their benefactor, all the party proud of him, happy in him, his praises on all their tongues.

We tried to arrange this, but it was beset with persistent and irreconcilable difficulties. We saw that Brown's shyness would not allow him to give up the lap-robe. This would offend Mary and her mother; and it would surprise the other ladies, partly because this stinginess toward the suffering Old People would be out of character with Brown, and partly because he was a special Providence and could not properly act so. If asked to explain his conduct, his shyness would not allow him to tell the truth, and lack of invention and practice would find him incapable of contriving a lie that would wash. We worked at the troublesome problem until three in the morning.

Meantime Mary was still reaching for the lap-robe. We gave it up, and decided to let her continue to reach. It is the reader's privilege to determine for himself how the thing came out.

CHAPTER III.

It is more trouble to make a maxim than it is to do right. — Pudd'nhead Wilson's New Calendar.

On the seventh day out we saw a dim vast bulk standing up out of the wastes of the Pacific and knew that that spectral promontory was Diamond Head, a piece of this world which I had not seen before for twenty-nine years. So we were nearing Honolulu, the capital city of the Sandwich Islands—those islands which to me were Paradise; a Paradise which I had been longing all those years to see again. Not any other thing in the world could have stirred me as the sight of that great rock did.

In the night we anchored a mile from shore. Through my port I could see the twinkling lights of Honolulu and the dark bulk of the mountain-range that stretched away right and left. I could not make out the beautiful Nuuana valley, but I knew where it lay, and remembered how it used to look in the old times. We used to ride up it on horseback in those days —we young people—and branch off and gather bones in a sandy region where one of the first Kamehameha's battles was fought. He was a remarkable man, for a king; and he was also a remarkable man for a savage. He was a mere kinglet and of little or no consequence at the time of Captain Cook's arrival in 1788; but about four years afterward he conceived the idea of enlarging his sphere of influence. That is a courteous modern phrase which means robbing your neighbor—for your neighbor's benefit; and the great theater of its benevolences is Africa. Kamehameha went to war, and in the course of ten years he whipped out all the other kings and made himself master of every one of the nine or ten islands that form the group. But he did more than that. He bought ships, freighted them with sandal wood and other native products, and sent them as far as South America and China; he sold to his savages the foreign stuffs and tools and utensils which came back in these ships, and started the march of civilization. It is doubtful if the match to this extraordinary thing is to be found in the history of any other savage. Savages are eager to learn from the white man any new way to kill each other, but it is not their habit to seize with avidity and apply with energy the larger and nobler ideas which he offers them. The details of Kamehameha's history show that he was always hospitably ready to examine the white man's ideas, and that he exercised a tidy discrimination in making his selections from the

samples placed on view.

A shrewder discrimination than was exhibited by his son and successor, Liholiho, I think. Liholiho could have qualified as a reformer, perhaps, but as a king he was a mistake. A mistake because he tried to be both king and reformer. This is mixing fire and gunpowder together. A king has no proper business with reforming. His best policy is to keep things as they are; and if he can't do that, he ought to try to make them worse than they are. This is not guesswork; I have thought over this matter a good deal, so that if I should ever have a chance to become a king I would know how to conduct the business in the best way.

When Liholiho succeeded his father he found himself possessed of an equipment of royal tools and safeguards which a wiser king would have known how to husband, and judiciously employ, and make profitable. The entire country was under the one scepter, and his was that scepter. There was an Established Church, and he was the head of it. There was a Standing Army, and he was the head of that; an Army of 114 privates under command of 27 Generals and a Field Marshal. There was a proud and ancient Hereditary Nobility. There was still one other asset. This was the tabu—an agent endowed with a mysterious and stupendous power, an agent not found among the properties of any European monarch, a tool of inestimable value in the business. Liholiho was headmaster of the tabu. The tabu was the most ingenious and effective of all the inventions that has ever been devised for keeping a people's privileges satisfactorily restricted.

It required the sexes to live in separate houses. It did not allow people to eat in either house; they must eat in another place. It did not allow a man's woman-folk to enter his house. It did not allow the sexes to eat together; the men must eat first, and the women must wait on them. Then the women could eat what was left—if anything was left—and wait on themselves. I mean, if anything of a coarse or unpalatable sort was left, the women could have it. But not the good things, the fine things, the choice things, such as pork, poultry, bananas, cocoanuts, the choicer varieties of fish, and so on. By the tabu, all these were sacred to the men; the women spent their lives longing for them and wondering what they might taste like; and they died without finding out.

These rules, as you see, were quite simple and clear. It was easy to remember them; and useful. For the penalty for infringing any rule in the whole list was death. Those women easily learned to put up with shark and taro and dog for a diet when the other things were so expensive.

It was death for any one to walk upon tabu'd ground; or defile a tabu'd thing with his touch; or fail in due servility to a chief; or step upon the king's shadow. The nobles and the King and the priests were always suspending little rags here and there and yonder, to give notice to the people that the decorated spot or thing was tabu, and death lurking near. The struggle for life was difficult and chancy in the islands in those days.

Thus advantageously was the new king situated. Will it be believed that the first thing he did was to destroy his Established Church, root and branch? He did indeed do that. To state the case figuratively, he was a prosperous sailor who burnt his ship and took to a raft. This Church was a horrid thing. It heavily oppressed the people; it kept them always trembling in the gloom of mysterious threatenings; it slaughtered them in sacrifice before its grotesque idols of wood and stone; it cowed them, it terrorized them, it made them slaves to its priests, and through the priests to the king. It was the best friend a king could have, and the most dependable. To a professional reformer who should annihilate so frightful and so devastating a power as this Church, reverence and praise would be due; but to a king who should do it, could properly be due nothing but reproach; reproach softened by sorrow; sorrow for his unfitness for his position.

He destroyed his Established Church, and his kingdom is a republic today, in consequence of that act.

When he destroyed the Church and burned the idols he did a mighty thing for civilization and for his people's weal—but it was not "business." It was unkingly, it was inartistic. It made trouble for his line. The American missionaries arrived while the burned idols were still smoking. They found the nation without a religion, and they repaired the defect. They offered their own religion and it was gladly received. But it was no support to arbitrary kingship, and so the kingly power began to weaken from that day. Forty-seven years later, when I was in the islands, Kainehameha V. was trying to repair Liholiho's blunder, and not succeeding. He had set up an Established Church and made himself the head of it. But it was only a pinchbeck thing, an imitation, a bauble, an empty show. It had no power, no value for a king. It could not harry or burn or slay, it in no way resembled the admirable machine which Liholiho destroyed. It was an Established Church without an Establishment; all the people were Dissenters.

Long before that, the kingship had itself become but a name, a show. At an early day the missionaries had turned it into something very much like a republic; and here lately the business whites have turned it into something exactly like it.

In Captain Cook's time (1778), the native population of the islands was estimated at 400,000; in 1836 at something short of 200,000, in 1866 at 50,000; it is to-day, per census, 25,000. All intelligent people praise Kamehameha I. and Liholiho for conferring upon their people the great boon of civilization. I would do it myself, but my intelligence is out of repair, now, from over-work.

When I was in the islands nearly a generation ago, I was acquainted with a young American couple who had among their belongings an attractive little son of the age of seven—attractive but not practicably companionable with me, because he knew no English. He had played from his birth with the little Kanakas on his father's plantation, and had preferred their language and would learn no other. The family removed to America a month after I arrived in the islands, and straightway the boy began to lose his Kanaka and pick up English. By the time he was twelve he hadn't a word of Kanaka left; the language had wholly departed from his tongue and from his comprehension. Nine years later, when he was twenty-one, I came upon the family in one of the lake towns of New York, and the mother told me about an adventure which her son had been having. By trade he was now a professional diver. A passenger boat had been caught in a storm on the lake, and had gone down, carrying her people with her. A few days later the young diver descended, with his armor on, and entered the berth-saloon of the boat, and stood at the foot of the companionway, with his hand on the rail, peering through the dim water. Presently something touched him on the shoulder, and he turned and found a dead man swaying and bobbing about him and seemingly inspecting him inquiringly. He was paralyzed with fright. His entry had disturbed the water, and now he discerned a number of dim corpses making for him and wagging their heads and swaying their bodies like sleepy people trying to dance. His senses forsook him, and in that condition he was drawn to the surface. He was put to bed at home, and was soon very ill. During some days he had seasons of delirium which lasted several hours at a time; and while they lasted he talked Kanaka incessantly and glibly; and Kanaka only. He was still very ill, and he talked to me in that tongue; but I did not understand it, of course. The doctor-books tell us that cases like this are not uncommon. Then the doctors ought to study the cases and find out how to multiply them. Many languages and things get mislaid in a person's head, and stay mislaid for lack of this remedy.

Many memories of my former visit to the islands came up in my mind while we lay at anchor in front of Honolulu that night. And pictures—pictures pictures—an enchanting procession of them! I was impatient for the morning to come.

When it came it brought disappointment, of course. Cholera had broken out in the town, and we were not allowed to have any communication with the shore. Thus suddenly did my dream of twenty-nine years go to ruin. Messages came from friends, but the friends themselves I was not to have any sight of. My lecture-hall was ready, but I was not to see that, either.

Several of our passengers belonged in Honolulu, and these were sent ashore; but nobody could go ashore and return. There were people on shore who were booked to go with us to Australia, but we could not receive them; to do it would cost us a quarantine-term in Sydney. They could have escaped the day before, by ship to San Francisco; but the bars had been put up, now, and they might have to wait weeks before any ship could venture to give them a passage any whither. And there were hardships for others. An elderly lady and her son, recreation-seekers from Massachusetts, had wandered westward, further and further from home, always intending to take the return track, but always concluding to go still a little further; and now here they were at anchor before Honolulu positively their last westward-bound indulgence—they had made up their minds to that—but where is the use in making up your mind in this world? It is usually a waste of time to do it. These two would have to stay with us as far as Australia. Then they could go on around the world, or go back the way they had come; the distance and the accommodations and outlay of time would be just the same, whichever of the two routes they might elect to take. Think of it: a projected excursion of five hundred miles gradually enlarged, without any elaborate degree of intention, to a possible twenty-four thousand. However, they were used to extensions by this time, and did not mind this new one much.

And we had with us a lawyer from Victoria, who had been sent out by the Government on an international matter, and he had brought his wife with him and left the children at home with the servants and now what was to be done? Go ashore amongst the cholera and take the risks? Most certainly not. They decided to go on, to the Fiji islands, wait there a fortnight for the next ship, and then sail for home. They couldn't foresee that they wouldn't see a homeward-bound ship again for six weeks, and that no word could come to them from the children, and no word go from them to the children in all that time. It is easy to make plans in this world; even a cat can do it; and when one is out in those remote oceans it is noticeable that a cat's plans and a man's are worth about the same. There is much the same shrinkage in both, in the matter of values.

There was nothing for us to do but sit about the decks in the shade of the awnings and look at the distant shore. We lay in luminous blue water; shoreward the water was green-green and brilliant; at the shore itself it broke in a long white ruffle, and with no crash, no sound that we could hear. The town was buried under a mat of foliage that looked like a cushion of moss. The silky mountains were clothed in soft, rich splendors of melting color, and some of the cliffs were veiled in slanting mists. I recognized it all. It was just as I had seen it long before, with nothing of its beauty lost, nothing of its charm wanting.

A change had come, but that was political, and not visible from the ship. The monarchy of my day was gone, and a republic was sitting in its seat. It was not a material change. The old imitation pomps, the fuss and feathers, have departed, and the royal trademark—that is about all that one could miss, I suppose. That imitation monarchy, was grotesque enough, in my time; if it had held on another thirty years it would have been a monarchy without subjects of the king's race.

We had a sunset of a very fine sort. The vast plain of the sea was marked off in bands of sharply-contrasted colors: great stretches of dark blue, others of purple, others of polished bronze; the billowy mountains showed all sorts of dainty browns and greens, blues and purples and blacks, and the rounded velvety backs of certain of them made one want to stroke them, as one would the sleek back of a cat. The long, sloping promontory projecting into the sea at the west turned dim and leaden and spectral, then became suffused with pink—dissolved itself in a pink dream, so to speak, it seemed so airy and unreal. Presently the cloud-rack was flooded with fiery splendors, and these were copied on the surface of the sea, and it made one drunk with delight to look upon it.

From talks with certain of our passengers whose home was Honolulu, and from a sketch by Mrs. Mary H. Krout, I was able to perceive what the Honolulu of to-day is, as compared with the Honolulu of my time. In my time it was a beautiful little town, made up of snow-white wooden cottages deliciously smothered in tropical vines and flowers and trees and shrubs; and its coral roads and streets were hard and smooth, and as white as the houses. The outside aspects of the place suggested the presence of a modest and comfortable prosperity—a general prosperity —perhaps one might strengthen the term and say universal. There were no fine houses, no fine furniture. There were no decorations. Tallow candles furnished the light for the bedrooms, a whale-oil lamp furnished it for the parlor. Native matting served as carpeting. In the parlor one would find two or three lithographs on the walls—portraits as a rule: Kamehameha IV., Louis Kossuth, Jenny Lind; and may be an engraving or two: Rebecca at the Well, Moses smiting the rock, Joseph's servants finding the cup in Benjamin's sack. There would be a center table, with books of a tranquil sort on it: The Whole Duty of Man, Baxter's Saints' Rest, Fox's Martyrs, Tupper's Proverbial Philosophy, bound copies of The Missionary Herald and of Father Damon's Seaman's Friend. A melodeon; a music stand, with 'Willie, We have Missed You', 'Star of the Evening', 'Roll on Silver Moon', 'Are We Most There', 'I Would not Live Alway', and other songs of love and sentiment, together with an assortment of hymns. A what-not with semi-globular glass paperweights, enclosing miniature pictures of ships, New England rural snowstorms, and the like; sea-shells with Bible texts carved on them in cameo style; native curios; whale's tooth with full-rigged ship carved on it. There was nothing reminiscent of foreign parts, for nobody had been abroad. Trips were made to San Francisco, but that could not be called going abroad. Comprehensively speaking, nobody traveled.

But Honolulu has grown wealthy since then, and of course wealth has introduced changes; some of the old simplicities have disappeared. Here is a modern house, as pictured by Mrs. Krout:

"Almost every house is surrounded by extensive lawns and gardens enclosed by walls of volcanic stone or by thick hedges of the brilliant hibiscus.

"The houses are most tastefully and comfortably furnished; the floors are either of hard wood covered with rugs or with fine Indian matting, while there is a preference, as in most warm countries, for rattan or bamboo furniture; there are the usual accessories of bric-a-brac, pictures, books, and curios from all parts of the world, for these island dwellers are indefatigable travelers.

"Nearly every house has what is called a lanai. It is a large apartment, roofed, floored, open on three sides, with a door or a draped archway opening into the drawing-room. Frequently the roof is formed by the thick interlacing boughs of the hou tree, impervious to the sun and even to the rain, except in violent storms. Vines are trained about the sides—the stephanotis or some one of the countless fragrant and blossoming trailers which abound in the islands. There are also curtains of matting that may be drawn to exclude the sun or rain. The floor is bare for coolness, or partially covered with rugs, and the lanai is prettily furnished with comfortable chairs, sofas, and tables loaded with flowers, or wonderful ferns in pots.

"The lanai is the favorite reception room, and here at any social function the musical program is given and cakes and ices are served; here morning callers are received, or gay riding parties, the ladies in pretty divided skirts, worn for convenience in riding astride, —the universal mode adopted by Europeans and Americans, as well as by the natives.

"The comfort and luxury of such an apartment, especially at a seashore villa, can hardly be imagined. The soft breezes sweep across it, heavy with the fragrance of jasmine and gardenia, and through the swaying boughs of palm and mimosa there are glimpses of rugged mountains, their summits veiled in clouds, of purple sea with the white surf beating eternally against the reefs, whiter still in the yellow sunlight or the magical moonlight of the tropics."

There: rugs, ices, pictures, lanais, worldly books, sinful bric-a-brac fetched from everywhere. And the ladies riding astride. These are changes, indeed. In my time the native women rode astride, but the white ones lacked the courage to adopt their wise custom. In my time ice was seldom seen in Honolulu. It sometimes came in sailing vessels from New England as ballast; and then, if there happened to be a man-of-war in port and balls and suppers raging by consequence, the ballast was worth six hundred dollars a ton, as is evidenced by reputable tradition. But the ice-machine has traveled all over the world, now, and brought ice within everybody's reach. In Lapland and Spitzbergen no one uses native ice in our day, except the bears and the walruses.

The bicycle is not mentioned. It was not necessary. We know that it is there, without inquiring. It is everywhere. But for it, people could never have had summer homes on the summit of Mont Blanc; before its day, property up there had but a nominal value. The ladies of the Hawaiian capital learned too late the right way to occupy a horse—too late to get much benefit from it. The riding-horse is retiring from business everywhere in the world. In Honolulu a few years from now he will be only a tradition.

We all know about Father Damien, the French priest who voluntarily forsook the world and went to the leper island of Molokai to labor among its population of sorrowful exiles who wait there, in slow-consuming misery, for death to cone and release them from their troubles; and we know that the thing which he knew beforehand would happen, did happen: that he became a leper himself, and died of that horrible disease. There was still another case of self-sacrifice, it appears. I asked after "Billy" Ragsdale, interpreter to the Parliament in my time—a half-white. He was a brilliant young fellow, and very popular. As an interpreter he would have been hard to match anywhere. He used to stand up in the Parliament and turn the English speeches into Hawaiian and the Hawaiian speeches into English with a readiness and a volubility that were astonishing. I asked after him, and was told that his prosperous career was cut short in a sudden and unexpected way, just as he was about to marry a beautiful half-caste girl. He discovered, by some nearly invisible sign about his skin, that the poison of leprosy was in him. The secret was his own, and might be kept concealed for years; but he would not be treacherous to the girl that loved him; he would not marry her to a doom like his. And so he put his affairs in order, and went around to all his friends and bade them good-bye, and sailed in the leper ship to Molokai. There he died the loathsome and lingering death that all lepers die.

In this place let me insert a paragraph or two from "The Paradise of the Pacific" (Rev. H. H. Gowen)—

"Poor lepers! It is easy for those who have no relatives or friends among them to enforce the decree of segregation to the letter, but who can write of the terrible, the heart-breaking scenes which that enforcement has brought about?

"A man upon Hawaii was suddenly taken away after a summary arrest, leaving behind him a helpless wife about to give birth to a babe. The devoted wife with great pain and risk came the whole journey to Honolulu, and pleaded until the authorities were unable to resist her entreaty that she might go and live like a leper with her leper husband.

"A woman in the prime of life and activity is condemned as an incipient leper, suddenly removed from her home, and her husband returns to find his two helpless babes moaning for their lost mother.

"Imagine it! The case of the babies is hard, but its bitterness is a trifle—less than a trifle—less than nothing—compared to what the mother must suffer; and suffer minute by minute, hour by hour, day by day, month by month, year by year, without respite, relief, or any abatement of her pain till she dies.

"One woman, Luka Kaaukau, has been living with her leper husband in the settlement for twelve years. The man has scarcely a joint left, his limbs are only distorted ulcerated stumps, for four years his wife has put every particle of food into his mouth. He wanted his wife to abandon his wretched carcass long ago, as she herself was sound and well, but Luka said that she was content to remain and wait on the man she loved till the spirit should be freed from its burden.

"I myself have known hard cases enough:—of a girl, apparently in full health, decorating the church with me at Easter, who before Christmas is taken away as a confirmed leper; of a mother hiding her child in the mountains for years

so that not even her dearest friends knew that she had a child alive, that he might not be taken away; of a respectable white man taken away from his wife and family, and compelled to become a dweller in the Leper Settlement, where he is counted dead, even by the insurance companies."

And one great pity of it all is, that these poor sufferers are innocent. The leprosy does not come of sins which they committed, but of sins committed by their ancestors, who escaped the curse of leprosy!

Mr. Gowan has made record of a certain very striking circumstance. Would you expect to find in that awful Leper Settlement a custom worthy to be transplanted to your own country? They have one such, and it is inexpressibly touching and beautiful. When death sets open the prison-door of life there, the band salutes the freed soul with a burst of glad music!

CHAPTER IV.

A dozen direct censures are easier to bear than one morganatic compliment. —Pudd'nhead Wilson's New Calendar.

Sailed from Honolulu.—From diary:

Sept. 2. Flocks of flying fish-slim, shapely, graceful, and intensely white. With the sun on them they look like a flight of silver fruit-knives. They are able to fly a hundred yards.

Sept. 3. In 9 deg. 50' north latitude, at breakfast. Approaching the equator on a long slant. Those of us who have never seen the equator are a good deal excited. I think I would rather see it than any other thing in the world. We entered the "doldrums" last night—variable winds, bursts of rain, intervals of calm, with chopping seas and a wobbly and drunken motion to the ship—a condition of things findable in other regions sometimes, but present in the doldrums always. The globe-girdling belt called the doldrums is 20 degrees wide, and the thread called the equator lies along the middle of it.

Sept. 4. Total eclipse of the moon last night. At 1.30 it began to go off. At total—or about that—it was like a rich rosy cloud with a tumbled surface framed in the circle and projecting from it—a bulge of strawberry-ice, so to speak. At half-eclipse the moon was like a gilded acorn in its cup.

Sept. 5. Closing in on the equator this noon. A sailor explained to a young girl that the ship's speed is poor because we are climbing up the bulge toward the center of the globe; but that when we should once get over, at the equator, and start down-hill, we should fly. When she asked him the other day what the fore-yard was, he said it was the front yard, the open area in the front end of the ship. That man has a good deal of learning stored up, and the girl is likely to get it all.

Afternoon. Crossed the equator. In the distance it looked like a blue ribbon stretched across the ocean. Several passengers kodak'd it. We had no fool ceremonies, no fantastics, no horse play. All that sort of thing has gone out. In old times a sailor, dressed as Neptune, used to come in over the bows, with his suite, and lather up and shave everybody who was crossing the equator for the first time, and then cleanse these unfortunates by swinging them from the yard-arm and ducking them three times in the sea. This was considered funny. Nobody knows why. No, that is not true. We do know why. Such a thing could never be funny on land; no part of the old-time grotesque performances gotten up on shipboard to celebrate the passage of the line would ever be funny on shore—they would seem dreary and less to shore people. But the shore people would change their minds about it at sea, on a long voyage. On such a voyage, with its eternal monotonies, people's intellects deteriorate; the owners of the intellects soon reach a point where they almost seem to prefer childish things to things of a maturer degree. One is often surprised at the juvenilities which grown people indulge in at sea, and the interest they take in them, and the consuming enjoyment they get out of them. This is on long voyages only. The mind gradually becomes inert, dull, blunted; it loses its accustomed interest in intellectual things; nothing but horse-play can rouse it, nothing but wild and foolish grotesqueries can entertain it. On short voyages it makes no such exposure of itself; it hasn't time to slump down to this sorrowful level.

The short-voyage passenger gets his chief physical exercise out of "horse-billiards"—shovel-board. It is a good game. We play it in this ship. A quartermaster chalks off a diagram like this-on the deck.

The player uses a cue that is like a broom-handle with a quarter-moon of wood fastened to the end of it. With this he shoves wooden disks the size of a saucer—he gives the disk a vigorous shove and sends it fifteen or twenty feet along the deck and lands it in one of the squares if he can. If it stays there till the inning is played out, it will count as many points in the game as the figure in the square it has stopped in represents. The adversary plays to knock that disk out and leave his own in its place—particularly if it rests upon the 9 or 10 or some other of the high numbers; but if it rests in the "10off" he backs it up—lands his disk behind it a foot or two, to make it difficult for its owner to knock it out of that damaging place and improve his record. When the inning is played out it may be found that each adversary has placed his four disks where they count; it may be found that some of them are touching chalk lines and not counting; and very often it will be found that there has been a general wreckage, and that not a disk has been left within the diagram. Anyway, the result is recorded, whatever it is, and the game goes on. The game is 100 points, and it takes from twenty minutes to forty to play it, according to luck and the condition of the sea. It is an exciting game, and the crowd of spectators furnish abundance of applause for fortunate shots and plenty of laughter for the other kind. It is a game of skill, but at the same time the uneasy motion of the ship is constantly interfering with skill; this makes it a chancy game, and the element of luck comes largely in.

We had a couple of grand tournaments, to determine who should be "Champion of the Pacific"; they included among the participants nearly all the passengers, of both sexes, and the officers of the ship, and they afforded many days of stupendous interest and excitement, and murderous exercise—for horse-billiards is a physically violent game.

The figures in the following record of some of the closing games in the first tournament will show, better than any description, how very chancy the game is. The losers here represented had all been winners in the previous games of the series, some of them by fine majorities:

Chase,102 Mrs. D.,57 Mortimer, 105 The Surgeon, 92 Miss C.,105 Mrs. T.,9 Clemens, 101 Taylor,92 Taylor,109 Davies,95 Miss C., 108 Mortimer,55 Thomas,102 Roper,76 Clemens, 111 Miss C.,89 Coomber, 106 Chase,98

And so on; until but three couples of winners were left. Then I beat my man, young Smith beat his man, and Thomas beat his. This reduced the combatants to three. Smith and I took the deck, and I led off. At the close of the first inning I was 10 worse than nothing and Smith had scored 7. The luck continued against me. When I was 57, Smith was 97 —within 3 of out. The luck changed then. He picked up a 10-off or so, and couldn't recover. I beat him.

The next game would end tournament No. 1.

Mr. Thomas and I were the contestants. He won the lead and went to the bat—so to speak. And there he stood, with the crotch of his cue resting against his disk while the ship rose slowly up, sank slowly down, rose again, sank again. She never seemed to rise to suit him exactly. She started up once more; and when she was nearly ready for the turn, he let drive and landed his disk just within the left-hand end of the 10. (Applause). The umpire proclaimed "a good 10," and the game-keeper set it down. I played: my disk grazed the edge of Mr. Thomas's disk, and went out of the diagram. (No applause.)

Mr. Thomas played again—and landed his second disk alongside of the first, and almost touching its right-hand side. "Good 10." (Great applause.)

I played, and missed both of them. (No applause.)

Mr. Thomas delivered his third shot and landed his disk just at the right of the other two. "Good 10." (Immense applause.)

There they lay, side by side, the three in a row. It did not seem possible that anybody could miss them. Still I did it. (Immense silence.)

Mr. Thomas played his last disk. It seems incredible, but he actually landed that disk alongside of the others, and just to the right of them-a straight solid row of 4 disks. (Tumultuous and long-continued applause.)

Then I played my last disk. Again it did not seem possible that anybody could miss that row—a row which would have been 14 inches long if the disks had been clamped together; whereas, with the spaces separating them they made a longer row than that. But I did it. It may be that I was getting nervous.

I think it unlikely that that innings has ever had its parallel in the history of horse-billiards. To place the four disks side by side in the 10 was an extraordinary feat; indeed, it was a kind of miracle. To miss them was another miracle. It will take a century to produce another man who can place the four disks in the 10; and longer than that to find a man who can't knock them out. I was ashamed of my performance at the time, but now that I reflect upon it I see that it was rather fine and difficult.

Mr. Thomas kept his luck, and won the game, and later the championship.

In a minor tournament I won the prize, which was a Waterbury watch. I put it in my trunk. In Pretoria, South Africa, nine months afterward, my proper watch broke down and I took the Waterbury out, wound it, set it by the great clock on the Parliament House (8.05), then went back to my room and went to bed, tired from a long railway journey. The parliamentary clock had a peculiarity which I was not aware of at the time —a peculiarity which exists in no other clock, and would not exist in that one if it had been made by a sane person; on the half-hour it strikes the succeeding hour, then strikes the hour again, at the proper time. I lay reading and smoking awhile; then, when I could hold my eyes open no longer and was about to put out the light, the great clock began to boom, and I counted ten. I reached for the Waterbury to see how it was getting along. It was marking 9.30. It seemed rather poor speed for a three-dollar watch, but I supposed that the climate was affecting it. I shoved it half an hour ahead; and took to my book and waited to see what would happen. At 10 the great clock struck ten again. I looked—the Waterbury was marking half-past 10. This was too much speed for the money, and it troubled me. I pushed the hands back a half hour, and waited once more; I had to, for I was vexed and restless now, and my sleepiness was gone. By and by the great clock struck 11. The Waterbury was marking 10.30. I pushed it ahead half an hour, with some show of temper. By and by the great clock struck 11 again. The Waterbury showed up 11.30, now, and I beat her brains out against the bedstead. I was sorry next day, when I found out.

To return to the ship.

The average human being is a perverse creature; and when he isn't that, he is a practical joker. The result to the other person concerned is about the same: that is, he is made to suffer. The washing down of the decks begins at a very early hour in all ships; in but few ships are any measures taken to protect the passengers, either by waking or warning them, or by sending a steward to close their ports. And so the deckwashers have their opportunity, and they use it. They send a bucket of water slashing along the side of the ship and into the ports, drenching the passenger's clothes, and often the passenger himself. This good old custom prevailed in this ship, and under unusually favorable circumstances, for in the blazing tropical regions a removable zinc thing like a sugarshovel projects from the port to catch the wind and bring it in; this thing catches the wash-water and brings it in, too—and in flooding abundance. Mrs. L, an invalid, had to sleep on the locker—sofa under her port, and every time she over-slept and thus failed to take care of herself, the deck-washers drowned her out.

And the painters, what a good time they had! This ship would be going into dock for a month in Sydney for repairs; but no matter, painting was going on all the time somewhere or other. The ladies' dresses were constantly getting ruined, nevertheless protests and supplications went for nothing. Sometimes a lady, taking an afternoon nap on deck near a ventilator or some other thing that didn't need painting, would wake up by and by and find that the humorous painter had been noiselessly daubing that thing and had splattered her white gown all over with little greasy yellow spots.

The blame for this untimely painting did not lie with the ship's officers, but with custom. As far back as Noah's time it became law that ships must be constantly painted and fussed at when at sea; custom grew out of the law, and at sea custom knows no death; this custom will continue until the sea goes dry.

Sept. 8.—Sunday. We are moving so nearly south that we cross only about two meridians of longitude a day. This morning we were in longitude 178 west from Greenwich, and 57 degrees west from San Francisco. To-morrow we shall be close to the center of the globe—the 180th degree of west longitude and 180th degree of east longitude.

And then we must drop out a day-lose a day out of our lives, a

day never to be found again. We shall all die one day earlier than from the beginning of time we were foreordained to die. We shall be a day behindhand all through eternity. We shall always be saying to the other angels, "Fine day today," and they will be always retorting, "But it isn't to-day, it's tomorrow." We shall be in a state of confusion all the time and shall never know what true happiness is.

Next Day. Sure enough, it has happened. Yesterday it was September 8, Sunday; to-day, per the bulletin-board at the head of the companionway, it is September 10, Tuesday. There is something uncanny about it. And uncomfortable. In fact, nearly unthinkable, and wholly unrealizable, when one comes to consider it. While we were crossing the 180th meridian it was Sunday in the stern of the ship where my family were, and Tuesday in the bow where I was. They were there eating the half of a fresh apple on the 8th, and I was at the same time eating the other half of it on the 10th—and I could notice how stale it was, already. The family were the same age that they were when I had left them five minutes before, but I was a day older now than I was then. The day they were living in stretched behind them half way round the globe, across the Pacific Ocean and America and Europe; the day I was living in stretched in front of me around the other half to meet it. They were stupendous days for bulk and stretch; apparently much larger days than we had ever been in before. All previous days had been but shrunk-up little things by comparison. The difference in temperature between the two days was very marked, their day being hotter than mine because it was closer to the equator.

Along about the moment that we were crossing the Great Meridian a child was born in the steerage, and now there is no way to tell which day it was born on. The nurse thinks it was Sunday, the surgeon thinks it was Tuesday. The child will never know its own birthday. It will always be choosing first one and then the other, and will never be able to make up its mind permanently. This will breed vacillation and uncertainty in its opinions about religion, and politics, and business, and sweethearts, and everything, and will undermine its principles, and rot them away, and make the poor thing characterless, and its success in life impossible. Every one in the ship says so. And this is not all—in fact, not the worst. For there is an enormously rich brewer in the ship who said as much as ten days ago, that if the child was born on his birthday he would give it ten thousand dollars to start its little life with. His birthday was Monday, the 9th of September.

If the ships all moved in the one direction—westward, I mean—the world would suffer a prodigious loss—in the matter of valuable time, through the dumping overboard on the Great Meridian of such multitudes of days by ships crews and passengers. But fortunately the ships do not all sail west, half of them sail east. So there is no real loss. These latter pick up all the discarded days and add them to the world's stock again; and about as good as new, too; for of course the salt water preserves them.

CHAPTER V.

Noise proves nothing. Often a hen who has merely laid an egg cackles as if she had laid an asteroid. —Pudd'nhead Wilson's New Calendar.

WEDNESDAY, Sept. 11. In this world we often make mistakes of judgment. We do not as a rule get out of them sound and whole, but sometimes we do. At dinner yesterday evening-present, a mixture of Scotch, English, American, Canadian, and Australasian folk—a discussion broke out about the pronunciation of certain Scottish words. This was private ground, and the non-Scotch nationalities, with one exception, discreetly kept still. But I am not discreet, and I took a hand. I didn't know anything about the subject, but I took a hand just to have something to do. At that moment the word in dispute was the word three. One Scotchman was claiming that the peasantry of Scotland pronounced it three, his adversaries claimed that they didn't—that they pronounced it 'thraw'. The solitary Scot was having a sultry time of it, so I thought I would enrich him with my help. In my position I was necessarily quite impartial, and was equally as well and as ill equipped to fight on the one side as on the other. So I spoke up and said the peasantry pronounced the word three, not thraw. It was an error of judgment. There was a moment of astonished and ominous silence, then weather ensued. The storm rose and spread in a surprising way, and I was snowed under in a very few minutes. It was a bad defeat for me—a kind of Waterloo. It promised to remain so, and I wished I had had better sense than to enter upon such a forlorn enterprise. But just then I had a saving thought—at least a thought that offered a chance. While the storm was still raging, I made up a Scotch couplet, and then spoke up and said:

"Very well, don't say any more. I confess defeat. I thought I knew, but I see my mistake. I was deceived by one of your Scotch poets."

"A Scotch poet! O come! Name him."

"Robert Burns."

It is wonderful the power of that name. These men looked doubtful—but paralyzed, all the same. They were quite silent for a moment; then one of them said—with the reverence in his voice which is always present in a Scotchman's tone when he utters the name.

"Does Robbie Burns say—what does he say?"

"This is what he says:

'There were nae bairns but only three —Ane at the breast, twa at the knee.'"

It ended the discussion. There was no man there profane enough, disloyal enough, to say any word against a thing which Robert Burns had settled. I shall always honor that great name for the salvation it brought me in this time of my sore need.

It is my belief that nearly any invented quotation, played with confidence, stands a good chance to deceive. There are people who think that honesty is always the best policy. This is a superstition; there are times when the appearance of it is worth six of it.

We are moving steadily southward-getting further and further down under the projecting paunch of the globe. Yesterday evening we saw the Big Dipper and the north star sink below the horizon and disappear from our world. No, not "we," but they. They saw it—somebody saw it—and told me about it. But it is no matter, I was not caring for those things, I am tired of them, any way. I think they are well enough, but one doesn't want them always hanging around. My interest was all in the Southern Cross. I had never seen that. I had heard about it all my life, and it was but natural that I should be burning to see it. No other constellation makes so much talk. I had nothing

against the Big Dipper —and naturally couldn't have anything against it, since it is a citizen of our own sky, and the property of the United States—but I did want it to move out of the way and give this foreigner a chance. Judging by the size of the talk which the Southern Cross had made, I supposed it would need a sky all to itself.

But that was a mistake. We saw the Cross to-night, and it is not large. Not large, and not strikingly bright. But it was low down toward the horizon, and it may improve when it gets up higher in the sky. It is ingeniously named, for it looks just as a cross would look if it looked like something else. But that description does not describe; it is too vague, too general, too indefinite. It does after a fashion suggest a cross across that is out of repair—or out of drawing; not correctly shaped. It is long, with a short cross-bar, and the cross-bar is canted out of the straight line.

It consists of four large stars and one little one. The little one is out of line and further damages the shape. It should have been placed at the intersection of the stem and the cross-bar. If you do not draw an imaginary line from star to star it does not suggest a cross—nor anything in particular.

One must ignore the little star, and leave it out of the combination—it confuses everything. If you leave it out, then you can make out of the four stars a sort of cross—out of true; or a sort of kite—out of true; or a sort of coffin-out of true.

Constellations have always been troublesome things to name. If you give one of them a fanciful name, it will always refuse to live up to it; it will always persist in not resembling the thing it has been named for. Ultimately, to satisfy the public, the fanciful name has to be discarded for a common-sense one, a manifestly descriptive one. The Great Bear remained the Great Bear—and unrecognizable as such—for thousands of years; and people complained about it all the time, and quite properly; but as soon as it became the property of the United States, Congress changed it to the Big Dipper, and now every body is satisfied, and there is no more talk about riots. I would not change the Southern Cross to the Southern Coffin, I would change it to the Southern Kite; for up there in the general emptiness is the proper home of a kite, but not for coffins and crosses and dippers. In a little while, now—I cannot tell exactly how long it will be—the globe will belong to the English-speaking race; and of course the skies also. Then the constellations will be re-organized, and polished up, and re-named—the most of them "Victoria," I reckon, but this one will sail thereafter as the Southern Kite, or go out of business. Several towns and things, here and there, have been named for Her Majesty already.

In these past few days we are plowing through a mighty Milky Way of islands. They are so thick on the map that one would hardly expect to find room between them for a canoe; yet we seldom glimpse one. Once we saw the dim bulk of a couple of them, far away, spectral and dreamy things; members of the Horne-Alofa and Fortuna. On the larger one are two rival native kings—and they have a time together. They are Catholics; so are their people. The missionaries there are French priests.

From the multitudinous islands in these regions the "recruits" for the Queensland plantations were formerly drawn; are still drawn from them, I believe. Vessels fitted up like old-time slavers came here and carried off the natives to serve as laborers in the great Australian province. In the beginning it was plain, simple man-stealing, as per testimony of the missionaries. This has been denied, but not disproven. Afterward it was forbidden by law to "recruit" a native without his consent, and governmental agents were sent in all recruiting vessels to see that the law was obeyed—which they did, according to the recruiting people; and which they sometimes didn't, according to the missionaries. A man could be lawfully recruited for a three-years term of service; he could volunteer for another term if he so chose; when his time was up he could return to his island. And would also have the means to do it; for the government required the employer to put money in its hands for this purpose before the recruit was delivered to him.

Captain Wawn was a recruiting ship-master during many years. From his pleasant book one gets the idea that the recruiting business was quite popular with the islanders, as a rule. And yet that did not make the business wholly dull and uninteresting; for one finds rather frequent little breaks in the monotony of it—like this, for instance:

"The afternoon of our arrival at Leper Island the schooner was lying almost becalmed under the lee of the lofty central portion of the island, about three-quarters of a mile from the shore. The boats were in sight at some distance. The recruiter-boat had run into a small nook on the rocky coast, under a high bank, above which stood a solitary hut backed by dense forest. The government agent and mate in the second boat lay about 400 yards to the westward.

"Suddenly we heard the sound of firing, followed by yells from the natives on shore, and then we saw the recruiter-boat push out with a seemingly diminished crew. The mate's boat pulled quickly up, took her in tow, and presently brought her alongside, all her own crew being more or less hurt. It seems the natives had called them into the place on pretence of friendship. A crowd gathered about the stern of the boat, and several fellows even got into her. All of a sudden our men were attacked with clubs and tomahawks. The recruiter escaped the first blows aimed at him, making play with his fists until he had an opportunity to draw his revolver. 'Tom Sayers,' a Mare man, received a tomahawk blow on the head which laid the scalp open but did not penetrate his skull, fortunately. 'Bobby Towns,' another Mare boatman, had both his thumbs cut in warding off blows, one of them being so nearly severed from the hand that the doctors had to finish the operation. Lihu, a Lifu boy, the recruiter's special attendant, was cut and pricked in various places, but nowhere seriously. Jack, an unlucky Tanna recruit, who had been engaged to act as boatman, received an arrow through his forearm, the head of which— apiece of bone seven or eight inches long—was still in the limb, protruding from both sides, when the boats returned. The recruiter himself would have got off scot-free had not an arrow pinned one of his fingers to the loom of the steering-oar just as they were getting off. The fight had been short but sharp. The enemy lost two men, both shot dead."

The truth is, Captain Wawn furnishes such a crowd of instances of fatal encounters between natives and French and English recruiting-crews (for the French are in the business for the plantations of New Caledonia), that one is almost persuaded that recruiting is not thoroughly popular among the islanders; else why this bristling string of attacks and bloodcurdling slaughter? The captain lays it all to "Exeter Hall influence." But for the meddling philanthropists, the native fathers and mothers would be fond of seeing their children carted into exile and now and then the grave, instead of weeping about it and trying to kill the kind recruiters.

CHAPTER VI.

He was as shy as a newspaper is when referring to its own merits. —Pudd'nhead Wilson's New Calendar.

Captain Wawn is crystal-clear on one point: He does not approve of missionaries. They obstruct his business. They make "Recruiting," as he calls it ("Slave-Catching," as they call it in their frank way) a trouble when it ought to be just a picnic and a pleasure excursion. The missionaries have their opinion about the manner in which the Labor Traffic is conducted, and about the recruiter's evasions of the law of the Traffic, and about the traffic itself—and it is distinctly uncomplimentary to the Traffic and to everything connected with it, including the law for its regulation. Captain Wawn's book is of very recent date; I have by me a pamphlet of still later date—hot from the press, in fact—by Rev. Wm. Gray, a missionary; and the book and the pamphlet taken together make exceedingly interesting reading, to my mind.

Interesting, and easy to understand—except in one detail, which I will mention presently. It is easy to understand why the Queensland sugar planter should want the Kanaka recruit: he is cheap. Very cheap, in fact. These are the figures paid by the planter: £20 to the recruiter for getting the Kanaka or "catching" him, as the missionary phrase goes; £3 to the Queensland government for "superintending" the importation; £5 deposited with the Government for the Kanaka's passage home when his three years are up, in case he shall live that long; about £25 to the Kanaka himself for three years' wages and clothing; total payment for the use of a man three years, £53; or, including diet, £60. Altogether, a hundred dollars a year. One can understand why the recruiter is fond of the business; the recruit costs him a few cheap presents (given to the recruit's relatives, not himself), and the recruit is worth £20 to the recruiter when delivered in Queensland. All this is clear enough; but the thing that is not clear is, what there is about it all to persuade the recruit. He is young and brisk; life at home in his beautiful island is one lazy, long holiday to him; or if he wants to work he can turn out a couple of bags of copra per week and sell it for four or five shillings a bag. In Queensland he must get up at dawn and work from eight to twelve hours a day in the canefields—in a much hotter climate than he is used to—and get less than four shillings a week for it.

I cannot understand his willingness to go to Queensland. It is a deep puzzle to me. Here is the explanation, from the planter's point of view; at least I gather from the missionary's pamphlet that it is the planter's:

"When he comes from his home he is a savage, pure and simple. He feels no shame at his nakedness and want of adornment. When he returns home he does so well dressed, sporting a Waterbury watch, collars, cuffs, boots, and jewelry. He takes with him one or more boxes—["Box" is English for trunk.]—well filled with clothing, a musical instrument or two, and perfumery and other articles of luxury he has learned to appreciate."

For just one moment we have a seeming flash of comprehension of, the Kanaka's reason for exiling himself: he goes away to acquire civilization. Yes, he was naked and not ashamed, now he is clothed and knows how to be ashamed; he was unenlightened; now he has a Waterbury watch; he was unrefined, now he has jewelry, and something to make him smell good; he was a nobody, a provincial, now he has been to far countries and can show off.

It all looks plausible—for a moment. Then the missionary takes hold of this explanation and pulls it to pieces, and dances on it, and damages it beyond recognition.

"Admitting that the foregoing description is the average one, the average sequel is this: The cuffs and collars, if used at all, are carried off by youngsters, who fasten them round the leg, just below the knee, as ornaments. The Waterbury, broken and dirty, finds its way to the trader, who gives a trifle for it; or the inside is taken out, the wheels strung on a thread and hung round the neck. Knives, axes, calico, and handkerchiefs are divided among friends, and there is hardly one of these apiece. The boxes, the keys often lost on the road home, can be bought for 2s. 6d. They are to be seen rotting outside in almost any shore village on Tanna. (I speak of what I have seen.) A returned Kanaka has been furiously angry with me because I would not buy his trousers, which he declared were just my fit. He sold them afterwards to one of my Aniwan teachers for 9d. worth of tobacco—a pair of trousers that probably cost him 8s. or 10s. in Queensland. A coat or shirt is handy for cold weather. The white handkerchiefs, the 'senet' (perfumery), the umbrella, and perhaps the hat, are kept. The boots have to take their chance, if they do not happen to fit the copra trader. 'Senet' on the hair, streaks of paint on the face, a dirty white handkerchief round the neck, strips of turtle shell in the ears, a belt, a sheath and knife, and an umbrella constitute the rig of returned Kanaka at home the day after landing."

A hat, an umbrella, a belt, a neckerchief. Otherwise stark naked. All in a day the hard-earned "civilization" has melted away to this. And even these perishable things must presently go. Indeed, there is but a single detail of his civilization that can be depended on to stay by him: according to the missionary, he has learned to swear. This is art, and art is long, as the poet says.

In all countries the laws throw light upon the past. The Queensland law for the regulation of the Labor Traffic is a confession. It is a confession that the evils charged by the missionaries upon the traffic had existed in the past, and that they still existed when the law was made. The missionaries make a further charge: that the law is evaded by the recruiters, and that the Government Agent sometimes helps them to do it. Regulation 31 reveals two things: that sometimes a young fool of a recruit gets his senses back, after being persuaded to sign away his liberty for three years, and dearly wants to get out of the engagement and stay at home with his own people; and that threats, intimidation, and force are used to keep him on board the recruiting-ship, and to hold him to his contract. Regulation 31 forbids these coercions. The law requires that he shall be allowed to go free; and another clause of it requires the recruiter to set him ashore—per boat, because of the prevalence of sharks. Testimony from Rev. Mr. Gray:

"There are 'wrinkles' for taking the penitent Kanaka. My first experience of the Traffic was a case of this kind in 1884. A vessel anchored just out of sight of our station, word was brought to me that some boys were stolen, and the relatives wished me to go and get them back. The facts were, as I found, that six boys had recruited, had rushed into the boat, the Government Agent informed me. They had all 'signed'; and, said the Government Agent, 'on board they shall remain.' I was assured that the six boys were of age and willing to go. Yet on getting ready to leave the ship I found four of the lads ready to come ashore in the boat! This I forbade. One of them jumped into the water and persisted in coming ashore in my boat. When appealed to, the Government Agent suggested that we

go and leave him to be picked up by the ship's boat, a quarter mile distant at the time!"

The law and the missionaries feel for the repentant recruit—and properly, one may be permitted to think, for he is only a youth and ignorant and persuadable to his hurt—but sympathy for him is not kept in stock by the recruiter. Rev. Mr. Gray says:

"A captain many years in the traffic explained to me how a penitent could be taken. 'When a boy jumps overboard we just take a boat and pull ahead of him, then lie between him and the shore. If he has not tired himself swimming, and passes the boat, keep on heading him in this way. The dodge rarely fails. The boy generally tires of swimming, gets into the boat of his own accord, and goes quietly on board."

Yes, exhaustion is likely to make a boy quiet. If the distressed boy had been the speaker's son, and the captors savages, the speaker would have been surprised to see how differently the thing looked from the new point of view; however, it is not our custom to put ourselves in the other person's place. Somehow there is something pathetic about that disappointed young savage's resignation. I must explain, here, that in the traffic dialect, "boy" does not always mean boy; it means a youth above sixteen years of age. That is by Queensland law the age of consent, though it is held that recruiters allow themselves some latitude in guessing at ages.

Captain Wawn of the free spirit chafes under the annoyance of "cast-iron regulations." They and the missionaries have poisoned his life. He grieves for the good old days, vanished to come no more. See him weep; hear him cuss between the lines!

"For a long time we were allowed to apprehend and detain all deserters who had signed the agreement on board ship, but the 'cast-iron' regulations of the Act of 1884 put a stop to that, allowing the Kanaka to sign the agreement for three years' service, travel about in the ship in receipt of the regular rations, cadge all he could, and leave when he thought fit, so long as he did not extend his pleasure trip to Queensland."

Rev. Mr. Gray calls this same restrictive cast-iron law a "farce." "There is as much cruelty and injustice done to natives by acts that are legal as by deeds unlawful. The regulations that exist are unjust and inadequate—unjust and inadequate they must ever be." He furnishes his reasons for his position, but they are too long for reproduction here.

However, if the most a Kanaka advantages himself by a three-years course in civilization in Queensland, is a necklace and an umbrella and a showy imperfection in the art of swearing, it must be that all the profit of the traffic goes to the white man. This could be twisted into a plausible argument that the traffic ought to be squarely abolished.

However, there is reason for hope that that can be left alone to achieve itself. It is claimed that the traffic will depopulate its sources of supply within the next twenty or thirty years. Queensland is a very healthy place for white people—death-rate 12 in 1,000 of the population —but the Kanaka death-rate is away above that. The vital statistics for 1893 place it at 52; for 1894 (Mackay district), 68. The first six months of the Kanaka's exile are peculiarly perilous for him because of the rigors of the new climate. The death-rate among the new men has reached as high as 180 in the 1,000. In the Kanaka's native home his death-rate is 12 in time of peace, and 15 in time of war. Thus exile to Queensland—with the opportunity to acquire civilization, an umbrella, and a pretty poor quality of profanity—is twelve times as deadly for him as war. Common Christian charity, common humanity, does seem to require, not only that these people be returned to their homes, but that war, pestilence, and famine be introduced among them for their preservation.

Concerning these Pacific isles and their peoples an eloquent prophet spoke long years ago—five and fifty years ago. In fact, he spoke a little too early. Prophecy is a good line of business, but it is full of risks. This prophet was the Right Rev. M. Russell, LL.D., D.C.L., of Edinburgh:

"Is the tide of civilization to roll only to the foot of the Rocky Mountains, and is the sun of knowledge to set at last in the waves of the Pacific? No; the mighty day of four thousand years is drawing to its close; the sun of humanity has performed its destined course; but long ere its setting rays are extinguished in the west, its ascending beams have glittered on the isles of the eastern seas . . . . And now we see the race of Japhet setting forth to people the isles, and the seeds of another Europe and a second England sown in the regions of the sun. But mark the words of the prophecy: 'He shall dwell in the tents of Shem, and Canaan shall be his servant.' It is not said Canaan shall be his slave. To the Anglo-Saxon race is given the scepter of the globe, but there is not given either the lash of the slave-driver or the rack of the executioner. The East will not be stained with the same atrocities as the West; the frightful gangrene of an enthralled race is not to mar the destinies of the family of Japhet in the Oriental world; humanizing, not destroying, as they advance; uniting with, not enslaving, the inhabitants with whom they dwell, the British race may," etc., etc.

And he closes his vision with an invocation from Thomson:

"Come, bright Improvement! on the car of Time, And rule the spacious world from clime to clime."

Very well, Bright Improvement has arrived, you see, with her civilization, and her Waterbury, and her umbrella, and her third-quality profanity, and her humanizing-not-destroying machinery, and her hundred-and-eighty death-rate, and everything is going along just as handsome!

But the prophet that speaks last has an advantage over the pioneer in the business. Rev. Mr. Gray says:

"What I am concerned about is that we as a Christian nation should wipe out these races to enrich ourselves."

And he closes his pamphlet with a grim Indictment which is as eloquent in its flowerless straightforward English as is the hand-painted rhapsody of the early prophet:

"My indictment of the Queensland-Kanaka Labor Traffic is this

"1. It generally demoralizes and always impoverishes the Kanaka, deprives him of his citizenship, and depopulates the islands fitted to his home.

"2. It is felt to lower the dignity of the white agricultural laborer in Queensland, and beyond a doubt it lowers his wages there.

"3. The whole system is fraught with danger to Australia and the islands on the score of health.

"4. On social and political grounds the continuance of the Queensland Kanaka Labor Traffic must be a barrier to the true federation of the Australian colonies.

"5. The Regulations under which the Traffic exists in Queensland are inadequate to prevent abuses, and in the nature of things they must remain so.

"6. The whole system is contrary to the spirit and doctrine of the Gospel of Jesus Christ. The Gospel requires us to help the weak, but the Kanaka is fleeced and trodden down.

"7. The bed-rock of this Traffic is that the life and liberty of a black man are of less value than those of a white man. And a Traffic that has grown out of 'slave-hunting' will certainly remain to the end not unlike its origin."

CHAPTER VII.

Truth is the most valuable thing we have. Let us economize it. —Pudd'nhead Wilson's New Calendar.

From Diary:—For a day or two we have been plowing among an invisible vast wilderness of islands, catching now and then a shadowy glimpse of a member of it. There does seem to be a prodigious lot of islands this year; the map of this region is freckled and fly-specked all over with them. Their number would seem to be uncountable. We are moving among the Fijis now—224 islands and islets in the group. In front of us, to the west, the wilderness stretches toward Australia, then curves upward to New Guinea, and still up and up to Japan; behind us, to the east, the wilderness stretches sixty degrees across the wastes of the Pacific; south of us is New Zealand. Somewhere or other among these myriads Samoa is concealed, and not discoverable on the map. Still, if you wish to go there, you will have no trouble about finding it if you follow the directions given by Robert Louis Stevenson to Dr. Conan Doyle and to Mr. J. M. Barrie. "You go to America, cross the continent to San Francisco, and then it's the second turning to the left." To get the full flavor of the joke one must take a glance at the map.

Wednesday, September 11.—Yesterday we passed close to an island or so, and recognized the published Fiji characteristics: a broad belt of clean white coral sand around the island; back of it a graceful fringe of leaning palms, with native huts nestling cosily among the shrubbery at their bases; back of these a stretch of level land clothed in tropic vegetation; back of that, rugged and picturesque mountains. A detail of the immediate foreground: a mouldering ship perched high up on a reef-bench. This completes the composition, and makes the picture artistically perfect.

In the afternoon we sighted Suva, the capital of the group, and threaded our way into the secluded little harbor—a placid basin of brilliant blue and green water tucked snugly in among the sheltering hills. A few ships rode at anchor in it—one of them a sailing vessel flying the American flag; and they said she came from Duluth! There's a journey! Duluth is several thousand miles from the sea, and yet she is entitled to the proud name of Mistress of the Commercial Marine of the United States of America. There is only one free, independent, unsubsidized American ship sailing the foreign seas, and Duluth owns it. All by itself that ship is the American fleet. All by itself it causes the American name and power to be respected in the far regions of the globe. All by itself it certifies to the world that the most populous civilized nation, in the earth has a just pride in her stupendous stretch of sea-front, and is determined to assert and maintain her rightful place as one of the Great Maritime Powers of the Planet. All by itself it is making foreign eyes familiar with a Flag which they have not seen before for forty years, outside of the museum. For what Duluth has done, in building, equipping, and maintaining at her sole expense the American Foreign Commercial Fleet, and in thus rescuing the American name from shame and lifting it high for the homage of the nations, we owe her a debt of gratitude which our hearts shall confess with quickened beats whenever her name is named henceforth. Many national toasts will die in the lapse of time, but while the flag flies and the Republic survives, they who live under their shelter will still drink this one, standing and uncovered: Health and prosperity to Thee, O Duluth, American Queen of the Alien Seas!

Row-boats began to flock from the shore; their crews were the first natives we had seen. These men carried no overplus of clothing, and this was wise, for the weather was hot. Handsome, great dusky men they were, muscular, clean-limbed, and with faces full of character and intelligence. It would be hard to find their superiors anywhere among the dark races, I should think.

Everybody went ashore to look around, and spy out the land, and have that luxury of luxuries to sea-voyagers—a land-dinner. And there we saw more natives: Wrinkled old women, with their flat mammals flung over their shoulders, or hanging down in front like the cold-weather drip from the molasses-faucet; plump and smily young girls, blithe and content, easy and graceful, a pleasure to look at; young matrons, tall, straight, comely, nobly built, sweeping by with chin up, and a gait incomparable for unconscious stateliness and dignity; majestic young men athletes for build and muscle clothed in a loose arrangement of dazzling white, with bronze breast and bronze legs naked, and the head a cannon-swab of solid hair combed straight out from the skull and dyed a rich brick-red. Only sixty years ago they were sunk in darkness; now they have the bicycle. We strolled about the streets of the white folks' little town, and around over the hills by paths and roads among European dwellings and gardens and plantations, and past clumps of hibiscus that made a body blink, the great blossoms were so intensely red; and by and by we stopped to ask an elderly English colonist a question or two, and to sympathize with him concerning the torrid weather; but he was surprised, and said:

"This? This is not hot. You ought to be here in the summer time once."

"We supposed that this was summer; it has the ear-marks of it. You could take it to almost any country and deceive people with it. But if it isn't summer, what does it lack?"

"It lacks half a year. This is mid-winter."

I had been suffering from colds for several months, and a sudden change of season, like this, could hardly fail to do me hurt. It brought on another cold. It is odd, these sudden jumps from season to season. A fortnight ago we left America in mid-summer, now it is midwinter; about a week hence we shall arrive in Australia in the spring.

After dinner I found in the billiard-room a resident whom I had known somewhere else in the world, and presently made, some new friends and drove with them out into the country to visit his Excellency the head of the State, who was occupying his country residence, to escape the rigors of the winter weather, I suppose, for it was on breezy high ground and much more comfortable than the lower regions, where the town is, and where the winter has full swing, and often sets a person's hair afire when he takes off his hat to bow. There is a noble and beautiful view of ocean and islands and castellated peaks from the governor's high-placed house, and its immediate surroundings lie drowsing in that dreamy repose and serenity which are the charm of life in the Pacific Islands.

One of the new friends who went out there with me was a large man, and I had been admiring his size all the way. I was still admiring it as he stood by the governor on the veranda, talking; then the Fijian butler stepped out there to announce tea, and dwarfed him. Maybe he did not quite dwarf him, but at any rate the contrast was quite striking. Perhaps that dark giant was a king in a condition of political suspension. I think that in the talk there on the veranda it was said that in Fiji, as in the Sandwich Islands, native kings and chiefs are of much grander size and build than the commoners. This man was clothed in flowing white vestments, and they were just the thing for him; they comported well with his great stature and his kingly port and dignity. European clothes would have degraded him and made him commonplace. I know that, because they do that with everybody that wears them.

It was said that the old-time devotion to chiefs and reverence for their persons still survive in the native commoner, and in great force. The educated young gentleman who is chief of the tribe that live in the region about the capital dresses in the fashion of high-class European gentlemen, but even his clothes cannot damn him in the reverence of his people. Their pride in his lofty rank and ancient lineage lives on, in spite of his lost authority and the evil magic of his tailor. He has no need to defile himself with work, or trouble his heart with the sordid cares of life; the tribe will see to it that he shall not want, and that he shall hold up his head and live like a gentleman. I had a glimpse of him down in the town. Perhaps he is a descendant of the last king—the king with the difficult name whose memory is preserved by a notable monument of cut-stone which one sees in the enclosure in the middle of the town. Thakombau—I remember, now; that is the name. It is easier to preserve it on a granite block than in your head.

Fiji was ceded to England by this king in 1858. One of the gentlemen present at the governor's quoted a remark made by the king at the time of the session—a neat retort, and with a touch of pathos in it, too. The English Commissioner had offered a crumb of comfort to Thakombau by saying that the transfer of the kingdom to Great Britain was merely "a sort of hermit-crab formality, you know." "Yes," said poor Thakombau, "but with this difference—the crab moves into an unoccupied shell, but mine isn't."

However, as far as I can make out from the books, the King was between the devil and the deep sea at the time, and hadn't much choice. He owed the United States a large debt—a debt which he could pay if allowed time, but time was denied him. He must pay up right away or the warships would be upon him. To protect his people from this disaster he ceded his country to Britain, with a clause in the contract providing for the ultimate payment of the American debt.

In old times the Fijians were fierce fighters; they were very religious, and worshiped idols; the big chiefs were proud and haughty, and they were men of great style in many ways; all chiefs had several wives, the biggest chiefs sometimes had as many as fifty; when a chief was dead and ready for burial, four or five of his wives were strangled and put into the grave with him. In 1804 twenty-seven British convicts escaped from Australia to Fiji, and brought guns and ammunition with them. Consider what a power they were, armed like that, and what an opportunity they had. If they had been energetic men and sober, and had had brains and known how to use them, they could have achieved the sovereignty of the archipelago twenty-seven kings and each with eight or nine islands under his scepter. But nothing came of this chance. They lived worthless lives of sin and luxury, and died without honor—in most cases by violence. Only one of them had any ambition; he was an Irishman named Connor. He tried to raise a family of fifty children, and scored forty-eight. He died lamenting his failure. It was a foolish sort of avarice. Many a father would have been rich enough with forty.

It is a fine race, the Fijians, with brains in their heads, and an inquiring turn of mind. It appears that their savage ancestors had a doctrine of immortality in their scheme of religion—with limitations. That is to say, their dead friend would go to a happy hereafter if he could be accumulated, but not otherwise. They drew the line; they thought that the missionary's doctrine was too sweeping, too comprehensive. They called his attention to certain facts. For instance, many of their friends had been devoured by sharks; the sharks, in their turn, were caught and eaten by other men; later, these men were captured in war, and eaten by the enemy. The original persons had entered into the composition of the sharks; next, they and the sharks had become part of the flesh and blood and bone of the cannibals. How, then, could the particles of the original men be searched out from the final conglomerate and put together again? The inquirers were full of doubts, and considered that the missionary had not examined the matter with—the gravity and attention which so serious a thing deserved.

The missionary taught these exacting savages many valuable things, and got from them one—a very dainty and poetical idea: Those wild and ignorant poor children of Nature believed that the flowers, after they perish, rise on the winds and float away to the fair fields of heaven, and flourish there forever in immortal beauty!

CHAPTER VIII.

It could probably be shown by facts and figures that there is no distinctly native American criminal class except Congress.
—Pudd'nhead Wilson's New Calendar.

When one glances at the map the members of the stupendous island wilderness of the Pacific seem to crowd upon each other; but no, there is no crowding, even in the center of a group; and between groups there are lonely wide deserts of sea. Not everything is known about the islands, their peoples and their languages. A startling reminder of this is furnished by the fact that in Fiji, twenty years ago, were living two strange and solitary beings who came from an unknown country and spoke an unknown language. "They were picked up by a passing vessel many hundreds of miles from any known land, floating in the same tiny canoe in which they had been blown out to sea. When found they were but skin and bone. No one could understand what they said, and they have never named their country; or, if they have, the name does not correspond with that of any island on any chart. They are now fat and sleek, and as happy as the day is long. In the ship's log there is an entry of the latitude and longitude in which they were found, and this is probably all the clue they will ever have

to their lost homes."—[Forbes's "Two Years in Fiji."]

What a strange and romantic episode it is; and how one is tortured with curiosity to know whence those mysterious creatures came, those Men Without a Country, errant waifs who cannot name their lost home, wandering Children of Nowhere.

Indeed, the Island Wilderness is the very home of romance and dreams and mystery. The loneliness, the solemnity, the beauty, and the deep repose of this wilderness have a charm which is all their own for the bruised spirit of men who have fought and failed in the struggle for life in the great world; and for men who have been hunted out of the great world for crime; and for other men who love an easy and indolent existence; and for others who love a roving free life, and stir and change and adventure; and for yet others who love an easy and comfortable career of trading and money-getting, mixed with plenty of loose matrimony by purchase, divorce without trial or expense, and limitless spreeing thrown in to make life ideally perfect.

We sailed again, refreshed.

The most cultivated person in the ship was a young English, man whose home was in New Zealand. He was a naturalist. His learning in his specialty was deep and thorough, his interest in his subject amounted to a passion, he had an easy gift of speech; and so, when he talked about animals it was a pleasure to listen to him. And profitable, too, though he was sometimes difficult to understand because now and then he used scientific technicalities which were above the reach of some of us. They were pretty sure to be above my reach, but as he was quite willing to explain them I always made it a point to get him to do it. I had a fair knowledge of his subject—layman's knowledge—to begin with, but it was his teachings which crystalized it into scientific form and clarity—in a word, gave it value.

His special interest was the fauna of Australasia, and his knowledge of the matter was as exhaustive as it was accurate. I already knew a good deal about the rabbits in Australasia and their marvelous fecundity, but in my talks with him I found that my estimate of the great hindrance and obstruction inflicted by the rabbit pest upon traffic and travel was far short of the facts. He told me that the first pair of rabbits imported into Australasia bred so wonderfully that within six months rabbits were so thick in the land that people had to dig trenches through them to get from town to town.

He told me a great deal about worms, and the kangaroo, and other coleoptera, and said he knew the history and ways of all such pachydermata. He said the kangaroo had pockets, and carried its young in them when it couldn't get apples. And he said that the emu was as big as an ostrich, and looked like one, and had an amorphous appetite and would eat bricks. Also, that the dingo was not a dingo at all, but just a wild dog; and that the only difference between a dingo and a dodo was that neither of them barked; otherwise they were just the same. He said that the only game-bird in Australia was the wombat, and the only song-bird the larrikin, and that both were protected by government. The most beautiful of the native birds was the bird of Paradise. Next came the two kinds of lyres; not spelt the same. He said the one kind was dying out, the other thickening up. He explained that the "Sundowner" was not a bird it was a man; sundowner was merely the Australian equivalent of our word, tramp. He is a loafer, a hard drinker, and a sponge. He tramps across the country in the sheep-shearing season, pretending to look for work; but he always times himself to arrive at a sheep-run just at sundown, when the day's labor ends; all he wants is whisky and supper and bed and breakfast; he gets them and then disappears. The naturalist spoke of the bell bird, the creature that at short intervals all day rings out its mellow and exquisite peal from the deeps of the forest. It is the favorite and best friend of the weary and thirsty sundowner; for he knows that wherever the bell bird is, there is water; and he goes somewhere else. The naturalist said that the oddest bird in Australasia was the, Laughing Jackass, and the biggest the now extinct Great Moa.

The Moa stood thirteen feet high, and could step over an ordinary man's head or kick his hat off; and his head, too, for that matter. He said it was wingless, but a swift runner. The natives used to ride it. It could make forty miles an hour, and keep it up for four hundred miles and come out reasonably fresh. It was still in existence when the railway was introduced into New Zealand; still in existence, and carrying the mails. The railroad began with the same schedule it has now: two expresses a week-time, twenty miles an hour. The company exterminated the moa to get the mails.

Speaking of the indigenous coneys and bactrian camels, the naturalist said that the coniferous and bacteriological output of Australasia was remarkable for its many and curious departures from the accepted laws governing these species of tubercles, but that in his opinion Nature's fondness for dabbling in the erratic was most notably exhibited in that curious combination of bird, fish, amphibian, burrower, crawler, quadruped, and Christian called the Ornithorhynchus—grotesquest of animals, king of the animalculae of the world for versatility of character and make-up. Said he:

"You can call it anything you want to, and be right. It is a fish, for it lives in the river half the time; it is a land animal, for it resides on the land half the time; it is an amphibian, since it likes both and does not know which it prefers; it is a hybernian, for when times are dull and nothing much going on it buries itself under the mud at the bottom of a puddle and hybernates there a couple of weeks at a time; it is a kind of duck, for it has a duck-bill and four webbed paddles; it is a fish and quadruped together, for in the water it swims with the paddles and on shore it paws itself across country with them; it is a kind of seal, for it has a seal's fur; it is carnivorous, herbivorous, insectivorous, and vermifuginous, for it eats fish and grass and butterflies, and in the season digs worms out of the mud and devours them; it is clearly a bird, for it lays eggs, and hatches them; it is clearly a mammal, for it nurses its young; and it is manifestly a kind of Christian, for it keeps the Sabbath when there is anybody around, and when there isn't, doesn't. It has all the tastes there are except refined ones, it has all the habits there are except good ones.

"It is a survival—a survival of the fittest. Mr. Darwin invented the theory that goes by that name, but the Ornithorhynchus was the first to put it to actual experiment and prove that it could be done. Hence it should have as much of the credit as Mr. Darwin. It was never in the Ark; you will find no mention of it there; it nobly stayed out and worked the theory. Of all creatures in the world it was the only one properly equipped for the test. The Ark was thirteen months afloat, and all the globe submerged; no land visible above the flood, no vegetation, no food for a mammal to eat, nor water for a mammal to drink; for all mammal food was destroyed, and when the pure floods from heaven and the salt oceans of the earth mingled their waters and rose above the mountain tops,

the result was a drink which no bird or beast of ordinary construction could use and live. But this combination was nuts for the Ornithorhynchus, if I may use a term like that without offense. Its river home had always been salted by the flood-tides of the sea. On the face of the Noachian deluge innumerable forest trees were floating. Upon these the Ornithorhynchus voyaged in peace; voyaged from clime to clime, from hemisphere to hemisphere, in contentment and comfort, in virile interest in the constant change Of scene, in humble thankfulness for its privileges, in ever-increasing enthusiasm in the development of the great theory upon whose validity it had staked its life, its fortunes, and its sacred honor, if I may use such expressions without impropriety in connection with an episode of this nature.

"It lived the tranquil and luxurious life of a creature of independent means. Of things actually necessary to its existence and its happiness not a detail was wanting. When it wished to walk, it scrambled along the tree-trunk; it mused in the shade of the leaves by day, it slept in their shelter by night; when it wanted the refreshment of a swim, it had it; it ate leaves when it wanted a vegetable diet, it dug under the bark for worms and grubs; when it wanted fish it caught them, when it wanted eggs it laid them. If the grubs gave out in one tree it swam to another; and as for fish, the very opulence of the supply was an embarrassment. And finally, when it was thirsty it smacked its chops in gratitude over a blend that would have slain a crocodile.

"When at last, after thirteen months of travel and research in all the Zones it went aground on a mountain-summit, it strode ashore, saying in its heart, 'Let them that come after me invent theories and dream dreams about the Survival of the Fittest if they like, but I am the first that has done it!

"This wonderful creature dates back like the kangaroo and many other Australian hydrocephalous invertebrates, to an age long anterior to the advent of man upon the earth; they date back, indeed, to a time when a causeway hundreds of miles wide, and thousands of miles long, joined Australia to Africa, and the animals of the two countries were alike, and all belonged to that remote geological epoch known to science as the Old Red Grindstone Post-Pleosaurian. Later the causeway sank under the sea; subterranean convulsions lifted the African continent a thousand feet higher than it was before, but Australia kept her old level. In Africa's new climate the animals necessarily began to develop and shade off into new forms and families and species, but the animals of Australia as necessarily remained stationary, and have so remained until this day. In the course of some millions of years the African Ornithorhynchus developed and developed and developed, and sluffed off detail after detail of its make-up until at last the creature became wholly disintegrated and scattered. Whenever you see a bird or a beast or a seal or an otter in Africa you know that he is merely a sorry surviving fragment of that sublime original of whom I have been speaking—that creature which was everything in general and nothing in particular—the opulently endowed 'e pluribus unum' of the animal world.

"Such is the history of the most hoary, the most ancient, the most venerable creature that exists in the earth today—Ornithorhynchus Platypus Extraordinariensis—whom God preserve!"

When he was strongly moved he could rise and soar like that with ease. And not only in the prose form, but in the poetical as well. He had written many pieces of poetry in his time, and these manuscripts he lent around among the passengers, and was willing to let them be copied. It seemed to me that the least technical one in the series, and the one which reached the loftiest note, perhaps, was his:

INVOCATION.

"Come forth from thy oozy couch, O Ornithorhynchus dear! And greet with a cordial claw The stranger that longs to hear

"From thy own own lips the tale Of thy origin all unknown: Thy misplaced bone where flesh should be And flesh where should be bone;

"And fishy fin where should be paw, And beaver-trowel tail, And snout of beast equip'd with teeth Where gills ought to prevail.

"Come, Kangaroo, the good and true Foreshortened as to legs, And body tapered like a churn, And sack marsupial, i' fegs,

"And tells us why you linger here, Thou relic of a vanished time, When all your friends as fossils sleep, Immortalized in lime!"

Perhaps no poet is a conscious plagiarist; but there seems to be warrant for suspecting that there is no poet who is not at one time or another an unconscious one. The above verses are indeed beautiful, and, in a way, touching; but there is a haunting something about them which unavoidably suggests the Sweet Singer of Michigan. It can hardly be doubted that the author had read the works of that poet and been impressed by them. It is not apparent that he has borrowed from them any word or yet any phrase, but the style and swing and mastery and melody of the Sweet Singer all are there. Compare this Invocation with "Frank Dutton"—particularly stanzas first and seventeenth—and I think the reader will feel convinced that he who wrote the one had read the other:

I.

"Frank Dutton was as fine a lad As ever you wish to see, And he was drowned in Pine Island Lake On earth no more will he be, His age was near fifteen years, And he was a motherless boy, He was living with his grandmother When he was drowned, poor boy."

XVII.

"He was drowned on Tuesday afternoon, On Sunday he was found, And the tidings of that drowned boy Was heard for miles around. His form was laid by his mother's side, Beneath the cold, cold ground, His friends for him will drop a tear When they view his little mound."

The Sentimental Song Book. By Mrs. Julia Moore, p. 36.

CHAPTER IX.

It is your human environment that makes climate. — Pudd'nhead Wilson's New Calendar.

Sept. 15—Night. Close to Australia now. Sydney 50 miles distant.

That note recalls an experience. The passengers were sent for, to come up in the bow and see a fine sight. It was very dark. One could not follow with the eye the surface of the sea more

than fifty yards in any direction it dimmed away and became lost to sight at about that distance from us. But if you patiently gazed into the darkness a little while, there was a sure reward for you. Presently, a quarter of a mile away you would see a blinding splash or explosion of light on the water—a flash so sudden and so astonishingly brilliant that it would make you catch your breath; then that blotch of light would instantly extend itself and take the corkscrew shape and imposing length of the fabled sea-serpent, with every curve of its body and the "break" spreading away from its head, and the wake following behind its tail clothed in a fierce splendor of living fire. And my, but it was coming at a lightning gait! Almost before you could think, this monster of light, fifty feet long, would go flaming and storming by, and suddenly disappear. And out in the distance whence he came you would see another flash; and another and another and another, and see them turn into sea-serpents on the instant; and once sixteen flashed up at the same time and came tearing towards us, a swarm of wiggling curves, a moving conflagration, a vision of bewildering beauty, a spectacle of fire and energy whose equal the most of those people will not see again until after they are dead.

It was porpoises—porpoises aglow with phosphorescent light. They presently collected in a wild and magnificent jumble under the bows, and there they played for an hour, leaping and frollicking and carrying on, turning summersaults in front of the stem or across it and never getting hit, never making a miscalculation, though the stem missed them only about an inch, as a rule. They were porpoises of the ordinary length — eight or ten feet—but every twist of their bodies sent a long procession of united and glowing curves astern. That fiery jumble was an enchanting thing to look at, and we stayed out the performance; one cannot have such a show as that twice in a lifetime. The porpoise is the kitten of the sea; he never has a serious thought, he cares for nothing but fun and play. But I think I never saw him at his winsomest until that night. It was near a center of civilization, and he could have been drinking.

By and by, when we had approached to somewhere within thirty miles of Sydney Heads the great electric light that is posted on one of those lofty ramparts began to show, and in time the little spark grew to a great sun and pierced the firmament of darkness with a far-reaching sword of light.

Sydney Harbor is shut in behind a precipice that extends some miles like a wall, and exhibits no break to the ignorant stranger. It has a break in the middle, but it makes so little show that even Captain Cook sailed by it without seeing it. Near by that break is a false break which resembles it, and which used to make trouble for the mariner at night, in the early days before the place was lighted. It caused the memorable disaster to the Duncan Dunbar, one of the most pathetic tragedies in the history of that pitiless ruffian, the sea. The ship was a sailing vessel; a fine and favorite passenger packet, commanded by a popular captain of high reputation. She was due from England, and Sydney was waiting, and counting the hours; counting the hours, and making ready to give her a heart-stirring welcome; for she was bringing back a great company of mothers and daughters, the long-missed light and bloom of life of Sydney homes; daughters that had been years absent at school, and mothers that had been with them all that time watching over them. Of all the world only India and Australasia have by custom freighted ships and fleets with their hearts, and know the tremendous meaning of that phrase; only they know what the waiting is like when this freightage is entrusted to the fickle winds, not steam, and what the joy is like when the ship that is returning this treasure comes safe to port and the long dread is over.

On board the Duncan Dunbar, flying toward Sydney Heads in the waning afternoon, the happy home-comers made busy preparation, for it was not doubted that they would be in the arms of their friends before the day was done; they put away their sea-going clothes and put on clothes meeter for the meeting, their richest and their loveliest, these poor brides of the grave. But the wind lost force, or there was a miscalculation, and before the Heads were sighted the darkness came on. It was said that ordinarily the captain would have made a safe offing and waited for the morning; but this was no ordinary occasion; all about him were appealing faces, faces pathetic with disappointment. So his sympathy moved him to try the dangerous passage in the dark. He had entered the Heads seventeen times, and believed he knew the ground. So he steered straight for the false opening, mistaking it for the true one. He did not find out that he was wrong until it was too late. There was no saving the ship. The great seas swept her in and crushed her to splinters and rubbish upon the rock tushes at the base of the precipice. Not one of all that fair and gracious company was ever seen again alive. The tale is told to every stranger that passes the spot, and it will continue to be told to all that come, for generations; but it will never grow old, custom cannot stale it, the heart-break that is in it can never perish out of it.

There were two hundred persons in the ship, and but one survived the disaster. He was a sailor. A huge sea flung him up the face of the precipice and stretched him on a narrow shelf of rock midway between the top and the bottom, and there he lay all night. At any other time he would have lain there for the rest of his life, without chance of discovery; but the next morning the ghastly news swept through Sydney that the Duncan Dunbar had gone down in sight of home, and straightway the walls of the Heads were black with mourners; and one of these, stretching himself out over the precipice to spy out what might be seen below, discovered this miraculously preserved relic of the wreck. Ropes were brought and the nearly impossible feat of rescuing the man was accomplished. He was a person with a practical turn of mind, and he hired a hall in Sydney and exhibited himself at sixpence a head till he exhausted the output of the gold fields for that year.

We entered and cast anchor, and in the morning went oh-ing and ah-ing in admiration up through the crooks and turns of the spacious and beautiful harbor—a harbor which is the darling of Sydney and the wonder of the world. It is not surprising that the people are proud of it, nor that they put their enthusiasm into eloquent words! A returning citizen asked me what I thought of it, and I testified with a cordiality which I judged would be up to the market rate. I said it was beautiful—superbly beautiful. Then by a natural impulse I gave God the praise. The citizen did not seem altogether satisfied. He said:

"It is beautiful, of course it's beautiful—the Harbor; but that isn't all of it, it's only half of it; Sydney's the other half, and it takes both of them together to ring the supremacy-bell. God made the Harbor, and that's all right; but Satan made Sydney."

Of course I made an apology; and asked him to convey it to his friend. He was right about Sydney being half of it. It would be beautiful without Sydney, but not above half as beautiful as it is now, with Sydney added. It is shaped somewhat like an oak-leaf—a roomy sheet of lovely blue water, with narrow off-shoots of water running up into the country on both sides between long fingers of land, high wooden ridges with sides sloped like graves. Handsome villas are perched here and there on these ridges, snuggling amongst the foliage, and one catches alluring glimpses of them as the ship swims by toward the city. The city clothes a cluster of hills and a ruffle of neighboring ridges with its undulating masses of masonry, and out of these masses spring towers and spires and other architectural dignities and grandeurs that break the flowing lines and give picturesqueness to the general effect.

The narrow inlets which I have mentioned go wandering out into the land everywhere and hiding themselves in it, and pleasure-launches are always exploring them with picnic parties on board. It is said by trustworthy people that if you explore them all you will find that you have covered 700 miles of water passage. But there are liars everywhere this year, and they will double that when their works are in good going order. October was close at hand, spring was come. It was really spring —everybody said so; but you could have sold it for summer in Canada, and nobody would have suspected. It was the very weather that makes our home summers the perfection of climatic luxury; I mean, when you are out in the wood or by the sea. But these people said it was cool, now—a person ought to see Sydney in the summer time if he wanted to know what warm weather is; and he ought to go north ten or fifteen hundred miles if he wanted to know what hot weather is. They said that away up there toward the equator the hens laid fried eggs. Sydney is the place to go to get information about other people's climates. It seems to me that the occupation of Unbiased Traveler Seeking Information is the pleasantest and most irresponsible trade there is. The traveler can always find out anything he wants to, merely by asking. He can get at all the facts, and more. Everybody helps him, nobody hinders him. Anybody who has an old fact in stock that is no longer negotiable in the domestic market will let him have it at his own price. An accumulation of such goods is easily and quickly made. They cost almost nothing and they bring par in the foreign market. Travelers who come to America always freight up with the same old nursery tales that their predecessors selected, and they carry them back and always work them off without any trouble in the home market.

If the climates of the world were determined by parallels of latitude, then we could know a place's climate by its position on the map; and so we should know that the climate of Sydney was the counterpart of the climate of Columbia, S. C., and of Little Rock, Arkansas, since Sydney is about the same distance south of the equator that those other towns are north of-it-thirty-four degrees. But no, climate disregards the parallels of latitude. In Arkansas they have a winter; in Sydney they have the name of it, but not the thing itself. I have seen the ice in the Mississippi floating past the mouth of the Arkansas river; and at Memphis, but a little way above, the Mississippi has been frozen over, from bank to bank. But they have never had a cold spell in Sydney which brought the mercury down to freezing point. Once in a mid-winter day there, in the month of July, the mercury went down to 36 deg., and that remains the memorable "cold day" in the history of the town. No doubt Little Rock has seen it below zero. Once, in Sydney, in mid-summer, about New Year's Day, the mercury went up to 106 deg. in the shade, and that is Sydney's memorable hot day. That would about tally with Little Rock's hottest day also, I imagine. My Sydney figures are taken from a government report, and are trustworthy. In the matter of summer weather Arkansas has no advantage over Sydney, perhaps, but when it comes to winter weather, that is another affair. You could cut up an Arkansas winter into a hundred Sydney winters and have enough left for Arkansas and the poor.

The whole narrow, hilly belt of the Pacific side of New South Wales has the climate of its capital—a mean winter temperature of 54 deg. and a mean summer one of 71 deg. It is a climate which cannot be improved upon for healthfulness. But the experts say that 90 deg. in New South Wales is harder to bear than 112 deg. in the neighboring colony of Victoria, because the atmosphere of the former is humid, and of the latter dry. The mean temperature of the southernmost point of New South Wales is the same as that of Nice—60 deg.—yet Nice is further from the equator by 460 miles than is the former.

But Nature is always stingy of perfect climates; stingier in the case of Australia than usual. Apparently this vast continent has a really good climate nowhere but around the edges.

If we look at a map of the world we are surprised to see how big Australia is. It is about two-thirds as large as the United States was before we added Alaska.

But where as one finds a sufficiently good climate and fertile land almost everywhere in the United States, it seems settled that inside of the Australian border-belt one finds many deserts and in spots a climate which nothing can stand except a few of the hardier kinds of rocks. In effect, Australia is as yet unoccupied. If you take a map of the United States and leave the Atlantic sea-board States in their places; also the fringe of Southern States from Florida west to the Mouth of the Mississippi; also a narrow, inhabited streak up the Mississippi half-way to its head waters; also a narrow, inhabited border along the Pacific coast: then take a brushful of paint and obliterate the whole remaining mighty stretch of country that lies between the Atlantic States and the Pacific-coast strip, your map will look like the latest map of Australia.

This stupendous blank is hot, not to say torrid; a part of it is fertile, the rest is desert; it is not liberally watered; it has no towns. One has only to cross the mountains of New South Wales and descend into the westward-lying regions to find that he has left the choice climate behind him, and found a new one of a quite different character. In fact, he would not know by the thermometer that he was not in the blistering Plains of India. Captain Sturt, the great explorer, gives us a sample of the heat.

"The wind, which had been blowing all the morning from the N.E., increased to a heavy gale, and I shall never forget its withering effect. I sought shelter behind a large gum-tree, but the blasts of heat were so terrific that I wondered the very grass did not take fire. This really was nothing ideal: everything both animate and inanimate gave way before it; the horses stood with their backs to the wind and their noses to the ground, without the muscular strength to raise their heads; the birds were mute, and the leaves of the trees under which we were sitting fell like a snow shower around us. At noon I took a thermometer graded to 127 deg., out of my box, and observed that the mercury was up to 125. Thinking that it had been unduly influenced, I put it in the fork of a tree close to me, sheltered alike from the wind and the sun. I went to examine it about an hour afterwards, when I found the mercury had risen to the-top of the instrument and had burst the bulb, a circumstance that I believe no traveler has ever before had to record. I cannot find language to convey to the reader's mind an idea of the intense and oppressive nature of the heat that prevailed."

That hot wind sweeps over Sydney sometimes, and brings with it what is called a "dust-storm." It is said that most Australian towns are acquainted with the dust-storm. I think I know what it is like, for the following description by Mr. Gape tallies very well with the alkali duststorm of Nevada, if you leave out the "shovel" part. Still the shovel part is a pretty important part, and seems to indicate that my Nevada storm is but a poor thing, after all.

"As we proceeded the altitude became less, and the heat proportionately greater until we reached Dubbo, which is only 600 feet above sea-level. It is a pretty town, built on an extensive plain . . . . After the effects of a shower of rain have passed away the surface of the ground crumbles into a thick layer of dust, and occasionally, when the wind is in a particular quarter, it is lifted bodily from the ground in one long opaque cloud. In the midst of such a storm nothing can be seen a few yards ahead, and the unlucky person who happens to be out at the time is compelled to seek the nearest retreat at hand. When the thrifty housewife sees in the distance the dark column advancing in a steady whirl towards her house, she closes the doors and windows with all expedition. A drawing-room, the window of which has been carelessly left open during a dust-storm, is indeed an extraordinary sight. A lady who has resided in Dubbo for some years says that the dust lies so thick on the carpet that it is necessary to use a shovel to remove it."

And probably a wagon. I was mistaken; I have not seen a proper duststorm. To my mind the exterior aspects and character of Australia are fascinating things to look at and think about, they are so strange, so weird, so new, so uncommonplace, such a startling and interesting contrast to the other sections of the planet, the sections that are known to us all, familiar to us all. In the matter of particulars—a detail here, a detail there—we have had the choice climate of New South Wales' seacoast; we have had the Australian heat as furnished by Captain Sturt; we have had the wonderful dust-storm; and we have considered the phenomenon of an almost empty hot wilderness half as big as the United States, with a narrow belt of civilization, population, and good climate around it.

CHAPTER X.

Everything human is pathetic. The secret source of Humor itself is not joy but sorrow. There is no humor in heaven. — Pudd'nhead Wilson's New Calendar.

Captain Cook found Australia in 1770, and eighteen years later the British Government began to transport convicts to it. Altogether, New South Wales received 83,000 in 53 years. The convicts wore heavy chains; they were ill-fed and badly treated by the officers set over them; they were heavily punished for even slight infractions of the rules; "the cruelest discipline ever known" is one historian's description of their life.—[The Story of Australasia. J. S. Laurie.]

English law was hard-hearted in those days. For trifling offenses which in our day would be punished by a small fine or a few days' confinement, men, women, and boys were sent to this other end of the earth to serve terms of seven and fourteen years; and for serious crimes they were transported for life. Children were sent to the penal colonies for seven years for stealing a rabbit!

When I was in London twenty-three years ago there was a new penalty in force for diminishing garroting and wife-beating—

25 lashes on the bare back with the cat-o'-nine-tails. It was said that this terrible punishment was able to bring the stubbornest ruffians to terms; and that no man had been found with grit enough to keep his emotions to himself beyond the ninth blow; as a rule the man shrieked earlier. That penalty had a great and wholesome effect upon the garroters and wife-beaters; but humane modern London could not endure it; it got its law rescinded. Many a bruised and battered English wife has since had occasion to deplore that cruel achievement of sentimental "humanity."

Twenty-five lashes! In Australia and Tasmania they gave a convict fifty for almost any little offense; and sometimes a brutal officer would add fifty, and then another fifty, and so on, as long as the sufferer could endure the torture and live. In Tasmania I read the entry, in an old manuscript official record, of a case where a convict was given three hundred lashes—for stealing some silver spoons. And men got more than that, sometimes. Who handled the cat? Often it was another convict; sometimes it was the culprit's dearest comrade; and he had to lay on with all his might; otherwise he would get a flogging himself for his mercy —for he was under watch—and yet not do his friend any good: the friend would be attended to by another hand and suffer no lack in the matter of full punishment.

The convict life in Tasmania was so unendurable, and suicide so difficult to accomplish that once or twice despairing men got together and drew straws to determine which of them should kill another of the group—this murder to secure death to the perpetrator and to the witnesses of it by the hand of the hangman!

The incidents quoted above are mere hints, mere suggestions of what convict life was like—they are but a couple of details tossed into view out of a shoreless sea of such; or, to change the figure, they are but a pair of flaming steeples photographed from a point which hides from sight the burning city which stretches away from their bases on every hand.

Some of the convicts—indeed, a good many of them—were very bad people, even for that day; but the most of them were probably not noticeably worse than the average of the people they left behind them at home. We must believe this; we cannot avoid it. We are obliged to believe that a nation that could look on, unmoved, and see starving or freezing women hanged for stealing twenty-six cents' worth of bacon or rags, and boys snatched from their mothers, and men from their families, and sent to the other side of the world for long terms of years for similar trifling offenses, was a nation to whom the term "civilized" could not in any large way be applied. And we must also believe that a nation that knew, during more than forty years, what was happening to those exiles and was still content with it, was not advancing in any showy way toward a higher grade of civilization.

If we look into the characters and conduct of the officers and gentlemen who had charge of the convicts and attended to their backs and stomachs, we must grant again that as between the convict and his masters, and between both and the nation at home, there was a quite noticeable monotony of sameness.

Four years had gone by, and many convicts had come. Respectable settlers were beginning to arrive. These two classes of colonists had to be protected, in case of trouble among themselves or with the natives. It is proper to mention the natives, though they could hardly count they were so scarce. At a time when they had not as yet begun to be much disturbed—not as yet being in the way—it was estimated that in New South Wales there was but one native to 45,000 acres of territory.

People had to be protected. Officers of the regular army did not want this service—away off there where neither honor nor distinction was to be gained. So England recruited and officered a kind of militia force of 1,000 uniformed civilians called the "New South Wales Corps" and shipped it.

This was the worst blow of all. The colony fairly staggered under it. The Corps was an object-lesson of the moral condition of England outside of the jails. The colonists trembled. It was feared that next there would be an importation of the nobility.

In those early days the colony was non-supporting. All the necessaries of life—food, clothing, and all—were sent out from England, and kept in great government store-houses, and given to the convicts and sold to the settlers—sold at a trifling advance upon cost. The Corps saw its opportunity. Its officers went into commerce, and in a most lawless way. They went to importing rum, and also to manufacturing it in private stills, in defiance of the government's commands and protests. They leagued themselves together and ruled the market; they boycotted the government and the other dealers; they established a close monopoly and kept it strictly in their own hands. When a vessel arrived with spirits, they allowed nobody to buy but themselves, and they forced the owner to sell to them at a price named by themselves—and it was always low enough. They bought rum at an average of two dollars a gallon and sold it at an average of ten. They made rum the currency of the country—for there was little or no money—and they maintained their devastating hold and kept the colony under their heel for eighteen or twenty years before they were finally conquered and routed by the government.

Meantime, they had spread intemperance everywhere. And they had squeezed farm after farm out of the settlers hands for rum, and thus had bountifully enriched themselves. When a farmer was caught in the last agonies of thirst they took advantage of him and sweated him for a drink. In one instance they sold a man a gallon of rum worth two dollars for a piece of property which was sold some years later for $100,000. When the colony was about eighteen or twenty years old it was discovered that the land was specially fitted for the wool-culture. Prosperity followed, commerce with the world began, by and by rich mines of the noble metals were opened, immigrants flowed in, capital likewise. The result is the great and wealthy and enlightened commonwealth of New South Wales.

It is a country that is rich in mines, wool ranches, trams, railways, steamship lines, schools, newspapers, botanical gardens, art galleries, libraries, museums, hospitals, learned societies; it is the hospitable home of every species of culture and of every species of material enterprise, and there is a, church at every man's door, and a race-track over the way.

CHAPTER XI.

We should be careful to get out of an experience only the wisdom that is in it—and stop there; lest we be like the cat that sits down on a hot stove-lid. She will never sit down on a hot stove-lid again—and that is well; but also she will never sit down on a cold one any more. —Pudd'nhead Wilson's New Calendar.

All English-speaking colonies are made up of lavishly hospitable people, and New South Wales and its capital are like the rest in this. The English-speaking colony of the United States of America is always called lavishly hospitable by the English traveler. As to the other English-speaking colonies throughout the world from Canada all around, I know by experience that the description fits them. I will not go more particularly into this matter, for I find that when writers try to distribute their gratitude here and there and yonder by detail they run across difficulties and do some ungraceful stumbling.

Mr. Gane ("New South Wales and Victoria in 1885 "), tried to distribute his gratitude, and was not lucky:

"The inhabitants of Sydney are renowned for their hospitality. The treatment which we experienced at the hands of this generous-hearted people will help more than anything else to make us recollect with pleasure our stay amongst them. In the character of hosts and hostesses they excel. The 'new chum' needs only the acquaintanceship of one of their number, and he becomes at once the happy recipient of numerous complimentary invitations and thoughtful kindnesses. Of the towns it has been our good fortune to visit, none have portrayed home so faithfully as Sydney."

Nobody could say it finer than that. If he had put in his cork then, and stayed away from Dubbo—but no; heedless man, he pulled it again. Pulled it when he was away along in his book, and his memory of what he had said about Sydney had grown dim:

"We cannot quit the promising town of Dubbo without testifying, in warm praise, to the kind-hearted and hospitable usages of its inhabitants. Sydney, though well deserving the character it bears of its kindly treatment of strangers, possesses a little formality and reserve. In Dubbo, on the contrary, though the same congenial manners prevail, there is a pleasing degree of respectful familiarity which gives the town a homely comfort not often met with elsewhere. In laying on one side our pen we feel contented in having been able, though so late in this work, to bestow a panegyric, however unpretentious, on a town which, though possessing no picturesque natural surroundings, nor interesting architectural productions, has yet a body of citizens whose hearts cannot but obtain for their town a reputation for benevolence and kind-heartedness."

I wonder what soured him on Sydney. It seems strange that a pleasing degree of three or four fingers of respectful familiarity should fill a man up and give him the panegyrics so bad. For he has them, the worst way—any one can see that. A man who is perfectly at himself does not throw cold detraction at people's architectural productions and picturesque surroundings, and let on that what he prefers is a Dubbonese dust-storm and a pleasing degree of respectful familiarity, No, these are old, old symptoms; and when they appear we know that the man has got the panegyrics.

Sydney has a population of 400,000. When a stranger from America steps ashore there, the first thing that strikes him is that the place is eight or nine times as large as he was expecting it to be; and the next thing that strikes him is that it is an English city with American trimmings. Later on, in Melbourne, he will find the American trimmings still more in evidence; there, even the architecture will often suggest America; a photograph of its stateliest business street might be passed upon him for a picture of the finest street in a large

American city. I was told that the most of the fine residences were the city residences of squatters. The name seemed out of focus somehow. When the explanation came, it offered a new instance of the curious changes which words, as well as animals, undergo through change of habitat and climate. With us, when you speak of a squatter you are always supposed to be speaking of a poor man, but in Australia when you speak of a squatter you are supposed to be speaking of a millionaire; in America the word indicates the possessor of a few acres and a doubtful title, in Australia it indicates a man whose landfront is as long as a railroad, and whose title has been perfected in one way or another; in America the word indicates a man who owns a dozen head of live stock, in Australia a man who owns anywhere from fifty thousand up to half a million head; in America the word indicates a man who is obscure and not important, in Australia a man who is prominent and of the first importance; in America you take off your hat to no squatter, in Australia you do; in America if your uncle is a squatter you keep it dark, in Australia you advertise it; in America if your friend is a squatter nothing comes of it, but with a squatter for your friend in Australia you may sup with kings if there are any around.

In Australia it takes about two acres and a half of pastureland (some people say twice as many), to support a sheep; and when the squatter has half a million sheep his private domain is about as large as Rhode Island, to speak in general terms. His annual wool crop may be worth a quarter or a half million dollars.

He will live in a palace in Melbourne or Sydney or some other of the large cities, and make occasional trips to his sheep-kingdom several hundred miles away in the great plains to look after his battalions of riders and shepherds and other hands. He has a commodious dwelling out there, and if he approve of you he will invite you to spend a week in it, and will make you at home and comfortable, and let you see the great industry in all its details, and feed you and slake you and smoke you with the best that money can buy.

On at least one of these vast estates there is a considerable town, with all the various businesses and occupations that go to make an important town; and the town and the land it stands upon are the property of the squatters. I have seen that town, and it is not unlikely that there are other squatter-owned towns in Australia.

Australia supplies the world not only with fine wool, but with mutton also. The modern invention of cold storage and its application in ships has created this great trade. In Sydney I visited a huge establishment where they kill and clean and solidly freeze a thousand sheep a day, for shipment to England.

The Australians did not seem to me to differ noticeably from Americans, either in dress, carriage, ways, pronunciation, inflections, or general appearance. There were fleeting and subtle suggestions of their English origin, but these were not pronounced enough, as a rule, to catch one's attention. The people have easy and cordial manners from the beginning — from the moment that the introduction is completed. This is American. To put it in another way, it is English friendliness with the English shyness and self-consciousness left out.

Now and then—but this is rare—one hears such words as piper for paper, lydy for lady, and tyble for table fall from lips whence one would not expect such pronunciations to come. There is a superstition prevalent in Sydney that this pronunciation is an Australianism, but people who have been "home"—as the native reverently and lovingly calls England—know better. It is "costermonger." All over Australasia this pronunciation is nearly as common among servants as it is in London among the uneducated and the partially educated of all sorts and conditions of people. That mislaid 'y' is rather striking when a person gets enough of it into a short sentence to enable it to show up. In the hotel in Sydney the chambermaid said, one morning:

"The tyble is set, and here is the piper; and if the lydy is ready I'll tell the wyter to bring up the breakfast."

I have made passing mention, a moment ago, of the native Australasian's custom of speaking of England as "home." It was always pretty to hear it, and often it was said in an unconsciously caressing way that made it touching; in a way which transmuted a sentiment into an embodiment, and made one seem to see Australasia as a young girl stroking mother England's old gray head.

In the Australasian home the table-talk is vivacious and unembarrassed; it is without stiffness or restraint. This does not remind one of England so much as it does of America. But Australasia is strictly democratic, and reserves and restraints are things that are bred by differences of rank.

English and colonial audiences are phenomenally alert and responsive. Where masses of people are gathered together in England, caste is submerged, and with it the English reserve; equality exists for the moment, and every individual is free; so free from any consciousness of fetters, indeed, that the Englishman's habit of watching himself and guarding himself against any injudicious exposure of his feelings is forgotten, and falls into abeyance—and to such a degree indeed, that he will bravely applaud all by himself if he wants to—an exhibition of daring which is unusual elsewhere in the world.

But it is hard to move a new English acquaintance when he is by himself, or when the company present is small and new to him. He is on his guard then, and his natural reserve is to the fore. This has given him the false reputation of being without humor and without the appreciation of humor.

Americans are not Englishmen, and American humor is not English humor; but both the American and his humor had their origin in England, and have merely undergone changes brought about by changed conditions and a new environment. About the best humorous speeches I have yet heard were a couple that were made in Australia at club suppers—one of them by an Englishman, the other by an Australian.

CHAPTER XII.

There are those who scoff at the schoolboy, calling him frivolous and shallow: Yet it was the schoolboy who said "Faith is believing what you know ain't so." —Pudd'nhead Wilson's New Calendar.

In Sydney I had a large dream, and in the course of talk I told it to a missionary from India who was on his way to visit some relatives in New Zealand. I dreamed that the visible universe is the physical person of God; that the vast worlds that we see twinkling millions of miles apart in the fields of space are the blood corpuscles in His veins; and that we and the other creatures are the microbes that charge with multitudinous life the corpuscles.

Mr. X., the missionary, considered the dream awhile, then said:

"It is not surpassable for magnitude, since its metes and bounds are the metes and bounds of the universe itself; and it seems to me that it almost accounts for a thing which is otherwise nearly unaccountable—the origin of the sacred legends of the Hindoos. Perhaps they dream them, and then honestly believe them to be divine revelations of fact. It looks like that, for the legends are built on so vast a scale that it does not seem reasonable that plodding priests would happen upon such colossal fancies when awake."

He told some of the legends, and said that they were implicitly believed by all classes of Hindoos, including those of high social position and intelligence; and he said that this universal credulity was a great hindrance to the missionary in his work. Then he said something like this:

"At home, people wonder why Christianity does not make faster progress in India. They hear that the Indians believe easily, and that they have a natural trust in miracles and give them a hospitable reception. Then they argue like this: since the Indian believes easily, place Christianity before them and they must believe; confirm its truths by the biblical miracles, and they will no longer doubt, The natural deduction is, that as Christianity makes but indifferent progress in India, the fault is with us: we are not fortunate in presenting the doctrines and the miracles.

"But the truth is, we are not by any means so well equipped as they think. We have not the easy task that they imagine. To use a military figure, we are sent against the enemy with good powder in our guns, but only wads for bullets; that is to say, our miracles are not effective; the Hindoos do not care for them; they have more extraordinary ones of their own. All the details of their own religion are proven and established by miracles; the details of ours must be proven in the same way. When I first began my work in India I greatly underestimated the difficulties thus put upon my task. A correction was not long in coming. I thought as our friends think at home—that to prepare my childlike wonder-lovers to listen with favor to my grave message I only needed to charm the way to it with wonders, marvels, miracles. With full confidence I told the wonders performed by Samson, the strongest man that had ever lived—for so I called him.

"At first I saw lively anticipation and strong interest in the faces of my people, but as I moved along from incident to incident of the great story, I was distressed to see that I was steadily losing the sympathy of my audience. I could not understand it. It was a surprise to me, and a disappointment. Before I was through, the fading sympathy had paled to indifference. Thence to the end the indifference remained; I was not able to make any impression upon it.

"A good old Hindoo gentleman told me where my trouble lay. He said 'We Hindoos recognize a god by the work of his hands—we accept no other testimony. Apparently, this is also the rule with you Christians. And we know when a man has his power from a god by the fact that he does things which he could not do, as a man, with the mere powers of a man. Plainly, this is the Christian's way also, of knowing when a man is working by a god's power and not by his own. You saw that there was a supernatural property in the hair of Samson; for you perceived that when his hair was gone he was as other men. It is our way, as I have said. There are many nations in the world, and each group of nations has its own gods, and will pay no worship to the gods of the others. Each group believes its own gods to be strongest, and it will not exchange them except for gods that shall be proven to be their superiors in power. Man is but a weak creature, and needs the help of gods—he cannot do without it. Shall he place his fate in the hands of weak gods when there may be stronger ones to be found? That would be foolish. No, if he hear of gods that are stronger than his own, he should not turn a deaf ear, for it is not a light matter that is at stake. How then shall he determine which gods are the stronger, his own or those that preside over the concerns of other nations? By comparing the known works of his own gods with the works of those others; there is no other way. Now, when we make this comparison, we are not drawn towards the gods of any other nation. Our gods are shown by their works to be the strongest, the most powerful. The Christians have but few gods, and they are new—new, and not strong; as it seems to us. They will increase in number, it is true, for this has happened with all gods, but that time is far away, many ages and decades of ages away, for gods multiply slowly, as is meet for beings to whom a thousand years is but a single moment. Our own gods have been born millions of years apart. The process is slow, the gathering of strength and power is similarly slow. In the slow lapse of the ages the steadily accumulating power of our gods has at last become prodigious. We have a thousand proofs of this in the colossal character of their personal acts and the acts of ordinary men to whom they have given supernatural qualities. To your Samson was given supernatural power, and when he broke the withes, and slew the thousands with the jawbone of an ass, and carried away the gate's of the city upon his shoulders, you were amazed—and also awed, for you recognized the divine source of his strength. But it could not profit to place these things before your Hindoo congregation and invite their wonder; for they would compare them with the deed done by Hanuman, when our gods infused their divine strength into his muscles; and they would be indifferent to them—as you saw. In the old, old times, ages and ages gone by, when our god Rama was warring with the demon god of Ceylon, Rama bethought him to bridge the sea and connect Ceylon with India, so that his armies might pass easily over; and he sent his general, Hanuman, inspired like your own Samson with divine strength, to bring the materials for the bridge. In two days Hanuman strode fifteen hundred miles, to the Himalayas, and took upon his shoulder a range of those lofty mountains two hundred miles long, and started with it toward Ceylon. It was in the night; and, as he passed along the plain, the people of Govardhun heard the thunder of his tread and felt the earth rocking under it, and they ran out, and there, with their snowy summits piled to heaven, they saw the Himalayas passing by. And as this huge continent swept along overshadowing the earth, upon its slopes they discerned the twinkling lights of a thousand sleeping villages, and it was as if the constellations were filing in procession through the sky. While they were looking, Hanuman stumbled, and a small ridge of red sandstone twenty miles long was jolted loose and fell. Half of its length has wasted away in the course of the ages, but the other ten miles of it remain in the plain by Govardhun to this day as proof of the might of the inspiration of our gods. You must know, yourself, that Hanuman could not have carried those mountains to Ceylon except by the strength of the gods. You know that it was not done by his own strength, therefore, you know that it was done by the strength of the gods, just as you know that Samson carried the gates by the divine strength and not by his own. I think you must concede two things: First, That in carrying the gates of the city upon his shoulders, Samson did not establish the superiority of his gods over ours; secondly, That his feat is not supported by any but verbal evidence, while Hanuman's is not only supported by verbal evidence, but this evidence is confirmed, established, proven, by visible, tangible evidence, which is the strongest of all testimony. We have the sandstone ridge, and while it remains we cannot doubt, and shall not. Have you the gates?'"

CHAPTER XIII.

The timid man yearns for full value and asks a tenth. The bold man strikes for double value and compromises on par.
—Pudd'nhead Wilson's New Calendar.

One is sure to be struck by the liberal way in which Australasia spends money upon public works—such as legislative buildings, town halls, hospitals, asylums, parks, and botanical gardens. I should say that where minor towns in America spend a hundred dollars on the town hall and on public parks and gardens, the like towns in Australasia spend a thousand. And I think that this ratio will hold good in the matter of hospitals, also. I have seen a costly and well-equipped, and architecturally handsome hospital in an Australian village of fifteen hundred inhabitants. It was built by private funds furnished by the villagers and the neighboring planters, and its running expenses were drawn from the same sources. I suppose it would be hard to match this in any country. This village was about to close a contract for lighting its streets with the electric light, when I was there. That is ahead of London. London is still obscured by gas—gas pretty widely scattered, too, in some of the districts; so widely indeed, that except on moonlight nights it is difficult to find the gas lamps.

The botanical garden of Sydney covers thirty-eight acres, beautifully laid out and rich with the spoil of all the lands and all the climes of the world. The garden is on high ground in the middle of the town, overlooking the great harbor, and it adjoins the spacious grounds of Government House—fifty-six acres; and at hand also, is a recreation ground containing eighty-two acres. In addition, there are the zoological gardens, the race-course, and the great cricket-grounds where the international matches are played. Therefore there is plenty of room for reposeful lazing and lounging, and for exercise too, for such as like that kind of work.

There are four specialties attainable in the way of social pleasure. If you enter your name on the Visitor's Book at Government House you will receive an invitation to the next ball that takes place there, if nothing can be proven against you. And it will be very pleasant; for you will see everybody except the Governor, and add a number of acquaintances and several friends to your list. The Governor will be in England. He always is. The continent has four or five governors, and I do not know how many it takes to govern the outlying archipelago; but anyway you will not see them. When they are appointed they come out from England and get inaugurated, and give a ball, and help pray for rain, and get aboard ship and go back home. And so the Lieutenant-Governor has to do all the work. I was in Australasia three months and a half, and saw only one Governor. The others were at home.

The Australasian Governor would not be so restless, perhaps, if he had a war, or a veto, or something like that to call for his reserve-energies, but he hasn't. There isn't any war, and there isn't any veto in his hands. And so there is really little or nothing doing in his line. The country governs itself, and prefers to do it; and is so strenuous about it and so jealous of its independence that it grows restive if even the Imperial Government at home proposes to help; and so the Imperial veto, while a fact, is yet mainly a name.

Thus the Governor's functions are much more limited than are a Governor's functions with us. And therefore more fatiguing. He is the apparent head of the State, he is the real head of Society. He represents culture, refinement, elevated sentiment, polite life, religion; and by his example he propagates these, and they spread and flourish and bear good fruit. He creates the fashion, and leads it. His ball is the ball of balls, and his countenance makes the horse-race thrive.

He is usually a lord, and this is well; for his position compels him to lead an expensive life, and an English lord is generally well equipped for that.

Another of Sydney's social pleasures is the visit to the Admiralty House; which is nobly situated on high ground overlooking the water. The trim boats of the service convey the guests thither; and there, or on board the flag-ship, they have the duplicate of the hospitalities of Government House. The Admiral commanding a station in British waters is a magnate of the first degree, and he is sumptuously housed, as becomes the dignity of his office.

Third in the list of special pleasures is the tour of the harbor in a fine steam pleasure-launch. Your richer friends own boats of this kind, and they will invite you, and the joys of the trip will make a long day seem short.

And finally comes the shark-fishing. Sydney Harbor is populous with the finest breeds of man-eating sharks in the world. Some people make their living catching them; for the Government pays a cash bounty on them. The larger the shark the larger the bounty, and some of the sharks are twenty feet long. You not only get the bounty, but everything that is in the shark belongs to you. Sometimes the contents are quite valuable.

The shark is the swiftest fish that swims. The speed of the fastest steamer afloat is poor compared to his. And he is a great gad-about, and roams far and wide in the oceans, and visits the shores of all of them, ultimately, in the course of his restless excursions. I have a tale to tell now, which has not as yet been in print. In 1870 a young stranger arrived in Sydney, and set about finding something to do; but he knew no one, and brought no recommendations, and the result was that he got no employment. He had aimed high, at first, but as time and his money wasted away he grew less and less exacting, until at last he was willing to serve in the humblest capacities if so he might get bread and shelter. But luck was still against him; he could find no opening of any sort. Finally his money was all gone. He walked the streets all day, thinking; he walked them all night, thinking, thinking, and growing hungrier and hungrier. At dawn he found himself well away from the town and drifting aimlessly along the harbor shore. As he was passing by a nodding shark-fisher the man looked up and said—

"Say, young fellow, take my line a spell, and change my luck for me."

"How do you know I won't make it worse?"

"Because you can't. It has been at its worst all night. If you can't change it, no harm's done; if you do change it, it's for the better, of course. Come."

"All right, what will you give?"

"I'll give you the shark, if you catch one."

"And I will eat it, bones and all. Give me the line."

"Here you are. I will get away, now, for awhile, so that my luck won't spoil yours; for many and many a time I've noticed that if—there, pull in, pull in, man, you've got a bite! I knew how it would be. Why, I knew you for a born son of luck the minute I saw you. All right—he's landed."

It was an unusually large shark—"a full nineteen-footer," the fisherman said, as he laid the creature open with his knife.

"Now you rob him, young man, while I step to my hamper for a fresh bait. There's generally something in them worth going for. You've changed my luck, you see. But my goodness, I hope you haven't changed your own."

"Oh, it wouldn't matter; don't worry about that. Get your bait. I'll rob him."

When the fisherman got back the young man had just finished washing his hands in the bay, and was starting away.

"What, you are not going?"

"Yes. Good-bye."

"But what about your shark?"

"The shark? Why, what use is he to me?"

"What use is he? I like that. Don't you know that we can go and report him to Government, and you'll get a clean solid eighty shillings bounty? Hard cash, you know. What do you think about it now?"

"Oh, well, you can collect it."

"And keep it? Is that what you mean?"

"Yes."

"Well, this is odd. You're one of those sort they call eccentrics, I judge. The saying is, you mustn't judge a man by his clothes, and I'm believing it now. Why yours are looking just ratty, don't you know; and yet you must be rich."

"I am."

The young man walked slowly back to the town, deeply musing as he went. He halted a moment in front of the best restaurant, then glanced at his clothes and passed on, and got his breakfast at a "stand-up." There was a good deal of it, and it cost five shillings. He tendered a sovereign, got his change, glanced at his silver, muttered to himself, "There isn't enough to buy clothes with," and went his way.

At half-past nine the richest wool-broker in Sydney was sitting in his morning-room at home, settling his breakfast with the morning paper. A servant put his head in and said:

"There's a sundowner at the door wants to see you, sir."

"What do you bring that kind of a message here for? Send him about his business."

"He won't go, sir. I've tried."

"He won't go? That's—why, that's unusual. He's one of two things, then: he's a remarkable person, or he's crazy. Is he crazy?"

"No, sir. He don't look it."

"Then he's remarkable. What does he say he wants?"

"He won't tell, sir; only says it's very important."

"And won't go. Does he say he won't go?"

"Says he'll stand there till he sees you, sir, if it's all day."

"And yet isn't crazy. Show him up."

The sundowner was shown in. The broker said to himself, "No, he's not crazy; that is easy to see; so he must be the other thing."

Then aloud, "Well, my good fellow, be quick about it; don't waste any words; what is it you want?"

"I want to borrow a hundred thousand pounds."

"Scott! (It's a mistake; he is crazy . . . . No—he can't be—not with that eye.) Why, you take my breath away. Come, who are you?"

"Nobody that you know."

"What is your name?"

"Cecil Rhodes."

"No, I don't remember hearing the name before. Now then—just for curiosity's sake—what has sent you to me on this extraordinary errand?"

"The intention to make a hundred thousand pounds for you and as much for myself within the next sixty days."

"Well, well, well. It is the most extraordinary idea that—sit down—you interest me. And somehow you—well, you fascinate me; I think that that is about the word. And it isn't your proposition—no, that doesn't fascinate me; it's something else, I don't quite know what; something that's born in you and oozes out of you, I suppose. Now then just for curiosity's sake again, nothing more: as I understand it, it is your desire to bor—"

"I said intention."

"Pardon, so you did. I thought it was an unheedful use of the word—an unheedful valuing of its strength, you know."

"I knew its strength."

"Well, I must say—but look here, let me walk the floor a little, my mind is getting into a sort of whirl, though you don't seem disturbed any. (Plainly this young fellow isn't crazy; but as to his being remarkable —well, really he amounts to that, and something over.) Now then, I believe I am beyond the reach of further astonishment. Strike, and spare not. What is your scheme?"

"To buy the wool crop—deliverable in sixty days."

"What, the whole of it?"

"The whole of it."

"No, I was not quite out of the reach of surprises, after all. Why, how you talk! Do you know what our crop is going to foot up?"

"Two and a half million sterling—maybe a little more."

"Well, you've got your statistics right, any way. Now, then, do you know what the margins would foot up, to buy it at sixty days?"

"The hundred thousand pounds I came here to get."

"Right, once more. Well, dear me, just to see what would happen, I wish you had the money. And if you had it, what would you do with it?"

"I shall make two hundred thousand pounds out of it in sixty days."

"You mean, of course, that you might make it if—"

"I said 'shall'."

"Yes, by George, you did say 'shall'! You are the most definite devil I ever saw, in the matter of language. Dear, dear, dear, look here! Definite speech means clarity of mind. Upon my word I believe you've got what you believe to be a rational reason, for venturing into this house, an entire stranger, on this wild scheme of buying the wool crop of an entire colony on speculation. Bring it out—I am prepared—acclimatized, if I may use the word. Why would you buy the crop, and why would you make that sum out of it? That is to say, what makes you think you—"

"I don't think—I know."

"Definite again. How do you know?"

"Because France has declared war against Germany, and wool has gone up fourteen per cent. in London and is still rising."

"Oh, in-deed? Now then, I've got you! Such a thunderbolt as you have just let fly ought to have made me jump out of my chair, but it didn't stir me the least little bit, you see. And for a very simple reason: I have read the morning paper. You can look at it if you want to. The fastest ship in the service arrived at eleven o'clock last night, fifty days out from London. All her news is printed here. There are no war-clouds anywhere; and as for wool, why, it is the low-spiritedest commodity in the English market. It is your turn to jump, now . . . . Well, why, don't you jump? Why do you sit there in that placid fashion, when—"

"Because I have later news."

"Later news? Oh, come—later news than fifty days, brought steaming hot from London by the—"

"My news is only ten days old."

"Oh, Mun-chausen, hear the maniac talk! Where did you get it?"

"Got it out of a shark."

"Oh, oh, oh, this is too much! Front! call the police bring the gun —raise the town! All the asylums in Christendom have broken loose in the single person of—"

"Sit down! And collect yourself. Where is the use in getting excited? Am I excited? There is nothing to get excited about. When I make a statement which I cannot prove, it will be time enough for you to begin to offer hospitality to damaging fancies about me and my sanity."

"Oh, a thousand, thousand pardons! I ought to be ashamed of myself, and I am ashamed of myself for thinking that a little bit of a circumstance like sending a shark to England to fetch back a market report—"

"What does your middle initial stand for, sir?"

"Andrew. What are you writing?"

"Wait a moment. Proof about the shark—and another matter. Only ten lines. There—now it is done. Sign it."

"Many thanks—many. Let me see; it says—it says oh, come, this is interesting! Why—why—look here! prove what you say here, and I'll put up the money, and double as much, if necessary, and divide the winnings with you, half and half. There, now—I've signed; make your promise good if you can. Show me a copy of the London Times only ten days old."

"Here it is—and with it these buttons and a memorandum book that belonged to the man the shark swallowed. Swallowed him in the Thames, without a doubt; for you will notice that the last entry in the book is dated 'London,' and is of the same date as the Times, and says, 'Ber confequentz der Kreigeseflarun, reife ich heute nach Deutchland ab, aur bak ich mein leben auf dem Ultar meines Landes legen mag'—, as clean native German as anybody can put upon paper, and means that in consequence of the declaration of war, this loyal soul is leaving for home to-day, to fight. And he did leave, too, but the shark had him before the day was done, poor fellow."

"And a pity, too. But there are times for mourning, and we will attend to this case further on; other matters are pressing, now. I will go down and set the machinery in motion in a quiet way and buy the crop. It will cheer the drooping spirits of the boys, in a transitory way. Everything is transitory in this world. Sixty days hence, when they are called to deliver the goods, they will think they've been struck by lightning. But there is a time for mourning, and we will attend to that case along with the other one. Come along, I'll take you to my tailor. What did you say your name is?"

"Cecil Rhodes."

"It is hard to remember. However, I think you will make it easier by and by, if you live. There are three kinds of people— Commonplace Men, Remarkable Men, and Lunatics. I'll classify you with the Remarkables, and take the chances."

The deal went through, and secured to the young stranger the first fortune he ever pocketed.

The people of Sydney ought to be afraid of the sharks, but for some reason they do not seem to be. On Saturdays the young men go out in their boats, and sometimes the water is fairly covered with the little sails. A boat upsets now and then, by accident, a result of tumultuous skylarking; sometimes the boys upset their boat for fun—such as it is with sharks visibly waiting around for just such an occurrence. The young fellows scramble aboard whole—sometimes—not always. Tragedies have happened more than once. While I was in Sydney it was reported that a boy fell out of a boat in the mouth of the Paramatta river and screamed for help and a boy jumped overboard from another boat to save him from the assembling sharks; but the sharks made swift work with the lives of both.

The government pays a bounty for the shark; to get the bounty the fishermen bait the hook or the seine with agreeable mutton; the news spreads and the sharks come from all over the Pacific Ocean to get the free board. In time the shark culture will be one of the most successful things in the colony.

CHAPTER XIV.

We can secure other people's approval, if we do right and try hard; but our own is worth a hundred of it, and no way has been found out of securing that. —Pudd'nhead Wilson's New Calendar.

My health had broken down in New York in May; it had remained in a doubtful but fairish condition during a succeeding period of 82 days; it broke again on the Pacific. It broke again in Sydney, but not until after I had had a good outing, and had also filled my lecture engagements. This latest break lost me the chance of seeing Queensland. In the circumstances, to go north toward hotter weather was not advisable.

So we moved south with a westward slant, 17 hours by rail to the capital of the colony of Victoria, Melbourne—that juvenile city of sixty years, and half a million inhabitants. On the map the distance looked small; but that is a trouble with all divisions of distance in such a vast country as Australia. The colony of Victoria itself looks small on the map—looks like a county, in fact—yet it is about as large as England, Scotland, and Wales combined. Or, to get another focus upon it, it is just 80 times as large as the state of Rhode Island, and one-third as large as the State of Texas.

Outside of Melbourne, Victoria seems to be owned by a handful of squatters, each with a Rhode Island for a sheep farm. That is the impression which one gathers from common talk, yet the wool industry of Victoria is by no means so great as that of New South Wales. The climate of Victoria is favorable to other great industries—among others, wheat-growing and the making of wine.

We took the train at Sydney at about four in the afternoon. It was American in one way, for we had a most rational sleeping car; also the car was clean and fine and new—nothing about it to suggest the rolling stock of the continent of Europe. But our baggage was weighed, and extra weight charged for. That was continental. Continental and troublesome. Any detail of railroading that is not troublesome cannot honorably be described as continental.

The tickets were round-trip ones—to Melbourne, and clear to Adelaide in South Australia, and then all the way back to Sydney. Twelve hundred more miles than we really expected to make; but then as the round trip wouldn't cost much more than the single trip, it seemed well enough to buy as many miles as one could afford, even if one was not likely to need them. A human being has a natural desire to have more of a good thing than he needs.

Now comes a singular thing: the oddest thing, the strangest thing, the most baffling and unaccountable marvel that Australasia can show. At the frontier between New South Wales and Victoria our multitude of passengers were routed out of their snug beds by lantern-light in the morning in the biting-cold of a high altitude to change cars on a road that has no break in it from Sydney to Melbourne! Think of the paralysis of intellect that gave that idea birth; imagine the boulder it emerged from on some petrified legislator's shoulders.

It is a narrow-gage road to the frontier, and a broader gauge thence to Melbourne. The two governments were the builders of the road and are the owners of it. One or two reasons are given for this curious state of things. One is, that it represents the jealousy existing between the colonies—the two most important colonies of Australasia. What the other one is, I have forgotten. But it is of no consequence. It could be but another effort to explain the inexplicable.

All passengers fret at the double-gauge; all shippers of freight must of course fret at it; unnecessary expense, delay, and annoyance are imposed upon everybody concerned, and no one is benefitted.

Each Australian colony fences itself off from its neighbor with a custom-house. Personally, I have no objection, but it must be a good deal of inconvenience to the people. We have something resembling it here and there in America, but it goes by another name. The large empire of the Pacific coast requires a world of iron machinery, and could manufacture it economically on the spot if the imposts on foreign iron were removed. But they are not. Protection to Pennsylvania and Alabama forbids it. The result to the Pacific coast is the same as if there were several rows of custom-fences between the coast and the East. Iron carted across the American continent at luxurious railway rates would be valuable enough to be coined when it arrived.

We changed cars. This was at Albury. And it was there, I think, that the growing day and the early sun exposed the distant range called the Blue Mountains. Accurately named. "My word!" as the Australians say, but it was a stunning color, that blue. Deep, strong, rich, exquisite; towering and majestic masses of blue—a softly luminous blue, a smouldering blue, as if vaguely lit by fires within. It extinguished the blue of the sky—made it pallid and unwholesome, whitey and washed-out. A wonderful color—just divine.

A resident told me that those were not mountains; he said they were rabbit-piles. And explained that long exposure and the over-ripe condition of the rabbits was what made them look so blue. This man may have been right, but much reading of books of travel has made me distrustful of gratis information furnished by unofficial residents of a country. The facts which such people give to travelers are usually erroneous, and often intemperately so. The rabbit-plague has indeed been very bad in Australia, and it could account for one mountain, but not for a mountain range, it seems to me. It is too large an order.

We breakfasted at the station. A good breakfast, except the coffee; and cheap. The Government establishes the prices and placards them. The waiters were men, I think; but that is not usual in Australasia. The usual thing is to have girls. No, not girls, young ladies—generally duchesses. Dress? They would attract attention at any royal levee in Europe. Even empresses and queens do not dress as they do. Not that they could not afford it, perhaps, but they would not know how.

All the pleasant morning we slid smoothly along over the plains, through thin—not thick—forests of great melancholy gum trees, with trunks rugged with curled sheets of flaking bark—erysipelas convalescents, so to speak, shedding their dead skins. And all along were tiny cabins, built sometimes of wood, sometimes of gray-blue corrugated iron; and the doorsteps and fences were clogged with children—rugged little simply-clad chaps that looked as if they had been imported from the banks of the Mississippi without breaking bulk.

And there were little villages, with neat stations well placarded with showy advertisements—mainly of almost too self-righteous brands of "sheepdip." If that is the name—and I think it is. It is a stuff like tar, and is dabbed on to places where the shearer clips a piece out of the sheep. It bars out the flies, and has healing properties, and a nip to it which makes the sheep skip like the cattle on a thousand hills. It is not good to eat. That is, it is not good to eat except when mixed with railroad coffee. It improves railroad coffee. Without it railroad coffee is too vague. But with it, it is quite assertive and enthusiastic. By itself, railroad coffee is too passive; but sheep-dip makes it wake up and get down to business. I wonder where they get railroad coffee?

We saw birds, but not a kangaroo, not an emu, not an ornithorhynchus, not a lecturer, not a native. Indeed, the land seemed quite destitute of game. But I have misused the word native. In Australia it is applied to Australian-born whites only. I should have said that we saw no Aboriginals—no "blackfellows." And to this day I have never seen one. In the great museums you will find all the other curiosities, but in the curio of chiefest interest to the stranger all of them are lacking. We have at home an abundance of museums, and not an American Indian in them. It is clearly an absurdity, but it never struck me before.

CHAPTER XV.

Truth is stranger than fiction—to some people, but I am measurably familiar with it. —Pudd'nhead Wilson's New Calendar.

Truth is stranger than fiction, but it is because Fiction is obliged to stick to possibilities; Truth isn't. —Pudd'nhead Wilson's New Calendar.

The air was balmy and delicious, the sunshine radiant; it was a charming excursion. In the course of it we came to a town whose odd name was famous all over the world a quarter of a century ago—Wagga-Wagga. This was because the Tichborne Claimant had kept a butcher-shop there. It was out of the midst of his humble collection of sausages and tripe that he soared up into the zenith of notoriety and hung there in the wastes of space a time, with the telescopes of all nations leveled at him in unappeasable curiosity—curiosity as to which of the two long-missing persons he was: Arthur Orton, the mislaid roustabout of Wapping, or Sir Roger Tichborne, the lost heir of a name and estates as old as English history. We all know now, but not a dozen people knew then; and the dozen kept the mystery to themselves and allowed the most intricate and fascinating and marvelous real-life romance that has ever been played upon the world's stage to unfold itself serenely, act by act, in a British court by the long and laborious processes of judicial development.

When we recall the details of that great romance we marvel to see what daring chances truth may freely take in constructing a tale, as compared with the poor little conservative risks permitted to fiction. The fiction-artist could achieve no success with the materials of this splendid Tichborne romance.

He would have to drop out the chief characters; the public would say such people are impossible. He would have to drop out a number of the most picturesque incidents; the public would say such things could never happen. And yet the chief characters did exist, and the incidents did happen.

It cost the Tichborne estates $400,000 to unmask the Claimant and drive him out; and even after the exposure multitudes of Englishmen still believed in him. It cost the British Government another $400,000 to convict him of perjury; and after the conviction the same old multitudes still believed in him; and among these believers were many educated and intelligent men; and some of them had personally known the real Sir Roger. The Claimant was sentenced to 14 years' imprisonment. When he got out of prison he went to New York and kept a whisky saloon in the Bowery for a time, then disappeared from view.

He always claimed to be Sir Roger Tichborne until death called for him. This was but a few months ago—not very much short of a generation since he left Wagga-Wagga to go and possess himself of his estates. On his death-bed he yielded up his secret, and confessed in writing that he was only Arthur Orton of Wapping, able seaman and butcher—that and nothing more. But it is scarcely to be doubted that there are people whom even his dying confession will not convince. The old habit of assimilating incredibilities must have made strong food a necessity in their case; a weaker article would probably disagree with them.

I was in London when the Claimant stood his trial for perjury. I attended one of his showy evenings in the sumptuous quarters provided for him from the purses of his adherents and well-wishers. He was in evening dress, and I thought him a rather fine and stately creature. There were about twenty-five gentlemen present; educated men, men moving in good society, none of them commonplace; some of them were men of distinction, none of them were obscurities. They were his cordial friends and admirers. It was "Sir Roger," always "Sir Roger," on all hands; no one withheld the title, all turned it from the tongue with unction, and as if it tasted good.

For many years I had had a mystery in stock. Melbourne, and only Melbourne, could unriddle it for me. In 1873 I arrived in London with my wife and young child, and presently received a note from Naples signed by a name not familiar to me. It was not Bascom, and it was not Henry; but I will call it Henry Bascom for convenience's sake. This note, of about six lines, was written on a strip of white paper whose end-edges were ragged. I came to be familiar with those strips in later years. Their size and pattern were always the same. Their contents were usually to the same effect: would I and mine come to the writer's country-place in England on such and such a date, by such and such a train, and stay twelve days and depart by such and such a train at the end of the specified time? A carriage would meet us at the station.

These invitations were always for a long time ahead; if we were in Europe, three months ahead; if we were in America, six to twelve months ahead. They always named the exact date and train for the beginning and also for the end of the visit.

This first note invited us for a date three months in the future. It asked us to arrive by the 4.10 p.m. train from London,

August 6th. The carriage would be waiting. The carriage would take us away seven days later-train specified. And there were these words: "Speak to Tom Hughes."

I showed the note to the author of "Tom Brown at Rugby," and be said: "Accept, and be thankful."

He described Mr. Bascom as being a man of genius, a man of fine attainments, a choice man in every way, a rare and beautiful character. He said that Bascom Hall was a particularly fine example of the stately manorial mansion of Elizabeth's days, and that it was a house worth going a long way to see—like Knowle; that Mr. B. was of a social disposition; liked the company of agreeable people, and always had samples of the sort coming and going.

We paid the visit. We paid others, in later years—the last one in 1879. Soon after that Mr. Bascom started on a voyage around the world in a steam yacht—a long and leisurely trip, for he was making collections, in all lands, of birds, butterflies, and such things.

The day that President Garfield was shot by the assassin Guiteau, we were at a little watering place on Long Island Sound; and in the mail matter of that day came a letter with the Melbourne post-mark on it. It was for my wife, but I recognized Mr. Bascom's handwriting on the envelope, and opened it. It was the usual note—as to paucity of lines—and was written on the customary strip of paper; but there was nothing usual about the contents. The note informed my wife that if it would be any assuagement of her grief to know that her husband's lecture-tour in Australia was a satisfactory venture from the beginning to the end, he, the writer, could testify that such was the case; also, that her husband's untimely death had been mourned by all classes, as she would already know by the press telegrams, long before the reception of this note; that the funeral was attended by the officials of the colonial and city governments; and that while he, the writer, her friend and mine, had not reached Melbourne in time to see the body, he had at least had the sad privilege of acting as one of the pall-bearers. Signed, "Henry Bascom."

My first thought was, why didn't he have the coffin opened? He would have seen that the corpse was an imposter, and he could have gone right ahead and dried up the most of those tears, and comforted those sorrowing governments, and sold the remains and sent me the money.

I did nothing about the matter. I had set the law after living lecture doubles of mine a couple of times in America, and the law had not been able to catch them; others in my trade had tried to catch their impostor-doubles and had failed. Then where was the use in harrying a ghost? None—and so I did not disturb it. I had a curiosity to know about that man's lecture-tour and last moments, but that could wait. When I should see Mr. Bascom he would tell me all about it. But he passed from life, and I never saw him again.. My curiosity faded away.

However, when I found that I was going to Australia it revived. And naturally: for if the people should say that I was a dull, poor thing compared to what I was before I died, it would have a bad effect on business. Well, to my surprise the Sydney journalists had never heard of that impostor! I pressed them, but they were firm—they had never heard of him, and didn't believe in him.

I could not understand it; still, I thought it would all come right in Melbourne. The government would remember; and the other mourners. At the supper of the Institute of Journalists I should find out all about the matter. But no—it turned out that they had never heard of it.

So my mystery was a mystery still. It was a great disappointment. I believed it would never be cleared up—in this life—so I dropped it out of my mind.

But at last! just when I was least expecting it—

However, this is not the place for the rest of it; I shall come to the matter again, in a far-distant chapter.

CHAPTER XVI.

There is a Moral sense, and there is an Immoral Sense. History shows us that the Moral Sense enables us to perceive morality and how to avoid it, and that the Immoral Sense enables us to perceive immorality and how to enjoy it. - Pudd'nhead Wilson's New Calendar.

Melbourne spreads around over an immense area of ground. It is a stately city architecturally as well as in magnitude. It has an elaborate system of cable-car service; it has museums, and colleges, and schools, and public gardens, and electricity, and gas, and libraries, and theaters, and mining centers, and wool centers, and centers of the arts and sciences, and boards of trade, and ships, and railroads, and a harbor, and social clubs, and journalistic clubs, and racing clubs, and a squatter club sumptuously housed and appointed, and as many churches and banks as can make a living. In a word, it is equipped with everything that goes to make the modern great city. It is the largest city of Australasia, and fills the post with honor and credit. It has one specialty; this must not be jumbled in with those other things. It is the mitred Metropolitan of the Horse-Racing Cult. Its race-ground is the Mecca of Australasia. On the great annual day of sacrifice—the 5th of November, Guy Fawkes's Day—business is suspended over a stretch of land and sea as wide as from New York to San Francisco, and deeper than from the northern lakes to the Gulf of Mexico; and every man and woman, of high degree or low, who can afford the expense, put away their other duties and come. They begin to swarm in by ship and rail a fortnight before the day, and they swarm thicker and thicker day after day, until all the vehicles of transportation are taxed to their uttermost to meet the demands of the occasion, and all hotels and lodgings are bulging outward because of the pressure from within. They come a hundred thousand strong, as all the best authorities say, and they pack the spacious grounds and grandstands and make a spectacle such as is never to be seen in Australasia elsewhere.

It is the "Melbourne Cup" that brings this multitude together. Their clothes have been ordered long ago, at unlimited cost, and without bounds as to beauty and magnificence, and have been kept in concealment until now, for unto this day are they consecrate. I am speaking of the ladies' clothes; but one might know that.

And so the grand-stands make a brilliant and wonderful spectacle, a delirium of color, a vision of beauty. The champagne flows, everybody is vivacious, excited, happy; everybody bets, and gloves and fortunes change hands right along, all the time. Day after day the races go on, and the fun and the excitement are kept at white heat; and when each day is done, the people dance all night so as to be fresh for the race in the morning. And at the end of the great week the swarms secure lodgings and transportation for next year, then flock

away to their remote homes and count their gains and losses, and order next year's Cup-clothes, and then lie down and sleep two weeks, and get up sorry to reflect that a whole year must be put in somehow or other before they can be wholly happy again.

The Melbourne Cup is the Australasian National Day. It would be difficult to overstate its importance. It overshadows all other holidays and specialized days of whatever sort in that congeries of colonies. Overshadows them? I might almost say it blots them out. Each of them gets attention, but not everybody's; each of them evokes interest, but not everybody's; each of them rouses enthusiasm, but not everybody's; in each case a part of the attention, interest, and enthusiasm is a matter of habit and custom, and another part of it is official and perfunctory. Cup Day, and Cup Day only, commands an attention, an interest, and an enthusiasm which are universal—and spontaneous, not perfunctory. Cup Day is supreme it has no rival. I can call to mind no specialized annual day, in any country, which can be named by that large name—Supreme. I can call to mind no specialized annual day, in any country, whose approach fires the whole land with a conflagration of conversation and preparation and anticipation and jubilation. No day save this one; but this one does it.

In America we have no annual supreme day; no day whose approach makes the whole nation glad. We have the Fourth of July, and Christmas, and Thanksgiving. Neither of them can claim the primacy; neither of them can arouse an enthusiasm which comes near to being universal. Eight grown Americans out of ten dread the coming of the Fourth, with its pandemonium and its perils, and they rejoice when it is gone— if still alive. The approach of Christmas brings harassment and dread to many excellent people. They have to buy a cart-load of presents, and they never know what to buy to hit the various tastes; they put in three weeks of hard and anxious work, and when Christmas morning comes they are so dissatisfied with the result, and so disappointed that they want to sit down and cry. Then they give thanks that Christmas comes but once a year. The observance of Thanksgiving Day—as a function—has become general of late years. The Thankfulness is not so general. This is natural. Two-thirds of the nation have always had hard luck and a hard time during the year, and this has a calming effect upon their enthusiasm.

We have a supreme day—a sweeping and tremendous and tumultuous day, a day which commands an absolute universality of interest and excitement; but it is not annual. It comes but once in four years; therefore it cannot count as a rival of the Melbourne Cup.

In Great Britain and Ireland they have two great days— Christmas and the Queen's birthday. But they are equally popular; there is no supremacy.

I think it must be conceded that the position of the Australasian Day is unique, solitary, unfellowed; and likely to hold that high place a long time.

The next things which interest us when we travel are, first, the people; next, the novelties; and finally the history of the places and countries visited. Novelties are rare in cities which represent the most advanced civilization of the modern day. When one is familiar with such cities in the other parts of the world he is in effect familiar with the cities of Australasia. The outside aspects will furnish little that is new. There will be new names, but the things which they represent will sometimes be found to be less new than their names. There may be shades of difference, but these can easily be too fine for detection by the incompetent eye of the passing stranger. In the larrikin he will not be able to discover a new species, but only an old one met elsewhere, and variously called loafer, rough, tough, bummer, or blatherskite, according to his geographical distribution. The larrikin differs by a shade from those others, in that he is more sociable toward the stranger than they, more kindly disposed, more hearty, more friendly. At least it seemed so to me, and I had opportunity to observe. In Sydney, at least. In Melbourne I had to drive to and from the lecture-theater, but in Sydney I was able to walk both ways, and did it. Every night, on my way home at ten, or a quarter past, I found the larrikin grouped in considerable force at several of the street corners, and he always gave me this pleasant salutation:

"Hello, Mark!"

"Here's to you, old chap!

"Say—Mark!—is he dead?"—a reference to a passage in some book of mine, though I did not detect, at that time, that that was its source. And I didn't detect it afterward in Melbourne, when I came on the stage for the first time, and the same question was dropped down upon me from the dizzy height of the gallery. It is always difficult to answer a sudden inquiry like that, when you have come unprepared and don't know what it means. I will remark here—if it is not an indecorum—that the welcome which an American lecturer gets from a British colonial audience is a thing which will move him to his deepest deeps, and veil his sight and break his voice. And from Winnipeg to Africa, experience will teach him nothing; he will never learn to expect it, it will catch him as a surprise each time. The war-cloud hanging black over England and America made no trouble for me. I was a prospective prisoner of war, but at dinners, suppers, on the platform, and elsewhere, there was never anything to remind me of it. This was hospitality of the right metal, and would have been prominently lacking in some countries, in the circumstances.

And speaking of the war-flurry, it seemed to me to bring to light the unexpected, in a detail or two. It seemed to relegate the war-talk to the politicians on both sides of the water; whereas whenever a prospective war between two nations had been in the air theretofore, the public had done most of the talking and the bitterest. The attitude of the newspapers was new also. I speak of those of Australasia and India, for I had access to those only. They treated the subject argumentatively and with dignity, not with spite and anger. That was a new spirit, too, and not learned of the French and German press, either before Sedan or since. I heard many public speeches, and they reflected the moderation of the journals. The outlook is that the English-speaking race will dominate the earth a hundred years from now, if its sections do not get to fighting each other. It would be a pity to spoil that prospect by baffling and retarding wars when arbitration would settle their differences so much better and also so much more definitely.

No, as I have suggested, novelties are rare in the great capitals of modern times. Even the wool exchange in Melbourne could not be told from the familiar stock exchange of other countries. Wool brokers are just like stockbrokers; they all bounce from their seats and put up their hands and yell in unison—no stranger can tell what—and the president calmly says "Sold to Smith & Co., threpence farthing—next!"—when probably nothing of the kind happened; for how should he know?

In the museums you will find acres of the most strange and fascinating things; but all museums are fascinating, and they do so tire your eyes, and break your back, and burn out your vitalities with their consuming interest. You always say you will never go again, but you do go. The palaces of the rich, in Melbourne, are much like the palaces of the rich in America, and the life in them is the same; but there the resemblance ends. The grounds surrounding the American palace are not often large, and not often beautiful, but in the Melbourne case the grounds are often ducally spacious, and the climate and the gardeners together make them as beautiful as a dream. It is said that some of the country seats have grounds—domains—about them which rival in charm and magnitude those which surround the country mansion of an English lord; but I was not out in the country; I had my hands full in town.

And what was the origin of this majestic city and its efflorescence of palatial town houses and country seats? Its first brick was laid and its first house built by a passing convict. Australian history is almost always picturesque; indeed, it is so curious and strange, that it is itself the chiefest novelty the country has to offer, and so it pushes the other novelties into second and third place. It does not read like history, but like the most beautiful lies. And all of a fresh new sort, no mouldy old stale ones. It is full of surprises, and adventures, and incongruities, and contradictions, and incredibilities; but they are all true, they all happened.

CHAPTER XVII.

The English are mentioned in the Bible: Blessed are the meek, for they shall inherit the earth. —Pudd'nhead Wilson's New Calendar.

When we consider the immensity of the British Empire in territory, population, and trade, it requires a stern exercise of faith to believe in the figures which represent Australasia's contribution to the Empire's commercial grandeur. As compared with the landed estate of the British Empire, the landed estate dominated by any other Power except one — Russia—is not very impressive for size. My authorities make the British Empire not much short of a fourth larger than the Russian Empire. Roughly proportioned, if you will allow your entire hand to represent the British Empire, you may then cut off the fingers a trifle above the middle joint of the middle finger, and what is left of the hand will represent Russia. The populations ruled by Great Britain and China are about the same—400,000,000 each. No other Power approaches these figures. Even Russia is left far behind.

The population of Australasia—4,000,000—sinks into nothingness, and is lost from sight in that British ocean of 400,000,000. Yet the statistics indicate that it rises again and shows up very conspicuously when its share of the Empire's commerce is the matter under consideration. The value of England's annual exports and imports is stated at three billions of dollars,—[New South Wales Blue Book.]—and it is claimed that more than one-tenth of this great aggregate is represented by Australasia's exports to England and imports from England. In addition to this, Australasia does a trade with countries other than England, amounting to a hundred million dollars a year, and a domestic intercolonial trade amounting to a hundred and fifty millions.

In round numbers the 4,000,000 buy and sell about $600,000,000 worth of goods a year. It is claimed that about half of this represents commodities of Australasian production. The products exported annually by India are worth a trifle over $500,000,000. Now, here are some faith-straining figures:

Indian production (300,000,000 population), $500,000,000.

Australasian production (4,000,000 population), $300,000,000.

That is to say, the product of the individual Indian, annually (for export some whither), is worth $1.15; that of the individual Australasian (for export some whither), $75! Or, to put it in another way, the Indian family of man and wife and three children sends away an annual result worth $8.75, while the Australasian family sends away $375 worth.

There are trustworthy statistics furnished by Sir Richard Temple and others, which show that the individual Indian's whole annual product, both for export and home use, is worth in gold only $7.50; or, $37.50 for the family-aggregate. Ciphered out on a like ratio of multiplication, the Australasian family's aggregate production would be nearly $1,600. Truly, nothing is so astonishing as figures, if they once get started.

We left Melbourne by rail for Adelaide, the capital of the vast Province of South Australia—a seventeen-hour excursion. On the train we found several Sydney friends; among them a Judge who was going out on circuit, and was going to hold court at Broken Hill, where the celebrated silver mine is. It seemed a curious road to take to get to that region. Broken Hill is close to the western border of New South Wales, and Sydney is on the eastern border. A fairly straight line, 700 miles long, drawn westward from Sydney, would strike Broken Hill, just as a somewhat shorter one drawn west from Boston would strike Buffalo. The way the Judge was traveling would carry him over 2,000 miles by rail, he said; southwest from Sydney down to Melbourne, then northward up to Adelaide, then a cant back northeastward and over the border into New South Wales once more—to Broken Hill. It was like going from Boston southwest to Richmond, Virginia, then northwest up to Erie, Pennsylvania, then a cant back northeast and over the border—to Buffalo, New York.

But the explanation was simple. Years ago the fabulously rich silver discovery at Broken Hill burst suddenly upon an unexpectant world. Its stocks started at shillings, and went by leaps and bounds to the most fanciful figures. It was one of those cases where the cook puts a month's wages into shares, and comes next mouth and buys your house at your own price, and moves into it herself; where the coachman takes a few shares, and next month sets up a bank; and where the common sailor invests the price of a spree, and next month buys out the steamship company and goes into business on his own hook. In a word, it was one of those excitements which bring multitudes of people to a common center with a rush, and whose needs must be supplied, and at once. Adelaide was close by, Sydney was far away. Adelaide threw a short railway across the border before Sydney had time to arrange for a long one; it was not worth while for Sydney to arrange at all. The whole vast trade-profit of Broken Hill fell into Adelaide's hands, irrevocably. New South Wales furnishes for Broken Hill and sends her Judges 2,000 miles—mainly through alien countries—to administer it, but Adelaide takes the dividends and makes no moan.

We started at 4.20 in the afternoon, and moved across level until night. In the morning we had a stretch of "scrub" country—the kind of thing which is so useful to the Australian novelist. In the scrub the hostile aboriginal lurks, and flits

mysteriously about, slipping out from time to time to surprise and slaughter the settler; then slipping back again, and leaving no track that the white man can follow. In the scrub the novelist's heroine gets lost, search fails of result; she wanders here and there, and finally sinks down exhausted and unconscious, and the searchers pass within a yard or two of her, not suspecting that she is near, and by and by some rambler finds her bones and the pathetic diary which she had scribbled with her failing hand and left behind. Nobody can find a lost heroine in the scrub but the aboriginal "tracker," and he will not lend himself to the scheme if it will interfere with the novelist's plot. The scrub stretches miles and miles in all directions, and looks like a level roof of bush-tops without a break or a crack in it —as seamless as a blanket, to all appearance. One might as well walk under water and hope to guess out a route and stick to it, I should think. Yet it is claimed that the aboriginal "tracker" was able to hunt out people lost in the scrub. Also in the "bush"; also in the desert; and even follow them over patches of bare rocks and over alluvial ground which had to all appearance been washed clear of footprints.

From reading Australian books and talking with the people, I became convinced that the aboriginal tracker's performances evince a craft, a penetration, a luminous sagacity, and a minuteness and accuracy of observation in the matter of detective-work not found in nearly so remarkable a degree in any other people, white or colored. In an official account of the blacks of Australia published by the government of Victoria, one reads that the aboriginal not only notices the faint marks left on the bark of a tree by the claws of a climbing opossum, but knows in some way or other whether the marks were made to-day or yesterday.

And there is the case, on records where A., a settler, makes a bet with B., that B. may lose a cow as effectually as he can, and A. will produce an aboriginal who will find her. B. selects a cow and lets the tracker see the cow's footprint, then be put under guard. B. then drives the cow a few miles over a course which drifts in all directions, and frequently doubles back upon itself; and he selects difficult ground all the time, and once or twice even drives the cow through herds of other cows, and mingles her tracks in the wide confusion of theirs. He finally brings his cow home; the aboriginal is set at liberty, and at once moves around in a great circle, examining all cow-tracks until he finds the one he is after; then sets off and follows it throughout its erratic course, and ultimately tracks it to the stable where B. has hidden the cow. Now wherein does one cow-track differ from another? There must be a difference, or the tracker could not have performed the feat; a difference minute, shadowy, and not detectible by you or me, or by the late Sherlock Holmes, and yet discernible by a member of a race charged by some people with occupying the bottom place in the gradations of human intelligence.

CHAPTER XVIII.

It is easier to stay out than get out. —Pudd'nhead Wilson's New Calendar.

The train was now exploring a beautiful hill country, and went twisting in and out through lovely little green valleys. There were several varieties of gum trees; among them many giants. Some of them were bodied and barked like the sycamore; some were of fantastic aspect, and reminded one of the quaint apple trees in Japanese pictures. And there was one peculiarly beautiful tree whose name and breed I did not know. The foliage seemed to consist of big bunches of pine-spines, the lower half of each bunch a rich brown or old-gold color, the upper half a most vivid and strenuous and shouting green. The effect was altogether bewitching. The tree was apparently rare. I should say that the first and last samples of it seen by us were not more than half an hour apart. There was another tree of striking aspect, a kind of pine, we were told. Its foliage was as fine as hair, apparently, and its mass sphered itself above the naked straight stem like an explosion of misty smoke. It was not a sociable sort; it did not gather in groups or couples, but each individual stood far away from its nearest neighbor. It scattered itself in this spacious and exclusive fashion about the slopes of swelling grassy great knolls, and stood in the full flood of the wonderful sunshine; and as far as you could see the tree itself you could also see the ink-black blot of its shadow on the shining green carpet at its feet.

On some part of this railway journey we saw gorse and broom—importations from England—and a gentleman who came into our compartment on a visit tried to tell me which—was which; but as he didn't know, he had difficulty. He said he was ashamed of his ignorance, but that he had never been confronted with the question before during the fifty years and more that he had spent in Australia, and so he had never happened to get interested in the matter. But there was no need to be ashamed. The most of us have his defect. We take a natural interest in novelties, but it is against nature to take an interest in familiar things. The gorse and the broom were a fine accent in the landscape. Here and there they burst out in sudden conflagrations of vivid yellow against a background of sober or sombre color, with a so startling effect as to make a body catch his breath with the happy surprise of it. And then there was the wattle, a native bush or tree, an inspiring cloud of sumptuous yellow bloom. It is a favorite with the Australians, and has a fine fragrance, a quality usually wanting in Australian blossoms.

The gentleman who enriched me with the poverty of his formation about the gorse and the broom told me that he came out from England a youth of twenty and entered the Province of South Australia with thirty-six shillings in his pocket—an adventurer without trade, profession, or friends, but with a clearly-defined purpose in his head: he would stay until he was worth £200, then go back home. He would allow himself five years for the accumulation of this fortune.

"That was more than fifty years ago," said he. "And here I am, yet."

As he went out at the door he met a friend, and turned and introduced him to me, and the friend and I had a talk and a smoke. I spoke of the previous conversation and said there something very pathetic about this half century of exile, and that I wished the £200 scheme had succeeded.

"With him? Oh, it did. It's not so sad a case. He is modest, and he left out some of the particulars. The lad reached South Australia just in time to help discover the Burra-Burra copper mines. They turned out £700,000 in the first three years. Up to now they have yielded £120,000,000. He has had his share. Before that boy had been in the country two years he could have gone home and bought a village; he could go now and buy a city, I think. No, there is nothing very pathetic about his case. He and his copper arrived at just a handy time to save South Australia. It had got mashed pretty flat under the collapse of a land boom a while before." There it is again; picturesque history —Australia's specialty. In 1829 South Australia hadn't a white man in it. In 1836 the British Parliament erected it—still a solitude—into a Province, and gave it a governor and other governmental machinery. Speculators took hold, now, and inaugurated a vast land scheme, and invited immigration, encouraging it with lurid promises of sudden wealth. It was well worked in London; and bishops, statesmen, and all ports of people made a rush for the land company's shares. Immigrants soon began to pour into the region of Adelaide and select town lots and farms in the sand and the mangrove swamps by the sea. The crowds continued to come, prices of land rose high, then higher and still higher, everybody was prosperous and happy, the boom swelled into gigantic proportions. A village of sheet iron huts and clapboard sheds sprang up in the sand, and in these wigwams fashion made display; richly-dressed ladies played on costly pianos, London swells in evening dress and patent-leather boots were abundant, and this fine society drank champagne, and in other ways conducted itself in this capital of humble sheds as it had been accustomed to do in the aristocratic quarters of the metropolis of the world. The provincial government put up expensive buildings for its own use, and a palace with gardens for the use of its governor. The governor had a guard, and maintained a court. Roads, wharves, and hospitals were built. All this on credit, on paper, on wind, on inflated and fictitious values—on the boom's moonshine, in fact. This went on handsomely during four or five years. Then of a sudden came a smash. Bills for a huge amount drawn the governor upon the Treasury were dishonored, the land company's credit went up in smoke, a panic followed, values fell with a rush, the frightened immigrants seized their grips and fled to other lands, leaving behind them a good imitation of a solitude, where lately had been a buzzing and populous hive of men.

Adelaide was indeed almost empty; its population had fallen to 3,000. During two years or more the death-trance continued. Prospect of revival there was none; hope of it ceased. Then, as suddenly as the paralysis had come, came the resurrection from it. Those astonishingly rich copper mines were discovered, and the corpse got up and danced.

The wool production began to grow; grain-raising followed—followed so vigorously, too, that four or five years after the copper discovery, this little colony, which had had to import its breadstuffs formerly, and pay hard prices for them—once $50 a barrel for flour—had become an exporter of grain.

The prosperities continued. After many years Providence, desiring to show especial regard for New South Wales and exhibit loving interest in its welfare which should certify to all nations the recognition of that colony's conspicuous righteousness and distinguished well-deserving, conferred upon it that treasury of inconceivable riches, Broken Hill; and South Australia went over the border and took it, giving thanks.

Among our passengers was an American with a unique vocation. Unique is a strong word, but I use it justifiably if I did not misconceive what the American told me; for I understood him to say that in the world there was not another man engaged in the business which he was following. He was buying the kangaroo-skin crop; buying all of it, both the Australian crop and the Tasmanian; and buying it for an American house in New York. The prices were not high, as there was no competition, but the year's aggregate of skins would cost him £30,000. I had had the idea that the kangaroo was about extinct in Tasmania and well thinned out on the continent. In America the skins are tanned and made into shoes. After the tanning, the leather takes a new name—which I have forgotten—I only remember that the new name does not indicate that the kangaroo furnishes the leather. There was a German competition for a while, some years ago, but that has ceased. The Germans failed to arrive at the secret of tanning the skins successfully, and they withdrew from the business. Now then, I suppose that I have seen a man whose occupation is really entitled to bear that high epithet—unique. And I suppose that there is not another occupation in the world that is restricted to the hands of a sole person. I can think of no instance of it. There is more than one Pope, there is more than one Emperor, there is even more than one living god, walking upon the earth and worshiped in all sincerity by large populations of men. I have seen and talked with two of these Beings myself in India, and I have the autograph of one of them. It can come good, by and by, I reckon, if I attach it to a "permit."

Approaching Adelaide we dismounted from the train, as the French say, and were driven in an open carriage over the hills and along their slopes to the city. It was an excursion of an hour or two, and the charm of it could not be overstated, I think. The road wound around gaps and gorges, and offered all varieties of scenery and prospect—mountains, crags, country homes, gardens, forests—color, color, color everywhere, and the air fine and fresh, the skies blue, and not a shred of cloud to mar the downpour of the brilliant sunshine. And finally the mountain gateway opened, and the immense plain lay spread out below and stretching away into dim distances on every hand, soft and delicate and dainty and beautiful. On its near edge reposed the city.

We descended and entered. There was nothing to remind one of the humble capital, of buts and sheds of the long-vanished day of the land-boom. No, this was a modern city, with wide streets, compactly built; with fine homes everywhere, embowered in foliage and flowers, and with imposing masses of public buildings nobly grouped and architecturally beautiful.

There was prosperity, in the air; for another boom was on. Providence, desiring to show especial regard for the neighboring colony on the west called Western Australia—and exhibit a loving interest in its welfare which should certify to all nations the recognition of that colony's conspicuous righteousness and distinguished well-deserving, had recently conferred upon it that majestic treasury of golden riches, Coolgardie; and now South Australia had gone around the corner and taken it, giving thanks. Everything comes to him who is patient and good, and waits.

But South Australia deserves much, for apparently she is a hospitable home for every alien who chooses to come; and for his religion, too. She has a population, as per the latest census, of only 320,000-odd, and yet her varieties of religion indicate the presence within her borders of samples of people from pretty nearly every part of the globe you can think of. Tabulated, these varieties of religion make a remarkable show. One would have to go far to find its match. I copy here this cosmopolitan curiosity, and it comes from the published census:

Church of England	89,271
Roman Catholic	47,179
Wesleyan	49,159
Lutheran	23,328
Presbyterian	18,206
Congregationalist	11,882
Bible Christian	15,762
Primitive Methodist	11,654

Baptist	17,547
Christian Brethren	465
Methodist New Connexion	39
Unitarian	688
Church of Christ	3,367
Society of Friends	100
Salvation Army	4,356
New Jerusalem Church	168
Jews	840
Protestants (undefined)	6,532
Mohammedans	299
Confucians, etc	3,884
Other religions	1,719
Object	6,940
Not stated	8,046
Total	320,431

The item in the above list "Other religions" includes the following as returned:

Agnostics, Atheists, Believers in Christ, Buddhists, Calvinists, Christadelphians, Christians, Christ's Chapel, Christian Israelites, Christian Socialists, Church of God, Cosmopolitans, Deists, Evangelists, Exclusive Brethren, Free Church, Free Methodists, Freethinkers, Followers of Christ, Gospel Meetings, Greek Church, Infidels, Maronites, Memnonists, Moravians, Mormons, Naturalists, Orthodox, Others (indefinite), Pagans, Pantheists, Plymouth Brethren, Rationalists, Reformers, Secularists, Seventh-day Adventists, Shaker, Shintoists, Spiritualists, Theosophists, Town (City) Mission, Welsh Church, Huguenot, Hussite, Zoroastrians, Zwinglian,

About 64 roads to the other world. You see how healthy the religious atmosphere is. Anything can live in it. Agnostics, Atheists, Freethinkers, Infidels, Mormons, Pagans, Indefinites they are all there. And all the big sects of the world can do more than merely live in it: they can spread, flourish, prosper. All except the Spiritualists and the Theosophists. That is the most curious feature of this curious table. What is the matter with the specter? Why do they puff him away? He is a welcome toy everywhere else in the world.

CHAPTER XIX.

Pity is for the living, Envy is for the dead. —Pudd'nhead Wilson's New Calendar.

The successor of the sheet-iron hamlet of the mangrove marshes has that other Australian specialty, the Botanical Gardens. We cannot have these paradises. The best we could do would be to cover a vast acreage under glass and apply steam heat. But it would be inadequate, the lacks would still be so great: the confined sense, the sense of suffocation, the atmospheric dimness, the sweaty heat—these would all be there, in place of the Australian openness to the sky, the sunshine and the breeze. Whatever will grow under glass with us will flourish rampantly out of doors in Australia.—[The greatest heat in Victoria, that there is an authoritative record of, was at Sandhurst, in January, 1862. The thermometer then registered 117 degrees in the shade. In January, 1880, the heat at Adelaide, South Australia, was 172 degrees in the sun.]

When the white man came the continent was nearly as poor, in variety of vegetation, as the desert of Sahara; now it has everything that grows on the earth. In fact, not Australia only, but all Australasia has levied tribute upon the flora of the rest of the world; and wherever one goes the results appear, in gardens private and public, in the woodsy walls of the highways, and in even the forests. If you see a curious or beautiful tree or bush or flower, and ask about it, the people, answering, usually name a foreign country as the place of its origin—India, Africa, Japan, China, England, America, Java, Sumatra, New Guinea, Polynesia, and so on.

In the Zoological Gardens of Adelaide I saw the only laughing jackass that ever showed any disposition to be courteous to me. This one opened his head wide and laughed like a demon; or like a maniac who was consumed with humorous scorn over a cheap and degraded pun. It was a very human laugh. If he had been out of sight I could have believed that the laughter came from a man. It is an odd-looking bird, with a head and beak that are much too large for its body. In time man will exterminate the rest of the wild creatures of Australia, but this one will probably survive, for man is his friend and lets him alone. Man always has a good reason for his charities towards wild things, human or animal when he has any. In this case the bird is spared because he kills snakes. If L. J. he will not kill all of them.

In that garden I also saw the wild Australian dog—the dingo. He was a beautiful creature—shapely, graceful, a little wolfish in some of his aspects, but with a most friendly eye and sociable disposition. The dingo is not an importation; he was present in great force when the whites first came to the continent. It may be that he is the oldest dog in the universe; his origin, his descent, the place where his ancestors first appeared, are as unknown and as untraceable as are the camel's. He is the most precious dog in the world, for he does not bark. But in an evil hour he got to raiding the sheep-runs to appease his hunger, and that sealed his doom. He is hunted, now, just as if he were a wolf. He has been sentenced to extermination, and the sentence will be carried out. This is all right, and not objectionable. The world was made for man— the white man.

South Australia is confusingly named. All of the colonies have a southern exposure except one—Queensland. Properly speaking, South Australia is middle Australia. It extends straight up through the center of the continent like the middle board in a center-table. It is 2,000 miles high, from south to north, and about a third as wide. A wee little spot down in its southeastern corner contains eight or nine-tenths of its population; the other one or two-tenths are elsewhere—as elsewhere as they could be in the United States with all the country between Denver and Chicago, and Canada and the Gulf of Mexico to scatter over. There is plenty of room.

A telegraph line stretches straight up north through that 2,000 miles of wilderness and desert from Adelaide to Port Darwin on the edge of the upper ocean. South Australia built the line; and did it in 1871-2 when her population numbered only 185,000. It was a great work; for there were no roads, no paths; 1,300 miles of the route had been traversed but once before by white men; provisions, wire, and poles had to be carried over immense stretches of desert; wells had to be dug along the route to supply the men and cattle with water.

A cable had been previously laid from Port Darwin to Java and thence to India, and there was telegraphic communication with England from India. And so, if Adelaide could make connection with Port Darwin it meant connection with the whole world. The enterprise succeeded. One could watch the London markets daily, now; the profit to the wool-growers of Australia was instant and enormous.

A telegram from Melbourne to San Francisco covers approximately 20,000 miles—the equivalent of five-sixths of the way around the globe. It has to halt along the way a good many times and be repeated; still, but little time is lost. These halts, and the distances between them, are here tabulated.— [From "Round the Empire." (George R. Parkin), all but the last two.]

Miles:

Melbourne-Mount Gambier	300
Mount Gambier-Adelaide	270
Adelaide-Port Augusta	200
Port Augusta-Alice Springs	1,036
Alice Springs-Port Darwin	898
Port Darwin-Banjoewangie	1,150
Banjoewangie-Batavia	480
Batavia-Singapore	553
Singapore-Penang	399
Penang-Madras	1,280
Madras-Bombay	650
Bombay-Aden	1,662
Aden-Suez	1,346
Suez-Alexandria	224
Alexandria-Malta	828
Malta-Gibraltar	1,008
Gibraltar-Falmouth	1,061
Falmouth-London	350
London-New York	2,500
New York-San Francisco	3,500

I was in Adelaide again, some months later, and saw the multitudes gather in the neighboring city of Glenelg to commemorate the Reading of the Proclamation—in 1836— which founded the Province. If I have at any time called it a Colony, I withdraw the discourtesy. It is not a Colony, it is a Province; and officially so. Moreover, it is the only one so named in Australasia. There was great enthusiasm; it was the Province's national holiday, its Fourth of July, so to speak. It is the pre-eminent holiday; and that is saying much, in a country where they seem to have a most un-English mania for holidays. Mainly they are workingmen's holidays; for in South Australia the workingman is sovereign; his vote is the desire of the politician—indeed, it is the very breath of the politician's being; the parliament exists to deliver the will of the workingman, and the government exists to execute it. The workingman is a great power everywhere in Australia, but South Australia is his paradise. He has had a hard time in this world, and has earned a paradise. I am glad he has found it. The holidays there are frequent enough to be bewildering to the stranger. I tried to get the hang of the system, but was not able to do it.

You have seen that the Province is tolerant, religious-wise. It is so politically, also. One of the speakers at the Commemoration banquet—the Minister of Public Works-was an American, born and reared in New England. There is nothing narrow about the Province, politically, or in any other way that I know of. Sixty-four religions and a Yankee cabinet minister. No amount of horse-racing can damn this community.

The mean temperature of the Province is 62 deg. The death-rate is 13 in the 1,000—about half what it is in the city of New York, I should think, and New York is a healthy city. Thirteen is the death-rate for the average citizen of the Province, but there seems to be no death-rate for the old people. There were people at the Commemoration banquet who could remember

Cromwell. There were six of them. These Old Settlers had all been present at the original Reading of the Proclamation, in 1536. They showed signs of the blightings and blastings of time, in their outward aspect, but they were young within; young and cheerful, and ready to talk; ready to talk, and talk all you wanted; in their turn, and out of it. They were down for six speeches, and they made 42. The governor and the cabinet and the mayor were down for 42 speeches, and they made 6. They have splendid grit, the Old Settlers, splendid staying power. But they do not hear well, and when they see the mayor going through motions which they recognize as the introducing of a speaker, they think they are the one, and they all get up together, and begin to respond, in the most animated way; and the more the mayor gesticulates, and shouts "Sit down! Sit down!" the more they take it for applause, and the more excited and reminiscent and enthusiastic they get; and next, when they see the whole house laughing and crying, three of them think it is about the bitter old-time hardships they are describing, and the other three think the laughter is caused by the jokes they have been uncorking—jokes of the vintage of 1836—and then the way they do go on! And finally when ushers come and plead, and beg, and gently and reverently crowd them down into their seats, they say, "Oh, I'm not tired—I could bang along a week!" and they sit there looking simple and childlike, and gentle, and proud of their oratory, and wholly unconscious of what is going on at the other end of the room. And so one of the great dignitaries gets a chance, and begins his carefully prepared speech, impressively and with solemnity—

"When we, now great and prosperous and powerful, bow our heads in reverent wonder in the contemplation of those sublimities of energy, of wisdom, of forethought, of—"

Up come the immortal six again, in a body, with a joyous "Hey, I've thought of another one!" and at it they go, with might and main, hearing not a whisper of the pandemonium that salutes them, but taking all the visible violences for applause, as before, and hammering joyously away till the imploring ushers pray them into their seats again. And a pity, too; for those lovely old boys did so enjoy living their heroic youth over, in these days of their honored antiquity; and certainly the things they had to tell were usually worth the telling and the hearing.

It was a stirring spectacle; stirring in more ways than one, for it was amazingly funny, and at the same time deeply pathetic; for they had seen so much, these time-worn veterans, end had suffered so much; and had built so strongly and well, and laid the foundations of their commonwealth so deep, in liberty and tolerance; and had lived to see the structure rise to such state and dignity and hear themselves so praised for honorable work.

One of these old gentlemen told me some things of interest afterward; things about the aboriginals, mainly. He thought them intelligent —remarkably so in some directions—and he said that along with their unpleasant qualities they had some exceedingly good ones; and he considered it a great pity that the race had died out. He instanced their invention of the boomerang and the "weet-weet" as evidences of their brightness; and as another evidence of it he said he had never seen a white man who had cleverness enough to learn to do the miracles with those two toys that the aboriginals achieved. He said that even the smartest whites had been obliged to confess that they could not learn the trick of the boomerang in perfection; that it had possibilities which they could not master. The white man could not control its motions, could not make it obey him; but the aboriginal could. He told me

710 *Following The Equator*

some wonderful things—some almost incredible things—which he had seen the blacks do with the boomerang and the weet-weet. They have been confirmed to me since by other early settlers and by trustworthy books.

It is contended—and may be said to be conceded—that the boomerang was known to certain savage tribes in Europe in Roman times. In support of this, Virgil and two other Roman poets are quoted. It is also contended that it was known to the ancient Egyptians.

One of two things either some one with is then apparent: a boomerang arrived in Australia in the days of antiquity before European knowledge of the thing had been lost, or the Australian aboriginal reinvented it. It will take some time to find out which of these two propositions is the fact. But there is no hurry.

CHAPTER XX.

It is by the goodness of God that in our country we have those three unspeakably precious things: freedom of speech, freedom of conscience, and the prudence never to practice either of them. —Pudd'nhead Wilson's New Calendar.

From diary:

Mr. G. called. I had not seen him since Nauheim, Germany—several years ago; the time that the cholera broke out at Hamburg. We talked of the people we had known there, or had casually met; and G. said:

"Do you remember my introducing you to an earl—the Earl of C.?"

"Yes. That was the last time I saw you. You and he were in a carriage, just starting—belated—for the train. I remember it."

"I remember it too, because of a thing which happened then which I was not looking for. He had told me a while before, about a remarkable and interesting Californian whom he had met and who was a friend of yours, and said that if he should ever meet you he would ask you for some particulars about that Californian. The subject was not mentioned that day at Nauheim, for we were hurrying away, and there was no time; but the thing that surprised me was this: when I induced you, you said, 'I am glad to meet your lordship gain.' The I again' was the surprise. He is a little hard of hearing, and didn't catch that word, and I thought you hadn't intended that he should. As we drove off I had only time to say, 'Why, what do you know about him?' and I understood you to say, 'Oh, nothing, except that he is the quickest judge of—' Then we were gone, and I didn't get the rest. I wondered what it was that he was such a quick judge of. I have thought of it many times since, and still wondered what it could be. He and I talked it over, but could not guess it out. He thought it must be fox-hounds or horses, for he is a good judge of those—no one is a better. But you couldn't know that, because you didn't know him; you had mistaken him for some one else; it must be that, he said, because he knew you had never met him before. And of course you hadn't had you?"

"Yes, I had."

"Is that so? Where?"

"At a fox-hunt, in England."

"How curious that is. Why, he hadn't the least recollection of it. Had you any conversation with him?"

"Some—yes."

"Well, it left not the least impression upon him. What did you talk about?"

"About the fox. I think that was all."

"Why, that would interest him; that ought to have left an impression. What did he talk about?"

"The fox."

It's very curious. I don't understand it. Did what he said leave an impression upon you?"

"Yes. It showed me that he was a quick judge of—however, I will tell you all about it, then you will understand. It was a quarter of a century ago 1873 or '74. I had an American friend in London named F., who was fond of hunting, and his friends the Blanks invited him and me to come out to a hunt and be their guests at their country place. In the morning the mounts were provided, but when I saw the horses I changed my mind and asked permission to walk. I had never seen an English hunter before, and it seemed to me that I could hunt a fox safer on the ground. I had always been diffident about horses, anyway, even those of the common altitudes, and I did not feel competent to hunt on a horse that went on stilts. So then Mrs. Blank came to my help and said I could go with her in the dog-cart and we would drive to a place she knew of, and there we should have a good glimpse of the hunt as it went by.

"When we got to that place I got out and went and leaned my elbows on a low stone wall which enclosed a turfy and beautiful great field with heavy wood on all its sides except ours. Mrs. Blank sat in the dog-cart fifty yards away, which was as near as she could get with the vehicle. I was full of interest, for I had never seen a fox-hunt. I waited, dreaming and imagining, in the deep stillness and impressive tranquility which reigned in that retired spot. Presently, from away off in the forest on the left, a mellow bugle-note came floating; then all of a sudden a multitude of dogs burst out of that forest and went tearing by and disappeared in the forest on the right; there was a pause, and then a cloud of horsemen in black caps and crimson coats plunged out of the left-hand forest and went flaming across the field like a prairie-fire, a stirring sight to see. There was one man ahead of the rest, and he came spurring straight at me. He was fiercely excited. It was fine to see him ride; he was a master horseman. He came like, a storm till he was within seven feet of me, where I was leaning on the wall, then he stood his horse straight up in the air on his hind toe-nails, and shouted like a demon:

"'Which way'd the fox go?'

"I didn't much like the tone, but I did not let on; for he was excited, you know. But I was calm; so I said softly, and without acrimony:

"'Which fox?'

"It seemed to anger him. I don't know why; and he thundered out:

"'WHICH fox? Why, THE fox? Which way did the FOX go?'

"I said, with great gentleness—even argumentatively:

"'If you could be a little more definite—a little less vague—because I am a stranger, and there are many foxes, as you will know even better than I, and unless I know which one it is that you desire to identify, and—'

"'You're certainly the damdest idiot that has escaped in a thousand years!' and he snatched his great horse around as easily as I would snatch a cat, and was away like a hurricane. A very excitable man.

"I went back to Mrs. Blank, and she was excited, too—oh, all alive. She said:

"'He spoke to you!—didn't he?'

"'Yes, it is what happened.'

"'I knew it! I couldn't hear what he said, but I knew be spoke to you! Do you know who it was? It was Lord C., and he is Master of the Buckhounds! Tell me—what do you think of him?'

"'Him? Well, for sizing-up a stranger, he's got the most sudden and accurate judgment of any man I ever saw.'

"It pleased her. I thought it would."

G. got away from Nauheim just in time to escape being shut in by the quarantine-bars on the frontiers; and so did we, for we left the next day. But G. had a great deal of trouble in getting by the Italian custom-house, and we should have fared likewise but for the thoughtfulness of our consul-general in Frankfort. He introduced me to the Italian consul-general, and I brought away from that consulate a letter which made our way smooth. It was a dozen lines merely commending me in a general way to the courtesies of servants in his Italian Majesty's service, but it was more powerful than it looked. In addition to a raft of ordinary baggage, we had six or eight trunks which were filled exclusively with dutiable stuff—household goods purchased in Frankfort for use in Florence, where we had taken a house. I was going to ship these through by express; but at the last moment an order went throughout Germany forbidding the moving of any parcels by train unless the owner went with them. This was a bad outlook. We must take these things along, and the delay sure to be caused by the examination of them in the custom-house might lose us our train. I imagined all sorts of terrors, and enlarged them steadily as we approached the Italian frontier. We were six in number, clogged with all that baggage, and I was courier for the party the most incapable one they ever employed.

We arrived, and pressed with the crowd into the immense custom-house, and the usual worries began; everybody crowding to the counter and begging to have his baggage examined first, and all hands clattering and chattering at once. It seemed to me that I could do nothing; it would be better to give it all up and go away and leave the baggage. I couldn't speak the language; I should never accomplish anything. Just then a tall handsome man in a fine uniform was passing by and I knew he must be the station-master—and that reminded me of my letter. I ran to him and put it into his hands. He took it out of the envelope, and the moment his eye caught the royal coat of arms printed at its top, he took off his cap and made a beautiful bow to me, and said in English:

"Which is your baggage? Please show it to me."

I showed him the mountain. Nobody was disturbing it; nobody was interested in it; all the family's attempts to get attention to it had failed—except in the case of one of the trunks containing the dutiable goods. It was just being opened. My officer said:

"There, let that alone! Lock it. Now chalk it. Chalk all of the lot. Now please come and show the hand-baggage."

He plowed through the waiting crowd, I following, to the counter, and he gave orders again, in his emphatic military way:

"Chalk these. Chalk all of them."

Then he took off his cap and made that beautiful bow again, and went his way. By this time these attentions had attracted the wonder of that acre of passengers, and the whisper had gone around that the royal family were present getting their baggage chalked; and as we passed down in review on our way to the door, I was conscious of a pervading atmosphere of envy which gave me deep satisfaction.

But soon there was an accident. My overcoat pockets were stuffed with German cigars and linen packages of American smoking tobacco, and a porter was following us around with this overcoat on his arm, and gradually getting it upside down. Just as I, in the rear of my family, moved by the sentinels at the door, about three hatfuls of the tobacco tumbled out on the floor. One of the soldiers pounced upon it, gathered it up in his arms, pointed back whence I had come, and marched me ahead of him past that long wall of passengers again—he chattering and exulting like a devil, they smiling in peaceful joy, and I trying to look as if my pride was not hurt, and as if I did not mind being brought to shame before these pleased people who had so lately envied me. But at heart I was cruelly humbled.

When I had been marched two-thirds of the long distance and the misery of it was at the worst, the stately station-master stepped out from somewhere, and the soldier left me and darted after him and overtook him; and I could see by the soldier's excited gestures that he was betraying to him the whole shabby business. The station-master was plainly very angry. He came striding down toward me, and when he was come near he began to pour out a stream of indignant Italian; then suddenly took off his hat and made that beautiful bow and said:

"Oh, it is you! I beg a thousands pardons! This idiot here—" He turned to the exulting soldier and burst out with a flood of white-hot Italian lava, and the next moment he was bowing, and the soldier and I were moving in procession again—he in the lead and ashamed, this time, I with my chin up. And so we marched by the crowd of fascinated passengers, and I went forth to the train with the honors of war. Tobacco and all.

CHAPTER XXI.

Man will do many things to get himself loved, he will do all things to get himself envied. —Pudd'nhead Wilson's New Calendar.

Before I saw Australia I had never heard of the "weet-weet" at all. I met but few men who had seen it thrown—at least I met but few who mentioned having seen it thrown. Roughly described, it is a fat wooden cigar with its butt-end fastened to a flexible twig. The whole thing is only a couple of feet long, and weighs less than two ounces. This feather—so to call it—is

not thrown through the air, but is flung with an underhanded throw and made to strike the ground a little way in front of the thrower; then it glances and makes a long skip; glances again, skips again, and again and again, like the flat stone which a boy sends skating over the water. The water is smooth, and the stone has a good chance; so a strong man may make it travel fifty or seventy-five yards; but the weet-weet has no such good chance, for it strikes sand, grass, and earth in its course. Yet an expert aboriginal has sent it a measured distance of two hundred and twenty yards. It would have gone even further but it encountered rank ferns and underwood on its passage and they damaged its speed. Two hundred and twenty yards; and so weightless a toy—a mouse on the end of a bit of wire, in effect; and not sailing through the accommodating air, but encountering grass and sand and stuff at every jump. It looks wholly impossible; but Mr. Brough Smyth saw the feat and did the measuring, and set down the facts in his book about aboriginal life, which he wrote by command of the Victorian Government.

What is the secret of the feat? No one explains. It cannot be physical strength, for that could not drive such a feather-weight any distance. It must be art. But no one explains what the art of it is; nor how it gets around that law of nature which says you shall not throw any two-ounce thing 220 yards, either through the air or bumping along the ground. Rev. J. G. Woods says:

"The distance to which the weet-weet or kangaroo-rat can be thrown is truly astonishing. I have seen an Australian stand at one side of Kennington Oval and throw the kangaroo rat completely across it." (Width of Kennington Oval not stated.) "It darts through the air with the sharp and menacing hiss of a rifle-ball, its greatest height from the ground being some seven or eight feet . . . . . . When properly thrown it looks just like a living animal leaping along . . . . . . Its movements have a wonderful resemblance to the long leaps of a kangaroo-rat fleeing in alarm, with its long tail trailing behind it."

The Old Settler said that he had seen distances made by the weet-weet, in the early days, which almost convinced him that it was as extraordinary an instrument as the boomerang.

There must have been a large distribution of acuteness among those naked skinny aboriginals, or they couldn't have been such unapproachable trackers and boomerangers and weet-weeters. It must have been race-aversion that put upon them a good deal of the low-rate intellectual reputation which they bear and have borne this long time in the world's estimate of them.

They were lazy—always lazy. Perhaps that was their trouble. It is a killing defect. Surely they could have invented and built a competent house, but they didn't. And they could have invented and developed the agricultural arts, but they didn't. They went naked and houseless, and lived on fish and grubs and worms and wild fruits, and were just plain savages, for all their smartness.

With a country as big as the United States to live and multiply in, and with no epidemic diseases among them till the white man came with those and his other appliances of civilization, it is quite probable that there was never a day in his history when he could muster 100,000 of his race in all Australia. He diligently and deliberately kept population down by infanticide—largely; but mainly by certain other methods. He did not need to practise these artificialities any more after the white man came. The white man knew ways of keeping down population which were worth several of his. The white man knew ways of reducing a native population 80 percent. in 20 years. The native had never seen anything as fine as that before.

For example, there is the case of the country now called Victoria—a country eighty times as large as Rhode Island, as I have already said. By the best official guess there were 4,500 aboriginals in it when the whites came along in the middle of the 'Thirties. Of these, 1,000 lived in Gippsland, a patch of territory the size of fifteen or sixteen Rhode Islands: they did not diminish as fast as some of the other communities; indeed, at the end of forty years there were still 200 of them left. The Geelong tribe diminished more satisfactorily: from 173 persons it faded to 34 in twenty years; at the end of another twenty the tribe numbered one person altogether. The two Melbourne tribes could muster almost 300 when the white man came; they could muster but twenty, thirty-seven years later, in 1875. In that year there were still odds and ends of tribes scattered about the colony of Victoria, but I was told that natives of full blood are very scarce now. It is said that the aboriginals continue in some force in the huge territory called Queensland.

The early whites were not used to savages. They could not understand the primary law of savage life: that if a man do you a wrong, his whole tribe is responsible—each individual of it—and you may take your change out of any individual of it, without bothering to seek out the guilty one. When a white killed an aboriginal, the tribe applied the ancient law, and killed the first white they came across. To the whites this was a monstrous thing. Extermination seemed to be the proper medicine for such creatures as this. They did not kill all the blacks, but they promptly killed enough of them to make their own persons safe. From the dawn of civilization down to this day the white man has always used that very precaution. Mrs. Campbell Praed lived in Queensland, as a child, in the early days, and in her "Sketches of Australian life," we get informing pictures of the early struggles of the white and the black to reform each other.

Speaking of pioneer days in the mighty wilderness of Queensland, Mrs. Praed says:

"At first the natives retreated before the whites; and, except that they every now and then speared a beast in one of the herds, gave little cause for uneasiness. But, as the number of squatters increased, each one taking up miles of country and bringing two or three men in his train, so that shepherds' huts and stockmen's camps lay far apart, and defenseless in the midst of hostile tribes, the Blacks' depredations became more frequent and murder was no unusual event.

"The loneliness of the Australian bush can hardly be painted in words. Here extends mile after mile of primeval forest where perhaps foot of white man has never trod—interminable vistas where the eucalyptus trees rear their lofty trunks and spread forth their lanky limbs, from which the red gum oozes and hangs in fantastic pendants like crimson stalactites; ravines along the sides of which the long-bladed grass grows rankly; level untimbered plains alternating with undulating tracts of pasture, here and there broken by a stony ridge, steep gully, or dried-up creek. All wild, vast and desolate; all the same monotonous gray coloring, except where the wattle, when in blossom, shows patches of feathery gold, or a belt of scrub lies green, glossy, and impenetrable as Indian jungle.

"The solitude seems intensified by the strange sounds of reptiles, birds, and insects, and by the absence of larger creatures; of which in the day-time, the only audible signs are the stampede of a herd of kangaroo, or the rustle of a wallabi, or a dingo stirring the grass as it creeps to its lair. But there are the whirring of locusts, the demoniac chuckle of the laughing jack-ass, the screeching of cockatoos and parrots, the hissing of the frilled lizard, and the buzzing of innumerable insects hidden under the dense undergrowth. And then at night, the melancholy wailing of the curlews, the dismal howling of dingoes, the discordant croaking of tree-frogs, might well shake the nerves of the solitary watcher."

That is the theater for the drama. When you comprehend one or two other details, you will perceive how well suited for trouble it was, and how loudly it invited it. The cattlemen's stations were scattered over that profound wilderness miles and miles apart—at each station half a dozen persons. There was a plenty of cattle, the black natives were always ill-nourished and hungry. The land belonged to them. The whites had not bought it, and couldn't buy it; for the tribes had no chiefs, nobody in authority, nobody competent to sell and convey; and the tribes themselves had no comprehension of the idea of transferable ownership of land. The ousted owners were despised by the white interlopers, and this opinion was not hidden under a bushel. More promising materials for a tragedy could not have been collated. Let Mrs. Praed speak:

"At Nie station, one dark night, the unsuspecting hut-keeper, having, as he believed, secured himself against assault, was lying wrapped in his blankets sleeping profoundly. The Blacks crept stealthily down the chimney and battered in his skull while he slept."

One could guess the whole drama from that little text. The curtain was up. It would not fall until the mastership of one party or the other was determined—and permanently:

"There was treachery on both sides. The Blacks killed the Whites when they found them defenseless, and the Whites slew the Blacks in a wholesale and promiscuous fashion which offended against my childish sense of justice.

"They were regarded as little above the level of brutes, and in some cases were destroyed like vermin.

"Here is an instance. A squatter, whose station was surrounded by Blacks, whom he suspected to be hostile and from whom he feared an attack, parleyed with them from his house-door. He told them it was Christmas-time—a time at which all men, black or white, feasted; that there were flour, sugar-plums, good things in plenty in the store, and that he would make for them such a pudding as they had never dreamed of—a great pudding of which all might eat and be filled. The Blacks listened and were lost. The pudding was made and distributed. Next morning there was howling in the camp, for it had been sweetened with sugar and arsenic!"

The white man's spirit was right, but his method was wrong. His spirit was the spirit which the civilized white has always exhibited toward the savage, but the use of poison was a departure from custom. True, it was merely a technical departure, not a real one; still, it was a departure, and therefore a mistake, in my opinion. It was better, kinder, swifter, and much more humane than a number of the methods which have been sanctified by custom, but that does not justify its employment. That is, it does not wholly justify it. Its unusual nature makes it stand out and attract an amount of attention which it is not entitled to. It takes hold upon morbid imaginations and they work it up into a sort of exhibition of cruelty, and this smirches the good name of our civilization, whereas one of the old harsher methods would have had no such effect because usage has made those methods familiar to us and innocent. In many countries we have chained the savage and starved him to death; and this we do not care for, because custom has inured us to it; yet a quick death by poison is loving-kindness to it. In many countries we have burned the savage at the stake; and this we do not care for, because custom has inured us to it; yet a quick death is loving-kindness to it. In more than one country we have hunted the savage and his little children and their mother with dogs and guns through the woods and swamps for an afternoon's sport, and filled the region with happy laughter over their sprawling and stumbling flight, and their wild supplications for mercy; but this method we do not mind, because custom has inured us to it; yet a quick death by poison is loving-kindness to it. In many countries we have taken the savage's land from him, and made him our slave, and lashed him every day, and broken his pride, and made death his only friend, and overworked him till he dropped in his tracks; and this we do not care for, because custom has inured us to it; yet a quick death by poison is loving-kindness to it. In the Matabeleland today—why, there we are confining ourselves to sanctified custom, we Rhodes-Beit millionaires in South Africa and Dukes in London; and nobody cares, because we are used to the old holy customs, and all we ask is that no notice-inviting new ones shall be intruded upon the attention of our comfortable consciences. Mrs. Praed says of the poisoner, "That squatter deserves to have his name handed down to the contempt of posterity."

I am sorry to hear her say that. I myself blame him for one thing, and severely, but I stop there. I blame him for, the indiscretion of introducing a novelty which was calculated to attract attention to our civilization. There was no occasion to do that. It was his duty, and it is every loyal man's duty to protect that heritage in every way he can; and the best way to do that is to attract attention elsewhere. The squatter's judgment was bad—that is plain; but his heart was right. He is almost the only pioneering representative of civilization in history who has risen above the prejudices of his caste and his heredity and tried to introduce the element of mercy into the superior race's dealings with the savage. His name is lost, and it is a pity; for it deserves to be handed down to posterity with homage and reverence.

This paragraph is from a London journal:

"To learn what France is doing to spread the blessings of civilization in her distant dependencies we may turn with advantage to New Caledonia. With a view to attracting free settlers to that penal colony, M. Feillet, the Governor, forcibly expropriated the Kanaka cultivators from the best of their plantations, with a derisory compensation, in spite of the protests of the Council General of the island. Such immigrants as could be induced to cross the seas thus found themselves in possession of thousands of coffee, cocoa, banana, and bread-fruit trees, the raising of which had cost the wretched natives years of toil whilst the latter had a few five-franc pieces to spend in the liquor stores of Noumea."

You observe the combination? It is robbery, humiliation, and slow, slow murder, through poverty and the white man's whisky. The savage's gentle friend, the savage's noble friend, the only magnanimous and unselfish friend the savage has ever had, was not there with the merciful swift release of his poisoned pudding.

There are many humorous things in the world; among them the white man's notion that he is less savage than the other savages.—[See Chapter on Tasmania, post.]

CHAPTER XXII.

Nothing is so ignorant as a man's left hand, except a lady's watch. —Pudd'nhead Wilson's New Calendar.

You notice that Mrs. Praed knows her art. She can place a thing before you so that you can see it. She is not alone in that. Australia is fertile in writers whose books are faithful mirrors of the life of the country and of its history. The materials were surprisingly rich, both in quality and in mass, and Marcus Clarke, Ralph Boldrewood, Cordon, Kendall, and the others, have built out of them a brilliant and vigorous literature, and one which must endure. Materials—there is no end to them! Why, a literature might be made out of the aboriginal all by himself, his character and ways are so freckled with varieties—varieties not staled by familiarity, but new to us. You do not need to invent any picturesquenesses; whatever you want in that line he can furnish you; and they will not be fancies and doubtful, but realities and authentic. In his history, as preserved by the white man's official records, he is everything—everything that a human creature can be. He covers the entire ground. He is a coward—there are a thousand fact to prove it. He is brave—there are a thousand facts to prove it. He is treacherous —oh, beyond imagination! he is faithful, loyal, true—the white man's records supply you with a harvest of instances of it that are noble, worshipful, and pathetically beautiful. He kills the starving stranger who comes begging for food and shelter there is proof of it. He succors, and feeds, and guides to safety, to-day, the lost stranger who fired on him only yesterday—there is proof of it. He takes his reluctant bride by force, he courts her with a club, then loves her faithfully through a long life—it is of record. He gathers to himself another wife by the same processes, beats and bangs her as a daily diversion, and by and by lays down his life in defending her from some outside harm—it is of record. He will face a hundred hostiles to rescue one of his children, and will kill another of his children because the family is large enough without it. His delicate stomach turns, at certain details of the white man's food; but he likes over-ripe fish, and brazed dog, and cat, and rat, and will eat his own uncle with relish. He is a sociable animal, yet he turns aside and hides behind his shield when his mother-in-law goes by. He is childishly afraid of ghosts and other trivialities that menace his soul, but dread of physical pain is a weakness which he is not acquainted with. He knows all the great and many of the little constellations, and has names for them; he has a symbol-writing by means of which he can convey messages far and wide among the tribes; he has a correct eye for form and expression, and draws a good picture; he can track a fugitive by delicate traces which the white man's eye cannot discern, and by methods which the finest white intelligence cannot master; he makes a missile which science itself cannot duplicate without the model—if with it; a missile whose secret baffled and defeated the searchings and theorizings of the white mathematicians for seventy years; and by an art all his own he performs miracles with it which the white man cannot approach untaught, nor parallel after teaching. Within certain limits this savage's intellect is the alertest and the brightest known to history or tradition; and yet the poor creature was never able to invent a counting system that would reach above five, nor a vessel that he could boil water in. He is the prize-curiosity of all the races. To all intents and purposes he is dead—in the body; but he has features that will live in literature.

Mr. Philip Chauncy, an officer of the Victorian Government, contributed to its archives a report of his personal observations of the aboriginals which has in it some things which I wish to condense slightly and insert here. He speaks of the quickness of their eyes and the accuracy of their judgment of the direction of approaching missiles as being quite extraordinary, and of the answering suppleness and accuracy of limb and muscle in avoiding the missile as being extraordinary also. He has seen an aboriginal stand as a target for cricket-balls thrown with great force ten or fifteen yards, by professional bowlers, and successfully dodge them or parry them with his shield during about half an hour. One of those balls, properly placed, could have killed him; "Yet he depended, with the utmost self-possession, on the quickness of his eye and his agility."

The shield was the customary war-shield of his race, and would not be a protection to you or to me. It is no broader than a stovepipe, and is about as long as a man's arm. The opposing surface is not flat, but slopes away from the centerline like a boat's bow. The difficulty about a cricket-ball that has been thrown with a scientific "twist" is, that it suddenly changes it course when it is close to its target and comes straight for the mark when apparently it was going overhead or to one side. I should not be able to protect myself from such balls for half-an-hour, or less.

Mr. Chauncy once saw "a little native man" throw a cricket-ball 119 yards. This is said to beat the English professional record by thirteen yards.

We have all seen the circus-man bound into the air from a spring-board and make a somersault over eight horses standing side by side. Mr. Chauncy saw an aboriginal do it over eleven; and was assured that he had sometimes done it over fourteen. But what is that to this:

"I saw the same man leap from the ground, and in going over he dipped his head, unaided by his hands, into a hat placed in an inverted position on the top of the head of another man sitting upright on horseback—both man and horse being of the average size. The native landed on the other side of the horse with the hat fairly on his head. The prodigious height of the leap, and the precision with which it was taken so as to enable him to dip his head into the hat, exceeded any feat of the kind I have ever beheld."

I should think so! On board a ship lately I saw a young Oxford athlete run four steps and spring into the air and squirm his hips by a side-twist over a bar that was five and one-half feet high; but he could not have stood still and cleared a bar that was four feet high. I know this, because I tried it myself.

One can see now where the kangaroo learned its art.

Sir George Grey and Mr. Eyre testify that the natives dug wells fourteen or fifteen feet deep and two feet in diameter at the bore—dug them in the sand—wells that were "quite circular, carried straight down, and the work beautifully executed."

Their tools were their hands and feet. How did they throw sand out from such a depth? How could they stoop down and get it, with only two feet of space to stoop in? How did they keep that sand-pipe from caving in on them? I do not know. Still, they did manage those seeming impossibilities. Swallowed the sand, may be.

Mr. Chauncy speaks highly of the patience and skill and alert intelligence of the native huntsman when he is stalking the emu, the kangaroo, and other game:

"As he walks through the bush his step is light, elastic, and noiseless; every track on the earth catches his keen eye; a leaf, or fragment of a stick turned, or a blade of grass recently bent by the tread of one of the lower animals, instantly arrests his attention; in fact, nothing escapes his quick and powerful sight on the ground, in the trees, or in the distance, which may supply him with a meal or warn him of danger. A little examination of the trunk of a tree which may be nearly covered with the scratches of opossums ascending and descending is sufficient to inform him whether one went up the night before without coming down again or not."

Fennimore Cooper lost his chance. He would have known how to value these people. He wouldn't have traded the dullest of them for the brightest Mohawk he ever invented.

All savages draw outline pictures upon bark; but the resemblances are not close, and expression is usually lacking. But the Australian aboriginal's pictures of animals were nicely accurate in form, attitude, carriage; and he put spirit into them, and expression. And his pictures of white people and natives were pretty nearly as good as his pictures of the other animals. He dressed his whites in the fashion of their day, both the ladies and the gentlemen. As an untaught wielder of the pencil it is not likely that he has had his equal among savage people.

His place in art—as to drawing, not color-work—is well up, all things considered. His art is not to be classified with savage art at all, but on a plane two degrees above it and one degree above the lowest plane of civilized art. To be exact, his place in art is between Botticelli and De Maurier. That is to say, he could not draw as well as De Maurier but better than Boticelli. In feeling, he resembles both; also in grouping and in his preferences in the matter of subjects. His "corrobboree" of the Australian wilds reappears in De Maurier's Belgravian ballrooms, with clothes and the smirk of civilization added; Botticelli's "Spring" is the "corrobboree" further idealized, but with fewer clothes and more smirk. And well enough as to intention, but—my word!

The aboriginal can make a fire by friction. I have tried that.

All savages are able to stand a good deal of physical pain. The Australian aboriginal has this quality in a well-developed degree. Do not read the following instances if horrors are not pleasant to you. They were recorded by the Rev. Henry N. Wolloston, of Melbourne, who had been a surgeon before he became a clergyman:

1. "In the summer of 1852 I started on horseback from Albany, King George's Sound, to visit at Cape Riche, accompanied by a native on foot. We traveled about forty miles the first day, then camped by a water-hole for the night. After cooking and eating our supper, I observed the native, who had said nothing to me on the subject, collect the hot embers of the fire together, and deliberately place his right foot in the glowing mass for a moment, then suddenly withdraw it, stamping on the ground and uttering a long-drawn guttural sound of mingled pain and satisfaction. This operation he repeated several times. On my inquiring the meaning of his strange conduct, he only said, 'Me carpenter-make 'em' ('I am mending my foot'), and then showed me his charred great toe, the nail of which had been torn off by a tea-tree stump, in which it had been caught

during the journey, and the pain of which he had borne with stoical composure until the evening, when he had an opportunity of cauterizing the wound in the primitive manner above described."

And he proceeded on the journey the next day, "as if nothing had happened"—and walked thirty miles. It was a strange idea, to keep a surgeon and then do his own surgery.

2. "A native about twenty-five years of age once applied to me, as a doctor, to extract the wooden barb of a spear, which, during a fight in the bush some four months previously, had entered his chest, just missing the heart, and penetrated the viscera to a considerable depth. The spear had been cut off, leaving the barb behind, which continued to force its way by muscular action gradually toward the back; and when I examined him I could feel a hard substance between the ribs below the left blade-bone. I made a deep incision, and with a pair of forceps extracted the barb, which was made, as usual, of hard wood about four inches long and from half an inch to an inch thick. It was very smooth, and partly digested, so to speak, by the maceration to which it had been exposed during its four months' journey through the body. The wound made by the spear had long since healed, leaving only a small cicatrix; and after the operation, which the native bore without flinching, he appeared to suffer no pain. Indeed, judging from his good state of health, the presence of the foreign matter did not materially annoy him. He was perfectly well in a few days."

But No. 3 is my favorite. Whenever I read it I seem to enjoy all that the patient enjoyed—whatever it was:

3. "Once at King George's Sound a native presented himself to me with one leg only, and requested me to supply him with a wooden leg. He had traveled in this maimed state about ninety-six miles, for this purpose. I examined the limb, which had been severed just below the knee, and found that it had been charred by fire, while about two inches of the partially calcined bone protruded through the flesh. I at once removed this with the saw; and having made as presentable a stump of it as I could, covered the amputated end of the bone with a surrounding of muscle, and kept the patient a few days under my care to allow the wound to heal. On inquiring, the native told me that in a fight with other black-fellows a spear had struck his leg and penetrated the bone below the knee. Finding it was serious, he had recourse to the following crude and barbarous operation, which it appears is not uncommon among these people in their native state. He made a fire, and dug a hole in the earth only sufficiently large to admit his leg, and deep enough to allow the wounded part to be on a level with the surface of the ground. He then surrounded the limb with the live coals or charcoal, which was replenished until the leg was literally burnt off. The cauterization thus applied completely checked the hemorrhage, and he was able in a day or two to hobble down to the Sound, with the aid of a long stout stick, although he was more than a week on the road."

But he was a fastidious native. He soon discarded the wooden leg made for him by the doctor, because "it had no feeling in it." It must have had as much as the one he burnt off, I should think.

So much for the Aboriginals. It is difficult for me to let them alone. They are marvelously interesting creatures. For a quarter of a century, now, the several colonial governments have housed their remnants in comfortable stations, and fed them well and taken good care of them in every way. If I had found this out while I was in Australia I could have seen some

of those people—but I didn't. I would walk thirty miles to see a stuffed one.

Australia has a slang of its own. This is a matter of course. The vast cattle and sheep industries, the strange aspects of the country, and the strange native animals, brute and human, are matters which would naturally breed a local slang. I have notes of this slang somewhere, but at the moment I can call to mind only a few of the words and phrases. They are expressive ones. The wide, sterile, unpeopled deserts have created eloquent phrases like "No Man's Land" and the "Never-never Country." Also this felicitous form: "She lives in the Never-never Country"—that is, she is an old maid. And this one is not without merit: "heifer-paddock"—young ladies' seminary. "Bail up" and "stick up" equivalent of our highwayman-term to "hold up" a stage-coach or a train. "New-chum" is the equivalent of our "tenderfoot"—new arrival.

And then there is the immortal "My word!" "We must import it." "M-y word!"

"In cold print it is the equivalent of our "Ger-rreat Caesar!" but spoken with the proper Australian unction and fervency, it is worth six of it for grace and charm and expressiveness. Our form is rude and explosive; it is not suited to the drawing-room or the heifer-paddock; but "M-y word!" is, and is music to the ear, too, when the utterer knows how to say it. I saw it in print several times on the Pacific Ocean, but it struck me coldly, it aroused no sympathy. That was because it was the dead corpse of the thing, the 'soul was not there—the tones were lacking—the informing spirit—the deep feeling—the eloquence. But the first time I heard an Australian say it, it was positively thrilling.

CHAPTER XXIII.

Be careless in your dress if you must, but keep a tidy soul. — Pudd'nhead Wilson's New Calendar.

We left Adelaide in due course, and went to Horsham, in the colony of Victoria; a good deal of a journey, if I remember rightly, but pleasant. Horsham sits in a plain which is as level as a floor—one of those famous dead levels which Australian books describe so often; gray, bare, sombre, melancholy, baked, cracked, in the tedious long drouths, but a horizonless ocean of vivid green grass the day after a rain. A country town, peaceful, reposeful, inviting, full of snug homes, with garden plots, and plenty of shrubbery and flowers.

"Horsham, October 17. At the hotel. The weather divine. Across the way, in front of the London Bank of Australia, is a very handsome cottonwood. It is in opulent leaf, and every leaf perfect. The full power of the on-rushing spring is upon it, and I imagine I can see it grow. Alongside the bank and a little way back in the garden there is a row of soaring fountain-sprays of delicate feathery foliage quivering in the breeze, and mottled with flashes of light that shift and play through the mass like flash-lights through an opal—a most beautiful tree, and a striking contrast to the cottonwood. Every leaf of the cottonwood is distinctly defined—it is a kodak for faithful, hard, unsentimental detail; the other an impressionist picture, delicious to look upon, full of a subtle and exquisite charm, but all details fused in a swoon of vague and soft loveliness."

It turned out, upon inquiry, to be a pepper tree—an importation from China. It has a silky sheen, soft and rich. I saw some that had long red bunches of currant-like berries ambushed among the foliage. At a distance, in certain lights, they give the tree a pinkish tint and a new charm.

There is an agricultural college eight miles from Horsham. We were driven out to it by its chief. The conveyance was an open wagon; the time, noonday; no wind; the sky without a cloud, the sunshine brilliant —and the mercury at 92 deg. in the shade. In some countries an indolent unsheltered drive of an hour and a half under such conditions would have been a sweltering and prostrating experience; but there was nothing of that in this case. It is a climate that is perfect. There was no sense of heat; indeed, there was no heat; the air was fine and pure and exhilarating; if the drive had lasted half a day I think we should not have felt any discomfort, or grown silent or droopy or tired. Of course, the secret of it was the exceeding dryness of the atmosphere. In that plain 112 deg. in the shade is without doubt no harder upon a man than is 88 or 90 deg. in New York.

The road lay through the middle of an empty space which seemed to me to be a hundred yards wide between the fences. I was not given the width in yards, but only in chains and perches—and furlongs, I think. I would have given a good deal to know what the width was, but I did not pursue the matter. I think it is best to put up with information the way you get it; and seem satisfied with it, and surprised at it, and grateful for it, and say, "My word!" and never let on. It was a wide space; I could tell you how wide, in chains and perches and furlongs and things, but that would not help you any. Those things sound well, but they are shadowy and indefinite, like troy weight and avoirdupois; nobody knows what they mean. When you buy a pound of a drug and the man asks you which you want, troy or avoirdupois, it is best to say "Yes," and shift the subject.

They said that the wide space dates from the earliest sheep and cattle-raising days. People had to drive their stock long distances —immense journeys—from worn-out places to new ones where were water and fresh pasturage; and this wide space had to be left in grass and unfenced, or the stock would have starved to death in the transit.

On the way we saw the usual birds—the beautiful little green parrots, the magpie, and some others; and also the slender native bird of modest plumage and the eternally-forgettable name—the bird that is the smartest among birds, and can give a parrot 30 to 1 in the game and then talk him to death. I cannot recall that bird's name. I think it begins with M. I wish it began with G. or something that a person can remember.

The magpie was out in great force, in the fields and on the fences. He is a handsome large creature, with snowy white decorations, and is a singer; he has a murmurous rich note that is lovely. He was once modest, even diffident; but he lost all that when he found out that he was Australia's sole musical bird. He has talent, and cuteness, and impudence; and in his tame state he is a most satisfactory pet—never coming when he is called, always coming when he isn't, and studying disobedience as an accomplishment. He is not confined, but loafs all over the house and grounds, like the laughing jackass. I think he learns to talk, I know he learns to sing tunes, and his friends say that he knows how to steal without learning. I was acquainted with a tame magpie in Melbourne. He had lived in a lady's house several years, and believed he owned it. The lady had tamed him, and in return he had tamed the lady. He was always on deck when not wanted, always having his own way, always tyrannizing over the dog, and always making the cat's life a slow sorrow and a martyrdom. He knew a number of tunes and could sing them in perfect time and tune; and

would do it, too, at any time that silence was wanted; and then encore himself and do it again; but if he was asked to sing he would go out and take a walk.

It was long believed that fruit trees would not grow in that baked and waterless plain around Horsham, but the agricultural college has dissipated that idea. Its ample nurseries were producing oranges, apricots, lemons, almonds, peaches, cherries, 48 varieties of apples—in fact, all manner of fruits, and in abundance. The trees did not seem to miss the water; they were in vigorous and flourishing condition.

Experiments are made with different soils, to see what things thrive best in them and what climates are best for them. A man who is ignorantly trying to produce upon his farm things not suited to its soil and its other conditions can make a journey to the college from anywhere in Australia, and go back with a change of scheme which will make his farm productive and profitable.

There were forty pupils there—a few of them farmers, relearning their trade, the rest young men mainly from the cities—novices. It seemed a strange thing that an agricultural college should have an attraction for city-bred youths, but such is the fact. They are good stuff, too; they are above the agricultural average of intelligence, and they come without any inherited prejudices in favor of hoary ignorances made sacred by long descent.

The students work all day in the fields, the nurseries, and the shearing-sheds, learning and doing all the practical work of the business—three days in a week. On the other three they study and hear lectures. They are taught the beginnings of such sciences as bear upon agriculture—like chemistry, for instance. We saw the sophomore class in sheep-shearing shear a dozen sheep. They did it by hand, not with the machine. The sheep was seized and flung down on his side and held there; and the students took off his coat with great celerity and adroitness. Sometimes they clipped off a sample of the sheep, but that is customary with shearers, and they don't mind it; they don't even mind it as much as the sheep. They dab a splotch of sheep-dip on the place and go right ahead.

The coat of wool was unbelievably thick. Before the shearing the sheep looked like the fat woman in the circus; after it he looked like a bench. He was clipped to the skin; and smoothly and uniformly. The fleece comes from him all in one piece and has the spread of a blanket.

The college was flying the Australian flag—the gridiron of England smuggled up in the northwest corner of a big red field that had the random stars of the Southern Cross wandering around over it.

From Horsham we went to Stawell. By rail. Still in the colony of Victoria. Stawell is in the gold-mining country. In the bank-safe was half a peck of surface-gold—gold dust, grain gold; rich; pure in fact, and pleasant to sift through one's fingers; and would be pleasanter if it would stick. And there were a couple of gold bricks, very heavy to handle, and worth $7,500 a piece. They were from a very valuable quartz mine; a lady owns two-thirds of it; she has an income of $75,000 a month from it, and is able to keep house.

The Stawell region is not productive of gold only; it has great vineyards, and produces exceptionally fine wines. One of these vineyards—the Great Western, owned by Mr. Irving—is regarded as a model. Its product has reputation abroad. It yields a choice champagne and a fine claret, and its hock took a prize in France two or three years ago. The champagne is kept in a maze of passages under ground, cut in the rock, to secure it an even temperature during the three-year term required to perfect it. In those vaults I saw 120,000 bottles of champagne. The colony of Victoria has a population of 1,000,000, and those people are said to drink 25,000,000 bottles of champagne per year. The dryest community on the earth. The government has lately reduced the duty upon foreign wines. That is one of the unkindnesses of Protection. A man invests years of work and a vast sum of money in a worthy enterprise, upon the faith of existing laws; then the law is changed, and the man is robbed by his own government.

On the way back to Stawell we had a chance to see a group of boulders called the Three Sisters—a curiosity oddly located; for it was upon high ground, with the land sloping away from it, and no height above it from whence the boulders could have rolled down. Relics of an early ice-drift, perhaps. They are noble boulders. One of them has the size and smoothness and plump sphericity of a balloon of the biggest pattern.

The road led through a forest of great gum-trees, lean and scraggy and sorrowful. The road was cream-white—a clayey kind of earth, apparently. Along it toiled occasional freight wagons, drawn by long double files of oxen. Those wagons were going a journey of two hundred miles, I was told, and were running a successful opposition to the railway! The railways are owned and run by the government.

Those sad gums stood up out of the dry white clay, pictures of patience and resignation. It is a tree that can get along without water; still it is fond of it—ravenously so. It is a very intelligent tree and will detect the presence of hidden water at a distance of fifty feet, and send out slender long root-fibres to prospect it. They will find it; and will also get at it even through a cement wall six inches thick. Once a cement water-pipe under ground at Stawell began to gradually reduce its output, and finally ceased altogether to deliver water. Upon examining into the matter it was found stopped up, wadded compactly with a mass of root-fibres, delicate and hair-like. How this stuff had gotten into the pipe was a puzzle for some little time; finally it was found that it had crept in through a crack that was almost invisible to the eye. A gum tree forty feet away had tapped the pipe and was drinking the water.

CHAPTER XXIV.

There is no such thing as "the Queen's English." The property has gone into the hands of a joint stock company and we own the bulk of the shares! —Pudd'nhead Wilson's New Calendar.

Frequently, in Australia, one has cloud-effects of an unfamiliar sort. We had this kind of scenery, finely staged, all the way to Ballarat. Consequently we saw more sky than country on that journey. At one time a great stretch of the vault was densely flecked with wee ragged-edged flakes of painfully white cloud-stuff, all of one shape and size, and equidistant apart, with narrow cracks of adorable blue showing between. The whole was suggestive of a hurricane of snow-flakes drifting across the skies. By and by these flakes fused themselves together in interminable lines, with shady faint hollows between the lines, the long satin-surfaced rollers following each other in simulated movement, and enchantingly counterfeiting the majestic march of a flowing sea. Later, the sea solidified itself; then gradually broke up its mass into innumerable lofty white pillars of about one size, and ranged these across the firmament, in receding and fading perspective, in the

similitude of a stupendous colonnade—a mirage without a doubt flung from the far Gates of the Hereafter.

The approaches to Ballarat were beautiful. The features, great green expanses of rolling pasture-land, bisected by eye contenting hedges of commingled new-gold and old-gold gorse—and a lovely lake. One must put in the pause, there, to fetch the reader up with a slight jolt, and keep him from gliding by without noticing the lake. One must notice it; for a lovely lake is not as common a thing along the railways of Australia as are the dry places. Ninety-two in the shade again, but balmy and comfortable, fresh and bracing. A perfect climate.

Forty-five years ago the site now occupied by the City of Ballarat was a sylvan solitude as quiet as Eden and as lovely. Nobody had ever heard of it. On the 25th of August, 1851, the first great gold-strike made in Australia was made here. The wandering prospectors who made it scraped up two pounds and a half of gold the first day-worth $600. A few days later the place was a hive—a town. The news of the strike spread everywhere in a sort of instantaneous way—spread like a flash to the very ends of the earth. A celebrity so prompt and so universal has hardly been paralleled in history, perhaps. It was as if the name BALLARAT had suddenly been written on the sky, where all the world could read it at once.

The smaller discoveries made in the colony of New South Wales three months before had already started emigrants toward Australia; they had been coming as a stream, but they came as a flood, now. A hundred thousand people poured into Melbourne from England and other countries in a single month, and flocked away to the mines. The crews of the ships that brought them flocked with them; the clerks in the government offices followed; so did the cooks, the maids, the coachmen, the butlers, and the other domestic servants; so did the carpenters, the smiths, the plumbers, the painters, the reporters, the editors, the lawyers, the clients, the barkeepers, the bummers, the blacklegs, the thieves, the loose women, the grocers, the butchers, the bakers, the doctors, the druggists, the nurses; so did the police; even officials of high and hitherto envied place threw up their positions and joined the procession. This roaring avalanche swept out of Melbourne and left it desolate, Sunday-like, paralyzed, everything at a stand-still, the ships lying idle at anchor, all signs of life departed, all sounds stilled save the rasping of the cloud-shadows as they scraped across the vacant streets.

That grassy and leafy paradise at Ballarat was soon ripped open, and lacerated and scarified and gutted, in the feverish search for its hidden riches. There is nothing like surface-mining to snatch the graces and beauties and benignities out of a paradise, and make an odious and repulsive spectacle of it.

What fortunes were made! Immigrants got rich while the ship unloaded and reloaded—and went back home for good in the same cabin they had come out in! Not all of them. Only some. I saw the others in Ballarat myself, forty-five years later—what were left of them by time and death and the disposition to rove. They were young and gay, then; they are patriarchal and grave, now; and they do not get excited any more. They talk of the Past. They live in it. Their life is a dream, a retrospection.

Ballarat was a great region for "nuggets." No such nuggets were found in California as Ballarat produced. In fact, the Ballarat region has yielded the largest ones known to history. Two of them weighed about 180 pounds each, and together were worth $90,000. They were offered to any poor person who would shoulder them and carry them away. Gold was so plentiful that it made people liberal like that.

Ballarat was a swarming city of tents in the early days. Everybody was happy, for a time, and apparently prosperous. Then came trouble. The government swooped down with a mining tax. And in its worst form, too; for it was not a tax upon what the miner had taken out, but upon what he was going to take out—if he could find it. It was a license-tax license to work his claim—and it had to be paid before he could begin digging.

Consider the situation. No business is so uncertain as surface-mining. Your claim may be good, and it may be worthless. It may make you well off in a month; and then again you may have to dig and slave for half a year, at heavy expense, only to find out at last that the gold is not there in cost-paying quantity, and that your time and your hard work have been thrown away. It might be wise policy to advance the miner a monthly sum to encourage him to develop the country's riches; but to tax him monthly in advance instead—why, such a thing was never dreamed of in America. There, neither the claim itself nor its products, howsoever rich or poor, were taxed.

The Ballarat miners protested, petitioned, complained—it was of no use; the government held its ground, and went on collecting the tax. And not by pleasant methods, but by ways which must have been very galling to free people. The rumblings of a coming storm began to be audible.

By and by there was a result; and I think it may be called the finest thing in Australasian history. It was a revolution—small in size; but great politically; it was a strike for liberty, a struggle for a principle, a stand against injustice and oppression. It was the Barons and John, over again; it was Hampden and Ship-Money; it was Concord and Lexington; small beginnings, all of them, but all of them great in political results, all of them epoch-making. It is another instance of a victory won by a lost battle. It adds an honorable page to history; the people know it and are proud of it. They keep green the memory of the men who fell at the Eureka Stockade, and Peter Lalor has his monument.

The surface-soil of Ballarat was full of gold. This soil the miners ripped and tore and trenched and harried and disembowled, and made it yield up its immense treasure. Then they went down into the earth with deep shafts, seeking the gravelly beds of ancient rivers and brooks—and found them. They followed the courses of these streams, and gutted them, sending the gravel up in buckets to the upper world, and washing out of it its enormous deposits of gold. The next biggest of the two monster nuggets mentioned above came from an old river-channel 180 feet under ground.

Finally the quartz lodes were attacked. That is not poor-man's mining. Quartz-mining and milling require capital, and staying-power, and patience. Big companies were formed, and for several decades, now, the lodes have been successfully worked, and have yielded great wealth. Since the gold discovery in 1853 the Ballarat mines—taking the three kinds of mining together—have contributed to the world's pocket something over three hundred millions of dollars, which is to say that this nearly invisible little spot on the earth's surface has yielded about one-fourth as much gold in forty-four years as all California has yielded in forty-seven. The Californian aggregate, from 1848 to 1895, inclusive, as reported by the Statistician of the United States Mint, is $1,265,215,217.

A citizen told me a curious thing about those mines. With all my experience of mining I had never heard of anything of the sort before. The main gold reef runs about north and south—of course for that is the custom of a rich gold reef. At Ballarat its course is between walls of slate. Now the citizen told me that throughout a stretch of twelve miles along the reef, the reef is crossed at intervals by a straight black streak of a carbonaceous nature—a streak in the slate; a streak no thicker than a pencil—and that wherever it crosses the reef you will certainly find gold at the junction. It is called the Indicator. Thirty feet on each side of the Indicator (and down in the slate, of course) is a still finer streak—a streak as fine as a pencil mark; and indeed, that is its name Pencil Mark. Whenever you find the Pencil Mark you know that thirty feet from it is the Indicator; you measure the distance, excavate, find the Indicator, trace it straight to the reef, and sink your shaft; your fortune is made, for certain. If that is true, it is curious. And it is curious anyway.

Ballarat is a town of only 40,000 population; and yet, since it is in Australia, it has every essential of an advanced and enlightened big city. This is pure matter of course. I must stop dwelling upon these things. It is hard to keep from dwelling upon them, though; for it is difficult to get away from the surprise of it. I will let the other details go, this time, but I must allow myself to mention that this little town has a park of 326 acres; a flower garden of 83 acres, with an elaborate and expensive fernery in it and some costly and unusually fine statuary; and an artificial lake covering 600 acres, equipped with a fleet of 200 shells, small sail boats, and little steam yachts.

At this point I strike out some other praiseful things which I was tempted to add. I do not strike them out because they were not true or not well said, but because I find them better said by another man—and a man more competent to testify, too, because he belongs on the ground, and knows. I clip them from a chatty speech delivered some years ago by Mr. William Little, who was at that time mayor of Ballarat:

"The language of our citizens, in this as in other parts of Australasia, is mostly healthy Anglo-Saxon, free from Americanisms, vulgarisms, and the conflicting dialects of our Fatherland, and is pure enough to suit a Trench or a Latham. Our youth, aided by climatic influence, are in point of physique and comeliness unsurpassed in the Sunny South. Our young men are well ordered; and our maidens, 'not stepping over the bounds of modesty,' are as fair as Psyches, dispensing smiles as charming as November flowers."

The closing clause has the seeming of a rather frosty compliment, but that is apparent only, not real. November is summer-time there.

His compliment to the local purity of the language is warranted. It is quite free from impurities; this is acknowledged far and wide. As in the German Empire all cultivated people claim to speak Hanovarian German, so in Australasia all cultivated people claim to speak Ballarat English. Even in England this cult has made considerable progress, and now that it is favored by the two great Universities, the time is not far away when Ballarat English will come into general use among the educated classes of Great Britain at large. Its great merit is, that it is shorter than ordinary English—that is, it is more compressed. At first you have some difficulty in understanding it when it is spoken as rapidly as the orator whom I have quoted speaks it. An illustration will show what I mean. When he called and I handed him a chair, he bowed and said:

"Q."

Presently, when we were lighting our cigars, he held a match to mine and I said:

"Thank you," and he said:

"Km."

Then I saw. 'Q' is the end of the phrase "I thank you" 'Km' is the end of the phrase "You are welcome." Mr. Little puts no emphasis upon either of them, but delivers them so reduced that they hardly have a sound. All Ballarat English is like that, and the effect is very soft and pleasant; it takes all the hardness and harshness out of our tongue and gives to it a delicate whispery and vanishing cadence which charms the ear like the faint rustling of the forest leaves.

CHAPTER XXV.

"Classic." A book which people praise and don't read. — Pudd'nhead Wilson's New Calendar.

On the rail again—bound for Bendigo. From diary:

October 23. Got up at 6, left at 7.30; soon reached Castlemaine, one of the rich gold-fields of the early days; waited several hours for a train; left at 3.40 and reached Bendigo in an hour. For comrade, a Catholic priest who was better than I was, but didn't seem to know it—a man full of graces of the heart, the mind, and the spirit; a lovable man. He will rise. He will be a bishop some day. Later an Archbishop. Later a Cardinal. Finally an Archangel, I hope. And then he will recall me when I say, "Do you remember that trip we made from Ballarat to Bendigo, when you were nothing but Father C., and I was nothing to what I am now?" It has actually taken nine hours to come from Ballarat to Bendigo. We could have saved seven by walking. However, there was no hurry.

Bendigo was another of the rich strikes of the early days. It does a great quartz-mining business, now—that business which, more than any other that I know of, teaches patience, and requires grit and a steady nerve. The town is full of towering chimney-stacks, and hoisting-works, and looks like a petroleum-city. Speaking of patience; for example, one of the local companies went steadily on with its deep borings and searchings without show of gold or a penny of reward for eleven years —then struck it, and became suddenly rich. The eleven years' work had cost $55,000, and the first gold found was a grain the size of a pin's head. It is kept under locks and bars, as a precious thing, and is reverently shown to the visitor, "hats off." When I saw it I had not heard its history.

"It is gold. Examine it—take the glass. Now how much should you say it is worth?"

I said:

"I should say about two cents; or in your English dialect, four farthings."

"Well, it cost £11,000."

"Oh, come!"

"Yes, it did. Ballarat and Bendigo have produced the three monumental nuggets of the world, and this one is the monumentalest one of the three. The other two represent 19,000 a piece; this one a couple of thousand more. It is small, and not much to look at, but it is entitled to (its) name—Adam. It is the Adam-nugget of this mine, and its children run up into the millions."

Speaking of patience again, another of the mines was worked, under heavy expenses, during 17 years before pay was struck, and still another one compelled a wait of 21 years before pay was struck; then, in both instances, the outlay was all back in a year or two, with compound interest.

Bendigo has turned out even more gold than Ballarat. The two together have produced $650,000,000 worth—which is half as much as California has produced.

It was through Mr. Blank—not to go into particulars about his name—it was mainly through Mr. Blank that my stay in Bendigo was made memorably pleasant and interesting. He explained this to me himself. He told me that it was through his influence that the city government invited me to the town-hall to hear complimentary speeches and respond to them; that it was through his influence that I had been taken on a long pleasure-drive through the city and shown its notable features; that it was through his influence that I was invited to visit the great mines; that it was through his influence that I was taken to the hospital and allowed to see the convalescent Chinaman who had been attacked at midnight in his lonely hut eight weeks before by robbers, and stabbed forty-six times and scalped besides; that it was through his influence that when I arrived this awful spectacle of piecings and patchings and bandagings was sitting up in his cot letting on to read one of my books; that it was through his influence that efforts had been made to get the Catholic Archbishop of Bendigo to invite me to dinner; that it was through his influence that efforts had been made to get the Anglican Bishop of Bendigo to ask me to supper; that it was through his influence that the dean of the editorial fraternity had driven me through the woodsy outlying country and shown me, from the summit of Lone Tree Hill, the mightiest and loveliest expanse of forest-clad mountain and valley that I had seen in all Australia. And when he asked me what had most impressed me in Bendigo and I answered and said it was the taste and the public spirit which had adorned the streets with 105 miles of shade trees, he said that it was through his influence that it had been done.

But I am not representing him quite correctly. He did not say it was through his influence that all these things had happened—for that would have been coarse; be merely conveyed that idea; conveyed it so subtly that I only caught it fleetingly, as one catches vagrant faint breaths of perfume when one traverses the meadows in summer; conveyed it without offense and without any suggestion of egoism or ostentation—but conveyed it, nevertheless.

He was an Irishman; an educated gentleman; grave, and kindly, and courteous; a bachelor, and about forty-five or possibly fifty years old, apparently. He called upon me at the hotel. He made me like him, and did it without trouble. This was partly through his winning and gentle ways, but mainly through the amazing familiarity with my books which his conversation showed. He was down to date with them, too; and if he had made them the study of his life he could hardly have been better posted as to their contents than he was. He made me better satisfied with myself than I had ever been before. It was plain that he had a deep fondness for humor, yet he never laughed; he never even chuckled; in fact, humor could not win to outward expression on his face at all. No, he was always grave—tenderly, pensively grave; but he made me laugh, all along; and this was very trying—and very pleasant at the same time—for it was at quotations from my own books.

When he was going, he turned and said:

"You don't remember me?"

"I? Why, no. Have we met before?"

"No, it was a matter of correspondence."

"Correspondence?"

"Yes, many years ago. Twelve or fifteen. Oh, longer than that. But of course you—" A musing pause. Then he said:

"Do you remember Corrigan Castle?"

"N-no, I believe I don't. I don't seem to recall the name."

He waited a moment, pondering, with the door-knob in his hand, then started out; but turned back and said that I had once been interested in Corrigan Castle, and asked me if I would go with him to his quarters in the evening and take a hot Scotch and talk it over. I was a teetotaler and liked relaxation, so I said I would.

We drove from the lecture-hall together about half-past ten. He had a most comfortably and tastefully furnished parlor, with good pictures on the walls, Indian and Japanese ornaments on the mantel, and here and there, and books everywhere-largely mine; which made me proud. The light was brilliant, the easy chairs were deep-cushioned, the arrangements for brewing and smoking were all there. We brewed and lit up; then he passed a sheet of note-paper to me and said—

"Do you remember that?"

"Oh, yes, indeed!"

The paper was of a sumptuous quality. At the top was a twisted and interlaced monogram printed from steel dies in gold and blue and red, in the ornate English fashion of long years ago; and under it, in neat gothic capitals was this—printed in blue:

The Mark Twain Club
Corrigan Castle
187

"My!" said I, "how did you come by this?"

"I was President of it."

"No!—you don't mean it."

"It is true. I was its first President. I was re-elected annually as long as its meetings were held in my castle—Corrigan—which was five years."

Then he showed me an album with twenty-three photographs of me in it. Five of them were of old dates, the others of various later crops; the list closed with a picture taken by Falk in Sydney a month before.

"You sent us the first five; the rest were bought."

This was paradise! We ran late, and talked, talked, talked—subject, the Mark Twain Club of Corrigan Castle, Ireland.

My first knowledge of that Club dates away back; all of twenty years, I should say. It came to me in the form of a courteous letter, written on the note-paper which I have described, and signed "By order of the President; C. PEMBROKE, Secretary." It conveyed the fact that the Club had been created in my honor, and added the hope that this token of appreciation of my work would meet with my approval.

I answered, with thanks; and did what I could to keep my gratification from over-exposure.

It was then that the long correspondence began. A letter came back, by order of the President, furnishing me the names of the members-thirty-two in number. With it came a copy of the Constitution and By-Laws, in pamphlet form, and artistically printed. The initiation fee and dues were in their proper place; also, schedule of meetings—monthly—for essays upon works of mine, followed by discussions; quarterly for business and a supper, without essays, but with after-supper speeches also, there was a list of the officers: President, Vice-President, Secretary, Treasurer, etc. The letter was brief, but it was pleasant reading, for it told me about the strong interest which the membership took in their new venture, etc., etc. It also asked me for a photograph —a special one. I went down and sat for it and sent it—with a letter, of course.

Presently came the badge of the Club, and very dainty and pretty it was; and very artistic. It was a frog peeping out from a graceful tangle of grass-sprays and rushes, and was done in enamels on a gold basis, and had a gold pin back of it. After I had petted it, and played with it, and caressed it, and enjoyed it a couple of hours, the light happened to fall upon it at a new angle, and revealed to me a cunning new detail; with the light just right, certain delicate shadings of the grass-blades and rush-stems wove themselves into a monogram—mine! You can see that that jewel was a work of art. And when you come to consider the intrinsic value of it, you must concede that it is not every literary club that could afford a badge like that. It was easily worth $75, in the opinion of Messrs. Marcus and Ward of New York. They said they could not duplicate it for that and make a profit. By this time the Club was well under way; and from that time forth its secretary kept my off-hours well supplied with business. He reported the Club's discussions of my books with laborious fullness, and did his work with great spirit and ability. As, a rule, he synopsized; but when a speech was especially brilliant, he short-handed it and gave me the best passages from it, written out. There were five speakers whom he particularly favored in that way: Palmer, Forbes, Naylor, Norris, and Calder. Palmer and Forbes could never get through a speech without attacking each other, and each in his own way was formidably effective—Palmer in virile and eloquent abuse, Forbes in courtly and elegant but scalding satire. I could always tell which of them was talking without looking for his name. Naylor had a polished style and a happy knack at felicitous metaphor; Norris's style was wholly without ornament, but enviably compact, lucid, and strong. But after all, Calder was the gem. He never spoke when sober, he spoke continuously when he wasn't. And certainly they were the drunkest speeches that a man ever uttered. They were full of good things, but so incredibly mixed up and wandering that it made one's head swim to follow him. They were not intended to be funny, but they were,—funny for the very gravity which the speaker put into his flowing miracles of incongruity. In the course of five years I came to know the styles of the five orators as well as I knew the style of any speaker in my own club at home.

These reports came every month. They were written on foolscap, 600 words to the page, and usually about twenty-five pages in a report—a good 15,000 words, I should say,—a solid week's work. The reports were absorbingly entertaining, long as they were; but, unfortunately for me, they did not come alone. They were always accompanied by a lot of questions about passages and purposes in my books, which the Club wanted answered; and additionally accompanied every quarter by the Treasurer's report, and the Auditor's report, and the Committee's report, and the President's review, and my opinion of these was always desired; also suggestions for the good of the Club, if any occurred to me.

By and by I came to dread those things; and this dread grew and grew and grew; grew until I got to anticipating them with a cold horror. For I was an indolent man, and not fond of letter-writing, and whenever these things came I had to put everything by and sit down—for my own peace of mind—and dig and dig until I got something out of my head which would answer for a reply. I got along fairly well the first year; but for the succeeding four years the Mark Twain Club of Corrigan Castle was my curse, my nightmare, the grief and misery of my life. And I got so, so sick of sitting for photographs. I sat every year for five years, trying to satisfy that insatiable organization. Then at last I rose in revolt. I could endure my oppressions no longer. I pulled my fortitude together and tore off my chains, and was a free man again, and happy. From that day I burned the secretary's fat envelopes the moment they arrived, and by and by they ceased to come.

Well, in the sociable frankness of that night in Bendigo I brought this all out in full confession. Then Mr. Blank came out in the same frank way, and with a preliminary word of gentle apology said that he was the Mark Twain Club, and the only member it had ever had!

Why, it was matter for anger, but I didn't feel any. He said he never had to work for a living, and that by the time he was thirty life had become a bore and a weariness to him. He had no interests left; they had paled and perished, one by one, and left him desolate. He had begun to think of suicide. Then all of a sudden he thought of that happy idea of starting an imaginary club, and went straightway to work at it, with enthusiasm and love. He was charmed with it; it gave him something to do. It elaborated itself on his hands;—it became twenty times more complex and formidable than was his first rude draft of it. Every new addition to his original plan which cropped up in his mind gave him a fresh interest and a new pleasure. He designed the Club badge himself, and worked over it, altering and improving it, a number of days and nights; then sent to London and had it made. It was the only one that was made. It was made for me; the "rest of the Club" went without.

He invented the thirty-two members and their names. He invented the five favorite speakers and their five separate styles. He invented their speeches, and reported them himself. He would have kept that Club going until now, if I hadn't deserted, he said. He said he worked like a slave over those reports; each of them cost him from a week to a fortnight's work, and the work gave him pleasure and kept him alive and willing to be alive. It was a bitter blow to him when the Club

died.

Finally, there wasn't any Corrigan Castle. He had invented that, too.

It was wonderful—the whole thing; and altogether the most ingenious and laborious and cheerful and painstaking practical joke I have ever heard of. And I liked it; liked to hear him tell about it; yet I have been a hater of practical jokes from as long back as I can remember. Finally he said—

"Do you remember a note from Melbourne fourteen or fifteen years ago, telling about your lecture tour in Australia, and your death and burial in Melbourne?—a note from Henry Bascomb, of Bascomb Hall, Upper Holywell Hants."

"Yes."

"I wrote it."

"M-y-word!"

"Yes, I did it. I don't know why. I just took the notion, and carried it out without stopping to think. It was wrong. It could have done harm. I was always sorry about it afterward. You must forgive me. I was Mr. Bascom's guest on his yacht, on his voyage around the world. He often spoke of you, and of the pleasant times you had had together in his home; and the notion took me, there in Melbourne, and I imitated his hand, and wrote the letter."

So the mystery was cleared up, after so many, many years.

CHAPTER XXVI.

There are people who can do all fine and heroic things but one! keep from telling their happinesses to the unhappy. — Pudd'nhead Wilson's New Calendar.

After visits to Maryborough and some other Australian towns, we presently took passage for New Zealand. If it would not look too much like showing off, I would tell the reader where New Zealand is; for he is as I was; he thinks he knows. And he thinks he knows where Hertzegovina is; and how to pronounce pariah; and how to use the word unique without exposing himself to the derision of the dictionary. But in truth, he knows none of these things. There are but four or five people in the world who possess this knowledge, and these make their living out of it. They travel from place to place, visiting literary assemblages, geographical societies, and seats of learning, and springing sudden bets that these people do not know these things. Since all people think they know them, they are an easy prey to these adventurers. Or rather they were an easy prey until the law interfered, three months ago, and a New York court decided that this kind of gambling is illegal, "because it traverses Article IV, Section 9, of the Constitution of the United States, which forbids betting on a sure thing." This decision was rendered by the full Bench of the New York Supreme Court, after a test sprung upon the court by counsel for the prosecution, which showed that none of the nine Judges was able to answer any of the four questions.

All people think that New Zealand is close to Australia or Asia, or somewhere, and that you cross to it on a bridge. But that is not so. It is not close to anything, but lies by itself, out in the water. It is nearest to Australia, but still not near. The gap between is very wide. It will be a surprise to the reader, as it was to me, to learn that the distance from Australia to New

Zealand is really twelve or thirteen hundred miles, and that there is no bridge. I learned this from Professor X., of Yale University, whom I met in the steamer on the great lakes when I was crossing the continent to sail across the Pacific. I asked him about New Zealand, in order to make conversation. I supposed he would generalize a little without compromising himself, and then turn the subject to something he was acquainted with, and my object would then be attained; the ice would be broken, and we could go smoothly on, and get acquainted, and have a pleasant time. But, to my surprise, he was not only not embarrassed by my question, but seemed to welcome it, and to take a distinct interest in it. He began to talk—fluently, confidently, comfortably; and as he talked, my admiration grew and grew; for as the subject developed under his hands, I saw that he not only knew where New Zealand was, but that he was minutely familiar with every detail of its history, politics, religions, and commerce, its fauna, flora, geology, products, and climatic peculiarities. When he was done, I was lost in wonder and admiration, and said to myself, he knows everything; in the domain of human knowledge he is king.

I wanted to see him do more miracles; and so, just for the pleasure of hearing him answer, I asked him about Hertzegovina, and pariah, and unique. But he began to generalize then, and show distress. I saw that with New Zealand gone, he was a Samson shorn of his locks; he was as other men. This was a curious and interesting mystery, and I was frank with him, and asked him to explain it.

He tried to avoid it at first; but then laughed and said that after all, the matter was not worth concealment, so he would let me into the secret. In substance, this is his story:

"Last autumn I was at work one morning at home, when a card came up—the card of a stranger. Under the name was printed a line which showed that this visitor was Professor of Theological Engineering in Wellington University, New Zealand. I was troubled—troubled, I mean, by the shortness of the notice. College etiquette required that he be at once invited to dinner by some member of the Faculty—invited to dine on that day—not, put off till a subsequent day. I did not quite know what to do. College etiquette requires, in the case of a foreign guest, that the dinner-talk shall begin with complimentary references to his country, its great men, its services to civilization, its seats of learning, and things like that; and of course the host is responsible, and must either begin this talk himself or see that it is done by some one else. I was in great difficulty; and the more I searched my memory, the more my trouble grew. I found that I knew nothing about New Zealand. I thought I knew where it was, and that was all. I had an impression that it was close to Australia, or Asia, or somewhere, and that one went over to it on a bridge. This might turn out to be incorrect; and even if correct, it would not furnish matter enough for the purpose at the dinner, and I should expose my College to shame before my guest; he would see that I, a member of the Faculty of the first University in America, was wholly ignorant of his country, and he would go away and tell this, and laugh at it. The thought of it made my face burn.

"I sent for my wife and told her how I was situated, and asked for her help, and she thought of a thing which I might have thought of myself, if I had not been excited and worried. She said she would go and tell the visitor that I was out but would be in in a few minutes; and she would talk, and keep him busy while I got out the back way and hurried over and make Professor Lawson give the dinner. For Lawson knew everything, and could meet the guest in a creditable way and save the reputation of the University. I ran to Lawson, but was disappointed. He did not know anything about New Zealand. He said that, as far as his recollection went it was close to Australia, or Asia, or somewhere, and you go over to it on a bridge; but that was all he knew. It was too bad. Lawson was a perfect encyclopedia of abstruse learning; but now in this hour of our need, it turned out that he did not know any useful thing.

"We consulted. He saw that the reputation of the University was in very real peril, and he walked the floor in anxiety, talking, and trying to think out some way to meet the difficulty. Presently he decided that we must try the rest of the Faculty—some of them might know about New Zealand. So we went to the telephone and called up the professor of astronomy and asked him, and he said that all he knew was, that it was close to Australia, or Asia, or somewhere, and you went over to it on—

"We shut him off and called up the professor of biology, and he said that all he knew was that it was close to Aus—.

"We shut him off, and sat down, worried and disheartened, to see if we could think up some other scheme. We shortly hit upon one which promised well, and this one we adopted, and set its machinery going at once. It was this. Lawson must give the dinner. The Faculty must be notified by telephone to prepare. We must all get to work diligently, and at the end of eight hours and a half we must come to dinner acquainted with New Zealand; at least well enough informed to appear without discredit before this native. To seem properly intelligent we should have to know about New Zealand's population, and politics, and form of government, and commerce, and taxes, and products, and ancient history, and modern history, and varieties of religion, and nature of the laws, and their codification, and amount of revenue, and whence drawn, and methods of collection, and percentage of loss, and character of climate, and—well, a lot of things like that; we must suck the maps and cyclopedias dry. And while we posted up in this way, the Faculty's wives must flock over, one after the other, in a studiedly casual way, and help my wife keep the New Zealander quiet, and not let him get out and come interfering with our studies. The scheme worked admirably; but it stopped business, stopped it entirely.

"It is in the official log-book of Yale, to be read and wondered at by future generations—the account of the Great Blank Day—the memorable Blank Day—the day wherein the wheels of culture were stopped, a Sunday silence prevailed all about, and the whole University stood still while the Faculty read-up and qualified itself to sit at meat, without shame, in the presence of the Professor of Theological Engineering from New Zealand:

"When we assembled at the dinner we were miserably tired and worn—but we were posted. Yes, it is fair to claim that. In fact, erudition is a pale name for it. New Zealand was the only subject; and it was just beautiful to hear us ripple it out. And with such an air of unembarrassed ease, and unostentatious familiarity with detail, and trained and seasoned mastery of the subject-and oh, the grace and fluency of it!

"Well, finally somebody happened to notice that the guest was looking dazed, and wasn't saying anything. So they stirred him up, of course. Then that man came out with a good, honest, eloquent compliment that made the Faculty blush. He said he was not worthy to sit in the company of men like these; that he had been silent from admiration; that he had been silent from another cause also—silent from shame—silent from ignorance! 'For,' said he, 'I, who have lived eighteen years in New Zealand and have served five in a professorship, and ought to know much about that country, perceive, now, that I know almost nothing about it. I say it with shame, that I have learned fifty times, yes, a hundred times more about New Zealand in these two hours at this table than I ever knew before in all the eighteen years put together. I was silent because I could not help myself. What I knew about taxes, and policies, and laws, and revenue, and products, and history, and all that multitude of things, was but general, and ordinary, and vague-unscientific, in a word—and it would have been insanity to expose it here to the searching glare of your amazingly accurate and all-comprehensive knowledge of those matters, gentlemen. I beg you to let me sit silent—as becomes me. But do not change the subject; I can at least follow you, in this one; whereas if you change to one which shall call out the full strength of your mighty erudition, I shall be as one lost. If you know all this about a remote little inconsequent patch like New Zealand, ah, what wouldn't you know about any other Subject!'"

CHAPTER XXVIL

Man is the Only Animal that Blushes. Or needs to. — Pudd'nhead Wilson's New Calendar.

The universal brotherhood of man is our most precious possession, what there is of it. —Pudd'nhead Wilson's New Calendar.

FROM DIARY:

November 1—noon. A fine day, a brilliant sun. Warm in the sun, cold in the shade—an icy breeze blowing out of the south. A solemn long swell rolling up northward. It comes from the South Pole, with nothing in the way to obstruct its march and tone its energy down. I have read somewhere that an acute observer among the early explorers—Cook? or Tasman?—accepted this majestic swell as trustworthy circumstantial evidence that no important land lay to the southward, and so did not waste time on a useless quest in that direction, but changed his course and went searching elsewhere.

Afternoon. Passing between Tasmania (formerly Van Diemen's Land) and neighboring islands—islands whence the poor exiled Tasmanian savages used to gaze at their lost homeland and cry; and die of broken hearts. How glad I am that all these native races are dead and gone, or nearly so. The work was mercifully swift and horrible in some portions of Australia. As far as Tasmania is concerned, the extermination was complete: not a native is left. It was a strife of years, and decades of years. The Whites and the Blacks hunted each other, ambushed each other, butchered each other. The Blacks were not numerous. But they were wary, alert, cunning, and they knew their country well. They lasted a long time, few as they were, and inflicted much slaughter upon the Whites.

The Government wanted to save the Blacks from ultimate extermination, if possible. One of its schemes was to capture them and coop them up, on a neighboring island, under guard. Bodies of Whites volunteered for the hunt, for the pay was good—£5 for each Black captured and delivered, but the success achieved was not very satisfactory. The Black was naked, and his body was greased. It was hard to get a grip on him that would hold. The Whites moved about in armed bodies, and surprised little families of natives, and did make captures; but it was suspected that in these surprises half a

dozen natives were killed to one caught—and that was not what the Government desired.

Another scheme was to drive the natives into a corner of the island and fence them in by a cordon of men placed in line across the country; but the natives managed to slip through, constantly, and continue their murders and arsons.

The governor warned these unlettered savages by printed proclamation that they must stay in the desolate region officially appointed for them! The proclamation was a dead letter; the savages could not read it. Afterward a picture-proclamation was issued. It was painted up on boards, and these were nailed to trees in the forest. Herewith is a photographic reproduction of this fashion-plate. Substantially it means:

1. The Governor wishes the Whites and the Blacks to love each other;

2. He loves his black subjects;

3. Blacks who kill Whites will be hanged;

4. Whites who kill Blacks will be hanged.

Upon its several schemes the Government spent £30,000 and employed the labors and ingenuities of several thousand Whites for a long time with failure as a result. Then, at last, a quarter of a century after the beginning of the troubles between the two races, the right man was found. No, he found himself. This was George Augustus Robinson, called in history "The Conciliator." He was not educated, and not conspicuous in any way. He was a working bricklayer, in Hobart Town. But he must have been an amazing personality; a man worth traveling far to see. It may be his counterpart appears in history, but I do not know where to look for it.

He set himself this incredible task: to go out into the wilderness, the jungle, and the mountain-retreats where the hunted and implacable savages were hidden, and appear among them unarmed, speak the language of love and of kindness to them, and persuade them to forsake their homes and the wild free life that was so dear to them, and go with him and surrender to the hated Whites and live under their watch and ward, and upon their charity the rest of their lives! On its face it was the dream of a madman.

In the beginning, his moral-suasion project was sarcastically dubbed the sugar plum speculation. If the scheme was striking, and new to the world's experience, the situation was not less so. It was this. The White population numbered 40,000 in 1831; the Black population numbered three hundred. Not 300 warriors, but 300 men, women, and children. The Whites were armed with guns, the Blacks with clubs and spears. The Whites had fought the Blacks for a quarter of a century, and had tried every thinkable way to capture, kill, or subdue them; and could not do it. If white men of any race could have done it, these would have accomplished it. But every scheme had failed, the splendid 300, the matchless 300 were unconquered, and manifestly unconquerable. They would not yield, they would listen to no terms, they would fight to the bitter end. Yet they had no poet to keep up their heart, and sing the marvel of their magnificent patriotism.

At the end of five-and-twenty years of hard fighting, the surviving 300 naked patriots were still defiant, still persistent, still efficacious with their rude weapons, and the Governor and the 40,000 knew not which way to turn, nor what to do.

Then the Bricklayer—that wonderful man—proposed to go out into the wilderness, with no weapon but his tongue, and no protection but his honest eye and his humane heart; and track those embittered savages to their lairs in the gloomy forests and among the mountain snows. Naturally, he was considered a crank. But he was not quite that. In fact, he was a good way short of that. He was building upon his long and intimate knowledge of the native character. The deriders of his project were right—from their standpoint—for they believed the natives to be mere wild beasts; and Robinson was right, from his standpoint—for he believed the natives to be human beings. The truth did really lie between the two. The event proved that Robinson's judgment was soundest; but about once a month for four years the event came near to giving the verdict to the deriders, for about that frequently Robinson barely escaped falling under the native spears.

But history shows that he had a thinking head, and was not a mere wild sentimentalist. For instance, he wanted the war parties called in before he started unarmed upon his mission of peace. He wanted the best chance of success—not a half-chance. And he was very willing to have help; and so, high rewards were advertised, for any who would go unarmed with him. This opportunity was declined. Robinson persuaded some tamed natives of both sexes to go with him—a strong evidence of his persuasive powers, for those natives well knew that their destruction would be almost certain. As it turned out, they had to face death over and over again.

Robinson and his little party had a difficult undertaking upon their hands. They could not ride off, horseback, comfortably into the woods and call Leonidas and his 300 together for a talk and a treaty the following day; for the wild men were not in a body; they were scattered, immense distances apart, over regions so desolate that even the birds could not make a living with the chances offered—scattered in groups of twenty, a dozen, half a dozen, even in groups of three. And the mission must go on foot. Mr. Bonwick furnishes a description of those horrible regions, whereby it will be seen that even fugitive gangs of the hardiest and choicest human devils the world has seen—the convicts set apart to people the "Hell of Macquarrie Harbor Station"—were never able, but once, to survive the horrors of a march through them, but starving and struggling, and fainting and failing, ate each other, and died:

"Onward, still onward, was the order of the indomitable Robinson. No one ignorant of the western country of Tasmania can form a correct idea of the traveling difficulties. While I was resident in Hobart Town, the Governor, Sir John Franklin, and his lady, undertook the western journey to Macquarrie Harbor, and suffered terribly. One man who assisted to carry her ladyship through the swamps, gave me his bitter experience of its miseries. Several were disabled for life. No wonder that but one party, escaping from Macquarrie Harbor convict settlement, arrived at the civilized region in safety. Men perished in the scrub, were lost in snow, or were devoured by their companions. This was the territory traversed by Mr. Robinson and his Black guides. All honor to his intrepidity, and their wonderful fidelity! When they had, in the depth of winter, to cross deep and rapid rivers, pass among mountains six thousand feet high, pierce dangerous thickets, and find food in a country forsaken even by birds, we can realize their hardships.

"After a frightful journey by Cradle Mountain, and over the lofty plateau of Middlesex Plains, the travelers experienced unwonted misery, and the circumstances called forth the best qualities of the noble little band. Mr. Robinson wrote afterwards to Mr. Secretary Burnett some details of this passage of horrors. In that letter, of Oct 2, 1834, he states that his Natives were very reluctant to go over the dreadful mountain passes; that 'for seven successive days we continued traveling over one solid body of snow;' that 'the snows were of incredible depth;' that 'the Natives were frequently up to their middle in snow.' But still the ill-clad, ill-fed, diseased, and way-worn men and women were sustained by the cheerful voice of their unconquerable friend, and responded most nobly to his call."

Mr. Bonwick says that Robinson's friendly capture of the Big River tribe remember, it was a whole tribe—"was by far the grandest feature of the war, and the crowning glory of his efforts." The word "war" was not well chosen, and is misleading. There was war still, but only the Blacks were conducting it—the Whites were holding off until Robinson could give his scheme a fair trial. I think that we are to understand that the friendly capture of that tribe was by far the most important thing, the highest in value, that happened during the whole thirty years of truceless hostilities; that it was a decisive thing, a peaceful Waterloo, the surrender of the native Napoleon and his dreaded forces, the happy ending of the long strife. For "that tribe was the terror of the colony," its chief "the Black Douglas of Bush households."

Robinson knew that these formidable people were lurking somewhere, in some remote corner of the hideous regions just described, and he and his unarmed little party started on a tedious and perilous hunt for them. At last, "there, under the shadows of the Frenchman's Cap, whose grim cone rose five thousand feet in the uninhabited westward interior," they were found. It was a serious moment. Robinson himself believed, for once, that his mission, successful until now, was to end here in failure, and that his own death-hour had struck.

The redoubtable chief stood in menacing attitude, with his eighteen-foot spear poised; his warriors stood massed at his back, armed for battle, their faces eloquent with their long-cherished loathing for white men. "They rattled their spears and shouted their war-cry." Their women were back of them, laden with supplies of weapons, and keeping their 150 eager dogs quiet until the chief should give the signal to fall on.

"I think we shall soon be in the resurrection," whispered a member of Robinson's little party.

"I think we shall," answered Robinson; then plucked up heart and began his persuasions—in the tribe's own dialect, which surprised and pleased the chief. Presently there was an interruption by the chief:

"Who are you?"

"We are gentlemen."

"Where are your guns?"

"We have none."

The warrior was astonished.

"Where your little guns?" (pistols).

"We have none."

A few minutes passed—in by-play—suspense—discussion among the tribesmen—Robinson's tamed squaws ventured to cross the line and begin persuasions upon the wild squaws. Then the chief stepped back "to confer with the old women—the real arbiters of savage war." Mr. Bonwick continues:

"As the fallen gladiator in the arena looks for the signal of life or death from the president of the amphitheatre, so waited our friends in anxious suspense while the conference continued. In a few minutes, before a word was uttered, the women of the tribe threw up their arms three times. This was the inviolable sign of peace! Down fell the spears. Forward, with a heavy sigh of relief, and upward glance of gratitude, came the friends of peace. The impulsive natives rushed forth with tears and cries, as each saw in the other's rank a loved one of the past.

"It was a jubilee of joy. A festival followed. And, while tears flowed at the recital of woe, a corrobory of pleasant laughter closed the eventful day."

In four years, without the spilling of a drop of blood, Robinson brought them all in, willing captives, and delivered them to the white governor, and ended the war which powder and bullets, and thousands of men to use them, had prosecuted without result since 1804.

Marsyas charming the wild beasts with his music—that is fable; but the miracle wrought by Robinson is fact. It is history—and authentic; and surely, there is nothing greater, nothing more reverence-compelling in the history of any country, ancient or modern.

And in memory of the greatest man Australasia ever developed or ever will develop, there is a stately monument to George Augustus Robinson, the Conciliator in—no, it is to another man, I forget his name.

However, Robertson's own generation honored him, and in manifesting it honored themselves. The Government gave him a money-reward and a thousand acres of land; and the people held mass-meetings and praised him and emphasized their praise with a large subscription of money.

A good dramatic situation; but the curtain fell on another:

"When this desperate tribe was thus captured, there was much surprise to find that the £30,000 of a little earlier day had been spent, and the whole population of the colony placed under arms, in contention with an opposing force of sixteen men with wooden spears! Yet such was the fact. The celebrated Big River tribe, that had been raised by European fears to a host, consisted of sixteen men, nine women, and one child. With a knowledge of the mischief done by these few, their wonderful marches and their widespread aggressions, their enemies cannot deny to them the attributes of courage and military tact. A Wallace might harass a large army with a small and determined band; but the contending parties were at least equal in arms and civilization. The Zulus who fought us in Africa, the Maories in New Zealand, the Arabs in the Soudan, were far better provided with weapons, more advanced in the science of war, and considerably more numerous, than the naked Tasmanians. Governor Arthur rightly termed them a noble race."

These were indeed wonderful people, the natives. They ought not to have been wasted. They should have been crossed with the Whites. It would have improved the Whites and done the

Natives no harm.

But the Natives were wasted, poor heroic wild creatures. They were gathered together in little settlements on neighboring islands, and paternally cared for by the Government, and instructed in religion, and deprived of tobacco, because the superintendent of the Sunday-school was not a smoker, and so considered smoking immoral.

The Natives were not used to clothes, and houses, and regular hours, and church, and school, and Sunday-school, and work, and the other misplaced persecutions of civilization, and they pined for their lost home and their wild free life. Too late they repented that they had traded that heaven for this hell. They sat homesick on their alien crags, and day by day gazed out through their tears over the sea with unappeasable longing toward the hazy bulk which was the specter of what had been their paradise; one by one their hearts broke and they died.

In a very few years nothing but a scant remnant remained alive. A handful lingered along into age. In 1864 the last man died, in 1876 the last woman died, and the Spartans of Australasia were extinct.

The Whites always mean well when they take human fish out of the ocean and try to make them dry and warm and happy and comfortable in a chicken coop; but the kindest-hearted white man can always be depended on to prove himself inadequate when he deals with savages. He cannot turn the situation around and imagine how he would like it to have a well-meaning savage transfer him from his house and his church and his clothes and his books and his choice food to a hideous wilderness of sand and rocks and snow, and ice and sleet and storm and blistering sun, with no shelter, no bed, no covering for his and his family's naked bodies, and nothing to eat but snakes and grubs and 'offal. This would be a hell to him; and if he had any wisdom he would know that his own civilization is a hell to the savage—but he hasn't any, and has never had any; and for lack of it he shut up those poor natives in the unimaginable perdition of his civilization, committing his crime with the very best intentions, and saw those poor creatures waste away under his tortures; and gazed at it, vaguely troubled and sorrowful, and wondered what could be the matter with them. One is almost betrayed into respecting those criminals, they were so sincerely kind, and tender, and humane; and well-meaning.

They didn't know why those exiled savages faded away, and they did their honest best to reason it out. And one man, in a like case in New South Wales, did reason it out and arrive at a solution:

"It is from the wrath of God, which is revealed from heaven against cold ungodliness and unrighteousness of men."

That settles it.

CHAPTER XXVIII.

Let us be thankful for the fools. But for them the rest of us could not succeed. —Pudd'nhead Wilson's New Calendar.

The aphorism does really seem true: "Given the Circumstances, the Man will appear." But the man musn't appear ahead of time, or it will spoil everything. In Robinson's case the Moment had been approaching for a quarter of a century—and meantime the future Conciliator was tranquilly laying bricks in Hobart. When all other means had failed, the

Moment had arrived, and the Bricklayer put down his trowel and came forward. Earlier he would have been jeered back to his trowel again. It reminds me of a tale that was told me by a Kentuckian on the train when we were crossing Montana. He said the tale was current in Louisville years ago. He thought it had been in print, but could not remember. At any rate, in substance it was this, as nearly as I can call it back to mind.

A few years before the outbreak of the Civil War it began to appear that Memphis, Tennessee, was going to be a great tobacco entrepot—the wise could see the signs of it. At that time Memphis had a wharf boat, of course. There was a paved sloping wharf, for the accommodation of freight, but the steamers landed on the outside of the wharfboat, and all loading and unloading was done across it, between steamer and shore. A number of wharfboat clerks were needed, and part of the time, every day, they were very busy, and part of the time tediously idle. They were boiling over with youth and spirits, and they had to make the intervals of idleness endurable in some way; and as a rule, they did it by contriving practical jokes and playing them upon each other.

The favorite butt for the jokes was Ed Jackson, because he played none himself, and was easy game for other people's— for he always believed whatever was told him.

One day he told the others his scheme for his holiday. He was not going fishing or hunting this time—no, he had thought out a better plan. Out of his $40 a month he had saved enough for his purpose, in an economical way, and he was going to have a look at New York.

It was a great and surprising idea. It meant travel immense travel—in those days it meant seeing the world; it was the equivalent of a voyage around it in ours. At first the other youths thought his mind was affected, but when they found that he was in earnest, the next thing to be thought of was, what sort of opportunity this venture might afford for a practical joke.

The young men studied over the matter, then held a secret consultation and made a plan. The idea was, that one of the conspirators should offer Ed a letter of introduction to Commodore Vanderbilt, and trick him into delivering it. It would be easy to do this. But what would Ed do when he got back to Memphis? That was a serious matter. He was good-hearted, and had always taken the jokes patiently; but they had been jokes which did not humiliate him, did not bring him to shame; whereas, this would be a cruel one in that way, and to play it was to meddle with fire; for with all his good nature, Ed was a Southerner—and the English of that was, that when he came back he would kill as many of the conspirators as he could before falling himself. However, the chances must be taken—it wouldn't do to waste such a joke as that.

So the letter was prepared with great care and elaboration. It was signed Alfred Fairchild, and was written in an easy and friendly spirit. It stated that the bearer was the bosom friend of the writer's son, and was of good parts and sterling character, and it begged the Commodore to be kind to the young stranger for the writer's sake. It went on to say, "You may have forgotten me, in this long stretch of time, but you will easily call me back out of your boyhood memories when I remind you of how we robbed old Stevenson's orchard that night; and how, while he was chasing down the road after us, we cut across the field and doubled back and sold his own apples to his own cook for a hat-full of doughnuts; and the time that we—" and so forth and so on, bringing in names of imaginary comrades, and detailing all sorts of wild and absurd and, of course, wholly imaginary schoolboy pranks and adventures, but putting them into lively and telling shape.

With all gravity Ed was asked if he would like to have a letter to Commodore Vanderbilt, the great millionaire. It was expected that the question would astonish Ed, and it did.

"What? Do you know that extraordinary man?"

"No; but my father does. They were schoolboys together. And if you like, I'll write and ask father. I know he'll be glad to give it to you for my sake."

Ed could not find words capable of expressing his gratitude and delight. The three days passed, and the letter was put into his bands. He started on his trip, still pouring out his thanks while he shook good-bye all around. And when he was out of sight his comrades let fly their laughter in a storm of happy satisfaction—and then quieted down, and were less happy, less satisfied. For the old doubts as to the wisdom of this deception began to intrude again.

Arrived in New York, Ed found his way to Commodore Vanderbilt's business quarters, and was ushered into a large anteroom, where a score of people were patiently awaiting their turn for a two-minute interview with the millionaire in his private office. A servant asked for Ed's card, and got the letter instead. Ed was sent for a moment later, and found Mr. Vanderbilt alone, with the letter—open—in his hand.

"Pray sit down, Mr. —er—"

"Jackson."

" Ah—sit down, Mr. Jackson. By the opening sentences it seems to be a letter from an old friend. Allow me—I will run my eye through it. He says he says—why, who is it?" He turned the sheet and found the signature. "Alfred Fairchild—hm—Fairchild—I don't recall the name. But that is nothing—a thousand names have gone from me. He says—he says-hm-hmoh, dear, but it's good! Oh, it's rare! I don't quite remember it, but I seem to it'll all come back to me presently. He says — he says—hm—hm-oh, but that was a game! Oh, spl-endid! How it carries me back! It's all dim, of course it's a long time ago—and the names—some of the names are wavery and indistinct—but sho', I know it happened—I can feel it! and lord, how it warms my heart, and brings back my lost youth! Well, well, well, I've got to come back into this work-a-day world now—business presses and people are waiting—I'll keep the rest for bed to-night, and live my youth over again. And you'll thank Fairchild for me when you see him—I used to call him Alf, I think —and you'll give him my gratitude for—what this letter has done for the tired spirit of a hard-worked man; and tell him there isn't anything that I can do for him or any friend of his that I won't do. And as for you, my lad, you are my guest; you can't stop at any hotel in New York. Sit. where you are a little while, till I get through with these people, then we'll go home. I'll take care of you, my boy—make yourself easy as to that."

Ed stayed a week, and had an immense time—and never suspected that the Commodore's shrewd eye was on him, and that he was daily being weighed and measured and analyzed and tried and tested.

Yes, he had an immense time; and never wrote home, but saved it all up to tell when he should get back. Twice, with proper modesty and decency, he proposed to end his visit, but the Commodore said, "No—wait; leave it to me; I'll tell you when to go."

In those days the Commodore was making some of those vast combinations of his—consolidations of warring odds and ends of railroads into harmonious systems, and concentrations of floating and rudderless commerce in effective centers—and among other things his farseeing eye had detected the convergence of that huge tobacco-commerce, already spoken of, toward Memphis, and he had resolved to set his grasp upon it and make it his own.

The week came to an end. Then the Commodore said:

"Now you can start home. But first we will have some more talk about that tobacco matter. I know you now. I know your abilities as well as you know them yourself—perhaps better. You understand that tobacco matter; you understand that I am going to take possession of it, and you also understand the plans which I have matured for doing it. What I want is a man who knows my mind, and is qualified to represent me in Memphis, and be in supreme command of that important business—and I appoint you."

"Me!"

"Yes. Your salary will be high—of course-for you are representing me. Later you will earn increases of it, and will get them. You will need a small army of assistants; choose them yourself—and carefully. Take no man for friendship's sake; but, all things being equal, take the man you know, take your friend, in preference to the stranger." After some further talk under this head, the Commodore said:

"Good-bye, my boy, and thank Alf for me, for sending you to me."

When Ed reached Memphis he rushed down to the wharf in a fever to tell his great news and thank the boys over and over again for thinking to give him the letter to Mr. Vanderbilt. It happened to be one of those idle times. Blazing hot noonday, and no sign of life on the wharf. But as Ed threaded his way among the freight piles, he saw a white linen figure stretched in slumber upon a pile of grain-sacks under an awning, and said to himself, "That's one of them," and hastened his step; next, he said, "It's Charley—it's Fairchild good"; and the next moment laid an affectionate hand on the sleeper's shoulder. The eyes opened lazily, took one glance, the face blanched, the form whirled itself from the sack-pile, and in an instant Ed was alone and Fairchild was flying for the wharf-boat like the wind!

Ed was dazed, stupefied. Was Fairchild crazy? What could be the meaning of this? He started slow and dreamily down toward the wharf-boat; turned the corner of a freight-pile and came suddenly upon two of the boys. They were lightly laughing over some pleasant matter; they heard his step, and glanced up just as he discovered them; the laugh died abruptly; and before Ed could speak they were off, and sailing over barrels and bales like hunted deer. Again Ed was paralyzed. Had the boys all gone mad? What could be the explanation of this extraordinary conduct? And so, dreaming along, he reached the wharf-boat, and stepped aboard nothing but silence there, and vacancy. He crossed the deck, turned the corner to go down the outer guard, heard a fervent—

"O lord!" and saw a white linen form plunge overboard.

The youth came up coughing and strangling, and cried out—

"Go 'way from here! You let me alone. I didn't do it, I swear I didn't!"

"Didn't do what?"

"Give you the—"

"Never mind what you didn't do—come out of that! What makes you all act so? What have I done?"

"You? Why you haven't done anything. But—"

"Well, then, what have you got against me? What do you all treat me so for?"

"I—er—but haven't you got anything against us?"

"Of course not. What put such a thing into your head?"

"Honor bright—you haven't?"

"Honor bright."

"Swear it!"

"I don't know what in the world you mean, but I swear it, anyway."

"And you'll shake hands with me?"

"Goodness knows I'll be glad to! Why, I'm just starving to shake hands with somebody!"

The swimmer muttered, "Hang him, he smelt a rat and never delivered the letter!—but it's all right, I'm not going to fetch up the subject." And he crawled out and came dripping and draining to shake hands. First one and then another of the conspirators showed up cautiously—armed to the teeth—took in the amicable situation, then ventured warily forward and joined the love-feast.

And to Ed's eager inquiry as to what made them act as they had been acting, they answered evasively, and pretended that they had put it up as a joke, to see what he would do. It was the best explanation they could invent at such short notice. And each said to himself, "He never delivered that letter, and the joke is on us, if he only knew it or we were dull enough to come out and tell."

Then, of course, they wanted to know all about the trip; and he said—

"Come right up on the boiler deck and order the drinks it's my treat. I'm going to tell you all about it. And to-night it's my treat again —and we'll have oysters and a time!"

When the drinks were brought and cigars lighted, Ed said:

"Well, when, I delivered the letter to Mr. Vanderbilt—"

"Great Scott!"

"Gracious, how you scared me. What's the matter?"

"Oh—er—nothing. Nothing—it was a tack in the chair-seat,"

said one.

"But you all said it. However, no matter. When I delivered the letter—"

"Did you deliver it?" And they looked at each other as people might who thought that maybe they were dreaming.

Then they settled to listening; and as the story deepened and its marvels grew, the amazement of it made them dumb, and the interest of it took their breath. They hardly uttered a whisper during two hours, but sat like petrifactions and drank in the immortal romance. At last the tale was ended, and Ed said—

"And it's all owing to you, boys, and you'll never find me ungrateful —bless your hearts, the best friends a fellow ever had! You'll all have places; I want every one of you. I know you—I know you 'by the back,' as the gamblers say. You're jokers, and all that, but you're sterling, with the hallmark on. And Charley Fairchild, you shall be my first assistant and right hand, because of your first-class ability, and because you got me the letter, and for your father's sake who wrote it for me, and to please Mr. Vanderbilt, who said it would! And here's to that great man—drink hearty!"

Yes, when the Moment comes, the Man appears—even if he is a thousand miles away, and has to be discovered by a practical joke.

CHAPTER XXIX.

When people do not respect us we are sharply offended; yet deep down in his private heart no man much respects himself. —Pudd'nhead Wilson's New Calendar.

Necessarily, the human interest is the first interest in the log-book of any country. The annals of Tasmania, in whose shadow we were sailing, are lurid with that feature. Tasmania was a convict-dump, in old times; this has been indicated in the account of the Conciliator, where reference is made to vain attempts of desperate convicts to win to permanent freedom, after escaping from Macquarrie Harbor and the "Gates of Hell." In the early days Tasmania had a great population of convicts, of both sexes and all ages, and a bitter hard life they had. In one spot there was a settlement of juvenile convicts—children—who had been sent thither from their home and their friends on the other side of the globe to expiate their "crimes."

In due course our ship entered the estuary called the Derwent, at whose head stands Hobart, the capital of Tasmania. The Derwent's shores furnish scenery of an interesting sort. The historian Laurie, whose book, "The Story of Australasia," is just out, invoices its features with considerable truth and intemperance: "The marvelous picturesqueness of every point of view, combined with the clear balmy atmosphere and the transparency of the ocean depths, must have delighted and deeply impressed" the early explorers. "If the rock-bound coasts, sullen, defiant, and lowering, seemed uninviting, these were occasionally broken into charmingly alluring coves floored with golden sand, clad with evergreen shrubbery, and adorned with every variety of indigenous wattle, she-oak, wild flower, and fern, from the delicately graceful 'maiden-hair' to the palm-like 'old man'; while the majestic gum-tree, clean and smooth as the mast of 'some tall admiral' pierces the clear air to the height of 230 feet or more."

It looked so to me. "Coasting along Tasman's Peninsula, what a shock of pleasant wonder must have struck the early mariner on suddenly sighting Cape Pillar, with its cluster of black-ribbed basaltic columns rising to a height of 900 feet, the hydra head wreathed in a turban of fleecy cloud, the base lashed by jealous waves spouting angry fountains of foam."

That is well enough, but I did not suppose those snags were 900 feet high. Still they were a very fine show. They stood boldly out by themselves, and made a fascinatingly odd spectacle. But there was nothing about their appearance to suggest the heads of a hydra. They looked like a row of lofty slabs with their upper ends tapered to the shape of a carving-knife point; in fact, the early voyager, ignorant of their great height, might have mistaken them for a rusty old rank of piles that had sagged this way and that out of the perpendicular.

The Peninsula is lofty, rocky, and densely clothed with scrub, or brush, or both. It is joined to the main by a low neck. At this junction was formerly a convict station called Port Arthur—a place hard to escape from. Behind it was the wilderness of scrub, in which a fugitive would soon starve; in front was the narrow neck, with a cordon of chained dogs across it, and a line of lanterns, and a fence of living guards, armed. We saw the place as we swept by—that is, we had a glimpse of what we were told was the entrance to Port Arthur. The glimpse was worth something, as a remembrancer, but that was all.

The voyage thence up the Derwent Frith displays a grand succession of fairy visions, in its entire length elsewhere unequaled. In gliding over the deep blue sea studded with lovely islets luxuriant to the water's edge, one is at a loss which scene to choose for contemplation and to admire most. When the Huon and Bruni have been passed, there seems no possible chance of a rival; but suddenly Mount Wellington, massive and noble like his brother Etna, literally heaves in sight, sternly guarded on either hand by Mounts Nelson and Rumney; presently we arrive at Sullivan's Cove—Hobart!

It is an attractive town. It sits on low hills that slope to the harbor —a harbor that looks like a river, and is as smooth as one. Its still surface is pictured with dainty reflections of boats and grassy banks and luxuriant foliage. Back of the town rise highlands that are clothed in woodland loveliness, and over the way is that noble mountain, Wellington, a stately bulk, a most majestic pile. How beautiful is the whole region, for form, and grouping, and opulence, and freshness of foliage, and variety of color, and grace and shapeliness of the hills, the capes, the, promontories; and then, the splendor of the sunlight, the dim rich distances, the charm of the water-glimpses! And it was in this paradise that the yellow-liveried convicts were landed, and the Corps-bandits quartered, and the wanton slaughter of the kangaroo-chasing black innocents consummated on that autumn day in May, in the brutish old time. It was all out of keeping with the place, a sort of bringing of heaven and hell together.

The remembrance of this paradise reminds me that it was at Hobart that we struck the head of the procession of Junior Englands. We were to encounter other sections of it in New Zealand, presently, and others later in Natal. Wherever the exiled Englishman can find in his new home resemblances to his old one, he is touched to the marrow of his being; the love that is in his heart inspires his imagination, and these allied forces transfigure those resemblances into authentic duplicates of the revered originals. It is beautiful, the feeling which works this enchantment, and it compels one's homage; compels it, and also compels one's assent—compels it always—

even when, as happens sometimes, one does not see the resemblances as clearly as does the exile who is pointing them out.

The resemblances do exist, it is quite true; and often they cunningly approximate the originals—but after all, in the matter of certain physical patent rights there is only one England. Now that I have sampled the globe, I am not in doubt. There is a beauty of Switzerland, and it is repeated in the glaciers and snowy ranges of many parts of the earth; there is a beauty of the fiord, and it is repeated in New Zealand and Alaska; there is a beauty of Hawaii, and it is repeated in ten thousand islands of the Southern seas; there is a beauty of the prairie and the plain, and it is repeated here and there in the earth; each of these is worshipful, each is perfect in its way, yet holds no monopoly of its beauty; but that beauty which is England is alone—it has no duplicate.

It is made up of very simple details—just grass, and trees, and shrubs, and roads, and hedges, and gardens, and houses, and vines, and churches, and castles, and here and there a ruin—and over it all a mellow dream-haze of history. But its beauty is incomparable, and all its own.

Hobart has a peculiarity—it is the neatest town that the sun shines on; and I incline to believe that it is also the cleanest. However that may be, its supremacy in neatness is not to be questioned. There cannot be another town in the world that has no shabby exteriors; no rickety gates and fences, no neglected houses crumbling to ruin, no crazy and unsightly sheds, no weed-grown front-yards of the poor, no back-yards littered with tin cans and old boots and empty bottles, no rubbish in the gutters, no clutter on the sidewalks, no outer-borders fraying out into dirty lanes and tin-patched huts. No, in Hobart all the aspects are tidy, and all a comfort to the eye; the modestest cottage looks combed and brushed, and has its vines, its flowers, its neat fence, its neat gate, its comely cat asleep on the window ledge.

We had a glimpse of the museum, by courtesy of the American gentleman who is curator of it. It has samples of half-a-dozen different kinds of marsupials—[A marsupial is a plantigrade vertebrate whose specialty is its pocket. In some countries it is extinct, in the others it is rare. The first American marsupials were Stephen Girard, Mr. Aston and the opossum; the principal marsupials of the Southern Hemisphere are Mr. Rhodes, and the kangaroo. I, myself, am the latest marsupial. Also, I might boast that I have the largest pocket of them all. But there is nothing in that.]—one, the "Tasmanian devil;" that is, I think he was one of them. And there was a fish with lungs. When the water dries up it can live in the mud. Most curious of all was a parrot that kills sheep. On one great sheep-run this bird killed a thousand sheep in a whole year. He doesn't want the whole sheep, but only the kidney-fat. This restricted taste makes him an expensive bird to support. To get the fat he drives his beak in and rips it out; the wound is mortal. This parrot furnishes a notable example of evolution brought about by changed conditions. When the sheep culture was introduced, it presently brought famine to the parrot by exterminating a kind of grub which had always thitherto been the parrot's diet. The miseries of hunger made the bird willing to eat raw flesh, since it could get no other food, and it began to pick remnants of meat from sheep skins hung out on the fences to dry. It soon came to prefer sheep meat to any other food, and by and by it came to prefer the kidney-fat to any other detail of the sheep. The parrot's bill was not well shaped for digging out the fat, but Nature fixed that matter; she altered the bill's shape, and now the parrot can dig out kidney-

fat better than the Chief Justice of the Supreme Court, or anybody else, for that matter—even an Admiral.

And there was another curiosity—quite a stunning one, I thought: Arrow-heads and knives just like those which Primeval Man made out of flint, and thought he had done such a wonderful thing—yes, and has been humored and coddled in that superstition by this age of admiring scientists until there is probably no living with him in the other world by now. Yet here is his finest and nicest work exactly duplicated in our day; and by people who have never heard of him or his works: by aborigines who lived in the islands of these seas, within our time. And they not only duplicated those works of art but did it in the brittlest and most treacherous of substances—glass: made them out of old brandy bottles flung out of the British camps; millions of tons of them. It is time for Primeval Man to make a little less noise, now. He has had his day. He is not what he used to be. We had a drive through a bloomy and odorous fairy-land, to the Refuge for the Indigent—a spacious and comfortable home, with hospitals, etc., for both sexes. There was a crowd in there, of the oldest people I have ever seen. It was like being suddenly set down in a new world—a weird world where Youth has never been, a world sacred to Age, and bowed forms, and wrinkles. Out of the 359 persons present, 223, were ex-convicts, and could have told stirring tales, no doubt, if they had been minded to talk; 42 of the 359 were past 80, and several were close upon 90; the average age at death there is 76 years. As for me, I have no use for that place; it is too healthy. Seventy is old enough—after that, there is too much risk. Youth and gaiety might vanish, any day—and then, what is left? Death in life; death without its privileges, death without its benefits. There were 185 women in that Refuge, and 81 of them were ex-convicts.

The steamer disappointed us. Instead of making a long visit at Hobart, as usual, she made a short one. So we got but a glimpse of Tasmania, and then moved on.

CHAPTER XXX.

Nature makes the locust with an appetite for crops; man would have made him with an appetite for sand. — Pudd'nhead Wilson's New Calendar.

We spent part of an afternoon and a night at sea, and reached Bluff, in New Zealand, early in the morning. Bluff is at the bottom of the middle island, and is away down south, nearly forty-seven degrees below the equator. It lies as far south of the line as Quebec lies north of it, and the climates of the two should be alike; but for some reason or other it has not been so arranged. Quebec is hot in the summer and cold in the winter, but Bluff's climate is less intense; the cold weather is not very cold, the hot weather is not very hot; and the difference between the hottest month and the coldest is but 17 degrees Fahrenheit.

In New Zealand the rabbit plague began at Bluff. The man who introduced the rabbit there was banqueted and lauded; but they would hang him, now, if they could get him. In England the natural enemy of the rabbit is detested and persecuted; in the Bluff region the natural enemy of the rabbit is honored, and his person is sacred. The rabbit's natural enemy in England is the poacher, in Bluff its natural enemy is the stoat, the weasel, the ferret, the cat, and the mongoose. In England any person below the Heir who is caught with a rabbit in his possession must satisfactorily explain how it got there, or he will suffer fine and imprisonment, together with extinction of his peerage; in Bluff, the cat found with a rabbit in its possession does not have to explain—everybody looks the other way; the person caught noticing would suffer fine and imprisonment, with extinction of peerage. This is a sure way to undermine the moral fabric of a cat. Thirty years from now there will not be a moral cat in New Zealand. Some think there is none there now. In England the poacher is watched, tracked, hunted—he dare not show his face; in Bluff the cat, the weasel, the stoat, and the mongoose go up and down, whither they will, unmolested. By a law of the legislature, posted where all may read, it is decreed that any person found in possession of one of these creatures (dead) must satisfactorily explain the circumstances or pay a fine of not less than £5, nor more than £20. The revenue from this source is not large. Persons who want to pay a hundred dollars for a dead cat are getting rarer and rarer every day. This is bad, for the revenue was to go to the endowment of a University. All governments are more or less short-sighted: in England they fine the poacher, whereas he ought to be banished to New Zealand. New Zealand would pay his way, and give him wages.

It was from Bluff that we ought to have cut across to the west coast and visited the New Zealand Switzerland, a land of superb scenery, made up of snowy grandeurs, anal mighty glaciers, and beautiful lakes; and over there, also, are the wonderful rivals of the Norwegian and Alaskan fiords; and for neighbor, a waterfall of 1,900 feet; but we were obliged to postpone the trip to some later and indefinite time.

November 6. A lovely summer morning; brilliant blue sky. A few miles out from Invercargill, passed through vast level green expanses snowed over with sheep. Fine to see. The green, deep and very vivid sometimes; at other times less so, but delicate and lovely. A passenger reminds me that I am in "the England of the Far South."

Dunedin, same date. The town justifies Michael Davitt's praises. The people are Scotch. They stopped here on their way from home to heaven-thinking they had arrived. The population is stated at 40,000, by Malcolm Ross, journalist; stated by an M. P. at 60,000. A journalist cannot lie.

To the residence of Dr. Hockin. He has a fine collection of books relating to New Zealand; and his house is a museum of Maori art and antiquities. He has pictures and prints in color of many native chiefs of the past—some of them of note in history. There is nothing of the savage in the faces; nothing could be finer than these men's features, nothing more intellectual than these faces, nothing more masculine, nothing nobler than their aspect. The aboriginals of Australia and Tasmania looked the savage, but these chiefs looked like Roman patricians. The tattooing in these portraits ought to suggest the savage, of course, but it does not. The designs are so flowing and graceful and beautiful that they are a most satisfactory decoration. It takes but fifteen minutes to get reconciled to the tattooing, and but fifteen more to perceive that it is just the thing. After that, the undecorated European face is unpleasant and ignoble.

Dr. Hockiu gave us a ghastly curiosity—a lignified caterpillar with a plant growing out of the back of its neck—a plant with a slender stem 4 inches high. It happened not by accident, but by design—Nature's design. This caterpillar was in the act of loyally carrying out a law inflicted upon him by Nature—a law purposely inflicted upon him to get him into trouble—a law which was a trap; in pursuance of this law he made the proper preparations for turning himself into a night-moth; that is to say, he dug a little trench, a little grave, and then stretched himself out in it on his stomach and partially buried himself—

then Nature was ready for him. She blew the spores of a peculiar fungus through the air with a purpose. Some of them fell into a crease in the back of the caterpillar's neck, and began to sprout and grow—for there was soil there—he had not washed his neck. The roots forced themselves down into the worm's person, and rearward along through its body, sucking up the creature's juices for sap; the worm slowly died, and turned to wood. And here he was now, a wooden caterpillar, with every detail of his former physique delicately and exactly preserved and perpetuated, and with that stem standing up out of him for his monument—monument commemorative of his own loyalty and of Nature's unfair return for it.

Nature is always acting like that. Mrs. X. said (of course) that the caterpillar was not conscious and didn't suffer. She should have known better. No caterpillar can deceive Nature. If this one couldn't suffer, Nature would have known it and would have hunted up another caterpillar. Not that she would have let this one go, merely because it was defective. No. She would have waited and let him turn into a night-moth; and then fried him in the candle.

Nature cakes a fish's eyes over with parasites, so that it shan't be able to avoid its enemies or find its food. She sends parasites into a star-fish's system, which clog up its prongs and swell them and make them so uncomfortable that the poor creature delivers itself from the prong to ease its misery; and presently it has to part with another prong for the sake of comfort, and finally with a third. If it re-grows the prongs, the parasite returns and the same thing is repeated. And finally, when the ability to reproduce prongs is lost through age, that poor old star-fish can't get around any more, and so it dies of starvation.

In Australia is prevalent a horrible disease due to an "unperfected tapeworm." Unperfected—that is what they call it, I do not know why, for it transacts business just as well as if it were finished and frescoed and gilded, and all that.

November 9. To the museum and public picture gallery with the president of the Society of Artists. Some fine pictures there, lent by the S. of A. several of them they bought, the others came to them by gift. Next, to the gallery of the S. of A.—annual exhibition—just opened. Fine. Think of a town like this having two such collections as this, and a Society of Artists. It is so all over Australasia. If it were a monarchy one might understand it. I mean an absolute monarchy, where it isn't necessary to vote money, but take it. Then art flourishes. But these colonies are republics—republics with a wide suffrage; voters of both sexes, this one of New Zealand. In republics, neither the government nor the rich private citizen is much given to propagating art. All over Australasia pictures by famous European artists are bought for the public galleries by the State and by societies of citizens. Living citizens—not dead ones. They rob themselves to give, not their heirs. This S. of A. here owns its buildings built it by subscription.

CHAPTER XXXI.

The spirit of wrath—not the words—is the sin; and the spirit of wrath is cursing. We begin to swear before we can talk. — Pudd'nhead Wilson's New Calendar.

November 11. On the road. This train-express goes twenty and one-half miles an hour, schedule time; but it is fast enough, the outlook upon sea and land is so interesting, and the cars so comfortable. They are not English, and not American; they are the Swiss combination of the two. A narrow and railed porch along the side, where a person can walk up and down. A lavatory in each car. This is progress; this is nineteenth-century spirit. In New Zealand, these fast expresses run twice a week. It is well to know this if you want to be a bird and fly through the country at a 20-mile gait; otherwise you may start on one of the five wrong days, and then you will get a train that can't overtake its own shadow.

By contrast, these pleasant cars call to mind the branch-road cars at Maryborough, Australia, and the passengers' talk about the branch-road and the hotel.

Somewhere on the road to Maryborough I changed for a while to a smoking-carriage. There were two gentlemen there; both riding backward, one at each end of the compartment. They were acquaintances of each other. I sat down facing the one that sat at the starboard window. He had a good face, and a friendly look, and I judged from his dress that he was a dissenting minister. He was along toward fifty. Of his own motion he struck a match, and shaded it with his hand for me to light my cigar. I take the rest from my diary:

In order to start conversation I asked him something about Maryborough. He said, in a most pleasant—even musical voice, but with quiet and cultured decision:

"It's a charming town, with a hell of a hotel."

I was astonished. It seemed so odd to hear a minister swear out loud. He went placidly on:

"It's the worst hotel in Australia. Well, one may go further, and say in Australasia."

"Bad beds?"

"No—none at all. Just sand-bags."

"The pillows, too?"

"Yes, the pillows, too. Just sand. And not a good quality of sand. It packs too hard, and has never been screened. There is too much gravel in it. It is like sleeping on nuts."

"Isn't there any good sand?"

"Plenty of it. There is as good bed-sand in this region as the world can furnish. Aerated sand—and loose; but they won't buy it. They want something that will pack solid, and petrify."

"How are the rooms?"

"Eight feet square; and a sheet of iced oil-cloth to step on in the morning when you get out of the sand-quarry."

"As to lights?"

"Coal-oil lamp."

"A good one?"

"No. It's the kind that sheds a gloom."

"I like a lamp that burns all night."

"This one won't. You must blow it out early."

"That is bad. One might want it again in the night. Can't find it in the dark."

"There's no trouble; you can find it by the stench."

"Wardrobe?"

"Two nails on the door to hang seven suits of clothes on if you've got them."

"Bells?"

"There aren't any."

"What do you do when you want service?"

"Shout. But it won't fetch anybody."

"Suppose you want the chambermaid to empty the slopjar?"

"There isn't any slop-jar. The hotels don't keep them. That is, outside of Sydney and Melbourne."

"Yes, I knew that. I was only talking. It's the oddest thing in Australia. Another thing: I've got to get up in the dark, in the morning, to take the 5 o'clock train. Now if the boots—"

"There isn't any."

"Well, the porter."

"There isn't any."

"But who will call me?"

"Nobody. You'll call yourself. And you'll light yourself, too. There'll not be a light burning in the halls or anywhere. And if you don't carry a light, you'll break your neck."

"But who will help me down with my baggage?"

"Nobody. However, I will tell you what to do. In Maryborough there's an American who has lived there half a lifetime; a fine man, and prosperous and popular. He will be on the lookout for you; you won't have any trouble. Sleep in peace; he will rout you out, and you will make your train. Where is your manager?"

"I left him at Ballarat, studying the language. And besides, he had to go to Melbourne and get us ready for New Zealand. I've not tried to pilot myself before, and it doesn't look easy."

"Easy! You've selected the very most difficult piece of railroad in Australia for your experiment. There are twelve miles of this road which no man without good executive ability can ever hope—tell me, have you good executive ability? first-rate executive ability?"

"I—well, I think so, but—"

"That settles it. The tone of—oh, you wouldn't ever make it in the world. However, that American will point you right, and you'll go. You've got tickets?"

"Yes—round trip; all the way to Sydney."

"Ah, there it is, you see! You are going in the 5 o'clock by Castlemaine—twelve miles—instead of the 7.15 by Ballarat—in order to save two hours of fooling along the road. Now then, don't interrupt—let me have the floor. You're going to save the government a deal of hauling, but that's nothing; your ticket is by Ballarat, and it isn't good over that twelve miles, and so—"

"But why should the government care which way I go?"

"Goodness knows! Ask of the winds that far away with fragments strewed the sea, as the boy that stood on the burning deck used to say. The government chooses to do its railway business in its own way, and it doesn't know as much about it as the French. In the beginning they tried idiots; then they imported the French—which was going backwards, you see; now it runs the roads itself—which is going backwards again, you see. Why, do you know, in order to curry favor with the voters, the government puts down a road wherever anybody wants it—anybody that owns two sheep and a dog; and by consequence we've got, in the colony of Victoria, 800 railway stations, and the business done at eighty of them doesn't foot up twenty shillings a week."

"Five dollars? Oh, come!"

"It's true. It's the absolute truth."

"Why, there are three or four men on wages at every station."

"I know it. And the station-business doesn't pay for the sheep-dip to sanctify their coffee with. It's just as I say. And accommodating? Why, if you shake a rag the train will stop in the midst of the wilderness to pick you up. All that kind of politics costs, you see. And then, besides, any town that has a good many votes and wants a fine station, gets it. Don't you overlook that Maryborough station, if you take an interest in governmental curiosities. Why, you can put the whole population of Maryborough into it, and give them a sofa apiece, and have room for more. You haven't fifteen stations in America that are as big, and you probably haven't five that are half as fine. Why, it's perfectly elegant. And the clock! Everybody will show you the clock. There isn't a station in Europe that's got such a clock. It doesn't strike—and that's one mercy. It hasn't any bell; and as you'll have cause to remember, if you keep your reason, all Australia is simply bedamned with bells. On every quarter-hour, night and day, they jingle a tiresome chime of half a dozen notes—all the clocks in town at once, all the clocks in Australasia at once, and all the very same notes; first, downward scale: mi, re, do, sol—then upward scale: sol, si, re, do—down again: mi, re, do, sol—up again: sol, si, re, do—then the clock—say at midnight clang—clang—clang—clang—clang-clang—clang—clang—clang —clang—and, by that time you're—hello, what's all this excitement about? a runaway—scared by the train; why, you think this train could scare anything. Well, when they build eighty stations at a loss and a lot of palace-stations and clocks like Maryborough's at another loss, the government has got to economize somewhere hasn't it? Very well look at the rolling stock. That's where they save the money. Why, that train from Maryborough will consist of eighteen freight-cars and two passenger-kennels; cheap, poor, shabby, slovenly; no drinking water, no sanitary arrangements, every imaginable inconvenience; and slow?—oh, the gait of cold molasses; no air-brake, no springs, and they'll jolt your head off every time they start or stop. That's where they make their little economies, you see. They spend tons of money to house you palatially while you wait fifteen minutes for a train, then degrade you to six hours' convict-transportation to get the foolish outlay back. What a rational man really needs is discomfort while he's waiting, then his journey in a nice train

would be a grateful change. But no, that would be common sense—and out of place in a government. And then, besides, they save in that other little detail, you know—repudiate their own tickets, and collect a poor little illegitimate extra shilling out of you for that twelve miles, and—"

"Well, in any case—"

"Wait—there's more. Leave that American out of the account and see what would happen. There's nobody on hand to examine your ticket when you arrive. But the conductor will come and examine it when the train is ready to start. It is too late to buy your extra ticket now; the train can't wait, and won't. You must climb out."

"But can't I pay the conductor?"

"No, he is not authorized to receive the money, and he won't. You must climb out. There's no other way. I tell you, the railway management is about the only thoroughly European thing here—continentally European I mean, not English. It's the continental business in perfection; down fine. Oh, yes, even to the peanut-commerce of weighing baggage."

The train slowed up at his place. As he stepped out he said:

"Yes, you'll like Maryborough. Plenty of intelligence there. It's a charming place—with a hell of a hotel."

Then he was gone. I turned to the other gentleman:

"Is your friend in the ministry?"

"No—studying for it."

CHAPTER XXXII.

The man with a new idea is a Crank until the idea succeeds. —Pudd'nhead Wilson's New Calendar.

It was Junior England all the way to Christchurch—in fact, just a garden. And Christchurch is an English town, with an English-park annex, and a winding English brook just like the Avon—and named the Avon; but from a man, not from Shakespeare's river. Its grassy banks are bordered by the stateliest and most impressive weeping willows to be found in the world, I suppose. They continue the line of a great ancestor; they were grown from sprouts of the willow that sheltered Napoleon's grave in St. Helena. It is a settled old community, with all the serenities, the graces, the conveniences, and the comforts of the ideal home-life. If it had an established Church and social inequality it would be England over again with hardly a lack.

In the museum we saw many curious and interesting things; among others a fine native house of the olden time, with all the details true to the facts, and the showy colors right and in their proper places. All the details: the fine mats and rugs and things; the elaborate and wonderful wood carvings— wonderful, surely, considering who did them wonderful in design and particularly in execution, for they were done with admirable sharpness and exactness, and yet with no better tools than flint and jade and shell could furnish; and the totem-posts were there, ancestor above ancestor, with tongues protruded and hands clasped comfortably over bellies containing other people's ancestors—grotesque and ugly devils, every one, but lovingly carved, and ably; and the stuffed natives were present, in their proper places, and looking as natural as life; and the housekeeping utensils were there, too, and close at hand the carved and finely ornamented war canoe.

And we saw little jade gods, to hang around the neck—not everybody's, but sacred to the necks of natives of rank. Also jade weapons, and many kinds of jade trinkets—all made out of that excessively hard stone without the help of any tool of iron. And some of these things had small round holes bored through them—nobody knows how it was done; a mystery, a lost art. I think it was said that if you want such a hole bored in a piece of jade now, you must send it to London or Amsterdam where the lapidaries are.

Also we saw a complete skeleton of the giant Moa. It stood ten feet high, and must have been a sight to look at when it was a living bird. It was a kicker, like the ostrich; in fight it did not use its beak, but its foot. It must have been a convincing kind of kick. If a person had his back to the bird and did not see who it was that did it, he would think he had been kicked by a wind-mill.

There must have been a sufficiency of moas in the old forgotten days when his breed walked the earth. His bones are found in vast masses, all crammed together in huge graves. They are not in caves, but in the ground. Nobody knows how they happened to get concentrated there. Mind, they are bones, not fossils. This means that the moa has not been extinct very long. Still, this is the only New Zealand creature which has no mention in that otherwise comprehensive literature, the native legends. This is a significant detail, and is good circumstantial evidence that the moa has been extinct 500 years, since the Maori has himself—by tradition—been in New Zealand since the end of the fifteenth century. He came from an unknown land—the first Maori did—then sailed back in his canoe and brought his tribe, and they removed the aboriginal peoples into the sea and into the ground and took the land. That is the tradition. That that first Maori could come, is understandable, for anybody can come to a place when he isn't trying to; but how that discoverer found his way back home again without a compass is his secret, and he died with it in him. His language indicates that he came from Polynesia. He told where he came from, but he couldn't spell well, so one can't find the place on the map, because people who could spell better than he could, spelt the resemblance all out of it when they made the map. However, it is better to have a map that is spelt right than one that has information in it.

In New Zealand women have the right to vote for members of the legislature, but they cannot be members themselves. The law extending the suffrage to them event into effect in 1893. The population of Christchurch (census of 1891) was 31,454. The first election under the law was held in November of that year. Number of men who voted, 6,313; number of women who voted, 5,989. These figures ought to convince us that women are not as indifferent about politics as some people would have us believe. In New Zealand as a whole, the estimated adult female population was 139,915; of these 109,461 qualified and registered their names on the rolls 78.23 per cent. of the whole. Of these, 90,290 went to the polls and voted—85.18 per cent. Do men ever turn out better than that— in America or elsewhere? Here is a remark to the other sex's credit, too—I take it from the official report:

"A feature of the election was the orderliness and sobriety of the people. Women were in no way molested."

At home, a standing argument against woman suffrage has

always been that women could not go to the polls without being insulted. The arguments against woman suffrage have always taken the easy form of prophecy. The prophets have been prophesying ever since the woman's rights movement began in 1848—and in forty-seven years they have never scored a hit.

Men ought to begin to feel a sort of respect for their mothers and wives and sisters by this time. The women deserve a change of attitude like that, for they have wrought well. In forty-seven years they have swept an imposingly large number of unfair laws from the statute books of America. In that brief time these serfs have set themselves free essentially. Men could not have done so much for themselves in that time without bloodshed—at least they never have; and that is argument that they didn't know how. The women have accomplished a peaceful revolution, and a very beneficent one; and yet that has not convinced the average man that they are intelligent, and have courage and energy and perseverance and fortitude. It takes much to convince the average man of anything; and perhaps nothing can ever make him realize that he is the average woman's inferior—yet in several important details the evidences seems to show that that is what he is. Man has ruled the human race from the beginning—but he should remember that up to the middle of the present century it was a dull world, and ignorant and stupid; but it is not such a dull world now, and is growing less and less dull all the time. This is woman's opportunity—she has had none before. I wonder where man will be in another forty-seven years?

In the New Zealand law occurs this: "The word person wherever it occurs throughout the Act includes woman."

That is promotion, you see. By that enlargement of the word, the matron with the garnered wisdom and experience of fifty years becomes at one jump the political equal of her callow kid of twenty-one. The white population of the colony is 626,000, the Maori population is 42,000. The whites elect seventy members of the House of Representatives, the Maoris four. The Maori women vote for their four members.

November 16. After four pleasant days in Christchurch, we are to leave at midnight to-night. Mr. Kinsey gave me an ornithorhynchus, and I am taming it.

Sunday, 17th. Sailed last night in the Flora, from Lyttelton.

So we did. I remember it yet. The people who sailed in the Flora that night may forget some other things if they live a good while, but they will not live long, enough to forget that. The Flora is about the equivalent of a cattle-scow; but when the Union Company find it inconvenient to keep a contract and lucrative to break it, they smuggle her into passenger service, and "keep the change."

They give no notice of their projected depredation; you innocently buy tickets for the advertised passenger boat, and when you get down to Lyttelton at midnight, you find that they have substituted the scow. They have plenty of good boats, but no competition—and that is the trouble. It is too late now to make other arrangements if you have engagements ahead.

It is a powerful company, it has a monopoly, and everybody is afraid of it—including the government's representative, who stands at the end of the stage-plank to tally the passengers and see that no boat receives a greater number than the law allows her to carry. This conveniently-blind representative saw the scow receive a number which was far in excess of its privilege, and winked a politic wink and said nothing. The passengers bore with meekness the cheat which had been put upon them, and made no complaint.

It was like being at home in America, where abused passengers act in just the same way. A few days before, the Union Company had discharged a captain for getting a boat into danger, and had advertised this act as evidence of its vigilance in looking after the safety of the passengers —for thugging a captain costs the company nothing, but when opportunity offered to send this dangerously overcrowded tub to sea and save a little trouble and a tidy penny by it, it forgot to worry about the passenger's safety.

The first officer told me that the Flora was privileged to carry 125 passengers. She must have had all of 200 on board. All the cabins were full, all the cattle-stalls in the main stable were full, the spaces at the heads of companionways were full, every inch of floor and table in the swill-room was packed with sleeping men and remained so until the place was required for breakfast, all the chairs and benches on the hurricane deck were occupied, and still there were people who had to walk about all night!

If the Flora had gone down that night, half of the people on board would have been wholly without means of escape.

The owners of that boat were not technically guilty of conspiracy to commit murder, but they were morally guilty of it.

I had a cattle-stall in the main stable—a cavern fitted up with a long double file of two-storied bunks, the files separated by a calico partition—twenty men and boys on one side of it, twenty women and girls on the other. The place was as dark as the soul of the Union Company, and smelt like a kennel. When the vessel got out into the heavy seas and began to pitch and wallow, the cavern prisoners became immediately seasick, and then the peculiar results that ensued laid all my previous experiences of the kind well away in the shade. And the wails, the groans, the cries, the shrieks, the strange ejaculations—it was wonderful.

The women and children and some of the men and boys spent the night in that place, for they were too ill to leave it; but the rest of us got up, by and by, and finished the night on the hurricane-deck.

That boat was the foulest I was ever in; and the smell of the breakfast saloon when we threaded our way among the layers of steaming passengers stretched upon its floor and its tables was incomparable for efficiency.

A good many of us got ashore at the first way-port to seek another ship. After a wait of three hours we got good rooms in the Mahinapua, a wee little bridal-parlor of a boat—only 205 tons burthen; clean and comfortable; good service; good beds; good table, and no crowding. The seas danced her about like a duck, but she was safe and capable.

Next morning early she went through the French Pass—a narrow gateway of rock, between bold headlands—so narrow, in fact, that it seemed no wider than a street. The current tore through there like a mill-race, and the boat darted through like a telegram. The passage was made in half a minute; then we were in a wide place where noble vast eddies swept grandly round and round in shoal water, and I wondered what they would do with the little boat. They did as they pleased with

her. They picked her up and flung her around like nothing and landed her gently on the solid, smooth bottom of sand—so gently, indeed, that we barely felt her touch it, barely felt her quiver when she came to a standstill. The water was as clear as glass, the sand on the bottom was vividly distinct, and the fishes seemed to be swimming about in nothing. Fishing lines were brought out, but before we could bait the hooks the boat was off and away again.

CHAPTER XXXIII.

Let us be grateful to Adam our benefactor. He cut us out of the "blessing of idleness," and won for us the "curse of labor."
—Pudd'nhead Wilson's New Calendar.

We soon reached the town of Nelson, and spent the most of the day there, visiting acquaintances and driving with them about the garden—the whole region is a garden, excepting the scene of the "Maungatapu Murders," of thirty years ago. That is a wild place—wild and lonely; an ideal place for a murder. It is at the base of a vast, rugged, densely timbered mountain. In the deep twilight of that forest solitude four desperate rascals—Burgess, Sullivan, Levy, and Kelley—ambushed themselves beside the mountain-trail to murder and rob four travelers—Kempthorne, Mathieu, Dudley, and De Pontius, the latter a New Yorker. A harmless old laboring man came wandering along, and as his presence was an embarrassment, they choked him, hid him, and then resumed their watch for the four. They had to wait a while, but eventually everything turned out as they desired.

That dark episode is the one large event in the history of Nelson. The fame of it traveled far. Burgess made a confession. It is a remarkable paper. For brevity, succinctness, and concentration, it is perhaps without its peer in the literature of murder. There are no waste words in it; there is no obtrusion of matter not pertinent to the occasion, nor any departure from the dispassionate tone proper to a formal business statement—for that is what it is: a business statement of a murder, by the chief engineer of it, or superintendent, or foreman, or whatever one may prefer to call him.

"We were getting impatient, when we saw four men and a pack-horse coming. I left my cover and had a look at the men, for Levy had told me that Mathieu was a small man and wore a large beard, and that it was a chestnut horse. I said, 'Here they come.' They were then a good distance away; I took the caps off my gun, and put fresh ones on. I said, 'You keep where you are, I'll put them up, and you give me your gun while you tie them.' It was arranged as I have described. The men came; they arrived within about fifteen yards when I stepped up and said, 'Stand! bail up!' That means all of them to get together. I made them fall back on the upper side of the road with their faces up the range, and Sullivan brought me his gun, and then tied their hands behind them. The horse was very quiet all the time, he did not move. When they were all tied, Sullivan took the horse up the hill, and put him in the bush; he cut the rope and let the swags—[A "swag" is a kit, a pack, small baggage.]—fall on the ground, and then came to me. We then marched the men down the incline to the creek; the water at this time barely running. Up this creek we took the men; we went, I daresay, five or six hundred yards up it, which took us nearly half-an-hour to accomplish. Then we turned to the right up the range; we went, I daresay, one hundred and fifty yards from the creek, and there we sat down with the men. I said to Sullivan, 'Put down your gun and search these men,' which he did. I asked them their several names; they told me. I asked them if they were expected at Nelson. They said, 'No.' If such their lives would have been spared. In money we took £60 odd. I said, 'Is this all you have? You had better tell me.' Sullivan said, 'Here is a bag of gold.' I said, 'What's on that pack-horse? Is there any gold ?' when Kempthorne said, 'Yes, my gold is in the portmanteau, and I trust you will not take it all.' 'Well,' I said, 'we must take you away one at a time, because the range is steep just here, and then we will let you go.' They said, 'All right,' most cheerfully. We tied their feet, and took Dudley with us; we went about sixty yards with him. This was through a scrub. It was arranged the night previously that it would be best to choke them, in case the report of the arms might be heard from the road, and if they were missed they never would be found. So we tied a handkerchief over his eyes, when Sullivan took the sash off his waist, put it round his neck, and so strangled him. Sullivan, after I had killed the old laboring man, found fault with the way he was choked. He said, 'The next we do I'll show you my way.' I said, 'I have never done such a thing before. I have shot a man, but never choked one.' We returned to the others, when Kempthorne said, 'What noise was that?' I said it was caused by breaking through the scrub. This was taking too much time, so it was agreed to shoot them. With that I said, 'We'll take you no further, but separate you, and then loose one of you, and he can relieve the others.' So with that, Sullivan took De Pontius to the left of where Kempthorne was sitting. I took Mathieu to the right. I tied a strap round his legs, and shot him with a revolver. He yelled, I ran from him with my gun in my hand, I sighted Kempthorne, who had risen to his feet. I presented the gun, and shot him behind the right ear; his life's blood welled from him, and he died instantaneously. Sullivan had shot. De Pontius in the meantime, and then came to me. I said, 'Look to Mathieu,' indicating the spot where he lay. He shortly returned and said, 'I had to "chiv" that fellow, he was not dead,' a cant word, meaning that he had to stab him. Returning to the road we passed where De Pontius lay and was dead. Sullivan said, 'This is the digger, the others were all storekeepers; this is the digger, let's cover him up, for should the others be found, they'll think he done it and sloped,' meaning he had gone. So with that we threw all the stones on him, and then left him. This bloody work took nearly an hour and a half from the time we stopped the men."

Anyone who reads that confession will think that the man who wrote it was destitute of emotions, destitute of feeling. That is partly true. As regarded others he was plainly without feeling—utterly cold and pitiless; but as regarded himself the case was different. While he cared nothing for the future of the murdered men, he cared a great deal for his own. It makes one's flesh creep to read the introduction to his confession. The judge on the bench characterized it as "scandalously blasphemous," and it certainly reads so, but Burgess meant no blasphemy. He was merely a brute, and whatever he said or wrote was sure to expose the fact. His redemption was a very real thing to him, and he was as jubilantly happy on the gallows as ever was Christian martyr at the stake. We dwellers in this world are strangely made, and mysteriously circumstanced. We have to suppose that the murdered men are lost, and that Burgess is saved; but we cannot suppress our natural regrets.

"Written in my dungeon drear this 7th of August, in the year of Grace, 1866. To God be ascribed all power and glory in subduing the rebellious spirit of a most guilty wretch, who has been brought, through the instrumentality of a faithful follower of Christ, to see his wretched and guilty state, inasmuch as hitherto he has led an awful and wretched life, and through the assurance of this faithful soldier of Christ, he has been led and also believes that Christ will yet receive and

cleanse him from all his deep-dyed and bloody sins. I lie under the imputation which says, 'Come now and let us reason together, saith the Lord: though your sins be as scarlet, they shall be as white as snow; though they be red like crimson, they shall be as wool.' On this promise I rely."

We sailed in the afternoon late, spent a few hours at New Plymouth, then sailed again and reached Auckland the next day, November 20th, and remained in that fine city several days. Its situation is commanding, and the sea-view is superb. There are charming drives all about, and by courtesy of friends we had opportunity to enjoy them. From the grassy crater-summit of Mount Eden one's eye ranges over a grand sweep and variety of scenery—forests clothed in luxuriant foliage, rolling green fields, conflagrations of flowers, receding and dimming stretches of green plain, broken by lofty and symmetrical old craters—then the blue bays twinkling and sparkling away into the dreamy distances where the mountains loom spiritual in their veils of haze.

It is from Auckland that one goes to Rotorua, the region of the renowned hot lakes and geysers—one of the chief wonders of New Zealand; but I was not well enough to make the trip. The government has a sanitorium there, and everything is comfortable for the tourist and the invalid. The government's official physician is almost over-cautious in his estimates of the efficacy of the baths, when he is talking about rheumatism, gout, paralysis, and such things; but when he is talking about the effectiveness of the waters in eradicating the whisky-habit, he seems to have no reserves. The baths will cure the drinking-habit no matter how chronic it is—and cure it so effectually that even the desire to drink intoxicants will come no more. There should be a rush from Europe and America to that place; and when the victims of alcoholism find out what they can get by going there, the rush will begin.

The Thermal-springs District of New Zealand comprises an area of upwards of 600,000 acres, or close on 1,000 square miles. Rotorua is the favorite place. It is the center of a rich field of lake and mountain scenery; from Rotorua as a base the pleasure-seeker makes excursions. The crowd of sick people is great, and growing. Rotorua is the Carlsbad of Australasia.

It is from Auckland that the Kauri gum is shipped. For a long time now about 8,000 tons of it have been brought into the town per year. It is worth about $300 per ton, unassorted; assorted, the finest grades are worth about $1,000. It goes to America, chiefly. It is in lumps, and is hard and smooth, and looks like amber—the light-colored like new amber, and the dark brown like rich old amber. And it has the pleasant feel of amber, too. Some of the light-colored samples were a tolerably fair counterfeit of uncut South African diamonds, they were so perfectly smooth and polished and transparent. It is manufactured into varnish; a varnish which answers for copal varnish and is cheaper.

The gum is dug up out of the ground; it has been there for ages. It is the sap of the Kauri tree. Dr. Campbell of Auckland told me he sent a cargo of it to England fifty years ago, but nothing came of the venture. Nobody knew what to do with it; so it was sold at 15 a ton, to light fires with.

November 26—3 P.M., sailed. Vast and beautiful harbor. Land all about for hours. Tangariwa, the mountain that "has the same shape from every point of view." That is the common belief in Auckland. And so it has —from every point of view except thirteen. Perfect summer weather. Large school of whales in the distance. Nothing could be daintier than the puffs of vapor they spout up, when seen against the pink glory of the sinking sun, or against the dark mass of an island reposing in the deep blue shadow of a storm cloud . . . . Great Barrier rock standing up out of the sea away to the left. Sometime ago a ship hit it full speed in a fog—20 miles out of her course—140 lives lost; the captain committed suicide without waiting a moment. He knew that, whether he was to blame or not, the company owning the vessel would discharge him and make a devotion—to—passengers' safety advertisement out of it, and his chance to make a livelihood would be permanently gone.

CHAPTER XXXIV.

Let us not be too particular. It is better to have old second-hand diamonds than none at all. —Pudd'nhead Wilson's New Calendar.

November 27. To-day we reached Gisborne, and anchored in a big bay; there was a heavy sea on, so we remained on board.

We were a mile from shore; a little steam-tug put out from the land; she was an object of thrilling interest; she would climb to the summit of a billow, reel drunkenly there a moment, dim and gray in the driving storm of spindrift, then make a plunge like a diver and remain out of sight until one had given her up, then up she would dart again, on a steep slant toward the sky, shedding Niagaras of water from her forecastle—and this she kept up, all the way out to us. She brought twenty-five passengers in her stomach—men and women mainly a traveling dramatic company. In sight on deck were the crew, in sou'westers, yellow waterproof canvas suits, and boots to the thigh. The deck was never quiet for a moment, and seldom nearer level than a ladder, and noble were the seas which leapt aboard and went flooding aft. We rove a long line to the yard-arm, hung a most primitive basketchair to it and swung it out into the spacious air of heaven, and there it swayed, pendulum-fashion, waiting for its chance—then down it shot, skillfully aimed, and was grabbed by the two men on the forecastle. A young fellow belonging to our crew was in the chair, to be a protection to the lady-comers. At once a couple of ladies appeared from below, took seats in his lap, we hoisted them into the sky, waited a moment till the roll of the ship brought them in overhead, then we lowered suddenly away, and seized the chair as it struck the deck. We took the twenty-five aboard, and delivered twenty-five into the tug—among them several aged ladies, and one blind one—and all without accident. It was a fine piece of work.

Ours is a nice ship, roomy, comfortable, well-ordered, and satisfactory. Now and then we step on a rat in a hotel, but we have had no rats on shipboard lately; unless, perhaps in the Flora; we had more serious things to think of there, and did not notice. I have noticed that it is only in ships and hotels which still employ the odious Chinese gong, that you find rats. The reason would seem to be, that as a rat cannot tell the time of day by a clock, he won't stay where he cannot find out when dinner is ready.

November 29. The doctor tells me of several old drunkards, one spiritless loafer, and several far-gone moral wrecks who have been reclaimed by the Salvation Army and have remained staunch people and hard workers these two years. Wherever one goes, these testimonials to the Army's efficiency are forthcoming . . . . This morning we had one of those whizzing green Ballarat flies in the room, with his stunning buzz-saw noise—the swiftest creature in the world except the lightning-flash. It is a stupendous force that is stored up in

that little body. If we had it in a ship in the same proportion, we could spin from Liverpool to New York in the space of an hour—the time it takes to eat luncheon. The New Zealand express train is called the Ballarat Fly . . . . Bad teeth in the colonies. A citizen told me they don't have teeth filled, but pull them out and put in false ones, and that now and then one sees a young lady with a full set. She is fortunate. I wish I had been born with false teeth and a false liver and false carbuncles. I should get along better.

December 2. Monday. Left Napier in the Ballarat Fly the one that goes twice a week. From Napier to Hastings, twelve miles; time, fifty-five minutes—not so far short of thirteen miles an hour . . . . A perfect summer day; cool breeze, brilliant sky, rich vegetation. Two or three times during the afternoon we saw wonderfully dense and beautiful forests, tumultuously piled skyward on the broken highlands—not the customary roof-like slant of a hillside, where the trees are all the same height. The noblest of these trees were of the Kauri breed, we were told the timber that is now furnishing the wood-paving for Europe, and is the best of all wood for that purpose. Sometimes these towering upheavals of forestry were festooned and garlanded with vine-cables, and sometimes the masses of undergrowth were cocooned in another sort of vine of a delicate cobwebby texture—they call it the "supplejack," I think. Tree ferns everywhere—a stem fifteen feet high, with a graceful chalice of fern-fronds sprouting from its top—a lovely forest ornament. And there was a ten-foot reed with a flowing suit of what looked like yellow hair hanging from its upper end. I do not know its name, but if there is such a thing as a scalp-plant, this is it. A romantic gorge, with a brook flowing in its bottom, approaching Palmerston North.

Waitukurau. Twenty minutes for luncheon. With me sat my wife and daughter, and my manager, Mr. Carlyle Smythe. I sat at the head of the table, and could see the right-hand wall; the others had their backs to it. On that wall, at a good distance away, were a couple of framed pictures. I could not see them clearly, but from the groupings of the figures I fancied that they represented the killing of Napoleon III's son by the Zulus in South Africa. I broke into the conversation, which was about poetry and cabbage and art, and said to my wife—

"Do you remember when the news came to Paris—"

"Of the killing of the Prince?"

(Those were the very words I had in my mind.) "Yes, but what Prince?"

"Napoleon. Lulu."

"What made you think of that?"

"I don't know."

There was no collusion. She had not seen the pictures, and they had not been mentioned. She ought to have thought of some recent news that came to Paris, for we were but seven months from there and had been living there a couple of years when we started on this trip; but instead of that she thought of an incident of our brief sojourn in Paris of sixteen years before.

Here was a clear case of mental telegraphy; of mind-transference; of my mind telegraphing a thought into hers. How do I know? Because I telegraphed an error. For it turned out that the pictures did not represent the killing of Lulu at all, nor anything connected with Lulu. She had to get the error from my head—it existed nowhere else.

CHAPTER XXXV.

The Autocrat of Russia possesses more power than any other man in the earth; but he cannot stop a sneeze. —Pudd'nhead Wilson's New Calendar.

WAUGANIUI, December 3. A pleasant trip, yesterday, per Ballarat Fly. Four hours. I do not know the distance, but it must have been well along toward fifty miles. The Fly could have spun it out to eight hours and not discommoded me; for where there is comfort, and no need for hurry, speed is of no value—at least to me; and nothing that goes on wheels can be more comfortable, more satisfactory, than the New Zealand trains. Outside of America there are no cars that are so rationally devised. When you add the constant presence of charming scenery and the nearly constant absence of dust—well, if one is not content then, he ought to get out and walk. That would change his spirit, perhaps? I think so. At the end of an hour you would find him waiting humbly beside the track, and glad to be taken aboard again.

Much horseback riding, in and around this town; many comely girls in cool and pretty summer gowns; much Salvation Army; lots of Maoris; the faces and bodies of some of the old ones very tastefully frescoed. Maori Council House over the river—large, strong, carpeted from end to end with matting, and decorated with elaborate wood carvings, artistically executed. The Maoris were very polite.

I was assured by a member of the House of Representatives that the native race is not decreasing, but actually increasing slightly. It is another evidence that they are a superior breed of savages. I do not call to mind any savage race that built such good houses, or such strong and ingenious and scientific fortresses, or gave so much attention to agriculture, or had military arts and devices which so nearly approached the white man's. These, taken together with their high abilities in boat-building, and their tastes and capacities in the ornamental arts modify their savagery to a semi-civilization—or at least to, a quarter-civilization.

It is a compliment to them that the British did not exterminate them, as they did the Australians and the Tasmanians, but were content with subduing them, and showed no desire to go further. And it is another compliment to them that the British did not take the whole of their choicest lands, but left them a considerable part, and then went further and protected them from the rapacities of landsharks—a protection which the New Zealand Government still extends to them. And it is still another compliment to the Maoris that the Government allows native representation—in both the legislature and the cabinet, and gives both sexes the vote. And in doing these things the Government also compliments itself; it has not been the custom of the world for conquerors to act in this large spirit toward the conquered.

The highest class white men Who lived among the Maoris in the earliest time had a high opinion of them and a strong affection for them. Among the whites of this sort was the author of "Old New Zealand;" and Dr. Campbell of Auckland was another. Dr. Campbell was a close friend of several chiefs, and has many pleasant things to say of their fidelity, their magnanimity, and their generosity. Also of their quaint notions about the white man's queer civilization, and their equally quaint comments upon it. One of them thought the missionary had got everything wrong end first and upside down. "Why, he wants us to stop worshiping and supplicating the evil gods, and go to worshiping and supplicating the Good One! There is no sense in that. A good god is not going to do us any harm."

The Maoris had the tabu; and had it on a Polynesian scale of comprehensiveness and elaboration. Some of its features could have been importations from India and Judea. Neither the Maori nor the Hindoo of common degree could cook by a fire that a person of higher caste had used, nor could the high Maori or high Hindoo employ fire that had served a man of low grade; if a low-grade Maori or Hindoo drank from a vessel belonging to a high-grade man, the vessel was defiled, and had to be destroyed. There were other resemblances between Maori tabu and Hindoo caste-custom.

Yesterday a lunatic burst into my quarters and warned me that the Jesuits were going to "cook" (poison) me in my food, or kill me on the stage at night. He said a mysterious sign was visible upon my posters and meant my death. He said he saved Rev. Mr. Haweis's life by warning him that there were three men on his platform who would kill him if he took his eyes off them for a moment during his lecture. The same men were in my audience last night, but they saw that he was there. "Will they be there again to-night?" He hesitated; then said no, he thought they would rather take a rest and chance the poison. This lunatic has no delicacy. But he was not uninteresting. He told me a lot of things. He said he had "saved so many lecturers in twenty years, that they put him in the asylum." I think he has less refinement than any lunatic I have met.

December 8. A couple of curious war-monuments here at Wanganui. One is in honor of white men "who fell in defence of law and order against fanaticism and barbarism." Fanaticism. We Americans are English in blood, English in speech, English in religion, English in the essentials of our governmental system, English in the essentials of our civilization; and so, let us hope, for the honor of the blend, for the honor of the blood, for the honor of the race, that that word got there through lack of heedfulness, and will not be suffered to remain. If you carve it at Thermopylae, or where Winkelried died, or upon Bunker Hill monument, and read it again "who fell in defence of law and order against fanaticism" you will perceive what the word means, and how mischosen it is. Patriotism is Patriotism. Calling it Fanaticism cannot degrade it; nothing can degrade it. Even though it be a political mistake, and a thousand times a political mistake, that does not affect it; it is honorable always honorable, always noble—and privileged to hold its head up and look the nations in the face. It is right to praise these brave white men who fell in the Maori war—they deserve it; but the presence of that word detracts from the dignity of their cause and their deeds, and makes them appear to have spilt their blood in a conflict with ignoble men, men not worthy of that costly sacrifice. But the men were worthy. It was no shame to fight them. They fought for their homes, they fought for their country; they bravely fought and bravely fell; and it would take nothing from the honor of the brave Englishmen who lie under the monument, but add to it, to say that they died in defense of English laws and English homes against men worthy of the sacrifice—the Maori patriots.

The other monument cannot be rectified. Except with dynamite. It is a mistake all through, and a strangely thoughtless one. It is a monument erected by white men to Maoris who fell fighting with the whites and against their own people, in the Maori war. "Sacred to the memory of the brave men who fell on the 14th of May, 1864," etc. On one side are the names of about twenty Maoris. It is not a fancy of mine; the monument exists. I saw it. It is an object-lesson to the rising generation. It invites to treachery, disloyalty, unpatriotism. Its lesson, in frank terms is, "Desert your flag, slay your people, burn their homes, shame your nationality—we honor such."

December 9. Wellington. Ten hours from Wanganui by the Fly. December 12. It is a fine city and nobly situated. A busy place, and full of life and movement. Have spent the three days partly in walking about, partly in enjoying social privileges, and largely in idling around the magnificent garden at Hutt, a little distance away, around the shore. I suppose we shall not see such another one soon.

We are packing to-night for the return-voyage to Australia. Our stay in New Zealand has been too brief; still, we are not unthankful for the glimpse which we have had of it.

The sturdy Maoris made the settlement of the country by the whites rather difficult. Not at first—but later. At first they welcomed the whites, and were eager to trade with them—particularly for muskets; for their pastime was internecine war, and they greatly preferred the white man's weapons to their own. War was their pastime—I use the word advisedly. They often met and slaughtered each other just for a lark, and when there was no quarrel. The author of "Old New Zealand" mentions a case where a victorious army could have followed up its advantage and exterminated the opposing army, but declined to do it; explaining naively that "if we did that, there couldn't be any more fighting." In another battle one army sent word that it was out of ammunition, and would be obliged to stop unless the opposing army would send some. It was sent, and the fight went on.

In the early days things went well enough. The natives sold land without clearly understanding the terms of exchange, and the whites bought it without being much disturbed about the native's confusion of mind. But by and by the Maori began to comprehend that he was being wronged; then there was trouble, for he was not the man to swallow a wrong and go aside and cry about it. He had the Tasmanian's spirit and endurance, and a notable share of military science besides; and so he rose against the oppressor, did this gallant "fanatic," and started a war that was not brought to a definite end until more than a generation had sped.

CHAPTER XXXVI.

There are several good protections against temptations, but the surest is cowardice. —Pudd'nhead Wilson's New Calendar.

Names are not always what they seem. The common Welsh name Bzjxxllwep is pronounced Jackson. —Pudd'nhead Wilson's New Calendar.

Friday, December 13. Sailed, at 3 p.m., in the 'Mararoa'. Summer seas and a good ship-life has nothing better.

Monday. Three days of paradise. Warm and sunny and smooth; the sea a luminous Mediterranean blue . . . . One lolls in a long chair all day under deck-awnings, and reads and smokes, in measureless content. One does not read prose at such a time, but poetry. I have been reading the poems of Mrs. Julia A. Moore, again, and I find in them the same grace and melody that attracted me when they were first published, twenty years ago, and have held me in happy bonds ever since.

"The Sentimental Song Book" has long been out of print, and has been forgotten by the world in general, but not by me. I carry it with me always—it and Goldsmith's deathless story.

Indeed, it has the same deep charm for me that the Vicar of Wakefield has, and I find in it the same subtle touch—the touch that makes an intentionally humorous episode pathetic and an intentionally pathetic one funny. In her time Mrs. Moore was called "the Sweet Singer of Michigan," and was best known by that name. I have read her book through twice today, with the purpose of determining which of her pieces has most merit, and I am persuaded that for wide grasp and sustained power, "William Upson" may claim first place:

WILLIAM UPSON.

Air—"The Major's Only Son." Come all good people far and near, Oh, come and see what you can hear, It's of a young man true and brave, That is now sleeping in his grave.

Now, William Upson was his name If it's not that, it's all the same He did enlist in a cruel strife, And it caused him to lose his life.

He was Perry Upson's eldest son, His father loved his noble son, This son was nineteen years of age When first in the rebellion he engaged.

His father said that he might go, But his dear mother she said no, "Oh! stay at home, dear Billy," she said, But she could not turn his head.

He went to Nashville, in Tennessee, There his kind friends he could not see; He died among strangers, so far away, They did not know where his body lay.

He was taken sick and lived four weeks, And Oh! how his parents weep, But now they must in sorrow mourn, For Billy has gone to his heavenly home.

Oh! if his mother could have seen her son, For she loved him, her darling son; If she could heard his dying prayer, It would ease her heart till she met him there.

How it would relieve his mother's heart To see her son from this world depart, And hear his noble words of love, As he left this world for that above.

Now it will relieve his mother's heart, For her son is laid in our graveyard; For now she knows that his grave is near, She will not shed so many tears.

Although she knows not that it was her son, For his coffin could not be opened It might be someone in his place, For she could not see his noble face.

December, 17. Reached Sydney.

December, 19. In the train. Fellow of 30 with four valises; a slim creature, with teeth which made his mouth look like a neglected churchyard. He had solidified hair—solidified with pomatum; it was all one shell. He smoked the most extraordinary cigarettes—made of some kind of manure, apparently. These and his hair made him smell like the very nation. He had a low-cut vest on, which exposed a deal of frayed and broken and unclean shirtfront. Showy studs, of imitation gold—they had made black disks on the linen.

Oversized sleeve buttons of imitation gold, the copper base showing through. Ponderous watch-chain of imitation gold. I judge that he couldn't tell the time by it, for he asked Smythe what time it was, once. He wore a coat which had been gay when it was young; 5-o'clock-tea-trousers of a light tint, and marvelously soiled; yellow mustache with a dashing upward whirl at the ends; foxy shoes, imitation patent leather. He was a novelty—an imitation dude. He would have been a real one if he could have afforded it. But he was satisfied with himself. You could see it in his expression, and in all his attitudes and movements. He was living in a dude dreamland where all his squalid shams were genuine, and himself a sincerity. It disarmed criticism, it mollified spite, to see him so enjoy his imitation languors, and arts, and airs, and his studied daintinesses of gesture and misbegotten refinements. It was plain to me that he was imagining himself the Prince of Wales, and was doing everything the way he thought the Prince would do it. For bringing his four valises aboard and stowing them in the nettings, he gave his porter four cents, and lightly apologized for the smallness of the gratuity —just with the condescendingest little royal air in the world. He stretched himself out on the front seat and rested his pomatum-cake on the middle arm, and stuck his feet out of the window, and began to pose as the Prince and work his dreams and languors for exhibition; and he would indolently watch the blue films curling up from his cigarette, and inhale the stench, and look so grateful; and would flip the ash away with the daintiest gesture, unintentionally displaying his brass ring in the most intentional way; why, it was as good as being in Marlborough House itself to see him do it so like.

There was other scenery in the trip. That of the Hawksbury river, in the National Park region, fine—extraordinarily fine, with spacious views of stream and lake imposingly framed in woody hills; and every now and then the noblest groupings of mountains, and the most enchanting rearrangements of the water effects. Further along, green flats, thinly covered with gum forests, with here and there the huts and cabins of small farmers engaged in raising children. Still further along, arid stretches, lifeless and melancholy. Then Newcastle, a rushing town, capital of the rich coal regions. Approaching Scone, wide farming and grazing levels, with pretty frequent glimpses of a troublesome plant—a particularly devilish little prickly pear, daily damned in the orisons of the agriculturist; imported by a lady of sentiment, and contributed gratis to the colony. Blazing hot, all day.

December 20. Back to Sydney. Blazing hot again. From the newspaper, and from the map, I have made a collection of curious names of Australasian towns, with the idea of making a poem out of them:

Tumut Takee Murriwillumba Bowral Ballarat Mullengudgery Murrurundi Wagga-Wagga Wyalong Murrumbidgee Goomeroo Wolloway Wangary Wanilla Worrow Koppio Yankalilla Yaranyacka Yackamoorundie Kaiwaka Coomooroo Tauranga Geelong Tongariro Kaikoura Wakatipu Oohipara Waitpinga Goelwa Munno Para Nangkita Myponga Kapunda Kooringa Penola Nangwarry Kongorong Comaum Koolywurtie Killanoola Naracoorte Muloowurtie Binnum Wallaroo Wirrega Mundoora Hauraki Rangiriri Teawamute Taranaki Toowoomba Goondiwindi Jerrilderie Whangaroa Wollongong Woolloomooloo Bombola Coolgardie Bendigo Coonamble Cootamundra Woolgoolga

Mittagong Jamberoo Kondoparinga Kuitpo Tungkillo Oukaparinga Talunga Yatala Parawirra Moorooroo Whangarei Woolundunga Booleroo Pernatty Parramatta Taroom

Narrandera Deniliquin Kawakawa.

It may be best to build the poem now, and make the weather help

A SWELTERING DAY IN AUSTRALIA.

(To be read soft and low, with the lights turned down.)

The Bombola faints in the hot Bowral tree, Where fierce Mullengudgery's smothering fires Far from the breezes of Coolgardie Burn ghastly and blue as the day expires;

And Murriwillumba complaineth in song For the garlanded bowers of Woolloomooloo, And the Ballarat Fly and the lone Wollongong They dream of the gardens of Jamberoo;

The wallabi sighs for the Murrubidgee, For the velvety sod of the Munno Parah, Where the waters of healing from Muloowurtie Flow dim in the gloaming by Yaranyackah;

The Koppio sorrows for lost Wolloway, And sigheth in secret for Murrurundi, The Whangeroo wombat lamenteth the day That made him an exile from Jerrilderie;

The Teawamute Tumut from Wirrega's glade, The Nangkita swallow, the Wallaroo swan, They long for the peace of the Timaru shade And thy balmy soft airs, O sweet Mittagong!

The Kooringa buffalo pants in the sun, The Kondoparinga lies gaping for breath, The Kongorong Camaum to the shadow has won, But the Goomeroo sinks in the slumber of death;

In the weltering hell of the Moorooroo plain The Yatala Wangary withers and dies, And the Worrow Wanilla, demented with pain, To the Woolgoolga woodlands despairingly flies;

Sweet Nangwarry's desolate, Coonamble wails, And Tungkillo Kuito in sables is drest, For the Whangerei winds fall asleep in the sails And the Booleroo life-breeze is dead in the west.

Mypongo, Kapunda, O slumber no more Yankalilla, Parawirra, be warned There's death in the air! Killanoola, wherefore Shall the prayer of Penola be scorned?

Cootamundra, and Takee, and Wakatipu, Toowoomba, Kaikoura are lost From Onkaparinga to far Oamaru All burn in this hell's holocaust!

Paramatta and Binnum are gone to their rest In the vale of Tapanni Taroom, Kawakawa, Deniliquin—all that was best In the earth are but graves and a tomb!

Narrandera mourns, Cameron answers not When the roll of the scathless we cry Tongariro, Goondiwindi, Woolundunga, the spot Is mute and forlorn where ye lie.

Those are good words for poetry. Among the best I have ever seen. There are 81 in the list. I did not need them all, but I have knocked down 66 of them; which is a good bag, it seems to me, for a person not in the business. Perhaps a poet laureate could do better, but a poet laureate gets wages, and that is different. When I write poetry I do not get any wages; often I lose money by it. The best word in that list, and the most musical and gurgly, is Woolloomoolloo. It is a place near Sydney, and is a favorite pleasure-resort. It has eight O's in it.

CHAPTER XXXVII.

To succeed in the other trades, capacity must be shown; in the law, concealment of it will do. —Pudd'nhead Wilson's New Calendar.

MONDAY,—December 23, 1895. Sailed from Sydney for Ceylon in the P. & O. steamer 'Oceana'. A Lascar crew mans this ship—the first I have seen. White cotton petticoat and pants; barefoot; red shawl for belt; straw cap, brimless, on head, with red scarf wound around it; complexion a rich dark brown; short straight black hair; whiskers fine and silky; lustrous and intensely black. Mild, good faces; willing and obedient people; capable, too; but are said to go into hopeless panics when there is danger. They are from Bombay and the coast thereabouts. Left some of the trunks in Sydney, to be shipped to South Africa by a vessel advertised to sail three months hence. The proverb says: "Separate not yourself from your baggage."

This 'Oceana' is a stately big ship, luxuriously appointed. She has spacious promenade decks. Large rooms; a surpassingly comfortable ship. The officers' library is well selected; a ship's library is not usually that . . . . For meals, the bugle call, man-of-war fashion; a pleasant change from the terrible gong . . . . Three big cats—very friendly loafers; they wander all over the ship; the white one follows the chief steward around like a dog. There is also a basket of kittens. One of these cats goes ashore, in port, in England, Australia, and India, to see how his various families are getting along, and is seen no more till the ship is ready to sail. No one knows how he finds out the sailing date, but no doubt he comes down to the dock every day and takes a look, and when he sees baggage and passengers flocking in, recognizes that it is time to get aboard. This is what the sailors believe. The Chief Engineer has been in the China and India trade thirty three years, and has had but three Christmases at home in that time . . . . Conversational items at dinner, "Mocha! sold all over the world! It is not true. In fact, very few foreigners except the Emperor of Russia have ever seen a grain of it, or ever will, while they live." Another man said: "There is no sale in Australia for Australian wine. But it goes to France and comes back with a French label on it, and then they buy it." I have heard that the most of the French-labeled claret in New York is made in California. And I remember what Professor S. told me once about Veuve Cliquot—if that was the wine, and I think it was. He was the guest of a great wine merchant whose town was quite near that vineyard, and this merchant asked him if very much V. C. was drunk in America.

"Oh, yes," said S., "a great abundance of it."

"Is it easy to be had?"

"Oh, yes—easy as water. All first and second-class hotels have it."

"What do you pay for it?"

"It depends on the style of the hotel—from fifteen to twenty-five francs a bottle."

"Oh, fortunate country! Why, it's worth 100 francs right here on the ground."

"No!"

"Yes!"

"Do you mean that we are drinking a bogus Veuve-Cliquot over there?"

"Yes—and there was never a bottle of the genuine in America since Columbus's time. That wine all comes from a little bit of a patch of ground which isn't big enough to raise many bottles; and all of it that is produced goes every year to one person—the Emperor of Russia. He takes the whole crop in advance, be it big or little."

January 4, 1898. Christmas in Melbourne, New Year's Day in Adelaide, and saw most of the friends again in both places . . . . Lying here at anchor all day—Albany (King George's Sound), Western Australia. It is a perfectly landlocked harbor, or roadstead—spacious to look at, but not deep water. Desolate-looking rocks and scarred hills. Plenty of ships arriving now, rushing to the new gold-fields. The papers are full of wonderful tales of the sort always to be heard in connection with new gold diggings. A sample: a youth staked out a claim and tried to sell half for £5; no takers; he stuck to it fourteen days, starving, then struck it rich and sold out for £10,000... About sunset, strong breeze blowing, got up the anchor. We were in a small deep puddle, with a narrow channel leading out of it, minutely buoyed, to the sea.

I stayed on deck to see how we were going to manage it with such a big ship and such a strong wind. On the bridge our giant captain, in uniform; at his side a little pilot in elaborately gold-laced uniform; on the forecastle a white mate and quartermaster or two, and a brilliant crowd of lascars standing by for business. Our stern was pointing straight at the head of the channel; so we must turn entirely around in the puddle—and the wind blowing as described. It was done, and beautifully. It was done by help of a jib. We stirred up much mud, but did not touch the bottom. We turned right around in our tracks—a seeming impossibility. We had several casts of quarter-less 5, and one cast of half 4—27 feet; we were drawing 26 astern. By the time we were entirely around and pointed, the first buoy was not more than.a hundred yards in front of us. It was a fine piece of work, and I was the only passenger that saw it. However, the others got their dinner; the P. & O. Company got mine . . . . More cats developed. Smythe says it is a British law that they must be carried; and he instanced a case of a ship not allowed to sail till she sent for a couple. The bill came, too: "Debtor, to 2 cats, 20 shillings." . . . News comes that within this week Siam has acknowledged herself to be, in effect, a French province. It seems plain that all savage and semi-civilized countries are going to be grabbed . . . . A vulture on board; bald, red, queer-shaped head, featherless red places here and there on his body, intense great black eyes set in featherless rims of inflamed flesh; dissipated look; a businesslike style, a selfish, conscienceless, murderous aspect—the very look of a professional assassin, and yet a bird which does no murder. What was the use of getting him up in that tragic style for so innocent a trade as his? For this one isn't the sort that wars upon the living, his diet is offal—and the more out of date it is the better he likes it. Nature should give him a suit of rusty black; then he would be all right, for he would look like an undertaker and would harmonize with his business; whereas the way he is now he is horribly out of true.

January 5. At 9 this morning we passed Cape Leeuwin (lioness) and ceased from our long due-west course along the southern shore of Australia. Turning this extreme southwestern corner, we now take a long straight slant nearly N. W., without a break, for Ceylon. As we speed northward it will grow hotter very fast—but it isn't chilly, now. . . . The vulture is from the public menagerie at Adelaide—a great and interesting collection. It was there that we saw the baby tiger solemnly spreading its mouth and trying to roar like its majestic mother. It swaggered, scowling, back and forth on its short legs just as it had seen her do on her long ones, and now and then snarling viciously, exposing its teeth, with a threatening lift of its upper lip and bristling moustache; and when it thought it was impressing the visitors, it would spread its mouth wide and do that screechy cry which it meant for a roar, but which did not deceive. It took itself quite seriously, and was lovably comical. And there was a hyena—an ugly creature; as ugly as the tiger-kitty was pretty. It repeatedly arched its back and delivered itself of such a human cry; a startling resemblance; a cry which was just that of a grown person badly hurt. In the dark one would assuredly go to its assistance—and be disappointed . . . . Many friends of Australasian Federation on board. They feel sure that the good day is not far off, now. But there seems to be a party that would go further —have Australasia cut loose from the British Empire and set up housekeeping on her own hook. It seems an unwise idea. They point to the United States, but it seems to me that the cases lack a good deal of being alike. Australasia governs herself wholly—there is no interference; and her commerce and manufactures are not oppressed in any way. If our case had been the same we should not have gone out when we did.

January 13. Unspeakably hot. The equator is arriving again. We are within eight degrees of it. Ceylon present. Dear me, it is beautiful! And most sumptuously tropical, as to character of foliage and opulence of it. "What though the spicy breezes blow soft o'er Ceylon's isle"—an eloquent line, an incomparable line; it says little, but conveys whole libraries of sentiment, and Oriental charm and mystery, and tropic deliciousness—a line that quivers and tingles with a thousand unexpressed and inexpressible things, things that haunt one and find no articulate voice . . . . Colombo, the capital. An Oriental town, most manifestly; and fascinating.

In this palatial ship the passengers dress for dinner. The ladies' toilettes make a fine display of color, and this is in keeping with the elegance of the vessel's furnishings and the flooding brilliancies of the electric light. On the stormy Atlantic one never sees a man in evening dress, except at the rarest intervals; and then there is only one, not two; and he shows up but once on the voyage—the night before the ship makes port—the night when they have the "concert" and do the amateur wailings and recitations. He is the tenor, as a rule . . . . There has been a deal of cricket-playing on board; it seems a queer game for a ship, but they enclose the promenade deck with nettings and keep the ball from flying overboard, and the sport goes very well, and is properly violent and exciting . . . . We must part from this vessel here.

January 14. Hotel Bristol. Servant Brompy. Alert, gentle, smiling, winning young brown creature as ever was. Beautiful shining black hair combed back like a woman's, and knotted at the back of his head —tortoise-shell comb in it, sign that he is a Singhalese; slender, shapely form; jacket; under it is a beltless and flowing white cotton gown—from neck straight to heel; he and his outfit quite unmasculine. It was an embarrassment to undress before him.

We drove to the market, using the Japanese jinriksha—our first acquaintanceship with it. It is a light cart, with a native to draw it. He makes good speed for half-an-hour, but it is hard work for him; he is too slight for it. After the half-hour there is no more pleasure for you; your attention is all on the man, just

as it would be on a tired horse, and necessarily your sympathy is there too. There's a plenty of these 'rickshas, and the tariff is incredibly cheap.

I was in Cairo years ago. That was Oriental, but there was a lack. When you are in Florida or New Orleans you are in the South—that is granted; but you are not in the South; you are in a modified South, a tempered South. Cairo was a tempered Orient—an Orient with an indefinite something wanting. That feeling was not present in Ceylon. Ceylon was Oriental in the last measure of completeness—utterly Oriental; also utterly tropical; and indeed to one's unreasoning spiritual sense the two things belong together. All the requisites were present. The costumes were right; the black and brown exposures, unconscious of immodesty, were right; the juggler was there, with his basket, his snakes, his mongoose, and his arrangements for growing a tree from seed to foliage and ripe fruitage before one's eyes; in sight were plants and flowers familiar to one on books but in no other way celebrated, desirable, strange, but in production restricted to the hot belt of the equator; and out a little way in the country were the proper deadly snakes, and fierce beasts of prey, and the wild elephant and the monkey. And there was that swoon in the air which one associates with the tropics, and that smother of heat, heavy with odors of unknown flowers, and that sudden invasion of purple gloom fissured with lightnings,—then the tumult of crashing thunder and the downpour and presently all sunny and smiling again; all these things were there; the conditions were complete, nothing was lacking. And away off in the deeps of the jungle and in the remotenesses of the mountains were the ruined cities and mouldering temples, mysterious relics of the pomps of a forgotten time and a vanished race—and this was as it should be, also, for nothing is quite satisfyingly Oriental that lacks the somber and impressive qualities of mystery and antiquity.

The drive through the town and out to the Galle Face by the seashore, what a dream it was of tropical splendors of bloom and blossom, and Oriental conflagrations of costume! The walking groups of men, women, boys, girls, babies—each individual was a flame, each group a house afire for color. And such stunning colors, such intensely vivid colors, such rich and exquisite minglings and fusings of rainbows and lightnings! And all harmonious, all in perfect taste; never a discordant note; never a color on any person swearing at another color on him or failing to harmonize faultlessly with the colors of any group the wearer might join. The stuffs were silk-thin, soft, delicate, clinging; and, as a rule, each piece a solid color: a splendid green, a splendid blue, a splendid yellow, a splendid purple, a splendid ruby, deep, and rich with smouldering fires they swept continuously by in crowds and legions and multitudes, glowing, flashing, burning, radiant; and every five seconds came a burst of blinding red that made a body catch his breath, and filled his heart with joy. And then, the unimaginable grace of those costumes! Sometimes a woman's whole dress was but a scarf wound about her person and her head, sometimes a man's was but a turban and a careless rag or two—in both cases generous areas of polished dark skin showing—but always the arrangement compelled the homage of the eye and made the heart sing for gladness.

I can see it to this day, that radiant panorama, that wilderness of rich color, that incomparable dissolving-view of harmonious tints, and lithe half-covered forms, and beautiful brown faces, and gracious and graceful gestures and attitudes and movements, free, unstudied, barren of stiffness and restraint, and—

Just then, into this dream of fairyland and paradise a grating dissonance was injected.

Out of a missionary school came marching, two and two, sixteen prim and pious little Christian black girls, Europeanly clothed—dressed, to the last detail, as they would have been dressed on a summer Sunday in an English or American village. Those clothes—oh, they were unspeakably ugly! Ugly, barbarous, destitute of taste, destitute of grace, repulsive as a shroud. I looked at my womenfolk's clothes—just full-grown duplicates of the outrages disguising those poor little abused creatures —and was ashamed to be seen in the street with them. Then I looked at my own clothes, and was ashamed to be seen in the street with myself.

However, we must put up with our clothes as they are—they have their reason for existing. They are on us to expose us—to advertise what we wear them to conceal. They are a sign; a sign of insincerity; a sign of suppressed vanity; a pretense that we despise gorgeous colors and the graces of harmony and form; and we put them on to propagate that lie and back it up. But we do not deceive our neighbor; and when we step into Ceylon we realize that we have not even deceived ourselves. We do love brilliant colors and graceful costumes; and at home we will turn out in a storm to see them when the procession goes by—and envy the wearers. We go to the theater to look at them and grieve that we can't be clothed like that. We go to the King's ball, when we get a chance, and are glad of a sight of the splendid uniforms and the glittering orders. When we are granted permission to attend an imperial drawing-room we shut ourselves up in private and parade around in the theatrical court-dress by the hour, and admire ourselves in the glass, and are utterly happy; and every member of every governor's staff in democratic America does the same with his grand new uniform—and if he is not watched he will get himself photographed in it, too. When I see the Lord Mayor's footman I am dissatisfied with my lot. Yes, our clothes are a lie, and have been nothing short of that these hundred years. They are insincere, they are the ugly and appropriate outward exposure of an inward sham and a moral decay.

The last little brown boy I chanced to notice in the crowds and swarms of Colombo had nothing on but a twine string around his waist, but in my memory the frank honesty of his costume still stands out in pleasant contrast with the odious flummery in which the little Sunday-school dowdies were masquerading.

CHAPTER XXXVIII.

Prosperity is the best protector of principle. —Pudd'nhead Wilson's New Calendar.

EVENING—11th. Sailed in the Rosetta. This is a poor old ship, and ought to be insured and sunk. As in the 'Oceana', just so here: everybody dresses for dinner; they make it a sort of pious duty. These fine and formal costumes are a rather conspicuous contrast to the poverty and shabbiness of the surroundings . . . . If you want a slice of a lime at four o'clock tea, you must sign an order on the bar. Limes cost 14 cents a barrel.

January 18th. We have been running up the Arabian Sea, latterly. Closing up on Bombay now, and due to arrive this evening.

January 20th. Bombay! A bewitching place, a bewildering place, an enchanting place—the Arabian Nights come again? It is a vast city; contains about a million inhabitants. Natives, they are, with a slight sprinkling of white people—not enough

to have the slightest modifying effect upon the massed dark complexion of the public. It is winter here, yet the weather is the divine weather of June, and the foliage is the fresh and heavenly foliage of June. There is a rank of noble great shade trees across the way from the hotel, and under them sit groups of picturesque natives of both sexes; and the juggler in his turban is there with his snakes and his magic; and all day long the cabs and the multitudinous varieties of costumes flock by. It does not seem as if one could ever get tired of watching this moving show, this shining and shifting spectacle . . . . In the great bazar the pack and jam of natives was marvelous, the sea of rich-colored turbans and draperies an inspiring sight, and the quaint and showy Indian architecture was just the right setting for it. Toward sunset another show; this is the drive around the sea-shore to Malabar Point, where Lord Sandhurst, the Governor of the Bombay Presidency, lives. Parsee palaces all along the first part of the drive; and past them all the world is driving; the private carriages of wealthy Englishmen and natives of rank are manned by a driver and three footmen in stunning oriental liveries—two of these turbaned statues standing up behind, as fine as monuments. Sometimes even the public carriages have this superabundant crew, slightly modified—one to drive, one to sit by and see it done, and one to stand up behind and yell—yell when there is anybody in the way, and for practice when there isn't. It all helps to keep up the liveliness and augment the general sense of swiftness and energy and confusion and pow-wow.

In the region of Scandal Point—felicitous name—where there are handy rocks to sit on and a noble view of the sea on the one hand, and on the other the passing and reprising whirl and tumult of gay carriages, are great groups of comfortably-off Parsee women—perfect flower-beds of brilliant color, a fascinating spectacle. Tramp, tramp, tramping along the road, in singles, couples, groups, and gangs, you have the working-man and the working-woman—but not clothed like ours. Usually the man is a nobly-built great athlete, with not a rag on but his loin-handkerchief; his color a deep dark brown, his skin satin, his rounded muscles knobbing it as if it had eggs under it. Usually the woman is a slender and shapely creature, as erect as a lightning-rod, and she has but one thing on—a bright-colored piece of stuff which is wound about her head and her body down nearly half-way to her knees, and which clings like her own skin. Her legs and feet are bare, and so are her arms, except for her fanciful bunches of loose silver rings on her ankles and on her arms. She has jewelry bunched on the side of her nose also, and showy clusterings on her toes. When she undresses for bed she takes off her jewelry, I suppose. If she took off anything more she would catch cold. As a rule she has a large shiney brass water jar of graceful shape on her head, and one of her naked arms curves up and the hand holds it there. She is so straight, so erect, and she steps with such style, and such easy grace and dignity; and her curved arm and her brazen jar are such a help to the picture indeed, our working-women cannot begin with her as a road-decoration.

It is all color, bewitching color, enchanting color—everywhere all around—all the way around the curving great opaline bay clear to Government House, where the turbaned big native 'chuprassies' stand grouped in state at the door in their robes of fiery red, and do most properly and stunningly finish up the splendid show and make it theatrically complete. I wish I were a 'chuprassy'.

This is indeed India! the land of dreams and romance, of fabulous wealth and fabulous poverty, of splendor and rags, of palaces and hovels, of famine and pestilence, of genii and giants and Aladdin lamps, of tigers and elephants, the cobra and the jungle, the country of a hundred nations and a hundred tongues, of a thousand religions and two million gods, cradle of the human race, birthplace of human speech, mother of history, grandmother of legend, great-grandmother of tradition, whose yesterdays bear date with the mouldering antiquities of the rest of the nations—the one sole country under the sun that is endowed with an imperishable interest for alien prince and alien peasant, for lettered and ignorant, wise and fool, rich and poor, bond and free, the one land that all men desire to see, and having seen once, by even a glimpse, would not give that glimpse for the shows of all the rest of the globe combined. Even now, after the lapse of a year, the delirium of those days in Bombay has not left me, and I hope never will. It was all new, no detail of it hackneyed. And India did not wait for morning, it began at the hotel —straight away. The lobbies and halls were full of turbaned, and fez'd and embroidered, cap'd, and barefooted, and cotton-clad dark natives, some of them rushing about, others at rest squatting, or sitting on the ground; some of them chattering with energy, others still and dreamy; in the dining-room every man's own private native servant standing behind his chair, and dressed for a part in the Arabian Nights.

Our rooms were high up, on the front. A white man—he was a burly German —went up with us, and brought three natives along to see to arranging things. About fourteen others followed in procession, with the hand-baggage; each carried an article—and only one; a bag, in some cases, in other cases less. One strong native carried my overcoat, another a parasol, another a box of cigars, another a novel, and the last man in the procession had no load but a fan. It was all done with earnestness and sincerity, there was not a smile in the procession from the head of it to the tail of it. Each man waited patiently, tranquilly, in no sort of hurry, till one of us found time to give him a copper, then he bent his head reverently, touched his forehead with his fingers, and went his way. They seemed a soft and gentle race, and there was something both winning and touching about their demeanor.

There was a vast glazed door which opened upon the balcony. It needed closing, or cleaning, or something, and a native got down on his knees and went to work at it. He seemed to be doing it well enough, but perhaps he wasn't, for the burly German put on a look that betrayed dissatisfaction, then without explaining what was wrong, gave the native a brisk cuff on the jaw and then told him where the defect was. It seemed such a shame to do that before us all. The native took it with meekness, saying nothing, and not showing in his face or manner any resentment. I had not seen the like of this for fifty years. It carried me back to my boyhood, and flashed upon me the forgotten fact that this was the usual way of explaining one's desires to a slave. I was able to remember that the method seemed right and natural to me in those days, I being born to it and unaware that elsewhere there were other methods; but I was also able to remember that those unresented cuffings made me sorry for the victim and ashamed for the punisher. My father was a refined and kindly gentleman, very grave, rather austere, of rigid probity, a sternly just and upright man, albeit he attended no church and never spoke of religious matters, and had no part nor lot in the pious joys of his Presbyterian family, nor ever seemed to suffer from this deprivation. He laid his hand upon me in punishment only twice in his life, and then not heavily; once for telling him a lie—which surprised me, and showed me how unsuspicious he was, for that was not my maiden effort. He punished me those two times only, and never any other member of the family at all; yet every now and then he cuffed

our harmless slave boy, Lewis, for trifling little blunders and awkwardnesses. My father had passed his life among the slaves from his cradle up, and his cuffings proceeded from the custom of the time, not from his nature. When I was ten years old I saw a man fling a lump of iron-ore at a slaveman in anger, for merely doing something awkwardly—as if that were a crime. It bounded from the man's skull, and the man fell and never spoke again. He was dead in an hour. I knew the man had a right to kill his slave if he wanted to, and yet it seemed a pitiful thing and somehow wrong, though why wrong I was not deep enough to explain if I had been asked to do it. Nobody in the village approved of that murder, but of course no one said much about it.

It is curious—the space-annihilating power of thought. For just one second, all that goes to make the me in me was in a Missourian village, on the other side of the globe, vividly seeing again these forgotten pictures of fifty years ago, and wholly unconscious of all things but just those; and in the next second I was back in Bombay, and that kneeling native's smitten cheek was not done tingling yet! Back to boyhood— fifty years; back to age again, another fifty; and a flight equal to the circumference of the globe-all in two seconds by the watch!

Some natives—I don't remember how many—went into my bedroom, now, and put things to rights and arranged the mosquito-bar, and I went to bed to nurse my cough. It was about nine in the evening. What a state of things! For three hours the yelling and shouting of natives in the hall continued, along with the velvety patter of their swift bare feet—what a racket it was! They were yelling orders and messages down three flights. Why, in the matter of noise it amounted to a riot, an insurrection, a revolution. And then there were other noises mixed up with these and at intervals tremendously accenting them—roofs falling in, I judged, windows smashing, persons being murdered, crows squawking, and deriding, and cursing, canaries screeching, monkeys jabbering, macaws blaspheming, and every now and then fiendish bursts of laughter and explosions of dynamite. By midnight I had suffered all the different kinds of shocks there are, and knew that I could never more be disturbed by them, either isolated or in combination. Then came peace—stillness deep and solemn and lasted till five.

Then it all broke loose again. And who re-started it? The Bird of Birds the Indian crow. I came to know him well, by and by, and be infatuated with him. I suppose he is the hardest lot that wears feathers. Yes, and the cheerfulest, and the best satisfied with himself. He never arrived at what he is by any careless process, or any sudden one; he is a work of art, and "art is long"; he is the product of immemorial ages, and of deep calculation; one can't make a bird like that in a day. He has been reincarnated more times than Shiva; and he has kept a sample of each incarnation, and fused it into his constitution. In the course of his evolutionary promotions, his sublime march toward ultimate perfection, he has been a gambler, a low comedian, a dissolute priest, a fussy woman, a blackguard, a scoffer, a liar, a thief, a spy, an informer, a trading politician, a swindler, a professional hypocrite, a patriot for cash, a reformer, a lecturer, a lawyer, a conspirator, a rebel, a royalist, a democrat, a practicer and propagator of irreverence, a meddler, an intruder, a busybody, an infidel, and a wallower in sin for the mere love of it. The strange result, the incredible result, of this patient accumulation of all damnable traits is, that be does not know what care is, he does not know what sorrow is, he does not know what remorse is, his life is one long thundering ecstasy of happiness, and he will go to his death untroubled, knowing that he will soon turn up again as an author or something, and be even more intolerably capable and comfortable than ever he was before.

In his straddling wide forward-step, and his springy side-wise series of hops, and his impudent air, and his cunning way of canting his head to one side upon occasion, he reminds one of the American blackbird. But the sharp resemblances stop there. He is much bigger than the blackbird; and he lacks the blackbird's trim and slender and beautiful build and shapely beak; and of course his sober garb of gray and rusty black is a poor and humble thing compared with the splendid lustre of the blackbird's metallic sables and shifting and flashing bronze glories. The blackbird is a perfect gentleman, in deportment and attire, and is not noisy, I believe, except when holding religious services and political conventions in a tree; but this Indian sham Quaker is just a rowdy, and is always noisy when awake—always chaffing, scolding, scoffing, laughing, ripping, and cursing, and carrying on about something or other. I never saw such a bird for delivering opinions. Nothing escapes him; he notices everything that happens, and brings out his opinion about it, particularly if it is a matter that is none of his business. And it is never a mild opinion, but always violent— violent and profane—the presence of ladies does not affect him. His opinions are not the outcome of reflection, for he never thinks about anything, but heaves out the opinion that is on top in his mind, and which is often an opinion about some quite different thing and does not fit the case. But that is his way; his main idea is to get out an opinion, and if he stopped to think he would lose chances.

I suppose he has no enemies among men. The whites and Mohammedans never seemed to molest him; and the Hindoos, because of their religion, never take the life of any creature, but spare even the snakes and tigers and fleas and rats. If I sat on one end of the balcony, the crows would gather on the railing at the other end and talk about me; and edge closer, little by little, till I could almost reach them; and they would sit there, in the most unabashed way, and talk about my clothes, and my hair, and my complexion, and probable character and vocation and politics, and how I came to be in India, and what I had been doing, and how many days I had got for it, and how I had happened to go unhanged so long, and when would it probably come off, and might there be more of my sort where I came from, and when would they be hanged,—and so on, and so on, until I could not longer endure the embarrassment of it; then I would shoo them away, and they would circle around in the air a little while, laughing and deriding and mocking, and presently settle on the rail and do it all over again.

They were very sociable when there was anything to eat— oppressively so. With a little encouragement they would come in and light on the table and help me eat my breakfast; and once when I was in the other room and they found themselves alone, they carried off everything they could lift; and they were particular to choose things which they could make no use of after they got them. In India their number is beyond estimate, and their noise is in proportion. I suppose they cost the country more than the government does; yet that is not a light matter. Still, they pay; their company pays; it would sadden the land to take their cheerful voice out of it.

CHAPTER XXXIX.

By trying we can easily learn to endure adversity. Another man's, I mean. —Pudd'nhead Wilson's New Calendar.

You soon find your long-ago dreams of India rising in a sort of vague and luscious moonlight above the horizon-rim of your opaque consciousness, and softly lighting up a thousand forgotten details which were parts of a vision that had once been vivid to you when you were a boy, and steeped your spirit in tales of the East. The barbaric gorgeousnesses, for instance; and the princely titles, the sumptuous titles, the sounding titles,—how good they taste in the mouth! The Nizam of Hyderabad; the Maharajah of Travancore; the Nabob of Jubbelpore; the Begum of Bhopal; the Nawab of Mysore; the Rance of Gulnare; the Ahkoond of Swat's; the Rao of Rohilkund; the Gaikwar of Baroda. Indeed, it is a country that runs richly to name. The great god Vishnu has 108—108 special ones—108 peculiarly holy ones—names just for Sunday use only. I learned the whole of Vishnu's 108 by heart once, but they wouldn't stay; I don't remember any of them now but John W.

And the romances connected with, those princely native houses—to this day they are always turning up, just as in the old, old times. They were sweating out a romance in an English court in Bombay a while before we were there. In this case a native prince, 16½ years old, who has been enjoying his titles and dignities and estates unmolested for fourteen years, is suddenly haled into court on the charge that he is rightfully no prince at all, but a pauper peasant; that the real prince died when two and one-half years old; that the death was concealed, and a peasant child smuggled into the royal cradle, and that this present incumbent was that smuggled substitute. This is the very material that so many oriental tales have been made of.

The case of that great prince, the Gaikwar of Baroda, is a reversal of the theme. When that throne fell vacant, no heir could be found for some time, but at last one was found in the person of a peasant child who was making mud pies in a village street, and having an innocent good time. But his pedigree was straight; he was the true prince, and he has reigned ever since, with none to dispute his right.

Lately there was another hunt for an heir to another princely house, and one was found who was circumstanced about as the Gaikwar had been. His fathers were traced back, in humble life, along a branch of the ancestral tree to the point where it joined the stem fourteen generations ago, and his heirship was thereby squarely established. The tracing was done by means of the records of one of the great Hindoo shrines, where princes on pilgrimage record their names and the date of their visit. This is to keep the prince's religious account straight, and his spiritual person safe; but the record has the added value of keeping the pedigree authentic, too.

When I think of Bombay now, at this distance of time, I seem to have a kaleidoscope at my eye; and I hear the clash of the glass bits as the splendid figures change, and fall apart, and flash into new forms, figure after figure, and with the birth of each new form I feel my skin crinkle and my nerve-web tingle with a new thrill of wonder and delight. These remembered pictures float past me in a sequence of contracts; following the same order always, and always whirling by and disappearing with the swiftness of a dream, leaving me with the sense that the actuality was the experience of an hour, at most, whereas it really covered days, I think.

The series begins with the hiring of a "bearer"—native man-servant—a person who should be selected with some care, because as long as he is in your employ he will be about as near to you as your clothes.

In India your day may be said to begin with the "bearer's" knock on the bedroom door, accompanied by a formula of, words—a formula which is intended to mean that the bath is ready. It doesn't really seem to mean anything at all. But that is because you are not used to "bearer" English. You will presently understand.

Where he gets his English is his own secret. There is nothing like it elsewhere in the earth; or even in paradise, perhaps, but the other place is probably full of it. You hire him as soon as you touch Indian soil; for no matter what your sex is, you cannot do without him. He is messenger, valet, chambermaid, table-waiter, lady's maid, courier—he is everything. He carries a coarse linen clothes-bag and a quilt; he sleeps on the stone floor outside your chamber door, and gets his meals you do not know where nor when; you only know that he is not fed on the premises, either when you are in a hotel or when you are a guest in a, private house. His wages are large—from an Indian point of view—and he feeds and clothes himself out of them. We had three of him in two and a half months. The first one's rate was thirty rupees a month that is to say, twenty-seven cents a day; the rate of the others, Rs. 40 (40 rupees) a month. A princely sum; for the native switchman on a railway and the native servant in a private family get only Rs. 7 per month, and the farm-hand only 4. The two former feed and clothe themselves and their families on their $1.90 per month; but I cannot believe that the farmhand has to feed himself on his $1.08. I think that the farm probably feeds him, and that the whole of his wages, except a trifle for the priest, go to the support of his family. That is, to the feeding of his family; for they live in a mud hut, hand-made, and, doubtless, rent-free, and they wear no clothes; at least, nothing more than a rag. And not much of a rag at that, in the case of the males. However, these are handsome times for the farm-hand; he was not always the child of luxury that he is now. The Chief Commissioner of the Central Provinces, in a recent official utterance wherein he was rebuking a native deputation for complaining of hard times, reminded them that they could easily remember when a farm-hand's wages were only half a rupee (former value) a month—that is to say, less than a cent a day; nearly $2.90 a year. If such a wage-earner had a good deal of a family—and they all have that, for God is very good to these poor natives in some ways—he would save a profit of fifteen cents, clean and clear, out of his year's toil; I mean a frugal, thrifty person would, not one given to display and ostentation. And if he owed $13.50 and took good care of his health, he could pay it off in ninety years. Then he could hold up his head, and look his creditors in the face again.

Think of these facts and what they mean. India does not consist of cities. There are no cities in India—to speak of. Its stupendous population consists of farm-laborers. India is one vast farm—one almost interminable stretch of fields with mud fences between. . . Think of the above facts; and consider what an incredible aggregate of poverty they place before you.

The first Bearer that applied, waited below and sent up his recommendations. That was the first morning in Bombay. We read them over; carefully, cautiously, thoughtfully. There was not a fault to find with them—except one; they were all from Americans. Is that a slur? If it is, it is a deserved one. In my experience, an American's recommendation of a servant is not usually valuable. We are too good-natured a race; we hate to say the unpleasant thing; we shrink from speaking the unkind truth about a poor fellow whose bread depends upon our verdict; so we speak of his good points only, thus not scrupling to tell a lie—a silent lie—for in not mentioning his bad ones we

as good as say he hasn't any. The only difference that I know of between a silent lie and a spoken one is, that the silent lie is a less respectable one than the other. And it can deceive, whereas the other can't—as a rule. We not only tell the silent lie as to a servant's faults, but we sin in another way: we overpraise his merits; for when it comes to writing recommendations of servants we are a nation of gushers. And we have not the Frenchman's excuse. In France you must give the departing servant a good recommendation; and you must conceal his faults; you have no choice. If you mention his faults for the protection of the next candidate for his services, he can sue you for damages; and the court will award them, too; and, moreover, the judge will give you a sharp dressing-down from the bench for trying to destroy a poor man's character, and rob him of his bread. I do not state this on my own authority, I got it from a French physician of fame and repute—a man who was born in Paris, and had practiced there all his life. And he said that he spoke not merely from common knowledge, but from exasperating personal experience.

As I was saying, the Bearer's recommendations were all from American tourists; and St. Peter would have admitted him to the fields of the blest on them—I mean if he is as unfamiliar with our people and our ways as I suppose he is. According to these recommendations, Manuel X. was supreme in all the arts connected with his complex trade; and these manifold arts were mentioned—and praised-in detail. His English was spoken of in terms of warm admiration—admiration verging upon rapture. I took pleased note of that, and hoped that some of it might be true.

We had to have some one right away; so the family went down stairs and took him a week on trial; then sent him up to me and departed on their affairs. I was shut up in my quarters with a bronchial cough, and glad to have something fresh to look at, something new to play with. Manuel filled the bill; Manuel was very welcome. He was toward fifty years old, tall, slender, with a slight stoop—an artificial stoop, a deferential stoop, a stoop rigidified by long habit—with face of European mould; short hair intensely black; gentle black eyes, timid black eyes, indeed; complexion very dark, nearly black in fact; face smooth-shaven. He was bareheaded and barefooted, and was never otherwise while his week with us lasted; his clothing was European, cheap, flimsy, and showed much wear.

He stood before me and inclined his head (and body) in the pathetic Indian way, touching his forehead with the finger-ends of his right hand, in salute. I said:

"Manuel, you are evidently Indian, but you seem to have a Spanish name when you put it all together. How is that?"

A perplexed look gathered in his face; it was plain that he had not understood—but he didn't let on. He spoke back placidly.

"Name, Manuel. Yes, master."

"I know; but how did you get the name?"

"Oh, yes, I suppose. Think happen so. Father same name, not mother."

I saw that I must simplify my language and spread my words apart, if I would be understood by this English scholar.

"Well—then—how—did—your—father—get—his name?"

"Oh, he,"—brightening a little—"he Christian—Portygee; live in

Goa; I born Goa; mother not Portygee, mother native-high-caste Brahmin—Coolin Brahmin; highest caste; no other so high caste. I high-caste Brahmin, too. Christian, too, same like father; high-caste Christian Brahmin, master—Salvation Army."

All this haltingly, and with difficulty. Then he had an inspiration, and began to pour out a flood of words that I could make nothing of; so I said:

"There—don't do that. I can't understand Hindostani."

"Not Hindostani, master—English. Always I speaking English sometimes when I talking every day all the time at you."

"Very well, stick to that; that is intelligible. It is not up to my hopes, it is not up to the promise of the recommendations, still it is English, and I understand it. Don't elaborate it; I don't like elaborations when they are crippled by uncertainty of touch."

"Master?"

"Oh, never mind; it was only a random thought; I didn't expect you to understand it. How did you get your English; is it an acquirement, or just a gift of God?"

After some hesitation—piously:

"Yes, he very good. Christian god very good, Hindoo god very good, too. Two million Hindoo god, one Christian god—make two million and one. All mine; two million and one god. I got a plenty. Sometime I pray all time at those, keep it up, go all time every day; give something at shrine, all good for me, make me better man; good for me, good for my family, dam good."

Then he had another inspiration, and went rambling off into fervent confusions and incoherencies, and I had to stop him again. I thought we had talked enough, so I told him to go to the bathroom and clean it up and remove the slops—this to get rid of him. He went away, seeming to understand, and got out some of my clothes and began to brush them. I repeated my desire several times, simplifying and re-simplifying it, and at last he got the idea. Then he went away and put a coolie at the work, and explained that he would lose caste if he did it himself; it would be pollution, by the law of his caste, and it would cost him a deal of fuss and trouble to purify himself and accomplish his rehabilitation. He said that that kind of work was strictly forbidden to persons of caste, and as strictly restricted to the very bottom layer of Hindoo society—the despised 'Sudra' (the toiler, the laborer). He was right; and apparently the poor Sudra has been content with his strange lot, his insulting distinction, for ages and ages—clear back to the beginning of things, so to speak. Buckle says that his name—laborer—is a term of contempt; that it is ordained by the Institutes of Menu (900 B.C.) that if a Sudra sit on a level with his superior he shall be exiled or branded—[Without going into particulars I will remark that as a rule they wear no clothing that would conceal the brand.—M. T.]. . . ; if he speak contemptuously of his superior or insult him he shall suffer death; if he listen to the reading of the sacred books he shall have burning oil poured in his ears; if he memorize passages from them he shall be killed; if he marry his daughter to a Brahmin the husband shall go to hell for defiling himself by contact with a woman so infinitely his inferior; and that it is forbidden to a Sudra to acquire wealth. "The bulk of the population of India," says Bucklet—[Population to-day, 300,000,000.] —"is the Sudras—the workers, the farmers, the

creators of wealth."

Manuel was a failure, poor old fellow. His age was against him. He was desperately slow and phenomenally forgetful. When he went three blocks on an errand he would be gone two hours, and then forget what it was he went for. When he packed a trunk it took him forever, and the trunk's contents were an unimaginable chaos when he got done. He couldn't wait satisfactorily at table—a prime defect, for if you haven't your own servant in an Indian hotel you are likely to have a slow time of it and go away hungry. We couldn't understand his English; he couldn't understand ours; and when we found that he couldn't understand his own, it seemed time for us to part. I had to discharge him; there was no help for it. But I did it as kindly as I could, and as gently. We must part, said I, but I hoped we should meet again in a better world. It was not true, but it was only a little thing to say, and saved his feelings and cost me nothing.

But now that he was gone, and was off my mind and heart, my spirits began to rise at once, and I was soon feeling brisk and ready to go out and have adventures. Then his newly-hired successor flitted in, touched his forehead, and began to fly around here, there, and everywhere, on his velvet feet, and in five minutes he had everything in the room "ship-shape and Bristol fashion," as the sailors say, and was standing at the salute, waiting for orders. Dear me, what a rustler he was after the slumbrous way of Manuel, poor old slug! All my heart, all my affection, all my admiration, went out spontaneously to this frisky little forked black thing, this compact and compressed incarnation of energy and force and promptness and celerity and confidence, this smart, smily, engaging, shiney-eyed little devil, feruled on his upper end by a gleaming fire-coal of a fez with a red-hot tassel dangling from it. I said, with deep satisfaction—

"You'll suit. What is your name?"

He reeled it mellowly off.

"Let me see if I can make a selection out of it—for business uses, I mean; we will keep the rest for Sundays. Give it to me in installments."

He did it. But there did not seem to be any short ones, except Mousawhich suggested mouse. It was out of character; it was too soft, too quiet, too conservative; it didn't fit his splendid style. I considered, and said—

"Mousa is short enough, but I don't quite like it. It seems colorless —inharmonious—inadequate; and I am sensitive to such things. How do you think Satan would do?"

"Yes, master. Satan do wair good."

It was his way of saying "very good."

There was a rap at the door. Satan covered the ground with a single skip; there was a word or two of Hindostani, then he disappeared. Three minutes later he was before me again, militarily erect, and waiting for me to speak first.

"What is it, Satan?"

"God want to see you."

"Who?"

"God. I show him up, master?"

"Why, this is so unusual, that—that—well, you see indeed I am so unprepared—I don't quite know what I do mean. Dear me, can't you explain? Don't you see that this is a most ex—"

"Here his card, master."

Wasn't it curious—and amazing, and tremendous, and all that? Such a personage going around calling on such as I, and sending up his card, like a mortal—sending it up by Satan. It was a bewildering collision of the impossibles. But this was the land of the Arabian Nights, this was India! and what is it that cannot happen in India?

We had the interview. Satan was right—the Visitor was indeed a God in the conviction of his multitudinous followers, and was worshiped by them in sincerity and humble adoration. They are troubled by no doubts as to his divine origin and office. They believe in him, they pray to him, they make offerings to him, they beg of him remission of sins; to them his person, together with everything connected with it, is sacred; from his barber they buy the parings of his nails and set them in gold, and wear them as precious amulets.

I tried to seem tranquilly conversational and at rest, but I was not. Would you have been? I was in a suppressed frenzy of excitement and curiosity and glad wonder. I could not keep my eyes off him. I was looking upon a god, an actual god, a recognized and accepted god; and every detail of his person and his dress had a consuming interest for me. And the thought went floating through my head, "He is worshiped—think of it—he is not a recipient of the pale homage called compliment, wherewith the highest human clay must make shift to be satisfied, but of an infinitely richer spiritual food: adoration, worship!—men and women lay their cares and their griefs and their broken hearts at his feet; and he gives them his peace; and they go away healed."

And just then the Awful Visitor said, in the simplest way— "There is a feature of the philosophy of Huck Finn which"— and went luminously on with the construction of a compact and nicely-discriminated literary verdict.

It is a land of surprises—India! I had had my ambitions—I had hoped, and almost expected, to be read by kings and presidents and emperors—but I had never looked so high as That. It would be false modesty to pretend that I was not inordinately pleased. I was. I was much more pleased than I should have been with a compliment from a man.

He remained half an hour, and I found him a most courteous and charming gentleman. The godship has been in his family a good while, but I do not know how long. He is a Mohammedan deity; by earthly rank he is a prince; not an Indian but a Persian prince. He is a direct descendant of the Prophet's line. He is comely; also young—for a god; not forty, perhaps not above thirty-five years old. He wears his immense honors with tranquil brace, and with a dignity proper to his awful calling. He speaks English with the ease and purity of a person born to it. I think I am not overstating this. He was the only god I had ever seen, and I was very favorably impressed. When he rose to say good-bye, the door swung open and I caught the flash of a red fez, and heard these words, reverently said—

"Satan see God out?"

"Yes." And these mis-mated Beings passed from view Satan in

the lead and The Other following after.

CHAPTER XL.

Few of us can stand prosperity. Another man's, I mean. — Pudd'nhead Wilson's New Calendar.

The next picture in my mind is Government House, on Malabar Point, with the wide sea-view from the windows and broad balconies; abode of His Excellency the Governor of the Bombay Presidency—a residence which is European in everything but the native guards and servants, and is a home and a palace of state harmoniously combined.

That was England, the English power, the English civilization, the modern civilization—with the quiet elegancies and quiet colors and quiet tastes and quiet dignity that are the outcome of the modern cultivation. And following it came a picture of the ancient civilization of India—an hour in the mansion of a native prince: Kumar Schri Samatsinhji Bahadur of the Palitana State.

The young lad, his heir, was with the prince; also, the lad's sister, a wee brown sprite, very pretty, very serious, very winning, delicately moulded, costumed like the daintiest butterfly, a dear little fairyland princess, gravely willing to be friendly with the strangers, but in the beginning preferring to hold her father's hand until she could take stock of them and determine how far they were to be trusted. She must have been eight years old; so in the natural (Indian) order of things she would be a bride in three or four years from now, and then this free contact with the sun and the air and the other belongings of out-door nature and comradeship with visiting male folk would end, and she would shut herself up in the zenana for life, like her mother, and by inherited habit of mind would be happy in that seclusion and not look upon it as an irksome restraint and a weary captivity.

The game which the prince amuses his leisure with—however, never mind it, I should never be able to describe it intelligibly. I tried to get an idea of it while my wife and daughter visited the princess in the zenana, a lady of charming graces and a fluent speaker of English, but I did not make it out. It is a complicated game, and I believe it is said that nobody can learn to play it well—but an Indian. And I was not able to learn how to wind a turban. It seemed a simple art and easy; but that was a deception. It is a piece of thin, delicate stuff a foot wide or more, and forty or fifty feet long; and the exhibitor of the art takes one end of it in his hands, and winds it in and out intricately about his head, twisting it as he goes, and in a minute or two the thing is finished, and is neat and symmetrical and fits as snugly as a mould.

We were interested in the wardrobe and the jewels, and in the silverware, and its grace of shape and beauty and delicacy of ornamentation. The silverware is kept locked up, except at meal-times, and none but the chief butler and the prince have keys to the safe. I did not clearly understand why, but it was not for the protection of the silver. It was either to protect the prince from the contamination which his caste would suffer if the vessels were touched by low-caste hands, or it was to protect his highness from poison. Possibly it was both. I believe a salaried taster has to taste everything before the prince ventures it—an ancient and judicious custom in the East, and has thinned out the tasters a good deal, for of course it is the cook that puts the poison in. If I were an Indian prince I would not go to the expense of a taster, I would eat with the cook.

Ceremonials are always interesting; and I noted that the Indian good-morning is a ceremonial, whereas ours doesn't amount to that. In salutation the son reverently touches the father's forehead with a small silver implement tipped with vermillion paste which leaves a red spot there, and in return the son receives the father's blessing. Our good morning is well enough for the rowdy West, perhaps, but would be too brusque for the soft and ceremonious East.

After being properly necklaced, according to custom, with great garlands made of yellow flowers, and provided with betel-nut to chew, this pleasant visit closed, and we passed thence to a scene of a different sort: from this glow of color and this sunny life to those grim receptacles of the Parsee dead, the Towers of Silence. There is something stately about that name, and an impressiveness which sinks deep; the hush of death is in it. We have the Grave, the Tomb, the Mausoleum, God's Acre, the Cemetery; and association has made them eloquent with solemn meaning; but we have no name that is so majestic as that one, or lingers upon the ear with such deep and haunting pathos.

On lofty ground, in the midst of a paradise of tropical foliage and flowers, remote from the world and its turmoil and noise, they stood—the Towers of Silence; and away below was spread the wide groves of cocoa palms, then the city, mile on mile, then the ocean with its fleets of creeping ships all steeped in a stillness as deep as the hush that hallowed this high place of the dead. The vultures were there. They stood close together in a great circle all around the rim of a massive low tower—waiting; stood as motionless as sculptured ornaments, and indeed almost deceived one into the belief that that was what they were. Presently there was a slight stir among the score of persons present, and all moved reverently out of the path and ceased from talking. A funeral procession entered the great gate, marching two and two, and moved silently by, toward the Tower. The corpse lay in a shallow shell, and was under cover of a white cloth, but was otherwise naked. The bearers of the body were separated by an interval of thirty feet from the mourners. They, and also the mourners, were draped all in pure white, and each couple of mourners was figuratively bound together by a piece of white rope or a handkerchief—though they merely held the ends of it in their hands. Behind the procession followed a dog, which was led in a leash. When the mourners had reached the neighborhood of the Tower — neither they nor any other human being but the bearers of the dead must approach within thirty feet of it—they turned and went back to one of the prayer-houses within the gates, to pray for the spirit of their dead. The bearers unlocked the Tower's sole door and disappeared from view within. In a little while they came out bringing the bier and the white covering-cloth, and locked the door again. Then the ring of vultures rose, flapping their wings, and swooped down into the Tower to devour the body. Nothing was left of it but a clean-picked skeleton when they flocked-out again a few minutes afterward.

The principle which underlies and orders everything connected with a Parsee funeral is Purity. By the tenets of the Zoroastrian religion, the elements, Earth, Fire, and Water, are sacred, and must not be contaminated by contact with a dead body. Hence corpses must not be burned, neither must they be buried. None may touch the dead or enter the Towers where they repose except certain men who are officially appointed for that purpose. They receive high pay, but theirs is a dismal life, for they must live apart from their species, because their commerce with the dead defiles them, and any who should associate with them would share their defilement. When they come out of the Tower the clothes they are wearing are exchanged for others, in a building within the grounds, and the ones which they have taken off are left behind, for they are contaminated, and must never be used again or suffered to go outside the grounds. These bearers come to every funeral in new garments. So far as is known, no human being, other than an official corpse-bearer—save one—has ever entered a Tower of Silence after its consecration. Just a hundred years ago a European rushed in behind the bearers and fed his brutal curiosity with a glimpse of the forbidden mysteries of the place. This shabby savage's name is not given; his quality is also concealed. These two details, taken in connection with the fact that for his extraordinary offense the only punishment he got from the East India Company's Government was a solemn official "reprimand"—suggest the suspicion that he was a European of consequence. The same public document which contained the reprimand gave warning that future offenders of his sort, if in the Company's service, would be dismissed; and if merchants, suffer revocation of license and exile to England.

The Towers are not tall, but are low in proportion to their circumference, like a gasometer. If you should fill a gasometer half way up with solid granite masonry, then drive a wide and deep well down through the center of this mass of masonry, you would have the idea of a Tower of Silence. On the masonry surrounding the well the bodies lie, in shallow trenches which radiate like wheel-spokes from the well. The trenches slant toward the well and carry into it the rainfall. Underground drains, with charcoal filters in them, carry off this water from the bottom of the well.

When a skeleton has lain in the Tower exposed to the rain and the flaming sun a month it is perfectly dry and clean. Then the same bearers that brought it there come gloved and take it up with tongs and throw it into the well. There it turns to dust. It is never seen again, never touched again, in the world. Other peoples separate their dead, and preserve and continue social distinctions in the grave—the skeletons of kings and statesmen and generals in temples and pantheons proper to skeletons of their degree, and the skeletons of the commonplace and the poor in places suited to their meaner estate; but the Parsees hold that all men rank alike in death—all are humble, all poor, all destitute. In sign of their poverty they are sent to their grave naked, in sign of their equality the bones of the rich, the poor, the illustrious and the obscure are flung into the common well together. At a Parsee funeral there are no vehicles; all concerned must walk, both rich and poor, howsoever great the distance to be traversed may be. In the wells of the Five Towers of Silence is mingled the dust of all the Parsee men and women and children who have died in Bombay and its vicinity during the two centuries which have elapsed since the Mohammedan conquerors drove the Parsees out of Persia, and into that region of India. The earliest of the five towers was built by the Modi family something more than 200 years ago, and it is now reserved to the heirs of that house; none but the dead of that blood are carried thither.

The origin of at least one of the details of a Parsee funeral is not now known—the presence of the dog. Before a corpse is borne from the house of mourning it must be uncovered and exposed to the gaze of a dog; a dog must also be led in the rear of the funeral. Mr. Nusserwanjee Byranjee, Secretary to the Parsee Punchayet, said that these formalities had once had a meaning and a reason for their institution, but that they were survivals whose origin none could now account for. Custom and tradition continue them in force, antiquity hallows them. It is thought that in ancient times in Persia the dog was a sacred animal and could guide souls to heaven; also that his

Following The Equator 749

eye had the power of purifying objects which had been contaminated by the touch of the dead; and that hence his presence with the funeral cortege provides an ever-applicable remedy in case of need.

The Parsees claim that their method of disposing of the dead is an effective protection of the living; that it disseminates no corruption, no impurities of any sort, no disease-germs; that no wrap, no garment which has touched the dead is allowed to touch the living afterward; that from the Towers of Silence nothing proceeds which can carry harm to the outside world. These are just claims, I think. As a sanitary measure, their system seems to be about the equivalent of cremation, and as sure. We are drifting slowly—but hopefully—toward cremation in these days. It could not be expected that this progress should be swift, but if it be steady and continuous, even if slow, that will suffice. When cremation becomes the rule we shall cease to shudder at it; we should shudder at burial if we allowed ourselves to think what goes on in the grave.

The dog was an impressive figure to me, representing as he did a mystery whose key is lost. He was humble, and apparently depressed; and he let his head droop pensively, and looked as if he might be trying to call back to his mind what it was that he had used to symbolize ages ago when he began his function. There was another impressive thing close at hand, but I was not privileged to see it. That was the sacred fire—a fire which is supposed to have been burning without interruption for more than two centuries; and so, living by the same heat that was imparted to it so long ago.

The Parsees are a remarkable community. There are only about 60,000 in Bombay, and only about half as many as that in the rest of India; but they make up in importance what they lack in numbers. They are highly educated, energetic, enterprising, progressive, rich, and the Jew himself is not more lavish or catholic in his charities and benevolences. The Parsees build and endow hospitals, for both men and animals; and they and their womenkind keep an open purse for all great and good objects. They are a political force, and a valued support to the government. They have a pure and lofty religion, and they preserve it in its integrity and order their lives by it.

We took a final sweep of the wonderful view of plain and city and ocean, and so ended our visit to the garden and the Towers of Silence; and the last thing I noticed was another symbol—a voluntary symbol this one; it was a vulture standing on the sawed-off top of a tall and slender and branchless palm in an open space in the ground; he was perfectly motionless, and looked like a piece of sculpture on a pillar. And he had a mortuary look, too, which was in keeping with the place.

CHAPTER XLI.

There is an old-time toast which is golden for its beauty. "When you ascend the hill of prosperity may you not meet a friend." —Pudd'nhead Wilson's New Calendar.

The next picture that drifts across the field of my memory is one which is connected with religious things. We were taken by friends to see a Jain temple. It was small, and had many flags or streamers flying from poles standing above its roof; and its little battlements supported a great many small idols or images. Upstairs, inside, a solitary Jain was praying or reciting aloud in the middle of the room. Our presence did not interrupt him, nor even incommode him or modify his fervor. Ten or twelve feet in front of him was the idol, a small figure in

a sitting posture. It had the pinkish look of a wax doll, but lacked the doll's roundness of limb and approximation to correctness of form and justness of proportion. Mr. Gandhi explained every thing to us. He was delegate to the Chicago Fair Congress of Religions. It was lucidly done, in masterly English, but in time it faded from me, and now I have nothing left of that episode but an impression: a dim idea of a religious belief clothed in subtle intellectual forms, lofty and clean, barren of fleshly grossnesses; and with this another dim impression which connects that intellectual system somehow with that crude image, that inadequate idol —how, I do not know. Properly they do not seem to belong together. Apparently the idol symbolized a person who had become a saint or a god through accessions of steadily augmenting holiness acquired through a series of reincarnations and promotions extending over many ages; and was now at last a saint and qualified to vicariously receive worship and transmit it to heaven's chancellery. Was that it?

And thence we went to Mr. Premchand Roychand's bungalow, in Lovelane, Byculla, where an Indian prince was to receive a deputation of the Jain community who desired to congratulate him upon a high honor lately conferred upon him by his sovereign, Victoria, Empress of India. She had made him a knight of the order of the Star of India. It would seem that even the grandest Indian prince is glad to add the modest title "Sir" to his ancient native grandeurs, and is willing to do valuable service to win it. He will remit taxes liberally, and will spend money freely upon the betterment of the condition of his subjects, if there is a knighthood to be gotten by it. And he will also do good work and a deal of it to get a gun added to the salute allowed him by the British Government. Every year the Empress distributes knighthoods and adds guns for public services done by native princes. The salute of a small prince is three or four guns; princes of greater consequence have salutes that run higher and higher, gun by gun,—oh, clear away up to eleven; possibly more, but I did not hear of any above eleven-gun princes. I was told that when a four-gun prince gets a gun added, he is pretty troublesome for a while, till the novelty wears off, for he likes the music, and keeps hunting up pretexts to get himself saluted. It may be that supremely grand folk, like the Nyzam of Hyderabad and the Gaikwar of Baroda, have more than eleven guns, but I don't know.

When we arrived at the bungalow, the large hall on the ground floor was already about full, and carriages were still flowing into the grounds. The company present made a fine show, an exhibition of human fireworks, so to speak, in the matters of costume and comminglings of brilliant color. The variety of form noticeable in the display of turbans was remarkable. We were told that the explanation of this was, that this Jain delegation was drawn from many parts of India, and that each man wore the turban that was in vogue in his own region. This diversity of turbans made a beautiful effect.

I could have wished to start a rival exhibition there, of Christian hats and clothes. I would have cleared one side of the room of its Indian splendors and repacked the space with Christians drawn from America, England, and the Colonies, dressed in the hats and habits of now, and of twenty and forty and fifty years ago. It would have been a hideous exhibition, a thoroughly devilish spectacle. Then there would have been the added disadvantage of the white complexion. It is not an unbearably unpleasant complexion when it keeps to itself, but when it comes into competition with masses of brown and black the fact is betrayed that it is endurable only because we are used to it. Nearly all black and brown skins are beautiful, but a beautiful white skin is rare. How rare, one may learn by walking down a street in Paris, New York, or London on a week-day particularly an unfashionable street—and keeping count of the satisfactory complexions encountered in the course of a mile. Where dark complexions are massed, they make the whites look bleached-out, unwholesome, and sometimes frankly ghastly. I could notice this as a boy, down South in the slavery days before the war. The splendid black satin skin of the South African Zulus of Durban seemed to me to come very close to perfection. I can see those Zulus yet— 'ricksha athletes waiting in front of the hotel for custom; handsome and intensely black creatures, moderately clothed in loose summer stuffs whose snowy whiteness made the black all the blacker by contrast. Keeping that group in my mind, I can compare those complexions with the white ones which are streaming past this London window now:

A lady. Complexion, new parchment. Another lady. Complexion, old parchment.

Another. Pink and white, very fine.

Man. Grayish skin, with purple areas.

Man. Unwholesome fish-belly skin.

Girl. Sallow face, sprinkled with freckles.

Old woman. Face whitey-gray.

Young butcher. Face a general red flush.

Jaundiced man—mustard yellow.

Elderly lady. Colorless skin, with two conspicuous moles.

Elderly man—a drinker. Boiled-cauliflower nose in a flabby face veined with purple crinklings.

Healthy young gentleman. Fine fresh complexion.

Sick young man. His face a ghastly white.

No end of people whose skins are dull and characterless modifications of the tint which we miscall white. Some of these faces are pimply; some exhibit other signs of diseased blood; some show scars of a tint out of a harmony with the surrounding shades of color. The white man's complexion makes no concealments. It can't. It seemed to have been designed as a catch-all for everything that can damage it. Ladies have to paint it, and powder it, and cosmetic it, and diet it with arsenic, and enamel it, and be always enticing it, and persuading it, and pestering it, and fussing at it, to make it beautiful; and they do not succeed. But these efforts show what they think of the natural complexion, as distributed. As distributed it needs these helps. The complexion which they try to counterfeit is one which nature restricts to the few—to the very few. To ninety-nine persons she gives a bad complexion, to the hundredth a good one. The hundredth can keep it—how long? Ten years, perhaps.

The advantage is with the Zulu, I think. He starts with a beautiful complexion, and it will last him through. And as for the Indian brown —firm, smooth, blemishless, pleasant and restful to the eye, afraid of no color, harmonizing with all colors and adding a grace to them all—I think there is no sort of chance for the average white complexion against that rich and perfect tint.

To return to the bungalow. The most gorgeous costume present were worn by some children. They seemed to blaze, so bright were the colors, and so brilliant the jewels strum over the rich materials. These children were professional nautch-dancers, and looked like girls, but they were boys, They got up by ones and twos and fours, and danced and sang to an accompaniment of weird music. Their posturings and gesturings were elaborate and graceful, but their voices were stringently raspy and unpleasant, and there was a good deal of monotony about the tune.

By and by there was a burst of shouts and cheers outside and the prince with his train entered in fine dramatic style. He was a stately man, he was ideally costumed, and fairly festooned with ropes of gems; some of the ropes were of pearls, some were of uncut great emeralds—emeralds renowned in Bombay for their quality and value. Their size was marvelous, and enticing to the eye, those rocks. A boy—a princeling —was with the prince, and he also was a radiant exhibition.

The ceremonies were not tedious. The prince strode to his throne with the port and majesty—and the sternness—of a Julius Caesar coming to receive and receipt for a back-country kingdom and have it over and get out, and no fooling. There was a throne for the young prince, too, and the two sat there, side by side, with their officers grouped at either hand and most accurately and creditably reproducing the pictures which one sees in the books—pictures which people in the prince's line of business have been furnishing ever since Solomon received the Queen of Sheba and showed her his things. The chief of the Jain delegation read his paper of congratulations, then pushed it into a beautifully engraved silver cylinder, which was delivered with ceremony into the prince's hands and at once delivered by him without ceremony into the hands of an officer. I will copy the address here. It is interesting, as showing what an Indian prince's subject may have opportunity to thank him for in these days of modern English rule, as contrasted with what his ancestor would have given them opportunity to thank him for a century and a half ago—the days of freedom unhampered by English interference. A century and a half ago an address of thanks could have been put into small space. It would have thanked the prince—

1. For not slaughtering too many of his people upon mere caprice;

2. For not stripping them bare by sudden and arbitrary tax levies, and bringing famine upon them;

3. For not upon empty pretext destroying the rich and seizing their property;

4. For not killing, blinding, imprisoning, or banishing the relatives of the royal house to protect the throne from possible plots;

5. For not betraying the subject secretly, for a bribe, into the hands of bands of professional Thugs, to be murdered and robbed in the prince's back lot.

Those were rather common princely industries in the old times, but they and some others of a harsh sort ceased long ago under English rule. Better industries have taken their place, as this Address from the Jain community will show:

"Your Highness,—We the undersigned members of the Jain community of Bombay have the pleasure to approach your

Highness with the expression of our heartfelt congratulations on the recent conference on your Highness of the Knighthood of the Most Exalted Order of the Star of India. Ten years ago we had the pleasure and privilege of welcoming your Highness to this city under circumstances which have made a memorable epoch in the history of your State, for had it not been for a generous and reasonable spirit that your Highness displayed in the negotiations between the Palitana Durbar and the Jain community, the conciliatory spirit that animated our people could not have borne fruit. That was the first step in your Highness's administration, and it fitly elicited the praise of the Jain community, and of the Bombay Government. A decade of your Highness's administration, combined with the abilities, training, and acquirements that your Highness brought to bear upon it, has justly earned for your Highness the unique and honourable distinction—the Knighthood of the Most Exalted Order of the Star of India, which we understand your Highness is the first to enjoy among Chiefs of your, Highness's rank and standing. And we assure your Highness that for this mark of honour that has been conferred on you by Her Most Gracious Majesty, the Queen-Empress, we feel no less proud than your Highness. Establishment of commercial factories, schools, hospitals, etc., by your Highness in your State has marked your Highness's career during these ten years, and we trust that your Highness will be spared to rule over your people with wisdom and foresight, and foster the many reforms that your Highness has been pleased to introduce in your State. We again offer your Highness our warmest felicitations for the honour that has been conferred on you. We beg to remain your Highness's obedient servants."

Factories, schools, hospitals, reforms. The prince propagates that kind of things in the modern times, and gets knighthood and guns for it.

After the address the prince responded with snap and brevity; spoke a moment with half a dozen guests in English, and with an official or two in a native tongue; then the garlands were distributed as usual, and the function ended.

CHAPTER XLII.

Each person is born to one possession which outvalues all his others—his last breath. —Pudd'nhead Wilson's New Calendar.

Toward midnight, that night, there was another function. This was a Hindoo wedding—no, I think it was a betrothal ceremony. Always before, we had driven through streets that were multitudinous and tumultuous with picturesque native life, but now there was nothing of that. We seemed to move through a city of the dead. There was hardly a suggestion of life in those still and vacant streets. Even the crows were silent. But everywhere on the ground lay sleeping natives-hundreds and hundreds. They lay stretched at full length and tightly wrapped in blankets, beads and all. Their attitude and their rigidity counterfeited death. The plague was not in Bombay then, but it is devastating the city now. The shops are deserted, now, half of the people have fled, and of the remainder the smitten perish by shoals every day. No doubt the city looks now in the daytime as it looked then at night. When we had pierced deep into the native quarter and were threading its narrow dim lanes, we had to go carefully, for men were stretched asleep all about and there was hardly room to drive between them. And every now and then a swarm of rats would scamper across past the horses' feet in the vague light—the forbears of the rats that are carrying the plague from house to house in Bombay now. The shops were but sheds, little booths open to the street; and the goods had been removed, and on the counters families were sleeping, usually with an oil lamp present. Recurrent dead watches, it looked like.

But at last we turned a corner and saw a great glare of light ahead. It was the home of the bride, wrapped in a perfect conflagration of illuminations,—mainly gas-work designs, gotten up specially for the occasion. Within was abundance of brilliancy—flames, costumes, colors, decorations, mirrors—it was another Aladdin show.

The bride was a trim and comely little thing of twelve years, dressed as we would dress a boy, though more expensively than we should do it, of course. She moved about very much at her ease, and stopped and talked with the guests and allowed her wedding jewelry to be examined. It was very fine. Particularly a rope of great diamonds, a lovely thing to look at and handle. It had a great emerald hanging to it.

The bridegroom was not present. He was having betrothal festivities of his own at his father's house. As I understood it, he and the bride were to entertain company every night and nearly all night for a week or more, then get married, if alive. Both of the children were a little elderly, as brides and grooms go, in India—twelve; they ought to have been married a year or two sooner; still to a, stranger twelve seems quite young enough.

A while after midnight a couple of celebrated and high-priced nautch-girls appeared in the gorgeous place, and danced and sang. With them were men who played upon strange instruments which made uncanny noises of a sort to make one's flesh creep. One of these instruments was a pipe, and to its music the girls went through a performance which represented snake charming. It seemed a doubtful sort of music to charm anything with, but a native gentleman assured me that snakes like it and will come out of their holes and listen to it with every evidence of refreshment And gratitude. He said that at an entertainment in his grounds once, the pipe brought out half a dozen snakes, and the music had to be stopped before they would be persuaded to go. Nobody wanted their company, for they were bold, familiar, and dangerous; but no one would kill them, of course, for it is sinful for a Hindoo to kill any kind of a creature.

We withdrew from the festivities at two in the morning. Another picture, then—but it has lodged itself in my memory rather as a stage-scene than as a reality. It is of a porch and short flight of steps crowded with dark faces and ghostly-white draperies flooded with the strong glare from the dazzling concentration of illuminations; and midway of the steps one conspicuous figure for accent—a turbaned giant, with a name according to his size: Rao Bahadur Baskirao Balinkanje Pitale, Vakeel to his Highness the Gaikwar of Baroda. Without him the picture would not have been complete; and if his name had been merely Smith, he wouldn't have answered. Close at hand on house-fronts on both sides of the narrow street were illuminations of a kind commonly employed by the natives — scores of glass tumblers (containing tapers) fastened a few in inches apart all over great latticed frames, forming starry constellations which showed out vividly against their black back grounds. As we drew away into the distance down the dim lanes the illuminations gathered together into a single mass, and glowed out of the enveloping darkness like a sun.

Then again the deep silence, the skurrying rats, the dim forms stretched every-where on the ground; and on either hand those open booths counterfeiting sepulchres, with counterfeit corpses sleeping motionless in the flicker of the counterfeit death lamps. And now, a year later, when I read the cablegrams I seem to be reading of what I myself partly saw—saw before it happened—in a prophetic dream, as it were. One cablegram says, "Business in the native town is about suspended. Except the wailing and the tramp of the funerals. There is but little life or movement. The closed shops exceed in number those that remain open." Another says that 325,000 of the people have fled the city and are carrying the plague to the country. Three days later comes the news, "The population is reduced by half." The refugees have carried the disease to Karachi; "220 cases, 214 deaths." A day or two later, "52 fresh cases, all of which proved fatal."

The plague carries with it a terror which no other disease can excite; for of all diseases known to men it is the deadliest—by far the deadliest. "Fifty-two fresh cases—all fatal." It is the Black Death alone that slays like that. We can all imagine, after a fashion, the desolation of a plague-stricken city, and the stupor of stillness broken at intervals by distant bursts of wailing, marking the passing of funerals, here and there and yonder, but I suppose it is not possible for us to realize to ourselves the nightmare of dread and fear that possesses the living who are present in such a place and cannot get away. That half million fled from Bombay in a wild panic suggests to us something of what they were feeling, but perhaps not even they could realize what the half million were feeling whom they left stranded behind to face the stalking horror without chance of escape. Kinglake was in Cairo many years ago during an epidemic of the Black Death, and he has imagined the terrors that creep into a man's heart at such a time and follow him until they themselves breed the fatal sign in the armpit, and then the delirium with confused images, and home-dreams, and reeling billiard-tables, and then the sudden blank of death:

"To the contagionist, filled as he is with the dread of final causes, having no faith in destiny, nor in the fixed will of God, and with none of the devil-may-care indifference which might stand him instead of creeds—to such one, every rag that shivers in the breeze of a plague-stricken city has this sort of sublimity. If by any terrible ordinance he be forced to venture forth, he sees death dangling from every sleeve; and, as he creeps forward, he poises his shuddering limbs between the imminent jacket that is stabbing at his right elbow and the murderous pelisse that threatens to mow him clean down as it sweeps along on his left. But most of all he dreads that which most of all he should love—the touch of a woman's dress; for mothers and wives, hurrying forth on kindly errands from the bedsides of the dying, go slouching along through the streets more willfully and less courteously than the men. For a while it may be that the caution of the poor Levantine may enable him to avoid contact, but sooner or later, perhaps, the dreaded chance arrives; that bundle of linen, with the dark tearful eyes at the top of it, that labors along with the voluptuous clumsiness of Grisi —she has touched the poor Levantine with the hem of her sleeve! From that dread moment his peace is gone; his mind for ever hanging upon the fatal touch invites the blow which he fears; he watches for the symptoms of plague so carefully, that sooner or later they come in truth. The parched mouth is a sign—his mouth is parched; the throbbing brain—his brain does throb; the rapid pulse—he touches his own wrist (for he dares not ask counsel of any man lest he be deserted), he touches his wrist, and feels how his frighted blood goes galloping out of his heart. There is nothing but the fatal swelling that is wanting to make his sad conviction complete; immediately, he has an odd feel under the arm—no pain, but a little straining of the skin; he would to God it were his fancy that were strong enough to give him that sensation; this is the worst of all. It now seems to him that he could be happy and contented with his parched mouth, and his throbbing brain, and his rapid pulse, if only he could know that there were no swelling under the left arm; but dares he try?—in a moment of calmness and deliberation he dares not; but when for a while he has writhed under the torture of suspense, a sudden strength of will drives him to seek and know his fate; he touches the gland, and finds the skin sane and sound but under the cuticle there lies a small lump like a pistol-bullet, that moves as he pushes it. Oh! but is this for all certainty, is this the sentence of death? Feel the gland of the other arm. There is not the same lump exactly, yet something a little like it. Have not some people glands naturally enlarged?—would to heaven he were one! So he does for himself the work of the plague, and when the Angel of Death thus courted does indeed and in truth come, he has only to finish that which has been so well begun; he passes his fiery hand over the brain of the victim, and lets him rave for a season, but all chance-wise, of people and things once dear, or of people and things indifferent. Once more the poor fellow is back at his home in fair Provence, and sees the sundial that stood in his childhood's garden—sees his mother, and the long-since forgotten face of that little dear sister—(he sees her, he says, on a Sunday morning, for all the church bells are ringing); he looks up and down through the universe, and owns it well piled with bales upon bales of cotton, and cotton eternal—so much so that he feels—he knows—he swears he could make that winning hazard, if the billiard-table would not slant upwards, and if the cue were a cue worth playing with; but it is not—it's a cue that won't move—his own arm won't move—in short, there's the devil to pay in the brain of the poor Levantine; and perhaps, the next night but one he becomes the 'life and the soul' of some squalling jackal family, who fish him out by the foot from his shallow and sandy grave."

CHAPTER XLIII.

Hunger is the handmaid of genius —Pudd'nhead Wilson's New Calendar.

One day during our stay in Bombay there was a criminal trial of a most interesting sort, a terribly realistic chapter out of the "Arabian Nights," a strange mixture of simplicities and pieties and murderous practicalities, which brought back the forgotten days of Thuggee and made them live again; in fact, even made them believable. It was a case where a young girl had been assassinated for the sake of her trifling ornaments, things not worth a laborer's day's wages in America. This thing could have been done in many other countries, but hardly with the cold business-like depravity, absence of fear, absence of caution, destitution of the sense of horror, repentance, remorse, exhibited in this case. Elsewhere the murderer would have done his crime secretly, by night, and without witnesses; his fears would have allowed him no peace while the dead body was in his neighborhood; he would not have rested until he had gotten it safe out of the way and hidden as effectually as he could hide it. But this Indian murderer does his deed in the full light of day, cares nothing for the society of witnesses, is in no way incommoded by the presence of the corpse, takes his own time about disposing of it, and the whole party are so indifferent, so phlegmatic, that they take their regular sleep as if nothing was happening and no halters hanging over them; and these five bland people close the episode with a religious service. The thing reads like a Meadows-Taylor Thug-tale of half a century ago, as may be seen by the official report of the trial:

"At the Mazagon Police Court yesterday, Superintendent

Nolan again charged Tookaram Suntoo Savat Baya, woman, her daughter Krishni, and Gopal Yithoo Bhanayker, before Mr. Phiroze Hoshang Dastur, Fourth Presidency Magistrate, under sections 302 and 109 of the Code, with having on the night of the 30th of December last murdered a Hindoo girl named Cassi, aged 12, by strangulation, in the room of a chawl at Jakaria Bunder, on the Sewriroad, and also with aiding and abetting each other in the commission of the offense.

"Mr. F. A. Little, Public Prosecutor, conducted the case on behalf of the Crown, the accused being undefended.

"Mr. Little applied under the provisions of the Criminal Procedure Code to tender pardon to one of the accused, Krishni, woman, aged 22, on her undertaking to make a true and full statement of facts under which the deceased girl Cassi was murdered.

"The Magistrate having granted the Public Prosecutor's application, the accused Krishni went into the witness-box, and, on being examined by Mr. Little, made the following confession:—I am a mill-hand employed at the Jubilee Mill. I recollect the day (Tuesday); on which the body of the deceased Cassi was found. Previous to that I attended the mill for half a day, and then returned home at 3 in the afternoon, when I saw five persons in the house, viz.: the first accused Tookaram, who is my paramour, my mother, the second accused Baya, the accused Gopal, and two guests named Ramji Daji and Annaji Gungaram. Tookaram rented the room of the chawl situated at Jakaria Bunder-road from its owner, Girdharilal Radhakishan, and in that room I, my paramour, Tookaram, and his younger brother, Yesso Mahadhoo, live. Since his arrival in Bombay from his native country Yesso came and lived with us. When I returned from the mill on the afternoon of that day, I saw the two guests seated on a cot in the veranda, and a few minutes after the accused Gopal came and took his seat by their side, while I and my mother were seated inside the room. Tookaram, who had gone out to fetch some 'pan' and betelnuts, on his return home had brought the two guests with him. After returning home he gave them 'pan supari'. While they were eating it my mother came out of the room and inquired of one of the guests, Ramji, what had happened to his foot, when he replied that he had tried many remedies, but they had done him no good. My mother then took some rice in her hand and prophesied that the disease which Ramji was suffering from would not be cured until he returned to his native country. In the meantime the deceased Casi came from the direction of an out-house, and stood in front on the threshold of our room with a 'lota' in her hand. Tookaram then told his two guests to leave the room, and they then went up the steps towards the quarry. After the guests had gone away, Tookaram seized the deceased, who had come into the room, and he afterwards put a waistband around her, and tied her to a post which supports a loft. After doing this, he pressed the girl's throat, and, having tied her mouth with the 'dhotur' (now shown in Court), fastened it to the post. Having killed the girl, Tookaram removed her gold head ornament and a gold 'putlee', and also took charge of her 'lota'. Besides these two ornaments Cassi had on her person ear-studs a nose-ring, some silver toe-rings, two necklaces, a pair of silver anklets and bracelets. Tookaram afterwards tried to remove the silver amulets, the ear-studs, and the nose-ring; but he failed in his attempt. While he was doing so, I, my mother, and Gopal were present. After removing the two gold ornaments, he handed them over to Gopal, who was at the time standing near me. When he killed Cassi, Tookaram threatened to strangle me also if I informed any one of this. Gopal and myself were then standing at the door of our room, and we both were threatened

by Tookaram. My mother, Baya, had seized the legs of the deceased at the time she was killed, and whilst she was being tied to the post. Cassi then made a noise. Tookaram and my mother took part in killing the girl. After the murder her body was wrapped up in a mattress and kept on the loft over the door of our room. When Cassi was strangled, the door of the room was fastened from the inside by Tookaram. This deed was committed shortly after my return home from work in the mill. Tookaram put the body of the deceased in the mattress, and, after it was left on the loft, he went to have his head shaved by a barber named Sambhoo Raghoo, who lives only one door away from me. My mother and myself then remained in the possession of the information. I was slapped and threatened by my paramour, Tookaram, and that was the only reason why I did not inform any one at that time. When I told Tookaram that I would give information of the occurrence, he slapped me. The accused Gopal was asked by Tookaram to go back to his room, and he did so, taking away with him the two gold ornaments and the 'lota'. Yesso Mahadhoo, a brother-in-law of Tookaram, came to the house and asked Taokaram why he was washing, the water-pipe being just opposite. Tookaram replied that he was washing his dhotur, as a fowl had polluted it. About 6 o'clock of the evening of that day my mother gave me three pice and asked me to buy a cocoanut, and I gave the money to Yessoo, who went and fetched a cocoanut and some betel leaves. When Yessoo and others were in the room I was bathing, and, after I finished my bath, my mother took the cocoanut and the betel leaves from Yessoo, and we five went to the sea. The party consisted of Tookaram, my mother, Yessoo, Tookaram's younger brother, and myself. On reaching the seashore, my mother made the offering to the sea, and prayed to be pardoned for what we had done. Before we went to the sea, some one came to inquire after the girl Cassi. The police and other people came to make these inquiries both before and after we left the house for the seashore. The police questioned my mother about the girl, and she replied that Cassi had come to her door, but had left. The next day the police questioned Tookaram, and he, too, gave a similar reply. This was said the same night when the search was made for the girl. After the offering was made to the sea, we partook of the cocoanut and returned home, when my mother gave me some food; but Tookaram did not partake of any food that night. After dinner I and my mother slept inside the room, and Tookaram slept on a cot near his brother-in-law, Yessoo Mahadhoo, just outside the door. That was not the usual place where Tookaram slept. He usually slept inside the room. The body of the deceased remained on the loft when I went to sleep. The room in which we slept was locked, and I heard that my paramour, Tookaram, was restless outside. About 3 o'clock the following morning Tookaram knocked at the door, when both myself and my mother opened it. He then told me to go to the steps leading to the quarry, and see if any one was about. Those steps lead to a stable, through which we go to the quarry at the back of the compound. When I got to the steps I saw no one there. Tookaram asked me if any one was there, and I replied that I could see no one about. He then took the body of the deceased from the loft, and having wrapped it up in his saree, asked me to accompany him to the steps of the quarry, and I did so. The 'saree' now produced here was the same. Besides the 'saree', there was also a 'cholee' on the body. He then carried the body in his arms, and went up the steps, through the stable, and then to the right hand towards a Sahib's bungalow, where Tookaram placed the body near a wall. All the time I and my mother were with him. When the body was taken down, Yessoo was lying on the cot. After depositing the body under the wall, we all returned home, and soon after 5 a.m. the police again came and took Tookaram away. About an hour after they returned and took me and my mother away. We were questioned about it, when I made a statement. Two hours later I was taken to the room, and I pointed out this waistband, the 'dhotur', the mattress, and the wooden post to Superintendent Nolan and Inspectors Roberts and Rashanali, in the presence of my mother and Tookaram. Tookaram killed the girl Cassi for her ornaments, which he wanted for the girl to whom he was shortly going to be married. The body was found in the same place where it was deposited by Tookaram."

The criminal side of the native has always been picturesque, always readable. The Thuggee and one or two other particularly outrageous features of it have been suppressed by the English, but there is enough of it left to keep it darkly interesting. One finds evidence of these survivals in the newspapers. Macaulay has a light-throwing passage upon this matter in his great historical sketch of Warren Hastings, where he is describing some effects which followed the temporary paralysis of Hastings' powerful government brought about by Sir Philip Francis and his party:

"The natives considered Hastings as a fallen man; and they acted after their kind. Some of our readers may have seen, in India, a cloud of crows pecking a sick vulture to death—no bad type of what happens in that country as often as fortune deserts one who has been great and dreaded. In an instant all the sycophants, who had lately been ready to lie for him, to forge for him, to pander for him, to poison for him, hasten to purchase the favor of his victorious enemies by accusing him. An Indian government has only to let it be understood that it wishes a particular man to be ruined, and in twenty-four hours it will be furnished with grave charges, supported by depositions so full and circumstantial that any person unaccustomed to Asiatic mendacity would regard them as decisive. It is well if the signature of the destined victim is not counterfeited at the foot of some illegal compact, and if some treasonable paper is not slipped into a hiding-place in his house."

That was nearly a century and a quarter ago. An article in one of the chief journals of India (the Pioneer) shows that in some respects the native of to-day is just what his ancestor was then. Here are niceties of so subtle and delicate a sort that they lift their breed of rascality to a place among the fine arts, and almost entitle it to respect:

"The records of the Indian courts might certainly be relied upon to prove that swindlers as a class in the East come very close to, if they do not surpass, in brilliancy of execution and originality of design the most expert of their fraternity in Europe and America. India in especial is the home of forgery. There are some particular districts which are noted as marts for the finest specimens of the forger's handiwork. The business is carried on by firms who possess stores of stamped papers to suit every emergency. They habitually lay in a store of fresh stamped papers every year, and some of the older and more thriving houses can supply documents for the past forty years, bearing the proper water-mark and possessing the genuine appearance of age. Other districts have earned notoriety for skilled perjury, a pre-eminence that excites a respectful admiration when one thinks of the universal prevalence of the art, and persons desirous of succeeding in false suits are ready to pay handsomely to avail themselves of the services of these local experts as witnesses."

Various instances illustrative of the methods of these swindlers are given. They exhibit deep cunning and total depravity on the part of the swindler and his pals, and more obtuseness on the part of the victim than one would expect to find in a country where suspicion of your neighbor must surely be one of the earliest things learned. The favorite subject is the young fool who has just come into a fortune and is trying to see how poor a use he can put it to. I will quote one example:

"Sometimes another form of confidence trick is adopted, which is invariably successful. The particular pigeon is spotted, and, his acquaintance having been made, he is encouraged in every form of vice. When the friendship is thoroughly established, the swindler remarks to the young man that he has a brother who has asked him to lend him Rs.10,000. The swindler says he has the money and would lend it; but, as the borrower is his brother, he cannot charge interest. So he proposes that he should hand the dupe the money, and the latter should lend it to the swindler's brother, exacting a heavy pre-payment of interest which, it is pointed out, they may equally enjoy in dissipation. The dupe sees no objection, and on the appointed day receives Rs.7,000 from the swindler, which he hands over to the confederate. The latter is profuse in his thanks, and executes a promissory note for Rs.10,000, payable to bearer. The swindler allows the scheme to remain quiescent for a time, and then suggests that, as the money has not been repaid and as it would be unpleasant to sue his brother, it would be better to sell the note in the bazaar. The dupe hands the note over, for the money he advanced was not his, and, on being informed that it would be necessary to have his signature on the back so as to render the security negotiable, he signs without any hesitation. The swindler passes it on to confederates, and the latter employ a respectable firm of solicitors to ask the dupe if his signature is genuine. He admits it at once, and his fate is sealed. A suit is filed by a confederate against the dupe, two accomplices being made co-defendants. They admit their Signatures as indorsers, and the one swears he bought the note for value from the dupe. The latter has no defense, for no court would believe the apparently idle explanation of the manner in which he came to endorse the note."

There is only one India! It is the only country that has a monopoly of grand and imposing specialties. When another country has a remarkable thing, it cannot have it all to itself—some other country has a duplicate. But India—that is different. Its marvels are its own; the patents cannot be infringed; imitations are not possible. And think of the size of them, the majesty of them, the weird and outlandish character of the most of them!

There is the Plague, the Black Death: India invented it; India is the cradle of that mighty birth.

The Car of Juggernaut was India's invention.

So was the Suttee; and within the time of men still living eight hundred widows willingly, and, in fact, rejoicingly, burned themselves to death on the bodies of their dead husbands in a single year. Eight hundred would do it this year if the British government would let them.

Famine is India's specialty. Elsewhere famines are inconsequential incidents—in India they are devastating cataclysms; in one case they annihilate hundreds; in the other, millions.

India had 2,000,000 gods, and worships them all. In religion all other countries are paupers; India is the only millionaire.

With her everything is on a giant scale—even her poverty; no other country can show anything to compare with it. And she has been used to wealth on so vast a scale that she has to shorten to single words the expressions describing great sums. She describes 100,000 with one word —a 'lahk'; she describes ten millions with one word—a 'crore'.

In the bowels of the granite mountains she has patiently carved out dozens of vast temples, and made them glorious with sculptured colonnades and stately groups of statuary, and has adorned the eternal walls with noble paintings. She has built fortresses of such magnitude that the show-strongholds of the rest of the world are but modest little things by comparison; palaces that are wonders for rarity of materials, delicacy and beauty of workmanship, and for cost; and one tomb which men go around the globe to see. It takes eighty nations, speaking eighty languages, to people her, and they number three hundred millions.

On top of all this she is the mother and home of that wonder of wonders caste—and of that mystery of mysteries, the satanic brotherhood of the Thugs.

India had the start of the whole world in the beginning of things. She had the first civilization; she had the first accumulation of material wealth; she was populous with deep thinkers and subtle intellects; she had mines, and woods, and a fruitful soil. It would seem as if she should have kept the lead, and should be to-day not the meek dependent of an alien master, but mistress of the world, and delivering law and command to every tribe and nation in it. But, in truth, there was never any possibility of such supremacy for her. If there had been but one India and one language—but there were eighty of them! Where there are eighty nations and several hundred governments, fighting and quarreling must be the common business of life; unity of purpose and policy are impossible; out of such elements supremacy in the world cannot come. Even caste itself could have had the defeating effect of a multiplicity of tongues, no doubt; for it separates a people into layers, and layers, and still other layers, that have no community of feeling with each other; and in such a condition of things as that, patriotism can have no healthy growth.

It was the division of the country into so many States and nations that made Thuggee possible and prosperous. It is difficult to realize the situation. But perhaps one may approximate it by imagining the States of our Union peopled by separate nations, speaking separate languages, with guards and custom-houses strung along all frontiers, plenty of interruptions for travelers and traders, interpreters able to handle all the languages very rare or non-existent, and a few wars always going on here and there and yonder as a further embarrassment to commerce and excursioning. It would make intercommunication in a measure ungeneral. India had eighty languages, and more custom-houses than cats. No clever man with the instinct of a highway robber could fail to notice what a chance for business was here offered. India was full of clever men with the highwayman instinct, and so, quite naturally, the brotherhood of the Thugs came into being to meet the long-felt want.

How long ago that was nobody knows-centuries, it is supposed. One of the chiefest wonders connected with it was the success with which it kept its secret. The English trader did business in India two hundred years and more before he ever heard of it; and yet it was assassinating its thousands all around him every year, the whole time.

CHAPTER XLIV.

The old saw says, "Let a sleeping dog lie." Right... Still, when there is much at stake it is better to get a newspaper to do it.
—Pudd'nhead Wilson's New Calendar.

FROM DIARY:

January 28. I learned of an official Thug-book the other day. I was not aware before that there was such a thing. I am allowed the temporary use of it. We are making preparations for travel. Mainly the preparations are purchases of bedding. This is to be used in sleeping berths in the trains; in private houses sometimes; and in nine-tenths of the hotels. It is not realizable; and yet it is true. It is a survival; an apparently unnecessary thing which in some strange way has outlived the conditions which once made it necessary. It comes down from a time when the railway and the hotel did not exist; when the occasional white traveler went horseback or by bullock-cart, and stopped over night in the small dak-bungalow provided at easy distances by the government—a shelter, merely, and nothing more. He had to carry bedding along, or do without. The dwellings of the English residents are spacious and comfortable and commodiously furnished, and surely it must be an odd sight to see half a dozen guests come filing into such a place and dumping blankets and pillows here and there and everywhere. But custom makes incongruous things congruous.

One buys the bedding, with waterproof hold-all for it at almost any shop —there is no difficulty about it.

January 30. What a spectacle the railway station was, at train-time! It was a very large station, yet when we arrived it seemed as if the whole world was present—half of it inside, the other half outside, and both halves, bearing mountainous head-loads of bedding and other freight, trying simultaneously to pass each other, in opposing floods, in one narrow door. These opposing floods were patient, gentle, long-suffering natives, with whites scattered among them at rare intervals; and wherever a white man's native servant appeared, that native seemed to have put aside his natural gentleness for the time and invested himself with the white man's privilege of making a way for himself by promptly shoving all intervening black things out of it. In these exhibitions of authority Satan was scandalous. He was probably a Thug in one of his former incarnations.

Inside the great station, tides upon tides of rainbow-costumed natives swept along, this way and that, in massed and bewildering confusion, eager, anxious, belated, distressed; and washed up to the long trains and flowed into them with their packs and bundles, and disappeared, followed at once by the next wash, the next wave. And here and there, in the midst of this hurly-burly, and seemingly undisturbed by it, sat great groups of natives on the bare stone floor,—young, slender brown women, old, gray wrinkled women, little soft brown babies, old men, young men, boys; all poor people, but all the females among them, both big and little, bejeweled with cheap and showy nose-rings, toe-rings, leglets, and armlets, these things constituting all their wealth, no doubt. These silent crowds sat there with their humble bundles and baskets and small household gear about them, and patiently waited—for what? A train that was to start at some time or other during the day or night! They hadn't timed themselves well, but that was no matter—the thing had been so ordered from on high, therefore why worry? There was plenty of time, hours and hours of it, and the thing that was to happen would happen — there was no hurrying it.

The natives traveled third class, and at marvelously cheap rates. They were packed and crammed into cars that held each about fifty; and it was said that often a Brahmin of the highest caste was thus brought into personal touch, and consequent defilement, with persons of the lowest castes—no doubt a very shocking thing if a body could understand it and properly appreciate it. Yes, a Brahmin who didn't own a rupee and couldn't borrow one, might have to touch elbows with a rich hereditary lord of inferior caste, inheritor of an ancient title a couple of yards long, and he would just have to stand it; for if either of the two was allowed to go in the cars where the sacred white people were, it probably wouldn't be the august poor Brahmin. There was an immense string of those third-class cars, for the natives travel by hordes; and a weary hard night of it the occupants would have, no doubt.

When we reached our car, Satan and Barney had already arrived there with their train of porters carrying bedding and parasols and cigar boxes, and were at work. We named him Barney for short; we couldn't use his real name, there wasn't time.

It was a car that promised comfort; indeed, luxury. Yet the cost of it —well, economy could no further go; even in France; not even in Italy. It was built of the plainest and cheapest partially-smoothed boards, with a coating of dull paint on them, and there was nowhere a thought of decoration. The floor was bare, but would not long remain so when the dust should begin to fly. Across one end of the compartment ran a netting for the accommodation of hand-baggage; at the other end was a door which would shut, upon compulsion, but wouldn't stay shut; it opened into a narrow little closet which had a wash-bowl in one end of it, and a place to put a towel, in case you had one with you—and you would be sure to have towels, because you buy them with the bedding, knowing that the railway doesn't furnish them. On each side of the car, and running fore and aft, was a broad leather-covered sofa to sit on in the day and sleep on at night. Over each sofa hung, by straps, a wide, flat, leather-covered shelf—to sleep on. In the daytime you can hitch it up against the wall, out of the way—and then you have a big unencumbered and most comfortable room to spread out in. No car in any country is quite its equal for comfort (and privacy) I think. For usually there are but two persons in it; and even when there are four there is but little sense of impaired privacy. Our own cars at home can surpass the railway world in all details but that one: they have no cosiness; there are too many people together.

At the foot of each sofa was a side-door, for entrance and exit. Along the whole length of the sofa on each side of the car ran a row of large single-plate windows, of a blue tint-blue to soften the bitter glare of the sun and protect one's eyes from torture. These could be let down out of the way when one wanted the breeze. In the roof were two oil lamps which gave a light strong enough to read by; each had a green-cloth attachment by which it could be covered when the light should be no longer needed.

While we talked outside with friends, Barney and Satan placed the hand-baggage, books, fruits, and soda-bottles in the racks, and the hold-alls and heavy baggage in the closet, hung the overcoats and sun-helmets and towels on the hooks, hoisted the two bed-shelves up out of the way, then shouldered their bedding and retired to the third class.

Now then, you see what a handsome, spacious, light, airy, homelike place it was, wherein to walk up and down, or sit and write, or stretch out and read and smoke. A central door in the forward end of the compartment opened into a similar compartment. It was occupied by my wife and daughter. About nine in the evening, while we halted a while at a station, Barney and Satan came and undid the clumsy big hold-alls, and spread the bedding on the sofas in both compartments—mattresses, sheets, gay coverlets, pillows, all complete; there are no chambermaids in India —apparently it was an office that was never heard of. Then they closed the communicating door, nimbly tidied up our place, put the night-clothing on the beds and the slippers under them, then returned to their own quarters.

January 31. It was novel and pleasant, and I stayed awake as long as I could, to enjoy it, and to read about those strange people the Thugs. In my sleep they remained with me, and tried to strangle me. The leader of the gang was that giant Hindoo who was such a picture in the strong light when we were leaving those Hindoo betrothal festivities at two o'clock in the morning—Rao Bahadur Baskirao Balinkanje Pitale, Vakeel to the Gaikwar of Baroda. It was he that brought me the invitation from his master to go to Baroda and lecture to that prince—and now he was misbehaving in my dreams. But all things can happen in dreams. It is indeed as the Sweet Singer of Michigan says—irrelevantly, of course, for the one and unfailing great quality which distinguishes her poetry from Shakespeare's and makes it precious to us is its stern and simple irrelevancy:

 My heart was gay and happy, This was ever in my mind, There is better times a coming, And I hope some day to find Myself capable of composing, It was my heart's delight To compose on a sentimental subject If it came in my mind just right.

—["The Sentimental Song Book," p. 49; theme, "The Author's Early Life," 19th stanza.]

Barroda. Arrived at 7 this morning. The dawn was just beginning to show. It was forlorn to have to turn out in a strange place at such a time, and the blinking lights in the station made it seem night still. But the gentlemen who had come to receive us were there with their servants, and they make quick work; there was no lost time. We were soon outside and moving swiftly through the soft gray light, and presently were comfortably housed—with more servants to help than we were used to, and with rather embarassingly important officials to direct them. But it was custom; they spoke Ballarat English, their bearing was charming and hospitable, and so all went well.

Breakfast was a satisfaction. Across the lawns was visible in the distance through the open window an Indian well, with two oxen tramping leisurely up and down long inclines, drawing water; and out of the stillness came the suffering screech of the machinery—not quite musical, and yet soothingly melancholy and dreamy and reposeful—a wail of lost spirits, one might imagine. And commemorative and reminiscent, perhaps; for of course the Thugs used to throw people down that well when they were done with them.

After breakfast the day began, a sufficiently busy one. We were driven by winding roads through a vast park, with noble forests of great trees, and with tangles and jungles of lovely growths of a humbler sort; and at one place three large gray apes came out and pranced across the road—a good deal of a surprise and an unpleasant one, for such creatures belong in the menagerie, and they look artificial and out of place in a wilderness.

We came to the city, by and by, and drove all through it. Intensely Indian, it was, and crumbly, and mouldering, and immemorially old, to all appearance. And the houses—oh, indescribably quaint and curious they were, with their fronts an elaborate lace-work of intricate and beautiful wood-carving, and now and then further adorned with rude pictures of elephants and princes and gods done in shouting colors; and all the ground floors along these cramped and narrow lanes occupied as shops —shops unbelievably small and impossibly packed with merchantable rubbish, and with nine-tenths-naked natives squatting at their work of hammering, pounding, brazing, soldering, sewing, designing, cooking, measuring out grain, grinding it, repairing idols—and then the swarm of ragged and noisy humanity under the horses' feet and everywhere, and the pervading reek and fume and smell! It was all wonderful and delightful.

Imagine a file of elephants marching through such a crevice of a street and scraping the paint off both sides of it with their hides. How big they must look, and how little they must make the houses look; and when the elephants are in their glittering court costume, what a contrast they must make with the humble and sordid surroundings. And when a mad elephant goes raging through, belting right and left with his trunk, how do these swarms of people get out of the way? I suppose it is a thing which happens now and then in the mad season (for elephants have a mad season).

I wonder how old the town is. There are patches of building—massive structures, monuments, apparently—that are so battered and worn, and seemingly so tired and so burdened with the weight of age, and so dulled and stupefied with trying to remember things they forgot before history began, that they give one the feeling that they must have been a part of original Creation. This is indeed one of the oldest of the princedoms of India, and has always been celebrated for its barbaric pomps and splendors, and for the wealth of its princes.

CHAPTER XLV.

It takes your enemy and your friend, working together, to hurt you to the heart; the one to slander you and the other to get the news to you. —Pudd'nhead Wilson's New Calendar.

Out of the town again; a long drive through open country, by winding roads among secluded villages nestling in the inviting shade of tropic vegetation, a Sabbath stillness everywhere, sometimes a pervading sense of solitude, but always barefoot natives gliding by like spirits, without sound of footfall, and others in the distance dissolving away and vanishing like the creatures of dreams. Now and then a string of stately camels passed by—always interesting things to look at—and they were velvet-shod by nature, and made no noise. Indeed, there were no noises of any sort in this paradise. Yes, once there was one, for a moment: a file of native convicts passed along in charge of an officer, and we caught the soft clink of their chains. In a retired spot, resting himself under a tree, was a holy person—a naked black fakeer, thin and skinny, and whitey-gray all over with ashes.

By and by to the elephant stables, and I took a ride; but it was by request—I did not ask for it, and didn't want it; but I took it, because otherwise they would have thought I was afraid, which I was. The elephant kneels down, by command—one end of him at a time—and you climb the ladder and get into the howdah, and then he gets up, one end at a time, just as a ship gets up over a wave; and after that, as he strides

monstrously about, his motion is much like a ship's motion. The mahout bores into the back of his head with a great iron prod and you wonder at his temerity and at the elephant's patience, and you think that perhaps the patience will not last; but it does, and nothing happens. The mahout talks to the elephant in a low voice all the time, and the elephant seems to understand it all and to be pleased with it; and he obeys every order in the most contented and docile way. Among these twenty-five elephants were two which were larger than any I had ever seen before, and if I had thought I could learn to not be afraid, I would have taken one of them while the police were not looking.

In the howdah-house there were many howdahs that were made of silver, one of gold, and one of old ivory, and equipped with cushions and canopies of rich and costly stuffs. The wardrobe of the elephants was there, too; vast velvet covers stiff and heavy with gold embroidery; and bells of silver and gold; and ropes of these metals for fastening the things on harness, so to speak; and monster hoops of massive gold for the elephant to wear on his ankles when he is out in procession on business of state.

But we did not see the treasury of crown jewels, and that was a disappointment, for in mass and richness it ranks only second in India. By mistake we were taken to see the new palace instead, and we used up the last remnant of our spare time there. It was a pity, too; for the new palace is mixed modern American-European, and has not a merit except costliness. It is wholly foreign to India, and impudent and out of place. The architect has escaped. This comes of overdoing the suppression of the Thugs; they had their merits. The old palace is oriental and charming, and in consonance with the country. The old palace would still be great if there were nothing of it but the spacious and lofty hall where the durbars are held. It is not a good place to lecture in, on account of the echoes, but it is a good place to hold durbars in and regulate the affairs of a kingdom, and that is what it is for. If I had it I would have a durbar every day, instead of once or twice a year.

The prince is an educated gentleman. His culture is European. He has been in Europe five times. People say that this is costly amusement for him, since in crossing the sea he must sometimes be obliged to drink water from vessels that are more or less public, and thus damage his caste. To get it purified again he must make pilgrimage to some renowned Hindoo temples and contribute a fortune or two to them. His people are like the other Hindoos, profoundly religious; and they could not be content with a master who was impure.

We failed to see the jewels, but we saw the gold cannon and the silver one—they seemed to be six-pounders. They were not designed for business, but for salutes upon rare and particularly important state occasions. An ancestor of the present Gaikwar had the silver one made, and a subsequent ancestor had the gold one made, in order to outdo him.

This sort of artillery is in keeping with the traditions of Baroda, which was of old famous for style and show. It used to entertain visiting rajahs and viceroys with tiger-fights, elephant-fights, illuminations, and elephant-processions of the most glittering and gorgeous character.

It makes the circus a pale, poor thing.

In the train, during a part of the return journey from Baroda, we had the company of a gentleman who had with him a remarkable looking dog. I had not seen one of its kind before, as far as I could remember; though of course I might have seen one and not noticed it, for I am not acquainted with dogs, but only with cats. This dog's coat was smooth and shiny and black, and I think it had tan trimmings around the edges of the dog, and perhaps underneath. It was a long, low dog, with very short, strange legs—legs that curved inboard, something like parentheses wrong way (. Indeed, it was made on the plan of a bench for length and lowness. It seemed to be satisfied, but I thought the plan poor, and structurally weak, on account of the distance between the forward supports and those abaft. With age the dog's back was likely to sag; and it seemed to me that it would have been a stronger and more practicable dog if it had had some more legs. It had not begun to sag yet, but the shape of the legs showed that the undue weight imposed upon them was beginning to tell. It had a long nose, and floppy ears that hung down, and a resigned expression of countenance. I did not like to ask what kind of a dog it was, or how it came to be deformed, for it was plain that the gentleman was very fond of it, and naturally he could be sensitive about it. From delicacy I thought it best not to seem to notice it too much. No doubt a man with a dog like that feels just as a person does who has a child that is out of true. The gentleman was not merely fond of the dog, he was also proud of it—just the same again, as a mother feels about her child when it is an idiot. I could see that he was proud of it, not-withstanding it was such a long dog and looked so resigned and pious. It had been all over the world with him, and had been pilgriming like that for years and years. It had traveled 50,000 miles by sea and rail, and had ridden in front of him on his horse 8,000. It had a silver medal from the Geographical Society of Great Britain for its travels, and I saw it. It had won prizes in dog shows, both in India and in England—I saw them. He said its pedigree was on record in the Kennel Club, and that it was a well-known dog. He said a great many people in London could recognize it the moment they saw it. I did not say anything, but I did not think it anything strange; I should know that dog again, myself, yet I am not careful about noticing dogs. He said that when he walked along in London, people often stopped and looked at the dog. Of course I did not say anything, for I did not want to hurt his feelings, but I could have explained to him that if you take a great long low dog like that and waddle it along the street anywhere in the world and not charge anything, people will stop and look. He was gratified because the dog took prizes. But that was nothing; if I were built like that I could take prizes myself. I wished I knew what kind of a dog it was, and what it was for, but I could not very well ask, for that would show that I did not know. Not that I want a dog like that, but only to know the secret of its birth.

I think he was going to hunt elephants with it, because I know, from remarks dropped by him, that he has hunted large game in India and Africa, and likes it. But I think that if he tries to hunt elephants with it, he is going to be disappointed.

I do not believe that it is suited for elephants. It lacks energy, it lacks force of character, it lacks bitterness. These things all show in the meekness and resignation of its expression. It would not attack an elephant, I am sure of it. It might not run if it saw one coming, but it looked to me like a dog that would sit down and pray.

I wish he had told me what breed it was, if there are others; but I shall know the dog next time, and then if I can bring myself to it I will put delicacy aside and ask. If I seem strangely interested in dogs, I have a reason for it; for a dog saved me from an embarrassing position once, and that has made me grateful to these animals; and if by study I could learn to tell some of the kinds from the others, I should be greatly pleased. I only know one kind apart, yet, and that is the kind that saved me that time. I always know that kind when I meet it, and if it is hungry or lost I take care of it. The matter happened in this way

It was years and years ago. I had received a note from Mr. Augustin Daly of the Fifth Avenue Theatre, asking me to call the next time I should be in New York. I was writing plays, in those days, and he was admiring them and trying to get me a chance to get them played in Siberia. I took the first train—the early one—the one that leaves Hartford at 8.29 in the morning. At New Haven I bought a paper, and found it filled with glaring display-lines about a "bench-show" there. I had often heard of bench-shows, but had never felt any interest in them, because I supposed they were lectures that were not well attended. It turned out, now, that it was not that, but a dog-show. There was a double-leaded column about the king-feature of this one, which was called a Saint Bernard, and was worth $10,000, and was known to be the largest and finest of his species in the world. I read all this with interest, because out of my school-boy readings I dimly remembered how the priests and pilgrims of St. Bernard used to go out in the storms and dig these dogs out of the snowdrifts when lost and exhausted, and give them brandy and save their lives, and drag them to the monastery and restore them with gruel.

Also, there was a picture of this prize-dog in the paper, a noble great creature with a benignant countenance, standing by a table. He was placed in that way so that one could get a right idea of his great dimensions. You could see that he was just a shade higher than the table—indeed, a huge fellow for a dog. Then there was a description which event into the details. It gave his enormous weight—150½ pounds, and his length 4 feet 2 inches, from stem to stern-post; and his height—3 feet 1 inch, to the top of his back. The pictures and the figures so impressed me, that I could see the beautiful colossus before me, and I kept on thinking about him for the next two hours; then I reached New York, and he dropped out of my mind.

In the swirl and tumult of the hotel lobby I ran across Mr. Daly's comedian, the late James Lewis, of beloved memory, and I casually mentioned that I was going to call upon Mr. Daly in the evening at 8. He looked surprised, and said he reckoned not. For answer I handed him Mr. Daly's note. Its substance was: "Come to my private den, over the theater, where we cannot be interrupted. And come by the back way, not the front. No. 642 Sixth Avenue is a cigar shop; pass through it and you are in a paved court, with high buildings all around; enter the second door on the left, and come up stairs."

"Is this all?"

"Yes," I said.

"Well, you'll never get in"

"Why?"

"Because you won't. Or if you do you can draw on me for a hundred dollars; for you will be the first man that has accomplished it in twenty-five years. I can't think what Mr. Daly can have been absorbed in. He has forgotten a most important detail, and he will feel humiliated in the morning when he finds that you tried to get in and couldn't."

"Why, what is the trouble?"

"I'll tell you. You see—"

At that point we were swept apart by the crowd, somebody detained me with a moment's talk, and we did not get together again. But it did not matter; I believed he was joking, anyway.

At eight in the evening I passed through the cigar shop and into the court and knocked at the second door.

"Come in!"

I entered. It was a small room, carpetless, dusty, with a naked deal table, and two cheap wooden chairs for furniture. A giant Irishman was standing there, with shirt collar and vest unbuttoned, and no coat on. I put my hat on the table, and was about to say something, when the Irishman took the innings himself. And not with marked courtesy of tone:

"Well, sor, what will you have?"

I was a little disconcerted, and my easy confidence suffered a shrinkage. The man stood as motionless as Gibraltar, and kept his unblinking eye upon me. It was very embarrassing, very humiliating. I stammered at a false start or two; then—

"I have just run down from—"

"Av ye plaze, ye'll not smoke here, ye understand."

I laid my cigar on the window-ledge; chased my flighty thoughts a moment, then said in a placating manner:

"I—I have come to see Mr. Daly."

"Oh, ye have, have ye?"

"Yes"

"Well, ye'll not see him."

"But he asked me to come."

"Oh, he did, did he?"

"Yes, he sent me this note, and—"

"Lemme see it."

For a moment I fancied there would be a change in the atmosphere, now; but this idea was premature. The big man was examining the note searchingly under the gas-jet. A glance showed me that he had it upside down—disheartening evidence that he could not read.

"Is ut his own handwrite?"

"Yes—he wrote it himself."

"He did, did he?"

"Yes."

"H'm. Well, then, why ud he write it like that?"

"How do you mean?"

"I mane, why wudn't he put his naime to ut?"

"His name is to it. That's not it—you are looking at my name."

I thought that that was a home shot, but he did not betray that he had been hit. He said:

"It's not an aisy one to spell; how do you pronounce ut?"

"Mark Twain."

"H'm. H'm. Mike Train. H'm. I don't remember ut. What is it ye want to see him about?"

"It isn't I that want to see him, he wants to see me."

"Oh, he does, does he?"

"Yes."

"What does he want to see ye about?"

"I don't know."

"Ye don't know! And ye confess it, becod! Well, I can tell ye wan thing—ye'll not see him. Are ye in the business?"

"What business?"

"The show business."

A fatal question. I recognized that I was defeated. If I answered no, he would cut the matter short and wave me to the door without the grace of a word—I saw it in his uncompromising eye; if I said I was a lecturer, he would despise me, and dismiss me with opprobrious words; if I said I was a dramatist, he would throw me out of the window. I saw that my case was hopeless, so I chose the course which seemed least humiliating: I would pocket my shame and glide out without answering. The silence was growing lengthy.

"I'll ask ye again. Are ye in the show business yerself?"

"Yes!"

I said it with splendid confidence; for in that moment the very twin of that grand New Haven dog loafed into the room, and I saw that Irishman's eye light eloquently with pride and affection.

"Ye are? And what is it?"

"I've got a bench-show in New Haven."

The weather did change then.

"You don't say, sir! And that's your show, sir! Oh, it's a grand show, it's a wonderful show, sir, and a proud man I am to see your honor this day. And ye'll be an expert, sir, and ye'll know all about dogs—more than ever they know theirselves, I'll take me oath to ut."

I said, with modesty:

"I believe I have some reputation that way. In fact, my business requires it."

"Ye have some reputation, your honor! Bedad I believe you! There's not a jintleman in the worrld that can lay over ye in the judgmint of a dog, sir. Now I'll venture that your honor'll know that dog's dimensions there better than he knows them his own self, and just by the casting of your educated eye upon him. Would you mind giving a guess, if ye'll be so good?"

I knew that upon my answer would depend my fate. If I made this dog bigger than the prize-dog, it would be bad diplomacy, and suspicious; if I fell too far short of the prizedog, that would be equally damaging. The dog was standing by the table, and I believed I knew the difference between him and the one whose picture I had seen in the newspaper to a shade. I spoke promptly up and said:

"It's no trouble to guess this noble creature's figures height, three feet; length, four feet and three-quarters of an inch; weight, a hundred and forty-eight and a quarter."

The man snatched his hat from its peg and danced on it with joy, shouting:

"Ye've hardly missed it the hair's breadth, hardly the shade of a shade, your honor! Oh, it's the miraculous eye ye've got, for the judgmint of a dog!"

And still pouring out his admiration of my capacities, he snatched off his vest and scoured off one of the wooden chairs with it, and scrubbed it and polished it, and said:

"There, sit down, your honor, I'm ashamed of meself that I forgot ye were standing all this time; and do put on your hat, ye mustn't take cold, it's a drafty place; and here is your cigar, sir, a getting cold, I'll give ye a light. There. The place is all yours, sir, and if ye'll just put your feet on the table and make yourself at home, I'll stir around and get a candle and light ye up the ould crazy stairs and see that ye don't come to anny harm, for be this time Mr. Daly'll be that impatient to see your honor that he'll be taking the roof off."

He conducted me cautiously and tenderly up the stairs, lighting the way and protecting me with friendly warnings, then pushed the door open and bowed me in and went his way, mumbling hearty things about my wonderful eye for points of a dog. Mr. Daly was writing and had his back to me. He glanced over his shoulder presently, then jumped up and said—

"Oh, dear me, I forgot all about giving instructions. I was just writing you to beg a thousand pardons. But how is it you are here? How did you get by that Irishman? You are the first man that's done it in five and twenty years. You didn't bribe him, I know that; there's not money enough in New York to do it. And you didn't persuade him; he is all ice and iron: there isn't a soft place nor a warm one in him anywhere. That is your secret? Look here; you owe me a hundred dollars for unintentionally giving you a chance to perform a miracle—for it is a miracle that you've done."

"That is all right," I said, "collect it of Jimmy Lewis."

That good dog not only did me that good turn in the time of my need, but he won for me the envious reputation among all the theatrical people from the Atlantic to the Pacific of being the only man in history who had ever run the blockade of Augustin Daly's back door.

CHAPTER XLVI.

If the desire to kill and the opportunity to kill came always together, who would escape hanging. —Pudd'nhead Wilson's New Calendar.

On the Train. Fifty years ago, when I was a boy in the then remote and sparsely peopled Mississippi valley, vague tales and rumors of a mysterious body of professional murderers came wandering in from a country which was constructively as far from us as the constellations blinking in space—India; vague tales and rumors of a sect called Thugs, who waylaid travelers in lonely places and killed them for the contentment of a god whom they worshiped; tales which everybody liked to listen to and nobody believed, except with reservations. It was considered that the stories had gathered bulk on their travels. The matter died down and a lull followed. Then Eugene Sue's "Wandering Jew" appeared, and made great talk for a while. One character in it was a chief of Thugs—"Feringhea"—a mysterious and terrible Indian who was as slippery and sly as a serpent, and as deadly; and he stirred up the Thug interest once more. But it did not last. It presently died again this time to stay dead.

At first glance it seems strange that this should have happened; but really it was not strange—on the contrary,. it was natural; I mean on our side of the water. For the source whence the Thug tales mainly came was a Government Report, and without doubt was not republished in America; it was probably never even seen there. Government Reports have no general circulation. They are distributed to the few, and are not always read by those few. I heard of this Report for the first time a day or two ago, and borrowed it. It is full of fascinations; and it turns those dim, dark fairy tales of my boyhood days into realities.

The Report was made in 1889 by Major Sleeman, of the Indian Service, and was printed in Calcutta in 1840. It is a clumsy, great, fat, poor sample of the printer's art, but good enough for a government printing-office in that old day and in that remote region, perhaps. To Major Sleeman was given the general superintendence of the giant task of ridding India of Thuggee, and he and his seventeen assistants accomplished it. It was the Augean Stables over again. Captain Vallancey, writing in a Madras journal in those old times, makes this remark:

"The day that sees this far-spread evil eradicated from India and known only in name, will greatly tend to immortalize British rule in the East."

He did not overestimate the magnitude and difficulty of the work, nor the immensity of the credit which would justly be due to British rule in case it was accomplished.

Thuggee became known to the British authorities in India about 1810, but its wide prevalence was not suspected; it was not regarded as a serious matter, and no systematic measures were taken for its suppression until about 1830. About that time Major Sleeman captured Eugene Sue's Thug-chief, "Feringhea," and got him to turn King's evidence. The revelations were so stupefying that Sleeman was not able to believe them. Sleeman thought he knew every criminal within his jurisdiction, and that the worst of them were merely thieves; but Feringhea told him that he was in reality living in the midst of a swarm of professional murderers; that they had been all about him for many years, and that they buried their dead close by. These seemed insane tales; but Feringhea said come and see—and he took him to a grave and dug up a hundred bodies, and told him all the circumstances of the killings, and named the Thugs who had done the work. It was a staggering business. Sleeman captured some of these Thugs and proceeded to examine them separately, and with proper precautions against collusion; for he would not believe any Indian's unsupported word. The evidence gathered proved the truth of what Feringhea had said, and also revealed the fact that gangs of Thugs were plying their trade all over India. The astonished government now took hold of Thuggee, and for ten years made systematic and relentless war upon it, and finally destroyed it. Gang after gang was captured, tried, and punished. The Thugs were harried and hunted from one end of India to the other. The government got all their secrets out of them; and also got the names of the members of the bands, and recorded them in a book, together with their birthplaces and places of residence.

The Thugs were worshipers of Bhowanee; and to this god they sacrificed anybody that came handy; but they kept the dead man's things themselves, for the god cared for nothing but the corpse. Men were initiated into the sect with solemn ceremonies. Then they were taught how to strangle a person with the sacred choke-cloth, but were not allowed to perform officially with it until after long practice. No half-educated strangler could choke a man to death quickly enough to keep him from uttering a sound—a muffled scream, gurgle, gasp, moan, or something of the sort; but the expert's work was instantaneous: the cloth was whipped around the victim's neck, there was a sudden twist, and the head fell silently forward, the eyes starting from the sockets; and all was over. The Thug carefully guarded against resistance. It was usual to to get the victims to sit down, for that was the handiest position for business.

If the Thug had planned India itself it could not have been more conveniently arranged for the needs of his occupation.

There were no public conveyances. There were no conveyances for hire. The traveler went on foot or in a bullock cart or on a horse which he bought for the purpose. As soon as he was out of his own little State or principality he was among strangers; nobody knew him, nobody took note of him, and from that time his movements could no longer be traced. He did not stop in towns or villages, but camped outside of them and sent his servants in to buy provisions. There were no habitations between villages. Whenever he was between villages he was an easy prey, particularly as he usually traveled by night, to avoid the heat. He was always being overtaken by strangers who offered him the protection of their company, or asked for the protection of his—and these strangers were often Thugs, as he presently found out to his cost. The landholders, the native police, the petty princes, the village officials, the customs officers were in many cases protectors and harborers of the Thugs, and betrayed travelers to them for a share of the spoil. At first this condition of things made it next to impossible for the government to catch the marauders; they were spirited away by these watchful friends. All through a vast continent, thus infested, helpless people of every caste and kind moved along the paths and trails in couples and groups silently by night, carrying the commerce of the country—treasure, jewels, money, and petty batches of silks, spices, and all manner of wares. It was a paradise for the Thug.

When the autumn opened, the Thugs began to gather together by pre-concert. Other people had to have interpreters at every turn, but not the Thugs; they could talk together, no matter how far apart they were born, for they had a language of their own, and they had secret signs by which they knew each other for Thugs; and they were always friends. Even their diversities of religion and caste were sunk in devotion to their calling, and the Moslem and the high-caste and low-caste Hindoo were staunch and affectionate brothers in Thuggery.

When a gang had been assembled, they had religious worship, and waited for an omen. They had definite notions about the omens. The cries of certain animals were good omens, the cries of certain other creatures were bad omens. A bad omen would stop proceedings and send the men home.

The sword and the strangling-cloth were sacred emblems. The Thugs worshiped the sword at home before going out to the assembling-place; the strangling-cloth was worshiped at the place of assembly. The chiefs of most of the bands performed the religious ceremonies themselves; but the Kaets delegated them to certain official stranglers (Chaurs). The rites of the Kaets were so holy that no one but the Chaur was allowed to touch the vessels and other things used in them.

Thug methods exhibit a curious mixture of caution and the absence of it; cold business calculation and sudden, unreflecting impulse; but there were two details which were constant, and not subject to caprice: patient persistence in following up the prey, and pitilessness when the time came to act.

Caution was exhibited in the strength of the bands. They never felt comfortable and confident unless their strength exceeded that of any party of travelers they were likely to meet by four or fivefold. Yet it was never their purpose to attack openly, but only when the victims were off their guard. When they got hold of a party of travelers they often moved along in their company several days, using all manner of arts to win their friendship and get their confidence. At last, when this was accomplished to their satisfaction, the real business began. A few Thugs were privately detached and sent forward in the dark to select a good killing-place and dig the graves. When the rest reached the spot a halt was called, for a rest or a smoke. The travelers were invited to sit. By signs, the chief appointed certain Thugs to sit down in front of the travelers as if to wait upon them, others to sit down beside them and engage them in conversation, and certain expert stranglers to stand behind the travelers and be ready when the signal was given. The signal was usually some commonplace remark, like "Bring the tobacco." Sometimes a considerable wait ensued after all the actors were in their places—the chief was biding his time, in order to make everything sure. Meantime, the talk droned on, dim figures moved about in the dull light, peace and tranquility reigned, the travelers resigned themselves to the pleasant reposefulness and comfort of the situation, unconscious of the death-angels standing motionless at their backs. The time was ripe, now, and the signal came: "Bring the tobacco." There was a mute swift movement, all in the same instant the men at each victim's sides seized his hands, the man in front seized his feet, and pulled, the man at his back whipped the cloth around his neck and gave it a twist the head sunk forward, the tragedy was over. The bodies were stripped and covered up in the graves, the spoil packed for transportation, then the Thugs gave pious thanks to Bhowanee, and departed on further holy service.

The Report shows that the travelers moved in exceedingly small groups —twos, threes, fours, as a rule; a party with a dozen in it was rare. The Thugs themselves seem to have been the only people who moved in force. They went about in gangs of 10, 15, 25, 40, 60, 100, 150, 200, 250, and one gang of 310 is mentioned. Considering their numbers, their catch was not extraordinary—particularly when you consider that they were not in the least fastidious, but took anybody they could get, whether rich or poor, and sometimes even killed children. Now and then they killed women, but it was considered sinful to do it, and unlucky. The "season" was six or eight months long. One season the half dozen Bundelkand and Gwalior gangs aggregated 712 men, and they murdered 210 people. One season the Malwa and Kandeish gangs aggregated 702 men, and they murdered 232. One season the Kandeish and Berar gangs aggregated 963 men, and they murdered 385 people.

Here is the tally-sheet of a gang of sixty Thugs for a whole season—gang under two noted chiefs, "Chotee and Sheik Nungoo from Gwalior":

"Left Poora, in Jhansee, and on arrival at Sarora murdered a traveler.

"On nearly reaching Bhopal, met 3 Brahmins, and murdered them.

"Cross the Nerbudda; at a village called Hutteea, murdered a Hindoo.

"Went through Aurungabad to Walagow; there met a Havildar of the barber caste and 5 sepoys (native soldiers); in the evening came to Jokur, and in the morning killed them near the place where the treasure-bearers were killed the year before.

"Between Jokur and Dholeea met a sepoy of the shepherd caste; killed him in the jungle.

"Passed through Dholeea and lodged in a village; two miles beyond, on the road to Indore, met a Byragee (beggar-holy mendicant); murdered him at the Thapa.

"In the morning, beyond the Thapa, fell in with 3 Marwarie travelers; murdered them.

"Near a village on the banks of the Taptee met 4 travelers and killed them.

"Between Choupra and Dhoreea met a Marwarie; murdered him.

"At Dhoreea met 3 Marwaries; took them two miles and murdered them.

"Two miles further on, overtaken by three treasure-bearers; took them two miles and murdered them in the jungle.

"Came on to Khurgore Bateesa in Indore, divided spoil, and dispersed.

"A total of 27 men murdered on one expedition."

Chotee (to save his neck) was informer, and furnished these facts. Several things are noticeable about his resume. 1. Business brevity; 2, absence of emotion; 3, smallness of the parties encountered by the 60; 4, variety in character and quality of the game captured; 5, Hindoo and Mohammedan chiefs in business together for Bhowanee; 6, the sacred caste of the Brahmins not respected by either; 7, nor yet the character of that mendicant, that Byragee.

A beggar is a holy creature, and some of the gangs spared him on that account, no matter how slack business might be; but other gangs slaughtered not only him, but even that sacredest of sacred creatures, the fakeer—that repulsive skin-and-bone thing that goes around naked and mats his bushy hair with dust and dirt, and so beflours his lean body with ashes that he looks like a specter. Sometimes a fakeer trusted a shade too far in the protection of his sacredness. In the middle of a tally-sheet of Feringhea's, who had been out with forty Thugs, I find a case of the kind. After the killing of thirty-nine men and one woman, the fakeer appears on the scene:

"Approaching Doregow, met 3 pundits; also a fakeer, mounted on a pony; he was plastered over with sugar to collect flies, and was covered with them. Drove off the fakeer, and killed the other three.

"Leaving Doregow, the fakeer joined again, and went on in company to Raojana; met 6 Khutries on their way from Bombay to Nagpore. Drove off the fakeer with stones, and killed the 6 men in camp, and buried them in the grove.

"Next day the fakeer joined again; made him leave at Mana. Beyond there, fell in with two Kahars and a sepoy, and came on towards the place selected for the murder. When near it, the fakeer came again. Losing all patience with him, gave Mithoo, one of the gang, 5 rupees ($2.50) to murder him, and take the sin upon himself. All four were strangled, including the fakeer. Surprised to find among the fakeer's effects 30 pounds of coral, 350 strings of small pearls, 15 strings of large pearls, and a gilt necklace."

It it curious, the little effect that time has upon a really interesting circumstance. This one, so old, so long ago gone down into oblivion, reads with the same freshness and charm that attach to the news in the morning paper; one's spirits go up, then down, then up again, following the chances which the fakeer is running; now you hope, now you despair, now you hope again; and at last everything comes out right, and you feel a great wave of personal satisfaction go weltering through you, and without thinking, you put out your hand to pat Mithoo on the back, when —puff! the whole thing has vanished away, there is nothing there; Mithoo and all the crowd have been dust and ashes and forgotten, oh, so many, many, many lagging years! And then comes a sense of injury: you don't know whether Mithoo got the swag, along with the sin, or had to divide up the swag and keep all the sin himself. There is no literary art about a government report. It stops a story right in the most interesting place.

These reports of Thug expeditions run along interminably in one monotonous tune: "Met a sepoy—killed him; met 5 pundits—killed them; met 4 Rajpoots and a woman—killed them"—and so on, till the statistics get to be pretty dry. But this small trip of Feringhea's Forty had some little variety about it. Once they came across a man hiding in a grave —a thief; he had stolen 1,100 rupees from Dhunroj Seith of Parowtee. They strangled him and took the money. They had no patience with thieves. They killed two treasure-bearers, and got 4,000 rupees. They came across two bullocks "laden with copper pice," and killed the four drivers and took the money. There must have been half a ton of it. I think it takes a double handful of pice to make an anna, and 16 annas to make a rupee; and even in those days the rupee was worth only half a dollar. Coming back over their tracks from Baroda, they had another picturesque stroke of luck: "'The Lohars of Oodeypore' put a traveler in their charge for safety." Dear, dear, across this abyssmal gulf of time we still see Feringhea's lips uncover his teeth, and through the dim haze we catch the incandescent glimmer of his smile. He accepted that trust, good man; and so we know what went with the traveler.

Even Rajahs had no terrors for Feringhea; he came across an

elephant-driver belonging to the Rajah of Oodeypore and promptly strangled him.

"A total of 100 men and 5 women murdered on this expedition."

Among the reports of expeditions we find mention of victims of almost every quality and estate.

Also a prince's cook; and even the water-carrier of that sublime lord of lords and king of kings, the Governor-General of India! How broad they were in their tastes! They also murdered actors—poor wandering barnstormers. There are two instances recorded; the first one by a gang of Thugs under a chief who soils a great name borne by a better man — Kipling's deathless "Gungadin":

"After murdering 4 sepoys, going on toward Indore, met 4 strolling players, and persuaded them to come with us, on the pretense that we would see their performance at the next stage. Murdered them at a temple near Bhopal."

Second instance:

"At Deohuttee, joined by comedians. Murdered them eastward of that place."

But this gang was a particularly bad crew. On that expedition they murdered a fakeer and twelve beggars. And yet Bhowanee protected them; for once when they were strangling a man in a wood when a crowd was going by close at hand and the noose slipped and the man screamed, Bhowanee made a camel burst out at the same moment with a roar that drowned the scream; and before the man could repeat it the breath was choked out of his body.

The cow is so sacred in India that to kill her keeper is an awful sacrilege, and even the Thugs recognized this; yet now and then the lust for blood was too strong, and so they did kill a few cow-keepers. In one of these instances the witness who killed the cowherd said, "In Thuggee this is strictly forbidden, and is an act from which no good can come. I was ill of a fever for ten days afterward. I do believe that evil will follow the murder of a man with a cow. If there be no cow it does not signify." Another Thug said he held the cowherd's feet while this witness did the strangling. He felt no concern, "because the bad fortune of such a deed is upon the strangler and not upon the assistants; even if there should be a hundred of them."

There were thousands of Thugs roving over India constantly, during many generations. They made Thuggee a hereditary vocation and taught it to their sons and to their son's sons. Boys were in full membership as early as 16 years of age; veterans were still at work at 70. What was the fascination, what was the impulse? Apparently, it was partly piety, largely gain, and there is reason to suspect that the sport afforded was the chiefest fascination of all. Meadows Taylor makes a Thug in one of his books claim that the pleasure of killing men was the white man's beast-hunting instinct enlarged, refined, ennobled. I will quote the passage:

CHAPTER XLVII.

Simple rules for saving money: To save half, when you are fired by an eager impulse to contribute to a charity, wait, and count forty. To save three-quarters, count sixty. To save it all, count sixty-five. —Pudd'nhead Wilson's New Calendar.

The Thug said:

"How many of you English are passionately devoted to sporting! Your days and months are passed in its excitement. A tiger, a panther, a buffalo or a hog rouses your utmost energies for its destruction—you even risk your lives in its pursuit. How much higher game is a Thug's!"

That must really be the secret of the rise and development of Thuggee. The joy of killing! the joy of seeing killing done—these are traits of the human race at large. We white people are merely modified Thugs; Thugs fretting under the restraints of a not very thick skin of civilization; Thugs who long ago enjoyed the slaughter of the Roman arena, and later the burning of doubtful Christians by authentic Christians in the public squares, and who now, with the Thugs of Spain and Nimes, flock to enjoy the blood and misery of the bullring. We have no tourists of either sex or any religion who are able to resist the delights of the bull-ring when opportunity offers; and we are gentle Thugs in the hunting-season, and love to chase a tame rabbit and kill it. Still, we have made some progress-microscopic, and in truth scarcely worth mentioning, and certainly nothing to be proud of—still, it is progress: we no longer take pleasure in slaughtering or burning helpless men. We have reached a little altitude where we may look down upon the Indian Thugs with a complacent shudder; and we may even hope for a day, many centuries hence, when our posterity will look down upon us in the same way.

There are many indications that the Thug often hunted men for the mere sport of it; that the fright and pain of the quarry were no more to him than are the fright and pain of the rabbit or the stag to us; and that he was no more ashamed of beguiling his game with deceits and abusing its trust than are we when we have imitated a wild animal's call and shot it when it honored us with its confidence and came to see what we wanted:

"Madara, son of Nihal, and I, Ramzam, set out from Kotdee in the cold weather and followed the high road for about twenty days in search of travelers, until we came to Selempore, where we met a very old man going to the east. We won his confidence in this manner: he carried a load which was too heavy for his old age; I said to him, 'You are an old man, I will aid you in carrying your load, as you are from my part of the country.' He said, 'Very well, take me with you.' So we took him with us to Selempore, where we slept that night. We woke him next morning before dawn and set out, and at the distance of three miles we seated him to rest while it was still very dark. Madara was ready behind him, and strangled him. He never spoke a word. He was about 60 or 70 years of age."

Another gang fell in with a couple of barbers and persuaded them to come along in their company by promising them the job of shaving the whole crew—30 Thugs. At the place appointed for the murder 15 got shaved, and actually paid the barbers for their work. Then killed them and took back the money.

A gang of forty-two Thugs came across two Brahmins and a shopkeeper on the road, beguiled them into a grove and got up a concert for their entertainment. While these poor fellows were listening to the music the stranglers were standing behind them; and at the proper moment for dramatic effect they applied the noose.

The most devoted fisherman must have a bite at least as often as once a week or his passion will cool and he will put up his tackle. The tiger-sportsman must find a tiger at least once a fortnight or he will get tired and quit. The elephant-hunter's enthusiasm will waste away little by little, and his zeal will perish at last if he plod around a month without finding a member of that noble family to assassinate.

But when the lust in the hunter's heart is for the noblest of all quarries, man, how different is the case! and how watery and poor is the zeal and how childish the endurance of those other hunters by comparison. Then, neither hunger, nor thirst, nor fatigue, nor deferred hope, nor monotonous disappointment, nor leaden-footed lapse of time can conquer the hunter's patience or weaken the joy of his quest or cool the splendid rage of his desire. Of all the hunting-passions that burn in the breast of man, there is none that can lift him superior to discouragements like these but the one—the royal sport, the supreme sport, whose quarry is his brother. By comparison, tiger-hunting is a colorless poor thing, for all it has been so bragged about.

Why, the Thug was content to tramp patiently along, afoot, in the wasting heat of India, week after week, at an average of nine or ten miles a day, if he might but hope to find game some time or other and refresh his longing soul with blood. Here is an instance:

"I (Ramzam) and Hyder set out, for the purpose of strangling travelers, from Guddapore, and proceeded via the Fort of Julalabad, Newulgunge, Bangermow, on the banks of the Ganges (upwards of 100 miles), from whence we returned by another route. Still no travelers! till we reached Bowaneegunge, where we fell in with a traveler, a boatman; we inveigled him and about two miles east of there Hyder strangled him as he stood—for he was troubled and afraid, and would not sit. We then made a long journey (about 130 miles) and reached Hussunpore Bundwa, where at the tank we fell in with a traveler—he slept there that night; next morning we followed him and tried to win his confidence; at the distance of two miles we endeavored to induce him to sit down—but he would not, having become aware of us. I attempted to strangle him as he walked along, but did not succeed; both of us then fell upon him, he made a great outcry, 'They are murdering me!' at length we strangled him and flung his body into a well. After this we returned to our homes, having been out a month and traveled about 260 miles. A total of two men murdered on the expedition."

And here is another case-related by the terrible Futty Khan, a man with a tremendous record, to be re-mentioned by and by:

"I, with three others, traveled for about 45 days a distance of about 200 miles in search of victims along the highway to Bundwa and returned by Davodpore (another 200 miles) during which journey we had only one murder, which happened in this manner. Four miles to the east of Noubustaghat we fell in with a traveler, an old man. I, with Koshal and Hyder, inveigled him and accompanied him that day within 3 miles of Rampoor, where, after dark, in a lonely place, we got him to sit down and rest; and while I kept him in talk, seated before him, Hyder behind strangled him: he made no resistance. Koshal stabbed him under the arms and in the throat, and we flung the body into a running stream. We got about 4 or 5 rupees each ($2 or $2.50). We then proceeded homewards. A total of one man murdered on this expedition."

There. They tramped 400 miles, were gone about three months, and harvested two dollars and a half apiece. But the mere pleasure of the hunt was sufficient. That was pay enough. They did no grumbling.

Every now and then in this big book one comes across that pathetic remark: "we tried to get him to sit down but he would not." It tells the whole story. Some accident had awakened the suspicion in him that these smooth friends who had been petting and coddling him and making him feel so safe and so fortunate after his forlorn and lonely wanderings were the dreaded Thugs; and now their ghastly invitation to "sit and rest" had confirmed its truth. He knew there was no help for him, and that he was looking his last upon earthly things, but "he would not sit." No, not that—it was too awful to think of!

There are a number of instances which indicate that when a man had once tasted the regal joys of man-hunting he could not be content with the dull monotony of a crimeless life afterward. Example, from a Thug's testimony:

"We passed through to Kurnaul, where we found a former Thug named Junooa, an old comrade of ours, who had turned religious mendicant and become a disciple and holy. He came to us in the serai and weeping with joy returned to his old trade."

Neither wealth nor honors nor dignities could satisfy a reformed Thug for long. He would throw them all away, someday, and go back to the lurid pleasures of hunting men, and being hunted himself by the British.

Ramzam was taken into a great native grandee's service and given authority over five villages. "My authority extended over these people to summons them to my presence, to make them stand or sit. I dressed well, rode my pony, and had two sepoys, a scribe and a village guard to attend me. During three years I used to pay each village a monthly visit, and no one suspected that I was a Thug! The chief man used to wait on me to transact business, and as I passed along, old and young made their salaam to me."

And yet during that very three years he got leave of absence "to attend a wedding," and instead went off on a Thugging lark with six other Thugs and hunted the highway for fifteen days!—with satisfactory results.

Afterwards he held a great office under a Rajah. There he had ten miles of country under his command and a military guard of fifteen men, with authority to call out 2,000 more upon occasion. But the British got on his track, and they crowded him so that he had to give himself up. See what a figure he was when he was gotten up for style and had all his things on: "I was fully armed—a sword, shield, pistols, a matchlock musket and a flint gun, for I was fond of being thus arrayed, and when so armed feared not though forty men stood before me."

He gave himself up and proudly proclaimed himself a Thug. Then by request he agreed to betray his friend and pal, Buhram, a Thug with the most tremendous record in India. "I went to the house where Buhram slept (often has he led our gangs!) I woke him, he knew me well, and came outside to me. It was a cold night, so under pretence of warming myself, but in reality to have light for his seizure by the guards, I lighted some straw and made a blaze. We were warming our hands. The guards drew around us. I said to them, 'This is Buhram,' and he was seized just as a cat seizes a mouse. Then Buhram said, 'I am a Thug! my father was a Thug, my grandfather was a Thug, and I have thugged with many!'"

So spoke the mighty hunter, the mightiest of the mighty, the Gordon Cumming of his day. Not much regret noticeable in it.—["Having planted a bullet in the shoulder-bone of an elephant, and caused the agonized creature to lean for support against a tree, I proceeded to brew some coffee. Having refreshed myself, taking observations of the elephant's spasms and writhings between the sips, I resolved to make experiments on vulnerable points, and, approaching very near, I fired several bullets at different parts of his enormous skull. He only acknowledged the shots by a salaam-like movement of his trunk, with the point of which he gently touched the wounds with a striking and peculiar action. Surprised and shocked to find that I was only prolonging the suffering of the noble beast, which bore its trials with such dignified composure, I resolved to finish the proceeding with all possible despatch, and accordingly opened fire upon him from the left side. Aiming at the shoulder, I fired six shots with the two-grooved rifle, which must have eventually proved mortal, after which I fired six shots at the same part with the Dutch six-pounder. Large tears now trickled down from his eyes, which he slowly shut and opened, his colossal frame shivered convulsively, and falling on his side he expired."—Gordon Cumming.]

So many many times this Official Report leaves one's curiosity unsatisfied. For instance, here is a little paragraph out of the record of a certain band of 193 Thugs, which has that defect:

"Fell in with Lall Sing Subahdar and his family, consisting of nine persons. Traveled with them two days, and the third put them all to death except the two children, little boys of one and a half years old."

There it stops. What did they do with those poor little fellows? What was their subsequent history? Did they purpose training them up as Thugs? How could they take care of such little creatures on a march which stretched over several months? No one seems to have cared to ask any questions about the babies. But I do wish I knew.

One would be apt to imagine that the Thugs were utterly callous, utterly destitute of human feelings, heartless toward their own families as well as toward other people's; but this was not so. Like all other Indians, they had a passionate love for their kin. A shrewd British officer who knew the Indian character, took that characteristic into account in laying his plans for the capture of Eugene Sue's famous Feringhea. He found out Feringhea's hiding-place, and sent a guard by night to seize him, but the squad was awkward and he got away. However, they got the rest of the family—the mother, wife, child, and brother—and brought them to the officer, at Jubbulpore; the officer did not fret, but bided his time: "I knew Feringhea would not go far while links so dear to him were in my hands." He was right. Feringhea knew all the danger he was running by staying in the neighborhood, still he could not tear himself away. The officer found that he divided his time between five villages where be had relatives and friends who could get news for him from his family in Jubbulpore jail; and that he never slept two consecutive nights in the same village. The officer traced out his several haunts, then pounced upon all the five villages on the one night and at the same hour, and got his man.

Another example of family affection. A little while previously to the capture of Feringhea's family, the British officer had captured Feringhea's foster-brother, leader of a gang of ten, and had tried the eleven and condemned them to be hanged. Feringhea's captured family arrived at the jail the day before

the execution was to take place. The foster-brother, Jhurhoo, entreated to be allowed to see the aged mother and the others. The prayer was granted, and this is what took place—it is the British officer who speaks:

"In the morning, just before going to the scaffold, the interview took place before me. He fell at the old woman's feet and begged that she would relieve him from the obligations of the milk with which she had nourished him from infancy, as he was about to die before he could fulfill any of them. She placed her hands on his head, and he knelt, and she said she forgave him all, and bid him die like a man."

If a capable artist should make a picture of it, it would be full of dignity and solemnity and pathos; and it could touch you. You would imagine it to be anything but what it was. There is reverence there, and tenderness, and gratefulness, and compassion, and resignation, and fortitude, and self-respect— and no sense of disgrace, no thought of dishonor. Everything is there that goes to make a noble parting, and give it a moving grace and beauty and dignity. And yet one of these people is a Thug and the other a mother of Thugs! The incongruities of our human nature seem to reach their limit here.

I wish to make note of one curious thing while I think of it. One of the very commonest remarks to be found in this bewildering array of Thug confessions is this:

"Strangled him and threw him an a well!" In one case they threw sixteen into a well—and they had thrown others in the same well before. It makes a body thirsty to read about it.

And there is another very curious thing. The bands of Thugs had private graveyards. They did not like to kill and bury at random, here and there and everywhere. They preferred to wait, and toll the victims along, and get to one of their regular burying-places ('bheels') if they could. In the little kingdom of Oude, which was about half as big as Ireland and about as big as the State of Maine, they had two hundred and seventy-four 'bheels'. They were scattered along fourteen hundred miles of road, at an average of only five miles apart, and the British government traced out and located each and every one of them and set them down on the map.

The Oude bands seldom went out of their own country, but they did a thriving business within its borders. So did outside bands who came in and helped. Some of the Thug leaders of Oude were noted for their successful careers. Each of four of them confessed to above 300 murders; another to nearly 400; our friend Ramzam to 604—he is the one who got leave of absence to attend a wedding and went thugging instead; and he is also the one who betrayed Buhram to the British.

But the biggest records of all were the murder-lists of Futty Khan and Buhram. Futty Khan's number is smaller than Ramzam's, but he is placed at the head because his average is the best in Oude-Thug history per year of service. His slaughter was 508 men in twenty years, and he was still a young man when the British stopped his industry. Buhram's list was 931 murders, but it took him forty years. His average was one man and nearly all of another man per month for forty years, but Futty Khan's average was two men and a little of another man per month during his twenty years of usefulness.

There is one very striking thing which I wish to call attention to. You have surmised from the listed callings followed by the victims of the Thugs that nobody could travel the Indian roads unprotected and live to get through; that the Thugs respected no quality, no vocation, no religion, nobody; that they killed every unarmed man that came in their way. That is wholly true—with one reservation. In all the long file of Thug confessions an English traveler is mentioned but once—and this is what the Thug says of the circumstance:

"He was on his way from Mhow to Bombay. We studiously avoided him. He proceeded next morning with a number of travelers who had sought his protection, and they took the road to Baroda."

We do not know who he was; he flits across the page of this rusty old book and disappears in the obscurity beyond; but he is an impressive figure, moving through that valley of death serene and unafraid, clothed in the might of the English name.

We have now followed the big official book through, and we understand what Thuggee was, what a bloody terror it was, what a desolating scourge it was. In 1830 the English found this cancerous organization imbedded in the vitals of the empire, doing its devastating work in secrecy, and assisted, protected, sheltered, and hidden by innumerable confederates —big and little native chiefs, customs officers, village officials, and native police, all ready to lie for it, and the mass of the people, through fear, persistently pretending to know nothing about its doings; and this condition of things had existed for generations, and was formidable with the sanctions of age and old custom. If ever there was an unpromising task, if ever there was a hopeless task in the world, surely it was offered here—the task of conquering Thuggee. But that little handful of English officials in India set their sturdy and confident grip upon it, and ripped it out, root and branch! How modest do Captain Vallancey's words sound now, when we read them again, knowing what we know:

"The day that sees this far-spread evil completely eradicated from India, and known only in name, will greatly tend to immortalize British rule in the East."

It would be hard to word a claim more modestly than that for this most noble work.

CHAPTER XLVIII.

Grief can take care of itself; but to get the full value of a joy you must have somebody to divide it with. —Pudd'nhead Wilson's New Calendar.

We left Bombay for Allahabad by a night train. It is the custom of the country to avoid day travel when it can conveniently be done. But there is one trouble: while you can seemingly "secure" the two lower berths by making early application, there is no ticket as witness of it, and no other producible evidence in case your proprietorship shall chance to be challenged. The word "engaged" appears on the window, but it doesn't state who the compartment is engaged, for. If your Satan and your Barney arrive before somebody else's servants, and spread the bedding on the two sofas and then stand guard till you come, all will be well; but if they step aside on an errand, they may find the beds promoted to the two shelves, and somebody else's demons standing guard over their master's beds, which in the meantime have been spread upon your sofas.

You do not pay anything extra for your sleeping place; that is where the trouble lies. If you buy a fare-ticket and fail to use it, there is room thus made available for someone else; but if the place were secured to you it would remain vacant, and yet your ticket would secure you another place when you were presently ready to travel.

However, no explanation of such a system can make it seem quite rational to a person who has been used to a more rational system. If our people had the arranging of it, we should charge extra for securing the place, and then the road would suffer no loss if the purchaser did not occupy it.

The present system encourages good manners—and also discourages them. If a young girl has a lower berth and an elderly lady comes in, it is usual for the girl to offer her place to this late comer; and it is usual for the late comer to thank her courteously and take it. But the thing happens differently sometimes. When we were ready to leave Bombay my daughter's satchels were holding possession of her berth—a lower one. At the last moment, a middle-aged American lady swarmed into the compartment, followed by native porters laden with her baggage. She was growling and snarling and scolding, and trying to make herself phenomenally disagreeable; and succeeding. Without a word, she hoisted the satchels into the hanging shelf, and took possession of that lower berth.

On one of our trips Mr. Smythe and I got out at a station to walk up and down, and when we came back Smythe's bed was in the hanging shelf and an English cavalry officer was in bed on the sofa which he had lately been occupying. It was mean to be glad about it, but it is the way we are made; I could not have been gladder if it had been my enemy that had suffered this misfortune. We all like to see people in trouble, if it doesn't cost us anything. I was so happy over Mr. Smythe's chagrin that I couldn't go to sleep for thinking of it and enjoying it. I knew he supposed the officer had committed the robbery himself, whereas without a doubt the officer's servant had done it without his knowledge. Mr. Smythe kept this incident warm in his heart, and longed for a chance to get even with somebody for it. Sometime afterward the opportunity came, in Calcutta. We were leaving on a 24-hour journey to Darjeeling. Mr. Barclay, the general superintendent, has made special provision for our accommodation, Mr. Smythe said; so there was no need to hurry about getting to the train; consequently, we were a little late.

When we arrived, the usual immense turmoil and confusion of a great Indian station were in full blast. It was an immoderately long train, for all the natives of India were going by it somewhither, and the native officials were being pestered to frenzy by belated and anxious people. They didn't know where our car was, and couldn't remember having received any orders about it. It was a deep disappointment; moreover, it looked as if our half of our party would be left behind altogether. Then Satan came running and said he had found a compartment with one shelf and one sofa unoccupied, and had made our beds and had stowed our baggage. We rushed to the place, and just as the train was ready to pull out and the porters were slamming the doors to, all down the line, an officer of the Indian Civil Service, a good friend of ours, put his head in and said:—

"I have been hunting for you everywhere. What are you doing here? Don't you know—"

The train started before he could finish. Mr. Smythe's opportunity was come. His bedding, on the shelf, at once changed places with the bedding—a stranger's—that was occupying the sofa that was opposite to mine. About ten o'clock we stopped somewhere, and a large Englishman of official military bearing stepped in. We pretended to be asleep. The lamps were covered, but there was light enough for us to note his look of surprise. He stood there, grand and fine, peering down at Smythe, and wondering in silence at the situation. After a bit be said:—

"Well!" And that was all.

But that was enough. It was easy to understand. It meant: "This is extraordinary. This is high-handed. I haven't had an experience like this before."

He sat down on his baggage, and for twenty minutes we watched him through our eyelashes, rocking and swaying there to the motion of the train. Then we came to a station, and he got up and went out, muttering: "I must find a lower berth, or wait over." His servant came presently and carried away his things.

Mr. Smythe's sore place was healed, his hunger for revenge was satisfied. But he couldn't sleep, and neither could I; for this was a venerable old car, and nothing about it was taut. The closet door slammed all night, and defied every fastening we could invent. We got up very much jaded, at dawn, and stepped out at a way station; and, while we were taking a cup of coffee, that Englishman ranged up alongside, and somebody said to him:

"So you didn't stop off, after all?"

"No. The guard found a place for me that had been, engaged and not occupied. I had a whole saloon car all to myself—oh, quite palatial! I never had such luck in my life."

That was our car, you see. We moved into it, straight off, the family and all. But I asked the English gentleman to remain, and he did. A pleasant man, an infantry colonel; and doesn't know, yet, that Smythe robbed him of his berth, but thinks it was done by Smythe's servant without Smythe's knowledge. He was assisted in gathering this impression.

The Indian trains are manned by natives exclusively. The Indian stations except very large and important ones—are manned entirely by natives, and so are the posts and telegraphs. The rank and file of the police are natives. All these people are pleasant and accommodating. One day I left an express train to lounge about in that perennially ravishing show, the ebb and flow and whirl of gaudy natives, that is always surging up and down the spacious platform of a great Indian station; and I lost myself in the ecstasy of it, and when I turned, the train was moving swiftly away. I was going to sit down and wait for another train, as I would have done at home; I had no thought of any other course. But a native official, who had a green flag in his hand, saw me, and said politely:

"Don't you belong in the train, sir?"

"Yes." I said.

He waved his flag, and the train came back! And he put me aboard with as much ceremony as if I had been the General Superintendent. They are kindly people, the natives. The face and the bearing that indicate a surly spirit and a bad heart seemed to me to be so rare among Indians—so nearly non-existent, in fact—that I sometimes wondered if Thuggee wasn't a dream, and not a reality. The bad hearts are there, but I

believe that they are in a small, poor minority. One thing is sure: They are much the most interesting people in the world—and the nearest to being incomprehensible. At any rate, the hardest to account for. Their character and their history, their customs and their religion, confront you with riddles at every turn-riddles which are a trifle more perplexing after they are explained than they were before. You can get the facts of a custom—like caste, and Suttee, and Thuggee, and so on—and with the facts a theory which tries to explain, but never quite does it to your satisfaction. You can never quite understand how so strange a thing could have been born, nor why.

For instance—the Suttee. This is the explanation of it:

A woman who throws away her life when her husband dies is instantly joined to him again, and is forever afterward happy with him in heaven; her family will build a little monument to her, or a temple, and will hold her in honor, and, indeed, worship her memory always; they will themselves be held in honor by the public; the woman's self-sacrifice has conferred a noble and lasting distinction upon her posterity. And, besides, see what she has escaped: If she had elected to live, she would be a disgraced person; she could not remarry; her family would despise her and disown her; she would be a friendless outcast, and miserable all her days.

Very well, you say, but the explanation is not complete yet. How did people come to drift into such a strange custom? What was the origin of the idea? "Well, nobody knows; it was probably a revelation sent down by the gods." One more thing: Why was such a cruel death chosen—why wouldn't a gentle one have answered? "Nobody knows; maybe that was a revelation, too."

No—you can never understand it. It all seems impossible. You resolve to believe that a widow never burnt herself willingly, but went to her death because she was afraid to defy public opinion. But you are not able to keep that position. History drives you from it. Major Sleeman has a convincing case in one of his books. In his government on the Nerbudda he made a brave attempt on the 28th of March, 1828, to put down Suttee on his own hook and without warrant from the Supreme Government of India. He could not foresee that the Government would put it down itself eight months later. The only backing he had was a bold nature and a compassionate heart. He issued his proclamation abolishing the Suttee in his district. On the morning of Tuesday—note the day of the week—the 24th of the following November, Ummed Singh Upadhya, head of the most respectable and most extensive Brahmin family in the district, died, and presently came a deputation of his sons and grandsons to beg that his old widow might be allowed to burn herself upon his pyre. Sleeman threatened to enforce his order, and punish severely any man who assisted; and he placed a police guard to see that no one did so. From the early morning the old widow of sixty-five had been sitting on the bank of the sacred river by her dead, waiting through the long hours for the permission; and at last the refusal came instead. In one little sentence Sleeman gives you a pathetic picture of this lonely old gray figure: all day and all night "she remained sitting by the edge of the water without eating or drinking." The next morning the body of the husband was burned to ashes in a pit eight feet square and three or four feet deep, in the view of several thousand spectators. Then the widow waded out to a bare rock in the river, and everybody went away but her sons and other relations. All day she sat there on her rock in the blazing sun without food or drink, and with no clothing but a sheet over her shoulders.

The relatives remained with her and all tried to persuade her to desist from her purpose, for they deeply loved her. She steadily refused. Then a part of the family went to Sleeman's house, ten miles away, and tried again to get him to let her burn herself. He refused, hoping to save her yet.

All that day she scorched in her sheet on the rock, and all that night she kept her vigil there in the bitter cold. Thursday morning, in the sight of her relatives, she went through a ceremonial which said more to them than any words could have done; she put on the dhaja (a coarse red turban) and broke her bracelets in pieces. By these acts she became a dead person in the eye of the law, and excluded from her caste forever. By the iron rule of ancient custom, if she should now choose to live she could never return to her family. Sleeman was in deep trouble. If she starved herself to death her family would be disgraced; and, moreover, starving would be a more lingering misery than the death by fire. He went back in the evening thoroughly worried. The old woman remained on her rock, and there in the morning he found her with her dhaja still on her head. "She talked very collectedly, telling me that she had determined to mix her ashes with those of her departed husband, and should patiently wait my permission to do so, assured that God would enable her to sustain life till that was given, though she dared not eat or drink. Looking at the sun, then rising before her over a long and beautiful reach of the river, she said calmly, 'My soul has been for five days with my husband's near that sun; nothing but my earthly frame is left; and this, I know, you will in time suffer to be mixed with his ashes in yonder pit, because it is not in your nature or usage wantonly to prolong the miseries of a poor old woman.'"

He assured her that it was his desire and duty to save her, and to urge her to live, and to keep her family from the disgrace of being thought her murderers. But she said she "was not afraid of their being thought so; that they had all, like good children, done everything in their power to induce her to live, and to abide with them; and if I should consent I know they would love and honor me, but my duties to them have now ended. I commit them all to your care, and I go to attend my husband, Ummed Singh Upadhya, with whose ashes on the funeral pile mine have been already three times mixed."

She believed that she and he had been upon the earth three several times as wife and husband, and that she had burned herself to death three times upon his pyre. That is why she said that strange thing. Since she had broken her bracelets and put on the red turban she regarded herself as a corpse; otherwise she would not have allowed herself to do her husband the irreverence of pronouncing his name. "This was the first time in her long life that she had ever uttered her husband's name, for in India no woman, high or low, ever pronounces the name of her husband."

Major Sleeman still tried to shake her purpose. He promised to build her a fine house among the temples of her ancestors upon the bank of the river and make handsome provision for her out of rent-free lands if she would consent to live; and if she wouldn't he would allow no stone or brick to ever mark the place where she died. But she only smiled and said, "My pulse has long ceased to beat, my spirit has departed; I shall suffer nothing in the burning; and if you wish proof, order some fire and you shall see this arm consumed without giving me any pain."

Sleeman was now satisfied that he could not alter her purpose.

He sent for all the chief members of the family and said he would suffer her to burn herself if they would enter into a written engagement to abandon the suttee in their family thenceforth. They agreed; the papers were drawn out and signed, and at noon, Saturday, word was sent to the poor old woman. She seemed greatly pleased. The ceremonies of bathing were gone through with, and by three o'clock she was ready and the fire was briskly burning in the pit. She had now gone without food or drink during more than four days and a half. She came ashore from her rock, first wetting her sheet in the waters of the sacred river, for without that safeguard any shadow which might fall upon her would convey impurity to her; then she walked to the pit, leaning upon one of her sons and a nephew—the distance was a hundred and fifty yards.

"I had sentries placed all around, and no other person was allowed to approach within five paces. She came on with a calm and cheerful countenance, stopped once, and casting her eyes upwards, said, 'Why have they kept me five days from thee, my husband?' On coming to the sentries her supporters stopped and remained standing; she moved on, and walked once around the pit, paused a moment, and while muttering a prayer, threw some flowers into the fire. She then walked up deliberately and steadily to the brink, stepped into the centre of the flame, sat down, and leaning back in the midst as if reposing upon a couch, was consumed without uttering a shriek or betraying one sign of agony."

It is fine and beautiful. It compels one's reverence and respect—no, has it freely, and without compulsion. We see how the custom, once started, could continue, for the soul of it is that stupendous power, Faith; faith brought to the pitch of effectiveness by the cumulative force of example and long use and custom; but we cannot understand how the first widows came to take to it. That is a perplexing detail.

Sleeman says that it was usual to play music at the suttee, but that the white man's notion that this was to drown the screams of the martyr is not correct; that it had a quite different purpose. It was believed that the martyr died prophecying; that the prophecies sometimes foretold disaster, and it was considered a kindness to those upon whom it was to fall to drown the voice and keep them in ignorance of the misfortune that was to come.

CHAPTER XLIX.

He had had much experience of physicians, and said "the only way to keep your health is to eat what you don't want, drink what you don't like, and do what you'd druther not." — Pudd'nhead Wilson's New Calendar.

It was a long journey—two nights, one day, and part of another day, from Bombay eastward to Allahabad; but it was always interesting, and it was not fatiguing. At first the, night travel promised to be fatiguing, but that was on account of pyjamas. This foolish night-dress consists of jacket and drawers. Sometimes they are made of silk, sometimes of a raspy, scratchy, slazy woolen material with a sandpaper surface. The drawers are loose elephant-legged and elephant-waisted things, and instead of buttoning around the body there is a drawstring to produce the required shrinkage. The jacket is roomy, and one buttons it in front. Pyjamas are hot on a hot night and cold on a cold night—defects which a nightshirt is free from. I tried the pyjamas in order to be in the fashion; but I was obliged to give them up, I couldn't stand them. There was no sufficient change from day-gear to night-gear. I missed the refreshing and luxurious sense, induced by the night-gown, of being undressed, emancipated, set free from restraints and trammels. In place of that, I had the worried, confined, oppressed, suffocated sense of being abed with my clothes on. All through the warm half of the night the coarse surfaces irritated my skin and made it feel baked and feverish, and the dreams which came in the fitful flurries of slumber were such as distress the sleep of the damned, or ought to; and all through the cold other half of the night I could get no time for sleep because I had to employ it all in stealing blankets. But blankets are of no value at such a time; the higher they are piled the more effectively they cork the cold in and keep it from getting out. The result is that your legs are ice, and you know how you will feel by and by when you are buried. In a sane interval I discarded the pyjamas, and led a rational and comfortable life thenceforth.

Out in the country in India, the day begins early. One sees a plain, perfectly flat, dust-colored and brick-yardy, stretching limitlessly away on every side in the dim gray light, striped everywhere with hard-beaten narrow paths, the vast flatness broken at wide intervals by bunches of spectral trees that mark where villages are; and along all the paths are slender women and the black forms of lanky naked men moving, to their work, the women with brass water-jars on their heads, the men carrying hoes. The man is not entirely naked; always there is a bit of white rag, a loin-cloth; it amounts to a bandage, and is a white accent on his black person, like the silver band around the middle of a pipe-stem. Sometimes he also wears a fluffy and voluminous white turban, and this adds a second accent. He then answers properly to Miss Gordon Cumming's flash-light picture of him—as a person who is dressed in "a turban and a pocket handkerchief."

All day long one has this monotony of dust-colored dead levels and scattering bunches of trees and mud villages. You soon realize that India is not beautiful; still there is an enchantment about it that is beguiling, and which does not pall. You cannot tell just what it is that makes the spell, perhaps, but you feel it and confess it, nevertheless. Of course, at bottom, you know in a vague way that it is history; it is that that affects you, a haunting sense of the myriads of human lives that have blossomed, and withered, and perished here, repeating and repeating and repeating, century after century, and age after age, the barren and meaningless process; it is this sense that gives to this forlorn, uncomely land power to speak to the spirit and make friends with it; to, speak to it with a voice bitter with satire, but eloquent with melancholy. The deserts of Australia and the ice-barrens of Greenland have no speech, for they have no venerable history; with nothing to tell of man and his vanities, his fleeting glories and his miseries, they have nothing wherewith to spiritualize their ugliness and veil it with a charm.

There is nothing pretty about an Indian village—a mud one— and I do not remember that we saw any but mud ones on that long flight to Allahabad. It is a little bunch of dirt-colored mud hovels jammed together within a mud wall. As a rule, the rains had beaten down parts of some of the houses, and this gave the village the aspect of a mouldering and hoary ruin. I believe the cattle and the vermin live inside the wall; for I saw cattle coming out and cattle going in; and whenever I saw a villager, he was scratching. This last is only circumstantial evidence, but I think it has value. The village has a battered little temple or two, big enough to hold an idol, and with custom enough to fat-up a priest and keep him comfortable. Where there are Mohammedans there are generally a few sorry tombs outside the village that have a decayed and neglected look. The villages interested me because of things which Major Sleeman says

about them in his books—particularly what he says about the division of labor in them. He says that the whole face of India is parceled out into estates of villages; that nine-tenths of the vast population of the land consist of cultivators of the soil; that it is these cultivators who inhabit the villages; that there are certain "established" village servants—mechanics and others who are apparently paid a wage by the village at large, and whose callings remain in certain families and are handed down from father to son, like an estate. He gives a list of these established servants: Priest, blacksmith, carpenter, accountant, washerman, basketmaker, potter, watchman, barber, shoemaker, brazier, confectioner, weaver, dyer, etc. In his day witches abounded, and it was not thought good business wisdom for a man to marry his daughter into a family that hadn't a witch in it, for she would need a witch on the premises to protect her children from the evil spells which would certainly be cast upon them by the witches connected with the neighboring families.

The office of midwife was hereditary in the family of the basket-maker. It belonged to his wife. She might not be competent, but the office was hers, anyway. Her pay was not high—25 cents for a boy, and half as much for a girl. The girl was not desired, because she would be a disastrous expense by and by. As soon as she should be old enough to begin to wear clothes for propriety's sake, it would be a disgrace to the family if she were not married; and to marry her meant financial ruin; for by custom the father must spend upon feasting and wedding-display everything he had and all he could borrow— in fact, reduce himself to a condition of poverty which he might never more recover from.

It was the dread of this prospective ruin which made the killing of girl-babies so prevalent in India in the old days before England laid the iron hand of her prohibitions upon the piteous slaughter. One may judge of how prevalent the custom was, by one of Sleeman's casual electrical remarks, when he speaks of children at play in villages—where girl-voices were never heard!

The wedding-display folly is still in full force in India, and by consequence the destruction of girl-babies is still furtively practiced; but not largely, because of the vigilance of the government and the sternness of the penalties it levies.

In some parts of India the village keeps in its pay three other servants: an astrologer to tell the villager when he may plant his crop, or make a journey, or marry a wife, or strangle a child, or borrow a dog, or climb a tree, or catch a rat, or swindle a neighbor, without offending the alert and solicitous heavens; and what his dream means, if he has had one and was not bright enough to interpret it himself by the details of his dinner; the two other established servants were the tiger-persuader and the hailstorm discourager. The one kept away the tigers if he could, and collected the wages anyway, and the other kept off the hailstorms, or explained why he failed. He charged the same for explaining a failure that he did for scoring a success. A man is an idiot who can't earn a living in India.

Major Sleeman reveals the fact that the trade union and the boycott are antiquities in India. India seems to have originated everything. The "sweeper" belongs to the bottom caste; he is the lowest of the low—all other castes despise him and scorn his office. But that does not trouble him. His caste is a caste, and that is sufficient for him, and so he is proud of it, not ashamed. Sleeman says:

"It is perhaps not known to many of my countrymen, even in India, that in every town and city in the country the right of sweeping the houses and streets is a monopoly, and is supported entirely by the pride of castes among the scavengers, who are all of the lowest class. The right of sweeping within a certain range is recognized by the caste to belong to a certain member; and if any other member presumes to sweep within that range, he is excommunicated—no other member will smoke out of his pipe or drink out of his jug; and he can get restored to caste only by a feast to the whole body of sweepers. If any housekeeper within a particular circle happens to offend the sweeper of that range, none of his filth will be removed till he pacifies him, because no other sweeper will dare to touch it; and the people of a town are often more tyrannized over by these people than by any other."

A footnote by Major Sleeman's editor, Mr. Vincent Arthur Smith, says that in our day this tyranny of the sweepers' guild is one of the many difficulties which bar the progress of Indian sanitary reform. Think of this:

"The sweepers cannot be readily coerced, because no Hindoo or Mussulman would do their work to save his life, nor will he pollute himself by beating the refractory scavenger."

They certainly do seem to have the whip-hand; it would be difficult to imagine a more impregnable position. "The vested rights described in the text are so fully recognized in practice that they are frequently the subject of sale or mortgage."

Just like a milk-route; or like a London crossing-sweepership. It is said that the London crossing-sweeper's right to his crossing is recognized by the rest of the guild; that they protect him in its possession; that certain choice crossings are valuable property, and are saleable at high figures. I have noticed that the man who sweeps in front of the Army and Navy Stores has a wealthy South African aristocratic style about him; and when he is off his guard, he has exactly that look on his face which you always see in the face of a man who has is saving up his daughter to marry her to a duke.

It appears from Sleeman that in India the occupation of elephant-driver is confined to Mohammedans. I wonder why that is. The water-carrier ('bheestie') is a Mohammedan, but it is said that the reason of that is, that the Hindoo's religion does not allow him to touch the skin of dead kine, and that is what the water-sack is made of; it would defile him. And it doesn't allow him to eat meat; the animal that furnished the meat was murdered, and to take any creature's life is a sin. It is a good and gentle religion, but inconvenient.

A great Indian river, at low water, suggests the familiar anatomical picture of a skinned human body, the intricate mesh of interwoven muscles and tendons to stand for water-channels, and the archipelagoes of fat and flesh inclosed by them to stand for the sandbars. Somewhere on this journey we passed such a river, and on a later journey we saw in the Sutlej the duplicate of that river. Curious rivers they are; low shores a dizzy distance apart, with nothing between but an enormous acreage of sand-flats with sluggish little veins of water dribbling around amongst them; Saharas of sand, smallpox-pitted with footprints punctured in belts as straight as the equator clear from the one shore to the other (barring the channel-interruptions)—a dry-shod ferry, you see. Long railway bridges are required for this sort of rivers, and India has them. You approach Allahabad by a very long one. It was now carrying us across the bed of the Jumna, a bed which did

not seem to have been slept in for one while or more. It wasn't all river-bed—most of it was overflow ground.

Allahabad means "City of God." I get this from the books. From a printed curiosity—a letter written by one of those brave and confident Hindoo strugglers with the English tongue, called a "babu"—I got a more compressed translation: "Godville." It is perfectly correct, but that is the most that can be said for it.

We arrived in the forenoon, and short-handed; for Satan got left behind somewhere that morning, and did not overtake us until after nightfall. It seemed very peaceful without him. The world seemed asleep and dreaming.

I did not see the native town, I think. I do not remember why; for an incident connects it with the Great Mutiny, and that is enough to make any place interesting. But I saw the English part of the city. It is a town of wide avenues and noble distances, and is comely and alluring, and full of suggestions of comfort and leisure, and of the serenity which a good conscience buttressed by a sufficient bank account gives. The bungalows (dwellings) stand well back in the seclusion and privacy of large enclosed compounds (private grounds, as we should say) and in the shade and shelter of trees. Even the photographer and the prosperous merchant ply their industries in the elegant reserve of big compounds, and the citizens drive in thereupon their business occasions. And not in cabs—no; in the Indian cities cabs are for the drifting stranger; all the white citizens have private carriages; and each carriage has a flock of white-turbaned black footmen and drivers all over it. The vicinity of a lecture-hall looks like a snowstorm,—and makes the lecturer feel like an opera. India has many names, and they are correctly descriptive. It is the Land of Contradictions, the Land of Subtlety and Superstition, the Land of Wealth and Poverty, the Land of Splendor and Desolation, the Land of Plague and Famine, the Land of the Thug and the Poisoner, and of the Meek and the Patient, the Land of the Suttee, the Land of the Unreinstatable Widow, the Land where All Life is Holy, the Land of Cremation, the Land where the Vulture is a Grave and a Monument, the Land of the Multitudinous Gods; and if signs go for anything, it is the Land of the Private Carriage.

In Bombay the forewoman of a millinery shop came to the hotel in her private carriage to take the measure for a gown—not for me, but for another. She had come out to India to make a temporary stay, but was extending it indefinitely; indeed, she was purposing to end her days there. In London, she said, her work had been hard, her hours long; for economy's sake she had had to live in shabby rooms and far away from the shop, watch the pennies, deny herself many of the common comforts of life, restrict herself in effect to its bare necessities, eschew cabs, travel third-class by underground train to and from her work, swallowing coal-smoke and cinders all the way, and sometimes troubled with the society of men and women who were less desirable than the smoke and the cinders. But in Bombay, on almost any kind of wages, she could live in comfort, and keep her carriage, and have six servants in place of the woman-of-all-work she had had in her English home. Later, in Calcutta, I found that the Standard Oil clerks had small one-horse vehicles, and did no walking; and I was told that the clerks of the other large concerns there had the like equipment. But to return to Allahabad.

I was up at dawn, the next morning. In India the tourist's servant does not sleep in a room in the hotel, but rolls himself up head and ears in his blanket and stretches himself on the veranda, across the front of his master's door, and spends the night there. I don't believe anybody's servant occupies a room. Apparently, the bungalow servants sleep on the veranda; it is roomy, and goes all around the house. I speak of menservants; I saw none of the other sex. I think there are none, except child-nurses. I was up at dawn, and walked around the veranda, past the rows of sleepers. In front of one door a Hindoo servant was squatting, waiting for his master to call him. He had polished the yellow shoes and placed them by the door, and now he had nothing to do but wait. It was freezing cold, but there he was, as motionless as a sculptured image, and as patient. It troubled me. I wanted to say to him, "Don't crouch there like that and freeze; nobody requires it of you; stir around and get warm." But I hadn't the words. I thought of saying 'jeldy jow', but I couldn't remember what it meant, so I didn't say it. I knew another phrase, but it wouldn't come to my mind. I moved on, purposing to dismiss him from my thoughts, but his bare legs and bare feet kept him there. They kept drawing me back from the sunny side to a point whence I could see him. At the end of an hour he had not changed his attitude in the least degree. It was a curious and impressive exhibition of meekness and patience, or fortitude or indifference, I did not know which. But it worried me, and it was spoiling my morning. In fact, it spoiled two hours of it quite thoroughly. I quitted this vicinity, then, and left him to punish himself as much as he might want to. But up to that time the man had not changed his attitude a hair. He will always remain with me, I suppose; his figure never grows vague in my memory. Whenever I read of Indian resignation, Indian patience under wrongs, hardships, and misfortunes, he comes before me. He becomes a personification, and stands for India in trouble. And for untold ages India in trouble has been pursued with the very remark which I was going to utter but didn't, because its meaning had slipped me: "Jeddy jow!" ("Come, shove along!")

Why, it was the very thing.

In the early brightness we made a long drive out to the Fort. Part of the way was beautiful. It led under stately trees and through groups of native houses and by the usual village well, where the picturesque gangs are always flocking to and fro and laughing and chattering; and this time brawny men were deluging their bronze bodies with the limpid water, and making a refreshing and enticing show of it; enticing, for the sun was already transacting business, firing India up for the day. There was plenty of this early bathing going on, for it was getting toward breakfast time, and with an unpurified body the Hindoo must not eat.

Then we struck into the hot plain, and found the roads crowded with pilgrims of both sexes, for one of the great religious fairs of India was being held, just beyond the Fort, at the junction of the sacred rivers, the Ganges and the Jumna. Three sacred rivers, I should have said, for there is a subterranean one. Nobody has seen it, but that doesn't signify. The fact that it is there is enough. These pilgrims had come from all over India; some of them had been months on the way, plodding patiently along in the heat and dust, worn, poor, hungry, but supported and sustained by an unwavering faith and belief; they were supremely happy and content, now; their full and sufficient reward was at hand; they were going to be cleansed from every vestige of sin and corruption by these holy waters which make utterly pure whatsoever thing they touch, even the dead and rotten. It is wonderful, the power of a faith like that, that can make multitudes upon multitudes of the old and weak and the young and frail enter without hesitation or complaint upon such incredible journeys and endure the

resultant miseries without repining. It is done in love, or it is done in fear; I do not know which it is. No matter what the impulse is, the act born of it is beyond imagination marvelous to our kind of people, the cold whites. There are choice great natures among us that could exhibit the equivalent of this prodigious self-sacrifice, but the rest of us know that we should not be equal to anything approaching it. Still, we all talk self-sacrifice, and this makes me hope that we are large enough to honor it in the Hindoo.

Two millions of natives arrive at this fair every year. How many start, and die on the road, from age and fatigue and disease and scanty nourishment, and how many die on the return, from the same causes, no one knows; but the tale is great, one may say enormous. Every twelfth year is held to be a year of peculiar grace; a greatly augmented volume of pilgrims results then. The twelfth year has held this distinction since the remotest times, it is said. It is said also that there is to be but one more twelfth year—for the Ganges. After that, that holiest of all sacred rivers will cease to be holy, and will be abandoned by the pilgrim for many centuries; how many, the wise men have not stated. At the end of that interval it will become holy again. Meantime, the data will be arranged by those people who have charge of all such matters, the great chief Brahmins. It will be like shutting down a mint. At a first glance it looks most unbrahminically uncommercial, but I am not disturbed, being soothed and tranquilized by their reputation. "Brer fox he lay low," as Uncle Remus says; and at the judicious time he will spring something on the Indian public which will show that he was not financially asleep when he took the Ganges out of the market.

Great numbers of the natives along the roads were bringing away holy water from the rivers. They would carry it far and wide in India and sell it. Tavernier, the French traveler (17th century), notes that Ganges water is often given at weddings, "each guest receiving a cup or two, according to the liberality of the host; sometimes 2,000 or 3,000 rupees' worth of it is consumed at a wedding."

The Fort is a huge old structure, and has had a large experience in religions. In its great court stands a monolith which was placed there more than 2,000 years ago to preach (Budhism) by its pious inscription; the Fort was built three centuries ago by a Mohammedan Emperor—a resanctification of the place in the interest of that religion. There is a Hindoo temple, too, with subterranean ramifications stocked with shrines and idols; and now the Fort belongs to the English, it contains a Christian Church. Insured in all the companies.

From the lofty ramparts one has a fine view of the sacred rivers. They join at that point—the pale blue Jumna, apparently clean and clear, and the muddy Ganges, dull yellow and not clean. On a long curved spit between the rivers, towns of tents were visible, with a multitude of fluttering pennons, and a mighty swarm of pilgrims. It was a troublesome place to get down to, and not a quiet place when you arrived; but it was interesting. There was a world of activity and turmoil and noise, partly religious, partly commercial; for the Mohammedans were there to curse and sell, and the Hindoos to buy and pray. It is a fair as well as a religious festival. Crowds were bathing, praying, and drinking the purifying waters, and many sick pilgrims had come long journeys in palanquins to be healed of their maladies by a bath; or if that might not be, then to die on the blessed banks and so make sure of heaven. There were fakeers in plenty, with their bodies dusted over with ashes and their long hair caked together with cow-dung; for the cow is holy and so is the rest of it; so holy that the good Hindoo peasant frescoes the walls of his hut with this refuse, and also constructs ornamental figures out of it for the gracing of his dirt floor. There were seated families, fearfully and wonderfully painted, who by attitude and grouping represented the families of certain great gods. There was a holy man who sat naked by the day and by the week on a cluster of iron spikes, and did not seem to mind it; and another holy man, who stood all day holding his withered arms motionless aloft, and was said to have been doing it for years. All of these performers have a cloth on the ground beside them for the reception of contributions, and even the poorest of the people give a trifle and hope that the sacrifice will be blessed to him. At last came a procession of naked holy people marching by and chanting, and I wrenched myself away.

CHAPTER L.

The man who is ostentatious of his modesty is twin to the statue that wears a fig-leaf. —Pudd'nhead Wilson's New Calendar.

The journey to Benares was all in daylight, and occupied but a few hours. It was admirably dusty. The dust settled upon you in a thick ashy layer and turned you into a fakeer, with nothing lacking to the role but the cow manure and the sense of holiness. There was a change of cars about mid-afternoon at Moghul-serai—if that was the name—and a wait of two hours there for the Benares train. We could have found a carriage and driven to the sacred city, but we should have lost the wait. In other countries a long wait at a station is a dull thing and tedious, but one has no right to have that feeling in India. You have the monster crowd of bejeweled natives, the stir, the bustle, the confusion, the shifting splendors of the costumes—dear me, the delight of it, the charm of it are beyond speech. The two-hour wait was over too soon. Among other satisfying things to look at was a minor native prince from the backwoods somewhere, with his guard of honor, a ragged but wonderfully gaudy gang of fifty dark barbarians armed with rusty flint-lock muskets. The general show came so near to exhausting variety that one would have said that no addition to it could be conspicuous, but when this Falstaff and his motleys marched through it one saw that that seeming impossibility had happened.

We got away by and by, and soon reached the outer edge of Benares; then there was another wait; but, as usual, with something to look at. This was a cluster of little canvas-boxes—palanquins. A canvas-box is not much of a sight—when empty; but when there is a lady in it, it is an object of interest. These boxes were grouped apart, in the full blaze of the terrible sun during the three-quarters of an hour that we tarried there. They contained zenana ladies. They had to sit up; there was not room enough to stretch out. They probably did not mind it. They are used to the close captivity of the dwellings all their lives; when they go a journey they are carried to the train in these boxes; in the train they have to be secluded from inspection. Many people pity them, and I always did it myself and never charged anything; but it is doubtful if this compassion is valued. While we were in India some good-hearted Europeans in one of the cities proposed to restrict a large park to the use of zenana ladies, so that they could go there and in assured privacy go about unveiled and enjoy the sunshine and air as they had never enjoyed them before. The good intentions back of the proposition were recognized, and sincere thanks returned for it, but the proposition itself met with a prompt declination at the hands of those who were authorized to speak for the zenana ladies.

Apparently, the idea was shocking to the ladies—indeed, it was quite manifestly shocking. Was that proposition the equivalent of inviting European ladies to assemble scantily and scandalously clothed in the seclusion of a private park? It seemed to be about that.

Without doubt modesty is nothing less than a holy feeling; and without doubt the person whose rule of modesty has been transgressed feels the same sort of wound that he would feel if something made holy to him by his religion had suffered a desecration. I say "rule of modesty" because there are about a million rules in the world, and this makes a million standards to be looked out for. Major Sleeman mentions the case of some high-caste veiled ladies who were profoundly scandalized when some English young ladies passed by with faces bare to the world; so scandalized that they spoke out with strong indignation and wondered that people could be so shameless as to expose their persons like that. And yet "the legs of the objectors were naked to mid-thigh." Both parties were clean-minded and irreproachably modest, while abiding by their separate rules, but they couldn't have traded rules for a change without suffering considerable discomfort. All human rules are more or less idiotic, I suppose. It is best so, no doubt. The way it is now, the asylums can hold the sane people, but if we tried to shut up the insane we should run out of building materials.

You have a long drive through the outskirts of Benares before you get to the hotel. And all the aspects are melancholy. It is a vision of dusty sterility, decaying temples, crumbling tombs, broken mud walls, shabby huts. The whole region seems to ache with age and penury. It must take ten thousand years of want to produce such an aspect. We were still outside of the great native city when we reached the hotel. It was a quiet and homelike house, inviting, and manifestly comfortable. But we liked its annex better, and went thither. It was a mile away, perhaps, and stood in the midst of a large compound, and was built bungalow fashion, everything on the ground floor, and a veranda all around. They have doors in India, but I don't know why. They don't fasten, and they stand open, as a rule, with a curtain hanging in the doorspace to keep out the glare of the sun. Still, there is plenty of privacy, for no white person will come in without notice, of course. The native men servants will, but they don't seem to count. They glide in, barefoot and noiseless, and are in the midst before one knows it. At first this is a shock, and sometimes it is an embarrassment; but one has to get used to it, and does.

There was one tree in the compound, and a monkey lived in it. At first I was strongly interested in the tree, for I was told that it was the renowned peepul—the tree in whose shadow you cannot tell a lie. This one failed to stand the test, and I went away from it disappointed. There was a softly creaking well close by, and a couple of oxen drew water from it by the hour, superintended by two natives dressed in the usual "turban and pocket-handkerchief." The tree and the well were the only scenery, and so the compound was a soothing and lonesome and satisfying place; and very restful after so many activities. There was nobody in our bungalow but ourselves; the other guests were in the next one, where the table d'hote was furnished. A body could not be more pleasantly situated. Each room had the customary bath attached—a room ten or twelve feet square, with a roomy stone-paved pit in it and abundance of water. One could not easily improve upon this arrangement, except by furnishing it with cold water and excluding the hot, in deference to the fervency of the climate; but that is forbidden. It would damage the bather's health. The stranger is warned against taking cold baths in India, but even the most intelligent strangers are fools, and they do not obey, and so they presently get laid up. I was the most intelligent fool that passed through, that year. But I am still more intelligent now. Now that it is too late.

I wonder if the 'dorian', if that is the name of it, is another superstition, like the peepul tree. There was a great abundance and variety of tropical fruits, but the dorian was never in evidence. It was never the season for the dorian. It was always going to arrive from Burma sometime or other, but it never did. By all accounts it was a most strange fruit, and incomparably delicious to the taste, but not to the smell. Its rind was said to exude a stench of so atrocious a nature that when a dorian was in the room even the presence of a polecat was a refreshment. We found many who had eaten the dorian, and they all spoke of it with a sort of rapture. They said that if you could hold your nose until the fruit was in your mouth a sacred joy would suffuse you from head to foot that would make you oblivious to the smell of the rind, but that if your grip slipped and you caught the smell of the rind before the fruit was in your mouth, you would faint. There is a fortune in that rind. Some day somebody will import it into Europe and sell it for cheese.

Benares was not a disappointment. It justified its reputation as a curiosity. It is on high ground, and overhangs a grand curve of the Ganges. It is a vast mass of building, compactly crusting a hill, and is cloven in all directions by an intricate confusion of cracks which stand for streets. Tall, slim minarets and beflagged temple-spires rise out of it and give it picturesqueness, viewed from the river. The city is as busy as an ant-hill, and the hurly-burly of human life swarming along the web of narrow streets reminds one of the ants. The sacred cow swarms along, too, and goes whither she pleases, and takes toll of the grain-shops, and is very much in the way, and is a good deal of a nuisance, since she must not be molested.

Benares is older than history, older than tradition, older even than legend, and looks twice as old as all of them put together. From a Hindoo statement quoted in Rev. Mr. Parker's compact and lucid Guide to Benares, I find that the site of the town was the beginning-place of the Creation. It was merely an upright "lingam," at first, no larger than a stove-pipe, and stood in the midst of a shoreless ocean. This was the work of the God Vishnu. Later he spread the lingam out till its surface was ten miles across. Still it was not large enough for the business; therefore he presently built the globe around it. Benares is thus the center of the earth. This is considered an advantage.

It has had a tumultuous history, both materially and spiritually. It started Brahminically, many ages ago; then by and by Buddha came in recent times 2,500 years ago, and after that it was Buddhist during many centuries—twelve, perhaps—but the Brahmins got the upper hand again, then, and have held it ever since. It is unspeakably sacred in Hindoo eyes, and is as unsanitary as it is sacred, and smells like the rind of the dorian. It is the headquarters of the Brahmin faith, and one-eighth of the population are priests of that church. But it is not an overstock, for they have all India as a prey. All India flocks thither on pilgrimage, and pours its savings into the pockets of the priests in a generous stream, which never fails. A priest with a good stand on the shore of the Ganges is much better off than the sweeper of the best crossing in London. A good stand is worth a world of money. The holy proprietor of it sits under his grand spectacular umbrella and blesses people all his life, and collects his commission, and grows fat and rich; and the stand passes from father to son, down and down and down through the ages, and remains a

permanent and lucrative estate in the family. As Mr. Parker suggests, it can become a subject of dispute, at one time or another, and then the matter will be settled, not by prayer and fasting and consultations with Vishnu, but by the intervention of a much more puissant power—an English court. In Bombay I was told by an American missionary that in India there are 640 Protestant missionaries at work. At first it seemed an immense force, but of course that was a thoughtless idea. One missionary to 500,000 natives—no, that is not a force; it is the reverse of it; 640 marching against an intrenched camp of 300,000,000—the odds are too great. A force of 640 in Benares alone would have its hands over-full with 8,000 Brahmin priests for adversary. Missionaries need to be well equipped with hope and confidence, and this equipment they seem to have always had in all parts of the world. Mr. Parker has it. It enables him to get a favorable outlook out of statistics which might add up differently with other mathematicians. For instance:

"During the past few years competent observers declare that the number of pilgrims to Benares has increased."

And then he adds up this fact and gets this conclusion:

"But the revival, if so it may be called, has in it the marks of death. It is a spasmodic struggle before dissolution."

In this world we have seen the Roman Catholic power dying, upon these same terms, for many centuries. Many a time we have gotten all ready for the funeral and found it postponed again, on account of the weather or something. Taught by experience, we ought not to put on our things for this Brahminical one till we see the procession move. Apparently one of the most uncertain things in the world is the funeral of a religion.

I should have been glad to acquire some sort of idea of Hindoo theology, but the difficulties were too great, the matter was too intricate. Even the mere A, B, C of it is baffling.

There is a trinity—Brahma, Shiva, and Vishnu—independent powers, apparently, though one cannot feel quite sure of that, because in one of the temples there is an image where an attempt has been made to concentrate the three in one person. The three have other names and plenty of them, and this makes confusion in one's mind. The three have wives and the wives have several names, and this increases the confusion. There are children, the children have many names, and thus the confusion goes on and on. It is not worth while to try to get any grip upon the cloud of minor gods, there are too many of them.

It is even a justifiable economy to leave Brahma, the chiefest god of all, out of your studies, for he seems to cut no great figure in India. The vast bulk of the national worship is lavished upon Shiva and Vishnu and their families. Shiva's symbol—the "lingam" with which Vishnu began the Creation—is worshiped by everybody, apparently. It is the commonest object in Benares. It is on view everywhere, it is garlanded with flowers, offerings are made to it, it suffers no neglect. Commonly it is an upright stone, shaped like a thimble-sometimes like an elongated thimble. This priapus-worship, then, is older than history. Mr. Parker says that the lingams in Benares "outnumber the inhabitants."

In Benares there are many Mohammedan mosques. There are Hindoo temples without number—these quaintly shaped and elaborately sculptured little stone jugs crowd all the lanes. The

Ganges itself and every individual drop of water in it are temples. Religion, then, is the business of Benares, just as gold-production is the business of Johannesburg. Other industries count for nothing as compared with the vast and all-absorbing rush and drive and boom of the town's specialty. Benares is the sacredest of sacred cities. The moment you step across the sharply-defined line which separates it from the rest of the globe, you stand upon ineffably and unspeakably holy ground. Mr. Parker says: "It is impossible to convey any adequate idea of the intense feelings of veneration and affection with which the pious Hindoo regards 'Holy Kashi' (Benares)." And then he gives you this vivid and moving picture:

"Let a Hindoo regiment be marched through the district, and as soon as they cross the line and enter the limits of the holy place they rend the air with cries of 'Kashi ji ki jai—jai—jai! (Holy Kashi! Hail to thee! Hail! Hail! Hail)'. The weary pilgrim scarcely able to stand, with age and weakness, blinded by the dust and heat, and almost dead with fatigue, crawls out of the oven-like railway carriage and as soon as his feet touch the ground he lifts up his withered hands and utters the same pious exclamation. Let a European in some distant city in casual talk in the bazar mention the fact that he has lived at Benares, and at once voices will be raised to call down blessings on his head, for a dweller in Benares is of all men most blessed."

It makes our own religious enthusiasm seem pale and cold. Inasmuch as the life of religion is in the heart, not the head, Mr. Parker's touching picture seems to promise a sort of indefinite postponement of that funeral.

CHAPTER LI.

Let me make the superstitions of a nation and I care not who makes its laws or its songs either. —Pudd'nhead Wilson's New Calendar.

Yes, the city of Benares is in effect just a big church, a religious hive, whose every cell is a temple, a shrine or a mosque, and whose every conceivable earthly and heavenly good is procurable under one roof, so to speak—a sort of Army and Navy Stores, theologically stocked.

I will make out a little itinerary for the pilgrim; then you will see how handy the system is, how convenient, how comprehensive. If you go to Benares with a serious desire to spiritually benefit yourself, you will find it valuable. I got some of the facts from conversations with the Rev. Mr. Parker and the others from his Guide to Benares; they are therefore trustworthy.

1. Purification. At sunrise you must go down to the Ganges and bathe, pray, and drink some of the water. This is for your general purification.

2. Protection against Hunger. Next, you must fortify yourself against the sorrowful earthly ill just named. This you will do by worshiping for a moment in the Cow Temple. By the door of it you will find an image of Ganesh, son of Shiva; it has the head of an elephant on a human body; its face and hands are of silver. You will worship it a little, and pass on, into a covered veranda, where you will find devotees reciting from the sacred books, with the help of instructors. In this place are groups of rude and dismal idols. You may contribute something for their support; then pass into the temple, a grim and stenchy place, for it is populous with sacred cows and with

beggars. You will give something to the beggars, and "reverently kiss the tails" of such cows as pass along, for these cows are peculiarly holy, and this act of worship will secure you from hunger for the day.

3. "The Poor Man's Friend." You will next worship this god. He is at the bottom of a stone cistern in the temple of Dalbhyeswar, under the shade of a noble peepul tree on the bluff overlooking the Ganges, so you must go back to the river. The Poor Man's Friend is the god of material prosperity in general, and the god of the rain in particular. You will secure material prosperity, or both, by worshiping him. He is Shiva, under a new alias, and he abides in the bottom of that cistern, in the form of a stone lingam. You pour Ganges water over him, and in return for this homage you get the promised benefits. If there is any delay about the rain, you must pour water in until the cistern is full; the rain will then be sure to come.

4. Fever. At the Kedar Ghat you will find a long flight of stone steps leading down to the river. Half way down is a tank filled with sewage. Drink as much of it as you want. It is for fever.

5. Smallpox. Go straight from there to the central Ghat. At its upstream end you will find a small whitewashed building, which is a temple sacred to Sitala, goddess of smallpox. Her under-study is there —a rude human figure behind a brass screen. You will worship this for reasons to be furnished presently.

6. The Well of Fate. For certain reasons you will next go and do homage at this well. You will find it in the Dandpan Temple, in the city. The sunlight falls into it from a square hole in the masonry above. You will approach it with awe, for your life is now at stake. You will bend over and look. If the fates are propitious, you will see your face pictured in the water far down in the well. If matters have been otherwise ordered, a sudden cloud will mask the sun and you will see nothing. This means that you have not six months to live. If you are already at the point of death, your circumstances are now serious. There is no time to lose. Let this world go, arrange for the next one. Handily situated, at your very elbow, is opportunity for this. You turn and worship the image of Maha Kal, the Great Fate, and happiness in the life to come is secured. If there is breath in your body yet, you should now make an effort to get a further lease of the present life. You have a chance. There is a chance for everything in this admirably stocked and wonderfully systemized Spiritual and Temporal Army and Navy Store. You must get yourself carried to the

7. Well of Long Life. This is within the precincts of the mouldering and venerable Briddhkal Temple, which is one of the oldest in Benares. You pass in by a stone image of the monkey god, Hanuman, and there, among the ruined courtyards, you will find a shallow pool of stagnant sewage. It smells like the best limburger cheese, and is filthy with the washings of rotting lepers, but that is nothing, bathe in it; bathe in it gratefully and worshipfully, for this is the Fountain of Youth; these are the Waters of Long Life. Your gray hairs will disappear, and with them your wrinkles and your rheumatism, the burdens of care and the weariness of age, and you will come out young, fresh, elastic, and full of eagerness for the new race of life. Now will come flooding upon you the manifold desires that haunt the dear dreams of the morning of life. You will go whither you will find

8. Fulfillment of Desire. To wit, to the Kameshwar Temple, sacred to Shiva as the Lord of Desires. Arrange for yours there.

And if you like to look at idols among the pack and jam of temples, there you will find enough to stock a museum. You will begin to commit sins now with a fresh, new vivacity; therefore, it will be well to go frequently to a place where you can get

9. Temporary Cleansing from Sin. To wit, to the Well of the Earring. You must approach this with the profoundest reverence, for it is unutterably sacred. It is, indeed, the most sacred place in Benares, the very Holy of Holies, in the estimation of the people. It is a railed tank, with stone stairways leading down to the water. The water is not clean. Of course it could not be, for people are always bathing in it. As long as you choose to stand and look, you will see the files of sinners descending and ascending—descending soiled with sin, ascending purged from it. "The liar, the thief, the murderer, and the adulterer may here wash and be clean," says the Rev. Mr. Parker, in his book. Very well. I know Mr. Parker, and I believe it; but if anybody else had said it, I should consider him a person who had better go down in the tank and take another wash. The god Vishnu dug this tank. He had nothing to dig with but his "discus." I do not know what a discus is, but I know it is a poor thing to dig tanks with, because, by the time this one was finished, it was full of sweat—Vishnu's sweat. He constructed the site that Benares stands on, and afterward built the globe around it, and thought nothing of it, yet sweated like that over a little thing like this tank. One of these statements is doubtful. I do not know which one it is, but I think it difficult not to believe that a god who could build a world around Benares would not be intelligent enough to build it around the tank too, and not have to dig it. Youth, long life, temporary purification from sin, salvation through propitiation of the Great Fate —these are all good. But you must do something more. You must

10. Make Salvation Sure. There are several ways. To get drowned in the Ganges is one, but that is not pleasant. To die within the limits of Benares is another; but that is a risky one, because you might be out of town when your time came. The best one of all is the Pilgrimage Around the City. You must walk; also, you must go barefoot. The tramp is forty-four miles, for the road winds out into the country a piece, and you will be marching five or six days. But you will have plenty of company. You will move with throngs and hosts of happy pilgrims whose radiant costumes will make the spectacle beautiful and whose glad songs and holy pans of triumph will banish your fatigues and cheer your spirit; and at intervals there will be temples where you may sleep and be refreshed with food. The pilgrimage completed, you have purchased salvation, and paid for it. But you may not get it unless you

11. Get Your Redemption Recorded. You can get this done at the Sakhi Binayak Temple, and it is best to do it, for otherwise you might not be able to prove that you had made the pilgrimage in case the matter should some day come to be disputed. That temple is in a lane back of the Cow Temple. Over the door is a red image of Ganesh of the elephant head, son and heir of Shiva, and Prince of Wales to the Theological Monarchy, so to speak. Within is a god whose office it is to record your pilgrimage and be responsible for you. You will not see him, but you will see a Brahmin who will attend to the matter and take the money. If he should forget to collect the money, you can remind him. He knows that your salvation is now secure, but of course you would like to know it yourself. You have nothing to do but go and pray, and pay at the

12. Well of the Knowledge of Salvation. It is close to the Golden Temple. There you will see, sculptured out of a single

piece of black marble, a bull which is much larger than any living bull you have ever seen, and yet is not a good likeness after all. And there also you will see a very uncommon thing—an image of Shiva. You have seen his lingam fifty thousand times already, but this is Shiva himself, and said to be a good likeness. It has three eyes. He is the only god in the firm that has three. "The well is covered by a fine canopy of stone supported by forty pillars," and around it you will find what you have already seen at almost every shrine you have visited in Benares, a mob of devout and eager pilgrims. The sacred water is being ladled out to them; with it comes to them the knowledge, clear, thrilling, absolute, that they are saved; and you can see by their faces that there is one happiness in this world which is supreme, and to which no other joy is comparable. You receive your water, you make your deposit, and now what more would you have? Gold, diamonds, power, fame? All in a single moment these things have withered to dirt, dust, ashes. The world has nothing to give you now. For you it is bankrupt.

I do not claim that the pilgrims do their acts of worship in the order and sequence above charted out in this Itinerary of mine, but I think logic suggests that they ought to do so. Instead of a helter-skelter worship, we then have a definite starting-place, and a march which carries the pilgrim steadily forward by reasoned and logical progression to a definite goal. Thus, his Ganges bath in the early morning gives him an appetite; he kisses the cow-tails, and that removes it. It is now business hours, and longings for material prosperity rise in his mind, and be goes and pours water over Shiva's symbol; this insures the prosperity, but also brings on a rain, which gives him a fever. Then he drinks the sewage at the Kedar Ghat to cure the fever; it cures the fever but gives him the smallpox. He wishes to know how it is going to turn out; he goes to the Dandpan Temple and looks down the well. A clouded sun shows him that death is near. Logically his best course for the present, since he cannot tell at what moment he may die, is to secure a happy hereafter; this he does, through the agency of the Great Fate. He is safe, now, for heaven; his next move will naturally be to keep out of it as long as he can. Therefore he goes to the Briddhkal Temple and secures Youth and long life by bathing in a puddle of leper-pus which would kill a microbe. Logically, Youth has re-equipped him for sin and with the disposition to commit it; he will naturally go to the fane which is consecrated to the Fulfillment of Desires, and make arrangements. Logically, he will now go to the Well of the Earring from time to time to unload and freshen up for further banned enjoyments. But first and last and all the time he is human, and therefore in his reflective intervals he will always be speculating in "futures." He will make the Great Pilgrimage around the city and so make his salvation absolutely sure; he will also have record made of it, so that it may remain absolutely sure and not be forgotten or repudiated in the confusion of the Final Settlement. Logically, also, he will wish to have satisfying and tranquilizing personal knowledge that that salvation is secure; therefore he goes to the Well of the Knowledge of Salvation, adds that completing detail, and then goes about his affairs serene and content; serene and content, for he is now royally endowed with an advantage which no religion in this world could give him but his own; for henceforth he may commit as many million sins as he wants to and nothing can come of it.

Thus the system, properly and logically ordered, is neat, compact, clearly defined, and covers the whole ground. I desire to recommend it to such as find the other systems too difficult, exacting, and irksome for the uses of this fretful brief life of ours.

However, let me not deceive any one. My Itinerary lacks a detail. I must put it in. The truth is, that after the pilgrim has faithfully followed the requirements of the Itinerary through to the end and has secured his salvation and also the personal knowledge of that fact, there is still an accident possible to him which can annul the whole thing. If he should ever cross to the other side of the Ganges and get caught out and die there he would at once come to life again in the form of an ass. Think of that, after all this trouble and expense. You see how capricious and uncertain salvation is there. The Hindoo has a childish and unreasoning aversion to being turned into an ass. It is hard to tell why. One could properly expect an ass to have an aversion to being turned into a Hindoo. One could understand that he could lose dignity by it; also self-respect, and nine-tenths of his intelligence. But the Hindoo changed into an ass wouldn't lose anything, unless you count his religion. And he would gain much—release from his slavery to two million gods and twenty million priests, fakeers, holy mendicants, and other sacred bacilli; he would escape the Hindoo hell; he would also escape the Hindoo heaven. These are advantages which the Hindoo ought to consider; then he would go over and die on the other side.

Benares is a religious Vesuvius. In its bowels the theological forces have been heaving and tossing, rumbling, thundering and quaking, boiling, and weltering and flaming and smoking for ages. But a little group of missionaries have taken post at its base, and they have hopes. There are the Baptist Missionary Society, the Church Missionary Society, the London Missionary Society, the Wesleyan Missionary Society, and the Zenana Bible and Medical Mission. They have schools, and the principal work seems to be among the children. And no doubt that part of the work prospers best, for grown people everywhere are always likely to cling to the religion they were brought up in.

CHAPTER LII.

Wrinkles should merely indicate where smiles have been. — Pudd'nhead Wilson's New Calendar.

In one of those Benares temples we saw a devotee working for salvation in a curious way. He had a huge wad of clay beside him and was making it up into little wee gods no bigger than carpet tacks. He stuck a grain of rice into each—to represent the lingam, I think. He turned them out nimbly, for he had had long practice and had acquired great facility. Every day he made 2,000 gods, then threw them into the holy Ganges. This act of homage brought him the profound homage of the pious—also their coppers. He had a sure living here, and was earning a high place in the hereafter.

The Ganges front is the supreme show-place of Benares. Its tall bluffs are solidly caked from water to summit, along a stretch of three miles, with a splendid jumble of massive and picturesque masonry, a bewildering and beautiful confusion of stone platforms, temples, stair-flights, rich and stately palaces—nowhere a break, nowhere a glimpse of the bluff itself; all the long face of it is compactly walled from sight by this crammed perspective of platforms, soaring stairways, sculptured temples, majestic palaces, softening away into the distances; and there is movement, motion, human life everywhere, and brilliantly costumed —streaming in rainbows up and down the lofty stairways, and massed in metaphorical flower-gardens on the miles of great platforms at the river's edge.

All this masonry, all this architecture represents piety. The palaces were built by native princes whose homes, as a rule, are far from Benares, but who go there from time to time to refresh their souls with the sight and touch of the Ganges, the river of their idolatry. The stairways are records of acts of piety; the crowd of costly little temples are tokens of money spent by rich men for present credit and hope of future reward. Apparently, the rich Christian who spends large sums upon his religion is conspicuous with us, by his rarity, but the rich Hindoo who doesn't spend large sums upon his religion is seemingly non-existent. With us the poor spend money on their religion, but they keep back some to live on. Apparently, in India, the poor bankrupt themselves daily for their religion. The rich Hindoo can afford his pious outlays; he gets much glory for his spendings, yet keeps back a sufficiency of his income for temporal purposes; but the poor Hindoo is entitled to compassion, for his spendings keep him poor, yet get him no glory.

We made the usual trip up and down the river, seated in chairs under an awning on the deck of the usual commodious hand-propelled ark; made it two or three times, and could have made it with increasing interest and enjoyment many times more; for, of course, the palaces and temples would grow more and more beautiful every time one saw them, for that happens with all such things; also, I think one would not get tired of the bathers, nor their costumes, nor of their ingenuities in getting out of them and into them again without exposing too much bronze, nor of their devotional gesticulations and absorbed bead-tellings.

But I should get tired of seeing them wash their mouths with that dreadful water and drink it. In fact, I did get tired of it, and very early, too. At one place where we halted for a while, the foul gush from a sewer was making the water turbid and murky all around, and there was a random corpse slopping around in it that had floated down from up country. Ten steps below that place stood a crowd of men, women, and comely young maidens waist deep in the water-and they were scooping it up in their hands and drinking it. Faith can certainly do wonders, and this is an instance of it. Those people were not drinking that fearful stuff to assuage thirst, but in order to purify their souls and the interior of their bodies. According to their creed, the Ganges water makes everything pure that it touches—instantly and utterly pure. The sewer water was not an offence to them, the corpse did not revolt them; the sacred water had touched both, and both were now snow-pure, and could defile no one. The memory of that sight will always stay by me; but not by request.

A word further concerning the nasty but all-purifying Ganges water. When we went to Agra, by and by, we happened there just in time to be in at the birth of a marvel—a memorable scientific discovery—the discovery that in certain ways the foul and derided Ganges water is the most puissant purifier in the world! This curious fact, as I have said, had just been added to the treasury of modern science. It had long been noted as a strange thing that while Benares is often afflicted with the cholera she does not spread it beyond her borders. This could not be accounted for. Mr. Henkin, the scientist in the employ of the government of Agra, concluded to examine the water. He went to Benares and made his tests. He got water at the mouths of the sewers where they empty into the river at the bathing ghats; a cubic centimetre of it contained millions of germs; at the end of six hours they were all dead. He caught a floating corpse, towed it to the shore, and from beside it he dipped up water that was swarming with cholera germs; at the end of six hours they were all dead. He added swarm after swarm of cholera germs to this water; within the six hours they always died, to the last sample. Repeatedly, he took pure well water which was bare of animal life, and put into it a few cholera germs; they always began to propagate at once, and always within six hours they swarmed—and were numberable by millions upon millions.

For ages and ages the Hindoos have had absolute faith that the water of the Ganges was absolutely pure, could not be defiled by any contact whatsoever, and infallibly made pure and clean whatsoever thing touched it. They still believe it, and that is why they bathe in it and drink it, caring nothing for its seeming filthiness and the floating corpses. The Hindoos have been laughed at, these many generations, but the laughter will need to modify itself a little from now on. How did they find out the water's secret in those ancient ages? Had they germ-scientists then? We do not know. We only know that they had a civilization long before we emerged from savagery. But to return to where I was before; I was about to speak of the burning-ghat.

They do not burn fakeers—those revered mendicants. They are so holy that they can get to their place without that sacrament, provided they be consigned to the consecrating river. We saw one carried to mid-stream and thrown overboard. He was sandwiched between two great slabs of stone.

We lay off the cremation-ghat half an hour and saw nine corpses burned. I should not wish to see any more of it, unless I might select the parties. The mourners follow the bier through the town and down to the ghat; then the bier-bearers deliver the body to some low-caste natives —Doms—and the mourners turn about and go back home. I heard no crying and saw no tears, there was no ceremony of parting. Apparently, these expressions of grief and affection are reserved for the privacy of the home. The dead women came draped in red, the men in white. They are laid in the water at the river's edge while the pyre is being prepared.

The first subject was a man. When the Doms unswathed him to wash him, he proved to be a sturdily built, well-nourished and handsome old gentleman, with not a sign about him to suggest that he had ever been ill. Dry wood was brought and built up into a loose pile; the corpse was laid upon it and covered over with fuel. Then a naked holy man who was sitting on high ground a little distance away began to talk and shout with great energy, and he kept up this noise right along. It may have been the funeral sermon, and probably was. I forgot to say that one of the mourners remained behind when the others went away. This was the dead man's son, a boy of ten or twelve, brown and handsome, grave and self-possessed, and clothed in flowing white. He was there to burn his father. He was given a torch, and while he slowly walked seven times around the pyre the naked black man on the high ground poured out his sermon more clamorously than ever. The seventh circuit completed, the boy applied the torch at his father's head, then at his feet; the flames sprang briskly up with a sharp crackling noise, and the lad went away. Hindoos do not want daughters, because their weddings make such a ruinous expense; but they want sons, so that at death they may have honorable exit from the world; and there is no honor equal to the honor of having one's pyre lighted by one's son. The father who dies sonless is in a grievous situation indeed, and is pitied. Life being uncertain, the Hindoo marries while he is still a boy, in the hope that he will have a son ready when the day of his need shall come. But if he have no son, he will adopt one. This answers every purpose.

Meantime the corpse is burning, also several others. It is a dismal business. The stokers did not sit down in idleness, but moved briskly about, punching up the fires with long poles, and now and then adding fuel. Sometimes they hoisted the half of a skeleton into the air, then slammed it down and beat it with the pole, breaking it up so that it would burn better. They hoisted skulls up in the same way and banged and battered them. The sight was hard to bear; it would have been harder if the mourners had stayed to witness it. I had but a moderate desire to see a cremation, so it was soon satisfied. For sanitary reasons it would be well if cremation were universal; but this form is revolting, and not to be recommended.

The fire used is sacred, of course—for there is money in it. Ordinary fire is forbidden; there is no money in it. I was told that this sacred fire is all furnished by one person, and that he has a monopoly of it and charges a good price for it. Sometimes a rich mourner pays a thousand rupees for it. To get to paradise from India is an expensive thing. Every detail connected with the matter costs something, and helps to fatten a priest. I suppose it is quite safe to conclude that that fire-bug is in holy orders.

Close to the cremation-ground stand a few time-worn stones which are remembrances of the suttee. Each has a rough carving upon it, representing a man and a woman standing or walking hand in hand, and marks the spot where a widow went to her death by fire in the days when the suttee flourished. Mr. Parker said that widows would burn themselves now if the government would allow it. The family that can point to one of these little memorials and say: "She who burned herself there was an ancestress of ours," is envied.

It is a curious people. With them, all life seems to be sacred except human life. Even the life of vermin is sacred, and must not be taken. The good Jain wipes off a seat before using it, lest he cause the death of some valueless insect by sitting down on it. It grieves him to have to drink water, because the provisions in his stomach may not agree with the microbes. Yet India invented Thuggery and the Suttee. India is a hard country to understand. We went to the temple of the Thug goddess, Bhowanee, or Kali, or Durga. She has these names and others. She is the only god to whom living sacrifices are made. Goats are sacrificed to her. Monkeys would be cheaper. There are plenty of them about the place. Being sacred, they make themselves very free, and scramble around wherever they please. The temple and its porch are beautifully carved, but this is not the case with the idol. Bhowanee is not pleasant to look at. She has a silver face, and a projecting swollen tongue painted a deep red. She wears a necklace of skulls.

In fact, none of the idols in Benares are handsome or attractive. And what a swarm of them there is! The town is a vast museum of idols—and all of them crude, misshapen, and ugly. They flock through one's dreams at night, a wild mob of nightmares. When you get tired of them in the temples and take a trip on the river, you find idol giants, flashily painted, stretched out side by side on the shore. And apparently wherever there is room for one more lingam, a lingam is there. If Vishnu had foreseen what his town was going to be, he would have called it Idolville or Lingamburg.

The most conspicuous feature of Benares is the pair of slender white minarets which tower like masts from the great Mosque of Aurangzeb. They seem to be always in sight, from everywhere, those airy, graceful, inspiring things. But masts is not the right word, for masts have a perceptible taper, while these minarets have not. They are 142 feet high, and only 8½ feet in diameter at the base, and 7½ at the summit—scarcely any taper at all. These are the proportions of a candle; and fair and fairylike candles these are. Will be, anyway, some day, when the Christians inherit them and top them with the electric light. There is a great view from up there—a wonderful view. A large gray monkey was part of it, and damaged it. A monkey has no judgment. This one was skipping about the upper great heights of the mosque —skipping across empty yawning intervals which were almost too wide for him, and which he only just barely cleared, each time, by the skin of his teeth. He got me so nervous that I couldn't look at the view. I couldn't look at anything but him. Every time he went sailing over one of those abysses my breath stood still, and when he grabbed for the perch he was going for, I grabbed too, in sympathy. And he was perfectly indifferent, perfectly unconcerned, and I did all the panting myself. He came within an ace of losing his life a dozen times, and I was so troubled about him that I would have shot him if I had had anything to do it with. But I strongly recommend the view. There is more monkey than view, and there is always going to be more monkey while that idiot survives, but what view you get is superb. All Benares, the river, and the region round about are spread before you. Take a gun, and look at the view.

The next thing I saw was more reposeful. It was a new kind of art. It was a picture painted on water. It was done by a native. He sprinkled fine dust of various colors on the still surface of a basin of water, and out of these sprinklings a dainty and pretty picture gradually grew, a picture which a breath could destroy. Somehow it was impressive, after so much browsing among massive and battered and decaying fanes that rest upon ruins, and those ruins upon still other ruins, and those upon still others again. It was a sermon, an allegory, a symbol of Instability. Those creations in stone were only a kind of water pictures, after all.

A prominent episode in the Indian career of Warren Hastings had Benares for its theater. Wherever that extraordinary man set his foot, he left his mark. He came to Benares in 1781 to collect a fine of £500,000 which he had levied upon its Rajah, Cheit Singly on behalf of the East India Company. Hastings was a long way from home and help. There were, probably, not a dozen Englishmen within reach; the Rajah was in his fort with his myriads around him. But no matter. From his little camp in a neighboring garden, Hastings sent a party to arrest the sovereign. He sent on this daring mission a couple of hundred native soldiers sepoys —under command of three young English lieutenants. The Rajah submitted without a word. The incident lights up the Indian situation electrically, and gives one a vivid sense of the strides which the English had made and the mastership they had acquired in the land since the date of Clive's great victory. In a quarter of a century, from being nobodies, and feared by none, they were become confessed lords and masters, feared by all, sovereigns included, and served by all, sovereigns included. It makes the fairy tales sound true. The English had not been afraid to enlist native soldiers to fight against their own people and keep them obedient. And now Hastings was not afraid to come away out to this remote place with a handful of such soldiers and send them to arrest a native sovereign.

The lieutenants imprisoned the Rajah in his own fort. It was beautiful, the pluckiness of it, the impudence of it. The arrest enraged the Rajah's people, and all Benares came storming about the place and threatening vengeance. And yet, but for an accident, nothing important would have resulted, perhaps. The mob found out a most strange thing, an almost incredible thing—that this handful of soldiers had come on this hardy errand with empty guns and no ammunition. This has been attributed to thoughtlessness, but it could hardly have been that, for in such large emergencies as this, intelligent people do think. It must have been indifference, an over-confidence born of the proved submissiveness of the native character, when confronted by even one or two stern Britons in their war paint. But, however that may be, it was a fatal discovery that the mob had made. They were full of courage, now, and they broke into the fort and massacred the helpless soldiers and their officers. Hastings escaped from Benares by night and got safely away, leaving the principality in a state of wild insurrection; but he was back again within the month, and quieted it down in his prompt and virile way, and took the Rajah's throne away from him and gave it to another man. He was a capable kind of person was Warren Hastings. This was the only time he was ever out of ammunition. Some of his acts have left stains upon his name which can never be washed away, but he saved to England the Indian Empire, and that was the best service that was ever done to the Indians themselves, those wretched heirs of a hundred centuries of pitiless oppression and abuse.

CHAPTER LIII.

True irreverence is disrespect for another man's god. — Pudd'nhead Wilson's New Calendar.

It was in Benares that I saw another living god. That makes two. I believe I have seen most of the greater and lesser wonders of the world, but I do not remember that any of them interested me so overwhelmingly as did that pair of gods.

When I try to account for this effect I find no difficulty about it. I find that, as a rule, when a thing is a wonder to us it is not because of what we see in it, but because of what others have seen in it. We get almost all our wonders at second hand. We are eager to see any celebrated thing—and we never fail of our reward; just the deep privilege of gazing upon an object which has stirred the enthusiasm or evoked the reverence or affection or admiration of multitudes of our race is a thing which we value; we are profoundly glad that we have seen it, we are permanently enriched from having seen it, we would not part with the memory of that experience for a great price. And yet that very spectacle may be the Taj. You cannot keep your enthusiasms down, you cannot keep your emotions within bounds when that soaring bubble of marble breaks upon your view. But these are not your enthusiasms and emotions—they are the accumulated emotions and enthusiasms of a thousand fervid writers, who have been slowly and steadily storing them up in your heart day by day and year by year all your life; and now they burst out in a flood and overwhelm you; and you could not be a whit happier if they were your very own. By and by you sober down, and then you perceive that you have been drunk on the smell of somebody else's cork. For ever and ever the memory of my distant first glimpse of the Taj will compensate me for creeping around the globe to have that great privilege.

But the Taj—with all your inflation of delusive emotions, acquired at second-hand from people to whom in the majority of cases they were also delusions acquired at second-hand—a thing which you fortunately did not think of or it might have made you doubtful of what you imagined were your own what is the Taj as a marvel, a spectacle and an uplifting and overpowering wonder, compared with a living, breathing, speaking personage whom several millions of human beings devoutly and sincerely and unquestioningly believe to be a

God, and humbly and gratefully worship as a God?

He was sixty years old when I saw him. He is called Sri 108 Swami Bhaskarananda Saraswati. That is one form of it. I think that that is what you would call him in speaking to him—because it is short. But you would use more of his name in addressing a letter to him; courtesy would require this. Even then you would not have to use all of it, but only this much:

Sri 108 Matparamahansrzpairivrajakacharyaswamibhaskaranandasaraswati.

You do not put "Esq." after it, for that is not necessary. The word which opens the volley is itself a title of honor "Sri." The "108" stands for the rest of his names, I believe. Vishnu has 108 names which he does not use in business, and no doubt it is a custom of gods and a privilege sacred to their order to keep 108 extra ones in stock. Just the restricted name set down above is a handsome property, without the 108. By my count it has 58 letters in it. This removes the long German words from competition; they are permanently out of the race.

Sri 108 S. B. Saraswati has attained to what among the Hindoos is called the "state of perfection." It is a state which other Hindoos reach by being born again and again, and over and over again into this world, through one re-incarnation after another—a tiresome long job covering centuries and decades of centuries, and one that is full of risks, too, like the accident of dying on the wrong side of the Ganges some time or other and waking up in the form of an ass, with a fresh start necessary and the numerous trips to be made all over again. But in reaching perfection, Sri 108 S. B. S. has escaped all that. He is no longer a part or a feature of this world; his substance has changed, all earthiness has departed out of it; he is utterly holy, utterly pure; nothing can desecrate this holiness or stain this purity; he is no longer of the earth, its concerns are matters foreign to him, its pains and griefs and troubles cannot reach him. When he dies, Nirvana is his; he will be absorbed into the substance of the Supreme Deity and be at peace forever.

The Hindoo Scriptures point out how this state is to be reached, but it is only once in a thousand years, perhaps, that candidate accomplishes it. This one has traversed the course required, stage by stage, from the beginning to the end, and now has nothing left to do but wait for the call which shall release him from a world in which he has now no part nor lot. First, he passed through the student stage, and became learned in the holy books. Next he became citizen, householder, husband, and father. That was the required second stage. Then—like John Bunyan's Christian he bade perpetual good-bye to his family, as required, and went wandering away. He went far into the desert and served a term as hermit. Next, he became a beggar, "in accordance with the rites laid down in the Scriptures," and wandered about India eating the bread of mendicancy. A quarter of a century ago he reached the stage of purity. This needs no garment; its symbol is nudity; he discarded the waist-cloth which he had previously worn. He could resume it now if he chose, for neither that nor any other contact can defile him; but he does not choose.

There are several other stages, I believe, but I do not remember what they are. But he has been through them. Throughout the long course he was perfecting himself in holy learning, and writing commentaries upon the sacred books. He was also meditating upon Brahma, and he does that now.

White marble relief-portraits of him are sold all about India. He lives in a good house in a noble great garden in Benares, all meet and proper to his stupendous rank. Necessarily he does not go abroad in the streets. Deities would never be able to move about handily in any country. If one whom we recognized and adored as a god should go abroad in our streets, and the day it was to happen were known, all traffic would be blocked and business would come to a standstill.

This god is comfortably housed, and yet modestly, all things considered, for if he wanted to live in a palace he would only need to speak and his worshipers would gladly build it. Sometimes he sees devotees for a moment, and comforts them and blesses them, and they kiss his feet and go away happy. Rank is nothing to him, he being a god. To him all men are alike. He sees whom he pleases and denies himself to whom he pleases. Sometimes he sees a prince and denies himself to a pauper; at other times he receives the pauper and turns the prince away. However, he does not receive many of either class. He has to husband his time for his meditations. I think he would receive Rev. Mr. Parker at any time. I think he is sorry for Mr. Parker, and I think Mr. Parker is sorry for him; and no doubt this compassion is good for both of them.

When we arrived we had to stand around in the garden a little while and wait, and the outlook was not good, for he had been turning away Maharajas that day and receiving only the riff-raff, and we belonged in between, somewhere. But presently, a servant came out saying it was all right, he was coming.

And sure enough, he came, and I saw him—that object of the worship of millions. It was a strange sensation, and thrilling. I wish I could feel it stream through my veins again. And yet, to me he was not a god, he was only a Taj. The thrill was not my thrill, but had come to me secondhand from those invisible millions of believers. By a hand-shake with their god I had ground-circuited their wire and got their monster battery's whole charge.

He was tall and slender, indeed emaciated. He had a clean cut and conspicuously intellectual face, and a deep and kindly eye. He looked many years older than he really was, but much study and meditation and fasting and prayer, with the arid life he had led as hermit and beggar, could account for that. He is wholly nude when he receives natives, of whatever rank they may be, but he had white cloth around his loins now, a concession to Mr. Parker's Europe prejudices, no doubt.

As soon as I had sobered down a little we got along very well together, and I found him a most pleasant and friendly deity. He had heard a deal about Chicago, and showed a quite remarkable interest in it, for a god. It all came of the World's Fair and the Congress of Religions. If India knows about nothing else American, she knows about those, and will keep them in mind one while.

He proposed an exchange of autographs, a delicate attention which made me believe in him, but I had been having my doubts before. He wrote his in his book, and I have a reverent regard for that book, though the words run from right to left, and so I can't read it. It was a mistake to print in that way. It contains his voluminous comments on the Hindoo holy writings, and if I could make them out I would try for perfection myself. I gave him a copy of Huckleberry Finn. I thought it might rest him up a little to mix it in along with his meditations on Brahma, for he looked tired, and I knew that if it didn't do him any good it wouldn't do him any harm.

He has a scholar meditating under him—Mina Bahadur Rana—but we did not see him. He wears clothes and is very imperfect. He has written a little pamphlet about his master, and I have that. It contains a wood-cut of the master and himself seated on a rug in the garden. The portrait of the master is very good indeed. The posture is exactly that which Brahma himself affects, and it requires long arms and limber legs, and can be accumulated only by gods and the india-rubber man. There is a life-size marble relief of Shri 108, S.B.S. in the garden. It represents him in this same posture.

Dear me! It is a strange world. Particularly the Indian division of it. This pupil, Mina Bahadur Rana, is not a commonplace person, but a man of distinguished capacities and attainments, and, apparently, he had a fine worldly career in front of him. He was serving the Nepal Government in a high capacity at the Court of the Viceroy of India, twenty years ago. He was an able man, educated, a thinker, a man of property. But the longing to devote himself to a religious life came upon him, and he resigned his place, turned his back upon the vanities and comforts of the world, and went away into the solitudes to live in a hut and study the sacred writings and meditate upon virtue and holiness and seek to attain them. This sort of religion resembles ours. Christ recommended the rich to give away all their property and follow Him in poverty, not in worldly comfort. American and English millionaires do it every day, and thus verify and confirm to the world the tremendous forces that lie in religion. Yet many people scoff at them for this loyalty to duty, and many will scoff at Mina Bahadur Rana and call him a crank. Like many Christians of great character and intellect, he has made the study of his Scriptures and the writing of books of commentaries upon them the loving labor of his life. Like them, he has believed that his was not an idle and foolish waste of his life, but a most worthy and honorable employment of it. Yet, there are many people who will see in those others, men worthy of homage and deep reverence, but in him merely a crank. But I shall not. He has my reverence. And I don't offer it as a common thing and poor, but as an unusual thing and of value. The ordinary reverence, the reverence defined and explained by the dictionary costs nothing. Reverence for one's own sacred things—parents, religion, flag, laws, and respect for one's own beliefs—these are feelings which we cannot even help. They come natural to us; they are involuntary, like breathing. There is no personal merit in breathing. But the reverence which is difficult, and which has personal merit in it, is the respect which you pay, without compulsion, to the political or religious attitude of a man whose beliefs are not yours. You can't revere his gods or his politics, and no one expects you to do that, but you could respect his belief in them if you tried hard enough; and you could respect him, too, if you tried hard enough. But it is very, very difficult; it is next to impossible, and so we hardly ever try. If the man doesn't believe as we do, we say he is a crank, and that settles it. I mean it does nowadays, because now we can't burn him.

We are always canting about people's "irreverence," always charging this offense upon somebody or other, and thereby intimating that we are better than that person and do not commit that offense ourselves. Whenever we do this we are in a lying attitude, and our speech is cant; for none of us are reverent—in a meritorious way; deep down in our hearts we are all irreverent. There is probably not a single exception to this rule in the earth. There is probably not one person whose reverence rises higher than respect for his own sacred things; and therefore, it is not a thing to boast about and be proud of, since the most degraded savage has that —and, like the best of us, has nothing higher. To speak plainly, we despise all

reverences and all objects of reverence which are outside the pale of our own list of sacred things. And yet, with strange inconsistency, we are shocked when other people despise and defile the things which are holy to us. Suppose we should meet with a paragraph like the following, in the newspapers:

"Yesterday a visiting party of the British nobility had a picnic at Mount Vernon, and in the tomb of Washington they ate their luncheon, sang popular songs, played games, and danced waltzes and polkas."

Should we be shocked? Should we feel outraged? Should we be amazed? Should we call the performance a desecration? Yes, that would all happen. We should denounce those people in round terms, and call them hard names.

And suppose we found this paragraph in the newspapers:

"Yesterday a visiting party of American pork-millionaires had a picnic in Westminster Abbey, and in that sacred place they ate their luncheon, sang popular songs, played games, and danced waltzes and polkas."

Would the English be shocked? Would they feel outraged? Would they be amazed? Would they call the performance a desecration? That would all happen. The pork-millionaires would be denounced in round terms; they would be called hard names.

In the tomb at Mount Vernon lie the ashes of America's most honored son; in the Abbey, the ashes of England's greatest dead; the tomb of tombs, the costliest in the earth, the wonder of the world, the Taj, was built by a great Emperor to honor the memory of a perfect wife and perfect mother, one in whom there was no spot or blemish, whose love was his stay and support, whose life was the light of the world to him; in it her ashes lie, and to the Mohammedan millions of India it is a holy place; to them it is what Mount Vernon is to Americans, it is what the Abbey is to the English.

Major Sleeman wrote forty or fifty years ago (the italics are mine):

"I would here enter my humble protest against the quadrille and lunch parties which are sometimes given to European ladies and gentlemen of the station at this imperial tomb; drinking and dancing are no doubt very good things in their season, but they are sadly out of place in a sepulchre."

Were there any Americans among those lunch parties? If they were invited, there were.

If my imagined lunch-parties in Westminster and the tomb of Washington should take place, the incident would cause a vast outbreak of bitter eloquence about Barbarism and Irreverence; and it would come from two sets of people who would go next day and dance in the Taj if they had a chance.

As we took our leave of the Benares god and started away we noticed a group of natives waiting respectfully just within the gate—a Rajah from somewhere in India, and some people of lesser consequence. The god beckoned them to come, and as we passed out the Rajah was kneeling and reverently kissing his sacred feet.

If Barnum—but Barnum's ambitions are at rest. This god will remain in the holy peace and seclusion of his garden, undisturbed. Barnum could not have gotten him, anyway. Still, he would have found a substitute that would answer.

CHAPTER LIV.

Do not undervalue the headache. While it is at its sharpest it seems a bad investment; but when relief begins, the unexpired remainder is worth $4 a minute. —Pudd'nhead Wilson's New Calendar.

A comfortable railway journey of seventeen and a half hours brought us to the capital of India, which is likewise the capital of Bengal—Calcutta. Like Bombay, it has a population of nearly a million natives and a small gathering of white people. It is a huge city and fine, and is called the City of Palaces. It is rich in historical memories; rich in British achievement— military, political, commercial; rich in the results of rise miracles done by that brace of mighty magicians, Clive and Hastings. And has a cloud kissing monument to one Ochterlony.

It is a fluted candlestick 250 feet high. This lingam is the only large monument in Calcutta, I believe. It is a fine ornament, and will keep Ochterlony in mind.

Wherever you are, in Calcutta, and for miles around, you can see it; and always when you see it you think of Ochterlony. And so there is not an hour in the day that you do not think of Ochterlony and wonder who he was. It is good that Clive cannot come back, for he would think it was for Plassey; and then that great spirit would be wounded when the revelation came that it was not. Clive would find out that it was for Ochterlony; and he would think Ochterlony was a battle. And he would think it was a great one, too, and he would say, "With three thousand I whipped sixty thousand and founded the Empire—and there is no monument; this other soldier must have whipped a billion with a dozen and saved the world."

But he would be mistaken. Ochterlony was a man, not a battle. And he did good and honorable service, too; as good and honorable service as has been done in India by seventy-five or a hundred other Englishmen of courage, rectitude, and distinguished capacity. For India has been a fertile breeding-ground of such men, and remains so; great men, both in war and in the civil service, and as modest as great. But they. have no monuments, and were not expecting any. Ochterlony could not have been expecting one, and it is not at all likely that he desired one—certainly not until Clive and Hastings should be supplied. Every day Clive and Hastings lean on the battlements of heaven and look down and wonder which of the two the monument is for; and they fret and worry because they cannot find out, and so the peace of heaven is spoiled for them and lost. But not for Ochterlony. Ochterlony is not troubled. He doesn't suspect that it is his monument. Heaven is sweet and peaceful to him. There is a sort of unfairness about it all.

Indeed, if monuments were always given in India for high achievements, duty straitly performed, and smirchless records, the landscape would be monotonous with them. The handful of English in India govern the Indian myriads with apparent ease, and without noticeable friction, through tact, training, and distinguished administrative ability, reinforced by just and liberal laws—and by keeping their word to the native whenever they give it.

England is far from India and knows little about the eminent services performed by her servants there, for it is the newspaper correspondent who makes fame, and he is not sent to India but to the continent, to report the doings of the

princelets and the dukelets, and where they are visiting and whom they are marrying. Often a British official spends thirty or forty years in India, climbing from grade to grade by services which would make him celebrated anywhere else, and finishes as a vice-sovereign, governing a great realm and millions of subjects; then he goes home to England substantially unknown and unheard of, and settles down in some modest corner, and is as one extinguished. Ten years later there is a twenty-line obituary in the London papers, and the reader is paralyzed by the splendors of a career which he is not sure that he had ever heard of before. But meanwhile he has learned all about the continental princelets and dukelets.

The average man is profoundly ignorant of countries that lie remote from his own. When they are mentioned in his presence one or two facts and maybe a couple of names rise like torches in his mind, lighting up an inch or two of it and leaving the rest all dark. The mention of Egypt suggests some Biblical facts and the Pyramids-nothing more. The mention of South Africa suggests Kimberly and the diamonds and there an end. Formerly the mention, to a Hindoo, of America suggested a name—George Washington—with that his familiarity with our country was exhausted. Latterly his familiarity with it has doubled in bulk; so that when America is mentioned now, two torches flare up in the dark caverns of his mind and he says, "Ah, the country of the great man Washington; and of the Holy City—Chicago." For he knows about the Congress of Religion, and this has enabled him to get an erroneous impression of Chicago.

When India is mentioned to the citizen of a far country it suggests Clive, Hastings, the Mutiny, Kipling, and a number of other great events; and the mention of Calcutta infallibly brings up the Black Hole. And so, when that citizen finds himself in the capital of India he goes first of all to see the Black Hole of Calcutta—and is disappointed.

The Black Hole was not preserved; it is gone, long, long ago. It is strange. Just as it stood, it was itself a monument; a ready-made one. It was finished, it was complete, its materials were strong and lasting, it needed no furbishing up, no repairs; it merely needed to be let alone. It was the first brick, the Foundation Stone, upon which was reared a mighty Empire— the Indian Empire of Great Britain. It was the ghastly episode of the Black Hole that maddened the British and brought Clive, that young military marvel, raging up from Madras; it was the seed from which sprung Plassey; and it was that extraordinary battle, whose like had not been seen in the earth since Agincourt, that laid deep and strong the foundations of England's colossal Indian sovereignty.

And yet within the time of men who still live, the Black Hole was torn down and thrown away as carelessly as if its bricks were common clay, not ingots of historic gold. There is no accounting for human beings.

The supposed site of the Black Hole is marked by an engraved plate. I saw that; and better that than nothing. The Black Hole was a prison—a cell is nearer the right word—eighteen feet square, the dimensions of an ordinary bedchamber; and into this place the victorious Nabob of Bengal packed 146 of his English prisoners. There was hardly standing room for them; scarcely a breath of air was to be got; the time was night, the weather sweltering hot. Before the dawn came, the captives were all dead but twenty-three. Mr. Holwell's long account of the awful episode was familiar to the world a hundred years ago, but one seldom sees in print even an extract from it in our day. Among the striking things in it is this. Mr. Holwell, perishing with thirst, kept himself alive by sucking the perspiration from his sleeves. It gives one a vivid idea of the situation. He presently found that while he was busy drawing life from one of his sleeves a young English gentleman was stealing supplies from the other one. Holwell was an unselfish man, a man of the most generous impulses; he lived and died famous for these fine and rare qualities; yet when he found out what was happening to that unwatched sleeve, he took the precaution to suck that one dry first. The miseries of the Black Hole were able to change even a nature like his. But that young gentleman was one of the twenty-three survivors, and he said it was the stolen perspiration that saved his life. From the middle of Mr. Holwell's narrative I will make a brief excerpt:

"Then a general prayer to Heaven, to hasten the approach of the flames to the right and left of us, and put a period to our misery. But these failing, they whose strength and spirits were quite exhausted laid themselves down and expired quietly upon their fellows: others who had yet some strength and vigor left made a last effort at the windows, and several succeeded by leaping and scrambling over the backs and heads of those in the first rank, and got hold of the bars, from which there was no removing them. Many to the right and left sunk with the violent pressure, and were soon suffocated; for now a steam arose from the living and the dead, which affected us in all its circumstances as if we were forcibly held with our heads over a bowl full of strong volatile spirit of hartshorn, until suffocated; nor could the effluvia of the one be distinguished from the other, and frequently, when I was forced by the load upon my head and shoulders to hold my face down, I was obliged, near as I was to the window, instantly to raise it again to avoid suffocation. I need not, my dear friend, ask your commiseration, when I tell you, that in this plight, from half an hour past eleven till near two in the morning, I sustained the weight of a heavy man, with his knees in my back, and the pressure of his whole body on my head. A Dutch surgeon who had taken his seat upon my left shoulder, and a Topaz (a black Christian soldier) bearing on my right; all which nothing could have enabled me to support but the props and pressure equally sustaining me all around. The two latter I frequently dislodged by shifting my hold on the bars and driving my knuckles into their ribs; but my friend above stuck fast, held immovable by two bars.

"I exerted anew my strength and fortitude; but the repeated trials and efforts I made to dislodge the insufferable incumbrances upon me at last quite exhausted me; and towards two o'clock, finding I must quit the window or sink where I was, I resolved on the former, having bore, truly for the sake of others, infinitely more for life than the best of it is worth. In the rank close behind me was an officer of one of the ships, whose name was Cary, and who had behaved with much bravery during the siege (his wife, a fine woman, though country born, would not quit him, but accompanied him into the prison, and was one who survived). This poor wretch had been long raving for water and air; I told him I was determined to give up life, and recommended his gaining my station. On my quitting it he made a fruitless attempt to get my place; but the Dutch surgeon, who sat on my shoulder, supplanted him. Poor Cary expressed his thankfulness, and said he would give up life too; but it was with the utmost labor we forced our way from the window (several in the inner ranks appearing to me dead standing, unable to fall by the throng and equal pressure around). He laid himself down to die; and his death, I believe, was very sudden; for he was a short, full, sanguine man. His strength was great; and, I imagine, had he not retired with me, I should never have been able to force my way. I was at this time sensible of no pain, and little

uneasiness; I can give you no better idea of my situation than by repeating my simile of the bowl of spirit of hartshorn. I found a stupor coming on apace, and laid myself down by that gallant old man, the Rev. Mr. Jervas Bellamy, who laid dead with his son, the lieutenant, hand in hand, near the southernmost wall of the prison. When I had lain there some little time, I still had reflection enough to suffer some uneasiness in the thought that I should be trampled upon, when dead, as I myself had done to others. With some difficulty I raised myself, and gained the platform a second time, where I presently lost all sensation; the last trace of sensibility that I have been able to recollect after my laying down, was my sash being uneasy about my waist, which I untied, and threw from me. Of what passed in this interval, to the time of my resurrection from this hole of horrors, I can give you no account."

There was plenty to see in Calcutta, but there was not plenty of time for it. I saw the fort that Clive built; and the place where Warren Hastings and the author of the Junius Letters fought their duel; and the great botanical gardens; and the fashionable afternoon turnout in the Maidan; and a grand review of the garrison in a great plain at sunrise; and a military tournament in which great bodies of native soldiery exhibited the perfection of their drill at all arms, a spectacular and beautiful show occupying several nights and closing with the mimic storming of a native fort which was as good as the reality for thrilling and accurate detail, and better than the reality for security and comfort; we had a pleasure excursion on the 'Hoogly' by courtesy of friends, and devoted the rest of the time to social life and the Indian museum. One should spend a month in the museum, an enchanted palace of Indian antiquities. Indeed, a person might spend half a year among the beautiful and wonderful things without exhausting their interest.

It was winter. We were of Kipling's "hosts of tourists who travel up and down India in the cold weather showing how things ought to be managed." It is a common expression there, "the cold weather," and the people think there is such a thing. It is because they have lived there half a lifetime, and their perceptions have become blunted. When a person is accustomed to 138 in the shade, his ideas about cold weather are not valuable. I had read, in the histories, that the June marches made between Lucknow and Cawnpore by the British forces in the time of the Mutiny were made weather—138 in the shade and had taken it for historical embroidery. I had read it again in Serjeant-Major Forbes-Mitchell's account of his military experiences in the Mutiny —at least I thought I had—and in Calcutta I asked him if it was true, and he said it was. An officer of high rank who had been in the thick of the Mutiny said the same. As long as those men were talking about what they knew, they were trustworthy, and I believed them; but when they said it was now "cold weather," I saw that they had traveled outside of their sphere of knowledge and were floundering. I believe that in India "cold weather" is merely a conventional phrase and has come into use through the necessity of having some way to distinguish between weather which will melt a brass door-knob and weather which will only make it mushy. It was observable that brass ones were in use while I was in Calcutta, showing that it was not yet time to change to porcelain; I was told the change to porcelain was not usually made until May. But this cold weather was too warm for us; so we started to Darjeeling, in the Himalayas—a twenty-four hour journey.

CHAPTER LV.

There are 869 different forms of lying, but only one of them has been squarely forbidden. Thou shalt not bear false witness against thy neighbor. —Pudd'nhead Wilson's New Calendar.

FROM DIARY:

February 14. We left at 4:30 P.M. Until dark we moved through rich vegetation, then changed to a boat and crossed the Ganges.

February 15. Up with the sun. A brilliant morning, and frosty. A double suit of flannels is found necessary. The plain is perfectly level, and seems to stretch away and away and away, dimming and softening, to the uttermost bounds of nowhere. What a soaring, strenuous, gushing fountain spray of delicate greenery a bunch of bamboo is! As far as the eye can reach, these grand vegetable geysers grace the view, their spoutings refined to steam by distance. And there are fields of bananas, with the sunshine glancing from the varnished surface of their drooping vast leaves. And there are frequent groves of palm; and an effective accent is given to the landscape by isolated individuals of this picturesque family, towering, clean-stemmed, their plumes broken and hanging ragged, Nature's imitation of an umbrella that has been out to see what a cyclone is like and is trying not to look disappointed. And everywhere through the soft morning vistas we glimpse the villages, the countless villages, the myriad villages, thatched, built of clean new matting, snuggling among grouped palms and sheaves of bamboo; villages, villages, no end of villages, not three hundred yards apart, and dozens and dozens of them in sight all the time; a mighty City, hundreds of miles long, hundreds of miles broad, made all of villages, the biggest city in the earth, and as populous as a European kingdom. I have seen no such city as this before. And there is a continuously repeated and replenished multitude of naked men in view on both sides and ahead. We fly through it mile after mile, but still it is always there, on both sides and ahead—brown-bodied, naked men and boys, plowing in the fields. But not woman. In these two hours I have not seen a woman or a girl working in the fields.

"From Greenland's icy mountains, From India's coral strand, Where Afric's sunny fountains Roll down their golden sand. From many an ancient river, From many a palmy plain, They call us to deliver Their land from error's chain."

Those are beautiful verses, and they have remained in my memory all my life. But if the closing lines are true, let us hope that when we come to answer the call and deliver the land from its errors, we shall secrete from it some of our high-civilization ways, and at the same time borrow some of its pagan ways to enrich our high system with. We have a right to do this. If we lift those people up, we have a right to lift ourselves up nine or ten grades or so, at their expense. A few years ago I spent several weeks at Tolz, in Bavaria. It is a Roman Catholic region, and not even Benares is more deeply or pervasively or intelligently devout. In my diary of those days I find this:

"We took a long drive yesterday around about the lovely country roads. But it was a drive whose pleasure was damaged in a couple of ways: by the dreadful shrines and by the shameful spectacle of gray and venerable old grandmothers toiling in the fields. The shrines were frequent along the roads—figures of the Saviour nailed to the cross and streaming with blood from the wounds of the nails and the thorns.

"When missionaries go from here do they find fault with the pagan idols? I saw many women seventy and even eighty years old mowing and binding in the fields, and pitchforking the loads into the wagons."

I was in Austria later, and in Munich. In Munich I saw gray old women pushing trucks up hill and down, long distances, trucks laden with barrels of beer, incredible loads. In my Austrian diary I find this:

"In the fields I often see a woman and a cow harnessed to the plow, and a man driving.

"In the public street of Marienbad to-day, I saw an old, bent, gray-headed woman, in harness with a dog, drawing a laden sled over bare dirt roads and bare pavements; and at his ease walked the driver, smoking his pipe, a hale fellow not thirty years old."

Five or six years ago I bought an open boat, made a kind of a canvas wagon-roof over the stern of it to shelter me from sun and rain; hired a courier and a boatman, and made a twelve-day floating voyage down the Rhone from Lake Bourget to Marseilles. In my diary of that trip I find this entry. I was far down the Rhone then:

"Passing St. Etienne, 2:15 P.M. On a distant ridge inland, a tall openwork structure commandingly situated, with a statue of the Virgin standing on it. A devout country. All down this river, wherever there is a crag there is a statue of the Virgin on it. I believe I have seen a hundred of them. And yet, in many respects, the peasantry seem to be mere pagans, and destitute of any considerable degree of civilization.

" .... We reached a not very promising looking village about 4 o'clock, and I concluded to tie up for the day; munching fruit and fogging the hood with pipe-smoke had grown monotonous; I could not have the hood furled, because the floods of rain fell unceasingly. The tavern was on the river bank, as is the custom. It was dull there, and melancholy—nothing to do but look out of the window into the drenching rain, and shiver; one could do that, for it was bleak and cold and windy, and country France furnishes no fire. Winter overcoats did not help me much; they had to be supplemented with rugs. The raindrops were so large and struck the river with such force that they knocked up the water like pebble-splashes.

"With the exception of a very occasional woodenshod peasant, nobody was abroad in this bitter weather—I mean nobody of our sex. But all weathers are alike to the women in these continental countries. To them and the other animals, life is serious; nothing interrupts their slavery. Three of them were washing clothes in the river under the window when I arrived, and they continued at it as long as there was light to work by. One was apparently thirty; another—the mother!—above fifty; the third—grandmother!—so old and worn and gray she could have passed for eighty; I took her to be that old. They had no waterproofs nor rubbers, of course; over their shoulders they wore gunnysacks—simply conductors for rivers of water; some of the volume reached the ground; the rest soaked in on the way.

"At last a vigorous fellow of thirty-five arrived, dry and comfortable, smoking his pipe under his big umbrella in an open donkey-cart-husband, son, and grandson of those women! He stood up in the cart, sheltering himself, and began to superintend, issuing his orders in a masterly tone of command, and showing temper when they were not obeyed swiftly enough.

"Without complaint or murmur the drowned women patiently carried out the orders, lifting the immense baskets of soggy, wrung-out clothing into the cart and stowing them to the man's satisfaction. There were six of the great baskets, and a man of mere ordinary strength could not have lifted any one of them. The cart being full now, the Frenchman descended, still sheltered by his umbrella, entered the tavern, and the women went drooping homeward, trudging in the wake of the cart, and soon were blended with the deluge and lost to sight.

"When I went down into the public room, the Frenchman had his bottle of wine and plate of food on a bare table black with grease, and was "chomping" like a horse. He had the little religious paper which is in everybody's hands on the Rhone borders, and was enlightening himself with the histories of French saints who used to flee to the desert in the Middle Ages to escape the contamination of woman. For two hundred years France has been sending missionaries to other savage lands. To spare to the needy from poverty like hers is fine and true generosity."

But to get back to India—where, as my favorite poem says—

"Every prospect pleases, And only man is vile."

It is because Bavaria and Austria and France have not introduced their civilization to him yet. But Bavaria and Austria and France are on their way. They are coming. They will rescue him; they will refine the vileness out of him.

Some time during the forenoon, approaching the mountains, we changed from the regular train to one composed of little canvas-sheltered cars that skimmed along within a foot of the ground and seemed to be going fifty miles an hour when they were really making about twenty. Each car had seating capacity for half-a-dozen persons; and when the curtains were up one was substantially out of doors, and could see everywhere, and get all the breeze, and be luxuriously comfortable. It was not a pleasure excursion in name only, but in fact.

After a while the stopped at a little wooden coop of a station just within the curtain of the sombre jungle, a place with a deep and dense forest of great trees and scrub and vines all about it. The royal Bengal tiger is in great force there, and is very bold and unconventional. From this lonely little station a message once went to the railway manager in Calcutta: "Tiger eating station-master on front porch; telegraph instructions."

It was there that I had my first tiger hunt. I killed thirteen. We were presently away again, and the train began to climb the mountains. In one place seven wild elephants crossed the track, but two of them got away before I could overtake them. The railway journey up the mountain is forty miles, and it takes eight hours to make it. It is so wild and interesting and exciting and enchanting that it ought to take a week. As for the vegetation, it is a museum. The jungle seemed to contain samples of every rare and curious tree and bush that we had ever seen or heard of. It is from that museum, I think, that the globe must have been supplied with the trees and vines and shrubs that it holds precious.

The road is infinitely and charmingly crooked. It goes winding in and out under lofty cliffs that are smothered in vines and foliage, and around the edges of bottomless chasms; and all

the way one glides by files of picturesque natives, some carrying burdens up, others going down from their work in the tea-gardens; and once there was a gaudy wedding procession, all bright tinsel and color, and a bride, comely and girlish, who peeped out from the curtains of her palanquin, exposing her face with that pure delight which the young and happy take in sin for sin's own sake.

By and by we were well up in the region of the clouds, and from that breezy height we looked down and afar over a wonderful picture—the Plains of India, stretching to the horizon, soft and fair, level as a floor, shimmering with heat, mottled with cloud-shadows, and cloven with shining rivers. Immediately below us, and receding down, down, down, toward the valley, was a shaven confusion of hilltops, with ribbony roads and paths squirming and snaking cream-yellow all over them and about them, every curve and twist sharply distinct.

At an elevation of 6,000 feet we entered a thick cloud, and it shut out the world and kept it shut out. We climbed 1,000 feet higher, then began to descend, and presently got down to Darjeeling, which is 6,000 feet above the level of the Plains.

We had passed many a mountain village on the way up, and seen some new kinds of natives, among them many samples of the fighting Ghurkas. They are not large men, but they are strong and resolute. There are no better soldiers among Britain's native troops. And we had passed shoals of their women climbing the forty miles of steep road from the valley to their mountain homes, with tall baskets on their backs hitched to their foreheads by a band, and containing a freightage weighing—I will not say how many hundreds of pounds, for the sum is unbelievable. These were young women, and they strode smartly along under these astonishing burdens with the air of people out for a holiday. I was told that a woman will carry a piano on her back all the way up the mountain; and that more than once a woman had done it. If these were old women I should regard the Ghurkas as no more civilized than the Europeans. At the railway station at Darjeeling you find plenty of cab-substitutes —open coffins, in which you sit, and are then borne on men's shoulders up the steep roads into the town.

Up there we found a fairly comfortable hotel, the property of an indiscriminate and incoherent landlord, who looks after nothing, but leaves everything to his army of Indian servants. No, he does look after the bill—to be just to him—and the tourist cannot do better than follow his example. I was told by a resident that the summit of Kinchinjunga is often hidden in the clouds, and that sometimes a tourist has waited twenty-two days and then been obliged to go away without a sight of it. And yet went not disappointed; for when he got his hotel bill he recognized that he was now seeing the highest thing in the Himalayas. But this is probably a lie.

After lecturing I went to the Club that night, and that was a comfortable place. It is loftily situated, and looks out over a vast spread of scenery; from it you can see where the boundaries of three countries come together, some thirty miles away; Thibet is one of them, Nepaul another, and I think Herzegovina was the other. Apparently, in every town and city in India the gentlemen of the British civil and military service have a club; sometimes it is a palatial one, always it is pleasant and homelike. The hotels are not always as good as they might be, and the stranger who has access to the Club is grateful for his privilege and knows how to value it.

Next day was Sunday. Friends came in the gray dawn with horses, and my party rode away to a distant point where Kinchinjunga and Mount Everest show up best, but I stayed at home for a private view; for it was very old, and I was not acquainted with the horses, any way. I got a pipe and a few blankets and sat for two hours at the window, and saw the sun drive away the veiling gray and touch up the snow-peaks one after another with pale pink splashes and delicate washes of gold, and finally flood the whole mighty convulsion of snow-mountains with a deluge of rich splendors.

Kinchinjunga's peak was but fitfully visible, but in the between times it was vividly clear against the sky—away up there in the blue dome more than 28,000 feet above sea level—the loftiest land I had ever seen, by 12,000 feet or more. It was 45 miles away. Mount Everest is a thousand feet higher, but it was not a part of that sea of mountains piled up there before me, so I did not see it; but I did not care, because I think that mountains that are as high as that are disagreeable.

I changed from the back to the front of the house and spent the rest of the morning there, watching the swarthy strange tribes flock by from their far homes in the Himalayas. All ages and both sexes were represented, and the breeds were quite new to me, though the costumes of the Thibetans made them look a good deal like Chinamen. The prayer-wheel was a frequent feature. It brought me near to these people, and made them seem kinfolk of mine. Through our preacher we do much of our praying by proxy. We do not whirl him around a stick, as they do, but that is merely a detail. The swarm swung briskly by, hour after hour, a strange and striking pageant. It was wasted there, and it seemed a pity. It should have been sent streaming through the cities of Europe or America, to refresh eyes weary of the pale monotonies of the circus-pageant. These people were bound for the bazar, with things to sell. We went down there, later, and saw that novel congress of the wild peoples, and plowed here and there through it, and concluded that it would be worth coming from Calcutta to see, even if there were no Kinchinjunga and Everest.

CHAPTER LVI.

There are two times in a man's life when he should not speculate: when he can't afford it, and when he can. — Pudd'nhead Wilson's New Calendar.

On Monday and Tuesday at sunrise we again had fair-to-middling views of the stupendous mountains; then, being well cooled off and refreshed, we were ready to chance the weather of the lower world once more.

We traveled up hill by the regular train five miles to the summit, then changed to a little canvas-canopied hand-car for the 35-mile descent. It was the size of a sleigh, it had six seats and was so low that it seemed to rest on the ground. It had no engine or other propelling power, and needed none to help it fly down those steep inclines. It only needed a strong brake, to modify its flight, and it had that. There was a story of a disastrous trip made down the mountain once in this little car by the Lieutenant-Governor of Bengal, when the car jumped the track and threw its passengers over a precipice. It was not true, but the story had value for me, for it made me nervous, and nervousness wakes a person up and makes him alive and alert, and heightens the thrill of a new and doubtful experience. The car could really jump the track, of course; a pebble on the track, placed there by either accident or malice, at a sharp curve where one might strike it before the eye could discover it, could derail the car and fling it down into India;

and the fact that the lieutenant-governor had escaped was no proof that I would have the same luck. And standing there, looking down upon the Indian Empire from the airy altitude of 7,000 feet, it seemed unpleasantly far, dangerously far, to be flung from a handcar.

But after all, there was but small danger-for me. What there was, was for Mr. Pugh, inspector of a division of the Indian police, in whose company and protection we had come from Calcutta. He had seen long service as an artillery officer, was less nervous than I was, and so he was to go ahead of us in a pilot hand-car, with a Ghurka and another native; and the plan was that when we should see his car jump over a precipice we must put on our break [sp.] and send for another pilot. It was a good arrangement. Also Mr. Barnard, chief engineer of the mountain-division of the road, was to take personal charge of our car, and he had been down the mountain in it many a time.

Everything looked safe. Indeed, there was but one questionable detail left: the regular train was to follow us as soon as we should start, and it might run over us. Privately, I thought it would.

The road fell sharply down in front of us and went corkscrewing in and out around the crags and precipices, down, down, forever down, suggesting nothing so exactly or so uncomfortably as a croaked toboggan slide with no end to it. Mr. Pugh waved his flag and started, like an arrow from a bow, and before I could get out of the car we were gone too. I had previously had but one sensation like the shock of that departure, and that was the gaspy shock that took my breath away the first time that I was discharged from the summit of a toboggan slide. But in both instances the sensation was pleasurable—intensely so; it was a sudden and immense exaltation, a mixed ecstasy of deadly fright and unimaginable joy. I believe that this combination makes the perfection of human delight.

The pilot car's flight down the mountain suggested the swoop of a swallow that is skimming the ground, so swiftly and smoothly and gracefully it swept down the long straight reaches and soared in and out of the bends and around the corners. We raced after it, and seemed to flash by the capes and crags with the speed of light; and now and then we almost overtook it—and had hopes; but it was only playing with us; when we got near, it released its brake, make a spring around a corner, and the next time it spun into view, a few seconds later, it looked as small as a wheelbarrow, it was so far away. We played with the train in the same way. We often got out to gather flowers or sit on a precipice and look at the scenery, then presently we would hear a dull and growing roar, and the long coils of the train would come into sight behind and above us; but we did not need to start till the locomotive was close down upon us —then we soon left it far behind. It had to stop at every station, therefore it was not an embarrassment to us. Our brake was a good piece of machinery; it could bring the car to a standstill on a slope as steep as a house-roof.

The scenery was grand and varied and beautiful, and there was no hurry; we could always stop and examine it. There was abundance of time. We did not need to hamper the train; if it wanted the road, we could switch off and let it go by, then overtake it and pass it later. We stopped at one place to see the Gladstone Cliff, a great crag which the ages and the weather have sculptured into a recognizable portrait of the venerable statesman. Mr. Gladstone is a stockholder in the road, and Nature began this portrait ten thousand years ago, with the idea of having the compliment ready in time for the event.

We saw a banyan tree which sent down supporting stems from branches which were sixty feet above the ground. That is, I suppose it was a banyan; its bark resembled that of the great banyan in the botanical gardens at Calcutta, that spider-legged thing with its wilderness of vegetable columns. And there were frequent glimpses of a totally leafless tree upon whose innumerable twigs and branches a cloud of crimson butterflies had lighted—apparently. In fact these brilliant red butterflies were flowers, but the illusion was good. Afterward in South Africa, I saw another splendid effect made by red flowers. This flower was probably called the torch-plant—should have been so named, anyway. It had a slender stem several feet high, and from its top stood up a single tongue of flame, an intensely red flower of the size and shape of a small corn-cob. The stems stood three or four feet apart all over a great hill-slope that was a mile long, and make one think of what the Place de la Concorde would be if its myriad lights were red instead of white and yellow.

A few miles down the mountain we stopped half an hour to see a Thibetan dramatic performance. It was in the open air on the hillside. The audience was composed of Thibetans, Ghurkas, and other unusual people. The costumes of the actors were in the last degree outlandish, and the performance was in keeping with the clothes. To an accompaniment of barbarous noises the actors stepped out one after another and began to spin around with immense swiftness and vigor and violence, chanting the while, and soon the whole troupe would be spinning and chanting and raising the dust. They were performing an ancient and celebrated historical play, and a Chinaman explained it to me in pidjin English as it went along. The play was obscure enough without the explanation; with the explanation added, it was (opake). As a drama this ancient historical work of art was defective, I thought, but as a wild and barbarous spectacle the representation was beyond criticism. Far down the mountain we got out to look at a piece of remarkable loop-engineering—a spiral where the road curves upon itself with such abruptness that when the regular train came down and entered the loop, we stood over it and saw the locomotive disappear under our bridge, then in a few moments appear again, chasing its own tail; and we saw it gain on it, overtake it, draw ahead past the rear cars, and run a race with that end of the train. It was like a snake swallowing itself.

Half-way down the mountain we stopped about an hour at Mr. Barnard's house for refreshments, and while we were sitting on the veranda looking at the distant panorama of hills through a gap in the forest, we came very near seeing a leopard kill a calf.—[It killed it the day before.] —It is a wild place and lovely. From the woods all about came the songs of birds,—among them the contributions of a couple of birds which I was not then acquainted with: the brain-fever bird and the coppersmith. The song of the brain-fever demon starts on a low but steadily rising key, and is a spiral twist which augments in intensity and severity with each added spiral, growing sharper and sharper, and more and more painful, more and more agonizing, more and more maddening, intolerable, unendurable, as it bores deeper and deeper and deeper into the listener's brain, until at last the brain fever comes as a relief and the man dies. I am bringing some of these birds home to America. They will be a great curiosity there, and it is believed that in our climate they will multiply like rabbits.

The coppersmith bird's note at a certain distance away has the ring of a sledge on granite; at a certain other distance the

hammering has a more metallic ring, and you might think that the bird was mending a copper kettle; at another distance it has a more woodeny thump, but it is a thump that is full of energy, and sounds just like starting a bung. So he is a hard bird to name with a single name; he is a stone-breaker, coppersmith, and bung-starter, and even then he is not completely named, for when he is close by you find that there is a soft, deep, melodious quality in his thump, and for that no satisfying name occurs to you. You will not mind his other notes, but when he camps near enough for you to hear that one, you presently find that his measured and monotonous repetition of it is beginning to disturb you; next it will weary you, soon it will distress you, and before long each thump will hurt your head; if this goes on, you will lose your mind with the pain and misery of it, and go crazy. I am bringing some of these birds home to America. There is nothing like them there. They will be a great surprise, and it is said that in a climate like ours they will surpass expectation for fecundity.

I am bringing some nightingales, too, and some cue-owls. I got them in Italy. The song of the nightingale is the deadliest known to ornithology. That demoniacal shriek can kill at thirty yards. The note of the cue-owl is infinitely soft and sweet—soft and sweet as the whisper of a flute. But penetrating—oh, beyond belief; it can bore through boiler-iron. It is a lingering note, and comes in triplets, on the one unchanging key: hoo-o-o, hoo-o-o, hoo-o-o; then a silence of fifteen seconds, then the triplet again; and so on, all night. At first it is divine; then less so; then trying; then distressing; then excruciating; then agonizing, and at the end of two hours the listener is a maniac.

And so, presently we took to the hand-car and went flying down the mountain again; flying and stopping, flying and stopping, till at last we were in the plain once more and stowed for Calcutta in the regular train. That was the most enjoyable day I have spent in the earth. For rousing, tingling, rapturous pleasure there is no holiday trip that approaches the bird-flight down the Himalayas in a hand-car. It has no fault, no blemish, no lack, except that there are only thirty-five miles of it instead of five hundred.

CHAPTER LVII.

She was not quite what you would call refined. She was not quite what you would call unrefined. She was the kind of person that keeps a parrot. —Pudd'nhead Wilson's New Calendar.

So far as I am able to judge, nothing has been left undone, either by man or Nature, to make India the most extraordinary country that the sun visits on his round. Nothing seems to have been forgotten, nothing over looked. Always, when you think you have come to the end of her tremendous specialties and have finished banging tags upon her as the Land of the Thug, the Land of the Plague, the Land of Famine, the Land of Giant Illusions, the Land of Stupendous Mountains, and so forth, another specialty crops up and another tag is required. I have been overlooking the fact that India is by an unapproachable supremacy—the Land of Murderous Wild Creatures. Perhaps it will be simplest to throw away the tags and generalize her with one all-comprehensive name, as the Land of Wonders.

For many years the British Indian Government has been trying to destroy the murderous wild creatures, and has spent a great deal of money in the effort. The annual official returns show that the undertaking is a difficult one.

These returns exhibit a curious annual uniformity in results; the sort of uniformity which you find in the annual output of suicides in the world's capitals, and the proportions of deaths by this, that, and the other disease. You can always come close to foretelling how many suicides will occur in Paris, London, and New York, next year, and also how many deaths will result from cancer, consumption, dog-bite, falling out of the window, getting run over by cabs, etc., if you know the statistics of those matters for the present year. In the same way, with one year's Indian statistics before you, you can guess closely at how many people were killed in that Empire by tigers during the previous year, and the year before that, and the year before that, and at how many were killed in each of those years by bears, how many by wolves, and how many by snakes; and you can also guess closely at how many people are going to be killed each year for the coming five years by each of those agencies. You can also guess closely at how many of each agency the government is going to kill each year for the next five years.

I have before me statistics covering a period of six consecutive years. By these, I know that in India the tiger kills something over 800 persons every year, and that the government responds by killing about double as many tigers every year. In four of the six years referred to, the tiger got 800 odd; in one of the remaining two years he got only 700, but in the other remaining year he made his average good by scoring 917. He is always sure of his average. Anyone who bets that the tiger will kill 2,400 people in India in any three consecutive years has invested his money in a certainty; anyone who bets that he will kill 2,600 in any three consecutive years, is absolutely sure to lose.

As strikingly uniform as are the statistics of suicide, they are not any more so than are those of the tiger's annual output of slaughtered human beings in India. The government's work is quite uniform, too; it about doubles the tiger's average. In six years the tiger killed 5,000 persons, minus 50; in the same six years 10,000 tigers were killed, minus 400.

The wolf kills nearly as many people as the tiger—700 a year to the tiger's 800 odd—but while he is doing it, more than 5,000 of his tribe fall.

The leopard kills an average of 230 people per year, but loses 3,300 of his own mess while he is doing it.

The bear kills 100 people per year at a cost of 1,250 of his own tribe.

The tiger, as the figures show, makes a very handsome fight against man. But it is nothing to the elephant's fight. The king of beasts, the lord of the jungle, loses four of his mess per year, but he kills forty—five persons to make up for it.

But when it comes to killing cattle, the lord of the jungle is not interested. He kills but 100 in six years—horses of hunters, no doubt —but in the same six the tiger kills more than 84,000, the leopard 100,000, the bear 4,000, the wolf 70,000, the hyena more than 13,000, other wild beasts 27,000, and the snakes 19,000, a grand total of more than 300,000; an average of 50,000 head per year.

In response, the government kills, in the six years, a total of 3,201,232 wild beasts and snakes. Ten for one.

It will be perceived that the snakes are not much interested in cattle; they kill only 3,000 odd per year. The snakes are much

more interested in man. India swarms with deadly snakes. At the head of the list is the cobra, the deadliest known to the world, a snake whose bite kills where the rattlesnake's bite merely entertains.

In India, the annual man-killings by snakes are as uniform, as regular, and as forecastable as are the tiger-average and the suicide-average. Anyone who bets that in India, in any three consecutive years the snakes will kill 49,500 persons, will win his bet; and anyone who bets that in India in any three consecutive years, the snakes will kill 53,500 persons, will lose his bet. In India the snakes kill 17,000 people a year; they hardly ever fall short of it; they as seldom exceed it. An insurance actuary could take the Indian census tables and the government's snake tables and tell you within sixpence how much it would be worth to insure a man against death by snake-bite there. If I had a dollar for every person killed per year in India, I would rather have it than any other property, as it is the only property in the world not subject to shrinkage.

I should like to have a royalty on the government-end of the snake business, too, and am in London now trying to get it; but when I get it it is not going to be as regular an income as the other will be if I get that; I have applied for it. The snakes transact their end of the business in a more orderly and systematic way than the government transacts its end of it, because the snakes have had a long experience and know all about the traffic. You can make sure that the government will never kill fewer than 110,000 snakes in a year, and that it will newer quite reach 300,000 too much room for oscillation; good speculative stock, to bear or bull, and buy and sell long and short, and all that kind of thing, but not eligible for investment like the other. The man that speculates in the government's snake crop wants to go carefully. I would not advise a man to buy a single crop at all—I mean a crop of futures for the possible wobble is something quite extraordinary. If he can buy six future crops in a bunch, seller to deliver 1,500,000 altogether, that is another matter. I do not know what snakes are worth now, but I know what they would be worth then, for the statistics show that the seller could not come within 427,000 of carrying out his contract. However, I think that a person who speculates in snakes is a fool, anyway. He always regrets it afterwards.

To finish the statistics. In six years the wild beasts kill 20,000 persons, and the snakes kill 103,000. In the same six the government kills 1,073,546 snakes. Plenty left.

There are narrow escapes in India. In the very jungle where I killed sixteen tigers and all those elephants, a cobra bit me but it got well; everyone was surprised. This could not happen twice in ten years, perhaps. Usually death would result in fifteen minutes.

We struck out westward or northwestward from Calcutta on an itinerary of a zig-zag sort, which would in the course of time carry us across India to its northwestern corner and the border of Afghanistan. The first part of the trip carried us through a great region which was an endless garden—miles and miles of the beautiful flower from whose juices comes the opium, and at Muzaffurpore we were in the midst of the indigo culture; thence by a branch road to the Ganges at a point near Dinapore, and by a train which would have missed the connection by a week but for the thoughtfulness of some British officers who were along, and who knew the ways of trains that are run by natives without white supervision. This train stopped at every village; for no purpose connected with business, apparently. We put out nothing, we took nothing aboard. The train bands stepped ashore and gossiped with friends a quarter of an hour, then pulled out and repeated this at the succeeding villages. We had thirty-five miles to go and six hours to do it in, but it was plain that we were not going to make it. It was then that the English officers said it was now necessary to turn this gravel train into an express. So they gave the engine-driver a rupee and told him to fly. It was a simple remedy. After that we made ninety miles an hour. We crossed the Ganges just at dawn, made our connection, and went to Benares, where we stayed twenty-four hours and inspected that strange and fascinating piety-hive again; then left for Lucknow, a city which is perhaps the most conspicuous of the many monuments of British fortitude and valor that are scattered about the earth.

The heat was pitiless, the flat plains were destitute of grass, and baked dry by the sun they were the color of pale dust, which was flying in clouds. But it was much hotter than this when the relieving forces marched to Lucknow in the time of the Mutiny. Those were the days of 138 deg. in the shade.

CHAPTER, LVIII.

Make it a point to do something every day that you don't want to do. This is the golden rule for acquiring the habit of doing your duty without pain. —Pudd'nhead Wilson's New Calendar.

It seems to be settled, now, that among the many causes from which the Great Mutiny sprang, the main one was the annexation of the kingdom of Oudh by the East India Company—characterized by Sir Henry Lawrence as "the most unrighteous act that was ever committed." In the spring of 1857, a mutinous spirit was observable in many of the native garrisons, and it grew day by day and spread wider and wider. The younger military men saw something very serious in it, and would have liked to take hold of it vigorously and stamp it out promptly; but they were not in authority. Old-men were in the high places of the army—men who should have been retired long before, because of their great age—and they regarded the matter as a thing of no consequence. They loved their native soldiers, and would not believe that anything could move them to revolt. Everywhere these obstinate veterans listened serenely to the rumbling of the volcanoes under them, and said it was nothing.

And so the propagators of mutiny had everything their own way. They moved from camp to camp undisturbed, and painted to the native soldier the wrongs his people were suffering at the hands of the English, and made his heart burn for revenge. They were able to point to two facts of formidable value as backers of their persuasions: In Clive's day, native armies were incoherent mobs, and without effective arms; therefore, they were weak against Clive's organized handful of well-armed men, but the thing was the other way, now. The British forces were native; they had been trained by the British, organized by the British, armed by the British, all the power was in their hands—they were a club made by British hands to beat out British brains with. There was nothing to oppose their mass, nothing but a few weak battalions of British soldiers scattered about India, a force not worth speaking of. This argument, taken alone, might not have succeeded, for the bravest and best Indian troops had a wholesome dread of the white soldier, whether he was weak or strong; but the agitators backed it with their second and best point prophecy—a prophecy a hundred years old. The Indian is open to prophecy at all times; argument may fail to convince him, but not prophecy. There was a prophecy that a hundred years from the

year of that battle of Clive's which founded the British Indian Empire, the British power would be overthrown and swept away by the natives.

The Mutiny broke out at Meerut on the 10th of May, 1857, and fired a train of tremendous historical explosions. Nana Sahib's massacre of the surrendered garrison of Cawnpore occurred in June, and the long siege of Lucknow began. The military history of England is old and great, but I think it must be granted that the crushing of the Mutiny is the greatest chapter in it. The British were caught asleep and unprepared. They were a few thousands, swallowed up in an ocean of hostile populations. It would take months to inform England and get help, but they did not falter or stop to count the odds, but with English resolution and English devotion they took up their task, and went stubbornly on with it, through good fortune and bad, and fought the most unpromising fight that one may read of in fiction or out of it, and won it thoroughly.

The Mutiny broke out so suddenly, and spread with such rapidity that there was but little time for occupants of weak outlying stations to escape to places of safety. Attempts were made, of course, but they were attended by hardships as bitter as death in the few cases which were successful; for the heat ranged between 120 and 138 in the shade; the way led through hostile peoples, and food and water were hardly to be had. For ladies and children accustomed to ease and comfort and plenty, such a journey must have been a cruel experience. Sir G. O. Trevelyan quotes an example:

"This is what befell Mrs. M—, the wife of the surgeon at a certain station on the southern confines of the insurrection. 'I heard,' she says, 'a number of shots fired, and, looking out, I saw my husband driving furiously from the mess-house, waving his whip. I ran to him, and, seeing a bearer with my child in his arms, I caught her up, and got into the buggy. At the mess-house we found all the officers assembled, together with sixty sepoys, who had remained faithful. We went off in one large party, amidst a general conflagration of our late homes. We reached the caravanserai at Chattapore the next morning, and thence started for Callinger. At this point our sepoy escort deserted us. We were fired upon by match-lockmen, and one officer was shot dead. We heard, likewise, that the people had risen at Callinger, so we returned and walked back ten miles that day. M— and I carried the child alternately. Presently Mrs. Smalley died of sunstroke. We had no food amongst us. An officer kindly lent us a horse. We were very faint. The Major died, and was buried; also the Sergeant-major and some women. The bandsmen left us on the nineteenth of June. We were fired at again by match-lockmen, and changed direction for Allahabad. Our party consisted of nine gentlemen, two children, the sergeant and his wife. On the morning of the twentieth, Captain Scott took Lottie on to his horse. I was riding behind my husband, and she was so crushed between us. She was two years old on the first of the month. We were both weak through want of food and the effect of the sun. Lottie and I had no head covering. M— had a sepoy's cap I found on the ground. Soon after sunrise we were followed by villagers armed with clubs and spears. One of them struck Captain Scott's horse on the leg. He galloped off with Lottie, and my poor husband never saw his child again. We rode on several miles, keeping away from villages, and then crossed the river. Our thirst was extreme. M— had dreadful cramps, so that I had to hold him on the horse. I was very uneasy about him. The day before I saw the drummer's wife eating chupatties, and asked her to give a piece to the child, which she did. I now saw water in a ravine. The descent was steep, and our only drinkingvessel was M—'s cap. Our horse got water, and I bathed my neck. I had no stockings, and my feet were torn and blistered. Two peasants came in sight, and we were frightened and rode off. The sergeant held our horse, and M— put me up and mounted. I think he must have got suddenly faint, for I fell and he over me, on the road, when the horse started off. Some time before he said, and Barber, too, that he could not live many hours. I felt he was dying before we came to the ravine. He told me his wishes about his children and myself, and took leave. My brain seemed burnt up. No tears came. As soon as we fell, the sergeant let go the horse, and it went off; so that escape was cut off. We sat down on the ground waiting for death. Poor fellow! he was very weak; his thirst was frightful, and I went to get him water. Some villagers came, and took my rupees and watch. I took off my wedding-ring, and twisted it in my hair, and replaced the guard. I tore off the skirt of my dress to bring water in, but was no use, for when I returned my beloved's eyes were fixed, and, though I called and tried to restore him, and poured water into his mouth, it only rattled in his throat. He never spoke to me again. I held him in my arms till he sank gradually down. I felt frantic, but could not cry. I was alone. I bound his head and face in my dress, for there was no earth to bury him. The pain in my hands and feet was dreadful. I went down to the ravine, and sat in the water on a stone, hoping to get off at night and look for Lottie. When I came back from the water, I saw that they had not taken her little watch, chain, and seals, so I tied them under my petticoat. In an hour, about thirty villagers came, they dragged me out of the ravine, and took off my jacket, and found the little chain. They then dragged me to a village, mocking me all the way, and disputing as to whom I was to belong to. The whole population came to look at me. I asked for a bedstead, and lay down outside the door of a hut. They had a dozen of cows, and yet refused me milk. When night came, and the village was quiet, some old woman brought me a leafful of rice. I was too parched to eat, and they gave me water. The morning after a neighboring Rajah sent a palanquin and a horseman to fetch me, who told me that a little child and three Sahibs had come to his master's house. And so the poor mother found her lost one, 'greatly blistered,' poor little creature. It is not for Europeans in India to pray that their flight be not in the winter."

In the first days of June the aged general, Sir Hugh Wheeler commanding the forces at Cawnpore, was deserted by his native troops; then he moved out of the fort and into an exposed patch of open flat ground and built a four-foot mud wall around it. He had with him a few hundred white soldiers and officers, and apparently more women and children than soldiers. He was short of provisions, short of arms, short of ammunition, short of military wisdom, short of everything but courage and devotion to duty. The defense of that open lot through twenty-one days and nights of hunger, thirst, Indian heat, and a never-ceasing storm of bullets, bombs, and cannon-balls—a defense conducted, not by the aged and infirm general, but by a young officer named Moore—is one of the most heroic episodes in history. When at last the Nana found it impossible to conquer these starving men and women with powder and ball, he resorted to treachery, and that succeeded. He agreed to supply them with food and send them to Allahabad in boats. Their mud wall and their barracks were in ruins, their provisions were at the point of exhaustion, they had done all that the brave could do, they had conquered an honorable compromise,—their forces had been fearfully reduced by casualties and by disease, they were not able to continue the contest longer. They came forth helpless but suspecting no treachery, the Nana's host closed around them, and at a signal from a trumpet the massacre began. About two hundred women and children were spared—for the present—

but all the men except three or four were killed. Among the incidents of the massacre quoted by Sir G. O. Trevelyan, is this:

"When, after the lapse of some twenty minutes, the dead began to outnumber the living;—when the fire slackened, as the marks grew few and far between; then the troopers who had been drawn up to the right of the temple plunged into the river, sabre between teeth, and pistol in hand. Thereupon two half-caste Christian women, the wives of musicians in the band of the Fifty-sixth, witnessed a scene which should not be related at second-hand. 'In the boat where I was to have gone,' says Mrs. Bradshaw, confirmed throughout by Mrs. Betts, 'was the school-mistress and twenty-two misses. General Wheeler came last in a palkee. They carried him into the water near the boat. I stood close by. He said, 'Carry me a little further towards the boat.' But a trooper said, 'No, get out here.' As the General got out of the palkee, head-foremost, the trooper gave him a cut with his sword into the neck, and he fell into the water. My son was killed near him. I saw it; alas! alas! Some were stabbed with bayonets; others cut down. Little infants were torn in pieces. We saw it; we did; and tell you only what we saw. Other children were stabbed and thrown into the river. The schoolgirls were burnt to death. I saw their clothes and hair catch fire. In the water, a few paces off, by the next boat, we saw the youngest daughter of Colonel Williams. A sepoy was going to kill her with his bayonet. She said, 'My father was always kind to sepoys.' He turned away, and just then a villager struck her on the head with a club, and she fell into the water. These people likewise saw good Mr. Moncrieff, the clergyman, take a book from his pocket that he never had leisure to open, and heard him commence a prayer for mercy which he was not permitted to conclude. Another deponent observed an European making for a drain like a scared water-rat, when some boatmen, armed with cudgels, cut off his retreat, and beat him down dead into the mud."

The women and children who had been reserved from the massacre were imprisoned during a fortnight in a small building, one story high—a cramped place, a slightly modified Black Hole of Calcutta. They were waiting in suspense; there was none who could foretaste their fate. Meantime the news of the massacre had traveled far and an army of rescuers with Havelock at its head was on its way—at least an army which hoped to be rescuers. It was crossing the country by forced marches, and strewing its way with its own dead men struck down by cholera, and by a heat which reached 135 deg. It was in a vengeful fury, and it stopped for nothing neither heat, nor fatigue, nor disease, nor human opposition. It tore its impetuous way through hostile forces, winning victory after victory, but still striding on and on, not halting to count results. And at last, after this extraordinary march, it arrived before the walls of Cawnpore, met the Nana's massed strength, delivered a crushing defeat, and entered.

But too late—only a few hours too late. For at the last moment the Nana had decided upon the massacre of the captive women and children, and had commissioned three Mohammedans and two Hindoos to do the work. Sir G. O. Trevelyan says:

"Thereupon the five men entered. It was the short gloaming of Hindostan—the hour when ladies take their evening drive. She who had accosted the officer was standing in the doorway. With her were the native doctor and two Hindoo menials. That much of the business might be seen from the veranda, but all else was concealed amidst the interior gloom. Shrieks and scuffing acquainted those without that the journeymen were earning their hire. Survur Khan soon emerged with his sword broken off at the hilt. He procured another from the Nana's house, and a few minutes after appeared again on the same errand. The third blade was of better temper; or perhaps the thick of the work was already over. By the time darkness had closed in, the men came forth and locked up the house for the night. Then the screams ceased, but the groans lasted till morning.

"The sun rose as usual. When he had been up nearly three hours the five repaired to the scene of their labors over night. They were attended by a few sweepers, who proceeded to transfer the contents of the house to a dry well situated behind some trees which grew hard by. 'The bodies,' says one who was present throughout, 'were dragged out, most of them by the hair of the head. Those who had clothing worth taking were stripped. Some of the women were alive. I cannot say how many; but three could speak. They prayed for the sake of God that an end might be put to their sufferings. I remarked one very stout woman, a half-caste, who was severely wounded in both arms, who entreated to be killed. She and two or three others were placed against the bank of the cut by which bullocks go down in drawing water. The dead were first thrown in. Yes: there was a great crowd looking on; they were standing along the walls of the compound. They were principally city people and villagers. Yes: there were also sepoys. Three boys were alive. They were fair children. The eldest, I think, must have been six or seven, and the youngest five years. They were running around the well (where else could they go to?), and there was none to save them. No one said a word or tried to save them.'

"At length the smallest of them made an infantile attempt to get away. The little thing had been frightened past bearing by the murder of one of the surviving ladies. He thus attracted the observation of a native who flung him and his companions down the well."

The soldiers had made a march of eighteen days, almost without rest, to save the women and the children, and now they were too late—all were dead and the assassin had flown. What happened then, Trevelyan hesitated to put into words. "Of what took place, the less said is the better."

Then he continues:

"But there was a spectacle to witness which might excuse much. Those who, straight from the contested field, wandered sobbing through the rooms of the ladies' house, saw what it were well could the outraged earth have straightway hidden. The inner apartment was ankle-deep in blood. The plaster was scored with sword-cuts; not high up as where men have fought, but low down, and about the corners, as if a creature had crouched to avoid the blow. Strips of dresses, vainly tied around the handles of the doors, signified the contrivance to which feminine despair had resorted as a means of keeping out the murderers. Broken combs were there, and the frills of children's trousers, and torn cuffs and pinafores, and little round hats, and one or two shoes with burst latchets, and one or two daguerreotype cases with cracked glasses. An officer picked up a few curls, preserved in a bit of cardboard, and marked 'Ned's hair, with love'; but around were strewn locks, some near a yard in length, dissevered, not as a keepsake, by quite other scissors."

The battle of Waterloo was fought on the 18th of June, 1815. I do not state this fact as a reminder to the reader, but as news to him. For a forgotten fact is news when it comes again.

Writers of books have the fashion of whizzing by vast and renowned historical events with the remark, "The details of this tremendous episode are too familiar to the reader to need repeating here." They know that that is not true. It is a low kind of flattery. They know that the reader has forgotten every detail of it, and that nothing of the tremendous event is left in his mind but a vague and formless luminous smudge. Aside from the desire to flatter the reader, they have another reason for making the remark-two reasons, indeed. They do not remember the details themselves, and do not want the trouble of hunting them up and copying them out; also, they are afraid that if they search them out and print them they will be scoffed at by the book-reviewers for retelling those worn old things which are familiar to everybody. They should not mind the reviewer's jeer; he doesn't remember any of the worn old things until the book which he is reviewing has retold them to him.

I have made the quoted remark myself, at one time and another, but I was not doing it to flatter the reader; I was merely doing it to save work. If I had known the details without brushing up, I would have put them in; but I didn't, and I did not want the labor of posting myself; so I said, "The details of this tremendous episode are too familiar to the reader to need repeating here." I do not like that kind of a lie; still, it does save work.

I am not trying to get out of repeating the details of the Siege of Lucknow in fear of the reviewer; I am not leaving them out in fear that they would not interest the reader; I am leaving them out partly to save work; mainly for lack of room. It is a pity, too; for there is not a dull place anywhere in the great story.

Ten days before the outbreak (May 10th) of the Mutiny, all was serene at Lucknow, the huge capital of Oudh, the kingdom which had recently been seized by the India Company. There was a great garrison, composed of about 7,000 native troops and between 700 and 800 whites. These white soldiers and their families were probably the only people of their race there; at their elbow was that swarming population of warlike natives, a race of born soldiers, brave, daring, and fond of fighting. On high ground just outside the city stood the palace of that great personage, the Resident, the representative of British power and authority. It stood in the midst of spacious grounds, with its due complement of outbuildings, and the grounds were enclosed by a wall—a wall not for defense, but for privacy. The mutinous spirit was in the air, but the whites were not afraid, and did not feel much troubled.

Then came the outbreak at Meerut, then the capture of Delhi by the mutineers; in June came the three-weeks leaguer of Sir Hugh Wheeler in his open lot at Cawnpore—40 miles distant from Lucknow—then the treacherous massacre of that gallant little garrison; and now the great revolt was in full flower, and the comfortable condition of things at Lucknow was instantly changed.

There was an outbreak there, and Sir Henry Lawrence marched out of the Residency on the 30th of June to put it down, but was defeated with heavy loss, and had difficulty in getting back again. That night the memorable siege of the Residency—called the siege of Lucknow—began. Sir Henry was killed three days later, and Brigadier Inglis succeeded him in command.

Outside of the Residency fence was an immense host of hostile and confident native besiegers; inside it were 480 loyal native soldiers, 730 white ones, and 500 women and children.

In those days the English garrisons always managed to hamper themselves sufficiently with women and children.

The natives established themselves in houses close at hand and began to rain bullets and cannon-balls into the Residency; and this they kept up, night and day, during four months and a half, the little garrison industriously replying all the time. The women and children soon became so used to the roar of the guns that it ceased to disturb their sleep. The children imitated siege and defense in their play. The women—with any pretext, or with none—would sally out into the storm-swept grounds. The defense was kept up week after week, with stubborn fortitude, in the midst of death, which came in many forms—by bullet, small-pox, cholera, and by various diseases induced by unpalatable and insufficient food, by the long hours of wearying and exhausting overwork in the daily and nightly battle in the oppressive Indian heat, and by the broken rest caused by the intolerable pest of mosquitoes, flies, mice, rats, and fleas.

Six weeks after the beginning of the siege more than one-half of the original force of white soldiers was dead, and close upon three-fifths of the original native force.

But the fighting went on just the same. The enemy mined, the English counter-mined, and, turn about, they blew up each other's posts. The Residency grounds were honey-combed with the enemy's tunnels. Deadly courtesies were constantly exchanged—sorties by the English in the night; rushes by the enemy in the night—rushes whose purpose was to breach the walls or scale them; rushes which cost heavily, and always failed.

The ladies got used to all the horrors of war—the shrieks of mutilated men, the sight of blood and death. Lady Inglis makes this mention in her diary:

"Mrs. Bruere's nurse was carried past our door to-day, wounded in the eye. To extract the bullet it was found necessary to take out the eye—a fearful operation. Her mistress held her while it was performed."

The first relieving force failed to relieve. It was under Havelock and Outram; and arrived when the siege had been going on for three months. It fought its desperate way to Lucknow, then fought its way through the city against odds of a hundred to one, and entered the Residency; but there was not enough left of it, then, to do any good. It lost more men in its last fight than it found in the Residency when it got in. It became captive itself.

The fighting and starving and dying by bullets and disease went steadily on. Both sides fought with energy and industry. Captain Birch puts this striking incident in evidence. He is speaking of the third month of the siege:

"As an instance of the heavy firing brought to bear on our position this month may be mentioned the cutting down of the upper story of a brick building simply by musketry firring. This building was in a most exposed position. All the shots which just missed the top of the rampart cut into the dead wall pretty much in a straight line, and at length cut right through and brought the upper story tumbling down. The upper structure on the top of the brigade-mess also fell in. The Residency house was a wreck. Captain Anderson's post had long ago been knocked down, and Innes' post also fell in.

These two were riddled with round shot. As many as 200 were picked up by Colonel Masters."

The exhausted garrison fought doggedly on all through the next month October. Then, November 2d, news came Sir Colin Campbell's relieving force would soon be on its way from Cawnpore.

On the 12th the boom of his guns was heard.

On the 13th the sounds came nearer—he was slowly, but steadily, cutting his way through, storming one stronghold after another.

On the 14th he captured the Martiniere College, and ran up the British flag there. It was seen from the Residency.

Next he took the Dilkoosha.

On the 17th he took the former mess-house of the 32d regiment—a fortified building, and very strong. "A most exciting, anxious day," writes Lady Inglis in her diary. "About 4 P.M., two strange officers walked through our yard, leading their horses"—and by that sign she knew that communication was established between the forces, that the relief was real, this time, and that the long siege of Lucknow was ended.

The last eight or ten miles of Sir Colin Campbell's march was through seas of, blood. The weapon mainly used was the bayonet, the fighting was desperate. The way was mile-stoned with detached strong buildings of stone, fortified, and heavily garrisoned, and these had to be taken by assault. Neither side asked for quarter, and neither gave it. At the Secundrabagh, where nearly two thousand of the enemy occupied a great stone house in a garden, the work of slaughter was continued until every man was killed. That is a sample of the character of that devastating march.

There were but few trees in the plain at that time, and from the Residency the progress of the march, step by step, victory by victory, could be noted; the ascending clouds of battle-smoke marked the way to the eye, and the thunder of the guns marked it to the ear.

Sir Colin Campbell had not come to Lucknow to hold it, but to save the occupants of the Residency, and bring them away. Four or five days after his arrival the secret evacuation by the troops took place, in the middle of a dark night, by the principal gate, (the Bailie Guard). The two hundred women and two hundred and fifty children had been previously removed. Captain Birch says:

"And now commenced a movement of the most perfect arrangement and successful generalship—the withdrawal of the whole of the various forces, a combined movement requiring the greatest care and skill. First, the garrison in immediate contact with the enemy at the furthest extremity of the Residency position was marched out. Every other garrison in turn fell in behind it, and so passed out through the Bailie Guard gate, till the whole of our position was evacuated. Then Havelock's force was similarly withdrawn, post by post, marching in rear of our garrison. After them in turn came the forces of the Commander-in-Chief, which joined on in the rear of Havelock's force. Regiment by regiment was withdrawn with—the utmost order and regularity. The whole operation resembled the movement of a telescope. Stern silence was kept, and the enemy took no alarm."

Lady Inglis, referring to her husband and to General Sir James Outram, sets down the closing detail of this impressive midnight retreat, in darkness and by stealth, of this shadowy host through the gate which it had defended so long and so well:

"At twelve precisely they marched out, John and Sir James Outram remaining till all had passed, and then they took off their hats to the Bailie Guard, the scene of as noble a defense as I think history will ever have to relate."

CHAPTER LIX.

Don't part with your illusions. When they are gone you may still exist but you have ceased to live. —Pudd'nhead Wilson's New Calendar.

Often, the surest way to convey misinformation is to tell the strict truth. —Pudd'nhead Wilson's New Calendar.

We were driven over Sir Colin Campbell's route by a British officer, and when I arrived at the Residency I was so familiar with the road that I could have led a retreat over it myself; but the compass in my head has been out of order from my birth, and so, as soon as I was within the battered Bailie Guard and turned about to review the march and imagine the relieving forces storming their way along it, everything was upside down and wrong end first in a moment, and I was never able to get straightened out again. And now, when I look at the battle-plan, the confusion remains. In me the east was born west, the battle-plans which have the east on the right-hand side are of no use to me.

The Residency ruins are draped with flowering vines, and are impressive and beautiful. They and the grounds are sacred now, and will suffer no neglect nor be profaned by any sordid or commercial use while the British remain masters of India. Within the grounds are buried the dead who gave up their lives there in the long siege.

After a fashion, I was able to imagine the fiery storm that raged night and day over the place during so many months, and after a fashion I could imagine the men moving through it, but I could not satisfactorily place the 200 women, and I could do nothing at all with the 250 children. I knew by Lady Inglis' diary that the children carried on their small affairs very much as if blood and carnage and the crash and thunder of a siege were natural and proper features of nursery life, and I tried to realize it; but when her little Johnny came rushing, all excitement, through the din and smoke, shouting, "Oh, mamma, the white hen has laid an egg!" I saw that I could not do it. Johnny's place was under the bed. I could imagine him there, because I could imagine myself there; and I think I should not have been interested in a hen that was laying an egg; my interest would have been with the parties that were laying the bombshells. I sat at dinner with one of those children in the Club's Indian palace, and I knew that all through the siege he was perfecting his teething and learning to talk; and while to me he was the most impressive object in Lucknow after the Residency ruins, I was not able to imagine what his life had been during that tempestuous infancy of his, nor what sort of a curious surprise it must have been to him to be marched suddenly out into a strange dumb world where there wasn't any noise, and nothing going on. He was only forty-one when I saw him, a strangely youthful link to connect the present with so ancient an episode as the Great Mutiny.

By and by we saw Cawnpore, and the open lot which was the scene of Moore's memorable defense, and the spot on the shore of the Ganges where the massacre of the betrayed garrison occurred, and the small Indian temple whence the bugle-signal notified the assassins to fall on. This latter was a lonely spot, and silent. The sluggish river drifted by, almost currentless. It was dead low water, narrow channels with vast sandbars between, all the way across the wide bed; and the only living thing in sight was that grotesque and solemn bald-headed bird, the Adjutant, standing on his six-foot stilts, solitary on a distant bar, with his head sunk between his shoulders, thinking; thinking of his prize, I suppose—the dead Hindoo that lay awash at his feet, and whether to eat him alone or invite friends. He and his prey were a proper accent to that mournful place. They were in keeping with it, they emphasized its loneliness and its solemnity.

And we saw the scene of the slaughter of the helpless women and children, and also the costly memorial that is built over the well which contains their remains. The Black Hole of Calcutta is gone, but a more reverent age is come, and whatever remembrancer still exists of the moving and heroic sufferings and achievements of the garrisons of Lucknow and Cawnpore will be guarded and preserved.

In Agra and its neighborhood, and afterwards at Delhi, we saw forts, mosques, and tombs, which were built in the great days of the Mohammedan emperors, and which are marvels of cost, magnitude, and richness of materials and ornamentation, creations of surpassing grandeur, wonders which do indeed make the like things in the rest of the world seem tame and inconsequential by comparison. I am not purposing to describe them. By good fortune I had not read too much about them, and therefore was able to get a natural and rational focus upon them, with the result that they thrilled, blessed, and exalted me. But if I had previously overheated my imagination by drinking too much pestilential literary hot Scotch, I should have suffered disappointment and sorrow.

I mean to speak of only one of these many world-renowned buildings, the Taj Mahal, the most celebrated construction in the earth. I had read a great deal too much about it. I saw it in the daytime, I saw it in the moonlight, I saw it near at hand, I saw it from a distance; and I knew all the time, that of its kind it was the wonder of the world, with no competitor now and no possible future competitor; and yet, it was not my Taj. My Taj had been built by excitable literary people; it was solidly lodged in my head, and I could not blast it out.

I wish to place before the reader some of the usual descriptions of the Taj, and ask him to take note of the impressions left in his mind. These descriptions do really state the truth—as nearly as the limitations of language will allow. But language is a treacherous thing, a most unsure vehicle, and it can seldom arrange descriptive words in such a way that they will not inflate the facts—by help of the reader's imagination, which is always ready to take a hand, and work for nothing, and do the bulk of it at that.

I will begin with a few sentences from the excellent little local guide-book of Mr. Satya Chandra Mukerji. I take them from here and there in his description:

"The inlaid work of the Taj and the flowers and petals that are to be found on all sides on the surface of the marble evince a most delicate touch."

That is true.

"The inlaid work, the marble, the flowers, the buds, the leaves, the petals, and the lotus stems are almost without a rival in the whole of the civilized world."

"The work of inlaying with stones and gems is found in the highest perfection in the Taj."

Gems, inlaid flowers, buds, and leaves to be found on all sides. What do you see before you? Is the fairy structure growing? Is it becoming a jewel casket?

"The whole of the Taj produces a wonderful effect that is equally sublime and beautiful."

Then Sir William Wilson Hunter:

"The Taj Mahal with its beautiful domes, 'a dream of marble,' rises on the river bank."

"The materials are white marble and red sandstone."

"The complexity of its design and the delicate intricacy of the workmanship baffle description."

Sir William continues. I will italicize some of his words:

"The mausoleum stands on a raised marble platform at each of whose corners rises a tall and slender minaret of graceful proportions and of exquisite beauty. Beyond the platform stretch the two wings, one of which is itself a mosque of great architectural merit. In the center of the whole design the mausoleum occupies a square of 186 feet, with the angles deeply truncated so also form an unequal octagon. The main feature in this central pile is the great dome, which swells upward to nearly two-thirds of a sphere and tapers at its extremity into a pointed spire crowned by a crescent. Beneath it an enclosure of marble trellis-work surrounds the tomb of the princess and of her husband, the Emperor. Each corner of the mausoleum is covered by a similar though much smaller dome erected on a pediment pierced with graceful Saracenic arches. Light is admitted into the interior through a double screen of pierced marble, which tempers the glare of an Indian sky while its whiteness prevents the mellow effect from degenerating into gloom. The internal decorations consist of inlaid work in precious stones, such as agate, jasper, etc., with which every squandril or salient point in the architecture is richly fretted. Brown and violet marble is also freely employed in wreaths, scrolls, and lintels to relieve the monotony of white wall. In regard to color and design, the interior of the Taj may rank first in the world for purely decorative workmanship; while the perfect symmetry of its exterior, once seen can never be forgotten, nor the aerial grace of its domes, rising like marble bubbles into the clear sky. The Taj represents the most highly elaborated stage of ornamentation reached by the Indo-Mohammedan builders, the stage in which the architect ends and the jeweler begins. In its magnificent gateway the diagonal ornamentation at the corners, which satisfied the designers of the gateways of Itimad-ud-doulah and Sikandra mausoleums is superseded by fine marble cables, in bold twists, strong and handsome. The triangular insertions of white marble and large flowers have in like manner given place to fine inlaid work. Firm perpendicular lines in black marble with well proportioned panels of the same material are effectively used in the interior of the gateway. On its top the Hindu brackets and monolithic architraves of Sikandra are replaced by Moorish carped arches, usually single blocks of red sandstone, in the Kiosks and pavilions which adorn the roof. From the pillared pavilions a magnificent view is obtained of the Taj

gardens below, with the noble Jumna river at their farther end, and the city and fort of Agra in the distance. From this beautiful and splendid gateway one passes up a straight alley shaded by evergreen trees cooled by a broad shallow piece of water running along the middle of the path to the Taj itself. The Taj is entirely of marble and gems. The red sandstone of the other Mohammedan buildings has entirely disappeared, or rather the red sandstone which used to form the thickness of the walls, is in the Taj itself overlaid completely with white marble, and the white marble is itself inlaid with precious stones arranged in lovely patterns of flowers. A feeling of purity impresses itself on the eye and the mind from the absence of the coarser material which forms so invariable a material in Agra architecture. The lower wall and panels are covered with tulips, oleanders, and fullblown lilies, in flat carving on the white marble; and although the inlaid work of flowers done in gems is very brilliant when looked at closely, there is on the whole but little color, and the all-prevailing sentiment is one of whiteness, silence, and calm. The whiteness is broken only by the fine color of the inlaid gems, by lines in black marble, and by delicately written inscriptions, also in black, from the Koran. Under the dome of the vast mausoleum a high and beautiful screen of open tracery in white marble rises around the two tombs, or rather cenotaphs of the emperor and his princess; and in this marvel of marble the carving has advanced from the old geometrical patterns to a trellis-work of flowers and foliage, handled with great freedom and spirit. The two cenotaphs in the center of the exquisite enclosure have no carving except the plain Kalamdan or oblong pen-box on the tomb of Emperor Shah Jehan. But both cenotaphs are inlaid with flowers made of costly gems, and with the ever graceful oleander scroll."

Bayard Taylor, after describing the details of the Taj, goes on to say:

"On both sides the palm, the banyan, and the feathery bamboo mingle their foliage; the song of birds meets your ears, and the odor of roses and lemon flowers sweetens the air. Down such a vista and over such a foreground rises the Taj. There is no mystery, no sense of partial failure about the Taj. A thing of perfect beauty and of absolute finish in every detail, it might pass for the work of genii who knew naught of the weaknesses and ills with which mankind are beset."

All of these details are true. But, taken together, they state a falsehood—to you. You cannot add them up correctly. Those writers know the values of their words and phrases, but to you the words and phrases convey other and uncertain values. To those writers their phrases have values which I think I am now acquainted with; and for the help of the reader I will here repeat certain of those words and phrases, and follow them with numerals which shall represent those values—then we shall see the difference between a writer's ciphering and a mistaken reader's—

Precious stones, such as agate, jasper, etc.—5.

With which every salient point is richly fretted—5.

First in the world for purely decorative workmanship—9.

The Taj represents the stage where the architect ends and the jeweler begins—5.

The Taj is entirely of marble and gems—7.

Inlaid with precious stones in lovely patterns of flowers—5.

The inlaid work of flowers done in gems is very brilliant (followed by a most important modification which the reader is sure to read too carelessly)—2.

The vast mausoleum—5.

This marvel of marble—5.

The exquisite enclosure—5.

Inlaid with flowers made of costly gems—5.

A thing of perfect beauty and absolute finish—5.

Those details are correct; the figures which I have placed after them represent quite fairly their individual, values. Then why, as a whole, do they convey a false impression to the reader? It is because the reader—beguiled by, his heated imagination—masses them in the wrong way. The writer would mass the first three figures in the following way, and they would speak the truth

Total—19

But the reader masses them thus—and then they tell a lie—559.

The writer would add all of his twelve numerals together, and then the sum would express the whole truth about the Taj, and the truth only—63.

But the reader—always helped by his imagination—would put the figures in a row one after the other, and get this sum, which would tell him a noble big lie:

559575255555.

You must put in the commas yourself; I have to go on with my work.

The reader will always be sure to put the figures together in that wrong way, and then as surely before him will stand, sparkling in the sun, a gem-crusted Taj tall as the Matterhorn.

I had to visit Niagara fifteen times before I succeeded in getting my imaginary Falls gauged to the actuality and could begin to sanely and wholesomely wonder at them for what they were, not what I had expected them to be. When I first approached them it was with my face lifted toward the sky, for I thought I was going to see an Atlantic ocean pouring down thence over cloud-vexed Himalayan heights, a sea-green wall of water sixty miles front and six miles high, and so, when the toy reality came suddenly into view—that beruiled little wet apron hanging out to dry—the shock was too much for me, and I fell with a dull thud.

Yet slowly, surely, steadily, in the course of my fifteen visits, the proportions adjusted themselves to the facts, and I came at last to realize that a waterfall a hundred and sixty-five feet high and a quarter of a mile wide was an impressive thing. It was not a dipperful to my vanished great vision, but it would answer.

I know that I ought to do with the Taj as I was obliged to do with Niagara—see it fifteen times, and let my mind gradually get rid of the Taj built in it by its describers, by help of my imagination, and substitute for it the Taj of fact. It would be noble and fine, then, and a marvel; not the marvel which it replaced, but still a marvel, and fine enough. I am a careless reader, I suppose—an impressionist reader; an impressionist reader of what is not an impressionist picture; a reader who overlooks the informing details or masses their sum improperly, and gets only a large splashy, general effect—an effect which is not correct, and which is not warranted by the particulars placed before me particulars which I did not examine, and whose meanings I did not cautiously and carefully estimate. It is an effect which is some thirty-five or forty times finer than the reality, and is therefore a great deal better and more valuable than the reality; and so, I ought never to hunt up the reality, but stay miles away from it, and thus preserve undamaged my own private mighty Niagara tumbling out of the vault of heaven, and my own ineffable Taj, built of tinted mists upon jeweled arches of rainbows supported by colonnades of moonlight. It is a mistake for a person with an unregulated imagination to go and look at an illustrious world's wonder.

I suppose that many, many years ago I gathered the idea that the Taj's place in the achievements of man was exactly the place of the ice-storm in the achievements of Nature; that the Taj represented man's supremest possibility in the creation of grace and beauty and exquisiteness and splendor, just as the ice-storm represents Nature's supremest possibility in the combination of those same qualities. I do not know how long ago that idea was bred in me, but I know that I cannot remember back to a time when the thought of either of these symbols of gracious and unapproachable perfection did not at once suggest the other. If I thought of the ice-storm, the Taj rose before me divinely beautiful; if I thought of the Taj, with its encrustings and inlayings of jewels, the vision of the ice-storm rose. And so, to me, all these years, the Taj has had no rival among the temples and palaces of men, none that even remotely approached it it was man's architectural ice-storm.

Here in London the other night I was talking with some Scotch and English friends, and I mentioned the ice-storm, using it as a figure—a figure which failed, for none of them had heard of the ice-storm. One gentleman, who was very familiar with American literature, said he had never seen it mentioned in any book. That is strange. And I, myself, was not able to say that I had seen it mentioned in a book; and yet the autumn foliage, with all other American scenery, has received full and competent attention.

The oversight is strange, for in America the ice-storm is an event. And it is not an event which one is careless about. When it comes, the news flies from room to room in the house, there are bangings on the doors, and shoutings, "The ice-storm! the ice-storm!" and even the laziest sleepers throw off the covers and join the rush for the windows. The ice-storm occurs in midwinter, and usually its enchantments are wrought in the silence and the darkness of the night. A fine drizzling rain falls hour after hour upon the naked twigs and branches of the trees, and as it falls it freezes. In time the trunk and every branch and twig are incased in hard pure ice; so that the tree looks like a skeleton tree made all of glass—glass that is crystal-clear. All along the underside of every branch and twig is a comb of little icicles—the frozen drip. Sometimes these pendants do not quite amount to icicles, but are round beads—frozen tears.

The weather clears, toward dawn, and leaves a brisk pure atmosphere and a sky without a shred of cloud in it—and everything is still, there is not a breath of wind. The dawn breaks and spreads, the news of the storm goes about the house, and the little and the big, in wraps and blankets, flock to the window and press together there, and gaze intently out upon the great white ghost in the grounds, and nobody says a word, nobody stirs. All are waiting; they know what is coming, and they are waiting waiting waiting for the miracle. The minutes drift on and on and on, with not a sound but the ticking of the clock; at last the sun fires a sudden sheaf of rays into the ghostly tree and turns it into a white splendor of glittering diamonds. Everybody catches his breath, and feels a swelling in his throat and a moisture in his eyes-but waits again; for he knows what is coming; there is more yet. The sun climbs higher, and still higher, flooding the tree from its loftiest spread of branches to its lowest, turning it to a glory of white fire; then in a moment, without warning, comes the great miracle, the supreme miracle, the miracle without its fellow in the earth; a gust of wind sets every branch and twig to swaying, and in an instant turns the whole white tree into a spouting and spraying explosion of flashing gems of every conceivable color; and there it stands and sways this way and that, flash! flash! flash! a dancing and glancing world of rubies, emeralds, diamonds, sapphires, the most radiant spectacle, the most blinding spectacle, the divinest, the most exquisite, the most intoxicating vision of fire and color and intolerable and unimaginable splendor that ever any eye has rested upon in this world, or will ever rest upon outside of the gates of heaven.

By, all my senses, all my faculties, I know that the icestorm is Nature's supremest achievement in the domain of the superb and the beautiful; and by my reason, at least, I know that the Taj is man's ice-storm.

In the ice-storm every one of the myriad ice-beads pendant from twig and branch is an individual gem, and changes color with every motion caused by the wind; each tree carries a million, and a forest-front exhibits the splendors of the single tree multiplied by a thousand.

It occurs to me now that I have never seen the ice-storm put upon canvas, and have not heard that any painter has tried to do it. I wonder why that is. Is it that paint cannot counterfeit the intense blaze of a sun-flooded jewel? There should be, and must be, a reason, and a good one, why the most enchanting sight that Nature has created has been neglected by the brush.

Often, the surest way to convey misinformation is to tell the strict truth. The describers of the Taj have used the word gem in its strictest sense—its scientific sense. In that sense it is a mild word, and promises but little to the eye-nothing bright, nothing brilliant, nothing sparkling, nothing splendid in the way of color. It accurately describes the sober and unobtrusive gem-work of the Taj; that is, to the very highly-educated one person in a thousand; but it most falsely describes it to the 999. But the 999 are the people who ought to be especially taken care of, and to them it does not mean quiet-colored designs wrought in carnelians, or agates, or such things; they know the word in its wide and ordinary sense only, and so to them it means diamonds and rubies and opals and their kindred, and the moment their eyes fall upon it in print they see a vision of glorious colors clothed in fire.

These describers are writing for the "general," and so, in order to make sure of being understood, they ought to use words in their ordinary sense, or else explain. The word fountain means one thing in Syria, where there is but a handful of people; it means quite another thing in North America, where there are 75,000,000. If I were describing some Syrian scenery, and should exclaim, "Within the narrow space of a quarter of a

mile square I saw, in the glory of the flooding moonlight, two hundred noble fountains—imagine the spectacle!" the North American would have a vision of clustering columns of water soaring aloft, bending over in graceful arches, bursting in beaded spray and raining white fire in the moonlight-and he would be deceived. But the Syrian would not be deceived; he would merely see two hundred fresh-water springs—two hundred· drowsing puddles, as level and unpretentious and unexcited as so many door-mats, and even with the help of the moonlight he would not lose his grip in the presence of the exhibition. My word "fountain" would be correct; it would speak the strict truth; and it would convey the strict truth to the handful of Syrians, and the strictest misinformation to the North American millions. With their gems—and gems—and more gems—and gems again—and still other gems—the describers of the Taj are within their legal but not their moral rights; they are dealing in the strictest scientific truth; and in doing it they succeed to admiration in telling "what ain't so."

CHAPTER LX.

SATAN (impatiently) to NEW-COMER. The trouble with you Chicago people is, that you think you are the best people down here; whereas you are merely the most numerous. — Pudd'nhead Wilson's New Calendar.

We wandered contentedly around here and there in India; to Lahore, among other places, where the Lieutenant-Governor lent me an elephant. This hospitality stands out in my experiences in a stately isolation. It was a fine elephant, affable, gentlemanly, educated, and I was not afraid of it. I even rode it with confidence through the crowded lanes of the native city, where it scared all the horses out of their senses, and where children were always just escaping its feet. It took the middle of the road in a fine independent way, and left it to the world to get out of the way or take the consequences. I am used to being afraid of collisions when I ride or drive, but when one is on top of an elephant that feeling is absent. I could have ridden in comfort through a regiment of runaway teams. I could easily learn to prefer an elephant to any other vehicle, partly because of that immunity from collisions, and partly because of the fine view one has from up there, and partly because of the dignity one feels in that high place, and partly because one can look in at the windows and see what is going on privately among the family. The Lahore horses were used to elephants, but they were rapturously afraid of them just the same. It seemed curious. Perhaps the better they know the elephant the more they respect him in that peculiar way. In our own case—we are not afraid of dynamite till we get acquainted with it.

We drifted as far as Rawal Pindi, away up on the Afghan frontier—I think it was the Afghan frontier, but it may have been Hertzegovina—it was around there somewhere—and down again to Delhi, to see the ancient architectural wonders there and in Old Delhi and not describe them, and also to see the scene of the illustrious assault, in the Mutiny days, when the British carried Delhi by storm, one of the marvels of history for impudent daring and immortal valor.

We had a refreshing rest, there in Delhi, in a great old mansion which possessed historical interest. It was built by a rich Englishman who had become orientalized—so much so that he had a zenana. But he was a broadminded man, and remained so. To please his harem he built a mosque; to please himself he built an English church. That kind of a man will arrive, somewhere. In the Mutiny days the mansion was the British general's headquarters. It stands in a great garden—

oriental fashion —and about it are many noble trees. The trees harbor monkeys; and they are monkeys of a watchful and enterprising sort, and not much troubled with fear. They invade the house whenever they get a chance, and carry off everything they don't want. One morning the master of the house was in his bath, and the window was open. Near it stood a pot of yellow paint and a brush. Some monkeys appeared in the window; to scare them away, the gentleman threw his sponge at them. They did not scare at all; they jumped into the room and threw yellow paint all over him from the brush, and drove him out; then they painted the walls and the floor and the tank and the windows and the furniture yellow, and were in the dressing-room painting that when help arrived and routed them.

Two of these creatures came into my room in the early morning, through a window whose shutters I had left open, and when I woke one of them was before the glass brushing his hair, and the other one had my note-book, and was reading a page of humorous notes and crying. I did not mind the one with the hair-brush, but the conduct of the other one hurt me; it hurts me yet. I threw something at him, and that was wrong, for my host had told me that the monkeys were best left alone. They threw everything at me that they could lift, and then went into the bathroom to get some more things, and I shut the door on them.

At Jeypore, in Rajputana, we made a considerable stay. We were not in the native city, but several miles from it, in the small European official suburb. There were but few Europeans—only fourteen but they were all kind and hospitable, and it amounted to being at home. In Jeypore we found again what we had found all about India—that while the Indian servant is in his way a very real treasure, he will sometimes bear watching, and the Englishman watches him. If he sends him on an errand, he wants more than the man's word for it that he did the errand. When fruit and vegetables were sent to us, a "chit" came with them—a receipt for us to sign; otherwise the things might not arrive. If a gentleman sent up his carriage, the chit stated "from" such-and-such an hour "to" such-and-such an hour—which made it unhandy for the coachman and his two or three subordinates to put us off with a part of the allotted time and devote the rest of it to a lark of their own.

We were pleasantly situated in a small two-storied inn, in an empty large compound which was surrounded by a mud wall as high as a man's head. The inn was kept by nine Hindoo brothers, its owners. They lived, with their families, in a one-storied building within the compound, but off to one side, and there was always a long pile of their little comely brown children loosely stacked in its veranda, and a detachment of the parents wedged among them, smoking the hookah or the howdah, or whatever they call it. By the veranda stood a palm, and a monkey lived in it, and led a lonesome life, and always looked sad and weary, and the crows bothered him a good deal.

The inn cow poked about the compound and emphasized the secluded and country air of the place, and there was a dog of no particular breed, who was always present in the compound, and always asleep, always stretched out baking in the sun and adding to the deep tranquility and reposefulness of the place, when the crows were away on business. White-draperied servants were coming and going all the time, but they seemed only spirits, for their feet were bare and made no sound. Down the lane a piece lived an elephant in the shade of a noble tree, and rocked and rocked, and reached about with his trunk,

begging of his brown mistress or fumbling the children playing at his feet. And there were camels about, but they go on velvet feet, and were proper to the silence and serenity of the surroundings.

The Satan mentioned at the head of this chapter was not our Satan, but the other one. Our Satan was lost to us. In these later days he had passed out of our life—lamented by me, and sincerely. I was missing him; I am missing him yet, after all these months. He was an astonishing creature to fly around and do things. He didn't always do them quite right, but he did them, and did them suddenly. There was no time wasted. You would say:

"Pack the trunks and bags, Satan."

"Wair good" (very good).

Then there would be a brief sound of thrashing and slashing and humming and buzzing, and a spectacle as of a whirlwind spinning gowns and jackets and coats and boots and things through the air, and then with bow and touch—

"Awready, master."

It was wonderful. It made one dizzy. He crumpled dresses a good deal, and he had no particular plan about the work—at first—except to put each article into the trunk it didn't belong in. But he soon reformed, in this matter. Not entirely; for, to the last, he would cram into the satchel sacred to literature any odds and ends of rubbish that he couldn't find a handy place for elsewhere. When threatened with death for this, it did not trouble him; he only looked pleasant, saluted with soldierly grace, said "Wair good," and did it again next day.

He was always busy; kept the rooms tidied up, the boots polished, the clothes brushed, the wash-basin full of clean water, my dress clothes laid out and ready for the lecture-hall an hour ahead of time; and he dressed me from head to heel in spite of my determination to do it myself, according to my lifelong custom.

He was a born boss, and loved to command, and to jaw and dispute with inferiors and harry them and bullyrag them. He was fine at the railway station—yes, he was at his finest there. He would shoulder and plunge and paw his violent way through the packed multitude of natives with nineteen coolies at his tail, each bearing a trifle of luggage—one a trunk, another a parasol, another a shawl, another a fan, and so on; one article to each, and the longer the procession, the better he was suited —and he was sure to make for some engaged sleeper and begin to hurl the owner's things out of it, swearing that it was ours and that there had been a mistake. Arrived at our own sleeper, he would undo the bedding-bundles and make the beds and put everything to rights and shipshape in two minutes; then put his head out at, a window and have a restful good time abusing his gang of coolies and disputing their bill until we arrived and made him pay them and stop his noise.

Speaking of noise, he certainly was the noisest little devil in India —and that is saying much, very much, indeed. I loved him for his noise, but the family detested him for it. They could not abide it; they could not get reconciled to it. It humiliated them. As a rule, when we got within six hundred yards of one of those big railway stations, a mighty racket of screaming and shrieking and shouting and storming would break upon us, and I would be happy to myself, and the family would say, with shame:

"There—that's Satan. Why do you keep him?"

And, sure enough, there in the whirling midst of fifteen hundred wondering people we would find that little scrap of a creature gesticulating like a spider with the colic, his black eyes snapping, his fez-tassel dancing, his jaws pouring out floods of billingsgate upon his gang of beseeching and astonished coolies.

I loved him; I couldn't help it; but the family—why, they could hardly speak of him with patience. To this day I regret his loss, and wish I had him back; but they—it is different with them. He was a native, and came from Surat. Twenty degrees of latitude lay between his birthplace and Manuel's, and fifteen hundred between their ways and characters and dispositions. I only liked Manuel, but I loved Satan. This latter's real name was intensely Indian. I could not quite get the hang of it, but it sounded like Bunder Rao Ram Chunder Clam Chowder. It was too long for handy use, anyway; so I reduced it.

When he had been with us two or three weeks, he began to make mistakes which I had difficulty in patching up for him. Approaching Benares one day, he got out of the train to see if he could get up a misunderstanding with somebody, for it had been a weary, long journey and he wanted to freshen up. He found what he was after, but kept up his pow-wow a shade too long and got left. So there we were in a strange city and no chambermaid. It was awkward for us, and we told him he must not do so any more. He saluted and said in his dear, pleasant way, "Wair good." Then at Lucknow he got drunk. I said it was a fever, and got the family's compassion, and solicitude aroused; so they gave him a teaspoonful of liquid quinine and it set his vitals on fire. He made several grimaces which gave me a better idea of the Lisbon earthquake than any I have ever got of it from paintings and descriptions. His drunk was still portentously solid next morning, but I could have pulled him through with the family if he would only have taken another spoonful of that remedy; but no, although he was stupefied, his memory still had flickerings of life; so he smiled a divinely dull smile and said, fumblingly saluting:

"Scoose me, mem Saheb, scoose me, Missy Saheb; Satan not prefer it, please."

Then some instinct revealed to them that he was drunk. They gave him prompt notice that next time this happened he must go. He got out a maudlin and most gentle "Wair good," and saluted indefinitely.

Only one short week later he fell again. And oh, sorrow! not in a hotel this time, but in an English gentleman's private house. And in Agra, of all places. So he had to go. When I told him, he said patiently, "Wair good," and made his parting salute, and went out from us to return no more forever. Dear me! I would rather have lost a hundred angels than that one poor lovely devil. What style he used to put on, in a swell hotel or in a private house—snow-white muslin from his chin to his bare feet, a crimson sash embroidered with gold thread around his waist, and on his head a great sea-green turban like to the turban of the Grand Turk.

He was not a liar; but he will become one if he keeps on. He told me once that he used to crack cocoanuts with his teeth when he was a boy; and when I asked how he got them into his mouth, he said he was upward of six feet high at that time, and had an unusual mouth. And when I followed him up and asked

him what had become of that other foot, he said a house fell on him and he was never able to get his stature back again. Swervings like these from the strict line of fact often beguile a truthful man on and on until he eventually becomes a liar.

His successor was a Mohammedan, Sahadat Mohammed Khan; very dark, very tall, very grave. He went always in flowing masses of white, from the top of his big turban down to his bare feet. His voice was low. He glided about in a noiseless way, and looked like a ghost. He was competent and satisfactory. But where he was, it seemed always Sunday. It was not so in Satan's time.

Jeypore is intensely Indian, but it has two or three features which indicate the presence of European science and European interest in the weal of the common public, such as the liberal water-supply furnished by great works built at the State's expense; good sanitation, resulting in a degree of healthfulness unusually high for India; a noble pleasure garden, with privileged days for women; schools for the instruction of native youth in advanced art, both ornamental and utilitarian; and a new and beautiful palace stocked with a museum of extraordinary interest and value. Without the Maharaja's sympathy and purse these beneficences could not have been created; but he is a man of wide views and large generosities, and all such matters find hospitality with him.

We drove often to the city from the hotel Kaiser-i-Hind, a journey which was always full of interest, both night and day, for that country road was never quiet, never empty, but was always India in motion, always a streaming flood of brown people clothed in smouchings from the rainbow, a tossing and moiling flood, happy, noisy, a charming and satisfying confusion of strange human and strange animal life and equally strange and outlandish vehicles.

And the city itself is a curiosity. Any Indian city is that, but this one is not like any other that we saw. It is shut up in a lofty turreted wall; the main body of it is divided into six parts by perfectly straight streets that are more than a hundred feet wide; the blocks of houses exhibit a long frontage of the most taking architectural quaintnesses, the straight lines being broken everywhere by pretty little balconies, pillared and highly ornamented, and other cunning and cozy and inviting perches and projections, and many of the fronts are curiously pictured by the brush, and the whole of them have the soft rich tint of strawberry ice-cream. One cannot look down the far stretch of the chief street and persuade himself that these are real houses, and that it is all out of doors—the impression that it is an unreality, a picture, a scene in a theater, is the only one that will take hold.

Then there came a great day when this illusion was more pronounced than ever. A rich Hindoo had been spending a fortune upon the manufacture of a crowd of idols and accompanying paraphernalia whose purpose was to illustrate scenes in the life of his especial god or saint, and this fine show was to be brought through the town in processional state at ten in the morning. As we passed through the great public pleasure garden on our way to the city we found it crowded with natives. That was one sight. Then there was another. In the midst of the spacious lawns stands the palace which contains the museum—a beautiful construction of stone which shows arched colonnades, one above another, and receding, terrace-fashion, toward the sky. Every one of these terraces, all the way to the top one, was packed and jammed with natives. One must try to imagine those solid masses of splendid color, one above another, up and up, against the blue sky, and the

Indian sun turning them all to beds of fire and flame.

Later, when we reached the city, and glanced down the chief avenue, smouldering in its crushed-strawberry tint, those splendid effects were repeated; for every balcony, and every fanciful bird-cage of a snuggery countersunk in the house-fronts, and all the long lines of roofs were crowded with people, and each crowd was an explosion of brilliant color.

Then the wide street itself, away down and down and down into the distance, was alive with gorgeously-clothed people not still, but moving, swaying, drifting, eddying, a delirious display of all colors and all shades of color, delicate, lovely, pale, soft, strong, stunning, vivid, brilliant, a sort of storm of sweetpea blossoms passing on the wings of a hurricane; and presently, through this storm of color, came swaying and swinging the majestic elephants, clothed in their Sunday best of gaudinesses, and the long procession of fanciful trucks freighted with their groups of curious and costly images, and then the long rearguard of stately camels, with their picturesque riders.

For color, and picturesqueness, and novelty, and outlandishness, and sustained interest and fascination, it was the most satisfying show I had ever seen, and I suppose I shall not have the privilege of looking upon its like again.

CHAPTER LXI.

In the first place God made idiots. This was for practice. Then He made School Boards. —Pudd'nhead Wilson's New Calendar.

Suppose we applied no more ingenuity to the instruction of deaf and dumb and blind children than we sometimes apply in our American public schools to the instruction of children who are in possession of all their faculties? The result would be that the deaf and dumb and blind would acquire nothing. They would live and die as ignorant as bricks and stones. The methods used in the asylums are rational. The teacher exactly measures the child's capacity, to begin with; and from thence onwards the tasks imposed are nicely gauged to the gradual development of that capacity, the tasks keep pace with the steps of the child's progress, they don't jump miles and leagues ahead of it by irrational caprice and land in vacancy—according to the average public-school plan. In the public school, apparently, they teach the child to spell cat, then ask it to calculate an eclipse; when it can read words of two syllables, they require it to explain the circulation of the blood; when it reaches the head of the infant class they bully it with conundrums that cover the domain of universal knowledge. This sounds extravagant—and is; yet it goes no great way beyond the facts.

I received a curious letter one day, from the Punjab (you must pronounce it Punjawb). The handwriting was excellent, and the wording was English —English, and yet not exactly English. The style was easy and smooth and flowing, yet there was something subtly foreign about it—A something tropically ornate and sentimental and rhetorical. It turned out to be the work of a Hindoo youth, the holder of a humble clerical billet in a railway office. He had been educated in one of the numerous colleges of India. Upon inquiry I was told that the country was full of young fellows of his like. They had been educated away up to the snow-summits of learning—and the market for all this elaborate cultivation was minutely out of proportion to the vastness of the product. This market consisted of some thousands of small clerical posts under the

government —the supply of material for it was multitudinous. If this youth with the flowing style and the blossoming English was occupying a small railway clerkship, it meant that there were hundreds and hundreds as capable as he, or he would be in a high place; and it certainly meant that there were thousands whose education and capacity had fallen a little short, and that they would have to go without places. Apparently, then, the colleges of India were doing what our high schools have long been doing —richly over-supplying the market for highly-educated service; and thereby doing a damage to the scholar, and through him to the country.

At home I once made a speech deploring the injuries inflicted by the high school in making handicrafts distasteful to boys who would have been willing to make a living at trades and agriculture if they had but had the good luck to stop with the common school. But I made no converts. Not one, in a community overrun with educated idlers who were above following their fathers' mechanical trades, yet could find no market for their book-knowledge. The same rail that brought me the letter from the Punjab, brought also a little book published by Messrs. Thacker, Spink & Co., of Calcutta, which interested me, for both its preface and its contents treated of this matter of over-education. In the preface occurs this paragraph from the Calcutta Review. For "Government office" read "drygoods clerkship" and it will fit more than one region of America:

"The education that we give makes the boys a little less clownish in their manners, and more intelligent when spoken to by strangers. On the other hand, it has made them less contented with their lot in life, and less willing to work with their hands. The form which discontent takes in this country is not of a healthy kind; for, the Natives of India consider that the only occupation worthy of an educated man is that of a writership in some office, and especially in a Government office. The village schoolboy goes back to the plow with the greatest reluctance; and the town schoolboy carries the same discontent and inefficiency into his father's workshop. Sometimes these ex-students positively refuse at first to work; and more than once parents have openly expressed their regret that they ever allowed their sons to be inveigled to school."

The little book which I am quoting from is called "Indo-Anglian Literature," and is well stocked with "baboo" English—clerkly English, hooky English, acquired in the schools. Some of it is very funny, —almost as funny, perhaps, as what you and I produce when we try to write in a language not our own; but much of it is surprisingly correct and free. If I were going to quote good English—but I am not. India is well stocked with natives who speak it and write it as well as the best of us. I merely wish to show some of the quaint imperfect attempts at the use of our tongue. There are many letters in the book; poverty imploring help—bread, money, kindness, office generally an office, a clerkship, some way to get food and a rag out of the applicant's unmarketable education; and food not for himself alone, but sometimes for a dozen helpless relations in addition to his own family; for those people are astonishingly unselfish, and admirably faithful to their ties of kinship. Among us I think there is nothing approaching it. Strange as some of these wailing and supplicating letters are, humble and even groveling as some of them are, and quaintly funny and confused as a goodly number of them are, there is still a pathos about them, as a rule, that checks the rising laugh and reproaches it. In the following letter "father" is not to be read literally. In Ceylon a little native beggar-girl embarrassed me by calling me father, although I knew she was mistaken. I was so new that I did not know that she was merely following the custom of the dependent and the supplicant.

"SIR,

"I pray please to give me some action (work) for I am very poor boy I have no one to help me even so father for it so it seemed in thy good sight, you give the Telegraph Office, and another work what is your wish I am very poor boy, this understand what is your wish you my father I am your son this understand what is your wish.

"Your Sirvent, P. C. B."

Through ages of debasing oppression suffered by these people at the hands of their native rulers, they come legitimately by the attitude and language of fawning and flattery, and one must remember this in mitigation when passing judgment upon the native character. It is common in these letters to find the petitioner furtively trying to get at the white man's soft religious side; even this poor boy baits his hook with a macerated Bible-text in the hope that it may catch something if all else fail.

Here is an application for the post of instructor in English to some children:

"My Dear Sir or Gentleman, that your Petitioner has much qualification in the Language of English to instruct the young boys; I was given to understand that your of suitable children has to acquire the knowledge of English language."

As a sample of the flowery Eastern style, I will take a sentence or two from along letter written by a young native to the Lieutenant-Governor of Bengal—an application for employment:

"HONORED AND MUCH RESPECTED SIR,

"I hope your honor will condescend to hear the tale of this poor creature. I shall overflow with gratitude at this mark of your royal condescension. The bird-like happiness has flown away from my nest-like heart and has not hitherto returned from the period whence the rose of my father's life suffered the autumnal breath of death, in plain English he passed through the gates of Grave, and from that hour the phantom of delight has never danced before me."

It is all school-English, book-English, you see; and good enough, too, all things considered. If the native boy had but that one study he would shine, he would dazzle, no doubt. But that is not the case. He is situated as are our public-school children—loaded down with an over-freightage of other studies; and frequently they are as far beyond the actual point of progress reached by him and suited to the stage of development attained, as could be imagined by the insanest fancy. Apparently—like our public-school boy—he must work, work, work, in school and out, and play but little. Apparently—like our public-school boy—his "education" consists in learning things, not the meaning of them; he is fed upon the husks, not the corn. From several essays written by native schoolboys in answer to the question of how they spend their day, I select one—the one which goes most into detail:

"66. At the break of day I rises from my own bed and finish my daily duty, then I employ myself till 8 o'clock, after which I employ myself to bathe, then take for my body some sweet meat, and just at 9½ I came to school to attend my class duty,

then at 2½ P. M. I return from school and engage myself to do my natural duty, then, I engage for a quarter to take my tithn, then I study till 5 P. M., after which I began to play anything which comes in my head. After 8½, half pass to eight we are began to sleep, before sleeping I told a constable just 11 o' he came and rose us from half pass eleven we began to read still morning."

It is not perfectly clear, now that I come to cipher upon it. He gets up at about 5 in the morning, or along there somewhere, and goes to bed about fifteen or sixteen hours afterward—that much of it seems straight; but why he should rise again three hours later and resume his studies till morning is puzzling.

I think it is because he is studying history. History requires a world of time and bitter hard work when your "education" is no further advanced than the cat's; when you are merely stuffing yourself with a mixed-up mess of empty names and random incidents and elusive dates, which no one teaches you how to interpret, and which, uninterpreted, pay you not a farthing's value for your waste of time. Yes, I think he had to get up at halfpast 11 P.M. in order to be sure to be perfect with his history lesson by noon. With results as follows—from a Calcutta school examination:

"Q. Who was Cardinal Wolsey? "Cardinal Wolsey was an Editor of a paper named North Briton. No. 45 of his publication he charged the King of uttering a lie from the throne. He was arrested and cast into prison; and after releasing went to France.

"3. As Bishop of York but died in disentry in a church on his way to be blockheaded.

"8. Cardinal Wolsey was the son of Edward IV, after his father's death he himself ascended the throne at the age of (10) ten only, but when he surpassed or when he was fallen in his twenty years of age at that time he wished to make a journey in his countries under him, but he was opposed by his mother to do journey, and according to his mother's example he remained in the home, and then became King. After many times obstacles and many confusion he become King and afterwards his brother."

There is probably not a word of truth in that.

"Q. What is the meaning of 'Ich Dien'?

"10. An honor conferred on the first or eldest sons of English Sovereigns. It is nothing more than some feathers.

"11. Ich Dien was the word which was written on the feathers of the blind King who came to fight, being interlaced with the bridles of the horse.

"13. Ich Dien is a title given to Henry VII by the Pope of Rome, when he forwarded the Reformation of Cardinal Wolsy to Rome, and for this reason he was called Commander of the faith."

A dozen or so of this kind of insane answers are quoted in the book from that examination. Each answer is sweeping proof, all by itself, that the person uttering it was pushed ahead of where he belonged when he was put into history; proof that he had been put to the task of acquiring history before he had had a single lesson in the art of acquiring it, which is the equivalent of dumping a pupil into geometry before he has learned the progressive steps which lead up to it and make its acquirement possible. Those Calcutta novices had no business with history. There was no excuse for examining them in it, no excuse for exposing them and their teachers. They were totally empty; there was nothing to "examine."

Helen Keller has been dumb, stone deaf, and stone blind, ever since she was a little baby a year-and-a-half old; and now at sixteen years of age this miraculous creature, this wonder of all the ages, passes the Harvard University examination in Latin, German, French history, belles lettres, and such things, and does it brilliantly, too, not in a commonplace fashion. She doesn't know merely things, she is splendidly familiar with the meanings of them. When she writes an essay on a Shakespearean character, her English is fine and strong, her grasp of the subject is the grasp of one who knows, and her page is electric with light. Has Miss Sullivan taught her by the methods of India and the American public school? No, oh, no; for then she would be deafer and dumber and blinder than she was before. It is a pity that we can't educate all the children in the asylums.

To continue the Calcutta exposure:

"What is the meaning of a Sheriff?"

"25. Sheriff is a post opened in the time of John. The duty of Sheriff here in Calcutta, to look out and catch those carriages which is rashly driven out by the coachman; but it is a high post in England.

"26. Sheriff was the English bill of common prayer.

"27. The man with whom the accusative persons are placed is called Sheriff.

"28. Sheriff—Latin term for 'shrub,' we called broom, worn by the first earl of Enjue, as an emblem of humility when they went to the pilgrimage, and from this their hairs took their crest and surname.

"29. Sheriff is a kind of titlous sect of people, as Barons, Nobles, etc.

"30. Sheriff; a tittle given on those persons who were respective and pious in England."

The students were examined in the following bulky matters: Geometry, the Solar Spectrum, the Habeas Corpus Act, the British Parliament, and in Metaphysics they were asked to trace the progress of skepticism from Descartes to Hume. It is within bounds to say that some of the results were astonishing. Without doubt, there were students present who justified their teacher's wisdom in introducing them to these studies; but the fact is also evident that others had been pushed into these studies to waste their time over them when they could have been profitably employed in hunting smaller game. Under the head of Geometry, one of the answers is this:

"49. The whole BD = the whole CA, and so-so-so-so-so-so-so."

To me this is cloudy, but I was never well up in geometry. That was the only effort made among the five students who appeared for examination in geometry; the other four wailed and surrendered without a fight. They are piteous wails, too, wails of despair; and one of them is an eloquent reproach; it comes from a poor fellow who has been laden beyond his strength by a stupid teacher, and is eloquent in spite of the poverty of its English. The poor chap finds himself required to

explain riddles which even Sir Isaac Newton was not able to understand:

"50. Oh my dear father examiner you my father and you kindly give a number of pass you my great father.

"51. I am a poor boy and have no means to support my mother and two brothers who are suffering much for want of food. I get four rupees monthly from charity fund of this place, from which I send two rupees for their support, and keep two for my own support. Father, if I relate the unlucky circumstance under which we are placed, then, I think, you will not be able to suppress the tender tear.

"52. Sir which Sir Isaac Newton and other experienced mathematicians cannot understand I being third of Entrance Class can understand these which is too impossible to imagine. And my examiner also has put very tiresome and very heavy propositions to prove."

We must remember that these pupils had to do their thinking in one language, and express themselves in another and alien one. It was a heavy handicap. I have by me "English as She is Taught"—a collection of American examinations made in the public schools of Brooklyn by one of the teachers, Miss Caroline B. Le Row. An extract or two from its pages will show that when the American pupil is using but one language, and that one his own, his performance is no whit better than his Indian brother's:

"ON HISTORY.

"Christopher Columbus was called the father of his Country. Queen Isabella of Spain sold her watch and chain and other millinery so that Columbus could discover America.

"The Indian wars were very desecrating to the country.

"The Indians pursued their warfare by hiding in the bushes and then scalping them.

"Captain John Smith has been styled the father of his country. His life was saved by his daughter Pochahantas.

"The Puritans found an insane asylum in the wilds of America.

"The Stamp Act was to make everybody stamp all materials so they should be null and void.

"Washington died in Spain almost broken-hearted. His remains were taken to the cathedral in Havana.

"Gorilla warfare was where men rode on gorillas."

In Brooklyn, as in India, they examine a pupil, and when they find out he doesn't know anything, they put him into literature, or geometry, or astronomy, or government, or something like that, so that he can properly display the assification of the whole system—

"ON LITERATURE.

"'Bracebridge Hall' was written by Henry Irving.

"Edgar A. Poe was a very curdling writer.

"Beowulf wrote the Scriptures.

"Ben Johnson survived Shakespeare in some respects.

"In the 'Canterbury Tale' it gives account of King Alfred on his way to the shrine of Thomas Bucket.

"Chaucer was the father of English pottery.

"Chaucer was succeeded by H. Wads. Longfellow."

We will finish with a couple of samples of "literature," one from America, the other from India. The first is a Brooklyn public-school boy's attempt to turn a few verses of the "Lady of the Lake" into prose. You will have to concede that he did it:

"The man who rode on the horse performed the whip and an instrument made of steel alone with strong ardor not diminishing, for, being tired from the time passed with hard labor overworked with anger and ignorant with weariness, while every breath for labor lie drew with cries full of sorrow, the young deer made imperfect who worked hard filtered in sight."

The following paragraph is from a little book which is famous in India —the biography of a distinguished Hindoo judge, Onoocool Chunder Mookerjee; it was written by his nephew, and is unintentionally funny-in fact, exceedingly so. I offer here the closing scene. If you would like to sample the rest of the book, it can be had by applying to the publishers, Messrs. Thacker, Spink & Co., Calcutta

"And having said these words he hermetically sealed his lips not to open them again. All the well-known doctors of Calcutta that could be procured for a man of his position and wealth were brought, —Doctors Payne, Fayrer, and Nilmadhub Mookerjee and others; they did what they could do, with their puissance and knack of medical knowledge, but it proved after all as if to milk the ram! His wife and children had not the mournful consolation to hear his last words; he remained sotto voce for a few hours, and then was taken from us at 6.12 P.m. according to the caprice of God which passeth understanding."

CHAPTER LXII.

There are no people who are quite so vulgar as the over-refined ones. —Pudd'nhead Wilson's New Calendar.

We sailed from Calcutta toward the end of March; stopped a day at Madras; two or three days in Ceylon; then sailed westward on a long flight for Mauritius. From my diary:

April 7. We are far abroad upon the smooth waters of the Indian Ocean, now; it is shady and pleasant and peaceful under the vast spread of the awnings, and life is perfect again—ideal.

The difference between a river and the sea is, that the river looks fluid, the sea solid—usually looks as if you could step out and walk on it.

The captain has this peculiarity—he cannot tell the truth in a plausible way. In this he is the very opposite of the austere Scot who sits midway of the table; he cannot tell a lie in an unplausible way. When the captain finishes a statement the passengers glance at each other privately, as who should say, "Do you believe that?" When the Scot finishes one, the look says, "How strange and interesting." The whole secret is in the manner and method of the two men. The captain is a little shy

and diffident, and he states the simplest fact as if he were a little afraid of it, while the Scot delivers himself of the most abandoned lie with such an air of stern veracity that one is forced to believe it although one knows it isn't so. For instance, the Scot told about a pet flying-fish he once owned, that lived in a little fountain in his conservatory, and supported itself by catching birds and frogs and rats in the neighboring fields. It was plain that no one at the table doubted this statement.

By and by, in the course of some talk about custom-house annoyances, the captain brought out the following simple everyday incident, but through his infirmity of style managed to tell it in such a way that it got no credence. He said:

"I went ashore at Naples one voyage when I was in that trade, and stood around helping my passengers, for I could speak a little Italian. Two or three times, at intervals, the officer asked me if I had anything dutiable about me, and seemed more and more put out and disappointed every time I told him no. Finally a passenger whom I had helped through asked me to come out and take something. I thanked him, but excused myself, saying I had taken a whisky just before I came ashore.

"It was a fatal admission. The officer at once made me pay sixpence import-duty on the whisky-just from ship to shore, you see; and he fined me £5 for not declaring the goods, another £5 for falsely denying that I had anything dutiable about me, also £5 for concealing the goods, and £50 for smuggling, which is the maximum penalty for unlawfully bringing in goods under the value of sevenpence ha'penny. Altogether, sixty-five pounds sixpence for a little thing like that."

The Scot is always believed, yet he never tells anything but lies; whereas the captain is never believed, although he never tells a lie, so far as I can judge. If he should say his uncle was a male person, he would probably say it in such a way that nobody would believe it; at the same time the Scot could claim that he had a female uncle and not stir a doubt in anybody's mind. My own luck has been curious all my literary life; I never could tell a lie that anybody would doubt, nor a truth that anybody would believe.

Lots of pets on board—birds and things. In these far countries the white people do seem to run remarkably to pets. Our host in Cawnpore had a fine collection of birds—the finest we saw in a private house in India. And in Colombo, Dr. Murray's great compound and commodious bungalow were well populated with domesticated company from the woods: frisky little squirrels; a Ceylon mina walking sociably about the house; a small green parrot that whistled a single urgent note of call without motion of its beak; also chuckled; a monkey in a cage on the back veranda, and some more out in the trees; also a number of beautiful macaws in the trees; and various and sundry birds and animals of breeds not known to me. But no cat. Yet a cat would have liked that place.

April 9. Tea-planting is the great business in Ceylon, now. A passenger says it often pays 40 per cent. on the investment. Says there is a boom.

April 10. The sea is a Mediterranean blue; and I believe that that is about the divinest color known to nature.

It is strange and fine—Nature's lavish generosities to her creatures. At least to all of them except man. For those that fly she has provided a home that is nobly spacious—a home which is forty miles deep and envelops the whole globe, and has not an obstruction in it. For those that swim she has provided a more than imperial domain—a domain which is miles deep and covers four-fifths of the globe. But as for man, she has cut him off with the mere odds and ends of the creation. She has given him the thin skin, the meagre skin which is stretched over the remaining one-fifth—the naked bones stick up through it in most places. On the one-half of this domain he can raise snow, ice, sand, rocks, and nothing else. So the valuable part of his inheritance really consists of but a single fifth of the family estate; and out of it he has to grub hard to get enough to keep him alive and provide kings and soldiers and powder to extend the blessings of civilization with. Yet man, in his simplicity and complacency and inability to cipher, thinks Nature regards him as the important member of the family—in fact, her favorite. Surely, it must occur to even his dull head, sometimes, that she has a curious way of showing it.

Afternoon. The captain has been telling how, in one of his Arctic voyages, it was so cold that the mate's shadow froze fast to the deck and had to be ripped loose by main strength. And even then he got only about two-thirds of it back. Nobody said anything, and the captain went away. I think he is becoming disheartened . . . . Also, to be fair, there is another word of praise due to this ship's library: it contains no copy of the Vicar of Wakefield, that strange menagerie of complacent hypocrites and idiots, of theatrical cheap-john heroes and heroines, who are always showing off, of bad people who are not interesting, and good people who are fatiguing. A singular book. Not a sincere line in it, and not a character that invites respect; a book which is one long waste-pipe discharge of goody-goody puerilities and dreary moralities; a book which is full of pathos which revolts, and humor which grieves the heart. There are few things in literature that are more piteous, more pathetic, than the celebrated "humorous" incident of Moses and the spectacles. Jane Austen's books, too, are absent from this library. Just that one omission alone would make a fairly good library out of a library that hadn't a book in it.

Customs in tropic seas. At 5 in the morning they pipe to wash down the decks, and at once the ladies who are sleeping there turn out and they and their beds go below. Then one after another the men come up from the bath in their pyjamas, and walk the decks an hour or two with bare legs and bare feet. Coffee and fruit served. The ship cat and her kitten now appear and get about their toilets; next the barber comes and flays us on the breezy deck. Breakfast at 9.30, and the day begins. I do not know how a day could be more reposeful: no motion; a level blue sea; nothing in sight from horizon to horizon; the speed of the ship furnishes a cooling breeze; there is no mail to read and answer; no newspapers to excite you; no telegrams to fret you or fright you—the world is far, far away; it has ceased to exist for you—seemed a fading dream, along in the first days; has dissolved to an unreality now; it is gone from your mind with all its businesses and ambitions, its prosperities and disasters, its exultations and despairs, its joys and griefs and cares and worries. They are no concern of yours any more; they have gone out of your life; they are a storm which has passed and left a deep calm behind. The people group themselves about the decks in their snowy white linen, and read, smoke, sew, play cards, talk, nap, and so on. In other ships the passengers are always ciphering about when they are going to arrive; out in these seas it is rare, very rare, to hear that subject broached. In other ships there is always an eager rush to the bulletin board at noon to find out what the "run" has been; in these seas the bulletin seems to attract no interest; I have seen no one visit it; in thirteen days I have visited it only once. Then I happened to notice the figures of the day's run. On that day there happened to be talk, at dinner,

about the speed of modern ships. I was the only passenger present who knew this ship's gait. Necessarily, the Atlantic custom of betting on the ship's run is not a custom here—nobody ever mentions it.

I myself am wholly indifferent as to when we are going to "get in"; if any one else feels interested in the matter he has not indicated it in my hearing. If I had my way we should never get in at all. This sort of sea life is charged with an indestructible charm. There is no weariness, no fatigue, no worry, no responsibility, no work, no depression of spirits. There is nothing like this serenity, this comfort, this peace, this deep contentment, to be found anywhere on land. If I had my way I would sail on for ever and never go to live on the solid ground again.

One of Kipling's ballads has delivered the aspect and sentiment of this bewitching sea correctly:

"The Injian Ocean sets an' smiles So sof', so bright, so bloomin' blue; There aren't a wave for miles an' miles Excep' the jiggle from the screw."

April 14. It turns out that the astronomical apprentice worked off a section of the Milky Way on me for the Magellan Clouds. A man of more experience in the business showed one of them to me last night. It was small and faint and delicate, and looked like the ghost of a bunch of white smoke left floating in the sky by an exploded bombshell.

Wednesday, April 15. Mauritius. Arrived and anchored off Port Louis 2 A. M. Rugged clusters of crags and peaks, green to their summits; from their bases to the sea a green plain with just tilt enough to it to make the water drain off. I believe it is in 56 E. and 22 S.—a hot tropical country. The green plain has an inviting look; has scattering dwellings nestling among the greenery. Scene of the sentimental adventure of Paul and Virginia.

Island under French control—which means a community which depends upon quarantines, not sanitation, for its health.

Thursday, April 16. Went ashore in the forenoon at Port Louis, a little town, but with the largest variety of nationalities and complexions we have encountered yet. French, English, Chinese, Arabs, Africans with wool, blacks with straight hair, East Indians, half-whites, quadroons —and great varieties in costumes and colors.

Took the train for Curepipe at 1.30—two hours' run, gradually uphill. What a contrast, this frantic luxuriance of vegetation, with the arid plains of India; these architecturally picturesque crags and knobs and miniature mountains, with the monotony of the Indian dead-levels.

A native pointed out a handsome swarthy man of grave and dignified bearing, and said in an awed tone, "That is so-and-so; has held office of one sort or another under this government for 37 years—he is known all over this whole island and in the other countries of the world perhaps —who knows? One thing is certain; you can speak his name anywhere in this whole island, and you will find not one grown person that has not heard it. It is a wonderful thing to be so celebrated; yet look at him; it makes no change in him; he does not even seem to know it."

Curepipe (means Pincushion or Pegtown, probably). Sixteen

miles (two hours) by rail from Port Louis. At each end of every roof and on the apex of every dormer window a wooden peg two feet high stands up; in some cases its top is blunt, in others the peg is sharp and looks like a toothpick. The passion for this humble ornament is universal.

Apparently, there has been only one prominent event in the history of Mauritius, and that one didn't happen. I refer to the romantic sojourn of Paul and Virginia here. It was that story that made Mauritius known to the world, made the name familiar to everybody, the geographical position of it to nobody.

A clergyman was asked to guess what was in a box on a table. It was a vellum fan painted with the shipwreck, and was "one of Virginia's wedding gifts."

April 18. This is the only country in the world where the stranger is not asked "How do you like this place?" This is indeed a large distinction. Here the citizen does the talking about the country himself; the stranger is not asked to help. You get all sorts of information. From one citizen you gather the idea that Mauritius was made first, and then heaven; and that heaven was copied after Mauritius. Another one tells you that this is an exaggeration; that the two chief villages, Port Louis and Curepipe, fall short of heavenly perfection; that nobody lives in Port Louis except upon compulsion, and that Curepipe is the wettest and rainiest place in the world. An English citizen said:

"In the early part of this century Mauritius was used by the French as a basis from which to operate against England's Indian merchantmen; so England captured the island and also the neighbor, Bourbon, to stop that annoyance. England gave Bourbon back; the government in London did not want any more possessions in the West Indies. If the government had had a better quality of geography in stock it would not have wasted Bourbon in that foolish way. A big war will temporarily shut up the Suez Canal some day and the English ships will have to go to India around the Cape of Good Hope again; then England will have to have Bourbon and will take it.

"Mauritius was a crown colony until 20 years ago, with a governor appointed by the Crown and assisted by a Council appointed by himself; but Pope Hennessey came out as Governor then, and he worked hard to get a part of the council made elective, and succeeded. So now the whole council is French, and in all ordinary matters of legislation they vote together and in the French interest, not the English. The English population is very slender; it has not votes enough to elect a legislator. Half a dozen rich French families elect the legislature. Pope Hennessey was an Irishman, a Catholic, a Home Ruler, M.P., a hater of England and the English, a very troublesome person and a serious incumbrance at Westminster; so it was decided to send him out to govern unhealthy countries, in hope that something would happen to him. But nothing did. The first experiment was not merely a failure, it was more than a failure. He proved to be more of a disease himself than any he was sent to encounter. The next experiment was here. The dark scheme failed again. It was an off-season and there was nothing but measles here at the time. Pope Hennessey's health was not affected. He worked with the French and for the French and against the English, and he made the English very tired and the French very happy, and lived to have the joy of seeing the flag he served publicly hissed. His memory is held in worshipful reverence and affection by the French.

"It is a land of extraordinary quarantines. They quarantine a ship for anything or for nothing; quarantine her for 20 and even 30 days. They once quarantined a ship because her captain had had the smallpox when he was a boy. That and because he was English.

"The population is very small; small to insignificance. The majority is East Indian; then mongrels; then negroes (descendants of the slaves of the French times); then French; then English. There was an American, but he is dead or mislaid. The mongrels are the result of all kinds of mixtures; black and white, mulatto and white, quadroon and white, octoroon and white. And so there is every shade of complexion; ebony, old mahogany, horsechestnut, sorrel, molasses-candy, clouded amber, clear amber, old-ivory white, new-ivory white, fish-belly white—this latter the leprous complexion frequent with the Anglo-Saxon long resident in tropical climates.

"You wouldn't expect a person to be proud of being a Mauritian, now would you? But it is so. The most of them have never been out of the island, and haven't read much or studied much, and they think the world consists of three principal countries—Judaea, France, and Mauritius; so they are very proud of belonging to one of the three grand divisions of the globe. They think that Russia and Germany are in England, and that England does not amount to much. They have heard vaguely about the United States and the equator, but they think both of them are monarchies. They think Mount Peter Botte is the highest mountain in the world, and if you show one of them a picture of Milan Cathedral he will swell up with satisfaction and say that the idea of that jungle of spires was stolen from the forest of peg-tops and toothpicks that makes the roofs of Curepipe look so fine and prickly.

"There is not much trade in books. The newspapers educate and entertain the people. Mainly the latter. They have two pages of large-print reading-matter-one of them English, the other French. The English page is a translation of the French one. The typography is super-extra primitive—in this quality it has not its equal anywhere. There is no proof-reader now; he is dead.

"Where do they get matter to fill up a page in this little island lost in the wastes of the Indian Ocean? Oh, Madagascar. They discuss Madagascar and France. That is the bulk. Then they chock up the rest with advice to the Government. Also, slurs upon the English administration. The papers are all owned and edited by creoles—French.

"The language of the country is French. Everybody speaks it—has to. You have to know French particularly mongrel French, the patois spoken by Tom, Dick, and Harry of the multiform complexions—or you can't get along.

"This was a flourishing country in former days, for it made then and still makes the best sugar in the world; but first the Suez Canal severed it from the world and left it out in the cold and next the beetroot sugar helped by bounties, captured the European markets. Sugar is the life of Mauritius, and it is losing its grip. Its downward course was checked by the depreciation of the rupee—for the planter pays wages in rupees but sells his crop for gold—and the insurrection in Cuba and paralyzation of the sugar industry there have given our prices here a life-saving lift; but the outlook has nothing permanently favorable about it. It takes a year to mature the canes—on the high ground three and six months longer —and there is always a chance that the annual cyclone will rip the profit out of the crop. In recent times a cyclone took the whole crop, as you may say; and the island never saw a finer one. Some of the noblest sugar estates in the island are in deep difficulties. A dozen of them are investments of English capital; and the companies that own them are at work now, trying to settle up and get out with a saving of half the money they put in. You know, in these days, when a country begins to introduce the tea culture, it means that its own specialty has gone back on it. Look at Bengal; look at Ceylon. Well, they've begun to introduce the tea culture, here.

"Many copies of Paul and Virginia are sold every year in Mauritius. No other book is so popular here except the Bible. By many it is supposed to be a part of the Bible. All the missionaries work up their French on it when they come here to pervert the Catholic mongrel. It is the greatest story that was ever written about Mauritius, and the only one."

CHAPTER LXIII.

The principal difference between a cat and a lie is that the cat has only nine lives. —Pudd'nhead Wilson's New Calendar.

April 20.—The cyclone of 1892 killed and crippled hundreds of people; it was accompanied by a deluge of rain, which drowned Port Louis and produced a water famine. Quite true; for it burst the reservoir and the water-pipes; and for a time after the flood had disappeared there was much distress from want of water.

This is the only place in the world where no breed of matches can stand the damp. Only one match in 16 will light.

The roads are hard and smooth; some of the compounds are spacious, some of the bungalows commodious, and the roadways are walled by tall bamboo hedges, trim and green and beautiful; and there are azalea hedges, too, both the white and the red; I never saw that before.

As to healthiness: I translate from to-day's (April 20) Merchants' and Planters' Gazette, from the article of a regular contributor, "Carminge," concerning the death of the nephew of a prominent citizen:

"Sad and lugubrious existence, this which we lead in Mauritius; I believe there is no other country in the world where one dies more easily than among us. The least indisposition becomes a mortal malady; a simple headache develops into meningitis; a cold into pneumonia, and presently, when we are least expecting it, death is a guest in our home."

This daily paper has a meteorological report which tells you what the weather was day before yesterday.

One is never pestered by a beggar or a peddler in this town, so far as I can see. This is pleasantly different from India.

April 22. To such as believe that the quaint product called French civilization would be an improvement upon the civilization of New Guinea and the like, the snatching of Madagascar and the laying on of French civilization there will be fully justified. But why did the English allow the French to have Madagascar? Did she respect a theft of a couple of centuries ago? Dear me, robbery by European nations of each other's territories has never been a sin, is not a sin to-day. To the several cabinets the several political establishments of the world are clotheslines; and a large part of the official duty of these cabinets is to keep an eye on each other's wash and grab what they can of it as opportunity offers. All the territorial possessions of all the political establishments in the earth—including America, of course—consist of pilferings from other people's wash. No tribe, howsoever insignificant, and no nation, howsoever mighty, occupies a foot of land that was not stolen. When the English, the French, and the Spaniards reached America, the Indian tribes had been raiding each other's territorial clothes-lines for ages, and every acre of ground in the continent had been stolen and re-stolen 500 times. The English, the French, and the Spaniards went to work and stole it all over again; and when that was satisfactorily accomplished they went diligently to work and stole it from each other. In Europe and Asia and Africa every acre of ground has been stolen several millions of times. A crime persevered in a thousand centuries ceases to be a crime, and becomes a virtue. This is the law of custom, and custom supersedes all other forms of law. Christian governments are as frank to-day, as open and above-board, in discussing projects for raiding each other's clothes-lines as ever they were before the Golden Rule came smiling into this inhospitable world and couldn't get a night's lodging anywhere. In 150 years England has beneficently retired garment after garment from the Indian lines, until there is hardly a rag of the original wash left dangling anywhere. In 800 years an obscure tribe of Muscovite savages has risen to the dazzling position of Land-Robber-in-Chief; she found a quarter of the world hanging out to dry on a hundred parallels of latitude, and she scooped in the whole wash. She keeps a sharp eye on a multitude of little lines that stretch along the northern boundaries of India, and every now and then she snatches a hip-rag or a pair of pyjamas. It is England's prospective property, and Russia knows it; but Russia cares nothing for that. In fact, in our day land-robbery, claim-jumping, is become a European governmental frenzy. Some have been hard at it in the borders of China, in Burma, in Siam, and the islands of the sea; and all have been at it in Africa. Africa has been as coolly divided up and portioned out among the gang as if they had bought it and paid for it. And now straightway they are beginning the old game again —to steal each other's grabbings. Germany found a vast slice of Central Africa with the English flag and the English missionary and the English trader scattered all over it, but with certain formalities neglected—no signs up, "Keep off the grass," "Trespassers-forbidden," etc.—and she stepped in with a cold calm smile and put up the signs herself, and swept those English pioneers promptly out of the country.

There is a tremendous point there. It can be put into the form of a maxim: Get your formalities right—never mind about the moralities.

It was an impudent thing; but England had to put up with it. Now, in the case of Madagascar, the formalities had originally been observed, but by neglect they had fallen into desuetude ages ago. England should have snatched Madagascar from the French clothes-line. Without an effort she could have saved those harmless natives from the calamity of French civilization, and she did not do it. Now it is too late.

The signs of the times show plainly enough what is going to happen. All the savage lands in the world are going to be brought under subjection to the Christian governments of Europe. I am not sorry, but glad. This coming fate might have been a calamity to those savage peoples two hundred years ago; but now it will in some cases be a benefaction. The sooner the seizure is consummated, the better for the savages.

The dreary and dragging ages of bloodshed and disorder and

oppression will give place to peace and order and the reign of law. When one considers what India was under her Hindoo and Mohammedan rulers, and what she is now; when he remembers the miseries of her millions then and the protections and humanities which they enjoy now, he must concede that the most fortunate thing that has ever befallen that empire was the establishment of British supremacy there. The savage lands of the world are to pass to alien possession, their peoples to the mercies of alien rulers. Let us hope and believe that they will all benefit by the change.

April 23. "The first year they gather shells; the second year they gather shells and drink; the third year they do not gather shells." (Said of immigrants to Mauritius.)

Population 375,000. 120 sugar factories.

Population 1851, 185,000. The increase is due mainly to the introduction of Indian coolies. They now apparently form the great majority of the population. They are admirable breeders; their homes are always hazy with children. Great savers of money. A British officer told me that in India he paid his servant 10 rupees a month, and he had 11 cousins, uncles, parents, etc., dependent upon him, and he supported them on his wages. These thrifty coolies are said to be acquiring land a trifle at a time, and cultivating it; and may own the island by and by.

The Indian women do very hard labor [for wages of (½ rupee) for twelve hours' work.] They carry mats of sugar on their heads (70 pounds) all day lading ships, for half a rupee, and work at gardening all day for less.

The camaron is a fresh water creature like a cray-fish. It is regarded here as the world's chiefest delicacy—and certainly it is good. Guards patrol the streams to prevent poaching it. A fine of Rs.200 or 300 (they say) for poaching. Bait is thrown in the water; the camaron goes for it; the fisher drops his loop in and works it around and about the camaron he has selected, till he gets it over its tail; then there's a jerk or something to certify the camaron that it is his turn now; he suddenly backs away, which moves the loop still further up his person and draws it taut, and his days are ended.

Another dish, called palmiste, is like raw turnip-shavings and tastes like green almonds; is very delicate and good. Costs the life of a palm tree 12 to 20 years old—for it is the pith.

Another dish—looks like greens or a tangle of fine seaweed—is a preparation of the deadly nightshade. Good enough.

The monkeys live in the dense forests on the flanks of the toy mountains, and they flock down nights and raid the sugar-fields. Also on other estates they come down and destroy a sort of bean-crop—just for fun, apparently—tear off the pods and throw them down.

The cyclone of 1892 tore down two great blocks of stone buildings in the center of Port Louis—the chief architectural feature-and left the uncomely and apparently frail blocks standing. Everywhere in its track it annihilated houses, tore off roofs, destroyed trees and crops. The men were in the towns, the women and children at home in the country getting crippled, killed, frightened to insanity; and the rain deluging them, the wind howling, the thunder crashing, the lightning glaring. This for an hour or so. Then a lull and sunshine; many ventured out of safe shelter; then suddenly here it came again from the opposite point and renewed and completed the

devastation. It is said the Chinese fed the sufferers for days on free rice.

Whole streets in Port Louis were laid flat—wrecked. During a minute and a half the wind blew 123 miles an hour; no official record made after that, when it may have reached 150. It cut down an obelisk. It carried an American ship into the woods after breaking the chains of two anchors. They now use four-two forward, two astern. Common report says it killed 1,200 in Port Louis alone, in half an hour. Then came the lull of the central calm—people did not know the barometer was still going down —then suddenly all perdition broke loose again while people were rushing around seeking friends and rescuing the wounded. The noise was comparable to nothing; there is nothing resembling it but thunder and cannon, and these are feeble in comparison.

What there is of Mauritius is beautiful. You have undulating wide expanses of sugar-cane—a fine, fresh green and very pleasant to the eye; and everywhere else you have a ragged luxuriance of tropic vegetation of vivid greens of varying shades, a wild tangle of underbrush, with graceful tall palms lifting their crippled plumes high above it; and you have stretches of shady dense forest with limpid streams frolicking through them, continually glimpsed and lost and glimpsed again in the pleasantest hide-and-seek fashion; and you have some tiny mountains, some quaint and picturesque groups of toy peaks, and a dainty little vest-pocket Matterhorn; and here and there and now and then a strip of sea with a white ruffle of surf breaks into the view.

That is Mauritius; and pretty enough. The details are few, the massed result is charming, but not imposing; not riotous, not exciting; it is a Sunday landscape. Perspective, and the enchantments wrought by distance, are wanting. There are no distances; there is no perspective, so to speak. Fifteen miles as the crow flies is the usual limit of vision. Mauritius is a garden and a park combined. It affects one's emotions as parks and gardens affect them. The surfaces of one's spiritual deeps are pleasantly played upon, the deeps themselves are not reached, not stirred. Spaciousness, remote altitudes, the sense of mystery which haunts apparently inaccessible mountain domes and summits reposing in the sky—these are the things which exalt the spirit and move it to see visions and dream dreams.

The Sandwich Islands remain my ideal of the perfect thing in the matter of tropical islands. I would add another story to Mauna Loa's 16,000 feet if I could, and make it particularly bold and steep and craggy and forbidding and snowy; and I would make the volcano spout its lava-floods out of its summit instead of its sides; but aside from these non-essentials I have no corrections to suggest. I hope these will be attended to; I do not wish to have to speak of it again.

CHAPTER LXIV.

When your watch gets out of order you have choice of two things to do: throw it in the fire or take it to the watch-tinker. The former is the quickest. —Pudd'nhead Wilson's New Calendar.

The Arundel Castle is the finest boat I have seen in these seas. She is thoroughly modern, and that statement covers a great deal of ground. She has the usual defect, the common defect, the universal defect, the defect that has never been missing from any ship that ever sailed—she has imperfect beds. Many ships have good beds, but no ship has very good ones. In the matter of beds all ships have been badly edited, ignorantly edited, from the beginning. The selection of the beds is given to some hearty, strong-backed, self-made man, when it ought to be given to a frail woman accustomed from girlhood to backaches and insomnia. Nothing is so rare, on either side of the ocean, as a perfect bed; nothing is so difficult to make. Some of the hotels on both sides provide it, but no ship ever does or ever did. In Noah's Ark the beds were simply scandalous. Noah set the fashion, and it will endure in one degree of modification or another till the next flood.

8 A.M. Passing Isle de Bourbon. Broken-up sky-line of volcanic mountains in the middle. Surely it would not cost much to repair them, and it seems inexcusable neglect to leave them as they are.

It seems stupid to send tired men to Europe to rest. It is no proper rest for the mind to clatter from town to town in the dust and cinders, and examine galleries and architecture, and be always meeting people and lunching and teaing and dining, and receiving worrying cables and letters. And a sea voyage on the Atlantic is of no use—voyage too short, sea too rough. The peaceful Indian and Pacific Oceans and the long stretches of time are the healing thing.

May 2, AM. A fair, great ship in sight, almost the first we have seen in these weeks of lonely voyaging. We are now in the Mozambique Channel, between Madagascar and South Africa, sailing straight west for Delagoa Bay.

Last night, the burly chief engineer, middle-aged, was standing telling a spirited seafaring tale, and had reached the most exciting place, where a man overboard was washing swiftly astern on the great seas, and uplifting despairing cries, everybody racing aft in a frenzy of excitement and fading hope, when the band, which had been silent a moment, began impressively its closing piece, the English national anthem. As simply as if he was unconscious of what he was doing, he stopped his story, uncovered, laid his laced cap against his breast, and slightly bent his grizzled head. The few bars finished, he put on his cap and took up his tale again, as naturally as if that interjection of music had been a part of it. There was something touching and fine about it, and it was moving to reflect that he was one of a myriad, scattered over every part of the globe, who by turn was doing as he was doing every hour of the twenty-four—those awake doing it while the others slept—those impressive bars forever floating up out of the various climes, never silent and never lacking reverent listeners.

All that I remember about Madagascar is that Thackeray's little Billie went up to the top of the mast and there knelt him upon his knee, saying, "I see

"Jerusalem and Madagascar, And North and South Amerikee."

May 3. Sunday. Fifteen or twenty Africanders who will end their voyage to-day and strike for their several homes from Delagoa Bay to-morrow, sat up singing on the afterdeck in the moonlight till 3 A.M. Good fun and wholesome. And the songs were clean songs, and some of them were hallowed by tender associations. Finally, in a pause, a man asked, "Have you heard about the fellow that kept a diary crossing the Atlantic?" It was a discord, a wet blanket. The men were not in the mood for humorous dirt. The songs had carried them to their homes, and in spirit they sat by those far hearthstones, and saw faces and heard voices other than those that were about them. And

so this disposition to drag in an old indecent anecdote got no welcome; nobody answered. The poor man hadn't wit enough to see that he had blundered, but asked his question again. Again there was no response. It was embarrassing for him. In his confusion he chose the wrong course, did the wrong thing—began the anecdote. Began it in a deep and hostile stillness, where had been such life and stir and warm comradeship before. He delivered himself of the brief details of the diary's first day, and did it with some confidence and a fair degree of eagerness. It fell flat. There was an awkward pause. The two rows of men sat like statues. There was no movement, no sound. He had to go on; there was no other way, at least none that an animal of his calibre could think of. At the close of each day's diary, the same dismal silence followed. When at last he finished his tale and sprung the indelicate surprise which is wont to fetch a crash of laughter, not a ripple of sound resulted. It was as if the tale had been told to dead men. After what seemed a long, long time, somebody sighed, somebody else stirred in his seat; presently, the men dropped into a low murmur of confidential talk, each with his neighbor, and the incident was closed. There were indications that that man was fond of his anecdote; that it was his pet, his standby, his shot that never missed, his reputation-maker. But he will never tell it again. No doubt he will think of it sometimes, for that cannot well be helped; and then he will see a picture, and always the same picture—the double rank of dead men; the vacant deck stretching away in dimming perspective beyond them, the wide desert of smooth sea all abroad; the rim of the moon spying from behind a rag of black cloud; the remote top of the mizzenmast shearing a zigzag path through the fields of stars in the deeps of space; and this soft picture will remind him of the time that he sat in the midst of it and told his poor little tale and felt so lonesome when he got through.

Fifty Indians and Chinamen asleep in a big tent in the waist of the ship forward; they lie side by side with no space between; the former wrapped up, head and all, as in the Indian streets, the Chinamen uncovered; the lamp and things for opium smoking in the center.

A passenger said it was ten 2-ton truck loads of dynamite that lately exploded at Johannesburg. Hundreds killed; he doesn't know how many; limbs picked up for miles around. Glass shattered, and roofs swept away or collapsed 200 yards off; fragment of iron flung three and a half miles.

It occurred at 3 p.m.; at 6, £65,000 had been subscribed. When this passenger left, £35,000 had been voted by city and state governments and £100,000 by citizens and business corporations. When news of the disaster was telephoned to the Exchange £35,000 were subscribed in the first five minutes. Subscribing was still going on when he left; the papers had ceased the names, only the amounts—too many names; not enough room. £100,000 subscribed by companies and citizens; if this is true, it must be what they call in Australia "a record"—the biggest instance of a spontaneous outpour for charity in history, considering the size of the population it was drawn from, $8 or $10 for each white resident, babies at the breast included.

Monday, May 4. Steaming slowly in the stupendous Delagoa Bay, its dim arms stretching far away and disappearing on both sides. It could furnish plenty of room for all the ships in the world, but it is shoal. The lead has given us 3½ fathoms several times and we are drawing that, lacking 6 inches.

A bold headland—precipitous wall, 150 feet high, very strong, red color, stretching a mile or so. A man said it was Portuguese blood—battle fought here with the natives last year. I think this doubtful. Pretty cluster of houses on the tableland above the red-and rolling stretches of grass and groups of trees, like England.

The Portuguese have the railroad (one passenger train a day) to the border—70 miles—then the Netherlands Company have it. Thousands of tons of freight on the shore—no cover. This is Portuguese all over — indolence, piousness, poverty, impotence.

Crews of small boats and tugs, all jet black woolly heads and very muscular.

Winter. The South African winter is just beginning now, but nobody but an expert can tell it from summer. However, I am tired of summer; we have had it unbroken for eleven months. We spent the afternoon on shore, Delagoa Bay. A small town—no sights. No carriages. Three 'rickshas, but we couldn't get them—apparently private. These Portuguese are a rich brown, like some of the Indians. Some of the blacks have the long horse beads and very long chins of the negroes of the picture books; but most of them are exactly like the negroes of our Southern States round faces, flat noses, good-natured, and easy laughers.

Flocks of black women passed along, carrying outrageously heavy bags of freight on their heads. The quiver of their leg as the foot was planted and the strain exhibited by their bodies showed what a tax upon their strength the load was. They were stevedores and doing full stevedores work. They were very erect when unladden—from carrying heavy loads on their heads—just like the Indian women. It gives them a proud fine carriage.

Sometimes one saw a woman carrying on her head a laden and top-heavy basket the shape of an inverted pyramid-its top the size of a soup-plate, its base the diameter of a teacup. It required nice balancing—and got it.

No bright colors; yet there were a good many Hindoos.

The Second Class Passenger came over as usual at "lights out" (11) and we lounged along the spacious vague solitudes of the deck and smoked the peaceful pipe and talked. He told me an incident in Mr. Barnum's life which was evidently characteristic of that great showman in several ways:

This was Barnum's purchase of Shakespeare's birthplace, a quarter of a century ago. The Second Class Passenger was in Jamrach's employ at the time and knew Barnum well. He said the thing began in this way. One morning Barnum and Jamrach were in Jamrach's little private snuggery back of the wilderness of caged monkeys and snakes and other commonplaces of Jamrach's stock in trade, refreshing themselves after an arduous stroke of business, Jamrach with something orthodox, Barnum with something heterodox—for Barnum was a teetaler. The stroke of business was in the elephant line. Jamrach had contracted to deliver to Barnum in New York 18 elephants for $360,000 in time for the next season's opening. Then it occurred to Mr. Barnum that he needed a "card" He suggested Jumbo. Jamrach said he would have to think of something else—Jumbo couldn't be had; the Zoo wouldn't part with that elephant. Barnum said he was willing to pay a fortune for Jumbo if he could get him. Jamrach said it was no use to think about it; that Jumbo was as popular as the Prince of Wales and the Zoo wouldn't dare to

sell him; all England would be outraged at the idea; Jumbo was an English institution; he was part of the national glory; one might as well think of buying the Nelson monument. Barnum spoke up with vivacity and said:

"It's a first-rate idea. I'll buy the Monument."

Jamrach was speechless for a second. Then he said, like one ashamed "You caught me. I was napping. For a moment I thought you were in earnest."

Barnum said pleasantly—

"I was in earnest. I know they won't sell it, but no matter, I will not throw away a good idea for all that. All I want is a big advertisement. I will keep the thing in mind, and if nothing better turns up I will offer to buy it. That will answer every purpose. It will furnish me a couple of columns of gratis advertising in every English and American paper for a couple of months, and give my show the biggest boom a show ever had in this world."

Jamrach started to deliver a burst of admiration, but was interrupted by Barnum, who said:

"Here is a state of things! England ought to blush."

His eye had fallen upon something in the newspaper. He read it through to himself, then read it aloud. It said that the house that Shakespeare was born in at Stratford-on-Avon was falling gradually to ruin through neglect; that the room where the poet first saw the light was now serving as a butcher's shop; that all appeals to England to contribute money (the requisite sum stated) to buy the house and repair it and place it in the care of salaried and trustworthy keepers had fallen resultless. Then Barnum said:

"There's my chance. Let Jumbo and the Monument alone for the present —they'll keep. I'll buy Shakespeare's house. I'll set it up in my Museum in New York and put a glass case around it and make a sacred thing of it; and you'll see all America flock there to worship; yes, and pilgrims from the whole earth; and I'll make them take their hats off, too. In America we know how to value anything that Shakespeare's touch has made holy. You'll see."

In conclusion the S. C. P. said:

"That is the way the thing came about. Barnum did buy Shakespeare's house. He paid the price asked, and received the properly attested documents of sale. Then there was an explosion, I can tell you. England rose! That, the birthplace of the master-genius of all the ages and all the climes—that priceless possession of Britain—to be carted out of the country like so much old lumber and set up for sixpenny desecration in a Yankee show-shop—the idea was not to be tolerated for a moment. England rose in her indignation; and Barnum was glad to relinquish his prize and offer apologies. However, he stood out for a compromise; he claimed a concession—England must let him have Jumbo. And England consented, but not cheerfully."

It shows how, by help of time, a story can grow—even after Barnum has had the first innings in the telling of it. Mr. Barnum told me the story himself, years ago. He said that the permission to buy Jumbo was not a concession; the purchase was made and the animal delivered before the public knew anything about it. Also, that the securing of Jumbo was all the advertisement he needed. It produced many columns of newspaper talk, free of cost, and he was satisfied. He said that if he had failed to get Jumbo he would have caused his notion of buying the Nelson Monument to be treacherously smuggled into print by some trusty friend, and after he had gotten a few hundred pages of gratuitous advertising out of it, he would have come out with a blundering, obtuse, but warm-hearted letter of apology, and in a postscript to it would have naively proposed to let the Monument go, and take Stonehenge in place of it at the same price.

It was his opinion that such a letter, written with well-simulated asinine innocence and gush would have gotten his ignorance and stupidity an amount of newspaper abuse worth six fortunes to him, and not purchasable for twice the money.

I knew Mr. Barnum well, and I placed every confidence in the account which he gave me of the Shakespeare birthplace episode. He said he found the house neglected and going-to decay, and he inquired into the matter and was told that many times earnest efforts had been made to raise money for its proper repair and preservation, but without success. He then proposed to buy it. The proposition was entertained, and a price named —$50,000, I think; but whatever it was, Barnum paid the money down, without remark, and the papers were drawn up and executed. He said that it had been his purpose to set up the house in his Museum, keep it in repair, protect it from name-scribblers and other desecrators, and leave it by bequest to the safe and perpetual guardianship of the Smithsonian Institute at Washington.

But as soon as it was found that Shakespeare's house had passed into foreign hands and was going to be carried across the ocean, England was stirred as no appeal from the custodians of the relic had ever stirred England before, and protests came flowing in—and money, too, to stop the outrage. Offers of repurchase were made—offers of double the money that Mr. Barnum had paid for the house. He handed the house back, but took only the sum which it had cost him—but on the condition that an endowment sufficient for the future safeguarding and maintenance of the sacred relic should be raised. This condition was fulfilled.

That was Barnum's account of the episode; and to the end of his days he claimed with pride and satisfaction that not England, but America —represented by him—saved the birthplace of Shakespeare from destruction.

At 3 P.M., May 6th, the ship slowed down, off the land, and thoughtfully and cautiously picked her way into the snug harbor of Durban, South Africa.

CHAPTER LXV.

In statesmanship get the formalities right, never mind about the moralities. —Pudd'nhead Wilson's New Calendar.

FROM DIARY:

Royal Hotel. Comfortable, good table, good service of natives and Madrasis. Curious jumble of modern and ancient city and village, primitiveness and the other thing. Electric bells, but they don't ring. Asked why they didn't, the watchman in the office said he thought they must be out of order; he thought so because some of them rang, but most of them didn't. Wouldn't it be a good idea to put them in order? He hesitated—like one who isn't quite sure—then conceded the point.

May 7. A bang on the door at 6. Did I want my boots cleaned? Fifteen minutes later another bang. Did we want coffee? Fifteen later, bang again, my wife's bath ready; 15 later, my bath ready. Two other bangs; I forget what they were about. Then lots of shouting back and forth, among the servants just as in an Indian hotel.

Evening. At 4 P.M. it was unpleasantly warm. Half-hour after sunset one needed a spring overcoat; by 8 a winter one.

Durban is a neat and clean town. One notices that without having his attention called to it.

Rickshaws drawn by splendidly built black Zulus, so overflowing with strength, seemingly, that it is a pleasure, not a pain, to see them snatch a rickshaw along. They smile and laugh and show their teeth—a good-natured lot. Not allowed to drink; 2s per hour for one person; 3s for two; 3d for a course—one person.

The chameleon in the hotel court. He is fat and indolent and contemplative; but is business-like and capable when a fly comes about —reaches out a tongue like a teaspoon and takes him in. He gums his tongue first. He is always pious, in his looks. And pious and thankful both, when Providence or one of us sends him a fly. He has a froggy head, and a back like a new grave—for shape; and hands like a bird's toes that have been frostbitten. But his eyes are his exhibition feature. A couple of skinny cones project from the sides of his head, with a wee shiny bead of an eye set in the apex of each; and these cones turn bodily like pivot-guns and point every-which-way, and they are independent of each other; each has its own exclusive machinery. When I am behind him and C. in front of him, he whirls one eye rearwards and the other forwards—which gives him a most Congressional expression (one eye on the constituency and one on the swag); and then if something happens above and below him he shoots out one eye upward like a telescope and the other downward—and this changes his expression, but does not improve it.

Natives must not be out after the curfew bell without a pass. In Natal there are ten blacks to one white.

Sturdy plump creatures are the women. They comb their wool up to a peak and keep it in position by stiffening it with brown-red clay—half of this tower colored, denotes engagement; the whole of it colored denotes marriage.

None but heathen Zulus on the police; Christian ones not allowed.

May 9. A drive yesterday with friends over the Berea. Very fine roads and lofty, overlooking the whole town, the harbor, and the sea-beautiful views. Residences all along, set in the midst of green lawns with shrubs and generally one or two intensely red outbursts of poinsettia—the flaming splotch of blinding red a stunning contrast with the world of surrounding green. The cactus tree—candelabrum-like; and one twisted like gray writhing serpents. The "flat-crown" (should be flat-roof) —half a dozen naked branches full of elbows, slant upward like artificial supports, and fling a roof of delicate foliage out in a horizontal platform as flat as a floor; and you look up through this thin floor as through a green cobweb or veil. The branches are japanesich. All about you is a bewildering variety of unfamiliar and beautiful trees; one sort wonderfully dense foliage and very dark green—so dark that you notice it at once, notwithstanding there are so many orange trees. The "flamboyant"—not in flower, now, but when in flower lives up to its name, we are told. Another tree with a lovely upright tassel scattered among its rich greenery, red and glowing as a firecoal. Here and there a gum-tree; half a dozen lofty Norfolk Island pines lifting their fronded arms skyward. Groups of tall bamboo.

Saw one bird. Not many birds here, and they have no music—and the flowers not much smell, they grow so fast.

Everything neat and trim and clean like the town. The loveliest trees and the greatest variety I have ever seen anywhere, except approaching Darjeeling. Have not heard anyone call Natal the garden of South Africa, but that is what it probably is.

It was when Bishop of Natal that Colenso raised such a storm in the religious world. The concerns of religion are a vital matter here yet. A vigilant eye is kept upon Sunday. Museums and other dangerous resorts are not allowed to be open. You may sail on the Bay, but it is wicked to play cricket. For a while a Sunday concert was tolerated, upon condition that it must be admission free and the money taken by collection. But the collection was alarmingly large and that stopped the matter. They are particular about babies. A clergyman would not bury a child according to the sacred rites because it had not been baptized. The Hindoo is more liberal. He burns no child under three, holding that it does not need purifying.

The King of the Zulus, a fine fellow of 30, was banished six years ago for a term of seven years. He is occupying Napoleon's old stand—St. Helena. The people are a little nervous about having him come back, and they may well be, for Zulu kings have been terrible people sometimes —like Tchaka, Dingaan, and Cetewayo.

There is a large Trappist monastery two hours from Durban, over the country roads, and in company with Mr. Milligan and Mr. Hunter, general manager of the Natal government railways, who knew the heads of it, we went out to see it.

There it all was, just as one reads about it in books and cannot believe that it is so—I mean the rough, hard work, the impossible hours, the scanty food, the coarse raiment, the Maryborough beds, the tabu of human speech, of social intercourse, of relaxation, of amusement, of entertainment, of the presence of woman in the men's establishment. There it all was. It was not a dream, it was not a lie. And yet with the fact before one's face it was still incredible. It is such a sweeping suppression of human instincts, such an extinction of the man as an individual.

La Trappe must have known the human race well. The scheme which he invented hunts out everything that a man wants and values—and withholds it from him. Apparently there is no detail that can help make life worth living that has not been carefully ascertained and placed out of the Trappist's reach. La Trappe must have known that there were men who would enjoy this kind of misery, but how did he find it out?

If he had consulted you or me he would have been told that his scheme lacked too many attractions; that it was impossible; that it could never be floated. But there in the monastery was proof that he knew the human race better than it knew itself. He set his foot upon every desire that a man has—yet he floated his project, and it has prospered for two hundred years, and will go on prospering forever, no doubt.

Man likes personal distinction—there in the monastery it is

obliterated. He likes delicious food—there he gets beans and bread and tea, and not enough of it. He likes to lie softly—there he lies on a sand mattress, and has a pillow and a blanket, but no sheet. When he is dining, in a great company of friends, he likes to laugh and chat—there a monk reads a holy book aloud during meals, and nobody speaks or laughs. When a man has a hundred friends about him, evenings, be likes to have a good time and run late—there he and the rest go silently to bed at 8; and in the dark, too; there is but a loose brown robe to discard, there are no night-clothes to put on, a light is not needed. Man likes to lie abed late there he gets up once or twice in the night to perform some religious office, and gets up finally for the day at two in the morning. Man likes light work or none at all—there he labors all day in the field, or in the blacksmith shop or the other shops devoted to the mechanical trades, such as shoemaking, saddlery, carpentry, and so on. Man likes the society of girls and women—there he never has it. He likes to have his children about him, and pet them and play with them —there he has none. He likes billiards—there is no table there. He likes outdoor sports and indoor dramatic and musical and social entertainments—there are none there. He likes to bet on things—I was told that betting is forbidden there. When a man's temper is up he likes to pour it out upon somebody there this is not allowed. A man likes animals—pets; there are none there. He likes to smoke—there he cannot do it. He likes to read the news—no papers or magazines come there. A man likes to know how his parents and brothers and sisters are getting along when he is away, and if they miss him—there he cannot know. A man likes a pretty house, and pretty furniture, and pretty things, and pretty colors—there he has nothing but naked aridity and sombre colors. A man likes—name it yourself: whatever it is, it is absent from that place.

From what I could learn, all that a man gets for this is merely the saving of his soul.

It all seems strange, incredible, impossible. But La Trappe knew the race. He knew the powerful attraction of unattractiveness; he knew that no life could be imagined, howsoever comfortless and forbidding, but somebody would want to try it.

This parent establishment of Germans began its work fifteen years ago, strangers, poor, and unencouraged; it owns 15,000 acres of land now, and raises grain and fruit, and makes wines, and manufactures all manner of things, and has native apprentices in its shops, and sends them forth able to read and write, and also well equipped to earn their living by their trades. And this young establishment has set up eleven branches in South Africa, and in them they are christianizing and educating and teaching wage-yielding mechanical trades to 1,200 boys and girls. Protestant Missionary work is coldly regarded by the commercial white colonist all over the heathen world, as a rule, and its product is nicknamed "rice-Christians" (occupationless incapables who join the church for revenue only), but I think it would be difficult to pick a flaw in the work of these Catholic monks, and I believe that the disposition to attempt it has not shown itself.

Tuesday, May 12. Transvaal politics in a confused condition. First the sentencing of the Johannesburg Reformers startled England by its severity; on the top of this came Kruger's exposure of the cipher correspondence, which showed that the invasion of the Transvaal, with the design of seizing that country and adding it to the British Empire, was planned by Cecil Rhodes and Beit—which made a revulsion in English feeling, and brought out a storm against Rhodes and the

Chartered Company for degrading British honor. For a good while I couldn't seem to get at a clear comprehension of it, it was so tangled. But at last by patient study I have managed it, I believe. As I understand it, the Uitlanders and other Dutchmen were dissatisfied because the English would not allow them to take any part in the government except to pay taxes. Next, as I understand it, Dr. Kruger and Dr. Jameson, not having been able to make the medical business pay, made a raid into Matabeleland with the intention of capturing the capital, Johannesburg, and holding the women and children to ransom until the Uitlanders and the other Boers should grant to them and the Chartered Company the political rights which had been withheld from them. They would have succeeded in this great scheme, as I understand it, but for the interference of Cecil Rhodes and Mr. Beit, and other Chiefs of the Matabele, who persuaded their countrymen to revolt and throw off their allegiance to Germany. This, in turn, as I understand it, provoked the King of Abyssinia to destroy the Italian army and fall back upon Johannesburg; this at the instigation of Rhodes, to bull the stock market.

CHAPTER LXVI.

Every one is a moon, and has a dark side which he never shows to anybody. —Pudd'nhead Wilson's New Calendar.

When I scribbled in my note-book a year ago the paragraph which ends the preceding chapter, it was meant to indicate, in an extravagant form, two things: the conflicting nature of the information conveyed by the citizen to the stranger concerning South African politics, and the resulting confusion created in the stranger's mind thereby.

But it does not seem so very extravagant now. Nothing could in that disturbed and excited time make South African politics clear or quite rational to the citizen of the country because his personal interest and his political prejudices were in his way; and nothing could make those politics clear or rational to the stranger, the sources of his information being such as they were.

I was in South Africa some little time. When I arrived there the political pot was boiling fiercely. Four months previously, Jameson had plunged over the Transvaal border with about 600 armed horsemen at his back, to go to the "relief of the women and children" of Johannesburg; on the fourth day of his march the Boers had defeated him in battle, and carried him and his men to Pretoria, the capital, as prisoners; the Boer government had turned Jameson and his officers over to the British government for trial, and shipped them to England; next, it had arrested 64 important citizens of Johannesburg as raid-conspirators, condemned their four leaders to death, then commuted the sentences, and now the 64 were waiting, in jail, for further results. Before midsummer they were all out excepting two, who refused to sign the petitions for release; 58 had been fined $10,000 each and enlarged, and the four leaders had gotten off with fines of $125,000 each with permanent exile added, in one case.

Those were wonderfully interesting days for a stranger, and I was glad. to be in the thick of the excitement. Everybody was talking, and I expected to understand the whole of one side of it in a very little while.

I was disappointed. There were singularities, perplexities, unaccountabilities about it which I was not able to master. I had no personal access to Boers—their side was a secret to me, aside from what I was able to gather of it from published

statements. My sympathies were soon with the Reformers in the Pretoria jail, with their friends, and with their cause. By diligent inquiry in Johannesburg I found out —apparently—all the details of their side of the quarrel except one—what they expected to accomplish by an armed rising.

Nobody seemed to know.

The reason why the Reformers were discontented and wanted some changes made, seemed quite clear. In Johannesburg it was claimed that the Uitlanders (strangers, foreigners) paid thirteen-fifteenths of the Transvaal taxes, yet got little or nothing for it. Their city had no charter; it had no municipal government; it could levy no taxes for drainage, water-supply, paving, cleaning, sanitation, policing. There was a police force, but it was composed of Boers, it was furnished by the State Government, and the city had no control over it. Mining was very costly; the government enormously increased the cost by putting burdensome taxes upon the mines, the output, the machinery, the buildings; by burdensome imposts upon incoming materials; by burdensome railway-freight-charges. Hardest of all to bear, the government reserved to itself a monopoly in that essential thing, dynamite, and burdened it with an extravagant price. The detested Hollander from over the water held all the public offices. The government was rank with corruption. The Uitlander had no vote, and must live in the State ten or twelve years before he could get one. He was not represented in the Raad (legislature) that oppressed him and fleeced him. Religion was not free. There were no schools where the teaching was in English, yet the great majority of the white population of the State knew no tongue but that. The State would not pass a liquor law; but allowed a great trade in cheap vile brandy among the blacks, with the result that 25 per cent. of the 50,000 blacks employed in the mines were usually drunk and incapable of working.

There—it was plain enough that the reasons for wanting some changes made were abundant and reasonable, if this statement of the existing grievances was correct.

What the Uitlanders wanted was reform—under the existing Republic.

What they proposed to do was to secure these reforms by, prayer, petition, and persuasion.

They did petition. Also, they issued a Manifesto, whose very first note is a bugle-blast of loyalty: "We want the establishment of this Republic as a true Republic."

Could anything be clearer than the Uitlander's statement of the grievances and oppressions under which they were suffering? Could anything be more legal and citizen-like and law-respecting than their attitude as expressed by their Manifesto? No. Those things were perfectly clear, perfectly comprehensible.

But at this point the puzzles and riddles and confusions begin to flock in. You have arrived at a place which you cannot quite understand.

For you find that as a preparation for this loyal, lawful, and in every way unexceptionable attempt to persuade the government to right their grievances, the Uitlanders had smuggled a Maxim gun or two and 1,500 muskets into the town, concealed in oil tanks and coal cars, and had begun to form and drill military companies composed of clerks, merchants, and citizens generally.

What was their idea? Did they suppose that the Boers would attack them for petitioning, for redress? That could not be.

Did they suppose that the Boers would attack them even for issuing a Manifesto demanding relief under the existing government?

Yes, they apparently believed so, because the air was full of talk of forcing the government to grant redress if it were not granted peacefully.

The Reformers were men of high intelligence. If they were in earnest, they were taking extraordinary risks. They had enormously valuable properties to defend; their town was full of women and children; their mines and compounds were packed with thousands upon thousands of sturdy blacks. If the Boers attacked, the mines would close, the blacks would swarm out and get drunk; riot and conflagration and the Boers together might lose the Reformers more in a day, in money, blood, and suffering, than the desired political relief could compensate in ten years if they won the fight and secured the reforms.

It is May, 1897, now; a year has gone by, and the confusions of that day have been to a considerable degree cleared away. Mr. Cecil Rhodes, Dr. Jameson, and others responsible for the Raid, have testified before the Parliamentary Committee of Inquiry in London, and so have Mr. Lionel Phillips and other Johannesburg Reformers, monthly-nurses of the Revolution which was born dead. These testimonies have thrown light. Three books have added much to this light:

"South Africa As It Is," by Mr. Statham, an able writer partial to the Boers; "The Story of an African Crisis," by Mr. Garrett, a brilliant writer partial to Rhodes; and "A Woman's Part in a Revolution," by Mrs. John Hays Hammond, a vigorous and vivid diarist, partial to the Reformers. By liquifying the evidence of the prejudiced books and of the prejudiced parliamentary witnesses and stirring the whole together and pouring it into my own (prejudiced) moulds, I have got at the truth of that puzzling South African situation, which is this:

1. The capitalists and other chief men of Johannesburg were fretting under various political and financial burdens imposed by the State (the South African Republic, sometimes called "the Transvaal") and desired to procure by peaceful means a modification of the laws.

2. Mr. Cecil Rhodes, Premier of the British Cape Colony, millionaire, creator and managing director of the territorially-immense and financially unproductive South Africa Company; projector of vast schemes for the unification and consolidation of all the South African States, one imposing commonwealth or empire under the shadow and general protection of the British flag, thought he saw an opportunity to make profitable use of the Uitlander discontent above mentioned—make the Johannesburg cat help pull out one of his consolidation chestnuts for him. With this view he set himself the task of warming the lawful and legitimate petitions and supplications of the Uitlanders into seditious talk, and their frettings into threatenings—the final outcome to be revolt and armed rebellion. If he could bring about a bloody collision between those people and the Boer government, Great Britain would have to interfere; her interference would be resisted by the Boers; she would chastise them and add the Transvaal to her South African possessions. It was not a foolish idea, but a rational and practical one.

After a couple of years of judicious plotting, Mr. Rhodes had his reward; the revolutionary kettle was briskly boiling in Johannesburg, and the Uitlander leaders were backing their appeals to the government—now hardened into demands—by threats of force and bloodshed. By the middle of December, 1895, the explosion seemed imminent. Mr. Rhodes was diligently helping, from his distant post in Cape Town. He was helping to procure arms for Johannesburg; he was also arranging to have Jameson break over the border and come to Johannesburg with 600 mounted men at his back. Jameson—as per instructions from Rhodes, perhaps—wanted a letter from the Reformers requesting him to come to their aid. It was a good idea. It would throw a considerable share of the responsibility of his invasion upon the Reformers. He got the letter—that famous one urging him to fly to the rescue of the women and children. He got it two months before he flew. The Reformers seem to have thought it over and concluded that they had not done wisely; for the next day after giving Jameson the implicating document they wanted to withdraw it and leave the women and children in danger; but they were told that it was too late. The original had gone to Mr. Rhodes at the Cape. Jameson had kept a copy, though.

From that time until the 29th of December, a good deal of the Reformers' time was taken up with energetic efforts to keep Jameson from coming to their assistance. Jameson's invasion had been set for the 26th. The Reformers were not ready. The town was not united. Some wanted a fight, some wanted peace; some wanted a new government, some wanted the existing one reformed; apparently very few wanted the revolution to take place in the interest and under the ultimate shelter of the Imperial flag —British; yet a report began to spread that Mr. Rhodes's embarrassing assistance had for its end this latter object.

Jameson was away up on the frontier tugging at his leash, fretting to burst over the border. By hard work the Reformers got his starting-date postponed a little, and wanted to get it postponed eleven days. Apparently, Rhodes's agents were seconding their efforts—in fact wearing out the telegraph wires trying to hold him back. Rhodes was himself the only man who could have effectively postponed Jameson, but that would have been a disadvantage to his scheme; indeed, it could spoil his whole two years' work.

Jameson endured postponement three days, then resolved to wait no longer. Without any orders—excepting Mr. Rhodes's significant silence—he cut the telegraph wires on the 29th, and made his plunge that night, to go to the rescue of the women and children, by urgent request of a letter now nine days old—as per date,—a couple of months old, in fact. He read the letter to his men, and it affected them. It did not affect all of them alike. Some saw in it a piece of piracy of doubtful wisdom, and were sorry to find that they had been assembled to violate friendly territory instead of to raid native kraals, as they had supposed.

Jameson would have to ride 150 miles. He knew that there were suspicions abroad in the Transvaal concerning him, but he expected to get through to Johannesburg before they should become general and obstructive. But a telegraph wire had been overlooked and not cut. It spread the news of his invasion far and wide, and a few hours after his start the Boer farmers were riding hard from every direction to intercept him.

As soon as it was known in Johannesburg that he was on his

way to rescue the women and children, the grateful people put the women and children in a train and rushed them for Australia. In fact, the approach of Johannesburg's saviour created panic and consternation; there, and a multitude of males of peaceable disposition swept to the trains like a sandstorm. The early ones fared best; they secured seats—by sitting in them—eight hours before the first train was timed to leave.

Mr. Rhodes lost no time. He cabled the renowned Johannesburg letter of invitation to the London press—the gray-headedest piece of ancient history that ever went over a cable.

The new poet laureate lost no time. He came out with a rousing poem lauding Jameson's prompt and splendid heroism in flying to the rescue of the women and children; for the poet could not know that he did not fly until two months after the invitation. He was deceived by the false date of the letter, which was December 20th.

Jameson was intercepted by the Boers on New Year's Day, and on the next day he surrendered. He had carried his copy of the letter along, and if his instructions required him—in case of emergency—to see that it fell into the hands of the Boers, he loyally carried them out. Mrs. Hammond gives him a sharp rap for his supposed carelessness, and emphasizes her feeling about it with burning italics: "It was picked up on the battle-field in a leathern pouch, supposed to be Dr. Jameson's saddle-bag. Why, in the name of all that is discreet and honorable, didn't he eat it!"

She requires too much. He was not in the service of the Reformers —excepting ostensibly; he was in the service of Mr. Rhodes. It was the only plain English document, undarkened by ciphers and mysteries, and responsibly signed and authenticated, which squarely implicated the Reformers in the raid, and it was not to Mr. Rhodes's interest that it should be eaten. Besides, that letter was not the original, it was only a copy. Mr. Rhodes had the original—and didn't eat it. He cabled it to the London press. It had already been read in England and America and all over Europe before, Jameson dropped it on the battlefield. If the subordinate's knuckles deserved a rap, the principal's deserved as many as a couple of them.

That letter is a juicily dramatic incident and is entitled to all its celebrity, because of the odd and variegated effects which it produced. All within the space of a single week it had made Jameson an illustrious hero in England, a pirate in Pretoria, and an ass without discretion or honor in Johannesburg; also it had produced a poet-laureatic explosion of colored fireworks which filled the world's sky with giddy splendors, and, the knowledge that Jameson was coming with it to rescue the women and children emptied Johannesburg of that detail of the population. For an old letter, this was much. For a letter two months old, it did marvels; if it had been a year old it would have done miracles.

CHAPTER LXVII.

First catch your Boer, then kick him. —Pudd'nhead Wilson's New Calendar.

Those latter days were days of bitter worry and trouble for the harassed Reformers.

From Mrs. Hammond we learn that on the 31st (the day after Johannesburg heard of the invasion), "The Reform Committee repudiates Dr. Jameson's inroad."

It also publishes its intention to adhere to the Manifesto.

It also earnestly desires that the inhabitants shall refrain from overt acts against the Boer government.

It also "distributes arms" at the Court House, and furnishes horses "to the newly-enrolled volunteers."

It also brings a Transvaal flag into the committee-room, and the entire body swear allegiance to it "with uncovered heads and upraised arms."

Also "one thousand Lee-Metford rifles have been given out"—to rebels.

Also, in a speech, Reformer Lionel Phillips informs the public that the Reform Committee Delegation has "been received with courtesy by the Government Commission," and "been assured that their proposals shall be earnestly considered." That "while the Reform Committee regretted Jameson's precipitate action, they would stand by him."

Also the populace are in a state of "wild enthusiasm," and "46 can scarcely be restrained; they want to go out to meet Jameson and bring him in with triumphal outcry."

Also the British High Commissioner has issued a damnifying proclamation against Jameson and all British abettors of his game. It arrives January 1st.

It is a difficult position for the Reformers, and full of hindrances and perplexities. Their duty is hard, but plain:

1. They have to repudiate the inroad, and stand by the inroader.

2. They have to swear allegiance to the Boer government, and distribute cavalry horses to the rebels.

3. They have to forbid overt acts against the Boer government, and distribute arms to its enemies.

4. They have to avoid collision with the British government, but still stand by Jameson and their new oath of allegiance to the Boer government, taken, uncovered, in presence of its flag.

They did such of these things as they could; they tried to do them all; in fact, did do them all, but only in turn, not simultaneously. In the nature of things they could not be made to simultane.

In preparing for armed revolution and in talking revolution, were the Reformers "bluffing," or were they in earnest? If they were in earnest, they were taking great risks—as has been already pointed out. A gentleman of high position told me in Johannesburg that he had in his possession a printed document proclaiming a new government and naming its president—one of the Reform leaders. He said that this proclamation had been ready for issue, but was suppressed when the raid collapsed. Perhaps I misunderstood him. Indeed, I must have misunderstood him, for I have not seen mention of this large incident in print anywhere.

Besides, I hope I am mistaken; for, if I am, then there is argument that the Reformers were privately not serious, but were only trying to scare the Boer government into granting the desired reforms.

The Boer government was scared, and it had a right to be. For if Mr. Rhodes's plan was to provoke a collision that would compel the interference of England, that was a serious matter. If it could be shown that that was also the Reformers' plan and purpose, it would prove that they had marked out a feasible project, at any rate, although it was one which could hardly fail to cost them ruinously before England should arrive. But it seems clear that they had no such plan nor desire. If, when the worst should come to the worst, they meant to overthrow the government, they also meant to inherit the assets themselves, no doubt.

This scheme could hardly have succeeded. With an army of Boers at their gates and 50,000 riotous blacks in their midst, the odds against success would have been too heavy—even if the whole town had been armed. With only 2,500 rifles in the place, they stood really no chance.

To me, the military problems of the situation are of more interest than the political ones, because by disposition I have always been especially fond of war. No, I mean fond of discussing war; and fond of giving military advice. If I had been with Jameson the morning after he started, I should have advised him to turn back. That was Monday; it was then that he received his first warning from a Boer source not to violate the friendly soil of the Transvaal. It showed that his invasion was known. If I had been with him on Tuesday morning and afternoon, when he received further warnings, I should have repeated my advice. If I had been with him the next morning—New Year's—when he received notice that "a few hundred" Boers were waiting for him a few miles ahead, I should not have advised, but commanded him to go back. And if I had been with him two or three hours later—a thing not conceivable to me—I should have retired him by force; for at that time he learned that the few hundred had now grown to 800; and that meant that the growing would go on growing.

For,—by authority of Mr. Garrett, one knows that Jameson's 600 were only 530 at most, when you count out his native drivers, etc.; and that the 530 consisted largely of "green" youths, "raw young fellows," not trained and war-worn British soldiers; and I would have told. Jameson that those lads would not be able to shoot effectively from horseback in the scamper and racket of battle, and that there would not be anything for them to shoot at, anyway, but rocks; for the Boers would be behind the rocks, not out in the open. I would have told him that 300 Boer sharpshooters behind rocks would be an overmatch for his 500 raw young fellows on horseback.

If pluck were the only thing essential to battle-winning, the English would lose no battles. But discretion, as well as pluck, is required when one fights Boers and Red Indians. In South Africa the Briton has always insisted upon standing bravely up, unsheltered, before the hidden Boer, and taking the results: Jameson's men would follow the custom. Jameson would not have listened to me—he would have been intent upon repeating history, according to precedent. Americans are not acquainted with the British-Boer war of 1881; but its history is interesting, and could have been instructive to Jameson if he had been receptive. I will cull some details of it from trustworthy sources mainly from "Russell's Natal." Mr. Russell is not a Boer, but a Briton. He is inspector of schools, and his history is a text-book whose purpose is the instruction of the Natal English youth.

After the seizure of the Transvaal and the suppression of the Boer government by England in 1877, the Boers fretted for

three years, and made several appeals to England for a restoration of their liberties, but without result. Then they gathered themselves together in a great mass-meeting at Krugersdorp, talked their troubles over, and resolved to fight for their deliverance from the British yoke. (Krugersdorp—the place where the Boers interrupted the Jameson raid.) The little handful of farmers rose against the strongest empire in the world. They proclaimed martial law and the re-establishment of their Republic. They organized their forces and sent them forward to intercept the British battalions. This, although Sir Garnet Wolseley had but lately made proclamation that "so long as the sun shone in the heavens," the Transvaal would be and remain English territory. And also in spite of the fact that the commander of the 94th regiment—already on the march to suppress this rebellion—had been heard to say that "the Boers would turn tail at the first beat of the big drum."—["South Africa As It Is," by F. Reginald Statham, page 82. London: T. Fisher Unwin, 1897.]

Four days after the flag-raising, the Boer force which had been sent forward to forbid the invasion of the English troops met them at Bronkhorst Spruit—246 men of the 94th regiment, in command of a colonel, the big drum beating, the band playing—and the first battle was fought. It lasted ten minutes. Result:

British loss, more than 150 officers and men, out of the 246. Surrender of the remnant.

Boer loss—if any—not stated.

They are fine marksmen, the Boers. From the cradle up, they live on horseback and hunt wild animals with the rifle. They have a passion for liberty and the Bible, and care for nothing else.

"General Sir George Colley, Lieutenant-Governor and Commander-in-Chief in Natal, felt it his duty to proceed at once to the relief of the loyalists and soldiers beleaguered in the different towns of the Transvaal." He moved out with 1,000 men and some artillery. He found the Boers encamped in a strong and sheltered position on high ground at Laing's Nek—every Boer behind a rock. Early in the morning of the 28th January, 1881, he moved to the attack "with the 58th regiment, commanded by Colonel Deane, a mounted squadron of 70 men, the 60th Rifles, the Naval Brigade with three rocket tubes, and the Artillery with six guns." He shelled the Boers for twenty minutes, then the assault was delivered, the 58th marching up the slope in solid column. The battle was soon finished, with this result, according to Russell—

British loss in killed and wounded, 174.

Boer loss, "trifling."

Colonel Deane was killed, and apparently every officer above the grade of lieutenant was killed or wounded, for the 58th retreated to its camp in command of a lieutenant. ("Africa as It Is.")

That ended the second battle.

On the 7th of February General Colley discovered that the Boers were flanking his position. The next morning he left his camp at Mount Pleasant and marched out and crossed the Ingogo river with 270 men, started up the Ingogo heights, and there fought a battle which lasted from noon till nightfall. He then retreated, leaving his wounded with his military chaplain, and in recrossing the now swollen river lost some of his men by drowning. That was the third Boer victory. Result, according to Mr. Russell—

British loss 150 out of 270 engaged.

Boer loss, 8 killed, 9 wounded—17.

There was a season of quiet, now, but at the end of about three weeks Sir George Colley conceived the idea of climbing, with an infantry and artillery force, the steep and rugged mountain of Amajuba in the night—a bitter hard task, but he accomplished it. On the way he left about 200 men to guard a strategic point, and took about 400 up the mountain with him. When the sun rose in the morning, there was an unpleasant surprise for the Boers; yonder were the English troops visible on top of the mountain two or three miles away, and now their own position was at the mercy of the English artillery. The Boer chief resolved to retreat—up that mountain. He asked for volunteers, and got them.

The storming party crossed the swale and began to creep up the steeps, "and from behind rocks and bushes they shot at the soldiers on the skyline as if they were stalking deer," says Mr. Russell. There was "continuous musketry fire, steady and fatal on the one side, wild and ineffectual on the other." The Boers reached the top, and began to put in their ruinous work. Presently the British "broke and fled for their lives down the rugged steep." The Boers had won the battle. Result in killed and wounded, including among the killed the British General:

British loss, 226, out of 400 engaged.

Boer loss, 1 killed, 5 wounded.

That ended the war. England listened to reason, and recognized the Boer Republic—a government which has never been in any really awful danger since, until Jameson started after it with his 500 "raw young fellows." To recapitulate:

The Boer farmers and British soldiers fought 4 battles, and the Boers won them all. Result of the 4, in killed and wounded:

British loss, 700 men.

Boer loss, so far as known, 23 men.

It is interesting, now, to note how loyally Jameson and his several trained British military officers tried to make their battles conform to precedent. Mr. Garrett's account of the Raid is much the best one I have met with, and my impressions of the Raid are drawn from that.

When Jameson learned that near Krugersdorp he would find 800 Boers waiting to dispute his passage, he was not in the least disturbed. He was feeling as he had felt two or three days before, when he had opened his campaign with a historic remark to the same purport as the one with which the commander of the 94th had opened the Boer-British war of fourteen years before. That Commander's remark was, that the Boers "would turn tail at the first beat of the big drum." Jameson's was, that with his "raw young fellows" he could kick the (persons) of the Boers "all round the Transvaal." He was keeping close to historic precedent.

Jameson arrived in the presence of the Boers. They—according to precedent—were not visible. It was a country of ridges, depressions, rocks, ditches, moraines of mining-tailings—not even as favorable for cavalry work as Laing's Nek had been in the former disastrous days. Jameson shot at the ridges and rocks with his artillery, just as General Colley had done at the Nek; and did them no damage and persuaded no Boer to show himself. Then about a hundred of his men formed up to charge the ridge-according to the 58th's precedent at the Nek; but as they dashed forward they opened out in a long line, which was a considerable improvement on the 58th's tactics; when they had gotten to within 200 yards of the ridge the concealed Boers opened out on them and emptied 20 saddles. The unwounded dismounted and fired at the rocks over the backs of their horses; but the return-fire was too hot, and they mounted again, "and galloped back or crawled away into a clump of reeds for cover, where they were shortly afterward taken prisoners as they lay among the reeds. Some thirty prisoners were so taken, and during the night which followed the Boers carried away another thirty killed and wounded—the wounded to Krugersdorp hospital." Sixty per cent. of the assaulted force disposed of—according to Mr. Garrett's estimate.

It was according to Amajuba precedent, where the British loss was 226 out of about 400 engaged.

Also, in Jameson's camp, that night, "there lay about 30 wounded or otherwise disabled" men. Also during the night "some 30 or 40 young fellows got separated from the command and straggled through into Johannesburg." Altogether a possible 150 men gone, out of his 530. His lads had fought valorously, but had not been able to get near enough to a Boer to kick him around the Transvaal.

At dawn the next morning the column of something short of 400 whites resumed its march. Jameson's grit was stubbornly good; indeed, it was always that. He still had hopes. There was a long and tedious zigzagging march through broken ground, with constant harassment from the Boers; and at last the column "walked into a sort of trap," and the Boers "closed in upon it." "Men and horses dropped on all sides. In the column the feeling grew that unless it could burst through the Boer lines at this point it was done for. The Maxims were fired until they grew too hot, and, water failing for the cool jacket, five of them jammed and went out of action. The 7-pounder was fired until only half an hour's ammunition was left to fire with. One last rush was made, and failed, and then the Staats Artillery came up on the left flank, and the game was up."

Jameson hoisted a white flag and surrendered.

There is a story, which may not be true, about an ignorant Boer farmer there who thought that this white flag was the national flag of England. He had been at Bronkhorst, and Laing's Nek, and Ingogo and Amajuba, and supposed that the English did not run up their flag excepting at the end of a fight.

The following is (as I understand it) Mr. Garrett's estimate of Jameson's total loss in killed and wounded for the two days:

"When they gave in they were minus some 20 per cent. of combatants. There were 76 casualties. There were 30 men hurt or sick in the wagons. There were 27 killed on the spot or mortally wounded."

Total, 133, out of the original 530. It is just 25 per cent.—[However, I judge that the total was really 150; for the number of wounded carried to Krugersdorp hospital was 53; not 30, as Mr. Garrett reports it. The lady whose guest I was in

Krugerdorp gave me the figures. She was head nurse from the beginning of hostilities (Jan. 1) until the professional nurses arrived, Jan. 8th. Of the 53, "Three or four were Boers"; I quote her words.]—This is a large improvement upon the precedents established at Bronkhorst, Laing's Nek, Ingogo, and Amajuba, and seems to indicate that Boer marksmanship is not so good now as it was in those days. But there is one detail in which the Raid-episode exactly repeats history. By surrender at Bronkhorst, the whole British force disappeared from the theater of war; this was the case with Jameson's force.

In the Boer loss, also, historical precedent is followed with sufficient fidelity. In the 4 battles named above, the Boer loss, so far as known, was an average of 6 men per battle, to the British average loss of 175. In Jameson's battles, as per Boer official report, the Boer loss in killed was 4. Two of these were killed by the Boers themselves, by accident, the other by Jameson's army—one of them intentionally, the other by a pathetic mischance. "A young Boer named Jacobz was moving forward to give a drink to one of the wounded troopers (Jameson's) after the first charge, when another wounded man, mistaking his intention; shot him." There were three or four wounded Boers in the Krugersdorp hospital, and apparently no others have been reported. Mr. Garrett, "on a balance of probabilities, fully accepts the official version, and thanks Heaven the killed was not larger."

As a military man, I wish to point out what seems to me to be military errors in the conduct of the campaign which we have just been considering. I have seen active service in the field, and it was in the actualities of war that I acquired my training and my right to speak. I served two weeks in the beginning of our Civil War, and during all that tune commanded a battery of infantry composed of twelve men. General Grant knew the history of my campaign, for I told it him. I also told him the principle upon which I had conducted it; which was, to tire the enemy. I tired out and disqualified many battalions, yet never had a casualty myself nor lost a man. General Grant was not given to paying compliments, yet he said frankly that if I had conducted the whole war much bloodshed would have been spared, and that what the army might have lost through the inspiriting results of collision in the field would have been amply made up by the liberalizing influences of travel. Further endorsement does not seem to me to be necessary.

Let us now examine history, and see what it teaches. In the 4 battles fought in 1881 and the two fought by Jameson, the British loss in killed, wounded, and prisoners, was substantially 1,300 men; the Boer loss, as far as is ascertainable, eras about 30 men. These figures show that there was a defect somewhere. It was not in the absence of courage. I think it lay in the absence of discretion. The Briton should have done one thing or the other: discarded British methods and fought the Boer with Boer methods, or augmented his own force until—using British methods—it should be large enough to equalize results with the Boer.

To retain the British method requires certain things, determinable by arithmetic. If, for argument's sake, we allow that the aggregate of 1,716 British soldiers engaged in the 4 early battles was opposed by the same aggregate of Boers, we have this result: the British loss of 700 and the Boer loss of 23 argues that in order to equalize results in future battles you must make the British force thirty times as strong as the Boer force. Mr. Garrett shows that the Boer force immediately opposed to Jameson was 2,000, and that there were 6,000 more on hand by the evening of the second day. Arithmetic

shows that in order to make himself the equal of the 8,000 Boers, Jameson should have had 240,000 men, whereas he merely had 530 boys. From a military point of view, backed by the facts of history, I conceive that Jameson's military judgment was at fault.

Another thing.—Jameson was encumbered by artillery, ammunition, and rifles. The facts of the battle show that he should have had none of those things along. They were heavy, they were in his way, they impeded his march. There was nothing to shoot at but rocks—he knew quite well that there would be nothing to shoot at but rocks—and he knew that artillery and rifles have no effect upon rocks. He was badly overloaded with unessentials. He had 8 Maxims—a Maxim is a kind of Gatling, I believe, and shoots about 500 bullets per minute; he had one 12 ½-pounder cannon and two 7-pounders; also, 145,000 rounds of ammunition. He worked the Maxims so hard upon the rocks that five of them became disabled—five of the Maxims, not the rocks. It is believed that upwards of 100,000 rounds of ammunition of the various kinds were fired during the 21 hours that the battles lasted. One man killed. He must have been much mutilated. It was a pity to bring those futile Maxims along. Jameson should have furnished himself with a battery of Pudd'nhead Wilson maxims instead, They are much more deadly than those others, and they are easily carried, because they have no weight.

Mr. Garrett—not very carefully concealing a smile—excuses the presence of the Maxims by saying that they were of very substantial use because their sputtering disordered the aim of the Boers, and in that way saved lives.

Three cannon, eight Maxims, and five hundred rifles yielded a result which emphasized a fact which had already been established—that the British system of standing out in the open to fight Boers who are behind rocks is not wise, not excusable, and ought to be abandoned for something more efficacious. For the purpose of war is to kill, not merely to waste ammunition.

If I could get the management of one of those campaigns, I would know what to do, for I have studied the Boer. He values the Bible above every other thing. The most delicious edible in South Africa is "biltong." You will have seen it mentioned in Olive Schreiner's books. It is what our plainsmen call "jerked beef." It is the Boer's main standby. He has a passion for it, and he is right.

If I had the command of the campaign I would go with rifles only, no cumbersome Maxims and cannon to spoil good rocks with. I would move surreptitiously by night to a point about a quarter of a mile from the Boer camp, and there I would build up a pyramid of biltong and Bibles fifty feet high, and then conceal my men all about. In the morning the Boers would send out spies, and then the rest would come with a rush. I would surround them, and they would have to fight my men on equal terms, in the open. There wouldn't be any Amajuba results.

—[Just as I am finishing this book an unfortunate dispute has sprung up between Dr. Jameson and his officers, on the one hand, and Colonel Rhodes on the other, concerning the wording of a note which Colonel Rhodes sent from Johannesburg by a cyclist to Jameson just before hostilities began on the memorable New Year's Day. Some of the fragments of this note were found on the battlefield after the fight, and these have been pieced together; the dispute is as to what words the lacking fragments contained. Jameson says the note promised him a reinforcement of 300 men from Johannesburg. Colonel Rhodes denies this, and says he merely promised to send out "some" men "to meet you."]

[It seems a pity that these friends should fall out over so little a thing. If the 300 had been sent, what good would it have done? In 21 hours of industrious fighting, Jameson's 530 men, with 8 Maxims, 3 cannon, and 145,000 rounds of ammunition, killed an aggregate of 1. Boer. These statistics show that a reinforcement of 300 Johannesburgers, armed merely with muskets, would have killed, at the outside, only a little over a half of another Boer. This would not have saved the day. It would not even have seriously affected the general result. The figures show clearly, and with mathematical violence, that the only way to save Jameson, or even give him a fair and equal chance with the enemy, was for Johannesburg to send him 240 Maxims, 90 cannon, 600 carloads of ammunition, and 240,000 men. Johannesburg was not in a position to do this. Johannesburg has been called very hard names for not reinforcing Jameson. But in every instance this has been done by two classes of persons—people who do not read history, and people, like Jameson, who do not understand what it means, after they have read it.]

CHAPTER LXVIII.

None of us can have as many virtues as the fountain-pen, or half its cussedness; but we can try. —Pudd'nhead Wilson's New Calendar.

The Duke of Fife has borne testimony that Mr. Rhodes deceived him. That is also what Mr. Rhodes did with the Reformers. He got them into trouble, and then stayed out himself. A judicious man. He has always been that. As to this there was a moment of doubt, once. It was when he was out on his last pirating expedition in the Matabele country. The cable shouted out that he had gone unarmed, to visit a party of hostile chiefs. It was true, too; and this dare-devil thing came near fetching another indiscretion out of the poet laureate. It would have been too bad, for when the facts were all in, it turned out that there was a lady along, too, and she also was unarmed.

In the opinion of many people Mr. Rhodes is South Africa; others think he is only a large part of it. These latter consider that South Africa consists of Table Mountain, the diamond mines, the Johannesburg gold fields, and Cecil Rhodes. The gold fields are wonderful in every way. In seven or eight years they built up, in a desert, a city of a hundred thousand inhabitants, counting white and black together; and not the ordinary mining city of wooden shanties, but a city made out of lasting material. Nowhere in the world is there such a concentration of rich mines as at Johannesburg. Mr. Bonamici, my manager there, gave me a small gold brick with some statistics engraved upon it which record the output of gold from the early days to July, 1895, and exhibit the strides which have been made in the development of the industry; in 1888 the output was $4,162,440; the output of the next five and a half years was (total: $17,585,894); for the single year ending with June, 1895, it was $45,553,700.

The capital which has developed the mines came from England, the mining engineers from America. This is the case with the diamond mines also. South Africa seems to be the heaven of the American scientific mining engineer. He gets the choicest places, and keeps them. His salary is not based upon what he would get in America, but apparently upon what a whole family of him would get there.

The successful mines pay great dividends, yet the rock is not rich, from a Californian point of view. Rock which yields ten or twelve dollars a ton is considered plenty rich enough. It is troubled with base metals to such a degree that twenty years ago it would have been only about half as valuable as it is now; for at that time there was no paying way of getting anything out of such rock but the coarser-grained "free" gold; but the new cyanide process has changed all that, and the gold fields of the world now deliver up fifty million dollars' worth of gold per year which would have gone into the tailing-pile under the former conditions.

The cyanide process was new to me, and full of interest; and among the costly and elaborate mining machinery there were fine things which were new to me, but I was already familiar with the rest of the details of the gold-mining industry. I had been a gold miner myself, in my day, and knew substantially everything that those people knew about it, except how to make money at it. But I learned a good deal about the Boers there, and that was a fresh subject. What I heard there was afterwards repeated to me in other parts of South Africa. Summed up—according to the information thus gained—this is the Boer:

He is deeply religious, profoundly ignorant, dull, obstinate, bigoted, uncleanly in his habits, hospitable, honest in his dealings with the whites, a hard master to his black servant, lazy, a good shot, good horseman, addicted to the chase, a lover of political independence, a good husband and father, not fond of herding together in towns, but liking the seclusion and remoteness and solitude and empty vastness and silence of the veldt; a man of a mighty appetite, and not delicate about what he appeases it with—well-satisfied with pork and Indian corn and biltong, requiring only that the quantity shall not be stinted; willing to ride a long journey to take a hand in a rude all-night dance interspersed with vigorous feeding and boisterous jollity, but ready to ride twice as far for a prayer-meeting; proud of his Dutch and Huguenot origin and its religious and military history; proud of his race's achievements in South Africa, its bold plunges into hostile and uncharted deserts in search of free solitudes unvexed by the pestering and detested English, also its victories over the natives and the British; proudest of all, of the direct and effusive personal interest which the Deity has always taken in its affairs. He cannot read, he cannot write; he has one or two newspapers, but he is, apparently, not aware of it; until latterly he had no schools, and taught his children nothing, news is a term which has no meaning to him, and the thing itself he cares nothing about. He hates to be taxed and resents it. He has stood stock still in South Africa for two centuries and a half, and would like to stand still till the end of time, for he has no sympathy with Uitlander notions of progress. He is hungry to be rich, for he is human; but his preference has been for riches in cattle, not in fine clothes and fine houses and gold and diamonds. The gold and the diamonds have brought the godless stranger within his gates, also contamination and broken repose, and he wishes that they had never been discovered.

I think that the bulk of those details can be found in Olive Schreiner's books, and she would not be accused of sketching the Boer's portrait with an unfair hand.

Now what would you expect from that unpromising material? What ought you to expect from it? Laws inimical to religious liberty? Yes. Laws denying, representation and suffrage to the intruder? Yes. Laws unfriendly to educational institutions? Yes. Laws obstructive of gold production? Yes. Discouragement of railway expansion? Yes. Laws heavily taxing the intruder and overlooking the Boer? Yes.

The Uitlander seems to have expected something very different from all that. I do not know why. Nothing different from it was rationally to be expected. A round man cannot be expected to fit a square hole right away. He must have time to modify his shape. The modification had begun in a detail or two, before the Raid, and was making some progress. It has made further progress since. There are wise men in the Boer government, and that accounts for the modification; the modification of the Boer mass has probably not begun yet. If the heads of the Boer government had not been wise men they would have hanged Jameson, and thus turned a very commonplace pirate into a holy martyr. But even their wisdom has its limits, and they will hang Mr. Rhodes if they ever catch him. That will round him and complete him and make him a saint. He has already been called by all other titles that symbolize human grandeur, and he ought to rise to this one, the grandest of all. It will be a dizzy jump from where he is now, but that is nothing, it will land him in good company and be a pleasant change for him.

Some of the things demanded by the Johannesburgers' Manifesto have been conceded since the days of the Raid, and the others will follow in time, no doubt. It was most fortunate for the miners of Johannesburg that the taxes which distressed them so much were levied by the Boer government, instead of by their friend Rhodes and his Chartered Company of highwaymen, for these latter take half of whatever their mining victims find, they do not stop at a mere percentage. If the Johannesburg miners were under their jurisdiction they would be in the poorhouse in twelve months.

I have been under the impression all along that I had an unpleasant paragraph about the Boers somewhere in my notebook, and also a pleasant one. I have found them now. The unpleasant one is dated at an interior village, and says—

"Mr. Z. called. He is an English Afrikander; is an old resident, and has a Boer wife. He speaks the language, and his professional business is with the Boers exclusively. He told me that the ancient Boer families in the great region of which this village is the commercial center are falling victims to their inherited indolence and dullness in the materialistic latter-day race and struggle, and are dropping one by one into the grip of the usurer—getting hopelessly in debt—and are losing their high place and retiring to second and lower. The Boer's farm does not go to another Boer when he loses it, but to a foreigner. Some have fallen so low that they sell their daughters to the blacks."

Under date of another South African town I find the note which is creditable to the Boers:

"Dr. X. told me that in the Kafir war 1,500 Kafirs took refuge in a great cave in the mountains about 90 miles north of Johannesburg, and the Boers blocked up the entrance and smoked them to death. Dr. X. has been in there and seen the great array of bleached skeletons—one a woman with the skeleton of a child hugged to her breast."

The great bulk of the savages must go. The white man wants their lands, and all must go excepting such percentage of them as he will need to do his work for him upon terms to be determined by himself. Since history has removed the element

of guesswork from this matter and made it certainty, the humanest way of diminishing the black population should be adopted, not the old cruel ways of the past. Mr. Rhodes and his gang have been following the old ways.—They are chartered to rob and slay, and they lawfully do it, but not in a compassionate and Christian spirit. They rob the Mashonas and the Matabeles of a portion of their territories in the hallowed old style of "purchase!" for a song, and then they force a quarrel and take the rest by the strong hand. They rob the natives of their cattle under the pretext that all the cattle in the country belonged to the king whom they have tricked and assassinated. They issue "regulations" requiring the incensed and harassed natives to work for the white settlers, and neglect their own affairs to do it. This is slavery, and is several times worse than was the American slavery which used to pain England so much; for when this Rhodesian slave is sick, super-annuated, or otherwise disabled, he must support himself or starve—his master is under no obligation to support him.

The reduction of the population by Rhodesian methods to the desired limit is a return to the old-time slow-misery and lingering-death system of a discredited time and a crude "civilization." We humanely reduce an overplus of dogs by swift chloroform; the Boer humanely reduced an overplus of blacks by swift suffocation; the nameless but right-hearted Australian pioneer humanely reduced his overplus of aboriginal neighbors by a sweetened swift death concealed in a poisoned pudding. All these are admirable, and worthy of praise; you and I would rather suffer either of these deaths thirty times over in thirty successive days than linger out one of the Rhodesian twenty-year deaths, with its daily burden of insult, humiliation, and forced labor for a man whose entire race the victim hates. Rhodesia is a happy name for that land of piracy and pillage, and puts the right stain upon it.

Several long journeys—gave us experience of the Cape Colony railways; easy-riding, fine cars; all the conveniences; thorough cleanliness; comfortable beds furnished for the night trains. It was in the first days of June, and winter; the daytime was pleasant, the nighttime nice and cold. Spinning along all day in the cars it was ecstasy to breathe the bracing air and gaze out over the vast brown solitudes of the velvet plains, soft and lovely near by, still softer and lovelier further away, softest and loveliest of all in the remote distances, where dim island-hills seemed afloat, as in a sea—a sea made of dream-stuff and flushed with colors faint and rich; and dear me, the depth of the sky, and the beauty of the strange new cloud-forms, and the glory of the sunshine, the lavishness, the wastefulness of it! The vigor and freshness and inspiration of the air and the sunwell, it was all just as Olive Schreiner had made it in her books.

To me the veldt, in its sober winter garb, was surpassingly beautiful. There were unlevel stretches where it was rolling and swelling, and rising and subsiding, and sweeping superbly on and on, and still on and on like an ocean, toward the faraway horizon, its pale brown deepening by delicately graduated shades to rich orange, and finally to purple and crimson where it washed against the wooded hills and naked red crags at the base of the sky.

Everywhere, from Cape Town to Kimberley and from Kimberley to Port Elizabeth and East London, the towns were well populated with tamed blacks; tamed and Christianized too, I suppose, for they wore the dowdy clothes of our Christian civilization. But for that, many of them would have been remarkably handsome. These fiendish clothes, together with the proper lounging gait, good-natured face, happy air, and easy laugh, made them precise counterparts of our American blacks; often where all the other aspects were strikingly and harmoniously and thrillingly African, a flock of these natives would intrude, looking wholly out of place, and spoil it all, making the thing a grating discord, half African and half American.

One Sunday in King William's Town a score of colored women came mincing across the great barren square dressed—oh, in the last perfection of fashion, and newness, and expensiveness, and showy mixture of unrelated colors,—all just as I had seen it so often at home; and in their faces and their gait was that languishing, aristocratic, divine delight in their finery which was so familiar to me, and had always been such a satisfaction to my eye and my heart. I seemed among old, old friends; friends of fifty years, and I stopped and cordially greeted them. They broke into a good-fellowship laugh, flashing their white teeth upon me, and all answered at once. I did not understand a word they said. I was astonished; I was not dreaming that they would answer in anything but American.

The voices, too, of the African women, were familiar to me sweet and musical, just like those of the slave women of my early days. I followed a couple of them all over the Orange Free State—no, over its capital —Bloemfontein, to hear their liquid voices and the happy ripple of their laughter. Their language was a large improvement upon American. Also upon the Zulu. It had no Zulu clicks in it; and it seemed to have no angles or corners, no roughness, no vile s's or other hissing sounds, but was very, very mellow and rounded and flowing.

In moving about the country in the trains, I had opportunity to see a good many Boers of the veldt. One day at a village station a hundred of them got out of the third-class cars to feed.

Their clothes were very interesting. For ugliness of shapes, and for miracles of ugly colors inharmoniously associated, they were a record. The effect was nearly as exciting and interesting as that produced by the brilliant and beautiful clothes and perfect taste always on view at the Indian railway stations. One man had corduroy trousers of a faded chewing gum tint. And they were new—showing that this tint did not come by calamity, but was intentional; the very ugliest color I have ever seen. A gaunt, shackly country lout six feet high, in battered gray slouched hat with wide brim, and old resin-colored breeches, had on a hideous brand-new woolen coat which was imitation tiger skin wavy broad stripes of dazzling yellow and deep brown. I thought he ought to be hanged, and asked the station-master if it could be arranged. He said no; and not only that, but said it rudely; said it with a quite unnecessary show of feeling. Then he muttered something about my being a jackass, and walked away and pointed me out to people, and did everything he could to turn public sentiment against me. It is what one gets for trying to do good.

In the train that day a passenger told me some more about Boer life out in the lonely veldt. He said the Boer gets up early and sets his "niggers" at their tasks (pasturing the cattle, and watching them); eats, smokes, drowses, sleeps; toward evening superintends the milking, etc.; eats, smokes, drowses; goes to bed at early candlelight in the fragrant clothes he (and she) have worn all day and every week-day for years. I remember that last detail, in Olive Schreiner's "Story of an African Farm." And the passenger told me that the Boers were justly noted for their hospitality. He told me a story about it. He said that his grace the Bishop of a certain See was once making a business-progress through the tavernless veldt, and

one night he stopped with a Boer; after supper was shown to bed; he undressed, weary and worn out, and was soon sound asleep; in the night he woke up feeling crowded and suffocated, and found the old Boer and his fat wife in bed with him, one on each side, with all their clothes on, and snoring. He had to stay there and stand it—awake and suffering—until toward dawn, when sleep again fell upon him for an hour. Then he woke again. The Boer was gone, but the wife was still at his side.

Those Reformers detested that Boer prison; they were not used to cramped quarters and tedious hours, and weary idleness, and early to bed, and limited movement, and arbitrary and irritating rules, and the absence of the luxuries which wealth comforts the day and the night with. The confinement told upon their bodies and their spirits; still, they were superior men, and they made the best that was to be made of the circumstances. Their wives smuggled delicacies to them, which helped to smooth the way down for the prison fare.

In the train Mr. B. told me that the Boer jail-guards treated the black prisoners—even political ones—mercilessly. An African chief and his following had been kept there nine months without trial, and during all that time they had been without shelter from rain and sun. He said that one day the guards put a big black in the stocks for dashing his soup on the ground; they stretched his legs painfully wide apart, and set him with his back down hill; he could not endure it, and put back his hands upon the slope for a support. The guard ordered him to withdraw the support and kicked him in the back. "Then," said Mr. B., "'the powerful black wrenched the stocks asunder and went for the guard; a Reform prisoner pulled him off, and thrashed the guard himself."

CHAPTER LXIX.

The very ink with which all history is written is merely fluid prejudice. —Pudd'nhead Wilsons's New Calendar.

There isn't a Parallel of Latitude but thinks it would have been the Equator if it had had its rights. —Pudd'nhead Wilson's New Calendar.

Next to Mr. Rhodes, to me the most interesting convulsion of nature in South Africa was the diamond-crater. The Rand gold fields are a stupendous marvel, and they make all other gold fields small, but I was not a stranger to gold-mining; the veldt was a noble thing to see, but it was only another and lovelier variety of our Great Plains; the natives were very far from being uninteresting, but they were not new; and as for the towns, I could find my way without a guide through the most of them because I had learned the streets, under other names, in towns just like them in other lands; but the diamond mine was a wholly fresh thing, a splendid and absorbing novelty. Very few people in the world have seen the diamond in its home. It has but three or four homes in the world, whereas gold has a million. It is worth while to journey around the globe to see anything which can truthfully be called a novelty, and the diamond mine is the greatest and most select and restricted novelty which the globe has in stock.

The Kimberley diamond deposits were discovered about 1869, I think. When everything is taken into consideration, the wonder is that they were not discovered five thousand years ago and made familiar to the African world for the rest of time. For this reason the first diamonds were found on the surface of the ground. They were smooth and limpid, and in the sunlight they vomited fire. They were the very things which an African savage of any era would value above every other thing in the world excepting a glass bead. For two or three centuries we have been buying his lands, his cattle, his neighbor, and any other thing he had for sale, for glass beads and so it is strange that he was indifferent to the diamonds—for he must have picked them up many and many a time. It would not occur to him to try to sell them to whites, of course, since the whites already had plenty of glass beads, and more fashionably shaped, too, than these; but one would think that the poorer sort of black, who could not afford real glass, would have been humbly content to decorate himself with the imitation, and that presently the white trader would notice the things, and dimly suspect, and carry some of them home, and find out what they were, and at once empty a multitude of fortune-hunters into Africa. There are many strange things in human history; one of the strangest is that the sparkling diamonds laid there so long without exciting any one's interest.

The revelation came at last by accident. In a Boer's hut out in the wide solitude of the plains, a traveling stranger noticed a child playing with a bright object, and was told it was a piece of glass which had been found in the veldt. The stranger bought it for a trifle and carried it away; and being without honor, made another stranger believe it was a diamond, and so got $125 out of him for it, and was as pleased with himself as if he had done a righteous thing. In Paris the wronged stranger sold it to a pawnshop for $10,000, who sold it to a countess for $90,000, who sold it to a brewer for $800,000, who traded it to a king for a dukedom and a pedigree, and the king "put it up the spout." —[handwritten note: "From the Greek meaning 'pawned it.'" M.T.]—I know these particulars to be correct.

The news flew around, and the South African diamond-boom began. The original traveler—the dishonest one—now remembered that he had once seen a Boer teamster chocking his wagon-wheel on a steep grade with a diamond as large as a football, and he laid aside his occupations and started out to hunt for it, but not with the intention of cheating anybody out of $125 with it, for he had reformed.

We now come to matters more didactic. Diamonds are not imbedded in rock ledges fifty miles long, like the Johannesburg gold, but are distributed through the rubbish of a filled-up well, so to speak. The well is rich, its walls are sharply defined; outside of the walls are no diamonds. The well is a crater, and a large one. Before it had been meddled with, its surface was even with the level plain, and there was no sign to suggest that it was there. The pasturage covering the surface of the Kimberley crater was sufficient for the support of a cow, and the pasturage underneath was sufficient for the support of a kingdom; but the cow did not know it, and lost her chance.

The Kimberley crater is roomy enough to admit the Roman Coliseum; the bottom of the crater has not been reached, and no one can tell how far down in the bowels of the earth it goes. Originally, it was a perpendicular hole packed solidly full of blue rock or cement, and scattered through that blue mass, like raisins in a pudding, were the diamonds. As deep down in the earth as the blue stuff extends, so deep will the diamonds be found.

There are three or four other celebrated craters near by a circle three miles in diameter would enclose them all. They are owned by the De Beers Company, a consolidation of diamond properties arranged by Mr. Rhodes twelve or fourteen years ago. The De Beers owns other craters; they are under the

grass, but the De Beers knows where they are, and will open them some day, if the market should require it.

Originally, the diamond deposits were the property of the Orange Free State; but a judicious "rectification" of the boundary line shifted them over into the British territory of Cape Colony. A high official of the Free State told me that the sum of $4,00,000 was handed to his commonwealth as a compromise, or indemnity, or something of the sort, and that he thought his commonwealth did wisely to take the money and keep out of a dispute, since the power was all on the one side and the weakness all on the other. The De Beers Company dig out $400,000 worth of diamonds per week, now. The Cape got the territory, but no profit; for Mr. Rhodes and the Rothschilds and the other De Beers people own the mines, and they pay no taxes.

In our day the mines are worked upon scientific principles, under the guidance of the ablest mining-engineering talent procurable in America. There are elaborate works for reducing the blue rock and passing it through one process after another until every diamond it contains has been hunted down and secured. I watched the "concentrators" at work big tanks containing mud and water and invisible diamonds—and was told that each could stir and churn and properly treat 300 car-loads of mud per day 1,600 pounds to the car-load—and reduce it to 3 car-loads of slush. I saw the 3 carloads of slush taken to the "pulsators" and there reduced to quarter of a load of nice clean dark-colored sand. Then I followed it to the sorting tables and saw the men deftly and swiftly spread it out and brush it about and seize the diamonds as they showed up. I assisted, and once I found a diamond half as large as an almond. It is an exciting kind of fishing, and you feel a fine thrill of pleasure every time you detect the glow of one of those limpid pebbles through the veil of dark sand. I would like to spend my Saturday holidays in that charming sport every now and then. Of course there are disappointments. Sometimes you find a diamond which is not a diamond; it is only a quartz crystal or some such worthless thing. The expert can generally distinguish it from the precious stone which it is counterfeiting; but if he is in doubt he lays it on a flatiron and hits it with a sledgehammer. If it is a diamond it holds its own; if it is anything else, it is reduced to powder. I liked that experiment very much, and did not tire of repetitions of it. It was full of enjoyable apprehensions, unmarred by any personal sense of risk. The De Beers concern treats 8,000 carloads —about 6,000 tons—of blue rock per day, and the result is three pounds of diamonds. Value, uncut, $50,000 to $70,000. After cutting, they will weigh considerably less than a pound, but will be worth four or five times as much as they were before.

All the plain around that region is spread over, a foot deep, with blue rock, placed there by the Company, and looks like a plowed field. Exposure for a length of time make the rock easier to work than it is when it comes out of the mine. If mining should cease now, the supply of rock spread over those fields would furnish the usual 8,000 car-loads per day to the separating works during three years. The fields are fenced and watched; and at night they are under the constant inspection of lofty electric searchlight. They contain fifty or sixty million dollars' worth' of diamonds, and there is an abundance of enterprising thieves around.

In the dirt of the Kimberley streets there is much hidden wealth. Some time ago the people were granted the privilege of a free wash-up. There was a general rush, the work was done with thoroughness, and a good harvest of diamonds was gathered.

The deep mining is done by natives. There are many hundreds of them. They live in quarters built around the inside of a great compound. They are a jolly and good-natured lot, and accommodating. They performed a war-dance for us, which was the wildest exhibition I have ever seen. They are not allowed outside of the compound during their term of service three months, I think it, is, as a rule. They go down the shaft, stand their watch, come up again, are searched, and go to bed or to their amusements in the compound; and this routine they repeat, day in and day out.

It is thought that they do not now steal many diamonds successfully. They used to swallow them, and find other ways of concealing them, but the white man found ways of beating their various games. One man cut his leg and shoved a diamond into the wound, but even that project did not succeed. When they find a fine large diamond they are more likely to report it than to steal it, for in the former case they get a reward, and in the latter they are quite apt to merely get into trouble. Some years ago, in a mine not owned by the De Beers, a black found what has been claimed to be the largest diamond known to the world's history; and, as a reward he was released from service and given a blanket, a horse, and five hundred dollars. It made him a Vanderbilt. He could buy four wives, and have money left. Four wives are an ample support for a native. With four wives he is wholly independent, and need never do a stroke of work again.

That great diamond weighs 971 carats. Some say it is as big as a piece of alum, others say it is as large as a bite of rock candy, but the best authorities agree that it is almost exactly the size of a chunk of ice. But those details are not important; and in my opinion not trustworthy. It has a flaw in it, otherwise it would be of incredible value. As it is, it is held to be worth $2,000,000. After cutting it ought to be worth from $5,000,000 to $8,000,000, therefore persons desiring to save money should buy it now. It is owned by a syndicate, and apparently there is no satisfactory market for it. It is earning nothing; it is eating its head off. Up to this time it has made nobody rich but the native who found it.

He found it in a mine which was being worked by contract. That is to say, a company had bought the privilege of taking from the mine 5,000,000 carloads of blue-rock, for a sum down and a royalty. Their speculation had not paid; but on the very day that their privilege ran out that native found the $2,000,000-diamond and handed it over to them. Even the diamond culture is not without its romantic episodes.

The Koh-i-Noor is a large diamond, and valuable; but it cannot compete in these matters with three which—according to legend—are among the crown trinkets of Portugal and Russia. One of these is held to be worth $20,000,000; another, $25,000,000, and the third something over $28,000,000.

Those are truly wonderful diamonds, whether they exist or not; and yet they are of but little importance by comparison with the one wherewith the Boer wagoner chocked his wheel on that steep grade as heretofore referred to. In Kimberley I had some conversation with the man who saw the Boer do that—an incident which had occurred twenty-seven or twenty-eight years before I had my talk with him. He assured me that that diamond's value could have been over a billion dollars, but not under it. I believed him, because he had devoted twenty-seven years to hunting for it, and was, in a position to know.

A fitting and interesting finish to an examination of the tedious and laborious and costly processes whereby the diamonds are gotten out of the deeps of the earth and freed from the base stuffs which imprison them is the visit to the De Beers offices in the town of Kimberley, where the result of each day's mining is brought every day, and, weighed, assorted, valued, and deposited in safes against shipping-day. An unknown and unaccredited person cannot, get into that place; and it seemed apparent from the generous supply of warning and protective and prohibitory signs that were posted all about, that not even the known and accredited can steal diamonds there without inconvenience.

We saw the day's output—shining little nests of diamonds, distributed a foot apart, along a counter, each nest reposing upon a sheet of white paper. That day's catch was about $70,000 worth. In the course of a year half a ton of diamonds pass under the scales there and sleep on that counter; the resulting money is $18,000,000 or $20,000,000. Profit, about $12,000,000.

Young girls were doing the sorting—a nice, clean, dainty, and probably distressing employment. Every day ducal incomes sift and sparkle through the fingers of those young girls; yet they go to bed at night as poor as they were when they got up in the morning. The same thing next day, and all the days.

They are beautiful things, those diamonds, in their native state. They are of various shapes; they have flat surfaces, rounded borders, and never a sharp edge. They are of all colors and shades of color, from dewdrop white to actual black; and their smooth and rounded surfaces and contours, variety of color, and transparent limpidity make them look like piles of assorted candies. A very light straw color is their commonest tint. It seemed to me that these uncut gems must be more beautiful than any cut ones could be; but when a collection of cut ones was brought out, I saw my mistake. Nothing is so beautiful as a rose diamond with the light playing through it, except that uncostly thing which is just like it—wavy sea-water with the sunlight playing through it and striking a white-sand bottom.

Before the middle of July we reached Cape Town, and the end of our African journeyings. And well satisfied; for, towering above us was Table Mountain—a reminder that we had now seen each and all of the great features of South Africa except Mr. Cecil Rhodes. I realize that that is a large exception. I know quite well that whether Mr. Rhodes is the lofty and worshipful patriot and statesman that multitudes believe him to be, or Satan come again, as the rest of the world account him, he is still the most imposing figure in the British empire outside of England. When he stands on the Cape of Good Hope, his shadow falls to the Zambesi. He is the only colonial in the British dominions whose goings and comings are chronicled and discussed under all the globe's meridians, and whose speeches, unclipped, are cabled from the ends of the earth; and he is the only unroyal outsider whose arrival in London can compete for attention with an eclipse.

That he is an extraordinary man, and not an accident of fortune, not even his dearest South African enemies were willing to deny, so far as I heard them testify. The whole South African world seemed to stand in a kind of shuddering awe of him, friend and enemy alike. It was as if he were deputy-God on the one side, deputy-Satan on the other, proprietor of the people, able to make them or ruin them by his breath, worshiped by many, hated by many, but blasphemed by none among the judicious, and even by the indiscreet in guarded whispers only.

What is the secret of his formidable supremacy? One says it is his prodigious wealth—a wealth whose drippings in salaries and in other ways support multitudes and make them his interested and loyal vassals; another says it is his personal magnetism and his persuasive tongue, and that these hypnotize and make happy slaves of all that drift within the circle of their influence; another says it is his majestic ideas, his vast schemes for the territorial aggrandizement of England, his patriotic and unselfish ambition to spread her beneficent protection and her just rule over the pagan wastes of Africa and make luminous the African darkness with the glory of her name; and another says he wants the earth and wants it for his own, and that the belief that he will get it and let his friends in on the ground floor is the secret that rivets so many eyes upon him and keeps him in the zenith where the view is unobstructed.

One may take his choice. They are all the same price. One fact is sure: he keeps his prominence and a vast following, no matter what he does. He "deceives" the Duke of Fife—it is the Duke's word—but that does not destroy the Duke's loyalty to him. He tricks the Reformers into immense trouble with his Raid, but the most of them believe he meant well. He weeps over the harshly—taxed Johannesburgers and makes them his friends; at the same time he taxes his Charter-settlers 50 per cent., and so wins their affection and their confidence that they are squelched with despair at every rumor that the Charter is to be annulled. He raids and robs and slays and enslaves the Matabele and gets worlds of Charter-Christian applause for it. He has beguiled England into buying Charter waste paper for Bank of England notes, ton for ton, and the ravished still burn incense to him as the Eventual God of Plenty. He has done everything he could think of to pull himself down to the ground; he has done more than enough to pull sixteen common-run great men down; yet there he stands, to this day, upon his dizzy summit under the dome of the sky, an apparent permanency, the marvel of the time, the mystery of the age, an Archangel with wings to half the world, Satan with a tail to the other half.

I admire him, I frankly confess it; and when his time comes I shall buy a piece of the rope for a keepsake.

CONCLUSION.

I have traveled more than anyone else, and I have noticed that even the angels speak English with an accent. — Pudd'nhead Wilson's New Calendar.

I saw Table Rock, anyway—a majestic pile. It is 3,000 feet high. It is also 17,000 feet high. These figures may be relied upon. I got them in Cape Town from the two best-informed citizens, men who had made Table Rock the study of their lives. And I saw Table Bay, so named for its levelness. I saw the Castle—built by the Dutch East India Company three hundred years ago—where the Commanding General lives; I saw St. Simon's Bay, where the Admiral lives. I saw the Government, also the Parliament, where they quarreled in two languages when I was there, and agreed in none. I saw the club. I saw and explored the beautiful sea-girt drives that wind about the mountains and through the paradise where the villas are: Also I saw some of the fine old Dutch mansions, pleasant homes of the early times, pleasant homes to-day, and enjoyed the privilege of their hospitalities.

And just before I sailed I saw in one of them a quaint old picture which was a link in a curious romance—a picture of a pale, intellectual young man in a pink coat with a high black collar. It was a portrait of Dr. James Barry, a military surgeon who came out to the Cape fifty years ago with his regiment. He was a wild young fellow, and was guilty of various kinds of misbehavior. He was several times reported to headquarters in England, and it was in each case expected that orders would come out to deal with him promptly and severely, but for some mysterious reason no orders of any kind ever came back—nothing came but just an impressive silence. This made him an imposing and uncanny wonder to the town.

Next, he was promoted-away up. He was made Medical Superintendent General, and transferred to India. Presently he was back at the Cape again and at his escapades once more. There were plenty of pretty girls, but none of them caught him, none of them could get hold of his heart; evidently he was not a marrying man. And that was another marvel, another puzzle, and made no end of perplexed talk. Once he was called in the night, an obstetric service, to do what he could for a woman who was believed to be dying. He was prompt and scientific, and saved both mother and child. There are other instances of record which testify to his mastership of his profession; and many which testify to his love of it and his devotion to it. Among other adventures of his was a duel of a desperate sort, fought with swords, at the Castle. He killed his man.

The child heretofore mentioned as having been saved by Dr. Barry so long ago, was named for him, and still lives in Cape Town. He had Dr. Barry's portrait painted, and gave it to the gentleman in whose old Dutch house I saw it—the quaint figure in pink coat and high black collar.

The story seems to be arriving nowhere. But that is because I have not finished. Dr. Barry died in Cape Town 30 years ago. It was then discovered that he was a woman.

The legend goes that enquiries—soon silenced—developed the fact that she was a daughter of a great English house, and that that was why her Cape wildnesses brought no punishment and got no notice when reported to the government at home. Her name was an alias. She had disgraced herself with her people; so she chose to change her name and her sex and take a new start in the world.

We sailed on the 15th of July in the Norman, a beautiful ship, perfectly appointed. The voyage to England occupied a short fortnight, without a stop except at Madeira. A good and restful voyage for tired people, and there were several of us. I seemed to have been lecturing a thousand years, though it was only a twelvemonth, and a considerable number of the others were Reformers who were fagged out with their five months of seclusion in the Pretoria prison.

Our trip around the earth ended at the Southampton pier, where we embarked thirteen months before. It seemed a fine and large thing to have accomplished—the circumnavigation of this great globe in that little time, and I was privately proud of it. For a moment. Then came one of those vanity-snubbing astronomical reports from the Observatory-people, whereby it appeared that another great body of light had lately flamed up in the remotenesses of space which was traveling at a gait which would enable it to do all that I had done in a minute and a half. Human pride is not worth while; there is always something lying in wait to take the wind out of it.

Breinigsville, PA USA
09 December 2009

228925BV00002B/42/A

9 780954 840181